THE FAMOUS FIVE

FIVE ON A TREASURE ISLAND

Have you read all THE FAMOUS FIVE books?

1. Five on a Treasure Island
2. Five Go Adventuring Again
3. Five Run Away Together
4. Five Go to Smuggler's Top
5. Five Go Off in a Caravan
6. Five on Kirrin Island Again
7. Five Go Off to Camp
8. Five Get Into Trouble
9. Five Fall Into Adventure
10. Five on a Hike Together
11. Five Have a Wonderful Time
12. Five Go Down to the Sea
13. Five Go to Mystery Moor
14. Five Have Plenty of Fun
15. Five on a Secret Trail
16. Five Go to Billycock Hill
17. Five Get Into a Fix
18. Five on Finniston Farm
19. Five Go to Demon's Rocks
20. Five Have a Mystery to Solve
21. Five Are Together Again

The Famous Five Colour Short Stories

1. Five and a Half-Term Adventure
2. George's Hair is Too Long
3. Good Old Timmy
4. A Lazy Afternoon
5. Well Done, Famous Five
6. Five Have a Puzzling Time
7. Happy Christmas, Five
8. When Timmy Chased the Cat

Enid Blyton®

THE FAMOUS FIVE

FIVE ON A TREASURE ISLAND

Illustrated by Eileen A. Soper

HODDER CHILDREN'S BOOKS

First published in Great Britain in 1942 by Hodder & Stoughton
This edition published in 2016

21

A CIP catalogue record for this book is available from the British Library.

ISBN: 978 1 444 93631 5

Printed and bound in Great Britain by Clays Ltd, Elcograf S.p.A.

The paper and board used in this book are made from wood from responsible sources

Hodder Children's Books
An imprint of
Hachette Children's Group
Part of Hodder & Stoughton
Carmelite House
50 Victoria Embankment
London EC4Y 0DZ

An Hachette UK Company
www.hachette.co.uk
www.hachettechildrens.co.uk

CONTENTS

1 A GREAT SURPRISE 1
2 THE STRANGE COUSIN 9
3 A PECULIAR STORY – AND A NEW FRIEND 19
4 AN EXCITING AFTERNOON 30
5 A VISIT TO THE ISLAND 41
6 WHAT THE STORM DID 53
7 BACK TO KIRRIN COTTAGE 64
8 EXPLORING THE WRECK 73
9 THE BOX FROM THE WRECK 84
10 AN ASTONISHING OFFER 97
11 OFF TO KIRRIN ISLAND 105
12 EXCITING DISCOVERIES 115
13 DOWN IN THE DUNGEONS 127
14 PRISONERS! 138
15 DICK TO THE RESCUE! 147
16 A PLAN – AND A NARROW ESCAPE 158
17 THE END OF THE GREAT ADVENTURE 171

CHAPTER ONE

A great surprise

'MOTHER HAVE you heard about our summer holidays yet?' said Julian, at the breakfast-table. 'Can we go to Polseath as usual?'

'I'm afraid not,' said his mother. 'They are quite full up this year.'

The three children at the breakfast-table looked at one another in great disappointment. They did so love the house at Polseath. The beach was so lovely there, too, and the bathing was fine.

'Cheer up,' said Daddy. 'I dare say we'll find somewhere else just as good for you. And anyway, Mother and I won't be able to go with you this year. Has Mother told you?'

'No!' said Anne. 'Oh, Mother – is it true? Can't you really come with us on our holidays? You always do.'

'Well, this time Daddy wants me to go to Scotland with him,' said Mother. 'All by ourselves! And as you are really getting big enough to look after yourselves now, we thought it would be rather fun for you to have a holiday on your own too. But now that you can't go to Polseath, I don't really quite know where to send you.'

'What about Quentin's?' suddenly said Daddy. Quentin was his brother, the children's uncle. They had only seen him once, and had been rather frightened of him. He was a very tall, frowning man, a clever scientist who spent all his time studying. He lived by the sea – but that was about all that the children knew of him!

'Quentin?' said Mother, pursing her lips. 'Whatever made you think of him? I shouldn't think he'd want the children messing about in his little house.'

'Well,' said Daddy, 'I had to see Quentin's wife in town the other day, about a business matter – and I don't think things are going too well for them. Fanny said that she would be quite glad if she could hear of one or two people to live with her for a while, to bring a little money in. Their house is by the sea, you know. It might be just the thing for the children. Fanny is very nice – she would look after them well.'

'Yes – and she has a child of her own too, hasn't she?' said the children's mother. 'Let me see – what's her name – something funny – yes, Georgina! How old would she be? About eleven, I should think.'

'Same age as me,' said Dick. 'Fancy having a cousin we've never seen! She must be jolly lonely all by herself. I've got Julian and Anne to play with – but Georgina is just one on her own. I should think she'd be glad to see us.'

'Well, your Aunt Fanny said that her Georgina would love a bit of company,' said Daddy. 'You know, I really think that would solve our difficulty, if we telephone to Fanny and arrange for the children to go there. It would help Fanny, I'm sure, and Georgina would love to have someone to play with in the holidays. And we should know that our three were safe.'

The children began to feel rather excited. It would be fun to go to a place they had never been to before, and stay with an unknown cousin.

'Are there cliffs and rocks and sands there?' asked Anne. 'Is it a nice place?'

'I don't remember it very well,' said Daddy. 'But I feel sure it's an exciting kind of place. Anyway, you'll love it! It's called Kirrin Bay. Your Aunt Fanny has lived there all her life, and wouldn't leave it for anything.'

'Oh, Daddy, do telephone to Aunt Fanny and ask her if we can go there!' cried Dick. 'I just feel as if it's the right place somehow. It sounds sort of adventurous!'

'Oh, you always say that, wherever you go!' said Daddy, with a laugh. 'All right – I'll ring up now, and see if there's any chance.'

They had all finished their breakfast, and they got up to wait for Daddy to telephone. He went out into the hall, and they heard him dialling.

'I hope it's all right for us!' said Julian. 'I wonder what Georgina's like. Funny name, isn't it? More like a boy's than a girl's. So she's eleven – a year younger than I am – same age as you, Dick – and a year older than you, Anne. She ought to fit in with us all right. The four of us ought to have a fine time together.'

Daddy came back in about ten minutes' time, and the

children knew at once that he had fixed up everything. He smiled round at them.

'Well, that's settled,' he said. 'Your Aunt Fanny is delighted about it. She says it will be awfully good for Georgina to have company, because she's such a lonely little girl, always going off by herself. And she will love looking after you all. Only you'll have to be careful not to disturb your Uncle Quentin. He is working very hard, and he isn't very good-tempered when he is disturbed.'

'We'll be as quiet as mice in the house!' said Dick.

'Honestly we will. Oh, goody, goody – when are we going, Daddy?'

'Next week, if Mother can manage it,' said Daddy.

Mother nodded her head. 'Yes,' she said, 'there's nothing much to get ready for them – just bathing suits and jerseys and jeans. They all wear the same.'

'How lovely it will be to wear jeans again,' said Anne, dancing round. 'I'm tired of wearing school tunics. I want to wear shorts, or a bathing suit, and go bathing and climbing with the boys.'

'Well, you'll soon be doing it,' said Mother, with a laugh. 'Remember to put ready any toys or books you want, won't you? Not many, please, because there won't be a great deal of room.'

'Anne wanted to take all her fifteen dolls with her last year,' said Dick. 'Do you remember, Anne? Weren't you funny?'

'No, I wasn't,' said Anne, going red. 'I love my dolls, and I just couldn't choose which to take – so I thought I'd take them all. There's nothing funny about that.'

And do you remember the year before, Anne wanted to take the rocking-horse?' said Dick, with a giggle.

Mother chimed in. 'You know, I remember a little boy called Dick who put aside one teddy bear, three toy dogs, two toy cats and his old monkey to take down to Polseath one year,' she said.

Then it was Dick's turn to go red. He changed the subject at once.

'Daddy, are we going by train or by car?' he asked.

'By car,' said Daddy. 'We can pile everything into the boot. Well – what about Tuesday?'

'That would suit me well,' said Mother. 'Then we could take the children down, come back, and do our own packing at leisure, and start off for Scotland on the Friday. Yes – we'll arrange for Tuesday.'

So Tuesday it was. The children counted the days eagerly, and Anne marked one off the calendar each night. The week seemed a very long time in going. But at last Tuesday did come. Dick and Julian, who shared a room, woke up at about the same moment, and stared out of the nearby window.

'It's a lovely day, hurrah!' cried Julian, leaping out of bed. 'I don't know why, but it always seems very important that it should be sunny on the first day of a holiday. Let's wake Anne.'

Anne slept in the next room. Julian ran in and shook her. 'Wake up! It's Tuesday! And the sun's shining.'

Anne woke up with a jump and stared at Julian joyfully. 'It's come at last!' she said. 'I thought it never would. Oh, isn't it an exciting feeling to go away for a holiday!'

They started soon after breakfast. Their car was a big one, so it held them all very comfortably. Mother sat in front with Daddy, and the three children sat behind, their feet on two suitcases. In the luggage-place at the back of the car were all kinds of odds and ends, and one small trunk. Mother really thought they had remembered everything.

Along the crowded London roads they went, slowly at first, and then, as they left the town behind, more quickly. Soon they were right into the open country, and the car sped along fast. The children sang songs to themselves, as they always did when they were happy.

'Are we picnicking soon?' asked Anne, feeling hungry all of a sudden.

'Yes,' said Mother. 'But not yet. It's only eleven o'clock. We shan't have lunch till at least half past twelve, Anne.'

'Oh, gracious!' said Anne. 'I know I can't last out till then!'

So her mother handed her some chocolate, and she and the boys munched happily, watching the hills, woods and fields as the car sped by.

The picnic was lovely. They had it on the top of a hill, in a sloping field that looked down into a sunny valley. Anne didn't very much like a big brown cow which came up close and stared at her, but it went away when Daddy told it to. The children ate enormously, and Mother said that instead of having a tea-picnic at half past four they would have to go to a tea-house somewhere, because they had eaten all the tea sandwiches as well as the lunch ones!

'What time shall we be at Aunt Fanny's?' asked Julian, finishing up the very last sandwich and wishing there were more.

'About six o'clock with luck,' said Daddy. 'Now who wants to stretch their legs a bit? We've another long spell in the car, you know.'

The car seemed to eat up the miles as it purred along. Tea-time came, and then the three children began to feel excited all over again.

'We must watch out for the sea,' said Dick. 'I can smell it somewhere near!'

He was right. The car suddenly topped a hill – and there was the shining blue sea, calm and smooth in the evening sun. The three children gave a yell.

'There it is!'

'Isn't it marvellous!'

'Oh, I want to bathe this very minute!'

'We shan't be more than twenty minutes now, before we're at Kirrin Bay,' said Daddy. 'We've made good time. You'll see the bay soon – it's quite a big one – with a funny sort of island at the entrance of the bay.'

The children looked out for it as they drove along the coast. Then Julian gave a shout.

'There it is – that must be Kirrin Bay. Look, Dick – isn't it lovely and blue?'

'And look at the rocky little island guarding the entrance of the bay,' said Dick. 'I'd like to visit that.'

'Well, I've no doubt you will,' said Mother. 'Now, let's look out for Aunt Fanny's house. It's called Kirrin Cottage.'

They soon came to it. It stood on the low cliff overlooking the bay, and was a very old house indeed. It wasn't really a cottage, but quite a big house, built of old white stone. Roses climbed over the front of it, and the garden was full of flowers.

'Here's Kirrin Cottage,' said Daddy, and he stopped the car in front of it. 'It's supposed to be about three hundred years old! Now – where's Quentin? Hallo, there's Fanny!'

CHAPTER TWO

The strange cousin

THE CHILDREN'S aunt had been watching for the car. She came running out of the old wooden door as soon as she saw it draw up outside. The children liked the look of her at once.

'Welcome to Kirrin!' she cried. 'Hallo, all of you! It's lovely to see you. And what big children!'

There were kisses all round, and then the children went into the house. They liked it. It felt old and rather mysterious somehow, and the furniture was old and very beautiful.

'Where's Georgina?' asked Anne, looking round for her unknown cousin.

'Oh, the naughty girl! I told her to wait in the garden for you,' said her aunt. 'Now she's gone off somewhere. I must tell you, children, you may find George a bit difficult at first – she's always been one on her own, you know, and at first may not like you being here. But you mustn't take any notice of that – she'll be all right in a short time. I was very glad for George's sake that you were able to come. She badly needs other children to play with.'

'Do you call her "George"?' asked Anne, in surprise. 'I thought her name was Georgina.'

'So it is,' said her aunt. 'But George hates being a girl, and we have to call her George, as if she were a boy. The naughty girl won't answer if we call her Georgina.'

The children thought that Georgina sounded rather exciting. They wished she would come. But she didn't. Their Uncle Quentin suddenly appeared instead. He was a most extraordinary-looking man, very tall, and with a rather fierce frown on his wide forehead.

'Hallo, Quentin!' said Daddy. 'It's a long time since I've seen you. I hope these three won't disturb you very much in your work.'

'Quentin is working on a very difficult book,' said Aunt Fanny. 'But I've given him a room all to himself on the other side of the house. So I don't expect he will be disturbed.'

Their uncle looked at the three children, and nodded to them. The frown didn't come off his face, and they all felt a little scared, and were glad that he was to work in another part of the house.

'Where's George?' he said, in a deep voice.

'Gone off somewhere again,' said Aunt Fanny, vexed. 'I told her she was to stay here and meet her cousins.'

'She wants a good talking to,' said Uncle Quentin. The children couldn't quite make out whether he was joking or not. 'Well, children, I hope you have a good time here, and maybe you will knock a little common-sense into George!'

There was no room at Kirrin Cottage for Mother and Daddy to stay the night, so after a hurried supper they left to stay at a hotel in the nearest town. They would drive back to London immediately after breakfast the next day. So they said goodbye to the children that night.

Georgina still hadn't appeared. 'I'm sorry we haven't seen Georgina,' said Mother. 'Just give her our love and tell her we hope she'll enjoy playing with Dick, Julian and Anne.'

Then Mother and Daddy went. The children felt a little bit lonely as they saw the big car disappear round the corner of the road, but Aunt Fanny took them upstairs to show them their bedrooms, and they soon forgot to be sad.

The two boys were to sleep together in a room with slanting ceilings at the top of the house. It had a marvellous view of the bay. The boys were really delighted with it. Anne was to sleep with Georgina in a smaller room, whose windows looked over the moors at the back of the house. But one side-window looked over the sea, which pleased Anne very much. It was a nice room, and red roses nodded their heads in at the window.

'I do wish Georgina would come,' Anne said to her aunt. 'I want to see what she's like.'

'Well, she's a funny little girl,' said her aunt. 'She can be very rude and haughty – but she's kind at heart, very loyal and absolutely truthful. Once she makes friends with you, she will always be your friend – but she finds it very difficult indeed to make friends, which is a great pity.'

Anne suddenly yawned. The boys frowned at her, because they knew what would happen next. And it did!

'Poor Anne! How tired you are! You must all go to bed straight away, and have a good night. Then you will wake up quite fresh tomorrow,' said Aunt Fanny.

'Anne, you *are* an idiot,' said Dick, crossly, when his aunt had gone out of the room. 'You know quite well what grown-ups think as soon as we yawn. I did want to go down on the beach for a while.'

'I'm so sorry,' said Anne. 'Somehow I couldn't help it. And anyway, *you're* yawning now, Dick – and Julian too!'

So they were. They were as sleepy as could be with their long drive. Secretly all of them longed to cuddle down into bed and shut their eyes.

'I wonder where Georgina is,' said Anne, when she said good night to the boys, and went to her own room. 'Isn't she odd – not waiting to welcome us – and not coming in to supper – and not even in yet! After all, she's sleeping in my room – goodness knows what time she'll be in!'

All the three children were fast asleep before Georgina came up to bed! They didn't hear her open Anne's door. They didn't hear her get undressed and clean her teeth. They didn't hear the creak of her bed as she got into it. They were so tired that they heard nothing at all until the sun awoke them in the morning.

When Anne awoke she couldn't at first think where she was. She lay in her little bed and looked up at the slanting ceiling, and at the red roses that nodded at the open window – and suddenly remembered all in a rush where she was! 'I'm at Kirrin Bay – and it's the holidays!' she said to herself, and screwed up her legs with joy.

Then she looked across at the other bed. In it lay the figure of another child, curled up under the bed-clothes. Anne could just see the top of a curly head, and that was all. When the figure stirred a little, Anne spoke.

'I say! Are you Georgina?'

The child in the opposite bed sat up and looked across at Anne. She had very short curly hair, almost as short as a boy's. Her face was burnt with the sun, and her very blue eyes looked as bright as forget-me-nots in her face. But her mouth was rather sulky, and she had a frown like her father's.

'No,' she said. 'I'm not Georgina.'

'Oh!' said Anne, in surprise. 'Then who are you?'

'I'm George,' said the girl. 'I shall only answer if you call me George. I hate being a girl. I won't be. I don't like doing the things that girls do. I like doing the things that boys do. I can climb better than any boy, and swim faster too. I can sail a boat as well as any fisher-boy on this coast. You're to call me George. Then I'll speak to you. But I shan't if you don't.'

'Oh!' said Anne, thinking that her new cousin was most extraordinary. 'All right! I don't care what I call you. George is a nice name, I think. I don't much like Georgina. Anyway, you look like a boy.'

'Do I really?' said George, the frown leaving her face for a moment. 'Mother was awfully cross with me when I cut my hair short. I had hair all round my neck; it was awful.'

The two girls stared at one another for a moment. 'Don't you simply hate being a girl?' asked George.

'No, of course not,' said Anne. 'You see – I do like pretty frocks – and I love my dolls – and you can't do that if you're a boy.'

'Pooh! Fancy bothering about pretty frocks,' said George, in a scornful voice. 'And dolls! Well, you *are* a baby, that's all I can say.'

Anne felt offended. 'You're not very polite,' she said. 'You won't find that my brothers take much notice of you if you act as if you know everything. They're *real* boys, not pretend boys, like you.'

'Well, if they're going to be nasty to me I shan't take any notice of *them*,' said George, jumping out of bed. 'I didn't want any of you to come, anyway. Interfering with my life here! I'm quite happy on my own. Now I've got to put up with a silly girl who likes frocks and dolls, and two stupid boy-cousins!'

Anne felt that they had made a very bad beginning. She said no more, but got dressed herself too. She put on her grey jeans and a red jersey. George put on jeans too, and a boy's jersey. Just as they were ready the boys hammered on their door.

'Aren't you ready? Is Georgina there? Cousin Georgina, come out and see us.'

George flung open the door and marched out with her head high. She took no notice of the two surprised boys at

all. She stalked downstairs. The other three children looked at one another.

'She won't answer if you call her Georgina,' explained Anne. 'She's awfully funny, I think. She says she didn't want us to come because we'll interfere with her. She laughed at me, and was rather rude.'

Julian put his arm round Anne, who looked a bit

doleful. 'Cheer up!' he said. 'You've got us to stick up for you. Come on down to breakfast.'

They were all hungry. The smell of bacon and eggs was very good. They ran down the stairs and said good-morning to their aunt. She was just bringing the breakfast to the table. Their uncle was sitting at the head, reading his paper. He nodded at the children. They sat down without a word, wondering if they were allowed to speak at meals. They always were at home, but their Uncle Quentin looked rather fierce.

George was there, buttering a piece of toast. She scowled at the three children.

'Don't look like that, George,' said her mother. 'I hope you've made friends already. It will be fun for you to play together. You must take your cousins to see the bay this morning and show them the best places to bathe.'

'I'm going fishing,' said George.

Her father looked up at once.

'You are not,' he said. 'You are going to show a few good manners for a change, and take your cousins to the bay. Do you hear me?'

'Yes,' said George, with a scowl exactly like her father's.

'Oh, we can go to the bay by ourselves all right, if George is going fishing,' said Anne, at once, thinking that it would be nice not to have George if she was in a bad temper.

'George will do exactly as she's told,' said her father. 'If she doesn't, I shall deal with her.'

So, after breakfast, four children got ready to go down to the beach. An easy path led down to the bay, and they ran down happily. Even George lost her frown as she felt the warmth of the sun and saw the dancing sparkles on the blue sea.

'You go fishing if you want to,' said Anne when they were down on the beach. 'We won't tell tales on you. We don't want to interfere with you, you know. We've got ourselves for company, and if you don't want to be with us, you needn't.'

'But we'd like you, all the same, if you'd like to be with us,' said Julian, generously. He thought George was rude and ill-mannered, but he couldn't help rather liking the look of the straight-backed, short-haired little girl, with her brilliant blue eyes and sulky mouth.

George stared at him. 'I'll see,' she said. 'I don't make friends with people just because they're my cousins, or something silly like that. I only make friends with people if I like them.'

'So do we,' said Julian. 'We may not like *you*, of course.'

'Oh!' said George, as if that thought hadn't occurred to her. 'Well – you may not, of course. Lots of people don't like me, now I come to think of it.'

Anne was staring out over the blue bay. At the entrance to it lay a curious rocky island with what looked like an old ruined castle on the top of it.

'Isn't that a funny place?' she said. 'I wonder what it's called.'

'It's called Kirrin Island,' said George, her eyes as blue as the sea as she turned to look at it. 'It's a lovely place to go to. If I like you, I may take you there some day. But I don't promise. The only way to get there is by boat.'

'Who does the funny island belong to?' asked Julian.

George made a most surprising answer. 'It belongs to *me*,' she said. 'At least, it *will* belong to me – some day! It will be my very own island – and my very own castle!'

CHAPTER THREE

A peculiar story – and a new friend

THE THREE children stared at George in the greatest surprise.

George stared back at them.

'What do you mean?' said Dick, at last. 'Kirrin Island can't belong to you. You're just boasting.'

'No, I'm not,' said George. 'You ask Mother. If you're not going to believe what I say I won't tell you another word more. But I don't tell untruths. I think it's being a coward if you don't tell the truth – and I'm not a coward.'

Julian remembered that Aunt Fanny had said that George was absolutely truthful, and he scratched his head and looked at George again. How could she be possibly telling the truth?

'Well, of course we'll believe you if you tell us the truth,' he said. 'But it does sound a bit extraordinary, you know. Really, it does. Children don't usually own islands, even funny little ones like that.'

'It *isn't* a funny little island,' said George, fiercely. 'It's lovely. There are rabbits there, as tame as can be – and the big cormorants sit on the other side – and all kinds of gulls go there. The castle is wonderful too, even if it *is* all in ruins.'

'It sounds fine,' said Dick. 'How does it belong to you, Georgina?'

George glared at him and didn't answer.

'Sorry,' said Dick, hastily. 'I didn't mean to call you Georgina. I meant to call you George.'

'Go on, George – tell us how the island belongs to you,' said Julian, slipping his arm through his sulky little cousin's.

She pulled away from him at once.

'Don't do that,' she said. 'I'm not sure that I want to make friends with you yet.'

'All right, all right,' said Julian, losing patience. 'Be enemies or anything you like. We don't care. But we like your mother awfully, and we don't want her to think we won't make friends with you.'

'Do you like my mother?' said George, her bright blue eyes softening a little. 'Yes – she's a dear, isn't she? Well – all right – I'll tell you how Kirrin Castle belongs to me. Come and sit down here in this corner where nobody can hear us.'

They all sat down in a sandy corner of the beach. George looked across at the little island in the bay.

'It's like this,' she said. 'Years ago my mother's family owned nearly all the land around here. Then they got poor, and had to sell most of it. But they could never sell that little island, because nobody thought it worth anything, especially as the castle has been ruined for years.'

'Fancy nobody wanting to buy a dear little island like that!' said Dick. 'I'd buy it at once if I had the money.'

'All that's left of what Mother's family owned is our own house, Kirrin Cottage, and a farm a little way off – and Kirrin Island,' said George. 'Mother says when I'm grown-up it will be mine. She says she doesn't want it now, either, so she's sort of given it to me. It belongs to me. It's my own private island, and I don't let anyone go there unless they get my permission.'

The three children stared at her. They believed every word George said, for it was quite plain that the girl was speaking the truth. Fancy having an island of your very own! They thought she was very lucky indeed.

'Oh, Georgina – I mean George!' said Dick. 'I do think you're lucky. It looks such a nice island. I hope you'll be friends with us and take us there one day soon. You simply can't imagine how we'd love it.'

'Well – I might,' said George, pleased at the interest she had caused. 'I'll see. I never have taken anyone there yet, though some of the boys and girls round here have begged me to. But I don't like them, so I haven't.'

There was a little silence as the four children looked out over the bay to where the island lay in the distance. The tide was going out. It almost looked as if they could wade over to the island. Dick asked if it was possible.

'No,' said George. 'I told you – it's only possible to get to it by boat. It's farther out than it looks – and the water is very, very deep. There are rocks all about too – you have to know exactly where to row a boat, or you bump into them. It's a dangerous bit of coast here. There are a lot of wrecks about.'

'Wrecks!' cried Julian, his eyes shining. 'I say! I've never seen an old wreck. Are there any to see?'

'Not now,' said George. 'They've all been cleared up. Except one, and that's the other side of the island. It's deep down in the water. You can just see the broken mast if you row over it on a calm day and look down into the water. That wreck really belongs to me too.'

This time the children really could hardly believe George. But she nodded her head firmly.

'Yes,' she said, 'it was a ship belonging to one of my great-great-great-grandfathers, or someone like that. He was bringing gold – big bars of gold – back in his ship – and it got wrecked off Kirrin Island.'

'Oooh – what happened to the gold?' asked Anne, her eyes round and big.

'Nobody knows,' said George. 'I expect it was stolen out of the ship. Divers have been down to see, of course, but they couldn't find any gold.'

'Golly – this does sound exciting,' said Julian. 'I wish I could see the wreck.'

'Well – we might perhaps go this afternoon when the tide is right down,' said George. 'The water is so calm and clear today. We could see a bit of it.'

'Oh, how wonderful!' said Anne. 'I do so want to see a real live wreck!'

The others laughed. 'Well, it won't be very alive,' said Dick. 'I say, George – what about a bathe?'

'I must go and get Timothy first,' said George. She got up.

'Who's Timothy?' said Dick.

'Can you keep a secret?' asked George. 'Nobody must know at home.'

'Well, go on, what's the secret?' asked Julian. 'You can tell us. We're not sneaks.'

'Timothy is my very greatest friend,' said George. 'I couldn't do without him. But Mother and Father don't like him, so I have to keep him in secret. I'll go and fetch him.'

She ran off up the cliff path. The others watched her go. They thought she was the most peculiar girl they had ever known.

'Who in the world can Timothy be?' wondered Julian. 'Some fisher-boy, I suppose, that George's parents don't approve of.'

The children lay back in the soft sand and waited. Soon they heard George's clear voice coming down from the cliff behind them.

'Come on, Timothy! Come on!'

They sat up and looked to see what Timothy was like. They saw no fisher-boy – but instead a big brown mongrel dog with an absurdly long tail and a big wide mouth that really seemed to grin! He was bounding all round George, mad with delight. She came running down to them.

'This is Timothy,' she said. 'Don't you think he is simply perfect?'

As a dog, Timothy was far from perfect. He was the wrong shape, his head was too big, his ears were too pricked, his tail was too long and it was quite impossible to say what kind of a dog he was supposed to be. But he was such a mad, friendly, clumsy, laughable creature that every one of the children adored him at once.

'Oh, you darling!' said Anne, and got a lick on the nose.

'I say – isn't he grand!' said Dick, and gave Timothy a friendly smack that made the dog bound madly all round him.

'I wish *I* had a dog like this,' said Julian, who really loved dogs, and had always wanted one of his own. 'Oh, George – he's fine. Aren't you proud of him?'

The little girl smiled, and her face altered at once, and became sunny and pretty. She sat down on the sand and her dog cuddled up to her, licking her wherever he could find a bare piece of skin.

'I love him awfully,' she said. 'I found him out on the moors when he was just a pup, a year ago, and I took him home. At first Mother liked him, but when he grew bigger he got terribly naughty.'

'What did he do?' asked Anne.

'Well, he's an awfully chewy kind of dog,' said George. 'He chewed up everything he could – a new rug Mother had bought – her nicest hat – Father's slippers – some of his papers, and things like that. And he barked too. I liked his bark, but Father didn't. He said it nearly drove him mad. He hit at Timothy and that made me angry, so I was awfully rude to him.'

'Did you get told off?' said Anne. 'I wouldn't like to be rude to your father. He looks fierce.'

George looked out over the bay. Her face had gone sulky again. 'Well, it doesn't matter what punishment I got,' she said, 'but the worst part of all was when Father said I couldn't keep Timothy any more, and Mother backed Father up and said Tim must go. I cried for days – and I never do cry, you know, because boys don't and I like to be like a boy.'

'Boys do cry sometimes,' began Anne, looking at Dick, who had been a bit of a cry-baby three or four years back. Dick gave her a sharp nudge, and she said no more.

George looked at Anne.

'Boys don't cry,' she said, obstinately. 'Anyway, I've never seen one, and I always try not to cry myself. It's so babyish. But I just couldn't help it when Timothy had to go. He cried too.'

The children looked with great respect at Timothy. They had not known that a dog could cry before.

'Do you mean – he cried real tears?' asked Anne.

'No, not quite,' said George. 'He's too brave for that. He cried with his voice – howled and howled and looked so miserable that he nearly broke my heart. And then I knew I couldn't possibly part with him.'

'What happened then?' asked Julian.

'I went to Alf, a fisher-boy I know,' said George, 'and I asked him if he'd keep Tim for me, if I paid him all the pocket-money I get. He said he would, and so he does. That's why I never have any money to spend – it all has to go on Tim. He seems to eat an awful lot – don't you, Tim?'

'Woof!' said Tim, and rolled over on his back, all his shaggy legs in the air. Julian tickled him.

'How do you manage when you want any sweets or ice-creams?' said Anne, who spent most of her pocket-money on things of that sort.

'I don't manage,' said George. 'I go without, of course.'

This sounded awful to the other children, who loved ice-creams, chocolates and sweets, and had a good many of them. They stared at George.

'Well – I suppose the other children who play on the beach share their sweets and ices with you sometimes, don't they?' asked Julian.

'I don't let them,' said George. 'If I can never give them any myself it's not fair to take them. So I say no.'

The tinkle of an ice-cream man's bell was heard in the distance. Julian felt in his pocket. He jumped up and rushed off, jingling his money. In a few moments he was back again, carrying four fat chocolate ice-cream bars. He gave one to Dick, and one to Anne, and then held out one to George. She looked at it longingly, but shook her head.

'No, thanks,' she said. 'You know what I just said. I haven't any money to buy them, so I can't share mine with you, and I can't take any from you. It's mean to take from people if you can't give even a little back.'

'You can take from us,' said Julian, trying to put the ice into George's tanned hand. 'We're your cousins.'

'No, thanks,' said George again. 'Though I do think it's nice of you.'

She looked at Julian out of her blue eyes and the boy frowned as he tried to think of a way to make the obstinate little girl take the ice. Then he smiled.

'Listen,' he said, 'you've got something we badly want to share – in fact you've got a lot of things we'd like to share, if only you'd let us. You share those with us, and let us share things like ices with you. See?'

'What things have I got that you want to share?' asked George, in surprise.

'You've got a dog,' said Julian, patting the big brown mongrel. 'We'd love to share him with you, he's such a darling. And you've got a lovely island. We'd be simply thrilled if you'd share it sometimes. And you've got a wreck. We'd like to look at it and share it too. Ices and sweets aren't so good as those things – but it would be nice to make a bargain and share with each other.'

George looked at the brown eyes that gazed steadily into hers. She couldn't help liking Julian. It wasn't her nature to share anything. She had always been an only child, a lonely, rather misunderstood little girl, fierce and hot-tempered. She had never had any friends of her own. Timothy looked up at Julian and saw that he was offering something nice and chocolatey to George. He jumped up and licked the boy with his friendly tongue.

'There you are, you see – Tim wants to be shared,' said Julian, with a laugh. 'It would be nice for him to have three new friends.'

'Yes – it would,' said George, giving in suddenly, and taking the chocolate bar. 'Thank you, Julian. I will share with you. But promise you'll never tell anyone at home that I'm still keeping Timothy?'

'Of course we'll promise,' said Julian. 'But I can't imagine that your father or mother would mind, so long as Tim doesn't live in their house. How's the ice? Is it nice?'

'Ooooh – the loveliest one I've ever tasted!' said George nibbling at it. 'It's so cold. I haven't had one this year. It's simply delicious!'

Timothy tried to nibble it too. George gave him a few crumbs at the end. Then she turned and smiled at the three children.

'You're nice,' she said. 'I'm glad you've come after all. Let's take a boat out this afternoon and row round the island to have a look at the wreck, shall we?'

'Rather!' said all three at once – and even Timothy wagged his tail as if he understood!

CHAPTER FOUR

An exciting afternoon

THEY ALL had a bathe that morning, and the boys found that George was a much better swimmer than they were. She was very strong and very fast, and she could swim under water, too, holding her breath for ages.

'You're jolly good,' said Julian, admiringly. 'It's a pity Anne isn't a bit better. Anne, you'll have to practise your swimming strokes hard, or you'll never be able to swim out as far as we do.'

They were all very hungry at lunch-time. They went back up the cliff-path, hoping there would be lots to eat – and there was! Cold meat and salad, plum-pie and custard, and cheese afterwards. How the children tucked in!

'What are you going to do this afternoon?' asked George's mother.

'George is going to take us out in a boat to see the wreck on the other side of the island,' said Anne. Her aunt looked most surprised.

'*George* is going to take you!' she said. 'Why, George – what's come over you? You've never taken a single person before, though I've asked you to dozens of times!'

George said nothing, but went on eating her plum-pie. She hadn't said a word all through the meal. Her father had not appeared at the table, much to the children's relief.

'Well, George, I must say I'm pleased that you want to try and do what your father said,' began her mother again. But George shook her head.

'I'm not doing it because I've got to,' she said. 'I'm doing it because I want to. I wouldn't have taken anyone to see my wreck, not even the Queen of England, if I didn't like them.'

Her mother laughed. 'Well, it's good news that you like your cousins,' she said. 'I hope they like you!'

'Oh yes!' said Anne, eagerly, anxious to stick up for her strange cousin. 'We do likc George – and we like Ti . . .'

She was just about to say that they liked Timothy too, when she got such a kick on her ankle that she cried out in pain and the tears came into her eyes. George glared at her.

'George! Why did you kick Anne like that when she was saying nice things about you?' cried her mother. 'Leave the table at once. I won't have such behaviour.'

George left the table without a word. She went out into the garden. She had just taken a piece of bread and cut herself some cheese. It was all left on her plate. The other three stared at it in distress. Anne was upset. How could she have been so silly as to forget she mustn't mention Tim?

'Oh, please call George back!' she said. 'She didn't mean to kick me. It was an accident.'

But her aunt was very angry with George. 'Finish your meal,' she said to the others. 'I expect George will go into a sulk now. Dear, dear, she *is* such a difficult child!'

The others didn't mind about George going into a sulk. What they did mind was that George might refuse to take them to see the wreck now!

They finished the meal in silence. Their aunt went to see if Uncle Quentin wanted any more pie. He was having his meal in the study by himself. As soon as she had gone out of the room, Anne picked up the bread and cheese from George's plate and went out into the garden.

The boys didn't scold her. They knew that Anne's tongue very often ran away with her – but she always tried to make up for it afterwards. They thought it was very brave of her to go and find George.

George was lying on her back under a big tree in the garden. Anne went up to her. 'I'm sorry I nearly made a mistake, George,' she said. 'Here's your bread and cheese. I've brought it for you. I promise I'll never forget not to mention Tim again.'

George sat up. 'I've a good mind not to take you to see the wreck,' she said. 'Stupid baby!'

Anne's heart sank. This was what she had feared. 'Well,' she said, 'you needn't take me, of course. But you might take the boys, George. After all, they didn't do anything silly. And anyway, you gave me an awful kick. Look at the bruise.'

George looked at it. Then she looked at Anne. 'But wouldn't you be miserable if I took Julian and Dick without you?' she asked.

'Of course,' said Anne. 'But I don't want to make them miss a treat, even if *I* have to.'

Then George did a surprising thing for her. She gave Anne a hug! Then she immediately looked most ashamed of herself, for she felt sure that no boy would have done that! And she always tried to act like a boy.

'It's all right,' she said, gruffly, taking the bread and cheese. 'You were nearly very silly – and I gave you a kick – so it's all square. Of course you can come this afternoon.'

Anne sped back to tell the boys that everything was all right – and in fifteen minutes' time four children ran down to the beach. By a boat was a suntanned fisher-boy, about fourteen years old. He had Timothy with him.

'Boat's all ready, George,' he said with a grin. 'And Tim's ready, too.'

'Thanks,' said George, and told the others to get in. Timothy jumped in, too, his big tail wagging nineteen to the dozen. George pushed the boat off into the surf and then jumped in herself. She took the oars.

She rowed splendidly, and the boat shot along over the blue bay. It was a wonderful afternoon, and the children loved the movement of the boat over the water. Timothy stood at the prow and barked whenever a wave reared its head.

'He's funny on a wild day,' said George, pulling hard. 'He barks madly at the big waves, and gets so angry if they splash him. He's an awfully good swimmer.'

'Isn't it nice to have a dog with us?' said Anne, anxious to make up for her mistake. 'I do so like him.'

'Woof,' said Timothy, in his deep voice and turned round to lick Anne's ear.

'I'm sure he knew what I said,' said Anne in delight.

'Of course he did,' said George. 'He understands every single word.'

'I say – we're getting near to your island now,' said

Julian, in excitement. 'It's bigger than I thought. And isn't the castle exciting?'

They drew near to the island, and the children saw that there were sharp rocks all round about it. Unless anyone knew exactly the way to take, no boat or ship could possibly land on the shore of the rocky little island. In the very middle of it, on a low hill, rose the ruined castle. It had been built of big white stones. Broken archways, tumbledown towers, ruined walls – that was all that was left of a once beautiful castle, proud and strong. Now the jackdaws nested in it and the gulls sat on the topmost stones.

'It looks awfully mysterious,' said Julian. 'How I'd love to land there and have a look at the castle. Wouldn't it be fun to spend a night or two here!'

George stopped rowing. Her face lit up. 'I say!' she said, in delight. 'Do you know, I never thought how lovely that would be! To spend a night on my island! To be there all alone, the four of us. To get our own meals, and pretend we really lived there. Wouldn't it be grand?'

'Yes, rather,' said Dick, looking longingly at the island. 'Do you think – do you suppose your mother would let us?'

'I don't know,' said George. 'She might. You could ask her.'

'Can't we land there this afternoon?' asked Julian.

'No, not if you want to see the wreck,' said George. 'We've got to get back for tea today, and it will take all the time to row round to the other side of Kirrin Island and back.'

'Well – I'd like to see the wreck,' said Julian, torn between the island and the wreck. 'Here, let me take the oars for a bit, George. You can't do all the rowing.'

'I can,' said George. 'But I'd quite enjoy lying back in the boat for a change! Look – I'll just take you by this rocky bit – and then you can take the oars till we come to another awkward piece. Honestly, the rocks around this bay are simply dreadful!'

George and Julian changed places in the boat. Julian rowed well, but not so strongly as George. The boat sped along rocking smoothly. They went right round the island, and saw the castle from the other side. It looked more ruined on the side that faced the sea.

'The strong winds come from the open sea,' explained George. 'There's not really much left of it this side, except piles of stones. But there's a good little harbour in a little cove, for those who know how to find it.'

George took the oars after a while, and rowed steadily out a little beyond the island. Then she stopped and looked back towards the shore.

'How do you know when you are over the wreck?' asked Julian, puzzled. 'I should never know!'

'Well, do you see that church tower on the mainland?' asked George. 'And do you see the tip of that hill over there? Well, when you get them exactly in line with one another, between the two towers of the castle on the island, you are pretty well over the wreck! I found that out ages ago.'

The children saw that the tip of the far-off hill and the church tower were practically in line, when they looked at them between the two old towers of the island castle. They looked eagerly down into the sea to see if they could spy the wreck.

The water was perfectly clear and smooth. There was hardly a wrinkle. Timothy looked down into it too, his head on one side, his ears cocked, just as if he knew what he was looking for! The children laughed at him.

'We're not exactly over it,' said George, looking down too. 'The water's so clear today that we should be able to see quite a long way down. Wait, I'll row a bit to the left.'

'Woof!' said Timothy, suddenly, and wagged his tail – and at the same moment the three children saw something deep down in the water!

'It's the wreck!' said Julian, almost falling out of the boat in his excitement. 'I can see a bit of broken mast. Look, Dick, look!'

All four children and the dog, too, gazed down earnestly into the clear water. After a little while they could make out the outlines of a dark hulk, out of which the broken mast stood.

'It's a bit on one side,' said Julian. 'Poor old ship. How it must hate lying there, gradually falling to pieces. George, I wish I could dive down and get a closer look at it.'

'Well, why don't you?' said George. 'You've got your

swimming trunks on. I've often dived down. I'll come with you, if you like, if Dick can keep the boat round about here. There's a current that is trying to take it out to sea. Dick, you'll have to keep working a bit with this oar to keep the boat in one spot.'

The girl stripped off her jeans and jersey and Julian did the same. They both had on bathing costumes underneath. George took a beautiful header off the end of the boat, deep down into the water. The others watched her swimming strongly downwards, holding her breath.

After a bit she came up, almost bursting for breath. 'Well, I went almost down to the wreck,' she said. 'It's just the same as it always is – seaweedy and covered with limpets and things. I wish I could get right into the ship itself. But I never have enough breath for that. You go down now, Julian.'

So down Julian went – but he was not so good at swimming deep under water as George was, and he couldn't go down so far. He knew how to open his eyes under water, so he was able to take a good look at the deck of the wreck. It looked very forlorn and strange. Julian didn't really like it very much. It gave him rather a sad sort of feeling. He was glad to go to the top of the water again, and take deep breaths of air, and feel the warm sunshine on his shoulders.

He climbed into the boat. 'Most exciting,' he said. 'Golly, wouldn't I just love to see that wreck properly – you know – go down under the deck into the cabins and

look around. And oh, suppose we could really find the boxes of gold!'

'That's impossible,' said George. 'I told you proper divers have already gone down and found nothing. What's the time? I say, we'll be late if we don't hurry back now!'

They did hurry back, and managed to be only about five

minutes late for tea. Afterwards they went for a walk over the moors, with Timothy at their heels, and by the time that bedtime came they were all so sleepy that they could hardly keep their eyes open.

'Well, good night, George,' said Anne, snuggling down into her bed. 'We've had a lovely day – thanks to you!'

'And *I've* had a lovely day, too,' said George, rather gruffly. 'Thanks to *you*. I'm glad you all came. We're going to have fun. And won't you love my castle and my little island!'

'Oooh, yes,' said Anne, and fell asleep to dream of wrecks and castles and islands by the hundred. Oh, when would George take them to her little island?

CHAPTER FIVE

A visit to the island

THE CHILDREN'S aunt arranged a picnic for them the next day, and they all went off to a little cove not far off where they could bathe and paddle to their hearts' content. They had a wonderful day, but secretly Julian, Dick and Anne wished they could have visited George's island. They would rather have done that than anything!

George didn't want to go for the picnic, not because she disliked picnics, but because she couldn't take her dog. Her mother went with the children, and George had to pass a whole day without her beloved Timothy.

'Bad luck!' said Julian, who guessed what she was brooding about. 'I can't think why you don't tell your mother about old Tim. I'm sure she wouldn't mind you letting someone else keep him for you. I know my mother wouldn't mind.'

'I'm not going to tell anybody but you,' said George. 'I get into awful trouble at home always. I dare say it's my fault, but I get a bit tired of it. You see, Daddy doesn't make much money with the learned books he writes, and he's always wanting to give mother and me things he can't afford. So that makes him bad-tempered. He wants to send me away to a good school but he hasn't got the money. I'm glad. I don't want to go away to school. I like being here. I couldn't bear to part with Timothy.'

'You'd like boarding school,' said Anne. 'We all go. It's fun.'

'No, it isn't,' said George obstinately. 'It must be awful to be one of a crowd, and to have other girls all laughing and yelling round you. I should hate it.'

'No, you wouldn't,' said Anne. 'All that is great fun. It would be good for you, George, I should think.'

'If you start telling me what is good for me, I shall hate you,' said George, suddenly looking very fierce. 'Mother and Father are always saying that things are good for me – and they are always the things I don't like.'

'All right, all right,' said Julian, beginning to laugh. 'My goodness, how you do go up in smoke! Honestly, I believe anyone could light a cigarette from the sparks that fly from your eyes!'

That made George laugh, though she didn't want to. It was really impossible to sulk with good-tempered Julian.

They went off to bathe in the sea for the fifth time that day. Soon they were all splashing about happily, and George found time to help Anne to swim. The little girl hadn't got the right stroke, and George felt really proud when she had taught her.

'Oh, thanks,' said Anne, struggling along. 'I'll never be as good as you – but I'd like to be as good as the boys.'

As they were going home, George spoke to Julian. 'Could you say that you want to go and buy a stamp or something?' she said. 'Then I could go with you, and just have a peep at old Tim. He'll be wondering why I haven't taken him out today.'

'Right!' said Julian. 'I don't want stamps, but I *could* do with an ice. Dick and Anne can go home with your mother and carry the things. I'll just go and tell Aunt Fanny.'

He ran up to his aunt. 'Do you mind if I go and buy some ice-creams?' he asked. 'We haven't had one today. I won't be long. Can George go with me?'

'I don't expect she will want to,' said his aunt. 'But you can ask her.'

'George, come with me!' yelled Julian, setting off to the little village at a great pace. George gave a sudden grin and ran after him. She soon caught him up and smiled gratefully at him.

'Thanks,' she said. 'You go and get the ice-creams, and I'll have a look at Tim.'

They parted, Julian bought four ice-creams, and turned to go home. He waited about for George, who came running up after a few minutes. Her face was glowing.

'He's all right,' she said. 'And you can't imagine how pleased he was to see me! He nearly jumped over my head! I say – another ice-cream for me. You really are a sport, Julian. I'll have to share something with you quickly. What about going to my island tomorrow?'

'Golly!' said Julian, his eyes shining. 'That would be marvellous. Will you really take us tomorrow? Come on, let's tell the others!'

The four children sat in the garden eating their ices. Julian told them what George had said. They all felt excited. George was pleased. She had always felt quite important before when she had haughtily refused to take any of the other children to see Kirrin Island – but it felt much nicer somehow to have consented to row her cousins there.

'I used to think it was much, much nicer always to do things on my own,' she thought, as she sucked the last bits of her ice. 'But it's going to be fun doing things with Julian and the others.'

The children were sent to wash themselves and to get tidy before supper. They talked eagerly about the visit to the island next day. Their aunt heard them and smiled.

'Well, I really must say I'm pleased that George is going to share something with you,' she said. 'Would you like to take your dinner there, and spend the day? It's hardly worthwhile rowing all the way there and landing unless you are going to spend some hours there.'

'Oh, Aunt Fanny! It would be marvellous to take our dinner!' cried Anne.

George looked up. 'Are you coming too, Mother?' she asked.

'You don't sound at all as if you want me to,' said her mother, in a hurt tone. 'You looked cross yesterday, too, when you found I was coming. No – I shan't come tomorrow – but I'm sure your cousins must think you are an odd girl never to want your mother to go with you.'

George said nothing. She hardly ever did say a word

when she was scolded. The other children said nothing too. They knew perfectly well that it wasn't that George didn't want her mother to go – it was just that she wanted Timothy with her!

'Anyway, I couldn't come,' went on Aunt Fanny. 'I've some gardening to do. You'll be quite safe with George. She can handle a boat like a man.'

The three children looked eagerly at the weather the next day when they got up. The sun was shining, and everything seemed splendid.

'Isn't it a marvellous day?' said Anne to George, as they dressed. 'I'm so looking forward to going to the island.'

'Well, honestly, I think really we oughtn't to go,' said George, unexpectedly.

'Oh, but why?' cried Anne, in dismay.

'I think there's going to be a storm or something,' said George, looking out to the south-west.

'But, George, why do you say that?' said Anne, impatiently. 'Look at the sun – and there's hardly a cloud in the sky!'

'The wind is wrong,' said George. 'And can't you see the little white tops of the waves out there by my island? That's always a bad sign.'

'Oh, George – it will be the biggest disappointment of our lives if we don't go today,' said Anne, who couldn't bear any disappointment, big or small. 'And besides,' she added, artfully, 'if we hang about the house, afraid of a storm, we shan't be able to have dear old Tim with us.'

'Yes, that's true,' said George. 'All right – we'll go. But mind – if a storm does come, you're not to be a baby. You're to try and enjoy it and not be frightened.'

'Well, I don't much like storms,' began Anne, but stopped when she saw George's scornful look. They went down to breakfast, and George asked her mother if they could take their dinner as they had planned.

'Yes,' said her mother. 'You and Anne can help to make the sandwiches. You boys can go into the garden and pick some ripe plums to take with you. Julian, you can go down to the village when you've done that and buy some bottles of lemonade or ginger-beer, whichever you like.'

'Ginger-pop for me, thanks!' said Julian, and everyone else said the same. They all felt very happy. It would be marvellous to visit the strange little island. George felt happy because she would be with Tim all day.

They set off at last, the food in two kit-bags. The first thing they did was to fetch Tim. He was tied up in the fisher-boy's backyard. The boy himself was there, and grinned at George.

''Morning, George,' he said. 'Tim's been barking his head off for you. I guess he knew you were coming for him today.'

'Of course he did,' said George, untying him. He at once went completely mad, and tore round and round the children, his tail down and his ears flat.

'He'd win any race if only he were a greyhound,' said Julian, admiringly. 'You can hardly see him for dust. Tim!

Hey, Tim! Come and say "Good-morning".'

Tim leapt up and licked Julian's left ear as he passed on his whirlwind way. Then he sobered down and ran lovingly by George as they all made their way to the beach. He licked George's bare legs every now and again, and she pulled at his ears gently.

They got into the boat, and George pushed off. The fisher-boy waved to them. 'You won't be very long, will you?' he called. 'There's a storm blowing up. Bad one it'll be, too.'

'I know,' shouted back George. 'But maybe we'll get back before it begins. It's pretty far off yet.'

George rowed all the way to the island. Tim stood at each end of the boat in turn, barking when the waves reared up at him. The children watched the island coming closer and closer. It looked even more exciting than it had the other day.

'George, where are you going to land?' asked Julian. 'I simply can't imagine how you know your way in and out of these awful rocks. I'm afraid every moment we'll bump into them!'

'I'm going to land at the little cove I told you about the other day,' said George. 'There's only one way to it, but I know it very well. It's hidden away on the east side of the island.'

The girl cleverly worked her boat in and out of the rocks, and suddenly, as it rounded a low wall of sharp rocks, the children saw the cove she had spoken of. It was like a natural little harbour, and was a smooth inlet of water running up to a stretch of sand, sheltered between high rocks. The boat slid into the inlet, and at once stopped rocking, for here the water was like glass, and had hardly a wrinkle.

'I say – this is fine!' said Julian, his eyes shining with delight. George looked at him and her eyes shone too, as bright as the sea itself. It was the first time she had ever taken anyone to her precious island, and she was enjoying it.

They landed on the smooth yellow sand. 'We're really on the island!' said Anne, and she capered about, Tim joining her and looking as mad as she did. The others laughed. George pulled the boat high up on the sand.

'Why so far up?' said Julian, helping her. 'The tide's almost in, isn't it? Surely it won't come as high as this.'

'I told you I thought a storm was coming,' said George. 'If one does, the waves simply tear up this inlet and we don't want to lose our boat, do we?'

'Let's explore the island, let's explore the island!' yelled Anne, who was now at the top of the little natural harbour, climbing up the rocks there. 'Oh do come on!'

They all followed her. It really was a most exciting place. Rabbits were everywhere! They scuttled about as the children appeared, but did not go into their holes.

'Aren't they awfully tame?' said Julian, in surprise.

'Well, nobody ever comes here but me,' said George, 'and I don't frighten them. Tim! Tim, if you go after the rabbits, I'll be furious.'

Tim turned big sorrowful eyes on to George. He and George agreed about every single thing except rabbits. To Tim rabbits were made for one thing – to chase! He never could understand why George wouldn't let him do this. But he held himself in and walked solemnly by the children, his eyes watching the lolloping rabbits longingly.

'I believe they would almost eat out of my hand,' said Julian.

But George shook her head.

'No, I've tried that with them,' she said. 'They won't. Look at those baby ones. Aren't they lovely?'

'Woof!' said Tim, agreeing, and he took a few steps towards them. George made a warning noise in her throat, and Tim walked back, his tail down.

'There's the castle!' said Julian. 'Shall we explore that now? I do want to.'

'Yes, we will,' said George. 'Look – that is where the entrance used to be – through that big broken archway.'

The children gazed at the enormous old archway, now half-broken down. Behind it were ruined stone steps leading towards the centre of the castle.

'It had strong walls all round it, with two towers,' said George. 'One tower is almost gone, as you can see, but the other is not so bad. The jackdaws build in that every year. They've almost filled it up with their sticks!'

As they came near to the better tower of the two the jackdaws circled round them with loud cries of 'Chack, chack, chack!' Tim leapt into the air as if he thought he could get them, but they only called mockingly to him.

'This is the centre of the castle,' said George, as they entered through a ruined doorway into what looked like a great yard, whose stone floor was now overgrown with grass and other weeds. 'Here is where the people used to live. You can see where the rooms were – look, there's one almost whole there. Go through that little door and you'll see it.'

They trooped through a doorway and found themselves in a dark, stone-walled, stone-roofed room, with a space at one end where a fireplace must have been. Two slit-like windows lit the room. It felt very strange and mysterious.

'What a pity it's all broken down,' said Julian, wandering out again. 'That room seems to be the only one quite whole. There are some others here – but all of them seem to have either no roof, or one or other of the walls gone. That room is the only livable one. Was there an upstairs to the castle, George?'

'Of course,' said George. 'But the steps that led up are gone. Look! You can see part of an upstairs room there, by the jackdaw tower. You can't get up to it, though, because I've tried. I nearly broke my neck trying to get up. The stones crumble away so.'

'Were there any dungeons?' asked Dick.

'I don't know,' said George. 'I expect so. But nobody could find them now – everywhere is so overgrown.'

It was indeed overgrown. Big blackberry bushes grew here and there, and a few gorse bushes forced their way into gaps and corners. The coarse green grass sprang everywhere, and pink thrift grew its cushions in holes and crannies.

'Well, I think it's a perfectly lovely place,' said Anne. 'Perfectly and absolutely lovely!'

'Do you really?' said George, pleased. 'I'm so glad.

Look! We're right on the other side of the island now, facing the sea. Do you see those rocks, with those peculiar big birds sitting there?'

The children looked. They saw some rocks sticking up, with great black shining birds sitting on them in strange positions.

'They are cormorants,' said George. 'They've caught plenty of fish for their dinner, and they're sitting there digesting it. Hallo – they're all flying away. I wonder why?'

She soon knew – for, from the south-west there suddenly came an ominous rumble.

'Thunder!' said George. 'That's the storm. It's coming sooner than I thought!'

CHAPTER SIX

What the storm did

THE FOUR children stared out to sea. They had all been so interested in exploring the exciting old castle that not one of them had noticed the sudden change in the weather.

Another rumble came. It sounded like a big dog growling in the sky. Tim heard it and growled back, sounding like a small roll of thunder himself.

'My goodness, we're in for it now,' said George, half-alarmed. 'We can't get back in time, that's certain. It's blowing up at top speed. Did you ever see such a change in the sky?'

The sky had been blue when they started. Now it was overcast, and the clouds seemed to hang very low indeed. They scudded along as if someone was chasing them – and the wind howled round in such a mournful way that Anne felt quite frightened.

'It's beginning to rain,' said Julian, feeling an enormous drop spatter on his outstretched hand. 'We had better shelter, hadn't we, George? We shall get wet through.'

'Yes, we will in a minute,' said George. 'I say, just look at these big waves coming! My word, it really *is* going to be a storm. Golly – what a flash of lightning!'

The waves were certainly beginning to run very high

indeed. It was amazing to see what a change had come over them. They swelled up, turned over as soon as they came to rocks, and then rushed up the beach of the island with a great roar.

'I think we'd better pull our boat up higher still,' said George suddenly. 'It's going to be a very bad storm indeed. Sometimes these sudden summer storms are worse than a winter one.'

She and Julian ran to the other side of the island where they had left the boat. It was a good thing they went, for great waves were already racing right up to it. The two children pulled the boat up almost to the top of the low cliff and George tied it to a stout gorse bush growing there.

By now the rain was simply pelting down, and George and Julian were soaked. 'I hope the others have been sensible enough to shelter in that room that has a roof and walls,' said George.

They were there all right, looking rather cold and scared. It was very dark there, for the only light came through the two slits of windows and the small doorway.

'Could we light a fire to make things a bit more cheerful?' said Julian, looking round. 'I wonder where we can find some nice dry sticks?'

Almost as if they were answering the question a small crowd of jackdaws cried out wildly as they circled in the storm. 'Chack, chack, chack!'

'Of course! There are plenty of sticks on the ground below the tower!' cried Julian. 'You know – where the jackdaws nest. They've dropped lots of sticks there.'

He dashed out into the rain and ran to the tower. He picked up an armful of sticks and ran back.

'Good,' said George. 'We'll be able to make a nice fire with those. Anyone got any paper to start it – or matches?'

'I've got some matches,' said Julian. 'But nobody's got paper.'

'Yes,' said Anne, suddenly. 'The sandwiches are wrapped in paper. Let's undo them, and then we can use the paper for the fire.'

'Good idea,' said George. So they undid the sandwiches, and put them neatly on a broken stone, rubbing it clean first. Then they built up a fire, with the paper underneath and the sticks arranged criss-cross on top.

It was fun when they lit the paper. It flared up and the sticks at once caught fire, for they were very old and dry. Soon there was a fine cracking fire going and the little ruined room was lit by dancing flames. It was very dark outside now, for the clouds hung almost low enough to touch the top of the castle tower! And how they raced by! The wind sent them off to the north-east, roaring behind them with a noise like the sea itself.

'I've never, never heard the sea making such an awful noise,' said Anne. 'Never! It really sounds as if it's shouting at the top of its voice.'

What with the howling of the wind and the crashing of the great waves all round the little island, the children could hardly hear themselves speak! They had to shout at one another.

'Let's have our dinner!' yelled Dick, who was feeling terribly hungry as usual. 'We can't do anything much while this storm lasts.'

'Yes, let's,' said Anne, looking longingly at the ham sandwiches. 'It will be fun to have a picnic round the fire in this dark old room. I wonder how long ago other people had a meal here? I wish I could see them.'

'Well, I don't,' said Dick, looking round half-scared as if he expected to see the old-time people walk in to share their picnic. 'It's quite a strange enough day without wanting things like that to happen.'

They all felt better when they were eating the sandwiches and drinking the ginger-beer. The fire flared up as more and more sticks caught, and gave out quite a pleasant warmth, for now that the wind had got up so strongly, the day had become cold.

'We'll take it in turns to fetch sticks,' said George. But Anne didn't want to go alone. She was trying her best not to show that she was afraid of the storm – but it was more than she could do to go out of the cosy room into the rain and thunder by herself.

Tim didn't seem to like the storm either. He sat close by George, his ears cocked, and growled whenever the thunder rumbled. The children fed him with titbits and he ate them eagerly, for he was hungry too.

All the children had four biscuits each. 'I think I shall give all mine to Tim,' said George. 'I didn't bring him any of his own biscuits, and he does seem so hungry.'

'No, don't do that,' said Julian. 'We'll each give him a biscuit – that will be four for him – and we'll still have three left each. That will be plenty for us.'

'You are really nice,' said George. 'Tim, don't you think they are nice?'

Tim did. He licked everyone and made them laugh. Then

he rolled over on his back and let Julian tickle him underneath.

The children fed the fire and finished their picnic. When it came to Julian's turn to get more sticks, he disappeared out of the room into the storm. He stood and looked around, the rain wetting his bare head.

The storm seemed to be right overhead now. The lightning flashed and the thunder crashed at the same moment. Julian was not a bit afraid of storms, but he couldn't help feeling rather over-awed at this one. It was so magnificent. The lightning tore the sky in half almost every minute, and the thunder crashed so loudly that it sounded almost as if mountains were falling down all around!

The sea's voice could be heard as soon as the thunder stopped – and that was magnificent to hear too. The spray flew so high into the air that it wetted Julian as he stood in the centre of the ruined castle.

'I really must see what the waves are like,' thought the boy. 'If the spray flies right over me here, they must be simply enormous!'

He made his way out of the castle and climbed up on to part of the ruined wall that had once run all round the castle. He stood up there, looking out to the open sea. And what a sight met his eyes!

The waves were like great walls of grey-green! They dashed over the rocks that lay all around the island, and spray flew from them, gleaming white in the stormy sky.

They rolled up to the island and dashed themselves against it with such terrific force that Julian could feel the wall beneath his feet tremble with the shock.

The boy looked out to sea, marvelling at the really great sight he saw. For half a moment he wondered if the sea might come right over the island itself? Then he knew that couldn't happen, for it would have happened before. He stared at the great waves coming in – and then he saw something rather strange.

There was something else out on the sea by the rocks besides the waves – something dark, something big, something that seemed to lurch out of the waves and settle down again. What could it be?

'It can't be a ship,' said Julian to himself, his heart beginning to beat fast as he strained his eyes to see through the rain and the spray. 'And yet it looks more like a ship than anything else. I hope it isn't a ship. There wouldn't be anyone saved from it on this dreadful day!'

He stood and watched for a while. The dark shape heaved into sight again and then sank away once more. Julian decided to go and tell the others. He ran back to the firelit room.

'George! Dick! There's something strange out on the rocks beyond the island!' he shouted, at the top of his voice. 'It looks like a ship – and yet it can't possibly be. Come and see!'

The others stared at him in surprise, and jumped to their feet. George hurriedly flung some more sticks on the fire to keep it going, and then she and the others quickly followed Julian out into the rain.

The storm seemed to be passing over a little now. The rain was not pelting down quite so hard. The thunder was rolling a little farther off, and the lightning did not flash so often. Julian led the way to the wall on which he had climbed to watch the sea.

Everyone climbed up to gaze out to sea. They saw a great tumbled, heaving mass of grey-green water, with waves rearing up everywhere. Their tops broke over the rocks and they rushed up to the island as if they would gobble it whole. Anne slipped her arm through Julian's. She felt rather small and scared.

'You're all right, Anne,' said Julian, loudly. 'Now just watch – you'll see something strange in a minute.'

They all watched. At first they saw nothing, for the waves reared up so high that they hid everything a little way out. Then suddenly George saw what Julian meant.

'Gracious!' she shouted. 'It *is* a ship! Yes, it is! Is it being wrecked? It's a big ship – not a sailing-boat, or fishing-smack!'

'Oh, is anyone in it?' wailed Anne.

The four children watched and Tim began to bark as he saw the strange dark shape lurching here and there in the enormous waves. The sea was bringing the ship nearer to shore.

'It will be dashed on to those rocks,' said Julian, suddenly. 'Look – there it goes!'

As he spoke there came a tremendous crashing, splintering sound, and the dark shape of the ship settled down on to the sharp teeth of the dangerous rocks on the south-west side of the island. It stayed there, shifting only slightly as the big waves ran under it and lifted it a little.

'She's stuck there,' said Julian. 'She won't move now.

The sea will soon be going down a bit, and then the ship will find herself held by those rocks.'

As he spoke, a ray of pale sunshine came wavering out between a gap in the thinning clouds. It was gone almost at once. 'Good!' said Dick, looking upwards. 'The sun will be out again soon. We can warm ourselves then and get dry – and maybe we can find out what that poor ship is. Oh, Julian – I do so hope there was nobody in it. I hope they've all taken to boats and got safely to land.'

The clouds thinned out a little more. The wind stopped roaring and dropped to a steady breeze. The sun shone out again for a longer time, and the children felt its welcome warmth. They all stared at the ship on the rocks. The sun shone on it and lighted it up.

'There's something odd about it somehow,' said Julian, slowly. 'Something awfully odd. I've never seen a ship quite like it.'

George was staring at it with a strange look in her eyes. She turned to face the three children, and they were astonished to see the bright gleam in her blue eyes. The girl looked almost too excited to speak.

'What is it?' asked Julian, catching hold of her hand.

'Julian – oh, Julian – it's my wreck!' she cried, in a high excited voice. 'Don't you see what's happened? The storm has lifted the ship up from the bottom of the sea, and has lodged it on those rocks. It's my wreck!'

The others saw at once that she was right. It was the old wrecked ship! No wonder it looked peculiar. No wonder it looked so old and dark, and such a strange shape. It was the wreck, lifted high out of its sleeping-place and put on the rocks nearby.

'George! We shall be able to row out and get into the wreck now!' shouted Julian. 'We shall be able to explore it from end to end. We may find the boxes of gold. Oh, *George*!'

CHAPTER SEVEN

Back to Kirrin Cottage

THE FOUR children were so tremendously surprised and excited that for a minute or two they didn't say a word. They just stared at the dark hulk of the old wreck, imagining what they might find. Then Julian clutched George's arm and pressed it tightly.

'Isn't this wonderful?' he said. 'Oh, George, isn't it an extraordinary thing to happen?'

Still George said nothing, but stared at the wreck, all kinds of thoughts racing through her mind. Then she turned to Julian.

'If only the wreck is still mine now it's thrown up like this!' she said. 'I don't know if wrecks belong to the queen or anyone, like lost treasure does. But after all, the ship did belong to our family. Nobody bothered much about it when it was down under the sea – but do you suppose people will still let me have it for my own now it's thrown up?'

'Well, don't let's tell anyone!' said Dick.

'Don't be silly,' said George. 'One of the fishermen is sure to see it when his ship goes slipping out of the bay. The news will soon be out.'

'Well, then, we'd better explore it thoroughly ourselves

before anyone else does!' said Dick, eagerly. 'No one knows about it yet. Only us. Can't we explore it as soon as the waves go down a bit?'

'We can't wade out to the rocks, if that's what you mean,' said George. 'We might get there by boat – but we couldn't possibly risk it now, while the waves are so big. They won't go down today, that's certain. The wind is still too strong.'

'Well, what about tomorrow morning, early?' said Julian. 'Before anyone has got to know about it? I bet if only *we* can get into the ship first, we can find anything there is to find!'

'Yes, I expect we could,' said George. 'I told you divers had been down and explored the ship as thoroughly as they could – but of course it is difficult to do that properly under water. We might find something they've missed. Oh, this is like a dream. I can't believe it's true that my old wreck has come up from the bottom of the sea like that!'

The sun was now properly out, and the children's wet clothes dried in its hot rays. They steamed in the sun, and even Tim's coat sent up a mist too. He didn't seem to like the wreck at all, and growled deeply at it.

'You are funny, Tim,' said George, patting him. 'It won't hurt you! What do you think it is?'

'He probably thinks it's a whale,' said Anne with a laugh. 'Oh, George – this is the most exciting day of my life! Oh, can't we possibly take the boat and see if we can get to the wreck?'

'No, we can't,' said George. 'I only wish we could. But it's quite impossible, Anne. For one thing, I don't think the wreck has quite settled down on the rocks yet, and maybe it won't till the tide has gone down. I can see it lifting a little still when an extra big wave comes. It would be dangerous to go into it yet. And for another thing I don't want my boat smashed to bits on the rocks, and us thrown into that wild water! That's what would happen. We must wait till tomorrow. It's a good idea to come early. I expect lots of grown-ups will think it's their business to explore it.'

The children watched the old wreck for a little time longer and then went all round the island again. It was certainly not very large, but it really was exciting, with its rocky little coast, its quiet inlet where their boat was, the ruined castle, the circling jackdaws, and the scampering rabbits everywhere.

'I do love it,' said Anne. 'I really do. It's just small enough to *feel* like an island. Most islands are too big to feel like islands. I mean, Britain is an island, but nobody living on it could possibly know it unless they were told. Now this island really *feels* like one because wherever you are you can see to the other side of it. I love it.'

George felt very happy. She had often been on her island before, but always alone except for Tim. She had always vowed that she never, never would take anyone there, because it would spoil her island for her. But it hadn't been spoilt. It had made it much nicer. For the first time George began to understand that sharing pleasures doubles their joy.

'We'll wait till the waves go down a bit then we'll go back home,' she said. 'I rather think there's some more rain coming, and we'll only get soaked through. We shan't be back till tea-time as it is, because we'll have a long pull against the out-going tide.'

All the children felt a little tired after the excitements of the morning. They said very little as they rowed home. Everyone took turns at rowing except Anne, who was not strong enough with the oars to row against the tide. They looked back at the island as they left it. They couldn't see the wreck because that was on the opposite side, facing the open sea.

'It's just as well it's there,' said Julian. 'No one can see it yet. Only when a boat goes out to fish will it be seen. And we shall be there as early as any boat goes out! I vote we get up at dawn.'

'Well, that's pretty early,' said George. 'Can you wake up? I'm often out at dawn, but you're not used to it.'

'Of course we can wake up,' said Julian. 'Well – here we are back at the beach again – and I'm jolly glad. My arms are awfully tired and I'm so hungry I could eat a whole larderful of things.'

'Woof,' said Tim, quite agreeing.

'I'll have to take Tim to Alf,' said George, jumping out of the boat. 'You get the boat in, Julian. I'll join you in a few minutes.'

It wasn't long before all four were sitting down to a good tea. Aunt Fanny had baked new scones for them, and had made a ginger cake with black treacle. It was dark brown and sticky to eat. The children finished it all up and said it was the nicest they had ever tasted.

'Did you have an exciting day?' asked their aunt.

'Oh yes!' said Anne, eagerly. 'The storm was grand. It threw up . . .'

Julian and Dick both kicked her under the table. George couldn't reach her or she would most certainly have kicked her too. Anne stared at the boys angrily, with tears in her eyes.

'Now what's the matter?' asked Aunt Fanny. 'Did somebody kick you, Anne? Well, really, this kicking under the table has got to stop. Poor Anne will be covered with bruises. What did the sea throw up, dear?'

'It threw up the most enormous waves,' said Anne, looking defiantly at the others. She knew they had thought she was going to say that the sea had thrown up the wreck – but they were wrong! They had kicked her for nothing!

'Sorry for kicking you, Anne,' said Julian. 'My foot sort of slipped.'

'So did mine,' said Dick. 'Yes, Aunt Fanny, it was a magnificent sight on the island. The waves raced up that little inlet, and we had to take our boat almost up to the top of the low cliff there.'

'I wasn't really afraid of the storm,' said Anne. 'In fact, I wasn't really as afraid of it as Ti . . .'

Everyone knew perfectly well that Anne was going to mention Timothy, and they all interrupted her at once, speaking very loudly. Julian managed to get a kick in again.

'Oooh!' said Anne.

'The rabbits were so tame,' said Julian, loudly.

'We watched the cormorants,' said Dick and George joined in too, talking at the same time.

'The jackdaws made such a noise, they said "Chack, chack, chack,' all the time.'

'Well, really, you sound like jackdaws yourselves, talking all at once like this!' said Aunt Fanny, with a laugh. 'Now, have you all finished? Very well, then, go and wash your sticky hands – yes, George, I know they're sticky, because *I* made that gingerbread, and you've had three slices! Then you had better go and play quietly in the other room, because it's raining, and you can't go out. But don't disturb your father, George. He's very busy.'

The children went to wash. 'Idiot!' said Julian to Anne. 'Nearly gave us away twice!'

'I didn't mean what you thought I meant the first time!' began Anne indignantly.

George interrupted her.

'I'd rather you gave the secret of the wreck away than my secret about Tim,' she said. 'I do think you've got a careless tongue.'

'Yes, I have,' said Anne, sorrowfully. 'I think I'd better not talk at meal-times any more. I love Tim so much I just can't seem to help wanting to talk about him.'

They all went to play in the other room. Julian turned a table upside down with a crash. 'We'll play at wrecks,' he said. 'This is the wreck. Now we're going to explore it.'

The door flew open and an angry, frowning face looked in. It was George's father!

'What was that noise?' he said. 'George! Did you overturn that table?'

'I did,' said Julian. 'I'm sorry. I quite forgot you were working.'

'Any more noise like that and I shall keep you all in tomorrow!' said his uncle Quentin. 'Georgina, keep your cousins quiet.'

The door shut and Uncle Quentin went out. The children looked at one another.

'Your father's awfully fierce, isn't he?' said Julian. 'I'm sorry I made that row. I didn't think.'

'We'd better do something really quiet,' said George. 'Or he'll keep his word – and we'll find ourselves inside tomorrow just when we want to explore the wreck.'

This was a terrible thought. Anne went to get one of her dolls to play with. She had managed to bring quite a number after all. Julian fetched a book. George took up a beautiful little boat she was carving out of a piece of wood. Dick lay back on a chair and thought of the exciting wreck. The rain poured down steadily, and everyone hoped it would have stopped by the morning.

'We'll have to be up most awfully early,' said Dick, yawning. 'What about going to bed in good time tonight? I'm tired with all that rowing.'

In the ordinary way none of the children liked going to bed early – but with such an exciting thing to look forward to, early bed seemed different that night.

'It will make the time go quickly,' said Anne, putting

down her doll. 'Shall we go now?'

'Whatever do you suppose Mother would say if we went just after tea?' said George. 'She'd think we were all ill. No, let's go after supper. We'll just say we're tired with rowing – which is perfectly true – and we'll get a good night's sleep, and be ready for our adventure tomorrow morning. And it *is* an adventure, you know. It isn't many people that have the chance of exploring an old, old wreck like that, which has always been at the bottom of the sea!'

So, by eight o'clock, all the children were in bed, rather to Aunt Fanny's surprise. Anne fell asleep at once. Julian and Dick were not long – but George lay awake for some time, thinking of her island, her wreck – and, of course, her beloved dog!

'I must take Tim too,' she thought, as she fell asleep. 'We can't leave old Tim out of this. He shall share in the adventure too!'

CHAPTER EIGHT

Exploring the wreck

JULIAN WOKE first the next morning. He awoke just as the sun was slipping over the horizon in the east, and filling the sky with gold. Julian stared at the ceiling for a moment, and then, in a rush, he remembered all that had happened the day before. He sat up straight in bed and whispered as loudly as he could.

'Dick! Wake up! We're going to see the wreck! Do wake up!'

Dick woke and grinned at Julian. A feeling of happiness crept over him. They were going on an adventure. He leapt out of bed and ran quietly to the girls' room. He opened the door. Both the girls were fast asleep, Anne curled up like a dormouse under the sheet.

Dick shook George and then dug Anne in the back. They awoke and sat up. 'Buck up!' whispered Dick. 'The sun is just rising. We'll have to hurry.'

George's blue eyes shone as she dressed. Anne skipped about quietly, finding her few clothes – just a bathing suit, jeans and jersey – and rubber shoes for her feet. It wasn't many minutes before they were all ready.

'Now, not a creak on the stairs – not a cough or a giggle!' warned Julian, as they stood together on the landing. Anne was a dreadful giggler, and had often given secret plans away by her sudden explosive choke. But this time the little girl was as solemn as the others, and as careful. They crept down the stairs and undid the little front door. Not a sound was made. They shut the door quietly and made their way down the garden path to the gate. The gate always creaked, so they climbed over it instead of opening it.

The sun was now shining brightly, though it was still low in the eastern sky. It felt warm already. The sky was so beautifully blue that Anne couldn't help feeling it had been freshly washed! 'It looks just as if it had come back from the laundry,' she told the others.

They squealed with laughter at her. She did say odd things at times. But they knew what she meant. The day had a lovely new feeling about it – the clouds were so pink in the bright blue sky, and the sea looked so smooth and fresh. It was impossible to imagine that it had been so rough the day before.

George got her boat. Then she went to get Tim, while the boys hauled the boat down to the sea. Alf, the fisher-boy, was surprised to see George so early. He was about to go with his father, fishing. He grinned at George.

'You going fishing, too?' he said to her. 'My, wasn't that a storm yesterday! I thought you'd be caught in it.'

'We were,' said George. 'Come on, Tim! Come on!'

Tim was very pleased to see George so early. He capered round her as she ran back to the others, almost tripping her up as she went. He leapt into the boat as soon as he saw it, and stood at the stern, his red tongue out, his tail wagging violently.

'I wonder his tail keeps on,' said Anne, looking at it. 'One day, Timothy, you'll wag it right off.'

They set off to the island. It was easy to row now, because the sea was so calm. They came to the island, and rowed around it to the other side.

And there was the wreck, piled high on some sharp rocks! It had settled down now and did not stir as waves slid under it. It lay a little to one side, and the broken mast, now shorter than before, stuck out at an angle.

'There she is,' said Julian, in excitement. 'Poor old wreck! I guess she's a bit more battered now. What a noise she made when she went crashing on to those rocks yesterday!'

'How do we get to her?' asked Anne, looking at the mass of ugly, sharp rocks all around. But George was not at all dismayed. She knew almost every inch of the coast around her little island. She pulled steadily at the oars and soon came near to the rocks in which the great wreck rested.

The children looked at the wreck from their boat. It was big, much bigger than they had imagined when they had peered at it from the top of the water. It was encrusted with shellfish of some kind, and strands of brown and green seaweed hung down. It smelt funny. It had great holes in its sides, showing where it had battered against rocks. There were holes in the deck too. Altogether, it looked a sad and forlorn old ship – but to the four children it was the most exciting thing in the whole world.

They rowed to the rocks on which the wreck lay. The tide washed over them. George took a look round.

'We'll tie our boat up to the wreck itself,' she said. 'And we'll get on to the deck quite easily by climbing up the side. Look, Julian! – throw this loop of rope over that broken bit of wood there, sticking out from the side.'

Julian did as he was told. The rope tightened and the boat was held in position. Then George clambered up the side of the wreck like a monkey. She was a marvel at climbing. Julian and Dick followed her, but Anne had to be helped up. Soon all four were standing on the slanting deck. It was slippery with seaweed, and the smell was very strong indeed. Anne didn't like it.

'Well, this was the deck,' said George, 'and that's where the men got up and down.' She pointed to a large hole. They went to it and looked down. The remains of an iron ladder were still there. George looked at it.

'I think it's still strong enough to hold us,' she said. 'I'll go first. Anyone got a torch? It looks pretty dark down there.'

Julian had a torch. He handed it to George. The children became rather quiet. It was mysterious somehow to look down into the dark inside of the big ship. What would they find? George switched on the torch and then swung herself down the ladder. The others followed.

The light from the torch showed a very strange sight. The under-parts of the ship were low-ceilinged, made of thick oak. The children had to bend their heads to get about. It seemed as if there were places that might have been cabins, though it was difficult to tell now, for everything was so battered, sea-drenched and seaweedy. The smell was really horrid, though it was mostly of drying seaweed.

The children slipped about on the seaweed as they went round the inside of the ship. It didn't seem so big inside after all. There was a big hold under the cabins, which the children saw by the light of their torch.

'That's where the boxes of gold would have been kept, I expect,' said Julian. But there was nothing in the hold except water and fish! The children couldn't go down because the water was too deep. One or two barrels floated in the water, but they had burst open and were quite empty.

'I expect they were water-barrels, or barrels of pork or biscuit,' said George. 'Let's go round the other part of the ship again – where the cabins are. Isn't it strange to see bunks there that sailors have slept in? – and look at that old wooden chair. Fancy it still being here after all these years! Look at the things on those hooks too – they are all rusty now, and covered with seaweedy stuff – but they must have been the cook's pans and dishes!'

It was a very weird trip round the old wreck. The children were all on the lookout for boxes which might contain bars of gold – but there didn't seem to be one single box of any kind anywhere!

They came to a rather bigger cabin than the others. It had a bunk in one corner, in which a large crab rested. An old bit of furniture looking rather like a table with two legs, all encrusted with greyish shells, lay against the bunk. Wooden shelves, festooned with grey-green seaweed, hung crookedly on the walls of the cabin.

'This must have been the captain's own cabin,' said Julian. 'It's the biggest one. Look, what's that in the corner?'

'An old cup!' said Anne, picking it up. 'And here's half of a saucer. I expect the captain was sitting here having a cup of tea when the ship went down.'

This made the children feel rather uneasy. It was dark and smelly in the little cabin, and the floor was wet and slippery to their feet. George began to feel that her wreck was really more pleasant sunk under the water than raised above it!

'Let's go,' she said, with a shiver. 'I don't like it much. It *is* exciting, I know – but it's a bit frightening too.'

They turned to go. Julian flashed his torch round the little cabin for the last time. He was about to switch it off and follow the others up to the deck above when he caught sight of something that made him stop. He flashed his torch on to it, and then called to the others.

'I say! Wait a bit. There's a cupboard here in the wall. Let's see if there's anything in it!'

The others turned back and looked. They saw what looked like a small cupboard set in level with the wall of the cabin. What had caught Julian's eye was the keyhole. There was no key there, though.

'There just *might* be something inside,' said Julian. He tried to prise open the wooden door with his fingers, but it wouldn't move. 'It's locked,' he said. 'Of course it would be!'

'I expect the lock is rotten by now,' said George, and she tried too. Then she took out her big strong pocket-knife and inserted it between the cupboard door and the cabin-wall. She forced back the blade – and the lock of the cupboard suddenly snapped! As she had said, it was quite rotten. The door swung open, and the children saw a shelf inside with a few curious things on it.

There was a wooden box, swollen with the wet sea-water in which it had lain for years. There were two or three things that looked like old, pulpy books. There was some sort of glass drinking-vessel, cracked in half – and two or three funny objects so spoilt by sea-water that no one could possibly say what they were.

'Nothing very interesting – except the box,' said Julian, and he picked it up. 'Anyway, I expect that whatever is inside is ruined. But we may as well try and open it.'

He and George tried their best to force the lock of the old wooden box. On the top of it were stamped initials – H.J.K.

'I expect those were the captain's initials,' said Dick.

'No, they were the initials of my great-great-great-grandfather!' said George, her eyes shining suddenly. 'I've heard all about him. His name was Henry John Kirrin. This was his ship, you know. This must have been his very private box in which he kept his old papers or diaries. Oh – we simply *must* open it!'

But it was quite impossible to force the lid up with the tools they had there. They soon gave it up, and Julian picked up the box to carry it to the boat.

'We'll open it at home,' he said, his voice sounding rather excited. 'We'll get a hammer or something, and get it open somehow. Oh, George – this really is a find!'

They all of them felt that they really had something mysterious in their possession. Was there anything inside the box – and if so, what would it be? They longed to get home and open it!

They went up on deck, climbing the old iron ladder. As soon as they got there they saw that others besides themselves had discovered that the wreck had been thrown up from the bottom of the sea!

'Golly! Half the fishing-smacks of the bay have discovered it!' cried Julian, looking round at the fishing-boats that had come as near as they dared to the wreck. The fishermen were looking at the wreck in wonder. When they saw the children on board they halloo-ed loudly.

'Ahoy there! What's that ship?'

'It's the old wreck!' yelled back Julian. 'She was thrown up yesterday in the storm!'

'Don't say any more,' said George, frowning. 'It's *my* wreck. I don't want sightseers on it!'

So no more was said, and the four children got into their boat and rowed home as fast as they could. It was past their breakfast-time. They might get a good scolding. They might even be sent to bed by George's fierce father – but what did they care? They had explored the wreck – and had come away with a box which *might* contain – well, if not bars of gold, one *small* bar, perhaps!

They did get a scolding. They had to go without half their breakfast, too, because Uncle Quentin said that children who came in so late didn't deserve hot bacon and eggs – only toast and marmalade. It was very sad.

They hid the box under the bed in the boys' room. Tim had been left with the fisher-boy – or rather, had been tied up in his backyard, for Alf had gone out fishing, and was even now gazing from his father's boat at the strange wreck.

'We can make a bit of money taking sightseers out to this wreck,' said Alf. And before the day was out scores of interested people had seen the old wreck from the decks of motor-boats and fishing-smacks.

George was furious about it. But she couldn't do anything. After all, as Julian said, anybody could have a look!

CHAPTER NINE

The box from the wreck

THE FIRST thing that the children did after breakfast was to fetch the precious box and take it out to the tool-shed in the garden. They were simply longing to force it open. All of them secretly felt certain that it would hold treasure of some sort.

Julian looked round for a tool. He found a chisel and decided that would be just the thing to force the box open. He tried, but the tool slipped and jabbed his fingers. Then he tried other things, but the box obstinately refused to open. The children stared at it crossly.

'I know what to do,' said Anne at last. 'Let's take it to the top of the house and throw it down to the ground. It would burst open then, I expect.'

The others thought over the idea. 'It might be worth trying,' said Julian. 'The only thing is it might break or spoil anything inside the box.'

But there didn't seem any other way to open the box, so Julian carried it up to the top of the house. He went to the attic and opened the window there. The others were down below, waiting. Julian hurled the box out of the window as violently as he could. It flew through the air and landed with a terrific crash on the crazy paving below.

At once the french window there opened and their Uncle Quentin came out like a bullet from a gun.

'Whatever are you doing?' he cried. 'Surely you aren't throwing things at each other out of the window? What's this on the ground?'

The children looked at the box. It had burst open and lay on the ground, showing a tin lining that was waterproof.

Whatever was in the box would not be spoilt! It would be quite dry!

Dick ran to pick it up.

'I said, what's this on the ground?' shouted his uncle and moved towards him.

'It's – it's something that belongs to us,' said Dick, going red.

'Well, I shall take it away from you,' said his uncle. 'Disturbing me like this! Give it to me. Where did you get it?'

Nobody answered. Uncle Quentin frowned till his glasses nearly fell off. 'Where did you get it?' he barked, glaring at poor Anne, who was nearest.

'Out of the wreck,' stammered the little girl, scared.

'Out of the *wreck*!' said her uncle, in surprise. 'The old wreck that was thrown up yesterday? I heard about that. Do you mean to say you've been in it?'

'Yes,' said Dick. Julian joined them at that moment, looking worried. It would be too awful if his uncle took the box just as they got it open. But that was exactly what he did do!

'Well, this box may contain something important,' he said, and he took it from Dick's hands. 'You've no right to go prying about in that old wreck. You might take something that mattered.'

'Well, it's my wreck,' said George, in a defiant tone. 'Please, Father, let us have the box. We'd just got it opened. We thought it might hold – a gold bar – or something like that!'

'A gold bar!' said her father, with a snort. 'What a baby you are! This small box would never hold a thing like that! It's much more likely to contain particulars of what happened to the bars! I have always thought that the gold was safely delivered somewhere – and that the ship, empty of its valuable cargo, got wrecked as it left the bay!'

'Oh, Father – please, please let us have our box,' begged George, almost in tears. She suddenly felt certain that it did contain papers that might tell them what had happened to the gold. But without another word her father turned and went into the house, carrying the box, burst open and cracked, its tin lining showing through under his arm.

Anne burst into tears. 'Don't blame me for telling him we got it from the wreck,' she sobbed. 'Please don't. He glared at me so. I just had to tell him.'

'All right, Baby,' said Julian, putting his arm round Anne. He looked furious. He thought it was very unfair of his uncle to take the box like that. 'Listen – I'm not going to stand this. We'll get hold of that box somehow and look into it. I'm sure your father won't bother himself with it, George – he'll start writing his book again and forget all about it. I'll wait my chance and slip into his study and get it, even if it means a telling off if I'm discovered!'

'Good!' said George. 'We'll all keep a watch and see if Father goes out.'

So they took it in turns to keep watch, but most annoyingly their Uncle Quentin remained in his study all the morning. Aunt Fanny was surprised to see one or two children always about the garden that day, instead of down on the beach.

'Why don't you all keep together and bathe or do something?' she said. 'Have you quarrelled with one another?'

'No,' said Dick. 'Of course not.' But he didn't say why they were in the garden!

'Doesn't your father *ever* go out?' he said to George, when it was her turn to keep watch. 'I don't think he leads a very healthy life.'

'Scientists never do,' said George, as if she knew all about them. 'But I tell you what – he may go to sleep this afternoon! He sometimes does!'

Julian was left behind in the garden that afternoon. He sat down under a tree and opened a book. Soon he heard a curious noise that made him look up. He knew at once what it was!

'That's Uncle Quentin snoring!' he said in excitement. 'It is! Oh – I wonder if I could possibly creep in at the french window and get our box!'

He stole to the windows and looked in. One was a little way open and Julian opened it a little more. He saw his uncle lying back in a comfortable armchair, his mouth a little open, his eyes closed, fast asleep! Every time he took a breath, he snored.

'Well, he really does look sound asleep,' thought the boy. 'And there's the box, just behind him, on that table. I'll risk it. I bet I'll get an awful telling off if I'm caught, but I can't help that!'

He stole in. His uncle still snored. He tiptoed by him to the table behind his uncle's chair. He took hold of the box.

And then a bit of the broken wood of the box fell to the floor with a thud! His uncle stirred in his chair and opened his eyes. Quick as lightning the boy crouched down behind his uncle's chair, hardly breathing.

'What's that?' he heard his uncle say. Julian didn't move. Then his uncle settled down again and shut his eyes. Soon there was the sound of his rhythmic snoring!

'Hurrah!' thought Julian. 'He's off again!'

Quietly he stood up, holding the box. On tiptoe he crept to the french window. He slipped out and ran softly down the garden path. He didn't think of hiding the box. All he wanted to do was to get to the other children and show them what he had done!

He ran to the beach where the others were lying in the sun. 'Hi!' he yelled. 'Hi! I've got it! I've got it!'

They all sat up with a jerk, thrilled to see the box in Julian's arms. They forgot all about the other people on the beach. Julian dropped down on the sand and grinned.

'Your father went to sleep,' he said to George. 'Tim, don't lick me like that! And George, I went in – and a bit of the box dropped on the floor – and it woke him up!'

'Golly!' said George. 'What happened?'

'I crouched down behind his chair till he went to sleep again,' said Julian. 'Then I fled. Now – let's see what's in here. I don't believe your father's even tried to see!'

He hadn't. The tin lining was intact. It had rusted with the years of lying in the wet, and the lid was so tightly fitted down that it was almost impossible to move it.

But once George began to work at it with her pocket-knife, scraping away the rust, it began to loosen – and in about a quarter of an hour it came off!

The children bent eagerly over it. Inside lay some old papers and a book of some kind with a black cover. Nothing else at all. No bar of gold. No treasure. Everyone felt a little bit disappointed.

'It's all quite dry,' said Julian, surprised. 'Not a bit damp. The tin lining kept everything perfect.'

He picked up the book and opened it. 'It's a diary your great-great-great-grandfather kept of the ship's voyages,' he said. 'I can hardly read the writing. It's so small and funny.'

George picked up one of the papers. It was made of thick parchment, quite yellow with age. She spread it out on the sand and looked at it. The others glanced at it too, but they couldn't make out what it was at all. It seemed to be a kind of map.

'Perhaps it's a map of some place he had to go to,' said Julian. But suddenly George's hands began to shake as she held the map, and her eyes gleamed brilliantly as she looked up at the others. She opened her mouth but didn't speak.

'What's the matter?' said Julian, curiously. 'What's up? Have you lost your tongue?'

George shook her head and then began to speak with a rush. 'Julian! Do you know what this is? It's a map of my old castle – of Kirrin Castle – when it wasn't a ruin. And it shows the dungeons! And look – just look what's written in this corner of the dungeons!'

She put a trembling finger on one part of the map. The others leaned over to see what it was – and, printed in old-fashioned letters was a curious word.

INGOTS

'Ingots!' said Anne, puzzled. 'What does that mean? I've never heard that word before.'

But the two boys had. 'Ingots!' cried Dick. 'Why – that must be the bars of gold. They were called ingots.'

'Most bars of metal are called ingots,' said Julian, going red with excitement. 'But as we know there is gold missing from that ship, then it really looks as if ingots here meant bars of gold. Oh golly! To think they may still be hidden somewhere under Kirrin Castle. George! George! Isn't it terribly, awfully exciting?'

George nodded. She was trembling all over with excitement. 'If only we could find it!' she whispered. 'If only we could!'

'We'll have a jolly good hunt for it,' said Julian. 'It will be awfully difficult because the castle is in ruins now, and so overgrown. But somehow or other we'll find those ingots. What a lovely word. Ingots! Ingots! Ingots!'

It sounded somehow more exciting than the word gold. Nobody spoke about gold any more. They talked about the ingots. Tim couldn't make out what the excitement was at all. He wagged his tail and tried hard to lick first one and then another of the children, but for once not one

of them paid any attention to him! He simply couldn't understand it, and after a while he went and sat down by himself with his back to the children, and his ears down.

'Oh, do look at poor Timothy!' said George. 'He can't understand your excitement. Tim! Tim, darling, it's all right, you're not in disgrace or anything. Oh, Tim, we've got the most wonderful secret in the whole world.'

Tim bounded up, his tail wagging, pleased to be taken notice of once more. He put his big paw on the precious map, and the four children shouted at him at once.

'Golly! We can't have that torn!' said Julian. Then he looked at the others and frowned. 'What are we going to do about the box?' he said. 'I mean – George's father will be sure to miss it, won't he? We'll have to give it back.'

'Well, can't we take out the map and keep it?' said Dick. 'He won't know it was there if he hasn't looked in the box. And it's pretty certain he hasn't. The other things don't matter much – they are only that old diary and a few letters.'

'To be on the safe side, let's take a copy of the map,' said Julian. 'Then we can put the real map back and replace the box.'

They all voted that a very good idea. They went back to Kirrin Cottage and traced out the map carefully. They did it in the tool-shed because they didn't want anyone to see them. It was a strange map. It was in three parts.

'This part shows the dungeons under the castle,' said Julian. 'And this shows a plan of the ground floor of the castle – and this shows the top part. My word, it was a fine place in those days! The dungeons run all under the castle. I bet they were pretty awful places. I wonder how people got down to them.'

'We'll have to study the map a bit more and see,' said George. 'It all looks rather muddled to us at present – but once we take the map over to the castle and study it there, we may be able to make out how to get down to the hidden dungeons. Ooooh! I don't expect any children ever had such an adventure as this.'

Julian put the traced map carefully into his jeans pocket. He didn't mean it to leave him. It was very precious. Then he put the real map back into the box and looked towards the house. 'What about putting it back now?' he said. 'Maybe your father is still asleep, George.'

But he wasn't. He was awake. Luckily he hadn't missed the box! He came into the dining-room to have tea with the family, and Julian took his chance. He muttered an excuse, slipped away from the table, and replaced the box on the table behind his uncle's chair!

He winked at the others when he came back. They felt relieved. They were all scared of Uncle Quentin, and were not at all anxious to be in his bad books. Anne didn't say one word during the whole of the meal. She was so terribly afraid she might give something away, either about Tim or the box. The others spoke very little too. While they were at tea the telephone rang and Aunt Fanny went to answer it.

She soon came back. 'It's for you, Quentin,' she said. 'Apparently the old wreck has caused quite a lot of excitement, and there are men from a London paper who want to ask you questions about it.'

'Tell them I'll see them at six,' said Uncle Quentin. The children looked at one another in alarm. They hoped that their uncle wouldn't show the box to the newspaper men. Then the secret of the hidden gold might come out!

'What a mercy we took a tracing of the map!' said Julian, after tea. 'But I'm jolly sorry now we left the real map in the box. Someone else may guess our secret!'

CHAPTER TEN

An astonishing offer

THE NEXT morning the papers were full of the extraordinary way in which the old wreck had been thrown up out of the sea. The newspaper men had got out of the children's uncle the tale of the wreck and the lost gold, and some of them even managed to land on Kirrin Island and take pictures of the old ruined castle.

George was furious. 'It's *my* castle!' she stormed to her mother. 'It's *my* island. You said it could be mine. You did, you did!'

'I know, George dear,' said her mother. 'But you really must be sensible. It can't hurt the island to be landed on, and it can't hurt the castle to be photographed.'

'But I don't want it to be,' said George, her face dark and sulky. 'It's mine. And the wreck is mine. You said so.'

'Well, I didn't know it was going to be thrown up like that,' said her mother. 'Do be sensible, George. What can it possibly matter if people go to look at the wreck? You can't stop them.'

George couldn't stop them, but that didn't make her any the less angry about it. The children were astonished at the interest that the cast-up wreck caused, and because of that, Kirrin Island became an object of great interest too.

Sightseers from the places all around came to see it, and the fishermen managed to find the little inlet and land the people there. George sobbed with rage, and Julian tried to comfort her.

'Listen, George! No one knows our secret yet. We'll wait till this excitement has died down, and then we'll go to Kirrin Castle and find the ingots.'

'If someone doesn't find them first,' said George, drying her eyes. She was furious with herself for crying, but she really couldn't help it.

'How could they?' said Julian. 'No one has seen inside the box yet! I'm going to wait my chance and get that map out before anyone sees it!'

But he didn't have a chance, because something dreadful happened. Uncle Quentin sold the old box to a man who bought antique things! He came out from his study, beaming, a day or two after the excitement began, and told Aunt Fanny and the children.

'I've struck a very good bargain with that man,' he said to his wife. 'You know that old tin-lined box from the wreck? Well, this fellow collects curious things like that, and he gave me a very good price for it. Very good indeed. More even that I could expect for the writing of my book! As soon as he saw the old map there and the old diary he said at once that he would buy the whole collection.'

The children stared at him in horror. The box was sold! Now someone would study that map and perhaps jump to what 'ingots' meant. The story of the lost gold had been put into all the newspapers now. Nobody could fail to know what the map showed if they studied it carefully.

The children did not dare to tell Uncle Quentin what they knew. It was true he was all smiles now, and was promising to buy them new shrimping-nets, and a raft for themselves – but he was such a changeable person. He might fly into a furious temper if he heard that Julian had taken the box and opened it himself, while his uncle was sleeping.

When they were alone the children discussed the whole matter. It seemed very serious indeed to them. They half-wondered if they should let Aunt Fanny into the secret – but it was such a precious secret, and so marvellous, that they felt they didn't want to give it away to anyone at all.

'Now listen!' said Julian, at last. 'We'll ask Aunt Fanny if we can go to Kirrin Island and spend a day or two there – sleep there at night too, I mean. That will give us a little time to poke round and see what we can find. The sightseers won't come after a day or two, I'm sure. Maybe we'll get in before anyone tumbles to our secret. After all, the man who bought the box may not even guess that the map shows Kirrin Castle.'

They felt more cheerful. It was so awful to do nothing. As soon as they had planned to act, they felt better. They decided to ask their aunt the next day if they might go and spend the weekend at the castle. The weather was gloriously fine, and it would be great fun. They could take plenty of food with them.

When they went to ask Aunt Fanny, Uncle Quentin was with her. He was all smiles again, and even clapped Julian on the back. 'Well!' he said. 'What's this deputation for?'

'We just wanted to ask Aunt Fanny something,' said Julian, politely. 'Aunt Fanny, as the weather is so fine, do you think you would let us go for the weekend to Kirrin Castle, please, and spend a day or two there on the island? You can't think how we would love to!'

'Well – what do you think, Quentin?' asked their aunt, turning to her husband.

'If they want to, they can,' said Uncle Quentin. 'They won't have a chance to, soon. My dears, we have had a marvellous offer for Kirrin Island! A man wants to buy it, rebuild the castle as a hotel, and make it into a proper holiday place! What do you think of that?'

All four children stared at the smiling man, shocked and horrified. Somebody was going to buy the island! Had their secret been discovered? Did the man want to buy the castle because he had read the map, and knew there was plenty of gold hidden there?

George gave a curious choke. Her eyes burned as if they were on fire. 'Mother! You can't sell my island! You can't sell my castle! I won't let them be sold.'

Her father frowned. 'Don't be silly, Georgina,' he said. 'It isn't really yours. You know that. It belongs to your mother, and naturally she would like to sell it if she could. We need the money very badly. You will be able to have a great many nice things once we sell the island.'

'I don't want nice things!' cried poor George. 'My castle and my island are the nicest things I could ever have. Mother! Mother! You know you said I could have them. You know you did! I believed you.'

'George dear, I did mean you to have them to play on, when I thought they couldn't possibly be worth anything,' said her mother, looking distressed. 'But now things are

different. Your father has been offered quite a good sum, far more than we ever thought of getting – and we really can't afford to turn it down.'

'So you only gave me the island when you thought it wasn't worth anything,' said George, her face white and angry. 'As soon as it is worth money you take it away again. I think that's horrid. It – it isn't honourable.'

'That's enough, Georgina,' said her father, angrily. 'Your mother is guided by me. You're only a child. Your mother didn't really mean what she said – it was only to please you. But you know well enough you will share in the money we get and have anything you want.'

'I won't touch a penny!' said George, in a low choking voice. 'You'll be sorry you sold it.'

The girl turned and stumbled out of the room. The others felt very sorry for her. They knew what she was feeling. She took things so very seriously. Julian thought she didn't understand grown-ups very well. It wasn't a bit of good fighting grown-ups. They could do exactly as they liked. If they wanted to take away George's island and castle, they could. If they wanted to sell it, they could! But what Uncle Quentin didn't know was the fact that there might be a store of gold ingots there! Julian stared at his uncle and wondered whether to warn him. Then he decided not to. There was just a chance that the four children could find the gold first!

'When are you selling the island, Uncle?' he asked quietly.

'The deeds will be signed in about a week's time,' was the answer. 'So if you really want to spend a day or two there, you'd better do so quickly, for after that you may not get permission from the new owners.'

'Was it the man who bought the old box who wants to buy the island?' asked Julian.

'Yes,' said his uncle. 'I was a little surprised myself, for I thought he was just a buyer of old things. It was astonishing to me that he should get the idea of buying the island to rebuild the castle as a hotel. Still, I dare say there will be big money in running a hotel there – very romantic, staying on a little island like that – people will like it. I'm no businessman myself, and I certainly shouldn't care to invest my money in a place like Kirrin Island. But I should think he knows what he is doing all right.'

'Yes, he certainly does,' thought Julian to himself, as he went out of the room with Dick and Anne. 'He's read that map – and has jumped to the same idea that we did – the store of hidden ingots is somewhere on that island – and he's going to get it! He doesn't want to build a hotel! He's after the treasure! I expect he's offered Uncle Quentin some silly low price that poor old uncle thinks is marvellous! Oh dear – this is a horrible thing to happen.'

He went to find George. She was in the tool-shed, looking quite green. She said she felt sick.

'It's only because you're so upset,' said Julian. He slipped his arm round her. For once George didn't push it away. She felt comforted. Tears came into her eyes, and she angrily tried to blink them away.

'Listen, George!' said Julian. 'We mustn't give up hope. We'll go to Kirrin Island tomorrow, and we'll do our very, very best to get down into the dungeons somehow and find the ingots. We'll jolly well stay there till we do. See? Now cheer up, because we'll want your help in planning everything. Thank goodness we took a tracing of the map.'

George cheered up a little. She still felt angry with her father and mother, but the thought of going to Kirrin Island for a day or two, and taking Timothy too, certainly seemed rather good.

'I do think my father and mother are unkind,' she said.

'Well, they're not really,' said Julian, wisely. 'After all, if they need money badly, they would be silly not to part with something they think is quite useless. And you know, your father did say you could have anything you want. I know what I would ask for, if I were you!'

'What?' asked George.

'Timothy, of course!' said Julian. And that made George smile and cheer up tremendously!

CHAPTER ELEVEN

Off to Kirrin Island

JULIAN AND George went to find Dick and Anne. They were waiting for them in the garden, looking rather upset. They were glad to see Julian and George and ran to meet them.

Anne took George's hands. 'I'm awfully sorry about your island, George,' she said.

'So am I,' said Dick. 'Bad luck, old girl – I mean, old boy!'

George managed to smile. 'I've been behaving like a girl,' she said, half-ashamed. 'But I did get an awful shock.'

Julian told the others what they had planned. 'We'll go tomorrow morning,' he said. 'We'll make out a list of all the things we shall need. Let's begin now.'

He took out a pencil and notebook. The others looked at him.

'Things to eat,' said Dick at once. 'Plenty because we'll be hungry.'

'Something to drink,' said George. 'There's no water on the island – though I believe there was a well or something, years ago, that went right down below the level of the sea, and was fresh water. Anyway, I've never found it.'

'Food,' wrote down Julian, 'and drink.' He looked at the others.

'Spades,' he said solemnly, and scribbled the word down.

Anne stared in surprise.

'What for?' she asked.

'Well, we'll want to dig about when we're hunting for a way down to the dungeons,' said Julian.

'Ropes,' said Dick. 'We may want those too.'

'And torches,' said George. 'It'll be dark in the dungeons.'

'Oooh!' said Anne, feeling a pleasant shiver go down her back at the thought. She had no idea what dungeons were like, but they sounded thrilling.

'Rugs,' said Dick. 'We'll be cold at night if we sleep in that little old room.'

Julian wrote them down. 'Mugs to drink from,' he said. 'And we'll take a few tools too – we may perhaps need them. You never know.'

At the end of half an hour they had quite a nice long list, and everyone felt pleased and excited. George was beginning to recover from her rage and disappointment. If she had been alone, and had brooded over everything, she would have been in an even worse sulk and temper – but somehow the others were so calm and sensible and cheerful. It was impossible to sulk for long if she was with them.

'I think I'd have been much nicer if I hadn't been on my

own so much,' thought George to herself, as she looked at Julian's bent head. 'Talking about things to other people does help a lot. They don't seem so dreadful then; they seem more bearable and ordinary. I like my three cousins awfully. I like them because they talk and laugh and are always cheerful and kind. I wish I were like them. I'm sulky and bad-tempered and fierce, and no wonder Father doesn't like me and scolds me so often. Mother's a dear, but I understand now why she says I am difficult. I'm different from my cousins – they're easy to understand, and everyone likes them. I'm glad they came. They are making me more like I ought to be.'

This was a long thought to think, and George looked very serious while she was thinking it. Julian looked up and caught her blue eyes fixed on him. He smiled.

'Penny for your thoughts!' he said.

'They're not worth a penny,' said George, going red. 'I was just thinking how nice you all are – and how I wished I could be like you.'

'You're an awfully nice person,' said Julian, surprisingly. 'You can't help being an only child. They're always a bit odd, you know, unless they're mighty careful. You're a most interesting person, I think.'

George flushed red again, and felt pleased. 'Let's go and take Timothy for a walk,' she said. 'He'll be wondering what's happened to us today.'

They all went off together, and Timothy greeted them at the top of his voice. They told him all about their plans for the next day, and he wagged his tail and looked up at them out of his soft brown eyes as if he understood every single word they said!

'He must feel pleased to think he's going to be with us for two or three days,' said Anne.

It was very exciting the next morning, setting off in the boat with all their things packed neatly at one end. Julian checked them all by reading out aloud from his list. It didn't seem as if they had forgotten anything.

'Got the map?' said Dick, suddenly.

Julian nodded.

'I put on clean jeans this morning,' he said, 'but you may be sure I remembered to pop the map into my pocket. Here it is!'

He took it out – and the wind at once blew it right out of his hands! It fell into the sea and bobbed there in the wind. All four children gave a cry of utter dismay. Their precious map!

'Quick! Row after it!' cried George, and swung the boat round. But someone was quicker than she was! Tim had seen the paper fly from Julian's hand, and had heard and understood the cries of dismay. With an enormous splash he leapt into the water and swam valiantly after the map.

He could swim well for a dog, for he was strong and powerful. He soon had the map in his mouth and was swimming back to the boat. The children thought he was simply marvellous!

George hauled him into the boat and took the map from his mouth. There was hardly the mark of his teeth on it he had carried it so carefully! It was wet, and the children looked anxiously at it to see if the tracing had been spoilt. But Julian had traced it very strongly, and it was quite all right. He placed it on a seat to dry, and told Dick to hold it there in the sun.

'That was a narrow squeak!' he said, and the others agreed.

George took the oars again, and they set off once more for the island, getting a perfect shower-bath from Timothy when he stood up and shook his wet coat. He was given a big biscuit as a reward, and crunched it up with great enjoyment.

George made her way through the reefs of rocks with a sure hand. It was marvellous to the others how she could slide the boat in between the dangerous rocks and never get a scratch. They thought she was really wonderful. She brought them safely to the little inlet, and they jumped out on to the sand. They pulled the boat high up, in case the tide came far up the tiny cove, and then began to unload their goods.

'We'll carry all the things to that little stone room,' said Julian. 'They will be safe there and won't get wet if it rains. I hope nobody comes to the island while we are here, George.'

'I shouldn't think they would,' said George. 'Father said it would be about a week before the deeds were signed, making over the island to that man. It won't be his till then. We've got a week, anyhow.'

'Well, we don't need to keep a watch in case anyone else arrives then,' said Julian, who had half thought that it would be a good idea to make someone stay on guard at the inlet, to give a warning to the others in case anyone else arrived. 'Come on! You take the spades, Dick. I'll take the food and drink with George. And Anne can take the little things.'

The food and drink were in a big box, for the children did not mean to starve while they were on the island! They had brought loaves of bread, butter, biscuits, jam, tins of fruit, ripe plums, bottles of ginger-beer, a kettle to make tea, and anything else they could think of! George and Julian staggered up the cliff with the heavy box. They had to put it down once or twice to give themselves a rest!

They put everything into the little room. Then they went back to get the collection of blankets and rugs from the boat. They arranged them in the corners of the little room, and thought that it would be most exciting to spend the night there.

'The two girls can sleep together on this pile of rugs,' said Julian. 'And we two boys will have this pile.'

George looked as if she didn't want to be put with Anne, and classed as a girl. But Anne didn't wish to sleep alone in her corner, and she looked so beseechingly at George that the bigger girl smiled at her and made no objection. Anne thought that George was getting nicer and nicer!

'Well, now we'll get down to business,' said Julian, and he pulled out his map. 'We must study this really carefully, and find out exactly under which spot the entrances to the dungeons are. Now – come around and let's do our best to find out! It's up to us to use our brains – and beat that man who's bought the island!'

They all bent over the traced map. It was quite dry now,

and the children looked at it earnestly. It was plain that in the old days the castle had been a very fine place.

'Now look,' said Julian, putting his finger on the plan of the dungeons. 'These seem to run all along under the castle – and here – and – here – are the marks that seem to be meant to represent steps or stairs.'

'Yes,' said George. 'I should think they are. Well, if so, there appear to be two ways of getting down into the dungeons. One lot of steps seems to begin somewhere near this little room – and the other seems to start under the tower there. And what do you suppose this thing is here, Julian?'

She put her finger on a round hole that was shown not only in the plan of the dungeons, but also in the plan of the ground floor of the castle.

'I can imagine what that is,' said Julian, puzzled. 'Oh yes, I know what it might be! You said there was an old well somewhere, do you remember? Well, that may be it, I should think. It would have to be very deep to get fresh water right under the sea – so it probably goes down through the dungeons too. Isn't this thrilling?'

Everyone thought it was. They felt happy and excited. There was something to discover – something they could and must discover within the next day or two.

They looked at one another. 'Well,' said Dick,' what are we going to start on? Shall we try to find the entrance to the dungeons – the one that seems to start round about this little room? For all we know there may be a big stone we can lift that opens above the dungeon steps!'

This was a thrilling thought, and the children jumped up at once. Julian folded up the precious map and put it into his pocket. He looked round. The stone floor of the little room was overgrown with creeping weeds. They must be cleared away before it was possible to see if there were any stones that looked as if they might be moved.

'We'd better set to work,' said Julian, and he picked up a spade. 'Let's clear away these weeds with our spades – scrape them off, look, like this – and then examine every single stone!'

They all picked up spades and soon the little stone room was full of a scraping sound as the four of them chiselled away at the close-growing weeds with their spades. It wasn't very difficult to get the stones clear of them, and the children worked with a will.

Tim got most excited about everything. He hadn't any idea at all what they were doing, but he joined in valiantly. He scraped away at the floor with his four paws, sending earth and plants flying high into the air!

'Hi, Tim!' said Julian, shaking a clod of earth out of his hair. 'You're being a bit too vigorous. My word, you'll send the stones flying into the air too, in a minute. George, isn't Tim marvellous the way he joins in everything?'

How they all worked! How they all longed to find the entrance to the underground dungeons! What a thrill that would be.

CHAPTER TWELVE

Exciting discoveries

SOON THE stones of the little room were clear of earth, sand and weeds. The children saw that they were all the same size – big and square, fitted well together. They went over them carefully with their torches, trying to find one that might move or lift.

'We should probably find one with an iron ring handle sunk into it,' said Julian. But they didn't. All the stones looked exactly the same. It was most disappointing.

Julian tried inserting his spade into the cracks between the various stones, to see if by any chance he could move one. But they couldn't be moved. It seemed as if they were all set in the solid ground. After about three hours' hard work the children sat down to eat a meal.

They were very hungry indeed, and felt glad to think there were so many things to eat. As they ate they discussed the problem they were trying to solve

'It looks as if the entrance to the dungeons was not under this little room after all,' said Julian. 'It's disappointing – but somehow I don't think now that the steps down to the dungeon started from here. Let's measure the map and see if we can make out exactly where the steps do start. It may be, of course, that the measurements aren't correct and won't be any help to us at all. But we can try.'

So they measured as best they could, to try and find out in exactly what place the dungeon steps seemed to begin. It was impossible to tell, for the plans of the three floors seemed to be done to different scales. Julian stared at the map, puzzled. It seemed rather hopeless. Surely they wouldn't have to hunt all over the ground floor of the castle! It would take ages.

'Look,' said George, suddenly, putting her finger on the hole that they all thought must be meant to represent the well. 'The entrance to the dungeons seems to be not very far off the well. If only we could find the well, we could hunt around a bit for the beginning of the dungeon steps. The well is shown in both maps. It seems to be somewhere about the middle of the castle.'

'That's a good idea of yours,' said Julian, pleased. 'Let's go out into the middle of the castle – we can more or less guess where the old well ought to be, because it definitely seems to be about the middle of the old yard out there.'

Out they all went into the sunshine. They felt very important and serious. It was marvellous to be looking for lost ingots of gold. They all felt perfectly certain that they really were somewhere beneath their feet. It didn't occur to any of the children that the treasure might not be there.

They stood in the ruined courtyard that had once been the centre of the castle. They paced out the middle of the yard and then stood there, looking around in vain for anything that might perhaps have been the opening of an old well. It was all so overgrown. Sand had blown in from the shore, and weeds and bushes of all kinds grew there. The stones that had once formed the floor of the big courtyard were now cracked and were no longer lying flat. Most of them were covered with sand or weeds.

'Look! There's a rabbit!' cried Dick, as a big sandy rabbit lolloped slowly across the yard. It disappeared into a hole on the other side. Then another rabbit appeared, sat up and looked at the children, and then vanished too. The children were thrilled. They had never seen such tame rabbits before.

A third rabbit appeared. It was a small one with absurdly big ears, and the tiniest white bob of a tail. It didn't even look at the children. It bounded about in a playful way, and then, to the children's enormous delight, it sat up on its hind legs, and began to wash its big ears, pulling down first one and then the other.

But this was too much for Timothy. He had watched the other two bound across the yard and then disappear without so much as barking at them. But to see this youngster actually sitting there washing its ears under his very nose was really too much for any dog. He gave an excited yelp and rushed full-tilt at the surprised rabbit.

For a moment the little thing didn't move. It had never been frightened or chased before, and it stared with big eyes at the rushing dog. Then it turned itself about and tore off at top speed, its white bobtail going up and down as it bounded away. It disappeared under a gorse bush near the children. Timothy went after it, vanishing under the big bush too.

Then a shower of sand and earth was thrown up as Tim tried to go down the hole after the rabbit and scraped and scrabbled with his strong front paws as fast as he could. He yelped and whined in excitement, not seeming to hear George's voice calling to him. He meant to get that rabbit! He went almost mad as he scraped at the hole, making it bigger and bigger.

'Tim! Do you hear me! Come out of there!' shouted George. 'You're not to chase the rabbits here. You know you mustn't. You're very naughty. Come out!'

But Tim didn't come out. He just went on and on scraping away madly. George went to fetch him. Just as she got up to the gorse bush the scraping suddenly stopped. There came a scared yelp – and no more noise was heard. George peered under the prickly bush in astonishment.

Tim had disappeared! He just simply wasn't there any more. There was the big rabbit-hole, made enormous by Tim – but there was no Tim.

'I say, Julian – Tim's gone,' said George in a scared voice. 'He surely can't have gone down the rabbit's hole, can he? I mean – he's such a big dog!'

The children crowded round the big gorse bush. There came the sound of a muffled whine from somewhere below it. Julian looked astonished.

'He *is* down the hole!' he said. 'How funny! I never

heard of a dog really going down a rabbit-hole before. How ever are we going to get him out?'

'We'll have to dig up the gorse bush, to begin with,' said George, in a determined voice. She would have dug up the whole of Kirrin Castle to get Tim back, that was certain! 'I can't have poor old Tim whining for help down there and not do what we can to help him.'

The bush was far too big and prickly to creep underneath. Julian was glad they had brought tools of all kinds. He went to fetch an axe. They had brought a small one with them and it would do to chop away the prickly branches and trunk of the gorse bush. The children slashed at it and soon the poor bush began to look a sorry sight.

It took a long time to destroy it, for it was prickly, sturdy and stout. Every child's hands were scratched by the time the bush had been reduced to a mere stump. Then they could see the hole quite well. Julian shone his torch down it.

He gave a shout of surprise. 'I know what's happened! The old well is here! The rabbits had a hole at the side of it – and Tim scraped away to make it bigger and uncovered a bit of the well-hole – and he's fallen down the well!'

'Oh no, oh no,' cried George, in panic. 'Oh Tim, Tim, are you all right?'

A distant whine came to their ears. Evidently Tim was there somewhere. The children looked at one another.

'Well, there's only one thing to do,' said Julian. 'We must get out spades now and dig out the hole of the well. Then maybe we can let a rope down or something and get Tim.'

They set to work with their spades. It was not really difficult to uncover the hole, which had been blocked only by the spreading roots of the big gorse bush, some fallen masonry, earth, sand and small stones. Apparently a big slab had fallen from part of the tower across the well-hole, and partly closed it. The weather and the growing gorse bush had done the rest.

It took all the children together to move the slab. Underneath was a very rotten wooden cover, which had plainly been used in the old days to protect the well. It had rotted so much that when Tim's weight had been pressed on it, it had given just there and made a hole for Tim to fall through.

Julian removed the old wooden cover and then the children could see down the well-hole. It was very deep and very dark. They could not possibly see the bottom. Julian took a stone and dropped it down. They all listened for the splash. But there was no splash. Either there was no longer any water there, or the well was too deep even to hear the splash!

'I think it's too deep for us to hear anything,' said Julian. 'Now – where's Tim?'

He shone his torch down – and there was Tim! Many years before a big slab had fallen down the well itself and had stuck a little way down, across the well-hole – and on this old cracked slab sat Tim, his big eyes staring up in fright. He simply could not imagine what had happened to him.

There was an old iron ladder fastened to the side of the well. George was on it before anyone else could get there! Down she went, not caring if the ladder held or not, and

reached Tim. Somehow she got him on to her shoulder and, holding him there with one hand, she climbed slowly up again. The other three hauled her out and Tim jumped round her, barking and licking for all he was worth!

'Well, Tim!' said Dick. 'You shouldn't chase rabbits – but you've certainly done us a good turn, because you've found the well for us! Now we've only got to look around a little to find the dungeon entrance!'

They set to work again to hunt for the dungeon entrance. They dug about with their spades under all the bushes. They pulled up crooked stones and dug their spades into the earth below, hoping that they might suddenly find them going through into space! It was really very thrilling.

And then Anne found the entrance! It was quite by accident. She was tired and sat down to rest. She lay on her front and scrabbled about in the sand. Suddenly her fingers touched something hard and cold in the sand. She uncovered it – and lo and behold, it was an iron ring! She gave a shout and the others looked up.

'There's a stone with an iron ring in it here!' yelled Anne, excitedly. They all rushed over to her. Julian dug about with his spade and uncovered the whole stone. Sure enough, it did have a ring in it – and rings are only set into stones that need to be moved! Surely this stone must be the one that covered the dungeon entrance!

All the children took turns at pulling on the iron ring, but the stone did not move. Then Julian tied two or three turns of rope through it and the four children put out their full strength and pulled for all they were worth.

The stone moved. The children distinctly felt it stir. 'All together again!' cried Julian. And all together they pulled. The stone stirred again and then suddenly gave way. It moved upwards – and the children fell over on top of one

another like a row of dominoes suddenly pushed down! Tim darted to the hole and barked madly down it as if all the rabbits of the world lived there!

Julian and George shot to their feet and rushed to the opening that the moved stone had disclosed. They stood there, looking downwards, their faces shining with delight. They *had* found the entrance to the dungeons! A steep flight of steps, cut out of the rock itself, led downwards into deep darkness.

'Come on!' cried Julian, snapping on his torch. 'We've found what we wanted! Now for the dungeons!'

The steps down were slippery. Tim darted down first, lost his footing and rolled down five or six steps, yelping with fright. Julian went after him, then George, then Dick and then Anne. They were all tremendously thrilled. Indeed, they quite expected to see piles of gold and all kinds of treasure everywhere around them!

It was dark down the steep flight of steps, and smelt very musty. Anne choked a little.

'I hope the air down here is all right,' said Julian. 'Sometimes it isn't good in these underground places. If anyone feels a bit funny they'd better say so and we'll go up into the open air again.'

But however funny they might feel, nobody would have said so. It was all far too exciting to worry about feeling strange.

The steps went down a long way. Then they came to an end. Julian stepped down from the last rock-stair and flashed his torch around. It was a weird sight that met his eyes.

The dungeons of Kirrin Castle were made out of the rock itself. Whether there were natural caves here, or whether they had been hollowed out by man the children could not tell. But certainly they were very mysterious, dark and full of echoing sounds. When Julian gave a sigh of excitement it fled into the rocky hollows and swelled out and echoed around as if it were a live thing. It gave all the children a very peculiar feeling.

'Isn't it strange?' said George, in a low voice. At once the echoes took up her words, and multiplied them and made them louder – and all the dungeon caves gave back the girl's words over and over again. 'Isn't it strange, ISN'T IT STRANGE, ISN'T IT STRANGE.'

Anne slipped her hand into Dick's. She felt scared. She didn't like the echoes at all. She knew they *were* only echoes – but they did sound exactly like the voices of scores of people hidden in the caves!

'Where do you suppose the ingots are?' said Dick. And at once the caves threw him back his words. INGOTS! INGOTS ARE! INGOTS ARE! ARE! ARE!

Julian laughed – and his laugh was split up into dozens of different laughs that came out of the dungeons and spun round the listening children. It really was the strangest thing.

'Come on,' said Julian. 'Maybe the echoes won't be so bad a little farther in.'

'FARTHER IN, said the echoes at once. 'FARTHER IN!'

They moved away from the end of the rocky steps and explored the nearby dungeons. They were really only rocky cellars stretching under the castle. Maybe wretched prisoners had been kept there many, many years before, but mostly they had been used for storing things.

'I wonder which dungeons was used for storing the ingots,' said Julian. He stopped and took the map out of his pocket. He flashed his torch on to it. But although it showed him quite plainly the dungeon where INGOTS were marked, he had no idea at all of the right direction.

'I say – look – there's a door here, shutting off the next dungeon!' suddenly cried Dick. 'I bet this is the dungeon we're looking for! I bet there are ingots in here!'

CHAPTER THIRTEEN

Down in the dungeons

FOUR TORCHES were flashed on to the wooden door. It was big and stout, studded with great iron nails. Julian gave a whoop of delight and rushed to it. He felt certain that behind it was the dungeon used for storing things.

But the door was fast shut. No amount of pushing or pulling would open it. It had a great keyhole – but no key there! The four children stared in exasperation at the door. Bother it! Just as they really thought they were near the ingots, this door wouldn't open!

'We'll fetch the axe,' said Julian, suddenly. 'We may be able to chop round the keyhole and smash the lock.'

'That's a good idea!' said George, delighted. 'Come on back!'

They left the big door, and tried to get back the way they had come. But the dungeons were so big and so rambling that they lost their way. They stumbled over old broken barrels, rotting wood, empty bottles and many other things as they tried to find their way back to the big flight of rock-steps.

'This is sickening!' said Julian, at last. 'I simply haven't any idea at all where the entrance is. We keep on going into one dungeon after another, and one passage after another, and they all seem to be exactly the same – dark and smelly and mysterious.'

'Suppose we have to stay here all the rest of our lives!' said Anne, gloomily.

'Idiot!' said Dick, taking her hand. 'We shall soon find the way out. Hallo! – what's this?'

They all stopped. They had come to what looked like a chimney shaft of brick, stretching down from the roof of the dungeon to the floor. Julian flashed his torch on to it. He was puzzled.

'I know what it is!' said George, suddenly. 'It's the well, of course! You remember it was shown in the plan of the dungeons, as well as in the plan of the ground floor. Well, that's the shaft of the well going down and down. I wonder if there's any opening in it just here – so that water could be taken into the dungeons as well as up to the ground floor.'

They went to see. On the other side of the well-shaft was a small opening big enough for one child at a time to put his head and shoulders through and look down. They shone their torches down and up. The well was so deep that it was still impossible to see the bottom of it. Julian dropped a stone down again, but there was no sound of either a thud or a splash. He looked upwards, and could see the faint gleam of daylight that slid round the broken slab of stone lying a little way down the shaft – the slab on which Tim had sat, waiting to be rescued.

'Yes,' he said, 'this is the well all right. Isn't it weird?

Well – now we've found the well we know that the entrance to the dungeons isn't very far off!'

That cheered them all up tremendously. They held hands and hunted around in the dark, their torches making bright beams of light here and there.

Anne gave a screech of excitement. 'Here's the entrance! It must be, because I can see faint daylight coming down!'

The children rounded a corner and sure enough, there was the steep, rocky flight of steps leading upwards. Julian took a quick look round so that he might know the way to go when they came down again. He didn't feel at all certain that he would find the wooden door!

They all went up into the sunshine. It was delicious to feel the warmth on their heads and shoulders after the cold air down in the dungeons. Julian looked at his watch and gave a loud exclamation.

'It's half past six! *Half past six!* No wonder I feel hungry. We haven't had any tea. We've been working, and wandering about those dungeons for hours.'

'Well, let's have a kind of tea-supper before we do anything else,' said Dick. 'I don't feel as if I've had anything to eat for about twelve months.'

'Well, considering you ate about twice as much as anyone else at dinner-time,' began Julian, indignantly. Then he grinned. 'I feel the same as you,' he said. 'Come on! – let's get a really good meal. George, what about boiling a kettle and making some cocoa, or something? I feel cold after all that time underground.'

It was fun boiling the kettle on a fire of dry sticks. It was lovely to lie about in the warmth of the evening sun and munch bread and cheese and enjoy cake and biscuits. They all enjoyed themselves thoroughly. Tim had a good meal too. He hadn't very much liked being underground, and had followed the others very closely indeed, his tail well down. He had been very frightened, too, of the curious echoes here and there.

Once he had barked, and it had seemed to Tim as if the whole of the dungeons were full of other dogs, all barking far more loudly than he could. He hadn't even dared to whine after that! But now he was happy again, eating the tit-bits that the children gave him, and licking George whenever he was near her.

It was past eight o'clock by the time that the children had finished their meal and tidied up. Julian looked at the others. The sun was sinking, and the day was no longer so warm.

'Well,' he said, 'I don't know what you feel. But I don't somehow want to go down into those dungeons again today, not even for the sake of smashing in that door with the axe and opening it! I'm tired – and I don't like the thought of losing my way in those dungeons at night.'

The others heartily agreed with him, especially Anne, who had secretly been dreading going down again with the night coming on. The little girl was almost asleep; she was so tired out with hard work and excitement.

'Come on, Anne!' said George, pulling her to her feet.

'Bed for you. We'll cuddle up together in the rugs on the floor of that little room – and in the morning when we wake we'll be simply thrilled to think of opening that big wooden door.'

All four children, with Tim close behind, went off to the little stone room. They curled up on their piles of rugs, and Tim crept in with George and Anne. He lay down on them, and felt so heavy that Anne had to push him off her legs.

He sat himself down on her again, and she groaned, half-asleep. Tim wagged his tail and thumped it hard against her ankles. Then George pulled him on to her own legs and lay there, feeling him breathe. She was very happy. She was spending the night on her island. They had almost found the ingots, she was sure. She had Tim with her, actually sleeping on her rugs. Perhaps everything would come right after all – somehow.

She fell asleep. The children felt perfectly safe with Tim on guard. They slept peacefully until the morning, when Tim saw a rabbit through the broken archway leading to the little room, and sped away to chase it. He awoke George as he got up from the rugs, and she sat up and rubbed her eyes.

'Wake up!' she cried to the others. 'Wake up, all of you! It's morning! And we're on the island!'

They all awoke. It was really thrilling to sit up and remember everything. Julian thought of the big wooden door at once. He would soon smash it in with his axe, he felt sure. And then what would they find?

They had breakfast, and ate just as much as ever. Then Julian picked up the axe they had brought and took everyone to the flight of steps. Tim went too, wagging his tail, but not really feeling very pleased at the thought of going down into the strange places where other dogs seemed to bark, and yet were not to be found. Poor Tim would never understand echoes!

They all went down underground again. And then, of course, they couldn't find the way to the wooden door! It was most tiresome.

'We shall lose our way all over again,' said George, desperately. 'These dungeons are about the most rambling spread-out maze of underground caves I've ever known! We shall lose the entrance again too!'

Julian had a bright idea. He had a piece of white chalk in his pocket, and he took it out. He went back to the steps, and marked the wall there. Then he began to put chalk-marks along the passages as they walked in the musty darkness. They came to the well, and Julian was pleased.

'Now,' he said, 'whenever we come to the well we shall at least be able to find the way back to the steps, because we can follow my chalk-marks. Now the thing is – which is the way next? We'll try and find it and I'll put chalk-marks along the walls here and there – but if we go the wrong way and have to come back, we'll rub out the marks, and start again from the well another way.'

This was really a very good idea. They did go the wrong way, and had to come back, rubbing out Julian's marks.

They reached the well, and set off in the opposite direction. And this time they did find the wooden door!

There it was, stout and sturdy, its old iron nails rusty and red. The children stared at it in delight. Julian lifted his axe.

Crash! He drove it into the wood and round about the keyhole. But the wood was still strong, and the axe only went in an inch or two. Julian drove it in once more. The axe hit one of the big nails and slipped a little to one side. A big splinter of wood flew out – and struck poor Dick on the cheek!

He gave a yell of pain. Julian jumped in alarm, and turned to look at him. Dick's cheek was pouring with blood!

'Something flew out of the door and hit me,' said poor Dick. 'It's a splinter, or something.'

'Golly!' said Julian, and he shone his torch on to Dick. 'Can you bear it a moment if I pull the splinter out? It's a big one, and it's still sticking into your poor cheek.'

But Dick pulled it out himself. He made a face with the pain, and then turned very white.

'You'd better get up into the open air for a bit,' said Julian. 'And we'll have to bathe your cheek and stop it bleeding somehow. Anne's got a clean hanky. We'll bathe it and dab it with that. We brought some water with us, luckily.'

'I'll go with Dick,' said Anne. 'You stay here with George. There's no need for us all to go.'

But Julian thought he would like to see Dick safely up into the open air first, and then he could leave him with Anne while he went back to George and went on with the smashing down of the door. He handed the axe to George.

'You can do a bit of chopping while I'm gone,' he said. 'It will take some time to smash that big door in. You get on with it – and I'll be down in a few minutes again. We can easily find the way to the entrance because we've only got to follow my chalk-marks.'

'Right!' said George, and she took the axe. 'Poor old Dick – you do look a sight.'

Leaving George behind with Tim, valiantly attacking the big door, Julian took Dick and Anne up to the open air. Anne dipped her hanky into the kettle of water and dabbed Dick's cheek gently. It was bleeding very much, as cheeks do, but the wound was not really very bad. Dick's colour soon came back, and he wanted to go down into the dungeons again.

'No, you'd better lie down on your back for a little,' said Julian. 'I know that's good for nose-bleeding – and maybe it's good for cheek-bleeding too. What about Anne and you going out on the rocks over there, where you can see the wreck, and staying there for half an hour or so? Come on – I'll take you both there, and leave you for a bit. You'd better not get up till your cheek's stopped bleeding, old boy.'

Julian took the two out of the castle yard and out on to the rocks on the side of the island that faced the open sea. The dark hulk of the old wreck was still there on the rocks. Dick lay down on his back and stared up into the sky, hoping that his cheek would soon stop bleeding. He didn't want to miss any of the fun!

Anne took his hand. She was very upset at the little accident, and although she didn't want to miss the fun either, she meant to stay with Dick till he felt better. Julian sat down beside them for a minute or two. Then he went back to the rocky steps and disappeared down them. He followed his chalk-marks, and soon came to where George was attacking the door.

She had smashed it well round the lock – but it simply would *not* give way. Julian took the axe from her and drove it hard into the wood.

After a blow or two something seemed to happen to the lock. It became loose, and hung a little sideways. Julian put down his axe.

'I think somehow that we can open the door now,' he said, in an excited voice. 'Get out of the way, Tim, old fellow. Now then, push, George!'

They both pushed – and the lock gave way with a grating noise. The big door opened creakingly, and the two children went inside, flashing their torches in excitement.

The room was not much more than a cave, hollowed out of the rock – but in it was something quite different from the old barrels and boxes the children had found before. At the back, in untidy piles, were curious, brick-shaped things of dull yellow-brown metal. Julian picked one up.

'George!' he cried. 'The ingots! These are real gold!' Oh,

I know they don't look like it – but they are, all the same. George, oh, George, there's a small fortune here in this cellar – and it's yours! We've found it at last!'

CHAPTER FOURTEEN

Prisoners!

GEORGE COULDN'T say a word. She just stood there, staring at the pile of ingots, holding one in her hands. She could hardly believe that these strange brick-shaped things were really gold. Her heart thumped fast. What a wonderful, marvellous find!

Suddenly Tim began to bark loudly. He stood with his back to the children, his nose towards the door – and how he barked!

'Shut up, Tim!' said Julian. 'What can you hear? Is it the others coming back?'

He went to the door and yelled down the passage outside. 'Dick! Anne! Is it you? Come quickly, because we've found the ingots! We've found them! Hurry! Hurry!'

Tim stopped barking and began to growl. George looked puzzled. 'Whatever *can* be the matter with Tim?' she said. 'He surely can't be growling at Dick and Anne.'

Then both children got a most tremendous shock – for a man's voice came booming down the dark passage, making strange echoes all around.

'Who is here? Who is down here?'

George clutched Julian in fright. Tim went on growling, all the hairs on his neck standing up straight. 'Do be quiet,

Tim!' whispered George, snapping off her torch. But Tim simply would *not* be quiet. He went on growling as if he were a small thunderstorm.

The children saw the beam of a powerful torchlight coming round the corner of the dungeon passage. Then the light picked them out, and the holder of the torch came to a surprised stop.

'Well, well, well!' said a voice. 'Look who's here! Two children in the dungeons of my castle.'

'What do you mean, *your* castle!' cried George.

'Well, my dear little girl, it *is* my castle, because I'm in the process of buying it,' said the voice. Then another voice spoke, more gruffly.

'What are you doing down here? What did you mean when you shouted out "Dick" and "Anne", and said you had found the ingots? What ingots?'

'Don't answer,' whispered Julian to George. But the echoes took his words and made them very loud in the passage. 'DON'T ANSWER! DON'T ANSWER!'

'Oh, so you won't answer,' said the second man, and he stepped towards the children. Tim bared his teeth, but the man didn't seem at all frightened of him. The man went to the door and flashed his torch inside the dungeon. He gave a long whistle of surprise.

'Jake! Look here!' he said. 'You were right. The gold's here all right. And how easy to take away! All in ingots – my word, this is the most amazing thing we've ever struck.'

'This gold is mine,' said George, in a fury. 'This island and the castle belong to my mother – and so does anything found here. This gold was brought here and stored by my great-great-great-grandfather before his ship got wrecked. It's not yours, and never will be. As soon as I get back home I shall tell my father and mother what we've found – and then you may be sure you won't be able to buy the castle or the island! You were very clever, finding out from the map in the old box about the gold – but just not clever enough for us. We found it first!'

The men listened in silence to George's clear and angry voice. One of them laughed. 'You're only a child,' he said. 'You surely don't think you can keep us from getting our way? We're going to buy this island – and everything in it – and we shall take the gold when the deeds are signed. And if by any chance we couldn't buy the island, we'd take the gold just the same. It would be easy enough to bring a ship here and transfer the ingots from here by boat to the ship. Don't worry – we shall get what we want all right.'

'You will not!' said George, and she stepped out of the door. 'I'm going straight home now – and I'll tell my father all you've said.'

'My dear little girl, you are not going home,' said the first man, putting his hands on George and forcing her back into the dungeon. 'And, by the way, unless you want me to shoot this unpleasant dog of yours, call him off, will you?'

George saw, to her dismay, that the man had a shining revolver in his hand. In fright she caught hold of Tim's collar and pulled him to her. 'Be quiet, Tim,' she said. 'It's all right.'

But Tim knew quite well that it wasn't all right. Something was very wrong. He went on growling fiercely.

'Now listen to me,' said the man, after he had had a hurried talk with his companion. 'If you are going to be sensible, nothing unpleasant will happen to you. But if you

want to be obstinate, you'll be very sorry. What we are going to do is this – we're going off in our motor-boat, leaving you nicely locked up here – and we're going to get a ship and come back for the gold. We don't think it's worthwhile buying the island now we know where the ingots are.'

'And you are going to write a note to your companions

above, telling them you've found the gold and they are to come down and look for it,' said the other man. 'Then we shall lock up all of you in this dungeon, with the ingots to play with, leaving you food and drink till we come back. Now then – here is a pencil. Write a note to Dick and Anne, whoever they are, and send your dog up with it. Come on.'

'I won't,' said George, her face furious. 'I won't. You can't make me do a thing like that. I won't get poor Dick and Anne down here to be made prisoners. And I won't let you have my gold, just when I've discovered it.'

'We shall shoot your dog if you don't do as you're told,' said the first man, suddenly. George's heart sank down and she felt cold and terrified.

'No, no,' she said in a low, desperate voice.

'Well, write the note then,' said the man, offering her a pencil and paper. 'Go on. I'll tell you what to say.'

'I can't!' sobbed George. 'I don't want to get Dick and Anne down here to be made prisoners.'

'All right – I'll shoot the dog then,' said the man, in a cold voice and he levelled his revolver at poor Tim. George threw her arms round her dog and gave a scream.

'No, no! I'll write the note. Don't shoot Tim, don't shoot him!'

The girl took the paper and pencil in a shaking hand and looked at the man. 'Write this,' he ordered. ' "Dear Dick and Anne. We've found the gold. Come on down at once and see it." Then sign your name, whatever it is.'

George wrote what the man had said. Then she signed her name. But instead of writing 'George' she put 'Georgina'. She knew that the others would feel certain she would never sign herself that – and she hoped it would warn them that something odd was up. The man took the note and fastened it to Tim's collar. The dog growled all the time, but George kept telling him not to bite.

'Now tell him to go and find your friends,' said the man.

'Find Dick and Anne,' commanded George. 'Go on, Tim. Find Dick and Anne. Give them the note.'

Tim did not want to leave George, but there was something very urgent in her voice. He took one last look at his mistress, gave her hand a lick and sped off down the passage. He knew the way now. Up the rocky steps he bounded and into the open air. He stopped in the old yard, sniffing. Where were Dick and Anne?

He smelt their footsteps and ran off, his nose to the ground. He soon found the two children out on the rocks. Dick was feeling better now and was sitting up. His cheek had almost stopped bleeding.

'Hallo,' he said in surprise, when he saw Tim. 'Here's Timothy! Why, Tim, old chap, why have you come to see us? Did you get tired of being underground in the dark?'

'Look, Dick – he's got something twisted into his collar,' said Anne, her sharp eyes seeing the paper there. 'It's a note. I expect it's from the others, telling us to go down. Isn't Tim clever to bring it?'

Dick took the paper from Tim's collar. He undid it and read it.

'"Dear Dick and Anne,"' he read out aloud. '"We've found the gold. Come on down at once and see it. Georgina."'

'Oooh!' said Anne, her eyes shining. 'They've found it. Oh, Dick – are you well enough to come now? Let's hurry.'

But Dick did not get up from the rocks. He sat and stared at the note, puzzled.

'What's the matter?' said Anne, impatiently.

'Well, don't you think it's funny that George should suddenly sign herself "Georgina"?' said Dick, slowly. 'You know how she hates being a girl, and having a girl's name. You know how she will never answer if anyone calls her Georgina. And yet in this note she signs herself by the name she hates. It does seem a bit funny to me. Almost as if it's a kind of warning that there's something wrong.'

'Oh, don't be so silly, Dick,' said Anne. 'What could be wrong? Do come on.'

'Anne, I'd like to pop over to that inlet of ours to make sure there's no one else come to the island,' said Dick. 'You stay here.'

But Anne didn't want to stay there alone. She ran round the coast with Dick, telling him all the time that she thought he was very silly.

But when they came to the little harbour, they saw that there was another boat there, as well as their own. It was a motor-boat! Someone else *was* on the island!

'Look,' said Dick, in a whisper. 'There *is* someone else here. And I bet it's the men who want to buy the island. I bet they've read that old map and know there's gold here. And they've found George and Julian and want to get us all together down in the dungeons so that they can keep us safe till they've stolen the gold. That's why they made George send us that note – but she signed it with a name she never uses – to warn us! Now – we must think hard. What are we going to do?'

CHAPTER FIFTEEN

Dick to the rescue!

DICK CAUGHT hold of Anne's hand and pulled her quickly away from the cove. He was afraid that whoever had come to the island might be somewhere about and see them. The boy took Anne to the little stone room where their things were and they sat down in a corner.

'Whoever has come has discovered Julian and George smashing in that door, I should think,' said Dick, in a whisper. 'I simply can't think what to do. We mustn't go down into the dungeons or we'll most certainly be caught. Hallo – where's Tim off to?'

The dog had kept with them for a while but now he ran off to the entrance of the dungeons. He disappeared down the steps. He meant to get back to George, for he knew she was in danger. Dick and Anne stared after him. They had felt comforted while he was there, and now they were sorry he had gone.

They really didn't know what to do. Then Anne had an idea. 'I know!' she said. 'We'll row back to the land in our boat and get help.'

'I'd thought of that,' said Dick, gloomily. 'But you know perfectly well we'd never know the way in and out of those awful rocks. We'd wreck the boat. I'm sure we're not strong enough either to row all the way back. Oh, dear – I do wish we could think what to do.'

They didn't need to puzzle their brains long. The men came up out of the dungeons and began to hunt for the two children! They had seen Tim when he came back and had found the note gone. So they knew the two children had taken it – and they couldn't imagine why they had not obeyed what George had said in the note, and come down to the dungeons!

Dick heard their voices. He clutched hold of Anne to make her keep quiet. He saw through the broken archway that the men were going in the opposite direction.

'Anne! I know where we can hide!' said the boy, excitedly. 'Down the old well! We can climb down the ladder a little way and hide there. I'm sure no one would ever look there!'

Anne didn't at all want to climb down the well even a little way. But Dick pulled her to her feet and hurried her off to the middle of the old courtyard. The men were hunting around the other side of the castle. There was just time to climb in. Dick slipped aside the old wooden cover of the well and helped Anne down the ladder. She was very scared. Then the boy climbed down himself and slipped the wooden cover back again over his head, as best he could.

The old stone slab that Tim had sat on when he fell down the well was still there. Dick climbed down to it and tested it. It was immovable.

'It's safe for you to sit on, Anne, if you don't want to keep clinging to the ladder,' he whispered. So Anne sat shivering on the stone slab across the well-shaft, waiting to see if they were discovered or not. They kept hearing the voices of the men, now near at hand and now far-off. Then the men began to shout for them.

'Dick! Anne! The others want you! Where are you? We've exciting news for you.'

'Well, why don't they let Julian and George come up and tell us then?' whispered Dick. 'There's something wrong, I know there is. I do wish we could get to Julian and George and find out what has happened.'

The two men came into the courtyard. They were angry. 'Where have those kids got to?' said Jake. 'Their boat is still in the cove, so they haven't got away. They must be hiding somewhere. We can't wait all day for them.'

'Well, let's take some food and drink down to the two we've locked up,' said the other man. 'There's plenty in that little stone room. I suppose it's a store the children brought over. We'll leave half in the room so that the other two kids can have it. And we'll take their boat with us so that they can't escape.'

'Right,' said Jake. 'The thing to do is to get the gold away as quickly as possible, and make sure the children are prisoners here until we've made a safe getaway. We won't bother any more about trying to buy the island. After all, it was only the idea of getting the ingots that put us up to the idea of getting Kirrin Castle and the island.'

'Well – come on,' said his companion. 'We will take the food down now, and not bother about the other kids. You stay here and see if you can spot them while I go down.'

Dick and Anne hardly dared to breathe when they heard all this. How they hoped that the men wouldn't think of looking down the well! They heard one man walk to the little stone room. It was plain that he was getting food and drink to take down to the two prisoners in the dungeons below. The other man stayed in the courtyard, whistling softly.

After what seemed a very long time to the hidden children, the first man came back. Then the two talked together, and at last went off to the cove. Dick heard the motor-boat being started up.

'It's safe to get out now, Anne,' he said. 'Isn't it cold down here? I'll be glad to get out into the sunshine.'

They climbed out and stood warming themselves in the hot summer sunshine. They could see the motor-boat streaking towards the mainland.

'Well, they're gone for the moment,' said Dick. 'And they've not taken our boat, as they said. If only we could rescue Julian and George, we could get help, because George could row us back.'

'Why *can't* we rescue them?' cried Anne, her eyes shining. 'We can go down the steps and unbolt the door, can't we?'

'No – we can't,' said Dick. 'Look!'

Anne looked to where he pointed. She saw that the two men had piled big, heavy slabs of broken stone over the dungeon entrance. It had taken all their strength to put the big stones there. Neither Dick nor Anne could hope to move them.

'It's quite impossible to get down the steps,' said Dick. 'They've made sure we shan't do that! And you know we haven't any idea where the second entrance is. We only know it was somewhere near the tower.'

'Let's see if we can find it,' said Anne eagerly. They set off to the tower on the right of the castle – but it was quite clear that whatever entrance there might have been once, it was gone now! The castle had fallen in very much just there, and there were piles of old broken stones everywhere, quite impossible to move. The children soon gave up the search.

'Blow!' said Dick. 'How I do hate to think of poor old Julian and George prisoners down below, and we can't even help them! Oh, Anne – can't *you* think of something to do?'

Anne sat down on a stone and thought hard. She was very worried. Then she brightened up a little and turned to Dick.

'Dick! I suppose – I suppose we couldn't *possibly* climb down the well, could we?' she asked. 'You know it goes past the dungeons – and there's an opening on the dungeon floor from the well-shaft, because don't you remember we were able to put in our heads and shoulders and look right up the well to the top? Could we get past that slab, do you think – the one that I sat on just now, that has fallen across the well?'

Dick thought it all over. He went to the well and peered down it. 'You know, I believe you are right, Anne,' he said at last. 'We might be able to squeeze past that slab. There's just about room. I don't know how far the iron ladder goes down though.'

'Oh, Dick – do let's try,' said Anne. 'It's our only chance of rescuing the others!'

'Well,' said Dick, 'I'll try it – but not you, Anne. I'm not going to have you falling down that well. The ladder might be broken half-way down – anything might happen. You must stay up here and I'll see what I can do.'

'You will be careful, won't you?' said Anne, anxiously. 'Take a rope with you, Dick, so that if you need one you won't have to climb all the way up again.'

'Good idea,' said Dick. He went to the little stone room and got one of the ropes they had put there. He wound it round and round his waist. Then he went back to Anne.

'Well, here goes!' he said, in a cheerful voice. 'Don't worry about me. I'll be all right.'

Anne was rather white. She was terribly afraid that Dick might fall right down to the bottom of the well. She watched him climb down the iron ladder to the slab of stone. He tried his best to squeeze by it, but it was very difficult. At last he managed it and after that Anne could see him no more. But she could hear him, for he kept calling up to her.

'Ladder's still going strong, Anne! I'm all right. Can you hear me?'

'Yes,' shouted Anne down the well, hearing her voice echo in a funny hollow manner. 'Take care, Dick. I do hope the ladder goes all the way down.'

'I think it does!' yelled back Dick. Then he gave a loud

exclamation. 'Blow! It's broken just here. Broken right off. Or else it ends. I'll have to use my rope.'

There was a silence as Dick unwound the rope from his waist. He tied it firmly to the last but one rung of the ladder, which seemed quite strong.

'I'm going down the rope now!' he shouted to Anne. 'Don't worry. I'm all right. Here I go!'

Anne couldn't hear what Dick said after that, for the well-shaft made his words go crooked and she couldn't make out what they were. But she was glad to hear him shouting even though she didn't know what he said. She yelled down to him too, hoping he could hear her.

Dick slid down the rope, holding on to it with hands, knees and feet, glad that he was so good at gym at school. He wondered if he was anywhere near the dungeons. He seemed to have gone down a long way. He managed to get out his torch. He put it between his teeth after he had switched it on, so that he might have both hands free for the rope. The light from the torch showed him the walls of the well around him. He couldn't make out if he was above or below the dungeons. He didn't want to go right down to the bottom of the well!

He decided that he must have just passed the opening into the dungeon-caves. He climbed back up the rope a little way and to his delight saw that he was right. The opening on to the dungeons was just by his head. He climbed up till he was level with it and then swung himself to the side of the well where the small opening was. He

managed to get hold of the bricked edge, and then tried to scramble through the opening into the dungeon.

It was difficult, but luckily Dick was not very big. He managed it at last and stood up straight with a sigh of relief. He was in the dungeons! He could now follow the chalk-marks to the room or cave where the ingots were – and where he felt sure that George and Julian were imprisoned!

He shone his torch on the wall. Yes – there were the chalk-marks. Good! He put his head into the well-opening and yelled at the top of his voice.

'Anne! I'm in the dungeons! Watch out that the men don't come back!'

Then he began to follow the white chalk-marks, his heart beating fast. After a while he came to the door of the store-room. As he had expected, it was fastened so that George and Julian couldn't get out. Big bolts had been driven home at the top and bottom, and the children inside could not possibly get out. They had tried their hardest to batter down the door, but it was no good at all.

They were sitting inside the store-cave, feeling angry and exhausted. The man had brought them food and drink, but they had not touched it. Tim was with them, lying down with his head on his paws, half-angry with George because she hadn't let him fly at the men as he had so badly wanted to. But George felt certain that Tim would be shot if he tried biting or snapping.

'Anyway, the other two had sense enough not to come down and be made prisoners too,' said George. 'They must have known there was something funny about that note when they saw I had signed myself Georgina instead of George. I wonder what they are doing. They must be hiding.'

Tim suddenly gave a growl. He leapt to his feet and went to the closed door, his head on one side. He had heard something, that was certain.

'I hope it's not those men back again already,' said George. Then she looked at Tim in surprise, flashing her torch on to him. He was wagging his tail!

A great bang at the door made them all jump out of their skins! Then came Dick's cheerful voice. 'Hi, Julian! Hi, George! Are you here?'

'Wuffffff!' barked Tim joyfully, and scratched at the door.

'Dick! Open the door!' yelled Julian in delight. 'Quick, open the door!'

CHAPTER SIXTEEN

A plan – and a narrow escape

DICK UNBOLTED the door at the top and bottom and flung it open. He rushed in and thumped George and Julian happily on the back.

'Hallo!' he said. 'How does it feel to be rescued?'

'Fine!' cried Julian, and Tim barked madly round them.

George grinned at Dick.

'Good work!' she said. 'What happened?'

Dick told them in a few words all that had happened. When he related how he had climbed down the old well, George and Julian could hardly believe their ears. Julian slipped his arm through his younger brother's.

'You're a brick!' he said. 'A real brick! Now quick – what are we going to do?'

'Well, if they've left us our boat I'm going to take us all back to the mainland as quickly as possible,' said George. 'I'm not playing about with men who brandish revolvers all the time. Come on! Up the well we go and find the boat.'

They ran to the well-shaft and squeezed through the small opening one by one. Up the rope they went and soon found the iron ladder. Julian made them go up one by one in case the ladder wouldn't bear the weight of all three at once.

It really wasn't very long before they were all up in the open air once more, giving Anne hugs, and hearing her exclaim gladly, with tears in her eyes, how pleased she was to see them all again.

'Now come on!' said George after a minute. 'Off to the boat. Quick! Those men may be back at any time.'

They rushed to the cove. There was their boat, lying

where they had pulled it, out of reach of the waves. But what a shock for them!

'They've taken the oars!' said George, in dismay. 'The beasts! They know we can't row the boat away without oars. They were afraid you and Anne might row off, Dick – so instead of bothering to tow the boat behind them, they just grabbed the oars. Now we're stuck. We can't possibly get away.'

It was a great disappointment. The children were almost ready to cry. After Dick's marvellous rescue of George and Julian, it had seemed as if everything was going right – and now suddenly things were going wrong again.

'We must think this out,' said Julian, sitting down where he could see at once if any boat came in sight. 'The men have gone off – probably to get a ship from somewhere in which they can put the ingots and sail away. They won't be back for some time, I should think, because you can't charter a ship all in a hurry – unless, of course, they've got one of their own.'

'And in the meantime we can't get off the island to get help, because they've got our oars,' said George. 'We can't even signal to any passing fishing-boat because they won't be out just now. The tide's wrong. It seems as if all we've got to do is wait here patiently till the men come back and take my gold! And we can't stop them.'

'You know – I've got a sort of plan coming into my head,' said Julian, slowly. 'Wait a bit – don't interrupt me. I'm thinking.'

The others waited in silence while Julian sat and frowned, thinking of his plan. Then he looked at the others with a smile.

'I believe it will work,' he said. 'Listen! We'll wait here in patience till the men come back. What will they do? They'll drag away those stones at the top of the dungeon entrance, and go down the steps. They'll go to the store-room, where they left us – thinking we are still there – and they will go into the room. Well, what about one of us being hidden down there ready to bolt *them* into the room? Then we can either go off in their motor-boat or our own boat if they bring back our oars – and get help.'

Anne thought it was a marvellous idea. But Dick and George did not look so certain. 'We'd have to go down and bolt that door again to make it seem as if we are still prisoners there,' said George. 'And suppose the one who hides down there doesn't manage to bolt the men in? It might be very difficult to do that quickly enough. They will simply catch whoever we plan to leave down there – and come up to look for the rest of us.'

'That's true,' said Julian, thoughtfully. 'Well – we'll suppose that Dick, or whoever goes down, doesn't manage to bolt them in and make them prisoners – and the men come up here again. All right – while they are down below we'll pile big stones over the entrance, just as they did. Then they won't be able to get out.'

'What about Dick down below?' said Anne, at once.

'I could climb up the well again!' said Dick, eagerly. 'I'll be the one to go down and hide. I'll do my best to bolt the men into the room. And if I have to escape I'll climb up the well-shaft again. The men don't know about that. So even if they are not prisoners in the dungeon room, they'll be prisoners underground!'

The children talked over this plan, and decided that it was the best they could think of. Then George said she thought it would be a good thing to have a meal. They were all half-starved and, now that the worry and excitement of being rescued was over, they were feeling very hungry!

They fetched some food from the little room and ate it in the cove, keeping a sharp lookout for the return of the men. After about two hours they saw a big fishing-smack appear in the distance, and heard the chug-chug-chug of a motor-boat too.

'There they are!' said Julian, in excitement, and he jumped to his feet. 'That's the ship they mean to load with the ingots, and sail away in safety – and there's the motor-boat bringing the men back! Quick, Dick, down the well, you, go and hide until you hear them in the dungeons!'

Dick shot off. Julian turned to the others. 'We'll have to hide,' he said. 'Now that the tide is out we'll hide over there, behind those uncovered rocks. I don't somehow think the men will do any hunting for Dick and Anne – but they might. Come on! Quick!'

They all hid themselves behind the rocks, and heard the motor-boat come chugging into the tiny harbour. They could

hear men calling to one another. There sounded to be more than two men this time. Then the men left the inlet and went up the low cliff towards the ruined castle.

Julian crept behind the rocks and peeped to see what the men were doing. He felt certain they were pulling away the slabs of stone that had been piled on top of the entrance to prevent Dick and Anne going down to rescue the others.

'George! Come on!' called Julian in a low tone. 'I think the men have gone down the steps into the dungeons now. We must go and try to put those big stones back. Quick!'

George, Julian and Anne ran softly and swiftly to the old courtyard of the castle. They saw that the stones had been pulled away from the entrance to the dungeons. The men had disappeared. They had plainly gone down the steps.

The three children did their best to tug at the heavy stones to drag them back. But their strength was not the same as that of the men, and they could not manage to get any very big stones across. They put three smaller ones, and Julian hoped the men would find them too difficult to move from below. 'If only Dick has managed to bolt them into that room!' he said to the others. 'Come on, back to the well now. Dick will have to come up there, because he won't be able to get out of the entrance.'

They all went to the well. Dick had removed the old wooden cover, and it was lying on the ground. The children leaned over the hole of the well and waited anxiously. What was Dick doing? They could hear nothing from the well and they longed to know what was happening.

There was plenty happening down below! The two men, and another, had gone down into the dungeons, expecting, of course, to find Julian, George and the dog still locked up in the store-room with the ingots. They passed the well-shaft not guessing that an excited small boy was hidden there, ready to slip out of the opening as soon as they had passed.

Dick heard them pass. He slipped out of the well-opening and followed behind quietly, his feet making no sound. He could see the beams made by the men's powerful torches, and with his heart thumping loudly he crept along the smelly old passage, between great caves, until the men turned into the wide passage where the store-cave lay.

'Here it is,' Dick heard one of the men say, as he flashed

his torch on to the great door. 'The gold's in there – so are the kids!'

The men unbolted the door at top and bottom. Dick was glad that he had slipped along to bolt the door, for if he hadn't done that before the men had come they would have known that Julian and George had escaped, and would have been on their guard.

The man opened the door and stepped inside. The second man followed him. Dick crept as close as he dared, waiting for the third man to go in too. Then he meant to slam the door and bolt it!

The first man swung his torch round and gave a loud exclamation. 'The children are gone! How strange! Where are they?'

Two of the men were now in the cave – and the third stepped in at that moment. Dick darted forward and slammed the door. It made a crash that went echoing round and round the caves and passages. Dick fumbled with the bolts, his hand trembling. They were stiff and rusty. The boy found it hard to shoot them home in their sockets. And meanwhile the men were not idle!

As soon as they heard the door slam they spun round. The third man put his shoulder to the door at once and heaved hard. Dick had just got one of the bolts almost into its socket. Then all three men forced their strength against the door, and the bolt gave way!

Dick stared in horror. The door was opening! He turned and fled down the dark passage. The men flashed their

torches on and saw him. They went after the boy at top speed.

Dick fled to the well-shaft. Fortunately the opening was on the opposite side, and he could clamber into it without being seen in the light of the torches. The boy only just had time to squeeze through into the shaft before the three men came running by. Not one of them guessed that the runaway was squeezed into the well-shaft they passed! Indeed, the men did not even know that there was a well there.

Trembling from head to foot, Dick began to climb the rope he had left dangling from the rungs of the iron ladder. He undid it when he reached the ladder itself, for he thought that perhaps the men might discover the old well and try to climb up later. They would not be able to do that if there was no rope dangling down.

The boy climbed up the ladder quickly, and squeezed round the stone slab near the top. The other children were there, waiting for him.

They knew at once by the look on Dick's face that he had failed in what he had tried to do. They pulled him out quickly. 'It was no good,' said Dick, panting with his climb. 'I couldn't do it. They burst the door open just as I was bolting it, and chased me. I got into the shaft just in time.'

'They're trying to get out of the entrance now!' cried Anne, suddenly. 'Quick! What shall we do? They'll catch us all!'

'To the boat!' shouted Julian, and he took Anne's hand to help her along. 'Come along! It's our only chance. The men will perhaps be able to move those stones.'

The four children fled down the courtyard. George darted into the little stone room as they passed it, and caught up an axe. Dick wondered why she bothered to do that. Tim dashed along with them, barking madly.

They came to the cove. Their own boat lay there without oars. The motor-boat was there too. George jumped into it and gave a yell of delight.

'Here are our oars!' she shouted. 'Take them, Julian, I've got a job to do here! Get the boat down to the water, quick!'

Julian and Dick took the oars. Then they dragged their boat down to the water, wondering what George was doing. All kinds of crashing sounds came from the motor-boat!

'George! George! Buck up. The men are out!' suddenly yelled Julian. He had seen the three men running to the cliff that led down to the cove. George leapt out of the motor-boat and joined the others. They pushed their boat out on to the water, and George took the oars at once, pulling for all she was worth.

The three men ran to their motor-boat. Then they paused in the greatest dismay – for George had completely ruined it! She had chopped wildly with her axe at all the machinery she could see – and now the boat could not possibly be started! It was damaged beyond any repair the men could make with the few tools they had.

'You wicked girl!' yelled Jake, shaking his fist at George. 'Wait till I get you!'

'I'll wait!' shouted back George, her blue eyes shining dangerously. 'And you can wait too! You won't be able to leave my island now!'

CHAPTER SEVENTEEN

The end of the great adventure

THE THREE men stood at the edge of the sea, watching George pull away strongly from the shore. They could do nothing. Their boat was quite useless.

'The fishing-smack they've got waiting out there is too big to use in that little inlet,' said George, as she pulled hard at her oars. 'They'll have to stay there till someone goes in with a boat. I guess they're as wild as can be!'

Their boat had to pass fairly near to the big fishing-boat. A man hailed them as they came by.

'Ahoy there! Have you come from Kirrin Island?'

'Don't answer,' said George. 'Don't say a word.' So no one said anything at all, but looked the other way as if they hadn't heard.

'Ahoy there!' yelled the man, angrily. 'Didn't you hear? Have you come from the island?'

Still the children said nothing at all, but looked away while George rowed steadily. The man on the ship gave it up, and looked in a worried manner towards the island. He felt sure the children had come from there – and he knew enough of his comrades' adventures to wonder if everything was right on the island.

'He may put out a boat from the smack and go and see

what's happening, said George. 'Well, he can't do much except take the men off – with a few ingots! I hardly think they'll dare to take any of the gold though, now that we've escaped to tell our tale!'

Julian looked behind at the ship. He saw after a time that the little boat it carried was being lowered into the sea. 'You're right,' he said to George. 'They're afraid something is up. They're going to rescue those three men. What a pity!'

Their little boat reached land. The children leapt out into the shallow water and dragged it up to the beach. Tim pulled at the rope too, wagging his tail. He loved to join in anything that the children were doing.

'Shall you take Tim to Alf?' asked Dick.

George shook her head. 'No,' she said, 'we haven't any time to waste. We must go and tell everything that has happened. I'll tie Tim up to the fence in the front garden.'

They made their way to Kirrin Cottage at top speed. Aunt Fanny was gardening there. She stared in surprise to see the hurrying children.

'Why,' she said, 'I thought you were not coming back till tomorrow or the next day! Has anything happened? What's the matter with Dick's cheek?'

'Nothing much,' said Dick.

The others chimed in.

'Aunt Fanny, where's Uncle Quentin? We have something important to tell him!'

'Mother, we've had such an adventure!'

'Aunt Fanny, we've an awful lot to tell you! We really have!'

Aunt Fanny looked at the untidy children in amazement. 'Whatever has happened?' she said. Then she turned towards the house and called 'Quentin! Quentin! The children have something to tell us!'

Uncle Quentin came out, looking rather cross, for he was in the middle of his work. 'What's the matter?' he asked.

'Uncle, it's about Kirrin Island,' said Julian, eagerly. 'Those men haven't bought it yet, have they?'

'Well, it's practically sold,' said his uncle. 'I've signed my part, and they are to sign their part tomorrow. Why? What's that to do with you?'

'Uncle, those men won't sign tomorrow,' said Julian. 'Do you know why they wanted to buy the island and the castle? Not because they really wanted to build an hotel or anything like that – but because they knew the lost gold was hidden there!'

'What nonsense are you talking?' said his uncle.

'It isn't nonsense, Father!' cried George indignantly. 'It's all true. The map of the old castle was in that box you sold – and in the map was shown where the ingots were hidden by my great-great-great-grandfather!'

George's father looked amazed and annoyed. He simply didn't believe a word! But his wife saw by the solemn and serious faces of the four children that something important really had happened. And then Anne suddenly burst into loud sobs! The excitement had been too much for her and she couldn't bear to think that her uncle wouldn't believe that everything was true.

'Aunt Fanny, Aunt Fanny, it's all true!' she sobbed. 'Uncle Quentin is horrid not to believe us. Oh, Aunt Fanny, the man had a revolver – and oh, he made Julian and George prisoners in the dungeons – and Dick had to climb down the well to rescue them. And George has smashed up their motor-boat to stop them escaping!'

Her aunt and uncle couldn't make head or tail of this, but Uncle Quentin suddenly seemed to think that the matter was serious and worth looking into. 'Smashed up a motor-boat!' he said. 'Whatever for? Come indoors. I shall have to hear the story from beginning to end. It seems quite unbelievable to me.'

They all trooped indoors. Anne sat on her aunt's knee and listened to George and Julian telling the whole story. They told it well and left nothing out. Aunt Fanny grew quite pale as she listened, especially when she heard about Dick climbing down the well.

'You might have been killed,' she said. 'Oh, Dick! What a brave thing to do!'

Uncle Quentin listened in the utmost amazement. He had never had much liking or admiration for any children – he always thought they were noisy, tiresome and silly. But now, as he listened to Julian's tale, he changed his mind about these four children at once!

'You've been very clever,' he said. 'And very brave too. I'm proud of you. Yes, I'm very proud of you all. No wonder you didn't want me to sell the island, George, when you knew about the ingots! But why didn't you tell me?'

The four children stared at him and didn't answer. They couldn't very well say, 'Well, firstly, you wouldn't have believed us. Secondly, you are bad-tempered and unjust and we are frightened of you. Thirdly, we didn't trust you enough to do the right thing.'

'Why don't you answer?' said their uncle. His wife answered for them, in a gentle voice.

'Quentin, you scare the children, you know, and I don't expect they liked to go to you. But now that they have, you will be able to take matters into your own hands. The children cannot do any more. You must ring up the police and see what they have to say about all this.'

'Right,' said Uncle Quentin, and he got up at once. He patted Julian on the back. 'You have all done well,' he said. Then he ruffled George's short curly hair. 'And I'm proud of you too, George,' he said.

'Oh, Father!' said George, going red with surprise and pleasure. She smiled at him and he smiled back. The children noticed that he had a very nice face when he smiled. He and George were really very alike to look at. Both looked ugly when they sulked and frowned – and both were good to look at when they laughed or smiled!

George's father went off to telephone the police and his lawyer too. The children sat and ate biscuits and plums, telling their aunt a great many little details they had forgotten when telling the story before.

As they sat there, there came a loud and angry bark from the front garden. George looked up. 'That's Tim,' she said, with an anxious look at her mother. 'I hadn't time to take him to Alf, who keeps him for me. Mother, Tim was such a comfort to us on the island, you know. I'm sorry he's barking now – but I expect he's hungry.'

'Well, fetch him in,' said her mother, unexpectedly. 'He's quite a hero, too – we must give him a good dinner.'

George smiled in delight. She sped out of the door and went to Tim. She set him free and he came bounding indoors, wagging his long tail. He licked George's mother and cocked his ears at her.

'Good dog,' she said, and actually patted him. 'I'll get you some dinner!'

Tim trotted out to the kitchen with her. Julian grinned at George. 'Well, look at that,' he said. 'Your mother's a brick, isn't she?'

'Yes – but I don't know what Father will say when he sees Tim in the house again,' said George, doubtfully.

Her father came back at that minute, his face grave. 'The police take a serious view of all this,' he said, 'and so does my lawyer. They all agree in thinking that you children have been remarkably clever and brave. And George – my lawyer says that the ingots definitely belong to us. Are there really a lot?'

'Father! There are hundreds!' cried George. 'Simply hundreds – all in a big pile in the dungeon. Oh, Father – shall we be rich now?'

'Yes,' said her father. 'We shall. Rich enough to give you and your mother all the things I've longed to give you for so many years and couldn't. I've worked hard enough for you – but it's not the kind of work that brings in a lot of money, and so I've become irritable and bad-tempered. But now you shall have everything you want!'

'I don't really want anything I haven't already got,' said George. 'But, Father, there is one thing I'd like more than anything else in the world – and it won't cost you a penny!'

'You shall have it, my dear!' said her father, slipping his arm around George, much to her surprise. 'Just say what it is – and even if it costs a hundred pounds you shall have it!'

Just then there came the pattering of big feet down the passage to the room they were in. A big hairy head pushed itself through the door and looked inquiringly at everyone there. It was Tim, of course!

Uncle Quentin stared at him in surprise. 'Why, isn't that Tim?' he asked. 'Hallo, Tim!'

'Father! Tim is the thing I want most in all the world,' said George, squeezing her father's arm. 'You can't think what a friend he was to us on the island – and he wanted to fly at those men and fight them. Oh, Father, I don't want any other present – I only want to keep Tim and have him here for my very own. We could afford to give him a proper kennel to sleep in now, and I'd see that he didn't disturb you, I really would.'

'Well, of course you can have him!' said her father – and Tim came right into the room at once, wagging his tail, looking for all the world as if he had understood every word that had been said. He actually licked Uncle Quentin's hand! Anne thought that was very brave of him.

But Uncle Quentin was quite different now. It seemed as if a great weight had been lifted off his shoulders. They were rich now – George could go to a good school – and his wife could have the things he had so much wanted her to have – and he would be able to go on with the work he loved without feeling that he was not earning enough to keep his family in comfort. He beamed round at everyone, looking as jolly a person as anyone could wish!

George was overjoyed about Tim. She flung her arms round her father's neck and hugged him, a thing she had not done for a long time. He looked astonished but very pleased. 'Well, well,' he said, 'this is all very pleasant. Hallo – is this the police already?'

It was. They came up to the door and had a few words with Uncle Quentin. Then one stayed behind to take down the children's story in his notebook and the others went off to get a boat to the island.

The men had gone from there! The boat from the fishing-smack had fetched them away! – and now both ship and boat had disappeared! The motor-boat was still there, quite unusable. The inspector looked at it with a grin.

'Fierce young lady, isn't she, that Miss Georgina?' he said. 'Done this job pretty well – no one could get away in this boat. We'll have to get it towed into harbour.'

The police brought back with them some of the ingots of gold to show Uncle Quentin. They had sealed up the door of the dungeon so that no one else could get in until the children's uncle was ready to go and fetch the gold. Everything was being done thoroughly and properly – though far too slowly for the children! They had hoped that the men would have been caught and taken to prison – and that the police would bring back the whole of the gold at once!

They were all very tired that night and didn't make any

fuss at all when their aunt said that they must go to bed early. They undressed and then the boys went to eat their supper in the girls' bedroom. Tim was there, ready to lick up any fallen crumbs.

'Well, I must say we've had a wonderful adventure,' said Julian, sleepily. 'In a way I'm sorry it's ended – though at times I didn't enjoy it very much – especially when you and I, George, were prisoners in that dungeon. That was awful.'

George was looking very happy as she nibbled her gingerbread biscuits. She grinned at Julian.

'And to think I hated the idea of you all coming here to stay!' she said. 'I was going to be such a beast to you! I was going to make you wish you were all home again! And now the only thing that makes me sad is the idea of you going away – which you will do, of course, when the holidays end. And then, after having three friends with me, enjoying adventures like this, I'll be all on my own again. I've never been lonely before – but I know I shall be now.'

'No, you won't,' said Anne, suddenly. 'You can do something that will stop you being lonely ever again.'

'What?' said George in surprise.

'You can ask to go to the same boarding school as I go to,' said Anne. 'It's such a lovely one – and we are allowed to keep our pets, so Tim could come too!'

'Gracious! Could he really?' said George, her eyes shining. 'Well, I'll go then. I always said I wouldn't – but I will because I see now how much better and happier it is to be with others than all by myself. And if I can have Tim, well, that's simply wonderful!'

'You'd better go back to your own bedroom now, boys,' said Aunt Fanny, appearing at the doorway. 'Look at Dick, almost dropping with sleep! Well, you should all have pleasant dreams tonight, for you've had an adventure to be proud of. George – is that Tim under your bed?'

'Well, yes it is, Mother,' said George, pretending to be surprised. 'Dear me! Tim, what are you doing here?'

Tim crawled out and went over to George's mother. He lay flat on his tummy and looked up at her most appealingly out of his soft brown eyes.

'Do you want to sleep in the girls' room tonight?' said George's mother, with a laugh. 'All right – just for once!'

'*Mother!*' yelled George, overjoyed. 'Oh, thank you, thank you, thank you! How did you guess that I just didn't want to be parted from Tim tonight? Oh, Mother! Tim, you can sleep on the rug over there.'

Four happy children snuggled down into their beds. Their wonderful adventure had come to a happy end. They had plenty of holidays still in front of them – and now that Uncle Quentin was no longer poor, he would give them the little presents he wanted to. George was going to school with Anne – and she had Tim for her own again! The island and castle still belonged to George – everything was marvellous!

'I'm so glad Kirrin Island wasn't sold, George,' said Anne, sleepily. 'I'm so glad it still belongs to you.'

'It belongs to three other people too,' said George. 'It belongs to me – and to you and Julian and Dick. I've discovered that it's fun to share things. So tomorrow I am going to draw up a deed, or whatever it's called, and put in it that I give you and the others a quarter-share each. Kirrin Island and Castle shall belong to us all!'

'Oh, George – how lovely!' said Anne, delighted. 'Won't the boys he pleased? I do feel so ha . . .'

But before she could finish, the little girl was asleep. So was George. In the other room the two boys slept, too, dreaming of ingots and dungeons and all kinds of exciting things.

Only one person was awake – and that was Tim. He had one ear up and was listening to the children's breathing. As soon as he knew they were asleep he got up quietly from his rug. He crept softly over to George's bed. He put his front paws up and sniffed at the sleeping girl.

Then, with a bound he was on the bed, and snuggled himself down into the crook of her legs. He gave a sigh, and shut his eyes. The four children might be happy – but Tim was happiest of all.

'Oh, Tim,' murmured George, half waking up as she felt him against her. 'Oh, Tim, you mustn't – but you do feel so nice. Tim – we'll have other adventures together, the five of us – won't we?'

They will – but that's another story!

Enid Blyton®

is one of the most popular children's authors of all time. Her books have sold over 500 million copies and have been translated into other languages more often than any other children's author.

Enid Blyton adored writing for children. She wrote over 700 books and about 2,000 short stories. *The Famous Five* books, now 75 years old, are her most popular. She is also the author of other favourites including *The Secret Seven*, *The Magic Faraway Tree*, *Malory Towers* and *Noddy*.

Born in London in 1897, Enid lived much of her life in Buckinghamshire and loved dogs, gardening and the countryside. She was very knowledgeable about trees, flowers, birds and animals. Dorset – where some of the Famous Five's adventures are set – was a favourite place of hers too.

Enid Blyton's stories are read and loved by millions of children (and grown-ups) all over the world. Visit enidblyton.co.uk to discover more.

Illustration by Laura Ellen Anderson.

THE FAMOUS FIVE

FIVE GO ADVENTURING AGAIN

Have you read all THE FAMOUS FIVE books?

1. Five on a Treasure Island
2. Five Go Adventuring Again
3. Five Run Away Together
4. Five Go to Smuggler's Top
5. Five Go Off in a Caravan
6. Five on Kirrin Island Again
7. Five Go Off to Camp
8. Five Get Into Trouble
9. Five Fall Into Adventure
10. Five on a Hike Together
11. Five Have a Wonderful Time
12. Five Go Down to the Sea
13. Five Go to Mystery Moor
14. Five Have Plenty of Fun
15. Five on a Secret Trail
16. Five Go to Billycock Hill
17. Five Get Into a Fix
18. Five on Finniston Farm
19. Five Go to Demon's Rocks
20. Five Have a Mystery to Solve
21. Five Are Together Again

The Famous Five Colour Short Stories

1. Five and a Half-Term Adventure
2. George's Hair is Too Long
3. Good Old Timmy
4. A Lazy Afternoon
5. Well Done, Famous Five
6. Five Have a Puzzling Time
7. Happy Christmas, Five
8. When Timmy Chased the Cat

Enid Blyton®

THE FAMOUS FIVE

FIVE GO ADVENTURING AGAIN

Illustrated by Eileen A. Soper

HODDER

HODDER CHILDREN'S BOOKS

First published in Great Britain in 1943 by Hodder & Stoughton
This edition published in 2016

21

A CIP catalogue record for this book is available from the British Library.

ISBN 978 1 444 93632 2

Printed and bound in Great Britain by Clays Ltd, Elcograf S.p.A.

The paper and board used in this book are made from wood from responsible sources.

Hodder Children's Books
An imprint of
Hachette Children's Group
Part of Hodder & Stoughton
Carmelite House
50 Victoria Embankment
London EC4Y 0DZ

An Hachette UK Company
www.hachette.co.uk
www.hachettechildrens.co.uk

CONTENTS

1 CHRISTMAS HOLIDAYS 1
2 ALL TOGETHER AGAIN 11
3 THE NEW TUTOR 20
4 AN EXCITING DISCOVERY 31
5 AN UNPLEASANT WALK 41
6 LESSONS WITH MR ROLAND 51
7 DIRECTIONS FOR THE SECRET WAY 62
8 WHAT HAPPENED ON CHRISTMAS NIGHT 73
9 A HUNT FOR THE SECRET WAY 83
10 A SHOCK FOR GEORGE AND TIM 95
11 STOLEN PAPERS 106
12 GEORGE IN TROUBLE 116
13 JULIAN HAS A SURPRISE 128
14 THE SECRET WAY AT LAST! 142
15 AN EXCITING JOURNEY AND HUNT 152
16 THE CHILDREN ARE DISCOVERED 164
17 GOOD OLD TIM! 173

CHAPTER ONE

Christmas holidays

IT WAS the last week of the Christmas term, and all the girls at Gaylands School were looking forward to the Christmas holidays. Anne sat down at the breakfast-table and picked up a letter addressed to her.

'Hallo, look at this!' she said to her cousin Georgina, who was sitting beside her. 'A letter from Daddy – and I only had one from him and Mummy yesterday.'

'I hope it's not bad news,' said George. She would not allow anyone to call her Georgina, and now even the mistresses called her George. She really was very like a boy with her short curly hair, and her boyish ways. She looked anxiously at Anne as her cousin read the letter.

'Oh, George – we can't go home for the holidays!' said Anne, with tears in her eyes. 'Mummy's got scarlet fever – and Daddy is in quarantine for it – so they can't have us back. Isn't it just too bad?'

'Oh, I *am* sorry,' said George. She was just as disappointed for herself as for Anne, because Anne's mother had invited George, and her dog Timothy, to stay for the Christmas holidays with them. She had been promised many things she had never seen before – the pantomime, and the circus – and a big party with a fine Christmas tree! Now it wouldn't happen.

'Whatever will the two boys say?' said Anne, thinking of Julian and Dick, her two brothers. 'They won't be able to go home either.'

'Well – what are you going to do for the holidays then?' asked George. 'Won't you come and stay at Kirrin Cottage with *me*? I'm sure my mother would love to have you again. We had such fun when you came to stay for the summer hols.'

'Wait a minute – let me finish the letter and see what Daddy says,' said Anne, picking up the note again. 'Poor Mummy – I do hope she isn't feeling very ill.'

She read a few more lines and then gave such a delighted exclamation that George and the other girls waited impatiently for her to explain.

'George! We *are* to come to you again – but oh blow, blow, blow! – we've got to have a tutor for the hols, partly to look after us so that your mother doesn't have too much bother with us, and partly because both Julian and Dick have been ill with flu twice this term and have got behind in their work.'

'A tutor! How sickening! That means I'll have to do lessons too, I'll bet!' said George, in dismay. 'When my mother and father see my report I guess they'll find out how little I know. After all, this is the first time I've ever been to a proper school, and there are heaps of things I don't know.'

'What horrid hols they'll be, if we have a tutor running after us all the time,' said Anne, gloomily. 'I expect I'll have quite a good report, because I've done well in the exams – but it won't be any fun for me not doing lessons with you three in the hols. Though, of course, I could go off with Timothy, I suppose. *He* won't be doing lessons!'

'Yes, he will,' said George, at once. She could not bear the idea of her beloved dog Timothy going off each morning with Anne, while she, George, sat and worked hard with Julian and Dick.

'Timothy can't do lessons, don't be silly, George,' said Anne.

'He can sit under my feet while *I'm* doing them,' said George. 'It will be a great help to feel him there. For goodness' sake eat up your sausages, Anne. We've all nearly finished. The bell will be going in a minute and you won't have had any breakfast.'

'I am glad Mummy isn't very bad,' said Anne, hurriedly finishing her letter. 'Daddy says he's written to Dick and Julian – and to your father to ask him to engage a tutor for us. Oh dash – this is an awful disappointment, isn't it? I don't mean I shan't enjoy going to Kirrin Cottage again – and seeing Kirrin Island – but after all there are no pantomimes or circuses or parties to look forward to at Kirrin.'

The end of the term came quickly. Anne and George packed up their trunks, and put on the labels, enjoying the noise and excitement of the last two days. The big school coaches rolled up to the door, and the girls clambered in.

'Off to Kirrin again!' said Anne. 'Come on, Timothy darling, you can sit between me and George.'

Gaylands School allowed the children to keep their own pets, and Timothy, George's big mongrel dog, had been a great success. Except for the time when he had run after the dustman, and dragged the dustbin away from him, all the way up the school grounds and into George's classroom, he had really behaved extremely well.

'I'm sure *you'll* have a good report, Tim,' said George, giving the dog a hug. 'We're going home again. Will you like that?'

'Woof,' said Tim, in his deep voice. He stood up, wagging his tail, and there was a squeal from the seat behind.

'George! Make Tim sit down. He's wagging my hat off!'

It was not very long before the two girls and Timothy were in London, being put into the train for Kirrin.

'I do wish the boys broke up today too,' sighed Anne. 'Then we could all have gone down to Kirrin together. That would have been fun.'

Julian and Dick broke up the next day and were to join the girls then at Kirrin Cottage. Anne was very much looking forward to seeing them again. A term was a long time to be away from one another. She had been glad to have her cousin George with her. The three of them had stayed with George in the summer, and had had some exciting adventures together on the little island off the coast. An old castle stood on the island and in the dungeons the children had made all kinds of wonderful discoveries.

'It will be lovely to go across to Kirrin Island again, George,' said Anne, as the train sped off towards the west.

'We shan't be able to,' said George. 'The sea is terribly rough round the island in the winter. It would be too dangerous to try and row there.'

'Oh, what a pity,' said Anne disappointed. 'I was looking forward to some more adventures there.'

'There won't be any adventures at Kirrin in the winter,' said George. 'It's cold down there – and when it snows we sometimes get frozen up completely – can't even walk to the village because the sea-wind blows the snow-drifts so high.'

'Oooh – that sounds rather exciting!' said Anne.

'Well, it isn't really,' said George. 'It's awfully boring – nothing to do but sit at home all day, or turn out with a spade and dig the snow away.'

It was a long time before the train reached the little station that served Kirrin. But at last it was there pulling in slowly and stopping at the tiny platform. The two girls jumped out eagerly, and looked to see if anyone had met them. Yes – there was George's mother!

'Hallo, George darling – hallo, Anne!' said George's mother, and gave both children a hug. 'Anne, I'm so sorry about your mother, but she's getting on all right, you'll be glad to know.'

'Oh, good!' said Anne. 'It's nice of you to have us, Aunt Fanny. We'll try and be good! What about Uncle Quentin? Will he mind having four children in the house in the winter-time? We won't be able to go out and leave him in peace as often as we did in the summer!'

George's father was a scientist, a very clever man, but rather frightening. He had little patience with children, and the four of them had felt very much afraid of him at times in the summer.

'Oh, your uncle is still working very hard at his book,' said Aunt Fanny. 'You know, he has been working out a secret theory – a secret idea – and putting it all into his book. He says that once it is all explained and finished, he is to take it to some high authority, and then his idea will be used for the good of the country.'

'Oh, Aunt Fanny – it does sound exciting,' said Anne. 'What's the secret?'

'I can't tell you that, silly,' said her aunt, laughing. 'Why, even I myself don't know it. Come along, now – it's cold standing here. Timothy looks very plump and well, George dear.'

'Oh Mother, he's had a marvellous time at school,' said George. 'He really has. He chewed up the cook's old slippers . . .'

'And he chased the cat that lives in the stables every time he saw her,' said Anne.

'And he once got into the larder and ate a whole steak pie,' said George; 'and once . . .'

'Good gracious, George, I should think the school will refuse to have Timothy next term,' said her mother, in horror. 'Wasn't he well punished? I hope he was.'

'No – he wasn't,' said George, going rather red. 'You see, Mother, we are responsible for our pets and their behaviour ourselves – so if ever Timothy does anything bad *I'm* punished for it, because I haven't shut him up properly, or something like that.'

'Well, you must have had quite a lot of punishments then,' said her mother, as she drove the little pony-trap along the frosty roads. 'I really think that's rather a good idea!' There was a twinkle in her eyes as she spoke. 'I think I'll keep on with the same idea – punish you every time Timothy misbehaves himself!'

The girls laughed. They felt happy and excited. Holidays were fun. Going back to Kirrin was lovely. Tomorrow the boys would come – and then Christmas would be there!

'Good old Kirrin Cottage!' said Anne, as they came in sight of the pretty old house. 'Oh – look, there's Kirrin Island!' The two looked out to sea, where the old ruined castle stood on the little island of Kirrin – what adventures they had had there in the summer!

The girls went into the house. 'Quentin!' called George's mother. 'Quentin! The girls are here.'

Uncle Quentin came out of his study at the other side of the house. Anne thought he looked taller and darker than ever. 'And frownier!' she said to herself. Uncle Quentin

might be very clever, but Anne preferred someone jolly and smiling like her own father. She shook hands with her uncle politely, and watched George kiss him.

'Well!' said Uncle Quentin to Anne. 'I hear I've got to get a tutor for you! At least, for the two boys. My word, you *will* have to behave yourself with a tutor, I can tell you!'

This was meant to be a joke, but it didn't sound very nice to Anne and George. People you had to behave well with were usually very strict and tiresome. Both girls were glad when George's father had gone back into his study.

'Your father has been working far too hard lately,' said George's mother to her. 'He is tired out. Thank goodness his book is nearly finished. He had hoped to finish it by Christmas so that he could join in the fun and games – but now he says he can't.'

'What a pity,' said Anne, politely, though secretly she thought it was a good thing. It wouldn't be much fun having Uncle Quentin to play charades and things like that! 'Oh, Aunt Fanny, I'm so looking forward to seeing Julian and Dick – and won't they be pleased to see Tim and George? Aunt Fanny, nobody calls George Georgina at school, not even our form mistress. I was rather hoping they would, because I wanted to see what would happen when she refused to answer to Georgina! George, you liked school, didn't you?'

'Yes,' said George, 'I did. I thought I'd hate being with a lot of others, but it's fun, after all. But, Mother, you won't find my report very good, I'm afraid. There were such a lot of things I was bad at because I'd never done them before.'

'Well, you'd never been to school before!' said her mother. 'I'll explain it to your father if he gets upset. Now, go along and get ready for a late tea. You must be very hungry.'

The girls went upstairs to their little room. 'I'm glad I'm not spending my hols by myself,' said George. 'I've had much more fun since I've known you and the boys. Hey, Timothy, where have you gone?'

'He's gone to smell all around the house to make sure it's his proper home!' said Anne, with a giggle. 'He wants to know if the kitchen smells the same – and the bathroom – and his basket. It must be just as exciting for him to come home for the holidays as it is for us!'

Anne was right. Timothy was thrilled to be back again. He ran round George's mother, sniffing at her legs in friendliness, pleased to see her again. He ran into the kitchen but soon came out again because someone new was there – Joanna the cook – a panting person who eyed him with suspicion.

'You can come into this kitchen once a day for your dinner,' said Joanna. 'And that's all. I'm not having meat and sausages and chicken disappearing under my nose if I can help it. I know what dogs are, I do!'

Timothy ran into the scullery and sniffed round there. He ran into the dining-room and the sitting-room, and was pleased to find they had the same old smell. He put his nose to the door of the study where George's father worked, and sniffed very cautiously. He didn't mean to go in. Timothy was just as wary of George's father as the other were!

He ran upstairs to the girl's bedroom again. Where was his basket? Ah, there it was by the window-seat. Good! That meant he was to sleep in the girls' bedroom once more. He curled himself up in his basket, and thumped loudly with his tail.

'Glad to be back,' said his tail, 'glad – to – be – back!'

CHAPTER TWO

All together again

THE NEXT day the boys came back. Anne and George went to meet them with Timothy. George drove the pony-trap, and Tim sat beside her. Anne could hardly wait for the train to stop at the station. She ran along the platform, looking for Julian and Dick in the carriages that passed.

Then she saw them. They were looking out of a window at the back of the train, waving and yelling.

'Anne! Anne! Here we are! Hallo, George! Oh, there's Timothy!'

'Julian! Dick!' yelled Anne. Timothy began to bark and leap about. It was most exciting.

'Oh, Julian! It's lovely to see you both again!' cried Anne, giving her two brothers a hug each. Timothy leapt up and licked them both. He was beside himself with joy. Now he had all the children around him that he loved.

The three children and the dog stood happily together, all talking at once while the porter got the luggage out of the train. Anne suddenly remembered George. She looked round her. She was nowhere to be seen, although she had come on the station platform with Anne.

'Where's old George?' said Julian. 'I saw her here when I waved out of the window.'

'She must have gone back to the pony-trap,' said Anne. 'Tell the porter to bring your trunks out to the trap, Julian. Come along! We'll go and find George.'

George was standing by the pony, holding his head. She looked rather gloomy, Anne thought. The boys went up to her.

'Hallo, George, old thing!' cried Julian, and gave her a hug. Dick did the same.

'What's up?' asked Anne, wondering at George's sudden silence.

'I believe George felt left out!' said Julian with a grin. 'Funny old Georgina!'

'*Don't* call me Georgina!' said the little girl fiercely. The boys laughed.

'Ah, it's the same fierce old George, all right,' said Dick, and gave the girl a friendly slap on the shoulder. 'Oh, George – it's good to see you again. Do you remember our marvellous adventures in the summer?'

George felt her awkwardness slipping away from her. She *had* felt left out when she had seen the great welcome that the two boys gave to their small sister – but no one could sulk for long with Julian and Dick. They just wouldn't let anyone feel left out or awkward or sulky.

The four children climbed into the trap. The porter heaved in the two trunks. There was only just room for them. Timothy sat on top of the trunks, his tail wagging nineteen to the dozen, and his tongue hanging out because he was panting with delight.

'You two girls were lucky to be able to take Tim to school with you,' said Dick, patting the big dog lovingly. 'No pets are allowed at our school. Awfully hard on those fellows who like live things.'

'Thompson Minor kept white mice,' said Julian. 'And one day they escaped and met Matron round a corner of the passage. She squealed the place down.'

The girls laughed. The boys always had funny tales to tell when they got home.

'And Kennedy keeps snails,' said Dick. 'You know, snails sleep for the winter – but Kennedy kept his in far too warm a place, and they all crawled out of their box and went up the walls. You should have heard how we laughed when the geography master asked Thompson to point out Cape Town on the map – and there was one of the snails in the very place!'

Everyone laughed again. It was so good to be all together once more. They were very much of an age – Julian was twelve. George and Dick were eleven, and Anne was ten. Holidays and Christmas time were in front of them. No wonder they laughed at everything, even the silliest little joke!

'It's good that Mummy is getting on all right, isn't it?' said Dick, as the pony went along the road at a great pace. 'I was disappointed not to go home, I must say – I did want to go to see *Aladdin and the Lamp*, and the circus – but still, it's good to be back at Kirrin Cottage again. I wish we could have some more exciting adventures. Not a hope of that this time, though.'

'There's one snag about these hols,' said Julian. 'And that's the tutor. I hear we've got to have one because Dick and I missed so much school this term, and we've got to take important exams next summer.'

'Yes,' said Anne. 'I wonder what he'll be like. I do hope he will be a sport. Uncle Quentin is going to choose one today.'

Julian and Dick made faces at one another. They felt sure that any tutor chosen by Uncle Quentin would be anything but a sport. Uncle Quentin's idea of a tutor would be somebody strict and gloomy and forbidding.

Never mind! He wouldn't come for a day or two. And he *might* be fun. The boys cheered up and pulled Timothy's thick coat. The dog pretended to growl and bite. *He* wasn't worried about tutors. Lucky Timothy!

They all arrived at Kirrin Cottage. The boys were really pleased to see their aunt, and rather relieved when she said that their uncle had not yet come back.

'He's gone to see two or three men who have answered the advertisement for a tutor,' she said. 'It won't be long before he's back.'

'Mother, I haven't got to do lessons in the hols too, have I?' asked George. Nothing had yet been said to her about this, and she longed to know.

'Oh yes, George,' said her mother. 'Your father has seen your report, and although it isn't really a bad one, and we certainly didn't expect a marvellous one, still it does show that you are behind your age in some things. A little extra coaching will soon help you along.'

George looked gloomy. She had expected this but it was tiresome all the same. 'Anne's the only one who won't have to do lessons,' she said.

'I'll do some too,' promised Anne. 'Perhaps not always, George, if it's a very fine day, for instance – but sometimes, just to keep you company.'

'Thanks,' said George. 'But you needn't. I shall have Timmy.'

George's mother looked doubtful about this. 'We'll have to see what the tutor says about that,' she said.

'Mother! If the tutor says I can't have Timothy in the room, I jolly well won't do holiday lessons!' began George, fiercely.

Her mother laughed. 'Well, well – here's our fierce, hot-tempered George again!' she said. 'Go along, you two boys, and wash your hands and do your hair. You seem to have collected all the grime on the railway.'

The children and Timothy went upstairs. It was such fun to be five again. They always counted Tim as one of themselves. He went everywhere with them, and really seemed to understand every single word they said.

'I wonder what sort of a tutor Uncle Quentin will choose,' said Dick, as he scrubbed his nails. 'If only he would choose the right kind – someone jolly and full of fun, who knows that holiday lessons are sickening to have, and tries to make up for them by being a sport out of lesson-time. I suppose we'll have to work every morning.'

'Hurry up. I want my tea,' said Julian. 'Come on down, Dick. We'll know about the tutor soon enough!'

They all went down together, and sat round the table. Joanna the cook had made a lovely lot of buns and a great big cake. There was not much left of either by the time the four children had finished!

Uncle Quentin returned just as they were finishing. He

seemed rather pleased with himself. He shook hands with the two boys and asked them if they had had a good term.

'Did you get a tutor, Uncle Quentin?' asked Anne, who could see that everyone was simply bursting to know this.

'Ah – yes, I did,' said her uncle. He sat down, while Aunt Fanny poured him out a cup of tea. 'I interviewed three applicants, and had almost chosen the last one, when another fellow came in, all in a hurry. Said he had only just seen the advertisement, and hoped he wasn't too late.'

'Did you choose him?' asked Dick.

'I did,' said his uncle. 'He seemed a most intelligent fellow. Even knew about me and my work! And he had the most wonderful letters of recommendation.'

'I don't think the children need to know all these details,' murmured Aunt Fanny. 'Anyway – you asked him to come?'

'Oh yes,' said Uncle Quentin. 'He's a good bit older than the others – they were rather young fellows – this one seems very responsible and intelligent. I'm sure you'll like him, Fanny. He'll fit in here very well. I feel I would like to have him to talk to me sometimes in the evening.'

The children couldn't help feeling that the new tutor sounded rather alarming. Their uncle smiled at the gloomy faces.

'You'll like Mr Roland,' he said. 'He knows how to handle youngsters – knows he's got to be very firm, and to see that you know a good bit more at the end of the holidays than you did at the beginning.'

This sounded even more alarming. All four children wished heartily that Aunt Fanny had been to choose the tutor, and not Uncle Quentin.

'When is he coming?' asked George.

'Tomorrow,' said her father. 'You can all go to meet him at the station. That will make a nice welcome for him.'

'We *had* thought of taking the bus and going to do a bit of Christmas shopping,' said Julian, seeing Anne looked very disappointed.

'Oh, no, you must certainly go and meet Mr Roland,' said his uncle. 'I told him you would. And mind you, you four – no nonsense with him! You've to do as you're told, and you must work hard with him, because your father is paying very high fees for his coaching. I'm paying a third, because I want him to coach George a little too – so George, you must do your best.'

'I'll try,' said George. 'If he's nice, I'll do my very best.'

'You'll do your best whether you think him nice or not!' said her father, frowning. 'He will arrive by the ten-thirty train. Be sure to be there in time.'

'I do hope he won't be too strict,' said Dick, that evening, when the five of them were alone for a minute or two. 'It's going to spoil the hols, if we have someone down on us all the time. And I do hope he'll like Timothy.'

George looked up at once. 'Like Timothy!' she said. 'Of course he'll like Timothy! How couldn't he?'

'Well – your father didn't like Timothy very much last summer,' said Dick. 'I don't see how anyone could *dislike*

darling Tim – but there are people who don't like dogs, you know, George.'

'If Mr Roland doesn't like Timothy, I'll not do a single thing for him,' said George. 'Not one single thing!'

'She's gone all fierce again!' said Dick, with a laugh. 'My word – the sparks will fly if Mr Roland dares to dislike our Timothy!'

CHAPTER THREE

The new tutor

NEXT MORNING the sun was out, all the sea-mist that had hung about for the last two days had disappeared, and Kirrin Island showed plainly at the mouth of Kirrin Bay. The children stared longingly at the ruined castle on it.

'I do wish we could get over to the castle,' said Dick. 'It looks quite calm enough, George.'

'It's very rough by the island,' said George. 'It always is at this time of year. I know Mother wouldn't let us go.'

'It's a lovely island, and it's all our own!' said Anne. 'You said you would share it with us for ever and ever, didn't you, George?'

'Yes, I did,' said George. 'And so I will, dungeons and all. Come on – we must get the trap out. We shall be late meeting the train if we stand here all day looking at the island.'

They got the pony and trap and set off down the hard lanes. Kirrin Island disappeared behind the cliffs as they turned inland to the station.

'Did all this land round about belong to your family once upon a time?' asked Julian.

'Yes, all of it,' said George. 'Now we don't own anything except Kirrin Island, our own house and that farm away over there – Kirrin Farm.'

She pointed with her whip. The children saw a fine old farmhouse standing on a hill a good way off, over the heather-clad common.

'Who lives there?' asked Julian.

'Oh, an old farmer and his wife,' said George. 'They were nice to me when I was smaller. We'll go over there one day, if you like. Mother says they don't make the farm pay any more, and in the summertime they take in people who want a holiday.'

'Listen! That's the train whistling in the tunnel!' said Julian, suddenly. 'Buck up, for goodness' sake, George. We shan't be there in time!'

The four children and Timothy looked at the train coming out of the tunnel and drawing in at the station. The pony cantered along swiftly. They would be just in time.

'Who's going on to the platform to meet him?' asked George, as they drew into the little station yard. 'I'm not. I must look after Tim and the pony.'

'I don't want to,' said Anne. 'I'll stay with George.'

'Well, we'd better go, then,' said Julian, and he and Dick leapt out of the trap. They ran on to the platform just as the train pulled up.

Not many people got out. A woman clambered out with a basket. A young man leapt out, whistling, the son of the baker in the village. An old man climbed down with difficulty. The tutor could be none of those!

Then, right at the front of the train, rather an odd-looking man got out. He was short and burly, and he had a beard rather like a sailor. His eyes were piercingly blue, and his thick hair was sprinkled with grey. He glanced up and down the platform, and then beckoned to the porter.

'That must be Mr Roland,' said Julian to Dick.

'Come on – let's ask him. There's no one else it could be.'

The boys went up to the bearded man. 'Are you Mr Roland, sir?' he asked.

'I am,' said the man. 'I suppose you are Julian and Dick?'

'Yes, sir,' answered the boys together. 'We brought the pony-trap for your luggage.'

'Oh, fine,' said Mr Roland. His bright blue eyes looked the boys up and down, and he smiled. Julian and Dick liked him. He seemed sensible and jolly.

'Are the other two here as well?' said Mr Roland, walking down the platform, with the porter trailing behind with his luggage.

'Yes – George and Anne are outside with the trap,' said Julian.

'George and Anne,' said Mr Roland, in a puzzled voice. 'I thought the others were girls. I didn't know there was a third boy.'

'Oh, George is a girl,' said Dick, with a laugh. 'Her real name is Georgina.'

'And a very nice name, too,' said Mr Roland.

'George doesn't think so,' said Julian. 'She won't answer

if she's called Georgina. You'd better call her George, sir!'

'Really?' said Mr Roland, in rather a chilly tone. Julian took a glance at him.

'Not quite so jolly as he looks!' thought the boy.

'Tim's out there too,' said Dick.

'Oh – and is Tim a boy or a girl?' inquired Mr Roland, cautiously.

'A dog, sir!' said Dick, with a grin.

Mr Roland seemed rather taken aback. 'A dog?' he said. 'I didn't know there was a dog in the household. Your uncle said nothing to me about a dog.'

'Don't you like dogs?' asked Julian, in surprise.

'No,' said Mr Roland, shortly. 'But I dare say your dog won't worry me much. Hallo, hallo – so here are the little girls! How do you do?'

George was not very pleased at being called a little girl. For one thing she hated to be spoken of as little, and for another thing she always tried to be a boy. She held out her hand to Mr Roland and said nothing. Anne smiled at him, and Mr Roland thought she was much the nicer of the two.

'Tim! Shake hands with Mr Roland!' said Julian to Timothy. This was one of Tim's really good tricks. He could hold out his right paw in a very polite manner. Mr Roland looked down at the big dog, and Tim looked back at him.

Then, very slowly and deliberately, Timothy turned his

back on Mr Roland and climbed up into the pony-trap! Usually he put out his paw at once when told to, and the children stared at him in amazement.

'Timothy! What's come over you?' cried Dick. Tim put his ears down and did not move.

'He doesn't like you,' said George, looking at Mr Roland. 'That's very strange. He usually likes people. But perhaps you don't like dogs?'

'No, I don't, as a matter of fact,' said Mr Roland. 'I was once very badly bitten as a boy, and somehow or other I've never managed to like dogs since. But I dare say your Tim will take to me sooner or later.'

They all got into the trap. It was a tight squeeze. Timothy looked at Mr Roland's ankles as if he would rather like to nibble them. Anne laughed.

'Tim *is* behaving strangely!' she said. 'It's a good thing you haven't come to teach him, Mr Roland!' She smiled up at the tutor, and he smiled back, showing very white teeth. His eyes were as brilliant a blue as George's.

Anne liked him. He joked with the boys as they drove him, and both of them began to feel that their Uncle Quentin hadn't made such a bad choice after all.

Only George said nothing. She sensed that the tutor disliked Timothy, and George was not prepared to like anyone who didn't take to Timothy at first sight. She thought it was very peculiar too, that Tim would not shake paws with the tutor. 'He's a clever dog,' she thought. 'He knows Mr Roland doesn't like him, so he won't shake hands. I don't blame you, Tim darling, I wouldn't shake hands with anyone who didn't like *me*!'

Mr Roland was shown up to his room when he arrived. Aunt Fanny came down and spoke to the children. 'Well! He seems very nice, youngish and jolly.'

'Youngish!' exclaimed Julian. 'Why, he's awfully old! Must be forty at the very least!'

Aunt Fanny laughed. 'Does he seem so old to you?' she said. 'Well, old or not, he'll be quite nice to you, I'm sure.'

'Aunt Fanny, we shan't begin lessons until after Christmas, shall we?' asked Julian, anxiously.

'Of course you will!' said his aunt. 'It is almost a week till Christmas – you don't suppose we have asked Mr Roland to come and do nothing till Christmas is over, do you?'

The children groaned. 'We wanted to do some Christmas shopping,' said Anne.

'Well, you can do that in the afternoon,' said her aunt. 'You will only do lessons in the morning, for three hours. That won't hurt any of you!'

The new tutor came downstairs at that moment, and Aunt Fanny took him to see Uncle Quentin. She came out after a while, looking very pleased.

'Mr Roland will be nice company for your uncle,' she said to Julian. 'I think they will get on very well together. Mr Roland seems to understand quite a bit about your uncle's work.'

'Let's hope he spends most of his time with him then!' said George, in a low voice.

'Come on out for a walk,' said Dick. 'It's so fine today. We shan't have lessons this morning, shall we, Aunt Fanny?'

'Oh, no,' said his aunt. 'You'll begin tomorrow. Go for a walk now, all of you – we shan't often get sunny days like this!'

'Let's go over to Kirrin Farm,' said Julian. 'It looks such a nice place. Show us the way, George.'

'Right!' said George. She whistled to Timothy, and he

came bounding up. The five of them set off together, going down the lane, and then on to a rough road over the common that led to the farm on the distant hill.

It was lovely walking in the December sun. Their feet rang on the frosty path, and Tim's blunt claws made quite a noise as he pattered up and down, overjoyed at being with his four friends again.

After a good long walk across the common the children came to the farmhouse. It was built of white stone, and stood strong and lovely on the hillside. George opened the farmgate and went into the farm-yard. She kept her hand on Tim's collar for there were two farm-dogs somewhere about.

Someone clattered round the barn near-by. It was an old man, and George hailed him loudly.

'Hallo, Mr Sanders! How are you?'

'Why, if it isn't George!' said the old fellow with a grin. George grinned too.

'These are my cousins,' shouted George. She turned to the others. 'He's hard of hearing,' she said. 'You'll have to shout to make him hear.'

'I'm Julian,' said Julian in a loud voice and the others said their names too. The farmer beamed at them.

'You come along in and see the Missis,' he said. 'She'll be rare pleased to see you all. We've known George since she was a baby, and we knew her mother when *she* was a baby too, and we knew her granny as well.'

'You must be very, very old,' said Anne.

The farmer smiled down at her.

'As old as my tongue and a little older than my teeth!' he said, chuckling. 'Come away in now.'

They all went into the big, warm farmhouse kitchen, where a little old woman, as lively as a bantam hen, was bustling about. She was just as pleased to see the four children as her husband was.

'Well, there now!' she said. 'I haven't seen you for months, George. I did hear that you'd gone away to school.'

'Yes, I did,' said George. 'But I'm home for the holidays now. Does it matter if I let Timothy loose, Mrs Sanders? I think he'll be friendly if your dogs are, too.'

'Yes, you let him loose,' said the old lady. 'He'll have a fine time in the farmyard with Ben and Rikky. Now what would you like to drink? Hot milk? Cocoa? Coffee? And I've some new shortbread baked yesterday. You shall have some of that.'

'Ah, my wife's very busy this week, cooking up all sorts of things,' said the old farmer, as his wife bustled off to the larder. 'We've company this Christmas!'

'Have you?' said George, surprised, for she knew that the old pair had never had any children of their own. 'Who is coming? Anyone I know?'

'Two artists from London Town!' said the old farmer. 'Wrote and asked us to take them for three weeks over Christmas – and offered us good money too. So my old wife's as busy as a bee.'

'Are they going to paint pictures?' asked Julian, who rather fancied himself as an artist, too. 'I wonder if I could come and talk to them some day. I'm rather good at pictures myself. They might give me a few hints.'

'You come along whenever you like,' said old Mrs Sanders, making cocoa in a big jug. She set out a plate of most delicious-looking shortbreads, and the children ate them hungrily.

'I should think the two artists will be rather lonely down here, in the depths of the country at Christmastime,' said George. 'Do they know anyone?'

'They say they don't know a soul,' said Mrs Sanders. 'But there – artists can be peculiar folk. I've had some here before. They seemed to like mooning about all alone. These two will be happy enough, I'll be bound.'

'They should be, with all the good things you're cooking up for them,' said her old husband. 'Well, I must be out after the sheep. Good-day to you, youngsters. Come again and see us sometime.'

He went out. Old Mrs Sanders chattered on to the children as she bustled about the big kitchen. Timothy ran in and settled down on the rug by the fire.

He suddenly saw a tabby cat slinking along by the wall, all her hairs on end with fear of the strange dog. He gave a delighted wuff and sprang at the cat. She fled out of the kitchen into the old panelled hall. Tim flew after her, taking no notice at all of George's stern shout.

The cat tried to leap on top of an old grandfather clock

in the hall. With a joyous bark Tim sprang too. He flung himself against a polished panel – and then a most extraordinary thing happened!

The panel disappeared – and a dark hole showed in the old wall! George, who had followed Tim out into the hall, gave a loud cry of surprise. 'Look! Mrs Sanders, come and look!'

CHAPTER FOUR

An exciting discovery

OLD MRS Sanders and the other three children rushed out into the hall when they heard George's shout.

'What's up?' cried Julian. 'What's happened?'

'Tim sprang at the cat, missed her, and fell hard against the panelled wall,' said George, 'and the panel moved, and look – there's a hole in the wall!'

'It's a secret panel!' cried Dick, in excitement, peering into the hole. 'Golly! Did you know there was one here, Mrs Sanders?'

'Oh yes,' said the old lady. 'This house is full of funny things like that. I'm very careful when I polish that panel, because if I rub too hard in the top corner, it always slides back.'

'What's behind the panel?' asked Julian. The hole was only about the width of his head, and when he stuck his head inside, he could see only darkness. The wall itself was about eight inches behind the panelling, and was of stone.

'Get a candle, do get a candle!' said Anne, thrilled. 'You haven't got a torch, have you, Mrs Sanders?'

'No,' said the old woman. 'But you can get a candle if you like. There's one on the kitchen mantelpiece.'

Anne shot off to get it. Julian lit it and put it into the

hole behind the panel. The others pushed against him to try and peep inside.

'Don't,' said Julian, impatiently. 'Wait your turn, sillies! Let me have a look.'

He had a good look, but there didn't really seem anything to see. It was all darkness behind, and stone wall. He gave the candle to Dick, and then each of the children had a turn at peeping. Old Mrs Sanders had gone back to the kitchen. She was used to the sliding panel!

'She said this house was full of strange things like that,' said Anne. 'What other things are there, do you think? Let's ask her.'

They slid the panel back into place and went to find Mrs Sanders. 'Mrs Sanders, what other funny things are there in Kirrin Farmhouse?' asked Julian.

'There's a cupboard upstairs with a false back,' said Mrs Sanders. 'Don't look so excited! There's nothing in it at all! And there's a big stone over there by the fireplace that pulls up to show a hidey-hole. I suppose in the old days people wanted good hiding-places for things.'

The children ran to the stone she pointed out. It had an iron ring in it, and was easily pulled up. Below was a hollowed-out place, big enough to take a small box. It was empty now, but all the same it looked exciting.

'Where's the cupboard?' asked Julian.

'My old legs are too tired to go traipsing upstairs this morning,' said the farmer's wife. 'But you can go yourselves. Up the stairs, turn to the right, and go into the second door you see. The cupboard is at the farther end. Open the door and feel about at the bottom till you come across a dent in the wood. Press it hard, and the false back slides to the side.'

The four children and Timothy ran upstairs as fast as they could, munching shortbread as they went. This really was a very exciting morning!

They found the cupboard and opened the door. All four went down on hands and knees to press round the bottom of the cupboard to find the dented place. Anne found it.

'I've got it!' she cried. She pressed hard, but her little fingers were not strong enough to work the mechanism of the sliding back. Julian had to help her.

There was a creaking noise, and the children saw the false back of the cupboard sliding sideways. A big space showed behind, large enough to take a fairly thin man.

'A jolly good hiding-place,' said Julian. 'Anyone could hide there and no one would ever know!'

'I'll get in and you shut me up,' said Dick. 'It would be exciting.'

He got into the space. Julian slid the back across, and Dick could no longer be seen!

'Bit of a tight fit!' he called. 'And awfully dark! Let me out again.'

The children all took turns at going into the space behind the back of the cupboard and being shut up. Anne didn't like it very much.

They went down to the warm kitchen again. 'It's a most

exciting cupboard, Mrs Sanders,' said Julian. 'I do wish we lived in a house like this, full of secrets!'

'Can we come and play in that cupboard again?' asked George.

'No, I'm afraid you can't, George,' said Mrs Sanders. 'That room where the cupboard is, is one the two gentlemen are going to have.'

'Oh!' said Julian, disappointed. 'Shall you tell them about the sliding back, Mrs Sanders?'

'I don't expect so,' said the old lady. 'It's only you children that get excited about things like that, bless you. Two gentlemen wouldn't think twice about it.'

'How funny grown-ups are!' said Anne, puzzled. 'I'm quite certain I shall be thrilled to see a sliding panel or a trapdoor even when I'm a hundred.'

'Same here,' said Dick. 'Could I just go and look into the sliding panel in the hall once more, Mrs Sanders? I'll take the candle.'

Dick never knew why he suddenly wanted to have another look. It was just an idea he had. The others didn't bother to go with him, for there really was nothing to see behind the panelling except the old stone wall.

Dick took the candle and went into the hall. He pressed on the panel at the top and it slid back. He put the candle inside and had another good look. There was nothing at all to be seen. Dick took out his head and put in his arm, stretching along the wall as far as his hand would reach. He was just about to take it back when his fingers found a hole in the wall.

'Funny!' said Dick. 'Why should there be a hole in the stone wall just there?'

He stuck in his finger and thumb and worked them about. He felt a little ridge inside the wall, rather like a bird's perch, and was able to get hold of it. He wriggled his fingers about the perch, but nothing happened. Then he got a good hold and pulled.

The stone came right out! Dick was so surprised that he let go the heavy stone and it fell to the ground behind the panelling with a crash!

The noise brought the others out into the hall. 'Whatever are you doing, Dick?' said Julian. 'Have you broken something?'

'No,' said Dick, his face reddening with excitement. 'I say – I put my hand in here – and found a hole in one of the stones the wall is made of – and I got hold of a sort of ridge with my finger and thumb and pulled. The stone came right out, and I got such a surprise I let go. It fell, and that's what you heard!'

'Golly!' said Julian, trying to push Dick away from the open panel. 'Let me see.'

'No, Julian,' said Dick, pushing him away. 'This is *my* discovery. Wait till I see if I can feel anything in the hole. It's difficult to get at!'

The others waited impatiently. Julian could hardly prevent himself from pushing Dick right away. Dick put his arm in as far as he could, and curved his hand round to get into the space behind where the stone had been. His fingers felt about and he closed them round something that felt like a book. Cautiously and carefully he brought it out.

'An old book!' he said.

'What's in it?' cried Anne.

They turned the pages carefully. They were so dry and brittle that some of them fell into dust.

'I think it's a book of recipes,' said Anne, as her sharp eyes read a few words in the old brown, faded handwriting. 'Let's take it to Mrs Sanders.'

The children carried the book to the old lady. She laughed at their beaming faces. She took the book and looked at it, not at all excited.

'Yes,' she said. 'It's a book of recipes, that's all it is. See the name in the front – Alice Mary Sanders – that must have been my husband's great-grandmother. She was famous for her medicines, I know. It was said she could cure any ill in man or animal, no matter what it was.'

'It's a pity it's so hard to read her writing,' said Julian, disappointed. 'The whole book is falling to pieces too. It must be very old.'

'Do you think there's anything else in that hidey-hole?' asked Anne. 'Julian, you go and put *your* arm in, it's longer than Dick's.'

'There didn't seem to be anything else at all,' said Dick. 'It's a very small place – just a few inches of hollow space behind that brick or stone that fell down.'

'Well, I'll just put my hand in and see,' said Julian. They all went back into the hall. Julian put his arm into the open panel, and slid it along the wall to where the stone had fallen out. His hand went into the space there, and his long fingers groped about, feeling for anything else that might be there.

There was something else, something soft and flat that felt like leather. Eagerly the boy's fingers closed over it and he drew it out carefully, half afraid that it might fall to pieces with age.

'I've got something!' he said, his eyes gleaming brightly. 'Look – what is it?'

The others crowded round. 'It's rather like Daddy's tobacco pouch,' said Anne, feeling it. 'The same shape. Is there anything inside?'

It was a tobacco pouch, very dark brown, made of soft leather and very much worn. Carefully Julian undid the flap, and unrolled the leather.

A few bits of black tobacco were still in the pouch but there was something else, too! Tightly rolled up in the last bit of pouch was a piece of linen. Julian took it out and unrolled it. He put it flat on the hall-table.

The children stared at it. There were marks and signs on the linen, done in black ink that had hardly faded. But the four of them could not make head or tail of the marks.

'It's not a map,' said Julian. 'It seems a sort of code, or something. I do wonder what it means. I wish we could make it out. It must be some sort of secret.'

The children stared at the piece of linen, very thrilled. It was so old – and contained some kind of secret. Whatever could it be?

They ran to show it to Mrs Sanders. She was studying the old recipe book, and her face glowed with pleasure as she raised it to look at the excited children.

'This book's a wonder!' she said. 'I can hardly read the writing, but here's a recipe for backache. I shall try it myself. My back aches so much at the end of the day. Now, you listen . . .'

But the children didn't want to listen to recipes for

backache. They pushed the piece of linen on to Mrs Sanders's lap.

'Look! What's this about, Mrs Sanders? Do you know? We found it in a kind of tobacco pouch in that place behind the panel.'

Mrs Sanders took off her glasses, polished them, and put them on again. She looked carefully at the piece of linen with its strange marks.

She shook her head. 'No – this doesn't make any sense to me. And what's this now? – it looks like an old tobacco pouch. Ah, my John would like that, I guess. He's got such an old one that it won't hold his tobacco any more! This is old too – but there's a lot of wear in it yet.'

'Mrs Sanders, do you want this piece of linen too?' asked Julian, anxiously. He was longing to take it home and study it. He felt certain there was some kind of exciting secret hidden there, and he could not bear the thought of leaving it with Mrs Sanders.

'You take it, Julian, if you want it,' said Mrs Sanders, with a laugh. 'I'll keep the recipes for myself, and John shall have the pouch. You can have the old rag if you want it, though it beats me why you think it's so fascinating! Ah, here's John!'

She raised her voice and shouted to the old man. 'Hey, John, here's a tobacco pouch for you. The children found it somewhere behind that panel that opens in the hall.'

John took it and fingered it. 'It's a strange one,' he said, 'but better than mine. Well, youngsters, I don't want to hurry you, but it's one o'clock now, and you'd better be going if it's near your dinner-time!'

'Gracious!' said Julian. 'We shall be late! Goodbye, Mrs Sanders, and thanks awfully for the shortbread and this old rag. We'll try our best to make out what's on it and tell you. Hurry, everyone! Where's Tim? Come on, Timothy, we're late!'

The five of them ran off quickly. They really were late, and had to run most of the way, which meant that it was difficult to talk. But they were so excited about their morning that they panted remarks to one another as they went.

'I wonder what this old rag says!' panted Julian. 'I mean to find out. I'm sure it's something mysterious.'

'Shall we tell anyone?' asked Dick.

'No!' said George. 'Let's keep it a secret.'

'If Anne starts to give away anything, kick her under the table, like we did last summer,' said Julian, with a grin. Poor Anne always found it difficult to keep a secret, and often had to be nudged or kicked when she began to give things away.

'I won't say a word,' said Anne, indignantly. 'And don't you dare to kick me. It only makes me cry out and then the grown-ups want to know why.'

'We'll have a good old puzzle over this piece of linen after dinner,' said Julian. 'I bet we'll find out what it says, if we really make up our minds to!'

'Here we are,' said George. 'Not too late. Hallo, Mother! We won't be a minute washing our hands! We've had a lovely time.'

CHAPTER FIVE

An unpleasant walk

AFTER DINNER the four children went upstairs to the boys' bedroom and spread out the bit of linen on a table there. There were words here and there, scrawled in rough printing. There was the sign of a compass, with E marked clearly for East. There were eight rough squares, and in one of them, right in the middle, was a cross. It was all very mysterious.

'You know, I believe these words are Latin,' said Julian, trying to make them out. 'But I can't read them properly. And I expect if I *could* read them, I wouldn't know what they meant. I wish we knew someone who could read Latin like this.'

'Could your father, George?' asked Anne.

'I expect so,' said George. But nobody wanted to ask George's father. He might take the curious old rag away. He might forget all about it, he might even burn it. Scientists were such peculiar people.

'What about Mr Roland?' said Dick. 'He's a tutor. He knows Latin.'

'We won't ask him till we know a bit more about him,' said Julian, cautiously. 'He *seems* jolly and nice – but you never know. Oh, blow – I wish we could make this out, I really do.'

'There are two words at the top,' said Dick, and he tried to spell them out. 'VIA OCCULTA.' What do you think they could mean, Julian?'

'Well – the only thing I can think of that they can mean is – Secret Way, or something like that,' said Julian, screwing up his forehead into a frown.

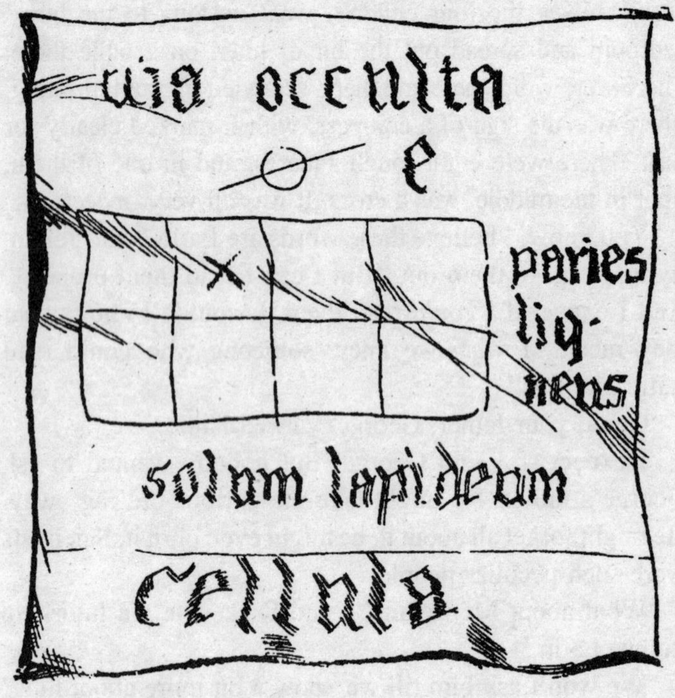

'Secret Way!' said Anne, her eyes shining. 'Oh, I hope it's that! Secret Way! How exciting. What sort of secret way would it be, Julian?'

'How do I know, Anne, silly?' said Julian. 'I don't even know that the words are meant to mean "Secret Way". It's really a guess on my part.'

'If they did mean that – the linen might have directions to find the Secret Way, whatever it is,' said Dick. 'Oh Julian, isn't it exasperating that we can't read it? Do, do try. You know more Latin than I do.'

'It's so hard to read the funny old letters,' said Julian, trying again. 'No – it's no good at all. I can't make them out.'

Steps came up the stairs, and the door opened. Mr Roland looked in.

'Hallo, hallo!' he said. 'I wondered where you all were. What about a walk over the cliffs?'

'We'll come,' said Julian, rolling up the old rag.

'What have you got there? Anything interesting?' asked Mr Roland.

'It's a—' began Anne, and at once all the others began to talk, afraid that Anne was going to give the secret away.

'It's a wonderful afternoon for a walk.'

'Come on, let's get our things on!'

'Tim, Tim, where are you?' George gave a piercing whistle. Tim was under the bed and came bounding out. Anne went red as she guessed why all the others had interrupted her so quickly.

'Idiot,' said Julian, under his breath. 'Baby.'

Fortunately Mr Roland said no more about the piece of linen he had seen Julian rolling up. He was looking at Tim.

'I suppose he must come,' he said. George stared at him in indignation.

'Of course he must!' she said. 'We never never go anywhere without Timothy.'

Mr Roland went downstairs, and the children got ready to go out. George was scowling. The very idea of leaving Tim behind made her angry.

'You nearly gave our secret away, you silly,' said Dick to Anne.

'I didn't think,' said the little girl, looking ashamed of herself. 'Anyway, Mr Roland seems very nice. I think we might ask him if he could help us to understand those funny words.'

'You leave that to me to decide,' said Julian, crossly. 'Now don't you dare to say a word.'

They all set out, Timothy too. Mr Roland need not have worried about the dog, for Timothy would not go near him. It was very strange, really. He kept away from the tutor, and took not the slightest notice of him even when Mr Roland spoke to him.

'He's not usually like that,' said Dick. 'He's a most friendly dog, really.'

'Well, as I've got to live in the same house with him, I must try and make him friends with me,' said the tutor. 'Hi, Timothy! Come here! I've got a biscuit in my pocket.'

Timothy pricked up his ears at the word 'biscuit', but did not even look towards Mr Roland. He put his tail down and went to George. She patted him.

'If he doesn't like anyone, not even a biscuit or a bone will make him go to them when he is called,' she said.

Mr Roland gave it up. He put the biscuit back into his pocket. 'He's a peculiar-looking dog, isn't he?' he said. 'A terrible mongrel! I must say I prefer well-bred dogs.'

George went purple in the face. 'He's *not* peculiar-looking!' she spluttered. 'He's not nearly so peculiar-looking as you! He's not a terrible mongrel. He's the best dog in the world!'

'I think you are being a little rude,' said Mr Roland, stiffly. 'I don't allow my pupils to be cheeky, Georgina.'

Calling her Georgina made George still more furious. She lagged behind with Tim, looking as dark as a thundercloud. The others felt uncomfortable. They knew what tempers George got into, and how difficult she could be. She had been so much better and happier since the summer, when they had come to stay for the first time. They did hope she wasn't going to be silly and get into rows. It would spoil the Christmas holidays.

Mr Roland took no more notice of George. He did not speak to her, but strode on ahead with the others, doing his best to be jolly. He could really be very funny, and the boys began to laugh at him. He took Anne's hand, and the little girl jumped along beside him, enjoying the walk.

Julian felt sorry for George. It wasn't nice to be left out of things, and he knew how George hated anything like that. He wondered if he dared to put in a good word for her. It might make things easier.

'Mr Roland, sir,' he began. 'Could you call my cousin by the name she likes – George – she simply hates Georgina. And she's very fond of Tim. She can't bear anyone to say horrid things about him.'

Mr Roland looked surprised. 'My dear boy, I am sure you mean well,' he said, in rather a dry sort of voice, 'but

I hardly think I want your advice about any of my pupils. I shall follow my own wishes in my treatment of Georgina, not yours. I want to be friends with you all, and I am sure we shall be – but Georgina has got to be sensible, as you three are.'

Julian felt rather squashed. He went red and looked at Dick. Dick gave him a squeeze on his arm. The boys knew George could be silly and difficult, especially if anyone didn't like her beloved dog – but they thought Mr Roland might try to be a bit more understanding too. Dick slipped behind and walked with George.

'You needn't walk with me,' said George at once, her blue eyes glinting. 'Walk with your friend Mr Roland.'

'He isn't my friend,' said Dick. 'Don't be silly.'

'I'm not silly,' said George, in a tight sort of voice. 'I heard you all laughing and joking with him. You go on and have a good laugh again. I've got Timothy.'

'George, it's Christmas holidays,' said Dick. 'Do let's all be friends. Do. Don't let's spoil Christmas.'

'I can't like anyone who doesn't like Tim,' said George, obstinately.

'Well, after all, Mr Roland did offer him a biscuit,' said Dick, trying to make peace as hard as he could.

George said nothing. Her small face looked fierce. Dick tried again.

'George! Promise to try and be nice till Christmas is over, anyway. Don't let's spoil Christmas, for goodness' sake! Come on, George.'

'All right,' said George, at last. 'I'll try.'

'Come and walk with us then,' said Dick. So George caught up the others, and tried not to look too sulky. Mr Roland guessed that Dick had been trying to make George behave, and he included her in his talk. He could not make her laugh, but she did at least answer politely.

'Is that Kirrin Farmhouse?' asked Mr Roland, as they came in sight of the farm.

'Yes. Do you know it?' asked Julian, in surprise.

'No, no,' said Mr Roland, at once, 'I've heard of it, and wondered if that was the place.'

'We went there this morning,' said Anne. 'It's an exciting place.' She looked at the others, wondering if they would mind if she said anything about the things they had seen that morning. Julian thought for a moment. After all, it couldn't matter telling him about the stone in the kitchen and the false back to the cupboard. Mrs Sanders would tell anyone that. He could speak about the sliding panel in the hall too, and say they had found an old recipe book there. He did not need to say anything about the old bit of marked linen.

So he told their tutor about the exciting things there had been at the old farmhouse, but said nothing at all about the linen and its strange markings. Mr Roland listened with the greatest interest.

'This is all very remarkable,' he said. 'Very remarkable indeed. Most interesting. You say the old couple live there quite alone?'

'Well, they are having two people to stay over Christmas,' said Dick. 'Artists. Julian thought he would go over and talk to them. He can paint awfully well, you know.'

'Can he really?' said Mr Roland. 'Well, he must show me some of his pictures. But I don't think he'd better go and worry the artists at the farmhouse. They might not like it.'

This remark made Julian feel obstinate. He made up his

mind at once that he *would* go and talk to the two artists when he got the chance!

It was quite a pleasant walk on the whole except that George was quiet, and Timothy would not go anywhere near Mr Roland. When they came to a frozen pond Dick threw sticks on it for Tim to fetch. It was so funny to see him go slithering about on his long legs, trying to run properly!

Everyone threw sticks for the dog, and Tim fetched all the sticks except Mr Roland's. When the tutor threw a stick the dog looked at it and took no more notice. It was almost as if he had said, 'What, *your* stick! No, thank you!'

'Now, home we go,' said Mr Roland, trying not to look annoyed with Tim. 'We shall just be in time for tea!'

CHAPTER SIX

Lessons with Mr Roland

NEXT MORNING the children felt a little gloomy. Lessons! How horrid in the holidays! Still, Mr Roland wasn't so bad. The children had not had him with them in the sitting-room the night before, because he had gone to talk to their uncle. So they were able to get out the mysterious bit of linen again and pore over it.

But it wasn't a bit of good. Nobody could make anything of it at all. Secret Way! What did it mean? Was it really directions for a Secret Way? And where was the way, and why was it secret? It was most exasperating not to be able to find out.

'I really feel we'll have to ask someone soon,' Julian had said with a sigh. 'I can't bear this mystery much longer. I keep on and on thinking of it.'

He had dreamt of it too that night, and now it was morning, with lessons ahead. He wondered what lesson Mr Roland would take – Latin perhaps. Then he could ask him what the words 'VIA OCCULTA' meant.

Mr Roland had seen all their reports and had noted the subjects they were weak in. One was Latin, and another was French. Maths were very weak in both Dick's report and George's. Both children must be helped on in those.

Geometry was Julian's weakest spot.

Anne was not supposed to need any coaching. 'But if you like to come along and join us, I'll give you some painting to do,' said Mr Roland, his blue eyes twinkling at her. He liked Anne. She was not difficult and sulky like George.

Anne loved painting. 'Oh, yes,' she said, happily, 'I'd love to do some painting. I can paint flowers, Mr Roland. I'll paint you some red poppies and blue cornflowers out of my head.'

'We will start at half-past nine,' said Mr Roland. 'We are to work in the sitting-room. Take your schoolbooks there, and be ready punctually.'

So all the children were there, sitting round a table, their books in front of them, at half-past nine. Anne had some painting water and her painting-box. The others looked at her enviously. Lucky Anne, to be doing painting while they worked hard at difficult things like Latin and maths!

'Where's Timothy?' asked Julian in a low voice, as they waited for their tutor to come in.

'Under the table,' said George, defiantly. 'I'm sure he'll lie still. Don't any of you say anything about him. I want him there. I'm not going to do lessons without Tim here.'

'I don't see why he shouldn't be here with us,' said Dick. 'He's very very good. Sh! Here comes Mr Roland.'

The tutor came in, his black beard bristling round his mouth and chin. His eyes looked very piercing in the pale winter sunlight that filtered into the room. He told the children to sit down.

'I'll have a look at your exercise books first,' he said, 'and see what you were doing last term. You come first, Julian.'

Soon the little class were working quietly together. Anne was very busy painting a bright picture of poppies and cornflowers. Mr Roland admired it very much. Anne thought he really was very nice.

Suddenly there was a huge sigh from under the table. It was Tim, tired of lying so still. Mr Roland looked up, surprised. George at once sighed heavily, hoping that Mr Roland would think it was she who had sighed before.

'You sound tired, Georgina,' said Mr Roland. 'You shall all have a little break at eleven.'

George frowned. She hated being called Georgina. She put her foot cautiously on Timothy to warn him not to make any more noises. Tim licked her foot.

After a while, just when the class was at its very quietest, Tim felt a great wish to scratch himself very hard on his back. He got up. He sat down again with a thump, gave a grunt, and began to scratch himself furiously. The children all began to make noises to hide the sounds that Tim was making.

George clattered her feet on the floor. Julian began to cough, and let one of his books slip to the ground. Dick jiggled the table and spoke to Mr Roland.

'Oh dear, this sum is so hard; it really is! I keep doing

it and doing it, and it simply *won't* come right!'

'Why all this sudden noise?' said Mr Roland in surprise. 'Stop tapping the floor with your feet, Georgina.'

Tim settled down quietly again. The children gave a sigh of relief. They became quiet, and Mr Roland told Dick to come to him with his Maths book.

The tutor took it, and stretched his legs out under the table, leaning back to speak to Dick. To his enormous surprise his feet struck something soft and warm – and then something nipped him sharply on the ankle! He drew in his feet with a cry of pain.

The children stared at him. He bent down and looked under the table. 'It's that dog,' he said, in disgust. 'The brute snapped at my ankles. He has made a hole in my trousers. Take him out, Georgina.'

Georgina said nothing. She sat as though she had not heard.

'She won't answer if you call her Georgina,' Julian reminded him.

'She'll answer me whatever I call her,' said Mr Roland, in a low and angry voice. 'I won't have that dog in here. If you don't take him out this very minute, Georgina, I will go to your father.'

George looked at him. She knew perfectly well that if she didn't take Tim out, and Mr Roland went to her father, he would order Timothy to live in the garden kennel, and that would be dreadful. There was absolutely nothing to be done but obey. Red in the face, a huge frown almost hiding her eyes, she got up and spoke to Tim.

'Come on, Tim! I'm not surprised you bit him. I would, too, if I were a dog!'

'There is no need to be rude, Georgina,' said Mr Roland, angrily.

The others stared at George. They wondered how she

dared to say things like that. When she got fierce it seemed as if she didn't care for anyone at all!

'Come back as soon as you have put the dog out,' said Mr Roland.

George scowled, but came back in a few minutes. She felt caught. Her father was friendly with Mr Roland, and knew how difficult George was – if she behaved as badly as she felt she would like to, it would be Tim who would suffer, for he would certainly be banished from the house. So for Tim's sake George obeyed the tutor – but from that moment she disliked him and resented him bitterly with all her fierce little heart.

The others were sorry for George and Timothy, but they did not share the little girl's intense dislike of the new tutor. He often made them laugh. He was patient with their mistakes. He was willing to show them how to make paper darts and ships, and to do funny little tricks. Julian and Dick thought these were fun, and stored them up to try on the other boys when they went back to school.

After lessons that morning the children went out for half an hour in the frosty sunshine. George called Tim.

'Poor old boy!' she said. 'What a shame to turn you out of the room! Whatever did you snap at Mr Roland for? I think it was a very good idea, Tim – but I really don't know what made you!'

'George, you can't play about with Mr Roland,' said Julian. 'You'll only get into trouble. He's tough. He won't stand much from any of us. But I think he'll be quite a good sport if we get on the right side of him.'

'Well, get on the right side of him if you like,' said George, in rather a sneering voice. 'I'm not going to. If I don't like a person, I don't – and I don't like *him*.'

'Why? Just because he doesn't like Tim?' asked Dick.

'Mostly because of that – but because he makes me feel prickly down my back,' said George. 'I don't like his nasty mouth.'

'But you can't see it,' said Julian. 'It's covered with his moustache and beard.'

'I've seen his lips through them,' said George, obstinately. 'They're thin and cruel. You look and see. I don't like thin-lipped people. They are always spiteful and hard. And I don't like his cold eyes either. You can suck up to him all you like. *I* shan't.'

Julian refused to get angry with the stubborn little girl. He laughed at her. 'We're not going to suck up to him,' he said. 'We're just going to be sensible, that's all. You be sensible too, George, old thing.'

But once George had made up her mind about something nothing would alter her. She cheered up when she heard that they were all to go Christmas shopping on the bus that afternoon – without Mr Roland! He was going to watch an experiment that her father was going to show him.

'I will take you into the nearest town and you shall shop to your hearts' content,' said Aunt Fanny to the children. 'Then we will have tea in a tea-shop and catch the six o'clock bus home.'

This was fun. They caught the afternoon bus and rumbled along the deep country lanes till they got to the town. The shops looked very colourful and bright. The children had brought their money with them, and were very busy indeed, buying all kinds of things. There were so many people to get presents for!

'I suppose we'd better get something for Mr Roland, hadn't we?' said Julian.

'I'm going to,' said Anne.

'Fancy buying Mr *Roland* a present!' said George, in her scornful voice.

'Why shouldn't she, George?' asked her mother, in surprise. 'Oh dear, I hope you are going to be sensible about him, and not take a violent dislike to the poor man. I don't want him to complain to your father about you.'

'What are you going to buy for Tim, George?' asked Julian, changing the subject quickly.

'The largest bone the butcher has got,' said George. 'What are *you* going to buy him?'

'I guess if Tim had money, he would buy us each a present,' said Anne, taking hold of the thick hair round Tim's neck, and pulling it lovingly, 'He's the best dog in the world!'

George forgave Anne for saying she would buy Mr Roland a present, when the little girl said that about Tim! She cheered up again and began to plan what she would buy for everyone.

They had a fine tea, and caught the six o'clock bus back. Aunt Fanny went to see if the cook had given the two men their tea. She came out of the study beaming.

'Really, I've never seen your uncle so jolly,' she said to Julian and Dick. 'He and Mr Roland are getting on like a house on fire. He has been showing your tutor quite a lot of his experiments. It's nice for him to have someone to talk to that knows a little about these things.'

Mr Roland played games with the children that evening. Tim was in the room, and the tutor tried again to make friends with him, but the dog refused to take any notice of him.

'As sulky as his little mistress!' said the tutor, with a laughing look at George, who was watching Tim refuse to go to Mr Roland, and looking rather pleased about it. She gave the tutor a scowl and said nothing.

'Shall we ask him whether "VIA OCCULTA" really does mean "Secret Way" or not, tomorrow?' said Julian to Dick, as they undressed that night. 'I'm just longing to know if it does. What do you think of Mr Roland, Dick?'

'I don't really quite know,' said Dick. 'I like lots of things about him, but then I suddenly don't like him at all. I don't like his eyes. And George is quite right about his lips. They are so thin there's hardly anything of them at all.'

'I think he's all right,' said Julian. 'He won't stand any nonsense, that's all. I wouldn't mind showing him the whole piece of rag and asking him to make out its meaning for us.'

'I thought you said it was to be a proper secret,' said Dick.

'I know – but what's the use of a secret we don't know the meaning of ourselves?' said Julian. 'I'll tell you what we *could* do – ask him to explain the words to us, and not show him the bit of linen.

'But we can't read some of the words ourselves,' said Dick. 'So that's no use. You'd have to show him the whole thing, and tell him where we got it.'

'Well, I'll see,' said Julian, getting into bed.

The next day there were lessons again from half-past nine to half-past twelve. George appeared without Tim. She was angry at having to do this, but it was no good being defiant and refusing to come to lessons without Tim. Now that he had snapped at Mr Roland, he had definitely put himself in the wrong, and the tutor had every right to refuse to allow him to come. But George looked very sulky indeed.

In the Latin lesson Julian took the chance of asking what he wanted to know. 'Please, Mr Roland,' he said, 'could you tell me what "VIA OCCULTA" means?'

'"VIA OCCULTA"' said Mr Roland, frowning. 'Yes – it means "Secret Path" or, "Secret Road". A hidden way – something like that. Why do you want to know?'

All the children were listening eagerly. Their hearts thumped with excitement. So Julian had been right. That funny bit of rag contained directions for some hidden way, some secret path – but where to! Where did it begin, and end?

'Oh – I just wanted to know,' said Julian. 'Thank you, sir.'

He winked at the others. He was as excited as they were. If only they could make out the rest of the markings, they might be able to solve the mystery. Well – perhaps he would ask Mr Roland in a day or two. The secret must be solved somehow.

'The "Secret Way",' said Julian to himself, as he worked out a problem in geometry. 'The "Secret Way". I'll find it somehow.'

CHAPTER SEVEN

Directions for the Secret Way

FOR THE next day or two the four children did not really have much time to think about the Secret Way, because Christmas was coming near, and there was a good deal to do.

There were Christmas cards to draw and paint for their mothers and fathers and friends. There was the house to decorate. They went out with Mr Roland to find sprays of holly, and came home laden.

'You look like a Christmas card yourselves,' said Aunt Fanny, as they walked up the garden path, carrying the red-berried holly over their shoulders. Mr Roland had found a group of trees with tufts of mistletoe growing from the top branches, and they had brought some of that too. Its berries shone like pale green pearls.

'Mr Roland had to climb the tree to get this,' said Anne. 'He's a good climber – as good as a monkey.'

Everyone laughed except George. She never laughed at anything to do with the tutor. They all dumped their loads down in the porch, and went to wash. They were to decorate the house that evening.

'Is Uncle going to let his study be decorated too?' asked Anne. There were all kinds of strange instruments and glass tubes in the study now, and the children looked at them with wonder whenever they ventured into the study, which was very seldom.

'No, my study is certainly not to be messed about,' said Uncle Quentin, at once. 'I wouldn't hear of it.'

'Uncle, why do you have all these funny things in your study?' asked Anne, looking round with wide eyes.

Uncle Quentin laughed. 'I'm looking for a secret formula!' he said.

'What's that?' said Anne.

'You wouldn't understand,' said her uncle. 'All these "funny things" as you call them, help me in my experiments, and I put down in my book what they tell me – and from all I learn I work out a secret formula, which will be of great use when it is finished.'

'You want to know a secret formula, and we want to know a secret way,' said Anne, quite forgetting that she was not supposed to talk about this.

Julian was standing by the door. He frowned at Anne. Luckily Uncle Quentin was not paying any more attention to the little girl's chatter. Julian pulled her out of the room.

'Anne, the only way to stop you giving away secrets is to sew up your mouth, like Brer Rabbit wanted to do to Mister Dog!' he said.

Joanna the cook was busy baking Christmas cakes. An enormous turkey had been sent over from Kirrin Farm, and was hanging up in the larder. Timothy thought it smelt glorious, and Joanna was always shooing him out of the kitchen.

There were boxes of crackers on the shelf in the sitting-room, and mysterious parcels everywhere. It was very, very Christmassy! The children were happy and excited.

Mr Roland went out and dug up a little spruce fir tree. 'We must have a Christmas tree,' he said. 'Have you any tree-ornaments, children?'

'No,' said Julian, seeing George shake her head.

'I'll go into the town this afternoon and get some for you,' promised the tutor. 'It will be fun dressing the tree. We'll put it in the hall, and light candles on it on Christmas Day after tea. Who's coming with me to get the candles and the ornaments?'

'I am!' cried three children. But the fourth said nothing. That was George. Not even to buy tree-ornaments would the obstinate little girl go with Mr Roland. She had never had a Christmas tree before, and she was very much looking forward to it – but it was spoilt for her because Mr Roland bought the things that made it so beautiful.

Now it stood in the hall, with coloured candles in holders clipped to the branches, and bright shining ornaments hanging from top to bottom. Silver strands of frosted string hung down from the branches like icicles, and Anne had put bits of white cotton-wool here and there to look like snow. It really was a lovely sight to see.

'Beautiful!' said Uncle Quentin, as he passed through the hall, and saw Mr Roland hanging the last ornaments on the tree. 'I say – look at the fairy doll on the top! Who's that for? A good girl?'

Anne secretly hoped that Mr Roland would give her the doll. She was sure it wasn't for George – and anyway, George wouldn't accept it. It was such a pretty doll, with its gauzy frock and silvery wings.

Julian, Dick and Anne had quite accepted the tutor now as teacher and friend. In fact, everyone had, their uncle and aunt too, and even Joanna the cook. George, of course, was the only exception, and she and Timothy kept away from Mr Roland, each looking as sulky as the other whenever the tutor was in the room.

'You know, I never knew a dog could look so sulky!' said Julian, watching Timothy. 'Really, he scowls almost like George.'

'And I always feel as if George puts her tail down like Tim, when Mr Roland is in the room,' giggled Anne.

'Laugh all you like,' said George, in a low tone. 'I think you're beastly to me. I know I'm right about Mr Roland. I've got a feeling about him. And so has Tim.'

'You're silly, George,' said Dick. 'You haven't *really* got a Feeling – it's only that Mr Roland will keep calling you Georgina and putting you in your place, and that he doesn't like Tim. I dare say he can't help disliking dogs. After all, there was once a famous man called Lord Roberts who couldn't bear cats.'

'Oh well, cats are different,' said George. 'If a person doesn't like dogs, especially a dog like our Timothy, then there really *must* be something wrong with him.'

'It's no use arguing with George,' said Julian. 'Once she's made up her mind about something, she won't budge!'

George went out of the room in a huff. The others thought she was behaving rather stupidly.

'I'm surprised really,' said Anne. 'She was so jolly last term at school. Now she's gone all strange, rather like she was when we first knew her last summer.'

'I do think Mr Roland has been decent digging up the Christmas tree and everything,' said Dick. 'I still don't like him awfully much sometimes, but I think he's a sport. What about asking him if he can read that old linen rag for us – I don't think I'd mind him sharing our secret, really.'

'I would *love* him to share it,' said Anne, who was busy doing a marvellous Christmas card for the tutor. 'He's most awfully clever. I'm sure he could tell us what the Secret Way is. Do let's ask him.'

'All right,' said Julian. 'I'll show him the piece of linen. It's Christmas Eve tonight. He will be with us in the sitting-room, because Aunt Fanny is going into the study with Uncle Quentin to wrap up presents for all of us!'

So, that evening, before Mr Roland came in to sit with them, Julian took out the little roll of linen and stroked it out flat on the table. George looked at it in surprise.

'Mr Roland will be here in a minute,' she said. 'You'd better put it away quickly.'

'We're going to ask him if he can tell us what the old Latin words mean,' said Julian.

'You're not!' cried George, in dismay. 'Ask him to share our secret! How ever can you?'

'Well, we want to know what the secret is, don't we?' said Julian. 'We don't need to tell him where we got this or anything about it except that we want to know what the markings mean. We're not exactly sharing the secret with him – only asking him to use his brains to help us.'

'Well, I never thought you'd ask *him*,' said George.

'And he'll want to know simply everything about it, you just see if he won't! He's terribly snoopy.'

'Whatever do you mean?' said Julian, in surprise. 'I don't think he's a bit snoopy.'

'I saw him yesterday snooping round the study when no one was there,' said George. 'He didn't see me outside the window with Tim. He was having a real poke round.'

'You know how interested he is in your father's work,' said Julian. 'Why shouldn't he look at it? Your father likes him too. You're just seeing what horrid things you can find to say about Mr Roland.'

'Oh shut up, you two,' said Dick. 'It's Christmas Eve. Don't let's argue or quarrel or say beastly things.'

Just at that moment the tutor came into the room. 'All as busy as bees?' he said, his mouth smiling beneath its moustache. 'Too busy to have a game of cards, I suppose?'

'Mr Roland, sir,' began Julian, 'could you help us with something? We've got an old bit of linen here with odd markings on it. The words seem to be in some sort of Latin and we can't make them out.'

George gave an angry exclamation as she saw Julian push the piece of linen over towards the tutor. She went out of the room and shut the door with a bang. Tim was with her.

'Our sweet-tempered Georgina doesn't seem to be very friendly tonight,' remarked Mr Roland, pulling the bit of linen towards him. 'Where in the world did you get this? What an odd thing!'

Nobody answered. Mr Roland studied the roll of linen, and then gave an exclamation. 'Ah – I see why you wanted to know the meaning of those Latin words the other day – the ones that meant "hidden path", you remember. They are at the top of this linen roll.'

'Yes,' said Dick. All the children leaned over towards Mr Roland, hoping he would be able to unravel a little of the mystery for them.

'We just want to know the meaning of the words, sir,' said Julian.

'This is really very interesting,' said the tutor, puzzling over the linen. 'Apparently there are directions here for finding the opening or entrance of a secret path or road.'

'That's what we thought!' cried Julian, excitedly. 'That's exactly what we thought. Oh, sir, do read the directions and see what you make of them.'

'Well, these eight squares are meant to represent wooden boards or panels, I think,' said the tutor, pointing to the eight rough squares drawn on the linen. 'Wait a minute – I can hardly read some of the words. This is most fascinating. *Solum lapideum – paries ligneus* – and what's this? – *cellula* – yes, *cellula*!'

The children hung on his words. 'Wooden panels!' That must mean panels somewhere at Kirrin Farmhouse.

Mr Roland frowned down at the old printed words. Then he sent Anne to borrow a magnifying glass from her uncle. She came back with it, and the four of them looked through the glass, seeing the words three times as clearly now.

'Well,' said the tutor at last, 'as far as I can make out the directions mean this: a room facing east; eight wooden panels, with an opening somewhere to be found in that marked one; a stone floor – yes, I think that's right, a stone floor, and a cupboard. It all sounds most extraordinary and very thrilling. Where *did* you get this from?'

'We just found it,' said Julian, after a pause. 'Oh, Mr

Roland, thanks awfully. We could never have made it out by ourselves. I suppose the entrance to the Secret Way is in a room facing east then.'

'It looks like it,' said Mr Roland, poring over the linen roll again. 'Where did you say you found this?'

'We didn't say,' said Dick. 'It's a secret really, you see.'

'I think you might tell me,' said the tutor, looking at Dick with his brilliant blue eyes. 'I can be trusted with secrets. You've no idea how many strange secrets I know.'

'Well,' said Julian, 'I don't really see why you shouldn't know where we found this, Mr Roland. We found it at Kirrin Farmhouse, in an old tobacco pouch. I suppose the Secret Way begins somewhere there! I wonder where and wherever can it lead to?'

'You found it at Kirrin Farmhouse!' exclaimed Mr Roland. 'Well, well – I must say that seems to be an interesting old place. I shall have to go over there one day.'

Julian rolled up the piece of linen and put it into his pocket. 'Well, thank you, sir,' he said. 'You've solved a bit of the mystery for us but set another puzzle! We must look for the entrance of the Secret Way after Christmas, when we can walk over to Kirrin Farmhouse.'

'I'll come with you,' said Mr Roland. 'I may be able to help a little. That is – if you don't mind me having a little share in this exciting secret.'

'Well – you've been such a help in telling us what the words mean,' said Julian, 'we'd like you to come if you want to, sir.'

'Yes, we *would*,' said Anne.

'We'll go and look for the Secret Way, then,' said Mr Roland. 'What fun we shall have, tapping round the panels, waiting for a mysterious dark entrance to appear!'

'I don't suppose George will go,' Dick murmured to Julian. 'You shouldn't have said Mr Roland could go with us, Ju. That means that old George will have to be left out of it. You know how she hates that.'

'I know,' said Julian, feeling uncomfortable. 'Don't let's worry about that now though. George may feel different after Christmas. She can't keep up this kind of behaviour for ever!'

CHAPTER EIGHT

What happened on Christmas night

IT WAS great fun on Christmas morning. The children awoke early and tumbled out of bed to look at the presents that were stacked on chairs near-by. Squeals and yells of delight came from everyone.

'Oh! a railway station! Just what I wanted! Who gave me this marvellous station?'

'A new doll – with eyes that shut! I shall call her Betsy-May. She looks just like a Betsy-May!'

'I say – what a whopping great book – all about aeroplanes. From Aunt Fanny! How decent of her!'

'Timothy! Look what Julian has given you – a collar with big brass studs all round – you *will* be grand. Go and lick him to say thank you!'

'Who's this from? I say, who gave me this? Where's the label? Oh – from Mr Roland. How decent of him! Look, Julian, a pocket-knife with three blades!'

So the cries and exclamations went on, and the four excited children and the equally excited dog spent a glorious hour before a late Christmas breakfast, opening all kinds and shapes of parcels. The bedrooms were in a fine mess when the children had finished!

'Who gave you that book about dogs, George?' asked

Julian, seeing rather a nice dog-book lying on George's pile.

'Mr Roland,' said George, rather shortly. Julian wondered if George was going to accept it. He rather thought she wouldn't. But the little girl, defiant and obstinate as she was, had made up her mind not to spoil Christmas Day by being 'difficult'. So, when the others thanked the tutor for their things she too added her thanks, though in rather a stiff little voice.

George had not given the tutor anything, but the others had, and Mr Roland thanked them all very heartily, appearing to be very pleased indeed. He told Anne that her Christmas card was the nicest he had ever had, and she beamed at him with joy.

'Well, I must say it's nice to be here for Christmas!' said Mr Roland, when he and the others were sitting round a loaded Christmas table, at the mid-day dinner. 'Shall I carve for you, Mr Kirrin? I'm good at that!'

Uncle Quentin handed him the carving knife and fork gladly. 'It's nice to have you here,' he said warmly. 'I must say you've settled in well – I'm sure we all feel as if we've known you for ages!'

It really was a jolly Christmas Day. There were no lessons, of course, and there were to be none the next day either. The children gave themselves up to the enjoyment of eating a great deal, sucking sweets, and looking forward to the lighting of the Christmas tree.

It looked beautiful when the candles were lighted. They

twinkled in the darkness of the hall, and the bright ornaments shone and glowed. Tim sat and looked at it, quite entranced.

'He likes it as much as we do,' said George. And indeed Tim had enjoyed the day just as much as any of them.

They were all tired out when they went to bed. 'I shan't be long before I'm asleep,' yawned Anne. 'Oh, George – it's been fun, hasn't it? I did like the Christmas tree.'

'Yes, it's been lovely,' said George, jumping into bed. 'Here comes Mother to say good-night. Basket, Tim, basket!'

Tim leapt into his basket by the window. He was always there when George's mother came into say good-night to the girls but as soon as she had gone downstairs, the dog took a flying leap and landed on George's bed. There he slept, his head curled round her feet.

'Don't you think Tim ought to sleep downstairs tonight?' said George's mother. 'Joanna says he ate such an enormous meal in the kitchen that she is sure he will be sick.'

'Oh *no*, Mother!' said George, at once. 'Make Tim sleep downstairs on Christmas night? Whatever would he think?'

'Oh, very well,' said her mother, with a laugh. 'I might have known it was useless to suggest it. Now to sleep quickly, Anne and George – it's late and you are all tired.'

She went into the boys' room and said good-night to them too. They were almost asleep.

Two hours later everyone else was in bed. The house was still and dark. George and Anne slept peacefully in their small beds. Timothy slept too, lying heavily on George's feet.

Suddenly George awoke with a jump. Tim was growling softly! He had raised his big shaggy head and George knew that he was listening.

'What is it, Tim?' she whispered. Anne did not wake. Tim went on growling softly. George sat up and put her hand on his collar to stop him. She knew that if he awoke her father, he would be cross.

Timothy stopped growling now that he had roused George. The girl sat and wondered what to do. It wasn't any good waking Anne. The little girl would be frightened. Why was Tim growling? He never did that at night!

'Perhaps I'd better go and see if everything is all right,' thought George. She was quite fearless, and the thought of creeping through the still, dark house did not disturb her at all. Besides she had Tim! Who could be afraid with Tim beside them!

She slipped on her dressing-gown. 'Perhaps a log has fallen out of one of the fire-places and a rug is burning,' she thought, sniffing as she went down the stairs. 'It would be just like Tim to smell it and warn us!'

With her hand on Tim's head to warn him to be quite quiet, George crept softly through the hall to the sitting-room. The fire was quite all right there, just a red glow. In the kitchen all was peace too. Tim's feet made a noise there, as his claws rattled against the linoleum.

A slight sound came from the other side of the house.

Tim growled quite loudly, and the hairs on the back of his neck rose up. George stood still. Could it possibly be burglars?

Suddenly Timothy shook himself free from her fingers and leapt across the hall, down a passage, and into the study beyond! There was the sound of an exclamation, and a noise as if someone was falling over.

'It *is* a burglar!' said George, and she ran to the study. She saw a torch shining on the floor, dropped by someone who was even now struggling with Tim.

George switched on the light, and then looked with the greatest astonishment into the study. Mr Roland was there in his dressing-gown, rolling on the floor, trying to get away from Timothy, who, although not biting him, was holding him firmly by his dressing-gown.

'Oh – it's you, George! Call your beastly dog off!' said Mr Roland, in a low and angry voice. 'Do you want to rouse all the household?'

'Why are you creeping about with a torch?' demanded George.

'I heard a noise down here, and came to see what it was,' said Mr Roland, sitting up and trying to fend off the angry dog. 'For goodness' sake, call your beast off.'

'Why didn't you put on the light?' asked George, not

attempting to take Tim away. She was very much enjoying the sight of an angry and frightened Mr Roland.

'I couldn't find it,' said the tutor. 'It's on the wrong side of the door, as you see.'

This was true. The switch was an awkward one to find if you didn't know it. Mr Roland tried to push Tim away again, and the dog suddenly barked.

'Well – he'll wake everyone!' said the tutor, angrily. 'I didn't want to rouse the house. I thought I could find out for myself if there was anyone about – a burglar perhaps. Here comes your father!'

George's father appeared, carrying a large poker. He stood still in astonishment when he saw Mr Roland on the ground and Timothy standing over him.

'What's all this?' he exclaimed. Mr Roland tried to get up, but Tim would not let him. George's father called to him sternly.

'Tim! Come here, sir!'

Timothy glanced at George to see if his mistress agreed with her father's command. She said nothing. So Timothy took no notice of the order and merely made a snap at Mr Roland's ankles.

'That dog's mad!' said Mr Roland, from the floor. 'He's already bitten me once before, and now he's trying to do it again!'

'Tim! Will you come here, sir!' shouted George's father. 'George, that dog is really disobedient. Call him off at once.'

'Come here, Tim!' said George, in a low voice. The dog at once came to her, standing by her side with the hairs on his neck still rising up stiffly. He growled softly as if to say, 'Be careful, Mr Roland, be careful!'

The tutor got up. He was very angry indeed. He spoke to George's father.

'I heard some sort of noise and came down with my

torch to see what it was,' he said. 'I thought it came from your study, and knowing you kept your valuable books and instruments here, I wondered if some thief was about. I had just got down, and into the room, when that dog appeared from somewhere and got me down on the ground! George came along too, and would not call him off.'

'I can't understand your behaviour, George; I really can't,' said her father, angrily. 'I hope you are not going to behave stupidly, as you used to behave before your cousins came last summer. And what is this I hear about Tim biting Mr Roland before?'

'George had him under the table during lessons,' said Mr Roland. 'I didn't know that, and when I stretched out my legs, they touched Tim, and he bit me. I didn't tell you before, sir, because I didn't want to trouble you. Both George and the dog have tried to annoy me ever since I have been here.'

'Well, Tim must go outside and live in the kennel,' said George's father. 'I won't have him in the house. It will be a punishment for him, and a punishment for you too, George. I will not have this kind of behaviour. Mr Roland has been extremely kind to you all.'

'I won't let Tim live outside,' said George furiously. 'It's such cold weather, and it would simply break his heart.'

'Well, his heart must be broken then,' said her father. 'It will depend entirely on your behaviour from now on whether Tim is allowed in the house at all these holidays.

I shall ask Mr Roland each day how you have behaved. If you have a bad report, then Tim stays outside. Now you know! Go back to bed but first apologise to Mr Roland!'

'I won't!' said George, and choked by feelings of anger and dismay, she tore out of the room and up the stairs. The two men stared after her.

'Let her be,' said Mr Roland. 'She's a very difficult child – and has made up her mind not to like me, that's quite plain. But I shall be very glad to know that that dog isn't in the house. I'm not at all certain that Georgina wouldn't set him on me, if she could!'

'I'm sorry about all this,' said George's father. 'I wonder what the noise was that you heard? – a log falling in the grate I expect. Now – what am I to do about that tiresome dog tonight? Go and take him outside, I suppose!'

'Leave him tonight,' said Mr Roland. 'I can hear noises upstairs – the others are awake by now! Don't let's make any more disturbance tonight.'

'Perhaps you are right,' said George's father, thankfully. He didn't at all want to tackle a defiant little girl and an angry big dog in the middle of a cold night!

The two men went to bed and slept. George did not sleep. The others had been awake when she got upstairs, and she had told them what had happened.

'George! You really are an idiot!' said Dick. 'After all, why shouldn't Mr Roland go down if he heard a noise! *You* went down! Now we shan't have darling old Tim in the house this cold weather!'

Anne began to cry. She didn't like hearing that the tutor she liked so much had been knocked down by Tim, and she hated hearing that Tim was to be punished.

'Don't be a baby,' said George. '*I'm* not crying, and it's *my* dog!'

But, when everyone had settled down again in bed, and slept peacefully, George's pillow was very wet indeed. Tim crept up beside her and licked the salt tears off her cheek. He whined softly. Tim was always unhappy when his little mistress was sad.

CHAPTER NINE

A hunt for the Secret Way

THERE WERE no lessons the next day. George looked rather pale, and was very quiet. Tim was already out in the yard-kennel, and the children could hear him whining unhappily. They were all upset to hear him.

'Oh, George, I'm awfully sorry about it all,' said Dick. 'I wish you wouldn't get so fierce about things. You only get yourself into trouble – and poor old Tim.'

George was full of mixed feelings. She disliked Mr Roland so much now that she could hardly bear to look at him – and yet she did not dare to be openly rude and rebellious because she was afraid that if she was, the tutor would give her a bad report, and perhaps she would not be allowed even to *see* Timothy. It was very hard for a defiant nature like hers to force herself to behave properly.

Mr Roland took no notice of her at all. The other children tried to bring George into their talks and plans, but she remained quiet and uninterested.

'George! We're going over to Kirrin Farmhouse today,' said Dick. 'Coming? We're going to try and find the entrance to the Secret Way. It must start somewhere there.'

The children had told George what Mr Roland had said about the piece of marked linen. They had all been thrilled about this, though the excitements of Christmas Day had made them forget about it for a while.

'Yes – of course I'll come,' said George, looking more cheerful. 'Timothy can come too. He wants a walk.'

But when the little girl found that Mr Roland was also going, she changed her mind at once. Not for anything would she go with the tutor! No – she would go for a walk alone with Timothy.

'But, George, think of the excitement we'll have trying to find the Secret Way,' said Julian, taking hold of her arm. George wrenched it away.

'I'm not going if Mr Roland is,' she said, obstinately, and the others knew that it was no good trying to coax her.

'I shall go alone with Tim,' said George. 'You go off together with your dear Mr Roland!'

She set out with Timothy, a lonely little figure going down the garden path. The others stared after her. This was horrid. George was being more and more left out, but what could they do about it?

'Well, children, are you ready?' asked Mr Roland. 'You start off by yourselves, will you? I'll meet you at the farmhouse later. I want to run down to the village first to get something.'

So the three children set off by themselves, wishing that George was with them. She was nowhere to be seen.

Old Mr and Mrs Sanders were pleased to see the three children, and sat them down in the big kitchen to eat ginger buns and drink hot milk.

'Well, have you come to find a few more secret things?' asked Mrs Sanders, with a smile.

'May we try?' asked Julian. 'We're looking for a room that's facing east, with a stone floor, and panelling!'

'All the rooms downstairs have stone floors,' said Mrs Sanders. 'You hunt all you like, my dears. You won't do any damage, I know. But don't go into the room upstairs with the cupboard that has a false back, will you, or the one next to it! Those are the rooms the two artists have.'

'All right,' said Julian, rather sorry that they were unable to fiddle about with the exciting cupboard again. 'Are the artists here, Mrs Sanders? I'd like to talk to them about pictures. I hope one day I'll be an artist too.'

'Dear me, is that so?' said Mrs Sanders. 'Well, well – it's always a marvel to me how people make any money at painting pictures.'

'It isn't making money that artists like, so much as the painting of the pictures,' said Julian, looking rather wise. That seemed to puzzle Mrs Sanders even more. She shook her head and laughed.

'They're peculiar folk!' she said. 'Ah well – you go along and have a hunt for whatever it is you want to find. You can't talk to the two artists today though, Julian – they're out.'

The children finished their buns and milk and then stood up, wondering where to begin their search. They must look for a room or rooms facing east. That would be the first thing to do.

'Which side of the house faces east, Mrs Sanders?' asked Julian. 'Do you know?'

'The kitchen faces due north,' said Mrs Sanders. 'So east will be over there,' she pointed to the left.

'Thanks,' said Julian. 'Come on, everyone!' The three children went out of the kitchen, and turned to the left. There were three rooms there – a kind of scullery, not much used now, a tiny room used as a den by old Mr Sanders, and a room that had once been a drawing-room, but which was now cold and unused.

'They've all got stone floors,' said Julian.

'So we'll have to hunt through all of the three rooms,' said Anne.

'No, we won't,' said Julian. 'We shan't have to look in this scullery, for one thing!'

'Why not?' asked Anne.

'Because the walls are of stone, silly, and we want panelling,' said Julian. 'Use your brains, Anne!'

'Well, that's one room we needn't bother with, then,' said Dick. 'Look – both this little room and the drawing-room have panelling, Julian. We must search in both.'

'There must be some reason for putting *eight* squares of panelling in the directions,' said Julian, looking at the roll of linen again. 'It would be a good idea to see whether there's a place with eight squares only – you know, over a window, or something.'

It was tremendously exciting to look round the two rooms! The children began with the smaller room. It was panelled all the way round in dark oak, but there was no place where only eight panels showed. So the children went into the next room.

The panelling there was different. It did not look so old, and was not so dark. The squares were rather a different size, too. The children tried each panel, tapping and pressing as they went, expecting at any moment to see one slide back as the one in the hall had done.

But they were disappointed. Nothing happened at all. They were still in the middle of trying when they heard footsteps in the hall, and voices. Somebody looked into the drawing-room. It was a man, thin and tall, wearing glasses on his long nose.

'Hallo!' he said. 'Mrs Sanders told me you were treasure-hunting, or something. How are you getting on?'

'Not very well,' said Julian, politely. He looked at the man, and saw behind him another one, younger, with rather screwed-up eyes and a big mouth. 'I suppose you are the two artists?' he asked.

'We are!' said the first man, coming into the room. 'Now, just exactly what are you looking for?'

Julian did not really want to tell him, but it was difficult not to. 'Well – we're just seeing if there's a sliding panel here,' he said at last. 'There's one in the hall, you know. It's exciting to hunt round.'

'Shall we help?' said the first artist, coming into the room. 'What are your names? Mine's Thomas, and my friend's name is Wilton.'

The children talked politely for a minute or two, not at all wanting the two men to help. If there was anything to be found, *they* wanted to find it. It would spoil everything if grown-ups solved the puzzle!

Soon everyone was tap-tap-tapping round the wooden panels. They were in the middle of this when a voice hailed them.

'Hallo! My word, we *are* all busy!'

The children turned, and saw their tutor standing in the doorway, smiling at them. The two artists looked at him.

'Is this a friend of yours?' asked Mr Thomas.

'Yes – he's our tutor, and he's very nice!' said Anne, running to Mr Roland and putting her hand in his.

'Perhaps you will introduce me, Anne,' said Mr Roland, smiling at the little girl.

Anne knew how to introduce people. She had often seen her mother doing it. 'This is Mr Roland,' she said to the two artists. Then she turned to Mr Roland. 'This is Mr Thomas,' she said, waving her hand towards him, 'and the other one is Mr Wilton.'

The men half-bowed to one another and nodded. 'Are you staying here?' asked Mr Roland. 'A very nice old farmhouse, isn't it?'

'It isn't time to go yet, is it?' asked Julian, hearing a clock strike.

'Yes, I'm afraid it is,' said Mr Roland. 'I'm later meeting you than I expected. We must go in about five minutes – no later. I'll just give you a hand in trying to find this mysterious secret way!'

But no matter how any one of them pressed and tapped around the panels in either of the two rooms, they could not find anything exciting. It really was most disappointing.

'Well, we really must go now,' said Mr Roland. 'Come and say good-bye to Mrs Sanders.'

They all went into the warm kitchen, where Mrs Sanders was cooking something that smelt most delicious.

'Something for our lunch, Mrs Sanders?' said Mr Wilton. 'My word, you really are a wonderful cook!'

Mrs Sanders smiled. She turned to the children. 'Well, dearies, did you find what you wanted?' she asked.

'No,' said Mr Roland, answering for them. 'We haven't been able to find the secret way, after all!'

'The secret way?' said Mrs Sanders, in surprise. 'What do you know about that now? I thought it had all been forgotten – in fact, I haven't believed in that secret way for many a year!'

'Oh, Mrs Sanders – do you know about it?' cried Julian. 'Where is it?'

'I don't know, dear – the secret of it has been lost for many a day,' said the old lady. 'I remember my old grandmother telling me something about it when I was smaller than any of you. But I wasn't interested in things like that when I was little. I was all for cows and hens and sheep.'

'Oh, Mrs Sanders – do, do try and remember something!' begged Dick. 'What *was* the secret way?'

'Well, it was supposed to be a hidden way from Kirrin Farmhouse to somewhere else,' said Mrs Sanders. 'I don't know where, I'm sure. It was used in the olden days when people wanted to hide from enemies.'

It was disappointing that Mrs Sanders knew so little. The children said good-bye and went off with their tutor, feeling that their morning had been wasted.

George was indoors when they got to Kirrin Cottage. Her cheeks were not so pale, now, and she greeted the children eagerly.

'Did you discover anything? Tell me all about it!' she said.

'There's nothing to tell,' said Dick, rather gloomily. 'We found three rooms facing east, with stone floors, but only two of them had wooden panelling, so we hunted round those, tapping and punching – but there wasn't anything to be discovered at all.'

'We saw the two artists,' said Anne. 'One was tall and thin and had a long nose with glasses on. He was called Mr Thomas. The other was younger, with little piggy eyes and an enormous mouth.'

'I met them out this morning,' said George. 'It must have been them. Mr Roland was with them, and they were all talking together. They didn't see me.'

'Oh, it couldn't have been the artists you saw,' said Anne, at once. 'Mr Roland didn't know them, I had to introduce them.'

'Well, I'm sure I heard Mr Roland call one of them Wilton,' said George, puzzled. 'He *must* have known them.'

'It couldn't have been the artists,' said Anne, again. 'They really didn't know Mr Roland. Mr Thomas asked if he was a friend of ours.'

'I'm sure I'm not mistaken,' said George, looking obstinate. 'If Mr Roland said he didn't know the two artists, he was telling lies.'

'Oh, you're always making out that he is doing something horrid!' cried Anne, indignantly. 'You just make up things about him!'

'Sh!' said Julian. 'Here he is.'

The door opened and the tutor came in. 'Well,' he said, 'it *was* disappointing that we couldn't find the secret way, wasn't it? Anyway, we were rather foolish to hunt about that drawing-room as we did – the panelling there wasn't really old – it must have been put in years after the other.'

'Oh – well, it's no good looking there again,' said Julian, disappointed. 'And I'm pretty sure there's nothing to be found in that other little room. We went all over it so thoroughly. Isn't it disappointing?'

'It is,' said Mr Roland. 'Well, Julian, how did you like the two artists? I was pleased to meet them – they seemed nice fellows, and I shall like to know them.'

George looked at the tutor. Could he possibly be telling untruths in such a truthful voice? The little girl was very puzzled. She felt sure it was the artists she had seen him with. But why should he pretend he didn't know them? She must be mistaken. But all the same, she felt uncomfortable about it, and made up her mind to find out the truth, if she could.

CHAPTER TEN

A shock for George and Tim

NEXT MORNING there were lessons again – and no Timothy under the table! George felt very much inclined to refuse to work, but what would be the good of that? Grown-ups were so powerful, and could dole out all kinds of punishments. She didn't care how much she was punished herself but she couldn't bear to think that Timothy might have to share in the punishments too.

So, pale and sullen, the little girl sat down at the table with the others. Anne was eager to join in the lessons – in fact she was eager to do anything to please Mr Roland, because he had given her the fairy doll from the top of the Christmas tree! Anne thought it was the prettiest doll she had ever seen.

George had scowled at the doll when Anne showed it to her. She didn't like dolls, and she certainly wasn't going to like one that Mr Roland had chosen, and given to Anne! But Anne loved it, and had made up her mind to do lessons with the others, and work as well as she could.

George did as little as she could without getting into trouble. Mr Roland took no interest in her or in her work. He praised the others, and took a lot of trouble to show Julian something he found difficult.

The children heard Tim whining outside as they worked. This troubled them very much, for Timothy was such a companion, and so dear to them all. They could not bear to think of him left out of everything, cold and miserable in the yard-kennel. When the ten minutes' break came, and Mr Roland went out of the room for a few minutes, Julian spoke to George.

'George! It's awful for us to hear poor old Tim whining out there in the cold. And I'm sure I heard him cough. Let me speak to Mr Roland about him. You must feel simply dreadful knowing that Tim is out there.'

'I thought I heard him cough, too,' said George, looking worried. 'I hope he won't get a cold. He simply doesn't understand why I have to put him there. He thinks I'm terribly unkind.'

The little girl turned her head away, afraid that tears might come into her eyes. She always boasted that she never cried – but it was very difficult to keep the tears away when she thought of Timothy out there in the cold.

Dick took her arm. 'Listen, George – you just hate Mr Roland, and I suppose you can't help it. But we can none of us bear Timothy being out there all alone – and it looks like snow today, which would be awful for him. Could you be awfully, awfully good today, and forget your dislike, so that when your father asks Mr Roland for your report, he can say you were very good – and then we'll ask Mr Roland if he wouldn't let Timmy come back into the house.'

'See?'

Timothy coughed again, out in the yard, and George's heart went cold. Suppose he got that awful illness called pneumonia – and she couldn't nurse him because he had to live in the kennel? She would die of unhappiness! She turned to Julian and Dick.

'All right,' she said. 'I do hate Mr Roland – but I love Timothy more than I hate the tutor – so for Tim's sake I'll pretend to be good and sweet and hard-working. And then you can beg him to let Timothy come back.'

'Good girl!' said Julian. 'Now here he comes – so do your best.'

To the tutor's enormous surprise, George gave him a smile when he came into the room. This was so unexpected that it puzzled him. He was even more puzzled to find that George worked harder than anyone for the rest of the morning, and she answered politely and cheerfully when he spoke to her. He gave her a word of praise.

'Well done, Georgina! I can see you've got brains.'

'Thank you,' said George, and gave him another wan smile – a very watery, poor affair, compared with the happy smiles the others had been used to – but still, it *was* a smile!

At dinner-time George looked after Mr Roland most politely – passed him the salt, offered him more bread, got up to fill his glass when it was empty! The others looked at her in admiration. George had plenty of pluck. She must be finding it very difficult to behave as if Mr Roland was a great friend, when she really disliked him so much!

Mr Roland seemed very pleased, and appeared to be quite willing to respond to George's friendliness. He made a little joke with her, and offered to lend her a book he had about a dog. George's mother was delighted to find that her difficult daughter seemed to be turning over a new leaf. Altogether things were very much happier that day.

'George, you go out of the room before your father comes in to ask Mr Roland about your behaviour tonight,' said Julian. 'Then, when the tutor gives you a splendid report, we will all ask if Timothy can come back. It will be easier if you are not there.'

'All right,' said George. She was longing for this difficult day to be over. It was very hard for her to pretend to be friendly, when she was not. She could never never do it, if it wasn't for Timothy's sake!

George disappeared out of the room just before six o'clock, when she heard her father coming. He walked into the room and nodded to Mr Roland.

'Well? Have your pupils worked well today?' he asked.

'Very well indeed,' said Mr Roland. 'Julian has really mastered something he didn't understand today. Dick has done well in Latin. Anne has written out a French exercise without a single mistake!'

'And what about George?' asked Uncle Quentin.

'I was coming to Georgina,' said Mr Roland, looking round and seeing that she was gone. 'She has worked better than anyone else today! I am really pleased with her.

She has tried hard – and she has really been polite and friendly. I feel she is trying to turn over a new leaf.'

'She's been a brick today,' said Julian, warmly. 'Uncle Quentin, she has tried awfully hard, she really has. And, you know, she's terribly unhappy.'

'Why?' asked Uncle Quentin in surprise.

'Because of Timothy,' said Julian. 'He's out in the cold, you see. And he's got a dreadful cough.'

'Oh, Uncle Quentin, please do let poor Timmy come indoors,' begged Anne.

'Yes, please do,' said Dick. 'Not only for George's sake, because she loves him so, but for us too. We hate to hear him whining outside. And George does deserve a reward, Uncle – she's been marvellous today.'

'Well,' said Uncle Quentin, looking doubtfully at the three eager faces before him, 'well – I hardly know what to say. If George is going to be sensible – and the weather gets colder – well . . .'

He looked at Mr Roland, expecting to hear him say something in favour of Timothy. But the tutor said nothing. He looked annoyed.

'What do you think, Mr Roland?' asked Uncle Quentin.

'I think you should keep to what you said and let the dog stay outside,' said the tutor. 'George is spoilt, and needs firm handling. You should really keep to your decision about the dog. There is no reason to give way about it just because she tried to be good for once!'

The three children stared at Mr Roland in surprise and

dismay. It had never entered their heads that he would not back them up!

'Oh, Mr Roland, you *are* horrid!' cried Anne. 'Oh do, do say you'll have Timothy back.'

The tutor did not look at Anne. He pursed up his mouth beneath its thick moustache and looked straight at Uncle Quentin.

'Well,' said Uncle Quentin, 'perhaps we had better see how George behaves for a whole week. After all – just one day isn't much.'

The children stared at him in disgust. They thought he was weak and unkind. Mr Roland nodded his head.

'Yes,' he said, 'a week will be a better test. If Georgina behaves well for a whole week, we'll have another word about the dog. But at present I feel it would be better to keep him outside.'

'Very well,' said Uncle Quentin, and went out of the room. He paused to look back. 'Come along into my study sometime,' he said. 'I've got a bit further with my formula. It's at a very interesting stage.'

The three children looked at one another but said nothing. How mean of the tutor to stop Uncle Quentin from having Timothy indoors again! They all felt disappointed in him. The tutor saw their faces.

'I'm sorry to disappoint you,' he said. 'But I think if you'd been bitten by Timothy once and snapped at all over when he got you on the floor, you would not be very keen on having him in either!'

He went out of the room. The children wondered what to say to George. She came in a moment later, her face eager. But when she saw the gloomy looks of the other three, she stopped short.

'Isn't Tim to come in?' she asked, quickly. 'What's happened? Tell me!'

They told her. The little girl's face grew dark and angry when she heard how the tutor had put his foot down about Timothy, even when her father had himself suggested that the dog might come indoors.

'Oh, what a beast he is!' she cried. 'How I do hate him! I'll pay him back for this. I will, I will, I will!'

She rushed out of the room. They heard her fumbling in the hall, and then the front door banged.

'She's gone out into the dark,' said Julian. 'I bet she's gone to Timmy. Poor old George. Now she'll be worse than ever!'

That night George could not sleep. She lay and tossed in her bed, listening for Timothy. She heard him cough. She heard him whine. He was cold, she knew he was. She had put plenty of fresh straw into his kennel and had turned it away from the cold north wind – but he must feel the bitter night terribly, after sleeping for so long on her bed!

Timothy gave such a hollow cough that George could bear it no longer. She must, she simply must, get up and go down to him. 'I shall bring him into the house for a little while and rub his chest with some of that stuff Mother uses for herself when she's got a cold on her chest,' thought the girl. 'Perhaps that will do him good.'

She quickly put a few clothes on and crept downstairs. The whole house was quiet. She slipped out into the yard and undid Tim's chain. He was delighted to see her and licked her hands and face lovingly.

'Come along into the warm for a little while,' whispered the little girl. 'I'll rub your poor chest with some oil I've got.'

Timmy pattered behind her into the house. She took him to the kitchen – but the fire was out and the room was cold. George went to look at the other rooms.

There was quite a nice fire still in her father's study. She

and Tim went in there. She did not put on the light, because the firelight was fairly bright. She had with her the little bottle of oil from the bathroom cupboard. She put it down by the fire to warm.

Then she rubbed the dog's hairy chest with the oil, hoping it would do him good. 'Don't cough now if you can help it, Tim,' she whispered. 'If you do, someone may hear you. Lie down here by the fire, darling, and get nice and warm. Your cold will soon be better.'

Timothy lay down on the rug. He was glad to be out of his kennel and with his beloved mistress. He put his head on her knee. She stroked him and whispered to him.

The firelight glinted on the curious instruments and glass tubes that stood around on shelves in her father's study. A log shifted a little in the fire and settled lower, sending up a cloud of sparks. It was warm and peaceful there.

The little girl almost fell asleep. The big dog closed his eyes too, and rested peacefully, happy and warm. George settled down with her head on his neck.

She awoke to hear the study clock striking six! The room was cold now, and she shivered. Goodness! Six o'clock! Joanna the cook would soon be awake. She must not find Timmy and George in the study!

'Tim darling! Wake up! We must put you back into your kennel,' whispered George. 'I'm sure your cold is better, because you haven't coughed once since you've been indoors. Get up – and don't make a noise. Sh!'

Tim stood up and shook himself. He licked George's hand. He understood perfectly that he must be quite quiet. The two of them slipped out of the study, went into the hall and out of the front door.

In a minute or two Timothy was on the chain, and in his kennel, cuddled down among the straw. George wished she could cuddle there with him. She gave him a pat and slipped back indoors again.

She went up to bed, sleepy and cold. She forgot that she was partly dressed and got into bed just as she was. She was asleep in a moment!

In the morning Anne was most amazed to find that George had on vest, knickers, jeans and jersey, when she got out of bed to dress.

'Look!' she said. 'You're half-dressed! But I *saw* you undressing last night.'

'Be quiet,' said George. 'I went down and let Tim in last night. We sat in front of the study fire and I rubbed him with oil. Now don't you dare to say a word to anyone! Promise!'

Anne promised – and she faithfully kept her word. Well, well – to think that George dared to roam about like that all night – what an extraordinary girl she was!

CHAPTER ELEVEN

Stolen papers

'GEORGE, DON'T behave fiercely today, will you?' said Julian, after breakfast. 'It won't do you or Timothy any good at all.'

'Do you suppose I'm going to behave well when I know perfectly well that Mr Roland will never let me have Tim indoors all these holidays?' said George.

'Well – they said a week,' said Dick. 'Can't you try for a week?'

'No. At the end of a week Mr Roland will say I must try for another week,' said George. 'He's got a real dislike for poor Tim. And for me too. I'm not surprised at that, because I know that when I try to be horrid, I really *am* horrid. But he shouldn't hate poor Timmy.'

'Oh, George – you'll spoil the whole hols if you are silly, and keep getting into trouble,' said Anne.

'Well, I'll spoil them then,' said George, the sulky look coming back on her face.

'I don't see why you have to spoil them for us, as well as for yourself,' said Julian.

'They don't need to be spoilt for you,' said George. 'You can have all the fun you want – go for walks with your dear Mr Roland, play games with him in the evening, and laugh and talk as much as you like. You don't need to take any notice of me.'

'You are a funny girl, George,' said Julian, with a sigh. 'We like you, and we hate you to be unhappy – so how can we have fun if we know you're miserable – and Timmy too?'

'Don't worry about *me*,' said George, in rather a choky voice. 'I'm going out to Tim. I'm not coming in to lessons today.'

'George! But you must!' said Dick and Julian together.

'There's no "must" about it,' said George. 'I'm just not coming. I won't work with Mr Roland till he says I can have Timothy indoors again.'

'But you know you can't do things like that – you'll be told off or something,' said Dick.

'I shall run away if things get too bad,' said George, in a shaky voice. 'I shall run away with Tim.'

She went out of the room and shut the door with a bang. The others stared after her. What could you do with a person like George? Anyone could rule her with kindness and understanding – but as soon as she came up against anyone who disliked her, or whom she disliked, she shied away like a frightened horse – and kicked like a frightened horse, too!

Mr Roland came into the sitting-room, his books in his hand. He smiled at the three children.

'Well? All ready for me, I see. Where's Georgina?'

Nobody answered. Nobody was going to give George away!

'Don't you know where she is?' asked Mr Roland in surprise. He looked at Julian.

'No, sir,' said Julian, truthfully. 'I've no idea where she is.'

'Well – perhaps she will come along in a few minutes,' said Mr Roland. 'Gone to feed that dog of hers, I suppose.'

They all settled down to work. The time went on and George did not come in. Mr Roland glanced at the clock and made an impatient clicking noise with his tongue.

'Really, it's too bad of Georgina to be so late! Anne, go and see if you can find her.'

Anne went. She looked in the bedroom. There was no George there. She looked in the kitchen. Joanna was there, making cakes. She gave the little girl a hot piece to eat. She had no idea where George was.

Anne couldn't find her anywhere. She went back and told Mr Roland. He looked angry.

'I shall have to report this to her father,' he said. 'I have never had to deal with such a rebellious child before. She seems to do everything she possibly can to get herself into trouble.'

Lessons went on. Break came, and still George did not appear. Julian slipped out and saw that the yard-kennel was empty. So George had gone out with Timmy! What a row she would get into when she got back!

No sooner had the children settled down after break to do the rest of the morning's lessons, than a big disturbance came.

Uncle Quentin burst in looking upset and worried.

'Have any of you children been into my study?' he asked.

'No, Uncle Quentin,' they all answered.

'You said we weren't to,' said Julian.

'Why? Has something been broken?' asked Mr Roland.

'Yes – the test-tubes I set yesterday for an experiment have been broken – and what is worse, three most important pages of my book have gone,' said Uncle Quentin. 'I can write them out again, but only after a great deal of work. I can't understand it. Are you *sure*, children, that none of you has been meddling with things in my study?'

'Quite sure,' they answered. Anne went very red – she suddenly remembered what George had told her. George said she had taken Timmy into Uncle Quentin's study last night, and rubbed his chest with oil! But George couldn't possibly have broken the test-tubes, and taken pages from her father's book!

Mr Roland noticed that Anne had gone red.

'Do you know anything about this, Anne?' he asked.

'No, Mr Roland,' said Anne, blushing even redder, and looking very uncomfortable indeed.

'Where's George?' suddenly said Uncle Quentin.

The children said nothing, and it was Mr Roland who answered:

'We don't know. She didn't come to lessons this morning.'

'Didn't come to lessons! Why not?' demanded Uncle Quentin, beginning to frown.

'She didn't say,' said Mr Roland dryly. 'I imagine she was upset because we were firm about Timothy last night, and this is her way of being defiant.'

'The naughty girl!' said George's father, angrily. 'I don't know what's come over her lately. Fanny! Come here! Did you know that George hasn't been in to her lessons today?'

Aunt Fanny came into the room. She looked very worried. She had a little bottle in her hand. The children wondered what it was.

'Didn't come in to lessons!' repeated Aunt Fanny. 'How extraordinary! Then where is she?'

'I don't think you need to worry about her,' said Mr Roland, smoothly. 'She's probably gone off with Timothy in a fit of temper. What is very much more important, is the fact that your work appears to have been spoilt by someone. I only hope it is not George, who has been spiteful enough to get back at you for not allowing her to have her dog in the house.'

'Of *course* it wasn't George!' cried Dick, angry that anyone should even think such a thing of his cousin.

'George would never, never do a thing like that,' said Julian.

'No, she never would,' said Anne, sticking up valiantly for her cousin, although a horrid doubt was in her mind. After all – George *had* been in the study last night!

'Quentin, I am sure George would not even *think* of such a thing,' said Aunt Fanny. 'You will find those pages somewhere – and as for the test-tubes that were broken, well, perhaps the wind blew the curtain against them, or something! When did you last see those pages?'

'Last night,' said Uncle Quentin. 'I read them over again, and checked my figures to make sure they were right. Those pages contain the very heart of my formula!

If they got into anyone else's hands, they could use my secret. This is a terrible thing for me! I *must* know what has happened to them.'

'I found this in your study, Quentin,' said Aunt Fanny, and she held up the little bottle she carried. 'Did you put it there? It was in the fender.'

Uncle Quentin took the bottle and stared at it. 'Camphorated oil!' he said. 'Of course I didn't take it there. Why should I?'

'Well – who took it there, then?' asked Aunt Fanny, puzzled. 'None of the children has a cold – and anyway, they wouldn't think of the camphorated oil, and take it into the study to use! It's most extraordinary!'

Everyone was astonished. Why should a bottle of camphorated oil appear in the study fender?

Only one person could think why. It suddenly came into Anne's mind in a flash. George had said she had taken Timmy into the study, and rubbed him with oil! He had had a cough, that was why. And she had left the oil in the study. Oh dear, oh dear – now what would happen? What a pity George had forgotten the oil!

Anne went very red again as she looked at the oil. Mr Roland, whose eyes seemed very sharp this morning, looked hard at the little girl.

'Anne! You know something about that oil!' he said suddenly. 'What do you know? Did you put it there?'

'No,' said Anne. 'I haven't been into the study. I said I hadn't.'

'Do you know anything about the oil?' said Mr Roland, again. 'You *do* know something.'

Everyone stared at Anne. She stared back. This was simply dreadful. She could not give George away. She could *not*. George was in quite enough trouble as it was, without getting into any more. She pursed up her little mouth and did not answer.

'Anne!' said Mr Roland, sternly. 'Answer when you are spoken to.'

Anne said nothing. The two boys stared at her, guessing that it was something to do with George. They did not know that George had brought Timothy in the night before.

'Anne, dear,' said her aunt, gently. 'Tell us if you know something. It might help us to find out what has happened to Uncle Quentin's papers. It is very, very important.'

Still Anne said nothing. Her eyes filled with tears. Julian squeezed her arm.

'Don't bother Anne,' he said to the grown-ups. 'If she thinks she can't tell you, she's got some very good reason.'

'I think she's shielding George,' said Mr Roland. 'Is that it, Anne?'

Anne burst into tears. Julian put his arms round his little sister, and spoke again to the three grown-ups.

'*Don't* bother Anne! Can't you see she's upset?'

'We'll let George speak for herself, when she thinks she will come in,' said Mr Roland. 'I'm sure she knows how that bottle got there – and if she put it there herself she must have been into the study – and she's the only person that *has* been there.'

The boys could not think for one moment that George would do such a thing as spoil her father's work. Anne feared it, and it upset her. She sobbed in Julian's arms.

'When George comes in, send her to me in my study,' said Uncle Quentin, irritably. 'How can a man work when these upsets go on? I was always against having children in the house.'

He stamped out, tall, cross and frowning. The children were glad to see him go. Mr Roland shut the books on the table with a snap.

'We can't do any more lessons this morning,' he said. 'Put on your things and go out for a walk till dinner-time.'

'Yes, do,' said Aunt Fanny, looking white and worried. 'That's a good idea.'

Mr Roland and their aunt went out of the room. 'I don't know if Mr Roland thinks he's coming out with us,' said Julian, in a low voice, 'but we've got to get out first and give him the slip. We've got to find George and warn her what's up.'

'Right!' said Dick. 'Dry your eyes, Anne darling. Hurry and get your things. We'll slip out of the garden door before Mr Roland comes down. I bet George has gone for her favourite walk over the cliffs. We'll meet her!' The three children threw on their outdoor things and crept out of the garden door quietly. They raced down the garden path, and out of the gate before Mr Roland even knew they

were gone! They made their way to the cliffs, and looked to see if George was coming.

'There she is – and Timothy, too!' cried Julian, pointing. 'George! George! Quick, we've got something to tell you!'

CHAPTER TWELVE

George in trouble

'WHAT'S THE matter?' asked George, as the three children tore up to her. 'Has something happened?'

'Yes, George. Someone has taken three most important pages out of your father's book!' panted Julian. 'And broken the test-tubes he was making an experiment with. Mr Roland thinks you might have had something to do with it!'

'The beast!' said George, her blue eyes deepening with anger. 'As if I'd do a thing like that! Why should he think it's me, anyway?'

'Well, George, you left that bottle of oil in the study fender,' said Anne. 'I haven't told anyone at all what you told me happened last night – but somehow Mr Roland guessed you had something to do with the bottle of oil.'

'Didn't you tell the boys how I got Timmy indoors?' asked George. 'Well, there's nothing much to tell, Julian. I just heard poor old Tim coughing in the night, and I half-dressed, went down, and took him into the study, where there was a fire. Mother keeps a bottle of oil that she uses to rub her chest with when she has a cough – so I thought it might do Timmy's cold good, too. I got the oil and rubbed him well – and we both fell asleep by the fire till six o'clock. I was sleepy when I woke up, and forgot the oil. That's all.'

'And you didn't take any pages from the book Uncle Quentin is writing, and you didn't break anything in the study, did you?' said Anne.

'Of course not, silly,' said George, indignantly. 'How can you ask me a thing like that? You must be mad.'

George never told a lie, and the others always believed her, whatever she said. They stared at her, and she stared back.

'I wonder who could have taken those pages then?' said Julian. 'Maybe your father will come across them, after all. I expect he put them into some safe place and then forgot all about them. And the test-tubes might easily have over-balanced and broken themselves. Some of them look very shaky to me.'

'I suppose I shall get into trouble now for taking Tim into the study,' said George.

'And for not coming into lessons this morning,' said Dick. 'You really are an idiot, George. I never knew anyone like you for walking right into trouble.'

'Hadn't you better stay out a bit longer, till everyone has calmed down a bit?' said Anne.

'No,' said George at once. 'If I'm going to get into a row, I'll get into it now! I'm not afraid!'

She marched over the cliff path, with Timmy running round her as usual. The others followed. It wasn't nice to think that George was going to get into such trouble.

They came to the house and went up the path.

Mr Roland saw them from the window and opened the door. He glanced at George.

'Your father wants to see you in the study,' said the tutor. Then he turned to the others, looking annoyed.

'Why did you go out without me? I meant to go with you.'

'Oh did you, sir? I'm sorry,' said Julian, politely, not looking at Mr Roland. 'We just went out on the cliff a little way.'

'Georgina, did you go into the study last night?' asked Mr Roland, watching George as she took off her hat and coat.

'I'll answer my father's questions, not yours,' said George.

'What you want is a good telling off,' said Mr Roland. 'And if I were your father I'd give it to you!'

'You're not my father,' answered George. She went to the study door and opened it. There was no one there.

'Father isn't here,' said George.

'He'll be there in a minute,' said Mr Roland. 'Go in and wait. And you others, go up and wash for lunch.'

The other three children felt almost as if they were deserting George as they went up the stairs. They could hear Timmy whining from the yard outside. He knew his little mistress was in trouble, and he wanted to be with her.

George sat down on a chair, and gazed at the fire, remembering how she had sat on the rug there with Tim last night, rubbing his hairy chest. How silly of her to have forgotten the bottle of oil!

Her father came into the room, frowning and angry. He looked sternly at George.

'Were you in here last night, George?' he asked.

'Yes, I was,' answered George at once.

'What were you doing in here?' asked her father. 'You know you children are forbidden to come into my study.'

'I know,' said George. 'But you see Timmy had a dreadful cough, and I couldn't bear it. So I crept down about one o'clock and let him in. This was the only room that was really warm, so I sat here and rubbed his chest with the oil Mother uses when she has a cold.'

'Rubbed the dog's chest with camphorated oil!' exclaimed her father, in amazement. 'What a mad thing to do! As if it would do him any good.'

'It didn't seem mad to me,' said George. 'It seemed sensible. And Timmy's cough is much better today. I'm sorry for coming into the study. I didn't touch a thing, of course.'

'George, something very serious has happened,' said her father, looking gravely at her. 'Some of my test-tubes with which I was doing an important experiment, have been broken – and, worse than that, three pages of my book have gone. Tell me on your honour that you know nothing of these things.'

'I know nothing of them,' said George, looking her father straight in the eyes. Her own eyes shone very blue

and clear as she gazed at him. He felt quite certain that George was speaking the truth. She could know nothing of the damage done. Then where were those pages?

'George, last night when I went to bed at eleven o'clock,

everything was in order,' he said. 'I read over those three important pages and checked them once more myself. This morning they are gone.'

'Then they must have been taken between eleven o'clock and one o'clock,' said George. 'I was here from that time until six.'

'But *who* could have taken them?' said her father. 'The window was fastened, as far as I know. And nobody knows that those three pages were so important but myself. It is most extraordinary.'

'Mr Roland probably knew,' said George, slowly.

'Don't be absurd,' said her father. 'Even if he did realise they were important, he would not have taken them. He's a very decent fellow. And that reminds me – why were you not at lessons this morning, George?'

'I'm not going to do lessons any more with Mr Roland,' said George. 'I simply hate him!'

'George! I will *not* have you talking like this!' said her father. 'Do you want me to say you are to lose Tim altogether?'

'No,' said George, feeling shaky about the knees. 'And I don't think it's fair to keep trying to force me to do things by threatening me with losing Timothy. If – if – you do a thing like that – I'll – I'll run away or something!'

There were no tears in George's eyes. She sat bolt upright on her chair, gazing defiantly at her father. How difficult she was! Her father sighed, and remembered that he too in his own childhood had been called 'difficult'.

Perhaps George took after him. She could be so good and sweet – and here she was being perfectly impossible!

Her father did not know what to do with George. He thought he had better have a word with his wife. He got up and went to the door.

'Stay here. I shall be back in a moment. I want to speak to your mother about you.'

'Don't speak to Mr Roland about me, will you?' said George, who felt quite certain that the tutor would urge terrible punishments for her and Timmy. 'Oh, Father, if only Timothy had been in the house last night, sleeping in my room as usual, he would have heard whoever it was that stole your secret – and he would have barked and roused the house!'

Her father said nothing, but he knew that what George had said was true. Timmy wouldn't have let anyone get into the study. It was funny he hadn't barked in the night, if anyone from outside had climbed in at the study window. Still, it was the other side of the house. Maybe he had heard nothing.

The door closed. George sat still on her chair, gazing up at the mantelpiece, where a clock ticked away the time. She felt very miserable. Everything was going wrong, every single thing!

As she gazed at the panelled overmantel, she counted the wooden panels. There were eight. Now, where had she heard of eight panels before? Of course – in that Secret Way. There were eight panels marked on the roll of linen.

What a pity there had not been eight panels in a wooden overmantel at Kirrin Farmhouse!

George glanced out of the window, and wondered if it faced east. She looked to see where the sun was – it was not shining into the room – but it did in the early morning – so it must face east. Fancy – here was a room facing east and with eight wooden panels. She wondered if it had a stone floor.

The floor was covered with a large thick carpet. George got up and went to the wall. She pulled up the edge of the carpet there – and saw that the floor underneath was made of large flat stones. The study had a stone floor too!

She sat down again and gazed at the wooden panels, trying to remember which one in the roll of linen was marked with a cross. But of course it couldn't be a room in Kirrin Cottage – it must be in Kirrin Farmhouse where the Secret Way began.

But just suppose it *was* Kirrin Cottage! Certainly the directions had been found in Kirrin Farmhouse – but that was not to say that the Secret Way had to begin there, even though Mrs Sanders seemed to think it did.

George was feeling excited. 'I must tap round about those eight panels and try to find the one that is marked on the linen roll,' she thought. 'It may slide back or something, and I shall suddenly see the entrance opening!'

She got up to try her luck – but at that moment the door opened again and her father came in looking very grave.

'I have been talking to your mother,' he said. 'She agrees with me that you have been very disobedient, rude and defiant. We can't let behaviour like that pass, George. You will have to be punished.'

George looked anxiously at her father. If only her punishment had nothing to do with Timothy! But, of course, it had.

'You will go to bed for the rest of the day, and you will not see Timothy for three days,' said her father. 'I will get Julian to feed him and take him for a walk. If you persist in being defiant, Timothy will have to go away altogether. I am afraid, strange as it may seem, that that dog has a bad influence on you.'

'He hasn't, he hasn't!' cried George. 'Oh, he'll be so miserable if I don't see him for three whole days.'

'There's nothing more to be said,' said her father. 'Go straight upstairs to bed, and think over all I have said to you, George. I am very disappointed in your behaviour these holidays. I really did think the influence of your three cousins had made you into a normal, sensible girl. Now you are worse then you have ever been.'

He held open the door and George walked out, holding her head high. She heard the others having their dinner in the dining-room. She went straight upstairs and undressed. She got into bed and thought miserably of not seeing Tim for three days. She couldn't bear it! Nobody could possibly know how much she loved Timothy!

Joanna came up with a tray of dinner. 'Well, it's a pity

to see you in bed,' she said cheerfully. 'Now you be a sensible girl and behave properly and you'll soon be downstairs again.'

George picked at her dinner. She did not feel at all hungry. She lay back on the bed, thinking of Tim and thinking of the eight panels over the mantelpiece. Could they possibly be the ones shown in the Secret Way directions? She gazed out of the window and thought hard.

'Golly, it's snowing!' she said suddenly, sitting up. 'I thought it would when I saw that leaden sky this morning. It's snowing hard! It will be quite thick by tonight – inches deep. Oh, poor Timothy. I hope Julian will see that his kennel is kept clear of the drifting snow.'

George had plenty of time to think as she lay in bed. Joanna came and took the tray away. No one else came to see her. George felt sure the other children had been forbidden to go up and speak to her. She felt lonely and left out.

She thought of her father's lost pages. Could Mr Roland have taken them? After all, he was very interested in her father's work and seemed to understand it. The thief must have been someone who knew which were the important pages. Surely Timothy would have barked if a thief had come in from outside, even though the study was the other side of the house. Timmy had such sharp ears.

'I think it must have been someone *in*side the house,' said George. 'None of us children, that's certain – and not Mother or Joanna. So that only leaves Mr Roland. And I did find him in the study that other night when Timmy woke me by growling.'

She sat up in bed suddenly. 'I believe Mr Roland had Timothy put out of the house because he wanted to go poking round the study again and was afraid Tim would bark!' she thought. 'He was so very insistent that Tim should go out of doors – even when everyone else begged for me to have him indoors. I believe – I really do believe – that Mr Roland is the thief!'

The little girl felt very excited. Could it be that the tutor had stolen the pages – and broken those important test-tubes? How she wished that the others would come and see her, so that she could talk things over with them!

CHAPTER THIRTEEN

Julian has a surprise

THE THREE children downstairs felt very sorry for George. Uncle Quentin had forbidden them to go up and see her.

'A little time for thinking out things all alone may do George good,' he said.

'Poor old George,' said Julian. 'It's too bad, isn't it? I say – look at the snow!'

The snow was falling very thickly. Julian went to the window and looked out. 'I shall have to go and see that Timmy's kennel is all right,' he said. 'We don't want the poor old fellow to be snowed up! I expect he is wondering what the snow is!'

Timothy was certainly very puzzled to see everywhere covered with soft white stuff. He sat in his kennel and stared out at the falling flakes, his big brown eyes following them as they fell to the ground. He was puzzled and unhappy. Why was he living out here by himself in the cold? Why didn't George come to him? Didn't she love him any more? The big dog was very miserable, as miserable as George!

He was delighted to see Julian. He jumped up at the boy and licked his face. 'Good old Tim!' said Julian. 'Are you all right? Let me sweep away some of this snow and swing your kennel round a bit so that no flakes fly inside. There – that's better. No, we're not going for a walk, old thing – not now.'

The boy patted the dog and fussed him a bit, then went indoors. The others met him at the sitting-room door.

'Julian! Mr Roland is going out for a walk by himself. Aunt Fanny is lying down, and Uncle Quentin is in his study. Can't we go up and see George?'

'We were forbidden to,' said Julian, doubtfully.

'I know,' said Dick. 'But I don't mind risking it for the sake of making George feel a bit happier. It must be so awful for her, lying up there all alone, knowing she can't see Tim for days.'

'Well – let me go up, as I'm the eldest,' said Julian. 'You two stay down here in the sitting-room and talk. Then Uncle Quentin will think we're all here. I'll slip up and see George for a few minutes.'

'All right,' said Dick. 'Give her our love and tell her we'll look after Timmy.'

Julian slipped quietly up the stairs. He opened George's door and crept inside. He shut the door, and saw George sitting up in bed, looking at him in delight.

'Sh!' said Julian. 'I'm not supposed to be here!'

'Oh, Julian!' said George joyfully. 'How good of you to come. I was so lonely. Come this side of the bed. Then if anyone comes in suddenly, you can duck down and hide.'

Julian went to the other side of the bed. George began to pour out to him all she had been thinking of.

'I believe Mr Roland is the thief, I really do!' she said. 'I'm not saying that because I hate him, Julian, really I'm not. After all, I *did* find him snooping round the study one afternoon – and again in the middle of the night. He may have got to hear of my father's work, and come to see if he could steal it. It was just lucky for him that we needed a tutor. I'm sure he stole those pages, and I'm sure he wanted Timmy out of the house so that he could do his stealing without Tim hearing him and growling.'

'Oh, George – I don't think so,' said Julian, who really could not approve of the idea of the tutor doing such a thing. 'It all sounds so far-fetched and unbelievable.'

'Lots of unbelievable things happen,' said George. 'Lots. And this is one of them.'

'Well, if Mr Roland *did* steal the pages, they must be somewhere in the house,' said Julian. 'He hasn't been out all day. They must be somewhere in his bedroom.'

'Of course!' said George, looking thrilled. 'I wish he'd go out! Then I'd search his room.'

'George, you can't do things like that,' said Julian, quite shocked.

'You simply don't know what things I can do, if I really want to,' said George, setting her mouth in a firm line. 'Oh – what's that noise?'

There was the bang of a door. Julian went cautiously to the window and peeped out. The snow had stopped falling for a time, and Mr Roland had taken the chance of going out.

'It's Mr Roland,' said Julian.

'Oooh – I could search his room now, if you'll keep watch at the window and tell me if he comes back,' said George, throwing back the bedclothes at once.

'No, George, don't,' said Julian. 'Honestly and truly, it's awful to search somebody's room like that. And anyway, I dare say he's got the pages with him. He may even be going to give them to somebody!'

'I never thought of that,' said George, and she looked at Julian with wide eyes. 'Isn't that sickening? Of course he may be doing that. He knows those two artists at Kirrin Farmhouse, for instance. They may be in the plot too.'

'Oh, George, don't be silly,' said Julian. 'You are making a mountain out of a mole-hill, talking of plots and goodness knows what! Anyone would think we were in the middle of a big adventure.'

'Well, I think we are,' said George, unexpectedly, and she looked rather solemn. 'I sort of feel it all round me – a Big Adventure!'

Julian stared at his cousin thoughtfully. Could there possibly be anything in what she said?

'Julian, will you do something for me?' said George.

'Of course,' said the boy, at once.

'Go out and follow Mr Roland,' said George. 'Don't let him see you. There's a white macintosh in the hall cupboard. Put it on and you won't be easily seen against the snow. Follow him and see if he meets anyone and gives them anything that looks like the pages of my father's book – you know those big pages he writes on. They're very large.'

'All right,' said Julian. 'But if I do, promise you won't go and search his room. You can't do things like that, George.'

'I can,' said George. 'But I won't, if you'll just follow

Mr Roland for me. I'm sure he's going to hand over what he has stolen to others who are in the plot! And I bet those others will be the two artists at Kirrin Farmhouse that he pretended not to know!'

'You'll find you're quite wrong,' said Julian, going to the door. 'I'm sure I shan't be able to follow Mr Roland, anyway – he's been gone five minutes now!'

'Yes, you will, silly – he'll have left his footmarks in the snow,' said George. 'And oh, Julian – I quite forgot to tell you something else exciting. Oh dear, there isn't time now. I'll tell you when you come back, if you can come up again then. It's about the Secret Way.'

'Really?' said Julian, in delight. It had been a great disappointment to him that all their hunting and searching had come to nothing. 'All right – I'll try and creep up again later. If I don't come, you'll know I can't, and you must wait till bed-time.'

He disappeared and shut the door quietly. He slipped downstairs, popped his head into the sitting-room and whispered to the others that he was going out after the tutor.

'Tell you why, later,' he said. He put the white macintosh around him and went out into the garden. Snow was beginning to fall again, but not yet heavily enough to hide Mr Roland's deep footsteps. He had had big wellington boots on, and the footmarks showed up well in the six-inch-deep snow.

The boy followed them quickly. The countryside was

very wintry-looking now. The sky was low and leaden, and he could see there was much more snow to come. He hurried on after Mr Roland, though he could not see a sign of the tutor.

Down the lane and over the path that led across the common went the double row of footmarks. Julian stumbled on, his eyes glued to the foot-prints. Suddenly he heard the sound of voices and stopped. A big gorse bush lay to the right and the voices came from there. The boy went nearer to the bush. He heard his tutor's voice, talking in low tones. He could not hear a word that was said.

'Whoever can he be talking to?' he wondered. He crept up closer to the bush. There was a hollow space inside. Julian thought he could creep right into it, though it would be very prickly, and peer out of the other side. Carefully the boy crept into the prickly hollow, where the branches were bare and brown.

He parted the prickly branches slowly and cautiously – and to his amazement he saw Mr Roland talking to the two artists from Kirrin Farmhouse – Mr Thomas and Mr Wilton! So George was right. The tutor had met them – and, as Julian watched, Mr Roland handed over to Mr Thomas a doubled-up sheaf of papers.

'They look just like pages from Uncle Quentin's book,' said Julian to himself. 'I say – this is mighty strange. It does begin to look like a plot – with Mr Roland at the centre of it!'

Mr Thomas put the papers into the pocket of his overcoat. The men muttered a few more words, which even Julian's sharp ears could not catch, and then parted. The artists went off towards Kirrin Farmhouse, and Mr Roland took the path back over the common. Julian crouched down in the hollow of the prickly gorse bush, hoping the tutor would not turn and see him. Luckily he didn't. He went straight on and disappeared into the snow, which was now falling thickly. It was also beginning to get dark and Julian, unable to see the path very clearly, hurried after Mr Roland, half-afraid of being lost in the snowstorm.

Mr Roland was not anxious to be out longer than he could help, either. He almost ran back to Kirrin Cottage. He came to the gate at last, and Julian watched him go into the house. He gave him a little time to take off his things and then, giving Timothy a pat as he went by, he went to the garden door. He took off his macintosh, changed his boots, and slipped into the sitting-room before Mr Roland had come down from his bedroom.

'What's happened?' asked Dick and Anne, seeing that Julian was in a great state of excitement. But he could not tell them, for just then Joanna came in to lay the tea.

Much to Julian's disappointment, he could not say a word to the others all that evening, because one or other of the grown-ups was always in the room. Neither could he go up to see George. He could hardly wait to tell his news, but it was no good, he had to.

'Is it still snowing, Aunt Fanny?' asked Anne.

Her aunt went to the front door and looked out. The snow was piled high against the step!

'Yes,' she said, when she came back. 'It is snowing fast

and thickly. If it goes on like this we shall be completely snowed up, as we were two winters ago! We couldn't get out of the house for five days then. The milkman couldn't get to us, nor the baker. Fortunately we had plenty of tinned milk, and I can bake my own bread. You poor children, you will not be able to go out tomorrow – the snow will be too thick!'

'Will Kirrin Farmhouse be snowed up too?' asked Mr Roland.

'Oh yes – worse than we shall be,' said Aunt Fanny. 'But they won't mind! They have plenty of food there. They will be prisoners just as much, and more, as we shall.'

Julian wondered why Mr Roland had asked that question. Was he afraid that his friends would not be able to send those pages away by the post – or take them anywhere by bus or car? The boy felt certain this was the reason for the question. How he longed to be able to talk over everything with the others.

'I'm tired!' he said, about eight o'clock. 'Let's go to bed.'

Dick and Anne stared at him in astonishment. Usually, as he was the eldest, he went to bed last of all. Tonight he was actually *asking* to go! Julian winked quickly at them, and they backed him up at once.

Dick yawned widely, and so did Anne. Their aunt put down the sewing she was doing. 'You *do* sound tired!' she said. 'I think you'd better all go to bed.'

'Could I just go out and see if Timmy is all right?' asked

Julian. His aunt nodded. The boy put on his rubber boots and coat, and slipped out through the garden door into the yard. It was very deep in snow, too. Tim's kennel was half-hidden in it. The dog had trampled a space in front of the kennel door, and stood there, looking for Julian as he came out of the house.

'Poor old boy, out here in the snow all alone,' said Julian. He patted the dog, and Timmy whined. He was asking to go back with the boy.

'I wish I *could* take you back with me,' said Julian. 'Never mind, Timothy. I'll come and see you tomorrow.'

He went indoors again. The children said good-night to their aunt and Mr Roland, and went upstairs.

'Undress quickly, put on dressing-gowns and meet in George's room,' whispered Julian to the others. 'Don't make a sound or we'll have Aunt Fanny up. Quick now!'

In less than three minutes the children were undressed, and were sitting on George's bed. She was very pleased to see them. Anne slipped into bed with her, because her feet were cold.

'Julian! Did you follow Mr Roland all right?' whispered George.

'Why did he follow him?' asked Dick, who had been dying to know.

Julian told them everything as quickly as he could – all that George suspected – and how he had followed the tutor – and what he had seen. When George heard how Julian had watched him giving a sheaf of papers to the two artists, her eyes gleamed angrily.

'The thief! They must have been the lost pages! And to think my father has been so friendly to him. Oh, what can we do? Those men will get the papers away as quickly as they can, and the secret Father has been working on for ages will be used by someone else – for some other country, probably!'

'They can't get the papers away,' said Julian. 'You've no idea how thick the snow is now, George. We shall be prisoners here for a few days, if this snow goes on, and so will the people in Kirrin Farmhouse. If they want to hide the papers, they will have to hide them in the farmhouse! If only we could get over there and hunt round!'

'Well, we can't,' said Dick. 'That's quite certain. We'd be up to our necks in snow!'

The four children looked gloomily at one another. Dick and Anne could hardly believe that the jolly Mr Roland was a thief – a spy perhaps, trying to steal a valuable secret from a friendly scientist. And they couldn't stop it.

'We'd better tell your father,' said Julian at last.

'No,' said Anne. 'He wouldn't believe it, would he, George?'

'He'd laugh at us and go straight and tell Mr Roland,' said George. 'That would warn him, and he mustn't be warned. He mustn't know that we guess anything.'

'Sh! Aunt Fanny's coming!' whispered Dick, suddenly. The boys slipped out of the room and into bed. Anne hopped across to her own little bed. All was peace and quiet when the children's aunt came into the bedroom.

She said good-night and tucked them up. As soon as she had gone down, the four children met together again in George's room.

'George, tell me now what you were going to say about the Secret Way,' said Julian.

'Oh, yes,' said George. 'Well, there may be nothing in my idea at all – but in the study downstairs, there are eight wooden panels over the mantelpiece – and the floor is of stone – and the room faces east! A bit odd, isn't it? Just what the directions said.'

'Is there a cupboard there too?' asked Julian.

'No. But there is everything else,' said George. 'And I was just wondering if by any chance the entrance to the Secret Way is in this house, not in the farmhouse. After all, they both belonged to my family at one time, you know. The people living in the farmhouse years ago must have known all about this cottage.'

'Golly, George – suppose the entrance *was* here!' said Dick. 'Wouldn't it be simply marvellous! Let's go straight down and look!'

'Don't be silly,' said Julian. 'Go down to the study when Uncle Quentin is there? I'd rather meet twenty lions than face Uncle! Especially after what has happened!'

'Well, we simply MUST find out if George's idea is right; we simply must,' said Dick, forgetting to whisper.

'Shut up, idiot!' said Julian, giving him a shove. 'Do you want to bring the whole household up here?'

'Sorry!' said Dick. 'But, oh golly, this *is* exciting. It's an Adventure again.'

'Just what I said,' said George, eagerly. 'Listen, shall we wait till midnight, and then creep down to the study when everyone is asleep, and try our luck? There may be nothing in my idea at all – but we'll have to find out now. I don't believe I could go to sleep till I've tried each one of those panels over the mantelpiece to see if something happens.'

'Well, I know I can't sleep a wink either,' said Dick. 'Listen – is that someone coming up? We'd better go. Come on, Julian! We'll meet in George's room at midnight – and creep down and try out George's idea!'

The two boys went off to their own room. Neither of them could sleep a wink. Nor could George. She lay awake, and went over and over in her mind all that had happened those holidays. 'It's like a jigsaw puzzle,' she thought. 'I couldn't understand a lot of things at first – but now they are fitting together, and making a picture.'

Anne was fast asleep. She had to be awakened at midnight. 'Come on!' whispered Julian, shaking her. 'Don't you want to share in this adventure?'

CHAPTER FOURTEEN

The Secret Way at last!

THE FOUR children crept downstairs through the dark and silent night. Nobody made a sound at all. They made their way to the study. George softly closed the door and then switched on the light.

The children stared at the eight panels over the mantelpiece. Yes – there were exactly eight, four in one row and four in the row above. Julian spread the linen roll out on the table, and the children pored over it.

'The cross is in the middle of the second panel in the top row,' said Julian in a low voice. 'I'll try pressing it. Watch, all of you!'

He went to the fireplace. The others followed him, their hearts beating fast with excitement. Julian stood on tiptoe and began to press hard in the middle of the second panel. Nothing happened.

'Press harder! Tap it!' said Dick.

'I daren't make too much noise,' said Julian, feeling all over the panel to see if there was any roughness that might tell of a hidden spring or lever.

Suddenly, under his hands, the panel slid silently back, just as the one had done at Kirrin Farmhouse in the hall! The children stared at the space behind, thrilled.

THE SECRET WAY AT LAST!

'It's not big enough to get into,' said George. 'It can't be the entrance to the Secret Way.'

Julian got out his torch from his dressing-gown pocket. He put it inside the opening, and gave a low exclamation.

'There's a sort of handle here – with strong wire or something attached to it. I'll pull it and see what happens.'

He pulled – but he was not strong enough to move the handle that seemed to be embedded in the wall. Dick put his hand in and the two boys then pulled together.

'It's moving – it's giving way a bit,' panted Julian. 'Go on, Dick, pull hard!'

The handle suddenly came away from the wall, and behind it came thick wire, rusty and old. At the same time a curious grating noise came from below the hearthrug in front of the fireplace, and Anne almost fell.

'Julian! Something is moving under the rug!' she said, frightened. 'I felt it. Under the rug, quick!'

The handle could not be pulled out any farther. The boys let go, and looked down. To the right of the fireplace, under the rug, something had moved. There was no doubt of that. The rug sagged down instead of being flat and straight.

'A stone has moved in the floor,' said Julian, his voice shaking with excitement. 'This handle works a lever, which is attached to this wire. Quick – pull up the rug, and roll back the carpet.'

With trembling hands the children pulled back the rug and the carpet – and then stood staring at a very strange thing. A big flat stone laid in the floor had slipped downwards, pulled in some manner by the wire attached to the handle hidden behind the panel! There was now a black space where the stone had been.

'Look at that!' said George, in a thrilling whisper.

'The entrance to the Secret Way!'

'It's here after all!' said Julian.

'Let's go down!' said Dick.

'No!' said Anne, shivering at the thought of disappearing into the black hole.

Julian flashed his torch into the black space. The stone had slid down and then sideways. Below was a space just big enough to take a man, bending down.

'I expect there's a passage or something leading from here, under the house, and out,' said Julian. 'Golly, I wonder where it leads to?'

'We simply must find out,' said George.

'Not now,' said Dick. 'It's dark and cold. I don't fancy going along the Secret Way at midnight. I don't mind just hopping down to see what it's like – but don't let's go along any passage till tomorrow.'

'Uncle Quentin will be working here tomorrow,' said Julian.

'He said he was going to sweep the snow away from the front door in the morning,' said George. 'We could slip into the study then. It's Saturday. There may be no lessons.'

'All right,' said Julian, who badly wanted to explore everything then and there. 'But for goodness' sake let's have a look and see if there *is* a passage down there. At present all we can see is a hole!'

'I'll help you down,' said Dick. So he gave his brother a hand and the boy dropped lightly down into the black space, holding his torch. He gave a loud exclamation.

It's the entrance to the Secret Way all right! There's a passage leading from here under the house – awfully low and narrow – but I can see it's a passage. I do wonder where it leads to!'

He shivered. It was cold and damp down there. 'Give me a hand up, Dick,' he said. He was soon out of the hole and in the warm study again.

The children looked at one another in the greatest joy and excitement. This *was* an Adventure, a real Adventure. It was a pity they couldn't go on with it now.

'We'll try and take Timmy with us tomorrow,' said George. 'Oh, I say – how are we going to shut the entrance up?'

'We can't leave the rug and carpet sagging over that hole,' said Dick. 'Nor can we leave the panel open.'

'We'll see if we can get the stone back,' said Julian. He stood on tiptoe and felt about inside the panel. His hand closed on a kind of knob, set deep in a stone. He pulled it, and at once the handle slid back, pulled by the wire. At the same time the sunk stone glided to the surface of the floor again, making a slight grating sound as it did so.

'Well, it's like magic!' said Dick. 'It really is! Fancy the mechanism working so smoothly after years of not being used. This is the most exciting thing I've ever seen!'

There was a noise in the bedroom above. The children stood still and listened.

'It's Mr Roland!' whispered Dick. 'He's heard us. Quick, slip upstairs before he comes down.'

They switched out the light and opened the study door softly. Up the stairs they fled, as quietly as church mice, their hearts thumping so loudly that it seemed as if everyone in the house must hear the beat.

The girls got safely to their rooms and Dick was able to slip into his. But Julian was seen by Mr Roland as he came out of his room with a torch.

'What are you doing, Julian!' asked the tutor, in surprise. 'Did you hear a noise downstairs? I thought I did.'

'Yes – I heard quite a lot of noise downstairs,' said Julian, truthfully. 'But perhaps it's snow falling off the roof, landing with a plop in the ground, sir. Do you think that's it?'

'I don't know,' said the tutor doubtfully. 'We'll go down and see.'

They went down, but of course there was nothing to be seen. Julian was glad they had been able to shut the panel and make the stone come back to its proper place again. Mr Roland was the very last person he wanted to tell his secret to.

They went upstairs and Julian slipped into his room. 'Is it all right?' whispered Dick.

'Yes,' said Julian. 'Don't let's talk. Mr Roland's awake, and I don't want him to suspect anything.'

The boys fell asleep. When they awoke in the morning, there was a completely white world outside. Snow covered everything and covered it deeply. Timothy's kennel could not be seen! But there were footmarks round about it.

George gave a squeal when she saw how deep the snow was. 'Poor Timothy! I'm going to get him in. I don't care what anyone says! I won't let him be buried in the snow!'

She dressed and tore downstairs. She went out to the

kennel, floundering knee deep in the snow. But there was no Timmy there!

A loud bark from the kitchen made her jump. Joanna the cook knocked on the kitchen window. 'It's all right! I couldn't bear the dog out there in the snow, so I fetched him in, poor thing. Your mother says I can have him in the kitchen but you're not to come and see him.'

'Oh, good – Timmy's in the warmth!' said George, gladly. She yelled to Joanna, 'Thanks awfully! You *are* kind!'

She went indoors and told the others. They were very glad. 'And *I've* got a bit of news for *you*,' said Dick. 'Mr Roland is in bed with a bad cold, so there are to be no lessons today. Cheers!'

'Golly, that *is* good news,' said George, cheering up tremendously. 'Timmy in the warm kitchen and Mr Roland kept in bed. I do feel pleased!'

'We shall be able to explore the Secret Way safely now,' said Julian. 'Aunt Fanny is going to do something in the kitchen this morning with Joanna, and Uncle is going to tackle the snow. I vote we say we'll do lessons by ourselves in the sitting-room, and then, when everything is safe, we'll explore the Secret Way!'

'But why must we do lessons?' asked George in dismay.

'Because if we don't, silly, we'll have to help your father dig away the snow,' said Julian.

So, to his uncle's surprise, Julian suggested that the four children should do lessons by themselves in the sitting-room. 'Well, I thought you'd like to come and help dig away the snow,' said Uncle Quentin. 'But perhaps you had better get on with your work.'

The children sat themselves down as good as gold in the sitting-room, their books before them. They heard Mr Roland coughing in his room. They heard their aunt go into the kitchen and talk to Joanna. They heard Timmy scratching at the kitchen door – then paws pattering down

the passage – then a big, inquiring nose came round the door, and there was old Timmy, looking anxiously for his beloved mistress!

'Timmy!' squealed George, and ran to him. She flung her arms round his neck and hugged him.

'You act as if you hadn't seen Tim for a year,' said Julian.

'It seems like a year,' said George. 'I say, there's my father digging away like mad. Can't we go to the study now? We ought to be safe for a good while.'

They left the sitting-room and went to the study. Julian was soon pulling the handle behind the secret panel. George had already turned back the rug and the carpet. The stone slid downward and sideways. The Secret Way was open!

'Come on!' said Julian. 'Hurry!'

He jumped down into the hole. Dick followed, then Anne, then George. Julian pushed them all into the narrow, low passage. Then he looked up. Perhaps he had better pull the carpet and rug over the hole, in case anyone came into the room and looked around. It took him a few seconds to do it. Then he bent down and joined the others in the passage. They were going to explore the Secret Way at last!

CHAPTER FIFTEEN

An exciting journey and hunt

TIMOTHY HAD leapt down into the hole when George had jumped. He now ran ahead of the children, puzzled at their wanting to explore such a cold, dark place. Both Julian and Dick had torches, which threw broad beams before them.

There was not much to be seen. The Secret Way under the old house was narrow and low, so that the children were forced to go in single file, and to stoop almost double. It was a great relief to them when the passage became a little wider, and the room a little higher. It was very tiring to stoop all the time.

'Have you any idea where the Secret Way is going?' Dick asked Julian. 'I mean – is it going towards the sea, or away from it?'

'Oh, not towards the sea!' said Julian, who had a very good sense of direction. 'As far as I can make out the passage is going towards the common. Look at the walls – they are rather sandy in places, and we know the common has sandy soil. I hope we shan't find that the passage has fallen in anywhere.'

They went on and on. The Secret Way was very straight, though occasionally it would round a rocky part in a curve.

'Isn't it dark and cold?' said Anne, shivering. 'I wish I had put on a coat. How many miles have we come, Julian?'

'Not even one, silly!' said Julian. 'Hallo – look here – the passage has fallen in a bit there!'

Two bright torches shone in front of them and the children saw that the sandy roof had fallen in. Julian kicked at the pile of sandy soil with his foot.

'It's all right,' he said. 'We can force our way through easily. It isn't much of a fall, and it's mostly sand. I'll do a bit of kicking!'

After some trampling and kicking, the roof-fall no longer blocked the way. There was now enough room for the children to climb over it, bending their heads low to avoid knocking them against the top of the passage. Julian shone his torch forward, and saw that the way was clear.

'The Secret Way is very wide just here!' he said suddenly, and flashed his torch around to show the others.

'It's been widened out to make a sort of little room,' said George. 'Look, there's a kind of bench at the back, made out of the rock. I believe it's a resting-place.'

George was right. It was very tiring to creep along the narrow passage for so long. The little wide place with its rocky bench made a very good resting-place. The four tired children, cold but excited, huddled together on the funny seat and took a welcome rest. Timmy put his head on George's knee. He was delighted to be with her again.

'Well, come on,' said Julian, after a few minutes. 'I'm

getting awfully cold. I do wonder where this passage comes out!'

'Julian – do you think it could come out at Kirrin Farmhouse?' asked George, suddenly. 'You know what Mrs Sanders said – that there was a secret passage leading from the farmhouse somewhere. Well, this may be the one – and it leads to Kirrin Cottage!'

'George, I believe you're right!' said Julian. 'Yes – the two houses belonged to your family years ago! And in the old days there were often secret passages joining houses, so it's quite plain this secret way joins them up together! Why didn't I think of that before?'

'I say!' squealed Anne, in a high, excited voice, 'I say! I've thought of something too!'

'What?' asked everyone.

'Well – if those two artists have got Uncle's papers, we may be able to get them away before the men can send them off by post, or take them away themselves!' squeaked Anne, so thrilled with her idea that she could hardly get the words out quickly enough. 'They're prisoners at the farmhouse because of the snow, just as we were at the cottage.'

'*Anne!* You're right!' said Julian.

'Clever girl!' said Dick.

'I *say* – if we *could* get those papers again – how wonderful it would be!' said George. Timmy joined in the general excitement, and jumped up and down in joy. Something had pleased the children, so he was pleased too!

'Come on!' said Julian, taking Anne's hand. 'This is thrilling. If George is right, and this Secret Way comes out at Kirrin Farmhouse somewhere, we'll somehow hunt through those men's rooms and find the papers.'

'You said that searching people's rooms was a shocking thing to do,' said George.

'Well, I didn't know then all I know now,' said Julian. 'We're doing this for your father – and maybe for our country too, if his secret formula is valuable. We've got to set our wits to work now, to outwit dangerous enemies.'

'Do you really think they are dangerous?' asked Anne rather afraid.

'Yes, I should think so,' said Julian. 'But you needn't worry, Anne, you've got me and Dick and Tim to protect you.'

'I can protect her too,' said George, indignantly.

'You're fiercer than any boy I know!' said Dick.

'Come on,' said Julian, impatiently. 'I'm longing to get to the end of this passage.'

They all went on again, Anne following behind Julian, and Dick behind George. Timmy ran up and down the line, squeezing by them whenever he wanted to. He thought it was a very peculiar way to spend a morning!

Julian stopped suddenly, after they had gone a good way. 'What's up?' asked Dick, from the back. 'Not another roof-fall, I hope!'

'No – but I think we've come to the end of the passage!' said Julian, thrilled. The others crowded as close to him as they could. The passage certainly had come to an end. There was a rocky wall in front of them, and set firmly in it were iron staples intended for footholds. These went up the wall and when Julian turned his torch upwards, the children saw that there was a square opening in the roof of the passage.

'We have to climb up this rocky wall now,' said Julian, 'go through that dark hole there, keep on climbing – and goodness knows where we come out! I'll go first. You wait here, everyone, and I'll come back and tell you what I've seen.'

The boy put his torch between his teeth, and then pulled himself up by the iron staples set in the wall. He set his feet on them, and then climbed up through the square dark hole, feeling for the staples as he went.

He went up for a good way. It was almost like going up a chimney shaft, he thought. It was cold and smelt musty.

Suddenly he came to a ledge, and he stepped on to it. He took his torch from his teeth and flashed it around him.

There was a stone wall behind him, at the side of him and stone above him. The black hole up which he had come, yawned by his feet. Julian shone his torch in front of him, and a shock of surprise went through him.

There was no stone wall in front of him, but a big wooden door, made of black oak. A handle was set about waist-high; Julian turned it with trembling fingers. What was he going to see?

The door opened outwards, over the ledge, and it was

difficult to get round it without falling back into the hole. Julian managed to open it wide, squeezed round it without losing his footing, and stepped beyond it, expecting to find himself in a room.

But his hand felt more wood in front of him! He shone his torch round, and found that he was up against what looked like yet another door. Under his searching fingers it suddenly moved sideways, and slid silently away!

And then Julian knew where he was! 'I'm in the cupboard at Kirrin Farmhouse – the one that has a false back!' he thought. 'The Secret Way comes up behind it! How clever! Little did we know when we played about in this cupboard that not only did it have a sliding back, but that it was the entrance to the Secret Way, hidden behind it!'

The cupboard was now full of clothes belonging to the artists. Julian stood and listened. There was no sound of anyone in the room. Should he just take a quick look round, and see if those lost papers were anywhere about?

Then he remembered the other four, waiting patiently below in the cold. He had better go and tell them what had happened. They could all come and help in the search.

He stepped into the space behind the sliding back. The sliding door slipped across again, and Julian was left standing on the narrow ledge, with the old oak door wide open to one side of him. He did not bother to shut it. He felt about his feet, and found the iron staples in the hole below him. Down he went, clinging with his hands and feet, his torch in his teeth again.

'Julian! What a time you've been! Quick, tell us all about it!' cried George.

'It's most terribly thrilling,' said Julian. 'Absolutely super! Where do you suppose all this leads to? Into the cupboard at Kirrin Farmhouse – the one that's got a false back!'

'Golly!' said Dick.

'I *say*!' said George.

'Did you go into the room?' cried Anne.

'I climbed as far as I could and came to a big oak door,' said Julian. 'It has a handle this side, so I swung it wide open. Then I saw another wooden door in front of me – at least, I thought it was a door, I didn't know it was just the false back of that cupboard. It was quite easy to slide back and I stepped through, and found myself among a whole lot of clothes hanging in the cupboard! Then I hurried back to tell you.'

'Julian! We can hunt for those papers now,' said George, eagerly. 'Was there anyone in the room?'

'I couldn't *hear* anyone,' said Julian. 'Now, what I propose is this – we'll all go up, and have a hunt round those two rooms. The men have the room next to the cupboard one too.'

'Oh good!' said Dick, thrilled at the thought of such an adventure. 'Let's go now. You go first, Ju. Then Anne, then George and then me.'

'What about Tim?' asked George.

'He can't climb, silly,' said Julian. 'He's a simply

marvellous dog, but he certainly can't climb, George. We'll have to leave him down here.'

'He won't like that,' said George.

'Well, we can't carry him up,' said Dick. 'You won't mind staying here for a bit, will you, Tim, old fellow?'

Tim wagged his tail. But, as he saw the four children mysteriously disappearing up the wall, he put his big tail down at once. What! Going without him? How could they?

He jumped up at the wall, and fell back. He jumped again and whined. George called down in a low voice.

'Be quiet, Tim dear! We shan't be long.'

Tim stopped whining. He lay down at the bottom of the wall, his ears well-cocked. This adventure was becoming more and more peculiar!

Soon the children were on the narrow ledge. The old oak door was still wide open. Julian shone his torch and the others saw the false back of the cupboard. Julian put his hands on it and it slid silently sideways. Then the torch shone on coats and dressing-gowns!

The children stood quite still, listening. There was no sound from the room. 'I'll open the cupboard door and peep into the room,' whispered Julian. 'Don't make a sound!'

The boy pushed between the clothes and felt for the outer cupboard door with his hand. He found it, and pushed it slightly. It opened a little and a shaft of daylight came into the cupboard. He peeped cautiously into the room.

There was no one there at all. That was good. 'Come on!' he whispered to the others. 'The room's empty!'

One by one the children crept out of the clothes cupboard and into the room. There was a big bed there, a wash-stand, chest of drawers, small table and two chairs. Nothing else. It would be easy to search the whole room.

'Look, Julian, there's a door between the two rooms,' said George, suddenly. 'Two of us can go and hunt there and two here – and we can lock the doors that lead on to the landing, so that no one can come in and catch us!'

'Good idea!' said Julian, who was afraid that at any moment someone might come in and catch them in their search. 'Anne and I will go into the next room, and you and Dick can search this one. Lock the door that opens on to the landing, Dick, and I'll lock the one in the other room. We'll leave the connecting-door open, so that we can whisper to one another.'

Quietly the boy and girl slipped through the connecting-door into the second room, which was very like the first. That was empty too. Julian went over to the door that led to the landing, and turned the key in the lock. He heard Dick doing the same to the door in the other room. He heaved a big sigh. Now he felt safe!

'Anne, turn up the rugs and see if any papers are hidden there,' he said. 'Then look under the chair-cushions and strip the bed to see if anything is hidden under the mattress.'

Anne set to work, and Julian began to hunt too. He started on the chest of drawers, which he thought would be a very likely place to hide things in. The children's hands were shaking, as they felt here and there for the lost papers. It was so terribly exciting.

They wondered where the two men were. Down in the warm kitchen, perhaps. It was cold up here in the bedrooms, and they would not want to be away from the warmth. They could not go out because the snow was piled in great drifts round Kirrin Farmhouse!

Dick and George were searching hard in the other room. They looked in every drawer. They stripped the bed. They turned up rugs and carpet. They even put their hands up the big chimney-place!

'Julian? Have you found anything?' asked Dick in a low voice, appearing at the door between the two rooms.

'Not a thing,' said Julian, rather gloomily. 'They've hidden the papers well! I only hope they haven't got them on them – in their pockets, or something!'

Dick stared at him in dismay. He hadn't thought of that. 'That *would* be sickening!' he said.

'You go back and hunt *everywhere* – simply *everywhere*!' ordered Julian. 'Punch the pillows to see if they've stuck them under the pillow-case!'

Dick disappeared. Rather a lot of noise came from his room. It sounded as if he were doing a good deal of punching!

Anne and Julian went on hunting too. There was simply nowhere that they did not look. They even turned the pictures round to see if the papers had been stuck behind one of them. But there was nothing to be found. It was bitterly disappointing.

'We can't go without finding them,' said Julian, in desperation. 'It was such a bit of luck to get here like this, down the Secret Way – right into the bedrooms! We simply *must* find those papers!'

'I say,' said Dick, appearing again, 'I can hear voices! Listen!'

All four children listened. Yes – there were men's voices – just outside the bedroom doors!

CHAPTER SIXTEEN

The children are discovered

'WHAT SHALL we do?' whispered George. They had all tiptoed to the first room, and were standing together, listening.

'We'd better go down the Secret Way again,' said Julian.

'Oh no, we . . .' began George, when she heard the handle of the door being turned. Whoever was trying to get in, could not open the door. There was an angry exclamation, and then the children heard Mr Wilton's voice. 'My door seems to have stuck. Do you mind If I come through your bedroom and see what's the matter with this handle?'

'Come right along!' came the voice of Mr Thomas. There was the sound of footsteps going to the outer door of the second room. Then there was the noise of a handle being turned and shaken.

'What's this!' said Mr Wilton, in exasperation. 'This won't open, either. Can the doors be locked?'

'It looks like it!' said Mr Thomas.

There was a pause. Then the children distinctly heard a few words uttered in a low voice. 'Are the papers safe? Is anyone after them?'

'They're in your room, aren't they?' said Mr Thomas.

There was another pause. The children looked at one another. So the men *had* got the papers – and what was more, they *were* in the room! The very room the children stood in! They looked round it eagerly, racking their brains to think of some place they had not yet explored.

'Quick! Hunt round again while we've time,' whispered Julian. 'Don't make a noise.'

On tiptoe the children began a thorough hunt once more. How they searched! They even opened the pages of the books on the table, thinking that the papers might have been slipped in there. But they could find nothing.

'Hi, Mrs Sanders!' came Mr Wilton's voice. 'Have you by any chance locked these two doors? We can't get in!'

'Dear me!' said the voice of Mrs Sanders from the stairs. 'I'll come along and see. I certainly haven't locked any doors!'

Once again the handles were turned, but the doors would not open. The men began to get very impatient.

'Do you suppose anyone is in our rooms?' Mr Wilton asked Mrs Sanders.

She laughed.

'Well now, who would be in your rooms? There's only me and Mr Sanders in the house, and you know as well as I do that no one can come in from outside, for we're quite snowed up. I don't understand it – the locks of the doors must have slipped.'

Anne was lifting up the wash-stand jug to look underneath, at that moment. It was heavier than she thought, and she had to let it down again suddenly. It struck the marble wash-stand with a crash, and water slopped out all over the place!

Everyone outside the door heard the noise. Mr Wilton banged on the door and rattled the handle.

'Who's there? Let us in or you'll be sorry! What are you doing in there?'

'Idiot, Anne!' said Dick. 'Now they'll break the door down!'

That was exactly what the two men intended to do! Afraid that someone was mysteriously in their room, trying to find the stolen papers, they went quite mad, and began to put their shoulders to the door, and heave hard. The door shook and creaked.

'Now, you be careful what you're doing!' cried the indignant voice of Mrs Sanders. The men took no notice. There came a crash as they both tried out their double strength on the door.

'Quick! We must go!' said Julian. 'We mustn't let the men know how we got here, or we shan't be able to come and hunt another time. Anne, George, Dick – get back to the cupboard quickly!'

The children raced for the clothes cupboard. 'I'll go first and help you down,' said Julian. He got out on to the narrow ledge and found the iron foot-holds with his feet. Down he went, torch held between his teeth as usual.

'Anne, come next,' he called. 'And Dick, you come third, and give a hand to Anne if she wants it. George is a good climber – she can easily get down herself.'

Anne was slow at climbing down. She was terribly excited, rather frightened, and so afraid of falling that she hardly dared to feel for each iron staple as she went down.

'Buck up, Anne!' whispered Dick, above her. 'The men have almost got the door down!'

There were tremendous sounds coming from the bedroom door. At any moment now it might break down, and the men would come racing in. Dick was thankful when he could begin to climb down the wall! Once they were all out, George could shut the big oak door, and they would be safe.

George was hidden among the clothes in the cupboard, waiting her turn to climb down. As she stood there, trying in vain to go over any likely hiding-place in her mind, her hands felt something rustly in the pocket of a coat she was standing against. It was a macintosh coat, with big pockets. The little girl's heart gave a leap.

Suppose the papers had been left in the pocket of the coat the man had on when he took them from Mr Roland? That was the only place the children had not searched – the pockets of the coats in the cupboard! With trembling fingers the girl felt in the pocket where the rustling was.

She drew out a sheaf of papers. It was dark in the cupboard, and she could not see if they were the ones she was hunting for, or not – but how she hoped they were! She stuffed them up the front of her jersey, for she had no big pocket, and whispered to Dick:

'Can I come now?'

CRASH! The door fell in with a terrific noise, and the two men leapt into the room. They looked round. It was empty! But there was the water spilt on the wash-stand

and on the floor. Someone must be there somewhere!

'Look in the cupboard!' said Mr Thomas.

George crept out of the clothes cupboard and on to the narrow ledge, beyond the place where the false back of the cupboard used to be. It was still hidden sideways in the wall. The girl climbed down the hole a few steps and then shut the oak door which was now above her head. She had not enough strength to close it completely, but she hoped that now she was safe!

The men went to the cupboard and felt about in the clothes for anyone who might possibly be hiding there. Mr Wilton gave a loud cry.

'The papers are gone! They were in this pocket! There's not a sign of them. Quick, we must find the thief and get them back!'

The men did not notice that the cupboard seemed to go farther back than usual. They stepped away from it now that they were sure no one was there, and began to hunt round the room.

By now all the children except George were at the bottom of the hole, standing in the Secret Way, waiting impatiently for George to come down. Poor George was in such a hurry to get down that she caught her clothing on one of the staples, and had to stand in a very dangerous position trying to disentangle it.

'Come on, George, for goodness' sake!' said Julian.

Timothy jumped up at the wall. He could feel the fear and excitement of the waiting children, and it upset him.

He wanted George. Why didn't she come? Why was she up that dark hole? Tim was unhappy about her.

He threw back his head and gave such a loud and mournful howl that all the children jumped violently.

'Shut up, Tim!' said Julian.

Tim howled again, and the weird sound echoed round and about in a strange manner. Anne was terrified, and she began to cry. Timothy howled again and again. Once he began to howl it was difficult to stop him.

The men in the bedroom above heard the extraordinary noise, and stopped in amazement.

'Whatever's that?' said one.

'Sounds like a dog howling in the depths of the earth,' said the other.

'Funny!' said Mr Wilton. 'It seems to be coming from the direction of that cupboard.'

He went over to it and opened the door. Tim chose that moment to give a specially mournful howl, and Mr Wilton jumped. He got into the cupboard and felt about at the back. The oak door there gave way beneath his hand, and he felt it open.

'There's something weird here,' called Mr Wilton. 'Bring my torch off the table.'

Tim howled again and the noise made Mr Wilton shiver! Tim had a peculiarly horrible howl. It came echoing up the hole, and burst out into the cupboard.

Mr Thomas got the torch. The men shone it at the back of the cupboard, and gave an exclamation.

'Look at that! There's a door here! Where does it lead to?'

Mrs Sanders, who had been watching everything in surprise and indignation, angry that her door should have been broken down, came up to the cupboard.

'My!' she said. 'I knew there was a false back to that cupboard – but I didn't know there was another door behind it too! That must be the entrance to the Secret Way that people used in the old days.'

'Where does it lead to?' rapped out Mr Wilton.

'Goodness knows!' said Mrs Sanders. 'I never took much interest in such things.'

'Come on, we must go down,' said Mr Wilton, shining his torch into the square black hole, and seeing the iron foot-holds set in the stone. 'This is where the thief went. He can't have got far. We'll go after him. We've got to get those papers back!'

It was not long before the two men had swung themselves over the narrow ledge and down into the hole, feeling with their feet for the iron staples. Down they went and down, wondering where they were coming to. There was no sound below them. Clearly the thief had got away!

George had got down at last. Tim almost knocked her over in his joy. She put her hand on his head. 'You old silly!' she said. 'I believe you've given our secret away! Quick, Ju – we must go, because those men will be after us in a minute. They could easily hear Tim's howling!'

Julian took Anne's hand. 'Come along, Anne,' he said. 'You must run as fast as you can. Hurry now! Dick, keep with George.'

The four of them hurried down the dark, narrow passage. What a long way they had to go home! If only the passage wasn't such a long one! The children's hearts were beating painfully as they made haste, stumbling as they went.

Julian shone his light steadily in front of him, and Dick shone his at the back. Half-leading, half-dragging Anne, Julian hurried along. Behind them they heard a shout.

'Look! There's a light ahead! That's the thief! Come on, we'll soon get him!'

CHAPTER SEVENTEEN

Good old Tim!

'HURRY, ANNE. Do hurry!' shouted Dick, who was just behind.

Poor Anne was finding it very difficult to get along quickly. Pulled by Julian and pushed by Dick, she almost fell two or three times. Her breath came in loud pants, and she felt as if she would burst.

'Let me have a rest!' she panted. But there was no time for that, with the two men hurrying after them! They came to the piece that was widened out, where the rocky bench was, and Anne looked longingly at it. But the boys hurried her on.

Suddenly the little girl caught her foot on a stone and fell heavily, almost dragging Julian down with her. She tried to get up, and began to cry.

'I've hurt my foot! I've twisted it! Oh, Julian, it hurts me to walk.'

'Well, you've just *got* to come along, darling,' said Julian, sorry for his little sister, but knowing that they would all be caught if he was not firm. 'Hurry as much as you can.'

But now it was impossible for Anne to go fast. She cried with pain as her foot hurt her, and hobbled along so slowly

that Dick almost fell over her. Dick cast a look behind him and saw the light of the men's torches coming nearer and nearer. Whatever were they to do?

'I'll stay here with Tim and keep them off,' said George, suddenly. 'Here, take these papers, Dick! I believe they're the ones we want, but I'm not sure till we get a good light to see them. I found them in a pocket of one of the coats in the cupboard.'

'Golly!' said Dick, surprised. He took the sheaf of papers and stuffed them up his jersey, just as George had stuffed them up hers. They were too big to go into his trouser pockets. 'I'll stay with you, George, and let the other two go on ahead.'

'No. I want the papers taken to safety, in case they are my father's,' said George. 'Go on, Dick! I'll be all right here with Tim. I shall stay here just where the passage curves round this rocky bit. I'll make Tim bark like mad.'

'Suppose the men have got revolvers?' said Dick doubtfully. 'They might shoot him.'

'I bet they haven't,' said George. '*Do* go, Dick! The men are almost here. There's the light of their torch.'

Dick sped after the stumbling Anne. He told Julian what George had suggested. 'Good for George!' said Julian. 'She really is marvellous – not afraid of anything! She will keep the men off till I get poor old Anne back.'

George was crouching behind the rocky bit, her hand on Tim's collar, waiting. 'Now, Tim!' she whispered. 'Bark your loudest. Now!'

Timothy had been growling up till now, but at George's command he opened his big mouth and barked. How he barked! He had a simply enormous voice, and the barks went echoing all down the dark and narrow passage. The hurrying men, who were near the rocky piece of the passage, stopped.

'If you come round this bend, I'll set my dog on you!' cried George.

'It's a child shouting,' said one man to another. 'Only a child! Come on!'

Timothy barked again, and pulled at his collar. He was longing to get at the men. The light of their torch shone round the bend. George let Tim go, and the big dog sprang joyfully round the curve to meet his enemies.

They suddenly saw him by the light of their torch, and he was a very terrifying sight! To begin with, he was a big dog, and now that he was angry all the hairs on the back of his neck had risen up, making him look even more enormous. His teeth were bared and glinted in the torch-light.

The men did not like the look of him at all. 'If you move one step nearer I'll tell my dog to fly at you!' shouted George. 'Wait, Tim, wait! Stand there till I give the word.'

The dog stood in the light of the torch, growling deeply. He looked an extremely fierce animal. The men looked at him doubtfully. One man took a step forward and George heard him. At once she shouted to Tim.

'Go for him, Tim, go for him!'

Tim leapt at the man's throat. He took him completely by surprise and the man fell to the ground with a thud, trying to beat off the dog. The other man helped.

'Call off your dog or we'll hurt him!' cried the second man.

'It's much more likely he'll hurt *you*!' said George, coming out from behind the rock and enjoying the fun. 'Tim, come off.'

Tim came away from the man he was worrying, looking up at his mistress as if to say, 'I was having *such* a good time! Why did you spoil it?'

'Who are you?' said the man on the ground.

'I'm not answering any of your questions,' said George. 'Go back to Kirrin Farmhouse, that's my advice to you. If you dare to come along this passage I'll set my dog on to you again – and next time he'll do more damage.'

The men turned and went back the way they had come. They neither of them wanted to face Tim again. George waited until she could no longer see the light of their torch, then she bent down and patted Timothy.

'Brave, good dog!' she said. 'I love you, darling Tim, and you don't know how proud I am of you! Come along – we'll hurry after the others now. I expect those two men will explore this passage some time tonight, and won't they get a shock when they find out where it leads to, and see who is waiting for them!'

George hurried along the rest of the long passage, with Tim running beside her. She had Dick's torch, and it did not take her long to catch the others up. She panted out to them what had happened, and even poor Anne chuckled in delight when she heard how Tim had flung Mr Wilton to the ground.

'Here we are,' said Julian, as the passage came to a stop below the hole in the study floor. 'Hallo – what's this?'

A bright light was shining down the hole, and the rug and carpet, so carefully pulled over the hole by Julian, were now pulled back again. The children gazed up in surprise.

Uncle Quentin was there, and Aunt Fanny, and when they saw the children's faces looking up at them from the hole, they were so astonished that they very nearly fell down the hole too!

'Julian! Anne! What in the wide world are you doing down there?' cried Uncle Quentin. He gave them each a hand up, and the four children and Timothy were at last safe in the warm study. How good it was to feel warm again! They got as near the fire as they could.

'Children – what *is* the meaning of this?' asked Aunt Fanny. She looked white and worried. 'I came into the study to do some dusting, and when I stood on that bit of the rug, it seemed to give way beneath me. When I pulled it up and turned back the carpet, I saw that hole – and the hole in the panelling too! And then I found that all of you had disappeared, and went to fetch your uncle. What *has* been happening – and where does that hole lead to?'

Dick took the sheaf of papers from under his jersey and gave them to George. She took them and handed them to her father. 'Are these the missing pages?' she asked.

Her father fell on them as if they had been worth more than a hundred times their weight in gold. 'Yes! Yes! They're the pages – all three of them! Thank goodness they're back. They took me three years to bring to perfection, and contained the heart of my secret formula. George, where did you get them?'

'It's a very long story,' said George. 'You tell it all, Julian, I feel tired.'

Julian began to tell the tale. He left out nothing. He told how George had found Mr Roland snooping about the study – how she had felt sure that the tutor had not wanted Timmy in the house because the dog gave warning of his movements at night – how George had seen him talking to the two artists, although he had said he did not know them. As the tale went on, Uncle Quentin and Aunt Fanny looked more and more amazed. They simply could not believe it all.

But after all, there were the missing papers, safely back. That was marvellous. Uncle Quentin hugged the papers as if they were a precious baby. He would not put them down for a moment.

George told the bit about Timmy keeping the men off the escaping children. 'So you see, although you made poor Tim live out in the cold, away from me, he really saved us all, and your papers too,' she said to her father, fixing her brilliant blue eyes on him.

Her father looked most uncomfortable. He felt very guilty for having punished George and Timothy. They had been right about Mr Roland and he had been wrong.

'Poor George,' he said, 'and poor Timmy. I'm sorry about all that.'

George did not bear malice once anyone had owned themselves to be in the wrong. She smiled at her father.

'It's all right,' she said. 'But don't you think that as I was punished unfairly, Mr Roland might be punished well and truly? He deserves it!'

'Oh, he shall be, certainly he shall be,' promised her father. 'He's up in bed with a cold, as you know. I hope he doesn't hear any of this, or he may try to escape.'

'He can't,' said George. 'We're snowed up. You could ring up the police, and arrange for them to come here as soon as ever they can manage it, when the snow has cleared. And I rather think those other two men will try to explore the Secret Way as soon as possible, to get the papers back. Could we catch them when they arrive, do you think?'

'Rather!' said Uncle Quentin, though Aunt Fanny looked as if she didn't want any more exciting things to happen! 'Now look here, you seem really frozen all of you, and you must be hungry too, because it's almost lunchtime. Go into the dining-room and sit by the fire, and Joanna shall bring us all a hot lunch. Then we'll talk about what to do.'

Nobody said a word to Mr Roland, of course. He lay in bed, coughing now and then. George had slipped up and locked his door. She wasn't going to have him wandering out and overhearing anything!

They all enjoyed their hot lunch, and became warm and cosy. It was nice to sit there together, talking over their adventure, and planning what to do.

'I will telephone to the police, of course,' said Uncle Quentin. 'And tonight we will put Timmy into the study to give the two artists a good welcome if they arrive!'

Mr Roland was most annoyed to find his door locked

that afternoon when he took it into his head to dress and go downstairs. He banged on it indignantly. George grinned and went upstairs. She had told the other children how she had locked the door.

'What's the matter, Mr Roland?' she asked, in a polite voice.

'Oh, it's you, George, is it?' said the tutor. 'See what's the matter with my door, will you? I can't open it.'

George had pocketed the key when she had locked the door. She answered Mr Roland in a cheerful voice.

'Oh, Mr Roland, there's no key in your door, so I can't unlock it. I'll see if I can find it!'

Mr Roland was angry and puzzled. He couldn't understand why his door was locked and the key gone. He did not guess that everyone knew about him now. Uncle Quentin laughed when George went down and told him about the locked door.

'He may as well be kept a prisoner,' he said. 'He can't escape now.'

'That night, everyone went to bed early, and Timmy was left in the study, guarding the hole. Mr Roland had become more and more angry and puzzled when his door was not unlocked. He had shouted for Uncle Quentin, but only George had come. He could not understand it. George, of course, was enjoying herself. She made Timothy bark outside Mr Roland's door, and this puzzled him too, for he knew that George was not supposed to see Timmy for three days. Wild thoughts raced through his head. Had that fierce, impossible child locked up her father and mother and Joanna, as well as himself? He could not imagine what had happened.

In the middle of the night Timmy awoke everyone by

barking madly. Uncle Quentin and the children hurried downstairs, followed by Aunt Fanny, and the amazed Joanna. A fine sight met their eyes!

Mr Wilton and Mr Thomas were in the study crouching behind the sofa, terrified of Timothy, who was barking for all he was worth! Timmy was standing by the hole in the stone floor, so that the two men could not escape down there. Artful Timmy! He had waited in silence until the men had crept up the hole into the study, and were exploring it, wondering where they were – and then the dog had leapt to the hole to guard it, preventing the men from escaping.

'Good evening, Mr Wilton, good evening, Mr Thomas,' said George, in a polite voice. 'Have you come to see our tutor Mr Roland?'

'So this is where he lives!' said Mr Wilton. 'Was it you in the passage today?'

'Yes – and my cousins,' said George. 'Have you come to look for the papers you stole from my father?'

The two men were silent. They knew they were caught. Mr Wilton spoke after a moment.

'Where's Mr Roland?'

'Shall we take these men to Mr Roland, Uncle?' asked Julian, winking at George. 'Although it's in the middle of the night I'm sure he would love to see them.'

'Yes,' said his uncle, jumping at once to what the boy meant to do. 'Take them up. Timmy, you go too.'

The men followed Julian upstairs, Timmy close at their

heels. George followed too, grinning. She handed Julian the key. He unlocked the door and the men went in, just as Julian switched on the light. Mr Roland was wide awake and gave an exclamation of complete amazement when he saw his friends.

Before they had time to say a word Julian locked the door again and threw the key to George.

'A nice little bag of prisoners,' he said. 'We will leave old Tim outside the door to guard them. It's impossible to get out of that window, and anyway, we're snowed up if they could escape that way.'

Everyone went to bed again, but the children found it difficult to sleep after such an exciting time. Anne and George whispered together and so did Julian and Dick. There was such a lot to talk about.

Next day there was a surprise for everyone. The police did arrive after all! The snow did not stop them, for somewhere or other they had got skis and had come skimming along valiantly to see the prisoners! It was a great excitement for everyone.

'We won't take the men away, sir, till the snow has gone,' said the Inspector. 'We'll just put the handcuffs on them, so that they don't try any funny tricks. You keep the door locked too, and that dog outside. They'll be safe there for a day or two. We've taken them enough food till we come back again. If they go a bit short, it will serve them right!'

The snow melted two days later, and the police took

away Mr Roland and the others. The children watched.

'No more lessons *these* hols!' said Anne gleefully.

'No more shutting Timothy out of the house,' said George.

'You were right and we were wrong, George,' said Julian. 'You were fierce, weren't you? – but it's a jolly good thing you were!'

'She is fierce, isn't she?' said Dick, giving the girl a sudden hug. 'But I rather like her when she's fierce, don't you, Julian? Oh, George, we do have marvellous adventures with you! I wonder if we'll have any more?'

They will – there isn't a doubt of that!

THE FAMOUS FIVE

FIVE RUN AWAY TOGETHER

Have you read all THE FAMOUS FIVE books?

1. Five on a Treasure Island
2. Five Go Adventuring Again
3. Five Run Away Together
4. Five Go to Smuggler's Top
5. Five Go Off in a Caravan
6. Five on Kirrin Island Again
7. Five Go Off to Camp
8. Five Get Into Trouble
9. Five Fall Into Adventure
10. Five on a Hike Together
11. Five Have a Wonderful Time
12. Five Go Down to the Sea
13. Five Go to Mystery Moor
14. Five Have Plenty of Fun
15. Five on a Secret Trail
16. Five Go to Billycock Hill
17. Five Get Into a Fix
18. Five on Finniston Farm
19. Five Go to Demon's Rocks
20. Five Have a Mystery to Solve
21. Five Are Together Again

The Famous Five Colour Short Stories

1. Five and a Half-Term Adventure
2. George's Hair is Too Long
3. Good Old Timmy
4. A Lazy Afternoon
5. Well Done, Famous Five
6. Five Have a Puzzling Time
7. Happy Christmas, Five
8. When Timmy Chased the Cat

Enid Blyton®

THE FAMOUS FIVE

FIVE RUN AWAY TOGETHER

Illustrated by Eileen A. Soper

HODDER

HODDER CHILDREN'S BOOKS

First published in Great Britain in 1944 by Hodder & Stoughton
This edition published in 2016

21

A CIP catalogue record for this book is available from the British Library.

ISBN 978 1 444 93633 9

Printed in Great Britain by Clays Ltd, Elcograf S.p.A.

The paper and board used in this book are made from wood from responsible sources.

Hodder Children's Books
An imprint of
Hachette Children's Group
Part of Hodder & Stoughton
Carmelite House
50 Victoria Embankment
London EC4Y 0DZ

An Hachette UK Company
www.hachette.co.uk
www.hachettechildrens.co.uk

CONTENTS

1 SUMMER HOLIDAYS 1
2 THE STICK FAMILY 10
3 A NASTY SHOCK 19
4 A FEW LITTLE UPSETS 28
5 IN THE MIDDLE OF THE NIGHT 37
6 JULIAN DEFEATS THE STICKS 46
7 BETTER NEWS 56
8 GEORGE'S PLAN 64
9 AN EXCITING NIGHT 74
10 KIRRIN ISLAND ONCE MORE! 85
11 ON THE OLD WRECK 93
12 THE CAVE IN THE CLIFF 101
13 A DAY ON THE ISLAND 109
14 DISTURBANCE IN THE NIGHT 118
15 WHO IS ON THE ISLAND? 128
16 THE STICKS GET A FRIGHT 136
17 A SHOCK FOR EDGAR 145
18 AN UNEXPECTED PRISONER 155
19 A SCREAM IN THE NIGHT 165
20 A RESCUE – AND A NEW PRISONER! 173
21 A VISIT TO THE POLICE STATION 183
22 BACK TO KIRRIN ISLAND! 193

CHAPTER ONE

Summer holidays

'GEORGE DEAR, do settle down and do something,' said George's mother. 'You keep wandering in and out with Timothy, and I am trying to have a rest.'

'Sorry, Mother,' said Georgina, taking hold of Timothy's collar. 'But I feel lonely without the others. Oh I do wish tomorrow would come. I've been without them for three whole weeks already.'

Georgina went to boarding school with her cousin Anne, and in the holidays she and Anne, and Anne's two brothers, Julian and Dick, usually joined up together and had plenty of fun. Now it was the summer holidays, and already three weeks had gone by. Anne, Dick and Julian had gone away with their father and mother, but Georgina's parents had wanted their little girl with them, so she had not gone.

Now her three cousins were coming the next day to spend the rest of the summer holidays with her at her old home, Kirrin Cottage.

'It will be lovely when they are here,' said George, as she was always called, to Timothy her dog. 'Simply lovely, Timothy. Don't you think so?'

'Woof,' said Timothy and licked George's hand.

George was dressed, as usual, exactly like a boy, in jeans and jersey. She had always wanted to be a boy, and would never answer if she was called Georgina. So everyone called her George. She had missed her cousins very much during the first weeks of the summer holidays.

'I used to think I liked best to be alone,' George said to Timothy, who always seemed to understand every word she said. 'But now I know that was silly. It's nice to be with others and share things, and make friends.'

Timothy thumped his tail on the ground. He certainly liked being with the other children too. He was longing to see Julian, Anne and Dick again.

George took Timothy down to the beach. She shaded her eyes with her hand, and looked out to the entrance of the bay. In the middle of it, almost as if it were guarding it, lay a small, rocky island, on which rose the ruins of an old castle.

'We'll visit you again this summer, Kirrin Island,' said George softly. 'I haven't been able to go to you yet this summer, because my boat was being mended – but it will be ready soon, then I'll come to you. And I'll look all round the old castle again. Oh, Tim – do you remember the adventures we had on Kirrin Island last summer?'

Tim remembered quite well, because he himself had shared in the thrilling adventures. He had been down in the dungeons of the castle with the others; he had helped to find treasure there, and had had just as grand a time as the four children he loved. He gave a little bark.

'You're remembering, aren't you, Tim?' said George, patting him. 'Won't it be fun to go there again? We'll go down into the dungeons again, shall we? And oh! – do you remember how Dick climbed down the deep well-shaft to rescue us?'

It was exciting, remembering all the things that had happened last year. It made George long all the more for the next day, when her three friends would arrive.

'I wish Mother would let us go and live on the island for a week,' thought George. 'That would be the greatest fun we could have. To live on my very own island!'

It *was* George's island. It really belonged to her mother,

but she had said, two or three years back, that George could have it, and George now thought of it as really her own. She felt that all the rabbits on it belonged to her, all the wild birds and other creatures.

'I'll suggest that we go there for a week, when the others come,' she thought, excitedly. 'We'll take our food and everything, and live there quite by ourselves. We shall feel like Robinson Crusoe.'

She went to meet her cousins the next day, driving the pony and trap by herself. Her mother wanted to come, but she said she did not feel very well. George felt a bit worried about her. So often lately her mother had said she didn't feel very well. Perhaps it was the heat of the summer. The weather had been so very hot lately. Day after day had brought nothing but blue sky and sunshine. George had been burnt, and her eyes were startlingly blue in her sunburnt face. She had had her hair cut even shorter than usual, and it really was difficult to know whether she was a boy or a girl.

The train came in. Three hands waved madly from a window, and George shouted in delight.

'Julian! Dick! Anne! You're here at last.'

The three children tumbled pell-mell out of their carriage. Julian yelled to a porter.

'Our bags are in the guard's van. Hallo, George! How are you? Golly, you've grown.'

They all had. They were all a year older and a year bigger than when they had had their exciting adventures on Kirrin

Island. Even Anne, the youngest, didn't look such a small girl now. She flung herself on George, almost knocking her over, and then went down on her knees beside Timothy, who was quite mad with joy to see his three friends.

There was a terrific noise. They all shouted their news at once, and Timothy barked without stopping.

'We thought the train would never get here!'

'Oh, Timothy, you darling, you're just the same as ever!'

'Woof, woof, woof!'

'Mother's sorry she couldn't come and meet you too.'

'George, how tanned you are! I say, aren't we going to have fun.'

'WOOF, WOOF!'

'Shut up, Tim darling, and do get down; you've bitten my tie almost in half. Oh, you dear old dog, it's grand to see you!'

'WOOF!'

The porter wheeled up their luggage, and soon it was in the pony-cart. George clicked to the waiting pony, and it cantered off. The five in the little cart all talked at once at the top of their voices, Tim far more loudly than anyone else, for his doggy voice was strong and powerful.

'I hope your mother isn't ill?' said Julian, who was fond of his Aunt Fanny. She was gentle and kind, and loved having them all.

'I think it must be the heat,' said George.

'What about Uncle Quentin?' asked Anne. 'Is he all right?'

The three children did not very much like George's father because he could get into very fierce tempers, and although he welcomed the three cousins to his house, he did not really care for children. So they always felt a little awkward with him, and were glad when he was not there.

'Father's all right,' said George, cheerfully. 'Only he's worried about Mother. He doesn't seem to notice her much when she's well and cheerful, but he gets awfully upset if anything goes wrong with her. So be a bit careful of him at the moment. You know what he's like when he's worried.'

The children did know. Uncle Quentin was best avoided when things went wrong. But not even the thought of a cross uncle could damp them today. They were on holiday; they were going to Kirrin Cottage; they were by the sea, and there was dear old Timothy beside them, and fun of all kinds in store for them.

'Shall we go to Kirrin Island, George?' asked Anne. 'Do let's! We haven't been there since last summer. The weather was too bad in the winter and Easter holidays. Now it's gorgeous.'

'Of course we'll go,' said George, her blue eyes shining. 'Do you know what I thought? I thought it would be marvellous to go and stay there for a whole week by ourselves! We are older now, and I'm sure Mother would let us.'

'Go and stay on your island for a week!' cried Anne. 'Oh! That would be too good to be true.'

'Our island,' said George, happily. 'Don't you remember I said I would divide it into four, and we'd all share it? Well, I meant it, you know. It's ours, not mine.'

'What about Timothy?' said Anne. 'Oughtn't he to have a share as well? Can't we make it five bits, one for him too?'

'He can share mine,' said George. She drew the pony to a stop, and the four children and the dog gazed out across the blue bay. 'There's Kirrin Island,' said George. 'Dear little island. I can hardly wait to get to it now. I haven't been able to go there yet, because my boat wasn't mended.'

'Then we can all go together,' said Dick. 'I wonder if the rabbits are just as tame as ever.'

'Woof!' said Timothy at once. He had only to hear the word 'rabbits' to get excited.

'It's no good your thinking about the rabbits on Kirrin,' said George. 'You know I don't allow you to chase them, Tim.'

Timothy's tail dropped and he looked mournfully at George. It was the only thing on which he and George did not agree. Tim was firmly convinced that rabbits were meant for him to chase, and George was just as firmly convinced that they were not.

'Get on!' said George to the pony, and jerked the reins. The little creature trotted on towards Kirrin Cottage, and very soon they were all opposite the front gate.

A sour-faced woman came out from the back door to

help them down with their luggage. The children did not know her.

'Who's she?' they whispered to George.

'The new cook,' said George. 'Joanna had to go and look after her mother, who broke her leg. Then Mother got this cook – Mrs Stick her name is.'

'Good name for her,' grinned Julian. 'She looks a real old stick! But all the same I hope she doesn't stick here for long. I hope Joanna comes back. I liked old Joanna, and she was nice to Timmy.'

'Mrs Stick has a dog too,' said George. 'A dreadful animal, smaller than Tim, all sort of mangy and motheaten. Tim can't bear it.'

'Where is it?' asked Anne, looking round.

'It's kept in the kitchen, and Tim isn't allowed near it,' said George. 'Good thing too, because I'm sure he'd eat it! He can't think what's in the kitchen, and goes sniffing round the shut door till Mrs Stick nearly goes mad.'

The others laughed. They had all climbed down from the pony-cart now, and were ready to go indoors. Julian had helped Mrs Stick in with all the bags. George took the pony-cart away, and the other three went in to say hello to their uncle and aunt.

'Well, dears,' said Aunt Fanny, smiling at them from the sofa where she was lying down. 'How are you all? I'm sorry I could not come to meet you. Uncle Quentin is out for a walk. You had better go upstairs, and wash and change. Then come down for tea.'

The boys went up to their old bedroom, with its funny slanting roof, and its window looking out over the bay. Anne went to the little room she shared with George. How good it was to be back again at Kirrin! What fun they would have these holidays with George and dear old Timmy!

CHAPTER TWO

The Stick family

IT WAS lovely to wake up the next morning at Kirrin Cottage and see the sun shining in at the windows, and to hear the far-off plash-plash-plash of the sea. It was gorgeous to leap out of bed and rush to see how blue the sea was, and how lovely Kirrin Island looked at the entrance of the bay.

'I'm going for a bathe before breakfast,' said Julian, and snatched up his bathing trunks. 'Coming, Dick?'

'You bet!' said Dick. 'Call the girls. We'll all go.'

So down they went, the four of them, with Tim galloping behind them, his tail wagging nineteen to the dozen, and his long pink tongue hanging out of his mouth. He went into the water with the others, and swam all round them. They were all good swimmers, but Julian and George were the best.

They put towels round themselves, rubbed their bodies dry and pulled on jeans and jerseys. Then back to breakfast they went, as hungry as hunters. Anne noticed a boy in the back garden and stared in surprise.

'Who's that?' she said.

'Oh, that's Edgar, Mrs Stick's boy,' said George. 'I don't like him. He does silly things, like putting out his tongue and calling rude names.'

Edgar appeared to be singing when the others went in at the gate. Anne stopped to listen.

'Georgie-porgie, pudding and pie!' sang Edgar, a silly look on his face. He seemed about thirteen or fourteen, a stupid, yet sly-looking youth. 'Georgie-porgie pudding and pie!'

George went red. 'He's always singing that,' she said, furiously. 'Just because I'm called "George," I suppose. He thinks he's clever. I can't bear him.'

Julian called out to Edgar. 'You shut up! You're not funny, only jolly silly!'

'Georgie-porgie,' began Edgar again, a silly smile on his wide red face. Julian made a step towards him, and he at once disappeared into the house.

'Shan't stand much of *him*,' said Julian, in a decided voice. 'I wonder *you* do, George. I wonder you haven't shoved him, stamped on his foot and done a few other things! You used to be so fierce.'

'Well – I am still, really,' said George. 'I *feel* frightfully fierce down inside me when I hear Edgar singing silly songs at me like that and calling out names – but you see, Mother really hasn't been well, and I know jolly well if I go for Edgar, Mrs Stick will leave, and poor old Mother would have to do all the work, and she really isn't fit to at present. So I just hold myself in, and hope that Timmy will do the same.'

'Good for *you* old thing!' said Julian, admiringly, for he

knew how hard it was for George to keep her temper at times.

'I think I'll just go up to Mother's room and see if she'd like breakfast in bed,' said George. 'Hang on to old Timmy a moment, will you? If Edgar appears again, he might go for him.'

Julian hung on to Timmy's collar. Timmy had growled when Edgar had been in the garden, now he stood stock still, his nose twitching as if he were trying to trace some smell.

Suddenly a mangy-looking dog appeared out of the kitchen door. It had a dirty white coat, out of which patches seemed to have been bitten, and its tail was well between its legs.

'Wooooof!' said Timmy, joyfully, and leapt at the dog. He pulled Julian over, for he was a big dog, and the boy let go his hold of the dog's collar. Timmy pounced excitedly on the other dog, who gave a fearful whine and tried to go into the kitchen door again.

'Timmy! Come here!' yelled Julian. But Timmy didn't hear. He was busy trying to snap off the other dog's ears – or at least, that is what he appeared to be doing. The other dog yelled for help, and Mrs Stick appeared at the kitchen door, a saucepan in her hand.

'Call off that dog!' she screeched. She hit out at Timmy with the saucepan, but he dodged and it hit her own dog instead, making it yelp all the more.

'Don't hit out with that!' said Julian. 'You'll hurt the dogs. Hi, Timmy, TIMMY!'

Edgar now appeared, looking very scared. He picked up a stone and seemed to be watching his chance to hurl it at Timmy. Anne shrieked.

'You're not to throw that stone; you're not to! You bad wicked boy!'

In the middle of all this turmoil Uncle Quentin appeared, looking angry and irritable.

'Good heavens! What is all this going on? I never heard such a row in my life.'

Then George appeared, flying out of the door like the wind, to rescue her beloved Timothy. She rushed to the two dogs and tried to pull Timmy away. Her father yelled at her.

'Come away, you little idiot! Don't you know better than to separate two fighting dogs with your bare hands? Where's the garden hose?'

It was fixed to a tap nearby. Julian ran to it and turned on the tap. He picked up the hose and turned it on the two dogs. At once the jet of water spurted out at them, and they leapt apart in surprise. Julian saw Edgar standing near, and couldn't resist swinging the hose a little so that the boy was soaked. He gave a scream and ran in at once.

'What did you do that for?' said Uncle Quentin, annoyed. 'George, tie Timothy up at once. Mrs Stick, didn't I tell you not to let your dog out of the kitchen unless you had him on a lead? I won't have this kind of thing happening. Where's the breakfast? Late as usual!'

Mrs Stick disappeared into the kitchen, muttering and grumbling, taking her drenched dog with her. George, looking sulky, tied Timothy up. He lay down in his kennel, looking beseechingly at his mistress.

'I've told you not to take any notice of that mangy-looking dog,' said George, severely. 'Now you see what happens! You put Father into a bad temper for the rest of the day, and Mrs Stick will be so angry she won't make any cakes for tea!'

Timmy gave a whine, and put his head down on his paws. He licked a few hairs from the corner of his mouth. It was sad to be tied up – but anyhow he had bitten a bit off the tip of one of that dreadful dog's ears!

They all went in to breakfast. 'Sorry I let Timmy go,' said Julian to George. 'But he nearly tore my arm off. I couldn't possibly hold him! He's grown into an awfully powerful dog, hasn't he?'

'Yes,' said George, proudly. 'He has. He could eat Mrs Stick's dog up in a mouthful if we'd let him. And Edgar too.'

'And Mrs Stick,' said Anne. 'All of them. I don't like any of them.'

Breakfast was rather a subdued meal, as Aunt Fanny was not there, but Uncle Quentin was – and Uncle Quentin in a bad temper was not a very cheerful person to have at the breakfast-table. He snapped at George and glared at the others. Anne almost wished they hadn't come to Kirrin Cottage! But her spirits rose when she thought of the rest of the day – they would take their dinner out, perhaps, and have it on the beach – or maybe even go out to Kirrin Island. Uncle Quentin wouldn't be with them to spoil things.

Mrs Stick appeared to take away the porridge plates and bring in the bacon. She banged the plates down on the table.

'No need to do that,' said Uncle Quentin, irritably. Mrs Stick said nothing. She was scared of Uncle Quentin, and no wonder! She put the next lot of plates down quietly.

'What are you going to do today?' asked Uncle Quentin, towards the end of breakfast. He was feeling a little better by that time, and didn't like to see such subdued faces round him.

'We thought we might go out for a picnic,' said George, eagerly. 'I asked Mother. She said we might, if Mrs Stick will make us sandwiches.'

'Well, I shouldn't think she'll try very hard,' said Uncle Quentin, trying to make a little joke. They all smiled politely. 'But you can ask her.'

There was a silence. Nobody liked the idea of asking Mrs Stick for sandwiches.

'I do wish she hadn't brought Stinker,' said George, gloomily. 'Everything would be easier if he wasn't here.'

'Is that the name of her son?' asked Uncle Quentin, startled.

George grinned. 'Oh no. Though it wouldn't be a bad

name for him, because he hardly ever has a bath, and he's jolly smelly. It's her dog I mean. She calls him Tinker, but I call him Stinker, because he really does smell awful.'

'I don't think it's a very nice name,' said her father, in the midst of the others' giggles.

'No, it isn't,' said George, 'but then, he isn't a very nice dog.'

In the end it was Aunt Fanny who saw Mrs Stick and arranged about the sandwiches. Mrs Stick went up to see Aunt Fanny, who was having breakfast in bed, and agreed to make sandwiches, though with a very bad grace.

'I didn't bargain for three more children to come traipsing along,' she said, sulkily.

'I told you they were coming, Mrs Stick,' said Aunt Fanny, patiently. 'I didn't know I should be feeling so ill myself when they came. If I had been well I could have made their sandwiches and done many more things. I can only ask you to help as much as you can till I feel better. I may be all right tomorrow. Let the children have a good time for a week or so, and then, if I still feel ill, I am sure they will all turn to and help a bit. But let them have a good time first.'

The children took their packets of sandwiches and set off. On the way they met Edgar, looking as stupid and sly as usual. 'Why don't you let me come along with you?' he said. 'Let's go to that island. I know a lot about it, I do.'

'No, you don't,' said George, in a flash. 'You don't know anything about it. And I'd never take *you*. It's *my* island, see? Well, *ours*. It belongs to all four of us and Timmy, too. We should never allow you to go.'

''Tisn't your island,' said Edgar. 'That's a lie, that is!'

'You don't know what you're talking about,' said George, scornfully. 'Come on, you others! We can't waste time talking to Edgar.'

They left him, looking sulky and angry. As soon as they were at a safe distance he lifted up his voice:

'Georgie-Porgie, pudding and pie,
She knows how to tell a lie,
Georgie-Porgie, pudding and pie!'

Julian started to go back after the rude Edgar, but George pulled him on. 'He'll only go and tell tales to his mother, and she'll walk out and there'll be no one to help Mother,' she said. 'I'll just have to put up with it. We'll try and think of some way to get our own back, though. Nasty creature! I hate his pimply nose and screwed-up eyes.'

'Woof!' said Timmy, feelingly.

'Timmy says he hates Stinker's miserable tail and silly little ears,' explained George, and they all laughed. That made them feel better. They were soon out of hearing of Edgar's silly song, and forgot all about him.

'Let's go and see if your boat is ready,' said Julian. 'Then maybe we could row out to the dear old island.'

CHAPTER THREE

A nasty shock

GEORGE'S BOAT was almost ready, but not quite. It was having a last coat of paint on it. It looked very nice, for George had chosen a bright red paint, and the oars were painted red too.

'Oh, can't we possibly have it this afternoon?' said George to Jim the boatman.

He shook his head.

'No, George,' he said, 'not unless you all want to be messed up with red paint. It'll be dry tomorrow, but not before.'

It always made the others smile to hear the boatmen and fishermen call Georgina 'George'. The local people all knew how badly she wanted to be a boy, and they knew, too, how plucky and straightforward she was, so they laughed to one another and said: 'Well, they reckoned she behaved like a boy, and if she wanted to be called "George" instead of "Georgina", she deserved it!'

So Georgina was George, and enjoyed strutting about in her jeans and jersey on the beach, using her boat as well as any fisher-boy, and swimming faster than them all.

'We'll go to the island tomorrow then,' said Julian. 'We'll just picnic on the beach today. Then we'll go for a walk.'

So they picnicked on the sands with Timothy sharing more than half their lunch. The sandwiches were not very nice. The bread was too stale; there was not enough butter inside, and they were far too thick. But Timothy didn't mind. He gobbled up as many as he could, his tail wagging so hard that it sent sand over everyone.

'Timothy, do take your tail out of the sand if you want to wag it,' said Julian, getting sand all over his hair for the fourth time. Timmy wagged his tail hard again, and sent another shower over him. Everyone laughed.

'Let's go for a walk now,' said Dick, jumping up. 'My legs could do with some good exercise. Where shall we go?'

'We'll walk along the cliff-top, where we can see the

island all the time, shall we?' said Anne. 'George, is the old wreck still there?'

George nodded. The children had once had a most exciting time with an old wreck that had lain at the bottom of the sea. A great storm had lifted it up and set it firmly on the rocks. They had been able to explore the wreck then, and had found a map of the castle in it, with instructions as to where hidden treasure was to be found.

'Do you remember how we found that old map in the wreck, and how we looked for the ingots of gold and found them?' said Julian, his eyes gleaming as he remembered it all. 'Isn't the wreck battered to pieces yet, George?'

'No,' said George. 'I don't think so. It's on the rocks on the other side of the island, you remember, so we can't see it from here. But we might have a look at it when we go on the island tomorrow.'

'Yes, let's,' said Anne. 'Poor old wreck! I guess it won't last many winters now.'

They walked along the cliff-top with Timothy capering ahead of them. They could see the island easily and the ruined castle rising up from the middle.

'There's the jackdaw tower,' said Anne, looking. 'The other tower's fallen down, hasn't it? Look at the jackdaws circling round and round the tower, George!'

'Yes. They build in it every year,' said George. 'Don't you remember the masses of sticks round about the tower that the jackdaws dropped when they built their nests? We picked some up and made a fire with them once.'

'I'd like to do that again,' said Anne. 'I would really. Let's do it each night if we stay a week on the island. George, did you ask your mother?'

'Oh yes,' said George. 'She said she thought we might, but she would see.'

'I don't like it when grown-ups say they'll see,' said Anne. 'It so often means they won't let you do something after all, but they don't like to tell you at the time.'

'Well, I expect she will let us,' said George. 'After all, we're much older than last year. Why, Julian is in his teens already, and I soon shall be and so will Dick. Only Anne is small.'

'I'm not,' said Anne, indignantly. 'I'm as strong as you are. I can't help being younger.'

'Hush, hush, baby!' said Julian, patting his little sister on the back and laughing at her furious face. 'Hallo – look! What's that over there on the island?'

He had caught sight of something as he was teasing Anne. Everyone swung round and gazed at Kirrin. George gave an exclamation.

'Golly – a spire of smoke! Surely it's smoke! Someone's on my island.'

'On *our* island,' corrected Dick. 'It can't be! That smoke must come from a steamer out beyond the island. We can't see it, that's all. But I bet the smoke comes from a steamer. We know no one can get to the island but us. They don't know the way.'

'If anyone's on my island,' began George, looking very

fierce and angry, 'if anyone's on my island, I'll–I'll–I'll . . .'

'You'll explode and go up in smoke!' said Dick. 'There – it's gone now. I'm sure it was only a steamer letting off steam or smoking hard, whatever they do.'

They watched Kirrin Island for some time after that, but they could see no more smoke. 'If only my boat was ready!' said George, restlessly. 'I'd go over this afternoon. I've a good mind to go and get my boat, even if the paint *is* wet.'

'Don't be an idiot!' said Julian. 'You know what an awful row we'd get into if we go home with all our things bright red. Have a bit of sense, George.'

George gave up the idea. She watched for a steamer to appear at one side of the island or another, to come into the bay, but none came.

'Probably anchored out there,' said Dick. 'Come on! Are we going to stand rooted to this spot for the rest of the day?'

'We'd better get back home,' said Julian, looking at his wristwatch. 'It's almost tea-time. I hope your mother is up, George. It's much nicer when she's at meals.'

'Oh, I expect she will be,' said George. 'Come on then, let's go back!'

They turned to go back. They watched Kirrin Island as they walked, but all they could see were jackdaws or gulls in the sky above it. No more spires of smoke appeared. It must have been a steamer!

'All the same, I'm going over tomorrow to have a look,' said George, firmly. 'If any day-trippers are visiting my island I'll turn them off.'

'*Our* island,' said Dick. 'George, I wish you'd remember you said you'd share it with us.'

'Well – I did share it out with you,' said George, 'but I can't help feeling it's still my island. Come on! I'm getting hungry.'

They came back at last to Kirrin Cottage. They went into the hall, and then into the sitting-room. To their great surprise Edgar was there, reading one of Julian's books.

'What are you doing here?' said Julian. 'And who told you you could borrow my book?'

'I'm not doing any harm,' said Edgar. 'If I want to have a quiet read, why shouldn't I?'

'You wait till my father comes in and finds you lolling about here,' said George. 'My goodness, if you'd gone into his study, you'd have been sorry.'

'I've been in there,' said Edgar, surprisingly. 'I've seen those funny instruments he's working with.'

'How *dare* you!' said George, going white with rage. 'Why, even *we* are not allowed to go into my father's study. As for touching his things – well!'

Julian eyed Edgar curiously. He could not imagine why the boy should suddenly be so insolent.

'Where's your father, George?' he said. 'I think we had better get him to deal with Edgar. He must be mad.'

'Call him if you like,' said Edgar, still lolling in the chair, and flicking over the pages of Julian's book in a most irritating way. 'He won't come.'

'What do you mean?' said George, feeling suddenly scared. 'Where's my mother?'

'Call her too, if you like,' said the boy, looking sly. 'Go on! Call her.'

The children suddenly felt afraid. What did Edgar mean? George flew upstairs to her mother's room, shouting loudly.

'Mother! Mother! Where are you?'

But her mother's bed was empty. It had not been made – but it was empty. George flew into all the other bedrooms, shouting desperately: 'Mother! Mother! Father! Where are you?'

But there was no answer. George ran downstairs, her face very white. Edgar grinned up at her.

'What did I tell you?' he said. 'I said you could call all you liked, but they wouldn't come.'

'Where are they?' demanded George. 'Tell me at once!'

'Find out yourself,' said Edgar.

There was a resounding slap, and Edgar leapt to his feet, holding his left cheek with his hand. George had flown at him and dealt him the hardest smack she could. Edgar lifted his hand to slap her back, but Julian stood in front.

'You're not fighting George,' he said. 'She's a girl. If you want a fight, I'll take you on.'

'I won't be a girl; I'm a boy!' shouted George, trying to push Julian away. 'I'll fight Edgar, and I'll beat him, you see if I don't.'

But Julian kept her off. Edgar began to edge towards the doorway, but he found Dick there.

'One minute,' said Dick. 'Before you go – where are our uncle and aunt?'

'Gr-r-r-r-r-r,' suddenly said Timothy, in such a threatening voice that Edgar stared at him in fright. The dog had bared his great teeth, and had put up the hackles on his neck. He looked very frightening.

'Hold that dog!' said Edgar, his voice trembling. 'He looks as if he's going to spring at me.'

Julian put his hand on Tim's collar. 'Quiet, Tim!' he said. 'Now, Edgar, tell us what we want to know, and tell us quickly, or you'll be sorry.'

'Well, there isn't much to tell,' said Edgar, keeping his eye on Timothy. He shot a look at George and went on. 'Your mother was suddenly taken very ill – with a terrible pain *here* – and they got the doctor and they've taken her away to hospital, and your father went with her. That's all!'

George sat down on the sofa, looking paler still and rather sick.

'Oh!' she said. 'Poor Mother! I wish I hadn't gone out today. Oh dear – how can we find out what's happened?'

Edgar had slipped out of the room, shutting the door behind him so that Timmy should not follow. The kitchen door was slammed, too. The children stared at one another, feeling sorry and dismayed. Poor George! Poor Aunt Fanny!

'There must be a note somewhere,' said Julian, and looked round the room. He saw a letter stuck into the rim of the big mirror there, addressed to George. He gave it to her. It was from George's father.

'Read it, quickly,' said Anne. 'Oh dear – this is really a horrid beginning to our holidays here!'

CHAPTER FOUR

A few little upsets

GEORGE READ the letter out loud. It was not very long, and had evidently been written in a great hurry.

> DEAR GEORGE,
>
> Your mother has been taken very ill. I am going with her to the hospital. I shall not leave her till she is getting better. That may be in a few days' time, or in a week's time. I will telephone to you each day at nine o'clock in the morning to tell you how she is. Mrs Stick will look after you all. Try to manage all right till I come back.
>
> Your loving
>
> FATHER

'Oh dear!' said Anne, knowing how dreadful George must feel. George loved her mother dearly, and for once the girl had tears in her eyes. George never cried – but it was terrible to come home and find her mother gone like this. And Father too! No one there but Mrs Stick and Edgar.

'I can't bear Mother going like this,' sobbed George, suddenly, and buried her head in a cushion. 'She – she might never come back.'

'Don't be silly, George,' said Julian, sitting down and putting his arm round her. 'Of course she will. Why shouldn't she? Didn't your father say he was staying with her till she was getting better – and that would be probably in a few days' time. Cheer up, George! It isn't like you to give way like this.'

'But I didn't say goodbye,' sobbed poor George. 'And I made her ask Mrs Stick for the sandwiches, instead of me. I want to go and find Mother and see how she is myself.'

'You don't know where they've taken her, and if you did, they wouldn't let you in,' said Dick, gently. 'Let's have some tea. We shall all feel better after that.'

'I couldn't eat *any*thing,' said George, fiercely. Timothy pushed his nose into her hands, and tried to lick them. They were under her buried face. The dog whined a little.

'Poor Timmy! He can't understand,' said Anne. 'He's awfully upset because you are unhappy, George.'

That made George sit up. She rubbed her hands over her eyes, and let Timmy lick the wet tears off them. He looked surprised at the salty taste. He tried to get on to George's knee.

'Silly Timmy!' said George, in a more ordinary voice. 'Don't be upset. I just got a shock, that's all! I'm better now, Timmy. Don't whine like that, silly! I'm all right. I'm not hurt.'

But Timothy felt certain George was really hurt or injured in some way to cry like that, and he kept whining, and pawing at George, and trying to get on to her knee.

Julian opened the door. 'I'm going to tell Mrs Stick we want our tea,' he said, and went out. The others thought he was rather brave to face Mrs Stick.

Julian went to the kitchen door and opened it. Edgar was sitting there, one side of his face scarlet, where George had slapped it. Mrs Stick was there, looking grim.

'If that girl slaps my Edgar again, I'll be after her,' she said, threateningly.

'Edgar deserved what he got,' said Julian. 'Can we have some tea, please?'

'I've a good mind to get you none,' said Mrs Stick. Her dog started up from its corner and growled at Julian. 'That's right, Tinker! You growl at folks that slap Edgar.'

Julian was not in the least afraid of Tinker. 'If you are not going to get us any tea, I'll get it myself,' said the boy. 'Where is the bread, and where are the cakes?'

Mrs Stick stared at Julian, and the boy looked back at her steadfastly. He thought she was a most unpleasant woman, and he certainly was not going to allow her to get the better of him. He wished he could tell her to go – but he had a feeling that she wouldn't, so it would be a waste of his breath.

Mrs Stick dropped her eyes first. 'I'll get your tea,' she said, 'but if I have any nonsense from you I'll get you no other meals.'

'And if I have any nonsense from you I shall go to the police,' said Julian, unexpectedly. He hadn't meant to say that. It came out quite suddenly, but it had a surprising effect on Mrs Stick. She looked startled and alarmed.

'Now, there's no call to be nasty,' she said in a much more polite voice. 'We've all had a bit of a shock, and we're upset, like – I'll get you your tea right now.'

Julian went out. He wondered why his sudden threat of going to the police had made Mrs Stick so much more polite. Perhaps she was afraid the police would get on to his Uncle Quentin and he would come tearing back. Uncle Quentin wouldn't care for a hundred Mrs Sticks!

He went back to the others. 'Tea's coming,' he said. 'So cheer up, everyone!'

It wasn't a very cheerful company that sat down to the tea Mrs Stick brought in. George was now feeling ashamed of her tears. Anne was still upset. Dick tried to make a few silly jokes to cheer everyone up, but they fell so flat that he soon gave it up. Julian was grave and helpful, suddenly very grown-up.

Timothy sat close beside George, his head on her knee. 'I do wish I had a dog who loved me like that,' thought Anne. Timmy kept gazing up at George out of big brown devoted eyes. He had no eyes or ears for anyone but his little mistress now she was sad.

Nobody noticed what they had for tea, but all the same it did them good, and they felt better after it. They didn't like to go out to the beach afterwards in case the telephone bell rang, and there was news of George's mother. So they sat about in the garden, keeping an ear open for the telephone.

From the kitchen came a song.

> '*Georgie-Porgie, pudding and pie,*
> *Sat herself down and had a good cry,*
> *Georgie-Porgie . . .*'

Julian got up. He went to the kitchen window and looked in. Edgar was there alone.

'Come on out here, Edgar!' said Julian, in a grim voice. 'I'll teach you to sing another song. Come along!'

Edgar didn't stir. 'Can't I sing if I want to?' he said.

'Oh yes,' said Julian, 'but not that song. I'll teach you another. Come along out!'

'No fear,' said Edgar. 'You want to fight me.'

'Yes, I do,' said Julian. 'I think a little bit of good honest fighting would be better for you than sitting singing nasty little songs about a girl who is miserable. Are you coming out? Or shall I come in and fetch you?'

'Ma!' called Edgar, suddenly feeling panicky. 'Ma! Where are you?'

Julian suddenly reached a long arm in at the window, caught hold of Edgar's over-long nose, and pulled it so hard that Edgar yelled in pain.

'Led go! Led go! You're hurding me! Led go by dose!'

Mrs Stick came hurrying into the kitchen. She gave a scream when she saw what Julian was doing. She flew at him. Julian withdrew his arm, and stood outside the window.

'How dare you!' yelled Mrs Stick. 'First that girl slaps Edgar, and then you pull his nose! What's the matter with you all?'

'Nothing,' said Julian, pleasantly, 'but there's an awful lot wrong with Edgar, Mrs Stick. We feel we just *must* put it right. It should be your job, of course, but you don't seem to have done it.'

'You're downright insolent,' said Mrs Stick, outraged and furious.

'Yes, I dare say I am,' said Julian. 'It's just the effect Edgar has on me. Stinker has the same effect.'

'Stinker!' cried Mrs Stick, getting angrier still. 'That's not my dog's name, and well you know it.'

'Well, it really ought to be,' said Julian, strolling off. 'Give him a bath, and maybe we'll call him Tinker instead.'

Leaving Mrs Stick muttering in fury, he went back to the others. They stared at him curiously. He somehow seemed a different Julian – a grim and determined Julian, a very grown-up Julian, a rather frightening Julian.

'I'm afraid the fat's in the fire now,' said Julian, sitting down on the grass. 'I pulled old Edgar's nose nearly off his face, and Ma saw me doing it. I guess it's open warfare now! We shan't have a very merry time from now on. I doubt if we'll get any meals.'

'We'll get them ourselves then,' said George. 'I hate

Mrs Stick. I wish Joanna would come back. I hate that horrid Edgar too, and that awful Stinker.'

'Look – there *is* Stinker!' suddenly said Dick, putting out his hand to catch Timothy, who had risen with a growl. But Timmy shook off his hand and leapt across the grass at once. Stinker gave a woeful howl and tried to escape.

But Timothy had him by the neck and was shaking him like a rat.

Mrs Stick appeared with a stick and lashed out, not seeming to mind which dog she hit at. Julian rushed for the hose again. Edgar skipped indoors at once, remembering what had happened to him before.

The water gushed out, and Timothy gave a gasp and let go the howling mongrel he held in his teeth. Stinker at once hurled himself on Mrs Stick, and tried to hide in her skirts, trembling with terror.

'I'll poison that dog of yours!' said Mrs Stick, furiously, to George. 'Always setting on to mine. You look out or I'll poison him.'

She disappeared indoors, and the four children went and sat down again. George looked really alarmed. 'Do you suppose she really *might* try to poison Timmy?' she asked Julian, in a scared voice.

'She's a nasty bit of work,' said Julian, in a low tone. 'I think it would be just as well to keep old Timmy close by us, day and night, and only to feed him ourselves, from our own plates.'

George pulled Timothy to her, horrified at the thought that anyone might want to poison him. But Mrs Stick really was awful – she might do anything like that, George thought. How she wished her father and mother were back! It was horrid to be on their own, like this.

The telephone bell suddenly shrilled out and made everyone jump. They all leapt to their feet and Timmy growled. George flew indoors and lifted the receiver. She heard her father's voice, and her heart began to beat fast.

'Is that you, George?' said her father. 'Are you all right? I haven't time to stay and tell you everything.'

'Father – what about Mother? Tell me quick – how is she?' said George.

'We shan't know till the day after next,' said her father. 'I'll telephone tomorrow morning and then the next morning too. I shan't come back till I know she's better.'

'Oh, Father – it's awful without you and Mother,' said poor George. 'Mrs Stick is so horrid.'

'Now, George,' said her father, rather impatiently, 'surely you children can see to yourselves and make do with Mrs Stick till I get back! Don't worry me about such things now. I've enough worry as it is.'

'When will you be back, do you think?' said George. 'Can I come and see Mother?'

'No,' said her father. 'Not for at least two weeks, they say. I'll be back as soon as I can. But I'm not going to leave your mother now. She needs me. Goodbye and be good, all of you.'

George put back the receiver. She turned to face the others. 'Shan't know about Mother till the day after next,' she said. 'And we've got to put up with Mrs Stick till Father comes back – and goodness knows when that will be! It's awful, isn't it?'

CHAPTER FIVE

In the middle of the night

MRS STICK was in such a bad temper that evening that there was no supper at all. Julian went to ask about some, but he found the kitchen door locked.

He went back to the others with a gloomy face, for they were all hungry. 'She's locked the door,' he said. 'She really is a dreadful creature. I don't believe we'll get any supper tonight.'

'We'll have to wait till she goes to bed,' said George. 'We'll go down and hunt in the larder then, and see what we can find.'

They went to bed hungry. Julian listened for Mrs Stick and Edgar to go to bed, too. When he heard them going upstairs, and was sure their doors had shut, he slipped down into the kitchen. It was dark there, and Julian was just about to put on the light when he heard the sound of someone breathing heavily. He wondered who it could be. Was it Stinker? No – it couldn't be the dog. It sounded like a human being.

Julian stood there, his hand over the light switch, puzzled and a little scared. It couldn't be a burglar, because burglars don't go to sleep in the house they have come to rob. It couldn't be Mrs Stick or Edgar. Then who was it?

He snapped on the light. The kitchen was flooded with radiance, and Julian's eyes fastened on the figure of a small man lying on the sofa. He was fast asleep, his mouth wide open.

He was not a very pleasant sight. He had not shaved for some days, and his cheeks and chin were bluish-black. He didn't seem to have washed for even longer than that, for his hands were dirty, and so were his fingernails. He had untidy hair and a nose exactly like Edgar's.

'Must be dear Edgar's father,' thought Julian to himself. 'What a sight! Well, poor Edgar hadn't much chance to be decent with a father and mother like his.'

The man snored. Julian wondered what to do. He badly wanted to go to the larder, but on the other hand he didn't particularly want to wake up the man and have a row. He didn't see how he could turn him out – for all he knew his aunt and uncle might have agreed to Mrs Stick's husband coming there now and again, though he hardly thought so.

Julian was very hungry. The thought of the good things in the larder made him snap off the light again and creep towards the larder door in the dark. He opened the door. He felt along the shelves. Good! – that felt like a pie of some sort. He lifted it up and sniffed. It smelt of meat. A meat-pie – good!

He felt along the shelf again and came to a plate on which were what he thought must be jam-tarts, for they were round and flat, and had something sticky in the middle. Well, a meat-pie and jam-tarts ought to be all right for four hungry children!

Julian picked up the meat-pie and the dish of tarts, and made his way carefully out of the larder. He pushed the door to with his foot. Then he turned to go out of the room.

But in the dark he went the wrong way, and by bad luck walked straight into the sofa! The dish of tarts got a sudden jerk and one of them fell off. It landed on the open mouth of the sleeping man, and woke him up with a start.

'Blow!' said Julian to himself, and began to back away quietly, hoping that the man would turn over and go to sleep again. But the sticky jam-tart sliding down his chin had startled the man, and he sat up with a jerk.

'Who's there? That you, Edgar? What are you doing down here?'

Julian said nothing but sidled towards what he hoped was the door. The man leapt up and lurched over to where he thought the light switch was. He found it and switched it on. He stared in the greatest astonishment at Julian.

'What are you doing here?' he demanded.

'Just what I was about to ask *you*,' said Julian, coolly. 'What do you think *you're* doing here, sleeping in my uncle's kitchen?'

'I've a right to be here,' said the man, in a rude voice. 'My wife's cook here, isn't she? My ship's in and I'm on leave. Your uncle arranged with my wife I could come here then, see?'

Julian had feared as much. How awful to have a Mr Stick as well as a Mrs and Master Stick in the house! It would be quite unbearable.

'I can ask my uncle about it when he telephones in the morning,' said Julian. 'Now get out of my way, please, I want to go upstairs.'

'Ho!' said Mr Stick, eyeing the meat-pie and jam-tarts that Julian was carrying. 'Ho! Stealing out of the larder, I see! Nice goings-on I must say.'

Julian was not going to argue with Mr Stick, who evidently felt that he was top-dog. 'Get out of my way,' he said. 'I will talk to you in the morning after my uncle has telephoned.'

Mr Stick didn't seem as if he was going to get out of the way at all. He stood there, a nasty little man, not much taller than Julian, a sarcastic smile on his unshaven face.

Julian pursed his lips and whistled. There came a bump on the floor above. That was Timothy jumping off George's bed! Then there came the pattering of feet down the stairs and up the kitchen passage. Timmy was coming!

He smelt Mr Stick in the doorway, put up his hackles, bared his teeth and growled. Mr Stick hastily removed himself from the doorway and then neatly banged the door in the dog's face. He grinned at Julian.

'Now what are you going to do?' he said.

'Shall I tell you?' said Julian, his temper suddenly rising. 'I'm going to hurl this nice juicy meat-pie straight into your grinning face!'

He raised his arms, and Mr Stick ducked.

'Now don't you do that,' he said. 'I'm only pulling your leg, see? Don't you waste that nice meat-pie. You can go upstairs if you want to.'

He moved away to the sofa. Julian opened the door and Timothy bounded in growling. Mr Stick eyed him uncomfortably.

'Don't you let that nasty great dog come near me,' he said. 'I don't like dogs.'

'Then I wonder you don't get rid of Stinker,' said Julian. 'Come here, Timmy! Leave him alone. He's not worth growling at.'

Julian went upstairs with Timothy close at his heels.

The others crowded round him, wondering what had happened, for they had heard the voices downstairs. They laughed when Julian told them how he had nearly thrown the meat-pie at Mr Stick.

'It would have served him right,' said Anne, 'though it would have been a great pity, because we shouldn't have been able to eat it. Well, Mrs Stick may be simply horrible, but she *can* cook. This pie is gorgeous.'

The children finished all the pie and the tarts, too. Julian told them all about Mr Stick coming on leave from his ship.

'Three Sticks are a lot too much,' said Dick thoughtfully. 'Pity we can't get rid of them all and manage for ourselves. George, can't you possibly persuade your father tomorrow to let us get rid of the Sticks and look after ourselves?'

'I'll try,' said George. 'But you know what he is – awfully difficult to argue with. But I'll try. Golly, I'm sleepy now. Come on, Timmy, let's get to bed! Lie on my feet. I'm hardly going to let you out of my sight now, in case those awful Sticks poison you!'

Soon the four children, now no longer hungry, were sleeping peacefully. They did not fear the Sticks coming up to their rooms, for they knew that Timmy would wake and warn them at once. Timmy was the best guard they could have.

In the morning Mrs Stick actually produced some sort of breakfast, which surprised the children very much.

'Guess she knows your father will telephone, George,' said Julian, 'and she wants to keep herself in the right. When did he say he would 'phone? Nine o'clock, wasn't it? Well, it's half past eight now. Let's go for a quick run down to the beach and back.'

So off they went, the five of them, ignoring Edgar, who stood in the back garden ready to make some of his silly faces at them. The children couldn't help thinking he must be a bit mad. He didn't behave at all like a boy of Julian's age.

When they came back it was about ten minutes to nine. 'We'll sit in the sitting-room till the telephone rings,' said Julian. 'We don't want Mrs Stick to answer it first.'

But to their great dismay, as they reached the house, they heard Mrs Stick using the telephone in the hall!

'Yes,' they heard her say, 'everything is quite all right. I can manage the children, even if they do make things a bit difficult. Yes, of course. Well it's lucky my husband is home on leave from his ship, because he can help me round, like, and it makes things easier. Don't you worry about anything, and don't you bother to come back till you're ready. I'll manage everything.'

George flew into the hall like a wild thing, and snatched the receiver out of Mrs Stick's hand.

'Father! It's me, George! How's Mother? Tell me quick!'

'No worse, George,' said her father's voice. 'But we shan't know anything definite till tomorrow morning. I'm glad to hear from Mrs Stick that everything is all right. I'm very upset and worried, and I'm glad to feel I can tell your mother that you are all right, and everything is going smoothly at Kirrin Cottage.'

'But it isn't,' said George, wildly. 'It isn't. It's all horrid. Can't the Sticks go and let us manage things by ourselves?'

'Good gracious me, of course not,' said her father's voice, surprised and annoyed. 'What can you be thinking of? I did hope, George, that you would be sensible and helpful. I must say . . .'

'*You* talk to him, Julian,' said George, helplessly, and thrust the receiver into Julian's hand. The boy put it to his ear and spoke into the telephone in his clear voice.

'Good morning. This is Julian! I'm glad my aunt is no worse.'

'Well, she will be if she thinks things are going wrong at Kirrin Cottage,' said Uncle Quentin, in an exasperated voice. 'Can't you manage George and make her see reason? Good gracious, can't she put up with the Sticks for a week or two? I tell you frankly, Julian, I am not going to sack the Sticks in my absence – I want the house ready for me to bring back your aunt. If you can't put up with them, you had better find out from your own parents if they can take you back for the rest of the holidays. But George is not to go with you. She is to stay at Kirrin Cottage. That's my last word on the subject.'

'But . . .' began Julian, wondering how in the world he could deal properly with his hot-tempered uncle, 'I must tell you that . . .'

There was a click at the other end of the 'phone. Uncle Quentin had put down his receiver and gone. There was no more to be said. Blow! Julian pursed up his mouth and looked round at the others, frowning.

'He's gone!' he said. 'Cut me off just as I was trying to reason with him!'

'Serves you right!' said Mrs Stick's harsh voice from the end of the hall. 'Now you know where you stand. I'm here and I'm staying here, on your uncle's orders. And you're all going to behave yourselves, or it'll be the worse for you.'

CHAPTER SIX

Julian defeats the Sticks

THERE WAS a slam. The kitchen door shut, and Mrs Stick could be heard telling the news triumphantly to Edgar and Mr Stick. The children went into the sitting-room, sat down and stared at one another gloomily.

'Father's awful!' said George, furiously. 'He never will listen to anything.'

'Well, after all, he is very upset,' said Dick, reasonably. 'It was a great pity that he rang before nine, so that Mrs Stick got her say in first.'

'What did Father say to you?' said George. 'Tell us exactly.'

'He said that if we couldn't put up with the Sticks, Anne and Dick and I were to go back to our own parents,' said Julian. 'But you were to stay here.'

George stared at Julian. 'Well,' she said at last, 'you *can't* put up with the Sticks, so you'd better all go back. I can look after myself.'

'Don't be an idiot!' said Julian, giving her arm a friendly shake. 'You know we wouldn't desert you. I can't say I look forward to the idea of being under the thumb of the amiable Sticks for a week or two, but there are worse things than that. We'll "stick" it together.'

But the feeble little joke didn't raise a smile, even from Anne. The idea of being under the Sticks' three thumbs was a most unpleasant prospect. Timothy put his head on George's knee. She patted him and looked round.

'You go back home,' she said to the others. 'I've got a plan of my own, and you're not in it. I've got Timmy, and he'll look after me. Telephone to your parents and go home tomorrow.'

George stared round defiantly. Her head was up, and there was no doubt but that she had made a plan of some sort.

Julian felt uneasy.

'Don't be silly,' he said. 'I tell you we all stand together in this. If you've got a plan, we'll come into it. But we're staying here with you, whatever happens.'

'Stay if you like,' said George, 'but my plan goes on, and you'll find you'll have to go home in the end. Come on, Timothy! Let's go to Jim and see if my boat is ready.'

'We'll go with you,' said Dick. He was sorry for George. He could see below her defiance, and he knew she was very unhappy, worried about her mother, angry with her father, and upset because she felt the others were staying on because of her, when they could go back home and have a lovely time.

It was not a happy day. George was very stand-offish, and kept on insisting that the others should go back home and leave her. She grew quite angry when they were as insistent that they would not.

'You're spoiling my plan,' she said at last. 'You *should* go back, you rcally should. I tell you, you're spoiling my plan completely.'

'Well, what *is* your plan?' said Julian impatiently. 'I can't help feeling you're just *pretending* you've got a plan, so that we'll go.'

'I'm *not* pretending,' said George, losing her temper. 'Do I ever pretend? You know I don't! If I say I've got a plan, I *have* got a plan. But I'm not giving it away, so it's no good asking me. It's my own secret, private plan.'

'Well, I really do think you might tell us,' said Dick, quite hurt. 'After all, we're your best friends, aren't we? And we're going to stick by you, plan or no plan – yes, even if we spoil your plan, as you say, we shall still stay here with you.'

'I shan't *let* you spoil my plan,' said George, her eyes flashing. 'You're mean. You're against me, just like the Sticks are.'

'Oh, George, don't,' said Anne, almost in tears. 'Don't let's quarrel. It's bad enough quarrelling with those awful Sticks, without *us* quarrelling too.'

George's temper died down as quickly as it had risen. She looked ashamed.

'Sorry!' she said. 'I'm an idiot. I won't quarrel. But I do mean what I say. I shall go on with my plan, and I shan't tell you what it is, because if I do, it will spoil the holidays for you. Please believe me.'

'Let's take our dinner out with us again,' said Julian,

getting up. 'We'll all feel better away from this house today. I'll go and tackle the old Stick.'

'Dear old Ju, isn't he brave!' said Anne, who would rather have died than go and face Mrs Stick at that moment.

Mrs Stick proved very difficult. She felt rather victorious at the time, and was also very annoyed to find that her beautiful meat-pie and jam-tarts had disappeared. Mr Stick was in the middle of telling her where they had gone when Julian appeared.

'How you can expect sandwiches for a picnic when you've stolen my meat-pie and jam-tarts, I *don't* know!' she began, indignantly. 'You can have dry bread and jam for your picnic, and that's all. And what's more, I wouldn't give you that either except that I'm glad to be rid of you.'

'Good riddance to bad rubbish,' murmured Edgar to himself. He was lying sprawled on the sofa, reading some kind of highly coloured comic.

'If you've anything to say to me, Edgar, come outside and say it,' said Julian, dangerously.

'You leave Edgar alone,' said Mrs Stick, at once.

'There's nothing I should like better,' said Julian, scornfully. 'Who wants to be with him? Cowardly little spotty-face!'

'Now, now, look 'ere!' began Mr Stick, from his corner.

'I don't want to look at you,' said Julian at once.

'Now, look '*ere*,' said Mr Stick, angrily, standing up.

'I've told you I don't want to,' said Julian. 'You're not a pleasant sight.'

'*Insolence*!' said Mrs Stick, rapidly losing her temper.

'No, not insolence – just the plain truth,' said Julian, airily. Mrs Stick glared at him. Julian defeated her. He had such a ready tongue, and he said everything so politely. The ruder his words were, the more politely he spoke. Mrs Stick didn't understand people like Julian. She felt that they were too clever for her. She hated the boy, and banged a saucepan viciously down on the sink, wishing that it was Julian's head under the saucepan instead of the sink.

Stinker jumped up and growled at the sudden noise.

'Hallo, Stinker!' said Julian. 'Had a bath yet? Alas, no! – as smelly as ever, aren't you?'

'You know that dog's name isn't Stinker,' said Mrs Stick, angrily. 'You get out of my kitchen.'

'Right!' said Julian. 'Pleased to go. Don't bother about the dry bread and jam. I'll manage something a bit better than that.'

He went out, whistling. Stinker growled, and Edgar repeated loudly what he had said before: 'Good riddance to bad rubbish!'

'What did you say?' said Julian, suddenly poking his head in at the kitchen door again. But Edgar did not dare to repeat it, so off went Julian again, whistling merrily, but not feeling nearly as merry as his whistle. He was worried. After all, if Mrs Stick was going to make meals as difficult as this, life was not going to be very pleasant at Kirrin Cottage.

‘Anyone feel inclined to have dry bread and jam for lunch?’ inquired Julian, when he returned to the others. ‘No? I rather thought so, so I turned down Mrs Stick’s kind offer. I vote we go and buy something decent. That shop in the village has good sausage-rolls.’

George was very silent all that day. She was worrying about her mother, the others knew. She was probably thinking about her plan too, they thought, and wondered whatever it could be.

‘Shall we go over to Kirrin Island today?’ asked Julian, thinking that it would take George’s mind off her worries, if they went to her beloved island.

George shook her head.

‘No,’ she said. ‘I don’t feel like it. The boat’s all ready, I know – but I just don’t feel like it. You see, till I know Mother is going to get better, I don’t feel I want to be out of reach of the house. If a telephone message came from Father, the Sticks could always send Edgar to look for me – and if I was on the island, he couldn’t find me.’

The children messed about that day, doing nothing at all. They went back to tea, and Mrs Stick provided them with bread and butter and jam, but no cake. The milk was sour too, and everyone had to have tea without milk, which they all disliked.

As they ate their tea, the children heard Edgar outside

the window. He held a tin bowl in his hand, and put it down on the grass outside.

'Your dog's dinner,' he yelled.

'He looks like a dog's dinner himself,' said Dick, in disgust. 'Messy creature!'

That made everyone laugh. 'Edgar, the Dog's Dinner!' said Anne. 'Any biscuits in that tin on the sideboard, do you think, George?'

George got up to see. Timothy slipped out of doors and went to the dish put down for him. He sniffed at it. George, coming back from the sideboard, looked out of the window as she passed and saw him. At once the thought of poison came back to her mind and she yelled to Timothy, making the others jump out of their skins.

'TIM! TIM! Don't touch it!'

Timothy wagged his tail as if to say he didn't mean to touch it, anyway. George rushed out of doors, and picked up the mess of raw meat. She sniffed at it.

'You haven't touched it, have you, Timothy?' she said, anxiously.

Dick leaned out of the window.

'No, he didn't eat any. I watched him. He sniffed all round and about it, but he wouldn't touch it. I bet it's been dosed with rat-poison or something.'

George was very white. 'Oh, Timmy!' she said. 'You're such a sensible dog. You wouldn't touch poisoned stuff, would you?'

'Woof!' said Timmy, decidedly. Stinker heard the bark and put his nose out of the kitchen door.

George called to him in a loud voice:

'Stinker, Stinker, come here! Timmy doesn't want his dinner. You can have it. Come along, Stinker, here it is!'

Edgar came rushing out behind Stinker. 'Don't you give that to him,' he said.

'Why not?' asked George. 'Go on, Edgar – tell me why not.'

'He doesn't eat raw meat,' said Edgar, after a pause. 'He only eats dog biscuits.'

'That's a lie!' said George, flaming up. 'I saw him eating meat yesterday. Here, Stinker – you come and eat this.'

Edgar snatched the bowl from George, almost snarling at her, and ran indoors at top speed. George was about to go after him, but Julian, who had jumped out of the window when Edgar came up, stopped her.

'No good, old thing!' he said. 'You won't get anything out of him. The meat's probably at the back of the kitchen fire by now. From now on, we feed Timothy ourselves with meat bought from the butcher with our own money. Don't be afraid that he'll eat poisoned stuff. He's too wise a dog for that.'

'He might, if he was terribly, awfully hungry, Julian,' said George, looking rather green now. She felt sick inside. 'I wasn't going to let Stinker eat that poisoned stuff, of course, but I guessed that if it *was* poisoned, one of the Sticks would come rushing out and stop Stinker eating it. And Edgar did. So it proves it was poisoned, doesn't it?'

'I rather think it does,' said Julian. 'But don't worry, George. Timmy won't be poisoned.'

'But he might, he might,' said George, putting her hand

on the big dog's head. 'Oh, I can't bear the thought of it, Julian. I can't, I really can't.'

'Don't think about it then,' said Julian, taking her indoors again. 'Here, have a biscuit!'

'You don't think the Sticks would poison *us*, do you?' said Anne, looking suddenly scared and gazing at her biscuit as if it might bite her.

'No, idiot. They only want to get Timmy out of the way because he guards us so well,' said Julian. 'Don't look so scared. All this will settle down in a day or two, and we'll have a grand time after all. You'll see!'

But Julian only said this to comfort his little sister. Secretly he was very worried. He wished he could take Anne, Dick and George back to his own home. But he knew George wouldn't come. And how could they leave her to the Sticks? It was quite impossible. Friends must stick together, and somehow they must face things until Aunt Fanny and Uncle Quentin came back.

CHAPTER SEVEN

Better news

'DO YOU think we'd better slip down after the Sticks have gone to bed and get some food out of the larder again?' said Dick, when no supper appeared that evening.

Julian didn't feel inclined to sneak down and confront Mr Stick again. Not that he was afraid of him, but the whole thing was so unpleasant. This was their house, the food was theirs – so why should they have to beg for it, or take it on the sly? It was ridiculous.

'Come here, Timothy!' said Julian. The dog left George's side and went to Julian, looking up at the boy inquiringly. 'You're going to come with me and persuade dear kind Mrs Stick to give us the best things out of the larder!' said Julian, with a grin.

The others laughed, cheering up at once.

'Good idea!' said Dick. 'Can we all come and see the fun.'

'Better not,' said Julian. 'I can manage fine by myself.'

He went down the passage to the kitchen. The radio was going inside, so no one in the kitchen heard Julian till he was actually standing inside the door. Then Edgar looked up and saw Timothy as well as Julian.

Edgar was scared of the big dog, who was now growling

fiercely. He went behind the kitchen sofa and stayed there, eyeing Timmy fearfully.

'What do you want?' said Mrs Stick, turning off the radio.

'Supper,' said Julian, pleasantly. 'Supper! The best things out of the larder – bought with my uncle's money, cooked on my aunt's stove with gas she pays for – yes, supper! Open the larder door and let's see what there is in there.'

'Well, of all the nerve!' began Mr Stick, in amazement.

'You can have a loaf of bread and some cheese,' said Mrs Stick, 'and that's my last word.'

'Well, it isn't my last word,' said Julian, and he went to the larder door. 'Timmy, keep to heel! Growl all you like, but don't bite anybody – yet!'

Timmy's growls were really frightful. Even Mr Stick put himself at the other end of the room. As for Stinker, he was nowhere to be seen. He had gone into the scullery at the very first growl, and was now shivering behind the wringer.

Mrs Stick's mouth went into a hard straight line. 'You take the bread and cheese and clear out,' she said.

Julian opened the larder door, whistling softly which annoyed Mrs Stick more than anything else. 'My word!' said Julian, admiringly. 'You do know how to stock a larder, I must say, Mrs Stick. A roast chicken! I thought I smelt one cooking. I suppose Mr Stick killed one of our chickens today. I thought I heard a lot of squawking. And what fine tomatoes! Best to be got from the village, I've no doubt. And oh, Mrs Stick – what a perfectly *marvellous* treacle tart! I must say you're a good cook, I really must.'

Julian picked up the chicken, the dish of tomatoes and then balanced the plate with the treacle tart on the top.

Mrs Stick yelled at him.

'You leave those things alone! That's our supper! You leave them there.'

'You've made a little mistake,' said Julian, politely. 'It's *our* supper! We've had very little to eat today, and we could do with a good supper. Thanks awfully!'

'Now look 'ere!' began Mr Stick, angrily, furious at seeing his lovely supper walking away.

'You surely don't want me to look at you *again*,' said Julian, in a tone of amazement. 'What for? Have you shaved yet – or washed? I'm afraid not. So, if you don't mind I think I'd rather *not* look at you.'

Mr Stick was speechless. He was not ready with his tongue at any time, and a boy like Julian took his breath away, and left him with nothing to say except his favourite 'Now, look 'ere!'

'Put those things down,' said Mrs Stick sharply. 'What do you think we're going to have for *our* supper if you walk off with them? You tell me that!'

'Easy!' said Julian. 'Let me offer you *our* supper – bread and cheese, Mrs Stick, bread and cheese!'

Mrs Stick made an angry noise, and started to go after Julian with her hand raised. But Timothy immediately

leapt at her, and his teeth snapped together with a loud click.

'Oh!' howled Mrs Stick. 'That dog of yours nearly took my hand off! The brute! I'll do for him one day, you see if I don't.'

'You had a good try today, didn't you?' said Julian, in a quiet voice, fixing his eyes straight on the woman's face. 'That's a matter for the police, isn't it? Be careful, Mrs Stick. I've a good mind to go to the police tomorrow.'

Just as before, the mention of the police seemed to frighten Mrs Stick. She cast a look at her husband and took a step backwards. Julian wondered if the man had done something wrong and was hiding from the police. He never seemed to put a foot out of doors.

The boy went up the passage triumphantly. Timmy followed at his heels, disappointed that he hadn't been able to get a nibble at Stinker. Julian marched into the sitting-room, and set the dishes carefully down on the table.

'What ho!' he said. 'Look what *I've* got – the Sticks' own supper!' Then he told the others all that had happened, and they laughed loudly.

'How do you think of all those things to say?' said Anne, admiringly. 'I don't wonder you make them feel wild, Ju. It's a good thing we've got Timmy to back us up.'

'Yes, I shouldn't feel nearly so bold without Timmy,' said Julian.

It was a very good supper. There were knives and forks in the sideboard, and the children made do with fruit plates from the sideboard too, rather than go and get plates from the kitchen. There was bread over from their tea, so they were able to make a very good meal. They enjoyed it thoroughly.

'Sorry we can't give you the chicken bones, Tim,' said George, 'but they might splinter inside you and injure you. You can have all the scraps. See you don't leave any for Stinker!'

Timmy didn't. With two or three great gulps he cleared his plate, and then sat waiting for any scraps of treacle tart that might descend his way.

The children felt cheerful after such a good meal. They had completely eaten the chicken. Nothing was left except a pile of bones. They had eaten all the tomatoes too, finished the bread, and enjoyed every scrap of the treacle tart.

It was late, Anne yawned, and then George yawned too, 'Let's go to bed,' she said. 'I don't feel like having a game of cards or anything.'

So they went to bed, and as usual Timothy lay heavily on George's feet. He lay there awake for some time, his ears cocked to hear noises from below. He heard the Sticks go up to bed. He heard doors closing. He heard a whine from Stinker. Then all was silence. Timmy dropped his head on to his paws and slept – but he kept one ear cocked for danger. Timothy didn't trust the Sticks any more than the children did!

The children awoke very early in the morning. Julian awoke first. It was a marvellous day. Julian went to the window and looked out. The sky was a very pale blue, and rosy-pink clouds floated about it. The sea was a clear blue too, smooth and calm. Julian remembered what Anne often said – she said that the world in the early morning always looked as if it had come back fresh from the laundry – so clean and new and fresh!

The children all bathed before breakfast, and this time they were back at half past eight, afraid that George's father might telephone early again. Julian saw Mrs Stick on the stairs and called to her.

'Has my uncle telephoned yet?'

'No,' said the woman, in a surly tone. She had been hoping that the telephone would ring while the children were out, then, as she had done the day before, she could answer it, and get a few words in first.

'We'll have breakfast now, please,' said Julian. 'A *good* breakfast, Mrs Stick. My uncle *might* ask us what we'd had for breakfast, mightn't he? You never know.'

Mrs Stick evidently thought that Julian might tell his uncle if she gave them only bread and butter for breakfast, so very soon the children smelt a delicious smell of bacon frying. Mrs Stick brought in a dish of it garnished with tomatoes. She banged it down on the table with the plates. Edgar arrived with a pot of tea and a tray of cups and saucers.

'Ah, here is dear Edgar!' said Julian, in a tone of amiable surprise. 'Dear old spotty-face!'

'Garn!' said Edgar, and banged down the teapot. Timmy growled, and Edgar fled for his life.

George didn't want any breakfast. Julian put hers back in the warm dish and put a plate over it. He knew that she was waiting for news. If only the telephone would ring – then she would know if her mother was really better or not.

It did ring as they were half-way through the meal. George was there before the bell had stopped pealing. She put the receiver to her ear. 'Father! Yes, it's George. How's Mother?'

There was a pause as George listened. All the children stopped eating and listened in silence, waiting for George to speak. They would know by her next words if the news was good or not.

'Oh – oh, I'm so glad!' they heard George say. 'Did she have the operation yesterday? Oh, you never told me! But it's all right now, is it? Poor Mother! Give her my love. I do want to see her. Oh, Father, can't I come?'

Evidently the answer was no. George listened for a while then spoke a few more words and said goodbye.

She ran into the sitting-room. 'You heard, didn't you?' she said, joyfully. 'Mother's better. She'll get all right now, and will be back home soon – in about ten days. Father won't come back till he brings her home. It's good news about Mother – but I'm afraid we can't get rid of the Sticks.'

CHAPTER EIGHT

George's plan

MRS STICK had overheard the conversation on the telephone – at least, she had heard George's side of it. She knew that George's mother was better and that her father would not return till her mother could be brought home. That would be in about ten days! The Sticks could have a fine time till then, no doubt about that!

George suddenly found that her appetite had come back. She ate her bacon hungrily, and scraped the dish round with a piece of bread. She had three cups of tea, and then sat back contentedly.

'I feel better,' she said. Anne slipped her hand in hers. She was very glad that her aunt was going to be all right. If it wasn't for those awful Sticks they could have a lovely time. Then George said something that made Julian cross.

'Well, now that I know Mother is going to be better, I can stand up to the Sticks all right by myself with Timmy. So I want you three to go back home and finish the hols without me. I shall be all right.'

'Shut up, George,' said Julian. 'We've argued this all out before. I've made up my mind – and I don't change it, any more than *you* do, when I've made it up. You make me cross.'

'Well,' said George, 'I told you I'd got a plan – and you don't come into it, I'm afraid – and you'll find you'll have to go back home whether you mean to or not.'

'Don't be so mysterious, George!' said Julian, impatiently. 'What is this strange plan? You'd better tell us, even if we're not in it. Can't you trust us?'

'Yes, of course. But you might try to stop me,' said George, looking sulky.

'Then you'd certainly better tell us,' said Julian feeling uneasy. George could be so reckless once she got ideas into her head. Goodness knows what she might do!

But George wouldn't say another word. Julian gave it up at last, but secretly made up his mind not to let George out of his sight that day. If she was going to carry out some wild plan, then she would have to do it under his, Julian's, eye!

But George didn't seem to be carrying out any wild plan. She bathed again with the others, went out for a walk with them, and went for a row on the sea. She didn't want to go to Kirrin Island, so the others didn't press her, thinking that she didn't want to be out of sight of the beach in case Edgar came with a message from her father.

It was quite a pleasant day. The children bought sausage rolls again, and fruit, and picnicked on the beach. Timmy had a large and juicy bone from the butcher's.

'I've got a bit of shopping to do,' said George, about tea-time. 'You others go and see if Mrs Stick is getting some tea for us, and I'll fly down to the shops and get what I want.'

Julian pricked up his ears at once. Was George sending them off so that she could be alone to carry out this mysterious plan of hers?

'I'll come with you,' said Julian, getting up. 'Dick can tackle Mrs Stick for once, and take Timmy with him.'

'No, you go,' said George. 'I won't be long.'

But Julian was determined not to go. In the end they all went with George, for Dick did not want to face Mrs Stick without Julian or George.

George went into the little general shop and got a new battery for her torch. She bought two boxes of matches, and a bottle of methylated spirit.

'Whatever do you want that for?' said Anne in surprise.

'Oh, it might come in useful,' said George, and said no more.

They all went back to Kirrin Cottage. Tea was actually on the table! True, it was not a thrilling tea, being merely bread and jam and a pot of hot tea – still it was there, and was edible.

It rained that evening. The children sat round the table and played cards. Their hearts were lighter now that they had had good news of George's mother. In the middle of the game Julian got up and rang the bell. The others stared at him in the greatest surprise.

'What are you ringing the bell for?' asked George, her eyes wide with astonishment.

'To tell Mrs Stick to bring some supper,' said Julian, with a grin. But no one answered the bell. So Julian rang again and then again.

The kitchen door opened at last and Mrs Stick came up the passage, evidently in a bad temper. She came into the sitting-room.

'You stop ringing that bell!' she said, angrily. 'I'm not answering any bells rung by you.'

'I rang it to tell you that we wanted some supper,' said Julian. 'And to say that if you would rather I came and got it myself from the larder – with Timmy – as I did last night, I'll come with pleasure. But if not, you can bring a decent supper to us yourself.'

'If you come stealing things out of my larder again, I'll – I'll . . .' began Mrs Stick.

'You'll call in the police!' Julian finished for her. 'Do. That would please us very much. I can see our local policeman taking down all the details in his note book. I could give him quite a few.'

Mrs Stick muttered something rude under her breath, glared at Julian as if she could get him, and went off down the passage again. By the sound of the clattering and crashing of crockery in the kitchen it was plain that Mrs Stick was getting some sort of supper for them, and Julian grinned to himself as he dealt out the cards.

Supper was not as good as the night before, but it was not bad. It was a little cold ham, cheese and the remains of a milk pudding. There was also a plate of cooked meat for Timmy.

George looked at it sharply. 'Take that away,' she said. 'I bet you've poisoned it again. Take it away!'

'No. On the contrary, leave it here,' said Julian. 'I'll take it down to the local chemist tomorrow and get him to test it. If, as George thinks, it's poisoned, the chemist might have a lot of interesting things to tell us.'

Mrs Stick took the meat away without a word. 'Horrible woman!' said George, pulling Timothy close to her. 'How I hate her! I feel so afraid for Timmy.'

Somehow that spoilt the evening. As it grew dark the children became sleepy. 'It's ten o'clock,' said Julian. 'Bed, I think, everyone! Anne ought to have gone long ago. She isn't nearly old enough to stay up as late as this.'

'*Well!*' began Anne, indignantly. 'I'm nearly as old as George, aren't I? I can't help being younger, can I?'

'All right, all right!' said Julian laughing. 'I shan't make you go off to bed by yourself, don't worry. We all keep together in this house while the Sticks are about. Come on! We'll go now, shall we?'

The children were tired. They had swum, walked and rowed that day. Julian tried to keep awake a little while, but he too fell asleep very quickly.

He awoke with a jump, thinking that he had heard a noise. But everything was quiet. What could the noise have been? Was it one of the Sticks creeping about? No – it couldn't be that, or Tim would have barked the house down. Then what was it? *Something* must have woken him.

'I suppose it's not old George doing anything about that plan of hers!' thought Julian, suddenly. He sat up. He felt about for his dressing-gown and put it on. Without waking Dick he crept to the girls' room, and switched on his torch to see that they were all right.

Anne was in her bed, sleeping peacefully. But George's bed was empty. George's clothes were gone!

'Blow!' said Julian, under his breath. 'Where has she gone? I bet she's run away to find where her mother is!'

His torch picked out a white envelope pinned to George's pillow. He stepped softly over to it.

It had his name printed on it in bold letters. 'JULIAN.' Julian ripped it open and read it.

'DEAR JULIAN,' said the note,

'Don't be angry with me, please. I daren't stay in Kirrin Cottage any longer in case the Sticks somehow poison Timmy. You know that would break my heart. So I've gone to live by myself on our island till Mother and Father come back. Please leave a note for Father and tell him to ask Jim to sail near Kirrin Island with his little red flag flying from the mast as soon as they are back. Then I'll come home. You and Dick and Anne must go back to your own parents now I've gone. It would be silly to stay at Kirrin Cottage with the Sticks now I'm not there.

Love from
GEORGE.'

Julian read the note through. 'Well, why didn't I *guess* that was her plan!' he said to himself. 'That's why we didn't come into it! She meant to go off by herself with Timmy. I can't let her do that. She can't live all by herself on Kirrin Island for so long. She might fall ill. She might slip on a rock and hurt herself, and no one would ever know!'

The boy was really worried about the determined little girl. He wondered what to do. That noise he heard must have been made by George. So she couldn't have got a very long start really. If he tore down to the beach, George might still be there, and he could stop her.

So, in his dressing-gown, he ran down the front path,

out of the gate, and took the road to the beach. The rain had stopped, and the stars were out. But it was not at all a light night.

'How can George expect to get through those rocks in the dark,' he thought. 'She's mad! She'll strike her boat on a rock, and sink.'

He tore on in the darkness, talking aloud to himself. 'No wonder she wanted a new battery for her torch, and matches – and I suppose the methylated spirit was for her little cooking stove! Why ever couldn't she tell us? It would have been fun to go with her.'

He came to the beach. He saw the light of a torch where George kept her boat. He ran to it, his feet sinking in the soft wet sand.

'George! Idiot! You're not to go off like this all alone, in the dead of night!' called Julian.

George was pushing her boat out into the water. She jumped when she heard Julian's voice. 'You can't stop me!' she said. 'I'm just off!'

But Julian caught hold of the boat, as he waded up to his waist in the water. 'George, listen to me! You can't go like this. You'll strike a rock. Come back!'

'No,' said George, getting cross. 'You can go back to your own home, Julian. I shall be all right. Let go my boat!'

'George, why didn't you tell me your plan?' said Julian, almost swept off his feet by a wave. 'Dash these waves! I shall have to get into the boat.'

He climbed in. He could not see George, but he felt quite certain she was glaring at him. Timmy licked his wet legs.

'You're spoiling everything,' said George, with a break

in her voice that meant she was upset.

'I'm not, silly!' said Julian, in a gentle voice. 'Listen! – you come back to Kirrin Cottage with me now, George, and I'll faithfully promise you something. Tomorrow we'll *all* go to the island with you. See? The whole lot of us. Why shouldn't we? Your mother said we could spend a week there, anyway, didn't she? We shall be out of the reach of those horrible Sticks. We shall enjoy ourselves, and have a marvellous time. So will you come back now, George, and let us go together tomorrow?'

CHAPTER NINE

An exciting night

THERE WAS a silence, except for the waves splashing round the boat. Then George's voice came out of the darkness, lifted joyfully.

'Oh, Julian – do you really mean it? Will you really come with me? I was afraid I'd get into trouble for doing this, because Father said I must stay at Kirrin Cottage till he came back – and you know how he hates disobedience. But I knew if I stayed there, you would too – and I didn't want you to be miserable with those horrid Sticks – so I thought I'd come away. I didn't think you'd come too, because of getting into trouble! I never even thought of asking you.'

'You're a very stupid person sometimes, aren't you, George?' said Julian. 'As if we'd care about getting into trouble, so long as we were all together, sticking by one another! Of course we'll come with you – and I'll take all the responsibility for this escape, and tell your father it's my fault.'

'Oh no you won't,' said George, quickly. 'I shall say it was my idea. If I do wrong, I'm not afraid to own up to it. You know that.'

'Well, we won't argue that now,' said Julian. 'We shall

have at least a week or ten days on Kirrin Island to do all the arguing we want to. The thing is – let's get back now, wake up the others for a bit, and have a nice quiet talk in the dead of night about this plan of yours. I must say it's a very, very good idea!'

George was overjoyed. 'I feel as if I could hug you, Julian,' she said. 'Where are the oars? Oh, here they are! The boat's floated quite a long way out.'

She rowed strongly back to the shore. Julian jumped out and pulled the boat up the beach, with George's help. He shone his torch into the boat and gave an exclamation.

'You've quite a nice little store of things here,' he said. 'Bread and ham and butter and stuff. How did you manage to get them without old Mr Stick seeing you tonight? I suppose you slipped down and got them out of the larder?'

'Yes, I did,' said George. 'But there was no one in the kitchen tonight. Perhaps Mr Stick has gone to sleep upstairs. Or maybe he has gone back to his ship. Anyway, there was no one there when I crept down, not even Stinker.'

'We'd better leave them here,' said Julian. 'Stuff them into that locker and shut down the lid. No one will guess there's anything there. We'll have to bring down a lot more stuff if we're all going to live on the island. Golly, this is going to be fun!'

The children made their way back to the house, feeling thrilled and excited. Julian's wet dressing-gown flapped round his legs, and he pulled it up high to be out of the way. Timothy gambolled round, not seeming at all surprised at the night's doings.

When they got back to the house they woke the other two, who listened in astonishment to what had happened that night. Anne was so excited to think that they were all going to live on the island that she raised her voice in joy.

'Oh! That's the loveliest thing that could happen! Oh, I do think . . .'

'Shut up!' said three furious voices in loud whispers. 'You'll wake the Sticks!'

'Sorry!' whispered Anne. 'But oh – it's so terribly, awfully exciting.'

They began to discuss the plans. 'If we go for a week or ten days, we must take plenty of stores,' said Julian.

'The thing is – can we possibly find food enough for so long? Even if we entirely empty the larder I doubt if that would be enough for a week or so. We all seem such hungry people, somehow.'

'Julian,' said George, suddenly remembering something, '*I* know what we'll do! Mother has a store-cupboard in her room. She keeps dozens and dozens of tins of food there, in case we ever get snowed up in the winter, and can't go to the village. That has happened once or twice, you know. And I know where Mother keeps the key! Can't we open the cupboard and get out some tins?'

'Of course!' said Julian, delighted. 'I know Aunt Fanny wouldn't mind. And anyway, we can make a list of what we take and replace them for her, if she does mind. It will be my birthday soon, and I am sure to get money then.'

'Where's the key?' whispered Dick.

'Let's go into Mother's room, and I'll show you where she keeps it,' said George. 'I only hope she hasn't taken it with her.'

But George's mother had felt far too ill when she left home to think of cupboard keys. George fumbled at the back of a drawer in the dressing-table and brought out two or three keys tied together with thin string. She fitted first one and then another into a cupboard set in the wall. The second one opened the door.

Julian shone his torch into the cupboard. It was filled with tins of food of all kinds, neatly arranged on the shelves.

'Golly!' said Dick, his eyes gleaming. 'Soup – tins of meat – tins of fruit – tinned milk – sardines – tinned butter – biscuits – tinned vegetables! There's everything we want here!'

'Yes,' said Julian, pleased. 'It's fine. We'll take all we can carry. Is there a sack or two anywhere about, George, do you know?'

Soon the tins were quietly packed into two sacks. The cupboard door was shut and locked again. The children stole to their own rooms once more.

'Well, that's the biggest problem solved – food,' said Julian. 'We'll raid the larder too, and take what bread there is – and cake. What about water, George? Is there any on the island?'

'Well, I suppose there is some in that old well,' said George, thinking, 'but as there's no bucket or anything, we can't get any. I was taking a big container of fresh water with me – but we'd better fill two or three more now you are all coming! I know where there are some, quite clean and new.'

So they filled some containers with fresh water, and put them with the sacks, ready to take to the boat. It was so exciting doing all these things in the middle of the night! Anne could hardly keep her voice down to a whisper, and it was a wonder that Timothy didn't bark for he sensed the excitement of the others.

There was a tin of cakes in the larder, freshly made, so those were added to the heap that was forming in the front garden. There was a large joint of meat too, and George wrapped it in a cloth and put that with the heap, telling Timmy in a fierce voice that if he so much as sniffed at it she would leave him behind!

'I've got my little stove for boiling water on, or heating up anything,' whispered George. 'It's in the boat. That's what I bought the methylated spirit for, of course. You didn't guess, did you? And the matches for lighting it. I say – what about candles? We can't use our torches all the time, the batteries would soon run out.'

They found a packet of candles in the kitchen cupboard, a kettle, a saucepan, some old knives and forks and spoons, and a good many other things they thought they might possibly want. They also came across some small bottles of ginger-beer, evidently stored for their own use by the Sticks.

'All bought out of my mother's money!' said George. 'Well, we'll take the ginger-beer too. It will be nice to drink it on a hot day.'

'Where are we going to sleep at night?' said Julian. 'In that ruined part of the old castle, where there is just one room with a roof left, and walls?'

'That's where I planned to sleep,' said George. 'I was going to make my bed of some of the heather that grows on the island, covered by a rug or two, which I've got down in the boat.'

'We'll take all the rugs we can find,' said Julian. 'And some cushions for pillows. I say, isn't this simply thrilling? I don't know when I've felt so excited. I feel like a prisoner escaping to freedom! Won't the Sticks be amazed when they find us gone!'

'Yes – we'll have to decide what to say to them,' said George, rather soberly. 'We don't want them sending people after us to the island, making us come back. I don't think they should know we've gone there.'

'We'll discuss that later,' said Dick. 'The thing is to get everything to the boat while it's dark. It will soon be dawn.'

'How are we going to get all this down to George's boat?' said Anne, looking at the enormous pile of goods by the light of her torch. 'We'll never be able to carry them all!'

Certainly it looked a great pile. Julian had an idea, as usual. 'Are there any barrows in the shed?' he asked George. 'If we could pile the things into a couple of barrows, we could easily take everything in one journey. We could wheel the barrows along on the sandy side of the road so that we don't make any noise.'

'Oh, good idea!' said George, delighted. 'I wish I'd thought of that before. I had to make about five journeys to and from the boat when I took my own things. There are two barrows in the shed. We'll get them. One has a squeaky wheel, but we'll hope no one hears it.'

Stinker heard the squeak, as he lay in a corner of

Mrs Stick's room. He pricked up his ears and growled softly. He did not dare to bark, for he was afraid of bringing Timothy up. Mrs Stick did not hear the growl. She slept soundly, not even stirring. She had no idea what was going on downstairs.

The things were all stowed into the boat. The children didn't like leaving them there unguarded. In the end they decided to leave Dick there, sleeping on the rugs. They stood thinking for a moment before they went back without Dick.

'I do hope we've remembered all we shall want,' said George, wrinkling up her forehead. 'Golly – I know! We haven't remembered a tin-opener – nor a thing to take off the tops of the ginger-beer bottles. They've got those little tin lids that have to be forced off by an opener.'

'We'll put those in our pockets when we get back to the house and find them,' said Julian. 'I remember seeing some in the sideboard drawer. Goodbye, Dick. We'll be down very early to row off. We must get some bread at the baker's as soon as he opens, because we've got hardly any, and we'll see if we can pick up a very large bone at the butcher's for Timmy. George has got a bag of biscuits in the boat for him too.'

The three of them set off back to the house with Timmy, leaving Dick curled up comfortably on the rugs. He soon fell asleep again, his face upturned to the stars that would soon fade from the sky.

The others talked about what to tell the Sticks. 'I think

we won't tell them anything,' said Julian, at last. 'I don't particularly want to tell them deliberate lies, and I'm certainly not going to tell them the truth. I know what we'll do – there is a train that leaves the station about eight o'clock, which would be the one we'd catch if we were going back to our own home. We'll find a timetable, leave it open on the dining-room table, as if we'd been looking up a train, and then we'll all set off across the moor at the back of the house, as if we were going to the station.'

'Oh yes – then the Sticks will think we've run away, and gone to catch the train back home,' said Anne. 'They will never guess we've gone to the island.'

'That's a good idea,' said George, pleased. 'But how shall we know when Father and Mother get back?'

'Is there anyone you could leave a message with – somebody you could really trust?' asked Julian.

George thought hard. 'There's Alf the fisher-boy,' she said at last. 'He used to look after Tim for me when I wasn't allowed to have him in the house. I know he'd not give us away.'

'We'll call on Alf before we go then,' said Julian. 'Now, let's look for that timetable and lay it open on the table at the right place.'

They hunted for the timetable, found the right page, and underlined the train they hoped that the Sticks would think they were catching. They found the tin and bottle openers and put them into their pockets. Julian found two or three more boxes of matches too. He thought two would not last long enough.

By this time dawn had come and the house was being flooded with early sunshine. 'I wonder if the baker is open,' said Julian. 'We might as well go and see. It's about six o'clock.'

They went to the baker. He was not open, but the new loaves had already been made. The baker was outside, sunning himself. He had baked his bread at night, ready to sell it new-made in the morning. He grinned at the children.

'Up early today,' he said. 'What, you want some of my loaves – how many? Six! Good gracious, whatever for?'

'To eat,' said George, grinning. Julian paid for six enormous loaves, and they went to the butcher's. His shop was not open either, but the butcher himself was sweeping the path outside. 'Could we buy a very big bone for Timmy, please?' asked George. She got an enormous one, and Timmy looked at it longingly. Such a bone would last him for days, he knew!

'Now,' said Julian, as they set off to the boat, 'we'll pack these things into the boat, then go back to the house, and make a noise so that the Sticks know we're there. Then we'll set off across the moors, and hope the Sticks will think we are making for the train.'

They woke Dick, who was still sleeping peacefully in the boat, and packed in the bread and bone.

'Take the boat into the next cove,' said George. 'Can

you do that? We shall be hidden there from anyone on the beach then. The fishermen are all out in their boats, fishing. We shan't be seen, if we set off in about an hour's time. We'll be back by then.'

They went back to the house and made a noise as if they were just getting up. George whistled to Timmy, and Julian sang at the top of his voice. Then, with a great banging of doors, they set out down the path and cut across the moors, in full sight of the kitchen window.

'Hope the Sticks won't notice Dick isn't with us,' said Julian, seeing Edgar staring out of the window. 'I expect they'll think he's gone ahead.'

They kept to the path until they came to a dip, where they were hidden from any watcher at Kirrin Cottage. Then they took another path that led them, unseen, to the cove where Dick had taken the boat. He was there, waiting anxiously for them.

'Ahoy there!' yelled Julian, in excitement. 'The adventure is about to begin.'

CHAPTER TEN

Kirrin Island once more!

THEY ALL clambered into the boat. Timothy leapt in lightly and ran to the prow, where he always stood. His tongue hung out in excitement. He knew quite well that something was up – and he was in it! No wonder he panted and wagged his tail hard.

'Off we go!' said Julian, taking the oars. 'Sit over there a bit, Anne. The luggage is weighing down the boat awfully the other end. Dick, sit by Anne to keep the balance better. That's right. Off we go!'

And off they went in George's boat, rocking up and down on the waves. The sea was fairly calm, but a good breeze blew through their hair. The water splashed round the boat and made a nice gurgly, friendly noise. The children all felt very happy. They were on their own. They were escaping from the horrid Sticks. They were going to stay on Kirrin Island, with the rabbits and gulls and jackdaws.

'Doesn't that new-made bread smell awfully good?' said Dick, feeling very hungry as usual. 'Can we just grab a bit, do you think?'

'Yes, let's,' said George. So they broke off bits of the warm brown crust, handed some to Julian, who was rowing, and chewed the delicious new-made bread. Timmy got a bit too, but his was gone as soon as it went into his mouth.

'Timmy's funny,' said Anne. 'He never eats his food as we do – he seems to *drink* it – just takes it into his mouth and swallows it, as if it was water!'

The others laughed. 'He doesn't drink his bones,' said George. 'He always eats those all right – chews on them for hours and hours. Don't you, Timothy?'

'Woof!' said Timmy, agreeing. He eyed the place where that enormous bone was, wishing he could have it now. But the children wouldn't let him. They were afraid it might go overboard, and that would be a pity.

'I don't believe anyone has noticed us going,' said Julian. 'Except Alf the fisher-boy, of course. We told him about going to the island, Dick, but nobody else.'

They had called at Alf's house on their way to the cove. Alf was alone in the yard at the back. His mother was away and his father was out fishing. They had told him their secret, and Alf had nodded his tousled head and promised faithfully to tell nobody at all. He was evidently very proud at being trusted.

'If my mother and father come back, you must let us know,' said George. 'Sail as near the island as you dare, and hail us. You can get nearer to it than anyone else.'

'I'll do that,' promised Alf, wishing he could go with them.

'So, you see, Dick,' said Julian, as he rowed out to the

island, 'if by any chance Aunt Fanny does return sooner than we expect, we shall know at once and come back. I think we've planned everything very well.'

'Yes, we have,' said Dick. He turned and faced the island, which was coming nearer. 'We shall soon be there. Isn't George going to take the oars and guide the boat in?'

'Yes,' said George. 'We've come to the difficult bit now, where we've got to weave our way in and out of the different rocks that keep sticking up. Give me the oars, Ju.'

She took the oars, and the others watched in admiration as the girl guided the big boat skilfully in and out of the hidden rocks. She certainly was very clever. They felt perfectly safe with her.

The boat slid into the little cove. It was a natural harbour, with the water running up to a stretch of sand. High rocks sheltered it. The children jumped out eagerly, and four pairs of willing hands tugged the boat quickly up the sand.

'Higher up still,' panted George. 'You know what awful storms suddenly blow up in this bay. We want to be sure the boat is quite safe, no matter how high the seas run.'

The boat soon lay on one side, high up the stretch of sand. The children sat down, puffing and blowing. 'Let's have breakfast here,' said Julian. 'I don't feel like unloading all those heavy things at the moment. We'll get what we want for breakfast, and have it here on this warm bit of sand.'

They got a loaf of new bread, some cold ham, a few tomatoes and a pot of jam. Anne found knives and forks and plates. Julian opened two bottles of ginger-beer.

'Funny sort of breakfast,' he said, setting the bottles down on the sand, 'but simply gorgeous when anyone is as hungry as we are.'

They ate everything except about a third of the loaf. Timmy was given his bone and some of his own biscuits. He crunched up the biscuits at once, and then sat down contentedly to gnaw the fine bone.

'How nice to be Timmy – with no plate or knife or fork or cup to bother about,' said Anne, lying on her back in the sun, feeling that she really couldn't eat anything more. 'Oh, if we are always going to have mixed-up meals like this on the island, I shall never want to go back. Who would have thought that ham and jam and ginger-beer would go so well together?'

Timmy was thirsty. He sat with his tongue hanging out wishing that George would give him a drink. He didn't like ginger-beer.

George eyed him lazily.

'Oh, Timmy – are you thirsty?' she said. 'Oh dear, I feel as if I really can't get up! You'll have to wait a few minutes, then I'll go to the boat and empty out some water for you.'

But Timothy couldn't wait. He went off to some nearby rocks, which were out of reach of the sea. In a hole in one of them he found some rain-water, and he lapped it up eagerly. The children heard him lapping it, and laughed.

'Isn't Timmy clever?' murmured Anne. 'I should never have thought of that.'

The children had been up half the night, and now they were full of good things, and were very sleepy. One by one they fell asleep on the warm sand. Timothy eyed them in astonishment. It wasn't night-time! Yet here were all the children sleeping tightly. Well, well – a dog could always go to sleep too at any time! So Timothy threw himself down beside George, put his head right on her middle, and closed his eyes.

The sun was high when the little company awoke. Julian awoke first, then Dick, feeling very hot indeed, for the sun was blazing down. They sat up, yawning.

'Goodness!' said Dick, looking at his arms. 'The sun has caught me properly. I shall be terribly sore by tonight. Did we bring any cream, Julian?'

'No. We never thought of it,' said Julian. 'Cheer up! You'll be burnt much more by the time this day ends. The sun's going to be hot – there's not a cloud in the sky!'

They woke up the girls. George pushed Timmy's head off her tummy. 'You give me nightmares when you put your heavy head there,' she complained. 'Oh, I say – we're on the island, aren't we? For a moment I thought I was back in bed at Kirrin Cottage!'

'Isn't it gorgeous? – here we are for ages, all by ourselves, with tons of nice things to eat, able to do just what we like!' said Anne, contentedly.

'I guess the old Sticks are glad we've gone.' said Dick. 'Spotty Face will be able to loll in the sitting-room and read all our books, if he wants to.'

'And Stinker-dog will be able to wander all over the house and lie on anybody's bed without being afraid that Timothy will eat him whole,' said George. 'Well, let him. I don't care about anything now that I've escaped.'

It was fun to lie there and talk about everything. But soon Julian, who could never rest for long, once he was awake, got up and stretched himself.

'Come on!' he said to the others. 'There is work to do, Lazy-Bones! Come along!'

'Work to do? What do you mean?' said George in astonishment.

'Well, we've got to unload the boat and pack everything somewhere where it won't get spoilt if the rain happens to come,' said Julian. 'And we've got to decide exactly where we're going to sleep, and get the heather for our beds and pile the rugs on them. There's plenty to do!'

'Oh, don't let's do it yet,' said Anne, not at all wanting to get up out of the warm sand. But the others pulled her up, and together they all set to work to unload the boat.

'Let's go and have a look at the castle,' said Julian. 'And find the little room where we'll sleep. It's the only one left whole, so it will have to be that one.'

They went right to the top of the inlet, climbed up on to the rocks and made their way towards the old ruined castle, whose walls rose up from the middle of the little island. They stopped to gaze at it.

'It's a fine old ruin,' said Dick. 'Aren't we lucky to have an island and castle of our own! Fancy, this is all ours!'

They gazed through a big broken-down archway, to old steps beyond. The castle had once had two fine towers, but now one was almost gone. The other rose high in the air, half-ruined. The black jackdaws collected there, talking loudly. 'Chack, chack, chack! Chack, chack, chack!'

'Nice birds,' said Dick. 'I like them. See the grey patch at the back of their heads, Anne? I wonder if they ever stop talking.'

'I don't think so,' said George. 'Oh, look at the rabbits – tamer than ever!'

The courtyard was full of big rabbits, who eyed them as they came near. It really seemed as if it would be possible to pat them, they were so tame – but one by one they edged away as the children approached.

Timothy was in a great state of excitement, and his tail quivered from end to end. Oh those rabbits! Why couldn't he chase them? Why was George so difficult about rabbits? Why couldn't he make them run a bit?

But George had her hand on his collar, and gave him a stern glance. 'Now, Timothy, don't you *dare* to chase even the smallest of these rabbits. They're mine, every one of them.'

'Ours!' corrected Anne at once. She wanted to share in the rabbits, as well as in the castle and the island.

'Ours!' said George. 'Let's go and have a look at the little dark room where we'll spend the nights.'

They made their way to where the castle did not seem to be quite so ruined. They came to a doorway and looked inside.

'Here it is!' said Julian, peeping in. 'I shall have to use my torch. The windows are only slits here, and it's quite dark.'

He turned on his torch – and the children all gazed into the old room where they proposed to store their goods and sleep.

George gave a loud exclamation. 'Golly! We can't use this room! The roof has fallen in since last summer.'

So it had. Julian's torch shone on to a heap of fallen stones, scattered all over the floor. It was quite impossible to use the old room now. In any case it might be dangerous to do so, for it looked as if more stones might fall at any moment.

'Blow!' said Julian. 'What shall we do about this? We shall have to find somewhere else for a storing and sleeping-place!'

CHAPTER ELEVEN

On the old wreck

IT WAS quite a shock to have their plans spoilt. They knew there was no other room in the ruined castle that was sufficiently whole to shelter them. And they must find some sort of shelter, for although the weather was fine at the moment, it might rain hard any day – or a storm might blow up.

'And storms round about Kirrin are so very violent,' said Julian, remembering one or two. 'Do you remember the storm that tossed your wreck up from the bottom of the sea, George?'

'Oh yes,' said George and Anne, together, and Anne added eagerly: 'Let's go and see the wreck today if we can. I'd love to see if it's still balanced on those rocks, as it was last year, when we explored it.'

'Well, first we must make up our minds where we are going to sleep,' said Julian, firmly. 'I don't know if you realise it, but it's about three o'clock in the afternoon! We slept for hours on the sand – tired out with our exciting night, I suppose. We really must find some safe place and put our things there at once, and make our beds.'

'Well, but where shall we go?' said Dick. 'There's no other place in the old castle.'

'There's the dungeon below,' said Anne, shivering. 'But I don't want to go there. It's so dark and mysterious.'

Nobody wanted to sleep down in the dungeons! Dick frowned and thought hard. 'What about the wreck?' he said. 'Any chance of living there?'

'We might go and see,' said Julian. 'I don't somehow fancy living on a damp old rotting wreck – but if it's still high on the rocks, maybe the sun will have dried it, and it might be possible to have our beds and stores there.'

'Let's go and see now,' said George. So they made their way from the ruined castle to the old wall that ran round it. From there they would be able to see the wreck. It had been cast up the year before, and had settled firmly on some rocks.

They stood on the wall and looked for the wreck, but it was not where they had expected it. 'It's moved,' said Julian, in surprise. 'There it is, look, on those rocks – nearer to the shore than it was before. Poor old wreck! It's been battered about a good bit this last winter, hasn't it? It looks much more of a real wreck than it did last summer.'

'I don't believe we shall be able to sleep there,' said Dick. 'It's dreadfully battered. We might be able to store food there, though. Do you know, I believe we could get to it from those rocks that run out from the island!'

'Yes, I believe we could,' said George. 'We could only reach it safely by boat last summer – but when the tide is down, I think we *could* climb out over the line of rocks, right to the wreck itself.'

'We'll try in about an hour,' said Julian, feeling excited. 'The tide will be off the rocks by then.'

'Let's go and have a look at the old well,' said Dick, and they made their way back to the courtyard of the castle. Here, the summer before, they had found the entrance to the well-shaft that ran deep down through the rock, past the dungeons below, lower than the level of the sea, to fresh water.

The children looked about for the well, and came to the old wooden cover. They drew it back.

'There are the rungs of the old iron ladder I went down last year,' said Dick, peering in. 'Now let's find the entrance to the dungeon. The steps down into it are somewhere near here.'

They found the entrance, but to their surprise some enormous stones had been pulled across it. 'Who did that?' said George, frowning. 'We didn't. Someone has been here!'

'Day-trippers, I suppose,' said Julian. 'Do you remember that we thought we saw a spire of smoke here the other day? I bet it was day-trippers. You know, the story of Kirrin Island, and its old castle and dungeons, and the treasure we found in it last year, was all in the newspapers. I expect one of the fishermen has been making money by taking day-trippers and landing them on *our* island.'

'How dare they?' said George, looking very fierce. 'I shall put up a board that says "Trespassers will be sent to prison". I won't have strangers on our island.'

'Well, don't worry about the stones pulled across the dungeon entrance,' said Julian. 'I don't think any of us want to go down there. Look at poor old Timmy! He's gazing at those rabbits most unhappily. Isn't he funny?'

Timothy was sitting down behind the children, looking most mournfully at the ring of rabbits all round the weed-grown courtyard. He looked at the rabbits and then he looked at George, then he looked back at the rabbits.

'No good, Timmy,' said George, firmly. 'I'm not going to change my mind about rabbits. You're not to chase them on our island.'

'I expect he thinks you're most unfair to him,' said Anne. 'After all, you said he might share your quarter of the island with you – and so he thinks he ought to have his share of your rabbits too!'

Everyone laughed. Timmy wagged his tail and looked hopefully at George. They all walked across the courtyard – and then Julian suddenly came to a stop.

'Look!' he said in surprise, pointing to something on the ground. 'Look! Someone *has* been here! This is where they built a fire!'

Everyone gazed at the ground. There was a heap of woodash there, quite evidently left from a fire. Stamped into the ground was a cigarette end, too. There was absolutely no doubt about it – someone had been on the island!

'If day-trippers come here I'll set Timmy on to them!' cried George, in a fury. 'This is our own place, it doesn't belong to anybody else at all. Timothy, you mustn't chase rabbits here, but you can chase anybody on two legs, except us! See?'

Timmy wagged his tail at once. 'Woof!' he said, quite agreeing. He looked all round as if he hoped to see somebody appearing that he could chase. But there was no one.

'I should think the tide is about off those rocks by now,' said Julian. 'Let's go and see. If it is we'll climb along them and see if we can get to the wreck. Anne had better not come. She might slip and fall, and the sea is raging all round the rocks.'

'Of course I'm coming!' cried Anne, indignantly. 'You're just as likely to fall as I am.'

'Well, I'll see if it looks too dangerous,' said Julian. They made their way over the castle wall, down to the line of rocks that ran out seawards, towards the wreck. Big waves did wash over the rocks occasionally, but it seemed fairly safe.

'If you keep between me and Dick, you can come, Anne,' said Julian. 'But you must let us help you over difficult parts, and not make a fuss. We don't want you to fall in and get washed away.'

They began to make their way along the line of rugged, slippery rocks. The tide went down even farther as they got nearer to the wreck, and soon there was very little danger of being washed off the rocks. It was possible now to get right to the wreck across the rocks – a thing they had not been able to do the summer before.

'Here we are!' said Julian at last, and he put his hand on the side of the old wreck. She was a big ship now that they were near to her. She towered above them, thick with shellfish and seaweed, smelling musty and old. The water washed round the bottom part of her, but the top part was right out of the water, even when the tide was at its highest.

'She's been thrown about a bit last winter,' said George, looking at her. 'There are a lot more new holes in her side, aren't there? And part of her old mast is gone, and some of the deck. How can we get up to her?'

'I've got a rope,' said Julian, and he undid a rope that he had wound round his waist. 'Half a minute – I'll make a loop and see if I can throw it round that post sticking out up there.'

He threw the rope two or three times, but could not get the loop round the post. George took it from him impatiently. At the first throw she got it round the post. She was very good indeed at things like that – better than a boy in some things, Anne thought admiringly.

She was up the rope like a monkey, and soon stood on the sloping slippery deck. She almost slipped, but caught at a broken piece of deck just in time. Julian helped Anne to go up, and then the two boys followed.

'It's a horrid smell, isn't it?' said Anne, wrinkling up her nose. 'Do all wrecks smell like this? I don't think I'll

go and look down in the cabins like we did last time. The smell would be worse there.'

So the others left Anne up on the half-rotten deck while they went to explore a bit. They went down to the smelly, seaweed-hung cabins, and into the captain's old cabin, the biggest of the lot. But it was quite plain that not only could they not sleep there, but they could certainly not hope to store anything there, either. The whole place was damp and rotten. Julian was half afraid his foot would go through the planking at any moment.

'Let's go up to the deck,' he said. 'It's nasty down here – awfully dark too.'

They were just going up, when they heard a shout from Anne. 'I say! Come here, quick! I've found something!'

They hurried up as fast as they could, slipping and sliding on the sloping deck. Anne was standing where they had left her, her eyes shining brightly. She was pointing to something on the opposite side of the ship.

'What is it?' said George. 'What's the matter?'

'Look – that wasn't here when we came here before, surely!' said Anne, still pointing. The others looked where she pointed. They saw an open locker at the other side of the deck, and stuffed into it was a small black trunk! How extraordinary!

'A little black trunk!' said Julian, in surprise. 'No – that wasn't there before. It's not been there long either – it's quite dry and new! Whoever does it belong to? And why should it be here?'

CHAPTER TWELVE

The cave in the cliff

CAUTIOUSLY THE children made their way down the slippery deck towards the locker. The door of this had evidently been shut on the trunk but had come open, so that the trunk was not hidden, as had been intended.

Julian pulled out the little black trunk. All the children were amazed. *Why* should anyone put a trunk there?

'Smugglers, do you think?' said Dick, his eyes gleaming.

'Yes – it might be,' said Julian, thoughtfully, trying to undo the straps of the trunk. 'This would be a very good place for smugglers. Ships that knew the way could put in, cast off a boat with smuggled goods, leave them here, and go on their way, knowing that people could come and collect the goods at their leisure.'

'Do you think there are smuggled goods inside the trunk?' asked Anne, in excitement. 'What would there be? Diamonds? Silks?'

'Anything that has a duty to be paid on it before it can get into the country,' said Julian. 'Blow these straps! I can't undo them.'

'Let *me* try,' said Anne, who had very deft little fingers. She began to work at the buckles, and in a short time had the straps undone. But a further disappointment awaited them. The trunk was well and truly locked! There were two good locks, and no keys!

'Blow!' said George. 'How sickening! How can we get the trunk open now?'

'We can't,' said Julian. 'And we mustn't smash it open, because it would warn whoever it belongs to that the goods had been found. We don't want to warn the smugglers that we have discovered their little game. We want to try and catch them!'

'Ooooh!' said Anne, going red with excitement. 'Catch the smugglers! Oh, Julian! Do you really think we could?'

'Why not?' said Julian. 'No one knows we are here. If we hid whenever we saw a ship approaching the island, we might see a boat coming to it, and we could watch and find out what is happening. I should think that the smugglers are using this island as a sort of dropping-place for goods. I wonder who comes and fetches them? Someone from Kirrin Village or the nearby places, I should think.'

'This is going to be awfully exciting,' said Dick. 'We always seem to have adventures when we come to Kirrin. It's absolutely *full* of them. This will be the third one we have had.'

'I think we ought to be getting back over the rocks,' said Julian, suddenly looking over the side of the ship and seeing that the tide had turned. 'Come on – we don't want to be caught by the tide and have to stay here for hours and hours! I'll go down the rope first. Then you come, Anne.'

They were soon climbing over the rocks again, feeling very excited. Just as they reached the last stretch of rocks leading to the rocky cliff of the island itself, Dick stopped.

'What's up?' said George, pushing behind him. 'Do get on!'

'Isn't that a cave, just beyond that big rock there?' said Dick, pointing. 'It looks awfully like one to me. If it was, it would be a simply lovely place to store our things in, and even to sleep in, if it was out of reach of the sea.'

'There aren't any caves on Kirrin,' began George, and then she stopped short. What Dick was pointing at really did look like a cave. It was worthwhile seeing if it was one. After all, George had never explored this line of rocks, and so had never been able to catch sight of the cave that lay just beyond. It could not possibly be seen from the land.

'We'll go and see,' she said. So they changed their direction, and instead of climbing back the way they had come, they cut across the mass of rock and made their way towards a jutting-out part of the cliff, in which the cave seemed to be.

They came to it at last. Steep rocks guarded the entrance, and half hid it. Except from where Dick had seen it, it was really impossible to catch sight of it, it was so well-hidden.

'It *is* a cave!' said Dick, in delight, stepping into it. 'And my, what a fine one!'

It really was a beauty. Its floor was spread with fine white sand, as soft as powder, and perfectly dry, for the cave was clearly higher than the tide reached, except, possibly, in a bad winter storm. Round one side of it ran a stone ledge.

'Exactly like a shelf made for us!' cried Anne, in joy. 'We can put all our things here. How lovely! Let's come and live here and sleep here. And look, Julian we've even got a skylight in the roof!'

The little girl pointed upwards, and the others saw that the roof of the cave was open in one part, giving on to the cliff-top itself. It was plain that somewhere on the heathery cliff above was a hole that looked down to the cave, making what Anne called a 'skylight'.

'We could drop all our things down through that hole,' said Julian, quickly making plans. 'We would have an awful time bringing them over the rocks. If we can find that hole up there when we are out on the cliff again, we can let down everything on a rope. It's not a very high "skylight", as Anne calls it, for the cliffs are low just here. I believe we could swing ourselves down a rope easily, so that we needn't have the bother of clambering over the rocks to the seaward entrance we have just come in by!'

This was a grand discovery. 'Our island is even more exciting than we thought,' said Anne, happily. 'We've got a beautiful cave to share now!'

The next thing to do, of course, was to go up on the cliff and find the hole that led to the roof of the cave. So out they all went, Timmy too. Timmy was funny on the slippery rocks. His feet slithered about, and two or three times he fell into the water. But he just swam across the pools he fell into, clambered out and went on again with his slithering.

'He's like George!' said Anne, with a laugh. 'He never gives up, whatever happens to him!'

They climbed up to the top of the cliff. It was easy to find the hole once they knew it was there.

'Pretty dangerous, really,' said Julian, when he had found it, and was peering down. 'Any one of us might have run on this cliff and popped down the hole by accident. See, it's all criss-crossed with blackberry brambles.'

They scratched their hands, trying to free the hole from the brambles. Once they had cleared the hole, they could look right down into the cave quite easily.

'It's not very far down,' said Anne. 'It looks almost as if we could jump down, if we let ourselves slide down this hole.'

'Don't you do anything of the sort,' said Julian. 'You'd break your leg. Wait till we get a rope fixed up, hanging down into the cave. Then we can manage to get in and out easily.'

They went back to the boat, and began unloading it. They took everything across to the seaward side of the island, where the cave was. Julian took a strong rope and knotted it thickly at intervals.

'To give our feet a hold as we go down,' he explained. 'If we drop down too quickly, we'll hurt our hands. These knots will stop us slipping and help us to climb up.'

'Let me go down first, and then you can lower all our things to me,' said George. So down she went, hand over

hand, her feet easily finding the thick knots, feeling for one after another. It was a good way to go down.

'How shall we get Timmy down?' said Julian. But Timothy, who had been whining anxiously at the edge of the hole, watching George sliding away from him, solved the difficulty himself.

He jumped into the hole and disappeared down it! There came a shriek from below.

'Oh! My goodness, what's this? Oh, *Timmy*! Have you hurt yourself?'

The sand was very soft, like a velvet cushion, and Tim had not hurt himself at all. He gave himself a shake and then barked joyfully. He was with George again! He wasn't going to have his mistress disappearing down mysterious holes without following her at once. Not Timmy!

Then followed the business of lowering down all the goods. Anne and Dick tied the things together in rugs, and Julian lowered them carefully. George untied the rope as soon as it reached her, took out the goods, and then back went the rope again to be tied round another bundle.

'Last one!' called Julian, after a long spell of really hard work. 'Then down we come too, and I don't mind telling you that before we make our beds or anything, our next job is to have a jolly good meal! It's hours and hours since we had a meal, and I'm starving.'

Soon they were all sitting on the warm soft floor of the

cave. They opened a tin of meat, cut huge slices of bread and made sandwiches. Then they opened a tin of pineapple chunks and ate those, spooning them out of the tin, full of sweetness and juice. After that they still felt hungry, so they opened two tins of sardines and dug them out with biscuits. It made a really grand meal.

'Ginger-pop to finish up with, please,' said Dick. 'My word, why don't people always have meals like this?'

'We'd better hurry up or we shan't be able to get heather for our beds,' said George, sleepily.

'Who wants heather?' said Dick. '*I* don't! This lovely soft sand is all *I* shall want – and a cushion and a rug or two. I shall sleep better here than ever I did in bed!'

So the rugs and cushions were spread out on the sandy floor of the cave. A candle was lit as it grew dark, and the four sleepy children looked at one another. Timmy, as usual, was with George.

'Goodnight,' said George. 'I can't keep awake another minute. Goodnight, ev . . . ery . . . body . . . good . . . night!

CHAPTER THIRTEEN

A day on the island

THE CHILDREN hardly knew where they were the next day when they woke up. The sun was pouring into the cave entrance, and fell first of all on George's sleeping face. It awoke her and she lay half-dozing, wondering why her bed felt rather less soft than usual.

'But I'm not in my bed – I'm on Kirrin Island, of course!' she thought suddenly to herself. She sat up and gave Anne a shove. 'Wake up, sleepy-head! We're on the island!'

Soon they were all awake rubbing the sleep from their eyes. 'I think I'm going to get heather today for my bed, after all,' said Anne. 'The sand feels soft at first, but it gets hard after a bit.'

The others agreed that they would all get heather for their beds, set on the sand, with rugs for covering. Then they would have really fine beds.

'It's fun to live in a cave,' said Dick. 'Fancy having a fine cave like this on our island, as well as a castle and dungeons! We are really very lucky.'

'I feel sticky and dirty,' said Julian. 'Let's go and have a bathe before we have breakfast. Then cold ham, bread, pickles and marmalade for me!'

'We shall be cold after our bathe,' said George. 'We'd better light my little stove and put the kettle on to boil while we're bathing. Then we can make some hot cocoa when we come back shivering!'

'Oh yes,' said Anne, who had never boiled anything on such a tiny stove before. 'Do let's. I'll fill the kettle with water from one of the containers. What shall we do for milk?'

'There's a tin of milk somewhere in the pile,' said Julian. 'We can open that. Where's the tin-opener?'

It was not to be found, which was most exasperating. But at last Julian discovered it in his pocket, so all was well.

The little stove was filled with methylated spirit, and lit. The kettle was filled and set on top. Then the children went off to bathe.

'Look! There's a simply marvellous pool in the middle of those rocks over there!' called Julian, pointing. 'We've never spotted it before. Golly, it's like a small swimming pool, made specially for us!'

'Kirrin Swimming Pool, twenty pence a dip!' said Dick. 'Free to the owners, though! Come on – it looks gorgeous! And see how the waves keep washing over the top of the rocks and splashing into the pool. Couldn't be better!'

It really was a lovely rock-pool, deep, clear and not too cold. The children enjoyed themselves thoroughly, splashing about and swimming and floating. George tried a dive off one of the rocks, and went in beautifully.

'George can do anything in the water,' said Anne, admiringly. 'I wish I could dive and swim like George. But I never shall.'

'We can see the old wreck nicely from here,' said Julian, coming out of the water. 'Blow! We didn't bring any towels.'

'We'll use one of the rugs, turn and turn about,' said Dick. 'I'll go and fetch the thinnest one. I say – do you remember that trunk we saw in the wreck yesterday? Odd, wasn't it?'

'Yes, very odd,' said Julian. 'I don't understand it. We'll have to keep a watch on the wreck and see who comes to collect the trunk.'

'I suppose the smugglers – if they are smugglers – will come slinking round this side of the island and quietly send off a boat to the wreck,' said George, drying herself vigorously. 'Well, we'd better keep a strict lookout, and see if anything appears on the sea out there in the way of a small steamer, boat or ship.'

'Yes. We don't want them to spot us,' said Dick. 'We shan't find out anything if they see us and are warned. They'd at once give up coming to the island. I vote we each of us take turns at keeping a lookout, so that we can spot anything at once and get under cover.'

'Good idea!' said Julian. 'Well, I'm dry, but not very warm. Let's race to the cave, and get that hot drink. And breakfast – golly, I could eat a whole chicken and probably a duck as well, to say nothing of a turkey.'

The others laughed. They all felt the same. They raced off to the cave, running over the sand and climbing over a few rocks, then down to the cave-beach and into the big entrance, still splashed with sunshine.

The kettle was boiling away merrily, sending a cloud of steam up from its tin spout. 'Get the ham out and a loaf of bread, and that jar of pickles we brought,' ordered Julian. 'I'll open the tin of milk. George, you take the tin of cocoa and that jug, and make enough for all of us.'

'I'm so terribly happy,' said Anne, as she sat at the entrance to the cave, eating her breakfast. 'It's a lovely feeling. It's simply gorgeous being on our island like this, all by ourselves, able to do what we like.'

They all felt the same. It was such a lovely day too, and the sky and sea were so blue. They sat eating and drinking, gazing out to sea, watching the waves break into spray over the rocks beyond the old wreck. It certainly was a very rocky coast.

'Let's arrange everything very nicely in the cave,' said Anne, who was the tidiest of the four, and always liked to play at 'houses' if she could. 'This shall be our house, our home. We'll make four proper beds. And we'll each have our own place to sit in. And we'll arrange everything tidily on that big stone shelf there. It might have been made for us!'

'We'll leave Anne to play "houses" by herself,' said George, who was longing to stretch her legs again. 'We'll go and get some heather for beds. And oh! – what about one of us keeping a watch on the old wreck, to see who comes there?'

'Yes – that's important,' said Julian at once. 'I'll take first watch. The best place would be up on the cliff just above this cave. I can find a gorse bush that will hide me all right from anyone out at sea. You others get the heather. We will take two-hourly watches. We can read if we like, so long as we keep on looking up.'

Dick and George went to get the heather. Julian climbed up the knotted rope that still hung down through the hole, tied firmly to the great old root of an enormous gorse bush. He pulled himself out on the cliff and lay on the heather panting.

He could see nothing out to sea at all except for some big steamer miles out on the sky-line. He lay down in the sun, enjoying the warmth that poured in to every inch of his body. This lookout job was going to be very nice!

He could hear Anne singing down in the cave as she tidied up her 'house'. Her voice came up through the cave roof hole, rather muffled. Julian smiled. He knew Anne was enjoying herself thoroughly.

So she was. She had washed the few bits of crockery they had used for breakfast, in a most convenient little rain-pool outside the cave. Timmy used it for drinking-water too, but he didn't seem to mind Anne using it for washing-up water, though she apologised to him for doing so.

'I'm sorry if I spoil your drinking water, Timmy darling,' she said, 'but you are such a sensible dog that I know if it suddenly tastes nasty to you, you will go off and find another rain-pool.'

'Woof!' said Timmy, and ran off to meet George, who was just arriving back with Dick, armed with masses of soft, sweet-smelling heather for beds.

'Put the heather outside the cave, please, George', said Anne. 'I'll make the beds inside when I'm ready.'

'Right!' said George. 'We'll go and get some more. Aren't we having fun?'

'Julian's gone up the rope to the top of the cliff,' said Anne. 'He'll yell if he sees anything unusual. I hope he does, don't you?'

'It would be exciting,' agreed Dick, putting down his heather on top of Timmy, and nearly burying him. 'Oh sorry, Timmy – are you there? Bad luck!'

Anne had a very happy morning. She arranged everything beautifully on the shelf – crockery and knives and forks and spoons in one place – saucepan and kettle in another – tins of meat next, tins of soup together, tins of fruit neatly piled on top of one another. It really was a splendid larder and dresser!

She wrapped all the bread up in an old tablecloth they had brought, and put it at the back of the cave in the coolest place she could find. The containers of water went there too, and so did all the bottles of drinks.

Then the little girl set to work to make the beds. She decided to make two nice big ones, one on each side of the cave.

'George and I and Tim will have the one this side,' she thought, busy patting down the heather into the shape of a bed. 'And Julian and Dick can have the other side. I shall want lots more heather. Oh, is that you, Dick? You're just in time! I want more heather.'

Soon the beds were made beautifully, and each had an old rug for an under-blanket, and two better rugs for covers. Cushions made pillows.

'What a pity we didn't bring night-things,' thought Anne. 'I could have folded them neatly and put them under the cushions. There! It all looks lovely. We've got a beautiful house.'

Julian came sliding down the rope from the cliff to the cave. He looked round admiringly. 'My word, Anne – the cave does look fine! Everything in order and looking so tidy. You are a good little girl.'

Anne was pleased to hear Julian's praise, though she didn't like him calling her a little girl.

'Yes, it does look nice, doesn't it?' she said. 'But why aren't you watching up on the cliff, Ju?'

'It's Dick's turn now,' said Julian. 'The two hours are up. Did we bring any biscuits? I feel as if I could do with one or two, and I bet the others could too. Let's all go up to the cliff-top and have some. George and Timmy are there with Dick.'

Anne knew exactly where to put her hand on the tin of biscuits. She took out ten and climbed up to the cliff-top. Julian went up the rope. Soon all five were sitting by the big gorse-bush, nibbling at biscuits, Timmy too. At least, he didn't nibble. He just swallowed.

The day passed very pleasantly and rather lazily. They took turns at being lookout, though Anne was severely scolded by Julian in the afternoon for falling asleep during her watch. She was very ashamed of herself and cried.

'You're too little to be a lookout, that's what it is,' said Julian. 'We three and Timmy had better do it.'

'Oh, no, do let me too,' begged poor Anne. 'I never, never will fall asleep again. But the sun was so hot and . . .'

'Don't make excuses,' said Julian. 'It only makes things worse if you do. All right – we'll give you another chance,

Anne, and see if you are really big enough to do the things we do.'

But though they all took their turns, and kept a watch on the sea for any strange vessel, none appeared. The children were disappointed. They did so badly want to know who had put that trunk on the wreck and why, and what it contained.

'Better go to bed now,' said Julian, when the sun sank low. 'It's about nine o'clock. Come on! I'm really looking forward to a sleep on those lovely heathery beds that Anne has made so nicely!'

CHAPTER FOURTEEN

Disturbance in the night

IT WAS dark in the cave, not really quite dark enough to light a candle, but the cave looked so nice by candlelight that it was fun to light one. So Anne took down the candlestick and lit the candle. At once strange shadows jumped all round the cave, and it became a rather exciting place, not at all like the cave they knew by daylight!

'I wish we could have a fire,' said Anne.

'We'd be far too hot,' said Julian. 'And it would smoke us out. You can't have a fire in a cave like this. There's no chimney.'

'Yes, there is,' said Anne, pointing to the hole in the roof. 'If we lit a fire just under that hole, it would act as a chimney, wouldn't it?'

'It might,' said Dick, thoughtfully. 'But I don't think so. We'd simply get the cave full of stifling smoke, and we wouldn't be able to sleep for choking.'

'Well, couldn't we light a fire at the cave entrance then?' said Anne who felt that a real home ought to have a fire somewhere. 'Just to keep away wild beasts, say! That's what the people of old times did. It says so in my history book. They lit fires at the cave entrance at night to keep away any wild animal that might be prowling around.'

'Well, what wild beasts do you think are likely to come and peep into this cave?' asked Julian, lazily, finishing up a cup of cocoa. 'Lions? Tigers? Or perhaps you are afraid of an elephant or two.'

Everyone laughed. 'No – I don't really think animals like that would come,' said Anne. 'Only – it would be nice to have a red, glowing fire to watch when we go to sleep.'

'Perhaps Anne thinks the rabbits might come in and nibble our toes or something,' said Dick.

'Woof!' said Tim, pricking up his ears as he always did at the mention of rabbits.

'I don't think we ought to have a fire,' said Julian, 'because it might be seen out at sea and give a warning to anyone thinking of coming to the island to do a bit of smuggling.'

'Oh no, Julian – the entrance to this cave is so well-hidden that I'm sure no one could see a fire out to sea,' said George, at once. 'There's that line of high rocks in front, which must hide it completely. I think it would be rather fun to have a fire. It would light up the cave so strangely and excitingly.'

'Oh good, George!' said Anne, delighted to find someone agreeing with her.

'Well, we can't possibly trek out and get sticks for it now,' said Dick, who was far too comfortable to move.

'You don't need to,' said Anne, eagerly. 'I got plenty myself today, and stored them at the back of the cave, in case we wanted a fire.'

'Isn't she a good housewife!' said Julian, in great admiration. 'She may go to sleep when she's lookout, but she's wide-awake enough when it comes to making a house for us out of a cave! All right, Anne – we'll make a fire for you!'

They all got up and fetched the sticks from the back of the cave. Anne had been to the jackdaw tower and had picked up armfuls that the birds had dropped when making their nests in the tower. They built them up to make a nice little fire. Julian got some dried seaweed too, to drop into it.

They lit the fire at the cave entrance, and the dry sticks blazed up at once. The children went back to their heather-beds, and lay down on them, watching the red flames leaping and crackling. The red glow lit up the cave and made it very weird and exciting.

'This is lovely,' said Anne, half-asleep. 'Really lovely. Oh, Timmy, move a bit, do. You're so heavy on my feet. Here, George, pull Timothy over to your side. You're used to him lying on you.'

'Goodnight,' said Dick, sleepily. 'The fire is dying down, but I can't be bothered to put any more wood on it. I'm sure all the lions and tigers and bears and elephants have been frightened away.'

'Silly!' said Anne. 'You needn't tease me about it – you've enjoyed it as much as I have! Goodnight.'

They all fell asleep and dreamed peacefully of many things. Julian awoke with a jump. Some strange noise had awakened him. He lay still, listening.

Timothy was growling deeply, right down in his throat. 'R-r-r-r-r-r,' he went. 'Gr-r-r-r-r-r-r-r!'

George awoke too, and put out her hand sleepily. 'What's the matter, Tim?' she said.

'He's heard something, George,' said Julian, in a low voice from his bed on the other side of the cave.

George sat up cautiously. Timmy was still growling. 'Sh!' said George and he stopped. He was sitting up straight, his ears well cocked.

'Perhaps it's the smugglers come in the night,' whispered George, and a funny prickly feeling ran down her back. Somehow smugglers in the day time were rather exciting and quite welcome – but at night they seemed different. George didn't at all want to meet any just then!

'I'm going out to see if I can spy anything,' said Julian, getting off his bed quietly, so as not to wake Dick. 'I'll go up the rope to the top of the cliff. I can see better from there.'

'Take my torch,' said George. But Julian didn't want it.

'No, thanks. I can feel the way up that knotted rope quite well, whether I can see or not,' he said.

He went up the rope in the dark, his body twisting round as the rope turned. He climbed up on to the cliff and looked out to sea. It was a very dark night, and he could see no ship at all, not even the wreck. It was far too dark.

'Pity there's no moon,' thought Julian. 'I might be able to see something then.'

He watched for a few minutes, and then George's voice came through the hole in the roof, coming out strangely at his feet.

'Julian! Is there anything to see? Shall I come up?'

'Nothing at all,' said Julian. 'Is Timmy still growling?'

'Yes, when I take my hand off his collar,' said George. 'I can't imagine what's upset him.'

Suddenly Julian caught sight of something. It was a light, a good way beyond the line of rocks. He watched in excitement. That would be just about where the wreck was! Yes – it must be someone on the wreck with a lantern!

'George! Come up!' he said, putting his head inside the hole.

George came up, hand over hand, like a monkey, leaving Timothy growling below. She sat by Julian on the cliff-top. 'See the wreck – look, over there!' said Julian. 'At least, you can't see the wreck itself, it's too dark – but you can see a lantern that someone has put there.'

'Yes – that's someone on our wreck, with a lantern!' said George, feeling excited. 'Oh, I wonder if it's the smugglers – coming to bring more things.'

'Or somebody fetching that trunk,' said Julian. 'Well, we'll know tomorrow, for we'll go and see. Look! – whoever is there is moving off now – the light of the lantern is going lower – they must be getting into a boat by the side of the wreck. And now the light's gone out.'

The children strained their ears to hear if they could discover the splash of oars or the sound of voices over the water. They both thought they could hear voices.

'The boat must have gone off to join a ship or something,' said Julian. 'I believe I can see a faint light right out there – out to sea, look! Maybe the boat is going to it.'

There was nothing more to see or hear, and soon the two of them slid down the knotted rope back to the cave. They didn't wake the others, who were still sleeping peacefully. Timothy leapt up and licked Julian and George, whining joyfully. He did not growl any more.

'You're a good dog, aren't you?' said Julian, patting him. 'Nothing ever escapes *your* sharp ears, does it?'

Timothy settled down on George's feet again. It was plain that whatever it was that had disturbed him had gone. It must have been the presence of the stranger or strangers on the old wreck. Well, they would go there in the morning and see if they could discover what had been taken away or brought there in the night.

Anne and Dick were most indignant the next morning when they heard Julian's tale. 'You *might* have woken us!' said Dick, crossly.

'We would have if there had been anything much to see,' said George. 'But there was only just the light from a lantern, and nothing else except that we thought we heard the sound of voices.'

When the tide was low enough the children and Timothy set off over the rocks to the wreck. They clambered up and stood on the slanting, slippery deck. They looked towards the locker where the little trunk had stood. The door of the locker was shut this time.

Julian slid down towards it and tried to pull it open. Someone had stuffed a piece of wood in to keep the locker from swinging open. Julian pulled it out. Then the door opened easily.

'Anything else in there?' said George, stepping carefully over the slimy deck to Julian.

'Yes,' said Julian. 'Look! Tins of food! And cups and plates and things – just as if someone was going to come and live on the island too! Isn't it funny? The trunk is still here too, locked as before. And here are some candles – and a little lamp – and a bundle of rags. Whatever *are* they here for?'

It really was a puzzle. Julian frowned for a few minutes, trying to think it out.

'It looks as if someone is going to come and stay on the island for a bit – probably to wait here and take in whatever goods are going to be smuggled. Well – we shall be on the lookout for them, day or night!'

They left the wreck, feeling excited. They had a fine hiding-place in their cave – no one could possibly find them there. And, from their hiding-place, they could watch anyone coming to and from the wreck, and from the wreck to the island.

'What about our cove, where we put our boat?' said George, suddenly. 'They might use that cove, you know – if they came in a boat. It's rather dangerous to reach the island from the wreck, if anyone tried to get to the rocky beach nearby.'

'Well – if anyone came to our cove, they'd see our boat,' said Dick, in alarm. 'We'd better hide it, hadn't we?'

'How?' said Anne, thinking that it would be a difficult thing to hide a boat as big as theirs.

'Don't know,' said Julian. 'We'll go and have a look.'

All four and Timmy went off to the cove into which

they had rowed their boat. The boat was pulled high up, out of reach of the waves. George explored the cove well, and then had an idea. 'Do you think we could pull the boat round this big rock? It would just about hide it, though anyone going round the rock would see it at once.'

The others thought it would be worthwhile trying, anyway. So, with much panting and puffing, they hauled the boat round the rock, which almost completely hid her.

'Good!' said George, going down into the cove to see if very much of the boat showed. 'A bit of her does show still. Let's drape it with seaweed!'

So they draped the prow of the boat with all the seaweed they could find at hand, and after that, unless anyone went

deliberately round the big rock, the boat really was not noticeable at all.

'Good!' said Julian, looking at his watch. 'I say – it's long past tea-time – and, you know, while we've been doing all this with the boat, we quite forgot to have someone on the lookout post on the cliff-top. What idiots we are!'

'Well, I don't expect anything has happened since we've been away from the cave,' said Dick, putting a fine big bit of seaweed on the prow of the boat, as a last touch. 'I bet the smugglers will only come at night.'

'I dare say you're right,' said Julian. 'I think we'd better keep a lookout at night, too. The lookout could take rugs up to the cliff-top and curl up there.'

'Timmy could be with whoever is keeping watch,' said Anne. 'Then if the lookout goes to sleep by mistake, Timmy would growl and wake them up if he saw anything.'

'You mean, when *you* go to sleep,' said Dick, grinning. 'Come on – let's get back to the cave and have some tea.'

And then Timothy suddenly began to growl again!

CHAPTER FIFTEEN

Who is on the island?

'SH!' SAID Julian, at once. 'Get down behind this bush, quick, everyone!'

They had left the cove and were walking towards the castle when Timmy growled. Now they all crouched behind a mass of brambles, their hearts beating fast.

'Don't growl, Timmy,' said George, in Timothy's nearest ear. He stopped at once, but he stood stiff and quivering, on the watch.

Julian peeped through the bush, parting the brambles and scratching his hands. He could just see somebody in the courtyard – one person – two persons – maybe three. He strained his eyes to try and see, but even as he looked, they disappeared.

'I believe they've moved those big stones over the entrance to the dungeons, and have gone down there,' he whispered. 'Stay here, and I'll creep out a bit and see. I won't let anyone spot me.'

He came back and nodded. 'Yes – they've gone down the dungeons. Do you think they can be the smugglers? Do you suppose they are storing their smuggled goods down there? It would be a marvellous place, of course.'

'Let's get back to the cave while they are underground,'

said George. 'I'm so afraid Timmy will give the game away by barking. He's just bursting himself trying not to make some sort of noise.'

'Come on, then!' said Julian. 'Don't go across the courtyard – make for the shore and we'll scramble round it till we get to the cave. Then one of us can pop up through the hole and hide behind that big gorse-bush there to see who the smugglers are. They must have come in by boat either from the wreck, or by rowing cleverly through the rocks off-shore.'

They got to the cave at last and went in. But no sooner had Julian shinned up the rope, helped by the others, than Timothy disappeared! He ran out of the cave while the others' backs were turned, and when George turned round there was no Timmy to be seen!

'Timmy!' she called in a low voice. 'Timmy! Where are you?'

But no answer came! Timmy had gone off on his own. If only the smugglers didn't see him! What a bad dog he was to do that!

But Timmy had smelt something exciting – he had smelt a smell he knew – a dog-smell – and he meant to find the owner of it and bite off his ears and tail! 'Gr-r-r-r-r!' Timmy was not going to allow dogs on *his* island!

Julian sat close beside the gorse-bush, watching all round. There was nothing to be seen on the wreck, and there was no ship out to sea. Probably the boat that had brought the strangers to the island was hidden down below among the rocks. Julian looked behind him, towards the castle – and even as he looked, he saw an astonishing sight!

A dog was sniffing about the bushes not far away – and creeping up behind him, all his hackles up, was Timothy! Timothy was stalking the dog as if he were a cat stalking a rabbit! The other dog suddenly heard him and leapt round, facing Timothy. Timmy flung himself on the dog with a blood-curdling howl, and the dog howled in fright.

Julian watched in horror, not knowing what to do. The two dogs made a fearful noise, especially the other dog whose howls of terror and yelps of rage resounded everywhere.

'This will bring the smugglers up, and they will see Timmy and know there's someone on the island,' thought Julian. 'Oh, blow you, Timmy! – why didn't you stay with George and keep quiet?'

From the walls of the ruined castle came three figures, running pell-mell to see what was happening to their dog – and Julian stared at them in the very greatest amazement – for the three people were no other than Mr Stick, Mrs Stick and Edgar!

'Golly!' said Julian, crawling round the bush to get to the hole quickly. 'They've come after us! They've guessed we've gone here and they've come to look for us, the beasts, to make us go back! Well, they won't find us! But oh, what a pity Timmy's given the show away!'

There came a shrill whistle from down below him. It was George, who, hearing the row from the dogs, was feeling worried, and had sent out her piercing whistle for Timmy. It was a whistle the dog always obeyed, and he let go his hold on the dog and shot off to the cliff-top at once, just as the three Sticks arrived on the scene, and picked up their bleeding, whining mongrel.

Edgar tore after Timmy, up to the cliff-top. Julian dropped down to the cave when he spotted Edgar appearing. Timmy ran to the hole and dropped bodily down, landing almost on top of Julian. He flung himself on George.

'Shut up, shut up!' said George, in an urgent whisper to the excited dog. 'Do you want to give our hiding-place away, you idiot?'

Edgar, panting and puffing, arrived on the cliff-top, and was completely amazed to see Timothy apparently disappear into the solid earth. He hunted about for a bit, but it was clear that the dog was no longer on the cliff.

Mr and Mrs Stick came up too. 'Where did that dog go?' shouted Mrs Stick. 'What was he like?'

'He looked awfully like that horrible dog of the children's,' said Edgar. His voice could clearly be heard by everyone down in the cave. The children kept as quiet as mice.

'But it *couldn't* be!' came Mrs Stick's voice. 'The children have gone home – we saw them, *and* the dog too, making off towards the railway. It must be some sort of stray dog left here by a day-tripper.'

'Well, where is he, then?' said Mr Stick's hoarse voice. 'Can't see any dog anywhere about now.'

'He disappeared into the earth,' said Edgar, in a surprised voice.

Mr Stick made a rude and scornful noise. 'You tell lovely tales, you do,' he said. 'Disappeared into the earth! What next? Fell over the cliff, I should think. Well, he got his teeth into poor Tinker good and proper. My word, if I see that dog, I'll get him!'

'He might have some hiding-place about this cliff,' said Mrs Stick. 'Let's have a look!'

The children sat as quiet as mice, George with a warning hand on Timmy's collar. They could hear that the Sticks were really very near. Julian expected one of them to fall down the hole at any moment!

But mercifully they didn't happen on the hole that led down to the cave. They stood quite near to it, though, while they were discussing the problem.

'If it's the children's dog, then those tiresome kids must have come to this island, instead of going home,' said Mrs Stick. 'That would upset our plan all right! We shall have to find out. I'll have no peace till I know.'

'We can soon find out,' said Mr Stick. 'No need to worry about that. Their boat will be here somewhere – and they'll all be about, too! It's impossible for four children, a dog and a boat to be hidden on this small island once anyone starts hunting for them! Edgar, you go round that way. Clara, you get along round about the castle. They may be hiding somewhere in the ruins. I'll have a look about here.'

The children crouched together in the cave. How they hoped that their boat would not be found! How they hoped that no one would find any traces of them at all! Timmy growled softly, wishing that he could go and find that Stinker-dog again! It had been lovely to bite his ears hard.

Edgar was half-scared of finding the children, and a good deal more scared of coming up against Timmy somewhere. So he did not make much of a search for either the children or the boat. He went into the cove where the boat had been pulled up, and although he saw traces where the vessel had been hauled up, barely smoothed out by the sea-water at high-tide, he did not notice the seaweedy prow of the boat sticking out round the rock behind which it was hidden.

'Nothing here!' he called to his mother, who was going round and about the ruins, looking into every likely nook. But she found nothing either, and neither did Mr Stick.

'Couldn't have been the children's dog,' said Mr Stick, at last. 'They'd be here if he was, and so would their boat, but there's no sign of them at all. That dog must have been some wild stray. Have to look out for him, no doubt about it. Gone wild, I should think.'

The children relaxed after about an hour, thinking that the Sticks must have given up looking for them. They boiled the kettle to make some tea, and Anne began to cut some sandwiches. Timmy was tied up in case he wandered out again to look for Stinker.

They ate their tea quietly, not speaking above a whisper. 'The Sticks haven't come here to look for us, after all,' said Julian. 'It's quite plain from what they said that they thought we had gone to catch the train home, taking George and Timmy with us.'

'Then what are they here for?' demanded George, fiercely. 'It's *our* island! They've no right here. Let's go and turn them off! They're scared of Timmy. We'll take him with us and say we'll set him on to them if they don't clear out.'

'No, George,' said Julian. 'Do be sensible. We don't want them rushing off and telling your father we are here, or he may lose his temper and come flying home to order us back. And – there's another thing I've thought of.'

'What?' asked the others, seeing Julian's eyes gleam in the way they did when he had an idea.

'Well,' said Julian, 'don't you think it's possible that the Sticks are something to do with the smugglers? Don't you think they may come here to take off smuggled goods, or to hide them till they can take them off in safety? Mr Stick is a sailor, isn't he? He would know all about smuggling. I bet he's in the pay of the smugglers all right.'

'I believe you're right!' said George, in excitement. 'Well – we'll wait till the Sticks have gone, and then we'll go down into the dungeons and see if they've hidden anything there! We'll find out their little game and stop it! It will be terribly thrilling, won't it?'

CHAPTER SIXTEEN

The Sticks get a fright

BUT THE Sticks didn't go! The children peeped out of the spy-hole at the top of the cave-roof every now and again, and saw one or other of the Sticks. The evening went on and it began to be dark. Still the Sticks didn't go. Julian ran down to the nearby shore and discovered a small boat there. So the Sticks had managed to find their way round the island, rowed near the wreck, maybe landed on it too, and then came to the shore, cleverly avoiding the rocks they might strike against.

'It looks as if the Sticks have come to stay for the night,' said Julian, gloomily. 'This is going to spoil our stay here, isn't it? We rush away here to escape from the Sticks – and lo and behold! the Sticks are on top of us again. It's too bad.'

'Let's frighten them,' said George, her eyes shining by the light of the one candle in the cave.

'What do you mean?' said Dick, cheering up. He always liked George's ideas, mad as they sometimes were.

'Well, I suppose they must be living down in one of the dungeon rooms, mustn't they?' said George. 'There is no place in the ruins to live in proper shelter, or we'd be there ourselves – and the only other place is down in the dungeons. I wouldn't care to sleep there myself, but I don't suppose the Sticks would mind.'

'Well, what about it?' said Dick. 'What's your idea?'

'Couldn't we creep down, and do a bit of shouting, so that the echoes start up all round?' said George. 'You know how frightening we found the echoes when we first went down into the dungeons. We only had to say one or two words, and the echoes began saying them over and over again shouting them back at us.'

'Oh yes, I remember,' said Anne. 'And wasn't Timmy frightened when he barked! The echoes barked back at him, and he thought there were thousands of dogs hiding down there! He was awfully frightened.'

'It's a good idea,' said Julian. 'Serve the Sticks right for coming to our island like this! If we can frighten them away, that would be one up to us! Let's do it.'

'What about Timothy?' said Anne. 'Hadn't we better leave him behind?'

'No. He can come and stand at the dungeon entrance to guard it for us,' said George. 'Then if any of the real smugglers happened to come, Timmy could give us warning. I'm not going to leave him behind.'

'Come on, then, let's go now!' said Julian. 'It would be a fine trick to play. It's quite dark, but I've got my torch, and as soon as we are certain that the Sticks are down in the dungeons, we can start to play our joke.'

There was no sign or sound of the Sticks anywhere about. No light of fire or candle was to be seen, no sound of voices to be heard. Either they had gone, or they were below in the dungeons. The stones had been taken from the entrance, so the children felt sure they were down there.

'Now, Timmy, you stay quite still and quiet here,' whispered George to Timmy. 'Bark if anyone comes, but not unless. We're going down into the dungeons.'

'I think perhaps I'll stay up here with Timothy,' said Anne, suddenly. She didn't like the dark look of the dungeon entrance. 'You see, George – Timmy might be frightened or lonely up here by himself.'

The others chuckled. They knew Anne was frightened. Julian squeezed her arm. 'You stay here, then,' he said, kindly. 'You keep old Timmy company.'

Then Julian, George and Dick went down the long flight of steps that led into the deep old dungeons of Kirrin Castle. They had been there the summer before, when they had been seeking for lost treasure; now here they were again!

They crept down the steps and came to the many cellars or dungeons cut out of the rock below the castle. There were scores of those, some big and some small, weird, damp underground rooms in which, maybe, unhappy prisoners had been kept in the olden days.

The children crept down the dark passages. Julian had a piece of white chalk with him, and drew a chalk line here and there on the rocky walls as he went, so that he might easily find the way back.

Suddenly they heard voices and saw a light. They stopped and whispered softly together in each other's ears.

'They're in that room where we found the treasure last year! That's where they're camping out! What noises shall we make?'

'I'll be a cow,' said Dick. 'I can moo awfully like a cow. I'll be a cow.'

'I'll be a sheep,' said Julian. 'George, you be a horse. You can whinny and hrrrumph just like a horse. Dick, you begin!'

So Dick began. Hidden behind a rocky pillar, he opened his mouth and mooed dolefully, like a cow in pain. At once the echoes took up the mooing, magnified it, sent it along all the underground passages, till it seemed as if a thousand cows had wandered there and were mooing together.

'Moo – oo – oo – oooooooo, ooo – oo – MOOOOOOO!'

The Sticks listened in amazement and fright at the sudden awful noise.

'What is it, Ma?' said Edgar, almost in tears. Stinker crouched at the back of the cave, terrified.

'It's cows,' said Mr Stick, amazed. 'I think it's cows. Can't you hear the moos? But how did cows get to be here?'

'Nonsense!' said Mrs Stick, recovering herself a little. 'Cows down these caves! You're mad! You'll be telling me there's sheep next!'

It was funny that she should have said that, for Julian chose that moment to begin baa-ing like a flock of sheep. His one long, bleating 'baa-baa-aa-aa' was taken up by the echoes at once, and it seemed suddenly as if hundreds of poor lost sheep were baa-ing their way down the dungeons!

Mr Stick jumped to his feet, as white as a sheet.

'Well, if it isn't sheep now!' he said. 'What's up? What's in these 'ere dungeons? I never did like them.'

'Baa-baa-baa-aa-AAAAAAAAAA!' went the mournful bleats all round and about. And then George started her whinnying and neighing, just like an impatient horse. The little girl tossed her head in the darkness and hrrrumphed exactly like a horse and then she stamped with her foot, and at once the echoes stamped too, sending her whinnying and neighing and stamping into the Sticks's cave twenty times louder than George had made them.

Poor Stinker began to whine pitifully. He was frightened almost out of his life. He pressed himself against the floor as if he would like to disappear into it. Edgar clutched his mother's arm. 'Let's go up,' he said. 'I can't stay here. There're hundreds of sheep and horses and cows roaming these dungeons, you can hear them. They're not real, but they've got voices and hoofs, and I'm scared of them.'

Mr Stick went to the door of the room they were in, and shouted loudly.

'Get out, you! Clear out! Whoever you are!'

George giggled. Then she shouted out in a very deep, hoarse voice.

'BE-WARE!' And the echoes thundered out all round.

''WARE! 'WARE! 'WARE-ARE-ARE!'

Mr Stick went back quickly into the cave-room, and lit another candle. He shut the big wooden door that led into the room. His hands were shaking.

'Peculiar goings-on,' he said. 'Shan't stay here much longer if we get this kind of thing happening every night.'

Julian, Dick and George were now in such a state of giggles that they could not imitate any more cows, horses or sheep. George did begin to be a pig, and gave such a realistic snort and grunt that Dick nearly died of laughing. The snorts and grunts were echoed everywhere.

'Come out,' gasped Julian, at last. 'I shall burst with trying not to laugh. Come out!'

'Come out!' whispered the echoes. 'Come out, out, out!'

They stumbled out, stuffing hankies into their mouths as they went, following Julian's chalk marks easily by the light of his torch. It was impossible to take the wrong passage if they followed his guiding lines.

They sat on the dungeon steps with Anne and Timmy, and choked with laughter as they related all they had done. 'We heard old Stick yelling to us to clear out,' said George, 'and he sounded scared stiff. As for Stinker, we never heard even the smallest growl from him. I bet the Sticks will clear off tomorrow after this! It must have given them a most terrible fright.'

'Oh, that was grand!' said Julian. 'It was a pity I began to laugh. I was just feeling I might trumpet like an elephant next. The echoes would like that!'

'Funny the Sticks all staying on the island like this,' said Dick, thoughtfully. 'They've left Kirrin Cottage – but they're not looking for us. They must be in league with the smugglers all right. Perhaps that's why Mrs Stick took the job with your mother, George – to be near the island when the time came – when the smugglers wanted their help.'

'We could really go back to Kirrin Cottage, couldn't we?' said Anne, who, much as she loved the island, was not nearly so keen on it now that the Sticks were there.

'Go back! Leave an adventure just when it's beginning!' said George, scornfully. 'How silly you are, Anne. Go back if you want to – but I'm sure nobody will go with you.'

'Oh, Anne will stay with us all right,' said Julian, knowing that Anne would feel hurt at the suggestion she should leave them. 'It will be the Sticks who have to go, don't worry!'

'Let's go back to the cave,' said Anne, thinking longingly of its safety and bright little candle. They got up and made their way across the courtyard to the little wall that ran round the castle. They climbed over it and turned their steps to the cliff. Julian switched on his torch when he thought it was safe, for it was impossible to see clearly in the dark, and he did not want any of them to fall down the hole, instead of climbing down properly by the rope.

Julian stood by the hole at last, shining his torch so that the others might climb down the rope in safety, one by one. He glanced up, looking over the dark sea as he stood there, and then stared intently.

There was a light out to sea, and it was signalling. It must have seen his torch-light! Julian watched, wondering if it was a ship that was signalling, and how far out it was, and why it was signalling.

'Perhaps they're going to put more stuff into the old wreck for the Sticks to find,' he thought. 'I wonder if they are. How I'd like to find out – but it would be dangerous to go there in daylight in case the Sticks see us.'

The signalling went on for a long time, as if a message was being flashed. Julian could not for the life of him make out what it was. It simply looked like the flash-flash-flash of a lantern to him. But it must mean a signal or message of some sort to the Sticks.

'Well, they won't get it tonight!' thought Julian, with a chuckle, when at last the signalling stopped. 'I rather think the Stick family will stay where they are tonight, too scared of sheep and cows and horses rushing about in those dungeons!'

Julian was quite right – the Sticks did stay where they were! Nothing would get them out of their underground room till morning.

CHAPTER SEVENTEEN

A shock for Edgar

THE CHILDREN slept well that night, and as Timothy did not growl at all, they were sure that nothing important could have happened. They had a fine breakfast of tongue, tinned peaches, bread and butter, golden syrup and ginger-beer.

'That's the end of the ginger-beer, I'm afraid,' said Julian, regretfully. 'I must say ginger-beer is a gorgeous drink – seems to go with simply everything.'

'That was the nicest meal I've ever had,' said Anne. 'It really was. We do have lovely meals on Kirrin Island. I wonder if the Sticks are having nice meals too.'

'You bet they are!' said Dick. 'I expect they have ransacked Aunt Fanny's cupboards and taken the best they can find.'

'Oh, the beasts!' said George, her eyes flashing. 'I never thought of that – they may have robbed the house and taken all kinds of things.'

'They probably have,' said Julian, and he frowned. 'I say, I never thought of that, somehow. How awful, George, if your mother came back, feeling ill and weak, and found half her belongings gone!'

'Oh dear!' said Anne, dismayed. 'George, wouldn't that be dreadful?'

'Yes,' said George, looking very angry. 'I would believe anything of those Sticks! If they have the cheek to come to our island and live here, they've the cheek to steal from my mother's house. I wish we could find out.'

'They could have brought quite a lot of things away in their boat,' said Julian. 'They must have come here by boat. If they did bring stolen goods, they must have put them somewhere – down in the dungeons, I suppose.'

'We might have a look round and see if we can spy anything, without the Sticks seeing us,' suggested Dick.

'Let's have a look round now,' said George, who always liked doing things at once. 'Anne, you do the washing-up and tidy our cave-house for us, will you?'

Anne was torn between wanting to go with the others, and longing to play 'house' again. She did so love arranging everything and making the beds and tidying up the cave. In the end she said she would stay and the others could go.

So up the rope they went. Timothy stayed with Anne, because they were afraid he might bark. Anne tied him up, and he whined a little, but did not make a terrible noise.

The other three lay flat on the cliff-top, looking down on the ruined castle. There seemed to be no one about, but, even as they watched, the three Sticks appeared, apparently coming up from the dungeons. They seemed glad to be in the sunshine, and the children were not surprised, for the dungeons were so cold and dark.

The Sticks looked all round. Stinker kept close to Mrs Stick, his tail well down.

'They're looking for the cows and sheep and horses they heard down in the dungeons last night!' whispered Dick to Julian.

The Sticks spoke together for a minute or two, and then went off in the direction of the shore that faced the wreck. Edgar went to the room in which the children had first planned to sleep – the one whose roof had fallen in.

'I'm going to stalk the two Sticks,' whispered Julian to the others. 'You two see what Edgar is up to.'

Julian disappeared, keeping behind bushes as he watched where the Sticks went, and followed them. George and Dick went cautiously and quietly over the cliff to the castle in the middle of the little island. They could hear Edgar whistling. Stinker was running about the courtyard of the castle.

Edgar appeared out of the ruined room, carrying a pile of cushions, which had evidently been stored there. George went red with rage and clutched Dick's arm fiercely.

'Mother's best cushions!' she whispered. 'Oh, the beasts!'

Dick felt angry too. It was quite plain that the Sticks had helped themselves to anything handy when they had left Kirrin Cottage. He picked up a clod of earth, took careful aim, and flung it into the air. It fell between Edgar and Stinker, breaking into a shower of earth.

Edgar dropped the cushions, and looked up into the air in fright. It was plain that he thought something had fallen from the sky. George picked up another clod, took aim, and flung it higher into the air. It fell all over Stinker, and the dog gave a yelp, and scuttled down the hole that led into the dungeons.

Edgar looked up into the sky and then all around and about him, his mouth wide open. What could be happening? Dick waited until he was looking in the opposite direction, and then once more sent a big clod into the air. It fell into his bits and scattered itself all over the startled Edgar.

Then Dick gave one of his realistic moos, exactly like a cow in pain, and Edgar stood rooted to the spot, almost frightened out of his skin. Those cows again! Where were they?

Dick mooed again, and Edgar gave a yell, found his feet, and almost fell down the dungeon steps. He disappeared with a dismal howl, leaving behind all the cushions on the ground.

'Quick!' said Dick, jumping to his feet. 'He won't be back for a few minutes, anyhow. He'll be too scared. Let's grab the cushions and bring them here. I don't see why the Sticks should use them down in those awful old dungeons.'

The two children raced to the courtyard, picked up the cushions and raced back to their hiding-place. Dick looked across to the room where Edgar had brought them from.

'What about slipping across there and seeing what else they've stored away?' he said. 'I don't see why they should be allowed to have anything that isn't theirs.'

'I'll go across, and you keep watch by the dungeon entrance,' said George. 'You've only got to moo again if you see Edgar, and he'll run for miles.'

'Right,' said Dick, with a grin, and went swiftly to the flight of steps that led underground to the dungeons. There was no sign of Edgar at all, nor of Stinker.

George went to the ruined room and gazed round in anger. Yes, the Sticks certainly *had* helped themselves to her mother's things, no doubt about that! There were blankets and silver and all kinds of food. Mrs Stick must have gone into the big cupboard under the stairs and taken out various things stored there for weekly use.

George ran to Dick. 'There are heaps of our things!' she said, in a fierce whisper. 'Come and help me to get them. We'll see if we can take them all before Edgar appears, or the Sticks come back.'

Just as they were whispering together, they heard a low whistle. They looked round, and saw Julian coming along. He joined them.

'The Sticks have rowed off to the wreck,' he said. 'They've got an old boat somewhere down among those rocks. Old Pa Stick must be a good sailor to be able to take the boat in and out of those awful hidden rocks.'

'Oh, then we've got time to do what we want to do,'

said Dick, pleased. He hurriedly told Julian of the things George had seen in the ruined room.

'Awful thieves!' said Julian, indignantly. 'They don't mean to go back to Kirrin Cottage, that's plain. They've got some business on with the smugglers here – and when that is done they'll go off with all their stolen goods, join a ship somewhere, and get off scot-free.'

'No, they won't,' said George at once. 'We are going to get everything and take it to the cave! Dick's going to keep watch for Edgar at the cave entrance, and you and I, Julian, can quickly carry the things away. We can drop them down the hole into the cave.'

'Hurry then!' said Julian. 'We must do it before the Sticks return, and I don't expect they'll be long. They've probably gone to fetch the trunk and anything else in the wreck. You know I saw a light out to sea last night – maybe that's a signal that the smugglers were leaving something in the wreck for the Sticks to fetch.'

George and Julian ran to the ruined room, piled their arms with the goods there, and then ran to hide them on the cliff, ready to take them to the hole when they had time. It looked as if the Sticks had just taken whatever was easiest to lay their hands on. They had even got the kitchen clock!

Edgar did not appear at all, so Dick had nothing to do but sit by the steps of the dungeon and watch the others. After some time Julian and George gave a sigh of relief and beckoned to Dick. He left his place and went to join them.

'We've got everything now,' said Julian. 'I'm just going to the cliff-edge to see if the Sticks are returning yet. If they're not we'll all carry the things to the hole in the roof of the cave.'

He soon returned. 'I can see their boat tied to the wreck,' he said. 'We're safe for some while yet. Come on, let's get the things to safety! This really is a bit of luck.'

They carried the things to the hole and called down it to Anne. 'Anne! We've got tons of things to put down the hole. Stand by to catch!'

Soon all kinds of things came down the hole into the cave! Anne was most astonished. The silver and anything that might be hurt by a fall was first wrapped up in the blankets, and then let down by a rope.

'My goodness!' said Anne. 'This cave will *really* look like a house soon, when I have arranged all these things too!'

Just as they were finishing their job the children heard voices in the distance.

'The Sticks are back!' said Julian, and looked cautiously over the cliff-top. He was right. They had returned to their boat, and were even now on their way back to the castle, carrying the trunk from the wreck.

'Let's follow them, and see what happens when they find everything gone,' grinned Julian. 'Come on, everyone!'

They wriggled over the cliff on their tummies, and came to a clump of bushes behind which they could hide and watch. The Sticks put the trunk down, and looked round for Edgar. But Edgar was nowhere to be seen.

'Where's that boy?' said Mrs Stick, impatiently. 'He's had plenty of time to do everything. Edgar! Edgar! Edgar!'

Mr Stick went to the ruined room and peeped inside. He came back to Mrs Stick.

'He's taken everything down,' he said. 'He must be down in the dungeon. That room's quite empty.'

'I told him to come up and sit in the sun when he'd finished,' said Mrs Stick. 'It isn't healthy down in those dungeons. EDGAR!'

This time Edgar heard, and his head appeared, looking out of the entrance to the dungeon. He looked extremely scared.

'Come on up!' said Mrs Stick. 'You've got all the things

down, and you'd better stay up here in the sunshine now.'

'I'm scared,' said Edgar. 'I'm not staying up here alone.'

'Why not?' said Mr Stick, astonished.

'It's those cows again!' said poor Edgar. 'Hundreds of them, Pa, all a-mooing round me, and throwing things at me. They're dangerous animals, they are, and I'm not coming up here alone!'

CHAPTER EIGHTEEN

An unexpected prisoner

THE STICKS stared at Edgar as if he was mad.

'Cows throwing things?' said Mrs Stick at last. 'What do you mean by that? Cows don't throw anything.'

'These ones did,' said Edgar, and then began to exaggerate in order to make his parents sympathise with him. 'They were dreadful cows, they were – hundreds of them, with horns as long as reindeer, and awful mooing voices. And they threw things at me and Tinker. He was really scared, and so was I. I dropped the cushions I was taking down, and rushed away to hide.'

'Where are the cushions?' said Mr Stick, looking round. 'I can't see any cushions. I suppose you'll tell us the cows ate them.'

'Didn't you take everything down into the dungeons?' demanded Mrs Stick. 'Because that room's empty now. There's not a thing in it.'

'I didn't take anything down at all,' said Edgar, coming cautiously out of the dungeon entrance. 'I dropped the cushions just about where you're standing. What's happened to them?'

'Look 'ere!' said Mr Stick, in amazement. 'Who's been 'ere since we've been gone? Someone's taken the cushions and everything else too. Where have they put them?'

'Pa, it was the cows,' said Edgar, looking all round as if he expected to see cows walking off with cushions and silver and blankets.

'Shut up about the cows,' said Mrs Stick, suddenly losing her temper. 'For one thing there aren't any cows on this island, and that we do know, for we looked all over it this morning. What we heard last night must have been strange sort of echoes rumbling round. No, my boy – there's something funny about all this. Looks as if there *is* somebody on the island!'

A dismal howl came echoing up from below the ground. It was Stinker, terrified at being alone below, and not daring to come up.

'Poor lamb!' said Mrs Stick, who seemed much fonder of Stinker than of anyone else.

'What's up with him?'

Stinker let out an even more doleful howl, and Mrs Stick hurried down the steps to go to him. Mr Stick followed her, and Edgar lost no time in going after them.

'Quick!' said Julian, standing up. 'Come with me, Dick. We may just have time to get that trunk! Run!'

The two boys ran quickly down to the courtyard of the ruined castle. Each took a handle of the small trunk, and lifted it between them. They staggered back to George with it.

'We'll take it to the cave,' whispered Julian. 'You stay here a few minutes and see what happens.'

The boys went over the cliff with the trunk. George flattened herself behind her bush and watched. Mr Stick appeared again in a few minutes, and looked round for the trunk. His mouth fell open in astonishment when he saw that it was gone. He yelled down the entrance to the dungeon.

'Clara! The trunk's gone!'

Mrs Stick was already on her way up, with Stinker close beside her and Edgar just behind. She climbed out and stared round.

'Gone?' she said, in enormous surprise. 'Gone! Where's it gone?'

'That's what *I'd* like to know!' said Mr Stick. 'We leave it here a few minutes – and then it goes. Walks off by itself – just like all the other things!'

'Look here! There's someone on this island,' said Mrs Stick. 'And I'm going to find out who it is. Got your gun, Pa?'

'I have,' said Mr Stick, slapping his belt. 'You get a good stout stick too, and we'll take Tinker. If we don't ferret out whoever's trying to spoil our plans, my name's not Stick!'

George slipped away quietly to warn the others. Before she slid down the rope into the cave, she pulled several bramble sprays across the hole. She dropped down to the floor of the cave, and told the others what had happened.

Julian had been trying to open the trunk, but it was still

locked. He looked up as George panted out her tale.

'We'll be all right here so long as no one falls down that hole in the roof!' he said. 'Now keep quiet everyone, and don't you dare to growl, Timmy!'

Nothing was heard for some time, and then Stinker's bark came in the distance. 'Quiet now,' said Julian. 'They are near here.'

The Sticks were up on the cliff once more, searching carefully behind every bush. They came to the great bush behind which the children often hid, and saw the flattened grass there.

'Someone's been here,' said Mr Stick. 'I wonder if they're in the middle of this bush – it's thick enough to hide half an army! I'll try and force my way in, Clara, while you stand by with my gun.'

Edgar wandered off by himself while this was happening, feeling certain that nobody would be foolish enough to live in the middle of such a prickly bush. He walked across the cliff – and then, to his awful horror, he found himself falling! His legs disappeared into a hole, he clutched at some thorny sprays but could not save himself. Down he went and down and down – and down – crash!

Edgar had fallen down the hole in the roof of the cave. He suddenly appeared before the children's startled eyes, and landed in a heap on the soft sand. Timmy at once pounced on him with a fearsome growl, but George pulled him off just in time.

Edgar was half-stunned with fright and his fall. He lay on the floor of the cave, groaning, his eyes shut. The children stared at him and then at one another. For a few moments they were completely taken aback and didn't know what to do or say. Timmy growled ferociously – so ferociously that Edgar opened his eyes in fright. He stared round at the four children and their dog in the utmost surprise and horror.

He opened his mouth to yell for help, but at once found Julian's large hand over it. 'Yell just once and Timmy shall have a bite out of any part of you he likes!' said Julian, in a voice as ferocious as Timothy's growl. 'See? Like to try it? Timmy's waiting to bite.'

'I shan't yell,' said Edgar, speaking in such a low whisper that the others could hardly hear him. 'Keep that dog off. I shan't yell.'

George spoke to Timothy. 'Now you listen, Timothy – if this boy shouts, you just go for him! Lie here by him and show him your big teeth. Bite him wherever you like if he yells.'

'Woof!' said Timmy, looking really pleased. He lay down by Edgar, and the boy tried to move away. But Timmy came nearer every time he moved.

Edgar looked round at the children. 'What are you doing on this island?' he said. 'We thought you'd gone home.'

'It's *our* island!' said George, in a very fierce voice. 'We've every right to be on it if we want to – but you have no right at all. None! What are you and your father and mother here for?'

'Don't know,' said Edgar, looking sulky.

'You'd better tell us,' said Julian. 'We know you're in league with smugglers.'

Edgar looked startled. 'Smugglers?' he said. 'I didn't know that. Pa and Ma don't tell me anything. I don't want anything to do with smugglers.'

'Don't you know *any*-thing?' said Dick. 'Don't you know why you've come to Kirrin Island?'

'I don't know anything,' said Edgar, in an injured tone. 'Pa and Ma are mean to me. They never tell me anything. I do as I'm told, that's all. I don't know anything about smugglers, I tell you that.'

It was quite plain to the children that Edgar really did not know anything of the reasons for his parents coming to the island. 'Well, I'm not surprised they don't let Spotty-Face into their secrets,' said Julian. 'He'd blab them if he could, I bet. Anyway, we know it's smuggling they're mixed up in.'

'You let me go,' said Edgar, sullenly. 'You've got no right to keep me here.'

'We're not going to let you go,' said George at once.

'You're our prisoner now. If we let you go back to your parents, you'd tell them all about us, and we don't want them to know we're here. We're going to spoil their pretty plans, you see.'

Edgar saw. He saw quite a lot of things. He felt rather sick. 'Was it you that took the cushions and things?'

'Oh no, dear Edgar,' said Dick. 'It was the cows, wasn't it? Don't you remember how you told your mother about the hundreds of cows that mooed at you and threw things and stole the cushions you dropped? Surely you haven't forgotten your cows already?'

'Funny, aren't you?' said Edgar, sulkily. 'What you going to do with me? I won't stay here, that's flat.'

'But you will, Spotty-Face,' said Julian. 'You will stay here till we let you go – and that won't be till we've cleared up this little smuggling mystery. And let me warn you that any nonsense on your part will be punished by Timmy.'

'Lot of beasts you are,' said Edgar, seeing that he could do nothing but obey the four children. 'My pa and ma won't half be furious with you.'

His ma and pa were feeling extremely astonished. There had, of course, been nobody hiding in the big thick bush, and when Mr Stick had wriggled out, scratched and bleeding, he had looked round for Edgar. And Edgar was not to be seen.

'Where's that dratted boy?' he said, and shouted for him. 'Edgar! ED-GAR!'

But Edgar did not answer. The Sticks spent a very long time looking for Edgar, both above ground and underground. Mrs Stick was convinced that poor Edgar was lost in the dungeons, and she tried to send Stinker to find him. But Stinker only went as far as the first cave. He remembered the peculiar noises of the night before and was not at all keen on exploring the dungeons.

Julian turned his attention to the little trunk, once Edgar had been dealt with. 'I'm going to open this somehow,' he said. 'I'm sure it's got smuggled goods in, though goodness knows what.'

'You'll have to smash the locks then,' said Dick. Julian got a small rock and tried to smash the two locks. He managed to wrench one open after a while, and then the other gave way too. The children threw back the lid.

On the top was a child's blanket, embroidered with white rabbits. Julian pulled it off, expecting to see the smuggled goods below. But to his astonishment there were a child's clothes!

He pulled them out. There were two blue jerseys, a blue skirt, some vests and knickers and a warm coat. At the bottom of the trunk were some dolls and a teddy bear!

'Golly!' said Julian, in amazement. 'What are all these for? Why did the Sticks bring these to the island – and why did the smugglers hide them in the wreck? It's a puzzler!'

Edgar appeared to be as astonished as the rest. He too had expected valuable goods of some kind. George and Anne pulled out the dolls. They were lovely ones. Anne cuddled them up to her. She loved dolls, though George scorned them.

'Who do they belong to?' she said. 'Oh won't they be sad not to have them! Julian, isn't it funny? *Why* should anyone bring a trunk full of clothes and dolls to Kirrin Island?

CHAPTER NINETEEN

A scream in the night

NOBODY COULD even guess the answers to Anne's surprised questions. The children stared into the trunk and puzzled over it. It seemed such a funny thing to smuggle. They remembered the other things in the wreck too – the tins of food. They were peculiar things to smuggle on to the island. There didn't seem any point in it.

'Funny,' said Dick, at last. 'It beats me. There's no doubt that strange things are afoot here, or the Sticks wouldn't be hanging around our island. And we've seen signals from a ship out to sea. Something's going on. We thought if we opened this trunk it might help us – but it's only made the mystery deeper.'

Just then the voices of the two parent Sticks could be heard shouting for Edgar. But Edgar did not dare to shout back. Timmy's nose was poked against his leg. He might be nipped at any time. Timmy growled every now and again to remind Edgar that he was still there.

'Do you know anything about the ship that signals to this island at night?' asked Julian, turning to Edgar.

The boy shook his head. 'Never heard of any signals,' he said. 'I just heard my mother saying that she expected the *Roamer* tonight, but I don't know what she meant.'

'The *Roamer*?' said George, at once. 'What's that – a man – or a boat – or what?'

'I don't know,' said Edgar. 'I'd only have got a clip on the ear if I'd asked. Find out yourself.'

'We will,' said Julian, grimly. 'We'll watch out for the *Roamer* tonight! Thanks for the information.'

The children spent a quiet and rather boring day in the cave – all but Anne, who had plenty of things to arrange again. Really, the cave looked most home-like when she had finished! She put the blankets on the bed, and used the rugs as carpets. So the cave really looked most imposing!

Edgar was not allowed to go out of the cave, and Timothy didn't leave him for a moment. He slept most of the time, complaining that 'those cows and things' had frightened him so much the night before that he'd not been able to sleep a wink.

The others discussed their plans in low voices. They decided to keep watch on the cliff-top, two and two together, that night. They would wait and see what happened. If the *Roamer* came, they would hurriedly make fresh plans then.

The sun sank. The night came up dark over the sea. Edgar snored softly, after a very good supper of sardines, corned beef sandwiches, tinned apricots and tinned milk. Anne and Dick went up to keep the first watch. It was about half past ten.

At half past twelve Julian and George climbed up the

knotted rope and joined the other two. They had nothing to report. They went down into the cave, got into their comfortable beds and went to sleep. Edgar was snoring away in his corner, Timmy still on guard.

Julian and George looked out to sea, watching for any sign of a ship. The moon was up that night, and things were not quite so dark. Suddenly they heard low voices, and saw shadowy figures down by the rocks below.

'The two Sticks,' whispered Julian. 'Going to row out to the wreck again, I suppose.'

There was the splash of oars, and the children saw a boat move out over the water. At the same time George nudged Julian violently and pointed out to sea. A light was being shown a good way out, from a ship that the children could barely see. Then the moon went behind a cloud, and they could see nothing for some time.

They watched breathlessly. Was that shadowy ship a good way out the *Roamer*? Or was the owner of it the 'Roamer'? Were the smugglers at work tonight?

'There's another boat coming – look!' said George. 'It must be coming from that ship out to sea. Now the moon has come out again, you can just see it. It is going to the old wreck. It must be a meeting-place, I should think.'

Then, most irritatingly, the moon went behind a cloud again, and remained there so long that the children grew impatient. At last it sailed out again and lit up the water.

'Both boats are leaving the wreck now,' said Julian excitedly. 'They've had their meeting – and passed over the smuggled goods, I suppose – and now one boat is returning to the ship, and the other, the Sticks' boat, is coming back here with the goods. We'll follow the Sticks when they get back and see where they put the goods.'

After a long time the Sticks' boat came to shore again. The children could not see anything then, but presently they saw the Sticks going back towards the castle. Mr Stick carried what looked like a large bundle, flung over his shoulder. They could not see if Mrs Stick carried anything.

The Sticks went into the courtyard of the castle, and came to the dungeon entrance. 'They're taking the smuggled goods down there,' whispered Julian to George. The children were now watching from behind a nearby wall. 'We'll go back and tell the others, and make some more plans. We must somehow or other get those goods ourselves, and take them back to the mainland and get in touch with the police!'

Just then a scream rang out in the night. It was a high-pitched, terrified scream, and frightened the watching children very much. They had no idea where it came from.

'Quick! It must be Anne!' said Julian, and the two ran as fast as they could to the hole that led down to the cave. They dropped down the rope and Julian looked round the quiet cave anxiously. What had happened to Anne to make her scream like that?

But Anne was peacefully asleep on her bed, and so was Dick. Edgar still snored and Timmy watched, his eyes gleaming green.

'Funny,' said Julian, still startled. 'Awfully funny. Who

screamed like that? It couldn't possibly have been Anne – because if she had screamed in her sleep like that, she would have woken the others.'

'Well, who screamed, then?' said George, feeling rather scared. 'Wasn't it weird, Julian? I didn't like it. It was somebody who was awfully frightened. But who could it be?'

They woke Dick and Anne and told them about the strange scream. Anne was very startled. Dick was interested to hear that two boats had met at the wreck, and that the Sticks had brought back smuggled goods of some sort, and taken them down in the dungeons.

'We'll get those tomorrow, somehow!' he said, cheerfully. 'We'll have good fun.'

'Why did you think it was me screaming?' asked Anne. 'Did you think it was a girl screaming?'

'Yes. It sounded like the scream you give when one of us jumps out at you suddenly,' said Julian.

'It's funny,' said Anne. She cuddled down into her bed again, and George got in beside her.

'Oh, Anne!' said George, in disgust. 'You've got our bed simply *full* of those dolls – and that teddy bear is here too! You really are a baby!'

'No, I'm not,' said Anne. 'The dolls and the bear are babies – they are frightened and lonely because they're not with the little girl they belong to. So I had them in bed with me instead! I'm sure the little girl would be glad.'

'The little girl!' said Julian, slowly. 'We thought we

heard a little girl scream tonight – we found a small trunk full of a little girl's clothes, and a little girl's dolls. What does it all mean?'

There was a silence – and then Anne spoke excitedly. 'I know! The smuggled goods are a little girl! They've stolen a little girl away – and these are her dolls, and those over there are her clothes that were stolen at the same time, for her to dress in and play with. The little girl's here, on this island now – you heard her scream tonight when those horrid Sticks carried her down into the dungeons!'

'Well – I do believe Anne has hit on the right idea,' said Julian. 'Clever girl, Anne! I think you're right. It isn't smugglers who are using this island – it's kidnappers!'

'What are kidnappers?' said Anne.

'People who steal away children or grown-ups and hide them somewhere till a large sum of money is paid out for them,' explained Julian. 'It's called a ransom. Till the ransom is paid, the prisoner is held by the captors.'

'Well, that's what's happened here then!' said George.

'I bet it has! Some poor little rich girl has been stolen away – and brought to the wreck by boat from some ship – and taken over by those horrible Sticks. Wicked creatures!'

'And we heard the poor little thing scream just as she was taken down underground,' said George. 'Julian, we've got to rescue her.'

'Yes, of course,' said Julian. 'We will, never fear! We'll rescue her tomorrow.'

Edgar woke up and joined in the conversation suddenly. 'What you talking about?' he said. 'Rescue who?'

'Never you mind,' said Julian.

George nudged him and whispered.

'All I hope is that Mrs Stick is feeling as upset about losing her dear Edgar as the mother of the little girl,' she said.

'Tomorrow we find the little girl somehow, and take her away,' said Julian. 'I expect the Sticks will be on guard, but we'll find a way.'

'I'm tired now,' said George, lying down. 'Let's go to sleep. We'll wake up nice and fresh. Oh, Anne, do put these dolls your side. I'm lying on at least three.'

Anne took the dolls and the bear and arranged them on her side of the bed. 'Don't feel lonely,' George heard her say. 'I'll look after you all right till you go back to your own mistress. Sleep tight!'

Soon they all slept – all but Timothy, who lay with one eye open all night long. There was no need to put anyone on guard while Timmy was there. He was the best guardian they could have.

CHAPTER TWENTY

A rescue – and a new prisoner!

THE NEXT day Julian was awake early and went up the rope to the cliff-top to see if the Sticks were about. He saw them coming up the steps that led from the dungeons. Mrs Stick looked pale and worried.

'We've got to find our Edgar,' she kept saying to Mr Stick. 'I tell you we've got to find our Edgar. He's not down in the dungeons. That I do know. We've yelled ourselves hoarse down there.'

'And he's not on the island,' said Mr Stick. 'We hunted all over it yesterday. I think whoever was here then, took our goods, caught Edgar, and made off with him and everything else in their boat. That's what I think.'

'Well, they've taken him to the mainland then,' said Mrs Stick. 'We'd better take our boat and go back there and ask a few questions. What I'd like to know is – who is it messing about here and interfering with our plans? It makes me scared. Just when things are going nicely too!'

'Is it all right to leave here just now?' said Mr Stick, doubtfully. 'Suppose whoever was here yesterday is still here – they might pop down into the dungeons when we're gone.'

'Well, they're not here,' said Mrs Stick, firmly. 'Use

your common sense, if you've got any – wouldn't our Edgar yell the place down if he was being kept prisoner on this little island – and wouldn't we hear him? I tell you he must have been taken off in a boat, together with all the other things that are gone. And I don't like it.'

'All right, all right!' said Mr Stick, in a grumbling tone. 'That boy's always a nuisance – always in silly trouble of some sort.'

'How can you talk of poor Edgar like that?' cried Mrs Stick. 'Do you think the poor child *likes* being captured! Goodness knows what he's going through – feeling frightened and lonely without me.'

Julian felt disgusted. Here was Mrs Stick talking like that about old Spotty-Face – and yet she had a little girl down in the dungeons – a child much younger than Edgar! What a beast she was.

'What about Tinker?' said Mr Stick, in a sulky tone. 'Better leave him here, hadn't we, to guard the entrance to the dungeons? Not that there will be anyone here, if what you say is right.'

'Oh, we'll leave Tinker,' said Mrs Stick, setting off to the boat. Julian saw them embark, leaving the dog behind. Tinker watched them rowing away, his tail well down between his legs. Then he turned and ran back to the courtyard, and lay down dolefully in the sun. He was very uneasy. His ears were cocked and he kept looking this way and that. He didn't like this strange island and its unexpected noises.

Julian tore back to the cave and dropped down the rope, startling Edgar very much. 'Come outside the cave and I'll tell you my plans,' said Julian to the others. He didn't want Edgar to hear them. They all went outside. Anne had got breakfast ready while Julian had been gone, and the kettle was boiling away merrily on the little stove.

'Listen!' said Julian. 'The Sticks have gone off in their boat back to the mainland to see if they can find their precious little darling Edgar. Mrs Stick is all hot and bothered because she thinks someone's gone off with him and she's afraid the poor boy will be feeling frightened and lonely!'

'Well!' said George. 'Doesn't she think that the little kidnapped girl must be feeling much worse? What a horrid woman she is!'

'You're right,' said Julian. 'Well, what I propose to do is this – we'll go down into the dungeons now and rescue the little girl – and bring her here to our cave for breakfast. Then we'll take her off in our boat, go to the police, find out where her parents are, and telephone to them that she is safe.'

'What shall we do with Edgar?' said Anne.

'I know!' said George at once. 'We'll put Edgar into the dungeon instead of the little girl! Think how astonished the Sticks will be to find the little girl gone and their dear Edgar shut up in the dungeon instead!'

'Oooh! – that *is* a good idea,' said Anne, and all the others laughed and agreed.

'You stay here, Anne, and cut some more bread and

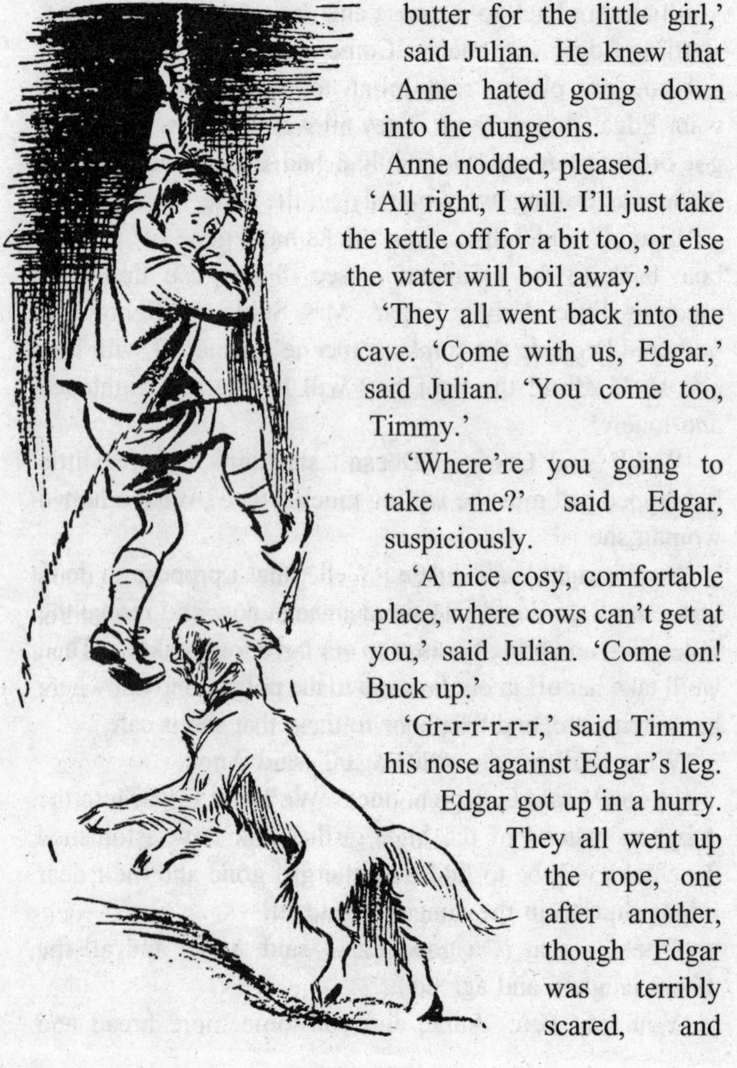

butter for the little girl,' said Julian. He knew that Anne hated going down into the dungeons.

Anne nodded, pleased. 'All right, I will. I'll just take the kettle off for a bit too, or else the water will boil away.'

'They all went back into the cave. 'Come with us, Edgar,' said Julian. 'You come too, Timmy.'

'Where're you going to take me?' said Edgar, suspiciously.

'A nice cosy, comfortable place, where cows can't get at you,' said Julian. 'Come on! Buck up.'

'Gr-r-r-r-r,' said Timmy, his nose against Edgar's leg. Edgar got up in a hurry.

They all went up the rope, one after another, though Edgar was terribly scared, and was sure he couldn't. But with Timmy snapping at his ankles below, he climbed up the rope remarkably quickly, and was hauled out at the top by Julian.

'Now, quick march!' said Julian, who wanted to get everything over before the Sticks thought of returning. And quick march it was, over the cliffs, over the low wall of the castle, and down into the courtyard.

'I'm not going down into those dungeons with you,' said Edgar, in alarm.

'You are, Spotty-Face,' said Julian, amiably.

'Where's my Pa and Ma?' said Edgar, looking anxiously all round.

'Those cows have got them, I expect,' said George. 'The ones that came and mooed at you and threw things, you know.'

Everyone giggled, except Edgar, who looked worried and pale. He did not like this kind of adventure at all. The children came to the dungeon entrance, and found that the Sticks had not only closed down the stone that opened the way to the dungeons, but had also dragged heavy rocks across it.

'Blow your parents!' said Julian, to Edgar. 'Making a lot of trouble for everybody. Come on, stir yourself all hands to these stones. Edgar, pull when we pull. Go on! You'll get into trouble if you don't.'

Edgar pulled with the rest, and one by one the rocks were moved away. Then the heavy trapdoor stone was hauled up too, and the flight of steps was exposed leading down into darkness.

'There's Tinker!' suddenly cried Edgar, pointing to a bush some distance away. Tinker was there, hiding, quite terrified at seeing Timothy again.

'Fat lot of good Stinker is,' said Julian. 'No, Timmy you're not to eat him. Stay here! He wouldn't taste nice if you did eat him!'

Timothy was sorry not to be able to chase Stinker round and round the island. If he couldn't chase rabbits, he might at least be allowed to chase Stinker!

They all went down into the dungeons. Julian's white chalk-marks were still on the rocky walls, so it was easy to find the way to the cave-like room where the children, last summer, had found piles of golden ingots. They felt sure that the little kidnapped girl had been put there, for this cave had a big wooden door that could be bolted on the outside.

They came to the door. It was well and truly bolted. There was no sound from inside. Everyone halted outside and Timmy scratched at the door, whining gently. He knew there was someone inside.

'Hallo there!' shouted Julian, in a loud and cheerful voice. 'Are you all right? We've come to rescue you.'

There was a scrambling noise, as if someone had got up from a stool. Then a small voice sounded from the cave.

'Hallo! Who are you? Oh, do please rescue me! I'm so lonely and frightened!'

'Just undoing the door!' called back Julian, cheerfully. 'We're all children out here, so don't be afraid. You'll soon be safe.'

He shot back the bolts, and flung open the door. Inside the cave, which was lit by a lantern, stood a small girl, with a scared little face, and large dark eyes. Dark red hair tumbled round her cheeks, and she had evidently been crying bitterly, for her face was dirty and tear-stained.

Dick went to her and put his arm round her. 'Everything's all right now,' he said. 'You're safe. We'll take you back to your mother.'

'I do want her, I do, I do,' said the little girl, and tears ran down her cheeks again. 'Why am I here? I don't like being here.'

'Oh, it's just an adventure you've had,' said Julian. 'It's over now – at least, nearly over. There's still a bit of it left – a nice bit, though. We want you to come and have breakfast with us in our cave. We've a lovely cave.'

'Oh, have you?' said the little girl, rubbing her eyes. 'I want to go with you, I like you, but I didn't like those other people.'

'Of course you didn't,' said George. 'Look! This is Timothy, our dog. He wants to be friends with you.'

'What a simply lovely dog!' said the little girl, and flung her arms around Timmy's neck. He licked her in delight. George was pleased. She put her arm round the little girl.

'What's your name?' she said.

'Jennifer Mary Armstrong,' said the little girl. 'What's yours?'

'George,' said George, and the little girl nodded, thinking that George was a boy, not a girl, for she was dressed in jeans just like Julian and Dick, and her hair was short, too, though very curly.

The others told her their names – and then she looked at Edgar, who had said nothing.

'This is Spotty-Face,' said Julian. 'He isn't a friend of

ours. It was his father and mother who put you here, Jennifer. Now we are going to leave him here in your place. It will be such a pleasant surprise for them, won't it?'

Edgar gave a yell of dismay and tried to back away – but Julian gave him a strong shove that sent him flying into the cave.

'There's only one way to teach people like you and your parents that wickedness doesn't pay!' said the boy, grimly. 'And that is to punish you hard. People like you don't understand kindness. You think it's just being soft and silly. All right – you can have a taste of what Jennifer has had. It will do you good, and do your parents a lot of good too! Goodbye!'

Edgar began to howl dismally as Julian bolted the big wooden door top and bottom. 'I shall starve!' he wailed.

'Oh no, you won't,' said Julian. 'There's plenty of food and water in there, so help yourself. It would do you good to go hungry for a while, all the same.'

'Mind the cows don't get you!' called Dick, and he gave a realistic moo that startled Jennifer very much, for the echoes came mooing round too.

'It's all right – only the echoes,' said George, smiling at her in the torch light. Edgar howled away in the cave, sobbing like a baby.

'Little coward, isn't he?' said Julian. 'Come on – let's get back. I'm awfully hungry for my breakfast.'

'So am I,' said Jennifer, slipping her small hand into

Julian's. 'I wasn't hungry at all in that cave – but now I am. Thank you for rescuing me.'

'Don't mention it,' said Julian, grinning at her. 'It's a real pleasure – and an even greater one to put old Spotty-Face there instead of you. Nice to give the Sticks a dose of their own medicine.'

Jennifer didn't know what he meant, but the others did, and they chuckled. They made their way back through the dark, musty passages of the dungeons, passing many caves, big and small, on the way. They came at last to the flight of steps and went up them into the dazzling sunlight.

'Oh!' said Jennifer, breathing in great gulps of the fresh, sea-smelling air. 'Oh! This is lovely! Where am I?'

'On our island,' said George. 'And this is our ruined castle. You were brought here last night in a boat. We heard you scream, and that's how we guessed you were being made a prisoner.'

They walked to the cliff, and Jennifer was amazed at the way they disappeared down the knotted rope. She was eager to try too, and soon slid down into the cave.

'Nice kid, isn't she?' said Julian to George. 'My word, she's had even more of an adventure than we have!'

CHAPTER TWENTY-ONE

A visit to the police station

ANNE LIKED Jennifer very much, and gave her a hug and a kiss. Jennifer looked round the well-furnished cave in amazement and wonder – and then she gave a scream of surprise and joy. She pointed to Anne's neatly made bed, on which sat a number of beautiful dolls, and a large teddy-bear.

'My dolls!' she said. 'Oh, and Teddy, too! Oh, oh, where did you get them? I've missed them so! Oh Josephine and Angela and Rosebud and Marigold, have you missed me?'

She flung herself on the dolls. Anne was very interested to hear their names. 'I've looked after them well,' she told Jennifer. 'They're quite all right.'

'Oh, thank you,' said the little girl, happily. 'I do think you're all nice. Oh, I say – what a lovely breakfast!'

It was. Anne had opened a tin of salmon, two tins of peaches, a tin of milk, cut some bread and butter, and made a big jug of cocoa. Jennifer sat down and began to eat. She was very hungry, and as she ate, she began to lose her paleness and look rosy and happy.

The children talked busily as they ate. Jennifer told them about herself.

'I was playing in the garden with my nanny,' she said,

'and suddenly, when nanny had gone indoors to fetch something, a man climbed over the wall, threw a shawl round my head, and took me away. We live by the sea, you know, and I soon heard the sound of the waves splashing on the shore, and I knew I was being put into a boat. I was taken to a big ship, and locked down in a cabin for two days. Then I suppose I was brought here one night. I was so frightened that I screamed.'

'That was the scream we heard,' said George. 'It was lucky we heard it. We had thought there was smuggling going on here, in our island – we didn't guess it was a case of kidnapping, till we heard you scream – though we had found your trunk with your clothes and toys.'

'I don't know how the man got those,' said Jennifer. 'Maybe one of our maids helped him. There was one I didn't like at all. She was called Sarah Stick.'

'Ah!' said Julian, at once. 'That's the one, then! It was Mr and Mrs Stick who brought you here. Sarah Stick, your maid, must be some relation of theirs. They must have been in the pay of someone else, I should think – someone who had a ship, and could bring you here to hide you.'

'Jolly good hiding-place, too,' said George. 'No one but us would ever have found it out.'

They ate all their breakfast, made some more cocoa, and discussed their future plans.

'We'll take our boat and go to the mainland this morning,' said Julian. 'We'll go straight to the police station with Jennifer. I expect the newspapers are full of her disappearance, and the police will recognise her at once.'

'I hope they catch the Sticks,' said George. 'I hope they won't disappear into into thin air as soon as they hear that Jennifer is found.'

'Yes – we must warn the police of that,' said Julian, thoughtfully. 'Better not spread the news abroad till the Sticks are caught. I wonder where they are?'

'Let's get the boat now,' said Dick. 'There's no point in waiting about. Jennifer's parents will be thrilled to know she is safe.'

'I don't really want to leave this lovely cave,' said Jennifer, who was thoroughly enjoying herself now. I wish I lived here, too. Are you going to come back to the island and live here, Julian?'

'Well, we shall come back for a few days more, I expect,' said Julian. 'You see, our aunt's home is empty at the moment because she is away ill and our uncle is with her. So we might as well stay on our island till they come back.'

'Oh, *could* I come back with you?' begged Jennifer, her small round face alight with joy at the thought of living in a cave on an island with these nice children and their lovely dog. 'Oh, do let me! I would so like it. And I do so love Timmy.'

'I don't expect your parents would let you, especially after you've just been kidnapped,' said Julian. 'But you can ask them, if you like.'

They all went to the boat and got in. Julian pushed off. George steered the boat in and out of the rocks. They saw the wreck, which interested Jenny very much indeed. She badly wanted to stop, but the others thought they ought to get to land as quickly as possible.

Soon they were near the beach. Alf, the fisher-boy was there. He saw them and waved. He ran to help them to pull in their boat.

'I was coming out in my boat this morning,' he said. 'Your father's back, George. But not your mother. She's getting better, they say, and will be back in a week's time.'

'Well, what's my father come back for?' demanded George, in surprise.

'He got worried because nobody answered the telephone,' explained Alf. 'He came down and asked me where you all were. I didn't tell him, of course. I kept your secret. But I was just coming out to warn you this morning. He got back last night – and wasn't he wild? No one there to give him any food – all the house upside down and half the things gone! He's at the police station now.'

'Golly!' said George. 'That's just where *we* are going too! We shall meet him there. Oh dear, I do hope he won't be in an awful temper. You just can't do anything with my father when he's cross.'

'Come on!' said Julian. 'It's a good thing, in a way, that your father is here, George – we can explain everything to him and to the police at the same time.'

They left Alf, who looked very surprised to see Jennifer with the others. He couldn't make out where she had come from. Certainly she had not started out to the island with them – but she had come back in their boat. How was that? It seemed very mysterious to Alf.

The children arrived at the police station and marched in, much to the surprise of the policeman there.

'Hallo!' he said. 'What's the matter? Been doing a burglary, or something, and come to own up?'

'Listen!' said George, suddenly, hearing a loud voice in the room next to theirs. 'That's Father's voice!'

She darted to the door. The policeman called to her, shocked. 'Now don't you go in there. The Inspector's in there. Come over here special, he has, and mustn't be interrupted.'

But George had flung open the door and gone inside. Her father turned and saw her. He rose to his feet. 'George! Where have you been? How dare you go away like this and leave the house and everything! It's been robbed right and left! I've just been telling the Inspector about all the things that have been stolen.'

'Don't worry, Father,' said George. 'Really don't worry. We've found them all. How's Mother?'

'Better, much better,' said her father, still looking amazed and angry. 'Thank goodness I can go back and tell her where you are. She kept asking me about you all, and I had to keep saying you were all right, so as not to worry her – but I hadn't any idea what was happening to

you or where you had gone. I feel very displeased with you. Where were you?'

'On the island,' said George, looking rather sulky, as she often did when her father was angry with her. 'Julian will tell you all about it.'

Julian came in, followed by Dick, Anne, Jennifer and Timothy. The Inspector, a big, clever-looking man with dark eyes under shaggy eyebrows, looked at them all closely. When he saw Jennifer, he stared hard – and then suddenly rose to his feet.

'What's your name, little girl?' he said.

'Jennifer Mary Armstrong,' said Jenny, in a surprised voice.

'Bless us all!' said the Inspector, in a startled voice. 'Here's the child the whole country is looking for – and she walks in here as cool as a cucumber! Lands sakes, where did she come from?'

'What do you mean?' said George's father, looking surprised. 'What child is the whole country looking for? I haven't read the papers for some days.'

'Then you don't know about little Jenny Armstrong being kidnapped?' said the Inspector, sitting down and pulling Jenny near him. 'She's the daughter of Harry Armstrong, the millionaire, you know. Well, somebody kidnapped her and wants a hundred thousand pounds ransom for her. My word, we've combed the country for her – and here she is, as merry as you please. Well, I'm blessed – this is the strangest thing I ever knew. Where have you been, little Missy?'

'On the island,' said Jenny. 'Julian – you tell it all.'

So Julian told the whole story from beginning to end. The policeman from outside came in, and took notes down as he spoke. Everyone listened in amazement. As for George's father, his eyes nearly fell out of his head. What adventures these children did have to be sure, and how well they managed everything!

'And do you happen to know who was the owner of the ship that brought little Jenny along – the one that sent a boat off to the wreck and put her there for the Sticks to take?' asked the Inspector.

'No,' said Julian. 'All we heard was that the *Roamer* was coming that night.'

'A-ha!' said the Inspector, with great satisfaction in his voice. 'Aha and oho! We know the *Roamer* all right – a ship we've been watching for some time – owned by somebody we're very, very suspicious of – we think he's dabbling in a whole lot of shady deals. Now this is very good news indeed. The thing is – where are the Sticks – and how can we catch them red-handed, now you've got Jenny out of their clutches? They'll probably deny everything.'

'I know how we could catch them,' said Julian quickly. 'We've left their nasty son, Edgar, locked in the same dungeon where they put Jenny. If only one of us could pass the word to the Sticks, that that is where Edgar is, they'd go back to the island all right, and go right in to the dungeons – so if you found them there, it wouldn't be much good them denying that they don't know anything about the island, and have never been there.'

'That would certainly make things a lot easier,' said the Inspector. He pressed a bell and another policeman came into the room. The Inspector gave him a full description of Mr and Mrs Stick, and told him to watch the countryside round about, and report when they were found.

'Then, Julian, you might like to go and have a little

conversation with them about their son, Edgar,' said the Inspector, smiling. 'If they do go back to the island, we shall follow them, and get all the evidence we want. Thank you for your very great help. Now we must telephone to Jenny's parents and tell them she is safe.'

'She can come back to Kirrin Cottage with us,' said George's father, still looking rather dazed at all that had happened. 'I've got Joanna, our old cook, to come back for a while to put things straight, so there will be someone there to see to the children. They must all come back.'

'Well, Father,' said George, firmly, 'we will come back just for today, but we plan to spend another week on Kirrin Island till Mother comes back. She said we could, and we are having such a fine time there. Let Joanna stay at Kirrin Cottage and keep it in order and get it ready for Mother when she comes home – she won't want the bother of looking after us too. We can look after ourselves on the island.'

'I certainly think these children deserve a reward for the good work they have done,' remarked the Inspector, and that settled the matter.

'Very well,' said George's father, 'you can all go off to the island again – but you must be back when your mother returns, George.'

'Of course I will,' said George. 'I badly want to see Mother. But home isn't nice without her. I would rather be on our island.'

'And I want to be there, too,' said Jenny, unexpectedly.

'Ask my parents to come to Kirrin, please – so that I can ask them if I can go with the other children.'

'I'll do my best,' said the Inspector, grinning at the five children. They liked him very much. George's father stood up.

'Come along!' he said. 'I want my lunch. All this has made me feel hungry. We'll go and see if Joanna has got anything for us.'

Off they all went, talking nineteen to the dozen, making George's poor father feel quite bewildered. He always seemed to get into the middle of some adventure when these children were about!

CHAPTER TWENTY-TWO

Back to Kirrin Island!

SOON EVERYONE was at Kirrin Cottage. Joanna, the old cook they had had before, gave them a good welcome, and listened to their adventures in astonishment, getting the lunch ready all the while.

It was while they were having lunch that Julian, looking out of the window, suddenly caught sight of a figure he knew very well – someone skulking along behind the hedge.

'Old Pa Stick!' he said, and jumped up. 'I'll go after him. Stay here, everyone.'

He went out of the house, ran round a corner and came face to face with Mr Stick.

'Do you want to know where Edgar is?' said Julian mysteriously.

Mr Stick looked startled. He stared at Julian not knowing what to say.

'He's down in the dungeons, locked in that cave,' said Julian, even more mysteriously.

'You don't know anything about Edgar,' said Mr Stick. 'Where have you been? Didn't you go home?'

'Never you mind,' said Julian. 'But if you want to find Edgar – look in that cave!'

Mr Stick gave the boy a glare and left him. Julian hurried indoors and rang up the police station. He felt sure that Mr Stick would tell Mrs Stick what he had said, and that Mrs Stick would insist on going back to the island to see if what he had said was true. So all that needed to be done was for the police to keep a watch on the boats along the shore and see when the Sticks left.

The children finished their dinner, and Uncle Quentin announced that he must return to his wife, who would want to know his news. 'I'll tell her you are having a fine time on the island,' he said, 'and we can tell her all the extraordinary details when she returns home, better.'

He left in a car, and the children wondered whether they

might now return to their island or not. But they decided to wait a little, for they did not know what to do with Jennifer.

Very soon a large car drove up and stopped outside the gate of Kirrin Cottage. Out jumped a tall man with dark red hair, and a pretty woman. 'They must be your father and mother, Jenny,' said Julian.

They were – and Jennifer got so many hugs and kisses that she quite lost her breath. She had to tell her story again and again, and her father could not thank Julian and the others enough for all they had done.

'Ask me for any reward you like,' he said, 'and you can have it. I shall never, never be able to tell you how grateful I am to you for rescuing our little Jenny.'

'Oh – we don't want anything, thank you,' said Julian, politely. 'We enjoyed it all very much. We like adventures.'

'Ah, but you *must* tell me something you want!' said Jenny's father.

Julian glanced round at the others. He knew that none of them wanted a reward. Jenny nudged him hard and nodded her head vigorously. Julian laughed.

'Well,' he said, 'there *is* one thing we'd all like very much.'

'It's granted before you ask it!' said Jenny's father.

'Will you let Jenny come and spend a week with us on our island?' said Julian. Jenny gave a squeal and pressed Julian's arm very hard between her two small hands.

Jenny's parents looked rather taken-aback. 'Well,' said

her father, 'well – she's just been kidnapped, you know – and we don't feel inclined to let her out of our sight at the moment – and . . .'

'You promised Julian you'd grant what he asked, you promised, Daddy,' said Jenny, urgently. 'Oh please do let me. I've always wanted to live on an island. And this one has got a perfectly marvellous cave, and a wonderful ruined castle, and the dungeons where I was kept, and—'

'And we take Timothy, our dog, with us,' said Julian. 'See what a big powerful fellow he is – nobody could come to much harm with Timmy about – could they, Tim?'

'Woof!' said Timothy, in his deepest voice.

'Well, you can go, Jenny, on one condition,' said the little girl's father at last, 'and that is that your mother and I come over tomorrow and spend the day on the island, to see that everything is all right for you.'

'Oh, thank you, thank you, Daddy!' cried Jenny, and danced round the room in delight. A whole week on the island with these new friends of hers, and Timmy the dog! What could be lovelier?

'Jenny can stay here the night, can't she?' said George. 'You'll be staying at the hotel, I suppose?'

Soon Jenny's parents left and went to the police station to get all the details of the kidnapping. The children went to see if Joanna was going to make cakes for tea.

Just about tea-time there came a knocking at the door. A large policeman stood outside.

'Is Julian here?' he said. 'Oh, you're the boy we want. The Sticks have just left for the island in their boat, and we've got ours on the beach to follow. But we don't think we know the way in and out of those hidden rocks that lie all round Kirrin Island. Could you or Georgina guide us, do you think?'

'I'm George, not Georgina,' said George in a cold voice.

'Sorry,' said the policeman, with a grin. 'Well, could you come too?'

'We'll all come!' said Dick, jumping up. 'I want to go back to the dear old island and sleep in our cave again tonight. Why should we miss a single night? We can fetch Jenny's people tomorrow in our own boat. We'll all come.'

The policeman was a little doubtful about the arrangement, but the children insisted, and as there was no time to waste, they all ended in crowding into the two boats, with three big policemen, George and Julian leading the way in their own boat. Timmy lay down at George's feet as usual.

George guided the boat as cleverly as ever, and soon they landed in the usual little sandy cove. The Sticks had evidently gone round by the wreck as usual, and landed on the rockier part.

'Now, no noise,' said Julian, warningly. They all went quietly towards the ruin, and came into the courtyard. There was no sign of the Sticks.

'We'll go down underground,' said Julian. 'I've got my

torch. I expect the Sticks are down there already, letting out dear Edgar.'

They went down the steps into the dark dungeons.

Anne went too, this time, holding on to the hand of one of the big policemen. They moved quietly through the long, dark, winding passages.

They came at last to the door of the cave in which they had imprisoned Edgar. It was still bolted at the top and bottom!

'Look!' said Julian, in a whisper, shining his torch on to the door. 'The Sticks haven't been down here yet.'

'Sh!' said George, as Timmy growled softly. 'There's someone coming. Hide! It's the Sticks, I expect.'

They all hid behind the wall that ran nearby. They could hear footsteps coming nearer, and then the voice of Mrs Stick raised in anger.

'If my Edgar's locked in there, I'll have something to say about it! Locking up a poor innocent boy like that. I don't understand it. If he's there, where's the girl? You answer me that. Where's the girl? It's my belief that the boss has done some double-crossing to do us out of our share of the money. Didn't he say that he'd give us two thousand pounds if we kept Jenny Armstrong for a week? Now I think he must have sent someone to this island, played tricks on us, taken the girl himself and locked up our Edgar.'

'You may be right, Clara,' said Mr Stick, his voice coming nearer and nearer. 'But how did this boy Julian know where Edgar was? There's a lot I don't understand about all this.'

Now the Sticks were right at the door of the cave, with Stinker at their heels. Stinker smelt the others in hiding and whined in fear. Mr Stick kicked him.

'Stop it! It's enough to hear our own voices echoing away all round without your whines too!'

Mrs Stick was calling out loudly: 'Edgar! Are you there? Edgar!'

'Ma! Yes, I'm here!' yelled Edgar. 'Let me out, quick! I'm scared. Let me out!'

Mrs Stick undid the bolts at once and flung open the door. By the light of the lantern in the cave she saw Edgar. He ran to her, half-crying.

'Who put you here?' demanded Mrs Stick. 'You tell your Pa and he'll knock their heads off, won't you, Pa? Putting a poor frightened child into a dark cave like this. It's a wicked thing to do!'

Suddenly the Stick family had the fright of their lives – for a large policeman stepped out of the shadows, torch in one hand and notebook in the other!

'Ah!' said the policeman, in a deep voice. 'You're right, Clara Stick. To shut up a poor frightened child in that cave *is* a wicked thing to do – and that's what you did, isn't it? You put Jenny Armstrong there! She's only a little girl. This boy of yours knew he wasn't coming to any harm – but that little girl was scared to death!'

Mrs Stick stood there, opening and shutting her mouth

like a goldfish, not finding a word to say. Mr Stick squealed like a rat caught in a corner.

'We're copped! It's a trap, that's it. We're copped!'

Edgar began to cry, sobbing like a four-year-old. The other children felt disgusted with him. The Sticks suddenly caught sight of all the children when Julian switched on his torch.

'Snakes alive, there's all the children – and there's Jenny Armstrong too!' said Mr Stick, in a tone of the greatest amazement. 'What's all this? What's happening? Who shut up Edgar?'

'We'll tell you the answers when we get to the police station,' said the big policeman. 'Now, are you coming quietly?'

The Sticks went quietly, Edgar sobbing away to himself. He imagined his mother and father in prison, and he himself sent to a hard and difficult school, not allowed to see his mother for years. Not that that would matter, for the Sticks, both mother and father, were no good to Edgar, and had taught him nothing but bad things. There might be a chance for the wretched boy if he were kept away from them, and set a good example instead of a bad one.

'We shan't be coming back with you,' said Julian, politely, to the policeman. 'We're staying here the night. You could go back in the Sticks's boat. They know the way all right. Take their dog with you. There he is – Stinker, we call him.' Then he added, 'I guess your colleagues could follow in the police boat!'

The Sticks's boat was found and the policeman, the two grown-up Sticks and Edgar got in. Stinker jumped in too, glad to get away from the glare of Timothy's green eyes.

Julian pushed the boat out. 'Goodbye!' he called, and

the other children waved goodbye, too. 'Goodbye, Mr Stick, don't go kidnapping any more children. Goodbye, Mrs Stick, look after Edgar better, in case *he* gets kidnapped again! Goodbye, Spotty-Face, try and be a better boy! Goodbye, Stinker, do get a bath as soon as possible. Goodbye!'

The policemen grinned and waved. The Sticks said not a word, nor did they wave. They sat sullen and angry, trying to work out in their minds what had happened to make things end up like this.

The boats rounded a high rock and were soon out of sight. 'Hurrah!' said Dick. 'They've gone – gone for ever! We've got our island to ourselves at last. Come on, Jenny, we'll show you all over it! What a lovely time we're going to have.'

They raced away, happy and carefree, five children and a dog, alone on an island they loved. And we will leave them there to enjoy their week's happiness. They really do deserve it!

THE FAMOUS FIVE

FIVE GO TO SMUGGLER'S TOP

Have you read all THE FAMOUS FIVE books?

1. Five on a Treasure Island
2. Five Go Adventuring Again
3. Five Run Away Together
4. Five Go to Smuggler's Top
5. Five Go Off in a Caravan
6. Five on Kirrin Island Again
7. Five Go Off to Camp
8. Five Get Into Trouble
9. Five Fall Into Adventure
10. Five on a Hike Together
11. Five Have a Wonderful Time
12. Five Go Down to the Sea
13. Five Go to Mystery Moor
14. Five Have Plenty of Fun
15. Five on a Secret Trail
16. Five Go to Billycock Hill
17. Five Get Into a Fix
18. Five on Finniston Farm
19. Five Go to Demon's Rocks
20. Five Have a Mystery to Solve
21. Five Are Together Again

The Famous Five Colour Short Stories

1. Five and a Half-Term Adventure
2. George's Hair is Too Long
3. Good Old Timmy
4. A Lazy Afternoon
5. Well Done, Famous Five
6. Five Have a Puzzling Time
7. Happy Christmas, Five
8. When Timmy Chased the Cat

Enid Blyton®

THE FAMOUS FIVE

FIVE GO TO SMUGGLER'S TOP

Illustrated by Eileen A. Soper

HODDER CHILDREN'S BOOKS

First published in Great Britain in 1945 by Hodder & Stoughton
This edition published in 2016

21

A CIP catalogue record for this book is available from the British Library.

ISBN 978 1 444 93634 6

Printed and bound in Great Britain by Clays Ltd, Elcograf S.p.A.

The paper and board used in this book are made from wood from responsible sources.

Hodder Children's Books
An imprint of
Hachette Children's Group
Part of Hodder & Stoughton
Carmelite House
50 Victoria Embankment
London EC4Y 0DZ

An Hachette UK Company
www.hachette.co.uk
www.hachettechildrens.co.uk

CONTENTS

1	BACK TO KIRRIN COTTAGE	1
2	A SHOCK IN THE NIGHT	9
3	UNCLE QUENTIN HAS AN IDEA	18
4	SMUGGLER'S TOP	27
5	SOOTY LENOIR	36
6	SOOTY'S STEPFATHER AND MOTHER	46
7	THE HIDDEN PIT	55
8	AN EXCITING WALK	64
9	WHO IS IN THE TOWER?	73
10	TIMMY MAKES A NOISE	84
11	GEORGE IS WORRIED	93
12	BLOCK GETS A SURPRISE	102
13	POOR GEORGE!	112
14	A VERY PUZZLING THING	122
15	STRANGE HAPPENINGS	130
16	NEXT MORNING	139
17	MORE AND MORE PUZZLING	149
18	CURIOUS DISCOVERIES	158
19	MR BARLING TALKS	167
20	TIMMY TO THE RESCUE	177
21	A JOURNEY THROUGH THE HILL	186
22	THINGS COME RIGHT AT LAST	193

CHAPTER ONE

Back to Kirrin Cottage

ONE FINE day, right at the beginning of the Easter holidays, four children and a dog travelled by train together.

'Soon be there now,' said Julian, a tall strong boy, with a determined face.

'Woof,' said Timothy the dog, getting excited, and trying to look out of the window too.

'Get down, Tim,' said Julian. 'Let Anne have a look.'

Anne was his younger sister. She put her head out of the window. 'We're coming into Kirrin Station!' she said. 'I do hope Aunt Fanny will be there to meet us.'

'Of course she will!' said Georgina, her cousin. She looked more like a boy than a girl, for she wore her hair very short, and it curled close about her head. She too had a determined face, like Julian. She pushed Anne away and looked out of the window.

'It's nice to be going home,' she said. 'I love school – but it will be fun to be at Kirrin Cottage and perhaps sail out to Kirrin Island and visit the castle there. We haven't been since last summer.'

'Dick's turn to look out now,' said Julian, turning to his younger brother, a boy with a pleasant face, sitting reading in a corner. 'We're just coming into sight of Kirrin, Dick. Can't you stop reading for a second?'

'It's such an exciting book,' said Dick, and shut it with a clap. 'The most exciting adventure story I've ever read!'

'Pooh! I bet it's not as exciting as some of the adventures *we've* had!' said Anne, at once.

It was quite true that the five of them, counting in Timmy the dog, who always shared everything with them, had had the most amazing adventures together. But now it looked as if they were going to have nice quiet holidays, going for long walks over the cliffs, and perhaps sailing out in George's boat to their island of Kirrin.

'I've worked jolly hard at school this term,' said Julian. 'I could do with a holiday!'

'You've gone thin,' said Georgina. Nobody called her that. They all called her George. She would never answer to any other name. Julian grinned.

'Well, I'll soon get fat at Kirrin Cottage, don't you worry! Aunt Fanny will see to that. She's a great one for trying to fatten people up. It will be nice to see your mother again, George. She's an awfully good sort.'

'Yes. I hope Father will be in a good temper these hols,' said George. 'He ought to be because he has just finished some new experiments, Mother says, which have been quite successful.'

George's father was a scientist, always working out new ideas. He liked to be quiet, and sometimes he flew into a temper when he could not get the peace he needed or things did not go exactly as he wanted them to. The children often thought that hot-tempered Georgina was very like her father! She too could fly into fierce tempers when things did not go right for her.

Aunt Fanny was there to meet them. The four children jumped out on the platform and rushed to hug her. George got there first. She was very fond of her gentle mother, who had so often tried to shield her when her father got angry with her. Timmy pranced round, barking in delight. He adored George's mother.

She patted him, and he tried to stand up and lick her face. 'Timmy's bigger than ever!' she said, laughing. 'Down, old boy! You'll knock me over.'

Timmy was certainly a big dog. All the children loved him, for he was loyal, loving and faithful. His brown eyes looked from one to the other, enjoying the children's excitement. Timmy shared in it, as he shared in everything.

But the person he loved most, of course, was his mistress, George. She had had him since he was a small puppy. She took him to school with her each term, for she and Anne went to a boarding school that allowed pets. Otherwise George would most certainly have refused to go!

They set off to Kirrin in the pony-trap. It was very windy and cold, and the children shivered and pulled their coats tightly round them.

'It's awfully cold,' said Anne, her teeth beginning to chatter. 'Colder than in the winter!'

'It's the wind,' said her aunt, and tucked a rug round her. 'It's been getting very strong the last day or two. The fishermen have pulled their boats high up the beach for fear of a big storm.'

The children saw the boats pulled right up as they passed the beach where they had bathed so often. They did not feel like bathing now. It made them shiver even to think of it.

The wind howled over the sea. Great scudding clouds raced overhead. The waves pounded on the beach and made a terrific noise. It excited Timmy, who began to bark.

'Be quiet, Tim,' said George, patting him. 'You will have to learn to be a good quiet dog now we are home again, or Father will be cross with you. Is Father very busy, Mother?'

'Very,' said her mother. 'But he's going to do very little work now you are coming home. He thought he would like to go for walks with you, or go out in the boat, if the weather calms down.'

The children looked at one another. Uncle Quentin was not the best of companions. He had no sense of humour, and when the children went off into fits of laughter, as they did twenty times a day or more, he could not see the joke at all.

'It looks as if these hols won't be quite so jolly if Uncle Quentin parks himself on us most of the time,' said Dick in a low voice to Julian.

'Sh,' said Julian, afraid that his aunt would hear, and be hurt. George frowned.

'Oh, Mother! Father will be bored stiff if he comes with us – and we'll be bored too.'

George was very outspoken, and could never learn to keep a guard on her tongue. Her mother sighed. 'Don't talk like that, dear. I daresay your father will get tired of going with you after a bit. But it does him good to have a bit of young life about him.'

'Here we are!' said Julian, as the trap stopped outside an old house. 'Kirrin Cottage! My word, how the wind is howling round it, Aunt Fanny!'

'Yes. It made a terrible noise last night,' said his aunt. 'You take the trap round to the back, Julian, when we've got the things out. Oh, here's your uncle to help!'

Uncle Quentin came out, a tall, clever-looking man, with rather frowning eyebrows. He smiled at the children and kissed George and Anne.

'Welcome to Kirrin Cottage!' he said. 'I'm quite glad your mother and father are away, Anne, because now we shall have you all here once again!'

Soon they were sitting round the table eating a big tea. Aunt Fanny always got ready a fine meal for their first one, for she knew they were very hungry after their long journey on the train.

Even George was satisfied at last, and leaned back in her chair, wishing she could manage just one more of her mother's delicious new-made buns.

Timmy sat close to her. He was not supposed to be fed at meal-times but it was really surprising how many titbits found their way to him under the table!

The wind howled round the house. The windows rattled, the doors shook, and the mats lifted themselves up and down as the draught got under them.

'They look as if they've got snakes wriggling underneath them,' said Anne. Timmy watched them and growled. He was a clever dog, but he did not know why the mats wriggled in such a strange way.

'I hope the wind will die down tonight,' said Aunt Fanny. 'It kept me awake last night. Julian dear, you look rather thin. Have you been working hard? I must fatten you up.'

The children laughed. 'Just what we thought you'd say, Mother!' said George. 'Goodness, what's that?'

They all sat still, startled. There was a loud bumping noise on the roof, and Timmy put up his ears and growled fiercely.

'A tile off the roof,' said Uncle Quentin. 'How tiresome! We shall have to get the loose tiles seen to, Fanny, when the storm is over, or the rain will come in.'

The children rather hoped that their uncle would retire to his study after tea, as he usually did, but this time he didn't. They wanted to play a game, but it wasn't much good with Uncle Quentin there. He really wasn't any good at all, not even at such a simple game as snap.

'Do you know a boy called Pierre Lenoir?' Uncle

Quentin suddenly asked, taking a letter from his pocket. 'I believe he goes to your school and Dick's, Julian.'

'Pierre Lenoir – oh you mean old Sooty,' said Julian. 'Yes – he's in Dick's form. Mad as a hatter.'

'Sooty! Now why do you call him that?' said Uncle Quentin. 'It seems a silly name for a boy.'

'If you saw him you wouldn't think so,' said Dick, with a laugh. 'Hair as black as soot, eyes like bits of coal, eyebrows that look as if they've been put in with charcoal.'

'But what a name to give anyone – *Sooty*!' said Uncle Quentin. 'Well, I've been having quite a lot of correspondence with this boy's father. He and I are interested in the same scientific matters. In fact, I've asked him whether he wouldn't like to come and stay with me a few days – and bring his boy, Pierre.'

'Oh really!' said Dick, looking quite pleased. 'Well it wouldn't be bad sport to have old Sooty here, Uncle. But he's quite mad. He never does as he's told, he climbs like a monkey, and he can be awfully cheeky. I don't know if you'd like him much.'

Uncle Quentin looked sorry he had asked Sooty after he had heard what Dick had to say. He didn't like cheeky boys. Nor did he like mad ones.

'Hm,' he said, putting the letter away. 'I wish I'd asked you about the boy first, before suggesting to his father that he might bring him with him. But perhaps I can prevent him coming.'

'No, don't, Father,' said George, who rather liked the

sound of Sooty Lenoir. 'Let's have him. He could come out with us and liven things up!'

'We'll see,' said her father, who had already made up his mind on no account to have the boy at Kirrin Cottage, if he was mad, climbed everywhere, and was cheeky. George was enough of a handful without a devil of a boy egging her on!

Much to the children's relief Uncle Quentin retired to read by himself about eight o'clock. Aunt Fanny looked at the clock.

'Time for Anne to go to bed,' she said. 'And you too, George.'

'Just one good game of Slap-Down Patience, all of us playing it together, Mother!' said George. 'Come on – you play it too. It's our first evening at home. Anyway, I shan't sleep for ages, with this gale howling round! Come on, Mother – one good game, then we'll go to bed. Julian's been yawning like anything already!'

CHAPTER TWO

A shock in the night

IT WAS nice to climb up the steep stairs to their familiar bedrooms that night. All the children were yawning widely. Their long train journey had tired them.

'If only this awful wind would stop!' said Anne, pulling the curtain aside and looking out into the night. 'There's a little moon, George. It keeps bobbing out between the scurrying clouds.'

'Let it bob!' said George, scrambling into bed. 'I'm jolly cold. Hurry, Anne, or you'll catch a chill at that window.'

'Don't the waves make a noise?' said Anne, still at the window. 'And the gale in the old ash tree is making a whistling, howling sound, and bending it right over.'

'Timmy, hurry up and get on my bed,' commanded George, screwing up her cold toes. 'That's one good thing about being at home, Anne. I can have Timmy on my bed! He's far better than a hot water bottle.'

'You're not supposed to have him on your bed at home, any more than you're supposed to at school,' said Anne, curling up in bed. 'Aunt Fanny thinks he sleeps in his basket over there.'

'Well, I can't stop him coming on my bed at night, can I, if he doesn't want to sleep in his basket?' said George.

'That's right, Timmy darling. Make my feet warm. Where's your nose? Let me pat it. Goodnight, Tim. Goodnight, Anne.'

'Goodnight,' said Anne, sleepily. 'I hope that Sooty boy comes, don't you? He does sound fun.'

'Yes. And anyway Father would stay in with Mr Lenoir, the boy's father, and not come out with us,' said George. 'Father doesn't mean to, but he does spoil things somehow.'

'He's not very good at laughing,' said Anne. 'He's too serious.'

A loud bang made both girls jump. 'That's the bathroom door!' said George, with a groan. 'One of the boys must have left it open. That's the sort of noise that drives Father mad! There it goes again!'

'Well, let Julian or Dick shut it,' said Anne, who was now beginning to feel nice and warm. But Julian and Dick were thinking that George or Anne might shut it, so nobody got out of bed to see to the banging door.

Very soon Uncle Quentin's voice roared up the stairs, louder than the gale.

'Shut that door, one of you! How can I work with that noise going on?'

All four children jumped out of bed like a shot. Timmy leapt off George's bed. Everyone fell over him as they rushed to the bathroom door. There was a lot of giggling and scuffling. Then Uncle Quentin's footsteps were heard on the stairs and the five fled silently to their rooms.

The gale still roared. Uncle Quentin and Aunt Fanny

came up to bed. The bedroom door flew out of Uncle Quentin's hand and slammed itself shut so violently that a vase leapt off a nearby shelf.

Uncle Quentin leapt too, startled. 'This wretched gale!' he said, fiercely. 'Never known one like it all the time we've been here. If it gets much worse the fishermen's boats will be smashed up, even though they've pulled them as high up the beach as possible.'

'It will blow itself out soon, dear,' said Aunt Fanny, soothingly. 'Probably by the time morning comes it will be quite calm.'

But she was wrong. The gale did not blow itself out that night. Instead it raged round the house even more fiercely, shrieking and howling like a live thing. Nobody could sleep. Timmy kept up a continuous low growling, for he did not like the shakes and rattles and howls.

Towards dawn the wind seemed in a fury. Anne thought it sounded as if it was in a horrible temper, out to do all the harm it could. She lay and trembled, half-frightened.

Suddenly there was a strange noise. It was a loud and woeful groaning and creaking, like someone in great pain. The two girls sat up, terrified. What could it be?

The boys heard it too. Julian leapt out of bed and ran to the window. Outside stood the old ash tree, tall and black in the fitful moonlight. It was gradually bending over!

'It's the ash! It's falling!' yelled Julian, almost startling Dick out of his wits. 'It's falling, I tell you. It'll crash on the house! Quick, warn the girls!'

Shouting at the top of his voice, Julian raced out of his door on to the landing. 'Uncle! Aunt! George and Anne! Come downstairs quickly. The ash tree is falling!'

George jumped out of bed, snatched at her dressing-gown, and raced to the door, yelling to Anne. The little

girl was soon with her. Timmy ran in front. At the door of Aunt Fanny's bedroom Uncle Quentin appeared, tall and amazed, wrapping his dressing-gown round him.

'What's all this noise? Julian, what's—?'

'Aunt Fanny! Come downstairs – the ash tree is falling! Listen to its terrible groans and creaks!' yelled Julian, almost beside himself with impatience. 'It'll smash in the roof and the bedrooms! Listen, here it comes!'

Everyone fled downstairs as, with an appalling wail, the great ash tree hauled up its roots and fell heavily on to Kirrin Cottage. There was a terrible crash, and the sound of tiles slipping to the ground everywhere.

'Oh dear!' said poor Aunt Fanny, covering her eyes. 'I knew something would happen! Quentin, we ought to have had that ash tree topped. I knew it would fall in a great gale like this. What has it done to the roof?'

After the great crash there had come other smaller noises, sounds of things falling, thuds and little smashing noises. The children could not imagine what was happening. Timmy was thoroughly angry, and barked loudly. Uncle Quentin slapped his hand angrily on the table, and made everyone jump.

'Stop that dog barking! I'll turn him out!' But nothing would stop Timmy barking or growling that night, and George at last pushed him into the warm kitchen, and shut the door on him.

'I feel like barking or growling myself,' said Anne, who

knew exactly what Timmy felt like. 'Julian, has the tree broken in the roof?'

Uncle Quentin took a powerful torch and went carefully up the stairs to the landing to see what damage had been done. He came down looking rather pale.

'The tree has crashed through the attic, smashed the roof in, and wrecked the girls' bedroom,' he said. 'A big branch has penetrated the boys' room too, but not badly. But the girls' room is ruined! They would have been killed if they had been in their beds.'

Everyone was silent. It was an awful thought that George and Anne had had such a narrow escape.

'Good thing I yelled my head off to warn them then,' said Julian, cheerfully, seeing how white Anne had gone. 'Cheer up, Anne – think what a tale you'll have to tell at school next term.'

'I think some hot cocoa would do us all good,' said Aunt Fanny, pulling herself together, though she felt very shaken. 'I'll go and make some. Quentin, see if the fire is still alight in your study. We want a little warmth!'

The fire was still alight. Everyone crowded round it. They welcomed Aunt Fanny when she came in with some steaming milky cocoa.

Anne looked curiously round the room as she sat sipping her drink. This was where her uncle did his work, his very clever work. He wrote his difficult books here, books which Anne could not understand at all. He drew his weird diagrams here, and made many strange experiments.

But just at the moment Uncle Quentin did not look very clever. He looked rather ashamed, somehow. Anne soon knew why.

'Quentin, it is a mercy none of us was hurt or killed,' said Aunt Fanny, looking at him rather sternly. 'I told you a dozen times you should get that ash tree topped. I knew it was too big and heavy to withstand a great gale. I was always afraid it would blow down on the house.'

'Yes, I know, my dear,' said Uncle Quentin, stirring his cup of cocoa very vigorously. 'But I was so busy these last months.'

'You always make that an excuse for not doing urgent things,' said Aunt Fanny, with a sigh. 'I shall have to manage things myself in the future. I can't risk our lives like this!'

'Well, a thing like this would only happen once in a blue moon!' cried Uncle Quentin, getting angry. Then he calmed down, seeing that Aunt Fanny was really shocked and upset, very near to tears. He put down his cocoa and slipped his arm round her.

'You've had a terrible shock,' he said. 'Don't you worry about things. Maybe they won't be so bad when morning comes.'

'Oh, Quentin – they'll be much worse!' said his wife. 'Where shall we sleep tonight, all of us, and what shall we do till the roof and upstairs rooms are repaired? The children have only just come home. The house will be full of workmen for weeks! I don't know how

I'm going to manage.'

'Leave it all to me!' said Uncle Quentin. 'I'll settle everything. Don't worry. I'm sorry about this, very sorry, particularly as it's my fault. But I'll straighten things out for everyone, you just see!'

Aunt Fanny didn't really believe him, but she was grateful for his comforting. The children listened in silence, drinking their hot cocoa. Uncle Quentin was so very clever, and knew so many things – but it was so like him to neglect something urgent like cutting off the top of the old ash tree. Sometimes he didn't seem to live in this world at all!

It was no use going up to bed! The rooms upstairs were either completely ruined, or so messed up with bits and pieces, and clouds of dust, that it was impossible to sleep there. Aunt Fanny began to pile rugs on sofas. There was one in the study, a big one in the sitting-room and a smaller one in the dining-room. She found a camp-bed in a cupboard and, with Julian's help, put that up too.

'We'll just have to do the best we can,' she said. 'There isn't much left of the night, but we'll get a little sleep if we can! The gale is not nearly so wild now.'

'No – it's done all the damage it can, so it's satisfied,' said Uncle Quentin, grimly. 'Well, we'll talk things over in the morning.'

The children found it very difficult to go to sleep after such an excitement, tired though they were. Anne felt worried. How could they all stay at Kirrin Cottage now?

It wouldn't be fair on Aunt Fanny. But they couldn't go home because her father and mother were both away and the house was shut up for a month.

'I hope we shan't be sent back to school,' thought Anne, trying to get comfortable on the sofa. 'It would be too awful, after having left there, and starting off so cheerfully for the holidays.'

George was afraid of that, too. She felt sure that they would all be packed back to their schools the next morning. That would mean that she and Anne wouldn't see Julian and Dick any more these holidays, for the boys, of course, went to a different school.

Timmy was the only one who didn't worry about things. He lay on George's feet, snoring a little, quite happy. So long as he was with George he didn't really mind *where* he went!

CHAPTER THREE

Uncle Quentin has an idea

NEXT MORNING the wind was still high, but the fury of the gale was gone. The fishermen on the beach were relieved to find that their boats had suffered very little damage. But word soon went round about the accident to Kirrin Cottage, and a few sightseers came up to marvel at the sight of the great, uprooted tree, lying heavily on the little house.

The children rather enjoyed the importance of relating

how nearly they had escaped with their lives. In the light of day it was surprising what damage the big tree had done. It had cracked the roof of the house like an eggshell, and the rooms upstairs were in a terrible mess.

The woman who came up from the village to help Aunt Fanny during the day exclaimed at the sight: 'Why, it'll take weeks to set that right!' she said. 'Have you got on to the builders? I'd get them up here right away and let them see what's to be done.'

'*I'm* seeing to things, Mrs Daly,' said Uncle Quentin. 'My wife has had a great shock. She is not fit to see to things herself. The first thing to do is to decide what is to happen to the children. They can't remain here while there are no usable bedrooms.'

'They had better go back to school, poor things,' said Aunt Fanny.

'No. I've a better idea than that,' said Uncle Quentin, fishing a letter out of his pocket. 'Much better. I've had a letter from that fellow Lenoir this morning – you know, the one who's interested in the same kind of experiments as I am. He says – er, wait a minute, I'll read you the bit. Yes, here it is.'

Uncle Quentin read it out: 'It is most kind of you to suggest my coming to stay with you and bringing my boy Pierre. Allow me to extend hospitality to you and your children also. I do not know how many you have, but all are welcome here in this big house. My Pierre will be glad of company, and so will his sister, Marybelle.'

Uncle Quentin looked up triumphantly at his wife. 'There you are! I call that a most generous invitation! It couldn't have come at a better time. We'll pack the whole of the children off to this fellow's house.'

'But, Quentin – you can't possibly do that! Why, we don't know anything about him or his family!' said Aunt Fanny.

'His boy goes to the same school as Julian and Dick, and I know Lenoir is a remarkable, clever fellow,' said Uncle Quentin, as if that was all that really mattered. 'I'll telephone him now. What's his number?'

Aunt Fanny felt helpless in the face of her husband's sudden determination to settle everything himself. He was ashamed because it was his forgetfulness that had brought on the accident to the house. Now he was going to show that he *could* see to things if he liked. She heard him telephoning, and frowned. How could they possibly send off the children to a strange place like that?

Uncle Quentin put down the receiver, and went to find his wife, looking jubilant and very pleased with himself.

'It's all settled,' he said. 'Lenoir is delighted, most delighted. Says he loves children about the place, and so does his wife, and his two will be thrilled to have them. If we can hire a car today, they can go at once.'

'But, Quentin – we *can't* let them go off like that to strange people! They'll hate it! I shouldn't be surprised if George refuses to go,' said his wife.

'Oh – that reminds me. She's not to take Timothy,' said Uncle Quentin. 'Apparently Lenoir doesn't like dogs.'

'Well then, you know George won't go!' said his wife. 'That's foolish, Quentin. George won't go anywhere without Timmy.'

'She'll have to, this time,' said Uncle Quentin, quite determined that George should not upset all his marvellous plans. 'Here are the children. I'll ask them what *they* feel about going, and see what they say!'

He called them into his study. They came in, feeling sure that they were to hear bad news – probably they were all to return to school!

'You remember that boy I spoke to you about last night?' began Uncle Quentin. 'Pierre Lenoir. You had some absurd name for him.'

'Sooty,' said Dick and Julian together.

'Ah yes, Sooty. Well, his father has kindly invited you all to go and stay with him at Smuggler's Top,' said Uncle Quentin.

The children were astonished.

'*Smuggler's Top!*' said Dick, his fancy caught by the peculiar name. 'What's Smuggler's Top?'

'The name of his house,' said Uncle Quentin. 'It's very old, built on the top of a strange hill surrounded by marshes over which the sea once flowed. The hill was once an island, but now it's just a tall hill rising up from the marsh. Smuggling went on there in the old days. It's a very peculiar place, so I've heard.'

All this made the children feel excited. Also Julian and Dick had always liked Sooty Lenoir. He was quite mad, but awfully good fun. They might have a first-rate time with him.

'Well – would you like to go? Or would you rather go back to school for the holidays?' asked Uncle Quentin impatiently.

'Oh *no* – not back to school!' said everyone at once.

'I'd *love* to go to Smuggler's Top,' said Dick. 'It sounds a thrilling place. And I always liked old Sooty, especially since he sawed half-way through one of the legs of our form-master's chair. It gave way at once when Mr Toms sat down!'

'Hm. I don't see that a trick like that is any reason for liking someone,' said Uncle Quentin, beginning to feel a little doubtful about Master Lenoir. 'Perhaps, on the whole, school would be best for you.'

'Oh no, no!' cried everyone. 'Let's go to Smuggler's Top! Do, do let's!'

'Very well,' said Uncle Quentin, pleased at their eagerness to follow his plan. 'As a matter of fact, I have already settled it. I telephoned a few minutes ago. Mr Lenoir was very kind about it all.'

'Can I take Timmy?' asked George, suddenly.

'No,' said her father. 'I'm afraid not. Mr Lenoir doesn't like dogs.'

'Then I shan't like *him*,' said George, sulkily. 'I won't go without Timmy.'

'You'll have to go back to school, then,' said her father, sharply. 'And take off that sulky expression, George. You know how I dislike it.'

But George wouldn't. She turned away. The others looked at her in dismay. Surely old George wasn't going to get into one of her moods, and spoil everything! It would be fun to go to Smuggler's Top. But, of course, it certainly wouldn't be so much fun without Timmy. Still – they couldn't all go back to school just because George wouldn't go anywhere without her dog.

They all went into the sitting-room. Anne put her arm through George's. George shook it off.

'George! You simply *must* come with us,' said Anne. 'I can't bear to go without you – it would be awful to see you going back to school all alone.'

'I shouldn't be all alone,' said George. 'I should have Timmy.'

The others pressed her to change her mind, but she shook them off. 'Leave me alone,' she said. 'I want to think. How are we supposed to get to Smuggler's Top, and where is it? Which road do we take?'

'We're going by car, and it's right up the coast somewhere, so I expect we'll take the coast-road,' said Julian. 'Why, George?'

'Don't ask questions,' said George. She went out with Timmy. The others didn't follow her. George was not very nice when she was cross.

Aunt Fanny began to pack for them, though it was

impossible to get some of the things from the girls' room. After a time George came back, but Timmy was not with her. She looked more cheerful.

'Where's Tim?' asked Anne, at once.

'Out somewhere,' said George.

'Are you coming with us, George?' asked Julian, looking at her.

'Yes. I've made up my mind to,' said George, but for some reason she wouldn't look Julian in the eyes. He wondered why.

Aunt Fanny gave them all an early lunch, and then a big car came for them. They packed themselves inside. Uncle Quentin gave them all sorts of messages for Mr Lenoir, and Aunt Fanny kissed them goodbye. 'I do hope you have a nice time at Smuggler's Top,' she said. 'Mind you write at once and tell me all about it.'

'Aren't we going to say goodbye to Timmy?' said Anne, her eyes opening wide in amazement at George, forgetting. 'George, surely you're not going without saying goodbye to old Timmy!'

'Can't stop now,' said Uncle Quentin, afraid that George might suddenly become awkward again. 'Right, driver! You can go off now. Don't drive too fast, please.'

Waving and shouting the children drove away from Kirrin Cottage, sad when they looked back and saw the smashed roof under the fallen tree. Never mind – they had not been sent back to school. That was the main thing.

Their spirits rose as they thought of Sooty and his oddly-named home, Smuggler's Top.

'Smuggler's Top! It sounds too exciting for words!' said Anne. 'I can picture it, an old house right on the top of a hill. Fancy being an island once. I wonder why the sea went back and left marshes instead.'

George said nothing for a while, and the car sped on. The others glanced at her once or twice, but came to the conclusion that she was grieving about Timmy. Still she didn't look very sad!

The car went over a hill and sped down to the bottom. When they got there George leaned forward and touched the driver's arm.

'Would you stop a moment, please? We have to pick somebody up here.'

Julian, Dick and Anne stared at George in surprise. The driver, also rather surprised, drew the car to a standstill. George opened the car door and gave a loud whistle.

Something shot out of the hedge and hurled itself joyfully into the car. It was Timmy! He licked everyone, trod on everyone's toes, and gave the little short barks that showed he was excited and happy.

'Well,' said the driver, doubtfully, 'I don't know if you're supposed to take that dog in. Your father didn't say anything about him.'

'It's all right,' said George, her face red with joy. 'Quite all right. You needn't worry. Start the car again, please.'

'You *are* a monkey!' said Julian, half-annoyed with George, and half-pleased because Timmy was with them after all. 'Mr Lenoir may send him back, you know.'

'Well, he'll have to send *me* back too,' said George, defiantly. 'Anyhow, the main thing is, we've got Timmy after all, and I am coming with you.'

'Yes – that's fine,' said Anne, and gave first George and then Timmy a hug. 'I didn't like going without Tim either.'

'On to Smuggler's Top!' said Dick, as the car started off again. 'On to Smuggler's Top. I wonder if we shall have any adventures there!'

CHAPTER FOUR

Smuggler's Top

THE CAR sped on, mostly along the coast, though it sometimes went inland for a few miles. But sooner or later it was in sight of the sea again. The children enjoyed the long drive. They were to stop somewhere for lunch, and the driver told them he knew of a good inn.

At half past twelve he drew up outside an old inn, and they all trooped in. Julian took charge, and ordered lunch. It was a very good one, and all the children enjoyed it. So did Timmy. The innkeeper liked dogs, and put down such a piled-up plate for Timmy that the dog hardly liked to begin on his meal in case it was not for him!

He looked up at George and she nodded to him. 'It's your dinner, Timmy. Eat it up.'

So he ate it, hoping that if they were going to stay anywhere they might be staying at the inn. Meals like this did not arrive every day for a hungry dog!

But after lunch the children got up. They went to find the driver, who was having his lunch in the kitchen with the innkeeper and his wife. They were old friends of his.

'Well, I hear you're going to Castaway,' said the innkeeper, getting up. 'You be careful there!'

'Castaway!' said Julian. 'Is that what the hill is called, where Smuggler's Top is?'

'That's its name,' said the innkeeper.

'Why is it called that?' said Anne. 'What a funny name! Were people cast away on it once, when it was an island?'

'Oh no. The old story goes that the hill was once joined to the mainland,' said the innkeeper. 'But it was the haunt of bad people, and one of the saints became angry with the place, and cast it away into the sea, where it became an island.'

'And so it was called Castaway,' said Dick. 'But perhaps it has got good again, because the sea has gone away from it, and you can walk from the mainland to the hill, can't you?'

'Yes. There's one good road you can take,' said the innkeeper. 'But you be careful of wandering away from it, if you go walking on it! The marsh will suck you down in no time if you set foot on it!'

'It does sound a most exciting place,' said George. 'Smuggler's Top on Castaway Hill! Only one road to it!'

'Time to get on,' said the driver, looking at the clock. 'You've got to be there before tea, your uncle said.'

They got into the car again, Timmy clambering over legs and feet to a comfortable place on George's lap. He was far too big and heavy to lie there but just occasionally he seemed to want to, and George never had the heart to refuse him.

They drove off once more. Anne fell asleep, and the

others felt drowsy too. The car purred on and on. It began to rain, and the countryside looked rather dreary.

The driver turned round after a while and spoke to Julian. 'We're coming near to Castaway Hill. We'll soon be leaving the mainland, and taking the road across the marsh.'

Julian woke Anne. They all sat up expectantly. But it was very disappointing after all! The marshes were full of mist! The children could not pierce through it with their eyes, and could only see the flat road they were on, raised a little higher than the surrounding flat marsh. When the mist shifted a little now and again the children saw a dreary space of flat marsh on either side.

'Stop a minute,' said Julian. 'I'd like to see what the marsh is like.'

'Well, don't step off the road,' warned the driver stopping the car. 'And don't you let that dog out. Once he runs off the road and gets into the marsh he'll be gone for good.'

'What do you mean – gone for good?' said Anne, her eyes wide.

'He means the marsh will suck down Timmy at once,' said Julian. 'Shut him in the car, George.'

So Timmy, much to his disgust, was shut safely in the car. He pawed at the door, and tried to look out of the window. The driver turned and spoke to him. 'It's all right. They'll be back soon, old fellow!'

But Timmy whined all the time the others were out of

the car. He saw them go to the edge of the road. He saw Julian jump down the couple of feet that raised the road above the marsh.

There was a line of raised stones running in the marsh alongside the road. Julian stood on one of these peering at the flat marsh.

'It's mud,' he said. 'Loose, squelchy mud! Look, when I touch it with my foot it moves! It would soon suck me down if I trod heavily on it.'

Anne didn't like it. She called to Julian. 'Come up on the road again. I'm afraid you'll fall in.'

Mists were wreathing and swirling over the salty marshes. It was a weird place, cold and damp. None of the children liked it. Timmy began to bark in the car.

'Tim will scratch the car to bits if we don't get back,' said George. So they all went back, rather silent. Julian wondered how many travellers had been lost in that strange sea-marsh.

'Oh, there're many that've never been heard of again,' said the driver, when they asked him. 'They say there're one or two winding paths that go to the hill from the mainland, that were used before the road was built. But unless you know every inch of them you're off them in a second, and find your feet sinking in the mud.'

'It's horrid to think about,' said Anne. 'Don't let's talk about it any more. Can we see Castaway Hill yet?'

'Yes. There it is, looming up in the mist,' said the driver. 'The top of it is out of the mist, see? Strange place, isn't it?'

The children looked in silence. Out of the slowly moving mists rose a tall, steep hill, whose rocky sides were as steep as cliffs. The hill seemed to swim in the mists, and to have no roots in the earth. It was covered with buildings which even at that distance looked old and quaint. Some of them had towers.

'That must be Smuggler's Top, right at the summit,' said Julian, pointing. 'It's like an old building of centuries ago – probably is! Look at the tower it has. What a wonderful view you'd get from it.'

The children gazed at the place where they were to stay. It looked exciting and picturesque, certainly – but it also looked rather forbidding.

'It's sort of – sort of *secret*, somehow,' said Anne, putting into words what the others were thinking. 'I mean – it looks as if it had kept all kinds of strange secrets down the centuries. I guess it could tell plenty of tales!'

The car drove on again, quite slowly, because the mists came down thickly. The road had a line of sparkling round buttons set all along the middle, and when the driver switched on his fog-lamp, they shone brightly and guided him well. Then as they neared Castaway Hill the road began to slope upwards.

'We go through a big archway soon,' said the driver. 'That used to be where the city gate once was. The whole town is surrounded by wall still, just as it used to be in olden times. It's wide enough to walk on, and if you start at a certain place, and walk long enough, you'll come round to the place you started at!'

All the children made up their minds to do this without fail. What a view they would have all round the hill, if they chose a fine day!

The road became steeper, and the driver put the engine into a lower gear. It groaned up the hill. Then it came to an archway, from which old gates were fastened back. It passed through, and the children were in Castaway.

'It's almost as if we've gone back through the centuries, and come to somewhere that existed ages ago!' said Julian, peering at the old houses and shops, with their cobbled streets, their diamond-paned windows, and stout old doors.

They went up the winding high street, and came at last to a big gateway, set with wrought-iron gates. The driver hooted and they opened. They swept into a steep drive, and at last stopped before Smuggler's Top.

They got out, feeling suddenly shy. The big old house seemed to frown down at them. It was built of brick and timber, and its front door was as massive as that of a castle.

Weird gables jutted here and there over the diamond-paned windows. The house's one tower stood sturdily at the east side of the house, with windows all round. It was not a square tower, but a rounded one, and ended in a point.

'Smuggler's Top!' said Julian. 'It's a good name for it somehow. I suppose lots of smuggling went on here in the old days.'

Dick rang the bell. To do this he had to pull down an iron handle, and a jangling at once made itself heard in the house.

There was the sound of running feet, and the door was opened. It opened slowly, for it was heavy.

Beyond it stood two children, one a girl of about Anne's age, and the other a boy of Dick's age.

'Here you are at last!' cried the boy, his dark eyes dancing. 'I thought you were never coming!'

'This is Sooty,' said Dick to the girls, who had not met him before. They stared at him.

Black hair, black eyes, black eyebrows, and a tanned face. In contrast to him the girl beside him looked pale and delicate. She had golden hair, blue eyes and her eyebrows were so faint they could hardly be seen.

'This is Marybelle, my sister,' said Sooty. 'I always think we look like Beauty and the Beast!'

Sooty was nice. Everyone liked him at once. George found herself twinkling at him in a way quite strange to her, for usually she was shy of strangers, and would not make friends for some time. But who could help liking Sooty with his dancing black eyes and his really wicked grin?

'Come in,' said Sooty. 'Driver, you can take the car round to the next door, and Block will take in the luggage for you and give you tea.'

Suddenly Sooty's face lost its smile and grew very solemn. He had seen Timmy!

'I say! I say – that's not your dog, is it?' he said.

'He's mine,' said George, and she laid a protecting hand on Timmy's head. 'I had to bring him. I can't go anywhere without him.'

'Yes, but – no dog's allowed at Smuggler's Top,' said Sooty, still looking very worried, and glancing behind him as if he was afraid someone might come along and see Timmy. 'My stepfather won't allow any dogs here. Once I brought in a stray one and he licked me till I couldn't sit down – my stepfather licked me, I mean, not the dog.'

Anne gave a frightened little smile at the poor joke. George looked stubborn and sulky.

'I thought – I thought maybe we could hide him somewhere while we were here,' she said. 'But if that's how you feel, I'll go back home with the car. Goodbye.'

She turned and went after the car, which was backing away. Timmy went with her. Sooty stared, and then he yelled after her. 'Come back, stupid! We'll think of *some*thing!'

CHAPTER FIVE

Sooty Lenoir

SOOTY RAN down the steps that led to the front door, and tore after George. The others followed. Marybelle went too, shutting the big front door behind her carefully.

There was a small door in the wall just where George was. Sooty caught hold of her and pushed her roughly through the door, holding it open for the others.

'Don't shove me like that,' began George, angrily. 'Timmy will bite you if you push me about.'

'No, he won't,' said Sooty, with a cheerful grin. 'Dogs like me. Even if I boxed your ears your dog would only wag his tail at me.'

The children found themselves in a dark passage. There was a door at the farther end. 'Wait here a minute and I'll see if the coast is clear,' said Sooty. 'I know my stepfather is in, and I tell you, if he sees that dog he'll pack you all into the car again, and send you back! And I don't want him to do that because I can't tell you how I've looked forward to having you all!'

He grinned at them, and their hearts warmed towards him again, even George's, though she still felt angry at being so roughly pushed. She kept Timmy close beside her.

All the same everyone felt a bit scared of Mr Lenoir. He sounded rather a fierce sort of person!

Sooty tiptoed to the door at the end of the passage and opened it. He peeped into the room there, and then came back to the others.

'All clear,' he said. 'We'll take the secret passage to my bedroom. No one will see us then, and once we're there we can make plans to hide the dog. Ready?'

A secret passage sounded thrilling. Feeling rather as if they were in an adventure story, the children went quietly to the door and into the room beyond. It was a dark, oak-panelled room, evidently a study of some sort, for there was a big desk there, and the walls were lined with books. There was no one there.

Sooty went to one of the oak panels in the wall, felt along it deftly, and pressed in a certain place. The panel slid softly aside. Sooty put in his hand and pulled at something. A much larger panel below slid into the wall, and left an opening big enough for the children to pass through.

'Come on,' said Sooty in a low voice. 'Don't make a noise.'

Feeling excited, the children all passed through the opening. Sooty came last, and did something that shut the opening and slid the first panel back into its place again.

He switched on a small torch, for it was pitch dark where the children were standing.

They were in a narrow stone passage, so narrow that two people could not possibly have passed one another unless both were as thin as rakes. Sooty passed his torch along to Julian, who was in front.

'Keep straight on till you come to stone steps,' he said. 'Go up them, turn to the right at the top, and keep straight on till you come to a blank wall, then I'll tell you what to do.'

Julian led the way, holding up the torch for the others. The narrow passage ran straight, and came to some stone steps. It was not only very narrow but rather low, so that Anne and Marybelle were the only ones who did not have to bend their heads.

Anne didn't like it very much. She never liked being in a very narrow enclosed space. It reminded her of dreams she sometimes had of being somewhere she couldn't get away from. She was glad when Julian spoke. 'The steps are here. Up we go, everyone.'

'Don't make a noise,' said Sooty, in a low voice. 'We're passing the dining-room now. There's a way into this passage from there too.'

Everyone fell silent, and tried to walk on tiptoe, though this was unexpectedly difficult when heads had to be bent and shoulders stooped.

They climbed up fourteen steps, which were quite steep, and curved round half-way. Julian turned to the right at the top. The passage ran upwards then, and was as narrow as before. Julian felt certain that a very large person could not possibly get along it.

He went on until, with a start, he almost bumped into a blank stone wall! He flashed his torch up and down it. A low voice came from the back of the line of children.

'You've got to the blank wall, Julian. Shine your torch up to where the roof of the passage meets the wall. You will see an iron handle there. Press down on it hard.'

Julian flashed his torch up and saw the handle. He put his torch into his left hand, and grasped the thick iron handle with his right. He pressed down as hard as he could.

And, quite silently, the great stone in the middle of the wall slid forward and sideways, leaving a gaping hole.

Julian was astonished. He let go of the iron handle and flashed his torch into the hole. There was nothing but darkness there!

'It's all right. It leads into a big cupboard in my bedroom!' called Sooty from the back. 'Get through, Julian, and we'll follow. There won't be anyone in my room.'

Julian crawled through the hole and found himself in a spacious cupboard, hung with Sooty's clothes. He groped his way through them and bumped against a door. He opened it and at once daylight flooded into the cupboard, lighting up the way from the passage into the room.

One by one the others clambered through the hole, lost themselves in clothes for a moment and then went thankfully into the room through the cupboard door.

Timmy, puzzled and silent, followed close beside George. He had not liked the dark, narrow passage very much. He was glad to be in daylight again!

Sooty, coming last, carefully closed the opening into the

passage by pressing the stone back. It worked easily, though Julian could not imagine how. 'There must be some sort of pivot,' he thought.

Sooty joined the others in his bedroom, grinning. George had her hand on Timmy's collar. 'It's all right George,' said Sooty. 'We're quite safe here. My room and Marybelle's are separate from the rest of the house. We're in a wing on our own, reached by a long passage!'

He opened the door and showed the others what he meant. There was a room next to his, which was Marybelle's. Beyond stretched a stone-floored, stone-walled passage, laid with mats. At the end of it a big window let in light. There was a door there, a great oak one, which was shut.

'See? We're quite safe here, all by ourselves,' said Sooty. 'Timmy could bark if he liked, and no one would know.'

'But doesn't anyone ever come?' said Anne surprised. 'Who keeps your rooms tidy, and cleans them?'

'Oh, Sarah comes and does that every morning,' said Sooty. 'But usually no one else comes. And anyway, I've got a way of knowing when anyone opens that door!'

He pointed to the door at the end of the passage. The others stared at him.

'How *do* you know?' said Dick.

'I've rigged up something that makes a buzzing noise here, in my room, as soon as that door is opened,' said Sooty, proudly. 'Look, I'll go along and open it, while you stay here and listen.'

He sped along the passage and opened the heavy door at the end. Immediately a low buzzing noise sounded somewhere in his room, and made everyone jump. Timmy was startled too, pricked up his ears, and growled fiercely.

Sooty shut the door and ran back. 'Did you hear the noise? It's a good idea, isn't it? I'm always thinking of things like that.'

The others thought they had come to rather a strange place! They stared round Sooty's bedroom, which was quite ordinary in its furnishings, and in its general untidiness. There was a big diamond-paned window, and Anne went to look out of it.

She gave a gasp. She had not expected to look down

such a precipice! Smuggler's Top was built at the summit of the hill, and, on the side where Sooty's bedroom was, the hill fell away steeply, down and down to the marsh below!

'Oh look!' she said. 'Look how steep it is! It really gives me a very funny feeling to look down there!'

The others crowded round and looked in silence, for it certainly was strange to gaze down such a long way.

The sun was shining up on the hill-summit, but all around, as far as they could see, mists hid the marsh and the far-off sea. The only bit of the marsh that could be seen was far down below, at the bottom of the steep hill.

'When the mists are away, you can see over the flat marshes to where the sea begins,' said Sooty. 'That's quite a fine sight. You can hardly tell where the marsh ends and sea begins except when the sea is very blue. Fancy, once upon a time, the sea came right up and around this hill, and it was an island.'

'Yes. The innkeeper told us that,' said George. 'Why did the sea go back and leave it?'

'I don't know,' said Sooty. 'People say it's going back farther and farther. There's a big scheme afoot to drain the marsh, and turn it into fields, but I don't know if that will ever happen.'

'I don't like that marsh,' said Anne, with a shiver. 'It looks wicked, somehow.'

Timmy whined. George remembered that they must hide him, and make plans for him. She turned to Sooty.

'Did you mean what you said about hiding Tim?' she asked. 'Where shall we put him? And can he be fed? And how can we exercise him? He's a big dog, you know.'

'We'll plan it all,' said Sooty. 'Don't you worry. I love dogs, and I shall be thrilled to have Timmy here. But I do warn you that if my stepfather ever finds out we shall probably all get a jolly good telling off, and you'll be sent home in disgrace.'

'But why doesn't your father like dogs?' said Anne puzzled. 'Is he afraid of them?'

'No, I don't think so. It's just that he won't have them here in the house,' said Sooty. 'I think he must have a reason for it, but I don't know what it is. He's an odd sort of man, my stepfather!'

'How is he odd?' asked Dick.

'Well – he seems full of secrets,' said Sooty. 'Strange people come here, and they come secretly without anyone knowing. I've seen lights shining in our tower on certain nights, but I don't know who puts them there or why. I've tried to find out, but I can't.'

'Do you think – do you think your father is a smuggler?' said Anne, suddenly.

'I don't think so,' said Sooty. 'We've got one smuggler here, and everyone knows him! See that house over there to the right, lower down the hill? Well, that's where he lives. He's as rich as can be. His name is Barling. Even the police know his goings-on, but they can't stop him! He is very rich and very powerful, so he does what he likes

– and he won't let anyone play the same game as he plays! No one else would dare to do any smuggling in Castaway, while *he* does it!'

'This seems rather an exciting place,' said Julian. 'I have a kind of feeling there might be an adventure somewhere about!'

'Oh no,' said Sooty. 'Nothing happens, really. It's only just a feeling you get here, because the place is so old, so full of secret ways and pits and passages. Why, the whole hill is mined with passages in the rock, used by the smugglers of olden times!'

'Well,' began Julian, and stopped very suddenly. Everyone stared at Sooty. His secret buzzer had suddenly barked from its hidden corner! Someone had opened the door at the end of the passage!

CHAPTER SIX

Sooty's stepfather and mother

'SOMEONE'S COMING!' said George, in a panic. 'What shall we do with Tim? Quick!'

Sooty took Timmy by the collar and shoved him into the old cupboard, and shut the door on him. 'Keep quiet!' he commanded, and Timmy stood still in the darkness, the hairs at the back of his neck standing up, his ears cocked.

'Well,' began Sooty, in a bright voice, 'perhaps I'd better show you where your bedrooms are now!'

The door opened and a man came in. He was dressed in black trousers and a white linen coat. He had a peculiar face. 'It's a shut face,' thought Anne to herself. 'You can't tell a bit what he's like inside, because his face is all shut and secret.'

'Oh hallo, Block,' said Sooty, airily. He turned to the others. 'This is Block, my stepfather's man,' he said. 'He's deaf, so you can say what you like, but it's better not to, because though he doesn't hear he seems to sense what we say.'

'Anyway, I think it would be beastly to say things we wouldn't say in front of him if he wasn't deaf,' said George, who had very strict ideas about things of that sort.

Block spoke in a curiously monotonous voice. 'Your

stepfather and your mother want to know why you have not brought your friends to see them,' he said. 'Why did you rush up here like this?'

Block looked all round as he spoke – almost as if he knew there was a dog, and wondered where he had gone to, George thought, in alarm. She did hope the car-driver had not mentioned Timmy.

'Oh – I was so pleased to see them I took them straight up here!' said Sooty. 'All right, Block. We'll be down in a minute.'

The man went, his face quite impassive. Not a smile, not a frown!

'I don't like him,' said Anne. 'Has he been with you long?'

'No – only about a year,' said Sooty. 'He suddenly appeared one day. Even Mother didn't know he was coming! He just came, and, without a word, changed into that white linen coat, and went to do some work in my stepfather's room. I suppose my stepfather was expecting him – but he didn't say anything to my mother, I'm sure of that. She seemed so surprised.'

'Is she your real mother, or a stepmother, too?' asked Anne.

'You don't have a stepmother *and* a stepfather!' said Sooty, scornfully. 'You only have one or the other. My mother is my real mother, and she's Marybelle's mother, too. But Marybelle and I are only half-brother and sister, because my stepfather is her *real* father.'

'It's rather muddled,' said Anne, trying to sort it out.

'Come on – we'd better go down,' said Sooty, remembering. 'By the way, my stepfather is always being very affable, always smiling and joking – but it isn't real, somehow. He's quite likely to fly into a furious temper at any moment.'

'I hope we shan't see very much of him,' said Anne, uncomfortably. 'What's your mother like, Sooty?'

'Like a frightened mouse!' said Sooty. 'You'll like her, all right. She's a darling. But she doesn't like living here; she doesn't like this house, and she's terrified of my stepfather. She wouldn't say so herself, of course, but I know she is.'

Marybelle, who was too shy to have joined in any talking until then, nodded her head.

'I don't like living here, either,' she said. 'I shall be glad when I go to boarding school, like Sooty. Except that I shall leave Mother all alone then.'

'Come on,' said Sooty, and led the way. 'We'd better leave Timmy in the cupboard till we come back, just in case Block does a bit of snooping. I'll lock the cupboard door and take the key.'

Feeling rather unhappy at leaving Timmy locked up in the cupboard, the children followed Sooty and Marybelle down the stone passage to the oak door. They went through, and found themselves at the top of a great flight of stairs, wide and shallow. They went down into a big hall.

At the right was a door, and Sooty opened it. He went in and spoke to someone.

'Here they all are,' he said. 'Sorry I rushed them off to

my bedroom like that, Father, but I was so excited to see them all!'

'Your manners still need a little polishing, Pierre,' said Mr Lenoir, in a deep voice. The children looked at him. He sat in a big oak chair, a neat, clever-looking man, with fair hair brushed upwards, and eyes as blue as Marybelle's. He smiled all the time, but with his mouth, not his eyes.

'What cold eyes!' thought Anne, when she went forward to shake hands with him. His hand was cold, too. He smiled at her, and patted her on the shoulder.

'What a nice little girl!' he said. 'You will be a good companion for Marybelle. Three boys for Sooty, and one girl for Marybelle. Ha ha!'

He evidently thought George was a boy, and she did look rather like one – she was wearing jeans and jersey as usual, and her curly hair was very short.

Nobody said that George wasn't a boy. Certainly George was not going to! She, Dick and Julian shook hands with Mr Lenoir. They had not even noticed Sooty's mother!

She was there, though, sitting lost in an armchair, a tiny woman like a doll, with mouse-coloured hair and grey eyes. Anne turned to her.

'Oh, how small you are!' she said, before she could stop herself.

Mr Lenoir laughed. He laughed no matter what anyone said. Mrs Lenoir got up and smiled. She was only as tall as Anne, and had the smallest hands and feet that Anne had ever seen on a grown-up. Anne liked her. She shook hands, and said, 'It's so nice of you to have us all here like this. You know, I expect, that a tree fell on the roof of our house and smashed it.'

Mr Lenoir's laugh came again. He made some kind of joke, and everyone smiled politely.

'Well, I hope you'll have a good time here,' he said. 'Pierre and Marybelle will show you the old town, and, if you promise to be careful, you can walk along the road to the mainland to go to the cinema there.'

'Thank you,' said everyone, and Mr Lenoir laughed his curious laugh again.

'Your father is a very clever man,' he said, suddenly

turning to Julian, who guessed that he had mistaken him for George. 'I am hoping he will come here to fetch you home again when you go, and then I shall have the pleasure of talking with him. He and I have been doing the same kind of experiments, but he has got further than I have.'

'Oh!' said Julian, politely. Then the doll-like Mrs Lenoir spoke in her soft voice.

'Block will give you all your meals in Marybelle's schoolroom, then you will not disturb my husband. He does not like talk at meal-times, and that would be rather hard on six children.'

Mr Lenoir laughed again. His cold blue eyes looked intently at all the children. 'By the way, Pierre,' he said suddenly, 'I forbid you to wander about the catacombs in this hill, as I have forbidden you before, and I also forbid you to do any of your dare-devil climbing, nor will I have you acting about on the city wall now that you have others here. I will not have them taking risks. Will you promise me this?'

'I don't act about on the city wall,' protested Sooty. 'I don't take risks, either.'

'You play the fools always,' said Mr Lenoir, and the tip of his nose turned quite white. Anne looked at it with interest. She did not know that it always did this when Mr Lenoir got angry.

'Oh, sir – I was top of my form last term,' said Sooty, in a most injured tone. The others felt certain that he was trying to lead Mr Lenoir away from his request – he was not going to promise him what he had asked!

Mrs Lenoir now joined in. 'He really did do well last term,' she said. 'You must remember—'

'Enough!' snapped Mr Lenoir, and the smiles and laughs he had so freely lavished on everyone vanished, entirely. 'Get out, all of you!'

Rather scared, Julian, Dick, Anne and George hurried from the room, followed by Marybelle and Sooty. Sooty was grinning as he shut the door.

'I didn't promise!' he said. 'He wanted to take all our fun away. This place isn't any fun if you don't explore it. I can show you heaps of strange places.'

'What are catacombs?' asked Anne, with a vague picture of cats and combs in her head.

'Winding, secret tunnels in the hill,' said Sooty. 'Nobody knows them all. You can get lost in them easily, and never get out again. Lots of people have.'

'Why are there so many secret ways and things here?' wondered George.

'Easy!' said Julian. 'It was a haunt of smugglers, and there must have been many a time when they had to hide not only their goods, but themselves! And, according to old Sooty, there still *is* a smuggler here! What did you say his name was – Barling, wasn't it?'

'Yes,' said Sooty. 'Come on upstairs and I'll show you your rooms. You've got a good view over the town.'

He took them to two rooms set side by side, on the

opposite side of the big staircase from his bedroom and Marybelle's. They were small but well-furnished, and had, as Sooty said, a marvellous view over the quaint roofs and towers of Castaway Hill. They also had a remarkably good view of Mr Barling's house.

George and Anne were to sleep in one room, and Julian and Dick in the other. Evidently Mrs Lenoir had taken the trouble to remember that there were two girls and two boys, not one girl and three boys, as Mr Lenoir imagined!

'Nice cosy rooms,' said Anne. 'I like these dark oak panels. Are there any secret passages in our rooms, Sooty?'

'You wait and see!' grinned Sooty. 'Look, there are your things, all unpacked from your suitcases. I expect Sarah did that. You'll like Sarah. She's a good sort, round and jolly – not a bit like Block!'

Sooty seemed to have forgotten all about Tim. George reminded him.

'What about Timmy? He'll have to be near me, you know. And we must arrange to feed him and exercise him. Oh, I do hope he'll be all right, Sooty. I'd rather leave straight away than have Timmy unhappy.'

'He'll be all right!' said Sooty. 'I'll give him the free run of that narrow passage we came up to my bedroom by, and we'll smuggle him out by a secret tunnel that opens half-way down the town, and give him plenty of exercise each morning. Oh, we'll have a grand time with Timmy!'

George wasn't so sure. 'Can he sleep with me at night?' she asked. 'He'll howl the place down if he can't.'

'Well – we'll try and manage it,' said Sooty, rather doubtfully. 'You've got to be jolly careful, you know. We don't want to land in serious trouble. You don't know what my stepfather can be like!'

They could guess, though. Julian looked curiously at Sooty. 'Was your own father's name Lenoir, too?' he asked.

Sooty nodded. 'Yes. He was my stepfather's cousin, and was as dark as all the Lenoirs usually are. My stepfather is an exception – he's fair. People say the fair Lenoirs are no good – but don't tell my stepfather that!'

'As if we should!' said George. 'Gracious, he'd cut off our heads or something! Come on – let's go back to Tim.'

CHAPTER SEVEN

The hidden pit

THE CHILDREN were all very glad to think that they were going to have meals by themselves in the old schoolroom. Nobody wanted to have much to do with Mr Lenoir! They felt sorry for Marybelle because she had such a peculiar father.

They soon settled down at Smuggler's Top. Once George was satisfied that Timmy was safe and happy, though rather puzzled about everything, she settled down too. The only difficulty was getting Timmy to her room at night. This had to be done in darkness. Block had a most tiresome way of appearing silently and suddenly, and George was terrified of him catching a glimpse of the big dog.

Timmy had a strange sort of life the next few days! While the children were indoors, he had to stay in the narrow secret passage, where he wandered about, puzzled and lonely, pricking his ears for a sound of the whistle that meant he was to come to the cupboard and be let out.

He was fed very well, for Sooty raided the larder every night. Sarah, the cook, was amazed at the way things like soup-bones disappeared. She could not understand it. But Timmy devoured everything that was given to him.

Each morning he was given good exercise by the children. The first morning this had been really very exciting!

George had reminded Sooty of his promise to take Timmy for walks each day. 'He simply must have exercise, or he'll be terribly miserable!' she said. 'But how can we manage it? We can't possibly take him through the house and out of the front door! We'd be certain to walk into your father!'

'I told you I knew a way that came out half-way down the hill, silly,' said Sooty. 'I'll show you. We shall be quite safe once we are down there, because even if we met Block or anyone else that knew us, they wouldn't know it was our dog. They would think it was just a stray we had picked up.'

'Well – show us the way,' said George, impatiently. They were all in Sooty's bedroom, and Timmy was lying on the mat beside George. They felt really safe in Sooty's room because of the buzzer that warned them when anyone opened the door at the end of the long passage.

'We'll have to go into Marybelle's room,' said Sooty. 'You'll get a shock when you see the way that leads down the hill, I can tell you!'

He looked out of the door. The door at the end of the passage was shut. 'Marybelle, slip along and peep through the passage door,' said Sooty. 'Warn us if anyone is coming up the stairs. If not, we'll all slip quickly into your room.'

Marybelle ran to the door at the end of the passage. She

opened it, and at once the warning buzzer sounded in Sooty's room, making Timmy growl fiercely. Marybelle looked through the doorway to the stair. Then she signalled to the others that no one was coming.

They all rushed out of Sooty's room into Marybelle's, and Marybelle came to join them. She was a funny little mouse of a girl, shy and timid. Anne liked her, and once or twice teased her for being so shy.

But Marybelle did not like being teased. Her eyes filled with tears at once, and she turned away. 'She'll be better when she goes to school,' Sooty said. 'She can't help being shy, shut up all the year round in this strange house. She hardly ever sees anyone of her own age.'

They crowded into the little girl's bedroom and shut the door. Sooty turned the key in the lock. 'Just in case friend Block comes snooping,' he said with a grin.

Sooty began to move the furniture in the room to the sides, near the walls. The others watched in surprise and then helped. 'What's the idea of the furniture removal?' asked Dick, struggling with a heavy chest.

'Got to get this heavy carpet up,' panted Sooty. 'It's put there to hide the trap-door below. At least, that's what I've always thought.'

Once the furniture stood by the walls, it was easy to drag up the heavy carpet. There was a felt lining under it too, and that had to be pulled aside as well. Then the children saw a trap-door, let flat into the floor, with a ring-handle to pull it up.

They felt excited. Another secret way! This house seemed full of them. Sooty pulled at the ring and the heavy door came up quite easily. The children peered down, but they could see nothing. It was pitch-dark.

'Are there steps down?' asked Julian, holding Anne back in case she fell.

'No,' said Sooty, reaching out for a big torch he had brought in with him. 'Look!'

He switched on his torch, and the children gave a gasp. The trap-door led down to a pit, far, far below!

'Why! It's miles below the foundations of the house, surely!' said Julian, surprised. 'It's just a hole down to a big pit. What's it for?'

'Oh, it was probably used to hide people – or to get rid of them!' said Sooty. 'Nice little place, isn't it? If you fell down there you'd land with an awful bump!'

'But – how in the world could we get Timmy down there – or get down ourselves?' said George. '*I'm* not going to fall down it, that's certain!'

Sooty laughed. 'You won't have to,' he said. 'Look here.' He opened a cupboard and reached up to a wide shelf. He pulled something down, and the children saw that it was a rope-ladder, fine but very strong.

'There you are! We can all get down by that,' he said.

'Timmy can't,' said George at once. 'He couldn't possibly climb up or down a ladder.'

'Oh, couldn't he?' said Sooty. 'He seems such a clever

dog – I should have thought he could easily have done a thing like that.'

'Well, he can't,' said George, decidedly. 'That's a silly idea.'

'I know,' said Marybelle, suddenly, going red at her boldness in breaking in on the conversation. 'I think I know! We could get the laundry basket and shut Timmy in it. And we would tie it with ropes, and let him down – and pull him up the same way!'

The others stared at her. 'Now that really *is* a brainwave!' said Julian, warmly. 'Good for you, Marybelle. Timmy would be quite safe in a basket. But it would have to be a big one.'

'There's a very big one in the kitchen,' said Marybelle. 'It's never used except when we have lots of people to stay, like now. We could borrow it.'

'Oh *yes*!' said Sooty. 'Of course we could. I'll go and get it now.'

'But what excuse will you give?' shouted Julian after him. Sooty had already unlocked the door and shot out! He was a most impatient person, and could never put off anything for a single minute.

Sooty didn't answer. He sped down the passage. Julian locked the door after him. He didn't want anyone coming in and seeing the carpet up and the yawning hole!

Sooty was back in two minutes, carrying a very heavy wicker laundry basket on his head. He banged on the door, and Julian unlocked it.

'Good!' said Julian. 'How did you get it? Did anyone mind?'

'Didn't ask them,' grinned Sooty. 'Nobody there to ask. Block's with Father, and Sarah has gone out shopping. I can always put it back if any awkward questions are asked.'

The rope-ladder was shaken out down the hole. It slipped like an uncoiling snake, down and down, and reached the pit at the bottom. Then Timmy was fetched from Sooty's room. He came in wagging his tail overjoyed at being with everyone again. George hugged him.

'Darling Timmy! I hate you being hidden away like this. But never mind, we're all going out together this morning!'

'I'll go down first,' said Sooty. 'Then you'd better let Timmy down. I'll tie his basket round with this rope. It's nice and strong, and there's plenty to let down. Better tie the other end to the end of the bed, then when we come up again we can easily pull him up.'

Timmy was made to get inside the big basket and lie down. He was surprised and barked a little. But George put her hand over his mouth.

'Sh! You mustn't say a word, Timmy,' she said. 'I know all this is very astonishing. But never mind, you'll have a marvellous walk at the end of it.'

Timmy heard the word 'Walk' and was glad. That was what he wanted – a really nice long walk in the open air and sunshine!

He didn't at all like having the lid shut down on him,

but as George seemed to think he must put up with all these strange happenings, Timmy did so, with a very good grace.

'He's really a marvellous dog,' said Marybelle. 'Sooty, get down the hole now, and be ready for when we let him down.'

Sooty disappeared down the dark hole, holding his torch between his teeth. Down and down he went, down and down. At last he stood safely at the bottom, and flashed his torch upwards. His voice came to them, sounding rather strange and far away.

'Come on! Lower Timmy down!'

The laundry basket, feeling extraordinarily heavy now, was pushed to the edge of the hole. Then down it went, knocking against the sides here and there. Timmy growled. He didn't like this game!

Dick and Julian had hold of the rope between them. They lowered Timmy as smoothly as they could. He reached the bottom with a slight bump, and Sooty undid the basket. Out leapt Timmy, barking! But his bark sounded very small and distant to the watchers at the top.

'Now come on down, one by one!' shouted up Sooty, waving his torch. 'Is the door locked, Julian?'

'Yes,' said Julian. 'Look out for Anne. She's coming now.'

Anne climbed down, a little frightened at first, but as her feet grew used to searching for and finding the rungs of the rope-ladder, she went down quite quickly.

Then the others followed, and soon they were all standing together at the bottom of the hole, in the enormous pit. They looked round curiously. It had a musty smell, and its walls were damp and greenish. Sooty swung his torch round, and the children saw various passages leading off here and there.

'Where do they all lead to?' asked Julian, in amazement.

'Well, I told you this hill was full of tunnels,' said Sooty. 'This pit is down in the hill and these tunnels lead into the catacombs. There are miles and miles of them. No one explores them now, because so many people have been lost in them and never heard of again. There used to be an old map of them, but it's lost.'

'It's weird!' said Anne, and shivered. 'I wouldn't like to be down here alone.'

'What a place to hide smuggled goods in,' said Dick. 'No one would ever find them here.'

'I guess the old-time smugglers knew every inch of these passages,' said Sooty. 'Come on! We'll take the one that leads out of the hillside. We'll have to do a bit of climbing when we get there. I hope you don't mind.'

'Not a bit,' said Julian. 'We're all good climbers. But I say, Sooty – you're sure you know the way? We don't want to be lost for ever down here!'

''Course I know the way! Come on!' said Sooty, and, flashing his torch in front of him, he led the way into the dark and narrow tunnel.

CHAPTER EIGHT

An exciting walk

THE TUNNEL ran slightly downwards, and smelt nasty in places. Sometimes it opened out into pits like the one they themselves had come from. Sooty flashed his torch up them.

'That one goes into Barling's house somewhere,' he said. 'Most of the old houses hereabouts have openings into pits, like ours. Jolly well hidden some of them are, too!'

'There's daylight or something in front!' said Anne, suddenly. 'Oh good! I hate this tunnel.'

Sure enough, it was daylight, creeping in through a kind of cave-entrance in the hillside. The children crowded there, and looked out.

They were outside the hill, and outside the town, somewhere on the steep cliff-side that ran down to the marsh. Sooty climbed out on to a ledge. He put his torch into his pocket.

'We've got to get to that path down there,' he said, pointing. 'That will lead us to a place where the city wall is fairly low, and we can climb over it. Is Timmy sure-footed? We don't want him tumbling into the marsh down there!'

The marsh lay a good way below, looking ugly and flat. George sincerely hoped Timmy would never fall into it.

Still, he was very sure-footed, and she didn't think he would slip. The path was steep and rocky, but quite passable.

They all went down it, clambering over rocks now and again. The path led them to the city wall, which, as Sooty had said, was fairly low just there. He climbed up to the top. He was like a cat for climbing!

'No wonder he's got such a name for climbing about everywhere at school!' said Dick to Julian. 'He's had good practice here. Do you remember how he climbed up to the roof of the school the term before last? Everyone was scared he'd slip and fall, but he didn't. He tied the Union Jack to one of the chimney-pots!'

'Come on!' called Sooty. 'The coast is clear. This is a lonely bit of the town, and no one will see us climbing up.'

Soon they were all over the wall, Timmy too. They set off for a good walk, swinging down the hill, enjoying themselves. The mist began to clear after a while, and the sun felt nice and warm.

The town was very old. Some of the houses seemed almost tumble-down, but there were people living in them, for smoke came from the chimneys. The shops were quaint, with their long narrow windows, and overhanging eaves. The children stopped to look into them.

'Look out – here's Block!' said Sooty suddenly in a low voice. 'Don't take any notice of Timmy at all. If he comes around licking us or jumping up, pretend to try and drive him off as if he were a stray.'

They all pretended not to see Block, but gazed earnestly into the window of a shop. Timmy, feeling rather out of it, ran up to George and pawed at her, trying to make her take notice of him.

'Go away, dog!' said Sooty, and flapped at the surprised Timmy. 'Go away! Following us about like this! Go home, can't you?'

Timmy thought this was some sort of a game. He barked happily, and ran round Sooty and George, giving them an occasional lick.

'Home, dog, home!' yelled Sooty, flapping hard again.

Then Block came up to them, no expression on his face

at all. 'The dog bothers you?' he said. 'I will throw a stone at him and make him go.'

'Don't you dare!' said George, immediately. 'You go home yourself! I don't mind the dog following us. He's quite a nice one.'

'Block's deaf, silly,' said Sooty. 'It's no good talking to him.' To George's horror Block picked up a big stone, meaning to throw it at Timmy. George flew at him, punched him hard on the arm, and made him drop the stone.

'How dare you throw stones at a dog!' yelled the little girl in a fury. 'I'll – I'll tell the police.'

'Now, now,' said a voice nearby. 'What's all this about? Pierre, what's the trouble?'

The children turned and saw a tall man standing near them, wearing his hair rather long. He had long, narrow eyes, a long nose and a long chin. 'He's long everywhere!' thought Anne, looking at his long thin legs and long narrow feet.

'Oh, Mr Barling! I didn't see you,' said Sooty, politely. 'Nothing's the matter, thanks. It's only that this dog is following us, and Block said he'd make it go away by chucking a stone at it. And George here is fond of dogs and got angry about that.'

'I see. And who are all these children?' said Mr Barling, looking at each one of them out of his long, narrow eyes.

'They've come to stay with us because their uncle's house has been damaged in a gale,' explained Sooty. 'George's father's house, I mean. At Kirrin.'

'Ah – at Kirrin?' said Mr Barling, and seemed to prick up his long ears. 'Surely that is where that very clever scientist friend of Mr Lenoir's lives?'

'Yes. He's my father,' said George. 'Why, do you know him?'

'I have heard of him – and of his very interesting experiments,' said Mr Barling. 'Mr Lenoir knows him well, I believe?'

'Not awfully well,' said George, puzzled. 'They just write to one another, I think. My father telephoned to Mr Lenoir to ask him if he could have us to stay while our own house is being mended.'

'And Mr Lenoir, of course, was only too delighted to have the whole company of you! said Mr Barling. '*Such* a good, generous fellow, your father, Pierre!'

The children stared at Mr Barling, thinking that it was strange of him to say nice things in such a nasty voice. They felt uncomfortable. It was plain that Mr Barling did not like Mr Lenoir at all. Well, neither did they, but they didn't like Mr Barling any better!

Timmy saw another dog and darted happily after him. Block had now disappeared, going up the steep high street with his basket. The children said goodbye to Mr Barling, not wanting to talk to him any more.

They went after Timmy, talking eagerly as soon as they had left Mr Barling behind.

'Goodness – that was a narrow escape from Block!' said Julian. 'Old beast – going to throw that enormous stone at

Timmy. No wonder you flew at him, George! But you very nearly gave the game away, though.'

'I don't care,' said George. 'I wasn't going to have Timmy's leg broken. It was a bit of bad luck meeting Block our very first morning out.'

'We'll probably never meet him again when we take Timmy out,' said Sooty, comfortingly. 'And if we do we'll simply say the dog always joins us when it meets us. Which is perfectly true.'

They enjoyed their walk. They went into a quaint old coffee shop and had steaming cups of delicious creamy coffee and jammy buns. Timmy had two of the buns and gobbled them greedily. George went off to buy some meat for him at the butcher's, choosing a shop that Sooty said Mrs Lenoir did not go to. She did not want any butcher telling Mrs Lenoir that the children had been buying dog-meat!

They went back the same way as they had come. They made their way up the steep cliff-path, and in at the tunnel-entrance, back through the winding tunnel to the pit, and there was the rope-ladder waiting for them. Julian and Dick went up first, while George packed the surprised Timmy into the basket again and tied the rope firmly round it. Then up went the whining Timmy, bumping against the sides of the hole, until the two panting boys pulled the basket into Marybelle's room and undid it.

It was ten minutes before the dinner-hour. 'Just time to shut the trap-door, pull back the carpet and wash our hands,' said Sooty. 'And I'll put old Timmy back into the secret passage behind the cupboard in my room, George. Where is that meat you bought? I'll put that in the passage too. He can eat it when he likes.'

'Did you put him a nice warm rug there, and a dish of fresh water?' asked George, anxiously, for the third or fourth time.

'You know I did. I keep telling you,' said Sooty. 'Look, we won't put back all the furniture except the chairs. We can say we want it left back because we like to play a game on the carpet. It'll be an awful bore if we have to move chests and things every time we exercise Tim.'

They were just in time for their dinner. Block was there to serve it, and so was Sarah. The children sat down hungrily, in spite of having had coffee and buns. Block and Sarah ladled out hot soup on to their plates.

'I hope you got rid of the unpleasant dog,' said Block in his monotonous voice. He gave George a rather nasty look. Evidently he had not forgotten how she had flown at him.

Sooty nodded. It was no good speaking an answer, for Block would not hear. Sarah bustled round, taking away the soup-plates and preparing to give them their second course.

The food was very good at Smuggler's Top. There was plenty of it, and the hungry visitors and Sooty ate everything put before them. Marybelle hadn't much appetite, but she was the only one. George tried to secrete titbits and bones whenever she could, for Timmy.

Two or three days went by, and the children fell into their new life quite happily. Timmy was taken out each morning for a long walk. The children soon got used to slipping down the rope-ladder, and making their way with Timmy to the cliff-side.

In the afternoons they went to either Sooty's room or Marybelle's, and played games or read. They could have Timmy there, because the buzzer always warned them if anyone was coming.

At night it was always an excitement to get Timmy to George's room without being seen. This was usually done when Mr and Mrs Lenoir were sitting at their dinner, and Block and Sarah were serving them. The children had a light supper first, and Mr and Mrs Lenoir had their dinner an hour later. It was quite the best time to smuggle Timmy along to George's room.

Timmy seemed to enjoy the smuggling. He ran silently beside George and Sooty, stopped at every corner, and scampered gladly into George's room as soon as he got there. He lay quietly under the bed till George was in bed herself, and then he came out to lie on her feet.

George always locked their door at night. She didn't want Sarah or Mrs Lenoir coming in and finding Timmy there! But nobody came, and as night after night went by, George grew more easy about Timmy.

Taking him back to Sooty's room in the morning was a bit of a nuisance, because it had to be done early, before anyone was up. But George could always wake herself at any time she chose, and each morning about half past six the little girl slipped through the house with Timmy. She went in at Sooty's door, and he jumped out of bed to deal with Timmy. He was always awakened by the buzzer that sounded when George opened the door at the end of the passage.

'I hope you are all enjoying yourselves,' Mr Lenoir said to the children, whenever they met him in the hall or on the stairs. And they always replied politely. 'Oh yes, Mr Lenoir, thank you.'

'It's quite a peaceful holiday after all,' said Julian. 'Nothing happens at all!'

And then things *did* begin to happen and once they had begun they never stopped!

CHAPTER NINE

Who is in the tower?

ONE NIGHT Julian was awakened by someone opening his door. He sat up at once. 'Who is it?' he said.

'Me, Sooty,' said Sooty's voice, very low. 'I say, I want you to come and see something.'

Julian woke Dick, and the two of them put on their dressing-gowns. Sooty led them quietly out of the room and took them to a peculiar little room, tucked away in an odd wing of the house. All kinds of things were kept here, trunks and boxes, old toys, chests of old clothes, broken vases that had never been mended, and many other worthless things.

'Look,' said Sooty, taking them to the window. They saw that the little room had a view of the tower belonging to the house. It was the only room in the house that did, for it was built at a strange angle.

The boys looked – and Julian gave an exclamation. Someone was signalling from the tower! A light there flashed every now and again. In and out – pause – flash, flash, in and out – pause. The light went regularly on and off in a certain rhythm.

'Now – who's doing that?' whispered Sooty.

'Your father?' wondered Julian.

'Don't think so,' said Sooty. 'I think I heard him snoring away in his room. We could go and find out though – see if he really is in his bedroom.'

'Well – for goodness' sake don't let's get caught,' said Julian, not at all liking the idea of prying about in his host's house.

They made their way to where Mr Lenoir had his room. It was quite plain he was there, for a regular low snoring came from behind the closed door.

'It may be Block up in the tower,' said Dick. 'He looks full of secrets. I wouldn't trust him an inch. I bet it's Block.'

'Well – shall we go to his room and see if it's empty?' whispered Sooty. 'Come on. If it's Block signalling, he's doing it without Father knowing.'

'Oh, your father might have told him to,' said Julian, who felt that he wouldn't trust Mr Lenoir much further than he would trust Block.

They went up the back-stairs to the wing where the staff slept. Sarah slept in a room there with Harriet the kitchen-maid. Block slept alone.

Sooty pushed open Block's door very softly and slowly. When he had enough room to put in his head, he did so. The room was full of moonlight. By the window was Block's bed. And Block was there! Sooty could see the humpy shape of his body, and the black round patch that was his head.

He listened, but he could not catch Block's breathing. He must sleep very quietly.

He withdrew his head, and pushed the other two boys quietly down the back-stairs.

'Was he there?' whispered Julian.

'Yes. So it can't be him, signalling up in our tower,' said Sooty. 'Well – who can it be then? I don't like it. It couldn't possibly be Mother or Sarah or Harriet. Is there a stranger in our house, someone we don't know, living here in secret?'

'Can't be!' said Julian, a little shiver running down his back. 'Look here – what about us going up to the tower and trying to peep through the door or something? We'd soon find out who it was then. Perhaps we ought to tell your father.'

'No. Not yet. I want to find out a whole lot more before I say anything to anyone,' said Sooty, sounding obstinate. 'Let's creep up to the tower. We shall have to be jolly careful though. You get to it by a spiral staircase, rather narrow. There's nowhere much to hide if anyone suddenly came down out of the tower.

'What's in the tower?' whispered Dick, as they made their way through the dark and silent house, thin streaks of moonlight coming in here and there between the crack of the closed curtains.

'Nothing much. Just a table and a chair or two, and a bookcase of books,' said Sooty. 'We use it on hot summer days when the breeze gets in strongly through the windows there, and we can see a long way all round us.'

They came to a little landing. From this a winding, narrow stairway of stone went up to the rounded tower. The boys looked up. Moonlight fell on the stairway from a slit-like window in the wall.

'We'd better not all go up,' said Sooty. 'We should find it so difficult to hurry down, three of us, if the person in the tower suddenly came out. I'll go. You stay down here and wait. I'll see if I can spy anything through the crack in the door or the key-hole.'

He crept softly up the stairway, soon lost to view as he rounded the first spiral. Julian and Dick waited in the shadows at the bottom. There was a thick curtain over one of the windows there, and they got behind it, wrapping its folds round them for warmth.

Sooty crept up to the top. The tower-room had a stout oak door, studded and barred. It was shut! It was no use trying to look through the crack, because there wasn't one. He bent down to peer through the key-hole.

But that was stuffed up with something, so he could not see through that either. He pressed his ear to it and listened.

He heard a series of little clicks. Click – click – click – click – click. Nothing else at all.

'That's the click of the light they're using,' thought Sooty. 'Still signalling like mad! What for? Who to? And who is in our tower-room, using it as a signalling-station? How I wish I knew!'

Suddenly the clicking stopped. There was the sound of someone walking across the stone floor of the tower. And almost at once the door opened!

Sooty had no time to hurry down the stairs. All he could do was to squeeze into a niche, and hope that the person would not see him or touch him as he went by. The moon went behind a cloud at that moment, and Sooty was thankful to know he was hidden in black shadow. Someone came down the stairs and actually brushed against Sooty's arm.

Sooty jumped almost out of his skin, expecting to be hauled out of his niche. But the person did not seem to

notice, and went on down the spiral stairway, walking softly.

Sooty did not dare to go down after him, for he was afraid the moon would come out, and cast his shadow down for the signaller to see.

So he stayed squeezed in his niche, hoping that Julian and Dick were well-hidden, and would not think it was he, Sooty, who was walking down the stairs!

Julian and Dick heard the soft footsteps coming, and thought at first it was Sooty. Then, not hearing his whisper, they stiffened behind the curtains, guessing that it was the signaller himself who was walking by!

'We'd better follow him!' whispered Julian to Dick. 'Come on. Quiet, now!'

But Julian got muddled up with the great curtains, and could not seem to find his way out. Dick, however, slipped out easily enough, and padded after the disappearing person. The moon was now out again, and Dick could catch glimpses of the signaller as he went past the moonlight streaks. Keeping well in the shadows himself, he darted quietly after him. Where was he going?

He followed him across the landing to a passage. Then across another landing and up the back-stairs! But those led to the staff bedrooms. Surely the man was not going there?

Dick, to his enormous surprise, saw the person disappear silently into Block's bedroom. He crept to the door, which had been left a little ajar. There was no light in the room except that of the moon. There was no sound of talking.

Nothing at all except a creak which might have come from the bed.

Dick peeped in, full of the most intense curiosity. Would he see the man waking up Block? Would he see him climbing out of the window?

He stared round the room. There was no one there at all, except Block lying in bed. The moonlight lit up the corners, and Dick could quite plainly see that the room was empty. Only Block lay there, and, as Dick watched, he heard him give a sigh and roll over in bed.

'Well! That's the strangest thing I ever saw,' thought Dick, puzzled. 'A man goes into a room and completely disappears, without a single sound! Where can he have gone?'

He went back to find the others. Sooty by this time had crept down the spiral staircase and had found Julian, who had explained that Dick had gone to follow the peculiar signaller.

They went to find Dick, and suddenly bumped into him, creeping along quietly in the darkness. They all jumped violently, and Julian almost cried out, but stifled his voice just in time.

'Golly! You gave me a scare, Dick!' he whispered. 'Well, did you see who it was and where he went?'

Dick told them of his strange experience. 'He simply went into Block's room and vanished,' he said. 'Is there any secret passage leading out of Block's room, Sooty?'

'No, none,' said Sooty. 'That wing is much newer than the rest of the house, and hasn't any secrets in at all. I simply can't imagine what happened to the man. How very odd! Who is he, and why does he come, and where on earth does he go?'

'We really must find out,' said Julian. 'It's such a mystery! Sooty, how did you know there was signalling going on from the tower?'

'Well, some time ago I found it out, quite by accident,' said Sooty. 'I couldn't sleep, and I went along to that funny little box-room place, and ferreted about for an old book I thought I'd seen there. And suddenly I looked up at the tower, and saw a light flashing there.'

'Funny,' said Dick.

'Well, I went along there at night a good many times

after that, to see if I could see the signals again,' said Sooty, 'and at last I did. The first time I had seen them there was a good moon, and the second time there was, too. So, I thought, next time there's a moon, I'll creep along to that old box-room and see if the signaller is at work again. And sure enough he was!'

'Where does that window look out on, that we saw the light flashing from?' asked Julian, thoughtfully. 'The seaward side – or the landward?'

'Seaward,' said Sooty at once. 'There's something or someone out at sea that receives those signals. Goodness knows who.'

'Some kind of smugglers, I suppose,' said Dick. 'But it can't be anything to do with your father, Sooty. I say – let's go up into the tower, shall we? We might find something there – or see something.'

They went back to the spiral staircase and climbed up to the tower-room. It was dark, for the moon was behind a cloud. But it came out after a while, and the boys looked out of the seaward window.

There was no mist at all that night. They could see the flat marshes stretching away to the sea. They gazed down in silence. Then the moon went in and darkness covered the marsh.

Suddenly Julian clutched the others, making them jump. 'I can see something!' he whispered. 'Look beyond there. What is it?'

They all looked. It seemed like a tiny line of very small

dots of light. They were so far away that it was difficult to see if they stayed still or moved. Then the moon came out again, flooding everywhere with silvery light, and the boys could not see anything except the moonshine.

But when the moon went in again, there was the line of tiny, pricking lights again! 'A bit nearer, surely!' whispered Sooty. 'Smugglers – coming over a secret path from the sea to Castaway Hill! Smugglers!'

CHAPTER TEN

Timmy makes a noise

THE THREE girls were very excited the next day when the boys told them their adventure of the night before.

'Gracious!' said Anne, her eyes wide with surprise. 'Who can it be signalling like that? And wherever did he go to? Fancy him going into Block's room, with Block there in bed!'

'It's very peculiar,' said George. 'I wish you had come and told me and Anne.'

'There wasn't time – and anyway, we couldn't have Timmy about at night. He might have flown at the signaller,' said Dick.

'The man must have been signalling to the smugglers,' said Julian, thoughtfully. 'Let me see – probably they came over from France in a ship – came as near to the marsh as they could – waited for a signal to tell them that the coast was clear – probably the signal from the tower – and then waded across a path they knew through the marsh. Each man must have carried a torch to prevent himself from leaving the path and falling into the marsh. No doubt there was someone waiting to receive the goods they brought – someone at the edge of the marsh below the hill.'

'But who?' said Dick. 'It can't have been Mr Barling,

who, Sooty says, is known to be a smuggler. Because the signal lights came from *our* house, not his. It's all very puzzling.'

'Well, we'll do our best to solve the mystery,' said George. 'There's some peculiar game going on in this very house, without your father's knowledge, Sooty. We'll keep a jolly good lookout and see if we can find out what it is.'

They were at breakfast alone, when they discussed the night's adventure. Block came in to see if they had finished at that moment. Anne did not notice him.

'What does Mr Barling smuggle?' she asked Sooty. Immediately she got a hard kick on her ankle, and stared in pain and surprise. 'Why did you . . . ?' she began, and got another kick, harder still. Then she saw Block.

'But he's deaf,' she said. 'He can't hear anything we say.'

Block began to clear away, his face as usual showing no expression. Sooty glared at Anne. She was upset and cross, but said no more. She rubbed her bruised ankle hard. As soon as Block went out of the room she turned on Sooty.

'You mean thing! You hurt my ankle like anything! Why shouldn't I say things in front of Block? He's quite deaf!' said Anne, her face very red.

'I know he's supposed to be,' said Sooty. 'And I think he is. But I saw a funny look come over his face when you asked me what Mr Barling smuggled – almost as if he had heard what you said, and was surprised.'

'You imagined it!' said Anne, crossly, still rubbing her

ankle. 'Anyway, don't kick me so hard again. A gentle push with your toe would have been enough. I won't talk in front of Block if you don't want me to, but it's quite plain he's deaf!'

'Yes, he's deaf all right,' said Dick. 'I dropped a plate off the table yesterday, by accident, just behind him, and it smashed to bits, if you remember. Well, he didn't jump or turn a hair, as he would have done if he could have heard.'

'All the same – I never trust Block, deaf or not,' said Sooty. 'I always feel he might read our lips or something. People can do that, you know.'

They went off to take Timmy for his usual morning walk. Timmy was quite used to being shut in the laundry basket by now, and lowered into the pit. In fact, he always jumped straight into the basket as soon as the lid was opened, and lay down.

That morning they again met Block, who stared with great interest at the dog. He plainly recognised it as the same dog as before.

'There's Block,' said Julian, in a low voice. 'Don't drive Timmy off this time. We'll pretend he's a stray who always meets us each morning.'

So they let Timmy run round them, and when Block came up, they nodded to him, and made as if to go on their way. But the man stopped them.

'That dog seems to be a friend of yours,' he said, in his curious monotone of a voice.

'Oh yes. He goes with us each morning now,' said

Julian, politely. 'He quite thinks he's our dog! Nice fellow, isn't he?'

Block stared at Timmy, who growled. 'Mind you do not bring that dog into the house,' said Block. 'If you do, Mr Lenoir will have him thrown out.'

Julian saw George's face beginning to turn red with fury. He spoke hurriedly. 'Why should we bring him to the house, Block? Don't be silly!'

Block, however, did not appear to hear. He gave Timmy a nasty look, and went on his way, occasionally turning round to look at the little company of children.

'Horrid fellow!' said George, angrily. 'How dare he say things like that?'

When they got back to Marybelle's bedroom that morning, they pulled Timmy up from the pit, and let him out of the basket. 'We'll put him into the secret passage as usual,' said George, 'and I'll put some biscuits in with him. I got some nice ones for him this morning, the sort he likes, all big and crunchy.'

She went to the door – but just as she was about to unlock it and take Timmy into Sooty's room next door, Timmy gave a small growl.

George took her hand away from the door at once. She turned to look at Timmy. He was standing stiffly, the hackles on his neck rising up, and he was staring fixedly at the door. George put her hand to her lips warningly, and whispered: 'Someone's outside. Timmy knows. He's smelt them. Will you all talk loudly, and pretend to be playing a game? I'll pop Timmy into the cupboard where the rope-ladder is kept.'

At once the others began to talk to one another, while George swiftly dragged Timmy to the cupboard, patted him to make him understand he was to be quiet, and shut him in.

'My turn to deal,' said Julian loudly, and took a pack of snap cards from the top of the chest. 'You won last time, Dick. Bet I'll win this time.'

He dealt swiftly. The others, still talking loudly, saying anything that came into their heads, began to play snap. They yelled 'snap' nearly all the time, pretending to be very jolly and hilarious. Anyone listening outside the door would never guess it was all pretence.

George, who was watching the door closely, saw that the handle was gradually turning, very slowly indeed. Someone meant to open the door without being heard, and come in unexpectedly. But the door was locked!

Soon the person outside, whoever it was, realised that the door was locked, and the handle slowly turned the other way again. Then it was still. There came no other sound. It was impossible to know if anyone was still outside the door or not.

But Timmy would know! Signing to the others to carry on with their shouting and laughing, George let Timmy out of the cupboard. He ran to the door of the room, and stood there, sniffing quietly. Then he turned and looked at George, his tail wagging.

'It's all right,' said George to the others. 'There's no one there now. Timmy always knows. We'd better quickly take him into your room, Sooty, while the coast is clear. Who could it have been, do you think, snooping outside?'

'Block, I should say,' said Sooty. He unlocked the door and peered out. There was no one in the passage. Sooty tiptoed to the door at the end and looked out there also. He waved to George to tell her it was all right to take Timmy into his room.

Soon Timmy was safely in the secret passage, crunching up his favourite biscuits. He had got quite used to his peculiar life now, and did not mind at all. He knew his way about the passage, and had explored other passages that led from it. He was quite at home in the maze of secret ways!

'Better go and have our dinner now,' said Dick. 'And mind, Anne – don't go and say anything silly in front of that horrid Block, in case he reads your lips.'

'Of course I shan't,' said Anne, indignantly. 'I wouldn't have before, but I never thought of him reading my lips. If he does, he's very clever.'

Soon they were all sitting down to lunch. Block was there, waiting to serve them. Sarah was out for the day and did not appear. Block served them with soup, and then went out.

Suddenly, to the children's intense surprise and fright, they heard Timmy barking loudly! They jumped violently.

'Listen! That's Timmy!' said Julian. 'He must be

somewhere near here, in that secret passage. How weird it sounds, his bark coming muffled and distant like that. But anyone would know it was a dog barking.'

'Don't say anything at all about it in front of Block,' said Sooty. 'Not a word. Pretend not to hear at all, if Timmy barks again. What on earth is he barking for?'

'It's the bark he uses when he's excited and pleased,' said George. 'I expect he's chasing a rat. He always goes right off his head when he sees a rat or a rabbit. There he goes again. Oh, dear, I hope he catches the rat quickly and settles down!'

Block came back at that moment. Timmy had again just stopped barking. But, in a moment or two, his doggy voice could be heard once more, very muffled. 'Woof! Woof-woof!'

Julian was watching Block closely. The man went on serving the meat. He said nothing, but looked round at the children intently, as if he wanted to see each child's expression, or see if they said anything.

'Jolly good soup that was today,' said Julian, cheerfully, looking round at the others. 'I must say Sarah is a wonderful cook.'

'I think her ginger buns are gorgeous,' said Anne. 'Especially when they are all hot from the oven.'

'Woof-woof,' said Timmy's voice from far away behind the walls.

'George, your mother makes the most heavenly fruit cake I ever tasted,' said Dick to George, wishing Timmy

would be quiet. 'I do wonder how they're all getting on at Kirrin Cottage, and if they've started mending the roof yet.'

'Woof!' said Timmy, joyfully chasing his rat down another bit of passage.

Block served everyone and then silently disappeared. Julian went to the door to make sure he had gone and was not outside.

'I hope old Block *is* deaf!' he said. 'I could have sworn I saw a surprised look come into those cold eyes of his, when Timmy barked.'

'Well, if he *could* hear him, which I don't believe,' said George, 'he must have been jolly surprised to see us talking away and not paying any attention to a dog's barking at all!'

The others giggled. They kept a sharp ear for Block's return. They heard footsteps after a time, and began to pile their plates together for him to take away.

The schoolroom door opened. But it was not Block who came in. It was Mr Lenoir! He came in, smiling as usual, and looked round at the surprised children.

'Ah! So you are enjoying your dinner, and eating it all up, like good children,' he said. He always irritated the children because he spoke to them as if they were very small. 'Does Block wait on you properly?'

'Oh yes, thank you,' said Julian, standing up politely. 'We are having a very nice time here. We think Sarah is a wonderful cook!'

'Ah, that's good, that's good,' said Mr Lenoir. The children waited impatiently for him to go. They were so afraid that Timmy would bark again. But Mr Lenoir seemed in no hurry.

And then Timmy barked again! 'Woof, woof, woof!'

CHAPTER ELEVEN

George is worried

MR LENOIR cocked his head on one side almost like a startled dog, when he heard the muffled barking. He looked at the children. But they made no sign of having heard anything. Mr Lenoir listened a little while, saying nothing. Then he turned to a drawing-book, belonging to Julian, and began to look at the sketches there.

The children felt somehow that he was doing it for the sake of staying in the schoolroom a little longer. Into Julian's mind came the quick suspicion that somehow Mr Lenoir must have been told of Timmy's barking and come to investigate it for himself. It was the first time he had ever come to the schoolroom!

Timmy barked again, a little more distantly. Mr Lenoir's nose grew white at the tip. Sooty and Marybelle knew the danger-sign, and glanced at one another. That white-tipped nose usually meant a storm of temper!

'Do you hear that noise?' said Mr Lenoir, snapping out the words.

'What noise?' asked Julian, politely.

Timmy barked again.

'Don't be foolish! There's the noise again!' said Mr

Lenoir. At that moment a gull called outside the window, circling in the sea-breeze.

'Oh – that gull? Yes, we often hear the gulls,' said Dick, brightly. 'Sometimes they seem to mew like a cat.'

'Pah!' said Mr Lenoir, almost spitting out the word. 'I suppose you will say they also bark like a dog?'

'Well, they might, I suppose,' agreed Dick, looking faintly surprised. 'After all, if they can mew like cats, there's no reason why they shouldn't bark like dogs.'

Timmy barked again very joyfully. Mr Lenoir faced the children, in a very bad temper indeed now.

'Can't you hear that? Tell me what *that* noise is!'

The children all put their heads on one side, and pretended to listen very carefully. 'I can't hear anything,' said Dick. 'Not a thing.'

'I can hear the wind,' said Anne.

'I can hear the gulls again,' said Julian, putting his hand behind one ear.

'I can hear a door banging. Perhaps that's the noise you mean,' said Sooty, with a most innocent expression. His stepfather gave him a poisonous look. He could really be very unpleasant.

'And there's a window rattling,' said Marybelle, eager to do her bit too, though she felt very frightened of her father, for she knew his sudden rages very well.

'I tell you, it's a dog, and you know it!' snapped Mr Lenoir, the tip of his nose so white now that it looked very strange indeed. 'Where's the dog? Whose is he?'

'What dog?' began Julian, frowning as if he were very puzzled indeed. 'There's no dog here that I can see.'

Mr Lenoir glared at him, and clenched his fingers. It was quite clear that he would have liked to box Julian's ears. 'Then listen!' he hissed. 'Listen and say what you think could make that barking, if not a dog?'

They were all forced to listen, for by now they felt scared of the angry man. But fortunately Timmy made no sound at all. Either he had let the rat escape, or was now gobbling it up. Anyway, there was not a single sound from him!

'Sorry, but *really* I can't hear a dog barking,' said Julian, in rather an injured tone.

'Nor can I!' said Dick, and the others joined in, saying the same. Mr Lenoir knew that this time they were speaking the truth, for he too could not hear anything.

'When I catch that dog I will have him poisoned,' he said, very slowly and clearly. 'I will not have dogs in my house.'

He turned on his heel and went out quickly, which was a very good thing, for George was quite ready to fly into one of *her* rages, and then there would have been a real battle! Anne put her hand on George's arm to stop her shouting after Mr Lenoir.

'Don't give the game away!' she whispered. 'Don't say anything, George!'

George bit her lip. She had gone first red with rage and then white. She stamped her foot.

'How dare he, how dare he?' she burst out.

'Shut up, silly,' said Julian. 'Block will be back in a minute. We must all pretend to be awfully surprised that Mr Lenoir thought there was a dog, because, if Block can read our lips, he mustn't know the truth.'

Block came in with the pudding at that moment, his face as blank as ever. It was the most curious face the children had ever seen, for there was never any change of expression on it at all. As Anne said, it might have been a wax mask!

'Funny how Mr Lenoir thought there was a dog barking!' began Julian, and the others backed him up valiantly. If Block could indeed read their lips he would be puzzled to know whether there had been a dog barking or not!

The children escaped to Sooty's room afterwards, and held a council of war. 'What are we to do about Timmy?' said George. 'Does your stepfather know the secret way behind the walls of Smuggler's Top, Sooty? Could he possibly get in and find Timmy? Timmy might fly at him, you know.'

'Yes, he might,' said Sooty, thoughtfully. 'I don't know if Father does know about the secret passages. I mean, I expect he knows, but I don't know if he guessed where the entrances are. I found them out quite by accident.'

'I'm going home,' said George, suddenly. 'I'm not going to risk Timmy being poisoned.'

'You can't go home alone,' said Julian. 'It would look funny. If you do, we'll all have to, and then we won't have a chance to solve this mystery with Sooty.'

'No, for goodness' sake don't go and leave me just now,' said Sooty, looking quite alarmed. 'It would make my father furious, simply furious.'

George hesitated. She didn't want to make trouble for Sooty, whom she liked very much. But, on the other hand, she certainly was not going to risk danger to Timmy.

'Well – I'll telephone my father and say I'm homesick and want to go back,' said George. 'I'll say I miss Mother. It's quite true. I do miss her. You others can stay on here and solve the mystery. It wouldn't be fair of you to try and keep me and Timmy here when you know I'd worry every moment in case someone got into the secret passage and put down poisoned meat for him to eat.'

The others hadn't thought of this. That would be terrible. Julian sighed. He would have to let George have her own way after all.

'All right. You telephone to your father,' he said. 'There's a phone downstairs. Do it now if you like. There won't be anyone about now, I don't suppose.'

George slipped down the passage, out of the door there, and down the stairs to where the telephone was enclosed in a dark little cupboard. She dialled the number she wanted.

There was a long wait. Then she heard the buzzing noise – brr – brr – brr – that told her that the telephone bell at Kirrin Cottage was ringing. She began to plan what she should say to her father. She must, she really must go home with Timmy. She didn't know how she was going to explain about Timmy – perhaps she needn't explain at all. But she meant to go home that day or the next!

'Brr – brr – brr – brr,' said the bell at the other end. It went on and on, and nobody answered it. She did not hear her father's familiar voice – only the bell that went on ringing. Why did nobody answer?

The operator at the exchange spoke to her. 'I'm sorry, there's no reply.'

George put down the receiver miserably. Perhaps her parents were out? She would have to try again later on.

Poor George tried three times, but each time with the

same result. No reply. As she was coming out of the telephone cupboard for the third time, Mrs Lenoir saw her.

'Have you been trying to telephone to your home?' she said. 'Haven't you heard any news?'

'I haven't had a letter yet,' said George. 'I've tried three times to telephone Kirrin Cottage but each time there is no reply.'

'Well, we heard this morning that it is impossible to live in Kirrin Cottage while the men are hammering and knocking everywhere,' said Mrs Lenoir, in her gentle voice. 'We heard from your mother. She said that the noise was driving your father mad, and they were going away for a week or so, till things were better. But Mr Lenoir at once wrote and asked them here. We shall know tomorrow, because we have asked them to telephone a reply. We could not get them on the telephone today, of course, any more than you could, because they have gone away already.'

'Oh,' said George, surprised at all this news, and wondered why her mother had not written to tell her too.

'Your mother said she had written to you,' said Mrs Lenoir. 'Maybe the letter will come by the next post. The posts are often most peculiar here. It will be a pleasure to have your parents if they can come. Mr Lenoir particularly wants to meet your clever father. He thinks he is quite a genius.'

George said no more but went back to the others, her

face serious. She opened Sooty's door, and the others saw at once that she had had news of some sort.

'I can't go home with Timothy,' said George. 'Mother and Father can't stand the noise the workmen make, and they have both gone away!'

'Bad luck!' said Sooty. 'All the same, I'm glad you'll have to stay here, George. I should hate to lose you or Timmy.'

'Your father has written to ask my mother and father to come and stay here too,' said George. 'What I shall do about Timmy I don't know! And they are sure to ask questions about him too. I can't tell a downright lie and say I left him with Alf the fisher-boy, or anything like that. I can't think *what* to do!'

'We'll think of something,' promised Sooty. 'Perhaps I can get one of the villagers to look after him for us. That would be a very good idea.'

'Oh yes!' said George, cheering up. 'Why didn't I think of that before? Let's ask someone quickly, Sooty.'

But it was impossible to do anything that day because Mrs Lenoir asked them to go down into the drawing-room after tea, and have a game with her. So none of them could go out to find someone to look after Timmy. 'Never mind,' thought George. 'He'll be safe tonight on my bed! Tomorrow will be soon enough.'

It was the first time that Mrs Lenoir had asked them down to be with her. 'You see, Mr Lenoir is out tonight on important business,' she explained. 'He has had to go to the mainland with the car. He doesn't like his evenings disturbed when he is at home, so I haven't been able to see as much of you all as I should have liked. But tonight I can.'

Julian wondered if Mr Lenoir had gone to the mainland on smuggling business! Somehow the smuggled goods must be taken across to the mainland and if all that signalling business the other night had to do with Mr Lenoir's smuggling then maybe he had now gone to dispose of the goods!

The telephone bell rang shrilly. Mrs Lenoir got up. 'I expect that is your mother or father on the phone,' she said to George. 'Maybe I shall have news for you! Perhaps your parents will be arriving here tomorrow.'

She went out into the hall. The children waited anxiously. Would George's parents come or not?

CHAPTER TWELVE

Block gets a surprise

MRS LENOIR came back after a time. She smiled at George.

'That was your father,' she said. 'He is coming tomorrow, but not your mother. They went to your aunt's, and your mother says she thinks she must stay and help her, because your aunt is not very well. But your father would like to come, because he wants to discuss his latest experiments with Mr Lenoir, who is very interested in them. It will be very nice to have him.'

The children would very much rather have had Aunt Fanny instead of Uncle Quentin, who could be very difficult at times. But still, he would probably be talking with Mr Lenoir most of the time, so that would be all right!

They finished their game with Mrs Lenoir and went up to bed. George was to get Timmy to take him to her room. Sooty went to see that the coast was clear. He could not see Block anywhere. His stepfather was still away from the house. Sarah was singing in the kitchen and the little kitchen-maid, Harriet, was knitting there in a corner.

'Block must be out,' thought Sooty, and went to tell George that the coast was clear. As he went across the landing to the long passage that led to his own room, the boy noticed two black lumps sticking out at the bottom of the thick curtains drawn across the landing window. He looked at them in surprise, and then recognised them. He grinned.

'So old Block suspects we have a dog, and he thinks it sleeps in George's room or Julian's, and he's posted himself there to watch!' he thought. 'Aha! I'll give friend Block a nasty shock!'

He ran to tell the others. George listened, alarmed. But Sooty, as usual, had a plan.

'We'll give Block an awful shock!' he said. 'I'll get a rope, and we'll all go down to the landing. I'll suddenly yell out that there's a robber hiding behind the curtains and I'll pounce on Block, and give him a few good shakes. Then, with your help, Julian and Dick, I'll fold him up well in the curtains – a good jerk will bring them down on top of him as well!'

The others began to laugh. It would be fun to play a trick on Block. He really was such an unpleasant fellow. A good lesson would do him no harm.

'While all the excitement is beginning I'll slip by with Timmy,' said George. 'I only hope he won't want to join in! He might give Block a good nip!'

'Well, hold on to Timmy firmly,' said Julian. 'Get him into your room quickly. Now – are we ready?'

They were. Feeling excited they crept down the long passage that led to the door which opened out on to the landing where Block was hiding. They saw the curtains move very slightly as they came along. Block was watching.

George waited with Timmy at the passage door, not showing herself at all. Then, with a yell from Sooty, a really blood-curdling yell that made both George and Timmy jump, things began to happen!

Sooty flung himself on the hidden Block with all his might. 'A robber! Help, a robber hiding here!' he shouted.

Block jumped, and began to struggle. Sooty got in two or three well-aimed punches. Block had often got him into trouble with his father, and now Sooty was getting a bit of his own back! Julian and Dick rushed to help.

A violent tug at the curtains brought them down on Block's head! Not only that, the curtain pole descended on him too, and knocked him sideways. Poor Block – he was completely taken by surprise, and could do nothing against the three determined boys. Even Anne gave a hand, though Marybelle stood apart, enjoying the fun though not daring to take part in it.

Just as it all began George slipped by with Timmy. But Timmy could not bear to miss the fun. He dragged behind George, and would not go with her.

She tried to force him, her hand on his collar. But Timmy had seen a nice leg waving about near him, protruding from the curtain. He pounced on it.

There was an agonised yell from Block. Certainly Timmy could nip hard with his sharp white teeth. He worried at the kicking leg for a few seconds, and then had

a sharp tap from George. Shocked, Timmy let go of the leg and humbly followed his mistress. She never tapped him! She must indeed be angry with him. With tail well down Timmy followed her into the bedroom and got under the bed at once. He poked his head out and looked beseechingly at George with big brown eyes.

'Oh, Timmy – I *had* to!' said George, and she knelt down by the big dog and patted his head. 'You see, you might have spoilt everything if you'd been seen. As it is I'm sure you bit Block and I don't know how we're going to explain that! Lie quietly now, old fellow. I'm going out to join the others.'

Timmy's tail thumped softly on the floor. George ran out of the room and joined the others on the landing. They were having a fine game with Block, who was yelling and wriggling and struggling for all he was worth. He was wrapped up in the curtains like a caterpillar inside a cocoon. His head was completely covered and he could see nothing.

Suddenly Mr Lenoir appeared in the hall below, with a very scared Mrs Lenoir beside him. 'What's all this?' thundered Sooty's stepfather. 'Have you gone mad? How dare you behave like this at this time of night?'

'We've caught a robber and tied him up,' panted Sooty.

Mr Lenoir ran up the stairs two steps at a time, amazed. He saw the kicking figure on the ground well-tied up in the heavy curtains. 'A robber! Do you mean a burglar? Where did you find him?'

'He was hiding behind the curtains!' said Julian. 'We managed to get hold of him and tie him up before he could escape. Could you call the police?'

An anguished voice came from inside of the curtains.

'Let me go! I've been bitten! Let me go!'

'Good heavens! You've got Block tied up there!' said Mr Lenoir, in amazement and anger. 'Untie him, quickly.'

'But – it can't be Block. He was hiding behind those curtains at the window,' protested Sooty.

'Do as you're told,' commanded Mr Lenoir, getting angry. Anne looked at the tip of his nose. Yes, it was turning white, as usual!

The boys reluctantly undid the ropes. Block angrily parted the curtains that enfolded him, and looked out, his usually blank face crimson with rage and fright.

'I won't stand this sort of thing!' he raged. 'Look here, at my leg, sir! I've been bitten. Only a dog could have done that. See my leg?'

Sure enough there were the marks of teeth on his leg, slowly turning purple. Timmy had taken a good nip, and almost gone through the skin.

'There's no dog here,' said Mrs Lenoir, coming timidly up the stairs at last. 'You couldn't have been bitten by a dog, Block.'

'Who bit him, then?' demanded Mr Lenoir, turning fiercely on poor Mrs Lenoir.

'Do you think *I* could have bitten him, in my excitement?' suddenly said Sooty, to the enormous surprise of the others, and to their immense amusement. He spoke very seriously with a worried look on his face. 'When I lose my temper, I hardly know what I do. Do you think I bit him?'

'Pah!' said Mr Lenoir, in disgust. 'Don't talk nonsense, boy! I'll have you punished if I think you go about biting people. Get up, Block. You're not badly hurt.'

'My teeth do feel a bit funny, now I come to think of it,' said Sooty, opening and shutting his mouth as if to see if they were all right. 'I think I'd better go and clean them. I feel as if I've got the taste of Block's ankle in my mouth. And it isn't nice.'

Mr Lenoir, driven to fury by Sooty's impudence, reached out swiftly to box the boy's ears. But Sooty dodged and ran back up the passage. 'Just going to clean my teeth!' he called, and the others tried to keep from laughing. The idea of Sooty biting anyone was absurd. It was quite obvious, however, that neither Mr nor Mrs Lenoir guessed what had bitten Block.

'Go to bed, all of you,' ordered Mr Lenoir. 'I hope I shall not have to complain about you to your father tomorrow when he comes – or your uncle, as it may be. I don't know which of you are his children, and which not. I'm surprised at you making such a nuisance of yourselves in somebody else's house. Tying up my servant! If he leaves, it will be your fault!'

The children hoped fervently that Block *would* leave. It would be marvellous to have the deaf blank-faced fellow out of the house. He was on the watch for Timmy, they felt sure. He would snoop about till he got Timmy or one of them into trouble.

But Block was still there next morning. He came into

the schoolroom with the breakfast, his face almost as blank as usual. He gave Sooty an evil look.

'You look out for yourself,' he said, in a curiously soft voice. 'You look out. Something's going to happen to you one of these days. Yes – and that dog too! I know you've got a dog, see? You can't deceive *me*.'

The children said nothing, but looked at one another. Sooty grinned, and rapped out a cheerful little tune on the table with his spoon.

'Dark, dire, dreadful threats!' he said. 'You look out for yourself too, Block. Any more snooping about, and you'll find yourself tied up again – yes, and I might bite you again too. You never know. My teeth feel quite ready for it this morning.'

He bared his teeth at Block, who made no reply at all, but merely looked as if he had not heard a word. The man went out, and closed the door softly behind him.

'Nasty bit of work, isn't he?' said Sooty. But George felt rather alarmed. She feared Block. There was something cold and clever and bad about those narrow eyes of his. She longed with all her heart to get Timmy out of the house.

She got a terrible shock that morning! Sooty came to her, looking agitated. 'I say! What do you think? Your father's going to have *my* room. I've got to sleep with Julian and Dick. Block is taking all my things from my room to theirs this very minute, with Sarah. I hope we shall have a chance to get him out all right, before your father comes!'

'Oh Sooty!' said George, in despair. 'I'll go and see if I can get him at once.'

She went off, pretending to go to Marybelle's room for something. But Block was still in Sooty's room. And there he stayed, cleaning it all morning!

George was very worried about Timmy. He would wonder why she hadn't fetched him. He would miss his walk. She hovered about the passage all morning, getting into Sarah's way as she carried clothes from Sooty's old room to Julian's.

Block gave George some curious looks. He walked with a limp to show that his leg was bad from the bite. He left the room at last and George darted in. But Block returned

almost at once and she dashed into Marybelle's room. Again Block left and went down the passage, and again the desperate little girl rushed into Sooty's room.

But Block was back before she could even open the cupboard door. 'What are you doing in this room?' he said, roughly. 'I haven't cleaned it all morning to have children in here messing it up again! Clear out of it!'

George went – and then once more waited for Block to go. He would have to see to the luncheon soon! He went at last. George rushed to the door of Sooty's room, eager to get poor Timmy.

But she couldn't open the door. It was locked – and Block had taken the key!

CHAPTER THIRTEEN

Poor George!

BY NOW George was in despair. She felt as if she was in a nightmare. She went to find Sooty. He was in Julian's room, next to hers, washing his hands ready for lunch.

'Sooty! I shall have to get into the secret passage the way you first took us in,' she said. 'Through that little study-room of your father's – you know, where the sliding panels are.'

'We can't,' said Sooty, looking rather alarmed. 'He uses it now, and he'd punish anyone who went in there. He's got the records of all his experiments there, and he's put them ready to show your father.'

'I don't care,' said George, desperately. 'I've got to get in there somehow. Timmy may starve!'

'Not Timmy! He'll live on the rats in the passages!' said Sooty. 'Timmy could always look after himself, I bet!'

'Well, he'd die of thirst then,' said George, obstinately. 'There's no water in those secret passages. You know that!'

George could hardly eat any lunch because she was so worried. She made up her mind somehow to get into that little study-room, and see if she could open the entrance into the wall behind the panels. Then she would slip in and get Timmy. She didn't care what happened; she was going to get Timmy.

'I shan't tell the others, though,' she thought. 'They would only try and stop me, or offer to do it themselves, and I don't trust anyone but myself to do this. Timmy's my dog, and *I'm* going to save him!'

After lunch, everyone went to Julian's room to discuss things. George went with them. But after a few minutes she left them. 'Back in a minute,' she said. They took no notice and went on discussing how to rescue Timmy. It really did seem as if the only way was to raid the study, and try and get into the secret passage without being seen.

'But my stepfather works there now,' said Sooty. 'And I shouldn't be surprised if he locks the door when he leaves the room.'

George didn't come back. After about ten minutes Anne grew puzzled.

'What can George be doing? It must be about ten minutes since she went.'

'Oh, she's probably gone to see if my old room is unlocked yet,' said Sooty, getting up. 'I'll peep out and see if she's about.'

She wasn't. She didn't seem to be anywhere! She wasn't in the passage that led to Sooty's old room; she couldn't be in that room because it was still locked, and she wasn't in Marybelle's room.

Sooty peeped in George's own room, the one she shared

with Anne. But that was empty too. He went downstairs and snooped around a bit. No George!

He went back to the others, puzzled.

'I can't find her anywhere,' he said. 'Where can she be?'

Anne looked alarmed. This was such a strange house, with strange happenings. She wished George would come.

'She's not gone into that little study-room, has she?' said Julian, suddenly. It would be just like George to try and get into the lion's den!'

'I didn't think of that,' said Sooty. 'Silly of me. I'll go and see.'

He went down the stairs. He made his way cautiously to his father's study. He stood quietly outside the shut door. There was no sound from inside. Was his father there or not?

Sooty debated whether to open the door and peep in or whether to knock. He decided to knock. Then, if his father answered he could rush back upstairs before the door could be opened, and his father would not know whom to scold for the interruption.

So he knocked, very smartly, rap-rap.

'Who's that?' came his stepfather's irritable voice. 'Come in! Am I to have no peace?'

Sooty fled upstairs at once. He went to the others. 'George can't be in the study,' he said. 'My stepfather's there, and he didn't sound in too good a temper either.'

'Then *where* can she be?' said Julian, looking worried. 'I do wish she wouldn't go off without telling us where she's going. She must be somewhere about. She wouldn't go very far from Timmy.'

They all had a good hunt over the house, even going into the kitchen. Block was there, reading a paper. 'What do you want?' he said. 'You won't get it, whatever it is.'

'We don't want anything from *you*,' said Sooty. 'How's your poor bad bitten leg?'

Block looked so unpleasantly at them that they all retreated from the kitchen in a hurry. Sooty put Julian and Dick on guard, and went up to the staff bedrooms to see if by any chance George had gone there. A silly idea, he knew, but George must be somewhere!

She wasn't there, of course. The children went back gloomily to Julian's room. 'This beastly house!' said Julian. 'I can't say I like it. Sorry to say so, Sooty, but it's a weird place with a funny feeling about it.'

Sooty was not hurt at all. 'Oh, I agree with you,' he said. 'I've always thought the same myself. So has Mother, and so has Marybelle. It's my stepfather that likes it.'

'Where *is* George?' said Anne. 'I keep on and on trying to think. There's only one place I'm certain she's not in – and that's your stepfather's study, Sooty. Even George wouldn't dare to go there while your stepfather was there.'

But Anne was wrong. The study was the very place where George was at that very moment!

The little girl had made up her mind that it was best to try and get in there, and wait for a chance to open the sliding panel. So she had slipped downstairs, gone across the hall, and tried the door of the study. It was locked.

'Blow!' said George, desperately. 'Everything is against me and Timmy. How can I get in? I must, I must!'

She slipped out of the side-door near the study and went into the little yard on to which the study-window looked. Could she get in there?

But the window was barred! So that was no good either. She went back again, wishing she could find the key to unlock the door. But it was nowhere to be seen.

Suddenly she heard Mr Lenoir's voice in the room across the hall. In a panic George lifted up the lid of a big wooden chest nearby, and climbed hurriedly into it. She closed the lid over her, and knelt there, waiting, heart beating fast.

Mr Lenoir came across the hall. He was going to his study. 'I shall get everything ready to show my visitor when he comes,' he called to his wife. 'Don't disturb me at all. I shall be very busy indeed.'

George heard the sound of a key being put into the study door. It turned. The door opened and shut with a click.

But it was not locked again from the inside. George knelt in the dark chest and considered matters. She meant to get into that study. She meant to get through the entrance into the secret passage, where Tim was. That passage led from the study to Sooty's old bedroom, and somewhere in that passage was Timmy.

What she was going to do once she had Timmy she didn't quite know. Perhaps Sooty would take him to someone who could look after him for her, someone on Castaway Hill.

She heard the sound of Mr Lenoir coughing. She heard the shuffling of papers. Then she heard the click of a cupboard being opened and shut. Mr Lenoir was evidently busy!

Then he gave an exclamation of annoyance. He said something in an irritable voice that sounded like 'Now where did I put that?'

Then the door opened very suddenly and Mr Lenoir came out. George had just time to close down the lid, which she had opened to let in fresh air. She knelt in the chest, trembling, as Mr Lenoir passed there and went on across the hall.

George suddenly knew that this was her chance. Mr Lenoir might be gone for a few minutes and give her time to open that panel in the wall! She lifted the lid of the chest, and jumped out quickly. She ran into the study, and went to the place where Sooty had pressed the panelling.

But before she could even run her fingers over the smooth brown oak, she heard returning footsteps! Mr Lenoir had hardly been half a minute. He was coming back at once.

In a panic poor George looked round for somewhere to hide. There was a large sofa against one wall. George crawled behind it, finding just room to crouch there without being seen. She was hardly there before Mr Lenoir entered the room, shut the door, and sat down at his desk.

He switched on a big lamp over it, and bent to look at some documents.

George hardly dared to breathe. Her heart bumped against her ribs and seemed to make a terrible noise. It was very uncomfortable behind the sofa, but she did not dare to move.

She could not think what in the world to do. It would be terrible to be there for hours! What would the others think? They would soon be looking for her.

They were. Even at that moment Sooty was outside the study door, pondering whether to go in or to knock. He knocked smartly – rap-rap – and George almost jumped out of her skin!

She heard Mr Lenoir's impatient voice. 'Who's that? Come in! Am I to have no peace?'

There was no answer. No one came in. Mr Lenoir called again. 'Come in, I say!'

Still no answer. He strode to the door and flung it open angrily. No one was there. Sooty had fled upstairs at once.

'Those tiresome children, I suppose,' muttered Mr Lenoir. 'Well, if any of them comes and knocks again and goes away, I'll punish them properly. Bed and bread and water for them!'

He sounded fierce. George wished she was anywhere but in his study. What would he say if he knew she was only three or four feet away from him?

Mr Lenoir worked for about half an hour, and poor George got stiffer and stiffer, and more and more uncomfortable. Then she heard Mr Lenoir yawn, and her heart felt lighter. Perhaps he would have a nap! That would be good luck. She might creep out then, and try to get into the secret passage.

Mr Lenoir yawned again. Then he pushed his papers aside and went to the sofa. He lay down on it and pulled the rug there over his knees. He settled himself down as if for a good sleep.

The sofa creaked under him. George tried to hold her breath again, afraid that now he was so near to her he would certainly hear her.

Soon a small snore came to her ears. Then another and another. Mr Lenoir was asleep! George waited for a few minutes. The snores went on, a little louder. Surely it would be safe now to creep from her hiding-place?

George began to move, very cautiously and quietly. She crept to the end of the sofa. She squeezed out from behind it. Still the snores went on.

She stood upright and went on tiptoe to the panel that had slid aside. She began to press here and there with her fingers, trying to find the spot that would move the panel to one side.

She couldn't seem to find it. She grew red with anxiety. She cast a glance at the sleeping Mr Lenoir, and worked feverishly at the panel. Where was the spot to press, oh, where was it?

Then a stern voice came from behind her, making her jump almost out of her skin.

'And what exactly do you think you are doing, my boy? How dare you come into my study and mess about like this?'

George turned round and faced Mr Lenoir. He always thought she was a boy! She didn't know what to say. He looked very angry indeed, and the tip of his nose was already white.

George was frightened. She ran to the door, but Mr Lenoir caught her before she opened it. He shook her hard.

'What were you doing in my study? Was it you who knocked and ran away? Do you think it is funny to play tricks like that? I'll soon teach you that it isn't!'

He opened the door and called loudly. 'Block! Come here! Sarah, tell Block I want him.'

Block appeared from the kitchen, his face as blank as usual. Mr Lenoir wrote something down quickly on a piece of paper and gave it to him to read. Block nodded.

'I've told him to take you to your room, lock you in, and give you nothing but bread and water for the rest of the day,' said Mr Lenoir, fiercely. 'That will teach you to behave yourself in the future. Any more nonsense and I'll whip you myself.'

'My father won't be very pleased when he hears you're punishing me like this,' began George in a trembling voice. But Mr Lenoir sneered.

'Pah! Wait till he hears from me how you have misbehaved yourself, and I am sure he will agree with me. Now go, and you will not be allowed out of your room till tomorrow. I will make your excuses to your father, when he comes.'

Poor George was propelled upstairs by Block, who was only too delighted to be punishing one of the children. As she came to the door of the room George shouted to the others who were in Julian's room next door.

'Julian! Dick! Help me! Quick, help me!'

CHAPTER FOURTEEN

A very puzzling thing

JULIAN, DICK, and the others rushed out at once, just in time to see Block shove George roughly into her room and shut the door. There was a click as he locked it.

'Here! What are you doing?' cried Julian, indignantly.

Block took no notice, but turned to go. Julian caught hold of his arm, and yelled loudly in his ear. 'Unlock that door at once! Do you hear?'

Block gave no sign whether he had or not. He shook off Julian's hand, but the boy put it back again at once, getting angry.

'Mr Lenoir gave me orders to punish that girl,' said Block, looking at Julian out of his cold, narrow eyes.

'Well, you jolly well unlock that door,' commanded Julian, and he tried to snatch the key from Block. With sudden vicious strength the man lifted his hand and struck Julian, sending him half across the landing. Then he went swiftly downstairs to the kitchen.

Julian looked after him, a little scared. 'The brute!' he said. 'He's as strong as a horse. George, George, whatever's happened?'

George answered angrily from the locked bedroom. She told the others everything, and they listened in silence.

'Bad luck, George,' said Dick. 'Poor old girl! Just as you were feeling for the opening to the passage too!'

'I must apologise for my stepfather,' said Sooty. 'He has such a terrible temper. He wouldn't have punished you like this if he had thought you were a girl. But he keeps thinking you're a boy.'

'I don't care,' said George. 'I don't care about any punishment. It's only that I'm so worried about Timmy. Well, I suppose I'll have to stay here now, till I'm let out tomorrow. I shan't eat anything that Block brings me, you can tell him. I don't want to see his horrid face again!'

'How shall I go to bed tonight?' wailed Anne. 'All my things are in your room, George.'

'You'll have to sleep with me,' said little Marybelle, who looked very frightened. 'I can lend you a nightie. Oh dear – what will George's father say when he comes? I hope he will say that George is to be set free at once.'

'Well, he won't,' said George, from behind the locked door. 'He'll just think I've been in one of my bad moods, and he won't mind my being punished at all. Oh dear – I wish Mother was coming too.'

The others were very upset about George, as well as about Timmy. Things seemed to be going very wrong indeed. At tea-time they went to the schoolroom to have tea, wishing they could take George some of the chocolate cake set ready for them.

George felt lonely when the others had gone to tea. It was five o'clock. She was hungry. She wanted Timmy. She was angry and miserable, and longed to escape. She went to the window and looked out.

Her room looked straight down the cliff-side, just as Sooty's old room did. Below was the city wall that ran round the town, going unevenly up and down as it followed the contours of the hillside.

George knew that she could not jump down to the wall. She might roll off it and fall straight down to the marsh below. That would be horrible. Then she suddenly remembered the rope-ladder that they used when they got down into the pit each day.

It had at first been kept in Marybelle's room, on the shelf in the cupboard, but since the children had been scared by knowing that someone had tried the handle of the door one morning, they had decided to keep the ladder in George's room for safety. They were afraid that perhaps Block might go snooping round Marybelle's room and find it. So George had smuggled it to her own room, and hidden it in her suitcase, which she had locked.

Now, her hands shaking a little with excitement, she unlocked her suitcase and took out the rope-ladder. She might perhaps escape out of the window with it. She looked out again, the rope in her hands.

But windows overlooked the city wall just there. The kitchen too must be just below, and maybe Block would see her climbing down. That would never do. She must wait till it was twilight.

When the others came back she told them what she was going to do, speaking in a low voice through the door.

'I'll get down on the wall, walk along it for some way, and then jump down and creep back,' she said. 'You get some food for me somehow, and I'll have it. Then tonight, when everyone has gone to bed I'll get into the study again and find the way through to the secret passage. Sooty can help me. Then I can get Timmy.'

'Right,' said Sooty. 'Wait till it's fairly dark before you go down the ladder, though. Block has gone to his room with a bad headache, but Sarah and Harriet are in the kitchen, and you don't want to be seen.'

So, when the twilight hung like a soft purple curtain over the house, George slid down the rope-ladder out of the window. She only needed to let about a quarter of it out for it was far too long for such a short distance.

She fastened it to the legs of her heavy little oak bed. Then she climbed out of the window and slid quietly down the rope-ladder.

She passed the kitchen window, which fortunately had its blinds drawn down now. She landed squarely on the old wall. She had brought a torch with her so that she could see.

She debated with herself what to do. She did not want to run any risk of coming up against either Block or Mr Lenoir. Perhaps it would be best to walk along the wall till she came to some part of the town she knew. Then she could jump off and make her way cautiously back up the hill, looking out for the others.

So she began to walk along the broad top of the old wall. It was very rough and uneven in places, and many stones were missing. But her torch showed a steady light and she did not miss her footing.

The wall ran round some stables, then round the backs of some quaint old shops. Then it ran round a big yard belonging to some house, and then round the house itself. Then down it went, around some more houses.

George could look into those windows that were not curtained. Lights shone out from them now. It was strange being able to see into the windows without being seen. A little family sat at a meal in one room, their faces cheerful and happy. An old man sat alone in another, reading and smoking.

A woman sat listening to a radio, knitting, as George

silently walked on the wall outside her window. Nobody heard her. Nobody saw her.

Then she came to another house, a big one. The wall ran close against it, for it was built where the cliff ran steeply down to the marsh just there.

There was a lit window there. George glanced in as she passed. Then she stood still in great surprise.

Surely, surely that was Block in there! He had his back to her, but she could have sworn it was Block. The same head, the same ears, the same shoulders!

Who was he talking to? George tried to see – and all at once she knew. He was talking to Mr Barling, whom everyone said was a smuggler – *the* smuggler of Castaway Hill!

But wait a minute – could it be Block? Block was deaf, and this man evidently wasn't. He was listening to Mr Barling, that was plain, and was answering him, though George could not hear the words, of course.

'I oughtn't to be snooping like this,' said George to herself. 'But it's very strange, very puzzling and very interesting. If only the man would turn round I'd know at once if it was Block!'

But he didn't turn. He just sat in his chair, his back to George. Mr Barling, his long face lit up by the nearby lamp, was talking animatedly, and Block, if it *was* Block, was listening intently and nodding his head in agreement every now and again.

George felt puzzled. If she only knew for certain that it was Block! But why should he be talking to Mr Barling

– and wasn't he deaf after all then?

George jumped down from the wall into a dark little passage and made her way through the town, up to Smuggler's Top. Outside the front door, hiding in the shadows was Sooty. He laid his hand on George's arm, making her jump.

'Come on in. I've left the side door open. We've got a fine spread for you!'

The two slipped in at the side door, tiptoed past the

study, across the hall, and up to Julian's bedroom. Truly there was a spread there!

'I went and raided the larder,' said Sooty, with satisfaction. 'Harriet was out, and Sarah had run along to the post. Block has gone to bed for a rest, because, he said, he had such an awful headache.'

'Oh,' said George, 'then it couldn't have been Block I saw. And yet I'm as certain as certain can be that it was!'

'Whatever do you mean?' asked the others, in surprise. George sat down on the floor and began to gobble up cakes and tarts, for she was terribly hungry. Between her mouthfuls she told them how she had got out of the window, walked along the city wall, and found herself unexpectedly by Mr Barling's house.

'And I looked into a lit window there, and saw Block talking to Mr Barling – and listening to him and answering him!' she said.

The others could not believe this. 'Did you see his face?' asked Julian.

'No,' said George. 'But I'm *certain* it was Block. Go and peep into his room and see if he's there, Sooty. He wouldn't be back yet from Mr Barling's, because he had a glass full of something or other, which would take him some time to drink. Go and peep.'

Sooty vanished. He came back quickly. 'He's in bed!' he said. 'I could see the shape of his body and the dark patch of his head. Are there *two* Blocks then? Whatever does this mean?'

CHAPTER FIFTEEN

Strange happenings

IT CERTAINLY was very puzzling – most of all to George, who felt so certain it had been Block talking to the well-known smuggler. The others did not feel so certain, especially as George admitted that she had not seen his face.

'Is my father here yet?' asked George, suddenly, remembering that he was supposed to come that evening.

'Yes. Just arrived,' said Sooty. 'Just before you came. I nearly got run over by the car! Just hopped aside in time. I was out there waiting for you.'

'What are our plans?' asked George. 'I'll have to get Timmy tonight, or he'll be frantic. I think I'd better go and climb back through my window again now, in case Block comes along and finds I've disappeared. I'll wait till everyone is in bed and then I'll slip out of the window again, and you must let me into the house, Sooty, please. Then I'll go to the study with you and you must open the secret way for me. Then I'll find Timmy and everything will be all right.'

'I don't see that everything will be all right,' said Sooty, doubtfully. 'But anyway, your plan is the only one to follow. You'd better get back into your room now, if you've had enough to eat.'

'I'll take a few buns back with me,' said George, stuffing

them into her pocket. 'Sooty, come and knock at my door when everyone is in bed and I'll know then that it's safe for me to slip out of the window, and come into the house again.'

It wasn't long before George was back in her room once more – just in time too, for Block appeared a little while after with a plate of dry bread and a glass of water. He unlocked the door and put them on the table.

'Your supper,' he said. George looked at his blank face and disliked it so much that she felt she must do something about it. So she took up the water and threw it deftly at the back of his head. It dripped down his neck and made him jump. Block took a step towards her, his eyes gleaming – but Julian and Dick were by the door, and he did not dare to strike her.

'I'll pay you back for that,' he said. 'See? You will never get that dog of yours back again!'

He went out and locked the door. Julian called through as soon as he had gone.

'What did you do that for, you idiot? He's a bad enemy to make.'

'I know. I just couldn't help it somehow,' said George, forlornly. 'I wish I hadn't now.'

The others had to go down to see Mr Lenoir. They left George feeling lonely. It was horrid to be locked up like this, even though she could escape through the window whenever she wanted to. She listened for the others to come back.

They soon did, and reported their meeting with George's father.

'Uncle Quentin is awfully tired and a bit cross, and frightfully annoyed with you for misbehaving,' said Julian, through the door. 'He said you were to be locked up the whole of tomorrow too, if you don't apologise.'

George didn't mean to apologise. She couldn't bear Mr Lenoir, with his false smiles and laughter, and his sudden odd rages. She said nothing.

'We've got to go and have our supper now,' said Sooty. 'We'll save you some of it as soon as Block goes out of the room. Look out for a knocking on your door tonight. It'll be me, telling you everyone's in bed.'

George lay on her bed, thinking. Many things puzzled her. She couldn't get them straight somehow. The signaller in the tower – the peculiar man, Block – Mr Barling's talk to a man who looked so like Block; but Block was all the time in his bed at home. As she lay thinking, her eyes closed, and she fell asleep.

Anne went up to bed with Marybelle, and came to whisper goodnight to her. The boys all went into the next room, for Sooty was now to share Julian's and Dick's bedroom. George woke up enough to say goodnight and then slept again.

At midnight she awoke with a jump. Someone was knocking softly and impatiently on her door. It was Sooty.

'Coming!' whispered George through the door, and took up her torch. She went to the window and was soon safely down the rope-ladder. She jumped down from the wall, and went to the side door of the house. Sooty was there. She slipped in thankfully.

'Everyone's gone to bed,' whispered Sooty. 'I thought your father and my stepfather were never going. They stayed talking in the study for ages!'

'Come on. Let's go there,' said George, impatiently. They went to the study door, and Sooty turned the handle.

It was locked again! He pushed hard, but it wasn't a bit of good. It was well and truly locked!

'We might have thought of that,' said George, in despair. 'Blow, blow, blow! What are we to do now?'

Sooty thought for a few moments. Then he spoke in a low voice, in George's ear.

'There's only one thing left to do, George. I must creep

into your father's room – my old bedroom – when he is asleep – and I must get into the cupboard there, open the entrance to the secret passage, and slip in that way. I'll find Timmy and bring him back the same way, hoping that your father won't wake!'

'Oh! Would you really do that for me?' said George gratefully. 'You *are* a good friend, Sooty! Would you rather I did it?'

'No. I know the way up and down that passage better than you do,' said Sooty. 'It's a bit frightening to be all alone there at midnight too. I'll go.'

George went with Sooty up the stairs, across the wide landing, to the door at the end of the passage that led to Sooty's old room, where George's father was now sleeping. When they got there, George pulled his arm.

'Sooty! The buzzer will go as soon as you open the door – and it will wake my father and warn him.'

'Idiot! I disconnected it as soon as I knew my room was to be changed,' said Sooty, scornfully. 'As if I wouldn't think of that!'

He opened the door that led into the passage. He crept up to his old room. The door was shut. He and George listened intently.

'Your father sounds a bit restless,' said Sooty. 'I'll wait my chance to creep in, George, and then, as soon as possible, I'll slip into the cupboard and open the secret passage to find Tim. As soon as I've got Timmy I'll bring him along to you. You could wait in Marybelle's room if you liked. Anne's there too.'

George crept into the room next door, where Anne and Marybelle lay fast asleep. She left the door open, so that she might hear when Sooty returned. How lovely it would be to have dear old Timmy again! He would lick her and lick her.

Sooty crept into the room where George's father lay, half-asleep. He made no sound. He knew every creaking board and avoided them. He made his way quietly to a big chair, meaning to hide behind it till he was certain George's father was sound asleep.

For some time the man in the bed tossed and turned. He was tired with his long journey, and his mind was excited with his talk with Mr Lenoir. He muttered now and again, and Sooty began to feel he would never be sound asleep! He grew sleepy himself, and yawned silently.

At last George's father grew quiet and peaceful. No more creaks came from the bed. Sooty cautiously moved out from behind the chair.

Then suddenly something startled him. He heard a sound over by the window! But what could it be? It was a very small sound, like a tiny creak of a door.

The night was rather dark, but the window, its curtains pulled right back, could easily be seen as a square of grey. Sooty fixed his eyes on it. Was someone opening the window?

No. The window did not move. But something strange was happening under it, near the sill.

A big window-seat was built in under the window, wide and comfortable. Sooty knew it well! He had sat on it hundreds of times to look out of the window. Now, what was happening to it?

It looked as if the top, or lid, of the seat was slowly moving upwards, bit by bit. Sooty was puzzled. He had never known it could be opened like that. It had always been screwed down, and he had thought it was just a seat and nothing else. But now it looked as if someone had unscrewed the top, and had hidden himself inside, lifting up the top like a lid when he thought it was safe.

Sooty stared at the upward-moving lid, quite fascinated. Who was in there? Why had he hidden? It was rather frightening, seeing the lid move slowly, bit by bit.

At last the lid was wide open and rested against the window-pane. A big figure cautiously and slowly got out, not making the slightest sound. Sooty felt his hair rising up on his head. He was afraid, terribly afraid. He could not utter a sound.

The figure tiptoed over to the bed. He made a quick and sudden movement, and there was a stifled sound from George's father. Sooty guessed he had been gagged, so that he could not cry out. Still the boy could not move or speak. He had never been so scared in all his life.

The intruder lifted the limp body from the bed, and went to the window-seat. He put George's father into the darkness there. What he had done to make him unable to struggle Sooty didn't know. He only knew that poor

George's father was being put down in the window-seat, and couldn't seem to move a hand to help himself!

The boy suddenly found his voice. 'Hi!' he yelled. 'Hi! What are you doing? Who are you?'

He remembered his torch and switched it on. He saw a face he knew, and cried out in surprise. 'Mr Barling!'

Then someone gave him a hard blow on the head and he remembered nothing more at all. He did not know that he was lifted into the window-seat too. He did not know that the intruder followed after him. He knew nothing.

George, awake in the next room, suddenly heard Sooty's voice crying out. 'Hi!' she heard. 'Hi! What are you doing? Who are you?' And then, as she slipped off the couch, she heard the next cry. 'Mr Barling!'

George was extremely startled. What was going on next door? She fumbled about for her torch. Anne and Marybelle were still asleep. George could not find her torch. She fell over a chair and banged her head.

When at last she had found her torch she tiptoed, trembling, to the door. She shone her torch and saw that the door next to hers was a little ajar, just as Sooty had left it, when he had crept inside. She listened. There was absolutely no sound at all now. She had heard a small bumping noise after Sooty's last cry, but she didn't know what it was.

She suddenly put her head round the door of her father's room, and shone her torch again. She stared in surprise. The bed was empty. The room was empty. There was no one there at all! She flashed her torch all round. She opened the cupboard door fearfully. She looked under the bed. She was, in fact, extremely brave.

At last she sank down on the window-seat, frightened and puzzled. Where was her father? Where was Sooty? Whatever had been happening here that night?

CHAPTER SIXTEEN

Next morning

AS GEORGE sat by the window, on the very seat into which everyone had unaccountably disappeared, though she did not know it, she heard a faint sound from the passage.

Quick as lightning the girl slipped under the bed. Someone was creeping down the long passage! George lay silently on the floor, lifting the valance a little to try and see who it was. What strange things were going on tonight!

Someone came in at the door. Someone stopped there, as if to look and listen. Then someone crept over to the window-seat.

George watched and listened, straining her eyes in the darkness. She dimly saw the someone outlined against the grey square of the window. He was bent over the window-seat.

He showed no light at all. But he made some curious little sounds. First came the sound of his fingers tapping about on the closed lid of the seat. Then came the clink of something metallic, and a very faint squeaking. George could not imagine what the man – if it was a man – was doing.

For about five minutes the someone worked away at his

task in the darkness. Then, as quietly as he had come, he went away. George couldn't help thinking it was Block, though his outline against the dark-grey of the window was too dim to recognise. But he had once given a little cough exactly like Block so often gave. It *must* be Block! But whatever was he doing in her father's room at night, on the window-seat?

George felt as if she was in a bad dream. The strangest things happened and kept on happening, and they didn't seem to make sense at all. Where was her father? Had he left his room and gone wandering over the house? Where was Sooty, and why had he called out? He wouldn't have shouted out like that, surely, if her father had been asleep in the room!

George lay under the bed, shivering, for a little while longer. Then she rolled out softly and went out of the door. She crept down the long passage to the end. She opened the door there and peeped out. The whole house was in darkness. Little sounds came to George's ears – a window rattling faintly, the creak of some bit of furniture – but nothing else.

She had only one thought in her mind, and that was to get to the boys' room and tell them the mysterious things that had happened. Soon she was across the landing, and had slipped through the door of Julian's bedroom. He and Dick were awake, of course, waiting for Sooty to come with Timmy and George.

But only George arrived. A scared George, with a very very curious story to tell. She wrapped herself in the eiderdown on Julian's bed, and told what had happened, in whispers.

They were amazed. Uncle Quentin gone! Sooty

disappeared! Someone creeping into the room and fiddling about on the window-seat! What did it all mean?

'We'll come to Uncle Quentin's room with you, straight away now,' said Julian, pulling on a dressing-gown, and hunting about for his slippers. 'I've got a feeling that things are getting pretty serious.'

They all padded off to the other rooms. They went into Marybelle's room and woke her and Anne. Both little girls felt scared. Soon all five children were in the next room, from which George's father and Sooty had so strangely vanished.

Julian shut the door, drew the curtains and switched on the light. At once they all felt better. It was so horrid to grope about in the dark with torches.

They looked round the silent room. There was nothing there to show them how the others had disappeared. The bed was crumpled and empty. On the floor lay Sooty's torch, where it had fallen.

George repeated again what she had thought she had heard Sooty call out, but it made no sense to anyone. 'Why call out Mr Barling's name, when there was only your father in the room?' said Julian. 'Surely Mr Barling wasn't hiding here – that would be nonsense. He has nothing to do with your father, George.'

'I know. But I'm sure it *was* Mr Barling's name that I heard Sooty call out,' said George. 'Do you think – oh yes, do you think Mr Barling could possibly have crept through the secret opening in the cupboard, meaning to do some dirty work or other – and have gone back the same way, taking the others with him because they discovered him?'

This seemed a likely explanation, though not a very good one. They all went to the cupboard and opened it. They groped between the clothes for the secret opening. But the little iron handle set there to pull on the stone at the back was gone! Someone had removed it – and now the secret passage could not be entered, for there was no way of opening it just there!

'Look at that!' said Julian in astonishment. 'Someone's been tampering with that too. No, George, the midnight visitor, whoever he was, didn't go back that way.'

George looked pale. She had been hoping to go and fetch Timmy, by slipping through the secret opening in the cupboard. Now she couldn't. She longed for Timmy with all her heart, and felt that if only the big faithful dog were with her things would seem much brighter.

'I'm sure Mr Lenoir is at the bottom of all this!' said Dick. 'And Block too. I bet that *was* Block you saw in here tonight, doing something in the dark, George. I bet he and Mr Lenoir are hand in glove with each other over something.'

'Well, then – we can't possibly go and tell them what has happened!' said Julian. 'If they are at the bottom of all these weird happenings it would be foolish to go and tell them what we know. And we can't tell your mother, Marybelle, because she would naturally go to your father about it. It's a puzzle to know what to do!'

Anne began to cry. Marybelle, frightened and puzzled, at once began to sob too. George felt tears pricking the backs of her eyelids, but she blinked them away. George never cried!

'I want Sooty,' wept Marybelle, who adored her cheeky, daring brother. 'Where's he gone? I'm sure he's in danger. I do want Sooty.'

'We'll rescue him tomorrow, don't you worry,' said Julian, kindly. 'We can't do anything tonight, though. There's nobody at Smuggler's Top we can possibly get advice or help from, as things are. I vote we go to bed, sleep on it, and make plans in the morning. By that time Sooty and Uncle Quentin may have turned up again. If they haven't, Mr Lenoir will have to be told by someone, and we'll see how he behaves! If he's surprised and upset, we'll soon know if he has had anything to do with this mystery or not. He'll have to do something – go to the police, or have the house turned upside down to find the missing people. We'll soon see what happens.'

Everyone felt a little comforted after this long speech. Julian sounded cheerful and firm, though he didn't feel at all happy, really. He knew, better than any of the others, that something very strange, and probably dangerous, was going on at Smuggler's Top. He wished the girls were not there.

'Now listen,' he said. 'George, you go and sleep with Anne and Marybelle next door. Lock your door and keep the light on. Dick and I will sleep here, in Sooty's old room, also with the light on, so you'll know we are quite nearby.'

It was comforting to know that the two boys were so near. The three girls went at last into Marybelle's room, tired out. Anne and Marybelle got into bed again, and George lay down again on the small but comfortable couch, pulling a thick rug over her. In spite of all the worry and excitement the girls were soon asleep, quite exhausted.

The boys talked a little, as they lay in Sooty's old bed, where their Uncle Quentin had been asleep some time before. Julian did not think anything more would happen that night. He and Dick fell asleep, but Julian was ready to wake at the slightest noise.

Next morning they were awakened by a most surprised Sarah, who had come in to draw the curtains and bring George's father a pot of early-morning tea. She could not believe her eyes when she saw the two boys in the visitor's bed – and no visitor!

'What's all this?' said Sarah, gaping. 'Where's your uncle? Why are you here?'

'Oh, we'll explain later,' said Julian, who did not want to enter into any details with Sarah, who was a bit of a chatterbox. 'You can leave the tea, Sarah. *We'd* like it!'

'Yes, but where's your uncle? Is he in *your* room?' said the puzzled Sarah. 'What's up?'

'You can go and look in our room if you like and see if he's there,' said Dick, wanting to get rid of the amazed woman. She disappeared, thinking that the household must be going mad. She left the hot tea behind, though, and the boys at once took it into the girls' room. George unlocked the door for them. They took it in turns to sip the hot tea from the one cup.

Presently Sarah came back, with Harriet and Block. Block's face was as blank as usual.

'There's nobody in your room, Julian,' began Sarah. Then Block gave a sudden exclamation and stared at George angrily. He had thought she was locked in her room – and here she was in Marybelle's room, drinking tea!

'How did you get out?' he demanded. 'I'll tell Mr Lenoir. You're in disgrace.'

'Shut up,' said Julian. 'Don't you dare to speak to my cousin like that. I believe you're mixed up in this curious business. Clear out, Block.'

Whether Block heard or not, he gave no sign of going. Julian got up, his face set.

'Clear out of this room,' he said, narrowing his eyes. 'Do you hear? I have a feeling that the police might be interested in you, Block. Now clear out!'

Harriet and Sarah gave little shrieks. The sudden mystery was too much for them. They gazed at Block and began to back out of the room. Fortunately Block went too, casting an evil look at the determined Julian.

'I shall go to Mr Lenoir,' said Block, and disappeared.

In a few minutes along came Mr and Mrs Lenoir to

Marybelle's room. Mrs Lenoir looked scared out of her life. Mr Lenoir looked puzzled and upset.

'Now, what's all this?' he began. 'Block has been to me with a most curious tale. Says your father has disappeared, George, and . . .'

'And so has Sooty,' suddenly wailed Marybelle, bursting into tears again. 'Sooty's gone. He's gone too.'

Mrs Lenoir gave a cry. 'What do you mean? How can he have gone? Marybelle, what do you mean?'

'Marybelle, I think I had better take charge of the telling,' said Julian, who was not going to let the little girl give away all the things they knew. After all, Mr Lenoir was probably at the bottom of everything, and it would be foolish to tell him what they suspected about him.

'Julian – tell me what has happened. Quickly!' begged Mrs Lenoir, looking really upset.

'Uncle Quentin disappeared from his bed last night, and Sooty has vanished too,' said Julian, shortly. 'They may turn up, of course.'

'Julian! You are keeping back something,' said Mr Lenoir, suddenly, watching the boy sharply. 'You will tell us *everything*, please. How dare you keep anything back at a moment like this?'

'Tell him, Julian, tell him,' wailed Marybelle. Julian looked obstinate, and glared at Marybelle.

The tip of Mr Lenoir's nose went white. 'I am going to the police,' he said. 'Perhaps you will talk to *them*, my boy. They will knock some sense into you!'

Julian was surprised. 'Why – I shouldn't have thought *you* would want to go to the police!' he blurted out. 'You've got too many secrets to hide!'

CHAPTER SEVENTEEN

More and more puzzling

MR LENOIR stared in the utmost amazement at Julian. There was a dead silence after this remark. Julian could have kicked himself for making it, but he couldn't unsay it now.

Mr Lenoir opened his mouth to say something at last, when footsteps came to the door. It was Block.

'Come in, Block!' said Mr Lenoir. 'There seem to have been peculiar happenings here.'

Block did not appear to hear, and remained outside the door. Mr Lenoir beckoned him in impatiently.

'No,' said Julian, firmly. 'What we have to say is not to be said in front of Block, Mr Lenoir. We don't like him and we don't trust him.'

'What do you mean?' cried Mr Lenoir, angrily. 'What do *you* know about my servants? I've known Block for years before he came into my service, and he's a most trustworthy fellow. He can't help being deaf, and that makes him irritable at times.'

Julian remained obstinate. He caught an angry gleam in Block's cold eyes, and glared back.

'Well, this is incredible!' said Mr Lenoir, trying not to lose his temper. 'I can't think what's come over everybody

– disappearing like this – and now you children talking to me as if I wasn't master in my own house. I insist that you tell me all you know.'

'I'd rather tell it to the police,' said Julian, his eye on Block. But Block showed no trace of expression on his face.

'Go away, Block,' said Mr Lenoir at last, seeing that there was no hope of getting anything out of Julian while the servant was there. 'You'd better all come down to my study. This is getting more and more mysterious. If the police have got to know, you may as well tell me first. I don't want to look a complete idiot in my own house in front of them.'

Julian couldn't help feeling a bit puzzled. Mr Lenoir was not behaving as he had thought he might behave. He seemed sincerely puzzled and upset, and he was evidently planning to get the police in himself. Surely he wouldn't do that if he had had a hand in the disappearances? Julian was lost in bewilderment again.

Mrs Lenoir was now crying quietly, with Marybelle sobbing beside her. Mr Lenoir put an arm round his wife and kissed Marybelle, suddenly appearing very much nicer than he had ever seemed before. 'Don't worry,' he said, in a gentle voice. 'We'll soon get to the bottom of this, if I have to get the whole of the police force in. I think I know who's at the bottom of it all!'

That surprised Julian even more. He and the others followed Mr Lenoir down to his study. It was still locked.

Mr Lenoir opened it and pushed aside a great pile of papers that were on his desk.

'Now – what do you know?' he said to Julian quietly. The children noticed that the top of his nose was no longer white. Evidently he had got over his burst of temper.

'Well, I think this is a strange house, with a lot of strange things happening in it,' said Julian, not quite knowing how to begin. 'I'm afraid you won't like me telling the police all I know.'

'Julian, don't speak in riddles!' said Mr Lenoir, impatiently. 'You act as if I were a criminal, in fear of the police. I'm not. What goes on in this house?'

'Well – the signalling from the tower, for instance,' said Julian, watching Mr Lenoir's face.

Mr Lenoir gaped. It was clear that he was immensely astonished. He stared at Julian, and Mrs Lenoir cried out suddenly: 'Signalling! What signalling?'

Julian explained. He told how Sooty had discovered the light-flashing first, and then how he and Dick had gone with him to the tower when they had seen the flashing again. He described the line of tiny, pricking lights across the marsh from the seaward side.

Mr Lenoir listened intently. He asked questions about dates and times. He heard how the boys had followed the signaller to Block's room, where he had disappeared.

'Got out of the window, I suppose,' said Mr Lenoir. 'Block's got nothing to do with this, you can rest assured of that. He is most faithful and loyal, and has been a great help to me while he has been here. I have an idea that Mr Barling is at the bottom of all this. He can't signal from his house to the sea because it's not quite high enough up the hill, and is in the wrong position. He must have been using *my* tower to signal from – coming himself to do it too! He knows all the secret ways of this house, better than I do! It would be easy for him to come here whenever he wanted to.'

The children thought at once that probably Mr Barling *had* been the signaller! They stared at Mr Lenoir. They were all beginning to think that he really and truly had nothing to do with the strange goings-on after all.

'I don't see why Block shouldn't know all this,' said Mr Lenoir, getting up. 'It's plain to me that Barling could explain a lot of the odd things that have been happening. I'll see if Block has ever suspected anything.'

Julian pursed his lips together. If Mr Lenoir was going to tell everything to Block, who certainly must be in the plot somehow, he wasn't going to tell him anything more!

'I'll see what Block thinks about everything, and then if we can't solve this mystery ourselves, we'll get in the police,' said Mr Lenoir, going out of the room.

Julian did not want to say anything much in front of Mrs Lenoir. So he changed the subject completely.

'What about breakfast?' he said. 'I'm feeling hungry!'

So they all went to have breakfast, though Marybelle could eat nothing at all, because she kept thinking of poor Sooty.

'I think,' said Julian, when they were alone at the table, 'I rather think we'll do a little mystery-solving ourselves. I'd like a jolly good look round that room of your father's, George, to begin with. There must be some other way of getting out of there, besides the secret passage we know.'

'What do you think happened there last night?' said Dick.

'Well, I imagine that Sooty went there and hid, to wait until it was safe to try and get into the secret passage as soon as Uncle Quentin was asleep,' said Julian, thoughtfully. 'And while he was hiding, someone came into that room from somewhere, to kidnap Uncle Quentin. Why, I don't know, but that's what I think. Then Sooty yelled out in surprise, and got knocked on the head or something. Then he and Uncle Quentin were kidnapped together, and taken off through some secret way we don't know.'

'Yes,' said George. 'And it was Mr Barling who kidnapped them! I distinctly heard Sooty yell out "Mr Barling". He must have switched on his torch and seen him.'

'They are quite probably hidden somewhere in Mr Barling's house,' said Anne, suddenly.

'Yes!' said Julian. 'Why didn't I think of that? Why, that's just where they would be, of course. I've a jolly good mind to go down and have a look!'

'Oh, let me come too,' begged George.

'No,' said Julian. 'Certainly not. This is rather a dangerous adventure, and Mr Barling is a bad and dangerous man. You and Marybelle are certainly not to come. I'll take Dick.'

'You are absolutely *mean*!' began George, her eyes flashing. 'Aren't I as good as a boy? I'm going to come.'

'Well, if you're as good as a boy, which I admit you are,' said Julian, 'can't you stay and keep an eye on Anne and Marybelle for us? We don't want them kidnapped too.'

'Oh, don't go, George,' said Anne. 'Stay here with us.'

'I think it's mad to go, anyhow,' said George. 'Mr Barling wouldn't let you in. And if you did get in you wouldn't be able to find all the secret places in his house. There must be as many, and more, as there are here.'

Julian couldn't help thinking George was right. Still, it was worth trying.

He and Dick set out after breakfast, and went down the hill to Mr Barling's. But when they got there they found the whole house shut up. Nobody answered their knocking and ringing. The curtains were drawn across the closed windows, and no smoke came from the chimney.

'Mr Barling's gone away for a holiday,' said the gardener who was working in the next door flowerbeds. 'Went this morning, he did. In his car. All his servants have got a holiday too.'

'Oh!' said Julian, blankly. 'Was there anyone with him in the car – a man and a boy, for instance?'

The gardener looked surprised at this question, and shook his head.

'No. He was alone, and drove off himself.'

'Thanks,' said Julian, and walked back with Dick to Smuggler's Top. This was most odd. Mr Barling had shut up the house and gone off without his captives! Then what had he done with them? And why on earth had he kidnapped Uncle Quentin? Julian remembered that Mr Lenoir had not put forward any reason for that. Did he know one, and hadn't wanted to say what it was? It was all most puzzling.

Meantime George had been doing a little snooping round on her own. She had slipped into Uncle Quentin's room, and had had a really good look round everywhere to see if by chance there was another secret passage Sooty hadn't known about.

She had tapped the walls. She had turned back the carpet and examined every inch of the floor. She had tried the cupboard again, and wished she could get through into the secret passage there and find Timmy. The study door downstairs was again locked, and she did not dare to tell Mr Lenoir about Timmy and ask his help.

George was just about to leave the quiet room when she noticed something on the floor near the window. She bent to pick it up. It was a small screw. She looked round. Where had it come from?

At first she couldn't see any screws of the same size at all. Then her eyes slid down to the window-seat. There were screws there, screwing down the top oaken plank to the under ones that supported it.

Had the screw come out of the window-seat? Why should it, anyway? The others there were all screwed down tightly. She examined one. Then she gave a low cry.

'One's missing. The one in the middle of this side. Now just let me think.'

She remembered last night. She remembered how someone had crept in, while she had hidden under the bed, and had fiddled about by the window, bending over the polished window-seat. She remembered the little noises – the metallic clinks and the tiny squeaks. It was screws being screwed into the seat!

'Someone screwed down the window-seat last night – and in the darkness, dropped one of the little screws,' thought George, beginning to feel excited. 'Why did he screw it down? To hide something? What's in this window-seat? It sounds hollow enough. It never lifted up. I know that. It was always screwed down, because I remember looking for a cupboard under it, like the one we have at home, and there wasn't one.'

George began to feel certain there was some secret about the window-seat. She rushed off to get a screw-driver. She found one and hurried back.

She shut the door and locked it behind her in case Block should come snooping around. Then she set to work with the screwdriver. What would she find in the window-seat? She could hardly wait to see!

CHAPTER EIGHTEEN

Curious discoveries

JUST AS she had unscrewed almost the last screw there came a tapping at the door. George jumped and stiffened. She did not answer, afraid that it was Block, or Mr Lenoir.

Then, to her great relief, she heard Julian's voice. 'George! Are you in here?'

The little girl hurried across to the door and unlocked it. The boys came in, looking surprised, followed by Anne and Marybelle. George shut the door and locked it again.

'Mr Barling's gone away and shut up the house,' said Julian. 'So that's that. What on earth are you doing, George?'

'Unscrewing this window-seat,' said George, and told them about the screw she had found on the floor. They all crowded round her, excited.

'Good for you, George!' said Dick. 'Here, let me finish the unscrewing.'

'No, thanks. This is *my* job!' said George. She took out the last screw. Then she lifted the edge of the window-seat. It came up like a lid.

Everyone peered inside, rather scared. What would they see? To their great surprise and disappointment they saw nothing but an empty cupboard! It was as if the window-seat was a box, with the lid screwed down for people to sit on.

'Well – what a disappointment!' said Dick. He shut down the lid. 'I don't expect you heard anyone screwing down the lid, really, George. It might have been your imagination.'

'Well, it wasn't, said George, shortly. She opened the lid again. She got right into the box-like window-seat and stamped, and pressed with her feet.

And quite suddenly, there came a small creaking noise, and the bottom of the empty window-seat fell downwards like a trap-door on a hinge!

George gasped and clutched at the side. She kicked about in air for a moment and then scrambled out. Everyone looked down in silence.

They looked down a straight yawning hole, which, however, came to an end only about eight feet down. There it appeared to widen out, and, no doubt, entered a secret passage which ran into one of the underground tunnels with which the whole hill was honeycombed. It might even run to Mr Barling's house.

'Look at that!' said Dick. 'Who would have thought of that? I bet even old Sooty didn't know about this.'

'Shall we go down?' said George. 'Shall we see where it goes to? We might find old Timmy.'

There came the noise of someone trying the handle of the door. It was locked. Then there was an impatient rapping, and a cross voice called out sharply:

'Why is this door locked? Open it at once! What are you doing in there?'

'It's Father!' whispered Marybelle, with wide eyes. 'I'd better unlock the door.'

George shut the lid of the window-seat down at once, quietly. She did not want Mr Lenoir to see their latest discovery. When the door was opened Mr Lenoir saw the children standing about, or sitting on the window-seat.

'I've had a good talk to Block,' he said, 'and, as I thought, he doesn't know a thing about all the goings-on here. He was most amazed to hear about the signalling from the tower. But he doesn't think it's Mr Barling. He thinks it may be a plot of some sort against *me*.'

'Oh!' said the children, who felt that *they* would not believe Block so readily as Mr Lenoir appeared to.

'It's quite upset Block,' said Mr Lenoir. 'He feels really sick, and I've told him to go and have a rest till we decide what to do next.'

The children felt that Block would not be so easily upset as all that. They all suspected at once that he would not really go to rest, but would probably sneak out on business of his own.

'I've some work to attend to for a little while,' said Mr Lenoir. 'I've rung up the police, but unluckily the Inspector is out. He will ring me directly he comes back. Now can you keep out of mischief till I've finished my work?'

The children thought that was a silly question. They

made no reply. Mr Lenoir gave one of his sudden smiles and little laughs, and went.

'I'm going to pop along to Block's room and see if he really *is* there,' said Julian, as soon as Mr Lenoir was out of sight.

He went to the wing where the staff bedrooms were, and stopped softly outside Block's. The door was a little ajar, and Julian could see through the crack. He saw the shape of Block's body in the bed, and the dark patch that was his head. The curtains were drawn across the window to keep out the light, but there was enough to see all this.

Julian sped back to the others. 'Yes, he's in bed all right,' he said. 'Well, he's safe for a bit. Shall we have a shot at getting down to the window-seat hole? I'd dearly like to see where it leads to!'

'Oh yes!' said everyone. But it was not an easy job to drop eight feet down without being terribly jolted! Julian went first and was very much jarred. He called up to Dick: 'We'll have to get a bit of rope and tie it to something up there, and let it hang down the hole – it's an awful business to let yourself drop down.'

But just as Dick went to find a rope, Julian called up again. 'Oh, it's all right! I've just seen something. There are niches carved into the sides of the hole – niches you can put foot or hand into. I didn't see them before. You can use them to help you down.'

So down went everyone, one after another, feeling for the niches and finding them. George missed one or two,

clawed wildly at the air, and dropped down the last few feet, landing with rather a bump, but she was not hurt.

As they had thought, the hole led to another secret passage in the house, but this one went straight downwards by means of steps, so that very soon they went well below the level of the house. Then they came into the maze of tunnels that honeycombed the hill. They stopped.

'Look here – we can't possibly go any farther,' said Julian. 'We shall get lost. We haven't got Sooty with us now, and Marybelle isn't any good at finding the way. It would be dangerous to wander about.'

They could hear the hollow sound of footsteps coming from a tunnel to the left of them. They all shrank back into the shadows, and Julian switched off his torch.

'It's *two* people!' whispered Anne, as two figures came out of the nearby tunnel. One was very tall and long. The other – yes, surely the other was Block! If it wasn't Block it was someone the exact image of him.

The men were talking in low voices, answering one another. How could it be Block, though, if he could hear as well as that? Anyway, Block was asleep in bed. It was hardly ten minutes since Julian had seen him there. Were there two Blocks, then? thought George, as she had once thought before.

The men disappeared into another tunnel, and the bright light of their lanterns disappeared gradually. The muffled rumble of their voices echoed back.

'Shall we follow them?' said Dick.

'Of course not,' said Julian. 'We might lose them – and lose ourselves too! And supposing they suddenly turned back and found us following them? We should be in a horrid fix.'

'I'm sure the first man was Mr Barling,' said Anne,

suddenly. 'I couldn't see his face because the light of the lantern wasn't on it – but he seemed just like Mr Barling – awfully tall and long everywhere!'

'But Mr Barling's gone away,' said Marybelle.

'*Supposed* to have gone away!' said George. 'It looks as if he's come back, if it *was* him. I wonder where those two have gone – to see my father and Sooty, do you think?'

'Quite likely,' said Julian. 'Come on, let's get back. We simply *daren't* wander about by ourselves in these old tunnels. They run for miles, Sooty said, and cross one another, and go up and down and round about – even right down to the marsh. We should never, never find our way out if we got lost.'

They turned to go back. They came to the end of the steps they had been climbing, and found themselves at the bottom of the window-seat hole. It was quite easy to pull themselves up by the niches in the sides of the hole.

Soon they were all in the room again, glad to see the sunshine streaming in at the window. They looked out. The marshes were beginning to be wreathed in mist once more, though up here the hill was golden with sunlight.

'I'm going to put the screws back into the window-seat again,' said Julian, picking up the screwdriver and shutting down the lid. 'Then if Block comes here he won't guess we've found this new secret place. I'm pretty certain that he unscrewed the seat so that Mr Barling could get into this room, and then screwed it down again so that no one would guess what had happened.'

He quickly put in the screws. Then he looked at his watch.

'Almost dinner-time, and I'm jolly hungry. I wish old Sooty was here – and Uncle Quentin. I do hope they're all right – and Timmy too,' said Julian. 'I wonder if Block is still in bed – or wandering about the tunnels. I'm going to have a peep again.'

He soon came back, puzzled. 'Yes, he's there all right, safe in bed. It's jolly funny.'

Block did not appear at lunch-time. Sarah said he had asked not to be disturbed, if he did not appear.

'He does get the most awful sick headaches,' she said. 'Maybe he'll be all right this afternoon.'

She badly wanted to talk about everything, but the children had decided not to tell her anything. She was very nice and they liked her, but somehow they didn't trust anyone at Smuggler's Top. So Sarah got nothing out of them at all, and retired in rather a huff.

Julian went down to speak to Mr Lenoir after the meal. He felt that even if the Inspector of Police was not at the police station, somebody else must be informed. He was very worried about his uncle and Sooty. He couldn't help wondering if Mr Lenoir had made up the bit about the Inspector being away, to put off time.

Mr Lenoir was looking cross when Julian knocked at his study-door. 'Oh, it's you!' he said to Julian. 'I was expecting Block. I've rung and rung for him. The bell rings in his room and I can't imagine why he doesn't come. I want him to come to the police station with me.'

'Good!' thought Julian. Then he spoke aloud. 'I'll go and hurry him up for you, Mr Lenoir. I know where his room is.'

Julian ran up the stairs and went to the little landing up which the back-stairs went to the staff bedrooms. He pushed open Block's door.

Block was apparently still asleep in bed! Julian called loudly, then remembered that Block was deaf. So he went over to the bed and put his hand rather roughly on the hump of the shoulder between the clothes.

But it was curiously soft! Julian drew his hand away, and looked down sharply. Then he got a real shock.

There was no Block in the bed! There was a big ball of some sort, painted black to look like a head almost under the sheets – and, when Julian threw back the covers, he saw instead of Block's body, a large lumpy bolster, cleverly moulded to look like a curved body!

'*That's* the trick Block plays when he wants to slip off anywhere, and yet pretend he's still here!' said Julian. 'So it *was* Block we saw in the tunnel this morning – and it *must* have been Block that George saw talking to Mr Barling yesterday, when she looked through the window. He's not deaf, either. He's a very clever – sly – double-faced – deceitful ROGUE!'

CHAPTER NINETEEN

Mr Barling talks

MEANTIME, WHAT was happening to Uncle Quentin and Sooty? Many strange things!

Uncle Quentin had been gagged, and drugged so that he could neither struggle nor make any noise, when Mr Barling had crept so unexpectedly into his room. It was easy to drop him down the hole in the window-seat. He fell with a thud that bruised him considerably.

Then poor Sooty had been dropped down too, and after them had come Mr Barling, climbing deftly down by the help of the niches in the sides.

Someone else was down there, to help Mr Barling. Not Block, who had been left to screw down the window-seat so that no one might guess where the victims had been taken, but a hard-faced servant belonging to Mr Barling.

'Had to bring this boy, too – it's Lenoir's son,' said Mr Barling. 'Snooping about in the room. Well, it will serve Lenoir right for working against me!'

The two were half-carried, half-dragged down the long flight of steps and taken into the tunnels below. Mr Barling stopped and took a ball of string from his pocket. He tossed it to his servant.

'Here you are. Tie the end to that nail over there, and

let the string unravel as we go. I know the way quite well, but Block doesn't, and he'll be coming along to bring food to our couple of prisoners tomorrow. Don't want him to lose his way! We can tie the string up again just before we get to the place I'm taking them to, so that they won't see it and use it to escape by.'

The servant tied the string to the nail that Mr Barling pointed out, and then as he went along he let the ball unravel. The string would then serve as a guide to anyone not knowing the way. Otherwise it would be very dangerous to wander about in the underground tunnels. For some of them ran for miles.

After about eight minutes the little company came to a kind of rounded cave, set in the side of a big, but rather low tunnel. Here had been put a bench with some rugs, a box to serve as a table, and a jug of water. Nothing else.

Sooty by now was coming round from his blow on the head. The other prisoner, however, still lay unconscious, breathing heavily.

'No good talking to him,' said Mr Barling. 'He won't be all right till tomorrow. We'll come and talk to him then. I'll bring Block.'

Sooty had been put on the floor. He suddenly sat up, and put his hand to his aching head. He couldn't imagine where he was.

He looked up and saw Mr Barling, and then suddenly he remembered everything. But how had he got there, in this dark cave?

'Mr Barling!' he said. 'What's all this? What did you hit me for? Why have you brought me here?'

'Punishment for a small boy who can't keep his nose out of things that don't concern him!' said Mr Barling, in a horrid sarcastic voice. 'You'll be company for our friend on the bench there. He'll sleep till the morning, I'm afraid. You can tell him all about it, then, and say I'll be back to have a little heart-to-heart talk with him! And see here, Pierre – you do know, don't you, the foolishness of trying to wander about these old passages? I've brought you to a little-known one, and if you want to lose yourself and never be heard of again, well, try wandering about, that's all!'

Sooty looked pale. He did know the danger of wandering about those lost old tunnels. This one he was in he was sure he didn't know at all. He was about to ask a few more questions when Mr Barling turned quickly on his heel and went off with his servant. They took the lantern with them and left the boy in darkness. He yelled after them.

'Hi, you beasts! Leave me a light!'

But there was no answer. Sooty heard the footfalls going farther and farther away, and then there was silence and darkness.

The boy felt in his pocket for his torch, but it wasn't there. He had dropped it in his bedroom. He groped his way over to the bench, and felt about for George's father. He wished he would wake up. It was so horrid to be there in the darkness. It was cold, too.

Sooty crept under the rugs and cuddled close to the unconscious man. He longed with all his heart for him to wake up.

From somewhere there sounded the drip-drip-drip of water. After a time Sooty couldn't bear it. He knew it was only drops dripping off the roof of the tunnel in a damp place, but he felt he couldn't bear it. Drip-drip-drip. Drip-drip-drip. If only it would stop!

'I'll have to wake George's father up!' thought the boy, desperately. 'I *must* talk to someone!'

He began to shake the sleeping man, wondering what to call him, for he did not know his surname. He couldn't call him 'George's father'! Then he remembered that the others called him Uncle Quentin, and he began yelling the name in the drugged man's ear.

'Uncle Quentin! Uncle Quentin! Wake up! Do wake up! Oh, won't you please wake up!'

Uncle Quentin stirred at last. He opened his eyes in the darkness, and listened to the urgent voice in his ear, feeling faintly puzzled.

'Uncle Quentin! Wake up and speak to me. I'm scared!' said the voice. 'UNCLE QUENTIN!'

The man thought vaguely that it must be Julian or Dick. He put his arm round Sooty and dragged him close to him. 'It's all right. Go to sleep,' he said. 'What's the matter, Julian? Or is it Dick? Go to sleep.'

He fell asleep again himself, for he was still half-drugged. But Sooty felt comforted now. He shut his eyes,

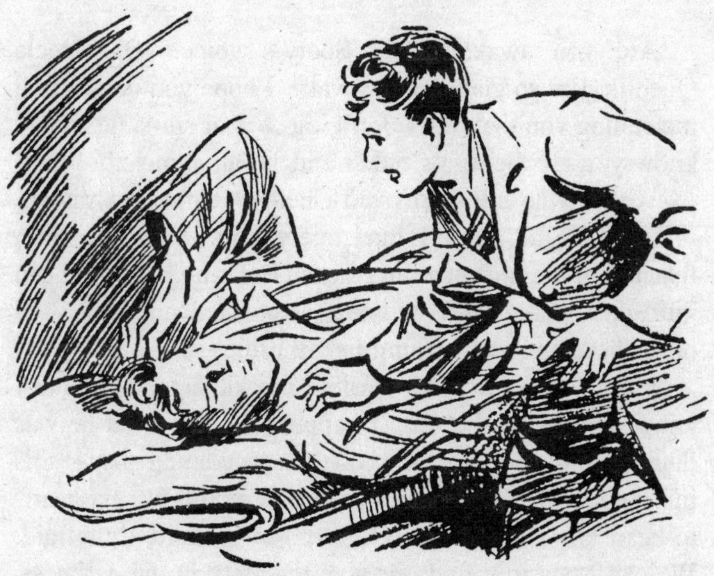

feeling certain that he couldn't possibly go to sleep. But he did, almost at once! He slept soundly all through the night, and was only awakened by Uncle Quentin moving on the bench.

The puzzled man was amazed to find his bed so unexpectedly hard. He was even more amazed to find someone in bed with him, for he remembered nothing at all. He stretched out his hand to switch on the reading-lamp which had been beside his bed the night before.

But it wasn't there! Strange! He felt about and touched Sooty's face. What was this beside him? He began to feel extremely puzzled. He felt ill, too. What *could* have happened?

'Are you awake?' said Sooty's voice. 'Oh, Uncle Quentin, I'm so glad you're awake. I hope you don't mind me calling you that, but I don't know your surname. I only know you are George's father and Julian's uncle.'

'Well – who are you?' said Uncle Quentin, in wonder.

Sooty began to tell him everything. Uncle Quentin listened in the utmost amazement. 'But *why* have we been kidnapped like this?' he said, astonished and angry. 'I never heard of such a thing in my life!'

'I don't know why Mr Barling has kidnapped *you* but I know he took me because I happened to see what he was doing,' said Sooty. 'Anyway, he's coming back this morning, with Block, and he said he would have a heart-to-heart talk with you. We'll have to wait here, I'm afraid. We can't possibly find our way to safety in the darkness, through this maze of tunnels.'

So they waited – and in due course Mr Barling did come, bringing Block with him. Block carried some food, which was very welcome to the prisoners.

'You beast, Block!' said Sooty, at once, as he saw the servant in the light of the lantern. 'How dare you help in this? You wait till my stepfather hears about it! Unless he's in it too!'

'Hold your tongue!' said Block.

Sooty stared at him. 'So you *can* hear!' he said. 'All this time you've been pretending you can't! What a sly fellow you are! What a lot of secrets you must have learnt, pretending to be deaf, and overhearing all kinds of things not meant for you. You're sly, Block, and you're worse things than that!'

'Whip him, Block, if you like,' said Mr Barling, sitting down on the box. 'I've no time for rude boys myself.'

'I will,' said Block, grimly, and he undid a length of rope from round his waist. 'I've often wanted to, cheeky little worm!'

Sooty felt alarmed. He leapt off the bench and put up his fists.

'Let me talk to our prisoner first,' said Mr Barling. 'Then you can give Pierre the punishment he deserves. It will be nice for him to wait for it.'

Uncle Quentin was listening quietly to all this. He looked at Mr Barling, and spoke sternly.

'You owe me an explanation for your strange behaviour. I demand to be taken to Smuggler's Top. You shall answer to the police for this!'

'Oh no, I shan't,' said Mr Barling, in a curiously soft voice. 'I have a very generous proposal to make to you. I know why you have come to Smuggler's Top. I know why you and Mr Lenoir are so interested in each other's experiments.'

'How do you know?' said Uncle Quentin. 'Spying, I suppose!'

'Yes – I bet Block's been spying and reading letters!' cried Sooty, indignantly.

Mr Barling took no notice of the interruption. 'Now, my dear sir,' he said to Uncle Quentin, 'I will tell you very shortly what I propose. I know you have heard that I am a smuggler. I am. I make a lot of money from it. It is easy to run a smuggling trade here, because no one can patrol the marshes, or stop men using the secret path that only I and a few others know. On favourable nights I send out a signal – or rather Block here does so, for me, using the convenient tower of Smuggler's Top . . .'

'Oh! So it *was* Block!' cried Sooty.

'Then when the goods arrive,' said Mr Barling, 'and again at a favourable moment I – er – dispose of them. I cover my tracks very carefully, so that no one can possibly accuse me because they never have any real proof.'

'Why are you telling me all this?' said Uncle Quentin scornfully. 'It's of no interest to me. I'm only interested in a plan for draining the marshes, not in smuggling goods across them!'

'Exactly, my dear fellow!' said Mr Barling, amiably. 'I know that. I have even seen your plans and read about your experiments and Mr Lenoir's. But the draining of the marsh means the end of my own business! Once the marsh is drained, once houses are built there, and roads made, once the mists have gone, my business goes too! A harbour may be built out there, at the edge of the marshes – my ships can no longer creep in unseen, bringing valuable cargoes! Not only will my money go, but all the excitement, which is more than life to me, will go too!'

'You're mad!' said Uncle Quentin, in disgust.

Mr Barling *was* a little mad. He had always felt a great satisfaction in being a successful smuggler in days when smuggling was almost at an end. He loved the thrill of knowing that his little ships were creeping in the mist towards the treacherous marshes. He liked to know that men were making their way over a small and narrow path over the misty marsh to the appointed meeting-place, bringing smuggled goods.

'You should have lived a hundred years or more ago!' said Sooty, also feeling that Mr Barling was a little mad. 'You don't belong to nowadays.'

Mr Barling turned on Sooty, his eyes gleaming dangerously in the light of the lantern.

'Another word from you and I'll drop you in the marshes!' he said. Sooty felt a shiver go down his back. He suddenly knew that Mr Barling really did mean what he said. He was a dangerous man. Uncle Quentin sensed it too. He looked at Mr Barling warily.

'How do I come into this?' he asked. 'Why have you kidnapped me?'

'I know that Mr Lenoir is going to buy your plans from you,' said Mr Barling. 'I know he is going to drain the marsh by using your very excellent ideas. You see, I know all about them! I know, too, that Mr Lenoir hopes to make a lot of money by selling the land once it is drained. It is all his, that misty marsh – and no use to anyone now except to me! But that marsh is not going to be drained – I am going to buy your plans, not Mr Lenoir!'

'Do *you* want to drain the marsh, then?' said Uncle Quentin, in surprise.

Mr Barling laughed scornfully. 'No! Your plans, and the results of your experiments, will be burnt! They will be mine, but I shall not want to use them. I want the marsh left as it is, secret, covered with mist, and treacherous to all but me and my men. So, my dear sir, you will please name your price to me, instead of to Mr Lenoir, and sign this document, which I have had prepared, making over all your plans to me!'

He flourished a large piece of paper in front of Uncle Quentin. Sooty watched breathlessly.

Uncle Quentin picked up the paper. He tore it into small pieces. He threw them into Mr Barling's face and said, scornfully: 'I don't deal with madmen, nor with rogues, Mr Barling!'

CHAPTER TWENTY

Timmy to the rescue

MR BARLING went very pale. Sooty gave a loud crow of delight. 'Hurrah! Good for *you*, Uncle Quentin!'

Block gave a loud exclamation, and darted to the excited boy. He took him by the shoulder, and raised the rope to thrash him.

'That's right,' said Mr Barling, in a funny kind of hissing voice. 'Deal with him first, Block, and then with this – this – stubborn – obstinate – fool! We'll soon bring them to their senses. A good thrashing now and again, a few days here in the dark, without any food – ah, that will make them more biddable!'

Sooty yelled at the top of his voice. Uncle Quentin leapt to his feet. The rope came down and Sooty yelled again.

Then there suddenly came the pattering of quick feet, and something flung itself on Block. Block gave a scream of pain and turned. He knocked the lantern over by accident, and the light went out. There was a sound of fierce growling. Block staggered about trying to keep off the creature that had fastened itself on to him.

'Barling! Help me!' he shouted.

Mr Barling went to his aid, but was attacked in his turn. Uncle Quentin and Sooty listened in amazement and fear.

What creature was this that had suddenly arrived? Would it attack them next? Was it a giant rat – or some fierce wild animal that haunted these tunnels?

The fierce animal suddenly barked. Sooty cheered.

'TIMMY! It's you, Timmy! Oh, good dog, good dog! Go for him, then, go for him! Bite him, Timmy, hard.'

The two frightened men could do nothing against the angry dog. Soon they were running down the tunnel as fast as they could go, feeling for the string for fear of being lost. Timmy chased them with much enjoyment, and then returned to Sooty and George's father, rather pleased with himself.

He had a tremendous welcome. George's father made a great fuss of him, and Sooty put his arms round the big dog's neck.

'How did you come here? Did you find your way out of the secret passage you've been in? Are you half-starved? Look, here's some food.'

Timmy ate heartily. He had managed to devour a few rats, but otherwise had had no food at all. He had licked the drops that here and there he had found dripping from the roof, so he had not been thirsty. But he had certainly been extremely puzzled and worried. He had never before been so long away from his beloved mistress!

'Uncle Quentin – Timmy could take us safely back to Smuggler's Top, couldn't he?' said Sooty, suddenly. He spoke to Timmy. 'Can you take us home, old boy? Home, to George?'

Timmy listened, with his ears cocked up. He ran down the passage a little way, but soon came back. He did not like the idea of going down there. He felt that enemies were waiting for them all. Mr Barling and Block were not likely to give in quite so easily!

But Timmy knew other ways about the tunnels that honeycombed the hillside. He knew, for instance, the way down to the marsh! So he set off in the darkness, with Uncle Quentin's hand on his collar, and Sooty following close behind, holding on to Uncle Quentin's coat.

It wasn't easy or pleasant. Uncle Quentin wondered at times if Timmy really did know where he was going. They went down and down, stumbling over uneven places, sometimes knocking their heads against an unexpected low piece of roof. It was not a pleasant journey for Uncle Quentin, for he had no shoes on his feet, and was dressed only in pyjamas and rugs.

After a long time they came out on the edge of the marsh itself, at the bottom of the hill! It was a desolate place, and the mists were over it, so that neither Sooty nor Uncle Quentin knew which way to turn!

'Never mind,' said Sooty, 'we can easily leave it to Timmy. He knows the way all right. He'll take us back to the town, and once there we'll know the way home ourselves!'

But suddenly, to their surprise and dismay, Timmy stopped dead, pricking up his ears, whined and would go no farther. He looked thoroughly miserable and unhappy. What could be the matter?

Then, with a bark, the big dog left the two by themselves, and galloped back into the tunnel they had just left.

He disappeared completely!

'Timmy!' yelled Sooty. 'Timmy! Come here! Don't leave us! TIMMY!'

But Timmy was gone; why, neither Sooty nor Uncle Quentin knew. They stared at one another.

'Well – I suppose we'd better try to make our way over this marshy bit,' said Uncle Quentin, doubtfully, putting a foot out to see if the ground was hard. It wasn't! He drew back his foot at once.

The mists were so thick that it was really impossible to see anything. Behind them was the opening to the tunnel. A steep rocky cliff rose up about it. There was no path that way, it was certain. Somehow they had to make their way round the foot of the hill to the main-road that entered the town – but the way lay over marshy ground!

'Let's sit down and wait for a bit to see if Timmy comes back,' said Sooty. So they sat down on a rock at the entrance to the tunnel and waited.

Sooty began to think of the others. He wondered what they had thought when they had discovered that both he and Uncle Quentin were missing. How astonished they must have been!

'I wonder what the others are doing?' he said, aloud. 'I'd love to know!'

The others, as we know, had been doing plenty. They had found the opening in the window-seat where Mr Barling had taken the captives, and they had gone down it and actually seen Mr Barling and Block on their way to talk to Uncle Quentin and Sooty!

They had found out, too, that Block hadn't been in his bed – he had left a dummy there instead. Now everyone was talking at once, and Mr Lenoir was suddenly convinced that Block had been a spy, put in his house by Mr Barling, and not the good servant he had appeared!

Once Julian felt that he was convinced of this he spoke to him more freely, and told him of the way through the window-seat, and of how they had seen Mr Barling and Block that very day, in the underground tunnels!

'Good heavens!' said Mr Lenoir, now looking thoroughly alarmed. 'Barling must be mad! I've always thought he was a bit strange – but he must be absolutely mad to kidnap people like this – and Block must be, too. This is a plot! They've heard what I've been planning with your uncle – and they've made up their minds to stop it because it will interfere with their smuggling. Goodness knows what they'll do now! This is serious!'

'If only we had Timmy!' suddenly said George.

Mr Lenoir looked astonished.

'Who's Timmy?'

'Well, you might as well know everything now,' said Julian, and he told Mr Lenoir about Timmy, and how they had hidden him.

'Very foolish of you,' said Mr Lenoir, shortly, looking displeased. 'If you'd told me I would have had someone in the town look after him. I can't help not liking dogs. I detest them, and never will have them in the house. But I would willingly have arranged for him to be boarded out, if I'd known you'd brought him.'

The children felt sorry and a little ashamed. Mr Lenoir was an odd, hot-tempered person, but he didn't seem nearly as horrid as they had thought he was.

'I'd like to go and see if I can find Timmy,' said George. 'You'll get the police in now, I suppose, Mr Lenoir, and perhaps we could go and find Timmy? We know the way into the secret passage from your study.'

'Oh – so *that's* why you were hiding there in the afternoon yesterday,' said Mr Lenoir. 'I thought you were a very bad boy. Well, go and try and find him if you like, but don't let him come anywhere near me. I really cannot bear dogs in the house.'

He went to telephone the police station again. Mrs Lenoir, her eyes red with crying, stood by him. George slipped away to the study, followed by Dick and Julian and Anne. Marybelle stayed beside her mother.

'Come on – let's get into that secret passage and try and find old Timmy,' said George. 'If we all go, and whistle and shout and call, he's sure to hear us!'

They found the way into the passage, by doing the things they had done before. The panel slid back, and then another, larger opening came as before. They all squeezed through it, and found themselves in the very narrow passage that led from the study up to Sooty's bedroom.

But Timmy was not there! The children were surprised, but George soon thought why.

'Do you remember Sooty telling us there was a way into this passage from the dining-room, as well as from the study and Sooty's bedroom? Well, I believe I saw a door or something there, as we passed where the dining-room must be, and it's likely Timmy may have pushed through it, and gone into another passage somewhere.'

They went back, one by one. They came to the dining-room – or rather, they walked behind the dining-room wall. There they saw the door that George had noticed as they passed – a door, small and set quite flat to the wall, so that it was difficult to see. George pushed it. It opened easily, and then flapped shut, with a little click. It could be opened from one side but not from the other.

'That's where Timmy's gone!' said George, and she pushed the door open again. 'He pushed against the door and it opened – he went through, and the door fastened itself so that he couldn't get back. Come on, we must find him.'

They all went through the small door. It was so low that they had to bend their heads to go through, even Anne. They found themselves in a passage rather like the one they had just left, but not quite so narrow. It suddenly began to go downwards. Julian called back to the others.

'I believe it goes down to the passages where we used to take Timmy when we let him down into that pit to go for a walk! Yes, look – we've come to where the pit itself is!'

They went on, calling Timmy, and whistling loudly, but

no Timmy came. George began to feel worried.

'Hallo! – Surely this is where we came out when we climbed down all those steps from the window-seat passage!' said Dick, suddenly. 'Yes, it is. Look, there's the tunnel where we saw Block and Mr Barling going!'

'Oh – do you think they've done something to Timmy?' said George, in a frightened voice. 'I never thought of that!'

Everyone felt alarmed. It was strange that Block and Mr Barling could go about unmolested by Timmy if Timmy was somewhere near! Could they have harmed him in any way? They had no idea that Timmy was at that very minute with George's father and Sooty!

'Look at this!' said Julian, suddenly, and he shone his torch on to something to show the others. 'String! String going right down this tunnel. Why?'

'It's the tunnel that Mr Barling and Block took!' said George. 'I believe it leads to where they've taken my father and Sooty! They're keeping them prisoners down here! I'm going to follow the string and find them! Who's coming with me?'

CHAPTER TWENTY-ONE

A journey through the hill

'I'M COMING!' said everyone at once. As if they would let George go alone!

So down the dark tunnel they went, feeling the string and following it. Julian ran it through his fingers, and the others followed behind, holding hands. It would not do for anyone to get lost.

After about ten minutes they came to the rounded cave where Sooty and George's father had been the night before. They were not there now, of course – they were on their way down to the marsh!

'Hallo, look! This is where they must have been!' cried Julian, shining his torch round. 'A bench – with tumbled rugs – and an over-turned lamp. And look here, scraps of paper torn into bits! Something's been happening here!'

Quick-witted George pieced it together in her mind. 'Mr Barling took them here and left them. Then he came back with some sort of proposal to Father, who refused it! There must have been a struggle of some sort and the lamp got broken. Oh – I do hope Father and Sooty got away all right.'

Julian felt gloomy. 'I hope to goodness they haven't gone wandering about these awful tunnels. Even Sooty doesn't know a quarter of them. I wish I knew what's happened.'

'Someone's coming!' suddenly said Dick. 'Snap out the light, Ju.'

Julian snapped off the torch he carried. At once they were all in darkness. They crouched at the back of the cave, listening.

Yes – footsteps were coming. Rather cautious footsteps. 'Sound like two or three people,' whispered Dick. They came nearer. Whoever was coming was plainly following the tunnel where the string was.

'Mr Barling perhaps – and Block,' whispered George. 'Come to have another talk with Father! But he's gone!'

A brilliant light flashed suddenly round the cave – and picked out the huddled children. There was a loud exclamation of astonishment.

'Good heavens! Who's here? What's all this?'

It was Mr Barling's voice. Julian stood up, blinking in the bright light.

'We came to look for my uncle and Sooty,' he said. 'Where are they?'

'Aren't they here?' said Mr Barling, seeming surprised. 'And is that horrible brute of a dog gone?'

'Oh – was Timmy here?' cried George, joyfully. 'Where is he?'

There were two other men with Mr Barling. One was Block. The other was his servant. Mr Barling put down the lantern he was carrying.

'Do you mean to say you don't know where the others are?' he said, uneasily. 'If they've gone off on their own, they'll never come back.'

Anne gave a little scream. 'It's all your fault, you horrid man!'

'Shut up, Anne!' said Julian. 'Mr Barling,' he said, turning to the angry smuggler, 'I think you'd better come back with us and explain things. Mr Lenoir is now talking to the police.'

'Oh, *is* he?' said Mr Barling. 'Then I think it would be as well for us all to stay down here for a while! Yes, you too! I'll make Mr Lenoir squirm! I'll hold you all prisoners – and this time you shall be bound so that you don't go wandering off like the others! Got some rope, Block?'

Block stepped forward with the other man. They caught hold of George first, very roughly.

She screamed loudly. 'Timmy! Timmy! Where are you? Timmy, come and help! Oh, TIMMY!'

But no Timmy came. She was soon in a corner with her hands tied behind her. Then they turned to Julian.

'You're mad,' Julian said to Mr Barling, who was standing nearby, holding the lantern. 'You *must* be mad to do things like this.'

'Timmy!' shouted George, trying to free her hands. 'Timmy, Timmy, Timmy!'

Timmy didn't hear. He was too far away. But the dog suddenly felt uneasy. He was with George's father and Sooty at the edge of the marsh, about to lead them round the hill to safety. But he stopped and listened. He could hear nothing of course. But Timmy knew that George was in danger. He knew that his beloved little mistress needed him.

His ears did not tell him, nor did his nose. But his heart told him. George was in danger!

He turned and fled back into the tunnel. He tore up the winding passages at top speed, panting.

And, quite suddenly, just as Julian was angrily submitting to have his hands tied tightly together, a furry thunderbolt arrived! It was Timmy!

He smelt his enemy, Mr Barling, again! He smelt Block. Grrrrrrrrr-rrrrrr!

'Here's that awful dog again!' yelled Block, and leapt away from Julian. 'Where's your gun, Barling?'

But Timmy didn't worry about guns. He leapt at Mr Barling and got him on the floor. He gave him a nip in the shoulder that made him yell. Then he leapt at Block, and got him down, too. The other man fled.

'Call your dog off. Call him off, or he'll kill us!' cried Mr Barling, struggling up, his shoulder paining him terribly. But nobody said a word. Let Timmy do what he liked!

It wasn't long before all three of the men had gone into the dark tunnel, staggering about without a light, trying to find their way back. But they missed the string, and went wandering away in the darkness, groaning and terrified.

Timmy came running back very pleased with himself.

He went to George and, whining with joy, he licked his little mistress from head to foot. And George, who never cried, was most astonished to find the tears pouring down her cheeks. 'But I'm glad, not sad!' she said. 'Oh, somebody undo my hands! I can't pat Timmy!'

Dick undid her hands and Julian's. Then they all had a marvellous time making a fuss of Timmy. And what a fuss he made of them too! He whined and barked, he rolled over and over, he licked them and butted them all with his head. He was wild with delight.

'Oh, Timmy – it's lovely to have you again,' said George, happily. 'Now you can lead us to the others. I'm sure you know where Father is, Timmy, and Sooty.'

Timmy did, of course. He set off, his tail wagging, George's hand on his collar, and the others behind in a line, holding hands.

They had the lantern with them and two torches, so they could see the way easily. But they would never have taken the right tunnels if Timmy hadn't been with them. The dog had explored them all thoroughly, and his sense of smell enabled him to go the right way without mistake.

'He's a marvellous dog,' said Anne. 'I think he's the best dog in the world, George.'

'Of course he is,' said George, who had always thought that ever since she had had Timmy as a puppy. 'Darling Tim – wasn't it wonderful when he came racing up and jumped at Block just as he was tying Julian's hands? He must have known we needed him!'

'I suppose he's taking us to wherever your father and Sooty are,' said Dick. 'He seems certain of the way. We're going steadily downhill. I bet we'll be at the marshes soon!'

When they at last came to the bottom of the hill, and emerged from the tunnel in the mists, George gave a yell. 'Look! There's Father – and Sooty too!'

'Uncle Quentin!' shouted Julian, Dick and Anne. 'Sooty! Hallo, here we are!'

Uncle Quentin and Sooty turned in the greatest surprise. They jumped up and went to meet the dog and the excited children.

'How *did* you get here?' said George's father, giving her a hug. 'Did Timmy go back for you? He suddenly deserted us and fled back into the tunnel.'

'What's happened?' asked Sooty, eagerly, knowing that the others would have plenty of news to tell him.

'Heaps,' said George, her face glowing. It was so nice all to be together again, Timmy too. She and Julian and Dick began to tell everything in turn, and then her father told his tale, too, interrupted a little by Sooty.

'Well,' said Julian at last, 'I suppose we ought to be getting back, or the police will be sending out blood-hounds to trace us all! Mr Lenoir will be surprised to see us all turning up together.'

'I wish I wasn't in pyjamas,' said his uncle, drawing the rugs about him. 'I shall feel most peculiar walking the streets like this!'

'Never mind – it's awfully misty now,' said George,

and she shivered a little, for the air was damp. 'Timmy – show us the way out of this place. I'm sure you know it.'

Timmy had never been out of the tunnel before, but he seemed to know what to do. He set off round the foot of the hill, the rest following, marvelling at the way Timmy found a dry path to follow. In the mist it was almost impossible to see which place was safe to walk on and which was not. The treacherous marsh was all around them!

'Hurrah! There's the road!' cried Julian, suddenly, as they came in sight of the roadway built over the marsh, running up the hill from the salty stretches of mud. They picked their way to it, their feet soaked with wet mud. Timmy tried to take a flying leap on to it.

But somehow or other he slipped! He fell back into the marsh, tried to find a safe foothold and couldn't. He whined.

'Timmy! Oh look, he's in the mud – and he's sinking!' screamed George, in panic. 'Timmy, Timmy, I'm coming!'

She was about to step down into the marsh to rescue Tim, but her father pulled her back roughly. 'Do you want to sink in, too?' he cried. 'Timmy will get out all right.'

But he wasn't getting out. He was sinking. 'Do something, oh, do something!' shouted George, struggling to get away from her father's hold. 'Oh, save Timmy, quick!'

CHAPTER TWENTY-TWO

Things come right at last

BUT WHAT could anyone do? In despair they all gazed at poor Timmy, who was struggling with all his might in the sinking mud. 'He's going down!' wept Anne.

Suddenly there came the sound of rumbling wheels along the road to the hill. It was a lorry carrying a load of goods – coal, coke, planks, logs, sacks of various things. George yelled to it.

'Stop, stop! Help us! Our dog's in the marsh.'

The lorry came to a stop. George's father ran his eye over the things it carried. In a trice he and Julian were dragging out some planks from the load. They threw these into the marsh, and, using them as stepping-stones, the two reached poor sinking Timmy.

The lorry-driver jumped down to help. Into the marsh, crosswise on the other planks, went some more wood, to make a safe path. The first lot were already sinking in the mud.

'Uncle Quentin's got Timmy – he's pulling him up! He's got him!' squealed Anne.

George had sat down suddenly at the edge of the road, looking white. She saw that Timmy would now be rescued, and she felt sick with shock and relief.

It was a difficult business getting Timmy right out, for the mud was strong, and sucked him down as hard as it could. But at last he was out, and he staggered across the sinking planks, trying to wag a very muddy tail.

Muddy as he was, George flung her arms round him.

'Oh, Timmy – what a fright you gave us all! Oh, how you smell – but I don't care a bit! I thought you were gone, poor, poor Timmy!'

The lorry-driver looked ruefully at his planks in the marsh. They were now out of sight beneath the mud. Uncle Quentin, feeling rather foolish in pyjamas and rugs, spoke to him.

'I've no money on me now, but if you'll call at Smuggler's Top sometime I'll pay you well for your lost planks and your help.'

'Well, I'm delivering some coal to the house next to Smuggler's Top,' said the man, eyeing Uncle Quentin's curious attire. 'Maybe you'd all like a lift? There's plenty of room at the back there.'

It was getting dark now, as well as being foggy, and everyone was tired. Thankfully they climbed up into the lorry, and it roared up the hill into Castaway. Soon they were at Smuggler's Top, and they all clambered down, suddenly feeling rather stiff.

'I'll be calling tomorrow, said the driver. 'Can't stop now. Good evening to you all!'

The little company rang the bell. Sarah came hurrying to the door. She almost fell over in surprise as she saw everyone standing there in the light of the hall-lamp.

'Lands' sakes!' she said. 'You're all back! My, Mr and Mrs Lenoir will be glad – they've got the police hunting everywhere for you! They've gone down secret passages, and they've been to Mr Barling's, and . . .'

Timmy bounced into the hall, the mud now drying on him, so that he looked most peculiar. Sarah gave a scream. 'What's that? Gracious, it can't be a dog!'

'Come here, Tim!' said George, suddenly remembering that Mr Lenoir detested dogs. 'Sarah, do you think you'd have poor Timmy in the kitchen with you? I really can't turn him out into the streets – you've no idea how brave he's been.'

'Come along, come along!' said her father, impatient with all this talk. 'Lenoir can put up with Timmy for a few minutes, surely!'

'Oh, *I'll* have him with pleasure!' said Sarah. 'I'll give him a bath. That's what he wants. Mr and Mrs Lenoir are in the sitting-room. Oh, shall I get you some clothes?'

The little party went in, and made their way to the sitting-room, while Timmy went docilely to the kitchen with the excited Sarah. Mr Lenoir heard the talking and flung open the sitting-room door.

Mrs Lenoir fell on Sooty, tears pouring down her cheeks. Marybelle pawed at him in delight, just as if she was a dog! Mr Lenoir rubbed his hands, clapped everyone on the back, and said: 'Well, well! Fine to see you all safe and sound. Well, well! What a tale you've got to tell, I'm sure!'

'It's a strange tale, Lenoir,' said George's father. 'Very strange. But I'll have to see to my feet before I tell it. I've walked miles in my bare feet, and they're very painful now!'

So, with bits of tales pouring out from everyone, the household bustled round and got hot water for bathing Uncle Quentin's feet, a dressing-gown for him, food for everyone, and hot drinks. It was really a most exciting time, and now that the thrills were all over, the children felt rather important to be able to relate so much.

Then the police came in, of course, and the Inspector at once asked a lot of questions. Everyone wanted to answer them, but the Inspector said that only George's father, Sooty and George were to tell the tale. They knew most about everything.

Mr Lenoir was perhaps the most surprised person there. When he heard how Mr Barling had actually offered to buy the plans for draining the marsh, and how he had frankly admitted to being a smuggler, he sat back in his chair, unable to say a word.

'He's mad, of course!' said the Inspector of Police. 'Doesn't seem to live in this world at all!'

'That's just what I said to him,' said Sooty. 'I told him he ought to have lived a hundred years ago!'

'Well, we've tried to catch him in the smuggling business many and many a time,' said the Inspector, 'but he was too artful. Fancy him planting Block here as a spy, sir – that was a clever bit of work – and Block using your tower as a signalling place! Bit of nerve, that! And Block isn't deaf, after all? That was clever, too – sending him about, pretending he was deaf, so that he could catch many a bit of knowledge not meant for his ears!'

'Do you think we ought to do something about Block and Mr Barling and the other man?' said Julian, suddenly. 'For all we know they're still wandering about in that maze of tunnels – and two of them are bitten by Timmy, we know.'

'Ah yes – that dog saved your lives, I should think,' said the Inspector. 'A bit of luck, that. Sorry you don't like dogs, Mr Lenoir, but I'm sure you'll admit it was a lucky thing for you all that he was wandering about!'

'Yes–yes, it was,' said Mr Lenoir. 'Of course, Block never wanted dogs here, either – he was afraid they might bark at his curious comings and goings, I suppose. By the way – where *is* this marvellous dog? I don't mind seeing him for a moment – though I do detest dogs, and always shall.'

'I'll get him,' said George. 'I only hope Sarah's done what she said, and bathed him. He was awfully muddy!'

She went out and came back with Timmy. But what a different Timmy! Sarah had given him a good hot bath, and had dried him well. He smelt sweet and fresh, his coat was springy and clean, and he had had a good meal. He was feeling very pleased with himself and everything.

'Timmy – meet a friend,' said George to him, solemnly. Timmy looked at Mr Lenoir out of his big brown eyes. He trotted straight up to him, and held up his right paw politely to shake hands, as George had taught him.

Mr Lenoir was rather taken aback. He was not used to good manners in dogs. He couldn't help putting out his

hand to Timmy – and the two shook hands in a most friendly manner. Timmy didn't attempt to lick Mr Lenoir or jump up at him. He took away his paw, gave a little wuff as if to say 'How-do-you-do?' and then went back to George. He lay down quietly beside her. 'Well – he doesn't seem like a *dog*!' said Mr Lenoir, in surprise.

'Oh, he *is*,' said George, at once, very earnestly. 'He's a real, proper dog, Mr Lenoir – only much, much cleverer than most dogs are. Could I keep him, please, while we stay here, and get someone in the town to look after him?'

'Well – seeing he is such a very fine fellow – and seems so sensible – I'll let you have him here,' said Mr Lenoir, making a great effort to be generous. 'Only – please keep him out of my way. I'm sure a sensible boy like you will see to that.'

Everyone grinned when Mr Lenoir called George a boy. He never seemed to realise she was a girl. She grinned, too. She wasn't going to tell him she wasn't a boy!

'You'll never see him!' she said, joyfully. 'I'll keep him right out of your way. Thank you very much. It's awfully good of you.'

The Inspector liked Timmy, too. He looked at him and nodded across to George. 'When you want to get rid of him, sell him to me!' he said. 'We could do with a dog like that in our police force! Soon round up the smugglers for us!'

George didn't even bother to reply! As if she would ever sell Timmy, or let him go into the police force!

All the same, the Inspector had to call on Timmy for help before long. When the next day came, and no one had found Mr Barling and his companions in the maze of tunnels, and they hadn't turned up anywhere, the Inspector asked George if she would let Timmy go down into the tunnels and hunt them out.

'Can't leave them there, lost and starving,' he said. 'Bad as they are we'll have to rescue them! Timmy is the only one who can find them.'

That was true, of course. So Timmy once more went underground into the hill, and hunted for his enemies. He found them after a while, lost in the maze of passages, hungry and thirsty, in pain and frightened.

He took them like sheep to where the police waited for them. And after that Mr Barling and his friends disappeared from public life for quite a long time!

'The police must be glad to have got them at last,' said Mr Lenoir. 'They have tried to stop this smuggling for a long time. They even suspected *me* at one time! Barling was a clever fellow, though I still think he was half mad. When Block found out my ideas about draining the marsh, Barling was afraid that once the mists and the marsh were gone, that would be the end of all his excitement – no more smuggling! No more waiting for his little ships to come creeping up in the fog – no more lines of men slipping across the secret ways of the marsh – no more signalling, no more hiding away of smuggled goods. Did you know that the police had found a cave full of them inside the hill?'

It was an exciting adventure to talk about, now that it was all over. The children felt sorry about one thing, though – they were sorry that they had thought Mr Lenoir so horrid. He was a strange man in many ways, but he could be kind and jolly too.

'Did you know we're leaving Smuggler's Top?' said Sooty. 'Mother was so terribly upset when I disappeared, that Father promised her he'd sell the place and leave Castaway, if I came back safe and sound. Mother's thrilled!'

'So am I,' said Marybelle. 'I don't like Smuggler's Top – it's so weird and secret and lonely!'

'Well, if it will make you all happy to leave it, I'm glad,' said Julian 'But *I* like it! I think it's a lovely place, set on a hill-top like this, with mists at its foot, and secret ways all about it. I'll be sorry never to come here again, if you leave.'

'So will I,' said Dick, and Anne and George nodded.

'It's an adventurous place!' said George, patting Timmy. 'Isn't it, Timmy? Do *you* like it, Timmy? Have *you* enjoyed your adventure here?'

'Woof!' said Timmy, and thumped his tail on the floor. Of course he had enjoyed himself. He always did, so long as George was anywhere about.

'Well – now perhaps we'll have a nice peaceful time!' said Marybelle. 'I don't want any more adventures.'

'Ah, but *we* do!' said the others. So no doubt they will get them. Adventures always come to the adventurous, there's no doubt about that!

THE FAMOUS FIVE

FIVE GO OFF IN A CARAVAN

Have you read all THE FAMOUS FIVE books?

1. Five on a Treasure Island
2. Five Go Adventuring Again
3. Five Run Away Together
4. Five Go to Smuggler's Top
5. Five Go Off in a Caravan
6. Five on Kirrin Island Again
7. Five Go Off to Camp
8. Five Get Into Trouble
9. Five Fall Into Adventure
10. Five on a Hike Together
11. Five Have a Wonderful Time
12. Five Go Down to the Sea
13. Five Go to Mystery Moor
14. Five Have Plenty of Fun
15. Five on a Secret Trail
16. Five Go to Billycock Hill
17. Five Get Into a Fix
18. Five on Finniston Farm
19. Five Go to Demon's Rocks
20. Five Have a Mystery to Solve
21. Five Are Together Again

The Famous Five Colour Short Stories

1. Five and a Half-Term Adventure
2. George's Hair is Too Long
3. Good Old Timmy
4. A Lazy Afternoon
5. Well Done, Famous Five
6. Five Have a Puzzling Time
7. Happy Christmas, Five
8. When Timmy Chased the Cat

Enid Blyton®

THE FAMOUS FIVE

FIVE GO OFF IN A CARAVAN

Illustrated by Eileen A. Soper

HODDER

HODDER CHILDREN'S BOOKS

First published in Great Britain in 1946 by Hodder & Stoughton
This edition published in 2016

21

A CIP catalogue record for this book is available from the British Library.

ISBN 978 1 444 93635 3

Printed and bound in Great Britain by Clays Ltd, Elcograf S.p.A.

The paper and board used in this book are made from wood from responsible sources.

Hodder Children's Books
An imprint of
Hachette Children's Group
Part of Hodder & Stoughton
Carmelite House
50 Victoria Embankment
London EC4Y 0DZ

An Hachette UK Company
www.hachette.co.uk
www.hachettechildrens.co.uk

CONTENTS

1 THE BEGINNING OF THE HOLIDAYS 1
2 GEORGE'S GREAT IDEA 11
3 THE CARAVANS ARRIVE 18
4 AWAY THEY GO! 28
5 THE WAY TO MERRAN LAKE 38
6 THE CIRCUS CAMP AND NOBBY 47
7 A TEA-PARTY – AND A VISIT IN THE NIGHT 57
8 UP IN THE HILLS 66
9 AN UNPLEASANT MEETING 75
10 A CURIOUS CHANGE OF MIND 84
11 FUN AT THE CIRCUS CAMP 93
12 A LOVELY DAY – WITH A HORRID END 102
13 JULIAN THINKS OF A PLAN 112
14 A VERY GOOD HIDING-PLACE 121
15 SEVERAL THINGS HAPPEN 130
16 A SURPRISING DISCOVERY 139
17 ANOTHER VISIT FROM LOU AND DAN 148
18 INSIDE THE HILL 157
19 PRISONERS UNDERGROUND 167
20 MORE EXCITEMENT 177

21 DICK HAS A GREAT IDEA! 188
22 THE END OF THE ADVENTURE 198
23 GOODBYE, NOBBY – GOODBYE, CARAVANNERS! 205

CHAPTER ONE

The beginning of the holidays

'I DO love the beginning of the summer hols,' said Julian. 'They always seem to stretch out ahead for ages and ages.'

'They go so nice and slowly at first,' said Anne, his little sister. 'Then they start to gallop.'

The others laughed. They knew exactly what Anne meant. 'Woof,' said a deep voice, as if someone else thoroughly agreed too.

'Timmy thinks you're right, Anne,' said George, and patted the big dog lying panting beside them. Dick patted him, too, and Timmy licked them both.

The four children were lying in a sunny garden in the first week of the holidays. Usually they went to their cousin Georgina's home for holidays, at Kirrin – but this time, for a change, they were all at the home of Julian, Dick and Anne.

Julian was the oldest, a tall, sturdy boy with a strong and pleasant face. Dick and Georgina came next. Georgina looked more like a curly-headed boy than a girl, and she insisted on being called George. Even the teachers at school called her George. Anne was the youngest, though, much to her delight, she was really growing taller now.

'Daddy said this morning that if we didn't want to stay

here all the hols we could choose what we wanted to do,' said Anne. 'I vote for staying here.'

'We could go off somewhere just for two weeks, perhaps,' said Dick. 'For a change.'

'Shall we go to Kirrin, and stay with George's mother and father for a bit?' said Julian, thinking that perhaps George would like this.

'No,' said George at once. 'I went home at half-term, and Mother said Father was just beginning one of his experiments in something or other – and you know what *that* means. If we go there we'd have to walk about on tiptoe, and talk in whispers, and keep out of his way the whole time.'

'That's the worst of having a scientist for a father,' said Dick, lying down on his back and shutting his eyes. 'Well, your mother couldn't cope with us and with your father, too, in the middle of one of his experiments, at the same time. Sparks would fly.'

'I like Uncle Quentin, but I'm afraid of him when he's in one of his tempers,' said Anne. 'He shouts so.'

'It's decided that we won't go to Kirrin, then,' said Julian, yawning. 'Not these hols, anyhow. You can always go and see your mother for a week or so, George, when you want to. What shall we do, then? Stay here all the time?'

They were now all lying down on their backs in the sun, their eyes shut. What a hot afternoon! Timmy sat up by George, his pink tongue hanging out, panting loudly.

'Don't, Timmy,' said Anne. 'You sound as if you have

been running for miles, and you make me feel hotter than ever.'

Timmy put a friendly paw on Anne's middle and she squealed. 'Oh, Timmy – your paw's heavy. Take it off.'

'You know, I think if we were allowed to go off by ourselves somewhere, it would be rather fun,' said George, biting a blade of grass and squinting up into the deep blue sky. 'The biggest fun we've ever had was when we were alone on Kirrin Island, for instance. Couldn't we go off somewhere all by ourselves?'

'But where?' said Dick. 'And how? I mean we aren't old enough to take a car – though I bet I could drive one. It wouldn't be much fun going on bicycles, because Anne can't ride as fast as we can.'

'And somebody always gets a puncture,' said Julian.

'It would be jolly good fun to go off on horses,' said George. 'Only we haven't got even one.'

'Yes, we have – there's old Dobby down in the field,' said Dick. 'He is ours. He used to draw the pony-cart, but we don't use it any more now he's turned out to grass.'

'Well, one horse wouldn't take four of us, silly,' said George. 'Dobby's no good.'

There was a silence, and everyone thought lazily about holidays. Timmy snapped at a fly, and his teeth came together with a loud click.

'Wish I could catch flies like that,' said Dick, flapping away a blue-bottle. 'Come and catch this one, Timmy, old thing.'

'What about a walking tour?' said Julian after a pause. There was a chorus of groans.

'What! In this weather! You're mad!'

'We shan't be allowed to.'

'How awful to walk for miles in this heat.'

'All right, all right,' said Julian. 'Think of a better idea, then.'

'I'd like to go somewhere where we could bathe,' said Anne. 'In a lake, for instance, if we can't to go the sea.'

'Sounds nice,' said Dick. 'My goodness, I'm sleepy. Let's hurry up and settle this matter, or I shall be snoring hard.'

But it wasn't easy to settle. Nobody wanted to go off to a hotel, or to rooms. Grown-ups would want to go with them and look after them. And nobody wanted to go walking or cycling in the hot July weather.

'Looks as if we'll have to stay at home all the hols, then,' said Julian. 'Well – I'm going to have a snooze.'

In two minutes they were all asleep on the grass except Timmy. If his family fell asleep like this, Timmy considered himself on guard. The big dog gave his mistress George a soft lick and sat up firmly beside her, his ears cocked, and his eyes bright. He panted hard, but nobody heard him. They were all snoozing deliciously in the sun, getting more and more tanned.

The garden sloped up a hillside. From where he sat Timmy could see quite a long way, both up and down the road that ran by the house. It was a wide road, but not a very busy one, for it was a country district.

Timmy heard a dog barking in the distance, and his ears twitched in that direction. He heard people walking down the road and his ears twitched again. He missed nothing, not even the robin that flew down to get a caterpillar on a bush not far off. He growled softly in his throat at the robin – just to tell it that he was on guard, so beware.

Then something came down the wide road, something that made Timmy shake with excitement, and sniff at the strange smells that came floating up to the garden. A big procession came winding up the road, with a rumble and clatter of wheels – a slow procession, headed by a very strange thing.

Timmy had no idea what it was that headed the procession. Actually it was a big elephant, and Timmy smelt its smelt, strange and strong, and didn't like it. He smelt the scent of the monkeys in their travelling cage, too, and he heard the barking of the performing dogs in their van.

He answered them defiantly. 'WOOF, WOOF, WOOF.'

The loud barking awoke all four children at once. 'Shut up, Timmy,' said George crossly. 'What a row to make when we're all having a nap.'

'WOOF,' said Timmy obstinately, and pawed at his mistress to make her sit up and take notice. George sat up. She saw the procession at once and gave a yell.

'Hey, you others. There's a circus procession going by. Look.'

They all sat up, wide awake now. They stared down at the caravans going slowly along, and listened to an animal howling, and the dogs barking.

'Look at that elephant, pulling the caravan along,' said Anne. 'He must be jolly strong.'

'Let's go down to the gate of the drive and watch,' said Dick. So they all got up and ran down the garden, then round the house and into the drive that led to the road. The procession was just passing the gates.

It was a colourful sight. The caravans were painted in brilliant colours, and looked spick and span from the outside. Little flowery curtains hung at the windows. At the front of each caravan sat the man or woman who owned it, driving the horse that pulled it. Only the front caravan was pulled by an elephant.

'Golly – doesn't it look exciting?' said George. 'I wish I belonged to a circus that went wandering all over the place all the year. That's just the sort of life I'd like.'

'Fat lot of good you'd be in the circus,' said Dick rudely. 'You can't even turn a cart-wheel.'

'What's a cart-wheel?' said Anne.

'What that boy's doing over there,' said Dick. 'Look.'

He pointed to a boy who was turning cart-wheels very quickly, going over and over on his hands and feet, turning himself like a wheel. It looked so easy, but it wasn't, as Dick very well knew.

'Oh, is he turning a cart-wheel?' said Anne admiringly. 'I wish I could do that.'

The boy came up to them and grinned. He had two terrier dogs with him. Timmy growled and George put her hand on his collar.

'Don't come too near,' she called. 'Timmy isn't quite sure about you.'

'We won't hurt him!' said the boy, and grinned again. He had an ugly, freckled face, with a shock of untidy hair. 'I won't let my dogs eat your Timmy.'

'As if they could!' began George scornfully, and then laughed. The terriers kept close to the boy's heels. He clicked and both dogs rose at once on their hind legs and walked sedately behind him with funny little steps.

'Oh – are they performing dogs?' said Anne. 'Are they yours?'

'These two are,' said the boy. 'This is Barker and this is Growler. I've had them from pups – clever as anything they are!'

'Woof,' said Timmy, apparently disgusted at seeing dogs walk in such a peculiar way. It had never occurred to him that a dog could get up on his hind legs.

'Where are you giving your next show?' asked George eagerly. 'We'd like to see it.'

'We're off for a rest,' said the boy. 'Up in the hills, where there's a blue lake at the bottom. We're allowed to camp there with our animals – it's wild and lonely and we don't disturb anybody. We just camp there with our caravans.'

'It sounds fine,' said Dick. 'Which is your caravan?'

'This one, just coming,' said the boy, and he pointed to a brightly painted van, whose sides were blue and yellow, and whose wheels were red. 'I live in it with my Uncle Dan. He's the chief clown of the circus. There he is, sitting on the front, driving the horse.'

The children stared at the chief clown, and thought that they had never seen anyone less like a clown. He was dressed in dirty grey flannel trousers and a dirty red shirt open at an equally dirty neck.

He didn't look as if he could make a single joke, or do anything in the least funny. In fact, he looked really bad-tempered, the children thought, and he scowled so fiercely as he chewed on an old pipe that Anne felt quite scared.

He didn't look at the children at all, but called in a sharp voice to the boy:

'Nobby! You come on along with us. Get in the caravan and make me a cup of tea.'

The boy Nobby winked at the children and ran to the caravan. It was plain that Uncle Dan kept him in order all right! He poked his head out of the little window in the side of the caravan nearest to the children.

'Sorry I can't ask you to tea too!' he called. 'And the dog. Barker and Growler wouldn't half like to know him!'

The caravan passed on, taking the scowling clown with it, and the grinning Nobby. The children watched the others going by, too; it was quite a big circus. There was a cage of monkeys, a chimpanzee sitting in a corner of a dark cage, asleep, a string of beautiful horses, sleek and shining, a great wagon carrying benches and forms and tents, caravans for the circus folk to live in, and a host of interesting people to see, sitting on the steps of their vans or walking together outside to stretch their legs.

At last the procession was gone and the children went slowly back to their sunny corner in the garden. They sat down – and then George announced something that made them sit up straight.

'*I* know what we'll do these hols! We'll hire a caravan and go off in it by ourselves. Do let's! Oh, do let's!'

CHAPTER TWO

George's great idea

THE OTHERS stared at George's excited face. She had gone quite red. Dick thumped on the ground.

'A jolly good idea! Why didn't we think of it before?'

'Oh, *yes*! A caravan to ourselves! It sounds too good to be true!' said Anne, and her face grew red too, and her eyes shone.

'Well, I must say it would be something we've never done before,' said Julian, wondering if it was really possible. 'I say – wouldn't it be gorgeous if we could go off into the hills – where that lake is that the boy spoke about? We could bathe there – and we could perhaps get to know the circus folk. I've always wanted to know about circuses.'

'Oh, *Julian*! That's a better idea still!' said George, rubbing her hands together in delight. 'I liked that boy Nobby, didn't you!'

'Yes,' said everyone.

'But I didn't like his uncle,' said Dick. 'He looked a nasty bit of work. I bet he makes Nobby toe the mark and do what he's told.'

'Julian, do you think we'd be allowed to go caravanning by ourselves?' asked Anne earnestly. 'It does seem to me to be the most marvellous idea we've ever had.'

'Well – we can ask and see,' said Julian. 'I'm old enough to look after you all.'

'Pooh!' said George. 'I don't want any looking after, thank you. And anyway, if we want looking after, Timmy can do that. I bet the grown-ups will be glad to be rid of us for a week or two. They always think the summer hols are too long.'

'We'll take Dobby with us to pull the caravan!' said Anne suddenly, looking down at the field where Dobby stood, patiently flicking away the flies with his long tail. 'Dobby would love that! I always think he must be lonely, living in that field all by himself, just being borrowed by people occasionally.'

'Of course – Dobby could come,' said Dick. 'That would be fine. Where could we get the caravan from? Are they easy to hire?'

'Don't know,' said Julian. 'I knew a chap at school – you remember him, Dick, that big fellow called Perry – he used to go caravanning every hols with his family. They used to hire caravans, I know. I might find out from him where he got them from.'

'Daddy will know,' said Anne. 'Or Mummy. Grown-ups always know things like that. I'd like a nice large caravan – red and blue – with a little chimney, and windows each side, and a door at the back, and steps to go up into the caravan, and . . .'

The others interrupted with their own ideas, and soon

they were all talking excitedly about it – so loudly that they didn't see someone walking up and standing near by, laughing at the excitement.

'Woof,' said Timmy politely. He was the only one who had ears and eyes for anything else at the moment. The children looked up.

'Oh, hallo, Mother!' said Julian. 'You've just come at the right moment. We want to tell you about an idea we've got.'

His mother sat down, smiling. 'You seem very excited about something,' she said. 'What is it?'

'Well, it's like this, Mummy,' said Anne, before anyone else could get a word in, 'we've made up our minds that we'd like to go off in a caravan for a holiday by ourselves! Oh, Mummy – it would be such fun!'

'By yourselves?' said her mother doubtfully. 'Well, I don't know about that.'

'Julian can look after us,' said Anne

'So can Timmy,' put in George at once, and Timmy thumped the ground with his tail. Of course he could look after them! Hadn't he done it for years, and shared all their adventures? Thump, thump, thump!

'I'll have to talk it over with Daddy,' said Mother. 'Now don't look so disappointed – I can't decide a thing like this all by myself in a hurry. But it may fit in quite well because I know Daddy has to go up north for a little while, and he would like me to go with him. So he might think a little caravanning quite a good idea. I'll talk to him tonight.'

'We could have Dobby to pull the caravan, Mummy,' said Anne, her eyes bright. 'Couldn't we? He'd love to come. He has such a dull life now.'

'We'll see, we'll see,' said her mother, getting up. 'Now you'd better all come in and wash. It's nearly tea-time. Your hair is terrible, Anne. What *have* you been doing? Standing on your head?'

Everyone rushed indoors to wash, feeling distinctly cheerful. Mother hadn't said NO. She had even thought it might fit in quite well. Golly, to go off in a caravan all alone – doing their own cooking and washing – having Dobby for company, and Timmy as well, of course. How simply gorgeous.

The children's father did not come home until late that evening, which was a nuisance, for nobody felt that they could wait for very long to know whether they might or might not go. Everyone but Julian was in bed when he came home, and even when he, too, came to bed he had nothing to report.

He stuck his head into the girls' bedroom. 'Daddy's tired and he's having a late supper, and Mother won't bother him till he's feeling better. So we shan't know till morning, worse luck!'

The girls groaned. How could they possibly go to sleep with thoughts of caravans floating deliciously in their heads – not knowing whether or not they would be allowed to go!

'Blow!' said George. 'I shan't go to sleep for ages. Get

off my feet, Timmy. Honestly, it's too hot to have you anywhere near me in this weather.'

In the morning good news awaited the four children. They sat down at the breakfast-table, all very punctual for once, and Julian looked expectantly at his mother. She smiled at him and nodded.

'Yes, we've talked it over,' she said. 'And Daddy says he doesn't see why you shouldn't have a caravan holiday. He thinks it would be good for you to go off and rough it a bit. But you will have to have two caravans, not one. We couldn't have all four of you, and Timmy too, living in one caravan.'

'Oh – but Dobby couldn't pull *two* caravans, Mummy,' said Anne.

'We can borrow another horse,' said Julian. 'Can't we, Mother? Thanks awfully, Daddy, for saying we can go. It's jolly sporting of you.'

'Absolutely super,' said Dick.

'Wizard!' said George, her fingers scratching Timmy's head excitedly. 'When can we go? Tomorrow?'

'Of course not!' said Julian. 'We've got to get the caravans – and borrow a horse – and pack – and all sorts of things.'

'You can go next week, when I take your mother up north with me,' said his father. 'That will suit us very well. We can give Cook a holiday, too, then. You will have to send us a card every single day to tell us how you are and where you are.'

'It does sound thrilling,' said Anne. 'I really don't feel as if I can eat any breakfast, Mummy.'

'Well, if that's the effect the idea of caravanning has on you, I don't think you'd better go,' said her mother. Anne hastily began to eat her shredded wheat, and her appetite soon came back. It was too good to be true – to have *two* caravans – and *two* horses – and sleep in bunks perhaps – and cook meals outside in the open air – and . . .

'You will be in complete charge, you understand, Julian,' said the boy's father. 'You are old enough now to be really responsible. The others must realise that you are in charge and they must do as you say.'

'Yes,' said Julian, feeling proud. 'I'll see to things all right.'

'And Timmy will be in charge, too,' said George. 'He's just as responsible as Julian.'

'Woof,' said Timmy, hearing his name, and thumping the floor with his tail.

'You're a darling, Timmy,' said Anne. 'I'll always do what *you* say, as well as what Julian says!'

'Idiot!' said Dick. He patted Timmy's head. 'I bet we wouldn't be allowed to go without you, Timothy. You are a jolly good guard for anyone.'

'You certainly wouldn't be allowed to go without Timmy,' said his mother. 'We know you'll be safe with him.'

It was all most exciting. The children went off to talk things over by themselves when breakfast was finished.

'I vote we go caravanning up into the hills that boy spoke of, where the lake lies at the bottom – and camp there,' said Julian. 'We'd have company then – jolly exciting company, too. We wouldn't live *too* near the circus camp – they might not like strangers butting in – but we'll live near enough to see the elephant going for his daily walk, and the dogs being exercised . . .'

'And we'll make friends with Nobby, won't we?' said Anne eagerly. 'I liked him. We won't go near his uncle, though. I think it's strange that such a bad-tempered looking man should be the chief clown in a circus.'

'I wonder when and where Mother will get the caravans!' said Julian. 'Gosh, won't it be fun when we see them for the first time!'

'Let's go and tell Dobby!' said Anne. 'He is sure to be excited, too!'

'Baby! He won't understand a word you tell him!' said George. But off she went with Anne just the same, and soon Dobby was hearing all about the wonderful holiday plan. Hrrrrumph! So long as it included him, too, he was happy!

CHAPTER THREE

The caravans arrive

AT LAST the great day came when the two caravans were due to arrive. The children stood at the end of the drive for hours, watching for them.

Mother had managed to borrow them from an old friend of hers. The children had promised faithfully to look after them well, and not to damage anything. Now they stood at the end of the drive, watching eagerly for the caravans to arrive.

'They are being drawn by cars today,' said Julian. 'But they are fitted up to be horse-drawn, too. I wonder what they are like – and what colour they are.'

'Will they be like travellers' caravans, on high wheels, do you think?' asked Anne. Julian shook his head.

'No, they're modern, Mother says. Streamlined and all that. Not too big either, because a horse can't draw too heavy a van.'

'They're coming, they're coming! I can see them!' suddenly yelled George, making them all jump. 'Look, isn't that them, far down the road?'

They all looked hard into the distance. No one had such good eyes as George, and all they could see was a blotch, a moving speck far away on the road. But George's eyes

saw two caravans, one behind the other.

'George is right,' said Julian, straining his eyes. 'It's our caravans. They're each drawn by a small car.'

'One's red and the other's green,' said Anne. 'Bags I the red one. Oh, hurry up, caravans!'

At last they were near enough to see properly. The children ran to meet them. They certainly were very nice ones, quite modern and 'streamlined', as Julian had said, well built and comfortable.

'They almost reach the ground!' said Anne. 'And look at the wheels, set so neatly into the side of the vans. I do like the red one, bags I the red one.'

Each van had a little chimney, long, narrow windows down the two sides, and tiny ones in front by the driver's seat. There was a broad door at the back and two steps down. Pretty curtains fluttered at the open windows.

'Red curtains for the green caravan, and green ones for the red caravan!' said Anne. 'Oh, I want to go inside!'

But she couldn't because the doors were locked. So she had to be content to run with the others up the drive after the two caravans, shouting loudly:

'Mummy! They're here, the caravans are here.'

Her mother came running down the steps to see. Soon the doors were unlocked and thc children went inside the caravans. Delighted shouts came from both vans.

'Bunks along one side – is that where we sleep? How gorgeous!'

'Look at this little sink – we can really wash up. And golly, water comes out of these taps!'

'There's a proper stove to cook on – but I vote we cook out of doors on a camp-fire. I say, look at the bright frying-pans – and all the cups and saucers hanging up!'

'It's like a proper little house inside. Doesn't it seem nice and *big*? Mother, isn't it beautifully planned? Don't you wish you were coming with us?'

'Hey, you girls! Do you see where the water comes from? Out of that tank on the roof. It must collect rainwater. And look at this gadget for heating water. Isn't it all super?'

The children spent hours examining their caravans and finding out all the secrets. They certainly were very well fitted, spotlessly clean, and very roomy. George felt as if she couldn't wait to start out. She really must get Dobby and set out at once!

'No, you must wait, silly,' said Julian. 'You know we've to get the other horse. He's not coming till tomorrow.'

The other horse was a sturdy little black fellow called Trotter. He belonged to the milkman, who often lent him out. He was a sensible little horse, and the children knew him very well and liked him. They all learnt riding at school, and knew how to groom and look after a horse, so there would be no difficulty over their managing Dobby and Trotter.

Mother was thrilled over the caravans, too, and looked very longingly at them. 'If I wasn't going with Daddy I should be most tempted to come with you,' she said. 'Don't look so startled, Anne dear – I'm not really coming!'

'We're jolly lucky to get such decent caravans,' said Julian. 'We'd better pack our things today, hadn't we, Mother – and start off tomorrow, now we've got the caravans.'

'You won't need to pack,' said his mother. 'All you have to do is to pop your things straight into the cupboards and drawers – you will only want clothes and books and a few games to play in case it's rainy.'

'We don't need any clothes except our night things, do we?' said George, who would have lived in a jersey and shorts all day and every day if she had been allowed to.

'You must take plenty of jerseys, another pair of shorts each, in case you get wet, your raincoats, bathing-things, towels, a change of shoes, night things, and some cool shirts or blouses,' said Mother. Everyone groaned.

'What a frightful lot of things!' said Dick. 'There'll never be room for all those.'

'Oh yes there will,' said Mother. 'You will be sorry if you take too few clothes, get soaked through, have nothing to change into, and catch fearful colds that will stop you from enjoying a lovely holiday like this.'

'Come on, let's get the things,' said Dick. 'Once Mother starts off about catching cold there's no knowing what else she'll make us take – is there, Mother?'

'You're a cheeky boy,' said his mother, smiling. 'Yes,

go and collect your things. I'll help you to put them into the cupboards and drawers. Isn't it marvellous how everything folds so neatly into the walls of the caravans – there seems to be room for everything, and you don't notice the cupboards.'

'I shall keep everything very clean,' said Anne. 'You know how I like *playing* at keeping house, don't you, Mother – well, it will be real this time. I shall have two caravans to keep clean, all by myself.'

'All by yourself!' said her mother. 'Well, surely the boys will help you – and certainly George must.'

'Pooh, the boys!' said Anne. 'They won't know how to wash and dry a cup properly – and George never bothers about things like that. If I don't make the bunks and wash the crockery, they would never be made or washed, I know that!'

'Well, it's a good thing that one of you is sensible!' said her mother. 'You'll find that everyone will share in the work, Anne. Now off you go and get your things. Bring all the raincoats, to start with.'

It was fun taking things down to the caravans and packing them all in. There were shelves for a few books and games, so Julian brought down snap cards, ludo, lexicon, happy families and dominoes, as well as four or five books for each of them. He also brought down some maps of the district, because he meant to plan out where they were to go, and the best roads to follow.

Daddy had given him a useful little book in which

were the names of farms that would give permission to caravanners to camp in fields for the night. 'You must always choose a field where there is a stream, if possible,' said his father, 'because Dobby and Trotter will want water.'

'Remember to boil every drop of water you drink,' said the children's mother. 'That's very important. Get as much milk from the farms as they will let you have. And remember that there is plenty of ginger-beer in the locker under the second caravan.'

'It's all so thrilling,' said Anne, peering down to look at the locker into which Julian had put the bottles of ginger-beer. 'I can't believe we're really going tomorrow.'

But it was true. Dobby and Trotter were to be taken to the caravans the next day and harnessed. 'How exciting for them, too,' Anne thought.

Timmy couldn't quite understand all the excitement, but he shared in it, of course, and kept his tail on the wag all day long. He examined the caravans thoroughly from end to end, found a rug he liked the smell of, and lay down on it. 'This is *my* corner,' he seemed to say. 'If you go off in these peculiar houses on wheels, this is my own little corner.'

'We'll have the red caravan, George,' said Anne. 'The boys can have the green one. They don't care what colour they have – but I love red. I say, won't it be fun to sleep in those bunks? They look jolly comfortable.'

At last tomorrow came – and the milkman brought the

sturdy little black horse, Trotter, up the drive. Julian fetched Dobby from the field. The horses nuzzled one another and Dobby went 'Hrrrumph' in a very civil horsy voice.

'They're going to like each other,' said Anne. 'Look at them nuzzling. Trotter, you're going to draw *my* caravan.'

The two horses stood patiently while they were harnessed. Dobby jerked his head once or twice as if he was impatient to be off and stamped a little.

'Oh, Dobby, I feel like that, too!' said Anne. 'Don't you, Dick, don't you, Julian?'

'I do rather,' said Dick with a grin. 'Get up there, Dobby – that's right. Who's going to drive, Julian – take it in turns, shall we?'

'I'm going to drive *our* caravan,' said George. 'Anne wouldn't be any good at it, though I'll let her have a turn at it sometimes. Driving is a man's job.'

'Well, you're only a girl!' said Anne indignantly. 'You're not a man, nor even a boy!'

George put on one of her scowls. She always wanted to be a boy, and even thought of herself as one. She didn't like to be reminded that she was a girl. But not even George could scowl for long that exciting morning! She soon began to caper round and about again, laughing and calling out with the others:

'We're ready! Surely we're ready!'

'Yes. Do let's go! JULIAN! He's gone indoors, the idiot, just when we want to start.'

'He's gone to get the cakes that Cook has baked this morning for us. We've heaps of food in the larder. I feel hungry already.'

'Here's Julian. Do come on, Julian. We'll drive off without you. Goodbye, Mother! We'll send you a card every single day, we faithfully promise.'

Julian got up on the front of the green caravan. He clicked to Dobby. 'Get on, Dobby! We're off! Goodbye, Mother!'

Dick sat beside him, grinning with pure happiness. The caravans moved off down the drive. George pulled at Trotter's reins and the little horse followed the caravan in front. Anne, sitting beside George, waved wildly.

'Goodbye, Mother! We're off at last on another adventure. Hurrah! Three cheers! Hurrah!'

CHAPTER FOUR

Away they go!

THE CARAVANS went slowly down the wide road. Julian was so happy that he sang at the top of his voice, and the others joined in the choruses. Timmy barked excitedly. He was sitting on one side of George and as Anne was on the other, George was decidedly squashed. But little things like that did not bother her at all.

Dobby plodded on slowly, enjoying the sunshine and the little breeze that raised the hairs on his mane. Trotter followed at a short distance. He was very much interested in Timmy, and always turned his head when the dog barked or got down for a run. It was fun to have two horses and a dog to travel with.

It had been decided that they should make their way towards the hills where they hoped to find the circus. Julian had traced the place on his map. He was sure it must be right because of the lake that lay in the valley at the foot of the hills.

'See?' he said to the others, pointing. 'There it is – Lake Merran. I bet we'll find the circus camp somewhere near it. It would be a very good place for all their animals – no one to interfere with the camp, plenty of water for both animals and men, and probably good farms to supply them with food.'

'We'll have to find a good farm ourselves tonight,' said Dick. 'And ask permission to camp. Lucky we've got that little book telling us where to go and ask.'

Anne thought with delight of the coming evening, when they would stop and camp, cook a meal, drowse over a camp-fire, and go to sleep in the little bunks. She didn't know which was nicer – ambling along down country lanes with the caravans – or preparing to settle in for the night. She was sure it was going to be the nicest holiday they had ever had.

'Don't you think so?' she asked George as they sat together on the driving-seat, with Timmy, for once, trotting beside the caravan, and leaving them a little more room than usual. 'You know, most of our hols have been packed with adventures – awfully exciting, I know – but I'd like an *ordinary* holiday now, wouldn't you – not *too* exciting.'

'Oh, I like adventures,' said George, shaking the reins and making Trotter do a little trot. 'I wouldn't a bit mind having another one. But we shan't this time, Anne. No such luck!'

They stopped for a meal at half past twelve, all of them feeling very hungry. Dobby and Trotter moved towards a ditch in which long, juicy grass grew, and munched away happily.

The children lay on a sunny bank and ate and drank. Anne looked at George. 'You've got more freckles these hols, George, than you ever had in your life before.'

'That doesn't worry *me*!' said George, who never cared in the least how she looked, and was even angry with her hair for being too curly, and making her look too much like a girl. 'Pass the sandwiches, Anne – the tomato ones – golly, if we always feel as hungry as this we'll have to buy eggs and bacon and butter and milk at every farm we pass!'

They set off again. Dick took his turn at driving Dobby, and Julian walked to stretch his legs. George still wanted to drive, but Anne felt too sleepy to sit beside her with safety.

'If I shut my eyes and sleep I shall fall off the seat,' she said. 'I'd better go into the caravan and sleep there.'

So in she went, all by herself. It was cool and dim inside the caravan, for the curtains had been pulled across the window to keep the inside cool. Anne climbed on to one of the bunks and lay down. She shut her eyes. The caravan rumbled slowly on, and the little girl fell asleep.

Julian peeped in at her and grinned. Timmy came and looked, too, but Julian wouldn't let him go in and wake Anne by licking her.

'You come and walk with me, Tim,' he said. 'You're getting round. Exercise will do you good.'

'He's *not* getting round!' called George, indignantly. 'He's a very nice shape. Don't you listen to him, Timmy.'

'Woof,' said Timmy, and trotted along at Julian's heels.

The two caravans covered quite a good distance that day, even though they went slowly. Julian did not miss the way once. He was very good indeed at map-reading. Anne was disappointed that they could not see the hills they were making for, at the end of the day.

'Goodness, they're miles and miles away!' said Julian. 'We shan't arrive for at least four or five days, silly! Now, look out for a farm, kids. There should be one near here, where we can ask permission to camp for the night.'

'There's one, surely,' said George, after a few minutes. She pointed to where a red-roofed building with moss-covered barns, stood glowing in the evening sun. Hens clucked about it, and a dog or two watched them from a gateway.

'Yes, that's the one,' said Julian, examining his map. 'Longman's Farm. There should be a stream near it. There it is, look – in that field. Now, if we could get permission to camp just here, it would be lovely.'

Julian went to the farm to see the farmer, and Anne went with him to ask for eggs. The farmer was not there, but the farmer's wife, who liked the look of the tall polite Julian very much, gave them permission at once to spend the night in the field by the stream.

'I know you won't leave a lot of litter, or go chasing the farm animals,' she said. 'Or leave the gates open like some campers do. And what's that you want, Missy – some new-laid eggs? Yes, of course, you can have some – and you can pick the ripe plums off that tree, too, to go with your supper!'

There was bacon in the larder of the caravans, and Anne

said she would fry that and an egg each for everyone. She was very proud of being able to cook them. She had taken a few lessons from Cook in the last few days, and was very anxious to show the others what she had learnt.

Julian said it was too hot to cook in the caravan, and he built her a fine fire in the field. Dick set the two horses free and they wandered off to the stream, where they stood knee-high in the cool water, enjoying it immensely. Trotter muzzled against Dobby, and then tried to nuzzle down to Timmy, too, when the big dog came to drink beside him.

'Doesn't the bacon smell lovely?' called Anne to George, who was busy getting plates and mugs out of the red caravan. 'Let's have ginger-beer to drink, George. I'm jolly thirsty. Watch me crack these eggs on the edge of this cup, everybody, so that I can get out the yolk and white and fry them.' Crack! The egg broke against the edge of the cup – but its contents unfortunately fell outside the cup instead of inside. Anne went red when everyone roared with laughter.

Timmy came and licked up the mess. He was very useful for that sort of thing. 'You'd make a good dustbin, Timmy,' said Anne. 'Here's a bit of bacon-rind, too. Catch!'

Anne fried the bacon and eggs really well. The others were most admiring, even George, and they all cleared their plates well, wiping the last bit of fat off with bread, so that they would be easy to wash.

'Do you think Timmy would like me to fry him a few dog-biscuits, instead of having them cold?' said Anne, suddenly. 'Fried things are so nice. I'm sure Timmy would like fried biscuits better than ordinary ones.'

'Well, he wouldn't,' said George. 'They would just make him sick.'

'How do you know?' said Anne. 'You can't possibly tell.'

'I always know what Timmy would really like and what he wouldn't,' said George. 'And he wouldn't like his biscuits fried. Pass the plums, Dick. They look super.'

They lingered over the little camp-fire for a long time, and then Julian said it was time for bed. Nobody minded, because they all wanted to try sleeping on the comfortable-looking bunks.

'Shall I wash at the stream or in the little sink where I washed the plates?' said Anne. 'I don't know which would be nicer.'

'There's more water to spare in the stream,' said Julian. 'Hurry up, won't you, because I want to lock your caravan door so that you'll be safe.'

'Lock our door!' said George, indignantly. 'You jolly well won't! Nobody's going to lock *me* in! I might think I'd like to take a walk in the moonlight or something.'

'Yes, but a tramp or somebody might . . .' began Julian. George interrupted him scornfully.

'What about Timmy? You know jolly well he'd never let anyone come *near* our caravans, let alone into them! I won't be locked in, Julian. I couldn't bear it. Timmy's better than any locked door.'

'Well, I suppose he is,' said Julian. 'All right, don't look so furious, George. Walk half the night in moonlight if you want to – though there won't be any moon tonight, I'm sure. Golly, I'm sleepy!'

They climbed into the two caravans, after washing in the stream. They all undressed, and got into the inviting bunks. There was a sheet, one blanket and a rug – but all the children threw off both blanket and rug and kept only a sheet over them that hot night.

At first Anne tried sleeping in the lower bunk, beneath George – but Timmy would keep on trying to clamber up to get to George. He wanted to lie on her feet as usual. Anne got cross.

'George! You'd better change places with me. Timmy keeps jumping on me and walking all over me trying to get up to your bunk. I'll never get to sleep.'

So George changed places, and after that Timmy made no more noise, but lay contentedly at the end of George's bunk on the rolled-up blanket, while Anne lay in the bunk above, trying not to go to sleep because it was such a lovely feeling to be inside a caravan that stood by a stream in a field.

Owls hooted to one another, and Timmy growled softly. The voice of the stream, contented and babbling, could be quite clearly heard now that everything was so quiet. Anne felt her eyes closing. Oh dear – she would simply *have* to go to sleep.

But something suddenly awoke her with a jump, and Timmy barked so loudly that both Anne and George almost fell out of their bunks in fright. Something bumped violently against the caravan, and shook it from end to end! Was somebody trying to get in?

Timmy leapt to the floor and ran to the door, which George had left open a little because of the heat. Then the voices of Dick and Julian were heard.

'What's up? Are you girls all right? We're coming!' And over the wet grass raced the two boys in their dressing-gowns. Julian ran straight into something hard and warm and solid. He yelled.

Dick switched on his torch and began to laugh helplessly. 'You ran straight into Dobby. Look at him staring at you! He must have lumbered all round our caravans making the bumps we heard. It's all right, girls. It's only Dobby.'

So back they all went again to sleep, and this time they slept till the morning, not even stirring when Trotter, too, came to nuzzle round the caravan and snort softly in the night.

CHAPTER FIVE

The way to Merran Lake

THE NEXT three or four days were absolutely perfect, the children thought. Blue skies, blazing sun, wayside streams to paddle or bathe in, and two houses on wheels that went rumbling for miles down roads and lanes quite new to them – what could be lovelier for four children all on their own?

Timmy seemed to enjoy everything thoroughly, too, and had made firm friends with Trotter, the little black horse. Trotter was always looking for Timmy to run beside him, and he whinnied to Timmy whenever he wanted him. The two horses were friends, too, and when they were set free at night they made for the stream together, and stood in the water side by side, nuzzling one another happily.

'I like this holiday better than any we've ever had,' said Anne, busily cooking something in a pan. 'It's exciting without being adventurous. And although Julian thinks he's in charge of us, *I* am really! You'd never get your bunks made, or your meals cooked, or the caravans kept clean if it wasn't for me!'

'Don't boast!' said George, feeling rather guilty because she let Anne do so much.

'I'm not boasting!' said Anne, indignantly. 'I'm just

telling the truth. Why, you've never even made your own bunk once, George. Not that I mind doing it. I love having two houses on wheels to look after.'

'You're a very good little housekeeper,' said Julian. 'We couldn't possibly do without you!'

Anne blushed with pride. She took the pan off the camp-fire and put the contents on to four plates. 'Come along!' she called, in a voice just like her mother's. 'Have your meal while it's hot.'

'I'd rather have mine when it's cold, thank you,' said George. 'It doesn't seem to have got a bit cooler, even though it's evening-time.'

They had been on the road four days now, and Anne had given up looking for the hills where they hoped to find the circus folk camping. In fact she secretly hoped they wouldn't find them, because she was so much enjoying the daily wanderings over the lovely countryside.

Timmy came to lick the plates. The children always let him do that now because it made them so much easier to wash. Anne and George took the things down to a little brown brook to rinse, and Julian took out his map.

He and Dick pored over it. 'We're just about here,' said Julian, pointing. 'And if so, it looks as if tomorrow we ought to come to those hills above the lake. Then we should see the circus.'

'Good!' said Dick. 'I hope Nobby will be there. He would love to show us round, I'm sure. He would show us a good place to camp, too, perhaps.'

'Oh, we can find that ourselves,' said Julian, who now rather prided himself on picking excellent camping-sites. 'Anyway, I don't want to be *too* near the circus. It might be a bit smelly. I'd rather be up in the hills some way above it. We'll get a place with a lovely view.'

'Right,' said Dick, and Julian folded up the map. The two girls came back with the clean crockery, and Anne put it neatly back on the shelves in the red caravan. Trotter came to look for Timmy, who was lying panting under George's caravan.

Timmy wouldn't budge, so Trotter tried to get under the caravan too. But he couldn't possibly, of course, for he was much too big. So he lay down on the shady side, as near to Timmy as he could get.

'Trotter's really a comic horse,' said Dick. 'He'd be quite good in a circus, I should think! Did you see him chasing Timmy yesterday – just as if they were playing "tag"?'

The word 'circus' reminded them of Nobby and his circus, and they began to talk eagerly of all the animals there.

'I liked the look of the elephant,' said George. 'I wonder what his name is. And wouldn't I like to hold a monkey!'

'I bet that chimpanzee's clever,' said Dick. 'I wonder what Timmy will think of him. I hope he'll get on all right with all the animals, especially the other dogs.'

'I hope we don't see much of Nobby's uncle,' said Anne. 'He looked as if he'd like to box anybody's ears if they so much as answered him back.'

'Well, he won't box *mine*,' said Julian. 'We'll keep out of his way. He doesn't look a very pleasant chap, I must say. Perhaps he won't be there.'

'Timmy, come out from under the caravan!' called George. 'It's quite cool and shady where we are. Come on!'

He came, panting. Trotter immediately got up and came with him. The little horse lay down beside Timmy and nuzzled him. Timmy gave his nose a lick and then turned away, looking bored.

'Isn't Trotter funny?' said Anne. 'Timmy, what *will* you think of all the circus animals, I wonder! I do hope we see the circus tomorrow. Shall we get as far as the hills, Julian? Though really I shan't mind a bit if we don't; it's so nice being on our own like this.'

They all looked out for the hills the next day as the caravans rumbled slowly down the lanes, pulled by Trotter and Dobby. And, in the afternoon, they saw them, blue in the distance.

'There they are!' said Julian. 'Those must be the Merran Hills – and Merran Lake must lie at the foot. I say, I hope the two horses are strong enough to pull the caravans a good way up. There should be an absolutely marvellous view over the lake if we get up high enough.'

The hills came nearer and nearer. They were high ones, and looked lovely in the evening light. Julian looked at his watch.

'We shan't have time to climb them and find a camping

site there tonight, I'm afraid,' he said. 'We'd better camp a little way on this evening, and then make our way up into the hills tomorrow morning.'

'All right,' said Dick. 'Anything you say, Captain! There should be a farm about two miles on, according to the book. We'll camp there.'

They came to the farm, which was set by a wide stream that ran swiftly along. Julian went as usual to ask permission to camp, and Dick went with him, leaving the two girls to prepare a meal.

Julian easily got permission, and the farmer's daughter, a plump jolly girl, sold the boys eggs, bacon, milk, and butter, besides a little crock of yellow cream. She also offered them raspberries from the garden if they liked to pick them and have them with the cream.

'Oh, I say, thanks awfully,' said Julian. 'Could you tell me if there's a circus camping in those hills? Somewhere by the lake.'

'Yes, it went by about a week ago,' said the girl. 'It goes camping there every year, for a rest. I always watch the caravans go by – quite a treat in a quiet place like this! One year they had lions, and at nights I could hear them roaring away. That fair frizzled my spine!'

The boys said goodbye and went off, chuckling to think of the farm-girl's spine being 'fair frizzled' by the roars of the distant lions.

'Well, it looks as if we'll pass the circus camp tomorrow all right,' said Julian. 'I shall enjoy camping up in the hills, won't you, Dick? It will be cooler up there, I expect – usually there's a breeze on the hills.'

'I hope we shan't get our spines fair frizzled by the noise of the circus animals at night,' grinned Dick. 'I feel fair frizzled up by the sun today, I must say!'

The next morning the caravans set off again on what the children hoped would be the last lap of their journey. They would find a lovely camping place and stay there till they had to go home.

Julian had remembered to send a postcard each day to his parents, telling them where he was, and that everything was fine. He had found out from the farm-girl the right address for that district, and he planned to arrange with the nearest post office to take in any letters for them that came. They had not been able to receive any post, of course, when they were wandering about in their caravans.

Dobby and Trotter walked sedately down the narrow country lane that led towards the hills. Suddenly George caught sight of something flashing blue between the trees.

'Look! There's the lake! Merran Lake!' she shouted. 'Make Dobby go more quickly, Ju. I'm longing to come out into the open and see the lake.'

Soon the lane ended in a broad cart-track that led over a heathery common. The common sloped right down to the edge of an enormous blue lake that lay glittering in the August sunshine.

'I say! Isn't it magnificent?' said Dick, stopping Dobby

with a pull. 'Come on, let's get down and go to the edge, Julian. Come on, girls!'

'It's lovely!' said Anne, jumping down from the driving-seat of the red caravan. 'Oh, do let's bathe straight away!'

'Yes, let's,' said Julian, and they all dived into their caravans, stripped off shorts and blouses and pulled on bathing-things. Then, without even a towel to dry themselves on, they tore down to the lakeside, eager to plunge into its blue coolness.

It was very warm at the edge of the water, but further in, where it was deep, the lake was deliciously cold. All the children could swim strongly, and they splashed and yelled in delight. The bottom of the lake was sandy, so the water was as clear as crystal.

When they were tired they all came out and lay on the warm sandy bank of the lake. They dried at once in the sun. Then as soon as they felt too hot in they went again, squealing with joy at the cold water.

'What gorgeous fun to come down here every day and bathe!' said Dick. 'Get away, Timmy, when I'm swimming on my back. Timmy's enjoying the bathe as much as we are, George.'

'Yes, and old Trotter wants to come in, too,' shouted Julian. 'Look at him – he's brought the red caravan right down to the edge of the lake. He'll be in the water with it if we don't stop him!'

They decided to have a picnic by the lake, and to set the horses free to have a bathe if they wanted one. But all they wanted was to drink and to stand knee-high in the water, swishing their tails to keep away the flies that worried them all day long.

'Where's the circus camp?' said George suddenly as they sat munching ham and tomato sandwiches. 'I can't see it.'

The children looked all round the edge of the lake, which stretched as far as they could see. At last George's sharp eyes saw a small spire of smoke rising in the air about a mile or so round the lake.

'The camp must be in that hollow at the foot of the hills over there,' she said. 'I expect the road leads round to it. We'll go that way, shall we, and then go up into the hills behind?'

'Yes,' agreed Julian. 'We shall have plenty of time to

have a word with Nobby, and to find a good camping place before night comes – and to find a farm, too, that will let us have food. Won't Nobby be surprised to see us?'

They cleared up, put the horses into their harness again and set off for the circus camp. Now for a bit of excitement!

CHAPTER SIX

The circus camp and Nobby

IT DID not take the caravans very long to come in sight of the circus camp. As George had said, it was in a comfortable hollow, set at the foot of the hills – a quiet spot, well away from any dwelling-places, where the circus animals could enjoy a certain amount of freedom and be exercised in peace.

The caravans were set round in a wide circle. Tents had been put up here and there. The big elephant was tied by a thick rope to a stout tree. Dogs ran about everywhere, and a string of shining horses was being paraded round a large field nearby.

'There they all are!' said Anne, excitedly, standing up on the driving-seat to see better. 'Golly, the chimpanzee is loose, isn't he? No, he isn't – someone has got him on a rope. Is it Nobby with him?'

'Yes, it is. I say, fancy walking about with a live chimp like that!' said Julian.

The children looked at everything with the greatest interest as their caravans came nearer to the circus camp. Few people seemed to be about that hot afternoon. Nobby was there with the chimpanzee, and one or two women were stirring pots over small fires – but that seemed to be all.

The circus dogs set up a great barking as the red and green caravans drew nearer. One or two men came out of the tents and looked up the track that led to the camp. They pointed to the children's caravans and seemed astonished.

Nobby, with the chimpanzee held firmly by the paw, came out of the camp in curiosity to meet the strange caravans. Julian hailed him.

'Hi, Nobby! You didn't think you'd see *us* here, did you?'

Nobby was amazed to hear his name called. At first he did not remember the children at all. Then he gave a yell.

'Jumping Jiminy, it's you kids I saw away back on the road! What are *you* doing here?'

Timmy growled ominously and George called to Nobby. 'He's never seen a chimpanzee before. Do you think they'll be friends?'

'Don't know,' said Nobby doubtfully. 'Old Pongo likes the circus dogs all right. Anyway, don't you let your dog fly at Pongo, or he'll be eaten alive! A chimp is very strong, you know.'

'Could I make friends with Pongo, do you think?' asked George. 'If he would shake hands with me, or something, Timmy would know I was friends with him and he'd be all right. Would Pongo make friends with me?'

'Course he will!' said Nobby. 'He's the sweetest-tempered chimp alive – aren't you, Pongo? Now, shake hands with the lady.'

Anne didn't feel at all inclined to go near the chimpanzee, but George was quite fearless. She walked up to the big animal and held out her hand. The chimpanzee took it at once, raised it to his mouth and pretended to nibble it, making friendly noises all the time.

George laughed. 'He's nice, isn't he?' she said. 'Timmy, this is Pongo, a friend. Nice Pongo, good Pongo!'

She patted Pongo on the shoulder to show Timmy that she liked the chimpanzee, and Pongo at once patted her on the shoulder, too, grinning amiably. He then patted her on the head and pulled one of her curls.

Timmy wagged his tail a little. He looked very doubtful indeed. What was this strange creature that his mistress appeared to like so much? He took a step towards Pongo.

'Come on, Timmy, say how do you do to Pongo,' said George. 'Like this.' And she shook hands with the chimpanzee again. This time he wouldn't let her hand go, but went on shaking it up and down as if he was pumping water with a pump-handle.

'He won't let go,' said George.

'Don't be naughty, Pongo,' said Nobby in a stern voice. Pongo at once dropped George's hand and covered his face with a hairy paw as if he was ashamed. But the children saw that he was peeping through his fingers with wicked eyes that twinkled with fun.

'He's a real monkey!' said George, laughing.

'You're wrong – he's an ape!' said Nobby. 'Ah, here comes Timmy to make friends. Jumping Jiminy, they're shaking paws!'

So they were. Timmy, having once made up his mind that Pongo was to be a friend, remembered his manners and held out his right paw as he had been taught. Pongo seized it and shook it vigorously. Then he walked round to the back of Timmy and shook hands with his tail. Timmy didn't know what to make of it all.

The children yelled with laughter, and Timmy sat down firmly on his tail. Then he stood up again, his tail wagging, for Barker and Growler had come rushing up. Timmy remembered them, and they remembered him.

'Well, *they're* making friends all right,' said Nobby, pleased. 'Now they'll introduce Timmy to all the other dogs, and there'll be no trouble. Hey, look out for Pongo, there!'

The chimpanzee had stolen round to the back of Julian and was slipping his hand into the boy's pocket. Nobby went to him and tapped the chimpanzee's paw hard.

'Naughty! Bad boy! Pickpocket!'

The children laughed again when the chimpanzee covered his face with his paws, pretending to be ashamed.

'You'll have to watch out when Pongo's about,' said Nobby. 'He loves to take things out of people's pockets. I say – do tell me – are those your caravans? Aren't they posh?'

'They're been lent to us,' said Dick. 'As a matter of fact, it was seeing your circus go by, with all its colourful caravans, that made us think of borrowing caravans, too, and coming away for a holiday.'

'And as you'd told us where you were going we thought we'd follow you and find you out, and get you to show us round the camp,' said Julian. 'Hope you don't mind.'

'I'm proud,' said Nobby, going a bright red. ''Tisn't often folks want to make friends with a circus fellow like me. I'll be proud to show you round – and you can make friends with every blessed monkey, dog and horse in the place!'

'Oh, thanks!' said all four at once.

'Jolly decent of you,' said Dick. 'Gosh, look at that chimp – he's trying to shake hands with Timmy's tail again. I bet he's funny in the circus ring, isn't he, Nobby?'

'He's a scream,' said Nobby. 'Brings the house down. You should see him act with my Uncle Dan. He's the chief clown, you know. Pongo is just as big a clown as my uncle is – it's a fair scream to see them act the fool together.'

'I wish we *could* see them,' said Anne. 'Acting in the ring, I mean. Will your uncle mind you showing us all the animals and everything?'

'Why should he?' said Nobby. 'Shan't ask him! But you mind and act polite to him, won't you? He's worse than a tiger when he's in a temper. They call him Tiger Dan because of his rages.'

Anne didn't like the sound of that at all – Tiger Dan! It sounded very fierce.

'I hope he isn't about anywhere now,' she said nervously, looking round.

'No. He's gone off somewhere,' said Nobby. 'He's a lonesome sort of chap – got no friends much in the circus, except Lou, the acrobat. That's Lou over there.'

Lou was a long-limbed, loose-jointed fellow with an ugly face, and a crop of black shining hair that curled tightly. He sat on the steps of a caravan, smoking a pipe and reading a paper. The children thought that he and

Tiger Dan would make a good pair – bad-tempered, scowling and unfriendly. They all made up their minds that they would have as little as possible to do with Lou the acrobat and Tiger Dan the clown.

'Is he a very good acrobat?' said Anne in a low voice, though Lou was much too far away to hear her.

'Fine. First class,' said Nobby with admiration in his voice. 'He can climb anything anywhere – he could go up that tree there like a monkey – and I've seen him climb a drainpipe straight up the side of a tall building just like a cat. He's a marvel. You should see him on the tight-rope, too. He can dance on it!'

The children gazed at Lou with awe. He felt their glances, looked up and scowled. 'Well,' thought Julian, 'he may be the finest acrobat that ever lived – but he's a jolly nasty-looking fellow. There's not much to choose between him and Tiger Dan!'

Lou got up, uncurling his long body like a cat. He moved easily and softly. He loped over to Nobby, still with the ugly scowl on his face.

'Who are these kids?' he said. 'What are they doing messing about here?'

'We're not messing about,' said Julian politely. 'We came to see Nobby. We've seen him before.'

Lou looked at Julian as if he was something that smelt nasty. 'Those your caravans?' he asked jerking his head towards them.

'Yes,' said Julian.

'Posh, aren't you?' said Lou sneeringly.

'Not particularly,' said Julian, still polite.

'Any grown-ups with you?' asked Lou.

'No. I'm in charge,' said Julian, 'and we've got a dog that flies at people he doesn't like.'

Timmy clearly didn't like Lou. He stood near him, growling in his throat. Lou kicked out at him.

George caught hold of Timmy's collar just in time. 'Down, Tim, down!' she cried. Then she turned on Lou, her eyes blazing.

'Don't you dare kick my dog!' she shouted. 'He'll have you down on the ground if you do. You keep out of his way, or he'll go for you now.'

Lou spat on the ground in contempt and turned to go. 'You clear out,' he said. 'We don't want any kids messing about here. And I'm not afraid of any dog. I've got ways of dealing with bad dogs.'

'What do you mean by that?' yelled George, still in a furious temper. But Lou did not bother to reply. He went up the steps of his caravan and slammed the door shut. Timmy barked angrily and tugged at his collar, which George was still holding firmly.

'Now you've torn it!' said Nobby dismally. 'If Lou catches you about anywhere he'll hoof you out. And you be careful of that dog of yours, or he'll disappear.'

George was angry and alarmed. 'Disappear! What do you mean? If you think Timmy would let anyone steal him, you're wrong.'

'All right, all right. I'm only telling you. Don't fly at me like that!' said Nobby. 'Jumping Jiminy, look at that chimp. He's gone inside one of your caravans!'

The sudden storm was forgotten as everyone rushed to the green caravan. Pongo was inside, helping himself liberally from a tin of sweets. As soon as he saw the children he groaned and covered his face with his paws – but he sucked hard at the sweets all the time.

'Pongo! Bad boy! Come here!' scolded Nobby. 'Shall I punish you?'

'Oh, no, don't,' begged Anne. 'He's a scamp, but I do like him. We've plenty of sweets to spare. You have some, too, Nobby.'

'Well, thank you,' said Nobby, and helped himself. He grinned round at everyone. 'Nice to have friends like you,' he said. 'Isn't it, Pongo?'

CHAPTER SEVEN

A tea-party – and a visit in the night

NOBODY PARTICULARLY wanted to see round the camp just then, as Lou had been so unpleasant. So instead they showed the admiring Nobby over the two caravans. He had never seen such beauties.

'Jumping Jiminy, they're like palaces!' he said. 'Do you mean to say them taps turn on and water comes out? Can I turn on a tap? I've never turned a tap in my life!'

He turned the taps on and off a dozen times, exclaiming in wonder to see the water come gushing out. He thumped the bunks to see how soft they were. He admired the colourful soft rugs and the shining crockery. He was, in fact, a very nice guest to have, and the children liked him more and more. They liked Barker and Growler, too, who were both well-behaved, obedient, merry dogs.

Pongo, of course, wanted to turn the taps on and off, too, and he threw all the coverings off the two bunks to see what was underneath. He also took the kettle off the stove, put the spout to his thick lips and drank all the water out of it very noisily indeed.

'You're forgetting your manners, Pongo!' said Nobby in horror, and snatched the kettle away from him. Anne squealed with laughter. She loved the chimpanzee, and he seemed to have taken a great fancy to Anne, too. He followed her about and stroked her hair and made funny affectionate noises.

'Would you like to stay and have tea here with us?' asked Julian, looking at his watch. 'It's about time.'

'Coo – I don't have tea as a rule,' said Nobby. 'Yes, I'd like to. Sure you don't mind me staying, though? I ain't got your manners. But you're real kind.'

'We'd love to have you stay,' said Anne in delight. 'I'll cut some bread and butter and make some sandwiches. Do you like potted meat sandwiches, Nobby?'

'Don't I just!' said Nobby. 'And Pongo does, too. Don't you let him get near them or he'll finish up the lot.'

It was a pleasant and amusing little tea-party. They all sat out on the heather, on the shady side of the caravan. Barker and Growler sat with Timmy. Pongo sat beside Anne, taking bits of sandwich from her most politely. Nobby enjoyed his tea immensely, eating more sandwiches than anyone and talking all the time with his mouth full.

He made the four children yell with laughter. He imitated his Uncle Dan doing some of his clown tricks. He turned cart-wheels all round the caravan while he was waiting for Anne to cut more sandwiches. He stood solemnly on his head and ate a sandwich like that, much to Timmy's amazement. Timmy walked round and round him, and sniffed at his face as if to say: 'Strange! No legs! Something's gone wrong.'

At last nobody could eat any more. Nobby stood up to

go, suddenly wondering if he had stayed too long.

'I was enjoying myself so much I forgot the time,' he said awkwardly. 'Bet I've stayed too long and you've been too polite to tell me to get out. Coo, that wasn't half a good tea! Thanks awfully for all those delicious sandwiches. 'Fraid my manners aren't like yours, kids, but thanks for a very good time.'

'You've got very good manners indeed,' said Anne, warmly. 'You've been a splendid guest. Come again, won't you?'

'Well, thanks, I will,' said Nobby, forgetting his sudden awkwardness, and beaming round. 'Where's Pongo? Look at that chimp! He's got one of your hankies, and he's blowing his nose!'

Anne squealed in delight. 'He can keep it!' she said. 'It's only an old one.'

'Will you be here camping for long?' asked Nobby.

'Well, not just exactly *here*,' said Julian. 'We thought of going up higher into the hills. It will be cooler there. But we might camp here just for tonight. We meant to go up higher this evening, but we might as well stay here and go tomorrow morning now. Perhaps we could see round the camp tomorrow morning.'

'Not if Lou's there you can't,' said Nobby. 'Once he's told people to clear out he means it. But it will be all right if he's not. I'll come and tell you.'

'All right,' said Julian. 'I'm not afraid of Lou – but we don't want to get *you* into any trouble, Nobby. If Lou's there tomorrow morning, we'll go on up into the hills, and you can always signal to us if he's out of the camp, and we can come down any time. And mind you come up and see us when you want to.'

'And bring Pongo,' said Anne.

'You bet!' said Nobby. 'Well – so long!'

He went off with Barker and Growler at his heels and with Pongo held firmly by the paw. Pongo didn't want to go at all. He kept pulling back like a naughty child.

'I do like Nobby and Pongo,' said Anne. 'I wonder what Mummy would say if she knew we'd made friends with a chimpanzee. She'd have a fit.'

Julian suddenly looked rather doubtful. He was wondering if he had done right to follow the circus and let Anne and the others make friends with them. But Nobby was so nice. He was sure his mother would like Nobby. And they could easily keep away from Tiger Dan and Lou the acrobat.

'Have we got enough to eat for supper tonight and breakfast tomorrow?' he asked Anne. 'Because there doesn't seem to be a farm near enough to go to just here. But Nobby says there's one up on the hill up there – the circus folk get their supplies from it, too – what they don't get from the nearest town. Apparently somebody goes in each day to shop.'

'I'll just see what we've got in the larder, Julian,' said Anne, getting up. She knew perfectly well what there was in the larder – but it made her feel grown-up and important to go and look. It was nice to feel like that when she so often felt small and young, and the others were big and knew so much.

She called back to them: 'I've got eggs and tomatoes and potted meat, and plenty of bread, and a cake we bought today, and a pound of butter.'

'That's all right then,' said Julian. 'We won't bother about going to the farm tonight.'

When darkness fell that night, there were clouds across the sky for the first time. Not a star showed and there was no moon. It was pitch-black, and Julian, looking out of the window of his caravan, before clambering into his bunk, could not even see a shimmer of water from the lake.

He got into his bunk and pulled the covers up. In the other caravan George and Anne were asleep. Timmy was, as usual, on George's feet. She had pushed him off them once or twice, but now that she was asleep he was undisturbed, and lay heavily across her ankles, his head on his paws.

Suddenly his ears cocked up. He raised his head cautiously. Then he growled softly in his throat. He had heard something. He sat there stiffly, listening. He could hear footsteps from two different directions. Then he heard voices – cautious voices, low and muffled.

Timmy growled again, more loudly. George awoke and reached for his collar. 'What's the matter?' she whispered. Timmy listened and so did she. They both heard the voices.

George slipped quietly out of the bunk and went to the half-open door of the caravan. She could not see anything outside at all because it was so dark. 'Don't make a noise, Tim,' she whispered.

Timmy understood. He did not growl again, but George could feel the hairs rising all along the back of his neck.

The voices seemed to come from not very far away. 'Two men must be talking together,' George thought. Then she heard a match struck, and in its light she saw two men lighting their cigarettes from the same match. She recognised them at once – they were Nobby's Uncle Dan and Lou the acrobat.

What were they doing there? Had they got a meeting-place there – or had they come to steal something from the caravans? George wished she could tell Julian and Dick – but she did not like to go out of her caravan in case the men heard her.

At first she could not hear anything the men said. They were discussing something very earnestly. Then one raised his voice.

'OK, then – that's settled.' Then came the sound of footsteps again, this time towards George's caravan. The men walked straight into the side of it, exclaimed in surprise and pain, and began to feel about to find out what they had walked into.

'It's those posh caravans!' George heard Lou exclaim. 'Still here! I told those kids to clear out!'

'What kids?' asked Tiger Dan, in surprise. Evidently he

had come back in the dark and did not know they had arrived.

'Some kids Nobby knows,' said Lou in an angry voice. He rapped loudly on the walls of the caravan, and Anne woke up with a jump. George, just inside the caravan with Timmy, jumped in fright, too. Timmy barked in rage.

Julian and Dick woke up. Julian flashed on his torch and went to his door. The light picked out the two men standing by George's caravan.

'What are you doing here at this time of night?' said Julian. 'Making a row like that! Clear off!'

This was quite the wrong thing to have said to Dan and Lou, both bad-tempered men who felt that the whole of the camping-ground around belonged to them and the circus.

'Who do you think you're talking to?' shouted Dan angrily. 'You're the ones to clear off! Do you hear?'

'Didn't I tell you to clear out this afternoon?' yelled Lou, losing his temper, too. 'You do as you're told, you young rogue, or I'll set the dogs on you and have you chased for miles.'

Anne began to cry. George trembled with rage. Timmy growled. Julian spoke calmly but determinedly.

'We're going in the morning, as we meant. But if you're suggesting we should go now, you can think again.' This is as much our camping-ground as yours. Now get off, and don't come disturbing us again.'

'I'll give you a leathering, you young cockerel!' cried

Lou, and began to unfasten the leather belt from round his waist.

George let go her hold of Timmy's collar. 'Go for them, Timmy,' she said. 'But don't bite. Just worry them!'

Timmy sprang down to the ground with a joyful bark. He flung himself at the two men. He knew what George wanted him to do, and although he longed to snap at the two rogues with his sharp teeth, he didn't. He pretended to, though, and growled so fiercely that they were scared out of their wits.

Lou hit out at Timmy, threatening to kill him. But Timmy cared for no threats of that kind. He got hold of Lou's right trouser-leg, pulled, and ripped it open from knee to ankle.

'Come on – the dog's mad!' cried Dan. 'He'll have us by the throat if we don't go. Call him off, you kids. We're going. But mind you clear out in the morning, or we'll see you do! We'll pay you out one day.'

Seeing that the men really meant to go, George whistled to Timmy. 'Come here, Tim. Stand on guard till they're really gone. Fly at them if they come back.'

But the men soon disappeared – and nothing would have made either of them come back and face Timmy again that night!

CHAPTER EIGHT

Up in the hills

THE FOUR children were upset and puzzled by the behaviour of the two men. George told how Timmy had woken her by growling and how she had heard the men talking together in low voices.

'I don't really think they had come to steal anything,' she said. 'I think they were just meeting near here for a secret talk. They didn't know the caravans were here and walked straight into ours.'

'They're bad-tempered brutes,' said Julian. 'And I don't care what you say, George, I'm going to lock your caravan door tonight. I know you've got Timmy – but I'm not running any risk of these men coming back, Timmy or no Timmy.'

Anne was so scared that George consented to let Julian lock the red caravan door. Timmy was locked in with them. The boys went back to their own caravan, and Julian locked his door, too, from the inside.

'I'll be glad to get away from here up into the hills,' he said. 'I shan't feel safe as long as we are quite so near the camp. We'll be all right up in the hills.'

'We'll go first thing after breakfast,' said Dick, settling down to his bunk again. 'Gosh, it's a good thing the girls had Timmy tonight. Those fellows looked as if they meant to go for you properly, Ju.'

'Yes. I shouldn't have had much chance against the two of them either,' said Julian. 'They are both hefty, strong fellows.'

The next morning all the four awoke early. Nobody felt inclined to lie and snooze – all of them were anxious to get off before Lou and Dan appeared again.

'You get the breakfast, Anne and George, and Dick and I will catch the horses and put them in the caravan shafts,' said Julian. 'Then we shall be ready to go off immediately after breakfast.'

They had breakfast and cleared up. They got up on to the driving-seats and were just about to drive away when Lou and Dan came down the track towards them.

'Oh, you're going, are you?' said Dan, with an ugly grin on his face. 'That's right. Nice to see kids so obedient. Where are you going?'

'Up into the hills,' said Julian. 'Not that it's anything to do with you where we go.'

'Why don't you go round the foot of the hills, instead of over the top?' said Lou. 'Silly way to go – up there, with the caravans dragging the horses back all the way.'

Julian was just about to say that he didn't intend to go right up to the top of the hills and over to the other side, when he stopped himself. No – just as well not to let these fellows know that he meant to camp up there, or they might come and worry them all again.

He clicked to Dobby. 'We're going the way we want to go,' he said to Lou in a curt voice. 'And that's up the hill. Get out of the way, please.'

As Dobby was walking straight at them, the men had to jump to one side. They scowled at the four children. Then they all heard the sound of running footsteps and along came Nobby, with Barker and Growler at his heels as usual.

'Hey, what are you going so early for?' he yelled. 'Let me come part of the way with you.'

'No, you don't,' said his uncle, and gave the surprised boy an unexpected cuff. 'I've told these kids to clear out, and they're going. I won't have any meddling strangers round this camp. And don't you kid yourself they want to make friends with you, see! Go and get out those dogs and exercise them, or I'll give you another box on the ears that'll make you see all the stars in the sky.'

Nobby stared at him, angry and afraid. He knew his uncle too well to defy him. He turned on his heel sullenly and went off back to the camp. The caravans overtook him on the way. Julian called to him in a low voice:

'Cheer up, Nobby. We'll be waiting for you up in the hills – don't tell Lou and your uncle about it. Let them think we've gone right away. Bring Pongo up sometime!'

Nobby grinned. 'Right you are!' he said. 'I can bring the dogs up to exercise them, too – but not today. I daren't today. And as soon as those two are safely out for the day

I'll bring you down to the camp and show you round, see? That all right?'

'Fine,' said Julian, and drove on. Neither Lou nor Dan had heard a word, or even guessed that this conversation was going on, for Nobby had been careful to walk on all the time and not even turn his face towards the children.

The road wound upwards into the hills. At first it was not very steep, but wound to and fro across the side of the hill. Half-way up the caravans crossed a stone bridge under which a very swift stream flowed.

'That stream's in a hurry!' said George, watching it bubble and gurgle downwards. 'Look – is that where it starts from – just there in the hillside?'

She pointed some way up the hill, and it seemed as if the stream really did suddenly start just where she pointed.

'But it can't suddenly start here – not such a big fast stream as this!' said Julian, stopping Dobby on the other side of the bridge. 'Let's go and see. I'm thirsty, and if there's a spring there, it will be very cold and clear – lovely to drink from. Come on, we'll go and see.'

But there was no spring. The stream did not 'begin' just there, but flowed out of a hole in the hillside, as big and as fast as it was just under the stone bridge. The children bent down and peered into the water-filled hole.

'It comes out from inside the hill,' said Anne, surprised. 'Fancy it running around in the hill itself. It must be glad to find a way out!'

They didn't like to drink it as it was not the clear, fresh spring they had hoped to find. But, wandering a little farther on, they came to a real spring that gushed out from beneath a stone, cold and crystal clear. They drank from this and voted that it was the nicest drink they had ever had in their lives. Dick followed the spring-water downwards and saw that it joined the little rushing stream.

'I suppose it flows into the lake,' he said. 'Come on. Let's get on and find a farm, Julian. I'm sure I heard the crowing of a cock just then, so one can't be far away.'

They went round a bend of the hill and saw the farm, a rambling collection of old buildings sprawling down the hillside. Hens ran about, clucking. Sheep grazed above the farm, and cows chewed the cud in fields nearby. A man was working not far off, and Julian hailed him. 'Good morning! Are you the farmer?'

'No. Farmer's over yonder,' said the man, pointing to a barn near the farmhouse. 'Be careful of the dogs.'

The two caravans went on towards the farm. The farmer heard them coming and came out with his dogs. When he saw that there were only children driving the two caravans he looked surprised.

Julian had a polite, well-mannered way with him that all the grown-ups liked. Soon he was deep in a talk with the man, with most satisfactory results. The farmer was willing to supply them with any farm produce they wanted, and they could have as much milk as they liked at any time. His wife, he was sure, would cook them anything they asked her to, and bake them cakes, too.

'Perhaps I could arrange payment with her?' said Julian. 'I'd like to pay for everything as I buy it.'

'That's right, son,' said the farmer. 'Always pay your way as you go along, and you won't come to any harm. You go and see my old woman. She likes children and she'll make you right welcome. Where are you going to camp?'

'I'd like to camp somewhere with a fine view over the lake,' said Julian. 'We can't see it from just here. Maybe a bit farther on we'll get just the view I want.'

'Yes, you go on about half a mile,' said the farmer. 'The track goes that far – and when you come to a clump of fine birch trees you'll see a sheltered hollow, set right in the hillside, with a wonderful fine view over the lake. You can pull your caravans in there, son, and you'll be sheltered from the winds.'

'Thanks awfully,' said all the children together, thinking what a nice man this old farmer was. How different from Lou and Dan, with their threats and rages!

'We'll go and see your wife first,' said Julian. 'Then we'll go on and pull into the hollow you suggest. We'll be seeing you again some time, I expect.'

They went to see the farmer's wife, a round-cheeked old woman, whose little curranty eyes twinkled with good humour. She made them very welcome, gave them hot buns from the oven and told them to help themselves to the little purple plums on the tree outside the old farmhouse.

Julian arranged to pay on the spot for anything they bought each day. The prices the farmer's wife asked seemed very low indeed, but she would not hear of taking any more money for her goods.

'It'll be a pleasure to see your bonny faces at my door!' she said. 'That'll be part of my payment, see? I can tell you're well-brought-up children by your nice manners and ways. You'll not be doing any damage or foolishness on the farm, *I* know.'

The children came away laden with all kinds of food, from eggs and ham to scones and ginger cakes. She pushed a bottle of raspberry syrup into Anne's hand when the little girl said goodbye. But when Julian turned back to pay her for it she was quite annoyed.

'If I want to make a present to somebody I'll do it!' she said. 'Go on with you . . . paying for this and paying for that. I'll have a little something extra for you each time, and don't you dare to ask to pay for it, or I'll be after you with my rolling pin!'

'Isn't she awfully nice?' said Anne as they made their way back to the caravans. 'Even Timmy offered to shake hands with her without you telling him to, George – and he hardly ever does that to anyone, does he?'

They packed the things away into the larder, got up into the driving-seats, clicked to Dobby and Trotter and set off up the track again.

Just over half a mile away was a clump of birch trees. 'We'll find that sheltered hollow near them,' said Julian.

'Yes, look – there it is – set back into the hill, a really cosy place! Just right for camping in – and oh, what a magnificent view!'

It certainly was. They could see right down the steep hillside to the lake. It lay spread out, flat and smooth, like an enchanted mirror. From where they were they could now see right to the opposite banks of the lake – and it was indeed a big stretch of water.

'Isn't it blue?' said Anne, staring. 'Bluer even than the sky. Oh, won't it be lovely to see this marvellous view every single day we're here?'

Julian backed the caravans into the hollow. Heather grew there, like a springy purple carpet. Harebells, pale as an evening sky, grew in clumps in crevices of the hill behind. It was a lovely spot for camping in.

George's sharp ears caught the sound of water and she went to look for it. She called back to the others. 'What do you think? There's another spring here, coming out of the hill. Drinking and washing water laid on! Aren't we lucky?'

'We certainly are,' said Julian. 'It's a lovely place – and nobody will disturb us here!'

But he spoke too soon!

CHAPTER NINE

An unpleasant meeting

IT REALLY was fun settling into that cosy hollow. The two caravans were backed in side by side. The horses were taken out and led to a big field where the farmer's horses were kept when they had done their day's work. Trotter and Dobby seemed very pleased with the green, sloping field. It had a spring of its own that ran into a stone trough and out of it, keeping it always filled with fresh cold water. Both horses went to take a long drink.

'Well, that settles the two horses all right,' said Julian. 'We'll tell the farmer he can borrow them if he wants to – he'll be harvesting soon and may like to have Dobby and Trotter for a few days. They will enjoy hobnobbing with other horses again.'

At the front of the hollow was a rocky ledge, hung with heathery tufts. 'This is the front seat for Lake View!' said Anne. 'Oh, it's warm from the sun! How lovely!'

'I vote we have all our meals on this ledge,' said George, sitting down too. 'It's comfortable and roomy – and flat enough to take our cups and plates without spilling anything – and honestly the view from here is too gorgeous for words. Can anyone see anything of the circus from up here?'

'There's a spire or two of smoke over yonder,' said Dick, pointing. 'I should think that's where the camp is. And look – there's a boat pushing out on the lake – doesn't it look tiny?'

'Perhaps Nobby is in it,' said Anne. 'Haven't we brought any field-glasses, Julian? I thought we had.'

'Yes – we have,' said Julian, remembering. 'I'll get them.' He went to the green caravan, rummaged about in the drawers, and came out with his field-glasses swinging on the end of their straps.

'Here we are!' he said, and set them to his eyes. 'Yes – I can see the boat clearly now – and it *is* Nobby in it – but who's with him? Golly, it's Pongo!'

Everyone had to look through the glasses to see Nobby and Pongo in the boat. 'You know, we could always get Nobby to signal to us somehow from his boat when he wanted to tell us that Lou and his uncle were away,' said Dick. 'Then we should know it was safe, and we could pop down to the camp and see round it.'

'Yes. Good idea,' said George. 'Give me the glasses, Dick. Timmy wants to have a turn at seeing, too.'

'He can't see through glasses like these, idiot,' said Dick, handing them to George. But Timmy most solemnly glued his eyes to the glasses, and appeared to be looking through them very earnestly indeed.

'Woof,' he remarked, when he took his eyes away at last.

'He says he's seen Nobby and Pongo, too,' said George,

and the others laughed. Anne half-believed that he had. Timmy was such an extraordinary dog, she thought, as she patted his smooth head.

It was a terribly hot day. Too hot to do anything – even to walk down to the lake and bathe! The children were glad they were up in the hills, for at least there was a little breeze that fanned them now and again. They did not expect to see Nobby again that day, but they hoped he would come up the next day. If not they would go down and bathe in the lake and hope to see him somewhere about there.

Soon the rocky ledge got too hot to sit on. The children retreated to the clump of birch trees, which at least cast some shade. They took books with them, and Timmy came along, too, panting as if he had run for miles. He kept going off to the little spring to drink. Anne filled a big bowl with the cold water, and stood it in a breezy place near by, with a cup to dip into it. They were thirsty all day long, and it was pleasant to dip a cup into the bowl of spring-water and drink.

The lake was unbelievably blue that day, and lay as still as a mirror. Nobby's boat was no longer in the water. He and Pongo had gone. There was not a single movement to be seen down by the lake.

'Shall we go down to the lake this evening, when it's cooler, and bathe there?' said Julian, at tea-time. 'We haven't had much exercise today, and it would do us good to walk down and have a swim. We won't take

Timmy in case we happen to come across Lou or Dan. He'd certainly fly at them today. We can always keep an eye open for those two and avoid them ourselves – but Timmy would go for them as soon as he spotted them. We might be in the water and unable to stop him.'

'Anyway, he'll guard the caravans for us,' said Anne. 'Well, I'll just take these cups and plates and rinse them in the stream. Nobody wants any more to eat, do they?'

'Too hot,' said Dick, rolling over on to his back. 'I wish we were by the lake at this moment – I'd go straight into the water now!'

At half past six it was cooler, and the four children set off down the hill. Timmy was angry and hurt at being left behind.

'You're to be on guard, Timmy,' said George firmly. 'See? Don't let anyone come near our caravans. On guard, Timmy!'

'Woof,' said Timmy dismally, and put his tail down. On guard! Didn't George know that the caravans wouldn't walk off by themselves, and that he wanted a good splash in the lake?

Still, he stayed behind, standing on the rocky ledge to see the last of the children, his ears cocked to hear their voices and his tail still down in disgust. Then he went and lay down beneath George's caravan, and waited patiently for his friends to return.

The children went down the hill with their bathing-things, taking short cuts, and leaping like goats over the steep bits. It had seemed quite a long way up when they had gone so slowly in the caravans with Dobby and Trotter – but it wasn't nearly so far when they could go on their own legs, and take rabbit-paths and short cuts whenever they liked.

There was one steep bit that forced them back on to the track. They went along it where the track turned a sharp corner round a cliff-like bend – and to their surprise and dismay they walked almost straight into Lou and Tiger Dan!

'Take no notice,' said Julian, in a low voice. 'Keep together and walk straight on. Pretend that Timmy is somewhere just behind us.'

'Tim, Tim!' called George, at once.

Lou and Dan seemed just as surprised to see the children as they had been to see the two men. They stopped and looked hard at them, but Julian hurried the others on.

'Hey, wait a minute!' called Dan. 'I thought you had gone off – over the hill-top!'

'Sorry we can't stop!' called back Julian. 'We're in rather a hurry!'

Lou looked round for Timmy. He wasn't going to lose his temper and start shouting in case that mad dog came at him again. He spoke to the children loudly, forcing himself to appear good-tempered.

'Where are your caravans? Are you camping up here anywhere?'

But the children still walked on, and the men had to go after them to make them hear.

'Hey! What's the matter? We shan't hurt you! We only want to know if you're camping here. It's better down below, you know.'

'Keep on walking,' muttered Julian. 'Don't tell them anything. Why do they tell us it's better to camp down below when they were so anxious for us to clear out yesterday? They're mad!'

'Timmy, Timmy!' called George, again, hoping that the men would stop following them if they heard her calling for her dog.

It did stop them. They gave up going after the children, and didn't shout any more. They turned angrily and went on up the track.

'Well, we've thrown them off all right,' said Dick, with relief. 'Don't look so scared, Anne. I wonder what they want up in the hills. They don't look the sort that would go walking for pleasure.'

'Dick – we're not going to have another adventure, are we?' said Anne suddenly, looking very woebegone. 'I don't want one. I just want a nice ordinary, peaceful holiday.'

''Course we're not going to have an adventure!' said Dick, scornfully. 'Just because we meet two bad-tempered fellows from a circus camp you think we're in for an adventure, Anne! Well, *I* jolly well wish we were! Every hols we've been together so far we've had adventures –

and you must admit that you love talking about them and remembering them.'

'Yes, I do. But I don't like it much when I'm in the *middle* of one,' said Anne. 'I don't think I'm a very adventurous person, really.'

'No, you're not,' said Julian, pulling Anne over a very steep bit. 'But you're a very nice little person, Anne, so don't worry about it. And, anyway, you wouldn't like to be left out of any of our adventures, would you?'

'Oh *no*,' said Anne. 'I couldn't bear it. Oh, look – we're at the bottom of the hill – and there's the lake, looking icy-cold!'

It wasn't long before they were all in the water – and suddenly there was Nobby too, waving and yelling. 'I'm coming in! Lou and my uncle have gone off somewhere. Hurray!'

Barker and Growler were with Nobby, but not Pongo the chimpanzee. Nobby was soon in the water, swimming like a dog, and splashing George as soon as he got up to her.

'We met Lou and your uncle as we came down,' called George. 'Shut up, Nobby, and let me talk to you. I said, we met Lou and your uncle just now – going up into the hills.'

'Up into the hills?' said Nobby, astonished. 'Whatever for? They don't go and fetch things from the farm. The women do that, early each morning.'

'Well, we met those two,' said Dick swimming up. 'They seemed jolly surprised to see us. I hope they aren't going to bother us any more.'

'I've had a bad day,' said Nobby. 'My uncle hit me like anything for making friends with you. He says I'm not to go talking to strangers any more.'

'Why ever not?' said Dick. 'What a surly, selfish fellow he is! Well, you don't seem to be taking much notice of him now!'

''Course not!' said Nobby. 'He's safe up in the hills, isn't he? I'll have to be careful he doesn't see me with you, that's all. Nobody else at the camp will split on me – they all hate Lou and Tiger Dan.'

'We saw you out in your boat with Pongo,' said Julian, swimming up to join in the conversation. 'We thought that if ever you wanted to signal to us you could easily do it by going out in your boat, and waving a handkerchief or something. We've got field-glasses, and we can easily see you. We could come along down if you signalled. We'd know it would be safe.'

'Right,' said Nobby. 'Come on, let's have a race. Bet you I'm on the shore first!'

He wasn't, of course, because he didn't swim properly. Even Anne could race him. Soon they were all drying themselves vigorously.

'Golly, I'm hungry!' said Julian. 'Come on up the hill with us, Nobby, and share our supper!'

CHAPTER TEN

A curious change of mind

NOBBY FELT very much tempted to go and have a meal up in the hills with the children. But he was afraid of meeting Lou and his uncle coming back from their walk.

'We can easily look out for them and warn you if we see or hear them,' said Dick, 'and you can flop under a bush and hide till they go past. You may be sure we'll be on the look-out for them ourselves, because *we* don't want to meet them either!'

'Well, I'll come,' said Nobby. 'I'll take Barker and Growler too. They'll like to see Timmy.'

So all five of them, with the two dogs, set off up the hill. They climbed up short cuts at first, but they were soon panting, and decided to take the track, which, although longer, was easier to follow.

They all kept a sharp look-out for the two men, but they could see no sign of them. 'We shall be at our caravans soon,' said Julian. Then he heard Timmy barking in the distance. 'Hallo! What's old Tim barking for? I wonder if those fellows have been up to our caravans?'

'Good thing we left Timmy on guard if so,' said Dick. 'We might have missed something if not.'

Then he went red, remembering that it was Nobby's

uncle he had been talking of. Nobby might feel upset and offended to hear someone speaking as if he thought Tiger Dan would commit a little robbery.

But Nobby wasn't at all offended. 'Don't you worry about what you say of my uncle,' he said, cheerfully. 'He's a bad lot. I know that. Anyway, he's not really my uncle, you know. When my father and mother died, they left a little money for me – and it turned out that they had asked Tiger Dan to look after me. So he took the money, called himself my uncle, and I've had to be with him ever since.'

'Was he in the same circus, then?' asked Julian.

'Oh yes. He and my father were both clowns,' said Nobby. 'Always have been clowns, in my family. But wait till I'm old enough, and I'll do a bunk – clear off and join another circus, where they'll let me look after the horses. I'm mad on horses. But the fellow at our circus won't often let me go near them. Jealous because I can handle them, I suppose!'

The children gazed at Nobby in wonder. He seemed an extraordinary boy to them – one who walked about with a tame chimpanzee, exercised hordes of performing dogs, lived with the chief clown in the circus, could turn the most marvellous cart-wheels, and whose only ambition was to work with horses! What a boy! Dick half-envied him.

'Haven't you ever been to school?' he asked Nobby.

The boy shook his head. 'Never! I can't write. And I can only read a bit. Most circus folk are like that, so nobody minds. Jumping Jiminy, I bet *you're* all clever, though! I bet even little Anne can read a book!'

'I've been able to read for *years*,' said Anne. 'And I'm up to fractions now in numbers.'

'Coo! What fractions?' said Nobby, impressed.

'Well – quarters and halves and seven-eighths, and things like that,' said Anne. 'But I'd rather be able to turn a cart-wheel like you can, Nobby, than know how to do fractions.'

'Whatever *is* Timmy barking for?' said George as they came near the clump of birch trees. Then she stopped suddenly, for she had seen two figures lying down in the grass below the trees. Lou – and Tiger Dan!

It was too late for Nobby to hide. The men saw him at once. They got up and waited for the children to come near. George felt thankful that Timmy was within whistling distance. He would come at the first call or whistle, she knew.

Julian looked at the men. To his surprise they appeared to be quite amiable. A faint scowl came over Tiger Dan's face when he caught sight of Nobby, but it passed at once.

'Good evening,' said Julian curtly, and would have passed on without another word, but Lou stepped up to him.

'We see you're camping up by here,' said Lou, and smiled showing yellow teeth. 'Aren't you going over the hill?'

'I don't need to discuss my affairs with either you or your friend,' said Julian, sounding extremely grown-up.

'You told us to clear out from down below, and we have. What we do now is nothing to do with you.'

'Ho yes, it is,' said Tiger Dan, sounding as if he was being polite with great difficulty. 'We come up here tonight to plan a place for some of our animals, see? And we don't want you to be in any danger.'

'We shan't be,' said Julian, scornfully. 'And there is plenty of room on these hills for you and your animals and for us, too. You won't scare us off, so don't think it. We shall stay here as long as we want to – and if we want help there's the farmer and his men quite near by – to say nothing of our dog.'

'Did you leave that there dog on guard?' asked Lou, as

he heard Timmy barking again. 'He ought to be destroyed, that dog of yours. He's dangerous.'

'He's only dangerous to rogues and scamps,' said George, joining in at once. 'You keep away from our caravans when Timmy's on guard. He'll maul you if you go near.'

Lou began to lose his temper. 'Well, are you going or aren't you?' he said. 'We've told you we want this here bit of the hill. You can come down and camp by the lake again if you want to.'

'Yes – you come,' said Tiger Dan to the children's growing astonishment. 'You come, see? You can bathe in the lake every day, then – and Nobby here can show you round the camp, and you can make friends with all the animals, see?'

Now it was Nobby's turn to look amazed.

'Jumping Jiminy! Didn't you beat me for making friends with these kids?' he demanded. 'What's the game, now? You've never had animals up in the hills before. You've . . .'

'Shut up,' said Tiger Dan in such a fierce voice that all the children were shocked. Lou nudged Dan, and he made an effort to appear pleasant again.

'We didn't want Nobby to make friends with posh folk like you,' he began again. 'But it seems as if you want to pal up with him – so it's OK with us. You come on down and camp by the lake, and Nobby'll show you everything in the circus. Can't say fairer than that.'

'You've got other reasons for making all these

suggestions,' said Julian, scornfully. 'I'm sorry – but our plans are made, and I am not going to discuss them with you.'

'Come on,' said Dick. 'Let's go and find Timmy. He's barking his head off because he can hear us, and it won't be long before he comes flying along here. Then we shall find it difficult to keep him off these two fellows.'

The four children began to move off. Nobby looked doubtfully at his uncle. He didn't know whether to go with them or not. Lou nudged Dan again.

'You go, too, if you want to,' said Tiger Dan, trying to grin amiably at the surprised Nobby. 'Keep your fine friends, see! Much good may they do you!' The grin vanished into a scowl, and Nobby skipped smartly out of reach of his uncle's hand. He was puzzled and wondered what was behind his uncle's change of mind.

He tore after the children. Timmy came to meet them, barking his head off, waving his plumy tail wildly in joy.

'Good dog, good dog!' said George, patting him. You keep on guard beautifully. You know I would have whistled for you if I'd wanted you, didn't you, Timmy? Good dog!'

'I'll get you some supper,' said Anne to everyone. 'We're all famished. We can talk while we eat. George, come and help. Julian, can you get some ginger-beer? And, Dick, do fill up the water-bowl for me.'

The boys winked at one another. They always thought that Anne was very funny when she took command like this, and gave her orders. But everyone went obediently to work.

Nobby went to help Anne. Together they boiled ten eggs hard in the little saucepan. Then Anne made tomato sandwiches with potted meat and got out the cake the farmer's wife had given them. She remembered the raspberry syrup, too – how lovely!

Soon they were all sitting on the rocky ledge, which was still warm, watching the sun go down into the lake. It was a most beautiful evening, with the lake as blue as a cornflower and the sky flecked with rosy clouds. They held their hard-boiled eggs in one hand and a piece of bread and butter in the other, munching happily. There was a dish of salt for everyone to dip their eggs into.

'I don't know why, but the meals we have on picnics always taste so much nicer than the ones we have indoors,' said George. 'For instance, even if we had hard-boiled eggs and bread and butter indoors, they wouldn't taste as nice as these.'

'Can everyone eat two eggs?' asked Anne. 'I did two each. And there's plenty of cake – and more sandwiches and some plums we picked this morning.'

'Best meal I've ever had in my life,' said Nobby, and picked up his second egg. 'Best company I've ever been in, too!'

'Thank you,' said Anne, and everyone looked pleased. Nobby might not have their good manners, but he always seemed to say just the right thing.

'It's a good thing your uncle didn't make you go back with him and Lou,' said Dick. 'Funny business – changing his mind like that!'

They began to talk about it. Julian was very puzzled indeed, and had even begun to wonder if he hadn't better find another camping site and go over the hill.

The others raised their voices scornfully.

'JULIAN! We're not cowards. We'll jolly well stay here!'

'What, leave now – why should we? We're in nobody's way, whatever those men say!'

'*I'm* not moving *my* caravan, whatever *anyone* says!' That was George, of course.

'No, don't you go,' said Nobby. 'Don't you take any notice of Lou and my uncle. They can't do anything to you at all. They're just trying to make trouble for you. Stay and let me show you over the camp, see?'

'It isn't that I *want* to give in to those fellows' ideas,' said Julian. 'It's just that – well, I'm in charge of us all – and I *don't* like the look of Lou and Tiger Dan – and, well . . .'

'Oh, have another egg and forget about it,' said Dick. 'We're going to stay here in this hollow, however much Dan and Lou want us out of it. And, what's more, I'd like to find out why they're so keen to push us off. It seems jolly strange to me.'

The sun went down in a blaze of orange and red, and the lake shimmered with its fiery reflection. Nobby got up regretfully, and Barker and Growler, who had been hobnobbing with Timmy, got up, too.

'I'll have to go,' said Nobby. 'Still got some jobs to do down there. What about you coming down tomorrow to see the animals? You'll like Old Lady, the elephant. She's a pet. And Pongo will be pleased to see you again.

'Your uncle may have changed his mind again by tomorrow, and not want us near the camp,' said Dick.

'Well – I'll signal to you,' said Nobby. 'I'll go out in the boat, see? And wave a hanky. Then you'll know it's all right. Well – so long! I'll be seeing you.'

CHAPTER ELEVEN

Fun at the circus camp

NEXT MORNING, while Anne cleared up the breakfast things with George, and Dick went off to the farm to buy whatever the farmer's wife had ready for him, Julian took the field-glasses and sat on the ledge to watch for Nobby to go out on the lake in his boat.

Dick sauntered along, whistling. The farmer's wife was delighted to see him, and showed him two big baskets full of delicious food.

'Slices of ham I've cured myself,' she said, lifting up the white cloth that covered one of the baskets. 'And a pot of brawn I've made. Keep it in a cool place. And some fresh lettuces and radishes I pulled myself this morning early. And some more tomatoes.'

'How gorgeous!' said Dick, eyeing the food in delight. 'Just the kind of things we love! Thanks awfully, Mrs Mackie. What's in the other basket?'

'Eggs, butter, milk, and a tin of shortbread I've baked,' said Mrs Mackie. 'You should do all right till tomorrow, the four of you! And in that paper there is a bone for the dog.'

'How much do I owe you?' asked Dick. He paid his bill and took up the baskets. Mrs Mackie slipped a bag into his pocket.

'Just a few home-made sweets,' she said. That was her little present. Dick grinned at her.

'Well, I won't offer to pay you for them because I'm afraid of that rolling-pin of yours,' he said. 'But thank you very, very much.'

He went off delighted. He thought of Anne's pleasure when she came to unpack the baskets. How she would love to put the things in the little larder – and pop the butter in a dish set in a bowl of cold water – and set the eggs in the little rack!

When he got back Julian called to him: 'Nobby's out in his boat. Come and look. He's waving something that can't possibly be a hanky. It must be the sheet off his bed!'

'Nobby doesn't sleep in sheets,' said Anne. 'He didn't know what they were when he saw them in our bunks. Perhaps it's a table-cloth.'

'Anyway, it's something big, to tell us that it's absolutely all right to come down to the camp,' said Julian. 'Are we ready?'

'Not quite,' said Anne, unpacking the baskets Dick had brought. 'I must put away these things – and do you want to take a picnic lunch with you? Because if so I must prepare it. Oh – look at all these gorgeous things!'

They all came back to look. 'Mrs Mackie is a darling,' said Anne. 'Honestly, these things are super – look at this gorgeous ham. It smells heavenly.'

'Here's her little present – home-made sweets,' said

Dick, remembering them and taking them out of his pocket. 'Have one!'

Anne had everything ready in half an hour. They had decided to take a picnic lunch with them for themselves and for Nobby as well. They took their bathing-things and towels, too.

'Are we going to take Timmy or not?' said George. 'I want to. But as these two men seem rather interested in our caravans, perhaps we had better leave him on guard again. We don't want to come back and find the caravans damaged or half the things stolen.'

'I should think not!' said Dick. 'They're not our things, nor our caravans. They belong to somebody else and we've got to take extra good care of them. I think we ought to leave Timmy on guard, don't you, Ju?'

'Yes, I do,' said Julian at once. 'These caravans are too valuable to leave at the mercy of any passing tramp – though I suppose we could lock them up. Anyway – we'll leave Timmy on guard today – poor old Timmy, it's a shame, isn't it?'

Timmy didn't answer. He looked gloomy and miserable. What! They were all going off without him again? He knew what 'on guard' meant – he was to stay here with these houses on wheels till the children chose to come back. He badly wanted to see Pongo again. He stood with his ears and tail drooping, the picture of misery.

But there was no help for it. The children felt that they couldn't leave the caravans unguarded while they were still so uncertain about Lou and Tiger Dan. So they all patted poor Timmy and fondled him, and then said goodbye. He sat down on the rocky ledge with his back to them and wouldn't even watch them go.

'He's sulking,' said George. 'Poor Timothy!'

It didn't take them very long to get down to the camp, and they found Nobby, Pongo, Barker and Growler waiting for them. Nobby was grinning from ear to ear.

'You saw my signal all right?' he said. 'Uncle hasn't changed his mind – in fact, he seems quite to have taken to you, and says I'm to show you all round and let you see anything you want to. That was his shirt I waved. I thought if I waved something enormous you'd know things were absolutely safe.'

'Where shall we put the bathing-things and the picnic baskets while we see round the camp?' asked Anne. 'Somewhere cool, if possible.'

'Put them in my caravan,' said Nobby, and led them to a caravan painted blue and yellow, with red wheels. The children remembered having seen it when the procession passed by their house a week or two before.

They peeped inside. It wasn't nearly so nice as theirs. It was much smaller, for one thing, and very untidy. It looked dirty, too, and had a nasty smell. Anne didn't like it very much.

'Not so good as yours!' said Nobby. 'I wish I had a caravan like yours. I'd feel like a prince. Now what do you want to see first? The elephant? Come on, then.'

They went to the tree to which Old Lady the elephant was tied. She curled her trunk round Nobby and looked at the children out of small, intelligent eyes.

'Well, Old Lady!' said Nobby. 'Want a bathe?'

The elephant trumpeted and made the children jump. 'I'll take you later on,' promised Nobby. 'Now then – hup, hup, hup!'

At these words the elephant curled her trunk tightly round Nobby's waist and lifting him bodily into the air, placed him gently on her big head!

Anne gasped.

'Oh! Did she hurt you, Nobby?'

'Course not!' said Nobby. 'Old Lady wouldn't hurt anyone, would you, big one?'

A small man came up. He had bright eyes that shone as if they had been polished, and a very wide grin. 'Good morning,' he said. 'How do you like my Old Lady? Like to see her play cricket?'

'Oh, *yes*!' said everyone, and the small man produced a cricket bat and held it out to Old Lady. She took it in her trunk and waved it about. Nobby slipped deftly off her head to the ground.

'I'll play with her, Larry,' he said, and took the ball from the small man. He threw it to Old Lady and she hit it smartly with the bat. It sailed over their heads!

Julian fetched the ball. He threw it at the elephant, and again the great creature hit the ball with a bang. Soon all the children were playing with Old Lady and enjoying the game very much.

Some small camp children came up to watch. But they were as scared as rabbits as soon as Julian or George spoke to them and scuttled off to their caravans at once.

Nobby went to fetch Pongo, who was dancing to and fro in his cage, making anguished sounds, thinking he was forgotten. He was simply delighted to see the children again, and put his arm right round Anne at once. Then he pulled George's hair and hid his face behind his paws, peeping out mischievously.

'He's a caution, aren't you, Pongo?' said Nobby. 'Now you keep with me, Pongo, or I'll put you back into your cage, see?'

They went to see the dogs and let them all out. They were mostly terrier dogs, or mongrels, smart, well-kept little things who jumped up eagerly at Nobby, and made a great fuss of him. It was clear that they loved him and trusted him.

'Like to see them play football?' asked Nobby. 'Here, Barker – fetch the ball. Go on, quick!'

Barker darted off to Nobby's caravan. The door was shut, but the clever little dog stood on his hind legs and jerked the handle with his nose. The door opened and in went Barker. He came out dribbling a football with his nose. Down the steps it went and into the camp field. All the dogs leapt on it with howls of delight.

'Yap-yap-yap! Yap-yap!' They dribbled the football to

and fro, while Nobby stood with his legs open to make a goal for them.

It was Barker's job and Growler's to score the goals, and the task of the other dogs to stop them. So it was a most amusing game to watch. Once, when Barker scored a goal by hurling himself on the ball and sending it rolling fast between Nobby's arched legs, Pongo leapt into the fray, picked up the ball and ran off with it.

'Foul, foul!' yelled Nobby and all the dogs rushed after the mischievous chimpanzee. He leapt on to the top of a caravan and began to bounce the ball there, grinning down at the furious dogs.

'Oh, this is such fun!' said Anne, wiping the tears of laughter from her eyes. 'Oh, dear! I've got such a pain in my side from laughing.'

Nobby had to climb up to the roof of the caravan to get the ball. Pongo jumped down the other side, but left the ball balanced neatly on the chimney. He was really a most mischievous chimpanzee.

Then they went to see the beautiful horses. All of them had shining satiny coats. They were being trotted round a big field by a slim, tall young fellow called Rossy, and they obeyed his slightest word.

'Can I ride Black Queen, Rossy?' asked Nobby eagerly. 'Do let me!'

'OK,' said Rossy, his black hair shining like the horses' coats. Then Nobby amazed the watching children, for he leapt on to a great black horse, stood up on her back and trotted all round the field like that!

'He'll fall!' cried Anne. But he didn't, of course. Then he suddenly swung himself down on to his hands and rode Black Queen standing upside down.

'Good, good!' cried Rossy. 'You are good with horses, young one! Now ride Fury!'

Fury was a small, fiery-looking little horse, whose gleaming eyes showed a temper. Nobby ran to her and leapt on her, bare-backed. She rose up, snorting and tried to throw him off. But he wouldn't be thrown off. No matter what she did, Nobby clung on like a limpet to a rock.

At last Fury tired of it, and began to canter round the field. Then she galloped – and suddenly she stopped absolutely dead, meaning to fling Nobby over her head!

But the boy was waiting for that trick and threw himself backwards at once. 'Good, good!' cried Rossy. 'She will soon eat out of your hand, Nobby! Good boy.'

'Nobby, Nobby, you're terribly clever!' yelled Anne. 'Oh, I wish I could do the things you do! I wish I could.'

Nobby slid off Fury's back, looking pleased. It was nice to show off a little to his 'posh' friends. Then he looked round and about. 'I say – where's that chimp? Up to some mischief, I'll be bound! Let's go and find him.'

CHAPTER TWELVE

A lovely day – with a horrid end

THEY SOON saw Pongo. He was coming round one of the caravans, looking exceedingly pleased with himself. He went to Anne and held out his paw to her, making little affectionate noises.

Anne took what he held. She looked at it. 'It's a hard-boiled egg! Oh, Nobby, he's been at the picnic baskets!'

So he had! Two of the eggs were gone, and some of the tomatoes! Nobby took him back to his cage. Pongo was very sad and made a noise as if he was crying, hiding his face in his paws. Anne was upset.

'Is he really crying? Oh, do forgive him, Nobby. He didn't mean to be naughty.'

'He's not crying. He's only pretending,' said Nobby. 'And he *did* mean to be naughty. I know him!'

The morning soon went in visiting the circus animals. It was dinner-time before they had had time to see the monkeys. 'We'll see them afterwards,' said Nobby. 'Let's have a meal now. Come on. We'll go and have it by the lake.'

The children hadn't seen Lou or Tiger Dan at all, much to their joy. 'Where are they?' asked Julian. 'Gone out for the day?'

'Yes, thank goodness,' said Nobby. 'Gone out on one of their mysterious jaunts. You know, when we're on the road, going from place to place, my uncle sometimes disappears at night. I wake up – and he's not there.'

'Where does he go?' asked George.

'I wouldn't dare to ask,' said Nobby. 'Anyway, he and Lou are out of the way today. I don't expect they'll be back till night.'

They had their meal by the lake. It glittered at their feet, calm and blue, and looked very inviting.

'What about a swim?' asked Dick when they had eaten as much as they could. Julian looked at his watch.

'Can't swim directly after a good meal,' he said. 'You know that, Dick. We'll have to wait a bit.'

'Right,' said Dick and lay down. 'I'll have a snooze – or shall we go and see the monkeys?'

They all had a short nap and then got up to go and see the monkeys. When they got back to the camp they found it alive with people, all excited and yelling.

'What's up? said Nobby. 'Jumping Jiminy, the monkeys are all loose!'

So they were. Wherever they looked the children saw a small brown monkey, chattering to itself, on the roof of a caravan or tent!

A woman with sharp eyes came up to Nobby. She caught him by the shoulder and shook him. 'See what that chimp of yours has done!' she said. 'You put him in his cage and couldn't have locked it properly. He got out and let all the monkeys loose. Drat that chimp – I'll take a broomstick to him if ever I catch him!'

'Where's Lucilla then?' asked Nobby, dragging himself away from the cross woman. 'Can't she get them in?'

'Lucilla's gone to the town,' scolded the woman. 'And fine and pleased she'll be to hear this when she comes back!'

'Aw, let the monkeys be!' said Nobby. 'They won't come to any harm. They'll wait for Lucilla all right!'

'Who's Lucilla?' asked Anne, thinking that life in a circus camp was very exciting.

'She owns the monkeys,' said Nobby. 'Oh, look – there's Lucilla coming back! Now we'll be all right!'

A little wizened old woman was hurrying towards the camp. She really looked rather like a monkey herself, Anne thought. Her eyes were bright and sharp, and her tiny hands clutched a red shawl round her. They looked like brown paws.

'Your monkeys are out!' yelled the camp children. 'LUCILLA! Your monkeys are out.'

Lucilla heard and, raising her voice, she scolded everyone in sight fully and shrilly. Then she stood still and held out her arms. She spoke some soft words in a language the children didn't know – magic words, Anne said afterwards.

One by one the wandering monkeys came scampering over to her, flinging themselves down from the caravan roofs, making little chattering sounds of love and welcome.

They leapt on to Lucilla's shoulders and into her arms, cuddling against her like tiny children. Not one monkey was left out – all went to Lucilla as if drawn by some enchantment.

She walked slowly towards their cage, murmuring her soft words as she went. Everyone watched in silence.

'She's an odd one,' said the woman to Nobby. 'She doesn't love anybody but her monkeys – and nobody loves her but them. You mind she doesn't go for that chimp of yours, letting out her precious monkeys!'

'I'll take him and Old Lady down to bathe,' said Nobby, hastily. 'By the time we're back, Lucilla will have forgotten.'

They fetched Old Lady and discovered where naughty Pongo was hiding under a caravan. As quickly as possible they went back to the lake, Old Lady stepping out well, looking forward to her bathe.

'I suppose things like that are always happening in a circus camp,' said Anne. 'It's not a bit like real life.'

'Isn't it?' said Nobby, surprised. 'It's real life all right to *me*!'

It was cool in the lake and they all enjoyed themselves very much, swimming and splashing. Pongo wouldn't go in very far, but splashed everyone who came within reach, laughing and cackling loudly. He gave Old Lady a shock by leaping up on to her back, and pulling one of her big ears.

She dipped her trunk into the lake, sucked up a lot of water, turned her trunk over her back, and squirted the water all over the startled chimpanzee! The children yelled with laughter, and roared again to see Pongo falling in fright off Old Lady's back. Splash! He went right in and got himself wet from head to foot – a thing he hated doing.

'Serves you right, you scamp!' shouted Nobby. 'Hey, Old Lady, stop it! Don't squirt at me!'

The elephant, pleased with her little joke, didn't want to stop it. So the children had to keep well away from her, for her aim was very good.

'I've never had such a lovely time in my life!' said Anne, as she dried herself. 'I shall dream all night of monkeys and elephants, horses, dogs and chimpanzees!'

Nobby turned about twenty cart-wheels by the edge of the lake from sheer good spirits – and Pongo at once did the same. He was even better at it than Nobby. Anne tried and fell down flop immediately.

They went back to the camp. 'Sorry I can't offer you any tea,' said Nobby, 'but we never seem to have tea, you know – we circus folk, I mean. Anyway, I'm not hungry after that enormous lunch. Are you?'

Nobody was. They shared out Mrs Mackie's home-made toffees, and gave one to Pongo. It stuck his teeth together and he looked so comically alarmed when he found that he couldn't open his mouth that the children roared at him.

He sat down, swayed from side to side, and began to groan dismally. But the toffee soon melted away, and he found that he could open his mouth after all. He

sucked the rest of the sweet noisily, but wouldn't have another.

They wandered round the camp, looking at the different caravans. Nobody took much notice of them now. They were just Nobby's 'posh' friends – that was all. Some of the smaller children peeped out and stuck out their little red tongues – but at Nobby's roar they vanished.

'Got no manners at all!' said Nobby. 'But they're all right really.'

They came to where big wagons stood, stored with all kinds of circus things. 'We don't bother to unpack these when we're resting in camp like this,' said Nobby. 'Don't need them here. One of my jobs is to help to unpack this stuff when we're camping to give a show. Have to get out all those benches and set them up in the big top – that's the circus tent, you know. We're pretty busy then, I can tell you!'

'What's in *this* cart?' asked Anne, coming to a small wagon with a tightly-fitting hood of tarpaulin.

'Don't know,' said Nobby. 'That cart belongs to my uncle. He won't ever let me unpack it. I don't know what he keeps there. I've wondered if it was things belonging to my dad and mum. I told you they were dead. Anyway, I thought I'd peep and see one day, but Uncle Dan caught me and half-killed me!'

'But if they belonged to your parents, they ought to be yours!' said George.

'Funny thing is, sometimes that cart's crammed full,' said Nobby. 'And sometimes it isn't. Maybe Lou puts some of his things there too.'

'Well, nobody could get anything else in there at the moment!' said Julian. 'It's full to bursting!'

They lost interest in the little wagon and wandered round to see the 'props' as Nobby called them. Anne pictured these as clothes-props, but they turned out to be gilt chairs and tables, the shining poles used for the tight-rope, brightly-painted stools for the performing dogs to sit on, and circus 'props' of that kind.

'*Prop*erties, Anne,' said Julian. 'Circus *prop*erties. Props for short. Look here, isn't it about time we went back? My watch has stopped. Whatever time is it?'

'Golly, it's quite late!' said Dick, looking at his watch. 'Seven o'clock. No wonder I feel jolly hungry. Time we went back. Coming with us, Nobby? You can have supper up there if you like. I bet you could find your way back in the dark.'

'I'll take Pongo with me, and Barker and Growler,' said Nobby, delighted at the invitation. 'If *I* lose the way back, *they* won't!'

So they all set off up the hill, tired with their long and exciting day. Anne began to plan what she would give the little company for supper. Ham, certainly – and tomatoes – and some of that raspberry syrup diluted with icy-cold spring-water.

They all heard Timmy barking excitedly as soon as they

came near the caravans. He barked without ceasing, loudly and determinedly.

'He sounds cross,' said Dick. 'Poor old Tim! He must think we've quite deserted him.'

They came to the caravans and Timmy flung himself on George as if he hadn't seen her for a year. He pawed her and licked her, then pawed her again.

Barker and Growler were pleased to see him too, and as for Pongo, he was delighted. He shook hands with Timmy's tail several times, and was disappointed that Timmy took no notice of him.

'Hallo! What's Barker gnawing at?' suddenly said Dick. 'Raw meat! How did it come here? Do you suppose the farmer has been by and given Timmy some? Well, why didn't he eat it, then?'

They all looked at Barker, who was gnawing some meat on the ground. Growler ran to it too. But Timmy would not go near it. Nor would Pongo. Timmy put his tail down and Pongo hid his furry face behind his paws.

'Funny,' said the children, puzzled at the strange behaviour of the two animals. Then suddenly they understood – for poor Barker suddenly gave a terrible whine, shivered from head to foot, and rolled over on his side.

'Jiminy – it's poisoned!' yelled Nobby, and kicked Growler away from the meat. He picked Barker up, and to the children's utter dismay they saw that Nobby was crying.

'He's done for,' said the boy, in a choking voice. 'Poor old Barker.'

Carrying Barker in his arms, with Growler and Pongo behind him, poor Nobby stumbled down the hill. No one liked to follow him. Poisoned meat! What a terrible thing.

CHAPTER THIRTEEN

Julian thinks of a plan

GEORGE WAS trembling. Her legs felt as if they wouldn't hold her up, and she sank down on the ledge. She put her arms round Timmy.

'Oh, Timmy! That meat was meant for you! Oh, thank goodness, thank goodness you were clever enough not to touch it! Timmy, you might have been poisoned!'

Timmy licked his mistress soberly. The others stood round, staring, not knowing what to think. Poor Barker! Would he die? Suppose it had been old Timmy? They had left him all alone, and he might have eaten the meat and died.

'I'll never, never leave you up here alone again!' said George.

'Who threw him the poisoned meat, do you think?' said Anne, in a small voice.

'Who do you suppose?' said George, in a hard, scornful voice. 'Lou and Tiger Dan!'

'They want to get us away from here, that's plain,' said Dick. 'But again – why?'

'What can there be about this place that makes the men want to get rid of us all?' wondered Julian. 'They're real rogues. Poor Nobby. He must have an awful life with them. And now they've gone and poisoned his dog.'

Nobody felt like eating very much that evening. Anne got out the bread and the butter and a pot of jam. George wouldn't eat anything. What a horrid end to a lovely day!

They all went to bed early, and nobody objected when Julian said he was going to lock both the caravans. 'Not that I think either Lou or Dan will be up here tonight,' he said. 'But you never know!'

Whether they came or not the children didn't know, for although Timmy began to bark loudly in the middle of the night, and scraped frantically at the shut door of George's caravan, there was nothing to be seen or heard when Julian opened his door and flashed on his torch.

Timmy didn't bark any more. He lay quite quietly sleeping with one ear cocked. Julian lay in bed and thought hard. Probably Lou and Dan had come creeping up in the dark, hoping that Timmy had taken the meat and been poisoned. But when they heard him bark, they knew he was all right, and they must have gone away again. What plan would they make next?

'There's something behind all this,' Julian thought, again and again. 'But what can it be? Why do they want us out of this particular spot?'

He couldn't imagine. He fell asleep at last with a vague plan in his mind. He would tell it to the others tomorrow. Perhaps if he could make Lou and Dan think they had all gone off for the day – with Timmy – but really, he, Julian, would be left behind, in hiding – maybe he could find out something, if Lou and Dan came along . . .

Julian fell asleep in the middle of thinking out his plan. Like the others, he dreamt of elephants squirting him with water, of Pongo chasing the monkeys, of the dogs playing football with excited yaps – and then into the dream came lumps of poisoned meat! Horrid.

Anne woke with a jump, having dreamt that someone had put poison into the hard-boiled eggs they were going to eat. She lay trembling in her bunk, and called to George in a small voice.

'George! I've been having an awful dream!'

George woke up, and Timmy stirred and stretched himself. George switched on her torch.

'I've been having beastly dreams, too,' she said. 'I dreamt that those men were after Timmy. I'll leave my torch on for a bit and we'll talk. I expect that with all the excitement we've had today, and the horrid end to it this evening, we're just in the mood for horrid dreams! Still – they are only dreams.'

'Woof,' said Timmy, and scratched himself.

'Don't,' said George. 'You shake the whole caravan when you do that, Timmy. Stop it.'

Timmy stopped. He sighed and lay down heavily. He put his head on his paws and looked sleepily at George, as if to say, 'Put that torch out. I want to go to sleep.'

The next morning was not so warm, and the sky was cloudy. Nobody felt very cheerful, because they kept thinking of Nobby and poor Barker. They ate their breakfast almost in silence, and then Anne and George began to stack the plates, ready to take them to the spring to rinse.

'*I'll* go to the farm this morning,' said Julian. 'You sit on the ledge and take the field-glasses, Dick. We'll see if Nobby goes out in his boat and waves. I've an idea that he won't want us down in the camp this morning. If he suspects his Uncle Dan and Lou of putting down the meat that poisoned Barker, he'll probably have had a frightful row with them.'

He went off to the farm with two empty baskets. Mrs Mackie was ready for him, and he bought a further supply of delicious-looking food. Her present this time was a round ginger cake, warm from the oven!

'Do the circus folk come up here often to buy food?' asked Julian, as he paid Mrs Mackie.

'They come sometimes,' said Mrs Mackie. 'I don't mind the women or the children – but it's the men I can't abide. There were two here last year, messing about in the hills, that my husband had to send off quickly.'

Julian pricked up his ears. 'Two men? What were they like?'

'Ugly fellows,' said Mrs Mackie. 'And one had the yellowest teeth I ever saw. Bad-tempered chaps, both of them. They came up here at night, and we were afraid our chickens would go. They swore they weren't after our chickens – but what else would they be up here at night for?'

'I can't imagine,' said Julian. He was sure that the two men Mrs Mackie spoke of were Lou and Tiger Dan. Why did they wander about in the hills at night?

He went off with the food. When he got near the camping place, Dick called to him excitedly.

'Hey, Julian! Come and look through the glasses. Nobby's out in his boat with Pongo, and I simply can't make out what it is they're both waving.'

Julian took the glasses and looked through them. Far down the hill, on the surface of the lake, floated Nobby's little boat. In it was Nobby, and with him was Pongo. Both of them were waving something bright red.

'Can't see what they're waving – but that doesn't matter,' said Julian. 'The thing is – what they're waving is red, not white. Red for danger. He's warning us.'

'Golly – I didn't think of that. What an idiot I am!' said Dick. 'Yes – red for danger. What's up, I wonder?'

'Well, it's clear we'd better not go down to the camp today,' said Julian. 'And it's also clear that whatever danger there is, is pretty bad – because both he *and* Pongo are waving red cloths – doubly dangerous!'

'Julian, you're jolly sharp,' said George, who was listening. 'You're the only one of us who worked that one out. Double-danger. What can it be?'

'Perhaps it means danger down the camp, and danger here too,' said Julian, thoughtfully. 'I hope poor old Nobby is all right. Tiger Dan is so jolly beastly to him. I bet he's had a beating or two since last night.'

'It's such a shame!' said Dick.

'Don't tell Anne we think there is double-danger about,' said Julian, seeing Anne coming back from the spring. 'She'll be scared. She was hoping we wouldn't have an adventure these hols – and now we seem to be plunged into the middle of one. Golly! I really think we ought to leave these hills and go on somewhere else.'

But he only said this half-heartedly, because he was burning to solve the curious mystery behind Lou's behaviour and Dan's. The others pounced on him at once.

'We can't leave! Don't be a coward, Ju!'

'I *won't* leave. Nor will Timmy.'

'Shut up,' said Julian. 'Here comes Anne.'

They said no more. Julian watched Nobby for a little while longer. Then the boy and the chimpanzee drew in to the shore and disappeared.

When they were all sitting together on the ledge, Julian proposed the plan he had been thinking out the night before.

'I'd like to find out what there is about this place that attracts Lou and Dan,' he said. 'There is *something* not far from here that makes the men want to get rid of us. Now suppose we four and Timmy go off down the hill and pass the camp, and yell out to Nobby that we're *all* – *all* of us – going to the town for the day – and you three do go, but I slip back up the hill – maybe Lou and Dan will come up here, and if I'm hiding I shall see what they're up to!'

'You mean, we'll all four pretend to go to town but really only three of us go, and you get back and hide,' said Dick. 'I see. It's a good idea.'

'And you'll hide somewhere and watch for the men to come,' said George. 'Well, for goodness' sake don't let them see you, Julian. You won't have Timmy, you know! Those men could make mincemeat of you if they wanted to.'

'Oh, they'd want to all right. I know that,' said Julian grimly. 'But you can be sure I'll be jolly well hidden.'

'I don't see why we can't have a good look round and see if we can't find the cave or whatever it is the men want to come to,' said Dick. 'If they can find it, we can, too!'

'We don't know that it *is* a cave,' said Julian. 'We haven't any idea at all what attracts the men up here. Mrs Mackie said they were up here last year, too, and the farmer had to drive them away. They thought the men were after the chickens – but I don't think so. There's *something* in these hills that makes the men want to get us away.'

'Let's have a good look round,' said George, feeling suddenly thrilled. 'I've gone all adventurous again!'

'Oh dear!' said Anne. But she couldn't help feeling rather thrilled, too. They all got up and Timmy followed, wagging his tail. He was pleased that his friends hadn't gone off and left him on guard by himself that morning.

'We'll all go different ways,' said Julian. 'Up, down and sideways. I'll go up.'

They separated and went off, George and Timmy together, of course. They hunted in the hillside for possible caves, or even for some kind of hiding-place. Timmy put his head down every rabbit hole and felt very busy indeed.

After about half an hour the others heard Julian yelling. They ran back to the caravans, sure that he had found something exciting.

But he hadn't. He had simply got tired of hunting and decided to give it up. He shook his head when they rushed up to him, shouting to know what he had found.

'Nothing,' he said. 'I'm fed up with looking. There's not a cave anywhere here. I'm sure of that! Anyone else found anything?'

'Not a thing,' said everyone in disappointment. 'What shall we do now?'

'Put our plan into action,' said Julian, promptly. 'Let the men themselves show us what they're after. Off we go down the hills, and we'll yell out to Nobby that we're off for the day – and we'll hope that Lou and Tiger Dan will hear us!'

CHAPTER FOURTEEN

A very good hiding-place

THEY WENT down the hill with Timmy. Julian gave Dick some instructions. 'Have a meal in the town,' he said. 'Keep away for the day, so as to give the men a chance to come up the hill. Go to the post office and see if there are any letters for us – and buy some tins of fruit. They'll make a nice change.'

'Right, Captain!' said Dick. 'And just you be careful, old boy. These men will stick at nothing – bad-tempered brutes they are.'

'Look after the girls,' said Julian. 'Don't let George do anything mad!'

Dick grinned. 'Who can stop George doing what she wants to? Not me!'

They were now at the bottom of the hills. The circus camp lay nearby. The children could hear the barking of the dogs and the shrill trumpeting of Old Lady.

They looked about for Nobby. He was nowhere to be seen. Blow! It wouldn't be any good setting off to the town and laying such a good plan if they couldn't tell Nobby they were going!

Nobody dared to go into the camp. Julian thought of the two red cloths that Nobby and Pongo had waved.

Double-danger! It would be wise not to go into the camp that morning. He stood still, undecided what to do.

Then he opened his mouth and yelled:

'Nobby! NOBBY!'

No answer and no Nobby. The elephant man heard him shouting and came up. 'Do you want Nobby? I'll fetch him.'

'Thanks,' said Julian.

The little man went off, whistling. Soon Nobby appeared from behind a caravan, looking rather scared. He didn't come near Julian, but stood a good way away, looking pale and troubled.

'Nobby! We're going into the town for the day,' yelled Julian at the top of his voice. 'We're . . .'

Tiger Dan suddenly appeared behind Nobby and grabbed his arm fiercely. Nobby put up a hand to protect his face, as if he expected a blow. Julian yelled again:

'We're going into the town, Nobby! We shan't be back till evening. Can you hear me? WE'RE GOING TO THE TOWN!'

The whole camp must have heard Julian. But he was quite determined that, whoever else didn't hear, Tiger Dan certainly should.

Nobby tried to shake off his uncle's hand, and opened his mouth to yell back something. But Dan roughly put his hand across Nobby's mouth and hauled him away, shaking him as a dog shakes a rat.

'HOW'S BARKER?' yelled Julian. But Nobby had

disappeared, dragged into his uncle's caravan by Dan. The little elephant man heard, however.

'Barker's bad,' he said. 'Not dead yet. But nearly. Never saw a dog so sick in my life. Nobby's fair upset!'

The children walked off with Timmy. George had had to hold his collar all the time, for once he saw Dan he growled without stopping, and tried to get away from George.

'Thank goodness Barker isn't dead,' said Anne. 'I do hope he'll get better.'

'Not much chance,' said Julian. 'That meat must have been chock-full of poison. Poor old Nobby. How awful to be under the thumb of a fellow like Tiger Dan.'

'I just simply can't *imagine* him as a clown – Tiger Dan, I mean,' said Anne. 'Clowns are always so merry and lively and jolly.'

'Well, that's just acting,' said Dick. 'A clown needn't be the same out of the ring as he has to be when he's in it. If you look at photographs of clowns when they're just being ordinary men, they've got quite sad faces.'

'Well, Tiger Dan hasn't got a sad face. He's got a nasty, ugly, cruel, fierce one,' said Anne, looking quite fierce herself.

That made the others laugh. Dick turned round to see if anyone was watching them walking towards the bus stop, where the buses turned to go to the town.

'Lou the acrobat is watching us,' he said. 'Good! Can he see the bus stop from where he is, Ju?'

Julian turned round. 'Yes, he can. He'll watch to see us all get into the bus – so I'd better climb in, too, and I'll get out at the first stop, double back, and get into the hills by some path he won't be able to see.'

'Right,' said Dick, enjoying the thought of playing a trick on Lou. 'Come on. There's the bus. We'll have to run for it.'

They all got into the bus. Lou was still watching, a small figure very far away. Dick felt inclined to wave cheekily to him, but didn't.

The bus set off. They took three tickets for the town and one for the nearest stop. Timmy had a ticket, too, which he wore proudly in his collar. He loved going in a bus.

Julian got out at the first stop. 'Well, see you this evening!' he said. 'Send Timmy on ahead to the caravans when you come back – just in case the men are anywhere about. I may not be able to warn you.'

'Right,' said Dick. 'Goodbye – and good luck!'

Julian waved and set off back down the road he had come. He saw a little lane leading off up into the hills and decided to take it. It led him not very far from Mrs Mackie's farm, so he soon knew where he was. He went back to the caravans, and quickly made himself some sandwiches and cut some cake to take to his hiding-place. He might have a long wait!

'Now – where shall I hide?' thought the boy. 'I want somewhere that will give me a view of the track so that I can see when the men come up it. And yet it must be somewhere that gives me a good view of their doings, too. What would be the best place?'

A tree? No, there wasn't one that was near enough or thick enough. Behind a bush? No, the men might easily come round it and see him. What about the middle of a thick gorse bush? That might be a good idea.

But Julian gave that up very quickly, for he found the bush far too prickly to force his way into the middle. He scratched his arms and legs terribly.

'Blow!' he said. 'I really must make up my mind, or the men may be here before I'm in hiding!'

And then he suddenly had a real brainwave, and he crowed in delight. Of course! The very place!

'I'll climb up on to the roof of one of the caravans!' thought Julian. 'Nobody will see me there – and certainly nobody would guess I was there! That really is a fine idea. I shall have a fine view of the track and a first-rate view of the men and where they go!'

It wasn't very easy to climb up on to the high roof. He had to get a rope, loop it at the end, and try to lasso the chimney in order to climb up.

He managed to lasso the chimney, and the rope hung down over the side of the caravan, ready for him to swarm up. He threw his packet of food up on to the roof and then climbed up himself. He pulled up the rope and coiled it beside him.

Then he lay down flat. He was certain that nobody could see him from below. Of course, if the men went higher up the hill and looked down on the caravans, he could easily be spotted – but he would have to chance that.

He lay there quite still, watching the lake, and keeping eyes and ears open for anyone coming up the hillside. He was glad that it was not a very hot sunny day, or he would have been cooked up on the roof. He wished he had thought of filling a bottle with water in case he was thirsty.

He saw spires of smoke rising from where the circus camp lay, far below. He saw a couple of boats on the lake, a good way round the water – people fishing, he supposed. He watched a couple of rabbits come out and play on the hillside just below.

The sun came out from behind the clouds for about ten minutes and Julian began to feel uncomfortably hot. Then it went in again and he felt better.

He suddenly heard somebody whistling and stiffened himself in expectation – but it was only someone belonging to the farm, going down the hill some distance away. The whistle had carried clearly in the still air.

Then he got bored. The rabbits went in, and not even a butterfly sailed by. He could see no birds except a yellow-hammer that sat on the topmost spray of a bush and sang: 'Little-bit-of-bread-and-no-cheese', over and over again in a most maddening manner.

Then it gave a cry of alarm and flew off. It had heard something that frightened it.

Julian heard something, too, and glued his eyes to the

track that led up the hill. His heart began to beat. He could see two men. Were they Lou and Dan?

He did not dare to raise his head to see them when they came nearer in case they spotted him. But he knew their voices when they came near enough!

Yes – it was Lou and Tiger Dan all right. There was no mistaking those two harsh, coarse voices. The men came right into the hollow, and Julian heard them talking.

'Yes, there's nobody here. Those kids have really gone off for the day at least – and taken that wretched dog with them!'

'I saw them get on the bus, dog and all, I told you,' growled Lou. 'There'll be nobody here for the day. We can get what we want to.'

'Let's go and get it, then,' said Dan.

Julian waited to see where they would go to. But they didn't go out of the hollow. They stayed there, apparently beside the caravans. Julian did not dare to look over the edge of the roof to see what they were up to. He was glad he fastened all the windows and locked the doors.

Then there began some curious scuffling sounds, and the men panted. The caravan on which Julian was lying began to shake a little.

'What *are* they doing?' thought Julian in bewilderment. In intense curiosity he slid quietly to the edge of the caravan roof and cautiously peeped over, though he had firmly made up his mind not to do this on any account.

He looked down on the ground. There was nobody there at all. Perhaps the men were the other side. He slid carefully across and peeped over the opposite side of the caravan, which was still shaking a little, as if the men were bumping against it.

There was nobody the other side either! How very extraordinary! 'Golly! They must be underneath the caravan!' thought Julian, going back to the middle of the roof. 'Underneath! What in the wide world for?'

It was quite impossible to see underneath the caravan from where he was, so he had to lie quietly and wonder about the men's doings. They grunted and groaned, and seemed to be scraping and scrabbling about, but nothing happened. Then Julian heard them scrambling out from underneath, angry and disappointed.

'Give us a cigarette,' said Lou in a disagreeable voice. 'I'm fed up with this. Have to shift this van. Those tiresome brats! What did they want to choose this spot for?'

Julian heard a match struck and smelt cigarette smoke. Then he got a shock. The caravan he was on began to move! Heavens! Were the men going to push it over the ledge and send it rolling down the hillside?

CHAPTER FIFTEEN

Several things happen

JULIAN WAS suddenly very scared. He wondered if he had better slide off the roof and run. He wouldn't have much chance if the caravan went hurtling down the hill! But he didn't move. He clung to the chimney with both hands, whilst the men shoved hard against the caravan.

It ran a few feet to the rocky ledge, and then stopped. Julian felt his forehead getting very damp, and he saw that his hands were trembling, but he couldn't stop them.

'Hey! Don't send it down the hill!' said Lou in alarm, and Julian's heart felt lighter. So they didn't mean to destroy the caravan in that way! They had just moved it to get at something underneath. But what could it be? Julian racked his brains to try and think what the floor of the hollow had been like when Dobby and Trotter pulled their caravans into it. As far as he could remember it was just an ordinary heathery hollow.

The men were now scrabbling away again by the back steps of the caravan. Julian was absolutely eaten up with curiosity, but he did not dare even to move. He could find out the secret when the men had gone. Meantime he really must be patient or he would spoil everything.

There was some muttered talking, but Julian couldn't

catch a word. Then, quite suddenly, there was complete and utter silence. Not a word. Not a bump against the caravan. Not a pant or even a grunt. Nothing at all.

Julian lay still. Maybe the men were still there. He wasn't going to give himself away. He lay for quite a long time, waiting and wondering. But he heard nothing.

Then he saw a robin fly to a nearby bramble spray. It flicked its wings and looked about for crumbs. It was a robin that came around when the children were having a meal – but it was not as tame as most robins, and would not fly down until the children had left the hollow.

Then a rabbit popped out of a hole on the hillside and capered about, running suddenly up to the hollow.

'Well,' thought Julian, 'it's plain the men aren't here now, or the birds and animals wouldn't be about like this. There's another rabbit. Those men have gone somewhere – though goodness knows where. I can peep over now and have a look, quite safely, I should think.'

He slid himself round and peered over the roof at the back end of the caravan. He looked down at the ground. There was absolutely nothing to be seen to tell him what the men had been doing, or where they had gone! The heather grew luxuriantly there as it did everywhere else. There was nothing to show what the men had been making such a disturbance about.

'This is really very strange,' thought Julian, beginning to wonder if he had been dreaming. 'The men are certainly gone – vanished into thin air, apparently! Dare

I get down and explore a bit? No, I daren't. The men may appear at any moment, and it's quite on the cards they'll lose their temper if they find me here, and chuck both me and the caravans down the hill! It's pretty steep just here, too.'

He lay there, thinking. He suddenly felt very hungry and thirsty. Thank goodness he had been sensible enough to take food up to the roof! He could at least have a meal while he was waiting for the men to come back – if they ever did!

He began to eat his sandwiches. They tasted very good indeed. He finished them all and began on the cake. That was good, too. He had brought a few plums up as well, and was very glad of them because he was thirsty. He flicked the plum stones from the roof before he thought what he was doing.

'Dash! Why did I do that? If the men notice them they may remember they weren't there before. Still, they've most of them gone into the heather!'

The sun came out a little and Julian felt hot. He wished the men would come again and go down the hill. He was tired of lying flat on the hard roof. Also he was terribly sleepy. He yawned silently and shut his eyes.

How long he slept he had no idea – but he was suddenly awakened by feeling the caravan being moved again! He clutched the chimney in alarm, listening to the low voices of the two men.

They were pulling the caravan back into place again.

Soon it was in the same position as before. Then Julian heard a match struck and smelt smoke again.

The men went and sat on the rocky ledge and took out food they had brought. Julian did not dare to peep at them, though he felt sure they had their backs to him. The men ate, and talked in low voices, and then, to Julian's dismay, they lay down and went to sleep! He knew that they were asleep because he could hear them snoring.

'Am I going to stay on this awful roof all day long?' he thought. 'I'm getting so cramped, lying flat like this. I want to sit up!'

'R-r-r-r-r!' snored Lou and Dan. Julian felt that surely it would be all right to sit up now that the men were obviously asleep. So he sat up cautiously, stretching himself with pleasure.

He looked down on the two men, who were lying on their backs with their mouths open. Beside them were two neat sacks, strong and thick. Julian wondered what was inside them. They certainly had not had them when they came up the track.

The boy gazed down the hillside, frowning, trying to probe the mystery of where the men had been, and what they were doing up here – and suddenly he jumped violently. He stared as if he could not believe his eyes.

A squat face was peering out from a bramble bush there. There was almost no nose, and an enormous mouth. Who could it be? Was it someone spying on Lou and Dan? But what a face! It didn't seem human.

A hand came up to rub the face – and Julian saw that it was hairy. With a start he knew who the face belonged to – Pongo the chimpanzee! No wonder he had thought it such an inhuman face. It was all right on a chimp, of course – quite a nice face – but not on a man.

Pongo stared at Julian solemnly, and Julian stared back, his mind in a whirl. What was Pongo doing there? Was Nobby with him? If so, Nobby was in danger, for at any moment the men might wake up. He couldn't think what to do. If he called out to warn Nobby, he would wake the men.

Pongo was pleased to see Julian, and did not seem to think the roof of a caravan a curious place to be in at all. After all, *he* often went up on the roofs of caravans. He nodded and blinked at the boy, and then scratched his head for a long time.

Then beside him appeared Nobby's face – a tear-stained face, bruised and swollen. He suddenly saw Julian looking over the roof of the caravan, and his mouth fell open in surprise. He seemed about to call out, and Julian shook his head frantically to stop him, pointing downwards to try and warn Nobby that somebody was there.

But Nobby didn't understand. He grinned and, to Julian's horror, began to climb up the hillside to the rocky ledge! The men were sleeping there, and Julian saw with dismay that Nobby would probably heave himself up right on top of them.

'Look out!' he said, in a low, urgent voice. 'Look out, you fathead!'

But it was too late. Nobby heaved himself up on to the ledge, and, to his utmost horror, found himself sprawling on top of Tiger Dan! He gave a yell and tried to slide away – but Dan, rousing suddenly, shot out a hand and gripped him.

Lou woke up, too. The men glared at poor Nobby, and the boy began to tremble, and to beg for mercy.

'I didn't know you were here, I swear it! Let me go, let me go! I only came up to look for my knife that I lost yesterday!'

Dan shook him savagely. 'How long have you been here? You been spying?'

'No, no! I've only just come! I've been at the camp all morning – you ask Larry and Rossy. I been helping them!'

'You been spying on us, that's what you've been doing!' said Lou, in a cold, hard voice that filled the listening Julian with dread. 'You've had plenty of beatings this week, but seemingly they aren't enough. Well, up here, there's nobody to hear your yells, see? So we'll show you what a real beating is! And if you can walk down to the camp after it, I'll be surprised.'

Nobby was terrified. He begged for mercy, he promised to do anything the men asked him, and tried to jerk his poor swollen face away from Dan's hard hands.

Julian couldn't bear it. He didn't want to give away the fact that it was he who had been spying, nor did he want to fight the men at all, for he was pretty certain he would get the worst of it. But nobody could lie in silence, watching two men treat a young boy in such a way. He made up his mind to leap off the roof right on to the men, and to rescue poor Nobby if he could.

Nobby gave anguished yell as Lou gave him a flick with his leather belt – but before Julian could jump down to help him, somebody else bounded up! Somebody who bared his teeth and made ugly animal noises of rage, somebody whose arms were far stronger than either Lou's or Dan's – somebody who loved poor Nobby, and wasn't going to let him be beaten any more!

It was Pongo. The chimpanzee had been watching the scene with his sharp little eyes. He had still hidden himself in the bush, for he was afraid of Lou and Dan – but now, hearing Nobby's cries, he leapt out of the brambles and flung himself on the astonished men.

He bit Lou's arm hard. Then he bit Dan's leg. The men yelled loudly, much more loudly than poor Nobby had. Lou lashed out with his leather belt, and it caught Pongo on the shoulder. The chimpanzee made a shrill chattering noise, and leapt on Lou with his arms open, clasping the man to him, trying to bite his throat.

Tiger Dan rushed down the hill at top speed, terrified of the angry chimpanzee. Lou yelled to Nobby:

'Call him off! He'll kill me!'

'Pongo!' shouted Nobby. 'Stop it! Pongo! Come here.'

Pongo gave Nobby a look of the greatest surprise. 'What!' he seemed to say. 'You won't let me punish this bad man who beat you? Well, well – whatever you say must be right!'

And the chimpanzee, giving Lou one last vicious nip, let the man go. Lou followed Dan down the hill at top speed, and Julian heard him crashing through the bushes as if a hundred chimpanzees were after him.

Nobby sat down, trembling. Pongo, not quite sure if his beloved friend was angry with him or not, crept up to him putting a paw on the boy's knee. Nobby put his arm round the anxious animal, and Pongo chattered with joy.

Julian slid down from the roof of the caravan and went to Nobby. He, too, sat down beside him. He put his arm round the trembling boy and gave him a hug.

'I was just coming to give you a hand, when Pongo shot up the hill,' he said.

'Were you really?' said Nobby, his face lighting up. 'You're a real friend, you are. Good as Pongo, here.'

And Julian felt quite proud to be ranked in bravery with the chimpanzee!

CHAPTER SIXTEEN

A surprising discovery

'LISTEN – SOMEBODY'S coming!' said Nobby, and Pongo gave an ugly growl. The sound of voices could be heard coming up the hill. Then a dog barked.

'It's all right. It's Timmy – and the others,' said Julian, unspeakably glad to welcome them back. He stood up and yelled.

'All right! Come along!'

George, Timmy, Dick and Anne came running up the track. 'Hallo!' shouted Dick. 'We thought it would be safe, because we saw Lou and Dan in the distance, running along at the bottom of the hill. I say – there's Pongo!'

Pongo shook hands with Dick, and then went to the back of Timmy, to shake hands with his tail. But Timmy was ready for him, and backing round, he held out his paw to Pongo instead. It was very funny to see the two animals solemnly shaking hands with one another.

'Hallo, Nobby!' said Dick. 'Goodness – what have you been doing to yourself? You look as if you've been in the wars.'

'Well, I have, rather,' said Nobby, with a feeble grin. He was very much shaken, and did not get up. Pongo ran to Anne and tried to put his arms round her.

'Oh, Pongo – you squeeze too hard,' said Anne. 'Julian, did anything happen? Did the men come? Have you any news?'

'Plenty,' said Julian. 'But what I want first is a jolly good drink. I've had none all day. Ginger-beer, I think.'

'We're all thirsty. I'll get five bottles – no, six, because I expect Pongo would like some.'

Pongo loved ginger-beer. He sat down with the children on the rocky ledge, and took his glass from Anne, just like a child. Timmy was a little jealous, but as he didn't like ginger-beer he couldn't make a fuss.

Julian began to tell the others about his day, and how he had hidden on the caravan roof. He described how the men had come – and had gone under the caravan – and then moved it. They all listened with wide eyes. What a story!

Then Nobby told his part. 'I butted in and almost gave the game away,' he said, when Julian had got as far as the men falling asleep and snoring. 'But, you see, I had to come and warn you. Lou and Dan swear they'll poison Timmy somehow, even if they have to dope him, put him into a sack and take him down to the camp to do it. Or they might knock him on the head.'

'Let them try!' said George, in her fiercest voice, and put her arm round Timmy. Pongo at once put his arm round Timmy too.

'And they said they'd damage your caravans too – maybe put a fire underneath and burn them up,' went on Nobby.

The four children stared at him in horror. 'But they wouldn't do a thing like that, surely?' said Julian, at last. 'They'd get into trouble with the police if they did.'

'Well, I'm just telling you what they said,' Nobby went on. 'You don't know Lou and Tiger Dan like I do. They'll stick at nothing to get their way – or to get anybody *out* of their way. They tried to poison Timmy, didn't they? And poor old Barker got it instead.'

'Is – is Barker – all right?' asked Anne.

'No,' said Nobby. 'He's dying, I think. I've given him to Lucilla to dose. She's a marvel with sick animals. I've put Growler with the other dogs. He's safe with them.'

He stared round at the other children, his mouth trembling, sniffing as if he had a bad cold.

'I daren't go back,' he said, in a low voice, 'I daren't. They'll half-kill me.'

'You're not going back, so that's settled,' said Julian, in a brisk voice. 'You're staying here with us. We shall love to have you. It was jolly decent of you to come up and warn us – and bad luck to have got caught like that. You're our friend now – and we'll stick together.'

Nobby couldn't say a word, but his face shone. He rubbed a dirty hand across his eyes, then grinned his old grin. He nodded his head, not trusting himself to speak, and the children all thought how nice he was. Poor old Nobby.

They finished their ginger-beer and then Julian got up. 'And now,' he said, 'we will do a little exploring and find out where those men went, shall we?'

'Oh yes!' cried George, who had sat still quite long enough. 'We *must* find out! Do we have to get under the caravan, Julian?'

''Fraid so,' said Julian. 'You sit there quietly, Nobby, and keep guard in case Lou or Dan come back.'

He didn't think for a moment that they would, but he could see that Nobby needed to sit quietly for a while. Nobby, however, had different ideas. He was going to share his adventure!

'Timmy's guard enough, and so is Pongo,' he said. 'They'll hear anyone coming half a mile away. I'm in on this!'

And he was. He went scrabbling underneath the lowslung base of the caravan with the others, eager to find out anything he could.

But it was impossible to explore down in the heather, with the caravan base just over their heads. They had no room at all. Like Dan and Lou they soon felt that they would have to move the van.

It took all five of them, with Pongo giving a shove, too, to move the caravan a few feet away. Then down they dropped to the thick carpet of heather again.

The tufts came up easily by the roots, because the men had already pulled them up once that day and then replanted them. The children dragged up a patch of heather about five feet square, and then gave an exclamation.

'Look! Boards under the heather!'

'Laid neatly across and across. What for?'

'Pull them up!'

The boys pulled up the planks one by one and piled them on one side. Then they saw that the boards had closed up the entrance of a deep hole. 'I'll get my torch,' said Julian. He fetched it and flashed it on.

The light showed them a dark hole, going down into the hillside, with footholds sticking out of one side. They all sat and gazed down in excitement.

'To think we went and put our caravan *exactly* over the entrance of the men's hiding-place!' said Dick 'No wonder they were wild! No wonder they changed their minds and told us we could go down to the lake and camp there instead of here!'

'Gosh!' said Julian, staring into the hole. 'So that's where the men went! Where does it lead to? They were down there a mighty long time. They were clever enough to replace the planks and drag some of the heather over them, too, to hide them when they went down.'

Pongo suddenly took it into his head to go down the hole. Down he went, feeling for the footholds with his hairy feet, grinning up at the others. He disappeared at the bottom. Julian's torch could not pick him out at all.

'Hey, Pongo! Don't lose yourself down there!' called Nobby, anxiously. But Pongo had gone.

'Blow him!' said Nobby. 'He'll never find his way back, if he goes wandering about underground. I'll have to go after him. Can I have your torch, Julian?'

'I'll come too,' said Julian. 'George, get me your torch as well, will you?'

'It's broken,' said George. 'I dropped it last night. And nobody else has got one.'

'What an awful nuisance!' said Julian. 'I want us to go and explore down there – but we can't with only one torch. Well, I'll just go down with Nobby and get Pongo – have a quick look round and come back. I may see something worth seeing!'

Nobby went down first, and Julian followed, the others all kneeling round the hole, watching them enviously. They disappeared.

'Pongo!' yelled Nobby. 'Pongo! Come here, you idiot!'

Pongo had not gone very far. He didn't like the dark down there very much, and he came to Nobby as soon as he saw the light of the torch. The boys found themselves in a narrow passage at the bottom of the hole, which widened as they went further into the hill.

'Must be caves somewhere,' said Julian, flashing his torch round. 'We know that a lot of springs run out of this hill. I daresay that through the centuries the water has eaten away the softer stuff and made caves and tunnels everywhere in the hill. And somewhere in a cave Lou and Dan store away things they don't want anyone to know about. Stolen goods, probably.'

The passage ended in a small cave that seemed to have no other opening out of it at all. There was nothing in it. Julian flashed his torch up and down the walls.

He saw footholds up one part, and traced them to a hole in the roof, which must have been made, years before, by running water. 'That's the way we go!' he said. 'Come on.'

'Wait!' said Nobby. 'Isn't your torch getting rather faint?'

'Goodness – yes!' said Julian in alarm, and shook his torch violently to make the light brighter. But the battery had almost worn out, and no better light came. Instead the light grew even fainter, until it was just a pin-prick in the torch.

'Come on – we'd better get back at once,' said Julian, feeling a bit scared. 'I don't want to wander about here in the pitch dark. Not my idea of fun at all.'

Nobby took firm hold of Pongo's hairy paw and equally firm hold of Julian's jersey. He didn't mean to lose either of them! The light in the torch went out completely. Now they must find their way back in black darkness.

Julian felt round for the beginning of the passage that led back to the hole. He found it and made his way up it, feeling the sides with his hands. It wasn't a pleasant experience at all, and Julian was thankful that he and Nobby had only gone a little way into the hill. It would have been like a nightmare if they had gone well in, and then found themselves unable to see the way back.

They saw a faint light shining further on and guessed it was the daylight shining down the entrance-hole. They stumbled thankfully towards it. They looked up and saw the anxious faces of the other three peering down at them, unable to see them.

'We're back!' called Julian, beginning to climb up. 'My torch went out, and we daren't go very far. We've got Pongo, though.'

The others helped to pull them out at the top of the hole.

Julian told them about the hole in the roof of the little cave.

'That's where the men went,' he said. 'And tomorrow, when we've all bought torches, and matches and candles, that's where we're going, too! We'll go down to the town and buy what we want, and come back and do a Really Good Exploration!'

'We're going to have an adventure after all,' said Anne, in rather a small voice.

''Fraid so,' said Julian. 'But you can stay at the farm with Mrs Mackie for the day, Anne dear. Don't you come with us.'

'If you're going on an adventure, I'm coming, too,' said Anne. 'So there! I wouldn't *dream* of not coming.'

'All right,' said Julian. 'We'll all go together. Golly, things are getting exciting!'

CHAPTER SEVENTEEN

Another visit from Lou and Dan

NOBODY DISTURBED the children that night, and Timmy did not bark once. Nobby slept on a pile of rugs in the boys' caravan, and Pongo cuddled up to him. The chimpanzee seemed delighted at staying with the caravanners. Timmy was rather jealous that another animal should be with them, and wouldn't take any notice of Pongo at all.

The next morning, after breakfast, the children discussed who was to go down to the town. 'Not Nobby and Pongo, because they wouldn't be allowed in the bus together,' said Julian. 'They had better stay behind.'

'Not by ourselves?' said Nobby, looking alarmed. 'Suppose Lou and Uncle Dan come up? Even if I've got Pongo I'd be scared.'

'Well, I'll stay here, too,' said Dick. 'We don't all need to go to buy torches. Don't forget to post that letter to Daddy and Mother, Julian.'

They had written a long letter to their parents, telling them of the exciting happenings. Julian put it into his pocket. 'I'll post it all right,' he said. 'Well, I suppose we might as well go now. Come on, girls. Keep a look-out, Dick, in case those rogues come back.'

George, Timmy, Anne and Julian went down the hill

together, Timmy running on in front, his tail wagging nineteen to the dozen. Pongo climbed up to the roof of the red caravan to watch them go. Nobby and Dick sat down in the warm sun on the ledge, their heads resting on springy clumps of heather.

'It's nice up here,' said Nobby. 'Much nicer than down below. I wonder what everyone is thinking about Pongo and me. I bet Mr Gorgio, the head of the circus, is wild that the chimpanzee's gone. I bet he'll send up to fetch us.'

Nobby was right. Two people were sent up to get him – Lou and Tiger Dan. They came creeping up through the bracken and heather, keeping a sharp eye for Timmy or Pongo.

Pongo sensed them long before they could be seen and warned Nobby. Nobby went very pale. He was terrified of the two scoundrels.

'Get into one of the caravans,' said Dick in a low voice. 'Go on. I'll deal with those fellows – if it *is* them. Pongo will help me if necessary.'

Nobby scuttled into the green caravan and shut the door. Dick sat where he was. Pongo squatted on the roof of the caravan, watching.

Lou and Dan suddenly appeared. They saw Dick, but did not see Pongo. They looked all round for the others.

'What do you want?' said Dick.

'Nobby and Pongo,' said Lou with a scowl. 'Where are they?'

They're going to stay on with us,' said Dick.

'Oh, no, they're not!' said Tiger Dan. 'Nobby's in my charge, see? I'm his uncle.'

'Funny sort of uncle,' remarked Dick. 'How's that dog you poisoned, by the way?'

Tiger Dan went purple in the face. He looked as if he would willingly have thrown Dick down the hill.

'You be careful what you say to me!' he said, beginning to shout.

Nobby, hidden in the caravan, trembled when he heard his uncle's angry yell. Pongo kept quite still, his face set and ugly.

'Well, you may as well say goodbye and go,' said Dick in a calm voice to Dan. 'I've told you that Nobby and Pongo are staying with us for the present.'

'Where *is* Nobby?' demanded Tiger Dan, looking as if he would burst with rage at any moment. 'Wait till I get my hands on him. Wait . . .'

He began to walk towards the caravans – but Pongo was not having any of that! He leapt straight off the roof on to the horrified man, and flung him to the ground. He made such a terrible snarling noise that Dan was terrified.

'Call him off!' he yelled. 'Lou, come and help.'

'Pongo won't obey *me*,' said Dick still sitting down looking quite undisturbed. 'You'd better go before he bites big pieces out of you.'

Dan staggered to the rock ledge, looking as if he would box Dick's ears. But the boy did not move, and somehow Dan did not dare to touch him. Pongo let him go and stood

glowering at him, his great hairy arms hanging down his sides, ready to fly at either of the men if they came near.

Tiger Dan picked up a stone – and as quick as lightning Pongo flung himself on him again and sent the man rolling down the hill. Lou fled in terror. Dan got up and fled, too, yelling furiously as he went. Pongo chased them in delight. He, too, picked up stones and flung them with a very accurate aim, so that Dick kept hearing yells of pain.

Pongo came back, looking extremely pleased with himself. He went to the green caravan, as Dick shouted to Nobby.

'All right, Nobby. They've gone. Pongo and I won the battle!'

Nobby came out. Pongo put his arm round him at once and chattered nonsense in his ear. Nobby looked rather ashamed of himself.

'Bit of a coward, aren't I?' he said. 'Leaving you out here all alone.'

'I enjoyed it,' said Dick truthfully. 'And I'm sure Pongo did!'

'You don't know what dangerous fellows Lou and Dan are,' said Nobby, looking down the hillside to make sure the men were really gone. 'I tell you they'd stick at nothing. They'd burn your caravans, hurl them down the hill, poison your dog, and do what harm they could to you, too. You don't know them like I do!'

'Well, as a matter of fact, we've had some pretty exciting adventures with men just as tough as Dan and Lou,' said Dick. 'We always seem to be falling into the middle of some adventure or other. Now, last hols we went to a place called Smuggler's Top – and, my word, the adventures we had there! You wouldn't believe them!'

'You tell me and Pongo,' said Nobby, sitting down beside Dick. 'We've plenty of time before the others come back.'

So Dick began to tell the tale of all the other thrilling adventures that the five of them had had, and the time flew. Both boys were surprised when they heard Timmy barking down the track, and knew that the others were back.

George came tearing up with Timmy at her heels. 'Are you all right? Did anything happen while we were away? Do you know, we saw Lou and Tiger Dan getting on the bus when we got off it! They were carrying bags as if they meant to go away and stay somewhere.'

Nobby brightened up at once. 'Did you really? Good! They came up here, you know, and Pongo chased them down the hill. They must have gone back to the camp, collected their bags, and gone to catch the bus. Hurrah!'

'We've got fine torches,' said Julian, and showed Dick his. 'Powerful ones. Here's one for you, Dick – and one for you, Nobby.'

'Oooh – thanks,' said Nobby. Then he went red. 'I haven't got enough money to pay you for such a grand torch,' he said awkwardly.

'It's a present for you,' said Anne at once, 'a present for a friend of ours, Nobby!'

'Coo! Thanks awfully,' said Nobby, looking quite overcome. 'I've never had a present before. You're decent kids, you are.'

Pongo held out his hand to Anne and made a chattering noise as if to say: 'What about one for me, too?'

'Oh – we didn't bring one for Pongo!' said Anne. 'Why ever didn't we?'

'Good thing you didn't,' said Nobby. 'He would have put it on and off all day long and wasted the battery in no time!'

'I'll give him my old torch,' said George. 'It's broken, but he won't mind that!'

Pongo was delighted with it. He kept pressing down the knob that should make the light flash – and when there was no light he looked all about on the ground as if the light must have dropped out! The children roared at him. He liked them to laugh at him. He did a little dance all round them to show how pleased he was.

'Look here – wouldn't it be a jolly good time to explore underground now that we know Lou and Dan are safely out of the way?' asked Julian suddenly. 'If they've got bags with them, surely that means they're going to spend the night somewhere and won't be back till tomorrow at least. We'd be quite safe to go down and explore.'

'Yes, we would,' said George eagerly. 'I'm longing to get down there and Make Discoveries!'

'Well, let's have something to eat first,' said Dick. 'It's long past our dinner-time. It must be about half past one. Yes, it is!'

'George and I will get you a meal,' said Anne. 'We called at the farm on our way up and got a lovely lot of food. Come on, George.'

George got up unwillingly. Timmy followed her, sniffing expectantly. Soon the two girls were busy getting a fine meal ready, and they all sat on the rocky ledge to eat it.

'Mrs Mackie gave us this enormous bar of chocolate for a present today,' said Anne, showing a great slab to Dick and Nobby. 'Isn't it lovely? No, Pongo, it's not for you. Eat your sandwiches properly, and don't grab.'

'I vote we take some food down into the hill with us,' said Julian. 'We may be quite a long time down there, and we shan't want to come back at tea-time.'

'Oooh – a picnic inside the hill!' said Anne. 'That would be thrilling. I'll soon pack up some food in the kit-bag. I won't bother to make sandwiches. We'll take a new loaf, butter, ham and a cake, and cut what we want. What about something to drink?'

'Oh, we can last out till we get back,' said Julian. 'Just take something to eat to keep us going till we have finished exploring.'

George and Nobby cleared up and rinsed the plates. Anne wrapped up some food in greased paper, and packed it carefully into the kitbag for Julian to carry. She popped the big bar of chocolate into the bag, too. It would be nice to eat at odd moments.

At last they were all ready. Timmy wagged his tail. He knew they were going somewhere.

The five of them pushed the caravan back a few feet to expose the hole. They had all tugged the van back into place the night before, in case Lou and Dan came to go down the hole again. No one could get down it if the caravan was over it.

The boards had been laid roughly across the hole and the boys took them off, tossing them to one side. As soon as Pongo saw the hole he drew back, frightened.

'He's remembered the darkness down there,' said George. 'He doesn't like it. Come on, Pongo. You'll be all right. We've all got torches!'

But nothing would persuade Pongo to go down the hole again. He cried like a baby when Nobby tried to make him.

'It's no good,' said Julian. 'You'll have to stop up here with him.'

'What – and miss all the excitement!' cried Nobby indignantly. 'I jolly well won't. We can tie old Pongo up to a wheel of the van so that he won't wander off. Lou and Dan are away somewhere, and no one else is likely to tackle a big chimp like Pongo. We'll tie him up.'

So Pongo was tied firmly to one of the caravan wheels. 'You stay there like a good chimp till we come back,' said Nobby, putting a pail of water beside him in case he should want a drink. 'We'll be back soon!'

Pongo was sad to see them go – but nothing would have made him go down that hole again! So he sat watching the children disappear one by one. Timmy jumped down, too, and then they were all gone. Gone on another adventure. What would happen now?

CHAPTER EIGHTEEN

Inside the hill

THE CHILDREN had all put on extra jerseys, by Julian's orders, for he knew it would be cold inside the dark hill. Nobby had been lent an old one of Dick's. They were glad of them as soon as they were walking down the dark passage that led to the first cave, for the air was very chilly.

They came to the small cave and Julian flashed his torch to show them where the footholds went up the wall to a hole in the roof.

'It's exciting,' said George, thrilled. 'I like this sort of thing. Where does that hole in the roof lead to, I wonder? I'll go first, Ju.'

'No, you won't,' said Julian firmly. 'I go first. You don't know what might be at the top!'

Up he went, his torch held in his mouth, for he needed both hands to climb. The footholds were strong nails driven into the rock of the cave-wall, and were fairly easy to climb.

He got to the hole in the roof and popped his head through. He gave a cry of astonishment.

'I say! There's a most *enormous* cavern here – bigger than six dance-halls – and the walls are all glittering with something – phosphorescence, I should think.'

He scrambled out of the hole and stood on the floor of

the immense cave. Its walls twinkled in their weird light, and Julian shut off his torch. There was almost enough phosphorescent light in the cavern to see by!

One by one the others came up and stared in wonder. 'It's like Aladdin's cave!' said Anne. 'Isn't that an odd light shining from the walls – and from the roof, too, Julian?'

Dick and George had rather a difficulty in getting Timmy up to the cavern, but they managed it at last. Timmy put his tail down at once when he saw the curious light gleaming everywhere. But it went up again when George patted him.

'What an enormous place!' said Dick. 'Do you suppose this is where the men hide their stuff, whatever it is?'

Julian flashed his torch on again and swung it round and about, picking out the dark, rocky corners. 'Can't see anything hidden,' he said. 'But we'd better explore the cave properly before we go on.'

So the five children explored every nook and cranny of the gleaming cave, but could find nothing at all. Julian gave a sudden exclamation and picked something up from the floor.

'A cigarette end!' he said. 'That shows that Lou and Dan have been here. Come on, let's see if there's a way out of this great cave.'

Right at the far end, half-way up the gleaming wall was a large hole, rather like a tunnel. Julian climbed up to it and called to the others. 'This is the way they went. There's a dead match just at the entrance to the tunnel or whatever this is.'

It was a curious tunnel, no higher than their shoulders in some places, and it wound about as it went further into the hill. Julian thought that at one time water must have run through it. But it was quite dry now. The floor of the tunnel was worn very smooth, as if a stream had hollowed it out through many, many years.

'I hope the stream won't take it into its head to begin running suddenly again!' said George. 'We should get jolly wet!'

The tunnel went on for some way, and Anne was beginning to feel it must go on for ever. Then the wall at one side widened out and made a big rocky shelf. Julian, who was first, flashed his torch into the hollow.

'I say!' he shouted. 'Here's where those fellows keep their stores! There's a whole pile of things here!'

The others crowded up as closely as they could, each of them flashing their torch brightly. On the wide, rocky shelf lay boxes and packages, sacks and cases. The children stared at them. 'What's in them?' said Nobby, full of intense curiosity. 'Let's see!'

He put down his torch and undid a sack. He slid in his hand – and brought it out holding a piece of shining gold plate!

'Coo!' said Nobby. 'So that's what the police were after last year when they came and searched the camp! And it was hidden safely here. Coo, look at all these things. Jumping Jiminy, they must have robbed the King himself!'

The sack was full of exquisite pieces of gold plate – cups, dishes, small trays. The children set them all out on the ledge. How they gleamed in the light of their torches!

'They're thieves in a very big way,' said Julian. 'No doubt about that. Let's look in this box.'

The box was not locked, and the lid opened easily. Inside was a piece of china, a vase so fragile that it looked as if it might break at a breath!

'Well, I don't know anything about china,' said Julian, 'but I suppose this is a very precious piece, worth thousands of pounds. A collector of china would probably give a very large sum for it. What rogues Lou and Dan are!'

'Look here!' suddenly said George, and she pulled leather boxes out of a bag. 'Jewellery!'

She opened the boxes. The children exclaimed in awe. Diamonds flashed brilliantly, rubies glowed, emeralds shone green. Necklaces, bracelets, rings, brooches – the beautiful things gleamed in the light of the five torches.

There was a tiara in one box that seemed to be made only of big diamonds. Anne picked it out of its box gently. Then she put it on her hair.

'I'm a princess! It's my crown!' she said.

'You look lovely,' said Nobby admiringly. 'You look as grand as Delphine the Bareback Rider when she goes into the ring on her horse, with jewels shining all over her!'

Anne put on necklaces and bracelets and sat there on the ledge like a little princess, shining brightly in the magnificent jewels. Then she took them off and put them carefully back into their satin-lined boxes.

'Well – what a haul those two rogues have made!' said Julian, pulling out some gleaming silver plate from another package. 'They must be very fine burglars!'

'*I* know how they work,' said Dick. 'Lou's a wonderful acrobat, isn't he? I bet he does all the climbing about up walls and over roofs and into windows – and Tiger Dan stands below and catches everything he throws down.'

'You're about right,' said Nobby, handling a beautiful silver cup. 'Lou could climb anywhere – up ivy, up pipes – even up the bare wall of a house, I shouldn't wonder! And jump! He can jump like a cat. He and Tiger Dan have been in this business for a long time, I expect. That's where Uncle Dan went at night, of course, when we were on tour, and I woke up and found him gone out of the caravan!'

'And I expect he stores the stolen goods in that wagon of his you showed us,' said Julian, remembering. 'You told us how angry he was with you once when you went and rummaged about in it. He probably stored it there, and then he and Lou came up here each year and hid the stuff underground – waiting till the police had given up the search for the stolen things – and then they come and get it and sell it somewhere safe.'

'A jolly clever plan,' said Dick. 'What a fine chance they've got – wandering about from place to place like that hearing of famous jewels or plate – slipping out at night – and Lou climbing up to bedrooms like a cat. I wonder how they found this place – it's a most wonderful hidy-hole!'

'Yes. Nobody would ever dream of it!' said George.

'And then we go and put our caravan bang on the top of the entrance – just when they want to put something in and take something out!' said Julian. 'It *must* have annoyed them.'

'What are we going to do about it?' said Dick.

'Tell the police, of course,' said Julian, promptly. 'What do you suppose? My word, I'd like to see the face of the policeman who first sees this little haul.'

They put everything back carefully. Julian shone his torch up the tunnel. 'Shall we explore a bit further, or not?' he said. 'It still goes on. Look!'

'Better get back,' said Nobby. 'Now we've found this we'd better do something about it.'

'Oh, let's just see where the tunnel goes to,' said George. 'It won't take a minute!'

'All right,' said Julian, who wanted to go up the tunnel as much as she did. He led the way, his torch shining brightly.

The tunnel came out into another cave, not nearly as big as the one they had left behind. At one end something gleamed like silver, and seemed to move. There was a curious sound there, too.

'What is it?' said Anne, alarmed. They stood and listened.

'Water!' said Julian, suddenly. 'Of course! Can't you hear it flowing along? It's an underground stream, flowing through the hill to find an opening where it can rush out.'

'Like that stream we saw before we came to our caravan camping place,' said George. 'It rushed out of the hill. Do you remember? This may be the very one!'

'I expect it is!' said Dick. They went over to it and watched it. It rushed along in its own hollowed out channel, close to the side of the cave-wall.

'Maybe at one time it ran across this cave and down the tunnel we came up by,' said Julian. 'Yes, look – there's a big kind of groove in the floor of the cave here – the stream must have run there once. Then for some reason it went a different way.'

'Let's get back,' said Nobby. 'I want to know if Pongo's all right. I don't somehow feel very comfortable about him. And I'm jolly cold, too. Let's go back to the sunshine and have something to eat. I don't want a picnic down here, after all.'

'All right,' said Julian, and they made their way back through the tunnel. They passed the rock shelf on which lay the treasure, and came at last to the enormous gleaming cavern. They went across it to the hole that led down into the small cave. Down they went, Julian and George trying to manage Timmy between them. But it was very awkward, for he was a big dog.

Then along the passage to the entrance-hole. They all felt quite pleased at the idea of going up into the sunshine again.

'Can't see any daylight shining down the hole,' said Julian puzzled. 'It would be near here.'

He came up against a blank wall, and was surprised. Where was the hole? Had they missed their way? Then he flashed his torch above him and saw the hole there – but there was no daylight shining in!

'I say!' said Julian, in horror. 'I say! What do you think's happened?'

'What?' asked everyone, in panic.

'The hole is closed!' said Julian. 'We can't get out! Somebody's been along and put those planks across – and I bet they've put the caravan over them, too. We can't get out!'

Everyone stared up at the closed entrance in dismay. They were prisoners.

'Whatever are we to do?' said George. 'Julian – what *are* we going to do?'

CHAPTER NINETEEN

Prisoners underground

JULIAN DIDN'T answer. He was angry with himself for not thinking that this might happen! Although Lou and Dan had been seen getting on the bus with bags, they might easily not have been spending the night away – the bags might contain things they wanted to sell – stolen goods of some kind.

'They came back quickly – and came up the hill, I suppose, to have another try at getting Nobby and Pongo back,' said Julian, out loud. 'What an idiot I am to leave things to chance like that. Well – I'll have a try at shifting these planks. I should be able to, with luck.'

He did his best, and did shift them to a certain extent – but, as he feared, the caravan had been run back over the hole, and even if he managed to shift some of the planks it was impossible to make a way out.

'Perhaps Pongo can help,' he said suddenly. He shouted loudly: 'Pongo! Pongo! Come and help!'

Everyone stood still, hoping that they would hear Pongo chattering somewhere near, or scraping at the planks above. But there was no sign or sound of Pongo.

Everyone called, but it was no use. Pongo didn't come. What had happened to him? Poor Nobby felt very worried.

'I wish I knew what has happened,' he kept saying. 'I feel as if something horrid has happened to poor old Pongo. Where can he be?'

Pongo was not very far away. He was lying on his side, his head bleeding. He was quite unconscious, and could not hear the frantic calls of the children at all. Poor Pongo!

What Julian had feared had actually happened. Lou and Dan had come back up the hill, bringing money with them to tempt Nobby and Pongo back. When they had got near to the hollow, they had stood still and called loudly.

'Nobby! Nobby! We've come to make friends, not to hurt you! We've got money for you. Be a sensible boy and come back to the camp. Mr Gorgio is asking for you.'

When there had been no reply at all, the men had gone nearer. Then they had seen Pongo and had stopped. The chimpanzee could not get at them because he was tied up. He sat there snarling.

'Where have those kids gone?' asked Lou. Then he saw that the caravan had been moved back a little, and he at once guessed.

'They've found the way underground! The interfering little brutes! See, they've moved one of the caravans off the hole. What do we do *now*!'

'This first,' said Tiger Dan, in a brutal voice, and he picked up an enormous stone. He threw it with all his force at poor Pongo, who tried to leap out of the way. But the rope prevented him, and the stone hit him full on the head.

He gave a loud scream and fell down at once, lying quite still.

'You've gone and killed him,' said Lou.

'So much the better!' said Tiger Dan. 'Now let's go and see if the entrance-hole is open. Those kids want their necks wringing!'

They went to the hollow and saw at once that the hole had been discovered, opened, and that the children must have gone down it.

'They're down there now,' said Tiger Dan, almost choking with rage. 'Shall we go down and deal with them – and get our stuff and clear off? We meant to clear off tomorrow, anyway. We might as well get the stuff out now.'

'What – in the daylight – with any of the farm men about to see us!' said Lou with a sneer. 'Clever, aren't you?'

'Well, have you got a better idea?' asked Tiger Dan.

'Why not follow our plan?' said Lou. 'Go down when it's dark and collect the stuff. We can bring our wagon up as we planned to do tonight. We don't need to bother about forcing the children to go now – they're underground – and we can make them prisoners till we're ready to clear off!'

'I see,' said Dan, and he grinned suddenly, showing his ugly teeth. 'Yes – we'll close up the hole and run the caravan back over it – and come up tonight in the dark with the wagon – go down – collect everything – and shut up the hole again with the children in it. We'll send a card to Gorgio when we're safe and tell him to go up and set the kids free.'

'Why bother to do that?' said Lou, in a cruel voice. 'Let 'em starve underground, the interfering little beasts. Serve 'em right.'

'Can't do that,' said Dan. 'Have the police after us worse than ever. We'll have to chuck some food down the hole, to keep them going till they're set free. No good starving them, Lou. There'd be an awful outcry if we do anything like that.'

The two men carefully put back the boards over the top of the hole and replaced the heather tufts. Then they ran the caravan back over the place. They looked at Pongo. The chimpanzee was still lying on his side, and the men could see what a nasty wound he had on his head.

'He ain't dead,' said Lou, and gave him a kick. 'He'll come round all right. Better leave him here. He might come to himself if we carried him back to camp, and fight us. He can't do us any harm tonight, tied up like that.'

They went away down the track. Not ten minutes afterwards the children came to the hole and found it blocked up! If only they hadn't stopped to explore that tunnel a bit further, they would have been able to get out and set Timmy on the two men.

But it was too late now. The hole was well and truly closed. No one could get out. No one could find poor Pongo and bathe his head. They were real prisoners.

They didn't like it at all. Anne began to cry, though she tried not to let the others see her. Nobby saw that she was upset, and put his arm round her.

'Don't cry, little Anne,' he said. 'We'll be all right.'

'It's no good staying here,' said Julian, at last. 'We might as well go somewhere more comfortable, and sit down and talk and eat. I'm hungry.'

They all went back down the passage, up through the hole in the roof, and into the enormous cavern. They found a sandy corner and sat down. Julian handed Anne the kitbag and she undid it to get the food inside.

'Better only have one torch going,' said Julian. 'We don't know how long we'll be here. We don't want to be left in the dark!'

Everybody immediately switched off their torches. The idea of being lost in the dark inside the hill wasn't at all nice! Anne handed out slices of bread and butter, and the children put thin slices of Mrs Mackie's delicious ham on them.

They felt distinctly better when they had all eaten a good meal. 'That was jolly good,' said Dick. 'No, we won't eat that chocolate, Anne. We may want it later on. Golly, I'm thirsty!'

'So am I,' said Nobby. 'My tongue's hanging out like old Timmy's. Let's go and get a drink.'

'Where from?' asked Anne, in surprise.

'Well, there was a stream in that other cave beyond the tunnel, wasn't there?' said Nobby. 'We can drink from that. It'll be all right.'

'Well, I hope it will,' said Julian. 'We were told not to drink water that wasn't boiled while we were caravanning – but we didn't know this sort of thing was going to happen! We'll go through the tunnel and get some water to drink from the stream.'

They made their way through the long, winding tunnel, and passed the shelf of stolen goods. Then on they went and came out into the cave through which the stream rushed so quickly. They dipped in their hands and drank thirstily. The water tasted lovely – so clear and cold.

Timmy drank too. He was puzzled at this adventure, but so long as he was with George he was happy. If his mistress suddenly took it into her head to live underground like a worm, that was all right – so long as Timmy was with her!

'I wonder if this stream *does* go to that hole in the hillside, and pours out there,' said Julian, suddenly. 'If it does, and we could follow it, we might be able to squeeze out.'

'We'd get terribly wet,' said George, 'but that wouldn't matter. Let's see if we can follow the water.'

They went to where the stream disappeared into a tunnel rather like the dry one they had come along. Julian shone his torch into it.

'We could wade along, I think,' he said. 'It is very fast but not very deep. I know – I'll go along it myself and see where it goes, and come back and tell you.'

'No,' said George, at once. 'If you go, we all go. You might get separated from us. That would be awful.'

'All right,' said Julian. 'I thought there was no sense in us all getting wet, that's all. Come on, we'll try now.'

One by one they waded into the stream. The current tugged at their legs, for the water ran very fast. But it was only just above the knees there. They waded along by the light of their torches, wondering where the tunnel would lead to.

Timmy half-waded, half-swam. He didn't like this water-business very much. It seemed silly to him. He pushed ahead of Julian and then a little further down, jumped up to a ledge that ran beside the water.

'Good idea, Tim,' said Julian, and he got up on to it too. He had to crouch down rather as he walked because his head touched the roof of the tunnel if he didn't – but at least his legs were out of the icy-cold water! All the others did the same, and as long as the ledge ran along beside the stream they all walked along it.

But at times it disappeared and then they had to wade in the water again, which now suddenly got deeper. 'Gracious! It's almost to my waist,' said Anne. 'I hope it doesn't get any deeper. I'm holding my clothes up as high as I can, but they'll get soaked soon.'

Fortunately the water got no deeper, but it seemed to go faster. 'We're going downhill a bit,' said Julian at last. 'Perhaps we are getting near to where it pours out of the hill.'

They were! Some distance ahead of him Julian suddenly saw a dim light, and wondered whatever it could be. He soon knew! It was daylight creeping in through the water that poured out of the hole in the hill-side – poured out in a torrent into the sunshine.

'We're almost there!' cried Julian. 'Come on.'

With light hearts the children waded along in the water. Now they would soon be out in the warm sunshine. They would find Pongo, and race down the hill in the warmth, catch the first bus, and go to the police station.

But nothing like that happened at all. To their enormous disappointment the water got far too deep to wade through, and Nobby stopped in fright. 'I daren't go no further,' he said. 'I'm almost off my feet now with the water rushing by.'

'I am, too,' said Anne, frightened.

'Perhaps I can swim out,' said Julian, and he struck out. But he gave it up in dismay, for the torrent of water was too much for him, and he was afraid of being hurled against the rocky sides and having his head cracked.

'It's no good,' he said, gloomily. 'No good at all. All that wading for nothing. It's far too dangerous to go any further – and yet daylight is only a few yards ahead. It's too sickening for words.'

'We must go back,' said George. 'I'm afraid Timmy will be drowned if we don't. Oh dear – we must go all that way back!'

CHAPTER TWENTY

More excitement

IT WAS a very sad and disappointed little company that made their way back to the cave. Along the tunnel they went, painfully and slowly, for it was not so easy against the current. Julian shivered; he was wet through with trying to swim.

At last they were back in the cave through which the stream flowed so swiftly. 'Let's run round and round it to get warm,' said Julian. 'I'm frozen. Dick, let me have one of your dry jerseys. I must take off these wet ones.'

The children ran round and round the cave, pretending to race one another, trying to get warm. They did get warm in the end, and sank down in a heap on some soft sand in a corner, panting. They sat there for a little while to get their breath.

Then they heard something. Timmy heard it first and growled. 'Jumping Jiminy, what's up with Timmy?' said Nobby, in fright. He was the most easily scared of the children, probably because of the frights he had had the last few days.

They all listened, George with her hand on Timmy's collar. He growled again, softly. The noise they all heard was a loud panting coming from the stream over at the other side of the cave!

'Someone is wading up the stream,' whispered Dick, in astonishment. 'Did they get in at the place where we couldn't get out? They must have!'

'But who is it?' asked Julian. 'Can't be Lou or Dan. They wouldn't come that way when they could come the right way. Sh! Whoever it is, is arriving in the cave. I'll shut off my torch.'

Darkness fell in the cave as the light from Julian's torch was clicked off. They all sat and listened, and poor Nobby shook and shivered. Timmy didn't growl any more, which was surprising. In fact, he even wagged his tail!

There was a sneeze from the other end of the cave – and then soft footsteps padded towards them. Anne felt as if she must scream. WHO was it?

Julian switched on his torch suddenly, and its light fell on a squat, hairy figure, halting in the bright glare. It was Pongo! 'It's *Pongo*!' everyone yelled, and leapt up at once. Timmy ran over to the surprised chimpanzee and sniffed round him in delight. Pongo put his arms round Nobby and Anne.

'Pongo! You've escaped! You must have bitten through your rope!' said Julian. 'How clever you are to find your way through the hole where the stream pours out. How did you know you would find us here! Clever Pongo.'

Then he saw the big wound on poor Pongo's head. 'Oh look!' said Julian. 'He's been hurt! I expect those brutes threw a stone at him. Poor old Pongo.'

'Let's bathe his head,' said Anne. 'I'll use my hanky.'

But Pongo wouldn't let anyone touch his wound, not even Nobby. He didn't snap or snarl at them but simply held their hands away from him, and refused to leave go. So nobody could bathe his head or bind it up.

'Never mind,' said Nobby at last, 'animals' wounds often heal up very quickly without any attention at all. He won't let us touch it, that's certain. I expect Lou and Dan hit him with a stone, and knocked him unconscious when they came. They then shut up the hole and made us prisoners. Beasts!'

'I say,' suddenly said Dick. 'I say! I've got an idea. I don't know if it will work – but it really *is* an idea.'

'What?' asked everyone, thrilled.

'Well – what about tying a letter round Pongo's neck and sending him out of the hole again, to take the letter to the camp?' said Dick. 'He won't go to Lou or Dan because he's scared of them – but he'd go to any of the others all right, wouldn't he? Larry would be the best one. He seems to be a good fellow.'

'Would Pongo understand enough to do all that, though?' asked Julian, doubtfully.

'We could try him,' said Nobby. 'I do send him here and there sometimes, just for fun – to take the elephant's bat to Larry, for instance – or to put my coat away in my caravan.'

'Well, we could certainly try,' said Dick. 'I've got a notebook and a pencil. I'll write a note and wrap it up in another sheet, pin it together and tie it round Pongo's neck with a bit of string.'

So he wrote a note. It said:

'*To whoever gets this note – please come up the hill to the hollow where there are two caravans. Under the red one is the entrance to an underground passage. We are prisoners inside the hill. Please rescue us soon.*

Julian, Dick, George, Anne and Nobby.'

He read it out to the others. Then he tied the note round Pongo's neck. Pongo was surprised, but fortunately did not try to pull it off.

'Now, you give him his orders,' said Dick to Nobby. So Nobby spoke slowly and importantly to the listening chimpanzee.

'Where's Larry? Go to Larry, Pongo. Fetch Larry, Go. GO!'

Pongo blinked at him and made a funny little noise as if he was saying: 'Please, Nobby, I don't want to go.'

Nobby repeated everything again. 'Understand Pongo? I think you do. GO, then, GO. GO!'

And Pongo turned and went! He disappeared into the

stream, splashing along by himself. The children watched him as far as they could by the light of their torches.

'He really is clever,' said Anne. 'He didn't want to go a bit, did he? Oh, I do hope he finds Larry, and that Larry sees the note and reads it and sends someone to rescue us.'

'I hope the note doesn't get all soaked and pulpy in the water,' said Julian, rather gloomily. 'Gosh, I wish I wasn't so cold. Let's run round a bit again, then have a piece of chocolate.'

They ran about and played 'tag' for a time till they all felt warm again. Then they decided to sit down and have some chocolate, and play some sort of guessing game to while away the time. Timmy sat close to Julian, and the boy was very glad.

'He's like a big hot-water bottle,' he said. 'Sit closer, Tim. That's right. You'll soon warm me up!'

It was dull after a time, sitting in the light of one torch, for they dared not use them all. Already it seemed as if Julian's torch was getting a little dim. They played all the games they could think of and then yawned.

'What's the time? I suppose it must be getting dark outside now. I feel quite sleepy.'

'It's nine o'clock almost,' said Julian. 'I hope Pongo has got down to the camp all right and found someone. We could expect help quite soon, if so.'

'Well, then, we'd better get along to the passage that leads to the hole,' said Dick, getting up. 'It's quite likely that if Larry or anyone else comes they'll not see the footholds leading up the wall out of that first little cave. They might not know where we were!'

This seemed very likely. They all made their way down the tunnel that led past the hidden store of valuables, and came out into the enormous cave. There was a nice sandy corner just by the hole that led down into the first small cave, and the children decided to sit there, rather than in the passage or in the first rocky and uncomfortable little cave. They cuddled up together for warmth, and felt hungry.

Anne and Nobby dozed off to sleep. George almost fell asleep, too. But the boys and Timmy kept awake, and talked in low voices. At least, Timmy didn't talk, but wagged his tail whenever either Dick or Julian said anything. That was his way of joining in their conversation.

After what seemed a long while Timmy growled, and the two boys sat up straight. Whatever it was that Timmy's sharp ears had heard, they had heard nothing at all. And they continued to hear nothing. But Timmy went on growling.

Julian shook the others awake. 'I believe help has come,' he said. 'But we'd better not go and see in case it's Dan and Lou come back. So wake up and look lively!'

They were all wide awake at once. Was it Larry come in answer to their note – or was it those horrid men, Tiger Dan and Lou the acrobat?

They soon knew! A head suddenly poked out of the hole nearby, and a torch shone on them. Timmy growled ferociously and struggled to fly at the head, but George held on firmly to his collar, thinking it might be Larry.

But it wasn't! It was Lou the acrobat, as the children knew only too well when they heard his voice. Julian shone his torch on him.

'I hope you've enjoyed your little selves,' came Lou's harsh voice. 'And you keep that dog under control, boy, or I'll shoot him. See? I'm not standing no nonsense from that dog this time. Have a look at this here gun!'

To George's horror she saw that Lou was pointing a gun at poor Timmy. She gave a scream and flung herself in front of him. 'Don't you dare to shoot my dog! I'll – I'll – I'll . . .'

She couldn't think of anything bad enough to do to the man who could shoot Timmy, and she stopped, choked by tears of rage and fear. Timmy, not knowing what the gun was, couldn't for the life of him understand why George wouldn't let him get at his enemy – such a nice position, too, with his head poking through a hole like that. Timmy felt he could deal with that head very quickly.

'Now, you kids, get up and go into that tunnel,' said Lou. 'Go on – go right ahead of me, and don't dare to stop. We've got work to do here tonight, and we're not going to have any more interference from kids like you. See?'

The children saw quite well. They began to walk towards the entrance of the tunnel. One by one they climbed into it. George first with Timmy. She dared not let his collar go

for an instant. A few paces behind them came Lou with his revolver, and Dan with a couple of big sacks.

The children were made to walk right past the shelf on which were the hidden goods.

Then Lou sat down in the tunnel, his torch switched on fully so that he could pick out each child. He still pointed his revolver at Timmy.

'Now we'll get on,' he said to Tiger Dan. 'You know what to do. Get on with it.'

Tiger Dan began to stuff the things into one of the big sacks he had brought. He staggered off with it. He came back in about ten minutes and filled the other sack. It was plain that the men meant to take everything away this time.

'Thought you'd made a very fine discovery, didn't you?' said Lou, mockingly, to the children. 'Ho, yes – very smart you were! See what happens to little smarties like you – you're prisoners – and here you'll stay for two or three days!'

'What do you mean?' said Julian, in alarm. 'Surely you wouldn't leave us here to starve?'

'Not to starve. We're too fond of you,' grinned Lou. 'We'll chuck you down some food into the tunnel. And in two or three days maybe someone will come and rescue you.'

Julian wished desperately that Pongo would bring help before Lou and Dan finished their business in the tunnel and went, leaving them prisoners. He watched Tiger Dan, working quickly, packing everything, carrying it off, coming back again, and packing feverishly once more. Lou sat still with his torch and revolver, enjoying the scared faces of the girls and Nobby. Julian and Dick put on a brave show which they were far from feeling.

Tiger Dan staggered away with another sackful. But he hadn't been gone for more than half a minute before a wail echoed through the tunnel.

'Lou! Help! Help! Something's attacking me! HELP.'

Lou rose up and went swiftly down the tunnel. 'It's Pongo, I bet it's old Pongo,' said Julian thrilled.

CHAPTER TWENTY-ONE

Dick has a great idea!

'LISTEN,' SAID Dick in an urgent voice. 'It may be Pongo by himself – he may not have gone back to the camp at all – he may have wandered about and at last gone down the entrance-hole by the caravans, and come up behind Tiger Dan. If so he won't have much chance because Lou's got a gun and will shoot him. And we shan't be rescued. So I'm going to slip down the tunnel while there's a chance and hide in a big cave.'

'What good will that do?' said Julian.

'Well, idiot, I may be able to slip down into the passage that leads to the entrance hole and hop out without the others seeing me,' said Dick, getting up. 'Then I can fetch help, see? You'd better all clear off somewhere and hide – find a good place, Julian, in case the men come after you when they find one of us is gone. Go on.'

Without another word the boy began to walk down the tunnel, past the rocky shelf on which now very few goods were left, and then came to the enormous cave.

Here there was a great noise going on, for Pongo appeared to have got hold of both men at once! Their torches were out, and Lou did not dare to shoot for fear of hurting Dan. Dick could see very little of this; he could only hear snarlings and shouting. He took a wide course round the heaving heap on the floor and made his way as quickly as he could in the dark to where he thought the hole was that led down into the first passage. He had to go carefully for fear of falling down it. He found it at last and let himself down into the cave below, and then, thinking it safe to switch on his torch in the passage, he flashed it in front of him to show him the way.

It wasn't long before he was out of the hole and was speeding round the caravans. Then he stopped. A thought struck him. He could fetch help all right – but the men would be gone by then! They had laid their plans for a getaway with all the goods; there was no doubt about that.

Suppose he put the boards over the hole, ramming them in with all his strength, and then rolled some heavy stones on top? He couldn't move the caravan over the boards, for it was far too heavy for a boy to push. But heavy stones would probably do the trick. The men would imagine that it was the caravan overhead again!

In great excitement Dick put back the boards, lugging them into place, panting and puffing. Then he flashed his torch round for stones. There were several small rocks nearby. He could not lift them, but he managed to roll them to the boards. Plonk! They went on to them one by one. Now nobody could move the boards at all.

'I know I've shut the others in with the men,' thought Dick. 'But I hope Julian will find a very safe hiding-place just for a time. Gosh, I'm hot! Now, down the hill I go – and I hope I don't lose my way in the darkness!'

Down below, the two men had at last freed themselves from the angry chimpanzee. They were badly bitten and mauled, but Pongo was not as strong and savage as usual because of his bad head-wound. The men were able to drive him off at last, and he went limping in the direction of the tunnel, sniffing out the children.

He would certainly have been shot if Lou could have found his revolver quickly enough. But he could not find it in the dark. He felt about for his torch, and found that although it was damaged, he could still put on the light by knocking it once or twice on the ground. He shone it on to Dan.

'We ought to have looked out for that ape when we saw he was gone,' growled Dan. 'He had bitten his rope through. We might have known he was somewhere about. He nearly did for me, leaping on me like that out of the darkness. It was lucky he flung himself on to my sack and not me.'

'Let's get the last of the things and clear out,' said Lou, who was badly shaken up. 'There's only one more load. We'll get back to the tunnel, scare the life out of those kids once more, shoot Pongo if we can, and then clear out. We'll chuck a few tins of food down the hole and then close it up.'

'I'm not going to risk meeting that chimp again,' said Dan. 'We'll leave the rest of the things. Come on. Let's go.

Lou was not particularly anxious to see Pongo again either. Keeping his torch carefully switched on and his revolver ready, he followed Dan to the hole that led down to the first cave. Down they went, and then along the passage, eager to get out into the night and go with their wagon down the track.

They got a terrible shock when they found that the hole was closed. Lou shone his torch upwards, and gazed in amazement at the underside of the boards. Someone had put them back into place again. *They* were prisoners now!

Tiger Dan went mad. One of his furious rages overtook him, and he hammered against those boards like a madman. But the heavy stones held them down, and the raging man dropped down beside Lou.

'Can't budge the boards! Someone must have put the caravan overhead again. We're prisoners!'

'But who's made us prisoners? Who's put back those boards?' shouted Lou, almost beside himself with fury. 'Could those kids have slipped by us when we were having that fight with the chimp?'

'We'll go and see if the kids are still there,' said Tiger Dan grimly. 'We'll find out. We'll make them very, very sorry for themselves. Come on.'

The two men went back again to the tunnel. The children were not there. Julian had taken Dick's advice and had gone off to try and find a good hiding-place. He had suddenly thought that perhaps Dick might get the idea of shutting up the entrance-hole – in which case the two men would certainly be furious!

So up the tunnel the children went, and into the cave with the stream. It seemed impossible to find any hiding-place there at all.

'I don't see where we can hide,' said Julian, feeling rather desperate. 'It's no good wading down that stream again – we shall only get wet and cold – and we have no escape from there at all if the men should come after us!'

'I can hear something,' said George, suddenly. 'Put your light out, Julian – quick!'

The torch was snapped off, and the children waited in the darkness. Timmy didn't growl. Instead George felt that he was wagging his tail.

'It's someone friendly,' she whispered. 'Over there. Perhaps it's Pongo. Put the torch on again.'

The light flashed out, and picked out the chimpanzee, who was coming towards them across the cave. Nobby gave a cry of joy.

'Here's old Pongo again!' he said. 'Pongo, did you go to the camp? Did you bring help?'

'No – he hasn't been down to the camp,' said Julian, his eyes catching sight of the note still tied round the chimpanzee's neck. 'There's our letter still on him. Blow!'

'He's clever – but not clever enough to understand a difficult errand like that,' said George.

'Oh, Pongo – and we were depending on you! Never

mind – perhaps Dick will escape and bring help. Julian, where *shall* we hide?'

'*Up* the stream?' suddenly said Anne. 'We've tried going *down* it. But we haven't tried going up it. Do you think it would be any good?'

'We could see,' said Julian, doubtfully. He didn't like this business of wading through water that might suddenly get deep. 'I'll shine my torch up the stream and see what it looks like.'

He went to the stream and shone his light up the tunnel from which it came. 'It seems as if we might walk along the ledge beside it,' he said. 'But we'd have to bend almost double – and the water runs so fast just here we must be careful not to slip and fall in.'

'I'll go first,' said Nobby. 'You go last, Julian. The girls can go in the middle with Pongo and Timmy.'

He stepped on to the narrow ledge inside the rocky tunnel, just above the rushing water. Then came Pongo. Then Anne, then George and Timmy – and last of all Julian.

But just as Julian was disappearing, the two men came into the cave, and by chance Lou's torch shone right on to the vanishing Julian. He gave a yell.

'There's one of them – look, over there! Come on!'

The men ran to where the stream came out of the tunnel, and Lou shone his torch up it. He saw the line of children, with Julian last of all. He grabbed hold of the boy and pulled him back.

Anne yelled when she saw Julian being pulled back. Nobby had a dreadful shock. Timmy growled ferociously, and Pongo made a most peculiar noise.

'Now look here,' came Lou's voice, 'I've got a gun, and I'm going to shoot that dog and that chimp if they so much as put their noses out of here. So hang on to them if you want to save their lives!'

He passed Julian to Tiger Dan, who gripped the boy firmly by the collar. Lou shone his torch up the tunnel again to count the children. 'Ho, there's Nobby,' he said, 'You come on out here, Nobby.'

'If I do, the chimp will come out too,' said Nobby. 'You know that. And he may get *you* before you get him!'

Lou thought about that. He was afraid of the big chimpanzee. 'You stay up there with him, then,' he said. And the girl can stay with you, holding the dog. But the other boy can come out here.'

He thought that George was a boy. George didn't mind. She liked people to think she was a boy. She answered at once.

'I can't come. If I do the dog will follow me, and I'm not going to have him shot.'

'You come on out,' said Lou, threateningly. 'I'm going to show you two boys what happens to kids who keep spying and interfering. Nobby knows what happens, don't you, Nobby? He's had his lesson. And you two boys are going to have yours, too.'

Dan called to him. 'There ought to be another girl there, Lou. I thought Nobby said there were two boys and two girls. Where's the other girl?'

'Gone further up the tunnel, I suppose,' said Lou, trying to see. 'Now, you boy – come on out!'

Anne began to cry. 'Don't go, George, don't go. They'll hurt you. Tell them you're a . . .'

'Shut up,' said George, fiercely. She added, in a whisper: 'If I say I'm a girl they'll know Dick is missing, and will be all the angrier. Hang on to Timmy.'

Anne clutched Timmy's collar in her trembling hand. George began to walk back to the cave. But Julian was not going to let George be hurt. He began to struggle.

Lou caught hold of George as she came out of the

tunnel – and at the same moment Julian managed to kick high in the air, and knocked Lou's torch right out of his hand. It flew up into the roof of the cave and fell somewhere with a crash. It went out. Now the cave was in darkness.

'Get back into the tunnel, George, with Anne,' yelled Julian. 'Timmy, Timmy, come on! Pongo, come here!'

'I don't want Timmy to be shot!' cried out George, in terror, as the dog shot past her into the cave.

Even as she spoke a shot rang out. It was Lou, shooting blindly at where he thought Timmy was. George screamed.

'Oh, Timmy, Timmy! You're not hurt, are you?'

CHAPTER TWENTY-TWO

The end of the adventure

NO, TIMMY wasn't hurt. The bullet zipped past his head and struck the wall of the cave. Timmy went for Lou's legs. Down went the man with a crash and a yell, and the revolver flew out of his hand. Julian heard it slithering across the floor of the cave, and he was very thankful.

'Put on your torch, George, quickly!' he yelled. 'We must see what we're doing. Goodness, here's Pongo now!'

Tiger Dan gave a yell of fright when the torch flashed on and he saw the chimpanzee making straight for him. He dealt the ape a smashing blow on the face that knocked him down, and then turned to run. Lou was trying to keep Timmy off his throat, kicking frantically at the excited dog.

Dan ran to the tunnel – and then stopped in astonishment. Four burly policemen were pushing their way out of the tunnel, led by Dick! One of them carried a revolver in his hand. Dan put his hands up at once.

'Timmy! Come off!' commanded George, seeing that there was now no need for the dog's delighted help. Timmy gave her a reproachful glance that said: 'Mistress! I'm really enjoying myself! Let me eat him all up!'

Then the dog caught sight of the four policemen and yelped furiously. More enemies! He would eat the lot.

'What's all this going on?' said the first man, who was an Inspector. 'Get up, you on the floor. Go on, get up!'

Lou got up with great difficulty. Timmy had nipped him in various places. His hair was over his eyes, his clothes were torn. He stared at the policemen, his mouth open in the utmost surprise. How had they come here? Then he saw Dick.

'So one of you kids slipped out – and shut the boards on us!' he said, savagely. 'I might have guessed. You . . .'

'Hold your tongue, Lewis Allburg,' rapped out the Inspector. 'You can talk when we tell you. You'll have quite a lot of talking to do, to explain some of the things we've heard about you.'

'Dick! How did you get here so soon?' cried Julian, going over to his brother. 'I didn't expect you for hours! Surely you didn't go all the way to the town and back?'

'No. I shot off to the farm, woke up the Mackies, used their telephone and got the police up here double-quick in their car,' said Dick, grinning. 'Everyone all right? Where's Anne? And Nobby?'

'There they are – just coming out of the tunnel, upstream,' said Julian, and swung his torch round. Dick saw Anne's white, scared face, and went over to her.

'It's all right,' he said. 'The adventure is over, Anne! You can smile again!'

Anne gave a watery sort of smile. Pongo took her hand

and made little affectionate noises, and that made her smile a little more. George called Timmy to her, afraid that he might take a last nip at Lou.

Lou swung round and stared at her. Then he looked at Dick and Julian. Then at Anne.

'So there *was* only one girl!' he said. 'What did you want to tell me there were two boys and two girls for?' he said to Nobby.

'Because there were,' answered Nobby. He pointed to George. 'She's a girl, though she looks like a boy. And she's as good as a boy any day.'

George felt proud. She stared defiantly at Lou. He was now in the grip of a stout policeman, and Tiger Dan was being hustled off by two more.

'I think we'll leave this rather gloomy place,' said the Inspector, putting away the notebook he had been hastily scribbling in. 'Quick march!'

Julian led the way down the tunnel. He pointed out the shelf where the men had stored their things, and the Inspector collected the few things that were still left. Then on they went, Tiger Dan muttering and growling to himself.

'Will they go to prison?' whispered Anne to Dick.

'You bet,' said Dick. 'That's where they ought to have gone long ago. Their burglaries have been worrying the police for four years!'

Out of the tunnel and into the cave with gleaming walls. Then down the hole and into the small cave and along the narrow passage to the entrance-hole. Stars glittered over the black hole, and the children were very thankful to see them. They were tired of being underground!

Lou and Dan did not have a very comfortable journey along the tunnels and passages, for their guards had a very firm hold of them indeed. Once out in the open they were handcuffed and put into the large police car that stood a little way down the track.

'What are you children going to do?' asked the big Inspector, who was now at the wheel of the car. 'Hadn't you better come down into the town with us after this disturbing adventure?'

'Oh, no thanks,' said Julian politely. 'We're quite used to adventures. We've had plenty, you know. We shall be all right here with Timmy and Pongo.'

'Well, I can't say I'd like a chimpanzee for company myself,' said the Inspector. 'We'll be up here in the morning, looking round and asking a few questions, which I'm sure you'll be pleased to answer. And many thanks for your help in capturing two dangerous thieves!'

'What about the wagon of goods?' asked Dick. 'Are you going to leave it up here? It's got lots of valuables in it.'

'Oh, one of the men is driving down,' said the Inspector, nodding towards a policeman, who stood nearby. 'He'll follow us. He can drive a horse all right. Well, look after yourselves. See you tomorrow!'

The car started up suddenly. The Inspector put her into gear, took off the brake and the car slid quietly down the hill, following the winding track. The policeman with the wagon followed slowly, clicking to the horse, which didn't seem at all surprised to have a new driver.

'Well, that's that!' said Julian thankfully. 'I must say we were well out of that. Gosh, Dick. I was glad to see you back with those bobbies so quickly. That was a brain wave of yours to telephone from the farm.'

Dick suddenly yawned. 'It must be frightfully late!' he said. 'Long past the middle of the night. But I'm so fearfully hungry that I simply must have something to eat before I fall into my bunk!'

'Got anything, Anne?' asked Julian.

Anne brightened up at once. 'I'll see,' she said. 'I can find something, I'm sure!'

And she did, of course. She opened two tins of sardines and made sandwiches, and she opened two tins of peaches, so they had a very nice meal in the middle of the night! They ate it sitting on the floor of George's caravan. Pongo had as good a meal as anyone, and Timmy crunched at one of his bones.

It didn't take them long to go to sleep that night. In fact they were all so sleepy when they had finished their meal that nobody undressed! They clambered into the bunks just as they were and fell asleep at once. Nobby curled up with Pongo, and Timmy, as usual, was on George's feet. Peace reigned in the caravans – and tonight no one came to disturb them!

All the children slept very late the next morning. They

were awakened by a loud knocking on Julian's caravan. He woke up with a jump and yelled out:

'Yes! Who is it?'

'It's us,' said a familiar voice, and the door opened. Farmer Mackie and his wife peeped in, looking rather anxious.

'We wondered what had happened,' said the farmer. 'You rushed out of the farmhouse when you had used the phone last night and didn't come back.'

'I ought to have slipped back and told you,' said Dick, sitting up with his hair over his eyes. He pushed it back. 'But I forgot. The police went down into the hills with us and got the two men. They're well-known burglars. The police got all the goods, too. It was a very thrilling night. Thanks most awfully for letting me use the phone.'

'You're very welcome,' said Mrs Mackie. 'And look – I've brought you some food.'

She had two baskets stacked with good things. Dick felt wide awake and very hungry when he saw them. 'Oh, thanks,' he said gratefully. 'You *are* a good sort!'

Nobby and Pongo suddenly uncurled themselves from their pile of rugs, and Mrs Mackie gave a squeal.

'Land-sakes, what's that? A monkey?'

'No, an ape, Mam,' said Nobby politely. 'He won't hurt you. Hey, take your hand out of that basket!'

Pongo, who had been hoping to find a little titbit unnoticed, covered his face with his hairy paw and looked through his fingers at Mrs Mackie.

'Look at that now – he's like a naughty child!' said Mrs Mackie. 'Isn't he, Ted?'

'He is that,' said the farmer. 'Strange sort of bed-fellow, I must say!'

'Well, I must be getting along,' said Mrs Mackie, nodding and smiling at George and Anne, who had now come out of their caravan with Timmy to see who the visitors were. 'You come along to the farm if you want anything. We'll be right pleased to see you.'

'Aren't they nice?' said Anne as the two farm-folk went down the cart-track. 'And oh, my goodness – what a breakfast we're going to have! Cold bacon – tomatoes – fresh radishes – curly lettuces – and who wants new honey?'

'Marvellous!' said Julian. 'Come on – let us have it now, before we clean up.'

But Anne made them wash and tidy themselves first! 'You'll enjoy it much more if you're clean,' she said. 'We all look as dirty as chimney sweeps! I'll give you five minutes – then you can come to a perfectly wonderful breakfast!'

'All right, Ma!' grinned Nobby, and he went off with the others to wash at the spring. Then back they all went to the sunny ledge to feast on the good things kind Mrs Mackie had provided.

CHAPTER TWENTY-THREE

Goodbye, Nobby – goodbye, caravanners!

BEFORE THEY had finished their breakfast the Inspector came roaring up the track in his powerful police car. There was one sharp-eyed policeman with him to take down notes.

'Hallo, hallo!' said the Inspector, eyeing the good things set out on the ledge. 'You seem to do yourselves well, I must say!'

'Have some new bread and honey,' said Anne in her best manner. 'Do! There's plenty!'

'Thanks,' said the Inspector, and sat down with the children. The other policeman wandered round the caravans, examining everything. The Inspector munched away at honey and bread, and the children talked to him, telling him all about their extraordinary adventure.

'It must have been a most unpleasant shock for those two fellows when they found that your caravan was immediately over the entrance to the place where they hid their stolen goods,' said the Inspector. 'Most unpleasant.'

'Have you examined the goods?' asked Dick eagerly. 'Are they very valuable?'

'Priceless,' answered the Inspector, taking another bit of bread and dabbing it thickly with honey. 'Quite priceless.

Those rogues apparently stole goods they knew to be of great value, hid them here for a year or two till the hue and cry had died down, then got them out and quietly disposed of them to friends in Holland and Belgium.'

'Tiger Dan used to act in circuses in Holland,' said Nobby. 'He often told me about them. He had friends all over Europe – people in the circus line, you know.'

'Yes. It was easy for him to dispose of his goods abroad,' said the Inspector. 'He planned to go across to Holland today, you know – got everything ready with Lou – or, to give him his right name, Lewis Allburg – and was going to sell most of those things. You just saved them in time!'

'What a bit of luck!' said George. 'They almost got away with it. If Dick hadn't managed to slip out when Pongo was attacking them, we'd still have been prisoners down in the hill, and Lou and Dan would have been half-way to Holland!'

'Smart bit of work you children did,' said the Inspector approvingly, and looked longingly at the honey-pot. 'That's fine honey, I must buy some from Mrs Mackie.'

'Have some more,' said Anne, remembering her manners. 'Do. We've got another loaf.'

'Well, I will,' said the Inspector, and took another slice of bread, spreading it with the yellow honey. It looked as if there wouldn't even be enough left for Pongo to lick out! Anne thought it was nice to see a grown-up enjoying bread and honey as much as children did.

'You know, that fellow Lou did some very remarkable burglaries,' said the Inspector. 'Once he got across from the third floor of one house to the third floor of another *across the street* – and nobody knows how!'

'That would be easy for Lou,' said Nobby, suddenly losing his fear of the big Inspector. 'He'd just throw a wire rope across, lasso something with the end of it, top of a gutter-pipe, perhaps, draw tight, and walk across! He's wonderful on the tight-rope. There ain't nothing he can't do on the tight-rope.'

'Yes – that's probably what he did,' said the Inspector.

'Never thought of that! No, thanks, I really won't have any more honey. That chimpanzee will eat me if I don't leave some for him to lick out!'

Pongo took away the jar, sat himself down behind one of the caravans, and put a large pink tongue into the remains of the honey. When Timmy came running up to see what he had got, Pongo held the jar high above his head and chattered at him.

'Yarra-yarra-yarra-yarra!' he said. Timmy looked rather surprised and went back to George. She was listening with great interest to what the Inspector had to tell them about the underground caves.

'They're very old,' he said. 'The entrance to them used to be some way down the hill, but there was a landslide and it was blocked up. Nobody bothered to unblock it because the caves were not particularly interesting.'

'Oh, but they *are*,' said Anne, 'especially the one with the gleaming walls.'

'Well, I imagine that quite by accident one day Dan and Lou found another way in,' said the Inspector. 'The way you know – a hole going down into the hill. They must have thought what a fine hiding-place it would make for any stolen goods – perfectly safe, perfectly dry, and quite near the camping place here each year. What could be better?'

'And I suppose they would have gone on burgling for years and hiding the stuff if we hadn't just happened to put our caravan over the very spot!' said Julian. 'What a bit of bad luck for them!'

'And what a bit of good luck for us!' said the Inspector. 'We did suspect those two, you know, and once or twice we raided the circus to try and find the goods – but they must always have got warning of our coming and got them away in time – up here!'

'Have you been down to the camp, mister?' asked Nobby suddenly.

The Inspector nodded. 'Oh, yes. We've been down already this morning – seen everyone and questioned them. We created quite a stir!'

Nobby looked gloomy.

'What's the matter, Nobby?' said Anne.

'I shan't half cop it when I get back to the camp,' said Nobby. 'They'll say it's all my fault the coppers going there. We don't like the bobbies round the camp. I shall get into a whole lot of trouble when I go back. I don't want to go back.'

Nobody said anything. They all wondered what would happen to poor Nobby now his Uncle Dan was in prison.

Then Anne asked him: 'Who will you live with now in the camp, Nobby?'

'Oh, somebody will take me in and work me hard,' said Nobby. 'I wouldn't mind if I could be with the horses – but Rossy won't let me. I know that. If I could be with horses I'd be happy. I love them and they understand me all right.'

'How old are you, Nobby?' asked the Inspector, joining in the talk. 'Oughtn't you to be going to school?'

'Never been in my life, mister,' said Nobby. 'I'm just over fourteen, so I reckon I never will go now!'

He grinned. He didn't look fourteen. He seemed more like twelve by his size. Then he looked solemn again.

'Reckon I won't go down to the camp today,' he said. 'I'll be proper set on by them all – about you going there and snooping round like. And Mr Gorgio, he won't like losing his best clown and best acrobat!'

'You can stay with us as long as you like,' said Julian. 'We'll be here a bit longer, anyway.'

But he was wrong. Just after the Inspector had left, taking his policeman with him, Mrs Mackie came hurrying up to them with a little orange envelope in her hand.

'The messenger boy's just been up,' she said. 'He was looking for you. He left this telegram for you. I hope it's not bad news.'

GOODBYE, NOBBY

Julian tore the envelope open and read the telegram out loud.

'AMAZED TO GET YOUR LETTER ABOUT THE EXTRAORDINARY HAPPENINGS YOU DESCRIBE. THEY SOUND DANGEROUS. COME HOME AT ONCE. DADDY.'

'Oh dear,' said Anne. 'Now we shall have to leave. What a pity!'

'I'd better go down to the town and telephone Daddy and tell him we're all right,' said Julian.

'You can phone from my house,' said Mrs Mackie, so Julian thought he would. They talked as they went along and suddenly a bright idea struck Julian.

'I say – I suppose Farmer Mackie doesn't want anyone to help him with his horses, does he?' he asked. 'He wouldn't want a boy who really loves and understands them and would work hard and well?'

'Well, now, I dare say he would,' said Mrs Mackie. 'He's a bit short-handed now. He was saying the other day he could do with a good lad, just leaving school.'

'Oh, *do* you think he'd try our friend Nobby from the circus camp?' said Julian. 'He's mad on horses. He can do anything with them. And he's been used to working very hard I'm sure he'd do well.'

Before Julian had left the farmhouse after telephoning to his amazed parents, he had had a long talk with Farmer Mackie – and now he was running back with the good news to the caravans.

'Nobby!' he shouted as he got near. 'Nobby! How

would you like to go and work for Farmer Mackie and help with the horses? He says you can start tomorrow if you like – and live at the farm!'

'Jumping Jiminy!' said Nobby, looking startled and disbelieving. 'At the farm? Work with the horses? Coo – I wouldn't half like that. But Farmer Mackie wouldn't have the likes of me.'

'He will. He says he'll try you,' said Julian. 'We've got to start back home tomorrow, and you can be with us till then. You don't need to go back to the camp at all.'

'Well – but what about Growler?' said Nobby. 'I'd have to have him with me. He's my dog. I expect poor old Barker's dead. Would the farmer mind me having a dog?'

'I shouldn't think so,' said Julian. 'Well, you'll have to go down to the camp, I suppose, to collect your few things – and to get Growler. Better go now, Nobby, and then you'll have the rest of the day with us.'

Nobby went off, his face shining with delight. 'Well, I never!' he kept saying to himself. 'Well, I never did! Dan and Lou gone, so they'll never hurt me again – and me not going to live in the camp any more – and going to have charge of them fine farm horses. Well, I never!'

The children had said goodbye to Pongo because he had to go back with Nobby to the camp. He belonged to Mr Gorgio, and Nobby could not possibly keep him. Anyway, it was certain that even if he could have kept him, Mrs Mackie wouldn't have let him live at the farm.

Pongo shook hands gravely with each one of them, even

with Timmy. He seemed to know it was goodbye. The children were really sorry to see the comical chimpanzee go. He had shared in their adventure with them and seemed much more like a human being than an animal.

When he had gone down the hill a little way he ran back to Anne. He put his arms round her and gave her a gentle squeeze, as if to say: 'You're all nice, the lot of you, but little Anne's the nicest!'

'Oh, Pongo, you're really a dear!' said Anne, and gave him a tomato. He ran off with it, leaping high for joy.

The children cleared up everything, put the breakfast things away, and cleaned the caravans, ready for starting off the next day. At dinner-time they looked out for Nobby. Surely he should be back soon?

They heard him whistling as he came up the track. He carried a bundle on his back. Round his feet ran two dogs. Two!

'Why – one of them is Barker!' shouted George in delight. 'He must have got better! How simply marvellous!'

Nobby came up, grinning. They all crowded round him, asking about Barker.

'Yes, it's fine, isn't it?' said Nobby, putting down his bundle of belongings. 'Lucilla dosed him all right. He almost died – then he started to wriggle a bit, she said, and the next she knew he was as lively as could be – bit weak on his legs at first – but he's fine this morning.'

Certainly there didn't seem anything wrong with Barker. He and Growler sniffed round Timmy, their tails wagging fast. Timmy stood towering above them, but his tail wagged, too, so Barker and Growler knew he was friendly.

'I was lucky,' said Nobby. 'I only spoke to Lucilla and Larry. Mr Gorgio has gone off to answer some questions at the police station, and so have some of the others. So I just told Larry to tell Mr Gorgio I was leaving, and I got my things and hopped it.'

'Well, now we can really enjoy our last day,' said Julian. 'Everybody's happy!'

And they did enjoy that last day. They went down to the lake and bathed. They had a fine farmhouse tea at Mrs Mackie's, by special invitation. They had a picnic supper on the rocky ledge, with the three dogs rolling over and over in play. Nobby felt sad to think he would so soon say goodbye to his 'posh' friends – but he couldn't help feeling proud and pleased to have a fine job of his own on the farm – with the horses he loved so much.

Nobby, Barker, Growler, Farmer Mackie and his wife all stood on the cart-track to wave goodbye to the two caravans the next morning.

'Goodbye!' yelled Nobby. 'Good luck! See you again some time!'

'Goodbye!' shouted the others. 'Give our love to Pongo when you see him.'

'Woof! woof!' barked Timmy, but only Barker and

Growler knew what *that* meant. It meant, 'Shake paws with Pongo for me!'

Goodbye, five caravanners . . . till your next exciting adventure!

Join the adventure!

If you can't wait to explore further with THE FAMOUS FIVE, read the next book in the series:

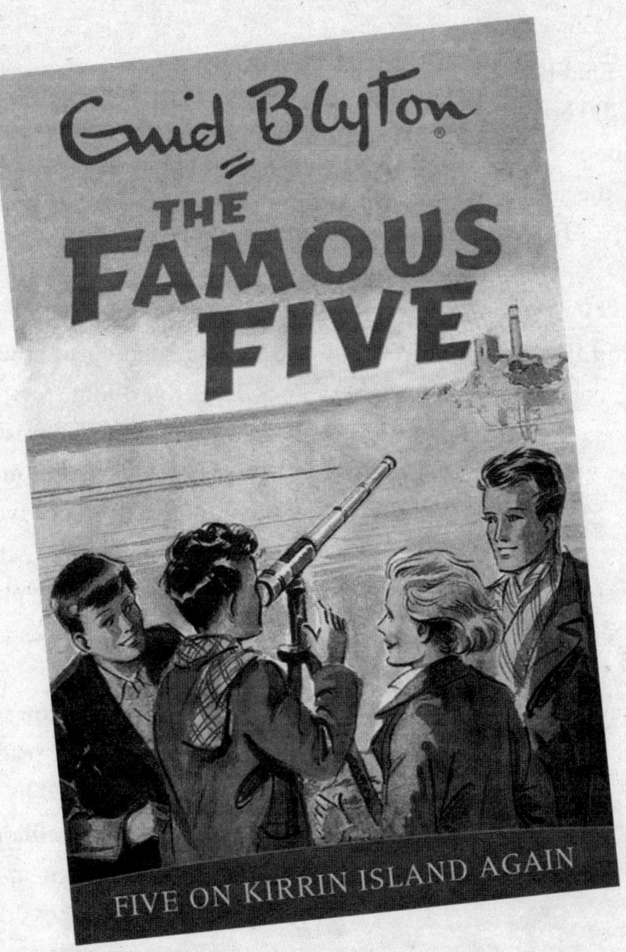

Enid Blyton®

is one of the most popular children's authors of all time. Her books have sold over 500 million copies and have been translated into other languages more often than any other children's author.

Enid Blyton adored writing for children. She wrote over 700 books and about 2,000 short stories. *The Famous Five* books, now 75 years old, are her most popular. She is also the author of other favourites including *The Secret Seven*, *The Magic Faraway Tree*, *Malory Towers* and *Noddy*.

Born in London in 1897, Enid lived much of her life in Buckinghamshire and loved dogs, gardening and the countryside. She was very knowledgeable about trees, flowers, birds and animals. Dorset – where some of the Famous Five's adventures are set – was a favourite place of hers too.

Enid Blyton's stories are read and loved by millions of children (and grown-ups) all over the world. Visit enidblyton.co.uk to discover more.

THE FAMOUS FIVE

FIVE ON KIRRIN ISLAND AGAIN

Have you read all THE FAMOUS FIVE books?

1. Five on a Treasure Island
2. Five Go Adventuring Again
3. Five Run Away Together
4. Five Go to Smuggler's Top
5. Five Go Off in a Caravan
6. Five on Kirrin Island Again
7. Five Go Off to Camp
8. Five Get Into Trouble
9. Five Fall Into Adventure
10. Five on a Hike Together
11. Five Have a Wonderful Time
12. Five Go Down to the Sea
13. Five Go to Mystery Moor
14. Five Have Plenty of Fun
15. Five on a Secret Trail
16. Five Go to Billycock Hill
17. Five Get Into a Fix
18. Five on Finniston Farm
19. Five Go to Demon's Rocks
20. Five Have a Mystery to Solve
21. Five Are Together Again

The Famous Five Colour Short Stories

1. Five and a Half-Term Adventure
2. George's Hair is Too Long
3. Good Old Timmy
4. A Lazy Afternoon
5. Well Done, Famous Five
6. Five Have a Puzzling Time
7. Happy Christmas, Five
8. When Timmy Chased the Cat

Enid Blyton®

THE FAMOUS FIVE

FIVE ON KIRRIN ISLAND AGAIN

Illustrated by Eileen A. Soper

HODDER CHILDREN'S BOOKS

First published in Great Britain in 1947 by Hodder & Stoughton
This edition published in 2016

21

A CIP catalogue record for this book is available from the British Library.

ISBN 978 1 444 93636 0

Printed and bound in Great Britain by Clays Ltd, Elcograf S.p.A.

The paper and board used in this book are made from wood from responsible sources.

Hodder Children's Books
An imprint of
Hachette Children's Group
Part of Hodder & Stoughton
Carmelite House
50 Victoria Embankment
London EC4Y 0DZ

An Hachette UK Company
www.hachette.co.uk
www.hachettechildrens.co.uk

CONTENTS

1	A LETTER FOR GEORGE	1
2	BACK AT KIRRIN COTTAGE	11
3	OFF TO KIRRIN ISLAND	20
4	WHERE IS UNCLE QUENTIN?	29
5	A MYSTERY	39
6	UP ON THE CLIFF	47
7	A LITTLE SQUABBLE	57
8	DOWN IN THE QUARRY	66
9	GEORGE MAKES A DISCOVERY – AND LOSES HER TEMPER	75
10	A SURPRISING SIGNAL	85
11	GEORGE MAKES A HARD CHOICE	94
12	THE OLD MAP AGAIN	103
13	AFTERNOON WITH MARTIN	112
14	A SHOCK FOR GEORGE	121
15	IN THE MIDDLE OF THE NIGHT	130
16	DOWN TO THE CAVES	140
17	TIMMY AT LAST	149
18	HALF PAST FOUR IN THE MORNING	161
19	A MEETING WITH MARTIN	169
20	EVERYTHING BOILS UP!	179
21	THE END OF THE ADVENTURE	189

CHAPTER ONE

A letter for George

ANNE WAS trying to do some of her prep in a corner of the common room when her cousin George came bursting in.

George was not a boy; she was a girl called Georgina, but because she had always wanted to be a boy she insisted on being called George. So George she was. She wore her curly hair cut short, and her bright blue eyes gleamed angrily now as she came towards Anne.

'Anne! I've just had a letter from home – and what do you think? Father wants to go and live on my island to do some special work – and he wants to build a sort of tower or something in the castle yard!'

The other girls looked up in amusement, and Anne held out her hand for the letter that George was waving at her. Everyone knew about the little island off Kirrin Bay that belonged to George. Kirrin Island was a tiny place with an old ruined castle in the middle of it: the home of rabbits and gulls and jackdaws.

It had underground dungeons in which George and her cousins had had one or two amazing adventures. It had once belonged to George's mother, and she had given it to George – and George was very fierce where her precious Kirrin Island was concerned! It was *hers*.

Nobody else must live there, or even land there without her permission.

And now, dear me, here was her father proposing to go to her island, and even build some sort of workshop there! George was red with exasperation.

'It's just like grown-ups; they go and give you things and then act as though the things were theirs all the time. I don't *want* Father living on my island, and building nasty messy sheds and things there.'

'Oh, George – you know your father is a very famous scientist, who needs to work in peace,' said Anne, taking the letter. 'Surely you can lend him your island for a bit?'

'There are plenty of other places where he can work in peace,' said George. 'Oh dear – I was so hoping we could go and stay there in the Easter hols – take our boat there, and food and everything, just like we've done before. Now we shan't be able to if Father really does go there.'

Anne read the letter. It was from George's mother.

'*My darling George,*

'I think I must tell you at once that your father proposes to live on Kirrin Island for some little time in order to finish some very important experiments he is making. He will have to have some kind of building erected there – a sort of tower, I believe. Apparently he needs a place where he can have absolute peace and isolation, and also, for some reason, where there is water

all around him. The fact of being surrounded by water is necessary to his experiment.

'Now, dear, don't be upset about this. I know that you consider Kirrin Island is your very own, but you must allow your family to share it, especially when it is for something as important as your father's scientific work. Father thinks you will be very pleased indeed to lend him Kirrin Island, but I know your funny feeling about it, so I thought I had better write and tell you, before you arrive home and see him installed there, complete with his tower.'

The letter then went on about other things, but Anne did not bother to read these. She looked at George.

'Oh, George! I don't see why you mind your father borrowing Kirrin Island for a bit! I wouldn't mind *my* father borrowing an island from me – if I was lucky enough to have one!'

'*Your* father would talk to you about it first, and ask your permission, and see if you minded,' said George, sulkily. 'My father never does anything like that. He just does exactly as he likes without asking anybody anything. I really do think he might have written to me himself. He just puts my back up.'

'You've got a back that is very easily put up, George,' said Anne, laughing. 'Don't scowl at me like that. *I'm* not borrowing your island without your gracious permission.'

But George wouldn't smile back. She took her letter and read it again gloomily. 'To think that all my lovely holiday plans are spoilt!' she said. 'You know how super Kirrin Island is at Easter time – all primroses and gorse and baby rabbits. And you and Julian and Dick were coming to stay, and we haven't stayed together since last summer when we went caravanning.'

'I know. It *is* hard luck!' said Anne. 'It would have been wizard to go and stay on the island these hols. But perhaps your father wouldn't mind if we did? We needn't disturb him.'

'As if living on Kirrin Island with Father there would be

the same as living there all by ourselves,' said George, scornfully. 'You know it would be horrid.'

Well, yes – Anne didn't think on the whole that Kirrin Island would be much fun with Uncle Quentin there. George's father was such a hot-tempered, impatient man, and when he was in the middle of one of his experiments he was quite unbearable. The least noise upset him.

'Oh dear – how he will yell at the jackdaws to keep quiet, and shout at the noisy gulls!' said Anne, beginning to giggle. 'He won't find Kirrin quite so peaceful as he imagines!'

George gave a watery sort of smile. She folded up the letter and turned away. 'Well, I think it's just the limit,' she said. 'I wouldn't have felt so bad if only Father had asked my permission.'

'He'd never do that!' said Anne. 'It just wouldn't occur to him. Now, George, don't spend the rest of the day brooding over your wrongs, for goodness' sake. Go down to the kennels and fetch Timmy. He'll soon cheer you up.'

Timothy was George's dog, whom she loved with all her heart. He was a big scruffy brown mongrel dog, with a ridiculously long tail, and a wide mouth that really seemed to smile. All the four cousins loved him. He was so friendly and loving, so lively and amusing, and he had shared so very many adventures with them all. The five of them had had many happy times together.

George went to get Timmy. Her school allowed the children to keep their own pets. If it hadn't allowed this, it is quite certain that George would not have gone to boarding school! She could not bear to be parted from Timmy for even a day.

Timmy began to bark excitedly as soon as she came near. George lost her sulky look and smiled. Dear Timmy, dear trustable Timmy – he was better than any person! He was always on her side, always her friend whatever she did,

and to Timmy there was no one in the world so wonderful as George.

They were soon going through the fields together, and George talked to Timmy as she always did. She told him about her father borrowing Kirrin Island. Timmy agreed with every word she said. He listened as if he understood everything, and not even when a rabbit shot across his path did he leave his mistress's side. Timmy always knew when George was upset.

He gave her hand a few little licks every now and again. By the time that George was back at school again she felt much better. She took Timmy into school with her, smuggling him in at a side door. Dogs were not allowed in the school building, but George, like her father, often did exactly as she liked.

She hurried Timmy up to her dormitory. He scuttled under her bed quickly and lay down. His tail thumped the floor gently. He knew what this meant. George wanted the comfort of his nearness that night! He would be able to jump on her bed, when lights were out, and snuggle into the crook of her knees. His brown eyes gleamed with delight.

'Now, lie quiet,' said George, and went out of the room to join the other girls. She found Anne, who was busy writing a letter to her brothers, Julian and Dick, at their boarding school.

'I've told them about Kirrin Island, and your father wanting to borrow it,' she said. 'Would you like to come and stay with *us*, George, these hols, instead of us coming to Kirrin? Then you won't feel cross all the time because your father is on your island.'

'No thanks,' said George, at once. 'I'm going home. I want to keep an eye on Father! I don't want him blowing up Kirrin Island with one of his experiments. You know he's messing about with explosives now, don't you?'

'Ooooh – atom bombs, or things like that?' said Anne.

'I don't know,' said George. 'Anyway, quite apart from keeping an eye on Father and my island, we ought to go and stay at Kirrin to keep Mother company. She'll be all alone if Father's on the island. I suppose he'll take food and everything there.'

'Well, there's one thing, we shan't have to creep about on tiptoe and whisper, if your father isn't at Kirrin Cottage!' said Anne. 'We can be as noisy as we like. Do cheer up, George!'

But it took George quite a long time to get over the fit of gloom caused by her mother's letter. Even having Timmy on her bed each night, till he was discovered by an angry teacher, did not quite make up for her disappointment.

The term ran swiftly on to its end. April came in, with sunshine and showers. Holidays came nearer and nearer! Anne thought joyfully of Kirrin, with its lovely sandy beach, its blue sea, its fishing-boats and its lovely cliffside walks.

Julian and Dick thought longingly of them too. This term both they and the girls broke up on the same day.

They could meet in London and travel down to Kirrin together. Hurrah!

The day came at last. Trunks were piled in the hall. Cars arrived to fetch some of the children who lived fairly near. The school coaches drew up to take the others down to the station. There was a terrific noise of yelling and shouting everywhere. The teachers could not make themselves heard in the din.

'Anyone would think that every single child had gone completely mad,' said one of them to another. 'Oh, thank goodness, they're getting into the coaches. George! *Must* you rush along the corridor at sixty miles an hour, with Timmy barking his head off all the time!'

'Yes, I must, I must!' cried George. 'Anne, where are you? Do come and get into the coach. I've got Timmy. He knows it's holidays now. Come on, Tim!'

Down to the station went the singing crowd of children. They piled into the train. 'Bags I this seat! Who's taken my bag? Get out, Hetty, you know you can't bring your dog in here with mine. They fight like anything. Hurrah, the guard's blowing his whistle! We're off!'

The engine pulled slowly out of the station, its long train of carriages behind it, filled to bursting with girls off for their holidays. Through the quiet countryside it went, through small towns and villages, and at last ran through the smoky outskirts of London.

'The boys' train is due in two minutes before ours,' said Anne, leaning out of the window, as the train drew slowly into the London station. 'If it was punctual, they might be on our platform to meet us. Oh look, George, look – there they are!'

George hung out of the window too. 'Hi, Julian!' she yelled. 'Here we are! Hi, Dick, Julian!'

CHAPTER TWO

Back at Kirrin Cottage

JULIAN, DICK, Anne, George and Timmy went straight away to have buns and ginger-beer at the station tearoom. It was good to be all together again. Timmy went nearly mad with joy at seeing the two boys. He kept trying to get on to their knees.

'Look here, Timmy, old thing, I love you very much and I'm jolly glad to see you,' said Dick, 'but that's twice you've upset my ginger-beer all over me. Has he behaved himself this term, George?'

'Fairly well,' said George, considering. 'Hasn't he, Anne? I mean – he only got the joint out of the larder once – and he didn't do so *much* harm to that cushion he chewed – and if people *will* leave their galoshes all over the place nobody can blame Timmy for having a good old game with them.'

'And that was the end of the galoshes, I suppose,' said Julian, with a grin. 'On the whole, Timmy, you have a rather poor report. I'm afraid our Uncle Quentin will not award you the usual twenty-five pence we get for good reports.'

At the mention of her father, George scowled. 'I see George has not lost her pretty scowl,' said Dick, in a teasing voice. 'Dear old George! We shouldn't know her unless she put on that fearsome scowl half a dozen times a day!'

'Oh, she's better than she was,' said Anne hurrying to George's defence at once. George was not so touchy as she had once been, when she was being teased. All the same, Anne knew that there might be sparks flying over her father taking Kirrin Island these holidays, and she didn't want George to fly into a temper too soon!

Julian looked at his cousin. 'I say, old thing, you're not going to take this business of Kirrin Island too much to heart, are you?' he said. 'You've just got to realise that your father's a remarkably clever man, one of the finest scientists we've got – and *I* think that those kind of fellows ought to be allowed as much freedom as they like, for their work. I mean – if Uncle Quentin wants to work on Kirrin Island for some peculiar reason of his own, then you ought to be pleased to say "Go ahead, Father!"'

George looked a little mutinous after this rather long speech; but she thought a great deal of Julian, and usually went by what he said. He was older than any of them, a tall, good-looking boy, with determined eyes and a strong chin. George scratched Timmy's head, and spoke in a low voice.

'All right. I won't go up in smoke about it, Julian. But I'm frightfully disappointed. I'd planned to go to Kirrin Island ourselves these hols.'

'Well, we're all disappointed,' said Julian. 'Buck up

with your bun, old thing. We've got to get across London and catch the train for Kirrin. We shall miss it if we don't look out.'

Soon they were in the train for Kirrin. Julian was very good at getting porters and taxis. Anne gazed admiringly at her big brother as he found them all corner-seats in a carriage. Julian did know how to tackle things!

'Do you think I've grown, Julian?' she asked him. 'I did hope I'd be as tall as George by the end of this term, but she grew too!'

'Well, I should think you might be a quarter of an inch taller than last term,' said Julian. 'You can't catch us up, Anne – you'll always be the smallest! But I like you small.'

'Look at Timmy, putting his head out of the window as usual!' said Dick. 'Timmy you'll get grit in your eye. Then George will go quite mad with grief!'

'Woof,' said Timmy, and wagged his tail. That was the nice part about Timmy. He always knew when he was being spoken to, even if his name was not mentioned, and he answered at once.

Aunt Fanny was at the station to meet them in the ponytrap. The children flung themselves on her, for they were very fond of her. She was kind and gentle, and did her best to keep her clever, impatient husband from finding too much fault with the children.

'How's Uncle Quentin?' asked Julian, politely, when they were setting off in the trap.

'He's very well,' said his aunt. 'And terribly excited.

Really, I've never known him to be so thrilled as he has been lately. His work has been coming along very successfully.'

'I suppose you don't know what his latest experiment is?' said Dick.

'Oh no. He never tells me a word,' said Aunt Fanny. 'He never tells anyone anything while he is at work, except his colleagues, of course. But I do know it's very important – and I know, of course, that the last part of the experiment has to be made in a place where there is deep water all round. Don't ask me why! I don't know.'

'Look! There's Kirrin Island!' said Anne, suddenly. They had rounded a corner, and had come in sight of the bay. Guarding the entrance to it was the curious little island topped by the old ruined castle. The sun shone down on the blue sea, and the island looked most enchanting.

George looked earnestly at it. She was looking for the building, whatever it was, that her father said he needed for his work. Everyone looked at the island, seeking the same thing.

They saw it easily enough! Rising from the centre of the castle, probably from the castle yard, was a tall thin tower, rather like a lighthouse. At the top was a glass-enclosed room, which glittered in the sun.

'Oh, Mother! I don't like it! It spoils Kirrin Island,' said George, in dismay.

'Darling, it can come down when your father has finished his work,' said her mother. 'It's a very flimsy,

temporary thing. It can easily be pulled down. Father promised me he would scrap it as soon as his work was done. He says you can go across and see it, if you like. It's really rather interesting.'

'Ooooh – I'd *love* to go and see it,' said Anne, at once. 'It looks so strange. Is Uncle Quentin all alone on Kirrin Island, Aunt Fanny?'

'Yes, I don't like him to be alone,' said her aunt. 'For one thing I am sure he doesn't get his meals properly, and for another, I'm always afraid some harm might come to him when he's experimenting – and if he's alone, how would I know if anything happened to him?'

'Well, Aunt Fanny, you could always arrange for him to signal to you each morning and night, couldn't you?' said Julian, sensibly. 'He could use that tower easily. He could flash a signal to you in the morning, using a mirror, you know – heliographing that he was all right – and at night he could signal with a lamp. Easy!'

'Yes. I did suggest that sort of thing,' said his aunt. 'I said I'd go over with you all tomorrow, to see him and perhaps, Julian dear, you could arrange something of the sort with your uncle? He seems to listen to you now.'

'Gracious! Do you mean to say Father wants us to invade his secret lair, and actually to see his strange tower?' asked George, surprised. 'Well – I don't think I want to go. After all, it's *my* island – and it's horrid to see someone else taking possession of it.'

'Oh, George, don't begin all that again,' said Anne, with a sigh. 'You and your island! Can't you even *lend* it to your own father! Aunt Fanny, you should have seen George when your letter came. She looked so fierce that I was quite scared!'

Everyone laughed except George and Aunt Fanny. She looked distressed. George was always so difficult! She found fault with her father, and got up against him time after time – but dear me, how very, very like him she was, with her scowls, her sudden temper, and her fierceness! If only George was as sweet-tempered and as easy-going as these three cousins of hers!

George looked at her mother's troubled face, and felt ashamed of herself. She put her hand on her knee. 'It's all right, Mother! I won't make a fuss. I'll try and keep my feelings to myself, really I will. I know Father's work is important. I'll go with you to the island tomorrow.'

Julian gave George a gentle clap on the back. 'Good old George! She's actually learnt, not only to give in, but to give in gracefully! George, you're more like a boy than ever when you act like that.'

George glowed. She liked Julian to say she was like a boy. But Anne looked a little indignant.

'It isn't *only* boys that can learn to give in decently, and things like that,' she said. 'Heaps of girls do. Well, I jolly well hope I do myself!'

'My goodness, here's another fire-brand!' said Aunt Fanny, smiling. 'Stop arguing now, all of you – here's

Kirrin Cottage. Doesn't it look sweet with all the primroses in the garden, and the wallflowers coming out, and the daffodils peeping everywhere?'

It certainly did. The four children and Timmy tore in at the front gate, delighted to be back. They clattered into the house, and, to their great delight, found Joanna, the old cook there. She had come back to help for the holidays. She beamed at the children, and fondled Timmy when he leapt round her barking.

'Well, there now! Haven't you all grown again? How big you are, Julian – taller than I am, I'd say. And little Anne, why, she's getting quite big.'

That pleased Anne, of course. Julian went back to the front door to help his aunt with the small bags in the trap. The trunks were coming later. Julian and Dick took everything upstairs.

Anne joined them, eager to see her old bedroom again. Oh, how good it was to be in Kirrin Cottage once more! She looked out of the windows. One looked on to the moor at the back. The other looked sideways on to the sea. Lovely! Lovely! She began to sing a little song as she undid her bag.

'You know,' she said to Dick, when he brought George's bag in, 'you know, Dick, I'm really quite pleased that Uncle Quentin has gone to Kirrin Island, even if it means we won't be able to go there much! I feel much freer in the house when he's away. He's a very clever man and he can be awfully nice – but I always feel a bit afraid of him.'

Dick laughed. 'I'm not afraid of him – but he's a bit of a wet blanket in a house, I must say, when we're here for the holidays. Funny to think of him on Kirrin Island all alone.'

A voice came up the stairs. 'Come down to tea, children, because there are hot scones for you, just out of the oven.'

'Coming, Aunt Fanny!' called Dick. 'Hurry, Anne. I'm awfully hungry. Julian, did you hear Aunt Fanny calling?'

George came up the stairs to fetch Anne. She was pleased to be home, and as for Timmy, he was engaged in going round every single corner of the house, sniffing vigorously.

'He always does that!' said George. 'As if he thought that there *might* be a chair or a table that didn't smell quite the same as it always did. Come on, Tim. Tea-time! Mother, as Father isn't here, can Timmy sit beside me on the floor? He's awfully well-behaved now.'

'Very well,' said her mother, and tea began. What a tea! It looked as if it was a spread for a party of twenty. Good old Joanna! She must have baked all day. Well, there wouldn't be much left when the Five had finished!

CHAPTER THREE

Off to Kirrin Island

NEXT DAY was fine and warm. 'We can go across to the island this morning,' said Aunt Fanny. 'We'll take our own food, because I'm sure Uncle Quentin will have forgotten we're coming.'

'Has he a boat there?' asked George. 'Mother – he hasn't taken *my* boat, has he?'

'No, dear,' said her mother. 'He's got another boat. I was afraid he would never be able to get it in and out of all those dangerous rocks round the island, but he got one of the fishermen to take him, and had his own boat towed behind, with all its stuff in.'

'Who built the tower?' asked Julian.

'Oh, he made out the plans himself and some men were sent down from the Ministry of Research to put the tower up for him,' said Aunt Fanny. 'It was all rather hush-hush really. The people here were most curious about it, but they don't know any more than I do! No local man helped in the building, but one or two fishermen were hired to take the material to the island, and to land the men and so on.'

'It's all very mysterious,' said Julian. 'Uncle Quentin leads rather an exciting life, really, doesn't he? I wouldn't mind being a scientist myself. I want to be something really worthwhile when I grow up – I'm not just going into somebody's office. I'm going to be on my own.'

'I think I shall be a doctor,' said Dick.

'I'm off to get my boat,' said George, rather bored with this talk. She knew what *she* was going to do when she was grown-up – live on Kirrin Island with Timmy!

Aunt Fanny had got ready plenty of food to take across to the island. She was quite looking forward to the trip. She had not seen her husband for some days, and was anxious to know that he was all right.

They all went down to the beach, Julian carrying the bag of food. George was already there with her boat. James, a fisher-boy friend of George's, was there too, ready to push the boat out for them.

He grinned at the children. He knew them all well. In the old days he had looked after Timmy for George when her father had said the dog must be given away. George had never forgotten James's kindness to Timmy, and always went to see him every holidays.

'Going off to the island?' said James. 'That's a strange thing in the middle of it, isn't it? Kind of lighthouse, it looks. Take my hand, and let me help you in.'

Anne took his hand and jumped into the boat. George was already there with Timmy. Soon they were all in. Julian and George took the oars. James gave them a shove and off they went on the calm, clear water. Anne could see every stone on the bottom!

Julian and George rowed strongly. They sent the boat along swiftly. George began to sing a rowing song and they all took it up. It was lovely to be on the sea in a boat again. Oh holidays, go slowly, don't rush away too fast!

'George,' said her mother nervously, as they came near to Kirrin Island, 'you *will* be careful of these awful rocks, won't you? The water's so clear today that I can see them all – and some of them are only just below the water.'

'Oh, Mother! You know I've rowed hundreds of times to Kirrin Island!' laughed George. 'I simply *couldn't* go on a rock! I know them all, really I do. I could almost row blindfold to the island now.'

There was only one place to land on the island in safety. This was a little cove, a natural little harbour running up to a stretch of sand. It was sheltered by high rocks all round. George and Julian worked their way to the east side of the island, rounded a low wall of very sharp rocks, and there lay the cove, a smooth inlet of water running into the shore!

Anne had been looking at the island as the others rowed. There was the old ruined Kirrin Castle in the centre, just the same as ever. Its tumbledown towers were full of jackdaws as usual. Its old walls were gripped by ivy.

'It's a lovely place!' said Anne, with a sigh. Then she gazed at the curious tower that now rose from the centre of the castle yard. It was not built of brick but some smooth, shiny material, which was fitted together in sections. Evidently the tower had been made in that way so that it might be brought to the island easily, and set up there quickly.

'Isn't it strange?' said Dick. 'Look at that little glass room at the top – like a look-out room! I wonder what it's for?

'Can anyone climb up inside the tower?' asked Dick, turning to Aunt Fanny.

'Oh yes. There is a narrow spiral staircase inside,' said his aunt. 'That's about all there is inside the tower itself. It's the little room at the top that is important. It has got some extraordinary wiring there, essential to your uncle's experiments. I don't think he *does* anything with the tower – it just has to be there, doing something on its own, which has a certain effect on the experiments he is making.'

Anne couldn't follow this. It sounded too complicated. 'I should like to go up the tower,' she said.

'Well, perhaps your uncle will let you,' said her aunt.

'If he's in a good temper,' said George.

'Now, George – you're not to say things like that,' said her mother.

The boat ran into the little harbour, and grounded softly. There was another boat there already – Uncle Quentin's.

George leapt out with Julian and they pulled it up a little further, so that the others could get out without wetting their feet. Out they all got, and Timmy ran up the beach in delight.

'Now, Timmy!' said George, warningly, and Timmy turned a despairing eye on his mistress. Surely she wasn't going to stop him looking to see if there were any rabbits? Only just *looking*! What harm was there in that?

Ah – there was a rabbit! And another and another! They sat all about, looking at the little company coming up from the shore. They flicked their ears and twitched their noses, keeping quite still.

'Oh, they're as tame as ever!' said Anne in delight. 'Aunty Fanny, aren't they lovely? Do look at the baby one over there. He's washing his face!'

They stopped to look at the rabbits. They really were astonishingly tame. But then very few people came to Kirrin Island, and the rabbits multiplied in peace, running about where they liked, quite unafraid.

'Oh, that one is . . .' began Dick, but then the picture was spoilt. Timmy, quite unable to do nothing but look, had suddenly lost his self-control and was bounding on the surprised rabbits. In a trice nothing could be seen but white bobtails flashing up and down as rabbit after rabbit rushed to its burrow.

'*Timmy!*' called George, crossly, and poor Timmy put his tail down, looking round at George miserably. 'What!' he seemed to say. 'Not even a scamper after the rabbits? What a hard-hearted mistress!'

'Where's Uncle Quentin?' asked Anne, as they walked to the great broken archway that was the entrance to the old castle. Behind it were the stone steps that led towards the centre. They were broken and irregular now. Aunt Fanny went across them carefully, afraid of stumbling, but the children, who were wearing rubber shoes, ran over them quickly.

They passed through an old ruined doorway into what looked like a great yard. Once there had been a stone-paved floor, but now most of it was covered by sand, and by close-growing weeds or grass.

The castle had had two towers. One was almost a complete ruin. The other was in better shape Jackdaws circled round it, and flew above the children's heads, crying ‘chack, chack, chack’.

‘I suppose your father lives in the little old room with the two slit-like windows,’ said Dick to George. ‘That’s the only place in the castle that would give him any shelter. Everywhere else is in ruins except that one room. Do you remember we once spent a night there?’

‘Yes,’ said George. ‘It was fun. I suppose that’s where Father lives. There’s nowhere else – unless he’s down in the dungeons!’

‘Oh, no one would live in the dungeons surely, unless they simply *had* to!’ said Julian. ‘They’re so dark and cold. Where *is* your father, George? I can’t see him anywhere.’

‘Mother, where would Father be?’ asked George. ‘Where’s his workshop – in that old room there?’ She pointed to the dark, stone-walled, stone-roofed room, which was really all that was left of the part in which people had long ago lived. It jutted out from what had once been the wall of the castle.

‘Well, really, I don’t exactly know,’ said her mother. ‘I suppose he works over there. He’s always met me down at the cove, and we’ve just sat on the sand and had a picnic and talked. He didn’t seem to want me to poke round much.’

‘Let’s call him,’ said Dick. So they shouted loudly.

‘Uncle QUEN-tin! Uncle QUEN-tin! Where are you?’

The jackdaws flew up in fright, and a few gulls, who had been sitting on part of the ruined wall, joined in the noise, crying ‘ee-oo, ee-oo, ee-oo’ over and over again.

Every rabbit disappeared in a trice.

No Uncle Quentin appeared. They shouted again.

'UNCLE QUENTIN! WHERE ARE YOU?'

'What a noise!' said Aunt Fanny, covering her ears. 'I should think that Joanna must have heard that at home. Oh dear – where is your uncle? This is most annoying of him. I *told* him I'd bring you across today.'

'Oh well – he must be somewhere about,' said Julian, cheerfully. 'If Mohammed won't come to the mountain, then the mountain must go to Mohammed. I expect he's deep in some book or other. We'll hunt for him.'

'We'll look in that little dark room,' said Anne. So they all went through the stone doorway, and found themselves in a little dark room, lit only by two slits of windows. At one end was a space, or recess, where a fireplace had once been, going back into the thick stone wall.

'He's not here,' said Julian in surprise. 'And what's more – there's nothing here at all! No food, no clothes, no books, no stores of any sort. This is not his workroom, nor even his store!'

'Then he must be down in the dungeons,' said Dick. 'Perhaps it's necessary to his work to be underground – and with water all round! Let's go and find the entrance. We know where it is – not far from the old well in the middle of the yard.'

'Yes. He must be down in the dungeons. Mustn't he, Aunt Fanny?' said Anne. 'Are you coming down?'

'Oh no,' said her aunt. 'I can't bear those dungeons. I'll

sit out here in the sun, in this sheltered corner, and unpack the sandwiches. It's almost lunch-time.'

'Oh good,' said everyone. They went towards the dungeon entrance. They expected to see the big flat stone that covered the entrance, standing upright, so that they might go down the steps underground.

But the stone was lying flat. Julian was just about to pull on the iron ring to lift it up when he noticed something peculiar.

'Look,' he said. 'There are weeds growing round the edges of the stone. Nobody has lifted it for a long time. Uncle Quentin isn't down in the dungeons!'

'Then where *is* he?' said Dick. 'Wherever *can* he be?'

CHAPTER FOUR

Where is Uncle Quentin?

THE FOUR of them, with Timmy nosing round their legs, stood staring down at the big stone that hid the entrance to the dungeons. Julian was perfectly right. The stone could not have been lifted for months, because weeds had grown closely round the edges, sending their small roots into every crack.

'No one is down there,' said Julian. 'We need not even bother to pull up the stone and go down to see. If it had been lifted lately, those weeds would have been torn up as it was raised.'

'And anyway, we know that no one can get *out* of the dungeon once the entrance stone is closing it,' said Dick. 'It's too heavy. Uncle Quentin wouldn't be silly enough to shut himself in! He'd leave it open.'

'Of course he would,' said Anne. 'Well – he's not there, then. He must be somewhere else.'

'But *where*?' said George. 'This is only a small island, and we know every corner of it. Oh – would he be in that cave we hid in once? The only cave on the island.'

'Oh yes – he might be,' said Julian. 'But I doubt it. I can't see Uncle Quentin dropping down through the hole in the cave's roof – and that's the only way of getting into it unless you're going to clamber and slide about the rocks on the shore for ages. I can't see him doing that, either.'

They made their way beyond the castle to the other side of the island. Here there was a cave they had once lived in. It could be entered with difficulty on the seaward side, as Julian had said, by clambering over slippery rocks, or it could be entered by dropping down a rope through a hole in the roof to the floor some way below.

They found the hole, half hidden in old heather. Julian felt about. The rope was still there. 'I'll slide down and have a look,' he said.

He went down the rope. It was knotted at intervals so that his feet found holding-places and he did not slide down too quickly and scorch his hands.

He was soon in the cave. A dim light came in from the seaward side. Julian took a quick look round. There was absolutely nothing there at all, except for an old box that they must have left behind when they were last here themselves.

He climbed up the rope again, his head appearing suddenly out of the hole. Dick gave him a hand.

'Well?' he said. 'Any sign of Uncle Quentin?'

'No,' said Julian. 'He's not there, and hasn't been there either, I should think. It's a mystery! Where is he, and if he's really doing important work where is all his stuff? I mean, we know that plenty of stuff was brought here because Aunt Fanny told us so.'

'Do you think he's in the tower?' said Anne, suddenly. 'He might be in that glass room at the top.'

'Well, he'd see us at once, if he were!' said Julian, scornfully. '*And* hear our yells too! Still, we might as well have a look.'

So back to the castle they went and walked to the peculiar tower. Their aunt saw them and called to them. 'Your lunch is ready. Come and have it. Your uncle will turn up, I expect.'

'But Aunt Fanny where is he?' said Anne, with a puzzled face. 'We've looked simply *everywhere*!'

Her aunt did not know the island as well as the children did. She imagined that there were plenty of places to shelter in, or to work in. 'Never mind,' she said, looking quite undisturbed. 'He'll turn up later. You come along and have your meal.'

'We think we'll go up the tower,' said Julian. 'Just in case he's up there working.'

The four children and Timmy went to where the tower rose up from the castle yard. They ran their hands over the smooth, shining sections, which were fitted together in curving rows. 'What's this stuff it's built of?' said Dick.

'Some kind of new plastic material, I should think,' said Julian. 'Very light and strong, and easily put together.'

'I should be afraid it would blow down in a gale,' said George.

'Yes, so should I,' said Dick. 'Look – here is the door.'

The door was small, and rounded at the top. A key was

in the keyhole. Julian turned it and unlocked the door. It opened outwards not inwards. Julian put his head inside and looked round.

There was not much room in the tower. A spiral staircase, made of the same shiny stuff as the tower itself, wound up and up and up. There was a space at one side of it, into which projected curious hook-like objects made of what looked like steel. Wire ran from one to the other.

'Better not touch them,' said Julian, looking curiously at them. 'Goodness, this is like a tower out of a fairy-tale. Come on – I'm going up the stairs to the top.'

He began to climb the steep, spiral stairway. It made him quite giddy to go up and round, up and round so many, many times.

The others followed him. Tiny, slit-like windows, set sideways not downwards, were let into the side of the tower here and there, and gave a little light to the stairway. Julian looked through one, and had a wonderful view of the sea and the mainland.

He went on up to the top. When he got there he found himself in a small round room, whose sides were of thick, gleaming glass. Wires ran right into the glass itself, and then pierced through it, the free ends waving and glittering in the strong wind that blew round the tower.

There was nothing in the little room at all! Certainly Uncle Quentin was not there. It was clearly only a tower meant to take the wires up on the hook-like things, and to run them through the strange, thick glass at the top, and set them free in the air. What for? Were they catching some kind of wireless waves? Was it to do with radar? Julian wondered, frowning, what was the meaning of the tower and the thin, shining wires?

The others crowded into the little room. Timmy came too, having managed the spiral stairs with difficulty.

'Gracious! What a weird place!' said George. 'My goodness, what a view we've got from here. We can see miles and miles out to sea – and on this other side we can see miles and miles across the bay, over the mainland to the hills beyond.'

'Yes. It's lovely,' said Anne. 'But – *where* is Uncle Quentin? We still haven't found him. I suppose he *is* on the island.'

'Well, his boat was pulled up in the cove,' said George. 'We saw it.'

'Then he must be here somewhere,' said Dick. 'But he's not in the castle, he's not in the dungeons, he's not in the cave and he's not up here. It's a first-class mystery.'

'The Missing Uncle. Where is he?' said Julian. 'Look, there's poor Aunt Fanny still down there, waiting with the lunch. We'd better go down. She's signalling to us.'

'I should like to,' said Anne. 'It's an awful squash in this tiny glass room. I say – did you feel the tower sway then, when that gust of wind shook it? I'm going down quickly, before the whole thing blows over!'

She began to go down the spiral stairs, holding on to a

little hand-rail that ran down beside them. The stairs were so steep that she was afraid of falling. She nearly *did* fall when Timmy pushed his way past her, and disappeared below at a remarkably fast pace.

Soon they were all down at the bottom. Julian locked the door again. 'Not much good locking a door if you leave the key in,' he said. 'Still – I'd better.'

They walked over to Aunt Fanny. 'Well, I thought you were never coming!' she said. 'Did you see anything interesting up there?'

'Only a lovely view,' said Anne. 'Simply magnificent. But we didn't find Uncle Quentin. It's very mysterious, Aunt Fanny – we really have looked everywhere on the island – but he's just not here.'

'And yet his boat is in the cove,' said Dick. 'So he can't have gone.'

'Yes, it does sound odd,' said Aunt Fanny, handing round the sandwiches. 'But you don't know your uncle as well as I do. He always turns up all right. He's forgotten I was bringing you, or he would be here. As it is, we may not see him, if he's quite forgotten about your coming. If he remembers, he'll suddenly turn up.'

'But where from?' asked Dick, munching a potted meat sandwich. 'He's done a jolly good disappearing trick, Aunt Fanny.'

'Well, you'll see where he comes from, I've no doubt, when he arrives,' said Aunt Fanny. 'Another sandwich, George? No, *not* you, Timmy. You've had three already.

Oh, George, do keep Timmy's head out of that plate.'

'He's hungry too, Mother,' said George.

'Well, I've brought dog biscuits for him,' said her mother.

'Oh, Mother! As if Timmy would eat *dog* biscuits when he can have sandwiches,' said George. 'He only eats dog biscuits when there's absolutely nothing else and he's so ravenous he can't help eating them.'

They sat in the warm April sunshine, eating hungrily. There was orangeade to drink, cool and delicious. Timmy wandered over to a rock pool he knew, where rain-water collected, and he could be heard lapping there.

'Hasn't he got a good memory?' said George proudly. 'It's ages since he was here – and yet he remembered that pool at once, when he felt thirsty.'

'It's funny Timmy hasn't found Uncle Quentin, isn't it?' said Dick, suddenly. 'I mean – when we were hunting for him, and got "Warm" you'd think Timmy would bark or scrape about or something. But he didn't.'

'I think it's jolly funny that Father can't be found anywhere,' said George. 'I do really. I can't think how you can take it so calmly, Mother.'

'Well, dear, as I said before, I know your father better than you do,' said her mother. 'He'll turn up in his own good time. Why, I remember once when he was doing some sort of work in the stalactite caves at Cheddar, he disappeared in them for over a week – but he wandered out all right when he had finished his experiments.'

'It's very strange,' began Anne, and then stopped suddenly. A curious noise came to their ears – a rumbling, grumbling, angry noise, like a giant hidden dog, growling in fury. Then there was a hissing noise from the tower, and all the wires that waved at the top were suddenly lit up as if by lightning.

'There now – I knew your father was somewhere about,' said George's mother. 'I heard that noise when I was here before – but I couldn't make out where it came from.'

'Where *did* it come from?' said Dick. 'It sounded almost as if it was underneath us, but it couldn't have been. Gracious, this is most mysterious.'

No more noises came. They each helped themselves to buns with jam in the middle. And then Anne gave a squeal that made them all jump violently.

'Look! *There's* Uncle Quentin! Standing over there, near the tower. He's watching the jackdaws! Wherever *did* he come from?'

CHAPTER FIVE

A mystery

EVERYONE STARED at Uncle Quentin. There he was, intently watching the jackdaws, his hands in his pockets. He hadn't seen the children or his wife.

Timmy leapt to his feet, and gambolled over to George's father. He barked loudly. Uncle Quentin jumped and turned round. He saw Timmy – and then he saw all the others, staring at him in real astonishment.

Uncle Quentin did not look particularly pleased to see anyone. He walked slowly over to them, a slight frown on his face. 'This *is* a surprise,' he said. 'I had no idea you were all coming today.'

'Oh, *Quentin*!' said his wife, reproachfully. 'I wrote it down for you in your diary. You know I did.'

'Did you! Well, I haven't looked at my diary since, so it's no wonder I forgot,' said Uncle Quentin, a little peevishly. He kissed his wife, George and Anne, and shook hands with the boys.

'Uncle Quentin – where did you come from?' asked Dick, who was eaten up with curiosity. 'We've looked for you for ages.'

'Oh, I was in my workroom,' said Uncle Quentin, vaguely.

'Well, but where's that?' demanded Dick. 'Honesty, Uncle, we can't imagine where you hid yourself. We even went up the tower to see if you were in that funny glass room at the top.'

'*What!*' exploded his uncle, in a sudden surprising fury. 'You dared to go up there? You might have been in great danger. I've just finished an experiment, and all those wires in there were connected with it.'

'Yes, we saw them acting a bit strangely,' said Julian.

'You've no business to come over here, and interfere with my work,' said his uncle, still looking furious. 'How did you get into that tower? I locked it.'

'Yes, it was locked all right,' said Julian. 'But you left the key in, you see, Uncle – so I thought it wouldn't matter if . . .'

'Oh, that's where the key is, is it?' said his uncle. 'I thought I'd lost it. Well, don't you ever go into that tower again. I tell you, it's dangerous.'

'Uncle Quentin, you haven't told us yet where your workroom is,' said Dick, who was quite determined to know. 'We can't imagine where you suddenly came from.'

'I told them you would turn up, Quentin,' said his wife. 'You look a bit thin, dear. Have you been having regular meals. You know, I left you plenty of good soup to heat up.'

'Did you?' said her husband. 'Well, I don't know if I've had it or not. I don't worry about meals when I'm working. I'll have some of those sandwiches now, though, if nobody else wants them.'

He began to devour the sandwiches, one after another, as if he was ravenous. Aunt Fanny watched him in distress.

'Oh, Quentin – you're starving. I shall come over here and stay and look after you!'

Her husband looked alarmed. 'Oh no! Nobody is to come here. I can't have my work interfered with. I'm working on an extremely important discovery.'

'Is it a discovery that nobody else knows about?' asked Anne, her eyes wide with admiration. How clever Uncle Quentin was!

'Well – I'm not sure about that,' said Uncle Quentin, taking two sandwiches at once. 'That's partly why I came over here – besides the fact that I wanted water round me and above me. I have a feeling that somebody knows a bit more than I want them to know. But there's one thing – they can't come here unless they're shown the way through all those rocks that lie round the island. Only a few of the fishermen know that, and they've been given orders not to bring anyone here at all. I think you're the only other person that knows the way, George.'

'Uncle Quentin – please do tell us where your workroom is,' begged Dick, feeling that he could not wait a single moment more to solve the mystery.

'Don't keep bothering your uncle,' said his aunt,

annoyingly. 'Let him eat his lunch. He can't have had anything for ages!'

'Yes, but Aunt Fanny, I . . .' began Dick and was interrupted by his uncle.

'You obey your aunt, young man. I don't want to be pestered by any of you. What does it matter where I work?'

'Oh, it doesn't really matter a bit,' said Dick, hurriedly. 'It's only that I'm awfully curious to know. You see, we looked for you simply everywhere.'

'Well, you're not quite so clever as you thought you were then,' said Uncle Quentin, and reached for a jammy bun. 'George, take this dog of yours away from me. He keeps breathing down my neck, hoping I shall give him a tit-bit. I don't approve of tit-bits at meal-times.'

George pulled Timmy away. Her mother watched her father gobbling up the rest of the food. Most of the sandwiches she had saved for tea-time had gone already. Poor Quentin! How very hungry he must be.

'Quentin, you don't think there's any danger for you here, do you?' she said. 'I mean – you don't think anyone would try to come spying on you, as they did once before?'

'No. How could they?' said her husband. 'No plane can land on this island. No boat can get through the rocks unless the way through is known, and the sea's too rough round the rocks for any swimmer.'

'Julian, see if you can make him promise to signal to me

night and morning,' said Aunt Fanny, turning to her nephew. 'I feel worried about him somehow.'

Julian tackled his uncle manfully. 'Uncle, it wouldn't be too much of a bother to you to signal to Aunt Fanny twice a day, would it?'

'If you don't, Quentin, I shall come over every single day to see you,' said his wife.

'And we might come too,' said Anne mischievously. Her uncle looked most dismayed at the idea.

'Well, I could signal in the morning and in the evening when I go up to the top of the tower,' he said. 'I have to go up once every twelve hours to re-adjust the wires. I'll signal then. Half past ten in the morning and half past ten at night.'

'How will you signal?' asked Julian. 'Will you flash with a mirror in the morning?'

'Yes – that would be quite a good idea,' said his uncle. 'I could do that easily. And I'll use a lantern at night. I'll shine it out six times at half past ten. Then perhaps you'll all know I'm all right and will leave me alone! But don't look for the signal tonight. I'll start tomorrow morning.'

'Oh, Quentin dear, you do sound cross,' said his wife. 'I don't like you being all alone here, that's all. You look thin and tired. I'm sure you're not . . .'

Uncle Quentin put on a scowl exactly like George sometimes put on. He looked at his wristwatch. 'Well I must go,' he said. 'Time to get to work again. I'll see you to your boat.'

'We're going to stay to tea here, Father,' said George.

'No, I'd rather you didn't,' said her father, getting up. 'Come on – I'll take you to your boat.'

'But, Father – I haven't been on my island for ages!' said George, indignantly. 'I want to stay here a bit longer. I don't see why I shouldn't.'

'Well, I've had enough interruption to my work,' said her father. 'I want to get on.'

'We shan't disturb you, Uncle Quentin,' said Dick, who was still terribly curious to know where his uncle had his workroom. Why wouldn't he tell them! Was he just being annoying? Or didn't he want them to know?

Uncle Quentin led them all firmly towards the little cove. It was plain that he meant them to go and to go quickly.

'When shall we come over and see you again, Quentin?' asked his wife.

'Not till I say so,' said her husband. 'It won't take me long now to finish what I'm on. My word, that dog's got a rabbit at last!'

'Oh, *Timmy*!' yelled George in distress. Timmy dropped the rabbit he had actually managed to grab. It scampered away unhurt. Timmy came to his mistress looking very sheepish.

'You're a very bad dog. Just because I took my eye off you for half a second! No, it's no good licking my hand like that. I'm cross.'

They all came to the boat. 'I'll push her off,' said Julian.

'Get in, all of you. Well, good-bye, Uncle Quentin. I hope your work goes well.'

Everyone got into the boat. Timmy tried to put his head on George's knee, but she pushed it away.

'Oh, be kind to him and forgive him,' begged Anne. 'He looks as if he's going to cry.'

'Are you ready?' cried Julian. 'Got the oars, George? Dick, take the other pair.'

He shoved the boat off and leapt in himself. He cupped his hands round his mouth. 'Don't forget to signal! We'll be watching out morning and evening!'

'And if you forget, I shall come over the very next day!' called his wife.

The boat slid away down the little inlet of water, and Uncle Quentin was lost to sight. Then round the low wall of rocks went the boat, and was soon on the open sea.

'Ju, watch and see if you can make out where Uncle Quentin is, when we're round these rocks,' said Dick. 'See what direction he goes in.'

Julian tried to see his uncle, but the rocks just there hid the cove from sight, and there was no sign of him at all.

'*Why* didn't he want us to stay? Because he didn't want us to know his hiding-place!' said Dick. 'And *why* doesn't he want us to know? Because it's somewhere *we* don't know, either!'

'But I thought we knew every single corner of my island,' said George. 'I think it's mean of Father not to tell me, if it's somewhere I don't know. I can't think *where* it can be!'

Timmy put his head on her knee again. George was so absorbed in trying to think where her father's hiding-place could be that she absent-mindedly stroked Timmy's head. He was almost beside himself with delight. He licked her fingers lovingly.

'Oh, Timmy – I didn't mean to pet you for ages,' said George. 'Stop licking my hands. You make them feel wet and horrid. Dick, it's very mysterious, isn't it – where *can* Father be hiding?'

'I can't imagine,' said Dick. He looked back at the island. A cloud of jackdaws rose up into the air calling loudly, 'Chack, chack, chack!'

The boy watched them. What had disturbed them? Was it Uncle Quentin? Perhaps his hiding-place was somewhere about that old tower then, the one the jackdaws nested in? On the other hand, the jackdaws often rose into the air together for no reason at all.

'Those jackdaws are making a bit of fuss,' he said. 'Perhaps Uncle's hiding-place is not far from where they roost together, by that tower.'

'Can't be,' said Julian. 'We went all round there today.'

'Well, it's a mystery,' said George, gloomily, 'and I think it's horrible having a mystery about my very own island – and to be forbidden to go to it, and solve it. It's really *too* bad!'

CHAPTER SIX

Up on the cliff

THE NEXT day was rainy. The four children put on their macintoshes and sou'westers and went out for a walk with Timmy. They never minded the weather. In fact Julian said that he really *liked* the feel of the wind and rain buffeting against his face.

'We forgot that Uncle Quentin couldn't flash to us if the weather wasn't sunny!' said Dick. 'Do you suppose he'll find some way to signal instead?'

'No,' said George. 'He just won't bother. He thinks we're awful fussers anyway, I'm sure. We'll have to watch at half past ten tonight to see if he signals.'

'I say! Shall I be able to stay up till then?' said Anne pleased.

'I shouldn't think so,' said Dick. 'I expect Julian and I will stay up – but you kids will have to buzz off to bed!'

George gave him a shove. 'Don't call us "*kids*"! I'm almost as tall as you are now.'

'It's not much use waiting about till half past ten now to see if Uncle signals to us in any way, is it?' said Anne. 'Let's go up on the cliff – it'll be lovely and blowy. Timmy will like that. I love to see him racing along in the wind, with his ears blown back straight!'

'Woof,' said Timmy.

'He says he likes to see you with yours blown back too,' said Julian, gravely. Anne gave a squeal of laughter.

'You really are an idiot, Ju! Come on – let's take the cliff-path!'

They went up the cliff. At the top it was very windy indeed. Anne's sou'wester was blown to the back of her head. The rain stung their cheeks and made them gasp.

'I should think we must be about the only people out this morning!' gasped George.

'Well, you're wrong,' said Julian. 'There are two people coming towards us!'

So there was. They were a man and a boy, both well wrapped up in macintoshes and sou'westers. Like the children, they too wore high rubber boots.

The children took a look at them as they passed. The man was tall and well built, with shaggy eyebrows and a determined mouth. The boy was about sixteen, also tall and well built. He was not a bad-looking boy, but he had rather a sullen expression.

'Good morning,' said the man, and nodded. 'Good morning,' chorused the children, politely. The man looked them over keenly, and then he and the boy went on.

'Wonder who they are?' said George. 'Mother didn't say there were any new people here.'

'Just walked over from the next village, I expect,' said Dick.

They went on for some way. 'We'll walk to the coastguard's cottage and then go back,' said Julian. 'Hey, Tim, don't go so near the cliff!'

The coastguard lived in a little whitewashed cottage on the cliff, facing the sea. Two other cottages stood beside it, also whitewashed. The children knew the coastguard well. He was a red-faced, barrel-shaped man, fond of joking.

He was nowhere to be seen when they came to his cottage. Then they heard his enormous voice singing a sea-shanty in the little shed behind. They went to find him.

'Hallo,' said Anne.

He looked up and grinned at the children. He was busy making something. 'Hallo to you!' he said. 'So you're back again are you? Bad pennies, the lot of you – always turning up when you're not wanted!'

'What are you making?' asked Anne.

'A windmill for my young grandson,' said the coastguard, showing it to Anne. He was very clever at making toys.

'Oh, it's *lovely*,' said Anne, taking it in her hands. 'Does the windmill part go round – oh yes – it's super!'

'I've been making quite a bit of money out of my toys,' said the old fellow, proudly. 'I've got some new neighbours in the next cottage – man and a boy – and the man's been buying all the toys I make. Seems to have a lot of nephews and nieces! He gives me good prices too.'

'Oh – would that be the man and the boy we met, I

wonder?' said Dick. 'Both tall, and well built – and the man had shaggy eyebrows.'

'That's right,' said the coastguard, trimming a bit of his windmill. 'Mr Curton and his son. They came here some weeks ago. You ought to get to know the son, Julian. He's about your age, I should think. Must be pretty lonely for him up here!'

'Doesn't he go to any school?' asked Julian.

'No. He's been ill, so his father said. Got to have plenty of sea-air and that sort of thing. Not a bad sort of boy. He comes and helps me with my toys sometimes. And he likes to mess about with my telescope.'

'I do too,' said George. 'I love looking through your telescope. Can I look through it now? I'd like to see if I can spot Kirrin Island.'

'Well, you won't see much in this weather,' said the coastguard. 'You wait a few minutes. See that break in the clouds? Well, it'll clear in a few minutes, and you'll be able to see your island easily. That's a funny thing your father's built there, isn't it? Part of his work, I suppose.'

'Yes,' said George. 'Oh, Timmy – look what he's done – he's upset that tin of paint. Bad boy, Timmy!'

'It's not my tin,' said the coastguard. 'It's a tin belonging to that young fellow next door. I told you he comes in to help me sometimes. He brought in that tin to help paint a little dolls' house I made for his father.'

'Oh dear,' said George, in dismay. 'Do you think he'll be cross when he knows Timmy spilt it?'

'Shouldn't think so,' said the coastguard. 'He's a funny boy though – quiet and a bit sulky. Not a bad boy, but doesn't seem very friendly like.'

George tried to clear up the mess of paint. Timmy had some on his paws, and made a little pattern of green paw-marks as he pattered about the shed.

'I'll tell the boy I'm sorry, if I meet him on the way back,' she said. 'Timmy if you dare to go near any more tins of paint you shan't sleep on my bed tonight.'

'The weather's a bit clearer now,' said Dick. 'Can we have a squint through the telescope?'

'Let *me* see my island first,' said George at once. She tilted the telescope in the direction of Kirrin Island. She looked through it earnestly, and a smile came over her face.

'Yes, I can see it clearly. There's the tower Father has had built. I can even see the glass room quite clearly, and there's nobody in it. No sign of Father anywhere.'

Everyone had a turn at looking through the telescope. It was fascinating to see the island appearing so close. On a clear day it would be even easier to see all the details. 'I can see a rabbit scampering,' said Anne, when her turn came.

'Don't you let that dog of yours squint through the telescope then,' said the coastguard at once. 'He'll try to get down it after that rabbit!'

Timmy cocked his ears up at the mention of the word rabbit. He looked all round and sniffed. No, there was no rabbit. Then why did people mention them?

'We'd better go now,' said Julian. 'We'll be up here again sometime, and we'll come and see what toys you've done. Thanks for letting us look through the telescope.'

'You're welcome!' said the old fellow. 'You're not likely to wear it out through looking! Come along any time you want to use it.'

They said good-bye and went off, Timmy capering round them. 'Couldn't we see Kirrin Island well!' said Anne. 'I wished I could see where your father was, George. Wouldn't it be fun if we spotted him just coming out of his hiding-place?'

The four children had discussed this problem a good deal since they had left the island. It puzzled them very much indeed. How did it happen that George's father knew a hiding-place that they didn't know? Why, they had been over every inch of the island! It must be quite a big hiding-place too, if he had got all his stuff for his experiments with him. According to George's mother, there had been quite a lot of this, to say nothing of stores of food.

'If Father knew a place I didn't know, and never told me about it, I think he's jolly mean,' George said half a dozen times. 'I do really. It's *my* island!'

'Well, he'll probably tell you when he's finished the work he's on,' said Julian. 'Then you'll know. We can all go and explore it then, wherever it is.'

After they left the coastguard's cottage they turned their

steps home. They made their way along the cliff, and then saw the boy they had met before. He was standing on the path looking out to sea. The man was not with him.

He turned as they came up and gave them a pale kind of smile. 'Hallo! Been up to see the coastguard?'

'Yes,' said Julian. 'Nice old fellow, isn't he?'

'I say,' said George, 'I'm sorry but my dog upset a tin

of green paint, and the coastguard said it was yours. Can I pay you for it, please?'

'Goodness, no!' said the boy. 'I don't mind. There wasn't much of it left anyway. That's a nice dog of yours.'

'Yes, he is,' said George, warmly. 'Best dog in the world. I've had him for years, but he's still as young as ever. Do you like dogs?'

'Oh yes,' said the boy, but he made no move to pat Timmy or fuss him, as most people did. And Timmy did not run round the boy and sniff at him as he usually did when he met anyone new. He just stood by George, his tail neither up nor down.

'That's an interesting little island,' said the boy, pointing to Kirrin. 'I wish I could go there.'

'It's *my* island,' said George, proudly. 'My very own.'

'Really?' said the boy, politely. 'Could you let me go over one day then?'

'Well – not just at present,' said George. 'You see, my father's there – working – he's a scientist.'

'Really?' said the boy again. 'Er – has he got some new experiment on hand, then?'

'Yes,' said George.

'Ah – and that weird tower is something to do with it, I suppose,' said the boy, looking interested for the first time. 'When will his experiment be finished?'

'What's that to do with you?' said Dick, suddenly. The others stared at him in surprise. Dick sounded rather rude, and it was not like him.

'Oh nothing!' said the boy, hastily. 'I only thought that if his work will soon be finished, perhaps your brother would take me over to his island!'

George couldn't help feeling pleased. This boy thought *she* was a boy! George was always gracious to people who made the mistake of thinking she was a boy.

'Of *course* I'll take you!' she said. 'It shouldn't be long before I do – the experiment is nearly done.'

CHAPTER SEVEN

A little squabble

A SOUND made them turn. It was the boy's father coming up. He nodded to the children. 'Making friends?' he said, amiably. 'That's right. My boy's pretty lonely here. I hope you'll come up and see us some time. Finished your conversation, son?'

'Yes,' said the boy. 'This boy here says that island is his, and he's going to take me over it when his father has finished his work there – and that won't be long.'

'And do you know the way through all those wicked rocks?' said the man. '*I* shouldn't care to try it. I was talking to the fishermen the other day, and not one of them appeared to know the way!'

This was rather astonishing. Some of the fishermen *did* know it. Then the children remembered that the men had all been forbidden to take anyone to the island while Uncle Quentin was at work there. It was clear that they had pretended not to know the way, in loyalty to their orders.

'Did you want to go to the island then?' asked Dick, suddenly.

'Oh no! But my boy here would love to go,' said the man. '*I* don't want to be seasick, bobbing up and down on those waves near the island. I'm a poor sailor. I never go on the sea if I can help it!'

'Well, we must go,' said Julian. 'We've got to do some shopping for my aunt. Good-bye!'

'Come and see us as soon as you can,' said the man. 'I've a fine television set that Martin here would like to show you. Any afternoon you like!'

'Oh thanks!' said George. She seldom saw television. 'We'll come!'

They parted, and the four children and Timmy went on down the cliff-path.

'Whatever made you sound so rude, Dick?' said George. 'The way you said "What's that to do with you?" sounded quite insulting.'

'Well – I just felt suspicious, that's all,' said Dick. 'That boy seemed to be so jolly interested in the island and in your father's work, and when it would be finished.'

'Why shouldn't he be?' demanded George. 'Everyone in the village is interested. They all know about the tower. And all the boy wanted to know was when he could go to my island – that's why he asked when Father's work would be finished. I liked him.'

'You only liked him because he was ass enough to think you were a boy,' said Dick. 'Jolly girlish-looking boy you are, that's all I can say.'

George flared up at once. 'Don't be mean! I'm *not* girlish-looking. I've far more freckles than you have, for one thing, and better eyebrows. *And* I can make my voice go deep.'

'You're just silly,' said Dick, in disgust. 'As if freckles are boyish! Girls have them just as much as boys. I don't believe that boy thought you were a boy at all. He was just sucking up to you. He must have heard how much you like playing at being what you aren't.'

George walked up to Dick with such a furious look on her face that Julian hastily put himself in between them. 'Now, no brawls,' he said. 'You're both too old to begin going at each other like kids in the nursery. Let me tell you, you're both behaving like babies, not like boys *or* girls!'

Anne was looking on with scared eyes. George didn't go off the deep end like this usually. And it *was* funny of Dick to have spoken so rudely to the boy on the cliff. Timmy gave a sudden little whine. His tail was down, and he looked very miserable.

'Oh, George – Timmy can't *bear* you to quarrel with Dick!' said Anne. 'Look at him! He's just miserable!'

'He didn't like that boy a bit,' said Dick. 'That was another thing I thought was funny. If Timmy doesn't like a person, *I* don't like him either.'

'Timmy doesn't *always* rush round new people,' said George. 'He didn't growl or snarl, anyway. All right, all right, Julian; I'm not going to start brawling. But I do think Dick is being silly. Making a mountain out of a molehill – just because someone was interested in Kirrin

Island and Father's work, and just because Timmy didn't caper all round him. He was such a solemn sort of boy that I'm not surprised Timmy wasn't all over him. He probably knew the boy wouldn't like it. Timmy's clever like that.'

'Oh, do stop,' said Dick. 'I give in – gracefully! I may be making a fuss. Probably am. I couldn't help my feelings, though.'

Anne gave a sigh of relief. The squabble was over. She hoped it wouldn't crop up again. George had been very touchy since she had been home. If only Uncle Quentin would hurry up and finish his work, and they could all go to the island as much as they liked, things would be all right.

'I'd rather like to see that television set,' said George. 'We might go up some afternoon.'

'Right,' said Julian. 'But on the whole, I think it would be best if we steered clear of any talk about your father's work. Not that we know much. Still, we do know that once before there were people after one of his theories. The secrets of the scientists are very, very important these days, you know, George. Scientists are VIP!'

'What's VIP?' asked Anne.

'Very Important People, baby!' said Julian, with a laugh. 'What did you think it meant? Violet, Indigo, Purple? I guess those are the colours Uncle Quentin would go if he knew anyone was trying to snoop into his secrets!'

Everyone laughed, even George. She looked affectionately at Julian. He was always so sensible and good-tempered. She really would go by what he said.

The day passed swiftly. The weather cleared and the sun came out strongly. The air smelt of gorse and primroses and the salt of the sea. Lovely! They went shopping for Aunt Fanny, and stopped to talk with James, the fisher-boy.

'Your father's got the island, I see,' he said to George with a grin. 'Bad luck, you won't be going over there so often. And nobody else will, either, so I've heard.'

'That's right,' said George. 'Nobody is allowed to go over there for some time. Did you help to take some of the stuff over, James?'

'Yes. I know the way, you see, because I've been with you,' said James. 'Well, how did you find your boat when you went across yesterday? I got her all ship-shape for you, didn't I?'

'Yes, you did, James,' said George, warmly. 'You made her look beautiful. You must come across to the island with us next time we go.'

'Thanks,' said James, his ready grin showing all his white teeth. 'Like to leave Timmy with me for a week or two? See how he wants to stay!'

George laughed. She knew James was only joking. He was very fond of Timmy, though, and Timmy adored James. He was now pushing himself hard against the fisher-boy's knees, and trying to put his nose into his tanned hand. Timmy had never forgotten the time when James looked after him so well.

The evening came, and the bay was softly blue. Little white horses flecked it here and there. The four gazed across to Kirrin Island. It always looked so lovely at this time of the evening.

The glass top of the tower winked and blinked in the sun. It looked almost as if someone was signalling. But there was no one in the little glass room. As the children watched they heard a faint rumbling sound, and suddenly the top of the tower was ablaze with a curious glare.

'Look! That's what happened yesterday!' said Julian, in excitement. 'Your father's at work all right, George. I do wonder what he's doing!'

Then there came a throbbing sound, almost like the noise of an aeroplane, and once more the glass top of the tower shone and blazed, as the wires became full of some curious power.

'Weird,' said Dick. 'A bit frightening too. Where's your father at this very moment, I wonder, George. How I'd like to know!'

'I bet he's forgotten all about meals again,' said George. 'Didn't he wolf our sandwiches – he must have been starving. I wish he'd let Mother go over there and look after him.'

Her mother came in at that moment. 'Did you hear the noise?' she said. 'I suppose that was your father at work again. Oh dear, I hope he doesn't blow himself up one of these days!'

'Aunt Fanny, can I stay up till half past ten tonight?' asked Anne, hopefully. 'To see Uncle Quentin's signal, you know?'

'Good gracious, no!' said her aunt. 'No one needs to stay up. I am quite capable of watching for it myself!'

'Oh, Aunt Fanny! Surely Dick and I can stay up!' said Julian. 'After all, we're not in bed till ten at school.'

'Yes – but this is *half past* ten, and you wouldn't even be in bed then,' said his aunt. 'There's no reason why you shouldn't lie in bed and watch for it though, if you want to – providing you haven't fallen asleep!'

'Oh yes – I can do that,' said Julian. 'My window looks across to Kirrin Island. Six flashes with a lantern? I shall count them carefully.'

So the four went to bed at the usual time. Anne was asleep long before half past ten, and George was so drowsy that she could not make herself get up and go into the boy's room. But Dick and Julian were both wide awake. They lay in their beds and looked out of the window. There was no moon, but the sky was clear, and the stars shone down, giving a faint light. The sea looked very black. There was no sign of Kirrin Island. It was lost in the darkness of the night.

'Almost half past ten,' said Julian, looking at his watch which had luminous hands. 'Now then, Uncle Quentin, what about it?'

Almost as if his uncle was answering him, a light shone out in the glass top of the tower. It was a clear, small light, like the light of a lantern.

Julian began to count. 'One flash.' There was a pause. 'Two flashes.' Another pause. 'Three . . . four . . . five . . . six!'

The flashes stopped. Julian snuggled down into bed. 'Well, that's that. Uncle Quentin's all right. I say, it's weird to think of him climbing that spiral stairway right to the top of the tower, in the dark of night, isn't it? – just to mess about with those wires.'

'Mmmmm,' said Dick sleepily. 'I'd rather he did it, than I! You can be a scientist if you like, Ju – but *I* don't want to climb towers in the dead of night on a lonely island. I'd like Timmy there, at least!'

Someone knocked on their door and it opened. Julian sat up at once. It was Aunt Fanny.

'Oh, Julian dear – did you see the flashes? I forgot to count them. Were there six?'

'Oh yes, Aunt Fanny! I'd have rushed down to tell you if anything was wrong. Uncle's all right. Don't you worry!'

'I wish I'd told him to do an *extra* flash to tell me if he's had some of that nice soup,' said his aunt. 'Well, good night, Julian. Sleep well!'

CHAPTER EIGHT

Down in the quarry

THE NEXT day dawned bright and sunny. The four tore down to breakfast, full of high spirits. 'Can we bathe? Aunt Fanny, it's *really* warm enough! Oh do say we can!'

'Of course not! Whoever heard of bathing in April!' said Aunt Fanny. 'Why, the sea is terribly cold. Do you want to be in bed for the rest of the holiday with a chill?'

'Well, let's go for a walk on the moors at the back of Kirrin Cottage,' said George. 'Timmy would love that. Wouldn't you, Tim?'

'Woof,' said Timmy, thumping his tail hard on the ground.

'Take your lunch with you if you like,' said her mother. 'I'll pack some for you.'

'You'll be glad to be rid of us for a little while, I expect, Aunt Fanny,' said Dick, with a grin. 'I know what we'll do. We'll go to the old quarry and look for prehistoric weapons! We've got a jolly good museum at school, and I'd like to take back some stone arrow-heads or something like that.'

They all liked hunting for things. It would be fun to go to the old quarry, and it would be lovely and warm in the hollow there.

'I hope we shan't find a poor dead sheep there, as we once did,' said Anne, with a shudder. 'Poor thing! It must have fallen down and baa-ed for help for ages.'

'Of course we shan't,' said Julian. 'We shall find stacks of primroses and violets though, growing down the sides of the quarry. They are always early there because it's sheltered from every wind.'

'And Timmy, of course, will hunt for rabbits, and will hope to bring home enough for you to decorate the larder from top to bottom,' said Dick, solemnly. Timmy looked thrilled and gave an excited little woof.

They waited for Uncle Quentin's signal at half past ten. It came – six flashes of a mirror in the sun. The flashes were quite blinding.

'Nice little bit of heliographing!' said Dick. 'Good morning and good-bye, Uncle! We'll watch for you tonight. Now, everybody ready?'

'Yes! Come on, Tim! Who's got the sandwiches? I say, isn't the sun hot!'

Off they all went. It was going to be a really lovely day!

The quarry was not really very far – only about a quarter of a mile. The children went for a walk beforehand, for Timmy's sake. Then they made for the quarry.

It was a strange place. At some time or other it had been deeply quarried for stone, and then left to itself. Now the sides were covered with small bushes and grass and plants of all kinds. In the sandy places heather grew.

The sides were very steep, and as few people came there, there were no paths to follow. It was like a huge rough bowl, irregular in places, and full of colour now where primroses opened their pale petals to the sky. Violets grew there by the thousands, both white and purple. Cowslips were opening too, the earliest anywhere.

'Oh, it's lovely!' said Anne, stopping at the top and looking down. 'Simply super! I never in my life saw so many primroses – nor such huge ones!'

'Be careful how you go, Anne,' said Julian. 'These sides are very steep. If you lose your footing you'll roll right down to the bottom – and find yourself with a broken arm or leg!'

'I'll be careful,' said Anne. 'I'll throw my basket down to the bottom, so that I can have two hands to cling to bushes with, if I want to.'

She flung the basket down, and it bounced all the way to the bottom of the quarry. The children climbed down to where they wanted to go – the girls to a great patch of big primroses, the boys to a place where they thought they might find stone weapons.

'Hallo!' said a voice, suddenly, from much lower down. The four stopped in surprise, and Timmy growled.

'Why – it's you!' said George, recognising the boy they had met the day before.

'Yes. I don't know if you know my name. It's Martin Curton,' said the boy.

Julian told him their names too. 'We've come to picnic

here,' he said. 'And to see if we can find stone weapons. What have you come for?'

'Oh – to see if I can find stone weapons too,' said the boy.

'Have you found any?' asked George.

'No. Not yet.'

'Well, you won't find any just there,' said Dick. 'Not in heather! You want to come over here, where the ground is bare and gravelly.'

Dick was trying to be friendly, to make up for the day before. Martin came over and began to scrape about with the boys. They had trowels with them, but he had only his hands.

'Isn't it hot down here?' called Anne. 'I'm going to take off my coat.'

Timmy had his head and shoulders down a rabbit hole. He was scraping violently, sending up heaps of soil behind him in a shower.

'Don't go near Timmy unless you want to be buried in earth!' said Dick. 'Hey, Timmy – is a rabbit really worth all that hard work?'

Apparently it was, for Timmy, panting loudly, went on digging for all he was worth. A stone flew high in the air and hit Julian. He rubbed his cheek. Then he looked at the stone that lay beside him. He gave a shout. 'Look at this – a jolly fine arrow-head! Thanks, Timmy, old fellow. Very good of you to go digging for me. What about a hammer-head next?'

The others came to see the stone arrow-head. Anne thought she would never have known what it was – but Julian and Dick exclaimed over it in admiration.

'Jolly good specimen,' said Dick. 'See how it's been shaped, George? To think that this was used thousands of years ago to kill the enemies of a cave-man!' Martin did not say much. He just looked at the arrow-head, which certainly was a very fine unspoilt specimen, and then turned away. Dick thought he was a strange fellow. A bit dull and boring. He wondered if they ought to ask him to their picnic. He didn't want to in the least.

But George did! 'Are you having a picnic here too?' she said. Martin shook his head.

'No. I haven't brought any sandwiches.'

'Well, we've plenty. Stay and have some with us when we eat them,' said George, generously.

'Thanks. It's very nice of you,' said the boy. 'And will you come and see my television this afternoon in return! I'd like you to.'

'Yes, we will,' said George. 'It would be something to do! Oh, Anne – just look at those violets! I've never seen such big white ones before.'

The boys went deeper down, scraping about with their trowels in any likely place. They came to where a shelf of stone projected out a good way. It would be a nice place to have their lunch. The stone would be warm to sit on, and was flat enough to take ginger-beer bottles and cups in safety.

At half past twelve they all had their lunch. They were very hungry. Martin shared their sandwiches, and became quite friendly over them.

'Best sandwiches I've ever tasted,' he said. 'I do like those sardine ones. Does your mother make them for you? I wish I had a mother. Mine died ages ago.'

There was a sympathetic silence. The four could not think of any worse thing to happen to a boy or girl. They offered Martin the nicest buns, and the biggest piece of cake immediately.

'I saw your father flashing his signals last night,' said Martin, munching a bun.

Dick looked up at once. 'How do you know he was signalling?' he asked. 'Who told you?'

'Nobody,' said the boy. 'I just saw the six flashes, and I thought it must be George's father.' He looked surprised at Dick's sharp tone. Julian gave Dick a nudge, to warn him not to go off the deep end again.

George scowled at Dick. 'I suppose you saw my father signalling this morning too,' she said to Martin. 'I bet scores of people saw the flashes. He just heliographs with a mirror at half past ten to signal that he's all right – and flashes a lantern at the same time at night.'

Now it was Dick's turn to scowl at George. Why give away all this information? It wasn't necessary. Dick felt sure she was doing it just to pay him back for his sharp question. He tried to change the subject.

'Where do you go to school?' he asked.

'I don't,' said the boy. 'I've been ill.'

'Well, where did you go to school before you were ill?' asked Dick.

'I–I had a tutor,' said Martin. 'I didn't go to school.'

'Bad luck!' said Julian. He thought it must be terrible not to go to school and have all the fun, the work and the games of school-life. He looked curiously at Martin. Was he one of those rather stupid boys who did no good at school, but had to have a tutor at home? Still he didn't *look* stupid. He just looked rather sullen and dull.

Timmy was sitting on the warm stone with the others. He had his share of the sandwiches, but had to be rationed, as Martin had to have some too.

He was funny with Martin. He took absolutely no notice of him at all. Martin might not have been there!

And Martin took no notice of Timmy. He did not talk to him, or pat him. Anne was sure he didn't really like dogs, as he had said. How could anyone be with Timmy and not give him even *one* pat?

Timmy did not even look at Martin, but sat with his back to him, leaning against George. It was really rather amusing, if it wasn't so odd. After all, George was talking in a friendly way to Martin; they were all sharing their food with him – and Timmy behaved as if Martin simply wasn't there at all!

Anne was just about to remark on Timmy's odd behaviour when he yawned, shook himself, and leapt down from the rock. 'He's going rabbiting again,' said

Julian. 'Hey, Tim – find me another arrow-head will you, old fellow?'

Timmy wagged his tail. He disappeared under the shelf of rock, and there came the sound of digging. A shower of stones and soil flew into the air.

The children lay back on the stone and felt sleepy. They talked for some minutes, and then Anne felt her eyes closing. She was awakened by George's voice.

'Where's Timmy? Timmy! Timmy! Come here! Where have you got to?'

But no Timmy came. There was not even an answering bark. 'Oh blow,' said George. 'Now he's gone down some extra-deep rabbit hole, I suppose. I must get him. Timmy! Wherever are you?'

CHAPTER NINE

George makes a discovery – and loses her temper

GEORGE SLIPPED down from the rock. She peered under it. There was a large opening there, scattered with stones that Timmy had loosened in his digging.

'Surely you haven't at last found a rabbit hole big enough to go down!' said George. 'TIMMY! Where are you?'

Not a bark, not a whine came from the hole. George wriggled under the shelf of rock, and peered down the burrow. Timmy had certainly made it very big. George called up to Julian.

'Julian! Throw me down your trowel, will you?'

The trowel landed by her foot. George took it and began to make the hole bigger. It might be big enough for Timmy, but it wasn't big enough for her!

She dug hard and soon got very hot. She crawled out and looked over on to the rock to see if she could get one of the others to help her. They were all asleep.

'Lazy things!' thought George, quite forgetting that she too would have been dozing if she hadn't wondered where Timmy had gone.

She slipped down under the rock again and began to dig hard with her trowel. Soon she had made the hole big enough to get through. She was surprised to find quite a large passage, once she had made the entrance big enough to take her. She could crawl along on hands and knees!

'I say – I wonder if this is just some animal's runway – or leads somewhere!' thought George. 'TIMMY! Where *are* you?'

From somewhere deep in the quarry side there came a faint whine. George felt thankful. So Timmy *was* there, after all. She crawled along, and then quite suddenly the tunnel became high and wide and she realised that she must be in a passage. It was perfectly dark, so she could not see anything, she could only feel.

Then she heard the sound of pattering feet, and Timmy pressed affectionately against her legs, whining. 'Oh, Timmy – you gave me a bit of a fright!' said George. 'Where have you been? Is this a real passage – or just a tunnel in the quarry, made by the old miners, and now used by animals?'

'Woof,' said Timmy, and pulled at George's jeans to make her go back to the daylight.

'All right, I'm coming!' said George. 'Don't imagine I want to wander alone in the dark! I only came to look for you.'

She made her way back to the shelf of rock. By this time Dick was awake, and wondered where George had gone. He waited a few minutes, blinking up into the deep blue sky, and then sat up.

'George!' There was no answer. So, in his turn Dick

slipped down from the rock and looked around. And, to his very great astonishment he saw first Timmy, and then George on hands and knees, appearing out of the hole under the rock. He stared open-mouthed, and George began to giggle.

'It's all right. I've only been rabbiting with Timmy!'

She stood beside him, shaking and brushing soil from her jersey and trousers. 'There's a passage behind the entrance to the hole under the rock,' she said. 'At first it's just a narrow tunnel, like an animal's hole – then it gets

wider – and then it becomes a proper high wide passage! I couldn't see if it went on, of course, because it was dark. Timmy was a long way in.'

'Good gracious!' said Dick. 'It sounds exciting.'

'Let's explore it, shall we?' said George. 'I expect Julian's got a torch.'

'No,' said Dick. 'We won't explore today.'

The others were now awake, and listening with interest. 'Is it a secret passage?' said Anne, thrilled. 'Oh do let's explore it!'

'No, not today,' said Dick again. He looked at Julian. Julian guessed that Dick did not want Martin to share this secret. Why should he? He was not a real friend of theirs, and they had only just got to know him. He nodded back to Dick.

'No, we won't explore today. Anyway, it may be nothing – just an old tunnel made by the quarrymen.'

Martin was listening with great interest. He went and looked into the hole. 'I wish we could explore,' he said. 'Maybe we could plan to meet again with torches and see if there really is a passage there.'

Julian looked at his watch. 'Nearly two o'clock. Well, Martin, if we're going to see that half past two programme of yours, we'd better be getting on.'

The girls began to climb up the steep side of the quarry. Julian took Anne's basket from her, afraid she might slip and fall. Soon they were all at the top. The air felt quite cool there after the warmth of the quarry.

They made their way to the cliff-path and before long were passing the coastguard's cottage. He was out in his garden, and he waved to them.

They went in the gateway of the next-door cottage. Martin pushed the door open. His father was sitting at the window of the room inside, reading. He got up with a broad, welcoming smile.

'Well, well, well! This *is* nice! Come along in, do. Yes, the dog as well. I don't mind dogs a bit. I like them.'

It seemed rather a crowd in the small room. They all shook hands politely. Martin explained hurriedly that he had brought the children to see a television programme.

'A good idea,' said Mr Curton, still beaming. Anne stared at his great eyebrows. They were very long and thick. She wondered why he didn't have them trimmed – but perhaps he liked them like that. They made him look very fierce, she thought.

The four looked round the little room. There was a television set standing at the far end, on a table. There was also a magnificent radio – and something else that made the boys stare with interest.

'Hallo! You've got a transmitting set, as well as a receiving set,' said Julian.

'Yes,' said Mr Curton. 'It's a hobby of mine. I made that set.'

'Well! You must be brainy!' said Dick.

'What's a transmitting set?' asked Anne. 'I haven't heard of one before.'

'Oh, it just means a set to send out messages by radio – like police cars have, when they send back messages to the police stations,' said Dick. 'This is a very powerful one, though.'

Martin was fiddling about with the television switches. Then the programme began.

It was great fun seeing the television programme. When it was over Mr Curton asked them to stay to tea.

'Now, don't say no,' he said. 'I'll ring up and ask your aunt, if you like, if you're afraid she might be worried.'

'Well – if you'd do that, sir,' said Julian. 'I think she *would* wonder where we'd gone!'

Mr Curton rang up Aunt Fanny. Yes, it was quite all right for them to stay, but they mustn't be too late back. So they settled down to an unexpectedly good tea. Martin was not very talkative, but Mr Curton made up for it. He laughed and joked and was altogether very good company.

The talk came round to Kirrin Island. Mr Curton said how beautiful it looked each evening. George looked pleased.

'Yes,' she said. '*I* always think that. I do wish Father hadn't chosen this particular time to work on my island. I'd planned to go and stay there.'

'I suppose you know every inch of it!' said Mr Curton.

'Oh yes!' said George. 'We all do. There are dungeons

there, you know – real dungeons that go deep down – where we once found gold ingots.'

'Yes – I remember reading about that,' said Mr Curton. 'That must have been exciting. Fancy *finding* the dungeons too! And there's an old well too you once got down, isn't there?'

'Yes,' said Anne, remembering. 'And there is a cave where we once lived – it's got an entrance through the roof, as well as from the sea.'

'And I suppose your father is conducting his marvellous experiments down in the dungeons?' said Mr Curton. 'Well, what a strange place to work in!'

'No – we don't . . .' began George, when she got a kick on the ankle from Dick. She screwed up her face in pain. It had been a very sharp kick indeed.

'What were you going to say?' said Mr Curton, looking surprised.

'Er – I was just going to say that – er – er – we don't know which place Father has chosen,' said George, keeping her legs well out of the way of Dick's feet.

Timmy gave a sudden sharp whine. George looked down at him in surprise. He was looking up at Dick, with a very hurt expression.

'What's the matter, Timmy!' said George anxiously.

'He's finding the room too hot, I think,' said Dick. 'Better take him out, George.'

George, feeling quite anxious, took him out. Dick joined her. She scowled at him. 'What did you want

to kick me for like that? I shall have a frightful bruise.'

'You know jolly well why I did,' said Dick. 'Giving away everything like that! Can't you see the chap's very interested in your father being on the island? There may be nothing in it at all, but you might at least keep your mouth shut. Just like a girl, can't help blabbing. I had to stop you somehow. I don't mind telling you I trod jolly hard on poor old Timmy's tail too, to make him yelp, so that you'd stop talking!'

'Oh – you beast!' said George, indignantly. 'How *could* you hurt Timmy?'

'I didn't want to. It was a shame,' said Dick, stopping to fondle Timmy's ears. 'Poor old Tim. I didn't want to hurt you, old fellow.'

'I'm going home,' said George, her face scarlet with anger. 'I hate you for talking to me like that – telling me I blab like a girl – and stamping on poor Timmy's tail. You can go back and say I'm taking Timmy home.'

'Right,' said Dick. 'And a jolly good thing too. The less you talk to Mr Curton the better. *I'm* going back to find out exactly what he is and what he does. I'm getting jolly suspicious. You'd better go before you give anything else away!'

Almost choking with rage, George went off with Timmy. Dick went back to make her apologies. Julian and Anne, sure that something was up, felt most uncomfortable. They rose to go, but to their surprise, Dick became very talkative and appeared to be suddenly very much interested in Mr Curton and what he did.

But at last they said good-bye and went. 'Come again, do,' said Mr Curton, beaming at the three of them. 'And tell the other boy – what's his name, George – that I hope his dog is quite all right again now. Such a nice, well-behaved dog! Well, good-bye! See you again, soon, I hope!'

CHAPTER TEN

A surprising signal

'WHAT'S UP with George?' demanded Julian, as soon as they were safely out of earshot. 'I know you kicked her at tea-time, for talking too much about the island – that was idiotic of her – but why has she gone home in a huff?'

Dick told them how he had trodden on poor Timmy's tail to make him whine, so that George would turn her attention to him and stop talking. Julian laughed, but Anne was indignant.

'That was *horrid* of you, Dick.'

'Yes, it was,' said Dick. 'But I couldn't think of any other way to head George off the island. I really honestly thought she was giving away to that fellow all the things he badly wanted to know. But now I think he wanted to know them for quite another reason.'

'What do you mean?' said Julian puzzled.

'Well, I thought at first he must be after Uncle Quentin's secret, whatever it is,' said Dick, 'and that was why he wanted to know all the ins and outs of everything. But now that he's told me he's a journalist – that's a man who writes for the newspapers, Anne – I think after all he only wants the information so that he can use it for his paper and make a splash when Uncle has finished his work.'

'Yes, I think that too,' said Julian thoughtfully. 'In fact, I'm pretty sure of it. Well, there's no harm in that but I don't see why we should sit there and be pumped all the time. He could easily say, "Look here, I'd be obliged if you'd spill the beans about Kirrin Island – I want to use it in a newspaper story." But he didn't say that.'

'No. So I was suspicious,' said Dick. 'But I see now he'd want all sorts of tit-bits about Kirrin Island to put in his newspaper, whatever it is. Blow! Now I shall have to explain to George I was wrong – and she really is in a temper!'

'Let's take the road to Kirrin Village and go to get some bones for Timmy at the butcher's,' said Julian. 'A sort of apology to Tim!'

This seemed a good idea. They bought two large meaty bones at the butcher's, and then went to Kirrin Cottage. George was up in her bedroom with Timmy. The three went up to find her.

She was sitting on the floor with a book. She looked up sulkily as they came in.

'George, sorry I was such a beast,' said Dick. 'I did it in a good cause, if you only knew it. But I've discovered that Mr Curton isn't a spy, seeking out your father's secret – he's only a journalist, smelling out a story for his paper! Look – I've brought these for Timmy – I apologise to him too.'

George was in a very bad temper, but she tried to respond to Dick's friendliness. She gave him a small smile.

'All right. Thanks for the bones. Don't talk to me tonight anybody. I feel mad, but I'll get over it.'

They left her sitting on the floor. It was always best to leave George severely alone when she was in one of her tempers. As long as Timmy was with her, she was all right, and he certainly would not leave her while she was cross and unhappy.

George did not come down to supper. Dick explained. 'We had a bit of a row, Aunt Fanny, but we've made it up. George still feels sore about it though. Shall I take her supper up?'

'No, I will,' said Anne, and she took up a tray of food.

'I'm not hungry,' said George, so Anne prepared to take it away again. 'Well, you can leave it,' said George hurriedly. 'I expect Timmy will like it.'

So Anne, with a secret smile to herself left the tray. All the dishes were empty by the time she climbed the stairs to fetch the tray again!

'Dear me – Timmy *was* hungry!' she said to George, and her cousin smiled sheepishly. 'Aren't you coming down now? We're going to play Monopoly.'

'No thanks. You leave me alone this evening, and I'll be all right tomorrow,' said George. 'Really I will.'

So Julian, Dick, Anne and Aunt Fanny played Monopoly without George. They went up to bed at the usual time and found George in bed, fast asleep, with Timmy curled up on her toes.

'I'll look out for Uncle Quentin's signal,' said Julian, as he got into bed. 'Gosh, it's a dark night tonight.'

He lay in bed and looked out of the window towards Kirrin Island. Then, at exactly half past ten, the six flashes came – flash, flash, flash, through the darkness. Julian buried his head in his pillow. Now for a good sleep!

He was awakened by a throbbing noise some time later. He sat up and looked out of the window, expecting to see the top of the tower ablaze with light, as it sometimes was when his uncle conducted a special experiment. But nothing happened. There was no flare of light. The throbbing died away and Julian lay down again.

'I saw Uncle's signals all right last night, Aunt Fanny,' he said next morning. 'Did you?'

'Yes,' said his aunt. 'Julian, do you think you would watch for them this morning, dear? I have to go and see the vicar about something, and I don't believe I would be able to see the tower from the vicarage.'

'Yes, of course I will, Aunt Fanny,' said Julian. 'What's the time now? Half past nine. Right. I'll write some letters sitting by the window in my room – and at half past ten I'll watch for the signals.'

He wrote his letters interrupted first by Dick, then by George, Anne and Timmy, who wanted him to go on the beach with them. George had quite recovered herself now, and was trying to be specially nice to make up for yesterday's temper.

'I'll come at half past ten,' said Julian. 'After I've seen the signals from the tower. They're due in ten minutes.'

At half past ten he looked at the glass top of the tower. Ah – there was the first signal, blazing brightly as the sun caught the mirror held by his uncle in the tower.

'One flash,' counted Julian. 'Two – three – four – five – six. He's all right.'

He was just about to turn away when another flash caught his eyes. 'Seven!' Then another came. Eight. Nine. Ten. Eleven. Twelve.

'How strange,' said Julian. 'Why twelve flashes? Hallo, here we go again!'

Another six flashes came from the tower, then no more at all. Julian wished he had a telescope, then he could see right into the tower! He sat and thought for a moment, puzzled. Then he heard the others come pounding up the stairs. They burst into the room.

'Julian! Father flashed eighteen times instead of six!'

'Did you count them, Ju?'

'Why did he do that? Is he in danger of some sort?'

'No. If he was he'd flash the SOS signal,' said Julian.

'He doesn't know Morse code!' said George.

'Well, I expect he just wants to let us know that he needs something,' said Julian. 'We must go over today and find out what it is. More food perhaps.'

So when Aunt Fanny came home they suggested they should all go over to the island. Aunt Fanny was pleased.

'Oh yes! That would be nice. I expect your uncle wants a message sent off somewhere. We'll go this morning.'

George flew off to tell James she wanted her boat. Aunt

Fanny packed up plenty of food with Joanna's help. Then they set off to Kirrin Island in George's boat.

As they rounded the low wall of rocks and came into the little cove, they saw Uncle Quentin waiting for them. He waved his hand, and helped to pull in the boat when it ran gently on to the sand.

'We saw your treble signal,' said Aunt Fanny. 'Did you want something, dear?'

'Yes, I did,' said Uncle Quentin. 'What's that you've got in your basket, Fanny? More of those delicious sandwiches. I'll have some!'

'Oh, Quentin – haven't you been having your meals properly again?' said Aunt Fanny. 'What about that lovely soup?'

'What soup?' said Uncle Quentin, looking surprised. 'I wish I'd known about it. I could have done with some last night.'

'But, *Quentin*! I told you about it before,' said Aunt Fanny. 'It will be bad by now. You must pour it away. Now, don't forget – pour it away! Where is it? Perhaps I had better pour it away myself.'

'No. I'll do it,' said Uncle Quentin. 'Let's sit down and have our lunch.'

It was much too early for lunch, but Aunt Fanny at once sat down and began to unpack the food. The children were always ready for a meal at any time, so they didn't in the least mind lunch being so early.

'Well, dear – how is your work getting on?' asked Aunt

Fanny, watching her husband devour sandwich after sandwich. She began to wonder if he had had anything at all to eat since she had left him two days ago.

'Oh very well indeed,' said her husband. 'Couldn't be better. Just got to a most tricky and interesting point. I'll have another sandwich, please.'

'Why did you signal eighteen times, Uncle Quentin?' asked Anne.

'Ah, well – it's difficult to explain, really,' said her uncle. 'The fact is – I can't help feeling there's somebody else on this island besides myself!'

'*Quentin!* What in the world do you mean?' cried Aunt Fanny, in alarm. She looked over her shoulder as if she half expected to see somebody there. All the children stared in amazement at Uncle Quentin.

He took another sandwich. 'Yes, I know it sounds mad. Nobody else could possibly have got here. But I know there *is* someone!'

'Oh don't, Uncle!' said Anne, with a shiver. 'It sounds horrid. And you're all alone at night too!'

'Ah, that's just it! I wouldn't mind a bit if I *was* all alone at night!' said her uncle. 'What worries me is that I don't think I *shall* be all alone.'

'Uncle, what makes you think there's somebody here?' asked Julian.

'Well, when I had finished the experiment I was doing last night – about half past three in the early morning it would be – but pitch-dark, of course,' said Uncle Quentin,

'I came into the open for a breath of fresh air. And I could swear I heard somebody cough – yes, cough twice!'

'Good gracious!' said Aunt Fanny, startled. 'But Quentin – you might have been mistaken. You do imagine things sometimes, you know, when you're tired.'

'Yes, I know,' said her husband. 'But I couldn't imagine *this*, could I?'

He put his hand into his pocket and took something out. He showed it to the others. It was a cigarette end, quite crisp and fresh.

'Now, I don't smoke cigarettes. Nor do any of you! Well then – who smoked that cigarette? And how did he come here? No one would bring him by boat – and that's the only way here.'

There was a silence. Anne felt scared. George stared at her father, puzzled. Who could be here? And why? And how had they got there?

'Well, Quentin – what are you going to do?' said his wife. 'What would be best?'

'I'll be all right if George will give her consent to something,' said Uncle Quentin. 'I want Timmy here, George! Will you leave him behind with me?'

CHAPTER ELEVEN

George makes a hard choice

THERE WAS a horrified silence. George stared at her father in complete dismay. Everyone waited to see what she would say.

'But, Father – Timmy and I have never been separated once,' she said at last, in a pleading voice. 'I do see you want him to guard you – and you *can* have him – but I'll have to stay here too!'

'Oh no!' said her father at once. 'You can't possibly stay, George. That's out of the question. As for never being separated from Timmy, well, surely you wouldn't mind that for once? If it was to ensure my safety?'

George swallowed hard. This was the most difficult decision she had ever had to make in her life. Leave Timmy behind on the island – where there was some unknown hidden enemy, likely to harm him if he possibly could!

And yet there was Father too – he might be in danger if there was no one to guard him.

'I shall just *have* to stay here, Father,' she said. 'I can't leave Timmy behind unless I stay too. It's no good.'

Her father began to lose his temper. He was like George – he wanted his own way, and if he didn't have it he was going to make a fuss!

'If I'd asked Julian or Dick or Anne this same thing, and they'd had a dog, they would all have said yes, at once!' he raged. 'But you, George, you must always make things difficult if you can! You and that dog – anyone would think he was worth a thousand pounds!'

'He's worth much more than that to me,' said George, in a trembling voice. Timmy crept nearer to her and pushed his nose into her hand. She held his collar as if she would not let him go for a moment.

'Yes. That dog's worth more to you than your father or mother or anyone,' said her father, in disgust.

'No, Quentin, I can't have you saying things like that,' said his wife, firmly. 'That's just silly. A mother and father are quite different from a dog – they're loved in different ways. But you are perfectly right, of course – Timmy *must* stay behind with you – and I shall certainly not allow George to stay with him. I'm not going to have *both* of you exposed to danger. It's bad enough to worry about *you*, as it is.'

George looked at her mother in dismay.

'Mother! Do tell Father I must stay here with Timmy.'

'Certainly not,' said her mother. 'Now, George, be unselfish. If it were left to Tim to decide, you know perfectly well that he would stay here – and stay *without* you. He would say to himself, "I'm needed here – my eyes are needed to spy out enemies, my ears to hear a quiet footfall – and maybe my teeth to protect my master. I shall be parted from George for a few days –

but she, like me, is big enough to put up with that!" That's what Timmy would say, George, if it were left to him.'

Everyone had been listening to this unexpected speech with great attention. It was about the only one that could persuade George to give in willingly!

She looked at Timmy. He looked back at her, wagging his tail. Then he did an extraordinary thing – he got up, walked over to George's father, and lay down beside him, looking at George as if to say 'There you are! Now you know what *I* think is right!'

'You see?' said her mother. 'He agrees with me. You've always said that Timmy was a good dog, and this proves it. He knows what his duty is. You ought to be proud of him.'

'I am,' said George, in a choky voice. She got up and walked off. 'All right,' she said over her shoulder. 'I'll leave him on the island with Father. I'll come back in a minute.'

Anne got up to go after poor George, but Julian pulled her down again. 'Leave her alone! She'll be all right. Good old Timmy – you know what's right and what's wrong, don't you? Good dog, splendid dog!'

Timmy wagged his tail. He did not attempt to follow George. No – he meant to stay by her father now, even though he would much rather be with his mistress. He was sorry that George was unhappy – but sometimes it was better to do a hard thing and be unhappy about it, than try to be happy without doing it.

'Oh, Quentin dear, I don't like this business of you being here and somebody else spying on you,' said his wife, 'I really don't. How long will it be before you've finished your work?'

'A few days more,' said her husband. He looked at Timmy admiringly. 'That dog might almost have known what you were saying, Fanny, just now. It was remarkable the way he walked straight over to me.'

'He's a very clever dog,' said Anne warmly. 'Aren't you, Tim? You'll be quite safe with him, Uncle Quentin. He's terribly fierce when he wants to be!'

'Yes. I shouldn't care to have him leaping at *my* throat,' said her uncle. 'He's so big and powerful. Are there any more pieces of cake?'

'Quentin, it's really too bad of you to go without your meals,' said his wife. 'It's no good telling me you haven't, because you wouldn't be as ravenous as this if you had had your food regularly.'

Her husband took no notice of what she was saying. He was looking up at his tower. 'Do you ever see those wires at the top blaze out?' he asked. 'Wonderful sight, isn't it?'

'Uncle, you're not inventing a new atom bomb, or anything are you?' asked Anne.

Her uncle looked at her scornfully. 'I wouldn't waste my time inventing things that will be used to harm and maim people! No – I'm inventing something that will be of the greatest use to mankind. You wait and see!'

George came back. 'Father,' she said, 'I'm leaving Timmy behind for you – but please will you do something for me?'

'What?' asked her father. 'No silly conditions now! I shall feed Timmy regularly, and look after him, if that's what you want to ask me. I may forget my own meals, but you ought to know me well enough to know I shouldn't neglect any animal dependent on me.'

'Yes – I know, Father,' said George, looking a bit doubtful all the same. 'What I wanted to ask you was this – when you go up in the tower to signal each morning, will you please take Timmy with you? I shall be up at the coastguard's cottage, looking through his telescope at the glass room in the tower – and I shall be able to see Timmy then. If I catch just a glimpse of him each day and know he's all right, I shan't worry so much.'

'Very well,' said her father. 'But I don't suppose for a moment that Timmy will be able to climb up the spiral stairway.'

'Oh, he can, Father – he's been up it once already,' said George.

'Good heavens!' said her father. 'Has the dog been up there too? All right, George – I promise I'll take him up with me each morning that I signal, and get him to wag his tail at you. There! Will that satisfy you?'

'Yes. Thank you,' said George. 'And you'll give him a

few kind words and a pat occasionally, Father, won't you . . . and . . . ?'

'And put his bib on for him at meal-times, I suppose, and clean his teeth for him at night!' said her father, looking cross again. 'I shall treat Timmy like a proper grown-up dog, a friend of mine, George – and believe me, that's the way he wants me to treat him. Isn't it, Timmy? You like all those frills to be kept for your mistress, don't you, not for me?'

'Woof,' said Timmy, and thumped his tail. The children looked at him admiringly. He really was a very sensible clever dog. He seemed somehow much more grown-up than George.

'Uncle, if anything goes wrong, or you want help or anything, flash eighteen times again,' said Julian. 'You ought to be all right with Timmy. He's better than a dozen policemen – but you never know.'

'Right. Eighteen flashes if I want you over here for anything,' said his uncle. 'I'll remember. Now you'd better all go. It's time I got on with my work.'

'You'll pour that soup away, won't you, Quentin?' said his wife, anxiously. 'You don't want to make yourself ill by eating bad soup. It must be green by now! It would be so like you to forget all about it while it was fresh and good – and only remember when it was bad!'

'What a thing to say!' said her husband, getting up. 'Anyone would think I was five years old, without a brain in my head, the way you talk to me!'

'You've plenty of brains dear, we all know that,' said his wife. 'But you don't seem very old sometimes! Now, look after yourself – and keep Timmy by you all the time.'

'Father won't need to bother about *that*,' said George. 'Timmy will keep by *him*! You're on guard, Timmy, aren't you? And you know what *that* means!'

'Woof,' said Timmy, solemnly. He went with them all to the boat, but he did not attempt to get in. He stood by George's father and watched the boat bob away over the water. 'Good-bye, Timmy!' shouted George, in a funny fierce voice. 'Look after yourself!'

Her father waved, and Timmy wagged his tail. George took one of the pairs of oars from Dick and began to row furiously, her face red with the hard work.

Julian looked at her in amusement. It was hard work for him, too, to keep up with the furious rowing, but he didn't say anything. He knew all this fury in rowing was George's way of hiding her grief at parting with Timmy. Funny old George! She was always so intense about things – furiously happy or furiously unhappy, in the seventh heaven of delight or down in the very depths of despair or anger.

Everyone talked hard so that George would think they were not noticing her feelings at parting with Timmy. The talk, of course, was mostly about the unknown man on the island. It seemed very mysterious indeed that he should suddenly have arrived.

'How did he get there? I'm sure not one of the fishermen would have taken him,' said Dick. 'He must have gone at night, of course, and I doubt if there is anyone but George who would know the way in the dark – or even dare to try and find it. These rocks are so close together, and so near the surface; one yard out of the right course and any boat would have a hole in the bottom!'

'No one could reach the island by swimming from the shore,' said Anne. 'It's too far, and the sea is too rough over these rocks. I honestly do wonder if there *is* anyone on the island after all. Perhaps that cigarette end was an old one.'

'It didn't look it,' said Julian. 'Well, it just beats me how anyone got there!'

He fell into thought, puzzling out all the possible and impossible ways. Then he gave an exclamation. The others looked at him.

'I've just thought – would it be possible for an aeroplane to parachute anyone down on the island? I did hear a throbbing noise one night – was it last night? It must have been a plane's engine, of course! *Could* anyone be dropped on the island?'

'Easily,' said Dick. 'I believe you've hit on the explanation, Ju! Good for you! But I say – whoever it is must be in deadly earnest, to risk being dropped on a small island like that in the dark of night!'

In deadly earnest! That didn't sound at all nice. A little shiver went down Anne's back. 'I *am* glad Timmy's there,' she said. And everyone felt the same – yes even George!

CHAPTER TWELVE

The old map again

IT WAS only about half past one when they arrived back, because they had had lunch so very early, and had not stayed long on the island. Joanna was most surprised to see them.

'Well, here you are again!' she said. 'I hope you don't all want another lunch, because there's nothing in the house till I go to the butcher's!'

'Oh no, Joanna – we've had our picnic lunch,' said George's mother, 'and it was a good thing we packed so much, because my husband ate nearly half the lunch! He still hasn't had that nice soup we made for him. Now it will be bad of course.'

'Oh, the men! They're as bad as children!' said Joanna.

'*Well!*' said George. 'Do you really think any of *us* would let your good soup go bad, Joanna? You know jolly well we'd probably eat it up before we ought to!'

'That's true – I wouldn't accuse any of you four – or Timmy either – of playing about with your food,' said Joanna. 'You make good work of it, the lot of you. But where is Timmy?'

'I left him behind to look after Father,' said George.

Joanna stared at her in surprise. She knew how passionately fond of Timmy George was.

'You're a very good girl – sometimes!' she said. 'See now – if you're still hungry because your father has eaten most of your lunch, go and look in the biscuit tin. I made you some of your favourite ginger biscuits this morning. Go and find them.'

That was always Joanna's way! If she thought anyone was upset, she offered them her best and freshest food. George went off to find the biscuits.

'You're a kind soul, Joanna,' said George's mother. 'I'm so thankful we left Timmy there. I feel happier about my husband now.'

'What shall we do this afternoon?' said Dick, when they had finished munching the delicious ginger biscuits. 'I say, aren't these good? You know, I do think good cooks deserve some kind of decoration, just as much as good soldiers or scientists, or writers. I should give Joanna the OBCBE.'

'Whatever's that?' said Julian.

'Order of the Best Cooks of the British Empire,' said Dick grinning. 'What did you think it was? "Oh Be Careful Before Eating"?'

'You really are an absolute donkey,' said Julian. 'Now, what *shall* we do this afternoon?'

'Go and explore the passage in the quarry,' said George.

Julian cocked an eye at the window. 'It's about to pour with rain,' he said. 'I don't think that clambering up and down the steep sides of that quarry in the wet would be very easy. No – we'll leave that till a fine day.'

'I'll tell you what we'll do,' said Anne suddenly. 'Do you remember that old map of Kirrin Castle we once found in a box? It had plans of the castle in it – a plan of the dungeons, and of the ground floor, and of the top part. Well, let's have it out and study it! Now we know there is another hiding-place somewhere, we might be able to trace it on that old map. It's sure to be on it somewhere – but perhaps we didn't notice it before!'

The others looked at her, thrilled. 'Now that really is a brilliant idea of yours, Anne,' said Julian, and Anne glowed with pleasure at his praise. 'A very fine idea indeed. Just the thing for a wet afternoon. Where's the map? I suppose you've got it somewhere safe, George?'

'Oh yes,' said George. 'It's still in that old wooden box, inside the tin lining. I'll get it.'

She disappeared upstairs and came down again with the map. It was made of thick parchment, and was yellow with age. She laid it out on the table. The others bent over it, eager to look at it once more.

'Do you remember how frightfully excited we were when we first found the box?' said Dick.

'Yes, and we couldn't open it, so we threw it out of the top window down to the ground below, hoping it would burst open!' said George.

'And the crash woke up Uncle Quentin,' said Anne,

with a giggle. 'And he came out and got the box and wouldn't let us have it!'

'Oh dear yes – and poor Julian had to wait till Uncle Quentin was asleep, and creep in and get the box to see what was in it!' finished Dick. 'And we found this map – and how we pored over it!'

They all pored over it again. It was in three parts, as Anne had said – a plan of the dungeons, a plan of the ground floor and a plan of the top part.

'It's no good bothering about the top part of the castle,' said Dick. 'It's all fallen down and ruined. There's practically none of it left except for that one tower.'

'I say!' said Julian, suddenly putting his finger on a certain spot in the map, 'do you remember there were *two* entrances to the dungeons? One that seemed to start somewhere about that little stone room – and the other that started where we did at last find the entrance? Well – we never found the other entrance, did we?'

'No! We didn't!' said George, in excitement. She pushed Julian's finger away from the map. 'Look – there are steps shown here – somewhere where that little room is – so there *must* be an entrance there! Here's the *other* flight of steps – the ones we did find, near the well.'

'I remember that we hunted pretty hard for the entrance in the little room,' said Dick. 'We scraped away the weeds from every single stone, and gave it up at last. Then we found the other entrance, and forgot all about this one.'

'And *I* think Father has found the entrance we *didn't* find!' said George, triumphantly. 'It leads underground, obviously. Whether or not it joins up with the dungeons we know I can't make out from this map. It's a bit blurred here. But it's quite plain that there *is* an entrance here, with stone steps leading underground somewhere! Look, there's some sort of passage or tunnel marked, leading from the steps. Goodness knows where it goes, it's so smeared.'

'It joins up with the dungeons, I expect,' said Julian. 'We never explored the whole of them, you know – they're so vast and weird. If we explored the whole place, we should probably come across the stone steps leading from somewhere near that little room. Still, they may be ruined or fallen in now.'

'No, they can't be,' said George. 'I'm perfectly *sure* that's the entrance Father has found. And I'll tell you something that seems to prove it, too.'

'What?' said everyone.

'Well, do you remember the other day when we first went to see Father?' said George. 'He didn't let us stay long, and he came to see us off at the boat. Well, we tried to see where he went, but we couldn't – but Dick said he saw the jackdaws rising up in a flock, as if they had been suddenly disturbed – and he wondered if Father had gone somewhere in that direction.'

Julian whistled. 'Yes – the jackdaws build in the tower, which is by the little room – and anyone going into the room would disturb them. I believe you're right, George.'

'It's been puzzling me awfully where Uncle Quentin could be doing his work,' said Dick. 'I simply could *not* solve the mystery – but now I think we have!'

'I wonder how Father found his hiding-place,' said George, thoughtfully. 'I still think it was mean of him not to tell me.'

'There must have been some reason,' said Dick,

sensibly. 'Don't start brooding again!'

'I'm not,' said George. 'I'm puzzled, that's all. I wish we could take the boat and go over to the island at once, and explore!'

'Yes. I bet we'd find the entrance all right now,' said Dick. 'Your father is sure to have left some trace of where it is – a stone a bit cleaner than the rest – or weeds scraped off – or something.'

'Do you suppose the unknown enemy on the island knows Uncle Quentin's hiding-place?' said Anne, suddenly. 'Oh, I do hope he doesn't! He could so easily shut him in if he did.'

'Well, he hasn't gone there to shut Uncle up – he's gone there to steal his secret, or find it out,' said Julian. 'Golly, I'm thankful he's got Timmy. Timmy could tackle a dozen enemies.'

'Not if they had guns,' said George, in a small voice. There was a silence. It was not a nice thought to think of Timmy at the wrong end of a gun. This had happened once or twice before in their adventures, and they didn't want to think of it happening again.

'Well, it's no good thinking silly things like that,' said Dick, getting up. 'We've had a jolly interesting half-hour. I think we've solved *that* mystery. But I suppose we shan't know for certain till your father's finished his experiment, George, and left the island – then we can go over and have a good snoop round.'

'It's still raining,' said Anne, looking out of the window.

'But it's a bit clearer. It looks as if the sun will be out soon. Let's go for a walk.'

'I shall go up to the coastguard's cottage,' said George, at once. 'I want to look through his telescope to see if I can just get a glimpse of Timmy.'

'Try the field-glasses,' suggested Julian. 'Go up to the top of the house with them.'

'Yes, I will,' said George. 'Thanks for the idea.'

She fetched the field-glasses, where they hung in the hall, and took them out of their leather case. She ran upstairs with them. But she soon came down again, looking disappointed.

'The house isn't high enough for me to see much of the island properly. I can see the glass top of the tower easily, of course – but the telescope would show it much better. It's more powerful. I think I'll go up and have a squint. You don't need to come if you don't want to.' She put the glasses back into their case.

'Oh, we'll all come and have a squint for old Timmy dog,' said Dick, getting up. 'And I don't mind telling you what we'll see!'

'What?' said George, in surprise.

'We'll see Timmy having a perfectly wonderful time, chasing every single rabbit on the island!' said Dick with a grin. 'My word – you needn't worry about Timmy not having his food regularly! He'll have rabbit for breakfast, rabbit for dinner, rabbit for tea – and rain-water from his favourite pool. Not a bad life for old Timmy!'

'You know perfectly well he'll do nothing of the sort,' said George. 'He'll keep close to Father and not think of rabbits once!'

'You don't know Timmy if you think that,' said Dick dodging out of George's way. She was turning red with exasperation. 'I bet that's why he wanted to stay. *Just* for the rabbits!'

George threw a book at him. It crashed to the floor. Anne giggled. 'Oh stop it, you two. We'll never get out. Come on Ju – we won't wait for the squabblers!'

CHAPTER THIRTEEN

Afternoon with Martin

BY THE time they reached the coastguard's cottage the sun was out. It was a real April day, with sudden showers and then the sun sweeping out, smiling. Everything glittered, especially the sea. It was wet underfoot, but the children had on their rubber boots.

They looked for the coastguard. As usual he was in his shed, singing and hammering.

'Good day to you,' he said, beaming all over his red face. 'I was wondering when you'd come and see me again. How do you like this railway station I'm making?'

'It's better than any I've ever seen in the shops,' said Anne in great admiration. The coastguard certainly had made it well, down to the smallest detail.

He nodded his head towards some small wooden figures of porters and guards and passengers. 'Those are waiting to be painted,' he said. 'That boy Martin said he'd come in and do them for me – very handy with his paints he is, a proper artist – but he's had an accident.'

'*Has* he? What happened?' said Julian.

'I don't quite know. He was half-carried home this morning by his father,' said the coastguard. 'Must have slipped and fallen somewhere. I went out to ask, but

Mr Curton was in a hurry to get the boy on a couch. Why don't you go in and ask after him? He's a funny sort of boy – but he's not a bad boy.'

'Yes, we will go and ask,' said Julian. 'I say – would you mind if we looked through your telescope again?'

'Now you go and look at all you want to!' said the old fellow. 'I tell you, you won't wear it out by looking! I saw the signal from your father's tower last night, George –

just happened to be looking that way. He went on flashing for a long time, didn't he?'

'Yes,' said George. 'Thank you. I'll go and have a look now.'

She went to the telescope and trained it on her island. But no matter where she looked she could not see Timmy, or her father. They must be down in his workroom, wherever it was. She looked at the glass room in the top of the tower. That was empty too, of course. She sighed. It would have been nice to see Timmy.

The others had a look through as well. But nobody saw Timmy. It was plain that he was keeping close to his master – a proper little guard!

'Well – shall we go in and see what's happened to Martin?' said Julian, when they had finished with the telescope. 'It's just about to pour with rain again – another April shower! We could wait next door till it's over.'

'Right. Let's go,' said Dick. He looked at George. 'Don't be afraid I shall be rude, George. Now that I know Mr Curton is a journalist, I shan't bother about him.'

'All the same – I'm not "blabbing" any more,' said George, with a grin. 'I see your point now – even if it doesn't matter, I still shan't "blab" any more.'

'Good for you!' said Dick, pleased. 'Spoken like a boy!'

'Ass!' said George, but she was pleased all the same.

They went through the front gateway of the next cottage. As they filed in, they heard an angry voice.

'Well, you can't! Always wanting to mess about with a brush and paint. I thought I'd knocked that idea out of your head. You lie still and get that ankle better. Spraining it just when I want your help!'

Anne stopped, feeling frightened. It was Mr Curton's voice they could hear through the open window. He was giving Martin a good talking-to about something, that was plain. The others stopped too, wondering whether to go in or not.

Then they heard a bang, and saw Mr Curton leaving the cottage from the back entrance. He walked rapidly down the garden, and made for the path, that led to the back of the cliff. There was a road there that went to the village.

'Good. He's gone. *And* he didn't see us!' said Dick. 'Who would have thought that such a genial, smiling fellow could have such a rough brutal voice when he loses his temper? Come on – let's pop in and see poor Martin while there's a chance.'

They knocked on the door. 'It's us!' called Julian, cheerfully. 'Can we come in?'

'Oh yes!' shouted Martin from indoors, sounding pleased. Julian opened the door and they all went in.

'I say! We heard you'd had an accident,' said Julian. 'What's up? Are you hurt much?'

'No. It's just that I twisted my ankle, and it was so painful to walk on that I had to be half-carried up here,' said Martin. 'Silly thing to do!'

'Oh – it'll soon be right if it's just a twist,' said Dick. 'I've often done that. The thing is to walk on it as soon as you can. Where were you when you fell?'

Martin went suddenly red, to everyone's surprise. 'Well – I was walking on the edge of the quarry with my father – and I slipped and rolled a good way down,' he said.

There was a silence. Then George spoke. 'I say,' she said, 'I hope you didn't go and give away our little secret to your father? I mean – it's not so much fun when grown-ups share a secret. They want to go snooping about themselves – and it's much more fun to discover things by ourselves. You didn't tell him about that hole under the shelf of rock, did you?'

Martin hesitated. 'I'm afraid I did,' he said at last. 'I didn't think it would matter. I'm sorry.'

'Blow!' said Dick. 'That was our own little discovery. We wanted to go and explore it this afternoon, but we thought it would be so wet we'd fall down the steep slope.'

Julian looked at Martin sharply. 'I suppose that's what happened to *you*?' he said. 'You tried clambering down and slipped!'

'Yes,' said Martin. 'I'm really sorry if you thought it was your secret. I just mentioned it to my father out of interest – you know – something to say – and he wanted to go down and see for himself.'

'I suppose journalists are always like that,' said Dick. 'Wanting to be on the spot if there's anything to be ferreted out. It's their job. All right, Martin – forget it. But do try and head your father off the quarry. We *would* like to do a bit of exploring, before he butts in. Though there may be nothing to be found at all!'

There was a pause. Nobody knew quite what to say. Martin was rather difficult to talk to. He didn't talk like any ordinary boy – he never made a joke, or said anything silly.

'Aren't you bored, lying here?' said Anne feeling sorry for him.

'Yes, awfully. I wanted my father to go in and ask the coastguard to bring in some little figures I said I'd paint for him,' said Martin. 'But he wouldn't let me. You know I simply love painting – even doing a little thing like that – painting clothes on toy porters and guards – so long as I can have a brush in my hand and colours to choose from!'

This was the longest speech Martin had ever made to the four children! His face lost its dull, bored look as he spoke, and became bright and cheerful.

'Oh – you want to be an artist, I suppose?' said Anne. 'I would like that too!'

'Anne! you can't even draw a cat that looks like one!' said Dick, scornfully. 'And when you drew a cow I thought it was an elephant.'

Martin smiled at Anne's indignant face. 'I'll show you some of my pictures,' he said. 'I have to keep them hidden away, because my father can't bear me to want to be an artist!'

'Don't get up if you don't want to,' said Julian. 'I'll get them for you.'

'It's all right. If it's good for me to try and walk, I will,' said Martin, and got off the couch. He put his right foot gingerly to the floor and then stood up. 'Not so bad after all!' he said. He limped across the room to a bookcase. He put his hand behind the second row of books and brought out a cardboard case, big and flat. He took it to the table. He opened it and spread out some pictures.

'Gracious!' said Anne. 'They're *beautiful*! Did you really do these?'

They were strange pictures for a young person to draw, for they were of flowers and trees, birds and butterflies – all drawn and coloured most perfectly, every detail put in lovingly.

Julian looked at them in surprise. This boy was certainly gifted. Why, these drawings were as good as any he had ever seen in exhibitions! He picked a few up and took them to the window.

'Do you mean to say your father doesn't think these are good – doesn't think it's worthwhile to let you train as an artist?' he said, in surprise.

'He hates my pictures,' said Martin, bitterly. 'I ran away from school, and went to an art-school to train – but he found me and forbade me to think of drawing any more. He thinks it's a weak, feeble thing for a man to do. So I only do it in secret now.'

The children looked at Martin with sympathy. It seemed

an awful thing to them that a boy who had no mother, should have a father who hated the thing his son most loved. No wonder he always looked dull and miserable and sullen!

'It's very bad luck,' said Julian at last. 'I wish we could do something to help.'

'Well – get me those figures and the paint tins from the coastguard,' said Martin, eagerly. 'Will you? Father won't be back till six. I'll have time to do them. And do stay and have tea with me. It's so dull up here. I hate it.'

'Yes, I'll get the things for you,' said Julian. 'I can't for the life of me see why you shouldn't have something to amuse yourself with if you want to. And we'll ring up my aunt and tell her we're staying here to tea – so long as we don't eat everything you've got!'

'Oh, that's all right,' said Martin, looking very cheerful indeed. 'There's plenty of food in the house. My father has an enormous appetite. I say, thanks most awfully.'

Julian rang up his aunt. The girls and Dick went to fetch the figures and the paint from the coastguard. They brought them back and arranged them on a table beside Martin. His eyes brightened at once. He seemed quite different.

'This is grand,' he said. 'Now I can get on! It's a silly little job, this, but it will help the old man next door, and I'm always happy when I'm messing about with a brush and paints!'

Martin was very, very clever at painting the little figures.

He was quick and deft, and Anne sat watching him, quite fascinated. George went to hunt in the larder for the tea-things. There was certainly plenty of food! She cut some bread and butter, found some new honey, brought out a huge chocolate cake and some ginger buns, and put the kettle on to boil.

'I say, this is really grand,' said Martin again. 'I wish my father wasn't coming back till eight. By the way – where's the dog? I thought he always went everywhere with you! Where's Timmy?'

CHAPTER FOURTEEN

A shock for George

DICK LOOKED at George. He didn't think it would matter telling Martin where Timmy was, so long as George didn't give the *reason* why he had been left on the island.

But George was going to hold her tongue now. She looked at Martin and spoke quite airily. 'Oh, Timmy? We left him behind today. He's all right.'

'Gone out shopping with your mother, I suppose, hoping for a visit to the butcher's!' said Martin. This was the first joke he had ever made to the children, and though it was rather a feeble one they laughed heartily. Martin looked pleased. He began to try and think of another little joke, while his deft hands put reds and blues and greens on the little wooden figures.

They all had a huge tea. Then, when the clock said a quarter to six the girls carried the painted figures carefully back to the coastguard, who was delighted with them. Dick took back the little tins of paint, and the brush stuck in a jar of turpentine.

'Well now, he's clever that boy, isn't he?' said the coastguard, eyeing the figures in delight. 'Looks sort of miserable and sulky – but he's not a bad sort of boy!'

'I'll just have one more squint through your telescope,' said George, 'before it gets too dark.'

She tilted it towards her island. But once more there was no sign of Timmy, or of her father either. She looked for some time, and then went to join the others. She shook her head as they raised their eyebrows inquiringly.

They washed up the tea-things, and cleared away neatly. Nobody felt as if they wanted to wait and see Mr Curton. They didn't feel as if they liked him very much, now they knew how hard he was on Martin.

'Thanks for a lovely afternoon,' said Martin, limping to the door with them. 'I enjoyed my spot of painting, to say nothing of your company.'

'You stick out for your painting,' said Julian. 'If it's the thing you've *got* to do, and you know it, you must go all out for it. See?'

'Yes,' said Martin, and his face went sullen again. 'But there are things that make it difficult – things I can't very well tell you. Oh well – never mind! I dare say it will all come right one day, and I'll be a famous artist with pictures in the Academy!'

'Come on, quickly,' said Dick, in a low voice to Julian. 'There's his father coming back!'

They hurried off down the cliff-path, seeing Mr Curton out of the corner of their eyes, coming up the other path.

'Horrid man!' said Anne. 'Forbidding Martin to do what he really longs to do. And he seemed so nice and jolly and all-over-us, didn't he?'

'Very all-over-us,' said Dick, smiling at Anne's new word. 'But there are a lot of people like that – one thing at home and quite another outside!'

'I hope Mr Curton hasn't been trying to explore that passage in the side of the quarry,' said George, looking back, and watching the man walk up to his back door. 'It would be too bad if he butted in and spoilt our fun. I mean – there may be nothing to discover at all – but it will be fun even finding there *is* nothing.'

'Very involved!' said Dick, with a grin. 'But I gather what you mean. I say, that was a good tea, wasn't it?'

'Yes,' said George, looking all round her in an absent-minded manner.

'What's up?' said Dick. 'What are you looking like that for?'

'Oh – how silly of me – I was just looking for Timmy,' said George. 'You know, I'm so used to him always being at my heels or somewhere near that I just can't get used to him not being here.'

'Yes, I feel a bit like that too,' said Julian. 'As if there was something missing all the time. Good old Tim! We shall miss him awfully, all of us – but you most of all, George.'

'Yes. Especially on my bed at night,' said George. 'I shan't be able to go to sleep for ages and ages.'

'I'll wrap a cushion up in a rug and plonk it down on your feet when you're in bed,' said Dick. 'Then it will feel like Timmy!'

'It won't! Don't be silly,' said George, rather crossly. 'And anyway it wouldn't *smell* like him. He's got a lovely smell.'

'Yes, a Timmy-smell,' agreed Anne. 'I like it too.'

The evening went very quickly, playing the endless game of Monopoly again. Julian lay in bed later, watching for his uncle's signal. Needless to say, George was at the window too! They waited for half past ten.

'Now!' said Julian. And just as he spoke there came the first flash from the lantern in the tower.

'One,' counted George, 'two – three – four – five – six!' She waited anxiously to see if there were any more, but there weren't.

'Now you can go to bed in peace,' said Julian to George. 'Your father is all right, and that means that Timmy is all right too. Probably he has remembered to give Timmy a good supper and has had some himself as well!'

'Well, Timmy would soon remind him if he forgot to feed him, that's one thing,' said George, slipping out of the room. 'Good night, Dick; good night, Ju! See you in the morning.'

And back she went to her own bed and snuggled down under the sheets. It was strange not to have Timmy on her feet. She tossed about for a while, missing him, and then fell asleep quite suddenly. She dreamt of her island. She was there with Timmy – and they were discovering ingots of gold down in the dungeon. What a lovely dream!

Next morning dawned bright and sunny again. The

April sky was as blue as the forget-me-nots coming out in the garden. George gazed out of the dining-room window at breakfast-time wondering if Timmy was running about her island.

'Dreaming about Tim?' said Julian, with a laugh. 'Never mind – you'll soon see him, George. Another hour or so and you'll feast your eyes on him through the coastguard's telescope!'

'Do you really think you'll be able to make out Tim, if he's in the tower with your father at half past ten?' asked her mother. 'I shouldn't have thought you would be able to.'

'Yes, I shall, Mother,' said George. 'It's a very powerful telescope, you know. I'll just go up and make my bed, then I'll go up the cliff-path. Anyone else coming?'

'I want Anne to help me with some turning out,' said her mother. 'I'm looking out some old clothes to give to the vicar's wife for her jumble sale. You don't mind helping me, Anne, do you?'

'No, I'd like to,' said Anne at once. 'What are the boys going to do?'

'I think I must do a bit of my holiday work this morning,' said Julian, with a sigh. 'I don't want to – but I've kept on putting it off. You'd better do some too, Dick. You know what you are – you'll leave it all to the last day if you're not careful!'

'All right. I'll do some too,' said Dick. 'You won't mind scooting up to the coastguard's cottage alone, will you, George?'

'Not a bit,' said George. 'I'll come back just after half past ten, as soon as I've spotted Timmy and Father.'

She disappeared to make her bed. Julian and Dick went to fetch some books. Anne went to make her bed too, and then came down to help her aunt. In a few minutes George yelled good-bye and rushed out of the house.

'What a hurricane!' said her mother. 'It seems as if George never walks if she can possibly run. Now, Anne, put the clothes in three piles – the very old, the not so old, and the quite nice.'

Just before half past ten Julian went up to his window to watch for the signal from his uncle. He waited patiently. A few seconds after the half-hour the flashes came – one, two, three, four, five, six – good! Now George would settle down for the day. Perhaps they could go to the quarry in the afternoon. Julian went back to his books and was soon buried in them, with Dick grunting by his side.

At about five minutes to eleven there was the sound of running feet and panting breath. George appeared at the door of the sitting-room where the two boys were doing their work. They looked up.

George was red in the face, and her hair was windblown. She fought to get her breath enough to speak. 'Julian! Dick! Something's happened – Timmy wasn't there!'

'What do you mean?' said Julian in surprise. George slumped down on a chair, still panting. The boys could see that she was trembling too.

'It's serious, Julian! I tell you Timmy wasn't in the tower when the signals came!'

'Well, it only means that your absent-minded father forgot to take him up with him,' said Julian, in his most sensible voice. 'What *did* you see?'

'I had my eye glued to the telescope,' said George, 'and suddenly I saw someone come into the little glass room at the top. I looked for Timmy, of course, at once – but I tell you, he wasn't there! The six flashes came, the man disappeared – and that was all. No, Timmy! Oh I do feel so dreadfully worried, Julian.'

'Well, don't be,' said Julian, soothingly. 'Honestly, I'm sure that's what happened. Your father forgot about Timmy. Anyway, if you saw *him*, obviously things are all right.'

'I'm not thinking about Father!' cried George. 'He must be all right if he flashed his signals – I'm thinking about Timmy. Why, even if Father forgot to take him, he'd go with him. You know that!'

'Your father might have shut the door at the bottom and prevented Timmy from going up,' said Dick.

'He might,' said George, frowning. She hadn't thought of that. 'Oh dear – now I shall worry all day long. *Why* didn't I stay with Timmy? What shall I do now?'

'Wait till tomorrow morning,' said Dick. 'Then probably you'll see old Tim all right.'

'Tomorrow morning! Why, that's *ages* away!' said poor George. She put her head in her hands and groaned. 'Oh, nobody understands how much I love Timmy. You would perhaps if you had a dog of your own, Julian. It's an awful feeling, really. Oh, Timmy, are you all right?'

'Of course he's all right,' said Julian, impatiently. 'Do pull yourself together, George.'

'I *feel* as if something's wrong,' said George, looking obstinate. 'Julian – I think I'd better go across to the island.'

'No,' said Julian at once. 'Don't be idiotic, George. Nothing is wrong, except that your father's been forgetful. He's sent his OK signal. That's enough! You're not to go and create a scene over there with him. That would be disgraceful!'

'Well – I'll try and be patient,' said George, unexpectedly meek. She got up, looking worried. Julian spoke in a kinder voice.

'Cheer up, old thing! You do like to go off the deep end, don't you?'

CHAPTER FIFTEEN

In the middle of the night

GEORGE DID not moan any more about her worries. She went about with an anxious look in her blue eyes, but she had the sense not to tell her mother how worried she was at not seeing Timmy in the glass room, when her father signalled.

She mentioned it, of course, but her mother took the same view as Julian did. 'There! I knew he'd forget to take Timmy up! He's so very forgetful when he's at work.'

The children decided to go to the quarry that afternoon and explore the tunnel under the shelf of rock. So they set off after their lunch. But when they came to the quarry, they did not dare to climb down the steep sides. The heavy rain of the day before had made them far too dangerous.

'Look,' said Julian, pointing to where the bushes and smaller plants were ripped up and crushed. 'I bet that's where old Martin fell down yesterday! He might have broken his neck!'

'Yes. I vote we don't attempt to go down till it's as dry as it was the other day,' said Dick.

It was very disappointing. They had brought torches, and a rope, and had looked forward to a little excitement. 'Well, what shall we do?' asked Julian.

'I'm going back home,' said George, unexpectedly. 'I'm tired. You others go for a walk.'

Anne looked at George. She did seem rather pale.

'I'll come back with you, George,' said Anne slipping her hand through her cousin's arm. But George shook it off.

'No thanks, Anne. I want to be alone.'

'Well – we'll go over to the cliff then,' said Julian. 'It'll be nice and blowy up there. See you later, George!'

They went off. George turned and sped back to Kirrin Cottage. Her mother was out. Joanna was upstairs in her bedroom. George went to the larder and took several things from it. She bundled them into a bag and then fled out of the house.

She found James the fisher-boy. 'James! You're not to tell a soul. I'm going over to Kirrin Island tonight – because I'm worried about Timmy. We left him there. Have my boat ready at ten o'clock!'

James was always ready to do anything in the world for George. He nodded and asked no questions at all. 'Right. It'll be ready. Anything you want put in it?'

'Yes, this bag,' said George. 'Now, don't split on me, James. I'll be back tomorrow if I find Tim's all right.'

She fled back to the house. She hoped Joanna would not notice the things she had taken from the larder shelf.

'I can't help it if what I'm doing is wrong,' she kept whispering to herself. 'I know something isn't right with Timmy. And I'm not at all sure about Father, either. He *wouldn't* have forgotten his solemn promise to me about taking Timmy up with him. I'll have to go across to the island. I can't help it if it's wrong!'

The others wondered what was up with George when they came back from their walk. She was so fidgety and restless. They had tea and then did some gardening for Aunt Fanny. George did some too, but her thoughts were far away, and twice her mother had to stop her pulling up seedlings instead of weeds.

Bedtime came. The girls got into bed at about a quarter to ten. Anne was tired and fell asleep at once. As soon as George heard her regular breathing she crept quietly out of bed and dressed again. She pulled on her warmest jersey, got her raincoat, rubber boots and a thick rug, and tiptoed downstairs.

Out of the side door she went and into the night. There was a bit of a moon in the sky, so it was not as dark as usual. George was glad. She would be able to see her way through the rocks a little now – though she was sure she could guide the boat even in the dark!

James was waiting for her. Her boat was ready. 'Everything's in,' said James. 'I'll push off. Now you be careful – and if you do scrape a rock, row like anything in case she fills and sinks. Ready?'

Off went George, hearing the lap-lap of the water against the sides of the boat. She heaved a sigh of relief, and began to row strongly away from the shore. She frowned as she rowed. Had she brought everything she

might want? Two torches. Plenty of food. A tin-opener. Something to drink. A rug to wrap herself in tonight.

Back at Kirrin Cottage Julian lay in bed watching for his uncle's signal. Half past ten. Now for the signal. Ah, here they were! One – two – three – four – five – six! Good. Six and no more!

He wondered why George hadn't come into his and Dick's room to watch for them. She had last night. He got up, padded to the door of George's room and put his head in. 'George!' he said softly. 'It's OK. Your father's signals have just come again.'

There was no reply. Julian heard regular breathing and turned to go back to bed. The girls must be asleep already! Well, George couldn't really be worrying much about Timmy now, then! Julian got into his bed and soon fell asleep himself. He had no idea that George's bed was empty – no idea that even now George was battling with the waves that guarded Kirrin Island!

It was more difficult that she had expected, for the moon did not really give very much light, and had an annoying way of going behind a cloud just when she badly needed every scrap of light she could get. But, deftly and cleverly, she managed to make her way through the passage between the hidden rocks. Thank goodness the tide was high so that most of them were well below the surface!

At last she swung her boat into the little cove. Here the water was perfectly calm. Panting a little, George pulled her boat up as far as she could. Then she stood in the darkness and thought hard.

What was she going to do? She did not know where her father's hiding-place was – but she felt certain the entrance to it must be somewhere in or near the little stone room. Should she make her way to that?

Yes, she would. It would be the only place to shelter in for the night, anyway. She would put on her torch when she got there, and hunt round for any likely entrance to the hiding-place. If she found it, she would go in – and what a surprise she would give her father! If old Timmy was there he would go mad with delight.

She took the heavy bag, draped the rug over her arm, and set off. She did not dare to put on her torch yet, in case the unknown enemy was lurking near. After all, her father had heard him cough at night!

George was not frightened. She did not even think about being frightened. All her thoughts were set on finding Timmy and making sure he was safe.

She came to the little stone room. It was pitch-dark in there, of course – not even the faint light of the moon pierced into its blackness. George had to put on her torch.

She put down her bundle by the wall at the back, near the old fireplace recess. She draped the rug over it and sat down to have a rest, switching off her torch.

After a while she got up cautiously and switched on her torch again. She began to search for the hiding-place. Where *could* the entrance be? She flashed her torch on to every flagstone in the floor of the room. But not one looked as if it had been moved or lifted. There was nothing to show where there might be an entrance underground.

She moved round the walls, examining those too in the light of her torch. No – there was no sign that a hidden way lay behind any of those stones either. It was most tantalising. If she only knew!

She went to wrap the rug round her, and to sit and think. It was cold now. She was shivering, as she sat there in the dark, trying to puzzle out where the hidden entrance could be.

And then she heard a sound! She jumped and then stiffened all over, holding her breath painfully. What was it?

There was a curious grating noise. Then a slight thud. It came from the recess where people long ago had built their big log fires! George sat perfectly still, straining her eyes and ears.

She saw a beam of light in the fireplace recess. Then she heard a man's cough!

Was it her father? He had a cough at times. She listened hard. The beam of light grew brighter. Then she heard another noise – it sounded as if someone had jumped down from somewhere! And then – a voice!

'Come on!'

It was not her father's voice! George grew cold with fear then. Not her father's voice! Then what had happened to him – and to Timmy?

Someone else jumped down into the recess, grumbling. 'I'm not used to this crawling about!'

That wasn't her father's voice either. So there were *two* unknown enemies! Not one. And they knew her father's secret workroom. George felt almost faint with horror. Whatever had happened to him and Timmy?

The men walked out of the little stone room without seeing George at all. She guessed they were going to the tower. How long would they be? Long enough for her to search for the place they had appeared from?

She strained her ears again. She heard their footsteps going into the great yard. She tiptoed to the doorway and looked out. Yes – there was the light of their torch near the tower! If they were going up, there would be plenty of time to look round.

She went back into the little stone room. Her hands were trembling and she found it difficult to switch on her torch. She went to the fireplace recess and flashed the light in it.

She gave a gasp! Half way up the recess at the back was a black opening! She flashed the light up there. Evidently there was a movable stone half way up that swung back and revealed an entrance behind. An entrance to what? Were there steps such as were shown in the old map?

Feeling quite breathless, George stood on tiptoe and flashed her light into the hole. Yes – there were steps! They went down into the wall at the back. She remembered that the little stone room backed on to one of the immensely thick old walls still left.

She stood there, uncertain what to do. Had she better go down and see if she could find Timmy and her father? But if she did, she might be made a prisoner too. On the other hand, if she stayed outside, and the men came back and shut up the entrance, she might not be able to open it. She would be worse off than ever!

'I'll go down!' she suddenly decided. 'But I'd better take my bag and the rug, in case the men come back and see them. I don't want them to know I'm on the island if

I can help it! I could hide them somewhere down there, I expect. I wonder if this entrance leads to the dungeons.'

She lifted up the rug and the bag and pushed them into the hole. She heard the bag roll down the steps, the tins inside making a muffled noise.

Then she climbed up herself. Gracious, what a long dark flight of steps! Wherever did they lead to?

CHAPTER SIXTEEN

Down to the caves

GEORGE WENT cautiously down the stone steps. They were steep and narrow. 'I should think they run right down in the middle of the stone wall,' thought George. 'Goodness, here's a narrow bit!'

It was so narrow that she had to go sideways. 'A large man would never get through there!' she thought to herself. 'Hallo – the steps have ended!'

She had got the rug round her shoulders, and had picked up her bag on the way down. In her other hand she held her torch. It was terribly dark and quiet down there. George did not feel scared because she was hoping to see Timmy at any moment. No one could feel afraid with Timmy just round the corner, ready to welcome them!

She stood at the bottom of the steps, her torch showing her a narrow tunnel. It curved sharply to the left. 'Now will it join the dungeons from here?' she wondered, trying to get her sense of direction to help her. 'They can't be far off. But there's no sign of them at the moment.'

She went down the narrow tunnel. Once the roof came down so low she almost had to crawl. She flashed her torch on it. She saw black rock there, which had evidently been too hard to be removed by the tunnel-builders long ago.

The tunnel went on and on and on. George was puzzled. Surely by now she must have gone by all the dungeons! Why – she must be heading towards the shore of the island! How very strange! Didn't this tunnel join the dungeons then? A little further and she would be under the bed of the sea itself.

The tunnel took a deep slope downwards. More steps appeared, cut roughly from rock. George climbed down them cautiously. Where in the world was she going?

At the bottom of the steps the tunnel seemed to be cut out of solid rock – or else it was a natural passage, not made by man at all. George didn't know. Her torch showed her black, rocky walls and roof, and her feet stumbled over an irregular rocky path. How she longed for Timmy beside her!

'I must be very deep down,' she thought, pausing to flash her torch round her once more. 'Very deep down and very far from the castle! Good gracious – whatever's that awful noise?'

She listened. She heard a muffled booming and moaning. Was it her father doing one of his experiments? The noise went on and on, a deep, never-ending boom.

'Why – I believe it's the sea!' said George, amazed. She stood and listened again. 'Yes – it *is* the sea – over my head! I'm under the rocky bed of Kirrin Bay!'

And now poor George did feel a bit scared! She thought

of the great waves surging above her, she thought of the restless, moving water scouring the rocky bed over her head, and felt frightened in case the sea should find a way to leak down into her narrow tunnel!

'Now don't be silly,' she told herself sternly. 'This tunnel has been here under the sea-bed for hundreds of years – why should it suddenly become unsafe just when *you* are in it, George?'

Talking to herself like this, to keep up her spirits, she went on again. It was very weird indeed to think she was walking under the sea. So this was where her father was at work! Under the sea itself.

And then George suddenly remembered something he had said to them all, the first time they had visited him on the island. What was it now? 'Oh yes! He said he had to have water *above* and *around* him!' said George. '*Now* I see what he meant! His workroom is somewhere down here – so the sea-water is *above* him – and it's all *round* the tower, because it's built on an island!'

Water above and water around – so that was why her father had chosen Kirrin Island for his experiment. How had he found the secret passage under the sea, though? 'Why, even I didn't know of that,' said George. 'Hallo – what am I coming to?'

She stopped. The passage had suddenly widened out into an enormous dark cave, whose roof was unexpectedly high, lost in dark shadows. George stared round. She saw strange things there that she didn't understand at all –

wires, glass boxes, little machines that seemed to be at work without a sound, whose centres were alive with funny, gleaming, shivering light.

Sudden sparks shot up now and again, and when that happened a funny smell crept round the cave. 'How weird all this is!' thought George. 'How ever can Father understand all these machines and things! I wonder where he is. I do hope those men haven't made him prisoner somewhere!'

From this strange Aladdin's cave another tunnel led. George switched on her torch again and went into it. It was much like the other one, but the roof was higher.

She came to another cave, smaller this time, and crammed with wires of all kinds. There was a curious humming sound here, like thousands of bees in a hive. George half-expected to see some flying round.

'It must be these wires making the noise,' she said. There was nobody in the cave at all, but it led into another one, and George hoped that soon she would find Timmy and her father.

She went into the next cave, which was perfectly empty and very cold. She shivered. Then down another passage, and into a small cave. The first thing she saw beyond this tiny cave was a light!

A light! Then perhaps she was coming to the cave her father must be in! She flashed her torch round the little cave she was now standing in and saw tins of food, bottles of beer, tins of sweets, and a pile of clothes of some sort. Ah, this was where her father kept his stores. She went on to the next cave, wondering why Timmy had not heard her and come to greet her.

She looked cautiously into the cave where the light came from. Sitting at a table, his head in his hands, perfectly still, was her father! There was no sign of Timmy.

'Father!' said George. The man at the table jumped violently and turned round. He stared at George as if he really could not believe his eyes. Then he turned back again, and buried his face in his hands.

'*Father!*' said George again, quite frightened because he did not say anything to her.

He looked round again, and this time he got up. He stared at George once more, and then sat down heavily. George ran to him. 'What's the matter? Oh, Father, what's the matter? Where's Timmy?'

'George! Is it *really* you, George? I thought I must be dreaming when I looked up and saw you!' said her father. 'How did you get here? Good gracious, it's impossible that you should be here!'

'Father are you all right? What's happened – and where's Timmy?' said George, urgently. She looked all round, but could see no sign of him. Her heart went cold. Surely nothing awful had happened to Timmy?

'Did you see two men?' asked her father. 'Where were they?'

'Oh, Father – we keep asking each other questions and not answering them!' said George. 'Tell me first – where is Timmy?'

'I don't know,' said her father. 'Did those two men go to the tower?'

'Yes,' said George. 'Father, what's happened?'

'Well, if they've gone to the tower, we've got about an hour in peace,' said her father. 'Now listen to me, George, very carefully. This is terribly important.'

'I'm listening,' said George. 'But do hurry up and tell me about Timmy.'

'These two men were parachuted down on to the island, to try and find out my secret,' said her father. 'I'll tell you what my experiments are for, George – they are to find a way of replacing all coal, coke and oil – an idea to give the world all the heat and power it wants, and to do away with mines and miners.'

'Good gracious!' said George. 'It would be one of the most wonderful things the world has ever known.'

'Yes,' said her father. 'And I should *give* it to the whole world – it shall not be in the power of any one country, or collection of men. It shall be a gift to the whole of mankind. But, George, there are men who want my secret for themselves, so that they may make colossal fortunes out of it.'

'How hateful!' cried George. 'Go on, Father – how did they hear of it?'

'Well, I was at work on this idea with some of my colleagues, my fellow-workers,' said her father. 'And one of them betrayed us, and went to some powerful businessmen to tell them of my idea. So when I knew this I decided to come away in secret and finish my experiments by myself. Then nobody could betray me.'

'And you came here!' said George. 'To my island.'

'Yes, because I needed water over me and water around me,' said her father. 'Quite by chance I looked at a copy of that old map, and thought that if the passage shown there – the one leading from the little stone room, I mean – if the passage there *really* did lead under the sea, as it seemed to show, that would be the ideal place to finish my experiments.'

'Oh, Father – and I made such a fuss!' said George, ashamed now, to remember how cross she had been.

'Did you?' said her father, as if he had forgotten all about that. 'Well, I got all my stuff and came here. And now these fellows have found me, and got hold of me!'

'Poor Father! Can't I help?' said George. 'I could go back and bring help over here, couldn't I?'

'Yes, you could!' said her father. 'But you mustn't let those men see you, George.'

'I'll do anything you want me to, Father, anything!' said George. 'But first do tell me what's happened to Timmy?'

'Well, he kept by me all the time,' said her father. 'Really, he's a wonderful dog, George. And then, this morning, just as I was coming out of the entrance in that little room to go up into the tower with Timmy to signal, the two men pounced on me and forced me back here.'

'But what happened to Timmy?' asked George,

impatiently. Would her father *never* tell her what she wanted to know?

'He flew at the men, of course,' said her father. 'But somehow or other one of them lassoed him with a noose of rope and caught him. They pulled the rope so tight round his neck that he almost choked.'

'Oh poor, poor Timmy,' said George, and the tears ran down her cheeks. 'Is he – do you think – he's all right, Father?'

'Yes. From what I heard the men saying afterwards I think they've taken him to some cave and shut him in there,' said her father. 'Anyway, I saw one of them getting some dog biscuits out of a bag this evening, so that looks as if he's alive and kicking – and hungry!'

George heaved a great sigh of relief. So long as Timmy was alive and all right! She took a few steps towards what she thought must be another cave. 'I'm going to find Timmy, Father,' she said. 'I *must* find him!'

CHAPTER SEVENTEEN

Timmy at last

'NO, GEORGE!' called her father sharply. 'Come back. There is something very important I want to say. Come here!'

George went over to him, filled with impatience to get to Timmy, wherever he was. She *must* find him!

'Now, listen,' said her father. 'I have a book in which I have made all my notes of this great experiment. The men haven't found it! I want you to take it safely to the mainland, George. Don't let it out of your sight! If the men get hold of it they would have all the information they needed!'

'But don't they know everything just by looking at your wires and machines and things?' asked George.

'They know a very great deal,' said her father, 'and they've found out a lot more since they've been here – but not quite enough. I daren't destroy my book of notes, because if anything should happen to me, my great idea would be completely lost. So, George, I must entrust it to you and you must take it to an address I will give you, and hand it to the person there.'

'It's an awful responsibility,' said George, a little scared of handling a book which meant so much, not only to her father, but possibly to the whole of the world. 'But I'll do my best, Father. I'll hide in one of the caves till the men come back, and then I'll slip back up the passage to the hidden entrance, get out, go to my boat and row back to the mainland. Then I'll deliver your book of notes without fail, and get help sent over here to you.'

'Good girl,' said her father, and gave her a hug. 'Honestly, George, I am proud of you.'

George thought that was the nicest thing her father had ever said to her. She smiled at him. 'Well, Father, I'll go and see if I can find Timmy now. I simply must see that he's all right before I go to hide in one of the other caves.'

'Very well,' said her father. 'The man who took the biscuits went in that direction – still further under the sea, George. Oh, by the way, how is it you're here, in the middle of the night?'

It seemed to strike her father for the first time that George also might have a story to tell. But George felt that she really couldn't waste any more time – she *must* find Timmy!

'I'll tell you later, Father,' she said. 'Oh, where's that book of notes?'

Her father rose and went to the back of the cave. He took a box and stood on it. He ran his hand along a dark ridge of rock, and felt about until he had found what he wanted.

He brought down a slim book, whose pages were of very thin paper. He opened the book and George saw many beautifully drawn diagrams, and pages of notes in her father's small neat handwriting.

'Here you are,' said her father, handing her the book. 'Do the best you can. If anything happens to me, this book will still enable my fellow-workers to give my idea to the world. If I come through this all right, I shall be glad to have the book, because it will mean I shall not have to work out all my experiments again.'

George took the precious book. She stuffed it into her macintosh pocket, which was a big one. 'I'll keep it safe, Father. Now I must go and find Timmy, or those two men will be back before I can hide in one of the other caves.'

She left her father's cave and went into the next one. There was nothing there at all. Then on she went down a passage that twisted and turned in the rock.

And then she heard a sound she longed to hear. A whine! Yes, really a whine!

'Timmy!' shouted George, eagerly. 'Oh, Timmy! I'm coming!'

Timmy's whine stopped suddenly. Then he barked joyously. 'Woof, woof, woof, woof!' George almost fell as she tried to run down the narrow tunnel. Her torch showed her a big boulder that seemed to be blocking up a small cave in the side of the tunnel. Behind the boulder Timmy barked, and scraped frantically!

George tugged at the stone with all her strength. 'Timmy!' she panted. 'Timmy! I'll get you out! I'm coming! Oh, Timmy!'

The stone moved a little. George tugged again. It was almost too heavy for her to move at all, but despair made her stronger than she had ever been in her life. The stone quite suddenly swung to one side, and George just got one of her feet out of its way in time, or it would have been crushed.

Timmy squeezed out of the space left. He flung himself on George, who fell on the ground with her arms tight round him. He licked her face and whined, and she buried her noise in his thick fur in joy. 'Timmy! What have they done to you? Timmy, I came as soon as I could!'

Timmy whined again and again in joy, and tried to paw and lick George as if he couldn't have enough of her. It would have been difficult to say which of the two was the happier.

At last George pushed Timmy away firmly. 'Timmy we've got work to do! We've got to escape from here and get across to the mainland and bring help.'

'Woof,' said Timmy. George stood up and flashed her torch into the tiny cave where Timmy had been. She saw that there was a bowl of water there and some biscuits. The men had not ill-treated him, then, except to lasso him and half-choke him when they caught him. She felt round his neck tenderly, but except for a swollen ridge there, he seemed none the worse.

'Now, hurry up – we'll go back to Father's cave – and then find another cave beyond his to hide in till the two men come back from the tower. Then we'll creep out into the little stone room and row back to the mainland,' said George. 'I've got a very, very important book here in my pocket, Timmy.'

Timmy growled suddenly, and the hairs on the back of his neck rose up. George stiffened, and stood listening.

A stern voice came down the passage. 'I don't know who you are or where you've come from, but if you have dared to let that dog loose he'll be shot! And, to show you that I mean what I say, here's something to let you know I've a revolver!'

Then there came a deafening crash, as the man pulled the trigger, and a bullet hit the roof somewhere in the passage. Timmy and George almost jumped out of their skins. Timmy would have leapt up the passage at once, but

George had her hand on his collar. She was very frightened, and tried hard to think what was best to do.

The echoes of the shot went on and on. It was horrid. Timmy stopped growling, and George stayed absolutely still.

'Well?' said the voice, 'did you hear what I said? If that dog is loose, he'll be shot. I'm not having my plans spoilt now. And you, whoever you are, will please come up the tunnel and let me see you. But I warn you, if the dog's with you, that's the end of him!'

'Timmy! Timmy, run away and hide somewhere!' whispered George suddenly. And then she remembered something else that filled her with despair. She had her father's precious book of notes with her – in her pocket! Suppose the man found it on her? It would break her father's heart to know that his wonderful secret had been stolen from him after all.

George hurriedly took the thin, flat little book from her pocket. She pushed it at Timmy. 'Put it in your mouth. Take it with you, Tim. And go and hide till it's safe to come. Quick! Go, Timmy, go! I'll be all right.'

To her great relief Timmy, with the book in his mouth, turned and disappeared down the tunnel that led further under the sea. How she hoped he would find a safe hiding-place! The tunnel must end soon – but maybe before it did, Timmy would settle down in some dark corner and wait for her to call him again.

'Will you come up the passage or not?' shouted the

voice angrily. 'You'll be sorry if I have to come and fetch you, because I shall shoot all the way along!'

'I'm coming!' called George, in a small voice, and she went up the passage. She soon saw a beam of light, and in a moment she was in the flash of a powerful torch. There was a surprised exclamation.

'Good heavens! A boy! What are you doing here, and where did you come from?'

George's short curly hair made the man with the torch think she was a boy, and George did not tell him he was wrong. The man held a revolver, but he let it drop as he saw George.

'I only came to rescue my dog, and to find my father,' said George, in a meek voice.

'Well, you can't move that heavy stone!' said the man. 'A kid like you wouldn't have the strength. And you can't rescue your father either! We've got him prisoner, as you no doubt saw.'

'Yes,' said George, delighted to think that the man was sure she had not been strong enough to move the big stone. She wasn't going to say a word about Timmy! If the man thought he was still shut up in that tiny cave, well and good!

Then she heard her father's voice, anxiously calling from somewhere beyond the man. 'George! Is that you? Are you all right?'

'Yes, Father!' shouted back George, hoping that he would not ask anything about Timmy. The man beckoned her to come to him. Then he pushed her in front of him and they walked to her father's cave.

'I've brought your boy back,' said the man. 'Silly little idiot, thinking he could set that savage dog free! We've got him penned up in a cave with a big boulder in front!'

Another man came in from the opposite end of the cave. He was amazed to see George. The other man explained.

'When I got down here, I heard a noise out beyond this cave, the dog barking and someone talking to him and found this kid there, trying to set the dog free. I'd have shot the dog, of course, if he *had* been freed.'

'But, how did this boy get here?' asked the other man, still amazed.

'Maybe *he* can tell us that!' said the other. And then, for the first time, George's father heard how George had got there and why.

She told them how she had watched for Timmy in the glass room of the tower and hadn't seen him, and that had worried her and made her suspicious. So she had come across to the island in her boat at night, and had seen where the men came from. She had gone down the tunnel, and kept on till she came to the cave, where she had found her father.

The three men listened in silence. 'Well, you're a tiresome nuisance,' one of the men said to George, 'but my word, you're a son to be proud of. It's not many boys would have been brave enough to run so much risk for anyone.'

'Yes. I'm really proud of you, George,' said her father. He looked at her anxiously. She knew what he was thinking – what about his precious book? Had she been sensible enough to hide it? She did not dare to let him know anything while the men were there.

'Now, this complicates matters,' said the other man, looking at George. 'If you don't go back home you'll soon be missed, and there will be all kinds of search-parties going on – and maybe someone will send over to the island here to tell your father you have disappeared! We don't want anyone here at present, not till we know what we want to know!'

He turned to George's father. 'If you will tell us what we want to know, and give us all your notes, we will set you free, give you whatever sum of money you ask us for, and disappear ourselves.'

'And if I still say I won't?' said George's father.

'Then I am afraid we shall blow up the whole of your machines and the tower – and possibly you will never be found again because you will be buried down here,' said the man, in a voice that was suddenly very hard.

There was a dead silence. George looked at her father. 'You couldn't do a thing like that,' he said at last. 'You would gain nothing by it at all!'

'It's all or nothing with us,' said the man. 'All or nothing. Make up your mind. We'll give you till half past ten tomorrow morning – about seven hours. Then either you tell us everything, or we blow the island sky-high!'

They went out of the cave and left George and her father together. Only seven hours! And then, perhaps, the end of Kirrin Island!

CHAPTER EIGHTEEN

Half past four in the morning

AS SOON as the men were out of earshot, George's father spoke in a low voice.

'It's no good. I'll have to let them have my book of notes. I can't risk having you buried down here, George. I don't mind anything for myself – workers of my sort have to be ready to take risks all their lives – but it's different now you're here!'

'Father, I haven't got the book of notes,' whispered George, thankfully. 'I gave them to Timmy. I *did* manage to get that stone away from the entrance to his little prison, though the men think I didn't! I gave the book to Timmy and told him to go and hide till I fetched him.'

'Fine work, George!' said her father. 'Well, perhaps if you got Timmy now and brought him here, he could deal with these two men before they suspect he is free! He is quite capable of getting them both down on the ground at once.'

'Oh yes! It's our only chance,' said George. 'I'll go and get him now. I'll go a little way along the passage and whistle. Father, why didn't *you* go and try and rescue Timmy?'

'I didn't want to leave my book,' said her father. 'I

dared not take it with me, in case the men came after me and found it. They've been looking in all the caves for it. I couldn't bear to leave it here, and go and look for the dog. I was sure he was all right, when I saw the men taking biscuits out of the bag. Now, do go, George, and whistle to Timmy. The men may be back at any moment.'

George took her torch and went into the passage that led to the little cave where Timmy had been. She whistled loudly, and then waited. But no Timmy came. She whistled again, and then went farther along the passage. Still no Timmy.

She called him loudly. 'TIMMY! TIMMY! COME HERE!' But Timmy did not come. There was no sound of scampering feet, no joyful bark.

'Oh bother!' thought George. 'I hope he hasn't gone so far away that he can't hear me. I'll go a little farther.'

So she made her way along the tunnel, past the cave where Timmy had been, and then on down the tunnel again. Still no Timmy.

George rounded a corner and then saw that the tunnel split into three. Three different passages, all dark, silent and cold. Oh dear! She didn't in the least know which to take. She took the one on the left.

But that also split into three a little way on! George stopped. 'I shall get absolutely lost in this maze of passages under the sea if I go on,' she thought. 'I simply daren't. It's too frightening. TIMMY! TIMMY!'

Her voice went echoing along the passage and sounded

very strange indeed. She retraced her steps and went right back to her father's cave, feeling miserable.

'Father, there's no sign of Timmy at all. He must have gone along one of the passages and got lost! Oh dear, this is awful. There are lots of tunnels beyond this cave. It seems as if the whole rocky bed of the sea is mined with tunnels!' George sat down and looked very downhearted.

'Quite likely,' said her father. 'Well, that's a perfectly good plan gone wrong. We must try and think of another.'

'I do wonder what Julian and the others will think when they wake up and find me gone,' said George, suddenly. 'They might even come and try to find me here.'

'That wouldn't be much good,' said her father. 'These men will simply come down here and wait, and nobody will know where we are. The others don't know of the entrance in the little stone room, do they?'

'No,' said George. 'If they came over here I'm sure they'd never find it! We've looked before. And that would mean they'd be blown up with the island. Father, this is simply dreadful.'

'If only we knew where Timmy was!' said her father, 'or if we could get a message to Julian to tell him not to come. What's the time? My word, it's half past three in the early morning! I suppose Julian and the others are fast asleep.'

Julian *was* fast asleep. So was Anne. Dick was in a deep sleep as well, so nobody guessed that George's bed was empty.

But, about half past four Anne awoke, feeling very hot. 'I really must open the window!' she thought. 'I'm boiling!'

She got up and went to the window. She opened it, and stood looking out. The stars were out and the bay shone faintly.

'George,' whispered Anne. 'Are you awake?'

She listened for a reply. But none came. Then she listened more intently. Why, she couldn't even hear George's breathing! Surely George was there?

She felt over George's bed. It was flat and empty. She

switched on the light and looked at it. George's pyjamas were still on the bed. Her clothes were gone.

'George has gone to the island!' said Anne, in a fright. 'All in the dark by herself!'

She went to the boys' room. She felt about Julian's bed for his shoulder, and shook him hard. He woke up with a jump. 'What is it? What's up?'

'Julian! George is gone. Her bed's not been slept in,' whispered Anne. Her whisper awoke Dick, and soon both boys were sitting up wide awake.

'Blow! I might have guessed she'd do a stupid thing like that,' said Julian. 'In the middle of the night too – and all those dangerous rocks to row round. *Now* what are we going to do about it? I *told* her she wasn't to go to the island – Timmy would be quite all right! I expect Uncle Quentin forgot to take him up to the tower with him yesterday, that's all. She might have waited till half past ten this morning, then she would probably have seen him.'

'Well, we can't do anything now, I suppose, can we?' said Anne, anxiously.

'Not a thing,' said Julian. 'I've no doubt she's safely on Kirrin Island by now, making a fuss of Timmy, and having a good old row with Uncle Quentin. Really, George is the limit!'

They talked for half an hour and then Julian looked at his watch. 'Five o'clock. We'd better try and get a bit more sleep. Aunt Fanny will be worried in the morning when she hears of George's latest escapade!'

Anne went back to her room. She got into bed and fell asleep. Julian could not sleep – he kept thinking of George and wondering where exactly she was. Wouldn't he give her a talking-to when she came back!

He suddenly heard a peculiar noise downstairs. Whatever could it be? It sounded like someone climbing in at a window. Was there one open? Yes, the window of the little wash-place might be open. Crash! What in the world was that? It couldn't be a burglar – no burglar would be foolish enough to make such a noise.

There was a sound on the stairs, and then the bedroom door was pushed open. In alarm Julian put out his hand to switch on the light, but before he could do something heavy jumped right on top of him!

He yelled and Dick woke up with a jump. He put on the light, then Julian saw what was on his bed – Timmy!

'Timmy! How did you get here? Where's George! Timmy, is it really you?'

'Timmy!' echoed Dick, amazed. 'Has George brought him back then? Is she here too?'

Anne came in, woken by the noise. 'Why, *Timmy*! Oh, Julian, is George back too, then?'

'No, apparently not,' said Julian, puzzled. 'I say, Tim, what's this you've got in your mouth? Drop it, old chap, drop it!'

Timmy dropped it. Julian picked it up from the bed. 'It's a book of notes – all in Uncle's handwriting! What *does* this mean? How did Timmy get hold of it – and why did

he bring it here? It's most extraordinary!'

Nobody could imagine why Timmy had suddenly appeared with the book of notes – and no George.

'It's very odd,' said Julian. 'There's something I don't understand here. Let's go and wake Aunt Fanny.'

So they went and woke her up, telling her all they knew. She was very worried indeed to hear that George was gone. She picked up the book of notes and knew at once that it was very important.

'I must put this into the safe,' she said. 'I know this is valuable. How *did* Timmy get hold of it?'

Timmy was acting strangely. He kept pawing at Julian and whining. He had been very pleased to see everyone, but he seemed to have something on his mind.

'What is it, old boy?' asked Dick. 'How did you get here? You didn't swim, because you're not wet. If you came in a boat, it must have been with George – and yet you've left her behind!'

'*I* think something's happened to George,' said Anne, suddenly. 'I think Timmy keeps pawing you to tell you to go with him and find her. Perhaps she brought him back in the boat, and then was terribly tired and fell asleep on the beach or something. We ought to go and see.'

'Yes, I think we ought,' said Julian. 'Aunt Fanny, would you like to wake Joanna and get something hot ready, in case we find George is tired out and cold? We'll go down to the beach and look. It will soon be daylight now. The eastern sky is just beginning to show its first light.'

'Well, go and dress then,' said Aunt Fanny, still looking very worried indeed. 'Oh, what a dreadful family I've got – always in some scrape or other!'

The three children began to dress. Timmy watched them, waiting patiently till they were ready. Then they all went downstairs and out of doors. Julian turned towards the beach, but Timmy stood still. He pawed at Dick and then ran a few steps in the opposite direction.

'Why, he doesn't *want* us to go the beach! He wants us to go another way!' cried Julian, in surprise. 'All right, Timmy, you lead the way and we'll follow!'

CHAPTER NINETEEN

A meeting with Martin

TIMMY RAN round the house and made for the moor behind. It was most extraordinary. Wherever was he going?

'This is awfully strange,' said Julian. 'I'm sure George can't be anywhere in this direction.'

Timmy went on swiftly, occasionally turning his head to make sure everyone was following him. He led the way to the quarry!

'The quarry! Did George come here then!' said Dick. 'But why?'

The dog disappeared down into the middle of the quarry, slipping and sliding down the steep sides as he went. The others followed as best they could. Luckily it was not as slippery as before, and they reached the bottom without accident.

Timmy went straight to the shelf of rock and disappeared underneath it. They heard him give a short sharp bark as if to say, 'Come on! This is the way! Hurry up!'

'He's gone into the tunnel under there,' said Dick. 'Where we thought we might explore and didn't. There must be a passage or something there, then. But is George there?'

'I'll go first,' said Julian, and wriggled through the hole. He was soon in the wider bit and then came out into the part where he could almost stand. He walked a little way in the dark, hearing Timmy bark impatiently now and then. But in a moment or two Julian stopped.

'It's no good trying to follow you in the dark, Timmy!' he called. 'We'll have to go back and get torches. I can't see a foot in front of me!'

Dick was just wriggling through the first part of the hole. Julian called to him to go back.

'It's too dark,' he said. 'We must go and get torches. If George for some reason is up this passage, she must have had an accident, and we'd better get a rope, and some brandy.'

Anne began to cry. She didn't like the idea of George lying hurt in that dark passage. Julian put his arm round her as soon as he was in the open air again. He helped her up the sides of the quarry, followed by Dick.

'Now don't worry. We'll get her all right. But it beats me why she went there – and I still can't imagine how Tim and she came from the island, if they are here, instead of on the beach!'

'Look – there's Martin!' suddenly said Dick in surprise. So there was! He was standing at the top of the quarry, and seemed just as surprised to see them as they were to see him!

'You're up early,' called Dick. 'And goodness me – are you going gardening or something? Why the spades?'

Martin looked sheepish and didn't seem to know what to say. Julian suddenly walked up to him and caught hold of his shoulder. 'Look here, Martin! There's some funny business going on here! What are you going to do with those spades? Have you seen George? Do you know where she is, or anything about her? Come on, tell me!'

Martin shook his shoulder away from Julian's grip looking extremely surprised.

'George? No! What's happened to him?'

'George isn't a him – she's a her,' said Anne, still crying. 'She's disappeared. We thought she'd gone to the island to find her dog – and Timmy suddenly appeared at Kirrin Cottage, and brought us here!'

'So it looks as if George might be somewhere near here,' said Julian. 'And I want to know if you've seen her or know anything of her whereabouts?'

'No, Julian. I swear I don't!' said Martin.

'Well, tell me what you're doing here so early in the morning, with spades,' said Julian, roughly. 'Who are you waiting for? Your father?'

'Yes,' said Martin.

'And what are you going to do?' asked Dick. 'Going exploring up the hole there?'

'Yes,' said Martin again, sullen and worried. 'No harm in that, is there?'

'It's all – very – strange!' said Julian, eyeing him and speaking slowly and loudly. 'But – let me tell you this – *we're* going exploring – not you! If there's anything odd up that hole, *we'll* find it! We shall not allow you or your father to get through the hole. So go and find him and tell him that!'

Martin didn't move. He went very white, and stared at Julian miserably. Anne went up to him, tears still on her face and put her hand on his arm.

'Martin, what is it? Why do you look like that? What's the mystery?'

And then, to the dismay and horror of everyone, Martin turned away with a noise that sounded very like a sob! He stood with his back to them, his shoulders shaking.

'Good gracious! What *is* up?' said Julian, in exasperation. 'Pull yourself together, Martin! Tell us what's worrying you.'

'Everything, everything!' said Martin, in a muffled voice. Then he swung round to face them. 'You don't know what it is to have no mother and no father – nobody who cares about you – and then . . .'

'But you *have* got a father!' said Dick at once.

'I haven't. He's not my father, that man. He's only my guardian, but he makes me call him father whenever we're on a job together.'

'A job? What sort of job?' said Julian.

'Oh any kind – all beastly,' said Martin. 'Snooping round and finding things out about people, and then getting money from them if we promise to say nothing – and receiving stolen goods and selling them – and helping people like the men who are after your uncle's secret . . .'

'*Oho!*' said Dick at once. 'Now we're coming to it. I *thought* you and Mr Curton were both suspiciously interested in Kirrin Island. What's this present job, then?'

'My guardian will punish me for telling all this,' said Martin. 'But, you see, they're planning to blow up the island – and it's about the worst thing I've ever been mixed up in – and I know your uncle is there – and perhaps George too now, you say. I can't go on with it!'

A few more tears ran down his cheeks. It was awful to see him crying like that, and the three felt sorry for Martin now. They were also full of horror when they heard him say that the island was to be blown up!

'How do you know this?' asked Julian.

'Well, Mr Curton's got a radio receiver and transmitter as you know,' explained Martin, 'and so have the fellows on the island – the ones who are after your uncle's secret – so they can easily keep in touch with one another. They mean to get the secret if they can – if not they are going to blow the whole place sky-high so that *nobody* can get the secret. But they can't get away by boat because they don't know the way through those rocks . . .'

'Well, how will they get away then?' demanded Julian.

'We feel sure this hole that Timmy found the other day, leads down to the sea, and under the sea-bed to Kirrin Island,' said Martin. 'Yes, I know it sounds too mad to be true, but Mr Curton's got an old map which clearly shows there was once a passage under the sea-bed. If there is – well, the fellows across on the island can escape down it, after making all preparations for the island to be blown up. See?'

'Yes,' said Julian, taking a long breath. 'I *do* see. I see it all very clearly now. I see something else too! *Timmy* has found his way from the island, using that same passage you have just told us about, and *that's* why he's led us back here – to take us to the island and rescue Uncle Quentin and George.'

There was a deep silence. Martin stared at the ground. Dick and Julian thought hard. Anne sobbed a little. It all seemed quite unbelievable to her. Then Julian put his hand on Martin's arm.

'Martin! You did right to tell us. We may be able to prevent something dreadful. But you must help. We may need those spades of yours and I expect you've got torches too. We haven't. We don't want to waste time going back and getting them, so will you come with us and help us? Will you lend us those spades and torches?'

'Would you trust me?' said Martin, in a low voice. 'Yes, I want to come and help you. And if we get in now, my guardian won't be able to follow, because he won't have a torch. We can get to the island and bring your uncle and George safely back.'

'Good for you!' said Dick. 'Well, come on then. We've been talking far too long. Come on down again, Ju. Hand him a spade and torch, Martin.'

'Anne, you're not to come,' said Julian to his little sister. 'You're to go back and tell Aunt Fanny what's happened. Will you do that?'

'Yes. I don't want to come,' said Anne. 'I'll go back now. Do be careful, Julian!'

She climbed down with the boys and then stood and watched till all three had disappeared into the hole. Timmy, who had been waiting impatiently during the talking, barking now and again, was glad to find that at last they were going to make a move. He ran ahead in the tunnel, his eyes gleaming green every time he turned to see if they were following.

Anne began to climb up the steep side of the quarry again. Then, thinking she heard a cough, she stopped and crouched under a bush. She peered through the leaves and saw Mr Curton. Then she heard his voice.

'Martin! Where on earth are you?'

So he had come to look for Martin and go up the tunnel with him! Anne hardly dared to breathe. Mr Curton called again and again, then made an impatient noise and began to climb down the side of the quarry.

Suddenly he slipped! He clutched at a bush as he passed, but it gave way. He rolled quite near Anne, and caught sight of her. He looked astonished, but then his look became one of fear as he rolled more and more quickly to the bottom of the deep quarry. Anne heard him give a deep groan as at last he came to a stop.

Anne peered down in fright. Mr Curton was sitting up, holding one of his legs and groaning. He looked up to see if he could spy Anne.

'Anne!' he called. 'I've broken my leg, I think. Can you fetch help? What are you doing here so early? Have you seen Martin?'

Anne did not answer. If he had broken his leg, then he couldn't go after the others! And Anne could get away quickly. She climbed carefully, afraid of rolling down to the bottom, and having to lie beside the horrid Mr Curton.

'Anne! Have you seen Martin? Look for him and get help for me, will you?' shouted Mr Curton, and then groaned again.

Anne climbed to the top of the quarry and looked down.

She cupped her hands round her mouth and shouted loudly:

'You're a very wicked man. I shan't fetch help for you. I simply can't *bear* you!'

And, having got all that off her chest, the little girl shot off at top speed over the moor.

'I must tell Aunt Fanny. She'll know what to do! Oh I hope the others are safe. What shall we do if the island blows up? I'm glad, glad, glad I told Mr Curton he was a very wicked man.'

And on she ran, panting. Aunt Fanny would know what to do!

CHAPTER TWENTY

Everything boils up!

MEANWHILE THE three boys and Timmy were having a strange journey underground. Timmy led the way without faltering, stopping every now and again for the others to catch up with him.

The tunnel at first had a low roof and the boys had to walk along in a stooping position, which was very tiring indeed. But after a bit the roof became higher and Julian, flashing his torch round, saw that the walls and floor, instead of being made of soil, were now made of rock. He tried to reckon out where they were.

'We've come practically straight towards the cliff,' he said to Dick. 'That's allowing for a few turns and twists. The tunnel has sloped down so steeply the last few hundred yards that I think we must be very far underground indeed.'

It was not until the boys heard the curious booming noise that George had heard in the caves, that they knew they must be under the rocky bed of the sea. They were walking under the sea to Kirrin Island. How strange, how unbelievably astonishing!

'It's like a peculiarly vivid dream,' said Julian. 'I'm not sure I like it very much! All right, Tim, we're coming. Hallo – what's this?'

They all stopped. Julian flashed his torch ahead and saw a pile of fallen rocks. Timmy had managed to squeeze himself through a hole in them and go through to the other side, but the boys couldn't.

'This is where the spades come in, Martin!' said Dick, cheerfully. 'Take a hand!'

By dint of pushing and shovelling, the boys at last managed to move the pile of fallen rocks enough to make a way past. 'Thank goodness for the spades!' said Julian.

They went on, and were soon very glad of the spades again, to move another heap of rock. Timmy barked impatiently when they kept him waiting. He was very anxious to get back to George.

Soon they came to where the tunnel forked into two. But Timmy took the right-hand passage without hesitation, and when that one forked into three, he again chose one without stopping to think for a moment.

'Marvellous, isn't he?' said Julian. 'All done by smell! He's been this way once, so he knows it again. We should be completely lost under here if we came by ourselves.'

Martin was not enjoying this adventure at all. He said very little, but laboured on after the others. Dick guessed he was worrying about what was going to happen when the adventure was over. Poor Martin. All he wanted to do was to draw, and instead of that he had been dragged into one horrible job after another, and used as a cat's-paw by his evil guardian.

'Do you think we're anywhere near the island?' said Dick, at last. 'I'm getting tired of this!'

'Yes, we must be,' said Julian. 'In fact I think we'd better be as quiet as we can, in case we come suddenly on the enemy!'

So, without speaking again, they went as quietly as they could – and then suddenly they saw a faint light ahead of them. Julian put out his hand to stop the others.

They were nearing the cave where George's father had his books and papers – where George had found him the night before. Timmy stood in front of them, listening too. He was not going to run headlong into danger!

They heard voices, and listened intently to see whose they were. 'George's – and Uncle Quentin's,' said Julian at last. And as if Timmy had also satisfied himself that those were indeed the two voices, the dog ran ahead and went into the lighted cave, barking joyfully.

'Timmy!' came George's voice, and they heard something overturn as she sprang up. 'Where have you been?'

'Woof,' said Timmy, trying to explain. 'Woof!'

And then Julian and Dick ran into the cave followed by Martin! Uncle Quentin and George stared in the very greatest amazement.

'Julian! Dick! And *Martin*! How did *you* get here?' cried George, while Timmy jumped and capered round her.

'I'll explain,' said Julian. 'It was Timmy that fetched us!' And he related the whole story of how Timmy had come into Kirrin Cottage in the early morning and had jumped on his bed, and all that had happened since.

And then, in their turn, Uncle Quentin and George told all that had happened to *them*!

'Where are the two men?' asked Julian.

'Somewhere on the island,' said George. 'I went scouting after them some time ago, and followed them up to where they get out into the little stone room. I think they're there until half past ten, when they'll go up and signal, so that people will think everything is all right.'

'Well, what are our plans?' said Julian. 'Will you come back down the passage under the sea with us? Or what shall we do?'

'Better not do that,' said Martin, quickly. 'My guardian may be coming – and he's in touch with other men. If he wonders where I am, and thinks something is up, he may call in two or three others, and we might meet them making their way up the passage.'

They did not know, of course, that Mr Curton was even then lying with a broken leg at the bottom of the quarry. Uncle Quentin considered.

'I've been given seven hours to say whether or not I will give the fellows my secret,' he said. 'That time will be up just after half past ten. Then the men will come down again to see me. I think between us we ought to be able to capture them – especially as we've got Timmy with us!'

'Yes, that's a good idea,' said Julian. 'We could hide

somewhere till they come and then set Timmy on them before they suspect anything!'

Almost before he had finished these words the light in the cave went out! Then a voice spoke out of the blackness.

'Keep still! One movement and I'll shoot.'

George gasped. What was happening? Had the men come back unexpectedly? Oh, why hadn't Timmy given them warning? She had been fondling his ears, so probably he had been unable to hear anything!

She held Timmy's collar, afraid that he would fly at the man in the darkness and be shot. The voice spoke again.

'Will you or will you not give us your secret?'

'Not,' said Uncle Quentin in a low voice.

'You will have this whole island, and all your work blown up then, and yourself too and the others.'

'Yes! You can do what you like!' suddenly yelled George. 'You'll be blown up yourself too. You'll never be able to get away in a boat – you'll go on the rocks!'

The man in the darkness laughed. 'We shall be safe,' he said. 'Now keep at the back of the cave. I have you covered with my revolver.'

They all crouched at the back. Timmy growled, but George made him stop at once. She did not know if the men knew he was free or not.

Quiet footsteps passed across the cave in the darkness. George listened, straining her ears. Two pairs of footsteps! Both men were passing through the cave. She knew where they were going! They were going to escape by the undersea passage – and leave the island to be blown up behind them!

As soon as the footsteps had died away, George switched on her torch. ‘Father! Those men are escaping now, down the sea-tunnel. We must escape too – but not that way. My boat is on the shore. Let’s get there quickly and get away before there’s any explosion.’

‘Yes, come along,’ said her father. ‘But if only I could get up into my tower, I could stop any wicked plan of theirs! They mean to use the power there, I know – but if I could get up to the glass room, I could undo all their plans!’

‘Oh do be quick then, Father!’ cried George, getting in quite a panic now. ‘Save my island if you can!’

They all made their way through the cave up to the passage that led to the stone flight of steps from the little stone room. And there they had a shock!

The stone could not be opened from the inside! The men had altered the mechanism so that it could now only be opened from the outside.

In vain Uncle Quentin swung the lever to and fro. Nothing happened. The stone would not move.

‘It’s only from outside it can be opened,’ he said in despair. ‘We’re trapped!’

They sat down on the stone steps in a row, one above the other. They were cold, hungry and miserable. What could they do now? Make their way back to the cave, and then go on down the under-sea tunnel?

'I don't want to do that,' said Uncle Quentin. 'I'm so afraid that if there is an explosion, it may crack the rocky bed of the sea, which is the roof of the tunnel – and then water would pour in. It wouldn't be pleasant if we happened to be there at that moment.'

'Oh no. Don't let's be trapped like that,' said George with a shudder. 'I couldn't bear it.'

'Perhaps I could get something to explode this stone away,' said her father, after a while. 'I've got plenty of stuff if only I've time to put it together.'

'Listen!' said Julian, suddenly. 'I can hear something outside this wall. Sh!'

They all listened intently. Timmy whined and scratched at the stone that would not move.

'It's voices!' cried Dick. 'Lots of them. Who can it be?'

'Be *quiet*,' said Julian, fiercely. 'We *must* find out!'

'I know, I know!' said George, suddenly. 'It's the fishermen who have come over in their boats! *That's* why the men didn't wait till half past ten! *That's* why they've gone in such a hurry! They saw the fisherboats coming!'

'Then Anne must have brought them!' cried Dick. 'She must have run home to Aunt Fanny, told her everything and given the news to the fishermen – and they've come to rescue us! Anne! ANNE! WE'RE HERE!'

Timmy began to bark deafeningly. The others encouraged him, because they felt certain that Timmy's bark was louder than their shouts!

'WOOF! WOOF! WOOF!'

Anne heard the barking and the shouting as soon as she ran into the little stone room. 'Where are you? Where are you?' she yelled.

'HERE! HERE! MOVE THE STONE!' yelled Julian,

shouting so loudly that everyone near him jumped violently.

'Move aside – I can see which stone it is,' said a man's deep voice. It was one of the fishermen. He felt round and about the stone in the recess, sure it was the right one because it was cleaner than the others through being used as an entrance.

Suddenly he touched the right place, and found a tiny iron spike. He pulled it down – and the lever swung back behind it, and pulled the stone aside!

Everyone hurried out, one on top of the other! The six fishermen standing in the little room stared in astonishment. Aunt Fanny was there too, and Anne. Aunt Fanny ran to her husband as soon as he appeared – but to her surprise he pushed her away quite roughly.

He ran out of the room, and hurried to the tower. Was he in time to save the island and everyone on it? Oh hurry, hurry!

CHAPTER TWENTY-ONE

The end of the adventure

'WHERE'S HE gone?' said Aunt Fanny, quite hurt. Nobody answered. Julian, George and Martin were watching the tower with anxious intensity. If only Uncle Quentin would appear at the top. Ah – there he was!

He had taken up with him a big stone. As everyone watched he smashed the glass round the tower with the stone. Crash! Crash! Crash!

The wires that ran through the glass were broken and split as the glass crashed into pieces. No power could race through them now. Uncle Quentin leant out of the broken glass room and shouted exultantly.

'It's all right! I was in time! I've destroyed the power that might have blown up the island – you're safe!'

George found that her knees were suddenly shaking. She had to sit down on the floor. Timmy came and licked her face wonderingly. Then he too sat down.

'What's he doing, smashing the tower up?' asked a burly fisherman. 'I don't understand all this.'

Uncle Quentin came down the tower and rejoined them. 'Another ten minutes and I should have been too late,' he said. 'Thank goodness, Anne, you all arrived when you did.'

'I ran all the way home, told Aunt Fanny, and we got the fishermen to come over as soon as they could get out their boats,' explained Anne. 'We couldn't think of any other way of rescuing you. Where are the wicked men?'

'Trying to escape down the under-sea tunnel,' said Julian. 'Oh – you don't know about that, Anne!' And he told her, while the fishermen listened open-mouthed.

'Look here,' said Uncle Quentin, when he had finished. 'As the boats are here, the men might as well take all my gear back with them. I've finished my job here. I shan't want the island any more.'

'Oh! Then *we* can have it!' said George, delighted. 'And there's plenty of the holidays left. We'll help to bring up what you want, Father.'

'We ought to get back as quickly as we can, so as to catch those fellows at the other end of the tunnel,' said one of the fishermen.

'Yes. We ought,' said Aunt Fanny.

'Gracious! They'll find Mr Curton there with a broken leg,' said Anne, suddenly remembering.

The others looked at her in surprise. This was the first they had heard of Mr Curton being in the quarry. Anne explained.

'And I told him he was a very wicked man,' she ended triumphantly.

'Quite right,' said Uncle Quentin, with a laugh. 'Well, perhaps we'd better get my gear another time.'

'Oh, two of us can see to that for you now,' said the

burly fisherman. 'George here, she's got her boat in the cove, and you've got yours. The others can go back with you, if you like – and Tom and me, we'll fix up your things and bring them across to the mainland later on. Save us coming over again.'

'Right,' said Uncle Quentin, pleased. 'You do that then. It's down in the caves through that tunnel behind the stone.'

They all went down to the cove. It was a beautiful day and the sea was very calm, except just round the island where the waters were always rough. Soon the boats were being sailed or rowed to the mainland.

'The adventure is over!' said Anne. 'How strange – I didn't think it was one while it was happening – but now I see it was!'

'Another to add to our long list of adventures,' said Julian. 'Cheer up, Martin, don't look so blue. Whatever happens, we'll see you don't come out badly over this. You helped us, and you threw in your lot with us. We'll see that you don't suffer – won't we, Uncle Quentin? We'd never have got through those falls of rock if we hadn't had Martin and his spades!'

'Well, thanks,' said Martin. 'If you can get me away from my guardian – and never let me see him again – I'll be happy!'

'It's quite likely that Mr Curton will be put somewhere safe where he won't be able to see his friends for quite a long time, said Uncle Quentin dryly. 'So I don't think you need worry.'

As soon as the boats reached shore, Julian, Dick, Timmy and Uncle Quentin went off to the quarry to see if Mr Curton was still there and to wait for the other two men to come out of the tunnel!

Mr Curton was there all right, still groaning and calling for help. Uncle Quentin spoke to him sternly.

'We know your part in this matter, Curton. You will be dealt with by the police. They will be along in a short while.'

Timmy sniffed round Mr Curton, and then walked away, nose in air, as if to say 'What a nasty bit of work!' The others arranged themselves at the mouth of the hole and waited.

But nobody came. An hour went by – two hours. Still nobody. 'I'm glad Martin and Anne didn't come,' said Uncle Quentin. 'I do wish we'd brought sandwiches.'

At that moment the police arrived, scrambling down the steep sides of the quarry. The police doctor was with them and he saw to Mr Curton's leg. Then, with the help of the others, he got the man to the top with great difficulty.

'Julian, go back and get sandwiches,' said Uncle Quentin at last. 'It looks as if we've got a long wait!'

Julian went back, and was soon down the quarry with neat packets of ham sandwiches and a thermos of hot coffee. The two policemen who were still left offered to stay and watch, if Uncle Quentin wanted to go home.

'Dear me, no!' he said. 'I want to see the faces of these two fellows when they come out. It's going to be one of the nicest moments of my life! The island is not blown up. My secret is safe. My book is safe. My work is finished. And I just want to tell these things to my two dear friends!'

'You know, Father, I believe they've lost their way underground,' said George. 'Julian said there were many different passages. Timmy took the boys through the right ones, of course – but they would have been quite lost if they hadn't had him with them!'

Her father's face fell at the thought of the men being lost underground. He did so badly want to see their dismayed faces when they arrived in the quarry!

'We could send Timmy in,' said Julian. 'He would soon find them and bring them out. Wouldn't you, Tim?'

'Woof,' said Timmy, agreeing.

'Oh yes, that's a good idea,' said George. 'They won't hurt him if they think he can show them the way out! Go in, Timmy. Find them boy; find them! Bring them here!'

'Woof,' said Timmy, obligingly, and disappeared under the shelf of rock.

Everyone waited, munching sandwiches and sipping coffee. And then they heard Timmy's bark again, from underground!

There was a panting noise, then a scraping sound as somebody came wriggling out from under the rock. He stood up – and then he saw the silent group watching him. He gasped.

'Good morning, Johnson,' said Uncle Quentin, in an amiable voice. 'How are you?'

Johnson went white. He sat down on the nearby heather. 'You win!' he said.

'I do,' said Uncle Quentin. 'In fact, I win handsomely. Your little plan went wrong. My secret is still safe – and next year it will be given to the whole world!'

There was another scraping sound and the second man arrived. He stood up too – and then he saw the quietly watching group.

'Good morning, Peters,' said Uncle Quentin. 'So nice to see you again. How did you like your underground walk? We found it better to come by sea.'

Peters looked at Johnson, and he too sat down suddenly. 'What's happened?' he said to Johnson.

'It's all up,' said Johnson. Then Timmy appeared, wagging his tail, and went to George.

'I bet they were glad when Timmy came up to them!' said Julian.

Johnson looked at him. 'Yes. We were lost in those hateful tunnels. Curton said he'd come to meet us, but he never came.'

'No. He's probably in the prison hospital by now, with a broken leg,' said Uncle Quentin. 'Well, constable – do your duty.'

Both men were at once arrested. Then the whole company made their way back over the moor. The two men were put into a police car and driven off. The rest of the company went into Kirrin Cottage to have a good meal.

'I'm most terribly hungry,' said George. 'Joanna, have you got anything nice for breakfast?'

'Not much,' said Joanna, from the kitchen. 'Only bacon and eggs and mushrooms!'

'Ooooh!' said Anne, 'Joanna, you shall have the OBCBE!'

'And what may that be?' cried Joanna, but Anne couldn't remember.

'It's a decoration!' she cried.

'Well, I'm not a Christmas tree!' shouted back Joanna. 'You come and help with the breakfast!'

It was a very jolly breakfast that the seven of them – no eight, for Timmy must certainly be counted – sat down to. Martin, now that he was free of his guardian, became quite a different boy.

The children made plans for him. 'You can stay with the coastguard, because he likes you – he kept on and on saying you weren't a bad boy! And you can come and play with us and go to the island. And Uncle Quentin will see if he can get you into an art-school. He says you deserve a reward for helping to save his wonderful secret!'

Martin glowed with pleasure. It seemed as if a load had fallen away from his shoulders. 'I've never had a chance till now,' he said. 'I'll make good. You see if I don't!'

'Mother! Can we go and stay on Kirrin Island and watch the tower being taken down tomorrow?' begged George. 'Do say yes! And can we stay there a whole week? We can sleep in that little room as we did before.'

'Well – I suppose you can!' said her mother, smiling at George's eager face. 'I'd rather like to have your father to myself for a few days and feed him up a bit.'

'Oh, that reminds me, Fanny,' said her husband, suddenly. 'I tried some soup you left for me, the night before last. And, my dear, it was horrible! Quite bad!'

'Oh *Quentin*! I told you to pour it away! You know I did,' said his wife, distressed. 'It must have been completely bad. You really are dreadful.'

They all finished their breakfast at last, and went out into the garden. They looked across Kirrin Bay to Kirrin Island. It looked lovely in the morning sun.

'We've had a lot of adventures together,' said Julian. 'More than most children. They *have* been exciting, haven't they?'

Yes, they have, but now we must say good-bye to the Five, and to Kirrin Island too. Good-bye, Julian, Dick, George, Anne – and Timmy. But only Timmy hears our good-bye, for he has such sharp ears.

'Woof! Good-bye!'

Join the adventure!

If you can't wait to explore further with THE FAMOUS FIVE, read the next book in the series:

Enid Blyton®

is one of the most popular children's authors of all time. Her books have sold over 500 million copies and have been translated into other languages more often than any other children's author.

Enid Blyton adored writing for children. She wrote over 700 books and about 2,000 short stories. *The Famous Five* books, now 75 years old, are her most popular. She is also the author of other favourites including *The Secret Seven*, *The Magic Faraway Tree*, *Malory Towers* and *Noddy*.

Born in London in 1897, Enid lived much of her life in Buckinghamshire and loved dogs, gardening and the countryside. She was very knowledgeable about trees, flowers, birds and animals. Dorset – where some of the Famous Five's adventures are set – was a favourite place of hers too.

Enid Blyton's stories are read and loved by millions of children (and grown-ups) all over the world. Visit enidblyton.co.uk to discover more.

Illustration by Laura Ellen Anderson.

THE FAMOUS FIVE

FIVE GO OFF TO CAMP

Have you read all THE FAMOUS FIVE books?

1. Five on a Treasure Island
2. Five Go Adventuring Again
3. Five Run Away Together
4. Five Go to Smuggler's Top
5. Five Go Off in a Caravan
6. Five on Kirrin Island Again
7. Five Go Off to Camp
8. Five Get Into Trouble
9. Five Fall Into Adventure
10. Five on a Hike Together
11. Five Have a Wonderful Time
12. Five Go Down to the Sea
13. Five Go to Mystery Moor
14. Five Have Plenty of Fun
15. Five on a Secret Trail
16. Five Go to Billycock Hill
17. Five Get Into a Fix
18. Five on Finniston Farm
19. Five Go to Demon's Rocks
20. Five Have a Mystery to Solve
21. Five Are Together Again

The Famous Five Colour Short Stories

1. Five and a Half-Term Adventure
2. George's Hair is Too Long
3. Good Old Timmy
4. A Lazy Afternoon
5. Well Done, Famous Five
6. Five Have a Puzzling Time
7. Happy Christmas, Five
8. When Timmy Chased the Cat

Enid Blyton®

THE FAMOUS FIVE

FIVE GO OFF TO CAMP

Illustrated by Eileen A. Soper

HODDER

HODDER CHILDREN'S BOOKS

First published in Great Britain in 1948 by Hodder & Stoughton
This edition published in 2016

21

A CIP catalogue record for this book is available from the British Library.

ISBN 978 1 444 93637 7

Printed and bound in Great Britain by Clays Ltd, Elcograf S.p.A.

The paper and board used in this book are made from wood from responsible sources.

Hodder Children's Books
An imprint of
Hachette Children's Group
Part of Hodder & Stoughton
Carmelite House
50 Victoria Embankment
London EC4Y 0DZ

An Hachette UK Company
www.hachette.co.uk
www.hachettechildrens.co.uk

CONTENTS

1 HOLIDAY TIME 1
2 UP ON THE MOORS 10
3 ANNE'S VOLCANO 21
4 SPOOK-TRAINS 31
5 BACK AT CAMP AGAIN 41
6 DAY AT THE FARM 51
7 MR ANDREWS COMES HOME 61
8 A LAZY EVENING 72
9 NIGHT VISITOR 82
10 HUNT FOR A SPOOK-TRAIN 91
11 MOSTLY ABOUT JOCK 104
12 GEORGE LOSES HER TEMPER 116
13 A THRILLING PLAN 127
14 JOCK COMES TO CAMP 138
15 GEORGE HAS AN ADVENTURE 149
16 IN THE TUNNEL AGAIN 161
17 AN AMAZING FIND 170
18 A WAY OF ESCAPE 182
19 WHAT AN ADVENTURE! 192

CHAPTER ONE

Holiday time

'TWO JOLLY fine tents, four groundsheets, four sleeping-bags – I say, what about Timmy? Isn't he going to have a sleeping-bag too?' said Dick, with a grin.

The other three children laughed, and Timmy, the dog, thumped his tail hard on the ground.

'Look at him,' said George. 'He's laughing, too! He's got his mouth stretched wide open.'

They all looked at Timmy. He really did look as if a wide grin stretched his hairy mouth from side to side.

'He's a darling,' said Anne, hugging him. 'Best dog in the world, aren't you, Timmy?'

'Woof!' said Timmy, agreeing. He gave Anne a wet lick on her nose.

The four children, Julian, tall and strong for his age, Dick, George and Anne were busy planning a camping holiday. George was a girl, not a boy, but she would never answer to her real name, Georgina. With her freckled face and short, curly hair she really did look more like a boy than a girl.

'It's absolutely wizard, being allowed to go on a camping holiday all by ourselves,' said Dick. 'I never thought our parents would allow it, after the terrific adventure we had last summer, when we went off in caravans.'

'Well – we shan't be *quite* all by ourselves,' said Anne. 'Don't forget we've got Mr Luffy to keep an eye on us. He'll be camping quite near.'

'Pooh! Old Luffy!' said Dick, with a laugh. 'He won't know if we're there or not. So long as he can study his precious moorland insects, he won't bother about us.'

'Well, if it hadn't been that he was going to camp, too, we wouldn't have been allowed to go,' said Anne. 'I heard Daddy say so.'

Mr Luffy was a master at the boys' school, an elderly, dreamy fellow with a passion for studying all kinds of insect-life. Anne avoided him when he carried about boxes of insect specimens, because sometimes they escaped and came crawling out. The boys liked him and thought him fun, but the idea of Mr Luffy keeping an eye on them struck them as very comical.

'It's more likely we'll have to keep an eye on *him*,' said Julian. 'He's the sort of chap whose tent will always be falling down on top of him, or he'll run out of water, or sit down on his bag of eggs. Old Luffy seems to live in the world of insects, not in our world!'

'Well, he can go and live in the world of insects if he likes, so long as he doesn't interfere with *us*,' said George, who hated interfering people. 'This sounds as if it will be a super holiday – living in tents on the high moors, away from everybody, doing exactly what we like, when we like and how we like.'

'Woof!' said Timmy, thumping his tail again.

'That means he's going to do as *he* likes, too,' said Anne. 'You're going to chase hundreds of rabbits, aren't you, Timmy, and bark madly at anyone who dares to come within two miles of us!'

'Now, be quiet a minute, Anne!' said Dick, picking up his list again. 'We really must check down our list and find out if we've got every single thing we want. Where did I get to – oh, four sleeping-bags.'

'Yes, and you wanted to know if Timmy was to have one,' said Anne, with a giggle.

'Of course he won't,' said George. 'He'll sleep where he always does – won't you, Timmy? On my feet.'

'Couldn't we get him just a *small* sleeping-bag?' asked Anne. 'He'd look sweet with his head poking out of the top.'

'Timmy hates looking sweet,' said George. 'Go on, Dick. I'll tie my hanky round Anne's mouth if she interrupts again.'

Dick went on down his list. It was a very interesting one. Things like cooking-stoves, canvas buckets, enamel plates and drinking-cups were on it and each item seemed to need a lot of discussion. The four children enjoyed themselves very much.

'You know, it's almost as much fun planning a holiday like this as having it,' said Dick. 'Well – I shouldn't think we've forgotten a thing, have we?'

'No. We've probably thought of too much!' said Julian. 'Well, old Luffy says he'll take all our things on the trailer behind his car, so we'll be all right. I shouldn't like to carry them ourselves!'

'Oh, I wish next week would come!' said Anne. 'Why is it that the time seems so long when you're waiting for something nice to happen, and so short when something nice *is* happening?'

'Yes, it seems the wrong way round, doesn't it?' said Dick, with a grin. 'Anyone got the map? I'd like to take another squint at the spot where we're going.'

Julian produced a map from his pocket. He opened it and the four children sprawled round it. The map showed a vast and lonely stretch of moorland, with very few houses indeed.

'Just a few small farms, that's all,' said Julian pointing to one or two. 'They can't get much of a living out of such poor land, though. See, that's about the place where we're going – just there – and on the opposite slope is a small farm where we shall get milk, eggs and butter when we need them. Luffy's been there before. He says it's a rather small farm, but jolly useful to campers.'

'These moors are awfully high, aren't they?' said George. 'I guess they'll be freezing cold in the winter.'

'They are,' said Julian. 'And they may be jolly windy and cold in the summer, too, so Luffy says we'd better take sweaters and things. He says in the winter they are covered with snow for months. The sheep have to be dug out when they get lost.'

Dick's finger followed a small winding road that

made its way over the wild stretch of moorland. 'That's the road we go,' he said. 'And I suppose we strike off here, look, where a cart-track is shown. That would go to the farm. We shall have to carry our stuff from wherever Luffy parks his car, and take it to our camping-place.'

'Not too near Luffy, I hope,' said George.

'Oh, no. He's agreed to keep an eye on us, but he'll forget all about us once he's settled down in his own tent,' said Julian. 'He will, really. Two chaps I know once went out in his car with him for a day's run, and he came back without them in the evening. He'd forgotten he had them

with him, and had left them wandering somewhere miles and miles away.'

'Good old Luffy,' said Dick. 'That's the sort of fellow we want! He won't come springing up to ask if we've cleaned our teeth or if we've got our warm jerseys on!'

The others laughed, and Timmy stretched his doggy mouth into a grin again. His tongue hung out happily. It was good to have all four of his friends with him again, and to hear them planning a holiday. Timmy went to school with George and Anne in term time, and he missed the two boys very much. But he belonged to George, and would not dream of leaving her. It was a good thing that George's school allowed pets, or George would certainly not have gone!

Julian folded up the map again. 'I hope all the things we've ordered will come in good time,' he said. 'We've got about six days to wait. I'd better keep on reminding Luffy that we're going with him, or he's quite likely to start without us!'

It was difficult to have to wait so long now that everything was planned. Parcels came from various stores and were eagerly opened. The sleeping-bags were fine.

'Super!' said Anne.

'Smashing!' said George, crawling into hers. 'Look! I can lace it up at the neck – and it's got a hood thing to come right over my head. Golly, it's warm! I shan't mind the coldest night if I'm sleeping in this. I vote we sleep in them tonight.'

'What? In our bedrooms?' said Anne.

'Yes. Why not? Just to get used to them,' said George, who felt that a sleeping-bag was a hundred times better than an ordinary bed.

So that night all four slept on the floor of their bedrooms in their sleeping-bags, and voted them very comfortable and as warm as toast.

'The only thing is, Timmy kept wanting to come right inside mine,' said George, 'and honestly there isn't enough room. Besides, he'd be cooked.'

'Well, he seemed to spend half the night on my tummy,' grumbled Julian. 'I shall jolly well keep the bedroom door shut if Timmy's going to spend the night flopping on everyone's bag in turn.'

'I don't mind the flopping, so much as the frightful habit he's got of turning himself round and round and round before he flops down,' complained Dick. 'He did that on me last night. Silly habit of his.'

'He can't help it,' said George at once. 'It's a habit that wild dogs had centuries and centuries ago – they slept in reeds and rushes, and they got into the way of turning themselves round and round in them, to trample them down and make themselves a good sleeping-place. And our dogs go on turning themselves round now, before they go to sleep, even though there aren't any rushes to trample down.'

'Well! I wish Timmy would forget his doggy ancestors were wild dogs with rushy beds, and just remember he's a nice tame dog with a basket of his own,' said Dick. 'You should see my tummy today! It's all printed over with his foot-marks.'

'Fibber!' said Anne. 'You do exaggerate, Dick. Oh, I do wish Tuesday would come. I'm tired of waiting.'

'It'll come all right,' said Julian. And so it did, of course. It dawned bright and sunny, with a sky that was a deep blue, flecked with tiny white clouds.

'Good-weather clouds,' said Julian, pleased. 'Now, let's hope old Luffy has remembered it's today we're starting off. He's due here at ten o'clock. We're taking sandwiches for the whole party. Mother thought we'd better, in case Luffy forgot his. If he's remembered them it won't matter, because we're sure to be able to eat them ourselves. And there's always Timmy to finish things up!'

Timmy was as excited as the four children. He always knew when something nice was going to happen. His tail was on the wag the whole time, his tongue hung out, and he panted as if he had been running a race. He kept getting under everyone's feet, but nobody minded.

Mr Luffy arrived half an hour late, just when everyone was beginning to feel he had forgotten to come. He was at the wheel of his big old car, beaming. All the children knew him quite well, because he lived not far away and often came to play bridge with their father and mother.

'Hallo, hallo!' he cried. 'All ready, I see! Good for you! Pile the things on the trailer, will you? Mine are there too but there's plenty of room. I've got sandwiches for everyone, by the way. My wife said I'd better bring plenty.'

'We'll have a fine feast today then,' said Dick, helping Julian to carry out the folded-up tents and sleeping-bags, while the girls followed with the smaller things. Soon everything was on the trailer and Julian made them safe with ropes.

They said goodbye to the watching grown-ups and climbed excitedly into the car. Mr Luffy started up his engine and put the lever into first gear with a frightful noise.

'Goodbye!' called all the grown-ups, and Julian's mother added a last word. 'DON'T get into any awful adventure this time!'

'Of course they won't!' called back Mr Luffy cheerfully. 'I'll see to that. There are no adventures to be found on a wild and deserted moor. Goodbye!'

Off they went, waving madly, and shouting goodbye all the way down the road. 'Goodbye! Goodbyeeeeee! Hurrah, we're off at last!'

The car raced down the road, the trailer bumping madly after it. The holiday had begun!

CHAPTER TWO

Up on the moors

MR LUFFY was not a good driver. He went too fast, especially round the corners, and many times Julian looked behind at the trailer in alarm, afraid that everything would suddenly leap off it at some sharp bend.

He saw the bundle of sleeping-bags jump high into the air, but fortunately they remained on the trailer. He touched Mr Luffy on the shoulder.

'Sir! Could you go a bit slower, please! The trailer will be empty by the time we arrive, if the luggage leaps about on it much more.'

'My word! I forgot we had a trailer,' said Mr Luffy, slowing down at once. 'Remind me if I go over thirty-five miles an hour, will you? Last time I took the trailer with me, I arrived with only half the goods on it. I don't want that to happen again.'

Julian certainly hoped it wouldn't. He kept a sharp eye on the speedometer, and when it veered towards forty he tapped Mr Luffy on the arm.

Mr Luffy looked supremely happy. He didn't like term time, but he loved holidays. Term time interfered with the study of his beloved insect-world. Now he was off with four nice children he liked, for a holiday on a moorland he

knew was alive with bees, beetles, butterflies and every other kind of insect he wanted. He looked forward to teaching the four children quite a lot. They would have been horrified if they guessed this, but they didn't.

He was an odd-looking fellow. He had very untidy, shaggy eyebrows over kind and gentle brown eyes that always reminded Dick of a monkey's. He had a rather large nose, which looked fiercer than it was because, unexpectedly, it had quite a forest of hairs growing out of the nostrils. He had an untidy moustache, and a round chin with a surprising dimple in the middle of it.

His ears always fascinated Anne. They were large and turned rather forward, and Mr Luffy could waggle the right one if he wanted to. To his great sorrow he had never been able to waggle the left one. His hair was thick and untidy, and his clothes always looked loose, comfortable and rather too big for him.

The children liked him. They couldn't help it. He was so odd and gentle and untidy and forgetful – and yet sometimes unexpectedly fierce. Julian had often told them the story of Tom Killin the bully.

Mr Luffy had once found Tom bullying a small new boy in the cloakroom, dragging him round and round it by his belt. With a roar like an angry bull, Mr Luffy had pounced on the big bully, got him by the belt, lifted him up and stuck him firmly on a peg in the cloakroom.

'There you stay till you get someone to lift you down!'

Mr Luffy had thundered. '*I* can get hold of a belt too, as you can see!'

And then he had stalked out of the cloakroom with the small, terrified boy beside him, leaving the bully hung up high on the peg, quite unable to free himself. And there he had to stay, because not one of the boys who came pouring in from a game of football would lift him down.

'And, if the peg hadn't given way under his weight, he'd be stuck up there still,' Julian had said with a grin. 'Good old Luffy! You'd never think he could be fierce like that, would you?'

Anne loved that story. Mr Luffy became quite a hero to her after that. She was pleased to sit next to him in the car, and chatter about all kinds of things. The other three were squashed at the back with Timmy on their feet. George firmly prevented him from climbing up on her knee because it was so hot. So he contented himself with trying to stand up with his paws on the window-ledge and his nose over the side.

They stopped about half past twelve for lunch. Mr Luffy had indeed provided sandwiches for everyone. And remarkably fine ones they were too, made the evening before by Mrs Luffy.

'Cucumber, dipped in vinegar! Ham and lettuce! Egg! Sardine! Oooh, Mr Luffy, your sandwiches are much nicer than ours,' said Anne, beginning on two together, one cucumber and the other ham and lettuce.

They were all very hungry. Timmy had a bit from

everyone, usually the last bite, and watched each sandwich eagerly till his turn came. Mr Luffy didn't seem to understand that Timmy had to have the last bite of any sandwich, so Timmy simply took it out of his hand, much to his surprise.

'A clever dog,' he said, and patted him. 'Knows what he wants and takes it. Very clever.'

That pleased George, of course. She thought that Timmy was the cleverest dog in the world, and indeed it did seem like it at times. He understood every word she said to him, every pat, every stroke, every gesture. He would be much, much better at keeping an eye on

the four children and guarding them than forgetful Mr Luffy.

They drank ginger beer and then ate some ripe plums. Timmy wouldn't have any plums, but he licked up some spilt ginger beer. Then he snuffed up a few odd crumbs and went to drink at a little stream nearby.

The party set off again in the car. Anne fell asleep. Dick gave an enormous yawn and fell asleep too. George wasn't sleepy, nor was Timmy, but Julian was. He didn't dare to take his eye off the speedometer, though, because Mr Luffy seemed to be very much inclined to speed along too fast again, after his good lunch.

'We won't stop for tea till we get there,' said Mr Luffy suddenly, and Dick woke up with a jump at the sound of his booming voice. 'We should be there about half past five. Look, you can see the moorland in the distance now – all ablaze with heather!'

Everybody looked ahead, except Anne, who was still fast asleep. Rising up to the left for miles upon miles was the heather-covered moorland, a lovely sight to see. It looked wild and lonely and beautiful, blazing with heather, and shading off into a purple-blue in the distance.

'We take this road to the left, and then we're on the moors,' said Mr Luffy, swinging violently to the left, and making the luggage in the trailer jump high again. 'Here we go.'

The car climbed the high moorland road steadily. It passed one or two small houses, and in the distance the children could see little farms in clearings. Sheep dotted the moorland, and some of them stood staring at the car as it drove by.

'We've got about twenty miles to go, I should think,' said Mr Luffy, jamming on his brakes suddenly to avoid two large sheep in the middle of the road. 'I wish these creatures wouldn't choose the centre of the road to gossip in. Hi, get on there! Let me pass!'

Timmy yelped and tried to get out of the car. The sheep hurriedly decided to move, and the car went on. Anne was thoroughly awake by now, having been almost jerked out of her seat by the sudden stop.

'What a shame to wake you!' said Mr Luffy, gazing down at her kindly, and almost running into a ditch by the side of the road. 'We're nearly there, Anne.'

They climbed steadily, and the wind grew a little cold. All around the children the moors stretched for mile upon mile, never-ending. Little streams sometimes splashed right down to the roadway, and ran beside it.

'We can drink the water in these streams,' said Mr Luffy. 'Crystal clear, and cold as ice! There's one quite near where we're going to camp.'

That was good news. Julian thought of the big canvas buckets they had brought. He didn't particularly want to carry those for miles. If there was a stream near their camping-place it would be easy to get the buckets filled with washing-water.

The road forked into two. To the right was a good road,

leading on and on. To the left it became not much more than a cart-track. 'That's the one we take,' said Mr Luffy, and the car jerked and jolted over it. He was forced to go slowly, and the children had time to see every little thing they passed.

'I shall leave the car here,' said Mr Luffy, bringing it to a standstill beside a great rock that stood up bare and grey out of the moor. 'It will be sheltered from the worst winds and rain. I thought we'd camp over yonder.'

There was a little slope just there, backed by some enormous gorse bushes. Thick heather grew everywhere. Julian nodded. It was a good place for camping. Those thick gorse bushes would provide fine shelter from the winds.

'Right, sir,' he said. 'Shall we have tea first, or unpack now?'

'Tea first,' said Mr Luffy. 'I've brought a very good little stove for boiling and cooking things. Better than a wood fire. That makes kettles and saucepans so black.'

'We've got a stove, too,' said Anne. She scrambled out of the car and looked all round. 'It's lovely here – all heather and wind and sun! Is that the farm over there – the one we shall go to for eggs and things?'

She pointed to a tiny farmhouse on the hill opposite. It stood in a small clearing. In a field behind it were three or four cows and a horse. A small orchard stood at the side, and a vegetable garden lay in front. It seemed odd to see such a trim little place in the midst of the moorland.

'That's Olly's Farm,' said Mr Luffy. 'It's changed hands, I believe, since I was here three years ago. I hope the new people are nice. Now – did we leave something to eat for our tea?'

They had, because Anne had wisely put away a good many sandwiches and bits of cake for tea-time. They sat in the heather, with bees humming all round them, and munched solidly for fifteen minutes. Timmy waited patiently for his bits, watching the bees that hummed round him. There were thousands of them.

'And now I suppose we'd better put up our tents,' said Julian. 'Come on, Dick – let's unpack the trailer. Mr Luffy, we don't intend to camp on top of you, sir, because you won't want four noisy children too near. Where would you like your tent put?'

Mr Luffy was about to say that he would like to have the four children and Timmy quite close, when it suddenly occurred to him that perhaps they might not want him too near. They might want to make a noise, or play silly games, and if he were near it would stop them enjoying themselves in their own way.

So he made up his mind not to be too close. 'I'll pitch my tent down there, where that old gorse bush is,' he said. 'And if you'd like to put yours up here, where there's a half-circle of gorse bushes keeping off the wind, you'd be well sheltered. And we shan't interfere with one another at all.'

'Right, sir,' said Julian, and he and Dick began to tackle

the tents. It was fun. Timmy got under everyone's feet as usual, and ran off with an important rope, but nobody minded.

By the time that dusk came creeping up the heather-covered moorland, all three tents were up, the ground-sheets were put down, and the sleeping-bags unrolled on them, two in each of the children's tents, and one in Mr Luffy's.

'I'm going to turn in,' said Mr Luffy. 'My eyes are almost shut. Good night, all of you. Sleep well!'

He disappeared into the dusk. Anne yawned widely, and that set the others off too. 'Come on – let's turn in, too,' said Julian. 'We'll have a bar of chocolate each, and a few biscuits. We can eat those in our sleeping-bags. Good night, girls. Won't it be grand to wake up tomorrow morning?'

He and Dick disappeared into their tent. The girls crawled into theirs with Timmy. They undressed, and got into their warm, soft sleeping-bags.

'This is super!' said George, pushing Timmy to one side. 'I never felt so cosy in my life. *Don't* do that, Timmy. Don't you know the difference between my feet and my middle? That's better.'

'Good night,' said Anne, sleepily. 'Look, George, you can see the stars shining through the opening of the tent. Don't they look enormous?'

But George didn't care whether they were enormous or not. She was fast asleep, tired out with the day's run.

Timmy cocked one ear when he heard Anne's voice, and gave a little grunt. That was his way of saying good night. Then he put his head down and slept.

'Our first night of camping,' thought Anne, happily. 'I shan't go to sleep. I shall lie awake and look at the stars and smell that heathery smell.'

But she didn't. In half a second she was sound asleep, too!

CHAPTER THREE

Anne's volcano

JULIAN AWOKE first in the morning. He heard a strange and lonely sound floating overhead. 'Coor-lie! Coor-lie!'

He sat up and wondered where he was and who was calling. Of course! He was in his tent with Dick – they were camping on the moors. And that wild cry overhead came from a curlew, the bird of the moorlands.

He yawned and lay down again. It was early in the morning. The sun put its warm fingers in at his tent opening, and he felt the warmth on his sleeping-bag. He felt lazy and snug and contented. He also felt hungry, which was a nuisance. He glanced at his watch.

Half past six. He really was too warm and comfortable to get up yet. He put out his hand to see if there was any chocolate left from the night before, and found a little piece. He put it into his mouth and lay there contentedly, listening to more curlews, and watching the sun climb a little higher.

He fell asleep again, and was awakened by Timmy busily licking his face. He sat up with a start. The girls were peering in at his tent, grinning. They were fully dressed already.

'Wake up, lazy!' said Anne. 'We sent Timmy in to get you up. It's half past seven. We've been up for ages.'

'It's a simply heavenly morning,' said George. 'Going to be a frightfully hot day. Do get up. We're going to find the stream and wash in it. It seems silly to lug heavy buckets of water to and fro for washing, if the stream's nearby.'

Dick awoke too. He and Julian decided to go and take a bathe in the stream. They wandered out into the sunny morning, feeling very happy and very hungry. The girls were just coming back from the stream.

'It's over there,' said Anne, pointing. 'Timmy, go with them and show them. It's a lovely little brown

stream, awfully cold, and it's got ferns along its banks. We've left the bucket there. Bring it back full, will you?'

'What do you want us to do that for, if you've already washed?' asked Dick.

'We want water for washing-up the dishes,' said Anne. 'I suddenly remembered we'd need water for that. I say, do you think we ought to wake up Mr Luffy? There's no sign of him yet.'

'No, let him sleep,' said Julian. 'He's probably tired out with driving the car so slowly! We can easily save him some breakfast. What are we going to have?'

'We've unpacked some bacon rashers and tomatoes,' said Anne, who loved cooking. 'How do you light the stove, Julian?'

'George knows,' said Julian. 'I say, did we pack a frying-pan?'

'Yes. I packed it myself,' said Anne. 'Do go and bathe if you're going to. Breakfast will be ready before you are!'

Timmy gravely trotted off with the boys and showed them the stream. Julian and Dick at once lay down in the clear brown bed, and kicked wildly. Timmy leapt in too, and there were yells and shrieks.

'Well – I should think we've woken up old Luffy now!' said Dick, rubbing himself down with a rough towel. 'How lovely and cold that was. The trouble is it's made me feel twice as hungry!'

'Doesn't that frying bacon smell good?' said Julian,

sniffing the air. They walked back to the girls. There was still no sign of Mr Luffy. He must indeed sleep very soundly!

They sat down in the heather and began their breakfast. Anne had fried big rounds of bread in the fat, and the boys told her she was the best cook in the world. She was very pleased.

'I shall look after the food side for you,' she said. 'But George must help with the preparing of the meals and washing-up. See, George?'

George didn't see. She hated doing all the things that Anne loved to do, such as making beds and washing-up. She looked sulky.

'Look at old George! Why bother about the washing-up when there's Timmy only too pleased to use his tongue to wash every plate?' said Dick.

Everyone laughed, even George. 'All right,' she said, 'I'll help of course. Only let's use as few plates as possible, then there won't be much washing-up. Is there any more fried bread, Anne?'

'No. But there are some biscuits in that tin,' said Anne. 'I say, boys, who's going to go to the farm each day for milk and things? I expect they can let us have bread, too, and fruit.'

'Oh, one or other of us will go,' said Dick. 'Anne, hadn't you better fry something for old Luffy now? I'll go and wake him. Half the day will be gone if he doesn't get up now.'

'I'll go and make a noise like an earwig outside his

tent,' said Julian, getting up. 'He might not wake with all our yells and shouts, but he'd certainly wake at the call of a friendly earwig!'

He went down to the tent. He cleared his throat and called politely: 'Are you awake yet, sir?'

There was no answer. Julian called again. Then, puzzled, he went to the tent opening. The flap was closed. He pulled it aside and looked in.

The tent was empty! There was nobody there at all.

'What's up, Ju?' called Dick.

'He's not here,' said Julian. 'Where can he be?'

There was silence. For a panic-stricken moment Anne thought one of their strange adventures was beginning. Then Dick called out again: 'Is his bug-tin gone? You know, the tin box with straps that he takes with him when he goes insect-hunting? And what about his clothes?'

Julian inspected the inside of the tent again. 'Okay!' he called, much to everyone's relief. 'His clothes are gone, and so has his bug-tin. He must have slipped out early before we were awake. I bet he's forgotten all about us and breakfast and everything!'

'That would be just like him,' said Dick. 'Well, we're not his keepers. He can do as he likes! If he doesn't want breakfast, he needn't have any. He'll come back when he's finished his hunting, I suppose.'

'Anne! Can you get on with the doings if Dick and I go to the farmhouse and see what food they've got?' asked

Julian. 'The time's getting on, and if we're going for a walk or anything today, we don't want to start too late.'

'Right,' said Anne. 'You go too, George. I can manage everything nicely, now that the boys have brought me a bucketful of water. Take Timmy. He wants a walk.'

George was only too pleased to get out of the washing-up. She and the boys, with Timmy trotting in front, set off to the farmhouse. Anne got on with her jobs, humming softly to herself in the sunshine. She soon finished them, and then looked to see if the others were coming back. There was no sign of them, or of Mr Luffy either.

'I'll go for a walk on my own,' thought Anne. 'I'll follow that little stream uphill and see where it begins. That would be fun. I can't possibly lose my way if I keep by the water.'

She set off in the sunshine and came to the little brown stream that gurgled down the hill. She scrambled through the heather beside it, following its course uphill. She liked all the little green ferns and the cushions of velvety moss that edged it. She tasted the water – it was cold and sweet and clean.

Feeling very happy all by herself, Anne walked on and on. She came at last to a big mound of a hill-top. The little stream began there, half-way up the mound. It came gurgling out of the heathery hillside, edged with moss, and made its chattering way far down the hill.

'So that's where you begin, is it?' said Anne. She flung herself down on the heather, hot with her climb. It was nice there, with the sun on her face, and the sound of the trickling water nearby.

She lay listening to the humming bees and the water. And then she heard another sound. She took no notice of it at all at first.

Then she sat up, frightened. 'The noise is underground! Deep, deep underground! It rumbles and roars. Oh, what is going to happen? Is there going to be an earthquake?'

The rumbling seemed to come nearer and nearer. Anne didn't even dare to get up and run. She sat there and trembled.

Then there came an unearthly shriek, and not far off a most astonishing thing happened. A great cloud of white smoke came right out of the ground and hung in the air before the wind blew it away. Anne was simply horrified. It was so sudden, so very unexpected on this quiet hillside. The rumbling noise went on for a while and then gradually faded away.

Anne leapt to her feet in a panic. She fled down the hill, screaming loudly: 'It's a volcano! Help! Help! I've been sitting on a volcano. It's going to burst, it's sending out smoke. Help, help, it's a VOLCANO!'

She tore down the hillside, caught her foot on a tuft of heather and went rolling over and over, sobbing. She came to rest at last, and then heard an anxious voice calling:

'Who's that? What's the matter?'

It was Mr Luffy's voice. Anne screamed to him in relief. 'Mr Luffy! Come and save me! There's a volcano here!'

There was such terror in her voice that Mr Luffy came

racing to her at once. He sat down beside the trembling girl and put his arm round her. 'Whatever's the matter?' he said. 'What's frightened you?'

Anne told him again. 'Up there – do you see? That's a volcano, Mr Luffy. It trembled and rumbled and then it shot up clouds of smoke. Oh quick, before it sends out red hot cinders!'

'Now, now!' said Mr Luffy, and to Anne's surprise and relief he actually laughed. 'Do you mean to tell me you don't know what that was?'

'No, I don't,' said Anne.

'Well,' said Mr Luffy, 'under this big moor run two or three long tunnels to take trains from one valley to another. Didn't you know? They make the rumbling noise you heard, and the sudden smoke you saw was the smoke sent up by a train below. There are big vent-holes here and there in the moor for the smoke to escape from.'

'Oh, good gracious me!' said Anne, going rather red. 'I didn't even *know* there were trains under here. What an extraordinary thing! I really did think I was sitting on a volcano, Mr Luffy. You won't tell the others will you? They would laugh at me dreadfully.'

'I won't say a word,' said Mr Luffy. 'And now I think we'll go back. Have you had breakfast? I'm terribly hungry. I went out early after a rather rare butterfly I saw flying by my tent.'

'We've had breakfast *ages* ago,' said Anne. 'But if

you'd like to come back with me now I'll cook you some bacon, Mr Luffy. And some tomatoes and fried bread.'

'Aha! It sounds good,' said Mr Luffy. 'Now – not a word about volcanoes. That's our secret.'

And off they went to the tents, where the others were wondering what in the world had become of Anne. Little did they know she had been 'sitting on a volcano'!

CHAPTER FOUR

Spook-trains

THE BOYS and George were full of talk about the farm. 'It's a nice little place,' said Julian, sitting down while Anne began to cook breakfast for Mr Luffy. 'Pretty farmhouse, nice little dairy, well-kept sheds. And even a grand piano in the drawing-room.'

'Gracious! You wouldn't think they'd make enough money to buy a thing like that, would you?' said Anne, turning over the bacon in the pan.

'The farmer's got a fine car,' went on Julian. 'Brand new. Must have cost him a pretty penny. His boy showed it to us. And he showed us some jolly good new farm machinery too.'

'Very interesting,' said Mr Luffy. 'I wonder how they make their money, farming that bit of land? The last people were hard-working folk, but they certainly couldn't have afforded a new car or a grand piano.'

'And you should have seen the lorries they've got!' said Dick. 'Beauties! Old army ones, I should think. The boy said his father's going to use them for carting things from the farm to the market.'

'What things?' said Mr Luffy, looking across at the little farmhouse. 'I shouldn't have thought they needed an army of lorries for that! An old farm wagon would carry all *their* produce.'

'Well, that's what he told us,' said Dick. 'Everything certainly looked very prosperous, I must say. He must be a jolly good farmer.'

'We got eggs and butter and fruit, and even some bacon,' said George. 'The boy's mother didn't seem worried about how much we had, and she hardly charged us anything. We didn't see the farmer.'

Mr Luffy was now eating his breakfast. He was certainly very hungry. He brushed away the flies that hung round his head, and when one settled on his right ear he waggled it violently. The fly flew off in surprise.

'Oh, do that again!' begged Anne. 'How do you do it? Do you think if I practised hard for weeks I could make my ear move?'

'No, I don't think so,' said Mr Luffy, finishing his breakfast. 'Well, I've got some writing to do now. What are you going to do? Go for a walk?'

'We might as well take a picnic lunch and go off somewhere,' said Julian. 'How about it?'

'Yes,' said Dick. 'Can you pack us dinner and tea, Anne? We'll help. What about hard-boiled eggs?'

It wasn't long before they had a picnic meal packed in greaseproof paper.

'You won't get lost, will you?' said Mr Luffy.

'Oh no, sir,' said Julian, with a laugh. 'I've got a compass, anyway, and a jolly good bump of locality, too. I usually know the way to go. We'll see you this evening, when we get back.'

'*You* won't get lost, Mr Luffy, will you?' asked Anne, looking worried.

'Don't be cheeky, Anne,' said Dick, rather horrified at Anne's question. But she really meant it. Mr Luffy was so absent-minded that she could quite well picture him wandering off and not being able to find his way back.

He smiled at her. 'No,' he said. 'I know my way about here all right – I know every stream and path and er – volcano!'

Anne giggled. The others stared at Mr Luffy, wondering what in the world he meant, but neither he nor Anne told them. They said goodbye and set off.

'It's heavenly walking today,' said Anne. 'Shall we follow a path if we find one or not?'

'Might as well,' said Julian. 'It'll be a bit tiring scrambling through heather all the day.'

So when they did unexpectedly come across a path they followed it. 'It's just a shepherd's path, I expect,' said Dick. 'I bet it's a lonely job, looking after sheep up on these desolate heathery hills.'

They went on for some way, enjoying the stretches of bright heather, the lizards that darted quickly away from their feet and the hosts of butterflies of all kinds that hovered and fluttered. Anne loved the little blue ones best and made up her mind to ask Mr Luffy what all their names were.

They had their lunch on a hill-top overlooking a vast stretch of heather, with grey-white blobs in it here and there – the sheep that wandered everywhere.

And, in the very middle of the meal, Anne heard the same rumbling she had heard before, and then, not far off, out spouted some white smoke from the ground. George went quite pale. Timmy leapt to his feet, growling and barking, his tail down. The boys roared with laughter.

'It's all right, Anne and George. It's only the trains underground here. We knew they ran under the moors and we thought we'd see what you did when you first heard them rumbling, and saw the smoke.'

'I'm not a bit frightened,' said Anne, and the boys looked at her, astonished. It was George who was the scared one! Usually it was quite the other way round.

George got back her colour and laughed. She called Timmy. 'It's all right, Tim. Come here. You know what trains are, don't you?'

The children discussed the trains. It really did seem strange to think of trains in those hollowed-out tunnels down below the moors – the people in them, reading their newspapers and talking – down in tunnels where the sun never shone at all.

'Come on,' said Julian, at last. 'Let's go on. We'll walk to the top of the next slope, and then I think we ought to turn back.'

They found a little path that Julian said must be a

rabbit-path, because it was so narrow, and set off, chattering and laughing. They climbed through the heather to the top of the next slope. And at the top they got quite a surprise.

Down in the valley below was a silent and deserted stretch of railway lines! They appeared out of the black hole of a tunnel-mouth, ran for about half a mile, and then ended in what seemed to be a kind of railway yard.

'Look at that,' said Julian. 'Old derelict lines – not used any more, I should think. I suppose that tunnel's out of date, too.'

'Let's go down and have a squint,' said Dick. 'Come on! We've got plenty of time, and we can easily go back a shorter way.'

They set off down the hill to the lines. They arrived some way from the tunnel-mouth, and followed the lines to the deserted railway yard. There seemed to be nobody about at all.

'Look,' said Dick, 'there are some old wagons on that set of lines over there. They look as if they haven't been used for a hundred years. Let's give them a shove and set them going!'

'Oh, no!' said Anne, afraid. But the two boys and George, who had always longed to play about with real railway trucks, ran over to where three or four stood on the lines. Dick and Julian shoved hard at one. It moved. It ran a little way and crashed into the buffers of another. It made a terrific noise in the silent yard.

A door flew open in a tiny hut at the side of the yard, and a terrifying figure came out. It was a one-legged man, with a wooden peg for his other leg, two great arms that might quite well belong to a gorilla, and a face as red as a tomato, except where grey whiskers grew.

He opened his mouth and the children expected a loud and angry yell. Instead out came a husky, hoarse whisper:

'What you doing? Ain't it bad enough to hear spook-trains a-running at night, without hearing them in the daytime, too?'

The four children stared at him. They thought he must

be quite mad. He came nearer to them, and his wooden leg tip-tapped oddly. He swung his great arms loosely. He peered at the children as if he could hardly see them.

'I've broken me glasses,' he said, and to their astonishment and dismay two tears ran down his cheeks. 'Poor old Wooden-Leg Sam, he's broken his glasses. Nobody cares about Wooden-Leg Sam now, nobody at all.'

There didn't seem anything to say to all this. Anne felt sorry for the funny old man, but she kept well behind Julian.

Sam peered at them again. 'Haven't you got tongues in your heads? Am I seeing things again, or are you there?'

'We're here and we're real,' said Julian. 'We happened to see this old railway yard and we came down to have a look at it. Who are you?'

'I told you – I'm Wooden-Leg Sam,' said the old man impatiently. 'The watchman, see? Though what there is to watch here, beats me. Do they think I'm going to watch for these spook-trains? Well, I'm not. Not me, Sam Wooden-Leg. I've seen many strange things in my life, yes, and been scared by them too, and I'm not watching for any more spook-trains.'

The children listened curiously. 'What spook-trains?' asked Julian.

Wooden-Leg Sam came closer. He looked all round as if he thought there might be someone listening, and then spoke in a hoarser whisper than usual.

'Spook-trains, I tell you. Trains that come out of that

tunnel at night all by themselves, and go back all by themselves. Nobody in them. One night they'll come for old Sam Wooden-Leg – but, see, I'm smart, I am. I lock myself into my hut and get under the bed. And I blow my candle out so those spook-trains don't know I'm there.'

Anne shivered. She pulled at Julian's hand. 'Julian! Let's go. I don't like it. It sounds all peculiar and horrid. What does he mean?'

The old man seemed suddenly to change his mood. He picked up a large cinder and threw it at Dick, hitting him on the head. 'You clear out! I'm watchman here. And what did they tell me? They told me to chase away anyone that came. Clear out, I tell you!'

In terror Anne fled away. Timmy growled and would have leapt at the strange old watchman, but George had her hand on his collar. Dick rubbed his head where the cinder had hit him.

'We're going,' he said soothingly to Sam. It was plain that the old fellow was a bit funny in the head. 'We didn't mean to trespass. You look after your spook-trains. We won't interfere with you!'

The boys and George turned away, and caught up with Anne. 'What did he mean?' she asked, scared. 'What are spook-trains? Trains that aren't real? Does he really see them at night?'

'He just imagines them,' said Julian. 'I expect being there all alone in that deserted old railway yard has made him think strange things. Don't worry, Anne. There are no

such things as spook-trains.'

'But he spoke as if there were,' said Anne, 'he really did. I'd hate to see a spook-train. Wouldn't you Ju?'

'No. I'd *love* to see one,' said Julian, and he turned to Dick. 'Wouldn't you, Dick? Shall we come one night and watch? Just to see?'

CHAPTER FIVE

Back at camp again

THE CHILDREN and Timmy left the deserted railway yard behind them and climbed up the heathery slope to find their way back to their camping-place. The boys could not stop talking about Wooden-Leg Sam and the strange things he said.

'It's a funny business altogether,' said Julian. 'I wonder why that yard isn't used any more – and where that tunnel leads to – and if trains ever do run there.'

'I expect there's quite an ordinary explanation,' said Dick. 'It's just that Wooden-Leg Sam made it all seem so weird. If there had been a proper watchman we shouldn't have thought there was anything strange about it at all.'

'Perhaps the boy at the farm would know,' said Julian. 'We'll ask him tomorrow. I'm afraid there aren't any spook-trains really – but, gosh, I'd love to go and watch for one, if there were any.'

'I wish you wouldn't talk like that,' said Anne, unhappily. 'You know, it makes me feel as if you want another adventure. And I don't.'

'Well, there won't be any adventure, so don't worry,' said Dick, comfortingly. 'And, anyway, if there was an adventure you could always go and hold old Luffy's hand.

He wouldn't see an adventure if it was right under his nose. You'd be quite safe with him.'

'Look – who's that up there?' said George, seeing Timmy prick up his ears, and then hearing him give a little growl.

'Shepherd or something, I should think,' said Julian. He shouted out cheerfully. 'Good afternoon! Nice day it's been!'

The old man on the path just above them nodded his head. He was either a shepherd or farm labourer of some sort. He waited for them to come up.

'Have you seen any of my sheep down along there?' he asked them. 'They've got red crosses on them.'

'No. There aren't any down there,' said Julian. 'But there are some further along the hill. We've been down to the railway yard and we'd have seen any sheep on the slope below.'

'Don't you go down there,' said the old shepherd, his faded blue eyes looking into Julian's. 'That's a bad place, that is.'

'Well, we've been hearing about spook-trains!' said Julian, with a laugh. 'Is that what you mean?'

'Ay. There're trains that nobody knows of running out of that tunnel,' said the shepherd. 'Many's the time I've heard them when I've been up here at night with my sheep. That tunnel hasn't been used for thirty years – but the trains, they still come out of it, just as they used to.'

'How do you know? Have you seen them?' asked Julian, a cold shiver creeping down his spine quite suddenly.

'No. I've only heard them,' said the old man. 'Choo, choo, they go, and they jangle and clank. But they don't whistle any more. Old Wooden-Leg Sam reckons they're spook-trains, with nobody to drive them and nobody to tend them. Don't you go down to that place. It's bad and scary.'

Julian caught sight of Anne's scared face. He laughed loudly. 'What a tale! I don't believe in spook-trains – and neither do you, shepherd. Dick, have you got the tea in your bag? Let's find a nice place and have some sandwiches and cake. Will you join us, shepherd?'

'No, thank you kindly,' said the old man, moving off. 'I'll be after my sheep. Always wandering they are, and they keep me wandering, too. Good day, sir, and don't go down to that bad place.'

Julian found a good spot out of sight of 'that bad place', and they all sat down. 'All a lot of nonsense,' said Julian, who wanted Anne to feel happier again. 'We can easily ask the farmer's boy about it tomorrow. I expect it's all a silly tale made up by that old one-legged fellow, and passed on to the shepherd.'

'I expect so,' said Dick. 'You noticed that the shepherd had never actually *seen* the trains, Julian? Only heard them. Well, sound travels far at night, and I expect what he heard was simply the rumblings of the trains that go underground here. There's one going somewhere now! I can feel the ground trembling!'

They all could. It was a peculiar feeling. The rumbling stopped at last and they sat and ate their tea, watching Timmy scraping at a rabbit-hole and trying his hardest to get down it. He covered them with sandy soil as he burrowed, and nothing would stop him.

'Look here, if we don't get Timmy out of that hole now he'll be gone down so far that we'll have to drag him out by his tail,' said Julian, getting up. 'Timmy! TIM-MY! The rabbit's miles away. Come on out.'

It took both George and Julian to get him out. He was most indignant. He looked at them as if to say: '*Well*, what spoil-sports! Almost got him and you drag me out!'

He shook himself, and bits of grit and sand flew out of his hair. He took a step towards the hole again, but George caught hold of his tail. 'No, Timmy. Home now!'

'He's looking for a spook-train,' said Dick, and that made everyone laugh, even Anne.

They set off back to the camping-place, pleasantly tired, with Timmy following rather sulkily at their heels. When they at last got back they saw Mr Luffy sitting waiting for them. The blue smoke from his pipe curled up into the air.

'Hallo, hallo!' he said, and his brown eyes looked up at them from under his shaggy eyebrows. 'I was beginning to wonder if you'd got lost. Still, I suppose that dog of yours would always bring you back.'

Timmy wagged his tail politely. 'Woof,' he agreed, and went to drink out of the bucket of water. Anne stopped him just in time.

'No, Timmy! You're not to drink out of our washing-up water. There's yours, in the dish over there.'

Timmy went to his dish and lapped. He thought Anne was very fussy. Anne asked Mr Luffy if he would like any supper.

'We're not having a proper supper,' she said. 'We had tea so late. But I'll cook you something if you like, Mr Luffy.'

'Very kind of you. But I've had an enormous tea,' said Mr Luffy. 'I've brought up a fruit cake for you, from my own larder. Shall we share it for supper? And I've got a bottle of lime juice, too, which will taste grand with some of the stream water.'

The boys went off to get some fresh stream water for drinking. Anne got out some plates and cut slices of the cake.

'Well,' said Mr Luffy. 'Had a nice walk?'

'Yes,' said Anne, 'except that we met a strange one-legged man who told us he saw spook-trains.'

Mr Luffy laughed. 'Well, well! He must be a cousin of a little girl I know who thought she was sitting on a volcano.'

Anne giggled. 'You're not to tease me. No, honestly, Mr Luffy, this old man was a watchman at a sort of old railway yard – not used now – and he said when the spook-trains came, he blew out his light and got under his bed so that they shouldn't get him.'

'Poor old fellow,' said Mr Luffy. 'I hope he didn't frighten you.'

'He did a bit,' said Anne. 'And he threw a cinder at Dick and hit him on the head. Tomorrow we're going to the farm to ask the boy there if he's heard of the spook-trains, too. We met an old shepherd who said he'd heard them but not seen them.'

'Well, well – it all sounds most interesting,' said Mr Luffy. 'But these exciting stories usually have a very tame explanation, you know. Now would you like to see what I found today? A very rare and interesting little beetle.'

He opened a small square tin and showed a shiny beetle

to Anne. It had green feelers and a red fiery spot near its tail-end. It was a lovely little thing.

'Now that's much more exciting to me than half a dozen spook-trains,' he told Anne. 'Spook-trains won't keep me awake at night – but thinking of this little beetle-fellow here certainly will.'

'I don't very much like beetles,' said Anne. 'But this one certainly is pretty. Do you really like hunting about all day for insects, and watching them, Mr Luffy?'

'Yes, very much,' said Mr Luffy. 'Ah, here come the boys with the water. Now we'll hand the cake round, shall we? Where's George? Oh, there she is, changing her shoes.'

George had a blister, and she had been putting a strip of plaster on her heel. She came up when the boys arrived and the cake was handed round. They sat in a circle, munching, while the sun gradually went down in a blaze of red.

'Nice day tomorrow again,' said Julian. 'What shall we do?'

'We'll have to go to the farm first,' said Dick. 'The farmer's wife said she'd let us have some more bread if we turned up in the morning. And we could do with more eggs if we can get them. We took eight hard-boiled ones with us today and we've only one or two left. And who's eaten all the tomatoes, I'd like to know?'

'All of you,' said Anne at once. 'You're perfect pigs over the tomatoes.'

'I'm afraid I'm one of the pigs,' apologised Mr Luffy. 'I think you fried me six for my breakfast, Anne.'

'That's all right,' said Anne. 'You didn't have as many as the others, even so! We can easily get some more.'

It was pleasant sitting there, eating and talking, and drinking lime juice and stream water. They were all tired, and it was nice to think of the cosy sleeping-bags. Timmy lifted his head and gave a vast yawn, showing an enormous amount of teeth.

'Timmy! I could see right down to your tail then!' said George. 'Do shut your mouth up. You've made us all yawn.'

So he had. Even Mr Luffy was yawning. He got up. 'Well, I'm going to turn in,' he said. 'Good night. We'll make plans tomorrow morning. I'll bring up some breakfast for you, if you like. I've got some tins of sardines.'

'Oh, thanks,' said Anne. 'And there's some of this cake left. I hope you won't think that's too funny a breakfast, Mr Luffy – sardines and fruit cake?'

'Not a bit. It sounds a most sensible meal,' came Mr Luffy's voice from down the hillside. 'Good night!'

The children sat there a few minutes longer. The sun went right out of sight. The wind grew a little chilly. Timmy yawned enormously again.

'Come on,' said Julian. 'Time we turned in. Thank goodness Timmy didn't come into our tent and walk all over me last night. Good night, girls. It's going to be a heavenly night – but as I shall be asleep in about two shakes of a duck's tail, I shan't see much of it!'

The girls went into their tent. They were soon in their

sleeping-bags. Just before they went to sleep Anne felt the slight shivering of the earth that meant a train was running underground somewhere. She could hear no rumbling sound. She fell asleep thinking of it.

The boys were not asleep. They, too, had felt the trembling of the earth beneath them, and it had reminded them of the old railway yard.

'Funny about those spook-trains, Dick,' said Julian, sleepily. 'Wonder if there *is* anything in it?'

'No. How could there be?' said Dick. 'All the same we'll go to the farm tomorrow and have a chat with that boy. He lives on the moors and he ought to know the truth.'

'The real truth is that Wooden-Leg Sam is potty, and imagines all he says, and the old shepherd is ready to believe in anything strange,' said Julian.

'I expect you're right,' said Dick. 'Oh my goodness, what's that?'

A dark shape stood looking in at the tent-flap. It gave a little whine.

'Oh, it's you, Timmy. Would you mind *not* coming and pretending you're a spook-train or something?' said Dick. 'And if you dare to put so much as half a paw on my middle, I'll scare you down the hill with a roar like a man-eating tiger. Go away.'

Timmy put a paw on Julian. Julian yelled out to George. 'George! Call this dog of yours, will you? He's just about to turn himself round twenty times on my middle, and curl himself up for the night.'

There was no answer from George. Timmy, feeling that he was not wanted, disappeared. He went back to George and curled himself up on her feet. He put his nose down on his paws and slept.

'Spooky Timmy,' murmured Julian, re-arranging himself. 'Timmy spooky – no, I mean – oh dear, what do I mean?'

'Shut up,' said Dick. 'What with you and Timmy messing about, I can't get – to – sleep!' But he could and he did – almost before he had finished speaking. Silence fell on the little camp, and nobody noticed when the next train rumbled underground – not even Timmy!

CHAPTER SIX

Day at the farm

THE NEXT day the children were up very early, as early as Mr Luffy, and they all had breakfast together. Mr Luffy had a map of the moorlands, and he studied it carefully after breakfast.

'I think I'll go off for the whole day,' he said to Julian, who was sitting beside him. 'See that little valley marked here – Crowleg Vale – well, I have heard that there are some of the rarest beetles in Britain to be found there. I think I'll take my gear and go along. What are you four going to do?'

'Five,' said George at once. 'You've forgotten Timmy.'

'So I have. I beg his pardon,' said Mr Luffy, solemnly. 'Well – what are you going to do?'

'We'll go over to the farm and get more food,' said Julian. 'And ask that farm-boy if he's heard the tale of the spook-trains. And perhaps look round the farm and get to know the animals there. I always like a farm.'

'Right,' said Mr Luffy, beginning to light his pipe. 'Don't worry about me if I'm not back till dusk. When I'm bug-hunting I lose count of the time.'

'You're sure you won't get lost?' said Anne, anxiously.

She didn't really feel that Mr Luffy could take proper care of himself.

'Oh yes. My right ear always warns me if I'm losing my way,' said Mr Luffy. 'It waggles hard.'

He waggled it at Anne and she laughed. 'I wish you'd tell me how you do that,' she said. 'I'm sure you know. You can't think how thrilled the girls at school would be if I learnt that trick. They'd think it was super.'

Mr Luffy grinned and got up. 'Well, so long,' he said. 'I'm off before Anne makes me give her a lesson in ear-waggles.'

He went off down the slope to his own tent. George and Anne washed-up, while the boys tightened some tent ropes that had come loose, and generally tidied up.

'I suppose it's quite all right leaving everything unguarded like this,' said Anne, anxiously.

'Well, we did yesterday,' said Dick. 'And who's likely to come and take anything up here in this wild and lonely spot, I'd like to know? You don't imagine a spook-train will come along and bundle everything into its luggage-van, do you, Anne?'

Anne giggled. 'Don't be silly. I just wondered if we ought to leave Timmy on guard, that's all.'

'Leave Timmy!' said George, amazed. 'You don't really think I'd leave Timmy behind every time we go off anywhere, Anne? Don't be an idiot.'

'No, I didn't really think you would,' said Anne. 'Well,

I suppose nobody will come along here. Throw over that tea-cloth, George, if you've finished with it.'

Soon the tea-cloths were hanging over the gorse bushes to dry in the sun. Everything was put away neatly in the tents. Mr Luffy had called a loud goodbye and gone. Now the Five were ready to go off to the farm.

Anne took a basket, and gave one to Julian too. 'To bring back the food,' said she. 'Are you ready to go now?'

They set off over the heather, their knees brushing through the honeyed flowers, and sending scores of busy bees into the air. It was a lovely day again, and the children felt free and happy.

They came to the trim little farm. Men were at work in the fields, but Julian did not think they were very industrious. He looked about for the farm-boy.

The boy came out of a shed and whistled to them. 'Hallo! You come for some more eggs? I've collected quite a lot for you.'

He stared at Anne. 'You didn't come yesterday. What's your name?'

'Anne,' said Anne. 'What's yours?'

'Jock,' said the boy, with a grin. He was rather a nice boy, Anne thought, with straw-coloured hair, blue eyes, and rather a red face which looked very good-tempered.

'Where's your mother?' said Julian. 'Can we get some bread and other things from her today? We ate an awful lot of our food yesterday, and we want to stock up our larder again!'

'She's busy just now in the dairy,' said Jock. 'Are you in a hurry? Come and see my pups.'

They all walked off with him to a shed. In there, right at the end, was a big box lined with straw. A collie dog lay there with five lovely little puppies. She growled at Timmy fiercely, and he backed hurriedly out of the shed. He had met fierce mother-dogs before, and he didn't like them!

The four children exclaimed over the little puppies, and Anne took one out very gently. It cuddled into her arms and made funny little whining noises.

'I wish it was mine,' said Anne. 'I should call it Cuddle.'

'What a frightful name for a dog,' said George scornfully. 'Just the kind of silly name you *would* think of, Anne. Let me hold it. Are they all yours, Jock?'

'Yes,' said Jock, proudly. 'The mother's mine, you see. Her name's Biddy.'

Biddy pricked up her ears at her name and looked up at Jock out of bright, alert eyes. He fondled her silky head.

'I've had her for four years,' he said. 'When we were at Owl Farm, old Farmer Burrows gave her to me when she was eight weeks old.'

'Oh – were you at another farm before this one, then?' asked Anne. 'Have you always lived on a farm? Aren't you lucky!'

'I've only lived on two,' said Jock. 'Owl Farm and this one. Mum and I had to leave Owl Farm when Dad died, and we went to live in a town for a year. I hated that. I was glad when we came here.'

'But I thought your father was here!' said Dick, puzzled.

'That's my stepfather,' said Jock. 'He's no farmer, though!' He looked round and lowered his voice. 'He doesn't know much about farming. It's my mother that tells the men what to do. Still, he gives her plenty of money to do everything well, and we've got fine machinery and wagons and things. Like to see the dairy? It's slap up-to-date and Mum loves working in it.'

Jock took the four children to the shining, spotless dairy. His mother was at work there with a girl. She nodded and smiled at the children. 'Good morning! Hungry again? I'll pack you up plenty of food when I've finished in the dairy. Would you like to stay and have dinner with my Jock? He's lonely enough here in the holidays, with no other boy to keep him company.'

'Oh, *yes* – do let's!' cried Anne, in delight. 'I'd like that. Can we, Ju?'

'Yes. Thank you very much, Mrs – er – Mrs . . .' said Julian.

'I'm Mrs Andrews,' said Jock's mother. 'But Jock is Jock Robins – he's the son of my first husband, a farmer. Well, stay to dinner all of you, and I'll see if I can give you a meal that will keep you going for the rest of the day!'

This sounded good. The four children felt thrilled, and Timmy wagged his tail hard. He liked Mrs Andrews.

'Come on,' said Jock, joyfully. 'I'll take you all round the farm, into every corner. It's not very big, but we're going to make it the best little farm on the moorlands. My stepfather doesn't seem to take much interest in the work of the farm, but he's jolly generous when it comes to handing out money to Mum to buy everything she wants.'

It certainly seemed to the children that the machinery on the farm was absolutely up-to-date. They examined the combine, they went into the little cowshed and admired the clean stone floor with white brick walls, they climbed into the red-painted wagons, and they wished they could try the two motor-tractors that stood side by side in a barn.

'You've got plenty of men here to work the farm,' said Julian. 'I shouldn't have thought there was enough for so many to do on this small place.'

'They're not good workers,' said Jock, his face creasing into frowns. 'Mum's always getting wild with them. They just don't know what to do. Dad gives her plenty of men to work the farm, but he always chooses the wrong ones! They don't seem to like farm-work, and they're always running off to the nearest town whenever they can. There's only one good fellow and he's old. See him over there? His name's Will.'

The children looked at Will. He was working in the little vegetable garden, an old fellow with a shrivelled face, a tiny nose and a pair of very blue eyes. They liked the look of him.

'Yes. He *looks* like a farm-worker,' said Julian. 'The others don't.'

'He won't work with them,' said Jock. 'He just says rude things to them, and calls them ninnies and idjits.'

'What's an idjit?' asked Anne.

'An idiot, silly,' said Dick. He walked up to old Will. 'Good morning,' he said. 'You're very busy. There's always a lot to do on a farm, isn't there?'

The old fellow looked at Dick out of his very blue eyes, and went on with his work. 'Plenty to do and plenty of folk to do it, and not much done,' he said, in a croaking kind of voice. 'Never thought I'd be put to work with ninnies and idjits. Not ninnies and idjits!'

'There! What did I tell you?' said Jock, with a grin. 'He's always calling the other men that, so we just have to let him work right away from them. Still, I must say he's about right – most of the fellows here don't know the first thing about work on a farm. I wish my stepfather would let us have a few proper workers instead of these fellows.'

'Where's your stepfather?' said Julian, thinking he must be rather peculiar to pour money into a little moorland farm like this, and yet choose the wrong kind of workers.

'He's away for the day,' said Jock. 'Thank goodness!' he added, with a sideways look at the others.

'Why? Don't you like him?' asked Dick.

'He's all right,' said Jock. 'But he's not a farmer, though he makes out he's always wanted to be – and what's more he doesn't like me one bit. I try to like him for Mum's sake. But I'm always glad when he's out of the way.'

'Your mother's nice,' said George.

'Oh, yes – Mum's grand,' said Jock. 'You don't know what it means to her to have a little farm of her own again, and to be able to run it with the proper machinery and all.'

They came to a large barn. The door was locked. 'I told you what was in here before,' said Jock. 'Lorries! You can peek through that hole here at them. Don't know why my stepfather wanted to buy up so many, but I suppose he got them cheap – he loves to get things cheap and sell them dear! He did say they'd be useful on the farm, to take goods to the market.'

'Yes – you told us that when we were here yesterday,' said Dick. 'But you've got heaps of wagons for that!'

'Yes. I reckon they weren't bought for the farm at all, but for holding here till prices went high and he could make a lot of money,' said Jock, lowering his voice. 'I don't tell Mum that. So long as she gets what she wants for the farm, I'm going to hold my tongue.'

The children were very interested in all this. They wished they could see Mr Andrews. He must be a peculiar sort of fellow, they thought. Anne tried to imagine what he was like.

'Big and tall and frowny,' she thought. 'Rather frightening and impatient, and he certainly won't like children. People like that never do.'

They spent a very pleasant morning poking about the little farm. They went back to see Biddy the collie and her pups. Timmy stood patiently outside the shed, with his tail down. He didn't like George to take so much interest in other dogs.

A bell rang loudly. 'Good! Dinner!' said Jock. 'We'd better wash. We're all filthy. Hope you feel hungry, because I guess Mum's got a super dinner for us.'

'I feel terribly hungry,' said Anne. 'It seems ages since we had breakfast. I've almost forgotten it!'

They all felt the same. They went into the farmhouse and were surprised to find a very nice little bathroom to wash in. Mrs Andrews was there, putting out a clean roller towel.

'Fine little bathroom, isn't it?' she said. 'My husband had it put in for me. First proper bathroom I've ever had!'

A glorious smell rose up from the kitchen downstairs. 'Come on!' said Jock, seizing the soap. 'Let's hurry. We'll be down in a minute, Mum!'

And they were. Nobody was going to dawdle over washing when a grand meal lay waiting for them downstairs!

CHAPTER SEVEN

Mr Andrews comes home

THEY ALL sat down to dinner. There was a big meat-pie, a cold ham, salad, potatoes in their jackets, and home-made pickles. It really was difficult to know what to choose.

'Have some of both,' said Mrs Andrews, cutting the meat-pie. 'Begin with the pie and go on with the ham. That's the best of living on a farm, you know – you do get plenty to eat.'

After the first course there were plums and thick cream, or jam tarts and the same cream. Everyone tucked in hungrily.

'I've never had such a lovely dinner in my life,' said Anne, at last. 'I wish I could eat some more but I can't. It was super, Mrs Andrews.'

'Smashing,' said Dick. That was his favourite word these holidays. 'Absolutely smashing.'

'Woof,' said Timmy, agreeing. He had had a fine plateful of meaty bones, biscuits and gravy, and he had licked up every crumb and every drop. Now he felt he would like to have a snooze in the sun and not do a thing for the rest of the day.

The children felt rather like that, too. Mrs Andrews handed them a chocolate each and sent them out of doors.

'You go and have a rest now,' she said. 'Talk to Jock. He doesn't get enough company of his own age in the holidays. You can stay on to tea, if you like.'

'Oh thanks,' said everyone, although they all felt that they wouldn't even be able to manage a biscuit. But it was so pleasant at the farm that they felt they would like to stay as long as they could.

'May we borrow one of Biddy's puppies to have with us?' asked Anne.

'If Biddy doesn't mind,' said Mrs Andrews, beginning to clear away. 'And if Timmy doesn't eat it up!'

'Timmy wouldn't dream of it!' said George at once. 'You go and get the puppy, Anne. We'll find a nice place in the sun.'

Anne went off to get the puppy. Biddy didn't seem to mind a bit. Anne cuddled the little thing against her, and went off to the others, feeling very happy. The boys had found a fine place against a haystack, and sat leaning against it, the sun shining down warmly on them.

'Those men of yours seem to take a jolly good lunch-hour off,' said Julian, not seeing any of them about.

Jock gave a snort. 'They're bone lazy. I'd sack the lot if I were my stepfather. Mum's told him how badly the men work, but he doesn't say a word to them. I've given up bothering. I don't pay their wages – if I did, I'd sack the whole lot!'

'Let's ask Jock about the spook-trains,' said George,

fonding Timmy's ears. 'It would be fun to talk about them.'

'Spook-trains? Whatever are they?' asked Jock, his eyes wide with surprise. 'Never heard of them!'

'Haven't you really?' asked Dick. 'Well, you don't live very far from them, Jock!'

'Tell me about them,' said Jock. 'Spook-trains – no, I've never heard of one of those.'

'Well, I'll tell you what we know,' said Julian. 'Actually we thought you'd be able to tell us much more about them than we know ourselves.'

He began to tell Jock about their visit to the deserted railway yard, and Wooden-Leg Sam, and his peculiar behaviour. Jock listened, enthralled.

'Coo! I wish I'd been with you. Let's all go there together, shall we?' he said. 'This was quite an adventure you had, wasn't it? You know, I've never had a single adventure in all my life, not even a little one. Have you?'

The four children looked at one another, and Timmy looked at George. Adventures! What didn't they know about them? They had had so many.

'Yes. We've had heaps of adventures – real ones – smashing ones,' said Dick. 'We've been down in dungeons, we've been lost in caves, we've found secret passages, we've looked for treasure – well, I can't tell you what we've done! It would take too long.'

'No, it wouldn't,' said Jock eagerly. 'You tell me. Go on. Did you all have the adventures? Little Anne, here, too?'

'Yes, all of us,' said George. 'And Timmy as well. He rescued us heaps of times from danger. Didn't you, Tim?'

'Woof, woof,' said Timmy, and thumped his tail against the hay.

They began to tell Jock about their many adventures. He was a very, very good listener. His eyes almost fell out of his head, and he went brick-red whenever they came to an exciting part.

'My word!' he said at last. 'I've never heard such things in my life before. Aren't you lucky? You just go about having adventures all the time, don't you? I *say* – do you think you'll have one here, these hols?'

Julian laughed. 'No. Whatever kind of adventure would there be on these lonely moorlands? Why, you yourself have lived here for three years, and haven't even had a tiny adventure.'

Jock sighed. 'That's true. I haven't.' Then his eyes brightened again. 'But see here – what about those spook-trains you've been asking me about? Perhaps you'll have an adventure with those?'

'Oh, no, I don't want to,' said Anne, in a horrified voice. 'An adventure with spook-trains would be simply horrid.'

'I'd like to go down to that old railway yard with you and see Wooden-Leg Sam,' said Jock longingly. 'Why, that would be a real adventure to me, you know – just talking to a funny old man like that, and wondering if he was suddenly going to throw cinders at us. Take me with you next time you go.'

'Well – I don't know that we meant to go again,' said Julian. 'There's really nothing much in his story except imagination – the old watchman's gone peculiar in the head through being alone there so much, guarding a yard where nothing and nobody ever comes. He's just remembering the trains that used to go in and out before the line was given up.'

'But the shepherd said the same as Sam,' said Jock. 'I *say* – what about going down there one night and watching for a spook-train!'

'NO!' said Anne, in horror.

'You needn't come,' said Jock. 'Just us three boys.'

'And me,' said George at once. 'I'm as good as any boy, and I'm not going to be left out. Timmy's coming, too.'

'Oh, please don't make these awful plans,' begged poor Anne. 'You'll *make* an adventure come, if you go on like this.'

Nobody took the least notice of her. Julian looked at Jock's excited face. 'Well,' he said, 'if we do go there again, we'll tell you. And if we think we'll go watching for spook-trains, we'll take you with us.'

Jock looked as if he could hug Julian. 'That would be terrific,' he said. 'Thanks a lot. Spook-trains! I *say*, just suppose we really did see one! Who'd be driving it? Where would it come from?'

'Out of the tunnel, Wooden-Leg Sam says,' said Dick. 'But I don't see how we'd spot it, except by the noise it made, because apparently the spook-trains only arrive in the dark of the night. Never in the daytime. We wouldn't *see* much, even if we were there.'

It was such an exciting subject to Jock that he persisted in talking about it all the afternoon. Anne got tired of listening, and went to sleep with Biddy's puppy in her arms. Timmy curled up by George and went to sleep too. He wanted to go for a walk, but he could see that there was no hope with all this talking going on.

It was tea-time before any of them had expected it. The bell rang, and Jock looked most surprised.

'Tea! Would you believe it? Well, I *have* had an exciting afternoon talking about all this. And look here, if you don't make up your minds to go spook-train hunting I'll jolly well go off by myself. If only I could have an adventure like the kind you've had, I'd be happy.'

They went in to tea, after waking Anne up with difficulty. She took the puppy back to Biddy, who received it gladly and licked it all over.

Julian was surprised to find that he was quite hungry again. 'Well,' he said, as he sat down at the table, 'I didn't imagine I'd feel hungry again for a week – but I do. What a marvellous tea, Mrs Andrews. Isn't Jock lucky to have meals like this always!'

There were home-made scones with new honey. There were slices of bread thickly spread with butter, and new-made cream cheese to go with it. There was sticky brown gingerbread, hot from the oven, and a big solid fruit cake that looked almost like a plum pudding when it was cut, it was so black.

'Oh dear! I wish now I hadn't had so much dinner,' sighed Anne. 'I don't feel hungry enough to eat a bit of everything and I would so like to!'

Mrs Andrews laughed. 'You eat what you can, and I'll give you some to take away, too,' she said. 'You can have some cream cheese, and the scones and honey – and some of the bread I made this morning. And maybe you'd like a slab of the gingerbread. I made plenty.'

'Oh, thanks,' said Julian. 'We'll be all right tomorrow

with all that. You're a marvellous cook, Mrs Andrews. I wish I lived on your farm.'

There was the sound of a car coming slowly up the rough track to the farmhouse, and Mrs Andrews looked up. 'That's Mr Andrews come back,' she said. 'My husband, you know, Jock's stepfather.'

Julian thought she looked a little worried. Perhaps Mr Andrews didn't like children and wouldn't be pleased to see them sitting round his table when he came home tired.

'Would you like us to go, Mrs Andrews?' he asked politely. 'Perhaps Mr Andrews would like a bit of peace for his meal when he comes in – and we're rather a crowd, aren't we?'

Jock's mother shook her head. 'No, you can stay. I'll get him a meal in the other room if he'd like it.'

Mr Andrews came in. He wasn't in the least like Anne or the others had imagined him to be. He was a short, little man, with a weak face and a nose much too big for it. He looked harassed and bad-tempered, and stopped short when he saw the five children.

'Hallo, dear,' said Mrs Andrews. 'Jock's got his friends here today. Would you like a bit of tea in your room? I can easily put a tray there.'

'Well,' said Mr Andrews, smiling a watery kind of smile, 'perhaps it would be best. I've had a worrying kind of day, and not much to eat.'

'I'll get you a tray of ham and pickles and bread,' said his wife. 'It won't take a minute. You go and wash.'

Mr Andrews went out. Anne was surprised that he seemed so small and looked rather stupid. She had imagined someone big and burly, strong and clever, who was always going about doing grand deals and making a lot of money. Well, he must be cleverer than he looked, to make enough money to give Mrs Andrews all she needed for her farm.

Mrs Andrews bustled about with this and that, laying a tray with a snow-white cloth, and plates of food. Mr Andrews could be heard in the bathroom, splashing as he washed. Then he came downstairs and put his head in at the door. 'My meal ready?' he asked. 'Well, Jock – had a good day?'

'Yes, thanks,' said Jock, as his stepfather took the tray from his mother and turned to go. 'We went all round the farm this morning – and we talked and talked this afternoon. And oh, I say – do you know anything about spook-trains, sir?'

Mr Andrews was just going out of the door. He turned in surprise. 'Spook-trains? What are you talking about?'

'Well, Julian says there's an old deserted railway yard a good way from here, and spook-trains are supposed to come out of the tunnel there in the dark of night,' said Jock. 'Have you heard of them?'

Mr Andrews stood stock still, his eyes on his step-son. He looked dismayed and shocked. Then he came back into the room and kicked the door shut behind him.

'I'll have my tea here after all,' he said. 'Well, to think

you've heard of those spook-trains! I've been careful not to mention them to your mother or to you, Jock, for fear of scaring you!'

'Gee!' said Dick. 'Are they really true then? They can't be.'

'You tell me all you know, and how you know about it,' said Mr Andrews, sitting down at the table with his tray. 'Go on. Don't miss out a thing. I want to hear everything.'

Julian hesitated. 'Oh – there's nothing really to tell, sir – just a lot of nonsense.'

'You tell it me!' almost shouted Mr Andrews. 'Then I'll tell *you* a few things. And I tell you, you won't go near that old railway yard again – no, that you won't!'

CHAPTER EIGHT

A lazy evening

THE FIVE children and Mrs Andrews stared in surprise at Mr Andrews, when he shouted at them. He repeated some of his words again.

'Go on! You tell me all you know. And then I'll tell *you*!'

Julian decided to tell, very shortly, what had happened at the old railway yard, and what Wooden-Leg Sam had said. He made the tale sound rather bald and dull. Mr Andrews listened to it with the greatest interest, never once taking his eyes off Julian.

Then he sat back and drank a whole cup of strong tea in one gulp. The children waited for him to speak, wondering what he had to say.

'Now,' he said, making his voice sound important and impressive, 'you listen to me. Don't any of you ever go down to that yard again. It's a bad place.'

'Why?' asked Julian. 'What do you mean – a bad place?'

'Things have happened there – years and years ago,' said Mr Andrews. 'Bad things. Accidents. It was all shut up after that and the tunnel wasn't used any more. See? Nobody was allowed to go there, and nobody did, because they were scared. They knew it was a bad place, where bad things happen.'

Anne felt frightened. 'But Mr Andrews – you don't mean there really are spook-trains, do you?' she asked, her face rather pale.

Mr Andrews pursed up his lips and nodded very solemnly indeed. 'That's just what I do mean. Spook-trains come and go. Nobody knows why. But it's bad luck to be there when they come. They might take you away, see?'

Julian laughed. 'Oh – not as bad as that, sir, surely! Anyway, you're frightening Anne, so let's change the subject. I don't believe in spook-trains.'

But Mr Andrews didn't seem to want to stop talking about the trains. 'Wooden-Leg Sam was right to hide himself when they come along,' he said. 'I don't know how he manages to stay on in a bad place like that. Never knowing when a train is going to come creeping out of that tunnel in the darkness.'

Julian was not going to have Anne frightened any more. He got up from the table and turned to Mrs Andrews.

'Thank you very much for a lovely day and lovely food!' he said. 'We must go now. Come along, Anne.'

'Wait a minute,' said Mr Andrews. 'I just want to warn you all very solemnly that you mustn't go down to that railway yard. You hear me, Jock? You might never come back. Old Wooden-Leg Sam's mad, and well he may be, with spook-trains coming along in the dead of night. It's a bad and dangerous place. You're not to go near it!'

'Well – thank you for the warning, sir,' said Julian, politely, suddenly disliking the small man with the big nose very much indeed. 'We'll be going. Goodbye, Mrs Andrews. Goodbye, Jock. Come along tomorrow and have a picnic with us, will you?'

'Oh, thanks! Yes, I will,' said Jock. 'But wait a minute – aren't you going to take any food with you?'

'Yes, of course they are,' said Mrs Andrews, getting up from her chair. She had been listening to the conversation with a look of puzzled wonder on her face. She went out into the scullery, where there was a big, cold larder. Julian followed her. He carried the two baskets.

'I'll give you plenty,' said Mrs Andrews, putting loaves, butter, and cream cheese into the baskets. 'I know what appetites you youngsters get. Now, don't you be too scared at what my husband's just been saying – I saw that little Anne was frightened. I've never heard of the spook-trains, and I've been here for three years. I don't reckon there's much in the tale, you know, for all my husband's so set on warning you not to go down to the yard.'

Julian said nothing. He thought that Mr Andrews had behaved rather oddly about the whole story. Was he one of the kind of people who believed in all sorts of silly things and got scared himself? He looked weak enough! Julian found himself wondering how a nice woman like Mrs Andrews could have married such a poor specimen of a man. Still, he was a generous fellow, judging by all Jock had said, and perhaps Jock's mother felt grateful to him for giving her the farm and the money to run it with. That must be it.

Julian thanked Mrs Andrews, and insisted on paying her, though she would have given him the food for nothing. She came into the kitchen with him and he saw that the others had already gone outside. Only Mr Andrews was left, eating ham and pickles.

'Goodbye, sir,' said Julian politely.

'Goodbye. And you remember what I've told you, boy,' said Mr Andrews. 'Bad luck comes to people who see the spook-trains – yes, terrible bad luck. You keep away from them.'

Julian gave a polite smile and went out. It was evening now and the sun was setting behind the moorland hills, though it still had a long way to go before it disappeared. He caught up with the others. Jock was with them.

'I'm just coming half-way with you,' said Jock. 'I say! My stepfather was pretty scary about those trains, wasn't he?'

'I felt pretty scary too, when he was warning us about them,' said Anne. 'I shan't go down to that yard again, ever. Will you, George?'

'If the boys did, I would,' said George, who didn't look very much as if she wanted to, all the same.

'*Are* you going to the yard again?' asked Jock, eagerly. 'I'm not scared. Not a bit. It would be an adventure to go and watch for a spook-train.'

'We might go,' said Julian. 'We'll take you with us, if we do. But the girls aren't to come.'

'Well, I like that!' said George angrily. 'As if you could leave me behind! When have I been scared of anything? I'm as brave as any of you.'

'Yes. I know. You can come as soon as we find out it's all a silly story,' said Julian.

'I shall come whenever you go,' flashed back George. 'Don't you dare to leave me out. I'll never speak to you again if you do.'

Jock looked most surprised at this sudden flare-up of temper from George. He didn't know how fierce she could be!

'I don't see why George shouldn't come,' he said. 'I bet she'd be every bit as good as a boy. I thought she was one when I first saw her.'

George gave him one of her sweetest smiles. He couldn't have said anything she liked better! But Julian would not change his mind.

'I mean what I say. The girls won't come if we do go, so that's that. For one thing, Anne certainly wouldn't want to come, and if George came without her she'd be left all alone up at the camp. She wouldn't like that.'

'She could have Mr Luffy's company,' said George, looking sulky again.

'Idiot! As if we'd want to tell Mr Luffy we were going off exploring deserted railway yards watched over by a mad, one-legged fellow who swears there are spook-trains!'

said Julian. 'He'd stop us going. You know what grown-ups are like. Or he'd come with us, which would be worse.'

'Yes. He'd see moths all the time, not spook-trains,' said Dick, with a grin.

'I'd better go back now,' said Jock. 'It's been a grand day. I'll come up tomorrow and picnic with you. Goodbye.'

They called goodbye to Jock, and went on their way to the camp. It was quite nice to see it again, waiting for them, the two tents flapping a little in the breeze. Anne pushed her way through the tent-flap, anxious to see that everything was untouched.

Inside the tent it was very hot. Anne decided to put the food they had brought under the bottom of the big gorse bush. It would be cooler there. She was soon busy about her little jobs. The boys went down to see if Mr Luffy was back, but he wasn't.

'Anne! We're going to bathe in the stream!' they called. 'We feel hot and dirty. Are you coming? George is coming too.'

'No, I won't come,' Anne called back. 'I've got lots of things to do.'

The boys grinned at one another. Anne did so enjoy 'playing house'. So they left her to it, and went to the stream, from which yells and howls and shrieks soon came. The water was colder than they expected, and nobody liked to lie down in it – but everyone was well and truly splashed, and the icy-cold drops falling on their hot bodies made them squeal and yell. Timmy didn't in the least mind the iciness of the water. He rolled over and over in it, enjoying himself.

'Look at him, showing off!' said Dick. 'Aha, Timmy, if I could bathe in a fur coat like you, I wouldn't mind the cold water either.'

'Woof,' said Timmy, and climbed up the shallow bank. He shook himself violently and thousands of icy-cold silvery drops flew from him and landed on the three shivering children. They yelled and chased him away.

It was a pleasant, lazy evening. Mr Luffy didn't appear at all. Anne got a light meal of bread and cream cheese and a piece of gingerbread. Nobody felt like facing another big meal that day. They lay in the heather and talked comfortably.

'This is the kind of holiday I like,' said Dick.

'So do I,' said Anne. 'Except for the spook-trains. That's spoilt it a bit for me.'

'Don't be silly, Anne,' said George. 'If they are not real it's just a silly story, and if they are real, well, it might be an adventure.'

There was a little silence. 'Are we going down to the yard again?' asked Dick lazily.

'Yes, I think so,' said Julian. 'I'm not going to be scared off it by weird warnings from Pa Andrews.'

'Then I vote we go one night and wait to see if a spook-train does come along,' said Dick.

'I shall come too,' said George.

'No, you won't,' said Julian. 'You'll stay with Anne.'

George said nothing, but everyone could feel mutiny in the air.

'Do we tell Mr Luffy, or don't we?' said Dick.

'You know we've said we wouldn't,' said Julian. He yawned. 'I'm getting sleepy. And the sun has gone, so it will soon be dark. I wonder where old Luffy is?'

'Do you think I'd better wait up and see if he wants something to eat?' said Anne, anxiously.

'No. Not unless you want to keep awake till midnight!' said Julian. 'He'll have got some food down in his tent. He'll be all right. I'm going to turn in. Coming, Dick?'

The boys were soon in their sleeping-bags. The girls lay in the heather for a little while longer, listening to the lonely-sounding cry of the curlews going home in the dusk. Then they, too, went into their own tent.

Once safely in their sleeping-bags, the two boys felt suddenly wide awake. They began to talk in low voices.

'Shall we take Jock down to see the yard in the daytime? Or shall we go one night and watch for the Train from Nowhere?' said Julian.

'I vote we go and watch at night,' said Dick. 'We'll never see a spook-train in the daytime. Wooden-Leg Sam is an interesting old chap, especially when he chucks cinders about – but I don't know that I like him enough to go and visit him again!'

'Well – if Jock badly wants to go and have a snoop round tomorrow morning when he comes, we'd better take him,' said Julian. 'We can always go one night, too, if we want to.'

'Right. We'll wait and see what Jock says,' said Dick. They talked a little longer and then felt sleepy. Dick was just dropping off when he heard something coming wriggling through the heather. A head was stuck through the opening of the tent.

'If you dare to come in, I'll push away your silly face,' said Dick, thinking it was Timmy. 'I know what you want, you perfect pest – you want to flop down on my tummy.

You just turn yourself round and go away! Do you hear?'

The head in the opening moved a little but didn't go away. Dick raised himself up on one elbow.

'Put one paw inside my tent and you'll be sent rolling down the hill!' he said. 'I love you very much in the daytime, but I'm not fond of you at night – not when I'm in a sleeping-bag anyway. Scoot!'

The head made a peculiar apologetic sound. Then it spoke. 'Er – you're awake, I see. Are all of you all right – the girls too? I'm only just back.'

'Gosh! It's Mr Luffy,' said Dick, filled with horror. 'I say, sir – I'm most awfully sorry – I thought you were Timmy, come to flop himself down on top of me, like he often does. So sorry, sir.'

'Don't mention it!' said the shadowy head with a chuckle. 'Glad you're all right. See you tomorrow!'

CHAPTER NINE

Night visitor

MR LUFFY slept very late the next morning and nobody liked to disturb him. The girls yelled with laughter when they heard how Dick had spoken to him the night before, thinking he was Timmy the dog.

'He was very decent about it,' said Dick. 'Seemed to think it was quite amusing. I hope he'll still think so this morning!'

They were all sitting eating their breakfast – ham, tomatoes, and the bread Mrs Andrews had given them the day before. Timmy collected the bits as usual, and wondered if George would let him have a lick of the cream cheese she was now putting on her bread. Timmy loved cheese. He looked at the lump in the dish and sighed all over George. He could easily eat that in one mouthful! How he wished he could.

'I wonder what time Jock will come up,' said George. 'If he came up pretty soon, we could go for a nice long walk over the moors, and picnic somewhere. Jock ought to know some fine walks.'

'Yes. We'll mess about till he comes, and then tell him he's to be our guide and take us to the nicest walk he knows,' said Anne. 'Oh, Timmy, you beast – you've taken my nice lump of cream cheese right out of my fingers!'

'Well, you were waving it about under his nose, so what could you expect?' said George. 'He thought you were giving it to him.'

'Well, he shan't have any more. It's too precious,' said Anne. 'Oh, dear – I wish we didn't eat so much. We keep bringing in stacks of food, and it hardly lasts any time.'

'I bet Jock will bring some more,' said Dick. 'He's a sensible sort of fellow. Did you get a peep into that enormous larder of his mother's? It's like a great cave, goes right back into the wall, with dozens of stone shelves – and all filled with food. No wonder Jock's plump.'

'Is he? I never noticed,' said Anne. 'Is that him whistling?'

It wasn't. It was a curlew, very high up. 'Too early for him yet,' said Julian. 'Shall we help you to clear up, Anne?'

'No. That's my job and George's,' said Anne firmly. 'You go down and see if Mr Luffy is awake. He can have a bit of ham and a few tomatoes, if he likes.'

They went down to Mr Luffy's tent. He was awake, sitting at the entrance, eating some kind of breakfast. He waved a sandwich at them.

'Hallo, there! I'm late this morning. I had a job getting back. I went much too far. Sorry I woke you up last night, Dick.'

'You didn't. I wasn't asleep,' said Dick, going rather red. 'Did you have a good day, Mr Luffy?'

'Bit disappointing. Didn't find quite all the creatures I'd hoped,' said Mr Luffy. 'What about you? Did you have a good day?'

'Fine,' said Dick, and described it. Mr Luffy seemed very interested in everything, even in Mr Andrews's rather frightening warning about the railway yard.

'Silly chap he sounds,' said Mr Luffy, shaking the crumbs off his front. 'All the same – I should keep away from the yard, if I were you. Stories don't get about for nothing, you know. No smoke without fire!'

'Why, sir – surely *you* don't believe there's anything spooky about the trains there?' said Dick, in surprise.

'Oh, no – I doubt if there *are* any trains,' said Mr Luffy. 'But when a place has got a bad name it's usually best to keep away from it.'

'I suppose so, sir,' said Dick and Julian together. Then they hastily changed the subject, afraid that Mr Luffy, like Mr Andrews, might also be going to forbid them to visit the railway yard. And the more they were warned about it and forbidden to go, the more they felt that they really must!

'Well, we must get back,' said Dick. 'We're expecting Jock – that's the boy at the farm – to come up for the day, and we thought we'd go out walking and take our food with us. Are you going out, too, sir?'

'Not today,' said Mr Luffy. 'My legs are tired and stiff with so much scrambling about yesterday, and I want to mount some of the specimens I found. Also I'd like to meet your farm friend – what's his name – Jock?'

'Yes, sir,' said Julian. 'Right. We'll bring him along as soon as he comes, then off we'll go. You'll be left in peace all day!'

But Jock didn't come. The children waited for him all the morning and he didn't turn up. They held up their lunch until they were too hungry to wait any longer, and then they had it on the heather in front of their tents.

'Funny,' said Julian. 'He knows where the camp is, because we pointed it out to him when he came half-way home with us yesterday. Perhaps he'll come this afternoon.'

But he didn't come in the afternoon either, nor did he come after tea. Julian debated whether or not to go and see what was up, but decided against it. There must be some good reason why Jock hadn't come, and Mrs Andrews wouldn't want them all visiting her two days running.

It was a disappointing day. They didn't like to leave the tents and go for even a short stroll in case Jock came. Mr Luffy was busy all day long with his specimens. He was sorry Jock had disappointed them. 'He'll come tomorrow,' he said. 'Have you got enough food? There's some in that tin over there if you want it.'

'Oh, no thank you, sir,' said Julian. 'We've plenty really. We're going to have a game of cards. Like to join us?'

'Yes, I think I will,' said Mr Luffy, getting up and stretching himself. 'Can you play rummy?'

They could – and they beat poor Mr Luffy handsomely, because he couldn't play at all. He blamed his luck on his bad cards, but he enjoyed the game immensely. He said the only thing that really put him off was the way that Timmy stood behind him and breathed down his neck all the time.

'I kept feeling certain that Timmy thought he knew how to play my cards better than I could,' he complained. 'And whenever I did something wrong, he breathed down my neck harder than usual.'

Everyone laughed, and George privately thought that Timmy would probably play very much better than Mr Luffy if only he could hold the cards.

Jock didn't come at all. They put the cards away when they could no longer see them, and Mr Luffy announced that he was going to bed. 'It was very late when I got back last night,' he said. 'I really must have an early night.'

The others thought they would go to bed too. The thought of their cosy sleeping-bags was always a nice one when darkness came on.

The girls crept into their bags and Timmy flopped down on George. The boys were in their bags about the same time and Dick gave a loud yawn.

'Good night, Ju,' he said, and fell fast asleep. Julian was soon asleep too. In fact, everyone was sound asleep when Timmy gave a little growl. It was such a small growl that neither of the girls heard it, and certainly Dick and Julian didn't, away in their tent.

Timmy raised his head and listened intently. Then he

gave another small growl. He listened again. Finally he got up, shook himself, still without waking George, and stalked out of the tent, his ears cocked and his tail up. He had heard somebody or something, and although he thought it was all right, he was going to make sure.

Dick was sound asleep when he felt something brushing against the outside of his tent. He awoke at once and sat up. He looked at the tent opening. A shadow appeared there and looked in.

Was it Timmy? Was it Mr Luffy? He mustn't make a mistake this time. He waited for the shadow to speak. But it didn't! It just stayed there as if it were listening for some movement inside the tent. Dick didn't like it.

'Timmy!' he said at last, in a low voice.

Then the shadow spoke: 'Dick? Or is it Julian? It's Jock here. I've got Timmy beside me. Can I come in?'

'*Jock!*' said Dick, in surprise. 'Whatever have you come at this time of night for? And why didn't you come today? We waited ages for you.'

'Yes. I know I'm awfully sorry,' said Jock's voice, and the boy wriggled himself into the tent. Dick poked Julian awake.

'Julian! Here's Jock – and Timmy. Get off me, Timmy. Here, Jock, see if you can squeeze inside my sleeping-bag – there's room for us both, I think.'

'Oh, thanks,' said Jock, and squeezed inside with difficulty. 'How warm it is! I say, I'm terribly sorry I didn't come today – but my stepfather suddenly announced he wanted me to go somewhere with him for the whole day. Can't think why. He doesn't bother about me as a rule.'

'That was mean of him, seeing that he knew you were to come on a picnic with us,' said Julian. 'Was it something important?'

'No. Not at all,' said Jock. 'He drove off to Endersfield – that's about forty miles away – parked me in the public library there, saying he'd be back in a few minutes – and he didn't come back till past tea-time! I had some sandwiches with me, luckily. I felt pretty angry about it, I can tell you.'

'Never mind. Come tomorrow instead,' said Dick.

'I can't,' said Jock in despair. 'He's gone and arranged for me to meet the son of some friend of his – a boy called Cecil Dearlove – what a name! I'm to spend the day with this frightful boy. The worst of it is Mum's quite pleased about it. She never thinks my stepfather takes enough notice of me – good thing he doesn't, *I* think.'

'Oh blow – so you won't be able to come tomorrow either,' said Julian. 'Well – what about the next day?'

'It should be all right,' said Jock. 'But I've feeling I'll have dear love of a Cecil plonked on me for the day – to show him the cows and the puppies, dear pet! Ugh! When I could be with you four and Timmy.'

'It's bad luck,' said Julian. 'It really is.'

'I thought I'd better come and tell you,' said Jock. 'It's the first chance I've had, creeping up here tonight. I've brought some more food for you, by the way. I guessed you'd want some. I feel down in the dumps about that adventure – you know, going to see the railway yard. I was going to ask you to take me today.'

'Well – if you can't come tomorrow either – and perhaps not the next day – what about going one night?' said Dick. 'Would you like to come up tomorrow night, about this time? We won't tell the girls. We'll just go off by ourselves, we three boys – and watch!'

Jock was too thrilled to say a word. He let out a deep breath of joy. Dick laughed.

'Don't get too thrilled. We probably shan't see a thing. Bring a torch if you've got one. Come to our tent and jerk my toe. I'll probably be awake, but if I'm not, that'll wake me all right! And don't say a word to anyone of course.'

'Rather not,' said Jock, overjoyed. 'Well – I suppose I'd better be going. It was pretty weird coming over the moorland in the dark. There's no moon, and the stars don't give much light. I've left the food outside the tent. Better look out that Timmy doesn't get it.'

'Right. Thanks awfully,' said Julian. Jock got out of Dick's sleeping-bag and went backwards out of the tent, with Timmy obligingly licking his nose all the way. Jock then found the bag of food and rolled it in to Julian, who put it safely under the groundsheet.

'Good night,' said Jock, in a low voice, and they heard him scrambling over the heather. Timmy went with him, pleased at this unexpected visitor, and the chance of a midnight walk. Jock was glad to have the dog's company.

Timmy went right to the farm with him and then bounded back over the moorland to the camping-place, longing to pounce on the rabbits he could smell here and there, but wanting to get back to George.

In the morning Anne was amazed to find the food in her 'larder' under the gorse bush. Julian had popped it there to surprise her. 'Look at this!' she cried, in astonishment. 'Meat-pies – more tomatoes – eggs, wherever did they come from?'

'Spook-train brought them in the night,' said Dick, with a grin.

'Volcano shot them up into the air,' said Mr Luffy, who was also there. Anne threw a tea-cloth at him.

'Tell me how it came here,' she demanded. 'I was worried about what to give you all for breakfast – and now there's more than we can possibly eat. Who put it there? George, do you know?'

But George didn't. She glanced at the smiling faces of the two boys. 'I bet Jock was here last night,' she said to them. 'Wasn't he?' And to herself she said: 'Yes – and somehow I think they've planned something together. You won't trick *me*, Dick and Julian. I'll be on the lookout from now on! Wherever you go, I go too!'

CHAPTER TEN

Hunt for a spook-train

THAT DAY passed pleasantly enough. The children, Timmy, and Mr Luffy all went off to a pool high up on the moorlands. It was called 'The Green Pool' because of its cucumber-green colour. Mr Luffy explained that some curious chemicals found there caused the water to look green.

'I hope we shan't come out looking green, too,' said Dick, getting into his bathing trunks. 'Are you going to bathe, Mr Luffy?'

Mr Luffy was. The children expected him to be a very poor swimmer and to splash about at the edge and do very little – but to their surprise he was magnificent in the water, and could swim faster even than Julian.

They had great fun, and when they were tired they came out to bask in the sun. The highroad ran alongside the green pool, and the children watched a herd of sheep being driven along, then a car or two came by, and finally a big army lorry. A boy sat beside the driver, and to the children's surprise he waved wildly at them.

'Who was that?' said Julian astonished. 'Surely he doesn't know us?'

George's sharp eye had seen who it was. 'It was Jock!

Sitting beside the driver. And, look, here comes his stepfather's fine new car. Jock's preferred to go with the lorry-driver instead of his stepfather! I don't blame him, either!'

The bright new car came by, driven by Mr Andrews. He didn't glance at the children by the wayside, but drove steadily on after the lorry.

'Going to market, I suppose,' said Dick, lying back again. 'Wonder what they're taking?'

'So do I,' said Mr Luffy. 'He must sell his farm produce at very high prices to be able to buy that fine car and all the machinery and gear you've told me about. Clever fellow Mr Andrews!'

'He doesn't look at all clever,' said Anne. 'He looks rather a weak, feeble sort of man, really, Mr Luffy. I can't even imagine him being clever enough to beat anyone down, or get the better of them.'

'Very interesting,' said Mr Luffy. 'Well, what about another dip before we have our dinner?'

It was a very nice day, and Mr Luffy was very good company. He could make fine jokes very solemnly indeed, and only the fact that his ear waggled violently showed the others that he too, was enjoying the joke. His right ear seemed to love to join in the joke, even if Mr Luffy's face was as solemn as Timmy's.

They arrived home at the camp about tea-time and Anne got a fine tea ready. They took it down to eat in front of Mr Luffy's tent. As the evening came on Julian and

Dick felt excitement rising in them. In the daytime neither of them really believed a word about the 'spook-trains', but as the sun sank and long shadows crept down the hills they felt pleasantly thrilled. Would they really see anything exciting that night?

It was a very dark night at first, because clouds lay across the sky and hid even the stars. The boys said good night to the girls and snuggled down into their sleeping-bags. They watched the sky through the tent opening.

Gradually the big clouds thinned out. A few stars appeared. The clouds thinned still more and fled away in rags. Soon the whole sky was bright with pin-points of light, and a hundred thousand stars looked down on the moorlands.

'We shall have a bit of starlight to see by,' whispered Julian. 'That's good. I don't want to stumble about over the heather and break my ankle in rabbit-holes in the pitch darkness. Nor do I want to use my torch on the way to the yard in case it's seen.'

'It's going to be fun!' Dick whispered back. 'I hope Jock comes. It will be maddening if he doesn't.'

He did come. There was a scrambling over the heather and once again a shadow appeared at the tent opening.

'Julian! Dick! I've come. Are you ready?'

It was Jock's voice, of course. Dick's thumb pressed the switch of his torch and for a moment its light fell on Jock's red, excited face, and then was switched off again.

'Hallo, Jock! So you were able to come,' said Dick. 'I

say, was that you in the lorry this morning, going by the green pool?'

'Yes. Did you see me? I saw you and waved like mad,' said Jock. 'I wanted to stop the lorry and get down and speak to you, but the driver's an awful bad-tempered sort of fellow. He wouldn't hear of stopping. Said my stepfather would be wild with him if he did. Did you see *him* – my stepfather, I mean? He was in his car behind.'

'Were you off to market or something?' asked Julian.

'I expect that's where the lorry was going,' said Jock. 'It was empty, so I suppose my stepfather was going to pick up something there. I came back in the car. The lorry was supposed to come later.'

'How did you like Cecil Dearlove?' asked Dick, grinning in the darkness.

'Awful! Worse than his name,' groaned Jock. 'Wanted me to play soldiers all the time! The frightful thing is I've got to have him at the farm for the day tomorrow. Another day wasted. What shall I do with him?'

'Roll him in the pig-sty,' suggested Dick. 'Or put him with Biddy's puppies and let him sleep there. Tell him to play soldiers with them.'

Jock chuckled. 'I wish I could. The worst of it is Mum is awfully pleased that my stepfather's got this Cecil boy for me to be friends with. Don't let's talk about it. Are you ready to start off?'

'Yes,' said Julian, and began to scramble quietly out of his bag. 'We didn't tell the girls. Anne doesn't want to come, and I don't want George to leave Anne by herself. Now, let's be very, very quiet till we're out of hearing.'

Dick got out of his bag too. The boys had not undressed that night, except for their coats, so all they had to do was to slip these on, and then crawl out of the tent.

'Which is the way – over there?' whispered Jock. Julian took his arm and guided him. He hoped he wouldn't lose his way in the starlit darkness. The moorland look so different at night!

'If we make for that hill you can dimly see over there against the starlit sky, we should be going in the right direction,' said Julian. So on they went, keeping towards the dark hill that rose up to the west.

It seemed very much farther to the railway yard at night than in the daytime. The three boys stumbled along, sometimes almost falling as their feet caught in tufts of heather. They were glad when they found some sort of path they could keep on.

'This is about where we met the shepherd,' said Dick, in a low voice. He didn't know why he spoke so quietly. He just felt as if he must. 'I'm sure we can't be very far off now.'

They went on for some way, and then Julian pulled Dick by the arm. 'Look,' he said. 'Down there, I believe that's the old yard. You can see the lines gleaming faintly here and there.'

They stood on the heathery slope above the old yard, straining their eyes. Soon they could make out dim shapes. Yes, it was the railway yard all right.

Jock clutched Julian's sleeve. 'Look – there's a light down there! Do you see it?'

The boys looked – and sure enough, down in the yard towards the other side of it, was a small yellow light. They stared at it.

'Oh – I think I know what it is,' said Dick, at last. 'It's the light in the watchman's little hut – old Wooden-Leg Sam's candle. Don't you think so, Ju?'

'Yes. You're right,' said Julian. 'I tell you what we'll do – we'll creep right down into the yard, and go over to the hut. We'll peep inside and see if old Sam is there. Then we'll hide somewhere about and wait for the spook-train to come!'

They crept down the slope. Their eyes had got used to the starlight by now, and they were beginning to see fairly well. They got right down to the yard, where their feet made a noise on some cinders there.

They stopped. 'Someone will hear us if we make a row like this,' whispered Julian.

'Who will?' whispered back Dick. 'There's no one here except old Sam in his hut!'

'How do you know there isn't?' said Julian. 'Good heavens, Jock, don't make such a row with your feet!'

They stood there, debating what was the best thing to do. 'We'd better walk right round the edge of the yard,' said Julian at last. 'As far as I remember, the grass has grown there. We'll walk on that.'

So they made their way to the edge of the yard. Sure

enough, there was grass there, and they walked on it without a sound. They went slowly and softly to where the light shone dimly in Sam's little hut.

The window was high and small. It was just about at the level of their heads, and the three boys cautiously eased themselves along to it and looked in.

Wooden-Leg Sam was there. He sat sprawled in a chair, smoking a pipe. He was reading a newspaper, squinting painfully as he did so. He obviously had not had his broken glasses mended yet. On a chair beside him was

his wooden leg. He had unstrapped it, and there it lay.

'He's not expecting the spook-train tonight, or he wouldn't have taken off his wooden leg,' whispered Dick.

The candlelight flickered and shadows jumped about the tiny hut. It was a poor, ill-furnished little place, dirty and untidy. A cup without saucer or handle stood on the table, and a tin kettle boiled on a rusty stove.

Sam put down his paper and rubbed his eyes. He muttered something. The boys could not hear it, but they felt certain it was something about his broken glasses.

'Are there many lines in this yard?' whispered Jock, tired of looking in at old Sam. 'Where do they go to?'

'About half a mile or so up there is a tunnel,' said Julian, pointing past Jock. 'The lines come from there and run here, where they break up in many pairs – for shunting and so on, in the old days, I suppose, when this place was used.'

'Let's go up the lines to the tunnel,' said Jock. 'Come on. There's nothing to be seen here. Let's walk up to the tunnel.'

'All right,' said Julian. 'We may as well. I don't expect we'll see much up there either! I think these spook-trains are all a tall story of old Sam's!'

They left the little hut with its forlorn candlelight, and made their way round the yard again. Then they followed the single-track line away from the yard and up towards the tunnel. It didn't seem to matter walking on cinders now, and making a noise. They walked along, talking in low voices.

And then things began to happen! A far-off muffled noise came rumbling out of the tunnel, which was now so near that the boys could see its black mouth. Julian heard it first. He stood still and clutched Dick.

'I say! Listen! Can you hear that?'

The others listened. 'Yes,' said Dick. 'But it's only a train going through one of the underground tunnels – the noise is echoing out through this one.'

'It isn't. That noise is made by a train coming through this tunnel!' said Julian. The noise grew louder and louder. A clanking made itself heard too. The boys stepped off the lines and crouched together by the side, waiting, hardly daring to breathe.

Could it be the spook-train? They watched for the light of an engine-lamp to appear like a fiery eye in the tunnel. But none came. It was darker than night in there! But the noise came nearer and nearer and nearer. Could there be the noise of a train without a train? Julian's heart began to beat twice as fast, and Dick and Jock found themselves clutching one another without knowing it.

The noise grew thunderous, and then out from the tunnel came something long and black, with a dull glow in front that passed quickly and was gone. The noise deafened the boys, and then the clanking and rumbling grew less as the train, or whatever it was, passed by. The ground trembled and then was still.

'Well, there you are,' said Julian, in a rather trembly voice. 'The spook-train – without a light or a signal! Where's it gone? To the yard, do you think?'

'Shall we go and see?' asked Dick. 'I didn't see anyone in the cab, even in the glow of what must have been the fire there – but there must be *someone* driving it! I say, what a weird thing, isn't it? It *sounded* real enough, anyway.'

'We'll go to the yard,' said Jock, who, of the three, seemed the least affected. 'Come on.'

They made their way very slowly – and then Dick gave a sharp cry. 'Blow! I've twisted my ankle. Half a minute!'

He sank down to the ground in great pain. It was only a sharp twist, not a sprain, but for a few minutes Dick could do nothing but groan. The others dared not leave him. Julian knelt by him, offering to rub the ankle, but Dick wouldn't let him touch it. Jock stood by anxiously.

It took about twenty minutes for Dick's ankle to be strong enough for him to stand on again. With the help of the others he got to his feet and tested his ankle. 'It's all right, I think. I can walk on it – slowly. Now we'll go to the yard and see what's happening!'

But even as they started to walk slowly back, they heard a noise coming up the lines from the far-away yard, 'Rumble, rumble, rumble, jangle, clank!'

'It's coming back again!' said Julian. 'Stand still. Watch! It'll be going back into the tunnel!'

They stood still and watched and listened. Again the noise came nearer and grew thunderous. They saw the glow of what might be the fire in the cab, and then it passed. The train disappeared into the blackness of the tunnel-mouth and they heard the echo of its rumblings for some time.

'Well, there you are! There *is* a spook-train!' said Julian, trying to laugh, though he felt a good deal shaken. 'It came and it went – where from or where to, nobody knows! But we've heard it and seen it, in the darkness of the night. And jolly creepy it was, too!'

CHAPTER ELEVEN

Mostly about Jock

THE THREE boys stood rather close together, glad to feel each other in the darkness. They couldn't believe that they had found what they had come looking for so doubtfully! What kind of a train was this that had come rumbling out of the tunnel so mysteriously, and then, after a pause at the yard, had gone just as mysteriously back again?

'If only I hadn't twisted my ankle, we could have followed the train down the lines to the yard, and have gone quite close to it there,' groaned Dick. 'What an ass I am, messing things up at the most exciting moment!'

'You couldn't help it,' said Jock. 'I *say*! We've seen the spook-train! I can hardly believe it. Does it go all by itself, with nobody to drive it? Is it a real train?'

'Judging by the noise it made, it's real all right,' said Julian. 'And it shot out smoke, too. All the same, it's jolly strange. I can't say I like it much.'

'Let's go and see what's happened to Wooden-Leg Sam,' said Dick. 'I bet he's under his bed!'

They made their way slowly back to the yard, Dick limping a little, though his ankle was practically all right again. When they came to the yard they looked towards Sam's hut. The light was there no longer.

'He's blown it out and got under the bed!' said Dick. 'Poor Sam! It really must be terrifying for him. Let's go and peep into his hut.'

They went over to it and tried to see in at the window. But there was nothing to be seen. The hut was in complete darkness. Then suddenly a little flare flashed out somewhere near the floor.

'Look – there's Sam! He's lighting a match,' said Julian. 'See – he's peeping out from under the bed. He looks scared stiff. Let's tap on the window and ask him if he's all right.'

But that was quite the wrong thing to do! As soon as Julian tapped sharply on the window, Sam gave an anguished yell and retired hurriedly under the bed again, his wavering match-light going out.

'It's come for to take me!' they heard him wailing. 'It's come for to take me! And me with my wooden leg off too.'

'We're only frightening the poor old fellow,' said Dick. 'Come on. Let's leave him. He'll have a fit or something if we call out to him. He honestly thinks the spook-train's come to get him.'

They wandered round the dark yard for a few minutes, but there was nothing to find out in the darkness. No more rumbling came to their ears. The spook-train was evidently not going to run again that night.

'Let's go back,' said Julian. 'That really was exciting! Honestly, my hair stood on end when that train came puffing out of the tunnel. Where on earth did it come from? And what's the reason for it?'

They gave it up, and began to walk back to the camp. They scrambled through the heather, tired but excited. 'Shall we tell the girls we've seen the train?' said Dick.

'No,' said Julian. 'It would only scare Anne, and George would be furious if she knew we'd gone without her. We'll wait and see if we discover anything more before we say anything, either to the girls or to old Luffy.'

'Right,' said Dick. 'You'll hold your tongue, too, won't you, Jock?'

'Course,' said Jock, scornfully. 'Who would I tell? My stepfather? Not likely! How furious he'd be if he knew we'd all pooh-poohed his warnings and gone down to see the spook-train after all!'

He suddenly felt something warm against his legs, and gave a startled cry: 'What's this? Get away!'

But the warm thing turned out to be Timmy, who had come to meet three boys. He pressed against each of them in turn and whined a little.

'He says, "Why didn't you take me with you?"' said Dick. 'Sorry, old thing, but we couldn't. George would never have spoken to us again if we'd taken you, and left her behind! How would you have liked spook-trains, Timmy? Would you have run into a corner somewhere and hidden?'

'Woof,' said Timmy, scornfully. As if he would be afraid of anything!

They reached their camping-place and began to speak in whispers. 'Goodbye, Jock. Come up tomorrow if you can. Hope you don't have that Cecil boy to cope with!'

'Goodbye! See you soon,' whispered Jock, and disappeared into the darkness, with Timmy at his heels. Another chance of a midnight walk? Good, thought Timmy, just what he'd like! It was hot in the tent, and a scamper in the cool night air would be fine.

Timmy growled softly when they came near to Olly's Farm, and stood still, the hackles on his neck rising up a little. Jock put his hand on the dog's head and stopped.

'What's the matter, old boy? Burglars or something?'

He strained his eyes in the darkness. Big clouds now covered the stars and there was no light at all to see by. Jock made out a dim light in one of the barns. He crept over to it to see what it was. It went out as he came near, and then he heard the sound of footsteps, the quiet closing of the barn door, and the click of a padlock as it was locked.

Jock crept nearer – too near, for whoever it was must have heard him and swung round, lashing out with his arm. He caught Jock on the shoulder, and the boy overbalanced. He almost fell, and the man who had struck him clutched hold of him. A flash-light was put on and he blinked in the sudden light.

'It's you, Jock!' said an astonished voice, rough and impatient. 'What are you doing out here at this time of night?'

'Well, what are *you* doing?' demanded Jock, wriggling free. He switched on his own torch and let the light fall on the man who had caught him. It was Peters, one of the farm men, the one in whose lorry he had ridden that very day.

'What's it to do with you?' said Peters, angrily. 'I had a breakdown, and I've only just got back. Look here – you're fully dressed! Where have you been at this time of night? Did you hear me come in and get up to see what was happening?'

'You never know!' said Jock cheekily. He wasn't going to say anything that might make Peters suspicious of him. 'You just never know!'

'Is that Biddy?' said Peters, seeing a dark shadow slinking away. 'Do you mean to say you've been out with Biddy? What in the world have you been doing?'

Jock thanked his lucky stars that Peters hadn't spotted it was Timmy, not Biddy. He moved off without saying another word. Let Peters think what he liked! It was bad luck, though, that Peters had had a breakdown and come in late. If the man told his stepfather he'd seen Jock, fully dressed in the middle of the night, there'd be questions asked by both his mother and his stepfather, and Jock, who was a truthful boy, would find things very difficult to explain.

He scuttled off to bed, climbing up the pear-tree outside his window, and dropping quietly into his room. He opened his door softly to hear if anyone was awake in the house, but all was dark and silent.

'Blow Peters!' thought Jock. 'If he splits on me, I'm for it!'

He got into bed, pondered over the curious happenings of the night for a few minutes, and then slid into an uneasy sleep, in which spook-trains, Peters, and Timmy kept doing most peculiar things. He was glad to awake in the bright, sunny morning and find his mother shaking him.

'Get up, Jock! You're very late. Whatever's made you so sleepy? We're half-way through breakfast!'

Peters, apparently, didn't say anything to Jock's step-father about seeing Jock in the night. Jock was very thankful. He began to plan how to slip off to the others at the camp. He'd take them some food! That would be a fine excuse.

'Mum, can I take a basket of stuff to the campers?' he said, after breakfast. 'They must be running short now.'

'Well, that boy is coming,' said his mother. 'What's his name – Cecil something? Your stepfather says he's such a nice boy. You did enjoy your day with him yesterday, didn't you?'

Jock would have said quite a lot of uncomplimentary things about dear Cecil if his stepfather had not been there, sitting by the window reading the paper. As it was, he shrugged his shoulders and made a face, hoping that his mother would understand his feelings. She did.

'What time is Cecil coming?' she said. 'Perhaps there's time for you to run to the camp with a basket.'

'I don't want him running off up there,' said

Mr Andrews, suddenly butting into the conversation, and putting down his newspaper. 'Cecil may be here at any minute – and I know what Jock is! He'd start talking to those kids and forget all about coming back. Cecil's father is a great friend of mine, and Jock's got to be polite to him, and be here to welcome him. There's to be no running off to that camp today.'

Jock looked sulky. Why must his stepfather suddenly interfere in his plans like this? Rushing him off to the town, making him take Cecil for a friend! Just when some other children had come into his rather lonely life and livened it up, too! It was maddening.

'Perhaps I can go up to the camp myself with some food,' said his mother, comfortingly. 'Or maybe the children will come down for some.'

Jock was still sulky. He stalked out into the yard and went to look for Biddy. She was with her pups who were now trying to crawl round the shed after her. Jock hoped the campers would come to fetch food themselves that day. Then at least he would get a word with them.

Cecil arrived by car. He was about the same age as Jock, though he was small for twelve years old. He had curly hair which was too long, and his grey flannel suit was very, very clean and well-pressed.

'Hallo!' he called to Jock. 'I've come. What shall we play at? Soldiers?'

'No. American Indians,' said Jock, who had suddenly

remembered his old American Indian head-dress with masses of feathers round it, and a trail of them falling down the back. He rushed indoors, grinning. He changed into the whole suit, and put on his head-dress. He took his paint-box and hurriedly painted a pattern of red, blue and green on his face. He would play at American Indians, and terrify that annoying boy!

Cecil was wandering round by himself. To his enormous horror, as he turned a corner, a most terrifying figure rose up from behind a wall, gave a horrible yell and pounced on him, waving what looked like a toy chopper.

Cecil turned and fled, howling loudly, with Jock leaping madly after him, whooping for all he was worth, and thoroughly enjoying himself. He had had to play at soldiers all the day before with dear Cecil. He didn't see why Cecil shouldn't play American Indians all day with him today!

Just at that moment, the four campers arrived to fetch food, with Timmy running beside them. They stopped in amazement at the sight of Cecil running like the wind, howling dismally, and a fully-dressed and painted American Indian leaping after him.

Jock saw them, did a dance all round them, much to Timmy's amazement, yelled dramatically, pretended to cut off Timmy's tail and then tore after the vanishing Cecil.

The children began to laugh helplessly. 'Oh dear!' said Anne, with tears of laughter in her eyes, 'that must be

Cecil he's after. I suppose this is Jock's revenge for having to play soldiers all day with him yesterday. Look, there they go round the pig-sty. Poor Cecil!'

Cecil disappeared into the farm kitchen, sobbing, and Mrs Andrews ran to comfort him. Jock made off back to the others, grinning all over his face.

'Hallo,' he said. 'I'm just having a nice quiet time with dear Cecil. I'm so glad to see you. I wanted to come over, but my stepfather said I wasn't to – I must play with Cecil. Isn't he frightful?'

'Awful,' everyone agreed.

'I say, will your mother be furious with you for frightening Cecil like that? Perhaps we'd better not ask her for any food yet?' said Julian.

'Yes, you'd better wait a bit,' said Jock, leading them to the sunny side of the haystack they had rested by before. 'Hallo, Timmy! Did you get back all right last night?'

Jock had completely forgotten that the girls didn't know of the happenings of the night before. Both Anne and George at once pricked up their ears. Julian frowned at Jock, and Dick gave him a secret nudge.

'What's up?' said George, seeing all this by-play. 'What happened last night?'

'Oh, I just came up to have a little night-talk with the boys – and Timmy walked back with me,' said Jock, airily. 'Hope you didn't mind him coming, George.'

George flushed an angry red. 'You're keeping something from me,' she said to the boys. 'Yes, you are. I know you are. I believe you went off to the railway yard last night! Did you?'

There was an awkward silence. Julian shot an annoyed look at poor Jock, who could have kicked himself.

'Go on – tell me,' persisted George, an angry frown on her forehead. 'You beasts! You did go! And you never woke me up to go with you! Oh, I do think you're mean!'

'Did you see anything?' said Anne, her eyes going from one boy to another. Each of the girls sensed that there had been some kind of adventure in the night.

'Well,' began Julian. And then there was an interruption.

Cecil came round the haystack, his eyes red with crying. He glared at Jock.

'Your father wants you,' he said. 'You're to go at once. You're a beast, and I want to go home. Can't you hear your father yelling for you? He's got a stick – but I'm not sorry for you! I hope he gets you hard!'

CHAPTER TWELVE

George loses her temper

JOCK MADE a face at Cecil and got up. He went slowly off round the haystack, and the others listened in silence for yells. But none came.

'He frightened me,' said Cecil, sitting down by the others.

'Poor icle ting,' said Dick at once.

'Darling baby,' said George.

'Mother's pet,' said Julian. Cecil glared at them all. He got up again, very red.

'If I didn't know my manners, I'd smack your faces,' he said, and marched off hurriedly, before his own could be smacked.

The four sat in silence. They were sorry for Jock. George was angry and sulky because she knew the others had gone off without her the night before. Anne was worried.

They all sat there for about ten minutes. Then round the haystack came Jock's mother, looking distressed. She carried a big basket of food.

The children all stood up politely. 'Good morning, Mrs Andrews,' said Julian.

'I'm sorry I can't ask you to stop today,' said

Mrs Andrews. 'But Jock has really behaved very foolishly. I wouldn't let Mr Andrews give him a punishment because it would only make Jock hate his stepfather, and that would never do. So I've sent him up to bed for the day. You won't be able to see him, I'm afraid. Here is some food for you to take. Oh, dear – I'm really very sorry about all this. I can't think what came over Jock to behave in such a way. It's not a bit like him.'

Cecil's face appeared round the haystack, looking rather smug. Julian grinned to himself.

'Would you like us to take Cecil for a nice long walk over the moors?' he said. 'We can climb hills and jump over streams and scramble through the heather. It would make such a nice day for him.'

Cecil's face immediately disappeared.

'Well,' said Mrs Andrews, 'that really would be very kind of you. Now that Jock's been sent upstairs for the day there's no one for Cecil to play with. But I'm afraid he's a bit of a mother's boy, you know. You'll have to go carefully with him. Cecil! Cecil! Where are you? Come and make friends with these children.'

But Cecil had gone. There was no answer at all. He didn't want to make friends with 'these children'. He knew better than that! Mrs Andrews went in search of him, but he had completely disappeared.

The four children were not at all surprised. Julian, Dick and Anne grinned at one another. George stood with her back to them, still sulky.

Mrs Andrews came back again, out of breath. 'I can't find him,' she said. 'Never mind. I'll find something for him to do when he appears again.'

'Yes. Perhaps you've got some beads for him to thread? Or a nice easy jigsaw puzzle to do?' said Julian, very politely. The others giggled. A smile appeared on Mrs Andrews's face.

'Bad boy!' she said. 'Oh dear – poor Jock. Well it's his own fault. Now goodbye, I must get on with my work.'

She ran off to the dairy. The children looked round the haystack. Mr Andrews was getting into his car. He would soon be gone. They waited a few minutes till they heard the car set off down the rough cart-track.

'That's Jock's bedroom – where the pear-tree is,' said Julian. 'Let's just have a word with him before we go. It's a shame.'

They went across the farmyard and stood under the pear-tree – all except George, who stayed behind the haystack with the food, frowning. Julian called up to the window above: 'Jock!'

A head came out, the face still painted terrifyingly in streaks and circles. 'Hallo! He didn't get me. Mum wouldn't let him. All the same, I'd rather he had – it's awful being stuck up here this sunny day. Where's dear Cecil?'

'I don't know. Probably in the darkest corner of one of the barns,' said Julian. 'Jock, if things are difficult in the daytime, come up at night. We've got to see you somehow.'

'Right,' said Jock. 'How do I look?'

Julian grinned. 'I wonder old Timmy knew you.'

'Where's George?' asked Jock.

'Sulking behind the haystack,' said Dick. 'We shall have an awful day with her now. You let the cat properly out of the bag, you idjit!'

'Yes. I'm a ninny and an idjit,' said Jock, and Anne giggled. 'Look – there's Cecil. You might tell him to beware of the bull, will you?'

'Is there a bull?' said Anne, looking alarmed.

'No. But that's no reason why he shouldn't beware of one,' grinned Jock. 'So long! Have a nice day!'

The three left him, and strolled over to Cecil, who had just appeared out of a dark little shed. He made a face at them, and stood ready to run to the dairy where Mrs Andrews was busy.

Julian suddenly clutched Dick and pointed behind Cecil. 'The bull! Beware of the bull!' he yelled suddenly.

Dick entered into the joke. 'The bull's loose! Look out! Beware of the bull!' he shouted.

Anne gave a shriek. It all sounded so real that, although she knew it was a joke, she felt half-scared. 'The bull!' she cried.

Cecil turned green. His legs shook. 'W-w-w-where is it?' he stammered.

'Look out behind you!' yelled Julian, pointing. Poor Cecil, convinced that a large bull was about to pounce on him from behind, gave an anguished cry and tore on tottering legs to the dairy. He threw himself against Mrs Andrews.

'Save me, save me! The bull's chasing me.'

'But there's no bull here,' said Mrs Andrews, in surprise. 'Really, Cecil! Was it a pig after you, or something?'

Helpless with laughter, the three children made their way back to George. They tried to tell her about the make-believe bull, but she turned away and wouldn't listen. Julian shrugged his shoulders. Best to leave George to herself when she was in one of her rages! She didn't lose her temper as often as she used to, but when she did she was very trying indeed.

They went back to the camp with the basket of food. Timmy followed soberly. He knew something was wrong with George and he was unhappy. His tail was down, and he looked miserable. George wouldn't even pat him.

When they got back to the camp, George flared up.

'How dare you go off without me when I told you I meant to come? Fancy taking Jock and not letting me go! I think you're absolute beasts. I never really thought you'd do a thing like that, you and Dick.'

'Don't be silly, George,' said Julian. 'I told you we didn't mean to let you and Anne go. I'll tell you all that happened – and it's pretty thrilling!'

'What? Tell me quickly!' begged Anne, but George obstinately turned away her head as if she was not interested.

Julian began to relate all the curious happenings of the night. Anne listened breathlessly. George was listening too, though she pretended not to. She was very angry and very hurt.

'Well, there you are,' said Julian, when he had finished. 'If that's what people mean by spook-trains, there was one puffing in and out of that tunnel all right! I felt pretty scared, I can tell you. Sorry you weren't there too, George – but I didn't want to leave Anne alone.'

George was not accepting any apologies. She still looked furious.

'I suppose Timmy went with you,' she said. 'I think that was horrid of him – to go without waking me, when he knew I'd like to be with you on the adventure.'

'Oh, don't be so silly,' said Dick, in disgust. 'Fancy being angry with old Tim, too! You're making him miserable. And anyway, he *didn't* come with us. He just came to meet us when we got back, and then went off to keep Jock company on his way back to the farm.'

'Oh,' said George, and she reached out her hand to pat Timmy, who was filled with delight. 'At least Timmy was loyal to me then. That's something.'

There was a silence. Nobody ever knew quite how to treat George when she was in one of her moods. It was really best to leave her to herself, but they couldn't very well go off and leave the camp just because George was there, cross and sulky.

Anne took hold of George's arm. She was miserable when George behaved like this. 'George,' she began, 'there's no need to be cross with me, too. *I* haven't done anything!'

'If you weren't such a little coward, too afraid to go with us, I'd have been able to go too,' said George unkindly, dragging her arm away.

Julian was disgusted. He saw Anne's hurt face and was angry with George.

'Shut up, George,' he said. 'You're being horrid, saying catty things like that! I'm astonished at you.'

George was ashamed of herself, but she was too proud to say so. She glared at Julian.

'And *I'm* astonished at *you*,' she said. 'After all the adventures we've had together, you try to keep me out of this one. But you *will* let me come next time, won't you, Julian?'

'What! After your frightful behaviour today?' said Julian, who could be just as obstinate as George when he wanted to. 'Certainly not. This is my adventure and Dick's – and perhaps Jock's. Not yours or Anne's.'

He got up and stalked down the hill with Dick. George sat pulling bits of heather off the stems, looking mutinous and angry. Anne blinked back tears. She hated this sort of thing. She got up to get dinner ready. Perhaps after a good meal they would all feel better.

Mr Luffy was sitting outside his tent, reading. He had already seen the children that morning. He looked up, smiling.

'Hallo! Come to talk to me?'

'Yes,' said Julian, an idea uncurling itself in his mind. 'Could I have a look at that map of yours, Mr Luffy? The big one you've got showing every mile of these moorlands?'

'Of course. It's in the tent somewhere,' said Mr Luffy.

The boys found it and opened it. Dick at once guessed why Julian wanted it. Mr Luffy went on reading.

'It shows the railways that run under the moorlands too, doesn't it?' said Julian. Mr Luffy nodded.

'Yes. There are quite a few lines. I suppose it was easier to tunnel under the moors from valley to valley rather than make a permanent way over the top of them. In any case, a railway over the moors would probably be completely snowed up in the winter-time.'

The boys bent their heads over the big map; it showed the railways as dotted lines when they went underground, but by long black lines when they appeared in the open air, in the various valleys.

They found exactly where they were. Then Julian's finger ran down the map a little and came to where a small line showed itself at the end of a dotted line.

He looked at Dick, who nodded. Yes – that showed where the tunnel was, out of which the 'spook-train' had come, and the lines to the deserted yard. Julian's finger

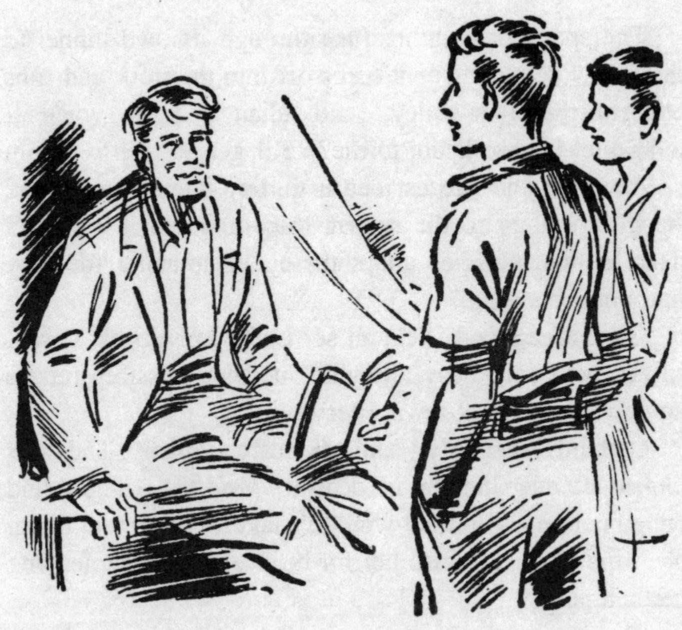

went back from the yard to the tunnel, where the dotted lines began. His finger traced the dotted lines a little way till they became whole lines again. That was where the train came out into another valley!

Then his finger showed where the tunnel that led from the yard appeared to join up with another one, that also ran for some distance before coming out into yet another valley. The boys looked at one another in silence.

Mr Luffy suddenly spotted a day-flying moth and got up to follow it. The boys took the chance of talking to one another.

'The spook-train either runs through its own tunnel to the valley beyond – or it turns off into this fork and runs along to the other valley,' said Julian, in a low voice. 'I tell you what we'll do, Dick. We'll get Mr Luffy to run us down to the nearest town to buy something – and we'll slip along to the station there and see if we can't make a few inquiries about these two tunnels. We may find out something.'

'Good idea,' said Dick, as Mr Luffy came back. 'I say, sir, are you very busy today? Could you possibly run us down to the nearest town after dinner?'

'Certainly, certainly,' said Mr Luffy, amiably. The boys looked at one another in delight. *Now* they might find out something! But they wouldn't take George with them. No – they would punish her for her bad temper by leaving her behind!

CHAPTER THIRTEEN

A thrilling plan

ANNE CALLED them to dinner. 'Come along!' she cried. 'I've got it all ready. Tell Mr Luffy there's plenty for him, too.'

Mr Luffy came along willingly. He thought Anne was a marvellous camp-housekeeper. He looked approvingly at the spread set out on a white cloth on the ground.

'Hm! Salad. Hard-boiled eggs. Slices of ham. And what's this – apple-pie! My goodness! Don't tell me you cooked that here, Anne.'

Anne laughed. 'No. All this came from the farm, of course. Except the lime juice and water.'

George ate with the others, but said hardly a word. She was brooding over her wrongs, and Mr Luffy looked at her several times, puzzled.

'Are you quite well, George?' he said, suddenly. George went red.

'Yes, thank you,' she said, and tried to be more herself, though she couldn't raise a smile at all. Mr Luffy watched her, and was relieved to see that she ate as much as the others. Probably had some sort of row, he guessed correctly. Well, it would blow over! He knew better than to interfere.

They finished lunch and drank all the lime juice. It was a hot day and they were very thirsty indeed. Timmy emptied all his dish of water and went and gazed longingly into the canvas bucket of washing-water. But he was too well-behaved to drink it, now that he knew he mustn't. Anne laughed, and poured some more water into his dish.

'Well,' said Mr Luffy, beginning to fill his old brown pipe, 'if anyone wants to come into town with me this afternoon, I'll be starting in fifteen minutes.'

'I'll come!' said Anne, at once. 'It won't take George and me long to wash-up these things. Will you come too, George?'

'No,' said George, and the boys heaved a sigh of relief. They had guessed she wouldn't want to come with them – but, if she'd known what they were going to try and find out, she would have come all right!

'I'm going for a walk with Timmy,' said George, when all the washing-up had been done.

'All right,' said Anne, who secretly thought that George would be much better left on her own to work off her ill-feelings that afternoon. 'See you later.'

George and Timmy set off. The others went with Mr Luffy to where his car was parked beside the great rock. They got in.

'Hi! The trailer's fastened to it,' called Julian. 'Wait a bit. Let me get out and undo it. We don't want to take an empty trailer bumping along behind us for miles.'

'Dear me. I always forget to undo the trailer,' said

Mr Luffy, vexed. 'The times I take it along without meaning to!'

The children winked at one another. Dear old Luffy! He was always doing things like that. No wonder his wife fussed round him like an old hen with one foolish chicken when he was at home.

They went off in the car, jolting over the rough road till they came to the smooth highway. They stopped in the centre of the town. Mr Luffy said he would meet them for tea at five o'clock at the hotel opposite the parking-place.

The three of them set off together, leaving Mr Luffy to go to the library and browse there. It seemed funny to be without George. Anne didn't much like it, and said so.

'Well, we don't like going off without George either,' said Julian. 'But honestly, she can't behave like that and get away with it. I thought she'd grown out of that sort of thing.'

'Well, you know how she adores an adventure,' said Anne. 'Oh dear – if I hadn't felt so scared you'd have taken me along, and George would have gone too. It's quite true what she said about me being a coward.'

'You're not,' said Dick. 'You can't help being scared of things sometimes – after all, you're the youngest of us – but being scared doesn't make you a coward. I've known you to be as brave as any of us when you've been scared stiff!'

'Where are we going?' asked Anne. The boys told her, and her eyes sparkled.

'Oh – are we going to find out where the spook-train comes from? It might come from one of two valleys then, judging from the map.'

'Yes. The tunnels aren't really very long ones,' said Julian. 'Not more than a mile, I should think. We thought we'd make some inquiries at the station and see if there's anyone who knows anything about the old railway yard and the tunnel beyond. We shan't say a word about the spook-train of course.'

They walked into the station. They went up to a railway plan and studied it. It didn't tell them much. Julian turned to a young porter who was wheeling some luggage along.

'I say! Could you help us? We're camping up on the moorlands, and we're quite near a deserted railway yard with lines that run into an old tunnel. Why isn't the yard used any more?'

'Don't know,' said the boy. 'You should ask old Tucky there – see him? He knows all the tunnels under the moors like the back of his hand. Worked in them all when he was a boy.'

'Thanks,' said Dick, pleased. They went over to where an old whiskered porter was sitting in the sun, enjoying a rest till the next train came in.

'Excuse me,' said Julian politely. 'I've been told that you know all about the moorland tunnels like the back of your hand. They must be very, very interesting.'

'My father and my grandfather built those tunnels,' said the old porter, looking up at the children out of small faded eyes that watered in the strong sunlight. 'And I've been guard on all the trains that ran through them.'

He mumbled a long string of names, going through all the list of tunnels in his mind. The children waited patiently till he had finished.

'There's a tunnel near where we're camping on the moorlands,' said Julian, getting a word in at last. 'We're not far from Olly's Farm. We came across an old deserted railway yard, with lines that led into a tunnel. Do you know it?'

'Oh yes, that's an old tunnel,' said Tucky, nodding his grey head, on which his porter's cap sat all crooked. 'Hasn't been used for many a long year. Nor the yard either. Wasn't enough traffic there, far as I remember. They shut up the yard. Tunnel isn't used any more.'

The boys exchanged glances. So it wasn't used any more! Well, they knew better.

'The tunnel joins another, doesn't it?' said Julian. The porter, pleased at their interest in the old tunnels he knew so well, got up and went into an office behind. He came out with a dirty, much-used map, which he spread out on his knee. His black finger-nail pointed to a mark on the map.

'That's the yard see? It was called Olly's Yard, after the farm. There're the lines to the tunnel. Here's the tunnel. It runs right through to Kilty Vale – there it is. And here's where it used to join the tunnel to Roker's Vale. But that was bricked up years ago. Something happened there – the roof fell in, I think it was – and the company decided not to use the tunnel to Roker's Vale at all.'

The children listened with the utmost interest. Julian reasoned things out in his mind. If that spook-train came from anywhere then it must come from Kilty Vale, because that was the only place the lines went to now, since the way to Roker's Vale had been bricked up where the tunnels joined.

'I suppose no trains run through the tunnel from Kilty Vale to Olly's Yard now, then?' he said.

Tucky snorted. 'Didn't I tell you it hasn't been used for years? The yard at Kilty Vale's been turned into something else, though the lines are still there. There's been no engine through that tunnel since I was a young man.'

This was all very, very interesting. Julian thanked old Tucky so profusely that he wanted to tell the children everything all over again. He even gave them the old map.

'Oh, thanks,' said Julian, delighted to have it. He looked at the others. 'This'll be jolly useful!' he said, and they nodded.

They left the pleased old man and went out into the town. They found a little park and sat down on a seat. They were longing to discuss all that Tucky had told them.

'It's jolly strange,' said Dick. 'No trains run there now – the tunnel's not been used for ages – and Olly's Yard must have been derelict for years.'

'And yet, there appear to be trains that come and go!' said Julian.

GO TO THE

'Then, they *must* be spook-trains,' said Anne, her eyes wide and puzzled. 'Julian, they must be, mustn't they?'

'Looks like it,' said Julian. 'It's most mysterious. I can't understand it.'

'Ju,' said Dick, suddenly. 'I know what we'll do! We'll wait one night again till we see the spook-train come out of the tunnel to the yard. Then one of us can sprint off to the *other* end of the tunnel – it's only about a mile long – and wait for it to come out the other side! Then we'll find out why a train still runs from Kilty Vale to Olly's Yard through that old tunnel.'

'Jolly good idea,' said Julian, thrilled. 'What about tonight? If Jock comes, he can go, too. If he doesn't, just you and I will go. *Not* George.'

They all felt excited. Anne wondered if she would be brave enough to go too, but she knew that when the night came she wouldn't feel half as brave as she did now! No, she wouldn't go. There was really no need for her to join in this adventure at present. It hadn't even turned out to be a proper one yet – it was only an unsolved mystery!

George hadn't come back from her walk when they reached the camp. They waited for her, and at last she appeared with Timmy, looking tired out.

'Sorry I was an ass this morning,' she said at once. 'I've walked my temper off! Don't know what came over me.'

'That's all right,' said Julian amiably. 'Forget it.'

They were all very glad that George had recovered her temper, for she was a very prickly person indeed when she was angry. She was rather subdued and said nothing at all about spook-trains or tunnels. So they said nothing either.

The night was fine and clear. Stars shone out brilliantly again in the sky. The children said good night to Mr Luffy at ten o'clock and got into their sleeping-bags. Julian and Dick did not mean to go exploring till midnight, so they lay and talked quietly.

About eleven o'clock they heard somebody moving cautiously outside. They wondered if it was Jock, but he did not call out to them. Who could it be?

Then Julian saw a familiar head outlined against the starlit sky. It was George. But what in the world was she doing? He couldn't make it out at all. Whatever it was she wasn't making any noise over it, and she obviously thought the boys were asleep. Julian gave a nice little snore or two just to let her go on thinking so.

At last she disappeared. Julian waited a few minutes and then put his head cautiously out of the tent opening. He felt about, and his fingers brushed against some string. He grinned to himself and got back into the tent.

'I've found out what George was doing,' he whispered. 'She's put string across the entrance of our tent, and I bet it runs to her tent and she's tied it to her big toe or something, so that if we go out without her she'll feel the pull of the string when we go through it and wake up and follow us!'

'Good old George,' chuckled Dick. 'Well, she'll be unlucky. We'll squeeze out under the sides of the tent!'

Which was what they did do at about a minute past twelve! They didn't disturb George's string at all. They were out on the heather and away down the slope while George was sleeping soundly in her tent beside Anne waiting for the pull on her toe which didn't come. Poor George!

The boys arrived at the deserted railway yard and looked to see if Wooden-Leg Sam's candle was alight. It was. So the spook-train hadn't come along *that* night, yet.

They were just scrambling down to the yard when they heard the train coming. There was the same rumbling noise as before, muffled by the tunnel – and then out of the tunnel, again with no lamps, came the spook-train, clanking on its way to the yard!

'Quick, Dick! You sprint off to the tunnel opening and watch for the train to go back in again. And I'll find my way across the moor to the other end of the tunnel. There was a path marked on that old map, and I follow that!' Julian's words tumbled over each other in his excitement. 'I'll jolly well watch for the spook-train to complete its journey, and see if it vanishes into thin air or what!'

And off he went to find the path that led over the moors to the other end of the tunnel. He meant to see what happened at the other end if he had to run all the way!

CHAPTER FOURTEEN

Jock comes to camp

JULIAN FOUND the path quite by chance and went along it as fast as he could. He used his torch, for he did not think he would meet anyone out on such a lonely way at that time of night. The path was very much overgrown, but he could follow it fairly easily, even running at times.

'If that spook-train stops about twenty minutes in the yard again, as it did before, it will give me just about time to reach the other end of the tunnel,' panted Julian. 'I'll be at Kilty's Yard before it comes.'

It seemed a very long way. But at last the path led downwards, and some way below him Julian could see what might be a railway yard. Then he saw that big sheds were built there – or what looked like big sheds in the starlight.

He remembered what the old porter had said. Kilty's Yard was used for something else now – maybe the lines had been taken up. Maybe even the tunnel had been stopped up, too. He slipped quickly down the path and came into what had once been the old railway yard. Big buildings loomed up on every side. Julian thought they must be workshops of some kind. He switched his torch on and off very quickly, but the short flash had shown him what he was looking for – two pairs of railway lines. They were old and rusty, but he knew they must lead to the tunnel.

He followed them closely, right up to the black mouth of the dark tunnel. He couldn't see inside at all. He switched his torch on and off quickly. Yes – the lines led right inside the tunnel. Julian stopped and wondered what to do.

'I'll sneak into the tunnel a little way and see if it's bricked up anywhere,' he thought. So in he went, walking between one pair of lines. He put on his torch, certain that no one would see its light and challenge him to say what he was doing out so late at night.

The tunnel stretched before him, a great yawning hole, disappearing into deep blackness. It was certainly not bricked up. Julian saw a little niche in the brickwork of the tunnel and decided to crouch in it. It was one of the niches made for workmen to stand in when trains went by in the old days.

Julian crouched down in the dirty old niche and waited. He glanced at the luminous face of his watch. He had been twenty minutes getting here. Maybe the train would be along in a few minutes. He would be very, very close to it! Julian couldn't help wishing that Dick was with him. It was so eerie waiting there in the dark for a mysterious train that apparently belonged to no one and came and went from nowhere to nowhere!

He waited and he waited. Once he thought he heard a

rumble far away down the tunnel, and he held his breath, feeling certain that the train was coming. But it didn't come. Julian waited for half an hour and still the train had not appeared. What had happened to it?

'I'll wait another ten minutes and then I'm going,' Julian decided. 'I've had about enough of hiding in a dark, dirty tunnel waiting for a train that doesn't come! Maybe it has decided to stay in Olly's Yard for the night.'

After ten minutes he gave it up. He left the tunnel, went into Kilty's Yard and then up the path to the moors. He hurried along it, eager to see if Dick was at the other end of the tunnel. Surely he would wait there till Julian came back!

Dick was there, tired and impatient. When he saw a quick flash from Julian's torch he answered it with his own. The two boys joined company thankfully.

'You *have* been ages!' said Dick, reproachfully. 'What happened? The spook-train went back into the tunnel ages and ages ago. It only stayed about twenty minutes in the yard again.'

'Went back into the tunnel!' exclaimed Julian. 'Did it really? Well, it never came out the other side! I waited for ages. I never even heard it – though I did hear a very faint rumble once, or thought I did.'

The boys fell silent, puzzled and mystified. What sort of a train was this that puffed out of a tunnel at dead of night, and went back again, but didn't appear out of the other end?

'I suppose the entrance to that second tunnel the porter told us about *is* really bricked up?' said Julian at last. 'If it wasn't, the train could go down there, of course.'

'Yes. That's the only solution, if the train's a real one and not a spook one,' agreed Dick. 'Well, we can't go exploring the tunnels now – let's wait and do it in the daytime. I've had enough tonight!'

Julian had had enough too. In silence the two boys went back to camp. They quite forgot the string in front of their tent, and scrambled right through it. They got into the sleeping-bags thankfully.

The string, fastened to George's big toe through a hole she had cut in her sleeping-bag, pulled hard, and George woke up with a jump. Timmy was awake, having heard the boys come back. He licked George when she sat up.

George had not undressed properly. She slipped quickly out of her bag and crawled out of her tent. Now she would catch the two boys going off secretly and follow them!

But there was no sign or sound of them anywhere around. She crawled silently to their tent. Both boys had fallen asleep immediately, tired out with their midnight trip. Julian snored a little, and Dick breathed so deeply that George could quite well hear him as she crouched outside, listening. She was very puzzled. Someone had pulled at her toe – so somebody must have scrambled through that string. After listening for a few minutes, she gave it up and went back to her tent.

In the morning, George was furious! Julian and Dick

related their night's adventure, and George could hardly believe that once again they had gone without her – and that they had managed to get away without disturbing the string! Dick saw George's face and couldn't help laughing.

'Sorry, old thing. We discovered your little trick and avoided it when we set out – but typically, we forgot all about it coming back. We must have given your toe a frightful tug. Did we? I suppose you *did* tie the other end of the string to your toe?'

George looked as if she could throw all the breakfast things at him. Fortunately for everyone Jock arrived at that moment. He didn't wear his usual beaming smile but seemed rather subdued.

'Hallo, Jock!' said Julian. 'Just in time for a spot of breakfast. Sit down and join us.'

'I can't,' said Jock. 'I've only a few minutes. Listen. Isn't it rotten – I'm to go away and stay with my stepfather's sister for two weeks! Two weeks! You'll be gone when I come back, won't you?'

'Yes. But, Jock, *why* have you got to go away?' said Dick, surprised. 'Has there been a row or something?'

'I don't know,' said Jock. 'Mum won't say, but she looks pretty miserable. My stepfather's in a frightful temper. It's my opinion they want me out of the way for some reason. I don't know this sister of my stepfather's very well – only met her once – but she's pretty awful.'

'Well, come over here and stay with us, if they want to

get rid of you,' said Julian, sorry for Jock. Jock's face brightened.

'I *say*, that's a fine idea!' he said.

'Smashing,' agreed Dick. 'Well, I don't see what's to stop you. If they want to get rid of you, it can't matter where you go for a fortnight. We'd love to have you.'

'Right. I'll come,' said Jock. 'I'll not say a word about it, though, to my stepfather. I'll let Mum into the secret. She was going to take me away today, but I'll just tell her I'm coming to you instead. I don't think she'll split on me, and I hope she'll square things with my step-aunt.'

Jock's face beamed again now. The others beamed back, even George, and Timmy wagged his tail. It would be nice to have Jock – and what a lot they had to tell him.

He went off to break the news to his mother, while the others washed up and cleared things away. George became sulky again when Jock was gone. She simply could not or would not realise that Julian meant what he said!

When they began to discuss everything that had happened the night before, George refused to listen. 'I'm not going to bother about your stupid spook-trains any more,' she said. 'You wouldn't let me join you when I wanted to, and now I shan't take any interest in the matter.'

And she walked off with Timmy, not saying where she was going.

'Well, let her go,' said Julian, exasperated and cross. 'What does she expect me to do? Climb down and say we'll let her come the next night we go?'

'We said we'd go in the daytime,' said Dick. 'She could come then, because if Anne doesn't want to come it won't matter leaving her here alone in the daytime.'

'You're right,' said Julian. 'Let's call her back and tell her.' But by that time George was out of hearing.

'She's taken sandwiches,' said Anne. 'She means to be gone all day. Isn't she an idiot?'

Jock came back after a time, with two rugs and an extra jersey and more food. 'I had hard work to persuade Mum,' he said. 'But she said yes at last. Though mind you, I'd have come anyhow! I'm not going to be shoved about by my stepfather just out of spite. I *say* – isn't this great! I never thought I'd be camping out with you. If there isn't room in your tent for me, Julian, I can sleep out on the heather.'

'There'll be room,' said Julian. 'Hallo, Mr Luffy! You've been out early!'

Mr Luffy came up and glanced at Jock. 'Ah, is this your friend from the farm? How do you do? Come to spend a few days with us? I see you have an armful of rugs!'

'Yes. Jock's coming to camp a bit with us,' said Julian. 'Look at all the food he's brought. Enough to stand a siege!'

'It is indeed,' said Mr Luffy. 'Well, I'm going to go through some of my specimens this morning. What are you going to do?'

'Oh, mess about till lunch-time,' said Julian. 'Then we might go for a walk.'

Mr Luffy went back to his tent and they could hear him whistling softly as he set to work. Suddenly Jock sat up straight and looked alarmed.

'What's the matter?' asked Dick. Then he heard what Jock had heard. A shrill whistle blown loudly by somebody some way off.

'That's my stepfather's whistle,' said Jock. 'He's whistling for me. Mum must have told him, or else he's found out I've come over here.'

'Quick – let's scoot away and hide,' said Anne. 'If you're not here he can't take you back! Come on! Maybe he'll get tired of looking for you, and go.'

Nobody could think of a better idea, and certainly nobody wanted to face a furious Mr Andrews. All four shot down the slope and made their way to where the heather was high and thick. They burrowed into it and lay still, hidden by some high bracken.

Mr Andrews's voice could soon be heard, shouting for Jock, but no Jock appeared. Mr Andrews came out by Mr Luffy's tent. Mr Luffy, surprised at the shouting, put his head out of his tent to see what it was all about. He didn't like the look of Mr Andrews at all.

'Where's Jock?' Mr Andrews demanded, scowling at him.

'I really do not know,' said Mr Luffy.

'He's got to come back,' said Mr Andrews, roughly. 'I won't have him hanging about here with those kids.'

'What's wrong with them?' inquired Mr Luffy. 'I

must say I find them very well-behaved and pleasant-mannered.'

Mr Andrews stared at Mr Luffy, and put him down as a silly, harmless old fellow who would probably help him to get Jock back if he went about it the right way.

'Now look here,' said Mr Andrews. 'I don't know who you are, but you must be a friend of the children's. And if so, then I'd better warn you they're running into danger. See?'

'Really? In what way?' asked Mr Luffy, mildly and disbelievingly.

'Well, there's bad and dangerous places about these moorlands,' said Mr Andrews. 'Very bad. I know them. And those children have been messing about in them. See? And if Jock comes here, he'll start messing about too, and I don't want him to get into any danger. It would break his mother's heart.'

'Quite,' said Mr Luffy.

'Well, will you talk to him and send him back?' said Mr Andrews. 'That railway yard now – that's a most dangerous place. And folks do say that there're spook-trains there. I wouldn't want Jock to be mixed up in anything of that sort.'

'Quite,' said Mr Luffy again, looking closely at Mr Andrews. 'You seem very concerned about this – er – railway yard.'

'Me? Oh, no,' said Mr Andrews. 'Never been near the horrible place. I wouldn't want to see spook-trains – make

me run a mile! It's just that I don't want Jock to get into danger. I'd be most obliged if you'd talk to him and send him home, when they all come back from wherever they are.'

'Quite,' said Mr Luffy again, most irritatingly. Mr Andrews gazed at Mr Luffy's bland face and suddenly wished he could smack it. 'Quite, quite, quite!' Gr-r-r-r-r-r!

He turned and went away. When he had gone for some time, and was a small speck in the distance, Mr Luffy called loudly.

'He's gone! Please send Jock here so that I can – er – address a few words to him.'

Four children appeared from their heathery hiding-place. Jock went over to Mr Luffy, looking mutinous.

'I just wanted to say,' said Mr Luffy, 'that I quite understand why you want to be away from your stepfather, and that I consider it's no business of mine where you go in order to get away from him!'

Jock grinned. 'Oh, thanks awfully,' he said. 'I thought you were going to send me back!' He rushed over to the others. 'It's all right,' he said. 'I'm going to stay, and, I say – what about going and exploring down that tunnel after lunch? We *might* find that spook-train then!'

'Good idea!' said Julian. 'We will! Poor old George – she'll miss that little adventure too!'

CHAPTER FIFTEEN

George has an adventure

GEORGE HAD gone off with one fixed idea in her mind. She was going to find out something about that mysterious tunnel! She thought she would walk over the moorlands to Kilty's Yard, and see what she could see there. Maybe she could walk right back through the tunnel itself!

She soon came to Olly's Yard. There it lay below her, with Wooden-Leg Sam pottering about. She went down to speak to him. He didn't see or hear her coming and jumped violently when she called to him.

He swung round, squinting at her fiercely. 'You clear off!' he shouted. 'I've been told to keep you children out of here, see? Do you want me to lose my job?'

'Who told you to keep us out?' asked George, puzzled as to who could have known they had been in the yard.

'*He* did, see?' said the old man. He rubbed his eyes, and then peered at George short-sightedly again. 'I've broken my glasses,' he said.

'Who's "he" – the person who told you to keep us out?' said George.

But the old watchman seemed to have one of his sudden strange changes of temper again. He bent down and picked up a large cinder. He was about to fling it at

George when Timmy gave a loud and menacing growl. Sam dropped his arm.

'You clear out,' he said. 'You don't want to get a poor old man like me into trouble, do you? You look a nice kind boy you do. You wouldn't get Wooden-Leg Sam into trouble, would you?'

George turned to go. She decided to take the path that led to the tunnel and peep inside. But when she got there there was nothing to see. She didn't feel that she wanted to walk all alone inside that dark mouth, so she took the path that Julian had taken the night before, over the top of the tunnel. But she left it half-way to look at a curious bump that jutted up from the heather just there.

She scraped away at the heather and found something hard beneath. She pulled at it but it would not give. Timmy, thinking she was obligingly digging for rabbits, came to help. He scrambled below the heather – and then he suddenly gave a bark of fright and disappeared!

George screamed: 'Timmy! What have you done? Where are you?'

To her enormous relief she heard Timmy's bark some way down. Where *could* he be? She called again, and once more Timmy barked.

George tugged at the tufts of heather, and then suddenly she saw what the curious mound was. It was a built-up vent-hole for the old tunnel – a place where the smoke came curling out in the days when trains ran there often. It had been barred across with iron, but the bars had rusted and fallen in, and heather had grown thickly over them.

'Oh, Timmy, you must have fallen down the vent,' said George, anxiously. 'But not very far down. Wait a bit and I'll see what I can do. If only the others were here to help!'

But they weren't, and George had to work all by herself to try and get down to the broken bars. It took her a very long time, but at last she had them exposed, and saw where Timmy had fallen down.

He kept giving short little barks, as if to say: 'It's all right. I can wait. I'm not hurt!'

George had to sit down and take a rest after her efforts. She was hungry, but she said to herself that she would *not*

eat till she had somehow got down to Timmy, and found out where he was. Soon she began her task again.

She climbed down through the fallen-in vent. It was very difficult, and she was terrified of the rusty old iron bars breaking off under her weight. But they didn't.

Once down in the vent she discovered steps made of great iron nails projecting out. Some of them had thin rungs across. There had evidently once been a ladder up to the top of the vent. Most of the rungs had gone, but the iron nails that supported them still stood in the brick walls of the old round vent. She heard Timmy give a little bark. He was quite near her now.

Cautiously she went down the great hole. Her foot touched Timmy. He had fallen on a collection of broken iron bars, which, caught in part of the old iron ladder, stuck out from it, and made a rough landing-place for the dog to fall on.

'Oh, Timmy,' said George, horrified. 'However am I going to get you out of here? This hole goes right down into the tunnel.'

She couldn't possibly pull Timmy up the hole. It was equally impossible to get him down. He could never climb down the iron ladder, especially as it had so many rungs missing.

George was in despair. 'Oh, Timmy! Why did I lose my temper and walk out on the others to do some exploring all by myself? Don't fall, Timmy. You'll break your legs if you do.'

Timmy had no intention of falling. He was frightened, but so far his curious landing-place felt firm. He kept quite still.

'Listen, Tim,' said George, at last. 'The only thing I can think of is to climb down round it somehow and see how far it is to the tunnel itself. There might even be someone there to help! No, that's silly. There can't be. But I might find an old rope – anything – that I could use to help you down with. Oh, dear, what a horrible nightmare!'

George gave Timmy a reassuring pat, and then began to feel about for the iron rungs with her feet. Further down they were all there, and it was easy to climb lower and lower. She was soon down in the tunnel itself. She had her torch with her and switched it on. Then she nearly gave a scream of horror.

Just near to her was a silent train! She could almost touch the engine. Was it – could it be – the spook-train itself? George stared at it, breathing fast.

It looked very, very old and out-of-date. It was smaller than the trains she was used to – the engine was smaller and so were the trucks. The funnel was longer and the wheels were different from those of ordinary trains. George stared at the silent train by the light of her torch, her mind in a muddle. She really didn't know *what* to think!

It *must* be the spook-train! It had come from this tunnel the night before, and had gone back again – and it hadn't run all the way through to Kilty's Yard, because Julian had watched for it, and it hadn't come out there. No – it

had run here, to the middle of the dark tunnel, and there it stood, waiting for night so that it might run again.

George shivered. The train belonged to years and years ago! Who drove it at night? Did anybody? Or did it run along without a driver, remembering its old days and old ways? No, that was silly. Trains didn't think or remember. George shook herself and remembered Timmy.

And just at that very moment, poor Timmy lost his foothold on the iron bars, and fell! He had stretched out to listen for George, his foot had slipped – and now he was hurtling down the vent! He gave a mournful howl.

He struck against part of the ladder and that stopped his headlong fall for a moment. But down he went again, scrabbling as he fell, trying to get hold of something to save himself.

George heard him howl and knew he was falling. She was so horror-stricken that she simply couldn't move. She stood there at the bottom of the vent like a statue, not even breathing.

Timmy fell with a thump beside her, and a groan was jerked out of him. In a trice George was down by him on her knees. 'Timmy! Are you hurt? Are you alive? Oh, Timmy, say something!'

'Woof,' said Timmy, and got up rather unsteadily on his four legs. He had fallen on a pile of the softest soot! The smoke of many, many years had sooted the walls of the vent, and the weather had sent it down to the bottom, until quite a pile had collected at one side. Timmy had fallen plump in the middle of it, and almost buried himself. He shook himself violently, and soot flew out all over George.

She didn't know or care. She hugged him, and her face and clothes grew as dark as soot! She felt about and found the soft pile that had saved Timmy from being hurt.

'It's soot! I came down the other side of the vent, so I didn't know the soot was there. Oh, Timmy, what a bit of luck for you! I thought you'd be killed – or at least badly hurt,' said George.

He licked her sooty nose and didn't like the taste of it.

George stood up. She didn't like the idea of climbing up that horrid vent again – and, anyway, Timmy couldn't. The only thing to do was to walk out of the tunnel. She wouldn't have fancied walking through the tunnel before, in case she met the spook-train – but here it was, close beside her, and she had been so concerned about Timmy that she had quite forgotten it.

Timmy went over to the engine and smelt the wheels. Then he jumped up into the cab. Somehow the sight of Timmy doing that took away all George's fear. If Timmy could jump up into the spook-train, there couldn't be much for her to be afraid of!

She decided to examine the trucks. There were four of them, all covered trucks. Shining her torch, she climbed up into one of them, pulling Timmy up behind her. She expected to find it quite empty, unloaded many, many years ago by long-forgotten railwaymen.

But it was loaded with boxes! George was surprised. Why did a spook-train run about with boxes in it? She shone her torch on to one – and then quickly switched it out!

She had heard a noise in the tunnel. She crouched down in the truck, put her hand on Timmy's collar, and listened. Timmy listened, too, the hackles rising on his neck.

It was a clanging noise. Then there came a bang. Then a light shone out, and the tunnel was suddenly as bright as day!

The light came from a great lamp in the side of the tunnel. George peeped cautiously out through a crack in the truck. She saw that this place must be where the tunnel forked. One fork went on to Kilty's Yard – but surely the other fork was supposed to be bricked up? George followed the lines with her eyes. One set went on down the tunnel to Kilty's Yard, the other set ran straight into a great wall, which was built across the second tunnel, that once led to Roker's Yard.

'Yes – it *is* bricked up, just as the old porter told Julian,' said George to herself. And then she stared in the greatest amazement, clutching the side of the truck, hardly believing her eyes.

Part of the wall was opening before her! Before her very eyes, a great mass of it slid back in the centre of the wall – back and back – until a strange-shaped opening, about the size of the train itself, showed in the thick wall. George gasped. Whatever could be happening?

A man came through the opening. George felt sure she

had seen him before somewhere. He came up to the engine of the train and swung himself into the cab.

There were all sorts of sounds then from the cab. What was the man doing? Starting the fire to run the train? George did not dare to try and see. She was trembling now, and Timmy pressed himself against her to comfort her.

Then came another set of noises – steam noises. The man must be going to start the engine moving. Smoke came from the funnel. More noises, and some clanks and clangs.

It suddenly occurred to George that the man might be going to take the train through that little opening in the

bricked-up wall. Then – supposing he shut the wall up again – George would be a prisoner! She would be in the truck, hidden behind that wall, and the wall would be closed so that she couldn't escape.

'I must get out before it's too late,' thought George, in a panic. 'I only hope the man doesn't see me!'

But just as she was about to try and get out, the engine gave a loud 'choo-choo', and began to move backwards! It ran down the lines a little way, then forward again, and this time its wheels were on the set of lines that led to the second tunnel, where the small opening now showed so clearly in the wall.

George didn't dare to get out of the moving train. So there she crouched as the engine steamed quickly to the hole in the wall that stretched right across the other tunnel. That hole just fitted it! It must have been made for it, thought George, as the train moved through it.

The train went right through and came out in another tunnel. Here there was a bright light, too. George peered out through the crack. There was more than a tunnel here! What looked like vast caves stretched away on each side of the tunnel, and men lounged about in them. Who on earth were they, and what were they doing with that old train?

There was a curious noise at the back of the train. The hole in the stout brick wall closed up once more! Now there was no way in or out. 'It's like the Open-Sesame trick in *Ali Baba and the Forty Thieves*,' thought George. 'And, like Ali Baba, I'm in the cave – and don't know the way to get myself out! Thank goodness Timmy is with me!'

The train was now at a standstill. Behind it was the thick wall – and then George saw that in front of it was a thick wall, too! This tunnel must be bricked up in two places – and in between was this extraordinary cavern, or whatever it was. George puzzled her head over the strange place, but couldn't make head or tail of it.

'Well! Whatever would the others say if they knew you and I were actually in the spook-train itself, tucked away in its hiding-place where nobody in the world can find it?' whispered George to Timmy. 'What are we to do, Timmy?'

Timmy wagged his tail cautiously. He didn't understand all this. He wanted to lie low for a bit and see how things turned out.

'We'll wait till the men have gone away, Timmy,' whispered George. 'That is, if they ever do! Then we'll get out and see if we can manage that Open-Sesame entrance and get away. We'd better tell Mr Luffy about all this. There's something very strange and very mysterious here – and we've fallen headlong into it!'

CHAPTER SIXTEEN

In the tunnel again

JOCK WAS really enjoying himself at the camp. He had a picnic lunch with the others, and ate as much as they did, looking very happy. Mr Luffy joined them, and Jock beamed at him, feeling that he was a real friend.

'Where's George?' asked Mr Luffy.

'Gone off by herself,' said Julian.

'Have you quarrelled, by any chance?' said Mr Luffy.

'A bit,' said Julian. 'We have to let George get over it by herself, Mr Luffy. She's like that.'

'Where's she gone?' said Mr Luffy, helping himself to a tomato. 'Why isn't she back to dinner?'

'She's taken hers with her,' said Anne. 'I feel a bit worried about her, somehow. I hope she's all right.'

Mr Luffy looked alarmed. 'I feel a bit worried myself,' he said. 'Still, she's got Timmy with her.'

'We're going off on a bit of exploring,' said Julian, when they had all finished eating. 'What are *you* going to do, Mr Luffy?'

'I think I'll come with you,' said Mr Luffy, unexpectedly. The children's hearts sank. They couldn't possibly go exploring for spook-trains in the tunnel if Mr Luffy was with them.

'Well – I don't think it will be very interesting for you, sir,' said Julian, rather feebly. However, Mr Luffy took the hint and realised he wasn't wanted that afternoon.

'Right,' he said. 'In that case I'll stay here and mess about.'

The children sighed with relief. Anne cleared up, with Jock helping her, and then they called goodbye to Mr Luffy and set off, taking their tea with them.

Jock was full of excitement. He was so pleased to be with the others, and he kept thinking of sleeping in the camp that night – what fun it would be! Good old Mr Luffy, taking his side like that. He bounded after the others joyfully as they went off to the old railway yard.

Wooden-Leg Sam was pottering about there as usual. They waved to him, but he didn't wave back. Instead he shook his fist at them and tried to bawl in his husky voice: 'You clear out! Trespassing, that's what you are. Don't you come down here or I'll chase you!'

'Well, we won't go down then,' said Dick, with a grin. 'Poor old man – thinking of chasing us with that wooden leg of his. We won't give him the chance. We'll just walk along here, climb down the lines and walk up them to the tunnel.'

Which is what they did, much to the rage of poor Sam. He yelled till his voice gave out, but they took no notice, and walked quickly up the lines. The mouth of the tunnel looked very round and black as they came near.

'Now we'll jolly well walk right through this tunnel and

see where that spook-train is that came out of it the other night,' said Julian. 'It didn't come out the other end, so it *must* be somewhere in the middle of the tunnel.'

'If it's a real spook-train, it might completely disappear,' said Anne, not liking the look of the dark tunnel at all. The others laughed.

'It won't have disappeared,' said Dick. 'We shall come across it somewhere, and we'll examine it thoroughly and try and find out exactly what it is, and why it comes and goes in such a mysterious manner.'

They walked into the black tunnel, and switched on their torches, which made little gleaming paths in front of them. They walked up the middle of one pair of lines, Julian in front keeping a sharp lookout for anything in the shape of a train!

The lines ran on and on. The children's voices sounded weird and echoing in the long tunnel. Anne kept close to Dick, and half wished she hadn't come. Then she remembered that George had called her a coward, and she put up her head, determined not to show that she was scared.

Jock talked almost without stopping. 'I've never done anything like this in my life. I call this a proper adventure, hunting for spook-trains in a dark tunnel. It makes me feel nice and shivery all over. I do hope we find the train. It simply *must* be here somewhere!'

They walked on and on and on. But there was no sign of any train. They came to where the tunnel forked into the second one, that used to run to Roker's Vale.

Julian flashed his torch on the enormous brick wall that stretched across the second tunnel.

'Yes, it's well and truly bricked up,' he said. 'So that only leaves this tunnel to explore. Come on.'

They went on again, little knowing that George and Timmy were behind that brick wall, hidden in a truck of the spook-train itself! They walked on and on down the lines, and found nothing interesting at all.

They saw a little round circle of bright light some way in front of them. 'See that?' said Julian. 'That must be the end of this tunnel – the opening that goes into Kilty's Yard. Well, if the train isn't between here and Kilty's Yard, it's gone!'

In silence they walked down the rest of the tunnel, and came out into the open air. Workshops were built all over Kilty's Yard. The entrance to the tunnel was weed-grown and neglected. Weeds grew even across the lines there.

'Well, no train has been out of this tunnel here for years,' said Julian, looking at the thick weeds. 'The wheels would have chopped the weeds to bits.'

'It's extraordinary,' said Dick, puzzled. 'We've been right through the tunnel and there's no train there at all, yet we know it goes in and out of it. What's happened to it?'

'It *is* a spook-train,' said Jock, his face red with excitement. 'Must be. It only exists at night, and then comes out on its lines, like it used to do years ago.'

'I don't like thinking that,' said Anne, troubled. 'It's a horrid thought.'

'What are we going to do now?' Julian asked. 'We seem to have come to a blank. No train, nothing to see, empty tunnel. What a dull end to an adventure.'

'Let's walk back all the way again,' said Jock – he wanted to squeeze as much out of this adventure as he could. 'I know we shan't see the train this time any more than we did the last time, but you never know!'

'I'm not coming through that tunnel again,' said Anne. 'I want to be out in the sun. I'll walk over the top of the tunnel, along the path there that Julian took the other night and you three can walk back, and meet me at the other end.'

'Right,' said Julian and the three boys disappeared into the dark tunnel. Anne ran up the path that led alongside the top of it. How good it was to be in the open air again! That horrid tunnel! She ran along cheerfully, glad to be out in the sun.

She got to the other end of the tunnel quite quickly, and sat down on the path above the yard to wait for the others. She looked for Wooden-Leg Sam. He was nowhere to be seen. Perhaps he was in his little hut.

She hadn't been there for more than two minutes when something surprising happened. A car came bumping slowly down the rough track to the yard! Anne sat up and watched. A man got out – and Anne's eyes almost fell out of her head. Why, it was – surely it was Mr Andrews, Jock's stepfather!

He went over to Sam's hut and threw open the door.

Anne could hear the sound of voices. Then she heard another noise – the sound of a heavy lorry coming. She saw it came cautiously down the steep, rough track. It ran into an old tumbledown shed and stayed there. Then three men came out and Anne stared at them. Where had she seen them before?

'Of course! They're the farm labourers at Jock's farm!' she thought. 'But what are they doing here? How very strange!'

Mr Andrews joined the men and, to Anne's dismay, they began to walk up the lines to the tunnel! Her heart almost stopped. Goodness, Julian, Dick and Jock were still in that tunnel, walking through it. They would bump right into Mr Andrews and his men – and then what would happen? Mr Andrews had warned them against going there, and had ordered Jock not to go.

Anne stared at the four men walking into the far-off mouth of the tunnel. What could she do? How could she warn the boys? She couldn't! She would just have to stay there and wait for them to come out – probably chased by a furious Mr Andrews and the other men. Oh dear, dear – if they were caught they would probably all get an awful telling off! What *could* she do?

'I can only wait,' thought poor Anne. 'There's nothing else to do. Oh, do come, Julian, Dick and Jock. I daren't do anything but wait for you.'

She waited and waited. It was now long past tea-time. Julian had the tea, so there was nothing for Anne to eat.

Nobody came out of the tunnel. Not a sound was heard. Anne at last decided to go down and ask Wooden-Leg Sam a few questions. So, rather afraid, the girl set off down to the yard.

Sam was in his hut, drinking cocoa, and looking very sour. Something had evidently gone wrong. When he saw Anne's shadow across the doorway he got up at once, shaking his fist.

'What, you children again! You went into that tunnel this afternoon, and so I went up and telephoned Mr Andrews to come and catch you all, poking your noses in all the time. How did you get out of that tunnel? Are the others with you? Didn't Mr Andrews catch you, eh?'

Anne listened to all this in horror. So old Sam had actually managed to telephone Mr Andrews, and tell tales on them – so that Jock's stepfather and his men had come to catch them. This was worse than ever.

'You come in here,' said Sam suddenly, and he darted his big arm at her. 'Come on. I don't know where the others are, but I'll get one of you!'

Anne gave a scream and ran away at top speed. Wooden-Leg Sam went after her for a few yards and then gave it up. He bent down and picked up a handful of cinders. A shower of them fell all round Anne, and made her run faster than ever.

She tore up the path to the heather, and was soon on the moors again, panting and sobbing. 'Oh, Julian! Oh, Dick!

What's happened to you? Oh, where's George? If only she would come home, she'd be brave enough to look for them, but I'm not. I must tell Mr Luffy. He'll know what to do!'

She ran on and on, her feet catching continually in the tufts of thick heather. She kept falling over and scrambling up again. She now had only one idea in her mind – to find Mr Luffy and tell him every single thing! Yes, she would tell him about the spook-trains and all. There was something strange and important about the whole thing now, and she wanted a grown-up's help.

She staggered on and on. 'Mr Luffy! Oh, Mr Luffy, where are you? MR LUFFY!'

But no Mr Luffy answered her. She came round the gorse bushes she thought were the ones sheltering the camp – but, alas, the camp was not there. Anne had lost her way!

'I'm lost,' said Anne, the tears running down her cheeks. 'But I mustn't get scared. I must try to find the right path now. Oh, dear, I'm quite lost! MR LUFFY!'

Poor Anne. She stumbled on blindly, hoping to come to the camp, calling every now and again. 'Mr Luffy. Can you hear me? MR LUFFFFFFFY!'

CHAPTER SEVENTEEN

An amazing find

IN THE meantime, what had happened to the three boys walking back through the tunnel? They had gone slowly along examining the lines to see if a train could have possibly run along them recently. Few weeds grew in the dark airless tunnel, so they could not tell by those.

But, when they came about half-way, Julian noticed an interesting thing. 'Look,' he said, flashing his torch on to the lines before and behind them. 'See that? The lines are black and rusty behind us now, but here this pair of lines is quite bright – as if they had been used a lot.'

He was right. Behind them stretched black and rusty lines, sometimes buckled in places – but in front of them, stretching to the mouth of the tunnel leading to Olly's Yard, the lines were bright, as if train-wheels had run along them.

'That's funny,' said Dick. 'Looks as if the spook-train ran only from here to Olly's Yard and back. But why? And where in the world is it now? It's vanished into thin air!'

Julian was as puzzled as Dick. Where *could* a train be if it was not in the tunnel? It had obviously run to the middle of the tunnel, and then stopped – but where had it gone now?

'Let's go to the mouth of the tunnel and see if the lines are bright all the way,' said Julian at last. 'We can't discover much here – unless the train suddenly materialises in front of us!'

They went on down the tunnel, their torches flashing on the lines in front of them. They talked earnestly as they went. They didn't see four men waiting for them, four men who crouched in a little niche at the side of the tunnel, waiting there in the dark.

'Well,' said Julian, 'I think—' and then he stopped, because four dark figures suddenly pounced on the three boys and held them fast. Julian gave a shout and struggled, but the man who had hold of him was far too strong to escape from. Their torches were flung to the ground. Julian's broke, and the other two torches lay there, their beams shining on the feet of the struggling company.

It didn't take more than twenty seconds to make each boy a captive, his arms behind his back. Julian tried to kick, but his captor twisted his arm so fiercely that he groaned in pain and stopped his kicking.

'Look here! What's all this about?' demanded Dick. 'Who are you, and what do you think you're doing? We're only three boys exploring an old tunnel. What's the harm in that?'

'Take them all away,' said a voice that everyone recognised at once.

'Mr Andrews! Is it you?' cried Julian. 'Set us free. You

know us – the boys at the camp. And Jock's here too. What do you think you're doing?'

Mr Andrews didn't answer, but he gave poor Jock a box on the right ear that almost sent him to the ground.

Their captors turned them about, and led them roughly up the tunnel, towards the middle. Nobody had a torch so it was all done in the darkness and the three boys stumbled badly, though the men seemed sure-footed enough.

They came to a halt after a time. Mr Andrews left them and Julian heard him go off somewhere to the left. Then there came a curious noise – a bang, a clank, and then a sliding, grating sound. What could be happening? Julian strained his eyes in the darkness, but he could see nothing at all.

He didn't know that Mr Andrews was opening the bricked-up wall through which the train had gone. He didn't know that he and the others were being pushed out of the first tunnel into the other one, through the curious hole in the wall. The three boys were shoved along in the darkness, not daring to protest.

Now they were in the curious place between the two walls which were built right across the place where the second tunnel forked from the first one. The place where the spook-train stood in silence – the place where George was, still hidden in one of the trucks with Timmy! But nobody knew that, of course; not even Mr Andrews guessed that a girl and a dog were listening in a truck nearby!

He put on a torch and flashed it in the faces of the three boys, who, although they were not showing any fear, felt rather scared all the same. This was so weird and unexpected, and they had no idea where they were at all.

'You were warned not to go down to that yard,' said the voice of one of the men. 'You were told it was a bad and dangerous place. So it is. And you've got to suffer for not taking heed of the warning! You'll be tied up and left here till we've finished our business. Maybe that'll be three days, maybe it'll be three weeks!'

'Look here, you can't keep us prisoner for all that time!' said Julian, alarmed. 'Why, there will be search parties out for us all over the place! They will be sure to find us.'

'Oh, no they won't,' said the voice. 'Nobody will find you here. Now, Peters – tie 'em up!'

Peters tied the three boys up. They had their legs tied, and their arms too, and were set down roughly against a wall. Julian protested again.

'What are you doing this for? We're quite harmless. We don't know a thing about your business, whatever it is.'

'We're not taking any chances,' said the voice. It was not Mr Andrews's voice, but a firm, strong one, full of determination and a large amount of annoyance.

'What about Mum?' said Jock suddenly, to his stepfather. 'She'll be worried.'

'Well, let her be worried,' said the voice again, answering before Mr Andrews could say a word. 'It's your own fault. You were warned.'

The feet of the four men moved away. Then there came the same noises again as the boys had heard before. They were made by the hole in the wall closing up, but the boys didn't know that. They couldn't imagine what they were. The noises stopped and there was dead silence. There was also pitch darkness. The three boys strained their ears, and felt sure that the men had gone.

'Well! The brutes! Whatever are they up to?' said Julian in a low voice, trying to loosen the ropes round his hands.

'They've got some secret to hide,' said Dick. 'Gosh, they've tied my feet so tightly that the rope is cutting into my flesh.'

'What's going to happen?' came Jock's scared voice. This adventure didn't seem quite so grand to him now.

'Sh!' said Julian suddenly. 'I can hear something!'

They all lay and listened. What was it they could hear?

'It's – it's a dog whining,' said Dick, suddenly.

It was. It was Timmy in the truck with George. He had heard the voices of the boys he knew, and he wanted to get to them. But George, not sure yet that the men had gone, still had her hand on his collar. Her heart beat for joy to think she was alone no longer. The three boys – and Anne, too, perhaps – were there, in the same strange place as she and Timmy were.

The boys listened hard. The whining came again. Then, George let go her hold of Timmy's collar, and he leapt headlong out of the truck. His feet pattered eagerly over the ground. He went straight to the boys in the darkness, and Julian felt a wet tongue licking his face. A warm body pressed against him, and a little bark told him who it was.

'Timmy! I say, Dick – it's Timmy!' cried Julian, in joy. 'Where did he come from? Timmy, is it really you?'

'Woof,' said Timmy, and licked Dick next and then Jock.

'Where's George then?' wondered Dick.

'Here,' said a voice, and out of the truck scrambled George, switching on her torch as she did so. She went over to the boys. 'Whatever's happened? How did you come here? Were you captured or something?'

'Yes,' said Julian. 'But, George – where are we? And what are *you* doing here too? It's like a peculiar dream!'

'I'll cut your ropes first, before I stop to explain anything,' said George, and she took out her sharp knife. In a few moments she had cut the boys' bonds, and they all sat up, rubbing their sore ankles and wrists, groaning.

'Thanks, George! Now I feel fine,' said Julian, getting up. 'Where *are* we? Gracious, is that an engine there? What's it doing here?'

'That, Julian, is the spook-train!' said George, with a laugh. 'Yes, it is, really.'

'But we walked all the way down the tunnel and out of the other end, without finding it,' said Julian puzzled. 'It's most mysterious.'

'Listen, Ju,' said George. 'You know where that second tunnel is bricked up, don't you? Well, there's a way in through the wall – a whole bit of it moves back in a sort of Open-Sesame manner! The spook-train can run in through the hole, on the rails. Once it's beyond the wall it stops, and the hole is closed up again.'

George switched her torch round to show the astonished boys the wall through which they had come. Then she swung her torch to the big wall opposite. 'See that?' she said. 'There are *two* walls across this second tunnel, with a big space in between – where the spook-train hides! Clever, isn't it?'

'It would be, if I could see any sense in it,' said Julian. 'But I can't. Why should anyone mess about with a silly spook-train at night?'

'That's what we've got to find out,' said George. 'And now's our chance. Look, Julian – look at all the caves stretching out on either side of the tunnel here. They would make wonderful hiding-places!'

'What for?' said Dick. 'I can't make head or tail of this!'

George swung her torch on the three boys and then asked a sudden question: 'I say – where's Anne?'

'Anne! She didn't want to come back with us through the tunnel, so she ran over the moorlands to meet us at the other end, by Olly's Yard,' said Julian. 'She'll be worried stiff, won't she, when we don't turn up? I only hope she doesn't come wandering up the tunnel to meet us – she'll run into those men if she does.'

Everyone felt worried. Anne hated the tunnel and she would be very frightened if people pounced on her in the darkness. Julian turned to George.

'Swing your torch round and let's see these caves. There doesn't seem to be anyone here now. We could have a snoop round.'

George swung her torch round, and Julian saw vast and apparently fathomless caves stretching out on either side, cut out of the sides of the tunnel. Jock saw something else. By the light of the torch he caught sight of a switch on the wall. Perhaps it opened the hole in the wall.

He crossed to it and pulled it down. Immediately the place was flooded with a bright light. It was a light-switch he had found. They all blinked in the sudden glare.

'That's better,' said Julian, pleased. 'Good for you, Jock! Now we can see what we're doing.'

He looked at the spook-train standing silently near them on its rails. It certainly looked very old and forgotten – as if it belonged to the last century, not to this.

'It's quite a museum piece,' said Julian, with interest. 'So that's what we heard puffing in and out of the tunnel at night – old Spooky!'

'I hid in that truck there,' said George, pointing, and she told them her own adventure. The boys could hardly believe she had actually puffed into this secret place, hidden on the spook-train itself!

'Come on – now let's look at these caves,' said Dick. They went over to the nearest one. It was packed with crates and boxes of all kinds. Julian pulled one open and whistled.

'All black market stuff, I imagine. Look here – crates of tea, crates of whisky and brandy, boxes and boxes of stuff – goodness knows what! This is a real black market hiding-place!'

The boys explored a little further. The caves were piled high with valuable stuff, worth thousands of pounds.

'All stolen, I suppose,' said Dick. 'But what do they *do* with it? I mean – how do they dispose of it? They bring it here in the train, of course, and hide it – but they must have some way of getting rid of it.'

'Would they repack it on the train and run it back to the yard when they had enough lorries to take it away?' said Julian.

'No!' said Dick. 'Of course not. Let me see – they steal it, pile it on to lorries at night, take it somewhere temporarily . . .'

'Yes – to my mother's farm!' said Jock, in a scared voice. 'All those lorries there in the barn – that's what they're used for! And they come down to Olly's Yard at night and the stuff is loaded in secret on the old train that comes puffing out to meet them – and then it's taken back here and hidden!'

'Wheeeee-ew!' Julian whistled. 'You're right, Jock! That's just what happens. What a cunning plot – to use a perfectly honest little farm as a hiding-place, to stock the farm with black-market men for labourers – no wonder they are such bad workers – and to wait for dark nights to run the stuff down to the yard and load it on the train!'

'Your stepfather must make a lot of money at this game,' said Dick to Jock.

'Yes. That's why he can afford to pour money into the farm,' said Jock, miserably. 'Poor Mum. This will break her heart. All the same, I don't think my stepfather's the chief one in this. There's somebody behind him.'

'Yes,' said Julian, thinking of the mean little Mr Andrews, with his big nose and weak chin. 'There probably is. Now – I've thought of something else. If this stuff is got rid of in any other way except down the tunnel it came up, there must somewhere be a way out of these caves!'

'I believe you're right,' said George. 'And if there is – we'll find it! And what's more, we'll escape that way!'

'Come on!' said Julian, and he switched off the glaring light. 'Your torch will give enough light now. We'll try this cave first. Keep your eyes open, all of you!'

CHAPTER EIGHTEEN

A way of escape

THE FOUR children and Timmy went into the big cave. They made their way round piles of boxes, chests and crates, marvelling at the amount the men must have stolen from time to time.

'These aren't man-made caves,' said Julian. 'They're natural. I expect the roof did perhaps fall in where the two tunnels met, and the entrance between them was actually blocked up.'

'But were *two* walls built then?' said Dick.

'Oh, no. We can't guess how it was that this black market hiding-place came into existence,' said Julian, 'but it might perhaps have been known there were caves here – and when someone came prospecting along the tunnel one day, maybe they even found an old train buried under a roof-fall or something like that.'

'And resurrected it, and built another wall secretly for a hiding-place – and used the train for their own purposes!' said Dick. 'Made that secret entrance, too. How ingenious!'

'Or it's possible the place was built during the last war,' said Julian. 'Maybe secret experiments were carried on here – and given up afterwards. The place might have been discovered by the black marketeers then, and used in this clever way. We can't tell!'

They had wandered for a good way in the cave by now, without finding anything of interest beyond the boxes and chests of all kinds of goods. Then they came to where a pile was very neatly arranged, with numbers chalked on boxes that were built up one on top of another. Julian halted.

'Now this looks as if these boxes were about to be shifted off somewhere,' he said. 'All put in order and numbered. Surely the exit must be somewhere here?'

He took George's torch from her and flashed it all round. Then he found what he wanted. The beam of light shone steadily on a strong roughly-made wooden door, set in the wall of the cave. They went over to it in excitement.

'This is what we want!' said Julian. 'I bet this is the exit to some very lonely part of the moors, not far from a road that lorries can come along to collect any goods carried out of here! There are some very deserted roads over these moors, running in the middle of miles of lonely moorland.'

'It's a clever organisation,' said Dick. 'Lorries stored at an innocent farm, full of goods for hiding in the tunnel-caves at a convenient time. The train comes out in the dark to collect the goods, and takes them back here, till the hue and cry after the goods has died down. Then out they go through this door to the moorlands, down to the lorries which come to collect them and whisk them away to the black market!'

'I told you how I saw Peters late one night, locking up the barn, didn't I?' said Jock, excitedly. 'Well, he must have got the lorry full of stolen goods then – and the next night he loaded them on to the spook-train!'

'That's about it,' said Julian, who had been trying the door to see if he could open it. 'I say, this door's maddening. I can't make it budge an inch. There's no lock that I can see.'

They all shoved hard, but the door would not give at all. It was very stout and strong, though rough and unfinished. Panting and hot, the four of them at last gave it up.

'Do you know what I think?' said Dick. 'I think the beastly thing has got something jammed hard against it on the outside.'

'Sure to have, when you come to think of it,' said Julian. 'It will be well hidden too – heather and bracken and stuff all over it. Nobody would ever find it. I suppose the lorry-drivers come across from the road to open the door when they want to collect the goods. And shut it and jam it after them.'

'No way of escape there, then,' said George in disappointment.

''Fraid not,' said Julian. George gave a sigh.

'Tired, old thing?' Julian asked kindly. 'Or hungry?'

'Both,' said George.

'Well, we've got some food somewhere, haven't we?' said Julian. 'I remember one of the men slinging my bag in after me. We've not had what we brought for tea yet. What about having a meal now? We can't seem to escape at the moment.'

'Let's have it here,' said George. 'I simply can't go a step further!'

They sat down against a big crate. Dick undid his kitbag. There were sandwiches, cake and chocolate. The four of them ate thankfully, and wished they had something to wash down the food with. Julian kept wondering about Anne.

'I wonder what she did,' he said. 'She'd wait and wait, I suppose. Then she might go back to the camp. But she doesn't know the way very well, and she might get lost. Oh dear – I don't know which would be worse for Anne, being lost on the moor or a prisoner down here with us!'

'Perhaps she's neither,' said Jock, giving Timmy his last bit of sandwich. 'I must say I'm jolly glad to have Timmy. Honest, George, I couldn't believe it when I heard Tim whine, and then heard your voice, too. I thought I must be dreaming.'

They sat where they were for a little longer and then decided to go back to the tunnel where the train was. 'It's just possible we might find the switch that works the Open-Sesame bit,' said Julian. 'We ought to have looked before, really, but I didn't think of it.'

They went back to where the train stood silently on its pair of lines. It seemed such an ordinary old train now that the children couldn't imagine why they had ever thought it was strange and spooky.

They switched on the light again, then they looked about for any lever or handle that might perhaps open the hole in the wall. There didn't seem to be anything at all. They tried a few switches, but nothing happened.

Then George suddenly came across a big lever low down in the brick wall itself. She tried to move it and couldn't. She called Julian.

'Ju! Come here. I wonder if this has got anything to do with opening that hole.'

The three boys came over to George. Julian tried to swing the lever down. Nothing happened. He pulled it but it wouldn't move. Then he and Dick pushed it upwards with all their strength.

And hey presto, there came a bang from somewhere, as

something heavy shifted, and then a clanking as if machinery was at work. Then came the sliding, grating noise and a great piece of the brick wall moved slowly back, and then swung round sideways and stopped. The way of escape was open!

'Open Sesame!' said Dick, grandly, as the hole appeared.

'Better switch off the light here,' said Julian. 'If there's anyone still in the tunnel they might see the reflection of it on the tunnel-wall beyond, and wonder what it was.'

He stepped back and switched it off, and the place was in darkness again. George put on her torch, and its feeble beam lighted up the way of escape.

'Come on,' said Dick, impatiently, and they all crowded out of the hole. 'We'll make for Olly's Yard.' They began to make their way down the dark tunnel.

'Listen,' said Julian, in a low voice. 'We'd better not talk at all, and we'd better go as quietly as we can. We don't know who may be in or out of this tunnel this evening. We don't want to walk bang into somebody.'

So they said nothing at all, but kept close to one another in single file, walking at the side of the track.

They had not gone more than a quarter of a mile before Julian stopped suddenly. The others bumped into one another, and Timmy gave a little whine as somebody trod on his paw. George's hand went down to his collar at once.

The four of them and Timmy listened, hardly daring to

breathe. Somebody was coming up the tunnel towards them! They could see the pin-point of a torch, and hear the distant crunch of footsteps.

'Other way, quick!' whispered Julian, and they all turned. With Jock leading them now, they made their way as quickly and quietly as they could back to the place where the two tunnels met. They passed it and went on towards Kilty's Yard, hoping to get out that way.

But alas for their hopes, a lantern stood some way down the tunnel there, and they did not dare to go on. There might be nobody with the lantern – on the other hand there might. What were they to do?

'They'll see that hole in the wall is open!' suddenly said Dick. 'We left it open. They'll know we've escaped then. We're caught again! They'll come down to find us, and here we'll be!'

They stood still, pressed close together, Timmy growling a little in his throat. Then George remembered something!

'Julian! Dick! We could climb up that vent that I came down,' she whispered. 'The one poor old Timmy fell down. Have we time?'

'Where is the vent?' said Julian, urgently. 'Quick, find it.'

George tried to remember. Yes, it was on the other side of the tunnel – near the place where the two tunnels met. She must look for the pile of soot. How she hoped the little light from her torch would not be seen. Whoever was coming up from Olly's Yard must be almost there by now!

She found the pile of soot that Timmy had fallen into. 'Here it is,' she whispered. 'But, oh, Julian! How can we take Timmy?'

'We can't,' said Julian. 'We must hope he'll manage to hide and then slink out of the tunnel by himself. He's quite clever enough.'

He pushed George up the vent first and her feet found the first rungs. Then Jock went up, his nose almost on George's heels. Then Dick – and last of all, Julian. But before he managed to climb the first steps, something happened.

A bright glare filled the tunnel, as someone switched on

the light that hung there. Timmy slunk into the shadows and growled in his throat. Then there came a shout.

'Who's opened the hole in the wall? It's open! Who's there?'

It was Mr Andrews's voice. Then came another voice, angry and loud: 'Who's here? Who's opened this place?'

'Those kids can't have moved the lever,' said Mr Andrews. 'We bound them up tightly.'

The men, three of them, went quickly through the hole in the wall. Julian climbed up the first few rungs thankfully. Poor Timmy was left in the shadows at the bottom.

Out came the men at a run. 'They've gone! Their ropes are cut! How could they have escaped? We put Kit down one end of the tunnel and we've been walking up this end. Those kids must be about here somewhere.'

'Or hiding in the caves,' said another voice. 'Peters, go and look, while we hunt here.'

The men hunted everywhere. They had no idea that the vent was nearby in the wall. They did not see the dog that slunk by them like a shadow, keeping out of their way, and lying down whenever the light from a torch came near him.

George climbed steadily, feeling with her feet for the iron nails whenever she came to broken rungs. Then she came to a stop. Something was pressing on her head. What was it? She put up her hand to feel. It was the collection of broken iron bars that Timmy had fallen on that morning. He had dislodged some of them, and they had then fallen in such a way that they had lodged across the vent, all twined into each other. George could climb no higher. She tried to move the bars, but they were heavy and strong – besides, she was afraid she might bring the whole lot on top of her and the others. They might be badly injured then.

'What's up, George? Why don't you go on?' asked Jock, who was next.

'There's some iron bars across the vent – ones that must have fallen when Timmy fell,' said George. 'I can't go any higher! I daren't pull too hard at the bars.'

Jock passed the message to Dick, and he passed it down to Julian. The four of them came to a full-stop!

'Blow!' said Julian. 'I wish I'd gone up first. What are we to do now?'

What indeed? The four of them hung there in the darkness, hating the smell of the sooty old vent, miserably uncomfortable on the broken rungs and nails.

'How do you like adventures now, Jock?' asked Dick. 'I bet you wish you were in your own bed at home!'

'I don't!' said Jock. 'I wouldn't miss this for worlds! I always wanted an adventure – and I'm not grumbling at this one!'

CHAPTER NINETEEN

What an adventure!

AND NOW, what had happened to Anne? She had stumbled on and on for a long time, shouting to Mr Luffy. And outside his tent Mr Luffy sat, reading peacefully. But, as the evening came, and then darkness, he became very worried indeed about the five children.

He wondered what to do. It was hopeless for one man to search the moors. Half a dozen or more were needed for that! He decided to get his car and go over to Olly's Farm to get the men from there. So off he went.

But when he got there he found no one at home except Mrs Andrews and the little maid. Mrs Andrews looked bewildered and worried.

'What is the matter?' said Mr Luffy gently, as she came running out to the car, looking troubled.

'Oh, it's you, Mr Luffy,' she said, when he told her who he was. 'I didn't know who you were. Mr Luffy, something strange is happening. All the men have gone – and all the lorries, too. My husband has taken the car and nobody will tell me anything. I'm so worried.'

Mr Luffy decided not to add to her worries by telling her the children were missing. He just pretended he had come to collect some milk. 'Don't worry,' he said comfortingly to Mrs Andrews. 'You'll find things are all right in the morning, I expect. I'll come and see you then. Now I must be off on an urgent matter.'

He went bumping along the road in his car, puzzled. He had known there was something funny about Olly's Farm, and he had puzzled his brains a good deal over Olly's Yard and the spook-trains. He hoped the children hadn't got mixed up in anything dangerous.

'I'd better go down and report to the police that they're missing,' he thought. 'After all, I'm more or less responsible for them. It's very worrying indeed.'

He told what he knew at the police station, and the sergeant, an intelligent man, at once mustered six men and a police car.

'Have to find those kids,' he said. 'And we'll have to look into this Olly's Farm business, sir, and these here spook-trains, whatever they may be. We've known there was something funny going on, but we couldn't put our finger on it. But we'll find the children first.'

They went quickly up to the moors and the six men began to fan out to search, with Mr Luffy at the head. And the first thing they found was Anne!

She was still stumbling along, crying for Mr Luffy, but in a very small, weak voice now. When she heard his voice calling her in the darkness she wept for joy.

'Oh, Mr Luffy! You must save the boys,' she begged him. 'They're in that tunnel – and they've been caught by

Mr Andrews and his men, I'm sure. They didn't come out and I waited and waited! Do come!'

'I've got some friends here who will certainly come and help,' said Mr Luffy gently. He called the men, and in a few words told them what Anne had said.

'In the tunnel?' said one of them. 'Where the spook-trains run? Well, come on, men, we'll go down there.'

'You stay behind, Anne,' said Mr Luffy. But she wouldn't. So he carried her as he followed the men who were making their way through the heather, down to Olly's Yard. They did not bother with Wooden-Leg Sam. They went straight to the tunnel and walked up it quietly. Mr

Luffy was a good way behind with Anne. She refused to stay with him in the yard.

'No,' she said, 'I'm not a coward. Really I'm not. I want to help to rescue the boys. I wish George was here. Where's George?'

Mr Luffy had no idea. Anne clung to his hand, scared but eager to prove that she was not a coward. Mr Luffy thought she was grand!

Meanwhile, Julian and the others had been in the vent for a good while, tired and uncomfortable. The men had searched in vain for them and were now looking closely into every niche at the sides of the tunnel.

And, of course, they found the vent! One of the men shone his light up it. It shone on to poor Julian's feet! The man gave a loud shout that almost made Julian fall off the rung he was standing on.

'Here they are! Up this vent. Who'd have thought it? Come on down or it'll be the worse for you!'

Julian didn't move. George pushed desperately at the iron bars above her head, but she could not move them. One of the men climbed up the vent and caught hold of Julian's foot.

He dragged so hard at it that the boy's foot was forced off the rung. Then the man dragged off the other foot, and Julian found himself hanging by his arms with the man tugging hard at his feet. He could hang on no longer. His tired arms gave way and he fell heavily down, landing half on the man and half on the pile of soot. Another man pounced on Julian at once, while the first climbed up the vent to find the next boy. Soon Dick felt his feet being tugged at, too.

'All right, all right. I'll come down!' he yelled, and climbed down. Then Jock climbed down, too. The men looked at them angrily.

'Giving us a chase like this! Who undid your ropes?' said Mr Andrews, roughly. One of the men put a hand on his arm and nodded up towards the vent. 'Someone else is coming down,' he said. 'We only tied up three boys, didn't we? Who's this, then?'

It was George, of course. She wasn't going to desert the three boys. Down she came, as dark as night with soot.

'Another boy!' said the men. 'Where did he come from?'

'Any more up there?' asked Mr Andrews.

'Look and see,' said Julian, and got a box on the ears for his answer.

'Treat them rough now,' ordered Peters. 'Teach them a lesson, the little pests. Take them away.'

The children's hearts sank. The men caught hold of them roughly. Blow! Now they would be made prisoners again.

Suddenly a cry came from down the tunnel: 'Police! Run for it!'

The men dropped the children's arms at once and stood undecided. A man came tearing up the tunnel. 'I tell you the police are coming!' he gasped. 'Didn't you hear? There's a whole crowd of them. Run for it! Somebody's split on us.'

'Get along to Kilty's Yard!' shouted Peters. 'We can get cars there. Run for it!'

To the children's dismay, the men tore down the tunnel to Kilty's Yard. They would escape! They heard the sound of the men's feet as they ran along the line.

George found her voice. 'Timmy! Where are you? After them, Timmy! Stop them!'

A black shadow came streaking by out of the hole in the wall, where Timmy had been hiding and watching for a chance to come to George. He had heard her voice and obeyed. He raced after the men like a greyhound, his tongue hanging out, panting as he went.

These were the men who had ill-treated George and the others, were they? Aha, Timmy knew how to deal with people like that!

The policemen came running up, and Mr Luffy and Anne came up behind them.

'They've gone down there, with Timmy after them,' shouted George. The men looked at her and gasped. She was covered all over. The others were filthy dirty too, with sooty faces in the light of the lamp that still shone down from the wall of the tunnel.

'George!' shrieked Anne in delight. 'Julian! Oh, are you all safe? I went back to tell Mr Luffy about you and I got lost. I'm so ashamed!'

'You've nothing to be ashamed of, Anne,' said Mr Luffy. 'You're a grand girl! Brave as a lion!'

From down the tunnel came shouts and yells and loud

barks. Timmy was at work! He had caught up with the men and launched himself on them one after another, bringing each one heavily to the ground. They were terrified to find a big animal growling and snapping all around them. Timmy held them at bay in the tunnel, not allowing them to go one step further, snapping at any man who dared to go near.

The police ran up. Timmy growled extra fiercely just to let the men know that it was quite impossible to get by him. In a trice each of the men was imprisoned by a pair of strong arms and they were being told to come quietly.

They didn't go quietly. For one thing Mr Andrews lost his nerve and howled dismally. Jock felt very ashamed of him.

'Shut up,' said a burly policeman. 'We know you're only the miserable little cat's-paw – taking money from the big men to hold your tongue and obey orders.'

Timmy barked as if to say, 'Yes, don't you dare call him a *dog's* paw! That would be too good a name for him!'

'Well, I don't think I ever in my life saw dirtier children,' said Mr Luffy. 'I vote we all go back to my car and I drive the lot of you over to Olly's Farm for a meal and a bath!'

So back they all went, tired, dirty, and also feeling very thrilled.

What a night! They told Anne all that had happened, and she told them her story, too. She almost fell asleep in the car as she talked, she was so tired.

Mrs Andrews was sensible and kind, though upset to hear that her husband had been taken off by the police. She got hot water for baths, and laid a meal for the hungry children.

'I wouldn't worry overmuch, Mrs Andrews,' said kindly Mr Luffy. 'That husband of yours needs a lesson, you know. This will probably keep him going straight in future. The farm is yours, and you can now hire proper farm-workers who will do what you want them to do. And I think Jock will be happier without a stepfather for the present.'

'You're right, Mr Luffy,' said Mrs Andrews, wiping her eyes quickly. 'Quite right. I'll let Jock help me with the farm, and get it going beautifully. To think that Mr Andrews was in with all those black marketeers! It's that friend of his, you know, who makes him do all this. He's so weak. He knew Jock was snooping about in that tunnel, and that's why he wanted him to go away – and kept making him have a boy here or go out with him. I knew there was something funny going on.'

'No wonder he was worried when Jock took it into his head to go and camp with our little lot,' said Mr Luffy.

'To think of that old yard and tunnel being used again!' said Mrs Andrews. 'And all those tales about spook-trains – and the way they hid that train, and hid all the stuff, too. Why, it's like a fairy tale isn't it!'

She ran to see if the water was hot for the baths. It was, and she went to call the children, who were in the big bedroom next door. She opened it and looked in. Then she called Mr Luffy upstairs.

He looked in at the door, too. The five, and Timmy, were lying on the floor in a heap, waiting for the bath-water. They hadn't liked to sit on chairs or beds, they were so filthy. And they had fallen asleep where they lay, their faces as dirty as a sweep's.

'Talk about black marketeers!' whispered Mrs Andrews. 'Anyone would think we'd got the whole lot of them here in the bedroom!'

They all woke up and went to have a bath one by one, and a good meal after that. Then back to camp with Mr Luffy, Jock with them, too.

It was glorious to snuggle down into the sleeping-bags. George called out to the three boys.

'Now, don't you dare to go off without me tonight, see?'

'The adventure is over,' called back Dick. 'How did you like it, Jock?'

'Like it?' said Jock, with a happy sigh. 'It was simply – smashing!'

Enid Blyton®

is one of the most popular children's authors of all time. Her books have sold over 500 million copies and have been translated into other languages more often than any other children's author.

Enid Blyton adored writing for children. She wrote over 700 books and about 2,000 short stories. *The Famous Five* books, now 75 years old, are her most popular. She is also the author of other favourites including *The Secret Seven*, *The Magic Faraway Tree*, *Malory Towers* and *Noddy*.

Born in London in 1897, Enid lived much of her life in Buckinghamshire and loved dogs, gardening and the countryside. She was very knowledgeable about trees, flowers, birds and animals. Dorset – where some of the Famous Five's adventures are set – was a favourite place of hers too.

Enid Blyton's stories are read and loved by millions of children (and grown-ups) all over the world. Visit enidblyton.co.uk to discover more.

THE FAMOUS FIVE

FIVE GET INTO TROUBLE

Have you read all THE FAMOUS FIVE books?

1. Five on a Treasure Island
2. Five Go Adventuring Again
3. Five Run Away Together
4. Five Go to Smuggler's Top
5. Five Go Off in a Caravan
6. Five on Kirrin Island Again
7. Five Go Off to Camp
8. Five Get Into Trouble
9. Five Fall Into Adventure
10. Five on a Hike Together
11. Five Have a Wonderful Time
12. Five Go Down to the Sea
13. Five Go to Mystery Moor
14. Five Have Plenty of Fun
15. Five on a Secret Trail
16. Five Go to Billycock Hill
17. Five Get Into a Fix
18. Five on Finniston Farm
19. Five Go to Demon's Rocks
20. Five Have a Mystery to Solve
21. Five Are Together Again

The Famous Five Colour Short Stories

1. Five and a Half-Term Adventure
2. George's Hair is Too Long
3. Good Old Timmy
4. A Lazy Afternoon
5. Well Done, Famous Five
6. Five Have a Puzzling Time
7. Happy Christmas, Five
8. When Timmy Chased the Cat

Enid Blyton®

THE FAMOUS FIVE

FIVE GET INTO TROUBLE

Illustrated by Eileen A. Soper

HODDER CHILDREN'S BOOKS

First published in Great Britain in 1949 by Hodder & Stoughton
This edition published in 2016

21

A CIP catalogue record for this book is available from the British Library.

ISBN 978 1 444 93638 4

Printed and bound in Great Britain by Clays Ltd, Elcograf S.p.A.

The paper and board used in this book are made from wood from responsible sources.

Hodder Children's Books
An imprint of
Hachette Children's Group
Part of Hodder & Stoughton
Carmelite House
50 Victoria Embankment
London EC4Y 0DZ

An Hachette UK Company
www.hachette.co.uk
www.hachettechildrens.co.uk

CONTENTS

1	FIVE MAKE A HOLIDAY PLAN	1
2	AWAY ON THEIR OWN	9
3	A LOVELY DAY – AND A LOVELY NIGHT	17
4	RICHARD	26
5	SIX INSTEAD OF FIVE	34
6	ODD HAPPENINGS	42
7	RICHARD TELLS AN ALARMING TALE	52
8	WHAT'S THE BEST THING TO DO?	60
9	MOONLIGHT ADVENTURE	68
10	OWL'S DENE ON OWL'S HILL	75
11	TRAPPED!	84
12	JULIAN LOOKS ROUND	94
13	STRANGE SECRET	103
14	ROOKY IS VERY ANGRY	112
15	PRISONERS	122
16	AGGIE – AND HUNCHY	132
17	JULIAN HAS A BRIGHT IDEA	140
18	HUNT FOR RICHARD!	148
19	RICHARD HAS HIS OWN ADVENTURE	157
20	THE SECRET ROOM	166
21	A VERY EXCITING FINISH!	175

CHAPTER ONE

Five make a holiday plan

'REALLY, QUENTIN, you are *most* difficult to cope with!' said Aunt Fanny to her husband.

The four children sat at the table, eating breakfast, and looking very interested. What had Uncle Quentin done now? Julian winked at Dick, and Anne kicked George under the table. Would Uncle Quentin explode into a temper, as he sometimes did?

Uncle Quentin held a letter in his hand, which his wife had just given back to him after she had read it. It was the letter that was causing all the trouble. Uncle Quentin frowned – and then decided not to explode. Instead he spoke quite mildly.

'Well, Fanny dear – how can I possibly be expected to remember exactly when the children's holidays come, and if they are going to be here with us or with your sister? You know I have my scientific work to do – and very important it is too, at the moment. *I* can't remember when the children's schools break up or go back!'

'You could always ask *me*,' said Aunt Fanny, exasperated. 'Really, Quentin, have you forgotten how we discussed having Julian, Dick and Anne here these Easter holidays because they all enjoy Kirrin and the sea so much at this time of the year? You said you would arrange to go off to your conferences *after* they had had their holidays – not in the very middle of them!'

'But they've broken up so late!' said Uncle Quentin. 'I didn't know they were going to do that.'

'Well, but you know Easter came late this year, so they broke up late,' said Aunt Fanny, with a sigh.

'Father wouldn't think of that,' said George. 'What's the matter, Mother? Does Father want to go away in the middle of our holidays, or what?'

'Yes,' said Aunt Fanny, and she stretched out her hand for the letter again. 'Let me see, he would have to go off in two days' time and I must certainly go with him. I can't possibly leave you children alone here, with nobody in the house. If Joanna were not ill it would be all right, but she won't be back for a week or two.'

Joanna was the cook. The children were all very fond of her, and had been sorry to find her missing when they had arrived for the holidays.

'We can look after ourselves,' said Dick. 'Anne is quite a good cook.'

'I can help too,' said George. Her real name was Georgina, but everyone called her George. Her mother smiled.

'Oh, George, last time you boiled an egg you left it in the saucepan till it boiled dry! I don't think the others would like your cooking very much.'

'It was just that I forgot the egg was there,' said George.

'I went to fetch the clock to time it, and on the way I remembered Timmy hadn't had his dinner, and . . .'

'Yes, we know all about that,' said her mother with a laugh. 'Timmy had his dinner, but your father had to go without his tea!'

'Woof,' said Timmy from under the table, hearing his name mentioned. He licked George's foot just to remind her he was there.

'Well, let's get back to the subject,' said Uncle Quentin, impatiently. 'I've got to go to these conferences, that's certain. I've to read some important papers there. You needn't come with me, Fanny – you can stay and look after the children.'

'Mother doesn't need to,' said George. 'We can do something we badly wanted to do, but thought we'd have to put off till the summer hols.'

'Oh *yes*,' said Anne, at once. 'So we could! Do let's!'

'Yes – I'd like that too,' said Dick.

'Well – *what* is it?' asked Aunt Fanny. 'I'm quite in the dark. If it's anything dangerous, I shall say no. So make up your minds about that!'

'When do we *ever* do anything dangerous?' cried George.

'Plenty of times,' said her mother. 'Now, what's this plan of yours?'

'It's nothing much,' said Julian. 'It's only that all our bikes happen to be in first-class order, Aunt Fanny, and you know you gave us two small tents for Christmas – so we just thought it would be great fun sometime to go off on our bikes, taking our tents with us and do a little exploring round the countryside.'

'It's grand weather now – we could have fine fun,' said Dick. 'After all, you must have meant us to use the tents, Aunt Fanny! Here's our chance!'

'I meant you to use them in the garden, or on the beach,' said Aunt Fanny. 'Last time you went camping you had Mr Luffy with you to look after you. I don't think I like the idea of you going off by yourselves with tents.'

'Oh, Fanny, if *Julian* can't look after the others he must be a pretty feeble specimen,' said her husband, sounding impatient. 'Let them go! I'd bank on Julian any time to keep the others in order and see they were all safe and sound.'

'Thanks, Uncle,' said Julian, who was not used to compliments from his uncle Quentin! He glanced round at the other children and grinned. 'Of course, it's easy to manage this little lot – though Anne sometimes is *very* difficult!'

Anne opened her mouth indignantly. She was the smallest and the only really manageable one. She caught Julian's grin – he was teasing her, of course. She grinned back. 'I promise to be easy to manage,' she said in an innocent voice to her uncle Quentin.

He looked surprised. 'Well, I must say I should have thought that George was the only difficult one to . . .' he began, but stopped when he saw his wife's warning frown. George *was* difficult, but it didn't make her any less difficult if that fact was pointed out!

'Quentin, you never know when Julian is pulling your leg or not, do you?' said his wife. 'Well – if you *really* think Julian can be put in charge – and we can let them go off on a cycling tour – with their new tents . . .'

'Hurray! It's settled then!' yelled George, and began to thump Dick on the back in joy. 'We'll go off tomorrow. We'll . . .'

'GEORGE! There's no need to shout and thump like that,' said her mother. 'You know your father doesn't like it – and now you've excited Timmy too. Lie down, Timmy – there he's off round the room like a mad thing!'

Uncle Quentin got up to go. He didn't like it when mealtimes turned into pandemonium. He almost fell over the excited Timmy, and disappeared thankfully out of the room. What a household it was when the four children and the dog were there!

'Oh, Aunt Fanny, can we really go off tomorrow?' asked Anne, her eyes shining. 'It *is* such lovely April weather – honestly it's as hot as July. We hardly need to take any thick clothes with us.'

'Well, if you think that, you won't go,' said Aunt Fanny, firmly. 'It may be hot and sunny today, but you can never trust April to be the same two days together. It may be pouring tomorrow, and snowing on the next day! I shall have to give you money, Julian, so that you can go to an hotel any night the weather is bad.'

The four children immediately made up their minds that the weather would never be too bad!

'Won't it be fun?' said Dick. 'We can choose our own sleeping-place every night and put our tents there. We can bike half the night if it's moonlight, and we want to!'

'Ooooh – biking in moonlight – I've never done that,' said Anne. 'It sounds super.'

'Well, it's a good thing there is something you want to do while we are away,' said Aunt Fanny. 'Dear me, I've been married all these years to Quentin, and still he makes this kind of muddle without my knowing! Well, well, we'd better get busy today, and decide what you're to take.'

Everything suddenly seemed very exciting. The four children rushed to do their morning jobs of making the beds and tidying their rooms, talking at the tops of their voices.

'Who would have thought we'd be off on our own tomorrow!' said Dick, pulling his sheets and blankets up in a heap together.

'Dick! *I'll* make your bed,' cried Anne, shocked to see it made in such a hurried way. 'You can't possibly make it like that!'

'Oh, *can't* I!' cried Dick. 'You just wait and see! And what's more I'm making Julian's like that too, so you clear off and do your own, Anne – tuck in every corner, smooth the pillow, pat the eiderdown – do what you like with your own bed, but leave me to make mine my own way! Wait till we're off on our biking tour – you won't want to bother about beds then – you'll roll up your sleeping-bag and that will be that!'

He finished his bed as he spoke, dragging on the cover all crooked, and stuffing his pyjamas under the pillow. Anne laughed and went to make her own. She was excited too. The days stretched before her, sunny, full of strange places, unknown woods, big and little hills, chattering streams, wayside picnics, biking in the moonlight – did

Dick really mean that? How wizard!

They were all very busy that day, packing up into rucksacks the things they would need, folding up the tents into as small a compass as possible to tie on to their carriers, ferreting in the larder for food to take, looking out the maps they would want.

Timmy knew they were going off somewhere, and, of course, felt certain he was going too, so he was as excited as they were, barking and thumping his tail, and generally getting into everyone's way all day long. But nobody minded. Timmy was one of them, one of the 'Five', he could do almost everything but speak – it was quite unthinkable to go anywhere without dear old Timmy.

'I suppose Timothy can keep up with you all right, when you bike for miles?' Aunt Fanny asked Julian.

'Goodness yes,' said Julian. 'He never minds how far we go. I hope you won't worry about us, Aunt Fanny. You know what a good guard Timmy is.'

'Yes, I know,' said his aunt. 'I wouldn't be letting you go off like this with such an easy mind if I didn't know Timmy would be with you! He's as good as any grown-up at looking after you!'

'Woof, woof,' agreed Timmy. George laughed. 'He says he's as good as *two* grown-ups, Mother!' she said, and Timmy thumped his big tail on the floor.

'Woof, woof, *woof*,' he said. Which meant, 'Not two – but *three*!'

CHAPTER TWO

Away on their own

THEY WERE all ready the next day. Everything was neatly packed and strapped to the bicycles, except for the rucksacks, which each child was to carry on his or her back. The baskets held a variety of food for that day, but when it had been eaten Julian was to buy what they needed.

'I suppose all their brakes are in order?' said Uncle Quentin, thinking he ought to take some interest in the proceedings, and remembering that when *he* was a boy and had a bicycle, the brakes would never work.

'Oh, Uncle Quentin, of course they're all right,' said Dick. 'We'd never dream of going out on our bikes if the brakes and things weren't in order. The Highway Code is very strict about things like that, you know – and so are we!'

Uncle Quentin looked as if he had never even heard of the Highway Code. It was quite likely he hadn't. He lived in a world of his own, a world of theories and figures and diagrams – and he was eager to get back to it! However, he waited politely for the children to make last-minute adjustments, and then they were ready.

'Good-bye, Aunt Fanny! I'm afraid we shan't be able to

write to you, as you won't be able to get in touch with us to let us know where you get fixed up. Never mind, enjoy yourselves,' said Julian.

'Good-bye, Mother! Don't worry about us – we'll be having a jolly good time!' called George.

'Good-bye, Aunt Fanny; good-bye, Uncle Quentin!'

'So long, Uncle! Aunt Fanny, we're off!'

And so they were, cycling down the lane that led away from Kirrin Cottage. Their aunt and uncle stood at the gate, waving till the little party had disappeared round the corner in the sunshine. Timmy was loping along beside George's bicycle, on his long, strong legs, overjoyed at the idea of a really good run.

'Well, we're off,' said Julian, as they rounded the corner. 'What a bit of luck, going off like this by ourselves. Good old Uncle Quentin! I'm glad he made that muddle.'

'Don't let's ride too many miles the first day – I always get so stiff if we do,' said Anne.

'We're not going to,' said Dick. 'Whenever you feel tired just say so – it doesn't matter where we stop!'

The morning was very warm. Soon the children began to feel wet with perspiration. They had sweaters on and they took them off, stuffing them in their baskets. George looked more like a boy than ever, with her short curly hair blown up by the wind. All of them wore shorts and thin jerseys except Julian, who had on jeans. He rolled up the sleeves of his jersey, and the others did the same.

They covered mile after mile, enjoying the sun and the

wind. Timmy galloped beside them, untiring, his long pink tongue hanging out. He ran on the grassy edge of the road when there was one. He really was a very sensible dog!

They stopped at a tiny village called Manlington-Tovey. It had only one general store, but it sold practically everything – or seemed to! 'Hope it sells ginger-beer!' said Julian. 'My tongue's hanging out like Timmy's!'

The little shop sold lemonade, orangeade, lime juice, grapefruit juice and ginger-beer. It was really difficult to choose which to have. It also sold ice-creams, and soon the children were sitting drinking ginger-beer and lime juice mixed, and eating delicious ices.

'Timmy must have an ice,' said George. 'He does so love them. Don't you, Timmy?'

'Woof,' said Timmy, and gulped his ice down in two big, gurgly licks.

'It's really a waste of ice-creams to give them to Timmy,' said Anne. 'He hardly has time to taste them, he gobbles them so. No, Timmy, get down. I'm going to finish up every single bit of mine, and there won't be even a lick for you!'

Timmy went off to drink from a bowl of water that the shopwoman had put down for him. He drank and he drank, then he flopped down, panting.

The children took a bottle of ginger-beer each with them when they went off again. They meant to have it with their lunch. Already they were beginning to think with pleasure of eating the sandwiches put up into neat packets for them.

Anne saw some cows pulling at the grass in a meadow as they passed. 'It must be awful to be a cow and eat nothing but tasteless grass,' she called to George. 'Think what a cow misses – never tastes an egg and lettuce sandwich, never eats a chocolate eclair, never has a boiled egg – and can't even drink a glass of ginger-beer! Poor cows!'

George laughed. 'You do think of silly things, Anne,' she said. 'Now you've made me want my lunch all the more – talking about egg sandwiches and ginger-beer! I know Mother made us egg sandwiches – and sardine ones too.'

'It's no good,' chimed in Dick, leading the way into a little copse, his bicycle wobbling dangerously, 'it's no good – we can't go another inch if you girls are going to jabber about food all the time. Julian, what about lunch?'

It was a lovely picnic, that first one in the copse. There were clumps of primroses all round, and from somewhere nearby came the sweet scent of hidden violets. A thrush was singing madly on a hazel tree, with two chaffinches calling 'pink-pink' every time he stopped.

'Band and decorations laid on,' said Julian, waving his hand towards the singing birds and the primroses. 'Very nice too. We just want a waiter to come and present us with a menu!'

A rabbit lolloped near, its big ears standing straight up inquiringly. 'Ah – the waiter!' said Julian, at once. 'What have you to offer us today, Bunny? A nice rabbit-pie?'

The rabbit scampered off at top speed. It had caught the

smell of Timmy nearby and was panic-stricken. The children laughed, because it seemed as if it was the mention of rabbit-pie that had sent it away. Timmy stared at the disappearing rabbit, but made no move to go after it.

'Well, *Timmy*! That's the first time you've ever let a rabbit go off on its own,' said Dick. 'You *must* be hot and tired. Got anything for him to eat, George?'

'Of course,' said George. 'I made his sandwiches myself.'

And so she had! She had bought sausage meat at the butcher's and had actually made Timmy twelve sandwiches with it, all neatly cut and packed.

The others laughed. George never minded taking trouble over Timmy. He wolfed his sandwiches eagerly, and thumped his tail hard on the mossy ground. They all sat and munched happily, perfectly contented to be together out in the open air, eating a wonderful lunch.

Anne gave a scream. 'George! Look what you're doing! You're eating one of Timmy's sandwiches!'

'Urhh!' said George. 'I thought it tasted a bit strong. I must have given Timmy one of mine and taken his instead. Sorry, Tim!'

'Woof,' said Tim politely, and accepted another of his sandwiches.

'At the rate he eats them he wouldn't really notice if he had twenty or fifty,' remarked Julian. 'He's had all his now, hasn't he? Well, look out, everybody – he'll be after ours. Aha – the band has struck up again!'

Everyone listened to the thrush. 'Mind how you go,' sang the thrush. 'Mind how you go! Mind how you do-it, do-it, do-it!'

'Sounds like a Safety First poster,' said Dick, and settled down with his head on a cushion of moss. 'All right, old bird – we'll mind how we go – but we're going to have a bit of a snooze now, so don't play the band too loudly!'

'It *would* be a good idea to have a bit of a rest,' said Julian, yawning. 'We've done pretty well, so far. We don't want to tire ourselves out the very first day. Get off my legs, Timmy – you're frightfully heavy with all those sandwiches inside you.'

Timmy removed himself. He went to George and flumped himself down beside her, licking her face. She pushed him away.

'Don't be so licky,' she said, sleepily, 'just be on guard like a good dog, and see that nobody comes along and steals our bikes.'

Timmy knew what 'on guard' meant, of course. He sat up straight when he heard the words, and looked carefully all round, sniffing as he did so. Anyone about? No. Not a sight, sound or smell of any stranger. Timmy lay down again, one ear cocked, and one eye very slightly open. George always thought it was marvellous the way he could be asleep with one ear and eye and awake with the others. She was about to say this to Dick and Julian when she saw that they were sound asleep.

She fell asleep too. Nobody came to disturb them. A

small robin hopped near inquisitively, and, with his head on one side, considered whether or not it would be a good thing to pull a few hairs out of Timmy's tail to line his new nest. The slit in Timmy's awake-eye widened a little – woe betide the robin if he tried any funny tricks on Timmy!

The robin flew off. The thrush sang a little more, and the rabbit came out again. Timmy's eye opened wide. The rabbit fled. Timmy gave a tiny snore. Was he awake or was he asleep? The rabbit wasn't going to wait and find out!

It was half past three when they all awoke one by one. Julian looked at his watch. 'It's almost tea-time!' he said, and Anne gave a little squeal.

'Oh no – why we've only just had lunch, and I'm still as full as can be!'

Julian grinned. 'It's all right. We'll go by our tummies for our meals, not by our watches, Anne. Come on, get up! We'll go without you if you don't.'

They wheeled their bicycles out of the primrose copse and mounted again. The breeze was lovely to feel on their faces. Anne gave a little groan.

'Oh dear – I feel a bit stiff already. Do you mean to go very many miles more, Ju?'

'No, not many,' said Julian. 'I thought we'd have tea somewhere when we feel like it and then do a bit of shopping for our supper and breakfast and then hunt about for a really good place to put up our tents for the night. I found a little lake on the map, and I thought we could have a swim in it if we can find it.'

This all sounded very good indeed. George felt she could cycle for miles if a swim in a lake was at the end of it.

'That's a very nice plan of yours,' she said, approvingly. 'Very nice indeed. I think our whole tour ought to be planned round lakes – so that we can always have a swim, night and morning!'

'Woof,' said Timmy, running beside George's bicycle. 'Woof!'

'Timmy agrees too,' said George, with a laugh. 'But oh dear – I don't believe he brought his bathing-towel!'

CHAPTER THREE

A lovely day – and a lovely night

THE FIVE of them had a lovely time that evening. They had tea about half past five, and then bought what they wanted for supper and breakfast. New rolls, anchovy paste, a big round jam-tart in a cardboard box, oranges, lime juice, a fat lettuce and some ham sandwiches – it seemed a very nice assortment indeed.

'Let's hope we don't eat it all for supper, and have no breakfast left,' said George, packing the sandwiches into her basket. 'Get down, Timmy. These sandwiches are not for you. I've bought you a whacking big bone – *that* will keep you busy for hours!'

'Well, don't let him have it when we settle down for the night,' said Anne. 'He makes such a row, crunching and munching. He'd keep me awake.'

'*Nothing* would keep *me* awake tonight,' said Dick. 'I believe I could sleep through an earthquake. I'm already thinking kindly of my sleeping-bag.'

'I don't think we need to put up our tents tonight,' said Julian, looking up at the perfectly clear sky. 'I'll ask someone what the weather forecast was on the radio at six. Honestly I think we could just snuggle into our sleeping-bags and have the sky for a roof.'

'How smashing!' said Anne. 'I'd love to lie and look at the stars.'

The weather forecast was good. 'Fine and clear and mild.'

'Good,' said Julian. 'That will save us a lot of trouble – we don't even need to unpack our tents. Come on – have we got everything now? Does anyone feel as if we ought to buy any more food?'

The baskets were all full. Nobody thought it advisable to try and get anything more into them.

'We could get lots more in if Timmy would only carry his own bones,' said Anne. 'Half my basket is crammed with enormous bones for him. Why can't you rig up something so that Timmy could carry his own food, George? I'm sure he's clever enough.'

'Yes, he's clever enough,' said George. 'But he's much too greedy, Anne. You know that. He'd stop and eat all his food at once if he had to carry it. Dogs seem to be able to eat anything at any time.'

'They're lucky,' said Dick. 'Wish I could. But I just *have* to pause between my meals!'

'Now for the lake,' said Julian, folding up the map which he had just been examining. 'It's only about five miles away. It's called the Green Pool, but it looks a good bit bigger than a pool. I could do with a bathe. I'm so hot and sticky.'

They came to the lake at about half past seven. It was in a lovely place, and had beside it a small hut which was obviously used in summer-time for bathers to change into bathing-suits. Now it was locked, and curtains were drawn across the windows.

'I suppose we can go in for a dip if we like?' said Dick rather doubtfully. 'We shan't be trespassing or anything, shall we?'

'No. It doesn't say anything about being private,' said Julian. 'The water won't be very warm, you know, because it's only mid-April! But after all, we're used to cold baths every morning, and I daresay the sun has taken the chill off the lake. Come on, let's get into bathing things.'

They changed behind the bushes and then ran down to the lake. The water was certainly very cold indeed. Anne skipped in and out, and wouldn't do any more than that.

George joined the boys in a swim, and they all came out glowing and laughing. 'Brrr, that was cold!' said Dick. 'Come on, let's have a sharp run. Look at Anne – dressed already. Timmy, where are you? *You* don't mind the cold water, do you?'

They all tore up and down the little paths by the Green Pool like mad things. Anne was getting the supper ready. The sun had disappeared now, and although the evening was still very mild the radiant warmth of the day had gone. Anne was glad of her sweater.

'Good old Anne,' said Dick, when at last he and the others joined her, dressed again, with their sweaters on for warmth. 'Look, she's got the food all ready. You're fantastic, Anne. I bet if we stayed here for more than one night Anne would have made some kind of larder, and have arranged a good place to wash everything – and be looking for somewhere to keep her dusters and broom!'

'You're so *silly*, Dick,' said Anne. 'You ought to be glad I like messing about with the food and getting it ready for you. Oh, TIMMY! Shoo! Get away! Look at him, he's shaken millions and millions of drops of lakewater all over the food. You ought to have dried him, George. You know how he shakes himself after a swim.'

'Sorry,' said George. 'Tim, say you're sorry. Why must you be so *violent* about everything? If I shook myself like that my ears and fingers would fly off into the air!'

It was a lovely meal, sitting there in the evening light, watching the first stars come out in the sky. The children and Timmy were all tired but happy. This was the beginning of their trip and beginnings were always lovely – the days stretched out before you endlessly, and somehow you felt certain that the sun would shine every single day!

They were not long in snuggling into their sleeping-bags when they had finished the meal. They had set them all together in a row, so that they could talk if they wanted to. Timmy was thrilled. He walked solemnly across the whole lot, and was greeted with squeals and threats.

'Timmy! How dare you! When I've had such a big supper too!'

'TIMMY! You brute! You put all your great big feet down on me at once!'

'George, you *really* might stop Timmy from walking all over us like that! I only hope he's not going to do it all night long.'

Timmy looked surprised at the shouts. He settled down beside George, after a vain attempt to get into her sleeping-bag with her. George turned her face away from his licks.

'Oh, Timmy, I do love you but I wish you wouldn't make my face so wet. Julian, look at that glorious star – like a little round lamp. What is it?'

'It's not a star really – it's Venus, one of the planets,' said Julian, sleepily. 'But it's called the Evening Star. Fancy you not knowing that, George. Don't they teach you anything at your school?'

George tried to kick Julian through her sleeping-bag, but she couldn't. She gave it up and yawned so loudly that she set all the others yawning too.

Anne fell asleep first. She was the smallest and was more easily tired with long walks and rides than the others, though she always kept up with them valiantly. George gazed unblinkingly at the bright evening star for a minute and then fell asleep suddenly. Julian and Dick talked quietly for a few minutes. Timmy was quite silent. He was tired out with his miles and miles of running.

Nobody stirred at all that night, not even Timmy. He took no notice of a horde of rabbits who played not far off. He hardly pricked an ear when an owl hooted nearby. He didn't even stir when a beetle ran over his head.

But if George had woken and spoken his name Timmy would have been wide awake at once, standing over George and licking her, whining gently! George was the centre of his world, night and day.

The next day was fair and bright. It was lovely to wake up and feel the warm sun on their cheeks, and hear a thrush singing his heart out. 'It might be the very same thrush,' thought Dick, drowsily. 'He's saying, "Mind how you do-it, do-it, do-it!" just like the other one did.'

Anne sat up cautiously. She wondered if she should get up and have breakfast ready for the others – or would they want a bathe first?

Julian sat up next and yawned as he wriggled himself half out of his sleeping-bag. He grinned at Anne.

'Hallo,' he said. 'Had a good night? I feel fine this morning!'

'I feel rather stiff,' said Anne. 'But it will soon wear off. Hallo, George – you awake?'

George grunted and snuggled down farther in her sleeping-bag. Timmy pawed at her, whining. He wanted her to get up and go for a run with him.

Shut up, Timmy,' said George from the depth of her bag. 'I'm asleep!'

'I'm going for a bathe,' said Julian. 'Anyone else coming?'

'I won't,' said Anne. 'It will be too cold for me this morning. George doesn't seem to want to, either. You two boys go by yourselves. I'll have breakfast ready for you when you come back. Sorry I shan't be able to have anything hot for you to drink – but we didn't bring a kettle or anything like that.'

Julian and Dick went off to the Green Pool, still looking sleepy. Anne got out of her sleeping-bag and dressed quickly. She decided to go down to the pool with her sponge and flannel and wake herself up properly with the cold water. George was still in her sleeping-bag.

The two boys were almost at the pool. Ah, now they could see it between the trees, shining a bright emerald green. It looked very inviting indeed.

They suddenly saw a bicycle standing beside a tree. They looked at it in astonishment. It wasn't one of theirs. It must belong to someone else.

Then they heard splashings from the pool, and they hurried down to it. Was someone else bathing?

A boy was in the pool, his golden head shining wet and smooth in the morning sun. He was swimming powerfully across the pool, leaving long ripples behind him as he went. He suddenly saw Dick and Julian, and swam over to them.

'Hallo,' he said, wading out of the water. 'You come for a swim too? Nice pool of mine, isn't it?'

'What do you mean? It isn't really your pool, is it?' said Julian.

'Well, it belongs to my father, Thurlow Kent,' said the boy.

Both Julian and Dick had heard of Thurlow Kent, one of the richest men in the country. Julian looked doubtfully at the boy.

'If it's a private pool we won't use it,' he said.

'Oh come on!' cried the boy, and splashed cold water all over them. 'Race you to the other side!'

And off all three of them went, cleaving the green waters with their strong tanned arms – what a fine beginning to a sunny day!

CHAPTER FOUR

Richard

ANNE WAS astonished to find three boys in the Green Pool instead of two. She stood by the water with her sponge and flannel, staring. Who was the third boy?

The three came back to the side of the pool where Anne stood. She looked at the strange boy shyly. He was not much older than she was, and not as big as Julian or Dick, but he was sturdily made, and had laughing blue eyes she liked. He smoothed back his dripping hair.

'This your sister?' he said to Julian and Dick. 'Hallo there!'

'Hallo,' said Anne and smiled. 'What's your name?'

'Richard,' he said. 'Richard Kent. What's yours?'

'Anne,' said Anne. 'We're on a biking tour.'

The boys had had no time to introduce themselves. They were still panting from their swim.

'I'm Julian and he's Dick, my brother,' said Julian, out of breath. 'I say – I hope we're not trespassing on your land as well as on your water!'

Richard grinned. 'Well, you are as a matter of fact. But I give you free permission! You can borrow my pool and my land as much as you like!'

'Oh thanks,' said Anne. 'I suppose it's your father's

property? It didn't say "Private" or anything, so we didn't know. Would you like to come and have breakfast with us? If you'll dress with the others they'll bring you to where we camped last night.'

She sponged her face and washed her hands in the pool, hearing the boys chattering behind the bushes where they had left their clothes. Then she sped back to their sleeping-place, meaning to tidy up the bags they had slept in, and put out breakfast neatly. But George was still fast asleep in her bag, her head showing at the top with its mass of short curls that made her look like a boy.

'George! Do wake up. Somebody's coming to breakfast,' said Anne, shaking her.

George shrugged away crossly, not believing her. It was just a trick to make her get up and help with the breakfast! Anne left her. All right – let her be found in her sleeping-bag if she liked!

She began to unpack the food and set it out neatly. What a good thing they had brought two extra bottles of lime juice. Now they could offer Richard one.

The three boys came up, their wet hair plastered down. Richard spotted George in the bag as Timmy came over to meet him. He fondled Timmy who, smelling that other dogs had been round Richard at home, sniffed him over with great interest.

'Who's that still asleep?' asked Richard.

'That's George,' said Anne. 'Too sleepy to wake up! Come on – I've got breakfast ready. Would you like to start off with rolls and anchovy and lettuce? And there's lime juice if you want it.'

George heard Richard's voice as he sat talking with the others and was astonished. Who was that? She sat up, blinking, her hair tousled and short. Richard honestly thought she was a boy. She looked like one and she was called George!

'Top of the morning to you, George,' he said. 'Hope I'm not eating your share of the breakfast.'

'Who are you?' demanded George. The boys told her.

'I live about three miles away,' said the boy. 'I biked over here this morning for a swim. I say – that reminds me – I'd better bring my bike up here and put it where I can see it. I've had two stolen already through not having them under my eye.'

He shot off to get his bike. George took the opportunity of getting out of her sleeping-bag and rushed off to dress. She was back before Richard was, eating her breakfast. He wheeled his bicycle as he came.

'Got it all right,' he said, and flung it down beside him. 'Don't want to have to tell my father this one's gone, like the others. He's pretty fierce.'

'My father's a bit fierce too,' said George.

'Does he hurt you?' asked Richard, giving Timmy a nice little titbit of roll and anchovy paste.

'Of course not,' said George. 'He's just got a temper, that's all.'

'Mine's got tempers and rages and furies, and if anyone

offends him or does him a wrong he's like an elephant – never forgets,' said Richard. 'He's made plenty of enemies in his lifetime. Sometimes he's had his life threatened, and he's had to take a bodyguard about with him.'

This all sounded extremely thrilling. Dick half-wished he had a father like that. It would be nice to talk to the other boys at school about his father's 'bodyguard'.

'What's his bodyguard like?' asked Anne, full of curiosity.

'Oh, they vary. But they're all big hefty fellows – they look like ruffians, and probably are,' said Richard, enjoying the interest the others were taking in him. 'One he had last year was awful – he had the thickest lips you ever saw, and such a big nose that when you saw him sideways you really thought he'd put a false one on just for fun.'

'Gracious!' said Anne. 'He sounds horrible. Has your father still got him?'

'No. He did something that annoyed Dad – I don't know what – and after a perfectly furious row my father chucked him out,' said Richard. 'That was the end of *him*. Jolly good thing too. I hated him. He used to kick the dogs around terribly.'

'*Oh!* What a beast!' said George, horrified. She put her arm round Timmy as if she was afraid somebody might suddenly kick him around too.

Julian and Dick wondered whether to believe all this. They came to the conclusion that the tales Richard told were very much exaggerated, and they listened with amusement, but not with such horror as the two girls, who hung on every word that Richard said.

'Where's your father now?' said Anne. 'Has he got a special bodyguard this very moment?'

'Rather! He's in America this week, but he's flying home soon – plus bodyguard,' said Richard, drinking the last of his lime juice from the bottle. 'Ummm, that's good. I say, aren't you lucky to be allowed to go off alone like this on your bikes and sleep where you like? My mother never will let *me* – she's always afraid something will happen to me.'

'Perhaps you'd better have a bodyguard too,' suggested Julian, slyly.

'I'd soon give him the slip,' said Richard. 'As a matter of fact I *have* got a kind of a bodyguard.'

'Who? Where?' asked Anne, looking all round as if she expected some enormous ruffian suddenly to appear.

'Well – he's supposed to be my holiday tutor,' said Richard, tickling Timmy round the ears. 'He's called Lomax and he's pretty awful. I'm supposed to tell him every time I go out – just as if I was a kid like Anne here.'

Anne was indignant. 'I don't have to tell anybody when I want to go off on my own,' she said.

'Actually I don't think we'd be allowed to rush off completely on our own unless we had old Timmy,' said Dick, honestly. 'He's better than any ruffianly bodyguard or holiday tutor. I wonder *you* don't have a dog.'

'Oh, I've got about five,' said Richard, airily.

'What are their names?' asked George, disbelievingly.

'Er – Bunter, Biscuit, Brownie, Bones – and er – Bonzo,' said Richard, with a grin.

'Silly names,' said George, scornfully. 'Fancy calling a dog *Biscuit.* You must be cracked.'

'You shut up,' said Richard, with a sudden scowl. 'I don't stand people telling me I'm cracked.'

'Well, you'll have to stand *me* telling you,' said George. 'I do think it's cracked to call a dog, a nice, decent dog, by a name like *Biscuit*!'

'I'll fight you then,' said Richard, surprisingly, and stood up. 'Come on – you stand up.'

George leapt to her feet. Julian shot out a hand and pulled her down again.

'None of that,' he said to Richard. 'You ought to be ashamed of yourself.'

'Why?' flared out Richard, whose face had gone very red. Evidently he and his father shared the same fierceness of temper!

'Well, you don't fight *girls*,' said Julian, scornfully. 'Or do you? Correct me if I'm wrong.'

Richard stared at him in amazement. 'What do you mean?' he said. 'Girls? Of course I don't fight girls. No decent boy hits a girl – but it's this boy here I want to fight – what do you call him? – George.'

To his great surprise Julian, Dick and Anne roared with laughter. Timmy barked madly too, pleased at the sudden ending of the quarrel. Only George looked mutinous and cross.

'What's up now?' asked Richard, aggressively. 'What's all the fun and games about?'

'Richard, George isn't a boy – she's a *girl*,' explained Dick at last. 'My goodness – she was just about to accept your challenge and fight you, too – two fierce little fox-terriers having a scrap!'

Richard's mouth fell open in even greater astonishment. He blushed redder than ever. He looked sheepishly at George.

'Are you *really* a girl?' he said. 'You behave so like a boy – and you look like one too. Sorry, George. Is your name *really* George?'

'No, Georgina,' said George, thawing a little at Richard's awkward apology, and pleased that he had honestly thought her a boy. She did so badly want to be a boy and not a girl.

'Good thing I *didn't* fight you,' said Richard, fervently. 'I should have knocked you flat!'

'Well, I like *that*!' said George, flaring up all over again. Julian pushed her back with his hand.

'Now, shut up, you two, and don't behave like idiots. Where's the map? It's time we had a squint at it and decided what we are going to do for today – how far we're going to ride, and where we're making for by the evening.'

Fortunately George and Richard both gave in with a good grace. Soon all six heads – Timmy's too – were bent over the map. Julian made his decision.

'We'll make for Middlecombe Woods – see, there they are on the map. That's decided then – it'll be a jolly nice ride.'

It might be a nice ride – but it was going to be something very much more than that!

CHAPTER FIVE

Six instead of five

'LOOK HERE,' said Richard, when they had tidied up everything, buried their bits of litter, and looked to see that no one had got a puncture in a tyre. 'Look here, I've got an aunt who lives in the direction of those woods – if I can get my mother to say I can come with you, will you let me? I can go and see my aunt on the way, then.'

Julian looked at Richard doubtfully. He wasn't very sure if Richard really *would* go and ask permission.

'Well – if you aren't too long about it,' he said. 'Of course we don't mind you coming with us. We can drop you at your aunt's on the way.'

'I'll go straight off now and ask my mother,' said Richard, eagerly, and he ran for his bicycle. 'I'll meet you at Croker's Corner – you saw it on the map. That will save time, because then I shan't have to come back here – it's not much farther than my home.'

'Right,' said Julian. 'I've got to adjust my brakes, and that will take ten minutes or so. You'll have time to go home and ask permission, and join us later. We'll wait for you; at least we'll wait for ten minutes, at Croker's Corner. If you don't turn up we'll know you didn't get permission. Tell your mother we'll have you safely at your aunt's.'

Richard shot off on his bicycle, looking excited. Anne began to clear up, and George helped her. Timmy got in everyone's way, sniffing about for dropped crumbs.

'Anyone would think he was half-starved!' said Anne. 'He had a lot more breakfast than I had. Timmy, if you walk through my legs again I'll tie you up!'

Julian adjusted his brakes with Dick's help. In about fifteen minutes they were ready to set off. They had planned where to stop to buy food for their lunch, and although the journey to Middlecombe Woods was a longer trip than they had made the day before, they felt able to cope with more miles on the second day. Timmy was eager to set off too. He was a big dog, and enjoyed all the exercise he was getting.

'It'll take a bit of your fat off,' said Dick to Timmy. 'We don't like round dogs, you know. They waddle and they puff.'

'Dick! Timmy's *never* been round!' said George, indignantly, and then stopped as she saw Dick's grin. He was pulling her leg as usual. She kicked herself. Why did she always rise like that, when Dick teased her through Timmy? She gave him a friendly punch.

They all mounted their bicycles. Timmy ran ahead, pleased. They came to a lane and rode down it, avoiding the ruts. They came out into a road. It was not a main road, for the children didn't like those; they were too full of traffic and dust. They liked the shady lanes or the country roads where they met only a few carts or a farmer's car.

'Now, don't let's miss Croker's Corner,' said Julian. 'It should be along this way somewhere, according to the map. George, if you get into ruts like that you'll be thrown off.'

'All right, I know that!' said George. 'I only got into one because Timmy swerved across my wheel. He's after a rabbit or something. Timmy! Don't get left behind, you idiot.'

Timmy bounded reluctantly after the little party. Exercise was wonderful, but it did mean leaving a lot of marvellous wayside smells unsniffed at. It was a dreadful waste of smells, Timmy thought.

They came to Croker's Corner sooner than they thought. The signpost proclaimed the name – and there, leaning against the post, sitting on his bicycle was Richard, beaming at them.

'You've been jolly quick, getting back home and then on to here,' said Julian. 'What did your mother say?'

'She didn't mind a bit so long as I was with *you*,' said Richard. 'I can go to my aunt's for the night, she said.'

'Haven't you brought pyjamas or anything with you?' asked Dick.

'There are always spare ones at my aunt's,' explained Richard. 'Hurray – it will be marvellous to be out on my own all day with you – no Mr Lomax to bother me with this and that. Come on!'

They all cycled on together. Richard would keep trying to ride three abreast, and Julian had to warn him that cyclists were not allowed to do that. 'I don't care!' sang Richard, who seemed in very high spirits. 'Who is there to stop us, anyway?'

'*I* shall stop you,' said Julian, and Richard ceased grinning at once. Julian could sound very stern when he liked. Dick winked at George, and she winked back. They had both come to the conclusion that Richard was very spoilt and liked his own way. Well, he wouldn't get it if he came up against old Julian!

They stopped at eleven for ice-creams and drinks. Richard seemed to have a lot of money. He insisted on buying ice-creams for all of them, even Timmy.

Once again they bought food for their lunch – new bread, farmhouse butter, cream cheese, crisp lettuce, fat red radishes and a bunch of spring onions. Richard bought a magnificent chocolate cake he saw in a first-class cake-shop.

'Gracious! That must have cost you a fortune!' said Anne. 'How are we going to carry it?'

'Woof,' said Timmy longingly.

'No, I certainly shan't let *you* carry it,' said Anne. 'Oh dear, we'll have to cut it in half, I think, and two people can share the carrying. It's such an enormous cake.'

On they went again, getting into the real country now, with villages few and far between. A farm here and there showed up on the hillsides, with cows and sheep and fowls. It was a peaceful, quiet scene, with the sun spilling down over everything, and the blue April sky above, patched with great white cotton-wool clouds.

'This is grand,' said Richard. 'I say, doesn't Timmy *ever* get tired? He's panting like anything now.'

'Yes, I think we ought to find somewhere for our lunch,' said Julian, looking at his watch. 'We've done a very good run this morning. Of course a lot of the way has been downhill. This afternoon we'll probably be slower, because we'll be getting into hilly country.'

They found a spot to picnic in. They chose the sunny side of a hedge, looking downhill into a small valley. Sheep and lambs were in the field they sat in. The lambs were very inquisitive, and one came right up to Anne and bleated.

'Do you want a bit of my bread?' asked Anne, and held it out to the lamb. Timmy watched indignantly. Fancy handing out food to those silly little creatures! He growled a little, and George shushed him.

Soon all the lambs were crowding round, quite unafraid, and one even tried to put its little front legs up on to George's shoulders! That was too much for Timmy! He gave such a sudden, fierce growl that all the lambs shot off at once.

'Oh, don't be so jealous, Timmy,' said George. 'Take this sandwich and behave yourself. Now you've frightened away the lambs, and they won't come back.'

They all ate the food and then drank their lime juice and ginger-beer. The sun was very hot. Soon they would all be burnt – and it was only April. How marvellous! Julian thought lazily that they were really lucky to have such weather – it would be awful to have to bike along all day in the pouring rain.

Once again the children snoozed in the afternoon sun, Richard too, and the little lambs skipped nearer and nearer. One actually leapt on to Julian as he slept, and he sat upright with a jerk. 'Timmy!' he began, 'if you leap on me again like that I'll . . .'

But it wasn't Timmy, it was a lamb! Julian laughed to himself. He sat for a few minutes and watched the little white creatures playing 'I'm king of the castle' with an old coop, then he lay down again.

'Are we anywhere near your aunt's house?' Julian asked Richard, when they once more mounted their bicycles.

'If we're anywhere near Great Giddings, we shall soon

be there,' said Richard, riding without holding his handlebars and almost ending up in the ditch. 'I didn't notice it on the map.'

Julian tried to remember. 'Yes, we should be at Great Giddings round about tea-time, say five o'clock or thereabouts. We'll leave you at your aunt's house for tea if you like.'

'Oh no, thank you,' said Richard, quickly. 'I'd much rather have tea with *you*. I *do* wish I could come on this tour with you. I suppose I couldn't possibly? You could telephone my mother.'

'Don't be an ass,' said Julian. 'You can have tea with us if you like but we drop you at your aunt's as arranged, see? No nonsense about that.'

They came to Great Giddings at about ten past five. Although it was called Great it was really very small. There was a little tea-place that said 'Home-made cakes and jams', so they went there for tea.

The woman who kept it was a plump, cheerful soul, fond of children. She guessed she would make very little out of the tea she served to five healthy children – but that didn't matter! She set to work to cut three big plates of well-buttered slices of bread, put out apricot jam, raspberry, and strawberry, and a selection of home-made buns that made the children's mouths water.

She knew Richard quite well, because he had sometimes been to her cottage with his aunt.

'I suppose you'll be going to stay with her tonight?' she

said to Richard, and he nodded, his mouth full of ginger cake. It was a lovely tea. Anne felt as if she wouldn't be able to eat any supper at all that night! Even Timmy seemed to have satisfied his enormous appetite.

'I think we ought to pay you double price for our gorgeous tea,' said Julian, but the woman wouldn't hear of it. No, no – it was lovely to see them all enjoying her cakes; she didn't want double price!

'Some people are so *awfully* nice and generous,' said Anne, as they mounted their bicycles to ride off again. 'You just can't help liking them. I do hope I can cook like that when I grow up.'

'If you do, Julian and I will always live with you and not dream of getting married!' said Dick, promptly, and they all laughed.

'Now for Richard's aunt,' said Julian. 'Do you know where the house is, Richard?'

'Yes, that's it over there,' said Richard, and rode up to a gate. 'Well, thanks awfully for your company. I hope I'll see you again soon! I have a feeling I shall! Good-bye!'

He rode up the drive and disappeared. 'What a sudden good-bye!' said George, puzzled. 'Isn't he *odd*?'

CHAPTER SIX

Odd happenings

THEY ALL thought it really was a little odd to disappear so suddenly like that, with just a casual good-bye. Julian wondered if he ought to have gone with him and delivered him safely on the door-step.

'Don't be an ass, Julian,' said Dick, scornfully. 'What *do* you think can happen to him from the front gate to the front door!'

'Nothing, of course. It's just that I don't trust that young fellow,' said Julian. 'You know I really wasn't sure he had asked his mother if he could come with us, to tell you the truth.'

'I thought that too,' said Anne. 'He did get to Croker's Corner so very quickly, didn't he? And he had quite a long way to go really, and he had to find his mother, and talk to her, and all that.'

'Yes, I've half a mind to pop up to the aunt's house and see if she expected him,' said Julian. But on second thoughts he didn't go. He would feel so silly if the aunt was there with Richard, and all was well – they would think that he and the others ought to be asked in.

So, after debating the matter for a few minutes they all rode off again. They wanted to get to Middlecombe

Woods fairly soon, because there were no villages between Great Giddings and Middlecombe, so they would have to find the woods and then go on to find a farmhouse somewhere to buy food for supper and breakfast. They hadn't been able to buy any in the shops at Great Giddings because it was early closing day, and they hadn't liked to ask the tea-shop woman to sell them anything. They felt they had taken quite enough of her food already!

They came to Middlecombe Woods, and found a very fine place to camp in for the night. It was in a little dell, set with primroses and violets, a perfectly hidden place, secure from all prying eyes, and surely unknown even to tramps.

'This is glorious,' said Anne. 'We must be miles away from anywhere: I hope we can find some farmhouse or something that will sell us food, though! I know we don't feel hungry now, but we shall!'

'I think I've got a puncture, blow it,' said Dick, looking at his back tyre. 'It's a slow one, fortunately. But I think I won't risk coming along to look for farmhouses till I've mended it.'

'Right,' said Julian. 'And Anne needn't come either. She looks a bit tired. George and I will go. We won't take our bikes. It's easier to walk through the woods. We may be an hour or so, but don't worry, Timmy will know the way back all right, so we shan't lose you!'

Julian and George set off on foot, with Timmy following. Timmy too was tired, but nothing would have made him stay behind with Anne and Dick. He must go with his beloved George!

Anne put her bicycle carefully into the middle of a bush. You never knew when someone might be about, watching to steal something! It didn't matter when Timmy was there, because he would growl if a tramp came within a mile of them. Dick called out that he would mend his puncture now. He had found the hole already, where a small nail had gone in.

She sat near to Dick, watching him. She was glad to rest. She wondered if the others had found a farmhouse yet.

Dick worked steadily at mending the puncture. They had been there together about half an hour when they heard sounds.

Dick lifted his head and listened. 'Can you hear something?' he said to Anne. She nodded.

'Yes. Somebody's shouting. I wonder why!'

They both listened again. Then they distinctly heard yells. 'Help! Julian! Where are you? Help!'

They shot to their feet. Who was calling Julian for help? It wasn't George's voice. The yells grew louder, to panic-stricken shrieks.

'JULIAN! Dick!'

'Why, it must be Richard,' said Dick, amazed. 'What in the world does he want? What's happened?'

Anne was pale. She didn't like sudden happenings like this. 'Shall we – shall we go and find him?' she said.

There was a crashing not far off, as if somebody was making his way through the undergrowth. It was rather dark among the trees, and Anne and Dick could see nothing at first. Dick yelled loudly.

'Hey! Is that you, Richard! We're here!'

The crashing noise redoubled. 'I'm coming!' squealed Richard. 'Wait for me, wait for me!'

They waited. Soon they saw Richard coming, stumbling as fast as he could between the trees. 'Here we are,' called Dick. 'Whatever's the matter?'

Richard staggered towards them. He looked frightened

out of his life. 'They're after me,' he panted. 'You must save me. I want Timmy. He'll bite them.'

'*Who*'s after you?' asked Dick, amazed.

'Where's Timmy? Where's Julian?' cried Richard, looking round in despair.

'They've gone to a farmhouse to get some food,' said Dick. 'They'll be back soon, Richard. Whatever's the *matter*? Are you mad? You look awful.'

The boy took no notice of the questions. 'Where has Julian gone? I want Timmy. Tell me the way they went. I can't stay here. They'll catch me!'

'They went along there,' said Dick, showing Richard the path. 'You can just see the tracks of their feet. Richard, whatever is . . . ?'

But Richard was gone! He fled down the path at top speed, calling at the top of his voice, 'Julian! Timmy!'

Anne and Dick stared at one another in surprise. What had happened to Richard? Why wasn't he at his aunt's house? He must be mad!

'It's no good going after him,' said Dick. 'We shall only lose the way and not be able to find this place again – and the others will miss us and go hunting and get lost too! What *is* the matter with Richard?'

'He kept saying somebody was after him – *they* were after him!' said Anne. 'He's got some bee in his bonnet about something.'

'Bats in the belfry,' said Dick. 'Mad, dippy, daft! Well, he'll give Julian and George a shock when he runs into them – if he does! The odds are he will miss them altogether.'

'I'm going to climb this tree and see if I can see anything of Richard or the others,' said Anne. 'It's tall, and it's easy to climb. You finish mending your puncture. I should just love to know what happens to Richard.'

Dick went back to his bicycle, puzzled. Anne climbed the tree. She climbed well, and was soon at the top. She gazed out over the countryside. There was an expanse of fields on one side, and woods stretched away on the other. She looked over the darkening fields, trying to see if a farmhouse was anywhere near. But she could see nothing.

Dick was just finishing his puncture when he heard another noise in the woods. Was it that idiot of a Richard coming back? He listened.

The noise came nearer. It wasn't a crashing noise, like Richard had made. It was a stealthy noise as if people were gradually closing in. Dick didn't much like it. Who was coming? Or perhaps – *what* was coming? Was it some wild animal – perhaps a badger and its mate? The boy stood listening.

A silence came. No more movements. No more rustling. Had he imagined it all? He wished Anne and the others were near him. It was eerie, standing there in the darkening wood, waiting and watching.

He decided that he had imagined it all. He thought it would be a very good idea if he turned on his bicycle lamp, then the light would soon dispel his silly ideas! He fumbled about for it on the front of his handlebars. He switched it on and a very comforting little glow at once spread a circle of light in the little dell.

Dick was just about to call up to Anne to tell her his absurd fears when the noises came again! There was absolutely no mistake about them this time.

A brilliant light suddenly pierced through the trees and fell on Dick. He blinked.

'Ah, so there you are, you little misery!' said a harsh voice, and someone came striding over to the dell. Somebody else followed behind.

'What do you mean?' asked Dick, amazed. He could not see who the men were because of the brilliant torch-light in his eyes.

'We've been chasing you for miles, haven't we? And you thought you'd get away. But we'd got you all the time!' said the voice.

'I don't understand this,' said Dick, putting on a bold voice. 'Who are you?'

'You know very well who we are,' said the voice. 'Didn't you run away screaming as soon as you saw Rooky? He went one way after you, and we went another – and we soon got you, didn't we? Now, you come along with us, my pretty!'

All this explained one thing clearly to Dick – that it was Richard they had been after, for some reason or other – and they thought *he* was Richard!

'I'm not the boy you're looking for,' he said. 'You'll get

into trouble if you touch *me*!'

'What's your name, then?' asked the first man.

Dick told him.

'Oh, so you're Dick – and isn't Dick short for Richard? You can't fool us with that baby-talk,' said the first man. 'You're the Richard we want, all right. Richard Kent, see?'

'I'm *not* Richard Kent!' shouted Dick, as he felt the man's hand clutching his arm suddenly. 'You take your hands off me. You wait till the police hear of this!'

'They *won't* hear of it,' said the man. 'They won't hear anything at all! Come on – and don't struggle or shout or you'll be sorry. Once you're at Owl's Dene we'll deal properly with you!'

Anne was sitting absolutely petrified up in the tree. She couldn't move or speak. She tried to call to poor Dick, but her tongue wouldn't say a word. She had to sit there and hear her brother being dragged away by two strange ruffians. She almost fell out of the tree in fright, and she heard him shouting and yelling when he was dragged away. She could hear the sound of crashing for a long time.

She began to cry. She didn't dare to climb down because she was trembling so much she was afraid she would lose her hold and fall.

She must wait for George and Julian to come back. Suppose they didn't? Suppose they had been caught too? She would be all by herself in the tree all night long. Anne sobbed up in the tree-top, holding on tightly.

The stars came out above her head, and she saw the very bright one again.

And then she heard the sound of footsteps and voices. She stiffened up in the tree. Who was it this time? Oh let it be Julian and George and Timmy; let it be Julian, George and Timmy!

CHAPTER SEVEN

Richard tells an alarming tale

JULIAN AND George had managed to find a little farmhouse tucked away in a hollow. A trio of dogs set up a terrific barking as they drew near. Timmy growled and the hair rose up on his neck. George put her hand on his collar.

'I won't go any nearer with Timmy,' she said. 'I don't want him to be set on by three dogs at once!'

So Julian went down to the farmhouse by himself. The dogs made such a noise and looked so fierce that he paused in the farmyard. He was not in the least afraid of dogs, but these looked most unpleasant, especially one big mongrel whose teeth were bared in a very threatening manner.

A voice called out to him. 'Clear off, you! We don't want no strangers here. When strangers come our eggs and hens go too!'

'Good evening,' called Julian, politely. 'We are four children camping out in the woods for the night. Could you let us have any food? I'll pay well for it.'

There was a pause. The man pulled his head in at the window he was shouting from, and was evidently speaking to someone inside.

He stuck it out again. 'I told you, we don't hold with strangers here, never did. We've only got plain bread and butter, and we can give you some hard-boiled eggs and milk and a bit of ham. That's all.'

'That'll do fine,' called Julian, cheerily. 'Just what we'd like. Shall I come and get it?'

'Not unless you want to be torn to pieces by those dogs,' came back the voice. 'You wait there. I'll be out when the eggs are done.'

'Blow,' said Julian, walking back to George. 'That means we'll have to kick our heels here for a while. What an unpleasant fellow! I don't think much of his place, do you?'

George agreed with him. It was ill-kept, the barn was falling to bits, rusty bits of machinery lay here and there in the thick grass. The three dogs kept up a continual barking and howling, but they did not come any nearer. George still kept her hand firmly on Timmy. He was bristling all over!

'What a lonely place to live in,' said Julian. 'No house within miles, I should think. No telephone. I wonder what they'd do if somebody was ill or had an accident and needed help.'

'I hope they'll hurry up with that food,' said George, getting impatient. 'It'll be dark soon. I'm getting hungry too.'

At last somebody came out of the tumbledown farmhouse. It was a bearded man, stooping and old, with long untidy hair and a pronounced limp. He had a grim and ugly face. Neither Julian nor George liked him.

‘Here you are,’ he said, waving his three dogs away behind him. ‘Get back, you!’ He aimed a kick at the nearest dog, and it yelped with pain.

‘Oh don’t!’ said George. ‘You hurt him.’

‘He’s my dog, isn’t he?’ said the man, angrily. ‘You mind your own business!’ He kicked out at another dog and scowled at George.

‘What about the food?’ said Julian, holding out his hand, anxious to be gone before trouble came between Timmy and the other dogs. ‘George, take Timmy back a bit. He’s upsetting the dogs.’

‘Well, I like that!’ said George. ‘It’s those other dogs that are upsetting *him*!’

She dragged Timmy back a few yards, and he stood there with all his hackles up on his neck, growling in a horrible way.

Julian took the food which was done up carelessly in old brown paper. ‘Thanks,’ he said. ‘How much?’

‘Five pounds,’ said the old man, surprisingly.

‘Don’t be silly,’ said Julian. He looked quickly at the food. ‘I’ll give you a pound for it, and that’s more than it’s worth. There’s hardly any ham.’

‘I said five pounds,’ said the man, sullenly. Julian looked at him. ‘He must be mad!’ he thought. He held out the food to the ugly old fellow.

‘Well, take it back,’ he said. ‘I haven’t got five pounds

to give you for food. A pound is the most I can spare. Good night.'

The old man pushed the food back, and held out his other hand in silence. Julian fished in his pocket and brought out a pound. He placed it in the man's dirty hand, wondering why on earth the fellow had asked him for such a ridiculous sum before. The man put the money in his pocket.

'Clear off,' he said, suddenly, in a growling voice. 'We don't want strangers here, stealing our goods. I'll set my dogs on you if you come again!'

Julian turned to go, half-afraid that the extraordinary old man *would* set his dogs on him. The fellow stood there in the half-dark, yelling abuse at Julian and George as they made their way out of the farmyard.

'Well! We'll never go *there* again!' said George, furious at their treatment. 'He's mad as a hatter.'

'Yes. And I don't much fancy his food, either,' said Julian. 'Still, it's all we'll get tonight!'

They followed Timmy back to the woods. They were glad they had him, because otherwise they might have missed the way. But Timmy knew it. Once he had been along a certain route Timmy always knew it again. He ran on now, sniffing here and there, occasionally waiting for the others to catch him up.

Then he stiffened and growled softly. George put her hand on his collar. Somebody must be coming.

Somebody *was* coming! It was Richard on his way to

find them. He was still shouting and yelling, and the noise he made had already come to Timmy's sharp ears. It soon came to Julian's, and George's too, as they stood there waiting.

'Julian! Where are you? Where's Timmy? I want Timmy! They're after me, I tell you; they're after me.'

'Listen – it sounds like *Richard*,' said Julian, startled. 'What in the world is he doing here? – and yelling like that too! Come on, we must find out. Something's happened. I hope Dick and Anne are all right.'

They ran up the path as fast as they could in the twilight. Soon they met Richard, who had now stopped shouting, and was stumbling along, half-sobbing.

'Richard! What's up?' cried Julian. Richard ran to him and flung himself against him. Timmy did not go to him, but stood there in surprise. George stared through the twilight, puzzled. What in the world had happened?

'Julian! Oh, Julian! I'm scared stiff,' panted Richard, hanging on to Julian's arm.

'Pull yourself together,' said Julian, in the calm voice that had made a good effect on Richard. 'I bet you're just making a silly fuss. What's happened? Did you find your aunt was out or something? And come racing after us?'

'My aunt's away,' said Richard, speaking in a calmer voice. 'She . . .'

'*Away!*' said Julian, in surprise. 'But didn't your mother know that when she said you could . . . ?'

'I didn't ask my mother's permission to come,' cried

Richard. 'I didn't even go back home when you thought I did! I just biked straight to Croker's Corner and waited for you. I wanted to come with you, you see and I knew my mother wouldn't let me.'

This was said with a great air of bravado. Julian was disgusted.

'I'm ashamed of you,' he said. 'Telling us lies like that!'

'I didn't know my aunt was away,' said Richard, all his sudden cockiness gone when he heard Julian's scornful voice. 'I thought she'd be there and I was going to tell her to telephone my mother and say I'd gone for a trip with *you*. Then I thought I'd come biking after you and – and . . .'

'And tell us your aunt was away, and could you come with us?' finished Julian, still scornfully. 'A deceitful and ridiculous plan. I'd have sent you back at once; you might have known that.'

'Yes, I know. But I might have had a whole night camping out with you,' said Richard, in a small voice. 'I've never done things like that. I . . .'

'What I want to know is, what were you scared of when you came rushing along, yelling and crying,' said Julian, impatiently.

'Oh, Julian – it was horrible,' said Richard, and he suddenly clutched Julian's arm again. 'You see, I biked down back to my aunt's gate and out into the lane and I was just going along the way to Middlecombe Woods when a car met me. And I saw who was in the car!'

'Well, *who*?' said Julian, feeling as if he could shake Richard.

'It was – it was Rooky!' said Richard, in a trembling voice.

'Who's he?' said Julian, and George gave an impatient click. Would Richard never tell his story properly?

'Don't you remember? I told you about him. He was the fellow that my father had for a bodyguard last year and he chucked him out,' said Richard. 'He always swore he'd have his revenge on my father – and on me too because I told tales about him to Dad and it was because of that he was sacked. So when I caught sight of him in the car I was terrified!'

'I *see*,' said Julian, seeing light. 'What happened then?'

'Rooky recognised me, and turned the car round and chased me on my bike,' said Richard, beginning to tremble again as he remembered that alarming ride. 'I pedalled for all I was worth and when I got to Middlecombe Woods I rode into the path there, hoping the car couldn't follow. It couldn't, of course – but the men leapt out – there were three of them, two I didn't know – and they chased me on foot. I pedalled and pedalled, and then I ran into a tree or something and fell off. I chucked my bike into a bush, and ran into the thick undergrowth to hide.'

'Go on,' said Julian, as Richard paused. 'What next?'

'The men split up then – Rooky went one way to find me, and the other two went another way. I waited till I thought they were gone, then I crept out and tore down the path again, hoping to find you. I wanted Timmy, you see, I thought he'd go for the men.'

Timmy growled. He certainly would have gone for them!

'Two of the men must have been hiding, waiting to hear me start up again,' went on Richard. 'And as soon as I began to run, they chased after me. I put them off the trail, though – I dodged and hid and hid and dodged – and then I came to Dick! He was mending a puncture. But you weren't with him – and it was you and Timmy I wanted – I knew the men would soon be catching me up, you see, so I tore on and on – and at last I found you. I've never been so glad in my life.'

It was a most extraordinary story – but Julian hardly paused to think about it. An alarming thought had come into his head. What about Dick and Anne? What would have happened to them if the men had suddenly come across them?

'Quick!' he said to George. 'We must get back to the others! Hurry!'

CHAPTER EIGHT

What's the best thing to do?

STUMBLING THROUGH the dark wood, Julian and George hurried as best they could. Timmy hurried too, knowing that something was worrying both his friends. Richard followed behind, half-crying again. He really had been very much afraid.

They came at last to the little dell where they had planned to spend the night. It was quite dark. Julian called loudly:

'Dick! Anne! Where are you?'

George had made her way to where she had hidden her bicycle. She fumbled for the lamp and switched it on. She took it off and flashed it round the dell. There was Dick's bicycle, with the puncture repair outfit on the ground beside it – but no Dick, and no Anne! What had happened?

'Anne!' yelled Julian, in alarm. 'Dick! Come here! We're back!'

And then a small trembling voice came down from the tree-top overhead.

'Oh, Julian! Oh Julian! I'm here.'

'It's Anne!' yelled Julian, his heart leaping in relief. 'Anne, where are you?'

'Up in this tree,' called back Anne, in a stronger voice. 'Oh, Ju, I've been so frightened, I didn't dare climb down in case I fell. Dick . . .'

'Where *is* Dick?' demanded Julian.

A sob came down to him. 'Two horrible men came – and they've taken him away. They thought he was Richard!'

Anne's voice became a wail. Julian felt that he must get her down from the tree so that she could be with them and be comforted. He spoke to George.

'Shine that lamp up here. I'm going up to fetch Anne.'

George silently shone the light of the lamp on the tree. Julian went up like a cat. He came to Anne who was still clinging tightly to a branch.

'Anne, I'll help you down. Come on, now – you can't

fall. I'm just below you. I'll guide your feet to the right branches.'

Anne was only too glad to be helped down. She was cold and miserable, and she longed to be with the others. Slowly she came down, with Julian's help, and he lifted her to the ground.

She clung to him, and he put his arm round his young sister. 'It's all right, Anne. I'm with you now. And here's George too – and old Timmy.'

'Who's *that*?' said Anne, suddenly seeing Richard in the shadows.

'Only Richard. He's behaved badly,' said Julian, grimly. 'It's all because of him and his idiotic behaviour that this has happened. Now, tell us slowly and carefully about Dick and the two men, Anne.'

Anne told him, not missing out anything at all. Timmy stood near her, licking her hand all the time. That was very comforting indeed! Timmy always knew when anyone was in trouble. Anne felt very much better when she had Julian's arm round her, and Timmy's tongue licking her!

'It's quite clear what's happened,' said Julian, when Anne had finished her alarming tale. 'This man Rooky recognised Richard, and he and the other two came after him, seeing a chance to kidnap him, and so get even with his father. Rooky was the only one who knew Richard, and he wasn't the man who caught Dick. The *others* got him – and they didn't know he wasn't Richard – and of course, hearing that his name was Dick they jumped to the conclusion that he was Richard – because Dick is short for Richard.'

'But Dick *told* them he wasn't Richard Kent,' said Anne, earnestly.

'Of course, but they thought he wasn't telling the truth,' said Julian. 'And they've taken him off. What did you say was the name of the place they were going to?'

'It sounded like Owl's Dene,' said Anne. 'Can we go there, Julian? If you told the men Dick was Dick and not Richard, they'd let him go, wouldn't they?'

'Oh yes,' said Julian. 'In any case, as soon as that fellow Rooky sets eyes on him he'll know there's a mistake been made. I think we can get old Dick away all right.'

A voice came out of the shadows nearby. 'What about *me*? Will you take me home first? *I* don't want to run into Rooky again.'

'I'm certainly not going to waste time taking *you* home,' said Julian, coldly. 'If it hadn't been for you and your tomfoolery we wouldn't have run into this trouble. You'll have to come with us. I'm going to find Dick first.'

'But I *can't* come with you – I'm afraid of Rooky!' wailed Richard.

'Well, stay here then,' said Julian, determined to teach Richard a lesson.

That was even worse. Richard howled loudly. 'Don't leave me here! Don't!'

'Now look here, if you come with us, you can always be dropped at a house somewhere, or at a police station and get yourself taken home somehow,' said Julian, exasperated. 'You're old enough to look after yourself. I'm fed up with you.'

Anne was sorry for Richard, although he had brought all this trouble on them. She knew how dreadful it was to feel really frightened. She put out a hand and touched him kindly.

'Richard! Don't be a baby. Julian will see that you're all right. He's just feeling cross with you now, but he'll soon get over it.'

'Don't you be too sure about that!' said Julian to Anne, pretending to be sterner than he really felt. 'What Richard wants is a jolly good scolding. He's untruthful and deceitful and an absolute baby!'

'Give me another chance,' almost wept poor Richard, who had never in his life been spoken to like this before. He tried to hate Julian for saying such things to him – but oddly enough he couldn't. He only respected and admired him all the more.

Julian said no more to Richard. He really thought the boy was too feeble for words. It was a nuisance that they had him with them. He would be no help at all – simply a tiresome nuisance.

'What are we going to do, Julian?' asked George, who had been very silent. She was fond of Dick, and was very worried about him. Where was Owl's Dene? How could they possibly find it in the night? And what about those awful men? How would they treat Julian if he demanded Dick back at once? Julian was fearless and straightforward – but the men wouldn't like him any the better for that.

'Well now, what *are* we going to do?' repeated Julian, and he fell silent.

'It's no good going back to that farm, and asking for help, is it?' said George, after a pause.

'Not a bit of good,' said Julian, at once. 'That old man wouldn't help anyone! And there's no telephone laid on, as we saw. No, that farm's no good. What a pity!'

'Where's the map?' said George, a sudden idea coming into her head. 'Would Owl's Dene be named on it, do you think?'

'Not if it's a house,' said Julian. 'Only places are named there. You'd want a frightfully big map to show every house.'

'Well, anyway – let's look at the map and see if it shows any more farms or villages,' said George, who felt as if she must *do* something, even if it was only looking at a map. Julian produced the map and unfolded it. He and the girls bent over it, by the light of the bicycle lamp, and Richard peered over their shoulders. Even Timmy tried to look, forcing his head under their arms.

'Get away, Tim,' said Julian. 'Look, here's where we are – Middlecombe Woods – see? My word, we *are* in a lonely spot! There isn't a village for miles!'

Certainly no village was marked. The countryside was shown, hilly and wooded, with a stream here and there, and third-class roads now and again – but no village, no church, no bridge even was marked anywhere.

Anne gave a sudden exclamation and pointed to the contour of a hill on the map. 'Look, see what that hill's called?'

'Owl's Hill,' read out Julian. 'Yes, I see what you're getting at, Anne. If a house was built on that hill it might be called Owl's Dene, because of the name of the hill. What's more, a building *is* marked there! It hasn't a name, of course. It might be a farmhouse, an old ruin – or a big house of some kind.'

'*I* think it's very likely that's where Owl's Dene is,' said George. 'I bet it's that very house. Let's take our bikes and go.'

A huge sigh from Richard attracted their attention. '*Now* what's the matter with you?' said Julian.

'Nothing. I'm hungry, that's all,' said Richard.

The others suddenly realised that they too were hungry. In fact, *terribly* hungry! It was a long, long time since tea.

Julian remembered the food he and George had brought from the farm. Should they have it now or should they eat some on their way to Owl's Hill?

'Better eat as we go,' said Julian. 'Every minute we waste means a minute of worry for Dick.'

'I wonder what they'd do with him, if Rooky sees him and says he's not me, not the boy they want,' said Richard, suddenly.

'Set him free, I should think,' said George. 'Ruffians like

that would probably turn him loose in a deserted countryside and not care tuppence if he found his way home or not. We've absolutely *got* to find out what's happened – whether he's at Owl's Dene, or been set free, or what.'

'I can't come with you,' suddenly wailed Richard.

'Why?' demanded Julian.

'Because I haven't got my bike,' said Richard, dolefully. 'I chucked it away, you remember – and goodness knows where it is. I'd never find it again.'

'He can have Dick's,' said Anne. 'There it is, over there – with the puncture mended too.'

'Oh yes,' said Richard, relieved. 'For one frightful moment I thought I'd have to be left behind.'

Julian secretly wished he *could* be left behind. Richard was more trouble than he was worth!

'Yes, you can take Dick's bike,' he said. 'But no idiotic behaviour with it, mind – no riding without handlebars, or any tricks like that. It's Dick's bike, not yours.'

Richard said nothing. Julian was always ticking him off. He supposed he deserved it – but it wasn't at all pleasant. He pulled at Dick's bike, and found the lamp was missing. Dick, of course, had taken it off. He hunted round for it and found it on the ground. Dick had let it fall, and the switch had turned itself off when the lamp hit the ground. When Richard pressed the switch down the lamp came on again. Good!

'Now, come on,' said Julian, fetching his bicycle too. 'I'll hand out food to eat as we go. We must try to find our way to Owl's Hill as quick as ever we can!'

CHAPTER NINE

Moonlight adventure

THE FOUR of them rode carefully down the rough, woodland path. They were glad when they came out into a lane. Julian stopped for a moment to take his bearings.

'Now, according to the map, we ought to go to the right here then take the left at the fork some way down, and then circle a hill by the road at the bottom, and then ride a mile or two in a little valley till we come to the foot of Owl's Hill.'

'If we meet anyone we could ask them about Owl's Dene,' said Anne, hopefully.

'We shan't meet anyone out at night in this district!' said Julian. 'For one thing it's far from any village, and there will be no farmer, no policeman, no traveller for miles! We can't hope to meet anyone.'

The moon was up, and the sky cleared as they rode down the lane. It was soon as bright as day!

'We could switch off our lamps and save the batteries,' said Julian. 'We can see quite well now we're out of the woods and in the moonlight. Rather weird, isn't it?'

'I always think moonlight's strange, because although it shines so brightly on everything, you can never see much *colour* anywhere,' said Anne. She switched off her lamp too. She glanced down at Timmy.

'Switch off your head-lamps, Timmy!' she said, which made Richard give a sudden giggle. Julian smiled. It was nice to hear Anne being cheerful again.

'Timmy's eyes *are* rather like head-lamps, aren't they?' said Richard. 'I say – what about that food, Julian?'

'Right,' said Julian, and he fished in his basket. But it was very difficult to get it out with one hand, and try to hand it to the others.

'Better stop for a few minutes, after all,' he said at last. 'I've already dropped a hard-boiled egg, I think! Come on let's stack our bikes by the side of the road for three minutes, and gulp down something just to satisfy us for now.'

Richard was only too pleased. The girls were so hungry that they too thought it a good idea. They leapt off their bicycles in the moonlit road and went to the little copse at the side. It was a pine-copse, and the ground below was littered with dry brown pine-needles.

'Let's squat here for a minute or two,' said Julian. 'I say, what's that over there?'

Everyone looked. 'It's a tumbledown hut or something,' said George, and she went nearer to see. 'Yes, that's all – some old cottage fallen to bits. There's only part of the walls left. Rather an eerie little place.'

They went to sit down under the pine-trees. Julian shared out the food. Timmy got his bit too, though not so much as he would have liked! They sat there in the pine shadows, munching hungrily as fast as they could.

'I say, can anyone hear what I hear?' said Julian, raising his head. 'It sounds like a car!'

They all listened. Julian was right. A car *was* purring quietly through the countryside! What a bit of luck!

'If only it comes this way!' said Julian. 'We could stop it and ask it for help. It could take us to the nearest police station at any rate!'

They left their food in the little copse and went to the roadside. They could see no headlights shining anywhere, but they could still hear the noise of the car.

'Very quiet engine,' said Julian. 'Probably a powerful car. It hasn't got its headlights on because of the bright moonlight.'

'It's coming nearer,' said George. 'It's coming down this lane. Yes – it is!'

So it was. The noise of the engine came nearer, and nearer. The children got ready to leap out into the road to stop the car.

And then the noise of the engine died away suddenly. The moon shone down on a big streamlined car that had stopped a little way down the lane. It had no lights at all, not even side-lights. Julian put out his hand to stop the others from rushing into the road and shouting.

'Wait,' he said. 'This is just a bit strange!'

They waited, keeping in the shadows. The car had stopped not far from the tumbledown hut. A door opened on the off-side. A man got out and rushed across the road to the shadow of the hedge there. He seemed to be carrying a bundle of some kind.

A low whistle sounded. The call of an owl came back. 'An answering signal!' thought Julian, intensely curious about all this. 'I wonder what's happening?'

'Keep absolutely quiet,' he breathed to the others. 'George, look after Timmy – don't let him growl.'

But Timmy knew when he had to be quiet. He didn't even give a whine. He stood like a statue, ears pricked, eyes watching the lane.

Nothing happened for a while. Julian moved very cautiously to the shelter of another tree, from where he could see better.

He could see the tumbledown shack. He saw a shadow moving towards it from some trees beyond. He saw a man waiting – the man from the car probably. Who were they? What in the world could they be doing here at this time of night?

The man from the trees came at last to the man from the car. There was a rapid interchange of words, but Julian could not hear what they were. He was sure that the men had no idea at all that he and the other children were near. He cautiously crept to yet another tree, and peered from the shadows to try and see what was happening.

'Don't be long,' he heard one man say. 'Don't bring your things to the car. Stuff them down the well.'

Julian could not see properly what the man was doing, but he thought he must be changing his clothes. Yes, now he was putting on the others – probably from the bundle the first man had brought from the car. Julian was more and more curious. What a funny business! Who was the second man? A spy?

The man who had changed his clothes now picked up his discarded ones and went to the back of the shack. He came back without them, and followed the first man across the lane to the waiting car.

Even before the door had closed, the engine was purring, and the car was away! It passed by the pine-copse where the children were watching, and they all shrank back as it raced by. Before it had gone very far it was travelling very fast indeed.

Julian joined the others. 'Well, what do you make of all that?' he said. 'Funny business, isn't it? I watched a man changing his clothes – goodness knows why. He's left them somewhere at the back of the shack – down a well, I think I heard them say. Shall we see?'

'Yes, let's,' said George, puzzled. 'I say, did you see the number on the car? I only managed to spot the letters – KMF.'

'I saw the numbers,' said Anne. '102. And it was a black Bentley.'

'Yes. Black Bentley, KMF 102,' said Richard. 'Up to some funny business, I'll be bound!'

They made their way to the ruined shack, and pushed through overgrown weeds and bushes into the backyard. There was a broken-down well there, most of its brick work missing.

It was covered by an old wooden lid. Julian removed it. It was still heavy, though rotten with age. He peered down the well, but there was nothing at all to be seen. It was far too deep to see to the bottom by the light of a bicycle lamp.

'Not much to be seen *there*,' said Julian, replacing the lid. 'I expect it *was* his clothes he threw down. Wonder why he changed them?'

'Do you think he could be an escaped prisoner?' said Anne, suddenly. 'He'd have to change his prison clothes, wouldn't he? – that would be the most important thing for him to do. Is there a prison near here?'

Nobody knew. 'Don't remember noticing one on the

map,' said Julian. 'No, somehow I don't think the man was an escaped prisoner – more likely a spy dropped down in this desolate countryside, and supplied with clothes – or perhaps a deserter from the army. That's even *more* likely!'

'Well, whatever he is I don't like it and I'm jolly glad the car's gone with the prisoner or deserter or spy,' said Anne. 'What a curious thing that we should just be nearby when this happened! The men would never, never guess there were four children and a dog watching just a few yards away.'

'Lucky for us they *didn't* know,' said Julian. 'They wouldn't have been at all pleased! Now, come on, we've wasted enough time. Let's get back to our food. I hope Timmy hasn't eaten it all. We left it on the ground.'

Timmy hadn't eaten even a crumb. He was sitting patiently by the food, occasionally sniffing at it. All that bread and ham and eggs waiting there and nobody to eat it!

'Good dog,' said George. 'You're very, very trustworthy, Timmy. You shall have a big bit of bread and ham for your reward.'

Timmy gulped it down in one mouthful, but there was no more for him to have. The others only just had enough for themselves, and ate every crumb. They rose to their feet in a very few minutes and went to get their bicycles.

'Now for Owl's Hill again,' said Julian. 'And let's hope we don't come across any more peculiar happenings tonight. We've had quite enough.'

CHAPTER TEN

Owl's Dene on Owl's Hill

OFF THEY went again, cycling fast in the brilliant moonlight. Even when the moon went behind a cloud it was still light enough to ride without lights. They rode for what seemed like miles, and then came to a steep hill.

'Is this Owl's Hill?' said Anne, as they dismounted to walk up it. It was too steep to ride.

'Yes,' said Julian. 'At least, I think so – unless we've come quite wrong. But I don't think we have. Now the thing is, shall we find Owl's Dene at the top or not? And how shall we know it *is* Owl's Dene!'

'We could ring the bell and ask,' said Anne.

Julian laughed. That was so like Anne. 'Maybe we'll have to do that!' he said. 'But we'll scout round a bit first.'

They pushed their bicycles up the steep road. Hedges bordered each side, and fields lay beyond. There were no animals in them that the children could see – no horses, sheep or cows.

'Look!' said Anne, suddenly. 'I can see a building – at least, I'm sure I can see chimneys!'

They looked where she pointed. Yes, certainly they were chimneys – tall, brick chimneys that looked old.

'Looks like an Elizabethan mansion, with chimneys like

that,' said Julian. He paused and took a good look. 'It must be a big place. We ought to come to a drive or something soon.'

They pushed on with their bicycles. Gradually the house came into view. It was more like a mansion, and in the moonlight it looked old, rather grand and very beautiful.

'There are the gates,' said Julian, thankfully. He was tired of pushing his bicycle up the hill. 'They're shut. Hope they're not locked!'

As they drew near to the great, wrought-iron gates, they slowly opened. The children paused in surprise. Why were they opening? Not for them, that was certain!

Then they heard the sound of a car in the distance. Of course, that was what the gates were opening for. The car, however, was not coming up the hill – it was coming down the drive on the other side of the gates.

'Get out of sight, quickly,' said Julian. 'We don't want to be seen yet.'

They crouched down in the ditch with their bicycles as a car came slowly out of the open gates. Julian gave an exclamation and nudged George.

'See that? It's the black Bentley again – KMF 102!'

'How mysterious!' said George, surprised. 'What's it doing rushing about the country at night and picking up stray men! Taking them to this place too. I wonder if it *is* Owl's Dene.'

The car went by and disappeared round a bend in the

hill. The children came out of the ditch with Timmy and their bicycles.

'Let's walk cautiously up to the gates,' said Julian. 'They're still open. Funny how they opened when the car came. I never saw anyone by them!'

They walked boldly up to the open gates.

'Look!' said Julian, pointing up to the great brick posts from which the gates were hung. They all looked, and exclaimed at the name shining there.

'Well! So it *is* Owl's Dene, after all!'

'There's the name in brass letters – Owl's Dene! We've found it!'

'Come on,' said Julian, wheeling his bicycle through the gateway. 'We'll go in and snoop round. We might be lucky enough to find old Dick somewhere about.'

They all went through the gates – and then Anne clutched Julian in fright. She pointed silently behind them.

The gates were closing again! But nobody was there to shut them. They closed silently and smoothly all by themselves. There was something very weird about that.

'Who's shutting them?' whispered Anne, in a scared voice.

'I think it must be done by machinery,' whispered back Julian. 'Probably worked from the house. Let's go back and see if we can find any machinery that works them.'

They left their bicycles by the side of the drive and walked back to the gates. Julian looked for a handle or latch to open them. But there was none.

He pulled at the gates. They did not budge. It was quite impossible to open them. They had been shut and locked by some kind of machinery, and nothing and nobody could open them but that special machinery.

'Blow!' said Julian, and he sounded so angry that the others looked at him in surprise.

'Well, don't you see? – we're locked in! We're as much prisoners here as Dick is, if he's here too. We can't get out through the gates, and if you take a look you'll see a high wall running round the property from the gates – and I don't mind betting it goes the *whole* way round. We can't get out even if we want to.'

They went back thoughtfully to their bicycles. 'Better wheel them a little way into the trees and leave them,' said Julian. 'They hinder us too much now. We'll leave them and go snooping quietly round the house. Hope there are no dogs.'

They left their bicycles well hidden among the trees at the side of the wide drive. The drive was not at all well-kept. It was mossy and weeds grew all over it. It was bare only where the wheels of cars had passed.

'Shall we walk up the drive or keep to the side?' asked George.

'Keep to the side,' said Julian. 'We should easily be seen in the moonlight, walking up the drive.'

So they kept to the side, in the shadows of the trees. They followed the curves of the long drive until the house itself came into sight.

It really was very big indeed. It was built in the shape of the letter E with the middle stroke missing. There was a courtyard in front, overgrown with weeds. A low wall, about knee high, ran round the courtyard.

There was a light in a room on the top floor, and another one on the ground floor. Otherwise from that side the house was dark.

'Let's walk quietly round it,' said Julian, in a low voice. 'Goodness – what's that?'

It was a weird and terrible screech that made them all jump in alarm. Anne clutched Julian in fright.

They stood and listened.

Something came down silently and brushed George's hair. She almost screamed, but before she could, that terrible screech came again, and she put out her hand to quieten Timmy, who was amazed and scared.

'What is it, Ju!' whispered George. 'Something touched me then. Before I could see what it was it was gone.'

'Listen, it's all right,' whispered back Julian. 'It's only an owl – a screech-owl!'

'Good gracious – so it was,' breathed back George, in great relief. 'What an ass I was not to think of it. It's a barn-owl – a screech-owl out hunting. Anne, were you scared?'

'I should just think I was!' said Anne, letting go her hold on Julian's arm.

'So was I,' said Richard, whose teeth were still chattering with fear. 'I nearly ran for my life! I would have too, if I could have got my legs to work – but they were glued to the ground!'

The owl screeched again, a little farther away, and another one answered it. A third one screeched, and the night was really made hideous with the unearthly calls.

'I'd rather have a brown owl any day, calling To-whooo-oo-oo,' said George. 'That's a nice noise. But this screeching is frightful.'

'No wonder it's called Owl's Hill,' said Julian. 'Perhaps it's always been a haunt of the screech-owls.'

The four children and Timmy began to walk quietly round the house, keeping to the shadows as much as they could. Everywhere was dark at the back except two long windows. They were leaded windows, and curtains were pulled across them. Julian tried to see through the cracks.

He found a place where two curtains didn't quite meet. He put his eye to the crack and looked in.

'It's the kitchen,' he told the others. 'An enormous place – lit with one big oil-lamp. All the rest of the room is in shadow. There's a great fire-place at the end, with a few logs burning in it.'

'Anyone there?' asked George, trying to see through the crack too. Julian moved aside and let her take her turn.

'No one that I can see,' he said. George gave an exclamation as she looked, and Julian pushed her aside to look in again.

He saw a man walking into the room – a short fellow. Behind him came a woman – thin, drab and the picture of misery.

The man flung himself into a chair and began to fill a pipe. The woman took a kettle off the fire and went to fill hot-water bottles in a corner.

'She must be the cook,' thought Julian. 'What a misery she looks! I wonder what the man is – man-of-all-work, I suppose. What an evil face he's got!'

The woman spoke timidly to the man in the chair. Julian, of course, could not hear a word from outside the window. The man answered her roughly, banging on the arm of the chair as he spoke.

The woman seemed to be pleading with him about something. The man flew into a rage, picked up a poker and threatened the woman with it. Julian watched in horror. Poor woman! No wonder she looked miserable if that was the sort of thing that kept happening.

However, the man did nothing with the poker except brandish it in temper, and he soon replaced it, and settled down in his chair again. The woman said no more at all, but went on filling the bottles. Julian wondered who they were for.

He told the others what he had seen. They didn't like it at all. If the people in the kitchen behaved like that whatever would those in the other part of the house be like?

They left the kitchen windows and went on round the house. They came to a lower room, lit inside. But there the curtains were tightly drawn, and there was no crack to look through.

They looked up to the one room high up that was lit. Surely Dick must be there? Perhaps he was locked up in the attic, all by himself? How they wished they knew!

Dared they throw up a stone? They wondered if they should try. There didn't seem any way at all of getting into the house. The front door was well and truly shut. There was a side door also tightly shut and locked, because they had tried it. Not a single window seemed to be open.

'I think I *will* throw up a stone,' said Julian at last. 'I feel sure Dick's up there, if he has been taken here – and you're certain you heard the men say "Owl's Dene", aren't you, Anne?'

'Quite certain,' said Anne. 'Do throw a stone, Julian. I'm getting so worried about poor Dick.'

Julian felt about on the ground for a stone. He found one embedded in the moss that was everywhere. He balanced it in his hand. Then up went the stone, but fell just short of the window. Julian got another. Up it went – and hit the glass of the window with a sharp crack. Somebody came to the pane at once.

Was it Dick? Everyone strained their eyes to see – but the window was too far up. Julian threw up another stone, and that hit the window too.

'I think it *is* Dick,' said Anne. 'Oh dear – no it isn't after all. Can't *you* see, Julian?'

But the person at the window, whoever he was, had now disappeared. The children felt a bit uncomfortable. Suppose it hadn't been Dick? Suppose it had been someone else who had now disappeared from the room to go and look for them?

'Let's get away from this part of the house,' whispered Julian. 'Get round to the other side.'

They made their way round quietly – and Richard suddenly pulled at Julian's arm. 'Look!' he said. 'There's a window open! Can't we get in there?'

CHAPTER ELEVEN

Trapped!

JULIAN LOOKED at the casement window. The moonlight shone on it. It certainly was a little ajar. 'How did we miss that when we went round before?' he wondered. He hesitated a little. Should they try to get in or not? Wouldn't it be better to rap on the back door and get that miserable-looking woman to answer it and tell them what they wanted to know?

On the other hand there was that evil-looking man there. Julian didn't like the look of him at all. No, on the whole it might be better to creep in at the window, see if it was Dick upstairs, set him free, and then all escape through the same open window. Nobody would know. The bird would have flown, and everything would be all right.

Julian went to the window. He put a leg up and there he was astride the window. He held out a hand to Anne. 'Come on, I'll give you a hand,' he said, and pulled her up beside him. He lifted her down on the floor inside.

Then George came, and then Richard. George was just leaning out to encourage Timmy to jump in through the window too, when something happened!

A powerful torchlight went on, and its beam shone right across the room into the dazzled eyes of the four children! They stood there, blinking in alarm. What was this?

Then Anne heard the voice of one of the men who had captured Dick. 'Well, well, well – a crowd of young burglars!'

The voice changed suddenly to anger. 'How *dare* you break in here! I'll hand you over to the police.'

From outside Timmy growled fiercely. He jumped up at the window and almost succeeded in leaping through. The man grasped what was happening at once, and went to the open window. He shut it with a bang. Now Timmy couldn't get in!

'Let my dog in!' said George, angrily, and stupidly tried to open the window again. The man brought his torch down sharply on her hand and she cried out in pain.

'That's what happens to boys who go against my wishes,' said the man, whilst poor George nursed her bruised hand.

'Look here,' began Julian, fiercely, 'what do you think you're doing? We're not burglars – and what's more we'd be very, very glad if you'd hand us over to the police!'

'Oh, you would, would you?' said the man. He went to the door of the room and yelled out in a tremendous voice: 'Aggie! AGGIE! Bring a lamp here at once.'

There was an answering shout from the kitchen, and almost immediately the light of a lamp appeared shining down the passage outside. It grew brighter, and the miserable-looking woman came in with a big oil-lamp. She stared in amazement at the little group of children. She seemed about to say something when the man gave her a rough push.

'Get out. And keep your mouth shut. Do you hear me?'

The woman scuttled out like a frightened hen. The man looked round at the children in the light of the lamp. The room was very barely furnished and appeared to be a sitting-room of some kind.

'So you don't mind being given up to the police?' said the man. 'That's very interesting. You think they'd approve of you breaking into my house?'

'I tell you, we *didn't* break in,' said Julian, determined to get that clear, at any rate. 'We came here because we had reason to believe that you've got my brother locked up somewhere in this house – and it's all a mistake. You've got the wrong boy.'

Richard didn't like this at all. He was terribly afraid of being locked up in place of Dick! He kept behind the others as much as possible.

The man looked hard at Julian. He seemed to be thinking. 'We haven't a boy here at all,' he said at last. 'I really don't know what you mean. You don't suggest that I go about the countryside picking boys up and making them prisoners, do you?'

'I don't know what you do,' said Julian. 'All I know is this – you captured Dick, my brother, this evening in Middlecombe Woods, thinking he was Richard Kent –

well, he's not, he's my brother Dick. And if you don't set him free at once, I'll tell the police what we know.'

'And dear me – *how* do you know all this?' asked the man. 'Were you there when he was captured, as you call it?'

'One of us was,' said Julian bluntly. 'In the tree overhead. That's how we know.'

There was a silence. The man took out a cigarette and lighted it. 'Well, you're quite mistaken,' he said. 'We've no boy held prisoner here. The thing is ridiculous. Now it's very, very late – would you like to bed down here for the night and get off in the morning? I don't like to send a parcel of kids out into the middle of the night. There's no telephone here, or I'd ring your home.'

Julian hesitated. He felt certain Dick was in the house. If he said he would stay for the night he might be able to find out if Dick was really there or not. He could quite well see that the man didn't want them tearing off to the police. There was something at Owl's Dene that was secret and sinister.

'We'll stay,' he said at last. 'Our people are away – they won't worry.'

He had forgotten about Richard for the moment. His people certainly *would* worry! Still, there was nothing to do about it. The first thing was to find Dick. Surely the men would be mad to hold him a prisoner once they were certain he wasn't the boy. Perhaps Rooky, the ruffian who knew Richard, hadn't yet arrived – hadn't seen Dick? That must be the reason that this man wanted them to stay the night. Of course, he'd wait till Rooky came, and when Rooky said, 'No, he's not the boy we want!' they'd let Dick go. They'd have to!

The man called for Aggie again. She came at once.

'These kids are lost,' said the man to her. 'I've said I'll put them up for the night. Get one of the rooms ready – just put down mattresses and blankets, that's all. Give them some food if they want it.'

Aggie was evidently tremendously astonished. Julian guessed that she was not used to this man being kind to lost children. He shouted at her.

'Well, don't stand dithering there. Get on with the job. Take these kids with you.'

Aggie beckoned to the four children. George hung back. 'What about my dog?' she said. 'He's still outside, whining. I can't go to bed without him.'

'You'll have to,' said the man, roughly. 'I won't have him in the house at any price, and that's flat.'

'He'll attack anyone he meets,' said George.

'He won't meet anyone out there,' said the man. 'By the way, how did you get in through the gates?'

'A car came out just as we got there and we slipped in before the gates closed,' said Julian. 'How do the gates shut? By machinery?'

'Mind your own business,' said the man, and went down the passage in the opposite direction.

'Pleasant, kindly fellow,' said Julian to George.

'Oh, a sweet nature,' answered George. The woman stared at them both in surprise. She didn't seem to realise that they meant the opposite to what they said! She led the way upstairs.

She came to a big room with a carpet on the floor, a small bed in a corner, and one or two chairs. There was no other furniture.

'I'll get some mattresses and put them down for you,' she said.

'I'll help you,' offered Julian, thinking it would be a good idea to see round a bit.

'All right,' said the woman. 'You others stay here.'

She went off with Julian. They went to a cupboard and the woman tugged at two big mattresses. Julian helped her. She seemed rather touched by his help.

'Well, thank you,' she said. 'They're pretty heavy.'

'Don't expect you have many children here, to stay, do you?' asked Julian.

'Well, it's funny that you should come just after . . .' the woman began. Then she stopped and bit her lip, looking anxiously up and down the passage.

'Just after what?' asked Julian. 'Just after the other boy came, do you mean?'

'Sh!' said the woman, looking scared to death. 'Whatever do you know about *that*? You shouldn't have said that. Mr Perton will skin me alive if he knew you'd said that. He'd be sure I'd told you. Forget about it.'

'That's the boy who's locked up in one of the attics at

the top of the house, isn't it?' said Julian, helping her to carry one of the mattresses to the big bedroom. She dropped her end in the greatest alarm.

'Now! Do you want to get me into terrible trouble – and yourselves too? Do you want Mr Perton to tell old Hunchy to get you all? You don't know that man! He's wicked.'

'When's Rooky coming?' asked Julian, bent on astonishing the woman, hoping to scare her into one admission after another. This was too much for her altogether. She stood there shaking at the knees, staring at Julian as if she couldn't believe her ears.

'What do you know about Rooky?' she whispered. 'Is he coming here? Don't tell me he's coming here!'

'Why? Don't you like him?' asked Julian. He put a hand on her shoulder. 'Why are you so frightened and upset? What's the matter? Tell me. I might be able to help you.'

'Rooky's bad,' said the woman. 'I thought he was in prison. Don't tell me he's out again. Don't tell me he's coming here.'

She was so frightened that she wouldn't say a word more. She began to cry, and Julian hadn't the heart to press her with any more questions. In silence he helped her to drag the mattresses into the other room.

'I'll get you some food,' said the poor woman, sniffing miserably. 'You'll find blankets in that cupboard over there if you want to lie down.'

She disappeared. Julian told the others in whispers what he had been able to find out. 'We'll see if we can find Dick as soon as things are quiet in the house,' he said. 'This is a bad house – a house of secrets, of strange comings and goings. I shall slip out of our room and see what I can find out later on. I think that man – Mr Perton is his name – is really waiting for Rooky to come and see if Dick is Richard or not. When he finds he isn't I've no doubt he'll set him free – and us too.'

'What about *me*?' said Richard. 'Once he sees me, I'm done for. I'm the boy he wants. He hates my father and he hates me too. He'll kidnap me, take me somewhere, and ask an enormous ransom for me, just to punish us!'

'Well, we must do something to prevent him seeing you,' said Julian. 'But I don't see why he *should* see you – it's only Dick he'll want to see. He won't be interested in what he thinks are Dick's brothers and sisters! Now for goodness' sake don't start to howl again, or honestly I'll give you up to Rooky myself! You really are a frightful little coward – haven't you any courage at all!'

'All this has come about because of your silly lies and deceit,' said George, quite fiercely. 'It's all because of you that our trip is spoilt, that Dick's locked up and poor Timmy's outside without me.'

Richard looked quite taken aback. He shrank into a corner and didn't say another word. He was very miserable. Nobody liked him, nobody believed him, nobody trusted him. Richard felt very, very small indeed.

CHAPTER TWELVE

Julian looks round

THE WOMAN brought them some food. It was only bread and butter and jam, with some hot coffee to drink. The four children were not really hungry, but they were very thirsty, and they drank the coffee eagerly.

George opened the window and called softly down to Timmy. 'Tim! Here's something for you!'

Timmy was down there all right, watching and waiting. He knew where George was. He had howled and whined for some time, but now he was quiet.

George was quite determined to get him indoors if she could. She gave him all her bread and jam, dropping it down bit by bit, and listening to him wolfing it up. Anyway, old Timmy would know she was thinking of him!

'Listen,' said Julian, coming in from the passage outside, where he had stood listening for a while. 'I think it would be a good idea if we put out this light, and settled down on the mattresses. But I shall make up a lump on mine to look like me, so that if anyones comes they'll think I'm there on the mattress. But I shan't be.'

'Where will you be, then?' asked Anne. 'Don't leave us!'

'I shall be hiding outside in that cupboard,' said Julian. 'I've a sort of feeling that our pleasant host, Mr Perton, will come along presently to lock us in – and I've no intention of being locked in! I think he'll flash a torch into the room, see that we're all four safely asleep on the mattresses, and then quietly lock the door. Well, *I* shall be able to unlock it when I come back from the cupboard outside and we shan't be prisoners at all!'

'Oh, that really is a good idea,' said Anne, cuddling herself up in a blanket. 'You'd better go and get into the cupboard now, Julian, before we're locked up for the night!'

Julian blew out the lamp. He tiptoed to the door and opened it. He left it ajar. He went into the passage and fumbled his way to where he knew the cupboard should be. Ah, there it was. He pulled the handle and the door opened silently. He slipped inside and left the door open just a crack, so that he would be able to see if anyone came along the wide passage.

He waited there about twenty minutes. The cupboard smelt musty, and it was very boring standing there doing absolutely nothing.

Then, through the crack in the door, he suddenly noticed that a light was coming. Ah, somebody was about!

He peered through the crack. He saw Mr Perton coming quietly along the corridor with a little oil-lamp held in his hand. He went to the door of the children's bedroom and pushed it a little. Julian watched him, hardly daring to breathe.

Would he notice that the figure on one of the mattresses

was only a lump made of a blanket rolled up and covered by another blanket? Julian fervently hoped that he wouldn't. All his plans would be spoilt if so.

Mr Perton held the lamp high in his hand and looked cautiously into the room. He saw four huddled-up shapes lying on the mattresses – four children – he thought.

They were obviously asleep. Softly, Mr Perton closed the door, and just as softly locked it. Julian watched anxiously to see if he pocketed the key or not. No – he hadn't! He had left it in the lock. Oh good!

The man went away again, treading softly. He did not go downstairs, but disappeared into a room some way down on the right. Julian heard the door shut with a click. Then he heard another click. The man evidently believed in locking himself in. Perhaps he didn't trust his other comrade, wherever he was – or Hunchy or the woman.

Julian waited a while and then crept out of the cupboard. He stole up to Mr Perton's room and looked through the keyhole to see if the room was in darkness or not. It was! Was Mr Perton snoring? Not that Julian could hear.

However Julian was not going to wait till he heard Mr Perton snore. He was going to find Dick – and he was pretty certain that the first place to look was in that attic upstairs!

'I bet Mr Perton was up there with Dick and heard me throwing stones at the window,' thought Julian. 'Then he slipped down and opened that window to trap us into getting in there, and we fell neatly into the trap! He must have been waiting inside the room for us. I don't like Mr Perton – too full of bright ideas!'

He was half-way up the flight of stairs that led to the attics now – going very carefully and slowly, afraid of making the stairs creak loudly. They did creak – and at every creak poor Julian stopped and listened to see if anyone had heard!

There was a long passage at the top turning at both ends into the side-wings. Julian stood still and debated – now which way ought he to go? Where exactly was that lit window? It was somewhere along this long passage, he was certain. Well, he'd go along the doors and see if a light shone out through the keyhole, or under the door anywhere.

Door after door was ajar. Julian peeped round each, making out bare dark attics, or box-rooms with rubbish in. Then he came to a door that was closed. He peered through the keyhole. No light came from inside the room.

Julian knocked gently. A voice came at once – Dick's voice. 'Who's there?'

'Sh! It's me – Julian,' whispered Julian. 'Are you all right, Dick?'

There came the creak of a bed, then the pattering of feet across a bare floor. Dick's voice came through the door, muffled and cautious.

'Julian! How did you get here? This is marvellous! Can you unlock the door and let me out?'

Julian had already felt for a key – but there was none. Mr Perton had taken *that* key, at any rate!

'No. The key's gone,' he said. 'Dick, what did they do to you?'

'Nothing much. They dragged me off to the car and shoved me in,' said Dick, through the door. 'The man called Rooky wasn't there. The others waited for him for some time, then drove off. They thought he might have gone off to see someone they meant to visit. So I haven't seen him. He's coming tomorrow morning. What a shock for him when he finds I'm not Richard!'

'Richard's here too,' whispered Julian. 'I wish he wasn't

– because if Rooky happens to see him he'll be kidnapped, I'm sure! The only hope is that Rooky will only see *you* – and as the other men think we're all one family, they may let us all go. Did you come straight here in the car, Dick?'

'Yes,' said Dick. 'The gates opened like magic when we got here, but I couldn't see anybody. I was shoved up here and locked in. One of the men came to tell me all the things Rooky was going to do to me when he saw me – and then he suddenly went downstairs and hasn't come back again.'

'Oh, I bet that was when we chucked stones up at your window,' said Julian at once. 'Didn't you hear them?'

'Yes, so that was the crack I heard! The man with me went across to the window at once and he must have seen you. Now, what about *you*, Ju? How on earth did you get here? Are you all really here? I suppose that was Timmy I heard howling outside.'

Julian quickly told him all his tale from the time he and George had met the howling Richard to the moment he had slipped up the stairs to find Dick.

There was a silence when he had finished his tale. Then Dick's voice came through the crack.

'Not much good making any plans, Julian. If things go all right, we'll be out of here by the morning, when Rooky finds I'm not the boy he wants. If things go wrong at least we're all together, and we can make plans then. I wonder what his mother will think when Richard doesn't get home tonight.'

'Probably think he's gone off to the aunt's,' said Julian.

'I should think he's a very unreliable person. Blow him! It was all because of him we got into this fix.

'I expect the men will have some cock-and-bull story tomorrow morning, about why they got hold of you, when they find you're not Richard,' went on Julian. 'They'll probably say you threw stones at their car or something, and they took you in hand – or found you hurt and brought you here to help you! Anyway, whatever they say, we won't make much fuss about it. We'll go quietly – and then we'll get things moving! I don't know what's going on here, but it's something fishy. The police ought to look into it, I'm certain.'

'Listen, that's Timmy again,' said Dick. 'Howling like anything for George, I suppose. You'd better go, Julian, in case he wakes up one of the men and they come out and find you here. Good night. I'm awfully glad you're near! Thanks awfully for coming to find me.'

'Good night,' said Julian, and went back along the corridor, walking over the patches of moonlight, looking fearfully into the dark shadows in case Mr Perton or somebody else was waiting for him!

But nobody was about. Timmy's howling died down. There was a deep silence in the house. Julian went down the stairs to the floor on which the bedroom was where the others lay asleep. He paused outside it. Should he do any further exploring? It really was such a chance!

He decided that he would. Mr Perton was fast asleep, he hoped. He thought probably Hunchy and the woman had gone to bed too. He wondered where the other man was, who had brought Dick to Owl's Dene. He hadn't seen him at all. Perhaps he had gone out in that black Bentley they had seen going out of the gate.

Julian went down to the ground floor. A brilliant thought had just occurred to him. Couldn't he undo the front door and get the others down, and send them out, free? He himself couldn't escape, because it would mean leaving Dick alone.

Then he gave up the idea. 'No,' he thought. 'For one thing George and Anne would refuse to go without me – and even if they agreed to get out of the front door, and go down the drive to the gates, how would they undo them? They're worked by some machinery from the house.'

So his brilliant idea came to nothing. He decided to look into all the rooms on the ground floor. He looked into the kitchen first. The fire was almost out. The moonlight came through the cracks of the curtains and lit up the dark silent room. Hunchy and the woman had evidently retired somewhere.

There was nothing of interest in the kitchen. Julian went into the room opposite. It was a dining-room, with a long polished table, candlesticks on the walls and mantelpiece, and the remains of a wood fire. Nothing of interest there either.

The boy went into another room. Was it a workroom, or what? There was a radio there, and a big desk. There was a stand with a curious instrument of some kind that had a stout wheel-like handle. Julian suddenly wondered if it would open the gates! Yes, that was what it was for. He saw a label attached to it. Left Gate. Right Gate. Both Gates.

'That's what it is – the machinery for opening either or both of the gates. If only I could get Dick out of that room I'd get us all out of this place in no time!' said Julian. He twisted the handle – what would happen?

CHAPTER THIRTEEN

Strange secret

A CURIOUS groaning, whining noise began, as some kind of strong machinery was set working. Julian hurriedly turned the handle back. If it was going to make all that noise, he wasn't going to try his hand at opening the gates! It would bring Mr Perton out of his room in a rush!

'Most ingenious, whatever it is,' thought the boy, examining it as well as he could in the moonlight that streamed through the window. He looked round the room again. A noise came to his ears and he stood still.

'It's somebody snoring,' he thought. 'I'd better not mess about here any more! Where are they sleeping? Somewhere not far from here, that's certain.'

He tiptoed cautiously into the next room and looked inside it. It was a lounge, but there was nobody there at all. He couldn't hear the snoring there either.

He was puzzled. There didn't seem to be any other room nearby where people could sleep. He went back to the workroom or study. Yes, now he could hear that noise again – and it *was* somebody snoring! Somebody quite near – and yet not near enough to hear properly, or to see. Most peculiar.

Julian walked softly round the room, trying to find a

place where the snoring sounded loudest of all. Yes, by this bookcase that reached to the ceiling. That was where the snoring sounded most of all. Was there a room behind this wall, next to the workroom? Julian went out to investigate. But there was no room behind the study at all – only the wall of the corridor, as far as he could see. It was more and more mysterious.

He went back to the study again, and over to the bookcase. Yes, there it was again. *Somebody* was asleep and snoring not far off – but WHERE?

Julian began to examine the bookcase. It was full of books jammed tightly together – novels, biographies, reference books – all higgledy-piggledy. He removed some from a shelf and examined the bookcase behind. It was of solid wood.

He put back the books and examined the big bookcase again. It was a very solid affair. Julian looked carefully at the books, shining in the moonlight. One shelf of books looked different from the others – less tidy – the books not so jammed together. Why should just one shelf be different?

Julian quietly took the books from that shelf. Behind them was the solid wood again. Julian put his hand at the back and felt about. A knob was hidden in a corner. A knob! Whatever was that there for?

Cautiously Julian turned the knob this way and that. Nothing happened. Then he pressed it. Still nothing happened. He pulled it – and it slid out a good six inches.

Then the whole of the back of that particular shelf slid quietly downwards, and left an opening big enough for somebody to squeeze through! Julian held his breath. A sliding panel! What was behind it?

A dim flickering light came from the space behind. Julian waited till his eyes were used to it after the bright moonlight. He was trembling with excitement. The snoring now sounded so loud that Julian felt as if the snorer must be almost within hand's reach!

Then gradually he made out a tiny room, with a small narrow bed, a table and a shelf on which a few articles could dimly be made out. A candle was burning in a corner. On the bed was the snorer. Julian could not see what he was like, except that he looked big and burly as he lay there, snoring peacefully.

'What a find!' thought Julian. 'A secret hiding-place – a place to hide all kinds of people, I suppose, who have enough money to pay for such a safe hole. This fellow ought to have been warned not to snore! He gave himself away.'

The boy did not dare to stay there any longer, looking into that curious secret room. It must be built in a space between the wall of the study and the wall of the corridor – probably a very old hiding-place made when the house was built.

Julian felt for the knob. He pushed it back into place, and the panel slid up again, as noiselessly as before. It was evidently kept in good working order!

The snoring was muffled again now. Julian replaced the books, hoping that they were more or less as he had found them.

He felt very thrilled. He had found one of the secrets of Owl's Dene, at any rate. The police would be *very* interested to hear about that secret hole – and perhaps they would be even more interested to hear about the person inside it!

It was absolutely essential now that he and the others should escape. Would it be all right if he went without Dick? No, if the men suspected any dirty work on his part – discovered that he knew of the secret hole, for instance – they might harm Dick. Regretfully Julian decided that there must be no escape for him unless everyone, including Dick, could come too.

He didn't explore any more. He suddenly felt very tired indeed and crept softly upstairs. He felt as if he simply must lie down and think. He was too tired to do anything else.

He went to the bedroom. The key was still in the lock outside. He went into the room and shut the door. Mr Perton would find the door unlocked the next morning, but probably he would think he hadn't turned the key properly. Julian lay down on the mattress beside Richard. All the others were fast asleep.

He meant to think out all his problems – but no sooner had he closed his eyes than he was fast asleep. He didn't hear Timmy howling outside once more. He didn't hear the screech-owl that made the night hideous on the hill. He didn't see the moon slide down the sky.

It was not Mr Perton who awoke the children next morning, but the woman. She came into the room and called to them.

'If you want breakfast you'd better come down and have it!'

They all sat up in a hurry, wondering where in the world they were. 'Hallo!' said Julian, blinking sleepily. 'Breakfast, did you say? It sounds good. Is there anywhere we can wash?'

'You can wash down in the kitchen,' said the woman, sullenly. 'I'm not cleaning any bathroom up after you!'

'Leave the door unlocked for us to get out!' said Julian, innocently. 'Mr Perton locked it last night.'

'So he said,' answered the woman, 'but he *hadn't* locked it! It wasn't locked when I tried the door this morning. Aha! You didn't know that, did you? You'd have been wandering all over the house, I suppose, if you'd guessed that.'

'Probably we should,' agreed Julian, winking at the others. They knew that he had meant to go and find Dick in the night, and snoop round a bit – but they didn't know all he had discovered. He hadn't had the heart to wake them and tell them the night before.

'Don't you be too long,' said the woman, and went out of the door, leaving it open.

'I hope she's taken some breakfast up to poor old Dick,'

said Julian, in a low voice. The others came close to him.

'Ju, did you find Dick last night?' whispered Anne. He nodded. Then, very quickly and quietly he told them all he had discovered – where Dick was, and then how he had heard the snoring, and discovered the secret panel, the hidden room, and the man who slept so soundly there, not knowing that Julian had seen him.

'Julian! How thrilling!' said George. 'Whoever would have thought of all that?'

'Oh yes, and I discovered the machinery that opens the gates too,' said Julian. 'It's in the same room. But come on, if we don't go down to the kitchen that woman will be after us again. I hope Hunchy won't be there, I don't like him.'

Hunchy, however, *was* there, finishing his breakfast at a small table. He scowled at the children, but they took absolutely no notice of him.

'You've been a long time,' grumbled the woman. 'There's the sink over there, if you want to wash, and I've put a towel out for you. You look pretty dirty, all of you.'

'We are,' said Julian, cheerfully. 'We could have done with a bath last night – but we didn't exactly get much of a welcome, you know.'

When they had washed they went to a big scrubbed table. There was no cloth on it. The woman had put out some bread and butter and some boiled eggs and a jug of steaming hot cocoa. They all sat down and began to help themselves. Julian talked cheerfully, winking at the others to make them do the same. He wasn't going to let that man think they were scared or worried in any way.

'Shut up, you,' said Hunchy, suddenly. Julian took no notice. He went on talking, and George backed him up valiantly, though Anne and Richard were too scared, after hearing the man's furious voice.

'Did you hear what I said?' suddenly yelled Hunchy, and got up from the little table where he had been sitting. 'Hold your tongues, all of you! Coming into my kitchen and making all that row! Hold your tongues!'

Julian rose too. 'I don't take orders from you, whoever you are,' he said, and he sounded just like a grown-up. 'You hold your tongue – or else be civil.'

'Oh, don't talk to him like that, don't,' begged the woman, anxiously. 'He's got such a temper – he'll take a stick to you!'

'I'd take a stick to *him* – except that I don't hit at fellows smaller than myself,' said Julian.

What would have happened if Mr Perton hadn't appeared in the kitchen at that moment nobody knew! He stalked in and glared round, sensing that there was a row going on.

'You losing your temper again, Hunchy?' he said. 'Keep it till it's needed. I'll ask you to produce it sometime today possibly – if these kids don't behave themselves!' He looked round at the children with a grim expression. Then he glanced at the woman.

'Rooky's coming soon,' he told her. 'And one or two others. Get a meal – a good one. Keep these children in here, Hunchy, and keep an eye on them. I may want them later.'

He went out. The woman was trembling. 'Rooky's coming,' she half-whispered to Hunchy.

'Get on with your work, woman,' said the man. 'Go out and get the vegetables in yourself – I've got to keep an eye on these kids.'

The poor woman scuttled about. Anne was sorry for her. She went over to her. 'Shall I clear away and wash up for you?' she asked. 'You're going to be busy and I've nothing to do.'

'We'll all help,' said Julian. The woman gave him an astonished and grateful glance. It was plain that she was not used to good manners or politeness of any sort.

'Yah!' said Hunchy, sneeringly. 'You won't get round *me* with your smarmy ways!'

Nobody took the slightest notice of him. All the children began to clear away the breakfast things, and Anne and George stacked them in the sink, and began to wash them.

'Yah!' said Hunchy again.

'And yah to you,' said Julian, pleasantly, which made the others laugh, and Hunchy scowl till his eyes disappeared under his brows!

CHAPTER FOURTEEN

Rooky is very angry

ABOUT AN hour later there was a curious grinding, groaning noise that turned to a whining. Richard, Anne and George jumped violently. But Julian knew what it was.

'The gates are being opened,' he told them, and they remembered how he had described the machinery that opened the gates – the curious wheel-like handle, labelled 'Left Gate. Right Gate. Both Gates'.

'How do *you* know that?' asked Hunchy at once, surprised and suspicious.

'Oh, I'm a good guesser,' replied Julian airily. 'Correct me if I'm wrong, but I couldn't help thinking the gates were being opened, and I'm guessing it's Rooky that's coming through them!'

'You're so sharp you'll cut yourself one day,' grumbled Hunchy, going to the door.

'So my mother told me when I was two years old,' said Julian, and the others giggled. If there was any answering back to be done, Julian could always do it!

They all went to the window. George opened it. Timmy was there, sitting just outside. George had begged the woman to let him in, but she wouldn't. She had thrown him some scraps, and told George there was a pond he could drink from, but beyond that she wouldn't go.

'Timmy,' called George, as she heard the sound of a car purring quietly up the drive, 'Timmy, stay there. Don't move!'

She was afraid that Timmy might perhaps run round to the front door, and go for anyone who jumped out of the car. Timmy looked up at her inquiringly. He was puzzled about this whole affair. Why wasn't he allowed inside the house with George? He knew there were some people who didn't welcome dogs into their houses – but George never went to those houses. It was a puzzle to him, too, to understand why she didn't come out to him.

Still, she was there, leaning out of the window; he could hear her voice; he could even lick her hand if he stood up on his hind legs against the wall.

'You shut that window and come inside,' said Hunchy, maliciously. He took quite a pleasure in seeing that George was upset at being separated from Timmy.

'Here comes the car,' said Julian. They all looked at it – and then glanced at each other. KMF 102 – of course!

The black Bentley swept by the kitchen windows and up to the front door. Three men got out. Richard crouched back, his face going pale.

Julian glanced round at him raising his eyebrows, mutely asking him if he recognised one of the men as Rooky. Richard nodded miserably. He was very frightened now.

The whining, groaning noise came again. The gates were being shut. Voices came from the hall, then the men went into one of the rooms, and there was the sound of a door being shut.

Julian wondered if he could slip out of the room unnoticed and go up to see if Dick was all right. He sidled to the door, thinking that Hunchy was engrossed in cleaning an array of dirty shoes. But his grating voice sounded at once.

'Where you going? If you don't obey orders I'll tell Mr Perton – and won't you be sorry!'

'There's quite a lot of people in this house going to be sorry for themselves soon,' said Julian, in an irritatingly cheerful voice. 'You be careful, Hunchy.'

Hunchy lost his temper suddenly and threw the shoe-brush he was using straight at Julian. Julian caught it deftly and threw it up on the high mantelpiece.

'Thanks,' he said. 'Like to throw another?'

'Oh don't,' said the woman, beseechingly. 'You don't know what he's like when he's in a real temper. Don't!'

The door of the room that the men had gone into opened, and somebody went upstairs. 'To fetch Dick,' thought Julian at once. He stood and listened.

Hunchy got another shoe-brush and went on polishing, muttering angrily under his breath. The woman went on preparing some food. The others listened with Julian. They too guessed that the man had gone to fetch Dick to show him to Rooky.

Footsteps came down the stairs again – two lots this time. Yes, Dick must be with the man, they could hear his voice.

'Let go my arm! I can come without being dragged!' they heard him say indignantly. Good old Dick! He wasn't going to be dragged about without making a strong protest.

He was taken into the room where the other three men were waiting. Then a loud voice was heard.

'He's not the boy! Fools, you've got the wrong boy!'

Hunchy and the woman heard the words too. They gaped at one another. Something had gone wrong. They went to the door and stood there silently. The children just stood behind them. Julian edged Richard away very gradually.

'Rub some soot over your hair,' he whispered. 'Make it as black as you can, Richard. If the men come out here to see us, they're not likely to recognise you so easily if your hair's black. Go on, quick, while the others aren't paying attention.'

Julian was pointing to the inside of the grate, where black soot hung. Richard put his trembling hands into it and covered them with it. Then he rubbed the soot over his yellow hair.

'More,' whispered Julian. 'Much more! Go on. I'll stand in front of you so that the others can't see what you're doing.'

Richard rubbed soot even more wildly over his hair.

Julian nodded. Yes, it looked black enough now. Richard looked quite different. Julian hoped Anne and George would be sensible enough not to exclaim when they saw him.

There was evidently some sharp argument going on in the room off the hall. Voices were raised, but not many words could be made out from where the children stood at the kitchen door. Dick's voice could be heard too. It suddenly sounded quite clearly.

'I TOLD you you'd made a mistake. Now you just let me go, see!'

Hunchy suddenly pushed everyone roughly away from the door – except poor Richard who was standing over in a dark corner, shaking with fright!

'They're coming,' he hissed. 'Get away from the door.'

Everyone obeyed. Hunchy took up a shoe-brush again, the woman went to peel potatoes, the children turned over the pages of some old magazines they had found.

Footsteps came to the kitchen door. It was flung open. Mr Perton was there – and behind him another man. No mistaking who *he* was!

Yes, he was the ruffian Rooky, once bodyguard to Richard's father, the man who hated Richard because he had told tales on him and who had been sent off in disgrace by the boy's father.

Richard cowered back in his corner, hiding behind the others. Anne and George had given him astonished stares when they had noticed his hair, but neither of them had said a word. Hunchy and the woman didn't seem to have noticed any change in him.

Dick was with the two men. He waved to the others. Julian grinned. Good old Dick!

Rooky glanced at all four children. His eyes rested for a moment on Richard, and then glanced away. He hadn't recognised him!

'Well, Mr Perton,' said Julian. 'I'm glad to see you've got my brother down from the room you locked him up in last night. I imagine that means he can come with us now. Why you brought him here as you did, and made him a prisoner last night I can't imagine.'

'Now look here,' said Mr Perton, in quite a different voice from the one he had used to them before. 'Now look here, quite frankly we made a mistake. You don't need to know why or how – that's none of your business. This isn't the boy we wanted.'

'We *told* you he was our brother,' said Anne.

'Quite,' said Mr Perton, politely. 'I am sorry I disbelieved you. These things happen. Now, we want to make you all a handsome present for any inconvenience you have suffered – er – ten pounds for you to spend on ice-creams and so on. You can go whenever you like.'

'And don't try and tell any fairy stories to anyone,' said Rooky suddenly, in a threatening voice. 'See? We made a mistake – but we're not having it talked about. If you say anything silly, we shall say that we found this boy lost in the woods, took pity on him and brought him here for the night – and that you kids were – found trespassing in the grounds. You understand?'

'I understand perfectly,' said Julian, in a cool rather scornful voice. 'Well, I take it we can all go now, then?'

'Yes,' said Mr Perton. He put his hand into his pocket and took out some coins. He handed two to each of the children. They glanced at Julian to see if they were to take them or not. Not one of them felt willing to accept Mr Perton's money. But they knew they must take them if Julian did.

Julian accepted the two coins handed to him, and pocketed them without a word of thanks. The others did the same. Richard kept his head down well all the time, hoping that the two men would not notice how his knees were shaking. He was really terrified of Rooky.

'Now clear out,' said Rooky when the ten pounds had been divided. 'Forget all this – or you'll be very sorry.'

He opened the door that led into the garden. The children trooped out silently, Richard well in their midst. Timmy was waiting for them. He gave a loud bark of welcome and flung himself on George, fawning on her, licking every bit of her he could reach. He looked back at the kitchen door and gave a questioning growl as if to say, 'Do you want me to go for anyone in there?'

'No,' said George. 'You come with us, Timmy. We'll get out of here as quickly as we can.'

'Give me your coins, quick,' said Julian in a low voice, when they had rounded a corner and were out of sight of the windows. They all handed them to him wonderingly. What was he going to do with them?

The woman had come out to watch them go. Julian beckoned to her. She came hesitatingly down the garden. 'For you,' said Julian, putting the coins into her hand. 'We don't want them.'

The woman took them, amazed. Her eyes filled with tears. 'Why, it's a fortune – no, no, you take them back. You're kind, though – so kind.'

Julian turned away, leaving the astonished and delighted woman standing staring after them. He hurried after the others.

'That was a very, very good idea of yours,' said Anne, warmly, and the others agreed. All of them had been sorry for the poor woman.

'Come on,' said Julian. 'We don't want to miss the opening of the gates! Listen, can you hear the groaning noise back at the house. Somebody has set the machinery working that opens the gates. Thank goodness we're free – and Richard too. That *was* a bit of luck!'

'Yes, I was so scared Rooky would recognise me, even though my hair was sooted black,' said Richard, who was now looking much more cheerful. 'Oh look, we can see the end of the drive now, and the gates are wide open. We're free!'

'We'll get our bikes,' said Julian. 'I know where we left them. You can ride on my crossbar, Richard, because we're a bike short. Dick must have his bike back now – you remember you borrowed it? Look, here they are.'

They mounted their bicycles and began to cycle down the drive – and then Anne gave a scream.

'Julian! Look, look – the gates are closing again. Quick, quick – we'll be left inside!'

Everyone saw in horror that the gates were actually closing, very slowly. They pedalled as fast as they could – but it was no use. By the time they got there the two great gates were fast shut. No amount of shaking would open them. And just as they were so very nearly out!

CHAPTER FIFTEEN

Prisoners

THEY ALL flung themselves down on the grass verge and groaned.

'What have they done that for, just as we were going out?' said Dick. 'Was it a mistake, do you think? I mean – did they think we'd had time to go out, or what?'

'Well, if it was a mistake, it's easy to put right,' said Julian. 'I'll just cycle back to the house and tell them they shut the gates too soon.'

'Yes, you do that,' said George. 'We'll wait here.'

But before Julian could even mount his bicycle there came the sound of the car purring down the long drive. All the children jumped to their feet. Richard ran behind a bush in panic. He was terrified of having to face Rooky again.

The car drew up by the children and stopped. 'Yes, they're still here,' said Mr Perton's voice, as he got out of the car. Rooky got out too. They came over to the children.

Rooky ran his eyes over them. 'Where's that other boy?' he asked quickly.

'I can't imagine,' said Julian, coolly. 'Dear me, I wonder if he had time to cycle out of the gateway. Why did you shut the gates so soon, Mr Perton?'

Rooky had caught sight of Richard's shivering figure behind the bush. He strode over to him and yanked him out. He looked at him closely. Then he pulled him over to Mr Perton.

'Yes, I thought so – *this* is the boy we want! He's sooted his hair or something, and that's why I didn't recognise him. But when he'd gone I felt sure there was something familiar about him – that's why I wanted another look.' He shook poor Richard like a dog shaking a rat.

'Well, what do you want to do about it?' asked Mr Perton, rather gloomily.

'Hold him, of course,' said Rooky. 'I'll get back at his father now – he'll have to pay a very large sum of money for his horrible son! That'll be useful, won't it? And I can pay this kid out for some of the lies he told his father about me. Nasty little rat.'

He shook Richard again. Julian stepped forward, white and furious.

'Now you stop that,' he said. 'Let the boy go. Haven't you done enough already – keeping my brother locked up for nothing – holding us all for the night – and now you talk about kidnapping! Haven't you just come out of prison? Do you want to go back there?'

Rooky dropped Richard and lunged out at Julian. With a snarl Timmy flung himself between them and bit the man's hand. Rooky let out a howl of rage and nursed his injured hand. He yelled at Julian.

'Call that dog to heel. Do you hear?'

'I'll call him to heel all right – if you talk sense,' said Julian, still white with rage. 'You're going to let us all go, here and now. Go back and open these gates.'

Timmy growled terrifyingly, and both Rooky and Mr Perton took some hurried steps backwards. Rooky picked up a very big stone.

'If you dare to throw that I'll set my dog on you again!' shouted George, in sudden fear. Mr Perton knocked the stone out of Rooky's hand.

'Don't be a fool,' he said. 'That dog could make mincemeat of us – great ugly brute. Look at his teeth. For goodness' sake let the kids go, Rooky.'

'Not till we've finished our plans,' said Rooky fiercely, still nursing his hand. 'Keep them all prisoners here! We shan't be long before our jobs are done. And what's more I'm going to take that little rat there off with me when I go! Ha! I'll teach him a few things – and his father too.'

Timmy growled again. He was straining at George's hand. She had him firmly by the collar. Richard trembled when he heard Rooky's threats about him. Tears ran down his face.

'Yes, you can howl all you like,' said Rooky, scowling at him. 'You wait till I get you! Miserable little coward, you never did have any spunk, you just ran round telling tales and misbehaving yourself whenever you could.'

'Look, Rooky, you'd better come up to the house and have that hand seen to,' said Mr Perton. 'It's bleeding badly. You ought to wash it and put some stuff on it – you know a dog's bite is dangerous. Come on. You can deal with these kids afterwards.'

Rooky allowed himself to be led back to the car. He shook his unhurt fist at the children as they watched silently.

'Interfering brats! Little . . .'

But the rest of his pleasant words were lost in the purring of the car's engine. Mr Perton backed a little, turned the car, and it disappeared up the drive. The five children sat themselves down on the grass verge. Richard began to sob out loud.

'Do shut up, Richard,' said George. 'Rooky was right when he said you were a little coward, with no spunk. So you are. Anne's much pluckier than you are. I wish to goodness we had never met you.'

Richard rubbed his hands over his eyes. They were sooty, and made his face look most peculiar with streaks of black soot mixed with his tears. He looked very woebegone indeed.

'I'm sorry,' he sniffed. 'I know you don't believe me – but I really am. I've always been a bit of a coward – I can't help it.'

'Yes you can,' said Julian, scornfully. 'Anybody can help being a coward. Cowardice is just thinking of your own miserable skin instead of somebody else's. Why, even little Anne is more worried about us than she is about herself – and that makes her brave. She couldn't be a coward if she tried.'

This was a completely new idea to Richard. He tried to wipe his face dry. 'I'll try to be like you,' he said, in a muffled voice. 'You're all so decent. I've never had friends like you before. Honestly, I won't let you down again.'

'Well, we'll see,' said Julian, doubtfully. 'It would certainly be a surprise if you turned into a hero all of a sudden – a very *nice* surprise, of course – but in the meantime it would be a help if you stopped howling for a bit and let us talk.'

Richard subsided. He really looked very peculiar with his soot-streaked face. Julian turned to the others.

'This is maddening!' he said. 'Just as we so nearly got out. I suppose they'll shut us up in some room and keep us there till they've finished whatever this "job" is. I imagine the "job" consists of getting that hidden fellow away in safety – the one I saw in the secret room.'

'Won't Richard's parents report his disappearance to the police?' said George, fondling Timmy, who wouldn't stop licking her now he had got her again.

'Yes, they will. But what good will that do? The police won't have the faintest notion where he is,' said Julian. 'Nobody knows where we are, either, come to that, but Aunt Fanny won't worry yet, because she knows we're off on a cycling tour, and wouldn't be writing to her anyway.'

'Do you think those men will really take me off with them when they go?' asked Richard.

'Well, we'll hope we shall have managed to escape

before that,' said Julian, not liking to say yes, certainly Richard would be whisked away!

'How *can* we escape?' asked Anne. 'We'd never get over those high walls. And I don't expect anyone ever comes by here – right at the top of this deserted hill. No tradesman would ever call.'

'What about the postman?' asked Dick.

'They probably arrange to fetch their post each day,' said Julian. 'I don't expect they want anyone coming here at all. Or, there may be a letter-box outside the gate. I never thought of that!'

They went to see. But although they craned their necks to see each side, there didn't seem to be any letter-box at all for the postman to slip letters in. So the faint hope that had risen in their minds, that they might catch the postman and give him a message, vanished at once.

'Hallo, here's the woman – Aggie, or whatever her name is,' said George, suddenly, as Timmy growled. They all turned their heads. Aggie was coming down the drive in a hurry – could she be going out? Would the gates open for her?

Their hopes died as she came near. 'Oh, there you are! I've come with a message. You can do one of two things – you can stay out in the grounds all day, and not put foot into the house at all – or you can come into the house and be locked up in one of the rooms.'

She looked round cautiously and lowered her voice. 'I'm sorry you didn't get out; right down upset I am. It's bad enough for an old woman like me, being cooped up here with Hunchy, but it's not right to keep children in this place. You're nice children too.'

'Thanks,' said Julian. 'Now, seeing that you think we're so nice – tell us, is there any way we can get out besides going through these gates?'

'No. No way at all,' said the woman. 'It's like a prison, once those gates are shut. Nobody's allowed in, and you're only allowed out if it suits Mr Perton and the others. So don't try to escape – it's hopeless.'

Nobody said anything to that. Aggie glanced over her shoulder as if she feared somebody might be listening – Hunchy perhaps – and went on in a low voice.

'Mr Perton said I wasn't to give you much food. And he said Hunchy's to put down food for the dog with poison in it, so don't you let him eat any but what I give you myself.'

'The brute,' cried George, and she held Timmy close against her. 'Did you hear that, Timmy? It's a pity you didn't bite Mr Perton too!'

'Sh!' said the woman, afraid. 'I didn't mean to tell you all this, you know that – but you're kind, and you gave me all that money. Right down nice you are. Now, you listen to me – you'd better say you'd rather keep out here in the grounds, because if you're locked up I wouldn't dare to bring you much food in case Rooky came in and saw it. But if you stay out here it's easier. I can give you plenty.'

'Thank you very much,' said Julian, and the others nodded too. 'In any case we'd rather be out here. I suppose Mr Perton is afraid we'd stumble on some of his strange secrets in the house if we had the free run there! All right, tell him we'll be in the grounds. What about our food? How shall we manage about that? We don't want to get you into trouble, but we're very hungry for our meals, and we really could do with a good dinner today.'

'I'll manage it for you,' said Aggie, and she actually smiled. 'But mind what I say now – don't you let that dog eat anything Hunchy puts down for him! It'll be poisoned.'

A voice shouted from the house. Aggie jerked her head up and listened. 'That's Hunchy,' she said. 'I must go.'

She hurried back up the drive. 'Well, well, well,' said Julian, 'so they thought they'd poison old Timmy, did they? They'll have to think again, old fellow, won't they?'

'Woof,' said Timmy, gravely, and didn't even wag his tail!

CHAPTER SIXTEEN

Aggie – and Hunchy

'I FEEL as if I want some exercise,' said George, when Aggie had gone. 'Let's explore the grounds. You never know what we might find!'

They got up, glad of something to do to take their minds off their surprising problems. Really, who would have thought yesterday, when they were happily cycling along sunny country roads, that they would be held prisoner like this today? You just never knew what would happen. It made life exciting, of course, but it did spoil a cycling tour!

They found absolutely nothing of interest in the grounds except a couple of cows, a large number of hens, and a brood of young ducklings. Evidently even the milkman didn't need to call at Owl's Dene! It was quite self-contained.

'I expect that black Bentley goes down each day to some town or other, to collect letters, and to buy meat, or fish,' said George. 'Otherwise Owl's Dene could keep itself going for months on end if necessary without any contact with the outside world. I expect they've got stacks and stacks of tinned food.'

'It's weird to find a place like this, tucked away on a deserted hill, forgotten by everyone – guarding goodness knows what secrets,' said Dick. 'I'd love to know who that man was you saw in the secret room, Julian – the snorer!'

'Someone who doesn't want to be seen even by Hunchy or Aggie,' said Julian. 'Someone the police would dearly love to see, I expect!'

'I *wish* we could get out of here,' said George, longingly. 'I hate the place. It's got such a nasty "feel" about it. And I hate the thought of somebody trying to poison Timmy.'

'Don't worry, he won't be poisoned,' said Dick. 'We won't let him be. He can have half *our* food, can't you, Timmy, old fellow?'

Timmy agreed. He woofed and wagged his tail. He wouldn't leave George's side that morning, but stuck to her like a leech.

'Well, we've been all round the grounds and there's nothing much to see,' said Julian, when they had come back near the house. 'I suppose Hunchy sees to the milking and feeds the poultry and brings in the vegetables. Aggie has to manage the house. I say – look – there's Hunchy now. He's putting down food for Timmy!'

Hunchy was making signs to them. 'Here's the dog's dinner!' he yelled.

'Don't say a word, George,' said Julian in a low voice. 'We'll pretend to let Timmy eat it, but we'll really throw it away somewhere – and he'll be frightfully astonished when Timmy is still all-alive-o tomorrow morning!'

Hunchy disappeared in the direction of the cowshed, carrying a pail. Anne gave a little giggle.

'I know what we'll pretend! We'll pretend that Timmy ate half and didn't like the rest so we gave it to the hens and ducks!'

'And Hunchy will be frightfully upset because he'll think they'll die and he'll get into a row,' said George. 'Serve him right! Come on, let's get the food now.'

She ran to pick up the big bowl of food. Timmy sniffed at it and turned away. It was obvious that he wouldn't have fancied it much even if George had allowed him to have it. Timmy was a very sensible dog.

'Quick, get that spade, Ju, and dig a hole before Hunchy comes back,' said George, and Julian set to work grinning. It didn't take him more than a minute to dig a large hole in the soft earth of a bed. George emptied all the food into the hole, wiped the bowl round with a handful of leaves and watched Julian filling in the earth. Now no animals could get at the poisoned food.

'Let's go to the hen-run now, and when we see Hunchy we'll wave to him,' said Julian. 'He'll ask us what we've been doing. Come on. He deserves to have a shock.'

They went to the hen-house, and stood looking through the wire surrounding the hen-run. As Hunchy came along they turned and waved to him. George pretended to scrape some scraps out of the dog's bowl into the run. Hunchy stared hard. Then he ran towards her, shouting.

'Don't do that, don't do that!'

'What's the matter?' asked George, innocently, pretending to push some scraps through the wire. 'Can't I give the hens some scraps?'

'Is that the bowl I put the dog's food down in?' asked Hunchy, sharply.

'Yes,' said George.

'And he didn't eat all the food – so you're giving it to my hens!' shouted Hunchy in a rage, and snatched the bowl out of George's hands. She pretended to be very angry.

'Don't! Why shouldn't your hens have scraps from the dog's bowl? The food you gave Timmy looked very nice – can't the hens have some?'

Hunchy looked into the hen-run with a groan. The hens were pecking about near the children for all the world as if they were eating something just thrown to them. Hunchy felt sure they would all be dead by the next day – and then, what trouble he would get into!

He glared at George. 'Idiot of a boy! Giving my hens that food! You deserve a good punishment.'

He thought George was a boy, of course. The others looked on with interest. It served Hunchy right to get into a panic over his hens, after trying to poison dear old Timmy.

Hunchy didn't seem to know what to do. Eventually he took a stiff brush from a nearby shed and went into the hen-run. He had evidently decided to sweep the whole place in case any poisoned bits of food were still left about. He swept laboriously and the children watched him, pleased that he should punish himself in this way.

'I've never seen anyone bother to sweep a hen-run before,' said Dick, in a loud and interested voice.

'Nor have I,' said George at once. 'He must be very anxious to bring his hens up properly.'

'It's jolly hard work, I should think,' said Julian. 'Glad I haven't got to do it. Pity to sweep up all the bits of food, though. An awful waste.'

Everyone agreed heartily to this.

'Funny he should be so upset about my giving the hens any scraps of the food he put down for Timmy,' said George. 'I mean, it seems a bit *suspicious*.'

'It does rather,' agreed Dick. 'But then perhaps he's a suspicious character.'

Hunchy could hear all this quite plainly. The children meant him to, of course. He stopped his sweeping and scowled evilly at them.

'Clear off, you little pests,' he said, and raised his broom as if to rush at the children with it.

'He looks like an angry hen,' said Anne, joining in.

'He's just going to cluck,' put in Richard, and the others laughed. Hunchy ran to open the gate of the hen-run, red with anger.

'Of course, it's just struck me – he *might* have put poison into Timmy's bowl of food,' said Julian, loudly.

'That's why he's so upset about his hens. Dear, dear, how true the old proverb is – he that digs a pit shall fall into it himself!'

The mention of poison stopped Hunchy's rush at once. He flung the broom into the shed, and made off for the house without another word.

'Well, we gave him a bit more than he bargained for,' said Julian.

'And you needn't worry, hens,' said Anne, putting her face to the wire-netting of the run. 'You're not poisoned – and we wouldn't *dream* of harming you!'

'Aggie's calling us,' said Richard. 'Look, perhaps she's got some food for us.'

'I hope so,' said Dick. 'I'm getting very hungry. It's funny that grown-ups never seem to get as hungry as children. I do pity them.'

'Why? Do you *like* being hungry?' said Anne as they walked over to the house.

'Yes, if I know there's a good meal in the offing,' said Dick. 'Otherwise it wouldn't be at all funny. Oh goodness – is this all that Aggie has provided?'

On the window-sill was a loaf of stale-looking bread and a piece of very hard yellow cheese. Nothing else at all. Hunchy was there, grinning.

'Aggie says that's your dinner,' he said, and sat himself down at the table to spoon out enormous helpings of a very savoury stew.

'A little revenge for our behaviour by the hen-run,'

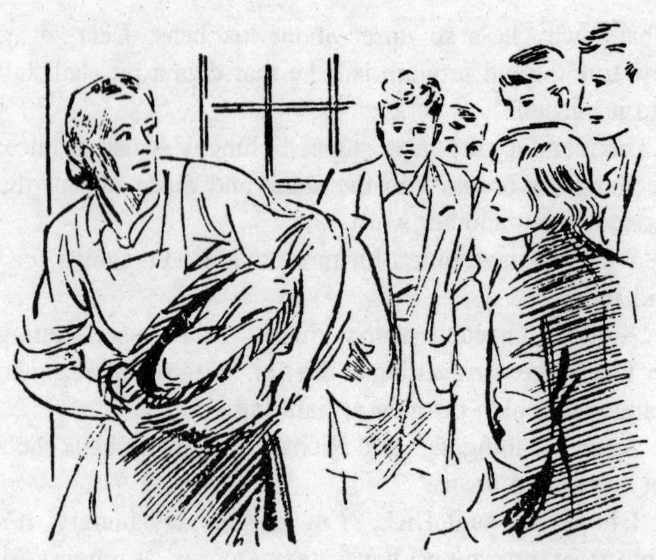

murmured Julian softly. 'Well, well, I thought better than this of Aggie. I wonder where she is.'

She came out of the kitchen door at that moment, carrying a washing-basket that appeared to be full of clothes. 'I'll just hang these out, Hunchy, and I'll be back,' she called to him. She turned to the children and gave them a broad wink.

'There's your dinner on the window-sill,' she said. 'Get it and take it somewhere to eat. Hunchy and I don't want you round the kitchen.'

She suddenly smiled and nodded her head down towards the washing-basket. The children understood immediately. Their real dinner was in there!

They snatched the bread and cheese from the sill and followed her. She set down the basket under a tree, where it was well-hidden from the house. A clothes-line stretched there. 'I'll be out afterwards to hang my washing,' she said, and with another smile that changed her whole face, she went back to the house.

'Good old Aggie,' said Julian, lifting up the top cloth in the basket. 'My word, just look here!'

CHAPTER SEVENTEEN

Julian has a bright idea

AGGIE HAD managed to pack knives, forks, spoons, plates and mugs into the bottom of the basket. There were two big bottles of milk. There was a large meat-pie with delicious-looking pastry on top, and a collection of buns, biscuits and oranges. There were also some home-made sweets. Aggie had certainly been very generous!

All the things were quickly whipped out of the basket. The children carried them behind the bushes, sat down and proceeded to eat a first-rate dinner. Timmy got his share of the meat-pie and biscuits. He also gobbled up a large part of the hard yellow cheese.

'Now, we'd better rinse everything under that garden tap over there, and then pack them neatly into the bottom of the basket again,' said Julian. 'We don't want to get Aggie into any sort of trouble for her kindness.'

The dishes were soon rinsed and packed back into the basket. The clothes were drawn over them – nothing could be seen!

Aggie came outside to them in about half an hour. The children went to her and spoke in low voices.

'Thanks, Aggie, that was super!'

'You *are* a brick. We did enjoy it!'

'I bet Hunchy didn't enjoy his dinner as much as *we* did!'

'Sh!' said Aggie, half-pleased and half-scared. 'You never know when Hunchy's listening. He's got ears like a hare! Listen, I'll be coming out to get the eggs from the hen-run at tea-time. I'll have a basket with me for the eggs – and I shall have your tea in it. I'll leave your tea in the hen-house when I get the eggs. You can fetch it when I've gone.'

'You're a wonder, Aggie!' said Julian, admiringly. 'You really are.'

Aggie looked pleased. It was plain that nobody had said a kind or admiring word to her for years and years. She was a poor, miserable, scared old woman – but she was quite enjoying this little secret. She was pleased at getting the better of Hunchy too. Perhaps she felt it was some slight revenge for all the years he had ill-treated her.

She hung out some of the clothes in the basket, left one in to cover the dinner things, and then went back into the house.

'Poor old thing,' said Dick. 'What a life!'

'Yes, *I* shouldn't like to be cooped up here for years and years with ruffians like Perton and Rooky,' said Julian.

'It looks as if we shall be if we don't hurry up and think of some plan of escape,' said Dick.

'Yes. We'd better think hard again,' said Julian. 'Come over to those trees there. We can sit on the grass under them and talk without being overheard anywhere.'

'Look, Hunchy is polishing the black Bentley,' said

George. 'I'll just pass near him with Timmy, and let Timmy growl. He'll see Timmy's all alive and kicking then.'

So she took Timmy near the Bentley, and of course he growled horribly when he came upon Hunchy. Hunchy promptly got into the car and shut the door. George grinned.

'Hallo!' she said. 'Going off for a ride? Can Timmy and I come with you?'

She made as if she was going to open the door, and Hunchy yelled loudly: 'Don't you let that dog in here! I've seen Rooky's hand – one finger's very bad indeed. I don't want that dog going for *me*.'

'Do take me for a ride with you, Hunchy,' persisted George. 'Timmy loves cars.'

'Go away,' said Hunchy, hanging on to the door handle for dear life. 'I've got to get this car cleaned up for Mr Perton this evening. You let me get out and finish the job.'

George laughed and went off to join the others.

'Well, he can see Timmy's all-alive-o,' said Dick, with a grin. 'Good thing too. We'd find ourselves in a much bigger fix if we hadn't got old Timmy to protect us.'

They went over to the clump of trees and sat down.

'What was it that Hunchy said about the car?' asked Julian. George told him. Julian looked thoughtful. Anne knew that look – it meant that Julian was thinking of a plan! She prodded him.

'Ju! You've got a plan, haven't you? What is it?'

'Well, I'm only just wondering about something,' said Julian, slowly. 'That car – and the fact that Mr Perton is going out in it tonight – which means he will go out through those gates . . .'

'What of it?' said Dick. 'Thinking of going with him?'

'Well, yes, I was,' said Julian, surprisingly. 'You see, if he's not going till dark, I think I could probably get into the boot and hide there till the car stops somewhere, and then I could open the boot, get out, and go off for help!'

Everyone looked at him in silence. Anne's eyes gleamed. 'Oh, Julian! It's a brilliant plan.'

'It sounds jolly good,' said Dick.

'The only thing is – I don't like being left here without Julian,' said Anne, suddenly feeling scared. 'Everything's all right if Julian's here.'

'*I* could go,' said Dick.

'Or I could,' said George, 'only there wouldn't be room for Timmy too.'

'The boot looks pretty big from outside,' said Julian. 'I wish I could take Anne with me. Then I'd know she was safe. You others would be all right so long as you had Timmy.'

They discussed the matter thoroughly. They dropped it towards tea-time when they saw Aggie coming out with a basket to collect the eggs. She made a sign to them not to come over to her. Possibly someone was watching. They stayed where they were, and watched her go into the hen-house. She remained there a short time, and then came out with a basketful of new-laid eggs. She walked to the house without looking at the children again.

'I'll go and see if she's left anything in the hen-house,' said Dick, and went over to it. He soon appeared again, grinning. His pockets bulged!

Aggie had left about two dozen potted-meat sandwiches, a big slab of cherry cake and a bottle of milk. The children went under the bushes and Dick unloaded his pockets. 'She even left a bone for old Tim,' he said.

'I suppose it's all right,' said George doubtfully. Julian smelt it.

'Perfectly fresh,' he said. 'No poison here at all! Anyway, Aggie wouldn't play a dirty trick like that. Come on, let's tuck in.'

They were very bored after tea, so Julian arranged some races and some jumping competitions. Timmy, of course, would have won them all if he had been counted as a proper competitor. But he wasn't. He went in for everything, though, and barked so excitedly that Mr Perton came to a window and yelled to him to stop.

'Sorry!' yelled back George. 'Timmy's so full of beans today, you see!'

'Mr Perton will be wondering why,' said Julian, with a grin. 'He'll be rowing Hunchy for not getting on with the poison job.'

When it began to grow dark the children went cautiously to the car. Hunchy had finished working on it. Quietly

Julian opened the boot and looked inside. He gave an exclamation of disappointment.

'It's only a small one! I can't get in there, I'm afraid. Nor can you, Dick.'

'I'll go then,' said Anne, in a small voice.

'Certainly not,' said Julian.

'Well – *I'll* go,' said Richard, surprisingly. 'I could just about squash in there.'

'*You!*' said Dick. 'You'd be scared stiff.'

Richard was silent for a moment. 'Yes, I should,' he admitted. 'But I'm still ready to go. I'll do my very best if you'd like me to try. After all, it's me or nobody. You won't let Anne go and there's not enough room for George and Timmy and not enough for either you or Julian, Dick.'

Everyone was astonished. It didn't seem a bit like Richard to offer to do an unselfish or courageous action. Julian felt very doubtful.

'Well, this is a serious thing, you know, Richard,' he said. 'I mean, if you're going to do it, you've got to do it properly – go right through with it, not get frightened in the middle and begin howling, so that the men hear you and examine the boot.'

'I know,' said Richard. 'I think I can do it all right. I do wish you'd trust me a bit.'

'I can't understand your offering to do a difficult thing like that,' said Julian. 'It doesn't seem a bit like you – you've not shown yourself to be at all plucky *so* far!'

'Julian, I think *I* understand,' said Anne suddenly, and she pulled at her brother's sleeve. 'He's thinking of *our* skins this time, not of his own – or at least he's trying to. Let's give him a chance to show he's got a bit of courage.'

'I only just want a chance,' said Richard in a small voice.

'All right,' said Julian. 'You shall have it. It'll be a very pleasant surprise if you take your chance and do something helpful!'

'Tell me exactly what I've got to do,' said Richard, trying to keep his voice from trembling.

'Well, once you're in the boot we'll have to shut you in. Goodness knows how long you'll have to wait there in the dark,' said Julian. 'I warn you it will be jolly stuffy and uncomfortable. When the car goes off it will be more uncomfortable still.'

'Poor Richard,' said Anne.

'As soon as the car stops anywhere and you hear the men get out, wait a minute to give them time to get out of sight and hearing – and then scramble out of the boot yourself and go straight to the nearest police station,' said Julian. 'Tell your story *quickly*, give this address – Owl's Dene, Owl's Hill, some miles from Middlecombe Woods – and the police will do the rest. Got all that?'

'Yes,' said Richard.

'Do you still want to go, now you know what you're in for?' asked Dick.

'Yes,' said Richard again. He was surprised by a warm hug from Anne.

'Richard, you're nice – and I didn't think you were!' said Anne.

He then got a thump on the back from Julian. 'Well, Richard, pull this off and you'll wipe out all the silly things you've done! Now, what about getting into the boot immediately? We don't know when the men will be coming out.'

'Yes. I'll get in now,' said Richard, feeling remarkably brave after Anne's hug and Julian's thump. Julian opened the boot. He examined the inside of the boot-cover. 'I don't believe Richard could open it from the inside,' he said. 'No, he couldn't. We mustn't close it tight, then – I'll have to wedge it a bit open with a stick or something. That will give him a little air, and he'll be able to push the boot open when he wants to. Where's a stick?'

Dick found one. Richard got into the boot and curled himself up. There wasn't very much room even for him! He looked extremely cramped. Julian shut the boot and wedged it with a stick so that there was a crack of half an inch all round.

Dick gave him a sharp nudge. 'Quick, someone's coming!'

CHAPTER EIGHTEEN

Hunt for Richard!

MR PERTON could be seen standing at the front door, outlined in the light from the lamp in the hall. He was talking to Rooky, who, apparently, was not going out. It seemed as if only Mr Perton was leaving in the car.

'Good luck, Richard,' Julian whispered, as he and the others melted into the shadows on the other side of the drive. They stood there in the darkness, watching Mr Perton walk over to the car. He got in and slammed the door. Thank goodness he hadn't wanted to put anything in the boot!

The engine started up and the car purred away down the drive. At the same time there came the grating sound of the gate machinery being used.

'Gates are opening for him,' muttered Dick. They heard the car go right down the drive and out of the gateway without stopping. It hooted as it went, evidently a signal to the house. The gates had been opened just at the right moment. They were now being shut, judging by the grinding noise going on.

The front door closed. The children stood in silence for a minute or two, thinking of Richard shut up in the boot.

'I'd never have thought it of him,' said George.

'No, but you just simply never know what is in anybody,' said Julian thoughtfully. 'I suppose even the worst coward, the most despicable crook, the most dishonest rogue *can* find some good thing in himself if he wants to badly enough.'

'Yes, it's the "wanting-to" that must be so rare, though,' said Dick. 'Look, there's Aggie at the kitchen door. She's calling us in.'

They went to her. 'You can come in now,' she said. 'I can't give you much supper, I'm afraid, because Hunchy will be here – but I'll put some cake up in your room, under the blankets.'

They went into the kitchen. It was pleasant with a log-fire and the mellow light from an oil-lamp. Hunchy was at the far end doing something with a rag and polish. He gave the children one of his familiar scowls. 'Take that dog out and leave him out,' he ordered.

'No,' said George.

'Then I'll tell Rooky,' said Hunchy. Neither he nor Aggie seemed to notice that there were only four children, not five.

'Well, if Rooky comes here I've no doubt Timmy will bite his other hand,' said George. 'Anyway, won't he be surprised to find Timmy still alive and kicking?'

Nothing more was said about Timmy. Aggie silently put the remains of a plum-pie on the table. 'There's your supper,' she said.

There was a very small piece each. As they were finishing, Hunchy went out. Aggie spoke in a whisper.

'I heard the radio at six o'clock. There was a police message about one of you – called Richard. His mother reported him missing and the police put it out on the radio.'

'Did they really?' said Dick. 'I say, they'll soon be here then!'

'But do they know where you are?' asked Aggie, surprised. Dick shook his head.

'Not yet – but I expect we'll soon be traced here.'

Aggie looked doubtful. 'Nobody's ever been traced here yet – nor ever will be, it's my belief. The police did come once, looking for somebody, and Mr Perton let them in, all polite-like. They hunted everywhere for the person they said they wanted, but they couldn't find him.'

Julian nudged Dick. He thought *he* knew where the police might have found him – in the little secret room behind that sliding panel.

'Funny thing,' said Julian. 'I haven't seen a telephone here. Don't they have one?'

'No,' said Aggie. 'No phone, no gas, no electricity, no water laid on, no nothing. Only just secrets and signs and comings and goings and threats and . . .'

She broke off as Hunchy came back, and went to the big fire-place, where a kettle was slung over the burning logs. Hunchy looked around at the children.

'Rooky wants the one of you that's called Richard,' he

said, with a horrible smile. 'Says he wants to teach him a few lessons.'

All the four felt extremely thankful that Richard was not there. They felt sure he wouldn't have liked the lessons that Rooky wanted to teach him.

They looked round at one another and then all round the room. 'Richard? Where *is* Richard?'

'What do you mean – where's Richard?' said Hunchy, in a snarling voice that made Timmy growl. 'One of you is Richard – that's all I know.'

'Why – there were five children – now there's only four!'

said Aggie, in sudden astonishment. 'I've only just noticed. Is Richard the missing one?'

'Dear me, *where's* Richard gone?' said Julian, pretending to be surprised. He called him. 'Richard! Hey, Richard, where are you?'

Hunchy looked angry. 'Now, none of your tricks. One of you is Richard. Which one?'

'Not one of us is,' answered Dick. 'Gracious, where *can* Richard be? Do you suppose we've left him in the grounds, Ju?'

'Must have,' said Julian. He went to the kitchen window and swung it wide open. 'RICHARD!' he roared. 'You're wanted, RICHARD!'

But no Richard answered or appeared, of course. He was miles away in the boot of the black Bentley!

There came the sound of angry footsteps in the hall and the kitchen door was flung open. Rooky stood there, scowling, his hand done up in a big bandage. With a delighted bark Timmy leapt forward. George caught him just in time.

'That dog! Didn't I say he was to be poisoned?' shouted Rooky, furiously. 'Why haven't you brought that boy to me, Hunchy?'

Hunchy looked afraid. 'He doesn't seem to be here,' he answered sullenly. 'Unless one of these here children is him, sir.'

Rooky glanced over them. 'No, he's not one of them. Where is Richard?' he demanded of Julian.

'I've just been yelling for him,' said Julian, with an air of amazement. 'Funny thing. He was out in the grounds all day with us, and now we're indoors, he just isn't here. Shall I go and hunt in the grounds?'

'I'll shout for him again,' said Dick, going to the window. 'RICHARD!'

'Shut up!' said Rooky. '*I'll* go and find him. Where's my torch? Get it, Aggie. And when I find him, he'll be sorry for himself, very, very sorry!'

'I'll come too,' said Hunchy. 'You go one way and I'll go another.'

'Get Ben and Fred too,' ordered Rooky. Hunchy departed to fetch Ben and Fred, whoever they were. The children supposed they must be the other men who had arrived with Rooky the night before.

Rooky went out of the kitchen door with his powerful torch. Anne shivered. She was very, very glad that Richard couldn't be found, however hard the men looked for him. Soon there came the sound of other voices in the grounds, as the four men separated into two parties, and began to search every yard.

'Where is he, the poor boy?' whispered Aggie.

'I don't know,' said Julian, truthfully. He wasn't going to give any secrets away to Aggie, even though she seemed really friendly to them.

She went out of the room and the children clustered together, speaking in low voices.

'I *say*, what a blessing it was Richard that went off in

the Bentley and not one of *us*,' whispered George.

'My word, yes – I didn't like the look on Rooky's face when he came into the kitchen just now,' said Julian.

'Well, Richard's got a little reward for trying to be brave,' said Anne. 'He's missed some ill-treatment from Rooky!'

Julian glanced at a clock in the kitchen. 'Look, it's almost nine. There's a radio on that shelf. Let's put it on and see if there's a message about Richard.'

He switched it on and twiddled the knob till he got the right station. After a minute or two of news, there came the message they wanted to hear.

'Missing from home since Wednesday, Richard Thurlow Kent, a boy of twelve, well-built, fair hair, blue eyes, wearing grey shorts and grey jersey. Probably on a bicycle.'

So the message went on, ending with a police telephone number that could be called. There was of course no message about Julian and the others. They were relieved. 'That means that Mother won't be worrying,' said George. 'But it also means that unless Richard can get help nobody can possibly find out we're here – if we're not missed we can't be searched for, and I don't really want to be here much longer.'

Nobody did, of course. All their hopes were now on Richard. He seemed rather a broken reed to rely on – but you never knew! He just might be successful in escaping unseen from the boot and getting to a police station.

After about an hour Rooky and the others came in, all in a furious temper. Rooky turned on Julian.

'What's happened to that boy? You must know.'

'Gr-r-r-r,' said Timmy at once. Rooky beckoned to Julian to come into the hall. He shut the kitchen door and shouted at Julian again.

'Well, you heard what I said – where's that boy?'

'Isn't he out in the grounds?' said Julian, putting on a very perturbed look. 'Good gracious, what *can* have happened to him? I assure you he was with us all day. Aggie will tell you that – and Hunchy too.'

'They've already told me,' said Rooky. 'He's not in the grounds. We've gone over every inch. Where is he?'

'Well, would he be somewhere in the house, then?' suggested Julian, innocently.

'How can he be?' raged Rooky. 'The front door's been closed and locked all day except when Perton went out. And Hunchy and Aggie swear he didn't come into the kitchen.'

'It's an absolute mystery,' said Julian. 'Shall I hunt all over the house? The others can help me. Maybe the dog will smell him out.'

'I'm not having that dog out of the kitchen,' said Rooky. 'Or any of *you*, either! I believe that boy's about somewhere, laughing up his sleeve at us all – and I believe you know where he is too!'

'I don't,' said Julian. 'And that's the truth.'

'When I *do* find him, I'll . . . I'll . . .' Rooky broke off, quite unable to think of anything bad enough to do to poor Richard.

He went to join the others, still muttering. Julian went thankfully back to the kitchen. He was very glad Richard was well out of the way. It was pure chance that he had gone – but what a very good thing! Where was Richard now? What was he doing? Was he still in the boot of the car? How Julian wished he knew!

CHAPTER NINETEEN

Richard has his own adventure

RICHARD HAD been having a much too exciting time. He had gone with the car, of course, crouching in the boot at the back, with a box of tools digging into him, and a can of petrol smelling horribly nearby, making him feel sick.

Through the gates went the car, and down the hill. It went at a good pace, and once stopped very suddenly. It had gone round a corner and almost collided with a stationary lorry, so that Mr Perton had put the brake on in a hurry. Poor Richard was terrified. He bumped his head hard on the back of the boot and gave a groan.

He sat curled up, feeling sick and scared. He began to wish he had not tried to be a hero and get help. Being any kind of a hero was difficult – but this was a dreadful way of being heroic.

The car went on for some miles; Richard had no idea where it was going. At first he heard no other traffic at all – then he heard the sound of many wheels on the road, and knew he must be getting near a town. Once they must have gone by a railway station or railway line because Richard could distinctly hear the noise of a train, and then a loud hooting.

The car stopped at last. Richard listened intently. Was it stopping just for traffic lights – or was Mr Perton getting out? If so, that was his chance to escape!

He heard the car door slam. Ah, Mr Perton was out of the car then. Richard pressed hard at the cover of the boot. Julian had wedged it rather tightly, but it gave at last, and the lid of the boot opened. It fell back with rather a noise.

Richard looked out cautiously. He was in a dark street. A few people were walking on the pavement opposite. A lamp-post was some way away. Could he get out now – or would Mr Perton be about and see him?

He stretched out a leg to slide from the boot and jump to the ground – but he had been huddled up in an awkward position for so long that he was too stiff to move. Cramp caught him and he felt miserably uncomfortable as he tried to straighten himself out.

Instead of jumping out and taking to his heels at once, poor Richard had to go very slowly indeed. His legs and arms would *not* move quickly. He sat for a half-minute on the open boot-lid, trying to make up his mind to jump down.

And then he heard Mr Perton's voice! He was running down the steps of the house outside which he had parked the car. Richard was horrified. It hadn't dawned on him that he would come back so quickly.

He tried to jump from the boot-cover, and fell sprawling to the ground. Mr Perton heard him, and, thinking someone was trying to steal something from his car he rushed up to the boot.

Richard scrambled up just in time to get away from his outstretched hand. He ran to the other side of the road as fast as he could, hoping that his stiff, cramped legs wouldn't let him down. Mr Perton tore after him.

'Hey, you, stop! What are you doing in my car?' shouted Mr Perton. Richard dodged a passer-by and tore on, panic-stricken. He mustn't be caught; he mustn't be caught!

Mr Perton caught up with him just under the lamp-post. He grabbed Richard's collar and swung him round roughly. 'You let me go!' yelled Richard, and kicked Mr Perton's ankles so hard that he almost fell over.

Mr Perton recognised him! 'Good gracious – it's you!' he cried. 'The boy Rooky wants! What are you doing here? How did you . . . ?'

But with a last despairing struggle, Richard was off again, leaving his coat in Mr Perton's hands! His legs were feeling better now, and he could run faster.

He tore round the corner, colliding with another boy. He was off and away before the boy could even call out. Mr Perton also tore round the corner and collided with the same boy – who, however, was a bit quicker than before, and clutched Mr Perton by the coat, in a real rage at being so nearly knocked over again.

By the time Mr Perton had got himself free from the angry boy, Richard was out of sight. Mr Perton raced to the corner of the road, and looked up and down the poorly lit road. He gave an exclamation of anger.

'Lost him! Little pest – how did he get here? Could he have been at the back of the car? Ah, surely that's him over there!'

It was. Richard had hidden in a garden, but was now being driven out by the barking of a dog. In despair he tore out of the gate and began running again. Mr Perton tore after him.

Round another corner, panting hard. Round yet another, hoping that no passer-by would clutch at him and stop him. Poor Richard! He didn't feel at all heroic, and didn't enjoy it a bit either.

He stumbled round the next corner and came into the main street of the town – and there, opposite, was a lamp that had a very welcome word shining on the glass.

POLICE

Thankfully Richard stumbled up the steps and pushed open the police station door. He almost fell inside. There was a kind of waiting-room there with a policeman sitting at a table. He looked up in astonishment as Richard came in in such a hurry.

'Now then, what's all this?' he asked the boy.

Richard looked fearfully back at the door, expecting Mr Perton to come in at any moment. But he didn't. The door remained shut. Mr Perton was not going to visit any police station if he could help it – especially with Richard pouring out a most peculiar story!

Richard was panting so much that he couldn't say a word at first. Then it all came out. The policeman listened in amazement, and very soon stopped Richard's tale, and called a big burly man in, who proved to be a most important police inspector.

He made Richard tell his tale slowly and as clearly as he could. The boy was now feeling much better – in fact he was feeling quite proud of himself! To think he'd done it – escaped in the boot of the car, got out, managed to get away from Mr Perton, and arrive safely at the police station. Marvellous!

'Where's this Owl's Dene?' demanded the Inspector, and the constable nearby answered.

'Must be that old place on Owl's Hill, sir. You remember we once went there on some kind of police business, but it seemed to be all right. Run by an old man and his sister for some man who is often away abroad – Perton, I think the name was.'

'That's right!' cried Richard. 'It was Mr Perton's car I came here in – a black Bentley.'

'Know the number?' said the Inspector, sharply.

'KMF 102,' said Richard at once.

'Good lad,' said the Inspector. He picked up a telephone and gave a few curt instructions for a police car to try to trace the Bentley immediately.

'So you're Richard Thurlow Kent,' he said. 'Your

mother is very upset and anxious about you. I'll see that she is telephoned straight away. You'd better be taken home now in a police car.'

'Oh but, sir, can't I go with you to Owl's Dene when you drive up there?' said Richard, deeply disappointed. 'You'll be going there, won't you? – because of all the others – Anne, Dick, George and Julian.'

'We'll be going all right,' said the Inspector, grimly. 'But you won't be with us. You've had enough adventures. You can go home and go to bed. You've done well to escape and come here. Quite the hero!'

Richard couldn't help feeling pleased – but how he wished he could race off to Owl's Dene with the police. What a marvellous thing it would be to march in with them and show Julian how well he had managed his part of the affair! Perhaps Julian would think better of him then.

The Inspector, however, was not having any boys in the cars that were to go to Owl's Dene, and Richard was taken off by the young constable, and told to wait till a car came to take him home.

The telephone rang, and the Inspector answered it. 'No trace of the Bentley? Right. Thanks.'

He spoke to the young constable. 'Didn't think they'd get him. He's probably raced back to Owl's Dene to warn the others.'

'We'll get there soon after!' said the constable with a grin. 'Our Wolseley's pretty well as fast as a Bentley!'

Mr Perton had indeed raced off, as soon as he saw Richard stumbling up the police station steps. He had gone back to his car at top speed, jumped in, slammed the door and raced away as fast as he could, feeling certain that the police would be on the look-out for KMF 102 immediately.

He tore dangerously round the corners, and hooted madly, making everyone leap out of the way. He was soon out in the country, and there he put on terrific speed, his powerful headlights picking out the dark country lanes for half a mile ahead.

As he came to the hill on which Owl's Dene stood, he hooted loudly. He wanted the gates opened quickly! Just as he got up to them they opened. Someone had heard his hooting signal – good! He raced up the drive and stopped at the front door. It opened as he jumped out. Rooky stood there, and two other men with him, all looking anxious.

'What's up, Perton? Why are you back so quickly?' called Rooky. 'Anything wrong?'

Mr Perton ran up the steps, shut the door and faced the three men in the hall.

'Do you know what's happened? That boy, Richard Kent, was in the car when I went out! See? Hidden in the back or in the boot, or somewhere! Didn't you miss him?'

'Yes,' said Rooky. 'Of course we missed him. Did you let him get away, Perton?'

'Well, seeing that I didn't know he was in hiding, and

had to leave the car to go in and see Ted, it was easy for him to get away!' said Mr Perton. 'He ran like a hare. I nearly grabbed him once, but he wriggled out of his coat. And as he ended up finally in the police station I decided to give up the chase and come back to warn you.'

'The police will be out here then, before you can say Jack Robinson,' shouted Rooky. 'You're a fool, Perton – you ought to have got that boy. There's our ransom gone west – and I was so glad to be able to get my hands on the little brute.'

'It's no good crying over spilt milk,' said Perton. 'What about Weston? Suppose the police find *him*. They're looking for him all right – the papers have been full of only two things the last couple of days – Disappearance of Richard Thurlow Kent and Escape from Prison of Solomon Weston! And we're mixed up with both these. Do you want to be shoved back into prison again, Rooky? You've only just come out, you know. What are we going to do?'

'We must think,' said Rooky, in a panic-stricken voice. 'Come in this room here. We must *think*.'

CHAPTER TWENTY

The secret room

THE FOUR children had heard the car come racing up the drive, and had heard Mr Perton's arrival. Julian went to the kitchen door, eager to find out what he could. If Mr Perton was back, then either Richard had played his part well, and had escaped – or he had been discovered, and had been brought back.

He heard every word of the excited talk out in the hall. Good, good good! – Richard had got away – and was even now telling his tale to the police. It surely wouldn't be very long before the police arrived at Owl's Dene then – and what surprising things they would find there!

He tiptoed out into the hall when he heard the men go into the room nearby. What were their plans! He hoped they would not vent their rage on him or the others. It was true they had Timmy, but in a real emergency Rooky would probably think nothing of shooting the dog straightaway.

Julian didn't at all like what he heard from the room where the men talked over their plans.

'I'm going to bang all those kids' heads together as hard as I can, to start with,' growled Rooky. 'That big boy – what's his name? – Julian or something – must have planned Richard Kent's escape – I'll give him a real good thrashing, the interfering little beast.'

'What about the sparklers, Rooky?' said another man's voice. 'We'd better put them in a safe hiding-place before the police arrive. We'll have to hurry.'

'Oh, it'll be some time before they find they can't open that gate,' said Rooky. 'And it'll take a little more time before they climb that wall. We'll have time to put the sparklers into the room with Weston. If *he's* safe there, they'll be safe too.'

'Sparklers!' thought Julian, excited. 'Those are diamonds – so they've got a haul of diamonds hidden somewhere. Whatever next?'

'Get them,' ordered Mr Perton. 'Take them to the secret room – and be quick about it, Rooky. The police may be here at any minute now.'

'We'll spin some tale about that kid Richard and his friends,' said the voice of a fourth man. 'We'll say they were caught trespassing, the lot of them, and kept here as a little punishment. Actually, if there's time, I think it would be best to let the rest of them go. After all – they don't *know* anything. They can't give away any secrets.'

Rooky didn't want to let them go. He had grim plans for them, but the others argued him over. 'All right,' he said sullenly. 'Let them go, then – if there's time! You take them down to the gate, Perton, and shove them out before the police arrive. They'll probably set off thankfully and get lost in the dark. So much the better.'

'You get the sparklers then, and see to them,' said Mr Perton, and Julian heard him getting up from his chair. The boy darted back to the kitchen.

It looked as if there would be nothing for it but to let themselves be led down to the gates and shoved out, and Julian decided that if that happened they would wait at the gateway till the police arrived. They wouldn't get lost in the dark, as Rooky hoped!

Mr Perton came into the kitchen. His eyes swept over the four children. Timmy growled.

'So you made a little plan, did you, and hid Richard in the car?' he said. 'Well, for that we're going to turn you all out into the night and you'll probably lose yourselves for days in the deserted countryside round here and I hope you do!'

Nobody said anything. Mr Perton aimed a blow at Julian, who ducked. Timmy sprang at the man, but George had hold of his collar, and he just missed snapping Mr Perton's arm in two!

'If that dog had stayed here a day longer I'd have shot him,' said Mr Perton, fiercely. 'Come on, all of you, get a move on.'

'Good-bye, Aggie,' said Anne. Aggie and Hunchy watched them go out of the kitchen door into the dark garden. Aggie looked very scared indeed. Hunchy spat after them and said something rude.

But, when they were half-way down the drive, there came the sound of cars roaring at top speed up the hill to the gates of Owl's Dene! Two cars, fast and powerful, with brilliant headlights. Police cars, without a doubt! Mr Perton stopped. Then he shoved the children roughly back towards the house. It was too late to set them free and hope they would lose themselves.

'You look out for Rooky,' he said to them. 'He goes mad when he's frightened – and he's going to be frightened now, with the police hammering at the gates!'

Julian and the others cautiously edged into the kitchen. They weren't going to risk meeting Rooky if they could help it. Nobody was there at all, not even Hunchy or Aggie. Mr Perton went through to the hall.

'Have you put those sparklers away?' he called, and a voice answered him: 'Yes. Weston's got them with him. They're OK. Did you get the kids out in time?'

'No – and the police are at the gates already,' growled Mr Perton.

A howl came from someone – probably Rooky. 'The police – already! If I had that kid Richard here I'd skin him alive. Wait till I've burnt a few letters I don't want found – then I'll go and get hold of the other kids. I'm going to put somebody through it for this, and I don't care who.'

'Don't be foolish, Rooky,' said Mr Perton's voice. 'Do you want to get yourself into trouble again through your violent temper? Leave the kids alone.'

Julian listened to all this and felt very uneasy indeed. He ought to hide the others. Even Timmy would be no protection if Rooky had a gun. But where could he hide them?

'Rooky will search the whole house from top to bottom if he loses his temper much more, and really makes up his mind to revenge himself on us,' thought Julian. 'What a pity there isn't another secret room – we could hide there and be safe!'

But even if there was one he didn't know of it. He heard Rooky go upstairs with the others. Now, if he and the other children were going to hide somewhere in safety, this was their chance. But WHERE could they hide?

An idea came to Julian – was it a brilliant one, or wasn't it? He couldn't make up his mind at first. Then he decided that brilliant or not they had got to try it.

He spoke to the others. 'We've got to hide. Rooky isn't safe when he's in a temper.'

'Where shall we hide?' said Anne, fearfully.

'In the secret room!' said Julian. They all gaped at him in amazement.

'But – but somebody else is already hidden there – you told us you saw him last night,' said George at last.

'I know. That can't be helped. He's the last person to give us away, if we share his hiding-place – he wouldn't want to be found himself!' said Julian. 'It will be a frightful squash, because the secret room is very, very small – but it's the safest place I can think of.'

'Timmy will have to come too,' said George firmly. Julian nodded.

'Of course. We may need him to protect us against the hidden man!' he said. 'He may be pretty wild at us all invading his hiding-place. We don't want to have him calling Rooky. We'll be all right once we're in the room, because Timmy will keep him quiet. And once we're in he won't call out because we'll tell him the police are here!'

'Fine,' said Dick. 'Let's go. Is the coast clear?'

'Yes. They're all upstairs for some reason or other,' said Julian. 'Probably destroying things they don't want found. Come on.'

Hunchy and Aggie were still not to be seen. They had probably heard what the scare was about and were hidden away themselves! Julian led the way quietly to the little study.

They stared at the big, solid wooden bookcase that

stretched from floor to ceiling. Julian went quickly to one shelf and emptied out the books. He felt for the knob.

There it was! He pulled it out, and the back panel of the shelf slid noiselessly downwards, leaving the large hole there, like a window into the secret room.

The children gasped. How strange! How very extraordinary! They blinked through the hole and saw the small room behind, lit by a little candle. They saw the hidden man too – and he saw them! He looked at them in the very greatest astonishment.

'Who are you?' he said, in a threatening voice. 'Who told you to open the panel? Where're Rooky and Perton?'

'We're coming through to join you,' said Julian quietly. 'Don't make a noise.'

He shoved George up first. She slid through the narrow opening sideways and landed feet-first on the floor. Timmy followed immediately, pushed through by Julian.

The man was up on his feet now, angry and surprised. He was a big burly fellow, with very small close-set eyes and a cruel mouth.

'Now, look here,' he began in a loud voice. 'I won't have this. Where's Perton? Hey, Per . . .'

'If you say another word I'll set my dog on you,' said George, at a sign from Julian. Timmy growled so ferociously that the man shrank back at once.

'I – I . . .' he began. Timmy growled again and bared all his magnificent teeth in a snarl. The man climbed up on the narrow bed and subsided, looking astonished and furious. Dick went through the opening next, then Anne. By that time the small room was uncomfortably crowded.

'I say,' said Julian, suddenly remembering something, 'I shall have to stay outside the room – because the books have got to be put back, otherwise Rooky will notice the shelf is empty and guess we're hiding in the secret room. Then we'll be at his mercy.'

'Oh, Ju, you must come in with us,' said Anne, frightened.

'I can't, Anne. I must shut the panel and put the books back,' said Julian. 'I can't risk your being discovered till the police have safely caught that madman Rooky! I shall be all right, don't you worry.'

'The police?' whispered the man in the secret room, his eyes almost falling out of his head. 'Are the police here?'

'At the gates,' answered Julian. 'So keep quiet if you don't want them on top of you at once!'

He pushed the knob. The panel slid back into place without a sound. Julian replaced the books on the shelf as fast as he could. Then he darted out of the study, so that the men would not even guess what he had been up to. He was very thankful that Rooky had kept away long enough for him to carry out his plan.

Where should he hide himself? How long would it take the police to get over the wall, or break down the great gates? Surely they would soon be here?

There came the sound of footsteps running down the

stairs. It was Rooky. He caught sight of Julian at once. 'Ah – there you are! Where are the others? I'll show you what . . .'

Rooky carried a whip in his hand and looked quite crazy. Julian was afraid. He darted back into the study and locked the door. Rooky began to hammer at it. Then such a crash came on the door that Julian guessed he was smashing it down with one of the hall chairs. The door would be down in a moment!

CHAPTER TWENTY-ONE

A very exciting finish!

JULIAN WAS a courageous boy, but just at that minute he felt very scared indeed. And what must the children hidden in the secret room beyond be thinking? Poor Anne must be feeling terrified at Rooky's shouts and the crashing on the door.

And then a really marvellous idea came to Julian. Why, oh why hadn't he thought of it before? He could open the gates himself for the police to come in! He knew how to do it – and there was the wheel nearby in the corner, that set the gate machinery working! Once he had the gates open it would not be more than a few minutes, surely, before the police were hammering at the front door.

Julian ran to the wheel-like handle. He turned it strongly. A grinding, whining noise came at once, as the machinery went into action.

Rooky was still crashing at the door with the heavy chair. Already he had broken in one panel of it. But when he suddenly heard the groaning of the machinery that opened the gates, he stopped in panic. The gates were being opened! The police would soon be there – he would be caught!

He forgot the beautiful stories he had arranged to tell,

forgot the plans that he and the others had made, forgot everything except that he must hide. He flung down the chair and fled.

Julian sat down in the nearest chair, his heart beating as if he had just been running a race. The gates were open – Rooky had fled – the police would soon be there! And, even as he sat thinking this, there came the sound of powerful cars roaring up the wide drive. Then the engines stopped, and car doors were thrown open.

Someone began to hammer at the front door. 'Open in the name of the law!' cried a loud voice, and then came another hammering.

Nobody opened the door. Julian unlocked the half-broken door of the study he was in, and peered cautiously into the hall. No one seemed to be about.

He raced to the front door, pulled back the bolts, and undid the heavy chain, afraid each moment that some of the men would come to shove him away. But they didn't.

The door was pushed open by the police, who swarmed in immediately. There were eight of them, and they looked surprised to see a boy there.

'Which boy's this?' said the Inspector.

'Julian, sir,' said Julian. 'I'm glad you've come. Things were getting pretty hot.'

'Where are the men?' asked the Inspector, walking right in.

'I don't know,' said Julian.

'Find them,' ordered the Inspector, and his men fanned

out up the hall. But before they could go into any room, a cool voice called to them from the end of the corridor.

'May I ask what all this is?'

It was Mr Perton, looking as calm as could be, smoking a cigarette. He stood at the door of his sitting-room, seeming quite unperturbed. 'Since when has a man's house been broken into for no reason at all?'

'Where are the rest of you?' demanded the Inspector.

'In here, Inspector,' drawled Mr Perton. 'We were having a little conference, and heard the hammering at the door. Apparently you got in somehow. I'm afraid you'll get into trouble for this.'

The Inspector advanced to the room where Mr Perton stood. He glanced into it.

'Aha – our friend Rooky, I see,' he said, genially. 'Only a day or two out of prison, Rooky, and you're mixed up in trouble again. Where's Weston?'

'I don't know what you mean,' said Rooky, sullenly. 'How should I know where he is? He was in prison last time I knew anything about him.'

'Yes. But he escaped,' said the Inspector. 'Somebody helped him, Rooky. Somebody planned his escape for him – friends of yours – and somebody knows where the diamonds are that he stole and hid. I've a guess that you're going to share them with him in return for getting your friends to help him. Where is Weston, Rooky?'

'I tell you I don't *know*,' repeated Rooky. 'Not here, if that's what you're getting at. You can search the whole house from top to bottom, if you like. Perton won't mind. Will you, Perton? Look for the sparklers, too, if you want to. I don't know anything about them.'

'Perton, we've suspected you for a long time,' said the Inspector, turning to Mr Perton, who was still calmly smoking his cigarette. 'We think you're at the bottom of all these prison escapes – that's why you bought this lonely old house, isn't it? – so that you could work from it undisturbed? You arrange the escapes, you arrange for a change of clothes, you arrange for a safe hiding-place till the man can get out of the country.'

'Utter nonsense,' said Mr Perton.

'And you only help criminals who have been known to do a clever robbery and hide the stuff before they're caught,' went on the Inspector, in a grim voice. 'So you know you'll make plenty of profit on your deals, Perton. Weston is here all right – and so are the diamonds. Where are they?'

'They're not here,' said Perton. 'You're at liberty to look and see. You won't get anything out of *me*, Inspector. I'm innocent.'

Julian had listened to all this in amazement. Why, they had fallen into the very middle of a nest of thieves and rogues! Well, *he* knew where Weston was – and the diamonds too! He stepped forward.

'Tell your story later, son,' said the Inspector. 'We've things to do now.'

'Well, sir, I can save you a lot of time,' said Julian. 'I

know where the hidden prisoner is – and the diamonds too!'

Rooky leapt to his feet with a howl. Mr Perton looked at Julian hard. The other men glanced uneasily at one another.

'You don't know anything!' shouted Rooky. 'You only came here yesterday.'

The Inspector regarded Julian gravely. He liked this boy with the quiet manners and honest eyes.

'Do you mean what you say?' he asked.

'Oh yes,' said Julian. 'Come with me, sir.'

He turned and went out of the room. Everyone crowded after him – police, Rooky and the others, but three of the policemen quietly placed themselves at the back.

Julian led them to the study. Rooky's face went purple, but Perton gave him a sharp nudge and he said nothing. Julian went to the bookcase and swept a whole shelf of books out at once.

Rooky gave a terrific yell and leapt at Julian. 'Stop that! What are you doing?'

Two policemen were on the infuriated Rooky at once. They dragged him back. Julian pulled out the knob and the panel slid noiselessly downwards, leaving a wide space in the wall behind.

From the secret room four faces gazed out – the faces of three children – and a man. Timmy was there too, but he was on the floor. For a few moments nobody said a single word. The ones in the hidden room were so surprised to see such a crowd of policemen looking in at them – and the ones in the study were filled with amazement to see so many children in the tiny room!

'WELL!' said the Inspector. 'Well, I'm blessed! And if that isn't Weston himself, large as life and twice as natural!'

Rooky began to struggle with the policemen. He seemed absolutely infuriated with Julian.

'That boy!' he muttered. 'Let me get at him. That boy!'

'Got the diamonds there, Weston?' asked the Inspector, cheerfully. 'May as well hand them over.' Weston was very pale indeed. He made no move at all. Dick reached under the narrow bed and pulled out a bag. 'Here they are,' he said, with a grin. 'Jolly good lot they feel – heavy as anything! Can we come out now, Ju?'

All three were helped out by policemen. Weston was handcuffed before he was brought out. Rooky found that he also had handcuffs on all of a sudden, and to Mr Perton's angry surprise he heard a click at his own wrists too!

'A very, very nice little haul,' said the Inspector, in his most genial voice, as he looked inside the bag. 'What happened to your prison clothes, Weston? That's a nice suit you've got on – but you weren't wearing that when you left prison.'

'I can tell you where they are,' said Julian, remembering. Everyone stared in amazement, except George and Anne, who also knew, of course.

'They're stuffed down a well belonging to an old

tumbledown shack in a lane between here and Middlecombe Woods,' said Julian. 'I could easily find it for you any time.'

Mr Perton stared at Julian as if he couldn't believe his ears. 'How do you know that?' he asked roughly. 'You can't know a thing like that!'

'I do know it,' said Julian. 'And what's more you took him a new suit of clothes, and arrived at the shack in your black Bentley, didn't you – KMF 102? I saw it.'

'That's got you, Perton,' said the Inspector, with a pleased smile. 'That's put you on the spot, hasn't it? Good boy, this – notices a whole lot of interesting things. I shouldn't be surprised if he joins the police force some day. We could do with people like him!'

Perton spat out his cigarette and stamped on it viciously, as if he wished he was stamping on Julian. Those children! If that idiot Rooky hadn't spotted Richard Kent and gone after him, none of this would have happened. Weston would have been safely hidden, the diamonds sold, Weston could have been sent abroad, and he, Perton, would have made a fortune. Now a pack of children had spoilt everything.

'Any other people in the house?' the Inspector asked Julian. 'You appear to be the one who knows more than anybody else, my boy – so perhaps you can tell me that.'

'Yes – Aggie and Hunchy,' said Julian, promptly. 'But don't be hard on Aggie, sir – she was awfully good to us, and she's terrified of Hunchy.'

'We'll remember what you say,' promised the Inspector. 'Search the house, men. Bring along Aggie and Hunchy too. We'll want them for witnesses, anyway. Leave two men on guard here. The rest of us will go.'

It needed the black Bentley as well as the two police cars to take everyone down the drive and on to the next town! The children's bicycles had to be left behind, as they could not be got on the cars anywhere. As it was, it was a terrific squash.

'You going home tonight?' the Inspector asked Julian. 'We'll run you back. What about your parents? Won't they be worried by all this?'

'They're away,' explained Julian. 'And we were on a cycling tour. So they don't know. There's really nowhere we can go for the night.'

But there was! There was a message awaiting the Inspector to say that Mrs Thurlow Kent would be very pleased indeed if Julian and the others would spend the night with Richard. She wanted to hear about their extraordinary adventures.

'Right,' said Julian. 'That settles that. We'll go there – and anyway, I want to bang old Richard on the back. He turned out quite a hero after all!'

'You'll have to stay around for a few days,' said the Inspector. 'We'll want you, I expect – you've a very fine tale to tell, and you've been a great help.'

'We'll stay around then,' said Julian. 'And if you could manage to have our bikes collected, sir, I'd be very grateful.'

Richard was at the front door to meet them all, although by now it was very late indeed. He was dressed in clean clothes and looked very spruce beside the dirty, bedraggled company of children that he went to greet.

'I wish I'd been in at the last!' he cried. 'I was sent off home, and I was wild. Mother – and Dad – here are the children I went off with.'

Mr Thurlow Kent had just come back from America. He shook hands with all of them. 'Come along in,' he said. 'We've got a fine spread for you – you must be ravenous!'

'Tell me what happened, tell me at once,' demanded Richard.

'We simply *must* have a bath first,' protested Julian. 'We're filthy.'

'Well, you can tell me while you're having a bath,' said Richard. 'I can't wait to hear!'

It was lovely to have hot baths and to be given clean clothes. George was solemnly handed out shorts like the boys, and the others grinned to see that both Mr and Mrs Kent thought she was a boy. George, of course, grinned too, and didn't say a word.

'I was very angry with Richard when I heard what he had done,' said Mr Kent, when they were all sitting at table, eating hungrily. 'I'm ashamed of him.'

Richard looked downcast at once. He gazed beseechingly at Julian.

'Yes – Richard made a fool of himself,' said Julian. 'And landed us all into trouble. He wants taking in hand, sir.'

Richard looked even more downcast. He went very red, and looked at the table-cloth.

'But,' said Julian, 'he more than made up for his silliness, sir – he offered to squash himself into the boot of the car, and escape that way, and go and warn the police. That took some doing, believe me! I think quite a bit of Richard now!'

He leant over and gave the boy a pat on the back. Dick and the others followed it up with thumps, and Timmy woofed in his deepest voice.

Richard was now red with pleasure. 'Thanks,' he said, awkwardly. 'I'll remember this.'

'See you do, my boy!' said his father. 'It might all have ended very differently!'

'But it didn't,' said Anne happily. 'It ended like this. We can all breathe again!'

'Till the next time,' said Dick, with a grin. 'What do *you* say, Timmy, old boy?'

'Woof,' said Timmy, of course, and thumped his tail on the floor. 'WOOF!'

Enid Blyton®

is one of the most popular children's authors of all time. Her books have sold over 500 million copies and have been translated into other languages more often than any other children's author.

Enid Blyton adored writing for children. She wrote over 700 books and about 2,000 short stories. *The Famous Five* books, now 75 years old, are her most popular. She is also the author of other favourites including *The Secret Seven*, *The Magic Faraway Tree*, *Malory Towers* and *Noddy*.

Born in London in 1897, Enid lived much of her life in Buckinghamshire and loved dogs, gardening and the countryside. She was very knowledgeable about trees, flowers, birds and animals. Dorset – where some of the Famous Five's adventures are set – was a favourite place of hers too.

Enid Blyton's stories are read and loved by millions of children (and grown-ups) all over the world. Visit enidblyton.co.uk to discover more.

THE FAMOUS FIVE

FIVE FALL INTO ADVENTURE

Have you read all THE FAMOUS FIVE books?

1. Five on a Treasure Island
2. Five Go Adventuring Again
3. Five Run Away Together
4. Five Go to Smuggler's Top
5. Five Go Off in a Caravan
6. Five on Kirrin Island Again
7. Five Go Off to Camp
8. Five Get Into Trouble
9. Five Fall Into Adventure
10. Five on a Hike Together
11. Five Have a Wonderful Time
12. Five Go Down to the Sea
13. Five Go to Mystery Moor
14. Five Have Plenty of Fun
15. Five on a Secret Trail
16. Five Go to Billycock Hill
17. Five Get Into a Fix
18. Five on Finniston Farm
19. Five Go to Demon's Rocks
20. Five Have a Mystery to Solve
21. Five Are Together Again

The Famous Five Colour Short Stories

1. Five and a Half-Term Adventure
2. George's Hair is Too Long
3. Good Old Timmy
4. A Lazy Afternoon
5. Well Done, Famous Five
6. Five Have a Puzzling Time
7. Happy Christmas, Five
8. When Timmy Chased the Cat

Enid Blyton®

THE FAMOUS FIVE

FIVE FALL INTO ADVENTURE

Illustrated by Eileen A. Soper

HODDER

HODDER CHILDREN'S BOOKS

First published in Great Britain in 1950 by Hodder & Stoughton
This edition published in 2016

21

A CIP catalogue record for this book is available from the British Library.

ISBN 978 1 444 93639 1

Printed in Great Britain by Clays Ltd, Elcograf S.p.A.

The paper and board used in this book are made from wood from responsible sources.

Hodder Children's Books
An imprint of
Hachette Children's Group
Part of Hodder & Stoughton
Carmelite House
50 Victoria Embankment
London EC4Y 0DZ

An Hachette UK Company
www.hachette.co.uk
www.hachettechildrens.co.uk

CONTENTS

1 AT KIRRIN COTTAGE AGAIN 1
2 A MEETING ON THE BEACH 9
3 FACE AT THE WINDOW 16
4 THE NEXT DAY 24
5 RAGAMUFFIN JO 32
6 WHAT HAPPENED IN THE NIGHT? 40
7 POLICEMEN IN THE HOUSE 48
8 WHERE CAN GEORGE BE? 56
9 AN EXTRAORDINARY MESSAGE – AND A PLAN 64
10 SID'S WONDERFUL EVENING 72
11 DICK MAKES A CAPTURE 81
12 JO BEGINS TO TALK 89
13 OFF TO FIND GEORGE 97
14 SIMMY'S CARAVAN 105
15 ANNE DOESN'T LIKE ADVENTURES 112
16 VISITOR IN THE NIGHT 120
17 OFF IN GEORGE'S BOAT 128
18 THINGS BEGIN TO HAPPEN 137
19 JO IS VERY SURPRISING 146
20 THE ADVENTURE BOILS UP 154
21 A FEW SURPRISES 162

22 JO IS VERY SMART 170
23 MARKHOFF GOES HUNTING 179
24 A GRAND SURPRISE 187
25 EVERYTHING OK 195

CHAPTER ONE

At Kirrin Cottage again

GEORGINA WAS at the station to meet her three cousins. Timmy her dog was with her, his long tail wagging eagerly. He knew quite well they had come to meet Julian, Dick and Anne, and he was glad. It was much more fun when the Five were all together.

'Here comes the train, Timmy!' said George. Nobody called her Georgina, because she wouldn't answer if they did. She looked like a boy with her short curly hair and her jeans and open-necked shirt. Her face was covered with freckles, and her legs and arms were very tanned.

There was the far-off rumble of a train, and as it came nearer, a short warning hoot. Timmy whined and wagged his tail. He didn't like trains, but he wanted this one to come.

Nearer and nearer it came, slowing down as it reached Kirrin station. Long before it came to the little platform three heads appeared out of one of the windows, and three hands waved wildly. George waved back, her face one big smile.

The door swung open almost before the train stopped. Out came a big boy, and helped down a small girl. Then came another boy, not quite so tall as the first one, with a bag in each hand. He dragged a third bag out, and then George and Timmy were on him.

'Julian! Dick! Anne! Your train's late; we thought you were never coming!'

'Hallo, George! Here we are at last. Get down, Timmy, don't eat me.'

AT KIRRIN COTTAGE AGAIN

'Hallo, George! Oh, Timmy, you darling – you're just as licky as ever!'

'Woof,' said Timmy joyfully, and bounded all round like a mad thing, getting into everybody's way.

'Any trunk or anything?' asked George. 'Only those three bags?'

'Well, we haven't come for long this time, worse luck,' said Dick. 'Only a fortnight! Still, it's better than nothing.'

'You shouldn't have gone off to France all those six weeks,' said George, half-jealously. 'I suppose you've gone all French now.'

Dick laughed, waved his hands in the air and went off into a stream of quick French that sounded just like gibberish to George. French was not one of her strong subjects.

'Shut up,' she said, giving him a friendly shove. 'You're just the same old idiot. Oh, I'm so glad you've come. It's been lonely and dull at Kirrin without you.'

A porter came up with a barrow. Dick turned to him, waved his hands again, and addressed the astonished man in fluent French. But the porter knew Dick quite well.

'Go on with you,' he said. 'Argy-bargying in double-Dutch like that. Do you want me to wheel these up to Kirrin Cottage for you?'

'Yes, please,' said Anne. 'Stop it, Dick. It isn't funny when you go on so long.'

'Oh, let him go on,' said George, and she linked her

arms in Anne's and Dick's. 'It's lovely to have you again. Mother's looking forward to seeing you all.'

'I bet Uncle Quentin isn't,' said Julian, as they went along the little platform, Timmy capering round them.

'Father's in quite a good temper,' said George. 'You know he's been to America with Mother, lecturing and hearing other scientists lecturing too. Mother says everyone made a great fuss of him, and he liked it.'

George's father was a brilliant scientist, well-known all over the world. But he was rather a difficult man at home, impatient, hot-tempered and forgetful. The children were fond of him, but held him in great respect. They all heaved a sigh of relief when he went away for a few days, for then they could make as much noise as they liked, tear up and down the stairs, play silly jokes and generally be as mad as they pleased.

'Will Uncle Quentin be at home all the time we're staying with you?' asked Anne. She was really rather afraid of her hot-tempered uncle.

'No,' said George. 'Mother and Father are going away for a tour in Spain – so we'll be on our own.'

'Wizard!' said Dick. 'We can wear our bathing costumes all day long then if we want to.'

'And Timmy can come in at meal-times without being sent out whenever he moves,' said George. 'He's been sent out every single meal-time this week, just because he snapped at the flies that came near him. Father goes absolutely mad if Timmy suddenly snaps at a fly.'

'Shame!' said Anne, and patted Timmy's rough-haired back. 'You can snap at every single fly you like, Timmy, when we're on our own.'

'Woof,' said Timmy, gratefully.

'There won't be time for any adventure these hols,' said Dick, regretfully, as they walked down the lane to Kirrin Cottage. Red poppies danced along the way, and in the distance the sea shone as blue as cornflowers. 'Only two weeks – and back we go to school! Well, let's hope the weather keeps fine. I want to bathe six times a day!'

Soon they were all sitting round the tea-table at Kirrin Cottage, and their Aunt Fanny was handing round plates of her nicest scones and tea-cake. She was very pleased to see her nephews and niece again.

'Now George will be happy,' she said, smiling at the hungry four. 'She's been going about like a bear with a sore head the last week or two. Have another scone, Dick? Take two while you're about it.'

'Good idea,' said Dick, and helped himself. 'Nobody makes scones and cakes like you do, Aunt Fanny. Where's Uncle Quentin?'

'In his study,' said his aunt. 'He knows it's tea-time, and he's heard the bell, but I expect he's buried in something or other. I'll have to fetch him in a minute. I honestly believe he'd go without food all day long if I didn't go and drag him into the dining-room!'

'Here he is,' said Julian, hearing the familiar impatient footsteps coming down the hall to the dining-room. The door was flung open. Uncle Quentin stood there, a newspaper in his hand, scowling. He didn't appear to see the children at all.

'Look here, Fanny!' he shouted. 'See what they've put in this paper – the very thing I gave orders was NOT to be put in! The dolts! the idiots! The . . .'

'Quentin! Whatever's the matter?' said his wife. 'Look – here are the children – they've just arrived.'

But Uncle Quentin simply didn't see any of the four children at all. He went on glaring at the paper. He rapped at it with his hand.

'*Now* we'll get the place full of reporters wanting to see me, and wanting to know all about my new ideas!' he said, beginning to shout. 'See what they've said! "This eminent scientist conducts all his experiments and works out all his ideas at his home, Kirrin Cottage. Here are his stack of notebooks, to which are now added two more – fruits of his visit to America, and here at his cottage are his amazing diagrams," and so on and so on.

'I tell you, Fanny, we'll have hordes of reporters down.'

'No, we shan't, dear,' said his wife. 'And, anyway, we are soon off to Spain. Do sit down and have some tea. And look, can't you say a word to welcome Julian, Dick and Anne?'

Uncle Quentin grunted and sat down. 'I didn't know they were coming,' he said, and helped himself to a scone. 'You might have told me, Fanny.'

'I told you three times yesterday and twice today,' said his wife.

Anne suddenly squeezed her uncle's arm. She was sitting next to him. 'You're just the same as ever, Uncle Quentin,' she said. 'You never, never remember we're coming! Shall we go away again?'

Her uncle looked down at her and smiled. His temper never lasted very long. He grinned at Julian and Dick. 'Well, here you are again!' he said. 'Do you think you can hold the fort for me while I'm away with your aunt?'

'You bet!' said all three together.

'We'll keep everyone at bay!' said Julian. 'With Timmy's help. I'll put up a notice: "*Beware, very fierce dog*".'

'Woof,' said Timmy, sounding delighted. He thumped

his tail on the floor. A fly came by his nose and he snapped at it. Uncle Quentin frowned.

'Have another scone, Father?' said George hurriedly. 'When are you and Mother going to Spain?'

'Tomorrow,' said her mother firmly. 'Now, don't look like that, Quentin. You know perfectly well it's been arranged for weeks, and you *need* a holiday, and if we don't go tomorrow all our arrangements will be upset.'

'Well, you might have *warned* me it was tomorrow,' said her husband, looking indignant. 'I mean – I've all my notebooks to check and put away, and . . .'

'Quentin, I've told you heaps of times that we leave on September the third,' said his wife, still more firmly. '*I* want a holiday, too. The four children will be quite all right here with Timmy – they'll love being on their own. Julian is almost grown-up now and he can cope with anything that turns up.'

Timmy snapped twice at a fly, and Uncle Quentin jumped. 'If that dog does that again,' he began, but his wife interrupted him at once.

'There, you see! You're as touchy and nervy as can be, Quentin, dear. It will do you good to get away – and the children will have a lovely two weeks on their own. Nothing can possibly happen, so make up your mind to leave tomorrow with an easy mind!'

Nothing can possibly happen? Aunt Fanny was wrong of course. *Anything* could happen when the Five were left on their own!

CHAPTER TWO

A meeting on the beach

IT REALLY was very difficult to get Uncle Quentin off the next day. He was shut up in his study until the last possible moment, sorting out his precious notebooks. The taxi arrived and hooted outside the gate. Aunt Fanny, who had been ready for a long time, went and rapped at the study door.

'Quentin! Unlock the door! You really must come. We shall miss the plane if we don't go now.'

'Just one minute!' shouted back her husband. Aunt Fanny looked at the four children in despair.

'That's the fourth time he's called out "Just one minute",' said George. The telephone shrilled out just then, and she picked up the receiver.

'Yes,' she said. 'No, I'm afraid you can't see him. He's off to Spain, and nobody will know where he is for the next two weeks. What's that? Wait a minute – I'll ask my mother.'

'Who is it?' said her mother.

'It's the *Daily Clarion*,' said George. 'They want to send a reporter down to interview Daddy. I told them he was going to Spain – and they said could they publish that?'

'Of course,' said her mother, thankfully. 'Once that's in

the papers nobody will ring up and worry you. Say, yes, George.'

George said yes, the taxi hooted more loudly than ever, and Timmy barked madly at the hooting. The study door was flung open and Uncle Quentin stood in the doorway, looking as dark as thunder.

'Why can't I have a little peace and quiet when I'm doing important work?' he began. But his wife made a dart at him and dragged him down the hall. She put his hat in one hand, and would have put his stick into the other if he hadn't been carrying a heavy despatch case.

'You're not doing important work, you're off on a holiday,' she said. 'Oh, Quentin, you're worse than ever! What's that case in your hand? Surely you are not taking work away with you?'

The taxi hooted again, and Timmy woofed just behind Uncle Quentin. He jumped violently, and the telephone rang loudly.

'That's another reporter coming down to see you, Father,' said George. 'Better go quickly!'

Whether that bit of news really did make Uncle Quentin decide at last to go, nobody knew – but in two seconds he was sitting in the taxi, still clutching his despatch case, telling the taxi-driver exactly what he thought of people who kept hooting their horns.

'Good-bye, dears,' called Aunt Fanny, thankfully. 'Don't get into mischief. We're off at last.'

The taxi disappeared down the lane. 'Poor Mother!'

said George. 'It's always like this when they go for a holiday. Well, there's one thing certain – I shall NEVER marry a scientist.'

Everyone heaved a sigh of relief at the thought that Uncle Quentin was gone. When he was over-worked he really was impossible.

'Still, you simply have to make excuses for anyone with a brain like his,' said Julian. 'Whenever our science master at school speaks of him, he almost holds his breath with awe. Worst of it is, he expects *me* to be brilliant because I've got a brilliant uncle.'

'Yes. It's difficult to live up to clever relations,' said Dick. 'Well – we're on our own, except for Joanna. Good old Joanna! I bet she'll give us some smashing meals.'

'Let's go and see if she's got anything we can have now,' said George. 'I'm hungry.'

'So am I,' said Dick. They marched down the hall into the kitchen, calling for Joanna.

'Now, you don't need to tell me what you've come for,' said Joanna, the smiling, good-tempered cook. 'And I don't need to tell you this – the larder's locked.'

'Oh, Joanna – what a mean thing to do!' said Dick.

'Mean or not, it's the only thing to do when all four of you are around, to say nothing of that great hungry dog,' said Joanna, rolling out some pastry vigorously. 'Why, last holidays I left a meat pie and half a tongue and a cherry tart and trifle sitting on the shelves for the next day's meals – and when I came back from my half-day's outing there wasn't a thing to be seen.'

'Well, we thought you'd left them there for our supper,' said Julian, sounding quite hurt.

'All right – but you won't get the chance of thinking anything like that again,' said Joanna, firmly. 'That larder door's going to be kept locked. Maybe I'll unlock it sometimes and hand you out a snack or two – but I'm the one that's going to unlock it, not you.'

The four drifted out of the kitchen again, disappointed. Timmy followed at their heels. 'Let's go down and have a bathe,' said Dick. 'If I'm going to have six bathes a day, I'd better hurry up and have my first one.'

'I'll get some ripe plums,' said Anne. 'We can take those down with us. And I expect the ice-cream man will come along to the beach too. We shan't starve! And we'd better wear our shirts and jeans over our bathing costumes, so we don't catch too much sun.'

Soon they were all down on the sand. They found a good place and scraped out comfortable holes to sit in. Timmy scraped his own.

'I can't imagine why Timmy bothers to scrape one,' said George. 'Because he always squeezes into mine sooner or later. Don't you, Timmy?'

Timmy wagged his tail, and scraped so violently that they were all covered with sand. 'Pooh!' said Anne, spitting sand out of her mouth. 'Stop it, Timmy. As fast as I scrape my hole, you fill it up!'

Timmy paused to give her a lick, and then scraped again, making a very deep hole indeed. He lay down in it, panting, his mouth looking as if he were smiling.

'He's smiling again,' said Anne. 'I never knew a dog that smiled like Timmy. Timmy, it's nice to have you again.'

'Woof,' said Timmy, politely, meaning that it was nice to have Anne and the others back again, too. He wagged his tail and sent a shower of sand over Dick.

They all wriggled down comfortably into their soft warm holes. 'We'll eat the plums first and then we'll have a bathe,' said Dick. 'Chuck me one, Anne.'

Two people came slowly along the beach. Dick looked at them out of half-closed eyes. A boy and a man – and what a ragamuffin the boy looked! He wore torn dirty jeans and a filthy jersey.

The man looked even worse. He slouched as he came, and dragged one foot. He had a straggly moustache and mean, clever little eyes that raked the beach up and down. The two were walking at the high-water mark and were obviously looking for anything that might have been cast up by the tide. The boy already had an old box, one wet shoe and some wood under his arm.

'What a pair!' said Dick to Julian. 'I hope they don't come near us. I feel as if I can smell them from here.'

The two walked along the beach and then back. Then, to the children's horror, they made a bee-line for where they were lying in their sandy holes, and sat down close beside them. Timmy growled.

The boy took no notice of Timmy's growling. But the man looked uneasy.

'Come on – let's have a bathe,' said Julian, annoyed at the way the two had sat down so close to them. After all, there was practically the whole of the beach to choose from – why come and sit almost on top of somebody else?

When they came back from their bathe the man had gone, but the boy was still there – and he had actually sat himself down in George's hole.

'Get out,' said George, shortly, her temper rising at once. 'That's my hole, and you jolly well know it.'

'Finders keepers,' said the boy, in a curious sing-song voice. 'It's my hole now.'

George bent down and pulled the boy roughly out of the hole. He was up in a trice, his fists clenched. George clenched hers, too.

Dick came up at a run. 'Now, George – if there's any fighting to be done, I'll do it,' he said. He turned to the scowling boy. 'Clear off! We don't want you here!'

The boy hit out with his right fist and caught Dick unexpectedly on the jawbone. Dick looked astounded. He hit out, too, and sent the tousle-headed boy flying.

'Yah, coward!' said the boy, holding his chin tenderly. 'Hitting someone smaller than yourself! I'll fight that first boy, but I won't fight *you*.'

'You can't fight him,' said Dick. 'He's a girl. You can't fight girls.'

'Says you!' said the dirty little ragamuffin, standing up

and doubling his fists again. 'Well, you look here – *I'm* a girl, too – so I can fight her all right, can't I?'

George and the ragamuffin stood scowling at one another, each with fists clenched. They looked so astonishingly alike, with their short, curly hair, suntanned freckled faces and fierce expressions that Julian suddenly roared with laughter. He pushed them firmly apart.

'Fighting's forbidden!' he said. He turned to the ragamuffin. 'Clear off!' he ordered. 'Do you hear me? Go on – off with you!'

The girl stared at him. Then she suddenly burst into tears and ran off howling.

'*She's* a girl all right,' said Dick, grinning at the howls. 'She's got some spunk though, facing up to me like that. Well, that's the last we'll see of *her*!'

But he was wrong. It wasn't!

CHAPTER THREE

Face at the window

THE FIVE curled up in their holes once more. Dick felt his jawbone. 'That ragamuffin of a girl gave me a good bang,' he said, half-admiringly. 'Little demon, isn't she! A bit of a live wire!'

'I can't see why Julian wouldn't let me have a go at her,' said George sulkily. 'It was my hole she sat in – she *meant* to be annoying! How dare she?'

'You can't go about fighting,' said Dick. 'Don't be an ass, George. I know you make out you're as tough as a boy, and you dress like a boy and climb trees – but it's really time you gave up thinking you're a boy.'

This sort of speech didn't please George at all. 'Well, anyway, I don't burst into howls if I'm beaten,' she said, turning her back on Dick.

'No, you don't,' agreed Dick. 'You've got as much spunk as any boy – much more than that other kid had. I'm sorry I sent her flying now. It's the first time I've ever hit a girl, and I hope it'll be the last.'

'I'm jolly glad you hit her,' said George. 'She's a nasty little beast. If I see her again I'll tell her what I think of her.'

'No, you won't,' said Dick. 'Not if I'm there, anyway. She had her punishment when I sent her flying.'

'Do shut up arguing, you two,' said Anne, and sent a shower of sand over them. 'George, don't go into one of your moods, for goodness' sake – we don't want to waste a single day of this two weeks.'

'Here's the ice-cream man,' said Julian, sitting up and feeling for the waterproof pocket in the belt of his bathing trunks. 'Let's have one each.'

'Woof,' said Timmy, and thumped his tail on the sand.

'Yes, all right – one for you, too,' said Dick. 'Though what sense there is in giving *you* one, I don't know. One lick, one swallow, and it's gone. It might be a fly for all you taste of it.'

Timmy gulped his ice-cream down at once and then went into George's hole, squeezing beside her, hoping for a lick of her ice, too. But she pushed him away.

'No, Timmy. Ice-cream's wasted on you! You can't even have a lick of mine. And do get back into your hole – you're making me frightfully hot.'

Timmy obligingly got out and went into Anne's hole. She gave him a little bit of her ice-cream. He sat panting beside her, looking longingly at the rest of the ice. 'You're melting it with your hot breath,' said Anne. 'Go into Julian's hole now!'

The five of them had a thoroughly lazy morning. As none of them had a watch they went in far too early for lunch, and were shooed out again by Joanna.

'How you can come in at ten past twelve for a one

o'clock lunch, I don't know!' she scolded. 'I haven't even finished the housework yet.'

'Well – it *felt* like one o'clock,' said Anne, disappointed to find there was so long to wait. Still, when lunch-time came, Joanna really did them well.

'Cold ham and tongue – cold baked beans – beetroot – crisp lettuce straight from the garden – heaps of tomatoes – cucumber – hard-boiled egg!' recited Anne in glee.

'Just the kind of meal I like,' said Dick, sitting down. 'What's for pudding?'

'There it is on the sideboard,' said Anne. 'Wobbly blancmange, fresh fruit salad and jelly. I'm glad I'm hungry.'

'Now, don't you give Timmy any of that ham and tongue,' Joanna warned George. 'I've got a fine bone for him. Coming, Timmy?'

Timmy knew the word 'bone' very well indeed. He trotted after Joanna at once, his feet sounding loudly in the hall. They heard Joanna talking kindly to him in the kitchen as she found him his bone.

'Good old Joanna,' said Dick. 'She's like Timmy – her bark is worse than her bite.'

'Timmy's got a good bite, though,' said George, helping herself to three tomatoes at once. 'And his bite came in useful heaps of times for us.'

They ate steadily, thinking of some of the hair-raising adventures they had had, when Timmy and his bite had certainly come in very useful. Timmy came in after a while, licking his lips.

'Nothing doing, old chap,' said Dick, looking at the empty dishes on the table. 'Don't tell me you've chomped up that bone already!'

Timmy had. He lay down under the table, and put his nose on his paws. He was happy. He had had a good meal, and he was with the people he loved best. He put his head as near George's feet as he could.

'Your whiskers are tickling me,' she said, and screwed up her bare toes. 'Pass the tomatoes, someone.'

'You *can't* manage any more tomatoes, surely!' said Anne. 'You've had five already.'

'They're out of my own garden,' said George, 'so I can eat as many as I like.'

After lunch they lazed on the beach till it was time for a bathe again. It was a happy day for all of them – warm, lazy, with plenty of running and romping about.

George looked out for the ragamuffin girl, but she didn't appear again. George was half sorry. She would have liked a battle of words with her, even if she couldn't have a fight!

They were all very tired when they went to bed that night. Julian yawned so loudly when Joanna came in with a jug of hot cocoa and some biscuits that she offered to lock up the house for him.

'Oh, no, thank you, Joanna,' said Julian at once. 'That's the man's job, you know, locking up the house. You can trust me all right. I'll see to every window and every door.'

'Right, Julian,' said Joanna, and bustled away to wind up the kitchen clock, rake out the fire, and go up to bed. The children went up, too, Timmy, as usual, at George's heels. Julian was left downstairs to lock up.

He was a very responsible boy. Joanna knew that he wouldn't leave a single window unfastened. She heard him trying to shut the little window in the pantry, and she called down:

'Julian! It's swollen or something, and won't shut properly. You needn't bother about it, it's too small for anyone to get into!'

'Right!' said Julian, thankfully, and went upstairs. He yawned a terrific yawn again, and set Dick off, too, as soon as he came into the bedroom they both shared. The girls, undressing in the next room, laughed to hear them.

'*You* wouldn't hear a burglar in the middle of the night, Julian and Dick!' called Anne. 'You'll sleep like logs!'

'Old Timmy can listen out for burglars,' said Julian, cleaning his teeth vigorously. 'That's his job, not mine. Isn't it, Timmy?'

'Woof,' said Timmy, clambering on to George's bed. He always slept curled up in the crook of her knees. Her mother had given up trying to insist that George didn't have Timmy on her bed at night. As George said, even if *she* agreed to that, Timmy wouldn't!

Nobody stayed awake for more than five seconds. Nobody even said anything in bed, except for a sleepy good-night. Timmy gave a little grunt and settled down, too, his head on George's feet. It was heavy, but she liked it there. She put out a hand and stroked Timmy gently. He licked one of her feet through the bed-clothes. He loved George more than anyone in the world.

It was dark outside that night. Thick clouds had come up and put out all the stars. There was no sound to be heard but the wind in the trees and the distant surge of the sea – and both sounded so much the same that it was hard to tell the difference.

Not another sound – not even an owl hooting to its mate, or the sound of a hedgehog pattering in the ditch.

Then why did Timmy wake up? Why did he open first one eye and then another? Why did he prick up his ears and lie there, listening? He didn't even lift his head at first. He simply lay listening in the darkness.

He lifted his head cautiously at last. He slid off the bed as quietly as a cat. He padded across the room and out of the door. Down the stairs he went, and into the hall, where his claws rattled on the tiled floor. But nobody heard him. Everyone in the house was fast asleep.

Timmy stood and listened in the hall. He knew he had heard something. Could it have been a rat somewhere? Timmy lifted his nose and sniffed.

And then he stiffened from head to tail, and stood as if turned into stone. Something was climbing up the wall of the house. Scrape, scrape, scrape – rustle, rustle! Would a rat dare to do that?

Upstairs, in her bed, Anne didn't know why she suddenly woke up just then, but she did. She was thirsty, and she thought she would get a drink of water. She felt for her torch, and switched it on.

The light fell on the window first, and Anne saw something that gave her a terrible shock. She screamed loudly, and dropped her torch in fright. George woke up at once. Timmy came bounding up the stairs.

'Julian!' wailed Anne. 'Come quickly. I saw a face at the window, a horrible, dreadful face looking in at me!'

George rushed to the window, switching on her torch as she did so. There was nothing there. Timmy went with her. He sniffed at the open window and growled.

'Listen – I can hear someone running quickly down the path,' said Julian, who now appeared with Dick. 'Come on, Timmy – downstairs with you and after them!'

And down they all went – Anne too. They flung the front door wide and Timmy sped out, barking loudly. A face at the window? He'd soon find out who it belonged to!

CHAPTER FOUR

The next day

THE FOUR children waited at the open front door, listening to Timmy's angry, excited barking. Anne was trembling, and Julian put his arm round her comfortingly.

'What was this dreadful face like?' he asked her. Anne shivered in his arm.

'I didn't see very much,' she said. 'You see, I just switched on my torch, and the beam was directed on the window nearby – and it lit up the face for a second. It had nasty gleaming eyes – oh, I *was* frightened!'

'Then did it disappear?' asked Julian.

'I don't know,' said Anne. 'I was so frightened that I dropped my torch and the light went out. Then George woke up and rushed to the window.'

'Where on earth was Timmy?' said Dick, feeling suddenly surprised that Timmy hadn't awakened them all by barking. Surely he must have heard the owner of the face climbing up to the window?

'I don't know. He came rushing into the bedroom when I screamed,' said Anne. 'Perhaps he *had* heard a noise and had gone down to see what it was.'

'That's about it,' said Julian. 'Never mind, Anne. It was a tramp, I expect. He found all the doors and windows downstairs fastened – and shinned up the ivy to see if he could enter by way of a bedroom. Timmy will get him, that's certain.'

But Timmy didn't get him. He came back after a time, with his tail down, and a puzzled look in his eyes. 'Couldn't you find him, Timmy?' said George, anxiously.

'Woof,' said Timmy, mournfully, his tail still down. George felt him. He was wet through.

'Goodness! Where have you been to get so wet?' she said, in surprise. 'Feel him, Dick.'

Dick felt him, and so did the others. 'He's been in the sea,' said Julian. 'That's why he's wet. I guess the burglar, or whatever he was, must have sprinted down to the beach, when he knew Timmy was after him – and jumped into a boat! It was his only chance of getting away.'

'And Timmy must have swum after him till he couldn't keep up any more,' said George. 'Poor old Tim. So you lost him, did you?'

Timmy wagged his tail a little. He looked very downhearted indeed. To think he had heard noises and thought it was a rat – and now, whoever it was had got away from him. Timmy felt ashamed.

Julian shut and bolted the front door. He put up the chain, too. 'I don't think the Face will come back again in a hurry,' he said. 'Now he knows there's a big dog here he'll keep away. I don't think we need worry any more.'

They all went back to bed again. Julian didn't go to sleep for some time. Although he had told the others not to worry, he felt worried himself. He was sorry that Anne had been frightened, and somehow the boldness of the burglar in climbing up to a bedroom worried him, too. He must have been determined to get in somehow.

Joanna, the cook, slept through all the disturbance. Julian wouldn't wake her. 'No,' he said, 'don't tell her anything about it. She'd want to send telegrams to Uncle Quentin or something.'

So Joanna knew nothing about the night's happenings, and they heard her cheerfully humming in the kitchen the next morning as she cooked bacon and eggs and tomatoes for their breakfast.

Anne was rather ashamed of herself when she woke up and remembered the fuss she had made. The Face was rather dim in her memory now. She half wondered if she had dreamt it all. She asked Julian if he thought she might have had a bad dream.

'Quite likely,' said Julian, cheerfully, very glad that Anne should think this. 'More than likely! I wouldn't worry about it any more, if I were you.'

He didn't tell Anne that he had examined the thickly-growing ivy outside the window, and had found clear traces of the night-climber. Part of the sturdy clinging ivy-stem had come away from the wall, and beneath the window were strewn broken-off ivy leaves. Julian showed them to Dick.

'There *was* somebody,' he said. 'What a nerve he had, climbing right up to the window like that. A real cat-burglar!'

There were no footprints to be seen anywhere in the garden. Julian didn't expect to find any, for the ground was dry and hard.

The day was very fine and warm again. 'I vote we do what we did yesterday – go off to the beach and bathe,' said Dick. 'We might take a picnic lunch if Joanna will give us one.'

'I'll help her to make it up for us,' said Anne, and she and George went off to beg for sandwiches and buns. Soon they were busy wrapping up a colossal lunch.

'Do for twelve, I should think!' said Joanna, with a laugh. 'Here's a bottle of home-made lemonade, too. You can take as many ripe plums as you like as well. I shan't prepare any supper for you tonight – you'll not need it after this lunch.'

George and Anne looked at her in alarm. No *supper*! Then they caught the twinkle in her eye and laughed.

'We'll make all the beds and do our rooms before we go,' said Anne. 'And is there anything you want from the village?'

'No, not today. You hurry up with your jobs and get along to the beach,' said Joanna. 'I'll be quite glad of a peaceful day to myself. I shall turn out the larder and the hall cupboards and the scullery, and enjoy myself in peace!'

Anne seemed quite to have forgotten her fright of the night before as they went down to the beach that day, chattering and laughing together. Even if she *had* thought about it, something soon happened that swept everything else from her mind.

The little ragamuffin girl was down on the beach again! She was alone. Her dreadful old father, or whatever he was, was not there.

George saw the girl first and scowled. Julian saw the scowl and then the girl, and made up his mind at once. He led the others firmly to where rocks jutted up from the beach, surrounded by limpid rock-pools.

'We'll be here today,' he said. 'It's so hot we'll be glad of the shade from the rocks. What about just here?'

'It's all right,' said George, half sulky and half amused at Julian for being so firm about things. 'Don't worry. I'm not having anything more to do with that smelly girl.'

'I'm glad to hear it,' said Julian. They had now turned a corner, and were out of sight of the girl. Big rocks ran in an upwards direction behind them, and jutted up all around them. Julian sat down in a lovely little corner, with rocks protecting them from the sun and the wind.

'Let's have a read before we bathe,' said Dick. 'I've got a mystery story here. I simply MUST find out who the thief is.'

He settled himself comfortably. Anne went to look for sea anemones in the pool. She liked the petal-like creatures that looked so like plants and weren't. She liked feeding them with bits of biscuit, seeing their 'petals' close over the fragments and draw them quickly inside.

George lay back and stroked Timmy. Julian began to

sketch the rocks around, and the little pools. It was all very peaceful indeed.

Suddenly something landed on George's middle and made her jump. She sat up, and so did Timmy.

'What was that?' said George indignantly. 'Did you throw something at me, Dick?'

'No,' said Dick, his eyes glued to his book.

Something else hit George on the back of the neck, and she put her hand up with an exclamation. 'What's happening? Who's throwing things?'

She looked to see what had hit her. Lying on the sand was a small roundish thing. George picked it up. 'Why – it's a damson stone,' she said. And 'Ping'! Another one hit her on the shoulder. She leapt up in a rage.

She could see nobody at all. She waited for another damson stone to appear, but none did.

'I just wish I could draw your face, George,' said Julian, with a grin. 'I never saw such a frown in my life. Ooch!'

The 'ooch!' was nothing to do with George's frown; it was caused by another damson stone that caught Julian neatly behind the ear. He leapt to his feet too. A helpless giggle came from behind a rock some way behind and above them. George was up on the ledge in a second.

Behind one of the rocks sat the ragamuffin girl. Her pockets were full of damsons, some of them spilling out as she rolled on the rocks, laughing. She sat up when she saw George, and grinned.

'What do you mean, throwing those stones at us?' demanded George.

'I wasn't throwing them,' said the girl.

'Don't tell lies,' said George scornfully. 'You know you were.'

'I wasn't. I was just spitting them,' said the awful girl. 'Watch!' She slipped a stone into her mouth, took a deep breath and then spat out the stone. It flew straight at George and hit her sharply and squarely on the nose. George looked so extremely surprised that Dick and Julian roared with laughter.

'Bet I can spit stones farther than any of you,' said the ragamuffin. 'Have some of my damsons and see.'

'Right!' said Dick promptly. 'If you win I'll buy you an ice-cream. If I do, you can clear off from here and not bother us any more. See?'

'Yes,' said the girl, and her eyes gleamed and danced. 'But I shall win!'

CHAPTER FIVE

Ragamuffin Jo

GEORGE WAS most astonished at Dick. How very shocking to see who could spit damson stones out the farthest.

'It's all right,' said Julian to her in a low voice. 'You know how good Dick is at that sort of game. He'll win – and we'll send the girl scooting off, well and truly beaten.'

'I think you're horrible, Dick,' said George, in a loud voice. 'Horrible!'

'Who used to spit cherry-stones out and try and beat me last year?' said Dick at once. 'Don't be so high-and-mighty, George.'

Anne came slowly back from her pool, wondering why the others were up on the rocks. Damson stones began to rain round her. She stopped in astonishment. Surely – surely it couldn't be the others doing that? A stone hit her on her bare arm, and she squealed.

The ragamuffin girl won handsomely. She managed to get her stones at least three feet farther than Dick. She lay back, laughing, her teeth gleaming very white indeed.

'You owe me an ice-cream,' she said, in her sing-song voice. Julian wondered if she was Welsh. Dick looked at her, marvelling that she managed to get her stones so far.

'I'll buy you the ice-cream, don't worry,' he said.

'Nobody's ever beaten me before like that, not even Stevens, a boy at school with a most enormous mouth.'

'I do think you really are dreadful,' said Anne. 'Go and buy her the ice-cream and tell her to go home.'

'I'm going to eat it here,' said the girl, and she suddenly looked exactly as mulish and obstinate as George did when she wanted something she didn't think she would get.

'You look like George now!' said Dick, and immediately wished he hadn't. George glared at him, furious.

'What! That nasty, rude tangly-haired girl like *me*!' stormed George. 'Pooh! I can't bear to go near her.'

'Shut up,' said Dick, shortly. The girl looked surprised.

'What does she mean?' she asked Dick. 'Am I nasty? You're as *rude* as I am, anyway.'

'There's an ice-cream man,' said Julian, afraid that the hot-tempered George would fly at the girl and slap her. He whistled to the man, who came to the edge of the rocks and handed out six ice-creams.

'Here you are,' said Julian, handing one to the girl. 'You eat that up and go.'

They all sat and ate ice-creams, George still scowling. Timmy gulped his at once as usual. 'Look – he's had all his,' marvelled the girl. 'I call that a waste. Here, boy – have a bit of mine!'

To George's annoyance, Timmy licked up the bit of ice-cream thrown to him by the girl. How *could* Timmy accept anything from her?

Dick couldn't help being amused by this odd, bold little girl, with her tangled short hair and sharp darting eyes. He suddenly saw something that made him feel uncomfortable.

On her chin the girl had a big bruise. 'I say,' said Dick, '*I* didn't give you that bruise yesterday, did I?'

'What bruise? Oh, this one on my chin?' said the girl, touching it. 'Yes, that's where you hit me when you sent me flying. *I* don't mind. I've had worse ones from my dad.'

'I'm sorry I hit you,' said Dick. 'I am honestly. What's your name?'

'Jo,' said the girl.

'But that's a *boy's* name,' said Dick.

'So's George. But you said she was a girl,' said Jo, licking the last bits of ice-cream from her fingers.

'Yes, but George is short for Georgina,' said Anne. 'What's Jo short for?'

'Don't know,' said Jo. 'I never heard. All I know is I'm a girl and my name is Jo.'

'It's probably short for Josephine,' said Julian. They all stared at the possible Josephine. The short name of Jo certainly suited her – but not the long and pretty name of Josephine.

'It's really strange,' said Anne, at last, 'but Jo *is* awfully like you, George – same short curly hair – only Jo's is terribly messy and tangly – same freckles, dozens of them – same turned-up nose . . .'

'Same way of sticking her chin up in the air, same scowl, same glare!' said Dick. George put on her fiercest glare at these remarks, which she didn't like at all.

'Well, all I can say is I hope I haven't her layers of dirt and her sm—' she began, angrily. But Dick stopped her.

'She's probably not got any soap or hair-brush or anything. She'd be all right cleaned up. Don't be unkind, George.'

George turned her back. How *could* Dick stick up for that awful girl? 'Isn't she ever going?' she said. 'Or is she going to park herself on us all day long?'

'I'll go when I want to,' said Jo, and put on a scowl, so exactly like George's that Julian and Dick laughed in surprise. Jo laughed, too, but George clenched her fists furiously. Anne looked on in distress. She wished Jo would go, then everything would be all right again.

'I like that dog,' said Jo, suddenly, and she leaned over to where Timmy lay beside George. She patted him with a hand that was like a little paw. George swung round.

'Don't touch my dog!' she said. '*He* doesn't like you, either!'

'Oh, but he does,' said Jo, surprisingly. 'All dogs like *me*. So do cats. I can make your dog come to me as easy as anything.'

'Try!' said George, scornfully. 'He won't go to *you*! Will you, Tim?'

Jo didn't move. She began to make a peculiar little whining noise down in her throat, like a forlorn puppy.

Timmy pricked up his ears at once. He looked inquiringly at Jo. Jo stopped making the noise and held out her hand.

Timmy looked at it and turned away – but when he heard the whining again he got up, listening. He stared intently at Jo. Was this a kind of god-girl, that she could so well speak his language?

Jo flung herself on her face and went on with the small, whining noises that sounded as if she were a small dog in pain or sorrow. Timmy walked over to her and sat down, his head on one side, puzzled. Then he suddenly bent down and licked the girl's half-hidden face. She sat up at once and put her arms round Timmy's neck.

'Come here, Timmy,' said George, jealously. Timmy shook off the tanned arms that held him and walked over to George at once.

Jo laughed.

'See? I made him come to me and give me one of his best licks! I can do that to any dog.'

'How can you?' asked Dick, in wonder. He had never seen Timmy make friends before with anyone who was disliked by George.

'I don't know, really,' said Jo, pushing back her hair again, as she sat up. 'I reckon it's in the family. My mother was in a circus, and she trained dogs for the ring. We had dozens – lovely they were. I loved them all.'

'Where is your mother?' asked Julian. 'Is she still in the circus?'

'No. She died,' said Jo. 'And I left the circus with my

dad. We've got a caravan. Dad was an acrobat till he hurt his foot.'

The four children remembered how the man had dragged his foot as he walked. They looked silently at little Jo. What a strange life she must have led!

'She's dirty, she's probably very good at telling lies and thieving, but she's got pluck,' thought Julian. 'Still, I'll be glad when she goes.'

'I wish I hadn't given her that awful bruise,' thought Dick. 'I wonder what she'd be like cleaned up and brushed? She looks as if a little kindness would do her good.'

'I'm sorry for her, but I don't much like her,' thought Anne.

'I don't believe a word she says!' thought George angrily. 'Not one word! She's a humbug. And I'm *ashamed* of Timmy for going to her. I feel very cross with him.'

'Where's your father?' said Julian at last.

'Gone off somewhere to meet somebody,' said Jo vaguely. 'I'm glad. He was in one of his tempers this morning. I went and hid under the caravan.'

There was a silence. 'Can I stay with you today till my dad comes back?' said Jo suddenly, in her sing-song voice. 'I'll wash myself if you like. I'm all alone today.'

'No. We don't want you,' said George, feeling as if she really couldn't bear Jo any longer. 'Do we, Anne?'

Anne didn't like hurting anyone. She hesitated. 'Well,' said at last, 'perhaps Jo *had* better go.'

'Yes,' said Julian. 'It's time you scooted off now, Jo.

You've had a long time with us.'

Jo looked at Dick with mournful eyes, and touched the bruise on her chin as if it hurt her. Dick felt most uncomfortable again. He looked round at the others.

'Don't you think she could stay and share our picnic?' he said. 'After all – she can't *help* being dirty and – and . . .'

'It's all right,' said Jo, suddenly scrambling up. 'I'm going! There's my dad!'

They saw the man in the distance, dragging his foot as he walked. He caught sight of Jo and gave a shrill and piercing whistle. Jo made a face at them all, an impudent, ugly, insolent face.

'I don't like you!' she said. Then she pointed at Dick. 'I only like *him* – he's nice. Yah to the rest of you!'

And off she went like a hare over the sand, her bare feet hardly touching the ground.

'What an extraordinary girl!' said Julian. 'I don't feel we've seen the last of her yet!'

CHAPTER SIX

What happened in the night?

THAT NIGHT Anne began to look rather scared as darkness fell. She was remembering the Face at the Window!

'It won't come again, Ju, will it?' she said to her big brother half a dozen times.

'No, Anne. But if you like I'll come and lie down on George's bed instead of George tonight, and stay with you all night long,' said Julian.

Anne considered this and then shook her head. 'No. I think I'd almost rather have George and Timmy. I mean – George and I – and even you – might be scared of Faces, but Timmy wouldn't. He'd simply leap at them.'

'You're quite right,' said Julian. 'He would. All right then, I won't keep you company – but you'll see, nothing whatever will happen tonight. Anyway, if you like, we'll all close our bedroom windows and fasten them, even if we are too hot for anything – then we'll know nobody can possibly get in.'

So that night Julian not only closed all the doors and windows downstairs as he had done the night before (except the tiny pantry window that wouldn't shut), but he also shut and fastened all the ones upstairs.

'What about Joanna's window?' asked Anne.

'She *always* sleeps with it shut, summer and winter,' said Julian, with a grin. 'Country folk often do. They think the night air's dangerous. Now, you've nothing at all to worry about, silly.'

So Anne went to bed with her mind at rest. George drew the curtains across their window so that even if the Face came again they wouldn't be able to see it!

'Let Timmy out for me, Julian, will you?' called George. 'Anne doesn't want me to leave her, even to take old Timmy out for his last walk. Just open the door and let him out. He'll come in when he's ready.'

'Right!' called Julian, and opened the front door. Timmy trotted out, tail wagging. He loved his last sniff round. He liked to smell the trail of the hedgehog who was out on his night-rounds; he liked to put his nose down a rabbit-hole and listen to stirrings down below; and he loved to follow the meanderings of rats and mice round by the thick hedges.

'Isn't Timmy in yet?' called George from the top of the stairs. 'Do call him, Ju. I want to go to bed. Anne's half-asleep already.'

'He'll be in in a moment,' said Julian, who wanted to finish his book. 'Don't fuss.'

But no Timmy appeared even when he had finished his book. Julian went to the door and whistled. He listened for Timmy to come. Then, hearing nothing, he whistled once more.

This time he heard the sound of pattering footsteps

coming up the path to the door. 'Oh there you are, Tim,' said Julian. 'What have you been up to? Chasing rabbits or something?'

Timmy wagged his tail feebly. He didn't jump up at Julian as he usually did. 'You look as if you've been up to some mischief, Tim,' said Julian. 'Go on – up to bed with you – and mind you bark if you hear the smallest sound in the night.'

'Woof,' said Timmy, in rather a subdued voice, and went upstairs. He climbed on to George's bed and sighed heavily.

'What a sigh!' said George. 'And what have you been eating, Timmy? Pooh – you've dug up some frightful old bone, I know you have. I've a good mind to push you off my bed. I suppose you suddenly remembered one you buried months ago. Pooh!'

Timmy wouldn't be pushed off the bed. He settled down to sleep, his nose on George's feet as usual. He snored a little, and woke George in about half an hour.

'Shut up, Timmy,' she said, pushing him with her feet. Anne woke up, alarmed.

'What is it, George?' she whispered, her heart thumping.

'Nothing. Only Timmy snoring. Hark at him. He won't stop,' said George, irritated. 'Wake up, Timmy, and stop snoring.'

Timmy moved sleepily and settled down again. He stopped snoring and George and Anne fell sound asleep. Julian woke once, thinking he heard something fall

– but hearing Timmy gently snoring again through the open doors of the two rooms, he lay down, his mind at rest.

If the noise had *really* been a noise Timmy would have heard it, no doubt about that. George always said that Timmy slept with one ear open.

Julian heard nothing more till Joanna went downstairs at seven o'clock. He heard her go into the kitchen and do something to the kitchen grate. He turned over and fell asleep again.

He was wakened suddenly twenty minutes later by loud screams from downstairs. He sat up and then leapt out of bed at once. He rushed downstairs. Dick followed him.

'Look at this! The master's study – turned upside down – those drawers ransacked! The safe's open, too. Mercy me, who's been here in the night – with all the doors locked and bolted, too!' Joanna wailed loudly and wrung her hands as she gazed at the untidy room.

'I say!' said Dick, horrified. 'Someone's been searching for something pretty thoroughly! Even got the safe open – and wrenched the drawer out.'

'How did he get in?' said Julian, feeling bewildered. He went round the house, looking at doors and windows. Except for the kitchen door, which Joanna said she had unlocked and unbolted herself as soon as she came down, not a window or door had been touched. All were fastened securely.

Anne came down, looking scared. 'What's the matter?' she said. But Julian brushed her aside. How did that burglar get in? That was what he wanted to know. Through one of the *upstairs* windows, he supposed – one that somebody had opened last night after he had fastened it. Perhaps in the girls' room?

But no – not one window was open. All were fastened securely, including Joanna's. Then a thought struck him as he looked into George's room. Why hadn't Timmy barked? After all, there must have been quite a bit of noise, however quiet the thief had been. He had himself heard something and had awakened. Why hadn't Timmy, then?

George was trying to pull Timmy off the bed. 'Ju, Ju! There's something wrong with Timmy. He won't wake up!' she cried. 'He's breathing so heavily, too – just listen to him! And what's the matter downstairs? What's happened?'

Julian told her shortly while he examined Timmy. 'Somebody got in last night – your father's study's in the most awful mess – absolutely ransacked from top to bottom, safe and all. Goodness knows how the fellow got in to do it.'

'How awful!' said George, looking very pale. 'And now something's wrong with Tim. He didn't wake up last night when the burglar came – he's ill, Julian!'

'No, he's not. He's been doped,' said Julian, pulling back Timmy's eyelids. 'So *that's* why he was so long outside last night! Somebody gave him some meat or something with dope in – some kind of drug. And he ate it, and slept so soundly that he never heard a thing – and isn't even awake yet.'

'Oh, Julian – will he be all right?' asked George anxiously, stroking Timmy's motionless body. 'But how *could* he take any food from a stranger in the night?'

'Maybe he picked it up – the burglar may have flung it down hoping that Timmy would eat it,' said Julian. 'Now I understand why he looked so sheepish when he came in. He didn't even jump up and lick me.'

'Oh, dear – Timmy, do, do wake up,' begged poor George, and she shook the big dog gently. He groaned a little and snuggled down again.

'Leave him,' said Julian. 'He'll be all right. He's not poisoned, only drugged. Come down and see the damage!'

George was horrified at the state of her father's study. 'They were after his two special books of American notes, I'm sure they were,' she said. 'Father said that any other country in the world would be glad to have those. Whatever are we to do?'

'Better get in the police,' said Julian, gravely. 'We can't manage this sort of thing ourselves. And do you know your father's address in Spain?'

'No,' wailed George. 'He and Mother said they were going to have a *real* holiday this time – no letters to be forwarded, and no address left till they had been settled somewhere for a few days. Then they'd telegraph it.'

'Well, we'll certainly have to get the police in, then,' said Julian, looking rather white and stern. George glanced at him. He seemed suddenly very grown-up indeed. She watched him go out of the room. He went into the hall and rang up the police station. Joanna was very relieved.

'Yes, get in the police, that's what we ought to do,' she said. 'There's that nice Constable Wilkins, and that other one with the red face, what's he called – Mr Donaldson. I'll be making some coffee for them when they come.'

She cheered up considerably at the thought of handing out cups of her good hot coffee to two interested policemen, who would ask her plenty of questions that she would be only too delighted to answer. She bustled off to the kitchen.

The four children stared silently at the ruins of the study. What a mess! Could it ever be cleared up? Nobody would know what was gone till Uncle Quentin came back. How furious he would be.

'I hope nothing very important has been taken,' said Dick. 'It looks as if somebody knew there was something valuable here, and meant to get it!'

'And has probably got it,' said Julian. 'Hallo – that must be the police! Come on – I can see it will be a long time before we get out breakfast this morning!'

CHAPTER SEVEN

Policemen in the house

THE POLICE were very, very thorough. The children got tired of them long before lunch-time. Joanna didn't. She made them cups of coffee and put some of her home-made buns on a plate and sent Anne to pick up ripe plums. She felt proud to think that it was she who had discovered the ransacked study.

There were two policemen. One was a sergeant, rather solemn and very correct. He interviewed each of the children and asked them exactly the same questions. The other man went over the study bit by bit, very thoroughly indeed.

'Looking for finger-prints, I suppose,' said Anne. 'Oh dear – when can we go and bathe?'

The thing that puzzled everyone, the police included, was – how did the thief or thieves get in? Both policemen went round the house, slowly and deliberately trying every door and window still locked or fastened. They stood and looked at the pantry window for some time.

'Got in there, I suppose,' said one of them.

'Must have been as small as a monkey then,' said the other. He turned to Anne, who was the smallest of the four children. 'Could you squeeze through there, Missy, do you think?'

'No,' said Anne. 'But I'll try if you like.' So she tried – but she stuck fast before she got even half-way through, and Julian had to pull hard to get her down again.

'Have you any idea what has been stolen?' the sergeant asked Julian, who seemed extraordinarily grown-up that morning.

'No, sergeant – none of us has,' said Julian. 'Not even George here, who knows her father's work better than any of us. The only thing we know is that my uncle went to America to lecture a short time ago – and he brought back two notebooks, full of valuable diagrams and notes. He did say that other countries might be very glad to get hold of those. I expect they were in that safe.'

'Well – they'll certainly be gone then,' said the sergeant, shutting his own fat notebook with a snap. 'Pity when people leave such things in an ordinary safe and then go off without leaving an address. Can't we possibly get in touch with him? This may be terribly important.'

'I know,' said Julian, looking worried. 'We shall have an address in a day or two – but I honestly don't see how we can get in touch before then.'

'Right,' said the sergeant. 'Well – we'll go now – but we'll bring back a photographer with us after lunch to photograph the room – then your cook can tidy it up. I know she's longing to.'

'Coming back *again*!' said Anne, when the two men had solemnly walked down the path, mounted very solid-looking bicycles, and gone sailing down the lane. 'Good gracious! Have we got to answer questions all over again?'

'Well, we'll go down to the beach and take a boat and go rowing,' said Julian, with a laugh. 'We'll be out of reach then. I don't see that we can give them any more help. I must say it's all very peculiar – I wish to goodness I knew how the thief got in.'

George had been very quiet and subdued all the morning. She had worried about Timmy, fearing that he had been poisoned, and not merely drugged, as Julian had said. But Timmy was now quite recovered, except that he seemed a bit sleepy still, and not inclined to gambol round in his usual ridiculous way. He looked extremely sheepish, too.

'I can't think why Timmy looks like that,' said George, puzzled. 'He usually only puts that look on when he's done something he's ashamed of – or got into mischief. He couldn't possibly know, could he, that whatever he picked up and ate last night was something he shouldn't eat?'

'No,' said Dick. 'He's sensible though, I think, not to touch poisoned meat – but he couldn't know if some harmless sleeping powder had been put into anything. It might have no smell and no taste. Perhaps he's just ashamed of being so sleepy!'

'If only he'd been awake!' groaned George. 'He would have heard any noise downstairs at once – and he'd have barked and woken us all, and flown downstairs himself to attack whoever was there! Why, oh why didn't I take him out myself last night as I usually do?'

'It was a chapter of accidents,' said Julian. 'You didn't take him out, so he was alone – and it happened that someone was waiting there with drugged food – which he either found or took from the thief . . .'

'*No*,' said George. 'Timmy would never, never take anything from someone he didn't know. I've always taught him that.'

'Well, he got it somehow – and slept through the very night he should have been awake,' said Julian. 'What I'm so afraid of, George, is that the thieves have got your father's two American notebooks. They seem to have left most of the stuff – piles and piles of books of all kinds, filled with your father's tiny handwriting.'

Joanna came in to say lunch was ready. She told the children that the policemen had eaten every one of her home-made buns. She still felt important and excited, and was longing to get out to the village and tell everyone the news.

'You'd better stay in and give the policemen a good tea,' said Julian. 'They're coming back with a photographer.'

'Then I'd better do another baking,' said Joanna, pleased.

'Yes. Make one of your chocolate cakes,' said Anne.

'Oh, do you think they'd like one?' said Joanna.

'Not for *them*, Joanna – for us, of course!' said George. 'Don't waste one of your marvellous chocolate cakes on policemen. Can you make us up a picnic tea? We're fed up with being indoors – we're going out in a boat.'

Joanna packed them a good tea after they had had their lunch and they all set off before the police came back. Timmy was much less sleepy now and did a little caper round them as they walked to the beach. George brightened up at once.

'He's getting better,' she said. 'Timmy, I simply shan't let you out of my sight now! If anyone's going to dope you again they'll have to do it under my very nose.'

They had a lovely time out in George's boat. They went half-way to Kirrin Island and bathed from the boat, diving in and having swimming races till they were tired out.

Timmy joined them, though he couldn't swim nearly as fast as they could.

'He doesn't really *swim*,' said Anne. 'He just tries to *run* through the water. I wish he'd let me ride on his back like a sea-dog – but he always slips away under me when I try.'

They got back about six o'clock to find that the policemen had eaten the whole of the chocolate cake that Joanna had made, besides an extraordinary amount of scones and buns.

Also the study was not tidied up, and a man had come to mend the safe. Everything was safely back there, though the police had told Joanna that if there was anything of real value it should be handed to them till George's father came back.

'But we don't know which of all those papers are valuable!' said Julian. 'Well – we'll have to wait till Uncle Quentin cables us – and that may not be for days. Anyway, I don't expect we'll be worried by the thief again – he's got what he wanted.'

The exciting happenings of the day had made them all tired except Julian. 'I'm off to bed,' said Dick, about nine o'clock. 'Anne, why don't you go? You look exhausted.'

'Yes, I will,' said Anne. 'Coming, George?'

'I'm going to take Timmy out for his last walk,' said George. 'I shall never let him go out alone at night again. Come on, Timmy. If you want to go to bed I'll lock up the front door, Ju.'

'Right,' said Julian. 'I'll go up in a minute. I don't fancy staying down here by myself tonight. I'll fasten everything and lock up, except the front door. Don't forget to put up the chain, too, George – though I'm pretty certain we don't need to expect any more burglaries!'

'Or faces at the window,' said Anne, at once.

'No,' said Julian. 'There won't be any more of those either. Good-night, Anne – sleep well!'

Anne and Dick went upstairs. Julian finished the paper he was reading, and then got up to go round the house and lock up. Joanna was already upstairs, dreaming of policemen eating her chocolate cakes.

George went out with Timmy. He ran eagerly to the gate and then set off down the lane for his usual night walk with George. At a gate in the lane he suddenly stood still and growled as if he saw something unusual.

'Silly, Timmy!' said George, coming up. 'It's only somebody camping in a caravan! Haven't you seen a caravan before? Stop growling!'

They went on, Timmy sniffing into every rat-hole and rabbit-hole, enjoying himself thoroughly. George was enjoying the walk, too. She didn't hurry – Julian could always go up to bed if he didn't want to wait.

Julian did go up to bed. He left the front door ajar, and went yawning upstairs, suddenly feeling sleepy. He got into bed quietly and quickly seeing that Dick was already asleep. He lay awake listening for George. When he was half asleep, he heard the front door shut.

'There she is,' he thought, and turned over to go to sleep.

But it wasn't George. Her bed was empty all that night, and nobody knew, not even Anne. George and Timmy didn't come back!

CHAPTER EIGHT

Where can George be?

ANNE WOKE up in the night, feeling thirsty. She whispered across the room:

'George! Are you awake?'

There was no answer, so, very cautiously and quietly Anne got herself a drink from the decanter on the washstand. George was sometimes cross if she was awakened in the middle of the night. Anne got back into bed, not guessing that George hadn't answered because she wasn't there!

She fell asleep and didn't wake till she heard Dick's voice. 'Hey, you two – get up; it's a quarter to eight. We're going for a bathe!'

Anne sat up, yawning. Her eyes went to George's bed. It was empty. More than that, it was all neat and tidy, as if it had just been made!

'*Well!*' said Anne in astonishment. 'George is up already, and has even made her bed. She *might* have woken me, and I could have gone out with her. It's such a lovely day. I suppose she's taken Timmy for an early morning walk, like she sometimes does.'

Anne slipped into her bathing costume and ran to join the boys. They went downstairs together, their bare feet padding on the carpet.

'George has gone out already,' said Anne. 'I expect she woke early and took Timmy; I never even heard her!'

Julian was now at the front door. 'Yes,' he said. 'The door isn't locked or bolted – George must have slipped down, undone it and then just pulled the door softly to. How very considerate of her! Last time she went out early she banged the door so hard that she woke everyone in the house!'

'She may have gone fishing in her boat,' said Dick. 'She said yesterday she'd like to some early morning when the tide was right. She'll probably arrive complete with stacks of fish for Joanna to cook.'

They looked out to sea when they got to the beach. There was a boat far out on the water with what looked like two people in it, fishing.

'I bet that's George and Timmy,' said Dick. He yelled and waved his hands, but the boat was too far away, and nobody waved back. The three of them plunged into the cold waves. Brrrr-rrr-rrr!

'Lovely!' said Anne, when they came out again, the drops of sea-water running down their bodies and glistening in the early morning sun. 'Let's have a run now.'

They chased one another up and down the beach, and then, glowing and very hungry, went back to breakfast.

'Where's George?' asked Joanna, as she brought in their breakfast. 'I see her bed's made and all – what's come over her?'

'I think she's out fishing with Timmy,' said Dick. 'She was up and about long before we were.'

'I never heard her go,' said Joanna. 'She must have been very quiet. There you are now – there's a fine breakfast for you – sausages and tomatoes and fried eggs!'

'O-o-o-o-h, lovely,' said Anne. 'And you've done the sausages just how I like them, Joanna – all bursting their skins. Do you think we'd better eat George's too? She's still out in the boat. She may not be back for ages.'

'Well, then you'd better eat her share,' said Joanna. 'I've no doubt she took something out of the larder before she went. Pity I didn't lock it last night, as usual!'

They finished George's share between them and then started on toast and marmalade. After that Anne went to help Joanna make the beds and dust and mop. Julian and Dick went off to the village to do the morning's shopping at the grocer's.

Nobody worried about George at all. Julian and Dick came back from their shopping and saw the little boat still out on the sea.

'George will be absolutely starving by the time she comes back,' said Julian. 'Perhaps she's got one of her moods on and wants to be alone. She was awfully upset about Timmy being drugged.'

They met the ragamuffin Jo. She was walking along the beach, collecting wood, and she looked sullen and dirtier than ever.

'Hallo, Jo!' called Dick. She looked up and came

towards them without a smile. She looked as if she had been crying. Her small face was streaked where the tears had run through the dirt.

'Hallo!' she said, looking at Dick. She looked so miserable that Dick felt touched.

'What's the matter, kid?' he said, kindly.

Tears trickled down Jo's face as she heard the kindness in his voice. She rubbed them away and smudged her face more than ever.

'Nothing,' she said. 'Where's Anne?'

'Anne's at home, and George is out in that boat with Timmy fishing,' said Dick, pointing out to sea.

'Oh!' said Jo, and turned away to go on with her collecting of wood. Dick went after her.

'Hey!' he said. 'Don't go off like that. You just tell me what's wrong with you this morning.'

He caught hold of Jo and swung her round to face him. He looked closely at her and saw that she now had two bruises on her face – one going yellow, that he had given her when he had sent her flying two or three days before – and a new one.

'Where did you get *that* bruise?' he said, touching it lightly.

'That was my dad,' said Jo. 'He's gone off and left me – taken the caravan and all! I wanted to go, too; but he wouldn't let me into the caravan. And when I hammered at the door, he came out and pushed me down the steps. That's when I got this bruise – and I've got another on my leg, too.'

Dick and Julian listened in horror. What kind of a life was this that Jo had to live? The boys sat down on the beach, and Dick pulled Jo down between them.

'But surely your father is coming back?' asked Julian. 'Is the caravan your only home?'

'Yes,' said Jo. 'I've never had another home. We've always lived in a caravan. Mum did, too, when she was alive. Things were better then. But this is the first time Dad's gone off without me.'

'But – how are you going to live?' asked Dick.

'Dad said Jake would give me money to buy food,' said Jo. 'But only if I do what he tells me. I don't like Jake. He's mean.'

'Who's Jake?' asked Julian, most astonished at all this.

'Jake's a traveller fellow. He knows my father,' said Jo. 'He's always turning up for a day or two, and going away again. If I wait about here, he'll come and give me five pence or so, I expect.'

'What will he tell you to do?' said Dick, puzzled. 'It all seems very strange and horrible to me. You're only a kid.'

'Oh, he may tell me to go poaching with him or – or – well, there's things we do that folks like you don't,' said Jo, suddenly realising that Dick and Julian would not at all approve of some of the things she did. 'I hope he gives me some money today, though. I haven't got any at all, and I'm hungry.'

Dick and Julian looked at one another. To think that in

these days there should be a forlorn waif like Jo, going in fear of others, and often hungry and lonely.

Dick put his hand in the shopping basket and pulled out a packet of chocolate and some biscuits. 'Here you are,' he said. 'Tuck into these – and if you'd like to go to the kitchen door some time today and ask Joanna, our cook, for a meal, she'll give you one. I'll tell her about you.'

'Folks don't like me at kitchen doors,' said Jo, cramming biscuits into her mouth. 'They're afraid I'll steal something.' She glanced up at Dick. 'And I do,' she said.

'You shouldn't do that,' said Dick.

'Well, wouldn't you, if you were so hungry you couldn't even bear to look at a baker's cart?' said Jo.

'No – I don't think so. At least, I hope not,' said Dick, wondering what he really would feel like if he were starving. 'Where's this Jake fellow?'

'I don't know. Somewhere about,' said Jo. 'He'll find me when he wants me. I've got to stay on the beach, Dad said. So I couldn't come to your house, anyway. I daren't leave here.'

The boys got up to go, worried about this little ragamuffin. But what could they do? Nothing, except feed her and give her money. Dick had slipped five pence into her hand, and she had pocketed it without a word, her eyes gleaming.

George was still not home by lunch-time; and now Julian for the first time began to feel anxious. He slipped out to the beach to see if the boat was still at sea. It was just pulling in – and with a sinking heart Julian saw that it was not George and Timmy who were in it, but two boys.

He went to look for George's boat – and there it was, high up on the boat-beach with many others. George had not been out in it at all!

He ran back to Kirrin Cottage and told the others. They were at once as anxious as he was. What *could* have become of George?

'We'll wait till tea-time,' said Julian. 'Then if she's not back we'll really have to do something about it – tell the police, I should think. But she *has* sometimes gone off for the day before, so we'll just wait a bit longer.'

Tea-time came – but no George, and no Timmy. Then they heard someone pattering up the garden path – was it Timmy? They leant out of the window to see.

'It's Jo,' said Dick, in disappointment. 'She's got a note or something. Whatever does *she* want?'

CHAPTER NINE

An extraordinary message – and a plan

JULIAN OPENED the front door. Jo silently gave him a plain envelope. Julian tore it open, not knowing what in the least to expect. Jo turned to go – but Julian put out his hand and caught hold of her firmly, whilst he read the note in complete amazement.

'Dick!' he called. 'Hold on to Jo. Don't let her go. Better take her indoors. This is serious.'

Jo wasn't going to be taken indoors. She squealed, and wriggled like an eel. Then she began to kick Dick viciously with her bare feet.

'Let me go! I'm not doing any harm. I only brought you that note!'

'Stop squealing and being silly,' said Dick. 'I don't want to hurt you, you know that. But you must come indoors.'

But Jo wouldn't stop wriggling and pulling and kicking. She looked scared out of her life. It was as much as Dick and Julian could do to get the little wriggler into the dining-room and shut the door. Anne followed, looking very frightened. Whatever was happening?

'Listen to this,' said Julian, when the door was shut. 'It's unbelievable!' He held out the typewritten note for the others to see as he read it out loud.

'We want the second notebook, the one with figures in, and we mean to have it. Find it and put it under the last stone on the crazy paving path at the bottom of the garden. Put it there tonight.

'We have got the girl and the dog. We will set them free when we have what we want from you. If you tell the police, neither the girl nor the dog will come back. The house will be watched to see that nobody leaves it to warn the police. The telephone wires are cut.

'When it is dark, put the lights on in the front room and all three of you sit there with the maid Joanna, so that we can keep a watch on you. Let the big boy leave the house at eleven o'clock, shining a torch and put the notebook where we said. He must then go back to the lighted room. You will hear a hoot like an owl when we have collected it. The girl and the dog will then be returned!'

This amazing and terrifying note made Anne burst into tears and cling to Julian's arm.

'Julian! Julian! George can't have come back from her walk with Timmy last night! She must have been caught then – and Timmy, too. Oh, why didn't we start hunting for her then?'

Julian looked very grim and white. He was thinking hard. 'Yes – someone was lying in wait, I've no doubt – and she and Timmy were kidnapped. Then the kidnappers – or one of them – came back to the house and shut the front door to make it seem as if George was back. And someone has probably been hanging round all day to find out whether we're worried about George, or just think she's gone off for the day!'

'Who gave you the note?' said Dick, sharply, to the scared Jo.

She trembled.

'A man,' she said.

'What sort of a man?' asked Julian.

'I don't know,' said Jo.

'Yes, you do,' said Dick. 'You *must* tell, Jo.'

Jo looked sullen. Dick shook her, and she tried to get away. But he held her far too tightly. 'Go on – tell us what the fellow was like,' he said.

'He was tall and had a long beard and a long nose and brown eyes,' rattled off Jo suddenly. 'And he was dressed in fisherman's clothes.'

The two boys looked sternly at her. 'I believe you're making all that up, Jo,' said Julian.

'I'm not,' said Jo sulkily. 'I'd never seen him before, so there.'

'Jo,' said Anne, taking Jo's little paw in hers, 'tell us truly anything you know. We're so worried about George.' Tears sprang out of her eyes as she spoke, and she gave a little wail.

'Serve that George-girl right if she's got taken away,' said Jo fiercely. 'She was rude to me – she's cruel and unkind. Serve her right, I say. I wouldn't tell you anything – not even if I knew something to tell.'

'You *do* know something,' said Dick. 'You're a bad little girl, Jo. I shan't have anything more to do with you. I felt sorry and unhappy about you, but now I don't.'

Jo looked sullen again, but her eyes were bright with tears. She turned away. 'Let me go,' she said. 'I tell you, that fellow gave me fifteen pence to bring this note to you, and that's all I know. And I'm *glad* George is in trouble. People like her deserve it, see!'

'Let her go,' said Julian wearily. 'She's like a savage little cat – all claws and spite. I thought there might be some good in her, but there isn't.'

'I thought so, too,' said Dick, letting go Jo's arm. 'I quite liked her. Well, go, Jo. We don't want you any more.'

Jo rushed to the door, wrenched it open, and fled down the hall and out of the house. There was silence after she had gone.

'Julian,' whispered Anne. 'What are we going to do?'

Julian said nothing. He got up and went into the hall. He picked up the telephone receiver and put his ear to it, listening for the faint crackling that would tell him it was connected. After a moment he put it back again.

'No connection,' he said. 'The wires have been cut, as the note said. And no doubt there's somebody on watch to see we don't slip out to give warning. This is all crazy. It can't be true.'

'But it is,' said Dick. 'Horribly true. Julian, do you know what notebook they want? I've no idea!'

'Nor have I,' said Julian. 'And it's impossible to go and hunt for it, because the safe has been mended and locked – and the police have the key.'

'Well, that's that, then,' said Dick. 'What are we going

to do? Shall I slip out and warn the police?'

Julian considered. 'No,' he said at last. 'I think these people mean business. It would be terrible if anything happened to George. Also, you might be caught and spirited away yourself. There are people watching the house, don't forget.'

'But, Julian – we can't just sit here and do nothing!' said Dick.

'I know. This will have to be thought about carefully,' said Julian. 'If only we knew where George had been taken to! We could rescue her then. But I can't see how we can find out.'

'If one of us went and hid down the bottom of the garden and waited to see whoever came to take up the notebook – we could follow the fellow and maybe he'd lead us to where George is hidden,' suggested Dick.

'You forget that we've all got to sit in the lighted front room, so it would easily be spotted if one of us were missing,' said Julian. 'Even Joanna has to sit there. This is all very stupid and melodramatic.'

'Does anyone come to the house this evening? Any of the tradesmen, for instance?' asked Anne, again in a whisper. She felt as if people must be all round the house, listening and watching!

'No. Else we could give them a note,' said Julian. Then he gave the table a rap that made the others jump. 'Wait a bit! Yes, of course – the paper-boy comes! Ours is almost the last house he delivers at. But perhaps it would be risky to give him a note. Can't we think of something better?'

'Listen,' said Dick, his eyes shining. 'I've got it! I know the paper-boy. He's all right. We'll have the front door open and yank him in as soon as he appears. And I'll go out immediately, with his cap on, and his satchel of papers, whistling – jump on his bike and ride away. And none of the watchers will know I'm not the boy! I'll come back when it's dark, sneak round the garden at the bottom and hide to watch who comes for the hidden notebook – and I'll follow him!'

'Good idea, Dick!' said Julian, turning it quickly over in his mind. 'Yes – it's possible. It would be better to watch and see who comes rather than tell the police – because if these kidnappers mean business, George would certainly be in trouble once they knew we'd been able to get in touch with the police.'

'Won't the newspaper boy think it's odd?' asked Anne.

'Not very. He's not that bright,' said Dick. 'He believes anything he's told. We'll make up something to satisfy him and give him such a good time that he'll want to keep visiting us!'

'About this notebook,' said Julian. 'We'd better get some kind of book out of one of the drawers and wrap it up with a note inside to say we hope it's the one. The fellow who comes to collect it will have some kind of parcel to take off with him to give the kidnappers. It isn't likely he'd undo it and look at it – or even know if it was the right one or not.'

'Go and hunt out a book, Anne,' said Dick. 'I'll be looking out for the newspaper boy. He's not due till half past seven, but I don't dare to risk missing him – and he may be early, you never know.'

Anne shot off to the study, thankful to have something to do. Her hands were trembling as she pulled out drawer after drawer to look for a big notebook that would do to wrap up in a parcel.

Julian went with Dick to the front door, to help him to deal with the unsuspecting newspaper boy. They stood there, patiently waiting, hearing the clock strike six o'clock, then half past, then seven.

'Here he comes!' said Dick, suddenly. 'Now – get ready to yank him in! Hallo, Sid!'

CHAPTER TEN

Sid's wonderful evening

SID, THE paper-boy, was most amazed to find himself yanked quickly through the front door by Julian. He was even more amazed to find his very lurid check cap snatched off his head, and his bag of papers torn from his shoulder.

'Here!' he said feebly. 'What are you doing?'

'It's all right, Sid,' said Julian, holding him firmly. 'Just a joke. We've got a little treat in store for you.'

Sid didn't like jokes of this sort. He struggled, but soon gave it up. Julian was big and strong and very determined. Sid turned and watched Dick stride out with his bright check cap sideways on his head, and his paper-bag over his shoulder. He gasped when he saw Dick leap on the bicycle that he, Sid, had left by the gate, and go sailing off up the lane on it.

'What's he doing?' he asked Julian, amazed. 'Funny sort of joke this.'

'I know. Hope you don't mind,' said Julian, leading him firmly into the sitting-room.

'Did somebody bet him he wouldn't deliver the papers?' said Sid. 'So he's taken the bet on?'

'You're clever, you are, Sid,' said Julian, and Sid beamed all over his round face.

'Well, I hope he'll deliver them all right,' he said. 'Anyway, there's only two more, up at the farm. Yours is the last house but one that I go to. When's he coming back?'

'Soon,' said Julian. 'Will you stay and have supper with us, Sid?'

Sid's eyes nearly fell out of his head. 'Supper with you folks?' he said. 'Coo! That'd be a rare treat!'

'All right. You sit and look at these books,' said Julian, giving him two or three story books belonging to Anne. 'I'll just go and tell our cook to make a specially nice supper for you.'

Sid was all at sea about this unexpected treat, but quite willing to accept a free meal and sit down. He sat beaming on the couch, turning over the pages of a fairy-story book. Coo! What would his mother say when she heard he'd had supper at Kirrin Cottage? 'She wouldn't half be surprised,' thought Sid.

And now Julian had to tackle Joanna, and get her to join in their little plot. He went into the kitchen and shut the door. He looked so grave that Joanna was startled.

'What's the matter?' she said.

Julian told her. He told her about the kidnapping of George, and the strange note. He gave it to her to read. She sat down, her knees beginning to shake.

'It's the kind of thing you read in the papers, Julian,' she said, in rather a shaky voice. 'But it's funny when it happens to *you*! I don't like it – that's flat, I don't.'

'Nor do we,' said Julian, and went on to tell Joanna all they had arranged to do. She smiled a watery smile when he told her how Dick had gone off as the paper-boy in order to watch who took the notebook that night, and described how surprised Sid was.

'That Sid!' she said. 'We'll never hear the last of it, down in the village – him being invited here to supper. He's a strange boy, but there's no harm in him.

'I'll get him a fine supper, don't you worry. And I'll come and sit with you tonight in the lighted room – we'll play a card game. One that Sid knows – he's never got much beyond Snap and Happy Families.'

'That's a very good idea,' said Julian, who had been wondering how in the world they could amuse Sid all the evening. 'We'll play Snap – and let him win!'

Sid was quite overcome at his wonderful evening. First there was what he called a 'smasher of a supper', with ham and eggs and chip potatoes followed by jam tarts and a big chocolate mould, of which Sid ate about three-quarters.

'I'm partial to chocolate mould,' he explained to Anne. 'Joanna knows that – she knows I'm partial to anything in the chocolate line. She's friendly with my mum, so she knows the things I'm partial to, that I like very much.'

Anne giggled and agreed. She was enjoying Sid, although she was very worried and anxious. But Sid was so comical. He didn't mean to be. He was just enjoying himself hugely, and he said so every other minute.

In fact, he was really a very nice guest to have. It wasn't everybody who could welcome everything with so much gusto and say how wonderful it was half a dozen times on end.

He went out to the kitchen after supper and offered to wash up for Joanna. 'I always do it for Mum,' he said. 'I won't break a thing.' So he did the washing up and Anne did the drying. Julian thought it was a good thing to give her as much to do as possible, to stop her worrying.

Sid looked a bit taken-aback when he was asked to play games later on. 'Well – I dunno,' he said. 'I'm not much good at games. I did try to learn draughts, but all that jumping over one another got me muddled. If I want to jump over things I'll play leap-frog and do the thing properly.'

'Well – we did think of playing Snap,' said Julian, and Sid brightened up at once.

'Snap! That's right up my street!' he said. And so it was. His habit of shouting snap and collecting all the cards at the same moment as his shout, led to his winning quite a lot of games. He was delighted.

'This is a smasher of an evening,' he kept saying. 'Don't know when I've enjoyed myself so much. Wonder how that brother of yours is getting on – hope he brings my bike back all right.'

'Oh, he will,' said Julian, dealing out the cards for the sixth game of Snap. They were all in the lighted sitting-room now, sitting round a table in the window – Julian,

Joanna, Anne and Sid. Anyone watching would see them clearly – and would certainly not guess that Sid, the fourth one, was the paper-boy and not Dick.

At eleven o'clock Julian left to put the parcel that Anne had carefully wrapped up under the stone at the bottom of the garden. She had found a big notebook she thought would do, one that didn't seem at all important, and had wrapped it in paper and tied it with string. Julian had slipped a note inside.

Here is the notebook. Please release our cousin at once. You will get into serious trouble if you hold her any longer.

He slipped down the garden and shone his torch on the crazy paving there. When he came to the last stone he found that it had been loosened. He lifted it up easily and put the parcel into a hollow that seemed to have been prepared ready for it. He took a cautious look round, wondering if Dick was hidden anywhere about, but could see no one.

He was back in the lighted sitting-room in under two minutes, yelling 'Snap' with the others. He played stupidly, partly because he wanted the delighted Sid to win and partly because he was wondering about Dick. Was he all right?

An outbreak of owls hooting loudly made them all jump. Julian glanced at Joanna and Anne, and they nodded. They guessed that it was the signal to tell them that the parcel had been found and collected. Now they could get rid of Sid, and wait for Dick.

Joanna disappeared and came back with cups of chocolate and some buns. Sid's eyes gleamed. Talk about an evening!

Another hour was spent in eating and drinking and hearing Sid relate details of all the most exciting games of Snap he had ever played. He then went on to talk of Happy Families and seemed inclined to stay a bit longer and have a game at that.

'Your mum will be getting worried about you,' said Julian, looking at the clock. 'It's very late.'

'Where's my bike?' said Sid, realising with sorrow that

his 'smasher of an evening' was now over. 'Hasn't that brother of yours come back yet? Well, you tell him to leave it at my house in time for my paper-round tomorrow morning. And my cap, too. That's my Special Cap, that is. I'm very partial to that cap – it's a bit of a smasher.'

'It certainly is,' agreed Julian, who was now feeling very tired. 'Now listen, Sid. It's very late, and there may be bad folks about. If anyone speaks to you, run for your life, and don't stop till you get home.'

'Coo,' said Sid, his eyes nearly falling out of his head. 'Yes, I'll run all right.'

He shook hands solemnly with each of them and departed. He whistled loudly to keep his spirits up. The village policeman came unexpectedly round a corner on rubber soles and made him jump.

'Now then, young Sid,' said the policeman, sternly. 'What are you doing out this time of night?'

Sid didn't wait to answer. He fled and when he got home there was his bicycle by the front gate, complete with checked cap and paper-bag. 'That was a bit of all right!' thought Sid.

He glanced in disappointment at the dark windows of his house. Mum was in bed and asleep. Now he would have to wait till morning to tell her of his most remarkable evening.

And now, what had happened to Dick? He had shot out of the house and sailed away on Sid's bicycle, with Sid's dazzling cap on his head. He thought he saw a movement in the hedge nearby and guessed someone was hidden there, watching. He deliberately slowed down, got off his bicycle and pretended to do something to the wheel. Let the watcher see his bag of papers and be deceived into thinking he was without any doubt the paper-boy.

He rode to the farm and delivered the two papers there, then down to the village where he left Sid's things outside his house. Then he went into the cinema for a long while – until it was dark and he could safely creep back to Kirrin Cottage.

He set off at last, going a very roundabout way indeed. He came to the back of Kirrin garden. Where should he hide? Was anyone already hidden there? If so, the game was up – and he'd be caught, too!

CHAPTER ELEVEN

Dick makes a capture

DICK STOOD and listened, holding his breath. He could hear no sound except for the rustling of the trees around, and the sudden squeak of a field-mouse. It was a dark night and cloudy. Was there anyone hidden nearby, or could he find a hiding-place in safety and wait?

He thought for a few minutes, and decided that there wouldn't be anyone watching the back of the house now that it was dark. Julian and the others would be in full view of any watcher at the front, seated as they were in the lighted sitting-room – there would be no need for anyone to watch the back.

He debated where to hide and then made a quick decision. 'I'll climb a tree,' he thought. 'What about that one just near the crazy paving path? If the clouds clear away I could perhaps catch a glimpse of what the man's like who comes to collect the parcel. Then I'll shin quietly down the tree and stalk him.'

He climbed up into an oak tree that spread its broad branches over the path. He wriggled down in a comfortable fork and set himself to wait patiently.

What time had that note said? Eleven o'clock. Yes – Julian was to go down at eleven o'clock and put the parcel under the stone. He listened for the church clock to strike. If the wind was in the right direction he would hear it clearly.

It struck just then. Half past ten. Half an hour to wait. The waiting was the worst part. Dick put his hand into his pocket and brought out a bar of half-melted chocolate. He began to nibble it very gently, to make it last a long time.

The church clock struck a quarter to eleven. Dick finished the chocolate, and wondered if Julian would soon be along. Just as the clock began to chime the hour at eleven, the kitchen door opened and Dick saw Julian outlined in the opening. He had the parcel under his arm.

He saw Julian go swiftly down the path and sensed him looking all about. He dared not give the slightest hint to him that he was just above his head!

He heard Julian scrabble about in the path, and then drop the big stone back into its place. He watched the light of Julian's torch bobbing back up the path to the kitchen door. Then the door shut with a bang.

And now Dick could hardly breathe! Who would come for the parcel? He listened, stiff with excitement. The wind blew and a leaf rustled against the back of his neck making him jump. It felt as if a finger had touched him.

Five minutes went by and nobody came. Then he heard the slightest sound. Was that somebody crawling through the hedge? Dick strained his eyes but could only make out a deeper shadow that seemed to be moving. Then he could most distinctly hear somebody breathing hard as they tugged at the heavy stone! The parcel was being collected as arranged!

The stone plopped back. A shadow crept over to the hedge again. Whoever had the parcel was now going off with it.

Dick dropped quietly down. He had rubber shoes on and made no noise. He slipped through a big gap in the hedge nearby and stood straining his eyes to find the man he wanted to follow. Ah – there was a shadow moving steadily down the field path to the stile. Dick followed, keeping close to the hedge.

He kept well behind the moving shadow till it reached the stile, got over it and went into the lane beyond. When it got there it stopped, and a perfect fusillade of loud owl-hoots came to Dick's startled ears.

Of course! That was the signal that the parcel had been collected. Dick admired the excellent imitation of a little owl's loud, excited hooting.

The shadow stopped hooting and went on again. It obviously did not suspect that it might be followed and, although it moved quietly, it did not attempt to keep under cover. Down the lane it went and into a field.

Dick was about to follow when he heard the sound of voices. They were very low, and he couldn't hear a word. He crouched in the shadow of the gate, which was swung right back, leaving an entry into the field.

A loud noise made him jump. Then a brilliant light dazzled him and he felt glad he could duck down behind the gate. There was a car in the field. A car that had just started up its engine and switched on its lights. It was going, moving slowly down to the gate!

Dick tried his hardest to see who was in the car. He could make out only one man, and he was driving. It didn't seem as if anyone else was in the car at all. Where was the other fellow, then – the one who must have collected the parcel and given it to the man in the car? Had he been left behind? If so, Dick had better be careful!

The car was soon out in the lane. It gained speed and then Dick heard it roaring off in the distance. He couldn't stalk a car, that was certain! He held his breath, listening for some movement of the other man who, he felt certain, was still there.

He heard a sniff and crouched lower still. Then a shadow passed quickly through the gate, turned back in the direction of Kirrin Cottage and was lost in the darkness of the lane.

In a trice Dick was after it again. At least he could track down *this* fellow! He must be going somewhere!

Down the lane to the stile. Over the stile and into the field. Across the field and back at the hedge that grew at the bottom of Kirrin Cottage.

Why was this fellow going back there? Dick was puzzled. He heard the shadow creeping through the hedge and he followed. He watched it go silently up the path and peer in at a darkened window.

'Going to get into the house again and ransack it, I

suppose!' thought Dick, in a rage. He considered the shadowy figure by the window. It didn't look big. It must be a small man – one that Dick could tackle and bring to the ground. He could yell loudly for Julian, and maybe he could hold the fellow down till Julian came.

'And then perhaps *we* could do a little kidnapping, and a little bargaining, too,' thought Dick grimly. 'If *they* hold George as a hostage, we'll hold one of them, too! Tit for tat!'

He waited till the shadow left the window, and then he pounced. His victim went down at once with a yell.

Dick was surprised how small he was – but how he fought! He bit and scratched and heaved and kicked, and the two of them rolled over and over and over, breaking down Michaelmas daisies in the beds, and scratching legs and arms and faces on rose bushes. Dick yelled for Julian all the time.

'Julian! JULIAN! Help! JULIAN!'

Julian heard. He tore out at once. 'Dick, Dick, where are you? What is it?'

He flashed his torch towards the shouting and saw Dick rolling on top of somebody. He ran to help at once, throwing his torch on the grass so that both hands were free.

It wasn't long before they had the struggling figure firmly in their grips and dragged it, wailing, to the back door. Dick recognised that wailing voice! Good gracious – no, it couldn't be – it couldn't be Jo!

But it was! When they dragged her inside she collapsed completely, sobbing and wailing, rubbing her scratched and bruised legs, calling both boys all the names she could think of. Anne and Joanna looked on in complete amazement. *Now* what had happened?

'Put her upstairs,' said Julian. 'Get her to bed. She's in an awful state now. So am I! I wouldn't have hit her like that if I'd known it was only Jo.'

'I never guessed,' said Dick, wiping his filthy face with his handkerchief. 'My word, what a wild-cat! See how she's bitten me!'

'I didn't know it was you, Dick; I didn't know,' wailed Jo. 'You pounced on me, and I fought back. I wouldn't have bitten you like that.'

'You're a savage, deceitful, double-dealing little wild-cat,' said Dick, looking at his bites and scratches. 'Pretending you know nothing about the man who gave you that note – and all the time you're in with that crooked lot of thieves and kidnappers, whoever they are.'

'I'm not in with them,' wept Jo.

'Don't tell lies,' shouted Dick, in a fury. 'I was up in a tree when you came and took that parcel from under the stone – yes, and I followed you right to that car – and followed you back again! You came back here to steal again, I suppose?'

Jo gulped. 'No, I didn't.'

'You did! You'll be handed over to the police tomorrow,' said Dick, still furious.

'I *didn't* come back to steal. I came back for something else,' insisted Jo, her eyes peering through her tangled hair like a frightened animal's.

'Ho! So you say! And what did you come back for? To find another dog to dope?' jeered Dick.

'No,' said Jo, miserably. 'I came back to tell you I'd take you to where George was, if you wouldn't tell on me. My dad would punish me if he thought I'd split on him. I know I took the parcel – I had to. I didn't know what it was or anything. I took it to the place I was told to. Jake told me. And then I came back to tell you all I could. And you set on me like that.'

Four pairs of eyes bored into Jo, and she covered her face. Dick took her hands away and made her look at him.

'Look here,' he said, 'this matters a lot to us, whether you are speaking the truth or not. Do you know where George is?'

Jo nodded.

'And will you take us there?' said Julian, his voice stern and cold.

Jo nodded again. 'Yes I will. You've been mean to me, but I'll show you I'm not as bad as you make out. I'll take you to George.'

CHAPTER TWELVE

Jo begins to talk

THE HALL clock suddenly struck loudly. 'DONG!'

'One o'clock,' said Joanna. 'One o'clock in the morning! Julian, we can't do any more tonight. This child here, she's not fit to take you traipsing out anywhere else. She's done for – she can hardly stand.'

'Yes, you're right Joanna,' said Julian, at once giving up the idea of going out to find George that night. 'We'll have to wait till tomorrow. It's a pity the telephone wires are cut. I do really think we ought to let the police know something about all this.'

Jo looked up at once. 'Then I won't tell you where George is,' she said. 'Do you know what the police will do to me if they get hold of me? They'll put me into a Home for Bad Girls, and I'll never get out again – because I *am* a bad girl and I do bad things. I've never had a chance.'

'Everyone gets a chance sooner or later,' said Julian gently. 'You'll get yours, Jo – but see you take it when it comes. All right – we'll leave the police out of it if you promise you'll take us to where George is. That's a bargain.'

Jo understood bargains. She nodded. Joanna pulled her to her feet and half led, half carried her upstairs.

'There's a couch in my room,' she told Julian. 'She can bed down there for the night – but late or not she's going to have a bath first. She smells like something the dog brought in!'

In half an hour's time Jo was tucked up on the couch in Joanna's room, perfectly clean, though marked with scratches and bruises from top to toe, hair washed, dried, and brushed so that it stood up in wiry curls like George's. A basin of steaming bread and milk was on a tray in front of her.

Joanna went to the landing and called across to Julian's room. 'Julian! Jo's in bed. She wants to say something to you and Dick.'

Dick and Julian put on dressing-gowns and went into Joanna's neat room. They hardly recognised Jo. She was wearing one of Anne's old nightgowns and looked very clean and childish and somehow pathetic.

Jo looked at them and gave them a very small smile. 'What do you want to say to us?' asked Julian.

'I've got some things to tell you,' said Jo, stirring the bread round and round in the basin. 'I feel good now – good and clean and – and all that. But maybe tomorrow I'll feel like I always do – and then I wouldn't tell you everything. So I'd better tell you now.'

'Go ahead,' said Julian.

'Well, I let the men into your house here, the night they came,' said Jo. Julian and Dick stared in astonishment. Jo went on stirring her bread round and round.

'It's true,' she said. 'I got in at that tiny window that was left unfastened, and then I went to the back door and opened it and let the men in. They did make a mess of that room, didn't they? I watched them. They took a lot of papers.'

'You couldn't possibly squeeze through that window,' said Dick at once.

'Well, I did,' said Jo. 'I've – I've squeezed through quite a lot of little windows. I know how to wriggle, you see. I can't get through such tiny ones as I used to, because I keep on growing. But yours was easy.'

'Phew!' said Julian, and let out a long breath. He hardly knew what to say. 'Well, go on. I suppose when the men had finished you locked and bolted the kitchen door after them and then squeezed out of the pantry window again?'

'Yes,' said Jo, and put a piece of milky bread into her mouth.

'What about Timmy? Who doped him so that he slept all that night?' demanded Dick.

'I did,' said Jo. 'That was easy, too.'

Both boys were speechless. To think that Jo did that, too! The wicked little misery!

'I made friends with Timmy on the beach, don't you remember?' said Jo. 'George was cross about it. I like dogs. We always had dozens till Mum died, and they'd do anything I told them. Dad told me what I was to do – make friends with Timmy so that I could meet him that night and give him meat with something in it.'

'I see. And it was very, very easy, because we sent Timmy out alone – straight into your hands,' said Dick bitterly.

'Yes. He came to me at once, he was glad to see me. I took him quite a long walk, letting him sniff the meat I'd got. When I gave it to him, he swallowed it all at once with hardly a chew!'

'And slept all night long so that your precious friends could break into the house,' said Julian. 'All I can say is that you are a hardened little rogue. Aren't you ashamed of anything?'

'I don't know,' said Jo, who wasn't really quite certain what feeling ashamed meant. 'Shall I stop telling you things?'

'No. For goodness' sake go on,' said Dick, hastily. 'Had you anything to do with George's kidnapping?'

'I just had to hoot like an owl when she and Timmy were coming,' said Jo. 'They were ready for her with a sack to put over her head – and they were going to bang Timmy on the head – with a stick to knock him out – then put him into a sack too. That's what I heard them say. But I didn't see them. I had to creep back here and shut the front door, so that if nobody missed George till morning they'd just think she'd gone out early somewhere.'

'Which is what we did think,' groaned Dick. 'What mutts we are! The only clever thing we thought of was to stalk the person who collected the parcel.'

'It was only me, though,' said Jo. 'And anyway, I was

coming back to tell you I would take you to George. Not because I like her – I don't. I think she's rude and horrible. I'd like her to stay kidnapped for years!'

'What a nice, kind nature!' said Julian to Dick, helplessly. 'What can you do with a kid like this?' He turned to Jo again. 'Seeing that you wish George would stay kidnapped for years, what made you decide to come and tell us where to find her?' he asked puzzled.

'Well, I don't like George – but I do like *him*!' said Jo, pointing with her spoon at Dick. 'He was nice to me, so I wanted to be nice back. I don't often feel like that,' she added hurriedly, as if being kind was some sort of weakness not really to be admired. 'I wanted him to go on liking me,' she said.

Dick looked at her. 'I shall like you if you take us to George,' he said. 'However, if you deceive us, I shall think you're like one of those sour damson stones – only fit to be spat out as far away as possible.'

'I'll take you tomorrow,' said Jo.

'Where *is* George?' asked Julian, bluntly, thinking it would be as well to know now, in case Jo changed her mind by the morning, and became her wicked little self again.

Jo hesitated. She looked at Dick. 'It would be very nice of you to tell us,' said Dick, in a kind voice. Jo loved a bit of kindness and couldn't resist this.

'Well,' she whispered, 'you know I told you my dad had gone off and left me to Jake. Dad didn't tell me why – but

Jake did. He shut George and Timmy into our caravan, harnessed Chestnut the horse, and drove away in the night with them both. And I guess I know where he's gone – where he always goes when he wants to hide.'

'Where?' asked Julian, feeling so astounded at these extraordinary revelations that he really began to wonder if he was dreaming.

'In the middle of Ravens Wood,' said Jo. 'You don't know where that is, but I do. I'll take you tomorrow. I can't tell you any more now.' She began to spoon up her bread and milk very fast indeed, watching the boys through her long eyelashes.

Dick considered her. He felt pretty sure she had told them the truth, though he was equally certain she would have told lies if she could have got more by doing so.

He thought her bad and cold-blooded, but he pitied her, and admired her unwillingly for her courage.

He caught sight of her bruises and grazes, and bit his lip as he remembered how he had pounced on her and pummelled her, giving her back kick for kick and blow for blow – he hadn't guessed for one moment it was Jo. 'I'm sorry I hurt you so,' he said. 'You know I didn't mean to. It was a mistake.'

Jo looked at him as a servant might look at a king. 'I don't mind,' she said. 'I'd do anything for you, straight I would. You're kind.'

Joanna knocked impatiently at the door. 'Aren't you ready yet, you boys?' she said. 'I want to come to bed.

Tell Jo to stop talking, and you come on out too, and go to bed.'

The boys opened the door. Joanna took one look at their solemn faces and guessed that what Jo had told them was important. She took the empty basin from the girl's hands and pushed her down on the couch.

'Now you go straight off to sleep – and mind, if I hear any hanky-panky from you in the night I'll get up and give you such a scolding you won't try it again,' she said roughly, but not unkindly.

Jo grinned. She understood that kind of talk. She snuggled down into the rugs, marvelling at the warmth and softness. She was already half-asleep. Joanna got into bed and switched off her light.

'Two o'clock in the morning!' she muttered as she heard the hall clock strike. 'Such goings-on! I'll never wake up in time to tell the milkman I want more milk.'

Soon only Julian was awake. He worried about whether he was doing right or not. Poor George – was she safe? Would that scamp of a Jo really lead them to the caravan next day – or might she lead them right into the lion's mouth, and get them all captured? Julian simply didn't know.

CHAPTER THIRTEEN

Off to find George

JOANNA WAS the only one in the household who woke up reasonably early the next morning – but even she was too late to catch the milkman. She scurried downstairs at half past seven, an hour later than usual, tying up her apron as she went.

'Half past seven – what a time to wake up!' she muttered, as she began to make breakfast. She thought of all the happenings of the night before – the strange evening with young Sid, Dick's capture of Jo – and Jo's extraordinary tale. She had had a look at Jo before she went down, half expecting that lively young rogue to have disappeared in the night.

But Jo was curled up like a kitten, her suntanned cheek on her paw, her hair, unusually bright and tidy, falling over her tightly-shut eyes. She didn't even stir when Joanna scurried about the bedroom, washing and dressing.

The others were fast asleep, too. Julian woke first, but not till eight o'clock. He remembered immediately all that had happened, and jumped out of bed at once.

He went to Joanna's room. He could hear Joanna downstairs talking to herself as usual. He peeped round the open door of her bedroom. Thank goodness – Jo was still there.

He went and shook her gently. She wriggled away, turned over and buried her face in the pillow. Julian shook her more vigorously. He meant to get her up and make her take them to where George was as soon as possible!

Most miraculously everyone was down at half past eight, eating porridge and looking rather subdued. Jo had hers in the kitchen, and the others could hear Joanna scolding her for her manners.

'Have you got to stuff yourself like that, as if the dog's going to come and lick your plate before you've finished? And who told you to stick your fingers into the syrup and lick them? I've eyes in the back of my head, so just you be careful what you're doing!'

Jo liked Joanna. She knew where she was with her. If she kept on Joanna's right side and did what she was told, Joanna would feed her well and not interfere too much – but if she didn't, then she could expect something else she understood very well indeed – scoldings and even punishments. Joanna was good-natured but impatient, and no child was ever afraid of her. Jo followed her about like a little dog when she had finished her breakfast.

Julian came out into the kitchen at nine o'clock. 'Where's Jo?' he said. 'Oh, there you are. Now, what about taking us to where your father's caravan is? You're sure you know the way?'

Jo laughed scornfully. 'Course I do! I know everywhere round here for miles.'

'Right,' said Julian, and he produced a map, which he spread out on the kitchen table. He put a finger on one spot. 'That's Kirrin,' he said. 'And here's a place called Ravens Wood. Is that the place you mean? How do you propose to get there – by this road, or that one?'

Jo looked at the map. It meant nothing to her at all. She gazed vaguely at the spot that Julian had pointed to.

'Well?' said Julian, impatiently. 'Is that the Ravens Wood you mean?'

'I don't know,' said Jo, helplessly. 'The one I mean is a real wood – I don't know anything about yours on this map.'

Joanna gave a little snort. 'Julian, maps are wasted on her. I don't expect she's ever seen one in her life! She can't even read!'

'*Can't* she?' said Julian, amazed. 'Then she can't write either.' He looked questioningly at Jo.

She shook her head. 'Mum tried to teach me to read,' she said, 'but Mum wasn't very good herself. What's the good of reading, anyway? Won't help you to trap rabbits or catch fish for your dinner, will it?'

'No. It's used for other things,' said Julian, amused. 'Well – maps are no good to *you*, I can see.' He rolled his map up, looking thoughtful. It was very difficult to know exactly how to deal with a person like Jo, who knew so little of some things and so much of others.

'I just know the way I have to go. And I don't go by the roads, either! They take too long to get to a place. I take the shortest way, see?' said Jo.

'How do you know it's the shortest way?' asked Anne.

Jo shrugged her thin shoulders. All this was very boring to her.

'Where's that other boy?' she said. 'Isn't he coming? I want to see him.'

'She's just crazy on Dick,' said Joanna, taking up

another saucepan. 'Here he is – now you can go and lick his boots if you want to, young Jo!'

'Hallo, Jo!' said Dick, with one of his amiable grins. 'Ready to take us travelling?'

'Better go at night,' said Jo, staring at Dick.

'Oh, no!' said Dick. 'We're going *now*. We're not going to be put off like that. *Now*, Jo, now!'

'If my dad sees us coming he'll be mad,' said Jo obstinately.

'Very well,' said Dick, looking at Julian. 'We'll go by ourselves. We've found Ravens Wood on the map. We can easily get there.'

'Pooh,' said Jo, rudely. 'You can get there all right – but it's a big place, Ravens Wood is – and nobody but me and Dad knows where we hide the caravan there. And if Dad wants to keep George quite safe, he'll take her to our hidey-hole in the middle of the wood, see? You can't go without me.'

'Right. Then we'll get the police to take us,' said Julian, quite cheerfully. 'They will help us to comb the wood from end to end. We'll soon find George.'

'No!' cried Jo, in alarm. 'You said you wouldn't! You promised!'

'*You* made a promise too,' said Julian. 'It was a bargain. But I see you're not really to be trusted. I'll just get on my bike and ride down to the police station.'

But before he could go out of the room Jo flung herself on him and clung to his arm like a cat. 'No, no! I'll take you. I'll keep my promise! But it *would* be best to go at night!'

'I'm not putting things off any more,' said Julian, shaking Jo off his arm. 'If you mean what you say, you'll come with us now. Make up your mind.'

'I'll come,' said Jo.

'Hadn't we better give her another pair of shorts or something?' said Anne, suddenly seeing a tremendous hole in Jo's grubby shorts. 'She can't go out like that. And look at her awful jersey. It's full of holes.'

The boys looked at it. 'She'd smell a bit better if she had clean clothes,' said Joanna. 'There's that old pair of shorts I washed for George last week, and mended up. Jo could have those. And there's an old shirt of hers she could have, too.'

In five minutes' time Jo was proudly wearing a pair of perfectly clean, much-mended shorts of George's, and a shirt like the one Anne had on. Anne looked at her and laughed.

'Now she's more like George than ever! They might be sisters.'

'Brothers, you mean,' said Dick. 'George and Jo – what a pair!'

Jo scowled. She didn't like George, and she didn't want to look like her.

'She's even got George's scowl!' said Anne. Jo turned her back at once, and Joanna then got the benefit of the scowl.

'My word, what an ugly creature you are!' said Joanna.

'You be careful the wind doesn't change – you might get your face stuck like that!'

'Oh, come on,' said Julian, impatiently. 'Jo! Do you hear me? Come along now and take us to Ravens Wood.'

'Jake might see us,' said Jo, sulkily. She was determined to put off going as long as she could.

'Yes, he might,' said Julian, who hadn't thought of that. 'Well – you go on a long way ahead, and we'll follow. We won't let Jake know you're leading us anywhere.'

At last they set off. Joanna had packed them up a meal

in case they wanted one. Julian slipped the package into a bag and slid it over his shoulder.

Jo slipped out the back way, went down to the bottom of the garden and made her way out to the lane through a little thicket. The others went out of the front gate and walked up the lane slowly, watching for Jo to appear.

'There she is,' said Julian. 'Come on. We must keep the little wretch in sight. I wouldn't be surprised if she gave us the slip even now!'

Jo danced on in front, a good way ahead. She took no notice of the others behind, and they followed steadily.

Then suddenly something happened. A dark figure strode out from the hedge, stood in front of Jo, and said something to her. She screamed and tried to dodge away. But the man caught hold of her and firmly pulled her into the hedge.

'It was Jake!' said Dick. 'I'm sure it was Jake. He was watching out for her. *Now* what do we do?'

CHAPTER FOURTEEN

Simmy's caravan

THEY ALL hurried up to the place where Jake had caught hold of Jo. There was absolutely nothing to be seen except a few broken twigs in the hedge. No Jake, no Jo. There was not a sound to be heard, either. Not a scream from Jo, not a shout from Jake. It was as if both had faded into the hedge and disappeared.

Dick squeezed through the hedge and into the field beyond. Nobody was there either, except a few cows who looked at him in surprise, their tails whisking.

'There's a little copse at the end of the field,' called back Dick. 'I bet they're there. I'll go and see.'

He ran across the field to the copse. But there was nobody there either. Beyond the copse was a row of huddled-up cottages. Dick looked along the untidy row, exasperated.

'I suppose Jake's taken her to one of those,' he thought, angrily. 'Probably lives there! Well, he won't let her go, that's certain. He most likely guesses that she's in with us now. Poor Jo!'

He went back to the others and they had a low-voiced conference in the lane. 'Let's tell the police now,' begged Anne.

'No. Let's go to Ravens Wood ourselves,' said Dick. 'We know where it is. We wouldn't be able to go the way Jo would have taken us – but at least we can go by the map.'

'Yes. I think we will,' said Julian. 'Come on, then. Quick march!'

They went on up the lane, took a field path and came out eventually on to a road. A bus passed them in the opposite direction to which they were going.

'When we come to a bus stop we'll find out if one goes anywhere near Ravens Wood,' said Julian. 'It would save a lot of time if we caught a bus. We'd be there long before Jake, if he thinks of going to warn Jo's father we're on the way! I bet Jo will tell him. You might as well trust a snake as that slippery little thing.'

'I hate Jo!' said Anne, almost in tears. 'I don't trust her a bit. Do you, Dick?'

'I don't know,' said Dick. 'I can't make up my mind. She hasn't really proved whether she's trustable or not yet. Anyway, she came back to tell us all she knew last night, didn't she?'

'I don't believe she *did* come back for that,' said Anne obstinately. 'I believe she was coming back to pry and snoop.'

'You may be right,' said Dick. 'Look, here's a bus stop – and a time-table!'

A bus did apparently go quite near Ravens Wood, and was due in five minutes' time. They sat down on the bus-stop seat and waited. The bus was punctual and came rumbling down the road, full of women going to Ravens Market. They all seemed very plump women and had enormous baskets, so it was difficult to squeeze inside.

Everyone got out at Ravens Market. Julian asked his way to Ravens Wood. 'There it is,' said the conductor, pointing down the hill to where trees grew thickly in the valley. 'It's a big place. Don't get lost!'

'Thanks,' said Julian, and the three of them set off down the hill into the valley. They came to the wood.

'It's a proper wood,' said Anne. 'Nothing but trees and trees. I should think it gets very thick in the middle – like a forest.'

They came to a clearing where there was a little camp. Three rather dirty-looking caravans stood together, and a crowd of children were playing some sort of a game with a rope. Julian took a quick look at the caravans. All had their doors open.

'No George here,' he said in a low voice to the others. 'I wish I knew exactly where to go! I suppose if we follow this broad pathway it would be best. After all, Jo's caravan must have a fairly broad way to go on.'

'Can't we ask if anyone knows if Jo's caravan is anywhere about?' said Anne.

'We don't know her father's name,' said Julian.

'But we could say it's a caravan drawn by a horse called Chestnut, and that a girl called Jo lives in it with her father,' said Anne.

'Yes. I'd forgotten the horse,' said Julian. He went up to

an old woman who was stirring something in a black pot over a fire of sticks. Julian thought she looked very like a witch. She peered up at him through tangled grey hair.

'Can you tell me if there's a caravan in the wood drawn by a horse called Chestnut?' he asked politely. 'A girl called Jo lives in it with her father. We want to see her.'

The old woman blinked. She took an iron spoon out of the pot and waved it to the right.

'Simmy's gone down-away there,' she said. 'I didn't see Jo this time – but the caravan door was shut so maybe she was inside. What do you want with Jo?'

'Oh – only just to see her,' said Julian, quite unable to think up a good reason for going to visit on the spur of the moment. 'Is Simmy her father?'

The old woman nodded and began to stir her pot again. Julian went back to the others.

'This way,' he said, and they went down the rutted path. It was just wide enough for a caravan to go down. Anne looked up. Tree branches waved overhead.

'I should think they brush against the roof of a caravan all the time,' she said. 'What a funny life to live – in a little caravan day in and day out, hiding yourself away in woods and fields!'

They walked on down the path, which wound about through the trees, following the clear spaces. Sometimes the trees were so close together that it seemed impossible for a caravan to go between. But the wheel-ruts showed that caravans did go down the path.

After a time the wood became thicker, and the sunlight

could hardly pierce through the branches. Still the path went on, but now it seemed as if only one set of wheel-ruts was marked on it. They were probably the wheels of Simmy's caravan.

Here and there a tree was shorn of one of its branches, and a bush uprooted and thrown to one side.

'Simmy meant to go deep into the wood last time he came,' said Julian, pointing to where a bush lay dying by the side of the path. 'He's cleared the way here and there. Actually we aren't on a proper path any longer – we're only following wheel-ruts.'

It was true. The path had faded out. They were now in a thick part of the wood, with only the ruts of the caravan wheels to guide them.

They fell silent. The wood was very quiet. There were no birds singing, and the branches of the trees were so thick that there was a kind of green twilight round them.

'I wish we had Timmy with us,' half-whispered Anne at last.

Julian nodded. He had been wishing that a long time. He was also wishing he hadn't brought Anne – but when they had started out, they had Jo with them to guide them, and warn them of any danger. Now they hadn't.

'I think we'd better go very cautiously,' he said, in a low voice. 'We may come on the caravan unexpectedly. We don't want Simmy to hear us and lie in wait.'

'I'll go a little way in front and warn you if I hear or see anything,' said Dick. Julian nodded to him and he went on ahead, peering round the trees when he came to any curve in the wheel-rut path. Julian began to think of what they would do when they reached the caravan. He was pretty certain that both George and Timmy would be found locked up securely inside.

'If we can undo the door and let them out, Timmy will do the rest,' he thought. 'He's as good as three policemen! Yes – that's the best plan.'

Dick suddenly stopped and lifted up his hand in warning. He peered round the trunk of a big tree, and then turned and nodded excitedly.

'He's found the caravan!' said Anne, and her heart began its usual thump-thump-thump of excitement.

'Stay here,' said Julian to Anne, and went on quietly to join Dick. Anne crept under a bush. She didn't like this dark, silent wood, with the green light all round. She peered out, watching the boys.

Dick had suddenly seen the caravan. It was small, badly needed painting, and appeared quite deserted. No fire burned outside. No Simmy was sitting anywhere about. Not even Chestnut the horse was to be seen.

The boys watched intently for a few minutes, not daring to move or speak. There was absolutely no sound or movement from the tiny clearing in which the caravan stood.

Windows and doors were shut. The shafts rested crookedly on the ground. The whole place seemed deserted.

'Dick,' whispered Julian at last, 'Simmy doesn't seem to be about. This is our chance! We'll creep over to the caravan and look into the window. We'll attract George's attention, and get her out as soon as we can. Timmy, too.'

'Funny he doesn't bark,' said Dick, also in a whisper. 'I suppose he can't have heard us. Well – shall we get over to the caravan now?'

They ran quietly to the little caravan, and Julian peered through the dirty window. It was too dark inside to see anything at all.

'George!' he whispered. 'George! Are you there?'

CHAPTER FIFTEEN

Anne doesn't like adventures

THERE WAS no answer from inside the caravan. Perhaps George was asleep – or drugged! And Timmy, too. Julian's heart sank. It would be dreadful if George had been ill-treated. He tried to peer inside the window again, but what with the darkness of the wood and the dirt on the pane, it really was impossible to see inside.

'Shall we bang on the door?' asked Dick.

'No. That would only bring Simmy if he's anywhere about – and if George is inside and awake, our voices would have attracted her attention,' said Julian.

They went quietly round the caravan to the door at the back. It had no key in the lock. Julian frowned.

Simmy must have got the key with him. That would mean breaking down the door and making a noise. He went up the few steps and pushed at the door. It seemed very solid indeed. How could he break it down, anyway? He had no tools, and it didn't look as if kicking and shoving would burst it in.

He knocked gently on the door – rap-rap-rap. Not a movement from inside. It seemed very strange. He tried the round handle, and it turned easily.

It not only turned easily – but the door opened! 'Dick!

It's not locked!' said Julian, forgetting to whisper in his surprise. He went inside the dark caravan, hardly hoping now to see George or Timmy.

Dick pushed in after him. There was a nasty sour smell and it was very untidy. Nobody was there. It was quite empty, as Julian had feared.

He groaned. 'All this way for nothing. They've taken George somewhere else. We're done now, Dick – we haven't a clue where to go next.'

Dick fished his torch out of his pocket. He flashed it over the untidy jumble of things in the caravan, looking for some sign that George had been there. But there was nothing at all that he could see to show him that either Timmy or George had been there.

'It's quite likely that Jo made the whole story up about her father taking George away,' he groaned. 'It doesn't look as if they've been here at all.'

His torch flashed on to the wooden wall of the caravan, and Dick saw something that caught his attention. Somebody had written something on the wall!

He looked more closely. 'Julian! Isn't that George's writing? Look! What's written there?'

Both boys bent towards the dirty wall. 'Red Tower, Red Tower, Red Tower,' was written again and again, in very small writing.

'Red Tower!' said Dick. 'What does that mean? *Is* it George's writing?'

'Yes, I think so,' said Julian. 'But why should she keep

writing that? Do you suppose that's where they have taken her to? She might have heard them saying something and scribbled it down quickly – just in *case* we found the caravan and examined it. Red Tower! It sounds most peculiar.'

'It must be a house with a red tower, I should think,' said Dick. 'Well – we'd better get back and tell the police now – and they'll have to hunt for a red tower somewhere.'

Bitterly disappointed the boys went back to Anne. She scrambled out from under her bush as they came.

'George is not there,' said Dick. 'She's gone. But she *has* been there – we saw some scribbled writing on the wall of the caravan inside.'

'How do you know it's hers?' said Anne.

'Well, she's written "Red Tower" ever so many times, and the R's and the T's are just like hers,' said Dick. 'We think she must have heard someone talking and say they were taking her to Red Tower, wherever that is. We're going straight back to the police now. I wish we hadn't trusted Jo. We've wasted such a lot of time.'

'Let's have something to eat,' said Julian. 'We won't sit down. We'll eat as we go. Come on.'

But somehow nobody wanted anything to eat. Anne said she felt sick. Julian was too worried to eat, and Dick was so anxious to go that he felt he couldn't even wait to unpack sandwiches! So they started back down the path, following the wheel-ruts as before.

It suddenly grew very dark indeed, and on the leaves of the trees heavy rain fell with a loud, pattering sound. Thunder suddenly rolled.

Anne caught hold of Julian's arm, startled. 'Julian! It's dangerous to be in a wood, isn't it, in a storm? Oh, Julian, we'll be struck by lightning.'

'No, we shan't,' said Julian. 'A wood's no more dangerous than anywhere else. It's sheltering under a lone tree somewhere that's dangerous. Look – there's a little clearing over there; we'll go to that, if you like.'

But when they got to the little clearing the rain was falling down in such heavy torrents that Julian could see that they would immediately be soaked through. He hurried Anne to a clump of bushes, and they crouched underneath, waiting for the storm to pass.

Soon the rain stopped, and the thunder rolled away to the east. There had been no lightning that they could see. The wood grew just a little lighter, as if somewhere above the thick green branches the sun might be shining!

'I hate this wood,' said Dick, crawling out from the bushes. 'Come on, for goodness' sake. Let's get back to the wheel-rut path.'

He led the way through the trees. Julian called to him. 'Wait, Dick. Are you sure this is right?'

Dick stopped, anxious at once. 'Well,' he said uncertainly. 'I thought it was. But I don't know. Do you?'

'*I* thought it was through those trees there,' said Julian. 'Where that little clearing is.'

They went to it. 'It's not the same clearing, though,' said Anne at once. 'The other clearing had a dead tree at one side. There's no dead tree here.'

'Blow!' said Julian. 'Well – try *this* way, then.'

They went to the left, and soon found themselves in a

thicker part of the wood than ever. Julian's heart went cold. What an absolute idiot he was! He might have known that it was madness to leave the only path they knew without marking it in some way.

Now he hadn't the very faintest idea where the wheel-rut way was. It might be in any direction! He hadn't even the sun to guide him.

He looked gloomily at Dick. 'Bad show!' said Dick. 'Well – we'll have to make up our minds which way to go! We can't just stay here.'

'We might go deeper and deeper and deeper,' said Anne, with a sudden little gulp of fear. Julian put his arm round her shoulder.

'Well, if we go deeper and deeper, we shall come out on the other side!' he said. 'It's not an endless wood, you know.'

'Well, let's go straight on through the wood, then,' said Anne. 'We'll *have* to come out the other side some time.'

The boys didn't tell her that it was impossible to go straight through a wood. It was necessary to go round clumps of bushes, to double back sometimes when they came to an impenetrable part, and to go either to the left or right when clumps of trees barred their way. It was quite impossible to go *straight* through.

'For all I know we're probably going round and round in circles, like people do when they're lost in the desert,' he thought. He blamed himself bitterly for having left the wheel-ruts.

They made their way on and on for about two or three hours, and then Anne stumbled and fell. 'I can't go on any further,' she wept. 'I must have a rest.'

Dick glanced at his watch and whistled. Where ever had the time gone? It was almost three o'clock. He sat down by Anne and pulled her close to him. 'What we want is a jolly good meal,' he said. 'We've had nothing since breakfast.'

Anne said she still wasn't hungry, but when she smelt the meat sandwiches that Joanna had made she changed her mind. She was soon eating with the others, and feeling much better.

'There's nothing to drink, unfortunately,' said Dick. 'But Joanna's packed tomatoes and plums, too – so we'll have those instead of a drink. They're nice and juicy.'

They ate everything, though secretly Julian wondered if it was a good thing to wolf all their food at once. There was no telling how long they might be lost in Ravens Wood! Joanna might get worried sooner or later and tell the police they had gone there, and a search would be made. But it might be ages before they were found.

Anne fell asleep after her meal. The boys talked softly over her head. 'I don't much like this,' said Dick. 'We set out to find George – and all we've done is to lose ourselves. We don't seem to be managing this adventure as well as we usually do.'

'If we don't get out before dark we'll have to make up some kind of bed under a bush,' said Julian. 'We'll have another go when Anne wakes – and we'll do a bit of yelling, too. Then if we're still lost, we'll bed down for the night.' But when darkness came – and it came very early in that thick wood – they were still as much lost as ever. They were all hoarse with shouting too.

In silence they pulled bracken from an open space and piled it under a sheltering bush. 'Thank goodness it's warm tonight,' said Dick, trying to sound cheerful. 'Well – we'll all feel much more lively in the morning. Cuddle up to me, Anne, and keep warm. That's right. Julian's on the other side of you! This is quite an adventure.'

'I don't like adventures,' said Anne, in a small voice, and immediately fell asleep.

CHAPTER SIXTEEN

Visitor in the night

IT TOOK a long time for Julian and Dick to fall asleep. They were both worried – worried about George and worried about themselves, too. They were also very hungry, and their hunger kept them awake as much as their anxiety.

Dick fell asleep at last. Julian still lay awake, hoping that Anne was nice and warm between them. He didn't feel very warm himself.

He heard the whisper of the leaves in the trees, and then the scamper of tiny paws behind his head. He wondered what animal it was – a mouse?

Something ran lightly over his hair and he shivered. A spider, perhaps. Well he couldn't move, or he would disturb Anne. If it wanted to make a web over his hair it would have to. He shut his eyes and began to doze off. Soon he was dreaming.

He awoke very suddenly, with a jump. He heard the hoot of an owl. That must have been what wakened him. Now it would be ages before he slept again.

He shut his eyes. The owl hooted again and Julian frowned, hoping that Anne would not wake. She stirred and muttered in her sleep. Julian touched her lightly. She felt quite warm.

He settled down again and shut his eyes. Then he opened them. He had heard something! Not an owl or the pattering of some little animal's feet – but another sound, a bigger one. He listened. There was a rustling going on somewhere. Some much bigger animal was about.

Julian was suddenly panic-stricken. Then he reasoned sternly with himself. There were no dangerous wild animals in this country, not even a wolf. It was probably a badger out on a nightly prowl. He listened for any snuffling sound, but he heard none, only the rustling as the animal moved about through the bushes.

It came nearer. It came right over to him! He felt warm breath on his ear and made a quick movement of revulsion. He sat up swiftly and put out his hand. It fell on something warm and hairy. He withdrew his hand at once, feeling for his torch in panic. To touch something warm and hairy in the pitch darkness was too much even for Julian!

Something caught hold of his arm, and he gave a yell and fought it off. Then he got the surprise of his life. The animal spoke.

'Julian!' said a voice. 'It's me!'

Julian, his hands trembling, flashed his torch round. The light fell on a face, with tangled hair over its eyes.

'Jo!' said Julian. 'JO! What on earth are you doing here? You scared me stiff. I thought you were some horrible hairy animal. I must have touched your head.'

'You did,' said Jo, squeezing in under the bush. Anne

and Dick, who had both woken up at Julian's yell, gazed at her, speechless with surprise. Jo of all people here in the middle of the wood! How had she got there?

'You're surprised to see me, aren't you?' said Jo. 'I got caught by Jake. But he didn't know you were following behind. He dragged me off to the cottage he lives in and locked me up. He knew I'd spent the night at Kirrin Cottage, and he said he was going to take me to my dad, who would give me the worst punishment I'd ever had in my life. So he would, too.'

'So that's what happened to you!' said Dick.

'Then I broke the window and got out,' said Jo. 'That Jake! I'll never do a thing he tells me again – locking me up like that. I hate that worse than anything! Well, then I came to look for you.'

'How did you find us?' said Julian, in wonder.

'Well, first I went to the caravan,' said Jo. 'Old Ma Smith – the one who always sits stirring a pot – she told me you'd been asking for my dad's caravan. I guessed you'd go off to find it. So along I went after you – but there was the caravan all by itself, and nobody there. Not even George.'

'Where *is* George, do you know?' asked Anne.

'No. I don't,' said Jo. 'Dad's taken her somewhere else. I expect he put her on Chestnut, because Chestnut's gone, too.'

'What about Timmy?' asked Dick.

Jo looked away. 'I reckon they've done Timmy in,' she said. Nobody said anything. The thought that Timmy might have come to harm was too dreadful to speak about.

'How did you find us here?' asked Julian at last.

'That was easy,' said Jo. 'I can follow anybody's trail. I'd have come quicker, but it got dark. My, you did wander round, didn't you?'

'Yes. We did,' said Dick. 'Do you mean to say you followed all our wanderings in and out and round about?'

'Oh, yes,' said Jo. 'Properly tired me out, you did, with all your messing round and round. Why did you leave the wheel-ruts?'

Julian told her. 'You're daft,' said Jo. 'If you're going somewhere off the path, just mark the trees with a nick as you go along – one here and one there – and then you can always find your way back.'

'We didn't even know we were lost till we were,' said Anne. She took Jo's hand and squeezed it. She was so very, very glad to see her. Now they would be able to get out of this horrible wood.

Jo was surprised and touched, but she withdrew her hand at once. She didn't like being fondled, though she would not have minded Dick taking her hand. Dick was her hero, someone above all others. He had been kind to her, and she was glad she had found him.

'We found something written on the caravan wall,' said Julian. 'We think we know where George has been taken. It's a place called Red Tower. Do you know it?'

'There's no place called Red Tower,' said Jo at once. 'It's . . .'

'Don't be silly, Jo. You can't possibly know if there's no place called Red Tower,' said Dick, impatiently. 'There may be hundreds of places with that name. That's the place we've got to find, anyway. The police will know it.'

Jo gave a frightened movement. 'You promised you wouldn't tell the police.'

'Yes – we promised that – but only if you took us to George,' said Dick. 'And you didn't. And anyway if you *had* taken us to the caravan George wouldn't have been there. So we'll jolly well have to call in the police now and find out where Red Tower is.'

'*Was* it Red Tower George had written down?' asked Jo. 'Well, then – I *can* take you to George!'

'How can you, when you say there's no place called Red Tower?' began Julian, exasperated. 'I don't believe a word you say, Jo. You're a fraud – and I half-believe you're still working for our enemies too!'

'I'm not,' said Jo. 'I'm NOT! You're mean. I tell you Red Tower isn't a place. Red Tower is a man.'

There was a most surprised silence after this astonishing remark. A man! Nobody had thought of that.

Jo spoke again, pleased at the surprise she had caused. 'His name's Tower, and he's got red hair, flaming red – so he's called Red Tower. See?'

'Are you making this up, by any chance?' asked Dick, after a pause. 'You have made up things before, you know.'

'All right. You can think I made it up, then,' said Jo, sulkily. 'I'll go. Get yourselves out of this the best you can. You're mean.'

She wriggled away, but Julian caught hold of her arm. 'Oh, no, you don't! You'll just stay with us now, if I have to tie you to me all night long! You see, we find it difficult to trust you, Jo – and that's your fault, not ours. But we'll trust you just this once. Tell us about Red Tower, and take us to where he lives. If you do that, we'll trust you for evermore.'

'Will Dick trust me, too?' said Jo, trying to get away from Julian's hand.

'Yes,' said Dick shortly. He felt as if he would dearly like to smack this unpredictable, annoying, extraordinary, yet somehow likeable ragamuffin girl. 'But I don't feel as if I *like* you very much at present. If you want us to like you as well as to trust you, you'll have to help us a lot more than you have done.'

'All right,' said Jo, and she wriggled down again. 'I'm tired. I'll show you the way out in the morning, and then I'll take you to Red's. But you won't like Red. He's a beast.'

She would say nothing more, so once again they tried to sleep. They felt happier now that Jo was with them and would show them the right way out of the wood. Julian hardly thought she would leave them in the lurch now. He shut his eyes and was soon dreaming.

Jo woke first. She uncurled like an animal and stretched, forgetting where she was. She woke up the others, and they all sat up, feeling stiff, dirty and hungry.

'I'm thirsty as well as hungry,' complained Anne. 'Where can we get something to eat and drink?'

'Better get back home for a wash and a meal, and to let Joanna know where we are,' said Julian. 'Come on, Jo – show us the way.'

Jo led the way immediately. The others wondered how in the world she knew it. They were even more astonished when they found themselves on the wheel-rut path in about two minutes.

'Gracious! We were as near to it as that!' said Dick. 'And yet we seemed to walk for miles through this horrible wood.'

'You did,' said Jo. 'You went round in an enormous circle, and you were almost back where you started. Come on – I'll take you *my* way back to your house now – it's much better than any bus!'

CHAPTER SEVENTEEN

Off in George's boat

JOANNA WAS extremely thankful to see them. She had been so worried the night before that if the telephone wires in the house had been mended, she would most certainly have rung up the police. As it was, she couldn't telephone, and the night was so dark that she was really afraid of walking all the way down to the village.

'I haven't slept all night,' she declared. 'This mustn't happen again, Julian. It's worrying me to death. And now you haven't got George or Timmy. I tell you, if they don't turn up soon I'll take matters into my own hands. I haven't heard from your uncle and aunt either – let's hope they're not lost, too!'

She bustled about after this outburst, and was soon frying sausages and tomatoes for them. They couldn't wait till they were cooked, and helped themselves to great hunks of bread and butter.

'I can't even go and wash till I've had something,' said Anne. 'I'm glad you know so many short cuts back here, Jo – the way didn't seem nearly so long as when we came by bus.'

It had really been amazing to see the deft, confident manner in which Jo had taken them home, through fields and little narrow paths, over stiles and across allotments. She was never once at a loss.

They had arrived not long after Joanna had got up, and she had almost cried with surprise and relief when she had seen them walking up the front path.

'And a lot of dirty little tatterdemalions you looked,' she said, as she turned their breakfast out on to a big dish. 'And still do, for that matter. I'll get the kitchen fire going for a bath for you. You might all be sister and brothers to that ragamuffin Jo.'

Jo didn't mind remarks of this sort at all. She chewed her bread and grinned. She wolfed the breakfast with no manners at all – but the others were nearly as bad, they were so hungry!

'It's a spade and trowel you want for your food this morning, not a knife and fork,' said Joanna, disapprovingly. 'You're just shovelling it in. No, I can't cook you any more, Julian. There's not a sausage left in the house nor a bit of bacon either. You fill up with toast and marmalade.'

The bath water ran vigorously after breakfast. All four had baths. Jo didn't want to, but Joanna ran after her with a carpet beater, vowing and declaring she would beat the dust and dirt out of her if she didn't bath. So Jo bathed, and quite enjoyed it.

They had a conference after breakfast. 'About this fellow, Red Tower,' said Julian. 'Who is he, Jo? What do you know about him?'

'Not much,' said Jo. 'He's rich, and I think he's mad. He gets fellows like Dad and Jake to do his dirty work for him.'

'What dirty work?' asked Dick.

'Oh – stealing and such,' said Jo, vaguely. 'I don't really know. Dad doesn't tell me much; I just do what I'm told, and don't ask questions. I don't want more punishments than I get!'

'Where does he live?' said Anne. 'Far away?'

'He's taken a house on the cliff,' said Jo. 'I don't know the way by land. Only by boat. It's an odd place – like a small castle almost, with very thick stone walls. Just the place for Red, my dad says.'

'Have you been there?' asked Dick, eagerly.

Jo nodded. 'Oh, yes,' she said. 'Twice. My dad took a big iron box there once, and another time he took something in a sack. I went with him.'

'Why?' asked Julian. 'I shouldn't have thought he'd wanted you messing round!'

'I rowed the boat,' said Jo. 'I told you, Red's place is up on the cliff. We got to it by boat; I don't know the way by road. There's a sort of cave behind a cove we landed at, and we went in there. Red met us. He came from his house on the cliff, he said, but I don't know how.'

Dick looked at Jo closely. 'I suppose you'll say next that there's a secret way from the cave to the house!' he said. 'Go on!'

'Must be,' said Jo. She suddenly glared at Dick. 'Don't you believe me? All right, find the place yourself!'

'Well – it does sound like a tale in a book,' said Julian. 'You're sure it *is* all true, Jo? We don't want to go on a wild-goose chase again, you know.'

'There's no wild goose in my story,' said Jo, puzzled. She hadn't the faintest idea what a wild-goose chase was. 'I'm telling you about Red. I'm ready to go when you are. We'll have to have a boat, though.'

'We'll take George's,' said Dick, getting up. 'Look, Jo – I think we'd better leave Anne behind this time. I don't like taking her into something that may be dangerous.'

'I want to come,' said Anne at once.

'No, you stay with me,' said Joanna. 'I want company

today. I'm getting scared of being by myself with all these things happening. You stay with me.'

So Anne stayed behind, really rather glad, and watched the other three go off together. Jo slipped into the hedge to avoid being seen by Jake, in case he was anywhere about. Julian and Dick went down to the beach and glanced round to make sure the traveller was nowhere in sight.

They beckoned to Jo, and she came swiftly from hiding, and leapt into George's boat. She lay down in it so that she couldn't be seen. The boys hauled the boat down to the sea. Dick jumped in, and Julian pushed off when a big wave came. Then he jumped in too.

'How far up the coast is it?' he asked Jo, who was still at the bottom of the boat.

'I don't know,' said Jo, with her usual irritating vagueness. 'Two hours, three hours, maybe.'

Time didn't mean the same to Jo as it did to the others. For one thing Jo had no wrist-watch as they had, always there to be glanced at. She wouldn't have found one any use if she had, because she couldn't tell the time. Time was just day and night to her, nothing else.

Dick put up the little sail. The wind was in their favour, so he thought he might as well use it. They would get there all the more quickly.

'Did you bring the lunch that Joanna put up for us?' said Julian to Dick. 'I can't see it anywhere.'

'Jo! You must be lying on it!' said Dick.

'It won't hurt it,' said Jo. She sat up as soon as they were well out to sea, and offered to take the tiller.

She was very deft with it, and the boys soon saw that they could leave her to guide the boat. Julian unfolded the map he had brought with him.

'I wonder whereabouts this place is where Red lives,' he said. 'It's pretty desolate all the way up to the next place, Port Limmersley. If there *is* a castle-like building, it must be a very lonely place to live in. There's not even a little fishing village shown for miles.'

The boat went on and on, scudding at times before a fairly strong wind. Julian took the tiller from Jo. 'We've come a long way already,' he said. 'Where *is* this place? Are you sure you'll know it, Jo?'

'Of course,' said Jo, scornfully. 'I think it's round that far-off rocky cliff.'

She was right. As they rounded the high cliff, which jutted fiercely with great slanting rocks, she pointed in triumph.

'There you are! See that place up there? That's Red's place.'

The boys looked at it. It was a dour, grey stone building, and was, as Jo had said, a little like a small castle. It brooded over the sea, with one square tower overlooking the waves.

'There's a cove before you come to the place,' said Jo. 'Watch out for it – it's very well hidden.'

It certainly was. The boat went right past it before they

saw it. 'There it is!' cried Jo, urgently.

They took the sail down and then rowed back. The cove lay between two high layers of rock that jutted out from the cliff. They rowed right into it. It was very quiet and calm there, and their boat merely rose and fell as the water swelled and subsided under it.

'Can anyone see us from the house above?' asked Dick, as they rowed right to the back of the cove.

'I don't know,' said Jo. 'I shouldn't think so. Look – pull the boat up behind that big rock. We don't know who else might come here.'

They dragged the boat up. Dick draped it with great armfuls of seaweed, and soon it looked almost like a rock itself.

'Now, what next?' said Julian. 'Where's this cave you were talking about?'

'Up here,' said Jo, and began to climb up the rocky cliff like a monkey. Both the boys were very good climbers, but soon they found it impossible to get any further. Jo scrambled down to them. 'What's the matter?' she said. 'If my dad can climb up, surely you can!'

'Your dad was an acrobat,' said Julian, sliding down a few feet, much too suddenly. 'Oooh! I don't much like this. I wish we had a rope.'

'There's one in the boat. I'll get it,' said Jo, and slithered down the cliff to the cove below at a most alarming rate. She climbed up again with the rope. She went on a good bit higher, and tied the rope to something.

It hung down to where Dick and Julian stood clinging for dear life.

It was much easier to climb up with the help of a rope. Both boys were soon standing on a ledge, looking into a curious-shaped cave. It was oval-shaped, and very dark.

'In here,' said Jo, and led the way. Dick and Julian followed stumblingly. Where in the world were they going to now?

CHAPTER EIGHTEEN

Things begin to happen

JO LED them into a narrow rocky tunnel, and then out into a wider cave, whose walls dripped with damp. Julian was thankful for his torch. It was eerie and chilly and musty. He shivered. Something brushed his face and he leapt back.

'What was that?' he said.

'Bats,' said Jo, 'there're hundreds of them here. That's why the place smells so sour. Come on. We go round this rocky bit here into a better cave.'

They squeezed round a rocky corner and came into a drier cave that did not smell so strongly of bats. 'I haven't been any farther than this,' said Jo. 'This is where me and Dad came and waited for Red. He suddenly appeared, but I don't know where from.'

'Well, he must have come from somewhere,' said Dick, switching on his torch, too. 'There's a passage probably. We'll soon find it.'

He and Julian began to hunt round the cave, looking for a passage or little tunnel, or even a hole that led into the cliff, upwards towards the house. Obviously Red must have come down some such passage to reach the cave. Jo stayed in a corner, waiting. She had no torch.

Suddenly the boys had a tremendous shock. A voice boomed into their cave, a loud and angry voice that made their hearts beat painfully.

'SO! YOU DARE TO COME HERE!'

Jo slipped behind a rock immediately, like an animal going to cover. The boys stood where they were, rooted to the spot. Where did that voice come from?

'Who are you?' boomed the voice.

'Who are *you*?' shouted Julian. 'Come out and show yourself! We've come to see a man called Red. Take us to him.'

There was a moment's silence, as if the owner of the voice was rather taken aback. Then it boomed out again.

'Why do you want to see Red? Who sent you?'

'Nobody. We came because we want our cousin back, and her dog, too,' boomed Julian, making a funnel of his hands and trying to outdo the other voice.

There was another astonished silence. Then two legs appeared out of a hole in the low ceiling, and someone leapt lightly down beside them. The boys started back in surprise. They hadn't expected that the voice came from the roof of the cave!

Julian flashed his torch on the man. He was a giant-like fellow with flaming red hair. His eyebrows were red, too, and he had a red beard that partly hid a cruel mouth. Julian took one look into the man's eyes and then no more.

'He's mad,' he thought. 'So this is Red Tower. What is he? A scientist like Uncle Quentin, jealous of uncle's work? Or a thief working on a big scale, trying to get important papers and sell them? He's mad, whatever he is.'

Red was looking closely at the two boys. 'So you think I have your cousin,' he said. 'Who told you such a stupid tale?'

Julian didn't answer. Red took a threatening step towards him. 'Who told you?'

'I'll tell you that when the police come,' said Julian, boldly.

Red stepped back.

'The police! What do they know? Why should they come here? Answer me, boy!'

'There's a lot to know about you, Mr Red Tower,' said Julian. 'Who sent men to steal my uncle's papers? Who sent a note to ask for another lot? Who kidnapped our cousin, so that she could be held till the papers were sent? Who brought her here from Simmy's old caravan? Who . . . ?'

'Aaaaaah!' said Red, and there was panic in his voice. 'How do you know all this? It isn't true! But the police – have they heard this fantastic tale, too?'

'What do you suppose?' said Julian, wishing with all his heart that the police *did* know, and that he was not merely bluffing. Red pulled at his beard. His green eyes gleamed as he thought quickly and urgently.

He suddenly called loudly, turning his head up to the hole in the ceiling. 'Markhoff! Come down!'

Two legs were swung down through the hole, and a short burly man leapt down beside the two startled boys.

'Go down the cliff. You will find a boat in the cove, somewhere – the boat we saw these boys coming in,' said Red sharply. 'Smash it to pieces. Then come back here and take the boys to the yard. Tie them up. We must leave quickly, and take the girl with us.'

The man stood listening, his face sullen. 'How can we go?' he said. 'You know the helicopter is not ready. You *know* that.'

'Make it ready, then,' snapped Red. 'We leave tonight. The police will be here – do you hear that? This boy knows everything – he has told me – and the police must know everything too. I tell you, we must go.'

'What about the dog?' said the man.

'Shoot it,' ordered Red. 'Shoot it before we go. It's a brute of a dog. We should have shot it before. Now go and smash the boat.'

The man disappeared round the rocky corner that led into the cave of bats. Julian clenched his fist. He hated to think of George's boat being smashed to bits. Red stood there waiting, his eyes glinting in the light of the torches.

'I'd take you with us too, if there was room!' he suddenly snarled at Julian. 'Yes, and drop you into the sea!

'You can tell your uncle he'll hear from me about his precious daughter – we'll make an exchange. If he wants her back he can send me the notes I want. And many thanks for coming to warn me. I'll be off before the police break in.'

He began to pace up and down the cave, muttering. Dick and Julian watched in silence. They felt afraid for George. Would Red really take her off in his helicopter? He looked mad enough for anything.

The sullen man came back at last. 'It's smashed,' he said.

'Right,' said Red. 'I'll go first. Then the boys. Then you. And boot them if they make any trouble.'

Red swung himself up into the hole in the roof. Julian and Dick followed, not seeing any point in resisting. The man behind was too sulky to stand any nonsense. He followed immediately.

There had been no sign of Jo. She had kept herself well hidden, scared stiff. Julian didn't know what to do about her. He couldn't possibly tell Red about her – and yet it seemed terrible to leave her behind all alone. Well – she was a sharp-brained little monkey. Maybe she would think up something for herself.

Red led the way through another cave into a passage with such a low roof that he had to walk bent almost double.

The man behind had now switched on a very powerful torch, and it was easier to see. The passage sloped upwards and was obviously leading to the building on the cliff. At one part it was so steep that a hand-rail had been put for the climber to help himself up.

Then came a flight of steps hewn out of the rock itself – rough, badly-shaped steps, so steep that it was quite an effort to climb from one to the next.

At the top of the steps was a stout door set on a broad ledge. Red pushed it open and daylight flooded in. Julian blinked. He was looking out on an enormous yard paved with great flat stones with weeds growing in all the crevices and cracks.

In the middle stood a helicopter. It looked very strange

and out-of-place in that old yard. The house, with its one tall square tower, was built round three sides of the yard. It was covered with creeper and thick-stemmed ivy.

A high wall ran along the fourth side, with an enormous gate in the middle. It was shut, and from where he stood Julian could see the huge bolts that were drawn across.

'It's almost like a small fort,' thought Julian, in astonishment. Then he felt himself seized and taken to a shed nearby. His arms were forced behind him and his wrists were tightly tied. Then the rope was run through an iron loop and tied again.

Julian glared at the burly fellow now doing the same to Dick. He twisted about to try to see how the rope was tied, but he couldn't even turn, he was so tightly tethered.

He looked up at the tower. A small, forlorn face was looking out of the window there. Julian's heart jumped and beat fast. That must be poor old George up there. He wondered if she had seen them. He hoped not, because she would know that he and Dick had been captured, and she would be very upset.

Where was Timmy? There seemed no sign of him. But wait a minute – what was that lying inside what looked like a summer-house on the opposite side of the yard? *Was* it Timmy? Surely he would have barked a welcome when he heard them coming into the yard, if it *was* Timmy!

'Is that my cousin's dog?' he asked the sullen man.

The man nodded. 'Yes. He's been doped half the time,

he barked so. Savage brute, isn't he? *Ought* to be shot, I reckon.'

Red had gone across the yard and had disappeared through a stone archway. The sullen man now followed him. Julian and Dick were left by themselves.

'We've muddled things again,' said Julian, with a groan. 'Now these fellows will be off and away, and take George

with them – they've been nicely warned!'

Dick said nothing. He felt very miserable, and his bound wrists hurt him, too. Both boys stood there, wondering what would happen to them.

'Pssssst!'

What was that? Julian turned round sharply and looked in the direction of the door that led from underground into the yard. Jo stood there, half-hidden by the archway over the door. 'Psssst! I'll come and untie you. Is the coast clear?'

CHAPTER NINETEEN

Jo is very surprising

'JO!' SAID the boys together, and their spirits lifted at once. 'Come on!'

There was no one about in the yard. Jo skipped lightly across from the doorway and slipped inside the shed.

'There's a knife in my back pocket,' said Julian. 'Get it out. It would be quicker to cut these ropes than to untie them. My word, Jo – I was never so pleased to see anyone in my life!'

Jo grinned as she hauled out Julian's sturdy pocket-knife. She opened it and ran her thumb lightly over the blade. It was beautifully sharp. She set to work to saw the blade across the thick rope. It cut easily through the fibres.

'I waited behind,' she said, rapidly. 'Then I followed when it was safe. But it was very dark and I didn't like it. Then I came to that door and peeped out. I was glad when I saw you.'

'Good thing the men didn't guess you were there,' said Dick. 'Good old Jo! I take back any nasty thing I've ever said about you!'

Jo beamed. She cut the last bit of rope that bound Julian, and he swung himself away from the iron loop and began to rub his stiff, aching wrists. Jo set to work on Dick's bonds. She soon had those cut through, too.

'Where's George?' she asked, after she had helped Dick to rub his wrists and arms.

'Up in that tower,' said Julian. 'If we dared to go out in that yard you could look up and see her. And there's poor old Tim, look – half-doped – lying in that summer-house place over there.'

'I shan't let him be shot,' said Jo. 'He's a nice dog. I shall go and drag him down into those caves underground.'

'Not now!' said Julian, horrified. 'If you're seen now, you'll spoil everything. We'll *all* be tied up then!'

But Jo had already darted over to the summer-house and was fondling poor old Timmy.

The slam of a door made the boys jump and sent Jo into the shadows at the back of the summer-house at once. It was Red, coming across the yard!

'Quick! He's coming over here!' said Dick, in a panic. 'Let's go back to the iron loops and put our hands behind us so that he thinks we're still bound.'

So, when Red came over to the door of the shed, it looked exactly as if the boys still had their hands tied behind them. He laughed.

'You can stay here till the police come!' he said. Then he shut the shed door and locked it. He strolled over to the helicopter and examined it thoroughly. Then back he went to the door he had come from, opened it, and slammed it shut. He was gone.

When everything was quiet Jo sped back from the summer-house to the shed. She unlocked the door of the shed. 'Come out,' she said. 'And we'll lock it again. Then nobody will know you aren't here. Hurry!'

There was nothing for it but to come out and hope there was nobody looking. Jo locked the shed door after them and hurried them back to the door that led underground. They slipped through it and half-fell down the steep steps.

'Thanks, Jo,' said Dick.

They sat down. Julian scratched his head, and for the life of him could not think of anything sensible to do. The police were *not* coming because they didn't know a thing about Red, or where George was or anything. And before long George would be flown off in that helicopter, and Timmy would be shot.

Julian thought of the high square tower and groaned. 'There's no way of getting George out of that tower,' he said aloud. 'It'll be locked and barred, or George would have got out at once. We can't even get to her. It's no good trying to make our way into the house – we'd be seen and caught at once.'

Jo looked at Dick. 'Do you badly want George to be rescued?' she said.

'That's a silly question,' said Dick. 'I want it more than anything else in the world.'

'Well – I'll go and get her, then,' said Jo, and she got up as if she really meant it.

'Don't make jokes now,' said Julian. 'This really is serious, Jo.'

'Well, so am I,' retorted Jo. 'I'll get her out, you see if I don't. Then you'll know I'm trustable, won't you? You think I'm mean and thieving and not worth a penny, and I expect you're right. But I can do some things you can't, and if you want this thing, I'll do it for you.'

'How?' said Julian, astonished and disbelieving.

Jo sat down again.

'You saw that tower, didn't you?' she began. 'Well, it's a big one, so I reckon there's more than one room in it – and if I can get into the room next to George's I could undo her door and set her free.'

'And how do you think you're going to get into the room next to hers?' said Dick, scornfully.

'Climb up the wall, of course,' said Jo. 'It's set thick with ivy. I've often climbed up walls like that.'

The boys looked at her. 'Were you the Face at the Window by any chance?' said Julian, remembering Anne's fright. 'I bet you were. You're like a monkey, climbing and darting about. But you can't climb up that great high wall, so don't think it. You'd fall and be killed. We couldn't let you.'

'Pooh!' said Jo, with great scorn. 'Fall off a wall like that! I've climbed up a wall without any ivy at all! There're always holes and cracks to hold on to. That one would be easy!'

Julian was quite amazed to think that Jo really meant all

this. Dick remembered that Jo's father was an acrobat. Perhaps that kind of thing was in the family.

'You just ought to see me on a tight-rope,' said Jo earnestly. 'I can dance on it – and I never have a safety-net underneath – that's baby-play! Well, I'm going.'

Without another word she climbed the steep steps lightly as a goat and stood poised in the archway of the door. All was quiet. Like a squirrel she leapt and bounded over the courtyard and came to the foot of the ivy-covered tower. Julian and Dick were now at the doorway that led into the yard, watching her.

'She'll be killed,' said Julian.

'Talk about pluck!' said Dick. 'I never saw such a kid in my life. There she goes – just like a monkey.'

And, sure enough, up the ivy went Jo, climbing lightly and steadily. Her hands reached out and tested each ivy-stem before she threw her weight on it, and her feet tried each one, too, before she stood on it.

Once she slipped when an ivy-stem came away from the wall. Julian and Dick watched, their hearts in their mouths. But Jo merely clutched at another piece of stem and steadied herself once. Then up she went again.

Up and up. Past the first storey, past the second, and up to the third. Only one more now and she would be up to the topmost one. She seemed very small as she neared the top.

'I can't bear to look and I can't bear not to,' said Dick, pretending to shield his eyes and almost trembling with nervousness. 'If she fell now – what should we do?'

'Do shut up,' said Julian, between his teeth. 'She won't fall. She's like a cat. There – she's making for the window next to George's. It's open at the bottom.'

Jo now sat triumphantly on the broad window-sill of the room next to George's. She waved impudently to the boys far below. Then she pushed with all her might at the window to open it a little more. It wouldn't budge.

So Jo laid herself flat, and by dint of much wriggling and squeezing, she managed to slip through the narrow space between the bottom of the window-pane and the sill. She disappeared from sight.

Both boys heaved heartfelt sighs of relief. Dick found that his knees were shaking. He and Julian retired into the underground passage below the steep steps and sat there in silence.

'Worse than a circus,' said Dick at last. 'I'll never be able to watch acrobats again. What's she doing now, do you suppose?'

Jo was very busy. She had fallen off the inside window-sill with a bump, and bruised herself on the floor below. But she was used to bruises.

She picked herself up and shot behind a chair in case anyone had heard her. Nobody seemed to have heard anything, so she peeped cautiously out. The room was furnished with enormous pieces of furniture, old and heavy. Dust was on everything, and cobwebs hung down from the stone ceiling.

Jo tiptoed to the door. Her feet were bare and made no

sound at all. She looked out. There was a spiral stone stairway nearby going downwards, and on each side was a door – there must be four rooms in the tower then, one for each corner, two windows in each. She looked at the door next to the room she was in. That must be the door of George's room.

There was a very large key in the lock, and a great bolt had been drawn across. Jo leapt across and dragged at the bolt. It made a loud noise and she darted back into the room again. But still nobody came. Back she went to the door again, and this time turned the enormous key. It was well oiled and turned easily.

Jo pushed open the door and put her head cautiously round. George was there – a thin and unhappy George, sitting by the window. She stared at Jo as if she couldn't believe her eyes!

'Psssst!' said Jo, enjoying all this very much indeed. 'I've come to get you out!'

CHAPTER TWENTY

The adventure boils up

GEORGE LOOKED as if she had seen a ghost. 'Jo!' she whispered. 'It can't really be you.'

'It is. Feel,' said Jo, and pattered across the room to give George quite a hard pinch. Then she pulled at her arm.

'Come on,' she said. 'We must go before Red comes. Hurry! I don't want to be caught.'

George got up as if she was in a dream. She went across to the door. She and Jo slipped out, and stood at the top of the spiral staircase.

'Have to go down here, I suppose,' said Jo. She cocked her head and listened. Then she went down a few steps and turned the first spiral bend.

But before she had gone down more than a dozen steps she stopped in fright. Somebody was coming up!

In panic Jo ran up again and pushed George roughly into the room she had climbed into first of all.

'Someone's coming,' she panted. 'Now we're finished.'

'It's that red-haired man, I expect,' said George. 'He comes up three or four times a day and tries to make me tell him about my father's work. But I don't know a thing. What are we to do?'

The slow steps came up and up, sounding hollowly on

the stone stairs. They could hear a panting breath now, too.

An idea came to Jo. She put her mouth close to George's ear. 'Listen! We look awfully alike. I'll let myself be caught and locked up in that room – and you take the chance to slip down and go to Dick and Julian. Red will never know I'm not you – we've even got the same clothes on now, because Joanna gave me old ones of yours.'

'No,' said George, astounded. 'You'll be caught. I don't want you to do that.'

'You've *got* to,' whispered Jo, fiercely. 'Don't be daft. I can open the window and climb down the ivy, easy as winking, when Red's gone. It's your only chance. They're going to take you off in that helicopter tonight.'

The footsteps were now at the top. Jo pushed George well behind a curtain and whispered fiercely again: 'Anyway, I'm not really doing this for you. I'm doing it for Dick. You keep there and I'll do the rest.'

There was a loud exclamation when the man outside discovered the door of George's room open. He went in quickly and found nobody there. Out he came and yelled down the stairs.

'Markhoff! The door's open and the girl's gone! Who opened the door?'

Markhoff came up two steps at a time, looking bewildered. 'No one! Who could? Anyway, the girl can't be far off! I've been in the room below all the time since I locked her in last time. I'd have seen her if she's gone.'

'Who unlocked the door?' screamed Red, quite beside himself with anger. 'We've *got* to have that girl to bargain with.'

'Well, she must be in one of the other rooms,' said Markhoff, stolidly, quite unmoved by his master's fury. He went into one on the opposite side to the room where Jo and George crouched trembling. Then he came into their room, and at once saw the top of Jo's head showing behind the chair.

He pounced on her and dragged her out. 'Here she is!' he said, and didn't seem to realise that it was not George at all, but Jo. With their short hair, freckled faces and their similar clothes they really were alike. Jo yelled and struggled most realistically. Nobody would have guessed that she had planned to be caught and locked up!

George shook and shivered behind the curtain, longing to go to Jo's help, but knowing that it wouldn't be of the least use. Besides – there might be a chance now of finding Timmy. It had almost broken George's heart to be parted from him for so long.

Jo was dragged yelling and kicking into the room and locked in again. Red and Markhoff began to quarrel about which of them must have left the door unlocked.

'You were there last,' said Red.

'Well, if I was, I tell you I didn't leave the door unlocked,' Markhoff raged back. 'I wouldn't be so fat-headed. That's the kind of thing *you* do.'

'That'll do,' snapped Red. 'Have you shot that dog yet? No, you haven't! Go down and do it before *he* escapes too!'

George's heart went stone-cold. Shoot Timmy! Oh *no*! Dear darling old Timmy. She couldn't let him be shot!

She didn't know what to do. She heard Red and Markhoff go down the stone stairway, their boots making a terrific noise at first, and then gradually becoming fainter.

She slipped down after them. They went into a nearby

room, still arguing. George risked being seen and shot past the open door. She came to another stairway, not a spiral one this time, and went down it so fast that she almost lost her footing. Down and down and down. She met nobody at all. What a very strange place this was!

She came into a dark, enormous hall that smelt musty and old. She ran to the great door at the front and tried to open it. It was very heavy, but at last it swung slowly back.

She stood there in the bright sunlight, peering out cautiously. She knew where Timmy was. She had been able to see him sometimes, flopping peculiarly in and out of the summer-house. She knew that because of his continual barking he had been doped. Red had told her that when she had asked him. He enjoyed making her miserable. Poor George!

She tore across the courtyard and came to the summer-house. Timmy was there, lying as if he were asleep. George flung herself on him, her arms round his thick neck.

'Timmy, oh, Timmy!' she cried, and couldn't see him for tears. Timmy, far away in some drugged dream, heard the voice he loved best in all the world. He stirred. He opened his eyes and saw George!

He was too heavy with his sleep to do more than lick her face. Then his eyes closed again. George was in despair. She was afraid Markhoff would come and shoot him in a very short time.

'Timmy!' she called in his ear. 'TIMMY! Do wake up. TIMMY!'

Tim opened his eyes again. What – his mistress still here! Then it couldn't be a dream. Perhaps his world would soon be right again. Timmy didn't understand at all what had been happening the last few days. He staggered to his feet somehow and stood swaying there, shaking his head. George put her hand on his collar. 'That's right, Tim,' she said. 'Now you come with me. Quick!'

But Timmy couldn't walk, though he had managed to stand. In despair George glanced over the courtyard, fearful that she would see Markhoff coming at any moment.

She saw somebody else. She saw Julian standing in an archway opposite, staring at her. She was too upset about Timmy even to feel much astonishment.

'Ju!' she called. 'Come and help me with Timmy. They're going to shoot him!'

In a trice Julian and Dick shot across the courtyard to George. 'What happened, Jo?' said Julian. 'Did you find George?'

'Ju – it's me, George!' said George, and Julian suddenly saw that indeed it was George herself. He had been so certain that it was still Jo that he hadn't known it was George!

'Help me with Timmy,' said George, and she pulled at the heavy dog. 'Where shall we hide him?'

'Down underground,' said Dick. 'It's the only place. Come on!'

How they managed it they never quite knew, but they

did drag the heavy, stupid Timmy all the way across the yard and into the archway. They opened the door and shoved him inside. Poor Timmy fell over and immediately rolled down the steep steps, landing at the bottom with a frightful thud. George gave a little scream.

'He'll be hurt!'

But astonishingly enough Timmy didn't seem to be hurt at all. In fact the shaking seemed to have done him good. He got up and looked round him in rather a surprised way. Then he whined and looked up at George. He tried to climb the steep steps, but wasn't lively enough.

George was down beside him in a moment, patting him and stroking him. The two boys joined in. Timmy began to feel that things might be all right again, if only he could get rid of the dreadful, heavy feeling in his head. He couldn't understand why he kept wanting to lie down and go to sleep.

'Bring him right down to the caves,' said Dick. 'Those men are sure to hunt for him and for us too when they find Timmy gone, and us not in the shed.'

So down the narrow passages and into the little cave with the hole in the roof they all went, Timmy feeling as if he didn't quite know which of his legs to use next.

They all sat down in a heap together when they got there, and George got as close to Timmy as she could. She was glad when the boys switched off their torches. She badly wanted to cry, and as she never did cry it was most embarrassing if anyone saw her.

She told the boys in a low voice all that had happened with Jo. 'She *made* me stay hidden so that she could be caught,' she said. 'She's wonderful. She's the bravest girl I ever knew. And she did it all even though she doesn't like me.'

'She's an odd one,' said Dick. 'She's all right at heart, though – very much all right.'

They talked quickly, in low voices, exchanging their news. George told them how she had been caught and taken to the caravan with Timmy, who had been knocked out with a cudgel.

'We saw where you had written Red's name,' said Dick. 'That gave us the clue to come here!'

'Listen,' said Julian, suddenly. 'I think we ought to make a plan quickly. I keep thinking I hear things. We're sure to be looked for soon, you know. What can we *do*?'

CHAPTER TWENTY-ONE

A few surprises

AS SOON as Julian had said that he kept hearing noises, the others felt as if they could hear some, too. They sat and listened intently, George's heart beating so loudly that she was certain the boys would be able to hear it.

'I think perhaps it's the sound of the sea, echoing in through the caves and the tunnels,' said Julian at last. 'In the ordinary way, of course, we wouldn't need to bother to listen – Timmy would growl at once! But, poor old chap, he's so doped and sleepy that I don't believe he hears anything.'

'Will he get all right again?' asked George, anxiously, fondling Timmy's silky ears.

'Oh, yes,' said Julian, sounding much more certain than he really felt. Poor Timmy – he really did seem ill! There wasn't even a growl in him.

'You've had an awful time these last few days, haven't you, George?' asked Dick.

'Yes,' said George. 'I don't much want to talk about it. If I'd had Timmy with me it wouldn't have been so bad, but at first, when they brought me here, all I knew of Timmy was hearing him bark and snarl and bark and snarl down below in the yard. Then Red told me he had doped him.'

'How did you get to Red's place?' asked Julian.

'Well, you know I was locked in that horrible-smelling caravan,' said George. 'Then suddenly a man called Simmy – he's Jo's father, I think – came and dragged us out. Timmy was all stupid with the blow they'd given him – and they put him in a sack and put us both on the caravan horse and took us through the wood and along a desolate path by the coast till we came here. That was in the middle of the night.'

'Poor old George!' said Julian. 'I wish Tim was himself again – I'd love to set him loose on Red and the other fellow!'

'I wonder what's happening to Jo,' said Dick, suddenly remembering that Jo was now imprisoned in the tower room where George had been kept so long.

'And do you suppose that Red and Markhoff have discovered that we've got out of that shed, and that Timmy has disappeared, too?' said Julian. 'They'll be in a fury when they do discover it!'

'Can't we get away?' said George, feeling suddenly scared. 'You came in a boat, didn't you? Well, can't we get away in that and go and fetch help for Jo?'

There was a silence. Neither of the boys liked to tell George that her beloved boat had been smashed to pieces by Markhoff. But she had to know, of course, and Julian told her in a few short words.

George said nothing at all. They all sat silently for a few minutes, hearing nothing but Timmy's heavy, almost snoring, breathing.

'Would it be possible, when it's dark, to creep up into the courtyard, and go round the walls to the big gate?' said Dick, breaking the silence. 'We can't escape anywhere down here, it's certain – not without a boat, anyhow.'

'Should we wait till Red and Markhoff have gone off in the helicopter?' said Julian. 'Then we'd be much safer.'

'Yes – but what about Jo?' asked Dick. 'They think she's George, don't they? – and they'll take her away with them, just as they planned to do with George. I don't see how we can try to escape ourselves without first trying to save Jo. She's been a brick about George.'

They talked round and round the idea of trying to save Jo, but nobody could think of any really sensible plan at all. Time went on, and they all felt hungry and rather cold.

'If only we could *do* something, it wouldn't be so bad!' groaned Dick. 'I wonder what's happening up at the house.'

Up at the grey stone house with its big square tower, plenty was happening!

To begin with, Markhoff had gone to shoot Timmy, as Red had ordered. But when he got to the summer-house there was no dog there!

Markhoff stared in the greatest amazement! The dog had been tied up, even though he was doped – and now, there was the loose rope, and no dog attached to it!

Markhoff gazed round the summer-house in astonishment. Who could have loosed Timmy? He darted across to the locked shed where he had tied Julian and

Dick with rope to the iron staples. The door was still locked, of course – and Markhoff turned the key and pushed it open.

'Here, you . . .' he began, shouting roughly. Then he stopped dead. Nobody was there! Again there was loose rope – this time cut here and there, so that it lay in short pieces – and again the prisoners had gone. No dog. No boys.

Markhoff couldn't believe his eyes. He looked all round the shed. 'But it was locked from the outside!' he muttered. 'What's all this? Who's freed the dog and the boys? What will Red say?'

Markhoff looked at the helicopter standing ready for flight in the middle of the yard, and half decided to desert Red and get away himself. Then, remembering Red's mad tempers, and his cruel revenges on anyone who dared to let him down, he changed his mind.

'We'd better get off now, before it's dark,' he thought. 'There's something strange going on here. There must be somebody else here that we know nothing about. I'd better find Red and tell him.'

He went in through the massive front door, and in the hall he came face to face with two men waiting there. At first he couldn't see who they were, and he stepped back hurriedly. Then he saw it was Simmy and Jake.

'What are you doing here?' shouted Markhoff. 'Weren't you told to keep watch on Kirrin Cottage and make sure the police weren't told anything?'

'Yes,' said Jake, sulkily. 'And we've come to say that

that cook woman called Joanna – went down to the police this morning. She had one of the kids with her – a girl. The boys don't seem to be about.'

'No. They're here – at least, they were,' said Markhoff. 'They've disappeared again. As for the police, we've heard they're on the way, and we've made our plans. You're a bit late with your news! Lot of good you are, with your spying! Clear off now – we're taking the girl off in the helicopter before the police come. How did anyone know where the girl was? Have you been spilling the beans?'

'Pah!' said Simmy, contemptuously. 'Think we want to be messed up with the police? You must be mad. We want some money. We've done all your dirty work, and you've only paid us half you promised. Give us the rest.'

'You can ask Red for it!' growled Markhoff. 'What's the good of asking me? Go and ask *him*!'

'Right. We will,' said Jake, his face as dark as thunder. 'We've done all he told us – took the papers for him, took the girl – and that savage brute of a dog too – see where he bit me on my hand? And all we get is half our money! I reckon we've only just come in time, too. Planning to go off in that heli-thing and do us out of our pay. Pah!'

'Where's Red?' demanded Simmy.

'Upstairs,' said Markhoff. 'I've got some bad news for him, so he won't be pleased to see you and your ugly mugs. Better let me find him for you and say what I've got to say – then you can chip in with your polite little speeches.'

'Funny, aren't you?' said Jake, in a dangerous voice.

Neither he nor Simmy liked Markhoff. They followed him up the broad stairway, and then up again till they came to the room that lay below the spiral staircase.

Red was there, scanning through the papers that had been stolen from the study of George's father. He was in a dark temper. He flung down the papers as Markhoff came in.

'These aren't the notes I wanted!' he began, loudly. 'Well, I'll hold the girl till I get . . . why, Markhoff, what's up? Anything wrong?'

'Plenty,' said Markhoff. 'The dog's gone – he wasn't there when I went to shoot him – and the two boys have gone too – yes, escaped out of a locked shed. Beats me!

'And here are two visitors for you – they want money! They've come to tell you what you already know – the police have been told about you.'

Red went purple in the face, and his strange eyes shone with rage. He stared first at Markhoff, then at Simmy and Jake. Markhoff looked uneasy, but Simmy and Jake looked back insolently.

'You – you – you *dare* to come here when I told you to keep away!' he shouted. 'You've BEEN paid. You can't blackmail me for any more money.'

What he would have said next nobody knew because from up the spiral stairs there came yells and screams and the noise of someone apparently trying to batter down a door.

'That's that girl, I suppose,' muttered Markhoff. 'What's

up with her? She's been quiet enough before.'

'We'd better get her out now and go,' said Red, his face still purple. 'Jake, go and get her. Bring her down here, and knock some sense into her if she goes on screaming.'

'Fetch her yourself,' said Jake, insolently.

Red looked at Markhoff, who immediately produced a revolver.

'My orders are always obeyed,' said Red in a suddenly cold voice. '*Always*, you understand?'

Not only Jake scuttled up the stairs then but also Simmy! They went to the locked and bolted room at the top and unlocked the door. They pulled back the bolt and door. Simmy stepped into the room to deal with the imprisoned girl.

But he stopped dead and gaped. He blinked, rubbed his eyes and gaped again. Jake gaped too.

'Hallo, Dad!' said Jo. 'You *do* seem surprised to see me!'

CHAPTER TWENTY-TWO

Jo is very smart

'JO,' SAID Simmy. 'Well, of all the . . . well . . . *JO*!' Jake recovered first. 'What's all this?' he said, roughly, to Simmy. 'What's Jo doing here? How did *she* get here? Where's the other kid, the one we caught?'

'How do *I* know?' said Simmy, still staring at Jo. 'Look here, Jo – what are you doing here? Go on, tell us. And where's the other kid?'

'Hunt round the room and see if you can find her!' said Jo, brightly, keeping on her toes in case her father or Jake was going to pounce on her. The two men looked hurriedly round the room. Jake went to a big cupboard.

'Yes – she might be in there,' said Jo, enjoying herself. 'You have a good look.'

The two bewildered men didn't know what to think. They had come to get George – and had only found Jo!

But how – why – what had happened? They didn't know what to do. Neither of them wanted to go back and tell Red. So they began to search the room feverishly, looking into likely and unlikely places, with Jo jeering at them all the time.

'Better take the drawers out of that chest and see if she's here. And don't forget to look under the rug. That's right,

Jake, poke your head up the chimney. Mind George doesn't kick soot into your eyes.'

'I'll get you in a minute!' growled Jake, furiously, opening a small cupboard door.

An angry voice came up the stairway. 'Jake! What are you doing up there? Bring that kid down.'

'She's not here!' yelled back Jake, suddenly losing his temper. 'What have you done with her? She's gone!'

Red came tearing up, two steps at a time, his eyes narrow with anger. The first thing he saw in the room was Jo – and, of course, he thought she was George.

'What do you mean – saying she's not here!' he raged. 'Are you mad?'

'Nope,' said Jake, his eyes narrow too. 'Not so mad as you are, anyway, Red. This kid isn't that fellow's daughter – the scientist chap we took the papers from – this is Simmy's kid – Jo.'

Red looked at Jake as if he had gone off his head. Then he looked at Jo. He could see no difference between Jo and the absent George at all – short hair, freckles, turned-up nose – he couldn't believe that she was Simmy's daughter.

In fact, he didn't believe it. He thought Jake and Simmy were suddenly deceiving him for some strange reason.

But Jo had a word to say, too. 'Yes, I'm Jo,' she said. 'I'm not Georgina. She's gone. I'm just Jo, and Simmy's my dad. You've come to save me, haven't you, Dad?'

Simmy hadn't come to do anything of the sort, of course. He stared helplessly at Jo, completely bewildered.

Red completely lost his temper. As soon as he heard Jo's voice he realised she was not George. Somehow or other he had been deceived – and seeing that this was Simmy's daughter, then it must be Simmy who had had a hand in the deception!

He went suddenly over to Simmy and struck him hard, his eyes blazing. 'Have you double-crossed me?' he shouted.

Simmy was sent flying to the floor. Jake came up immediately to help him. He tripped up Red, and leapt on him.

Jo looked at the three struggling, shouting men, and shrugged her shoulders. Let them fight! They had forgotten all about her, and that suited her very well. She ran to the door and was just going down the stairs, when an idea came into her sharp little mind. With an impish grin she turned back. She pulled the door to quietly – and then she turned the key in the lock, and shot the bolt.

The three men inside heard the key turn, and in a trice Jake was at the door, pulling at the handle.

'She's locked us in!' he raged. 'And shot the bolt, too.'

'Yell for Markhoff!' shouted Red, trembling with fury. And Markhoff, left down in the room at the bottom of the stairs, suddenly heard yells and shouts and tremendous hammerings at the door! He tore up at once, wondering what in the world had happened.

Jo was hiding in the next room. As soon as Markhoff went to the door and shot back the bolt she slipped out and was down the spiral stairway in a trice, unseen by Markhoff. She grinned to herself and hugged something to her thin little chest.

It was the big key belonging to the door upstairs. Nobody could unlock that door now – the key was missing. Jo had it!

'Unlock the door!' shouted Red. 'That kid's gone.'

'There's no key!' yelled back Markhoff. 'She must have taken it. I'll go after her.'

But it was one thing to go after Jo and quite another to find her. She seemed to have disappeared into thin air.

Markhoff raged through every room, but she was nowhere to be seen. He went out into the courtyard and looked round there.

Actually she had made her way to the kitchen and found the larder. She was very hungry and wanted something to eat. There was nobody in the kitchen at all, though a fine fire burned in the big range there.

She slipped into the larder, took the key from the outer side of the door and locked herself in. She saw that there was a small window, and she carefully unfastened it so that she could make her escape if anyone discovered that she was locked in the larder.

Then she tucked in. Three sausage rolls, a large piece of cheese, a hunk of bread, half a meat pie and two jam tarts went the same way. After that Jo felt a lot better. She remembered the others and thought how hungry they must be feeling, too.

She found a rush basket hanging on a nail and slipped some food into it – more sausage rolls, some rockbuns, some cheese and bread. Now, if only she could find the others, how they would welcome her!

Jo put the big key at the bottom of the rush basket. She was feeling very, very pleased with herself. Red and Simmy and Jake were all nicely locked up and out of the way. She didn't fear Markhoff as much as Red. She was sure she could get away from him.

She wasn't even sorry for her father, Simmy.

She had no love for him and no respect, because he was everything that a father shouldn't be.

She heard Markhoff come raging into the kitchen and she clambered quickly up on the larder shelf, ready to drop out of the window if he tried the door. But he didn't. He raged out again, and she heard him no more.

Jo unlocked the door very cautiously. There was now an old woman in the kitchen, standing by the table, folding some clothes she had brought in from the clothes line in the yard. She stared in the greatest surprise at Jo peeping out of the larder.

'What . . . ?' she began, indignantly; but Jo was out of the room before she had even got out the next word. The old dame waddled over to the larder and began to wail as she saw all the empty plates and dishes.

Jo went cautiously into the front hall. She could hear Markhoff upstairs, still tearing about. She smiled delightedly and slipped over to the door.

She undid it and pulled it open. Then, keeping to the wall, she sidled like a weasel to the door that led underground. She opened it and went through, shutting it softly behind her.

Now to find the others. She felt sure they must be down in the caves. How pleased they would be with the food in her basket!

She half-fell down the steep steps, and made her way as quickly as she could down the slanting passage. She had no torch and had to feel her way in the dark. She wasn't in the least afraid. Only when she trod on a sharp stone with her bare foot did she make a sound.

The other three – Julian, Dick and George – were still sitting crouched together with Timmy in the centre. Julian had been once up to the door that led into the yard and had cautiously peered out to see what was to be seen – but had seen nothing at all except for an old woman hanging out some clothes on a line.

The three had decided to wait till night before they did anything. They thought maybe Timmy might have recovered a little then, and would be of some help in protecting them against Red or Markhoff. They half-dozed, sitting together for warmth, enjoying the heat of Timmy's big body.

Timmy growled! Yes, he actually growled – a thing he hadn't done at all so far. George put a warning hand on him. They all sat up, listening. A voice came to them.

'Julian! Dick! Where are you? I've lost my way!'

'It's Jo!' cried Dick, and switched on his torch at once. 'Here we are, Jo! How did you escape? What's happened?'

'Heaps,' said Jo, and came gladly over to them. 'My, it was dark up in those passages without a torch. Somehow I went the wrong way. That's why I yelled. But I hadn't gone far wrong. Have a sausage roll?'

'*What?*' cried three hungry voices, and even Timmy lifted his head and began to sniff at the rush basket that Jo carried.

Jo laughed and opened the basket. She handed out all the food and the three of them fell on it like wolves. 'Jo, you're the eighth wonder of the world,' said Dick. 'Is there anything left in the basket?'

'Yes,' said Jo, and took out the enormous key. 'This, look! I locked Red and Jake and Simmy into that tower room, and here's the key. What do you think of *that*?'

CHAPTER TWENTY-THREE

Markhoff goes hunting

GEORGE TOOK the big key and looked at it with awe. 'Jo! Is this really the key – and you've locked them all in? Honestly, I think you're a marvel.'

'She is,' said Dick, and to Jo's enormous delight he gave her a sudden quick hug. 'I never knew such a girl in my life. Never. She's got the pluck of twenty!'

'It was easy, really,' said Jo, her eyes shining joyfully in the light of the torch. 'You trust me now, Dick, don't you? You won't be mean to me any more, any of you, will you?'

'Of course not,' said Julian. 'You're our friend for ever!'

'Not George's,' said Jo at once.

'Oh yes you are,' said George. 'I take back every single mean thing I said about you. You're as good as a boy.'

This was the very highest compliment that George could ever pay any girl. Jo beamed and gave George a light punch.

'I did it all for Dick, really,' she said. 'But next time I'll do it for you!'

'Goodness, I hope there won't *be* a next time,' said George, with a shiver. 'I can't say I enjoyed one single minute of the last few days.'

Timmy suddenly put his head on Jo's knee. She stroked

him. ‘Look at that!’ she said. ‘He remembers me. He’s better, isn’t he, George?’

George carefully removed Timmy’s head from Jo’s knee to her own. She felt decidedly friendly towards Jo now, but not to the extent of having Timmy put his head on Jo’s knee. She patted him.

‘Yes, he’s better,’ she said. ‘He ate half the sausage roll I gave him, though he sniffed at it like anything first. I think he knows something has been put into his food and now he’s suspicious of it. Good old Timmy.’

They all felt much more lively and cheerful now that they were no longer so dreadfully empty. Julian looked at his watch. ‘It’s getting on towards evening now,’ he said. ‘I wonder what all those fellows are doing?’

Three of them were still locked up! No matter how Markhoff had tried to batter in the door, it held. It was old and immensely strong, and the lock held without showing any sign of giving way even half an inch. Two other men had been called in from the garage to help, but except that the door looked decidedly worse for wear, it stood there just the same, sturdy and unbreakable.

Simmy and Jake watched Red as he walked up and down the tower room like a caged lion. They were glad they were two against one. He seemed like a madman to them as he raged and paced up and down.

Markhoff, outside with the other two men he had brought up to help, was getting very worried. No police had arrived as yet (and wouldn’t either, because Joanna hadn't been able to tell them anything except that she knew Julian and Dick had gone to see a man called Red – but where he lived she had no idea!).

But Red and Markhoff didn't know this – they felt sure that a police ambush was somewhere nearby. If only they could get away in the helicopter before anything else happened!

'Markhoff! Take Carl and Tom and go down into those underground caves,' ordered Red at last. 'Those children are sure to be there – it's the only place for them to hide. They can't get out of here because the front gate is locked and bolted, and the wall's too high to climb. Get hold of the kids and search them for the key.'

So Markhoff and two burly fellows went downstairs and out of the door. They crossed the yard to the door that led to the caves.

They got down the steep steps and were soon stumbling along the narrow, slanting passage, their nailed boots making a great noise as they went. They hung on to the hand-rail when they came to the difficult stretch of tunnel, and finally came out into the cave that had the hole in the floor.

There was nobody there. The children had heard the noise of the coming men, and had hurriedly swung themselves down through the hole into the cave below.

They ran through into another cave, the sour-smelling one where bats lived and slept. Then round the rocky corner into the first cave, the curious oval-shaped one that led out to the ledge of rock overlooking the steep cliff.

'There's nowhere to hide,' groaned Julian. He looked back into the cave. At least it was better in there than out on this ledge, outlined by the daylight. He pulled the others back into the cave, and shone his torch up and down the walls to find some corner that they could squeeze behind.

Half-way up the wall was a shelf of rock. He hoisted George up there, and she dragged Timmy up too. Poor Timmy – he wasn't much use to them; he was still so bemused and so very sleepy. He had growled at the noise made by the coming men, but had dropped his head again almost immediately.

Dick got up beside George. Julian found a jutting-out rock and tried to hide behind it, while Jo lay down in a hole beside one wall and covered herself cleverly with sand. Julian couldn't help thinking how sharp Jo was. She always seemed to know the best thing to do.

But as it happened, Jo was the only one to be discovered! It was quite by accident – Markhoff trod on her. He and the other two men had let themselves down through the hole into the cave below, had then gone into the cave of bats, seen no sign of anyone there, and were now in the cave that led to the cliff.

'Those kids aren't here,' said one of the men. 'They've gone to hide somewhere else. What a horrible place this is – let's go back.'

Markhoff was flashing his torch up and down the walls to see if any of the children were crouching behind a jutting rock – and he trod heavily on Jo's hand. She gave an agonised yell, and Markhoff almost dropped his torch!

In a trice he had pulled the girl out of her bed of sand and was shaking her like a rat. 'This is the one we want!' he said to the others. 'She's got the key. Where is it, you little rat? Give it to me or I'll throw you down the cliff!'

Julian was horrified. He felt quite certain that Markhoff really would throw Jo down the cliff, and he was just about to jump down to help her, when he heard her speak.

'All right. Let me go, you brute. Here's the key! You go and let my dad out before the police come! I don't want him caught!'

Markhoff gave an exclamation of triumph, and snatched a shining key out of Jo's hand. He gave her a resounding box on the ear.

'You little toad! You can just stay down here with the others, and it'll be a very, very long stay! Do you know what we're going to do? We're going to roll a big rock over the hole in that other cave's roof – and you'll be prisoners!

'You can't escape upwards – and you won't be able to escape downwards. You'll be dashed on the rocks by the sea if you try to swim away. That'll teach you to interfere!'

The other two men guffawed. 'Good idea, Mark,' said one. 'They'll all be nicely boxed up here and nobody will know where they are! Come on – we've no time to lose. If Red isn't unlocked soon he'll go mad!'

They made their way into the heart of the cliff again, and the listening children heard their footsteps getting fainter. Finally they ceased altogether, as one by one the men levered themselves up through the hole in the roof of the last cave, and disappeared up the narrow, low-roofed tunnel that led to the courtyard.

Julian came out from his hiding-place, looking grim and rather scared. 'That's done it!' he said. 'If those fellows really do block up that hole – and I bet they have already – it looks as if we're here for keeps! As he said, we can't get up, and we can't escape down – the sea's too rough for us to attempt any swimming, and the cliff's unclimbable above the ledge!'

'I'll go and have a look and see if they *have* blocked up that hole,' said Dick. 'They may be bluffing.'

But it hadn't been bluff. When Julian and Dick shone their torches on to the hole in the roof, they saw that a great rock was now blocking it up.

They could not get through the hole again. It was impossible to move the rock from below. They went soberly back to the front cave and sat out on the ledge in the light of the sinking sun.

'It's a pity poor Jo was found,' said George. 'And an even greater pity she had to give up the key! Now Red and the others will go free.'

'They won't,' said Jo, surprisingly. 'I didn't give them the key of the tower room. I'd another key with me – the key of the kitchen larder! And I gave them that.'

'Well, I'm blessed!' said Julian, astounded. 'The things you do, Jo! But how on earth did you happen to have the key of the *larder*?'

Jo told them how she had taken it out and locked herself

in when she was having a meal there.

'I had to unlock the door to get out again, of course,' she said. 'And I thought I'd take that key, too, because, who knows? – I might have wanted to get into that larder again and lock myself in with the food!'

'No one will ever get the better of you, Jo,' said Dick with the utmost conviction. 'Never. You're as cute as a bagful of monkeys. So you've still got the right key with you?'

'Yes,' said Jo. 'And Red and my dad and Jake are still locked up in the tower room!'

But suddenly a most disagreeable thought struck Dick. 'Wait a bit!' he said. 'What's going to happen when they find they've got the *wrong* key? They'll be down here again, and my word, what'll happen to us all then!'

CHAPTER TWENTY-FOUR

A grand surprise

THE THOUGHT that the men might soon return even angrier than they had been before was most unpleasant.

'As soon as Markhoff tries the key in the door of the tower room he'll find it won't unlock it, and he'll know that Jo has tricked him!' said George.

'And then he'll be in such a fury that he'll tear down here again, and goodness knows what will happen to us!' groaned Julian. 'What shall we do? Hide again?'

'No,' said Dick. 'Let's get out of here and climb down the cliff to the sea. I'd feel safer there than up here in this cave. We might be able to find a better hiding-place down on the rocks in that little cove.'

'It's a pity my boat's smashed,' said George, with a sigh for her lovely boat. 'And, I say – how are we going to get old Timmy down?'

There was a conference about this. Timmy couldn't climb down, that was certain. Jo remembered the rope still hanging down the side of the cliff to the ledges below – the one she had tied there to help Julian and Dick climb up the steep sides of the cliff.

'I know,' she said, her quick mind working hard again. 'You go down first, Julian, then Dick. Then George can go

– each of you holding on to the rope as you climb down, in case you fall.

'Then I'll haul up the rope and tie old Timmy to it, round his waist – and I'll lower him down to you. He's so sleepy still, he won't struggle. He won't even know what's happening!'

'But what about you?' said Dick. 'You'll be last of all. Will you mind? You'll be all alone up on this ledge, with the men coming behind you at any minute.'

'No, I don't mind,' said Jo. 'But let's be quick.'

Julian went down first, glad of the rope to hold to as his feet and hands searched for crevices and cracks. Then came Dick, almost slipping in his anxiety to get down.

Then George climbed down, slowly and anxiously, not at all liking the steep cliff. Once she glanced down to the sea below, and felt sick. She shut her eyes for a moment and clung with one hand to the rope.

It was a dreadful business getting Timmy down. George stood below, anxiously waiting. Jo found it very difficult to tie Timmy safely. He was big and heavy, and didn't like being tied up at all, though he really seemed hardly to know what was going on. At last Jo had got the knots well and securely tied, and called out to the others.

'Here he comes. Watch out that the rope doesn't break. Oh, dear – I wish he wouldn't struggle – now he's bumped himself against the cliff!'

It was not at all a nice experience for poor Timmy. He

swung to and fro on the rope as he was slowly let down, and was amazed to find that he was suspended in mid air. Above him Jo panted and puffed.

'Oh, he's so awfully heavy! I hope I shan't have to let go. Look out for him!' she screamed.

The weight was too much for her just at the last, and the rope was let out with rather a rush. Fortunately Timmy was only about six feet up then, and Julian and George managed to catch him as he suddenly descended.

'I'm coming now,' called Jo, and without even holding the rope, or looking at it, she climbed down like a monkey, seeming to find handholds and footholds by magic. The others watched her admiringly. Soon she was standing beside them. George was untying Timmy.

'Thanks awfully, Jo,' said George, looking up gratefully at Jo. 'You're a wonder. Tim must have been frightfully heavy.'

'He was,' said Jo, giving him a pat. 'I nearly dropped him. Well – what's the next move?'

'We'll hunt round this peculiar little cove a bit and see if there's any place we can hide,' said Julian. 'You go that way, George, and we'll go this.'

They parted, and began to hunt for a hiding-place. As far as Julian and Dick could see there was none at all, at least on the side they were exploring. The sea swept into the cove, swelling and subsiding – and just outside the great waves battered on to the rocks. There was certainly no chance of swimming out.

There was suddenly an excited shriek from George. 'JU! Come here. Look what I've found!'

They all rushed round to where George was standing, behind a big ledge of rock. She pointed to a great mass of something draped with seaweed.

'A boat! It's covered with seaweed – but it's a boat!'

'It's *your* boat!' yelled Dick, suddenly, and began to pull the fronds of seaweed madly off the hidden boat. 'Markhoff *didn't* smash it! It's here, perfectly all right. He couldn't find it – it was hidden so well with seaweed – so he just came back to Red and told him a lie.'

'He didn't smash it!' shouted Jo, and she, too, began to pull away the seaweed. 'It's quite all right – there's nothing wrong with it. He didn't smash it!'

The four children were so tremendously surprised and joyful that they thumped each other ridiculously on the back, and leapt about like mad things. They had their boat after all – George's good, sound boat. They could escape, hip hip hurrah!

A roar from above made them fall silent.

They gazed up, startled. Markhoff and the other two men were on the ledge far above, shouting and shaking their fists.

'You wait till we get you!' yelled Markhoff.

'Quick, quick!' said Julian, urgently, pulling at the boat. 'We've got just a chance. Pull her down to the water, pull hard!'

Markhoff was now coming down the cliff, and Jo

wished she had untied the rope before she herself had climbed down, for Markhoff was finding it very useful. She tugged at the boat with the others, wishing it wasn't so heavy.

The boat was almost down to the water when something happened. Timmy, who had been gazing at everything in a most bewildered manner, suddenly slid off the ledge he was on and fell straight into the sea. George gave a scream.

'Oh, Timmy! He's in the water, quick, quick – he's too doped to swim! He'll drown!'

Julian and Dick didn't dare to stop heaving at the boat, because they could see that Markhoff would soon be down beside them. George rushed to Timmy, who was splashing around in the waves, still looking surprised and bemused.

But the water had an amazing effect on him. It was cold and it seemed to bring him to his senses quite suddenly. He became much more lively and swam strongly to the rock off which he had slipped. He clambered out with George's help, barking loudly.

The boat slid into the water, and Julian grabbed at George. 'Come on. In you get. Buck up!'

Jo was in the boat and so was Dick. George, trying to clutch at Timmy, was hauled in, too. Julian took a despairing look at Markhoff, who was almost at the end of the rope, about to jump down. They just wouldn't get off in time!

Timmy suddenly slipped out of George's grasp and tore madly over to the cliff barking warningly. He seemed to

be perfectly all right. The sudden coldness of the sea had washed away all his dopeyness and sleepiness. Timmy was himself again!

Markhoff was about five feet above the ledge when he heard Timmy barking. He looked down in horror and saw the big dog trying to jump up at him. He tried to climb up quickly, out of Timmy's reach.

'Woof!' barked Timmy. 'Woof, woof, woof! Grrrrrrr!'

'Look out – he'll have your foot off!' yelled one of the men above on the ledge.

'He's mad – angry – he's savage. Look out, Mark!'

Markhoff *was* looking out! He was terrified. He clambered up another few feet, and then found that Timmy was making runs at the cliff to try and get up after him. He went up a bit further and clung to the rope with one hand, afraid of falling and being pounced on by the furious Timmy.

'Come on, Timmy!' suddenly cried George. 'Come on!'

The four of them had now got the boat on the waves, and if only they had Timmy they could set off and row round the rocks at the cave entrance before Markhoff could possibly reach them.

'Timmy! Timmy!'

Timmy heard, cast a last regretful look at Markhoff's legs, and bounded across to the boat. He leapt right in and stood there, still barking madly.

Markhoff dropped down the rope to the ledge – but he was too late. The boat shot out to the entrance of the cove and rounded it. In half a minute it had disappeared round the rocky corner and was out at sea.

Julian and Dick rowed steadily. George put her arms round Timmy and buried her face in his fur. Jo did the same.

'He's all right again, quite all right,' said George, happily.

'Yes, falling into the cold water did it,' agreed Jo, ruffling up his fur. 'Good old Timmy!'

Timmy was now snuffling about in the bottom of the boat joyfully. He had smelt a lovely smell. Jo wondered what he had found. Then she knew.

'It's the packet of sandwiches we brought with us in the boat and never ate!' she cried. 'Good old Timmy – he's wolfing the lot!'

'Let him!' said Julian, pulling hard at the oars. 'He deserves them all! My word, it's nice to hear his bark again and see his tail wagging.'

And wag it certainly did. It never stopped. The world had come right again for Timmy, he could see and hear properly again, he could bark and caper and jump – and he had his beloved George with him once more.

'Now for home,' said Julian. 'Anne *will* be pleased to see us. Gosh, what a time we've had!'

CHAPTER TWENTY-FIVE

Everything OK

IT WAS getting dark as George's boat came into Kirrin Bay. It had seemed a very long pull indeed, and everyone was tired out. The girls had helped in the rowing when the boys had almost collapsed from exhaustion, and Timmy had cheered everyone up by his sudden high spirits.

'Honestly, his tail hasn't stopped wagging since he got into the boat,' said George. 'He's so pleased to be himself again!'

A small figure was on the beach as they came in, half-lost in the darkness. It was Anne. She called out to them in a trembling voice.

'Is it really you? I've been watching for you all day long! Are you all right?'

'Yes! And we've got George and Timmy, too!' shouted back Dick, as the boat scraped on the shingle. 'We're fine!'

They jumped out, Timmy too, and hauled the boat up the beach. Anne gave a hand, almost crying with joy to have them all again.

'It's bad enough being in the middle of an adventure,' she said, 'but it's much, much worse when you're left out. I'll never be left out again!'

'Woof,' said Timmy, wagging his tail in full agreement. He never wanted to be left out of adventures either!

They all went home – rather slowly, because they were so tired. Joanna was on the look-out for them, as she had been all day. She screamed for joy when she saw George. 'George! You've got George at last! Oh, you bad children, you've been away all day and I didn't know where and I've been worried to death. George, are you all right?'

'Yes, thank you,' said George, who felt as if she was about to fall asleep at any moment. 'I just want something to eat before I fall absolutely sound asleep!'

'But where have you been all day? What have you been doing?' cried Joanna as she bustled off to get them a meal.

'I got so worked up I went to the police – and what a silly I felt – I couldn't tell them where you'd gone or anything. All I could say was you'd gone to find a man called Red, and had rowed away in George's boat!'

'The police have been up and down the coast in a motorboat ever since,' said Anne. 'Trying to spot you, but they couldn't.'

'No. Our boat was well hidden,' said Dick. 'And so were we! So well hidden that I began to think we'd stay hidden for the rest of our lives.'

The telephone rang. Julian jumped. 'Oh, good – you've had the telephone mended. I'll go and phone the police when you've answered this call, Joanna.'

But it was the police themselves on the telephone,

very pleased to hear Joanna saying excitedly that all the children were back safely. 'We'll be up in ten minutes,' they said.

In ten minutes' time the five children and Timmy were tucking into a good meal. 'Don't stop,' said the police sergeant, when he came into the room with the constable the children had seen before. 'Just talk while you're eating.'

So they talked. They told about every single thing. First George told a bit, then Jo, then Dick, then Julian. At first the sergeant was bewildered, but then the bits of information began to piece themselves together in his mind like a jigsaw puzzle.

'Will my father go to prison?' asked Jo.

'I'm afraid so,' said the sergeant.

'Bad luck, Jo,' said Dick.

'I don't mind,' said Jo. 'I'm better off when he's away – I don't have to do things he tells me then.'

'We'll see if we can't fix you up with a nice home,' said the sergeant, kindly. 'You've run wild, Jo – you want looking after.'

'I don't want to go to a Home for Bad Girls,' said Jo, looking scared.

'I shan't let you,' said Dick. 'You're one of the pluckiest kids I've ever known. We'll none of us let you go to a home. We'll find someone who'll be kind to you, someone like – like . . .'

'Like *me*,' said Joanna, who was listening, and she put her arm round Jo and gave her a squeeze. 'I've got a cousin who'd like a ragamuffin like you – a bad little girl with a very good heart. Don't you fret. We'll look after you.'

'I wouldn't mind living with somebody like you,' said Jo, in an offhand way. 'I wouldn't be mean any more then, and I daresay I wouldn't be bad. I'd like to see Dick and all of you sometimes, though.'

'You will if you're good,' said Dick, with a grin. 'But mind – if I ever hear you've got in at anyone's pantry window again, or anything like that, I'll never see you again!'

Jo grinned. She was very happy. She suddenly remembered something and put her hand into the little rush basket she still carried. She took out an enormous key.

'Here you are,' she said to the sergeant. 'Here's the key to the tower room. I bet Red and the others are still locked up there, ready for you to catch! My, won't they get a shock when *you* unlock the door and walk in!'

'Quite a lot of people are going to get shocks,' said the sergeant, putting away his very full notebook. 'Georgina, you're lucky to get away unharmed, you and your dog. By the way, we got in touch with a friend of your father's, when we tried to find out about those papers that were stolen. He says your father gave him all his important American papers before he went – so this fellow Red hasn't anything of value at all. He went to all his trouble for nothing.'

'Do you know anything about Red?' asked Julian. 'He seemed a bit mad to me.'

'If he's the fellow we think he is, he's not very sane,' said the sergeant. 'We'll be glad to have him under lock and key – and that man Markhoff too. He's not as clever as Red, but he's dangerous.'

'I hope he hasn't escaped in that helicopter,' said Dick. 'He meant to go tonight.'

'Well, we'll be there in under an hour or so,' said the sergeant. 'I'll just use your telephone, if I may, and set things going.'

Things were certainly set going that night! Cars roared

up to Red's house, and the gate was broken in when no one came to open it. The helicopter was still in the yard – but alas! it was on its side, smashed beyond repair. The children were told afterwards that Markhoff and the other two men had tried to set off in it, but there was something wrong – and it had risen some way and then fallen back to the yard.

The old woman was trying to look after the three hurt men, who had crawled from their seats and gone to bathe their cuts and bruises. Markhoff had hurt his head, and showed no fight at all.

'And what about Red?' the sergeant asked Markhoff. 'Is he still locked up?'

'Yes,' said Markhoff, savagely. 'And a good thing, too. You'll have to break that door down with a battering-ram to get him and the others out.'

'Oh no, we shan't,' said the sergeant, and produced the key. Markhoff stared at it.

'That kid!' he said. 'She gave me the key of the larder. Wait till I get her – she'll be sorry.'

'It'll be a long wait, Markhoff,' said the sergeant. 'A long, long wait. We'll have to take you off with us, I'm afraid.'

Red, Simmy and Jake were still locked up, and were mad with rage. But they saw that the game was up, and it wasn't long before all of them were safely tucked away in police cars.

'A very, very nice little haul,' said the sergeant to one

of his men. 'Very neat, too – three of them all locked up ready for us!'

'What about that kid, Jo?' said the man. 'She seems a bad lot, and as clever as they make them!'

'She's going to have a chance now,' said the sergeant. 'Everybody has a chance sometimes, and this is hers. She's just about half-and-half, I reckon – half bad and half good. But she'll be all right now she's got a chance!'

Jo was sleeping in Joanna's room again. The rest were in their own bedrooms, getting ready for bed. They suddenly didn't feel sleepy any more. Timmy especially was very lively, darting in and out of the rooms, and sending the landing mats sliding about all over the place.

'Timmy! If you jump on my bed again I'll slam the door on you!' threatened Anne. But she didn't, of course. It was so lovely to see old Timmy quite himself once more.

The telephone bell suddenly rang, and made everyone jump.

'*Now* what's up?' said Julian, and went down in the hall to answer it. A voice spoke in his ear.

'Is that Kirrin 011? This is Telegrams. There is a cable for you, with reply prepaid. I am now going to read it.'

'Go ahead,' said Julian.

'It is from Seville in Spain,' said the voice, 'and reads as follows:

"HERE IS OUR ADDRESS PLEASE CABLE BACK SAYING IF EVERYTHING ALL RIGHT – UNCLE QUENTIN".'

Julian repeated the message to the others, who had now crowded round him in the hall. 'What reply shall I give?' he asked. 'No good upsetting them now everything is over!'

'Not a bit of good,' said Dick. 'Say what you like!'

'Right!' said Julian, and turned to the telephone again. 'Hallo – here is the reply message, please. Ready?

"HAVING A MOST EXCITING TIME WITH LOTS OF FUN AND GAMES EVERYTHING OK – JULIAN".'

'Everything OK,' repeated Anne, as they went upstairs to bed once more. 'That's what I like to hear at the end of an adventure. Everything OK.'

THE FAMOUS FIVE

FIVE ON A HIKE TOGETHER

Have you read all THE FAMOUS FIVE books?

1. Five on a Treasure Island
2. Five Go Adventuring Again
3. Five Run Away Together
4. Five Go to Smuggler's Top
5. Five Go Off in a Caravan
6. Five on Kirrin Island Again
7. Five Go Off to Camp
8. Five Get Into Trouble
9. Five Fall Into Adventure
10. Five on a Hike Together
11. Five Have a Wonderful Time
12. Five Go Down to the Sea
13. Five Go to Mystery Moor
14. Five Have Plenty of Fun
15. Five on a Secret Trail
16. Five Go to Billycock Hill
17. Five Get Into a Fix
18. Five on Finniston Farm
19. Five Go to Demon's Rocks
20. Five Have a Mystery to Solve
21. Five Are Together Again

The Famous Five Colour Short Stories

1. Five and a Half-Term Adventure
2. George's Hair is Too Long
3. Good Old Timmy
4. A Lazy Afternoon
5. Well Done, Famous Five
6. Five Have a Puzzling Time
7. Happy Christmas, Five
8. When Timmy Chased the Cat

Enid Blyton®

THE FAMOUS FIVE

FIVE ON A HIKE TOGETHER

Illustrated by Eileen A. Soper

HODDER

HODDER CHILDREN'S BOOKS

First published in Great Britain in 1951 by Hodder & Stoughton
This edition published in 2016

21

A CIP catalogue record for this book is available from the British Library.

ISBN 978 1 444 93640 7

Printed and bound in Great Britain by Clays Ltd, Elcograf S.p.A.

The paper and board used in this book are made from wood from responsible sources.

Hodder Children's Books
An imprint of
Hachette Children's Group
Part of Hodder & Stoughton
Carmelite House
50 Victoria Embankment
London EC4Y 0DZ

An Hachette UK Company
www.hachette.co.uk
www.hachettechildrens.co.uk

CONTENTS

1 A LETTER FROM JULIAN 1
2 SETTING OFF 10
3 ACROSS THE COUNTRYSIDE 19
4 GEORGE IS WORRIED 28
5 ANNE AND DICK 37
6 IN THE MIDDLE OF THE NIGHT 47
7 IN THE MORNING 55
8 ALL TOGETHER AGAIN 64
9 DICK SURPRISES THE OTHERS 72
10 AN ANGRY POLICEMAN AND A FINE LUNCH 81
11 JULIAN'S IDEA 90
12 A HIDING PLACE AT TWO-TREES 98
13 A NIGHT IN THE CELLAR 107
14 WHERE IS THE *SAUCY JANE*? 115
15 MAGGIE – AND DIRTY DICK 124
16 OUT ON THE RAFT 133
17 TIT FOR TAT! 143
18 A VERY EXCITING TIME 152
19 MAGGIE AND DICK ARE ANNOYED 160
20 IN THE MOONLIGHT 169
21 THE SACK AT LAST! 177
22 AN EXCITING FINISH 186

CHAPTER ONE

A letter from Julian

'ANNE!' SHOUTED George, running after her cousin as she went along to her classroom. 'Anne! I've just been down to the letterboard and there's a letter from your brother Julian. I've brought it for you.'

Anne stopped. 'Oh thanks,' she said. 'What *can* Julian want? He only wrote a few days ago – it's most extraordinary for him to write again so soon. It must be something important.'

'Well, open it and see,' said George. 'Hurry up – I've got a maths class to go to.'

Anne ripped open the envelope. She pulled out a sheet of notepaper and read it quickly. She looked up at George, her eyes shining.

'George! Julian and Dick have got a few days off at our half-term weekend! Somebody's won a wonderful scholarship or something, and the boys have got two days tacked on to a weekend to celebrate! They want us to join them in a hike, and all go off together.'

'What a glorious idea!' said George. 'Good old Julian. I bet he thought of that. Let's read the letter, Anne.'

But before she could read it a mistress came along. 'Georgina! You should be in class – and you too, Anne.'

George scowled. She hated to be called by her full name. She went off without a word. Anne tucked the letter into her pocket and rushed off joyfully. Half-term with her brothers, Julian and Dick – and with George and Timmy the dog. Could anything be better?

She and George talked about it again after morning school. 'We get from Friday morning till Tuesday,' said George. 'The boys are getting the same. What luck! They don't usually have a half-term in the winter term.'

'They can't go home because the painters are in our house,' said Anne. 'That's why I was going home with you, of course. But I'm sure your mother won't mind if we go off with the boys. Your father never likes us in the middle of the term.'

'No, he doesn't,' said George. 'He's always deep in the middle of some wonderful idea, and he hates to be disturbed. It will suit everyone if we go off on a hike.'

'Julian says he will telephone to us tonight and arrange everything,' said Anne. 'I hope it will be a nice fine weekend. It will still be October, so there's a chance of a bit of warm sunshine.'

'The woods will be beautiful,' said George. 'And won't Timmy enjoy himself? Let's go and tell him the news.'

The boarding school that the two girls were at was one that allowed the children to bring their own pets to school. There were kennels down in the yard for various

dogs, and Timmy lived there during term-time. The two girls went to get him.

He heard their footsteps at once and began to bark excitedly. He scraped at the gate of the kennel yard, wishing for the thousandth time that he could find out how to open it.

He flung himself on the two girls, licking and pawing and barking.

'Silly dog. Mad dog!' said George, and thumped his back affectionately. 'Listen, Tim – we're going off for the weekend with Julian and Dick! What do you think of that? We're going on a hike, so you'll love it. All through the woods and up the hills and goodness knows where!'

Timmy seemed to understand every word. He cocked up his ears, put his head on one side and listened intently while George was speaking.

'Woof,' he said, at the end, as if he approved thoroughly. Then off he went with the girls for his walk, his plumy tail wagging happily. He didn't like term-time nearly as much as the holidays – but he was quite prepared to put up with kennel life so long as he could be near his beloved George.

Julian rang up that night as he had promised. He had got everything planned already. Anne listened, thrilled.

'It sounds super,' she said. 'Yes – we can meet where you say, and we'll be there as near as we can on time. Anyway, we can wait about if you others aren't there. Yes – we'll bring the things you say. Oh, Julian, won't it be fun?'

'What's he say?' asked George impatiently when at last Anne put the receiver down. 'You might have let me have a word with Julian. I wanted to tell him all about Timmy.'

'He doesn't want to waste an expensive telephone call listening to you raving about Timmy,' said Anne. 'He asked how he was and I said "fine", and that's all he wanted to know about Tim. He's made all the arrangements. I'll tell you what they are.'

The girls went off to a corner of their common room and sat down. Timmy was there too. He was allowed in at certain times, and so were three other dogs belonging to the girls. Each dog behaved well – he knew that if he didn't he would be taken back to the kennels at once!

'Julian says that he and Dick can get off immediately after breakfast,' said Anne. 'So can we, so that's all right. He says we've got to take very little with us – just night things, toothbrush, hairbrush and flannel and a rolled-up mac. And any biscuits or chocolate we can buy. Have you any money left?'

'A bit,' said George. 'Not much. Enough to buy a few bars of chocolate, I think. Anyway, you've got all the biscuits your mother sent last week. We can take some of those.'

'Yes. And the barley sugar one of my aunts sent,' said Anne. 'But Julian says we're not to take much because this is to be a proper hike, and we'll get tired if we have to carry a heavy load. Oh, he said put in two pairs of extra socks.'

'Right,' said George, and she patted Timmy who was lying close beside her. 'There's going to be a long walky-walk, Tim. Won't you love that!'

Timmy grunted comfortably. He wondered if there would be any rabbits on the walk. A walk wasn't really exciting unless there were rabbits all over the place. Timmy thought it was a pity that rabbits were allowed to live down holes. They always disappeared most unfairly just when he had nearly caught one!

Anne and George went to see their housemistress to tell

her that they were not going to Kirrin Cottage after all, but were going walking.

'My brother says he has written to you,' said Anne. 'So you'll know all about it tomorrow, Miss Peters. And George's mother will be writing too. We can go, can't we?'

'Oh, yes – it will be a lovely half-term for you!' said Miss Peters. 'Especially if this sunny weather lasts. Where are you going?'

'Over the moors,' said Anne. 'In the very loneliest, most deserted parts that Julian can find! We might see deer and wild ponies and perhaps even a few badgers. We shall walk and walk.'

'But where will you sleep if the parts you are going to are so very lonely?' asked Miss Peters.

'Oh Julian is arranging all that,' said George. 'He's been looking up little inns and farmhouses on the map, and we shall make for those at night. It will be too cold to sleep out of doors.'

'It certainly will!' said Miss Peters. 'Well, don't get into trouble, that's all. I know what you five are when you get together. I imagine Timmy is going with you too?'

'Of *course*!' said George. 'I wouldn't go if he didn't go! I couldn't leave him here alone.'

The two girls got their things ready as Friday came near. The biscuits were taken out of the tin and put into paper bags. The barley sugar was put into a bag too, and the bars of chocolate.

Both girls had rucksacks with straps for their shoulders. They packed and repacked them several times. One by one more and more things were added. Anne felt she must take a book to read. George said they must each take a torch with a new battery.

'And what about biscuits for Timmy?' she said. 'I simply must take something for him. He'd like a bone too – a big one that he can chew and chew and that I can put back into the bag for another time.'

'Well, let me carry all the biscuits and chocolate then if you're going to put a smelly old bone into your bag,' said Anne. 'I don't see why you want to take *anything* for Timmy – he can always have something to eat when we do – wherever we have a meal.'

George decided not to take the bone. She had fetched one from his kennel, and it certainly was big and heavy, and equally certainly it was smelly. She took it back to the kennel again, Timmy following her rather puzzled. Why keep carrying his bone here and there? He didn't approve at all.

It seemed a long time till Friday, but at last it came. Both girls woke up very early indeed. George was out in the kennels before breakfast, brushing and combing Timmy to make him look spruce and tidy for Julian and Dick. He knew it was the day they were to set off and he was as excited as the two girls.

'We'd better eat a good breakfast,' said Anne. 'We might have to wait some time before our next meal. Let's slip off immediately after breakfast. It's lovely to feel free of school and bells and timetables – but I shan't feel *really* free till I'm outside the school grounds!'

They ate an enormous breakfast though really they were too excited to want much. Then they got their rucksacks, ready-packed the night before, said goodbye to Miss Peters, and went to fetch Timmy.

He was waiting impatiently for them, and barked madly when they came near. In a trice he was out of his kennel-yard and capering round them, almost tripping them up.

'Goodbye, Anne and George!' yelled one of their friends. 'Have a good time on your hike – and it's no good coming back on Tuesday and telling us you've had one of your usual hair-raising adventures, because we just shan't believe it!'

'Woof,' said Timmy. 'Woof, woof!' Which meant that *he* was going to have adventures with hundreds of rabbits, anyway!

CHAPTER TWO

Setting off

JULIAN AND Dick were also on their way, very pleased to have such an unexpectedly long weekend.

'I never liked Willis or Johnson much,' said Julian, as they walked out of the school grounds. 'Awful swotters they were – never had any time for games or fun. But I take my hat off to them today! Because of their swotting they've won medals and scholarships and goodness knows what – and we've got a weekend off in celebration! Good old Willis and Johnson!'

'Hear hear,' said Dick. 'But I bet they'll sit in a corner with their books all the weekend – they won't know if it's a brilliant day like this, or pouring with rain like yesterday! Poor mutts!'

'They'd hate to go off on a hike,' said Julian. 'It would be utter misery to them. Do you remember how awful Johnson was at rugger? He never knew which goal he was playing against – always ran the wrong way!'

'Yes. But he must have got terrific brains,' said Dick. 'Why are we talking about Willis and Johnson? I can think of plenty of more interesting things. Anne and George, for instance – and old Tim. I hope they'll manage to get off in time all right.'

Julian had carefully looked up a large-scale map of the moors that lay between the two schools that he and the girls went to. They were vast stretches of lonely heathery land, dotted with farms here and there, with a few small cottages, and some inns.

'We'll keep right off the main roads, and the second-and third-grades,' he said. 'We'll take the little lanes and paths. I wonder what Timmy will say if we see deer. He'll wonder what in the world they are!'

'He'll only be interested in rabbits,' said Dick. 'I hope he's not as fat as he was last hols. I think we must have given him too many ice-creams and too much chocolate!'

'Well, he won't get that in term-time!' said Julian. 'The girls don't get as much pocket money as we do. Buck up – there's the bus!'

They ran for the little country bus that rumbled along the country lanes, taking people to market, or to the tiny villages that lay here and there tucked away in the moor. It stopped most obligingly for them, and they leapt in.

'Ha! Running away from school?' said the conductor. 'Have to report you, you know!'

'Very funny,' said Julian, bored at this joke, which the conductor produced regularly every time a boy got on board with a rucksack over his shoulders.

They had to get out at the next village and cut across country to get to another bus route. They managed to catch a bus there easily and settled down comfortably in their seats. It was half an hour's run from there to where they had planned to meet the girls.

'Here you are, young sirs,' called the conductor, as the bus ran into a village. It had a wide green on which geese cackled, and a small pond for ducks. 'You wanted Pippin Village, didn't you? We don't go any farther – we just turn round and go back.'

'Thanks,' said the boys and got out. 'Now – are the girls here or not?' said Julian. 'They have to walk from a tiny railway station about two miles away.'

They were not there. Julian and Dick went to have a drink of orangeade at the village store. They had hardly finished when they saw the two girls looking in at the door.

'Julian! Dick! We guessed you'd be eating or drinking!' said Anne, and she rushed at her brothers. 'We came as quickly as we could. The engine broke down – it was such a funny little train! All the passengers got out and advised the engine-driver what to do!'

'Hallo!' said Julian, and gave Anne a hug. He was very fond of his young sister. 'Hallo, George! My, you've grown bigger, haven't you?'

'I have not,' said George, indignantly. 'And Timmy isn't fat either, so don't tell him he is.'

'Julian's pulling your leg as usual,' said Dick, giving George a friendly slap on the back. 'All the same, you've grown a bit – you'll soon be as tall as I am. Hallo, Timmy! Good dog, fine dog! Tongue as wet as usual? Yes, it is! I never knew a dog with a wetter tongue than yours!'

Timmy went nearly mad with joy at being with all four of his friends. He leapt round them, barking, wagging his long tail and sending a pile of tins crashing to the floor in his delight.

'Now, now!' said the shop-woman, emerging from a dark little room at the back. 'Take that dog out. He's gone mad!'

'Don't you girls want a drink of ginger-beer or something?' asked Julian, getting hold of Timmy's collar. 'You'd better, because we don't want to have to carry heavy bottles of drinkables with us.'

'Where are we going to set off to?' asked George. 'Yes, I'd like ginger-beer please. Get down, Timmy. Anyone would think you'd been away from Julian and Dick for at least ten years!'

'It probably does seem like ten years to him,' said Anne. 'I say – are those sandwiches?'

She pointed to a ledge at the back of the counter. There was a little pile of sandwiches there, looking most appetising.

'Yes, they're sandwiches, Miss,' said the shop-woman, opening two bottles of ginger-beer. 'I've made them for my son who works over at Blackbush Farm – he'll be in for them soon.'

'I suppose you couldn't make *us* some, could you?' asked Julian. 'We wouldn't need to bother about trying to get to some village at lunch time then. They look jolly good.'

'Yes. I can make you all you want,' said the shop-woman, putting two glasses down in front of the girls. 'What do you want – cheese, egg, ham or pork?'

'Well – we'd like some of all of those,' said Julian. 'The bread looks so nice too.'

'I make it myself,' said the woman, pleased. 'All right – I'll go and make you some. You tell me if anyone comes into the shop while I'm gone.'

She disappeared. 'That's good,' said Julian. 'If she makes plenty of those we can avoid villages all day and have a really good day of exploration – treading where no foot has trod before and all that!'

'How many can you manage each?' asked the woman, suddenly reappearing. 'My son, he has six – that's twelve rounds of bread.'

'Well – could you manage eight sandwiches for each of us?' said Julian. The woman looked astonished. 'It's to last us all day,' he explained, and she nodded and disappeared again.

'That's a nice little sum for her,' said Anne. 'Eight sandwiches each, making sixteen rounds of bread – for four people!'

'Well, let's hope she's got a bread-cutting machine!' said Dick. 'Or we'll be here for keeps! Hallo – who's this?'

A tall man appeared at the entrance of the shop, a bicycle in his hand. 'Ma!' he called.

The children guessed who he was at once – the son who worked over at Blackbush Farm. He had come for his sandwiches!

'Your mother is hard at work cutting sixty-four rounds of bread,' said Dick. 'Shall I get her for you?'

'No. I'm in a hurry,' said the man, and he set his bicycle by the door, came in, reached over the counter for his sandwiches and then went back to his bicycle.

'Tell my mother I've been in,' he said. 'And you might tell her I'll be late home today – got to take some stuff to the prison.'

He was off at once, sailing away down the road on his bicycle. The old woman suddenly came in, a knife in one hand, a loaf in the other.

'Did I hear Jim?' she said. 'Oh yes – he's got his sandwiches. You should have told me he was in!'

'He said he was in a hurry,' explained Julian. 'And he said we were to tell you he'd be late today because he had to take some stuff to the prison.'

'I've got another son there,' said the woman. The four looked at her. Did she mean he was a prisoner? And what prison?

She guessed their thoughts and smiled. 'Oh, my Tom isn't a prisoner!' she said. 'He's a warder – a fine fellow. Not a nice job there though – I'm always afraid of those men in prison – a fierce lot, a bad lot!'

'Yes – I've heard there is a big prison on this moor,' said Julian. 'It's marked on our map too. We're not going near it, of course.'

'No. Don't you take the girls near there,' said the woman, disappearing again. 'If I don't get on with your sandwiches you'll not have them before tomorrow morning.'

Only one customer came in while the children were waiting – a solemn old man smoking a clay pipe. He looked round the shop, couldn't see the woman, took a packet of blancmange powder, which he slipped into his pocket, and put the money down on the counter.

'Tell 'er when 'er comes,' he mumbled with his pipe still in his mouth, and out he shuffled. Timmy growled. The old man smelt very unwashed and Timmy didn't like him.

At last the sandwiches were finished and the old woman appeared again. She had packed them up neatly in four parcels of greaseproof paper, and had pencilled on each what they were. Julian read what she had written and winked at the others.

'My word – we're in for a grand time!' he said. 'Cheese, Pork, Ham and Egg – and what's this?'

'Oh, that's four slices of my home-made fruit cake,' said the old woman. 'I'm not charging you for that. It's just so that you can taste it!'

'It looks like half the cake!' said Julian, touched. 'But we shall pay for it, with many thanks. How much is all that?'

She told him. Julian put down the money and added five pence for the cake. 'There you are, and many thanks,' he said. 'And that money there was left by an old fellow with a clay pipe who took a packet of blancmange powder.'

'That would be Old Gupps,' said the woman. 'Well, I hope you'll enjoy your tour. Come back here if you want any more sandwiches cut! If you eat all those today you won't do badly!'

'Woof,' said Timmy, hoping that he too would share a few. The woman produced a bone for him, and he took it up in his mouth.

'Thanks!' Julian said. 'Come on – now we'll really start!'

CHAPTER THREE

Across the countryside

THEY SET off at last, Timmy running in front. School already seemed far behind them. The October sun shone down warmly, and the trees in the village glowed yellow and red and golden, dressed in their autumn colourings. A few leaves floated down in the breeze, but not until there was a real frost would many come whirling down.

'It's a heavenly day,' said George. 'I wish I hadn't got my blazer on. I'm cooked already.'

'Well, take it off and carry it over your shoulder,' said Julian. 'I'm going to do the same. Our jerseys are quite warm enough today!'

They took off their thick blazers and carried them. Each of them had a rucksack, a mac rolled up tightly and tied to it, and now a blazer to carry. But none of them noticed the weight at the outset of their day.

'I'm glad you girls took my advice and wore your thickest shoes,' said Julian, looking with approval at their brogues. 'Some of our walking may be wet. Have you got changes of socks?'

'Yes. We brought everything you told us to,' said Anne. 'Your rucksack looks a bit fuller than ours, Ju!'

'Well, I've got maps and things in it,' said Julian. 'It's

a strange place, this moor – miles and miles and miles of it! Strange names on it too – Blind Valley – Rabbit Hill – Lost Lake – Coney Copse!'

'Rabbit Hill! Timmy would love that,' said George, and Timmy pricked up his ears. Rabbits? Ah, that was the kind of place he liked!

'Well, actually we're going towards Rabbit Hill now,' said Julian. 'And after that there's Coney Copse, and as "coney" is a country word for rabbit, Timmy ought to enjoy himself!'

'Woof,' said Timmy joyfully and bounded ahead. He felt very happy. His four friends were with him, their rucksacks were full of delicious-smelling sandwiches, and a long, long walk lay ahead, teeming, he hoped with rabbits!

It was lovely walking along in the sun. They soon left the little village behind and took a winding lane. The hedges on either side became so high that the four couldn't see over the tops at all.

'What a sunken lane!' said Dick. 'I feel as if I'm walking in a tunnel! And how narrow! I wouldn't like to drive a car along this lane. If I met another car I might have to back up for miles!'

'We shan't meet anyone much,' said Julian. 'It's only in the summer that cars come along these lanes – people on holiday, touring round the countryside. Look – we take that path now – it leads to Rabbit Hill, according to the map!'

They climbed over a stile in the high hedge and walked over a field towards a curious little hill. Timmy suddenly went mad with excitement. He could smell rabbits – and he could see them too!

'You don't often see so many rabbits out in the day-time,' said George, surprised. 'Big ones and little ones too – what a scampering.'

They came to the hill and sat down quietly to watch the rabbits. But it was quite impossible to make Timmy do the same. The sight and smell of so many made him quite wild. He pulled away from George's hand and went bounding madly up the hill, scattering rabbits by the dozen.

'Timmy!' yelled George, but for once Timmy paid no attention. He rushed here and rushed there, getting very angry as first one rabbit and then another neatly popped down a hole.

'It's no use calling him,' said Dick. 'He won't catch one, anyway – see how nippy they are. It's my belief they're having a game with our Timmy!'

It did look rather like it. As soon as Timmy had chased two or three rabbits down one hole, a few more would pop up from another behind him. The children laughed. It was as good as a pantomime.

'Where do you mean to have lunch?' asked Anne. 'If we stay here much longer I shall really have to have something to eat – and it's not nearly time yet. I wish I didn't always feel so hungry in the open air.'

'Well, come on then,' said Julian. 'We've got some way to go before we get to our lunch-place. I've made a pretty good timetable of our tour – we're going to go all round the moors and finish at the place we started at! I've really marked it all out pretty well.'

'Do we sleep at farmhouses or something at night?' asked George. 'I should like that. Will they mind having us, do you think? Or do we go to inns?'

'Farmhouses for two nights and inns for the other nights,' said Julian. 'I've marked them all.'

They went up Rabbit Hill and down the other side. There were just as many rabbits there. Timmy chased them till he panted like an engine going uphill! His tongue hung out, dripping wet.

'You've had enough, Tim,' said George. 'Be sensible now.'

But Timmy couldn't be sensible with so many rabbits about. So they left him to chase and dart and race at top speed and went on down the hill. Timmy came rushing after them when they got to the bottom.

'*Now* perhaps you'll stop tearing about like a mad thing and walk with us,' scolded George. But she spoke too soon, for soon they were in a small wood which Julian informed them was Coney Copse.

'And as I told you, "coney" means rabbit, so you can't expect Timmy to stop being mad just yet,' said Julian.

They very nearly lost Timmy in Coney Copse. A rabbit disappeared down a very big hole, and Timmy was actually able to get down a little way. Then he got stuck. He scrabbled violently with his feet but it was no good. He was well and truly stuck.

The others soon discovered he wasn't with them and went back, calling. Quite by chance they came on the hole he was in and heard the sound of panting and scraping. A shower of sand flew out of the hole.

'There he is! The idiot, he's down a hole,' said George in alarm. 'Timmy! TIMMY! Come on out!'

There was nothing that Timmy would have liked better, but he couldn't come out, however much he tried. A root of a tree had got wedged into his back, and he couldn't seem to push himself out again, past the annoying root.

It took the four children twenty minutes to get Timmy out. Anne had to lie down and wriggle in a little way to reach him. She was the only one small enough to get into the hole.

She caught hold of Timmy's back legs and pulled hard. Somehow the root slid off his back and he came backwards. He whined loudly.

'Oh, Anne, you're hurting him, you're hurting him!' shouted George. 'Let him go!'

'I can't!' yelled back Anne. 'He'll only go down deeper, if I leave go his legs. Can you pull me out? If so Timmy will come too – he'll have to because I've got his legs!'

Poor Anne was pulled out by her legs, and poor Timmy came too, pulled by his. He whined and went to George.

'He's hurt himself somewhere,' said George anxiously. 'I know he has. He wouldn't whine like that if he wasn't hurt.'

She ran her fingers over him, pressing here and there. She examined each leg and each paw. She looked at his head. Still he whined. Where could he have hurt himself?

'Leave him,' said Julian, at last. 'I can't see that he's hurt anywhere – except in his feelings! He probably didn't like Anne hauling him out by his hind legs. Most undignified!'

George wasn't satisfied. Although she could find nothing wrong, she couldn't help being sure that Timmy had hurt himself somewhere. Ought he to see a vet?

'Don't be silly, George,' said Julian. 'Vets don't grow on trees in moorland country like this! Let's go on walking. You'll see Timmy will follow quite all right, and soon forget to whine. I tell you, he's hurt his doggy feelings, that's all. His vanity is wounded!'

They left Coney Copse and went on, George rather silent. Timmy trotted beside her, also rather quiet. Still, there really didn't seem anything the matter with him, except that he gave sudden little whines now and again.

'Now here's where I thought we might have our lunch,' said Julian, at last. 'Fallaway Hill! It's a good name for it too – it falls away steeply, and we've got a marvellous view.'

So they had. They had come to the top of a steep hill, not guessing that it fell away on the other side. They could sit on the top and see the sun shining on miles and miles of lonely heather-grown moor. They might see shy deer in the distance – or little wild ponies.

'This is heavenly,' said Anne, sitting down on a great tuft of heather. 'It's as warm as summer too! I do hope it's like this all over the weekend. We shall all be burnt!'

'It will also be heavenly having some of those sandwiches,' said Dick, choosing a lump of heather too. 'What comfortable seats are provided for us! I've a good mind to take a tuft of this heather back to school with me to put on the very hard chair that goes with my desk!'

Julian put the four packets of sandwiches down in the heather. Anne undid them. They looked wonderful!

'Super!' said Anne. 'What do you want first?'

'Well, speaking for myself I'm going to have one of each, put them all on top of one another, and have a huge bite of cheese, ham, pork and egg at once,' said Dick. Anne laughed.

'Even *your* mouth isn't big enough for that,' she said. But somehow Dick managed, though it was difficult.

'Disgusting behaviour,' he said, when he had managed the first mouthful. 'I think on the whole that one at a time is more economical. Hie, Timmy – have a bit?'

Timmy obliged. He was very quiet, and George was still anxious about him. Still, his appetite seemed remarkably good, so nobody but George wondered any more if he had hurt himself. He lay beside George, occasionally putting a great paw on her knee if he wanted another bit of sandwich.

'Timmy does jolly well,' said Dick, with his mouth full. 'He gets bits from us all. I bet he eats more than any of us. I say – did anyone ever taste such smashing sandwiches? Have you tried the pork? It must have come from a super pig!'

It was lovely sitting there in the sun, looking over miles of countryside, eating hungrily. They all felt very happy. Except George. *Was* there anything wrong with Timmy? It would spoil the whole weekend if so!

CHAPTER FOUR

George is worried

THEY LAZED for some time in the sun after they had finished their meal. There were three sandwiches each left, and half a piece each of the fruit cake. No one had been able to manage a whole piece, much as they would have liked to.

Timmy seemed to think he could finish all the cake that was left, but Julian said no. 'It's such a gorgeous cake it would be really wasted on Timmy,' he said. 'You've had enough, Tim. Greedy dog!'

'Woof,' said Timmy, wagging his tail, and eyeing the cake watchfully. He sighed when he saw it being packed up. He had only had a bit of George's half-slice – what a cake!

'I'll pack three sandwiches and a half-slice of the cake into each of four bags,' said Julian. 'Anyone can eat his or hers whenever they like. I expect we shall have a good meal at the farmhouse I've chosen for tonight, so you can eat when you like before then.'

'I don't feel as if I could eat anything till tomorrow morning,' said Anne, putting her bag of food into her rucksack. 'But it's odd how hungry you keep on getting, even if you feel you can't possibly be for hours and hours.'

'Well, Timmy can wolf anything you don't want,' said Julian. 'Nothing wasted when Tim's about. Now, are we all ready? We're going through a little village soon, where we'll stop for a drink. I could do with a ginger-beer. And then on we go to our farmhouse. We ought to try and arrive about five, because it gets dark so soon.'

'What's the farmhouse called?' asked Anne.

'Blue Pond Farm,' said Julian. 'Nice name, isn't it? I hope it's still got a blue pond.'

'Suppose they haven't room for us?' said Anne.

'Oh, they can always put a couple of girls somewhere,' said Julian. 'Dick and I can sleep in a barn if necessary. We're not particular!'

'*I'd* like to sleep in a barn too,' said Anne. 'I'd love to. Let's not ask for a bedroom, let's all sleep in a barn – on straw or hay or something.'

'No,' said Julian. 'You girls will have to be in the house. It gets cold at night, and we've brought no rugs. We boys will be all right with our macs over us. I'm not letting you two girls do that.'

'It's *stupid* being a girl!' said George, for about the millionth time in her life. 'Always having to be careful when boys can do as they like! I'm going to sleep in a barn, anyway. I don't care what you say, Ju!'

'Oh yes you do,' said Julian. 'You know quite well that if ever you go against the orders of the chief – that's me, my girl, in case you didn't know it – you won't come out with us again. You may look like a boy and behave like a boy, but you're a girl all the same. And like it or not, girls have got to be taken care of.'

'I should have thought that boys hated having to take care of girls,' said George, sulkily. 'Especially girls like me who don't like it.'

'Well, decent boys like looking after their girl cousins or their sisters,' said Julian. 'And oddly enough decent girls like it. But I won't count you as a girl, George, decent or otherwise. I'll merely count you as a boy who's got to have an eye on him – my eye, see? So take that look off your face, and don't make yourself any more difficult than you already are.'

George couldn't help laughing, and the sulky look went at once. She gave Julian a shove. 'All right. You win. You're so jolly domineering these days I feel quite afraid of you!'

'You're not afraid of anyone,' said Dick. 'You're the bravest girl I ever knew! Aha! That's made old George blush like a girl! Let me warm my hands, George!'

And Dick held his hands up in front of George's scarlet face, pretending to warm them at her fiery blush. She didn't know whether to be pleased or angry. She pushed his hands away and got up, looking more like a boy than ever with her short, tousled hair and her well-freckled face!

The others got up and stretched. Then they settled their rucksacks on their backs again, with their macs fastened to them, threw their blazers over their shoulders and set off down Fallaway Hill.

Timmy followed, but he didn't bound about as usual. He went slowly and carefully. George looked round for him, and frowned.

'What *is* the matter with Timmy?' she said. 'Look at him! Not a jump or a scamper in him!'

They all stopped and watched him. He came towards them and they saw that he was limping slightly with his left hind leg. George dropped down beside him and felt the leg carefully.

'I think he must have twisted it – sprained it or something, when he was down that rabbit hole,' she said. She patted him gently on the back and he winced.

'What's the matter, Tim?' said George, and she parted the hair on his back, examining the white skin underneath to see why he had winced when she had patted him.

'He's got an awful bruise here,' she said at last, and the others bent to see. 'Something must have hurt his back down in that hole. And Anne must have hurt one of his legs when she held on to them and dragged him out. I *told* you not to hold on to his legs, Anne.'

'Well, how were we to get him out if I didn't?' demanded Anne, feeling cross but rather guilty. 'Did you want him to stick there for days and days?'

'I don't think there's much damage done,' said Julian, feeling the hind leg. 'I honestly think he's only just twisted it a bit, George. He'll be all right after tonight, I'm sure.'

'But I must be *certain*,' said George. 'Did you say we come to a village soon, Ju?'

'Yes – Beacons Village,' said Julian. 'We can ask if there's a vet anywhere in the district if you like. He'll look at Timmy's leg and tell you if there's anything much wrong. But I don't think there is.'

'We'll go on to the village then,' said George. 'Oh dear – the only time I *ever* wish Timmy was a *little* dog is when he's hurt – because he's so very, very heavy to carry.'

'Well, don't think of carrying him yet,' said Dick. 'He can walk on three legs even if he can't on four! He's not as bad as all that, are you, Timmy?'

'Woof,' said Timmy, mournfully. He was rather enjoying all the fuss. George patted his head. 'Come on,' she said, 'we'll soon get that leg put right. Come on, Tim.'

They all went on, looking round to see how Timmy was getting on. He followed slowly, and then began to limp more badly. Finally he lifted his left hind leg up from the ground and ran on three legs only.

'Poor boy,' said George. 'Poor Timmy! I do hope his leg will be all right tomorrow. I can't possibly go on with the hike if it isn't.'

It was rather a gloomy company that came to Beacons Village. Julian made his way to a little inn that stood in the middle, called Three Shepherds.

A woman was shaking a duster out of a window. Julian called up to her.

'I say! Is there a vet anywhere in this district? I want someone to have a look at our dog's leg.'

'No. No vet here,' answered the woman. 'Not one nearer than Marlins over six miles away.'

George's heart sank. Timmy would never be able to walk six miles.

'Is there a bus?' she called.

'No. Not to Marlins,' said the woman. 'No bus goes there, missy. But if you want your dog's leg seen to, you go up to Spiggy House, up along there. Mr Gaston lives there with his horses, and he knows about dogs too. You take the dog there. He'll know what to do.'

'Oh *thank* you,' said George, gratefully. 'Is it very far?'

'About half a mile,' said the woman. 'See that hill? You go up there, take the turning to the right and you'll see a big house. That's Spiggy House. You can't mistake it because of the stables built all round it. Ask for Mr Gaston. He's nice, he is. Maybe you'll have to wait a little if he's out with his horses though – he may not be in till it's almost dark.'

The four put their heads together. 'We'd better go up to this Mr Gaston's, I think,' said Julian. 'But I think you and Anne, Dick, should go on to the farmhouse I planned to stay in for the night, and make arrangements for us. We don't want to leave it till the last minute. I'll go with George and Timmy, of course.'

'Right,' said Dick. 'I'll take Anne now. It will be dark pretty soon. Got your torch, Julian?'

'Yes,' said Julian. 'And I'm pretty good at finding my way, as you know. I shall come back to this village after we've been to Mr Gaston's, and then make straight for the farmhouse. It's about a mile and a half away.'

'Thanks awfully for saying you'll come with me, Julian,' said George. 'Let's go now, shall we? Well, Dick and Anne – see you later!'

Julian set off with George and Timmy up the hill to Spiggy House. Timmy went on three legs, and still seemed very sorry for himself. Anne and Dick watched him, feeling sorry for him too.

'I hope he's all right tomorrow,' said Dick. 'It will spoil our weekend if he's not, no doubt about that!'

They turned away and walked through the little village of Beacons. 'Now for Blue Pond Farmhouse,' said Dick. 'Julian didn't give me very clear directions. I think I'll ask someone exactly where it is.'

But they met nobody except a man driving a little cart. Dick hailed him and he pulled up his horse.

'Are we on the right road for Blue Pond Farmhouse?' shouted Dick.

'Ar,' answered the man, nodding his head.

'Is it straight on – or do we take any paths or little lanes?' asked Dick.

'Ar,' said the man, nodding again.

'What does he mean – "ar"?' said Dick. He raised his voice again.

'Is it this way?' And he pointed.

'Ar,' said the man again. He raised his whip and pointed up the road where the two were going, and then across to the west.

'Oh, I see – we turn to the right up there?' called Dick.

'Ar,' said the man, nodding, and drove on so suddenly that the horse almost stepped on Dick's foot.

'Well – if we find the farmhouse after all those "ar"s we'll be clever,' said Dick. 'Come on!'

CHAPTER FIVE

Anne and Dick

IT BEGAN to get dark very suddenly. The sun had gone, and a big black cloud slid smoothly over the sky. 'It's going to rain,' said Dick. 'Blow! I thought it was going to be a lovely evening.'

'We'd better hurry,' said Anne. 'I hate sheltering under a hedge in the pouring rain, with drips down my neck, and puddles round my feet!'

They hurried. They went up the road that led out of the village and then came to a turning on the right. This must be the one the man had meant. They stopped and looked down it. It seemed to be like one of the sunken lanes they had walked down in the morning, and it looked rather dark and tunnel-like now, in the twilight.

'I hope it's right,' said Dick. 'We'll ask the very first person we meet.'

'If we *do* meet anyone!' said Anne, feeling that they never would in this curious deep lane. They went up it. It would round and about and then went downhill into a very muddy bit indeed. Anne found herself sloshing about in thick mud.

'A stream or something must run across the lane here,' she said. 'Ugh! The water's got into my shoes! I'm sure we don't go this way, Dick. The water's quite deep farther on, I'm certain. I was up to my ankles just now.'

Dick looked about in the deepening twilight. He made out something above him in the high hedge that grew on the steep bank each side.

'Look – is that a stile?' he said. 'Where's my torch? At the bottom of my rucksack, of course! Can you get it out, Anne, to save me taking the thing off?'

Anne found the torch and gave it to Dick. He switched it on, and immediately the shadows round them grew blacker, and the lane seemed more tunnel-like than ever. Dick flashed the torch upwards to what he had thought was a stile.

'Yes – it is a stile,' he said. 'I expect that leads up to the farmhouse – a shortcut, probably. I've no doubt this lane is the one used by the farm carts, and probably goes right round to the farm – but if this is a shortcut we might as well take it. It must lead somewhere, anyway!'

They scrambled up the bank to the stile. Dick helped Anne over, and they found themselves in a wide field. In front of them was a narrow path, running between crops of some sort.

'Yes – this is obviously a shortcut,' said Dick, pleased. 'I expect we'll see the lights of the farmhouse in a minute.'

'Or fall into the blue pond first,' said Anne, rather dismally. It was just beginning to rain and she was wondering if it was worthwhile to untie her mac from her shoulder and put it on. Or was the farmhouse really nearby? Julian had said it wasn't very far.

They walked across the field and came to another stile. The rain was coming down fast now. Anne decided to put on her mac. She stood under a thick bush and Dick helped her on with it. She had a small sou'wester in the pocket and put that on too. Dick put his on and they set off again.

The second stile led into another endless field, and the path then came at last to a big field-gate. They climbed over it and found themselves on what looked like a heathery moor – wild and uncultivated land! No farmhouse was to be seen – though, indeed, they could not have seen anything of one unless they had been very close to it, because the night was on them, dark and rainy.

'If only we could see lights somewhere – shining out of a window,' said Dick. He shone his torch on to the moor in front of them. 'I don't quite know what to do. There doesn't seem to be a path here – and I just hate the idea of going all the way back across those wet fields, and into that dark little lane.'

'Oh no – don't let's,' said Anne, with a shiver. 'I really didn't like that lane. There *must* be a path somewhere! It's silly for a gate to open on to moorland!'

And then, as they stood there, with the rain dripping on them and not much else to be heard, another noise came to their ears.

It was so unexpected and so very startling that both of them clutched the other in a start of alarm. It was certainly a strange noise to hear in that deserted bit of country.

Bells! Wild, clanging bells sounding without a stop, jangling out over the dark countryside in peal after peal. Anne held on tightly to Dick.

'What is it? Where are those bells? What are they ringing for?' whispered Anne.

Dick had no idea. He was as startled as Anne to hear this extraordinary noise. It sounded some distance away, but every now and again the wind blew hard and then the noise of the jangling swept round them, close to them it seemed.

'I wish they'd stop. Oh, I wish they'd stop!' said Anne, her heart beating fast. 'I don't like them. They frighten me. They're not church bells.'

'No. They're certainly not church bells,' said Dick. 'They're a warning of some kind. I'm sure – but what for? Fire? We'd see fire if there was one anywhere near us. War? No – bells and beacons were used to warn people of war long, long ago. Not now.'

'That village was called Beacons,' said Anne, suddenly remembering. 'Do you suppose it has that name because long ago there was a nearby hill where people lighted a beacon, to send a warning to other towns telling them that the enemy was coming? Did they ring bells too? Are we hearing long-ago bells, Dick? They don't sound like bells I've ever heard in my life before.'

'Good gracious! They're certainly not long-ago bells!' said Dick, speaking cheerfully, though he was really just as puzzled and alarmed as Anne. 'Those bells are being rung now, at this very minute!'

Quite suddenly the bells stopped and an enormous silence took the place of the wild ringing. The two children stood and listened for a minute or two and then heaved a sigh of relief.

'They've stopped at last,' said Anne. 'I hated them! *Why* did they ring out on this dark, dark night? Oh do let's find Blue Pond Farmhouse as soon as ever we can, Dick. I don't like being lost in the dark like this, with bells ringing madly for nothing at all!'

'Come on,' said Dick. 'Keep close to the hedge. As long as we follow that we must come to somewhere. We won't wander out on to the moorland.'

He took Anne's arm and the two of them kept close to the hedge. They came to another path at last and followed it. That led to a lane, but not a sunken one this time – and then, oh wonderful sight – not far off they saw a light shining!

'That must be Blue Pond Farmhouse!' said Dick, thankfully. 'Come on, Anne – not much farther now!'

They came to a low stone wall and followed it till they came to a broken-down gate. It opened with a squeak, and Anne stepped through – right into an enormous puddle!

'Blow!' she said. 'Now I'm wetter than ever! For a

moment I thought I must have stepped into the blue pond!'

But it was only a puddle. They went round it and followed a muddy path to a little door set in a white stone wall. Dick thought it must be the back door. Nearby was a window, and in it shone the light they had seen so thankfully.

An old woman sat near the light, her head bent over some sewing. The children could see her quite clearly as they stood by the door.

Dick looked for a bell or knocker but there was none. He knocked with his bare knuckles. Nobody answered. The door remained shut. They looked at the old woman by the lamp, and saw that she was still sewing.

'Perhaps she's deaf,' said Dick and he knocked again, much more loudly. Still the old woman sewed on placidly. She must indeed be deaf!

'We'll never get in at this rate!' said Dick, impatiently. He tried the handle of the door – it opened at once!

'We'll just have to walk in and announce ourselves,' said Dick, and he stepped on to the worn mat inside the door. He was in a narrow little passage that led to a stone stairway, steep and narrow at the farther end.

On his right was a door, a little ajar. It opened into the room where the old woman was sitting. The two children could see a streak of light coming through the crack.

Dick pushed the door open and walked boldly in,

followed by Anne. Still the old woman didn't look up. She pushed her needle in and out of her sewing and seemed to hear and see nothing else whatsoever.

Dick had to walk right up to her before she knew he was in the room. Then she leapt up in such a fright that her chair fell over with a bang.

'I'm sorry,' said Dick, upset at frightening the old lady. 'We knocked but you didn't hear!'

She stared at them, her hand over her heart. 'You give me such a fright,' she said. 'Where did you come from this dark night?'

Dick picked up her chair, and she sat down in it, panting a little.

'We've been looking for this place,' said Dick. 'Blue Pond Farmhouse, isn't it? We wondered if we could stay the night here – and two others of us as well.'

The old woman pointed to her ears and shook her head. 'I'm deaf,' she said. 'No good talking to me, my dear. You've lost your way, I suppose?'

Dick nodded.

'Well, you can't stay here,' said the old woman. 'My son won't have no one here at all. You'd best be gone before he comes. He have a nasty temper, he have.'

Dick shook his head. Then he pointed out to the dark, rainy night, then pointed to Anne's wet shoes and clothes. The old woman knew what he meant.

'You've lost your way, you're wet and tired, and you don't want me to turn you out,' she said. 'But there's my son, you see. He don't like strangers here.'

Dick pointed to Anne, and then to a sofa in a corner of the room. Then he pointed to himself, and then outside. Again the old woman understood at once.

'You want me to give your sister shelter, but you'll go out into the night?' she said. Dick nodded. He thought he could easily find some shed or barn for himself. But Anne really must be indoors.

'My son mustn't see either of you,' said the old woman, and she pulled Anne to what the girl thought was a cupboard. But when the door opened, she saw a very small, steep wooden staircase leading upwards into the roof.

'You go up there,' said the old woman to Anne. 'And don't you come down till I call you in the morning. I'll get into trouble if my son knows you're here.'

'Go up, Anne,' said Dick, rather troubled. 'I don't know what you'll find there. If it's too bad, come down. See if there's a window or something you can call out from, and then I'll know if you're all right.'

'Yes,' said Anne, in rather a trembling voice, and she went up the steep, dirty wooden stairs. They led straight into a little loft. There was a mattress there, fairly clean, and a chair. A rug was folded up on the chair and a jug of water stood on a shelf. Otherwise the room was bare.

A tiny window opened out on one side. Anne went to it and called out. 'Dick! Are you there? Dick!'

'Yes, I'm here,' said Dick. 'What's it like, Anne? Is it all right? Listen, I'll find somewhere nearby to shelter in – and you can always call me if you want me!'

CHAPTER SIX

In the middle of the night

'IT'S NOT bad,' said Anne. 'There's a fairly clean mattress and a rug. I'll be all right. But what about if the others come, Dick? Will you look out for them? I almost think George will have to sleep in a barn with you and Julian if she comes. That old woman won't let anyone else in, I'm sure!'

'I'll look out for them and arrange something,' said Dick. 'You eat the rest of your sandwiches and your cake, and see if you can dry your wet feet and make yourself really comfortable. There's a shed or something out here. I shall be quite all right. Yell for me if you want me.'

Anne went back into the room. She felt wet and tired, hungry and thirsty. She ate all her food, and had a drink from the jug. Then she felt sleepy and lay down on the mattress, throwing the rug over herself. She meant to listen for the others to come, but she was too tired. She fell fast asleep!

Dick was prowling about down below. He was careful because he didn't want to run into the old woman's son. He didn't like the sound of him somehow! He came to a small barn with piles of straw in one corner. He flashed his torch cautiously round.

'This will do for me,' he thought. 'I can be quite comfortable here in that straw. Poor Anne! I wish old George was with her. I'd better wait about and watch for the other two, or I'll fall asleep and miss them, once I bed down in that straw! It's only about six o'clock too – but we've had a long day. I wonder how Timmy is. I wish he was here!'

Dick thought that probably George and Julian would come in through the same gate as he and Anne had used. He found a broken-down shed near the gate and sat down on a box there, waiting for them to come.

He ate his sandwiches while he waited. They were very comforting! He ate every one and then the cake. He yawned. He felt very sleepy indeed, and his feet were wet and tired.

No one arrived at all – not even the old woman's son. She could still be seen sewing under the lamp. But after about two hours, when it was almost eight o'clock, and Dick was beginning to be very worried about George and Julian, the old woman got up and put away her workbasket.

She disappeared out of Dick's sight, and didn't come back. But the light was still there, shining out of the window. Left for her son, probably, thought Dick.

He tiptoed to the window. The rain had stopped now and the night was much clearer. The stars were out and a moon was coming up. Dick's spirits rose.

He peered in at the lighted room. Then he saw the old

woman lying on a broken-down sofa in a corner. A blanket was pulled right up to her chin and she seemed to be asleep. Dick went back to his shed, but now he felt there was no use in watching for George and Julian. They must have lost their way completely! Or else Mr Gaston, or whatever his name was, must have had to do something to Timmy's leg, and Julian had decided to stay at the inn in Beacons Village for the night.

He yawned again. 'I'm too sleepy to watch any more,' he decided. 'I shall fall off this box with sleep if I don't go and lie down in that straw. Anyway I think I'd hear if the others came.'

Using his torch cautiously, he made his way to the barn. He shut the door behind him and bolted it roughly from the inside by running a stick through two hasps. He didn't know why he did that – perhaps because he was still thinking of the old woman's bad-tempered son!

He flung himself down on the straw, and immediately fell asleep. Outside the sky became clearer and clearer. The moon came up, not fully, but large enough to give some light. It shone down on the desolate little stone house and ill-kept outbuildings.

Dick slept soundly. He lay in the soft straw and dreamt of Timmy and George and Blue Ponds and bells. Especially bells.

He awoke suddenly, and lay for a moment wondering where he was. What was this prickly stuff round him? Then he remembered – of course, it was straw and he was in a barn! He was about to cuddle down again when he heard a noise.

It was only a small noise – a scratching on the wooden walls of the barn perhaps. Dick sat up. Were there rats there? He hoped not!

He listened. The scratching seemed to come from *outside* the barn, not inside. Then it stopped. After an interval it began again. Then there came a gentle tapping at the broken window just above Dick's head.

He felt very startled. Rats scratched and scrabbled about – but they didn't tap on windows. Who was tapping so very cautiously on the little window? He held his breath and listened, straining his ears.

And then he heard a voice – a hoarse whisper.

'Dick! Dick!'

Dick was amazed. Could it be Julian? If so, how in the world did he know that he, Dick, was in the barn? He sat listening, stiff with surprise.

The tapping came again, and then the voice, a little louder. 'Dick! I know you're there. I saw you go in. Come here to the window – quiet, now!'

Dick didn't know the voice. It wasn't Julian's, and it certainly wasn't either George's or Anne's. Then how did the owner know *his* name and that he was there? It was astounding. Dick didn't know what to do!

'Buck up!' said the voice. 'I've got to go in half a tick. I've got that message for you.'

Dick decided to go nearer to the window. He was quite

certain that he didn't want whoever it was outside to come into the barn. He cautiously knelt up in the straw and spoke just underneath the window.

'I'm here,' he said, trying to make his voice deep and grown-up.

'You've been long enough coming,' grumbled the one outside, and then Dick saw him through the window – just a face, dim and wild-eyed, with a round, bullet-like head. He crouched back, thankful that the face couldn't see him in the darkness of the barn.

'Here's the message from Nailer,' said the voice. 'Two-Trees. Gloomy Water. Saucy Jane. And he says Maggie knows. He sent you this. Maggie's got one too.'

A bit of paper fluttered in at the broken pane. Dick picked it up in a daze. What *was* all this? Was he dreaming?

The voice came again, insistent and urgent. 'You heard all that, Dick? Two-Trees. Gloomy Water. Saucy Jane. And Maggie knows too. Now I'm going.'

There came the sound of someone cautiously creeping round the barn – and then there was silence. Dick sat amazed and bewildered. Who was this wild-eyed fellow, who called him by his name in the middle of the night and gave him extraordinary messages that meant nothing at all to a sleepy boy? But Dick was wide awake now. He stood up and looked out of the window. There was nothing and no one to be seen except the lonely house and the sky.

Dick sat down again and thought. He put his torch on cautiously and looked at the piece of paper he had picked up. It was a dirty half-sheet, with pencil marks on it that meant nothing to Dick at all. Words were printed here and there, but they were all nonsense to him. He simply couldn't make head or tail of his visitor, his message or the bit of paper!

'I'm sure I must be dreaming,' thought Dick, and put the paper into his pocket. He lay back in his straw, cuddling in deep, because he had got cold by the window. He lay and thought for a while, puzzling over the curious happenings, and then he felt his eyes closing.

But before he was quite asleep, he heard cautious footsteps again! Was that fellow back once more? This time someone tried the door – but the wooden stick was in the hasps. Whoever it was outside shook the door and the stick fell out at once. The man shook the door again as if thinking it had stuck, and then opened it. He came inside and shut the door behind him.

Dick caught a quick glimpse of him. No – this wasn't the same man as before. This was a man with a head of thick hair, Dick hoped and prayed that he wouldn't come over to the straw.

He didn't. He sat down on a sack and waited. He talked to himself after a while, but Dick could only make out a word or two.

'What's happened?' he heard. 'How much longer do I wait?' Then there was a mumble and Dick could not catch a word.

'Wait, wait – that's all I do,' muttered the man, and he stood up and stretched himself. Then he went to the door and looked out. He came back and sat down on the sack again.

He sat still and quiet then, and Dick found his eyes closing once more. Was this part of a dream too? He didn't have time to think it out because he was suddenly in a real dream, walking along ringing bells and seeing trees in twos everywhere round him!

He slept heavily all night long. When morning came he awoke suddenly and sat up. He was alone in the barn. Where had the second visitor gone? Or *could* it all have been a dream?

CHAPTER SEVEN

In the morning

DICK STOOD up and stretched himself. He felt dirty and untidy. Also he was very hungry. He wondered if the old woman would let him buy some bread and cheese and a glass of milk.

'Anne must be hungry too,' he thought. 'I wonder if she's all right.' He went cautiously outside and looked up at the tiny window of the loft where Anne had spent the night. Her anxious face was already there, watching for Dick!

'Are you all right, Anne?' called Dick, in a low tone. She pushed open the tiny window and smiled at him.

'Yes. But I daren't go down because that son is downstairs. I can hear him shouting at the deaf old woman every now and again. He sounds very bad-tempered.'

'I'll wait for him to go out to his work then, before I go and see the old woman,' said Dick. 'I must pay her something for letting you sleep up in that loft – and perhaps I can persuade her to let us have something to eat.'

'I wish you could,' said Anne. 'I've eaten all the chocolate I had in my bag. Shall I wait till I hear you call me?'

Dick nodded and disappeared into the barn in a hurry. He had heard footsteps!

A man came into sight – a broad, short, hunched-up man, with a shock of untidy hair. He was the man that Dick had seen in the barn the night before. He was muttering to himself and looked very bad-tempered indeed. Dick decided to keep out of his way. He crouched down in the barn.

But the man did not go in there. He walked past, still muttering. Dick listened for his footsteps to die away. He heard the opening of a gate somewhere, then it crashed behind the man.

'I'd better take my chance now,' thought Dick, and he went quickly out of the barn and up to the little white house. It looked very tumbledown and neglected in the daylight, and had a more forlorn air.

Dick knew that it was no good knocking, because the old woman wouldn't hear him. So he walked right into the house and found the woman washing up a few dishes in a cracked old sink. She stared at him in dismay.

'I'd forgotten about you! And the girl too! Is she still up there? Get her down quickly before my son comes back! And then go, both of you!'

'Can you sell us some bread and cheese?' shouted Dick. But the old woman really was deaf, and all she did was to push Dick away towards the door, jabbing at him with the wet cloth in her hand. Dick slipped aside and pointed to some bread on a table.

'No, no – I tell you, you're to go,' said the old woman, obviously terrified in case her son should come back. 'Get the girl, quickly!'

But before Dick could do anything, there were footsteps outside and in came the hunched-up fellow with the shock of hair! He was back already, holding some eggs he had been to find.

He walked into the kitchen and stared at Dick. 'Clear out!' he said, angrily. 'What do you want here?'

Dick thought he had better not say he had slept the night in the barn. There were strange goings-on here, and the man might be very fierce if he knew Dick had slept the night nearby.

'I wanted to know if your mother could sell us some bread,' he said, and could have bitten his tongue out. He had said 'us'! Now the man would guess there was someone with him.

'Us? Who's "us"?' said the man, looking round. 'You fetch him and I'll tell you both what I do to boys who come stealing my eggs!'

'I'll go and fetch him,' said Dick, seizing the chance to get away. He ran to the door. The man made a clumsy dart at him and almost caught him. But Dick was out and away, running down the path. He hid behind a shed, his heart thumping. He had to wait for Anne. Somehow he had to go back and get her.

The man stood at the door, shouting angrily after Dick. But he didn't chase him. He went back into the house and

after a while came out again with a pail of steaming food. Dick guessed he was going to feed the chickens wherever they were.

He had to take this chance of fetching Anne. He waited till he heard the crash of the distant gate again and then he rushed to the house. Anne's face was at the window, scared. She had heard all that the man had said to Dick, and then to his mother about allowing boys to come to the house.

'Anne! Come down at once. He's gone,' shouted Dick. 'Hurry!'

Anne's face disappeared from the window. She ran to the door, tumbled quickly down the stairs, and ran through the kitchen. The old woman flapped a cloth at her, screaming at her.

Dick ran into the kitchen and put a pound coin on the table. Then he caught Anne's arm and both children tore out of the house and down the path. They came to the hedge they had followed the night before.

Anne was quite scared. 'That awful man!' she said. 'Oh Dick – what a horrible place. Honestly I think Julian must be mad to choose a place like that to sleep in for the night – horrible little house! And it didn't look a bit like a farm. There were no cows or pigs that I could see and not even a farm dog!'

'You know, Anne, I don't think it could possibly have been Blue Pond Farmhouse,' said Dick, as they walked beside the hedge, looking for the gate that they had come through the night before. 'We made a mistake. It was an ordinary cottage. If we hadn't lost our way we'd have come to the proper Blue Pond Farmhouse I'm sure.'

'Whatever will George and Julian be thinking?' said Anne. 'They'll be dreadfully worried, won't they, wondering what has become of us? Do you suppose they're at the real Blue Pond Farmhouse?'

'We'll have to find out,' said Dick. 'Do I look very messy and untidy, Anne? I feel awful.'

'Yes. Haven't you a comb?' said Anne. 'Your hair's all up on end. And your face is very dirty. Look, there's a little stream over there. Let's get our flannels out and wash our hands and faces with them.'

They did a little washing in the cold water of the stream, and Dick combed back his hair.

'You look a lot better,' said Anne. 'Oh dear – I wish we could have some breakfast. I'm really starving! I didn't sleep awfully well, did you, Dick? My mattress was so hard, and I was rather scared, up in that funny little room all alone.'

Before Dick could answer, a boy came whistling through the gate. He looked astonished to see Dick and Anne.

'Hallo!' he said. 'You hiking?'

'Yes,' said Dick. 'Can you tell me if that place up there is Blue Pond Farmhouse?'

He pointed back to the old woman's house. The boy laughed.

'That's no farmhouse. That's Mrs Taggart's place, and a dirty old place it is. Don't you go there, or her son will drive you off. Dirty Dick we call him – he's a terror! Blue Pond Farmhouse is down along there, see? Past the Three Shepherds Inn and away up to the left.'

'Thanks,' said Dick, feeling very angry indeed with the man who had said 'ar' and sent them all wrong the day before. The boy waved, and set off across a moorland path.

'We certainly went the wrong way last night,' said Dick, as they walked over the fields they had crossed in the dark the night before. 'Poor Anne! Dragging you all that way in the dark and the rain to a horrible place that wasn't Blue Pond Farmhouse after all. I can't think what Julian is going to say to me.'

'Well, it was my fault too,' said Anne. 'Dick, let's go down to the Three Shepherds and telephone Blue Pond Farmhouse from there, shall we? If it's on the phone, that is. I don't somehow feel as if I want to walk for miles and perhaps not find Blue Pond Farmhouse again.'

'Good idea,' said Dick. 'The Three Shepherds was where that woman was shaking a duster out of the window, wasn't it? She told Julian the way to Spiggy House. I wonder how old Timmy is. I hope he's better. I say – this hike isn't as good as we hoped it would be, is it?'

'Well, there's still time for it to be all right!' said Anne, much more cheerfully than she felt. She so badly wanted her breakfast that she felt quite bad-tempered!

'We'll telephone to Julian from the Three Shepherds to say what happened to us,' said Dick, as they came to the lane where they had floundered in the mud the night before. He helped Anne over the stile and they jumped down to the narrow road. 'And what's more, we'll have breakfast at the Three Shepherds – and I bet we eat more than ever the Three Shepherds did, whoever they were!'

Anne felt more cheerful at once. She had thought they would have to walk all the way to find Blue Pond Farmhouse before they had breakfast!

'See – a stream does flow right across the road here,' she said. 'No wonder I got my feet wet yesterday! Come on – the thought of breakfast makes my legs want to run!'

They at last arrived in Beacons Village, and made their way to the inn. On the sign three shepherds were painted, looking rather gloomy.

'They look like I feel,' said Anne, 'but I shall soon feel different. Oh Dick – think of porridge – and bacon and eggs – and toast and marmalade!'

'We must telephone first,' said Dick, firmly – and then he suddenly stopped, just as he was going into the inn. Someone was calling him.

'DICK! DICK! ANNE! Look, there they are! Hey, Dick, DICK!'

It was Julian's voice! Dick swung round in delight. He saw Julian, George and Timmy racing along the village street, shouting and waving. Timmy was first to reach them of course – and there was no sign of limping either!

He leapt on them, barking madly, and licked every bare part of them he could reach.

'Oh, Ju! I'm so glad to see you!' said Anne, in rather a trembling voice. 'We lost our way last night. George, is Timmy all right?'

'Quite. Absolutely,' said George. 'You see . . .'

'Have you had breakfast? interrupted Julian. 'We haven't. We were so worried about you we were just going to see the police. But now we can all have breakfast together and tell our news!'

CHAPTER EIGHT

All together again

IT WAS wonderful to be all together again. Julian took hold of Anne's arm and squeezed it. 'All right, Anne?' he said, rather worried at her pale face.

Anne nodded. She felt better at once, now she had Julian, George and Timmy, as well as Dick. 'I'm only just terribly hungry,' she said.

'I'll ask for breakfast straight away,' said Julian. 'All news later!'

The woman who had leant out of the window shaking a duster the evening before, came up to them. 'I expect it's a bit late for you,' said Julian. 'But we haven't had any breakfast. What have you got?'

'Porridge and cream,' said the woman. 'And our own cured bacon and our own eggs. Our own honey and the bread I bake myself. Will that do? And coffee with cream?'

'I could hug you,' said Julian, beaming at her. The others felt the same. They went into a small, cosy dining-room and sat down to wait. Soon a smell of frying bacon and hot strong coffee would come into the room – what joy!

'Your news first,' said Dick, patting Timmy. 'Did you get to Spiggy House? Was Mr Gaston there?'

'No, he wasn't,' said Julian. 'He was out somewhere.

He had a very nice wife who made us wait for him, and said he wouldn't mind in the least looking at Timmy when he came back. So we waited and waited.'

'We waited till half past seven!' said George. 'And we felt rather awkward because we thought it might be getting near their meal-time. And then at last Mr Gaston came.'

'He was awfully kind,' said Julian. 'He looked at Timmy's leg, and then he did something, I don't know what – put it back into place, I suppose – and Timmy gave a yell and George flung herself on him, and Mr Gaston roared with laughter at George . . .'

'Well, he was very *rough* with Timmy's leg,' said George. 'But he knew what he was doing, of course, and now Timmy is perfectly all right, except for that bruise on his back, and even that is getting better. He can run as well as ever.'

'I'm glad,' said Anne. 'I kept thinking of poor old Tim all last night.' She patted him, and he licked her lavishly and wetly.

'What did you do then?' asked Dick.

'Well, Mrs Gaston insisted on us staying to supper,' said Julian. 'She simply wouldn't take no for an answer, and I must say that by that time we were jolly hungry. So we stayed – and we had a jolly good meal too. So did Timmy! You should have seen his tummy afterwards – as round as a barrel. Good thing it's gone down today or I was thinking of changing his name to Tummy.' They all laughed, George especially.

'Idiot,' she said. 'Well, we didn't leave till about nine o'clock. We didn't worry about you because we felt sure you would be safely at Blue Pond Farmhouse and would guess we'd had to wait about with Timmy. And when we got there and found you hadn't arrived – well, we *were* in a state!'

'And then we thought you must have found somewhere else for the night,' said Julian, 'but we thought if we heard nothing we'd go down to the police first thing this morning and report your disappearance!'

'So down we came – without any breakfast either!' said

George. 'That shows how worried we were! Blue Pond Farmhouse was nice. They gave us a bed each in two tiny little rooms, and Timmy slept with me, of course.'

A wonderful smell came creeping into the little dining-room, followed by the inn-woman carrying a large tray. On it was a steaming tureen of porridge, a bowl of golden syrup, a jug of very thick cream, and a dish of bacon and eggs, all piled high on crisp brown toast. Little mushrooms were on the same dish.

'It's like magic!' and Anne, staring. 'Just the very things I longed for!'

'Toast, marmalade and butter to come, and the coffee and hot milk,' said the woman, busily setting everything out. 'And if you want any more bacon and eggs, just ring the bell.'

'Too good to be true!' said Dick, looking at the table. 'For goodness' sake, help yourselves quickly, girls, or I shall forget my manners and grab.'

It was a wonderful breakfast – extra wonderful because they were all so ravenously hungry. There wasn't a word said as they spooned up their porridge and cream, sweetened with golden syrup. Timmy had a dishful too – he loved porridge, though he didn't like the syrup – it made his whiskers sticky!

'I feel better,' said Anne, looking at the porridge dish. 'The thing is – shall I have some more porridge and risk not enjoying my bacon and eggs so much – or shall I go straight on with bacon and eggs?'

'A difficult question,' said Dick. 'And one that I am faced with too. On the whole I think I'll go on with bacon and eggs – we can always have more of those if we want to – and those little mushrooms really do make my mouth water! Aren't we greedy? But how can anyone help that when they're so hungry?'

'You haven't told us a single word of what happened to *you* last night,' said Julian, serving out the bacon and eggs with a generous hand. 'Now that you've got something inside you, perhaps you feel able to tell us exactly why you ignored my instructions and didn't arrive where you were supposed to last night.'

'You sound like our headmaster at school!' said Dick. 'The plain fact is – we got lost! And when we did finally arrive somewhere, we thought it was Blue Pond Farmhouse, and we stayed the night there.'

'I see,' said Julian. 'But didn't the people there tell you it wasn't the right place? Just so that you could have let us know? You must have known that we would worry about you.'

'Well, the old woman there was deaf,' explained Anne, attacking her bacon and eggs vigorously. 'She didn't understand a word we said, and as we thought it *was* Blue Pond Farmhouse, we stayed there – though it was a horrible place. And *we* were worried because *you* didn't arrive!'

'A chapter of accidents,' said Julian. 'All's well that ends well, however.'

'Don't sound so pompous!' said Dick. 'Actually we had

a pretty poor time, Ju. Poor Anne had to sleep in a little loft, and I slept in straw in a barn – not that I minded that – but – well, peculiar things happened in the night. At least – I *think* they did. I'm not really sure it wasn't all a dream.'

'What peculiar things?' asked Julian at once.

'Well – I think perhaps I'll tell you when we're on our way again,' said Dick. 'Now I think about it in full daylight I feel that either it was all a silly dream – or – well, as I said – something very peculiar.'

'You never told me, Dick!' said Anne, in surprise.

'Well, to tell you the truth I forgot about it because other things happened,' said Dick. 'Having to get away from that man, for instance – and wondering about Julian and George – and feeling so hungry.'

'You don't sound as if you had a good night at all,' said George. 'It must have been awful, too, trying to find your way in the dark. It poured with rain, didn't it?'

'Yes,' said Anne, 'but oh – the thing that frightened me more than anything was the bells! Did you hear them Julian? They suddenly clanged out, and they made me terribly scared. I couldn't think what they were! Whatever were they ringing out for? They were so loud.'

'Didn't you know what they were ringing for?' said Julian. 'They were bells rung from the prison that nice old woman told us about – they were rung to tell everyone in the countryside that a prisoner had escaped! Lock your doors. Guard your folk.'

Anne stared at Julian in silence. So that was why the bells

had made such a clamour and clangour. She shivered.

'I'm glad I didn't know that,' she said. 'I would have slept in the straw with Dick if I'd known there was an escaped prisoner. Have they caught him?'

'I don't know,' said Julian. 'We'll ask the inn-woman when she comes.'

They asked her, and she shook her head. 'No. He's not caught yet. But he will be. All the roads from the moor are guarded and everyone is on the watch. He was a robber who broke into houses and attacked anyone who tried to prevent him. A dangerous fellow.'

'Julian – is it all right to go hiking on the moors if there's an escaped prisoner about?' said Anne. 'I shan't feel very comfortable.'

'We've got Timmy,' said Julian. 'He would be strong enough to protect us from three prisoners if necessary! You needn't worry.'

'Woof,' agreed Timmy, at once, and thumped his tail on the floor.

At last everyone had finished breakfast. Even starving Anne couldn't manage the last bit of toast. She sighed happily. 'I feel myself again,' she announced. 'I can't say I feel very much like walking – but I know it would be good for me after that enormous meal.'

'Good or not, we're going on our way,' said Julian, getting up. 'I'll buy some sandwiches first.'

The inn-woman was delighted with their hearty praises. She gave them some packets of sandwiches and waved goodbye. 'You come again whenever you can,' she said. 'I'll always have something nice for you.'

The four went down the street and took a lane at the bottom. It wound about for a short way and then came into a valley. A stream ran down the middle of the valley. The children could hear it gurgling from where they stood.

'Lovely!' said Anne. 'Are we going along by the stream? I'd like to.'

Julian looked at his map. 'Yes – we could,' he said. 'I've marked the path to follow, and the stream joins it some way on. So if you like we could go along by it, though it will be very rough walking.'

They made their way to the stream. 'Now, Dick,' said Julian, when they had left the path. 'What about telling us all those peculiar things that happened in the night? There's nobody about to hear – not a soul in sight. Let's hear everything. We'll soon tell you whether it was a dream or not.'

'Right,' said Dick. 'Well, here's the tale. It does sound pretty peculiar. Listen . . .'

CHAPTER NINE

Dick surprises the others

DICK BEGAN his tale – but it was really very difficult to hear it because they couldn't walk four abreast, as there was no path to follow.

In the end Julian stopped and pointed to a thick clump of heather. 'Let's go and sit there and hear Dick's story properly. I keep missing bits. No one can hear us if we sit here.'

They sat down and Dick started again. He told about the old woman who was afraid her son would be angry if she let them stay the night. He told about his bed in the straw.

'And now here comes the bit I think must have been a dream,' he said. 'I woke up to hear a scratching noise on the wooden walls of the barn . . .'

'Rats or mice?' said George, and Timmy leapt up at once, of course. He was sure she had said the words to him!

'I thought that too,' said Dick. 'But then I heard a gentle tap-tap-tapping on the window.'

'How horrid,' said Anne. 'I shouldn't have liked that at all.'

'Neither did I,' said Dick. 'But the *next* thing I heard was my name being called! "Dick! Dick!" Just like that.'

'It *must* have been a dream then,' said Anne. 'There was no one there who knew your name.'

Dick went on. 'Well, then the voice said – "Dick! I know you're there. I saw you go in!" And it told me to go to the window.'

'Go on,' said Julian. He was puzzled. No one in the world but Anne could have known that Dick was in the barn – and it certainly wasn't Anne out there in the night!

'Well, I went to the window,' said Dick, 'and I saw, rather dimly, of course, a wild-eyed looking fellow. He couldn't see me in the darkness of the barn. I just mumbled, "I'm here," hoping he would think I was whoever he wanted.'

'What did he say next?' said George.

'He said something that sounded stuff and nonsense,' said Dick. 'He said it twice. It was "Two-Trees. Gloomy Water. Saucy Jane." And he said "Maggie knows." Just like that!'

There was silence. Then George laughed. 'Two-Trees! Gloomy Water! Saucy Jane – and Maggie knows about it! Well, it *must* have been a dream, Dick! You know it must. What do you think, Julian?'

'Well – it does sound a bit nonsensical to have someone come in the middle of the night and call Dick by name and give him a strange message that doesn't mean a thing to him!' said Julian. 'It sounds more dreamlike than real. I'd say it was a dream too.'

Dick began to think they were right – and then a sudden thought struck him. He sat up straight. 'Wait a bit!' he said. 'I've remembered something! The man slipped a bit of paper through the broken pane of the window, and I picked it up!'

'Ah – that's different,' said Julian. 'Now – if you can't find that paper, it's all a dream and you dreamt the paper too – but if you *can* find it, well the whole thing is true. Very peculiar indeed – but true.'

Dick searched quickly in his pockets. He felt paper in one of them, and drew it out. It was a dirty, crumpled piece, with a few words on it and a few lines. He held it out to the others in silence, his eyes shining.

'Is this the paper?' asked Julian. 'My word – so you didn't dream it after all, then!'

He took the paper. Four heads bent over it to examine it. No, five – because Timmy wanted to see what they were all so interested in. He thrust his hairy head between Julian's and Dick's.

'I can't make any sense of this paper,' said Julian. 'It's a plan of some kind, I think – but what of, or where, it's impossible to know.'

'The fellow said that Maggie had one of these bits of paper too,' said Dick, remembering.

'Who in the wide world *is* Maggie?' said George, 'and why should Maggie know?'

'Any more to tell?' asked Julian, intensely interested now.

'Well – the son of the deaf old woman came into the barn later on,' said Dick. 'And he sat and waited and waited, and muttered and muttered – and then when I woke up he wasn't there. So I thought I must have dreamt him too. He didn't see me, of course.'

Julian pursed up his lips and frowned. Then Anne spoke excitedly.

'Dick! Ju! I think I know why the second man came into the barn. It was the *second* man that the wild-eyed man wanted to give the message to, and the bit of paper – not to Dick. He didn't want *Dick.* But he had seen him creep into the barn, and I suppose he thought Dick was the man he really wanted and that he was in the barn waiting for him!'

'That's all very well – but how did he know my name?' asked Dick.

'He didn't know it! He didn't know it was you at all!' said Anne, excitedly. 'The other man's name must have been Dick too! Don't you *see*? They must have planned to meet there, the wild-eyed man and the old woman's son – and the first man saw Dick go in, so he waited a bit and then went and tapped on the window! And when he called "Dick! Dick!" of course Dick thought it was he that he wanted, and he took the message and everything! And then the other man, the real Dick came along – and was too late to meet the first one. *Our* Dick had met him and got the message!'

Anne was quite breathless after this long speech. She sat and stared at the others eagerly. Didn't they think she was right?

They did, of course. Julian clapped her on the back. 'Well worked out, Anne! Of course that's what happened.'

Dick suddenly remembered the boy they had met on the way down from the old woman's cottage to Beacons Village – the whistling boy. What had he said about the old woman and her son?

'Anne – what did that whistling boy say? Wait a bit – he said that was Mrs Taggart's place – and he said we'd better not go there or her son would drive us off. And he said – yes, I remember now – he said "Dirty Dick we call him – he's a terror!" Dirty *Dick*! His name *must* be Dick then! Why didn't I think of it before?'

'That proves that Anne is right,' said Julian, pleased. Anne looked pleased too. It wasn't often that she thought of something clever before the others did!

They all sat thinking. 'Would this have anything to do with the escaped prisoner?' said George at last.

'It might,' said Julian. 'He might have been the prisoner himself, that fellow who came with the message. Did he say who the message was from?'

'Yes,' said Dick, trying to remember. 'He said it was from Nailer. I think that was the name – but it was all given in whispers, you know.'

'A message from Nailer,' said Julian. 'Well – perhaps Nailer is in prison – a friend of the man who escaped. And maybe when he knew this fellow was going to make a dash for it, he gave him a message for someone – the man at that old cottage, the son of the old woman. They may have had a prearranged plan.'

'How do you mean?' asked Dick, looking puzzled.

'Well – the old woman's son, Dirty Dick, may have known that when the bells rang out, this fellow was making a run for it – and would come to bring him a message. He was to wait in the barn at night if the bells rang, just in case it was Nailer's friend who had escaped.'

'Yes, I see,' said Dick. 'I think you're right. Yes, I'm sure you are. My word, I'm glad I didn't know that fellow at the window was an escaped convict!'

'And *you've* got the message from Nailer!' said Anne. 'What a peculiar thing! Just because we lost our way and went to the wrong place, you get a message from a prisoner given you by one who's escaped! It's a pity we don't know what the message means – or the paper either.'

'Had we better tell the police?' said George. 'I mean – it may be important. It might help them to catch that man.'

'Yes,' said Julian. 'I think we *should* tell the police. Let's have a look at our map. Where's the next village?'

He looked at the map for a minute. 'I think really we might as well go on with what I had planned,' he said. 'I planned we should reach this village here – Reebles, look – in time for lunch, in case we hadn't got sandwiches. We'd have gone there for drinks anyway. So I vote we just carry on with our ramble, and call in at Reebles police station – if there is one – and tell them our bit of news.'

They all got up. Timmy was glad. He didn't approve of this long sit-down so soon after breakfast. He bounded ahead in delight.

'His leg's *quite* all right,' said Anne, pleased. 'Well, I

hope it teaches him not to go down rabbit holes again!'

It didn't, of course. He had his head down half a dozen within the next half-hour, but fortunately he could get no farther, and he was able to pull himself out quite easily.

The four saw little wild ponies that day. They came trotting over a hillock together, small and brown, with long manes and tails, looking very busy indeed. The children stopped in delight. The ponies saw them, tossed their pretty heads, turned one way all together and galloped off like the wind.

Timmy wanted to go after them, but George held his collar tightly. No one must chase those dear little wild ponies!

'Lovely!' said Anne. 'Lovely to meet them as suddenly as that. I hope we meet some more.'

The morning was as warm and sunny as the day before. Once again the four of them had to take off their blazers, and Timmy's tongue hung out, wet and dripping. The heather and wiry grass was soft underfoot. They followed the stream closely, liking its brown colour and its soft gurgling voice.

They bathed their hot feet in it as they ate one of their sandwiches at half past eleven. 'This is bliss!' said George, lying back on a tuft of heather with her feet lapped by the water. 'The stream is tickling my feet, and the sun is warming my face – lovely! Oh, get away, Timmy, you idiot! Breathing down my neck like that, and making my face so wet!'

The stream at last joined the path that led to the village of Reebles. They walked along it, beginning to think of dinner. It would be fun to have it in a little inn or perhaps a farmhouse, and keep their sandwiches for tea-time.

'But first we must find the police station,' said Julian. 'We'll get our tale told, and then we'll be ready for our meal!'

CHAPTER TEN

An angry policeman and a fine lunch

THERE *WAS* a police station at Reebles, a small one with a house for the policeman attached. As the one policeman had four villages under his control he felt himself to be rather an important fellow.

He was in his house having his dinner when the children walked up to the police station. They found nobody there, and walked out again. The policeman had seen them from his window and he came out, wiping his mouth. He wasn't very pleased at having to come out in the middle of a nice meal of sausage and onions.

'What do you want?' he said, suspiciously. He didn't like children of any sort. Nasty little things, he thought them – always full of mischief and cheek. He didn't know which were worse, the small ones or the big ones!

Julian spoke to him politely. 'We've come to report something rather strange, which we thought perhaps the police ought to know. It might help them to catch the prisoner who escaped last night.'

'Ha!' said the policeman scornfully. 'You've seen him too, I suppose? You wouldn't believe how many people have seen him. 'Cording to them he's been in every part of the moor at one and the same time. Clever fellow he must be to split himself up like that.'

'Well, one of us saw him last night,' said Julian politely. 'At least, we think it must have been him. He gave a message to my brother here.'

'Ho, he did, did he?' said the policeman, eyeing Dick in a most disbelieving manner. 'So he runs about giving messages to schoolboys, does he? And what message did he give you, may I ask?'

The message sounded extremely silly when Dick repeated it to the police. 'Two-Trees. Gloomy Water. Saucy Jane. And Maggie knows.'

'Really?' said the policeman, in a sarcastic voice. 'Maggie knows as well, does she? Well, you tell Maggie to come along here and tell me too. I'd like to meet Maggie – specially if she's a friend of yours.'

'She's not,' said Dick feeling annoyed. 'That was in the message. I don't know who Maggie is! How should I? We thought perhaps the police could unravel the meaning. We couldn't. The fellow gave me this bit of paper too.'

He handed the piece of dirty paper to the policeman, who looked at it with a crooked smile. 'So he gave you this too, did he?' he said. 'Now wasn't that kind of him? And what do you suppose all this is, scribbled on the paper?'

'We don't know,' said Dick. 'But we thought our report might help the police to catch the prisoner, that's all.'

'The prisoner's caught,' said the policeman, with a smirk on his face. 'You know so much – but you didn't know that! Yes, he's caught – four hours ago – and he's safe back in prison now. And let me tell you youngsters this – I'm not taken in by any silly school-boy spoofing, see?'

'It's not spoofing,' said Julian, in a very grown-up manner. 'You should learn to see the difference between the truth and a joke.'

That didn't please the policeman at all. He turned on Julian at once, his face reddening.

'Now, you run away!' he said. 'I'm not having any cheek from you! Do you want me to take your names and addresses and report you?'

'If you like,' said Julian, in disgust. 'Have you got a notebook there? I'll give you all our names, and I myself will make a report to the police in our district when I get back.'

The policeman stared at him. He couldn't help being impressed by Julian's manner, and he calmed down a little.

'You go away, all of you,' he said, his voice not nearly so fierce. 'I shan't report you this time. But don't you go spreading silly stories like that or you'll get into trouble. Serious trouble too.'

'I don't think so,' said Julian. 'Anyway, seeing that you are not going to do anything about our story, may we have back our bit of paper, please?'

The policeman frowned. He made as if he would tear the paper up, but Dick snatched at it. He was too late. The aggravating policeman had torn it into four pieces and thrown it into the road!

'Don't you have laws against scattering litter in your village?' asked Dick, severely, and carefully picked up the four pieces of paper. The policeman glared at Dick as he put the bits into his pocket. Then he made a peculiar snorting noise, turned on his heel and marched back to his sausages and onions.

'And I hope his dinner's gone cold!' said George. 'Horrid fellow! Why should he think we're telling a lot of untruths?'

'It is rather an odd story of ours,' said Julian. 'After all – we found it a bit difficult to believe when Dick first told it. I don't blame the policeman for disbelieving it – I blame him for his manner. It's a good thing most of our police aren't the same. Nobody would ever report anything.'

'He told us one bit of good news, anyway,' said Anne. 'That escaped prisoner is back in prison again! I'm so relieved to know that.'

'I am too,' said Dick. 'I didn't like the look of him at all. Well, Ju – what do we do now? Forget the whole business? Do *you* think there's anything in that message to follow up? And if so – can we do anything?'

'I don't know,' said Julian. 'We must think a bit. Let's go and see if we can scrounge a meal in some farmhouse somewhere. There seem to be plenty around.'

They asked a little girl if there was a farmhouse anywhere near that would give them dinner. She nodded and pointed.

'See that farmhouse up on the hill there? That's my

gran's place. She'll give you dinner, I expect. She used to give dinner in the summer to trippers, and I expect she would give you some too, if you ask her, though it's late in the season.'

'Thanks,' said Julian, and they all went up the lane that curved round the hillside. Dogs barked loudly as they came near and Timmy's hackles went up at once. He growled.

'Friends, Timmy, friends,' said George. 'Dinner here, Timmy. Dinner, perhaps a nice bone for you. Bone!'

Timmy understood. The fur down his neck lay flat again and he stopped growling. He wagged his tail at the two dogs near the farm gate who sniffed his doggy smell suspiciously even when he was some distance away.

A man hailed them. 'What do you kids want? Mind those dogs!'

'We wondered if we could get a meal here!' called back Julian. 'A little girl down in the village said we might.'

'I'll ask my mother,' said the man, and he yelled in an enormous voice to the farmhouse nearby. 'Ma! MA! Four kids out here want to know if you can give them a meal.'

A very plump old lady appeared, with twinkling eyes and red cheeks like an apple. She took one glance at the four by the gate, and nodded her head. 'Yes. They look decent children. Tell them to come along in. Better hold their dog's collar though.'

The four walked to the farmhouse, George holding Timmy firmly. The other two dogs came up, but as

Timmy was hoping for a bone, he was determined to be friendly, and not a single growl came from him, even when the two dogs growled suspiciously. He wagged his tail, and let his tongue hang out.

The other dogs soon wagged theirs, and then it was safe to let Timmy go. He bounded over to them and there was a mad game of 'chase-me-roll-me-over' as George called it.

'Come your ways in,' said the plump old lady. 'Now you'll have to take what we've got. I'm busy today and haven't had time for cooking. You can have a bit of homemade meat pie, or a slice or two of ham and tongue, or hard-boiled eggs and salad. Bless you, you look as pleased as Punch! I'll put the lot on the table for you and you can help yourselves! Will that do? There's no vegetables though. You'll have to make do with pickled cabbage and my own pickled onions and beetroot in vinegar.'

'It sounds too marvellous for words,' said Julian. 'We shan't want any sweet after that!'

'There's no pudding today,' said the old lady. 'But I'll open a bottle or two of our own raspberries and you can have them with cream if you like. And there's the cream cheese I made yesterday too.'

'Don't tell us any more!' begged Dick. 'It makes me feel too hungry. Why is it that people on farms always have the most delicious food? I mean, surely people in towns can bottle raspberries and pickle onions and make cream cheese?'

'Well, either they can't or they don't,' said George. 'My

mother does all those things – and even when she lived in a town she did. Anyway, *I'm* going to when I'm grown-up. It must be so wonderful to offer home-made things by the score when people come to a meal!'

It was extraordinary to think that any children could possibly eat the meal the four did, after having had such a huge breakfast. Timmy ate an enormous dinner too, and then lay down with a sigh. How he wished he could live at that farmhouse! How lucky those other two dogs were!

A small girl came in shyly as they ate. 'I'm Meg,' she said. 'I live with my gran. What are your names?'

They told her. Then Julian had an idea. 'We're walking over your moor,' he said. 'We've been to lots of nice places. But there's one we haven't been to yet. Do you know it? It's called Two-Trees.'

The little girl shook her head. 'Gran would know,' she said. 'Gran! Where's Two-Trees?'

The old lady looked in at the door. 'What's that? Two-Trees? Oh, that was a lovely place once, but it's all in ruins now. It was built beside a strange dark lake, in the middle of the moors. Let's see now – what was it called?'

'Gloomy Water?' said Dick.

'Yes! That's right. Gloomy Water,' said the old lady. 'Are you thinking of going by there? You be careful then, there's marshland around there, just when you least expect it! Now – would you like anything more?'

'No thank you,' said Julian, regretfully, and paid the

very modest bill. 'It's the nicest lunch we've ever had. Now we must be off.'

'Off to Two-Trees and Gloomy Water, I hope!' George whispered to Dick. 'That would be really exciting.'

CHAPTER ELEVEN

Julian's idea

ONCE OUTSIDE the farmhouse Julian looked round at the others. 'We'll find out how far Two-Trees is and see if we've got time to pay it visit,' he said. 'If we have, we'll go along there and snoop round. If we haven't we'll go tomorrow.'

'How can we find out how far it is?' said Dick eagerly. 'Will it be on your map?'

'It may be marked there if the lake is big enough,' said Julian. They walked down the hill, and took a path that led once more over the moors. As soon as they were out of sight and hearing of anyone Julian stopped and took out his big map. He unfolded it and the four of them crouched over it as he spread it out on the heather.

'That nice old lady said it was in the middle of the moors,' said Julian. 'Also we know there's a lake or at any rate a big pool of some kind.'

His finger traced its way here and there on the map. Then George gave a cry and dabbed her finger down.

'There, look! It's not really in the middle. See – Gloomy Water! That must be it. Is Two-Trees marked as well?'

'No,' said Julian. 'But perhaps it wouldn't be if it's in ruins. Ruins aren't marked on maps unless they are important in some way. This can't be important. Well – that's certainly Gloomy Water marked there. What do you say? Shall we have a shot at going there this afternoon? I wonder exactly how far it is.'

'We could ask at the post-office,' said George. 'Probably once upon a time the postman had to take letters there. They might know. They could tell us the way to go.'

They went back to the village and found the post-office. It was part of the village store. The old man who kept it looked over the top of his glasses at the children.

'Gloomy Water! Now what be you wanting that for? A real miserable place it is, and it used to be so fine.'

'What happened to it?' asked Dick.

'It was burnt,' said the old man. 'The owner was away, and only a couple of servants were there. It flared up one night, no one knows how or why – and was burnt almost to a shell. Couldn't get a fire-engine out there, you see. There was only a cart-track to the place.'

'And wasn't it ever built up again?' asked Julian. The old man shook his head.

'No. It wasn't worth it. The owner just let it fall to rack and ruin. The jackdaws and the owls nest there now, and the wild animals snuggle in the ruins. It's a peculiar place. I once went out to see it, hearing tales of lights being seen there. But there was nothing to see but the shell of the place, and the dark blue water. Ah, Gloomy Water's a good name for that lake!'

'Could you tell us the way? And how long would it take us to get there?' asked Julian.

'What for do you want to go and gaze at a poor old ruin?' said the old man. 'Or do you want to bathe in the lake? Well, don't you do so – it's freezing cold!'

'We just thought we'd go and see Gloomy Water,' said Julian. 'Such a strange name. Which is the way, did you say?'

'I didn't say,' said the old fellow. 'But I will if you're so set on it. Where's your map? Is that one in your hand?'

Julian spread it out. The old fellow took a pen from his waistcoat pocket and began to trace a path over the moor. He put crosses here and there.

'See them crosses? They mark marshland. Don't go treading there, or you'll be up to your knees in muddy water! You follow these paths I've inked in for you and you'll be all right. Keep your eyes open for deer – there's plenty about those parts, and pretty things they are too.'

'Thank you very much,' said Julian, folding up the map. 'How long would it take us to get there from here?'

'Matter of two hours or more,' said the old man. 'Don't you try to go this afternoon. You'll find yourselves in darkness coming back, and with them dangerous marshy bits you're in danger all the time!'

'Right,' said Julian. 'Thanks very much. Er – we're thinking of doing a bit of camping, as the weather is so beautiful. I suppose you couldn't hire us a groundsheet or two and a few rugs?'

The other three stared at him in astonishment. Camping

out? Where? Why? What was Julian thinking of all of a sudden?

Julian winked at them. The old man was ferreting about in a cupboard. He pulled out two large rubber groundsheets and four old rugs. 'Thought I had them somewhere!' he said. 'Well, better you camping out in October than me! Be careful you don't catch your deaths of cold!'

'Oh thanks – just what we want,' said Julian, pleased. 'Roll them up, you others. I'll settle up for them.'

Dick, Anne and George folded up the groundsheets and the rugs in astonishment. Surely – surely Julian wasn't thinking of camping out by Gloomy Water? He must think the message that Dick had been given was very important!

'Julian!' said Dick, as soon as they got outside. 'What's up? What's all this for?'

Julian looked a little sheepish. 'Well – something suddenly came over me in the store,' he said. 'I suddenly felt we ought to go to Gloomy Water and snoop round. I felt excited somehow. And as we've got so little time this weekend I thought if we took things and camped out in the ruin we might make more of our few days.'

'What an idea!' said George. 'Not go on with our hiking, do you mean?'

'Well,' said Julian. 'If we find nothing, we *can* go on with our hike, of course. But if there's anything interesting, it's up to us to unearth it. I'm quite sure there's something up at Two-Trees.'

'We might meet Maggie there!' said Anne, with a giggle.

'We might!' said Julian. 'I feel quite free to go and investigate on our own seeing that we've made our report to the police, and it's been turned down with scorn. *Somebody* ought to follow up that message – besides Maggie!'

'Dear Maggie,' said Dick. 'I wonder who in the wide world she is!'

'Somebody worth watching if she's the friend of convicts,' said Julian, more soberly. 'Look, this is what I thought we'd do – buy some extra food, and go along to Gloomy Water this afternoon, arriving there before dark. We'll find a good place to shelter in – there must be some good spot in the old ruin – and get heather or bracken for beds. Then tomorrow we can be up bright and early to have a look round.'

'It sounds smashing,' said Dick, pleased. 'Sort of thing we like. What do you say, Tim?'

'Woof,' said Tim, solemnly, bumping his tail to and fro across Dick's legs.

'And if we find there's absolutely nothing of interest, well, we can come back here with the things we've borrowed, and go on with our hike,' said Julian. 'But we'll have to sleep the night there because it will be dark by the time we've had a look round.'

They bought some loaves of bread, some butter and potted meat, and a big fruit cake. Also some more chocolate and some biscuits. Julian bought a bottle of orangeade as well.

'There's sure to be a well,' he said. 'Or a spring of some sort. We can dilute the orangeade and drink it when we're thirsty. Now I think we're ready. Come on!'

They couldn't go as fast as usual because they were carrying so many things. Timmy was the only one that ran as fast as ever – but then Timmy carried nothing but himself!

It was a really lovely walk over the moorlands. They climbed fairly high and had wonderful views all over the autumn countryside. They saw wild ponies again, in the distance this time, and a little herd of dappled deer, which sped away immediately.

Julian was very careful to take the right paths – the ones traced so carefully on the map by the old man in the post office. 'I expect he knew the way well because he was once a postman and had to take letters to Two-Trees!' said Dick, bending over the map. 'We're getting on, Ju – halfway there!'

The sun began to sink low. The children hurried as much as they could because once the sun had gone darkness would soon come. Fortunately the sky was very clear, so twilight would be later than it had been the night before.

'It looks as if the moorland near here gives way soon to a little bit of wooded country, according to the map,' said Julian. 'We'll look out for clumps of trees.'

After another little stretch of moorland Julian pointed to the right. 'Look!' he said. 'Trees! Quite a lot – a proper little wood.'

'And isn't that water over there?' said Anne. They stood still and gazed hard. Was it Gloomy Water? It might be. It looked such a dark blue. They hurried on eagerly. It didn't look very far now. Timmy ran ahead, his long tail waving in the air.

They went down a little winding path and joined a cart-track that was very much overgrown – so overgrown that it hardly looked like a track. 'This must lead to Two-Trees,' said Julian. 'I wish the sun wasn't going down so quickly. We'll hardly have any time to look round!'

They entered a wood. The track wound through it. The trees must have been cleared at some time to make a road through the wood. And then, quite suddenly, they came on what had once been the lovely house of Two-Trees.

It was a desolate ruin, blackened and scorched with fire. The windows had no glass, the roof had gone, except for a few rafters here and there. Two birds flew up with a loud cry as the children went near.

'Two Maggies!' said Anne, with a laugh. They were black and white magpies, their long tails stretched out behind them. 'I wonder if they know the message too.'

The house stood on the edge of the lake. Gloomy Water was indeed a good name for it. It lay there, smooth and dark, a curious deep blue. No little waves lapped the edge. It was as still as if it were frozen.

'I don't like it,' said Anne. 'I don't like this place at all! I wish we hadn't come!'

CHAPTER TWELVE

A hiding place at Two-Trees

NOBODY PARTICULARLY liked the place. They all stared round and Julian pointed silently to something. At each end of the house was the great burnt trunk of a big tree.

'Those must be the two trees that gave the place its name,' said Julian. 'How horrid they look now, so stiff and black. Two-Trees and Gloomy Water – all so lonely and desolate now.'

The sun disappeared and a little chill came on the air. Julian suddenly became very busy. 'Come on – we must see if there's anywhere to shelter at all in this old ruin!'

They went to the silent house. The upper floors were all burnt out. The ground floor was pretty bad too, but Julian thought it might be possible to find a sheltered corner.

'This might do,' he said, coming out of a blackened room and beckoning the others to him. 'There is even a mouldy carpet still on the floor! And there's a big table. We could sleep under it if it rained – which I don't think it will do!'

'What a horrid room!' said Anne, looking round. 'I don't like its smell, either. I don't want to sleep here.'

'Well, find somewhere else then, but be quick about it,' said Julian. 'It will soon be dark. I'm going to collect heather and bracken straight away, before it's too dark. Coming, Dick and George?'

The three of them went off and came back with vast armfuls of heather and brown bracken. Anne met them, looking excited.

'I've found somewhere. Somewhere much better than this horrid room. Come and look.'

She took them to what once had been the kitchen. A door lay flat on the floor at the end of the room, and a stone stairway led downwards.

'That leads down to the cellars,' said Anne. 'I came in here and saw that door. It was locked and I couldn't open it. Well, I tugged and tugged and the whole door came off its rusty old hinges and tumbled down almost on top of me! And I saw there were cellars down there!'

She stared at Julian beseechingly. 'They'll be dry. They won't be burnt and black like everywhere else. We'll be well-sheltered. Can't we sleep down there? I don't like the feel of these horrid burnt rooms.'

'It's an idea,' said Julian. He switched on his torch and let the beam light up the cellar below. It seemed spacious and smelt all right.

He went down the steps, Timmy just in front. He called up in surprise.

'There's a proper room down here, as well as cellars all round. Maybe it was a kind of sitting-room for the staff. It's wired for electricity too – they must have had their own electricity generator. Yes – we'll certainly come down here.'

It was a strange little room. Moth-eaten carpets were on the floor, and the furnishings were moth-eaten too and covered with dust. Spiders had been at work and George slashed fiercely at the long cobwebs that hung down and startled her by touching her face.

'There are still candles in the candlesticks on this shelf!' said Dick, surprised. 'We can light them and have a bit of brightness when it's dark. This isn't bad at all. I must say I agree with Anne. There's something hateful about those burnt-out rooms.'

They piled heather and bracken into the cellar room on the floor. The furniture was so old and moth-eaten that it gave beneath their weight, and was useless for sitting on. The table was all right though. They soon set out their food on it after George had wiped it free of dust. She caused them all to have fits of choking because she was so vigorous in her dusting! They were driven up into the kitchen till the dust had settled.

It was dark outside now. The moon was not yet up. The wind rustled the dry leaves left on the trees around, but there was no lap-lap of water. The lake was as still as glass.

There was a cupboard in the cellar room. Julian opened it to see what was there. 'More candles – good!' he said, bringing out a bundle. 'And plates and cups. Did anyone see a well outside? If so we could dilute some orangeade and have a drink with our supper.'

No one had noticed a well – but Anne suddenly

remembered something peculiar she had seen in a corner of the kitchen, near the sink.

'I believe I saw a pump up there!' she said. 'Go and see, Ju. If so, it might still work.'

He went up the cellar steps with a candle. Yes – Anne was right. That *was* an old pump over there in the corner. It probably pumped water into a tank and came out of the kitchen taps.

He turned on a big tap which was over the large sink. Then he took the handle of the pump and worked it vigorously up and down. Splash! Splash! Water came flooding through the big tap and splashed into the sink! That was good.

Julian pumped and pumped, feeling that he had better get rid of any water running into the tank for the first time for years. The tank might be dirty or rusty – he must wash it round with a good deal of pumped water first.

The water seemed to be clean and clear, and was certainly as cold as ice! Julian held a cup from the cellar cupboard under the tap, and then tasted the water. It was delicious.

'Good for you, Anne!' he called, going down the cellar steps with a cupful of water. 'Dick, you find some more cups – or a jug or something in that cupboard, and we'll wash them out and fill them with water for our orangeade.'

The cellar room looked very cheerful as Julian came down the steps. George and Anne had lit six more candles, and stuck them about here and there. The light they gave was very pleasant, and they also warmed the room a little.

'Well, I suppose as usual, everyone wants a meal?' said Julian. 'Good thing we bought that bread and potted meat and stuff. I can't say I'm as hungry as I was at breakfast, but I'm getting that way.'

The four squatted round on their beds of heather and bracken. They had put down their groundsheets first in case the floor was damp, though it didn't seem to be. Over bread and butter and potted meat they discussed their plans. They would sleep there for the night and then have all the next day to examine Two-Trees and the lake.

'What exactly are we looking for?' asked Anne. 'Do you suppose there's some secret here, Julian?'

'Yes,' said Julian. 'And I think I know what it is!'

'What?' asked George and Anne, surprised. Dick thought he knew. Julian explained.

'Well, we know that a prisoner called Nailer sent an important message by his escaped friend to two people – one he wanted to send to Dirty Dick – but he didn't get it – and the other to Maggie, whoever she is. Now what secret does he want to tell them?'

'I think I can guess,' said Dick. 'But go on.'

'Now suppose that Nailer has done some big robberies,' said Julian. 'I don't know what. Jewellery robberies probably, because they are the commonest with big criminals. All right – he does a big robbery – he hides the stuff till he hopes the hue and cry will be over – but he's caught and put into prison for a number of years. But he doesn't tell where the stuff is hidden! He daren't even write a letter to tell his friends outside the prison where it is. All his letters are read before they leave the prison. So what is he to do?'

'Wait till someone escapes and then give him a message,' said Dick. 'And that's just what happened, isn't it, Julian? That round-headed man I saw was the escaped prisoner, and he was sent to tell Dirty Dick and Maggie where the stolen goods were hidden – so that they could get them before anyone else did!'

'Yes. I'm sure that's it,' said Julian. 'His friend, the escaped prisoner, probably wouldn't understand the message at all – but Dirty Dick and Maggie would, because they knew all about the robbery. And now Maggie will certainly try to find out where the stuff is.'

'Well, we must find it first!' said George, her eyes gleaming with excitement. 'We're here first, anyway. And tomorrow, as early as possible we'll begin to snoop round. What was the next clue in the message, Dick? After Two-Trees and Gloomy Water.'

'Saucy Jane,' said Dick.

'Sounds a silly sort of clue,' said Anne. 'Do you suppose Maggie and Jane are *both* in the secret?'

'Saucy Jane sounds more like a boat to me,' said Dick.

'Of *course*!' said George. 'A boat! Why not? There's a lake here, and I imagine that people don't build a house beside a lake unless they want to go boating and bathing and fishing. I bet we shall find a boat called *Saucy Jane* tomorrow – and the stolen goods will be inside it.'

'Too easy!' said Dick. 'And not a very clever place either. Anyone could come across goods hidden in a boat. No – *Saucy Jane* is a clue, but we shan't find the stolen goods in her. And remember, there's that bit of paper as well. It must have something to do with the hiding place too, I should think.'

'Where is it?' asked Julian. 'That wretched policeman! He tore it up. Have you still got the pieces, Dick?'

'Of course,' said Dick. He fished in his pocket and brought them out. 'Four little pieces! Anyone got some gummed paper?'

Nobody had – but George produced a small roll of plaster. Strips were cut and stuck behind the four portions of paper. Now it was whole again. They all examined it carefully.

'Look – four lines drawn, meeting in the centre,' said Julian. 'At the outer end of each line there's a word, so faintly written I can hardly read one of them. What's this one? "Tock Hill." And this next one is "Steeple". Whatever are the others?'

They made them out at last. ' "Chimney," ' said Anne. 'That's the third.'

'And "Tall Stone" is the fourth,' said George. 'Whatever do they all mean? We shall never, never find out!'

'We'll sleep on it,' said Julian, cheerfully. 'It's wonderful what good ideas come in the night. It will be a very interesting little problem to solve tomorrow!'

CHAPTER THIRTEEN

A night in the cellar

THE PIECE of paper was carefully folded and this time Julian took it for safe keeping. 'I can't imagine what it means, but it's clearly important,' he said. 'We may quite suddenly come on something – or think of something – that will give us a clue to what the words and the lines mean on the paper.'

'We mustn't forget that dear Maggie has a copy of the paper too,' said Dick. 'She probably knows better than we do what it all means!'

'If she does, she will pay a visit to Two-Trees too,' said Anne. 'We ought to keep a lookout for her. Should we have to hide if we saw her?'

Julian considered this. 'No,' he said, 'I certainly don't think we should hide. Maggie can't *possibly* guess that we have had the message from Nailer, and the paper too. We had better just say we are on a hike and found this place and thought we would shelter here. All perfectly true.'

'And we can keep an eye on her, and see what she does if she comes!' said Dick, with a grin. 'Won't she be annoyed!'

'She wouldn't come alone,' said Julian, thoughtfully. 'I should think it quite likely that she would come with Dirty Dick! He didn't get the message, but she did – and probably part of her message was the statement that Dirty Dick would know everything too. So she would get in touch with him.'

'Yes – and be surprised that he hadn't got the message or the paper,' said George. 'Still, they'd think that the escaped fellow hadn't been able to get to Dirty Dick.'

'All very complicated,' said Anne, yawning. 'I can't follow any more arguments and explanations – I'm half asleep. How long are you going to be before you settle down?'

Dick yawned too. 'I'm coming now,' he said. 'My bed of bracken and heather looks inviting. It's not at all cold in here, is it?'

'The only thing I don't like is the thought of those cellars beyond this little underground room,' said Anne. 'I keep thinking that Maggie and her friends might be there, waiting to pounce on us when we are asleep.'

'You're silly,' said George, scornfully. '*Really* silly! Do you honestly suppose that Timmy would lie here quietly if there was anyone in those cellars? You know jolly well he would be barking his head off!'

'Yes. I know all that,' said Anne, snuggling down in her heathery bed. 'It's just my imagination. You haven't got any, George, so you don't bother about imaginary fears. I'm not *really* scared while Timmy is here. But I do think it's funny the way we always plunge into something peculiar when we're together.'

'Adventures always do come to some people,' said Dick.

'You've only got to read the lives of explorers and see how they simply *walk* into adventures all the time.'

'Yes, but I'm not an explorer,' said Anne. 'I'm an ordinary person, and I'd be just as pleased if things *didn't* keep happening to me.'

The others laughed. 'I don't expect anything much will happen this time,' said Julian, comfortingly. 'We go back to school on Tuesday and that's not far off. Not much time for anything to happen!'

He was wrong of course. Things can happen one after the other in a few minutes! Still, Anne cuddled down feeling happier. This was better than last night when she was all alone in that horrid little loft. Now she had all the others with her, Timmy too.

Anne and George had one big bed between them. They drew their two rugs over themselves, and put their blazers on top too. Nobody had undressed because Julian had said that they might be too cold in just their night things.

Timmy as usual put himself on George's feet. She moved them because he was heavy. He wormed his way up the bed and found a very comfortable place between the knees of the two girls. He gave a heavy sigh.

'That means he's planning to go to sleep!' said George. 'Are you quite comfortable, Anne?'

'Yes,' said Anne, sleepily. 'I like Timmy there. I feel safe!'

Julian was blowing out the candles. He left just one

burning. Then he got into his bed of bracken and heather beside Dick. He felt tired too.

The four slept like logs. Nobody moved except Timmy, who got up once or twice in the night and sniffed round inquiringly. He had heard a noise in the cellars. He stood at the closed door that led to the cellars and listened, his head on one side.

He sniffed at the crack. Then he went back to bed, satisfied. It was only a toad! Timmy knew the smell of toads. If toads liked to crawl about in the night, they were welcome to!

The second time he awoke he thought he heard something up in the kitchen above. He padded up the steps, his paws making a click-click-click as he went. He stood in the kitchen silently, his eyes gleaming like green lamps, as the moon shone on him.

An animal with a long bushy tail began to slink away outside the house. It was a fine fox. It had smelt unusual smells near the old ruin – the scent of people and of a dog, and it had come to find out what was happening.

It had slunk into the kitchen and then smelt the strong scent of Timmy in the room below. As quietly as a cat it had slunk out again – but Timmy had awakened!

Now the dog stood watching and waiting – but the fox had gone! Timmy sniffed its scent and padded to the door. He debated whether to bark and go after the fox.

The scent grew very faint, and Timmy decided not to make a fuss. He padded back to the steps that led down to the cellar room, and curled up on George's feet again. He was very heavy, but George was too tired to wake up and push him off. Timmy lay with one ear cocked for a while, and then went to sleep again, with his ear still cocked. He was a good sentinel!

It was dark in the cellar when the one candle went out. There was no daylight or sunshine to wake the children down in that dim little room, and they slept late.

Julian woke up first. He found his bed suddenly very hard, and he turned over to find a comfortable place. The heather and bracken had been flattened with his weight, and the floor below was very hard indeed! The movement woke him up, and he lay blinking in the darkness. Where was he?

He remembered at once and sat up. Dick woke too and yawned. 'Dick! It's half past eight!!' said Julian, looking at the luminous hands of his wristwatch. 'We've slept for hours and hours!'

They rolled out of their heathery bed. Timmy leapt off George's feet and came over to them, his tail wagging gladly. He had been half-awake for a long time and was very glad to see Julian and Dick awake too, because he was thirsty.

The girls awoke – and soon there was a great deal of noise and activity going on. Anne and George washed at the big stone sink, the cold water making them squeal. Timmy lapped up a big bowlful of water gladly. The boys debated whether or not to have a splash in the lake. They felt very dirty.

Dick shivered at the thought. 'Still, I think we ought to,' he said. 'Come on, Ju!'

The two boys went down to the lakeside and leapt in. It was icy-cold! They swam out strongly and came back glowing and shouting.

By the time they were back the girls had got breakfast in the cellar room. It was darker than the kitchen, but all of them disliked the look of the burnt, scorched rooms above. The bread and butter, potted meat, cake and chocolate went down well.

In the middle of the meal a sound came echoing into the old house – bells! Anne stopped eating, and her heart beat fast.

But they were not the clanging warning bells she had heard before!

'Church bells,' said Julian at once, seeing Anne's sudden look of fright. 'Lovely sound I always think!'

'Oh *yes*,' said Anne, thankfully. 'So it is. It's Sunday and people are going to church. I'd like to go too, on this lovely sunny October day.'

'We might walk across the moor to the nearest village if you like,' said Dick, looking at his watch. 'But we should be very late.'

It was decided that it was much too late. They pushed their plates aside and planned what to do that day.

'The first thing, of course, is to see if there's a boathouse and find out if there's a boat called *Saucy Jane*,' said Julian. 'Then we'd better try and puzzle out what that plan means. We could wander here and there and see if we can find Tall Stone – and I'll look at the map to see if Tock Hill is marked. That was on the plan too, wasn't it?'

'You boys go and get some more heather and bracken while we clear away and wash up,' said Anne. 'That is if you mean us to camp here another night.'

'Yes. I think we will,' said Julian. 'I think we may find things rather interesting here this weekend!'

Julian went out with Dick and they brought in a great deal more bedding. Everyone had complained that the hard floor came through the amount of heather and bracken they had used the night before, and poor George was quite stiff.

The girls took the dirty things up to the big sink to wash them. There was nothing to dry them with but that didn't matter. They laid them on the old, worn draining board to dry.

They wiped their hands on their hankies and then felt ready for exploring round outside. The boys were ready too.

With Timmy bounding here and there they went down to the lake. A path had once led down to it, with a low wall on each side. But now the wall was broken, moss had crept everywhere, and the path was choked with tufts of heather and even with small bushes of gorse.

The lake was as still and dark as ever. Some moorhens chugged across it quickly, disappearing under the water when they saw the children.

'Now, what about the boathouse?' said Dick at last. 'Is there one – or not?'

CHAPTER FOURTEEN

Where is the Saucy Jane?

THEY WALKED beside the lake as best they could. It was difficult because bushes and trees grew right down to the edge. It seemed as if there was no boathouse at all.

And then George came to a little backwater, leading off the lake. 'Look!' she called. 'Here's a sort of river running from the lake.'

'It's not a river. It's only a little backwater,' said Dick. 'Now we *may* find a boathouse somewhere here.'

They followed the backwater a little way, and then Julian gave an exclamation. 'There it is! But it's so covered up with ivy and brambles that you can hardly see it!'

They all looked where he pointed. They saw a long, low building built right across the backwater, where it narrowed and came to an end. It was almost impossible to tell that it was a building, it was so overgrown.

'That's it!' said Dick, pleased. 'Now for the *Saucy Jane*!'

They scrambled through bushes and brambles to get to the entrance of the building. It had to be entered by the front, which was over the water and completely open. A broad ledge ran right round the boathouse inside, and the steps that went up to it from the bank outside were all broken away, completely rotted.

'Have to tread warily here,' said Julian. 'Let me go first.'

He tried the old wooden steps, but they gave way beneath him at once. 'Hopeless!' he said. 'Let's see if there's any other way into the boathouse.'

There wasn't – but at one side some of the wooden boards that made the wall of the boathouse were so rotten that they could be pulled away to make an opening. The boys pulled them down and then Julian squeezed through the opening into the dark, musty boathouse.

He found himself on the broad ledge that went round the great shed. Below him was the dark, quiet water with not even a ripple on it. He called to the others.

'Come along in! There's a wooden ledge to stand on here, and it's hardly rotted at all. It must be made of better wood.'

They all went through the opening and stood on the ledge, peering down. Their eyes had to get used to the darkness at first, because the only light came through the big entrance at the farther end – and that was obscured by big trails of ivy and other creepers hanging down from roof to water.

'There *are* boats here!' said Dick, excited. 'Tied up to posts. Look – there's one just below us. Let's hope one of them is the *Saucy Jane*!'

There were three boats. Two of them were half full of

water, and their bows were sunk right down. 'Must have got holes in them,' said Julian, peering about. He had got out his torch and was shining it all round the old boathouse.

Oars were strung along the walls. Dirty, pulpy masses of something lay on the shelves too – rotted cushions probably. A boat-hook stood in one corner. Ropes were in coils on a shelf. It was a dreary, desolate sight, and Anne didn't like the strange echoes of their voices in the damp-smelling, lonely boathouse.

'Let's see if any of the boats are called *Saucy Jane*,' said Dick. He flashed his torch on to the nearest one. The name was almost gone.

'What is it?' said Dick, trying to decipher the faded letters. '*Merry* something.'

'*Meg*!' said Anne. '*Merry Meg*. Well, she may be a sister of *Saucy Jane*. What's the next boat's name?'

The torch shone steadily on to it. The name there was easier to read. They all read it at once.

'*Cheeky Charlie*!'

'Brother to *Merry Meg*!' said Dick. 'Well, all I can say is that these poor old boats look anything but merry or cheeky.'

'I'm sure the last one must be *Saucy Jane*!' said Anne, excited. 'I do hope it is!'

They went along the broad ledge and tried to read the name on the half-sunk boat there. 'It begins with C,' said George, disappointed. 'I'm sure it's C.'

CHARLIE
MEG

Julian took out his handkerchief and dipped it in the water. He rubbed at the name to try and clean it and make it clearer.

It could be read then – but it wasn't *Saucy Jane*!

'*Careful Carrie*!' read the four, mournfully. 'Blow!'

'*Merry Meg, Cheeky Charlie, Careful Carrie*,' said Julian. 'Well, it's quite obvious that *Saucy Jane* belongs to the family of boats here – but where oh where is she?'

'Sunk out of sight?' suggested Dick.

'Don't think so,' said Julian. 'The water is pretty shallow in this boathouse – it's right at the very end of the little backwater, you see. I think we should be able to spot a boat sunk to the bottom. We can see the sandy bottom of the backwater quite clearly by the light of our torches.'

Just to make quite sure, they walked carefully all round the broad wooden ledge and flashed their torches on the water that filled the boathouse. There was no completely sunken boat there at all.

'Well, that's that,' said Dick. 'The *Saucy Jane* is gone. Where? Why? And when?'

They flashed their torches round the walls of the boathouse once more. George's eye was caught by a large, flat wooden thing standing upright on the ledge at one side of the house.

'What's that?' she said. 'Oh – a raft, isn't it? That's what those paddles are for, then, that I saw on the shelf above.'

They went and examined the raft. 'Yes – and in quite

good condition too,' said Julian. 'It would be rather fun to see if it would carry us on the water.'

'Ooooh *yes*!' said Anne, thrilled. 'That would be super. I always like rafts. I'd rather try that raft than any of those boats.'

'Well, there's only one boat that is possible to use,' said Julian. 'The others are obviously no good – they must have big holes in them to sink down like that.'

'Hadn't we better look into them carefully just to make sure there's no loot hidden there?' said Dick.

'If you like,' said Julian. 'But *I* think it's *Saucy Jane* that's got the loot – otherwise why mention it by name in that message?'

Dick felt that Julian was right. All the same he went to examine the three boats most methodically. But except for rotted and burst cushions and coils of rope there was nothing to be seen in the boats at all.

'Well – where's the *Saucy Jane*?' said Dick, puzzled. 'All the family are here but her. Can she be hidden anywhere on the banks of the lake?'

'*That's* an idea!' said Julian, who was trying to shift the big raft. 'That's a really good idea! I think we ought to explore all round the lake and see if we can find the *Saucy Jane* hidden anywhere.'

'Let's leave the raft for a bit then,' said George, feeling thrilled at the thought of possibly finding the *Saucy Jane* tucked away somewhere, all the loot hidden in her. 'Let's go now!'

They made their way round the wooden ledge to the opening they had made in the side of the boathouse, and jumped down. Timmy leapt down gladly. He hadn't liked the dark boathouse at all. He ran into the warm sunshine, wagging his tail.

'Now which side of the lake shall we go to first?' said Anne. 'The left or the right?'

They went down to the edge of the silent water and looked to left and right. They both seemed to be equally thick with bushes!

'It's going to be difficult to keep close to the edge of the water,' said Julian. 'Anyway, we'll try. The left side looks a bit easier. Come on!'

It was fairly easy at first to keep close to the water, and examine any tiny creek or look under overhanging bushes. But after about a quarter of a mile the undergrowth became so very thick and grew so close to the water's edge that it was quite impossible to force their way through it without completely ruining their clothes.

'I give up!' said Julian at last. 'I shall have no jersey left in a minute! These spiteful brambles! My hands are ripped to bits.'

'Yes – they *are* spiteful!' said Anne. 'I felt that too!'

Timmy was the only one really enjoying himself. He couldn't *imagine* why the four were scrambling through such thick undergrowth, but as it was just what he liked he was very pleased. He was disappointed when they decided to give up and go back.

'Shall we try the right-hand side of the lake, do you think?' said Julian, as they went back, rather disheartened.

'No. Don't let's,' said Anne. 'It looks even worse than this side. It's only a waste of time. I'd rather go out on the raft!'

'Well – that would surely be a better way of exploring the banks of the lake than scrambling through prickly bushes, wouldn't it?' said George. 'We'd only need to paddle along slowly and squint into all the little creeks and under overhanging trees – it would be easy!'

'Of course,' said Dick. 'We were silly not to think of it

before. It would be a lovely way of spending the afternoon, anyway.'

They came through the trees and saw the ruined house in the distance. Timmy suddenly stopped. He gave a low growl, and all the others stopped too.

'What's up, Timmy?' said George in a low voice. 'What is it?'

Timmy growled again. The others cautiously retreated behind bushes and looked intently towards the house. They could see nothing out of the way. Nobody seemed to be about. Then what was Timmy growling at?

And then a woman came in sight, and with her was a man. They were talking earnestly together.

'Maggie! I bet it's Maggie!' said Julian.

'And the other is Dirty Dick,' said Dick. 'I recognise him – yes – it's Dirty Dick.'

CHAPTER FIFTEEN

Maggie – and Dirty Dick

THEY WATCHED the couple in the distance, and thought quickly. Julian had been expecting them, so he was not surprised. Dick was looking at Dirty Dick, recognising the broad, short man, with his hunched-up shoulders and shock of hair. He didn't like the look of him any more than when he had seen him up at the old cottage!

Anne and George didn't like the look of the woman either! She was wearing trousers and had a jacket draped round her shoulders. She was also wearing sunglasses, and smoking a cigarette. She walked quickly and they could hear her voice. It was sharp and determined.

'So that's Maggie,' thought Julian. 'Well, I don't like her. She looks as hard as nails – a good companion for Nailer!'

He moved cautiously towards the other three. George had her hand on Timmy's collar, afraid that he might show himself.

'Listen,' said Julian. 'You're none of you to turn a hair! We'll just walk out into the open, talking cheerfully together and let them see us. If they ask us what we're doing, you all know what to say. Chatter nonsense as much as you like – put them off and make them think we're a bunch of harmless kids. If there are any leading questions asked us – leave *me* to answer them. Ready?'

They nodded. Then Julian swung out from the bushes and walked into the open, calling to Dick. 'Here we are again – there's the old house! My word, it looks worse than ever this morning!'

George and Timmy came bounding out together, and Anne followed, her heart beating fast. She wasn't as good as the others at this sort of thing!

The man and the woman stopped abruptly when they saw the children. They said a few words to one another very rapidly. The man scowled.

The children went towards them, chattering all the time as Julian had ordered. The woman called sharply to them.

'Who are you?' What are you doing here?'

'Just hiking,' said Julian, stopping. 'It's our half-term.'

'What do you want to come *here* for then?' asked the woman. 'This is private property.'

'Oh no,' said Julian. 'It's only a burnt-out ruin. Anyone can come. We want to explore this strange lake – it looks exciting.'

The man and the woman looked at one another. It was clear that the idea of the children exploring the lake was surprising and annoying to them. The woman spoke again.

'You can't explore this lake. It's dangerous. People are forbidden to bathe in it or use a boat.'

'We weren't told that,' said Julian, looking astonished. 'We were told how to get here, and no one said the lake was forbidden. You've been told wrongly.'

'We want to watch the moorhens, you see,' put in Anne, suddenly seeing a moorhen on the water. 'We're fond of nature.'

'And we've been told there are deer near here,' said George.

'And wild ponies,' said Dick. 'We saw some yesterday. They were really lovely. Have you seen any?'

This sudden burst of chatter seemed to annoy the man and the woman more than Julian's answers. The man spoke roughly.

'Stop this nonsense. People aren't allowed here. Clear out before we make you!'

'Why are *you* here, then, if people aren't allowed?' asked Julian, and a hard tone came into his voice. 'Don't talk to us like that.'

'You clear off, I say!' cried the man, suddenly shouting loudly as he lost his temper. He took two or three steps towards them, looking very threatening indeed. George loosed her hold on Timmy's collar.

Timmy also took two or three steps forward. His hackles went up and he emitted a most fearsome growl. The man stopped suddenly, and then retreated.

'Take hold of that dog's collar,' he ordered. 'He looks savage.'

'Then he looks what he is,' said George. 'I'm not taking

hold of his collar while you're about. Don't think it!'

Timmy took two or three more steps forward, growling loudly, walking stiffly and menacingly. The woman called out at once.

'It's all right, children. My friend here just lost his temper for a moment. Call your dog back.'

'Not while you are about,' said George. 'How long are you staying?'

'What's that to do with you?' growled the man, but he didn't say any more because Timmy at once growled back.

'Let's go and have something to eat,' said Julian, loudly, to the others. 'After all, we have as much right to be here as these people have. We don't need to take any notice of them – and we shan't be in *their* way!'

The four children marched forward. Timmy was still loose. He barked savagely once or twice as he came close to the unpleasant couple, and they shrank back at once. Timmy was such a big dog and he looked so very powerful! They eyed the children angrily as they went by, and watched them go into the ruined house.

'On guard, Timmy,' said George, as soon as they were in, pointing to the ruined doorway. Timmy understood at once, and stood in the doorway, a menacing figure with hackles up and snarling mouth. The children went down to the cellar room. They looked round to see if anyone had been there while they were away, but nothing seemed to have been moved.

'They probably haven't even noticed the cellars,' said Julian. 'I hope there's plenty of bread left. I'm hungry. I wish to goodness we were going to have a dinner like the one we had yesterday! I say – what an unpleasant pair Maggie and Dick are!'

'Yes. Very,' said Dick. 'I can't bear Maggie. Horrid mean voice and hard face. Ugh!'

'I think Dirty Dick is worse,' said Anne. 'He looks like a gorilla or something with his broad, hunched-up body. And WHY doesn't he cut his hair?'

'Fancies himself like that, I expect,' said George, cutting a loaf of bread. 'His surname ought to be Hairy. Or Tarzan. I'm jolly glad we've got Timmy.'

'So am I,' said Anne. 'Good old Timmy. He hated them, didn't he? I bet they won't come near the doorway with Timmy there!'

'I wonder where they are,' said Dick picking up a great hunk of bread and butter and potted meat. 'I'm going to look.'

He came back in half a minute. 'They've gone to the boathouse, I think,' he said. 'I just caught a sight of one of them moving in that direction. Looking for *Saucy Jane*, I expect.'

'Let's sit down and eat and talk over what we'll do next,' said Julian. 'And what we think *they* will do next! That's quite important. They may be able to read the clues on that paper better than we can. If we watch what they do it may give us a guide as to what *we* must do.'

'That's true,' said Dick. 'I imagine that the plan Nailer sent must mean something to Dirty Dick and Maggie, just as the message did.' He chewed at his bread, thinking hard, trying once more to fathom the meaning of that mysterious piece of paper.

'I think on the whole we will follow out our original plan for this afternoon,' said Julian, after a little silence. 'We'll get out that raft and go on the lake with it. It's a harmless-looking thing to do. We can examine the banks as we go – and if Maggie and Dick are out in a boat too, we can keep an eye on them as well.'

'Yes. Good idea,' said George. 'It's a heavenly afternoon anyway. I'd love to paddle about on the lake with that raft. I hope it's good and sound.'

'Sure to be,' said Dick. 'The wood it's made of is meant to last. Pass the cake, George – and *don't* save Timmy any. It's wasted on him.'

'It isn't!' said George. 'You know he loves it.'

'Yes. But I still say it's wasted on him,' said Dick. 'Good thing we got such an enormous cake! Are there any biscuits left?'

'Plenty,' said Anne. 'And chocolate too!'

'Good,' said Dick. 'I only hope our food will last us out. It won't if George has her usual colossal appetite.'

'What about yours?' said George, indignantly, rising every time to Dick's lazy teasing.

'Shut up, you two,' said Julian. 'I'm going to fill the

water jug and have some orangeade. Give me something to take to old Tim.'

They spent about half an hour over their lunch. Then they decided to go and tackle the raft in the boathouse, and see if they could possibly launch it on the lake. It would be heavy, they knew.

They left the old house and went off to the boathouse. Julian suddenly caught sight of something out on the lake.

'Look!' he said, 'they've got one of the boats out of the boathouse – the one that wasn't half-sunk, I suppose! Dirty Dick is rowing hard. I BET they're looking for the *Saucy Jane*!'

They all stood still and watched. Dick's heart sank. Would Maggie and Dirty Dick get there first, and find what he and the other three were looking for? Did they know where the *Saucy Jane* was?

'Come on,' said Julian. 'We'd better get going if we want to keep an eye on them. They may be rowing to where the *Saucy Jane* is hidden!'

They climbed in through the wooden side of the boathouse and went to the raft. Julian saw at once that one of the boats had gone – *Merry Meg*. It was the only boat that was fit to take.

The four began to manhandle the big raft. They took it to the edge of the ledge. It had rope handles on each side, which the children held on to.

'Now – ease her gently,' said Julian. 'Gently does it. Down she goes!'

And down she went, landing with a big splash in the water. She bobbed there gently, a strong, sound raft, eager to go out on the lake!

'Get the paddles,' said Julian. 'Then we'll be off.'

CHAPTER SIXTEEN

Out on the raft

THERE WERE four little paddles. Dick got them, and gave everyone one each. Timmy looked down solemnly at the raft. What was it? Surely he was not expected to ride on that bobbing, floating thing?

Julian was on the raft already, holding it steady for the others. He helped Anne on and then George stepped down. Dick came last – well, not quite last, because Timmy was not yet on.

'Come on, Tim!' said George. 'It's all right! It's not the kind of boat you're used to, but it acts in the same way. Come *on*, Timmy!'

Timmy jumped down and the raft bobbed violently. Anne sat down suddenly with a giggle. 'Oh dear – Timmy is so *sudden*! Keep still, Tim – there isn't enough room on this raft for you to walk all over it.'

Julian pushed the raft out of the boathouse. It knocked against the wooden ledge as it went, and then swung out on to the backwater outside. It floated very smoothly.

'Here we go!' said Julian, paddling deftly. 'I'll steer, Dick. None of you need to paddle till I say so. I can paddle and steer at the moment, till we get on to the lake itself.'

They were all sitting on the raft except Timmy, who was standing up. He was very interested in seeing the water flow past so quickly. *Was* this a boat then? He was used to boats – but in boats the water was never quite so near. Timmy put out a paw into the water. It was pleasantly cool and tickled him. He lay down with his nose almost in the water.

'You're a funny dog, Timmy!' said Anne. 'You won't get up too suddenly, will you, or you'll knock me overboard.'

Julian paddled down the little backwater and the raft swung out on to the lake itself. The children looked to see if there was any sign of Maggie and Dirty Dick.

'There they are!' said Julian. 'Out in the middle, rowing hard. Shall we follow them? If they know where the *Saucy Jane* is they'll lead us to it.'

'Yes. Follow them,' said Dick. 'Shall *we* paddle now? We'll have to be quick or we may lose them.'

They all paddled hard, and the raft suddenly swung to and fro in a most alarming manner.

'Hey, stop!' shouted Julian. 'You're all paddling against one another. We're going round in circles. Dick and Anne go one side and George the other. That's better. Watch how we're going, all of you, and stop paddling for a moment if the raft swings round too much.'

They soon got into the way of paddling so that the raft went straight ahead. It was fun. They got very hot and wished they could take off their jerseys. The sun was quite warm, and there was no wind at all – it was really a perfect October afternoon.

'They've stopped rowing,' said George, suddenly. 'They're looking at something – do you suppose they have got a bit of paper like the one we have, with the same marks, and are examining it? I *wish* I could see!'

They all stopped paddling and looked towards the boat in which Maggie and Dirty Dick sat. They were certainly examining something very carefully – their heads were close together. But they were too far away for the children to see if they were holding a piece of paper.

'Come on – we'll get as close to them as we can!' said Julian, beginning to paddle again. 'I expect it will make them absolutely mad to see us so close, but we can't help that!'

They paddled hard again, and at last came up to the boat. Timmy barked. Maggie and Dirty Dick at once looked round and saw the raft and the four children. They stared at them fiercely.

'Hallo!' cried Dick, waving a paddle. 'We took the raft out. It goes well. Does your boat go all right?'

Maggie went red with rage. 'You'll get into trouble for taking that raft without permission,' she shouted.

'Whose permission did *you* ask when you took that boat?' shouted back Julian. 'Tell us and we'll ask their permission to use this raft!'

George laughed. Maggie scowled, and Dirty Dick looked as if he would like to throw his oars at them.

CHEEKY CHARLIE

'Keep away from us!' he shouted. 'We don't want you kids spoiling our afternoon!'

'We like to be friendly!' called Dick, and made George laugh again.

Maggie and Dirty Dick had a hurried and angry conversation. They glared at the raft and then Maggie gave an order to Dirty Dick. He took up the oars again, and began to row, looking rather mutinous.

'Come on – follow,' said Julian, so the four began to paddle again following after the boat. 'Maybe we'll learn something now.'

But they didn't. Dirty Dick rowed the boat towards the west bank, and the raft followed. Then he swung out into the middle again, and again the raft followed, the children panting in their efforts to keep up.

Dirty Dick rowed right across to the east bank and stayed there till the children came up. Then he rowed off again.

'Having some nice exercise, aren't you?' called the woman in her harsh voice. 'So good for you all!'

The boat swung out to the middle of the lake again. Dick groaned. 'Blow! My arms are so tired I can hardly paddle. What are they doing?'

'I'm afraid they're just leading us on a wild goose chase,' said Julian, ruefully. 'They have evidently made up their minds that they won't look for the *Saucy Jane* while we're about – they're just tiring us out!'

'Well, if *that's* what they're doing I'm not playing!'

said Dick, and he put down his paddle and lay flat on his back, his knees drawn up, panting hard.

The others did the same. They were all tired. Timmy licked each one sympathetically and then sat down on George. She pushed him off so violently that he nearly fell into the water.

'Timmy! Right on my middle!' cried George, surprised and indignant. 'You great clumsy dog, you!'

Timmy licked her all over, shocked at being scolded by George. She was too exhausted to push him away.

'What's happened to the boat?' asked Anne at last. 'I'm too tired to sit up and see.'

Julian sat up, groaning. 'Oh, my back! Now where is that wretched boat? Oh, there it is – right away down the lake, making for the landing-place by the house – or for the boathouse probably. They've given up the search for the *Saucy Jane* for the time being anyway.'

'Thank goodness,' said Anne. 'Perhaps we can give it up too – till tomorrow anyhow! Stop snuffling down my neck, Timmy. What do you want us to do, Julian?'

'I think we'd better get back,' said Julian. 'It's too late now to start searching the banks of the lake – and anyway somehow I think it wouldn't be much use. The two in the boat didn't appear to be going anywhere near the banks – except when they began to play that trick on us to make us tired out!'

'Well, let's get back then,' said George. 'But I simply

must have a rest first. Timmy, I shall push you into the water if you keep sitting on my legs.'

There was a sudden splash. George sat up in alarm. Timmy was not on the raft!

He was swimming in the water, looking very pleased with himself.

'There! He thought he'd rather jump in than be pushed,' said Dick, grinning at George.

'*You* pushed him in!' said George, looking fierce.

'I didn't,' said Dick. 'He just took a header. He's having a jolly good time. I say – what about putting a rope round him and getting him to pull us to shore? It would save an awful lot of paddling.'

George was just about to say what she thought of *that* idea, when she caught Dick's sly grin. She kicked out at him.

'Don't keep baiting me, Dick. I'll push *you* in, in a minute.'

'Like to try?' asked Dick, at once. 'Come on. I'd like a wrestle to see who'd go into the water first.'

George, of course, always rose to a challenge. She never could resist one. She was up in a moment and fell on Dick, who very nearly went overboard at once.

'Shut up, you two!' said Julian, crossly. 'We haven't got a change of clothing, you know that. And I don't want to take you back with bronchitis or pneumonia. Stop it, George.'

George recognised the tone in his voice and she stopped. She ran her hand through her short curls and gave a sudden grin.

'All right, teacher!' she said, and sat down meekly. She picked up her paddle.

Julian picked up his. 'We'll get back,' he said. 'The sun's sinking low. It seems to slide down the sky at a most remarkable speed in October.'

They took a very wet Timmy on board and began to

paddle back. Anne thought it was a truly lovely evening. She gazed dreamily round as she paddled. The lake was a wonderful dark blue, and the ripples they made turned to silver as they ran away from the raft. Two moorhens said 'crek-crek' and swam round the raft in curiosity, their heads bobbing like clockwork.

Anne gazed over the tops of the trees that grew at the lakeside. The sky was turning pink. Away in the distance, on a high slope about a mile away she saw something that interested her.

It looked like a high stone. She pointed at it. 'Look, Julian,' she said. 'What's that stone? Is it a boundary mark, or something? It must be very big.'

Julian looked where she was pointing. 'Where?' he said. 'Oh, that. I can't imagine what it is.'

'It looks like a very tall stone,' said Dick, suddenly catching sight of it too.

'A tall stone,' repeated Anne, wondering where she had heard that before. 'A tall . . . oh, of *course*! It was printed on that plan, wasn't it – on the piece of paper Dick was given. Tall Stone! Don't you remember?'

'Yes. So it was,' said Dick and he stared at the far-away stone monument with interest. Then as the raft swung onwards, high trees hid the stone. It was gone.

'Tall Stone,' said Julian. 'It may be only a coincidence, of course. It wants a bit of thinking about, though. Funny we should suddenly spot it.'

'Would the loot be buried there?' asked George,

doubtfully. Julian shook his head. 'Oh, no,' he said, 'it is probably hidden in some position explained by that mysterious map. Paddle up, everyone! We really must get back.'

CHAPTER SEVENTEEN

Tit for tat!

WHEN THEY arrived at the boathouse there was no sign of Maggie or Dick. But their boat was in the shed, tied up in front of the other two, where it had been before.

'They're back all right,' said Julian. 'I wonder where they are. Don't let's drag this clumsy, heavy raft into the boathouse. I don't feel as if I've any strength left in my arms. Let's drag it under a bush and tie it there.'

They thought this a good idea. They pulled the raft up to some thick bushes and tied it firmly to a root that was sticking out of the ground.

Then they made their way to the ruined house, keeping a sharp lookout for Maggie and Dick. There was still no sign of them.

They went in, Timmy first. He didn't growl so they knew it was safe. He led the way to the cellar steps. Then he growled!

'What's up?' said Julian. 'Are they down there, Tim?'

Timmy ran straight down the steps into the cellar room. He growled again, but it was not the fierce growl he always gave when he wanted to warn that enemies or strangers were near. It was an angry, annoyed growl as if something was wrong.

'I expect dear Maggie and Dirty Dick have been down here and found out where our headquarters are!' said Julian, following Timmy down the steps. He switched on his torch.

The beds of heather and bracken were there as they had left them, and their macs and rugs and rucksacks. Nothing seemed to have been disturbed. Julian lit the candles on the mantelpiece and the dark little underground room came to life at once.

'What's the matter with Timmy?' asked George, coming down into the room. 'He's still growling. Timmy, what's up?'

'I expect he can smell that the others have been down here,' said Dick. 'Look at him sniffing all round. It's quite clear that *someone* has been here.'

'Anyone hungry?' asked Anne. 'I could do with some cake and biscuits.'

'Right,' said Julian, and opened the cupboard where they had put the food they had bought.

There was none there! Except for the crockery and one or two odds and ends that had been in the cupboard before, there was nothing. The bread had gone, the biscuits, the chocolate – everything!

'Blow!' said Julian, angrily. 'Look at that! The beasts! They've taken all our food – every bit. Not even a biscuit left. We were mad not to think they might do that!'

'Clever of them,' said Dick. 'They know we can't stay here long without food. It's a good way of chasing us out.

It's too late to go and get any tonight, anyway – and if we go tomorrow for some, they'll do what they have come to do in their own good time . . . when we're not here.'

Everyone felt distinctly down in the dumps. They were hungry and tired, and a good meal would have made all the difference. Anne sank down on her bed of heather and sighed.

'I wish I'd left some chocolate in my rucksack,' she said. 'But I didn't leave any there at all. And poor Tim – he's hungry too! Look at him sniffing in the cupboard and looking round at George. Tim, there's nothing for you. The cupboard is bare!'

'Where have those two wretches gone?' suddenly said Julian, fiercely. 'I'll tick them off! I'll tell them what I think of people who come and rifle cupboards and take away all the food.'

'Woof,' said Timmy, in full agreement.

Julian went angrily up the stairs. He wondered again where Maggie and Dirty Dick were. He went to the empty doorway and looked out. Then he saw where they were.

Two small tents had been put up under some thickly growing trees! So that's where the two were going to sleep. He debated whether or not to go and tell them what he thought of people who stole food. He decided that he would.

But when he got over to the tents with Timmy, there was no one there! Rugs were laid inside, and there was a primus stove and a kettle and other odds and ends. At the back of one tent was a pile of something, covered by a cloth.

Julian had a good look into each tent, and then went to see if he could find out where Maggie and Dirty Dick had gone. He saw them at last, walking through the trees. They must have gone for an evening stroll, he thought.

They didn't come back to the tents, but sat down by the lake. Julian gave up the thought of tackling them and went back to the others. Timmy was left behind, snuffling about happily.

'They've got tents,' Julian informed the others when he was back in the cellar room again. 'They're obviously staying put till they've got what they came for. They aren't in the tents – they're out by the lake.'

'Where's Timmy?' asked George. 'You shouldn't have left him behind, Ju. They might do something to him.'

'Here he is!' said Julian, as a familiar noise of claws clattering on the floor came to their ears. Timmy came down the stone steps and ran to George.

'He's got something in his mouth!' said George, in surprise. Timmy dropped it into her lap. She gave a yell.

'It's a tin of shortbread! Where did he get it from?'

Julian began to laugh. 'He must have taken it from one of the tents!' he said. 'I saw something covered up with a cloth in one tent – their food, I imagine! Well, well – tit for tat – they took our food and now Timmy is taking theirs!'

'Fair exchange is no robbery,' grinned Dick. 'Serves them right! I say – Tim's gone again!'

He was back in a minute with something large and paper-covered. It was a big cake! The four roared with laughter. 'Timmy! You're a wonder! You really are!'

Timmy was pleased at this praise. Off he went again and brought back a cardboard box in which was a fine pork pie. The children could hardly believe their eyes.

'It's a miracle!' said Anne. 'Just as I had made up my mind to starve for hours! A pork pie of all things! Let's have some.'

'Well, I have no second thoughts about it,' said Julian,

firmly. 'They took our food and we deserve some of theirs. Good gracious – don't say Tim's gone again.'

He had! He was enjoying himself thoroughly. He arrived this time with a packet of ham, and the children couldn't *imagine* how he had stopped himself from eating some on the way.

'Fancy carrying it in his mouth and not even *tasting* a bit!' said Dick. 'Tim's a better person than I am. I'd just have to have had a lick.'

'I say – we ought to stop him now,' said Julian, as Timmy ran up the steps again, his tail wagging nineteen to the dozen. 'We're getting a bit too much in exchange!'

'Oh, do see what he brings back this time,' begged Anne. 'Then stop him.'

He came back carrying an old flour bag in which something had been packed. Timmy carried it cleverly by the neck so that nothing had fallen out. George undid the bag.

'Home-made scones – and buns,' she said. 'Timmy, you are very, very clever, and you shall have a wonderful supper. But you are not to go and take any more things, because we've got enough. See? No more. Lie down and be a good dog and eat your supper.'

Timmy was quite willing. He wolfed ham and scones and a slice of cake, and then he went up into the kitchen, jumped into the sink and lapped the water lying there. He then jumped down and went to the doorway to look out. He barked. Then he growled loudly.

The children rushed up the stone steps at once. Outside, at a safe distance, was Dirty Dick.

'Have you been taking anything of ours?' he shouted.

'No more than you have been taking of ours!' shouted back Julian. 'Fair exchange, you know, and all that.'

'How dare you go into our tents?' raged the man, his shock of hair making him look very peculiar in the twilight.

'We didn't. The dog fetched and carried for us,' said Julian. 'And don't you come any nearer. He's just longing to fly at you! And I warn you, he'll be on guard tonight, so don't try any funny tricks. He's as strong and savage as a lion.'

'Grrrr,' said Timmy, so fiercely that the man started back in fright. He went off without another word, shaking with anger.

Julian and the others went back to finish a very delicious supper. Timmy went with them – but he planted himself at the top of the cellar steps.

'Not a bad place for him to be in tonight,' said Julian. 'I don't trust that couple an inch. We can give him one of our blazers to lie on. I say – this has boiled up into quite an adventure, hasn't it? It seems frightful to think we'll be back at school on Tuesday!'

'We *must* find the loot first!' said Anne. 'We really must. Let's get out that plan again, Ju. Let's make sure that Tall Stone is marked on it.'

They got it out and put it on the table. They bent over it once more.

'Yes – Tall Stone is marked at the end of one of the lines,' said Julian. 'Tock Hill is at the end of the opposite line. Let's get the map and see if there *is* a Tock Hill.'

They got the map, and studied it. Anne suddenly put her finger down on it. 'There it is. On the opposite side of the lake from where we saw the Tall Stone. Tock Hill on one side. Tall Stone on the other. Surely that *means* something.'

'It does, of course,' said Julian. 'It is bearings given to show the whereabouts of the hidden goods. There are four bearings given – Tall Stone. Tock Hill. Chimney. And Steeple.'

'Listen!' said Dick, suddenly. 'LISTEN! *I* know how to read that map. It's easy.'

The others looked at him in surprise and doubt.

'Read it, then,' said Julian. 'Tell us what it all means. I don't believe you can!'

CHAPTER EIGHTEEN

A very exciting time

'LET'S TAKE all the clues we know,' said Dick, looking excited. 'Two-Trees. That's here. Gloomy Water. That's where the hidden stuff must be. *Saucy Jane*. It's a boat that contains the stuff, hidden somewhere on Gloomy Water.'

'Go on,' said Julian, as Dick paused to think.

'Maggie is the next clue – well she's here, probably an old friend of Nailer's,' said Dick. 'She knows all the clues too.'

He jabbed his finger at the piece of paper. 'Now for *these* clues. Listen! We saw Tall Stone when we were out on the lake, didn't we? Very well. There must be SOME spot on the lake where we can see not only Tall Stone, but also Tock Hill, Chimney and Steeple, whatever they are! There must be only one spot from which we can see all those four things at the same time – and *that's* the spot to hunt in for the treasure!'

There was an astonished silence after this. Julian drew a long breath and clapped Dick on the back.

'Of course! What idiots we were not to see it before. The *Saucy Jane* must be somewhere on – or in – the lake at the spot where all four clues are seen at the same time. We've only got to explore and find out!'

'Yes – but don't forget that Maggie and Dirty Dick know what these clues mean too! They'll be there first if they possibly can!' said Dick. 'And what's more if they get the goods we can't do anything about it. We're not the police! They'll be off and away with their find and disappear completely.'

Everyone began to feel intensely excited. 'I think we'd better set off early tomorrow morning,' said Julian. 'As soon as it's light. Otherwise Maggie and Dick will get in first. I wish to goodness we had an alarm clock.'

'We'll go on the raft, and we'll paddle about till we see Tall Stone again – then we'll keep that in sight till we see Tock Hill, whatever that is,' said Dick. 'And once we've spotted that we'll keep both Tall Stone *and* Tock Hill in sight and paddle round to find out where we can see a steeple – and then a chimney. I should think that would be the one chimney left on Two-Trees house! Did you notice there is just one left, sticking up high?'

'Yes, I noticed,' said Anne. 'What a clever way to hide anything, Dick. Nobody could possibly know what the clues meant unless they knew something of the secret. This is *awfully* exciting!'

They talked about it for some time and then Julian said they really must try and go to sleep or they would never wake up early enough in the morning.

They settled down in their beds of heather and

bracken. Timmy lay on Julian's blazer on the top step of the stairs leading down to the cellar room. He seemed to think it was quite a good idea to sleep there that night.

They were all tired and they fell asleep very quickly. Nothing disturbed them in the night. The fox came again and looked into the old house, but Timmy didn't stir. He merely gave a small growl and the fox fled, his bushy tail spread behind him.

The morning came and daylight crept in at the burnt-out doorway and windows. Timmy stirred and went to the door. He looked towards the two tents. No one was about there. He went to the cellar steps and clattered down waking Dick and Julian at once.

'What's the time?' said Julian, remembering immediately that he was to wake early. 'Half past seven. Wake up, everyone! It's daylight. We've heaps to do!'

They washed hurriedly, combed out their hair, cleaned their teeth, and tried to brush down their clothes. Anne got ready some snacks for them – ham, scones and a piece of shortbread each. They all had a drink of water and then they were ready to go.

There was no sign of anyone near the two tents. 'Good,' said Julian. 'We'll be there first!'

They dragged the raft out and got on to it, taking up the paddles. Then off they went, Timmy too, all feeling tremendously excited.

'We'll paddle out to where we think we were last night

when Anne caught sight of Tall Stone,' said Julian. So they paddled valiantly, though their arms were stiff with yesterday's paddling and it was really very painful to use the tired muscles all over again!

They paddled out to the middle of the lake and looked for Tall Stone. It didn't seem anywhere to be seen! They strained their eyes for it, but for a long time it was not to be spotted at all. Then Dick gave a cry. 'It's just come into sight. Look, when we passed those tall trees on the bank over there, Tall Stone came into view. It was behind them before that.'

'Good,' said Julian. 'Now I'm going to stop paddling and keep Tall Stone in sight. If it goes out of sight I'll tell you and you must back-paddle. Dick, can you possibly paddle and look out for something that could be Tock Hill on the opposite side? I daren't take my eyes off Tall Stone in case it disappears.'

'Right,' said Dick, and paddled while he looked earnestly for Tock Hill.

'Got it!' he said suddenly. 'It must be it! Look, over there – a funny little hill with a pointed top. Julian, can you still see Tall Stone?'

'Yes,' said Julian. 'Keep your eyes on Tock Hill. Now it's up to the girls. George, paddle away and see if you can spot Steeple.'

'I can see it now, already!' said George, and for one moment the boys took their eyes off Tall Stone and Tock Hill and looked where George pointed. They saw the steeple of a faraway church glinting in the morning sun.

'Good, good, good,' said Julian. 'Now, Anne – look for Chimney – look down towards the end of the lake where the house is. Can you see its one chimney?'

'Not quite,' said Anne. 'Paddle just a bit to the left – the left, I said, George! Yes – yes, I can see the one chimney. Stop paddling everyone. We're here!'

They stopped paddling but the raft drifted on, and Anne lost the chimney again! They had to paddle back a bit until it came into sight. By that time George had lost her steeple!

At last all four things were in view at once, and the raft seemed to be still and unmoving on the quiet waters of the lake.

'I'm going to drop something to mark the place,' said Julian, still keeping his eyes desperately on Tall Stone. 'George, can you manage to watch Tall Stone and Steeple at the same time? I simply must look what I'm doing for the moment.'

'I'll try,' said George, and fixed her eyes first on Tall Stone, then on Steeple, then on Tall Stone again, hoping and praying that neither would slip out of sight if the raft moved on the water.

Julian was busy. He had taken his torch and his pocket-knife out of his pocket and had tied them together with string. 'I haven't enough string, Dick,' he said. 'You've got some, haven't you?'

Dick had, of course. He put his hand into his pocket, still keeping his eyes on Tock Hill and passed his string over to Julian.

Julian tied it to the end of the string that joined together the knife and torch. Then he dropped them into the water, letting out the string as they went down with their weight. The string slid through his hands. It stopped in a short while and Julian knew that the knife and torch had reached the bed of the lake.

He felt in his pockets again. He knew he had a cork somewhere that he had carved into a horse's head. He found it and tied the end of the string firmly round it. Then he dropped the cork thankfully into the water. It bobbed there, held by the string, which led right down to the knife and torch on the lake-bed below.

'It's done!' he said, with a sigh of relief. 'Take your eyes off everything! I've marked the place now, so we don't need to glue our eyes on the four bearings!'

He told them how he had tied together his knife and torch and dropped them on string to the bottom of the lake, and then had tied a cork to the other end, so that it would bob and show them the place.

They all looked at it. 'Jolly clever, Ju,' said Dick. 'But once we slid away from this spot, and it would be an easy thing to do, we'd find it jolly difficult to find that cork again! Hadn't we better tie something else to it?'

'I haven't got anything else that will float,' said Julian. 'Have you?'

'I have,' said George, and she handed him a little wooden box. 'I keep the five pence pieces I collect in that,' she said, putting the money into her pocket. 'You can have the box. It will be much easier to see than the cork.'

Julian tied the box to the cork. It was certainly a good deal easier to see! 'Fine!' he said. 'Now we're quite all right. We must be right over the loot!'

They all bent over the edge of the raft and looked down – and they saw a most surprising sight! Below them, resting on the bottom of the lake, was a boat! It lay there in the shadows of the water, its outline blurred by the ripples the raft made – but quite plainly it was a boat!

'The *Saucy Jane*!' said Julian, peering down, feeling amazed and awed to think that they had read the bearings so correctly that they were actually over the *Saucy Jane* herself! 'The Nailer must have come here with the stolen goods – got out the *Saucy Jane* and rowed her to this spot. He must have taken his bearings very carefully indeed, and then holed the boat so that she sank down with the loot in her. Then I suppose he swam back to shore.'

'Most ingenious,' said Dick. 'Really, he must be a jolly clever fellow. But I say, Julian – how on earth are we going to get the boat up?'

'I can't imagine,' said Julian. 'I simply – can't – imagine! I hadn't even thought of that.'

Timmy suddenly began to growl. The four looked up quickly to see why.

They saw a boat coming over the water towards them – the *Merry Meg*, with Maggie and Dirty Dick in it. And the children felt quite certain that both were reading the bearings on their piece of paper in exactly the same way as they themselves had!

They were so engrossed in watching for Tall Stone, Tock Hill, Chimney and Steeple that they took no notice of the children at all. 'I don't think they guess for one moment that we've read the bearings and marked the place,' said Julian. 'How wild they'll be when they find we are right over the place they're looking for! Watch out for trouble!'

CHAPTER NINETEEN

Maggie and Dick are annoyed

THE BOAT in which Maggie and Dirty Dick were rowing went this way and that as the two searched for the same objects that the children had already spotted. The four watched them, and George put her hand on Timmy to stop him barking.

The boat came nearer and nearer. Maggie was trying to keep in view two or three of the bearings at once and her head twisted from side to side continually. The children grinned at one another. It had been hard enough for the four of them to keep all the bearings in view – it must be very difficult for Maggie, especially as Dirty Dick didn't seem to be helping very much.

They heard Maggie give sharp orders as the boat swung this way and that. Then it headed for them. Dirty Dick growled something to Maggie, who had her back to them, and she turned round sharply, losing the view of the things she was looking for.

Her face was full of anger when she saw the raft so near – and in the place where she wanted *her* boat to go! Afraid of completely losing the view of the things she was keeping her eyes on, she turned back again and hastily looked to see if Tock Hill, Tall Stone and Steeple were still all to be seen together. She said something in a furious voice to Dirty Dick, and he nodded with a sour face.

The boat came nearer and they heard Maggie say, 'I think I can see it now – yes – a bit farther to the right, please.'

'She's spotted one Chimney now,' whispered Anne. 'I expect they've got all the bearings. Oh dear – the boat will bump right into us!'

It did! Dirty Dick rowed viciously at them and the bows of the boat gave them a terrific jolt. Anne would have fallen into the water if Julian hadn't grabbed at her.

He yelled at Dirty Dick. 'Look out, you ass! You nearly had us over! What on earth do you think you're doing?'

'Get out of the way then,' growled Dirty Dick. Timmy began to bark savagely, and the boat at once drew away from the raft.

'There's plenty of room on this lake,' shouted Julian. 'What do you want to come and disturb us for? We aren't doing any harm.'

'We're going to report you to the police,' called the woman, her face red with anger. 'Taking a raft that doesn't belong to you, sleeping in a house where you've no right to be – and stealing our food.'

'Don't talk nonsense,' cried Julian. 'And don't you dare to ram us again. If you do I'll send our dog after you. He's longing to come.'

'Grrrr!' said Timmy, and showed his magnificent set of gleaming white teeth. Dirty Dick muttered something quickly to Maggie. She turned round again and called to them.

'Now, look here, you kids – be sensible. My friend and I have come down here for a quiet weekend, and it isn't nice to find you four everywhere we go. Go back and keep out of our way and we won't report you at all. That's a fair bargain – we won't even say anything about your stealing our food.'

'We're going back when we think we will,' answered Julian. 'And no threats or bargains will make any difference to us.'

There was a silence. Then Maggie spoke hurriedly to Dirty Dick again. He nodded.

'Is this your half-term?' she called. 'When do you have to go back?'

'Tomorrow,' said Julian. 'You'll be rid of us then. But we're going to enjoy ourselves on this raft while we can.'

There was another hurried conference between the two. Then Dirty Dick rowed round a little, and Maggie began to peer down into the water. She suddenly looked up, nodded at Dirty Dick, and he rowed away again towards the end of the lake! Not another word did the couple say.

'I can see what they've decided to do,' said Julian, in a pleased voice. 'They think we'll be gone by tomorrow, so they'll wait till the coast is clear and then they'll come and collect the loot in peace. Did you see Maggie looking down into the water to spot the boat? I was afraid she would also spot our mark – the cork and the box! But she didn't.'

'I don't know why you sound so pleased,' said George. 'We can't get the boat up, you know that – and *I* don't feel pleased that we'll have to leave tomorrow and let that horrid pair collect the loot. I imagine they'll have some clever grown-up way of pulling up the boat from the bed of the lake – which they will do when we've gone tomorrow.'

'You're not very bright today, George,' said Julian, watching the boat being rowed farther and farther away. 'I told them we'd be gone tomorrow, hoping they would clear off and wait – and leave us time to get the loot ourselves. I think we can!'

'How?' said three voices at once, and Timmy looked inquiringly at Julian too.

'Well, we don't need to pull up the *boat*,' said Julian. 'We only want the loot. What's to prevent us from going down and getting it? I'm quite prepared to strip and dive down to the bottom there and feel about for any sack or bag or box. If I find one I'll come up for air, borrow a bit of rope from the raft and go down again – tie the rope to the sack and you can haul it up to the surface!'

'Oh, Julian – it sounds so easy – but is it really?' said Anne. George and Dick considered the proposal carefully. They were most impressed by Julian's idea.

'Well, it may turn out to be much more difficult than it

sounds, but I'm jolly well going to try it,' said Julian, and began to strip off his jersey.

Anne felt the water. It was very cold to her warm hand. 'Ugh! I'd hate to dive down to the bottom of this horrid, cold, dark lake,' she said. 'I think you're brave, Ju.'

'Don't talk rubbish!' said Julian.

He was ready to go in now. He dived neatly into the water with hardly a splash. The other three craned over the edge of the raft to watch. They could see him down, deep down in the water, a ghostly figure. He stayed down such a long time that Anne got worried.

'He can't hold his breath all that time!' she said. 'He can't!'

But Julian could. He was one of the star swimmers and divers at his school, and this was easy to him. He came up again at last, and panted hard, trying to make up for holding his breath so long. The others waited patiently. At last his breathing grew more even and he grinned at them.

'Ah – that's better! Well – it's there!' he said, triumphantly.

'*Is* it!' said everyone, thrilled. 'Oh, Julian!'

'Yes. I dived right down to the boat – almost got there with the force of my dive – had to swim just a couple of strokes perhaps. And there was the poor old boat, rotting to bits. And in one end is a waterproof bag – almost a sack, it's so big. I ran my hands over it, and it's waterproof all right – so the loot must be packed in there.'

'Did it feel heavy?' asked Dick.

'I gave it a tug and couldn't move it,' said Julian. 'Either it's wedged in somehow or is really heavy. Anyway we can't fetch it out by diving down for it. I'll have to dive down again, fix a rope to it, then come up – and we'll give a heave-ho and up she'll come!'

Julian was shivering. Anne picked up the blazer she had brought and gave it to him to dry himself with. Dick looked hurriedly over the raft. There were certainly bits and pieces of rope sticking out here and there, some of it half-rotten; and a short length was tucked into a space between two planks of the raft.

It was much too short though – and surely the other bits and pieces would never join to make a long enough rope?

'The bits of rope we've got won't do, Julian,' said Dick. Julian was drying himself and looking towards the end of the lake, where Two-Trees stood. He was frowning. The others looked too.

The boat had reached the bank there, and had been pulled up. One of the couple, the children couldn't see which, was standing up on the bank – and something was glinting in the sun, something he or she was holding!

'See that glint?' said Julian. 'Well, that's either Maggie or Dirty Dick using field-glasses. They're going to keep an eye on us while we're here – just to make sure we don't suddenly spot the boat, I suppose! They don't guess we've already found it. I bet they were worried when they saw I'd taken a header into the water just over the sunken boat!'

'Oh – so that's what the flash is,' said George. 'The glint of field-glasses! Yes – they're watching us. Blow! That will put an end to us trying to haul up the loot, Ju. They'd see it and wait for us!'

'Yes. No good trying for that now,' said Julian. 'Anyway, as Dick says, we've not got enough rope. We'll have to get some from the boathouse.'

'But when do you propose to get the bag out of the sunken boat?' asked Dick. 'They'll keep those field-glasses on us even if we go out again this afternoon.'

'There's only one time to go when they *won't* have their

glasses watching us,' said Julian, beginning to dress himself very rapidly, 'and that's tonight. We'll go tonight! My word – what an adventure!'

'Don't let's,' said Anne, in a small voice.

'There'll be a moon,' said George, excited.

'Smashing idea!' said Dick, thumping Julian on the back. 'Let's go back now so that they won't have any suspicions of us, and make our plans for tonight. And we'd better keep an eye on them too in case they row out to this spot themselves this afternoon.'

'They won't,' said Julian. 'They daren't run any risk of us spotting what they're doing. They will be sure to wait till we've gone.'

'And till the loot is gone!' said George with a laugh. 'I say – I do hope those two wretches haven't gone and taken our food again!'

'I hid it down in the cellars beyond our room – and locked the door leading there – and here's the key,' grinned Julian, holding up a large key.

'You never told us!' said George. 'Julian, you're a genius! How do you manage to think of things like that?'

'Oh – just brains!' said Julian, pretending to look modest, and then laughing. 'Come on – if I don't get warm quickly I'll have a most almighty chill!'

CHAPTER TWENTY

In the moonlight

THEY PADDLED rapidly away. Dick took a last glance back to make sure that the cork and the box were still bobbing on the water to mark the place where the sunken boat lay. Yes – they were still there.

'It'll be maddening if it's cloudy tonight and the moon doesn't come out,' said George, as they paddled. 'We shouldn't be able to see Tock Hill, Tall Stone and the rest – and we might paddle for ages in the dark without spotting our cork-and-box mark.'

'Don't cross your bridges before you come to them,' said Dick.

'I'm not,' said George. 'I was only just *hoping* that wouldn't happen.'

'It won't,' said Julian, looking at the sky. 'The weather's set fine again.'

As soon as Maggie saw the children coming back again, she and Dirty Dick disappeared into their tents. Julian grinned. 'They've heaved a sigh of relief and gone to have a snack,' he said. 'I could do with one myself.'

Everyone felt the same. Paddling was hard work, and the air on the lake was chilly – quite enough to give anyone a large appetite!

They pushed the raft into its hiding place again. Then they made their way to the old house. They went down into the cellar room. Timmy growled and sniffed about again.

'I bet Maggie and Dirty Dick have been here, snooping round again,' said George. 'Looking for their pork pie and ham! Good thing you locked it up, Ju!'

Julian unlocked the door into the cellars beyond, and brought out the food. 'A large toad was looking at it with great interest,' he said, as he brought it back. 'Timmy also looked at the toad with interest – but he's wary of toads by now. They taste much too nasty when pounced on!'

They took the meal up into the sunshine and enjoyed it. The orangeade was finished so they drank the cold clear water, pumping some vigorously.

'Do you know it's a quarter to three?' said Julian amazed. 'Where has the time gone? In a couple of hours or so it will be dark. Let me see – the moon will be well up about eleven o'clock. That's the time to go, I think.'

'Please don't let's,' said Anne. Julian put his arm round her.

'Now you know you don't mean that, Anne,' he said. 'You know you'll enjoy it all when the time comes. You couldn't bear to be left out of it! Could you?'

'No. I suppose I couldn't,' said Anne. 'But I *don't* like Maggie and Dirty Dick!'

'Nor do we,' said Julian, cheerfully. 'That's why we're going to beat them at their own game. We're on the side of the right, and it's worthwhile running into a bit of danger for that. Now let's see – perhaps we'd better just keep an eye on that couple till it's dark – just in *case* they try any funny tricks – and then we'll have a snooze, if we can, so as to be sure to be lively tonight.'

'There they are!' said Anne. As she spoke Maggie and her companion came out of their tents. They had a few words together and then walked off to the moorland.

'Taking their usual stroll, I suppose,' said Dick. 'Let's have a game of cricket. There's a bit of wood over there for a bat, and I've got a ball in my rucksack.'

'Good idea,' said Julian. 'I still feel a bit chilled from my bathe. Brrrrrr! That water was cold. I don't feel very thrilled at the thought of diving in tonight!'

'I'll do that,' said Dick, at once. 'My turn this time!'

'No. I know exactly where to spot the loot,' said Julian. 'I'll have to go down. But you can come down too, if you like, and help to tie the rope on to it.'

'Right,' said Dick. 'Now look out – I'm going to bowl!'

They enjoyed their game. The sun sank lower and lower, then it disappeared. A cloud came over the sky and darkness came quickly. George looked up at the sky anxiously.

'It's all right,' said Julian. 'It'll clear. Don't you worry!'

Before they went back into the house Julian and Dick slipped down to the boathouse for the coil of rope they would want that night. They found it quite easily enough and came back, pleased. It was quite a good strong rope, frayed only in one place.

Julian was right about the weather. The sky cleared again in about an hour, and the stars shone crisply. Good! Julian put Timmy on guard at the doorway. Then he and the others went into the dark cellar room and lit a couple of candles. They all snuggled down into their beds of heather.

'I shan't be able to snooze,' complained Anne. 'I feel much too excited.'

'Don't snooze then,' said Dick. 'Just have a rest and wake us up at the right time!'

Anne was the only one who didn't fall into a comfortable doze. She lay awake, thinking of this new adventure of theirs. Some children always had adventures and some didn't. Anne thought it would be much nicer to *read* about adventures than to have them. But then probably the ones who only read about them simply longed to have the adventures themselves! It was all very difficult.

Anne woke the others at ten to eleven. She shook George first, and then the boys. They were all in such a comfortable sleep that it was hard to wake them.

But soon they were up and about, whispering. 'Where's the rope? Good, here it is. Better put on blazers *and* macs. It'll be freezing on the lake. Everyone ready? Now – not a sound!'

Timmy had come to the cellar room as soon as he had heard them stirring. He knew he had to be quiet so he didn't give even one small bark. He was thrilled to find they were going out into the night.

The moon was well up now, and although it was not full, it was very bright. Small clouds swam across the sky, and every now and again the moon went behind one of them and the world became dark. But that was only for a minute or two, then out it came again, as brilliant as ever.

'Any sign of the others?' whispered Dick. Julian stood at the doorway and looked towards the tents. No – all was quiet there. Still, it would be better if he and the others crept round the side of the house and kept in the shadows.

'We don't want to run any risk of them spotting us now,' whispered Julian, giving his orders. 'Keep out of the moonlight, whatever you do. And see that Tim walks to heel, George.'

Keeping well in the shadows the Five crept down to the lakeside. The water gleamed in the moonlight, and a bright moon-path ran all down it, lovely to see. The lake looked very dark and brooding. Anne wished it had a voice of some kind – even the little lap-lap-lap of waves at the edge. But there was none.

They pulled out the raft and threw the coil of rope on to it. Then they clambered on, enjoying its smooth bob-bob-bobbing as they paddled out on the water. They were off!

Timmy was thrilled. He kept licking first one of the four, then another. He loved going out in the night. The moon shone down on the little company and turned every little ripple to silver as the raft bobbed over the water.

'It's a heavenly night,' said Anne, looking round at the silent trees that lined the banks. 'The whole place is so quiet and peaceful.'

An owl immediately hooted very loudly indeed from the trees and Anne jumped violently.

'Now don't start all the owls hooting by talking about how quiet everything is,' teased Julian. 'I agree though that it really is a heavenly evening. How calm and mirror-like this lake is. I wonder if it ever produces a wave of any sort! Do you suppose it stays like this even in a storm?'

'It's a weird sort of lake,' said Dick. 'Look out, Timmy – that's my ear. Don't lick it all away. I say – anyone looking out for our four bearings?'

'Well, we know more or less where we've got to paddle

the raft to,' said Julian. 'We'll go in that direction and then see if we're spotting the bearings. I'm sure we're going right at the moment.'

They were. George soon saw Tall Stone, and then Tock Hill came into sight. It wasn't long before Steeple was seen too, shining in the moonlight.

'I bet the Nailer came and hid his loot out here on a moonlit night,' said Julian. 'All the bearings can be seen so very clearly – even Tall Stone. We really must find out sometime what it is. It looks like a great stone pointer of some sort, put up in memory of something or somebody.'

'There's the Chimney now,' said Anne. 'We have got them all in view – we should be near our mark.'

'We are!' said Dick, pointing to a little dark bobbing thing nearby. 'The cork and the box. How extremely clever we are! I really have a great admiration for the Five!'

'Idiot!' said Julian. 'Go on, strip now, Dick – we'll do our job straight away. Brrrrrrr! It's cold!'

Both boys stripped quickly, putting their clothes into a neat pile in the middle of the raft. 'Look after them, Anne,' said Julian. 'Got the rope, Dick? Come on, then, in we go. We can't see the boat now, the waters are so dark – but we know it's just below the cork and the box!'

The boys dived in one after the other. Splash! Splash! They were both beautiful divers. The raft rocked as they plunged in and Timmy nearly went in too.

Julian had dived in first. He opened his eyes under the water and found that he could see the sunken boat just below him. With two strong strokes he reached it, and tugged at the waterproof bag there. Dick was beside him almost at once, the rope in his hands. The boys twisted it tightly round the top part of the bag.

Before they could finish the job they had to rise up to the surface to breathe. Dick couldn't hold his breath under water as long as Julian and he was up first, gasping painfully. Then Julian shot up and the night was full of great, painful breaths, as the boys gasped in the air they longed for.

The girls knew better than to ask anything just then. They waited anxiously till the boys' breathing grew easier. Julian turned and grinned at them.

'Everything's all right!' he said. 'Now – down we go again!'

CHAPTER TWENTY-ONE

The sack at last!

DOWN WENT the boys again and once more the raft jerked violently. The girls peered anxiously over the edge, waiting for them to return.

Julian and Dick were down at the sunken boat in a matter of a second or two. They finished the task of tying the rope to the waterproof bag. Julian gave it a hard jerk, hoping to free it if it were wedged tightly into the boat. He took the rest of the rope length in his hands in order to take it up to the surface.

Then, bursting for breath again, the two boys shot up to the raft, popping out of the water with loud gasps. They climbed on board.

They took a minute to get their breath and then Dick and Julian took the rope together. The girls watched, their hearts beating fast. Now was the test! Would that waterproof sack come up – or not?

The boys pulled strongly but without jerking. The raft slanted and Anne made a grab at the pile of clothes in the middle. Dick fell off into the water again.

He climbed back, spluttering. 'Have to pull more smoothly,' he said. 'I felt the sack give a bit, didn't you?'

Julian nodded. He was shivering with cold, but his eyes were shining with excitement. Anne put a macintosh round his shoulders and one round Dick's too. They never even noticed!

'Now – pull again,' said Julian. 'Steady does it – steady – steady! It's coming! Gosh, it's really coming. Pull, Dick, pull!'

As the heavy bag came up on the end of the rope, the raft slanted again, and the boys pushed themselves back to the other side of the raft, afraid of upsetting everyone into the water. Timmy began to bark excitedly.

'Be quiet, Timmy,' said George at once. She knew how easily sound travels over water, and she was afraid the couple in the tents might hear him.

'It's coming – it's there, look – just below the surface!' said Anne. 'One more pull, boys!'

But it was impossible to pull the heavy bag on board without upsetting the raft. As it was, the girls got very wet when the water splashed over the raft as it jerked and slanted.

'Look – let's paddle back to the shore and let the sack drag behind us,' said Julian, at last. 'We shall only upset the raft. Dress again, Dick, and we'll get back to the old house and open the sack in comfort. I'm so cold now that I can hardly feel my fingers.'

The boys dressed as quickly as they could. They were shivering, and were very glad to take up their paddles and work hard to get the raft back to shore. They soon felt a welcome warmth stealing through their bodies, and in ten minutes had stopped shivering. They felt very pleased with themselves indeed.

They looked back at the bulky object following them, dragging along just under the surface. What was in that bag? Excitement crept over all of them again, and the paddles struck through the water at top speed as all the four strained to get back as quickly as possible. Timmy felt the excitement too, and wagged his long tail without ceasing as he stood in the middle of the raft, watching the thing that bobbed along behind them.

They came at last to the end of the lake. Making as little noise as possible they dragged the raft under its usual bush. They did not want to leave it out on the bank in case Maggie and Dirty Dick saw that it had been used again, and started wondering.

Dick and Julian dragged the waterproof sack out of the water. They carried it between them as they went cautiously back to the house. It looked a most miserable, grotesque place with its burnt-out roof, doorways and windows – but the children didn't notice its forlorn appearance in the moonlight – they were far too excited!

They walked slowly up the overgrown path between the two broken-down walls, their feet making no sound on the soft mossy ground. They came to the doorway and dragged the bundle into the kitchen.

'Go and light the candles in the cellar room,' said Julian to George. 'I just want to make sure that that couple are not snooping anywhere about.'

George and Anne went to light the candles, flashing their torches before them down the stone steps. Julian and Dick stood at the open doorway, facing the moonlight, listening intently. Not a sound was to be heard, not a shadow moved!

They set Timmy on guard and left him there, dragging the dripping, heavy bundle across the stone floor of the kitchen. They bumped it down the cellar steps – and at last had it before them, ready to be opened!

Julian's fingers fumbled at the knots of the rope. George couldn't bear waiting. She took a pocket-knife and handed it to Julian.

'For goodness' sake, cut the rope!' she said. 'I simply can't wait another moment.'

Julian grinned. He cut the rope – and then he looked to see how to undo the waterproof wrapping.

'I see,' he said. 'It's been folded over and over the goods, and then sewn up to make a kind of bag. It must have kept the loot absolutely waterproof.'

'Buck *up*!' said George. 'I shall tear it open myself in a minute!'

Julian cut the strong stitches that closed the covering. They began to unwrap the bundle. There seemed to be yards and yards of waterproof covering! But at last it was off – and there, in the middle of the mass of waterproof, were scores of little boxes – leather-covered boxes that everyone knew at once were jewel-boxes!

'It *is* jewellery then!' said Anne, and she opened a box. They all exclaimed in wonder.

A magnificent necklace glittered on black velvet. It shone and glinted and sparkled in the candlelight as if it were on fire. Even the two boys gazed without a word. Why – it was fit for a queen!

'It must be that wonderful necklace stolen from the Queen of Fallonia,' said George at last. 'I saw a picture of it in the papers. What diamonds!'

'Oooh – are they *diamonds*?' said Anne, in awe. 'Oh Julian – what a lot of money they must be worth! A hundred pounds, do you think?'

'A hundred thousand pounds more likely, Anne,' said Julian, soberly. 'My word – no wonder the Nailer hid these stolen goods carefully, in such an ingenious place. No wonder Maggie and Dirty Dick were longing to find them. Let's see what else there is.'

Every box contained precious stones of some kind – sapphire bracelets, ruby and diamond rings, a strange and wonderful opal necklace, earrings of such enormous diamonds that Anne was quite sure no one would be able to bear the weight of them!

'I would never, never dare to own jewellery like this,' said Anne. 'I should always be afraid of its being stolen. Did it all belong to the Queen of Fallonia?'

'No. Some to a princess who was visiting her,' said Julian. 'These jewels are worth a king's ransom. I just hate the thought of being in charge of them, even for a little while.'

'Well, it's better that we should have them, rather than Maggie or Dirty Dick,' said George. She held a string of diamonds in her hands and let them run through her fingers. How they sparkled! No one could have imagined that they had been at the bottom of a lake for a year or two!

'Now let's see,' said Julian, sitting down on the edge of the table. 'We're due back at school tomorrow afternoon, Tuesday – or is it Tuesday already? It must be past midnight – gosh, yes, it's almost half past two! Would you believe it?'

'I feel as if I'd believe anything,' said Anne, blinking at the glittering treasure on the table.

'We'd better start off fairly early tomorrow,' went on Julian. 'We've got to get these things to the police . . .'

'*Not* to that awful policeman we saw the other day!' said George, in horror.

'Of course not. I think our best course would be to ring up that nice Mr Gaston and tell him that we've got important news for the police and see which police station he recommends us to go to,' said Julian. 'He might even arrange a car for us, so that we don't need to take this stuff about in buses. I'm not particularly keen on carrying it about with me!'

'Have we got to carry all these boxes?' said George, in dismay.

'No. That would be asking for trouble if anyone spotted them,' said Julian. 'I fear we'll just have to wrap up the jewels in our hankies and stuff them down into the bottom of our rucksacks. We'll leave the boxes here. The police can collect them afterwards if they want to.'

It was all decided. The four divided up the glittering jewellery and wrapped it carefully into four handkerchiefs, one for each of them. They stuffed the hankies into their rucksacks.

'We'd better use them for pillows,' said Dick. 'Then they'll be quite safe.'

'What! These horrid rough bags!' said Anne. 'Why? Timmy's on guard, isn't he? I'll put mine beside me under the rug but I just won't put my head on it.'

Dick laughed. 'All right, Anne. Timmy won't let any robber through, I'm quite sure. Now – we start off first thing in the morning, do we, Julian?'

'Yes. As soon as we wake,' said Julian. 'We can't have much to eat. There're only a few biscuits and a bit of chocolate left.'

'I shan't mind,' said Anne. 'I'm so excited that at the moment I don't feel I'll ever eat anything again!'

'You'll change your mind tomorrow,' said Julian with a laugh. 'Now – to bed, everyone.'

They lay down on their heather and bracken, excited and pleased. What a weekend! And all because Dick and Anne had lost their way and Dick slept in the wrong barn!

'Good-night,' said Julian, yawning. 'I feel very, very rich – richer than I'll ever be in my life again. Well – I'll enjoy the feeling while I can!'

CHAPTER TWENTY-TWO

An exciting finish

THEY AWOKE to hear Timmy barking. It was daylight already. Julian leapt up the steps to see what was the matter. He saw Maggie not very far away.

'Why do you keep such a fierce dog?' she called. 'I just came to see if you wanted to take any food with you. We'll give you some if you like.'

'It's *too* kind of you, all of a sudden!' said Julian. How anxious Maggie was to get rid of them! She would even give them food to get rid of them quickly. But Julian didn't want any food from Maggie or Dirty Dick!

'Do you want some, then?' asked the woman. She couldn't make Julian out. He looked a youngster, and yet his manner was anything but childish. She was rather afraid of him.

'No thanks,' said Julian. 'We're just about to go. Got to get back to school today, you know.'

'Well, you'd better hurry then,' said the woman. 'It's going to rain.'

Julian turned on his heel, grinning. It wasn't going to rain. Maggie would say anything to hurry them away! Still, that was just what Julian wanted – to get away as quickly as possible!

In ten minutes' time the four children were ready to go. Each had rucksack and mac on their backs – and each had jewels worth thousands of pounds in their charge! What a very extraordinary thing.

'It will be a lovely walk across the moors,' said Anne, as they went along. 'I feel like singing now everything's turned out all right. The only thing is – nobody at school will believe George or me when we tell them what's happened.'

'We shall probably be set a composition to do – "What did you do on your half-term?"' said George. 'And Miss Peters will read ours and say "Quite well-written, but *rather* far-fetched, don't you think?"'

Everyone laughed. Timmy looked round with his tongue out and what George called 'his *smiling* face'. Then his 'smile' vanished, and he began to bark, facing to the rear of the children.

They looked round, startled. 'Gosh – it's Maggie and Dirty Dick – rushing along like fury!' said Dick. 'What's up? Are they sorry we've gone and want us back again?'

'They're trying to cut us off,' said Julian. 'Look – they've left the path and they're going to take a shortcut to come across us. There is marshland all round, so we can't leave our own path. What idiots they are! Unless they know this bit of marsh-moor country they'll get bogged.'

Maggie and Dirty Dick were yelling and shouting in a

fury. Dirty Dick shook his fists, and leapt from tuft to tuft like a goat.

'They look as if they have gone quite mad,' said Anne, suddenly afraid. 'What's the matter with them?'

'I know!' said George. 'They've been into our cellar room – and they've found that waterproof covering and all those empty boxes. They've found out that we've got the goods!'

'Of course!' said Julian. 'We should have thrown all the boxes into the cellars beyond. No wonder they're in a fury. They've lost a fortune to us four!'

'What do they think they can do now, though?' said Dick. 'We've got Timmy. He'll certainly fly at them if they come too near. But Dirty Dick looks mad enough to fight even Timmy. Honestly, I think he's gone off his head.'

'I think he has,' said Julian, startled by the man's mad shouts and behaviour.

He looked at Anne, who had gone white. Julian felt sure that Timmy would go for Dirty Dick and bring him to the ground, and he didn't want Anne to see dog and man fighting. There was no doubt that Dirty Dick was quite out of his mind with rage and disappointment.

Timmy began to bark fiercely. He snarled, and looked very savage. He could see that the man was spoiling for a fight with someone. All right – Timmy didn't mind!

'Let's hurry on,' said Julian. 'But no shortcuts for us, mind – we'll keep strictly to the path. Maggie is in difficulties already.'

So she was. She was floundering ankle deep in marshy ground, yelling to Dirty Dick to help her. But he was too intent on cutting right across the children's path.

And then *he* got into difficulties too! He suddenly sank up to his knees! He tried to clamber out and reach a tuft of some sort. He missed his footing and went down again. He gave an anguished yell. 'My ankle! I've broken it! Maggie, come over here!'

But Maggie was having her own difficulties and paid no attention. The children stopped and looked at Dirty Dick. He was sitting on a tuft, nursing his foot, and even from where the children stood they could see that his face was deathly white. He certainly had done something to his ankle.

'Ought we to help him?' said Anne, trembling.

'Good gracious no!' said Julian. 'He may be pretending for all we know – though I don't think so. The chase is over, anyway. And if, as I think, Dirty Dick really has injured his ankle, he won't be able to get far out of that marsh – and nor will Maggie by the look of her – down she goes again, look! It may be that the police will find it very easy to pick up that unpleasant couple when they come along to look for them.'

'Nicely embedded in the marsh,' said Dick. 'Well, personally, I don't feel sorry for either of them. They're bad lots.'

They went on their way again, Timmy gloomy because he hadn't had a fight with Dirty Dick after all. They walked all the way to Reebles. It took them two hours.

'We'll go to the post office, and telephone from there,' said Julian.

The old man was pleased to see them again. 'Had a nice time?' he said. 'Did you find Two-Trees?'

Julian left him talking to the others while he went to look up Mr Gaston's telephone number. He found it – and hoping devoutly that Mr Gaston wouldn't mind giving his help, he rang him up.

Mr Gaston answered the telephone himself. 'Hallo? Who? Oh, yes, of course I remember you. You want a bit of help? Well, what can I do for you?'

Julian told him. Mr Gaston listened in amazement.

'WHAT? You've found the Fallonia jewels! I can't believe it! In your rucksacks now, you say! Bless us all! You're not spoofing me, are you?'

Julian assured him that he wasn't. Mr Gaston could hardly believe his ears. 'Right. Right – of course I'll put you in touch with the police. We'd better go to Gathercombe – I know the inspector there, a fine fellow. Where are you? Oh yes, I know it. Wait there and I'll fetch you in my car – in about half an hour, say.'

He rang off and Julian went to find the others, delighted that he had thought of getting in touch with Mr Gaston. Some grown-ups were so jolly decent – and they knew exactly what to do. The other three were delighted too, when he told them.

'Well, I must say that although it's nice to have things happening to us, it's a sort of safe, comfortable feeling when we hand over to the grown-ups,' said George. 'Now I only want one thing – breakfast!'

'We'd better have a mixture of breakfast and lunch,' said Julian. 'It's so late.'

'Oh yes – let's have brunch!' said Anne, delighted. 'I love brunch.'

So they had some 'brunch' – sandwiches, buns, biscuits and ginger-beer, which they bought at a little shop down the road. And just as they were finishing, up swept Mr Gaston in an enormous car!

The four children grinned at him with pleasure. Julian introduced Anne and Dick. Timmy was thrilled to see him again and offered him a polite paw, which Mr Gaston shook heartily.

'Nice manners your dog's got,' he said, and pressed down the accelerator. Whoooosh! Away they went at top speed, with Timmy sticking his head out of the window as he always did in a car.

They told their extraordinary story as they went. Mr Gaston was full of admiration for all they had done. 'You're a bunch of plucky kids!' he kept saying. 'My word, I wish you were mine!'

They came to the police station. Mr Gaston had already warned the inspector they were coming, and he was waiting for them.

'Come along into my private room,' he said. 'Now first of all – where are these jewels? Have you really got them with you? Let's have a look at them before you tell your story.'

The children undid their rucksacks – and out of the hankies inside they poured the shining, glittering jewellery on to the oak table.

The inspector whistled and exchanged a look with Mr Gaston. He picked up the diamond necklace.

'You've got them!' he said. 'The very jewels! And to think the police everywhere have been hunting for them for months and months and months. Where did you find them, youngsters?'

'It's rather a long story,' said Julian. He began to tell it, and he told it well, prompted by the others, when he forgot anything. Mr Gaston and the inspector listened with amazement on their faces. When Julian came to the bit where Dirty Dick and Maggie had been left floundering in the marshes, the inspector interrupted him.

'Wait! Would they still be there? They would? Right. Half a minute!'

He pressed a bell and a policeman appeared. 'Tell Johns to take his three men and the car, and go to the Green Marshes, near Gloomy Water,' ordered the inspector. 'He's to pick up two people floundering there – man and woman. Our old friends Dirty Dick and Maggie Martin! Look sharp!'

The policeman disappeared. Anne hugged herself. Now that awful couple would be put into safe custody for some time, thank goodness – till she had forgotten about them! Anne hadn't liked them a bit.

Julian's tale came to an end. The inspector looked across at the tousle-headed, dirty, untidy group and smiled. He held out his hand. 'Shake!' he said. 'All of you! You're the kind of kids we want in this country – plucky, sensible, responsible youngsters who use your brains and never give up! I'm proud to meet you!'

They all shook hands with him solemnly. Timmy held up his paw too, and the inspector grinned and shook that too.

'And now – what's your programme?' asked Mr Gaston, getting up.

'Well – we're supposed to be back at school by three

o'clock,' said Julian. 'But I don't think we can arrive looking like this. We'd get into awful rows! Is there a hotel where we can have a bath and clean ourselves up a bit?'

'You can do that here,' said the inspector. 'And if you like I'll run you back to your schools in the police car. We can't do too much for people who produce the Fallonia jewels out of rucksacks, you know. Bless us all – I can't believe it!'

Mr Gaston said goodbye and went, saying that he was very proud to have made friends with them. 'And don't you get stuck down any more rabbit holes!' he said to Timmy, who woofed happily at him.

They bathed and washed every inch of themselves. They found their clothes neatly folded and brushed, and felt grateful. They brushed their hair and arrived looking very clean and tidy in the inspector's private room. He had a man there, inspecting the jewels and labelling them before he put them away into boxes.

'You'll be interested to know that we have picked up your couple,' he told them. 'The man had a broken ankle and couldn't stir a step. The woman was thigh deep in the marsh when we found her. They quite welcomed the police, they were so fed up with everything!'

'Oh *good*!' said the four, and Anne beamed with relief. That settled Maggie and Dirty Dick then!

'And these *are* the Fallonia jewels,' said the inspector. 'Not that I had any doubt of it. They are now being checked and labelled. I've no doubt the Queen of Fallonia and her titled friend will be extremely pleased to hear of your little exploit.'

A clock struck half past two. Julian looked at it. Half an hour only to get back in time. Would they do it?

'It's all right,' said the inspector, with his wide grin. 'Car's at the door. I'll come and see you off. You'll all be back at your schools in good time – and if anyone believes your tale I'll be surprised. Come along!'

He saw them into the car, Timmy too. 'Good-bye,' he said, and saluted them all smartly. 'I'm proud to have met you – good luck to you, Famous Five!'

Yes, good luck to you, Famous Five – and may you have many more adventures!

Join the adventure!

If you can't wait to explore further with **THE FAMOUS FIVE**, read the next book in the series:

Enid Blyton®

is one of the most popular children's authors of all time. Her books have sold over 500 million copies and have been translated into other languages more often than any other children's author.

Enid Blyton adored writing for children. She wrote over 700 books and about 2,000 short stories. *The Famous Five* books, now 75 years old, are her most popular. She is also the author of other favourites including *The Secret Seven*, *The Magic Faraway Tree*, *Malory Towers* and *Noddy*.

Born in London in 1897, Enid lived much of her life in Buckinghamshire and loved dogs, gardening and the countryside. She was very knowledgeable about trees, flowers, birds and animals. Dorset – where some of the Famous Five's adventures are set – was a favourite place of hers too.

Enid Blyton's stories are read and loved by millions of children (and grown-ups) all over the world. Visit enidblyton.co.uk to discover more.

THE FAMOUS FIVE

FIVE HAVE A WONDERFUL TIME

Have you read all THE FAMOUS FIVE books?

1. Five on a Treasure Island
2. Five Go Adventuring Again
3. Five Run Away Together
4. Five Go to Smuggler's Top
5. Five Go Off in a Caravan
6. Five on Kirrin Island Again
7. Five Go Off to Camp
8. Five Get Into Trouble
9. Five Fall Into Adventure
10. Five on a Hike Together
11. Five Have a Wonderful Time
12. Five Go Down to the Sea
13. Five Go to Mystery Moor
14. Five Have Plenty of Fun
15. Five on a Secret Trail
16. Five Go to Billycock Hill
17. Five Get Into a Fix
18. Five on Finniston Farm
19. Five Go to Demon's Rocks
20. Five Have a Mystery to Solve
21. Five Are Together Again

The Famous Five Colour Short Stories

1. Five and a Half-Term Adventure
2. George's Hair is Too Long
3. Good Old Timmy
4. A Lazy Afternoon
5. Well Done, Famous Five
6. Five Have a Puzzling Time
7. Happy Christmas, Five
8. When Timmy Chased the Cat

Enid Blyton®

THE FAMOUS FIVE

FIVE HAVE A WONDERFUL TIME

Illustrated by Eileen A. Soper

HODDER

HODDER CHILDREN'S BOOKS

First published in Great Britain in 1952 by Hodder & Stoughton
This edition published in 2016

20

A CIP catalogue record for this book is available from the British Library.

ISBN 978 1 444 93641 4

Printed and bound in Great Britain by Clays Ltd, Elcograf S.p.A.

The paper and board used in this book are made from wood from responsible sources.

Hodder Children's Books
An imprint of
Hachette Children's Group
Part of Hodder & Stoughton
Carmelite House
50 Victoria Embankment
London EC4Y 0DZ

An Hachette UK Company
www.hachette.co.uk
www.hachettechildrens.co.uk

CONTENTS

1 GEORGE IS ALL ALONE 1
2 ALL TOGETHER AGAIN 9
3 A PLEASANT MORNING 18
4 THE FAIR-FOLK ARRIVE 26
5 NIGHT AND MORNING 35
6 UNFRIENDLY FOLK 44
7 A LETTER – A WALK – AND A SHOCK 53
8 WHERE ARE THE CARAVANS? 62
9 A GREAT SURPRISE 70
10 BACK WITH THE FAIR-FOLK AGAIN 79
11 A VERY STRANGE THING 88
12 FIRE-EATING AND OTHER THINGS! 96
13 OFF TO THE CASTLE 105
14 FAYNIGHTS CASTLE 114
15 AN INTERESTING DAY 123
16 SECRET WAYS 131
17 EXCITEMENT AND SHOCKS 140
18 JO HAS AN ADVENTURE ON HER OWN 149
19 JO JOINS IN 158
20 A LOT OF EXCITEMENT 167
21 IN THE TOWER ROOM 175
22 BEAUTY AND JO ENJOY THEMSELVES 183
23 HAVING A WONDERFUL TIME! 193

CHAPTER ONE

George is all alone

'I DO think it's *mean*,' said George, fiercely. 'Why can't I go when the others do? I've had two weeks at home, and haven't seen the others since school broke up. And now they're off for a wonderful fortnight and I'm not with them.'

'Don't be silly, George,' said her mother. 'You can go as soon as that cold of yours is better.'

'It's better now,' said George, scowling. 'Mother, you know it is!'

'That's enough, Georgina,' said her father, looking up from his newspaper. 'This is the third breakfast-time we've had this argument. Be quiet.'

George would never answer anyone when she was called Georgina – so, much as she would have liked to say something back, she pursed up her mouth and looked away.

Her mother laughed. 'Oh, George, dear! Don't look so terribly fierce. It was your own fault you got this cold – you *would* go and bathe and stay in far too long and after all, it's only the third week in April!'

'I always bathe in April,' said George, sulkily.

'I said "BE QUIET",' said her father, banging down his

paper on the table. 'One more word from you, George, and you won't go to your three cousins' at all.'

'Woof,' said Timmy, from under the table. He didn't like it when anyone spoke angrily to George.

'And don't *you* start arguing with me, either,' said George's father, poking Timmy with his toe, and scowling exactly like George.

His wife laughed again. 'Oh, be quiet, the two of you,' she said. 'George, be patient dear. I'll let you go off to your cousins as soon as ever I can – tomorrow, if you're good, and don't cough much today.'

'Oh, Mother – why didn't you say so before?' said George, her scowl disappearing like magic. 'I didn't cough once in the night. I'm perfectly all right today. Oh, if I can go off to Faynights Castle tomorrow, I *promise* I won't cough once today!'

'What's this about Faynights Castle?' demanded her father, looking up again. 'First I've heard of it!'

'Oh no, Quentin dear, I've told you at least three times,' said his wife. 'Julian, Dick and Anne have been lent two funny old caravans by a school friend. They are in a field near Faynights Castle.'

'Oh. So they're not *staying* in a castle, then,' said George's father. 'Can't have that. I won't have George coming home all high and mighty.'

'George couldn't *possibly* be high and mighty,' said his wife. 'It's as much as I can do to get her to keep her nails clean and wear clean jeans. Do be sensible,

Quentin. You know perfectly well that George and her cousins always like to go off on extraordinary holidays together.'

'And have adventures,' grinned George, who was in a very good temper indeed at the thought of going to join her cousins the next day.

'No. You're not to have any of those awful adventures this time,' said her mother. 'Anyway, I don't see how you can, staying in a peaceful place like the village of Faynights Castle, living in a couple of old caravans.'

'I wouldn't trust George anywhere,' said her husband. 'Give her just a *sniff* of an adventure, and she's after it. I never knew anyone like George. Thank goodness we've only got one child. I don't feel as if I could cope with two or three Georges.'

'There are plenty of people like George,' said his wife. 'Julian and Dick for instance. Always in the middle of something or other – with Anne tagging behind, longing for a peaceful life.'

'Well, I've had enough of this argument,' said George's father, pushing his chair out vigorously, and accidentally kicking Timmy under the table. He yelped.

'That dog's got no brains,' said the impatient man. 'Lies under the table at every meal and expects me to remember he's there! Well, I'm going to do some work.'

He went out of the room. The dining-room door banged. Then the study door banged. Then a window was shut with a bang. A fire was poked very vigorously.

There was the creak of an armchair as someone sat down in it heavily. Then there was silence.

'Now your father's lost to the world till lunchtime,' said George's mother. 'Dear, oh dear – I've told him at *least* three times about Faynights Castle, where your cousins are staying, bless him. Now, George, I do really think you can go tomorrow, dear – you look so much better today. You can get your things ready and I'll pack them this afternoon.'

'Thank you, Mother,' said George, giving her a sudden hug. 'Anyway, Father will be glad to have me out of the house for a bit! I'm too noisy for him!'

'You're a pair!' said her mother, remembering the slammed doors and other things. 'You're both a perfect nuisance at times, but I couldn't bear to do without you! Oh, Timmy, are you still under the table? I wish you wouldn't leave your tail about so! Did I hurt you?'

'Oh, he doesn't mind *you* treading on it, Mother,' said George, generously. 'I'm going to get my things ready this very minute. How do I get to Faynights Castle? By train?'

'Yes. I'll take you to Kirrin Station, and you can catch the ten-forty,' said her mother. 'You change at Limming Ho, and take the train that goes to Faynights. If you send a card to Julian, he'll get it tomorrow morning and will meet you.'

'I'll write it now,' said George, happily. 'Oh, Mother, I began to be afraid this awful cold would hang on all through the holidays! I shan't bathe again on such a cold day in April.'

'You said that last year – and the year before that too,' said her mother. 'You have a very short memory, George!'

'Come on, Timmy!' said George, and the two of them went out of the door like a whirlwind. It slammed behind them, and the house shook.

At once the study door opened and an angry voice yelled loudly: 'Who's that slamming doors when I'm at work? Can't ANYBODY in this house shut a door quietly?'

George grinned as she fled upstairs. The biggest slammer-of-doors was her father, but he only heard the slams made by other people. George turned her writing-case inside out to find a postcard. She must post it at once or Julian

wouldn't get it – and it *would* be so nice to have all her three cousins meeting her!

'We're off tomorrow,' she told Timmy, who looked up at her and wagged his tail vigorously. 'Yes, you're coming too, of course – then the Five will all be together again. The Famous Five! You'll like that, won't you, Tim? So shall I!'

She scribbled the postcard and flew down to post it. Slam went the front door, and her father almost jumped out of his skin. He was a very clever and hardworking scientist, impatient, hot-tempered, kindly and very forgetful. How he wished his daughter was not so exactly like him, but was like his quiet, gentle little niece Anne!

George posted the card. It was short and to the point.

> Cold gone. Coming tomorrow. Arriving 12.05 so make sure you all meet me and Timmy. Our tails are well up, I can tell you!
>
> GEORGE.

George turned out her drawers and began to pick out the things she wanted to take with her. Her mother came to help. There was always an argument about packing, because George wanted to take as little as possible, and no warm things at all, and her mother had exactly opposite ideas.

However, between the two of them they managed to pack the suitcase full of quite sensible things. George refused as usual to take a dress of any sort.

'I wonder when you'll grow out of wanting to be a boy, and of acting like one!' said her mother, exasperated. 'All right, all right – take those awful old jeans if you want to, and that red jersey. But you *are* to pack those warm vests. I put them in once, and you took them out. And you must take a warm rug, Julian says. The caravans are not very warm in this weather.'

'I wonder what they're like,' said George, stuffing the vests in. 'They're funny, old-fashioned ones, Julian said in his letter. Perhaps they're like the ones the travellers have – not the modern, streamlined ones that are pulled along by cars.'

'You'll see tomorrow,' said her mother. 'Oh, George – you're coughing again!'

'Just the dust, that's all,' said George going purple in the face trying to hold back the tickle in her throat. She drank a glass of water in a hurry. It would be too dreadful if her mother said she wasn't to go after all!

However, her mother really did think that George was better. She had been in bed for a week, making a terrible fuss, and being a very difficult patient. Now, after being up for a few days she really seemed herself again.

'It will do her good to get down to Faynights and its good, strong air,' thought her mother. 'She needs company again, too – she doesn't like having to be all alone, knowing the others are holidaying without her.'

George felt happy that evening. Only one more night

and she would be off to a fortnight's caravanning! If only the weather was good, what a fine time they would have!

Suddenly the telephone shrilled out. R-r-r-r-r-ring! R-r-r-r-r-ring!

George's mother went to answer it. 'Hallo!' she said. 'Oh – it's you, Julian. Is everything all right?'

George sped out into the hall at once. Oh, surely, surely, nothing had happened! Surely Julian wasn't ringing to tell her not to come! She listened breathlessly.

'What's that you say, Julian? I can't make out what you're talking about, dear. Yes, of course, your uncle is all right. Why shouldn't he be? No, he hasn't disappeared. Julian, what *are* you talking about?'

George listened impatiently. What *was* all this? But it turned out to be something quite ordinary, really. When at last her mother put down the receiver, she told George.

'Don't hop about like that, George. It's *quite* all right, you can go tomorrow. Julian was only ringing up to make sure that your father wasn't one of the scientists who have suddenly disappeared. Apparently in tonight's paper there is a short report about two that have completely vanished – and dear old Julian wanted to make sure your father was here safely!'

'As if Father would vanish!' said George, scornfully. 'Julian must be mad! It's just two more of those silly scientists who are disloyal to this country, and disappear to another country to sell our secrets! *I* could have told Julian that!'

CHAPTER TWO

All together again

NEXT MORNING, on a dewy hillside a good distance from Kirrin, where George lived, two boys leapt down the steps of a caravan, and went to one nearby. They rapped on the door.

'Anne! Are you awake? It's a heavenly day!'

'Of course I'm awake!' cried a voice. 'The door's unlocked. Come in. I'm getting breakfast.'

Julian and Dick pushed open the blue-painted door. Anne was standing at a little stove at one end of her caravan, boiling eggs in a saucepan.

'I can't look round,' she said. 'I'm timing them by my watch. One minute more to go.'

'The postman has just brought a card from George,' said Julian. 'She says her tail and Timmy's are both well up! I'm glad she's coming at last – and old Timmy too.'

'We'll all go and meet her,' said Anne, still with her eyes on her watch. 'Twenty seconds more.'

'We only came here ourselves three days ago,' said Dick. 'So she hasn't really missed much. Surely those eggs will be hard-boiled, Anne!'

Anne stopped looking at her watch. 'No, they won't. They'll be just right.' She scooped them out of the little saucepan with a big spoon. 'Put them in the egg-cups, Dick. There they are – just under your nose.'

Dick picked an egg up from the plate on which Anne had placed them. It was so hot that he dropped it with a yell, and it broke its shell. Yolk flowed out of it.

'DICK! You *saw* me take it out of boiling water!' said Anne. 'Now I've got to do another. It's a pity old Timmy isn't here. He'd soon have licked that broken egg up from the floor and saved me clearing up the mess.'

'We'll eat our breakfast sitting on the steps of your caravan, Anne,' said Julian. 'The sun's so lovely.'

So they all sat there, eating boiled eggs, well-buttered bread with chunky, home-made marmalade afterwards, and then juicy apples. The sun shone down and Julian took off his coat.

Their two caravans were set on a sloping, grassy hillside. A tall hedge grew behind, and kept off the wind. Primroses ran in a pale gold streak under the hedge, and brilliant celandines shone in the sun, turning their polished faces towards it.

Not far off were three more caravans, but they were modern ones. The people staying in those were not yet up, and the doors were fast shut. The three children had had no chance of making friends with them.

On the opposite hill rose an old, ruined castle, whose great walls still defied the gales that sometimes blew over the hills. It had four towers. Three were very much broken, but the fourth looked almost complete. The windows were

slit-holes, made centuries back when archers shot their arrows from them.

A very steep pathway led up to the castle. At the top of it was a gateway, enormously strong, built of big white blocks of stone. The gateway was now filled by a great screen of wrought iron to prevent anyone entering, and the only entrance was by a small tower in which was a narrow door. Here there was a turnstile through which visitors might go to see the old castle.

A high, strong wall ran all round the castle, still standing after so many years. Bits of the top of it had fallen down the hill and lay half-buried in grass and weeds. It had once been a magnificent old castle, built on the high, steep hill for safety, a place from which the castle guards might see the country easily for miles around.

As Julian said, anyone up in one of the towers, or even on the wall, would be able to see enemies approaching from seven counties. There would be plenty of time to shut the great gate, man the walls, and get ready to withstand quite a long siege if necessary.

The three of them sat on the steps, lazing in the sun, when they had finished their breakfast. They looked at the ruined old castle, and watched the jackdaws circling round the four towers.

'There must be about a thousand jackdaws there,' said Dick. 'I wish we had field-glasses so that we could watch them. It would be as good as a circus. I love the way they all fly up together, and circle round and round and yet never bump into one another.'

'Do they nest in that old castle?' asked Anne.

'Oh, yes – they fill up the towers with big sticks,' said Dick, 'and put their nests on the top. I bet we'd find the ground beneath the towers strewn ankle-deep in sticks if we went to see.'

'Well, let's go one day when George is here,' said Anne. 'It only costs five pence to go in. I like old castles. I like the *feel* of old places.'

'So do I,' said Julian. 'I hope George brings the field-glasses she had for her birthday. We could take them up into the castle with us and see all round the countryside for miles and miles. We could count the seven counties!'

'I must wash up,' said Anne, getting up. 'I must tidy the caravans too before George comes.'

'You don't really think old George will notice if they're tidy or not, do you?' said Dick. 'It will be a waste of your time, Anne!'

But Anne always enjoyed tidying things and putting them away in cupboards or on shelves. She liked having the two caravans to look after. She had just got used to them nicely and was looking forward to showing George round them.

She skipped over to the hedge and picked a great bunch of primroses. Back she went and divided them into two. She stuffed half into one little blue bowl, set their green crinkled leaves round them, and then put the other half into a second bowl.

'There – you go with the green and yellow curtains!' she said. She was soon very busy sweeping and dusting. She debated whether to send Dick to the stream to wash the breakfast things, and decided not to. Dick wasn't too good with crockery, and it was not theirs to break – it belonged to the owner of the caravans.

By the time it was half past eleven the caravans were spick and span. George's sheets and blankets were on the shelf above her bunk, which, in the daytime, let down neatly against the wall to make more room. Anne had a bunk on the opposite side.

'This is the kind of holiday I *like*,' said Anne to herself. 'Somewhere small to live, fields and hills just outside, picnicky meals – and not too much adventure!'

'What are you murmuring about, Anne?' said Dick peeping in at the window. 'Did I hear something about adventure? Are you looking for one already?'

'Good gracious no!' said Anne. 'It's the last thing I want! And the last thing we'll get too, in this quiet little place, thank goodness.'

Dick grinned. 'Well, you never know,' he said. 'Are you ready to come and meet George, Anne? It's about time we went.'

Anne went down the steps and joined Dick and Julian. 'Better lock the door,' said Dick. 'We've locked ours.' He locked Anne's door and the three set off down the grassy hillside to the stile that led into the lane below. The old castle on the opposite hill seemed to tower up higher and higher as they went down towards the village.

'It will be lovely to see Timmy again,' said Anne. 'And I'll be jolly glad to have George too, in my caravan. I didn't really *mind* being alone at night – but it's always nice to have George near me, and Timmy grunting in his sleep.'

'You want to share a room with Dick if you like grunts and snorts and moans,' said Julian. 'What *do* you dream about, Dick? You must have more nightmares than anyone else in the kingdom!'

'I *never* grunt or snort or moan,' said Dick indignantly. 'You want to hear yourself! Why . . .'

'Look – isn't that the train coming in – isn't that it curving round the line in the distance?' said Anne. 'It must be! There's only one train in the morning here! We'd better run!'

They ran at top speed. The train drew in at the station just as they raced on to the platform. A head of short, curly hair looked out from a window – and then another brown head just below it.

'George – and Timmy!' yelled Anne.

'Hallo!' shouted George, almost falling out of the door.

'WOOF!' barked Timmy, and leapt down to the platform almost on top of Dick. Down jumped George, her eyes shining. She hugged Anne, and gave Julian and Dick a playful shove each. 'I'm here!' she said. 'I felt awful knowing you were away camping without me. I gave poor old Mother a dreadful time.'

'I bet you did,' said Julian, and linked his arm in hers. 'Let me take that suitcase. We'll just slip into the village first and have a few ice-creams to celebrate. There's a shop here that has some jolly decent ones.'

'Good. I feel exactly like ice-creams,' said George, happily. 'Look, Timmy knows what you said. His tongue is hanging out for an ice-cream already. Timmy, aren't you pleased we're all together again?'

'Woof,' said Timmy, and licked Anne's hand for the twentieth time.

'I really ought to bring a towel with me when I meet Timmy,' said Anne. 'His licks are so very wet. Oh no, not *again*, Timmy – go and use your tongue on Julian!'

'I say, look – George *has* brought her field-glasses with her!' said Dick, suddenly noticing that the brown strap over George's shoulder did not belong to a camera but to a very fine leather case that held the new field-glasses. 'Good! We wanted to watch the jackdaws with them – and there are some herons down on the marsh too.'

'Well, I thought I *must* bring them,' said George. 'It's the first hols I've had a chance to use them. Mother wouldn't let me take them to school. I say – how much further is this ice-cream shop?'

'In the dairy here,' said Julian, marching her in. 'And I advise you to start off with vanilla, go on to strawberry and finish up with chocolate.'

'You do have good ideas!' said George. 'I hope you've got some money as well, if we're going to eat ice-creams at this rate. Mother didn't give me very much to spend.'

They sat down and ordered ice-creams. The plump little shop-woman smiled at them. She knew them by now. 'This is very good weather for you,' she said. 'Are there many caravanners up on Faynights Field?'

'No, not many,' said Julian, beginning his ice.

'Well, you're going to have a few more,' said the little plump lady. 'I hear there's some fair-folk coming – they usually camp up in your field. You'll have some fun if so.'

'Oh, good!' said Dick. 'We'll really be able to make a few friends then. We like fair-folk, don't we, Timmy?'

CHAPTER THREE

A pleasant morning

'IS THERE going to be a fair near here then?' asked George, starting on her strawberry ice. 'What sort of a fair? A circus or something?'

'No. Just a mixed-up show,' said the shop-woman. 'There's to be a fire-eater, and that'll bring the villagers to the show faster than anything. A fire-eater! Did you ever hear of such a thing? I wonder that anyone cares to make a living at that!'

'What else is there to be?' asked Anne. She didn't somehow fancy watching anyone eating fire!

'Well, there's a man who can get himself free in under two minutes, no matter how tightly he's tied up with rope,' said the woman. 'Fair miracle he must be! And there's a man called Mr India-rubber, because he can bend himself anywhere, and wriggle through drainpipes and get in at a window if it's left open just a crack!'

'Gracious! He'd make a good burglar!' said George. 'I wish I was like india-rubber! Can this man bounce when he falls down?'

Everyone laughed. 'What else?' said Anne. 'This sounds very exciting.'

'There's a man with snakes,' said the plump little lady with a shudder. 'Snakes! Just fancy! I'd be afraid they would bite me. I'd run a mile if I saw a snake coming at me.'

'Are they poisonous snakes that he has, I wonder?' said Dick. 'I don't somehow fancy having a caravan next to ours with lashings of poisonous snakes crawling round.'

'Don't!' said Anne. 'I should go home at once.'

Another customer came in and the shop-woman had to leave the children and go to serve her. The four felt rather thrilled. What a bit of luck to have such exciting people in the same field as they were!

'A fire-eater!' said Dick. 'I've always wanted to see one. I bet he doesn't *really* eat fire! He'd burn the whole of his mouth and throat.'

'Has everyone finished?' asked Julian, getting some money out of his pocket. 'If so, we'll take George up to the field and show her our painted caravans. They aren't a bit like the ones we once went caravanning in, George – they are old-fashioned travellers' ones. You'll like them. Colourful and very picturesque.'

'Who lent you them?' asked George, as they left the shop. 'Some school friend, wasn't it?'

'Yes. He and his family always go and camp in their caravans in the Easter and summer hols,' said Julian. 'But this Easter they're going to France – and rather than leave them empty, they thought they'd lend them out – and we're the lucky ones!'

They walked up the lane and came to the stile. George looked up at the towering castle, gleaming in the sun on the hill opposite.

'Faynights Castle,' she said. 'Hundreds of years old! How I'd love to know all the things that happened there through the centuries. I do love old things. I vote we go and explore it.'

'We will. It only costs five pence,' said Dick. 'We'll all have a good five pence worth of castle. I wonder if there are any dungeons. Dark, damp, drear and dreadful!'

They went up the grassy hillside to the field where their caravans were. George exclaimed in delight. 'Oh! Are *those* our caravans? Aren't they lovely? They're just like the caravans the travellers use – only these look cleaner and brighter.'

'The red caravan, picked out with black and yellow, is ours,' said Dick. 'The blue one, picked out in black and yellow, is yours and Anne's.'

'Woof,' said Timmy at once.

'Oh, sorry – yours *too*, Timmy,' said Dick at once, and everyone chuckled. It was funny the way Timmy suddenly made a woofish remark, just as if he really understood every word that was said. George was quite certain he did, of course.

The caravans stood on high wheels. There was a window on each side. The door was at the front, and so were the steps, of course. Bright curtains hung at the windows, and a line of bold carving ran round the edges of the out-jutting roof.

'They are old traveller caravans painted and made really up to date,' said Julian. 'They're jolly comfortable inside too – bunks that fold down against the walls in the daytime

– a little sink for washing-up, though we usually use the stream, because it's such a bore to fetch water – a small larder, cupboards and shelves – cork carpet on the floor with warm rugs so that no draught comes through . . .'

'You sound as if you are trying to sell them to me!' said George, with a laugh. 'You needn't! I love them both, and I think they're miles nicer than the modern caravans down there. Somehow these seem *real*!'

'Oh, the others are real enough,' said Julian. 'And they've got more space – but space doesn't matter to us because we shall live outside most of the time.'

'Do we have a camp-fire?' asked George, eagerly. 'Oh, yes – I see we do. There's the ashy patch where you had your fire. Oh, Julian, do let's have a fire there at night and sit round it in the darkness!'

'With midges biting us and bats flapping all round,' said Dick. 'Yes, certainly we will! Come inside, George.'

'She's to come into my caravan first,' said Anne, and pushed George up the steps. George was really delighted. She was very happy to think she was going to have a peaceful two weeks here with her three cousins and Timmy. She pulled her bunk up and down to see how it worked. She opened the larder and cupboard doors. Then she went to see the boys' caravan.

'How *tidy*!' she said, in surprise. 'I expected Anne's to be tidy – but yours is just as spick and span. Oh dear – I hope you haven't all turned over a new leaf and become models of neatness – *I* haven't!'

'Don't worry,' said Dick, with a grin. 'Anne has been at work – you know how she loves to put everything in its place. We don't need to worry about anything when she's about. Good old Anne!'

'All the same, George will have to help,' said Anne, firmly. 'We've all got to tidy up and cook and do things like that.'

George groaned. 'All right, Anne, I'll do my share – sometimes. I say – there won't be much room for Timmy on my bunk at nights, will there?'

'Well, he's not coming on mine,' said Anne. 'He can sleep on the floor on a rug. Can't you, Timmy?'

'Woof,' said Timmy, without wagging his tail at all. He looked very disapproving.

'There you are – he says he wouldn't *dream* of doing such a thing!' said George. 'He *always* sleeps on my feet.'

They went outside again. It really was a lovely day. The primroses opened more and more of their little yellow flowers, and a blackbird suddenly burst into a fluting song on the bough of a hawthorn tree in the hedge nearby.

'Did anyone get a paper in the village?' asked Dick. 'Oh, you did, Julian. Good. Let's have a look at the weather forecast. If it's good we might go for a long walk this afternoon. The sea is not really very far off.'

Julian took the folded paper from his pocket and threw it over to Dick. He sat down on the steps of the caravan and opened it.

He was looking for the paragraph giving the weather forecast when headlines caught his eye. He gave an exclamation.

‘Hallo! Here’s a bit more about those two vanished scientists, Julian!’

‘Oh!’ said George, remembering Julian’s telephone call of the night before. ‘Julian, whatever in the world made you think my father could be one of the vanished scientists? As if he would ever be disloyal to his country and take his secrets anywhere else!’

‘Oh, I didn’t think that,’ said Julian, at once. ‘Of *course* I didn’t! I’d never think Uncle Quentin would do a thing like that. No – in yesterday’s paper it just said that two of our most famous scientists had disappeared – and I thought perhaps they had been kidnapped. And as Uncle Quentin is really very famous, I just thought I'd ring up to make sure.'

'Oh,' said George. 'Well, as Mother hadn't heard a thing about them she was awfully astonished when you asked her if Father had disappeared. Especially as he was banging about just then in the study, looking for something he had lost.'

'Which he was sitting on as usual, I suppose,' said Dick with a grin. 'But listen to this – it doesn't look as if the two men have been kidnapped – it looks as if they just walked out and took important papers with them! Beasts! There's too much of that sort of thing nowadays, it seems to me!'

He read out a paragraph or two.

> 'Derek Terry-Kane and Jeffrey Pottersham have been missing for two days. They met at a friend's house to discuss a certain aspect of their work, and then left together to walk to the Underground. Since then they have not been seen.
>
> 'It has, however, been established that Terry-Kane had brought his passport up to date and had purchased tickets for flying to Paris. No news of his arrival there has been reported.'

'There! Just what I said to Mother!' exclaimed George. 'They've gone off to sell their secrets to another country. Why do we let them?'

'Uncle Quentin won't be pleased about that,' said Julian. 'Didn't he work with Terry-Kane at one time?'

'Yes, I believe he did,' said George. 'I'm jolly glad I'm not at home today – Father will be rampaging round like anything, telling Mother hundreds of times what he thinks about scientists who are traitors!'

'He certainly will,' said Julian. 'I don't blame him either. That's a thing I don't understand – to be a traitor to one's own country. It leaves a nasty taste in my mouth to think of it. Come on – let's think about dinner, Anne. What are we going to have?'

'Fried sausages and onions, potatoes, a tin of sliced peaches, and I'll make a custard,' said Anne, at once.

'I'll fry the sausages,' said Dick. 'I'll light the fire out here and get the frying-pan. Anyone like their sausages split in the cooking?'

Everyone did. 'I like mine nice and *burnt*,' said George. 'How many do we have each? I've only had those ice-creams since breakfast.'

'There are twelve,' said Anne, giving Dick the bag. 'Three each. None for Timmy! But I've got a large, juicy bone for him. Julian, will you get me some water, please? There's the pail, over there. I want to peel the potatoes. George, can you possibly open the peaches without cutting yourself like you did last time?'

'Yes, Captain!' said George, with a grin. 'Ah – this is like old times. Good food, good company and a good time. Three cheers for Us!'

CHAPTER FOUR

The fair-folk arrive

THAT FIRST day they were all together was a lovely one. They enjoyed it thoroughly, especially George, who had fretted all by herself for two weeks at home. Timmy was very happy too. He tore after rabbits, most of them quite imaginary, up and down the field and in and out the hedges till he was tired out.

Then he would come and fling himself down by the four, panting like a steam-engine going uphill, his long pink tongue hanging out of his mouth.

'You make me feel hot just to *look* at you, Timmy,' said Anne, pushing him away. 'Look, George – he's so hot he's steaming! One of these days, Timmy, you'll blow up!'

They went for a walk in the afternoon, but didn't quite get to the sea. They saw it from a hill, sparkling blue in the distance. Little white yachts dotted the blue water like far-off swans with wings outspread. They had tea at a farmhouse, watched by a couple of big-eyed farm children.

'Do you want to take some of my home-made jam with you?' asked the farmer's jolly, red-faced wife, when they paid her for their tea.

'Oh, yes, rather!' said Dick. 'And I suppose you couldn't sell us some of that fruit cake? We're camping in caravans in Faynights Field, just opposite the castle – so we're having picnic meals each day.'

'Yes, you can have a whole cake,' said the farmer's wife. 'I did my baking yesterday, so there's plenty. And would you like some ham? And I've some good pickled onions too.'

This was wonderful! They bought all the food very cheaply indeed, and carried it home gladly. Dick took off the lid of the pickled onions halfway back to the caravans, and sniffed.

'Better than any scent!' he said. 'Have a sniff, George.'

It didn't stop at sniffs, of course. Everyone took out a large pickled onion – except Timmy who backed away at once. Onions were one thing he really couldn't bear. Dick put back the lid.

'I think somebody else ought to carry the onions, not Dick,' said Anne. 'There won't be many left by the time we reach our caravans!'

When they climbed over the stile at the bottom of the field the sun was going down. The evening star had appeared in the sky and twinkled brightly. As they trudged up to their caravans Julian stopped and pointed.

'Hallo! Look! There are two more caravans here – rather like ours. I wonder if it's the fair-folk arriving.'

'And there's another one, see – coming up the lane,' said Dick. 'It will have to go to the field-gate because it can't come the way we do – over the stile. There it goes.'

'We shall soon have plenty of exciting neighbours!' said Anne, pleased. They went up to their own caravans and looked curiously at the one that stood near theirs. It was yellow, picked out with blue and black, and could have done with a new coat of paint. It was very like their own caravans, but looked much older.

There didn't seem to be anyone about the newly arrived vans. The doors and windows were shut. The four stood and looked curiously at them.

'There's a big box under the nearest caravan,' said Julian. 'I wonder what's in it!'

The box was long, shallow and wide. On the sides were round holes, punched into it at intervals. George went to the caravan and bent down to look at the box, wondering if there was anything alive in it.

Timmy went with her, sniffing at the holes in curiosity. He suddenly backed away, and barked loudly. George put her hand on his collar to drag him off but he wouldn't go with her. He barked without stopping!

A noise came from inside the box – a rustling, dry, sliding sort of noise that made Timmy bark even more frantically.

'Stop it, Timmy! Stop it!' said George, tugging at him. 'Julian, come and help me. There's something in that box that Timmy has never met before – goodness knows what – and he's half-puzzled and half-scared. He's barking defiance – and he'll never stop unless we drag him away!'

An angry voice came from the bottom of the field by the stile. 'Hey you! Take that dog away! What do you mean by poking into my business – upsetting my snakes!'

'Oooh – snakes!' said Anne, retiring quickly to her own caravan. 'George, it's snakes in there. Do get Timmy away.'

Julian and George managed to drag Timmy away, half-choking him with his collar, though he didn't seem to notice this at all. The angry voice was now just behind them. George turned and saw a little man, middle-aged, with gleaming black eyes. He was shaking his fist, still shouting.

'Sorry,' said George, pulling Timmy harder. 'Please stop shouting, or my dog will go for you.'

'Go for me! He will go for me! You keep a dangerous dog like that, which smells out my snakes and will go for me!' yelled the angry little man, dancing about like a boxer on his toes. 'Ahhhhhh! Wait till I let out my snakes – and then your dog will run and run, and will never be seen again!'

This was a most alarming threat. With an enormous heave, Julian, Dick and George at last got Timmy under control, dragged him up the steps of Anne's caravan, and shut the door on him. Anne tried to quieten him, while the other three went out to the angry little man again.

He had dragged out the big, shallow box, and had opened the lid. The three watched, fascinated. What snakes had he in there? Rattlesnakes? Cobras? They were all ready to run for their lives if the snakes were as angry as their owner.

A great head reared itself out of the box, and swung itself from side to side. Two unblinking dark eyes gleamed – and then a long, long body writhed out and glided up the man's legs, round his waist and round his neck. He fondled it, talking in a low, caressing voice.

George shivered. Julian and Dick watched in amazement. 'It's a python,' said Julian. 'My, what a monster. I've never seen one so close before. I wonder it doesn't wind itself round that fellow and squeeze him to death.'

'He's got hold of it near the tail,' said Dick, watching. 'Oh, look – there's another one!'

Sure enough a second python slid out of the box, coil upon gleaming coil. It too wreathed itself round its owner, making a loud hissing noise as it did so. Its body was thicker than Julian's calf.

Anne was watching out of her caravan window, hardly able to believe her eyes. She had never in her life seen snakes as big as these. She didn't even know what they were. She began to wish their caravans were miles and miles away.

The little man quieted his snakes at last. They almost hid him with their great coils! From each side of his neck came a snake's head, flat and shining.

Timmy was now watching out of the window also, his head beside Anne's. He was amazed to see the gliding snakes, and stopped barking at once. He got down from the window and went under the table. Timmy didn't think he liked the look of these new creatures at all!

The man fondled the snakes and then, still speaking to them lovingly, got them back into their box again. They glided in, and piled themselves inside, coil upon coil. The man shut down the lid and locked it.

Then he turned to the three watching children. 'You see

how upset you make my snakes?' he said. 'Now you keep away, you hear? And you keep your dog away too. Ah, you children! Interfering, poking your noses, staring! I do not like children and nor do my snakes. You KEEP AWAY, SEE?'

He shouted the last words so angrily that the three jumped. 'Look here,' said Julian, 'we only came to say we were sorry our dog barked like that. Dogs always bark at strange things they don't know or understand. It's only natural.'

'Dogs, too, I hate,' said the little man, going into his caravan. 'You will keep him away from here, especially when I have my snakes out, or one might give him too loving a squeeze. Ha!'

He disappeared into his van and the door shut firmly.

'Not so good,' said Julian. 'We seem to have made a bad start with the fair-folk – and I had hoped they would be friendly and let us into some of their secrets.'

'I don't like the last thing he said,' said George, worried. 'A "loving squeeze" by one of those pythons would be the end of Timmy. I shall certainly keep him away when I see that funny little man taking out his snakes. He really seemed to *love* them, didn't he?'

'He certainly did,' said Julian. 'Well, I wonder who lives in the second newly arrived caravan. I feel I hardly dare even to look at it in case it contains gorillas or elephants or hippos, or . . .'

'Don't be an idiot,' said George. 'Come on, it's getting

dark. Hallo, here comes the caravan we saw down in the lane just now!'

It came slowly up the grassy hillside, bumping as it went. On the side was painted a name in large, scarlet letters.

'Mister India-rubber.'

'Oh – the rubber-man!' said George. 'Dick – is he the driver, do you think?'

They all stared at the driver. He was long and thin and droopy, and he looked as if he might burst into tears at any moment. His horse looked rather the same.

'Well – he *might* be Mr India-rubber,' said Julian. 'But certainly there doesn't seem to be much *bounce* in him! Look – he's getting down.'

The man got down with a supple, loose grace that didn't seem to fit his droopy body at all. He took the horse out of the shafts and set it loose in the field. It wandered away, pulling here and there at the grass, still looking as sad and droopy as its master.

'Bufflo!' suddenly yelled the man. 'You in?'

The door of the second caravan opened and a young man looked out – a huge young man with a mop of yellow hair, a bright red shirt and a broad smile.

'Hiya, Rubber!' he called. 'We got here first. Come along in – Skippy's got some food ready.'

Mr India-rubber walked sadly up the steps of Bufflo's caravan. The door shut.

'This is really rather exciting,' said Dick. 'An india-rubber man – Bufflo and Skippy, whoever they may be – and a man with tame snakes next to us. Whatever next!'

Anne called to them. 'Do come in. Timmy's whining like anything.'

They went up the steps of her caravan and found that Anne had got ready a light supper for them – a ham sandwich each, a piece of fruit cake and an orange.

'I'll have a pickled onion with my sandwich, please,' said Dick. 'I'll chop it up and put it in with the ham. What wonderful ideas I do have, to be sure!'

CHAPTER FIVE

Night and morning

As they had their supper they talked about the strange new arrivals. Timmy sat close to George, trying to tell her that he was sorry for causing such a disturbance. She patted him and scolded him at the same time.

'I quite understand that you don't like the snakes, Timmy – but when I tell you to stop barking and come away you MUST do as you're told! Do you understand?'

Timmy's tail dropped and he put his big head on George's knee. He gave a little whine.

'I don't think he'll ever go near that box again, now he's seen the snakes that came out of it,' said Anne. 'You should have seen how scared he was when he looked out of the window with me and saw them. He went and hid under the table.'

'It's a pity we've made a bad start with the fair-folk,' said Julian. 'I don't expect they like children much, because as a rule the kids would make themselves an awful nuisance – peering here and poking there.'

'I think I can hear more caravans arriving,' said George, and Timmy pricked up his ears and growled. 'Be quiet, Timmy. We're not the only ones allowed in this field!'

Dick went to the window and peered out into the twilight. He saw some large, dark shapes in another part of the field, looming out of the darkness. A little camp-fire burned brightly in front of one, showing a small figure bending over it.

'These are jolly good sandwiches, Anne,' said Dick. 'What about another pickled onion, everyone?'

'No, Dick,' said Anne firmly. 'You've eaten your sandwich.'

'Well, I can eat a pickled onion *without* a sandwich,

can't I?' said Dick. 'Hand over, Anne.'

Anne wouldn't. 'I've hidden them,' she said. 'You want some for tomorrow, don't you? Don't be greedy, Dick. Have a biscuit if you're still hungry.'

'I meant to ask if we could have a camp-fire outside tonight,' said George, remembering. 'But somehow I feel so sleepy I think I'd nod off if I sat by it!'

'I feel sleepy too,' said Anne. 'Let's clear up, George, and snuggle into our bunks. The boys can go to their caravan and read or play games if they want to.'

Dick yawned. 'Well – I might read for a bit,' he said. 'I hope you've got enough water, Anne, for the various things you use it for – because I do NOT intend to stumble over this dark field to the stream, and fall over snakes and anything else the fair-folk may have strewn carelessly about the grass!'

'You don't think those snakes could get loose, do you?' said Anne, anxiously.

'Of course not!' said Julian. 'Anyway, Timmy will bark the place down if even a hedgehog comes roving by, so you don't need to worry about snakes!'

The boys said good night and went off to their own caravan. The girls saw a light suddenly shine out there, and shadows moved across the curtains drawn over the windows.

'Dick's lit their lamp,' said Anne. Theirs was already lit, and the caravan looked cosy and friendly. Anne showed George how to put up her bunk. It clicked into place, felt nice and firm and was most inviting-looking.

The girls made their beds in the bunks, putting in sheets and blankets and rugs. 'Where's my pillow?' asked George. 'Oh – it's a cushion in the daytime, is it? What a good idea!'

She and Anne took the covers off the two cushions in the chairs, and underneath were the pillowcases over the pillows, ready for the night!

They undressed, washed in stream water in the little sink, cleaned their teeth and brushed their hair. 'Does the water go under the caravan when I pull the plug out of the sink?' said George. 'Here goes!'

The water gurgled out and splashed on the ground under the van. Timmy pricked up his ears and listened. He could see that he would have to get used to quite a lot of new noises here!

'Got your torch?' said Anne when at last they had both got into their bunks. 'I'm going to blow out the lamp. If you want anything in the night you'll have to put on your torch, George. Look at Timmy sitting on the floor still! He doesn't realise we've gone to bed! Tim – are you waiting for us to go upstairs?'

Timmy thumped his tail on the floor. That was just exactly what he *was* waiting for. When George went to bed she *always* went upstairs, whether she was at school or at home – and though he hadn't managed to discover any stairs in the caravan yet, he was sure that George knew where they were!

It took Timmy a few minutes to realise that George was going to sleep for the night in the bunk she had put up against the wall. Then, with one bound he was on top of her, and settled down on her legs. She gave a groan.

'Oh, Timmy – you *are* rough! Get off my legs – get further down – get into the curve of my knees.'

Timmy found the bunk too small to be really comfortable. However he managed to curl himself up in as small a space as possible, put his head down on one of George's knees, gave one of his heavy sighs, and fell asleep.

He had one ear open all the time, though – an ear for a rat that for some peculiar reason ran over the roof – an ear for a daring rabbit that nibbled the grass under the caravan – and a very alert ear for a big cockchafer that flew straight into the glass pane of the right-hand window, just above George's bunk.

Plang! It collided with the pane, and fell back, stunned. Timmy couldn't for the life of him think what it was, but soon fell asleep again, still with one ear open. The blackbird in the hawthorn tree woke him up early. It had thought of a perfectly new melody, and was trying it out very loudly and deliberately. A thrush nearby joined in.

'Mind how you do it, mind how you do it!' sang the thrush at the top of its voice. Timmy sat up and stretched. George woke up at once, because Timmy trod heavily on her middle.

She couldn't think where she was at first, then she remembered and smiled. Of course – in a caravan, with

Anne. How that blackbird sang – a better song than the thrush! Cows mooed in the distance, and the early morning sun slid in through the window and picked out the clock and the bowl of primroses.

Timmy settled down. If George wasn't going to get up neither was he! George shut her eyes and fell asleep again too. Outside, the camp began to awake. Caravan doors opened. Fires were lit. Somebody went down to the stream to get water.

The boys came banging at the door of the girls' caravan. 'Come on, sleepyheads! It's half past seven, and we're hungry!'

'Goodness!' said Anne, sitting up, bright-eyed with sleep. 'George! Wake up!'

It wasn't long before they were all sitting round a little fire, from which came a very nice smell. Dick was frying bacon and eggs, and the smell made everyone very hungry. Anne had boiled a kettle on her little stove, and made some tea. She came down the steps with a tray on which she had put the teapot and hot water.

'Anne always does things properly,' said Dick. 'Here, hold your plate out, Ju – your bacon's done. Take your nose out of the way, Timmy, you silly dog – you'll get it splashed with hot fat again. Do look after Timmy when I'm cooking, George. He's already wolfed one slice of bacon.'

'Well, it saved you cooking it,' said George. 'I say, aren't there a lot of caravans here now? They must have come last night.'

They stared round at the field. Besides the snake-man's caravan, and Bufflo's and Mr India-rubber's, there were four or five more.

One interested the children very much. It was a brilliant yellow with red flames painted on the sides. The name on it was 'Alfredo, the Fire-Eater'.

'I imagine him to be a great big, fierce chap,' said Dick. 'A regular fire-eater, with a terribly ferocious temper, an enormous voice and a great stride when he walks.'

'He will probably be a skinny little fellow who trots along like a pony,' said Julian.

'There's someone coming out of his caravan now,' said George. 'Look.'

'It's a woman,' said Anne. 'His wife, I expect. How tiny she is – rather sweet. She looks Spanish.'

'*This* must be the fire-eater, coming behind her,' said George. 'Surely it is! And he's JUST like you imagined him, Dick. How clever of you!'

A great big fellow came down the steps behind his tiny wife. He certainly looked very fierce, for he had a lion-like mane of tawny hair, and a big red face with large, gleaming eyes. He took enormous strides as he went, and his wife had to run to keep up with him.

'*Just* my idea of a fire-eater,' said Dick, pleased. 'I think we'll keep out of his way until we know if he also dislikes children, like the snake-man. What a tiny wife he has! I bet he makes her run around him, and wait on him hand and foot.'

'Well, he's fetching water from the stream for her, anyway,' said Anne. 'Two huge pails. My word, he really does look like a fire-eater, doesn't he?'

'There's somebody else, look,' said Dick. 'Now who would *he* be? Look at him going to the stream – he walks like a tiger or a cat – all slinky and powerful.'

'The man who can set himself free from ropes no matter how he's tied!' said Anne. 'I'm sure he is.'

It was most exciting to watch the new arrivals. They all seemed to know one another. They stopped to talk, they laughed, they visited one another's caravans, and finally three of the women set off together with baskets.

'Going off to shop,' said Anne. 'That's what *I* ought to do. Coming, George? There's a bus that goes down to the village in about ten minutes. We can easily clear up when we come back.'

'Right,' said George, and got up too. 'What are the boys going to do while we're gone?'

'Oh, fetch more water, find sticks for the fire, and see to their own bunks,' said Anne, airily.

'Are we *really*?' said Dick, grinning. 'Well, we might. On the other hand, we might not. Anyway, you two go, because food is getting rather low. A very serious thought, that! Anne, get me some more toothpaste, will you? And if you can spot some of those doughnuts at the dairy, bring a dozen back with you.'

'Yes – and see if you can get a tin of pineapple,' said Julian. 'Don't forget we want milk too.'

'If you want many more things you'll have to come and help us carry them,' said Anne. 'Anything else?'

'Call at the post office and see if there are any letters,' said Dick. 'And don't forget to buy a paper. We may as well find out if anything has happened in the outside world! Not that I feel I can take much interest in it at the moment.'

'Right,' said Anne. 'Come on, George – we shall miss that bus!' And off they went with Timmy at their heels.

CHAPTER SIX

Unfriendly folk

THE TWO boys decided they *would* fetch the water and stack up some firewood while the girls were gone. They 'made' their bunks too, by the simple process of dragging off all the clothes and bundling them on the shelf, and then letting down the bunks against the wall.

That done there didn't seem much else to do except wait for the girls. So they took a walk round the field. They kept a good distance from the snake-man, who was doing something peculiar to one of his pythons.

'It *looks* as if he's polishing it, but he surely can't be,' said Julian. 'I'd like to go near enough to watch but he's such a hot-tempered little fellow he might quite well set one of those enormous pythons on to us!'

The snake-man was sitting on a box, with one snake spread over his knee, some of its coils round one of his legs, the other coils round his waist. The head appeared to be under his armpit. The man was rubbing away hard at the snake's scaly body, and it really seemed as if the python was enjoying it!

Bufflo was doing something with a whip. It had a magnificent handle, set with semi-precious stones that caught the sun and glittered in many colours.

'Look at the lash,' said Julian. 'Yards and yards long! I'd like to see him crack it!'

Almost as if he heard him, Bufflo got to his feet, and swung the great whip in his hand. Then he raised it – and a moment later there was a sound exactly like a pistol-shot! The lash cracked as it was whipped through the air, and the two boys jumped, not expecting such a loud noise.

Bufflo cracked it again. Then he whistled and a small plump woman came to the steps of his caravan.

'You mended it yet?' she called.

'Perhaps,' said Bufflo. 'Get a cigarette, Skippy. Hurry!'

Skippy put her hand into the caravan, felt along a shelf, and brought out a packet of cigarettes. She didn't go down the steps, but stood there, holding out the cigarette between her finger and thumb.

Bufflo swung his whip. CRACK! The cigarette disappeared as if by magic! The boys stared in amazement. Surely the end of the lash hadn't whipped that cigarette from Skippy's fingers? It didn't seem possible.

'There it is,' said Bufflo, pointing some distance away. 'Hold it again, Skippy. I reckon this whip is OK now.'

Skippy picked up the cigarette and put it in her mouth!

'No!' called Bufflo. 'I ain't sure enough of this lash yet. You hold it like you did.'

Skippy took it out of her mouth and held out the cigarette in her finger and thumb once more.

CRACK! Like a pistol-shot the whip cracked again, and once more the cigarette disappeared.

'Aw, Bufflo – you've gone and broken it in half,' said Skippy, reproachfully, pointing to where it lay on the ground, neatly cut in half. 'That was real careless of you.'

Bufflo said nothing. He merely turned his back on Skippy, and set to work on his lash again, though what he was doing neither of the boys could make out. They went a little nearer to see.

Bufflo had his back to them but he must have heard them coming. 'You clear out,' he said, hardly raising his voice. 'No kids allowed round here. Clear out – or I'll crack my whip and take the top hairs off your head!'

Julian and Dick felt perfectly certain he would be able to carry out his threat, and they retreated with as much dignity as they could. 'I suppose the snake-man told him what a disturbance old Timmy made yesterday with the snakes,' said Dick. 'I hope it won't spoil things for us with all the fair-folk.'

They went across the field and on the way met Mr India-rubber. They couldn't help staring at him. He honestly looked as if he were made of rubber – he was a curious grey, the grey of an ordinary school rubber, and his skin looked rubbery too.

He scowled at the two boys. 'Clear out,' he said. 'No kids allowed in our field.'

Julian was annoyed. 'It's our field as much as yours,' he said. 'We've got a couple of caravans here – those over there.'

'Well, this has always *been* our field,' said Mr India-rubber. 'So you clear out to the next one.'

'We haven't any horses to pull our caravans, even if we wanted to go, which we don't,' retorted Julian, angrily. 'Anyway, why should you object to us? We'd like to be friendly. We shan't do you any harm, or make a nuisance of ourselves.'

'Us-folk and you-folk don't mix,' said the man, obstinately. 'We don't want you here – nor them posh caravans down there, neither,' and he pointed to the three modern caravans in one corner of the field. 'This has always been *our* field.'

'Don't let's argue about it,' said Dick, who had been looking at the man with the greatest curiosity. 'Are you really so rubbery that you can wriggle in and out of pipes and things? Do you—'

But he didn't have time to finish his question because the rubber-man flung himself down on the ground, did a few strange contortions, flicked himself between the boys' legs – and there they both were, flat on the ground! The rubber-man was walking off, looking quite pleased with himself.

'Well!' said Dick, feeling a bump on his head. 'I tried to grab his legs and they honestly felt like rubber! I say – what a pity these people resent us being in their field. It's not going to be very pleasant to have them all banded against us. Not fair either. I should *like* to be friendly.'

'Well, perhaps it's just a case of us-folk and you-folk,' said Julian. 'There's a lot of that kind of feeling about these days, and it's so silly. We're all the same under the skin. We've always got on well with anyone before.'

They hardly liked to go near the other caravans, though they longed to have a closer view of Alfredo the Fire-Eater.

'He looked so *exactly* like what I imagined a fire-eater ought to be,' said Dick. 'I should think he's probably chief of all the fair-folk here – if they've got a chief.'

'Look – here he comes!' said Julian. And sure enough, round the corner came Alfredo, running fast. He came towards the boys, and Julian at first thought that he was coming to chase them away. He didn't mean to run from Alfredo, but it wasn't very pleasant standing still, either, with this enormous fellow racing towards them, his cheeks as red as fire, his great mane of hair flopping up and down.

And then they saw why Alfredo was running! After him came his wife. She was shrieking at him in another language, and was chasing him with a saucepan!

Alfredo lumbered by the two boys, looking scared out of his life. He went down to the stile, leapt over it and disappeared down the lane.

The woman watched him go. When he turned to look round she waved the saucepan at him.

'Big bad one!' she cried. 'You burn breakfast again! Again, again! I bang you with saucepan, big bad one. Come, Alfredo, come!'

ALFREDO

But Alfredo had no intention of coming. The angry woman turned to the two boys. 'He burn breakfast,' she said. 'He no watch, he burn always.'

'It seems odd for a fire-eater to burn something he's cooking,' said Julian. 'Though, on second thoughts, perhaps it's not!'

'Poof! Fire-eating, it is easy!' said Alfredo's hot-tempered wife. 'Cooking is not so easy. It needs brains and eyes and hands. But Fredo, he has no brains, his hands are clumsy – he can only eat fire, and what use is that?'

'Well – I suppose he makes money by it,' said Dick, amused.

'He is my big bad one,' said the woman. She turned to go and then turned back again with a sudden smile. 'But he is very good sometimes,' she said.

She went back to her caravan. The boys looked at one another. 'Poor Alfredo,' said Dick. 'He looks as brave as a lion, and he's certainly a giant of a man – but he's as timid as a mouse. Fancy running away from that tiny woman.'

'Well, I'm not so sure I wouldn't too, if she came bounding over the field after me, brandishing that dangerous-looking saucepan,' said Julian. 'Ah – who's this?'

The man that Anne had thought might be the one who could set himself free when bound with ropes was coming up from the stile. He walked easily and lightly, really very like a cat. Julian glanced at his hands – they were small but looked very strong. Yes – he could certainly undo knots with hands like that. They gazed at him curiously.

'No kids allowed here,' said the man, as he came up.

'Sorry, but we're caravanners too,' said Dick. 'I say – are you the fellow that can undo ropes when he's tied up in them?'

'Could be,' said the man, and walked on. He turned round suddenly. 'Like me to tie *you* up?' he called. 'I've a good mind to try. Don't you try interfering with us, or I'll do it!'

'Dear me – what a nice, pleasant lot they are!' said Julian. 'Quite different from the other circus folk we've known. I begin to feel we shan't make friends as fast as I thought!'

'We'd better be careful, I think,' said Dick. 'They seem to resent us, goodness knows why. They may make things jolly unpleasant. Don't let's snoop round any more this morning. Let's keep away from them till they get a bit used to us. Then perhaps they'll be more friendly.'

'We'll go and meet the girls,' said Julian. So they went down to the stile and walked to the bus stop. The bus came panting up the hill at that very moment, and the girls stepped off, with the three fair-women behind them.

The girls joined the boys. 'We've done a lot of shopping,' said Anne. 'Our baskets are awfully heavy. Thanks, Julian, if you'll carry mine. Dick can take George's. Did you see those women who got off with us?'

'Yes,' said Julian. 'Why?'

'Well, we tried to talk to them but they were very unfriendly,' said Anne. 'We felt quite uncomfortable. And

Timmy growled like anything, of course, which made things worse. I don't think he liked the smell of them.'

'*We* didn't get on too well either, with the rest of the fair-folk,' said Julian. 'In fact I can't say that Dick and I were a success at all. All they wanted us to do was to clear out.'

'I got a paper for you,' said Anne, 'and George found a letter at the post office from her mother. It's addressed to all of us so we didn't open it. We'll read it when we get to the caravans.'

'I *hope* it's nearly time for dinner,' said George. 'What do *you* think, Timmy?'

Timmy knew the word dinner! He gave a joyful bark and led the way. Dinner? There couldn't be a better idea!

CHAPTER SEVEN

A letter – a walk – and a shock

GEORGE OPENED her mother's letter when they had finished their meal. Everyone voted that it was a truly wizard lunch – two hard-boiled eggs each, fresh lettuce, tomatoes, mustard and cress, and potatoes baked in the fire in their jackets – followed by what Julian had asked for – slices of tinned pineapple, very sweet and juicy.

'Very nice,' said Julian, lying back in the sun. 'Anne, you're a jolly good housekeeper. Now, George, let's hear what Aunt Fanny has got to say in her letter.'

George unfolded the notepaper and smoothed it out. 'It's to all of us,' she said.

'DEAR GEORGE, ANNE, JULIAN AND DICK,

'I hope George arrived safely and that you all met her. I am really writing to remind George that it is her grandmother's birthday on Saturday, and she must write to her. I forgot to remind George before she went, so thought I must quickly send a letter.

'George, your father is very much upset to read about those two missing scientists. He knows Derek Terry-Kane very well, and worked with him for some time. He says he is absolutely sure that he isn't a traitor to his country; he thinks he has been spirited away somewhere, and Jeffrey Pottersham too – probably in a plane miles away by now, in a country that will force them to give up their secrets. It's just as well you went off today, because this afternoon your father is striding about all over the place, talking nineteen to the dozen, and banging every door he comes to, bless him.

'If you write, please don't mention scientists, as I am hoping he will calm down soon. He really is very upset, and keeps on saying, "What is the world coming to?" when he knows quite well that it's coming to exactly what the scientists plan it to come to.

'Have a good time, all of you, and DON'T forget to write to your grandmother, George!

'Your loving,

MOTHER (AUNT FANNY).'

'I can just see Father striding about like a – like a . . .'

'Fire-eater,' said Julian with a grin, as George stopped for a word. 'He'll drive Aunt Fanny into chasing him around with a saucepan one day! Funny business about these scientists though, isn't it? After all, Terry-Kane *had* planned to leave the country – got his aeroplane ticket and everything – so although your father believes in him, George, it honestly looks a bit fishy, doesn't it?'

'Anything in the paper about it?' asked Dick, and shook it open. 'Yes – here we are:

MISSING SCIENTISTS

It is now certain that Jeffrey Pottersham was in the pay of a country unfriendly to us, and was planning to join Terry-Kane on his journey abroad. Nothing has been heard of the two men, although reports that they have been seen in many places abroad have been received.

'That rather settles it,' said Julian. 'Two Really Bad Eggs. Look – here are their photographs.'

The four leant over the paper, looking at the pictures of the two men. 'Well, I should have thought *anyone* would recognise Terry-Kane if they saw him,' said Anne. 'Those big, thick, arched eyebrows, and that enormous forehead. If I saw anyone with eyebrows like that I'd think they weren't real!'

'He'll shave them off,' said Dick. 'Then he'll look completely different. Probably stick them on his upper lip upside down and use them for moustaches!'

'Don't be silly,' said George, with a giggle. 'The other fellow is very ordinary-looking, except for his dome of a head. Pity none of us four have got great foreheads – I suppose we must be rather stupid people!'

'We're not so bad,' said Julian. 'We've had to use our brains many times in all our adventures – and we haven't come off so badly!'

'Let's clear up and then go for a walk again,' said Anne. 'If we don't I shall fall asleep. This sun is so gloriously hot, it's really cooking me.'

'Yes – we'd better go for a walk,' said Julian, getting up. 'Shall we go and see the castle, do you think? Or shall we leave that for another day?'

'Leave it,' said Anne. 'I honestly don't feel like clambering up that steep hill just now. I think the morning would be a better time!'

They cleared up and then locked the two caravans and set out. Julian looked back. Some of the fair-folk were sitting together, eating a meal. They watched the children in silence. It wasn't very pleasant somehow.

'They don't exactly love us, do they?' said Dick. 'Now you listen, Timmy – don't you go accepting any titbits from people here, see?'

'Oh, Dick!' said George, in alarm. 'You surely don't think they would harm Timmy?'

'No, I don't really,' said Dick. 'But we might as well be careful. As the rubber-man pointed out to us this morning, us-folk and his-folk think differently about some things. It just can't be helped. But I do wish they'd let us be friendly. I don't like this kind of thing.'

'Well, anyway, I shall keep Timmy to heel all the time,' said George, making up her mind firmly. 'Timmy, to heel!' Please understand that as long as we are in the caravan field you must walk to heel! *Do* you understand?'

'Woof-woof,' said Timmy, and immediately kept so close to George's ankles that his nose kept bumping into them.

They decided to catch the bus to Tinkers' Green, and then walk from there to the sea. They would have time to get there and back before dark. The bus was waiting at the corner, and they ran to catch it. It was about two miles to Tinkers' Green, which was a dear little village, with a proper green and a duck-pond with white ducks swimming on it.

'Shall we have an ice-cream?' suggested Dick as they came to a grocer's shop with an ice-cream sign outside it.

'No,' said Julian firmly. 'We've just had an enormous lunch, and we'll save up ice-cream for tea-time. We shall never get down to the sea if we sit and eat ice-creams half the afternoon!'

It was a lovely walk, down violet-studded lanes, and then over a heathery common with clumps of primroses in the hollows – and even a few very, very early bluebells, much to Anne's delight.

'There's the sea! Oh, what a dear little bay!' said Anne,

in delight. 'And isn't it blue – as blue as cornflowers. We could almost bathe.'

'You wouldn't like it if you did,' said Julian. 'The sea would be as cold as ice! Come on – let's get down to the little jetty and have a look at the fishing boats.'

They went down to the sun-warmed stone jetty and began talking to the fishermen there. Some were sitting in the sun mending their nets, and were very willing to talk.

'How nice to have a bit of friendliness shown us instead of the stares and rudeness of the fair-folk!' said Dick to Julian, who nodded and agreed.

A fisherman took them on his boat, and explained a lot of things they already knew and some they didn't. It was nice to sit and listen to his broad speech, and to watch his bright blue eyes as he talked. He was as tanned as an oak-apple.

'Could we ever hire a boat here if we wanted to?' asked Julian. 'Is there one we could manage by ourselves? We are quite good at sailing.'

'Old Joseph there has a boat he could hire out if you wanted one,' said the man they were talking to. 'He hired it out the other day, and I expect he'd hire it out to you too if you think you can really manage it.'

'Thanks. We'll ask him, if we ever decide to go out,' said Julian. He looked at his watch. 'We'd better go and get some tea somewhere. We want to be home before dark. We're camping over at Faynights Castle.'

'Oh ay?' said the fisherman. 'You've got the fair-folk there now, haven't you? They were here two weeks since.

My, that fire-eater is a fair treat, he is! And that rope-man – well! I tell you this – I tied him up in my fishing-line – you can see it here, strong as two ropes it is! I tied him up with all the knots I know – and in under a minute he stood up and the line fell off him, knots and all!'

'Ay, that is so,' said the old fellow called Joseph. 'A wonder he is, that man. So is the rubber fellow. He called for a drainpipe, narrow as this, see? And he wriggled through it, quick as an eel. Fair scared me, it did, to see him wriggling out of the other end.'

'We'll go and see them perform when they begin their show,' said Julian. 'At the moment they're not very friendly towards us. They don't like us being in their field.'

'They keeps themselves to themselves,' said Joseph. 'They had a heap of trouble at the place they were in before they came to us – someone set the police on them, and now they won't make friends with anyone.'

'Well, we must go,' said Julian, and they said goodbye to the friendly fishermen and went. They stopped and had tea at a little teashop, and then made their way home. 'Anyone want to take the bus?' said Julian. 'We can easily get home before dark if we walk – but if the girls are tired we'll bus from Tinkers' Green.'

'Of *course* we're not tired!' said George, indignantly. 'Have you *ever* known me say I'm tired, Julian?'

'All right, all right – it was just a bit of politeness on my part,' said Julian. 'Come on – let's get going.'

The way was longer than they had thought. It was getting dark when they got to the stile that led into the caravan field. They climbed over it and made their way slowly to their corner.

And then they suddenly stopped and stared. They looked all round and stared again.

Their two caravans were gone! They could see the places

where they had stood, and where their fire had been. But no caravans stood there now!

'*Well!*' said Julian, astounded. 'This beats everything! Are we dreaming? I can't see a sign of our caravans anywhere!'

'Yes – but – *how* could they go?' said Anne, almost stammering in her surprise. 'I mean – we had no horses to pull them away anywhere! They couldn't go just by themselves.'

There was a silence. The four were completely bewildered. How could two large, solid caravans disappear into thin air?

'Look – there are wheel-marks in the grass,' said Dick suddenly. 'See – our caravans went this way – come on, follow. Down the hillside, look!'

In the greatest astonishment the four children and Timmy followed the wheel-marks. Julian glanced back once, feeling that they were being watched. But not one of the fair-folk was to be seen. 'Perhaps they are watching silently behind their caravan curtains,' Julian thought, uncomfortably.

The wheel-marks went right down the field and reached the gate. It was shut now, but it must have been opened for the two caravans, because there were marks in the grass by the gate, marks that passed through it and then were lost in the lane.

'What are we to do?' said Anne, scared. 'They're gone! We've nowhere to sleep. Oh, Julian – what are we going to *do*?'

CHAPTER EIGHT

Where are the caravans?

For once in a way Julian was quite at a loss what to do! It looked as if someone had stolen the two caravans – taken them right away somewhere!

'I suppose we'd better ring up the police,' he said. 'They'll watch out for the two caravans, and arrest the thieves. But that won't help us much for tonight! We've got to find somewhere to sleep.'

'I think we ought to go and tackle one or two of the fair-folk,' said Dick. 'Even if they have got nothing to do with the theft they *must* have seen the caravans being taken away.'

'Yes. I think you're right,' said Julian. 'They must know *something* about it. George, you stay here with Anne, in case the fair people are rude. We'll take Timmy – he may be useful!'

George didn't want to stay behind – but she could see that Anne did! So she stayed with her, straining her eyes after the two boys as they went back up the hill with Timmy close behind.

'Don't let's go to the snake-man,' said Dick. 'He might be playing with his snakes in his caravan!'

'What possible game can you play with snakes?' said Julian. 'Or are you thinking of snakes and ladders?'

'Funny joke,' said Dick, politely. 'Look – there's somebody by a camp-fire – Bufflo, I think. No, it's Alfredo. Well, we know he isn't as fierce as he looks – let's tackle *him* about the caravans.'

They went up to the big fire-eater, who was sitting smoking by the fire. He didn't hear them coming and jumped violently when Julian spoke to him.

'Mr Alfredo,' began Julian, 'could you tell us where our two caravans have gone? We found them missing when we got back just now.'

'Ask Bufflo,' said Alfredo, gruffly, not looking at them.

'But don't *you* know anything about them?' persisted Julian.

'Ask Bufflo,' said Alfredo, blowing out clouds of smoke.

Julian and Dick turned away, annoyed, and went over to Bufflo's caravan. It was shut. They knocked on the door, and Bufflo appeared, his mop of golden hair gleaming in the lamplight.

'Mr Bufflo,' began Julian politely again, 'Mr Alfredo told us to come and ask you about our caravans, which are missing, and . . .'

'Ask the rubber-man,' said Bufflo, shortly, and slammed the door. Julian was angry. He knocked again. The window opened and Skippy, Bufflo's wife, looked out.

'You go and ask Mr India-rubber,' she called, and shut the window with what sounded suspiciously like a giggle.

'Is this a silly trick they're playing on us?' said Dick fiercely.

'Looks like it,' said Julian. 'Well, we'll try the rubber-man. Come on. He's the last one we'll try, though!'

They went to the rubber-man's caravan, and rapped smartly on the door. 'Who's there?' came the voice of Mr India-rubber.

'Come out – we want to ask you something,' said Julian.

'Who's there?' said the rubber-man again.

'You know jolly well who we are,' said Julian, raising his voice. 'Our caravans have been stolen, and we want to find out who took them. If you won't give us any help, we're going to telephone the police.'

The door opened and the rubber-man stood on the top of the steps, looking down at Julian. 'Nobody has stolen them,' he said. 'Nobody at all. You go and ask the snake-man.'

'If you think we're going round asking every single person in this camp, you're mistaken!' said Julian, angrily. 'I don't *want* to go to the police – we wanted to be friends with you fair-folk, not enemies. This is all very silly. If the caravans *are* stolen we've no choice but to go to the police – and I don't imagine you want them after you again! We know they were put on to you a few weeks back.'

'You know too much,' said the rubber-man, in a very surly voice. 'Your caravans are *not* stolen. I will show you where they are.'

He came lightly down the steps of his caravan and walked in front of the two boys in the half-darkness. He went across the grassy hillside, making for where the children's caravans had stood.

'Where are you taking us?' called Julian. 'We know the vans are not there! Please don't act the idiot – there's been enough of that already.'

The man said nothing, but walked on. The boys and Timmy could do nothing but follow. Timmy was not happy. He kept up a continuous low growling, like far-off thunder. The rubber-man took not the slightest notice. Julian wondered idly if he didn't fear dogs because they wouldn't be able to bite rubber!

The man took them to the hedge that ran at one side of the field, beyond where the two caravans had stood. Julian began to feel exasperated. He knew perfectly well that the two vans had been taken down to the field-gate and out into the lane – so why was this fellow leading them in the opposite direction?

The rubber-man forced his way through the hedge, and the boys followed – and there, just the other side, two big, dark shapes loomed up in the twilight – the caravans!

'Well!' said Julian, taken aback. 'What *was* the idea of putting the caravans here, in the next field?'

'Us-folk and you-folk don't mix,' said the man. 'We don't like kids messing about. Three weeks ago we had a canary-man, with over a hundred canaries that gave a show with him – and some kids opened all the cages one night and set them loose.'

'Oh,' said Julian. 'They'd die, of course, if they were set loose – they don't know how to look for their own food. That was bad luck. But *we* don't do things like that.'

'No kids allowed with us now,' said the rubber-man. 'That's why we put horses into your vans, took them down to the field-gate, and up into the next field – and here they are. We thought you'd be back in the daylight and would see them.'

'Well, it's nice to find you can be chatty, all of a sudden,' said Julian. 'Don't growl any more, Timmy. It's all right. We've found our vans!'

The rubber-man disappeared without another word. They heard him squeezing easily through the hedge. Julian took out the key to his caravan, went up the steps and opened the door. He rummaged about and found his torch. He switched it on and shone it round. Nothing had been disturbed.

'Well – so that's that,' he said. 'Just a bit of spite on the part of the fair-folk, I suppose – punishing us for what those horrid kids did to the canaries. I must say it was a shame to open those cages – half the poor little creatures must have died. I don't *like* birds put in cages – but canaries can't live in this country unless they are looked after, it's cruel to let them go loose, and starve.'

'I agree with you,' said Dick. They were now walking down the hillside to a gap in the hedge through which the vans must have been pulled up the hill. George and Anne would be most relieved to hear they had found the caravans!

Julian gave a whistle, and George answered it at once. 'We're still here, Julian! What's happened?'

'We've got the caravans,' shouted back Julian, cheerily. 'They're in this field.'

The girls joined them at once, most surprised to hear this news. Julian explained.

'The fair-folk really have got a hate on against children,' he said. 'Apparently they had a canary-man, whose show consisted of singing canaries – and some kids set all the birds loose one night – so half of them died. And now the fair-folk won't have children anywhere near them.'

'I suppose the snake-man is afraid of us setting his snakes loose,' said Dick, with a chuckle. 'Well, thank goodness we've found the vans. I had a feeling we might have to sleep in a haystack tonight!'

'I wouldn't have minded that,' said George. 'I like haystacks.'

'We'll light a fire and cook something,' said Julian. 'I feel hungry after all this upset.'

'I don't,' said Anne. 'I hate feeling that the fair-folk won't be friends. It's silly of them. We're not used to that.'

'Yes – but they're rather like children themselves,' said Julian. 'Somebody does something unkind to them, so they get sulky, and wait for a chance to hit back – and then someone set the police on them, too, don't forget – they're very touchy at the moment, I imagine.'

'Well, it's a pity,' said George, watching Dick light a camp-fire very efficiently. 'I was looking forward to having a good time with them. Do you suppose the farmer will mind us being here?'

'Oh – I never thought of that.' said Julian. 'This may not be a camping field. I hope to goodness we don't have an angry farmer shouting at us tomorrow!'

'And, oh dear, we are so far away from the stream now,' said Anne. 'It's on the other side of the field where we were – and we do badly want water.'

'We'll have to do without it tonight,' said Dick firmly. 'I don't want the top of my hair taken off by Bufflo, or a rope tying up my legs, thrown by the rope-man, or a snake wriggling after me. I bet those fair-folk will be on the watch for us to fetch water. This is all very silly.'

They had rather a solemn meal. Things had suddenly begun to seem rather complicated. They *couldn't* go to the police about such a silly thing – nor did they want to. But if the farmer wanted to turn them out of this field, how could they go back to their first camping place? Nobody wanted to live in a camp surrounded by enemies!

'We'll sleep on it,' said Julian, at last. 'Don't worry, you girls. We'll find a way out of this problem. We are pretty good at getting out of difficulties. Never say die!'

'Woof,' said Timmy, agreeing heartily. George patted him.

'That's one of *your* mottoes, isn't it, Timmy?' she said.

'And another motto of his is "Let sleeping dogs lie",' said Dick, with a broad grin. 'He hates being woken up when he's having a nice nap, dreaming of millions of rabbits to catch!'

'Well, talking of naps, what about getting into our bunks?' said Julian, with a yawn. 'We've had a good long walk today, and I'm tired. I'm going to lie in my bunk and read.'

Everyone thought this a very good idea. They cleared up the supper things, and the girls said good night to the boys. They went into the caravan with Timmy.

'I do hope this holiday isn't going to be a failure,' said Anne, as she got into her bunk. George gave one of her snorts.

'A failure! You wait and see! I've a feeling it will turn out to be *super*.'

CHAPTER NINE

A great surprise

It didn't seem as if George's feeling that the holiday was going to be 'super' was at all correct the next morning. A loud rapping came on the door of the boys' caravan before they were even awake!

Then a large, red face looked in at the window, startling Julian considerably.

'Who gave you permission to camp here?' said the face, looking as dark as thunder.

Julian went to the door in his pyjamas. 'Do you own this field?' he said, politely. 'Well, we were camping in the next field, and . . .'

'That's let for campers and caravanners,' said the man, who was dressed like a farmer. 'This isn't.'

'As I said, we were in the next field,' repeated Julian, 'and for some reason the fair-folk there didn't like us – and when we were out they brought our caravans here! As we've no horses to take them away, we couldn't do anything else but stay!'

'Well, you *can't* stay,' said the farmer. 'I don't let out this field. I use it for my cows. You'll have to go today, or I'll put your caravans out into the road.'

'Yes, but look here . . .' began Julian, and then stopped.

The farmer had walked off, a determined figure in riding-breeches and tweed coat. The girls opened their window and called to Julian.

'We heard what he said. Isn't he mean? *Now* what are we going to do?'

'We're going to get up and have breakfast,' said Julian. 'And then I'm going to give the fair-folk one more chance – they'll have to lend us two horses – and pull us back into our rightful place. Otherwise I very much fear I shall have to get help from the police!'

'Oh, dear,' said Anne. 'I do hate this kind of thing. We were having such a lovely time before the fair people arrived. But it seems quite impossible to get them to be friends with us.'

'Quite,' said Julian. 'I'm not so sure *I* want to be friendly now, either. I'd rather give up this holiday altogether and go back home than have continual trouble going on round us! Dick and I will go and tackle the fair-folk after breakfast.'

Breakfast was just as solemn as supper had been. Julian was rather silent. He was thinking what was best to say to the sullen folk in the next field. 'You must take Timmy with you,' said George, voicing the thoughts of everyone.

Julian and Dick set off with Timmy about half past eight. All the fair people were up and about, and the smoke of their fires rose up in the morning air.

Julian thought he would go and tackle the fire-eater, so the two boys went towards his caravan. The other fair people looked up, and one by one left their vans or their fires and closed round the boys. Timmy bared his teeth and growled.

'Mr Alfredo,' began Julian, 'the farmer is turning us out of that field. We must come back here. We want you to lend us two horses for our vans.'

A ripple of laughter spread through the listening people. Mr Alfredo answered politely, with a large smile on his face. 'What a pity! We don't hire out our horses!'

'I don't want to hire them from you,' said Julian, patiently. 'It's up to you to let us have them to bring back our vans. Otherwise – well, I shall *have* to go and ask the police for help. Those caravans don't belong to us, you know.'

There was an angry murmur from the listening crowd. Timmy growled more loudly. One or two of the fair-folk stepped back hurriedly when they heard him.

CRACK! Julian turned quickly. The fair people ran back, and the two boys found that they were facing Bufflo, who, with a large and unpleasant grin on his face, was swinging his whip in his hand.

CRACK! Julian jumped violently, for a few hairs from the top of his head were suddenly whisked off into the air – the end of the lash had neatly cut them away!

The crowd laughed loudly. Timmy bared his white teeth, and snarled.

Dick put his hand down on the dog's collar. 'Do that again and I shan't be able to hold the dog!' he called, warningly.

Julian stood there, at a loss to know what to do next. He couldn't *bear* turning tail and going off to the accompaniment of jeers and howls. He was so full of rage that he couldn't say a word.

And then something happened. Something so utterly unexpected that nobody did anything at all except let it happen!

A boyish figure came running up the grass hillside – someone very like George, with short curly hair and a very freckled face – someone dressed, however, in a short grey skirt, and not in jeans, like George.

She came racing up, yelling at the top of her voice. 'Dick! DICK! Hey, DICK!'

Dick turned and stared in amazement.

'Why – it's Jo! JO! The traveller girl who once got mixed up with us in an adventure! Julian, it's Jo!'

There was no doubt about it at all. It *was* Jo! She came tearing up, her face glowing with the utmost delight and flung herself excitedly on Dick. She had always liked him best.

'Dick! I didn't know *you* were here! Julian! Are the others here too? Oh, Timmy, dear old Timmy! Dick, are you camping here? Oh, this is really too marvellous to be true!'

Jo seemed to be about to fling herself on Dick again, and he fended her off. 'Jo! Where in the world have you come from?'

'Well, you see,' said Jo, 'I've got school holidays like you – and I thought I'd go and visit you at Kirrin Cottage. So I did. But you had all gone away together. That was yesterday.'

'Go on,' said Dick, as Jo stopped, out of breath.

'Well, I didn't want to go back home again straight away,' said Jo. 'So I thought I'd pay a visit to my uncle – he's my mother's brother – and I knew he was camping here so I hitchhiked all the way yesterday, and came late last night.'

'Well, I'm blessed,' said Julian. 'And who is your uncle, may I ask?'

'Oh Alfredo – the fire-eater,' was Jo's astonishing reply. 'Didn't you know? Oh, Dick! Oh, Julian! Can I stay here while you're here? Do, DO say I can! You haven't forgotten me, have you?'

'Of course not,' said Dick, thinking that nobody could

possibly forget this wild little girl, with her mad ways and her staunch affection.

Then for the first time Jo realised that something was going on! What was this crowd doing round Julian and Dick?

She looked round, and immediately sensed that the fair people were not friendly to the two boys – although the main expression on their faces now was one of astonishment!

How did Jo know these boys? they wondered. How was it she was so very friendly with them? They were puzzled and suspicious.

'Uncle Alfredo, where are you?' demanded Jo, looking all round. 'Oh, there you are! Uncle, these are my very best friends – and so are the girls too, wherever they are. I'll tell you all about them, and how nice they were to me! I'll tell everybody!'

'Well,' said Julian, feeling rather embarrassed at what Jo might reveal, 'well, you tell them, Jo, and I'll just pop back and break the news to George and Anne. They *will* be surprised to find you are here – and that Alfredo is your uncle!'

The two boys and Timmy turned to go. The little crowd opened to let them pass. It closed up again round the excited Jo, whose high voice the boys could hear all the way across the field.

'Well, well, well!' said Dick, as they got through the hedge. 'What an astonishing thing! I couldn't believe my eyes when young Jo appeared, could you? I hope George won't mind. She was always rather jealous of Jo and the things she could do.'

The two girls were amazed at the boys' news. George was not too pleased. She preferred Jo at a distance rather than near. She liked and admired her but rather unwillingly. Jo was too like George herself for George to give her complete friendliness!

'Well, fancy *Jo*, Jo herself being here!' said Anne, smiling. 'Oh, Julian – it was a good thing she arrived when she did! I don't like that bit about Bufflo cracking his whip at you. He might have made you bald on the top!'

'Oh, it was only a few hairs,' said Julian. 'But it gave me quite a shock. And I think it gave the fair people a shock too when Jo arrived like a little hurricane, yelling at the top of her voice, and flinging herself on poor old Dick. She almost knocked him over!'

'She's not a bad kid,' said Dick, 'but she never stops to think. I wonder if the people she stays with know where she's gone. I wouldn't be a bit surprised if she just disappeared without a word.'

'Like the two scientists,' said Julian, with a grin. 'Gosh, I can't get over it! Jo was the very last person I would expect here.'

'Well, not really, if you think a bit,' said Anne. 'Her father is a traveller, isn't he – and her mother was in a circus, she told us so. She trained dogs, don't you remember, Julian? So it's quite natural for Jo to have relations like the fair people. But just fancy having a fire-eater for an uncle!'

'Yes – I'd forgotten that Jo's mother was in a circus,' said Julian. 'I expect she's got relations all over the country! I wonder what she's telling them about us.'

'She's singing *Dick's* praises anyway,' said George. 'She always thought the world of Dick. Perhaps the fair people won't be *quite* so unfriendly if they know that Jo is fond of us.'

'Well, we're in a bit of a fix,' said Dick. 'We can't stay in this field, or the farmer will be after us again – and I can't see the fair people lending us their horses – and without horses we can't leave this field!'

'We could ask the farmer to lend us his horses,' suggested Anne.

'We'd have to pay him, though, and I don't see why we should,' said Julian. 'After all, it isn't *our* fault that our caravans were moved here.'

'I think this is a horrid and unfriendly place,' said Anne. 'And I don't want to stay here another day. I'm not enjoying it a bit.'

'Cheer up!' said Dick. 'Never say die!'

'Woof,' said Timmy.

'Look – someone's coming through that gap in the hedge down there by the lane,' said George, pointing. 'It's Jo!'

'Yes – and my goodness me, she's got a couple of horses with her!' cried Dick. 'Good old Jo! She's got Alfredo's horses!'

CHAPTER TEN

Back with the fair-folk again

THE FOUR of them, with Timmy capering behind, ran to meet Jo. She beamed at everyone.

'Hallo, Anne, hallo, George! Pleased to meet you again. This isn't half a surprise!'

'Jo! How did you get those horses?' said Dick, taking one by the bridle.

'Easy,' grinned Jo. 'I just told Uncle Fredo all about you – what wonders you were – and all you did for me – and wasn't I shocked when I heard they'd turned you out of your field! I let go then! I told them just what I thought of them, treating my best friends like that!'

'Did you really, Jo?' said George, doubtfully.

'Didn't you hear me?' demanded Jo. 'I yelled like anything at Uncle Fredo, and then his wife, my Aunt Anita, she yelled at him too – and then we both yelled at everyone.'

'It must have been quite a yelling match,' said Julian. 'And the result was that you got your way, and got the horses to take back our caravans, Jo?'

'Well, when Aunt Anita told me they'd taken your caravans into the next field and left them there, and wouldn't lend you horses to bring them back, I told them all a few things,' said Jo. 'I said – no, I'd better not tell you what I said. I wasn't very polite.'

'I bet you weren't,' said Dick, who had already had a little experience of Jo's wild tongue the year before.

'And when I told them how my father went to prison, and you got me a home with somebody nice who looks after me, they were sorry they'd treated you roughly,' said Jo. 'And so I told Uncle Fredo I was going to catch two horses and bring your caravans back into the field again.'

'I see,' said Julian. 'And the fair-folk just let you?'

'Oh, yes,' said Jo. 'So let's hitch them in, Julian, and go back at once. Isn't that the farmer coming over there?'

It was, and he looked pretty grim. Julian hurriedly put one horse into the shafts of the girls' caravan, and Dick backed the other horse into the shafts of the second caravan. The farmer came up and watched.

'So you thought you'd get horses after all, did you?' he said. 'I thought you would. Telling me a lot of poppycock about being stranded here and not being able to get away!'

'Grrrrrrr,' said Timmy at once, but he was the only one who made any reply!

'Gee-up!' said Jo, taking the reins of the horse pulling the girls' caravan. 'Hup there! Git along, will you?'

The horse got along, and Jo wickedly drove him so near to the farmer that he had to move back in a hurry. He growled something at her. Timmy, appearing round the caravan, growled back. The farmer stood back further, and watched the two caravans going down the hillside, out through the wide gap in the hedge, and down the lane.

They came to the field-gate and Anne opened it. In went the horses, straining now, because they were going uphill,

and the vans were heavy. At last they arrived in the corner where the vans had stood before. Julian backed them over the same bit of ground.

He unhitched the horses, and threw the reins of the second horse to Dick. 'We'll take them back ourselves,' he said.

So the two boys walked the horses over to Alfredo, who was pegging up some washing on a line. It seemed a most unsuitable thing for a fire-eater to do, but Alfredo didn't seem to mind.

'Mr Alfredo, thank you for lending us the horses,' said Julian, in his politest tones. 'Shall we tie them up anywhere, or set them loose?'

Alfredo turned round, and took some pegs out of his large mouth. He looked rather ashamed.

'Set them loose,' he said. He hesitated before he put the pegs back into his mouth. 'We didn't know you were friends with my niece.' he said. 'She told us all about you. You should have told us you knew her.'

'And how could he do that when he didn't know she was your niece?' shouted Mrs Alfredo from the caravan door. 'Fredo, you have no brains, not a single brain do you have. Ahhhhhh! Now you drop my best blouse on the ground!'

She ran out at top speed, and Alfredo stared in alarm. Fortunately she had no saucepan with her this time. She turned to the two amused boys.

'Alfredo is sorry he took your caravans away,' she said. 'Are you not, Fredo?'

'Well! It was *you* who . . .' began Alfredo, with a look of astonishment. But he wasn't allowed to finish. His wife gave him a violent nudge, and spoke again herself, her words tumbling over one another.

'Pay no attention to this big bad man! He has no brains. He can only eat fire, and that is a poor thing to do! Now, Jo, she has brains. Now, are you not glad that you are back again in your corner?'

'I should have felt gladder if you had all been friendly to us,' said Julian. 'I'm afraid we don't feel like stopping here any longer, though. We shall probably leave tomorrow.'

'Now there, Fredo, see what you have done! You have chased away these nice children!' cried Mrs Alfredo. 'They have manners, these boys, a thing you know nothing about, Fredo. You should learn from them, Fredo, you should . . .'

Fredo took some pegs from his mouth to make an indignant answer, but his wife suddenly gave a shriek and ran to her caravan. 'Something burns! Something burns!'

Alfredo gave a hearty laugh, a loud guffaw that surprised the boys. 'Ha! She bakes today, and burns her cake! She has no brains, that woman! No brains at all!'

Julian and Dick turned to go. Alfredo spoke to them in a low voice. 'You can stay here now, here in this field. You are Jo's friend. That is enough for us.'

'It may be,' said Julian. 'But it's not quite enough for *us*, I'm afraid. We shall leave tomorrow.'

The boys went back to the caravans. Jo sat on the grass with George and Anne, eagerly telling them of her life with a very nice family. 'But they won't let me wear jeans or be a boy,' she ended sadly. 'That's why I wear a skirt now. Could you lend me some jeans, George?'

'No, I couldn't,' said George, firmly. Jo was quite enough like her as it was, without wearing jeans! 'Well, you seem to have turned over a new leaf, Jo. Can you read and write yet?'

'Almost,' said Jo, and turned her eyes away. She found lessons very difficult, for she had never been to school when she lived with her traveller father. She looked back again with bright eyes. 'Can I stay with you?' she said. 'My foster-mother would let me, I know – if it was you I was with.'

'Didn't you tell her you were coming here?' said Dick. 'That was unkind, Jo.'

'I never thought,' said Jo. 'You send her a card for me, Dick.'

'Send one yourself,' said George at once. 'You said you could write.'

Jo took no notice of that remark. '*Can* I stay with you?' she said. 'I won't sleep in the caravans, I'll doss down underneath. I always did that when the weather was fine, and I lived with my dad in his caravan. It would be a change for me now not to live in a house. I like lots of things in houses, though I never thought I would – but I shall always like sleeping rough best.'

'Well – you *could* stay here with us, if we were going to stay,' said Julian. 'But I don't much feel inclined to, now we've had such an unfriendly welcome from everyone.'

'I'll tell everyone to be kind to you,' said Jo at once, and got up as if she meant to go then and there to force everyone into kindness!

Dick pushed her down. 'No. We'll stay here one more day and night, and make up our minds tomorrow. What do you say, Julian?'

'Right,' said Julian. He looked at his watch. 'Let's go and celebrate Jo's coming with a few ice-creams. And I expect you two girls have got some shopping to do, haven't you?'

'Yes,' said Anne, and fetched the shopping bags. They set off down the hill, the five of them and Timmy. As they passed the snake-man he called out cheerily to them: 'Good morning! Nice day, isn't it?'

After the surliness and sulkiness the children had got from the fair-folk up till then, this came as a surprise. Anne smiled, but the boys and George merely nodded and passed by. They were not so forgiving as Anne!

They passed the rubber-man, bringing back water. Behind him came the rope-man. Both of them nodded to the children, and the sad-looking rubber-man actually gave a brief grin.

Then they saw Bufflo, practising with his whip – crack-crack-crack! He came over to them. 'If you'd like a crack

with my whip, you're welcome any time,' he said to Julian.

'Thanks,' said Julian, politely but stiffly. 'But we're probably leaving tomorrow.'

'Keep your hair on!' said Bufflo, feeling snubbed.

'I would if you'd let me,' said Julian at once, rubbing his hand over the top of his head where Bufflo had stripped off a few up-standing hairs.

'Ho, ho!' guffawed Bufflo and then stopped abruptly, afraid he had given offence. Julian grinned at him. He rather liked Bufflo, with his mop of yellow hair and lazy drawl.

'You stay on with us,' said Bufflo. 'I'll lend you a whip.'

'We're probably leaving tomorrow,' repeated Julian. He nodded to him, and went on with the others.

'I'm beginning to feel I'd rather like to stay after all,' said George. 'It makes such a difference if people are friendly.'

'Well, we're not staying,' said Julian, shortly. 'I've practically made up my mind – but we'll just wait till tomorrow. It's a – matter of pride with me. You girls don't understand quite how I feel about the whole thing.'

They didn't. Dick understood, though, and he agreed with Julian. They went on down to the village and made their way to the ice-cream shop.

They had a very pleasant day. They had a wonderful lunch on the grass by their caravans – and to their surprise Mrs Alfredo presented them with a sponge sandwich she had made. Anne thanked her very much indeed to make up for a certain stiffness in the thanks of the two boys.

'You *might* have said a bit more,' she said reproachfully to them. 'She really is a kind woman. Honestly I wouldn't mind staying on now.'

But Julian was curiously obstinate about it. He shook his head. 'We go tomorrow,' he said. 'Unless something unexpected happens to *make* us stay. And it won't.'

But Julian was quite wrong. Something unexpected *did* happen. Something really very peculiar indeed.

CHAPTER ELEVEN

A very strange thing

THE UNEXPECTED happening came that evening after tea. They had all had rather a late tea, and a very nice one. Bread and butter and honey – new doughnuts from the dairy – and the sponge cake that Mrs Alfredo had presented them with, which had a very rich filling indeed.

'I can't eat a thing more,' said George. 'That sponge cake was too rich for words. I don't even feel as if I can get up and clear away – so don't start suggesting it, Anne.'

'I'm not,' said Anne. 'There's plenty of time. It's a heavenly evening – let's sit for a while. There goes that blackbird again. He has a different tune every time he sings.'

'That's what I like about blackbirds,' said Dick, lazily. 'They're proper composers. They make up their own tunes – not like the chaffinch who just carols the same old song again and again and again. Honestly there was one this morning that said it fifty times without stopping.'

'Chip-chip-chip, cherry-erry-erry, chippee-OO-EE-Ar!' shouted a chaffinch, rattling it all off as if he had learnt it by heart. 'Chip-chip-chip . . .'

'There he goes again,' said Dick. 'If he doesn't say that, he shouts "pink-pink-pink" as if he'd got that colour on the brain. Look at him over there – isn't he a beauty?'

He certainly was. He flew down to the grass beside the children and began to peck up the crumbs, even venturing on to Anne's knee once. She sat still, really thrilled.

Timmy growled, and the chaffinch flew off. 'Silly, Timmy,' said George. 'Jealous of a chaffinch! Oh, look, Dick – are those herons flying down to the marsh on the east side of the castle hill?'

'Yes, said Dick, sitting up. 'Where are your field-glasses, George? We could see the big birds beautifully through them.'

George fetched them from her caravan. She handed them to Dick. He focused them on the marsh. 'Yes – four herons – gosh, what long legs they've got, haven't they? They are wading happily about – now one's struck down at something with its great beak. What's it got? Yes, it's a frog. I can see its back legs!'

'You can't!' said George, taking the field-glasses from him. 'You're a fibber. The glasses aren't powerful enough to see a frog's legs all that way off!'

But they *were* powerful enough. They were really magnificent ones, far too good for George, who wasn't very careful with valuable things.

She was just in time to see the poor frog's legs disappearing into the big, strong beak of the heron. Then something frightened the birds, and before the others could have a look at them they had all flapped away.

'How slowly they flap their wings,' said Dick. 'They

must surely flap them more slowly than any other bird. Give me the glasses again, George. I'll have a squint at the jackdaws. There are thousands of them flying again over the castle – their evening jaunt, I suppose.'

He put them to his eyes, and moved the glasses to and fro, watching the endless whirl and swoop of the black jackdaws. The sound of their many voices came loudly over the evening air. 'Chack-chack-chack-chack!'

Dick saw some fly down to the only complete tower of the castle. He lowered the glasses to follow them. One jackdaw flew down to the sill of the slit-window near the top of the tower, and Dick followed its flight. It rested for half a second on the sill and then flew off as if frightened.

And then Dick saw something that made his heart suddenly jump. His glasses were trained on the window-slit and he saw something most astonishing there! He gazed as if he couldn't believe his eyes.

Then he spoke in a low voice to Julian.

'Ju! Take the glasses, will you? Train them on the window-slit near the top of the only complete tower – and tell me if you see what I see. Quick!'

Julian held out his hand in astonishment for the glasses. The others stared in surprise. What could Dick have seen? Julian put the glasses to his eyes and focused them on the window Dick had been looking at. He stared hard.

'Yes. Yes, I can. What an extraordinary thing. It must be an effect of the light, I think.'

By this time the others were in such a state of curiosity

that they couldn't bear it. George snatched the glasses from Julian. 'Let *me* see!' she said, quite fiercely. She trained them on to the window. She gazed and gazed and gazed.

Then she lowered the glasses and stared at Julian and Dick. 'Are you being funny?' she said. 'There's nothing there – nothing but an empty window!'

Anne snatched the glasses from her just before Dick

tried to take them again. She too trained them on the window. But there was absolutely nothing there to see.

'There's nothing,' said Anne, disgusted, and Dick took the glasses from her at once, focusing them once more on the window. He lowered them.

'It's gone,' he said to Julian. 'Nothing there now.'

'DICK! If you don't tell us what you saw we'll roll you down the hill,' said George, crossly. 'Are you making something up? *What* did you see?'

'Well,' said Dick, looking at Julian. '*I* saw a face. A face not far from the window, staring out. What did you see, Ju?'

'The same,' said Julian. 'It made me feel pretty peculiar, too.'

'A *face*!' said George, Anne and Jo all together. 'What do you mean?'

'Well – just what we said,' replied Dick. 'A face – with eyes and nose and mouth.'

'But nobody lives in the castle. It's a ruin,' said George. 'Was it someone exploring, do you think?'

Julian looked at his watch. 'No, it couldn't have been a visitor, I'm sure – the castle shuts at half past five and it's gone six. Anyway – it looked a – a – sort of *desperate* face!'

'Yes. I thought so too,' said Dick. 'It's – well, it's very peculiar, isn't it, Julian? There may be some kind of ordinary explanation for it, but I can't help feeling there's something *odd* about it.'

'Was it a man's face?' asked George. 'Or a woman's?'

'A man's, I think,' said Dick. 'I couldn't see any hair against the darkness inside the window. Or clothes. But it *looked* a man's face. Did you notice the eyebrows, Ju?'

'Yes, I did,' said Julian. 'They were very pronounced, weren't they?'

This rang a bell with George! 'Eyebrows!' she said at once. 'Don't you remember – the picture of that scientist, Terry-Kane, showed that he had thick black eyebrows – you said he'd shave them off and use them upside down for moustaches, don't you remember, Dick?'

'Yes. I do remember,' said Dick, and looked at Julian. Julian shook his head. 'I didn't recognise the likeness,' he said, 'but after all it's a very long way away. It is only because George's glasses are so extraordinarily good that we managed to spot a face looking out of a window so very far away. Actually I think there will be an ordinary explanation – it's just that we were so startled – and that made us think it was very strange.'

'I *wish* I'd seen the face,' sighed George. 'They're my glasses, too – and I never saw the face!'

'Well, you can keep on looking and see if it comes back,' said Dick, handing over the glasses. 'It may do.'

So Anne, George, and Jo took turn and turn about, gazing earnestly through the field-glasses – but they saw no face. In the end it got so dark that it was quite difficult to make out the tower, let alone the window or a face!

'I tell you what we might do,' said Julian. 'We could go and see over the castle ourselves tomorrow. And we could go up into that tower. Then we should certainly see if there's a face there.'

'But I thought we were leaving tomorrow,' said Dick.

'Oh – yes, we did think of leaving, didn't we?' said Julian, who had quite forgotten this idea of his in his excitement. 'Well – I don't feel as if we can go before we've explored that castle, and found the explanation of the face.'

'Of *course* we can't,' said George. 'Fancy seeing a thing like that and rushing off without finding out about it. I couldn't possibly.'

'*I'm* going to stay anyhow,' announced Jo. 'I could stop with my Uncle Alfredo, if you go, and I'll let you know if the face comes again – if George will leave me her glasses.'

'Well, I shan't,' said George, with much determination. 'If I go, my glasses go with me. But I'm not going. You *will* stay now, won't you, Julian?'

'We'll stay and find out about the face,' said Julian. 'I honestly feel awfully puzzled about it. Hallo, who's this coming?'

A big figure loomed up in the twilight. It was Alfredo, the fire-eater. 'Jo! Are you there?' he said. 'Your aunt invites you to supper – and all your friends too. Come along.'

There was a pause. Anne looked expectantly across at Julian. Was he still going to be high and mighty and proud? She hoped not.

'Thanks,' said Julian, at last. 'We'd be pleased to come. Do you mean now?'

'That would be nice,' said Alfredo, with a little bow. 'I

fire-eat for you? Anything you say!'

This was too tempting to resist. Everyone got up at once and followed the big Alfredo over the hillside to his caravan. Outside there was a really good fire, and on it was a big black pot that gave out a wonderful smell.

'Supper is not quite ready,' said Alfredo. The five children were relieved. After their big tea they didn't feel ready even for a meal that smelt as good as the one in the pot! They sat down by it.

'Will you really eat fire for us?' asked Anne. 'How do you do it?'

'Ah, very difficult!' said Alfredo. 'I do it only if you promise me not to try it by yourselves. You would not like blisters all over your mouth inside, would you?'

Everyone felt certain that they wouldn't. 'I don't want you to have blisters in *your* mouth, either,' added Anne.

Alfredo looked shocked. 'I am a very good fire-eater,' he assured her. 'No good ones ever make blisters in their mouths. Now – you sit still and I will fetch my torch and eat fire for you.'

Someone else sat down beside them. It was Bufflo. He grinned at them. Skippy came and sat down too. Then the snake-man came up, and he sat down on the opposite side of the fire.

Alfredo came back carrying a few things in his hands. 'Quite a family circle!' he said. 'Now watch – I will eat fire for you!'

CHAPTER TWELVE

Fire-eating and other things!

ALFREDO SAT down on the grass, some way back from the fire. He set a little metal bowl in front of him, that smelt of petrol. He held up two things to show the children.

'His torches,' said Mrs Alfredo, proudly. 'He eats fire from them.'

Alfredo called out something to the snake-man, dipping his two torches into the bowl. They were not alight yet, and to the children they looked like very large button-hooks, with a wad of wool caught in the hook part.

The snake-man leant forward and took a burning twig out of the fire. With a deft throw he pitched it right into the metal bowl. Immediately it set light to the petrol there, and flames shot up in the darkness.

Alfredo had held his torches out of the way, but now he thrust first one and then another into the burning petrol in the bowl.

They flared alight at once, and red flames shot up as he held one in each hand. His eyes gleamed in the brilliant light, and the five children sat still, spellbound.

Then Alfredo leant back his head – back and back – and opened his great mouth wide. He put one of the lighted torches into it, and closed his mouth over it, so that his

cheeks gleamed a strange and unbelievable red from the flames inside his mouth. Anne gave a little scream and George gasped. The two boys held their breath. Only Jo watched unconcerned. She had seen her uncle do this many times before!

Alfredo opened his mouth, and flames rushed out of it, gushing like a fiery waterfall. What with the other torch flaring in his left hand, the burning petrol in the bowl, the torch in his right hand and the flames from his mouth, it really was an extraordinary scene!

He did the same with the other torch, and once more his cheeks glowed like a lamp. Then fire came from his mouth again, and was blown this way and that by the night breeze.

Alfredo closed his mouth. He swallowed. Then he looked round, opened his mouth to show that he no longer had any flames there, and smiled broadly.

'Ah – you like to see me eat fire?' he said, and put out his torches. The bowl was no longer flaming, and now only the fire light lit the scene.

'It's marvellous,' said Julian, with great admiration. 'But don't you burn your mouth?'

'What me? No, never!' laughed Alfredo. 'At first maybe, yes – when I begin years and years ago. But now, no. It would be a shameful thing to burn my mouth – I would hang my head, and go away.'

'But – how is it you *don't* burn your mouth?' asked Dick, puzzled.

Alfredo refused to give any explanation. That was part of the mystery of his act and he wasn't going to give it away.

'*I* can fire-eat too,' announced Jo, casually and most unexpectedly. 'Here, Uncle, let me have one of your torches.'

'You! You will do nothing of the sort!' roared Alfredo. 'Do you want to burn to bits?'

'No. And I shan't either,' said Jo. 'I've watched you and I know just how it's done. I've tried it.'

'Fibber!' said George at once.

'Now you listen to me,' began Alfredo again. 'If you fire-eat I will whip you till you beg me for mercy. I will . . .'

'Now, Fredo,' said his wife, 'you'll do nothing of the sort. I'll deal with Jo if she starts any nonsense here. As for fire-eating – well, if there's to be anyone else fire-eating here, *I* will do it, I, your wife.'

'You will *not* fire-eat,' said Alfredo obstinately, evidently afraid that his hot-tempered wife might try to do it.

Anne suddenly gave a scream of fright. A long, thick body glided between her and Julian – one of the snake-man's pythons! He had brought one with him, and the children hadn't known. Jo caught hold of it and held on for dear life.

'Let him be,' said the snake-man. 'He will come back to me. He wants a run.'

'Let me hold him for a bit,' begged Jo. 'He feels so smooth and cold. I like snakes.'

Julian put out his hand gingerly and touched the great snake. It did feel unexpectedly smooth, and quite cool. How extraordinary! It looked so scaly and rough.

The snake slithered all the way up Jo and then began to pour itself down her back. 'Now, don't you let him get his

tail round you,' warned the snake-man. 'I've told you that before.'

'I'll wear him round my neck,' said Jo, and proceeded to pull the snake's long body until in the end he hung round her neck like a scarf. George watched in unwilling admiration. Anne had removed herself as far from Jo as possible. The boys gazed in astonishment, and felt a new respect for the little traveller girl.

Someone struck up a soft melody on a guitar. It was Skippy, Bufflo's wife. She hummed a sad little song that had a jolly little chorus in which all the fair-folk joined. Practically all the camp had come along now, and there were quite a few the children hadn't seen before.

It was exciting sitting there round the glowing fire, listening to the thrum of the guitar, and the sound of Skippy's low, clear voice – sitting near a fire-eater too, and within arm's length of a snake who also seemed to be enjoying the music! He swayed about in time to the chorus, and then suddenly poured himself all down the front of Jo, and glided like magic to his master, the snake-man.

'Ah, my beauty,' said the funny little man, and let the python slide between his hands, its coils pulsing powerfully as it went. 'You like the music, my beauty?'

'He really loves his snake,' whispered Anne to George. 'How can he?'

Alfredo's wife got up. 'It is time to go,' she told the audience. 'Alfredo needs his supper. Is it not so, my big bad man?'

Alfredo agreed that it was so. He placed the heavy iron pot over the glowing fire again, and in a few seconds such a glorious smell came from it that all the five children began to sniff expectantly.

'Where's Timmy?' said George, suddenly. He was nowhere to be seen!

'He crept away with his tail down when he saw the snake,' said Jo. 'I saw him go. Timmy, come back! It's all right! Timmy, Timmy!'

'I'll call him, thank you,' said George. 'He's *my* dog. Timmy!'

Timmy came, his tail still down. George fondled him and so did Jo. He licked them both in turn. George tried to drag him away from Jo. She didn't like Timmy to show affection for the little traveller girl – but he always did! He loved her.

The supper was lovely. '*What* is in your pot?' asked Dick, accepting a second helping. 'I've never tasted such a delicious stew in my life.'

'Chicken, duck, beef, bacon, rabbit, hare, hedgehog, onions, turnips . . .' began Alfredo's wife. 'I put there everything that comes. It cooks and I stir, it cooks and I stir. Perhaps a partridge goes in one day, and a pheasant the next, and . . .'

'Hold your tongue, wife,' growled Alfredo, who knew quite well that the farmers round about might well ask questions about some of the things in that stew.

'You tell me to hold my tongue!' cried little Mrs Alfredo angrily, flourishing a spoon. 'You tell me that!'

'Woof,' said Timmy, receiving some nice tasty drops on his nose, and licking them off. 'Woof!' He got up and went towards the spoon, hoping for a few more.

'Oh, Aunt Nita, do give Timmy a spoonful out of the stew,' begged Jo, and to Timmy's great joy he got a big plateful all to himself. He could hardly believe it!

'Thank you very much for a very nice supper,' said Julian, feeling that it really was time to go. He got up and the others followed his example.

'And thank you for fire-eating for us, Alfredo,' said George. 'It doesn't seem to have spoilt your appetite!'

'Poof!' said Alfredo, as if such a thing would never

enter his head. 'Jo – are you going to stay with us again tonight? You are welcome.'

'I'd just like an old rug, that's all, Aunt Nita,' said Jo. 'I'm going to sleep under George's caravan.'

'You can sleep on the floor inside, if you like,' said George. But Jo shook her head.

'No. I've had enough of sleeping indoors for a bit. I want to sleep out. Under the caravan will be a fine place for me. Travellers often sleep there when the weather is warm.'

They went back over the dark hillside. A few stars were out, but the moon was not yet up. 'That was a jolly interesting evening,' said Dick. 'I enjoyed it. I like your aunt and uncle, Jo.'

Jo was delighted. She always loved praise from Dick. She went under the girls' caravan, and rolled herself up in the rug. She had been taught to clean her teeth and wash and do her hair but all that was forgotten now.

'In a day or two she'll be the dirty, tangly-haired, rude girl she was when we first knew her,' said George, combing out her own hair extra well. 'I'm glad we're going to stay here after all, aren't you, Anne? I really do think the fair people are friendly towards us now.'

'Thanks to Jo,' said Anne. George said nothing. She didn't like being under obligation to Jo! She finished preparing herself for bed and got into her bunk.

'I wish *we'd* seen that face at the window, don't you, Anne?' she said. 'I do wonder whose it was – and why it was there, looking out.'

'I don't think I want to talk about faces at windows just now,' said Anne, getting into her bunk. 'Let's change the subject.' She blew out the lamp and settled down. They talked for a few minutes, and then George heard something outside the caravan. What could it be? Timmy raised his head and gave a little growl.

George looked at the window opposite. A lone star shone through it – and then something came in front of the star, blotted it out, and pressed itself against the glass pane. Timmy growled again, but not very loudly. Was it someone he knew?'

George flashed on her torch, and immediately saw what it was. She gave a little giggle. Then she called to Anne.

'Anne! Anne! Quick, there's a face at the window. Anne, wake up!'

'I'm not asleep,' said Anne's voice, and she sat up, scared. 'What face? Where? You're not just frightening me, are you?'

'No – there it is, look!' said George and shone her torch at the window. A big, long face looked in, and Anne gave a shriek. Then she laughed. 'You beast, George – it's only Alfredo's horse. Oh, you *did* give me a fright. I've a good mind to pull you out of your bunk on to the floor. Go away, you silly staring horse – shoo, go away!'

CHAPTER THIRTEEN

Off to the castle

NEXT MORNING, as they had breakfast, the children discussed the face at the castle window again. They had levelled the field-glasses time and again at the window, but there was nothing to be seen.

'Let's go and see over the castle as soon as it opens,' said Dick. 'But mind – nobody is to mention faces at windows – you hear me, Jo? You're the one who can't keep your tongue still sometimes.'

Jo flared up. 'I'm not! I can keep a secret!'

'All right, fire-eater,' said Dick with a grin. He looked at his watch. 'It's too soon to go yet.'

'I'll go and help Mr Slither with his snakes,' said Jo. 'Anyone else coming?'

'Mr Slither! What a marvellous name for a man who keeps snakes,' said Dick. 'I don't mind coming to watch, but I'm not keen on the way they pour themselves up and down people.'

They all went to Mr Slither's caravan except Anne, who said she would much rather clear up the breakfast things.

The snake-man had both his snakes out of their box. 'He *is* polishing them,' said George, sitting down nearby. 'See how he makes their brown bodies shine.'

'Here, Jo – you mop Beauty for me,' said Mr Slither. 'The stuff is in that bottle over there. He's got those nasty little mites again under his scales. Mop him with that stuff and that will soon get rid of them.'

Jo seemed to know what to do. She got a rag, tipped up the bottle of yellow stuff and began to pat one of the snakes gently, letting the lotion soak round his scales.

George, not to be outdone, offered to help in the polishing of the other snake. 'You hold him then,' said Mr Slither, and slid the snake over to George. He got up and went into his caravan. George hadn't quite bargained for this. The snake lay across her knees, and then began to wind round her body. 'Don't you let him get a hold of you with his tail,' Jo warned her.

The boys soon got tired of seeing Jo and George vying with one another over the pythons, and went off to where Bufflo was practising spinning rope rings. He spun loop after loop of rope, making wonderful patterns in the air with it. He grinned at the boys.

'Like a try?' he said. But neither of them could do anything with the rope at all.

'Let's see you snap off something with the whip-lash,' said Dick. 'I think you're a marvel at that.'

'What do you want me to hit?' asked Bufflo, picking up his magnificent whip. 'The topmost leaves on that bush?'

'Yes,' said Dick. Bufflo looked at them, swung his whip once or twice, lifted it – and cracked it.

Like magic the topmost leaves disappeared off the bush.

The boys gazed in admiration. 'Now pick off that daisy-head over there,' said Julian, pointing.

Crack! The daisy-head vanished. 'That's easy,' said Bufflo. 'Look, you hold a pencil or something in your hand, one of you. I'll pick it out without touching your fingers!'

Julian hesitated. But Dick dived his hand into his pocket and brought out a red pencil, not very long. He held out his hand, with the pencil between finger and thumb. Bufflo looked at it with half-closed eyes, as if measuring the distance. He raised his whip.

Crack! The tip-end of the lash curled itself round the pencil and pulled it clean out of Dick's hand. It flew up into the air, and Bufflo reached out his hand and caught it!

'Jolly good,' said Dick, lost in admiration. 'Does it take long to learn a thing like that?'

'Matter of twenty years or so,' said Bufflo. 'But you want to begin when you're a nipper – about three years old, say. My pa taught me – and if I didn't learn fast enough he'd take the skin off the tips of my ears with his whip-lash! You soon learn if you know that's going to happen to you!'

The boys gazed at Bufflo's big ears. They certainly did look a bit rough at the edges!

'I throw knives too,' said Bufflo, basking in the boys' admiration. 'I put Skippy up against a board, and throw knives all round her – so that when she walks away from the board at the end, there's her shape all outlined in knives. Like to see me?'

'Well, no, not now,' said Julian, looking at his watch. 'We're going to see over the castle. Have you ever seen over it, Bufflo?'

'No. Who wants to waste time going over a ruined old castle?' said Bufflo, scornfully. 'Not me!'

He went off to his caravan, spinning rope rings as he went with an ease that Dick couldn't help envying from the bottom of his heart. What a pity he hadn't begun to learn these things early enough. He was afraid he would never be really good at them now. He was too old!

'George! Jo! It's time we went,' called Julian. 'Put down those snakes, and come along. Anne! Are you ready?'

Mr Slither went to collect his snakes. They glided over him in delight, and he ran his hands over their smooth, gleaming bodies.

'I must wash my hands before I go,' said George. 'They're a bit snaky. Coming, Jo?'

Jo didn't really see why it was necessary to wash snaky hands, but she went with George to the stream and they rinsed them thoroughly. George wiped her hands on a rather dirty hanky, and Jo wiped hers on a much dirtier skirt. She looked at George's jeans enviously. What a pity to have to wear skirts!

They didn't lock up the caravans. Julian felt sure that the fair-folk were now really friendly to them, and would not take anything from them themselves, nor permit anyone else to do so. They all walked down the hillside, Timmy bounding along joyfully, under the impression that he was going to take them for a nice long walk.

They climbed over the stile, walked up the lane a little way, and came to the wooden gate that opened on to the steep path up to the castle. Now that it was so near to them it looked almost as if it might fall on top of them!

They went up the path and came to the small tower in which was the little door giving entrance to the castle. An old woman was there, looking a little like a witch. If she had had green eyes Anne would most certainly have set her down as a descendant of a witch! But she had eyes like black beads. She had no teeth at all and it was difficult to understand what she said.

'Five, please,' said Julian, giving her twenty-five pence.

'You can't take the dog in,' said the old woman, mumbling so much that they couldn't make out what she said. She pointed to the dog and repeated her remark again, shaking her head all the time.

'Oh – can't we really take our dog?' said George. 'He won't do any harm.'

The old woman pointed to a set of rules: 'DOGS NOT ALLOWED IN.'

'All right. We'll leave him outside then,' said George, crossly. 'What a silly rule! Timmy, stay here. We won't be long.'

Timmy put his tail down. He didn't approve of this. But he knew that he was not allowed into certain places, such as churches, and he imagined this place must be an enormous church – the kind of place into which George so often disappeared on Sundays. He lay down in a sunny corner.

The five children went in through the clicking turnstile. They opened the door beyond and went into the castle grounds. The door shut behind them.

'Wait – we ought to get a guidebook,' said Julian. 'I want to know something about that tower.'

He went back and bought one for another five pence. They stood in the great castle yard and looked at the book. It gave the history of the old place – a history of peace and war, quarrels and truces, family feuds, marriages and all the other things that make up history.

'It would be an exciting story if it was written up properly,' said Julian. 'Look – here's the plan. There *are* dungeons!'

'Not open to the public,' quoted Dick, in disappointment. 'What a pity.'

'It was once a very strong and powerful castle,' said Julian, looking at the plan. 'It always had the strong wall that is still round it – and the castle itself is built in the middle of a great courtyard that runs all round. It says the walls of the castle itself are eight feet thick. Eight feet thick! No wonder most of it is still standing!'

They looked at the silent ruins in awe. The castle towered up, broken here and there, with sometimes a whole wall missing, and with all the doorways misshapen.

'There were four towers, of course,' said Julian, still with his nose glued to the guidebook. 'It says three are almost completely ruined now – but the fourth one is in fairly good condition, though the stone stairway that led up to the top has fallen in.'

'Well then – you couldn't have seen a face at that window,' said George, looking up at the fourth tower. 'If the stairway has fallen in, no one could get up there.'

'Hm. We'll see how much fallen in it is,' said Julian. 'It may be dangerous to the public, and perhaps we'll find a notice warning us off – but it might be quite climbable in places.'

'Shall we go up it if so?' said Jo, her eyes shining. 'What shall we do if we find the Face?'

'We'll wait till we find it first!' said Julian. He shut the guidebook and put it into his pocket. 'Well, we seem to be the only people here. Let's get going. We'll walk round the courtyard first.'

They walked round the courtyard that surrounded the castle. It was strewn with great white stones that had fallen from the walls of the castle itself. In one place a whole wall had fallen in, and they could see the inside of the castle, dark and forbidding.

They came round to the front of it again. 'Let's go in at the front door – if you can call that great stone archway that,' said Julian. 'I say – can't you imagine knights on horseback riding round this courtyard, impatient to be off to some tournament, their horses' hoofs clip-clopping all the time?'

'Yes!' said Dick. 'I can just imagine it!'

They went in at the arched entrance, and wandered through room after room with stone floors and walls, and with small slit-like windows that gave very little light indeed.

'They had no glass for panes in those days,' said Dick. 'I bet they were glad on cold windy days that the windows were so tiny. Brrrrrrr! This must have been a terribly cold place to live in.'

'The floors used to be covered with rushes, and tapestry was hung on the walls,' said Anne, remembering a history lesson. 'Julian – let's go and look for the stairway to that tower now. Do let's! I'm longing to find out whether there really *is* a face up in that tower!'

CHAPTER FOURTEEN

Faynights Castle

'CHACK-CHACK-CHACK! Chack-chack-chack!' The jack-daws circled round the old castle, calling to one another in their cheerful, friendly voices. The five children looked up and watched them.

'You can see the grey at the backs of their necks,' said Dick. 'I wonder how many years jackdaws have lived round and about this castle.'

'I suppose the sticks lying all over this courtyard must have been dropped by them,' said Julian. 'They make their nests of big twigs – really, they must drop as many as they use! Just look at that pile over there!'

'Very wasteful of them!' said Dick. 'I wish they would come and drop some near our caravan to save me going to get firewood each day for the fire!'

They were standing at the great archway that made the entrance to the castle. Anne grew impatient. 'Do let's look at the towers now,' she said.

They went to the nearest one, but it was almost impossible to realise that it *had* been a tower. It was just a great heap of fallen stones, piled one on top of another.

They went to the only good tower. They had hoped to find some remains of a stone stairway, but to their great disappointment they could not even look up into the tower! One of the inner walls had fallen in, and the floor was piled up, completely blocked. There was no sign of a stairway. Either it too had fallen in, or it was covered by the stones of the ruined wall.

Julian was astonished. It was obvious that nobody could possibly climb up the tower from the inside! Then how in the world could there have been a face at the tower window? He began to feel rather uncomfortable. Was it a real face? If not, what could it have been?

'This is odd,' said Dick, thinking the same as Julian, and pointing to the heaped-up stones on the ground floor of the tower. 'It does look absolutely impossible for anyone to get up into the top of the tower. Well – what about that face then?'

'Let's go and ask that old woman if there *is* any way at all of getting up into the tower,' said Julian. 'She might know.'

So they left the castle, walked across the courtyard, back to the little tower in the outer wall that guarded the big gateway. The old woman was sitting by the turnstile, knitting.

'Could you tell us, please, if there is any way of getting up into the tower over there?' asked Julian

The old woman answered something, but it was difficult to understand a word she said. However, as she shook her head vigorously, it was plain that there *was* no way up to the tower. It was very puzzling.

'Is there a better plan of the castle than this?' asked Julian, showing his guidebook. 'A plan of the dungeons for instance – and a plan of the towers as they once were, before they were ruined?'

The old lady said something that sounded like 'Society of Reservation of something-or-other.'

'What did you say?' asked Julian, patiently.

The witch-like woman was evidently getting tired of these questions. She opened a big book that showed the amount of people and fees paid, and looked down it. She put her finger on something written there, and showed it to Julian.

'Society for Preservation of Old Buildings,' he read. 'Oh – did somebody come from them lately? Would they know more than it says in the guidebook?'

'Yes,' said the old woman. 'Two men came. They spent all day here – last Thursday. You ask that Society what you want to know – not me. I only take the money.'

She sounded quite intelligible all of a sudden. Then she relapsed into mumbles again, and no one could understand a word.

'Anyway, she's told us what we want to know,' said Julian. 'We'll telephone the Society and ask them if they can tell us any more about the castle. There may be secret passages and things not shown in the guidebook at all.'

'How exciting!' said George, thrilled. 'I say, let's go back to that tower and look at the *outside* of it. It might be climbable there.'

They went back to see – but it *wasn't* climbable. Although the stones it was built of were uneven enough to form slight footholds and handholds it would be much too dangerous for anyone to try to climb up – even the cat-footed Jo. For one thing it would not be possible to tell which stones were loose and crumbling until the climber caught hold – and then down he would go!

All the same, Jo was willing to try. 'I might be able to do it,' she said, slipping off one of her shoes.

'Put your shoe on,' said Dick at once. 'You are NOT

going to try any tricks of that sort. There isn't even ivy for you to cling to.'

Jo put back her shoe sulkily, looking astonishingly like George as she scowled. And then, to everyone's enormous astonishment, who should come bounding up to them but Timmy!

'Timmy! Wherever have you come from?' said George, in surprise. 'There's no way in except through the turnstile – and the door behind it is shut. We shut it ourselves! *How* did you get in?

'Woof,' said Timmy, trying to explain. He ran to the good tower, made his way over the blocks of stone lying about and stopped by a small space between three or four of the fallen stones. 'Woof,' he said again, and pawed at one of the stones.

'He came out there,' said George. She tugged at a big stone, but she couldn't move it an inch, of course. 'I don't know how in the world Timmy squeezed himself out of this space – it doesn't look big enough for a rabbit. Certainly none of *us* could get inside!'

'What puzzles *me*,' said Julian, 'is how Timmy got in from the outside. We left him right outside the castle – so he must have run round the outer wall somewhere and found a small hole. He must have squeezed into that.'

'Yes. That's right,' said Dick. 'We know the walls are eight feet thick, so he must have found a place where a bit of it had broken at the bottom, and forced his way in. But

– would there be a hole right through the whole thickness of eight feet?'

This was really puzzling. They all looked at Timmy, and he wagged his tail expectantly. Then he barked loudly and capered round as if he wanted a game.

The door behind the turnstile opened at once and the old lady appeared. 'How did that dog get here?' she called. 'He's to go out at once!'

'We don't know how he got in,' said Dick. 'Is there a hole in the outer wall?'

'No,' said the old woman. 'Not one. You must have let that dog in when I wasn't looking. He's to go out. And you too. You've been here long enough.'

'We may as well go,' said Julian. 'We've seen all there is to see – or all that we are *allowed* to see. I'm quite sure there is some way of getting up into that tower although the stairway is in ruins. I'm going to ring up the Society for the Preservation of Old Buildings and ask them to put me in touch with the fellows who examined the castle last week. They must have been experts.'

'Yes. They would probably have a complete plan,' said Dick. 'Secret passages, dungeons, hidden rooms and all – if there are any!'

They took Timmy by the collar, and went out through the turnstiles, click-click-click. 'I feel like having a couple of doughnuts at the dairy,' said George. 'And some lemonade. Anyone else feel the same?'

Everyone did, including Timmy, who barked at once.

'Timmy's silly over those doughnuts,' said George. 'He just wolfs them down.'

'It's a great waste,' said Anne. 'He ate four last time – more than anyone else had.'

They walked down to the village. 'You go and order what we want,' said Julian, 'and I'll just go and look up this Society. It may have an office somewhere in this district.'

He went to the post office to use the telephone there, and the rest of them trooped in at the door of the bright little dairy. The plump shop-woman welcomed them beamingly. She considered them her best customers, and they certainly were.

They were each on their second doughnut when Julian came back. 'Any news?' asked Dick.

'Yes,' said Julian. 'Peculiar news, though. I found the address of the Society – they've got a branch about fifty miles from here – that deals with all the old buildings for a radius of a hundred miles. I asked if they had any recent booklet about the castle.'

He stopped to take a doughnut, and bit into it. The others waited patiently while he chewed.

'They said they hadn't. The last time they had checked over Faynights Castle was two years ago.'

'But – but what about those two men who came from the Society last week, then?' said George.

'Yes. That's what *I* said,' answered Julian, taking another bite. 'And here's the peculiar bit. They said they

didn't know what I was talking about, nobody had been sent there from the Society, and who was I, anyhow?'

'Hmm!' said Dick, thinking hard. 'Then – those men were examining and exploring the castle for their own reasons!'

'I agree,' said Julian. 'And I can't help thinking that the face at the window and those two men have something to do with one another. It's quite clear that the men had nothing whatever to do with any official society – they merely gave it as an excuse because they wanted to find out what kind of hiding place the castle had.'

The others stared at him, feeling a familiar excitement rising in them – what George called the 'adventure feeling'.

'Then there *was* a real face at that tower window, and there *is* a way of getting up there,' said Anne.

'Yes,' said Julian. 'I know it sounds very far-fetched, but I do think there is just a possibility that those two scientists have gone there. I don't know if you read it in the paper, but one of them, Jeffrey Pottersham, has written a book on famous ruins. He would know all about Faynights Castle, because it's a very well-known one. If they wanted to hide somewhere till the hue and cry had died down, and then escape to another country, well . . .'

'They could hide in the tower, and then quietly slip out from the castle one night, go down to the sea, and hire a fishing boat!' cried Dick, taking the words out of Julian's mouth. 'They'd be across the Channel in no time.'

'Yes. That's what I'd worked out too,' said Julian. 'I rather think I'll telephone Uncle Quentin about this. I'll describe the face as well as I can to him. I feel this is all rather too important to manage quite on our own. Those men may have extremely important secrets.'

'It's an adventure again,' said Jo, her face serious, but her eyes very bright. 'Oh – I'm *glad* I'm in it too!'

CHAPTER FIFTEEN

An interesting day

EVERYONE BEGAN to feel distinctly excited. 'I think I'll catch the bus into the next town,' said Julian. 'The telephone-box here is too easily overheard. I'd rather go to a kiosk somewhere in a street, where nobody can hear what I'm saying.'

'All right. You go,' said Dick. 'We'll do some shopping and go back to the caravans. I wonder what Uncle Quentin will say!'

Julian went off to the bus stop. The others wandered in and out of the few village shops, doing their shopping. Tomatoes, lettuces, mustard and cress, sausage rolls, fruit cake, tins of fruit, and plenty of creamy milk in big quart bottles.

They met some of the fair-folk in the street, and everyone was very friendly indeed. Mrs Alfredo was there with an enormous basket, nearly as big as herself. She beamed and called across to them.

'You see I have to do my shopping myself! That big bad man is too lazy to do it for me. And he has no brains. I tell him to bring back meat and he brings fish, I tell him to buy cabbage and he brings lettuce. He has no brains!'

The children laughed. It was strange to find great big

Alfredo, a real fire-eater, ordered about and grumbled at by his tiny wife.

'It's a change to find them all so friendly,' said George, pleased. 'Long may it last. There's the snake-man, Mr Slither – he hasn't got his snakes with him, though.'

'He'd have the whole village to himself if he did!' said Anne. 'I wonder what he buys to feed his snakes on.'

'They're only fed once a fortnight,' said Jo. 'They swallow . . .'

'No, don't tell me,' said Anne, hastily. 'I don't really want to know. Look, there's Skippy.'

Skippy waved cheerily. She carried bags filled to bursting too. The fair-folk certainly did themselves well.

'They must make a lot of money,' said Anne.

'Well, they spend it when they have it,' said Jo. 'They never save. It's either a good time for them or a very bad time. They must have had a good run at the last show-place – they all seem very rich!'

They went back to the camp and spent a very interesting day, because the fair-folk, eager to make up for their unfriendly behaviour, made them all very welcome. Alfredo explained his fire-eating a little more, and showed how he put wads of cotton wool at the hook-end of his torches, and then soaked them in petrol to flare easily.

The rubber-man obligingly wriggled in and out of the wheel-spokes of his caravan, a most amazing feat. He also doubled himself up, and twisted his arms and legs together in such a peculiar manner that he seemed to be more like a four-tentacled octopus than a human being.

He offered to teach Dick how to do this, but Dick couldn't even bend himself properly double. He was disappointed because he couldn't help thinking what a marvellous trick it would be to perform in the playing field at school.

Mr Slither gave them a most entertaining talk about snakes, and ended up with some information about poisonous snakes that he said they might find very useful indeed.

'Take rattlers now,' he said, 'or mambas, or any poisonous snake. If you want to catch one to tame, don't go after it with a stick, or pin it to the ground. That frightens it and you can't do anything with it.'

'What do you have to do then?' asked George.

'Well, you want to watch their forked tongues,' said Mr Slither, earnestly. 'You know how they put them out, and make them quiver and shake?'

'Yes,' said everyone.

'Well, now, if a poisonous snake makes its tongue go all stiff without a quiver in it, just be careful,' said Mr Slither, solemnly. 'Don't you touch it then. But if its tongue is nice and quivery, just slide your arms along its body, and it will let you pick it up.' He went through the motions he described, picking up a pretend snake and letting its body slither through his arms. It was fascinating to watch, but very weird.

'Thanks most awfully,' said Dick. 'Whenever I pick up poisonous snakes, I'll do exactly as you say.'

The others laughed. Dick sounded as if he went about picking up poisonous snakes every day! Mr Slither was pleased to have such an appreciative audience. George and Anne, however, had firmly made up their minds that they were not going even to *look* at a snake's tongue if it put it out – they were going to run for miles!

There were a few more fair-folk there that the children didn't know much about – Dacca, the tap-dancer, who put on high boots and tap-danced for the children on the top step of her caravan – Pearl, who was an acrobat and could walk on wire-rope, dance on it, and turn somersaults over it, landing back safely each time – and others who belonged to the show but only helped with the crowds and the various turns.

Jo didn't know them all, but she was soon so much one of them that the children began to wonder if she would ever go back to her foster-mother again!

'She's exactly like them all now,' said George. 'Cheerful, slapdash and generous, lazy and yet hardworking too! Bufflo practises for hours at his rope-spinning, but he lies about for hours too. They're strange folk, but I really do like them very much.'

The others agreed with her heartily. They had their lunch without Julian, because he hadn't come back. Why was he so long? He only had to telephone his uncle!

He came back at last. 'Sorry I'm so late,' he said, 'but

first of all I couldn't get any answer at all, so I waited a bit in case Aunt Fanny and Uncle Quentin were out – and I had lunch while I waited. Then I telephoned again, and Aunt Fanny was in, but Uncle Quentin had gone to London and wouldn't be back till night.'

'To London!' said George, astonished. 'He hardly ever goes to London.'

'Apparently he went up about these two missing scientists,' said Julian. 'He's so certain that his friend Terry-Kane isn't a traitor, and he went up to tell the authorities so. Well, I couldn't wait till night, of course.'

'Didn't you report our news then?' said Dick, disappointed.

'Yes. But I had to tell Aunt Fanny,' said Julian. 'She said she would repeat it all to Uncle Quentin when he came back tonight. It's a pity I couldn't get hold of him and find out what he thinks. I asked Aunt Fanny to tell him to write to me at once.'

After tea they sat on the hillside again, basking in the sun. It really was wonderful weather for them. Julian looked over to the ruined castle opposite. He fixed his eyes on the tower where they had seen the face. It was so far away that he could only just make out the window-slit.

'Get your glasses, George,' he said. 'We may as well have another squint at the window. It was about this time that we saw the face.'

George fetched them. She would not give them to Julian first though – she put them to her own eyes and gazed at the window. At first she saw nothing – and then, quite suddenly, a face appeared at the window! George was so astonished that she cried out.

Julian snatched the glasses from her. He focused them on the window and saw the face at once. Yes – the same as yesterday – eyebrows and all!

Dick took the glasses, and then each of them in turn gazed at the strange face. It did not move at all, as far as they could see, but simply stared. Then, when Anne was looking at it, it suddenly disappeared and did not come back again.

'Well – we *didn't* imagine it yesterday then,' said Julian. 'It's there all right. And where there's a face, there should be a body. Er – did any of you think that the face had a – a sort of – despairing expression?'

'Yes,' said Dick and the others agreed. 'I thought so yesterday, too,' said Dick. 'Do you suppose the fellow, whoever he is, is being kept prisoner up there?'

'It looks like it,' said Julian. 'But how in the world did he get there? It's a marvellous place to put him, of course. Nobody would ever dream of a hiding place like that – and if it hadn't been for us looking at the jackdaws through very fine field-glasses, we'd never have seen him looking out. It was a chance in a thousand that we saw him.'

'In a *million*,' said Dick. 'Look here, Ju – I think we ought to go up to the castle and yell up to the fellow – he might be able to yell back, or throw a message out.'

'He would have thrown out a message before now if he'd been able to,' said Julian. 'As for yelling, he'd have to lean right out of that thick-walled window to make himself heard. He's right at the back of it, remember, and the slit is very deep.'

'Can't we go and find out something?' said George, who was longing to take some action. 'After all, Timmy got in somewhere, and we might be able to as well.'

'That's quite an idea,' said Julian. 'Timmy *did* find a way in – and it may be the way that leads up to the top of the tower.'

'Let's go then,' said George at once.

'Not now,' said Julian. 'We'd be seen if we scrambled about on the hill outside the castle walls. We'd have to go at night. We could go when the moon comes up.'

A shiver of excitement ran through the whole five. Timmy thumped his tail on the ground. He had been listening all the time, just as if he understood.

'We'll take you too, Timmy,' said George, 'just in case we run into any trouble.'

'We shan't get into trouble,' said Julian. 'We're only going to explore – and I don't think for a minute we'll find much, because I'm sure we shan't be able to get up into the tower. But I expect you all feel like I do – you can't leave this mystery of the face at the window alone – you want to *do* something about it, even if it's only scrambling round the old walls at night.'

'Yes. That's *exactly* how I feel,' said George. 'I wouldn't be able to go to sleep tonight, I know. Oh, Julian – isn't this exciting?'

'Very,' said Julian. 'I'm glad we didn't leave today, after all! We should have, if we hadn't seen that face at the window.'

The sun went down and the air grew rather cold. They went into the boys' caravan and played cards, not feeling at all sleepy. Jo was very bad at cards, and soon stopped playing. She sat watching, her arm round Timmy's neck.

They had a supper of sausage rolls and tinned strawberries. 'It's a pity they don't have meals like this at school,' said Dick. 'No trouble to prepare, and most delicious to eat. Julian – is it time to go?'

'Yes,' said Julian. 'Put on warm things – and we'll set off! Here's to a really adventurous night!'

CHAPTER SIXTEEN

Secret ways

THEY WAITED till the moon went behind a cloud, and then, like moving shadows, made their way down the hillside as fast as they could. They did not want any of the fair-folk to see them. They clambered over the stile and went up the lane. They made their way up the steep path to the castle, but when they came to the little tower where the turnstile was they went off to the right, and walked round the foot of the great, thick walls.

It was difficult to walk there, because the slope of the hill was so steep. Timmy went with them, excited at this unexpected walk.

'Now, Timmy, listen – we want you to show us how you got in,' said George. 'Are you listening, Timmy? Go in, Timmy, go in where you went this morning.'

Timmy waved his long tail, panted, and let his tongue hang out in the way he did when he wanted to show he was being as helpful as he could. He ran in front, sniffing.

Then he suddenly stopped and looked back. He gave a little whine. The others hurried to him.

The moon most annoyingly went behind a cloud. Julian took out his torch and shone it where Timmy stood. The dog stood there, looking very pleased.

'Well, what is there to be pleased about, Timmy?' said Julian, puzzled. 'There's no hole there – nowhere you

could possibly have got in. What are you trying to show us?'

Timmy gave a little bark. Then suddenly leapt about four feet up the uneven stones of the wall, and disappeared!

'Hey – where's he gone?' said Julian, startled. He flashed his torch up. 'I say, look! There's a stone missing up there, quite a big block – and Timmy's gone in at the hole.'

'There's the block – fallen down the hillside,' said Dick, pointing to a big white stone, roughly square in shape. 'But how has Timmy gone in, Ju? This wall is frightfully thick, and even if one stone falls out, there must be plenty more behind!'

Julian climbed up. He came to the space where the great fallen stone had been and flashed his torch there. 'I say – this is interesting!' he called. 'The wall is hollow just here. Timmy's gone into the hollow!'

At once a surge of excitement went through the whole lot. 'Can we get in and follow Timmy?' called George. 'Shout to him, Julian, and see where he is.'

Julian called into the hollow. 'Timmy! Timmy, where are you?'

A distant, rather muffled bark answered him, and then Timmy's eyes suddenly gleamed up at Julian. The dog was standing down in the small hollow behind the fallen stone. 'He's here,' called back Julian. 'I tell you what I think we've hit on. When this enormous wall was built, a space was left inside – either to save stones, or to make a hidden passage, I don't know which. And that fallen stone has exposed a bit of the hollow. Shall we explore?'

'Oh, *yes*,' came the answer at once. Julian climbed down into the middle of the wall. He flashed his torch into the space he was standing in. 'Yes,' he called, 'it's a kind of passage. It's small, though. We'll have to bend almost double to get along it. Anne, you come next, then I can help you.'

'Will the air be all right?' called Dick into the passage.

'It smells a bit musty,' said Julian. 'But if it really *is* a passage, there must be secret air-holes somewhere to keep the air fresh in here. That's right, Anne – you hang on to me. Jo, you come next, then George, then Dick.'

Soon they were all in the curious passage, which ran along in the centre of the wall. It certainly was very small. They all got tired of going along bent double. It was pitch dark too, and although they all had torches, except Jo, it was very difficult to see.

Anne hung on to Julian's jacket for dear life. She wasn't enjoying this very much, but she wouldn't have been left out of it for anything.

Julian suddenly stopped, and everyone bumped into the one in front. 'What's up?' called Dick, from the back.

'Steps here!' shouted back Julian. 'Steps going down very, very steeply – almost like a stone ladder. Be careful, everybody!'

The steps were certainly steep. 'Better go down

backwards,' decided Julian. 'Then we can have handholds as well as footholds. Anne, wait till I'm down and I'll help you.'

The steps went down for about ten feet. Julian got down safely, then Anne turned herself round and went down backwards too, as if she were on a ladder instead of on stairs. It was much easier that way.

At the bottom was another passage, wider and higher, for which everyone was devoutly thankful. 'Where does *this* lead to?' said Julian, stopping to think. 'This passage is at right angles to the wall – we've left the wall now – we're going underneath part of the courtyard, I should think.'

'I bet we're not far from that tower,' called Dick. 'I say – I do hope this leads to the tower.'

Nobody could possibly tell where it was going to lead to! Anyway, it seemed to run quite straight, and after about eighty feet of it, Julian stopped again.

'Steps up again!' he called. 'Just as steep as the others. I think we may be going up into the inside of the castle walls. This is possibly a secret way into one of the old rooms of the castle.'

They went carefully up the steep stone steps and found themselves, not in a passage, but in a very small room that appeared to be hollowed out of the wall of the castle itself. Julian stopped in surprise, and everyone crowded into the tiny room. It really wasn't much larger than a big cupboard. A narrow bench stood at one side, with a shelf above it. An old pitcher stood on the shelf, with a broken lip, and on the bench was a small dagger, rusty and broken.

'I *say*! Look here! This is a secret room – like they used to have in old places, so that someone might hide if necessary,' said Julian. 'We're inside one of the walls of the castle itself – perhaps the wall of an old bedroom!'

'And there's the old pitcher that had water in,' said George. 'And a dagger. Who hid here – and how long ago?'

Dick flashed his torch round to see if he could spot anything else. He gave a sudden exclamation, and kept his torch fixed on a corner of the room.

'What is it?' said Julian.

'Paper – red and blue silver paper,' said Dick. 'Chocolate wrapping! How many times have we bought this kind of chocolate, wrapped in silver paper patterned with red and blue!'

He picked it up and straightened it out. Yes – there was the name of the chocolate firm on it!

Everyone was silent. This could only mean one thing. *Someone* had been in this room lately – someone who ate chocolate – someone who had thrown down the wrapping never expecting it to be found!

'Well,' said Julian, breaking the silence. 'This *is* surprising. Someone else knows this way in. Where does it lead to? Up to that tower, I imagine!'

'Hadn't we better be careful?' said Dick, lowering his voice. 'I mean – whoever was here might quite well be wandering about somewhere near.'

'Yes. Perhaps we'd better go back,' said Julian, thinking of the girls.

'No,' said George, in a fierce whisper. 'Let's go on. We can be very cautious.'

A passage led from the strange hidden room. It went along on the level for a little way, and then they arrived at a spiral stairway that ran straight upwards like a corkscrew.

At the top they came to a small, very narrow door. It had a great, old-fashioned iron ring for a handle.

Julian stood hesitating. Should he open it or not? He stood for half a minute, trying to make up his mind. He whispered back to the others. 'I've come to a little door. Shall I open it?'

'Yes,' came back the answering whispers. Julian cautiously took hold of the iron ring. He turned it, and it made no noise. He wondered if the door was locked on the other side. But it wasn't. It opened silently.

Julian looked through it, expecting to see a room, but there wasn't one. Instead he found himself on a small gallery that seemed to run all the way round the inside of the tower. The moon shone in through a slit-window, and Julian could just make out that he must be looking down from a gallery into the darkness of a tower room on the second or third floor of the tower – the third, probably.

He pulled Anne out and the other three followed. There was no sound to be heard. Julian whispered to the others.

'We've come out on to a gallery, which overlooks one of the rooms inside the tower. It may be a second-floor room, because we know that the ceiling of the first floor has fallen in. Or perhaps it's even the third floor.'

'Must be the third,' said Dick. 'We're pretty high.' His whisper went all round the gallery and came back to them. He had spoken more loudly than Julian. It made them jump.

'How do we get higher still?' whispered George.

'Is there any way up from this gallery?'

'We'll walk round it and see,' said Julian. 'Be as quiet as you can. I don't *think* there's anyone here, but you never know. And watch your step, in case the stone isn't sound – it's very crumbly here and there.'

Julian led the way round the curious little gallery. Had this tower room been used for old plays or mimes? Was the gallery for spectators? He wished he could turn back the years and lean over the gallery to see what had been going on in the room below, when the castle was full of people.

About three-quarters of the way round the gallery a little flight of steps led downwards into the room below. But just beyond where the steps began there was another door set in the wall, very like the one they had just come through.

It too had an iron ring for a handle. Julian turned it slowly. It didn't open. Was it locked? There was a great key standing in the iron lock, and Julian turned it. But still the door didn't open. Then he saw that it was bolted.

The bolt was securely pushed home. So somebody was a prisoner on the other side! Was it the man who owned the Face? Julian turned and whispered very softly in Anne's ear.

'There's a door here bolted on my side. Looks as if we're coming to the Face. Tell George to send Timmy right up to me.'

Anne whispered to George, and George pushed Timmy forward. He squeezed past Anne's legs and stood by Julian, sensing the sudden excitement.

'We're probably coming to stairs that lead up to the top tower room, where that window is with the Face,' thought Julian, as he slid back the bolt very cautiously. He pushed the door, and it opened. He stood listening, his torch switched off. Then he switched it on.

Just as he had thought, another stone stairway led up steeply. At the top must be the prisoner, whoever he was.

'We'll go up,' said Julian softly. 'Quiet, everybody!'

CHAPTER SEVENTEEN

Excitement and shocks

TIMMY STRAINED forward, but Julian had his hand on the dog's collar. He went up the stone stairway, very steep and narrow. The others followed with hardly a sound. All of them but Jo had on their rubber shoes; she had bare feet. Timmy made the most noise, because his claws clicked on the stone.

At the top was another door. From behind it came a curious noise – guttural and growling. Timmy growled in his throat. At first Julian couldn't think what the noise was. Then he suddenly knew.

'Somebody snoring! Well, that's lucky. I can take a peep in and see who it is. We must be at the top of the tower now.'

The door in front of him was not locked. He pushed it open and looked inside, his hand still on Timmy's collar.

The moonlight struck through a narrow window and fell on the face of a sleeping man. Julian stared at it in rising excitement. Those eyebrows! Yes – this was the man whose face had appeared at the window!

'And I know who he is too – it *is* Terry-Kane!' thought Julian, moving like a shadow into the room. 'He's exactly like the picture we saw in the papers. Perhaps the other man is here too.'

He looked cautiously round the room but could see no one else, although it was possible there might be someone in the darkest shadows. He listened.

There was only the snoring of the man lying in the moonlight. He could not hear the breathing of anyone else. With his hand still on Timmy's collar he switched on his torch and swept it round the tower room, its beam piercing the black corners.

No one was there except the one man – and, with a sudden shock, Julian saw that he was tied with ropes! His arms were bound behind him and his legs were tied together too. If this was Terry-Kane then his uncle must be right. The man was no traitor – he had been kidnapped and was a prisoner.

Everyone was now in the room, staring at the sleeping man. He had his mouth open, and he still snored loudly.

'What are you going to do, Julian?' whispered George. 'Wake him up?'

Julian nodded. He went over to the sleeping man and shook him by the shoulder. He woke up at once and stared in amazement at Julian, who was full in the moonlight. He struggled up to a sitting position.

'Who are you?' he said. 'How did you get here – and who are those over in the shadows there?'

'Listen – are you Mr Terry-Kane?' asked Julian.

'Yes. I am. But who are you?'

'We are staying on the hill opposite the castle,' said Julian. 'And we saw your face at the window, through our field-glasses. So we came to find you.'

'But – but how do you know who I am?' said the man, still amazed.

'We read about you in the papers,' said Julian. 'And we saw your picture. We couldn't help noticing your eyebrows, sir – we even saw them through the glasses.'

'Look here – can you undo me?' said the man, eagerly. 'I must escape. Tomorrow night my enemies are smuggling me out of here, into a car and down to the sea – and a boat is being hired to take me across to the Continent. They want me to tell them what I know about my latest experiments. I shan't, of course – but life wouldn't be at all pleasant for me!'

'I'll cut the ropes,' said Julian, and he took out his pocket-knife. He cut the knots that tied Terry-Kane's wrists together and then freed his legs. Timmy stood and watched, ready to pounce if the man did anything fierce!

'That's better,' said the man, stretching his arms out.

'How did you manage to get to the window?' asked Julian, watching the man rub his arms and knees.

'Each evening one of the men who brought me here comes to bring me food and drink,' said Terry-Kane. 'He undoes my hands so that I can feed myself. He sits and smokes while I eat, taking no notice of me. I drag myself over to the window to have a breath of fresh air. I can't stay there long because I am soon tied up again, of course. I can't imagine how anyone could see my face at this deep-set slit-window!'

'It was our field-glasses,' said Julian. 'They are such fine ones. It's a good thing you *did* get to the window for a breath of air or we'd never have found you!'

'Julian – I can hear a noise,' said Jo, suddenly. She had ears like a cat, able to pick up the slightest sound.

'Where?' said Julian, turning sharply.

'Downstairs,' whispered Jo. 'Wait – I'll go and see.'

She slipped out of the door and down the steep little stairs. She came to the door at the bottom, the one that led into the gallery.

Yes – someone was coming! Coming along the gallery too. Jo thought quickly. If she darted back up the stairs to warn the others, this newcomer might go up there too, and they would all be caught. He could bolt the door at the top and would have six prisoners instead of one! She decided to crouch down on the floor of the gallery a little beyond the door that led upwards.

Footsteps came loudly along the gallery and up to the door. Then the stranger obviously found the door unbolted, and stopped in consternation. He stood perfectly still, listening. Jo thought he really must be able to hear her heart beating, it was thumping so loudly. She didn't dare to call out to try and warn the others – if she did they would walk straight into his arms!

And then Jo heard Julian's voice calling quietly down the stone stairs. 'Jo! Jo! Where are you?' And then, oh dear, she thought she could hear Julian coming down the stairs to find her. 'Don't come, Julian,' she said under her breath. 'Don't come.'

But Julian came right down – and behind him came Terry-Kane and Dick, with the girls following with Timmy, on their way to escaping.

The stranger down at the door was even more amazed to hear voices and footsteps. He slammed the door suddenly and rammed the stout bolt home. The footsteps on the stairs stopped in alarm.

'Hey, Jo! Is that you?' called Julian's voice. 'Open the door!'

The stranger spoke angrily. 'The door's bolted. Who are you?'

There was a silence – then Terry-Kane answered. 'So you're back again, Pottersham! Open that door at once.'

'Oho!' thought Julian. 'So the other scientist is here too – Jeffrey Pottersham. He must have got Terry-Kane here by kidnapping him. What can have happened to Jo?'

The man at the door stood there as if he didn't quite know what to do. Jo crouched down in the gallery and listened intently. The man spoke again.

'Who set you free? Who's that with you?'

'Now, listen, Pottersham,' said Terry-Kane's voice. 'I've had enough of this nonsense. You must be out of your mind, acting like this! Doping me, and kidnapping me, telling me we're going to go off by fishing boat to the Continent, and the rest of it! There are four children here, who saw my face at the window and came to investigate, and . . .'

'*Children!*' said Pottersham, taken aback. 'What, in the middle of the night! How did they get up to this tower? I'm the only one that knows the way in.'

'Pottersham, open the door!' shouted Terry-Kane, furiously. He gave it a kick, but the old door was sturdy and strong.

'You can go back to the tower, all of you,' said Pottersham. 'I'm going off to get fresh orders. It looks as if we'll have to take those kids with us, Terry-Kane – they'll be sorry they saw your face at the window. They won't like life where we're going!'

Pottersham turned and went back the way he had come. Jo guessed that he knew the same way in as they had happened on. She waited until she felt that it was perfectly safe, and then she ran to the door again. She hammered on it.

'Dick! Dick! Come down. Where are you?' She heard an answering shout from up the stairs behind the door, and then Dick came running down.

'Jo! Unbolt the door, quick!'

Jo unbolted it – but it wouldn't open. Julian had now come down too, and he called to Jo: 'Turn the key, Jo. It may be locked too.'

'Julian, the key's gone!' cried Jo, and she tugged in vain at the door. 'He must have locked it as well as bolted it – and he's taken the key. Oh, how can I get you out?'

'You can't,' said Dick. 'Still, *you're* free, Jo. You can go and tell the police. Buck up, now. You know the way, don't you?'

'I haven't got a torch,' said Jo.

'Oh dear – well, we can't possibly get one of ours out to you,' said Dick. 'You'd better wait till morning, then, Jo. You may lose yourself down in those dark passages. Yes – wait till morning.'

'The passages will still be dark!' said poor Jo. 'I'd better go now.'

'No – you're to wait till morning,' said Julian, fearing that Jo might wander off in the strange passages, and be lost for ever! She might even find herself down in the dungeons. Horrible thought.

'All right,' said Jo. 'I'll wait till morning. I'll curl up on the gallery here. It's quite warm.'

'It will be very hard!' said Dick. 'We'll go back to the room upstairs, Jo. Call us if you want us. What a blessing you're free!'

Jo curled up on the gallery, but she couldn't sleep. For one thing the floor was very hard, and the stone was very, very cold. She suddenly thought of the little room where they had seen the pitcher, the dagger and the chocolate wrapping paper. That would be a far better place to sleep! She could lie on the bench!

She stood up and thought out the way. All she had to do was to go round the gallery till she came to the little door that opened on to the corkscrew staircase leading from the gallery to the little hidden room.

She made her way cautiously to the door. She felt for the iron ring, turned it and opened the door. It was very, very dark, and she could see nothing at all in front of her. She put out her foot carefully. Was she at the top of the spiral staircase?

She found that she was. She held out her hands on either side, touching the stone walls of the curious little stairway, and went slowly down, step by step.

'Oh dear – am I going the right way? The stairs seem to be going on so long!' thought Jo. 'I don't like it – but I MUST go on!'

CHAPTER EIGHTEEN

Jo has an adventure on her own

Jo came to the end of the spiral stairway at last. She found herself on the level once more, and remembered the little straight passage that led to the secret room from the stairway. Good, good, good! Now she would soon be in the room and could lie down on the bench.

She went through the doorway of the secret room without knowing it, because it was so dark. She groped her way along, and suddenly felt the edge of the bench.

'Here at last,' she said thankfully, out loud.

And then poor Jo got a dreadful shock! A pair of strong arms went round her and held her fast! She screamed and struggled, her heart beating in wild alarm. Who was it? Oh, if only she had a light!

And then a torch was switched on, and held to her face. 'Oho! You must be Jo, I suppose,' said Pottersham's voice. 'I wondered who you were when one of those kids yelled out for you! I thought you must be wandering somewhere about. I guessed you'd come this way, and I sat on the bench and waited for you.'

'Let me go,' said Jo fiercely and struggled like a wild cat. The man only held her all the more tightly. He was very strong.

Jo suddenly put down her face and bit his hand. He gave a shout and loosened his hold. Jo was almost free when he caught her again, and shook her like a rat. 'You little wild cat! Don't you do that again!'

Jo did it again, even more fiercely, and the man dropped her on to the ground, nursing his hand. Jo made for the entrance of the room, but again the man was too quick and she found herself held again.

'I'll tie you up,' said the man, furiously. 'I'll rope you so that you won't be able to move! And I'll leave you here in the dark till I come back again.'

He took a rope from round his waist and proceeded to tie Jo up so thoroughly that she could hardly move. Her hands were behind her back, her legs were tied at the knees and ankles. She rolled about the floor, calling the man all the names she knew.

'Well, you're safe for the time being,' said Pottersham, sucking his bitten hand. 'Now I'm going. I wish you joy of the hard, cold floor and the darkness, you little wild cat!'

Jo heard his footsteps going in the distance. She could have kicked herself for not having guessed he might have been lying in wait for her. Now she couldn't get help for the others. In fact, she was much worse off than they were because she was tied up, and they weren't.

Poor Jo! She dozed off, exhausted by the night's excitement and her fierce struggle. She lay against the wall, so uncomfortable that she kept waking from her doze every few minutes.

And then a thought came into her head. She remembered the rope-man, all tied up in length after length of knotted rope. She had watched him set himself free so many times. Could any of his tricks help her now?

'The rope-man would be able to get himself free of this rope in two minutes!' she thought, and began to wriggle and struggle again. But she was not the rope-man, and after about an hour she was so exhausted again that she went into a doze once more.

When she awoke, she felt better. She forced herself into a sitting position, and made herself think clearly and slowly.

'Work one knot free first,' she said to herself, remembering what the rope-man had told her. 'At first you won't know which knot is best. When you know that you will always be able to free yourself in two minutes. But find that one knot first!'

She said all this to herself as she tried to find a knot that might be worked loose. At last one seemed a little looser than the others. It was one that bound her left wrist to her right. She twisted her wrist round and got her thumb to the knot. She picked and pulled and at last it loosened a little. She had more control over that hand now. If only she had a knife somewhere! She could manage to get it between her finger and thumb now and perhaps use it to cut another knot.

She suddenly lost her patience and flung her head back on the bench, straining and pulling at the rope. She knocked against something and it fell to the stone floor with a clatter. Jo wondered what it was – and then she knew.

'That dagger! The old, rusty dagger! Oh, if I could find it I might do something with it!'

She swung herself round on the floor till she felt the dagger under her. She rolled over on her back and tried to pick it up with her free finger and thumb, and at last she managed to hold it.

She sat up, bent forward and did her best to force the rusty dagger up and down a little on the rope that tied her hands behind her. She could hardly move it at all because her hands were still so tightly tied. But she persevered.

She grew so tired that she had to give it up for a long while. Then she tried again, then had another long rest. The third time she was lucky! The rope suddenly frayed and broke! She pulled her hands hard, found them looser and picked at a knot.

It took Jo a long time to free her hands, but she did it at last. She couldn't manage to undo her legs at first, because her hands were trembling so much. But after another long rest she undid the tight knots, and shook her legs free. 'Well, thank goodness I learnt a few hints from the rope-man,' she said, out loud. 'I'd never have got free if I hadn't!'

She wondered what the time was. It was pitch dark in the little room, of course. She stood up and was surprised to find that her legs were shaky. She staggered a few steps and then sat down again. But her legs soon felt better and she stood up once more. 'Now to find my way out,' she said. 'How I wish I had a torch!'

She went carefully down the flight of stone steps that

led down from the room, and then came to the wide passage that ran under the courtyard. She went along it, glad it was level, and then came once again to stone steps that led upwards. Up she climbed, knowing that she was going the right way, although she was in the dark.

Now she came to the small passage where she had to bend almost double, the one that ran through the centre of the thick outer walls. Jo heaved a sigh of relief. Surely she would soon come to where the stone had fallen out and would be able to see daylight!

She saw daylight before she came to the place where the stone was missing. She saw it some way in front of her, a misty little patch that made her wonder what it was at first. Then she knew.

'Daylight! Oh, thank goodness!' She stumbled along to it and climbed up to the hole from which the stone had fallen. She sat there, drinking in the sunlight. It was bright and warm and very comforting.

After the darkness of the passages Jo felt quite dazed. Then she suddenly realised how very high the sun was in the sky! Goodness, it must be afternoon!

She looked cautiously out of the hole in the wall. Now that she was so near freedom she didn't want to be caught by anyone watching out for her! There was nobody. Jo leapt down from the hole and ran down the steep hillside. She went as sure-footed as a goat, leaping along till she came to the lane. She crossed it and made her way to the caravan field.

She was just about to go over the stile when she stopped. Julian had said she was to go to the police. But Jo, like the other traveller folk, was afraid of the police. No traveller ever asked the police for help. Jo felt herself shrivelling up inside when she thought of talking to big policemen.

'No. I'll go to Uncle Fredo,' she thought. 'He will know what to do. I will tell him about it.'

She was going up the field when she saw someone strange there! Who was it? Could it be that horrid man who had tied her up? She had not seen him at all clearly, and she was afraid it might be. She saw that he was talking urgently to some of the fair-folk. They were listening politely, but Jo could see that they thought he was rather mad.

She went a bit nearer, and found that he was asking where Julian and the rest were. He was becoming very angry with the fair people because they assured him that they did not know where the children had gone.

'It's the man they called Pottersham,' said Jo to herself, and dived under a caravan. 'He's come to find out how much we've told anyone about that Face.'

She hid till he had gone away down the hillside to the lane, very red in the face, and shouting out that he would get the police.

Jo crawled out, and the fair-folk crowded round her at once. 'Where have you been? Where are the others? That man wanted to know all about you. He sounds quite mad!'

'He's a *bad* man,' said Jo. 'I'll tell you all about him – and where the others are. We've got to rescue them!'

Whereupon Jo launched into her story with the greatest zest, beginning in the middle, then going back to the beginning, putting in things she had forgotten, and thoroughly muddling everyone. When she ended they all stared at her in excitement. They didn't really know what it was all about but they had certainly gathered a few things.

'You mean to say that those kids are locked up in that

tower over there?' said Alfredo, amazed. 'And a spy is with them!'

'No – *he's* not a spy – he's a good man,' explained Jo. 'What they call a scientist, very, very, clever.'

'That man who left just now, he said he was a – a scientist,' said Skippy, stumbling over the unfamiliar word.

'Well, he's a *bad* man,' said Jo, firmly. 'He is probably a spy. He kidnapped the good man, up in the tower there, to take him away to another country. And he tied me up too, like I told you. See my wrists and ankles?'

She displayed them, cut and bruised. The fair-folk looked at them in silence. Then Bufflo cracked his whip and made everyone jump.

'We will rescue them!' he said. 'This is no police job. It is our job.'

'I say, look – that scientist comes back,' said Skippy suddenly. And sure enough, there he was, coming hurriedly up the field to ask some more questions!

'We will get him,' muttered Bufflo. All the fair-folk waited in silence for the man to come up. Then they closed round him solidly and began to walk up the hill. The man was taken with them. He couldn't help himself! He was walked behind a caravan, and before the crowd had come apart again he was on the ground, neatly roped by the rope-man!

'Well, we've got *you*,' said the rope-man. 'And now we'll get on to the next bit of business!'

CHAPTER NINETEEN

Jo joins in

THE 'SCIENTIST', as Skippy persisted in calling him, was put into an empty caravan with windows and doors shut, because he shouted so loudly. When the snake-man opened the door and slid in one of his pythons the scientist stopped shouting at once and lay extremely still.

The snake-man opened the door and his python glided out again. But the man in the caravan had learnt his lesson. Not another sound came from him!

Then everyone in the camp held a conference. There was no hurry about it at all, because it had been decided that nothing should be done before night-time.

'If we make a rescue in the daylight, then the police will come,' said Alfredo. 'They will interfere. They will not believe a word we say. They never do.'

'How shall we rescue them?' said Skippy. 'Do we go through these strange passages and up steep stone stairs? It does not sound nice to me.'

'It isn't at all nice,' Jo assured her. 'And anyway it wouldn't be sensible. The door leading to the tower room is locked, I told you. And that man has got the key.'

'Ah!' said Bufflo, springing up at once. 'You didn't tell us that before! He has the key? Then I will get it from him!'

'I didn't think of that,' said Jo, watching Bufflo leap up the caravan steps.

He came out in a minute or two and joined them again. 'He has no key on him,' he said. 'He says he never had. He says we are all mad, and he will get the police.'

'He will find it hard to get the police just yet,' said Mrs Alfredo, and gave a high little laugh. 'He has thrown away the key – or given it to a friend, perhaps?'

'Well, it's settled we can't get in through the door that leads to the tower room, then,' said the snake-man, who seemed to have a better grasp of things than the others. 'Right. Is there any other way into the room?'

'Only by the window,' said Jo. 'That slit-window there, see? Too high for any ladder, of course. Anyway, we've got to get into the courtyard first. We'll have to climb over the high castle wall.'

'That is easy,' said the rubber-man. 'I can climb any wall. But not, perhaps, one so high as the tower wall.'

'Can anyone get into or out of the slit of a window?' asked Bufflo, screwing up his eyes to look at the tower.

'Oh, yes – it's bigger than you think,' said Jo. 'It's very *deep* – the walls are so thick, you see – though I don't think they are so thick up there as they are down below. But Bufflo, how can anyone get up to that window?'

'It can be done,' said Bufflo. 'That is not so difficult! You can lend us a peg-rope, Jekky?' he said to the rope-man.

'Yes,' said Jekky. Jo knew what that was – a thick rope with pegs thrust through the strands to act as footholds.

'But how will you get the peg-rope up?' said Jo, puzzled.

'It can be done,' said Bufflo again, and the talking went on. Jo suddenly began to feel terribly hungry and got up to get herself a meal. When she got back to the conference everything was apparently settled.

'We set off tonight as soon as darkness comes,' Bufflo told her. 'You will not come, Jo. This is man's business.'

'Of course I'm coming!' said Jo, amazed that anyone should think she wasn't. 'They're my friends, aren't they? I'm coming all right!'

'You are not,' said Bufflo, and Jo immediately made up her mind to disappear before the men set off and hide somewhere so that she might follow them.

By this time it was about six o'clock. Bufflo and the rope-man disappeared into Jekky's caravan and became very busy there. Jo went peeping in at the door to see what they were doing but they ordered her out.

'This is not your business any more,' they said, and turned her out when she refused to go.

When darkness came, a little company set out from the camp. They had searched for Jo to make sure she was not coming, but she had disappeared. Bufflo led the way down the hill, looking extremely large because he was wound about with a great deal of peg-rope. Then came Mr Slither with one of his pythons draped round him. Then the rubber-man with Mr Alfredo.

Bufflo also carried his whip though nobody quite knew why. Anyway, Bufflo always did carry a whip, it was part of him, so nobody questioned him about it.

Behind them, like a little shadow, slipped Jo. What were they going to do? She had watched the tower-window for the last two hours, and when darkness came she saw a light there – a light that shone on and off, on and off.

'That's Dick or Julian signalling,' she thought. 'They will have wondered why I haven't brought help sometime today. They don't know that I was captured and tied up! I'll have something to tell them when we're all together again!'

The little company went over the stile, into the lane and up the path to the castle. They came to the wall. The rubber-man took a jump at it, and literally seemed to run up it, fling himself on to the top, roll over and disappear!

'He's over,' said Bufflo. 'What it is to be made of rubber! I don't believe that fellow ever feels hurt!'

There was a low whistle from the other side of the wall. Bufflo unwound a thin rope from his waist, tied a stone to it and flung it over. The rope slithered after the stone and over the wall like a long thin worm.

Thud! They heard the stone fall on the ground on the other side. Another low whistle told them that the rubber-man had it. Bufflo then undid the peg-rope from his waist, and he and the others held out its length between them, standing one behind the other. One end was fastened to the thin rope whose other end held the stone.

The rubber-man, on the other side of the wall, began to pull on the thin rope. When all the slack was taken in, the peg-rope began to go up the wall too, because it was tied to the thin rope and had to follow it! Up went the peg-rope and up, looking like a great thick caterpillar with tufts sticking out of its sides.

Jo watched. Yes, that was clever. A good and easy way of getting over the thick high wall. But to get the peg-rope up to the slit-window would not be so easy.

A whistle came again. Bufflo let go the peg-rope, and it swung flat against his side of the wall. He tugged it. It was firm. Evidently the rubber-man had tied it fast to something. It was safe to go up. It would bear anyone's weight without slipping down the wall.

Bufflo went up first, using the pegs as footholds and pulling himself up by the rope between the pegs. Each of the men was quick and deft in the way he climbed. Jo waited till the last one had started up, and then leapt for the rope too!

Up she went like a cat and landed beside Bufflo on the other side of the wall. He was astounded and gave her a cuff. She dodged away, and stood aside, watching. She wondered how the men intended to reach the topmost window of the high tower. Perhaps she would be of some help. If only she could be!

The four men stood in the moonlight, looking up at the tower. They talked in low tones, while the rubber-man undid the thin rope from the peg-rope, and neatly coiled it into loops. The peg-rope was left on the wall.

Jo heard a car going up the lane at the bottom of the castle hill. She heard it stop and back somewhere. Part of her attention was on the four men and the other part on the car.

The car stopped its engine. There was no further sound. Jo forgot it for a few minutes, and then was on the alert again – was that voices she heard somewhere? She listened intently. The sound came again on the night air – a low murmur that came nearer.

Jo held her breath – could that horrid man – what was his name – Pottersham – could he have arranged for his equally horrid friends to fetch Mr Terry-Kane and all the children out of the tower that night, and take them off to the coast? Perhaps they had already hired a fishing boat from Joseph the old fisherman, and they would all be away and never heard of again!

So the thoughts ran in Jo's alert mind. Mr Pottersham would have had plenty of time to get fresh orders, and arrange everything before he had gone to the camp and got himself locked up in a caravan! Oh dear – dare she go and warn her Uncle Alfredo, where he stood in the moonlight, holding a little conference with the others?

'He'll cuff me as soon as I go near,' thought Jo, rubbing her left ear, which still stung from Bufflo's cuff. 'They won't listen to me, I know. Still, I'll try.'

She went up to the group of men cautiously. She saw Bufflo take out a dagger-knife from his belt, and tie it to the end of the thin rope that the rubber-man held. She guessed in a moment what he was about to do, and ran to him.

'No, Bufflo, no! Don't throw that knife up – you'll hurt someone – you might wound one of them! No, Bufflo, no!'

'Clear out,' said Bufflo, angrily and raised his hand to slap her. She dodged away.

She went round the group to her uncle. 'Uncle Fredo,' she said, beseechingly, 'listen. I can hear voices – I think those . . .'

Alfredo pushed her away roughly. 'Will you stop this, Jo? Do you want a good punishing? You behave like a buzzing fly!'

Mr Slither called her. 'See here, Jo – if you want to be useful, hold Beauty for me. He will be in the way in a minute.'

He draped the great snake over her shoulders, and Beauty hissed loudly. He began to coil himself round Jo, and she caught hold of his tail. She liked Beauty, but just at that moment she didn't want him at all!

She stood back and watched what Bufflo was going to do. She knew, of course, and her heart beat fearfully. He was going to throw his knife through that high slit-window, a thing that surely only Bufflo, with his unerring aim, could possibly do!

'But if he gets it through the window, it may stick into one of the four up there – or into Mr Terry-Kane,' she thought, in a panic. 'It might wound Dick – or Timmy! Oh, I wish Bufflo wouldn't do it!'

She heard low voices again – this time they came from just the other side of the wall! Men were going to follow those secret passages, and go right up to the tower room! Jo knew they were! They would be there before Bufflo and the others had followed out their rescue plan. She pictured the four children being dragged down the stairs, and Terry-Kane, too. Would Timmy defend them? He would – but the men would certainly deal with him. They knew there was a dog there, because Timmy had barked the night before.

'Oh, dear,' thought Jo, in despair. 'I must do something! But what can I DO?'

CHAPTER TWENTY

A lot of excitement

Jo SUDDENLY made up her mind. She would follow the men through those passages, and see if she could warn the others by shouting when she came near enough to the tower room. She would help them *somehow*. Bufflo and the others would be too late to save them now.

Jo ran to the wall. She was up the peg-rope left there and down the other side in a trice. She made her way to where the missing stone left the gap in the old wall.

Beauty, the python, was surprised to find himself pulled off and thrown on the ground, just before Jo ran for the wall. He wasn't used to that sort of treatment. He lay there, coiling and uncoiling himself. Where had that nice girl gone? Beauty liked Jo – she knew how to treat him!

He glided after her. He too went up the wall and over, quite easily, though he did not need to use the peg-rope like Jo. He glided after Jo quickly. It was amazing to see his speed when he really wanted to be quick!

He came to the hole in the wall. Ah, he liked holes. He glided in after Jo. He caught up with her just as she had reached the end of the small passage, through which she had had to walk bent double. He pushed against her legs and then twined himself round her.

She gave a small scream, and then realised what it was. 'Beauty! You'll get into trouble with Mr Slither, coming after me like this. Go back! Stop twining yourself round me – I've got important things to do.'

But Beauty was not like Timmy. He obeyed only when he thought he would, and he was not going to obey this time!

'All right – come with me if you want to,' said Jo, at last, having in vain tried to push the great snake back. 'You'll be company, I suppose. Stop hissing like that, Beauty! You sound like an engine letting off steam in this narrow passage.'

Soon Jo had gone down the steep steps that led to the level passage under the courtyard. Beauty slithered down them too, rather surprised at the sudden drop. Along the wider passage they went, Beauty now in front, and Jo sometimes tripping over his powerful tail.

Up steps again, and into the thick wall of the castle itself. Something shining ahead made Jo suddenly stop. She listened but heard nothing. She went forward cautiously and found that in the little secret room was a small lantern, left there probably by one of the men in front.

She saw the rusty dagger lying on the floor where she had left it the night before and grinned. The rope was there too, that she had untied from her arms and legs.

Jo went on, along the passage that led to the spiral stairway. Now she thought she could hear something. She climbed the steep stairs, cross with Beauty because he

pushed by her and almost sent her headlong down them. She came to the door that opened on to the little gallery. Dare she open it? Suppose the men were just outside?

She opened it slowly. It was pitch dark on the other side, of course, but Jo knew she was about to step out on the little gallery. Beauty suddenly slithered up her and coiled himself lovingly round her. Jo could not make the snake uncoil, and she stepped out on the small gallery with Beauty firmly wrapped about her.

And then, what a noise she heard! She stood quite aghast. Whatever could be going on? She heard excited voices – surely one was Bufflo's? And was that crack a pistol-shot?

What had happened down below in the courtyard when Jo had disappeared over the wall with Beauty? None of the men noticed her go. They were all too intent on their plan.

Bufflo was to use his gift for knife-throwing – but in quite a different way from usual! He was to throw the knife high into the air, and make it curve in through the slit-window at the top of the tower!

Bufflo was an expert at knife-throwing, or, indeed, at any kind of throwing. He stood there in the courtyard, looking up at the high window. He half-closed his eyes, getting the distance and the direction fixed in his mind. The moon suddenly went in, and he lowered his hand. He could not throw accurately in the dark!

The moon sailed out again, quite brilliant. Bufflo lost no time. Once more he took aim, his eyes narrowed – and then the knife flew high into the air, gleaming as it went – taking behind it a long tail of very thin rope.

It struck the sill of the slit-window and fell back. Bufflo caught it deftly. The moonlight showed plainly that the knife was not sharp-pointed – Bufflo had filed off the point, and it was now quite blunt. Jo need not have worried about someone in the tower being hurt by a sharp dagger!

Once more Bufflo took aim, and once more the knife sailed up, swift as a swallow, shining silver as it went. This time it fell cleanly in at the window-opening, slithered all the way across the stone ledge inside, and fell to the floor of the tower room with a thud.

It caused the greatest astonishment there. Mr Terry-Kane, the four children and Timmy were all huddled together for warmth in one corner. They were hungry and cold. No one had brought them food, and they had nothing to keep them warm except a rug belonging to Terry-Kane. All that day they had been in the tower room, sometimes looking from the window, sometimes shouting all together at the tops of their voices. But nobody heard them, and nobody saw them.

'Why doesn't Jo bring help?' they had said a hundred times that long, long day. They didn't know that poor Jo was spending hours trying to free herself from the knots round her legs and wrists.

They had looked out of the window at the camp on the opposite hill, where the fair-folk went about their business, looking like ants on the far-off green slope. Was Jo there? It was too far-off to make out anyone for certain.

When darkness came Julian had flashed his torch from the window on and off – on and off. Then, cold and miserable, they had all huddled together, with Timmy licking first one and then another, not at all understanding why they should stay in this one room.

'Timmy will be so thirsty,' said George. 'He keeps

licking round his mouth in the way he does when he wants a drink.'

'Well, I feel like licking round *my* mouth too,' said Dick.

They were half asleep when the knife came thudding into the room. Timmy leapt up at once and barked madly. He stood and stared at the knife that lay gleaming in the moonlight, and barked without stopping.

'A knife!' said George, in amazement. 'A knife with a string tied on the end!'

'It's blunt,' said Julian, picking it up. 'The tip has been filed off. What's the meaning of it? And why the string tied to it?'

'Be careful that another knife doesn't come through,' warned Terry-Kane.

'It won't,' said Julian. 'I think this is something to do with Jo. She hasn't gone to the police. She has got the fair-folk to help us. This is Bufflo's knife, I'm sure!'

They were all round him, examining it now. 'I'm going to the window,' said Julian. 'I'll look right out into the courtyard. Hold my legs, Dick.'

He climbed up on the stone sill and crawled a little forward through the deep-set slit. He came to the outer edge of the window and looked down. Dick hung on to his legs, afraid that the sill might crumble away and Julian would fall.

'I can see four people down in the courtyard,' said Julian. 'Oh, good – one is Alfredo, one is Bufflo – and I can't make out the other two. AHOY down there!'

The four men below were standing looking up intently. They saw Julian's head appear outside the window, and waved to him.

'Pull in the rope!' shouted Bufflo. He had now tied the end of a second peg-rope to the thin rope, and he and the others lifted it so that it might run easily up the wall.

Julian slid back into the tower room. He was excited. 'This string on the knife runs down the wall and is tied to a thicker rope,' he said. 'I'll pull it up – and up will come a rope that we can climb down!'

He pulled on the string, and more and more of it appeared through the window. Then Julian felt a heavier weight and he guessed the thicker rope was coming up. Now he had to pull more slowly. Dick helped him.

Over the windowsill, in at the window, appeared the first length of the peg-rope. The children had never seen one like it before, they were used to the more ordinary rope-ladder. But Terry-Kane knew what it was.

'A peg-rope,' he said. 'Circus people and fair people make them – they are lighter and easier to manage than rope-ladders. We'll have to fix the end to something really strong, so that it will hold our weight.'

Anne looked at the peg-rope in dismay. She didn't at all like the idea of climbing down that, swinging on it all the way down the high stone wall of the tower! But the others looked at it with pleasure and excitement – a way of escape – a good, strong rope to climb down out of this hateful cold room!

Terry-Kane looked about for something to fasten the rope to. In the wall at one side was a great iron ring, embedded in the stone. What it had been used for once upon a time nobody could imagine – but certainly it would be of great use now!

There were no pegs in the first yard or so of the rope. Terry-Kane and Julian cut off the string that had pulled it up, and then dragged it right through until the first peg stopped it. Then they twisted the rope-end round upon itself and made great strong knots that could not slip.

Julian took hold of the rope, and leant back hard on it, pulling it with all his strength. 'It would hold a dozen of us at once!' he said, pleased. 'Shall I go first, sir? I can help everyone else down then, if I'm at the bottom. Dick and you can see to the girls when they climb out.'

'What about Timmy?' asked George, at once.

'We'll wrap him up in the rug, tie him firmly and lower him down on the string,' said Dick. 'It's very strong string – thin rope, really.'

'I'll go down now,' said Julian, and went to the window. Then he stopped. Someone was clattering up the stone steps that led to the tower. Someone was at the door! Who could it be?

CHAPTER TWENTY-ONE

In the tower room

THE DOOR was flung open, and a man stood there, panting. Behind him came three others.

'Pottersham!' said Terry-Kane. 'So you're back!'

'Yes. I'm back,' said the panting man.

Timmy began to bark and try to escape from George's hand. He showed his teeth and all his hackles rose up on his neck. He looked a very savage dog indeed.

Pottersham backed away. He didn't like the look of Timmy at all! 'If you let that dog go, I'll shoot him,' he said, and as if by magic a gun appeared in his right hand.

George tried her hardest to restrain the furious Timmy, and called to Julian to help her. 'Julian, hold him as well. He'll fling himself on that man, he's so angry.'

Julian went to help. Between them they forced the furious dog back into a corner, where George tried in vain to pacify him. She was terrified that he might be shot.

'You can't behave like this, Pottersham,' began Terry-Kane, but he was cut short.

'We've no time to lose. We're taking you, Terry-Kane, and one of the kids. We can use him for a hostage if too much fuss is made about your disappearance. We'll take this boy,' and he grabbed at Dick. Dick gave him a punch

on the jaw immediately, thanking his stars that he had learnt boxing at school. But he at once found himself on the floor! These men were not standing for any nonsense. They were in a hurry!

'Get him,' said Pottersham, to one of the men behind him, and Dick was pounced on. Then Terry-Kane was taken too, and his arms held behind him.

'What about these other kids?' he said, angrily. 'You're surely not going to lock them up in this room and leave them.'

'Yes, we are,' said Pottersham. 'We're leaving a note for the old turnstile woman to tell her they're up here. Let the police rescue them if they can!'

'You always were a . . .' began Terry-Kane, and then ducked to avoid a blow.

Timmy barked madly all the time, and almost choked himself trying to get away from George and Julian. He was mad with rage, and when he saw Dick being roughly treated he very nearly did manage to get loose. 'Take them,' ordered Pottersham. 'And hurry. Go on – down the steps with them.'

The three men forced Terry-Kane and Dick to the stone stairs – and then everyone shot round in astonishment! A loud voice suddenly came from the window!

Anne gasped. Bufflo was there! He hadn't been able to understand why nobody came down the peg-rope, so he had come up to find out. And to his enormous surprise there appeared to be quite an upset going on!

'Hey there! WHAT'S UP?' he yelled, and slid into the room, looking most out of place with his mop of yellow hair, bright checked shirt and whip!

'BUFFLO!' shouted all four of the children, and Timmy changed his angry bark to a welcoming one. Terry-Kane looked on in astonishment, his arms still pinioned behind him.

'Who in the world is this?' shouted Pottersham, alarmed at Bufflo's sudden appearance through the window. 'How did he get through there?'

Bufflo eyed the gun in Pottersham's hand and lazily cracked his small whip once or twice. 'Put that thing away,' he said, in his drawling voice. 'You ought to know better than to wave a thing like that about when there's kids around. Go on – put it away!'

He cracked his whip again. Pottersham pointed the gun at him angrily. And then a most amazing thing happened.

The gun disappeared from Pottersham's hand, flew right up into the air, and was neatly caught by Bufflo! And all by the crack of a whip!

Crack! Just that – and the gun had been flicked from his hand by the powerful lash-end – and had stung Pottersham's fingers so much he was now howling in pain and bending double to nurse his injured hand.

Terry-Kane gasped. What a neat trick – but how dangerous! The gun might have gone off. Now the tables were indeed turned, for it was Bufflo who held the gun, not Pottersham. And Pottersham looked very pale indeed!

He stared as if he hardly knew what to do. 'Let go of them,' ordered Bufflo, nodding his head towards Terry-Kane and Dick. The three men released them and stood back.

'Seems as if we got to get the police after all,' remarked Bufflo, in a perfectly ordinary voice, as if these happenings were not at all unusual. 'You can let that dog go now, if you want, Julian.'

'No! NO!' cried Pottersham in terror – and at that moment the moon went behind a cloud, and the tower room was plunged in darkness – except for the lantern that Pottersham had set down on the floor when he had first arrived.

He saw one slight chance for himself and the others. He suddenly kicked the lantern, which flew into the air and hit Bufflo, then went out, and left the entire place in pitch darkness. Bufflo did not dare to fire. He might hit the wrong person!

'Set the dog loose!' he roared – but it was too late. By the time Timmy had got to the door, it was slammed shut – and the bolt was shot home on the other side! There was the sound of hurried steps slipping and stumbling down the stone stairway in the dark.

'Hrrr!' said Bufflo, when the moon came out again, and showed him the astonished and dismayed faces of the five in the room. 'We slipped up somewhere, didn't we? They've gone!'

'Yes. But without *us*,' said Terry-Kane, letting Dick untie his arms. 'They've probably gone down through those passages. They'll be out before we've escaped ourselves, more's the pity. And now we've got to try this rope trick down the tower wall, seeing that the door is locked!'

'Come on, then,' said Julian. 'Let's go before anything else happens.' He went to the window, slid to the outer

edge, and took hold of the rope. It was perfectly easy to climb down, though it wasn't very pleasant to look below him into the courtyard. It seemed so very far away.

Anne went next, very much afraid, but not showing it. She was quite a good climber so she didn't find the rope difficult. She was very, very glad when she at last stood safely beside Julian.

Then came George, with a bit of news. 'I can't think what's happening to the four men,' she said. 'They still seem to be about – and they're yelling like anything. It sounds as if they are rushing round that gallery that runs along the walls of the tower room below.'

'Well, let them,' said Julian. 'If they stay there long enough, we'll have time to go to the hole in the outer wall, and wait for them to come out one by one! That would be very, very nice.'

'Timmy's coming now,' said George. 'I've wrapped him up well in that rug and tied it all round him, and put a kind of rope harness on him. Dick's going to lower him down. We doubled the rope to make sure it would hold. Look – here he comes! Poor darling Timmy! He can't think what in the world is happening!'

Timmy came down slowly, swinging a little, and bumping into the stone wall now and again. He gave a little yelp each time, and George was sure he would be covered with bruises! She watched in great suspense as he came lower and lower.

'Timmy ought to be used to this sort of thing by now,'

said Julian. 'He's had plenty of it in the adventures he's shared with us. Hey there, Tim! Slowly does it! Good dog, then! I guess you're glad to be standing on firm ground again!'

Timmy certainly was. He allowed himself to be untied from his rug by George, and then tried a few steps to see if the ground was really firm beneath his feet. He leapt up at George joyfully, very glad to be out in the open air again.

'Here comes Dick,' said Julian. The peg-rope swayed a little, and Alfredo went to hold it steady. He and the rubber-man and Mr Slither were now extremely concerned about something, so concerned that they had hardly a word to say to Julian and George and Anne.

They had suddenly missed Jo and the snake! The snake-man didn't care tuppence about Jo – but he did care about his precious, beloved, magnificent python! He had already hunted all round the courtyard for it.

'If Jo's taken it back to camp with her, I'll pull her hair off!' muttered the snake-man, unhappily, and Julian looked at him in astonishment. What *was* he muttering about?

Terry-Kane came next, and last of all, Bufflo, who seemed to slide down in a most remarkable way, not using the pegs at all. He leapt down beside them, grinning.

'There's a tremendous upset up aloft!' he said. 'Yelling and shouting and scampering about. What do you suppose is the matter with those fellows? We'll be able to get them nicely, if we go to the hole in the wall. They'll be out there soon, I reckon. Come on!'

CHAPTER TWENTY-TWO

Beauty and Jo enjoy themselves

SOMETHING CERTAINLY had happened to upset Pottersham and his three friends. After the door of the tower room had been slammed and bolted, the men had gone clattering down the stone steps. They had come to the door that led into the gallery, and had opened it and gone out on to the gallery itself.

But before they could find the spiral staircase a little way along, Pottersham had tripped over something – something that hissed like an engine letting off steam, and had wound itself round his legs.

He yelled, and struck out at whatever it was. At first he had thought it was a man lying in wait for him, who had pounced at his legs – but he knew it wasn't a man now. No man could hiss like that!

One of the men shone a torch down to see what was the matter with Pottersham. What he saw made him yell and almost drop the torch.

'A snake! A snake bigger than any I've ever seen! It's got you, Pottersham!'

'Help me, man, help me!' shouted Pottersham, hitting down at the snake as hard as he could. 'It's squeezing my legs together in its coils.'

The other men ran to help him. As soon as they began to tug, Beauty uncoiled and glided off into the shadows.

'Where's the horrible thing gone?' panted Pottersham.

'It nearly crushed my legs to powder! Quick, let's go before it comes back. Where in the world did it come from?'

They took a few steps – but the snake was lying in wait for them! It tripped them all up by gliding in and out of their legs, and then began to coil itself round one of the men's waists.

Such a shouting and yelling and howling began then! If ever there were frightened men, those four were! No matter where they went, that snake seemed to be there, coiling and uncoiling, gliding, writhing, squeezing!

It was Jo who had set the python on to them, of course. Jo had stayed in the gallery while all the disturbance upstairs had been going on, Beauty draped round her neck. The girl tried in vain to make out what was happening.

And then she had heard a door slam, a bolt shot home, and men's feet pouring down the stone stairs! She guessed it must be the four whose voices she had heard earlier in the evening, the men who had gone through the passage.

'Beauty! Now it's *your* turn to do something,' said Jo, and she pulled the snake off her shoulders. He poured himself down her and flowed on to the ground in one beautiful movement. He glided towards the men, who were now coming out of the gallery. After that, the python had the time of his life. The more the men howled the more excited the big snake became.

Jo was huddled in a corner, laughing till the tears ran down her cheeks. She knew the snake was quite harmless unless he gave one of the men too tight a squeeze. She couldn't see what was going on, but she could hear.

'Oh dear – there's another one down!' she thought, as she heard one of the men tripped up by Beauty. 'And there goes another! I shall die of laughing. Good old Beauty! He's never allowed to behave like this in the usual way. He *must* be enjoying himself!'

At last the men could bear it no more. 'Come up to that tower room!' yelled Pottersham. 'I'm not going back through those dark passages with snakes after me. There must be dozens of them here. We'll be bitten soon!'

Jo laughed out loud. Dozens of them! Well, probably Beauty did seem like a dozen snakes to the bewildered men falling over one another in the dark. But Beauty would not bite – he was not poisonous.

Somehow the men got up into the tower room, and left the snake behind. Beauty was tired of the game now, and went to Jo when the girl called to him. She draped him round her neck, and listened.

The door up in the tower room had slammed. Jo slipped up the steps, felt for the door-bolt in the darkness and neatly and quietly pulled it across. Now, unless the men liked to risk going down the peg-rope, which she guessed Bufflo had put up against the wall to rescue the others, they were nicely trapped. And if they *did* go down the rope they would be sure to find a few people waiting for them at the bottom!

'Come on, Beauty, let's go,' said Jo, and went down the

steps, wishing she had a torch. She remembered the little lantern that had been left in the hidden room, and felt more cheerful. She would be able to take that with her down all those dark passages. Good!

Beauty slithered in front of her. He knew the way all right! They came to the little room, and Jo thankfully picked up the lantern. She looked down at the big python and he stared up at her with gleaming, unwinking eyes. His long body coiled and uncoiled, shining brown and polished in the light.

'I wouldn't mind you for a pet, if you were a bit smaller,' Jo told him. 'I don't know why people don't like snakes. Oh, Beauty – it makes me laugh to think of the way you treated those men!'

She chuckled as she went along the secret ways, holding the lantern high, except when she came to the last passage of all, and had to walk bent double. Beauty waited for her when she came to the hole in the wall. He had heard noises outside.

Jo climbed out first, and was immensely surprised to find herself pounced on and held. She wriggled and shouted and struggled, and finally bit the hand that was holding her.

Then a torch was shone on her and a shout went up. 'It's Jo! Jo, where have you been? And look here, if you bite like that I'll scrag you!'

'Bufflo! I'm sorry – but what did you want to go and pounce on me for?' cried Jo. The moon suddenly came out

and lit up the scene. She saw Julian and the rest there, coming up eagerly.

'Jo! Are you all right?' said her uncle. 'We were worried about you. Where have you been?'

Jo took no notice. She ran up to Dick and the others. 'You escaped!' she cried. 'Did you all get safely down the peg-rope?'

'There's no time to tell about that now,' said Bufflo, watching the hole in the wall. 'What about those fellows? We're waiting for them here. Did you hear anything of them, Jo?'

'Oh, yes. I followed them. Oh, Bufflo, it was so funny . . .' said Jo, and began to laugh. Bufflo shook her, but she couldn't stop. And then who should come gliding out through the hole but Beauty!

Mr Slither saw him at once and gave a yell. 'Beauty! Jo, did you take him with you? You wicked girl! Come here, my Beauty!'

The snake glided to him and wound himself lovingly round him.

'I'm not wicked,' said Jo, indignantly. 'Beauty wanted to come with me and he did – and oh, he got mixed up with all those men, and . . .'

She went off into peals of laughter again. Dick grinned in sympathy. Jo was very funny when she couldn't stop laughing.

Alfredo shook her roughly and made her stop. 'Tell us what you know about those men,' he commanded. 'Are they coming out this way? Where are they?'

'Oh – the men,' said Jo, wiping her eyes and trying to stop laughing. 'They're all right. Beauty chased them back to the tower room, and I bolted them in. They're still there, I expect – unless they dare to get down the peg-rope, which I bet they won't!'

Bufflo gave a short laugh. 'You did well, Jo,' he said. 'You and Beauty!'

He gave a sharp order to Alfredo and the rubber-man, who went back over the wall and into the courtyard to watch if the men slid down the peg-rope.

'I think it would be a good idea to get the police now,' said Terry-Kane, beginning to feel that he must be in some kind of extraordinary dream, with peg-ropes and whips and knives and snakes turning up in such a peculiar manner. 'That fellow Pottersham is dangerous. He's a traitor, and must be caught before he gives away all that he knows about the work he and I have been doing.'

'Right,' said Bufflo. 'We've got another fellow locked up too – in an empty caravan.'

'But – didn't he escape, then?' said Jo, surprised. 'I thought that man Pottersham, who's up in the tower room now, was the one we locked up.'

'The one we locked up is *still* locked up,' said Bufflo grimly.

'But who is *he*, then?' said Terry-Kane, bewildered.

'We'll soon find out,' said Bufflo. 'Come on, let's get going now. It's very late, you kids must be dying of hunger, somebody ought to go to the police, and I want to get back to camp.'

'Alfredo and the rubber-man will keep guard on the peg-rope,' said Mr Slither, still fondling Beauty. 'There is no need to stay here any longer.'

So down the hill they went, talking nineteen to the dozen. Terry-Kane went off to the police station and to telephone what he vaguely called 'the high-up authorities'. The five children began to think hungrily of something to eat and drink! Timmy ran to the stream as soon as they reached the field and began to lap thirstily.

'Let's just find out if you know the fellow we've got locked up in this caravan,' said Bufflo, when they got to the camp. 'He seems the only unexplained bit so far.'

He unlocked the caravan, and called loudly: 'Come on out. We want to know who you are!' He held up a lamp, and the man inside came slowly to the door.

There was a shout of amazement from all the children. 'Uncle Quentin!' cried Julian, Dick and Anne. 'Father!' shouted George. 'What ARE you doing here?'

CHAPTER TWENTY-THREE

Having a wonderful time!

THERE WAS a minute or two of silence. Everyone was most astonished. To think that George's father had been locked up like that! It had been Jo's mistake, of course – she had been so sure he was Mr Pottersham.

'Julian,' said Uncle Quentin, very much on his dignity, and also very angry, 'I must ask you to go and get the police here. I was set on and locked up in this caravan for no reason at all.'

Bufflo began to look most disturbed. He turned on Jo.

'Why didn't you tell us he was George's father?' he said.

'I didn't know it *was*,' said Jo. 'I've never seen him, and anyhow I thought . . .'

'It doesn't matter what you thought,' said Uncle Quentin, looking at the little girl in disgust. 'I insist on the police being fetched.'

'Uncle Quentin, I'm sure it's all been a mistake,' said Julian, 'and anyway Mr Terry-Kane has gone to the police himself.'

His uncle stared at him as if he couldn't believe his ears. '*Terry-Kane?* Where is he? What has happened? Is he found?'

'Yes. It's rather a long story,' said Julian. 'It all began when we saw that face at the window. I told Aunt Fanny all about that, Uncle, and she said she would tell you when you got back from London. Well – it *was* Mr Terry-Kane at the window!'

'I thought so! I told your Aunt Fanny I had a feeling it was!' said his uncle. 'That's why I came as soon as ever I could – but you were none of you here. What happened to you?'

'Well, that's part of the story, Uncle,' said Julian, patiently. 'But I say, do you mind if we have something to eat? We're practically dead from starvation – haven't had anything since yesterday!'

That ended the interview for the time being! Mrs Alfredo bustled about, and soon there was a perfectly glorious meal set in front of the five half-starved children. They sat round a camp-fire and ate and ate and ate.

Mrs Alfredo practically emptied her big pot for them. Timmy was surrounded by plates of scraps and big bones brought by every member of the camp! Almost every minute someone loomed up out of the darkness with a plate of something or other either for the hungry children, or for Timmy.

At last they really could eat no more, and Julian began to tell their extraordinary story. Dick took it up, and George added quite a few bits. Jo interrupted continually and even Timmy put in a few barks. Only Anne said nothing. She was leaning against her uncle, fast asleep.

'I never heard such a tale in my life,' said Uncle Quentin, continually. 'Never! Fancy that fellow Pottersham going off with Terry-Kane like that. I *knew* Terry-Kane was all right – *he* wouldn't let his country down. Now, Pottersham I never did like. Well, go on.'

The fair-folk were as enthralled as Uncle Quentin with the tale. They came closer and closer as the story of the secret passages, the hidden room, the stone stairways and the rest was unfolded.

They got very excited when they learnt how Bufflo had appeared in the tower room and had flicked the gun out of Pottersham's hand. Uncle Quentin threw back his head and roared when he heard that bit.

'What a shock for that fellow!' he said. 'I'd like to have seen his face. Well, well – I never heard such a tale in my life!'

And then it was Jo's turn to tell how she had followed the four men into the secret passages, and had set Beauty, the python, on to the men. She began to laugh again as she told her tale, and soon all the fair-folk were laughing in sympathy, rocking to and fro, with tears streaming down their faces.

Only Uncle Quentin looked rather solemn at this point. He remembered how he had felt when, because of his shouting, the fair-folk had sent the python into his caravan, and almost frightened him out of his life.

'Mr Slither, please do get Beauty,' begged Jo. 'He ought to listen to his part of the story. He was wonderful. He enjoyed it all too. I'm sure he would have laughed if only snakes *could* laugh.'

Poor Uncle Quentin didn't like to object when the snake-man fetched his beloved python – in fact, he fetched both of them, and they had never had such a fuss made of them before. They were patted and rubbed and pulled about in a way they both seemed to enjoy hugely.

'Let me hold Beauty, Mr Slither,' said Jo, at last, and she draped him round her neck like a long, shiny scarf. Uncle Quentin looked as if he was going to be sick. He would certainly have got up and gone away if it hadn't been that his favourite niece Anne was fast asleep against his shoulder.

'What extraordinary people George seems to be friends with,' he thought. 'I suppose they are all right – but really! What with whips and knives and snakes I must say I find all this very peculiar.'

'Somebody's coming up the field,' said Jo, suddenly. 'It's – yes, it's Mr Terry-Kane, and he's got three policemen with him.'

Immediately almost all the fair-folk melted away into the darkness. They knew quite well why the police had come – not for them, but because of Mr Pottersham and his unpleasant friends. But all the same they wanted nothing to do with the three burly policemen walking up the hill with Terry-Kane.

Uncle Quentin leapt to his feet as soon as he saw Terry-

Kane. He ran to meet him joyfully, and pumped his arm up and down, up and down, shaking hands so vigorously that Terry-Kane felt quite exhausted.

'My dear fellow,' said Uncle Quentin, 'I'm so glad you're safe. I told everyone you weren't a traitor, and never could be – everyone! I went up to London and told them. I'm glad you're all right.'

'Well – it's thanks to these children,' said Terry-Kane, who looked very tired. 'I expect you've heard the peculiar and most extraordinary tale of the Face at the Window.'

'Yes – it's all so extraordinary that I shouldn't believe it if I read it in a book,' said Uncle Quentin. 'And yet it all happened! My dear fellow, you must be very tired!'

'I am,' said Terry-Kane. 'But I'm not going to lie down and sleep until those other fellows are safely under lock and key – Pottersham and his fine friends! Do you mind if I leave you for a bit, and go off to the castle again? We simply must catch those fellows. I came to ask if one of the children could go with us, because I hear we have to creep through all kinds of passages and galleries and up spiral stairways and goodness knows what.'

'But – didn't *you* go that way when Pottersham first took you there and hid you in that room?' asked Dick, surprised.

'Yes. I must have gone that way,' said Mr Terry-Kane. 'But I was blindfolded and half-doped with something they had made me drink. I've no idea of the way. Of course, Pottersham knew every inch – he's written books about all these old castles, you know – nobody knows more about them and their secrets than he does. He certainly put his knowledge to good use this week!'

'I'll go with you,' said Jo. 'I've been up and down those passages four times now. I know them by heart! The others have only been once.'

'Yes, you go,' said Bufflo.

'Take Timmy,' said George most generously, for usually she would never let Timmy go with Jo.

'Or take a snake,' suggested Dick, with a grin.

'I won't take anything,' said Jo. 'I'll be all right with three big policemen! So long as they're not after *me*, I like them!'

She didn't really, but she couldn't help boasting a little. She set off with Terry-Kane and the three policemen, strutting a little, and feeling quite a heroine.

The others all went to their caravans, tired out. Uncle Quentin sat by the camp-fire, waiting for the arrival of Pottersham and his three friends.

'Good night,' said Julian to the girls. 'I'd like to wait till the crowd come back – complete with the rubber-man and Alfredo – but I shall fall asleep standing on my feet in a minute. I say, wasn't that a smashing supper?'

'Super!' said the others. 'Well – see you tomorrow.'

They all slept very late the next day. Jo was back long before they awoke, very anxious to tell them how they had captured Pottersham and the others, and how they had been marched off to the police station, with her following all the way. But Mrs Alfredo would not let her wake the four children up.

However, they did awake at last, and got up eagerly, remembering all the exciting moments of the day before. Soon they were jumping down the steps of the two caravans, eager to hear the latest news.

'Hallo, Father!' shouted George, seeing him not far off.

'Hallo, Uncle Quentin! Hallo, Jo!' called the others, and soon heard the latest bits of information from Jo who was very proud of being in at the finish.

'But they didn't put up any fight at all,' she said, rather disappointed. 'I think Beauty scared all the fight out of them last night – they just gave in without a word.'

'Now you children!' called Mrs Alfredo, 'I have kept a little breakfast for you. You like to come?'

They did like to come! Jo went too, though she had already had one breakfast. Uncle Quentin went to sit down with them. He gazed around amazed at all the goings-on of the camp.

Bufflo was doing some remarkable rope-spinning and whip-cracking. The rubber-man was wriggling in and out of the wheel-spokes of his caravan without stopping. Mr Slither was polishing his snakes. Dacca was step-dancing on a board, click-click-clickity-click.

Alfredo came up with his buttonhook-like torches, and his metal bowl. 'I give you a treat,' he announced to Uncle Quentin. 'You would like to see me fire-eat?'

Uncle Quentin stared at him as if he thought he had gone raving mad.

'He's a fire-eater, Uncle,' explained Dick.

'Oh. No, thank you, my good man. I would rather not see you eat fire,' said Uncle Quentin, politely but very firmly. Alfredo was most disappointed. He had meant to give this man a real treat to make up for locking him into the caravan! He went away sadly, and Mrs Alfredo screamed after him.

'You foolish man. Who wants to see you fire-eat? You have no brains. You are a big, silly bad man. You keep away with your fire-eating!' She disappeared into her caravan, and Uncle Quentin looked after her, astonished at her sudden outburst.

'This is really a very extraordinary place,' he said. 'And *most* extraordinary people. I'm going back home today, George. Wouldn't you all like to come with me? I don't really feel it's the right thing for you to get mixed up in so many funny doings.'

'Oh *no*, Father,' said George, in horror. 'Go home when we've only just settled in! Of *course* not. None of us wants to leave – do we, Julian?' she said, looking round beseechingly at him.

Julian answered at once. 'George is right, Uncle. We're just beginning to enjoy ourselves here. I think we're *all* agreed on that!'

'We are,' said everyone, and Timmy thumped his tail hard and gave a very loud 'WOOF'.

'Very well,' said Uncle Quentin, getting up. 'I must go, I suppose. I'll catch the bus down to the station. Come down with me.'

They went to see him off on the bus. It came up well on time and he got in.

'Goodbye,' he said. 'What message shall I give your mother, George? She'll expect to hear something from the five of you.'

'Well,' shouted everyone, as the bus rumbled off, 'well – just tell her the FIVE ARE HAVING A WONDERFUL TIME! Goodbye, Uncle Quentin, goodbye!'

Enid Blyton®

is one of the most popular children's authors of all time. Her books have sold over 500 million copies and have been translated into other languages more often than any other children's author.

Enid Blyton adored writing for children. She wrote over 700 books and about 2,000 short stories. *The Famous Five* books, now 75 years old, are her most popular. She is also the author of other favourites including *The Secret Seven*, *The Magic Faraway Tree*, *Malory Towers* and *Noddy*.

Born in London in 1897, Enid lived much of her life in Buckinghamshire and loved dogs, gardening and the countryside. She was very knowledgeable about trees, flowers, birds and animals. Dorset – where some of the Famous Five's adventures are set – was a favourite place of hers too.

Enid Blyton's stories are read and loved by millions of children (and grown-ups) all over the world. Visit enidblyton.co.uk to discover more.

THE FAMOUS FIVE

FIVE GO DOWN TO THE SEA

Have you read all THE FAMOUS FIVE books?

1. Five on a Treasure Island
2. Five Go Adventuring Again
3. Five Run Away Together
4. Five Go to Smuggler's Top
5. Five Go Off in a Caravan
6. Five on Kirrin Island Again
7. Five Go Off to Camp
8. Five Get Into Trouble
9. Five Fall Into Adventure
10. Five on a Hike Together
11. Five Have a Wonderful Time
12. Five Go Down to the Sea
13. Five Go to Mystery Moor
14. Five Have Plenty of Fun
15. Five on a Secret Trail
16. Five Go to Billycock Hill
17. Five Get Into a Fix
18. Five on Finniston Farm
19. Five Go to Demon's Rocks
20. Five Have a Mystery to Solve
21. Five Are Together Again

The Famous Five Colour Short Stories

1. Five and a Half-Term Adventure
2. George's Hair is Too Long
3. Good Old Timmy
4. A Lazy Afternoon
5. Well Done, Famous Five
6. Five Have a Puzzling Time
7. Happy Christmas, Five
8. When Timmy Chased the Cat

Enid Blyton®

THE FAMOUS FIVE

FIVE GO DOWN TO THE SEA

Illustrated by Eileen A. Soper

HODDER

HODDER CHILDREN'S BOOKS

First published in Great Britain in 1953 by Hodder & Stoughton
This edition published in 2016

20

A CIP catalogue record for this book is available from the British Library.

ISBN 978 1 444 93642 1

Printed in Great Britain by Clays Ltd, Elcograf S.p.A.

The paper and board used in this book are made from wood from responsible sources.

Hodder Children's Books
An imprint of
Hachette Children's Group
Part of Hodder and Stoughton
Carmelite House
50 Victoria Embankment
London EC4Y 0DZ

An Hachette UK Company
www.hachette.co.uk
www.hachettechildrens.co.uk

CONTENTS

1	THE HOLIDAY BEGINS	1
2	TREMANNON FARM	10
3	THE FIRST EVENING	21
4	DOWN IN THE COVE	31
5	YAN – AND HIS GRANDAD	42
6	A STRANGE TALE	54
7	OUT IN THE NIGHT	64
8	HERE COME THE BARNIES!	75
9	THE LIGHT IN THE TOWER	86
10	GETTING READY FOR THE SHOW	97
11	THE BARNIES – AND CLOPPER	107
12	A TRIP TO THE TOWER	118
13	IN THE WRECKERS' TOWER	128
14	THE SECRET PASSAGE	139
15	LOCKED IN THE CAVE	148
16	WRECKERS' WAY	158
17	LONG AFTER MIDNIGHT!	169
18	DICK GETS AN IDEA!	180
19	MOSTLY ABOUT CLOPPER	189

CHAPTER ONE

The holiday begins

'BLOW! I'VE got a puncture!' said Dick. 'My tyre's going flat. Worst time it could possibly happen!'

Julian glanced down at Dick's back tyre. Then he looked at his watch. 'You've just got time to pump it up and hope for the best,' he said. 'We've got seven minutes before the train goes.'

Dick jumped off and took his pump. The others got off their bicycles, too, and stood round, watching to see if the tyre blew up well or not.

They were on their way to Kirrin Station to catch the train, bicycles and all. Their luggage had gone on in advance, and they thought they had left plenty of time to ride to the station, get their bicycles labelled and put in the luggage van, and catch the train comfortably.

'We *can't* miss the train!' said George, putting on her best scowl. She always hated it when things went wrong.

'We can. Easiest thing in the world!' said Julian, grinning at George's fierce face. 'What do *you* say, Timmy?'

Timmy barked sharply, as if to say he certainly agreed. He licked George's hand and she patted him. The scowl left her face as she saw Dick's tyre coming up well. They'd just do it! Dick felt his tyre, gave a sigh of relief, and put his pump back in its place.

'Phew! That was hot work,' he said, mounting his bicycle. 'Hope it will last till we get to the station. I was afraid you'd have to go without me.'

'Oh, *no*,' said Anne. 'We'd have caught the next train. Come on, Timmy!'

The four cousins and Timmy the dog raced on towards the station. They cycled into the station yard just as the signal went up to show the train was due. The porter came towards them, his big round face red and smiling.

'I sent your luggage off for you,' he said. 'Not much between you, I must say – just one small trunk!'

'Well, we don't wear much on holidays,' said Julian. 'Can you label our bikes quickly for us? I see the train is due.'

The porter began to label the four bicycles. He didn't hurry. He wouldn't let the train go off again till he had done his job, that was certain. There it was now, coming round the bend.

'You going off to Cornwall, I see?' said the porter. 'And to Tremannon, too. You want to be careful of bathing there. That's a fierce coast and a hungry sea.'

'Oh, do you know it?' said Anne, surprised. 'Is it a nice place?'

'Nice? Well, I dunno about that,' said the porter, raising his voice as the train came rumbling in. 'I used to go out in my uncle's fishing boat all round there, and it's wild and lonely. I shouldn't have thought it was much of a place for a holiday – no pier, no ice-cream sellers, no concert parties, no cinema, no . . .'

'Good,' said Julian. 'We can do without all those, thank you. We mean to bathe, and hire a boat, and fish, and bike all round about. That's *our* kind of holiday!'

'Woof!' said Timmy, wagging his tail.

'Yes, and yours too,' said George, rubbing his big head. 'Come on, we'd better get into a carriage.'

'I'll see to your bikes,' said the porter. 'Have a good holiday, and if you see my uncle tell him you know me.

His name's same as mine, John Polpenny.'

' "By Tre, Pol and Pen, you may know the Cornishmen",' quoted Julian, getting into a carriage with the others. 'Thanks, John. We'll look up your uncle if we can!'

They each took a corner seat, and Timmy went to the opposite door, put his feet up on the ledge and his nose out of the window. He meant to stand like that all the way! He loved the rush of air past his nose.

'Timmy, come down,' said George.

Timmy took no notice. He was happy. It was the holidays again, and he was with everybody he loved. They were going away together. There might be rabbits to chase. Timmy had never yet caught a rabbit, but he went on hoping!

'Now, we're off again!' said Julian, settling into his corner. 'Gosh, how I do like the beginnings of a holiday, getting ready, looking at maps, planning how to get there, and then at last setting off!'

'On a lovely fine day like this!' said Anne. 'George, how did your mother hear of Tremannon Farm?'

'Well, it was Father who heard about it, really,' said George. 'You know Father's got a lot of scientist friends who like to go off to lonely places and work out all kinds of ideas in peace and quiet. Well, one of them went to Tremannon Farm because he heard it was one of the quietest places in the country. Father said his friend went there all skin and bone and came back as plump as a Christmas goose, and Mother said that sounded *just* the place for us to go these hols!'

'She's right!' said Dick. 'I feel a bit skin-and-bonish myself after working hard at school for three months. I could do with fattening up!'

They all laughed. 'You may *feel* skin-and-bonish, but you don't look it,' said Julian. 'You want a bit of exercise. We'll get it, too. We'll walk and bike and bathe and climb . . .'

'And eat,' said George. 'Timmy, you must be polite to farm dogs, or you'll have a bad time.'

'And you must remember that when you go out to play, you'll have to ask the other dogs' permission before you can chase their rabbits,' said Dick solemnly.

Timmy thumped his tail against Dick's knees and opened his mouth to let his tongue hang out. He looked exactly as if he were laughing.

'That's right. Grin at my jokes,' said Dick. 'I'm glad you're coming, Tim, it would be awful without you.'

'He always *has* come with us, on every holiday,' said George. 'And he's shared in every single adventure we've ever had.'

'Good old Timmy,' said Julian. 'Well, he may share in one this time, too. You never know.'

'I'm not going to have any adventures this time,' said Anne in a firm voice. 'I just want a holiday, nothing more. Let's have a jolly good time, and not go on looking for anything strange or mysterious or adventurous.'

'Right,' said Julian. 'Adventures are *off* this time.

Definitely off. And if anything does turn up, we pooh-pooh it and walk off. Is that agreed?'

'Yes,' said Anne.

'All right,' said George, doubtfully.

'Fine,' said Dick.

Julian looked surprised. 'Gosh, you're a poor lot, I must say. Well, I'll fall in with you, if you're all agreed. Even if we find ourselves right in the very middle of Goodness Knows What, we say "No, thank you" and walk away. That's agreed.'

'Well,' began George, 'I'm not sure if . . .' But what she wasn't sure about nobody knew because Timmy chose that moment to fall off the seat. He yelped as he hit the floor with a bang, and immediately went back to his post at the window, putting his head right out.

'We'll have to get him in and shut the windows,' said George. 'He might get something in his eye.'

'No, I'm not going to cook slowly to a cinder in this hot carriage with all the windows shut, not even for the sake of Timmy's eyes,' said Julian, firmly. 'If you can't make him obey you and come inside, he can jolly well get something in his eye.'

However, the problem was solved very quickly because at that moment the train gave a most unearthly shriek and disappeared headlong into utter blackness. Timmy, astounded, fell back into the carriage and tried to get on to George's knee, terrified.

'Don't be a baby, Timmy,' said George. 'It's only a tunnel!

Ju, haul him off me. It's too hot to try and nurse a heavy dog like Timmy. Stop it, Timmy, I tell you it's only a *tunnel*!'

The journey seemed very long. The carriage was so hot, and they had to change twice. Timmy panted loudly and hung his tongue out; George begged the porters for water at each changing place.

They had their lunch with them, but somehow they weren't hungry. They got dirtier and dirtier, and thirstier and thirstier, for they very quickly drank the orangeade they had brought with them.

'Phew!' said Julian, fanning himself with a magazine. 'What wouldn't I give for a bathe? Timmy, don't pant all over me. You make me feel hotter still.'

'What time do we get there?' asked Anne.

'Well, we have to get out at Polwilly Halt,' said Julian. 'That's the nearest place to Tremannon Farm. We bike from there. With luck, we should be there by tea-time.'

'We ought to have brought masses more to drink,' said Dick. 'I feel like a man who's been lost in a sun-scorched desert for weeks.'

They were all extremely glad when they at last arrived at Polwilly Halt. At first they didn't think it was a halt, but it was. It was nothing but a tiny wooden stage built beside the railway. The children sat and waited. They hadn't even seen the little wooden stage or the small sign that said 'Polwilly Halt'.

The sound of impatient feet came along the little platform. The guard's perspiring face appeared at the window.

'Well? Didn't you want to get out here? You going to sit there all day?'

'Gosh! Is this Polwilly?' said Julian, leaping up. 'Sorry. We didn't know it was a halt. We'll be out in half a tick.'

The train started off almost before they had banged the door. They stood there on the funny little staging, all alone save for their four bicycles at the other end. The little halt seemed lonely and lost, set in the midst of rolling fields and rounded hills. Not a building was in sight!

But not far off to the west George's sharp eyes saw something lovely. She pulled Julian's arm. 'Look, the sea! Over there, between the hills, in the dip. Can't you see it? I'm sure it's the sea. What a heavenly blue.'

'It's always that gorgeous blue on the Cornish coast,' said Dick. 'Ah, I feel better when I see that. Come on, let's get our bikes and find our way to Tremannon Farm. If I don't get something to drink soon I shall certainly hang my tongue out, like Timmy.'

They went to get their bikes. Dick felt his back tyre. It was a bit soft, but not too bad. He could easily pump it up again. 'How far is it to Tremannon Farm?' he asked.

Julian looked at his notes. '"Get out at Polwilly Halt. Then bike four miles to Tremannon Farm, along narrow lanes. Tremannon Village is about one mile before you get to the farm." Not too bad. We might get some lemonade, or even an ice-cream, in the village.'

'Woof, woof,' said Timmy, who knew the word ice-cream very well indeed.

'Poor Tim!' said Anne. 'He'll be so hot running beside our bikes. We'd better go slowly.'

'Well, if anyone thinks I'm going to tear along, he can think again,' said Dick. 'I'll go as slowly as you like, Anne!'

They set off with Timmy down a funny little lane, deep-set between high hedges. They went slowly for Timmy's sake. He panted along valiantly. Good old Timmy! He would never give up as long as he was with the four children.

It was about five o'clock and a very lovely evening. They met nobody at all, not even a slow old farm cart. It was even too hot for the birds to sing. No wind blew. There seemed a curious silence and loneliness everywhere.

Julian looked back at the other three with a grin. 'Adventure is in the air! I feel it. We're all set for adventure! But no, we'll turn our backs on it and say: "Away with you!" That's agreed!'

CHAPTER TWO

Tremannon Farm

IT CERTAINLY was a lovely ride to Tremannon Farm. Poppies blew by the wayside in hundreds, and honeysuckle threw its scent out from the hedges as they passed. The corn stood high in the fields, touched with gold already, and splashed with the scarlet of the poppies.

They came to Tremannon Village at last. It was really nothing but a winding street, set with a few shops and houses, and beyond that, straggling out, were other houses. Farther off, set in the hills, were a few farmhouses, their grey stone walls gleaming in the sun.

The four children found the general store and went in. 'Any ice-cream?' said Julian hopefully. But there was none. What a blow! There was orangeade and lemonade, however, quite cool through being kept down in the cellar of the store.

'Are you the folks that old Mrs Penruthlan is having in?' said the village shopkeeper. 'She's expecting you. Foreigners, aren't you?'

'Well, not exactly,' said Julian, remembering that to many Cornish folk anyone was a foreigner who did not belong to Cornwall. 'My mother had a great-aunt who lived in Cornwall all her life. So we're not *exactly* "foreigners", are we?'

'You're foreigners all right,' said the bent little shopkeeper, looking at Julian with bird-like eyes. 'Your talk is foreign-like, too. Like that man Mrs Penruthlan had before. We reckoned he was mad, though he was harmless enough.'

'Really?' said Julian, pouring himself out a third lemonade. 'Well, he was a scientist, and if you're going to be a really *good* one you have to be a bit mad, you know. At least, so I've heard. Golly, this lemonade is good. Can I have another bottle, please?'

The old woman suddenly laughed, sounding just like an amused hen. 'Well, well, Marty Penruthlan's got a fine meal ready for you, but seems like you won't be able to eat a thing, not with all that lemonade splashing about in your innards!'

'Don't say you can hear the splashing,' said Julian earnestly. 'Very bad manners, that! Foreigners' manners, I'm sure. Well, how much do we owe you? That was jolly good lemonade.'

He paid the bill and they all mounted their bicycles once more, having been given minute directions as to how to get to the farm. Timmy set off with them, feeling much refreshed, having drunk steadily for four minutes without stopping.

'I should think you've had about as much water as would fill a horse-trough, Timmy,' Julian told him. 'My word, if this weather holds we're going to get really tanned!'

It was an uphill ride to Tremannon Farm, but they got

there at last. As they cycled through the open gates, a fusillade of barks greeted them, and four large dogs came flying to meet them. Timmy put up his hackles at once and growled warningly. He went completely stiff, and stood there glaring.

A woman came out behind the dogs, her face one large smile. 'Now, Ben; now, Bouncer! Here, Nellie, here! Bad dog, Willy! It's all right, children, that's their way of saying "Welcome to Tremannon Farm!"'

The dogs now stood in a ring round the four children, their tongues out, three collies and one small black Scottie. Timmy eyed them one by one. George had her hand on his collar, just in case he should feel foolhardy all of a sudden and imagine he could take on all four dogs single-handed.

But he didn't. He behaved like a perfect gentleman! His tail wagged politely, and his hackles went down. The little Scottie ran up to him and sniffed his nose. Timmy sniffed back, his tail wagging more vigorously.

Then the three sheepdogs ran up, beautiful collies with plumy tails, and the children heaved sighs of relief to see that the farm dogs evidently were not going to regard Timmy as a 'foreigner'!

'They're all right now,' said Mrs Penruthlan. 'They've introduced themselves to one another. Now come along with me. You must be tired and dirty – and hungry and thirsty. I've high tea waiting for you.'

She didn't talk in the Cornish way. She was pleased to

see them and gave them a grand welcome. She took them upstairs to a bathroom, big but primitive. There was one tap only and that was for cold water. It ran very slowly indeed!

But it was really cold, and was lovely and soft to wash in. The tired children cleaned themselves and combed their hair.

They had two bedrooms between them, one for the girls and one for the boys. They were rather small, with little windows that gave a meagre amount of light, so that the rooms looked dark even in the bright evening sunshine.

They were bare little rooms, with two beds in each, one chair, one chest of drawers, one cupboard and two small rugs. Nothing else! But, oh! the views out of the windows!

Miles and miles of countryside, set with cornfields, pasture land, tall hedges and glimpses of winding lanes; heather was out on some of the hills, blazing purple in the sun; and, gleaming in the distance was the dark blue brilliance of the Cornish sea. Lovely!

'We'll bike to the sea as soon as we can,' said Dick, trying to flatten the few hairs that would stick up straight on the top of his head. 'There are caves on this coast. We'll explore them. I wonder if Mrs Penruthlan would give us picnic lunches so that we can go off for the day when we want to.'

'Sure to,' said Julian. 'She's a pet. I've never felt so

welcome in my life. Are we ready? Come on down, then. I'm beginning to feel very empty indeed.'

The high tea that awaited them was truly magnificent. A huge ham gleaming as pink as Timmy's tongue; a salad fit for a king. In fact, as Dick said, fit for *several* kings, it was so enormous. It had in it everything that anyone could possibly want.

'Lettuce, tomatoes, onions, radishes, mustard and cress, carrot grated up – this *is* carrot, isn't it, Mrs Penruthlan?' said Dick. 'And lashings of hard-boiled eggs.'

There was an enormous tureen of new potatoes, all gleaming with melted butter, scattered with parsley. There was a big bottle of home-made salad cream.

'Look at that cream cheese, too,' marvelled Dick, quite overcome. 'And that fruit cake. And are those drop-scones, or what? Are we supposed to have something of everything, Mrs Penruthlan?'

'Oh, yes,' said the plump little woman, smiling at Dick's pleasure. 'And there's a cherry tart made with our own cherries, and our own cream with it. I know what hungry children are. I've had seven of my own, all married and gone away. So I have to make do with other people's when I can get them.'

'I'm jolly glad you happened to get hold of *us*,' said Dick, beginning on ham and salad. 'Well, we'll keep you busy, Mrs Penruthlan. We've all got big appetites!'

'Ah, I've not met any children yet that could eat like mine,' said Mrs Penruthlan, sounding really sorry. 'Same as I've not met any man that can eat like Mr Penruthlan. He's a fine eater, he is. He'll be in soon.'

'I hope we shall leave enough for him,' said Anne, looking at the ham and the half-empty salad dish. 'No wonder my uncle's friend, the man who came to stay here, went away as fat as butter, Mrs Penruthlan.'

'Oh, the poor man!' said their hostess, who was now filling up their glasses with rich, creamy milk. 'Thin as my husband's old rake, he was, and all his bones showing and creaking. He said "No" to this and "No" to that, but I took no notice of him at all. If he didn't eat his dinner, I'd take his tray away and tidy it up, and then in ten minutes I'd take it back again and say: "Dinner-time, sir, and I hope you're hungry!" And he'd start all over again, and maybe that time he'd really tuck in!'

'But didn't he know you'd already taken him his dinner-tray once?' said Julian, astonished. 'Goodness, he *must* have been a dreamer.'

'I took his tray in three times once,' said Mrs Penruthlan. 'So you be careful in case I do the same kind of thing to you!'

'I should love it!' grinned Julian. 'Yes, please, I'd like some more ham. *And* more salad.'

Footsteps came outside the room, on the stone floor of the hall. The door opened and the farmer himself came in. The children stared at him in awe.

He was a strange and magnificent figure of a man – tall, well over six feet and broadly built. His mane of hair

was black and curly, and his eyes were as black as his hair.

'This is Mr Penruthlan,' said his wife, and the children stood up to shake hands, feeling half afraid of this giant.

He nodded his head and shook hands. His hand was enormous, and was covered with hairs so thick and black that it was like fur. Anne felt that it would be quite nice and soft to stroke, like a cat's back!

He didn't say a word, but sat down and let his wife serve him. 'Well, Mr Penruthlan,' she said, 'and how's the cow getting along?'

'Ah,' said the farmer, taking a plate of ham. The children gazed at the slices in awe, seven or eight of them. Goodness!

'Oh, I'm glad she's all right,' said Mrs Penruthlan, stacking up some dirty plates. 'And is the calf a dear little thing – and what's the colour?'

'Ah,' said Mr Penruthlan, nodding his head.

'Red and white, like its mother! That's good, isn't it?' said his wife, who seemed to have a miraculous way of interpreting his 'Ahs'. 'What shall we call it?'

Everybody badly wanted to say 'Ah', but nobody dared. However, Mr Penruthlan didn't say 'Ah' that time, but something that sounded like 'Ock'.

'Yes, we'll call it Buttercup, then,' said his wife, nodding her head. 'You always have such good ideas, Mr Penruthlan.'

It sounded odd to hear her call her husband by his surname like that, and yet, somehow, the children couldn't imagine this giant of a fellow even *owning* a name like Jack or Jim. They went on with their own meal, enjoying every minute of it, watching Mr Penruthlan shovel in great mouthfuls, and working his way quickly through every dish. Mrs Penruthlan saw them watching him.

'He's a grand eater, isn't he?' she said, proudly. 'So were all my children. When they were at home, I was kept really busy, but now, with only Mr Penruthlan to feed, I feel quite lost. That's why I like people here. You'll tell me if you don't have enough to eat, won't you?'

They all laughed, and Timmy barked. He had had a wonderful meal, too; it was the remains of Mrs Penruthlan's big stock-pot, and was very tasty indeed. He had also got the largest bone he had ever had in his life. The only thing that really worried the well-fed Timmy now was, where could he put the bone out of the way of the farm dogs?

Mr Penruthlan suddenly made a peculiar noise and began undoing a trouser pocket at the back. 'Oo-ah!' he said, and brought out a dirty, folded piece of paper. He handed it to his wife, who unfolded it and read it. She looked up at the children, smiling.

'Now, *here's* a bit of excitement!' she said. 'The Barnies will be along this week! You'll love them.'

'What *are* the Barnies?' asked George, puzzled at Mrs Penruthlan's evident pleasure and excitement.

'Oh, they're travelling players that wander round the countryside and play and act in our big barns,' said Mrs Penruthlan. 'We've no cinemas for miles, you know, so the Barnies are always very welcome.'

'Oh, you call them Barnies because they use your barns for their shows,' said Anne, seeing light. 'Yes, we shall love to see them, Mrs Penruthlan. Will they play in *your* barn?'

'Yes. We'll have all the village here when the Barnies come,' said Mrs Penruthlan, her cheeks going red with delight. 'And maybe people from Trelin Village, too. Now, there's a treat for you!'

'Ah,' said Mr Penruthlan, and nodded his great head. Evidently he liked the Barnies, too. He gave a sudden laugh and said something short and quite incomprehensible.

'He says you'll like Clopper the horse,' said his wife, laughing. 'The things he does! The way he sits down and crosses his legs. Well, you wait and see. That horse!'

This sounded rather astonishing. A horse that sat down and crossed its legs? Julian winked at Dick. They would most certainly see the Barnies!

CHAPTER THREE

The first evening

AFTER THEIR wonderful high tea the four children didn't really feel like doing very much. Dick thought he ought to mend his puncture, but wasn't sure that he could bend over properly!

Mrs Penruthlan began to stack the dishes and clear away. George and Anne offered to help her. 'Well, that's kind of you, Anne and Georgina,' said the farmer's wife. 'But you're tired tonight. You can give me a hand some other time. By the way, which of you is which?'

'I'm Anne,' said Anne.

'And I'm George, not Georgina,' said George. 'So please don't call me that. I hate it. I always wanted to be a boy, so I only like to be called George.'

'What she really means is that she won't answer unless you *do* call her George,' said Anne. 'Well, if you really are sure you don't need our help, we'll go out with the boys.'

So out they went, George really looking far more like a boy than a girl, with her grey jeans and shirt and her short, curly hair and freckled face. She put her hands in her pockets and tried to walk like Dick!

Dick soon found his puncture and mended it. Mr Penruthlan came by with some straw for his cow and new calf. The boys watched him in awe, for he was carrying almost a wagonload of straw tied up in bales! What strength he had! He nodded to them and passed without a word.

'Why doesn't he talk?' wondered Dick. 'I suppose all his seven children take after their talkative mother, and he never had a chance to get a word in. And it's too late now, he's forgotten how to!'

They laughed. 'What a giant of a man,' said Julian. 'I hope I grow as big as that.'

'I don't. I'd hate to have my bare feet poking out of the bottom of the bed every night,' said Dick. 'There. I've finished that puncture. See the nail that made it? I must have run over it on the way to the station this morning.'

'Do look at Timmy,' said Julian. 'He's having the time of his life with those farm dogs, acting just like a puppy!'

So he was, bounding here and there, rushing round the dogs and then rushing away, jumping on first one and then another, till they all went down in an excited, yapping scrum, the little Scottie doing his best to keep up with everything!

'Timmy's going to have a good time here,' said Dick. 'And he'll soon lose his beautiful waistline if he eats as well as we do!'

'We'll take him on long bike rides,' said Julian. 'He can't grow much tummy if he runs for miles!'

The girls came up just then. A few feet behind trotted an odd little boy, bare-footed, shock-headed and very dirty.

'Who's this?' said Dick.

'I don't know,' said George. 'He suddenly appeared behind us and has been following us ever since. He just won't go away!'

The boy wore a ragged pair of jeans and an old pullover. He was black-eyed and burnt by the sun. He stood a few feet away and stared.

'Who are you?' said Dick. The boy went back a few steps in fright. He shook his head.

'I said, who are you?' said Dick again. 'Or, if you prefer it another way, what's your name?'

'Yan,' said the boy.

'Yan?' said Dick. 'That's a funny name.'

'He probably means *Jan*,' said George.

The boy nodded. 'Yes. Yan,' he said.

'All right, Jan. You can go now,' said Anne.

'I want to stay,' said the boy solemnly.

And stay he did, following them about everywhere, gazing at all they did with the utmost curiosity, as if he had never in his life seen children before!

'He's like a mosquito,' said Dick. 'Always buzzing around. I'm getting tired of it. Hey, Yan!'

'Yes?'

'Clear out now! Understand? Get away, go, run off, vamoose, bunk, scoot!' explained Dick sternly. Yan stared.

Mrs Penruthlan came out and heard all this. 'Jan bothering you?' she said. 'He's as full of curiosity as a cat.

Go home, Jan. Take this to your old grandad. And here's some for you.'

Jan came up eagerly and took the packet of food Mrs Penruthlan held out to him, and the slice of cake. He ran off without a word, his bare feet making no sound.

'Who is he?' asked George. 'What a little scarecrow!'

'He's a poor little thing,' said the farmer's wife. 'He's got no kith or kin except for his old great-grandad, and there's more than eighty years between them! The old man is our shepherd. Do you see that hill over there, well, he's got a hut on the other side, and there he lives, winter and summer alike, and that child with him.'

'Surely he ought to go to school?' said Julian. 'Perhaps he does?'

'No,' said Mrs Penruthlan. 'He plays truant nearly all the time. You ought to go and talk to his old great-grandad. His father was one of the Wreckers on this coast, and he can tell you some strange stories about those dreadful days.'

'We'll certainly go and talk to him,' said Dick. 'I'd forgotten that this Cornish coast was the haunt of Wreckers. They shone false lights to bring ships in close to shore, so that they would be smashed to pieces on the rocks, didn't they?'

'Yes, and then they robbed the poor, groaning ship when she was helpless,' said Mrs Penruthlan. 'And it's said they paid no heed to the drowning folk, either. Those were wicked days.'

'How far is it to cycle to the sea?' said George. 'I can see it from my bedroom window.'

'Oh, it won't take you more than ten minutes,' said the farmer's wife. 'Go tomorrow, if you like. You all look very tired now. Why don't you take a short walk and go to bed? I'll have a snack ready for you when you come in.'

'Oh, we couldn't *possibly* eat any more tonight, thank you,' said Dick, hurriedly. 'But the walk is quite a good idea. We'd like to see round the farm.'

Mrs Penruthlan left them, and Dick looked round at the others. 'A snack!' he said. 'I never thought I'd groan at the thought. But I bet Mr Penruthlan will want a jolly good snack when he comes in. Come on, let's go up by those sheds.'

They went off together, Timmy following behind with his four friends, their tails wagging amiably. It was still a lovely evening, and a cool breeze came down from the hills, making it lovelier still. The children wandered round, enjoying the familiar farm sights, the ducks on the pond, a few hens still clucking round, the grey sheep dotting the hills. Cows were peacefully grazing and an old farm horse came to a gate to stare at them.

They rubbed his velvety nose, and he bent down to sniff at Timmy, whom he didn't know. Timmy sniffed solemnly back.

They went into the barns and looked around, big, dark, sweet-smelling places, stored with many things. Dick was sure that the biggest one would be the one used by the Barnies. What fun!

'I bet they'll be pretty awful, but good fun, all the same,' he said. 'It must be grand to wander round the countryside with all your belongings done up in a parcel or two, and then amaze the country people with your songs and dances and acting. I wouldn't mind trying it myself! I'm pretty good at a spot of conjuring, for instance!'

'Yes, you are,' said Anne. 'Wouldn't it be fun if we could give a little show too, if the Barnies would let us join them just for one evening?'

'We wouldn't be allowed to because we're "foreigners",' said Dick grinning. 'I say, what's that, over there, behind that sack?'

Timmy at once went over to see, and stood there barking. The others went over to look.

'It's that kid Yan again,' said Julian in disgust. He pulled the boy out from his hiding place. 'What are you following us around for, you little idiot?' he demanded. 'We don't like it. See? Go and find your old grandad before you eat all the food Mrs Penruthlan gave you. Go on now.'

He pushed the boy out of the barn, and watched him go into the next field. 'That's got rid of him,' he said. 'I think he's a bit simple. We'll go and see that grandad of his one day and see if he really *has* got anything interesting to say about the old Wreckers.'

'Let's go back now,' said Dick, yawning. 'I've seen enough of this place to know I'm going to like it a lot. I'm going to like my bed tonight too. Coming, Ju?'

They all felt the same as Dick. His yawn had set them yawning too, and they thought longingly of bed. They made their way back to the farm, followed closely by Timmy at their heels, and the other four dogs a respectful distance away.

They said good night to the two Penruthlans, who were sitting peacefully listening to their radio. Mrs Penruthlan wanted to come up with them but they wouldn't let her.

They said good night to the farmer, who grunted 'Ah!' without even looking at them, and went on listening to the radio programme. Then up the stairs they went, and into their rooms.

When Julian was in bed and almost asleep he heard a scrabbling noise outside his window. He half-opened his eyes, and listened. He hoped it wasn't rats! If it was, Anne would probably hear them too, and be scared, and Timmy would hear them and bark the place down!

The scrabbling noise came again. Julian spoke softly to Dick. 'Dick! Are you awake? Did you hear that noise at the window?'

No answer. Dick was sound asleep, dreaming that he had a puncture in his foot and couldn't walk till it was mended! Julian lay and listened. Yes, there it was again, and now surely there was someone trying to peep in at the tiny window?

He slid out of bed and went to the side of the window.

Thick ivy grew outside. Somebody was still there for Julian could see the leaves shaking.

He put his head suddenly out of the window, and a scared face, quite close to his, stared in fright.

'Yan! What do you think you're doing?' said Julian, fiercely. 'I'll get very angry with you if you go on like this, staring and peeping! What's so strange about us?'

Yan was terrified. He suddenly slithered down the ivy like a cat, landed with a slight thud on the ground and then ran off into the twilight at top speed.

'I hope he's not going to follow us around all the time,' thought Julian, getting into bed again. 'I'll teach him a lesson if he does. Blow him! Now he's made me wide awake!'

But it wasn't long before Julian was sleeping as soundly as Dick. Neither of them stirred until a cock outside their window decided that it was time the whole world woke up, and crowed at the top of his voice.

'Cock-a-doodle-DOO!'

The boys woke with a jump. The early sun streamed into the room, and Julian glanced at his watch. How early it was! And yet he could hear movements downstairs that told him Mrs Penruthlan was up and about, and so was her giant of a husband.

He fell asleep again, and was awakened by a loud knock at his door, and Mrs Penruthlan's voice. 'It's half past seven, and breakfast will be on the table for you at eight. Wake up!'

How lovely to wake in a strange place at the beginning of a holiday, to think of bathing and biking and picnicking and eating and drinking, forgetting all about exams and rules and punishments! The four children and Timmy stretched themselves and stared at the sunshine outside. What a day!

Downstairs breakfast awaited them. 'Super!' said Dick, eyeing the bacon and fried eggs, the cold ham, and the home-made jam and marmalade. 'Mrs Penruthlan, your seven children must have been very sorry to marry and leave home. I feel, if I'd been one of them, I'd have stayed with you for the rest of my life!'

CHAPTER FOUR

Down in the cove

THE FIRST three days at Tremannon Farm were lazy uneventful days, full of sunshine, good food, dogs – and of little Yan.

He really was a perfect nuisance. The four children seemed to have a real fascination for him, and he trailed them everywhere, following them bare-footed. He turned up behind hedges, along lanes, at their picnicking places, his dark eyes watching them intently.

'What's the good of telling him to go?' groaned Julian. 'He disappears behind one hedge and appears out of another. You'd think he'd get bored, doing this shadowing business all the time. What's the point of it, anyway?'

'No point,' said George. 'Just curiosity. What I can't understand is why Timmy puts up with him. You'd think he'd bark or growl or something, but he's quite silly with Yan, lets him play with him, and roll him over as if he was a mad puppy.'

'Well, I'm going to find this great-grandad of his tomorrow, and tell him to keep Yan with him,' said Julian. 'He's maddening. I feel I want to swat him like a gnat, always buzzing round us. Gosh, there he is again!'

So he was. A pair of dark eyes were gazing round a tree-trunk, half hidden by a sheaf of leaves. Timmy bounded up to him in glee, and made such a fuss of Yan that George was quite disgusted.

'Timmy! Come here!' she called, imperiously. 'Don't you understand that you ought to chase Yan away when he comes and not encourage him? I'm ashamed of you!'

Timmy put his tail down and went to her. He sat down beside her with a bump. Dick laughed.

'He's sulking! He won't look at you, George! He's turning his head away on purpose!'

Julian chased Yan away, threatening him with all sorts of things if he caught him, but the boy was as fast as a hare, and seemed suddenly to disappear into thin air. He had a wonderful way of vanishing, and an equally remarkable way of appearing again.

'I don't like that kid,' said Julian. 'He makes me shiver down my back whenever I see him suddenly peeping somewhere.'

'He can't be a bad kid, though, because Timmy likes him so much,' said Anne, who had great faith in Timmy's judgement. 'Timmy never likes anyone horrid.'

'Well, he's made a mistake this time, then,' said George, who was cross with Timmy. 'He's being very stupid. I'm not pleased with you, Timmy!'

'Let's go down to the sea and bathe,' said Dick. 'We'll go on our bikes and Yan won't be able to pop up and watch us there.'

They took their bicycles and rode off to the coast. Mrs Penruthlan made them sandwiches and gave them fruit cake and drinks to take with them. They saw Yan watching them from behind a hedge as they went.

They took the road to the sea. It was no more than a narrow lane, and wound about like a stream, twisting and turning so that they couldn't get up any speed at all.

'Look – the sea!' cried Dick as they rounded one last bend. The lane had run down between two high, rocky cliffs, and in front of them was a cove into which raced enormous breakers, throwing spray high into the air.

They left their bicycles at the top of the cove, and went behind some big rocks to change into bathing things. When they came out, Julian looked at the sea. It was calm beyond the rocks, but over these the waters raged fiercely and it was impossible to venture in.

They walked a little way round the cliffs, and came to a great pool lying in a rock hollow. 'Just the thing!' cried George and plunged in. 'Gosh, it's cold!'

It should have been hot from the sun, but every now and again an extra large wave broke right into the pool itself, bringing in cooler water. It was fun when that happened. The four of them swam to their hearts' content, and Timmy had a fine time too.

They picnicked on the rocks, with spray flying round them, and then went to explore round the foot of the cliffs.

'This is exciting,' said George. 'Caves, and more caves, and yet more caves! And cove after cove, all as lovely as the one before. I suppose when the tide's in, all these coves are shoulder-high in water.'

'My word, yes,' said Julian, who was keeping a very sharp eye indeed on the tide. 'And a good many of these caves would be flooded too. No wonder Mrs Penruthlan warned us so solemnly about the tides here! I wouldn't want to try and climb up these cliffs if we were caught!'

Anne looked up and shivered. They were so very steep and high. They frowned down at her as if to say 'We stand no nonsense from anyone! So look after yourself!'

'Well, I'm blessed! Look there, isn't that the tiresome

little wretch of a Yan?' said Dick, suddenly. He pointed to a rock covered with seaweed. Peeping from behind it was Yan!

'He must have run all the way here, and found us,' said Julian in disgust. 'Well, we'll leave him here. It's time we went. The tide's coming in. It'll serve him right to find us gone as soon as he arrives. He must be mad!'

'Do you think he knows about the tide?' said Anne, looking worried. 'I mean, knows that it's coming in and might catch him?'

'Of course he knows!' said Julian. 'Don't be silly. But we'll wait and have our tea at the top part of the cove, if you like. That's the only way back, if he wants to escape the tide, short of climbing the cliff, which no one would be mad enough to try!'

They had put aside some cake and biscuits for their tea, and they found a good picnicking place at the top of the cove where they had left their bicycles. They settled down to munch the solid fruit cake that Mrs Penruthlan had given them. There was no doubt about it, she was a wonderful cook!

The tide swept in at a great rate, and soon the noise of enormous waves pounding on the rocks grew louder. 'Yan hasn't appeared yet,' said Anne. 'Do you think he's all right?'

'He must be having a good old wetting if he's still there,' said Dick. 'I think we'd better go and see. Much as I dislike him I don't want him to be drowned.'

The two boys went down the cove as far as they could, peering round the cliff to where they had seen Yan hiding. But how different it all looked now!

'Gosh, the beach is gone already!' said Julian, startled. 'I can see how easily anyone could get caught by the tide now. See that last wave, it swept right into that cave we explored!'

'What's happened to Yan?' said Dick. 'He's nowhere to be seen. He didn't come out of the cove; we've been sitting there all the time. Where is he?'

Dick spoke urgently, and Julian began to feel scared too. He hesitated. Should they wade over the rocks a little way? The next wave decided him. It would be folly to do any such thing! Another wave like that and both he and Dick would be flung off the rock they were standing on!

'Look out, here comes an even bigger one!' yelled Julian, and the two boys leapt off their rock and raced back up the cove. Even so, the wave lapped right up to their feet.

They went back to the girls. 'Can't see him anywhere,' said Julian, speaking more cheerfully than he felt. 'The whole beach is covered with the tide now, more than covered. The lower caves are full too.'

'He – he won't be drowned, will he?' said Anne, fearfully.

'Oh, I expect he can look after himself,' said Julian. 'He's used to this coast. Come on, it's time we went.'

They all rode off, Timmy running beside their bicycles.

Nobody said anything. They couldn't help feeling worried about Yan. Whatever could have happened to him?

They arrived at the farm and put their bicycles away. They went in to find Mrs Penruthlan. They told her about Yan, and how he had disappeared.

'You don't think he might have been swept off his feet and drowned, do you?' asked Anne.

Mrs Penruthlan laughed. 'Good gracious, no! That boy knows his way about the countryside and the seashore blindfold. He's cleverer than you think. He never misses anything! He's a poor little thing, but he looks after himself all right!'

This was rather comforting. Perhaps Yan would turn up again, with his dark eyes fixed unblinking on them!

After a high tea as good as any they had had, they went for a walk down the honeysuckle-scented lanes, accompanied as usual by the five dogs. They sat on a stile, and Dick handed round some barley sugar.

'Look!' said George suddenly. 'Do you see what I see? Look!' She nodded her head towards an oak tree in the hedge, not far off. The others stared up into it.

Two dark eyes stared back. Yan! He had followed them as usual, and had hidden himself to watch them. Anne was so tremendously relieved to see him that she called to him in delight.

'Oh, Yan! Have a barley sugar?'

Yan slithered down the tree at top speed and came up. He held out his hand for the barley sugar. For the first time he smiled, and his dirty, sullen face lit up enchantingly. Anne stared at him. Why, he was all right after all! His eyes shone and twinkled, and a dimple came in each cheek.

'Here you are, here's a couple more sweets for you,' Dick said, very glad to see that the small boy hadn't been drowned. Yan almost snatched them from him! It was plain that he very, very seldom had any sweets! Timmy was making a fuss of him as usual. He lay down on his back and rolled over Yan's feet. He licked his fingers, and jumped up at him, almost knocking the boy down. Yan laughed and fell on Timmy, rolling over and over with him. Julian, Dick and Anne watched and laughed.

But George was not pleased. Timmy was her dog, and she didn't like him to make a fuss of anyone she disapproved of. She was glad that Yan was safe but she still didn't like him! So she scowled, and Julian nudged Dick to make him see the scowl. George saw him and scowled worse than ever.

'You'll be sorry you gave him sweets,' she said. 'He'll be round us worse than ever now.'

Yan came up after a minute or two, sucking all three sweets at once, so that his right cheek was very swollen indeed.

'Come and see my grandad,' he said, earnestly, talking even worse than usual because of the sweets. 'I've told him about you all. He'll tell you many things.'

He stared at them all seriously. 'Grandad likes sweets too,' he added, solemnly. 'Yes. Yes, he does.'

Julian laughed. 'All right. We'll come and see him tomorrow afternoon. Now you clear off or you won't get any more sweets. Understand?'

'Yes,' said Yan, nodding his head. He took the three sweets out of his mouth, looked at them to see how much he had sucked them, and then put them back again.

'Clear off now,' said Julian again. 'But wait a bit, I've just thought; how did you get away from that beach this afternoon? Did you climb that cliff?'

'No,' said Yan, shifting his sweets to the other cheek. 'I came the Wreckers' Way. My grandad showed me.'

He was off and away before anyone could ask him another question. The four looked at one another. 'Did you hear that?' said Julian. 'He went the Wreckers' Way. What's that, do you suppose? We must have been on one of the beaches the Wreckers used long, long ago.'

'Yes. But how did he get off that beach, and away into safety?' said Dick. 'I'd like to know more about the Wreckers' Way! I certainly think we'd better pay a visit to old Great-Grandad tomorrow. He might have some very interesting things to tell us.'

'Well, we'll go and see him,' said George, getting up. 'But just you remember what I said. Yan will pester us more than ever now we've encouraged him.'

'Oh well, he doesn't seem such a bad kid after all,' said Dick, remembering that sudden smile and the eager acceptance of a few sweets. 'And if he persuades Grandad to let us into the secret of Wreckers' Way, we might have some fun doing a bit of exploring. Don't you think so, Ju?'

'It might even lead to an adventure,' said Julian, laughing at Anne's serious face. 'Cheer up, Anne. I can't even *smell* an adventure in Tremannon. I'm just pulling your leg!'

'I think you're wrong,' said Anne. 'If *you* can't smell one somewhere, I can. I don't want to, but I can!'

CHAPTER FIVE

Yan – and his grandad

THE NEXT day was Sunday. It made no difference to the time that the two Penruthlans got up, however. As Mrs Penruthlan said, the cows and horses, hens and ducks didn't approve of late Sunday breakfasts! They wanted attending to at exactly the same time each day!

'Will you be going to church?' asked Mrs Penruthlan. 'It's a beautiful walk across the fields to Tremannou Church, and you'd like Parson. He's a good man, he is.'

'Yes, we're all going,' said Julian. 'We can tie Timmy up outside. He's used to that. And we thought we'd go up and see your old shepherd this afternoon, Mrs Penruthlan, and see what tales he has to tell.'

'Yan will show you the way,' said the farmer's wife, bustling off to her cooking. 'I'll get you a fine Sunday dinner. Do you like fresh fruit salad with cream?'

'You bet!' said everyone at once.

'Can't we help you to do something?' said Anne. 'I've just seen all the peas you're going to shell. Piles of them! And don't you want help with those redcurrants? I love getting the currants off their stalks with a fork!'

'Well, you'll have a few odd minutes before you go

to church, I expect,' said Mrs Penruthlan, looking pleased. 'It *would* be a bit of help today. But the boys needn't help.'

'I like that!' said George, indignantly. 'How unfair! Why shouldn't they, just because they're boys?'

'Don't fly off the handle, George,' grinned Dick. 'We're going to help, don't worry. We like podding peas too! You're not going to have all the treats!'

Dick had a very neat way of turning the tables on George when he saw her flying into a tantrum. She smiled unwillingly. She was always jealous of the boys because she so badly wanted to be one herself, and wasn't! She hitched up her jeans, and went to get a pan of peas to shell.

Soon the noise of the popping of pods was to be heard, a very pleasant noise, Anne thought. The four of them sat on the big kitchen step, out in the sun, with Timmy sitting beside them, watching with interest. He didn't stay with them long though.

Up came his four friends, the little Scottie trotting valiantly behind, trying to keep up with the longer legs of the others. 'Woof!' said the biggest collie. Timmy wagged his tail politely, but didn't stir.

'Woof!' said the collie again, and pranced around invitingly.

'Timmy! He says "Will you come and play?" ' said George. 'Aren't you going? You aren't the least help with shelling peas, and you keep breathing down my neck.'

Timmy gave George a flying lick and leapt off the step joyfully. He pounced on the Scottie, rolled him over, and then took on all three collies at once. They were big, strong dogs, but no match for Timmy!

'Look at him,' said George, proudly. 'He can manage the whole lot single-handed.'

'Single-footed!' said Dick. 'He's faster than even that biggest collie and stronger than the whole lot. Good old Tim. He's come in jolly useful in some of our adventures!'

'I've no doubt he will again,' said Julian. 'I'd rather have one Timmy than two police dogs.'

'I should think his ears are burning, the way we're talking about him!' said Anne. 'Oh, sorry, Dick, that pod popped unexpectedly!'

'That's the second lot of peas you've shot all over me,' said Dick, scrabbling inside his shirt. 'I *must* just find one that went down my neck, or I shall be fidgeting all through church.'

'You always do,' said Anne. 'Look – isn't that Yan?'

It was! He came sidling up, looking as dirty as ever, and gave them a quick smile that once more entirely changed his sullen little face. He held out his hand, palm upwards, and said something.

'What's he saying?' said Dick. 'Oh, he's asking for a sweet.'

'Don't give him one,' said Julian, quickly. 'Don't turn him into a little beggar. Make him *work* for a sweet this

time. Yan, if you want a sweet, you can help pod these peas.'

Mrs Penruthlan appeared at once. 'But see he washes those filthy hands first,' she commanded, and disappeared again. Yan looked at his hands, then put them under his armpits.

'Go and wash them,' said Julian. But Yan shook his head, and sat down a little way away from them.

'All right. Don't wash your hands. Don't shell the peas. Don't have a sweet,' said George.

Yan scowled at George. He didn't seem to like her any more than she liked him. He waited till someone split a pod, and a few peas shot out on the ground instead of into the dish. Then he darted at them, picked them up and ate them. He was as quick as a cat.

'My grandad says come and see him,' announced Yan. 'I'll take you.'

'Right,' said Julian. 'We'll come this afternoon. We'll get Mrs Penruthlan to pack us up a basket, and we'll have a tea in the hills. You can share it if you wash your hands and face.'

'I shouldn't think he's ever washed himself in his life,' said George. 'Oh, here's Timmy come back. I *will* not have him fawn round that dirty little boy. Here, Timmy!'

But Timmy darted to Yan with the greatest delight and pawed at him to come and have a game. They began to roll over and over like two puppies.

'If you're going to church, you'd better get ready,' said Mrs Penruthlan, appearing again, this time with arms floured up to the elbow. 'My, what a lot of peas you've done for me!'

'I wish I had time to do the redcurrants,' said Anne. 'We've practically finished the peas, anyway, Mrs Penruthlan. We've done thousands, I should think!'

'Ah, Mr Penruthlan is very fond of peas,' said the farmer's wife. 'He can eat a whole tureen at one sitting.'

She disappeared again. The children went to get

ready for church, and then off they went. It certainly was a lovely walk over the fields, with honeysuckle trailing everywhere!

The church was small and old and lovely. Yan went with them, trailing behind, right to the church door. When he saw George tying Timmy up to a railing, he sat down beside him and looked pleased. George didn't look pleased, however. Now Timmy and Yan would play about together all the time she was in church! How annoying!

The church was cool and dark, except for three lovely stained-glass windows through which the sun poured, its brilliance dimmed by the colours of the glass. 'Parson' was as nice as Mrs Penruthlan had said, a simple friendly person whose words were listened to by everyone, from an old, old woman bent almost double in a corner to a solemn-eyed five-year-old clutching her mother's hand.

It was dazzling to come out into the sun again from the cool dimness of the church. Timmy barked a welcome. Yan was still there, sitting with his arm round Timmy's neck. He gave them his sudden smile, and untied Timmy, who promptly went mad and tore out of the churchyard at sixty miles an hour. He always did that when he had been tied up.

'Come and see Grandad,' said Yan to Dick, and pulled at his arm.

'This afternoon,' said Dick. 'You can show us the way. Come after dinner.'

So, after the children had had a dinner of cold boiled beef and carrots, with a dumpling each, and 'lashings' of peas and new potatoes, followed by a truly magnificent fruit salad and cream, Yan appeared at the door to take them to see his grandad.

'Did you see the amount of peas that Mr Penruthlan got through?' said Anne, in awe. 'I should think he really *did* manage a tureen all to himself. I wish he'd say something besides "Ah" and "Ock" and the other peculiar sounds he makes. Conversation is awfully difficult with him.'

'Is Yan taking you up to Grandad?' called Mrs Penruthlan. 'I'll put a few cakes in the basket for him, too, then, and for Grandad.'

'*Don't* make us up a big tea,' begged Dick. 'We only want a snack, just to keep us going till high tea.'

But all the same the basket was quite heavy when Mrs Penruthlan had finished packing it!

It was a long walk over the fields to the shepherd's hut. Yan led the way proudly. They crossed the fields and climbed stiles, walked up narrow cart-paths, and at last came to a cone-shaped hill on which sheep grazed peacefully. Half-grown lambs, wearing their woolly coats, unlike the shorn sheep, gambolled here and there – then remembered that they were nearly grown up, and walked sedately.

The old shepherd was sitting outside his hut, smoking a clay pipe. He wasn't very big, and he seemed shrivelled up, like an apple stored too long. But there was still sweetness in him, and the children liked him at once. He had Yan's sudden smile, that lit up eyes that were still as blue as the summer sky above.

His face had a thousand wrinkles that creased and ran into one another when he smiled. His shaggy eyebrows, curly beard and hair were all grey, as grey as the woolly coats of the sheep he had lived with all his life.

'You're welcome,' he said, in his slow Cornish voice. 'Yan told me about you.'

'We've brought our tea to share with you,' said Dick. 'We'll have it later on. Is it true that your father was one of the Wreckers in the old days?'

The old fellow nodded his head. Julian got out a bag of boiled sweets, and offered them to the old man. He took one eagerly. Yan edged up at once and was given one too.

Judging by the crunching that went on old Grandad still had plenty of teeth! When the sweet had gone, he began to talk. He talked slowly and simply, almost as Yan might have done, and sometimes paused to find a word he wanted.

'Living with sheep all his life doesn't make for easy talking,' thought Julian, interested in this old man with the wise, keen eyes. 'He must be much more at home with sheep than with human beings.'

Grandad certainly had some interesting things to tell them: dreadful things, Anne thought.

'You've seen the rocks down on Tremannon coast,'

began Grandad. 'Wicked rocks they are, hungry for ships and men. Many a ship has been wrecked on purpose! Ay, you can look disbelieving-like, but it's true.'

'How did they get wrecked on purpose?' asked Dick. 'Were they lured here by a false light, or something?'

The old man lowered his voice as if he was afraid of being overheard.

'Way back up the coast, more than a hundred years ago, there was a light set to guide the ships that sail round here,' said Grandad. 'They were to sail towards that light, and then hug the coast and avoid the rocks that stood out to sea. They were safe then. But, on wild nights, a light was set two miles farther down the coast, to bemuse lost ships, and drag them to the rocks round Tremannon coves.'

'How wicked!' said Anne and George together. 'How *could* men do that?'

'It's amazing what men will do,' said Grandad, nodding his head. 'Take my old dad now – a kind man he was and went to church, and took me with him. But he was the one that set the false light burning every time, and sent men to watch the ship coming in on the rocks – crashing over them and breaking into pieces.'

'Did you – did you ever see a ship crashing to its death?' asked Dick, imagining the groaning of the sailing ships, and the groaning of the men flung into the raging sea.

'Ay, I did,' said Grandad, his eyes taking on a very faraway look. 'I was sent to the cove with the men, and had to hold a lantern to bemuse the ship again when she came to the rocks. Poor thing, she groaned like a live thing when she ran into those wicked rocks, and split into pieces. And the next day I went to the cove to help get the goods that were scattered all around the cove. There were lots drowned that night, and . . .'

'Don't tell us about that,' said Dick, feeling sick. 'Where did they flash the false light from? From these hills, or from the cliff somewhere?'

'I'll show you where my dad flashed it from,' said Grandad, and he got up slowly. 'There's only one place on these hills where you could see the light flashing. The Wreckers had to find somewhere well hidden, so that their wicked light couldn't be seen from inland, or the police would stop it, but it could be seen plainly by any ship on the sea near this coast!'

He took them round his hill, and then pointed towards the coast. Set between two hills there the roof of a house could just be seen, and from it rose a tower. It could only be seen from that one spot! Dick took a few steps to each side of it, and at once the house disappeared behind one or other of the hills on each side of it.

'I was the only one who ever knew the false light could be seen from inland,' said Grandad, pointing with his pipe-stem towards the far-off square tower. 'I was watching lambs one night up here, and I saw the light flashing. 'And I heard there was a ship wrecked down in Tremannon cove that night so I reckoned it was the Wreckers at work.'

'Did you often see the light flashing over there, when

you watched the sheep?' asked George.

'Oh yes, many a time,' said the shepherd. 'And always on wild, stormy nights, when ships were labouring along, and in trouble, looking for some light to guide them into shore. Then a light would flare out over there, and I'd say to myself "Now may the Good God help those sailors tonight, for it's sure that nobody else will!"'

'How horrible!' said George, quite appalled at such wickedness. 'You must be glad that you never see that false light shining there on stormy nights now!'

Grandad looked at George, and his eyes were scared and strange. He lowered his voice and spoke to George as if she were a boy.

'Young man,' he said, 'that light still flares on dark and stormy nights. The place is a ruin, and jackdaws build in the tower. But three times this year I've seen that light again! Come a stormy night it'll flare again! I know it in my bones, I know it in my bones!'

CHAPTER SIX

A strange tale

THE FOUR children shivered suddenly in the hot sun, as they listened to the shepherd's strange words. Were they true? Did the Wreckers' light still flash in the old tower on wild and stormy nights? But why should it? Surely no Wreckers any longer did their dreadful work on this lonely rocky coast?

Dick voiced the thoughts of the others. 'But surely there are no wrecks on this coast now? Isn't there a good lighthouse farther up, to warn ships to keep right out to sea?'

Grandad nodded his grey head. 'Yes. There's a lighthouse, and there's not been a wreck along this coast for more years than I can remember. But I tell you that light flares up just as it used to do. I see it with my own eyes, and there's nothing wrong with them yet!'

'I've seen it too,' put in Yan, suddenly.

Grandad looked at Yan, annoyed. 'You hold your tongue,' he commanded. 'You've never seen the light. You sleep like a babe at night.'

'I've seen it,' said Yan, obstinately, and moved out of Grandad's way quickly as the old man raised his hand to cuff the small boy.

Dick changed the subject. 'Grandad, do you know anything about the Wreckers' Way?' he asked. 'Is it a secret way to get down to the coves from inland? Was it used by the Wreckers?'

Grandad frowned. 'That's a secret,' he said shortly. 'My dad showed it to me, and I swore I would never tell. We all had to swear and promise that.'

'But Yan here said that you taught the way to him,' said Dick, puzzled.

Yan promptly removed himself from the company and disappeared round a clump of bushes. His old great-grandad glared round at the disappearing boy.

'Yan! That boy! He doesn't know anything about the Wreckers' Way. It's lost and forgotten by every man living. I'm the last one left who knows of it. Yan! He's dreaming! Maybe he's heard tell of an old Wreckers' Way, but that's all.'

'Oh!' said Dick, disappointed. He had hoped that Grandad would tell them the old way, and then they could go and explore it. Perhaps they could go and search for it, anyhow! It would be fun to do that.

Julian came back to the question of the light flashing from the old tower by the coast. He was puzzled. 'Who could possibly flash that light?' he said to Grandad. 'You say the place is a ruin. Are you sure it wasn't lightning you saw? You said it came on a wild and stormy night.'

'It wasn't lightning,' said the old man shortly. 'I first saw that light near ninety years ago, and I tell you I saw it again three times this year, same place, same light, same weather! And if you told me it wasn't flashed by mortal hands, I'd believe you.'

There was a silence after this extraordinary statement. Anne looked over towards the far-off tower that showed just between the two distant hills. How strange that this spot where they were standing was the only place from which the tower could be seen from inland. The Wreckers had been clever to choose a spot like that to flash a light from. No one but old Grandad up on the hills could possibly have seen the light and guessed what was going on, no one but the callous Wreckers themselves.

Grandad delved deep into more memories stored in his mind. He poured them out, tales of the old days, strange unbelievable stories. One was about an old woman who was said to be a witch. The things she did!

The four stared at the old shepherd, marvelling to think they were, in a way, linked with the witches, the Wreckers and the killers of long-ago days, through this old, old man.

Yan appeared again as soon as Julian opened the tea-basket. They had now gone back to the hut, and sat outside in the sunshine, surrounded by nibbling sheep. One or two of the half-grown lambs came up, looking hot in their unshorn woolly coats. They nosed round the old shepherd, and he rubbed their woolly noses.

'These are lambs I fed from a bottle,' he explained. 'They always remember. Go away now, Woolly. Cake's wasted on you.'

Yan wolfed quite half the tea. He gave Anne a quick grin of pure pleasure, showing both his dimples at once. She smiled back. She liked this funny little boy now, and felt sorry for him. She was sure that his old Grandad didn't give him enough to eat!

The church bells began to ring, and the sun was now sliding down the sky. 'We must go,' said Julian, reluctantly. 'It's quite a long walk back. Thanks for a most interesting afternoon, Grandad. I expect you'll be glad to be rid of us now, and smoke your pipe in peace with your sheep around you.'

'Ay, I will,' said Grandad, truthfully. 'I'm one for my own company, and I like to think my own thoughts. Long thoughts they are, too, going back nearly a hundred years. If I want to talk, I talk to my sheep. It's rare and wonderful how they listen.'

The children laughed, but Grandad was quite solemn, and meant every word he said. They packed up the basket, and said goodbye to the old man.

'Well, what do you think he meant when he talked about the light still flashing in the old tower?' said Dick, as they went over the hills back to the farm. 'What an extraordinary thing to say. Was it true, do you suppose?'

'There's only one way to find out!' said George, her eyes dancing. 'Wait for a wild and stormy night and go and see!'

'But what about our agreement?' said Julian, solemnly. 'If anything exciting seems about to happen we turn our backs on it. That's what we decided. Don't you remember?'

'Pooh!' said George.

'We ought to keep the agreement,' said Anne, doubtfully. She knew quite well that the others didn't think so!

'Look! Who are all these people?' said Dick, suddenly. They were just climbing over a stile to cross a lane to another field.

They sat on the stile and stared. Some carts were going by, open wagons, their canvas tops folded down. They were the most old-fashioned carts the children had ever seen, not in the least like travellers' caravans.

Ten or eleven people were with the wagons, dressed in the clothes of other days! Some rode in the wagons and some walked. Some were middle-aged, some were young, but they all looked cheerful and bright.

The children stared. After Grandad's tales of long ago these old-time folk seemed just right! For a few moments Anne felt herself back in Grandad's time, when he was a boy. He must have seen people dressed like these!

'Who are they?' she said, wonderingly. And then the children saw red lettering painted on the biggest cart:

THE BARNIES

'Oh! It's the Barnies! Don't you remember Mrs Penruthlan telling us about them?' said Anne. 'The strolling players,

THE BARNIES

who play to the country folk around, in the barns. What fun!'

The Barnies waved to the watching children. One man, dressed in velvet and lace, with a sword at his side, and a wig of curly hair, threw a leaflet or two to them. They read them with interest.

THE BARNIES ARE COMING

They will sing, they will dance, they will fiddle.
They will perform plays of all kinds.
Edith Wells, the nightingale singer.
Bonnie Carter, the old-time dancer.
Janie Coster and her fiddle.
John Walters, finest tenor in the world.
George Roth – he'll make you laugh!
And Others.
We also present Clopper, the Funniest Horse in
the World!

THE BARNIES ARE COMING

'This'll be fun! said George, pleased. She called out to the passing wagons: 'Will you be playing at Tremannon Farm?'

'Oh, yes!' called a man with bright, merry eyes. 'We always play there. You staying there?'

'Yes,' said George. 'We'll look out for you all. Where are you going now?'

'To Poltelly Farm for the night,' called the man. 'We'll be at Tremannon soon.'

The wagons passed, and the cheerful, oddly-dressed players went out of sight. 'Good,' said Dick. 'Their show may not be first-rate, but it's sure to be funny. They looked a merry lot.'

'All but the man driving the front cart. Did you see him?' said Anne. 'He looked pretty grim, I thought.'

Nobody else had noticed him. 'He was probably the owner of the Barnies,' said Dick. 'And has got all the organisation on his shoulders. Well, come on. Where's Timmy?'

They looked round for him, and George frowned. Yan had followed them as usual, and Timmy was playing with him. Bother Yan! Was he going to trail them all day and every day?

They went back to the peaceful farmhouse. Hens were still clucking around and ducks were quacking. A horse stamped somewhere nearby, and the grunting of pigs came on the air. It all looked quite perfect.

Footsteps came through the farmyard, and Mr Penruthlan came by. He grunted at them and went into a barn.

Anne spoke in almost a whisper. 'I can imagine *him* living in the olden days and being a Wrecker. I can really!'

'Yes! I know what you mean,' said Dick. 'He's so fierce-looking and determined. What's the word I want? *Ruthless!* I'm sure he would have made a good Wrecker!

'Do you suppose there *are* any Wreckers now, and that

light really *is* flashed to make ships go on the rocks?' said George.

'Well, I shouldn't have thought there were any Wreckers in *this* country, anyway,' said Dick. 'I can't imagine that such a thing would be tolerated for an instant. But if that light *is* flashed, what is it flashed for?'

'Old Grandad said there hadn't been any wrecks on this coast for ages,' said Julian. 'I think really that the old man is wandering a bit in his mind about that light!'

'But Yan said he had seen it, too,' said Anne.

'I'm not sure that Yan's as truthful as he might be!' said Julian.

'Why did Grandad say that the light isn't flashed by mortal hands now?' asked George. 'It must be! I can't imagine any other hands working it! He surely doesn't think that his father is still doing it?'

There was a pause. 'We could easily find out if we popped over to that tower and had a look at it,' said Dick.

There was another pause. 'I thought we said we wouldn't go poking about in anything mysterious,' said Anne.

'This isn't really mysterious,' argued Dick. 'It's just a story an old man remembers, and I really *can't* believe that that light still flashes on a wild, stormy night. Grandad must have seen lightning or something. Why don't we settle the matter for good and all and go and explore the old house with the tower?'

'I should like to,' said George firmly. 'I never was keen on this "Keep away from anything unusual" idea we suddenly had. We've got Timmy with us – we can't possibly come to any harm!'

'All right,' said Anne, with a sigh. 'I give up. We'll go if you want to.'

'Good old Anne,' said Dick, giving her a friendly slap on the back. 'But *you* needn't come, you know. Why don't you stay behind and hear our story when we come back?'

'Certainly *not*,' said Anne, quite cross. 'I may not want to go as much as you do, but I'm not going to be left out of anything, so don't think it!'

'All right. It's settled then,' said Julian. 'We take our opportunity and go as soon as we can. Tomorrow, perhaps.'

Mrs Penruthlan came to the door and called them. 'Your high tea is ready. You must be hungry. Come along indoors.'

The sun suddenly went in. Julian looked up at the sky in surprise. 'My word, look at those black clouds!' he said. 'There's a storm coming! Well, I thought there might be, it's been so terribly hot all day!'

'A storm!' said George. 'That light flashes on wild and stormy nights! Oh, Julian, do you think it will flash tonight? Can't we – *can't* we go and see?'

CHAPTER SEVEN

Out in the night

Before the children had finished their high tea, the big kitchen-sitting-room was quite dark. Thunder clouds had moved up from the west, gathering together silently, frowning and sinister. Then, from far off, came the first rumble of thunder.

The little Scottie came and cowered against Mrs Penruthlan's skirts. He hated storms. The farmer's wife comforted him, and her big husband gave a little unexpected snort of laughter. He said something that sounded like 'oose'.

'He's *not* as timid as a mouse,' said his wife, who was really marvellous at interpreting her husband's peculiar noises. 'He just doesn't like the thunder. He never did. He can sleep with us in our room tonight.'

There were a few more sounds from Mr Penruthlan to which his wife listened anxiously. 'Very well, if you have to get up and see to Jenny the horse in the night, I'll see Benny doesn't bark the house down,' she said. She turned to the children. 'Don't worry if you hear him barking,' she said. 'It will only be Mr Penruthlan stirring.'

The thunder crashed and rumbled again, this time a little nearer, and then lightning flashed. Then down came the rain. How it poured! It rattled and clattered on the roof in enormous drops, and then settled down into a steady downpour.

The four children got out their cards and played games by the light of the oil lamp. There was no electricity at Tremannon. Timmy sat with his head on George's knee. He didn't mind the thunder but he didn't particularly like it.

'Well, I think we'd better go to bed,' said Julian at last. He knew that the Penruthlans liked to go to bed early because they got up so early, and as they did not go upstairs until after the children did, Julian saw to it that they, too, went early.

They said good night and went up to their bare little rooms. The windows were still open and the small curtains drawn back, so that the hills, lit now and again by lightning, showed up clearly. The children went and stood there, watching. They all loved a storm, especially Dick. There was something powerful and most majestic about this kind of storm, sweeping over hills and sea, rumbling all round, and tearing the sky in half with flashes of lightning.

'Julian, is it possible to go up to that place the shepherd showed us and see if the light flashes tonight?' said George. 'You only laughed when I asked you before.'

'Well, I laugh again!' said Julian. 'Of course not! We'd be drenched, and I don't fancy being out in this lightning on those exposed hills, either.'

'All right,' said George. 'Anyway, I don't feel *quite* such an urge to go now that it's so pitch dark.'

'Just as well,' said Julian. 'Come on, Dick, let's go to bed.'

The storm went on for some time, rumbling all round the hills again, as if it were going round in a circle. The girls fell asleep, but the boys tossed about, feeling hot and sticky.

'Dick,' said Julian, suddenly, 'let's get up and go out. It's stopped raining. Let's go and see if that light is flashing tonight. It should be just the night for it, according to old Grandad.'

'Right,' said Dick, and sat up, feeling for his clothes. 'I simply can't go to sleep, even though I felt really sleepy when I undressed.'

They pulled on as few clothes as possible, for the night was still thundery and hot. Julian took his torch and Dick hunted for his.

'Got it,' he said at last. 'Are you ready? Come on, then. Let's tiptoe past the Penruthlans' door, or we may wake that Scottie dog! He's sleeping there tonight, don't forget.'

They tiptoed along the passage, past the Penruthlans' door and down the stairs. One stair creaked rather alarmingly, and they stopped in dismay, wondering if Ben the Scottie would break out into a storm of barking.

But he didn't. Good! Down they went again, switching on their torches to see the way. They came to the bottom of the stairs. 'Shall we go out by the front door or back door, Ju?' whispered Dick.

'Back,' said Julian. 'The front door's so heavy to open. Come on.'

So they went down the passage to the back door that led out from the kitchen. It was locked and bolted, but the two boys opened it without too much noise.

They stepped out into the night. The rain had now stopped, but the sky was still dark and overclouded. The thunder rumbled away in the distance. A wind had got up and blew coolly against the boys' faces.

'Nice cool breeze,' whispered Dick. 'Now – do we go

through the farmyard? Is that the shortest way to the stile we have to climb over into that first field?'

'Yes, I think so,' said Julian. They made their way across the silent farmyard, where, in the daytime, such a lot of noise went on, clucking, quacking, grunting, clip-clopping, and shouting!

Now it was dark and deserted. They passed the barns and the stables. A little 'hrrrrrrumph'ing came from one of the stables. 'That's Jenny, the horse that's not well,' said Julian, stopping. 'Let's just have a look at her and see if she's all right. She was lying down feeling very sorry for herself when I saw her last.'

They flashed their torch over the top half of the stable door, which was pulled back to let in air. They looked in with interest.

Jenny was no longer lying down. She was standing up, munching something. Goodness, she must be quite all right again! She whinnied to the two boys.

They left her and went on. They came to the stile and climbed over. The rain began drizzling again, and if the boys had not had their torches with them they would not have been able to see a step in front of them, it was so dark.

'I say, Ju – did you hear that?' said Dick, stopping suddenly.

'No. What?' said Julian, listening.

'Well, it sounded like a cough,' said Dick.

'One of the sheep,' suggested Julian. 'I heard one old sheep coughing just like Uncle Quentin does sometimes, sort of hollow and mournful.'

'No. It wasn't a sheep,' said Dick. 'Anyway, there aren't any in this field.'

'You imagined it,' said Julian. 'I bet there's nobody idiotic enough to be out on a night like this, except ourselves!'

They went on cautiously over the field. The thunder began again, a little nearer. Then came a flash, and again the thunder. Dick stopped dead once more and clutched Julian's arm.

'There's somebody a good way in front of us, the lightning just lit him up for half a second. He was climbing over that stile, the one we're making for. Who do you suppose it is on a night like this?'

'He's apparently going the same way that we are,' said Julian. 'Well, I suppose if we saw *him* he's quite likely to have seen *us*!'

'Not unless he was looking backwards,' said Dick. 'Come on, let's see where he's going.'

They went on cautiously towards the stile. They came to it and climbed over. And then a hand suddenly clutched hold of Dick's shoulder!

He jumped almost out of his skin! The hand gripped him so hard and so fiercely that Dick shouted in pain and tried to wriggle away from the powerful grip.

Julian felt a hand lunge at him, too, but dodged and pressed himself into the hedge. He switched off his torch at once and stood quite still, his heart thumping.

'Let me go!' shouted Dick, wriggling like an eel. His shirt was almost torn off his back in his struggles. He kicked out at the man's ankles and for one moment his captor loosened his grasp. That was enough for Dick. He ripped himself away and left his shirt in the man's hand!

He ran up the lane into which the stile had led and flung himself under a bush in the darkness, panting. He heard his captor coming along, muttering, and Dick pressed himself farther into the bush. A torchlight swept the ground near him, but missed him.

Dick waited till the footsteps had gone and then crawled out. He went quietly down the lane. 'Julian!' he whispered, and jumped as a voice answered almost in his ear, just above his head!

'I'm here. Are you all right?'

Dick looked up into the darkness of a tree, but could see nothing. 'I've dropped my torch somewhere,' he said. 'Where are you, Ju? Up in the tree?'

A hand groped out and felt his head. 'Here I am, on the first branch,' said Julian. 'I hid in the hedge first and then climbed up here. I daren't put on my torch in case that fellow's anywhere around and sees it.'

'He's gone up the lane,' said Dick. 'My word, he nearly wrenched my shoulder off. Half my shirt's gone! Who was he? Did you see?'

'No. I didn't,' said Julian, clambering down. 'Let's find your torch before we go home. It's too good to lose. It must be by that stile.'

They went to look. Julian still didn't like to put on his torch, so that it was more a question of *feeling* for Dick's torch, not looking! Dick suddenly trod on it and picked it up thankfully.

'Listen, there's that fellow coming back again. I'm sure!' said Dick. 'I heard the same dry little cough! What shall we do?'

'Well, I don't now feel like going up to the shepherd's hill to see if that light is flashing from the tower,' said Julian. 'I vote we hide and follow this chap to see where he goes. I don't think anyone who is wandering out tonight can be up to any good.'

'Yes. Good idea,' said Dick. 'Squash into the hedge again. Blow, there are nettles here! Just my luck.'

The footsteps came nearer, and the cough came again. 'I seem to know that cough,' whispered Dick. 'Sh!' said Julian.

The man came up to the stile, and they heard him climbing over it. After a short time both boys followed cautiously. They couldn't hear the man's footsteps across the grass, but the sky had cleared a little and they could just make out a moving shadow ahead of them.

They followed him at a distance, holding their breath whenever they kicked against a stone or cracked a twig beneath their feet. Now and again they heard the cough.

'He's making for the farm,' whispered Julian. He could just see the outline of the big barns against the sky. 'Do you think he's one of the labourers? They live in cottages round about.'

The man came to the farmyard and walked through it, trying to make as little sound as possible. The boys followed. He went round the barns and into the little garden that Mrs Penruthlan tended herself. Still the boys followed.

Round to the front door went the man, and the boys held their breath. Was he going to burgle the farm-house? They tiptoed nearer. There came the sound of a soft click, and then of bolts being shot home! After that there was silence.

'He's gone in,' said Julian in amazement.

'Don't you know who it was? Can't you guess now?' said Dick. 'We both ought to have known when we heard that cough! It was Mr Penruthlan! No wonder he almost dislocated my shoulder with his strong hand!'

'*Mr Penruthlan* – gosh, yes, you're right,' said Julian, astonished, almost forgetting to speak in a whisper. 'We didn't notice that the front door was undone because we went out the back way. So it was him we followed. How silly! But what was he doing out on the hills? He didn't go to see the horse, she wasn't ill.'

'Perhaps he likes a walk at night,' suggested Dick. 'Come on, let's go in ourselves. I feel a bit chilly with practically no shirt on!'

They crept round to the back door. It was still open, thank goodness! They went inside, bolted and locked it, and tiptoed upstairs. They heaved sighs of relief when they were safely in their room again.

'Switch on your torch, Julian, and see if my shoulder is bruised,' said Dick. 'It feels jolly painful.'

Julian flashed his torch on Dick's shoulder. He gave a low whistle. 'My word, you've got a wonderful bruise all down your right shoulder. He must have given you an awful wrench.'

'He did,' said poor Dick. 'Well, I can't say we had a very successful time. We followed our host through the night, got caught by him, and then followed him all the way back here. *Not* very clever!'

'Well, never mind, I bet no light flashed in that tower,' said Julian, getting into bed. 'We haven't lost much by not going all the way to see!'

CHAPTER EIGHT

Here come the Barnies!

THE TWO boys looked curiously at Mr Penruthlan the next morning. It seemed strange to think of their little adventure the night before with him, and *he* didn't even know it was them he had tried to catch! He gave the curious little dry cough again, and Julian nudged Dick and grinned.

Mrs Penruthlan was beaming at the head of the breakfast table as usual. 'The storm soon died down, didn't it?'

Mr Penruthlan got up, said: 'Ah, ock, oooh!' or something that sounded like that, and went out.

'What did he say?' asked Anne curiously. She could *not* think how anyone could possibly understand Mr Penruthlan's extraordinary speech. Julian had said that he thought he must talk in shorthand!

'He said he might not be back for dinner,' said Mrs Penruthlan. 'I hope he'll get some somewhere. He had his breakfast at half past six, and that's very early. I'm glad he came in and had a cup of your breakfast tea now. The poor man had a very bad night, I'm sorry to say.'

The boys pricked up their ears. 'What happened?' asked Julian at once.

'Oh, he had to get up and go and spend two hours with poor Jenny,' said Mrs Penruthlan. 'I woke when he left, but luckily Benny didn't bark, and it wasn't till two hours later he came back, he'd been sitting with the horse all that time, poor man.'

Julian and Dick did not feel at all sympathetic. They knew quite well where Mr Penruthlan had been: not with the horse, that was certain! Anyway, Jenny hadn't been ill when they had looked at her in the night. What a lot of untruths!

They were puzzled. Why should Mr Penruthlan deceive his wife and tell her what wasn't true? What had he been doing that he didn't even want *her* to know?

They told the girls everything immediately after breakfast, when they went to pick currants, raspberries and plums for a fruit salad. Anne and George listened in surprise.

'You never told us you were going,' said George, reproachfully. 'I'd like to have come with you.'

'I always thought Mr Penruthlan looked sort of strange and – and *sinister*,' said Anne. 'I'm sure he's up to no good. What a pity. His wife is so very nice.'

They went on picking the endless redcurrants. Anne suddenly got the feeling that somebody was hiding somewhere near. She looked round uncomfortably. Yes, there was someone in the tall raspberry canes, she was sure! She watched.

It was Yan, of course. She might have guessed! He flashed his smile at her and came towards her. He liked Anne best of all! He held out his hand.

'No, I've no sweets,' said Anne. 'How did you get on last night in the storm, Yan? Were you frightened?'

Yan shook his head. Then he came nearer and spoke softly.

'I saw the light last night!'

Anne stared at him, astonished. What light?

'You don't mean – the light that flashes in that old hidden tower?' she said.

He nodded. Anne went quickly to Julian and Dick, who were picking whitecurrants and eating just about as many as they put into the basket!

'Julian! Dick! Yan says he saw that light flashing last night, the one in the tower!'

'Gosh!' said the boys together. They turned to Yan, who had followed Anne. 'You saw that light?' said Julian.

Yan nodded. 'Big light. Very big,' he said. 'Like – like a fire.'

'Shining from the tower?' said Dick, and Yan nodded again.

'Did your grandad see it?' asked Dick.

Yan nodded. 'He saw it, too.'

'Are you telling the truth?' demanded Julian, wondering how far he could believe Yan.

Yan nodded again.

'What time was this?' asked Dick. But that Yan couldn't tell him. He had no watch, and if he had had, he wouldn't have been able to use it. He couldn't tell the time.

'Blow!' said Julian to Dick. 'We missed it. If Yan's telling the truth we would have seen that light last night.'

'Yes. Well, we'll go tonight and watch for it,' said Dick, determined. 'It's a wild enough day, all wind and scurrying clouds. If that light is used at night in weather like this, we'll be able to see it again. But I'm blessed if I can understand why the Wreckers' tower should be used nowadays. No ship would take any notice of an odd light like that when they've got the lighthouse signalling hard all the time!'

'I'll come, too,' nodded Yan, who had overheard this.

'No, you won't,' said Julian. 'You stay with Grandad. He'll wonder where you are if you're not there.'

It began to rain. 'Blow!' said George. 'I do hope the weather hasn't broken up. It's been so gorgeous. It's quite cold today with this tearing wind. Come on, let's go in, Anne. We've got enough now to feed an army, I should think!'

They all went in, just as the rain came down properly. Mrs Penruthlan greeted them in excitement.

'The Barnies want our barn for tomorrow night!' she said. 'They're giving their first show in our barn, and after that they go to another place. Would you like to help clear out the barn and get ready?'

'You bet!' said Julian. 'We'll go now. There's a lot of stuff to clear out. Where shall we put it? In the other barn?'

The Barnies arrived in about twenty minutes and went straight to the barn, which they had been lent several times before for their shows. They were pleased to see the children and were glad of their help.

They were no longer dressed in fancy clothes, as they had been when the children had seen them on the Sunday evening. They were practically all dressed in slacks, the women, too, ready for the hard work of clearing the barn and setting up a simple stage and background.

Julian caught sight of a horse's head being carried in by a little nimble fellow who pranced along with it comically.

'What's that for?' he said. 'Oh, is that Clopper's head?

The horse that can sit down and cross its legs?'

'That's right,' said the little fellow. 'I'm in charge of it. Never let it out of my sight! Guv'nor's orders!'

'Who's the Guv'nor?' asked Julian. 'The fellow over there?' He nodded to a grim-faced man who was supervising the moving of some bales of straw.

'That's him,' said the little man with a grin. 'His lordship himself! What do you think of my horse?'

Julian looked at the horse's head. It was beautifully made and had a most comical look in its eye. Its mouth could open and shut, and so could its big eyes.

'I'm only the hind legs,' said the little man regretfully. 'But I work his tail, too. Mr Binks over there is his front legs, and works his head, the horse's head, I mean. You should see old Clopper when he performs! My, there isn't a horse like him in the world. He can do everything short of fly!'

'Where are his back and front legs – and – er – his body part?' asked Dick, coming up and looking with great interest at the horse's head.

'Over there,' said the little man. 'By the way, my name's Sid. What's yours, and how is it you're here?'

Julian introduced himself and Dick, and explained that they were helping because they were staying at the farm. He caught hold of a bale of straw, thinking it was about time he did some work.

'Like to give me a hand?' he asked.

Sid shook his head.

'Sorry. Orders are I'm not to put this horse's head down anywhere. Where I go, it goes! I can tell you, Clopper and I are quite attached to one another!'

'Why? Is it so valuable?' asked Dick.

'It's not so much that,' said Sid. 'It's just that Clopper's so popular, you know. And he's important. You see, whenever we think the show's flopping a bit, we bring Clopper on, and then we get the laughs and the claps, and the audience is in a good temper. Oh, Clopper's saved the show many times. He's a jolly good horse.'

Mr Binks came up. He was bigger than Sid and much stronger. He grinned at the two boys. 'Admiring old Clopper?' he said. 'Did Sid tell you about the time Clopper's head dropped off the wagon and we didn't miss him till we were miles away? My word, what a state the Guv'nor was in! Said we couldn't give a show without Clopper, and nearly gave us all the sack!'

'We're important, we are,' said Sid, throwing out his chest and doing a funny little strut with the horse's head in front of him. 'Me and Binks and Clopper – there'd be no show without us!'

'Don't you put that horse down even for a moment,' warned Mr Binks. 'The Guv'nor's got his eye on you, Sid. Look, he's calling you.'

Sid went over to the Guv'nor, looking rather alarmed. He carried the horse's head safely under his arm.

The grim-faced man said a few sharp words and Sid nodded. Julian went up to him when he came back. 'Let me feel how heavy the horse's head is,' he said. 'I've often wondered, when I've seen something like this on the stage.'

Sid immediately put the horse under his other arm, and glared at Julian, looking around quickly to see if the Guv'nor had heard.

'That's a stupid thing to ask me,' he said. 'After I've told you I'm not allowed to put the horse down! And didn't the Guv'nor just this minute say to me "Keep away from those kids, you know what tricks they're up to. They'll have that horse away from you if you're not careful." See? Do you want me to lose my job?'

Julian laughed. 'Don't be silly. You wouldn't lose your job for that! When are you and Mr Binks going to do a bit of practice? We want to see you!'

'Oh well, we could manage that all right,' said Sid, calming down. 'Here, Binks. Bit of practice wanted. Get the legs.'

Binks and Sid went to a cleared space in the big barn and proceeded to clothe themselves in the horse's canvas skin and legs. Sid showed the boys how he worked the tail with one of his hands when he wanted to.

Binks put on the head and the front legs. His head only went into the neck of the horse, no farther. He was able to use his hands for pulling strings to open the horse's mouth and work its rolling eyes.

Sid got his legs in the horse's back legs, bent over and put his head and arms over towards Binks, so making the

horse's back. Somebody came up and zipped up the two halves of the horse's 'skin'.

'Oh! What a jolly good horse!' said Dick, delighted. It looked a lively, comical, extremely supple beast, and the two men inside at once proceeded to make it do ridiculous things. It marched – left-right, left-right, left-right. It did a little tap-dance with its front feet, which then remained perfectly still, and then the back feet did the same little tap-dance.

The back feet got themselves entangled and fell over, and the horse's head looked round at itself in astonishment.

All four children were now watching, and Yan was peeping in at the door. They roared with laughter at the ridiculous horse.

It took its tail in its mouth and marched round and round itself. It stood up on its hind legs only. It jumped like a kangaroo, and made peculiar noises. The whole company stood and watched and even the grim-faced Guv'nor had to smile.

Then it sat down on its hind legs and crossed its front ones in the air, looking round comically. It then gave an enormous yawn that showed dozens of large teeth.

'Oh, don't do any more!' cried Anne, who was weak with laughing. 'Don't! Oh, I can quite well see how important you are, Clopper! You'll be the best part of the show!'

It was a mad, happy morning, for the Barnies were full of chatter and jokes and laughter. Sid and Binks took off their horse garments, and then Sid went about as before, the horse's head, grinning comically, tucked safely under his arm.

Mrs Penruthlan called the children in to dinner. Yan ran after Julian, and caught hold of his arm.

'I saw that light,' he said, urgently. 'Come and see it tonight. Don't forget. I saw that light!'

Julian *had* forgotten it in the excitement of the morning. He grinned down at the small boy.

'All right, all right. I won't forget. We're coming along tonight, but you're not coming, Yan, so get that out of your head! Look, here's a sweet for you. Now, scoot!'

CHAPTER NINE

The light in the tower

BY THE end of the day the big barn was quite transformed! It had been cleared of all straw, sacks of corn, bags of fertiliser and odd machines that had been stored in it. It looked enormous now, and the Barnies were very pleased with it.

'We've been here plenty of times,' they told the children. 'It's the best barn in the district. We don't get the best audience, though, because it's rather a lonely spot here, and there are only two villages near enough to send people to see us. Still, we have a good time, and Mrs Penruthlan gives us a marvellous supper afterwards!'

'I bet she does!' said Dick, grinning. 'I bet that's why you come to this lonely spot, too, to taste Mrs Penruthlan's cooking. I don't blame you. I'd come a good few miles myself!'

A stage had been set up, made of long boards, supported on barrels. A backcloth had been unrolled and hung over the wooden wall of the barn at the back of the stage. It showed a country scene, and had been painted by the company themselves, bit by bit.

'That's my bit,' said Sid, showing Dick a horse standing in one of the fields painted on the backcloth. 'I had to put old Clopper in! See him?'

The Barnies had plenty of scenery, which they were used to changing several times during their performance. This was all home-made too, and they were very proud of it, especially some that represented a castle with a tower.

The tower reminded the boys of the one Yan had said he had seen flashing a light the night before. They looked at one another secretly, and Julian nodded slightly. They would certainly watch to see that light themselves. Then they would know for certain whether Grandad and Yan were telling the truth.

Julian wondered if they would have to look out for Mr Penruthlan again that night. Jenny the horse was quite better now, if she had ever been ill, and was out in the fields again. So Mr Penruthlan had no excuse for creeping about the countryside at night again!

Neither of the boys could *imagine* what had taken him out the night before, on such a wild night too! Was he meeting somebody? He hadn't had time to go up to see the shepherd about anything, and there wouldn't have been much point in that anyway. He had seen Grandad in the morning already.

Mrs Penruthlan came to see the barn now that it was almost ready for the show the next night. She looked red and excited. This was a grand time for her, the Barnies in her barn, the villagers all coming up the next night, a grand supper to be held afterwards. What an excitement!

She was very busy in her kitchen, cooking, cooking, cooking! Her enormous larder was already full of the most appetising-looking pies, tarts, hams and cheeses. The children took turns at looking into it and sniffing in delight. Mrs Penruthlan laughed at them and shooed them out.

'You'll have to help me tomorrow,' she said. 'Shelling peas, scraping potatoes, stringing beans, picking currants and raspberries, and you'll find hundreds of wild strawberries in the copse too, which can go to add a flavour to the fruit salad.'

'We shall love to help,' said Anne. 'All this is grand fun!

But surely you aren't going to do all the supper single-handed, Mrs Penruthlan?'

'Oh, one or two of the villagers will stay behind to help me serve it,' said the plump little farmer's wife, who looked as happy as could be in the midst of so much hard work. 'Anyway, I'll be up at five o'clock tomorrow morning. I'll have plenty of time!'

'You'd better go to bed early tonight then!' said George.

'We all will,' said Mrs Penruthlan. 'We'll be up early and abed late tomorrow, and we'll need some sleep tonight. It's no trouble to get Mr Penruthlan to bed early. He's always ready to go!'

The children felt sure he would be ready to go early that night because he had spent so much time out in the storm the night before! Julian and Dick were tired too, but they were quite determined to go up to the shepherd's hill and find the place where they could watch and see if that light really did flash out!

They had a high tea as usual, at which Mr Penruthlan was present. He ate solidly and solemnly, not saying a word except something that sounded like 'Ooahah, ooh.'

'Well, I'm glad you like the pie, Mr Penruthlan,' said his wife. 'Though I say it myself, it's a good one.'

It really was wonderful the way she understood her husband's speech. It was also very strange to hear her speak to her husband as if he was someone to whom she had to be polite, and call Mister! Anne wondered if she called him Mr Penruthlan when they were alone together.

She looked at him earnestly. What a giant he was – and how he ate!

He looked up and saw Anne watching him. He nodded at her and said 'Ah! Oooh, ock, ukker.' It might have been another language for all Anne could understand! She looked startled and didn't know what to say.

'Now, Mr Penruthlan, don't you tease the child!' said his wife. 'She doesn't know what to answer. Do you, Anne?'

'Well – I – er – I didn't really catch what he said,' said Anne, going scarlet.

'There now, Mr Penruthlan – see how badly you talk without your teeth in!' said the farmer's wife scoldingly. 'Haven't I told you you should wear your teeth when you want to make conversation! *I* understand you all right, but others don't. It must sound just a mumble to them!'

Mr Penruthlan frowned and muttered something. The children all stared at him, surprised to hear that he had no teeth. Goodness gracious – HOW did he manage to eat all he did, then? He seemed to chew and munch and crunch, and yet he had no teeth!

'So that's why he speaks so oddly,' thought Dick, amused. 'But fancy eating as much as he does, with no teeth in his head! Goodness, what would he eat if he *had* got all his teeth?'

Mrs Penruthlan changed the conversation because it was clear that her husband was annoyed with her. She talked brightly about the Barnies.

'That horse Clopper! You wait till you see him prance on to the stage, and fall off it. You'll see Mr Penruthlan almost fall out of his seat he laughs so much. He loves that horse. He's seen it a dozen times, and it tickles him to death.'

'I think it's jolly funny myself,' said Julian. 'I've always thought I'd like to put on an act like that at our end-of-term concert at school. Dick and I could do it all right. I wish Sid and Mr Binks would let us try.'

The meal was finished at last. Most of the dishes were empty, and Mrs Penruthlan looked pleased. 'There now – you've done really well,' she said. 'That's what I do like to see, people finishing up everything put before them.'

'It's easy when it's food *you* put before us,' said George. 'Isn't it, Timmy? I bet Timmy wishes he lived here always, Mrs Penruthlan! I'm sure he keeps telling your dogs how lucky they are!'

After the washing-up, in which everyone but Mr Penruthlan helped, they went to sit down for a while, and read. But the farmer kept giving such enormous yawns that he set everyone else yawning too, and Mrs Penruthlan began to laugh.

'Come on, to bed, all of you!' she said. 'I've never heard so many yawns in my life! Poor Mr Penruthlan. He's tired out with sitting up with Jenny the horse half the night.'

The children exchanged glances. They knew better!

Everyone went up to bed, and the children laughed to hear Mr Penruthlan still yawning loudly in his room. Julian looked out of his window. It was a dark, blustery night, with sudden spurts of sharp rain. The wind howled and Julian almost thought he could hear the great waves crashing on the rocks in the nearest coves! How enormous they would be in this wind!

'A good night for Wreckers, if there were any nowadays!' he said to Dick. 'Not much chance for any ship that went too near those coves tonight! They'd be on the rocks, and dashed to pieces in half an hour! The beach would be strewn with thousands of pieces of wreckage the next day.'

'We'd better wait a bit before we go,' said Dick. 'It's really very early. On a bright sunny evening the hills would still be full of daylight, but this stormy evening is very dark. Let's light our torches and read.'

The wind became even stronger, and grew almost to a gale. It made a howling noise round the old farmhouse, and sounded angry and in pain. Not a very nice night to go out on the hills!

'We'll go now, I think,' said Julian, at last. 'It's quite dark, and getting late. Come on.'

They hadn't undressed, so they went down the stairs at once, and out of the back door as before, closing it silently behind them. They made their way through the farmyard, not daring to shine their torches till they were well away from the house.

They had had a quick look at the front door, when they had stood in the hall. It was locked and bolted!

Mr Penruthlan was not out tonight, that was certain.

They walked steadily through the gale, gasping when it caught them full in the face. They each had their warm jerseys on, for it was quite cold, and the wind blew all the time.

Across the fields. Over one stile after another. Across more fields. The boys stopped once or twice to make sure they were right. They were relieved when they came to the great flock of sheep, and knew they must be near the shepherd's hut.

'There's the hut,' whispered Julian, at last. 'You can just see its dark outline. We must go quietly now.'

They stole by the hut. Not a sound came from inside, and no candlelight showed through the cracks. Old Grandad must be fast asleep! Julian pictured Yan curled up with him on their bed of old sheepskins.

The boys went quietly along. Now, they must make for the spot from which the old tower could be seen, and it must be the *exact* spot, for the tower could be seen from nowhere else.

They couldn't find it, or, if they *had* found it, and were standing on it, they were unable to see the tower far off in the darkness.

'If it didn't happen to be flashing a light, we wouldn't know if we were looking in the right direction or not!' said Julian. 'We'd never see it in the dark. Why didn't we think of that? Somehow I thought we'd see the tower whether it was lit up or not. We're asses.'

They wandered about a little, continually looking in the direction where they thought the tower should be but saw nothing at all. What a waste of a long walk!

Then Julian suddenly gave an exclamation. 'Who's that? I saw someone there! Who is it?'

Dick jumped. What was this now? Then someone sidled up against them both, and a voice spoke timidly.

'It's me, Yan!'

'Good gracious! You turn up everywhere!' said Julian. 'I suppose you were watching out for us.'

'Yes. Come with me,' said Yan, and tugged at Julian's arm. The two boys went with him, a few yards to the right, then higher up the hill. Then Yan stopped.

The boys saw the distant light at once. There was no doubt about it at all! It flashed continually, rather like a small lighthouse light. Each time it flashed they could see the faint outline of the tower.

'It seems to be some kind of signal,' said Julian. 'Flash – flash-flash-flash – flash-flash – flash. My word, how weird. Who's doing it, and why? Surely there are no Wreckers nowadays!'

'Grandad says it's his old dad,' said Yan, in an awed voiced. Julian laughed.

'Don't be silly! All the same, it's a bit of a mystery, isn't it, Dick? *Could* any ship out at sea be deceived and come near to the shore, and be wrecked? It's a wicked night, just the night for great waves to pound a ship to pieces if it came near this coast.'

'Yes. Well, we shall hear tomorrow if there *has* been a wreck,' said Dick soberly. 'I hope there won't be. I can't bear thinking of it, anyway. Surely, *surely* there aren't Wreckers here now!'

'If there are, they will be creeping down the hidden Wreckers' Way, wherever it is,' said Julian. 'And watching for the ship to crash to pieces. Then they will collect sacks upon sacks of booty and creep away back.'

Dick felt a chill of horror. 'Shut up, Ju!' he said, sharply. 'Don't talk like that. Now, what are we going to do about that light?'

'I'll tell you,' said Julian, firmly. 'We're going to find that tower and see what's going on. That's what we're going to do! And as soon as ever we can too, maybe tomorrow!'

CHAPTER TEN

Getting ready for the show

JULIAN AND Dick watched the light for a little longer, and then turned to go back to the farm. The wind was so strong and so cold that even on that summer's night they found themselves shivering.

'I'm glad you found us, Yan,' said Dick, putting an arm round the small, shivering boy. 'Thanks for your help. We're going to explore the old tower. Would you like to show us the way to it?'

Yan shivered all the more, from fright as much as cold. 'No. I'm frightened,' he said. 'I'm frightened of that tower now.'

'All right, Yan,' said Dick. 'You needn't come. It *is* pretty peculiar, I must admit. Now, go back to your hut.'

Yan shot off in the dark like a scared rabbit. The boys made their way home, not very cautiously, for they felt sure they were the only people out at night. But when they came to the farmyard they saw something that made them stop suddenly.

'There's a light in the big barn!' whispered Dick. 'It's gone, no, there it is again. It's somebody with a torch, flashing it on and off. Who is it?'

'One of the Barnies, perhaps,' whispered back Julian.

'Let's go and see. We know the Barnies are sleeping in the nearby sheds tonight.'

They tiptoed to the barn and looked through a crack. They saw nothing at first. Then a torch flashed, shedding its light on some of the properties of the Barnies, stacked in a corner, scenery, dresses, coats, and other things.

'Somebody's going through the pockets!' said Julian, indignantly. 'Look at that! A thief!'

'Who is it?' said Dick. 'One of the Barnies pick-pocketing?'

For a moment or two the torch lit up the back of the intruder's hand in the barn, and the boys stifled an exclamation. They knew that hand! It was covered with black hairs almost as thick as fur!

'Mr Penruthlan!' whispered Dick. 'Yes, I see it's him now. Look at his enormous shadow. What's he doing? He must be mad, walking about at night on the hills, stealing into the barn, going through pockets. Look what he's doing now! Looking in the drawers of that chest the Barnies are going to use in one of their scenes. Yes, he's mad!'

Julian felt most uncomfortable. He didn't like spying on his host like this. What a strange man he was! He told untruths, he crept about at night, he went through people's pockets. Yes, he must be mad! Did Mrs Penruthlan know? She couldn't know, or she would be unhappy, and she really seemed the most cheerful, happy little person in the world!

'Come on,' said Julian, in Dick's ear. 'He's going through everything! Though what he expects to find in the Barnies' stage clothes and properties, I don't know. He's weird! Come on, I really don't want to spot him taking something, stealing it. It would be so awkward if we had to say we saw him stealing.'

They left the barn and went back to the farmhouse, creeping in once more at the back door. They looked at the front door. It was shut, but no longer locked or bolted.

The boys went upstairs, puzzled. What a strange night! The howling wind, the flashing light, the furtive man in the barn, they didn't know what to make of it!

'Let's wake the girls and tell them,' said Julian. 'I feel as if I can't wait till the morning.'

George was awake and so was Timmy. Timmy had heard them going out, and had lain awake waiting for them to come back. He had stirred and had awakened George. She was quite prepared to hear a whisper at the door!

'Anne! George! We've got some news!' whispered Julian. Timmy gave a little welcoming whine and leapt off the bed. Soon Anne was awake, too, and the girls were listening in amazement to the boys' news.

They were almost as surprised to hear about Mr Penruthlan in the barn as to hear about the light actually flashing in the tower.

'So it *was* true what old Grandad said, then?' whispered Anne. 'He *had* seen the light again. I do think it's weird, all this. Julian, you don't think we'll hear of a wreck tomorrow, do you? I couldn't bear it!'

'Nor could I,' said George, listening to the wind howling outside. 'Fancy being wrecked on a night like this, and being dashed on the rocks by those pounding waves. I feel as if we ought to rush off to the coves here and now and see if we can do any rescuing!'

'We wouldn't be much use,' said Dick. 'I doubt if we could even get near the cove on a night like this. The waves would run right up to the road that leads down to it.'

They talked and talked about everything. Then George yawned. 'We'd better stop,' she said. 'We'll never wake up tomorrow morning. We can't go and explore that tower tomorrow, Julian. The Barnies will be here, and we've promised Mrs Penruthlan to help her.'

'It'll have to be the next day, then,' said Julian. 'But I'm determined to go. Yan said he wouldn't show us the way. He said he was too frightened!'

'I feel pretty frightened myself,' said George, settling down. 'I should have jumped out of my skin if I'd seen that light tonight.'

The boys stole back to their room. Soon they were in bed and asleep. The wind still howled round the house, but they didn't hear it. They were tired out with their long walk over the hills.

The next day was so busy that it was quite difficult to find time to remember the night's happenings! They were reminded of it by one thing, though.

Mrs Penruthlan was seeing to their breakfast, and making bright conversation as usual. She was never at a loss for words, and chattered all day long either to the children or to the dogs.

'Did you sleep well with that howling gale blowing all night long?' she asked. 'I slept like a top. So did Mr Penruthlan! He told me he never moved all night, he was that tired!'

The children kicked each other under the table, but said nothing. They knew quite a lot more about her husband's nights than she did!

After that they had very little time to think of anything but picking fruit, podding peas, rushing here and there, carrying things for the Barnies, helping them to put up benches, barrels, boxes and chairs for the audience to sit on, and even mending tears in some of the stage clothes! Anne had offered to sew on a button, and at once found herself overwhelmed with requests to mend this, that and the other!

It was an extremely busy day. Yan appeared as usual and was greeted uproariously by Timmy, of course. All the dogs loved him, but Timmy was quite silly with him. Mrs Penruthlan sent Yan on endless errands, which he ran quickly and willingly.

'He may be a bit simple, but he's quick enough when he thinks there's some food he's going to share!' she said. So it was 'Fetch this, Yan!', 'Do that, Yan!' all day long.

The Barnies worked hard, too. They had a quick rehearsal in which every single thing went wrong; the Guv'nor raved and raged and stamped, making Anne wonder why they didn't all run away and stay away!

First there was to be a kind of concert party. Then there was to be a play, most heart-rending and melodramatic, with villains and heroes and a heroine who was very harshly treated. But everything came right for her in the end, Anne was relieved to find!

Clopper the horse was to have no definite performance of his own. He just wandered on and off the stage to get laughs and to please everyone, or to fill awkward gaps. There was no doubt he would do this to perfection!

Julian and Dick watched Mr Binks and Sid doing a small rehearsal on their own in a corner of the farmyard. How well those back legs and front legs worked together! How that horse danced, trotted, galloped, marched, fell over, tied itself into knots, sat down, got up, went to sleep, and, in fact, did every comical thing that Sid and Mr Binks could think of. They really were very, very funny.

'Let me try the head on, Mr Binks,' begged Julian. 'Do let me. Just to feel what it's like.'

But it was no good. Sid wouldn't let him. Mr Binks had no say in the matter at all. 'Orders are orders,' said Sid, picking up the head as soon as Mr Binks took it off. 'I don't want to lose my job. The Guv'nor says if this horse's head is mislaid again, I'll be mislaid, too! So hands off Clopper!'

'Do you sleep with Clopper?' asked Dick, curiously. 'Having to take charge of a horse's head all the time must be a bore!'

'You get used to it,' said Sid. 'Yes, I sleep with old Clopper. Him and me have our heads on the pillow together. He sleeps sound, does old Clopper!'

'He's the best part of the show,' grinned Julian. 'You'll bring the barn down with Clopper tonight!'

'We always do,' said Mr Binks. 'He's the most important member of the Barnies, and he gets paid the worst. Shame.'

'Yes, back legs and front legs are badly paid,' said Sid. 'They only count as one player, see, so we get half pay. Still, we like the life, so there you are!'

They went off together, Sid carrying the horse's head as usual under his arm. He really was a funny little man, cheery and silly and bright.

Julian suddenly remembered something at dinner-time. 'Mrs Penruthlan,' he said, 'I suppose that awful wind didn't cause any wrecks last night, did it?'

The farmer's wife looked surprised. 'No, Julian. Why should it? Ships keep right out to sea round these coasts now. The lighthouse warns them, you know. The only way any ship could come in now would be to nose into one of the coves at full tide, and then she'd have to be very careful of rocks. The fishermen know the rocks as well as they know the backs of their hands, and they come into the coves at times. But no other craft come now.'

Everyone heaved a sigh of relief. The flashing light hadn't caused a wreck last night, then. That was a mercy! They went on with their meal. Mr Penruthlan was there, eating away as usual, and saying nothing at all. His jaws worked vigorously up and down, and it was impossible to think he had no teeth to chew with. Julian glanced at his hands, covered with black hairs. Yes, he had seen those hands last night, no doubt about that! Not wielding a knife and fork, but sliding into pockets.

The evening came at last. Everything was ready. A big table was placed in the kitchen, made of strong trestles and boards. Mrs Penruthlan gave the two girls a most enormous white cloth to lay over it. It was bigger than any cloth they had ever seen!

'It's the one I use at harvest-time,' said the farmer's wife, proudly. 'We have a wonderful harvest supper then, on that same table, but we put it out in the big barn because there's not enough room here in the kitchen for all the farm workers. And we clear the table away afterwards and have a dance.'

'What fun!' said Anne. 'I do think people are lucky to live on a farm. There's always something going on!'

'Town folk wouldn't say that!' said Mrs Penruthlan. 'They think the country is a dead-and-alive place, but, my word, there's more life about a farm than anywhere else in the world. Farm life's the *real* thing, I always say!'

'It is,' agreed Anne, and George nodded, too. They had now spread out the snowy-white cloth and it looked lovely.

'That cloth's the real thing, too,' said Mrs Penruthlan. 'It belonged to my great-great-great-grandmother, and it's nearly two hundred years old! As white as ever and not a darn in it! It's seen more harvest suppers than any cloth, and that's the truth!'

The table was laid with plates and knives and forks, cruets and glasses. All the Barnies had been invited, and there were the children, too, of course. One or two of the villagers were staying as well, to help. What a feast they would all have!

The larder was so crammed with food that it was difficult to get into it. Meat pies, fruit pies, hams, a great round tongue, pickles, sauces, jam tarts, stewed and fresh fruit, jellies, a great trifle, jugs of cream – there was no end to the things Mrs Penruthlan had got ready. She laughed when she saw the children peeping there and marvelling.

'You won't get any high tea today,' she told them. 'You'll get nothing from dinner till supper, so that you can get up a good appetite and really eat well!'

Nobody minded missing high tea with that wonderful supper to come. The excitement grew as the time came near for the show. 'Here come the first villagers!' cried Julian, who was at the barn door to help to sell the tickets. 'Hurrah! It will soon begin! Walk up, everyone! Finest show in the world. Come along in your hundreds! Come along!'

CHAPTER ELEVEN

The Barnies – and Clopper

WHEN THE big barn was full of villagers, and a few more boxes had been fetched for some of the extra children, the noise was tremendous. Everyone was laughing and talking, some of the children were clapping for the show to begin, and the excited farm dogs were yapping and barking at the top of their voices!

Timmy was excited, too. He welcomed everyone with a bark and a vigorous wag. Yan was with him, and George was sure that he was pretending that Timmy was his dog! Yan looked cleaner than usual. Mrs Penruthlan had actually given him a bath!

'You don't come to the show and you don't come to the supper unless you bath yourself,' she threatened. But he wouldn't. He said he was frightened of the bath.

'I'll be drowned in there,' he said, backing away from it hurriedly. It was already half full of water for him!

'Frightened, are you?' said Mrs Penruthlan grimly, lifting him up and plunging him into the water, clothes and all. 'Well, you'll be more frightened now! Take your clothes off in the water and I'll wash them in the bath when you're clean. Oh, the dirty little so-and-so that you are!'

Yan screamed the place down as Mrs Penruthlan

scrubbed him and soaped him and flannelled him. He felt very much at her mercy, and decided not to annoy her in any way while he was in that dreadful bath!

She washed his ragged pants and shirt, too, and set them to dry. She wrapped him in an old shawl, and told him to wait till his things dried and then put them on.

'One of these days I'll make you some decent clothes,' she said. 'Little rapscallion that you are! What a mite of a body you've got. I'll need to feed you up a bit!'

Yan brightened up considerably. Feeding up was the kind of treatment he really liked!

Now he was down in the barn, welcoming everyone with Timmy and feeling quite important. He yelled with delight when he saw his old great-grandfather coming along!

'Grandad! You said you were coming, but I didn't believe you. Come on in. I'll find you a chair.'

'And what's come over you, the way you look tonight?' said the old man, puzzled. 'What've you done to yourself?'

'I've had a bath,' said Yan, sounding proud. 'Yes. I took a bath, Grandad. As you ought to.'

Grandad aimed a cuff at him, and then nodded to various people he knew. He had his big old shepherd's crook with him, and he held on to it even when he sat down on a chair.

'Well, Grandad, it must be twenty years since we saw you down here,' said a big, red-faced villager. 'What've you been doing with yourself all these years?'

'Minding my business and minding my sheep,' said Grandad, in his slow, Cornish voice. 'Yes, and it might be twenty years before you see me again, Joe Tremayne. And if you want to know something I'll tell you this. It isn't the show I've come for, it's the supper.'

Everyone roared with laughter, and Grandad looked as pleased as Punch. Yan looked at him proudly. His old grandad was as good as anyone, any day!

'Sh! Sh! Show's going to begin!' said somebody, when they saw the curtain twitching. At once the talking and shuffling stopped, and all eyes turned to the stage. A faded, rather torn blue curtain was drawn across.

There came a chord from a fiddle behind the scenes, and then a lively tune sounded out. The curtain was drawn back slowly, halting on its rings here and there, and the audience gave a long sigh of delight. They had seen the Barnies many times but they never tired of them.

All the Barnies were on the stage, and the fiddler fiddled away as they struck up a rousing song with a chorus that all the villagers joined in most heartily. Old Grandad beat time, banging his crook on the floor.

Everything was applauded heartily. Then someone called out loudly: 'Where's old Clopper? Where is he?'

And old Clopper the horse came shyly on, looking out of the sides of his eyes at the audience, and being so very bashful that old Grandad almost fell off his chair with laughing.

The fiddle struck up again and Clopper marched in time

to it. It grew quicker, and he ran. It grew quicker still and he galloped, and fell right off the stage.

'Hoo-hoo-hoo-hoo!' roared someone. 'HOO-HOO-HOO-HOO!' It was such an enormous guffaw that everyone turned round. It came from Mr Penruthlan, who was writhing and wriggling in his seat as if he was in great pain. But he was only laughing at Clopper.

Clopper heard the giant of a laugh and put a hoof behind one ear to listen to it. Grandad promptly fell off his seat with joy. Clopper caught his back legs in his front legs and fell over too. There was such a pandemonium of screams and guffaws and yells from the delighted audience that it was surprising the roof didn't fall in.

'Off now,' said a firm voice at the side of the stage. Julian looked to see who it was, as Clopper obediently turned to shuffle off, waving one back leg to the admiring villagers. The voice came from the Guv'nor who was standing where he could watch the whole show in detail. His face was still unsmiling, even after Clopper's antics!

The show was a great success, although it could not have been simpler. The jokes were old, the play acted was even older, the singing was a bit flat, and the dancing not as good as the third form of a girls' school, but it was so merry and smiling and idiotic and good-natured that it went with a terrific swing from start to finish.

As for Clopper, it was his evening! Every time his head so much as looked in on the stage, the audience rocked with joy. They would, in fact, have been delighted to have had one actor only, all the evening, and that actor, Clopper, of course. Julian and Dick watched him, fascinated. How they both longed to try on those back and front legs, and put on the head, and do a little 'cloppering' themselves!

'Sid and Binks are awfully good, aren't they?' said Dick. 'Gosh, I wish we could get hold of legs and a head and do that act at the Christmas school concert, Ju! We'd bring the house down. Let's ask Sid if we can have a shot some time.'

'He won't lend us the head,' said Julian. 'Still, we could do without that, and just try the legs. I bet we could think of some funny things to do, Dick!'

Everybody was sad when the curtain went across the stage, and the show was over. The fiddle struck up 'God Save the Queen', and everyone rose loyally to stand and sing every word lustily.

'Three cheers for the Barnies!' yelled a child, and the hip-hurrahing rose to the rafters. Grandad waved his crook too vigorously and hit a very large farmer on the back of his neck.

'Now, old Grandad!' said the farmer, rubbing his neck, 'are you trying to pick a fight with me? No, no, I'd be afraid to take you on. You'd get me by my hind leg with that crook like you do your sheep, and down I'd go!'

Grandad was delighted. He hadn't had such an evening for forty years! Maybe fifty. And now for that supper. That was what he had really come for. He'd show some of these sixty-year-old youngsters how to eat!

The villagers went home, talking and laughing. Two or three of the women stayed on to help. The Barnies didn't bother to change out of their acting clothes, but came into the kitchen as they were, greasepaint running down their cheeks in the heat. The barn had got very hot with so many people packed in close together.

The children were simply delighted with everything. They had laughed so much at Clopper that they felt quite weak. The play had amused them too, with its sighings and groanings and threats and tears and stridings around. Now they were more than ready for their supper!

The Barnies crowded round the loaded table, cracking jokes, complimenting Mrs Penruthlan, clapping everyone on the back, and generally behaving like a lot of school children out for a treat. Julian looked round at them all. What a jolly lot! He looked for the Guv'nor. Surely for once he too would be smiling and cheerful.

But he wasn't there. Julian looked and looked again. No, he certainly wasn't there.

'Where's the Guv'nor?' he asked Sid, who was sitting next to him.

'The Guv'nor? Oh, he's sitting in solitary state in the barn,' said Sid, attacking an enormous slice of meat pie laced with hard-boiled eggs. 'He never feeds with us, not even after a show. Keeps himself to himself, he does! He'll be having a whacking great tray of food all on his own. Suits me all right! I never did get on with the Guv'nor.'

'Where's Clopper – the horse's head, I mean?' asked

Julian. He couldn't see it beside Sid anywhere. 'Is it under the table?'

'No. The Guv'nor's got it tonight. Said he wasn't going to have it rolled about under the table, or have jelly or gravy dropped all over it,' said Sid, taking six large pickled onions. 'My, Mrs Penruthlan is a wonder! Why don't I marry someone like her, instead of getting thinner and thinner inside Clopper's back legs?'

Julian laughed. He wondered who was going to take the Guv'nor's tray into the barn. He noticed that Mrs Penruthlan was getting one ready, and he went over to her.

'Is that for the Guv'nor?' he asked. 'Shall I take it for you?'

'Oh, thank you, Julian,' said the busy farmer's wife, gratefully. 'Here it is, and ask Dick to carry in a bottle and a glass for him, will you? There's no more room on the tray.'

So Julian and Dick together went out to the barn with the food and drink. The wind still blew strongly and rain was beginning to fall again.

'There's no one here,' said Julian, looking round. He set down the tray, puzzled. Then he saw a note pinned on the curtain. He went to read it.

'Back in an hour,' he read. 'Gone for a walk. The Guv'nor.'

'Oh well, we'll leave the tray then,' said Julian. He and Dick were just turning to go when they caught sight of

something, the back and front legs of Clopper the horse! They stopped, each with the same thought in his mind.

'Everyone at supper! The Guv'nor gone for an hour. Nobody would know if we tried on the legs!'

They looked at one another, and read each other's mind. 'Let's have a go at being Clopper!'

'Come on, quick,' said Julian. 'You be the back legs and I'll be the front ones. Quick!'

They got into them hurriedly, and Julian managed to do up most of the zip. But it wasn't right without the head. Had the Guv'nor taken it with him? Surely not? It would be quite safe in the barn.

'There it is, on that chair under the shawl,' said Dick, and they galloped over to get it. Julian picked it up. It was rather heavier than he had imagined. He looked inside it to see how far his head went in it, wondering how to work the eyes and mouth.

He put his hand inside, and scrabbled about. A lid fell open in the side of the neck, and out came some cigarettes, scattering over the floor. 'Blow!' said Julian. 'I didn't know Mr Binks kept his cigarettes in Clopper. Pick them up, Dick, and I'll put them back. Thanks.'

He put the cigarettes back in the little space, and shut the lid on them. Then he put the head carefully over his own. It felt extremely strange.

'There are eyeholes in the neck,' he said to Dick. 'That's how Mr Binks knew where he was going. I kept wondering why he didn't bump into things more than he did! Now – I'm ready. The head seems to be on firmly. I'll count – one-two, one-two – and we'll walk in time. Don't let's start any funny tricks till we're used to Clopper. Does my voice sound funny inside the neck?'

'*Most* peculiar,' said Dick, who was now bending over so that his back made the horse's back, and his arms were round Julian's waist. 'I say, what's that?'

'Someone's coming, it's the Guv'nor coming back!' said Julian in alarm. 'Quick, gallop out of the door before we're caught.'

And so, to the Guv'nor's enormous surprise, Clopper galloped very clumsily out of the barn door just as he was

coming in, almost knocking him over. At first he didn't realise it was Clopper, then he let out a loud roar and gave chase.

'I can't *see*,' panted poor Julian. 'Where am I going? Oh thank goodness, it's an empty stable! Quick, let's unzip ourselves, and you'll have to take this head off for me, I can't manage it myself.'

But alas and alack! The zip got stuck and wouldn't come undone. The boys tugged and pulled but it wasn't a bit of good. It looked as if they had got to be Clopper for the rest of the evening!

CHAPTER TWELVE

A trip to the tower

'BLOW THIS zip!' said Julian, desperately. 'It's got *absolutely* stuck! It's so difficult for us to undo it from the inside of the beastly horse. Oh, this head. I *must* get it off.'

He pushed at the head but somehow or other it had got wedged on him, and Julian felt that short of pulling his own head off he would certainly never get Clopper's off!

The horse sat down, exhausted, looking a very peculiar shape. Julian leant the head against the wall of the stable and panted. 'I'm so *hot*,' he complained. 'Dick, for goodness' sake think of something. We'll have to get help. But I daren't go back to the barn because of the Guv'nor, and we really can't appear in the kitchen like this. Everyone would have a fit, and Sid and Mr Binks would be furious with us.'

'I think we were asses to try this,' said Dick, pulling viciously at the zip again. 'Ugh! What use are zips, I'd like to know. I feel most uncomfortable. Can't you get in some other position, Ju? I seem to be standing on my head or something.'

'Let's go and scout round the kitchen,' said Julian trying to get up. Dick tried to get up too, but they both fell down on top of one another. They tried again and this time stood up rather shakily.

'It's not as easy as it looks, is it, to be a two-man horse,' said Julian. 'I wish I could get these eyeholes in the right place. I can't see!'

However, he managed to adjust them at last, and the two boys made their way cautiously and clumsily out of the stable. They went carefully over the farmyard, Julian counting one-two, one-two, under his breath so that they walked in time with one another.

They came to the kitchen door and debated whether to try and catch someone's attention without going in. There was a fairly large window nearby, open because of the warmth of the kitchen. Julian decided to take a look through to see if George or Anne were anywhere near. If so, he could call them outside.

But he reckoned without the clumsiness of the big head! It knocked against the window frame, and everyone looked up. There were shrieks at once.

'A horse! Farmer Penruthlan, one of your horses is loose!' cried a villager who was helping with the supper. 'He looked in at the window!'

The farmer went out at once. Julian and Dick backed hurriedly away and trotted in very good style over the farmyard. Where now? The farmer saw their moving figure in the darkness and went after them.

Trot-trot-trot went the horse desperately then gallop-gallop-gallop! But that finished them, because the back and front legs didn't gallop together, got entangled and down went the horse! The farmer ran up in alarm, thinking that his horse had fallen.

'Take your knee out of my mouth,' mumbled an angry voice, and the farmer stopped suddenly, astounded to hear a human voice coming from the horse. Then he realised what was happening – it was the stage horse with two people in it! Who? It sounded like Julian and Dick. He gave the horse a gentle kick.

'Don't,' said Dick's voice. 'For goodness' sake whoever it is, unzip us! We're suffocating!'

The farmer let out a terrific guffaw, bent down and felt for the zip. One good pull and the horse's canvas skin came in half as the zip was undone.

The boys clambered out thankfully. 'Oh – er – thanks awfully, Mr Penruthlan,' said Julian, rather embarrassed. 'We – er – we were just having a canter round.'

Mr Penruthlan gave another hearty roar and went off towards the kitchen to finish his meal. Dick and Julian felt very thankful. They carried the legs and head of the horse cautiously towards the barn. They peeped in at a window. The Guv'nor was there, striding up and down, looking extremely angry.

Julian waited till he was at the far end of the barn, and then hurriedly pushed the legs and head in the door, as quietly as he could. When the Guv'nor turned round to stride angrily back the first thing he saw was the bundle that was Clopper! He raced over to it at once, and looked out of the door.

But Julian and Dick had gone. They could own up the next day when things were not quite so exciting! They slid quietly into the kitchen, feeling hot and untidy, hoping that nobody would notice them.

George and Anne saw them at once. George came over. 'What have you been doing? You've been ages and ages. Do you want any more to eat before everything is finished up?'

'Tell you everything afterwards,' said Julian. 'Yes, we do want something to eat. I've hardly had a thing yet. I'm starving!'

Mr Penruthlan was back in his place eating again. He pointed with his knife at the boys sliding into their seats. 'Ock-ock-oo,' he said, beginning to laugh, and added a few more equally puzzling words.

'Oh, they've been to help you catch the horse that peeped in at the window, have they?' said Mrs Penruthlan, nodding. 'Which horse was it?'

'Clopper!' said the farmer, quite clearly, and gave a loud guffaw again. Nobody understood what he meant, so nothing more was said. George and Anne guessed, though, and grinned at the two boys.

It was a wonderful evening altogether, and everyone was sorry that it had to come to an end. The village women and the two girls stacked the dirty dishes and plates and the boys carried them to the sink to be washed. The

Barnies gave a hand where they could, and the big kitchen was full of chatter and laughter. It was very pleasant indeed.

But at last the kitchen was empty again, and the big lamp turned out. The village women went home, the Barnies departed. Old Grandad took Yan's hand and went back to his sheep, saying dolefully that he'd 'et a mort' too much and wouldn't be able to sleep a wink, so he wouldn't.

'Never mind. It was worth it, Grandad,' said Mrs Penruthlan, and shut and locked the kitchen door. She looked round, tired but happy. There was nothing she liked better than to spend hours upon hours preparing delicious dishes for people and then see them eaten in no time at all! The children thought she was truly wonderful.

They were soon all in bed and asleep. The Penruthlans were asleep, too. Only the kitchen cat was awake, watching for mice in the kitchen. She didn't like a crowd. She liked the kitchen to herself!

Next day was fair and warm, though a stiff breeze still blew. Mrs Penruthlan spoke to the four children at breakfast-time.

'I'll be busy today cleaning up the mess. How would you like to take a picnic lunch of some of the remains of the supper and stay out all day? It's a nice day, and you'll enjoy it.'

Nothing could be better! Julian had already planned to make his way to the old tower once used by the Wreckers, and explore it. Now they would have all day to do it in!

'Oh, yes, Mrs Penruthlan, we'd love to do that,' he said. 'We'll get the picnic ready. You've plenty to do!'

But no, Mrs Penruthlan wouldn't let anyone deal with food but herself. She proceeded to pack up enough food for twelve people, or so Julian thought when he saw her preparations!

They set off together happily, with Timmy at their heels. The four farm dogs accompanied them for some way, tearing on in front and then tearing back trying to make Timmy as mad as they were. But Timmy was sedate, walking along as if to say, 'I'm taking these children for a walk, I've not time to play with you. You're only farm dogs!'

'Do we want Yan with us if he turns up?' asked George. 'Do we particularly want him to know what we are doing today?'

Julian considered. 'No, I don't think we *do* want him with us. We may find out something we don't want him to know, or to spread around.'

'Right,' said George. 'Well, just you send him off, then, if he comes. I'm fed up with him. Thank goodness he's a bit cleaner than he was!'

Yan did appear, of course. He came up silently on his bare feet. Nobody would have known he was trotting behind if it hadn't been for Timmy. Timmy quite happily left George's heels and went to say how-do-you-do to Yan, jumping up at him in delight.

George turned round to see where Timmy was, and saw Yan. 'Julian, there's Yan!' she said.

'Hallo, Yan,' said Julian. 'Buzz off today. We're going somewhere alone.'

'I'm coming too,' said Yan, strutting along behind. He still looked fairly clean.

'No, you don't come too,' said Julian. 'You buzz off. See? Off you go. We don't want you today.'

Yan's face took on a sullen look. He turned to Anne. 'Can't I come too?' he said, pleadingly.

Anne shook her head. 'No, not today,' she said. 'Another time. Take this sweet, Yan, and go away.'

Yan took the sweet and turned away, his face sulky. He disappeared over the field and was soon lost to sight.

The four children and Timmy went on together, glad of their warm pullovers when the wind blew strongly. Julian gave a sudden groan.

'I shall be jolly glad when we've had our lunch,' he said. 'This bag of food is so heavy it's cutting into my shoulders.'

'Well, let's wait till we get to the tower and we can put the bags down,' said Dick. 'We'll do a little exploring before we have our lunch. I should think Mrs Penruthlan meant us to stay out to dinner, tea and supper, the amount she's packed for us!'

They hoped they were going in the right direction. They had looked at a map, and found various lanes which they thought would eventually lead to the tower, and had worked out which was the best direction to take.

Julian had his compass and was going by that, leading them down lanes, across fields, along little paths, and sometimes along no paths at all! He felt sure, however, that they were going right. They were making for the coast, anyway.

'Look, there are two hills side by side, or cliffs, are they?' said Anne, pointing. 'I believe they are the hills between which we saw that tower.'

'Yes, you're right,' said Dick. 'We're nearly there. I wonder how people got there when the tower and house were lived in. There appears to be no proper road at all.'

They walked on, over a rough field. They soon found themselves in a very narrow, overgrown lane, deep-set between hedges that almost met overhead.

'A green tunnel,' said Anne, pleased. 'Look out for those enormous nettles, Ju.'

At the end of the lane an overgrown path swung sharply right, and there, not far from them, was the tower! They stood and stared at it. This was where the light had flashed a hundred years ago to bring ships to their doom, and where the light had flashed only the other night.

'The tower's falling into ruins,' said Dick. 'Large pieces have dropped out of it. And I should think the house is in ruins, too, though we can't see enough of it at the moment, just a bit of the roof. Come on. This is going to be fun!'

The tower didn't look the frightening thing it had seemed on the stormy night when the boys saw the flashing light. It just looked a poor old ruin. They made their way to it through high thistles, nettles and willow-herb.

'Doesn't *look* as if anyone has been here for years,' said Julian, rather puzzled. 'I rather wish we'd brought a scythe to cut down these enormous weeds! We can hardly get through them. I'm stung all over with nettles, too.'

They came to the house at last, and a poor, tumbledown ruin it was! The doors had fallen in, the windows were out of shape, and had no glass, the roof was full of holes. An enormous climbing rose rambled everywhere, throwing masses of old-fashioned white roses over walls and roof to hide the ugliness of the ruin.

Only the tower seemed still strong, except at the top, where parts of the wall had crumbled away and fallen. Julian forced his way through the broken doorway into the house. Weeds grew in the floor.

'There's a stone stairway going up the tower!' he called. 'And I say, look here! What's this on each stair?'

'Oil,' said George. 'Someone's been carrying oil up in a can, or a lamp, and has spilt it. Julian, we'd better be careful. That somebody may be here still!'

CHAPTER THIRTEEN

In the Wreckers' tower

DICK AND Anne came hurriedly up to the old stone stairway when they heard what Julian and George had said. Oil! That could only mean one thing: a lamp in the tower.

They all stood and looked at the big splashes of oil on each step.

'Come on up,' said Julian at last. 'I'll go first. Be careful how you go because the tower's in a very crumbly state.'

The tower was built at one end of the old house, and its walls were thicker than the house walls. The only entry to it was by a doorway inside the house. In the tower was a stone stairway that went very steeply up in a spiral.

'This must once have been the door of the tower,' said Dick, kicking at a great, thick slab of wood that lay mouldering away beside the stone doorway. 'The tower doesn't seem to hold anything but this stone stairway, just a lookout, I suppose.'

'Or a place for signalling to ships to entice them on the rocks,' said George. 'Oh, Timmy, don't push past like that; you nearly made me fall, these stone steps are so steep.'

As Dick said, the tower seemed to hold nothing but a stairway spiralling up steeply. Julian came to the top first and gave a gasp. The view over the sea was astonishing. He could see for miles over the dark cornflower-blue waters. Near the coast the churning of the waves into white breakers and spray showed the hidden rocks that waited for unwary ships.

George came up beside him and stared in wonder, too. What a marvellous sight: blue sky, blue sea, waves pounding over the rocks, and white gulls soaring on the stiff breeze.

Then Dick came up, and Julian gave him a warning. 'Be careful. Don't lean on the walls at all, they're crumbling badly.'

Julian put out his hand and touched the top of the tower wall near him. It crumbled and bits fell away below.

Big pieces had fallen away here and there, leaving great gaps in the wall round the top of the tower. When Anne came up also, Julian took her arm, afraid that with such a crowd up there someone might stumble against a crumbling wall and fall from the tower.

George had hold of Timmy's collar and made him stand quite still. 'Don't you go putting your great paws up on the wall,' she warned him. 'You'll find yourself down in the nettles below in no time if you do!'

'You can quite well see what a wonderful place this is for flashing a light at night over the sea,' said Dick. 'It could be seen for miles. In the old days, when sailing ships got caught in the storms that rage round this coast at times, they would be thankful to see a guiding light.'

'But what a light!' said Julian. 'A light that guided them straight on to those great rocks! Let me see now. Are those the rocks near those coves we went to the other day?'

'Yes, I think so,' said Dick. 'But there are rocks and rocks, and coves and coves round here. It's difficult to tell if they are the same ones we saw.'

'The ships that sailed towards the light must have been wrecked on the rocks down there,' said Julian, pointing. 'How did the Wreckers get there? There must have been a path from here somewhere.'

'The Wreckers' Way, do you think?' said Dick.

Julian considered. 'Well, I don't know. I imagine that the Wreckers' Way must have been a way leading to the sea from inland somewhere, certainly a way that was convenient for the villagers to use. No. I'll tell you what *I* think happened!'

'What?' said everyone.

'I think, on a stormy night long ago, the people who lived here in this house went up into the tower and flashed their false light to any ship that was sailing out on the waters. Then, in great excitement, they watched it sailing nearer and nearer, perhaps shown up by the lightning, perhaps by the moon.'

Everyone imagined such a ship, and George shivered. Poor wretched ship!

'When the ship reached the rocks and crashed on them, the signallers in the tower gave a different signal, a signal to a watcher up there on the hills,' said Julian, pointing behind him. 'A watcher who was standing on the only spot from which the flash could be seen! Maybe the light gleamed steadily to entice a ship in, but was flashed in code to the watcher on the hills, and the flashing said, 'Ship on rocks. Tell the others, and come to the feast!'

'How simply horrible!' said Anne. 'I can't believe it!'

'It *is* difficult to think anyone could be so heartless,' said Julian. 'But I think that's what happened. And then, I think, the people who lived in this house went down from here to the nearby coves and waited for their friends to come along the other way, the Wreckers' Way, wherever that is.'

'It must be a secret way,' said Dick. 'It must have been a way known only to those villagers who *were* Wreckers. After all, wrecking was against the law, and so this whole business of showing lights and wrecking ships must have been kept a dead secret. We heard what old Grandad said, that every Wrecker who knew the way had to vow he would tell no one else.'

'Old Grandad's father probably lived in this very house, and climbed the stone stairway on a wild night, and lit the lamp that shone out over the stormy sea,' said Julian.

'That's why Yan said he was frightened of this tower,' said George. 'He thinks his grandad's dad still lights it! Well, we know better. Somebody else lights it, somebody who can't be up to any good either!'

'And, don't let's forget, somebody who may still be about somewhere!' said Julian, lowering his voice suddenly.

'Gosh! yes,' said Dick, looking round the little tower as if he expected to see a stranger there, listening. 'I wonder where he keeps his lamp. It's not here.'

'The oil splashes are on almost every one of the stone steps,' said Anne. 'I noticed as I came up. I bet it's a big lamp. It has to give a light far out to sea!'

'Look, it must have been stood on this bit of the wall,' said Dick. 'There are some oily patches here.'

They all looked at the oily patches. Dick bent down and smelt them. 'Yes, paraffin oil,' he said.

George was looking at the wall on the other side of the tower. She called to the other three.

'And here's a patch on *this* side!' she said. 'I know what happened! Once a ship had been caught by the light and was on its way in, the men with the lamp put it on the *other* side of the tower to signal to the watcher on the hills, to tell him the ship was caught!'

'Yes. That's it,' said Anne. 'But who could it be? I'm sure nobody lives *here*, the place is an absolute ruin, open to the wind and the rain. It must be somebody who knows the way here, sees to the light, and does the signalling.'

There was a pause. Dick looked at Julian. The same thought came into their minds. *They* had seen somebody wandering out in the stormy night, twice!

'Could it be Mr Penruthlan, do you suppose?' said Dick. 'We couldn't *imagine* why he was out here in the storm the first night we came out to watch for the light.'

'No, he's not the man with the light, *he's the watcher on the hills*!' said Julian. 'That's it! That's why he goes out on wild nights, to see if there's a signal from the tower, flashing to say that a ship is coming in!'

There was an even longer pause. Nobody liked that idea at all.

'We know he tells lies, we know he goes through people's pockets, because we saw him,' went on Julian after a few moments. 'He fits in well. He's the man who goes and stands in that special spot on the hills and watches for a light!'

'What does he do after that?' said Anne. 'Didn't we

hear that there were no wrecks here now, because of the lighthouse higher up the coast? What's the point of it all, if there isn't a wreck?'

'Smuggling,' said Julian shortly. 'That's the point. Probably by motorboat. They choose a wild night of storm and wind, when they will be neither seen nor heard, wait out at sea for the signalling light to show them all's clear, and then come into one of these coves.'

'Yes, and I bet the Wreckers' secret way is used by someone who steals down to the cove and takes the smuggled goods!' said Dick, excited. 'Three or four people, perhaps, if the goods are heavy. Gosh! I'm sure we're right.'

'And it's the watcher on the hill who tells his friends, and down they go to the coves together. It's most ingenious,' Julian said. 'Nobody sees the light on the tower except the boat waiting, and nobody sees the signal inland except the one watcher on the hills. Absolutely foolproof.'

'We are lucky to stumble on it,' said Dick. 'But what puzzles me is this. I'm pretty certain that the man who lights the lamp didn't come the way *we* came – we'd have seen trodden-down weeds or something. We should certainly have found some sort of a path his feet had made.'

'Yes. And there wasn't anything, not even a broken thistle,' said Anne. 'There must be some other way into this old house.'

'Of course there is! We've already said there must be a

way for the man who lights the lamp to get down to the coves from here!' said George. 'Well, that's the way he gets here, of course. He comes up the passage from the cove. How stupid we are!'

This idea excited them all. Where was the passage? Nobody could imagine! It certainly wasn't in the tower, there was no room for anything in that small tower except for the spiral staircase leading to the top.

'Let's go down,' said Anne, and began to descend the steps. A slight noise below made her stop. 'Go on,' said George, who was just behind her. Anne turned a scared face to her.

'I heard a noise down there,' she whispered.

George turned to Julian immediately. 'Anne thinks there's somebody down there,' she said, in a low voice.

'Come back, Anne,' ordered Julian at once. Anne climbed back, still looking scared.

'Would it be the man who does the lamp?' she whispered. 'Do be careful, Julian. He can't be a nice man!'

'Nice! He must be a beast!' said George, scornfully. 'Are you going down, Ju? Look out, then.'

Julian peered down the stone steps. There was really nothing for it but to go down and see who was there. They couldn't possibly stay up in the tower all day long, hoping that whoever it was would go away!

'What sort of noise did you hear?' Julian asked Anne.

'Well, a sort of scuffling noise,' said Anne. 'It might have been a rat, of course, or a rabbit. It was just a noise, that's all. Something's down there, or somebody!'

'Let's sit down for a moment or two and wait,' said Dick. 'We'll listen hard and see if we can hear anyone.'

So they sat down cautiously, George with her hand on Timmy's collar. They waited and they listened. They heard the wind blowing round the old tower. They heard the distant gulls calling, 'ee-oo, ee-oo, ee-oo'. They heard the thistles rustling their prickles together down below.

But they heard nothing from the kitchen at the foot of the tower. Julian looked at Anne. 'No sound to be heard now,' he said. 'It must have been a rabbit!'

'Perhaps it was,' said Anne, feeling rather foolish. 'What shall we do then? Go down?'

'Yes. I'll go first though, with Timmy,' said Julian.

'If anyone is lying in wait he'll be annoyed to see our Timmy. And Timmy will be even more annoyed to see him!'

Just as Julian was getting up, a noise was quite distinctly heard from below. It was, as Anne had described, a kind of scuffle, then silence.

'Well, here goes!' said Julian, and began to descend the steps. The others watched breathlessly. Timmy went with Julian, trying to press past him. He hadn't seemed worried about the noise at all! So perhaps it *was* only a rat or rabbit!

Julian went down slowly. Who was he going to find – an enemy, or a friend? Careful now, Julian, there may be somebody lying in wait!

CHAPTER FOURTEEN

The secret passage

JULIAN PAUSED on the last step of the spiral staircase and listened. Not a sound came from the nearby room. 'Who's there?' said Julian, sharply. 'I know you're there! I heard you!'

Still not a sound! The kitchen, overgrown with weeds and dark with ivy and the white rambling rose, seemed to be listening to him, but there was no answer!

Julian stepped right into the room and looked round. Nothing was there – nobody was there! The place was absolutely empty and quiet. Julian went through a doorway into another room. That was empty, too. The old house only had four rooms altogether, two of them very tiny, and every one of them was empty. Timmy didn't seem disturbed at all, either, nor did he bark as he certainly would have done if there had been any intruder there.

'Well, Timmy, it's a false alarm,' said Julian, relieved. 'Must have been a rabbit, or even a bit of wall crumbling and falling. What are you sniffing at there?'

Timmy was sniffing with interest at a corner near the doorway. He stood and looked at Julian as if he would like to tell him something. Julian went over to see what it was.

There was nothing there except for some rather flattened

weeds, growing through the floor. Julian couldn't think why Timmy should be interested. However, Timmy soon wandered away and went all round the place, wondering why they had come to such a peculiar house.

'Dick! Bring the girls down!' shouted Julian up the stone stairway. 'There doesn't seem to be anyone here, after all. It must have been some small animal that Anne heard.'

The others clattered down in relief. 'I'm sorry I gave you all a shock,' said Anne. 'But it did sound like somebody down there! However, I'm sure Timmy would have barked if so! He didn't seem at all disturbed.'

'No. I think we can safely say that it was a false alarm,' said Dick. 'What do we do next? Have our lunch? Or hunt about to see if we can find the entrance to the passage that leads from here down to the coves?'

Julian looked at his watch. 'It's not really time for lunch yet, unless you're all frightfully hungry,' he said.

'Well, I'm *beginning* to feel jolly hungry,' said Dick. 'But, on the other hand, I feel I can't wait to find that passage! Where on earth is the entrance?'

'I've been in all four rooms,' said Julian. 'None of them seems to have anything but weeds in them, no old door leading out of the walls, no trapdoor. It's a puzzle.'

'Well, we'll all have a jolly good hunt,' said George. 'This is the sort of thing I like. Timmy, you hunt, too!'

They began to explore the four rooms of the old house. As weeds grew more or less all over the floor they felt that there could be no trapdoor. If there had been, and the man with the lamp used it, the weeds would surely have shown signs of it. But they grew quite undisturbed.

'Listen,' said Julian at last. 'I've got an idea. We'll make Timmy find the entrance.'

'How?' said George at once.

'Well, we'll make him smell the oil drips on the steps, and follow with his nose any others that have dripped in the weeds,' said Julian. 'I don't suppose the lamp dripped only on the steps. It must have dripped all the way from the passage entrance, wherever it is, to the top of the tower. Couldn't Timmy sniff them out? They would lead us to the entrance we're trying to find!'

'All right. But I'm beginning to believe there *is* no entrance,' said George, getting hold of Timmy's collar. 'We've looked over every single inch of this house. Come on, Tim, you've got to perform a miracle!'

Timmy's nose was firmly placed over the oil-drip on the bottom stair. 'Sniff it, Timmy, and follow,' said George.

Timmy knew perfectly well what she meant. George had trained him well! He sniffed hard at the oil and then started up the stone steps for the next oil patch. But George pulled him back.

'No, Tim. Not that way. This way. There must be other oil drips on the floor of the house.'

Timmy amiably turned the other way. He found an oil drip at once, on a patch of weeds growing on the floor. He sniffed it and went on to another and another.

'Good old Timmy,' said George, delighted. 'Isn't he

clever, Ju? He's following where the man walked when he carried that lamp! Go on, Timmy, where's the next drip?'

It was an easy, strong-smelling trail for Timmy to follow! He followed it, sniffing, out of one room into another, smaller one. Then into a third, bigger one, which must have been the main room, for it had a very big fireplace, his nose to the ground. In fact, he went right into the hearth, and there came to a stop. He looked round at George and barked.

'He says the trail ends here,' said George, in excitement. 'So the entrance to the secret passage must be in this big fireplace!'

The others crowded to the hearth. Julian produced his torch and shone it up the chimney. It was an enormous one, though part of the top of it had now fallen away. 'Nothing there,' said Julian. 'But – hallo – what's this?'

He now shone his torch to the side of the big fireplace and saw a small, dark cavity there, barely big enough for a man to get into. 'Look!' he said, excited, 'I believe we've found it. See that small hole? Well, I bet if we crawl through that we'll find it's the way to the secret passage! Good old Timmy!'

'We shall get absolutely *filthy*,' said Anne.

'You *would* say that!' said George, scornfully. 'Who cares? This could be very important, couldn't it, Ju?'

'Rather!' said Julian. 'If we're on to what we think we are, and that's Smuggling with a big S, it *is* important. Well, what about it? Lunch first, or exploring that hole?'

'Exploring, of course,' said Dick. 'What about letting old Tim go first? I'll give him a leg-up.'

Timmy was hoisted up to the black hole, and disappeared into it with delight. Rabbits? Rats? What were the children after? This was a fine game!

'Now I'll go,' said Julian, and clambered up. 'It's a bit difficult to squeeze into. Dick, you help Anne and George up next, and then you come.'

He disappeared, and one by one the others also hoisted themselves to the hole and crawled in, too.

The hole was merely an entrance to a narrow standing-place at the side of the chimney. Julian got down from the hole, and stood still for a moment, wondering if this was just an old hiding place, and not an entrance to anywhere, after all. But then, just to the right of his feet, he saw another hole that dropped sharply down.

He flashed his torch down, and saw iron hand-grips at one side. He called back and told the others. Then he descended into the hole, at first using the grips for his feet and then for his hands as well.

The hole went down as straight as a well. It came to a sudden end, and Julian found himself standing on solid ground. He turned round, flashing his torch.

There was the passage in front of him! It must be the one that led down to the coves, the one that the man with the lamp must have used long ago, when he went to gloat over the groaning ships on the rocks.

Julian could hear the others coming down the shaft. He suddenly thought of Timmy. Where was he? He must have fallen headlong down the hole and found himself suddenly at the bottom. Poor Tim! Julian hoped he hadn't hurt himself, but as he hadn't yelped, perhaps he had fallen like a cat, on his feet!

He called up to the others. 'I've found the passage. It starts at the bottom of the shaft. I'll go along it a little way and wait for you all to come. Then we can keep together in a line.'

Soon everyone was safely down the shaft. George began to worry about Timmy. 'He *must* have hurt himself, Ju! Falling all that way; oh, dear, where is he?'

'We'll soon come across him, I expect,' said Julian. 'Now, keep close together, everybody. The path goes downwards pretty steeply, as you might expect.'

It certainly did. In places the four children almost slithered along. Then Julian discovered iron staples fixed here and there in the steepest places, and after that they held on to them in the most slippery spots.

'These iron staples would be jolly useful to anyone coming *up*,' said Julian. 'It would be almost impossible to climb up this passage without something to help the climber to pull himself up. Ah, here's a more level stretch.'

The level part soon became much wider. And then, quite suddenly, it became a cave! The four came out into it in surprise. It was rather low-roofed, and the walls were made of black rock that glistened in the light of the torch.

'I wish I could find Timmy,' said George, uneasily. 'I can't even hear him anywhere!'

'We'll go on till we come to the cove,' said Julian. 'This must lead us right down to the shore, probably to the very cove where the ships were wrecked. Look, there's a kind of rocky arch leading out of this cave.'

They went through the archway and into yet another passage that wound between jutting rocks, which made it rather difficult to get through at times. Then suddenly the passage divided into two. One fork went meandering off towards the seaward side, the other into the cliff.

'Better take the seaward side,' said Julian. They were just going to take the right-hand passage when George stopped and clutched at Julian. 'Listen!' she said. 'I can hear Timmy!'

They all stopped and listened. George had the sharpest ears of the lot, and she could hear him barking. So could the others after a few moments. Bark-bark-bark! Bark-bark-bark! Yes, it was Timmy all right!

'Timmy!' yelled George, making the others jump almost out of their skins. 'TIMMY!'

'He can't hear you all this way away,' said Dick. 'Gosh, you made me jump. Come on, we'll have to take the cliff passage. Timmy's barking comes from that direction, not this.'

'Yes, I agree,' said Julian. 'We'll go and collect him, and then come back and take the other passage. I'm sure it leads down to the sea.'

They made their way along the left-hand passage. It was not difficult, because it was much wider than the one they had already come down. Timmy's barking became louder and louder as they went down. George whistled piercingly, hoping that Timmy would come rushing up. But he didn't.

'It's funny that he doesn't come,' said George, worried. 'I think he must be hurt. TIMMY!'

The passage wound round a corner, and then once more divided into two. To the children's surprise they saw a rough door set into the rocky wall of the passage on the left-hand side. A door! How very extraordinary!

'Look, a door!' said Dick, amazed. 'And a jolly stout one, too.'

'Timmy's behind it!' said George. 'He must have gone through it and it shut behind him. Timmy! We're here! We're coming!'

She pushed at the door, but it didn't open. She saw that it was lightly latched, and lifted the old iron latch. The door opened easily and all four went through into a curious cave beyond. It was more like a low-roofed room!

Timmy flung himself at them as soon as they came through the door. He wasn't hurt. He was so pleased to see them that he barked the place down! 'Woof! WOOOOOF!'

'Oh, Timmy, how did you get here?' said George, hugging him. 'Did the door click behind you? My word, what a strange place this is! It's a storeroom – look at all the boxes and crates and things!'

They looked round the strange cave, and at that moment there was a soft click. Then something slid smoothly into place. Julian leapt to the door and tried to open it.

'It's locked! Somebody's locked it, and bolted it! I heard them. Let us out, let us *out*!'

CHAPTER FIFTEEN

Locked in the cave

DICK, GEORGE and Anne looked at one another in dismay. Someone must have been lying in wait for them, someone must have captured Timmy and shut him up. And now they were captured, too!

Timmy began to bark when Julian shouted. He ran to the door. Julian was hammering on it and even kicking it.

A voice came from the other side of the door, a drawling voice, sounding rather amused.

'You came at an awkward time, that's all, and you must remain where you are till tomorrow.'

'Who are you?' said Julian fiercely. 'How dare you lock us in like this!'

'I believe you have food and drink with you,' said the voice. 'I noticed the packs on your backs, which I presume contain food. That is lucky for you! Now be sensible. You must pay the penalty for being inquisitive!'

'You let us out!' shouted Julian, enraged at the cool voice with its impertinent tone. He kicked the door again out of temper, though he knew that it wasn't the slightest use!

There was no reply. Whoever it was outside the cave door had gone. Julian gave the door one last furious kick and looked round at the others.

'That man must have been watching us from somewhere. Probably followed us all the way to the old house, and saw the packs on our backs then. It must have been him that you heard down in the house when we were in the tower, Anne.'

Timmy barked again. He was still at the door. George called him. 'Tim! It's no use! The door's locked. Oh dear, why did we let you go into that hole first? If you hadn't run on ahead and somehow got yourself caught, you'd have been able to protect us when those men lay in wait!'

'Well, what do we do now?' said Anne, trying to sound brave.

'What *can* we do?' said George. 'Nothing at all! Here we are, locked and bolted in a cave inside the cliff, with nobody near except the fellow who locked us in. If anybody's got any ideas I'd like to hear them!'

'You do sound cross!' said Anne. 'I suppose there isn't anything to do but wait till we're let out. I only hope that man remembers we're here. Nobody else knows where we are.'

'Horrid thought!' said Dick. 'Still, I've no doubt that Mrs Penruthlan would raise the alarm, and a search-party would set out to find us.'

'What a hope they'd have!' said George. 'Even if they did trace us to the old tower, they wouldn't know the secret entrance to the passage!'

'Well, let's look on the cheerful side,' said Julian,

undoing the pack from his back. 'Let's have some food.'

Everybody cheered up at once. 'I feel quite hungry,' said Anne in surprise. 'It must be past our dinner-time now. Well, anyway, eating will be something to do!'

They had a very good meal and felt thankful that Mrs Penruthlan had packed up so much food. If they were not going to be let out till the next day they would need plenty to eat!

They examined the boxes and crates. Some were very old. All were empty. There was a big seaman's chest there, too, with 'Abram Trelawny' painted on it. They lifted the lid. That was empty too, save for one old brass button.

'Abram Trelawny,' said Dick, looking at the name. 'He must have been a sailor on one of the ships that the Wreckers enticed to the rocks. This chest must have been rolled up on the beach by the waves and brought up here. I dare say this cave was the place where the man who owned that old house took his share of the booty and hid it.'

'Yes, I think you're right,' said Julian. 'That is why it has a door that can be locked. The Wreckers probably stored quite a lot of valuable things here from different wrecks, and didn't want any other Wrecker to creep up from the cave and take them. What a hateful lot they must have been! Well, there doesn't seem anything of real interest here.'

LOCKED IN THE CAVE

It was very, very boring in the cave. The children used only one torch because they were afraid that if they used the others they had brought they might exhaust all the batteries, and then have to be in the dark.

Julian examined the cave from top to bottom to see if there was any possible way of escape. But there wasn't. That was quite clear. The cave walls were made of solid rocks, and there wasn't a hole anywhere through which to escape, big or small!

'That man said we'd come at an awkward time,' said Julian, throwing himself down on the ground. 'Why? Are they expecting some smuggled goods tonight? They've signalled out to sea twice already this week, as *we* know. Hasn't the boat they expected come along yet? If so, they must be expecting it tonight, and so we've come at an awkward time!'

'If only we weren't locked in this beastly cave!' said George. 'We might have spied on them and seen what they were up to, and might even have been able to stop them somehow, or get word to the police.'

'Well, we can't now,' said Dick gloomily. 'Timmy, you were an ass to get caught; you really were.'

Timmy put his tail down and looked as gloomy as Dick. He didn't like being in this low-roofed cave. Why didn't they open the door and go out? He went to the door and whined, scraping at it with his feet.

'No good, Tim. It won't open,' said Anne. 'I think he's thirsty, George.'

There was nothing for Timmy to drink except homemade lemonade, and he didn't seem to like that very much.

'Don't waste it on him if he doesn't like it,' said Julian, hastily. 'We may be jolly glad of it ourselves tomorrow.'

Dick glanced at his watch. 'Only half past two!' he groaned. 'Hours and hours to wait. Let's have a game of some sort, noughts and crosses would be better than nothing.'

They played noughts and crosses till they were sick of them. They played word games and guessing games. They had a light tea at five o'clock and began to wonder what Mrs Penruthlan would think when they didn't turn up that evening.

'If Mr Penruthlan is mixed up in this affair, and it's pretty certain that he is,' said Julian, 'he'll not be best pleased to be told to fetch the police to look for *us*! It's just the one night he won't want the police about!'

'I think you're wrong,' said George. 'I think he'd be delighted to have the police looking for lost children, and not poking their noses into *his* affairs tonight!'

'I hadn't thought of that,' said Julian. How slowly the time went by. They yawned, talked, fell silent, argued and played with Timmy. Julian's torch flickered out and they took Dick's instead.

'Good thing we brought more than one torch!' said Anne.

Half past nine came and they all began to feel sleepy.

'I vote we try to go to sleep,' said Dick, yawning hugely.

'There's a sandy spot over there, softer to lie on than this rock. What about trying to sleep?'

They all thought it was a good idea and went to the sandy spot. It certainly was better than the hard rock. They wriggled about in the sand and made dents for their bodies to lie in.

'It's still hard,' complained George. 'Oh, Timmy darling, *don't* snuffle all round my face. Lie down beside me and Anne and go to sleep, too!'

Timmy lay down on George's legs. He put his nose on his paws and heaved a huge sigh.

'I hope Timmy's not going to do *that* all night,' said Anne. 'What a draught!'

Although they thought they couldn't possibly go to sleep, they did. Timmy did, too, though he kept one ear open and one eye ready to open. He was on guard! No one could open that door or even come near it without Timmy hearing!

At about eleven o'clock Timmy opened one eye and cocked both ears. He listened, not taking his head off George's legs. He opened the other eye.

Then he sat up and listened harder. George woke up when he moved and stretched out a hand to Timmy. 'Tim, lie down,' she whispered. But Timmy didn't. He gave a small whine.

George sat up, fully awake. Why was Timmy whining? Was there something going on outside the door, men passing perhaps, on their way to the cove? Had the light been flashing out to sea and had it brought in the boat the men were waiting for?

She put her hand on Timmy's collar. 'What is it?' she whispered, expecting Timmy to growl when he next heard something. But he didn't growl. He whined again.

Then he shook off George's hand and went to the door. George switched on her torch, puzzled. Timmy scraped at the door and whined again. But he still didn't growl.

'Ju! I believe someone is at the door!' called George, suddenly, in a low voice. 'I believe Timmy can hear a search party or something. Wake up!'

Everyone awoke suddenly. George repeated her words again. 'Timmy's not growling. That means it's not our enemies he hears,' she added. 'He'd growl like anything at the man who locked us in.'

'Be quiet for a moment and listen,' said Julian. 'Let's see if we can hear anything ourselves. We haven't got Timmy's sharp ears, but we might be able to hear *some*thing.'

They sat absolutely still, listening. Then Julian nudged Dick. He had heard something. 'Quiet!' he breathed. They listened again, hardly breathing.

They heard a little scrabbling noise at the door. Then it stopped. George expected Timmy to break out into a fusillade of barks at once, but he didn't. He stood there with his head on one side and his ears cocked. He gave an excited little whine and suddenly scraped at the door again.

Somebody whispered outside the door, and Timmy whined and ran to George and then back to the door again. Everyone was puzzled.

Julian got up and went to the door himself, his feet making no sound. Yes, there was most certainly somebody outside, two people, perhaps, whispering to one another.

'Who's there?' said Julian suddenly. 'I can hear you outside. Who is it?'

There was dead silence for a moment, and then a small familiar voice answered softly:

'It's me. Yan.'

'Yan! Gosh! Is it really you?'

'Yes.'

There was an amazed silence in the cave. Yan! Yan at this time of night outside the door of the very cave they were locked in! Were they dreaming?

Timmy went mad when he heard Yan speaking to Julian. He flung himself at the door, barking and yelping. Julian puts his hand on his collar. 'Be quiet, idiot! You'll spoil everything! Be *quiet*!'

Timmy stopped. Julian spoke to Yan again. 'Yan, have you got a light?'

'No, no light. It is dark here,' said Yan. 'Can I come to you?'

'Yes, of course. Listen, Yan. Do you know how to unlock and unbolt a door?' asked Julian, wondering whether the half-wild boy knew even such simple things.

'Yes,' said Yan. 'Are you locked in?'

'Yes,' said Julian. 'But the key may be in the lock. Feel and see. Feel for the bolts, too. Slide them back and turn the key if there is one.'

The four in the cave held their breath as they heard Yan's hands wandering over the stout door in the dark, tapping here and there to find the bolts and the lock.

Then they heard the bolts being slid smoothly back. How they hoped their captor had left the key in the lock!

'Here is a key,' said Yan's voice suddenly. 'But it is so stiff. My hand isn't strong enough to turn it.'

'Try both hands at once,' said Julian urgently.

They heard Yan trying, panting with his efforts. But the key would not turn.

'Blow!' said Dick. 'So near and yet so far!'

Anne pushed Dick out of the way, an idea suddenly flooding into her mind. 'Yan! Listen to me, Yan. Take the key out of the lock and push it under the bottom of the door. Do you hear me?'

'Yes, I heard,' said Yan, and they heard him tugging at the key. There was a sharp noise as it came suddenly out of the lock. Then, lo and behold! it appeared under the bottom of the door, slid through carefully by Yan!

Julian snatched it up and put it into the lock on his side. He turned the key, and unlocked the door. What a wonderful bit of luck!

CHAPTER SIXTEEN

Wreckers' Way

Julian flung open the door. Timmy leapt past him and yelped with delight to find Yan standing outside. He fawned on the boy and licked him, and Yan laughed.

'Let's get out of here, quick!' said Dick. 'That man may be along at any moment, you can't tell.'

'Right. Explanations later,' said Julian. He hustled everyone out, took the key from the inside lock and shut the door. He inserted the key into the outside lock and turned it. He shot the bolts, took out the key and put it into his pocket. He grinned at Dick.

'Now if that man comes along to see how we are he won't even know we're gone! He won't be able to get in to see if we're there or not.'

'Where shall we go now?' asked Anne, feeling as if she was in a peculiar kind of dream.

Julian stood and considered. 'It would be madness to go back up the passage and into the old house,' he said. 'If there's any signalling going on, and there's pretty certain to be, we shall be caught again. We'd be sure to make a noise scrambling out of that hole in the fireplace.'

'Well, let's take that other passage we saw, the

right-hand one,' said George. 'Look, there it is.' She shone her torch on it. 'Where does it lead to, Yan?'

'To the beach,' said Yan. 'I went down it when I was looking for you all, but you weren't there, so I came back and found that door. There is nobody on the beach.'

'Well, let's go down there, then,' said Dick. 'Once we feel we're out of danger's way we can plan what's best to do.'

They went along the other passage, their torch showing them the way. It was a steep tunnel, and they found it rather difficult going. Anne managed to give Yan a squeeze.

'You were clever to find us!' she said, and Yan gave her a smile which she couldn't see because of the dark.

They heard the sound of waves at last and came out into the open air. It was a windy night but stars were shining in the sky, and gave quite a fair light after the darkness of the passage.

'Where are we exactly?' said Dick, looking round. Then he saw they were on the same beach as they had been a few days before, but a good way farther along.

'Can we get back to the farm from here?' said Julian, stopping to consider exactly where they were. 'Gosh! I think we'd better hurry. The tide's coming in! We'll be cut off if we don't look out!'

A wave ran up the sand almost to their feet. Julian took a quick look at the cliff behind them. It was very steep.

They certainly couldn't climb it in the darkness! Would there be time to look for a cave to sit in till the tide went out again?

Another wave ran up, and Julian's feet felt suddenly wet. 'Blow!' he said. 'This is getting serious. The next big one will sweep us off our feet. I wish the moon was out. These stars give such a faint light.'

'Yan, is there a cave we can go to, a cave open to the air, not inside the cliff?' said George, anxiously.

'I'll take you back by the Wreckers' Way,' said Yan, surprisingly. 'Come with me.'

'Of course, you said you knew the Wreckers' Way,' said Julian, remembering. 'If it comes out near here, we're in luck's way! Lead on, Yan. You're a marvel! But do hurry, our feet got wet again just then, and at any moment a giant of a wave may come!'

Yan took the lead. He led them into cove after cove, and then came to a larger one than usual. He took them to the back of the cove, and led them a little way up a cliff path.

He came to a great rock. He squeezed behind it and the others followed one by one. Nobody could ever have guessed that there was a way into the cliff behind that rock.

'Now we are in the Wreckers' Way,' said Yan proudly, and led them on again. But suddenly he stopped and the others all bumped into one another. Timmy gave a short, warning bark, and George put her hand on his collar.

'Somebody's coming!' whispered Yan, and pushed them back. Sure enough, they could hear voices in the distance. They turned and hurried back. They didn't want to walk into any more trouble!

Yan got to the front and led them back to the big rock. He was trembling. They all squeezed out behind it, and Yan went along the cliff face to a tiny cave, really only a big ledge with an overhanging roof. 'Sssssssss!' he said warningly, sounding like a snake!

They sat down and waited. Two men came out from behind the rock, one a big man, and one a small one. Nobody could see them clearly, but Julian hissed into Dick's ear: 'I'm sure that's Mr Penruthlan! See how enormous he is!'

Dick nodded. It was no surprise to him to think that the giant farmer should be mixed up in this. The five children held their breath and watched.

Yan nudged Dick and pointed out to sea. 'Boat coming!' he whispered.

Dick could see and hear nothing. But in a few moments he did hear something, the whirr of a fast motorboat! What sharp ears Yan must have! The others heard the noise, too, through the crashing of the waves on the rocks.

'No light,' whispered Yan, as the noise of the boat grew louder.

'He'll be on the rocks!' said Dick. But before the boat got to the rocks, the engine stopped. The children could just make out the boat now, swaying up and down beyond the barrier of rocks. Evidently it was not going to try and come any farther in.

Now the watchers could hear voices again. The two men who had come down Wreckers' Way were standing below the big rock that hid the entrance, talking. One leapt down to a rock farther down, and disappeared. The other man was left standing alone.

'It was the big man who leapt down,' whispered Julian. 'Where's he gone? Ah, there he is! You can just see him moving behind that rock down there. What's he got?'

'A boat!' whispered Yan. 'He has a boat down there, pulled up high out of reach of the big waves. There is a pool there. He is going to row out to the other boat.'

The children strained their eyes to watch. The sky was quite clear, but the only light they had was from the stars, and it was difficult to see anything more than moving shadows or outlines.

Then there came the sound of oars in rowlocks, and a moving black shadow of a rowing boat and man could be seen faintly, going over the waves.

'Does he know the way through that mass of rocks?' wondered Dick. 'He must know this coast well to risk rowing out through the rocks at high tide in the dead of night!'

'Why is he doing it?'

'He's getting smuggled goods from the motorboat,' said Julian. 'Goodness knows what! There, I've lost him in the darkness.'

So had everyone. They could no longer hear the oars either, for the crashing of the waves on the rocks drowned every other sound.

Beyond the rocks lay the motorboat, but only Yan's sharp eyes could see it even faintly in the starlight. Once, in a sudden silence of the waves, there came the exchange of voices over the water.

'He's reached the motorboat,' said Dick. 'He'll be back in a minute.'

'Look! The second man is going down to the cove now, going to help the first one in, I expect,' said Julian. 'What about us escaping through the Wreckers' Way while we've got the chance?'

'Good idea,' said George, scrambling up. 'Come on, Timmy! Home!'

They went to the great rock and squeezed behind it once more into the entrance of the Wreckers' Way. Then, Yan once more leading, they went up the secret passage, flicking on the torch very thankfully.

'Where does the Wreckers' Way come out?' asked Anne.

'In a shed at Tremannon Farm,' said Yan, to the astonishment of everyone.

'Goodness, so it's very nice and handy for Mr Penruthlan!' said George. 'I wonder how many times he has been up on the hills at night, and has been warned by the tower light to go down Wreckers' Way to the cove and collect smuggled goods from some boat or other! A very good scheme, it seems to me, and impossible for anyone to find out.'

'Except us!' said Dick in a pleased voice. 'We got on to it pretty well. There's not much we don't know about Mr Penruthlan now!'

They went on and on. The passage was fairly straight and had probably been the bed of an underground stream at some time. The way was quite smooth to the feet.

'We've walked about a mile, I should think!' groaned Dick, at last. 'How far now, Yan? Shall we soon be back?'

'Yes,' said Yan.

Anne suddenly remembered that nobody knew how it was that Yan had found them that night. She turned to him.

'Yan, how did you find us tonight? It seemed like a miracle when we woke up to find you outside that locked door!'

'It was easy,' said Yan. 'You said to me: "Go away. Do not come with us today." So I went back a little way. But I followed you. I followed you to the old house, though I was frightened.'

'I guess you were frightened!' said Dick with a grin. 'Well, go on.'

'I hid,' said Yan. 'You went up into the tower a long time. I came out into the room below, and . . .'

'It was *you* we heard scuffling there, then!' said Anne. 'We wondered who it was!'

'Yes,' said Yan. 'I sat down on some weeds in a corner,

and waited till you came down, and then I hid again: but I watched you through a hole from outside. I saw you go through the fireplace. One minute you were there. The next you were gone. I was frightened.'

'So it was you who flattened down that patch of weeds that Timmy sniffed at?' said Dick. 'Well, what did you do next?'

'I was going to come too,' said Yan. 'But the hole was so dark and black. I stood in the fireplace for a long time, hoping you would come back.'

'Then what happened?' said Dick.

'Then I heard voices,' said Yan. 'I thought it was you all coming back. But it wasn't. It was men. So I ran away and hid in the nettles.'

'What a place to choose!' said George.

'Then I was hungry,' said Yan, 'and I went back to Grandad's hut for food. He cuffed me for leaving him, and he made me work for him all day. He was angry with me.'

'My word! So you've been on the hills all day, knowing we were down in that passage!' said Julian. 'Didn't you say anything to anyone?'

'I went down to Tremannon Farm to see if you were back when it grew dark,' said Yan. 'But you weren't there. Only the Barnies were there, giving another show. I didn't see Mr or Mrs Penruthlan. I knew then that you must still be down in that dark hole. I was afraid the men had hurt you.'

'So you came all the way again in the dark!' said Julian, astonished. 'Well, you've got pluck, I must say!'

'I was very frightened,' said Yan. 'My legs shook at the knees like my old Grandad's. I climbed in at the hole, and at last I found you.'

'With no torch to light the way!' said Dick, and clapped the small boy on the back. 'You're a real friend, Yan! Timmy knew you all right when you came to the locked door. He didn't even bark! He knew it was you.'

'I wanted to save Timmy too,' said Yan. 'Timmy is my friend.'

George said nothing to that. She was thinking rather unwillingly that Yan was a remarkably brave young man, and that she had been silly and unkind to resent Timmy's

liking for him. What a good thing he *had* liked Yan!

Yan suddenly stopped. 'We are there,' he said. 'We are at Tremannon Farm. Look above your heads.'

Julian flashed his torch upwards, and stared. An open trapdoor was just above them.

'The trapdoor is open!' he said. 'Someone came down here tonight!'

'And we know who!' said Dick, grimly. 'Mr Penruthlan and his friend! Where does that trapdoor lead to, Yan?'

'Into a corner of the machine shed,' said Yan. 'When the trapdoor is shut, it is covered with sacks of corn or onions. They have been moved to open the way down.'

They all climbed out. Julian flashed the torch round the shed. Yes, there were the machines and the tools. Well, who would have thought that the sacks he had seen in here the other day were hiding the trapdoor that led to the Wreckers' Way!

CHAPTER SEVENTEEN

Long after midnight!

A RAT suddenly shot out from a corner of the shed, and tore across to the open trapdoor. Timmy gave a bark and leapt after it. He just stopped himself from taking a header through the trapdoor by sliding along on all four feet and coming to a stop at the entrance.

He stood up and looked down the hole, his head cocked to one side.

'Look, he's listening,' said Anne. 'Is there someone coming, those men, perhaps, with the smuggled goods?'

'No, he's only listening for the rat,' said Julian. 'I'll tell you what we'll do! We'll shut the trapdoor and pile sacks and boxes and everything on top of it! Then when the men come up, they'll find themselves trapped. They won't be able to get out. If we can get the police in time, they'll be able to catch them easily.'

'Good idea!' said Dick. 'Super! How mad those two men will be when they come to the trapdoor and find it shut! They can't get out the other way because the tide's up.'

'I'd like to see Mr Penruthlan's face when he sees the trapdoor shut, and feels a whole lot of things piled on top of it!' said Julian. 'He'll make a few more of his peculiar noises!'

'Ooh – ah – ock,' said Dick, solemnly. 'Come on, help me with the trapdoor, Ju, it's heavy.'

They shut the big trapdoor and then began to drag sacks, boxes and even some kind of heavy farm machine on top of the trapdoor. Now certainly nobody could open it from underneath.

They were hot and very dirty by the time they had finished. They were also beginning to feel very tired. 'Phew!' said Dick. 'I'm glad that's done. Now we'd better go to the farmhouse and show ourselves to Mrs Penruthlan.'

'Oh dear, do we tell her about her husband, and how he's mixed up in this horrid business?' said Anne. 'I do so like her. I expect she's very worried about us, too.'

'Yes. It's going to be a bit difficult,' said Julian, soberly. 'Better let me do most of the talking. Come on, we'll go. Don't make too much row or we'll set the dogs barking. I'm surprised they haven't yelled their heads off already!'

It *was* rather surprising. Usually the farm dogs barked the place down if there was any unusual noise in the night. The five children and Timmy left the machine shed and made their way towards the farmhouse. George pulled at Julian's arm.

'Look,' she said, in a low voice. 'See those lights up in the hills? What are they?'

Julian looked. He could see moving lights here and there up on the hills. He was puzzled. Then he made a guess. 'I bet Mrs Penruthlan has sent out searchers for us,' he said, 'and they've got lanterns. They're hunting for us on the hills. Gosh, I hope all the Barnies aren't out after us too.'

They came to the farmyard, moving very quietly. The big barn, used by the Barnies for their show, was in darkness. Julian pictured it full of benches, left from that night's show. The memory of Mr Penruthlan turning out the pockets of the clothes left and hunting through the drawers in the chest used by the Barnies, came into his mind.

A sharp whisper made them stop very suddenly. George put her hand on Timmy's collar to stop him growling or barking. Who was this now?

None of the little company answered or moved. The whisper came again.

'Here! I'm here!'

Still nobody moved. They were all puzzled. Who was waiting there in the shadows, and for whom was he waiting? The whisper came again, a little louder.

'Here! Over here!'

And then, as if too impatient to wait any longer, the whisperer moved out into the yard. Julian couldn't see who it was in the dark, and he quickly flashed his torch on the man.

It was the Guv'nor, grim-faced as ever! He flinched as the light fell on his face, took a few steps back and disappeared round a corner. Timmy growled.

'Well! How many *more* people wander about at night here?' said Dick. 'That was the Guv'nor. What was *he* doing?'

'I give it up,' said Julian. 'I'm getting too tired to think straight. I shouldn't be in the least surprised to see Clopper the horse peering round a corner at us, and saying "Peep-bo, chaps!"'

Everyone chuckled. It was just the kind of thing Clopper *would* do if he were really alive!

They came to the farmhouse. It was full of light, upstairs and downstairs. The curtains were not drawn across the kitchen window and the children looked in as they passed. Mrs Penruthlan was sitting there, her hands clasped, looking extremely worried.

They opened the kitchen door and trooped in. Yan too. Mrs Penruthlan leapt up at once and ran to them. She hugged Anne, she tried to hug George, she said all kinds of things at top speed, and to the children's dismay they saw that she was crying.

'Oh, where *have* you been?' she said, tears pouring down her face. 'The men are out looking for you, and all the dogs, and the Barnies too. They've been looking for ages! And Mr Penruthlan's not home, either. I don't know where *he* is, he's gone too! Oh, what a terrible evening. But thank goodness you're safe!'

Julian saw that she was terribly upset. He took her arm gently and led her to a chair. 'Don't worry,' he said. 'We're all safe. We're sorry you've been upset.'

'But where have you *been*?' wept Mrs Penruthlan. 'I pictured you drowned, or lost on the hills, or fallen into quarries. And where is Mr Penruthlan? He went out at seven and there's been not a sign of him since!'

The children felt uncomfortable. They thought they knew where Mr Penruthlan was, getting smuggled goods from the motorboat, and carrying them back with his friend, up the Wreckers' Way!

'Now just you tell me what you've been doing,' said Mrs Penruthlan, drying her eyes, and sounding unexpectedly determined. 'Upsetting everybody like this!'

'Well,' said Julian, 'it's a long story, but I'll try to make it short. Strange things have been happening, Mrs Penruthlan.'

He plunged into the whole story, the old tower, Grandad's tale of the flashing light, their journey to explore the tower, the secret passage to the Wreckers' cove, their imprisonment and escape, and then Julian stopped.

How was he to tell poor Mrs Penruthlan that one of the smugglers was her husband? He glanced at the others desperately. Anne began to cry, and George felt very much like it, too. It was Yan who suddenly spoke and broke the news.

'We saw Mr Penruthlan in the cove,' he said, glad of a chance to put in a word. 'We saw him!'

Mrs Penruthlan stared at Yan, and then at the embarrassed, anxious faces of the other children.

'You saw him in the cove?' she said. 'You didn't! What was he doing there?'

'We think, we think he must be one of the smugglers,' said Julian, awkwardly. 'We think we saw him get into a boat and row to the motorboat beyond the rocks. If so, he – well – he may get into trouble, Mrs Penr—'

He didn't finish, because, to his enormous surprise, Mrs Penruthlan jumped up from her chair in a rage.

'You wicked boy!' panted Mrs Penruthlan, sounding suddenly out of breath. 'You bad, wicked boy, saying things like that about Mr Penruthlan, who's the straightest, honestest, most God-fearing man who ever lived! Him a smuggler! Him in with those wicked men! I'll box your ears till you eat your words and serve you right!'

Julian was amazed at the change in the cheerful little farmer's wife. Her face was red, her eyes were blazing,

and somehow she seemed to be taller. He had never seen anyone so angry in his life! Yan went promptly under the table.

Timmy growled. He liked Mrs Penruthlan, but he felt he really couldn't allow her to set about his friends. She faced Julian, trembling with anger.

'Now you apologise!' she said. 'Or I'll give you such a drubbing as you've never had in your life before. And you just wait and see what Mr Penruthlan will say when he comes back and hears the things you've said about him!'

Julian was much too big and strong for the farmer's wife to 'give him a drubbing' but he felt certain she would try, if he didn't apologise! What a tiger she was!

He put his hand on her arm. 'Don't get so upset,' he said. 'I'm very sorry to have made you so angry.'

Mrs Penruthlan shook his hand off her arm. 'Angry! I should just think I *am* angry!' she said. 'To think anyone should say those things about Mr Penruthlan. That wasn't him down in Wreckers' Cove. I know it wasn't. I only wish I knew *where* he was! I'm that worried!'

'He's down Wreckers' Way,' announced Yan from his safe vantage point under the table. 'We put the trapdoor down over him.'

'Down Wreckers' Way!' cried Mrs Penruthlan and to the children's great relief she sank down into a chair again. She turned to Julian, questioningly.

He nodded. 'Yes. We came up that way from the beach

– Yan knew it. It comes up in a corner of the machine shed, through a trapdoor. We – er – we shut the trapdoor and piled sacks and things on it. I'm afraid, well, I'm rather afraid Mr Penruthlan can't get out!'

Mrs Penruthlan's eyes almost dropped out of her head. She opened and shut her mouth several times, rather like a goldfish gasping for breath. All the children felt most uncomfortable and extremely sorry for her.

'I don't believe it,' she said at last. 'It's a bad dream. It's not real. Mr Penruthlan will come walking in here at any moment, at any moment, I tell you! He's not down in the Wreckers' Way. He's NOT a bad man. He'll come walking in, you just see!'

There was silence after this, and in the silence a sound could be heard. The sound of big boots walking over the farmyard. Clomp-clomp-clomp-clomp!

'I'm frightened!' squealed Yan, suddenly, and made everyone jump. The footsteps came round the kitchen wall, and up to the kitchen door.

'I know who that is!' said Mrs Penruthlan, jumping up. 'I know who that is.'

The door opened and somebody walked in. Mr Penruthlan!

His wife ran to him and flung her arms round him. 'You've come walking in! I said you would. Praise be that you've come!'

Mr Penruthlan looked tired, and the children, quite struck with amazement at seeing him, saw that he was wet through. He looked round at them in great surprise.

'What are these children up for?' he said, and they all gaped in surprise. Why, he was talking properly! His words were quite clear, except that he lisped over his S's.

'Oh, Mr Penruthlan, the tales these bad children have told about you!' cried his wife. 'They said you were a smuggler. They said they'd seen you in Wreckers' Cove going out to a motorboat to get smuggled goods, they said you were trapped in Wreckers' Way, they'd put the trapdoor down, and . . .'

Mr Penruthlan pushed his wife away from him and swung round on the astounded children. They were most alarmed. How had he escaped from Wreckers' Way? Surely even his great strength could not lift up all the things they had piled on top of the trapdoor? How fierce this giant of a man looked, with his mane of black hair, his shaggy eyebrows drawn over his deep-set eyes, and his dense black beard!

'What's all this?' he demanded, and they gaped again at his speech. They were so used to his peculiar noises that it seemed amazing he could speak properly after all.

'Well,' began Julian, awkwardly, 'we – er – we've been exploring that tower – and – er – finding out a bit about the smugglers, and we *really* thought we recognised you in Wreckers' Cove, and we thought we'd trapped you, and your friend, by shutting the trapdoor and—'

'This is important,' said Mr Penruthlan, and his voice

sounded urgent. 'Forget all this about thinking I'm a smuggler. You've got things wrong. I'm working with the police. It was someone else down in the cove, not me. I've been on the coast, it's true, watching out, and getting drenched, as you can see, all to no purpose. What do you know? What's this about the trapdoor? Did you really close it, and trap those men?'

All this was so completely astonishing that for a moment nobody could say a word. Then Julian leapt up.

'Yes, sir! We did put the trapdoor down, and if you want to catch those fellows, send for the police, and we'll do it! We've only got to wait beside the trapdoor till the smugglers come!'

'Right,' said Mr Penruthlan. 'Come along. Hurry!'

CHAPTER EIGHTEEN

Dick gets an idea!

In the greatest surprise and excitement the five children rushed to the kitchen door to follow Mr Penruthlan. Yan had scrambled out from beneath the table, determined not to miss anything. But at the door the farmer turned round.

'Not the girls,' he said. 'Nor you, Yan.'

'I'll keep the girls here with me,' said Mrs Penruthlan, who had forgotten her dismay and anger completely in this new excitement. 'Yan, come here.'

But Yan had slipped out with the others. Nothing in the world would keep him from missing this new excitement! Timmy had gone too, of course, as excited as the rest.

'What goings-on in the early hours of the morning!' said Mrs Penruthlan, sitting down suddenly again. 'To think that Mr Penruthlan never told me he was working to find those smugglers! We knew it was going on, around this coast, and to think he was keeping a watch, and never told me!'

Julian and Dick had quite forgotten that they felt tired. They hurried over the farmyard with Mr Penruthlan, Yan a little way behind, and Timmy leaping round like a mad thing. They came to the machine shed and went in.

'We piled . . .' began Julian, and then suddenly stopped. Mr Penruthlan's powerful torch was shining on the corner where the trapdoor was fixed.

It was open! Unbelievably open! The sacks and boxes that the children had dragged over it were now scattered to one side.

'Look at that!' said Julian, amazed. 'Who's opened it? The smugglers have got out, with their smuggled goods, and they've gone. We're beaten!'

Mr Penruthlan made a very angry noise, and flung the trapdoor shut with a resounding bang. He was about to say something more when there came the sound of voices not far off. It was the Barnies returning from their search for the children.

They saw the light in the shed and peered in. When they saw Julian and Dick they cried out in delight. 'Where were you? We've searched everywhere for you!'

Julian and Dick were so disappointed at finding their high hopes dashed that they could hardly respond to the Barnies' delighted greetings. They felt suddenly very tired again, and Mr Penruthlan seemed all at once in a very bad temper. He answered the Barnies gruffly, said that everything was all right now, and any talking could be done tomorrow. As for him, he was going to bed!

The Barnies dispersed at once, still talking. Mr Penruthlan silently led the way back to the farmhouse with Julian and Dick trailing behind. Yan had gone like a shadow. As he was not at the farmhouse when they walked wearily into the kitchen, Julian guessed that he had scampered back up the hills to old Grandad.

'Five past three in the morning,' said Mr Penruthlan, looking at the clock. 'I'll sleep down here for an hour or two, then I'll be up to milk the cows. Send these children to bed. I'm too weary to talk. Good night.'

And with that he put his hand to his mouth and quite solemnly took out his false teeth, putting them into a glass of water on the mantelpiece.

'Oooh – ock,' he said to his wife, and stripped off his wet coat. Mrs Penruthlan hustled Julian and the rest upstairs. They were almost dropping with exhaustion now. The girls managed to undress, but the two boys flopped on their beds and were asleep in half a second. They didn't stir when the cocks crowed, or when the cow lowed, or even when the wagons of the Barnies came trundling out into the yard to be packed with their things. They were going off to play in another village barn that night.

Julian awoke at last. It took him a few moments to realise why he was still fully dressed. He lay and thought for a while, and a feeling of dejection came over him when he remembered how all the excitement of the day before had ended in complete failure.

If only they knew who had opened that trapdoor! WHO could it be?

And then something clicked in his mind, and he knew. Of course! Why hadn't he thought of it before? Why hadn't he remembered to tell Mr Penruthlan about the

Guv'nor standing in the shadows, and his whispered message: 'Here! I'm here!'

He must have been waiting for the smugglers to come to him, of course, he probably used local fishermen to row through the rocks to the motorboat that had slunk over to the Cornish coast, and those fishermen used the Wreckers' Way so that no one knew what they were doing.

The Barnies often came to play at Tremannon Barn. Nothing could be easier than for the Guv'nor to arrange for the smuggling to take place then, for the Wreckers' Way actually had an entrance in the shed near the big barn! If a stormy night came, all the better! No one would be about. He could go up on the hills and wait for the signal from the tower which would tell him that at last the boat was coming.

Yes, and he would arrange with the signaller too, to flash out the news that he, the Guv'nor, was at Tremannon again, and waiting! Who was the signaller? Probably another of the fishermen, descendants of the old Wreckers, and glad of a bit of excitement.

Everything fell into place, all the odd bits and pieces of happenings fitted together like a jigsaw puzzle. Julian saw the clear picture.

Who would ever have thought of the owner of the Barnies being involved in smuggling? Smugglers were clever, but the Guv'nor was cleverer than most!

Julian heard the noise outside, and got up to see what it was. When he saw the Barnies piling their furniture on the wagons, he rushed downstairs, yelling to wake Dick as he went. He must tell Mr Penruthlan about the Guv'nor! He must get him arrested! He had probably got the smuggled goods somewhere in one of the boxes on the wagons. What an easy way of getting it away unseen! The Guv'nor was cunning, there was no doubt about that.

With Dick at his heels, puzzled and surprised, Julian went to find Mr Penruthlan. There he was, watching the Barnies getting ready to go, looking very dour and grim. Julian ran up to him.

'I've remembered something, something important! Can I speak to you?'

They went into a nearby field, and there Julian poured out all he had surmised about the Guv'nor.

'He was waiting in the dark last night for the smugglers,' said Julian. 'I'm sure he was. He must have heard us and thought we were the men. And it must have been he who opened the trapdoor. When they didn't come, he must have gone to the trapdoor and found it shut, with things piled on it. And he opened it, and waited there till the men came and handed him the goods. And now he's got them hidden somewhere in those wagons!'

'Why didn't you tell me this last night?' said Mr Penruthlan. 'We may be too late now! I'll have to get the police here to search those wagons, but if I try to stop the Barnies going now, the Guv'nor will suspect something and go off at once!'

Julian was relieved to see that Mr Penruthlan had his

teeth in again and could speak properly! The farmer pulled at his black beard and frowned. 'I've searched many times through the Barnies' properties to find the smuggled goods,' he said. 'Each time they've been here I've gone through everything in the dead of night.'

'Do you know what it is they're smuggling?' asked Julian. The farmer nodded.

'Yes. Dangerous drugs. Drugs that are sold at enormously high prices on the black market. The parcel wouldn't need to be very big. I've suspected one or other of the Barnies of being the receiver before this, and I've searched and searched. No good.'

'If it's a small parcel it could be hidden easily,' said Dick, thoughtfully. 'But it's a dangerous thing to hide. The Guv'nor wouldn't have it on him, would he?'

'Oh no, he would be afraid of being searched,' said Mr Penruthlan. 'Well, I reckon I must let them go this time, and I must warn the police. If they like to search the wagons on the road, they're welcome. I can't get the police here in time to stop the wagons going off. We've got no telephone at the farm.'

Mr Binks came up at that moment, carrying Clopper's front and back legs. He grinned at the boys. 'You led us a fine dance last night!' he said. 'What happened?'

'Yes,' said Sid, coming up with Clopper's ridiculous head under his arm as usual. 'Clopper was right worried about you!'

'Gosh, you didn't carry old Clopper's head all over the

hills last night, did you?' said Dick, astonished.

'No. I left it with the Guv'nor,' said Sid. 'He took charge of his precious Clopper while I went gallivanting over the hills and far away, looking for a pack of tiresome kids!'

Dick stared at the horse's head, with its comical rolling eyes. He stared at it very hard indeed. And then he did a most peculiar thing!

He snatched the head away from the surprised Sid, and tore across the farmyard with it! Julian looked after him in amazement.

Sid gave an angry yell. 'Now then! What do you think you're doing? Bring that horse back at once!'

But Dick didn't. He tore round a corner and disappeared. Sid went after him, and so did somebody else!

The Guv'nor raced across the yard at top speed, looking furious! He shouted, he yelled, he shook his fist. But when he and Sid got to the corner, Dick had disappeared!

'What's got into him?' said Mr Penruthlan, amazed. 'What does he want to rush off with Clopper's head for? The boy must be mad.'

Julian suddenly saw light. He knew why Dick had snatched Clopper's head. He knew!

'Mr Penruthlan, why does the Guv'nor always have someone in charge of Clopper's head?' he said. 'Maybe he hides something precious there, something he doesn't want anyone to find! Quick, let's go and see!'

CHAPTER NINETEEN

Mostly about Clopper

AT THAT moment Dick appeared again, round another corner, still holding Clopper's head, with Sid and the Guv'nor hard on his heels. He hadn't been able to stop for a moment, or even to hide anywhere. He panted up to Mr Penruthlan, and thrust the head at him.

'Take it. I bet it's got the goods in it!'

Then Sid and the Guv'nor raced up too, both in a furious rage. The Guv'nor tried to snatch Clopper away from the big farmer. But he was a small man and Mr Penruthlan was well over six feet. He calmly held the horse's head out of reach with his strong right hand, and fended off the Guv'nor with the other.

Everyone ran up at once. The Barnies surrounded the little group in excitement, and one or two farm men came up too. Mrs Penruthlan and the girls, who were now up, heard the excitement and came running out as well. Hens scattered away, clucking, and the four dogs and Timmy barked madly.

The Guv'nor was beside himself with fury. He tried to hit the farmer, but was immediately pulled away by Mr Binks.

Then one of the farm men shouldered his way through

the excited crowd, and put his great hand on to the Guv'nor's shoulder. He held him in a grip of iron.

'Don't let him go,' said the farmer. He lowered Clopper's head and looked round at the puzzled Barnies.

'Fetch that barrel,' he said to Julian, and the boy got it at once, placing it in front of the farmer. The Guv'nor watched, his face going white.

'You leave that horse alone,' he said. 'It's my property. What do you think you're doing?'

'You say this horse is your property?' said the farmer. 'Is it entirely your property, inside as well as outside?'

The Guv'nor said nothing. He looked very worried indeed. Mr Penruthlan turned the head upside down, and looked into the neck. He put his hand in and scrabbled about. He found the little lid and opened it. Out fell about a dozen cigarettes.

'They're mine,' said Mr Binks. 'I keep them there. Anything wrong with that, sir? It's a little place the Guv'nor had made for me.'

'Nothing wrong with that, Mr Binks,' said the farmer, and put his hand in again. He pulled at the lid, and ran his finger round the hole where Mr Binks kept his cigarettes. The Guv'nor watched, breathing quickly.

'I can feel something, Guv'nor,' said Mr Penruthlan, watching the man's face. 'I can feel a false bottom to this clever little space. How do I get it open, Guv'nor? Will you tell me, or do I smash Clopper up to find it?'

'Don't smash him!' said Sid and Mr Binks together.

They turned to the Guv'nor, puzzled. 'What's up?' said Sid. 'We never knew there was a secret about Clopper.'

'There isn't,' said the Guv'nor, stubbornly.

'Ah, I've found the trick!' said Mr Penruthlan, suddenly. 'Now I've got it!' He worked his fingers about in the space that he had suddenly hit on, behind the place where Mr Binks had his cigarettes. He pulled out a package done up in white paper, a small package, but worth many hundreds of pounds!

'What's this, Guv'nor?' he asked the white-faced man. 'Is it one of the many packets of drugs you've handled

round this coast? Was it because of this secret of yours that you told Sid never to let Clopper out of his sight? Shall I open this packet, Guv'nor, and see what's inside?'

A murmur arose from the Barnies, a murmur of horror. Sid turned fiercely on the Guv'nor. 'You made me guard your horrible drugs, not Clopper! To think I've been helping you all this time, helping a man who's only fit for prison! I'll never work with Clopper again! Never!'

Almost in tears poor Sid pushed his way through the amazed Barnies and went off by himself. After a few moments Mr Binks followed him.

Mr Penruthlan put the white package into his pocket. 'Lock the Guv'nor up in the small barn,' he ordered. 'And you, Dan, get on your bike and get the police. As for you, Barnies, I don't know rightly what to say. You've lost your Guv'nor, but it's good riddance, I'll tell you that.'

The Barnies stared after the Guv'nor as he was dragged away by two farm men, over to the small barn.

'We never liked him,' said one. 'But he had money to tide us over bad times. Money from smuggling in those wicked drugs! He used us Barnies as a screen for his goings-on. It's good riddance, you're right.'

'We'll manage,' said another Barnie. 'We'll get along. Hey, Sid, come back. Cheer up!'

Sid and Mr Binks came back, looking rather solemn. 'We're not going to use Clopper any more,' said Sid. 'He'll bring us bad luck. We'll get a donkey instead and work up another act. Mr Binks says he couldn't wear

Clopper again, and I feel the same.'

'Right,' said the farmer, picking up Clopper's head. 'Get the back and front legs. I'll take charge of old Clopper. I've always been fond of him, and he won't bring any bad luck to *me*!'

There was nothing more to be done. The Barnies said rather a forlorn goodbye. Sid and Mr Binks shook hands solemnly with each of the children. Sid gave Clopper one last pat and turned away.

'We'll go off now,' said Mr Binks. 'Thanks for everything, Mr Penruthlan. So long!'

'See you again when next you're by here,' said Mr Penruthlan. 'You can have my barn any time, Sid.'

The Guv'nor was safely locked up, waiting for the police. Mr Penruthlan picked Clopper up, legs and all, and looked down at the five children, for Yan was now with them.

He smiled at them all, looking suddenly quite a different man. 'Well, that's all finished up!' he said. 'Dick, I thought you'd gone mad when you went off with old Clopper's head!'

'It was certainly a bit of a brainwave,' said Dick, modestly. 'It came over me all of a sudden. Only just in time, too, the Barnies were nearly on their way again!'

They went over to the farmhouse. Mrs Penruthlan had already run across. The girls guessed why, and they were right!

'I'm getting a meal for you!' she cried, as they came in.

'Poor children, not a mite to eat have you had today. No breakfast, nothing. Come away in and help me. You can turn out the whole larder if you like!'

They very nearly did! Ham and tongue and pies went on the table. Anne picked crisp lettuces from the garden and washed them. Julian piled tomatoes in a dish. George cooked a dozen hard-boiled eggs at the stove. A fruit tart and a jam tart appeared as if by magic and two great jugs of creamy milk were set at each end of the table.

Yan hovered around, getting into everybody's way, his eyes nearly falling out of his head at the sight of the food. Mrs Penruthlan laughed.

'Get away from under my feet, you dirty little ruffian! Do you want to eat with us?'

'Yes,' said Yan, his eyes sparkling. 'Yes!'

'Then go upstairs and wash those dirty hands!' said the farmer's wife. And, marvel of marvels, Yan went off upstairs as good as gold, and came down with hands that really were almost clean!

They all sat down. Julian solemnly put a chair beside him, and arranged Clopper in such a way that it looked as if he were sitting down too! Anne giggled.

'Oh, Clopper! You look quite real. Mr Penruthlan, what are you going to do with him?'

'I'm going to give him away,' said the farmer, munching as hard with his teeth as he did without them. 'To friends of mine.'

'Lucky friends!' said Dick, helping himself to a hard-boiled egg and salad. 'Do they know how to work the back and front legs, sir?'

'Oh yes,' said the farmer. 'They know fine. They'll do well with Clopper. There's only one thing they don't know. Haw – haw-haw!'

The children looked at him in surprise. Why the sudden guffaw?

Mr Penruthlan choked, and his wife banged him on the back. 'Careful now, Mr Penruthlan,' she said. 'Mr Clopper's looking at you!'

The farmer guffawed again. Then he looked round at the listening children. 'I was telling you,' he said, 'there's only one thing these friends of mine don't know.'

'What's that?' asked George.

'Well, they don't know how to undo the zip!' said the farmer, and roared again till the tears came into his eyes. 'They don't know how to – how to – haw-haw-haw-haw – undo the ZIP!'

'Mr Penruthlan now, behave yourself!' said his amused wife. 'Why don't you say straight out that you're giving Clopper to Julian and Dick, instead of spluttering away like that?'

'Gosh, are you really?' said Dick, thrilled. 'Thanks most awfully!'

'Well, you got me what I wanted, so it's only right and fair I should give you what *you* wanted,' said the farmer, taking another plate of ham. 'You'll do well with Clopper, you and your brother. You can give us a show one day before you leave for home. Haw-haw – Clopper's a funny one, see him looking at us now!'

'He winked!' said George, in an astonished voice, and Timmy came out from under the table to stare at Clopper with the others. 'I saw him wink!'

Well, it wouldn't be surprising if he did wink. He's really had a most exciting time!

Join the adventure!

If you can't wait to explore further with **THE FAMOUS FIVE**, read the next book in the series:

Enid Blyton®

is one of the most popular children's authors of all time. Her books have sold over 500 million copies and have been translated into other languages more often than any other children's author.

Enid Blyton adored writing for children. She wrote over 700 books and about 2,000 short stories. *The Famous Five* books, now 75 years old, are her most popular. She is also the author of other favourites including *The Secret Seven*, *The Magic Faraway Tree*, *Malory Towers* and *Noddy*.

Born in London in 1897, Enid lived much of her life in Buckinghamshire and loved dogs, gardening and the countryside. She was very knowledgeable about trees, flowers, birds and animals. Dorset – where some of the Famous Five's adventures are set – was a favourite place of hers too.

Enid Blyton's stories are read and loved by millions of children (and grown-ups) all over the world. Visit enidblyton.co.uk to discover more.

Illustration by
Laura Ellen Anderson.

THE FAMOUS FIVE

FIVE GO TO MYSTERY MOOR

Have you read all THE FAMOUS FIVE books?

1. Five on a Treasure Island
2. Five Go Adventuring Again
3. Five Run Away Together
4. Five Go to Smuggler's Top
5. Five Go Off in a Caravan
6. Five on Kirrin Island Again
7. Five Go Off to Camp
8. Five Get Into Trouble
9. Five Fall Into Adventure
10. Five on a Hike Together
11. Five Have a Wonderful Time
12. Five Go Down to the Sea
13. Five Go to Mystery Moor
14. Five Have Plenty of Fun
15. Five on a Secret Trail
16. Five Go to Billycock Hill
17. Five Get Into a Fix
18. Five on Finniston Farm
19. Five Go to Demon's Rocks
20. Five Have a Mystery to Solve
21. Five Are Together Again

The Famous Five Colour Short Stories

1. Five and a Half-Term Adventure
2. George's Hair is Too Long
3. Good Old Timmy
4. A Lazy Afternoon
5. Well Done, Famous Five
6. Five Have a Puzzling Time
7. Happy Christmas, Five
8. When Timmy Chased the Cat

Enid Blyton®

THE FAMOUS FIVE

FIVE GO TO MYSTERY MOOR

Illustrated by Eileen A. Soper

HODDER CHILDREN'S BOOKS

First published in Great Britain in 1954 by Hodder & Stoughton
This edition published in 2016

20

A CIP catalogue record for this book is available from the British Library.

ISBN 978 1 444 93643 8

Printed in Great Britain by Clays Ltd, Elcograf S.p.A.

The paper and board used in this book are made from wood from responsible sources.

Hodder Children's Books
An imprint of
Hachette Children's Group
Part of Hodder & Stoughton
Carmelite House
50 Victoria Embankment
London EC4Y 0DZ

An Hachette UK Company
www.hachette.co.uk
www.hachettechildrens.co.uk

CONTENTS

1	AT THE STABLES	1
2	JULIAN, DICK – AND HENRY	11
3	SNIFFER	21
4	A BED IN THE STABLE	31
5	GEORGE GETS A HEADACHE!	40
6	A GRAND DAY	49
7	GEORGE, SNIFFER AND LIZ	59
8	SNIFFER MAKES A PROMISE	68
9	THE BLACKSMITH TELLS A TALE	77
10	SNIFFER'S PATRINS	86
11	A NICE LITTLE PLAN	95
12	THE LITTLE RAILWAY	104
13	A NOISE IN THE NIGHT	113
14	THE TRAVELLERS ARE NOT PLEASED	122
15	A STARTLING NIGHT	131
16	THE TERRIBLE MIST	140
17	PRISONERS TOGETHER	149
18	GEORGE'S TRICK	159
19	GOOD OLD TIM!	168
20	EXCITEMENT IN THE MORNING	179
21	THE END OF THE MYSTERY	188

CHAPTER ONE

At the stables

'WE'VE BEEN here a week and I've been bored every single minute!' said George.

'You haven't,' said Anne. 'You've enjoyed all the rides we've had, and you know you've enjoyed messing about the stables when we haven't been out riding.'

'I tell you, I've been bored every single *minute*,' said George, quite fiercely. 'I ought to know, oughtn't I? That awful girl Henrietta too. Why do we have to put up with her?'

'Oh – Henry!' said Anne, with a laugh. 'I should have thought you'd find a lot in common with another girl like yourself, who would rather be a boy, and tries to act like one!'

The two girls were lying by a haystack eating sandwiches. Round them in a field were many horses, most of which the girls either rode or looked after. Some way off was an old rambling building, and by the front entrance was a great board,

Captain Johnson's Riding School

Anne and George had been staying there for a week, while Julian and Dick had gone to camp with other boys from their school. It had been Anne's idea. She was fond of horses, and had heard so much from her friends at school what fun it was to spend day after day at the stables, that she had made up her mind to go herself.

George hadn't wanted to come. She was sulky because the two boys had gone off somewhere without her and Anne, for a change. Gone to camp! George would have liked that, but girls were not allowed to go camping with the boys from Julian's school, of course. It was a camp just for the boys alone.

'You're silly to keep feeling cross because you couldn't go camping too,' said Anne. 'The boys don't want us girls round them all the time.'

George thought differently. 'Why not? I can do anything that Dick and Julian can do,' she said. 'I can climb, and bike for miles, I can walk as far as they can, I can swim, I can beat a whole lot of boys at most things.'

'That's what Henry says!' said Anne, with a laugh. 'Look, there she is, striding about as usual, hands in her jodhpur pockets, whistling like the stable boy!'

George scowled. Anne had been very much amused to see how Henrietta and George hated one another at sight – and yet both had so very much the same ideas. George's real name was Georgina, but she would only answer to George. Henry's real name was Henrietta, but she would only answer to Henry, or Harry to her *very* best friends!

She was about as old as George, and her hair was short too, but it wasn't curly. 'It's a pity yours is curly,' she said to George, pityingly. 'It looks so *girlish*, doesn't it?'

'Don't be an ass,' George said, curtly. 'Plenty of boys have curly hair.'

The maddening part was that Henrietta was a wonderful rider, and had won all kinds of cups. George hadn't enjoyed herself a bit during that week at the stables, because for once another girl had outshone her. She couldn't bear to see Henrietta striding about, whistling, doing everything so competently and quickly.

Anne had had many a quiet laugh to herself, especially when the two girls had each made up their minds not to call one another Henry and George, but to use their full names, Henrietta and Georgina! This meant that neither of them would answer the other when called, and Captain Johnson, the big, burly owner of the riding stables, got very tired of both of them.

'What are you behaving like this for?' he demanded one morning, seeing their sulky looks at one another at breakfast-time. 'Behaving like a couple of idiotic schoolgirls!'

That made Anne laugh! A couple of idiotic school*girls*. My goodness, how annoyed both girls were with Captain Johnson. Anne was a bit scared of him. He was hot-tempered, outspoken, and stood no nonsense at all, but he was a wonder with the horses, and loved a good, hearty laugh. He and his wife took either boys or girls for the holidays, and worked them hard, but the children always enjoyed their stay immensely.

'If it hadn't been for Henry, you'd have been perfectly happy this week,' said Anne, leaning back against the haystack. 'We've had heavenly April weather, the horses are lovely, and I like Captain and Mrs Johnson very much.'

'I wish the boys were here,' said George. 'They would soon put that silly Henrietta in her place. I wish I'd stayed at home now.'

'Well, you had the choice,' said Anne, rather cross. 'You could have stayed at Kirrin Cottage with your father and mother, but you chose to come here with me, till the boys came back from camp. You shouldn't make such a fuss if things aren't exactly to your liking. It spoils things for *me*.'

'Sorry,' said George. 'I'm being a pig, I know, but I do miss the boys. We can only be with them in the hols and it seems funny without them. There's just *one* thing that pleases me here, you'll be glad to know . . .'

'You needn't tell me, I know what it is!' said Anne, with a laugh. 'You're glad that Timmy won't have anything to do with Henry!'

'With Henrietta,' corrected George. She grinned suddenly. 'Yes, old Timmy's got some sense. He just can't stick her. Here, Timmy boy, leave those rabbit holes alone and come and lie down for a bit. You've run for miles this morning when we took the horses out, and you've snuffled down about a hundred rabbit holes. Come and be peaceful.'

Timmy left his latest rabbit hole reluctantly and came to flop down beside Anne and George. He gave George a hearty lick and she patted him.

'We're just saying, Timmy, how sensible you are not to make friends with that awful Henrietta,' said George. She stopped suddenly at a sharp nudge from Anne. A shadow fell across them as someone came round the haystack.

It was Henrietta. By the annoyed look on her face it was clear that she had heard George's remark. She held out an envelope to George.

'A letter for you, Georgina,' she said, stiffly. 'I thought I'd better bring it in case it was important.'

'Oh, thanks, Henrietta,' said George, and took the envelope. She tore it open, read it and groaned.

'Look at that!' she said to Anne and passed it to her. 'It's from Mother.'

Anne took the letter and read it. 'Please stay another week. Your father is not well. Love from Mother.'

'What bad luck!' said George, a familiar scowl on her face. 'Just when I thought we'd be going home in a day or two, and the boys would join us at Kirrin. Now we'll be stuck here by ourselves for ages! What's the matter with Father? I bet he's only got a headache or something, and doesn't want us stamping about in and out of the house and making a noise.'

'We could go to *my* home,' said Anne. 'That's if you don't mind its being a bit upside down because of the decorating we're having done.'

'No. I know you want to stay here with the horses,' said George. 'Anyway your father and mother are abroad, we'd only be in the way. Blow, blow, blow! Now we'll have to do without the boys for another week. They'll stay on in camp, of course.'

Captain Johnson said yes, certainly the two girls could stay on. It was possible that they might have to do a bit of camping out if one or two extra children came, but they wouldn't mind that, would they?

'Not a bit,' said George. 'Actually we'd rather like to be

on our own, Anne and I. We've got Timmy, you see. So long as we could come in to meals and do a few jobs for you, we'd love to go off on our own.'

Anne smiled to herself. What George really meant was that she wanted to see as little of Henrietta as possible! Still, it *would* be fun to camp out if the weather was fine. They could easily borrow a tent from Captain Johnson.

'Bad luck, Georgina!' said Henry, who was listening to all this. 'Very bad luck! I know you're terribly bored here. It's a pity you don't really like horses. It's a pity that you—'

'Shut up,' said George, rudely and went out of the room. Captain Johnson glared at Henrietta, who stood whistling at the window, hands in pockets.

'You two girls!' he said. 'Why don't you behave yourselves? Always aping the boys, pretending you're so mannish! Give me Anne here, any day! What you want is your ears boxing. Did you take that bale of straw to the stables?'

'Yes,' said Henrietta, without turning.

Suddenly, a small boy came running in. 'There's a traveller kid outside with a horse, a skewbald, a mangy-looking thing. He says can you help him – the horse has got something wrong with its leg.'

'Those travellers again!' said Captain Johnson. 'All right, I'll come.'

He went out and Anne went with him, not wanting to

be left alone with the angry Henrietta. She found George outside with a traveller boy and a patient little skewbald horse, its brown and white coat looking very flea-bitten.

'What have you done to your horse *this* time?' said Captain Johnson, looking at its leg. 'You'll have to leave it here, and I'll see to it.'

'I can't do that,' said the boy. 'We're off to Mystery Moor again.'

'Well, you'll have to,' said Captain Johnson. 'It's not fit to walk. Your caravan can't go with the others, this horse isn't fit to pull it. I'll get the police to your father if you try to work this horse before it's better.'

'Don't do that!' said the boy. 'It's just that my dad says we've *got* to go tomorrow.'

'What's the hurry?' said Captain Johnson. 'Can't your caravan wait a day or two? Mystery Moor will still be there in two days' time! It beats me why you go there, a desolate place like that, not even a farm or cottage for miles!'

'I'll leave the horse,' said the boy, and stroked the skewbald's nose. It was clear that he loved the ugly little horse. 'My father will be angry, but the other caravans can go on without us. We'll have to catch them up.'

He gave a kind of half-salute to the captain and disappeared from the stable yard, a skinny little sunburnt figure. The skewbald stood patiently.

'Take it round to the small stable,' said Captain

Johnson to George and Anne. 'I'll come and see to it in a minute.'

The girls led the little horse away. 'Mystery Moor!' said George. 'What an odd name! The boys would like that, they'd be exploring it at once, wouldn't they?'

'Yes. I do wish they were coming here,' said Anne. 'Still, I expect they'll like the chance of staying on in camp. Come on, you funny little creature, here's the stable!'

The girls shut the door on the traveller's pony and turned to go back. William, the boy who had brought the message about the horse, yelled to them.

'Hey, George and Anne! There's *another* letter for you!'

The two hurried into the house at once. 'Oh, I hope Father is better and we can go home and join the boys at Kirrin!' said George. She tore open the envelope and then gave a yell that made Anne jump. 'Look, see what it says. They're coming *here*!'

Anne snatched the letter and read it. 'Joining you tomorrow. We'll camp out if no room. Hope you've got a nice juicy adventure ready for us! Julian and Dick.

'They're coming! They're coming!' said Anne, as excited as George. '*Now* we'll have some fun!'

'It's a pity we've no adventure to offer them,' said George. 'Still, you simply never know!'

CHAPTER TWO

Julian, Dick – and Henry

GEORGE WAS quite a different person now that she knew her two cousins were coming the next day. She was even polite to Henrietta!

Captain Johnson scratched his head when he heard that the boys were arriving. 'We can't have them in the house, except for meals,' he said. 'We're full up. They can either sleep in the stables or have a tent. I don't care which.'

'There will be ten altogether then,' said his wife. 'Julian, Dick, Anne, George, Henry – and John, Susan, Alice, Rita and William. Henry may have to camp out too.'

'Not with us,' said George, at once.

'I think you're rather unkind to Henry,' said Mrs Johnson. 'After all, you and she are very alike, George. You both think you ought to have been boys, and . . .'

'I'm not a *bit* like Henrietta!' said George, indignantly. 'You wait till my cousins come, Mrs Johnson. *They* won't think she's like me. I don't expect they'll want anything to do with her.'

'Oh well, you'll just have to shake down together somehow, if you want to stay here,' said Mrs Johnson. 'Let me see, I'd better get some rugs out. The boys will want them, whether they sleep in the stables or in a tent. Come and help me to look for them, Anne.'

Anne, George and Henry were a good bit older than the other five children staying at the stables, but all of them, small or big, were excited to hear about the coming of Julian and Dick. For one thing George and Anne had related so many of the adventures they had had with them, that everyone was inclined to think of them as heroes.

Henrietta disappeared after tea that day and could not be found. 'Wherever have you been?' demanded Mrs Johnson when she at last turned up.

'Up in my room,' said Henrietta. 'Cleaning my shoes and my jods, and mending my riding jacket. You keep telling me to, and now I've done it!'

'Aha! Preparing for the heroes!' said Captain Johnson, and Henry immediately put on a scowl very like the one George often wore.

'Nothing of the sort!' she said. 'I've been meaning to do it for a long time. If Georgina's cousins are anything like *her* I shan't be very interested in them.'

'But you might like my brothers,' said Anne, with a laugh. 'If you don't there'll be something wrong with you.'

'Don't be silly,' said Henrietta. 'Georgina's cousins and your brothers are the same people!'

'How clever of you to work that out,' said George. But she felt too happy to keep up the silly bickering for long. She went out with Timmy, whistling softly.

'They're coming tomorrow, Tim,' she said. 'Julian and

Dick. We'll all go off together, like we always do, the five of us. You'll like that, won't you, Timmy?'

'Woof,' said Timmy approvingly and waved his plumy tail. He knew quite well what she meant.

Next morning George and Anne looked up the trains that arrived at the station two miles away. 'This is the one they'll come by,' said George, her finger on the timetable. 'It's the only one this morning. It arrives at half past twelve. We'll go and meet them.'

'Right,' said Anne. 'We'll start at ten minutes to twelve

– we'll be in plenty of time then. We can help them with their things. They won't bring much.'

'Take the ponies up to Hawthorn Field, will you?' called Captain Johnson. 'Can you manage all four of them?'

'Oh yes,' said Anne, pleased. She loved the walk to Hawthorn Field, up a little narrow lane set with celandines, violets and primroses, and the fresh green of the budding hawthorn bushes. 'Come on, George. Let's catch the ponies and take them now. It's a heavenly morning.'

They set off with the four frisky ponies, Timmy at their heels. He was quite a help with the horses at the stable, especially when any had to be caught.

No sooner had they left the stables and gone on their way to Hawthorn Field than the telephone rang. It was for Anne.

'Oh, I'm sorry, she's not here,' said Mrs Johnson, answering it. 'Who is it speaking? Oh, Julian her brother? Can I give her a message?'

'Yes, please,' said Julian's voice. 'Tell her we are arriving at the bus stop at Milling Green at half past eleven, and is there a little hand-cart she and George could bring, because we've got our tent with us and other odds and ends?'

'Oh, we'll send the little wagon,' said Mrs Johnson. 'The one that always goes to meet the train or the bus. I'll get George to meet you with Anne, they can drive it in. We're pleased you are coming. The weather's very good and you'll enjoy yourselves!'

'You bet!' said Julian. 'Thanks awfully for putting us up. We won't be any trouble, in fact we'll help all we can.'

Mrs Johnson said goodbye and put down the receiver. She saw Henrietta passing outside the window, looking much cleaner and tidier than usual. She called to her.

'Henry! Where are George and Anne? Julian and Dick are arriving at the bus stop at Milling Green at eleven-thirty and I've said we'll meet them in the little wagon. Will you tell George and Anne? They can put Winkie into the cart and trot him down to the bus stop.'

'Right,' said Henry. Then she remembered that George and Anne had been sent up to Hawthorn Field with four ponies.

'I say, they won't be back in time!' she called. 'Shall *I* take the wagon and meet them?'

'Yes, do. That would be kind of you, Henry,' said Mrs Johnson. 'You'd better hurry, though. Time's getting on. Where's Winkie? In the big field?'

'Yes,' said Henry and hurried off to get him. Soon he was in the wagon shafts, and Henry was in the driving seat. She drove off smartly, grinning to herself to think how cross George and Anne would be to find they had missed meeting the two boys after all.

Julian and Dick had already arrived at the bus stop when Henry drove up. They looked hopefully at the wagon, thinking that perhaps one of the girls was driving in to meet them.

'No go,' said Dick. 'It's somebody else, driving into the village. I wonder if the girls got our message. I thought they would meet us at the bus stop here. Well, we'll wait a few minutes more.'

They had just sat down on the bus stop seat again when the wagon stopped nearby. Henry saluted them.

'Are you Anne's brothers?' she called. 'She didn't get your telephone message, so I've come with the wagon instead. Get in!'

'Oh, jolly nice of you,' said Julian, dragging his things to the wagon. 'Er – I'm Julian – and this is Dick. What's your name?'

'Henry,' said Henrietta, helping Julian with his things. She heaved them in valiantly, then clicked to Winkie to stand still and not fidget. 'I'm glad you've come. There are rather a lot of small kids at the stables. We'll be glad of you two! I say, Timmy will be pleased to see you, won't he?'

'Good old Tim,' said Dick, heaving his things in. Henry gave them a shove too. She wasn't very big but she was wiry and strong. She grinned round at the boys. 'All set! Now we'll get back to the stables. Or do you want to have an ice-cream or anything before we start? Dinner's not till one.'

'No. We'll get on, I think,' said Julian. Henry leapt into the driver's seat, took the reins and clicked to Winkie. The boys were behind in the wagon. Winkie set off at a spanking pace.

'Nice boy!' said Dick to Julian, in a low voice, as they

drove off. 'Decent of him to meet us.'

Julian nodded. He was disappointed that Anne and George hadn't come with Timmy, but it was good to be met by *someone*! It wouldn't have been very funny to walk the long road to the farm carrying their packs by themselves.

They arrived at the stables and Henry helped them down with their things. Mrs Johnson heard them arriving and came to the door to welcome them.

'Ah, there you are. Come along in. I've a mid-morning snack for you, because I guessed you'd have had breakfast early. Leave the things there, Henry. If the boys sleep in one of the stables, there's no sense in bringing them into the house. Now, are George and Anne still not back? What a pity!'

Henry disappeared to put away the wagon. The boys went into the pleasant house and sat down to lemonade and home-made biscuits. They had hardly taken a bite before Anne came running in. 'Henry told me you'd come! Oh, I'm sorry we didn't meet you! We thought you'd come by train!'

Timmy came racing in, his tail waving madly. He leapt at the two boys, who were just giving Anne a hug each. Then in came George, her face one big beam.

'Julian! Dick! I *am* so glad you've come! It's been dull as ditch-water without you! Did anyone meet you?'

'Yes. An awfully nice boy,' said Dick. 'Gave us quite a welcome and dragged our packs into the wagon, and was very friendly. You never told us about him.'

'Oh, was that William?' said Anne. 'Well, he's only little. We didn't bother about telling you of the juniors here.'

'No, he wasn't little,' said Dick. 'He was quite big, very strong too. You didn't mention him at all.'

'Well, we told you about the other *girl* here,' said George. 'Henrietta, awful creature! Thinks she's like a boy and goes whistling about everywhere. She makes us laugh! You'll laugh too.'

A sudden thought struck Anne. 'Did the – er – boy who met you, tell you his name?' she asked.

'Yes, what was it now, Henry,' said Dick. 'Nice chap. I'm going to like him.'

George stared as if she couldn't believe her ears. '*Henry!* Did *she* meet you?'

'No – not she – *he*,' corrected Julian. 'Fellow with a big grin.'

'But that's *Henrietta*!' cried George, her face flaming red with anger. 'The awful girl I told you about, who tries to act like a boy, and whistles and strides about all over the place. Don't tell me she took you in! She calls herself Henry, instead of Henrietta, and wears her hair short, and . . .'

'Gosh, she sounds very like *you*, George,' said Dick. 'Well, I never! It never occurred to me that he was a girl. Jolly good show she put up. I must say I liked him – her, I mean.'

'*Oh!*' said George, really furious. 'The beast! She goes

and meets you and never says a word to us, and makes you think she's a boy – and – and – spoils everything!'

'Hold your horses, George, old thing,' said Julian, surprised. 'After all, you've often been pleased when people take *you* for a boy, though goodness knows why. I thought you'd grown out of it a bit. Don't blame us for thinking Henry was a boy, and liking him – her, I mean.'

George stamped out of the room. Julian scratched his head and looked at Dick. 'Now we've put our foot in it,' he said. 'What an ass George is! I should have thought she'd have liked someone like Henry, who had exactly the same ideas as she has. Well, she'll get over it, I suppose.'

'It's going to be a bit awkward,' said Anne, soberly.

She was right. It was going to be *very* awkward!

CHAPTER THREE

Sniffer

As soon as George had gone out of the room, a scowl on her face, Henry walked in, hands in jodhpur pockets.

'Hallo!' said Dick, at once. '*Henrietta!*'

Henry grinned. 'Oh, so they've told you, have they? I was tickled pink when you took me for a boy.'

'You've even got your riding jacket buttons buttoning up the wrong way,' said Anne, noticing for the first time. 'You really are an idiot, Henry. You and George are a pair!'

'Well, I look more like a real boy than George does, anyway,' said Henry.

'Only because of your hair,' said Dick. 'It's straight.'

'Don't say that in front of George,' said Anne. 'She'll immediately have hers cut like a convict or something, all shaven and shorn.'

'Well, anyway, it was jolly decent of Henry to come and meet us and lug our things about,' said Julian. 'Have a biscuit, anyone?'

'No thanks,' said Anne and Henry.

'Are we supposed to leave any for politeness' sake?' said Dick, eyeing the plate. 'They're home-made and quite super. I could wolf the lot.'

'We aren't especially polite here,' said Henry, with a grin. 'We aren't especially clean and tidy, either. We have to change out of our jods at night for supper, which is an awful nuisance, especially as Captain Johnson never bothers to change his.'

'Any news?' asked Julian, drinking the last of the lemonade. 'Anything exciting happened?'

'No, nothing,' said Anne. 'The only excitement is the horses, nothing more. This is quite a lonely place, really, and the only exciting thing we've heard is the name of the big, desolate moor that stretches from here to the coast. Mystery Moor it's called.'

'Why?' asked Dick. 'Some long-ago mystery gave it that name, I suppose?'

'I don't know,' said Anne. 'I think only travellers go there now. A little traveller boy came in with a lame horse yesterday, and said his people had to go to Mystery Moor. Why they wanted to go to such a deserted stretch of land I don't know – no farms there, not even a cottage.'

'Travellers have amazing ideas sometimes,' said Henry. 'I must say I like the way they leave messages for any traveller following – patrins, they're called.'

'Patrins? Yes, I've heard of those,' said Dick. 'Sticks and leaves arranged in certain patterns, or something, aren't they?'

'Yes,' said Henry. 'I know our gardener at home showed me an arrangement of sticks outside our back gate once, which he said was a message to any traveller following. He told me what it meant, too!'

'What did it mean?' asked Julian.

'It meant "Don't beg here. Mean people. No good!"' said Henry, with a laugh. 'That's what he *said*, anyway!'

'We might ask the little traveller boy who came with the skewbald horse,' said Anne. 'He'll probably show us some messages. I'd like to learn some. You never know when anything like that could come in useful!'

'Yes. And we'll ask him why the travellers go to Mystery Moor,' said Julian, getting up and dusting the crumbs off his coat. 'They don't go there for nothing, you may be sure!'

'Where's old George gone?' asked Dick. 'I do hope she's not going to be silly.'

George was in one of the stables, grooming a horse so vigorously that it was most surprised. Swish-swish-swish-swish! What a brushing! George was working her intense annoyance out of herself. She mustn't spoil things for the boys and Anne! But oh, that horrible Henrietta, meeting them like that, pretending to be a boy. Heaving their luggage about, playing a joke on them! But surely they might have guessed!

'Oh, there you are, George,' said Dick's voice at the stable door. 'Let me help. Gosh, aren't you tanned! Just as many freckles as ever!'

George grinned unwillingly. She tossed Dick the brush. 'Here you are, then! Do you and Ju want to go riding at all? There are plenty of horses to choose from here.'

Dick was relieved to see that George appeared to have got over her rage. 'Yes. It might be fun to go off for the day. What about tomorrow? We might explore a little of Mystery Moor.'

'Right,' said George. She began to heave some straw about. 'But not with That Girl,' she announced, from behind the straw she was carrying.

'What girl?' asked Dick, innocently. 'Oh, Henry, you mean? I keep thinking of her as a boy. No, we won't have her with us. We'll be just the Five as usual.'

'That's all right then,' said George happily. 'Oh, here's Julian. Give a hand, Ju!'

It was lovely to have the two boys again, joking, laughing, teasing. They all went out in the fields that afternoon and heard the tales of the camp. It was just like old times, and Timmy was as pleased as anyone else. He went first to one of the four, then to another, licking each one as he went, his tail wagging vigorously.

'That's three times you've smacked me in the face with your tail, Timmy,' said Dick, dodging it. 'Can't you look behind yourself and see where my face is?'

'Woof,' said Timmy happily, and turned round to lick Dick, wagging his tail in Julian's face this time!

Somebody squeezed through the hedge behind them. George stiffened, feeling sure that it was Henrietta. Timmy barked sharply.

It wasn't Henrietta. It was the little traveller boy. He came up to them. There were tear streaks down his face.

'I've come for the horse,' he said. 'Do you know where he is?'

'He's not ready for walking yet,' said George. 'Captain Johnson told you he wouldn't be. What's the matter? Why have you been crying?'

'My father punished me,' said the boy. 'He knocked me right over.'

'Whatever for?' said Anne.

'Because I left the horse,' said the boy. 'My father said all it wanted was a bit of ointment and a bandage. He has to start off with the other caravans today, you see.'

'Well, you really *can't* have the horse yet,' said Anne.

'It isn't fit to walk, let alone drag a caravan. You don't want Captain Johnson to tell the police you're working it when it's not fit, do you? You know he means what he says?'

'Yes. But I must have the horse,' said the small boy. 'I daren't go back without it. My father would punish me.'

'I suppose he doesn't care to come himself, so he sends you instead,' said Dick, in disgust.

The boy said nothing, and rubbed his sleeve across his face. He sniffed.

'Get your hanky,' said Dick.

'Please let me have my horse,' said the boy. 'I tell you, I'll be punished if I go back without him.' He began to cry again.

The children felt sorry for him. He was such a thin, skinny misery of a boy, and goodness, how he sniffed all the time!

'What's your name?' asked Anne.

'Sniffer,' said the boy. 'That's what my father calls me.'

It was certainly a good name for him; but what a horrid father he must have!

'Haven't you got a proper name?' asked Anne.

'Yes. But I've forgotten it,' said Sniffer. 'Let me have my horse. I tell you, my father's waiting.'

Julian got up. 'I'll come and see your father and put some sense into him. Where is he?'

'Over there,' said Sniffer with a big sniff, and he pointed over the hedge. 'I'll come too,' said Dick. In the end everyone got up and went with Sniffer. They walked

through the gate and saw a surly-looking man standing motionless not far off. His thick, oily hair was curly, and he wore enormous gold rings hanging from his ears. He looked up as the little company came near.

'Your horse isn't fit to walk yet, said Julian. 'You can have it tomorrow or the next day, the captain says.'

'I'll have it now,' said the man, in a surly tone. 'We're starting off tonight or tomorrow over the moor. I can't wait.'

'But what's the hurry?' said Julian. 'The moor will wait for you!'

The man scowled and shifted from one foot to another. 'Can't you stay for another night or two and then go after the others?' said Dick.

'Listen, Father! You go with the other caravans,' said Sniffer, eagerly. 'Go in Moses' caravan and leave ours here. I can put our horse into the shafts tomorrow, or maybe the next day, and follow after!'

'But how would you know the way?' said George.

Sniffer made a scornful movement with his hand. 'Easy! They'll leave me patrins to follow,' he said.

'Oh yes,' said Dick, remembering. He turned to the silent traveller. 'Well, what about it? It seems that Sniffer here has quite a good idea, and you most certainly can't have the horse today anyway.'

The man turned and said something angry and scornful to poor Sniffer, who shrank away from the words as if they were blows. The four children couldn't understand a word, for it was all poured out in a language that they could not follow. Then the man turned on his heel and without so much as a look at them, slouched away, his earrings gleaming as he went.

'What did he say?' asked Julian.

Sniffer gave one of his continual sniffs. 'He was very angry. He said he'd go with the others, and I could come on with Clip the horse, and drive our caravan,' he said. 'I'll be all right there tonight with Liz.'

'Who's Liz?' asked Anne, hoping that it was someone who would be kind to this poor little wretch.

'My dog,' said Sniffer, smiling for the first time. 'I left her behind because she sometimes goes for hens, and Captain Johnson doesn't like that.'

'I bet he doesn't,' said Julian. 'All right, that's settled then. You can come for Clip, or Clop, or whatever your horse is called, tomorrow, and we'll see if it's fit to walk.'

'I'm glad,' said Sniffer, rubbing his nose. 'I don't want Clip to go lame, see? But my father's very fierce.'

'So we gather,' said Julian, looking at a bruise on Sniffer's face. 'You come tomorrow and you can show us some of the patrins, the messages, that you use. We'd like to know some.'

'I'll come,' promised Sniffer, nodding his head vigorously. 'And you will come to see my caravan? I shall be all alone there, except for Liz.'

'Well, I suppose it would be something to do,' said Dick. 'Yes, we'll come.'

'I will show you patrins there and Liz will show you her tricks. She is very, very clever. Once she belonged to a circus,' said Sniffer.

'We must certainly take Timmy to see this clever dog,' said Anne, patting Timmy, who had been hunting for rabbits and had only just come back. 'Timmy, would you like to go and visit a very clever dog called Liz?'

'Woof,' said Timmy, wagging his tail politely.

'Right,' said Dick. 'I'm glad you approve, Tim. We'll all try and come tomorrow, Sniffer, after you've been to see how Clip is getting on. I don't somehow think you'll be able to have him then, though. We'll see!'

CHAPTER FOUR

A bed in the stable

THE BOYS slept in one of the stables that night. Captain Johnson said they could either have mattresses sent out, or could sleep in the straw, with rugs.

'Oh, straw and rugs, please,' said Julian. 'That's fine. We'll be as snug as anything with those.'

'I wish Anne and I could sleep in a stable too,' said George, longingly. 'We never have. Can't we, Captain Johnson?'

'No. You've got beds that you're paying for,' said the captain. 'Anyway, girls can't do that sort of thing, not even girls who try to be boys, George!'

'I've *often* slept in a stable,' said Henrietta. 'At home when we've too many visitors, I always turn out and sleep in the straw.'

'Bad luck on the horses!' said George.

'Why?' demanded Henry at once.

'Because you must keep them awake all night with your snoring!' said George.

Henry snorted crossly and went out. It was maddening that she should snore at night, but she simply couldn't help it.

'Never mind!' George called after her. 'It's a nice *manly* snore, Henrietta!'

'Shut up, George,' said Dick, rather shocked at this sudden display of pettiness on George's part.

'Don't tell *me* to shut up,' said George. 'Tell Henrietta!'

'George, don't be an ass,' said Julian. But George didn't like that either, and stalked out of the room in just the same stiff, offended way that Henry had done!

'Oh dear!' said Anne. 'It's been like this all the time. First Henry, then George, then George, then Henry! They really are a couple of idiots!'

She went to see where the boys were to sleep. They had been told to use a small stable, empty except for the traveller's horse that lay patiently down, its bandaged leg stretched out on the floor. Anne patted it and stroked it. It was an ugly little thing but its patient brown eyes were lovely.

The boys had heaps of straw to burrow into, and some old rugs. Anne thought it all looked lovely. 'You can wash and everything at the house,' she said. 'Then just slip over here to sleep. Doesn't it smell nice? All straw and hay and horse! I hope the horse won't disturb you. He may be a bit restless if his leg hurts him.'

'Nothing will disturb *us* tonight!' said Julian. 'What with camp life and open air and wind-on-the-hills and all that kind of thing, we're sure to sleep like logs. I think we're going to enjoy it here, Anne, very quiet and peaceful!'

George looked in at the door. 'I'll lend you Timmy if you like,' she said, anxious to make up for her display of temper.

'Oh, hallo, George! No thanks. I don't particularly want old Tim climbing over me all night long, trying to find the softest part of me to sleep on!' said Julian. 'I say, look, he's showing me how to make a good old burrow to sleep in! Hey, Tim, come out of my straw!'

Timmy had flung himself into the straw and was turning vigorously round and round in it as if he were making a bed for himself. He stood and looked up at them, his mouth open and his tongue hanging out at one side.

'He's laughing,' said Anne, and it did indeed look as if Timmy was having a good old laugh at them. Anne gave him a hug and he licked her lavishly, and then began to burrow round and round in the straw again.

Someone came up, whistling loudly, and put her head in at the door. 'I've brought you a couple of old pillows. Mrs Johnson said you'd better have something for your heads.'

'Oh thanks awfully, Henry,' said Julian, taking them.

'How kind of you, Henri*etta*,' said George.

'It's a pleasure, Geor*gina*,' said Henry, and the boys burst out laughing. Fortunately the supper-bell went just then and they all went across the yard at once. Somehow everyone was always hungry at the stables!

The girls looked very different in the evening, because they had to change out of their dirty, smelly jodhpurs or breeches and put on dresses. Anne, Henry and George hurried to change before Mrs Johnson rang the supper-bell again. She always gave them ten minutes' grace, knowing that they might sometimes have a job to finish with the horses, but everyone was supposed to be at the table when the second supper-bell had finished ringing.

George looked nice, because her curly hair went with a skirt and blouse quite well, but Henry looked quite wrong, somehow, in her frilly dress.

'You look like a boy dressed up!' said Anne, and this pleased Henry, but not George. The talk at the supper-table was mainly about all the wonderful things that Henry had done in her life. Apparently she had three brothers and did everything with them, and according to her own tales, she was considerably better than they were!

They had sailed a ship up to Norway. They had hiked from London to York.

'Was Dick Turpin with you?' inquired George, sarcastically. 'On his horse, Black Bess? I expect you got there long before *him*, didn't you?'

Henry took no notice. She went on with wonderful tales of her family's exploits, swimming across wide rivers, climbing Snowdon to the top, goodness, there wasn't a single thing she didn't seem to have done!

'You certainly ought to have been a boy, Henry,' said Mrs Johnson, which was exactly what Henry wanted everyone to say!

'Henry, when you've told us the story of how you climbed Mount Everest and got there before anyone else, perhaps you would finish your plateful,' said Captain Johnson, who got very tired of Henry's tongue.

George roared with laughter, not that she thought it was very funny, but because she loved any chance to laugh at Henry. Henry tackled the rest of her food at top speed. How she did love to hold everyone spellbound with her extraordinary tales! George didn't believe a word, but Dick and Julian thought it quite likely that this tall, wiry girl *could* do things just as well as her brothers.

There were a few jobs to be done after supper, and Henry kept well away from George, knowing quite well that she would have a few cutting things to say. Well, *she* didn't care! Everyone else thought she was marvellous! She tore off her frilly dress and put on jodhpurs again, although it would only be a short time before they all went to bed.

George and Anne went with the boys to their stable. They were in pyjamas and dressing-gowns, both yawning as they went. 'Got your torches?' said George. 'We're not allowed to have candles in the stables, because of the straw, you know. Good night! Sleep well! And I hope that that idiot of a Henry doesn't come along early in the morning, whistling like a paperboy, and wake you up!'

'Nothing will wake me up tonight, nothing at all,' said Julian, with a huge yawn. He lay down in the straw and pulled an old rug over him. 'Oh, what a bed! Give me stable straw every time to sleep in!'

The girls laughed. The boys really *did* look very comfortable. 'Sleep tight,' said Anne, and walked off with George to the house.

Soon all the lights were out everywhere. Henry was asleep and snoring as usual. She had to have a separate room, otherwise she kept everyone awake! But even so, Anne and George could hear her, snoring away – rrrumph – rrrumph! rrrumph – RRRRUMPH!

'Blow Henrietta!' said George, sleepily. 'What a row she makes. Anne, she's not to come with us when we go riding tomorrow. Do you hear, Anne?'

'Not very well,' murmured Anne, trying to open her eyes. 'G'night, George!'

Timmy was on George's feet as usual. He lay snuggled

there, eyes shut and ears asleep too. He got as tired as everyone else, running over the hills all day, scrabbling at scores of rabbit holes, chasing dozens of remarkably fleet-footed rabbits. But at night he too slept like a log.

Out in the stable the two boys slept peacefully, covered by the old rug. Nearby the little skewbald horse moved restlessly, but they heard nothing. An owl came swooping over the stable, looking for mice down below. It screeched loudly, hoping to scare a mouse into sudden flight. Then it would swoop down and take it into its talons.

Not even the screech awakened the boys. They slept dreamlessly, tired out.

The door of the stable was shut and latched. Clip, the horse, suddenly stirred and looked round at the door. The latch was moving! Someone was lifting it from the outside. Clip's pricked ears heard the sound of a little shuffle.

He watched the door. Who was coming? He hoped it was Sniffer, the boy he liked so much. Sniffer was always kind to him. He didn't like being away from Sniffer. He listened for the sniff-sniff that always went with the little boy, but he didn't hear it.

The door opened very slowly indeed. It gave no creak. Clip saw the night sky outside, set with stars. He made out a figure outlined against the darkness of the starry night, a black shadow.

Someone came into the stable, and whispered 'Clip!'

The horse gave a little whinny. It wasn't Sniffer's voice. It was his father's. Clip did not like him, he was too free with cuffs and kicks, and slashes with the whip. He lay still, wondering why the traveller had come.

The man had no idea that Dick and Julian were sleeping in the stable. He had come in quietly because he had thought there might be other horses there, and he did not want to startle them and make them stamp about in fright. He had no torch, but his keen eyes made out Clip at once, lying in his straw.

He tiptoed across to him and fell over Julian's feet, sticking out from the straw bed he was lying on. He fell with a thud, and Julian sat up very suddenly indeed, awake at once.

'Who's there! What is it?'

The traveller shrank down beside Clip, keeping silent. Julian began to wonder if he had been dreaming. But his foot distinctly hurt him. Surely somebody had trodden on it, or fallen over it? He woke Dick.

'Where's the torch? Hallo, look, the stable door is open! Quick, Dick, where on earth is the torch?'

They found it at last and Julian clicked it on. At first he saw nothing, for the man was in Clip's stall, lying down behind the horse. Then the torch picked him out.

'Hallo! Look there – it's that traveller, Sniffer's father!' said Julian. 'Get up, you! What on earth are you doing here, in the middle of the night?'

CHAPTER FIVE

George gets a headache!

THE MAN got up sullenly. His earrings shone in the light of the torch. 'I came to get Clip,' he said. 'He's my horse, isn't he?'

'You were told he wasn't fit to walk yet,' said Julian. 'Do you want him to go lame for life? You ought to know enough about horses to know when one can be worked or not!'

'I've got my orders,' said the man. 'I've got to take my caravan with the others.'

'Who said so?' said Dick, scornfully.

'Barney Boswell,' said the man. 'He's boss of our lot here. We've got to start off together tomorrow.'

'But why?' said Julian, puzzled. 'What's so urgent about all this? What's the mystery?'

'There isn't any mystery,' said the man, still sullen. 'We're just going to the moor.'

'What are you going to do there?' asked Dick, curiously. 'It doesn't seem to me to be the place to take a lot of caravans to. There's nothing there at all, is there? Or so I've heard.'

The man shrugged his shoulders and said nothing. He turned to Clip as if to get him up. But Julian rapped out at him at once.

'Oh no, you don't! If you don't care about injuring a horse, I do! You've only got to be patient for a day or two more, and he'll be quite all right. You're not to take him tonight. Dick, go and wake Captain Johnson. He'll know what to do.'

'No,' said the man, scowling. 'Don't wake anybody. I'll go. But just see that Clip is given to Sniffer as soon as it's possible, or I'll know the reason why! See?'

He looked at Julian in a threatening way.

'Take that scowl off your face,' said Julian. 'I'm glad you've seen sense. Clear out now. Go off with the others tomorrow and I'll see that Sniffer has the horse in a short time.'

The man moved to the door and slid out like a shadow. Julian went to watch him across the yard, wondering whether, out of spite, the man might try to steal a hen, or one of the ducks sleeping beside the pond.

But there was no sudden clucking, no loud quack. The man had gone as silently as he had come.

'Most peculiar, all this!' said Julian, latching the door again. He tied a piece of thick string over it his side, so that it could not be lifted from outside. 'There! Now if the traveller comes again, he'll find he can't get in. What a nerve, coming here in the middle of the night like that!'

He got back into the straw. 'He must have fallen right over my foot,' he said, snuggling down. 'He woke me up with an awful jump. Good thing for Clip that we were sleeping out here tonight, or he'd be dragging along a heavy caravan tomorrow, and going lame again. I don't like that fellow!'

He fell asleep again and so did Dick. Clip slept too, his leg feeling easier. How glad he had been that day not to have to drag along the heavy caravan!

The boys told Captain Johnson next morning about the traveller's midnight visit. He nodded. 'Yes, I ought to have warned you that he might come. They're not always very good to their horses. Well, I'm glad you sent him off. I don't reckon Clip's leg will be ready for walking on till the day after tomorrow. There's no harm in giving the poor creature a few days' rest. Sniffer can easily take the caravan on after the others.'

It looked as if that day was going to be fun. After all the horses had been seen to, and many odd jobs done, the four, with Timmy, planned to set out for a day's ride. Captain Johnson said he would let Julian ride his own sturdy cob and Dick took a bonny chestnut horse, with four white socks. The girls had the horses they usually rode.

Henry hung about, looking very mournful. The boys felt quite uncomfortable. 'We *really* ought to tell her to come along too,' said Dick to Julian. 'It seems jolly mean to leave her behind with those little kids.'

'Yes, I know. I agree with you,' said Julian. 'Anne, come here! Can't you suggest to George that we take Henry too? She's longing to come, I know.'

'Yes, she is,' said Anne. 'I feel awful about it. But George will be mad if we ask Henry. They really do get on each other's nerves. I simply daren't ask George to let Henry come, Ju.'

'But this is *silly*!' said Julian. 'To think we don't *dare* to ask George to let somebody come! George will have to learn sense. I like Henry. She's boastful, and I don't believe half the tales she tells, but she's a sport and good fun. Hey, Henry!'

'Coming!' yelled Henry, and came running, looking very hopeful.

'Would you like to come with us!' said Julian. 'We're all going off for the day. Have you got any jobs to do, or can you come?'

'Can I *come*! You bet!' said Henry, joyfully. 'But – does George know?'

'I'll soon tell her,' said Julian, and went in search of George. She was helping Mrs Johnson to get saddle bags ready, full of food.

'George,' said Julian, boldly, 'Henry is coming too. Will there be enough food for everyone?'

'Oh! How *nice* of you to ask her!' said Mrs Johnson, sounding very pleased. 'She's dying to come. She's been so good this week, too, while we've been short-handed. She deserves a treat. Isn't that *nice*, George?'

George muttered something peculiar and went out of the room, her face scarlet. Julian stared after her, his eyebrows cocked in a comical manner.

'I don't somehow feel that George thinks it's nice,' he said. 'I feel as if we are in for an awkward day, Mrs Johnson.'

'Oh, don't take any notice of George when she's silly,' said Mrs Johnson, comfortably, filling another paper bag with delicious-looking sandwiches. 'And don't take any notice of Henry, either, when she's idiotic. There! If you get through all this food, I shall be surprised!'

William, one of the younger ones, came in just then.

'What a lot of food you've given them,' he said. 'Will there be enough left for *us* to have today?'

'Good gracious, yes!' said Mrs Johnson. 'You think of nothing but your tummy, William! Go and find George and tell her the food is ready for her to put into the saddle bags.'

William disappeared and then came back. 'George says she's got a headache and doesn't think she'll go on the ride,' he announced.

Julian looked startled and upset. 'Now listen to me, Julian,' said Mrs Johnson, beginning to insert the parcels of food carefully into the saddle-bags, 'just leave her to her imaginary headache. Don't go fussing round her, and begging her to come and saying you won't have Henry. Just believe quite firmly in her headache, and go off by yourselves. It's the quickest way to make George see sense, believe *me*!'

'Yes, I think you're right,' said Julian, frowning. To think that George should behave like a sulky little girl, after all the adventures they had been through together! Just because of Henry. It really was absurd.

'Where *is* George?' he said to William.

'Up in her room,' said William, who had been engrossed in picking up and eating all the crumbs he could. Julian went out of the room and into the yard. He knew which window belonged to the room where George and Anne slept. He yelled up.

'George! Sorry about your headache! Sure you don't feel like coming?'

'No!' came back an answering shout, and the window was shut down with a slam.

'OK! Awfully disappointed and all that!' shouted Julian. 'Do hope your head will soon be better! See you later!'

No other reply came from the window, but, as Julian went across the yard to the stables, a very surprised face watched him go, from behind the bedroom curtains. George was extremely astonished to have been taken at her word, shocked at being left behind after all, and angry with Henry and everyone else for putting her into this fix!

Julian told the others that George had a headache and wasn't coming. Anne was most concerned and wanted to go and comfort her but Julian forbade her to.

'No. She's up in her room. Leave her alone, Anne. That's an order – OK?'

'All right,' said Anne, half-relieved. She felt sure that George's headache was mostly temper, and she didn't at all want to go and argue with her for half an hour. Henry hadn't said a word. She had flushed with surprise when Julian had announced that George was not coming, and she knew at once that there was no real headache! *She* was George's headache, she knew that!

She went up to Julian. 'Look, I guess it's because you've asked *me* to come, that Georgina won't come with us. I don't want to spoil things. You go and tell her I'm not going after all.'

Julian looked at Henry gratefully. 'That's jolly nice of

you,' he said. 'But we're taking George at her word. Anyway, we didn't ask you out of politeness. We *wanted* you to come!'

'Thanks,' said Henry. 'Well, let's go before anything else happens! Our horses are ready. I'll fix the saddle-bags.'

Soon all four were on their horses, and were walking over the yard to the gate. George heard the clippity-clop-clippity-clop of the hooves and peeped out of the window again. They were going after all! She hadn't thought they really *would* go without her. She was horrified.

'Why did I behave like that? I've put myself in the wrong!' thought poor George. 'Now Henrietta will be with them all day and will be as nice as possible, just to show me up. What an ass I am!'

'Timmy, I'm an ass and an idiot, and a great big idiot! Aren't I?'

Timmy didn't think so. He had been puzzled to hear the others going off without him and George, and had gone to the door and whined. Now he came back to George and put his head on her knee. He knew George was not happy.

'*You* don't care how I behave, do you, Tim?' said George, stroking the soft, furry head. 'That's the best thing about a dog! You don't care if I'm in the wrong or not, you just love me all the same, don't you? Well, you shouldn't love me today, Tim. I've been an idiot!'

There was a knock at her door. It was William again. 'George! Mrs Johnson says, if your headache is bad, undress and get into bed. But if it's better, come down and help with Clip, the traveller's horse.'

'I'll come down,' said George, flinging away her sulks at one go. 'Tell Mrs Johnson I'll go to the stable at once.'

'All right,' said the stolid William, and trotted off like a reliable little pony.

George went downstairs with Timmy, and into the yard. She wondered how far the others had gone. She couldn't see them in the distance. Would they have a good day together, with that horrid Henry? Ugh!

The others were almost a mile away, cantering easily. What *fun*! A whole day before them, on Mystery Moor!

CHAPTER SIX

A grand day

'I THINK it's a jolly good name, Mystery Moor,' said Dick, as the four of them went along. 'Look at it stretching for miles, all blazing with gorse.'

'I don't think it looks at all mysterious,' said Henry, surprised.

'Well, it's got a sort of quietness and broodiness,' said Anne, 'as if something big happened long ago in the past and it's waiting for something to happen again.'

'Quiet and broody? It sounds like one of the farmyard hens sitting on her eggs!' said Henry with a laugh. 'I think it might be a bit frightening and mysterious at night, but it's just an ordinary stretch of country in the daytime, fine for riding over. I can't think why it's called Mystery Moor.'

'We'll have to look it up in some book that tells about this part of the country,' said Dick. 'I expect it was called that because of some strange happening or other, hundreds of years ago, when people believed in witches and things like that.'

They followed no road or path, but rode where they pleased. There were great stretches of wiry grass, masses of heather springing up afresh, and, blazing its gold everywhere on this lovely April day, was the gorse.

Anne sniffed continually as they rode past the gorse bushes. Dick looked at her.

'You sound like Sniffer!' he said. 'Have you got a cold?'

Anne laughed. 'No, of course not. But I do so love the smell of the gorse. What does it smell of? Vanilla? Hot coconut? It's a lovely *warm* smell!'

'Look! What's that moving over there?' said Julian, suddenly reining in his horse. They all strained their eyes to see.

'It's caravans!' said Julian, at last. 'Of course! They were setting out today, weren't they? Well, they must find it very rough going, that's all I can say. There's no real road anywhere, as far as I can see.'

'Where can they be going?' wondered Anne. 'What's over in that direction?'

'They'll come to the coast if they keep on the way they are going,' said Julian, considering. 'Let's ride over and have a look at them, shall we?'

'Yes. Good idea!' said Dick. So they turned their horses' heads to the right, and rode towards the far-away caravans. These made quite a splash of colour as they went along. There were four of them – two red ones, a blue one and a yellow one. They went very slowly indeed, each pulled by a small, wiry horse.

'They all look like skewbalds, brown and white,' said Dick. 'It's funny that so many travellers have skewbald horses. I wonder why it is?'

They heard shouting as they came near the caravans, and saw one man pointing them out to another. It was Sniffer's father!

'Look, that's the fellow who woke us up in the stable last night,' said Julian to Dick. 'Sniffer's father! What a nasty bit of work he is! Why doesn't he get a haircut?'

'Good morning!' called Dick, as they rode up to the caravans on their horses. 'Nice day!'

There was no answer. The travellers driving their caravans, and those walking alongside, looked sourly at the four riders.

'Where are you going?' asked Henry. 'To the coast?'

'It's nothing to do with you,' said one of the travellers, an old man with curly grey hair.

'Surly folk, aren't they?' said Dick to Julian. 'I suppose they think we're spying on them, or something. I wonder how they manage about food on this moor, no shops or anything. I suppose they take it all with them.'

'I'll ask them,' said Henry, not at all put off by the surly looks. She rode right up to Sniffer's father.

'How do you manage about food, and water?' she asked.

'We've got food there,' said Sniffer's father, jerking his head back towards one of the caravans. 'As for water, we know where the springs are.'

'Are you camping on the moor for a long time?' asked Henry, thinking that a traveller's life might be a fine one, for a time! Fancy living out here on this lovely moor with gorse blazing gold all around, and primroses by the thousand in the sheltered corners!

'That's nothing to do with *you*!' shouted the old man with curly grey hair. 'Clear off and leave us alone!'

'Come on, Henry,' said Julian, swinging round to go off. 'They don't like us asking them questions. They think it's prying, not interest. Maybe they have lots of things to hide, and don't want us poking around – one or two chickens from a farm, a duck or so from the pond. They live from hand-to-mouth, these folk.'

Some bright-eyed children peered from the vans as they went by. One or two were running outside, but they sheered off like frightened rabbits when Henry cantered towards them.

'Oh well, they simply don't *want* to be friendly,' she said, and went to join the other three. 'What an unusual life they lead, in their houses on wheels! Never staying anywhere for long, always on the move. Get up, there, Sultan. Go after the others!'

Her horse obediently followed the other three, taking care not to step into any rabbit holes! What fun it was to be out here in the sunshine, jogging up and down on the horse's back, without a care in the world! Henry was very happy.

The other three were enjoying their day, but they were not quite so happy. They kept wondering about George. They missed Timmy too. He should be trotting beside them, enjoying the day as well!

They lost sight of the caravans after a time. Julian kept track of the way they went, half-afraid of being lost. He had a compass with him, and checked their direction continually. 'It would never do to have to spend a night out here!' he said. 'Nobody would ever find us!'

They had a magnificent lunch about half past twelve. Really, Mrs Johnson had surpassed herself! Egg and sardine sandwiches, tomato and lettuce, ham – there seemed no end to them! Great slices of cherry cake were added too, and a large, juicy pear each.

'I like this kind of cherry cake,' said Dick, looking at his enormous slice. 'The cherries have all gone to the bottom. They make a very nice last mouthful!'

'Any drinks?' said Henry, and was handed a bottle of ginger-beer. She drank it thirstily.

'Why does ginger-beer taste so nice on a picnic?' she said. '*Much* nicer than drinking it sitting down in a shop, even if it's got ice in it!'

'There's a spring or something nearby,' said Julian. 'I can hear it bubbling.'

They all listened. Yes, there was a little bubbling, tinkling noise. Anne got up to trace it. She found it in a few minutes and called the others. There was a round pool, cool and blue, lying two or three feet down, and into it, from one side, fell a crystal clear spring of water, tinkling as it fell.

'One of the springs that the travellers use, when they come to this deserted moor, I expect,' said Julian. He cupped his hands under the falling water and got his palms full. He carried the water to his mouth and sipped it.

'Delicious! Cool as an ice-box,' he said. 'Taste it, Anne.'

They rode a little farther, but the moor seemed the same everywhere: heather, wiry grass, gorse, a clear spring falling into a pool or tiny stream here and there, and a few trees, mostly silver birch.

Larks sang all the time, soaring high in the air, almost too far up to see.

'Their song falls down like raindrops,' said Anne, holding out her hands as if to catch it. Henry laughed. She liked this family, and was very glad they had asked her to come out with them. She thought George was silly to have stayed at the stables.

'I think we ought to get home,' said Julian at last, looking at his watch. 'We're a good way away. Let me see now. We want to make more or less for the setting sun. Come on!'

He led the way, his horse picking its own path over the heather. The others followed. Dick stopped after a while.

'Are you sure we're quite right, Ju? I don't somehow feel that we are. The moor is different here, rather sandy and not so much gorse.'

Julian stopped his horse and looked round and about. 'Yes, it does look a bit different,' he said. 'But yet we seem to be going in the right direction. Let's go a bit more to the west. If only there was something on the horizon to guide us. But this moor hasn't a thing that stands out anywhere!'

They went on again, and then Henry gave an exclamation. 'I say! What's this? Do come here.'

The two boys and Anne swerved over to Henry. She was now off her horse, and was bending over, scraping away at the heather.

'Look, it seems like rails, or something,' said Henry. 'Very old and rusty. But they can't be, surely?'

Everyone was now down on their knees, scraping sand and heather away. Julian sat back and considered.

'Yes, it's rails. Old ones, as you say. But what in the world were rails laid down here for?'

'I can't think,' said Henry. 'I only caught sight of them by chance, they're so overgrown. I couldn't believe my eyes!'

'They must lead from somewhere *to* somewhere!' said Dick. 'Perhaps there was a quarry, or something on the moor and they ran little engines with trucks there, to fetch the sand, and take it back to town to sell.'

'That's about it,' said Julian. 'It's very sandy here, as we noticed. Good, fine sand. Maybe there is a quarry on the moor. Well, *that* way, behind us, goes right out on the moor, so *this* way must lead back to some town or village, probably Milling Green or somewhere like that.'

'Yes. You're right,' said Dick. 'In which case, if we follow the lines along, we'll get back to civilisation sooner or later!'

'Well, seeing that we seem to be more or less lost, that would be quite a good idea!' said Henry. She mounted her horse again and rode along the lines.

'They're fairly easy to see!' she called. 'If you ride between them, that is, because they go so straight.'

The lines ran steadily over the moor, sometimes very overgrown, and in about half an hour's time Henry gave a cry and pointed forward. 'Houses! I thought we'd soon come to some place!'

'It *is* Milling Green!' said Julian, as the rails came to a sudden end, and they rode out into a small cart road.

'Well, we haven't far to go now, to get to the stables,' said Henry, pleased. 'I say, wouldn't it be fun to follow those lines all across the moor and see where they really lead to?'

'Yes. We might do that one day,' said Julian. 'Gosh, it's getting late. I wonder how old George has been getting on today!'

They walked quickly along to the stables, thinking of George. Would she have retired to bed? Would she still be cross, or worse still, hurt and grieved? It was anybody's guess!

CHAPTER SEVEN

George, Sniffer and Liz

George had had quite an interesting day. First she had gone down to help Captain Johnson do Clip's leg again and bandage it up. The little skewbald stood very patiently, and George felt a sudden liking for the ugly little creature.

'Thanks, George,' said Captain Johnson, who, to her relief, had said nothing about her not having gone riding with the others. 'Now would you like to come and put jumps up for the youngsters? They're longing to do some more jumping.'

George found that it was quite amusing to teach the younger ones how to jump. They were so very, very proud of themselves when they went over even a foot-high jump on their little ponies.

After that Sniffer arrived accompanied by a peculiar little mongrel called Liz. Liz was a bit of a spaniel, a bit of a poodle, and odd bits of something else – and looked rather like a small, walking hearth rug of black curly fur.

Timmy was amazed to see this walking mat, and sat and watched Liz sniffing here and there for some time, before he came to the conclusion that it really *was* some kind of dog. He gave a sharp little bark to see what this comical creature would do when she heard it.

Liz took no notice at all. She had unearthed a small bone, which smelt extremely interesting. Timmy considered that all bones within the radius of at least a mile belonged to him and him alone. So he ran over to Liz at once and gave a small, warning growl.

Liz immediately dropped the bone humbly at his feet, then sat up on her hind legs and begged. Timmy eyed her in astonishment. Then Liz stood up on her hind legs and walked daintily all round Timmy and back again.

Timmy was astounded. He had never seen a dog do that before. *Could* this hearth-rug affair be a dog after all?

Liz saw that Timmy was really impressed, and went on with yet another trick she had learnt during the time she had been with the circus.

She turned head-over-heels, yapping all the time. Timmy retreated a few steps into the bushes. This was going *too* far! What was this animal doing? Trying to stand on its head?

Liz went on turning head-over-heels very rapidly and ended up almost on Timmy's front paws. He had now backed into the bush as far as he could.

Liz remained on her back, paws in the air, tongue hanging out, panting. She gave a very small, beseeching whine.

Timmy bent his head down and sniffed at her paws. Behind him his tail began to move a little – yes, it had a wag in it! He sniffed again. Liz leapt on to her four feet and pranced all round Timmy, yapping as if to say 'Come on and play! Do come!'

And then suddenly Timmy fell upon the absurd little creature and pretended to worry it. Liz gave a delighted volley of yaps and rolled over and over. They had a marvellous game, and when it was all over, Timmy sank down panting for breath, in a sunny corner of the yard and Liz settled herself between his front paws, as if she had known him all her life!

When George came out of the stable with Sniffer, she could hardly believe her eyes. 'What's that Timmy's got between his paws?' she said. 'It's surely not a *dog*!'

'It's Liz,' said Sniffer. 'She can get round any dog there is, George! Liz! You're a monkey, aren't you! Walk, then, walk!'

Liz left Timmy and ran over to Sniffer, walking daintily on her hind legs. George laughed. 'What a funny little creature, like a bit cut out of a furry hearth rug!'

'She's clever,' said Sniffer and patted Liz. 'Well, George, when can I have Clip, do you think? My father has gone off with the other caravans and he's left me with ours. So it doesn't matter whether it's today or tomorrow, or even the next day.'

'Well, it won't be today, that's certain,' said George. 'It might perhaps be tomorrow. Haven't you got a hanky, Sniffer? I never in my life heard anyone sniff as often as you do?'

Sniffer rubbed his sleeve across his nose. 'I've never had a hanky,' he said. 'But I've got my sleeve!'

'I think you're quite disgusting,' said George. 'I'm going to give you one of my own hankies, and you're to use it. You're *not* to keep sniffing like that.'

'Didn't know I did,' said Sniffer, half sulkily. 'What does it matter, anyway?'

But George had gone indoors and up the stairs. She chose a large hanky, in red and white stripes. That would do nicely for Sniffer! She took it down to him. He looked at it in surprise.

'That's a scarf for my neck!' he said.

'No, it isn't. It's a hanky for your nose,' said George. 'Haven't you a pocket to put it in? That's right. Now, use it instead of sniffing, for goodness' sake!'

'Where are the others?' asked Sniffer, putting the

hanky carefully into his pocket, almost as if it were made of glass.

'Gone riding,' said George, shortly.

'They said they would come and see my caravan,' said Sniffer. 'They said so!'

'Well, they won't be able to today,' said George. 'They'll be back too late, I expect. I'll come and see it, though. There's nobody in it, is there?'

George was not keen on meeting Sniffer's father or any other of his relations! He shook his head. 'No, it's empty. My father's gone, I told you, and my aunt and my grandma too.'

'What do you *do* on the moor?' asked George, as she followed Sniffer across the field and up the hill to where the caravans had stood. Now only one was left – Sniffer's.

'Play around,' said Sniffer, and gave an enormous sniff. George gave him a shove in the back.

'Sniffer! What did I give you the hanky for? *Don't* do that! It gets on my nerves!'

Sniffer used his sleeve at once, but fortunately George didn't notice. She had now come to the caravan and was staring at it. She thought of Sniffer's answer to her question a minute or two back.

'You said you just played around on the moor. But what does your *father* do, and your uncle and grandad and all the rest of the men? There's nothing to do there at all, as far as I can see, and no farmhouse to beg eggs or milk or anything from.'

Sniffer shut up like a clam. He was just about to sniff and thought better of it. He stared at George, his mouth set in an obstinate line.

George looked at him impatiently. 'Captain Johnson said you and your caravans went there every three months,' she said. 'What for? There must be *some* reason?'

'Well,' said Sniffer, looking away from her, 'we make pegs, and baskets, and . . .'

'I know that! All travellers make things to sell,' said George. 'But you don't need to go into the middle of a deserted moor to make them. You can do them just as well in a village, or sitting in a field near a farmhouse. *Why* go to such a lonely place as the moor?'

Sniffer said nothing, but bent over an odd little arrangement of sticks set on the path beside his caravan. George saw them and bent over them too, her question forgotten.

'Oh! Is that a patrin? A traveller message! What does it mean?'

There were two sticks, one long and one short, neatly arranged in the shape of a cross. A little farther up on the path were a few single, straight sticks, all pointing in the same direction.

'Yes,' said Sniffer, very glad to have the subject changed. 'It's our way of telling things to those who may come after us. See the sticks in the shape of the cross? That's a patrin that says we've been along this way and we're going in the direction that the long stick points.'

'I see,' said George. 'How simple! But what about these four straight sticks, all pointing the same way too. What do *they* mean?'

'They mean that the travellers went in caravans,' said Sniffer, giving a sudden sniff. 'See, four sticks, four caravans, going that way!'

'I *see*,' said George, making up her mind that she herself would evolve quite a few 'patrins' for use at school when they went for walks. 'Are there any more "patrins", Sniffer?'

'Plenty,' said the boy. 'Look, when I leave here, I shall put a patrin like this!' He picked a large leaf from a nearby tree, and then a small one. He placed them side by side, and weighted them down with small stones.

'What in the world does that mean?' said George.

'Well, it's a patrin, a message, to say that me and my little dog have gone in the caravan too,' said Sniffer, picking up the leaves. 'Suppose my father came back to find me, and he saw those leaves there, he'd know I'd gone on with my dog. It's simple. Big leaf for me, little leaf for my dog!'

'Yes. I like it,' said George, pleased. 'Now let's look at the caravan.'

It was an old-fashioned kind of caravan, not very big, and with huge wheels. The door and the steps down were in front. The shafts rested on the ground waiting for Clip to come back. The caravan was black with red designs on it here and there.

George went up the steps. 'I've been inside a few caravans,' she said. 'But never one quite like this.'

She peeped in curiously.

'It's not smelly, is it?' said Sniffer, quite anxiously. 'I tidied it up today, seeing as how I thought you were all visiting me. That's our bed at the back. We all sleep on it.'

George stared at the big bunk-like bed stretched at the end of the caravan, covered with a bright quilt. She imagined the whole family sleeping there, close together. Well, at least they would be warm in the winter.

'Don't you get hot in the summer, sleeping in this small caravan?' asked George.

'Oh no, only my grandma sleeps here then,' said Sniffer, swallowing a sniff in a hurry, before George could hear it. 'Me and the others sleep under the caravan. Then if it rains it doesn't matter.'

'Well, thanks for showing me so many things,' said George, looking round at the cupboards, the little locker-seats, and the over-big chest of drawers. 'How you all get in here is a miracle.'

'Come and see us tomorrow, Sniffer,' she said, going down the steps. 'Clip may be all right by then. And Sniffer, don't you forget you've got a hanky now.'

'I won't forget,' said Sniffer proudly. 'I'll keep it as clean as can be, George!'

CHAPTER EIGHT

Sniffer makes a promise

GEORGE WAS feeling very lonely by the time the evening came. How had the others got on without her? Had they missed her at all? Perhaps they hadn't even *thought* of her!

'Anyway, they didn't have *you*, Timmy!' said George. 'You wouldn't go off and leave me, would you?'

Timmy pressed against her, glad to see that she was happier again. He wondered where the others were, and where they had gone to all day.

There was suddenly a clattering of hooves in the stable yard and George flew to the door. Yes, they were back! How should she behave? She felt cross and relieved and rather humble and glad all at once! She stood there, not knowing whether to frown or to smile.

The others made up her mind for her. 'Hallo, George!' shouted Dick. 'We did miss you!'

'How's your head?' called Anne. 'I hope it's better!'

'Hallo!' called Henry. 'You ought to have come. We've had a super day!'

'Come and help us stable the horses, George,' shouted Julian. 'Tell us what you've been doing!'

Timmy had sped over to them, barking in delight.

George found her legs running towards them too, a welcoming smile on her face.

'Hallo!' she called. 'Let me help! Did you really miss me? I missed you too.'

The boys were very relieved to see that George was herself again. Nothing more was said about her headache! She busied herself unsaddling the horses and listening to their story of the day. Then she told them about Sniffer and his patrins, and how she had given him a brand-new handkerchief.

'But I'm sure he thinks he's got to keep it spotlessly clean!' she said. 'He never used it once when I was with him. There's the supper-bell, we'll only *just* be in time! Are you hungry?'

'You bet we are!' said Dick. 'Though after Mrs Johnson's sandwiches I never thought I'd be able to eat any supper at all. How's Clip?'

'Never mind now. I'll tell you everything at supper,' said George. 'Do you want any help, Henry?'

Henry was surprised to hear George call her Henry instead of Henrietta. 'No thanks – er – George,' she said. 'I can manage.'

It was a very jolly supper-time that evening. The youngsters were set at a table by themselves, so the older ones talked to their heart's content.

Captain Johnson was very interested to hear about the old railway they had found. 'I never knew there was anything like that on the moors,' he said. 'Though of course, we've only been here about fifteen years, so we don't know a great deal of the local history. You want to go and ask old Ben the blacksmith about that. He's lived here all his life, and a long life it is, for he's over eighty!'

'Well, we've got to take some of the horses to be shod tomorrow, haven't we?' said Henry, eagerly. 'We could ask him then! Why, he might even have helped to make the rails!'

'We saw the caravans, George, when we had got pretty far out on the moor,' said Julian. 'Goodness knows where they were heading for, towards the coast, I should think. What's the coast like beyond the moor, Captain Johnson?'

'Wild,' said the captain. 'Great, unclimbable cliffs, and reefs or rocks stretching out to sea. Only the birds live there. There's no bathing, no boating, no beach.'

'Well, it beats me where those caravans are going,' said Dick. 'It's a mystery. They go every three months, don't they?'

'About that,' said Captain Johnson. 'I've no idea what the attraction of the moor is for the travellers. It just beats me! Usually they won't go anywhere there aren't a few farms, or at least a small village where they can sell their goods.'

'I'd like to go after them and see where they are and what they're doing,' said Julian, eating his third hard-boiled egg.

'All right. Let's,' said George.

'But how? We don't know where they've gone,' said Henry.

'Well, Sniffer's going to join them tomorrow, or as soon as Clip is all right for walking,' said George. 'And he's got to follow the patrins left on the way by the others. He says that he looks at the places where fires have been made on the way, and beside them somewhere he will see the patrins, the sticks that point in the direction he must follow.'

'He's sure to destroy them,' said Dick. '*We* couldn't follow them!'

'We'll ask him to leave his *own* patrins,' said George. 'I think he will. He's not a bad little boy, really. I could ask him to leave *plenty* of patrins, so that we could easily find the way.'

'Well, it might be fun to see if we could read the right road to go, just as easily as the travellers do,' said Julian. 'We could make it a day's ride. It would be interesting!'

Henry gave a most enormous yawn, and that made Anne yawn too, though hers was a very polite one.

'Henry!' said Mrs Johnson.

'Sorry,' said Henry. 'It just came almost like a sneeze does. I don't know why, but I feel almost asleep.'

'Go to bed then,' said Mrs Johnson. 'You've had such a day of air and sunshine! You all look very suntanned too. The April sun has been as hot as July today.'

The five of them, and Timmy, went out for a last look at the horses, and to do one or two small jobs. Henry yawned again, and that set everyone else off, even George.

'Me for the straw!' said Julian, with a laugh. 'Oh, the

thought of that warm, comfy straw bed is too good for words! You girls are welcome to the beds!'

'I hope Sniffer's pa doesn't come in the middle of the night again,' said Dick.

'I shall tie up the latch,' said Julian. 'Well, let's go and say good night to Mrs Johnson.'

It wasn't long before the three girls were in bed and the two boys cuddled down in the straw of the stable. Clip was there still, but he no longer fidgeted. He lay down quietly, and did not once move his bad leg. It was getting much better. He would certainly be able to go after the others the next day!

Julian and Dick fell asleep at once. No one came creeping in at the stable door that night. Nothing disturbed them until the morning, when a cock got into the stable through a window, sat on a rafter just above them, and crowed loudly enough to wake both boys with a jump.

'What's that!' said Dick. 'That awful screeching in my ear! Was it you, Ju?'

The cock crowed again and the boys laughed. 'Blow him!' said Julian, settling down again. 'I could do with another couple of hours' sleep!'

That morning Sniffer came slipping in at the gate again. He never came boldly in, he slid through the hedge, or crept in at the gate, or appeared round a corner. He saw George and went over to her.

'George,' he called. 'Is Clip better?'

'Yes!' called back George. 'Captain Johnson says you

can take him today. But wait a bit, Sniffer, I want to ask you something before you go.'

Sniffer was pleased. He liked this girl who had presented him with such a magnificent handkerchief. He took it carefully out of his pocket, hoping to please her.

'See,' he said. 'How clean it is! I have kept it very carefully.' He sniffed loudly.

'You're an idiot,' said George, exasperated. 'I gave it to you to *use*, not to keep clean in your pocket. It's to stop your *sniffing*. Honestly, you're a bit of a mutt, Sniffer. I shall take that hanky away if you don't use it!'

Sniffer looked alarmed. He shook it out carefully and then lightly touched his nose with it. He then folded it up conscientiously in the right creases and put it back into his pocket again.

'Now, NO sniffing!' commanded George, trying not to laugh. 'Listen, Sniffer, you know those patrins you showed me yesterday?'

'Yes, George,' said Sniffer.

'Well, will the other travellers who have gone in front, leave you patrins to follow, so that you will know the way?' said George.

Sniffer nodded. 'Yes, but not many, because I have been that way twice before. They will only leave them in places where I might go wrong.'

'I see,' said George. 'Now Sniffer, we want to have a sort of game. We want to see which of us can follow patrins, and we want you to lay patrins for us quite often, on your way to your family today. Will you?'

'Oh yes, I will,' said Sniffer, quite proud to have a favour asked of him. 'I will lay the ones I showed you, the cross, the long sticks, and the big and little leaf.'

'Yes, do,' said George. 'That will mean that you have passed in a certain direction and you are a boy and a dog. That's right, isn't it?'

'Yes,' said Sniffer, nodding his head. 'You have remembered!'

'Right. And we're going to have a kind of game, trying to pretend we are travellers following others who have passed,' said George.

'You must not show yourselves when you come up to our caravans,' said Sniffer, looking suddenly alarmed. 'I should get into trouble for laying patrins for you.'

'All right. We'll be careful,' said George. 'Now let's go and get Clip.'

They fetched the patient little skewbald who came out gladly. He no longer limped, and his rest seemed to have done him good. He went off at a good pace with Sniffer. The last George heard of them was a very loud sniff indeed!

'Sniffer!' she shouted, warningly. He put his hand in his pocket and pulled out the hanky. He waved it happily in the air, a sudden grin lighting up his face.

George went to find the others. 'Sniffer has taken Clip,' she said. 'What about going down to the blacksmith, and taking those horses that want shoeing?'

'Good idea,' said Julian. 'We can ask him all about Mystery Moor then, and the strange little railway line, or whatever it is! Come on.'

They took the horses that needed shoeing. There were six of them, so they each rode one, and Julian led the sixth. Timmy ran happily along beside them. He loved the horses, and they regarded him as a real friend, bending their long noses down to sniff at him, whenever he came near.

They went slowly down the long lane to the blacksmith's. 'There it is!' said George. 'A proper old smithy with a lovely fire! And there's the smith!'

Old Ben was a mighty figure of a man, even though he was over eighty. He didn't shoe many horses now, but sat in the sun, watching all that was going on. He had a great mane of white hair, and eyes that were as black as the coal he had so many times heated to a fiery flame.

'Good morning, young masters and Miss,' he said and Julian grinned. That would please George and Henry!

'We've got some questions to ask you,' said George dismounting.

'Ask away!' said the old man. 'If it's about this place, there's nothing much old Ben can't tell you! Give Jim your horses. Now, ask away!'

CHAPTER NINE

The blacksmith tells a tale

'WELL,' BEGAN Julian, 'we went riding on Mystery Moor yesterday, and for one thing we'd like to know if there is any reason for the curious name. *Was* there ever a mystery on that moor?'

'Oh, there were plenty of mysteries away there,' said Old Ben. 'People lost and never come back again, noises that no one could find the reason of . . .'

'What kind of noises?' said Anne, curiously.

'Ah now, when I was a boy, I spent nights up on that moor,' said old Ben, solemnly, 'and the noises that went on there! Screeches and howls and the like, and moans and the sweep of big wings . . .'

'Well, all that might have been owls and foxes and things like that,' said Dick. 'I've heard a barn owl give a screech just over my head which made me nearly jump out of my skin. If I hadn't known it was an owl I'd have run for miles!'

Ben grinned and his face ran into a score of creases and wrinkles.

'Why is it called *Mystery* Moor?' persisted Julian. 'Is it a very old name?'

'When my grandad was a boy it was called *Misty* Moor,'

said the old blacksmith, remembering. 'See, *Misty*, not *Mystery*. And that was because of the sea-fogs that came stealing in from the coast, and lay heavy on the moor, so that no man could see his hand in front of his face. Yes, I've been lost in one of those mists, and right scared I was too. It swirled round me like a live thing, and touched me all over with its cold damp fingers.'

'How horrid!' said Anne with a shiver. 'What did you do?'

'Well, first I ran for my life,' said Ben, getting out his pipe and looking into the empty bowl. 'I ran over heather and into gorse. I fell a dozen times, and all the time the mist was feeling me with its damp fingers, trying to get me, that's what the old folk used to say of that mist, it was always trying to get you!'

'Still, it was only a mist,' said George, feeling that the old man was exaggerating. 'Does it still come over the moor?'

'Oh ay,' said Ben, ramming some tobacco into his pipe. 'Autumn's the time, but it comes suddenly at any moment of the year. I've known it come at the end of a fine summer's day, creeping in stealthily, and my, if you don't happen to see it soon enough, it gets you!'

'What do you mean, it *gets* you?' said George.

'Well, it may last for days,' said old Ben. 'And if you're lost on the moors, you're really lost, and you never come back. Ah, smile if you like, young man, but I *know*!' He went off into memories of long ago, looking down at his pipe. 'Let's see now, there was old Mrs Banks, who went bilberry-picking with her basket on a summer's afternoon, and no one ever heard of her again, after the mist came down. And there was young Victor who played truant and went off to the moor, and the mist got him too.'

'I can see we'd better watch out for the mist if we go riding there,' said Dick. 'This is the first I've heard of it.'

'Yes. You keep your eyes skinned,' said old Ben. 'Look away to the coast side and watch there, that's where it comes from. But there aren't many mists nowadays, though I don't know why. No, now I think of it, there hasn't been a mist, not a proper wicked one, for nearly three years.'

'What I'd like to know is why was the name changed to *Mystery* Moor,' said Henry. 'I can understand its being called Misty Moor, but now everyone calls it *Mystery*, not Misty.'

'Well now, that must have been about seventy years ago, when I was a boy,' said Ben, lighting his pipe and puffing hard. He was enjoying himself. He didn't often get such an interested audience as this, five of them, including a dog who sat and listened too!

'That was when the Bartle family built the little railway over the moor,' he began, and stopped at the exclamations of his five listeners.

'Ah! We wanted to know about that!'

'Oh! You know about the railway then?'

'Do go on!'

The blacksmith seemed to get some trouble with his pipe and pulled at it for an exasperatingly long time. George wished she was a horse and could stamp her foot impatiently!

'Well, the Bartle family was a big one,' said Ben at last. 'All boys, but for one ailing little girl. Big, strong fellows they were, I remember them well. I was scared of them, they were so free with their fists. Well, one of them, Dan, found a mighty good stretch of sand out there on the moor . . .'

'Oh yes, we *thought* there might have been a sand-quarry,' said Anne. Ben frowned at the interruption.

'And as there were nine or ten good strong Bartles, they reckoned to make a fine do of it,' said Ben. 'They got wagons and they went to and from the quarry they dug, and they sold their sand for miles around, good, sharp sand it was . . .'

'We saw some,' said Henry. 'But what about the rails?'

'Don't hurry him,' said Dick, with a frown.

'They made a great deal of money,' said Ben, remembering. 'And they set to work and built a little railway to carry an engine and trucks to the quarry and back, to save labour. My, my, that was a nine days' wonder, that railway! Us youngsters used to follow the little engine, puffing along, and we all longed to drive it. But we never did. Those Bartles kept a big stick, each one of them, and they whipped the hide off any boy that got too near them. Fierce they were, and quarrelsome.'

'Why did the railway fall into ruin?' asked Julian. 'The rails are all overgrown with heather and grass. You can hardly see them.'

'Well, now we come to the Mystery you keep on about,' said Ben, taking an extra big puff at his pipe. 'Those Bartles fell foul of the travellers up on the moor . . .'

'Oh, were there travellers on the moor *then*?' said Dick. 'There are some now!'

'Oh ay, there's always been travellers on the moor, long as I can remember,' said the blacksmith. 'Well, it's said those travellers quarrelled with the Bartles, and it wasn't hard to do that, most people did! And the travellers pulled up bits of the line, here and there, and the little engine toppled over and pulled the trucks with it.'

The children could quite well imagine the little engine puffing along, coming to the damaged rails and falling over. What a to-do there must have been up on the moor then!

'The Bartles weren't ones to put up with a thing like that,' said Ben, 'so they set about to drive all the travellers off the moor, and they swore that if so much as one caravan went there, they'd set fire to it and chase the travellers over to the coast and into the sea!'

'They *must* have been a fierce family,' said Anne.

'You're right there,' said Ben. 'All nine or ten of them were big upstanding men, with great shaggy eyebrows that almost hid their eyes, and loud voices. Nobody dared to cross them. If they did, they'd have the whole family on

their doorstep with sticks. They ruled this place, they did, and my, they were hated! Us children ran off as soon as we saw one coming round a corner.'

'What about the travellers? Did the Bartles manage to drive them off the moor?' asked George, impatiently.

'Now let me go my own pace,' said Ben, pointing at her with his pipe. 'You want a Bartle after you, young man, that's what you want!' He thought she was a boy, of course. He did something to his pipe and made them all wait a little. Julian winked at the others. He liked this old fellow with his long, long memories.

'Now, you can't cross the travellers for long,' said Ben, at last. 'That's a fact, you can't. And one day all the Bartles disappeared and never come back home. No, not one of them. All that was left of the family was little Agnes, their sister.'

Everyone exclaimed in surprise and old Ben looked round with satisfaction. Ah, he could tell a story, he could!

'But what happened?' said Henry.

'Well, no one rightly knows,' said Ben. 'It happened in a week when the mist came swirling over the moors and blotted everything out. Nobody went up there except the Bartles, and they were safe because all they had to do was to follow their railway lines there and back. They went up to the quarry each day the mist was there, and worked the same as usual. Nothing stopped those Bartles from working!'

He paused and looked round at his listeners. He dropped his voice low, and all five of the children felt little shivers up their backs.

'One night somebody in the village saw twenty or more travellers' caravans slinking through the village at dead of night,' said Ben. 'Up on the moor they went in the thick mist. Maybe they followed the railway; nobody knows. And next morning, up to the quarry went the Bartles as usual, swallowed up in the mist.'

He paused again. 'And they never came back,' he said. 'No, not one of them. Never heard of again!'

'But what *happened*?' said George.

'Search parties were sent out when the mist cleared,' said old Ben. 'But not one of the Bartles did they find, alive or dead. Not one! And they didn't find any travellers' caravans either. They'd all come creeping back the next night, and passed through the village like shadows. I reckon the travellers set upon the Bartles in the mist that day, fought them and defeated them, and took them and threw them over the cliffs into the roaring sea!'

'How horrible!' said Anne, feeling sick.

'Don't worry yourself!' said the blacksmith. 'It all happened a long time ago, and there weren't many that mourned those Bartles, I can tell you. Funny thing was, their weakly little sister, Agnes, she lived to be a hale old woman of ninety-six, and only died a few years ago! And to think those strong, fierce brothers of hers went all together like that!'

'It's a most interesting story, Ben,' said Julian. 'So Misty Moor became *Mystery* Moor then, did it? And nobody ever *really* found out what happened, so the mystery was never solved. Didn't anyone work the railway after that, or get the sand?'

'No, not a soul,' said Ben. 'We were all scared, you see, and young Agnes, she said the railway and the trucks and engine could rot, for all she cared. I never dared to go near them after that. It was a long time before anyone but the travellers set foot on Misty Moor again. Now it's all forgotten, the tale of the Bartles, but those travellers still remember, I've no doubt! They've got good memories, they have.'

'Do you know why they come to Mystery Moor every so often?' asked Dick.

'No. They come and they go,' said Ben. 'They've their own funny ways. They don't belong anywhere, those folk. What they do on the moor is their own business, and I wouldn't want to poke *my* nose into it. I'd remember those old Bartles, and keep away!'

A voice came from inside the smithy, where Jim, the blacksmith's grandson, had been shoeing the horses. 'Grandad! Stop jabbering away there, and let the children come and talk to *me*! I've shod nearly all the horses.'

Ben laughed. 'Go along,' he said to the children. 'I know you'd like to be in there and see the sparks fly, and the shoes made. I've wasted your time, I have, telling you long-ago things. Go along into the smithy. And just remember two things – watch out for that mist, and keep away from the travellers on the moor!'

CHAPTER TEN

Sniffer's patrins

IT WAS fun in the smithy, working the bellows, seeing the fire glow, and watching the red-hot shoes being shaped. Jim was quick and clever, and it was a pleasure to watch him.

'Have you been hearing Grandad's old stories?' he said. 'It's all he's got to do now, sit there and remember, though when he wants to he can make a horseshoe as well as I can! There, that's the last one. Stand still, Sultan. That's right!'

The five children were soon on their way back again. It was a lovely morning, and the banks and ditches they passed were bright gold with thousands of celandines.

'All beautifully polished!' said Anne, picking two or three for her buttonhole. It *did* look as if someone had polished the inside of each petal, for they gleamed like enamel.

'What a strange tale the old man told,' said Julian. 'He told it well!'

'Yes. He made me feel I don't want to go up on the moor again!' said Anne.

'Don't be feeble!' said George. 'It all happened ages ago. Jolly interesting too. I wonder if the travellers who are there now know the story. Maybe their great-grandparents were the ones who set on the Bartles that misty day!'

'Well, Sniffer's father looked sly enough to carry out a plan like that,' said Henry. 'What about us having a shot at following the way they went, and seeing if we can make out the patrins that Sniffer told George he would leave?'

'Good idea,' said Julian. 'We'll go this afternoon. I say, what's the time? I should think it must be half past lunch-time!'

They looked at their watches. 'Yes, we're late, but we always are when we get back from the blacksmith,' said George. 'Never mind, I bet Mrs Johnson will have an extra-special meal for us!'

She had! There was an enormous plate of stew for everyone, complete with carrots, onions, parsnips and turnips, and a date pudding to follow. Good old Mrs Johnson!

'You three girls must wash up for me afterwards,' she said. 'I've such a lot to do today.'

'Why can't the boys help?' said George at once.

'*I'll* do all the washing-up!' said Anne with a sudden grin. 'You four *boys* can go out to the stables!'

Dick gave her a good-natured shove. 'You know we'll help, even if we're not good at it. I'll dry. I hate those bits and pieces that float about in the washing-bowl.'

'Will it be all right if we go up on the moors this afternoon?' asked George.

'Yes, quite all right. But if you want to take your tea, you'll have to pack it yourselves,' said Mrs Johnson. 'I'm taking the small children out for a ride, and there's one on the leading-rein still, as you know.'

They were ready to set off at three o'clock, their tea packed and everything. The horses were caught in the field and got ready too. They set off happily.

'Now we'll see if we are as clever as we think we are, at reading traveller patrins!' said George. 'Timmy, don't chase *every* rabbit you see, or you'll be left behind!'

They cantered up on to the moor, passing the place where the caravans had stood. They knew the direction they had taken, and here and there they saw wheel-marks. It was fairly easy to follow their trail, because five caravans made quite a path to follow.

'Here's where they camped first,' said Julian, riding up to a blackened spot that showed where a fire had been lit. 'We ought to find a message left somewhere here.'

They searched for one. George found it. 'It's here, behind this tree!' she called. 'Out of the wind.'

They dismounted and came round George. On the ground was the patrin, the shape of a cross, the long stick pointing forwards, in the direction they were going. Other single sticks lay there, to show that a caravan had gone that way, and beside them were the large and the small leaf, weighted with tiny stones.

'What did those leaves show now, oh yes, Sniffer and his dog!' said Dick. 'Well, we're on the right way, though we'd know that anyhow, by the fire!'

They mounted again and went on. It proved quite easy

to find and follow the patrins. Only once did they find any difficulty and that was when they came to a place, marked by two trees, where there was no apparent sign in the heather of any caravan marks.

'The heather's so jolly thick here that it's taken the caravans as if it were a feather bed, springing up when they had gone, and giving no sign of where they had passed,' said Julian. He dismounted and had a good look round. No, there was no sign.

'We'll go on a little way,' he said. 'We may come to a camping place, then we'll know.'

But they came to no old camping place, and stopped at last in bewilderment. 'We've lost the trail,' said Dick. 'We're not such good travellers after all!'

'Let's go back to those two trees,' said George. 'We can still just see them. If it's so easy to lose the way there, there *might* be a patrin, although there are no camp marks. After all, a patrin is left to show the way, in case the ones following take the wrong route.'

So back they rode to the two trees, and there, sure enough, was Sniffer's patrin! Henry found it set carefully between the trees, so that nothing could disturb it.

'Here's the cross, and the single sticks, and the leaves!' she said. 'But look, the long stick of the cross points to the east and we went off to the north. No wonder we found no signs of the caravans!'

They set off to the east this time, across the thick, springy heather, and almost at once found signs of the passing of caravans, twigs broken off the bushes, a wheel rut on a soft piece of ground.

'We're right, now,' said Julian, pleased. 'I was beginning to think it was all too easy for words! But it isn't!'

They rode for two hours, and then decided to have tea. They sat down in a little glade of silver birches, with an unexpected copse of pale primroses behind. Timmy had to make up his mind which to choose, a rabbit chase, or titbits from the children's tea!

He chose both, racing after an imaginary rabbit, and then coming back for a sandwich!

'You know, it's a lot better for us when Mrs Johnson makes sandwiches of tomato or lettuce or something like that,' said Henry. 'We do get them all then, but when we have meat or sardine or egg sandwiches Timmy gets as much as we do!'

'Well, surely you don't mind that, Henrietta,' said George at once. 'You make Timmy sound very greedy. After all, you don't need to give him any of *your* sandwiches!'

'Now, Georgina!' murmured Dick, in her ear.

'Sorry, Georgina,' said Henry, with a grin. 'I just can't *help* giving him a sandwich or two when he comes and sits down and looks at me so longingly.'

'Woof,' said Timmy, and at once sat down in front of Henry, his tongue out, and his eyes fixed unblinkingly on her.

'He sort of *hypnotises* me,' complained Henry. 'Make

him go away, George, I shan't be able to keep a single sandwich or bit of cake for myself. Go and stare at someone else, Timmy, for goodness' sake!'

Julian looked at his watch. 'I don't think we ought to spend *too* long over tea,' he said. 'I know we've got summertime now, and the evenings are nice and light, but we haven't reached the travellers' camp yet, and after that we've got to go all the way back. What about starting off again?'

'Right,' said everyone and remounted their horses. They set off through the heather. Soon they found it unexpectedly easy to follow the caravan route, because the soil became sandy, and there were many bare patches on which the marks of the wheels could plainly be seen.

'Goodness, if we go to the east much more, we'll come to the sea!' said Dick.

'No, it's still some miles away,' said Julian. 'Hallo, there's a little hill or something in the distance. First time we've seen anything but complete flatness!'

The wheel-marks led steadily towards the little hill, which, as they came near, seemed to grow considerably bigger. 'I bet the caravans are there,' said George. 'That hill would give a nice bit of shelter from the wind that came from the sea. I believe I can see one!'

George was right. The caravans were there. They showed up well against the hill, in their bright colours.

'They've even got up a washing line as usual!' said Anne. 'Clothes flapping in the wind!'

'Let's go and ask if Clip is all right,' said Julian. 'It will be a very good excuse for going right up to the camp.' So they cantered straight up to the little group of five

caravans. Four or five men appeared as soon as they heard the sound of hooves. They looked silent and rather forbidding. Sniffer ran out and shouted.

'Hallo! Clip's fine! Quite all right again!'

His father gave him a push and said something sharp to him. He disappeared under the nearest caravan.

Julian rode up to Sniffer's father. 'Did I hear Sniffer say that Clip was quite all right?' he asked. 'Where is he?'

'Over there,' said the man, with a nod of his head. 'No need for you to see him. He's mended fine.'

'All right, all right! I'm not going to take him away from you!' said Julian. 'This is a nice, sheltered place you've got, isn't it? How long are you staying?'

'What's that to do with you?' said an old traveller, unpleasantly.

'Nothing,' said Julian, surprised. 'Just a polite question, that's all!'

'How do you get water?' called George. 'Is there a good spring here?'

There was no reply at all. The four or five men had now been joined by others, and there were three dogs growling round. Timmy was beginning to growl back.

'You'd better go before our dogs get you,' said Sniffer's father, sourly.

'Where's Liz?' said George, remembering Sniffer's dog, but before she got an answer the three dogs suddenly made an attack on Timmy! They pounced on him and he had hard work to keep them off. He was far bigger than they were, but they were nippy little things.

'Call off those dogs!' yelled Julian, seeing that George was dismounting to go to Timmy's help. She would get bitten. 'Do you hear me? Call off those dogs.'

Sniffer's father whistled. The three dogs reluctantly left Timmy and went over to the men, their tails down. George had reached Tim and had now got her hand on his collar to stop him from chasing the other three dogs.

'Mount your horse, whistle Timmy, and we'll go,' shouted Julian, not at all liking the silent, sour-looking travellers. George did as she was told. Timmy ran beside her, and they all cantered away from the unpleasant camp.

The men stood watching them in complete silence. 'What's up with them?' said Dick, puzzled. 'Anyone would think they were planning another Bartle affair!'

'Don't!' said Anne. 'They're planning *some*thing, all alone out here, far away from anywhere! I shan't go near them again.'

'They thought we were prying and spying,' said Dick. 'That's all. Poor old Sniffer. What a life he has!'

'We couldn't even tell him that we found his patrins useful,' said George. 'Oh well, there's probably nothing in it, not even an adventure!'

Was she right or wrong? Julian looked at Dick and Dick looked back, his eyebrows raised. They didn't know. Oh well, time would tell!

CHAPTER ELEVEN

A nice little plan

THE FIVE of them told Captain and Mrs Johnson about their afternoon's experience, as they were having supper.

'Patrins!' said Mrs Johnson. 'So Sniffer told you about those? But I really don't think you should visit the travellers' camp. Those particular travellers are a surly, bad-tempered lot.'

'Did you ever hear the tale of the Big Bartles?' said Henry, getting ready to relate it, and add little bits of her own, here and there!

'No. But it can wait, I'm sure,' said Mrs Johnson, knowing Henry's habit of leaving her food quite uneaten once she began on some marvellous tale. 'Is it one of your tales? You can tell it after supper.'

'It's *not* Henry's tale,' said George, annoyed that Henry should get all the limelight again, and take the blacksmith's tale for her own. 'It's one old Ben told us. Ju, *you* tell it!'

'Nobody is to tell it *now*,' said Captain Johnson. 'You came in late for supper, we waited for you, and the least you can do is to get on with your eating.'

The five juniors at the other table were disappointed.

They had hoped to hear another of Henry's marvellous stories. But Captain Johnson was hungry and tired.

'Old Ben is a great age, as you said,' began Henry, after a few mouthfuls. 'He—'

'Not another word, please, Henrietta,' said the captain, curtly. Henry went red and George grinned, kicking at Dick under the table. Unfortunately she kicked Henry instead, and the girl glared at her for a whole minute.

'Oh dear!' thought Anne. 'Just as we'd had such a lovely day! I suppose we're all tired and scratchy.'

'*Why* did you kick me?' began Henry in a cross voice, as soon as she and George left the table with the others.

'Shut up, you two,' said Julian. 'She probably meant to kick me or Dick, not you.'

Henry shut up. She didn't like Julian to tick her off. George looked mutinous and went off with Timmy.

Dick yawned. 'What jobs are there to do, if any?' he said. 'Don't say there's washing-up again. I feel I might break a few things.'

Mrs Johnson heard him and laughed. 'No, there's no washing-up. The woman has come in to do it tonight. Have a look at the horses – and see that Jenny the mare is not with Flash, you know she doesn't like her for some reason, and *will* kick out at her. She must always be kept in another field.'

'That's all right, Mrs Johnson,' said William, suddenly appearing, stolid and competent as ever. 'I've seen to that. I've seen to everything, really.'

'You're better than any stable boy, William,' said Mrs Johnson, smiling at him. 'I wish you'd take a permanent job here!'

'I wish you meant that,' said William, earnestly. There was nothing he would have liked better! He went off looking pleased.

'I think you'd better all go to bed then, as William appears to have done everything necessary,' said Mrs Johnson. 'Any plans for tomorrow?'

'Not yet,' said Julian, trying to stop a yawn. 'So if you want anything done, we'll do it.'

'We'll see what tomorrow brings,' said Mrs Johnson and said good night. The boys said good night to the three girls and went off to the stable.

'Gosh, we've forgotten to undress and wash and everything,' said Julian, half-asleep. 'What's the matter with us at this place? I can't seem to keep my eyes open after half past eight!'

The next day certainly brought a few things. It brought a letter for Henry that filled her with disgust. It brought two letters for Mrs Johnson that made her start fussing and worrying. It brought a letter for Captain Johnson that sent him down to the station at once.

Henrietta's letter was from two of her great-aunts. They announced that as they would be near the stables that day and the following, they would like to fetch her and take her out with them.

'Blow!' said Henrietta, ungratefully. 'Great-Aunts

Hannah and Lucy *would* choose this very week to come along and see me! Just when Julian and Dick are here, and everything is such fun. Can't I phone and say I'm too busy, Mrs Johnson?'

'Certainly not,' said Mrs Johnson, shocked. 'That would be very rude, Henry, and you know it. You're having the whole of the Easter holidays here, and yet you think you can't spare two days. As a matter of fact I shall be glad if your aunts *do* take you off my hands for a couple of days.'

'Why?' asked Henry, astonished. 'Have I been a nuisance?'

'Oh no, but I've had two letters this morning telling me that four children are coming unexpectedly,' said Mrs Johnson. 'They were not supposed to come till three of the others left this weekend, but there you are! These things happen. *Where* I am to put them I really don't know!'

'Oh dear!' said Anne. 'Do you think Dick and Julian ought to go home, Mrs Johnson? You didn't plan for them, you know, they just came.'

'Yes, I know,' said Mrs Johnson. 'But we're more or less used to that, and I do like having bigger boys, I must say, they're such a help. Now let me see. What *can* we do?'

Captain Johnson came in, looking hurried. 'I've just had a letter, dear,' he said. 'I've got to go down to the station. Those two new horses have arrived. Two days before I wanted them – what a nuisance!'

'This is one of those *days*!' said Mrs Johnson, desperately. 'Good gracious, how many shall we be in the house? And however many horses shall we have? No, I can't count this morning. I'm all muddle-headed!'

Anne felt that it was a pity that she and George and the boys couldn't immediately pack and go home. After all, poor Mrs Johnson had thought that she and George *would* have gone home three or four days ago, and instead of that they had stayed on and the boys had arrived as well!

Anne hurried to find Julian. He would know what to do. She found him with Dick, carrying straw for the stables.

'Julian! Listen! I want to talk to you,' said Anne. Julian let the load of straw slip to the ground, and turned to Anne.

'What's up?' he said. '*Don't* tell me it's a row between George and Henry again, because I shan't listen!'

'No. Nothing like that,' said Anne. 'It's Mrs Johnson. She's got four children coming unexpectedly, before the others go. She's in a great state about it, and I wondered what we could do to help. You see, she didn't expect any of *us* four to be here this week.'

'No. That's true,' said Julian, sitting down on his straw. 'Let's think hard.'

'It's easy!' said Dick. 'We'll simply take our tents, some food, and go and camp out on the moor by some spring. WHAT could be nicer?'

'Oh *yes*!' said Anne, her eyes shining. 'Oh Dick, that's a *marvellous* idea! Mrs Johnson will get rid of us all and Timmy too, then, and we would have a lovely time all by ourselves!'

'Killing quite a lot of birds with one stone!' said Julian. 'We've got a couple of tents in our kit, Anne. Very small ones, but they'll do. And we can borrow rubber sheets to put on the heather, though it's as dry as a bone, as far as I can see!'

'I'll go and tell George!' said Anne, joyfully. 'Let's go today, Julian, and be out of the way before the new children come. Captain Johnson's got two new horses coming too. He'll be very glad to have a few of us out of the way!'

She flew off to tell George. George was busy polishing some harness, a job she liked very much. She listened to Anne's excited tale. Henry was there too, looking gloomy. She looked gloomier still at the end.

'It's too bad,' she said, when Anne had finished. 'I could have come with you if it hadn't been for these great-aunts of mine. *WHY* did they have to come just at this very moment? Don't you think it's maddening?'

Neither Anne nor George thought it was maddening. They were secretly very pleased indeed to think that they could once more go off entirely on their own, with Timmy, as they had so often done before. But they would have *had* to ask Henry if her aunts hadn't written at this very lucky moment!

George didn't like to show how delighted she was to think of going off camping on the moor. She and Anne did a little comforting of poor Henry and then went off to make arrangements with Mrs Johnson.

'Well, that's a very bright idea of Dick's!' she said in delight. 'It solves a whole lot of problems. And I know you don't mind. You're thrilled at the chance, aren't you! It's really very helpful. I only wish poor Henry could go too, but she *must* go out with her old great-aunts. They adore her!'

'Of course she must,' said George, solemnly. She and Anne exchanged a look. Poor Henry! But really, it would be very nice to be without her for a little while.

Everyone began to be suddenly very busy. Dick and

Julian undid their packs to find out exactly what was in them. Mrs Johnson looked out rubber sheets and old rugs. She was a wonder at producing things like that!

William wanted to go with them and help to carry the things, but nobody wanted his help. They just wanted to be off and away by themselves, just the Five and nobody else! Timmy caught the excitement too and his tail thumped and wagged the whole morning.

'You'll be pretty well loaded,' said Mrs Johnson, doubtfully. 'It's a good thing that fine weather is forecast, or you'd have to take macs as well. Still, I imagine you won't go very far on the moors, will you? You can easily get back to the stable if you have forgotten anything, or want more food.'

They were ready at last, and went to find Henry to say goodbye. She stared at them mournfully. She had changed into a smart little coat and dress. She looked completely different and very gloomy.

'What part of the moor are you going to?' she asked eagerly. 'Up the railway?'

'Yes. We thought we would,' said Julian. 'Just to see where it goes to. And it's a nice straight way to follow. We can't lose our way if we keep near the railway!'

'Have a good time, Henry,' said George, with a grin. 'Do they call you Henrietta?'

'Yes,' said poor Henry, putting on a pair of gloves. 'Well, goodbye. For goodness' sake don't stay away too long. Thank goodness you're all such a hungry lot. You'll simply have to come back and get more food in a couple of days!'

They grinned and left her, Timmy at their heels. They made their way to the moor, intending to cut out the part of the railway that ran to Milling Green, and join it some way before that.

'Now we're off,' said George, contentedly. 'Without that chatterbox of a Henry.'

'She's *really* not too bad,' said Dick. 'All the same, it's fine to be on our own, just the Famous Five together!'

CHAPTER TWELVE

The little railway

IT WAS a very hot day. The five had had their lunch before they started, as Mrs Johnson said it would be easier to carry that inside than outside!

Even Timmy carried something. George said that he ought to do his share, and had neatly fastened a bag of his pet biscuits on his back.

'There now!' she said. 'You've got your load too. No, don't try and sniff the biscuits all the time, Timmy. You can't walk with your head screwing round like that. You ought to be used to the smell of biscuits by this time!'

They set off to the railway line, or where they hoped it would be. It took a little time to discover it running under the heather. Julian was glad. He didn't want to walk right into Milling Green to find the beginning of it and then walk all the way up again!

Anne found it by tripping over it! 'Oh!' she said. 'Here it is! I caught my foot in a bit of rusty line. Look you can hardly see it!'

'Good,' said Julian, and stepped in between the narrow pair of old, rusty lines. In some places they had rusted away, and there were gaps. In other places the heather had grown completely over the lines, and unless the children had known that they must keep straight forward, they would have lost them completely. As it was they sometimes missed them and once had to do quite a bit of scrabbling about in the heather to see if they could feel them.

It was very hot. Their packs began to feel distinctly heavy. Timmy's biscuits began to slide round his body and eventually hung below his tummy. He didn't like that, and George suddenly spied him sitting down trying to prise open the bag with his teeth!

She put down her own pack and adjusted Timmy's. 'If only you didn't keep chasing rabbits, and making your pack swing about, it wouldn't slip,' she said. 'There now, it's all right again, Tim. Walk to heel and it won't slip any more.'

They went on and on up the railway lines. Sometimes the rails took a curve round an unexpected rock. Soon the soil began to look sandy, and the heather did not grow so thickly. It was easier to see the lines, though in some places the sand had sifted over them and hidden them.

'I really *must* have a rest!' said Anne, sitting down in some heather. 'I feel I want to pant and hang my tongue out like Timmy!'

'I wonder how far these lines go,' said Dick. 'It's so very sandy now underfoot that I feel we must be getting near the quarry!'

They lay back in the heather and felt very sleepy. Julian yawned and sat up.

'This really won't do!' he said. 'If we fall asleep we'll never want to start off with our heavy packs again. Stir yourselves, lazy-bones!'

They all got up again. Timmy's biscuits had slithered round to his tummy once more, and George had to put them right again. Timmy stood quietly, panting, his tongue hanging out. He thought the biscuits were a great nuisance. It would be much easier to eat them!

The sand got deeper and soon there were big sandy patches with no heather or grass at all. The wind blew the sand up in the air, and the Five found that they had to shut their eyes against it.

'I say! The lines end here!' said Julian, stopping suddenly. 'Look, they're broken, wrenched out of place, the engine couldn't go any farther.'

'They may appear again a bit farther on,' said Dick, and went to look. But he couldn't find any, and came back to look at the lines again.

'It's funny,' he said. 'We aren't at any quarry yet, are we? I quite thought that the line would run right to the quarry, the trucks would fill up there, and the engine would pull them back to Milling Green. *Where* is the quarry? Why do the lines stop so suddenly here?'

'Yes. The quarry *should* be near here, shouldn't it?' said Julian. 'Well, there simply must be more lines somewhere! Ones that go to the quarry. Let's look for the quarry first, though. We ought to see that easily enough!'

But it wasn't really very easy to find because it was

behind a great mass of thick tall gorse bushes. Dick rounded them and stopped. Behind the enormous spread of bushes was a great pit, a sandy pit quarried and hollowed for its beautiful sand.

'Here it is!' called Dick. 'Come and look! My word, there's been some quarrying here for sand. They must have taken tons and tons out of it!'

The others came to look. It certainly was an enormous pit, deep and wide. They put their packs beside it and leapt down. Their feet sank into the fine sand.

'The sides are pitted with holes,' said Dick. 'I bet hundreds of sand-martins nest here in May!'

'There are even some caves,' said George, in surprise. 'Sand caves! Well, we can easily shelter here if we have rain. Some of these caves seem to go quite a long way back.'

'Yes. But I'd be a bit afraid of the sand falling in and burying me, if I crawled in,' said Anne. 'It's quite loose, look!' She scraped some down with her hand.

'I've found the lines!' called Julian. 'Here, look. The sand has almost covered them. I trod on a rail and it was so rotten it broke beneath my foot!'

The others went to see, Timmy too. He was quite delighted with this place. The rabbit holes in it! What fun he was going to have!

'Let's follow these lines,' said Julian. So they kicked away the sand from the rails and followed them slowly out of the quarry and towards the ends of the other broken lines.

About ten yards from these the lines they were following were wrenched apart. Some were flung into the nearby heather, and could be seen there, bent and rusty.

The children stared at them. 'I guess the travellers did that, when the Bartles were here years ago,' said Dick. 'The day they attacked them perhaps. I say, look, what*ever's* that great lump over there, with gorse growing over it?'

They went to see. Timmy saw the lump and couldn't make it out. He growled warningly at it.

Julian took up a broken piece of rail and forced back the gorse bush that had grown over and around the great lump, almost hiding it.

'See what it is?' he said, startled.

They all stared. 'Why, it's the engine! The little engine old Ben the blacksmith told us about!' said Dick. 'It must have run right off the broken lines and overturned here, and through the years these great gorse bushes grew up and hid it. Poor old engine!'

Julian forced the gorse back a little more. 'What a funny, old-fashioned affair!' he said. 'Look at the funnel, and the fat little boiler. And see, there's the small cab. It can't have had much more power, only just enough to puff along with a few trucks!'

'What happened to the trucks?' wondered Anne.

'Well, they would be easy enough to set upright again and put on the rails, and hand-push to Milling Green,' said Dick. 'But this engine couldn't be lifted, except by

some kind of machinery. Not even a dozen men could lift it and set it on the rails!'

'The travellers must have set on the Bartles in the mist, having first broken up the lines so that the engine would run off and overturn,' said Julian. 'They may even have used the broken rails to attack them with. Anyway, they won the battle, because not one of the Bartles ever returned.'

'Some of the villagers must have gone to see what became of them and have got the trucks back on the lines and pushed them to Milling Green,' said George, trying to reconstruct the long-ago happenings in her mind. 'But they couldn't do anything about the engine.'

'That's about it,' said Julian. 'My word, what a shock for the Bartles when they saw the travellers creeping out at them from the mist, like shadows!'

'I hope we don't dream about this tonight,' said Anne.

They went back to the quarry. 'This wouldn't be a bad place to camp in,' said Dick. 'The sand is so dry and so soft. We could make lovely beds for ourselves. We wouldn't need the tents up, either, because the sides of the quarry shelter us beautifully from the wind.'

'Yes. Let's camp here,' said Anne, pleased. 'There are quite a lot of nice holes to store our things in.'

'What about water?' asked George. 'We want to be fairly near it, don't we? Timmy, find some water! Drink, Timmy, drink! Aren't you thirsty? Your tongue looks as if it is, the way you are hanging it out like a flag!'

Timmy put his head on one side as George talked to him. Water? Drink? He knew what both those words meant! He ran off, sniffing the air. George watched him.

He disappeared round a bush and was away for about half a minute. When he came back George gave a pleased shout.

'He's found some water! Look – his mouth is all wet! Timmy, where is it?'

Timmy wagged his tail vigorously, glad that George was pleased with him. He ran round the bush again and the others followed.

He led them to a little green patch and stopped. A spring bubbled up like a small fountain, dancing a little in the sunshine. The water fell from it into a little channel it had made for itself in the sand, ran away for a short distance, and then disappeared underground again.

'Thank you, Tim,' said George. 'Julian, is the water all right to drink here?'

'Well, I can see some that *is*!' said Julian, pointing to the right. 'The Bartles must have put a pipe in that bank, look, and caught another spring there, a much bigger one. It's as clear as can be. That will do fine for us!'

'Good,' said Anne, pleased. 'It's hardly any way from the quarry. It's as cold as ice, too – feel!'

They felt, and then they drank from their palms. How cold and pure! The moor must be full of these little bubbling springs, welling up from underground. That explained the brilliant green patches here and there.

'Now let's sit down and have some tea,' said Anne, unpacking the bag she had carried. 'It's too hot to feel really hungry.'

'Oh no, it isn't,' said Dick. 'Speak for yourself, Anne!'

They sat in the sunny quarry, the sand warm to their legs. 'Far away from anybody!' said Anne, pleased. 'Nobody near us for miles!'

But she wasn't quite right. There was somebody much nearer than she thought!

CHAPTER THIRTEEN

A noise in the night

It was Timmy who first knew there was somebody not far off. He pricked up his ears and listened. George saw him.

'What is it, Tim?' she said. 'Nobody is coming here, surely?'

Timmy gave a tiny growl, as if he were not quite sure of himself. Then he leapt up, his tail wagging, and tore out of the quarry!

'Where's he gone to?' said George, astonished. 'Gosh, here he is, back again!'

So he was, and with him was a funny little hearth rug of a dog – yes, Liz! She was not quite sure of her welcome and crawled up to the children on her tummy, looking more like a hearth rug than ever!

Timmy leapt round her in delight. She might have been his very best friend, he was so delighted! George patted the funny little dog and Julian looked thoughtful.

'I hope this doesn't mean that we are anywhere near the travellers' camp,' he said. 'It's quite likely that the lines might end somewhere near them. I've rather lost my sense of direction.'

'Oh goodness, I do HOPE we're not near their camp!' said Anne, in dismay. 'Those old-time travellers must have camped pretty near to the Bartles' quarry before they attacked them, so perhaps the present camp is near too.'

'Well, what's it matter if it is?' said Dick. 'Who's afraid of them? *I'm* not!'

They all sat still, thinking hard, Liz licking Anne's hand. And in the silence they heard an all-too-familiar sound.

Sniff! Sniff!

'Sniffer!' called George. 'Come on out, wherever you are hiding. I can hear you!'

A pair of legs stuck out from a great clump of heather at the edge of the quarry, and then the whole of Sniffer's wiry little body slithered out and down into the sand. He sat there, grinning at them, half-afraid to come any nearer in case they were cross with him.

'What are *you* doing here?' said Dick. 'Not spying on us, I hope?'

'No,' said Sniffer. 'Our camp isn't very far away. Liz heard you, I think, and ran off. I followed her.'

'Oh blow. We hoped we weren't near anyone else,' said George. 'Does anyone at your camp know we're here?'

'Not yet,' said Sniffer. 'But they'll find out. They always do. I won't tell, though, if you don't want me to.'

Dick tossed him a biscuit. 'Well, keep your mouth shut if you can,' he said. 'We're not interfering with anyone and we don't want anyone interfering with us. See?'

Sniffer nodded. He suddenly put his hand in his pocket and pulled out the red and white hanky that George had given him. It was still clean and beautifully folded.

'Not dirty yet!' he said to George.

'Well, it ought to be,' said George. 'It's for your sniffs. No, *don't* use your coat-sleeve.'

Sniffer simply could *not* understand why he should use a beautiful clean hanky when he had a dirty coat-sleeve. He put the hanky carefully back into his pocket.

Liz ran to him and fawned on him. Sniffer fondled the peculiar little creature, and then Timmy went over and played with them both. The four finished their tea, threw Sniffer one last biscuit, and got up to put their things away safely. Now that Sniffer was about, and the travellers' camp near, they didn't feel it was terribly safe to leave anything unguarded or unhidden.

'Scoot off, now, Sniffer,' said Julian. 'And no spying on

us, mind! Timmy will know immediately you arrive anywhere near, and come hunting for you. If you want to see us, give a whistle when you get near. No creeping or slipping into the quarry. Understand?'

'Yes,' said Sniffer, standing up. He took the hanky from his pocket again, waved it at George, and disappeared with Liz at his heels.

'I'm just going to see exactly how near to the travellers' camp we are,' Julian said. He walked to the entrance of the quarry and up on to the moor. He looked in the direction that Sniffer had gone. Yes, there was the hill in the shelter of which the travellers had their caravans. It wasn't more than a quarter of a mile away. Blow! Still, it was far enough for the travellers not to discover them, unless by chance.

'Or unless Sniffer gives the game away,' thought Julian. 'Well, we'll spend the night here, anyway, and we can move off somewhere else tomorrow if we feel like it.'

They felt rather energetic that evening and played a ball game in the quarry, in which Timmy joined wholeheartedly. But as he always got the ball before anyone else did they had to tie him up in order to get a game themselves. Timmy was very cross. He turned his back on them and sulked.

'He looks like you now, George,' said Dick, grinning, and got the ball bang on the side of his head from an angry George!

Nobody wanted much supper. Julian took a little

aluminium jug to the spring and filled it once for everyone. It really was lovely water from that bubbling spring!

'I wonder how Henry's getting on,' said Anne. 'Spoilt to bits by her great-aunts, I expect. Didn't she look odd in proper clothes!'

'Yes, she ought to have been a boy,' said Dick. 'Like you, George,' he added hastily. 'Both of you are real sports, plucky as anything.'

'How do you know Henry's plucky?' said George, scornfully. 'Only by her silly tales! I bet they're all made up and exaggerated.'

Julian changed the subject. 'Shall we want rugs tonight, do you think?' he said.

'You bet! It may be warm now, and the sand is hot with the sun, but it won't be quite so nice when it's gone down,' said Anne. 'Anyway we can always creep into one of those cosy little caves if we feel chilly. They're as warm as toast. I went into one, so I know.'

They settled down quite early to sleep. The boys took one side of the quarry, the girls the other. Tim, as usual, was on George's feet, much to Anne's discomfort.

'He's on mine too,' she complained to George. 'He's *so long*, he stretches over my feet as well. Move him, George.'

So George moved him, but as soon as Anne was asleep he stretched out again and lay on both girls' legs. He slept with one ear open.

He heard a scurrying hedgehog. He heard all the rabbits out for a night-time game. He heard the frogs in a far-off pool croaking in the night. His sharp ear even heard the tinkle of the little spring outside the pit.

Nobody moved in the quarry. There was a small moon but it gave very little light. The stars that studded the sky seemed to give more light than the moon.

Timmy's one open ear suddenly pricked itself right up. Then the other ear stood up too. Timmy was still asleep but his ears were both listening very hard!

A low, humming sound came slowly over the night. It came nearer and nearer. Timmy awoke properly and sat up, listening, his eyes wide open now.

The sound was now very loud indeed. Dick awoke and listened. What *was* that noise? An aeroplane? It must be jolly low! Surely it wasn't about to land on the moor in the dark!

He woke Julian and they both got up and went out of the quarry. 'It's an aeroplane all right,' said Dick, in a low voice. 'What's it doing? It doesn't seem to be going to land. It's gone round in a low circle two or three times.'

'Is it in trouble, do you think?' asked Julian. 'Here it comes again.'

'Look, what's that light over there?' suddenly said Dick, pointing to the east. 'See, that sort of glow. It's not very far from the travellers' camp.'

'I don't know,' said Julian, puzzled. 'It's not a fire, is it? We can't see any flames and it doesn't seem to flicker like a fire would.'

'I think it may be some sort of guide to that plane,' said Dick. 'It seems to be circling round and about over the glow. Let's watch it.'

They watched it. Yes, it did seem to be circling round the glow, whatever it was, and then, quite suddenly it rose in the air, circled round once more and made off to the east.

'There it goes,' said Dick, straining his eyes. 'I can't tell what kind it is, except that it's very small.'

'What can it have been doing?' said Julian, puzzled. 'I thought the glow might have been to guide it in landing, though where it could land here in safety I simply don't know. But it didn't land at all, it just circled and made off.'

'Where would it have come from?' said Dick. 'From the coast, I suppose, from over the sea, do you think?'

'I simply don't know,' said Julian. 'It beats me! And why should the travellers have anything to do with it? Travellers and planes don't seem to mix, somehow.'

'Well, we don't know that they do have anything to do with the plane, except that we saw that glow,' said Dick. 'And that's going now, look.'

Even as they watched, the bright glow died completely away. Now the moor lay in darkness again.

'Funny,' said Julian, scratching his head. 'I can't make it out. It's true that the travellers may be up to something, the way they come out here secretly, apparently for no purpose at all, and also they don't want us snooping round, that's clear.'

'I think we'd better try and find out what that glow is,' said Dick. 'We could have a bit of a snoop tomorrow. Or perhaps Sniffer could tell us.'

'He might,' said Julian. 'We'll try him. Come on, let's get back into the quarry. It's cold out here!'

The quarry felt quite warm to them as they went down into it. The girls were sound asleep still. Timmy, who had been with them, did not wake them. He had been as puzzled as Julian and Dick over the low-flying plane, but he had not barked at all. Julian had been glad about that, Timmy's bark might have carried right over to the travellers' camp and warned them that someone was camping near.

They got back under their rug, keeping close to one another for warmth. But they soon lost their shivers, and Dick threw off his share of the rug. In a few minutes they were asleep.

Timmy awoke first and stretched himself out in the warm morning sunshine. Anne sat up with a little scream. 'Oh, Timmy, *don't*! You nearly squashed me to bits. Do that to George if you must stretch yourself all over somebody!'

The boys awoke then, and went to the spring to splash their faces and bring back a jugful of water to drink. Anne got the breakfast, and over it the boys told the girls of the aeroplane in the night.

'How strange!' said Anne. 'And that glow too. It must have been a guide of some sort to the plane. Let's go and see where it was. It must have been a fire of *some* kind!'

'Right,' said Dick. 'I vote we go this morning, but we'll take Tim with us in case we meet those travellers!'

CHAPTER FOURTEEN

The travellers are not pleased

JULIAN AND Dick went to stand where they had stood the night before, trying to see exactly in what direction the glow had been.

'I *think* it was beyond the travellers' camp, to the left,' said Julian. 'What do you think, Dick?'

'Yes. That's about it,' said Dick. 'Shall we go now?' He raised his voice. 'We're going, George and Anne. Are you coming? We can leave our stuff here, tucked away in the caves because we shan't be very long.'

George called back. 'Julian, I think Timmy's got a thorn in his foot or something. He's limping. Anne and I think we'll stay here with him and try to get it out. You go, but for goodness' sake don't get into trouble with the travellers!'

'We shan't,' said Julian. 'We've as much right on this moor as they have and they know it. All right, we'll leave you two here then with Timmy. Sure you don't want any help with his paw?'

'Oh no,' said George. 'I can manage, thank you.'

The two boys went off, leaving Anne and George fussing over Timmy's paw. He had leapt into a gorse bush after a rabbit and a thorn had gone right into his left fore-paw. Then it had broken off, leaving the point in poor Timmy's pad. No wonder he limped. George was going to have quite a time trying to ease out the bit of thorn.

Julian and Dick set off over the moor. It was a day like summer, far too warm for April. There was not a single cloud to be seen in the sky, which was as blue as forget-me-nots. The boys felt too hot in their pullovers and longed to take them off. But that would mean carrying them, which would be an awful nuisance.

The travellers' camp was not really far away. They soon came near to the curious hill that stood up from the flatness of the moor. The caravans still stood in its shelter, and the boys saw that a little group of men were sitting together, talking earnestly.

'I bet they're having a jaw about that aeroplane last night,' said Dick. 'And I bet it was they who set the light or fire, or whatever it was, to guide it. I wonder why it didn't land.'

They kept in the shelter of big gorse bushes, as they skirted the camp. They were not particularly anxious to be seen. The dogs, sitting round the group of men, apparently did not see or hear them, which was lucky.

The boys made their way towards the place where they thought they had seen the glow, some way to the left of the camp, and beyond it.

'Doesn't seem to be anything out of the ordinary anywhere,' said Julian, stopping and looking round. 'I was expecting to see a big burnt patch, or something.'

'Wait – what's in that dip over there?' said Dick, pointing to where the ground seemed to dip downwards. 'It looks like another old quarry, rather like the one we're camping in, but smaller, much smaller. I bet that's where the fire was!'

They made their way to the quarry. It was much more overgrown than theirs was, and was evidently one that had been worked at an earlier time. It dipped down to quite a pit in the middle, and set there was something unusual. What was it?'

The boys scrambled down into the pit-like quarry and made their way to the middle. They stared at the big thing that was set there, pointing to the sky.

'It's a lamp, a powerful lamp of some kind,' said Dick. 'Like those we see making a flare-path at an aerodrome, guiding planes in to land. Fancy seeing one here!'

'How did the travellers get it?' wondered Dick, puzzled. 'And why signal to a plane that doesn't land? It looked as if it wanted to, circling round low like that.'

'Maybe the travellers signalled that it wasn't safe to land for some reason,' said Julian. 'Or perhaps they were going to give something to the pilot and it wasn't ready.'

'Well, it's a puzzle,' said Dick. 'I can't *imagine* what's going on. Something is, that's certain. Let's snoop round a bit.'

They found nothing else, except a trail that led to the lamp and back. Just as they were examining it, a shout came to their ears. They swung round – and saw the figure of a traveller at the edge of the pit.

'What are you doing here?' he shouted, in a harsh voice. He was joined by a few others, and they all looked threateningly at Julian and Dick as they climbed out of the pit.

Julian decided to be honest. 'We're camping out on the moor for a night or two,' he said, 'and we heard a plane last night, circling low. We also saw a glow that appeared to be guiding it, and we came along to see what it was. Did *you* hear the plane?'

'Maybe we did and maybe we didn't,' said the nearest traveller, who was Sniffer's father. 'What of it? Planes fly over this moor any day!'

'We found that powerful lamp,' said Dick, pointing back at it. 'Do you know anything about *that*?'

'Nothing,' said the traveller, scowling. 'What lamp?'

'Well, as far as I can see there's no charge for looking at it,' said Julian. 'Go and have a squint, if you don't know anything about it! But I can't believe that you didn't see the light it gave last night! It's a jolly good place to hide it, I must say.'

'We don't know anything about any lamp,' said another traveller, the old one with grey hair. 'This is our usual camping place. We don't interfere with anything or anybody – unless they interfere with us. Then we make them sorry for it.'

The boys at once thought of the long-ago mystery of

the disappearance of the Bartles. They felt quite uncomfortable.

'Well, we're going now, so don't worry,' said Julian. 'We're only camping for a night or two, as I said. We won't come near here again, if you object to us.'

He saw Sniffer creeping up behind the men, with Liz, who for some reason of her own, was walking sedately on her hind legs. Sniffer pulled at his father's arm.

'They're all right,' he said. 'You know our Clip got his leg made better at the stables. They're all right!'

All he got was a harsh cuff that sent him to the ground, where he rolled over and over. Liz dropped down on all fours and went to lick him.

'Hey!' said Julian, shocked. 'Leave that kid alone! You've no right to hit him like that!'

Sniffer set up such a yelling that some of the women left the caravans not far off and came running to see what was up. One of them began to shout at Sniffer's father and he shouted back. Soon there was quite a row going on between the men and the angry women, one of whom had picked up poor Sniffer and was dabbing his head with a wet cloth.

'Come on, it's a good time to go,' said Julian to Dick. 'What an unfriendly lot they are, except poor Sniffer, and he was doing his best for us, poor kid.'

The two boys went off quickly, glad to be away from the men and their dogs. They were puzzled about everything. The men said they knew nothing about the lamp, but they *must* know something about it. Nobody but a traveller could have lit it last night.

They went back to the girls and told them what had happened. 'Let's get back to the stables,' said Anne. 'There's something funny going on. We'll be in the middle of an adventure before we know where we are!'

'We'll stay one more night,' said Julian. 'I want to see if that plane comes again. Those travellers don't know where we're camping and though Sniffer knows, I'm pretty sure he won't tell. It was plucky of him to try and stick up for us to his father.'

'All right. We'll stay,' said George. 'I'm not particularly anxious for Timmy to have that long walk home today. I *think* I've got most of that thorn out of his pad, but he still won't put his foot to the ground.'

'He's jolly clever at running about on three legs,' said Dick, watching Timmy tearing round the quarry, sniffing as usual for rabbits.

'The amount of quarrying that Timmy has done in this pit already is colossal!' said Julian, staring round at the places where Timmy had tried to get in at some rabbit hole and scrabbled out big heaps of sand. 'He would have been a great help to the Bartles when they dug out sand! Poor old Tim – your bad foot has stopped you scraping for rabbits, hasn't it!'

Timmy ran over on three legs. He enjoyed all the fussing he got when anything happened to him. He meant to make the most of his bad foot!

They had a very lazy day indeed. It really was too hot to do anything much. They went to the little spring and sat with their feet in the rivulet it made – it was deliciously cool! They went and had a look at the old engine again, lying on its side, half-buried.

Dick scraped away a lot of the sand that had seeped into the cab. Soon they were all helping. They uncovered the old handles and levers and tried to move them. But they couldn't of course.

'Let's go round to the other side of the gorse bush and see if we can see the funnel again,' said Dick, at last.

'Blow these thorns. I'm getting pricked all over. Timmy's very sensible, sitting there, not attempting to examine this old Puffing Billy!'

They had to cut away some of the gorse before they could examine the funnel properly. Then they exclaimed in wonder.

'Look! It's very like the long funnel that Puffing Billy had. You know, one of the first engines ever made!'

'It's filled with sand,' said Dick, and tried to scrape it out. It was fairly loose, and soon he was able to peer down the funnel quite a long way.

'Funny to think of smoke puffing out of this strange old funnel,' said Dick. 'Poor old engine, lying here for years, quite forgotten. I'd have thought *someone* would rescue it!'

'Well, you know what the blacksmith told us,' said George. 'The Bartle sister that was left wouldn't have anything more to do with the railway or the engine or the quarry. And certainly nobody could move this great thing on their own.'

'I shouldn't be surprised if we're the only people in the world who know where the old engine is,' said Anne. 'It's so overgrown that nobody could see it except by accident!'

'I feel jolly hungry, all of a sudden,' said Dick, stopping his work of getting sand off the engine. 'What about something to eat?'

'We've got enough to last for a day or two more,' said

Anne. 'Then we'll have to get something else – or go back to the stables.'

'I *must* spend one more night here,' said Julian. 'I want to see if that plane returns again.'

'Right. We'll all watch this time,' said George. 'It will be fun. Come on, let's go and get something to eat. Don't you think that's a good idea, Timmy?'

Timmy certainly did. He limped off at top speed on three legs, though really his left fore-paw no longer hurt him. Timmy, you're a fraud!

CHAPTER FIFTEEN

A startling night

NO TRAVELLERS came near them that day, not even Sniffer. The evening was as lovely as the day had been, and almost as warm.

'It's extraordinary!' said Dick, looking up into the sky. 'What weather for April! The bluebells will be rushing out soon if the sun goes on being as hot as this!'

They lay on the sand in the quarry and watched the evening star shine in the sky. It looked very big and bright and round.

Timmy scrabbled round in the sand. 'His paw is much better,' said George. 'Though I notice that he still sometimes holds it up.'

'Only when he wants you to say "Poor Timmy, does it hurt!"' said Dick. 'He's a baby, likes to be fussed!'

They talked for a while and then Anne yawned. 'It's early, I know – but I believe I'm going to sleep.'

There was soon a trek to the spring, and everyone sluiced themselves in the cool water. There was only one towel between them, but that did very well. Then they settled down in their sandy beds. The sand was beautifully warm and they did not bother about putting down the rubber sheets. There could not possibly be any dampness in that quarry after it had been baked so much by the hot sun!

'I hope we wake when the plane comes, if it does come,' said Julian to Dick, as they lay without any covering in their soft, sandy bed. 'My goodness, isn't it hot! No wonder Timmy's panting over there!'

They went to sleep at last, but Dick awoke suddenly, feeling much too hot. Phew! What a night! He lay looking up at the brilliant stars, and then shut his eyes again. But it was no use, he couldn't go to sleep.

He sat up cautiously, so as not to awake Julian. 'I think I'll just go and have a squint to see if that big lamp is lit again, down in that pit by the travellers' camp,' he thought.

He went to the edge of the quarry and climbed up. He looked towards the travellers' camp and gave a sudden exclamation. 'Yes!' he thought. 'It's glowing again! I can't see the lamp, of course, but its light is so powerful that I can easily see the glow it makes. It must be very bright, looked down on from the sky. I wonder if the plane is due to come now that the lamp is lit.'

He listened, and yes, he could distinctly hear a low humming noise from the east. It must be the plane coming again. Would it land this time, and if so, who was in it?

He ran to wake Julian and the girls. Timmy was alert at once, wagging his tail excitedly. He was always ready for anything, even in the middle of the night! Anne and George got up too, very thrilled.

'Is the lamp really alight again? And I can hear the plane too now! Oh, I say! This is exciting! George, Timmy won't bark and give us away, will he?'

'No. I've told him to be quiet,' said George. 'He won't make a sound. Listen, the plane is coming nearer!'

The noise was now loud enough for them to search the starry sky for the plane. Julian gave Dick a nudge. 'Look, you can just see it, straight over where the travellers' camp is!'

Dick managed to pick it out. 'It's very small,' he said. 'Smaller even than I thought it was last night. Look, it's coming down!'

But it wasn't. It merely swept low, and then went round in a circle, as it had done the night before. It rose a little again and then came in low once more, almost over the boys' heads.

Then something extraordinary happened. Something fell not far from Julian, something that bounced and then came to rest! It made a thud as it fell, and all four jumped. Timmy gave a startled whine.

Thud! Something else fell. Thud, thud, thud! Anne gave a squeal. 'Are they trying to bomb us or something? Julian, what are they doing?'

Thud! Thud! Julian ducked at the last two thuds, they sounded so near. He took hold of Anne and pulled her down into the quarry, calling to Dick and George.

'Get down here, quickly! Force yourselves into the caves somewhere! We shall get hit!'

They ran across the quarry as the plane swooped round in a circle once more and then again began dropping the things that went 'thud! thud!'. Some even fell into the quarry this time. Timmy got the shock of his life when one bounced in front of his nose and rolled away. He yelped and tore after George.

Soon they were all safely squeezed into the little caves

that lined the sides of the quarry. The plane swept round once more, up and then round, and the thud-thudding began again. The four could hear that some of the thuds were actually in the quarry again and they were thankful they were well sheltered.

'Well, nothing is exploding,' said Dick, thankfully. 'But what on earth is the plane dropping? And why? This is a most peculiar adventure to have.'

'It's probably a dream,' said Julian, and laughed. 'No, not even a dream could be so mad. Here we are, snuggling into sandy caves in a quarry on Mystery Moor, while a plane drops something all round us in the middle of the night! Quite mad.'

'I believe the plane's going away now,' said Dick. 'It's circled round but hasn't dropped anything. Now it's climbing, it's going away! The engine doesn't sound nearly so loud. Goodness, when we were standing out there at the edge of the quarry, I almost thought the plane would take my head off, it was so low!'

'I thought that too,' said Anne, very glad that there was to be no more swooping down and dropping dozens of unknown things. 'Is it safe to go out?'

'Oh yes,' said Julian, scrambling out of the sand. 'Come on. We shall easily hear if the plane comes back again. I want to see what it has dropped!'

In great excitement they ran to get the parcels. The stars gave so much light on that clear night that the four did not even need a torch.

Julian picked up something first. It was a firm, flattish parcel, done up well, sewn into a canvas covering. He examined it.

'No name. Nothing,' he said. 'This is most exciting. Let's have three guesses what's inside.'

'Bacon for breakfast, I hope!' said Anne at once.

'Idiot,' said Julian, getting out a knife to slit the string threads that sewed up the canvas. 'I guess it's smuggled goods of some sort. That's what that plane was doing, I should think, flying over from France, and dropping smuggled goods in a pre-arranged place, and I suppose the travellers pick them up, and take them away, well hidden in their caravans, to deliver them somewhere. Very clever!'

'Oh, Julian, is *that* the explanation?' said Anne. 'What would be in the parcels then, cigarettes?'

'No,' said Julian. 'The parcels wouldn't be so heavy if they only contained cigarettes. There, I've slit the threads at last!'

The others crowded round to see. George took her torch out of her pocket so that they could see really well. She flashed it on.

Julian ripped off the canvas covering. Next came some strong brown paper. He ripped that off too. Then came strong cardboard, tied round with string. That was undone as well, and the cardboard fell to the ground.

'Now, what have we got?' said Julian, excited. Thin sheets of paper, dozens and dozens of them packed together. Shine your torch nearer, George.'

There was a silence as all the four craned over Julian's hands.

'Whew! I say! Gosh, do you see what they are?' said Julian, in awe. 'American money, dollar notes. But look what they are, *one-hundred*-dollar notes! 'And, my word, there are scores and scores of them in this one packet!'

The four stared in amazement as Julian riffled through the packet of notes. However much would they be worth?

'Julian, how much is a hundred-dollar note worth in our money?' asked George.

'About fifty pounds I think,' said Julian. 'Yes, just about that. Gosh, and there are scores in this one packet, and we know they dropped *dozens* of the packets too. Whatever is it all about?'

'Well, there must be thousands and thousands of dollars lying around us, here in the quarry and outside it,' said George. 'I *say*! Surely this *isn't* a dream?'

'Well, I must say it's a very *extravagant* kind of dream, if so,' said Dick. 'A dream worth thousands of pounds isn't very usual. Ju, hadn't we better get busy picking up these parcels?'

'Yes. We certainly had,' said Julian. 'I'm beginning to see it all now. The smugglers come over in a plane from France, say, having previously arranged to drop these packets in a lonely spot on this moor. The travellers are in the plot to the extent that they light the guiding lamp and pick up the parcels.'

'I see, and then they quietly pack them into their caravans, slip off the moor, and deliver them to somebody else, who pays them well for their trouble,' said Dick. 'Very smart!'

'That's about it,' said Julian. 'But I can't for the life of me see why *dollar* notes have to be smuggled here. They can be brought freely enough into the country – why *smuggle* them?'

'Stolen ones, perhaps?' said George. 'Oh well, it's quite beyond *me*. What a thing to do! No wonder the travellers didn't want us around.'

'Better buck up and collect all these parcels and clear off back to the stables with them,' said Julian, picking up one near him. 'The travellers will be after them, there's no doubt about that! We must be gone before they come.'

The four of them went about looking for the parcels. They found about sixty of them, and they made quite a heavy load.

'We'll put them somewhere safe, I think,' said Julian. 'What about stuffing them into one of the sand caves? I don't very well see how we can carry them like this.'

'We could put them in the rugs and tie up the ends and carry them like that,' said George. 'It would be mad to leave them hidden somewhere in this quarry. It's the first place the travellers would search.'

'All right. We'll follow your idea,' said Julian. 'I think we've about collected all the packets there are. Get the rugs.'

George's idea proved to be a good one. Half the parcels were rolled into one rug, and tied up, and half into the other.

'Good thing the rugs are nice and big,' said Dick, tying his up strongly. 'Now I can just about manage mine nicely on my back. You all right, Ju?'

'Yes, come along, you girls,' said Julian. 'Follow behind us. We'll go down the railway line. Leave everything else here. We can easily get it another time. We *must* leave before the travellers come.'

Timmy began to bark suddenly. 'That must mean the travellers are coming,' said Dick. 'Come on, quick! Yes, I can hear their voices – for goodness' sake, HURRY!'

CHAPTER SIXTEEN

The terrible mist

YES, THE travellers were certainly coming! Their dogs were with them, barking. The four children hurried out of the quarry with Timmy at their heels, quite silent.

'Those fellows may not know we were camping in the quarry,' panted Dick. 'They may just be coming to find the parcels, and while they are hunting around, we may be able to get a good start. Buck up!'

They set off to where the lines ended, near where the old engine lay half-buried. The travellers' dogs heard them and set up a yelping and howling. The travellers stopped to see what had excited them.

They spied shadows moving in the distance, the four children slipping away from the quarry. One of the men shouted loudly.

'Hey you – stop! Who are you? Stop, I say!'

But the Five didn't stop. They were now stumbling between the railways lines, glad of George's torch and Anne's. The boys could not have held one for it was all they could do to hang on to the heavy-laden rugs.

'Quick, oh quick!' whispered Anne, but it was impossible to go very quickly.

'They must be catching us up,' said Julian, suddenly. 'Look round and see, George.'

George looked round. 'No, I can't see anyone,' she said. 'Julian, everywhere looks peculiar. What's happening? Julian, stop. Something strange is happening!'

Julian stopped and looked round. His eyes had been fixed on his feet, trying to see where he was going without stumbling. Anne had shone her torch down for him but it was still difficult to get along properly. Julian gazed all round, wondering what George meant.

Then he gave a gasp. 'Gosh! How strange! There's a mist come up, look. It's even blotted out the stars. No wonder it seems so jolly dark all of a sudden.'

'A mist!' said Anne, scared. 'Not that *awful* mist that sometimes covers the moor! Oh, Julian, is it?'

Julian and Dick watched the swirling mist in astonishment. 'It's come from the sea,' Julian said. 'Can't you smell the salt in it? It's come just as suddenly as we've been told it comes, and look, it's getting thicker every minute!'

'What a good thing we're on the railway lines!' said George. 'What shall we do? Go on?'

Julian stood and thought. 'The travellers won't come after us in this mist,' he said. 'I've a good mind to hide this money somewhere, and then walk back to get the police. If we keep on the lines we can't go wrong. But we must be sure not to leave them, or we'll be completely lost!'

'Yes, let's do that,' said Dick, who was heartily sick already of lugging along his heavy load. 'But where do you propose to hide them, Ju? Not in the quarry! We'd have to walk through this awful mist to do that, and we'd get lost at once.'

'No. I've thought of a fine place,' said Julian, and he lowered his voice. 'Remember that old engine, fallen on its side? Well, what about stuffing these packets all the way down that great long funnel, and then stopping the top of it up with sand? I bet you anything you like that nobody would find the packets there.'

'Grand idea!' said Dick. 'The travellers will be sure we've gone off carrying the money, and they'll not hunt about for it long, once they find the dropped packets are all gone. We'll be halfway home by the time they try to catch us, if they dare to brave this mist.'

Anne and George thought Julian's idea was first-rate, a stroke of genius. 'I'd never, never have thought of the engine funnel!' said Anne.

'Now, there's no need for you two girls and Timmy to walk all the way to the engine with us,' said Julian. 'You sit down here on the lines and wait for us to come back. We shan't be long. We'll walk straight up the railway, find the engine, pack the money into the funnel, and walk back.'

'Right,' said George, squatting down. 'Bring the rugs back with you, though. It's cold now!'

Julian and Dick went off together, with Anne's torch. George kept hers. Timmy pressed close against her, astonished at the thick mist that had so suddenly swirled up and around them.

'That's right. Keep close to us and keep us warm, Tim,' said George. 'It's jolly cold now. This mist is damp!'

Julian stumbled along, keeping a lookout for the travellers. He could see nothing of them, but then, if they had been only two feet away he could not have seen anything of them in the mist! It seemed to get thicker and thicker.

'I know what old Ben meant now, when he said that it had damp fingers,' thought Julian, feeling little touches like fingers on his face, hands and legs as the mist wreathed itself round him.

Dick nudged him. 'Here we are,' he said. 'The lines are broken here. The engine should be just over there, a yard or two away.'

They stepped cautiously away from the lines. The big gorse bush could not be seen, but it could be felt! Julian felt thorns pricking his legs, and knew he was beside it.

'Shine your torch here, Dick,' he whispered. 'That's right. There's the cab of the engine, see? Now let's circle the bush, and we'll come to the funnel.'

'Here it is,' said Dick, in a few moments. 'Look! Now then, let's do a bit of work, shoving these packets down. Gosh, what a lot of them there are! I hope the funnel will take them all.'

They spent ten minutes ramming the packets into the wide funnel. Down they went to the bottom! More and more followed and then, at last, the final one was shoved in and rammed down.

'That's the lot,' said Dick, relieved. 'Now we'll pack some sand in. Gosh, isn't this bush full of prickles! It's really spiteful!'

'The packets *almost* fill the funnel,' said Julian. 'Hardly any room for sand. Still, we can put in enough to hide the money all right. There, that's done. Now pull this gorse branch over the top of the funnel. My word, I never knew a bush so set with spines! I'm scratched to bits!'

'Can you hear anything of the travellers?' asked Dick, in a low voice, as they prepared to go back to the lines.

They listened. 'Not a thing,' said Julian. 'It's my belief they're scared of this mist, and are lying low till it clears.'

'They may be in the quarry,' said Dick. 'Waiting there in safety. Well, long may they be there! They won't get the money now!'

'Come on,' said Julian, and walked round the bush. 'It's just about here that we step out to get to the lines. Take my arm. We mustn't get separated. Did you ever see such a mist in your life? It's the thickest fog I ever knew. We can't even see our feet in the light of the torch now.'

They took a few steps and then felt about for the rails. They couldn't feel even one. 'A bit farther, I think,' said Julian. 'No, this way.'

But they still couldn't find the railway lines. Where *were* the wretched things? A small feeling of panic came into Julian's mind. Which way should they step now, to find the rails? How had they gone wrong?

Now both boys were on hands and knees, feeling for the broken rails. 'I've got one,' said Dick. 'No, blow, it isn't. It's a bit of wood, or something. For goodness' sake, keep close to me, Ju.'

After ten minutes' search, the two boys sat back on their

heels, the little torch between them.

'Somehow we've just missed those two or three correct steps from the gorse bush to the rails,' said Julian. 'Now we're done for! I don't see anything for it but to wait till the mist clears.'

'But what about the two girls?' said Dick, anxiously. 'Let's try a bit longer. Look, the mist is clearing a little there. Let's go forward and hope we'll stumble over the lines soon. If the mist does clear, we shall soon be able to get our bearings.'

So they went forward hopefully, seeing the mist clear a little in front of them, so that the torch made a longer beam for them to see by. Now and again, when their feet knocked against something hard, they felt for the rails. But they could not find even one!

'Let's shout,' said Julian, at last. So they shouted loudly. 'George! Anne! Can you hear us?'

They stood and listened. No answer.

'GEORGE!' yelled Dick. 'TIMMY!'

They thought they heard a far-off bark. 'That was Timmy!' said Julian. 'Over there!'

They stumbled along and then shouted again. But this time there was no bark at all. Not a sound came out of that dreadful mist, which had now closed tightly round them again.

'We'll be walking in it all night long,' said Julian, desperately. 'Why did we leave the girls? Suppose this frightful fog doesn't clear by tomorrow? Sometimes it lasts for days.'

'What a horrible idea,' said Dick, lightly, sounding much more cheerful than he felt. 'I don't think we need worry about the girls, Ju. Timmy's with them and he can easily take them back to the stables across the moor, in the mist. Dogs don't mind fogs.'

Julian felt most relieved. He hadn't thought of that. 'Oh yes, I'd forgotten old Tim,' he said. 'Well, seeing that the girls will probably be all right with Timmy to guide them, let's sit down somewhere and have a rest. I'm tired out!'

'Here's a good thick bush,' said Dick. 'Let's get into the middle of it if we can, and keep the damp out of us. Thank goodness it's not a gorse bush!'

'I wish I knew if the girls had had the sense not to wait for us any longer, but to try to find their way back down the lines,' said Julian. 'I wonder where they are now?'

Anne and George were no longer where Julian and Dick had left them! They had waited and waited, and then had become very anxious indeed.

'Something's happened,' said George. 'I think we ought to go and get help, Anne. We can easily follow the railway down to where we have to break off for the stable. Timmy will know, anyway. Don't you think we ought to go back and get help?'

'Yes, I do,' said Anne, getting up. 'Come on George. Gosh, this mist is worse than ever! We'll have to be careful we don't lose the lines! Even Timmy might find it hard to smell his way in this fog!'

They got up. Anne followed George and Timmy followed behind, looking puzzled. He couldn't understand this night-time wandering about at all!

Anne and George kept closely to the railway lines, walking slowly along, shining the light of the torch downwards, and following carefully.

After a time George stopped, puzzled. 'This line's broken here,' she said. 'There's no more of it. That's funny, I don't remember it being as badly broken as this. The lines simply stop. I can't see any more.'

'Oh *George*!' said Anne, peering down. 'Do you know what we've done? We've come all the way *up* the lines again – instead of going down them, homewards! How *could* we have been so mad? Look, this is where they break off, so the old engine must be somewhere near, and the quarry!'

'Blow!' said George, quite in despair. 'What asses we are. It shows how we can lose our sense of direction in a mist like this.'

'I can't see or hear anything of the boys,' said Anne, fearfully. 'George, let's go to the quarry and wait there till daylight comes. I'm cold and tired. We can squeeze into one of those warm sand caves.'

'All right,' said George, very much down in the dumps. 'Come along, and for goodness' sake don't let's lose our way to the quarry!'

CHAPTER SEVENTEEN

Prisoners together

THE TWO girls and Timmy made their way carefully, hoping to come across the lines that led to the quarry. They were lucky. They went across the gap in the lines where once long ago the travellers had wrenched out the rails, and came to where they began again, and led to the edge of the quarry.

'Here they are!' said George, thankfully. 'Now we're all right. We've only just got to follow these and we'll be in the quarry. I hope it will be warmer than here. Brrr! This mist is terribly cold and clammy.'

'It came up so *suddenly*,' said Anne, shining her torch downwards. 'I couldn't believe my eyes when I looked round and saw it creeping up on us. I . . .'

She stopped suddenly. Timmy had given a low growl. 'What's up, Tim?' whispered George. He stood quite still, his hackles up and his tail motionless. He looked steadfastly into the mist.

'Oh dear. What can be the matter now?' whispered Anne. 'I can't hear a thing, can you?'

They listened. No, there was nothing to hear at all. They went on into the quarry, thinking that Timmy might have heard a rabbit or hedgehog, and growled at it as he sometimes did.

Timmy heard a sound and ran to the side, lost in the mist at once. He suddenly yelped loudly, then there was a heavy thud, and no more sound from Timmy!

'Timmy! What's happened? Timmy, come here!' shouted George, at the top of her voice. But no Timmy came. The girls heard the sound of something heavy being dragged away, and George ran after the sound.

'Timmy! Oh, Timmy, what's happened!' she cried. 'Where are you? Are you hurt?'

The mist swirled round, and she tried to beat against it with her fists, angry that she could not see. 'Tim! Tim!'

Then a pair of hands took her arms from behind and a voice said, 'Now you come with me! You were warned not to snoop about on the moor!'

George struggled violently, less concerned for herself than for Timmy.

'Where's my dog?' she cried. 'What have you done to him?'

'I knocked him on the head,' said the voice, which sounded very like Sniffer's father. 'He's all right, but he won't feel himself for a bit! You can have him back if you're sensible.'

George wasn't sensible. She kicked and fought and wriggled and struggled. It was no use. She was held in a grip like iron. She heard Anne scream once and knew that she had been caught too.

When George was too tired to struggle any more, she was led firmly out of the quarry with Anne.

'Where's my dog?' she sobbed. 'What have you done with him?'

'He's all right,' said the man behind her. 'But if you make any more fuss I'll give him another blow on the head. NOW will you be quiet?'

George was quiet at once. She was taken with Anne across the moor for what seemed like miles, but was really only the fairly short distance between the quarry and the travellers' camp.

'Are you bringing my dog?' asked George, unable to contain her fears about Timmy.

'Yes. Somebody's got him,' said her captor. 'You shall have him back safe and sound, if you do what you're told!'

George had to be content with that. What a night! The boys gone, Timmy hurt, she and Anne captured, and this horrible, wreathing mist all the time!

The mist cleared a little as they came near to the travellers' camp. The hill behind seemed to keep it off. George and Anne saw the light of a fire, and of a few lanterns here and there. More men were gathered together, waiting. Anne thought she could see Sniffer and Liz in the background but she couldn't be sure.

'If only I could get hold of Sniffer,' she thought. 'He would soon find out if Timmy is really hurt. Oh, Sniffer, do come nearer if it's you!'

Their captors took them to the little fire, and made both girls sit down. One of the men there exclaimed in surprise.

'But these are not those two boys! This is a boy and a

girl, not as tall as the others were!'

'We're two girls,' said Anne, thinking that the men might treat George less roughly if they knew she was not a boy. 'I'm a girl and so is she.'

She got a scowl from George, but took no notice. This was not the time to pretend anything. These men were ruthless, and very angry. They thought their plans had gone wrong, all because of two boys. Perhaps when they found they had got two girls, they would let them go.

The men began to question them. 'Where are the boys then?'

'We've no idea! Lost in the mist,' said Anne. 'We all went out to go back home, and got separated, so George, I mean Georgina, and I went back to the quarry.'

'Did you hear the plane?'

'Of course!'

'Did you see or hear it dropping anything?'

'We didn't *see* anything drop, we heard it,' said Anne. George stared at her furiously. Why was Anne giving all this away? Perhaps she thought that Timmy would be given back to them if they proved helpful? George immediately changed her mind about feeling cross with Anne. If only Timmy were all right!

'Did you pick up what the plane dropped?' The man rapped out the question so sharply that Anne jumped. What should she say?

'Oh yes,' she heard herself saying. 'We picked up a few strange parcels. What was in them, do you know?'

'Never you mind,' said the man. 'What did you do with the parcels?'

George stared at Anne, wondering what she was going to say? Surely, surely she wouldn't give *that* secret away?

'I didn't do anything with them,' said Anne, in an innocent voice. 'The boys said they would hide them. So they went off into the mist with them, but they didn't come back. So George and I went to the quarry again. That's when you caught us.'

The men talked among themselves in low voices. Then Sniffer's father turned to the girls again.

'Where did the boys hide these packets?'

'How do I know?' said Anne. 'I didn't go with them. I didn't see what they did with them.'

'Do you think they will still have got them with them?' asked the man.

'Why don't you go and *find* the boys and ask them?' said Anne. 'I haven't seen or heard of the boys since they left us and went into the mist. I don't know *what* became of them or the parcels!'

'They're probably lost somewhere on the moors,' said the old, grey-haired traveller. 'With the packets! We'll look for the boys tomorrow. They won't get home in this! We'll fetch them back here.'

'They wouldn't come,' said George. 'As soon as they saw you, they'd run. You'd never catch them. Anyway they'd get back home as soon as the mist cleared.'

'Take these girls away,' said the old traveller, sounding tired of them. 'Put them in the far cave, and tie them up.'

'Where's my dog?' shouted George, suddenly. 'You bring me my dog!'

'You haven't been very helpful,' said the old traveller. 'We'll question you again tomorrow, and if you are *more* helpful, you shall have your dog.'

Two men took the girls away from the fire and over to the hill. A large opening led into the strange hill. One of the men had a lantern and led the way, the other man walking behind.

A passage led straight into the hill. There was sand underfoot, and it seemed to Anne as if even the walls were made of sand. How strange!

The hill was honeycombed with passages. They criss-crossed and forked like burrows in a rabbit warren. Anne wondered however the men could find their way!

They came at last to a cave that must have been right in the heart of the hill, a cave with a sandy floor, and a post that was driven deeply into the ground.

Ropes were fastened firmly to it. The two girls looked at them in dismay. Surely they were not going to be tied up like prisoners!

But they were! The ropes were fastened firmly round their waists and knotted at the back. The knots were travellers' knots, firm, tight and complicated. It would take the girls hours to unpick those, even supposing they could manage to reach right round to their backs!

'There you are,' said the men, grinning at the two angry girls. 'Maybe in the morning you will remember where those packets were put!'

'You go and get my dog,' ordered George. But they only laughed loudly and went out of the cave.

It was stuffy and hot in there. George was worried to death about Timmy, but Anne was almost too tired to think.

She fell asleep, sitting up uncomfortably with the ropes round her waist, and the knots digging into her back.

George sat brooding. Timmy – where was he? Was he badly hurt? George was very miserable indeed.

She didn't go to sleep. She sat there, worrying, wide awake. She made an attempt to get at the knots behind her, but it was no use, she couldn't.

Suddenly she thought she heard a noise. Was that someone creeping up the passage to the cave? She felt frightened. Oh, if only Timmy were here!

Sniff! Sniff!

'Gracious goodness, it must be Sniffer!' thought George, and at that moment she almost loved the little traveller boy!

'Sniffer!' she called quietly, and put on her torch. Sniffer's head appeared and then his body. He was crawling quietly up the passage on all fours.

He came right into the cave, and stared at her and the sleeping Anne. 'I've sometimes been tied up here too,' he said.

'Sniffer, how is Timmy?' asked George, anxiously. 'Tell me, quickly!'

'He's all right,' said Sniffer. 'He's just got a bad cut on his head. I bathed it for him. *He's* tied up too, and he's mad about it!'

'Sniffer, listen, go and get Timmy and bring him to me,' said George, breathlessly. 'And bring me a knife too, to cut these ropes. Will you? Can you?'

'Oooh, I dunno,' said Sniffer, looking frightened. 'My father would punish me!'

'Sniffer, is there anything you want, anything you've *always* wanted?' said George. 'I'll give it to you if you do this for me, I promise you!'

'I want a bike,' said Sniffer, surprisingly. 'And I want to live in a house, and ride my bike to school.'

'I'll see that you have what you want, Sniffer,' said George, wildly. 'Only, do, do go and get Timmy, and a knife! You got here without being seen, you can surely get back again safely with Timmy. Think of that bike!'

Sniffer thought of it. Then he nodded and disappeared down the passage as silently as he had come.

George waited and waited. Would he bring dear old Timmy to her, or would he be caught?

CHAPTER EIGHTEEN

George's trick

GEORGE SAT in the darkness of the cave, hearing Anne's peaceful breathing nearby, waiting for Sniffer to come back. She was longing to see Timmy again. Was the cut on his head *very* bad?

A thought came into her mind. She would send Timmy back to the stables with a note! He was very clever, he knew what to do when he had a note tied to his collar. Then help would come very quickly indeed. Timmy would know his way all right out of this hill, once he had been in it!

Ah, here was Sniffer coming back again. Was Timmy with him? She heard Sniffer's sniff-sniff-sniff, but no sound of Timmy. Her heart sank.

Sniffer appeared cautiously in the cave.

'I didn't dare to take Timmy,' he said. 'My father has him tied up too near to him, and I'd have woken him. But I've brought you a knife, look.'

'Thank you, Sniffer,' said George, taking the knife and putting it into her pocket. 'Listen, there's something important I'm going to do and you've got to help.'

'I'm scared,' said Sniffer. 'I'm really scared.'

'Think of that bicycle,' said George. 'A red one, perhaps with silver handles?'

Sniffer thought of it. 'All right,' he said. 'What are you going to do?'

'I'm going to write a note,' said George, feeling in her pocket for her notebook and pencil. 'And I want you to tie it on to Timmy's collar, under his chin, and set him free somehow. Will you do that? He'll run off back to the stables with the note, and then Anne and I will be rescued, and you will get the most beautiful bicycle in the world!'

'And a house to live in,' said Sniffer, at once. 'So that I can ride my bike to school?'

'All right,' said George, hoping that somehow he could have that too. 'Now, wait a minute.'

She scribbled the note, but she had hardly written more than a few words, when a sound came up the passage. Someone was coughing.

'It's my father!' said Sniffer, in fright. 'Listen, if you cut your ropes and escape, can you find your way out from here? It's very twisty and turny.'

'I don't know. I don't think I can!' whispered George, in a panic.

'I'll leave patrins for you!' said Sniffer. 'Look out for them! Now I'm going to slip into the cave next door, and wait till my father's finished talking to you. Then I'll go back to Timmy.'

He slipped out just in time. The lantern shone into George's cave and Sniffer's father stood there.

'Have you seen Sniffer?' he asked. 'I missed him when

I woke just now. If I catch him in here I'll whip him till he squeals.'

'Sniffer? He's not here,' said George, trying to sound surprised. 'Look round the cave and see!'

The man caught sight of the notebook and pencil in George's hand. 'What's that you're writing?' he said suspiciously and took it from her.

'So you're writing for help, are you!' he said. 'And how do you think you're going to get help, I'd like to know?

Who's going to take this note home for you? Sniffer?'

'No,' said George, truthfully.

The man frowned as he looked again at the note. 'Look here,' he said, 'you can write another note, to those two boys. And I'll tell you what to say.'

'No,' said George.

'Oh yes, you will,' said the man. 'I'm not going to hurt those boys. I'm just going to get back those packets from wherever they are hidden. Do you want your dog back safely?'

'Yes,' said George, with a gulp.

'Well, if you don't write this note you won't see him again,' said the man. 'Now then, take your pencil and write in that notebook of yours.'

George took up her pencil. 'This is what you must write,' said the man, frowning as he thought hard.

'Wait a minute,' said George. 'How are you going to get this note to the boys? You don't know where they are! You won't be able to find them if this mist still goes on.'

The man scratched his head and thought.

'The only way to get the note to them is to tie it on my dog's collar and send him to find them,' said George. 'If you bring him here to me I can make him understand. He always does what I tell him.'

'You mean he'll take the note to whoever you tell him to take it?' said the man, his eyes gleaming. 'Well, write it then. Say this:

'"We are prisoners. Follow Timmy and he will bring you to us and you can save us." Then sign your name, whatever it is.'

'It's Georgina,' said George, firmly. 'You go and get my dog while I write the note.'

The man turned and went. George looked after him, her eyes bright. *He* thought he was making her play a trick on Julian and Dick, to bring them here so that they could be threatened and questioned about the packets, and where they were hidden!

'But *I'm* going to play a trick on him,' thought George. 'I'm going to tell Timmy to take the note to *Henry*, and she'll be suspicious and get Captain Johnson to follow Tim back here, and that will give the travellers an *awful* shock! I expect the captain will be sensible enough to get the police as well. Aha, *I'm* playing a trick too!'

In ten minutes' time Sniffer's father returned with Timmy. It was a rather subdued Timmy, with a very bad cut on his head, which really needed stitching. He pattered soberly across to George, and she flung her arms round his neck and cried into his thick hair.

'Does your head hurt you?' she said. 'I'll take you to the vet when I get back, Tim.'

'You can get back as soon as we've got those two boys here and they've told us where those packets are hidden,' said the man.

Timmy was licking George as if he would never stop, and his tail waved to and fro, to and fro. He couldn't understand what was happening at all! Why was George here? Never mind, he was with her again. He settled down on the floor with a thump and put his head on her knee.

'Write the note,' said the man, 'and tie it on to his collar, on the top, so that it can easily be seen.'

'I've written it,' said George. The traveller held out a hand for it and read it.

> '*We are prisoners. Follow Timmy and he will bring you to us and you can save us.*
>
> GEORGINA.'

'Is that really your name, Georgina?' asked the man. George nodded. It was one of the few times she ever owned to a girl's name!

She tied the note firmly to Timmy's collar, on the top of his neck. It was quite plainly to be seen. Then she gave him a hug and spoke urgently to him.

'Go to Henry, Tim, go to HENRY. Do you understand, Timmy dear, take this note to HENRY.' She tapped the paper on his collar as he listened to her. Then she gave him a push. 'Go along. Don't stay here any longer. Go and find HENRY.'

'Hadn't you better tell him the other boy's name too?' said the man.

'Oh no, I don't want to *muddle* Timmy,' said George hastily. 'Henry, Henry, HENRY!'

'Woof,' said Timmy, and George knew that he understood. She gave him another push.

'Go, then,' she said. 'Hurry!'

Timmy gave her rather a reproachful look as if to say, 'You haven't let me stay with you very long!' Then he padded off down the passage, the note showing clearly on his collar.

'I'll bring the boys up here as soon as they come with the dog,' said the man, and he turned on his heel, and went out. George wondered if Sniffer was still about and she called him. But there was no answer. He must have slipped away down the passages back to his caravan.

Anne woke up then, and wondered where she was. George switched on her torch again and explained all that had happened.

'You should have woken me,' said Anne. 'Oh blow these ropes. They're *so* uncomfortable.'

'I've got a knife now,' said George. 'Sniffer gave it to me. Shall I cut our ropes?'

'Oh yes!' said Anne, in delight. 'But don't let's try and escape yet. It's still night-time and if that mist is about, we'll only get lost. We can pretend we're still tied up if anyone comes.'

George cut her own ropes with Sniffer's exceedingly blunt knife. Then she cut Anne's. Oh, what a relief to lie down properly, and not to have to sit up all the time and feel the knots at the back!

'Now do remember, if we hear anyone coming, we must

tie the ropes loosely round us,' she said. 'We will stay here till we know it's day, and perhaps we can find out if the mist is still about, or if it's gone. If it's gone, we'll go.'

They fell asleep on the sandy floor, both glad to lie down flat. Nobody came to disturb them, and they slept on and on, tired out.

Where were the boys? Still under the bush, half-sleeping, half-waking, for they were could and uncomfortable. They hoped the girls were now safely at home. 'They must have gone right down the railway, and made their way back to the stables,' thought Julian, every time he awoke. 'I do hope they are safe, and Timmy too. Thank goodness he is with them.'

But Timmy wasn't with them, of course. He was padding across the misty moor all by himself, puzzled, and with a badly aching head. Why had George sent him to Henry? He didn't like Henry. He didn't think that George did, either. And yet she had sent him to find her. Very strange!

Still, George had given him his orders, and he loved her and always obeyed her. He padded over the heather and grass. He didn't bother about keeping to the railway line. He knew the way back without even thinking about it!

It was still night, though soon the dawn would come. But the mist was so thick that even the dawn would not be able to break through it. The sun would have to remain hidden behind the thick swathes of mist.

Timmy came to the stables. He paused to remember which was Henry's bedroom. Ah yes, it was upstairs, next to the room that Anne and George had had.

Timmy leapt into the kitchen through a window left open for the cat. He padded upstairs and came to Henry's room. He pushed at the door and it opened.

In he went and put his paws on her bed. 'Woof,' he said in her ear. 'Woof! Woof! Woof!'

CHAPTER NINETEEN

Good old Tim!

HENRY HAD been fast asleep and snoring. She awoke with a tremendous jump when she felt Timmy's paw on her arm and heard his sharp little bark.

'Oooh! What is it?' she said, sitting up straight in bed and fumbling for her torch. She was quite panic-stricken. She switched on the torch with trembling fingers and then saw Timmy, his big brown eyes looking at her beseechingly.

'Why, Timmy!' said Henry, in amazement. '*Timmy!* Whatever are you doing here? Have the others come back? No, they couldn't have, not in the middle of the night! Why have *you* come then, Timmy?'

'Woof,' said Timmy, trying to make her understand that he was bringing a message. Henry put out her hand to pat his head, and suddenly caught sight of the paper tied to his collar at the back.

'What's this on your collar?' she said, and reached out for it. 'Why, it's paper. Tied on, too. It must be a message!'

She untied the piece of paper and unrolled it. She read it.

'We are prisoners. Follow Timmy and he will bring you to us and you can save us.

GEORGINA.'

Henry was astounded. She looked at Timmy and he looked back, wagging his tail. He pawed at her arm impatiently. Henry read the note again. Then she pinched herself to make sure she was not dreaming.

'Oooh, no I'm awake all right,' she said. 'Timmy, is this note true? *Are* they prisoners? And who does "we" mean? George and Anne, or the whole four? Oh, Timmy I *do* wish you could speak!'

Timmy wished the same! He pawed energetically at Henry. She suddenly saw the cut on his head and was horrified.

'You're hurt, Timmy! Oh, you poor, poor thing. Who did that to you? You ought to have that wound seen to!'

Timmy certainly had a very outsize headache, but he couldn't bother to think about that. He gave a little whine and ran to the door and back.

'Yes, I know you want me to follow you, but I've got to *think*,' said Henry. 'If Captain Johnson was here I'd go and fetch him. But he's away for the night, Timmy. And I'm sure Mrs Johnson would have the fright of her life if I fetched her. I simply don't know what to do.'

'Woof,' said Timmy, scornfully.

'It's all very well to say "Woof" like that,' said Henry, 'but I'm not as brave as you are. I *pretend* I am, Timmy, but I'm not really. I'm afraid of following you! I'm afraid of going to find the others. I might be caught too. And there's a terrible mist, Timmy, you know.

Henry slid out of bed, and Timmy looked suddenly

hopeful. Was this silly girl going to make up her mind at last?

'Timmy, there's no grown-up here tonight except Mrs Johnson, and I really *can't* wake her,' said Henry. 'She's had such a very hard, busy day. I'm going to dress, and then get William. He's only eleven, I know, but he's very sensible.'

She dressed quickly in her riding things and then set off to William's room. He slept by himself across the landing. Henry walked in and switched on her torch.

William awoke at once. 'Who's there?' he demanded, sitting up at once. 'What do you want?'

'It's me. Henry,' said Henry. 'William, a most extraordinary thing has happened. Timmy has arrived in my room with a note on his collar. Read it!'

William took the note and read it. He was most astonished. 'Look,' he said, 'George has signed herself *Georgina*. She wouldn't do that unless things were very urgent. She never, never lets herself be called anything but George. We'll have to follow Tim and go, at once, too!'

'But I can't walk miles in a mist over the moor,' said Henry, in a panic.

'We don't need to. We'll saddle our horses and go on those,' said William, beginning to dress, and sounding very sensible indeed. 'Timmy will lead the way. You go and get the horses out. *Do* buck up, Henry. The others may be in danger. You're acting like a Henrietta!'

That made Henry cross. She went out of the room at once and down into the yard. What a pity Captain Johnson happened to be away just that night. He would have decided everything at once.

Courage came to her when she got the horses. They were surprised but quite willing to go for a night-time ride, even in this thick mist! William came up in a very short time with Timmy behind him. Timmy was delighted to have William with him. He liked him, but he was not very fond of Henry.

He ran forward, just in front of the horses, and they followed behind. Both Henry and William had excellent torches, and kept them shining downwards, so that they should not miss Timmy. He did go out of sight once or twice, but came back immediately, when he heard the horses stopping.

Over the moor they rode. They didn't follow the railway, of course. Timmy didn't need to. He knew the way perfectly!

Once he stopped and sniffed the air. What had he smelt? Henry and William had no idea, but Timmy was puzzled by what he had smelt on the misty air.

Surely he had smelt the smell of the two boys, Julian and Dick? It had come on the air for a moment or two, and Timmy was half-inclined to follow it and see if the smell was right. Then he remembered George and Anne and went on through the swirling mist.

The boys were actually not very far away when Timmy

smelt them. They were still in the middle of the bush, trying to keep warm, and sleep. If only they had known that Timmy was near, with Henry and William! But they didn't.

Timmy led the way. Soon they came to the quarry, but did not see it because of the mist. They went round it, led by Timmy, and rode towards the travellers' camp. Timmy slowed down, and they took warning.

'He's getting near wherever he wants to take us,' whispered William. 'Had we better dismount and tie the horses up, do you think? Their hooves may give a warning that we are near.'

'Yes. Yes, William,' said Henry, thinking that the boy was really very sensible. They dismounted quietly and tied the horses to a nearby birch tree.

They were quite near the hill in front of which was the travellers' camp. The mist was not so thick here, and the two suddenly caught sight of a dark, shadowy caravan, outlined against a camp-fire, left burning nearby. 'We'll have to be very quiet,' whispered William. 'Timmy's brought us to the travellers' camp on the moor. I had an idea that he would. The others must be held prisoner somewhere near – be as quiet as you can.'

Timmy hung his head, panting, his tail down. His head was hurting him very much, and he felt decidedly strange and giddy. But he must get to George, he must!

He led the way to the opening in the hill. William and Henry were most astonished. They followed Timmy through the maze of passages, wondering how he knew the way so surely. But Timmy didn't falter. He only needed to go somewhere once, and after that he never forgot the way!

He was going very slowly now, and his legs felt peculiar and shaky. He wanted to lie down and put his aching head on his paws. But no, he must find George. He must find George.

George and Anne were lying in the little cave, asleep. They were uncomfortable, and the cave was hot, so they were restless, waking up every few minutes. But both were asleep when Timmy walked slowly into the cave, and flopped down beside George.

George awoke when she heard William and Henry come into the cave. She thought it might be Sniffer's father coming back, and she hastily put the ropes round her waist so that she would look as if she were still tied up. Then she heard Timmy panting, and switched on her torch eagerly.

It showed her Timmy, and Henry and William! Henry was full of amazement when she saw George and Anne with ropes round their waists. She gaped at them.

'Oh, Timmy darling, you fetched help!' said George, putting her arms round his neck. 'Oh, Henry, I'm *so* glad you've come. But didn't you bring Captain Johnson too?'

'No. He's away,' said Henry. 'But William's here. We rode, and Timmy guided us. What*ever's* happened, George?'

Anne awoke just then, and couldn't believe her eyes when she saw the visitors! There was a hasty discussion, and then William spoke firmly.

'If you want to escape, you'd better come now, while the travellers' camp is asleep. Timmy can guide us out of this rabbit warren of a hill. We'd never be able to find our way out alone. Come on!'

'Come on, Tim,' said George, shaking him gently. But poor old Timmy was feeling very peculiar. He couldn't see things properly. George's voice sounded blurred to him. His head felt as heavy as lead, and somehow his legs wouldn't carry him. The blow on his head was taking real effect now, and the hurried journey over the moor and back was making it worse.

'He's ill!' said George, in a panic. 'He can't get up! Oh Timmy, what's the matter?'

'It's that cut on his head,' said William. 'It's pretty bad, and he's worn out with coming to fetch us and running all the way back again. He can't possibly guide us back, George. We'll have to do the best we can by ourselves.'

'Oh, poor, poor Timmy!' said Anne, horrified at seeing the dog stretched out quite limp on the floor of the cave. 'George, can you carry him?'

'I think so,' said George, and she lugged him up in her arms. 'He's awfully heavy, but I think I can just manage him. Perhaps the fresh air will revive him when we get outside.'

'But, George, we don't know our way out of here,' said

Anne, fearfully. 'If Timmy can't lead us, we're lost! We'd end up by wandering miles and miles inside the hill and never getting out!'

'Well, we'll simply *have* to make a shot at it,' said William. 'Come on, I'll lead the way. We really MUST go!'

He went out of the cave and down a passage; the others followed, George carrying the limp Timmy. But very soon William came to a fork and stopped.

'Oh dear – do we go to the left or the right?' he wondered.

Nobody knew. George shone her torch here and there, trying to remember. The beam of light picked up something on the ground nearby.

It was two sticks, one short and one long, in the shape of a cross! George gave an exclamation.

'Look – a patrin! Left by Sniffer to show us the way out. We have to take the passage that the long stick points to! Oh, I hope that Sniffer has left patrins at every corner and every fork!'

They took the right-hand way and went on, their torches making long beams in the darkness, and at every place where they might go wrong, they saw a patrin, a message left by Sniffer to show them the right way to go.

'Another cross, we go *this* way,' said Anne.

'Here's a patrin again, we take *this* fork!' said George. And so it went on until they came safely to the entrance of the hill. How thankful they were to see the mist. At least it meant that they were in the open air!

'Now to get to the horses,' said William. 'They will each have to carry two of us at once, I'm afraid.'

And then, just as they were making their way to where they had left the horses, the travellers' dogs began to bark the place down!

'They've heard us!' said William, desperately. 'Buck up! We'll be stopped if we don't get off at once!'

Then a voice shouted loudly. 'I can see you over there, with your torches! Stop at once! Do you hear me? STOP!'

CHAPTER TWENTY

Excitement in the morning

THE DAWN was coming now. The mist was no longer full of darkness, but was white, and thinning rapidly. The four children hurried to the horses, which were stamping impatiently by the trees. George couldn't go very fast because of Timmy. He really was very heavy.

Suddenly he began to struggle. The fresh, cool air had revived him and he wanted to be set down. George put him down thankfully, and he began to bark defiantly at the travellers who were now coming out of their caravans, their dogs with them.

The four children mounted hurriedly and the horses were surprised at the double weight. William swung his horse's head round and set off with George sitting behind him. Henry took Anne. Timmy, feeling much better, ran after them, his legs no longer feeling so shaky.

The travellers ran too, shaking their fists and shouting. Sniffer's father was amazed beyond measure. Why, there were the two girls he had tied up – and that dog he had sent off to trick the other two boys on the moor.

Then who were these on horseback, and how had they found their way to the hill? How had the prisoners been able to find their way *out* of the hill, too? That was a real puzzle to Sniffer's father.

The travellers tore after the horses, but the dogs contented themselves with excited barks. Not one of them dared to go after Timmy. They were afraid of him.

The horses went off as fast as they dared in the mist, Timmy running in front. He seemed very much better, though George was afraid it was only the excitement that now kept him going. She glanced back at the travellers. They would never catch up now, thank goodness!

Somewhere behind the mist the sun was shining. Soon it would disperse the strange fog that had come up so suddenly from the sea. She glanced down at her watch. Good gracious, could it really be almost six o'clock in the morning? It was tomorrow now!

She wondered what had happened to Julian and Dick. She thought of Sniffer gratefully, and all those patrins he had left in the hill. They would never have got out but for those. She thought of Henry and William, and gave William a sudden tight hug round the waist for coming out in the middle of the night and rescuing them!

'Where are Julian and Dick, do you suppose?' she said to William. 'Do you think they are still lost on the moor? Ought we to shout, and look for them?'

'No,' called back William over his shoulder 'We're going straight back to the stables. They can look after themselves!'

* * *

Dick and Julian had certainly tried to look after themselves, that cold, misty night, but not very successfully. By the time that their torch showed them that it was a quarter to five by their watches, they had had enough of the bush they were in. If only they had known it, Henry and William, with Timmy, were just then riding over the moor, not a great distance from where they were!

They got out of the bush, damp and stiff. They stretched themselves and looked into the dark night, still full of mist.

'Let's walk,' said Julian. 'I can't bear keeping still in this mist. I've got my compass. If we walk due west we should surely come to the edge of the moor, not far from Milling Green.'

They set off, stumbling in the now dim light of the torch, whose battery was getting low. 'It will give out soon,' groaned Dick, giving it a shake. 'Blow the thing! It hardly gives us any light now, and we simply must keep looking at the compass.'

Julian tripped against something hard and almost fell. He snatched the torch from Dick. 'Quick, let me have it!'

He shone it on what had tripped him and gave a delighted exclamation. 'Look, it's a rail! We're on the railway line again. What a bit of luck!'

'I should *think* so!' said Dick, relieved. 'This torch is just about finished. Now, for GOODNESS' sake don't let's lose this railway line. Stop at once if you can't feel it with your foot.'

'To think we were so jolly near the line after all, and didn't know it!' groaned Julian. 'We could have been back at the stables ages ago. I do hope the girls got back safely and didn't alarm anyone about us. They'd know we would come back as soon as it was daylight, anyhow, if we could follow the lines!'

They stumbled in at the stables' entrance about six o'clock, tired out. Nobody was yet up, it seemed. They found the garden door open, left ajar by William and Henry, and went up to the girls' room, hoping to find them in bed.

But the beds were empty of course. They went to Henry's room, to ask her if she had heard anything of the girls, but her bed, though slept in, was empty too!

They went across the landing to William's room. '*He's* gone as well!' said Dick, in great astonishment. 'Where are they all?'

'Let's wake Captain Johnson,' said Julian, who had no idea that the captain was away for the night. So they awakened a very startled Mrs Johnson, and almost scared the life out of her, for she thought they were far away, camping on the moor!

She was even more startled when she heard their tale and realised that George and Anne were missing. 'Where *are* the girls, then!' she said, flinging on a dressing-gown. 'This is serious, Julian. They might be completely lost on the moor, or those travellers might have got them! I must telephone my husband, and the police too. Oh dear, oh dear, why did I ever let you go camping out!'

She was in the middle of telephoning, with Julian and Dick beside her, looking very anxious indeed, when the sound of horses' hooves came in the yard below.

'Now goodness me! Who's that?' said Mrs Johnson. 'Horses! Who's riding them at this time of the morning?'

They all went to the window and looked down into the yard. Dick gave a yell that almost made Mrs Johnson fall out of the window!

'Anne! George! Look, there they are, and Timmy too. And gosh, there's Henry, and William! What is all this?'

Anne heard the yell and looked up. Tired as she was, she gave a cheerful wave and a grin. George gave a shout.

'Oh, Julian! Oh, Dick, you're back then! We did hope you would be. After you left us we went back up the lines the wrong way and arrived at the quarry again!'

'And the travellers took us prisoner!' yelled Anne.

'But – but – how do Henry and William come into this?' said poor Mrs Johnson, thinking she must really still be asleep. 'And what's the matter with Timmy?'

Timmy had suddenly flopped on the ground. The excitement was over, they were home, now he could put his poor aching head on his paws and sleep!

George was off her horse immediately. 'Timmy! Darling Timmy! *Brave* Timmy! Help me, William. I'll take him upstairs to my room and see to that cut.'

By this time all the other children were awake and there was such a pandemonium going on that Mrs Johnson couldn't make herself heard.

Children in dressing-gowns and without, children shouting and yelling, children pouring into the yard and asking questions; William trying to quiet the two horses which were getting very excited at all this sudden clamour; and all the cocks round about crowing their heads off! *What* an excitement!

The sun suddenly shone out brilliantly, and the last wisps of mist disappeared. 'Hurrah! That mist has gone!' shouted George. 'The sun's out. Cheer up, Timmy. We'll all be all right now!'

Timmy was half-carried, half-dragged up the stairs by William and George. George and Mrs Johnson examined his cut head carefully, and bathed it.

'It really should have been stitched up,' said Mrs Johnson, 'but it seems to be healing already. How wicked to hit a dog like that!'

Soon there was the sound of horse's hooves again in the yard, and Captain Johnson arrived, looking very anxious. At almost the same moment a car slid in at the gates, a police car, with two policemen who had been sent to inquire about the missing girls! Mrs Johnson had forgotten to telephone again to say they had arrived.

'Oh dear, I'm so sorry to have bothered you,' said Mrs Johnson to the police sergeant. 'The girls have just arrived back, but I still don't know what has really happened. Still, they're safe, so please don't bother any more.'

'Wait!' said Julian, who was in the room, too. 'I think we *shall* need the police! Something very peculiar has been happening up on the moor.'

'Really? What's that?' said the sergeant, taking out a notebook.

'We were camping there,' said Julian. 'And a plane came over, very low, guided by a lamp set in a sandpit by the travellers.'

'A lamp set by the *travellers*!' said the sergeant, surprised. 'But why should they need to guide a plane? I suppose it landed?'

'No. It didn't,' said Julian. 'It came again the next night, and did exactly the same thing, swooping low and circling.

But this time it dropped packages!'

'Oh, it did, did it?' said the sergeant, more interested. 'For the travellers to pick up, by any chance?'

'Yes,' said Julian. 'But the plane's aim wasn't very good, and the packets fell all round *us* and almost hit us. We ran for shelter, because we didn't know if there were any explosives or not!'

'Did you pick up any of the packages?' asked the sergeant. Julian nodded.

'Yes, we did, and I opened one.'

'What was in it?'

'Paper money, dollars!' said Julian. 'In one packet alone there were scores of notes and each note was for a hundred dollars, about fifty pounds a time! Thousands of pounds' worth thrown all around us!'

The sergeant looked at his companion. 'Ha! Now we know! This explains a lot that has been puzzling us, doesn't it, Wilkins?'

Wilkins, the other policeman, nodded grimly. 'It certainly does. So that's what happens! That's how the gang get the dollars over here, from that printing press in northern France. Just a nice little run in a plane!'

'But why do they throw the packets down for the *travellers* to collect?' asked Julian. 'Is it so that they can give them to someone else? Why don't they bring them openly into the country? Surely anyone can bring *dollars* here?'

'Not *forged* ones, my lad,' said the sergeant. 'These will

all be forged, you mark my words. The gang have got a headquarters near London, and as soon as those packets are handed over to them by one of the travellers, they will set to work passing them off as real ones, paying hotel bills with them, buying all kinds of goods and paying for them in notes that aren't worth a penny!'

'Whew!' said Julian. 'I never thought of them being forged!'

'Oh yes. We've known of this gang for some time, but all we knew was that they had a printing press to print the notes in northern France, and that somehow the rest of the gang here, near London, received them and passed them off as real ones,' said the sergeant. 'But we didn't know how they were brought here, nor who took them to the gang near London.'

'But now we know all right!' said Wilkins. 'My word, this is a pretty scoop, Sergeant. Good kids these, finding out what we've been months trying to discover!'

'Where are these packages?' said the sergeant. 'Did you hide them? Did the travellers get them?'

'No, we hid them,' said Julian. 'But I guess the travellers will be hunting all over the place for them today, so we'd better get on the moors quick, Sergeant.'

'Where did you hide them?' said the sergeant. 'In a safe place, I hope!'

'Oh very!' said Julian. 'I'll call my brother, Sergeant. He'll come with us. Hey, Dick! Come on in here, and you'll hear a very interesting bit of news!'

CHAPTER TWENTY-ONE

The end of the mystery

MRS JOHNSON was amazed to hear that the police wanted Julian and Dick to go out on the moors again.

'But they're tired out!' she said. 'They need something to eat. Can't it wait?'

'I'm afraid not,' said the sergeant. 'You needn't worry, Mrs Johnson. These boys are tough!'

'Well, actually I don't think that the travellers can *possibly* find the packets,' said Julian. 'So it wouldn't matter if we had a bite to eat. I'm ravenous!'

'All right,' said the big policeman, putting away his notebook. 'Have a snack and we'll go afterwards.'

Well, of course, George, Anne and Henry all wanted to go too, as soon as they heard about the proposed jaunt over the moors!

'What! Leave us out of *that*!' said George, indignantly. 'What a hope! Anne wants to come too.'

'So does Henry,' said Anne, looking at George, 'even though she didn't help to find the packages of notes.'

'Of *course* Henry must come,' said George at once, and Henry beamed. George had been very struck indeed with Henry's courage in coming with William to rescue her and Anne, and very pleased that she hadn't boasted about it!

But Henry knew that William was the one mostly to praise, and she had been unexpectedly modest about the whole affair.

It was quite a large party that set off after everyone had made a very good breakfast. Mrs Johnson had set to work cooking huge platefuls of bacon and egg, exclaiming every now and again when she thought of all that had happened up on the moors.

'Those travellers! And fancy that plane coming like that – dropping money all over the place! And the travellers tying up Anne and George in that hill. I never heard anything like it in my life!'

Captain Johnson went with the party too. He could hardly believe the extraordinary tale that the four had to tell – five, with old Timmy! Timmy now had a beautiful patch on his head, and was feeling extremely important. Wait till Liz saw that!

Ten people set out, including Timmy, for William had been included in the party too. He tried to guess where Julian had hidden the notes, but he couldn't, of course. Julian firmly refused to tell anyone. He wanted it to be a real surprise.

They came to the quarry at last, having walked all the way up the old railway line. Julian stood on the edge of the quarry and pointed out the travellers' camp.

'Look, they're leaving,' he said. 'I bet they were afraid we'd spread the news of their behaviour, after the girls escaped.'

Sure enough, the caravans were moving slowly away.

'Wilkins, as soon as you get back, give word to have every traveller watched if he leaves the caravans,' said the sergeant. 'One of them is sure to have arranged a meeting place to give the gang the packets dropped from the plane, and if we watch those caravans, and every traveller in them, we'll soon be able to put our hands on the gang that spends the forged notes.'

'I bet it's Sniffer's father,' said Dick. 'He's the ring-leader, anyway.'

They watched the caravans move away one by one. Anne wondered about Sniffer. So did George. What had she promised him last night, if he would help them? A bicycle, and to live in a house so that he could ride it to school! Well, it wasn't likely she would ever see the little boy again, but if she did she would certainly have to keep her word!

'Now, where's this wonderful hiding-place?' asked the sergeant, as Julian turned from watching the caravans. He had tried to make out Sniffer and Liz, but the vans were too far away.

'Follow me!' said Julian, with a sudden grin and led the way back up the lines to where they broke off. The gorse bush was there, and the old engine lay on its side as before, almost hidden.

'Whatever's that?' said the sergeant, surprised.

'It's the old Puffing Billy that used to pull the trucks of sand from the quarry,' said Dick. 'Apparently there was a quarrel long ago between the owners of the quarry and the travellers, and the travellers pulled up the lines and the engine ran off and fell over. There it's been ever since, as far as I can see!'

Julian went round to the funnel end, and bent back the prickly gorse branch that hid it. The sergeant looked on in surprise. Dick scraped the sand out of the top of the funnel and then pulled out one of the packages. He had been afraid they would not be there.

'Here you are!' he said, and tossed the packet to the sergeant. 'There are plenty more. I'll come to the one we opened in a minute – yes – here it is.'

The sergeant and Wilkins were amazed to see the packages hauled up from such a peculiar hiding-place. No wonder the travellers hadn't found them. Nobody would ever have looked down the funnel of the old engine, even if they had spotted it, half-buried as it was.

The sergeant looked at the hundred-dollar notes in the opened parcel and whistled. 'My word, this is it! We've seen these before, beautiful forgeries they are! If the gang had got rid of *this* lot, a great many people would have suffered. The money is worth nothing! How many packets did you say there were?'

'Dozens!' said Dick, and pulled more of them out of the funnel. 'Gosh, I can't reach the ones at the bottom.'

'Never mind,' said the sergeant. 'Put some sand in to hide them and I'll send a man to poke the rest out with a stick. The travellers have gone and they are the only people likely to hunt for them. This is a wonderful scoop! You kids have certainly put us on to something.'

'I'm glad,' said Julian. 'I say, we'd better collect all the things we left here yesterday, hadn't we? We went off in rather a hurry, you see, Sergeant, and left our things in the quarry.'

He and George went into the quarry to collect the things they had left there. Timmy went with them. He suddenly growled, and George stopped, her hand on his collar.

'What's up, Tim? Ju, there must be somebody here! Is it one of the travellers, do you think?'

Then Timmy stopped growling and wagged his tail. He dragged away from George's hand and ran over to one of the little caves in the sandy walls. He looked most peculiar with the patch on his head.

Out of the cave came Liz! As soon as she saw Timmy she began to turn head-over-heels as fast as she could. Timmy stared in wonder – what a dog! How could she turn somersaults like that?

'Sniffer!' called George. 'Come on out. I know you're there!'

A pale, worried face looked out of the cave. Then Sniffer's thin, wiry little body followed, and soon he was standing in the quarry, looking scared.

'I got away from them,' he said, nodding his head towards where the travellers' camp had been. He went up to George, and gave a sniff.

'You said I could have a bike,' he said.

'I know,' said George. 'You *shall* have one, Sniffer. If you hadn't left us patrins in that hill, we'd never have escaped!'

'And you said I could live in a house and ride my bike to school,' said Sniffer urgently. 'I can't go back to my father, he'd punish me now. He saw those patrins I left in the hill and he chased me all over the moor for miles. But he didn't catch me. I hid.'

'We'll do the best we can for you,' promised Julian, sorry for this little waif. Sniffer sniffed.

'Where's that hanky?' demanded George. He pulled it out of his pocket, still clean and folded. He beamed at her.

'You're quite hopeless,' said George. 'Listen, if you want to go to school, you'll *have* to stop that awful sniff and use your hanky. See?'

Sniffer nodded, but put the hanky carefully back into his pocket. Then the sergeant came into the quarry and Sniffer fled at the sight of him!

'Funny little thing,' said Julian. 'Well, I should imagine that his father will be sent to prison for his share in this affair, so Sniffer will be able to get his wish and leave the caravan life to live in a house. We might be able to get him into a good home.'

'And I shall keep my word, and take some money out of my savings bank and buy him a bicycle,' said George. 'He deserves it! Oh, do look at Liz – simply *adoring* Timmy and his patch. Don't look so important, Tim – it's only a patch on your cut!'

'Sniffer!' called Julian. 'Come back. You needn't be afraid of this policeman. He is a friend of ours. He'll help us to choose a bicycle for you.'

The sergeant looked extremely surprised at this remark, but at any rate it brought Sniffer back at once!

'Well, we'll go back now,' said the sergeant. 'We've got what we want, and Wilkins has already started back to get somebody on to watching the travellers. Once we find out who they have to report to about this forged money we shall feel happy.'

'I hope Wilkins went along down the railway,' said Julian. 'It's so easy to get lost on this moor.'

'Yes. He had the sense to do that, after hearing how *you* got lost!' said the sergeant. 'It's wonderful up here, isn't it, so peaceful and quiet and calm.'

'Yes, you'd never think that mysteries could happen up here, would you?' said Dick. 'Old ones, and new ones! Well, I'm glad we happened to be mixed up in the newest one. It was quite an adventure!'

They all went back to the stables, to find that it was now almost lunch-time and that everyone had a large appetite to match the very large lunch that Mrs Johnson had got ready. The girls went upstairs to wash. George went into Henry's room.

'Henry,' she said, 'thanks most awfully. You're as good as a boy any day!'

'Thanks, George,' said Henry, surprised. 'You're *better* than a boy!'

Dick was passing the door and heard all this. He laughed, and stuck his head in at the door.

'I say, do let me share in these compliments!' he said. 'Just tell me I'm as good as a girl, will you?'

But all he got was a well-aimed hairbrush and a shoe, and he fled away, laughing.

Anne gazed out of her bedroom window over the moor. It looked so peaceful and serene under the April sun. No mystery about it now!

'All the same, it's a good name for you,' said Anne. 'You're full of mystery and adventure, and your last adventure waited for *us* to come and share it. I really think I'd call this adventure "Five Go To Mystery Moor".'

It's a good name, Anne. We'll call it that too!

Join the adventure!

If you can't wait to explore further with **THE FAMOUS FIVE**, read the next book in the series:

Do you want to solve a mystery?

Enid Blyton

The Secret Seven

Join Peter, Janet, Jack, Barbara, Pam, Colin, George and Scamper as they solve puzzles and mysteries, foil baddies, and rescue people from danger – all without help from the grown-ups. Enid Blyton wrote fifteen stories about the Secret Seven. These editions contain brilliant illustrations by Tony Ross, plus extra fun facts and stories to read and share.

More classic stories from the world of

Enid Blyton

The Naughtiest Girl

Elizabeth Allen is spoilt and selfish. When she's sent away to boarding school she makes up her mind to be the naughtiest pupil there's ever been! But Elizabeth soon finds out that being bad isn't as simple as it seems. There are ten brilliant books about the Naughtiest Girl to enjoy.

Enid Blyton®

is one of the most popular children's authors of all time. Her books have sold over 500 million copies and have been translated into other languages more often than any other children's author.

Enid Blyton adored writing for children. She wrote over 700 books and about 2,000 short stories. *The Famous Five* books, now 75 years old, are her most popular. She is also the author of other favourites including *The Secret Seven*, *The Magic Faraway Tree*, *Malory Towers* and *Noddy*.

Born in London in 1897, Enid lived much of her life in Buckinghamshire and loved dogs, gardening and the countryside. She was very knowledgeable about trees, flowers, birds and animals. Dorset – where some of the Famous Five's adventures are set – was a favourite place of hers too.

Illustration by Laura Ellen Anderson.

Enid Blyton's stories are read and loved by millions of children (and grown-ups) all over the world. Visit enidblyton.co.uk to discover more.

THE FAMOUS FIVE

FIVE HAVE PLENTY OF FUN

Have you read all THE FAMOUS FIVE books?

1. Five on a Treasure Island
2. Five Go Adventuring Again
3. Five Run Away Together
4. Five Go to Smuggler's Top
5. Five Go Off in a Caravan
6. Five on Kirrin Island Again
7. Five Go Off to Camp
8. Five Get Into Trouble
9. Five Fall Into Adventure
10. Five on a Hike Together
11. Five Have a Wonderful Time
12. Five Go Down to the Sea
13. Five Go to Mystery Moor
14. Five Have Plenty of Fun
15. Five on a Secret Trail
16. Five Go to Billycock Hill
17. Five Get Into a Fix
18. Five on Finniston Farm
19. Five Go to Demon's Rocks
20. Five Have a Mystery to Solve
21. Five Are Together Again

The Famous Five Colour Short Stories

1. Five and a Half-Term Adventure
2. George's Hair is Too Long
3. Good Old Timmy
4. A Lazy Afternoon
5. Well Done, Famous Five
6. Five Have a Puzzling Time
7. Happy Christmas, Five
8. When Timmy Chased the Cat

Enid Blyton®

THE FAMOUS FIVE

FIVE HAVE PLENTY OF FUN

Illustrated by Eileen A. Soper

HODDER

HODDER CHILDREN'S BOOKS

First published in Great Britain in 1955 by Hodder & Stoughton
This edition published in 2016

20

A CIP catalogue record for this book is available from the British Library.

ISBN 978 1 444 93644 5

Printed and bound in Great Britain by Clays Ltd, Elcograf S.p.A.

The paper and board used in this book are made from wood from responsible sources.

Hodder Children's Books
An imprint of
Hachette Children's Group
Part of Hodder & Stoughton
Carmelite House
50 Victoria Embankment
London EC4Y 0DZ

An Hachette UK Company
www.hachette.co.uk
www.hachettechildrens.co.uk

CONTENTS

1 AT KIRRIN COTTAGE 1
2 A VISITOR IN THE NIGHT 10
3 ANNOYING NEWS 20
4 BERTA 29
5 IN THE MORNING 38
6 A FEW UPSETS 47
7 A LITTLE CONFERENCE 56
8 A TRANSFORMATION 65
9 A SUDDEN TELEPHONE CALL 74
10 A PUZZLING THING 83
11 ON KIRRIN ISLAND AGAIN 93
12 VERY SUSPICIOUS 102
13 A HORRID SHOCK 111
14 WHERE IS GEORGE? 120
15 DISCOVERIES IN THE WOOD 129
16 JO! 138
17 TO GRINGO'S FAIR 147
18 SPIKY IS VERY HELPFUL 156
19 AN EXCITING PLAN 165
20 A THRILLING TIME 173
21 MOST UNEXPECTED! 183
22 'THESE KIDS SURE ARE WUNNERFUL!' 191

CHAPTER ONE

At Kirrin Cottage

'I FEEL as if we've been at Kirrin for about a month already!' said Anne, stretching herself out on the warm sand, and digging her toes in. 'And we've only just come!'

'Yes – it's funny how we settle down at Kirrin so quickly,' said Dick. 'We only came yesterday, and I agree with you, Anne – it seems as if we've been here ages. I love Kirrin.'

'I hope this weather lasts out the three weeks we've got left of the holiday,' said Julian, rolling away from Timmy, who was pawing at him, trying to make him play. 'Go away, Timmy. You're too energetic. We've bathed, had a run, played ball – and that's quite enough for a little while. Go and play with the crabs!'

'Woof!' said Timmy, disgusted. Then he pricked up his ears as he heard a tinkling noise from the promenade. He barked again.

'Trust old Timmy to hear the ice-cream man,' said Dick. 'Anyone want an ice-cream?'

Everyone did, so Anne collected the money and went off to get the ice-creams, Timmy close at her heels. She came back with five cartons of ice-cream, Timmy jumping up at her all the way.

'I can't think of anything nicer than lying down on hot sand with the sun on every part of my body, eating an ice-cream, and knowing there are still three weeks' holiday in front of us – at Kirrin too!' said Dick.

'Yes. It's heaven,' said Anne. 'It's a pity your father has visitors today, George. Who are they? Have we got to dress up for them?'

'I don't think so,' said George. 'Timmy, you've eaten your ice-cream in one gulp. What a frightful waste!'

'When are these people coming?' asked Dick.

'About half past twelve,' said George. 'They're coming

to lunch – but thank goodness Father told Mother he didn't want a pack of children gobbling all round him and his friends at lunch, so Mother said we could go in at half past twelve, say how-do-you-do and then clear off again with a picnic basket.'

'I must say I think your father has some good ideas at times,' said Dick. 'I suppose they are some scientist friends of his?'

'Yes. Father's working on some great scheme with these two men,' said George. 'One of them's a genius, apparently, and has hit on an idea that's too wonderful for words.'

'What kind of modern idea is it?' said Julian, lazily, holding out his fingertips for Timmy to lick off smears of ice-cream. 'Some spaceship to take us on day trips to the moon – or some new bomb to set off – or . . .'

'No, I *think* it's something that will give us heat, light and power for almost nothing!' said George. 'I heard Father say that it's the simplest and best idea anyone had ever worked out, and he's awfully excited about it. He called it a "gift to mankind" and said he was proud to have anything to do with it.'

'Uncle Quentin is very clever, isn't he?' said Anne. George's father was the uncle of Julian, Dick and Anne, and they were cousins to George – short for Georgina. Once more they had all come down to Kirrin for part of their holiday, the last three weeks.

George's father was certainly clever. All the same,

George sometimes wished that he was a more *ordinary* parent, one who would play cricket or tennis with children, and not be so horrified at shouting and laughter and silly jokes. He always made a fuss when George's mother insisted that George should have her cousins to stay.

'Noisy, rowdy, yelling kids!' he said. 'I shall lock myself in my study and stay there!'

'All right, dear,' said his wife. 'You do that. But you know perfectly well that they will be out practically all day long. George *must* have other children to stay sometimes, and her three cousins are the nicest ones I know. George loves having them here.'

The four cousins were very careful not to upset George's father. He had a very hot temper and shouted at the top of his voice when he was angry. Still, as Julian said, he really couldn't *help* being a genius, and geniuses weren't ordinary people.

'Especially *scientific* geniuses who might easily blow up the whole world in a fit of temper,' said Julian, solemnly.

'Well, I wish he wouldn't keep blowing *me* up if I let a door bang, or set Timmy barking,' said George.

'That's only to keep his hand in,' said Dick. 'Just a bit of practice at blowing up!'

'Don't be an ass,' said George. 'Does anyone feel like another bathe?'

'No. But I don't mind going and lying in the very edge of the sea, and letting the waves there just curl over me,' said Dick. 'I'm absolutely baked lying here.'

'It *sounds* lovely,' said Anne. 'But the hotter you are the colder the water feels.'

'Come on!' said Dick, getting up. 'I shall hang my tongue out and pant like Timmy soon.'

They all went down to the edge of the water and lay down flat in the tiny curling waves there. Anne gave a little shriek.

'It feels icy! I knew it would. I can't lie down in it yet – I can only sit up!'

However they were soon all lying full-length in the shallow waves at the edge of the sea, sliding down the sand a little every now and again as the tide ebbed farther from them. It was lovely to feel the cool fingers of the sea on every part of them.

Suddenly Timmy barked. He was not in the water with them, but was just at the edge. He thought that lying down in the sea was quite unnecessary! George raised her head.

'What's the matter?' she said. 'There's nobody coming.'

But Dick had heard something too. He sat up hurriedly. 'Gosh, I believe that's someone ringing a bell for us. It sounds like the bell from Kirrin Cottage!'

'But it *can't* be dinner-time yet!' said Anne in dismay.

'It must be,' said Julian, leaping up. 'Blow! This is what comes of leaving my watch in my anorak pocket! I ought to have remembered that time at Kirrin goes more quickly than anywhere else!'

He ran up the beach to his anorak and took his

wristwatch from the pocket. 'It's one o'clock!' he yelled. 'In fact, it's a minute past. Buck up, we'll be awfully late!'

'Blow!' said George. 'Mother won't be at all pleased with us, because those two scientist people will be there!'

They collected their anoraks and tore up the beach. It was not very far to Kirrin Cottage, fortunately, and they were soon running in at the front gate. There was a very large car outside, one of the latest American models. But there was no time to examine it!

They trailed in quietly at the garden door. George's mother met them, looking rather cross.

'Sorry, Aunt Fanny,' said Julian. 'Please forgive us. It was my fault entirely. I'm the only one with a watch.'

'Are we *awfully* late?' asked Anne. 'Have you begun lunch yet? Would you like us just to take our picnic basket and slip off without interrupting?'

'No,' said her aunt. 'Fortunately your uncle is still shut up in his study with his friends. I've sounded the gong once but I don't expect they've even *heard* it! I rang the bell for you because I thought that any moment they might come out, and your uncle would be cross if you weren't there just to say how-do-you-do!'

'But Father's friends don't *usually* want to see us,' said George, surprised.

'Well, one of them has a girl a bit younger than you, George – younger than Anne too, I think,' said her mother. 'And he specially asked to see you all, because his daughter is going to your school next term.'

'We'd better buck up and have a bit of a wash then,' said Julian – but at that very moment the study door opened, and his Uncle Quentin came out with two men.

'Hallo – are these your kids?' said one of the men, stopping.

'They've just come in from the beach,' said Aunt Fanny hurriedly. 'I'm afraid they are not really fit to be seen. I . . .'

'Great snakes!' said the man. 'Don't you dare to apologise for kids like these! I never saw such a fine lot in my life – they're wunnerful!'

He spoke with an American accent, and beamed all over his face. The children warmed to him at once. He turned to George's father. 'These all yours?' he asked. 'I bet you're proud of them!'

'They're not all mine,' said Uncle Quentin, looking quite horrified at the thought. 'Only this one is mine,' and he put his hand on George's shoulder. 'The others are nephews and a niece.'

'Well, I must say you've got a fine boy,' said the American, ruffling George's short curls. As a rule she hated people who did that, but because he mistook her for a boy, she grinned happily!

'My girl's going to your school,' he said to Anne. 'Give her a bit of help, will you? She'll be scared stiff at first.'

'Of course I will,' said Anne, taking a liking to the

huge, loud-voiced American. He didn't look a bit like a scientist. The other man did, though. He was round-shouldered and wore owl-like glasses, and, as Uncle Quentin often did, he stared into the distance as if he was not hearing a single word that anyone said.

Uncle Quentin thought this gossiping had lasted long enough. He waved the children away.

'Come and have lunch,' he said to the other men. The second man followed him at once, but the big American stayed behind. He thrust his hand into his pocket and brought out a pound coin. He gave it to Anne.

'Spend that on yourselves,' he said. 'And be kind to my Berta, won't you?'

He disappeared into the dining-room and shut the door with a loud bang. 'Goodness – what will Father say to a bang like *that*!' said George, with a sudden giggle. 'I like him, don't you? That must be *his* car outside. I can't imagine the other man even riding a bicycle, let alone driving a car!'

'Children – take your picnic basket and *go*!' said Aunt Fanny, urgently. 'I *must* run and see that everything is all right!'

She thrust a big basket into Julian's hands, and disappeared into the dining-room. Julian grinned as he felt the weight of the basket.

'Come along,' he said. 'This feels good! Back to the beach, everyone!'

CHAPTER TWO

A visitor in the night

THE FIVE were on the beach in two minutes, and Julian undid the basket. It was full of neatly packed sandwiches, and packets of biscuits and chocolate. A bag contained ripe plums, and there were two bottles of lemonade.

'Home-made!' said Dick, taking it out. 'And icy-cold. And what's this? A fruit cake – a *whole* fruit cake – we're in luck.'

'Woof,' said Timmy, approvingly, and sniffed inside the basket.

Wrapped in brown paper were some biscuits and a bone, together with a small pot of paste. George undid the packet. '*I* packed these for you, Timmy,' she said. 'Say thank you!'

Timmy licked her so lavishly that she cried out for mercy. 'Pass me the towel, Ju!' she said. 'Timmy's made my face all wet. Get away now, Timmy – you've thanked me quite enough! Get *away*, I said. How can I spread paste on your biscuits if you stick your nose into the pot all the time?'

'You spoil Timmy dreadfully,' said Anne. 'All right, all right – you needn't scowl at me, George! I agree that he's *worth* spoiling. Take your bone a *bit* farther away from me, Tim – it's smelly!'

They were soon eating sardine sandwiches with tomatoes, and egg-and-lettuce sandwiches after that. Then they started on the fruit cake and the lemonade.

'I can't think why people ever have table-meals when they can have picnics,' said Dick. 'Think of Uncle and Aunt and those two men tucking into a hot meal indoors on a day like this. Phew!'

'I liked that big American,' said George.

'Aha! We all know why,' said Dick, annoyingly. 'He thought you were a boy. Will you ever grow out of that, George?'

'Timmy's trying to get at the cake!' said Anne. 'Quick, George, stop him!'

They all lay back on the sand after their picnic, and Julian began a long story of some trick that he and Dick had played on their form-master at school. He was most annoyed because nobody laughed at the funny part, and sat up to see why.

'All asleep!' he said, in disgust. Then he cocked his head just as Timmy pricked up his ears. A loud roaring noise came to him.

'Just the American revving up his car, do you think, Tim?' said Julian. The boy stood up and saw the great car tearing down the sea road.

The day was too hot to do anything but laze. The Five were quite content to do that on their first day together again. Soon they would want to plan all kinds of things, but the first day at Kirrin was a day for picking up old threads, teasing Timmy, getting into the 'feel' of things again, as Dick said.

Dick and Julian had been abroad for four weeks, and Anne had been away to camp and had had a school friend to stay with her at home afterwards. George had been alone at Kirrin so it was wonderful to all the Five to meet together once more for three whole summer weeks. At Kirrin too, Kirrin by the sea, with its lovely beach, its fine boating – and its exciting little island across Kirrin Bay!

As usual the first day or two passed in a kind of dream, and then the children began to plan exciting things to do.

'We'll go to Kirrin Island again,' said Dick. 'We haven't been there for ages.'

'We'll go fishing in Lobster Cove,' said Julian.

'We'll go and explore some of the caves in the cliffs,' said George. 'I meant to do that these hols, but somehow it's no fun going alone.'

On the third day, just as they were finishing making their beds, the telephone rang.

'I'll go!' yelled Julian to his aunt, and went to answer it. An urgent voice spoke at the other end.

'Who's that? Oh, you, Julian – you're Quentin's nephew, aren't you? Listen, tell your uncle I'm coming over tonight – yes, tonight. Latish, say. Tell him to wait up for me. It's important.'

'But, won't you speak to him yourself?' said Julian, surprised. 'I'll fetch him, if you'll . . .'

But the line had gone dead. Julian was puzzled. The man hadn't even given his name – but Julian had recognised the voice. It was the big, cheery American who had come to see his uncle two days before! What had happened? What was all the excitement about?

He went to find his uncle but he was not in his study. So he found his aunt instead.

'Aunt Fanny,' he said, 'I *think* that was the big American on the phone – the one who came to lunch the other day. He said I was to tell Uncle Quentin that he was coming here tonight – late, he said – and that Uncle was to wait up for him, because it was important.'

'Dear me!' said his aunt, startled. 'Is he going to stay the night then? We've no bedroom free now you and the others are here.'

'He didn't say, Aunt Fanny,' said Julian. 'I'm awfully sorry not to be able to tell you any details – but just as I was saying I'd fetch Uncle Quentin, he rang off – in the very middle of what I was saying.'

'How mysterious!' said his aunt. 'And how annoying. *How* can I put him up, if he wants to stay? I suppose he'll come roaring down at midnight in that enormous car of his. I only hope nothing's gone wrong with this latest work your uncle is doing. I know it's tremendously important.'

'Perhaps Uncle will know the American's telephone number and he can ring him up to find out a bit more,' said Julian, helpfully. 'Where is Uncle?'

'He's gone down to the post office, I think,' said his aunt. 'I'll tell him when he gets back.'

Julian told the others about the mysterious phone call. Dick was pleased.

'I didn't have a chance of getting a good look at that enormous car the other day,' he said. 'I think I'll keep awake tonight till the American comes and then nip down and have a look at it. I bet it's got more gadgets on the dashboard than any car I've ever seen!'

Uncle Quentin appeared to be as surprised as anyone else at the phone call, and was inclined to blame Julian for not finding out more details.

'What's he want now?' he demanded, almost as if Julian ought to know! 'I fixed everything up with him the other day. *Every*thing! Each of us three has his own part to do. Mine's the least important, as it happens – and his is the most important. He took all the papers away with him; he can't have left any behind. Coming down in the middle of the night like this – quite extraordinary!'

None of the children except Dick meant to stay awake and listen for the American's coming. Dick put on his bedside light and took up a book to read. He knew he would fall asleep and not wake up for any noise, if he didn't somehow keep himself wide awake!

He listened as he read, his ear alert to hear the coming of any car. Eleven o'clock came – then midnight struck. He listened to the twelve dongs from the big grandfather clock in the hall. Goodness – Uncle Quentin wouldn't be at all pleased that his visitor was so late!

He yawned, and turned over his page. He read on and on. Half past twelve. One o'clock. Then he thought he heard a sound downstairs and opened his door. Yes – it was Uncle Quentin in his study. Dick could hear his voice.

'Poor old Aunt Fanny must be up too,' he thought. 'I can hear their voices. Gosh, I shall soon fall asleep over my book. I'll slip down and out into the garden for a breath of fresh air. I shall keep awake then.'

He put on his dressing-gown and went quietly down the stairs. He undid the bolt of the garden door and slipped out. He stood listening for a moment, wondering if he would hear the roar of the American's car in the stillness of the night.

But all he heard was the sound of the tyres of a bicycle on the road outside. A bicycle! Who was riding about at this time of night? Perhaps it was the village policeman?

Dick stood in the shadows and watched. A man was on the bicycle. Dick could just make him out dimly, a big black shadow in the starlit night. To the boy's enormous surprise, he heard the sound of the man dismounting, then the swish of the leaves in the hedge as the bicycle was slung there.

Then someone came quietly up the path and went round to the window of the study. It was the only room in the house that was lit. Dick heard a tapping on the window, and then it was opened cautiously. His uncle's head appeared.

'Who is it?' he said, in a low tone. 'Is it you, Elbur?'

It apparently was. Dick saw that it was the big American who had visited his uncle two days before. 'I'll open the door,' said his aunt, but Elbur was already putting his leg across the windowsill!

Dick went back to bed, puzzled. How strange! Why should the American come so secretly in the night, why should he ride a bicycle instead of driving his car? He fell asleep still wondering.

He did not know whether the American rode away again, or whether his aunt made a bed for him on a couch downstairs. In fact, when he awoke the next morning, he really wondered if it had all been a dream.

He asked his aunt, when he went down to breakfast. 'Did that man who telephoned come last night?' he said.

His aunt nodded her head. 'Yes. But please say nothing about it. I don't want anyone to know. He's gone now.'

'Was it important?' asked Dick. 'Julian seemed to think it was, when he answered the phone.'

'Yes – it was important,' said Aunt Fanny. 'But not in the way you think. Don't ask me anything now, Dick. And keep out of your uncle's way. He's rather cross this morning.'

'Then something must have gone wrong with this new work he's doing,' thought Dick, and went to warn the others.

'It sounds rather exciting,' said Julian. 'I wonder what's up?'

They kept out of Uncle Quentin's way. They heard him grumbling loudly to his wife about something, they heard him slam down his desk-lid as he always did when he was bad-tempered, and then he settled down to his morning's work.

Anne came running to the others after a time, looking surprised. 'George! I've just been into our room and what do you think! Aunt Fanny's put a camp-bed over in the corner – a camp-bed made up with blankets and everything! It looks an awful squash with two other beds as well in the room – mine and yours!'

'Gosh – someone else is coming to stay then – a girl,' said Dick. 'Or a woman. Aha! I expect it's a governess engaged to look after you and Anne, George, to see that you behave like little ladies!'

'Don't be an idiot,' said George, surprised and cross at the news. 'I'm going to ask Mother what it's all about. I won't have anyone else in our room. I just will *not*!'

But just as she was marching off to tell her mother this, the study door downstairs opened and her father bellowed into the hall, calling his wife.

'Fanny! Tell the children I want them. Tell them to come to my study AT ONCE!'

'Gracious – he does sound cross. Whatever can we have done?' said Anne, scared.

CHAPTER THREE

Annoying news

The four children and Timmy trooped down the stairs together. George's mother was in the hall, just going to call them.

'Oh, there you are,' she said. 'Well, I suppose you heard that you're wanted in the study. I'm coming too. And listen – *please* don't make any more fuss than you can help. I've had quite enough fuss made by Quentin!'

This was very mysterious! What had Aunt Fanny to do with whatever trouble there was? Into the study went the Five, Timmy too, and saw Uncle Quentin standing on the hearthrug looking as dark as thunder.

'Quentin, *I* could have told the children,' began his wife, but he silenced her with a scowl exactly like the one George sometimes put on.

'I've got something to say to you,' he began. 'You remember those two friends of mine – scientists working on a scheme with me – you remember the big American?'

'Yes,' said everyone.

'He gave us a whole pound,' said Anne.

Uncle Quentin took no notice of that remark. 'Well,' he said, 'he's got a daughter – let's see now – she's got some silly name . . .'

'Berta,' said his wife.

'Don't interrupt me,' said Uncle Quentin. 'Yes, Berta. Well, Elbur, her father, has been warned that she's going to be kidnapped.'

'Whatever for?' said Julian, amazed.

'Because it so happens that her father knows more secrets about a new scheme we're planning than anyone else in the world,' said his uncle. 'And he says, quite frankly, that if this girl – what's her name now . . .'

'Berta,' said everyone, obligingly.

'That if this Berta is kidnapped, he will give away every single secret he knows to get her back,' said Uncle Quentin. 'Pah! What's he made of? Traitor to us all! How can he even *think* of giving away secrets for the sake of a silly girl?'

'Quentin, she's his only child and he adores her,' said Aunt Fanny. 'I should feel the same about George.'

'Women are always soft and silly,' said her husband, in a tone of great disgust. 'It's a good thing *you* don't know any secrets – you'd give them away to the milkman!'

This was so ridiculous that the children laughed. Uncle Quentin glared at them.

'This is no laughing matter. It has been a great shock to me to be told by one of the leading scientists of the world that he feels certain he might give all our secrets to the enemy if this – this . . .'

'Berta,' said everyone again, at once.

'If this Berta was kidnapped,' went on Uncle Quentin.

'So he came to ask if we'd take this – this Berta into our own home for three weeks. By that time the scheme will be finished and launched, and our secrets will be safe.'

There was a silence. Nobody looked very pleased. In fact, George looked furious. She burst out at last.

'So *that's* who the bed is for in our room! Mother, have we *got* to be squashed up with nowhere to move about the room, for three whole weeks? It's too bad.'

'For once you and I agree, George,' said her father. 'But I'm afraid you'll have to put up with it. Elbur is in such a state about this kidnapping warning that he couldn't be reasoned with. In fact he threatened to tear up all his figures and diagrams and burn them, if I didn't agree to this. That

would mean we couldn't get on with the scheme.'

'But why has she got to come *here*?' said George, fiercely. 'Why put her on to *us*? Hasn't she any relations or friends she can go to?'

'George, don't be so fierce,' said her mother. 'Apparently Berta has no mother, and has been everywhere with her father. They have no relations in this country – and no friends they can trust. He won't send her back to America because he has been warned by the police that she might be followed there – and at the moment he can't leave this country himself to go with her.'

'But why choose *us*?' said George again. 'He doesn't know a thing about us!'

'Well,' said her mother, with a small smile, 'he met you all the other day, you know – and he was apparently very struck with you – and especially with *you*, George, though I can't imagine why. He said he'd rather his Berta was with you four than with any other family in the world.'

She paused and looked at the four, a harassed expression on her face. Julian went over to her.

'Don't you worry!' he said. 'We'll look after Berta! I won't pretend I'm pleased at having a strange girl to join us these last three precious weeks – but I can see her father's point of view – he's scared for Berta, and he's scared he might find himself spilling the beans if anything happened to her! It might be the only way he could get her back.'

'To think of such a thing!' burst out Uncle Quentin. 'All the work of the last two years! The man must be mad!'

'Now, Quentin, don't think any more about it,' said his wife. 'I'm glad to have the child here. I would hate George to be kidnapped, and I know exactly how he feels. You won't even notice she's here. One more will make no difference.'

'So you say,' grumbled her husband. 'Anyway, it's settled.'

'When is she coming?' asked Dick.

'Tonight. By boat,' said his uncle. 'We'll have to let Joanna the cook into the secret – but nobody else. That's understood, isn't it?'

'Of course,' said the four at once. Then Uncle Quentin sat down firmly at his desk, and the children went hurriedly out of the room, Aunt Fanny behind them, and Timmy pushing between their ankles.

'It's such a pity, and I'm so sorry,' said Aunt Fanny. 'But I do feel we can't do anything else.'

'I bet Timmy will hate her,' said George.

'Now don't you go and make things difficult, George, old thing,' said Julian. 'We're all agreed it can't be helped, so we might as well make the best of it.'

'I hate making the best of things,' said George, obstinately.

'Well,' said Dick, amiably, 'Julian and Anne and I could go back home and take Berta with us if you hate everything so much. I don't particularly want to stay here for three weeks if you're going to put on a Hate all the time.'

'All right, I won't,' said George. 'I'm only letting off steam. You know that.'

'I'm never sure, with you,' said Dick, with a grin. 'Well, look – let's not spoil this one day when we *will* be by ourselves!'

They all tried valiantly to have as good a time as possible, and went out in George's boat for a long row to Lobster Cove. They didn't do any fishing there, but bathed from the boat instead, in water as green and clear as in an open-air bath. Timmy didn't approve of bathing from boats. It was quite easy to jump out of the boat into the water – but he found it extremely difficult to jump in again!

Aunt Fanny had again packed them a wonderful lunch. 'An extra good one to make up for disappointment,' she said, smiling. Anne had given her a hug for that. Here they had all been making such a fuss about having someone extra – and Aunt Fanny had been the only one to feel a real kindness for a child in danger.

They had enough food for tea too, and did not get home until the evening. The sea was calm and blue, and the children could see almost to the bottom of the water, when they leant over the side of the boat. The sky was the colour of harebells as they rowed into the bay and up to the beach.

'Will Berta be there yet, do you suppose?' said George, mentioning the girl for the first time since they had set out that morning.

'I shouldn't think so,' said Julian. 'Your father said she would be coming tonight – and I imagine that as she's coming by boat, it will be dark – so that she won't be seen.'

'I expect she'll be feeling very scared,' said Anne. 'It must be horrid to be sent away to a strange place, to strange people. I should hate it!'

They beached the boat and left it high and dry. Then they made their way to Kirrin Cottage. Aunt Fanny was pleased to see them.

'You *are* in nice time for supper,' she said. 'Though if you ate all I gave you today for your picnics, you'll surely find it difficult to eat very much supper.'

'Oh, I'm *terribly* hungry,' said Dick. He sniffed, holding his nose up in the air just as Timmy often did. 'I believe you've been making your special tomato soup, with real tomatoes, Aunt Fanny!'

'You're too good at guessing,' said his aunt with a laugh. 'It was meant to be a surprise! Now go and wash and make yourselves tidy.'

'Berta hasn't come yet, I suppose, has she?' asked Julian.

'No,' said his aunt. 'And we'll have to think of another name for her, Julian. It would never do to call her Berta now.'

Uncle Quentin didn't appear for supper. 'He is having his in the study by himself,' said Aunt Fanny.

There was a sigh of relief. Nobody had looked forward to seeing Uncle Quentin that night. It took him quite a long time to get over any annoyance!

'How sunburnt you all are!' said Aunt Fanny, looking round the table. 'George, your nose is beginning to peel.'

'I know,' said George. 'I wish it didn't. Anne's never does. Gosh, I'm sleepy!'

'Well, go to bed as soon as you've finished your supper,' said her mother.

'I'd like to. But what about this Berta?' said George. 'What time is she coming? It would be rather mean to be in bed when she arrives.'

'I've no idea what time she will come,' said her mother. 'But I shall wait up, of course. There's no need for anyone else to. I expect she'll be tired and scared, so I shall give her something to eat – some of the tomato soup, if you've left any! – and then pop her into bed. I expect she would be quite glad not to have to meet any of you tonight.'

'Well – *I* shall go to bed,' said Dick. 'I heard Mr Elbur arriving last night, Aunt Fanny, and it was pretty late, wasn't it? I can hardly keep my eyes open tonight.'

'Come on, then – let's all go up,' said Julian. 'We can read if we can't sleep. Good night, Aunt Fanny. Thank you for that lovely picnic food again!'

All the four went upstairs, Anne and Dick yawning loudly, and setting the others off too. Timmy padded behind them, quite glad that George was going to bed so early.

They were all asleep in ten minutes. The boys slept like logs and didn't stir at all. The girls fell fast asleep for about four hours – and then George was awakened by hearing Timmy growl. She sat up at once.

'What is it?' she said. 'Oh – is it Berta arriving, Tim? Let's keep quiet and see what she's like!'

After a minute Timmy growled again. George heard the sound of quiet footsteps on the stairs. Then the bedroom door was slid softly open, and two people stood in the light of the landing lamp. One was Aunt Fanny.

The other, of course, was Berta.

CHAPTER FOUR

Berta

George sat up in bed and stared at Berta. She looked very peculiar indeed. For one thing she was so bundled up in coats and wraps that it was difficult to see if she was big or small, tall or short, and for another thing she was crying so bitterly that her face was all screwed up.

Anne didn't wake up. Timmy was so astonished that, like George, he simply sat and stared.

'Tell Timmy not to make a sound,' whispered George's mother, afraid that the dog might bark the house down, once he began.

George laid a warning hand on Timmy. Her mother gave Berta a little push farther into the room.

'She's been terribly seasick, poor child,' she told George. 'And she's scared and upset. I want her to get into bed as soon as possible.'

Berta was still sobbing, but the sobs grew quieter as she began to feel less sick. George's mother was so kind and sensible that she felt comforted.

'Let's take these things off,' she said to Berta. 'My word, you *are* bundled up! But if you came in an open motorboat I expect you needed them.'

'What am I to call you?' asked Berta, with one last sniff.

'You'd better call me Aunt Fanny, as the others do, I think,' said George's mother. 'I expect you know why you've come to stay with us for a while, don't you?'

'Yes,' said Berta. 'I didn't want to come. I wanted to stay with my father. I'm not afraid of being kidnapped. I've got Sally to look after me.'

'Who's Sally, dear?' asked Aunt Fanny, taking a coat or two off Berta.

'My dog,' said Berta. 'She's downstairs in the basket I was carrying.'

George pricked up her ears at *that* bit of news! 'A dog!' she said. 'We can't have a dog here. Mine would never allow that. Would you, Timmy?'

Timmy gave a small wuff. He was watching this night arrival with great interest. Who was she? He was longing to get down from George's bed and go to sniff at her, but George had her hand on his collar.

'Well, I've brought my dog, and I just reckon she'll have to stay now,' said Berta. 'The boat's gone back. Anyway, I wouldn't go anywhere without Sally. I told my father that, and he said all right then, take her with you! So I did.'

'Mother, tell her how fierce Timmy is and that he would fight any other dog who came here,' said George, urgently. 'I won't have anybody else's dog at Kirrin Cottage.'

To George's annoyance her mother took not the slightest notice. She went on helping Berta take off scarves, thick socks and goodness knows what. George wondered how anyone could possibly exist in all those clothes on a warm summer's night.

At last Berta stood in a simple jersey and skirt, a slim, pretty little girl with large blue eyes and wavy golden hair.

She shook back her hair and rubbed her face with a hanky.

'Thank you,' she said. 'Can I get Sally my dog now?'

'Not tonight,' said Aunt Fanny. 'You see, you are to sleep in that little camp-bed over in the corner – and I can't let you have your dog here too, because she and Timmy might fight unless we introduce them to one another properly. And there is no time to bother about that tonight. Do you feel hungry now? Would you like some tomato soup and biscuits?'

'Yes, please. I do feel a bit hungry,' said Berta. 'I've been so sick on that awful bumpy boat that I don't expect there's anything left inside me at all!'

'Well, look – you unpack your little night-case, and have a wash in the bathroom if you want to, and then get into your pyjamas,' said Aunt Fanny. 'Then hop into bed and I'll bring you up some soup.'

But one look at the scowling George made her change her mind. Better not leave poor Berta with an angry George on her very first night!

'I think perhaps I won't get the soup myself,' she said. 'George, you go and get it, will you? It's warming up in the saucepan on the stove downstairs. You'll see the little soup-cup on the table, and some biscuits too.'

George got out of bed, still looking very mutinous. She watched Berta shake out a nightdress from her night-case and pursed up her lips.

'She doesn't even wear pyjamas!' she thought. 'What a ninny! And she's had the nerve to bring her own dog, too

– spoilt little thing! I wonder where it is? I've a good mind to have a look at it when I'm downstairs.'

But her mother had an idea that George might do that and she went to the door after her. 'George!' she said, warningly, 'I don't want you to open the dog's basket downstairs. I'm not having any dogfights tonight. I shall put him in Timmy's kennel outside before I go to bed.'

George said nothing but went on downstairs. The soup was just about to boil and she whipped it off the stove at once. She poured it into the little soup-cup, placed it on the saucer, and put some biscuits on the side.

She heard a small whimpering sound, and turned round. It came from a fairly large basket over in the corner. George was terribly tempted to go and undo it – but she knew perfectly well that if the new dog ran upstairs to find its mistress, Timmy would bark and wake everybody up! It wasn't worth risking.

She took up the soup. Berta was now in the camp-bed and looked very cosy. Anne was still sleeping peacefully, quite undisturbed by all that was going on. Timmy had taken the opportunity of jumping off George's bed and had gone to examine this newcomer. He sniffed her delicately, and Berta put out her hand and stroked his head.

'What lovely eyes he's got,' she said. 'But he's a mongrel, isn't he? A sort of mixture-dog.'

'Don't you say anything like that to George,' said

Aunt Fanny. 'She adores Timmy. Now – do you feel better? I hope you'll be happy with us, Berta, dear – I am sure you didn't want to come – but your father was so worried. And it will be nice for you to get to know Anne and Georgina before you go to their school next term.'

'Oh – was that Georgina – the one you called George?' said Berta in surprise. 'I wasn't really sure if she was a boy or not. My father told me there were three boys here and one girl – and that's the girl, isn't it – in bed there?'

She pointed to Anne. Aunt Fanny nodded. 'Yes, that's Anne. Your father thought George was a boy, that's why he told you there were three boys and only one girl here, I suppose. The two boys are in the next room.'

'I don't like George very much,' said Berta. 'She doesn't want me here, does she – or my dog?'

'Oh, you'll find George great fun when you get to know her,' said Aunt Fanny. 'Here she comes now with your soup.'

George came in with the soup, and was not at all pleased to see Timmy standing by the camp-bed, being petted by Berta. She set the soup down sharply and pushed Timmy away.

'Thank you,' said Berta, and took the soup-cup eagerly into her hands. 'What *lovely* soup!' she said. George got into bed and turned over on her side. She knew she was behaving badly, but the thought of someone daring to

bring another *dog* to live at Kirrin Cottage was more than she could bear.

Timmy leapt up to lie at her feet as usual. Berta looked at this with much approval.

'I'll have Sally on *my* feet tomorrow!' she said. 'That's an awfully good idea. Pops – that's my father – always let me have Sally in my room, but she had to be in her basket, not on my bed. Tomorrow night she can sleep on my feet, like Timmy does on George's.'

'She will not,' said George, in a fierce voice. 'No dog sleeps in my bedroom except Timmy.'

'Now don't talk any more,' said Aunt Fanny, hurriedly. 'We can settle everything tomorrow when you're not so tired. I'll look after Sally tonight for you, I promise. Lie down now and go to sleep. You look as if you're half-asleep already!'

Berta was suddenly overcome with sleep and flopped down into bed. Her eyes closed, but she managed to force them open and look up at George's mother.

'Good night, Aunt Fanny,' she said, sleepily. 'That's what I was to call you, wasn't it? Thank you for being so kind to me.'

She was asleep almost before she had finished speaking. Aunt Fanny took up the soup-cup and went to the door. 'Are you awake, George?' she said.

George lay absolutely still. She knew that her mother was not pleased with her. It would be better to pretend to be fast asleep!

'I am sure you are awake,' said her mother. 'And I hope you are ashamed of yourself. I shall expect you to make up for this silly behaviour in the morning. It is a pity to behave in such a childish manner!'

She went out of the room, closing the door softly. George put out her hand to Timmy. She *was* ashamed of herself, but she wasn't at all certain that she would behave better in the morning. That silly, soppy girl! Her dog would be as silly as herself, she was sure! And Timmy would simply *hate* having another dog in the house. He would probably growl and snarl to such a degree that Berta would be forced to send her dog away.

'And a good thing too,' murmured George, as Timmy

licked her fingers lovingly. '*You* don't want another girl in the house or another dog either, do you, Timmy? Especially a girl like that!'

Aunt Fanny saw to Berta's dog, and put her safely into Timmy's kennel outside. It had a little door to it, which could be shut, so the dog was safe there, and would not be able to run out.

She went back into the house, cleared up Berta's belongings a little, for they had been thrown higgledy-piggledy into the room, and then turned out the light.

She went upstairs to bed. Her husband had slept soundly all through Berta's late arrival. He had been very sure that he would wake up and welcome the girl as well as his wife, but he hadn't even stirred!

Aunt Fanny was glad. It was much easier for her to deal with a seasick, frightened girl by herself. She climbed thankfully into bed and lay down with a sigh. 'Oh dear – I don't look forward to the morning! What will happen then, with George in this mood, and two dogs to sort out? Berta seems a nice little thing. Well – perhaps they will all get on better than I think!'

Yes – things wouldn't be too easy in the morning. That was quite certain!

CHAPTER FIVE

In the morning

GEORGE WAS the first to wake up in the morning. She at once remembered the events of the night before and looked across at Berta in the camp-bed. The girl was asleep, her wavy golden hair spread over the pillow. George leant across Anne's bed and gave her a sharp nudge.

Anne woke up at once and gazed sleepily at George. 'What's the matter, George? Is it time to get up?'

'Look over there,' whispered George, nodding her head towards Berta. Anne turned over and looked. Unlike George she liked the look of Berta. Her sleeping face was pleasant and open, and her mouth turned up, not down. Anne couldn't bear people whose mouths turned down.

'She looks all right,' whispered back Anne. George frowned.

'She howled like anything when she came,' she told Anne. 'She's a real baby. *And* she's brought a dog!'

'Goodness – Timmy won't like that,' said Anne, startled. 'Where is it?'

'Down in Timmy's kennel,' said George, still whispering. 'I haven't seen it. It was in a closed basket last night and

I didn't dare open it in case it tore upstairs and had a fight with Tim. But it can't be very big. I expect it's a horrible peke, or some silly little lap-dog.'

'Pekes aren't horrible,' said Anne. 'They may be small and have funny little pug noses, but they're awfully brave. Fancy having another dog! I can't *think* what Timmy will say!'

'It's a pity Berta isn't our kind,' said George. 'Look at her pale face – not a scrap of suntan! And she looks *weedy*, doesn't she? I'm sure she couldn't climb a tree or row a boat, or . . .'

'Sh! She's waking up,' said Anne warningly.

Berta yawned and stretched herself. Then she opened her eyes and looked round. At first she had no idea where she was, and then she suddenly remembered. She sat up.

'Hallo!' said Anne, and smiled at her. 'You weren't there when I came to bed last night. I was surprised to see you this morning.'

Berta took an immediate liking to Anne. 'She's got kind eyes,' she thought. 'She's not like the other girl. I like this one!'

She smiled back at Anne. 'Yes – I came in the middle of the night,' she said. 'I came by motorboat and the sea was so bumpy that I was frightfully sick. My father didn't come with me but a friend of his did and he carried me from the boat to Kirrin Cottage. Even my legs felt seasick!'

'Bad luck!' said Anne. 'You didn't really enjoy the adventure then!'

'No. I can do without adventures!' said Berta. 'I'm not keen on them. Especially when Pops gets all excited and worried about me – he fusses round me like a hen, dear old Pops. I shall hate being away from him.'

George was listening to all this. Not keen on adventures! Well, a girl like that wouldn't be, of course!

'*I'm* not very keen on adventures either,' said Anne. 'We've had plenty. I prefer adventures when they're all over!'

George exploded. 'Anne! How *can* you talk like that! We've had some *smashing* adventures, and we've enjoyed every one of them. If you feel like that we'll leave you out of the next one.'

Anne laughed. 'You won't! An adventure comes up all of a sudden, like a wind blowing up in the sky, and we're all in it, whether we like it or not. And you know that I like sharing things with you. I say – isn't it time we got up?'

'Yes,' said George, looking at the clock on the mantelpiece. 'Unless Berta wants to have her breakfast in bed? I bet she always does at home.'

'No, I don't. I hate meals in bed,' said Berta. 'I'm going to get up.'

She leapt out of bed and went to the window. Immediately she saw the wide sweep of the bay, sparkling in the morning sun, as blue as cornflowers. The sea-sparkle was reflected into the bedroom, and made it very bright indeed.

'Oh. I *wondered* why our room was so full of brilliant

light,' said Berta. 'Now I know! What a view! Oh, how lovely the sea looks this morning! And what's that little island out there? What a lovely place it looks.'

'That's Kirrin Island,' said George, proudly. 'It belongs to *me*.'

Berta laughed, thinking that George was joking. 'Belongs to *you*! I bet you wish it did. It's really wunnerful!'

'*Wunnerful!*' said George imitating her. 'Can't you say "wonderful"? It's got a D in the middle, you know.'

'Yes. I'm always being told things like that,' said Berta, still staring out of the window. 'I had an English governess and she tried to make me speak like you do. I do try, because I've got to go to an English school. My, my – I wish that island belonged to *me*. I wonder if my pops could buy it.'

George exploded again. '*Buy* it! You donkey, I *told* you it was mine, didn't I?'

Berta turned round in surprise. 'But – you didn't *mean* it, did you?' she said. '*Yours?* But how could it be?'

'It *is* George's,' said Anne. 'It has always belonged to the Kirrin family. That's Kirrin Island. George's father gave it to her, after an adventure we once had.'

Berta stared at George in awe. 'Great snakes! So it *is* yours! Aren't you the lucky one! Will you take me to visit it?'

'I'll see,' said George gruffly, glad to have impressed this American girl so much. Getting her 'Pops' to buy the island indeed! George snorted to herself. What next!

A shout came from the next room. It was Julian. 'Hey, you girls! Are you getting up? We're all too late for a bathe before breakfast this morning. Dick and I have only just woken up.'

'Berta's here!' shouted back Anne. 'We'll get dressed, all of us, and then we'll introduce Berta to you.'

'Are they your brothers?' asked Berta. 'I haven't got any. Or sisters either. I shall be pretty scared of them.'

'You won't be scared of Julian and Dick,' said Anne, proudly. 'You'll wish you had brothers like them. Won't she, George?'

'Yes,' said George, shortly. She was feeling rather annoyed just then because Timmy was standing by Berta, wagging his plumy tail. 'Come here, Timmy. Don't make a nuisance of yourself.'

'Oh, he's not,' said Berta, and patted his big head. 'I like him. He seems simply ENORMOUS after my Sally. But you'll love Sally, George, you really will. Everyone says how sweet she is – and I've trained her beautifully.'

George took no interest in these remarks at all. She flounced off to wash in the bathroom, but Julian and Dick were there, and there was a lot of yelling and shouting as George tried to make them hurry up and get out. Berta laughed.

'That sounds nice and family-like,' she said. 'You don't get that sort of thing if you're an only child. What do I wear here?'

'Oh – something very simple,' said Anne, looking at the suitcase open on the floor, showing a collection of Berta's clothes. 'That shirt and those jeans will do.'

They were ready just as the gong rang for breakfast. A delicious smell of frying bacon and tomatoes came up the stairs, and Berta sniffed in delight.

'I do like English breakfast,' she said. 'We haven't

gotten around to a proper breakfast in America yet! That's bacon and tomatoes I smell, isn't it? My English governess always said that bacon and eggs made the best breakfast in the world, but I guess the one we're going to have will taste pretty good.'

Uncle Quentin was at the table when the children came down. He looked most surprised to see Berta, having quite forgotten that she was coming. 'Who's this?' he said.

'Now, Quentin – don't pretend you don't know!' said his wife. 'It's Elbur's girl – your friend Elbur. She came in the middle of the night, but I didn't wake you, you were so sound asleep.'

'Ah yes,' said Uncle Quentin, and he shook hands with the rather scared Berta. 'Glad to have you here, er – let me see now – what's your name?'

'Berta,' said everyone in a chorus.

'Yes, yes – Berta. Sit down, my dear. I know your father well. He's doing some wonderful work.'

Berta beamed. 'He's always at work!' she said. 'He works all through the night sometimes.'

'Does he? Well, what a thing to do!' said Uncle Quentin.

'It's a thing you often do yourself, Quentin,' said his wife, pouring out coffee. 'Though I don't suppose you even realise it.'

Uncle Quentin looked surprised. 'Do I really? Bless us all! Don't I go to bed some nights then?'

Berta laughed. 'You're like my pops! Sometimes he doesn't know what day of the week it is, even! And yet he's supposed to be one of the cleverest guys in the world!'

'Guy?' said Uncle Quentin, surprised, immediately thinking of Firework Night. Everyone laughed. Anne patted her uncle's knee. 'It's all right, Uncle,' she said, 'he's not going to sit on the top of a bonfire!'

But Uncle Quentin was not listening. He had suddenly seen a letter marked 'IMPORTANT' on the top of his pile of correspondence, and he picked it up.

'Well, unless I'm much mistaken, here's a letter from your father,' he said to Berta. 'I'll see what it says.'

He opened the letter and read it to himself. Then he looked up. 'It's all about you – er . . .'

'Her name's Berta,' said Aunt Fanny, patiently.

'About you, Berta,' said Uncle Quentin. 'But I must say your father has some very strange ideas. Yes, very strange.'

'What are they?' asked his wife.

'Well – he says she must be disguised – in case anyone comes to find her here,' said Uncle Quentin. 'And he wants her name changed – and, bless us all, he wants us to buy her boy's clothes – and cut her hair short – and dress her up as a boy!'

Everyone listened in surprise. Berta gave a little squeal.

'I won't! I WON'T be dressed up as a boy! I *won't* have my hair cut off. Don't you dare to make me! I WON'T!'

CHAPTER SIX

A few upsets

BERTA LOOKED so upset that Aunt Fanny acted quickly and firmly. 'Don't bother about that letter now, Quentin,' she said. 'We'll go through it afterwards and decide what to do. Let's have our breakfast in peace.'

'I *won't* have my hair cut off,' said Berta, again. Uncle Quentin was not used to being defied openly like this, and he scowled. He looked at his wife.

'Surely you are not going to let this – er what's her name now – Bertha . . .'

'Berta,' said everyone automatically.

'I said that we would not discuss this till after breakfast,' said Aunt Fanny, in the kind of voice that made everyone, including Uncle Quentin, quite certain that she meant what she said. Her husband folded up the letter and opened the next one, frowning. The children looked at one another.

Berta to be a boy! Goodness! If ever anyone looked less like a boy it was Berta! George was most annoyed. She loved to dress like a boy, but she didn't feel inclined to urge anyone else to! She looked at Berta, who was eating her breakfast with tears in her eyes. What a baby! She wouldn't even *look* like a boy, if she was dressed in boys' clothes. She would just look absolutely silly.

Julian began a conversation with his aunt about the garden. She was grateful to him for breaking up the sudden awkwardness caused by the letter. She was very fond of Julian. 'I can always depend on him,' she thought, and talked gladly of the garden fruit, and who would pick the raspberries for lunch and whether the wasps would eat *all* the plums or not!

Dick joined in, and Anne, and soon Berta did too. Only George and her father remained gloomy. They both looked so exactly alike with solemn, rather frowning expressions that Julian nudged Dick and nodded towards them.

Dick grinned. 'Like father, like daughter!' he said. 'Cheer up, George. Don't you like your breakfast?'

George was just about to answer crossly when Anne gave an exclamation. 'Oh, *look* at Uncle Quentin! He's putting mustard on his toast – Aunt Fanny, stop him – he's just going to eat it!'

Everyone roared with laughter. Aunt Fanny managed to smack her husband's hand down from his mouth, just as he was putting his toast and mustard up to it, reading a letter at the same time.

'Hey – what's the matter?' he said, startled.

'*Quentin* – that's the second time this month you've spread your toast with mustard instead of with marmalade,' said his wife. 'Do have a little sense.'

After that everyone became very cheerful. Uncle Quentin laughed at himself, and George saw the funny side and laughed loudly too, which made Timmy bark, and Berta giggled. Aunt Fanny was quite relieved that her husband had done such a silly thing.

'Do you remember when Father poured custard all over his fried fish once?' George said, entering into the talk for the first time. 'And he said it was the best egg-sauce he had ever tasted?'

The conversation was very animated after that, and Aunt Fanny felt happier. 'You children can clear away and wash up the breakfast things for Joanna,' she said. 'Or two of you can and the others can make the beds with me.'

'What about my little dog?' said Berta, suddenly remembering her again. 'I haven't seen her yet, because I was only just in time for breakfast. Where is she?'

'You can go and get her now,' said Aunt Fanny. 'We've all finished. Are you going to start your work, Quentin?'

'Yes, I am,' said her husband. 'So I don't want any yelling or shouting or barking outside my study door.'

He got up and went out of the room. Berta stood up too. 'Where's the kennel?' she said.

'I'll show you,' said Anne. 'We'll go and get your dog and introduce it to Timmy. Coming, George?'

'You can bring the dog in here, and we'll see what Timmy says,' said George, going all gloomy again. 'If he doesn't like the dog – and he won't – it will have to live out in the kennel.'

'Oh *no*,' said Berta, at once.

'Well, you don't want Timmy to *eat* it, do you?' said

George. 'He's very jealous of other dogs in the house. He might go for yours and savage it.'

'Oh *no*!' said Berta, again, looking upset. 'Timmy's nice. He's not a fierce dog.'

'That's all *you* know!' said George. 'We'll, I've warned you.'

'Come on,' said Anne, pulling at Berta's sleeve. 'Let's go and fetch Sally. She must be wondering why nobody bothers about her. I bet Timmy won't mind *terribly*.'

As soon as the two had gone out, George spoke in Timmy's ear. 'You don't like strange dogs who want to come and live here, do you, Tim? You'll growl and snarl like anything, won't you? Growl your very fiercest! I know you won't bite but if you could just growl your loudest, that will be enough. Berta will make that Sally-dog live out of doors then!'

Soon she heard footsteps returning, and Anne's voice exclaiming in delight.

'Oh, she's sweet! Oh, what a darling! Sally, you're a pet! Julian, Dick, Aunt Fanny – do come and see Berta's dog!'

Everyone came into the room, led by Berta and Anne. Berta held the dog in her arms.

It was a tiny black poodle, whose woolly fur was cut away here and there to give it a very funny look. Sally was certainly an attractive little thing! Her sharp little nose sniffed all the time she was carried into the room, and her quick little eyes looked everywhere.

Berta put her down, and the little poodle stood there,

poised on her dainty feet like a ballet dancer about to perform. Everyone but George exclaimed in delight.

'She's a poppet!'

'Sally! Sally, you're a pet!'

'Oh, a poodle! I do love poodles! They look so knowing.'

Timmy stood by George, sniffing hard to get the smell of this new dog. George had her hand on his collar in case he sprang. His tail was as stiff as a ramrod.

The poodle suddenly saw him. She stared at him out of bright little eyes, quite unafraid. Then she pulled away from Berta's hand and trotted right over to Timmy, her funny little tail wagging merrily.

Timmy backed a little in surprise. The poodle danced all round him on her toes, and gave a little whimpering bark, which said as plainly as possible 'I want to play with you!'

Timmy sprang. He leapt in the air and came down with a thud on his big paws, and the little poodle dodged. Timmy's tail began to wag wildly. He sprang again in play, and almost knocked the little poodle over. He barked as if to say 'Sorry, I didn't mean that!'

Then he and the poodle played a most ridiculous game of dodge and run, and although one or two chairs went flying nobody minded – they were all laughing so much at the sight of the quick little poodle leading Timmy such a dance.

At last Sally was tired and sat down in a corner. Timmy

pranced about in front of her, showing off. Then he went up to her and sniffed her nose. He licked it gently, and then lay down in front of her, gazing at her adoringly.

Anne gave a little squeal of laughter. 'He's gazing at Sally exactly as he gazes at you, George!' she cried.

But George was not at all pleased. In fact she was quite astounded. To think that Timmy should *welcome* another dog! To think that he should behave like this when she had told him to do the opposite!

'Aren't they sweet together?' said Berta, pleased. 'I *thought* Timmy would like Sally. Of course Sally is a pedigree dog, and cost a lot of money – and Timmy's only a mongrel. I expect he thinks she's *wunnerful*.'

'Oh, Tim may be a mongrel, but he's absolutely wunnerful too,' said Dick, hastily, pronouncing the word like Berta, to try and get a laugh. He saw George's scowl, and knew how cross she felt at hearing her beloved Timmy compared with a pedigree dog. 'He's a magnificent fellow, aren't you, Timmy?' went on Dick. 'Sally may be a darling, but you're worth more than a *hundred* darlings, aren't you?'

'I think he's beautiful,' said Berta, looking down at Timmy. 'He's got the loveliest eyes I ever did see.'

George began to feel a little better. She called Timmy. 'You're making rather a fool of yourself,' she said to him.

'Now that Timmy and Sally are going to be friends, can I have Sally to sleep on my bed at night, like George has Timmy?' said Berta. 'Please say yes, Aunt Fanny.'

'No,' said George at once. 'Mother, I won't have that. I won't!'

'Well, we'll see what we can do about it,' said her mother. 'Sally was quite happy in the kennel last night, I must say.'

'I'm going to have her sleep with me,' said Berta, scowling at George. 'My father will pay you a lot of money to make me happy. He told me he would.'

'Don't be silly, Berta,' said Aunt Fanny, firmly. 'This isn't a question of money. Now, leave this for a little while, please, and go and do your jobs, all of you. And then we must consider your father's letter, Berta, and see exactly what he wants done. We must certainly try to follow his advice about you.'

'But I don't want to . . .' began Berta, and then felt a firm hand on her arm. It was Julian.

'Come on, kid,' he said. 'Be your age! Remember you're a guest here and put on a few of your best manners. We like American children – but not *spoilt* ones!'

Berta had quite a shock to hear Julian speaking like this. She looked up at him and he grinned down at her. She felt near tears, but she smiled back.

'You haven't any brothers to keep you in your place,' said Julian, linking his arm in hers. 'Well, from now on, while you're here, Dick and I are your brothers, and you've got to toe the line, just like Anne. See? What about it?'

Berta felt that there was nothing in the world she would like better than having Julian for a brother! He was big and tall and had twinkling kindly eyes that made Berta feel he was as responsible and trustable as her father.

Aunt Fanny smiled to herself. Julian always knew the best thing to say and do. Now he would take Berta in hand and see that she didn't upset the household too much. She was glad. It wasn't easy to run a big family like this, with a scientist husband to cope with, unless everyone pulled together!

'You go and help Aunt Fanny with the beds,' said Julian to Berta. 'And take your Sally-dog with you. She's great! But so is Timmy, and don't you forget it!'

CHAPTER SEVEN

A little conference

PEACE REIGNED in the house for a little while. George and Anne went to help the cook with the washing-up. Joanna was pleased, because with eight people in the house, including herself, there was a lot to do.

She had been very astonished that morning to find a fifth child added to the household, but had been told that after breakfast she could go into the sitting-room and hear an explanation! Joanna must certainly be in the secret too!

Upstairs Berta was helping with the beds – not very successfully because she was not used to doing things for herself. But she was very willing to learn and Aunt Fanny was quite pleased with her. Timmy and Sally darted about together and made things rather more difficult than they need have been, popping under beds and out again at top speed.

'I'm glad Timmy likes Sally,' said Berta. 'I knew he would. I can't think why George thought he wouldn't. George is funny, I think.'

'Not really,' said Aunt Fanny. 'She hasn't any brothers or sisters to rub off her corners, and she didn't even know her three cousins till a few years ago, or go to school.

Lonely people aren't so easy to get on with as others – but she is great fun now, as you will soon find out.'

'I'm an only child too,' said Berta. 'But I've always had plenty of other children to play with. My pop saw to that. He's wunnerful – I mean wonDERful. I'll say that word "wonDERful" twenny times, then maybe, I'll get it right.'

'Well, say the word "twenty" as well!' said Aunt Fanny. 'It has a letter T at the end as well as at the beginning, you know. It's "twenTY" not "twenny". But don't make yourself *too* English. It's nice to have a change!'

'WonDERful, wonDERful, wonDERful! TwenTY, twenTY!' chanted Berta, as she made the beds. Dick looked into the room and chuckled.

'Great snakes!' he said, with a grin, and an American accent. 'You shore are wunnerful, baby!'

'Don't be so silly, Dick,' said his aunt, laughing. 'Now – I think we've finished all we have to do, Berta. We'll go downstairs and have a conference. Tell the others, will you?'

Berta, followed closely by Sally, who was also followed closely by an adoring Timmy, went to tell Dick and Julian, and then George and Anne. George was not too pleased with Timmy.

'Where have you been?' she said. 'Can't you stop running about after Sally? She'll get very very tired of you!'

'Wuff!' said Sally, in a high little bark, not at all like Timmy's deep 'Woof!'

Soon all five children and the two dogs, and also Joanna, were in the sitting-room with Aunt Fanny. Berta began to look a little nervous.

Aunt Fanny had the letter that Berta's father had sent. She did not read it out to the children, but told them what was in it. She also explained to Joanna about Berta.

'Joanna, you have always known what important work my husband does,' she said. 'Well, Berta's father does the same kind of work in America, and he and Quentin are working on a great new scheme together.'

'Oh yes,' said Joanna, very much interested.

'Berta's father has been warned by the police that it is possible Berta may be kidnapped and held to ransom, not for money, but for the scientific secrets that he knows,' went on Aunt Fanny. 'So she has been sent to us to be kept safe for three weeks. By that time the scheme will be finished and made public. Berta is going to the same school as Anne and George, and it is a good idea to let them know one another first.'

Joanna nodded. 'I understand that,' she said. 'I think we can keep Berta safe, don't you?'

'Yes,' said Aunt Fanny. 'But her father has now put up some further ideas that he wants us to follow. He says it would be best to disguise her as a boy . . .'

'Jolly good idea,' interrupted Dick.

'And to give her another name – a boy's name,' said Aunt Fanny. 'He wants her to have her hair cut short and . . .'

'Oh please not that!' begged Berta, shaking back her fair, wavy hair. 'I'd hate it. Girls with short hair like boys look so silly, they . . .'

Anne nudged her and frowned. Berta stopped hurriedly, remembering that George had curly hair cut as short as any boy.

'I think we'll have to do what your father says,' said Aunt Fanny. 'This is very important, Berta. You see, if anyone *should* come here looking for you, thinking of kidnapping, they would never recognise you if you were looking exactly like a boy.'

'But my hair,' said Berta, almost in tears. 'How *could* Pops says I'm to have my hair off? He always said it was wunnerful!'

Nobody liked to point out that there was a D in wonderful just then! Berta was really so very upset about her hair.

'Your hair will grow quickly enough,' said Aunt Fanny.

'Her *head's* a good shape,' said Julian, looking at it consideringly. 'She should look nice with short hair.'

Berta cheered up. If Julian thought that, then it wouldn't be so bad.

'But what about clothes?' she said, remembering this point with a look of horror. 'Girls look frightful in boys' clothes. Pops always said so till now.'

'You won't look any worse than George does,' said Dick. 'She's got on a boy's jersey, boy's jeans and boy's shoes this very minute!'

'I think she looks awful,' said Berta, obstinately, and George scowled.

'Well, I think *you*'d look horrible,' she said. 'You wouldn't even *look* like a boy, you'd look little-girlish, silly little sissy-boy. *I* think it's a stupid idea to put you into boy's clothes!'

'Aha! Our George wants to be the only one!' said Dick, slyly, and quickly got out of the way of a punch from the furious George.

'Well,' said Julian. 'I'll go out and buy some things for Berta this morning, so that's settled. What about her hair? Shall *I* cut it short?'

Aunt Fanny was amused at Julian's high-handed way of dealing with Berta and her troubles, and even more amused to see that Berta did not even argue with Julian.

'You can certainly go shopping for Berta if you like,' she said. 'But I'd rather you didn't cut her hair. You'd make her look a scarecrow!'

'I don't mind if Julian cuts it,' said Berta, surprisingly meek all at once.

'I shall cut it for you myself,' said Aunt Fanny. 'Now – what about a boy's name? We can't call you Berta any more, that's certain.'

'I'd rather not have a boy's name,' said Berta. 'It's silly for a girl to be called by a boy's name, like George.'

'If you *mean* to be rude to me, I'll . . .' began George, but got no farther. Julian and Dick had burst into laughter.

'Oh, George – you and Berta will be the death of us!' said Julian. 'Here are you doing all you can to *pretend* to be a boy – and here is Berta doing all she can to get *out* of it! For goodness' sake, let's settle the matter without any more bickering. We'll call Berta Robert.'

'No – that's too like Berta,' said Dick. 'It ought to be a completely different name. We'll call her a good plain boy's name like Jim or Tom or John.'

'No,' said Berta. 'I don't like any of them. Let me have my second name, please.'

'What's that? Another girl's name?' asked Julian.

'Yes. But it's used for a boy too, only then it's spelt differently,' said Berta. 'It's Lesley. It's a nice name, I think.'

'Lesley. Yes – it rather suits you,' said Julian. 'It suits you better than Berta. We'll call you Lesley – and people will think it's Leslie spelt l-i-e at the end, and not l-e-y. All right. Everything's settled.'

'Not quite,' said his aunt. 'I just want to say that you mustn't let Berta – I mean Lesley – out of your sight at all. And you must report at once any mysterious happening or any stranger you see. The local police here know that we have Lesley with us, and why – and anything can be reported to them at once. They also are keeping a good lookout, of course.'

'This almost sounds as if we're in the middle of an adventure!' said Dick, looking pleased.

'I hope not,' said his aunt. 'I don't imagine that anyone will ever guess Berta – I mean Lesley – is anything more than she will appear to be – a boy friend of yours and Julian's, come to stay for a while. Dear me, it's going to be difficult to refer to her as him all the time!'

'It certainly is,' said Julian, standing up. 'If you'll give me some money, Aunt Fanny, I'll go and do a little shopping for Lesley. What size do you think HE needs?'

Everyone laughed. 'HE wears size three shoes,' said Joanna smiling. 'I noticed that this morning.'

'And HE will have to get used to doing his coat buttons up on the right-hand side instead of on the left,' said Anne, joining in the fun.

'SHE will soon get used to that,' said George. 'Won't SHE, Timmy?'

'Don't spoil it all now, George,' said Julian. 'A slip of the tongue, saying SHE instead of HE, might lead to danger for Ber – I mean Lesley.'

'Yes, I know,' said George. 'It's just that she'll never look like a boy, and . . .'

'I don't *want* to look like a boy,' said Berta. 'I think *you* look . . .'

'Here we go again!' said Julian. 'Stop it, Lesley, stop it, George. George, you'd better come out and help me to get the things for Lesley. Come on. And take that scowl off your face. You look like a sulky girl!'

That made George alter her face at once. She couldn't help grinning at the artful Julian.

'I'm coming,' she said. 'Goodbye, Berta. When we come back, you'll be Leslie, haircut and all!'

She and Julian went off. Anne fetched her aunt's sharpest scissors and draped a big towel round Berta's shoulders. Berta looked as if she was going to cry.

'Cheer up,' said Dick. 'You're going to look angelic with short hair! Begin, Aunt Fanny. Let's see what she's like with shorn locks.'

'Sit quite still,' said Aunt Fanny and began. Clip-clip-clip! The wavy golden hair fell to the floor in big strands and Berta began to weep in earnest. 'My hair! I can't bear this. Oh, my hair!'

Soon most of it was on the floor, and Aunt Fanny began to clip what was left as best she could, to make it look as boyish as possible. She made a very good job of it indeed. Dick and Anne watched with the greatest interest.

'There! It's done!' said Aunt Fanny at last. 'Stop crying, Lesley – and let's have a look at you!'

CHAPTER EIGHT

A transformation

BERTA STOOD in the middle of the floor, blinking her tears away. Anne gave a gasp.

'You know – it's *very* odd – but she does look rather like a boy – a very, very good-looking boy!'

'An angelic boy,' said Dick. 'A choirboy or something. She looks smashing! Who would have thought it?'

Aunt Fanny was very struck with Berta's appearance too. 'It's certainly very odd,' she said. 'But there's no doubt about it – when she's – I mean he's – dressed in boy's clothes, he'll make a fine boy. Better than George, actually, because her hair's *really* too curly for a boy.'

Berta went to the looking-glass on the wall. She gave a wail. 'I look awful! I don't know myself! Nobody would EVER recognise me!'

'Splendid!' said Dick, at once. 'You've hit the nail right on the head. Nobody *would* recognise you now. Your father was quite right to say cut your hair off and dress up as a boy. Any prowling kidnapper would never think *you* were Berta, the pretty little girl.'

'I'd rather be kidnapped than look like this,' wept Berta. 'What will the girls at your school say, Anne, when they see me?'

'They don't say anything to George about her short hair, and they won't say anything to you,' said Anne.

'Stop crying, Bert – er – Lesley,' said Aunt Fanny. 'You make me feel quite miserable. You've been very good to sit so still all that time. Now I really must think of a little reward for you.'

Berta stopped crying at once. 'Please,' she said, 'there's only one thing I want now. I want Sally-dog to sleep with me.'

'Oh dear, Ber – er Lesley – I really *can't* have another dog in that little bedroom,' said poor Aunt Fanny. 'And George would make things most unpleasant if I did.'

'Aunt Fanny – Sally is a very very good guard for me,' said Berta. 'She barks at the very slightest sound. I'd feel safe with her in the bedroom.'

'I'd like you to have her,' said Aunt Fanny, 'but . . .'

Joanna had come into the room to put away some things and had heard the conversation. She stared in admiration at Berta's neat golden head, and then made a suggestion.

'Berta could have her camp-bed in *my* room,' she said. 'I don't mind the dog a bit, she can have her and welcome, she's a pet, that little poodle. It's very crowded in the girls' room now, with three beds in it, and my room's a nice big one. So, if Berta doesn't mind sharing it, she's welcome.'

'Oh, Joanna – that's good of you,' said Aunt Fanny, relieved at such a simple solution. 'Also, your room is up in the attic – it would be *very* difficult for kidnappers to find their way there – and nobody would think of looking into your room for one of the children.'

'*Thank* you, Joanna, you're just *wunnerful*!' said Berta in delight. 'Sally, do you hear that? You'll be sleeping on my feet tonight, like Timmy does on George's.'

'I don't really approve of that, you know, Berta,' said Aunt Fanny. 'Oh dear – I called you Berta again. Lesley, I mean. What a muddle I'm going to get into! Anne, get the dustpan and sweep up the hair on the floor.'

When Julian and George came back there was no sign of the golden hair on the floor. They put their parcels down on the table and shouted for Aunt Fanny. 'Mother!' called George. 'Aunt Fanny!' shouted Julian.

She came running downstairs with Berta and Anne and Dick. Julian and George looked at Berta, thunderstruck. 'Gosh – is it *really* you, Berta?' said Julian. 'I simply didn't recognise you!'

'Why – you *do* look like a boy!' said George. 'I never thought you would.'

'A jolly good-looking boy,' said Julian. 'Well, your father was right. It's the best disguise you could have!'

'Where are the clothes?' asked Berta, rather pleased at all the interest in her looks. They opened the parcels and pulled out the things.

They were not really very exciting – a boy's anorak in navy blue, two pairs of boy's jeans, two grey jerseys, a few shirts, a tie and a pullover without sleeves.

'And shoes and socks,' said George. 'But we decided you'd got plenty of socks that would do, so we only bought one pair of those. Oh – and here's a boy's cap! We bought it just for fun.'

Berta put on the cap at once. There were squeals of laughter from everyone. 'It suits her! She's got it on at just the right angle. She looks a real boy!'

'*You* put it on, George,' said Berta, and George took it, eager to share in the admiration. But it looked ridiculous on her curls, and wouldn't sit down flat as it should. Everyone hooted.

'It makes you look a girl! Take it off!'

George took it off in disappointment. How very aggravating that this girl Berta should make a better boy than she did! She threw the cap on the table, half-cross that they had bought it.

'Go upstairs and put some of the things on,' said Aunt Fanny, amused at all these goings-on. Up went Berta obediently, and soon came down again, neatly arrayed in jeans, grey shirt and blue tie.

Everyone roared with laughter. Berta was now quite enjoying herself and paraded round the room, her cap tilted on one side of her head.

'She looks like a very tidy, neat little boy, a good and most angelic child!' said Julian. 'Dear Lesley, you must get yourself just a little dirty – you look too good to be true.'

'I don't like getting dirty,' said Berta. 'I think . . .'

But what she thought nobody knew because at that moment the door opened and Uncle Quentin came into the room.

'I'd like to know how you think I can do my work with

all this hooting and cackling going on,' he began, and then he suddenly saw Berta, and stopped.

'Who's this?' he said, looking Berta up and down.

'Don't you know, Father?' said George.

'Of course not. Never seen him in my life before!' said her father. 'Don't tell me it's somebody else come to stay.'

'It's Berta,' said Anne, with a giggle.

'Berta – now who's Berta?' said Uncle Quentin, frowning. 'I seem to have heard that name before.'

'The girl you thought might be kidnapped,' explained Dick.

'Oh *Berta* – Elbur's girl!' said Uncle Quentin. 'I remember *her* all right. But who's *this*? This boy? I've never seen *him* before. What's your name, boy?'

'Lesley,' said Berta. 'But I was Berta when you saw me at breakfast.'

'Good heavens!' said Uncle Quentin, amazed. 'What a – what a transformation! Why, your own father wouldn't know you. I hope I remember who you are. Keep reminding me, if I don't.'

Off he went, back to his study. The children laughed, and Aunt Fanny had to laugh too.

'By the way,' she said, 'I want you all to have lunch at home today, because it's really too late now to start making sandwiches for a picnic; it's only cold ham and salad, so don't get *too* hungry, will you?'

'Is there time for a bathe?' asked Julian, looking at his watch.

'Yes – if you'll come in about twelve o'clock and pick the fruit for a pudding for lunch,' said his aunt. 'It takes ages to pick enough for eight people, and Joanna and I have a lot to do today.'

'Right. We'll go for a bathe now, and then we'll ALL pick fruit,' said Julian. 'Bags I pick the plums. The raspberries are such fiddly little things.'

'Have you a swimsuit, Berta, I mean Lesley?' asked George.

'Yes. It's an absolutely plain one, so I'll be all right in it,' said Berta. 'Hurray, I shan't need to wear a cap. Boys never do.'

Berta's cases were now all in Joanna's big room and she ran to get into her swimsuit.

'Bring your anorak and a towel,' yelled George, and went into her own room with Anne.

'I bet Berta can't swim,' she said. 'That will be a pity. We'll have to teach her.'

'Well, don't duck her too often!' said Anne, seeing a look in George's eye that was not too kindly. 'Blow – my swimsuit isn't here – I'm sure I brought it in from the clothes-line.'

It took quite a while to find it, and the boys and Berta had already gone down to the beach with Sally by the time Anne and George were ready to follow with the impatient Timmy.

They were down on the beach at last, and there was Sally-dog guarding the anoraks belonging to Julian, Dick

and Berta. She was lying on them, and she even dared to growl at Timmy when he came near.

George laughed. 'Growl back, Timmy! Don't let a little snippet like that cheek you. Growl back!'

But Timmy wouldn't. He just sat down out of reach of Sally, and looked at her sadly. Wasn't she friends with him any more?

'Where are the others?' said Anne, shading her eyes from the glare of the sun and looking out to sea. 'Goodness, how far out they've swum! That *can't* be Berta with them, surely!'

George looked out over the stretch of blue sea at once. She saw three heads bobbing. Yes, Berta *was* out there!

'She must be a jolly good swimmer,' said Anne,

admiringly. 'I couldn't swim out as far as that. We were wrong about Berta. She swims like a fish!'

George said nothing. She ran to the waves, plunged through a big one just as it was curling over, and swam out strongly. She couldn't *believe* that it was Berta out there! And if it was, the boys must be helping her!

But it *was* Berta. Her golden head glistened wet in the water, and she shouted in glee as she swam.

'This is great! This is wunnerful! Gee, I'm enjoying this! Hi there, George – isn't the water warm?'

Julian and Dick grinned at the panting George. 'Lesley's a fine swimmer,' said Dick. 'Gosh, I thought she was going to race me at one time. She'd beat *you*, George!'

'She wouldn't,' said George, but all the same she didn't challenge Berta to race!

It was fun to be five, fun to chase one another in the sea, to swim under the water and grab somebody's leg. And Anne laughed till she choked when she saw somebody heave themselves out of the water right on to George's back, and duck her well and truly.

It was Berta! And what was more, the angry George couldn't catch her afterwards. Berta could swim much too fast!

CHAPTER NINE

A sudden telephone call

BERTA SOON settled down happily with the Five. George couldn't bear to think that the girl had to be dressed like a boy, but her jealousy wore off a little as the days went by – though she couldn't help feeling annoyed that Berta proved to be such a good swimmer!

She could dive well too, and swim under water even longer than the boys could, much to their surprise.

'Oh well, you see, back home, we've got a pool in our garden,' she said. 'A wonDERful pool, gee, you should see it. And I learnt to swim in it when I was two. Pops always called me a water-baby.'

Berta ate just as much as the others, although she was not so sturdy and well built. She was loud in her praise of the meals, and this pleased Aunt Fanny and Joanna very much.

'You're getting fatter, Lesley,' said Aunt Fanny a week later, looking at her as she sat eating her lunch with the others. 'And what is better still – you're getting a really good suntan. You're almost as tanned as the others!'

'Yes. I thought so too,' said Berta, pleased.

'It's a good thing you caught the sun so easily,' said

Aunt Fanny. 'Now, if any kidnappers come round looking for a long-haired, pale-faced American girl, they would take one look at the lot of you and off they would go! Nobody would guess you were Berta!'

'All the same, I'd much rather *be* Berta,' said Berta. 'I still don't like pretending to be a boy. It's silly, and it makes me *feel* silly. Anyway, thank goodness my hair's growing a bit longer. I don't look *quite* so much like a boy now!'

'Dear me, you're right,' said Aunt Fanny, and everyone looked at Berta. 'I shall have to cut it short again.'

'Gosh!' said Berta. 'Why did I say that? You wouldn't have noticed if I hadn't mentioned it. Let it grow again, please, Aunt Fanny. I've been here a week and there isn't even a *smell* of a kidnapper – and I reckon there won't be either!'

But Aunt Fanny was firm about the hair, and after the meal she made Berta sit still while she clipped it a little shorter. It was not a bit curly like George's, and now that it was short, the wave had almost gone from it. She really did look like a good, clean little boy!

'Rather a wishy-washy one!' said George, unkindly, but everyone knew what she meant.

Sally the poodle was a great success. Even George couldn't go on disliking the happy, dancing little dog. She trotted and capered about on her slim little legs, and Timmy was her adoring servant.

'She always looks as if she's running about on tiptoe,'

said Anne, and so she did. She made friends with everyone, even the paperboy, who was really scared of dogs.

Uncle Quentin was the only one who didn't get used to Berta and Sally. When he met them together, Berta so like a small boy, Sally at her heels, he stopped and stared.

'Now let me see – who are you?' he said. 'Yes – you're Berta!'

'No – he's LESLEY!' everyone would say.

'You must *not* call her Berta, dear,' said his wife. 'You really must not. It's a funny thing that you never could remember she was Berta, and now that we've made her into Lesley, you immediately remember she's Berta!'

'Well, I must say you've made her look exactly like a boy,' said Uncle Quentin, much to George's annoyance. George was beginning to be afraid that Berta looked more boyish than she did! 'Well, I hope you're having a good time with the others, er – er . . .'

'*Lesley* is the name,' said Aunt Fanny with a little laugh. 'Quentin, do try and remember.'

Another day passed peacefully by, and the five children and two dogs were out of doors all day long, swimming, boating, exploring, really enjoying themselves.

Berta wanted to go over to Kirrin Island, but George kept making excuses not to go. 'Don't be mean,' said Dick. 'We *all* want to go. It's ages since we went. It's just that you don't want to let Lesley do something she'd like to do!'

'It isn't,' said George. 'Perhaps we'll go tomorrow.'

A SUDDEN TELEPHONE CALL

But when tomorrow came something happened that upset their plans for going to Kirrin Island. A telephone call came for Uncle Quentin, and immediately he was in a panic.

'Fanny! Fanny, where are you?' he called. 'Pack my bag at once. At once, do you hear?'

His wife came running down the stairs at top speed. 'Quentin, why? What's happened?'

'Elbur's found a mistake in our calculations,' said Uncle Quentin. 'What nonsense! There's no mistake. None at all.'

'But why can't he come *here* and work it out with you?' asked his wife. 'Why have *you* got to rush off like this? Tell him to come here, Quentin. I'll find him a bed somehow.'

'He says he doesn't want to, while his daughter – his daughter – what's her name now?'

'*Lesley*,' said his wife. 'All right, don't bother to explain. I see now that it would be foolish for him to come while Lesley's here – she'd be calling him Pops, and . . .'

'Pops?' said her husband, startled. 'What do you mean – Pops?'

'It's what she calls her father, dear,' said Aunt Fanny, patiently. 'Anyway, he's quite right. It would be foolish to hide Lesley here so well, and then have everyone hear her calling him Pops, and him calling her Berta – if any kidnappers followed him, they would soon find out where his daughter was – here, with our four!'

'Yes – that's what I was trying to tell you,' said her husband, impatiently. 'Anyway I must go to Elbur straight away. So pack my bag, please. I'll be back in two days' time.'

'In that case I'll go with you, Quentin,' said his wife. 'I could do with a quiet two days – and you're not much good when you're alone, are you – losing your socks, and forgetting to have your shoes cleaned, and . . .'

Her husband gave a sudden smile that lit up his face and made him seem quite young. 'Will you really come with me? I thought you'd hate to leave the children.'

'It's only for two days,' said his wife. 'And Joanna is

very good with them. I'll arrange that they shall go out on all-day picnics in the boat – they'll be quite safe then. If any kidnappers *were* around they'd find it difficult to snatch Lesley out of a boat! But I'm beginning not to believe that tale of Elbur's. He just got into a panic when he heard the rumour, I expect.'

The children were told of the sudden decision when they got back to lunch that day. Joanna had to tell them, because Aunt Fanny and her husband had already departed, complete with two suitcases, one containing precious papers and the other clothes for two days.

'Gosh!' said Julian, surprised. 'I hope nothing horrid's happened.'

'Oh no – it was just a sudden telephone call from Lesley's father,' said Joanna, smiling at Berta. 'He had to see your uncle in a hurry – about some figures.'

'Why didn't Pops come down here – then he could have seen *me*?' demanded Berta at once.

'Because everyone would have known who you are, then,' said Dick. 'We're *hiding* you, don't forget!'

'Oh yes – well I do believe I *had* forgotten,' said Berta, rather surprised at herself. 'It's so *lovely* down here in Kirrin with you all. The days seem to *swim* by!'

'Your mother said you had better go off on all-day picnics in the boat,' said Joanna to George. 'That was to make things easy for me, of course. But I don't mind what you do – you can come back to lunch each day, if you like.'

'I do so like you, Joanna!' said Berta, giving the surprised cook a sudden hug. 'You're a real honey!'

'In fact, she's quite wunnerful!' said Dick. 'It's all right, Joanna – we'll go out for the midday meal, *and* for tea, till my aunt comes back. And we'll make the sandwiches and pack up everything ourselves.'

'Well, that's nice of you,' said Joanna. 'Why don't you go across to Kirrin Island for the day? Lesley keeps wanting to go.'

Berta grinned at Joanna.

'We'll go if the boat is ready,' said George, rather reluctantly. 'You know James is mending one of the rowlocks. We'll go and see if it's finished.'

They all went to see, but James was not there. His father was working on another boat, over by the jetty, and he called to them.

'Do you want my James? He's gone off in his uncle's boat for a day's fishing. He said to tell you the rowlock's not mended yet, but he'll do it for certain tonight when he comes back.'

'Right. Thank you,' called back Julian. Berta looked very disappointed. 'Cheer up,' he said. 'We'll be able to go tomorrow.'

'We shan't,' said Berta, mournfully. 'Something else will happen to prevent us – or George will think of another excuse not to go. Gee, if I had a wunnerful – wonDERful – island like that, I'd go and *live* on it.'

They went back to Kirrin Cottage and packed up a very

good lunch for themselves. Berta's father had sent down a parcel of American goodies three days before, and they meant to try them.

'Snick-snacks!' said Dick, reading the name on a tin. 'Shrimp, lobster, crab and a dozen other things all in one tin. Sounds good. We'll make sandwiches with this!'

'Gorgies,' said Anne, reading the name on another tin. 'What a peculiar name! Oh – I suppose it's something you *gorge* yourself with. Let's open it.'

They opened half a dozen tins with most exciting names and made themselves so many sandwiches that Joanna exclaimed in amazement. 'How ever many have you made for each of you?'

'Twenny each – I mean twenTY,' said Berta. 'But we won't be back to lunch *or* tea, Joanna. I guess we'll be plenny hungry.'

'PlenTY!' chorused everyone, and Berta obediently repeated the word, a grin on her suntanned face.

What a day they had! They walked for miles and picnicked in a shady wood near a little stream that bubbled along nearby, sounding very cool and enticing. They decided to sit with their feet in it as they ate, and Anne gave continual little squeals because she said the water tickled the soles of her feet.

They were so tired when they got home that night that it was all they could do to eat their supper and stagger upstairs to bed.

'I shan't wake till half past twelve tomorrow morning,'

yawned Dick. 'Oh my poor feet! Gosh, I'm so tired I shall probably fall asleep cleaning my teeth.'

'What a peaceful night!' said Anne, looking out of her window. 'Well – sleep tight, everyone. I don't expect any of us will open an eye till late tomorrow morning. I know I shan't!'

But she did. She opened both eyes very wide indeed in the middle of the night.

CHAPTER TEN

A puzzling thing

ALL WAS quiet at Kirrin Cottage. The two boys slept soundly in their room, and George and Anne slept without stirring in theirs. Berta was up in Joanna's attic room, and hadn't moved since she had flopped into bed.

Timmy was on George's feet, as usual, and Sally the poodle was curled up in the crook of Berta's knees, looking like a ball of black wool! Nobody stirred.

A black cloud crept up the sky and blotted out the stars one by one. Then a low roll of thunder came. It was far off, and only a rumble, but it woke both the dogs, and it woke Anne too.

She opened her eyes, wondering what the noise was. Then she knew – it was thunder.

'Oh, I hope a storm won't come and break up this wonderful weather!' she thought, as she lay and listened. She turned towards the open window and looked for the stars, but there were none to see.

'Well, if a storm's coming, I'll go and watch it at the window,' thought Anne. 'It should be a magnificent sight over Kirrin Bay. I'm so hot too – I'd like a breath of fresh air at the window!'

She got quietly out of bed and padded over to the open

window. She leant out, sniffing the cool air outside. The night was very dark indeed, because of the great black cloud.

The thunder came again, but not very near – just a low growl. Timmy jumped off George's bed and went to join Anne. He put his great paws up on the windowsill and looked out solemnly over the bay.

And then both he and Anne heard another sound – a faraway chug-chug-chug-chug-chug.

'It's a motorboat,' said Anne, listening. 'Isn't it, Timmy? Someone's having a very late trip! Can you see any ship-lights, Tim? I can't.'

The engine of the motorboat cut out just then, and there was complete silence except for the swish-swash-swish of the waves on the beach. Anne strained her eyes to see if she could spot any light anywhere to show where the motorboat was. It sounded quite far out in the bay. Why had it stopped on the water? Why hadn't it gone to the jetty?

Then she did see a light, but a very faint one, right out at the entrance of the bay, about the middle. It shone for a while, moved here and there, and then disappeared. Anne was puzzled.

'Surely that's just about where Kirrin Island is?' she whispered to Timmy. 'Is anyone there? Has the motorboat gone there, do you suppose? Well, we'll listen to see if it leaves again and goes away.'

But no further sound came from across the bay, and no light shone either. 'Perhaps the motorboat is *behind* Kirrin Island,' thought Anne, suddenly. 'And then I wouldn't be able to see any lights on it – the island would hide the boat *and* its lights. But what was that *moving* light I saw? *Was* it someone on the island? Oh dear, my eyes are getting so sleepy again that I can hardly keep them open. Perhaps I didn't hear or see anything after all!'

There was no more thunder, and no lightning at all. The big black cloud began to thin out and one or two stars appeared in the gaps. Anne yawned and crawled into bed. Timmy jumped back on George's bed and curled himself up with a little sigh.

In the morning Anne had almost forgotten her watch at the open window the night before. It was only when Joanna mentioned that a big storm had burst over a town fifty miles away that Anne remembered the thunder she had heard.

'Oh!' she said, suddenly. 'Yes – *I* heard thunder too, and I got out of bed, hoping to watch a storm. But it didn't come. And I heard a motorboat far out in the bay, but I couldn't see any lights – except for a faint, moving one I thought was on Kirrin Island.'

George sat up in her chair as if she had had an electric shock. 'On Kirrin Island! Whatever do you mean? Nobody's there. *Nobody's* allowed there!'

'Well – I may have been mistaken,' said Anne. 'I was so very sleepy. I didn't hear the motorboat go away. I just went back to bed.'

'You *might* have woken me, if you thought you saw a light on my island,' said George. 'You really might!'

'Oh, Anne – it wouldn't be kidnappers, would it!' said Joanna, at once.

Julian laughed. 'No, Joanna. What would be the use of them going to Kirrin Island? They couldn't do any kidnapping there, in full view of all the houses round the bay!'

'I guess it was only a dream, Anne,' said Berta. 'I guess you heard the thunder in your sleep, and it turned into the sound of a motorboat chugging – dreams *do* that sort of thing. I know once I left the tap running in my basin when I went to sleep, and I dreamed all night long I was riding over the Niagara Falls!'

Everyone laughed. Berta could be very droll at times. 'If the boat's ready, we'll certainly go over to Kirrin Island today,' said George. 'If any trippers are there I'll send Timmy after them!'

'There will only be the rabbits,' said Dick. 'I wonder if there are still hundreds there – my word, last time we went they were so tame that we nearly fell over them!'

'Yes – but we didn't have Timmy with us,' said Anne. 'George, it *will* be nice to go to Kirrin Island again. We'll have to tell Lesley about the adventures we've had there.'

They washed up after breakfast, made the beds and did their rooms. Joanna put her head round Julian's bedroom door.

'Will you want a packed lunch for a picnic again, Julian?' she said. 'If you don't, I can get you a nice bit of cold ham for lunch. The grocer's just rung up.'

'If the boat's mended, we're going over to the island, Joanna,' said Julian. 'And then we'd like a packed lunch.

But if we don't go, we'll stay for lunch. It will be easier for you in a way, won't it? We all got up so late this morning that there's not much time to make sandwiches and pick fruit and so on.'

'Well, you tell me, as soon as you know about the boat,' said Joanna, and disappeared.

George came in. 'I'm going to see if the boat is mended,' she said. 'I'll only be gone a minute. Joanna wants to know.'

She was back almost at once. 'It's not ready,' she said, disappointed. 'But it will be ready at two o'clock this afternoon. So we'll have lunch here, shall we, and then go over to the island afterwards? We'll pack up a picnic tea.'

'Right,' said Julian. 'I vote we bathe from the beach this morning, then. The tide will be nice and high and we can have some fun with the big breakers.'

'And also keep an eye on James to see that he keeps his word about the boat,' said Dick.

So, when all their jobs were finished – and they were very conscientious about them – the five children and the two dogs went off down to the beach. It was a little cooler after the thunder, but not much, and they were quite warm enough in their swimsuits, with an anorak to wear after a bathe.

'There's nothing nicer than to feel hot and go into the sea and get cool, and then come out and get hot in the sun again, and then go back into the sea,' began Berta.

'You say that every single day!' said George. 'It's like

a record! Still, I must say that I agree with you! Come on – let's have a jolly good swim!'

They all plunged through the big, curling breakers, squealing as the water dashed over their bodies, cold and stinging. They chased one another, swam under water and grabbed at the legs swimming there, floated on their backs, and wished they hadn't forgotten to bring the big red rubber ball with them. But nobody wanted to go and fetch it so they had to do without it.

Timmy and Sally raced about in the shallow waves at the edge of the sea. Timmy was a fine swimmer, but Sally

didn't much like the water, so they always played together at the edge. They really were most amusing to watch.

The dogs were glad when the children came panting out of the water. They lay down on the warm beach and Timmy flopped down beside George. She pushed him away.

'You smell of seaweed,' she said. 'Pooh!'

After a while Dick sat up to pull on his anorak. He gazed over the bay to where Kirrin Island lay basking in the sun and gave a sudden exclamation.

'I say! Look, all of you!'

Everyone sat up. 'There's someone on Kirrin Island, though I can't see them,' said Dick. 'Someone lying down, looking through binoculars at our beach. Can you see the sun glittering on the glasses?'

'Yes!' said Julian. 'You're right! Someone must be using binoculars to examine this beach. We can't see them as you say – but it's easy enough to see the sunlight glinting on the glasses. Gosh, what cheek!'

'Cheek!' said George, her face crimson with rage. 'It's a lot more than cheek! How *dare* people go on my island and use it to spy on people on the beach? Let's spy on *them*! Let's get our own field-glasses and look through them. We'll see who it is, then!'

'I'll get them,' said Dick and ran off to Kirrin Cottage. He felt worried. It seemed a strange thing to do – to spy on people sitting on the beach round the bay, using binoculars on Kirrin Island. What was the reason?

He came back with the binoculars, and handed them to Julian. 'I think they're gone now, whoever it was,' said Julian. 'I don't mean gone off the island, but gone somewhere else on it. We can't see the glint of the sun on their glasses any more.'

'Well, buck up and see if you can spy anyone through *our* glasses,' said George, impatiently.

Julian adjusted them, and gazed through them earnestly. The island seemed very near indeed when seen through the powerful glasses. Everyone watched him anxiously.

'See anyone?' asked Dick.

'Not a soul,' said Julian, disappointed. He handed the glasses to the impatient George, who put them to her eyes at once. 'Blow!' she said. 'There's not a thing to be seen, not a thing. Whoever it was has gone into hiding somewhere. If it's trippers having a picnic there I'll be absolutely furious. If we see smoke rising we'll know it *is* trippers!'

But no smoke arose. Dick had a turn at looking through the glasses, and he looked puzzled. He took them down from his eyes and turned to the others.

'We ought to be able to see the rabbits running about,' he said. 'But I can't see a single one. Did either of you, Julian and George?'

'Well – now I come to think of it – no, I didn't,' said Julian, and George said the same.

'They were frightened by whoever was there, of course,'

said Dick. 'I suppose it will be all right to take Lesley with us when we go to the island this afternoon? I mean – it's just a bit *odd* that anyone should be using the island to spy from.'

'Yes. I see what you mean,' said Julian. 'If it occurred to the kidnappers, whoever they are, that Berta *might* be down here with us, it would be quite a good idea on their part to land on the island and use it as a place from which to spy on the beach. They would guess we would come down to bathe every day.'

'Yes. And they would see five children instead of four and would begin to make enquiries about the fifth!' said Dick. 'They would hope actually to *see* Berta on the beach – they've probably got a photograph of her – and they would be looking for a girl with long wavy hair.'

'And there isn't one!' said Anne. 'Mine's not wavy and it's not right down to my shoulders as Lesley's was. How muddled they would be!'

'There's one thing that would tell them that Berta was here though,' said Julian, suddenly. He pointed to Sally.

'Good gracious, yes!' said Dick. 'Sally would give the game away all right! Whew! We'll have to think about all this!'

CHAPTER ELEVEN

On Kirrin Island again

GEORGE WANTED to get her boat and go across to the island immediately. She was so furious at the thought of anyone else being there without permission that all she wanted to do was to chase them away.

But Julian said no. 'For one thing the boat won't be ready till two,' he said. 'For another thing we've got to consider whether it's a sensible thing to do, to go to the island *if* possible kidnappers are here, on the lookout for Berta – Lesley, I mean.'

'We could go without her,' said George. 'We could leave her safely with Joanna.'

'That would be a foolish thing to do,' said Dick. 'Anyone watching us coming across in the boat would see that one of the five was missing, and would guess at once it was Berta. If we go, *all* of us must go.'

'Actually I think it might be a good thing to do,' said Julian. 'Carry the war right into the enemy's camp, so to speak – if there *are* enemies! It would be a most useful thing if we could see what they are like and give a description to the police. I rather vote we go.'

'Oh *yes*!' said Dick. 'Anyway, we'll have Tim with us.

He can deal with any bad behaviour on the part of the intruders!'

'I don't really think it's anybody but trippers,' said Julian. 'I think we're making too much of the whole thing just because someone gazed at the beach through glasses!'

'Remember that I think I saw a light on the island last night,' Anne reminded him.

'Yes, I'd forgotten that,' said Julian, looking at his watch. 'It's almost lunch-time. Let's go and have something to eat, and then fetch the boat. James is working on it now. We'll give him a shout to see if it will be ready at two.'

James was hailed, and he shouted back. 'Yes! Be ready sharp at two o'clock, if you want her. I've done one or two little jobs on her besides the rowlock.'

'That's good,' said Dick, and they walked back to Kirrin Cottage. 'Well, we'll soon find out who's on your island, George – and if they are obstinate about leaving, we'll have a little fun with Timmy! He can round them up all right, can't you, Tim!'

'So could Sally,' said Berta. 'Sally's teeth aren't very big, but they're sharp. She once went for a man who accidentally pushed into me, and you should have seen the nips she gave him, all down his leg!'

'Yes. Sally would come in useful,' said Dick. George looked rather scornful. 'That silly little poodle!' she thought. 'A fat lot of good *she* would be! Timmy's worth a hundred of her!'

Joanna had a fine lunch ready for them – ham and salad and new potatoes piled high in a big dish. There were firm red tomatoes from the greenhouse, and lettuces with enormous yellow-green hearts, crisp radishes, and a whole cucumber ready for anyone to cut as they liked. Slices of hard-boiled egg were mixed in with the salad, and Joanna had put in tiny boiled carrots and peas as well.

'What a salad!' said Dick. 'Fit for a king!'

'And big enough for *several* kings!' said Anne. 'How many potatoes, Ju? Small or large ones?'

Julian looked at the piled-up dish. 'Ha – I can really go for these potatoes!' he said. 'I'll have three large and four small.'

'What's for pudding?' asked Berta. 'I like this kind of salad so much that I might not have room for a stodgy sort of pudding.'

'It's fresh raspberries from the garden, sugar and home-made ice-cream,' said Joanna. 'I didn't think you'd want a hot pudding. My sister came to see me this morning, so I got her to pick the raspberries for me.'

'I can't think of a nicer meal than this,' said Berta, helping herself to the salad. 'I really can't. I like your meals better than the ones we have at home in America.

'We'll turn you into a proper little English boy before you know where you are!' said Dick.

They told Joanna about what they had seen that morning on the island. She took a grave view of it at once.

'Now you know what your aunt said, Julian,' she said.

'The police have got to have a report of anything suspicious. You'd better ring them up.'

'I will when we've been over to the island and back,' said Julian. 'I don't want to look an ass, Joanna. If it's only harmless trippers who don't know any better there's no need to bother the police. I *promise* to ring the police if we find anything suspicious.'

'I think you ought to ring them *now*,' said Joanna. 'And what's more I don't think you ought to go over to the island if you're suspicious of the people there.'

'We'll have Timmy with us,' said Dick. 'Don't worry.'

'And Sally too,' added Berta at once.

Joanna said no more, but went out to get the raspberries and ice-cream, looking worried. She brought in an enormous glass dish of fresh red raspberries and another dish of creamy-looking ice-cream blocks from the refrigerator.

A sigh of admiration went up from everyone. 'Who could want anything better?' said Dick. 'And that ice-cream – how do you get it like that, Joanna – not too frozen and not too melty? Just how I like it. I do hope some American doesn't get hold of you and whisk you away across the ocean – you're worth your weight in gold!'

Joanna laughed. 'You say such extravagant things, Dick – and all because of an ordinary dish like raspberries and ice-cream. Get along with you! Lesley will tell you there's nothing clever about raspberries and cream.'

'I agree with every word the others say,' said Berta fervently. 'You're wunnerful, you're a honey, you're . . .'

But Joanna had run out of the room, laughing, very pleased. She didn't mind what she did for children like these!

After they had finished lunch, they went down to the beach. James was still with the boat.

'She's finished!' he called. 'You going out in her now? I'll give you a hand down with her, then.'

Soon all five children and the dogs as well were in George's boat. The boys took the oars and began to pull hard towards the island. Timmy stood at the prow as he loved to do, fore-paws on the edge of the boat, looking out across the water.

'He fancies himself as a figurehead,' said Dick. 'Ah, here comes Sally – she wants to be one too. Mind you don't fall overboard, Sally, and get your pretty feet wet. You'll have to learn to swim if you do!'

Sally stood close beside Timmy, and both dogs looked eagerly towards the island – Timmy because he knew there were hundreds of rabbits there, and Sally because for her it was still quite an adventure to go out in a boat like this.

Berta, too, gazed eagerly at the little island as they drew near. She had heard so many tales about it now! She looked especially at the old castle rising up from it. It was in ruins, and Berta thought it must be very old indeed. Like so many Americans, she loved old buildings and old customs. How lucky George was to own an island like this!

Rocks guarded the island, and the sea ran strongly over them, sending up spray and foam.

'How ever are we going to get safely to the shore of the island?' said Berta, rather alarmed at the array of fierce-looking rocks that guarded it.

'There's a little cove we always use,' said George. She was at the tiller, and she steered the boat cleverly in and out of the rocks.

They rounded a low wall of very sharp rocks and Berta suddenly saw the little cove.

'Oh – is that the cove you mean?' she said. 'Why, it's like a little harbour going right up to that stretch of sand!'

There was a smooth inlet of water running between rocks, making a natural little harbour, as Berta said. The boat slid smoothly into the inlet and up to the beach of sand.

Dick leapt out and pulled it up the shore. 'She's safe here,' he told Berta. 'Welcome to Kirrin Island!'

Berta laughed. She felt very happy. What a truly wonderful place to come to!

George led the way up the sandy beach to the rocks behind, and they climbed over them. They stopped at the top, and Berta exclaimed in amazement.

'Rabbits! Thousands of them! Simply thousands. My, my, I never saw such tame ones in my life. Will they let me pick them up?'

'No,' said George. 'They're not as tame as that! They'll run away when we go near – but they will probably not go into their holes. They know us – we've so often been here.'

Sally the poodle was amazed at the rabbits. She couldn't believe her eyes. She stood close beside Berta, staring at the scuttling rabbits, her nose twitching as she tried to get their smell. She simply couldn't understand why Timmy didn't run at them.

Timmy stood quite still beside George, his tail down, looking very mournful. A visit to Kirrin Island was not such a pleasure to him as to the children, because he wasn't allowed to hunt the rabbits. *What* a waste of rabbits!

'Poor old Tim! Look at him!' said Julian. 'He looks the picture of misery. Look at Sally, too – she's longing to go after the rabbits, but she doesn't think it's good manners to chase them till Timmy does!'

Good manners or not, little Sally could bear it no longer! She suddenly made a dart at a rabbit who had come temptingly near, and it leapt into the air in fright.

'Sally!' called George, in a most peremptory manner. 'NO! You're not to chase my rabbits! Tim – go and fetch her here!'

Timmy went off to Sally and gave a tiny little growl. Sally looked at him in amazement. Could her friend Timmy *really* be growling at her? Timmy began to push himself against her and she found herself shepherded over to George.

'Good dog, Timmy,' said George, pleased to have shown everyone how obedient he was. 'Sally, you mustn't chase these rabbits, because they are too tame! They haven't learnt to run away properly yet, because not many people come here and frighten them.'

'Whoever was here this morning scared them all right,'

said Julian, remembering. 'Gosh, don't let's forget there may be people here. Well – I can't see anyone so far!'

They went cautiously forward, towards the old castle, Timmy running ahead. Then Julian stopped and pointed to the ground.

'Cigarette ends – look! Fresh ones, too. There *are* people here, that's certain. Walk ahead of us, Tim.'

But at that moment there came the sound that Anne had heard the night before – the sound of a motorboat's engine. R-r-r-r-r-r-r!

'They're escaping!' cried Dick. 'Quick, run to the other side of the island! We may see them then!'

CHAPTER TWELVE

Very suspicious

THE CHILDREN, with the two dogs barking excitedly, ran to the other, seaward side of the island. Great rocks lay out there, and the sea splashed over them.

'There it is – a motorboat!' cried Dick. They all stood and watched the boat riding over the sea at a very fast speed.

'Where are the glasses – did we bring them with us?' said Julian. 'I'd like to focus them on the boat and see if I can read the name – or even see the men in it!'

But the glasses had been left behind at Kirrin Cottage – what a pity!

'They must have anchored their motorboat out there, and somehow clambered inshore over the rocks,' said George. 'It's a dangerous thing to do if you don't know the best way.'

'Yes – and if they came last night, as I think they must have done, because I'm sure now it was the engine of the motorboat that I heard,' said Anne, 'if they came last night, they must have clambered to the shore in the dark. I wonder they managed it!'

'It must have been the light of a lantern or a torch you saw on the island in the night,' said Julian. 'They probably didn't want to be seen arriving on the island, and that's why they went to the other side, the seaward side. I wonder if they *were* men spying to find out if Berta is with us or not.'

'Let's snoop around a bit more and see if we can find anything else,' said Anne. 'The motorboat is almost out of sight now.'

They went back to the other side of the island. Berta looked with awe at the old castle in the middle. Jackdaws circled round a tower, calling loudly. 'Chack-chack-chack!'

'Once upon a time my castle had strong walls all round it,' said George. 'And there were two great towers. One's almost in ruins, as you can see, but the other is fairly good. Come right into the castle.'

Berta followed the others in, left speechless with awe. To think that this island, and this wonderful old ruined castle, belonged to George! How very, very lucky she was!

She went through a great doorway, and found herself in a dark room, with stone walls enclosing it. Two narrow, slit-like windows brought in all the light there was.

'It's strange and old and mysterious,' said Berta, half to herself. 'It's asleep and dreaming of the old days when people lived here. It doesn't like us being here!'

'Wake up!' said Dick. 'You look quite dopey!' Berta shook herself and looked round again. Then she went on through the castle and looked at other rooms, some without roofs, some without one or two of their walls.

'It's a honey of a castle!' she said to George. 'A real honey. Wunnerful. WonDERful.'

They wandered all round, showing the awe-struck Berta everything. 'We'll show you the dungeons too,' said George, very pleased to be impressing Berta so much.

'Dungeons! You've got dungeons too – oh, of course, you told me about them,' said Berta. '*Dungeons!* You don't say! My my, I'll never forget this afternoon.'

As they walked over the old courtyard Timmy suddenly growled and stood still, his tail down, the hackles on his neck rising. Everyone automatically stood still too.

'What is it, Tim?' asked George, in a whisper. Timmy's nose was pointing towards the little harbour where they had left their boat.

'There must be someone there,' said Dick. 'Don't say they're going off with our boat!'

George gave a scream. Her boat! Her precious boat! She set off at top speed with Timmy bounding in front.

'Come back, George – there may be danger!' shouted Julian, but George didn't listen. She ran over the rocks that led down to the little harbour beach, and then stopped still in surprise.

Two policemen were walking up the sandy beach! Their boat was drawn up beside George's. They saluted her and grinned.

'Afternoon, George!'

'What are you doing on my island?' demanded George, recognising them. 'Why have you come here?'

'Someone reported suspicious people on the island,' said the first policeman.

'*Who* did?' said George. 'Nobody knew about it but us!'

'I bet I know who reported it,' said Dick suddenly. 'Joanna did! She didn't like us going off by ourselves; she said we ought to telephone the police.'

'That's right,' said the policeman. 'So we came to see for ourselves. Found anyone?'

Julian took command then, and related how they had first seen the cigarette ends, and then heard the motorboat starting up, and had gone to see it roaring away from the island.

'Ah,' said the policeman, profoundly. 'Ah!'

'What do you mean – "AH"?' asked Dick.

'Fred here heard a motorboat somewhere in the bay in the night,' said the first man. 'What was it doing there, I'd like to know?'

'So would we,' said Julian. '*We* saw someone on the island looking through binoculars at the beach this morning.'

This brought forth two more 'Ahs', and the policemen exchanged glances.

'Good thing you've got a couple of dogs with you,' said the one called Fred. 'Well – we'll just have a bit of a look round, and then we'll go back on our beats again. And mind you ring us up next time anything turns up, George, see?'

Off they went together, looking closely at the ground. They found the cigarette ends and picked them up. Then on they went again.

'Let's go back,' said George, in a low voice. 'It spoils things if other people are on the island. I don't want to have a picnic here now. We'll go off in the boat somewhere and have a picnic tea in a cove.'

So they dragged the boat down to the water and jumped in. Sally was very pleased to be back in the boat and ran from end to end wagging her stiff tail in delight. Timmy followed her up and down and got in everyone's way.

'How can I row if you keep on jumping over me, Timmy?' complained Dick. 'Sally, you're just as bad. Berta, are you all right? You look a bit green?'

'It's only excitement and the bumpy bit past the rocks,' said Berta, anxious not to appear seasick in front of the others. 'I'll be all right as soon as we get on to calm waters.'

But she wasn't, so it was regretfully decided that they must row to the shore. They had a lazy tea on the beach, and Berta recovered enough to join in heartily.

'Anyone got room for an ice-cream?' asked Anne. 'Because if so I'll stroll down to the shops and get some. I want to buy a new pair of shoelaces too. One of mine broke this morning.'

Everyone appeared to have room for an ice-cream, so Anne set off with Sally, who wanted to come with her. She went to the draper's and got the laces, and then went to the teashop that sold ices.

'Seven, please,' she said. The girl in the shop smiled.

'Seven! You used to ask for five.'

'Yes, I know. But we've got someone staying with us

– and another dog,' explained Anne. 'And both dogs like ice-creams.'

'That reminds me – someone was in my shop yesterday asking about your uncle,' said the girl. 'He said he knew him. He wanted to know how many children were staying at Kirrin Cottage, and I thought only the four of you were there – and Timmy, of course. He seemed surprised, and said, surely there was another girl?'

'Good gracious!' said Anne, startled. 'Did he really? How inquisitive! What did you say then?'

'I just said there were two boys and a girl, and a girl who liked to dress as a boy,' said the girl.

Anne was glad to think the shop-girl hadn't known about Berta. 'What was the man like?' she asked.

'Quite ordinary,' said the girl, trying to remember. 'He wore dark glasses like so many visitors do in the bright sun. I noticed he had a large gold ring on his finger when he paid my bill. That's all I can remember.'

'Well, if anyone else asks you about us, just say we've got a friend staying with us called Lesley,' said Anne. 'Goodbye.'

She went off at top speed, anxious to tell the others. The man in the teashop must have been one of those who had gone to the island to watch the beach – he might have been staring at the five of them as they had played together. He must be one of the men now in the motorboat. Anne didn't like it, and it made her feel very uneasy.

She told the others what the shop-girl had said as they

sat in the sand and ate their ice-creams. Timmy gobbled his almost at once, and sat patiently watching Sally deal with hers, hoping that she would leave some.

All the four listened intently to Anne's little story. 'That settles it,' said Dick. 'Those men are certainly snooping round trying to find out if Lesley is here.'

'They are getting uncomfortably close,' said Julian.

'Still, your uncle and aunt come back tomorrow,' said Berta. 'We'll tell them, and maybe they'll have some good plan.'

'I hope those men don't know that they are away,' said Dick, uneasily. 'I think we'll have to keep a pretty close watch from now on. I wonder if Berta ought to stay on here with us.'

'See what Father says tomorrow,' said George. So it was decided that nothing should be done except to keep a sharp lookout until George's parents came back. They all went back rather soberly to Kirrin Cottage and told Joanna what had happened on the island.

'You telephoned the police, Joanna!' said Dick, shaking his finger at her.

'I did. And I was right to,' said Joanna. 'And what's more, Lesley's bed is going to be moved away from the window tonight *and* the window's going to be fastened even if we melt, *and* the door will be locked.'

'I'll lend you Timmy, too, if you like,' said George. 'He can sleep in the room with Sally. You ought to be safe then!'

She really only meant it as a joke, but to her surprise Joanna accepted at once. 'Thank you,' she said. 'I'd be glad of Timmy. I feel all of a dither, left on my own like this, and kidnappers closing in on us!'

Julian laughed. 'Oh, it's not so bad as that, Joanna. Only one more night and Uncle Quentin and Aunt Fanny will be back.'

'Oh – I quite forgot to tell you,' said Joanna. 'A letter's arrived. They're staying away a whole week! That's why I feel so scared. A week – well, a lot can happen in a week!'

CHAPTER THIRTEEN

A horrid shock

JULIAN WAS not very happy to hear that his aunt and uncle were staying away for a week. He picked up the letter. It was addressed to George, but Joanna had opened it.

'Not returning for a week,' it said. 'Complications have arisen. Hope all goes well. Love from Mother.'

There was no address. How annoying! Now Julian couldn't even let them *know* that he was feeling uneasy. He made up his mind to guard Berta every minute! Thank goodness they had Timmy. Nobody would dare to do any kidnapping under Timmy's eye!

He thought it was a good idea to put Timmy in Joanna's room that night with Berta. In fact, if George would agree, it would be best to do that each night. He thought it would not be wise to ask George now, though, because he could see that she was half sorry she had made the offer to Joanna!

Julian was quite fussy that evening. He insisted on the blinds being drawn when they sat down to play cards after their supper. He would not let Berta take Sally out for a run, but took her himself, watching for any strange person as he went down the lane.

'You're making me feel quite scared!' said Anne with a

laugh. 'Oh, Ju, it's so hot in this room. Do, do let's have the blind up for a few minutes and let some air in. I shall begin to sizzle if we don't. Timmy would soon growl if there was anyone outside.'

'All right,' said Julian and drew up the blind. It was dark outside now, and the light streamed out.

'That's better,' said Anne, mopping her wet forehead. 'Now, whose turn is it? Yours, George.'

They sat round the table, playing. Julian and Berta sat side by side, as Julian was helping her in a new game of cards. She looked exactly like a very earnest little boy, with her straight close-cut fair hair. George sat opposite

the window with Dick on one side of her and Anne on the other.

'Your turn, Dick,' said George. 'Do buck up, you're slow tonight.' She sat and waited, looking out of the window into the darkness.

Then suddenly she slammed down her cards and leapt up, shouting. Everyone jumped almost out of their skins.

'What is it, what is it, George?' cried Julian.

'Out there – look – a face! I saw a face peeping in at us – the light of the window just caught it! Timmy, Timmy! Quick, go after him!'

But Timmy wasn't there! Nor was Sally. George called frantically again. 'TIMMY! Come here, quickly. Oh, blow him, that fellow will get away. TIM!'

Timmy came bounding up the hall and into the sitting-room, barking. Sally followed behind.

'Where were you! Idiot!' cried George furiously. 'Jump out of the window – go on – chase him, find him!'

Timmy leapt out of the window and Sally tried to do the same, but couldn't. She barked and yelped, trying again and again to jump out. Joanna came running in, panic-stricken, wondering what was happening.

'*Listen*,' said Julian, suddenly. 'Shut up, Sally. *Listen*!'

They were all suddenly quiet, Sally too. There was the sound of a car being revved up down the lane, and then the sound died down as the car sped away.

'He's got away, whoever he was,' said Dick, and sat down suddenly. 'Gosh, I feel as if I'd been running a mile.

You nearly scared the life out of me when you slammed down your cards like that, George, and yelled in my ear.'

Timmy leapt in at the window at that moment and Dick almost jumped out of his skin again. So did everyone else, including Sally, who fled behind the sofa in panic.

'*What's* all this about?' said Joanna, quite fiercely. 'Really!'

George was in a tearing rage – with Timmy of all things! She shouted at the surprised dog and he put his tail down at once.

'Where were you? Why did you slink out of the room into the kitchen? How dare you leave me and go off like that? Just when we needed you! I'm ashamed of you, Timmy – you could have caught that fellow easily!'

'Oh don't,' said Berta, almost in tears. 'Poor Timmy! Don't, George!'

Then George turned on Berta. 'You just let me scold my own dog if he needs it! And you go and scold yours too. I bet Timmy followed your horrid little woolly pet out into the kitchen – it was *her* fault, not his!'

'Shut up, George,' said Julian. 'Your temper gets us nowhere. Calm down and let's hear what you saw. CALM DOWN, I say.'

George stared at him, about to retort with something defiant. Then Timmy gave a small whimper – his heart was almost broken to hear George – George, his beloved mistress – rave at him in such anger. He had no idea what he had done to displease her.

The whimper brought George to her senses. 'Oh, Timmy!' she said, and knelt down and flung her arms round his neck. 'I didn't mean to shout at you. I was so angry because we missed our chance of getting that man who was peeping in at us. Oh, Timmy, it's all right, it really is.'

Timmy was extremely glad to hear it. He licked George lavishly, and then lay down by her very soberly. He wished he knew what all the excitement was about.

So did Joanna. She thumped on the table to get everyone's attention, and at last got Julian to explain everything to her. She stared out of the window, half-thinking that she could see faces in the darkness outside. She drew the blind down sharply.

'We'll go to bed,' she said. 'All of us. I don't like this. I shall ring up the police and warn them. Lesley, you come with me straight away now.'

'I think perhaps you're right, Joanna,' said Julian. 'I'll lock up everywhere. Come on, girls.'

Timmy was astonished and upset to find himself handed over to Joanna and Berta. Was George still cross with him then? It was a very, very long time since he had slept away from her at night. He cheered up a little when he saw that Sally was going to be with him, and trotted rather mournfully up the attic stairs to Joanna's room.

Joanna soon got Berta into bed, and then undressed herself. She fastened the window and locked the door. She gave Timmy a rug in a corner, and Sally jumped up on Berta's bed as usual.

'Now we ought to be quite safe!' said Joanna, and settled creakingly into her bed.

On the floor below the two boys followed the same procedure, and so did Anne and George. Doors were locked and windows fastened, though it was a hot night and they were all sure they would be melted by the morning. George couldn't bear to think of Timmy with Berta and Joanna – especially as she had been so very cross with him. She lay in bed, full of remorse. Dear, kind, faithful Timmy – how *could* she have shouted at him like that?

'Do you suppose Timmy is feeling very upset?' she said, when she and Anne were in bed.

'A bit, perhaps,' said Anne. 'But dogs are very forgiving.'

'I know. That somehow makes it worse,' said George.

'Well, you really *shouldn't* get into such tempers,' said Anne, seizing the opportunity to tell George a few home truths. 'I thought you were getting over the tantrums you used to have. But these hols you've been pretty bad. Because of Berta, I suppose.'

'I wish I could go up and say good night to Timmy,' George began again, after a few minutes' silence.

'Oh for goodness' sake, George!' said Anne, sleepily. 'Do be sensible. You *can't* go and bang on Joanna's door and ask for Timmy – you'd scare them to death!'

Anne fell asleep, but George didn't. Then suddenly she heard the sound of a door being unlocked, and sat up. It sounded as if it came from the attic. Was it Joanna unlocking her door? What did she want?

A cautious little knock came at George's door. 'Who is it?' said George.

'Me. Joanna,' said Joanna's voice. 'I've brought Sally down, George. Timmy keeps trying to get up on Berta's bed to be with Sally, and she simply *can't* go to sleep, her camp-bed is too small to hold all three of them. So will you have Sally, please?'

'Oh blow!' said George, and went to open her door. 'How's Timmy?' she said, in a low voice.

'All right,' said Joanna. 'He'll be annoyed I've taken Sally away. I'm glad to have him up there tonight with all these goings-on!'

'Is he – is he happy, Joanna?' asked George, but Joanna had turned away and didn't hear. George sighed. *Why* had she offered to let Joanna and Berta have Timmy tonight of all nights, when she had scolded him so unfairly? Now she had to have this silly little Sally instead!

Sally whimpered. She didn't like being away from Berta, and she was not fond of George. She wriggled out of George's arms and ran round the room, still whimpering.

Anne woke up with a jump. 'Whatever's going on?' she said. 'Why – it's Sally in the room! How did *she* get here?'

George told her, sounding very cross. 'Well, I hope she'll settle down,' said Anne. 'I don't want her to whimper and run round the bedroom all night long.'

But Sally wouldn't settle down. Her whimpering became

louder, and when she took a flying jump on to George's bed and landed right on George's middle, the girl had had

enough of it. She sat up and spoke in a fierce whisper.

'You little idiot! I'm jolly well going to take you downstairs and put you into Timmy's kennel!'

'Good idea,' said Anne, sleepily. George picked up the lively little poodle and went out of the room, shutting the door softly. Anne promptly went to sleep again.

George crept down the stairs and went to the garden door. She undid it and walked out in dressing-gown and pyjamas, her curly hair all tousled, carrying the whimpering little dog.

Suddenly she felt Sally stiffen in her arms, and growl. Grrrrrrr! George stood quite still. What had Sally heard?

Then things happened very suddenly indeed. A torch was flashed in her face, and before she could cry out, a cloth was thrown over her head so that she could not make a sound.

'This is the one!' said a low voice. 'The one with curly hair! And this is her dog, the poodle. Put him in that kennel, quick, before he barks the place down.'

Sally, too scared even to growl, was pushed into the kennel and the door shut on her. George, struggling and trying vainly to call out, was lifted off her feet and carried swiftly down to the front gate.

The garden door swung creaking to and fro in the night wind. Sally whimpered in her kennel. But no one heard either door or dog. Everyone in Kirrin Cottage was sound asleep!

CHAPTER FOURTEEN

Where is George?

NEXT MORNING, about half past seven, Joanna went downstairs as usual. Berta was awake and decided to fetch Sally from George's bedroom. She put on her dressing-gown and padded downstairs with Timmy behind her, to George's room on the floor below. The door was shut, and she knocked gently.

'Come in,' said Anne's sleepy voice. 'Oh, it's you, Berta.'

'Yes. I've come for Sally,' said Berta. 'Hallo – where's George?'

Anne looked at the empty bed beside hers. 'I don't know. The last thing I heard of her was in the middle of the night when we got cross because Sally wouldn't settle down, and George said she would take her down to the kennel.'

'Oh. Well, probably George has gone down to fetch her back,' said Berta. 'I'll go up and dress. It's a heavenly morning again. Are you going to bathe before breakfast, because if so I'll just put on my swimsuit.'

'Yes. I think we might today – we're nice and early,' said Anne, scrambling out of bed. 'Go and wake the boys. Timmy, go down and find George.'

Dick and Julian were awake, and quite ready for a

before-breakfast bathe. Anne joined them as they went downstairs. Berta had already gone down and had discovered Sally in the kennel, most excited to see her. She pranced round barking happily.

Timmy came up to the children, looking puzzled. He had hunted everywhere for George and hadn't found her. 'Woof,' he said to Anne. 'Woof, woof!' It was just as if he were saying, 'Please, where is George?'

'Haven't you found George yet?' said Anne in surprise. She called to Joanna. 'Joanna, where's George? Has she gone down to bathe already?'

'I haven't seen her,' said Joanna. 'But I expect she has because the garden door was open when I came down, and I guessed one of you had gone for an early bathe.'

'Well, George must be down on the beach, then,' said Anne, feeling rather puzzled. Why hadn't George woken her and told her to come too?

Soon all four were on the beach with the two dogs, Sally very happy to be with Berta again, and Timmy very downcast and puzzled. He stood staring up the beach and down, looking quite lost.

'I can't see George anywhere,' said Dick, suddenly feeling scared. 'She's not in the sea.'

They all gazed over the water, but no one was bathing that morning. Anne turned to Julian in sudden panic.

'Ju! Where is she?'

'I wish I knew,' said Julian, anxiously. 'She's not here.

And she hasn't gone out in her boat – it's over there. Let's go back to the house.'

'I don't think George would have gone for an early bathe without telling me,' said Anne. 'And I also think I would surely have woken up just for a moment when she came back after taking Sally down – oh, Julian, I think something happened when she went downstairs with Sally late last night!'

'I've been thinking that too,' said Julian soberly. 'We know that there was someone about last night, because George saw a face outside the window. Let's go back to the house and see if we can spot anything to help us near the garden door or the kennel.'

They went back, looking very anxious. As soon as they began to look about near the kennel, Anne gave an exclamation and bent down. She picked up something and held it out to the others without a word.

'What is it – gosh, it's the girdle off George's dressing-gown!' said Dick, startled. 'That proves it! George was caught when she came down to put Sally into her kennel!'

'They must have thought she was *me*,' said Berta, in tears. 'You see – she was carrying Sally and they know Sally belongs to me – and she has short hair too and dresses like a boy in the daytime.'

'That's it!' said Julian. 'Actually you *look* like a boy in your boy's things, but George doesn't – and the kidnappers are looking for a girl dressed as a boy – and George fitted the bill nicely, especially as she had the poodle with her. She's been kidnapped!'

'And will my father get the usual note to say his daughter will not be harmed if he does what the kidnappers want, and hands over this new secret?' said Berta.

'Sure to,' said Julian.

'What will they say when they know they've got George, not me?' asked Berta.

'Well . . .' said Julian, considering. 'I really don't know. They might try the same thing with Uncle Quentin, but of course, he hasn't got the figures they want.'

'What about *Berta* now?' asked Dick. 'Once those men find they've got the wrong girl, they'll be after Berta in a trice!'

'George won't tell them,' said Anne, at once. 'She'll know that Berta would be in immediate danger if she did tell them – so she'll say nothing as long as she can.'

'Would she really?' said Berta, wonderingly. 'She's brave, isn't she? She could get herself set free at once if she said she wasn't me, and proved it. Gee, she's wunnerful if she could do a thing like that!'

'George is brave all right,' said Dick. 'As brave as anything when she's in a fix! Julian, let's go and tell Joanna. We've GOT to make up our minds what we are going to do about this – and also, we *must* safeguard Berta somehow. She can't possibly wander round with us any more.'

Berta all at once began to feel scared. George's sudden disappearance had brought home to her the very real danger she was in. She had not really believed in it before. She looked over her shoulder and all round and about as if she expected someone to pounce on her.

'It's all right, Berta – there's no one here at present!' said Dick, comfortingly. 'But you'd better get indoors, all the same. I don't *think* George would give away the fact that she wasn't you, but the men might find out some other way – and back they would come, hotfoot!'

Berta raced indoors as if someone was chasing her! Julian shut and locked the garden door and called Joanna.

They had a very serious conference indeed. Joanna was

horrified. She wept when she heard that George must have been kidnapped in the middle of the night. She wiped her eyes with her apron.

'I *said* we must lock the doors and the windows, I *said* we must tell the police – and then George has to go down all by herself into the garden!' she said. 'If only she hadn't had the poodle with her! No wonder they thought she was Berta, with Sally in her arms.'

'Listen, Joanna,' said Julian. 'There are a lot of things to do. First we must tell the police. Then somehow we must contact Aunt Fanny and Uncle Quentin – it's so like them not to give us an address! Then we must most certainly decide about Berta. She must be well hidden away somewhere.'

'Yes. That's certain,' said Joanna wiping her eyes again. She sat and thought for a minute, and then her face lightened.

'I know where we could hide her!' she said. 'You remember Jo – the little traveller girl you've had one or two adventures with?'

'Yes,' said Julian. 'She lives with your cousin now, doesn't she?'

'She does,' said Joanna. 'And my cousin would have Berta straight away if she knew about this. She lives in a quiet little village where nothing ever happens, and nobody would think anything of my cousin having a child to stay with Jo. She often does.'

'It really seems an idea,' said Dick. 'Doesn't it, Julian?

We've simply *got* to get Berta away at once. We could trust Jo to look after her, too – Jo's as sharp as a packet of needles!'

'The police would know, too,' said Julian, 'and would keep an eye on her as well. Joanna, can you ring up and get a taxi and take Berta now, this very minute?'

'It'll be a surprise for my cousin, my arriving this time of the morning,' said Joanna, standing up and taking off her apron, 'but she's quick on the uptake, and she'll do it, I know. Lesley, get a few things together – nothing posh, mind, like your silver hairbrush.'

Berta looked extremely scared by now, and was inclined to refuse to go. Julian put his arm round her.

'Look,' he said, 'I bet George is holding her tongue so that we can get you away in safety before the men tumble to the fact that they've got the wrong boy – so you can play up, too, can't you, and be brave?'

'Yes,' said Berta, looking up at Julian's kind, serious face. 'I'll do what you say – but what's this Jo like? Joanna said she was a little traveller girl. I might not like her.'

'You'll like this one all right,' said Julian. 'She's a pickle and a scamp and a scallywag – but her heart's in the right place – isn't it, Joanna?'

Joanna nodded. She had always been fond of the reckless, cheeky little Jo, and it was she who had found a home for her when Jo's father had had to go to prison. 'Come on, Lesley,' she said. 'We must hurry. Julian, is she to go as a girl or a boy now – we've got to decide that too.'

'A girl, please, please, a girl!' said Berta, at once.

Julian considered. 'Yes, I think you're right,' he said. 'You'd better be a girl now – but for goodness' sake don't call yourself Berta yet.'

'She can be Jane,' said Joanna, firmly. 'That's a nice name, but quite ordinary enough for nobody to notice. Berta is too noticeable a name. Come along, now – we'll have to pick out your simplest clothes!'

'Now I'll ring up the police,' said Julian, 'and also ring for a taxi.'

'No, don't get a taxi for us,' said Joanna. 'I don't want to arrive at my cousin's little cottage in a taxi, and make everyone stare! Jane and I will catch the market bus and people will think I'm going off to market. We can get another bus there, that will take us almost all the way to my cousin's. We've only to walk down the lane then.'

'Good idea,' said Julian, and went to the telephone. He got hold of the police sergeant, and told his tale. The man showed not the least excitement but took down quickly all that Julian told him. 'I'll be up in ten minutes,' he said. 'Wait in till I come.'

Julian put down the receiver. Dick and Anne were watching him with troubled eyes. What was happening to George? Was she frightened – or furious – or perhaps hurt?

Timmy was absolutely miserable. He knew by now that something had happened to George. He had gone a dozen times to the place where her dressing-gown girdle had been found, and had sniffed round disconsolately.

Sally knew he was unhappy and trotted after him soberly. When he lay down she lay down beside him. When he got up, she got up too. It would have been amusing to watch if anyone had felt like being amused. But nobody felt that way!

Footsteps came up the path. 'The police!' said Julian 'They've not been long!'

CHAPTER FIFTEEN

Discoveries in the wood

THE SERGEANT had come, and also a constable. Anne felt comforted when she saw the big, solid, responsible-looking men. Julian took them into the sitting-room, and began to tell all that had happened.

In the middle of it there came the sound of footsteps racing down the stairs, and up the hall. 'We're just off!' shouted Joanna's voice. 'Can't stop to say goodbye, or we shall miss the bus!'

Down the garden path rushed Joanna, carrying a small suitcase of her own, which she had lent Berta, because Berta's was too grand. In it she had packed the very simplest of Berta's clothes, but secretly she had thought that she would tell her cousin to dress Berta in some of Jo's things.

Berta ran behind her – a different Berta now, dressed in a frock instead of jeans and jersey. She waved to the others as she went, trying to smile.

'Good old Berta!' said Dick. 'She's got quite a lot in her, that kid.'

'In fact, she's quite a honey!' said Julian, trying to make Anne smile.

'What's all that?' said the sergeant, in surprise, nodding

his head towards the front path, down which Joanna and Berta had just rushed.

Julian explained. The sergeant frowned. 'You shouldn't have arranged about that till you'd consulted us,' he said. Julian was quite taken aback.

'Well, you see,' he said, 'it seemed to me that I must get Berta out of the house and hidden away at once in case the kidnappers realised quickly that they'd got the wrong girl.'

'That's so,' said the sergeant. 'Still, you *should* have consulted us. It seems quite a good idea to put her in that quiet village, with Jo to see to her – she's sharp, that Jo. I wouldn't put it past her to hoodwink the kidnappers any day! But this is a very serious business, you realise, Julian – it can't be dealt with by children.'

'Can you get George back?' asked Anne, breaking in with the question she had been longing to ask ever since the police came.

'Maybe,' said the sergeant. 'Now I'll get in touch with your aunt and uncle, Julian, and with Mr Elbur Wright, and . . .'

The telephone rang just then and Anne answered it. 'It's for you, Sergeant,' she said, and he took the receiver from her.

'Ha. Hm. Just so. Yes, yes. Right. Ha. Hm.' The sergeant replaced the receiver and went back to Julian and the others. 'News has just come in that the kidnappers have contacted Mr Elbur Wright, and told him they've got his daughter Berta,' he said.

'Oh! And have they demanded that he shall tell them the secret figures he knows?' asked Julian.

The sergeant nodded. 'Yes. He's almost off his head with shock! He's promised to give them all they want. Very foolish!'

'Gosh – you'd better tell him it's *not* Berta they've got, but George,' said Dick. 'Then he'll sit tight!'

The sergeant frowned. 'Now, you leave this to *us*,' he said, ponderously. 'You'll only hinder us if you interfere or try meddling on your own. You just sit back and take things easy.'

'What! With George kidnapped and in danger?' exploded Dick. 'What are *you* going to do to get her back?'

'Now, now!' said the sergeant, annoyed. 'She is in no danger – she's not the person they want. They will free her as soon as they realise that.'

'They won't,' said Dick. 'They'll get on to her father and make *him* give up a few secrets!'

'Well, that will give us a little more time to find these men,' said the irritating sergeant, and he stood up, big and burly in his navy blue uniform. 'Let me know *at once* if you have any other news, and please do not try to meddle. I assure you that we know the right things to do.'

He went out with the constable. Julian groaned. 'He doesn't see that this is *urgent*. It's so complicated too – the wrong girl kidnapped, the wrong father informed, the right one not at all inclined to give up powerful secrets – and poor old George not knowing what is happening!'

'Well, thank goodness we got *Berta* out of the way,' said Dick. 'Anne, you look funny – are you all right?'

'Yes. I think I'm just shocked – and oh dear, I feel awfully *empty*!' said Anne, pressing her tummy.

'Gosh – we forgot all about breakfast!' said Dick, staring at the clock. 'And it's almost ten o'clock now! What *have* we been doing all this time? Come on, Anne – get us some food, there's a dear. We shall all feel better then.'

'I'm so sorry for poor old Timmy and little Sally,' said Anne, going into the kitchen. 'Timmy, darling, don't look at me like that! I don't know *where* your beloved George is, or I'd take you to her straight away! And Sally, you will have to put up with me for a little while, because although I do know where Berta is, I can't possibly take you there!'

They were soon sitting down to a plain breakfast of boiled eggs, toast and butter. It seemed strange only to be three. Dick tried to make conversation, but the other two were very quiet. Timmy sat under the table with his head on Anne's foot, and Sally stood beside her, paws on her knee. Anne comforted both the mournful dogs as best she could!

After breakfast Anne went to wash up and make the beds, and the boys went outside to have another look at the place where George's dressing-gown girdle had been found. Sally and Timmy came with them.

Timmy sniffed around a good bit, and then, nose to ground went down the garden path to the front gate, and then pushed it open and went through it. Nose to ground he went down the lane and turned off into a little path.

'Dick – he's following some kind of trail,' said Julian. 'I'm certain it's George's. Even if somebody *carried* her away, Timmy is clever enough to know George might be with him – he might just get a whiff of her.'

'Come on – let's follow Timmy,' said Dick, and the boys and Sally went along the little path, hot on Timmy's track. Timmy began to run, and Dick called to him.

'Not so fast, old boy! We're coming too.'

But Timmy did not slow down. Whatever it was he smelt, the scent was quite strong. The boys ran after him, beginning to feel excited.

But soon Timmy came to a full stop, in a little clearing in the wood. Dick and Julian panted up to where he was nosing round. He looked up at them forlornly. Evidently the scent came to an end there.

'Car-tracks!' said Dick, pointing down to where the dampish grass under a great oak tree had been rutted with big tyre-marks. 'See? The men brought a car here and hid it, then crept through the woods to Kirrin Cottage, and waited for a chance to get Berta. They got George instead – but they wouldn't have got *anyone* if only George hadn't been ass enough to take Sally to the kennel! The house was well and truly locked and bolted!'

Julian was looking at the wheel-tracks. 'These tracks were made by very big tyres,' he said. 'It was a car – and I rather think these are *American* tyre-marks. I can check that when I get back – I'll go and ask Jim at the local garage – he'll know. I'll just sketch one quickly.'

He took out a notebook and pencil and began to sketch. Dick bent down and looked more carefully at the tracks. 'There is quite a lot of criss-crossing of tracks,' he said. 'I think the men came here and waited. Then, when they got George, they must have pushed her into the car, and turned it to go back the way they came – see, the tracks lead down that wide path over there. They made a mess of the turning, though – bumped into this tree, look – there's a mark right across it.'

'Where?' said Julian at once. 'Yes – a bright blue mark – the car was that colour – or the wings were, at any rate. Well, that's something we've learnt! A big blue car, probably American. Surely the police could trace that?'

'Timmy's still nosing round, the picture of misery,' said Dick. 'Poor old Tim. I expect he knows George was pushed into a car just there. Hallo – he's scraping at something!'

They ran to see what it was. Timmy was trying to get at some small object embedded in a car-rut. Evidently, in turning, the car had run over whatever it was.

Dick saw something broken in half – something green. He picked up the halves. 'A comb! Did George have a little green comb like this?'

'Yes. She did,' said Julian. 'She must have thrown it down when she got near to the car – to show us she was taken here – hoping we would find it. And look, what's that?'

It was a handkerchief hanging on a gorse bush. Julian ran to it. It had the initial G. on it in blue.

'Yes, it's George's,' he said. 'She's got six of these, all

with different-coloured initials. She must have thrown this out too. Quick, Dick, look for anything else she might have thrown out of the car, while they were trying to turn it. They would probably put her in the back, and she would just have had a chance to throw out anything she had in her dressing-gown pocket, to let us know she was here if we came along this way.'

They searched for a long time. Timmy found one more thing, again embedded in a car-rut – a boiled sweet wrapped in cellophane paper.

'Look!' said Dick, picking it up. 'One of the sweets we

all had the other night! George must have had one in her dressing-gown pocket! If only she had had a pencil and bit of paper – she might have had time to write a note too!'

'That's an idea!' said Julian. 'We'll hunt even more carefully!'

But although they searched every bit of ground and every bush, there was no note to be found. It was too much to hope for!

'Let's just follow the car-tracks and make sure they reached the road,' said Julian. So they followed them down the wide woodland path.

At the side a little way along, a piece of paper blew in the wind, hopping an inch or two each time the breeze flapped it. Dick picked it up – and then looked at Julian excitedly.

'She *did* have time to write a note! This is her writing. But there's only one word, look – whatever does it mean?'

Julian and Dick frowned over the piece of paper. Yes, it was George's writing – the G was exactly like the way she always wrote the big G at the beginning of her signature.

'Gringo,' read Julian. 'Just that one word. Gringo! What *does* it mean? It's something she heard them say, I suppose – and she just had time to write it and throw out the paper. Gringo! Timmy, what does *Gringo* mean?

CHAPTER SIXTEEN

Jo!

DICK AND Julian went back to Kirrin Cottage with the two disconsolate dogs. They showed Anne the things they had found, and she too puzzled over the word Gringo.

'We'll have to tell the police what you have discovered,' she said. 'They might trace the car, and they might know who or what Gringo is.'

'I'll telephone them now,' said Julian. 'Dick, you go down to the garage with this sketch of the tyre-mark, and see if it's an American design.'

The police were interested but not helpful. The sergeant said he would send his constable up to examine the place where the car had stood in the clearing, and gave it as his opinion that the bit of paper wasn't much use, as the boys had found it some way from the turning place of the car.

'Your cousin wouldn't be able to throw it out of the window once the car was going,' he said. 'There would be sure to be someone in the back with her. The only reason she could throw things out at the clearing would be because the second fellow – and there would certainly be two – would be guiding the other man in the turning of the car.'

'The wind might have blown the note along the path,' said Julian. 'Anyway, I've given you the information.'

It was a very miserable day, although the sun shone down warmly, and the sea was blue and most inviting. But nobody wanted to bathe, nobody really wanted to do anything but talk and talk about George and what had happened, and where she could be at that moment!

Joanna came back in time to get their lunch, and was pleased to find that Anne had done the potatoes and prepared a salad, and that Dick had managed to pick some raspberries. They were very glad to see Joanna. She was someone sensible and comforting and matter-of-fact.

'Well, Jane is now safely in my cousin's cottage,' she said. 'She was very miserable but I told her she must smile and play about, else the neighbours would wonder about her. I put her into some of Jo's clothes – they fitted her all right. Hers are too expensive-looking, and would make people talk!'

They told Joanna what they had discovered in the clearing that morning. She took the note and looked at it. 'Gringo!' she said. 'That's a funny word – sounds like a traveller word to me. It's a pity Jo isn't here – she might tell us what it means!'

'Did you see Jo?' asked Dick.

'No. She was out shopping,' said Joanna, lifting the lid to look at the potatoes. 'I only hope she gets on with Jane all right. Really, it's getting very difficult to remember that child's change of names!'

The only fresh news that day was a worried telephone call from Aunt Fanny. She was shocked and amazed at the news she had heard. 'Your uncle has collapsed!' she said. 'He has been working very hard, you know, and now this news of George has been quite the last straw. He's very ill. I can't leave him at the moment – but anyway we couldn't *do* anything! Only the police can help now. To think those horrible men took George by mistake!'

'Don't worry too much, Aunt Fanny,' said Julian. 'We've hidden Berta away safely, and I expect the men will free George as soon as she tells them she's the wrong girl.'

'If she *does* tell them!' said Dick, under his breath. 'She might not, for Berta's sake, for a few days at any rate!'

Everyone went miserable to bed that night. Anne took Timmy and Sally with her, for both were so forlorn that she couldn't bear to do anything else. Timmy wouldn't eat anything at all, and Anne was worried about him.

Julian could not go to sleep. He tossed and turned, thinking about George. Hot-tempered, courageous, impatient, independent George! He worried and worried about her, wishing he could *do* something!

A small stone suddenly rattled against his window! He sat up, alert at once. Then something fell right into the room, and rolled over the floor. Julian was at the window in a trice. Who was throwing pebbles at his window?

He leant out. A voice came up to him at once. 'Is it you, Dick?'

'Jo! What *are* you doing here?' said Julian, startled. 'It's Julian speaking. Dick's asleep. I'll wake him, and let you in.'

But he did not need to go down and let Jo in. She was up a tree outside the window and across some ivy and on

his windowsill before he had even shaken Dick awake!

She slid into the room. Julian switched on his light. There was Jo, sitting at the end of Dick's bed, the familiar cheeky grin on her face! She was very tanned, but still showed her freckles, and her hair was as short and curly as ever.

'I *had* to come,' she said. 'When I got home from shopping, there was this girl Jane. She told me all about how George had been captured in mistake for her – and when I said to her, "You go straight away and say you're safe and sound, and it's all a mistake, and George has got to be set free!" she wouldn't! She just wouldn't! All she did was to sit and cry. Little coward!'

'No, no, Jo,' said Dick, and tried to explain everything to the indignant girl. But he could not convince her.

'If I was that girl Jane I wouldn't let someone stay kidnapped because of *me*,' she said. 'I don't like her, she's silly. And I'm supposed to keep an eye on her! Phoo! Not me! I'd *like* her to be kidnapped, the way she's behaving about George.'

Julian looked at Jo. She was very, very loyal to the Five, and proud of being their friend. She had been in two adventures with them now, a crafty little girl, but a very loyal friend. Her father was in prison, and she was living with a cousin of Joanna's, and, for the first time in her life, going to school to learn lessons!

'Listen, Jo – we've found out a few more things since Berta – I mean Lesley – no, I don't, I mean Jane . . .'

'What *do* you mean?' said Jo, puzzled.

'I mean Jane,' said Julian. 'We've found out something else since Joanna parked Jane with her cousin this morning.'

'Go on, tell me,' said Jo. 'Have you found out where George is? I'll go and break in and get her out, if you have!'

'Oh, Jo – it's no use just being fierce,' said Dick. 'Things are not so easy as all that!'

'George threw out a bit of paper with this written on it,' said Julian, and he put it before Jo. 'See? Just that one word – "Gringo". Does it mean anything to you?'

'Gringo?' said Jo. 'That rings a bell! Let's see now – *Gringo*!'

She frowned as she thought hard. Then she nodded. 'Oh yes, I remember now. A fair came to the town a few weeks back – the big town not far from our village. It was called Gringo's Great Fair.'

'Where did it go?' asked Dick, eagerly.

'It was going to Fallenwick, then to Granton,' said Jo. 'I made friends with the boy whose father owned the roundabout, and gosh, I had about a hundred free rides.'

'You *would*!' said both boys together, and Jo grinned.

'Do you suppose this Gringo, who runs the fair, could be anything to do with the name Gringo that George wrote on this paper?' said Julian.

'*I* dunno!' said Jo. 'But if you like I can go and find the fair and get hold of Spiky – that's the roundabout boy – and see if I can find out anything. I know Spiky said Gringo was a real horror to work for, and thought himself as good as a lord!'

'Had he a car – a big car?' asked Dick, suddenly.

'I dunno that either,' said Jo. 'I can find out. Here – I'll go *now*! You lend me a bike and I'll bike to Granton!'

'Certainly not,' said Julian, startled at the idea of Jo biking the twelve miles to Granton in the middle of the night.

'All right,' said Jo, rather sulkily. 'I just thought you'd like me to help. It might be that this Gringo has got George somewhere. He was the kind of fellow who was a go-between, if you know what I mean.'

'How?' asked Dick.

'Well, Spiky said that if anyone wanted something dirty done, this Gringo just held out his hand, and if a wad of notes was put into it, he'd do it, and nothing said!' said Jo.

'I see,' said Julian. 'Hm – it sounds as if kidnapping would be right up his street, then.'

Jo laughed scornfully. 'That would be nothing to him – chicken-feed. Come on, Julian – let me have a lend of your bike.'

'NO,' said Julian. 'Thanks very, very much, but I'm not letting anyone ride to a fair in the middle of the night to find out if a fellow called Gringo has anything to do with George. I can't believe he has, either – it's too far-fetched.'

'All right. But you *asked* me if the name meant anything

to me,' said Jo, sounding offended. 'Anyway, it's a common enough nickname in the circus world and the fair world too. There's probably a thousand Gringos about!'

'It's time you went back home,' said Julian, looking at his watch. 'And be decent to Berta – I mean Jane – *please*, Jo. You can come over tomorrow to see if there's any more news. How did you get here tonight, by the way?'

'Walked,' said Jo. 'Well – ran, I mean. Not by the roads, though – they take too long. I go like the birds do – as straight as I can, and it's *much* shorter!'

Dick had a sudden picture of the valiant little Jo speeding through woods and fields, over hills and through valleys, as straight as a crow flying homewards. How did she find her way like that? He knew *he* would never be able to!

Jo slipped out over the windowsill, and down the tree, as easily as a cat. 'Bye!' she said. 'See you soon.'

'Give our love to Jane,' whispered Dick.

'Shan't!' said Jo, much too loudly, and disappeared.

Julian switched out the light. 'Whew!' he said, 'I always feel as if I've been blown about by a strong, fresh wind when I see Jo. What a girl! Fancy wanting to ride all the way to Granton tonight, after running all the way here from Berta's!'

'Yes. I'm jolly glad you wouldn't let her take your bike,' said Dick. 'It's a good thing she wouldn't dare to disobey you!'

He got into bed – and just at that very moment the two boys heard a loud ringing noise. Dick sat up straight away.

'Well I'm blowed!' he said. 'The little wretch!'

'What's up?' said Julian, and then he too realised what the ringing was – a bicycle bell. Yes, a bell rung loudly and defiantly by someone cycling swiftly along the sea-road towards Granton!

'It's *Jo*!' said Dick. 'And she's taken *my* bike! I know its bell. Gosh, won't I rub her face in the mud when I get hold of her!'

Julian gave a loud guffaw. 'She's a monkey, a gallant, plucky, loyal, aggravating *monkey*. What a cheek she's got! She didn't dare to take *my* bike when I'd said no – so she took yours. Well – we can't do a thing about it now. What that roundabout boy is going to think when he's woken in the middle of the night by Jo, I cannot imagine.'

'He's probably used to her,' said Dick. 'Well, let's go to sleep. I wonder if George is asleep or awake? I hate to think of her a prisoner somewhere.'

'I bet Timmy hates it more than we do,' said Dick, hearing a long-drawn whimper from the next room. 'Poor old Tim. He can't go to sleep either!'

Dick and Julian managed to go to sleep at last, both thinking of a speedy little figure on a bicycle, racing through the night to ask questions of a roundabout boy called Spiky!

CHAPTER SEVENTEEN

To Gringo's Fair

AT HALF past seven next morning Joanna came running upstairs to Julian's bedroom, a piece of paper in her hand. She knocked on the door.

'Julian! A dirty little note was on the front doormat when I got down this morning. It's folded over with your name on the outside.'

Julian was out of bed in a trice. A note from the kidnappers perhaps? No – it couldn't be. They wouldn't write to *him*!

It was from Jo! She had scribbled it so badly that Julian could hardly read it.

'Julian, I saw Spiky, he's coming to the beach at eleven. I took Dick's bike to go home on. I will bring it back at eleven, don't be too cross. Jo.'

'Little scallywag,' said Dick. 'I hope she hasn't damaged my bike in any way.'

Jo hadn't. She had actually managed to find time to clean it before she left home, and arrived with it so bright and gleaming that Dick hadn't the heart to scold her!

She was early so she came to the house instead of the beach. She rode through the gate and up the front path and Timmy ran to greet her with a volley of delighted

barks. He liked Jo – in fact he really loved the little girl. She certainly had a way with animals! Sally followed, dancing on her tiptoes as usual, ready to welcome as a friend anyone that Timmy liked.

Dick hailed Jo from the front door as she came up.

'Hallo, bicycle-stealer! My word, what's happened to my bike – have you spring-cleaned it?'

Jo grinned, looking at Dick warily. 'Yes. I'm sorry I took it, Dick.'

'You're not a bit sorry – but I'll forgive you,' said Dick, grinning too. 'So you got to the fair safely after all?'

'Oh yes – and I woke up Spiky – he wasn't half

surprised,' said Jo. 'But his pa was sleeping in the same caravan as he was, so I couldn't say much. I just told him to be on Kirrin Beach at eleven. Then I rode back home. I ought to have left your bike on the way back, but I was a bit tired, so I rode home, instead of walking.'

'You can't have had much sleep last night,' said Julian, looking at the sunburnt girl with her untidy curly hair. 'Hallo – who's that?'

A short, plump boy was hurrying past the gate. He had a mop of black hair which stuck up into curious spikes of hair at the crown.

'Oh – that's Spiky!' said Jo. 'He's on time, isn't he? He's called Spiky because of his hair. You won't believe it, but he spends a fortune on hair-oil, trying to make those spiky bits go flat. But they won't.' She called loudly.

'Spiky! Hey, SPIKY!'

Spiky turned at once. He had a pleasant, rather lopsided face, and eyes as black as currants. He stood staring at Jo and the boys. 'I'm just off to the beach,' he said.

'Right. We're coming too,' said Jo, and she and the boys went to join him. They met the ice-cream man on the way and Julian bought an ice-cream for each of them.

'Coo – thanks,' said Spiky, pleased. He was rather shy of Dick and Julian, and wondered very much why he had been asked to come.

They sat down on the beach. 'I wasn't half scared when you came tapping at the window last night,' he said to Jo, licking his ice-cream with a very pink tongue. 'What's it all about?'

'Well,' said Julian, cautiously, 'we're interested in somebody called Gringo.'

'Old Gringo?' said Spiky. 'A lot of people're interested in Gringo. Do you know what we say at the fair? We say Gringo ought to put up a notice. 'All dirty work done here!' He's a bad lot, Gringo is – but he pays us well, even if he makes us work like servants.'

'He owns the fair, doesn't he?' said Julian, and Spiky nodded. 'I expect he uses it as a cover for all his other, bigger jobs,' Julian said to Dick. He looked at the plump, black-eyed boy, wondering how far he could trust him. Jo saw the look and knew what it meant.

'He's all right,' she said, nodding towards Spiky. 'You can say what you like. He's an oyster, he is. Aren't you, Spiky?'

Spiky grinned his lopsided grin. Julian decided to trust him, and speaking in a low voice that really thrilled Spiky, he told him about the kidnapping of George. Spiky's eyes nearly fell out of his head.

'Coo!' he said. 'I bet old Gringo's at the bottom of that. Last week he went off up to London – he told my pa he was on to a big job – an American job, he said it was.'

'Yes – it sounds as if it all fits,' said Julian. 'Spiky, this kidnapping happened the night before last. Did anything unusual occur in the fair camp, do you know? It must have happened in the middle of the night.'

Spiky considered. He shook his head. 'No – I don't think so. Gringo's big double-caravan is still there – so he can't have gone. He had it moved right away from the camp yesterday morning – said there was too much noise for his old ma, who lives in his posh caravan and looks after him. We was all glad it was moved – now he can't spy on us so easily!'

'I suppose you . . .' began Julian, and then stopped as Dick gave an exclamation.

'I've got an idea!' he said. 'Suppose that caravan was moved for *another* reason – suppose someone was making a row inside the van – someone shouting for help, say! Gringo would have to move it away from the rest of the camp in case that someone was heard.'

There was a pause, and then Spiky nodded. 'Yes. It could be,' he said. 'I've never known Gringo move his caravan away from the camp before. Shall I do a bit of snooping for you?'

'Yes,' said Julian, excited. 'My word – it *would* be a bit of luck if we could find George so quickly – and so near us too! A fair camp would be a fine place to hide her, of course. Thank goodness we found that bit of paper with "Gringo" written on it!'

'Let's all go to the fair this afternoon,' said Dick. 'Timmy too. He'd smell out George at once.'

'Hadn't we better tell the police first?' said Julian. At once Spiky and Jo got up in alarm. Spiky looked as if he were going to run away immediately!

'Don't you get the police, Julian!' said Jo urgently. 'You won't get anything more out of Spiky, if you do. Not a thing.'

'I'm going,' said Spiky, still looking terrified.

'No you're not,' said Dick, and caught hold of him. 'We shan't go to the police. They might frighten off Gringo and make him smuggle George away at once. I've no doubt he has plans to do so at any minute. We shan't say a word, so sit down and be sensible.'

'You can believe him,' Jo told Spiky. 'He's straight, see?'

Spiky sat down, still looking wary. 'If you're coming to the fair, come at four,' he said. 'It's half-day closing today for the towns around, and the place will be packed. If you want to do any snooping, you won't be noticed in that crowd.'

'Right,' said Julian. 'We'll be there. Look out for us, Spiky, in case you've got any news.'

Spiky then left, and the boys couldn't help smiling at his back view – the spikes of hair at the top of his head were so very noticeable!

'You'd better stay to lunch with us, Jo,' said Dick, and the delighted girl beamed all over her face.

'Will Joanna's cousin mind you not being back to dinner?' asked Julian.

'No. I said I wouldn't be back all day,' said Jo. 'It's still school holidays, you see. Anyway, I can't stand that Jane – she moons about all the time – and she's got some of my clothes on, too.'

Jo sounded so indignant about Berta that the boys had to laugh. They all went back to Kirrin Cottage, and found Joanna and Anne hard at work in the house.

'Well, you monkey!' said Joanna to Jo. 'Up to tricks as usual, I hear. Throwing stones at people's windows in the middle of the night. You just try that on *my* window and see what happens to you! Now, put on that apron, and help round a bit. How's Jane?'

Joanna was most excited to hear about the boys' latest ideas as to where George might be. Julian gave her a warning.

'But no ringing up the police behind our backs *this* time, Joanna,' he said. 'This is something best done by Dick and me.'

'Can't I come with Sally?' asked Anne.

'We can't *possibly* take Sally,' said Dick, 'in case Gringo's about and recognises her. So you'd better stay and look after her, and we'll take Timmy. He would be sure to smell where George is, if she's hidden anywhere in the camp. But I think she's probably in Gringo's own caravan.'

Timmy pricked up his ears every time he heard George's name mentioned. He was a very miserable dog indeed, and kept running to the front gate, hoping to see George coming along. Whenever they missed him, they knew where to find him – lying mournfully on George's empty bed – probably with an equally mournful Sally beside him!

The boys and Jo set off to the fair about half past three, on their bicycles. Jo rode Anne's this time, and Timmy ran valiantly beside them. Jo glanced at Dick's bicycle from time to time, proud of its brilliant look – how well she had cleaned it that morning!

They came to the fair. 'You can put your bikes up against Spiky's caravan,' said Jo. 'They'll be safe there. Will you pay, and then we'll get in straight away? You needn't pay for me – I'm going through the gap in the hedge. I'm Spiky's friend, so it's all right.'

She gave Dick her bicycle and disappeared. Julian paid and went in at the gate. They saw Jo waving wildly to them from the side of the big field and wheeled the three bicycles over to her. Timmy followed closely at their heels.

'Hallo!' said Spiky, appearing suddenly. 'See you soon!' I've got to go and tend to the roundabout. I've got a bit of news, but not much. That's Gringo's caravan over there, the double one, big van in front, little van behind.'

He nodded his head to where a most magnificent caravan stood, right away from the rest of the camp. There were people milling about all round the other vans, but there was nobody at all by Gringo's. Evidently no one dared to go too near.

'I vote we buy a ball at one of the stands, and then go and play near Gringo's caravan,' said Dick, in a low voice. 'Then one of us will throw the ball too hard and it will go near the van – and we'll somehow manage to get a peep inside. Timmy can go sniffing round while we play. If George is there he'll bark the place down.'

'Jolly good idea!' said Julian. 'Come on, Jo! And keep your eyes open all the time in case you've got to warn us of danger.'

CHAPTER EIGHTEEN

Spiky is very helpful

THE TWO boys and Jo, with Timmy at their heels, wandered round the fair to find somewhere to buy a ball. There seemed to be none for sale, so they had a go at a hoop-la stall, and Julian managed to get a ring round a small red ball. Just the thing!

It was a big and noisy fair, and hundreds of people from the nearby towns had come on this shops' closing day to enjoy the fun. The roundabout played its loud, raucous music all the time, swings went to and fro, the dodgem cars banged and bumped one another as usual, and men went round shouting their wares.

'Balloons! Giant balloons! Fifty pence each!'

'Ice-cream! All flavours.'

'Tell your fortune, lady? I'll tell it true as can be!'

Jo was very much at home in the fair. She had been brought up in one, and knew all the tricks of the trade. Timmy was rather amazed at the noise, and kept close to the boys, his tail still down because he could not forget that George was missing.

'Now let's play our little game of ball,' said Julian. 'Come on, Tim – and if we get into any trouble, just growl and show your teeth, see?'

The three of them, with Timmy, went to the clear space of field that separated the magnificent caravan from the rest of the camp. A man at a nearby stall called to them.

'Hey! You'll get into trouble if you play there!' But they took no notice and he shrugged his shoulders and began to shout his wares.

They threw the ball to one another, and then Julian flung it so wildly that it ran right up to the wheels of the front caravan of the pair. In a trice Dick and Jo were after it. Jo leapt up on a wheel and looked in at the big window, while Dick ran to the small van that was attached behind the big one.

A quick glance assured Jo that the big caravan was empty. The interior was furnished in a most luxurious way and looked like a very fine bed-sitting-room. She leapt down.

Dick peered into the window of the smaller van. At first he thought there was no one there – and then he saw a pair of very fierce, angry eyes looking at him – the eyes of a small, bent old woman with untidy hair. She looked rather like a witch, Dick thought. She was sitting sewing on a bunk, and, as he looked in, she shook her fist at him and called out something he couldn't hear.

He jumped down and joined the others. 'No one at all in the big van,' said Jo.

'Only a witch-like old woman in the other,' reported Dick, in deep disappointment. 'Unless George is pushed under a bunk or squashed into a cupboard, she's certainly not there!'

'Timmy doesn't seem interested in the caravans at all, does he?' said Julian. 'I'm sure if George really *was* in one of those caravans, he'd bark and try to get inside.'

'Yes – I think he would,' said Dick. 'Hallo, there's somebody coming out of the second van. It's the old lady! She's in a fine old temper!'

So she was! She came down the steps to the van, shouting and shaking her fist at them. 'Tim – go and find, go and find – in that van!' said Julian, suddenly, as the old woman came towards them.

The three of them stood their ground as the old woman came right up. They couldn't understand a word she said, partly because she had no teeth, and partly because she spoke a mixture of many languages. Anyway, it was quite obvious that she was ticking them off for daring to play near the two vans.

Timmy had understood what Julian had said, and had slipped inside the second van. He was there for half a minute, and then he barked. The boys jumped, and Dick made a move towards the van.

Then Timmy appeared, dragging something behind him with his teeth. He tried to bark at the same time, but he couldn't. He dragged the coat-like thing right down to the ground before the old woman was on him, screaming in a high voice, and hitting at him. She pulled the garment away and went up the steps, kicking out at the surprised

Timmy as he tried to pull it away. The door slammed.

'If that old woman hadn't been old, Timmy would have soon shown her he was top dog!' said Dick. 'Whatever was he pulling out of the van?'

'Come over here, out of sight of the van,' said Julian, urgently. 'Didn't you recognise it, Dick? It was *George's dressing-gown*!'

'My word!' said Dick, stopping in surprise. 'Yes, you're right – it was. Whew! What does that mean exactly? George certainly isn't in those vans, or Timmy would have found her.'

'I sent him in to see if he could *smell* that George had been hidden there,' said Julian. 'I thought he would bark excitedly if he smelt her scent anywhere – on the bunk, perhaps. I never guessed he'd find her *dressing-gown* and drag it out to show us!'

'Good old Timmy! Clever old Timmy!' said Dick, patting the dog, whose tail was now at half-mast instead of right down. He had at least found George's dressing-gown – but how surprising to find it in that caravan!

'Why on earth didn't they take the dressing-gown with them, when they took George off?' wondered Julian. 'There's no doubt that she has *been* in that caravan – she was taken straight there the night before last, I expect. Where is she now?'

'She must have been dressed differently,' said Dick. 'They must have had to dress her properly, when they took her somewhere else. After all, she was only in pyjamas and dressing-gown.'

Jo was listening to all this, puzzled and worried. She nudged Dick. 'Spiky's beckoning to us,' she said. They went over to the roundabout boy, whose father was now in charge of the noisy machine.

Spiky took them into his caravan, a small and rather dirty one, in which he lived with his father.

'I saw Gringo's old ma chasing you!' he said with his lopsided grin. 'What was your dog dragging out of the van?'

They told him. He nodded. 'I've been asking round a bit, cautiously,' he said, 'just to see if anyone had heard anything from Gringo's caravan – and the fellow whose caravan is nearest told me he heard shouts and yells two nights ago. He reckoned it was someone in Gringo's van – but he's too scared of Gringo to go and interfere, of course.'

'That would be George yelling,' said Dick.

'Well, then Gringo's vans were moved the next day right away from the other vans,' said Spiky. 'And this afternoon, before the fair opened, Gringo got his car and towed the little van – the second one – out of the field, and set off with it. We all wondered why, but he told somebody it needed repairing.'

'Whew! And George was inside!' said Dick. 'What a cunning way of moving her off to another hiding place.'

'When did the van come back?' asked Julian.

'Just before you came,' said Spiky. 'I don't know where it went. It was gone an hour, I should think.'

'An hour,' said Dick. 'Well, suppose it goes at an average of twenty-five miles an hour – you can't go very fast if you are towing something – that would mean he had gone somewhere about twelve miles or so away, and come back the same distance – making about an hour's drive, allowing for a stop when they arrived at the place they had to leave her at.'

'Yes,' said Julian. 'But there are lots of places within the radius of twelve miles!'

'Where's Gringo's *car*?' said Dick suddenly.

'Over there, under that big tarpaulin,' said Spiky. 'It's a silver-grey one – American and very striking. He thinks the world of it, Gringo does.'

'I'm going to have a peep at it,' said Julian, and strode off. He came to the tarpaulin, which covered the car right to the ground. He lifted it and was just about to look under it when a man ran up, shouting.

'Here, you! Leave that alone! You'll be turned out of the fair if you mess about with things that don't concern you!'

But Timmy was with Julian, and he turned and growled so fiercely that the man stopped in a hurry. Julian had plenty of time to take a good look under the tarpaulin!

Yes – the car was silver-grey, a big American one – and the wings were bright blue! Julian took a quick look at the two left-hand ones and saw a deep scratch on one of them. Before he dropped the tarpaulin he had time to glance at the tyres. He was sure they had the same pattern as those shown in the wheel-tracks he had sketched! He had checked the sketch with Jim, at Kirrin Garage, who had told him they were an American design.

Yes – this was the car that had hidden in the clearing the night before last – the car that had turned with difficulty and made those deep ruts – the car that had taken George away, and this afternoon had towed away the caravan with her inside, to hide her somewhere else.

He dropped the tarpaulin and walked back to the others, excited, taking no notice of the rude things that the nearby man called out to him.

'It's the car, all right,' said Julian. 'Now – WHERE did it go this afternoon? If only we could find out!'

'It's such a very striking car that anyone would notice it – especially as it was towing a rather nice little caravan,' said Dick.

'Yes – but we can't go round the countryside asking everyone we meet if they've noticed a silver-grey car with blue wings,' said Julian.

'Let's go back home and get a map and see the lie of the country round about,' said Dick. 'Spiky, which way did the car turn when it went out of the field-gate?'

'Towards the east,' said Spiky. 'On the road to Big Twillingham.'

'Well, that's something to know,' said Dick. 'Come on, let's get our bikes. Thanks a lot, Spiky. You've been a terrific help. We'll let you know what happens.'

'Call on me if ever you want more help,' said Spiky, proudly, and gave them a smart little salute, bobbing his head so that his spikes of hair shook comically.

The three of them rode off, with Timmy running beside them again. As soon as they got home they told Anne and Joanna all they had found out. Joanna was for ringing up the police at once again, but Julian stopped her.

'I think perhaps we can do this next bit of work better than they can,' he said. 'We're going to try and find out where the car went, Joanna. Now – where are the maps of the district?'

They found them and began to pore over them. Jo was quite lost when it came to map-reading. She could find her way anywhere, day or night – but not with a map!

'Now – here's the road to Big Twillingham and Little Twillingham,' he said. 'Let's list carefully all the roads the car could take from there. My word – it's a job!'

CHAPTER NINETEEN

An exciting plan

AFTER FIFTEEN minutes they had six towns on their list, all of which could have been reached in about half an hour from Big Twillingham, which was two miles away from the fair.

'And *now* what do you propose to do, Ju?' asked Dick. 'Bike over to all the towns and ask if anyone has seen the car?'

'No. We can't possibly do that,' said Julian. 'I'm going down to the garage to see our friend Jim, and get *his* help! I'm going to ask him to ring up any friends he has in the garages in those towns, and ask if they've seen the car passing through.'

'Won't he think it's a bit funny?' asked Anne.

'Yes. But he won't mind how funny it is if we pay for the telephone calls and give him some money for his trouble!' said Julian, folding up the map. 'And what's more he won't ask any questions either. He'll probably think it's some silly bet we've got on with one another.'

Jim was quite willing to ring up the garages for them. He knew boys working in main garages in four of the towns, and he knew the hall porter of a hotel in the fifth town. But he knew no one in the sixth.

'That doesn't matter!' he said. 'We'll ring up the garage in the High Street there, and just ask whoever comes to the phone.'

Jim rang up the garage in Hillingford, and had a rather cheeky conversation with his friend there. He put the receiver down. 'No go,' he said. 'He says no car like that came through Hillingford, or he'd have noticed it that time of day. I'll ring up Jake at Green's Garage in Lowington now.'

'That's no go, either,' he said, after a minute's telephone conversation. 'I'll try my hall porter now. He's a cousin of mine.'

The hall porter had some news. 'Yes!' Jim kept saying. 'Yes, that's the one! Yes, yes! You heard him say that, did you? Thanks a lot.'

'What is it?' asked Dick, eagerly, when Jim at last put down the receiver.

'Pat – that's the hall porter – says he was off duty this afternoon, and went to buy some cigarettes at a little shop in the main street of Graysfield, where his hotel is – and as he stood talking to the fellow in the shop an enormous car drew up at the kerb – silver-grey, with blue wings – an American car, left-hand drive and all.'

'Yes – what next?' said Julian, eagerly.

'Well, the driver got out to get some cigarettes at the shop. He had dark glasses on, and a big gold ring on his finger – Pat noticed that . . .'

'That must be the man who asked about us at the teashop in Kirrin!' said Julian, remembering. 'Go on, Jim – this is wonderful!'

'Well, Pat's interested in big cars, so he went out and had a good look at it,' said Jim. 'He said the car had its blinds drawn down at the back, so he couldn't see inside. The fellow with the dark glasses came out and got into the driver's seat again. He called out to whoever was behind and said "Which way now?"'

'Yes, yes – did he hear the answer?' said Julian.

'Somebody called back and said, "Not far now. Into Twining, turn to the left, and it's the house on the hill."'

'*Well!* Of all the luck!' said Dick. 'Would that be where G . . .' He stopped at a sharp nudge from Julian, and remembered that he mustn't give too much away to the helpful Jim.

Julian passed over a pound to the pleased garage boy, who pocketed it at once, grinning. 'Now, you just come along to me if you want to know about any more cars,' he said. 'I'll phone all over the place for you! Thanks a lot!'

They sped back to Kirrin Cottage, too excited even to talk. They flung their bicycles against the wall and ran in to tell Anne and Joanna. Timmy and Sally sensed their excitement and danced round, barking loudly.

'We know where George is!' cried Dick. 'We know, we know!'

Joanna and Anne listened eagerly. 'Well, Julian,' said Joanna, in admiration, 'it was really smart of you to make

Jim phone up like that. The police couldn't have done better. What are you going to do now? Ring up that sergeant?'

'No,' said Julian. 'I'm so afraid that if the police get moving on this now, they'll alarm Gringo and he'll spirit George away somewhere else. Dick and I will go to this place tonight, and see if we can't get hold of George and bring her back! After all – it's only an ordinary house, I imagine – and as Gringo doesn't suspect that anyone knows where George is, he won't be on the lookout!'

'Good!' said Dick. 'Good, good, good!'

'I'm coming too,' said Jo.

'You are not,' said Julian, at once. 'That's flat – you are NOT COMING, Jo. But I shall take Timmy, of course.'

Jo said no more, but looked so sulky that Anne laughed. 'Cheer up, Jo. You can keep me and Sally company. Oh Julian – wouldn't it be *wonderful* to find George and rescue her!'

There was more map-reading as the boys decided which was the best way to bicycle over to Graysfield. 'Look out the best torches we've got, Anne, will you?' said Dick. 'And let me see – how can we bring George back once we've got her? On my bike-step, I think, though I know it's not allowed. But this is very urgent. We can't very well take a third bike with us. Gosh, isn't this exciting!'

'We really ought to ring up the police,' said Joanna, who kept saying this at intervals.

'Joanna, you sound like a parrot!' said Julian. 'If we're not back by morning you can ring up all the police in the country if you want to!'

'There's been another phone call from your aunt today, Julian – I nearly forgot to tell you,' said Joanna. 'Your uncle is better and they are coming home as soon as possible.'

'Not this evening, I hope,' said Julian, in alarm. 'Did they tell you anything about Mr Elbur Wright – Berta's father?'

'Oh, he's hanging on to his secrets quite happily now that he knows it isn't Berta who is kidnapped,' said Joanna. 'I don't know if the kidnappers even know they've got the wrong girl yet. It's all very hush-hush. Even your uncle and aunt are having to obey the police. Your poor aunt is so terribly upset about George.'

'Yes. She must be frightfully worried,' said Julian, soberly. 'We've had so much excitement today that I've almost forgotten to worry. And anyway when you're able to *do* something, things don't seem so bad.'

'Be careful you don't go and do too much and land yourself in trouble,' said Joanna, darkly.

'I'll be careful!' said Julian, winking at Dick. 'I say – isn't it nearly supper-time? I feel awfully hungry.'

'Well, we haven't had any tea. No wonder we're hungry.'

'Would you like bacon and eggs for a treat?' said Joanna, and there was a chorus of approval at once. Timmy and Sally wagged their tails as if Joanna's question applied to them too!

'We'll set off as soon as it's dark,' said Julian. 'Jo, you'd better go home after supper. They'll be worrying about you.'

'All right,' said Jo, pleased to have been asked to supper, but still sulky at being forbidden to go with Julian and Dick that night.

Jo disappeared after supper, with many messages to Berta from Dick, Julian, Anne and Sally.

'And I bet she doesn't give a single one of them!' said Dick. 'Now, let's have a game before we set off, Julian. Just to take our minds off the excitement. I'm getting all worked up!'

Joanna went up to bed at ten because she was tired. Anne stayed up to see the boys off. 'You *will* be careful,' she kept saying. 'You *will* be careful, won't you? Oh dear, I think it's almost worse to stay behind and wonder what's happening to you, than to go with you and find out!'

At last the time came for the boys to go. It was a quarter to twelve and, except for a small moon, was a dark night, with great clouds looming up, often hiding the moon.

'Come on, Timmy,' said Dick. 'We're going to find George.'

'Woof!' said Timmy, delighted. Sally wuffed too, and was most disappointed at being left behind. The boys wheeled their bicycles to the front gate.

'So long, Anne!' said Dick. 'Go to bed – and hope to see George when you wake up!'

They set off on their bicycles, with Timmy loping along beside them. They soon arrived at the field where the fair was, and went swinging away to the east, following the road the silver-grey car had gone that afternoon.

They knew the way by heart, for they had studied the map so well. As they passed the signposts they felt their excitement beginning to mount. 'Graysfield next,' said Dick at last. 'Soon be there, Timmy! You're not getting tired, are you?'

They came into Graysfield silently. The town was asleep, and not a single light showed in any window. A policeman suddenly loomed up out of the shadows, but when he saw two boys cycling, he did not stop them.

'Now – into Twining Village, turn to the left – and look for the house on the hill!' said Dick.

They rode through the tiny, silent village of Twining, and took the lane to the left. It led up a steep, narrow lane. The boys had to get off and walk because the hill was too much for them.

'There's the house!' said Julian, suddenly whispering. 'Look – through those trees. My word, it looks a dark and lonely one!'

They came to some enormous iron gates, but when they tried to open them, they found them locked. A great wall ran completely round the grounds. They followed it a little way, leaving their bicycles against a tree by the gate, but it was soon certain that nobody could climb a wall like that!

'Blow!' said Julian. 'Blow!'

'What about the gates?' whispered Dick. Then he glanced round him nervously, hearing a twig crack. 'Did your hear that? There's nobody following us, is there?'

'No! Don't get the jitters, for goodness' sake!' said Julian. 'What was it you were saying?'

'I said "What about the gates?"' said Dick. 'I don't see why we can't climb over them, do you? Nobody would do that in the daytime, they'd be seen – but I can't see why we can't do it *now* – they didn't look too difficult – just ordinary wrought-iron ones.'

'Yes! Of course!' said Julian. 'That's a brainwave. Come on!'

CHAPTER TWENTY

A thrilling time

THE TWO boys went back to the gates. Dick turned round and looked behind him two or three times. 'I do hope nobody *is* shadowing us!' he said. 'I keep on feeling somebody's watching us all the time.'

'Oh, stuff!' said Julian, impatiently. 'Look – here are the gates. Give me a leg-up and I'll be over in a jiffy.'

Dick gave him a shove, and Julian climbed over the gates without much difficulty. They were bolted, not locked. He slid the great bolts carefully, and opened one gate a little for Dick and Timmy. 'Timmy can't be left behind!' he said. 'And he certainly couldn't climb this gate!'

They kept to the shadowed side of the drive as they walked up towards the house. The small moon came out from behind a cloud as they came near. It was an old house, with high chimneys, an ugly house with narrow windows that seemed like watching eyes.

Dick glanced behind him suddenly and Julian saw him. 'Got the jitters again?' he said, impatiently. 'Dick, don't be an ass. You know perfectly well that if anyone was shadowing us, Timmy would hear them and go for them at once.'

'Yes, I know,' said Dick. 'I'm an idiot – but I've just got that feeling tonight – the feeling that someone else *is* there!'

They came right up to the house. 'How shall we get in?' whispered Julian. 'The doors are all sure to be locked. We'll have to try the windows.'

They tiptoed silently round the big house. As Julian had

said, the doors were all locked. The windows were all fastened too – well and truly fastened. Not one was open or could be opened.

'If this is a house belonging to Gringo he must be able to hide plenty of things in absolute safety – bolted gates, high walls, locked doors, fastened windows!' said Dick. 'No burglar could possibly get in.'

'And neither can we,' said Julian, desperately. 'We've been all round the house three times now! There's no door, no window we can get in. No balcony to climb up to – no ivy to hang on to – nothing!'

'Let's go round once more,' said Dick. 'We *might* have missed something.'

So once more they went round – and discovered something curious when they got to the kitchen quarters. The moon came out, and showed them a round black hole in the ground! Whatever could it be?

They tiptoed to it just as the moon went in again. They shone their torches on it briefly.

'It's a coal-hole!' said Dick, astonished. '*Why* didn't we see it before? Look, there's the lid just beside it. It's been left open. I suppose the moon was in last time we came by this part of the house. I can't think how we didn't notice it.'

Julian was uneasy. 'I didn't see it before, certainly. It's strange. Could it be a trap, do you think?'

'I don't see how it could be,' said Dick. 'Come on – let's get down. At least it's a way in.' He shone his torch into the hole. 'Yes, look – there's a whole lot of coke down there – we can easily jump on to it. Tim, you go first and spy out the land.'

Timmy jumped down at once, the coke slithering away from beneath his four paws. 'He's down all right,' said Julian. 'I'll go next. Then you.'

Down they jumped, and the coke slithered away again, making what seemed to be a very loud noise in the silent night. Julian shone his torch around.

They were standing on a very large heap of coke in the middle of a big cellar. At the end was a door.

'Hope it's not locked,' said Dick, in a whisper. 'Now, Tim, keep to heel, for goodness' sake, and don't make a sound!'

They went to the door, treading on gritty bits of coke. Julian turned the dirty handle – and the door opened inwards! 'It's not locked!' said Julian, thankfully.

They crept through it, Timmy treading on their heels, and found themselves in another cellar, set with stone shelves on which were piled tins and boxes and crates. 'Enough food here to stand a siege!' whispered Dick. 'Where are the cellar steps? We've got to get out.'

'Over there,' said Julian. Then he stopped and put out his torch. He had heard something.

'Did you hear that?' he whispered. 'It sounded like somebody treading on the coke in the coal cellar! Gosh, I hope nobody *is* shadowing us. We'll soon be prisoners if so.'

They listened but heard nothing further. Up the stone steps they went and undid the door at the top. A big kitchen lay beyond, lit by the dim moon. A shadow rose suddenly in front of them and Timmy growled. Dick's heart almost stopped beating. What in the world was that, crawling silently over the floor and disappearing in the shadows? He clutched at Julian and made him jump.

'Don't do that, ass! That was only the kitchen cat you saw,' whispered Julian. 'Gosh, you made me jump. Wasn't it a good thing that Timmy didn't go for the cat? There would have been an awful yowling!'

'Where do you suppose George will be?' asked Dick. 'Somewhere at the top of the house?'

'I've no idea. We'll just have to look into every room,' said Julian. So they looked into every room on the ground floor, but they were empty. They were huge rooms, ugly and over-furnished.

'Come on – up the stairs!' said Dick, and up they went. They came to an enormous landing, hung with tapestry curtains at the windows. Timmy suddenly gave a small growl and in a trice both boys had hidden themselves in the folds of the long window-curtains. Timmy went with them, feeling surprised. Dick peeped out after a minute.

'I think it was that cat again,' he whispered. 'Look, there it is, up on that chest. It's following us, wondering what on earth we're doing, I expect!'

'Blow it!' said Julian. '*I'm* getting the jitters now, being watched by a shadowy cat. I suppose it *is* real?'

'Timmy thinks so!' said Dick. 'Come on – there are any amount of bedroom doors on this landing.'

They tiptoed into the rooms whose doors were open, but no one was sleeping in the beds there. They came to a closed door and listened. Someone was snoring inside!

'That's not George,' said Dick. 'Anyway, she'd be locked in, and the key is in this door.'

They went to the next door, which was also shut. They listened and could hear someone breathing heavily.

'Not George,' said Dick, and they went on up to the next flight of stairs. There were four more rooms there, two of them not even furnished. The doors of the other two were ajar, and it was clear that people were sleeping in them, because once more there was loud breathing to be heard.

'There don't seem to be any more rooms,' said Dick, in dismay, as they flashed their torches carefully round the top landing. 'Blow! Where's George then?'

'Look – there's a little wooden door there,' said Julian, in Dick's ear. 'A door leading into the cistern room, I should think.'

'She wouldn't be there,' said Dick. 'But wait – look, there's a strong bolt on the door! And cistern rooms don't have bolts on their doors, or even locks. This one hasn't a lock, but it *has* a bolt.'

'Sh! Not so loud!' said Julian. 'Yes, that's funny, I must say. How can we get the door open without waking the people in those other two rooms?'

'We'll shut their doors very quietly, and we'll lock them!' said Dick, excited. 'I'll go and do it.'

He drew the doors gently to, and then locked first one and then the other, having taken the keys from the other side of the doors to do so. Except that one made a slight click as he locked it, there was no noise. Nobody stirred in the two rooms, and the boys breathed freely again.

They went to the little wooden door opposite. They pulled gently at the bolt, afraid that it might squeak. But it didn't. It was obviously quite new, and ran easily. The door opened outwards with a small creak. There was pitch darkness inside, and the sound of trickling water from the cistern.

Dick flashed his torch on and off quickly. In that second he saw something that made his heart jump!

There was a small mattress on the floor of the little cistern room, and someone was lying on it, rolled so completely in blankets that even the head was covered! Julian had seen it too, and he put his arm on Dick's, afraid that it might not be George, afraid that it might be someone who would give the alarm, perhaps another prisoner.

But Timmy knew who it was! Timmy ran straight in with a small, loving whimper and flung himself on the sleeping figure!

Dick shut the cistern room door at once, afraid of the noise being heard. Timmy might bark with joy in a moment, or George might shout!

The figure gave a grunt and sat up. The blanket fell away from the head – and there was George's curly nob, and her startled face.

'Sh!' said Dick, raising his finger warningly. 'SH!'

Timmy was licking George from head to foot, wild with delight, but extraordinarily silent – clever old Timmy knew that this was one of the times when joy must be quiet!

'Oh!' said George, hugging Timmy anywhere she could. 'Oh, Timmy! I missed you so! Darling, darling, Tim! Oh Timmy!'

Dick stood by the closed door, listening to find out if anyone was stirring in the other rooms. He heard nothing at all. Julian went to George.

'Are you all right, George?' he asked. 'Have you been treated well?'

'Not very,' said George. 'But then I didn't behave very well! I did quite a lot of kicking and biting – so they locked me in here!'

'Poor old George!' said Julian. 'Well, we'll hear everything when we've got out of here. So far, we've been jolly lucky. Can you come now?'

'Yes,' said George and got off the mattress. She was dressed in an odd selection of clothes, and looked rather peculiar. 'That awful old woman – Gringo's mother – found these for me when I was taken to the caravan,' she said. 'Gosh, I've got a lot to tell you!'

'Sh!' said Dick, at the door. 'Not a sound, now! I'm going to open the door!'

He opened it slowly. All was quiet. 'Now we'll go down the stairs,' he said. 'Not a sound!'

They went down the first flight of stairs and on to the enormous landing. Then, just as Dick put his foot on to the next stair down, he trod on something soft that yowled, spat and scratched. It was that cat!

Dick fell halfway down the stairs, and Timmy could not stop himself from chasing the cat up the landing and up the top stairs to the cistern room. Nor could he stop himself from barking!

Shouts came from two of the nearby bedrooms and two men appeared in pyjamas. One switched on the landing light, and then both of them tore down the stairs after the three children. Dick picked himself up, but he had ricked his ankle and could not even walk!

'Run, George – I'll see to Dick!' yelled Julian. But George stopped too – and in a trice the two men were on to them, catching hold of Dick and Julian, and jerking them into a nearby room.

'Tim! TIM!' shouted George. 'Help, Timmy!'

But before Timmy could come pelting down the stairs from the attic George was shoved into the room too, and the door locked.

'Look out for the dog!' shouted one of the men. 'He's dangerous!'

Timmy certainly was! He came tearing towards the men, snarling, his eyes blazing, showing all his teeth.

The men darted into the room next to the one into which they had locked the children, and banged the door. Timmy flung himself against it in rage, snarling and growling in a most terrifying manner. If only he could get at those men! If only he could!

CHAPTER TWENTY-ONE

Most unexpected!

SOON THERE was real pandemonium in the old house! The sleepers in the rooms on the top landing awoke suddenly and found their doors locked, and began to bang on them and shout. The three children in the locked room on the ground floor shouted and banged too – and Timmy nearly went mad!

Only the men in the room next to the children were silent. They were terrified at Timmy's growling and snarling. They would have liked to lock themselves in, but the key was on the other side of the door – and they certainly didn't dare to open it to get the key!

Soon the children quietened down. Dick sat on a chair, exhausted. 'That cat! That wretched, prowling, sly old cat! Gosh, I stepped on it and it scratched me to the bone – to say nothing of pitching me headlong down the stairs and making me wrench my ankle!'

'We so *nearly* managed to escape!' groaned Julian.

'I can't *think* what will happen now!' said George. 'Timmy's out there and can't get in to us, and we can't possibly get out to him because the door's locked – and those men won't dare to set a foot outside *their* door while Tim's there!'

'And we've locked the people into their rooms upstairs!' said Julian. 'Well, it's certain that nobody can get out of their rooms to help anyone else – so it looks as if we'll all be here till Doomsday!'

It certainly did seem a very poor lookout. The only people who were not behind locked doors were the two men, whoever they were – and they simply dared not put a foot outside their room. Timmy roamed about, occasionally whimpering and scratching outside the children's door, but more often growling outside the next door, sometimes flinging his heavy body against it as if he would break it down.

'I bet the men are shaking with fright,' said Dick. 'They won't even dare to try and get out of a window in case they meet Timmy outside somewhere!'

'Serve them right,' said George. 'Gosh, I'm glad you came! Wasn't I an absolute ass to take Sally down to the kennel that night?'

'You were,' said Julian, 'I agree wholeheartedly. The men were waiting for a chance to get Berta, of course, and they saw you, complete with Berta's dog, and thought you were the girl they wanted!'

'Yes. They flung something all over my head so that I couldn't make a sound,' said George. 'I fought like anything, and my dressing-gown girdle must have slipped off – did you find it?'

'Yes,' said Dick. 'We were jolly glad to find a few other things too – the comb – the hanky – the sweet – and of course the note!'

'They carried me quite a way to somewhere in the wood,' said George. 'Then they plonked me down in the back of the car. But they had to turn it and it was difficult – and I had the bright thought of throwing out all the things in my dressing-gown pocket just in *case* you came along and saw them.'

'What about that note – with the word Gringo on?' asked Julian. 'That was a terrific help. We wouldn't be here tonight if it hadn't been for that.'

'Well, I heard one of the men call the other Gringo,' said George. 'And it was such an unusual name I thought I'd scribble it on a bit of paper and throw that out too – it was just on chance I did it.'

'A jolly good chance!' said Dick. 'Good thing you had a notebook and pencil with you!'

'I hadn't,' said George. 'But one of the men had left his coat in the back of the car and there was a notebook with a pencil in the breast pocket. I just used that!'

'Jolly good!' said Julian.

'Well, they whizzed me off in the car to some fairground or other,' said George. 'I heard the roundabout music next day. There was a horrid old witch-like woman in the caravan; she didn't seem at all pleased to see me. I had to sleep in a chair that night, and I got so wild that I yelled and shouted and threw things about and smashed quite a lot of cups and saucers. I enjoyed that.'

The boys couldn't help laughing. 'Yes – I bet you did,' said Dick. 'They had to move the caravan away from the fair itself, because they were afraid people would hear you. In fact, I expect that's why Gringo decided to hide you here!'

'Yes. I suddenly felt a jolt, and found the caravan we were in was being towed away!' said George. 'I was awfully surprised. I waved at the windows and shouted as we drove through the streets, but nobody seemed to notice anything wrong – in fact some people waved back to me! Then we swung in through some gates, and came here – and, as I told you, they put me up here because I made such a nuisance of myself!'

'Did you tell them you weren't Berta?' asked Dick.

'No,' said George. 'Of course not. For two reasons – I knew there would be no fear of Berta's father giving those secrets away, because he'd be told by you that *I* had been kidnapped, not his precious Berta. So he'd hang on to them. And also I thought *Berta* would be safe, so long as I didn't tell the men they'd got the wrong person.'

'You're a good kid, George,' said Julian, and slapped her gently on the back. 'A – very – good – kid. I'm jolly proud of you. There's nobody like our George!'

'Don't be an idiot,' said George, but she was very pleased all the same.

'Well, there's no more to tell,' she said, 'except that the cistern room was most frightfully draughty, and I had to wrap my head up as well as my body when I lay down. And the cistern made awful noises – sort of *rude* noises, that made me want to say "I beg your pardon!" all the time! Of course I knew you'd rescue me, so I wasn't awfully worried!'

'And we *haven't* rescued you!' said Julian. 'All we've done is to get ourselves locked up as well as you!'

'Tell me how you found out I was here,' said George. So the boys told her everything and she listened, thrilled.

'So Berta went to stay with Jo!' she said. 'I bet Jo didn't like that.'

'She didn't, said Julian. 'But she's been quite a help. I only wish she were here now, and could do one of her ivy-climbing stunts, or something!'

'I say – Timmy's very quiet all of a sudden!' said George, listening. 'What's happened?'

They listened. Timmy was not barking or whimpering. There was no sound from him at all. What was happening? George's heart sank – perhaps those men had managed to do something to him?

But suddenly they heard him again, whimpering – but whimpering gladly and excitedly. And then a familiar voice came to their ears.

'Dick! Julian! Where are you?'

'Gosh – it's JO!' said Dick, astounded. He limped to the door. 'We're in here, Jo. Unlock the door!'

Jo unlocked it and looked in, grinning, Timmy tore in like a whirlwind and flung himself on George, almost knocking her over. Dick limped out of the room immediately Jo rushed in, much to everyone's astonishment. Then he returned, looking rather pleased with himself.

'Let's go while the going's good,' he said.

'Yes – but, be careful, those men will be out, now that Timmy isn't there to guard them!' cried Julian, suddenly realising that the two angry fellows could easily escape while Timmy was in with them – and might lock the door on the lot of them, Timmy too!

'It's all right – there's no desperate hurry!' said Dick. 'I thought of that. I slipped out and locked their door on *them*, as soon as Jo rushed in to us. And there they can stay till the police arrive in the morning. They can then collect the whole lot – the men upstairs too.'

'And I'm sure the police will be quite pleased to search the house and the cellars,' said Julian. 'There will be plenty of stuff here that they will be interested in! Well, let's go at once.'

They called a cheery goodbye to the two men. 'We're off!' shouted Dick. 'You'd better look out for the dog in case he gets you!' They all went down the hall, Dick hobbling, for his ankle was still painful.

'We might as well leave in style,' said Julian, and unbolted and unlocked the front door. 'Also it would be as well to leave this door open for the police to come in by – I don't expect *they* will want to come in through the coal-hole! It was a good idea of yours to let the men think we were leaving Tim behind to guard them, Dick – they won't dare even to climb out of the windows in case he's waiting for them!'

'We've left a good many lights on,' said George, looking

back. 'Never mind – we're not paying the bill! Come on, Timmy, out into the dark, dark night!'

They went down the front steps and into the dark drive. Everyone felt safe with Timmy running ahead.

'Jo – exactly how did you get here?' said Dick, suddenly. 'You were forbidden to come.'

'I know,' said Jo. 'Well, I just took Anne's bike and followed you, that's all. And I walked in through the front gates when you'd left them open, of course. That was easy.'

'Gosh – I kept *feeling* there was someone behind me!' said Dick. 'And there was – it was *you*, you little horror! No wonder Timmy didn't bother to bark or growl.'

'Yes, it was me,' said Jo. 'And I followed you round and round the house, while you were trying to get in – and I thought you never *would* see that coal-hole – so I took the lid off and put it on the ground, hoping you'd see it then. And you did!'

'So *you* did that!' said Dick. 'I must say I was astonished to see it. I knew we must have passed it before. So that was you too! You want a good telling-off, you disobedient, cheeky little wretch!'

Jo laughed. 'I couldn't bear you to go off without me,' she said. 'It's a good thing I *did* come! I waited and waited inside that coal-hole for you to come back with George – and when you didn't, I left the coal-hole and got into the house. And Timmy heard me and came running down the stairs. He nearly knocked me over, he was that pleased!'

'Here are the gates at last,' said George. 'What are we going to do about bikes? There isn't one for me.'

'Jo can stand behind on my step and hold on to my shoulder,' said Julian. 'You take Anne's bike, George. We'll leave these gates open. The police ought to be pleased with us for saving them so much trouble!'

Off they went down the steep hill, Timmy running behind, his tail wagging happily. He had got George back again. All was well again in his doggy world!

CHAPTER TWENTY-TWO

'These kids sure are wunnerful!'

WHAT SHRIEKS and shouts there were from Joanna and Anne when the four arrived at Kirrin Cottage at last, at half past three in the morning! Joanna was awake, but Anne had just gone to sleep. She was sleeping in Joanna's room for company and Sally was there too.

The stories had to be told again and again. First Dick, then Julian, then George, then Jo – they all talked without stopping, excited and happy. Sally ran from one to the other, and followed Timmy about – but sometimes her little stiff tail drooped when she remembered that Berta was not there.

'I *say*,' said Dick, suddenly drawing back the sitting-room curtains '– it's daylight! The sun's up! And all the time I've been thinking it was still night!'

'No use going to bed, then,' said Jo, at once. She was so much enjoying this that she felt as if she never wanted it to stop!

'Well, I suppose it isn't,' said Joanna. 'I know what we'll do – we'll have a big breakfast now, a very big one to celebrate – and then we'll all go back to bed and sleep till lunch-time. We're tired out really – just look at our black-rimmed eyes and pale cheeks!'

'Joanna! We're all as sunburnt as can be, you're just making that up!' said George. 'Come on – let's get this celebration breakfast going! Bacon – eggs – tomatoes – fried bread. Oh, and mushrooms too – have you any mushrooms, Joanna? And lots and lots of hot coffee, and toast and marmalade. I'm ravenous.'

They discovered that they all were, and twenty minutes later they sat at the table tucking in as if they had eaten nothing for a month.

'I can't eat a thing more,' said Dick, 'and I don't know what's happened to my eyes – they keep closing!'

'So do mine,' said George, with an enormous yawn. 'Joanna – don't say we've got to do the washing-up, will you?'

'Of course not!' said Joanna. 'Go on up to your beds now – don't even bother to undress.'

'I feel as if there's something I ought to do – but I can't remember it,' said Julian, sleepily, staggering upstairs. 'I – just – can't remember!'

He flopped on his bed and was asleep as soon as his head fell on the pillow. In two minutes everyone but Joanna was asleep too. Joanna stopped to give Timmy a drink, and then he bounded up to George and curled up in the crook of her knees as usual.

Joanna went to lie down too, thinking she would just have a rest, but not go to sleep. But in half a second she slept too.

The sun rose higher in the sky. The milkman came

whistling up the path and left four bottles of milk on the step. The gulls in the bay circled and soared and called loudly. But nobody stirred in Kirrin Cottage.

A car came up to the front gate, and another one followed. Out of the first stepped Uncle Quentin, Aunt Fanny, Mr Elbur Wright – and Berta! Out of the second car stepped the sergeant and his constable.

Berta flew to the front door, but it was shut. She raced round to the garden door. That was locked too – and so was the kitchen door!

'Pops! We'll have to ring – all the doors are locked!' she called. And then, from up above came a sound of excited barking, and Sally's head appeared at a bedroom window. When she saw it really was Berta down below, she tore down the stairs and scraped at the front door.

'What's happened? Where *is* everyone?' said Aunt Fanny in amazement. '*All* the doors locked? But it's ten o'clock in the morning. Where are the children?'

'I've got my key,' said Uncle Quentin, and he put it into the front door lock. He opened the door and Sally leapt straight into Berta's arms, licking her face from forehead to chin!

Aunt Fanny went into the hall and called, 'Anyone at home?'

No answer. Timmy heard her call, but as George did not stir, he didn't either. He was not going to leave George for a minute, not even to go downstairs!

Aunt Fanny walked into all the rooms on the ground floor. Nobody there! She marvelled at the remains of the meal spread all over the dining-room table, and even more at the dirty pans and dishes in the kitchen. What was Joanna thinking of? WHERE was everybody? She did not expect George to be there, because she knew George had been kidnapped – but where in the world were all the others?

She went upstairs and her husband followed with Berta and her father. They were all feeling most astonished now. They went into Julian's room – good gracious he *was* there, then! And Dick too – lying floppily on their beds, absolutely sound asleep! Aunt Fanny couldn't understand it.

And then she went into the girls' room – and there was Anne fast asleep too – and GOOD GRACIOUS, could that be *George*? But surely George was kidnapped – then how – why – where . . .

Her mother suddenly put her arms round the sleeping George and kissed her and hugged her. She had worried so much about her – and now here she was, safe and sound after all!

George awoke at once. She sat up and gazed at her mother and father in astonishment.

'Oh – you're back! Oh, how lovely! When did you come?'

'Just now,' said her mother. 'But, George – why is everyone asleep – and how did *you* get here – we thought you were . . .'

'Oh, Mother – yes, of course you don't know half the story, do you?' said George. 'Gosh, there's Berta here too – and your pops, Berta! Hallo, everyone.'

She was still so sleepy that she was not quite sure whether this was a dream or not. But then Anne woke up and squealed, and that woke Julian and Dick. They came into the very crowded bedroom, and soon there was such a noise that Joanna and Jo, in the room above, awoke too.

Down they came, looking very dishevelled, Joanna full of apologies. She rushed downstairs to put some coffee on and bumped into the two policemen in the hall. She screamed.

'Excuse me,' said the sergeant to Joanna. 'Isn't anyone ever coming down again? We're supposed to be guarding Berta.'

'Oh my – you don't need to do that now!' said Joanna. 'Didn't Julian telephone you last night – this morning, I mean – I thought he was going to.'

'What about?' said the sergeant.

'About the kidnappers. Everything's all right,' explained Joanna to the two astonished policemen. 'We've got George back – and oh, bless us all, there's those kidnappers – you haven't been told they're all locked up and waiting for you, have you?'

'Look here, what *are* you talking about?' said the sergeant, bewildered. 'This is too bad – what do you *mean* – kidnappers locked up and waiting!'

'Julian!' called Joanna, 'the police are here – and you forgot to telephone and tell them what happened last night. They'd better go to that house and get the men, hadn't they?'

'I *knew* there was something I'd forgotten,' said Julian, running down the stairs. 'I did mean to telephone, but I was so tired that I forgot.'

Everyone then came downstairs and went into the sitting-room. Jo was shy with so many people there, and wouldn't sit anywhere near the two policemen.

'I've just been told, Mr Wright, that there's no need to guard your daughter now,' said the sergeant, rather stiffly. 'Seems as if the police are the last to hear about anything!'

'Well, the fact of the matter is that we found out that Gringo, who owns the fair called Gringo's Fair, was paid to kidnap Berta,' said Julian. 'He kidnapped George instead, by mistake. We found out where Gringo had taken her and went to rescue her last night. You go on, Dick.'

'And we left Gringo and somebody else locked up in a room on the ground floor, and two other people locked up in a top-floor room – and we've left the front door open for you and the drive gates open too,' said Dick. 'So don't be too annoyed about it, Sergeant, because we really have tried to make things easy for you! We've rescued George, as you see – and now *you* can get the men.'

The sergeant looked as if he found it difficult to believe a single word! Uncle Quentin tapped him sharply on the shoulder.

'Well, look alive, man – they'll escape before you can get them if you don't hurry.'

'What's the address?' said the sergeant, stolidly.

'I don't know the name of the house, or the lane it's in,' said Julian. 'But you go through the village of Twining, turn to the left, and it's the house up on the hill.'

'How did you find out all this?' said the sergeant.

'It's too long to tell you now!' said Dick. 'We'll write it all down in a book, and send you a copy. We'll call it – er – we'll call it – what *shall* we call it, you others? It's a peculiar adventure really – it ended with everyone fast asleep in bed!'

'I want some coffee,' announced Uncle Quentin. 'I think we've talked enough. Do go and catch your kidnappers, my good men.'

The policemen disappeared. Mr Elbur Wright beamed round happily, Berta on his knee.

'Well, this is a very happy ending!' he said. 'And I can take my little Berta back with me after all!'

'Oh no!' wailed Berta, much to her father's surprise.

'What do you mean?' he asked.

'Gee, Pops, be a honey and let me stay on here,' begged Berta. 'These kids sure are wunnerful.'

'WonDERful, wonDERful, wonDERful!' chanted the others.

'Of course let her stay on if she'd like to,' said Aunt Fanny. 'But as a girl this time, not a boy!'

George heaved a sigh of relief. That was all right then. She wouldn't mind Berta as a girl, even though she was a *silly* girl!

'Woof!' said Timmy suddenly, and made everyone jump.

'He says he's jolly pleased you're staying, Berta, because now Sally-dog will have to stay too,' said Dick. 'So *he'll* have someone to play with as well!'

'Shall we really send the sergeant a book about this adventure?' said Anne. 'Did you *really* mean it, Dick?'

'Rather!' said Dick. 'Our fourteenth adventure – and may we have many more! What shall we call the book?'

'I know!' said George, at once. 'I know! Let's call it "FIVE HAVE PLENTY OF FUN".'

Well, they did – and they hope you like it!

Join the adventure!

If you can't wait to explore further with THE FAMOUS FIVE, read the next book in the series:

Enid Blyton®

is one of the most popular children's authors of all time. Her books have sold over 500 million copies and have been translated into other languages more often than any other children's author.

Enid Blyton adored writing for children. She wrote over 700 books and about 2,000 short stories. *The Famous Five* books, now 75 years old, are her most popular. She is also the author of other favourites including *The Secret Seven*, *The Magic Faraway Tree*, *Malory Towers* and *Noddy*.

Born in London in 1897, Enid lived much of her life in Buckinghamshire and loved dogs, gardening and the countryside. She was very knowledgeable about trees, flowers, birds and animals. Dorset – where some of the Famous Five's adventures are set – was a favourite place of hers too.

Enid Blyton's stories are read and loved by millions of children (and grown-ups) all over the world. Visit enidblyton.co.uk to discover more.

THE FAMOUS FIVE

FIVE ON A SECRET TRAIL

Have you read all THE FAMOUS FIVE books?

1. Five on a Treasure Island
2. Five Go Adventuring Again
3. Five Run Away Together
4. Five Go to Smuggler's Top
5. Five Go Off in a Caravan
6. Five on Kirrin Island Again
7. Five Go Off to Camp
8. Five Get Into Trouble
9. Five Fall Into Adventure
10. Five on a Hike Together
11. Five Have a Wonderful Time
12. Five Go Down to the Sea
13. Five Go to Mystery Moor
14. Five Have Plenty of Fun
15. Five on a Secret Trail
16. Five Go to Billycock Hill
17. Five Get Into a Fix
18. Five on Finniston Farm
19. Five Go to Demon's Rocks
20. Five Have a Mystery to Solve
21. Five Are Together Again

The Famous Five Colour Short Stories

1. Five and a Half-Term Adventure
2. George's Hair is Too Long
3. Good Old Timmy
4. A Lazy Afternoon
5. Well Done, Famous Five
6. Five Have a Puzzling Time
7. Happy Christmas, Five
8. When Timmy Chased the Cat

Enid Blyton®

THE FAMOUS FIVE

FIVE ON A SECRET TRAIL

Illustrated by Eileen A. Soper

HODDER CHILDREN'S BOOKS

First published in Great Britain in 1956 by Hodder & Stoughton
This edition published in 2016

20

A CIP catalogue record for this book is available from the British Library.

ISBN 978 1 444 93645 2

Printed in Great Britain by Clays Ltd, Elcograf S.p.A.

The paper and board used in this book are made from wood from responsible sources.

Hodder Children's Books
An imprint of
Hachette Children's Group
Part of Hodder & Stoughton
Carmelite House
50 Victoria Embankment
London EC4Y 0DZ

An Hachette UK Company
www.hachette.co.uk
www.hachettechildrens.co.uk

CONTENTS

1	GEORGE IS RATHER DIFFICULT	1
2	ANNE JOINS THE LITTLE CAMP	10
3	THE OLD COTTAGE – AND A SURPRISE	18
4	THAT NIGHT	27
5	THAT BOY AGAIN!	36
6	STORM IN THE NIGHT	45
7	STRANGE HAPPENINGS	55
8	ALL TOGETHER AGAIN!	65
9	A LITTLE EXPLORATION	74
10	WHAT CAN BE HAPPENING?	83
11	INTERESTING DISCOVERIES – AND A PLAN	92
12	A GOOD HIDING-PLACE	100
13	ON WATCH IN THE COTTAGE	108
14	AN EXCITING NIGHT – AND A SURPRISING MORNING	117
15	WELL DONE, GEORGE!	127
16	THE SECRET WAY	136
17	FULL OF SURPRISES	145
18	THE WAY OUT	154
19	BACK TO KIRRIN COTTAGE	164
20	THE ADVENTURE ENDS – AS IT BEGAN!	172

CHAPTER ONE

George is rather difficult

'MOTHER! MOTHER, where are you?' shouted George, rushing into the house. 'Mother, quick!'

There was no answer. George's mother was out in the garden at the back of Kirrin Cottage, picking flowers. George yelled again, this time at the top of her very strong voice.

'MOTHER! MOTHER! Where are you? IT'S URGENT.'

A door was flung open nearby and George's father stood there, glaring at her.

'George! What's this row about? Here am I in the middle of some very difficult . . .'

'Oh, Father! Timmy's hurt!' said George. 'He went . . .'

Her father looked down at Timmy, standing meekly behind George. He gave a little snort.

'Hurt! He seems all right to me. I suppose he's got a thorn in his paw again – and you think it's the end of the world or something, and come yelling in here and . . .'

'Timmy *is* hurt!' said George, with tears in her voice. 'Look!'

But her father had gone back into his study again, and the door slammed. George glared at it, looking exactly like her hot-tempered father.

'You're unkind!' she shouted, 'and . . . oh there's MOTHER. MOTHER!'

'Dear me, George, whatever *is* the matter?' said her mother, putting down the flowers. 'I heard your father shouting, and then you.'

'Mother – Timmy's hurt!' said George. 'Look!'

She knelt down by the dog, and gently pulled forward one ear. Behind it was a big cut. Timmy whined. Tears came into George's eyes, and she looked up at her mother.

'It's all right, George,' said Mrs Kirrin. 'It's only a cut. How did he do it?'

'He tried to jump over a ditch, and he didn't see some old barbed wire there,' said George. 'And a rusty piece caught his ear, and ripped that awful cut. I can't stop it bleeding.'

Her mother looked at it. It certainly was quite deep. 'Take him to the vet, George,' she said. 'Perhaps it ought to be stitched. It does look rather deep. Poor old Timmy-boy – well, it's a good thing it wasn't his eye, George.'

'I'll take him to the vet at once,' said George, getting up. 'Will he be in, Mother?'

'Oh yes – it's his surgery hour,' said her mother. 'Take him along now.'

So Timmy was hurried along the country lanes to the pretty little house where the vet lived. George, very anxious indeed, was most relieved to see that the vet seemed quite unconcerned.

'A couple of stitches and that cut will heal well,' he said. 'Hold him, will you, while I do the job? He'll hardly feel it. There, old boy – stand still – that's right.'

In five minutes' time George was thanking the vet wholeheartedly. 'Thank you! I *was* worried! Will he be all right now?'

'Good gracious, yes – but you mustn't let him scratch that wound,' said the vet, washing his hands. 'If he does, it may go wrong.'

'Oh. But how can I stop him?' asked George anxiously. 'Look – he's trying to scratch it now.'

'Well, you must make him a big cardboard collar,' said

the vet. 'One that sticks out right round his neck, so that his paw can't get near that cut, however much he tries to reach it.'

'But – but Timmy won't like that a bit,' said George. 'Dogs look silly wearing cardboard collars like great ruffs round their necks. I've seen them. He'll hate one.'

'Well, it's the only way of stopping him from scratching that wound,' said the vet. 'Get along now, George – I've more patients waiting.'

George went home with Timmy. He padded along quietly, pleased at the fuss that George was making of him. When he was nearly home, he suddenly sat down and put up his hind leg to scratch his bad ear.

'No, Timmy! NO!' cried George, in alarm. 'You must NOT scratch. You'll get the plaster off in no time, and break the stitches. NO, Timmy!'

Timmy looked up in surprise. Very well. If scratching was suddenly upsetting George, he would wait till he was alone.

But George could read Timmy's thoughts as easily as he could read hers! She frowned.

'Blow! I'll *have* to make him that cardboard collar. Perhaps Mother will help me.'

Her mother was quite willing to help. George was not good at things of that sort, and she watched her mother cutting out a big cardboard collar, fitting it round the surprised Timmy's head, and then lacing the edges together with thread so that he could not get it off. Timmy was most surprised, but he stood very patiently.

As soon as the collar was finished, and safely round his neck, he walked away. Then he raised his hind leg to scratch at his smarting ear – but, of course, he couldn't get it over the collar, and merely scratched the cardboard.

'Never mind, Timmy,' said George. 'It will only be for a few days.'

The study door nearby opened and her father came out. He saw Timmy in his collar and stopped in surprise. Then he roared with laughter.

'Hey, Timmy – you look like Queen Elizabeth the First in a fine big ruff!' he said.

'Don't laugh at him, Father,' said George. 'You know that dogs can't bear being laughed at.'

Timmy certainly looked offended. He turned his back on George's father and stalked off to the kitchen. A little squeal of laughter came from there and then a loud guffaw from someone at the kitchen door – the milkman.

'Oh, Timmy – whatever have you got that collar on for?' said the cook's voice. 'You do look peculiar!'

George was angry. She remained angry all that day and made everyone most uncomfortable. How *mean* of people to jeer at poor Timmy! Didn't they realise how terribly uncomfortable a collar like that was – and Timmy had to wear it night and day! He couldn't even lie down comfortably. George mooned about looking so angry and miserable that her mother felt worried.

'George dear, don't be silly about this. You will make your father cross. Timmy will have to wear that collar for at least a week, you know, and he *does* look a bit comical when you first see him. He's getting used to it, he soon won't notice it.'

'Everybody laughs at him,' said George, in an angry voice. 'He went into the garden and a lot of kids hung over the wall and laughed like anything. And the postman told me it was cruel. And Father thinks it's funny. And . . .'

'Oh dear, George, don't get into one of your moods,' said her mother. 'Remember, Anne is coming soon. She won't enjoy things much if you behave like this.'

George bore it for one day more. Then, after two upsets with her father over Timmy, another with a couple of boys who laughed at him, and one with the paper boy, she decided she wouldn't stay at Kirrin Cottage for one day longer!

'We'll take my little tent, and go off by ourselves somewhere,' she told Timmy. 'Some place where nobody can see you till your ear is better and that hateful collar is off. Don't you think that's a good idea, Timmy?'

'Woof,' said Timmy. He thought that any of George's ideas were good, though the collar puzzled him very much.

'You know the *dogs* laugh at you too, Timmy,' said George, earnestly. 'Did you see how that silly little poodle belonging to Mrs Janes up the lane stood and stared at you? He looked *exactly* as if he was laughing. I won't have you laughed at. I know you hate it.'

Timmy certainly didn't like it, but he really was not as upset about the collar as George seemed to be. He followed her as she went up to her bedroom and watched her as she began to put a few things into a small bag.

'We'll go to that lonely little spot on the common,' she said to him. 'We'll pitch our tent near a little stream, and we'll jolly well stay there till your ear's better. We'll go tonight. I'll take my bike, and strap everything on to the back.'

So, in the middle of the night, when Kirrin Cottage was dark and quiet, George stole downstairs with Timmy. She left a note on the dining-room table, and then went to get her bicycle. She strapped her little tent on it, and the bag containing food and other odds and ends.

'Come on!' she whispered to the surprised Timmy. 'We'll go. I'll ride slowly and you can run beside me. Don't bark for goodness' sake!'

They disappeared into the darkness, Timmy running like a black shadow beside the bicycle. Nobody guessed they were gone. Kirrin Cottage was quiet and undisturbed – except for the creaking of the kitchen door, which George had forgotten to shut.

But in the morning, what a disturbance! Joanna the cook found George's note first and wondered what a letter in George's writing was doing on the dining-room table. She ran straight up to George's room and looked inside.

The bed was empty. There was no George and Timmy's

CHAPTER TWO

Anne joins the little camp

AUNT FANNY soon told Anne about Timmy's ear and the big collar of cardboard that had caused all the trouble. Anne couldn't help smiling.

'Oh, Aunt Fanny – George is quite crazy about old Tim, isn't she? I'll go and meet her at twelve, and of course I'll camp with her for a day or two. It's lovely weather and I'd like to. I expect Uncle Quentin will be glad to have us out of the house!'

'How are Julian and Dick?' asked her aunt. She was very fond of Anne's two brothers, George's cousins. 'Will they be coming down here at all these holidays?'

'I don't know,' said Anne. 'They're still in France, you know, on a schoolboys' tour. I feel funny without them! George will be cross to hear they probably won't be coming to Kirrin. She'll just have to put up with *me*!'

At twelve o'clock Anne was standing patiently at the end of Carters Lane. It ran to the common and then ended in a small, winding path that led to nowhere in particular. Big gorse bushes grew here and there, and slender birch trees. Anne, her belongings strapped to her back, and a bag in her hand, looked over the common to see if she could spy George coming.

There was no sign of her. 'Blow!' said Anne. 'I suppose she's changed her mind or something. Perhaps her watch has stopped and she doesn't know the time. She ought to, though, by looking at the sun! How long shall I wait?'

She sat down by a big gorse bush, out of the hot sun. She hadn't been there for more than a minute when she heard a hissing sound.

'Pssssst!'

Anne sat up at once. The sound came from the other side of the bush, and she got up and walked round it. Half-hidden under a prickly branch were George and Timmy!

'Hallo!' said Anne, surprised. 'Didn't you see me when I arrived? Hallo, Tim darling! How's your poor old ear? Oh, doesn't he look a quaint old dear in that collar, George?'

George scrambled out of the bush. 'I hid here just in case Father or Mother should come with you and try to make me come back,' she said. 'I wanted to make quite sure they weren't waiting somewhere a little way away. I'm glad you've come, Anne.'

'Of course I've come,' said Anne. 'I wouldn't stay alone at Kirrin Cottage while you were camping out. Besides, I understand how you feel about Timmy. The collar's a jolly good idea, of course – but it does make him look comical. I think he looks rather a dear in it, I do really.'

George was almost relieved that Anne had not laughed at Timmy as most people had. She smiled at her cousin, and Timmy licked her till Anne really had to push him away.

'Let's go,' said George, scrambling up. 'I've got a lovely camping place, Anne. You'll like it. It's near a little spring too, so there's plenty of water for Timmy to drink – and us too. Did you bring any more food? I didn't really bring much.'

'Yes. I've brought heaps,' said Anne. 'Aunt Fanny made me. She's not cross with you, George. I didn't see your father. He was shut up in his study.'

George's spirits suddenly rose. She gave Anne a friendly push. 'This is going to be fun! Timmy's ear will soon be better, and he loves camping out as much as we do. I've really found a good place – about the loneliest on the common! Nobody near us for miles!'

They set off together, Timmy at their heels, darting off every now and again when he smelt rabbit.

'When are Julian and Dick coming down?' asked George. 'In a few days? Timmy's ear will be all right then and we can go back to Kirrin Cottage to welcome the boys, and have some fun there.'

'They may not be coming down at all these hols,' said Anne, and George's face fell at once. She stopped and stared at Anne in dismay.

'Not coming! But they *always* come in the hols – or we go away somewhere together!' she said. 'They *must* come! I shall be miserable without Ju and Dick.'

'Well – they're still in France, on a tour or something,' said Anne. 'We shall hear if they're staying on there or coming down to Kirrin when we get back to the cottage. Don't look so woebegone, George!'

But George felt woebegone. The holidays stretched before her, suddenly seeming long and dreary. Her two boy cousins were always such fun – they had had such wonderful adventures together. And now – now they weren't coming!

'We shan't have any adventures at all if the boys don't come,' she said, in a small voice.

'I shan't mind that,' said Anne. 'I'm the peaceful one, not always on the look-out for something to happen, like you and the boys! Perhaps these holidays will be quite unexciting without even the *smell* of an adventure! Oh, George – cheer up! *Don't* look so mournful. You'd better send a letter to Julian and Dick if you feel so badly about it.'

'I've a good mind to!' said George. 'I can't *imagine* hols without the boys. Why – we shan't be the Five – the Famous Five – if they don't come!'

'Woof!' said Timmy, quite agreeing. He sat down and tried to scratch his ear, but the big collar prevented him. He didn't seem to mind and ran off after a rabbit quite happily.

'I think *you* are more upset about that collar than Timmy,' said Anne, as they walked along. 'Are we getting near this place of yours, George? It's a jolly long way.'

'We go up this hill in front of us – and then drop down to a little copse,' said George. 'There's a funny old cottage nearby – quite ruined and empty. At first I thought perhaps people lived there, but when I went nearer I saw that it was ruined. There's a big old rose-rambler climbing all over it, even inside. I suppose the people who used to live there planted it.'

They walked up the little hill and down again, following curving rabbit paths. 'Better look out for adders,' said Anne. 'This is just the kind of place for them. My word, it's hot, George. Is there anywhere to bathe near here – a pool or anything?'

'I don't know. We could explore and see,' said George. 'I did bring my swimsuit just in case. Look, you can see part of the old cottage now. My camp is fairly near there. I thought I'd better camp near the spring.'

They were soon at George's rough little camp. Her tent was up, and she had made a bed inside of the springy heather. A mug, a bag of dog biscuits, a few tins, and a loaf of bread were at one end of the tent. It didn't seem to Anne as if George had brought very much, and she felt glad that she had managed to pack such a lot of things.

'Aunt Fanny cut dozens and dozens of sandwiches,' said Anne. 'She said if we kept them in this tin they wouldn't go stale, and would last us a day or two till we went back. I'm hungry. Shall we have some now?'

They sat out in the sun, munching the ham sandwiches. Anne had brought tomatoes too, and they took a bite at a sandwich and then a bite at a tomato. Timmy had to make do with a handful of dog biscuits and half a sandwich every now and again. After a bit he got up and wandered off.

'Where's he going?' asked Anne. 'To look for a rabbit?'

'No. Probably to get a drink,' said George. 'The spring is in the direction he's gone. I'm thirsty too – let's take the mug and get a drink ourselves.'

They went off with the mug, Anne following George through the thick heather. The little spring was a lovely one. It had evidently been used by the people who had once lived in the old cottage, and was built round with big white stones, so that the spring ran through a little stony channel, as clear as crystal.

'Oooh – it's as cold as ice!' said Anne. 'Simply delicious! I could drink gallons of this!'

They lay on the heather out in the sun, talking, when they came back from the spring. Timmy wandered off by himself again.

'It's so peaceful here,' said Anne. 'Nobody near us for miles. Just the birds and the rabbits. This is what I like!'

'There's hardly a sound,' said George, yawning.

And then, just as she said that, there came a noise in the distance. A sharp sound, like metal on stone. It came again and again and then stopped.

'What's that, do you suppose?' said George, sitting up.

'I can't imagine,' said Anne. 'Anyway, it's a long way away – everything is so still that sounds carry from quite a distance.'

The sharp noises began again in a little while and then stopped. The girls shut their eyes, and slept. There wasn't a sound now except the pop-pop-pop of gorse pods exploding in the sun and sending out their little black seeds.

George woke up when Timmy came back. He sat down heavily on her feet and she woke up with a jump.

'Timmy! Don't!' she said. 'Get off my feet, you made me jump!' Timmy obligingly removed himself and then picked up something he had dropped, lay down and began gnawing it. George looked to see what it was.

'Timmy! That's a bone! Where did you get it?' she said. 'Anne, did you bring a bone for Tim?'

'What? What did you say?' said Anne, half asleep. 'A bone. No, I didn't. Why?'

'Because Timmy's found one,' said George, 'and it's a bone that has had cooked meat on it, so it's not a rabbit or anything Timmy's caught. Timmy, where did you get it?'

'Woof,' said Timmy, offering the bone to George, thinking that she too might like a gnaw, as she seemed so interested in it.

'Do you suppose anyone else is camping near us?' asked Anne, sitting up and yawning. 'After all, bones don't grow in the heather. That's quite a good meaty one, too. Timmy, have you stolen it from another dog?'

Timmy thumped his tail on the ground and went on with his bone. He looked pleased with himself.

'It's rather an old bone,' said George. 'It's smelly. Go away, Tim – take it further off.'

The sharp metallic noises suddenly began again and George frowned. 'I believe there *is* someone camping near us, Anne. Come on – let's do a bit of exploring and find out. I vote we move our camp if there are other people near. Come on, Timmy – that's right, bury that horrible bone! This way, Anne!'

CHAPTER THREE

The old cottage – and a surprise

THE TWO girls, with Timmy at their heels, left their camping place and set off in the hot sun. Anne caught sight of the ruined cottage and stopped.

'Let's have a look at it,' she said. 'It must be awfully old, George.'

They went in at the wide doorway. There was no door left, only the stone archway. Inside was a big room, whose floor had once been paved with slabs of white stone. Now grass and other weeds had grown between the cracks, and had actually lifted up some of the slabs so that the whole floor was uneven.

Here and there parts of the walls had fallen away and the daylight came through. One window was still more or less intact, but the others had fallen out. A small crooked stairway of stone led upwards in one corner.

'To rooms above, I suppose,' said Anne. 'Oh, here's another doorway, leading into a second room – a small one. It's got an old sink in it, look – and this must be the remains of a pump.'

'There's not much to see, really,' said George, looking round. 'The top rooms must be quite ruined, because half the roof is off. Hallo, here's another door – a back door.

It's actually a *door* too, not just a doorway.'

She gave a push at the stout wood – and the old door promptly fell off its hinges and crashed outwards into an overgrown yard.

'Goodness!' said George, startled. 'I didn't know it was quite so rotten. It made poor Tim jump almost out of his skin!'

'There are outhouses here – or the remains of them,' said Anne, exploring the back-yard. 'They must have kept pigs and hens and ducks. Here's a dried-up pond, look.'

Everything was falling to pieces. The best preserved corner of the old place was what must have been a small stable. Rusted mangers were still there and the floor was of stone. An old, old piece of harness hung on a big nail.

'It's got quite a nice "*feel*" about it, this old place,' said Anne. 'Sometimes I don't like the feel of places – they give me an uneasy feeling, a feeling that horrid things may have happened there. But this is quite different. I think people have been happy here, and led peaceful lives. I can almost hear hens clucking and ducks quacking, and pigs gr—'

'Quack, quack, quack! Quack!'

'*Cuck*-cuk-cuk-cuk-cuk! *Cuck*-cuk-cuk-cuk-cuk!'

Anne clutched George and the two girls looked extremely startled to hear the sudden loud noise of quacking and clucking. They stood and listened.

'What was it?' said Anne. 'It *sounded* like hens and ducks – though I'm not quite sure. But there aren't any here, surely. We shall hear a horse whinnying next!'

They didn't hear a whinny – but they heard the snorting of a horse at once. 'Hrrrrr-umph! Hrrrrr-umph!'

Both girls were now quite alarmed. They looked for Timmy. He was nowhere to be seen! Wherever could he have got to?

'*Cuck*-cuk-cuk-cuk-cuk!'

'This is silly,' said George. 'Are we imagining things? Anne, there *must* be hens near. Come round the back of these stables and look. Timmy, where are you? TIMMY!'

She whistled shrilly – and immediately an echo came – or so it seemed!

'Phee-phee-phee-phee-phee!'

'TIMMY!' yelled George, beginning to feel as if she was in a dream.

Timmy appeared, looking rather sheepish. He wagged his tail – and to the girls' enormous amazement, they saw that he had a ribbon tied on it. A ribbon – a bright blue one at that!

'Timmy! Your tail – the ribbon – Timmy, what's all this about?' said George, really startled.

Timmy went to her, still looking sheepish, and George tore the ribbon off his tail. 'Who tied it there?' she demanded. 'Who's here? Timmy, where have you been?'

The two girls searched the old buildings thoroughly, and found nothing and nobody. Not a hen, not a duck, not a pig – and certainly not a horse. Then – what was the explanation? They stared at one another in bewilderment.

'And where did Timmy get that silly ribbon?' said

George, exasperated. '*Someone* must have tied it on.'

'Perhaps it was a hiker passing by – perhaps he heard us here and saw Timmy and played a joke,' said Anne. 'But it's strange that Old Tim *let* him tie on the ribbon. I mean – Timmy's not overfriendly with strangers, is he?'

The girls gave up the idea of exploring any further and went back to their little camp. Timmy went with them. He lay down – and then suddenly got up again, making for a thick gorse bush. He tried to squirm underneath.

'*Now* what's he after?' said George. 'Really, I think Timmy's gone mad. Timmy, you *can't* get under there with that great collar on. TIMMY, do you hear me!'

Timmy backed out reluctantly, the collar all crooked. After him came a peculiar little mongrel dog with one blind eye and one exceedingly bright and lively one. He was white and black, and had a ridiculously long thin tail, which he waved about merrily.

'*Well!*' said George, amazed. 'What's that dog doing there? And how did Timmy get so friendly with him? Timmy, I can't make you out.'

'Woof,' said Timmy, and brought the mongrel dog over to Anne and George. He then proceeded to dig up the smelly bone he had buried, and actually offered it to the little dog, who looked away and took no interest in it at all.

'This is all very peculiar,' said Anne. 'I shall expect to see Timmy bring a cat to us next!'

At once there came a pathetic mewing.

'Mee-ew! Mee-ew-ee-ew-ee-ew!'

Both dogs pricked up their ears, and rushed to the bush. Timmy was once again kept back by his big collar and barked furiously.

George got up and marched to the bush. 'If there's a cat there, it won't have much chance against two dogs,' she called to Anne. 'Come away, Tim. Hey, you little dog, come away, too.'

Timmy backed out, and George pulled out the small dog very firmly indeed. 'Hold him, Anne!' she called. 'He's quite friendly. He won't bite. I'm going to find that cat.'

Anne held on to the small mongrel, who gazed at her excitedly with his one good eye and wagged his tail violently. He was a most friendly little fellow. George began to crawl into the bare hollow space under the big gorse bush.

She looked into it, not able to see anything at first, because it was dark there after the bright sunlight. Then she got a tremendous shock.

A round, grinning face stared back at her, a face with very bright eyes and tousled hair falling on to the forehead. The mouth was set in a wide smile, showing very white teeth.

'Mee-ew-ee-ew-ee-ew!' said the face.

George scrambled back at top speed, her heart thumping. 'What is it?' called Anne.

'There's somebody hiding there,' said George. 'Not a cat. An idiot of a boy who is doing the mewing.'

'Mew-ee-ew-ee-ew!'

'Come out!' called Anne. 'Come out and let's see you. You must be crazy.'

There was a scrambling noise and a boy came head first from the hollow space under the bush. He was about twelve or thirteen, short, sturdily built, and with the cheekiest face Anne had ever seen.

Timmy rushed at him and licked him lovingly. George stared in amazement.

'How does my dog know you?' she demanded.

'Well, he came growling at me yesterday when I was in my own camp,' said the boy. 'And I offered him a nice meaty bone. Then he saw my little dog Jet – short for jet-propelled, you know – and made friends with him – and with me too.'

'I see,' said George, still not at all friendly. 'Well, I don't like my dog to take food from strangers.'

'Oh, I couldn't agree more,' said the boy. 'But I thought I'd rather he ate the bone than ate *me*. He's a nice dog, yours. He feels a bit of an idiot wearing that collar, doesn't he? You should have heard Jet laugh when he first saw it!'

George frowned. 'I came here to be alone so that Timmy shouldn't be jeered at,' she said. 'He's got a bad ear. I suppose *you* were the fathead who tied a blue ribbon on his tail?'

'Just for a joke,' said the boy. '*You* like frowning and glaring, I can see. Well, *I* like joking and tricking! Your Timmy didn't mind a bit. He took to my dog right away. But everyone likes Jet! I wanted to find out who owned Timmy – because, like you, *I* don't like strangers messing about when I'm camping out. So I came along.'

'I see. And you did all the clucking and quacking and hrrr-umphing?' said Anne. She liked this idiot of a boy, with his broad friendly grin. 'What are you doing – just camping – or hiking – or botanising?'

'I'm digging,' said the boy. 'My father's an archaeologist – he loves old buildings more than anything else in the world. I take after him, I suppose. There was once an old Roman camp on this common, you know – and I've found a place where part of it must have been, so I'm digging for anything I can find – pottery, weapons, anything like that. See, I found this yesterday – look at the date on it!'

He suddenly thrust an old coin at them – a strange, uneven one, rather heavy to hold.

'Its date is 292,' he said. 'At least, as far as I can make out. So the camp's pretty old, isn't it?'

'We'll come and see it,' said Anne, excited.

'No, don't,' said the boy. 'I don't like people messing round me when I'm doing something serious. Please don't come. I won't bother you again. I promise.'

'All right. We won't come,' said Anne, quite understanding. 'But don't you play any more silly tricks on us, see?'

'I promise,' said the boy. 'I tell you, I won't come near you again. I only wanted to see whose dog this was. Well, I'm off. So long!'

And, whistling to Jet, he set off at a furious pace. George turned to Anne.

'What a peculiar boy!' she said. 'Actually – I'd rather *like* to see him again. Wouldn't you?'

CHAPTER FOUR

That night

It was now tea-time, according to Anne's watch and also according to everyone's feelings, including Timmy's. Timmy felt the heat very much and was always wandering off to the little spring to lap the crystal-cold water. Anne wished that she and George had a big jug that they could fill – it was such a nuisance to have to keep running to and fro with just a mug.

They had tea – biscuits, a sandwich each, and a bar of rather soft chocolate. George examined Timmy's ear for the hundredth time that day, and pronounced it very much better.

'Well, don't take off that collar yet,' said Anne. 'He'll only open the wound by scratching if you do.'

'I'm not *going* to take it off!' said George, touchily. 'What shall we do now, Anne? Go for a walk?'

'Yes,' said Anne. 'Listen – you can hear those sharp, metallic noises again – that's the boy at work again, I expect. Funny boy he must be – coming to dig about all on his own with his comical little dog. I wish we could see what he's doing.'

'We promised we wouldn't,' said George. 'So I don't feel that we even ought to go and peep.'

'Of course not!' said Anne. 'Come on – let's go in the opposite direction, George – right away from the boy. I hope we shan't get lost!'

'Not while Timmy's with us, silly!' said George. 'You'd find your way home from the moon, wouldn't you, Tim?'

'Woof,' agreed Timmy.

'He always says yes to whatever you say, George,' said Anne. 'I say – isn't it a lovely evening? I wonder what Julian and Dick are doing?'

George immediately looked downcast. She felt that her two cousins had no right to go rushing across France when she wanted them at Kirrin. Didn't they like Kirrin? Would they be having magnificent adventures abroad, and not want to spend even a week at Kirrin? She looked so lost in miserable thoughts that Anne laughed at her.

'Cheer up! At least *I* am here with you – though I agree that compared with Ju and Dick I'm very poor company, and not at all adventurous!'

They had a lovely walk, and sat down halfway to watch hordes of rabbits playing together. Timmy was very unhappy about this. Why *sit down* to watch silly rabbits? Rabbits were made to *chase*, weren't they? Why did George always put a restraining hand on his collar when she sat down to watch rabbits? He whined continually, as he watched with her.

'Shut up, Timmy, you ass,' said George. 'You'd only spoil the entertainment if you sent them to their holes.'

They watched for a long while and then got up to go

back to the camp. When they came near, they heard the sound of low whistling. Someone was about that evening, quite near their camp. Who was it?

They came round a big gorse bush, and almost bumped into a boy. He got out of their way politely, but said nothing.

'Why – it's *you*!' said George, in surprise. 'I don't know your name. What are you doing here? You said you wouldn't come near us.'

The boy stared, looking very surprised. His tousled hair fell right across his forehead, and he brushed it back.

'I said nothing of the sort,' he said.

'Oh, you *did*!' said Anne. 'You know you did. Well, if you break your promise, there's no reason for us to keep ours. We shall come and visit *your* camp.'

'I never made you any promise,' said the boy, looking quite startled. 'You're mad!'

'Don't be an idiot!' said George, getting cross. 'I suppose you'll be saying next that you didn't act like a hen, and a duck, and a horse this afternoon . . .'

'And a cat,' said Anne.

'Barmy!' said the boy, looking at them pityingly. 'Quite barmy.'

'Are you coming here again?' demanded George.

'If I want to,' said the boy. 'The water in this spring is better than the one over by my camp.'

'Then we shall come and explore *your* camp,' said George, firmly. 'If you don't keep your promise, we shan't keep ours.'

'By all means come if you want to,' said the boy. 'You seem quite mad, but I daresay you're harmless. But don't bring your dog. He might eat mine.'

'You know he wouldn't eat Jet!' said Anne. 'They're good friends.'

'I don't know anything of the sort,' said the boy, and went off, brushing his hair out of his eyes again.

'What do you make of *that*?' said George, staring after him. 'Not a bit the same as he was this afternoon. Do you think he really *had* forgotten about his promise and everything?'

'I don't know,' said Anne, puzzled. 'He was so perky and jolly and full of fun before – grinning all the time – but just now he seemed quite serious – not a smile in him!'

'Oh well – perhaps he's a bit crazy,' said George. 'Are you sleepy, Anne? I am, though I can't think why!'

'Not very – but I'd like to lie down on this springy heather and watch the stars gradually come sparkling into the sky,' said Anne. 'I don't think I'll sleep in the tent, George. You'll want Timmy with you, and honestly there's so little room inside the tent that I'm quite sure Timmy would lie on my legs all night long.'

'I'll sleep in the open air as well,' said George. 'I only slept in the tent last night because it looked a bit like rain. Let's get some more heather and make a kind of mattress of it. We can put a rug on top of it, and lie on that.'

The two of them pulled a lot of heather and carried it to their 'bed'. Soon they had a fine pile, and Timmy went to lie on it.

'Hey – it's not for you!' cried George. 'Get off – you'll flatten it right down. Where's the rug, Anne?'

They laid the rug on the heather pile and then went to the spring to wash and clean their teeth. Timmy immediately got on to the heather bed again, and shut his eyes.

'You old fraud!' said George, lugging him off. 'You're not asleep. Keep off our bed! Look – there's a nice soft patch of grass for you. That's your bed!'

George lay down on the rug, and the heathery bed sank a little beneath her weight. 'Very comfortable!' said George. 'Shall we want a rug over us, Anne?'

'Well, I did bring one,' said Anne. 'But I don't think we'll want it, the night's so hot. Look – there is a star already!'

Soon there were six or seven – and then gradually hundreds more pricked through the evening sky as the twilight deepened. It was a wonderful night.

'Don't the stars look big and bright?' said Anne, sleepily. 'They make me feel very small, they're such millions of miles away. George, are you asleep?'

There was no answer. George hadn't heard a word. She was fast asleep. Her hand fell down the side of the heather and rested on the ground below. Timmy moved a little nearer and gave it a small lick. Then he too fell asleep, and gave some small doggy snores.

The night darkened. There was no moon but the stars shone out well from the midnight sky. It was very quiet out there on the common, far away from streets and villages and towns. Not even an owl hooted.

Anne didn't quite know why she awoke. At first she had no idea where she was, and she lay gazing up at the stars in astonishment, thinking she must still be asleep.

She suddenly felt very thirsty. She groped about in the nearby tent for the mug, couldn't find it and gave it up.

'I'll drink from my cupped hands,' she thought, and set off for the little spring. Timmy wondered whether to follow her. No – he would stay with George. She wouldn't like it if she awoke and found him gone with Anne. So he settled his head down on his paws again and slept, leaving one ear open for Anne.

Anne found the little spring. Its tinkling gurgling sound guided her as soon as she heard it. She sat down on one of the stones nearby, and held out her cupped hands. How very cold the water was – and how delicious to drink on this hot night! She sipped thirstily, slopping some of the water down her front.

She got up to go back, and walked a few steps in the starlight. Then she stopped. Wait – was she going in the right direction? She wasn't sure.

'I *think* I am!' she decided, and went on, carefully and quietly. Surely she must be near their little camp now?

Then all at once she stood still, and felt herself stiffen. She had suddenly seen a light. It had flashed and disappeared. Ah – there it was again! Whatever could it be?

Then, as her eyes strained through the starlit darkness,

she suddenly saw that she *had* taken the wrong way – she had gone in the direction of the old ruined cottage, and not the camp – and the light had come from there!

She didn't dare go any nearer. She felt glued to the grass she was standing on! Now she could hear sounds – whispering sounds – and the noise of a footfall on the stone floor of the cottage – and then the flash of a light came again! Yes, it *was* from the old cottage!

Anne began to breathe fast. Who was it in the old cottage? She simply dared not go and see. She must go back to George, and to Timmy's protection. As fast and as

silently as she could she found her way back to the spring – and then, almost stumbling now, made her way to where George was still lying peacefully asleep.

'Woof,' said Timmy, sleepily, and tried to lick her hand. Anne climbed on to the heathery bed beside George, her heart still beating fast.

'George!' she whispered. 'George, do wake up. I've something strange to tell you!'

CHAPTER FIVE

That boy again!

GEORGE WOULD not wake up. She grunted when Anne poked her and prodded her, and then she turned over, almost falling off the small heather bed.

'Oh, George – *please* do wake!' begged Anne, in a whisper. She was afraid of speaking out loud in case anyone should hear her. Who knew what might happen if she drew attention to their little camp?

George awoke at last and was cross. 'Whatever is it, Anne?' she said, her voice sounding loud in the night.

'Sh!' said Anne. 'Sh!'

'Why? We're all alone here! We can make as much noise as we like!' said George, surprised.

'George, do listen! There's someone in that old cottage!' said Anne, and at last George heard and understood. She sat up at once.

Anne told her the whole story – though it didn't really seem very much of a tale when she related it. George spoke to Timmy.

'Tim!' she said, keeping her voice low. 'We'll go and do a little exploring, shall we? Come on, then – and keep quiet!'

She slid off the rug and stood up. 'You stay here,' she

said to Anne. 'Timmy and I will be very quiet and careful, and see what we can find out.'

'Oh no – I couldn't stay here *alone*!' said Anne in alarm, and got up hurriedly. 'I shall have to come too. I don't mind a bit now Timmy's with us. I wonder he didn't bark at the people in the old cottage, whoever they were.'

'He probably thought it was you messing about,' said George, and Anne nodded. Yes, of course, Timmy must have thought that any noises he heard had been made by her.

They took the path that led to the old cottage. George had Timmy well to heel. He knew he must not push forward unless told to. His ears were pricked now, and he was listening hard.

They came cautiously to the cottage. They could see its dark outline in the starlight, but little else. There was no light flashing there. Nor did there seem to be any noises at all.

All three stood still and quiet for about five minutes. Then Timmy moved restlessly. This was boring! Why wouldn't George let him run forward and explore everywhere if she wanted to know if intruders were about?

'I don't think there's a soul here!' whispered George into Anne's ear. 'They must have gone – unless you dreamt it all, Anne!'

'I didn't!' whispered back Anne indignantly. 'Let's go forward a bit and send Timmy into the cottage. He'll soon bark if there's anyone there.'

George gave Timmy a little shove. 'Go on, then!' she said. 'Find, Timmy, find!'

Timmy gladly shot forward into the darkness. He trotted into the cottage, though it was impossible even to see him go to it. The two girls stood and listened, their heartbeats sounding very loud to them! There was not a sound to be heard, except occasionally the rattle of Timmy's strong claws on a stony slab.

'There can't be anyone there,' said George at last, 'else Timmy would have sniffed them out. You're an ass, Anne – you dreamt it all!'

'I did not!' said Anne, indignant again. 'I *know* there was someone there – in fact, more than one person, because I'm sure I heard whispering!'

George raised her voice. 'Timmy!' she called loudly, making Anne jump violently. 'Timmy! Come along. We've sent you on a silly wild goose chase – but now we'll go back to bed!'

Timmy came trotting out of the cottage and went obediently to George. She heard him yawn as he stood beside her, and she laughed.

'Anne had a bad dream, that's all, Timmy,' she said.

Anne felt cross – very cross. She said no more and they left the old cottage and went back to their heather bed. Anne climbed on to her side and turned over with her back to George. All right – let George think it was a dream if she liked!

But when Anne awoke in the morning and remembered

the happenings of the night before, she too began to wonder uneasily if she *had* dreamt what she had seen and heard in the old cottage.

'After all – Timmy would certainly have caught anyone who was there,' she thought. 'And he wasn't at all excited, so there can't have *been* anyone in the cottage. And anyway, why would they come? It's just silly!'

So, when George talked about Anne's dreaming in the middle of the night, Anne did not defend herself. She really could *not* be sure that it had really happened. So she stuck out her tongue when George teased her, and said nothing.

'Let's go and see that boy and his camp,' George said when they had eaten a few rather stale sandwiches and some shortbread biscuits. 'I'm beginning to feel bored, aren't you? I wish Timmy's ear would quite heal up. I'd go back home like a shot then.'

They set off in the direction of the camp with Timmy. They heard a chip-chipping noise as they came near, and then something small and hairy shot out from a bush and rushed up, barking a welcome.

'Hallo, Jet!' said Anne. 'Don't you let Timmy have any more of your bones!'

The chipping noise had stopped. The two girls went on and came to a very messy piece of common. It had been well dug over, in some places very deeply. Surely that boy couldn't have done so much excavating by himself?

'Hey! Where are you?' called George. Then she saw the

boy below her, examining something in a trench he had dug out. He jumped and looked upwards.

Then he scowled. 'Look – you promised not to come and disturb me!' he shouted. 'You're mean. You broke your promise.'

'Well! I like *that*!' said George amazed. 'It was *you* who broke yours! Who came messing round *our* camp yesterday evening I'd like to know?'

'Not me!' said the boy at once. 'I always keep my promises. Now go away and keep yours. Pooh!'

'Well, I can't say we think much of *you*,' said George, disgusted. 'We're going. *We* don't want to see anything of your silly digging. Goodbye!'

'Goodbye and good riddance!' called the boy rudely, and turned back to his work.

'I think he must be *quite* mad,' said Anne. 'First he makes a promise – then last evening he broke his promise and even said he hadn't made one – and now today he says he *did* make a promise and that he'd kept his and we'd broken ours. Idiotic!'

They went up a little rabbit path, and into a small copse of birch trees. Someone was sitting there reading. He looked up as they came.

The two girls stopped in amazement. It was that boy *again*! But how had he got here? They had just left him behind in a trench! Anne looked at the title of the book he was reading. Goodness – what a learned title – something about Archaeology.

'Another little trick of yours, I suppose?' said George, sarcastically, stopping in front of him. 'You must be a jolly good runner, I must say, to have got here so quickly. Funny boy, aren't you – very very funny!'

'Good gracious – it's those potty girls again,' groaned the boy. 'Can't you leave me alone? You talked a lot of rubbish yesterday – and now you're talking it again.'

'How did you get here so quickly?' said Anne, puzzled.

'I didn't get here quickly. I came very slowly, reading my book as I went,' said the boy.

'Fibber!' said George. 'You must have run at top speed. Why do you pretend like this? It's only a minute or so ago that we saw you.'

'Now *you're* the fibber!' said the boy. 'I do think you two girls are awful. Go away and leave me alone and never let me see you again!'

Timmy didn't like the tone of the boy's voice and he growled. The boy scowled at him. 'And just you shut up too,' he said.

Anne pulled at George's sleeve. 'Come on,' she said, 'it's no good staying here arguing. The boy's mad – we'll never get any sense out of him!'

The two girls walked off together, Timmy following. The boy took absolutely no notice. His face was turned to his book and he was quite absorbed in it.

'I've never met anyone *quite* so mad before!' said Anne, rather puzzled. 'By the way, George – you don't suppose it could have been that idiotic boy last night in the cottage?'

'No. I tell you I think you dreamt it,' said George, firmly. 'Though that boy is quite idiot enough to explore an old cottage in the middle of the night. He would probably think it a very good time to do so. Oh, Anne, look – there's a pool – in that hollow there. Do you think we could bathe in it?'

It certainly shone very temptingly. They went down to have a closer look. 'Yes – we'll have a swim this afternoon,' said George. 'And then I really think, Anne, we ought to go back to Kirrin Cottage and get a few more provisions. The sandwiches we've got left are so dry that we really shan't enjoy eating them – and as Timmy's ear isn't healed, it looks as if we'll have to stay a bit longer.'

'Right!' said Anne, and they went on back to the camp. They changed into their swimsuits in the afternoon and went off to the little pool. It was fairly deep, very warm and quite clean. They spent a lovely hour swimming and basking and swimming again – then they reluctantly dressed and began to think of going off on the long journey to Kirrin Cottage.

George's mother was very surprised to see the two girls and Timmy. She said yes, of course they could have some more food, and sent them to ask Joanna for all she could spare.

'By the way, I've heard from Julian and Dick,' she said. 'They're back from France – and may be here in a day or two! Shall I tell them to join you or will you come back here?'

'Tell them to come and fetch us as soon as they get here!' said George, delighted. Her face shone. Ah – the Five would be together again. How wonderful!

'Leave me directions to give them so that they can find you,' said her mother. 'Then you can all come back – together. The boys can help to carry everything.'

What fun, what fun! Julian and Dick again, now things would be exciting, things would happen, as they always did. What FUN!

CHAPTER SIX

Storm in the night

IT WAS fun to go back to their little camping place again. It was growing dark, as they had stayed to have a good meal at Kirrin Cottage, and Timmy had eaten a most enormous plate of meat, vegetables and gravy. Then he had sat down and sighed as if to say 'That was jolly good! I could do with some more!'

However, nobody took any notice of this, so he trotted off to have a good look round the garden to make sure it was just the same as when he had left it a day or two before. Then it was time to start back to the camping place, and Timmy heard George's whistle.

'Well, nobody laughed at Timmy this evening!' said Anne. 'Not even your father!'

'Oh, I expect Mother had told him not to,' said George. 'Anyway, I *said* I would stay away till Tim's ear is better, and I mean to.'

'Well, I'm quite willing,' said Anne. 'The only thing I'm a bit worried about is – do you suppose there will be anyone snooping about in that old cottage again?'

'You dreamt it all!' said George. 'You admitted you did!'

'Well, yes, I did wonder if I *had* dreamt it,' said Anne,

as they walked up the long Carters Lane to the moor. 'But now that it will soon be dark, I'm beginning to think I *didn't* dream it – and it isn't a very nice feeling.'

'Oh, don't be silly!' said George impatiently. 'You can't chop and change about like that. Anyway, we've got Timmy – no one would dare to upset Timmy! Would they, Tim?'

But Timmy was ahead, hoping against hope that he might for once in a while catch a rabbit. There were so many about on the common at this time of the evening, peeping at him here, making fun of him there, and showing their little white bobtails as soon as he moved in their direction.

The two girls got safely back to their camp. The tent was still up, their heather bed out in the open, covered with the old rug. They put down their loads thankfully, and went to the little spring for a drink.

George yawned. 'I'm tired. Let's get to bed at once, shall we? Or wait – perhaps it would be a good idea to have a look in at that cottage to make sure no one is there to disturb us tonight.'

'Oh no – I don't want to look,' said Anne. 'It's getting dark now.'

'All right – I'll go with Timmy,' said George, and off she went. She came back in about five minutes, her little torch shining in front of her, for it was now almost dark.

'Nothing to report,' she said. 'Nothing whatever – except one bat flying round that big room. Timmy nearly went mad when it flew down and almost touched his nose.'

'Oh. That's when he barked, I suppose,' said Anne, who was now curled up on the heather bed. 'I heard him. Come on, George – I'm sleepy.'

'I must just look at Timmy's ear once more,' said George and shone her torch on it.

'Well, buck up, then,' said Anne. 'That's about the thousandth time today you've examined it.'

'It does seem much better,' said George, and she patted Timmy. 'I *shall* be glad when I can take this awful collar off him. I'm sure he hates it.'

'I don't believe he even *notices* it now,' said Anne. 'George, are you coming or not? I really can't keep awake one minute more.'

'I'm coming,' said George. 'No, Tim – you are *not* sleeping on our bed. I told you that last night. There's hardly enough room for Anne and me.'

She climbed carefully on to the heather bed, and lay looking up at the twinkling stars. 'I feel happy tonight,' she said, 'because Julian and Dick are coming. I was down in the dumps when I thought they might not be coming at all these hols. When do you suppose they'll be here, Anne?'

There was no answer. Anne was asleep. George sighed. She would have liked to plan what they were going to do when the boys came. Timmy's ear would surely be all right in a day or two – and the boys could carry everything back from this little camp to Kirrin Cottage – and then long days of swimming and boating and fishing and all kinds of fun could begin – begin – begin – be . . .

And now George was asleep too! She didn't feel a small spider running over her hand, wondering whether or not to spin a web between her finger and thumb. She didn't hear the scramble of a hedgehog not far off – though Timmy did and pricked one ear. It was a very peaceful night indeed.

Next day the girls were very cheerful. They made a good breakfast of some of the food they had brought, and then spent some time getting more heather for their bed, which, under the weight of their two bodies, was now rather flat and uncomfortable.

'Now for a swim!' said George. They put on their swimsuits, threw cardigans over their shoulders and set off to the little pool. On the way they saw Jet, the little mongrel dog, in the distance, and the boy with him. Jet tore up to them and danced round Timmy excitedly.

The boy called to them. 'It's all right, don't worry, I'm not going near your place! I'm still keeping *my* promise! Jet – come here!'

The girls took no notice of the grinning boy, but couldn't resist patting the little one-eyed mongrel. Jet really was like a piece of quicksilver, darting in and out and round about. He shot back to the boy at once.

The girls went on to the pool – and stopped in dismay when they came near. Someone was already there, swimming vigorously!

'Who is it?' said Anne. 'Dear me, this lonely common seems absolutely *crowded* with people!'

George was staring at the swimmer in utmost amazement. 'Anne – it's that boy!' she said. 'Look – tousled hair and everything! But – but . . .'

'But we've just met him going in the opposite direction!' said Anne, also amazed. 'How extraordinary! No, it *can't* be the boy!'

They went a little nearer. Yes – it *was* the boy. He called out to them. 'I'm just going out. I shan't be a minute!'

'How did you get here?' shouted George. 'We never saw you turn back and run.'

'I've been here for about ten minutes,' shouted back the boy.

'Fibber!' yelled back George at once.

'Ah – barmy as usual!' yelled the boy. 'Same as yesterday!'

He got out and walked off, dripping wet, in the direction of the trenches and pits which he was digging. George looked about for Jet, but she couldn't see him. 'Perhaps he's in the pool too,' she said. 'Come on, Anne – let's swim. I must say that that boy is extraordinary! I suppose he thinks it's funny to meet people, then double back and appear again!'

'He was nicer the first time of all that we saw him,' said Anne. 'I liked him then. I just don't understand him now. Ooooh – isn't this water lovely and warm!'

They had a long swim, got out and basked in the sun, lying on the heather, and then swam again. Then they began to feel hungry and went back to their little camping place.

The day passed quickly. They saw no more of the puzzling boy, or of Jet. They occasionally heard the sharp noise of metal on stone, or of chipping, from the place where the boy was presumably still digging in the old Roman camp.

'Or what he *hopes* is an old Roman camp,' said George. 'Personally I think he's so mad that I don't suppose he would know the difference between a Roman camp and a Boy Scouts' camp!'

They settled down on their heather bed that night but saw no stars twinkling above them this time. Instead there were rather heavy clouds, and it was not nearly so warm.

'Gosh – I hope it's not going to rain!' said George. 'Our tent wouldn't be much good against a real downpour! We could squeeze into it all right, but it's not a proper waterproof tent. Do you think it's going to rain, Anne?'

'No,' said Anne, sleepily. 'Anyway, I'm not getting up till I have to! I'm tired.'

She went to sleep, and so did George. Timmy didn't, though. He had heard the far-off growl of thunder, and he was uneasy. Timmy was not afraid of thunderstorms, but he didn't like them. They were things that growled like enormous dogs in the sky, and flashed angrily – but he never could get at them, or frighten them!

He closed both eyes, and put down one ear, leaving the other one up, listening.

Another thunder growl came, and one large and heavy drop of rain fell on Timmy's black nose. Then another fell on his cardboard collar and made a very loud noise indeed, startling him. He sat up, growling.

The rain came closer, and soon large drops, the size of ten-penny pieces, peppered the faces of the two sleeping girls. Then came such a crash of thunder that they both awoke in a fright.

'Blow! It's a thunderstorm!' said George. 'And pouring rain too. We shall be soaked.'

'Better get into the tent,' said Anne, as a flash of lightning forked down the sky and lit up everything with a quick brilliance.

'No good,' said George. 'It's soaked already. There's nothing for it but to get into the cottage, Anne. At least we'll have a roof over our heads or rather, a ceiling, for the roof's gone. Come on.'

Anne didn't in the least want to shelter in the old cottage, but there was absolutely nothing else to do. The girls grabbed their rug and ran through the rain, George flashing her torch to guide them. Timmy ran too, barking.

They came to the doorway of the cottage and went inside. What a relief to get out of the rain! The two girls huddled down into a corner, the rug round them – but soon they were too hot and threw it off.

The storm passed overhead with a few terrific crashes and much lightning. Gradually the rain grew less and soon stopped. One star came out, and then others followed as the thunder-clouds swept away in the wind.

'We can't go back to the tent – we'll have to stay here,' said George. 'I'll go and get our bags for pillows. We can lie on the rug.'

Anne went with her, and carried a bag back too. Soon the girls were lying in a corner of the rug, their heads on the bags, and Timmy close beside them.

'Good night,' said Anne. 'We'll try to go to sleep again! Blow that storm!'

Soon they were both asleep – but Timmy wasn't. Timmy

was uneasy. Very uneasy! And quite suddenly he broke into a volley of such loud barks that both girls woke up in a panic.

'Timmy! What's the matter? Oh, Tim, what is it?' cried George. She clutched his leather collar and held on to him.

'Don't leave us! Timmy, what's scared you?'

CHAPTER SEVEN

Strange happenings

TIMMY STOPPED barking and tried to get away from George's hand on his collar. But she would not let him. George was not easily frightened, but what with the thunderstorm, the strange old cottage and now Timmy's sudden excitement, she wanted him near her.

'What is it?' asked Anne, in a scared whisper.

'I don't know. I can't even imagine,' said George, also in a low voice. 'Perhaps it's nothing – just the thunderstorm that has upset him and made him nervous. We'll keep awake a bit, and see if we hear anything peculiar.'

They lay quietly in their corner, and George kept a firm hand on Timmy. He growled once or twice, but did not bark any more. George began to think it really must have been the storm that had upset him.

A rumble of thunder came again – the storm was returning, or else another one was blowing up!

George felt relieved. 'It's all right, Anne. It must have been the thunder and lightning in the distance that upset Timmy. You're silly, Timmy – scaring us like that!'

Crash – rumble – crash! Yes, certainly the storm was gathering force again! Timmy barked angrily.

'Be quiet! You make more noise than the thunder!' said

George, crossly. 'No you can't go out into the rain, Timmy. It's begun again, as bad as before. You'd only get dripping wet – and then you'd want to come and sit as close to me as possible and make me wet too. I know you!'

'No – don't let him go, George,' said Anne. 'I like him here with us. My word – what a storm! I hope it won't strike this cottage.'

'Well, considering that it must have stood here for three or four hundred years, and have seen thousands of storms, I expect it will come safely through one more!' said George. 'Where are you going, Anne?'

'Just to look out of the window,' said Anne. 'Or out of the place where the window used to be! I like to see the countryside suddenly lit up for just one moment in a lightning flash – and then go back to darkness again.'

She went to stand at the window. There came the crash of thunder, not far away, and a brilliant flash of lightning. Anne stared over the countryside, which had suddenly become visible in the flash – and then disappeared like magic in a second!

Anne gave a sudden cry and stumbled back to George. 'George – George . . .'

'Whatever's the matter?' asked George, alarmed.

'There's someone out there – people!' said Anne, clutching George and making her jump. 'I saw them just for an instant, when the lightning flashed.'

'People? What sort of people?' said George, astonished. 'How many?'

'I don't know. It was all so quick. I think there were two – or maybe three. They were standing some way off – quite still, out there in the storm.'

'Anne, those are *trees*!' said George, scornfully. 'There are two or three small trees standing against the sky out there – I noticed them the other day.'

'These weren't trees,' said Anne. 'I know they weren't. What are people doing out there in this storm? I'm frightened.'

George was absolutely certain that Anne had seen the group of little trees that she knew were there – they would look just like people, in a quick flash of lightning. No sooner did you see something in a storm than it was gone!

She comforted Anne. 'Don't worry, Anne! It's the easiest thing in the world to imagine seeing things in a lightning flash. Timmy would bark if there were people around. He would . . .'

'Well, he *did* bark, didn't he?' said Anne. 'He woke us both up with his barking.'

'Ah yes – but that was just because he heard the storm coming up again,' said George. 'And you know he gets angry when he hears the thunder growling.'

Just at that moment the thunder crashed again – then the lightning flashed its weird and brilliant light.

This time *both* the girls screamed, and Timmy gave an enormous bark, trying his hardest to get away from George.

'There! Did you see *that*?' said Anne, in a shaky voice.

'Yes. Yes, I did. Oh, Anne, you're right! Someone was looking in at the window! And if we saw him, he must have seen *us*! Whatever is he doing here in the middle of the night?'

'Well, I told you I saw two or three people,' said Anne, still shakily. 'I expect it was one of them. Maybe they saw the cottage in one of the lightning flashes, and thought they might shelter here – and sent one of their number to see.'

'Maybe. But what in the world is anyone *doing*, wandering about here at night?' said George. 'They can't possibly be up to any good. Let's go home tomorrow,

Anne. I wish the boys were here! They'd know what to do, they would have some good plan!'

'The storm's going off again,' said Anne. 'Timmy has stopped barking too, thank goodness. Don't let him go, George. You never know – those people, whoever they are, might do him harm. Anyway, I feel safer when he's with us!'

'I wouldn't dream of letting him go,' said George. 'You're trembling, Anne! You needn't be as scared as that! Timmy won't let you come to any harm.'

'I know! But it wasn't very nice suddenly seeing somebody looking in at the window like that, outlined in a lightning flash!' said Anne. 'I can't possibly go to sleep again. Let's play some silly game to take our minds off it.'

So they played the Alphabet game with Animals. Each had to think in turn of an animal beginning with A, and a mark went to the one who could keep it up longest! Then they went on to B and to C and to D.

They were doing the Es when they heard a loud and very comforting sound.

'Timmy's snoring,' said George. 'He's fast asleep. What an elephantine snore, Tim!'

'E for elephant,' said Anne, quickly.

'Cheat! That should have been *my* E!' said George. 'All right. E for Eland.'

'E for Egg-Eater,' said Anne, after a pause.

'Not allowed – you made that up!' said George. 'My mark!'

By the time they got to M, Anne was two marks ahead, and the dawn was breaking. It was a great relief to the two girls to see the silvering of the sky in the east and to know that soon the sun would be up. They immediately felt much better. George even stood up and went bravely to the window, where there was nothing to be seen but the quiet countryside outside, with its stretches of heather, gorse bushes and silver birches.

'We were silly to be so scared,' said George. 'I don't think we'll go back home today after all, Anne. I hate running away from anything. The boys would laugh at us.'

'I don't care if they do,' said Anne. 'I'm going back. If the boys were here, I'd stay – but goodness knows when they'll come – it might not be till next week! I'm just NOT staying here another night.'

'All right, all right,' said George. 'Do as you like – but for goodness' sake tell the boys it was *you* who wanted to run away, not me!'

'I will,' said Anne. 'Oh dear – now I feel sleepy all over again. I suppose it's because daylight is here and everything seems safe, so I know I can fall asleep.'

George felt the same! They cuddled down together on the rug again and immediately fell asleep. They did not wake till quite late – and even then something woke them, or they might have slept on for hours, tired out with their broken night and the fright they had had.

They were awakened by something scuttling round them,

making a very loud noise indeed. Then Timmy barked.

The girls awoke and sat up, rather dazed. 'Oh, it's *Jet*!' said Anne. 'Jet, have you come to see if we're all right, you dear, funny little one-eyed thing!'

'Wuff-wuff!' said Jet and rolled over on his back to be tickled, his long thin tail wagging all the time. Timmy leapt on him and pretended to eat him. Then a loud voice called to them.

They looked up. The boy was standing at the door, grinning widely.

'Hallo, sleepy-heads! I came to see if you were all right after that awful storm. I know I promised I wouldn't come here, but I felt a bit worried about you.'

'Oh. Well, that's nice of you,' said Anne, getting up and brushing the dust from her skirt. 'We're quite all right – but we had rather a peculiar night. We—'

She got a hard nudge from George and stopped suddenly. George was warning her not to say anything about the people they had seen – or the person at the window. Did she think they might have anything to do with this boy? Anne said no more and George spoke instead.

'Wasn't it a dreadful storm? How did you get on?'

'All right. I sleep down in a trench, and the rain can't get at me. Well – so long! Come on, Jet!'

The boy and the dog disappeared. 'That was nice of him,' said Anne. He doesn't seem crazy this morning, does he – quite normal! He didn't even contradict us. I think I quite like him after all.'

They went to their soaked tent and got a tin of sardines out to eat with bread and butter. Just as they were opening it, they heard someone whistling and looked up.

'Here comes that boy again!' said Anne.

'Good morning. I don't want to butt in – but I just wondered if you were all right after the storm,' said the boy, without even a smile. The girls stared at him in amazement.

'Look – don't start being crazy all over again!' said George. 'You know jolly well we're all right. We've already told you.'

'You haven't. And I *didn't* know!' said the boy. 'Well, I only came out of politeness. Sorry to see you are still barmy!'

And off he went. 'There!' said Anne, vexed. 'Just as we thought he was nice again, and not crazy, he starts all over again. I suppose he thinks it's funny. Silly ass!'

They set their things out to dry in the sun, and it was half past twelve before they were ready to pack and go back to Kirrin Cottage. George was rather cross about going, but Anne was quite firm. She was NOT going to spend another night on the common.

George was just strapping a package on her bicycle, when the two girls heard the sound of voices – and then Timmy went quite mad! He barked wildly, and set off down a path at top speed, his tail wagging nineteen to the dozen!

'Oh! It can't be – surely it can't be Julian and Dick!'

shouted George, in sudden delight, and she shot off after Timmy.

It was! It *was* Julian and Dick! There they came, packs on their backs, grinning all over their faces! Hurrah! The Famous Five were all together once more!

CHAPTER EIGHT

All together again!

THERE WAS such excitement at the arrival of the boys that at first nobody could make themselves heard. Timmy barked at the top of his very loud voice and simply would *not* stop! George shouted, and Dick and Julian laughed. Anne hugged them, and felt proud of two such tanned, good-looking brothers.

'Ju! We never guessed you'd come so soon!' said the delighted George. 'Gosh, I'm pleased to see you!'

'We got fed up with French food,' said Dick. 'I came out in spots and Julian was sick, and it was SO hot. Phew! Next time I go there I'll go when it's cooler.'

'And we kept on thinking of Kirrin and the bay, and you two girls and Timmy,' said Julian, giving George a friendly grin. 'I think we *really* got a bit homesick. So we packed up before we should, and flew home.'

'Flew?' said George. 'You lucky things! And then did you come straight down here?'

'We spent the night with Mother and Dad at home,' said Julian, 'and then caught the first train here that we possibly could this morning – only to find that you weren't at Kirrin!'

'So we packed camping-out things in smaller bags and

came straight along to you!' said Dick. 'I say, George, old thing, do you think you could possibly make Timmy stop barking?'

'Shut up, Tim,' ordered George. 'Let other people bark a bit. Do you notice his collar, Julian?'

'Can't help seeing it!' said Julian. 'He looks a scream in it, doesn't he? Ha ha! You're an Elizabethan dog with a ruff, Timmy – that's what Uncle Quentin told us – and that's what you look like, old fellow!'

'He looks most comical, I must say,' said Dick. 'Enough to make a cat laugh, hey, Timmy!'

Anne looked at George. Goodness, what would she say to hear *Julian and Dick* laughing at Timmy and making fun of him! Would she lose her temper at once?

But George only grinned. In fact she gave a little laugh herself. 'Yes – he does look funny, doesn't he? But he doesn't mind a bit!'

'You know, we came here to camp because George couldn't bear people laughing at . . .' began Anne, thinking that she wouldn't let George get away with this! But George gave her such a beseeching look, that she stopped at once. George could never bear to look small in front of Julian and Dick. She prided herself on being just like a boy – and she was suddenly certain that her two cousins would think she was 'just like a *girl*' if they heard the fuss she had made about people laughing at Timmy's collar.

'I say – you two seem to be packing up,' said Julian,

looking at the package strapped to the back of George's bicycle. 'What's happened?'

'Well – it got a bit lonely and Anne was . . .' and then in her turn George caught a beseeching look from Anne! She knew what it meant. 'I didn't tell tales on *you* – so don't tell tales on *me* – *don't* say I was scared!'

'Er – Anne was certain that there was something funny going on here,' went on George, who had quite meant to say that Anne was scared and insisted on going home. 'And we didn't feel that we could tackle it ourselves – though if you had been here we wouldn't have *dreamt* of going home, of course.'

'What do you mean – something funny?' asked Dick.

'Well – you see – it began like this,' said George, but Julian interrupted.

'If there's a tale to tell, let's have it over a meal, shall we? We've had nothing to eat since six o'clock this morning, Dick and I – and we're ravenous!'

'Yes. Good idea,' said Dick, and began to undo a big package which he took out of his bag. 'I've a picnic lunch here from your mother, George – a jolly good one, I can tell you. I think she was so relieved to think that she was going to get rid of us that she really surpassed herself! We've got a marvellous piece of boiled ham – look! It'll last us for ages – if we don't give bits to Timmy. Get away, Tim. This is *not* for you! Grrrrr!'

George suddenly felt so happy that she could hardly speak. It had been fun camping with Anne – but what a difference the boys made! So confident of themselves, so merry, full of jokes, so idiotic, and yet so dependable. She felt that she wanted to sing at the top of her voice!

The sun had been hot again that morning and had dried the common beautifully. It wasn't long before the Five were sitting down in the heather with a very fine feast before them.

'I wouldn't sell anyone my hunger for a hundred pounds,' said Dick. 'Now then – who's going to carve this magnificent piece of gammon?'

There were no plates, so they had to make sandwiches of the ham. Dick had actually brought some mustard, and dabbed it generously over the slices of ham before George put them between pieces of bread. 'Aha, Tim – this is one way of making sure you won't get even a *bite* of these wonderful ham sandwiches!' said Dick. 'You can't bear mustard, can you? Ju, where's the meat we brought for Tim?'

'Here. Pooh – it smells a bit strong,' said Julian. 'Do you mind taking it to a nice secluded corner, Tim?'

Timmy immediately sat down close to Julian. 'Now – don't be so disobedient!' said Julian, and gave Timmy a friendly push.

'He doesn't understand the word "secluded",' said George, with a grin. 'Tim – buzz off a bit!'

Timmy understood that and took his meat a little way away. Everyone took a ripe red tomato, and a little lettuce heart from a damp cloth brought by Julian, and settled down happily to munch sandwiches.

'Lovely!' said Anne, contentedly. 'Goodness gracious – I can hardly believe we had such a peculiar time last night!'

'Ah – tell us all about it!' said Dick.

So first Anne, then George related all that had happened. Anne told of the night she had seen a light in the old cottage and had heard whispers and footfalls inside.

'We did think I might have been dreaming,' she said, 'but now we don't think I was. We think I really did see and hear those things.'

'What next?' asked Julian, taking his third sandwich.

'This all sounds most interesting. Quite Famous Five-ish, in fact!'

George told of the storm in the night, and how they had had to leave their heather bed and go to shelter in the old cottage – and how, in the flashes of lightning, Anne had seen two or three people standing outside – and then how they had *both* seen someone standing silently, looking in at the window.

'Strange,' said Julian, puzzled. 'Yes – something is up. I wonder what? I mean – there's absolutely nothing on this lonely bit of common that's at all interesting.'

'Well – there are the remains of an old Roman camp,' said Anne. 'And a boy there who is examining them to see if he can find anything old and interesting.'

'A completely *mad* boy,' said George. 'He doesn't seem to know what he says or doesn't say. Contradicts himself all the time – or to put it another way, tells the most idiotic fibs.'

'And he apparently thinks it's awfully funny to meet us somewhere, and then double round on his tracks and appear suddenly somewhere else,' said Anne. 'Sometimes I can't help liking him – other times he's too idiotic for words.'

'He's got a little one-eyed dog called Jet,' said George, and Timmy gave a sudden bark as he heard the name. 'You like Jet, don't you, Tim?'

'This all sounds most interesting,' said Dick. 'Pass me the tomato bag, Ju, before you eat the lot. Thanks. As I said, *most* interesting – a one-eyed dog, a mad boy, Roman remains – and people who come to an old ruined cottage in the dead of night and look into windows!'

'I wonder you two girls didn't pack up and go home,' said Julian. 'You must be braver without us than I thought possible!'

George caught Anne's eye and grinned mischievously, but said nothing. Anne owned up, red in the face.

'Well – I did tell George I was going home this very morning, I was so scared last night. George didn't want to, of course, but she was coming, all the same. But now you've turned up, things are different.'

'Ah – well, do we stay on, or don't we, Ju?' said Dick. 'Are we scared or are we not?'

Everyone laughed. 'Well – if you go back *I* shall stay on alone!' said Anne. 'Just to show you!'

'Good old Anne!' said Dick. 'We all stay, of course. It may be nothing – it may be something – we can't tell. But we'll certainly find out. And the first thing to do is to have a look at the Roman remains and the mad boy. I'm looking forward to meeting him, I must say! After that we'll tackle the ruined cottage!'

Timmy came up to see if he could get any tit-bits. Julian waved him away. 'You smell of too-strong meat, Timmy,' he said. 'Go and get a drink. By the way, *is* there anything to drink here, George?'

'Oh yes,' said George. 'A lovely spring. Not far off, either. Let's take the remains of our meal there, and the mug. We've only got one unfortunately, so it's no good getting water unless we all sit by the spring and take turns at the mug. Come on!'

The boys thought that the spring was a really splendid one. They grouped themselves around it and took turns at filling the mug and drinking from it. They were now eating slabs of Joanna's fruit cake and it was very good.

'Now, you girls unpack again,' said Dick, when they had finished their meal. 'Goodness, I did enjoy that! We'd better unpack too, Julian.'

'Right. Where shall we put our things?' asked Julian, looking around. 'I don't somehow like to leave everything under that little tent, with a mad boy about, and a one-eyed dog. I feel that both of them might like the rest of that ham.'

'Oh, it's too hot to leave ham out in this sun,' said George. 'We'll have to put it into the old cottage, on a shelf. We'll put *everything* there, shall we? Move in properly, in case it rains again at night. It's so tiresome to have to bundle everything indoors in the dark and the rain.'

'I agree,' said Dick. 'Right. We'll move into the ruined cottage. What fun! Come on, everyone!'

They spent the next half-hour taking their things into the cottage and putting them in corners or on shelves. George found a dark corner behind the fireplace where she put the food, for she was half-afraid that Jet, nice little dog though he seemed, might perhaps smell the ham and gobble up most of their food.

'Now!' said Julian. 'Are we ready to go and see the Roman remains and the Mad Boy? Here we go, then – the Famous Five are off again, and who knows what will happen!'

CHAPTER NINE

A little exploration

THE FIVE walked off together, Timmy at the back, delighted to have all his friends with him again. He kept nudging first one person's heels and then another, just to remind them that he was there.

As they came near the old camp, they saw a boy sitting beside a bush, reading.

'There's that boy we told you of!' said George. 'See?'

'He looks fairly ordinary,' said Dick. 'Very absorbed in his book, I must say. Determined to take no notice of us!'

'I'll speak to him,' said George. So, as they drew near, she called to the boy.

'Hallo! Where's Jet?'

The boy looked up, annoyed. 'How do I know?'

'Well, he was with you this morning,' said George.

'He was not,' said the boy. 'He's never with me! Please don't disturb me, I'm reading.'

'There you are!' said George to the others. 'He came to see us this morning with Jet – and now he says the little dog is never with him. Quite, quite mad!'

'Or plain rude,' said Dick. 'Not worth bothering about, anyway. Well, if he's not doing any excavating in his

Roman camp, perhaps we can explore it without being ordered off!'

They walked on slowly and came to the camp, and at once heard a cheerful whistling going on, and the sound of someone digging. George looked over the top of the dug-out trench in surprise. She almost toppled in, she was so amazed at what she saw!

The boy was there, digging carefully, whistling as he did so! He brushed his tousled hair from his hot forehead and caught sight of George and the others. He looked rather astonished.

'How on earth did you get down here so quickly?' said George. 'Do you have wings or something?'

'I've been down here all the afternoon,' said the boy. 'For at least an hour, I should think.'

'Fibber!' said George. The boy looked very angry, and shouted back at once.

'I'm tired of you two girls – and now you've brought your friends too, I suppose you think you can come and aggravate me even more!'

'Don't be an idiot,' said Dick, feeling as puzzled about this boy as George and Anne had been. How in the world had he run around them and got down in the trench so quickly? Did he enjoy playing tricks like that? He really didn't *look* mad!

'Is this your property, this old camp?' asked Julian.

'No. Of course not. Don't be daft!' said the boy. 'As if I could own a whole camp like this! It was discovered by my father some time ago, and he gave me permission to work here for the hols. It's pretty exciting, I can tell you. See my finds?'

He pointed to a rough shelf where stood a broken pot, something that looked like an old brooch, a long pinlike thing, and part of a stone head. Julian was at once interested. He leapt down into the trench.

'I say – you've certainly got something there!' he said. 'Any coins too?'

'Yes – three,' said the boy and put his hand in his pocket. 'I found this one first – then these two close together yesterday. They must be hundreds and hundreds of years old.'

By this time all the others were down in the trench too. They looked about with much interest. Evidently the place had been well excavated by experts, and now the boy was working here and there on his own, hoping to find something that had been overlooked.

Dick went out of the trench and began to clamber about over the great stones and rocks. A small animal suddenly caught his eye – a young rabbit.

It stared at him in fright and then disappeared behind a slab of stone. It peeped out at Dick again, and he was amused. He went cautiously over to the slab, and the little rabbit disappeared – but soon two or three whiskers poked out. Dick got down on hands and knees and looked behind the slab. A dark hole was there.

Dick pulled out his torch and flashed it into the hole,

wondering if the small rabbit was hiding there, or whether it was the entrance to a burrow.

To his surprise there was a very big hole indeed – a hole that seemed to go down and down and down – his torch could make out no bottom to it.

'It's far too wide for a rabbit hole,' thought Dick. 'I wonder where it leads to. I'll ask that boy.'

He went back to where the boy was still showing his things to Julian, talking eagerly. 'I say,' began Dick, 'there's a most interesting hole behind one of the stone slabs over there – what is it?'

'Oh that – my father says it was explored and that it was only a place for storage – meat in hot weather, or loot, or something like that. Actually nothing whatever was found there – most uninteresting. As a matter of fact it may be nothing to do with the camp at all.'

'I say, look – here's another shelf with things on it,' said George, suddenly spying a little collection of things on a rough shelf in another part of the trench. 'Are these yours too?'

'Those? No,' said the boy. 'Nothing to do with me at all. Don't touch them, please.'

'Whose are they then?' asked George, curiously. The boy took no notice whatever of her question and went on talking to Julian. George took down a beautiful little round pot.

'Hey! I told you NOT to touch those!' yelled the boy, so suddenly and angrily that George almost dropped the pot. 'Put it back – and clear out if you can't do what you're told.'

'Easy, old man, easy!' said Julian. 'No need to yell at her like that. You scared that little dog of yours and made him jump almost out of his skin! We'd better go, I think.'

'Well – I don't like being disturbed too much,' said the boy. 'People always seem to be wandering around. I've turned off quite a lot.'

'People?' said Julian, remembering Anne's story of two or three figures standing outside the cottage the night before, and of someone looking in. 'What kind of people?'

'Oh – nosey ones – wanting to get down and explore – disturbing me – it's surprising how many idiots there are wandering about this lonely place,' said the boy, picking up a tool again and setting to work. He grinned suddenly. 'I don't mean you. You really *know* something about this kind of thing.'

'Was anyone about last night?' asked Julian.

'Well – I rather think so,' said the boy. 'Because Jet here barked like mad. But it might have been the storm that frightened him – not that he's *usually* frightened of storms.'

'What's your name?' asked Dick.

'Guy Lawdler,' said the boy, and Dick whistled.

'My word – is your father the famous explorer Sir John Lawdler?' he asked. The boy nodded.

'Well, no wonder you're so keen on archaeology!' said

Dick. 'Your father's done pretty well in that line, hasn't he?'

'Come on, Dick!' said George. 'Let's go now. We might have time for a swim in the pool. We forgot to tell you about that.'

'Right,' said Dick. 'Come on, Julian. Goodbye, Guy!'

They left the rather desolate old camp and went back to the cottage to get their swimsuits and change. It wasn't long before they were running over the heather to the pool.

'Hallo – Guy's having a swim!' said Dick, in surprise. Sure enough, a boy was there, his hair falling over his forehead as usual.

'Hey, Guy!' shouted George. 'Have a swim with us!'

But the boy was already getting out of the water. Dick shouted. 'Wait a minute – don't go. We'd like to have a swim with you, Guy!'

But the boy turned defiantly. 'Don't be an ass!' he said. 'My name's not Guy!'

And, leaving four astonished people behind him, he ran lightly over the heather and disappeared.

'There you are – he's mad after all!' said Anne. 'Don't bother about him. Come on in – the water's lovely and warm.'

They lazed about afterwards and began to feel hungry. 'Though how *any* of us could feel hungry after eating about fifty sandwiches between us at lunch-time, I don't know!' said Dick. 'Race you back to the cottage, Ju!'

They changed back into ordinary clothes and then had tea – fruit cake, shortbread biscuits and tinned pineapple on bread. They kept the juice and diluted it with cold spring water – it was simply delicious.

'Now let's explore the cottage,' said Dick.

'We already have, Anne and I,' said George. 'So I don't expect you'll find anything much.'

They went methodically through the old house, and even up the old stone stairway to the two rooms, upstairs – though they could hardly be called rooms, for they had very little roof and not much wall!

'Nothing much here, that's certain,' said Dick, clattering down the stone stairway. 'Now let's go to the outbuildings – not that there's much left of them either!'

They examined everything, and came last of all to the old stables. It was dark inside, for the windows were very small, and it was some seconds before anyone could see properly.

'Old mangers,' said Dick, touching them. 'I wonder how long ago it is since they were used – and . . .'

'I say!' said George, suddenly. 'There's something funny here. Anne, look – this bit of floor was undisturbed yesterday, wasn't it?'

Anne looked down at the big white flagstone on which George was standing. It was quite obvious that it had been lifted, for the edges were not as green with moss as the others were, and the stone had been put back a little crookedly.

'Yes – someone's been interested in this stone – or in what is beneath it!' said Dick. 'I bet something is buried underneath!'

'Those men last night – that's what they came about!' said George. 'They went into these stables and lifted this stone. Why?'

'We'll soon find out!' said Julian. 'Come on, everyone, loosen it with your fingers – then we'll heave it up!'

CHAPTER TEN

What can be happening?

FORTY FINGERS and thumbs were very hard at work trying to loosen the heavy stone. At last Julian got hold of a corner which could be held more easily than any other part of the stone. He tried to lift it and it came away a little.

'Help me this side, Dick,' said Julian, and Dick put his strong fingers there too. 'Heave-ho!' he said – and up came the stone.

It went over with a crash and Timmy barked loudly, jumping aside. Everyone peered down – and then looked exceedingly disappointed!

There was nothing there at all. Not even a hole! The black earth, hard as iron, lay underneath, and nothing else.

They all stared down at the dry, hard earth, puzzled. George looked up at Julian.

'Well – that's strange, isn't it? Why should anyone lift up this heavy stone if there is nothing hidden underneath?'

'Well, it's clear that whoever was here didn't find anything – nor did he *hide* anything either,' said Julian. 'Dear me – why should anyone lift up a heavy stone and put it back – just for nothing?'

'He was obviously looking for something that wasn't here,' said Anne. 'The wrong stone, probably!'

'Yes. I think Anne's right,' said Dick. 'It's the wrong stone! Probably there is something very interesting under the *right* stone! But which one is it?'

They all sat and looked at one another, and Timmy sat too, wondering why all this fuss was made about a flat white stone. Julian thought hard.

'From what you've told me, Anne – about seeing a light in the cottage that first night you were here – and hearing voices – and then seeing those figures outside last night in the storm – it looks as if someone is urgently hunting for something round about here.'

'Yes – something under a stone. Treasure of some sort, do you think?' said George.

Julian shook his head. 'No. I hardly think that much treasure would be hidden anywhere about this old cottage – all the people who lived here must have been fairly poor. The most they would have hidden would have been a few pieces of gold, and that would have been found long ago.'

'Well – someone modern might have hidden something valuable here – even something stolen,' said Anne.

'Yes. We can't tell. It's obviously important and urgent to somebody,' said Dick. 'I wonder if the people that Guy said came bothering him were anything to do with this?'

'They may have been,' said Julian. 'But they have clearly decided that what they are looking for is here now, whatever it is. And they must have been most annoyed to find you and Anne here last night, George. That's why someone came and looked in at the window, I expect – to make sure you were asleep! And you weren't.'

'I don't know whether I want to stay on here or not now,' said Anne, alarmed. 'If they haven't found what they want, they'll probably come again – in the night too.'

'Who cares?' said Dick. 'We've got Timmy, haven't we? I'm not turning out of here because somebody's got a habit of turning up big stones!'

Julian laughed. 'Nor am I. Let's stay on! And I don't see why we shouldn't do a bit of pulling up of stones ourselves! We might come across something very interesting!'

'Right. It's decided that we stay on then, is it?' said Dick. 'What about you, Anne?'

'Oh yes – of course I'll stay,' said Anne, not wanting to in the least, but knowing that she simply could not bear not to be with the others.

The Five walked round and about the cottage for a while, trying to make out where the people that the girls had seen the night before had come from – from what direction did they come and where did they go?

'The figures I saw first in the lightning stood about there,' said Anne, pointing. 'Let's go and see if there are any footprints. It was pouring with rain and the ground must have been very muddy.'

'Good idea,' said Dick, and off they went to where Anne had pointed. But it was a heathery piece of ground, and difficult to tell even if anyone *had* trodden there, for the heather was thick and springy.

'Let's look just outside the window now – the one where Anne saw someone looking in,' said Dick. And there they had a find! Just in front of the window were two quite deeply printed footmarks. One was slightly blurred as if the maker of them had turned his foot sideways as he waited. The other was very clear indeed.

Dick got out a piece of paper. 'I rather think I'll measure these,' he said, 'and make a note of the pattern on the soles. They had rubber soles and heels – look at the markings – crêpe rubber I should think.'

He measured the prints. 'Size eight shoes,' he said.

'Same as yours, Ju.' Then he carefully drew an exact picture of the sole and heel markings.

'You're quite a detective, Dick,' said Anne, admiringly, and he laughed.

'Oh, anyone can copy footprints!' he said. 'The thing is to match them up with the owner!'

'I have a feeling it's getting on for supper-time – if anyone *wants* any supper,' said George. 'It's half past eight! Would you believe that the time could fly so fast?'

'I don't *really* feel very hungry,' said Dick. 'We've done pretty well today.'

'Well, don't waste our precious food if you don't feel hungry,' said George. 'We shall have to keep going home for more if we eat everything too quickly.'

Nobody felt terribly hungry. They made a cosy corner in the cottage and had a slice of cake and a biscuit each, with a drink of pineapple juice and spring-water. George had had the bright idea of filling the big empty pineapple tin, and they each filled a mug from it in turn, and drank.

'It's getting dark,' said Julian. 'Are we going to sleep inside the cottage or out?'

'In,' said Dick, promptly. 'We'll make things just as difficult for any night prowlers as possible!'

'Right,' said Julian. 'I bet they won't be pleased to find old Timmy here too. Shall we go out and get some heather for beds? I don't fancy sharing a thin rug between the four of us.'

Soon they were all dragging in armfuls of the springy heather. They laid it in the front room, in two corners, for the boys thought they would rather be in the same room as the girls, in case of danger.

'You need an awful lot of heather to make a *soft* bed,' said Dick, trying his. 'My bones seem to go right through the clumps and rub against the floor!'

'We can put our anoraks over our heather,' said Julian. 'That will help. The girls can have the rug. We shan't need any covering, it's so hot.'

By the time they had finished, it was dark. George lay on her heather and yawned. 'I'm going to sleep,' she announced. 'We don't need to keep guard or anything like that, do we? Timmy will bark if anyone comes near.'

'You're right. I really don't think we need take turns at keeping awake,' said Julian. 'Move up, Dick – you've left me no room.'

Julian was the last to go to sleep. He lay awake puzzling over the lifted stone slab. It was clear that someone had expected to find something under it. How did they know it was that particular slab? Had they a map? If so, it must have shown the wrong stone – or perhaps the searchers read the map wrong?

Before he could work it out any further, he was asleep. Timmy was asleep too, happy because all the others were under his care. He had one ear open as usual, but not *very* much open!

It was enough to let him hear a small mouse of some kind run across the floor. It was even enough for him to hear a beetle scraping its way up the wall. After a while his ear dropped down and he didn't even hear a hedgehog outside.

But something caused his ear to listen again and it pricked up. A noise crept inside the cottage – a noise that got louder and louder – a weird and puzzling noise!

Timmy woke up and listened. He pawed at George, not knowing whether to bark or not. He knew he should not bark at owls, but this was not an owl. Perhaps George would know.

'Don't, Timmy,' said George sleepily, but Timmy went on pawing her. Then she too heard the noise and sat up in a hurry.

What a truly horrible sound! It was a whining and a wailing, rising and falling through the night. A sound of misery and woe, that went on and on.

'Julian! Dick! Wake up!' called George, her heart beating wildly. 'Something's happening.'

The boys awoke at once and so did Anne. They sat and listened to the weird noise. What in the world could it be? There it went again – wailing high in the air, and then dying away with a moan, only to begin again a few seconds later.

Dick felt the roots of his hair pricking. He leapt off the heather bed and ran to the window. 'Quick! Come and look at this!' he cried. 'What is it?'

They all crowded to the window, Timmy barking now as loudly as he could. In silence the others gazed at a very strange sight.

Blue and green lights were shining here and there, sometimes dimly, sometimes brightly. A curious round white light was travelling slowly in the air, and Anne clutched George, breathing fast.

'It won't come here,' she said. 'It won't, will it? I don't like it. What is happening, Julian?'

'I wish that awful wailing, whining noise would stop,' said Dick. 'It gets right inside my head. Do you make anything of all this, Julian?'

'Something very strange is going on,' said Julian. 'I'll go out with Timmy and see what I can find.' And before anyone could stop him, out he went, Timmy barking beside him.

'Oh, Julian – come back!' called Anne, listening as his footsteps became distant. They all waited tensely at the window – and then suddenly the wailing noise stopped and the strange lights gradually began to fade.

Then they heard Julian's footsteps coming back firmly in the darkness.

'Ju! What was it?' called Dick, as his brother came in at the doorway.

'I don't know, Dick,' said Julian, sounding very puzzled. 'I simply – don't – know! Perhaps we can find out in the morning.'

CHAPTER ELEVEN

Interesting discoveries – and a plan

THE FOUR sat in the dark and talked over the horrible noises and the weird blue and green and white lights. Anne sat close to Julian. She really was frightened.

'I want to go back to Kirrin,' she said. 'Let's go tomorrow. I don't like this.'

'I didn't see a thing just now,' said Julian, puzzled, his arm close round Anne. 'I seemed to go quite close to those wailing sounds – and then they stopped as soon as I got fairly near. But although Timmy barked and ran around, there didn't seem to be anyone there.'

'Did you get near the lights?' asked Dick.

'Yes, fairly near. But the odd thing was that they seemed high up when I got near them – not near the ground as I expected. And *again* Timmy couldn't find anyone. You would have thought if there was anyone about, playing the fool, that Timmy would have found them. But he didn't.'

'Woof,' said Timmy, dolefully. He didn't like this funny business at all!

'Well, if *nobody's* making the noises and lights, it makes it even worse,' said Anne. 'Do let's go home, Julian. Tomorrow.'

'All right,' said Julian. 'I don't feel particularly thrilled about all this myself. But there is *one* idea I've got in my mind which I'd like to sort out tomorrow.'

'What's that?' said Dick.

'Well – it may quite well be that somebody very badly wants us out of here for some reason,' said Julian. 'And that somebody may want to come and lift other stones and have a thorough search all over the place – which he can't do with us around. So he's trying to frighten us out!'

'Yes, I believe you are right, Julian,' said Dick. 'Those noises – and lights – they would be enough to scare anyone out of a place. Too eerie for words! Well, let's have a good snoop round in the daylight, to see if we can find any trace of a trickster!'

'We will – but it's extremely odd that *Timmy* didn't find him,' said Julian. 'Timmy can smell anyone out of any hiding-place! Yes – we'll have a very very good hunt round tomorrow.'

'And if you find nothing and nobody, we'll go home?' asked Anne.

'Yes, we will. I promise you,' said Julian, hugging Anne. 'Don't worry. You shan't have to stay here one night longer, unless you want to! Now, let's try and go to sleep again!'

It took the four a long time to go to sleep after all this excitement in the middle of the night. Anne kept listening for the wailing noises again, but none came. She kept her eyes shut tightly in case she should happen to see any more of the strange lights outside the window.

George and the boys lay awake too, puzzling out the problems of lights and noises which were not apparently caused by anyone! Julian especially was puzzled.

Only Timmy was unconcerned. He went to sleep before anyone else, though he kept one ear *wide* open – and up went the other one when George moved, or Dick whispered to Julian.

The excitement of the night made them all sleep late. Julian awoke first, and stared at the low ceiling in surprise. Now – where was he? In France? No. Ah, of course he was in the old ruined cottage!

He woke Dick, who yawned and stretched. 'Remember those strange lights and noises last night?' asked Dick. 'What a fright they gave us! It seems silly to think we were all so puzzled and scared, now that the sun is shining in at the window, and we can see the countryside around for miles!'

'I'm pretty certain someone is trying to scare us away,' said Julian. 'We are in their way here – they want to do some thorough explorations and they can't, because of us! I've a good mind to take the girls home, Dick, and come back here with you.'

'Anne might go, but George wouldn't,' said Dick. 'You know what old George is – she doesn't like to miss out. Let's not decide anything till we have had a look round this morning. I don't really believe there's anything spooky about this at all – I agree with you that it's just a few tricks to frighten us away.'

'Right,' said Julian. 'Let's wake the girls. Hey, George! Anne! Sleepyheads! Get up and get us breakfast!'

George sat up, looking furious, as Julian intended. 'You jolly well get your own b—' she began, and then laughed as she saw Julian's amused face.

'I was only just striking a little match to set you alight!' said Julian. 'Come on – let's all go for a swim in the pool!'

They set off together happily in the warm sunshine, Timmy padding along, his tail waving vigorously. As soon as they got to the pool, they saw the boy there, floating lazily on his back.

'There's Guy!' said Anne.

'I wonder if he will admit to his name or not this morning!' said George. 'Remember how he told us his name was Guy – and then said it wasn't a little while after? Silly ass! I can't make out if he's quite mad, or just thinks it's funny to keep playing the fool!'

They came to the pool. The boy waved to them, grinning. 'Come on in – it's fine!'

'Is your name Guy this morning or not?' called George.

The boy looked surprised. 'Of course it's Guy!' he said. 'Don't be idiotic! Come on in and have a game.'

They had a fine swim and a mad one. Guy was like an eel, swimming under the water, catching their legs, splashing, swimming away fast, doubling round and going underwater just as they got up to him!

At last they all sat panting on the edge of the pond, the sun shining down warmly on them.

'I say, Guy – did you hear anything strange last night?' asked Dick. 'Or see anything?'

'I didn't *see* anything strange – but I thought I heard somebody wailing and crying in the distance,' said Guy. 'Just now and again when the wind brought the sound this way. Jet didn't like it at all – did you, Jet? He went and hid under my legs!'

'We heard it too – quite near us,' said Julian. 'And saw strange lights.'

They discussed the matter for some time, but Guy could not really help them, because he had not been near enough to the noises to hear them as clearly as the others had.

'I'm getting hungry,' said George, at last. 'I keep thinking of ham and tomatoes and cheese. Let's go back to the cottage.'

'Right,' said Julian. 'Goodbye, Guy – see you sometime soon. Goodbye, Jet, you mad little thing.'

They went off together, their swimsuits almost dry already in the sun.

'Well, Guy was perfectly sensible this morning,' said Anne. 'Funny! I wonder why he's so silly sometimes.'

'See – isn't that him – running down the path there – to the right, look!' said George, suddenly. 'Now how did he get there so quickly? We left him by the pool!'

It certainly looked like Guy! They called to him, but he didn't even look round or wave, though he must have heard

them. They went on, puzzled. How could one person be so different each time – and why? What was the point?

They had a good breakfast and then went out to look round and see if they could find anything to explain the strange happenings of the night before.

'The noises seemed to come from about here, when I came out last night,' said Julian, stopping near the little group of trees. 'And the lights seemed to start about here too – but not near the ground – they were high up, above my head.'

'Above your head?' said Dick, puzzled. 'That seems odd.'

'It doesn't!' said Anne. 'Not a *bit* odd! What about those trees there? Couldn't somebody climb up them and do the wailing and whining there, with some strange instrument – and set off the weird lights?'

Julian stared up at the trees and then round at Anne. He grinned suddenly.

'Anne's got it! Clever girl! Of course someone was up there – or maybe two people – one doing the noises with some weird instrument and the other playing about with fireworks of some kind. Not the noisy kind – just coloured fire or balloons lit up from inside.'

'Yes! *That's* why the lights seemed to be so high up, when you came out!' said Dick. 'They were sent out by someone up in a tree!'

'And floated away to scare us,' said Anne. 'Golly – I *do* feel glad that it was silly tricks like that that frightened us so. They wouldn't frighten me *again*!'

'It explains something else too,' said George. 'It explains why Timmy didn't find anyone! They were safely up trees! I bet they hardly breathed when they knew Tim was down below.'

'Yes. Of course! That puzzled me too,' said Julian. 'It was too spooky for words when even old Tim couldn't find anyone real about – just noises and lights!'

'Here's something, look – a wrinkled little rubber-skin – pale green!' said Dick, picking something up from the ground. 'That's what those lights were – balloons lit up from inside in some way and sent floating away in the air.'

'Most ingenious,' said Julian. 'I expect they had quite a

lot of funny tricks at their disposal last night. Yes – they certainly mean to scare us away!'

'Well, they won't,' said Anne, unexpectedly. '*I'm* not going, for one. I won't be scared away by stupid tricks!'

'Good old Anne!' said Julian, and clapped her on the back. 'Right – we'll all stay – but I've got an idea.'

'What?' asked everyone.

'We'll *pretend* to go!' said Julian. 'We'll pack up everything – remove our things from here – and go and camp somewhere else. But Dick and I will *hide* somewhere here tonight – and watch to see if anyone comes, and where they look for whatever it is they're hunting for, and why!'

'That's a fantastic plan,' said Dick, pleased. 'We'll do it! Roll on, tonight! Adventure is about – and we'll be ready for it!'

CHAPTER TWELVE

A good hiding-place

THE FIVE spent quite a pleasant day, but when late afternoon came, they decided that it was time to carry out their plan and pack as if they were leaving.

'I imagine someone is spying on our doings,' said Dick. 'And won't he be pleased to see us apparently on the point of leaving!'

'How can anyone be spying?' asked Anne, looking all round as if she expected to see someone behind a bush. 'Timmy would be sure to sniff out anyone in hiding.'

'Oh, he won't be near enough for Timmy to smell out,' said Dick. 'He'll be a long way off.'

'Then how can he possibly see us – or know that we're leaving?' asked Anne.

'Anne – I don't know if you've heard of field-glasses,' began Dick, solemnly. 'Well, they're things that can spot anything half a mile away . . .'

Anne went red and gave Dick a shove. 'Don't be an ass! Of course – that's it! Field-glasses used by someone on a hillside somewhere – trained on the old cottage.'

'Actually I think I know where the someone is,' said Dick. 'I've caught sight of a little flash every now and again on the hill over there – the kind of flash that is made by the sun on glass – and I somehow think that our spy is sitting near the top of the hill, watching us carefully.'

Anne turned to look at the hill, but Julian at once spoke sharply. 'No – don't stand and stare up there, anyone. We don't want the watcher to know that *we* know we are being watched.'

They went on with their packing, and soon began to stagger out with their bundles. George was told to strap her things on her bicycle, and stand well out in the open as she did so, so that the watcher on the hill would be able to observe all her doings.

Julian was in the midst of carefully folding up his things to go into his knapsack, when Anne gave a sudden exclamation.

'Someone's coming!'

Everyone looked round, imagining that they would see someone peculiar.

But all they saw was a countrywoman hurrying along, a shawl over her head, and a basket under her arm. She wore glasses, had no make-up on, and her hair was pulled straight back under the shawl. She stopped when she saw the Five.

'Good afternoon,' said Julian, politely. 'Isn't it glorious weather!'

'Beautiful,' said the woman. 'Are you camping out – you've certainly chosen a very good time!'

'No – actually we're packing,' said Julian. 'We've been

sleeping in the old cottage, but we've decided to move out. Is it very, very old?'

'Oh yes – and it's supposed to have strange things happening in it at nights,' said the woman.

'We know that!' said Julian. 'My word – we were pretty scared last night, I can tell you – weird noises and horrible, ghostly lights. We decided not to stay there any longer.'

'That's right,' said the woman. 'Don't you stay! You get as far from this place as you can! I can tell you, *I* wouldn't come by it at night. Where are you going?'

'Well, our home is at Kirrin,' said Julian, evading the question. 'You know – on Kirrin Bay.'

'Ah yes – a fine place,' said the woman. 'Well, don't you stay another night! Goodbye!'

She hurried off, and was soon lost to sight.

'Go on packing,' said Julian to the others.

'The watcher is still up in the hills. I caught sight of a flash again just then.'

'Julian, why did you tell all that to the woman?' asked Anne. 'You don't usually say so much when we are in the middle of something funny!'

'My dear, unsuspecting Anne – do you mean to say that you thought that woman was really what she pretended to be – a woman from a nearby farm?' said Julian.

'Well – wasn't she?' said Anne, surprised. 'She looked like one – no make-up – and that old shawl – and she knew all about the old cottage!'

'Anne – farm women don't have gold fillings in their

teeth,' said Julian. 'Didn't you notice them when she smiled?'

'And her hair was dyed,' said George. 'I noticed it was blonde at the roots and black above.'

'*And* what about her hands?' said Dick. 'A farmer's wife does a great deal of hard, rough work, and her hands are never clean and smooth – they are rough and weathered. This woman's hands were like a princess's!'

'Well yes, I did notice them,' said Anne. 'And I did notice too that she sometimes spoke with an accent and sometimes without.'

'Well, there you are!' said Julian. 'She's one of the unpleasant gang that tried to scare us last night – and when the watcher on the hill reported that we appeared to be packing up and going, she was told to go and make sure. So she pretended to be a country-woman and came by – but unfortunately we weren't quite so stupid as she thought we would be!'

'You certainly fooled her!' said Dick, with a grin. 'The gang will be down here tonight, digging up all the big stones they can find. You and I will have a marvellous time, snooping round them.'

'You'll be careful they don't see you, won't you?' said Anne. 'Where will you hide?'

'We haven't planned that yet,' said Dick. 'Now come on and we'll make a new camp somewhere that won't be easily seen. You and George and Timmy can sleep there tonight, and Ju and I will come and watch here.'

'I want to come too,' said George at once. 'Anne will be all right with Timmy.'

'You aren't joining us this time, George,' said Ju. 'The fewer people watching the better. Sorry, old thing – but you'll have to stay with Anne.'

George scowled and looked sulky at once. Julian laughed and clapped her on the shoulder. 'What a *lovely* scowl! One of your best! I haven't seen it for quite a long time. Keep it up, George – go on, scowl a bit harder, it suits you!'

George grinned unwillingly, and pulled herself together. She hated being left out of anything, but she did see that it was no use having a crowd of people watching that night. All right, she would stay with Anne and keep her company.

It seemed as if the watcher on the hills must have gone, because there were no more sudden flashes such as came when he lifted his field-glasses to watch the Five.

'That disguised countrywoman has convinced the watcher that we're going! Any ideas, anyone, where we can go? Not too far away – but somewhere where the watcher can't follow us with his glasses, if he's still up there.'

'I know a place,' said George. 'There's a simply colossal gorse bush on the other side of the spring. And underneath it is all hollow and dry. It's almost like a kind of gorse cave.'

'Sounds all right,' said Julian. 'Let's go and find it.'

George led the way, trying to remember exactly where

it was. Timmy followed, still in his enormous cardboard collar, which was now rather the worse for wear. George stopped when they had gone a little way past the spring.

'It was somewhere here,' she said. 'I know I could still hear the sound of the spring when I found the hollow under the bush. Ah – there it is!'

It certainly was a great bush, green and spiky outside, with a few yellow blooms on it still. Under it was a big hollow place, where the ground was soft and fine, scattered with dry old prickles.

The main trunk – for it was almost a trunk that supported the big bush – was not quite in the middle, so there was a good bit of room. Julian caught hold of the branches that hid the hollow, using a folded sheet of paper to hold them by, for the bush was very prickly.

'This is fine,' he said. 'Plenty of room for you two girls – and Timmy. My word, he'll have difficulty with his collar though, won't he – squeezing in and out!'

'Take it off!' said Dick. 'His ear really is practically healed now. Even if he scratches it, he can't do much damage. Dear old Timmy, we simply shan't *know* you without your collar.'

'Right,' said George. She took a quick look at the ear. It was still covered by a piece of elastoplast, but it was quite obvious that the ear was healthy. She cut the thread that bound the two ends of the circular collar and then bent it so that it came off.

They all stared at Timmy, who looked most surprised. He wagged his tail gently as if to say 'Well – so you've taken that thing off – I wonder why?'

'Oh, Tim – you look sort of *undressed* without that collar now!' said Anne. 'It *is* nice to see you without it, though. Good old Tim! You'll guard me and George tonight, won't you? *You* know that we're in the Middle of Something again, don't you?'

'Woof,' said Timmy, wagging his tail violently. 'Woof!' Yes – he knew all right!

CHAPTER THIRTEEN

On watch in the cottage

IT WAS getting dark – and under the gorse bush it was very dark indeed! All the Five had managed to squeeze in there, and Timmy too. One torch only was allowed to be used at a time, to save the batteries of the others.

The Five were having supper. The ham was now practically finished, but there were still a few tomatoes and plenty of cake.

Julian opened the last tin of sardines, and made some sandwiches for himself and Dick to take with them. He also wrapped up two enormous chunks of cake and pocketed two slabs of chocolate each.

'We shall need something to while away the time when we're on the watch tonight!' he said, with a grin. 'I don't know if the Weepies and Wailies and Floating Lights will be along to give us a show – but I fear not. They would be wasted on an empty cottage!'

'I do hope you'll be careful,' said Anne.

'Anne – that's the seventh time you've said that,' said Dick. 'Don't be an ass. Don't you understand that Ju and I are going to *enjoy* ourselves? You'll be the one that has to be careful.'

'How?' asked Anne, surprised.

'Well – you'll have to be careful of that big black beetle squatting over there,' said Dick. 'And mind that a hedgehog doesn't sit down on your bare legs. And be careful in case a snake wants to share this nice safe warm place with you . . .'

'Now *you're* being an ass!' said Anne, giving him a shove. 'When will you be back?'

'We shall be back at exactly the moment you hear us squeezing under here,' said Julian. 'Now, Dick – what about it? I think we might be going, don't you?'

'Right,' said Dick, and began to squeeze out carefully so as not to be pricked more than he could help. 'Oh – why are gorse bushes so horribly spiteful! Jab jab –

anyone would think the bush was *trying* to prick me!'

The two girls sat quite still when the boys had gone from the bush. They tried to hear their footsteps, but they couldn't. Dick and Julian trod too softly on the wiry grass.

'I do so hope they'll be . . .' began Anne, and George groaned.

'If you say that again I shall get cross, Anne! Honestly I shall.'

'I *wasn't* saying it,' said Anne, 'I was only going to say that I hope they'll be *successful* tonight. I'd like to get back to Kirrin and have some fun bathing and boating, wouldn't you?'

'Yes. And some of Joanna's marvellous cooking,' said George. 'Sausages and mash – and tomatoes with it.'

'Yes. And fried plaice fresh from the sea with Joanna's best chipped potatoes,' said Anne. 'I can almost smell it.'

'Woof,' said Timmy, sniffing hard.

'There! He thought I meant it!' said Anne. 'Isn't Timmy clever?'

They had a pleasant talk about how very very clever Timmy was, and Timmy listened and wagged his tail so hard that he made it quite dusty in the gorse hollow.

'Let's go to sleep,' said Anne. 'We can't talk all night – and keeping awake won't help the boys!'

They curled up on the rug they had brought and cuddled together – not so much for warmth, because it was a hot night, but because there was so little room! Anne put out her torch, and the little place immediately became black and dark. Timmy put his head on George's tummy. She groaned.

'Oh, Tim – be careful, please! I had rather a lot of supper!'

Anne giggled and pulled Timmy's head close to her. It was comforting to have old Timmy there. She agreed with George that he was the best dog in the whole world.

'I wonder what the boys are doing now,' she said, after a while. 'Do you suppose they are in the middle of something exciting? Perhaps they are!'

But they weren't! Julian and Dick were feeling extremely bored at that minute. They had gone cautiously to the cottage when they had left the girls, not using their torches at all, for fear of giving anyone warning that they were about. They had debated beforehand where would be the best place to hide, and had decided that it would be a good idea to climb up the little stone stair and hide in the roofless rooms above.

'There's no roof there – and hardly any walls,' said Dick. 'We can peep over any side to watch – and no one would guess that anyone was above them, spying down! It's a good thing it's such a starry night – once we get used to the dim light, we shall be able to see fairly well. Pity there's no moon.'

They had approached the cottage very cautiously indeed, stopping at every step and listening with bated breath for any sound. But there was none.

'Not even the light of somebody's torch, either,' said Dick in Julian's ear. 'I don't think anyone is here yet. Let's get into the cottage and up those stairs as soon as we can.'

They tiptoed into the cottage, not daring to put on their torches. They fumbled across to the little stone stairway, and climbed it with as little sound as they could. Holding their breath made their hearts thump loudly.

'Can you hear my heart thumping?' Dick whispered to Julian, as they at last stood on the floor of the roofless rooms above.

'No. Mine's just the same, thumping away! Well, we're safely here. Let's just shuffle to and fro and see if there are any loose stones we might fall over, and so give ourselves away!'

They cleared away a few loose stones, and then sat down silently on the low broken wall of the two ruined rooms. The wind blew gently but warmly. Everything was still except the rose-rambler climbing over the old house. It moved a little in the wind and made a faint scraping noise. Dick caught his hand on a thorn, and sucked his finger. The rambler was everywhere, across the floor, and over the walls and even up what was left of the little chimney.

The boys had been there for about three-quarters of an hour when Julian gave Dick a slight nudge.

'Here they come!' he whispered. 'See – over there!'

Dick looked round and about and then caught sight of a

small, moving light, just a prick in the darkness. It cast a faint glow before it.

'A torch!' he whispered. 'And another – and another! Quite a procession! A slow one, too.'

The procession made very little noise. It made its way to the cottage, and then split up.

'Having a look to see if we really *are* gone,' whispered Julian. 'Hope they won't think of coming up here.'

'Let's get behind the chimney, in case,' whispered back Dick. So very quietly they rose and made their way to where the remains of the chimney stood, a dark shadow in the starry night. The chimney was quite big, though rather crumbly. The two boys crouched close to it, on the side farthest from where the stone stairway came up in the corner.

'Someone *is* coming up!' whispered Dick, his sharp ears catching the sound of someone's feet on the stone stairs. 'I hope he gets caught by the rambler – there's a big spray near the top!'

'Sh!' said Julian.

Someone came right up the stairway, and gave a sharp exclamation of annoyance near the top. 'Good!' thought Dick. 'He *has* got caught by the rambler!'

A torch shone out over the ruined rooms, the crumbling walls and the remains of the chimney. The boys held their breath, and stood like statues. The light of the torch played over the place for one second and then a voice called down the stairs.

'No one here. The kids have gone. We can get on with the job!'

The boys let out a long breath. Good – they were safe – for the time being at any rate! The visitors down below were no longer cautious – they spoke in ordinary voices and torches flashed all over the place. Then someone lit two lanterns, and the little cottage shone quite brightly.

'Where do we start?' said a voice. 'Here, Jess – where's that plan?'

'I've got it. I'll spread it on the floor,' said a voice that the boys recognised at once. It was the voice of the 'countrywoman' who had spoken to them that day! 'Not that it's much use. Paul's no good at drawing!'

Evidently the searchers were now leaning over the plan. Voices came up the stone stairway.

'All we know for certain is that we have to find that white stone slab – and we know the size. But we don't know the place, except that we think it *must* be here. After all – we've searched the old Roman camp, and there are no slabs there that size!'

Julian nudged Dick. So some of the visitors that Guy had complained of must have been these searchers! Whatever was it they were looking for, hidden behind a slab of stone?

He knew a minute later! A drawling voice said: 'If we have to get up every great slab in this neighbourhood, we will. I'm going to find that secret way if it's the last thing I do! If we don't find that, we don't find those blueprints

– and if we don't find *them*, we might as well go into the poorhouse for the rest of our lives.'

'Or prison!' said someone.

'Not prison,' said the drawling voice. 'It'll be Paul who goes to prison. *He* managed to steal them, we didn't!'

'Can't you get Paul to draw a better plan than this?' said the voice of the 'countrywoman'. 'I can't understand half that's written here.'

'He's ill – almost off his head, too,' said someone. 'No good asking him. He had such a time escaping with those prints, he nearly died. No good asking him, I say.'

'I can't make out this word here,' said the woman. '"W-A-D-E-R" – whatever does it mean?'

'I don't know – wait, though, I do! It might be W-A-T-E-R – water. T not D in the middle. Where's the well? Anywhere in this kitchen? That's it, that's it. *Water!* I bet there's a slab over the well. That's the way to the secret hiding-place!'

Julian clutched Dick. He was as excited as the man down below. They listened eagerly, straining their ears.

'Here's the old sink – and this must be the remains of the pump. The well's underneath this slab – and see the stone is just about the right size. Get busy! Buck up, get busy!'

CHAPTER FOURTEEN

An exciting night – and a surprising morning

SOON THERE came the sound of loud breathing and grunts, as the searchers tried to prise up the stone by the pump. It was obviously very heavy, and very difficult to move, for it had become almost part of the floor itself, through the centuries!

'Drat the thing! It's tearing my hands to pieces!' said a voice. 'Lend me that jemmy, Tom – you don't seem to be doing much good with it!'

After a lot more struggling and panting the stone was loosened. 'Up she comes!' said a voice, and up came the stone so suddenly that it sounded as if most of those pulling at it had sat down very hard on the floor!

The two hidden boys were beside themselves with interest and excitement. How they wished they could go and watch! But it was impossible. They must just listen and try to make out what was happening from what the men said below them.

'Is it a well down there? Yes, it is! My, the water's pretty far down – and black as pitch too.'

There was a silence as the well was examined in the light of torches. Then an exasperated voice, the one with the drawl, said: '*This* is no secret way! Who's going to get through that water! It's just an ordinary small well, and nothing else. That word *can't* have meant Water.'

'All right, boss. What *does* it mean then?' said the woman. '*I* don't know. This isn't a plan, it's a riddle! Why couldn't Paul have made it clear where the stone slab is – he just goes and does a lot of scribble round it – and all we can make out is that it's on this common, somewhere near here – and the secret way is behind the slab!'

'And all we have to do is to go and look behind dozens of heavy slabs!' said someone else. 'I'm fed up. We've lifted slabs in that wretched camp – we've lifted some here – and we still don't know if we're anywhere near the right one.'

'Shut up,' said the voice of the drawler but now the voice was sharp and angry. 'If we have to pull this cottage down, if we have to lift every slab there is, if we have to take over that camp, I'll do it! I tell you, this makes all the difference between wealth and poverty! Anyone who wants to back out can do so – but he'd better be careful!'

'Now, boss, now, boss, don't you fly off the handle!' said the woman. 'We're all in this! We'll do all you say. Look, let's start by lifting a few more slabs. There are not so very many that are the size that Paul figured on this plan.'

Then began a boring time for the two hidden boys, as slab after slab was lifted and put back. Nothing was found under any of them, apparently.

The men went to the outbuildings too, leaving the

woman in the cottage. The boys thought she had gone as well, and Julian moved a little, feeling rather cramped after being still for so long. The woman's ears must have been sharp for she called out at once.

'Who's there? Is it you, Tom?'

The boys stiffened and stood like statues. The woman said no more. It was not long before the men came back, talking among themselves. It sounded as if there were three of them.

'No go,' said the drawler. 'I think we'll have to search that camp really well again.'

'That's going to be difficult with someone already there,' said the woman.

'We'll deal with him,' said a voice, grimly. Julian frowned. Did that mean that Guy was in danger? He had better warn him!

'I'm fed up with this place,' said the woman. 'Let's go. I don't think the slab is anywhere here! We're wasting our time!'

To the boys' great relief, the four searchers left the cottage and went off together. Julian and Dick leant over the crumbling wall of the room they stood in, and watched the lights of the torches and lanterns getting dimmer and dimmer over the common. Good! Now they could go back to the girls!

'I'm stiff!' said Dick, stretching himself.

'Well, Ju – we know a lot more now, don't we? It's clear that someone called Paul had stolen some valuable blueprints of something – maybe a new plane, or battleship perhaps – and has hidden them in some secret place he knew of about here – and to get to it you have to lift a slab of stone of a certain size.'

'Yes. And we know the size because we've already seen the one they lifted in the old stables,' said Julian. 'I vote we go there and measure it – or measure the one by the sink. I should think that the right slab will be somewhere in the old camp. We'd better tell Guy and let him into the secret. He'll help us to search!'

'What a peculiar business this is to find ourselves mixed up in,' said Dick. 'All because George didn't like people

laughing at old Timmy with a cardboard collar round his neck! Timmy's the cause of this!'

The boys went down the stone stairs, and, of course, Dick quite forgot about the rambler, which caught him neatly round the ankle and almost tripped him headlong down the stairs!

'Blow!' he said, clutching Julian and nearly making him topple too. 'Sorry. It was that rambler again. It's ripped my ankle all round. Put on the torch for goodness' sake.'

They carefully measured the stone slab by the sink and then made their way out of the cottage and up towards the spring, hoping that they would find the great gorse bush in the dark. They tried to get under the wrong one at first, but at last found the right one. They heard a small welcome bark from Timmy.

'Oh! Julian! Dick! Is it you?' said Anne's voice, as the boys squeezed through into the hollow middle. 'Oh, what AGES you've been! We haven't slept a wink. Keep still, Timmy, do – this place is too small for you to rampage about in!'

The boys settled down and torches were put on. Julian related the curious happenings to the two interested girls. George was thrilled.

'Oh I *say*! Fancy all this springing up out of the blue so suddenly! What are you going to do?'

'Warn Guy first thing in the morning – and then get in touch with the police, I think,' said Julian. 'We ourselves can't stop the men searching the camp, and as soon as they *do* find the slab they're looking for, they can easily get what they want and go off with it!'

'Well, it's really thrilling,' said George. 'I wish I'd been with you. I'll never go to sleep tonight!'

But they did manage to drop off to sleep, for they were all very tired. After a few hours, just as dawn was breaking, Timmy lifted his head and growled. George awoke at once.

'What is it, Tim? I can't hear anything.'

But Timmy could, that was certain. George woke Julian, and made him listen to Timmy's continuous growling.

'What do you think he's growling at?' she asked. 'He keeps on and on. I can't hear a thing, can you?'

'No,' said Julian, listening. 'Well, it's no use my creeping out and going searching in the dark for whatever Timmy's growling at. It might be something silly like a weasel or a hedgehog or a stoat. Shut up, Tim. That's enough.'

Although it was as dark as night under the thick old gorse bush, outside it was just getting light. What *was* Timmy growling at? Were there people about again? Or was it just one of the hedgehogs he so heartily disliked?

He stopped growling at last and put his head down on his paws, closing his eyes. George patted him.

'Well, whatever it was, it's gone. Are you comfy, Julian? It's very cramped in here – and hot too, isn't it?'

'Yes. We'll get up fairly early and go to warn Guy –

then we'll have a swim,' said Julian, yawning. He switched off his torch and went to sleep again.

It was late when they awoke. Dick was the first, and he looked at his watch. He gave an exclamation.

'Gosh! It's half past eight! Hey, Ju – Anne – George wake up, it's almost afternoon!'

Everyone felt stiff and cramped, and they went off to have a swim and to warn Guy. As they came near the camp, they stopped in amazement.

Someone was howling down in the trench, howling so miserably and so broken-heartedly that the Five felt quite panic-stricken. Whatever in the world could have happened? They ran to the edge of the excavations and looked down into the trench.

The boy was there, lying on his face, sobbing. He kept lifting his head and howling, then putting it down again.

'Guy! GUY! Whatever's happened?' shouted Julian. He leapt down beside the boy. 'Are you hurt? Is Jet hurt? What's the matter?'

'It's Guy! He's gone! They've taken him,' howled the boy. 'And I was so awful to him. Now he's gone. He'll never come back, I know he won't!'

'Guy's gone? But – but *you're* Guy!' said Julian in astonishment. 'What do you mean?'

He felt sure that the boy really *was* mad now – quite mad – talking about himself like that. He patted him on the shoulder. 'Look, you're ill. You come along with us. You need a doctor.'

The boy sprang to his feet, his face swollen and stained. 'I'm not ill! I tell you Guy's gone. I'm *not* Guy. He's my twin. There are two of us.'

Everyone gasped. It took half a minute to think about this and get everything straight – and then, of course many things were clear! There was not one mad boy, there were two ordinary boys – but they were twins! There wasn't, as they had thought, just *one* boy who contradicted himself all the time, who seemed continually to appear suddenly and unexpectedly, and who was sometimes nice and sometimes not.

'Twins! Why on earth didn't we think of that before?' said Julian. 'We thought there was only one of you. You were never together.'

'No. We quarrelled – quarrelled bitterly,' said the boy, tears in his eyes again. 'And when twins quarrel, *really* quarrel, it's worse than any quarrel there is! We hated one another then – we really did! We wouldn't be with one another, we wouldn't eat together, or dig together, or sleep together. We've often quarrelled before, but not like this – not like this! I just pretended that he didn't exist – and he did the same with me!'

'What a to-do!' said Julian, astonished and worried. 'Well now, what's happened to make you so upset? Tell me!'

'Guy wanted to be friends with me again last night,' said the boy. 'And I wouldn't. I shoved him and walked away. Then this morning I was sorry and went to find him and be friends – and – and . . .'

He stopped and howled again. Everyone felt very sad and uncomfortable. 'Go on, tell us,' said Julian, gently.

'I was just in time to see him fighting two men, and screaming at them, and kicking – then they hustled him away somewhere!' said the boy. 'I fell down in the trench and hurt my leg – and by the time I dragged myself up, Guy had gone – and so had everyone else!'

He turned away and wept again. 'I'll never forgive myself, never! If I'd made friends last night I could have helped him – and I didn't!'

CHAPTER FIFTEEN

Well done, George!

IT WAS Anne who comforted the boy. She went to him and pulled him down on a stone beside her. 'Let me look at your leg,' she said. 'It's pretty bad, isn't it? Look, I'll bind it up for you. Don't be so upset – we'll help you. I think we know what's happened, don't we Julian?'

The boy looked at Anne gratefully, and sniffed hard. When she offered him her handkerchief, he took it and wiped his face. Dick gave Anne his big hanky to bind up the boy's cut and bruised leg. He must have fallen right into the trench in his fright at seeing his brother fighting and being taken away.

'How do *you* know what's happened?' he said to Julian. 'Can you get Guy back? Do say you can! I'll never forgive myself for this. My twin brother – and I wasn't there to fight by his side when he needed me!'

'Now don't soak my hanky all over again!' said Anne. He gave her a forlorn little smile and turned to Julian again.

'My name's Harry Lawdler, and Guy and I are mad on old camps and buildings and things. We spend almost all our holidays together, digging and finding all kinds of things, like these.' He nodded his head towards the little shelf of relics that the four had seen before.

'Yes, Guy told us,' said Dick. 'But he never said a word about you. We were often very puzzled – we thought you and he were one boy – not two, you see – and we couldn't understand a lot of things you both said. You're so very, very alike.'

'Well, I tell you, we each pretended that the other didn't even exist,' said Harry. 'We're like that. We love each other best in the world, and we hate each other worst – when we quarrel. We're simply *horrible* then!'

'Can you tell us a bit about the people that Guy was fighting?' asked Dick.

'Yes. They were some that came before, wanting Guy to clear out while they had a look round,' said Harry, wiping his face again. 'Guy was pretty rude to them. In fact I heard him say that if they messed about his camp he would throw stones at them – he's like that, you know, very fierce, when he's roused.'

'And you think these were the same people?' said Dick. 'Which way did they go with Guy?'

'That way,' said Harry, pointing. 'I've hunted the whole camp round, but they're gone – disappeared into thin air! It's extraordinary!'

'Let's have a hunt round,' said Julian. 'We might find something. But I imagine that the searchers have taken Guy off with them because he knew too much – perhaps they found here what they were looking for, and saw Guy watching.'

'Oh! Then we're too late!' said George, in deep disappointment. 'They've got what they want – and they'll disappear now and never be caught. I expect by now they are speeding away in a fast car – and have taken Guy with them to make sure he doesn't talk before they're safely in another country!'

'Oh no!' cried Harry. 'He's not kidnapped, is he? Don't say that!'

'Come on – let's have a hunt,' said Julian, and they all made their way among the various trenches and pits, looking for they hardly knew what.

They gave it up after a while. There were too many slabs and stones of all sizes! Besides, what good would it be even if they found the right one? The birds had flown – presumably with what they had come for! In fact, if Guy hadn't come along and seen the searchers, nobody would even have known that they had been in the camp and made a successful search!

'It's no good,' said Julian, at last. 'This is too big a place to know where to look for anything that might help us. Let's go back to the gorse bush and collect our things, return to Kirrin and go to the police. It's the only sensible thing left to do!'

'Come along, Harry,' said Anne, to the miserable twin. He was so full of remorse that her handkerchief was now soaked for the third time! 'You'd better come with us and tell all you know.'

'I'll come,' said Harry. 'I'll do anything to get Guy

back. I'll never quarrel with him again. Never. To think that . . .'

'Now don't go all through that again,' said Anne. 'Look, you're upsetting Timmy so much that his tail is down all the time!'

Harry gave another forlorn little smile. They all left the camp and made their way back to the gorse bush. It was only when they got there, and began pulling out the tins of food, as well as the rug and other things, that they realised how extremely hungry they were!

'We've had no breakfast. We've been up for ages, and it's very late. I'm simply starving!' said George.

'Well, if we finish up all the food, we shan't have to carry the tins!' said Dick. 'Let's have a meal. Ten minutes more here can't make much difference.'

They were thankful not to have to sit under the gorse bush again. They sat outside in the sun, and discussed everything.

'I believe when Timmy began to growl and growl about six o'clock this morning, it was because he could hear those people coming quietly by to go to search the camp,' said George.

'I think you're right,' said Julian. 'I bet they searched the camp well – till Guy woke and came on the scene and fought like fury. It's a pity I didn't squeeze out from under the bush and follow them, when Timmy growled.'

'Anyone want a drink?' said George. 'I'll go and fetch some water from the spring. Where's the pineapple tin?'

Anne passed it to her. George got up and took the little rabbit path that led to the spring. She could hear it gurgling and bubbling as she came near – a very pleasant noise.

'Water always sounds nice,' said George to herself. 'I love the sound of water.'

Water! Now why did that ring a bell in her mind just then? Who had been talking about water? Oh – Dick and Julian, of course, when they had come back from the old cottage last night. They had told Anne and herself about the word on the plan – the word that might have been *water*, not *wader*.

'I wonder which it was,' said George to herself as she idly held the pineapple tin to the gurling water. She gazed at the beautiful little spring, jutting up from the stony slabs – and then another bell rang loudly in the mind.

'Stone slabs! Water! Why – I wonder – I just wonder – if one of *these* slabs is the one! This one just here is about the right size!'

She stared at it. It was set firmly in a high little bank at the back of the place where the spring gurgled up and then ran into the clean stony channel. *Did* it hide anything behind it?

George suddenly dropped the tin and ran back to the others at full speed. 'Julian! Julian! I believe I've found the slab! It's been staring us in the face the whole time!'

Julian was very startled. So were the others. They stared up at George in astonishment.

'What do you mean, George?' said Julian, jumping to his feet. 'Show me!'

Followed by everyone, George ran back to the spring. She pointed to the white slab behind the water. 'There!' she said. 'That's the right size, isn't it? And it's beside *water* – just as it said in the plan you told us about – only the people thought it was *wader*.'

'Gosh, I wonder if you're right, George,' said Julian, excited. 'You might be – you never know. Sometimes springs come from underground passages – secret hidden ways into the earth.'

'Let's try and move it,' said Dick, his face red with sudden excitement. 'It looks pretty hefty to me.'

They began to struggle with the stone, getting extremely wet as they splashed about in the spring. But nobody minded that. This was too exciting for words. Harry helped too, heaving and tugging. He was very strong indeed.

The stone slab moved a little. It slid to one side and stuck. More tugging. More pulling. More panting and puffing!

'I believe we'll have to get help,' said Julian at last. 'It really is too heavy and well-embedded.'

'I'll go and get some of my tools,' said Harry. 'I'm used to heaving stones about with them. We can easily move it if we have the right tools.'

He flew off at top speed. The others sat down and mopped their streaming foreheads.

'Phew!' said Julian. 'What a job this is for a hot day! I'm

glad Harry remembered his tools. Just what we want!'

'How funny that he and Guy are twins!' said George. 'I never even thought of such a thing!'

'Well, they behaved so idiotically,' said Julian. 'Always pretending there was just one of them, and neither of them even mentioning the other. I wonder where Guy has been taken to. I don't think he'll come to much harm – but it will be worrying for his family.'

'Here comes Harry,' said Anne, after a pause. 'One of us ought to have gone with him to help him. He's brought dozens of tools!'

The things he had fetched proved very useful indeed, especially a big jemmy-like tool. The stone soon began to move when this was applied by Julian and Harry!

'It's slipping – it's coming away – look out, it will fall right down into the spring!' cried Dick. 'Look out, you girls!'

The stone was prised right out, and fell into the stony channel where the water ran. The five children stared at the opening it left.

Julian leant forward and looked into it. 'Yes – there's a big hole behind,' he said. 'Let me shine my torch in.'

In great excitement he flashed his torch into the opening. He turned round, his face glowing.

'Yes! I think we've got it! There's a tunnel behind, going down and down. It widens out behind this hole!'

Everyone was too thrilled for words. George gave Dick a clap on the back, and Anne patted Timmy so hard that he whined. Harry beamed round, all his woes forgotten.

'Do we go down now?' asked Dick. 'We'll have to make the opening a bit wider. Earth and roots have narrowed it very much. Let's make it bigger.'

'Then we'll explore it!' said George, her eyes shining. 'A secret tunnel only known to us! Quick – let's explore it!'

CHAPTER SIXTEEN

The secret way

ALL THE children were so excited that they got into each other's way. Julian pushed them back.

'Let's be sensible! We can't *all* make the opening wider – let Harry and me get at it with the tools – and we'll soon make it bigger!'

It took only a minute to hack away at the sides of the hole to make it big enough for even Julian to climb through. He stood there panting, smiling broadly.

'There – it's done! I'll get in first. Everyone got torches? We shall need them! It's going to be dark in there!'

He clambered up and into the hole. He had to crawl on hands and knees for a little way, and then the hole suddenly went downwards and became considerably bigger. Julian could walk in it, if he bent down, for at that point the tunnel was about three feet high.

He called back to the others. 'Follow me! Take hold of each other's shirts or jerseys and hang on. It's pitch black in here!'

George followed after Julian, then Anne, then Dick, then Harry. Timmy went with George, of course, pushing and shoving like all the rest. Everyone was excited, and nobody could talk in a normal voice. They all shouted!

'I'll give you a hand! One good shove and you're in!'

'I say – isn't it dark!'

'What a crawl! I feel like a fox going into its den!'

'Timmy, don't butt me from behind like that! I can't crawl any faster!'

'Ah – thank goodness I can stand up now! What size of rabbit do you think made *this* burrow!'

'It was made by water at some time perhaps. Don't *shove*, Timmy!'

'Water doesn't run uphill, ass! Hang on to my jersey, Harry. Don't get left behind.'

Julian, bent almost double at times, walked carefully along the narrow tunnel, which went steadily downwards. Soon it widened and became higher, and then it was easier to walk in comfort.

'Do you suppose this is the right secret way?' called George, after a time. 'We don't seem to be getting anywhere.'

'I can't tell. In fact we shan't know till we find something hidden somewhere – if we ever do!'

A sudden scuttering noise in front of him made Julian stop suddenly. Immediately everyone bumped into the one in front, and there were shouts at once.

'What's up, Ju?'

Julian's torch shone on to two pairs of bright, frightened eyes. He gave a laugh.

'It's all right – just a couple of rabbits using our burrow! There are small holes running out of the tunnel which, I imagine, are rabbit burrows. I bet we're giving the bunnies a shock!'

The tunnel wound about a good deal, and then suddenly the rather soft ground they were treading on turned to rock. The passage was now not so high, and the children had to bend down again. It was most uncomfortable.

Julian stopped once more. He had heard another sound. What was it?

'Water!' he said. 'There must be an underground stream here! How thrilling! Everyone all right?'

'Yes!' shouted those behind him. 'Get on, Julian – let's see the water!'

The tunnel suddenly ended, and Julian found himself in a big cave with a fairly high roof. Almost in the middle of it ran a stream – not a very big one, and not a very fast one. It gurgled along in a small channel of rock, which it had carved out for itself through hundreds of years.

Julian shone his torch on it. The water looked very black and glittered in the light of the torch. The others came one by one out of the tunnel and stared at the underground stream. It looked rather mysterious, slipping through the cave, gurgling quietly as it disappeared through a hole at one end.

'Strange,' said Dick.

'It's not unusual, this,' began Harry. 'In some parts of the country round about here, the ground below our feet is honeycombed with many little streams. Some come up as springs, of course, some join other streams when they come out into the open, others just run away goodness knows where!'

Julian was looking up round the cave. 'Does our tunnel end here?' he wondered. 'Is this where we have to look for whatever is hidden?'

'We'll have a look round the cave and see if there are any exits,' said Dick. Using their torches the five separated, Timmy keeping close to George, not seeming in the least surprised at this underground adventure.

'I've found another tunnel over here, leading out of the cave!' called Dick. No sooner had he said that than Anne called out too.

'There's one here as well!'

'Now – which do we take?' said Julian. 'How annoying that there should be two!'

'Would the fellow – what's his name – Paul – have marked the correct underground way on his plan?' said George. 'I mean – I don't see how he could possibly expect either himself or anyone else to find what he had hidden, if there are numbers of passages to choose from down here!'

'You're right!' said Julian. 'Let's look about and see if we can find anything to help us.'

It wasn't long before Dick gave another shout. 'It's all right! This is the passage to take, over here – the one I found just now. There's an arrow drawn in white chalk on the wall.'

Everyone crowded over to Dick, stepping across the little stream as they did so. Dick held his torch up and they all saw the white arrow, drawn roughly on the wall.

Julian was pleased. 'Good. That helps a lot! It shows we're going the right way – and that this *is* the secret way that Paul chose. Come on!'

They entered the tunnel, left the little stream behind, and went on again. 'Anyone got any idea in which direction we're going?' called Dick. 'East, west, north, south?'

Harry had a compass. He looked at it. 'I think we're going rather in the direction of the old Roman camp,' he said.

'Ah – that's interesting,' said Julian. 'This tunnel was probably used in olden times.'

'Guy and I have seen the plan of the camp as it probably used to be,' said Harry. 'And there are plenty of tunnels and caves and holes shown on it – just roughed in, not a proper plan of them. Gosh, I never thought I'd be exploring one! My father warned me not to, in case of roof-falls and things like that.'

The tunnel suddenly forked into two. One passage was nice and wide, the other narrow. Julian took the wide one, thinking that the other was really too narrow to get through. But after a minute or two, he stopped, puzzled.

'There's a blank wall of rock here – the tunnel's ended! We'll have to turn back! I suppose we should have taken that very narrow opening.'

They went back, Harry leading the way now. Timmy suddenly took it into his head that *he* would like to lead,

too, and made himself a real nuisance, pushing his way between everyone's legs!

They came back to the fork. Harry shone his torch in at the second opening, the very narrow one. There, clearly marked on the right hand wall, was a white arrow in chalk!

'We're idiots,' said Dick. 'We don't even look for the signposts! Lead the way, Julian!'

This tunnel was very narrow indeed, and had rough, jutting rocky sides. There were loud 'aahs!' and 'oohs!' as elbows and ankles were knocked against hard rock.

And then again there came a blank wall of rock in front of Julian, and again he had to stop!

'Can't go this way either!' he said. 'There's a blank wall again – this is a blind alley too!'

There were cries of dismay at once.

'Blow! It can't be!'

'What's gone wrong? Look all round, Ju – flash your torch down at your feet and above your head!'

Julian shone his torch over his head, and gave an exclamation.

'There's a hole above my head!'

'Is there a white arrow anywhere?' called Harry.

'Yes! And it's pointing up, instead of forwards!' called back Julian. 'We're still all right – we've got to go upwards now – but how?'

George, who was just behind him, shone her torch on the side walls. 'Look!' she said. 'We can easily get up to the hole. There are rough, natural steps up – made by ledges of rock. Look, Julian!'

'Yes,' said Julian. 'We can manage to get up quite easily, I think. George, you go first – I'll give you a boost up.'

George was delighted to go first. She put her torch between her teeth, and began to climb up the ledges, Julian pushing her as best he could. She came to the hole and immediately saw that it would be quite easy to hoist herself through.

'One more boost and I'll be through!' she called to Julian. And with one last heave George was up, rolling on the floor of a small cave above! She called down in excitement to the others.

'I believe this is the place where those things are hidden! I can see something on a ledge. Oh, do buck up!'

The others followed eagerly. Dick slipped off the rocky ledges in his excitement and almost squashed poor Harry as he fell on him. However, everyone was up at last, even Timmy, who was the most difficult of all to heave through! He seemed to have far too many vigorous legs!

Harry found no difficulty at all. 'I'm used to this kind of thing,' he said. 'Guy and I have explored a whole lot of tunnels and caves in hills and other places.'

George was pointing her torch at a broad ledge of rock. On it was a brown leather bag, and beside it, marked on the rock, was a very large arrow indeed.

Julian was overjoyed. He picked up the bag at once. 'My word – I hope there's something in it!' he said. 'It feels jolly light – as if it's empty!'

'Open it!' cried everyone – but Julian couldn't. It was locked – and alas, there wasn't a key!

CHAPTER SEVENTEEN

Full of surprises

'IT'S LOCKED – we can't open the bag,' said Julian, and shook it vigorously as if that might make it fly open and spill whatever contents it had!

'We don't know if it's got anything of value in it or not,' said Dick, in deep disappointment. 'I mean – it might be some trick on that fellow Paul's part – he might have taken the blueprints, or whatever they were he hid, for himself, and left the bag just to trick the others.'

'Can we cut it open?' asked George.

'No. I don't think so. It's made of really strong leather. We would need a special knife to cut through it – an ordinary pen-knife wouldn't be any use,' said Julian. 'I think we'll just have to assume that we've got the goods, and hope for the best. If they're not in here, it's just bad luck. Someone else has got them, if so.'

They all looked at the tantalising bag.

Now they would have to wait for ages before they found out whether their efforts had been successful or not!

'Well – what do we do now?' said George, feeling suddenly flat. 'Go back all through that long tunnel once more? I'll be glad to be in the open air again, won't you?'

'You bet!' said Julian. 'Well – I suppose we'd better get down through that hole again.'

'Wait!' said Anne, her sharp eyes catching sight of something. 'Look – what does all this mean?'

She shone her torch on to various signs on the wall. Again there were arrows drawn in white chalk – but very oddly, a line of them ran downwards across the wall of the little rocky room, right to the edge of the hole – and another line of arrows pointing the *other* way, ran horizontally across the wall!

'Well, do you suppose that's just meant to muddle people?' said Dick, puzzled. 'We know jolly well that the way out of this room is down that hole, because that's the way we came into it.'

'Perhaps the other line of arrows means that there's a second way out,' suggested George. They all looked round the little rocky room. There didn't seem any way out at all.

'Where's Timmy?' said Anne, suddenly, flashing her torch round. 'He's not here! Has he fallen down the hole? I never heard him yelp!'

At once there was a great to-do. 'Timmy, Timmy, Timmy! TIMMY! Where are you?'

George whistled shrilly, and the noise echoed round and round the little room. Then, from somewhere, there was a bark. How relieved everyone was.

'Where is he? Where did that bark come from?' said Dick. 'It didn't sound as if it came from below, down that hole!'

There came another welcome bark, and the sound of Timmy's feet. Then to everyone's amazement, he appeared in the little rocky room as if by magic – appearing straight out of the wall, it seemed!

'Timmy! Where were you? Where have you come from?' cried George, and ran to see. She came to a standstill and exclaimed loudly.

'Oh! What idiots we are! Why, just behind this big jutting-out piece of rock, there's another passage!'

So there was! A very, very narrow one, it is true – and completely hidden from the children because of the enormous slab of rock that jutted out from the wall that hid it! They stood and stared at it, shining their torches on the narrow way. The arrows ran round the wall to it.

'We never even looked properly!' said Dick. 'Still – it's a passage that would be extremely difficult to spot – hidden round the corner of that rock – and very narrow at that. Well, I do know one thing for certain about that man called Paul!'

'What?' asked Anne.

'He's thin – thin as a rake!' said Dick. 'No one but a skinny fellow could squeeze through *this* opening! I doubt if *you* can, Julian – you're the biggest of us.'

'Well, what about trying?' said George. 'What does everyone say? This might be an easier, shorter way out – or it might be a harder, longer one.'

'It won't be longer,' said Harry. 'By my reckoning we must be pretty well near the camp now. It's likely that the way leads straight there – though where it comes out I can't imagine. Guy and I have explored the camp pretty thoroughly.'

Dick suddenly thought of something he had noticed at the camp – the big hole behind the slab of stone, where he had seen the baby rabbit a day or two before! What had Guy said about that? He had said there was a great hole underground, which had been explored – but that it was probably just an ancient storage place for food or for loot! He turned eagerly to Harry.

'Harry, would this lead to that enormous hole underground – the one that Guy once told me had been explored, but was of no interest – probably just an old store place?'

'Let me see,' said Harry. 'Yes – yes, it *might* lead to that. Most of these underground ways are throughways – ways that led from one place to another. They don't as a rule stop suddenly, but have usually been of use as secret escape routes or something of that kind. I think you may be right, Dick – we're fairly near the camp, I'm sure, and we may quite well find that if we go on, instead of going back, we shall come into the camp itself – probably through that great hole!'

'Then come on,' said Julian. 'It will certainly be a shorter way!'

They tried to squeeze through the narrow opening that led out of the little rocky room. Dick got through all right, and so did the others – but poor Julian found it very very difficult and almost gave up.

'You shouldn't eat so much,' said Dick, unkindly. 'Go on – one more try, Ju – I'll haul on your arm at the same time!'

Julian got through, groaning. 'I'm squashed flat!' he said. 'Now, if anyone makes any more jokes about too much breakfast, I'll pull his nose!'

The passage grew wider immediately, and everyone was thankful. It ran fairly straight, and then went steeply downwards, so that the five slithered about, and Timmy found himself suddenly running. Then it came to a stop – a complete stop! This time it was not a blank wall of rock that faced them – it was something else.

'A roof-fall!' groaned Dick. 'Look at that! Now we're done!'

It certainly looked most formidable. Earth, rocks and stones had fallen from the roof and blocked up the whole passageway. There was no use in going on – they would just have to turn and go back!

'Blow it!' said Dick, and kicked at the mass of earth. 'Well, there's no use staying here – we'd better turn back. My torch isn't too good now, and neither is yours, George. We don't want to lose any time – if our torches give out, we shall find things very difficult.'

They turned to go back, feeling very despondent. 'Come on, Timmy!' said George. But Timmy didn't come. He stood beside the roof-fall, looking very puzzled, his ears cocked and his head on one side. Then he suddenly gave a sharp bark.

It made everyone jump almost out of their skins, for the sound echoed round and about in a very strange way.

'Don't, Timmy!' said George, almost angrily. 'Whatever's the matter? Come along!'

But Timmy didn't come. He began to paw at the pile of earth and rocks in front of him, and barked without stopping. Wuff-wuff-wuff-wuff-wuff-WUFF!

'What's up?' said Julian, startled. 'Timmy, what on *earth's* the matter?'

Timmy took absolutely no notice, but went on feverishly scraping at the roof-fall, sending earth and stones flying all over the others.

'There's something he wants to get at – something behind this roof-fall,' said Dick. 'Or perhaps *somebody* – make him stop barking, George, and we'll listen ourselves and see if we can hear anything.'

George silenced Timmy with difficulty, and made him stand quiet and still. Then they all listened intently – and a sound came at once to their ears.

'Yap-yap-wuff-wuff-wuff!'

'It's Jet!' yelled Harry, making everyone jump violently again. 'Jet! Then Guy must be with him. He never leaves Guy! What's Guy doing here? He may be hurt. GUY! GUY! JET!'

Timmy began to bark wildly again and to scrape more furiously than ever. Julian shouted to the others above the barking.

'If we can hear Jet barking, this roof-fall can't be very

big. We'd better try and get through it. Two of us can work in turn with Timmy. We can't all work at once, the passage is too narrow.'

Then began some very hard work – but it didn't last as long as Julian feared, because, quite suddenly, the mass of rubble and rock shifted as they worked, and a gap appeared at the top of the heap, between it and the roof.

Dick began to scramble up, but Julian called to him at once. 'Be careful, ass! The roof can't be too good here – it may come down again, and you'll be buried. Go carefully!'

But before Dick could go any further, a little figure appeared on the top of the rubble over their heads, and slid down to them yapping loudly, and waving a long wiry tail!

'Jet! Oh, Jet! Where's Guy?' cried Harry, as the little dog leapt into his arms and licked his face lavishly, barking joyfully in between the licks.

'GUY!' yelled Julian. 'Are you there?'

A weak voice came back. 'Yes! Who's that?' An absolute volley of voices answered him.

'It's us! And Harry! We're coming to you, we shan't be long!'

And it wasn't long, either, before the roof-fall was slowly and carefully climbed by each one – though Timmy, of course, scrambled up, over and down at top speed!

On the other side of the roof-fall was a passage, of

course, the continuation of the one the children had come along. Guy was there, sitting down, looking very pale. Jet flung himself on him and licked him as if he hadn't seen him for a month, instead of just a minute or two before!

'Hallo!' said Guy, in a small voice. 'I'm all right. It's just my ankle, that's all. I'm jolly glad to . . .'

But before he could say a word more, Harry was beside him, his arms round him, his voice choking.

'Guy! Oh, Guy! I've been a beast. I wouldn't be friends! What happened to you? Are you really all right? Oh, Guy, we *are* friends again, aren't we?'

'Look out, Harry old son,' said Julian gently. 'He's fainted. Now just let's be sensible and everything will come all right. Flap your hanky at him, Dick, and give him a little air. It's only the excitement!'

In half a minute Guy opened his eyes and smiled weakly. 'Sorry!' he said. 'I'm all right now. I only hope this isn't a dream, and that you really *are* here!'

'You bet we are!' said Dick. 'Have a bit of chocolate, then you'll know we're real!'

'Good idea!' said Julian. 'We'll all have some – and I've some biscuits in my pocket too. We'll eat and talk – and we'll make plans at the same time. Catch, Guy – here's a biscuit!'

CHAPTER EIGHTEEN

The way out

GUY SOON told his story. It was much as the others had imagined.

'I was fast asleep this morning, with Jet curled up to me,' he said. 'He began to bark and I wondered why, so I got up to see – and I saw four people in the camp.'

'The four we know!' said Dick, and Julian nodded. 'Go on, Guy.'

'They were looking all over the place,' said Guy, 'prising up rocks, messing about – so I yelled at them. But they only laughed. Then one of the men, who was trying to prise up a slab – the slab that covers that great hole underground, Harry – you remember it? – well, this man gave a yell and said "I've got it! This is the way in – down here, behind this slab!" '

Guy stopped, looking very angry. Jet licked him comfortingly. 'Well,' he went on. 'I set Jet on them, and they kicked him – so I went for them.'

'You're a plucky one, aren't you!' said Dick, admiringly. 'Did you knock them all out, by any chance?'

'No. Of course not,' said Guy. 'One of the men pretty well knocked *me* out though. He hit me on the head and I went down, dazed. I heard him say "drat this kid – he'll be fetching help, and we shan't be able to get down and hunt for the goods." And then another man said "We'll take him with us then", and they got hold of me and dragged me through the opening.'

'But how did they get down into that great hole?' said Harry in wonder. 'There is such a steep drop into it. You need a rope.'

'Oh, they had a rope all right,' said Guy, munching his biscuit and chocolate and looking decidedly better. 'One of the men had one tied round and round his waist. They knotted it fast round a rock – that big one we can't move, Harry – and then they swung down on it. All except the woman. She said she'd stay at the top and keep watch. She hid behind a bush some way off.'

'I never saw her when I came along!' said Harry. 'I never thought of looking there! What about you? Did you get down too?'

'Yes. I screamed and shouted and kicked and howled, but it wasn't a bit of good. They made me swing down the rope – and I fell off halfway down and hurt my ankle. I howled at the top of my voice for help, and they hurried me along with them, shaking me like a rat.'

'The beasts!' said Harry, fervently. 'Oh, the beasts!'

'I heard one of them say that there should be a tunnel out of the hole somewhere, it was marked on Paul's plan – whatever that may be – and then I think I must have fainted – the pain of my ankle, you know. And when I came to myself again, we were all here, the three men and

I – beside this roof-fall – though I really don't know how we got here. They must have dragged me along with them!'

'And that's all, is it?' asked Julian.

'Not quite. They were furious when they saw the roof-fall, but as soon as they began to scrabble in it a rock rolled down and hit one of the men quite a crack – and after that they were afraid to do anything. They stood and talked for a bit – and then they decided to go and get some tools, and come down again to see if they could remove all this stuff and get through it.'

'Good gracious!' said Julian, startled. 'Then they may be back at any moment!'

'I suppose so. They left me here because they couldn't think of anything else to do with me! They knew I couldn't walk, because of my ankle. I think it's broken. So of course I couldn't possibly find my way out myself! And here I've been waiting for those brutes to come back, and to hack through the rubble to go after whatever it is they want!'

Everyone began to feel rather uncomfortable at the thought that three violent men might be appearing at any moment. 'Is it very far to the opening you came down?' asked Julian. But Guy didn't know. He had fainted, as he had said, and he didn't even know what way they had come.

'It can't be far,' said Harry. 'I think it would be worth while trying to find the opening, see if the men have left the rope there, and get out that way. If Guy's ankle really is broken, he couldn't possibly manage to go back the long way we've come.'

'No. That's true,' said Julian, thoughtfully. 'Well, that's what we'll do then. But we'll go jolly cautiously, without a sound, because it might be just our luck to meet those fellows on their way back here!'

'Shall we start?' said George. 'What about Guy?'

Julian knelt down beside the boy, and gently examined his ankle. 'I've done my first aid training, like everybody else!' he said. 'And I *ought* to know if his ankle is broken or just sprained.'

He examined the swollen ankle carefully. 'It's not

broken. I believe I could bandage it tightly with a couple of large hankies. Give me yours, Dick.'

The others watched admiringly as Julian deftly and confidently bandaged Guy's swollen ankle. 'There!' he said. 'You can perhaps hobble on it now, Guy. It may hurt, but I don't think it will damage it. Try. You'll have to go barefoot because your ankle is too swollen for your shoe to go on.'

Very gingerly Guy stood up, helped by Harry. He tried his hurt foot, and it certainly seemed all right to hobble on, though it was very painful. He grinned round at the others' anxious faces.

'It's fine!' he said. 'Come on, let's go! We don't want to bump into those fellows if we can help it. Thank goodness we've got Jet and Timmy.'

They set off down the passage, flashing their torches in front as usual, to show them the way. The tunnel was quite wide and high here, and in a very short time came out into an enormous pit underground.

'Ah – this is the hole I saw down behind the slab where the rabbit went,' said Dick. 'We weren't very far from the camp, as we thought. I'm surprised that when this pit was explored, the underground passages were not discovered, Guy.'

'I expect the men exploring it came to the roof-fall and thought there was nothing beyond,' said Guy. 'Or maybe they were afraid of going further in case of further falls. They can be very dangerous, you know. Many a man has been buried under one and never heard of again.'

They looked round the enormous hole – it was really a huge round pit. Daylight showed in the roof at one place.

'That's the opening into it,' said Guy, eagerly. 'The one I came through, on the rope.'

He limped a few steps forward to look for the rope. Harry held him by the arm, thankful that the ankle was holding up so well. Guy pointed upwards.

'Yes. I can see the rope. The men have left it there, thank goodness. They must have been certain that I couldn't get to it!'

The rope hung down from the little opening high above their heads. Julian looked round at Anne.

'Can you manage to climb up the rope, Anne?' he said, doubtfully.

'Of course!' said Anne, scornfully. 'We do rope-climbing in the gym at school often enough. Don't we, George?'

'Yes, but our gym rope is a bit thicker!' said George.

'I'll go up first,' said Harry. 'We've got a much thicker rope, Guy and I, that we use when we want to haul on very heavy stones. I'll find it, and let it down.'

'Well, we can't afford to waste any time, in case those fellows come back,' said Julian. 'I daresay the girls can manage all right. George, you go up first.'

George went up like a monkey, hand over hand, her legs

twisted round the rope. She grinned down when she got to the top.

'Easy!' she said. 'Come on up next, Anne, and show the boys how to do it!'

Before the boys could leap to the rope, Anne was on it, pulling herself up lithely. Julian laughed. He called up to George.

'George! You might have a squint round and see if there's any sign of people about. If they were going to borrow *Guy's* tools, they would have been back long ago, so I think probably they've had to go to Kirrin or some farmhouse to borrow them.'

'They wouldn't get my tools,' said Guy, 'or Harry's. We had them stolen once, and now we always hide them where no one can possibly find them.'

'That settles it then,' said Julian. 'They've had to go a good way, I expect, to get satisfactory tools to tackle that roof-fall. They probably imagine that it's a pretty *big* fall! All the same, keep a watch out, George, till we're all up.'

It was difficult to get Guy up, for he was feeling weak, but they managed it at last. The two dogs had to have the boys' shirts tied round them so that the rope would not cut them when they were hauled up. They didn't seem to mind at all. Timmy was very heavy to pull up because he appeared to think that he had to try and make his legs do a running action all the time – just to help! All that happened was that he began to spin round and round, as he went up!

Everyone was up in the open air at long last, hot and perspiring. Julian had the precious bag safely under his arm. Timmy sat down panting. Then he suddenly stopped panting, and pricked up his ears.

'Woof,' he said warningly, and stood up.

'Quiet, Tim, quiet, Jet,' said Julian, at once aware that somebody must be about. 'Hide, everyone – quickly. It may be those fellows coming back!'

'Wuff,' began Jet, but Guy stopped him immediately. The six children separated and went into hiding at once, each choosing the best place he or she could see. There were plenty of hiding-places in the old camp!

They heard voices coming near. Nobody dared to peep out and see who was coming – but Julian and Dick recognised the drawling voice of one of the men!

'What a time we've been!' said the man. 'Just chuck the spades and things down the hole – then we'll all climb down again. Buck up! We've wasted too much time already. Anyone might come on the scene at any moment!'

The spades and jemmies went hurtling down the hole. Then one by one the men went down the rope. The children could not hear the woman's voice. They thought she must have been left behind.

Julian gave a low whistle and all the others popped up their heads. 'We'll spring for it!' said Julian. 'Buck up!'

They all shot out of their hiding-places at once and made off – except Julian. He stayed behind for a minute or two. What *could* he be doing?

Julian was doing something very simple indeed! He was hauling up the rope that dangled underground! He slipped it off the rock that held it and tied it round his waist, looking suddenly very bulky.

He grinned a very wide grin and went after the others. How very, very angry those men were going to be!

CHAPTER NINETEEN

Back to Kirrin Cottage

JULIAN RAN AFTER the others. 'What were you doing?' said George. 'Calling rude names down to the men?'

'No. I hope they'll go and dig for hours if they want to!' said Julian. 'They'll soon find that when they've got through it, that roof-fall is nothing much, and they'll go on till they come to the little room – and what they'll say when they find that the bag is gone, I really don't know!'

'I wish I could be there!' said Dick.

'What are we going to do about Guy?' asked Harry. 'He really can't walk *very* far on that bad foot.'

'If he can walk as far as the gorse bush where we've left our things, I've got a bike there,' said George. 'He could pedal with one foot, I should think.'

'Oh yes, I could easily do that,' said Guy, pleased. He had dreaded the thought of having to walk all the way to Kirrin – but neither did he want to be left behind!

He limped along, helped by Harry, who couldn't do enough for him. Jet ran along beside them, excited and happy at being with so many people. Timmy sometimes wuffed a little bark to him, which made Jet as proud as Punch. He thought the big Timmy was wonderful!

They came to the gorse bush, and found their things all

safe. The bicycle was there, with its packages strapped to it. George unstrapped them, meaning to carry them herself, so that Guy would not have too heavy a weight to pedal with his one foot. They all started off together, Guy riding ahead on the bicycle.

'We will go to Kirrin, dump our things at the cottage, and get Aunt Fanny to ring the police and ask them if they'll come along and collect this bag from us,' said Julian. 'I don't want to leave it at the police station – I want to see it opened in front of us!'

'I do hope it won't be empty,' said Anne. 'It does feel terribly light!'

'Yes. It does,' said Julian, swinging it to and fro. 'I can't help fearing that Paul, who drew the plan that the men found so difficult to understand, may have double-crossed his friends – drawn a deliberately difficult plan – and then left the bag quite empty in the place he marked on the plan! It would be the kind of hoax that a trickster loves to play – and would give him time to get away in safety.'

'But they said he was ill,' said Dick. 'Still – perhaps he might have been pretending that too! It's a mystery!'

'How are you getting on, Guy?' called George, as they overtook the boy. He kept riding on by himself for a little way, and then resting, waiting for them to catch up with him before he pedalled on again with his one good foot.

'Very well indeed, thank you,' said Guy. 'This bike was a very good idea of yours. What a blessing you had it with you!'

'Your foot doesn't seem any more swollen,' said Anne. 'I expect you'll be able to walk on it properly in a day or two. Oh, dear – it does make me laugh when I think how puzzled we all were when we thought there was just one of you, not twins!'

'We met first one of you, then the other, and thought you were the same boy,' said George, with a chuckle. 'We were absolutely wild with you sometimes, you seemed so mad and contradictory!'

'Don't remind us of it,' said Harry. 'I can't bear thinking that if I'd only been with Guy, all this trouble of his would never have happened.'

'Oh well – it's an ill wind that blows nobody any good! said George. 'The bad and the good have fitted together very well this time, and made a most exciting adventure!'

'Here's Carters Lane at last,' said Anne. 'What a long walk it seemed over the common. It will be much easier for you to ride that bike when you're on a proper road, Guy. It won't go bumping over heather clumps now.'

They went down the long lane and came into Kirrin at last, realising that they were all very hungry indeed. 'It must be well past lunch-time,' said George, looking at her watch. 'Good gracious – it's a quarter to two! Would you believe it! I hope there's some lunch left over for us – Mother doesn't know we're coming.'

'We'll raid Joanna's larder!' said Dick. 'She never minds so long as she's there to grumble at us while we do it!'

They went in at the gate of Kirrin Cottage and up to the front door, which was open. George shouted.

'Mother! Where are you? We've come back!'

Nobody answered. George yelled again. 'Mother! We've come home!'

The door of the study opened and her father looked out, red in the face and frowning.

'George! How many times am I to tell you not to shout when I'm working? Oh, my goodness me, who are all these?'

'Hallo, Father!' said George, mildly. 'Surely you know

Anne and Julian and Dick! *Don't* say you've forgotten them already!'

'Of course not! But who are these?' and George's father pointed to the startled twins. 'They're as like as peas. Where did *they* come from? I haven't seen them before, have I?'

'No, Father. They're just friends of ours,' said George. 'Where's Mother? We've just had an adventure and we want to tell her. Oh, and we want to ring the police – and I think we ought to get a doctor to see to Guy's foot – and, Father, look, Timmy's ear is healed!'

'Bless us all! There's never any peace when you are about, George,' said her father, groaning. 'Your mother's at the bottom of the garden, picking raspberries – or it might have been strawberries.'

'Oh no, Father – it's August, not June!' said George. 'You always . . .'

Julian thought he had better get his uncle safely back in his study before a row blew up between him and George. Uncle Quentin did *not* like being disturbed in his complicated work!

'Let's go and find Aunt Fanny,' he said, 'we can tell her everything out in the garden. Come on!'

'Wuff-wuff!' said Jet.

'Good gracious – that's not *another* dog, is it?' said George's father, scowling. 'How many times have I said that . . .'

'We won't disturb you any more, Uncle,' said Julian,

hurriedly, seeing Guy's scared face. 'We'll go and find Aunt Fanny.'

They all went thankfully out in the garden, hearing the house echo to the slam of Uncle Quentin's study door. George shouted.

'Mother! Where are you?'

'Shut up, George – we don't want to make your father leap out of the window after us!' said Dick. 'Ah – there's Aunt Fanny!'

His aunt was very surprised to see him and the others advancing on her. She went to greet them, a basket of raspberries on her arm.

'Well! I thought you wanted to stay away for longer than this!'

'We did – but an adventure descended on us!' said Dick. 'We'll tell you all about it in detail later on, Aunt Fanny.'

'But just now we want two things – can we ring the police – or will *you* – and ask them to come here?' said Julian, very grown-up all of a sudden. 'There's something that might be very important for them to know. And also do you think we should let a doctor see Guy's foot – he's sprained his ankle, I think?'

'Oh dear!' said Aunt Fanny, distressed to see the boy's swollen foot. 'Yes, he ought to have that seen to properly. Who is he? Dear me – there's another of them! Aren't they alike?'

'Twins,' said George. 'I don't know how I shall be able

to tell one from t'other when Guy's bad foot is better.'

'I'm going to ring the police,' said Julian, seeing that his aunt could now only think of Guy's swollen foot. He went off indoors, and they heard him speaking on the telephone. He put it down and came out again.

'The inspector himself is coming,' said Julian. 'Shall I ring the doctor now, Aunt Fanny?'

'Oh yes. His number is 042,' said his aunt. 'How *did* you get such an ankle, Guy?'

'Mother, you don't seem at all interested in our adventure,' complained George.

'Oh, I am, dear,' said her mother. 'But you do have such a lot, you know. What have you been up to this time?'

But before George could do more than begin, a black police car drew up at the front gate, and the inspector of police got out and marched up to the front door. He knocked extremely loudly on the knocker.

Which, of course, had the immediate result of bringing George's father hotfoot out of his study in another rage! He flung open the front door.

'Hammering at the door like that! What's the matter? I've a good mind to report you to the police! Oh – er – h'm – good afternoon, Inspector. Do come in. Are we expecting you?'

Smiling broadly, the inspector came in. By this time Julian had come back in the house again and greeted him. His uncle went back into his study, rather red in the face, and actually closed the door quietly!

'You wanted me to come along at once, because of something important?' said the inspector. 'What is it?'

The others came into the room now, with Julian's aunt behind them. Julian nodded round at them. 'They're all in this – except my aunt, of course. We've brought something we think may be important. Quite a lot of people were looking for it – but we managed to get hold of it first!'

He put the brown bag on the table. The inspector's eyes went to it at once. 'What is it? What's inside? Stolen goods?'

'Yes – blueprints of some kind, I think. But I don't know what of, of course.'

'Open the bag, my boy! I'll examine them,' said the inspector.

'I can't open it,' said Julian. 'It's locked – and there's no key!'

'Well – we'll soon manage *that*!' said the inspector, and took out a small, strong-looking tool. He forced the lock, and the bag opened. Everyone leant forward eagerly, even Timmy. What was in the bag?

There was nothing there! Absolutely nothing! Julian groaned in bitter disappointment.

'No wonder it felt so light. It's empty after all. Would you believe it!'

CHAPTER TWENTY

The adventure ends – as it began!

IT WAS a moment of great disappointment for all the children. Although they had talked about the possibility of the bag being empty, everyone had secretly felt certain that something exciting would be inside.

The inspector was astonished. He looked round sharply. 'Where did you get this bag? What made you think it had stolen goods inside – and what kind of blueprints were they?'

'Well – it's rather a long story,' said Julian.

'I'm afraid you'll have to tell it to me,' said the inspector, taking out his notebook. 'Now – how did this all begin?'

'Well – it really began with Timmy hurting his ear and having to wear a cardboard collar,' said George.

The inspector looked most surprised. He turned to Julian. '*You'd* better tell it,' he said. 'I don't want to waste time on cardboard collars!'

George went red and put on a scowl. Julian grinned at her, and began the story, making it as clear and short as he could.

The inspector became more and more interested. He laughed when Julian came to the weird noises and lights.

'They certainly wanted to get rid of you,' he said. 'You

were plucky to stay on. Go on – there's something behind all this, that's certain!'

He jotted down the names 'Paul', 'Tom' and 'Jess', the name of the woman. He noted that one man had a drawl. 'Any other clues to them?' he asked.

'Only this,' said Julian and handed his drawing of the crêpe-soled shoe to the inspector. This was carefully folded and put into the notebook too. 'Might be of use. Might not,' said the inspector. 'You never know!'

He listened intently to the tale of the underground passages, and picked up the bag again.

'I can't understand why it's empty,' he said. 'It isn't really like a crook deliberately to mislead his friends when they know quite well where he is and can get at him whenever they like.' He shook the bag hard. Then he began to examine it very very carefully.

Finally he took out a sharp knife and gently slit the lining at the bottom of the bag. He turned it back.

Something was there – under the lining! Something blue, folded very carefully. Something covered with thousands of minute figures, thousands of lines, thousands of strange little designs!

'Wheeeeeew!' whistled the inspector. 'So the bag's *not* empty, after all! Now what is this? It's a blueprint of some project – but what?'

'My father would know!' said George, at once. 'He's a scientist, you know, Inspector – one of the cleverest in the world. Shall I get him?'

'Yes,' said the inspector, laying out the blueprint on the table. 'Get him at once.'

George flew off and returned with her father, who didn't look very pleased.

'Good afternoon, once more. Sorry to disturb you,' said the inspector. 'But do you happen to know whether this document is of any importance?'

George's father took it up. He ran his eyes over it, and then gave a loud exclamation.

'Why – why – no, it's IMPOSSIBLE! Good heavens, it's – no, no, it can't be! Am I dreaming?'

Everyone gazed at him, surprised and anxious. What did he mean? What could it be, this blueprint?

'Er – it's important then?' said the inspector.

'Important? *Important?* My dear fellow, there are only two of these prints in existence – and at the moment I have the second one, which I am checking very carefully indeed. Where did this come from? Why – I simply can't believe it! Sir James Lawton-Harrison has the other. There isn't a third!'

'But – but – there must be if you have one here and Sir James has the other!' said the inspector. 'It's obvious there is a third!'

'You're wrong. It isn't obvious!' shouted George's father. 'What *is* obvious is that Sir James hasn't got his! I'll ring him up – this very minute. Astounding! Most disturbing! Bless us all, what will happen next?'

The children did not dare say a word. They were full of astonishment. To think that the blueprint was so important – and that George's father actually had the pair to this one. What was its importance?

They heard George's father shouting into the telephone, evidently angry and disturbed. He slammed it down and came back.

'Yes. Sir James's copy has been stolen – but it's been kept very hush-hush because of its importance. Good heavens – they never even let *me* know! And to think I spilt a bottle of ink over mine yesterday – gross carelessness. Stolen! A thing like that – stolen out of his safe under his very nose. Now there's only my one copy left!'

'Two,' said the inspector, tapping the copy on the table. 'You're so upset to hear that Sir James's copy has gone that you've forgotten we have it here!'

'Bless us all! Thank goodness! Yes, I *had* forgotten for the moment!' said Uncle Quentin. 'My word, I even forgot to tell Sir James it was here.' He leapt up to go to the telephone again, but the inspector caught his arm.

'No. Don't telephone again. I think we should keep this as quiet as possible.'

'Father – what *is* this a blueprint of?' said George, voicing the thoughts of everyone there, the inspector included.

'This blueprint? I'm certainly not going to tell you!' said her father. 'It's too big a thing even to speak of to you children – or the inspector either for that matter. It's one of the biggest secrets we have. Here, give it to me.'

The inspector placed his big hand on it at once. 'No. I think I must take it with me, and send a secret messenger to Sir James with it. It wouldn't do to have the only two copies in one place. Why, your house might catch fire and both prints might go up in flames!'

'Take it, then, take it! We can't possibly risk such a thing!' said George's father. He glared round at the children. 'I still don't understand how *you* came to possess it!' he said, looking suddenly amazed.

'Sit down, won't you, and listen to their tale,' said the inspector. 'They've done very well. They haven't finished their story.'

Julian went on with it. The inspector sat up straight when he heard where the three men were – down in the great pit below the Roman camp.

'You saw them go down into that pit?' he said. 'Watched them swing down on the rope? They may be there now!' He glanced at his watch. 'No, they won't. They'll be gone.'

He groaned loudly. 'And to think we might easily have caught three clever rogues. They've slipped through our hands again!'

'They haven't!' said Julian, his voice rising exultantly. 'They're still there!'

'How do you know?' said the inspector.

'Because I pulled up their rope and took it away – look, I've got it round me!' said Julian. 'They can't get out without a rope – and they won't know how to escape any other way. They're still there – waiting for you, Inspector!'

The inspector slapped the table so hard that everyone jumped and the two dogs barked.

'Good work!' he boomed. 'Magnificent! I must go at once and send some men out there. I'll let you know what happens!'

And out he went at a run, the precious blueprint buttoned safely in his pocket. He leapt into the driving seat and the police car roared away at top speed down the lane.

'Whew!' said Julian, flopping back into his chair. 'It's too exciting for words!'

Everyone felt the same, and began to talk at the tops of their voices. Poor Aunt Fanny couldn't make herself heard. But when Joanna came in and asked if anyone wanted anything to eat, they heard her at once!

The doctor came to see Guy's foot, and rebandaged it. 'Rest it for a day or two,' he said. 'It will soon be all right.'

'Well, you'll have to stay here with George and the others, Guy,' said George's mother. 'You can't go excavating in that camp of yours again yet. Harry can stay too. So can Jet.'

The twins beamed. They liked this jolly family, and the adventurous life they seemed to lead. It would be fun to stay with them for a while. They thought it would be even *more* fun when Joanna arrived with a truly wonderful meal!

'Home-made veal-and-ham-pie! Stuffed tomatoes! And what a salad – what's in it, Joanna? Radishes, cucumber, carrot, beetroot, hard-boiled eggs, tomatoes, peas – Joanna, you're a marvel! What is the pudding?' George asked.

Soon they were all sitting down enjoying themselves,

and talking over their adventure. Just as they were finishing, the telephone bell rang. Julian went to answer it. He came back looking thrilled.

'That was the inspector. They've got all three men! When they got to the pit, one of the men called up for help – said some idiot of a boy or some hoaxer must have taken their rope away. So the police – all in plain-clothes, so that of course the three men suspected nothing – the police let down a rope, and up came the men one by one . . .'

'And were arrested as soon as they popped out of the hole, I suppose!' said George, delighted. 'Oh, I wish I'd been there! What a joke!'

'The inspector's awfully pleased with us,' said Julian. 'And so is Sir James Lawton-Harrison too, apparently. We're to get a reward – very hush-hush, though. We mustn't say anything about it. There's to be something for each of us.'

'And for Timmy too?' said George at once.

Julian looked round at Timmy. 'Well, I can see what old Timmy ought to ask for,' he said. 'A new cardboard collar. He's scratching his ear to bits!'

George screamed and rushed to bend over Timmy. She lifted a woebegone face. 'Yes! He's scratched so hard he's made his ear bad again. Oh, Timmy! You really are a stupid dog! Mother! Mother! Timmy's messed up his ear again!'

Her mother looked into the room. 'Oh, George, what a

pity! I *told* you not to take off that collar till his ear was absolutely healed!'

'It's maddening!' said George. 'Now everyone will laugh at him again.'

'Oh no they won't,' said Julian, and he smiled at George's scowling face. 'Cheer up – it's a very peculiar thing, George – this adventure *began* with Timmy and a cardboard collar – and bless me if it hasn't *ended* with Timmy and a cardboard collar. Three cheers for old Timmy!'

Yes – three cheers for old Timmy! Get your ear well before the next adventure, Tim – you really *can't* wear a cardboard collar again!

Join the adventure!

If you can't wait to explore further with **THE FAMOUS FIVE**, read the next book in the series:

Do you want to solve a mystery?

Enid Blyton

The Secret Seven

Join Peter, Janet, Jack, Barbara, Pam, Colin, George and Scamper as they solve puzzles and mysteries, foil baddies, and rescue people from danger – all without help from the grown-ups. Enid Blyton wrote fifteen stories about the Secret Seven. These editions contain brilliant illustrations by Tony Ross, plus extra fun facts and stories to read and share.

More classic stories from the world of

Enid Blyton

The Naughtiest Girl

Elizabeth Allen is spoilt and selfish. When she's sent away to boarding school she makes up her mind to be the naughtiest pupil there's ever been! But Elizabeth soon finds out that being bad isn't as simple as it seems. There are ten brilliant books about the Naughtiest Girl to enjoy.

Enid Blyton®

is one of the most popular children's authors of all time. Her books have sold over 500 million copies and have been translated into other languages more often than any other children's author.

Enid Blyton adored writing for children. She wrote over 700 books and about 2,000 short stories. *The Famous Five* books, now 75 years old, are her most popular. She is also the author of other favourites including *The Secret Seven*, *The Magic Faraway Tree*, *Malory Towers* and *Noddy*.

Born in London in 1897, Enid lived much of her life in Buckinghamshire and loved dogs, gardening and the countryside. She was very knowledgeable about trees, flowers, birds and animals. Dorset – where some of the Famous Five's adventures are set – was a favourite place of hers too.

Enid Blyton's stories are read and loved by millions of children (and grown-ups) all over the world. Visit enidblyton.co.uk to discover more.

THE FAMOUS FIVE

FIVE GO TO BILLYCOCK HILL

Have you read all THE FAMOUS FIVE books?

1. Five on a Treasure Island
2. Five Go Adventuring Again
3. Five Run Away Together
4. Five Go to Smuggler's Top
5. Five Go Off in a Caravan
6. Five on Kirrin Island Again
7. Five Go Off to Camp
8. Five Get Into Trouble
9. Five Fall Into Adventure
10. Five on a Hike Together
11. Five Have a Wonderful Time
12. Five Go Down to the Sea
13. Five Go to Mystery Moor
14. Five Have Plenty of Fun
15. Five on a Secret Trail
16. Five Go to Billycock Hill
17. Five Get Into a Fix
18. Five on Finniston Farm
19. Five Go to Demon's Rocks
20. Five Have a Mystery to Solve
21. Five Are Together Again

The Famous Five Colour Short Stories

1. Five and a Half-Term Adventure
2. George's Hair is Too Long
3. Good Old Timmy
4. A Lazy Afternoon
5. Well Done, Famous Five
6. Five Have a Puzzling Time
7. Happy Christmas, Five
8. When Timmy Chased the Cat

Enid Blyton®

THE FAMOUS FIVE

FIVE GO TO BILLYCOCK HILL

Illustrated by Eileen A. Soper

HODDER CHILDREN'S BOOKS

First published in Great Britain in 1957 by Hodder & Stoughton
This edition published in 2016

20

A CIP catalogue record for this book is available from the British Library.

ISBN 978 1 444 93646 9

Printed and bound in Great Britain by Clays Ltd, Elcograf S.p.A.

The paper and board used in this book are made from wood from responsible sources.

Hodder Children's Books
An imprint of
Hachette Children's Group
Part of Hodder & Stoughton
Carmelite House
50 Victoria Embankment
London EC4Y 0DZ

An Hachette UK Company
www.hachette.co.uk
www.hachettechildrens.co.uk

CONTENTS

1 A WEEK'S HOLIDAY 1
2 OFF TO BILLYCOCK HILL 9
3 BILLYCOCK FARM 18
4 A FINE CAMPING PLACE 28
5 THE FIRST NIGHT – AND A MORNING VISITOR 36
6 THE BUTTERFLY FARM 45
7 MRS JANES – A SPIDER – AND A POOL 53
8 A SPOT OF TROUBLE 62
9 COUSIN JEFF 71
10 BUTTERFLY FARM AGAIN 80
11 A STORMY NIGHT 88
12 WHAT HAPPENED IN BILLYCOCK CAVES 97
13 A DREADFUL SHOCK 105
14 MR GRINGLE IS ANNOYED 113
15 MORE NEWS – AND A NIGHT TRIP 121
16 LOOKING THROUGH WINDOWS 129
17 QUITE A LOT HAPPENS 139
18 NOBODY KNOWS WHERE TO LOOK 148
19 A MORNING OF WORK 156
20 A PECULIAR MESSAGE 164
21 AN EXCITING FINISH 174

CHAPTER ONE

A week's holiday

'WHERE'S THE map?' said Julian. 'Is that it, George? Good! Now – where shall we spread it?'

'On the floor,' said Anne. 'A map is always easiest to read on the floor. I'll push the table out of the way.'

'Well, be careful, for goodness' sake,' said George. 'Father's in his study, and you know what happened before when someone pushed the table right over!'

Everyone laughed. George's father so often came pouncing out of his study if any sudden noise was made when he was working.

The table was pushed out of the way and the big map unfolded and spread out over the floor. Timmy was surprised to see the four children kneeling down around it, and barked, imagining this was some kind of new game.

'Be quiet, Timmy!' said Dick. 'You've got into trouble once this morning already for making a row. And stop brushing my face with your tail.'

'Wuff,' said Timmy and lay down heavily on the map.

'Get up, idiot,' said Dick. 'Don't you know we're in a hurry? We want to trace our route to Billycock Hill . . .'

'Billycock Hill – what a lovely name!' said Anne. 'Is that where we're going?'

'Yes,' said Julian, poring over the map. 'It's near some caves we want to see – and there's a butterfly farm not far off, and . . .'

'A butterfly farm!' said George, surprised. 'Whatever's that?'

'Just what it sounds like!' said Dick. 'A farm for butterflies! Toby, a friend of ours at school, told me about it. He lives quite near it and he says it's a most interesting place – they breed butterflies – and moths, too – from eggs, and sell them to collectors.'

'Do they really?' said Anne. 'Well, I must say I used to enjoy keeping caterpillars and seeing what they turned into – it was like magic to see a lovely butterfly or moth creep out of the chrysalis. But a *farm* for them – can we really go and see it?'

'Oh yes – Toby says the men who run it are very happy to show anyone round,' said Julian. 'Apparently Billycock Hill is a good place for rare butterflies too – that's why they've got their farm there. They rush about with nets half the time – and at night they go moth-hunting.'

'It sounds exciting,' said Dick. 'Well, what with caves to see, and a butterfly farm, and Toby to visit, and . . .'

'And just Five together again on a sunny week's holiday!' said George, giving Timmy a sudden thump of joy. 'Hurrah for Whitsun – and thank goodness our two schools had a week's holiday at the same time!'

The four cousins sprawled on the floor, looking with great interest at the map, following out a route with their

fingers. As they traced out the way, there came an angry noise from the study, where George's father was at work.

'Who's been tidying my desk? Where are those papers I left here? Fanny, Fanny – come here!'

'He wants Mother – I'll get her,' said George. 'No, I can't – she's gone shopping.'

'Why can't people leave my papers alone?' came her father's voice again. 'Fanny! FANNY!'

Then the study door was flung open and Mr Kirrin came striding out, muttering to himself. He didn't see the four children on the floor and fell right over them. Timmy barked in delight and leapt at him, thinking that for once George's father was actually having a game with them!

'Oooh!' said George, as her father's hand came over her face. 'Don't! What *are* you doing, Father?'

'Uncle Quentin – sorry you fell over us!' said Julian. 'Shut up, Timmy – this isn't a game!'

He helped his uncle up and waited for the explosion. His uncle brushed himself down and glared at Julian. 'Have you *got* to lie on the floor? Get down, will you, Timmy! Where's your mother, George? Get up, for goodness' sake! Where's Joanna? If she's been tidying my desk again I'll give her her notice!'

Joanna the cook appeared at the doorway, wiping her floury hands on her apron. 'Whatever's all this noise about?' she began. 'Oh sorry – I didn't know it was you. I . . .'

'Joanna – have you been tidying my desk again?' barked George's father.

'No. Have you lost something? Never you mind, I'll come along and find it,' said Joanna, who was used to Mr Kirrin's ways. 'Pick up that map, you four – and put the table back. Stop barking, Timmy. George, take him out for goodness' sake, or your father will go mad.'

'He's only excited because we're all together again,' said George, and took Timmy into the garden. The others followed, Julian folding up the map, grinning.

'We ought to put Uncle Quentin into a play,' said Dick. 'He'd bring the house down! Well – do we know the way, Julian? And when do we start?'

'Here's Mother,' said George as someone came to the front gate with a basket.

Julian ran to open it. He was very fond of his kindly, pleasant-faced aunt. She smiled round at them all.

'Well – have you decided where to go – and what to take with you? You'll be able to camp out this beautiful weather – what a lovely Whitsun it's going to be!'

'Yes,' said Julian, taking his aunt's basket from her and carrying it indoors. 'We're going to Billycock Hill, and as our friend Toby lives at the bottom of it, at Billycock Farm, he's going to lend us all the camping gear we need.'

'So we shan't need to load our bikes with tents and mattresses and things,' said Dick.

'Oh – good!' said his aunt. 'What about food? You can get it at Toby's farm, I suppose?'

'You bet! We shan't *eat* there, of course,' said Julian. 'But we shall buy any eggs or milk or bread we need – and

Toby says the strawberries are already ripening!'

Aunt Fanny smiled. 'Well, I needn't worry about your meals, then. And you'll have Timmy with you, too. He'll look after you all, won't you, Timmy? You won't let them get into any trouble, will you?'

'Woof,' said Timmy, in his deepest voice, and wagged his tail. 'Woof.'

'Good old Tim,' said George, patting him. 'If it wasn't for you we'd never be allowed to go off so much on our own, *I* bet!'

'Uncle Quentin's a bit on the warpath, Aunt Fanny,' said Dick. 'He wants to know who's been tidying his desk. He came rushing out of the study, didn't see us lying on the floor round our map – and fell right over us.'

'Oh dear – I'd better go and find out what papers he's lost *now*,' said his aunt. 'I expect he forgot that he had a tidying fit last night, and tidied his desk himself. He's probably put a lot of his most precious papers into the waste-paper basket!'

Everyone laughed as Mrs Kirrin hurried into the study.

'Well, let's get ready,' said Julian. 'We won't need to take much, as old Toby's going to help us. Anoraks, of course – and don't forget yours, Timmy! And sweaters. And one or two maps.'

'And torches,' said Anne, 'because we want to explore those caves. Oh, and let's take our swimsuits in *case* we find somewhere to bathe. It's warm enough!'

'And candles and matches,' said George, slapping the

pocket of her jeans. 'I've got those. I got Joanna to give me three boxes. And let's take some sweets.'

'Yes. That tin of humbugs,' said Julian. 'And I vote we take our little portable radio!'

'Oh yes – that's a good idea,' said Anne, pleased. 'We can hear our favourite programmes then – and the news. I don't suppose we shall be able to buy newspapers.'

'I'll get out the bikes from the shed,' said Julian.

'Dick, get the sandwiches from Joanna – she said she'd make us some because we shan't get to Toby's farm till after our dinner-time – and I bet we'll be hungry!'

'Wuff,' said Timmy, who knew that word very well.

'He says remember biscuits for him,' said Anne with a laugh. 'I'll go and get some now, Tim – though I expect you can share meals with the dogs at Billycock Farm.'

Joanna had two large packets of sandwiches and cake ready for them, and two bottles of orangeade. 'There you are,' she said, handing them over. 'And if you get through all those you'll no longer feel hungry. And here are Timmy's biscuits – *and* a bone.'

'You're a star, Joanna,' said Dick, and put his arm round her to give her one of the sudden hugs she liked. 'Well, you'll soon be rid of us – a whole week at Whitsun – isn't that luck – and with such glorious weather, too.'

'Buck up!' called Julian. 'I've got the bikes – and no one's had a puncture, for a change. Bring my anorak, Dick.'

In three minutes everything was packed into the bicycle

carriers. Timmy made sure that his biscuits and bone were packed by sniffing at each pack until he came to the smell he was hoping for. Then he wagged his tail and bounded round excitedly. The Five were together again – and who knew what might happen? Timmy was ready for anything!

'Goodbye, dears,' said Mrs Kirrin, standing at the gate to see them go. 'Julian, take care of the girls – and Tim, take care of everyone!'

Uncle Quentin suddenly appeared at the window. 'What's all the noise about?' he began impatiently. 'Oh – they're off at last, are they? Now we'll have a little peace and quiet! Goodbye – and behave yourselves!'

'Grown-ups always say that,' said Anne as the Five set off happily, ringing their bells in farewell. 'Hurrah – we're off on our own again – yes, you too, Timmy. What fun!'

CHAPTER TWO

Off to Billycock Hill

THE SUN shone down hotly as the Five sped down the sandy road that ran alongside Kirrin Bay. Timmy loped easily beside them, his tongue hanging out quite a long way. Anne always said that he had the longest tongue of any dog she had ever known!

The sea was as blue as forget-me-nots as they cycled along beside it. Across the bay they could see little Kirrin Island, with Kirrin Castle towering up.

'Doesn't it look fine?' said Dick. 'I half wish we were going to spend Whitsun at Kirrin Cottage, and were going bathing, and rowing across to George's little island over there.'

'We can do that in the summer hols,' said Julian. 'It's fun to explore other parts of the country when we can. Toby says the caves in Billycock Hill are marvellous.'

'What's Toby like?' asked George. 'We've never seen him, Anne and I.'

'He's a bit of a joker,' said Dick. 'Likes to put caterpillars down people's necks and so on – and beware if he has a magnificent rose in his buttonhole and asks you to smell it.'

'Why?' asked Anne, surprised.

'Because when you bend down to smell it you'll get a squirt of water in your face,' said Dick. 'It's a trick rose.'

'I don't think I'm going to like him much,' said George, who didn't take kindly to tricks of this sort. 'I'll probably bash him on the head if he does things like that to me.'

'That won't be any good,' said Dick cheerfully. 'He won't bash you back – he'll just think up some worse trick. Don't scowl, George – we're on holiday! Toby's all right – a bit of an ass, that's all.'

They had now left Kirrin Bay behind and were cycling down a country lane, set with hawthorn hedges each side. The may was over now, and the first wild roses were showing pink here and there. A little breeze got up, and was very welcome indeed.

'We'll have an ice when we come to a village,' said Julian after they had cycled about six miles.

'*Two* ices,' said Anne. 'Oh dear – this hill – what a steep one we've come to. I don't know whether it's worse to ride up slowly and painfully, or to get off and push my bike to the top.'

Timmy tore up to the top in front of them and then sat down to wait in the cool breeze there, his tongue hanging out longer than ever. Julian came to the top first and looked down the other side.

'There's a village there,' he said. 'Right at the bottom. Let's see – yes, it's Tennick village – we'll stop and ask if it sells ices.'

It did, of course, strawberry and vanilla. The four children sat on a seat under a tree outside the small village shop, and dug little wooden spoons into ice-tubs. Timmy sat nearby, watching hopefully. He knew that at least he would be able to lick out the empty tubs.

'Oh, Tim – I didn't mean to buy you one, because you really are a bit fat,' said George, looking at the beseeching brown eyes fixed on her ice-cream. 'But as you'll probably get very thin running so far while we're cycling, I'll buy you a whole one for yourself.'

'Wuff,' said Timmy, bounding into the little shop at once and putting his great paws up on the counter, much to the surprise of the woman behind it.

'It's a waste, really, giving Timmy an ice,' said Anne when George and the dog came out. 'He just loosens it with his tongue and gulps it down. I sometimes wonder he doesn't chew up the cardboard tub, too!'

After ten minutes' rest they all set off again, feeling nice and cool inside. It really was lovely cycling through the June countryside – the trees were so fresh and green still, and the fields they passed were golden with buttercups – thousands and thousands of them, nodding their polished heads in the wind.

There was very little traffic on these deserted country roads – an occasional farm-cart, and sometimes a car, but little else. The Five kept to the lanes as much as they could, for they all preferred their quaint winding curves set with hedges of all kinds to the wide, dusty main roads, straight and uninteresting.

'We ought to get to Billycock Farm about four o'clock,' said Dick. 'Or maybe sooner. What time do we have our lunch, Julian? And where?'

'We'll find a good place about one o'clock,' said Julian. 'And not a minute before. So it's no good anyone saying they are hungry yet. It's only twelve.'

'I'm more thirsty than hungry,' said Anne. 'And I'm sure old Timmy must be dying of thirst! Let's stop at the next stream so that he can have a drink.'

'There's one,' said Dick, pointing to where a stream wound across a nearby field. 'Hey, Tim – go and have a drink, old fellow!'

Timmy shot through the hedge to the stream and began to lap. The others dismounted and stood waiting. Anne picked a spray of honeysuckle and put it through a buttonhole of her blouse. 'Now I can sniff it all the time,' she said. 'Delicious!'

'Hey, Tim – leave some water for the fishes!' shouted Dick. 'George, stop him drinking any more. He's swelling up like a balloon.'

'He's *not*,' said George. 'Timmy! That's enough! Here, boy, here!'

Timmy took one last lap and then raced over to George. He pranced round her, barking joyfully.

'There – he feels much better now,' said George, and away they all went again, groaning as they cycled slowly up the many hills in that part of the country, and shouting with delight as they sped furiously down the other side.

Julian had decided where to have their midday meal – on the top of a high hill! Then they could see all the country for miles around, and there would also be a nice cooling breeze.

'Cheer up,' he said as they came to the steepest hill they had so far encountered. 'We'll have our lunch at the top of this hill – and a good long rest!'

'Thank goodness,' panted Anne. 'We'll be as stiff as anything tomorrow!'

It really was lovely at the top of the hill! It was so high that they could see the countryside spreading for miles and miles around them.

'You can see five counties from here,' said Julian. 'But

don't ask me which – I've forgotten! Let's lie in this heather and have a bit of a rest before we have our lunch.'

It was soft and comfortable lying in the springy heather, but Timmy did not approve of a rest before lunch. He wanted his bone! He went to where George had put her bicycle down, and sniffed in her carrier. Yes – his bone was most certainly there! He glanced round to make sure that everyone was resting, and nobody watching him. Then he began to nuzzle a paper parcel.

Anne was lying nearest to him, and she heard the crackling of the paper and sat up. '*Timmy!*' she said, shocked. 'Oh, Timmy – fancy helping yourself to our sandwiches!'

George sat up at once, and Timmy put his tail down, still wagging it a little as if to say, 'Sorry – but after all, it *is* my bone!'

'Oh – he just wants his bone,' said George. 'He's not after our sandwiches. As if he *would* take them, Anne! You might have known he wouldn't!'

'I feel rather like having mine now,' said Anne. 'Julian, can't we have some? – and I *do* really want a drink.'

The idea of a drink made everyone long to begin lunch and soon they were unwrapping ham and tomato sandwiches, and enormous slices of Joanna's fruit cake. Julian found the little cardboard drinking cups, and poured out the orangeade carefully.

'This is fine,' said Dick, munching his sandwiches and gazing out over the rolling countryside, with its moorlands,

its stretches of farmland with the fields of green corn, and its sloping hills. 'Look – see that hill far away in the distance, Julian – over there – would that be Billycock Hill, do you think? It's rather a funny shape.'

'I'll look through my field-glasses,' said Julian, and took them from their leather case. He put them to his eyes and stared hard at the faraway hill that lay to the north of them.

'Yes – I think it probably is Billycock Hill,' he said. 'It's got such an odd-shaped top; it looks a bit like an old Billycock hat.'

He handed the glasses round, and everyone looked at the far-off hill. George put the glasses to Timmy's eyes. 'There you are!' she said. 'Have a squint, Timmy! Julian, it doesn't look so very far away.'

'It's not, as the crow flies,' said Julian, taking back his glasses and surveying the countryside around them again. 'But it's a long, long way through those hundreds of little winding lanes. Any more sandwiches, anyone?'

'There aren't any more left,' said Dick. 'Or fruit cake either. Have a humbug if you're still hungry.'

The humbugs were passed round and Timmy waited hopefully for his turn. George gave him one. 'Not that it's much use to you,' she said. 'You just swallow it without even one suck!'

'We'll rest for half an hour more,' said Julian. 'Gosh, I do feel sleepy!'

They all snuggled down into the soft clumps of heather,

and soon they were asleep in the warm sun. Even Timmy snoozed, with one ear half up just in case someone came by. But nobody did. In fact it was so very quiet on the top of the hill that three-quarters of an hour went by before anyone awoke. Anne felt something crawling up her arm and woke with a jump.

'Ugh – a big beetle!' she said, and shook it off. She glanced at her watch. 'Dick! Ju! Wake up! We must get on, or we'll never be there by tea-time!'

Soon they were once more on their way, tearing down the hill at top speed, shouting as they went, with Timmy barking madly beside them. Really, the start of a holiday was the happiest thing in the world!

CHAPTER THREE

Billycock Farm

THE FIVE certainly cycled fast that afternoon, and would have arrived at Billycock Hill even sooner than they did if it hadn't been for Timmy. He panted so much in the heat that they stopped for brief rests every fifteen minutes.

'It's a pity he's so big and heavy,' said Anne. 'If he had been a small dog we could have taken turns at carrying him on our bikes.'

Billycock Hill was soon very near. It certainly was a strange shape, very like an old-fashioned hat. It was partly heather-clad and partly sloping meadow land. Cows grazed in the meadows, and farther up the hill, where there was shorter, wiry grass, the farmer had put a good many sheep.

Nestling down at the foot of the hill was a rambling old farm-building, with out-houses and stables and a big greenhouse. 'That must be Billycock Farm,' said Julian. 'Well, we've made very good time, you know – it's only half past three. Let's wash our faces in that stream over there – we all look rather hot and dirty. Timmy, you can have a bathe if you want to!'

The water was cool and silky to the touch, and the children splashed it over their faces and necks, wishing they could do as Timmy was doing – lying down in the stream and letting the water flow over him!

'That's better,' said Dick, mopping his face with an enormous handkerchief. 'Now let's go and present ourselves at Billycock Farm. I hope Toby's remembered that we're coming – he *promised* to lend us all we wanted for camping out.'

They combed their hair, brushed down their clothes with their hands, and then, feeling more respectable, made their way across a field path to a farm gate. The field was bumpy, so they rode slowly.

Soon they were in a big farmyard, with hens pecking around them, and ducks swimming on a round duck-pond. Farm dogs began barking from somewhere – and then something ran round the corner of the old house – something very small and pink.

'Whatever is it?' said Anne. 'Oh – it's a pigling! What a pet! Oh, it's come right up to us – little pigling, have you escaped from your sty? How clean you are!'

The tiny pig gave funny little squeals, and ran up to Timmy, who sat back on his haunches in surprise, staring at this unexpected little creature. He thought it must be some sort of dog without any hair.

The pigling butted Timmy gently and Timmy retreated backwards. Julian laughed. 'Tim can't make it out!' he said. 'No don't growl, Timmy – it's quite harmless!'

'Hallo – who's this?' said Dick as a small figure came round the house. It stopped when it saw the Five.

'What a dear little boy!' said Anne. 'Is he Toby's brother?'

The child didn't look more than five years old. He had a head of bright yellow curls, big brown eyes, and a grin just like his big brother's.

'That's my pig,' he said, coming slowly towards them. 'He runned away from me.'

Anne laughed. 'What's your pig's name?' she said.

'Curly,' said the small boy, and pointed at the pigling's tail. 'He's got a curly tail. It won't go straight.'

'It's a nice tail,' said Anne. The pigling ran to the small boy, and he grabbed it by its tail. 'You runned away again,' he said. Then he picked up the pig and walked off.

'Hey! Is this Billycock Farm?' called Julian. 'Have you got a brother called Toby?'

'Toby? Yes, Toby's over there,' said the boy, and he pointed to a big barn. 'Toby's ratting with Binky.'

'Right,' said Julian. The little boy disappeared with his funny pet, and Julian laughed. 'He's rather a pet himself,' he said. 'Come on – let's go and find Toby and Binky. Perhaps Binky is another brother.'

'Or a dog,' said George, and put her hand on Timmy's collar. 'Better be careful. He might go for Tim.'

'Yes – Binky might be a dog, of course – probably a good ratter,' said Julian. 'Dick and I will go to the barn and you two girls stay here with Timmy.'

They went off to the barn. A great noise came from inside as the two boys approached. Shouts and barks and the rap of a stick came to their ears.

'Get him, Binky – look, he went under that sack! Oh, you fathead, you've lost him again!'

Wuff-wuff-wuff! Rap-rap! More yells! In great curiosity Julian and Dick peered into the rather dark old barn. They saw Toby there, prodding under sacks, with a most excited collie beside him, barking incessantly.

'Hey, Toby!' yelled Julian, and Toby stood up and turned a red and perspiring face towards the two boys.

'Oh – you've arrived!' he said, going quickly to the door. 'I thought you were never coming. Glad to see you! But are there only two of you? I got out tents and things for four.'

'There *are* four of us – five counting Timmy,' said

Julian. 'We've left the two girls over there with him – he's our dog. Will yours be friendly or not?'

'Oh, yes, so long as I introduce them,' said Toby and they all went out of the barn. As soon as Binky, Toby's dog, saw Timmy, he stood still, made himself stiff, and growled, while the hackles on his neck slowly rose up.

'It's all right,' shouted Toby to the girls. 'Bring your dog here. He'll be all right with Binky in half a minute.'

Rather doubtfully George brought Timmy across. Timmy was a bit doubtful himself of this big collie! Toby bent down and spoke into Binky's ear.

'Binky, shake paws with this nice girl – she's a friend.'

He nodded at George. 'Hold out your hand,' he said.

George bent down to the collie and held out her hand. At once the dog put up his paw and allowed her to shake it solemnly.

'Now you,' said Toby to Anne, and she did the same. She liked this dog Binky, with his bright brown eyes and long, sleek nose.

'Does *your* dog shake hands, too?' asked Toby. George nodded. 'He does? Right – tell him to shake paws with Binky. Binky, shake!'

'Timmy, shake,' commanded George, and very politely and solemnly the two dogs shook paws, eyeing each other cautiously. Timmy gave a sudden little whine – and then the two were tearing round the yard together, barking furiously, chasing one another, rolling over, and having a wonderful game.

'That's all right, then,' said Toby, pleased. 'Binky's quite all right with anyone, human or animal, so long as he can shake hands with them. I've taught him that. But he's a dud ratter! He just can't seem to nip a rat. Well – let's go and see my mother. She's expecting you. She's got a whopping great tea.'

This was all very satisfactory! Just the kind of welcome the Five liked. Anne looked sideways at Toby. She thought he was rather nice. George wasn't so sure. He had a rose in his buttonhole – was it a trick one, and was he going to ask her to smell it?

'We saw a little yellow-haired boy just now,' said Anne. 'With a tiny pigling.'

'Oh, that's Benny with his pet pig,' said Toby, laughing. 'He calls it Curly – and he adores it! We've offered him a kitten or a puppy – but no, he wants that pigling. They go everywhere together – like Mary and her lamb! Benny's a pet – he really is. Kid brothers are usually a nuisance, you know, but Benny isn't.'

'Kid sisters are a bit of a nuisance sometimes too,' said Dick, glancing slyly at Anne, who at once gave him a determined punch. 'Still – Anne's not too bad, is she, Ju?'

Toby's mother, Mrs Thomas, was a plump and jolly woman, with a smile as wide as Toby's and Benny's. She made them all very welcome.

'Come along in,' she said. 'Toby's pleased you're going to camp hereabouts – he's got all the tents and rugs you'll need – and you can come every day and get eggs and milk and bread and butter and anything else you need from here. Don't be afraid to ask!'

There was suddenly the scamper of little hooves and Curly the pigling came running indoors.

'There, now!' said Toby's mother. 'There's that pigling again. Benny, Benny – you are NOT to let Curly come indoors. Cats I don't mind, nor dogs – but pigs I won't have. Benny!'

Benny appeared, looking most apologetic. 'Sorry, Mum – but he's lively today. Oooh, I say – what a tea! Can we have some yet?'

'I'll just make the tea – unless you'd rather have some of our creamy milk?' said Toby's mother.

'Oh, milk, please, Mrs Thomas,' said Anne, and they all said the same. Nothing could be nicer than icy-cold, creamy farm milk from the dairy on a hot day like this.

They all sat down to tea, and the four visitors wished they had not had such a big lunch! A large ham sat on the table, and there were crusty loaves of new bread. Crisp lettuces, dewy and cool, and red radishes were side by side in a big glass dish. On the sideboard was an enormous cake, and beside it a dish of scones. Great slabs of butter and jugs of creamy milk were there, too, with honey and home-made jam.

'I wish I was hungry, *really* hungry,' said Dick. 'This is just the kind of meal for a hungry day.'

'I didn't think you'd have had much lunch,' said Mrs Thomas. 'Now then, Toby – you're the host. See to your

guests, please – and, Benny, take the pigling off your knee. I will *not* have him at the table.'

'Curly will be very upset if he sees that ham,' said Toby slyly. 'That's his grandfather!'

Benny put Curly down hurriedly, afraid that his feelings might be hurt. The pigling went to sit beside Timmy, who, very much surprised, but rather pleased, at once made room for him.

It was a very happy meal, and Toby was a good host. Anne sat beside little Benny, and found herself liking him more than ever. 'He's like a little boy out of a story,' she said to George. 'He and Curly ought to be put into a book!'

'Well now,' said Mrs Thomas after everyone had eaten their fill, 'what are your plans? Toby, show them where you have put their tents and everything. Then they can decide where they are going to camp.'

'Come on, then,' said Toby, and Benny and Curly and Binky all came along, too. 'You can help to carry everything – and we'll go up on Billycock Hill and find a fine camping place. How I wish I could camp out with you too!'

Away they all went, feeling rather full but very happy. Where should they camp? How lovely to sleep out at nights, and see the stars through the opening in the tent!

CHAPTER FOUR

A fine camping place

TOBY HAD put all the camping-out gear in a nearby barn. He took the Five there, with Benny and the pigling trailing after. Binky came, too, so friendly now with Timmy that they trotted along side by side, occasionally pushing against each other like schoolboys!

Julian and Dick looked at the pile of canvas, the pegs and the ropes. Yes, these two tents would do very well, though if the weather stayed like this they would hardly need tents! They could lay their rugs out on the springy heather.

'This is fine, Toby,' said Julian gratefully. 'You've even provided a kettle and a frying-pan.'

'Well, you might want to cook a meal,' said Toby. 'Or boil soup. There's a saucepan for that – ah, here it is!'

He picked it up and promptly put it on Benny's head, where it stuck tightly on his yellow curls. Benny yelled and ran at Toby, hitting at him with his fists. The little pig rushed away in fright and disappeared round a corner.

Anne took the saucepan off poor Benny's head. 'You're all right!' she said. 'It was a funny hat to wear, wasn't it?'

'Curly runned away again!' wept Benny, and he pummelled the laughing Toby. 'I hate you, I hate you!'

'You go and find him,' said Toby, fending off the angry small boy, and Benny ran off on his fat little legs.

'Well, we've got rid of him for a few minutes,' said Toby. 'Now – is there anything I've forgotten? You've got torches, I suppose? What about candles – and matches?'

'We've got those, too,' said Dick. 'And we've brought sweaters and swimsuits – but that's about all. I see you've put a couple of rugs here as well in case we're cold!'

'Well, it *might* turn wet and chilly,' said Toby. 'Of course, if it snows, or anything like that, you'll have to come and borrow some more rugs! Now, shall I help you to fix them on your bikes?'

It was too difficult to fix anything on to the four bikes, and in the end Toby found a hand-cart and the children piled everything into that.

'We'll fetch our bikes some other time,' said Julian.

'Leave them here!' said Toby. 'They'll be all right. Are you going now? Well, I'll get a package Mother's got ready for you – you know, ham and new-laid eggs and bread and butter and the rest.'

'It's most awfully good of her,' said Julian gratefully. 'Well, let's start – we've got everything in the hand-cart now. We'll just wait for the food. Dick, you and I can push this hand-cart together. It will need two of us up the hill – and I vote we camp on the side of the slope somewhere, so that we can get a good view.'

Toby came back with an enormous package of food.

Benny came with him, Curly trotting behind. Benny carried a basket of ripe strawberries.

'I picked them for you,' he said, and handed them to Anne.

'What beauties!' she said, and gave the smiling child a hug. 'We shall enjoy them, Benny.'

'Can I come and see your camp when you've built it?' he asked. 'Can I bring Curly? He's never seen a camp.'

'Yes, of course you can,' said Anne. 'Are we ready now, Julian? What about milk? Mrs Thomas said we could take some.'

'Oh yes – I forgot that,' said Toby. 'It's in the dairy.' He sped off with Binky, and the others arranged everything neatly in the useful little hand-cart. Toby came back with the milk – two big bottles. They were stacked carefully in a corner of the cart.

'Well, we're ready now, I think,' said Julian, and he and Dick began to push the cart down the path to the gate. Timmy and Binky trotted on ahead, and everyone else followed. Benny came as far as the gate with Curly, then Toby sent him back.

'You know what Mother said, Benny,' he said. 'You're not to come with us now – it'll be too late when Binky and I come back.'

Benny's mouth went down, but he didn't attempt to follow them. He picked Curly up in his arms in case the pigling should run away after the others.

'Benny's a pet,' said Anne. 'I wish I had a little brother like that.'

'He's all right,' said Toby. 'A bit of a cry-baby, though. I'm *trying* to bring him up properly – teasing him out of his babyishness, and making him stand on his own feet.'

'He seems to be able to do that all right,' said Dick. 'My word – the way he went for you when you put that saucepan on his head! He pummelled you right and left!'

'Benny's a funny little kid,' said Toby, giving a hand with the cart as they reached the slope of the hill. 'He's always having funny pets. Two years ago he had a lamb that followed him everywhere. Last year he had two goslings that followed him about – and when they grew into geese they still followed him! They waddled all the way upstairs one day!'

'And this year he's got a pig!' said George, who, like Anne, was very much amused with Benny. 'Don't you think Timmy was very funny with Curly? I'm sure he still thinks it's a puppy without any hair!'

They made their way up the hill, following a narrow sheep-path. The hand-cart bumped and wobbled, and soon it needed four or five pairs of hands to push it.

'How much farther?' panted Toby at last. 'Surely you're not going right to the top?'

'No,' said Julian. 'About halfway up. We do want to have a good view, Toby. Not very much farther up, I should think. But let's have a bit of rest, shall we?'

They sat down, glad to get their breath. Certainly the view was magnificent. Far away on the horizon were purplish hills, and in front of them stretched miles and

miles of green and golden countryside. Green for growing corn and grass – gold for the buttercups, which were at their best in this sunny week of June.

'I like those silvery threads here and there winding about the green fields,' said Anne. 'Little streams – or rivers – curving like snakes all about! And I like the dark green patches that are woods.'

'What's that just down there?' asked George, pointing to what looked like an enormous field with great sheds in the centre.

'That's an airfield,' said Toby promptly. 'A bit hush-hush. Secret planes tried out, and all that. I know all about it because a cousin of mine is there – he's a flight-lieutenant. He comes to see us sometimes and tells me things. It's an experimental place.'

'What's that, exactly?' asked Anne.

'Well – where new ideas are tried out,' said Toby. 'They deal mostly with very small planes down there – one-man fighter planes, I think. Don't be scared if you hear noises from the airfield sometimes – bangs and bursts. I don't know what they are, of course – it's all to do with their experiments.'

'I wish I could visit the airfield,' said Dick. 'I'm keen on planes. I'm going to fly one when I'm older.'

'You'd better meet my cousin, then,' said Toby. 'He might take you up in one.'

'I *should* like to meet him,' said Dick, delighted. 'So would Julian.'

'We'd better get on now,' said Julian, standing up. 'We won't go much higher – the view can't be much better anywhere else!'

George and Anne went on ahead to find a good camping place, while the three boys pushed the cart slowly over the heather. But it was Timmy who found the right place! He ran on ahead, feeling thirsty, so when he heard the sound of running water he ran to it at once.

From under a jutting rock gushed a little spring. It rippled down a rocky shelf and lost itself in a mass of lush greenery below. Rushes grew to mark the way it went, and George's sharp eyes could follow its path for quite a long way down the hill, outlined by the dark line of rushes.

'Julian! Look what Timmy's found!' she called as she watched him lap from the clear spring water. 'A little spring gushing out of the hillside! Hadn't we better camp near it?'

'Good idea!' shouted back Julian, and left the hand-cart to come and see. 'Yes, this is just the place! A fine view – plenty of springy heather to camp on – and water laid on quite near!'

Everyone agreed that it was a fine place, and soon all the gear was taken from the hand-cart. The tents were not erected, for everyone meant to sleep under the stars that night, the evening was so warm. Nobody wanted to lie in a stuffy tent!

Anne unpacked the food parcel, wondering where would be the coolest place for a 'larder'. She went over to the rock from which gushed the crystal-clear spring water. She pushed away the rushes around and discovered a kind of small cave hollowed out of the rock below the spring.

'It would be as cool as anything in there,' thought Anne, and put her hand through the falling water into the cavelike hole. 'Yes, it was icy cold! Was it big enough to hold the milk bottles and everything? Just about,' she thought.

Anne loved arranging anything, and she was soon at work putting away the food and the milk into her odd larder. George laughed when she saw it.

'Just like you, Anne!' she said. 'Well, we'd better put a towel by the spring, for certainly we shall get soaked every time we get out any food!'

'Tell Timmy he's *not* to try and poke his head into my larder,' said Anne, pushing Timmy away. 'Oh, now he's all wet. Go and shake yourself somewhere else, Timmy – you're showering me with drops of water!'

Toby had to leave them, for it was already past his supper-time. 'See you tomorrow!' he said. 'How I wish I was staying up here with you! So long!'

Away he went down the hill with Binky at his heels. The Five looked at one another and grinned.

'He's nice – but it's good to be alone again – just us Five,' said George. 'Come on – let's settle in. This is the best camp we've ever had!'

CHAPTER FIVE

The first night – and a morning visitor

'WHAT'S THE time?' said Julian, looking at his watch. 'Good gracious – it's almost eight o'clock. Anyone feel tired?'

'Yes,' said Dick, Anne and George, and even Timmy joined in with his deepest 'Woof'.

'With all that bicycling and then pushing that heavy cart up the hill, I can hardly move!' said Dick. 'I vote we have a simple supper – something out of Anne's little larder – and then spread our rugs over some thick heather and sleep under the sky. Even up here, with a breeze, it's warm. I should be stifled in a tent.'

'Well, we're all agreed on that,' said Julian. 'Anne, what do you suggest for a light supper?'

'Bread, butter and some of Mrs Thomas's farm cheese,' said Anne promptly. 'With a tomato or two if you like and icy-cold milk and Benny's strawberries to finish with. That is – if the milk has had time to get cold in the little hole under the spring.'

'Sounds jolly good,' said Julian. 'What do *you* think, Timmy? Anne, if you and George get the supper ready, Dick and I will prepare our heathery beds. Then we can all turn in as soon as possible. I honestly feel that once I sit down or lie down I'll not be able to get up again!'

'Same here,' said Dick, and went off with Julian to find the best place for sleeping. They soon found one. They came across a giant of a gorse bush, thick, prickly and still full of golden blooms. In front of it was a stretch of very close-set heather, as springy as the best mattress in the world. Dick sat down on it and grinned at Julian.

'Just made for us!' he said. 'We shall sleep like logs here. We hardly need a rug to lie on, it's so close-grown. Help me up – legs won't do anything now I've sat down!'

Julian pulled him up and they called to the girls: 'Anne! George! Bring the supper here. We've found a good place. It's by this giant gorse bush.'

The girls came along with the meal, and the boys fetched a couple of rugs from the pile of things that they had brought in the hand-cart. They spread them on the heather.

'I say! This certainly is a good place,' said George, coming up with Anne and Timmy carrying a loaf of bread, a pat of butter and tomatoes. Anne had the milk and the cheese. Timmy was carrying a little bag of his own biscuits.

'The gorse bush will shelter us from too much wind,' said Dick, taking the milk from Anne. 'It's an ideal spot – and the view is superb.'

It was a very happy supper they had, sitting in the heather, while the sun sank lower and lower in the west. The evenings were very light now, and certainly they would not need candles! They finished up everything, and then went to wash at the little spring that bubbled out so cheerfully.

They lay down on their rugs in the heather while it was still daylight. 'Goodnight!' said Dick, and promptly fell fast asleep. 'Goodnight!' called Julian and lay for a few seconds looking at the view which was now becoming dim and blue.

Timmy kept the two girls awake for a minute or two, trying to squeeze in between them. 'Do keep still, Timmy,' said George. 'And just remember you're on guard, even though I don't expect there is anyone nearer than a mile – and that will be at Billycock Farm! Lie still now, or I'll push you off the rug! Goodnight, Anne.'

George was soon asleep, and so was Timmy, tired out with so many miles of running. Anne lay awake for a few minutes, looking at the evening star which shone large and golden in the sky. She felt very happy. 'I don't want to grow up,' she thought. 'There can't be anything nicer in the world than this – being with the others, having fun with them. No – I don't want to grow up!'

Then she, too, fell asleep, and night came quietly down, with stars brilliant in the sky, and very little noise to be heard anywhere – just the gurgling of the spring some way away, and the far-off bark of some dog – perhaps Binky at the farm. The breeze died down, so that even that could not be heard.

No one except Timmy awoke at all that night. Timmy

put up one ear when he heard a squeak just above his head. It came again and he opened one eye. It was a small black bat circling and swooping, hunting for insects. Its squeak was so high that only Timmy's quick ear caught it. He put down his listening ear and went to sleep again.

Nobody stirred until a very loud noise awakened them. R-r-r-r-r-r-r-r-r! R-r-r-r-r-r-r-r-r! They all woke up with a jump and the boys sat up straight, startled. What could it be?

'It's a plane,' said Julian, staring up at a small aeroplane flying over the hill. 'It must be one from that airfield down there! I say – it's five past nine! Five past nine – we've slept for nearly twelve hours!'

'Well, I'm going to sleep for some more,' said Dick, snuggling down into his heathery bed again and shutting his eyes.

'No, you're not,' said Julian, giving him a shove. 'It's too good a day to waste in any more sleep. Hey, you girls – are you awake?'

'Yes,' called George, sitting up, rubbing her eyes. 'That aeroplane woke me. Anne's awake, too – and you can see that Timmy is; he's gone after a rabbit or something.'

'We'll go and wash at the spring,' said Anne, scrambling off the rug. 'And George and I will get breakfast. Anyone like a boiled egg?'

The sun shone down out of a blue sky, and the little breeze awoke and began to blow again. They washed in the cold water, and Timmy drank it, lapping it thirstily as it splashed down over his nose. Then they had their breakfast.

It was easy to make a little fire in the shelter of the giant gorse bush, and boil the eggs in the saucepan. Bread and butter and tomatoes completed the simple meal, with cold creamy milk to wash it down.

In the middle of this Timmy began to bark frantically, but as his tail was wagging all the time, the others guessed that it must be Toby coming. They heard Binky's answering bark, and then the dog himself appeared, panting and excited. He greeted Timmy first of all, and then ran round to give everyone a lick.

'Hallo, hallo, hallo!' came Toby's voice, and he appeared

round the gorse bush. 'Had a good night? I say, aren't you late – *still* having your breakfast? My word, you're sleepy-heads! I've been up since six. I've milked cows and cleaned out a shed, and fed the hens and collected the eggs.'

The Five immediately felt ashamed of themselves! They gazed at Toby in admiration – why, he was quite a farmer!

'I've brought you some more milk, bread and eggs and cake,' he said, and put down a basket.

'Jolly good of you,' said Julian. 'We must pay for any food we get from your farm, you know that. Any idea of how much we owe for yesterday's food and for what you've brought today?'

'Well, my mother says you don't *need* to pay her,' said Toby. 'But I know you mean to – so I suggest that you pay *me* each time and I'll put the money into a box and buy my mother a smashing present at the end – from you all. Will that do?'

'That's a good idea,' said Julian. 'We couldn't possibly accept food if we didn't pay for it – but I know what mothers are – they don't like being paid in money for their kindness! So we'll do what you say. Now, reckon up what we owe so far, and I'll pay you.'

'Right,' said Toby in a business-like way. 'I'll charge you market prices, not top prices. I'll just tot up the bill while you're clearing up and putting away what I've brought.'

The girls washed up in the spring, and the boys carried everything there for Anne to put in her 'larder'. Toby presented Julian with a neatly written bill, which he at once paid. Toby receipted the bill and gave it back.

'There you are – all business-like,' he said. 'Thanks very much. What are you going to do today? There are super caves to be explored if you like – or there's the butterfly farm – or you can just come down to *our* farm for the day.'

'No, not today,' said Julian, afraid that they might make themselves a nuisance to Mrs Thomas. 'I don't feel like seeing caves this morning either – so dark and eerie on such a sunny day. What shall we do, girls?'

But before they could decide Binky and Timmy began to bark, each dog standing quite still, facing the same way – towards the giant gorse bush.

'Who is it, Tim?' asked George. 'Go and see! Go on then!'

Timmy ran behind the bush, followed by Binky, and then the children heard a surprised voice.

'Hallo, Binky! What are *you* doing all the way up here? And who's your friend?'

'It's Mr Gringle,' said Toby. 'One of the men who own the butterfly farm. He's often up here with his net, because it's a wonderful place for butterflies.'

A man came round the gorse bush – rather a peculiar figure, untidy, with glasses slipping down his nose, and his hair much too long. He carried a big butterfly net and stopped when he saw the five children.

'Hallo!' he said. 'Who are all these, Toby? Quite a crowd!'

'Friends of mine, Mr Gringle,' said Toby solemnly. 'Allow me to introduce them. Julian Kirrin, Dick Kirrin, Anne Kirrin, George Kirrin, their cousin – and their dog Timothy.'

'Ha – pleased to meet you!' said Mr Gringle, and came shambling forward, his big butterfly net over his shoulder. Behind his glasses shone curiously bright eyes. He nodded his head to each of the four cousins. 'Three boys – and a girl. Very nice lot, too. You don't look as if you'll leave litter about or start fires in this lovely countryside.'

'We shouldn't dream of it,' said George, delighted that he had thought she was a boy. Nothing pleased George as much as that! 'Mr Gringle – *could* we see your butterfly farm, please? We would so like to!'

'Of course, my dear boy, of course,' said Mr Gringle, and his eyes shone as if he were pleased. 'We don't often have visitors, so it's quite an event when somebody comes along. This way, this way!'

CHAPTER SIX

The butterfly farm

MR GRINGLE led the way down the hill by a little path so overgrown that it was hardly possible to see it. Halfway down the little company heard a squealing noise – and then an excited little voice.

'Toby, Toby! I'm here! Can I come with you?'

'It's Benny – and the pigling!' said Anne, amused at the little couple making their way excitedly towards them. Timmy ran to Curly and sniffed him all over, still not quite sure that he wasn't some kind of strange puppy.

'What are you doing up here?' said Toby sternly. 'You know you're not supposed to wander too far from the farm. You'll get lost one of these days, Benny.'

'Curly runned away,' said Benny, looking up at his big brother with wide brown eyes.

'You mean you wanted to find out where I'd gone so you came after me with Curly,' said Toby.

'Curly runned away, he runned fast!' said Benny, looking as if he was going to cry.

'You're a scoundrel, Benny,' said Toby. 'You make that pigling of yours an excuse for getting about all over the place. You wait till Dad hears it – you'll get such a scolding. Well – tail on to us now – we're going to the butterfly farm. And if Curly runs away, let him! I'm tired of that pig.'

'I'll carry him,' said Benny, and picked up the little creature in his arms. But he soon had to put him down, for Curly squealed so loudly that Timmy and Binky both leapt round him in great concern.

'Hm – well – shall we proceed?' asked Mr Gringle, walking on in front. 'Quite a party we have today.'

'Are your butterflies afraid of pigs or dogs?' asked Benny, trotting beside him. 'Shall we leave them outside?'

'Don't ask idiotic questions, Benny,' said Toby. Then he gave a cry and caught Mr Gringle's arm. 'I say – look at that butterfly. Don't you want to catch it? Is it rare?'

'No,' said Mr Gringle rather coldly. 'It's a meadow brown – very common indeed. Don't they teach you anything at school? Fancy not knowing that!'

'Julian, do we have any butterfly lessons?' asked Toby with a grin. 'I say, Mr Gringle, what about you coming and teaching us about cabbage butterflies and cauliflower moths, and red admirals and blue captains and peacock butterflies and ostrich moths and . . .'

'Don't be an ass, Toby,' said Julian, seeing that Mr Gringle had no sense of humour at all, and did not think this in the least funny. 'Mr Gringle, are there many rare butterflies about here?'

'Oh, yes, yes,' said the butterfly man. 'But not only that – there are so many of *all* kinds here, and it is easy to catch as many as I want for breeding purposes. One butterfly means hundreds of eggs, you know – and we hatch them out and sell them.'

He suddenly made a dart to one side, almost knocking George over. 'Sorry, boy!' he said, making the others smile. 'Sorry! There's a brown argus there – a lovely specimen, first I've seen this year! Stand clear, will you.'

The children – and the dogs too – stood still as he tiptoed towards a small dark brown butterfly spreading its tiny wings as it sat on a flowering plant. With a swift downwards swoop the net closed over the plant, and in a trice the butterfly man had caught the fluttering insect. He pinched the net inwards, and showed the children the tiny creature.

'There you are – a female brown argus, one of the family of the Blue butterflies you see so often in full summer. She'll lay me plenty of eggs and they'll all hatch into fat little slug-like caterpillars, and . . .'

'But this isn't a blue butterfly,' said Anne, looking through the fine net. 'It's dark brown, with a row of pretty orange spots along the margins of its wings.'

'All the same, it belongs to the Blue butterfly family,' said Mr Gringle, taking it out with the gentlest of fingers and putting it into a tin case slung round his shoulders. 'It's probably come up from one of those hay meadows down in the valley there. In you go, my little beauty!'

'Mr Gringle, quick – here's a most lovely butterfly!' called George. 'It's got greeny-black front wings with red spots, and lovely red back wings with dark green borders. Oh, quick – I'm sure you want this one!'

'That's not a butterfly,' said Dick, who knew a good deal about them.

'I should think not!' said Mr Gringle, getting his net poised ready to swoop. 'It's a moth – a lovely little thing!' Down went his net and the pretty little red and green insect fluttered in surprise inside it.

'But moths don't fly in the daytime,' argued George. 'Only at night.'

'Rubbish!' said Mr Gringle, looking at the moth through the thick lenses of his glasses. 'What are boys coming to nowadays? In *my* boyhood nearly every boy knew that there are night-time *and* daytime ones as well!'

'But,' began George again, and stopped as Mr Gringle gave her quite a glare.

'This is a six-spot burnet day-flying moth,' he said speaking slowly as if he were addressing a very small child. 'It loves to fly in the hot sunshine. Please do not argue with me. I don't like ignorance of this sort.'

George looked rather mutinous and Dick nudged her. 'He's right, fathead,' he said in a low voice. 'You don't know much about moths, so say nothing, George, or he won't let us go with him.'

'I'd like two or three more of these six-spots – highly coloured and unusually large. Perhaps you would see if you can find any more, all of you.'

Everybody began to look here and there, and to shake

any little bush or clump of grass they passed. Timmy and Binky were most interested in this and began a hunt on their own, sniffing and snuffling everywhere, not quite sure what they were looking for, but enjoying it all the same.

Mr Gringle took a long time to get to his butterfly farm, and the children began to wish they hadn't asked to go. There was so much side-stepping to see this and that, so much examining when a specimen was caught, so much 'talky-talk', as Dick whispered to Anne.

'Do you keep your butterflies and moths in those glasshouses?' asked Julian.

'Yes,' said Mr Gringle. 'Come along – I'll show you what I and my friend Mr Brent do. He's away today, so you can't meet him.'

It was certainly a strange place. The cottage looked as if it were about to fall down at any moment. Two of the windows were broken and some tiles had fallen off the roof. But the glasshouses were in good repair, and the glass panes were perfectly clean. Evidently the butterfly men thought more of their butterflies and moths than they did of themselves.

'Do you live here all alone with Mr Brent, your friend?' asked Dick curiously, thinking that it must be a strange and lonely life.

'Oh, no. Old Mrs Janes lives here too,' said Mr Gringle. 'And sometimes her son comes to do my small repairs, and to clean all the glass of the butterfly houses. There's

the old lady, look. She can't bear insects of any sort, so she never comes into the glasshouses.'

An old woman, looking exactly like a witch, peered out at them through a window in the cottage. Anne was quite scared to see her. Toby grinned. 'She's quite harmless,' he said to Anne. 'Our cook knows her because she often comes to us for eggs and milk. She's got no teeth at all, so she mutters and mumbles and that makes her seem more like a witch than ever.'

'I don't much like the look of her,' said Anne, going thankfully into the first of the butterfly houses. 'Oh – what a lot of butterflies!'

There certainly were! Hundreds were flying about loose,

and many others were in little compartments either by themselves or with another butterfly to match.

The children saw that many bushes and plants were growing in the glasshouse, and on some of them were placed long sleeves made of muslin, tied in at each end.

'What's in these long sleeves of fine muslin?' asked Dick. 'Oh – I see. They are full of caterpillars! My word, how they are eating, too!'

'Yes. I told you we breed butterflies and moths,' said Mr Gringle, and he opened the end of one of the muslin bags, so that the visitors could see the caterpillars better. 'These are the caterpillars of one kind of butterfly; they feed on this particular plant.'

The children gazed at scores of green caterpillars, marked with red and yellow spots, all eating greedily on the leaves of the twig enclosed there. Mr Gringle undid another of the muslin bags and showed them some huge caterpillars, each of them green, with purple stripes on the side and a curious black horn on the tail end.

'Privet hawk-moth caterpillars,' said Mr Gringle, and Julian and Dick nodded. They knew these big green caterpillars quite well.

'Why is the moth called privet *hawk*?' asked Anne. 'There are so many different hawk-moths, I know. I've often wondered why they are all called *hawk*.'

Mr Gringle beamed at Anne, evidently thinking that this was a quite intelligent question. 'Haven't you ever seen a hawk-moth flying?' he said. 'No? Well, it flies very strongly indeed. Oh, a most striking flight – like the flight of the *bird* called a hawk, you know.'

'You're not feeding the caterpillars on privet, though,' said George. 'But you *said* they were privet hawks.'

'There isn't any privet growing near here,' said Mr Gringle. 'So I give them elder – this is an elder bush which I planted in the glasshouse. They like it just as much.'

The butterfly farm was certainly interesting, and the children wandered about the glasshouse watching caterpillars of all kinds, admiring the lovely specimens of butterflies, and marvelling at the collection of curious-shaped chrysalides and cocoons that Mr Gringle kept carefully in boxes, waiting for the perfect insect, moth or butterfly, to emerge.

'Like magic,' he said in an awed voice, his eyes shining behind his glasses. 'Sometimes, you know, I feel like a magician myself – and my butterfly net is a wand!'

The children felt rather uncomfortable as he said this, waving his butterfly net to and fro like a wand. He really was rather an odd person.

'It's terribly hot in here,' said Julian suddenly. 'Let's get into the fresh air. I've had enough. Goodbye, Mr Gringle, and thank you!'

Out they all went and drew in deep breaths of fresh air. And then they heard a croaking voice behind them.

'Get out of here!' said the voice. 'Get out!'

CHAPTER SEVEN

Mrs Janes – a spider – and a pool

TIMMY GROWLED, and so did Binky. The children swung round and saw the old witch-like woman standing there, her wispy grey hair hanging over her face.

'What's the matter, Mrs – er – Mrs Janes?' said Julian, fortunately remembering the name Mr Gringle had told them. 'We're not doing any harm.'

'My son doesn't like strangers here,' said Mrs Janes, mumbling so much that the children could hardly understand what she was saying.

'But this place belongs to Mr Gringle surely, and his friend,' said Dick, puzzled.

'I tell you my son doesn't like strangers here,' mumbled the old woman again and shook her fist at them.

Timmy didn't like this, and growled. She at once pointed her finger at him and muttered a long string of strange-sounding words so that Anne shrank back, afraid. Really, Mrs Janes did look exactly like a witch – and sounded like one, too.

Timmy acted strangely. He put his tail down, stopped growling and crept close to George. She was most astonished.

'It looks as if she's trying to put a spell on old Tim,'

said Dick, half laughing, but that was too much for Anne and George.

Taking Timmy by the collar, George rushed off quickly with Anne following. The boys laughed. Binky ran after Timmy, and Toby spoke boldly to the funny old woman.

'Your son isn't even here – so what business is it of his to tell you to give orders to visitors?'

Tears suddenly began to pour down the old woman's face and she wrung her bony hands together. 'He'll hit me,' she wept. 'He'll twist my arm! Go away! Do go away! If he comes, he'll chase you off. He's a bad man, my son!'

'She's mad, poor old thing,' said Toby, feeling sorry for old Mrs Janes. 'Our cook often says so, though she's harmless enough. Her son's not too bad – he's quite handy at repairs, and we used to have him come to the farm to mend roofs and things like that. But he's not so good as he used to be. Come on – let's go. Mr Gringle's a bit peculiar, too, isn't he?'

They went off after the two girls, Toby still feeling uncomfortable and distressed.

'What's Mr Gringle's friend like – the one who helps him?' Julian asked.

'I don't know. I've never seen him,' said Toby. 'He's away mostly, doing the business side, I think – selling specimens of eggs, caterpillars and so on – and the perfect moths and butterflies too, of course.'

'I'd like to see that butterfly house again, but Mr Gringle gets on my nerves,' said Dick. 'Those brilliant eyes behind those thick glasses. You'd think that if they were as bright and piercing as that he wouldn't need to wear any glasses at all!'

'Hey, George – Anne!' shouted Julian. 'Wait for us – we're just coming.' They caught up with the girls and Julian grinned at George.

'You thought old Timmy was going to be changed into a black beetle or something, didn't you?' he said.

'No, of course not,' said George, going red. 'I just didn't like her very much – pointing her finger like that at Timmy. No wonder he growled.'

'You didn't hear what she said about her son,' said Dick. 'She began to cry like anything after you'd gone, and say that her son would beat her and twist her arm if we didn't go – and he's not even there!'

'She's mad,' said George. 'I don't want to go there again. What are we going to do now?'

'Go up to our camping place and have our lunch,' said Julian promptly. 'Come with us, Toby – or have you got jobs to do at the farm?'

'No. I've done them all,' said Toby. 'I'd love to have a meal with you up on the hill.'

It wasn't very long before they were back at their camping place. Everything was as they had left it – anoraks neatly under the gorse bush with the rugs and other little things – and the food in Anne's 'larder' waiting for them.

The meal was very hilarious, as Toby was in one of his silly moods, and produced some idiotic jokes. The most successful one was a large imitation spider with shaky legs, which, while Anne and George had gone to get the food, he hung by a thin nylon thread to a spray on the nearby gorse bush. Dick grinned broadly.

'Wait till Anne sees that!' he said. 'George always says

she doesn't mind spiders, but a big one like that is distinctly creepy.'

It certainly was. Anne didn't spot it until she was eating her strawberries, covered with some of the cream that Toby's mother had generously sent. Then she suddenly spied it, shaking slightly in the breeze, hanging by its thread just over George's head.

'Ooooooooh!' she squealed. 'Ooooh, George – be careful! There's a MONSTER spider just over your head!'

'What – is George scared of spiders?' cried Toby at once. 'Just like a girl!'

George glared at him. 'I don't mind them at all,' she said coldly.

'*George* – do move!' cried Anne, upsetting her strawberries in her anxiety. 'It's almost on your head, I tell you – its legs are wobbling as if they are going to settle on your hair. George, it's an ENORMOUS one! It might even be one of those tarantulas or something!'

The wind blew a little just then and the spider moved about on the thread most realistically. Even Dick was glad it wasn't alive!

George couldn't resist looking up, pretending to be quite unmoved – but when she saw the enormous creature just above her she shot straight out of her place and landed on Toby's legs, making him spill his strawberries and cream.

'Now, now, Georgina,' said the annoying Toby, picking up his strawberries. 'You said you didn't *mind* spiders. I'll remove it for you, and you can go back to your place.'

'No, no – don't touch it – ugh!' cried Anne. But Toby, putting on a very brave face, leant over and neatly took the spider off the gorse bush, still swinging by its thread. He swung it near to Anne, who scrambled up at once.

Then he made it 'walk' over Dick's knee, and Timmy came to investigate at once. Binky came too, and snapped at it, breaking the nylon thread that held it.

'Ass!' said Toby, giving him a tap. 'My beautiful spider – my spinner of webs – my tame catcher of flies!'

'What – is it a *tame* one?' said Anne in horror.

'More or less,' said Toby, and put it carefully into his pocket, grinning all over his round face.

'That's enough, Toby,' said Julian. 'Joke's finished.'

George stared at Toby, her face growing crimson. 'A joke? A JOKE! You wait till I pay you back, Toby! I don't call that a joke . . . I call it a mean trick. You knew Anne hated spiders.'

'Let's change the subject,' said Dick hastily. 'What are we going to do this afternoon?'

'I know what I'd *like* to do,' said Julian longingly. 'I'd like a bathe. It's so jolly hot. If we were at Kirrin I'd be in the sea all the afternoon.'

'I wish we *were* at Kirrin,' said George sulkily.

'Well – if you really do want a bathe, I can take you to a pool,' said Toby, anxious to get into everyone's good books again.

'A pool? Where?' said Dick eagerly.

'Well – see that airfield down there?' said Toby pointing. 'And see this spring here, where you get your water? It goes on and on running down the hill, joins two or three more little rivulets, and ends in a smashing pool not far from the airfield. Cold as ice it is, too. I've often bathed there.'

'It sounds jolly good,' said Julian, pleased. 'Well, we can't bathe immediately after a meal. We'll do the washing-up, and put the rest of the food away. Then we'll sit here and have a bit of a rest, and then go and find this pool.'

Everyone agreed to this and they all set to work. The girls hurried off to the little spring.

'If Toby has any more idiotic tricks like that I'll play a few on *him*!' said George. 'In fact I've a good mind to pull him under in the pool.'

'He's all right, George,' said Anne. 'He's just like that at school, Dick says. He must drive the masters mad!'

They soon joined the boys and had a short rest, while Timmy and Binky went off amiably together to do a little hunting – sniffing down holes and under bushes, looking very serious indeed. They came back immediately George whistled.

'We're going, Timmy,' said George. 'Here's your swimsuit, Dick, and yours, Julian. Good thing we brought them with us!'

'What about you, Toby? You haven't a swimsuit with you,' said Julian.

'We have to pass fairly near the farm,' said Toby. 'I'll

leave you when we're near there and get mine – it won't take more than five minutes if I run all the way back.'

They set off down the hill towards the airfield. Except for the plane they had heard that morning, they had heard and seen none. It seemed a very quiet airfield.

'Wait till they start experimenting with the new fighter planes my cousin told me about!' said Toby. 'You'll hear a noise then – they're so fast they break the sound barrier every time they go up!'

'Would your cousin let us look over the airfield one day?' asked Julian. 'I'd like to do that. Look – isn't that your farm, Toby? We've got here jolly quickly – but it's all downhill, of course.'

'Yes,' said Toby. 'Come on, Binky – race you home and back. Shan't be long, Julian! Keep straight ahead and walk towards that big pine tree you can see in the distance. I'll be with you by the time you're there.'

He raced off at top speed, while the others went on slowly towards the pine trees in the distance. It would be heavenly to bathe in a cool pool!

Toby was certainly a fast runner! Just before they reached the pine tree he came up behind them, his swimsuit over his shoulder, so out of breath that he could hardly speak!

'It's over there,' he panted. 'Look – the pool!'

And sure enough, there was the pool – deep blue, cool and as smooth as glass. Trees surrounded it on one side, and heather grew right down to the edge.

The five children went towards it gladly – but suddenly they came to a big notice, nailed to a tree:

KEEP OUT

DANGER

CROWN PROPERTY

'I say – what does *that* mean?' said Dick in dismay. 'We can't bathe after all!'

'Oh, take no notice of that,' said Toby. 'It doesn't mean a thing!'

But it did as they were very soon to find out!

CHAPTER EIGHT

A spot of trouble

'WHAT DO you mean by saying that the notice doesn't mean a thing?' said Julian. 'Why put it up, then?'

'Oh, there are notices like that all round the airfield,' said Toby airily. 'Telling you to KEEP OUT, there's DANGER. But there isn't. Only aeroplanes are here, no guns, no bombs, nothing. It's a jolly lonely place, too, tucked away at the foot of this hill.'

'Why don't you ask your cousin *why* they put up the notices?' asked Dick. 'There must be *some* reason!'

'I tell you those notices have been up for ages,' said Toby, sounding cross. 'Ages! They might have been some use at some time or other, but not now. We can bathe here and do what we like.'

'All right – but I hope you know what you're talking about,' said Julian. 'I must say I can't see any sense myself in putting notices here – there's no wire or fencing to keep anyone out.'

'Let's get into our bathing things, then,' said Dick. 'You girls can have that bush over there and we'll have this one. Buck up!'

They were soon changed into their swimsuits, and dived into the pool, which was surprisingly deep. It was also deliciously cool, and silky to the touch, just as the spring water had been. The two dogs leapt in gladly and swam vigorously round and round. The children splashed them, and Timmy began to bark excitedly.

'Shut up, Timmy!' said Toby at once.

'Why should he?' demanded George, swimming up.

'Well – someone at the airfield might hear him,' said Toby.

'You said it didn't matter us being here!' said George. 'Look out for yourself!' She dived underwater and got hold of Toby's legs, pulling him down. He yelled and kicked and spluttered, but George was strong and she gave him a very, very good ducking! He came up purple in the face.

'I said I'd pay you back for the spider!' yelled George, and swam strongly away. Toby swam after her, and she led him a fine dance round the pool, for she was a splendid swimmer. The others laughed at the contest.

'I back old George,' said Dick. 'She'd outswim most boys. Well, she's put Toby in his place all right. He won't be so free with spiders and silly jokes for a while!'

Timmy began to bark again when he saw Toby chasing George, and Binky joined in.

'Shut up, Binky!' shouted Toby, 'I tell you *stop barking*!'

Before Binky had obeyed, something happened. A very loud voice came across the pool.

'What's all this! You're trespassing on Crown property. Didn't you see the notice?'

KEEP OUT
DANGER

A SPOT OF TROUBLE

The dogs stopped barking and the five children looked round to see who was shouting. Their heads bobbed on the surface of the water as they gazed about to find the shouter.

It was a man in Air Force uniform, a big man, burly and red-faced.

'What's the matter?' called Julian, swimming towards him. 'We're only bathing. We're not doing any harm.'

'Didn't you see the notice?' shouted the man, pointing over to it.

'Yes. But we couldn't see much danger here,' called back Julian, wishing now that he hadn't believed Toby.

'You come on out!' roared the man. 'All of you. Come on.'

They all waded out of the cool pond, Anne feeling scared. The dogs splashed out, too, and stood eyeing the man grimly. He calmed down a little when he saw them.

'Those your dogs I heard barking? Well, now, I see you're all kids – though one of you's big enough to know better!' and he pointed to Julian. 'I thought maybe you were day-trippers – thinking you could come wandering on the airfield and not get into trouble!'

'Day-trippers don't come here,' said Toby, squeezing the water out of his hair.

'Nor do sensible children,' retorted the man. 'I've had trouble from you before, haven't I? Yes. Didn't you come walking round the hangars bold as brass one day? And that dog with you, too?'

'I only went to see my cousin, Flight-Lieutenant Thomas,' said Toby. 'I wasn't doing any harm – I wasn't spying. I tell you I only went to see my cousin!'

'Well, I shall report you to him,' said the man, 'and tell him to give you a proper ticking off. We've strict instructions to warn off anyone – there's notices everywhere.'

'Is something hush-hush going on then?' said Toby with a sudden grin.

'As if I'd tell you if there was!' said the man in disgust. 'Far as I can see, there's nothing much doing here – dull as ditch-water this place – and as far as I'm concerned I'd welcome a *horde* of day-trippers – it would liven up the place no end. But orders are orders, as you very well know.'

Julian thought it was about time that he should join in. The man was only doing his duty, and Toby was an ass to have said that the notices meant nothing.

'Well, we apologise for trespassing,' he said in his clear, pleasant voice. 'We shan't bathe here again, I promise you. Sorry to have made you come all this way to warn us off.'

The RAF guard looked at Julian with respect.

There was something about the boy that reassured people, and the man now felt quite sure that it was all Toby's fault. He smiled.

'That's all right,' he said. 'Sorry to cut your bathe short this hot day. And – er – if that rogue of a boy here' – he pointed to Toby – 'if he cares to ask Flight-Lieutenant Thomas for permission to bathe in this pool at certain hours, it's OK by me. I shan't come running then when I hear dogs barking and a lot of shouting if I know you're allowed here at certain hours.'

'Thanks,' said Julian. 'But anyway we're only here for a few days.'

'So long,' said the man and walked off smartly.

'Well,' said Toby, quite unashamed, 'what did he want to come messing about here for, spoiling our bathe? He *said* there wasn't anything secret going on, so why . . .'

'Oh shut up!' said Dick. 'You heard what he said about orders being orders? He's not a silly schoolboy trying to be clever and getting out of doing his work – yes, like *you* do at school, Toby, and a good many of the others! He's a man in uniform. You'd better grow up a bit, young Toby.'

'I agree,' said Julian. 'So don't let's hear any more about it. You slipped up, Toby, and that's all there is to it. Now let's dry ourselves and go to the farm and ask your nice kind mother if she'll let us have some more food to take back to our camp with us. I'm as hungry as a hunter after our bathe.'

Toby was rather subdued after all this. He glanced at George to see if she was gloating over his ticking off, but George was never one to exult over anyone's downfall, and Toby felt relieved.

'*Shall* I ask my cousin if he'll get permission for us to bathe in the pool?' he said as they went away from the water, dry and dressed again.

'I think not,' said Julian. 'But I'd like to meet your cousin some time all the same.'

'He *might* take us up in a plane,' said Toby hopefully, his spirits rising at the thought. 'Oh, look there – here's that little wretch Benny again – *and* the pigling!'

Benny panted up, carrying the little pig. 'You look like Tom, Tom the Piper's Son,' said Julian, ruffling the yellow curls. 'He stole a pig and ran away, carrying it under his arm.'

'But this is my own pig,' said Benny, surprised. 'I didn't steal him. I came to find you, because my mother says come to tea.'

'You *have* got a nice mother!' said Anne, taking the small boy's hand. 'Why don't you put the pig down? He must be so heavy.'

'He runned away again,' said Benny severely. 'So I carried him.'

'Put a collar on his neck, with a lead,' suggested Dick.

'He hasn't got a neck,' said Benny, and indeed the pigling was so plump that his head joined his body without any neck at all.

The little procession made its way to the farm, and the pigling at once ran in front, squealing. It seemed surprised and delighted to find it was home again. Timmy pricked up his ears when it squealed. He thought that it must be in pain, and he was worried! He ran beside the little creature, trying to nuzzle it.

Mrs Thomas saw them through the window. 'Come along in!' she said. 'I thought you might like to have tea here again today, because I've a visitor you'd like to meet!'

'Who is it?' cried Toby, running indoors. 'Oh! it's you, Cousin Jeff. Hey, Julian, Dick – look, it's my Cousin Jeff from the airfield – Flight-Lieutenant Thomas! The one I told you about! Cousin Jeff, meet my friends – Julian, Dick, Anne, Georgina – er, I mean George – and Timmy!'

A tall, good-looking young man stood up, smiling. The Five gazed at him, liking him very much indeed. They all envied Toby at that moment. No wonder he had boasted about him so much!

'Hallo to you!' said Cousin Jeff. 'Glad to see you all. 'Hey – look at this dog!'

And well might everyone look, for Timmy had marched

straight up to him and then held up a paw. 'Wuff!' he said, which, of course, meant 'Shake'!

'How do you do?' said Cousin Jeff solemnly, and shook paws with Timmy at once.

'Timmy's *never* done that before!' said George, astonished. 'Well – what a surprising thing! He must like you *very* much!'

CHAPTER NINE

Cousin Jeff

'I LIKE dogs,' said Jeff, and patted Timmy on the head. 'This is a fine one – as smart as can be, too, isn't he?'

George nodded, pleased. She loved anyone to praise Timmy. 'Yes, he's very clever. He's been in heaps of adventures with us. He can be very fierce if he thinks anyone is going to attack us. Oh, look – he wants to shake hands *again*! Isn't he funny!'

Jeff shook paws once more and then Timmy settled down beside him, almost as if he considered himself to be his dog. George didn't mind. She liked Cousin Jeff as much as Timmy did!

'Tell us about your job,' begged Dick. 'It's such a strange airfield, the one you're at – no fencing round it, hardly any planes, nobody about the field! Do you do much flying?'

'Not much at the moment,' said Cousin Jeff. 'But don't be misled by the fact that there's no fencing round the airfield! Believe me, the commanding officer knows immediately if any stranger comes into the district, and – er – well, let us say that extra precautions are taken.'

'*Really?*' said George. 'Do you mean to say, for instance, that your commanding officer knows *we've* arrived?'

'You bet he does,' said Jeff, laughing. 'You've probably been given the once-over already, though you didn't know it. I expect someone has been detailed to find out who you are and why you're here, and you may even have been watched for a few hours – though you had no idea of it.'

This was rather a creepy thought. Watched? How? By whom? And where did they hide to watch? Dick asked Jeff these questions, but the young airman shook his head.

'Sorry. Can't answer,' he said. 'But you needn't worry, *you're* all right. Maybe my aunt here has said a few words about you – you never know!'

Mrs Thomas smiled, but said nothing. She beckoned to Anne and George to help her to bring in the tea – just as good a one as they had had before. The girls bustled about, setting out cups and saucers, while the boys talked to Cousin Jeff and asked him eager questions about planes and flying and how this was done and that.

'I suppose you wouldn't take us up some time, Cousin Jeff, would you?' asked Toby at last.

'I don't think I'd be allowed to,' said Jeff. 'In fact I don't think I can even ask. You see, the planes there are pretty special – you can't go joy-riding in them and . . .'

'Of course we see,' said Julian hurriedly, afraid of embarrassing the friendly young airman. 'We wouldn't *dream* of bothering you. When are you going up next? Can we watch you from our camping place?'

'Yes, I should think you could see me with field-glasses,' said Jeff, considering. 'I'll tell you the number of my plane – it's painted underneath it, of course, so you'll know it's me if you see it circling over the hill. But I shan't do any stunts, I'm afraid – like coming down low to you, or anything like that. Only silly beginners do that.'

'We'll look out for you,' said Dick, quite envious of Toby for having such a fine young cousin. 'I don't expect you'll see us – but we'll wave anyway!'

Tea was now ready and they all drew up their chairs. Benny wandered in with his pigling under his arm, and set it down in the cat's basket, where it stayed quite peacefully, falling asleep and making tiny, grunting snores.

'Does the cat mind?' asked George, astonished, looking at the basket.

'Not a bit,' said Mrs Thomas. 'It had to put up with two goslings last year in its basket – and something the year before . . .'

'A lamb,' said Toby.

'Oh yes – and old Tabby – that's the cat – didn't seem to worry at all,' said Mrs Thomas, pouring out creamy milk for everyone, even Cousin Jeff. 'I once found her curled up round the goslings one morning, purring loudly.'

'Good old Tabby!' said Toby. 'Where is she? I'd like to see what she thinks of Curly. She couldn't cuddle *him* – he takes up nearly all the basket, he's so plump.'

Tea was a merry meal, with Toby playing the fool, putting a spoonful of sifted sugar on the side of Anne's plate to eat with her crisp radishes instead of salt, and offering the salt to George to eat with her strawberries.

Both girls were listening so intently to Cousin Jeff that they didn't even notice what Toby had done, and he almost fell off his chair with laughing when he saw their faces. Salt with strawberries – ugh! Sugar and radishes – ugh!

'Funny boy, aren't you?' said George, annoyed at being tricked. 'You wait!' But Toby was too wily to be tricked and George had to give it up. Anyway, she couldn't bother with Toby when Cousin Jeff was talking about planes, his eyes shining with pleasure. Flying was his great love, and in listening to him all three boys there made up their minds to take it up as soon as ever they could!

Benny didn't listen much. He was more interested in animals than in planes. He ate his tea solemnly and watched his pigling in the cat's basket, occasionally leaning over to tap his mother's hand when he wanted to speak to her.

'Curly runned away again,' he told her solemnly. 'Right up to the horse-pond.'

'I thought I had told you not to go there,' said his mother. 'You fell in last time.'

'But Curly *runned* there,' said Benny, his big eyes looking very wide and innocent. 'I had to go after him, didn't I? He's my pigling.'

'Well, I shall scold Curly if he takes you to places you've been told not to go to,' said his mother. 'I can't let him grow up disobedient, can I?'

This needed thinking over, and Benny ate his tea with a serious face, ignoring the others. Anne looked at him several times, delighted with the solemn little boy and his funny ways. How nice it would be to have a small brother like that!

'Well, I must be off,' said Jeff when the meal was finished. 'Thanks most awfully for a super tea, Aunt Sarah – but then your teas always *are* super! I was jolly lucky to be stationed here so near to Billycock Farm! Well, so long, everyone! So long, Timmy!'

Everyone went with him to the gate, Timmy and Binky as well, and Benny awoke his little pig and carried him to the gate too, squealing and kicking. They all watched the tall, sturdy young airman striding away round the hill.

'Do you like him?' asked Toby proudly. 'Isn't he super? I'm awfully proud of him. He's supposed to be one of the cleverest flying men in the kingdom – did you know?'

'No, we didn't,' said Dick. 'But I'm not surprised. He's got eyes as keen as a hawk's, and he's heart and soul in his work! How lucky for you that he is stationed so near!'

'We'd better get back to our camp when we've helped your mother to clear away and wash-up,' said Julian, anxious not to outstay his welcome at the farm. 'Toby, can you pack us up a bit more food in case we don't see you tomorrow?'

'Right,' said Toby, and went off, whistling.

Benny appeared again with Curly running round his feet.

'Hallo!' said Dick with a grin. 'Is that pigling of yours running away again?'

Benny grinned back. 'If he runned away to your camp, would you be cross?' he asked, looking most innocently up at Dick.

'He mustn't do that,' said Dick seriously, guessing what was in the little boy's mind; he meant to go to find the camp himself, and then say that it was Curly who had 'runned away' there! 'You see, you might lose your way if you went so far.'

Benny said no more, but wandered off with his comical pet running in front of him. The boys went to find Toby to see if they could help him to pack food into a basket. 'We must pay his bill, too,' said Julian, feeling for his purse. 'It was a good idea of his to save up the money to buy his mother a present. She really is a darling.'

Soon the Five were on their way back to their camp again. Toby was left behind to do his usual jobs of collecting the eggs, washing them and grading them into sizes for the market. 'I'll be up tomorrow!' he called after them. 'We'll plan something good to do – maybe visit the caves if you like!'

The four children went up the steep slope of Billycock Hill, talking, while Timmy ranged in front, sniffing everywhere as usual. And then suddenly a large butterfly sailed through the air, and came to rest on a flower of a blossoming elder bush, just in front of George – a butterfly that none of them had ever seen before.

'Look at that! What is it?' cried Anne in delight. 'Oh, what a beauty! Julian, what is it?'

'I've absolutely no idea!' said Julian, astonished. 'It may be an unusual fritillary, though it's early in the year for those. That butterfly man – what's his name now? – Mr Gringle – said that this hill was famous for rare butterflies, and I imagine this is pretty uncommon. It *is* a beauty, isn't it?'

They watched the butterfly opening and shutting its magnificent wings on the white blossom. 'We ought to try and catch it,' said Dick. 'I'm sure that Mr Gringle would be thrilled. It might lay eggs for him and start a whole breed of uncommon butterflies in this country.'

'I've got a very thin hanky,' said Anne. 'I think I can catch it without harming its wings – and we'll put it into the little box that Toby filled with sugar lumps for us. Get it and empty it, Dick.'

In half a minute the butterfly was inside the box, quite unharmed, for Anne had been very deft in catching it.

'What a magnificent creature!' said Dick, shutting the box. 'Now come on – we'll give Mr Gringle a surprise!'

'What about that witch woman – you know, Mrs Janes, who looks exactly like a witch?' said Anne. 'I don't want to meet her again.'

'I'll tell her to jump on her broomstick and fly away!' said Julian with a laugh. 'Don't be silly, Anne – she can't hurt you.'

They went off round the hill, taking the little path down

which Mr Gringle had guided them. Soon they saw the reflection of the sun glittering on the glasshouses. Anne and George hesitated as they came near, and Timmy stopped, too, his tail down.

'Well, stay there, then,' said Dick impatiently. 'Ju and I won't be long!' And off went the two boys together, while George and Anne waited in the distance.

'I hope they *won't* be long!' said Anne, worried. 'I don't know *why* I feel creepy here, but I do!'

CHAPTER TEN

Butterfly farm again

DICK AND Julian went to the glasshouses where the butterflies and caterpillars lived. They peered through the panes, but could see nobody there.

'Mr Gringle must be in the cottage,' said Julian. 'Let's stand outside and call – he'll come out then. I don't much like Mrs Janes.'

So they stood outside the tumbledown cottage and shouted: 'Mr Gringle! Mr Gringle!'

Nobody answered. No Mr Gringle came out, but somebody pulled aside the corner of a window curtain upstairs and peeped out. The boys shouted again, waving at the window.

'Mr Gringle! We've got a rare butterfly for you!'

The window opened and old Mrs Janes looked out, seeming more witch-like than ever.

'Mr Gringle's away!' she mumbled.

'What about his friend Mr Brent – the one we didn't see?' shouted Dick. 'Is he in?'

The old woman stared at them, mumbled something else, and then disappeared very suddenly indeed from the window.

Dick looked at Julian in surprise.

'Why did she go so suddenly? Almost as if somebody pulled her roughly away? Julian, I don't like it.'

'Why? Do you think that son of hers is here – the one she said was cruel to her?' asked Julian, who was puzzled, too.

'I don't know,' said Dick. 'Let's snoop round a bit. Perhaps Mr Gringle *is* somewhere about, whatever old Mrs Janes says!'

They went round the corner of the house and peered into a shed. Nobody there. Then they heard footsteps and turned round hurriedly. A man was coming towards them, small and thin, with a pinched-looking face, and dark glasses. He carried a butterfly net, and nodded at the two boys.

'My friend Gringle is away,' he said. 'Can I do anything for you?'

'Oh – you're Mr Brent then?' said Dick. 'Look – we've found a rare butterfly. That's why we came!'

He undid the box in which the butterfly was peacefully resting, having found a tiny grain of sugar to feed on. Mr Brent looked at it through his dark glasses.

'Hm! Hm!' he said, peering closely at it. 'Yes, very fine indeed. I'll buy it off you for fifty pence.'

'Oh, you can have it for nothing,' said Dick. 'What is it?'

'Can't say without examining it closely,' said Mr Brent, and took the box and put the lid on again.

'But isn't it some kind of fritillary?' asked Julian. 'We thought it was.'

'Quite likely,' said Mr Brent, and suddenly produced a fifty pence piece and shoved it at Dick. 'Here you are. Much obliged. I'll tell Mr Gringle you came.'

He turned abruptly and went off, his butterfly net still over his shoulder.

Dick stared at the fifty pence piece in his hand, then at the receding back of Mr Brent.

'What a peculiar fellow!' he said. 'Well, I must say that he and Mr Gringle are a pair! What are we to do with this money, Julian? I don't want it!'

'Let's see if we can give it to that poor Mrs Janes,' said Julian, always generous. 'She looks as if they paid her only about ten pence a week, poor soul.'

They went round to the front of the house, hoping to find the old woman, and after a little hesitation knocked at the door. It opened and she stood there, mumbling as before.

'You go away! My son's coming back. He'll hit me. He doesn't like strangers. You go away, I say!'

'All right,' said Dick. 'Look – here's something for you,' and he pressed the fifty pence into her clawlike hand. She looked at it as if she couldn't believe her eyes, and then, amazingly quickly she slipped the money into one of her broken-down shoes. When she stood up her eyes were full of tears.

'You're kind,' she whispered, and gave them a little push. 'Yes, you're kind. Keep away from here. My son's a bad man. Keep away!'

The boys went off silently, not knowing what to make of it. After all, Toby knew the son – they had employed him at the farm. Why did the old woman keep saying he was bad and cruel? She must be at least a little mad to talk like that!

'It must be a strange household,' said Julian as they went to join the waiting girls. 'Two butterfly men, both rather peculiar. One old witch-like woman, *very* peculiar. And a son who seems to terrify her out of her wits! I vote we don't go there again.'

'So do I,' said Dick. 'Hallo, you two – did we keep you waiting for long?'

'You did rather,' said Anne. 'We were just about to

send Timmy to look for you! We thought you might have been turned into mice, or something!'

The boys told the two girls about Mr Brent and the fifty pence and old Mrs Janes. 'A funny household altogether,' said Dick. 'We think we'll give it a miss now, however many rare butterflies we spot! I'm pretty certain that the one we found was a kind of fritillary, aren't you, Julian?'

'Yes, I was surprised Mr Brent didn't say so,' said Julian. 'I have a feeling that Mr Gringle is the expert of the two. Mr Brent probably does the donkey-work – sees to the caterpillars and so on.'

They came to their camp at last, and Timmy at once went to the 'larder'. But Anne shook her head. 'No, Tim – it's not nearly supper-time. Bad luck!'

'What shall we do?' asked Dick, flinging himself down on the heather. 'It's another heavenly evening!'

'Yes – but I don't much like the look of the sky over to the west tonight,' said Julian. 'See those clouds there coming up slowly against the wind? It looks like rain tomorrow to me!'

'Blow!' said George. 'The weather might have lasted for just one week! Whatever shall we do if it pours? Sit in our tents all day, I suppose!'

'Cheer up – we could go and see the caves,' said Dick. 'I know what we'll do now! We'll get out our portable radio and turn it on. If there's some decent music, it will sound glorious up here!'

'All right. But for goodness' sake have it on softly,' said

Anne. 'I *loathe* people who take radios out into the country with them, and switch them on loudly, so that it spoils the peace and quiet for everyone else. I could go and kick their radios to pieces!'

'Gracious, Anne – you do sound fierce!' said George, looking at her cousin in surprise.

'You don't know our quiet sister Anne quite as well as we do, George,' said Julian, with a twinkle in his eyes. 'She can be really fierce if she thinks anyone is spoiling things for others. I had to stop her once from going up to scold people at a picnic – they actually had a gramophone going full-pelt, in spite of the angry looks from people all round. I do believe she meant to take off the gramophone record and break it over somebody's head!'

'Oh, *Julian*! How can you say such a thing!' said Anne. 'I did feel like it – but I didn't do it.'

'All right, young Anne!' said Julian affectionately and patted her head. Both he and Dick thought the world of their quiet, kind little sister and looked after her well. She smiled at them.

'Well – let's have some music, then,' she said. 'There's the Pastoral Symphony on sometime this evening, I know, because I made a note of it. It would sound beautiful out here in this lovely countryside with that view spreading for miles in front of us. But softly, *please*.'

Julian fetched the little radio set and took it out of its waterproof case. He switched on, and a voice came loudly from the set. Julian lowered the volume to make it softer.

'It's the seven o'clock news,' he said. 'We'll hear it, shall we?'

But it was almost the end of the news, and the voice soon stopped to give way to an announcer. Yes – it was going to be the Pastoral Symphony now. Soon the first notes came softly from the little radio, and it seemed to set the countryside around to music. The four settled down in the heather to listen, lying half-propped up to watch the changing colours of the view in front of them as the sun sank lower.

The bank of cloud on the horizon was higher now, and the sun would soon slip behind it, for it was coming up fast. What a pity!

And then, cutting across the music, came another sound – the sound of an aeroplane.

R-r-r-r-r-r-r! R-r-r-r-r-r! R-r-r-r-r-r!

It sounded so very loud that Dick and Julian leapt to their feet, and Timmy began to bark loudly.

'Where is it?' said Dick, puzzled. 'It sounds so jolly near. I wonder if it's Cousin Jeff's!'

'There it is – coming up over the back of the hill!' said Julian, and as he spoke a small aeroplane appeared over the brow of the hill, and circled once before it flew down to the airfield.

The four children could plainly see the number painted underneath. '5–6–9,' began Julian, and Dick gave a shout.

'It's Jeff's plane! It is – that's his number! Wave, everybody, wave!'

So they all waved madly, though they felt sure that Jeff wouldn't see them, tucked away in their camp on the hillside. They watched the plane fly down to the airfield, circle round, and land neatly on the runway. It came to a stop.

Julian looked through his glasses and saw a small figure leap from the plane. 'I bet it's Jeff,' he said. 'Gosh – I do wish *I* had a plane to fly over the hills and far away!'

CHAPTER ELEVEN

A stormy night

THE FIVE soon began to prepare for their evening meal and Timmy trotted about pretending to help, always hopeful of being allowed to carry a loaf of bread or piece of cold ham in his mouth. But he was never lucky!

As they sat eating their meal, Julian glanced uneasily at the western sky again. 'The rain's certainly coming,' he said. 'That cloud has covered half the sky now, and swallowed up the evening sun. I think we ought to put up the tents.'

'Blow! I suppose we ought,' said George.

'*And* we'd better do it quickly,' said Dick. 'I distinctly felt a nasty cold wind just then – the first really cold air since we came here. We shall certainly want to roll up in our rugs tonight!'

'Well, let's get the things out from under the old gorse bush,' said Julian. 'It won't take long to put up the tents if we all get to work.'

In three-quarters of an hour the tents were up, set nicely in the shelter of the giant gorse bush. 'A good, business-like job,' said Dick, pleased. 'It would take a hurricane to blow the tents away – we'll be quite all right here. Let's pull up some more heather and pile it in the tents. We shall want our rugs to wrap ourselves in, not to lie on tonight, so we might as well make our beds as soft as possible.'

They piled heather into the tents, spread their anoraks there, too, and then looked at the sky. Yes, there was no doubt about it – there was rain coming and probably a storm! Still, it might clear tomorrow, and be as fine as ever. If it wasn't they would go and explore the caves that Toby had told them about.

It was now almost dark and the children decided that they would all get into one tent and have the radio on again. They called Timmy, but he preferred to be outside.

They set the radio going – but almost immediately Timmy began to bark. George switched off at once.

'That's the bark he gives when somebody is coming,' she said. 'I wonder who it is?'

'Toby, to say we'd better go to the farm for the night,' guessed Dick.

'Mr Gringle hunting for moths!' said Anne with a giggle.

'Old Mrs Janes looking for things to make spells with!' said George.

Everyone laughed. 'Idiot!' said Dick. 'Though I must say this looks a night for witches!'

Timmy went on barking, and Julian put his head out of the tent. 'What's up, Tim?' he said. 'Who's coming?'

'Wuff, wuff,' said Timmy, not turning his head to Julian, but seeming to watch something or someone in the half-light.

'It may be a hedgehog he's seen,' said George from inside the tent. 'He always barks at them because he knows he can't pick them up.'

'Well – maybe you're right,' said Julian. 'But I think I'll just go out and get Timmy to take me to whatever it is he's barking at. I feel I'd like to know. He obviously hears or sees something!'

He slid out of the tent opening and went to Timmy. 'Come on, Tim,' he said. 'Who is it? What's upsetting you?'

Timmy wagged his tail and ran in front of Julian. He obviously had no doubts about where he was going. Julian followed him, stumbling over the heather and wishing he had brought his torch, for it was now half-dark.

Timmy ran some way down the hill towards the airfield, then rounded a clump of birch trees and stopped. He barked loudly again. Julian saw a dark shadow moving there and called out.

'Who's there? Who is it?'

'It's only me – Mr Brent,' said an annoyed voice, and Julian caught sight of a long stick with a shadowy net on the end. 'I've come out to examine our honey-traps before the rain comes and washes away the moths feeding there.'

'Oh,' said Julian. 'I might have thought of that when Timmy barked. Is Mr Gringle about, too?'

'Yes – so if your dog barks again you'll know it's only us,' said Mr Brent. 'We're often prowling around at night – this is just as good a hill for moths at night as it is for

butterflies by day. Can't you stop that dog barking at me? Really, he's very badly trained.'

'Shut up, Tim,' ordered Julian, and Timmy obediently closed his mouth, but still stood stiffly, staring at the man in the darkness.

'I'm going on to our next honey-trap,' said the man. 'So you can take that noisy dog back to wherever you are camping.' Mr Brent began to move away, flashing a torch in front of him.

'We're just up the hill,' said Julian. 'About a hundred yards. Oh – you've got a torch, I see. I wish I'd brought mine.'

The man said nothing more, but went slowly on his way, the beam of his torch growing fainter. Julian began to climb back up the hill to the tents, but in the growing darkness it was not easy! He missed his way and went much too far to the right. Timmy was puzzled and went to him, tugging gently at his sleeve.

'Am I going wrong?' said Julian. 'Blow! I'd soon get lost on this lonely hillside. Dick! George! Anne! Give a shout, will you? I don't know where I am.'

But he had wandered so far off the path that the three didn't hear him – and Timmy had to guide him for a good way before he saw the torches of the others flashing up above. He felt most relieved. He had no wish to be caught in a heavy rainstorm on the exposed side of Billycock Hill!

'Is that you, Julian?' called Anne's anxious voice. 'What a long time you've been! Did you get lost?'

'Almost!' said Julian. 'Like an idiot I went without my torch – but Timmy here knew the way all right. I'm glad I'm back – it's just beginning to rain!'

'Who was Tim barking at?' asked George.

'One of the butterfly men – Mr Brent, the one Dick and I saw today,' said Julian. 'I just caught the glint of his dark glasses in the half-light, and saw the butterfly net he carried. He said Mr Gringle was out, too.'

'But whatever for, with a storm coming?' marvelled Anne. 'All the moths would be well in hiding.'

'They've come out to examine their moth-traps, as they call them,' said Julian. 'They spread sticky stuff like honey or something round the trunks of trees – and the moths fly down to it by the score. Then they come along and collect any they want to take back.'

'I see – and I suppose Mr Brent was afraid the rain might wash away the clinging moths,' said Dick. 'Well, they'll both be caught in the storm, that's certain. Listen to the rain pelting down on the tent now!'

Timmy squeezed into the tent, not liking the sting of the heavy raindrops. He sat down by George and Anne.

'You do take up a lot of room in a small tent, Tim,' said George. 'Can't you make yourself a bit smaller?'

Timmy couldn't. He was a big dog, and rather a sprawly one. He put his wet head on George's knee and heaved a heavy sigh. George patted him.

'Humbug!' she said. 'What are you sighing about? Because you've finished your bone? Because it's raining and you can't go and sit and bark at anything moving on the hill?'

'What shall we do now?' said Julian, setting his torch on the radio set, so that it more or less lit up the tent. 'There's nothing on the radio we want to hear.'

'I've got a pack of cards somewhere,' said George, much to everybody's joy, and she found them and got them out. 'Let's have a game of some sort.'

It was rather difficult in the small tent, with Timmy sometimes getting up just when all the cards were neatly dealt, and upsetting the piles. The storm grew fiercer and the rain tried its best to lash its way through the canvas of the little tent.

Then Timmy began to bark again, startling everyone very much. He climbed over legs and knees and poked his head out of the tent opening, barking loudly.

'Good gracious – you almost gave me a heart attack!' said Dick, pulling him back. 'You'll get soaked out there, Tim. Come back – it's only those mad mothmen out there picking moths off rain-soaked honey-traps. Don't worry about *them*. They're probably enjoying themselves enormously.'

But Timmy simply would NOT stop barking, and even growled when Julian tried to drag him into the tent.

'Whatever's up with him?' said Julian, bewildered. 'Oh, stop it, Timmy! You're deafening us!'

'Something's upsetting him – something unusual,' said George. 'Listen – was that a yell?'

Everyone listened, but the rain was pelting down so hard that it was impossible to hear anything but the slashing rain and the wind.

'Well, we can't do much about it, whatever it is that's upsetting Timmy,' said Dick. 'We can't possibly go wandering about in this storm – we'd get soaked through and probably lost!'

Timmy was still barking, and George grew cross. 'Timmy! Stop! Do you hear me? I won't have it.'

It was so seldom that George was angry with him that Timmy turned in surprise. George pounced at his collar and dragged him forcibly into the tent. 'Now – be QUIET!' she commanded. 'Whatever it is, we can't do anything about it!'

Just then another noise rose above the howling of the wind and the torrents of rain, and the Five pricked up their ears at once, sitting absolutely still.

'R-r-r-r-r-r-r-r! R-r-r-r-r-r-r-r-r-r! R-R-R-R-R-R-R-R-R-R-R! R-R-R-R-R-R-R-R-R-R!'

They all looked round at one another. 'Aeroplanes!' said Dick. '*Aeroplanes!* In this weather, too. Whatever *is* going on?'

CHAPTER TWELVE

What happened in Billycock Caves

THE LITTLE company in the tent were amazed. Why should aeroplanes take off from the airfield in the middle of a stormy night?

'For experiments in storms, perhaps?' said Dick. 'No – that would be rather unnecessary.'

'Perhaps they were aeroplanes *landing* there, not leaving,' suggested Anne.

'Possibly – perhaps seeking the shelter of the airfield when they were caught in this storm,' said Dick. But Julian shook his head.

'No,' he said. 'This airfield is too far off the ordinary air-routes – nobody would bother about it; it's so small for one thing – more a little experimental station than anything else. Any aeroplane in difficulties could easily go to a first-class airfield for shelter or help.'

'I wonder if Jeff went up in one of the two we heard,' said George.

Anne yawned. 'What about bedding down?' she said. 'This tent is so hot and stuffy that I feel half-asleep.'

'Yes – it's getting late,' said Julian, looking at his watch. 'You two girls and Timmy can have this tent – it will save you going out into the rain. Fasten the flap after we've gone – and yell if you want anything.'

'Right. Goodnight, Ju, goodnight, Dick,' said the girls, and the boys scrambled out into the rain. Anne fastened the flap of the tent, and wrapped her rug round her. She burrowed into her heathery bed and made herself comfortable. George did the same.

'Goodnight,' said Anne, sleepily. 'Keep Tim on your side. I can't bear him on my legs, he's so heavy.'

The Five slept soundly and awoke the next morning to a dismal scene of rain and dark clouds.

'*How* disappointing!' said Dick, peering out of his tent. 'We ought to have listened to the weather forecast to see if it would clear today. What's the time, Julian?'

'Just gone eight,' said Julian. 'My word, we *are* sleepy these days! Well, it's not raining so very hard now – let's see if the girls are awake, and put on our anoraks and go and wash at the spring.'

They all had breakfast – not quite so merry as usual, because it was a bit of a crowd in the tent and not nearly so much fun as having it in the sunshine. Still, the day might clear, and then they could go down to see Toby at the farm.

'I suppose we'd better go and explore those caves this morning,' said Dick, after breakfast. 'There's nothing else to do, and I refuse to play cards all morning.'

'We *all* refuse!' said George. 'Let's put on our anoraks and see if we can find the caves.'

'We can look at the map,' said Julian. 'It's a large-scale one. There must be a road or lane to them – they are quite well-known. They're probably round the hill – a bit lower down.'

'Well, never mind – we'll see if we can find them, and if we can't it won't matter. We shall have been for a walk!' said Dick.

They set off in a fine drizzle, walking through the damp heather, Timmy leaping in front.

'Everyone got torches?' said Dick suddenly. 'I've got mine. We'll need them in the caves!'

Yes, everyone had a torch – except Timmy of course, and he, as Anne pointed out, had eyes that were far better for seeing in the dark than any torch could ever be!

They made their way down the hill and then veered off to the north side – and came suddenly upon a wide rather chalky path, where the heather had been cut well back.

'This rather looks as if it led somewhere,' said Julian, stopping.

'It might lead to an old chalk quarry,' said Dick, kicking some loose white lumps of chalk. 'Like the one near Kirrin.'

'Well, let's follow it up and see,' said George, and they went along it, kicking the lumps of chalk as they went. They rounded a corner and saw a notice.

To Billycock Caves

Warning

Keep only to the roped ways.

Beware of losing your way in the unroped tunnels.

'This sounds good,' said Julian. 'Let's see – what did Toby tell us about the caves?'

'They're thousands of years old – they've got stalagmites and stalactites,' said George.

'Oh – I know what those are,' said Anne. 'They look like icicles hanging from the roof – while below, on the floor of the cave, other icicles seem to grow upwards to meet them!'

'Yes – the roof ones are stalac*tites* and the ground ones are stalag*mites*,' said Dick.

'I simply *never* can remember which is which,' said Anne.

'It's easy!' said Julian. 'The stalac*tite* icicles have to hold *tight* to the roof – and the stalag*mite* ones *might* some day join with the ones above them!'

The others laughed.

'I shall never forget which are which now,' said Anne.

The path they were following altered as they came near to the caves, and lost its chalky look. Just in front of the entrance the way was properly paved, and was no longer rough. The entrance was only about six feet high, and had over it a white board with two words painted very large in black.

BILLYCOCK CAVES

The warning they had read on the first notice they had come to was repeated on another one just inside the entrance. 'Read it, Tim,' said George, seeing him looking at it. 'And keep close to us!'

They went right in, and had to switch on their torches at once. Timmy was amazed to see the walls around him glittering suddenly in the light of the four torches. He began to bark, and the noise echoed all around in a very weird manner.

Timmy didn't like it, and he pressed close to George. She laughed. 'Come on, silly. These are only caves. You've been in plenty in your life, Timmy! Goodness, don't they feel cold! I'm glad of my anorak!'

They passed through one or two small and ordinary caves and then came to a magnificent one, full of what looked like gleaming icicles. Some hung down from the roof, others rose up from the ground. In some places the one below had reached to the one hanging down, so that they had joined, making it look as if the cave was held up by great shining pillars.

'Oh!' said Anne, catching her breath. 'What a wonderful sight! How they gleam and shine!'

'It reminds me of cathedrals I have seen,' said Julian, looking up at the roof of the cave. 'I don't know why. All these finely wrought pillars . . . come along, let's go into the next cave.'

The next one was smaller, but contained some splendid coloured 'icicles' that shone and gleamed in the light of the torches. 'It's like a cave in Fairyland,' said Anne. 'Full of rainbow colours!'

The following cave had no colour, but was of a dazzling white, walls, roof, floor and pillars. So many stalactites and stalagmites had joined that they almost formed a snow-white screen through which the children peered – only to see even more of the strange 'icicles'.

They came to a threefold forking of the ways. The centre one was roped, but the other two tunnels were not. The children looked down the unroped tunnels, stretching away so dark and quiet, and shivered. How awful to go down one and lose the way, never to be found again, perhaps!

'Let's go down the roped way,' said George. 'Just to see where it leads to – more caves, probably.'

Timmy ran sniffing down one of the other ways, and George called him, 'Tim! You'll get lost! Come back.'

But Timmy didn't come back. He ran off into the darkness and the others felt cross. 'Blow him,' said Dick. 'What's he after? TIM! TIM!' The echoes took up the last word and sent it repeatedly up and down the passage.

Timmy barked in answer, and at once the place was full of weird barking, echoing everywhere and making Anne put her fingers to her ears.

'Woof-oof-oof-oof!' said the echoes, sounding as if a gang of dogs were barking madly in the caves. Then Timmy appeared in the light of their torches, looking extremely surprised at the enormous noise he had created with his barking.

'I shall put you on the lead, Timmy,' scolded George.

'Keep to heel now. Surely you understand what that word means after all these years?'

Timmy did. He kept faithfully to heel as the little company went along a narrow, roped tunnel and came out into a succession of dazzling caves, all linked together by little passages or tunnels. They kept only to those that were roped. Many of them were not, and the Five longed to see where they led to, but were sensible enough not to try.

And then, as they were examining what looked like a frozen pool, which reflected the snowy roof above like a mirror, a curious noise came to their ears. They straightened themselves and listened.

It was a whistling sound, high-pitched and shrill, that filled the cave, and filled their eardrums, too, until they felt like bursting. It rose high, then died down – then rose again till the children were forced to put their hands to their heads – and died away.

Timmy couldn't bear it. He barked frantically and ran round and round like a mad thing. And then the second noise began – a howling! A howling that seemed to be tossed to and fro, and grew louder as the echoes threw it about from cave to cave! Anne clutched Dick, terrified.

'What is it?' she said. 'Quick, let's go!' And, led by an extremely scared Timmy, the Five raced pell-mell out of Billycock Caves as if a hundred dogs were after them!

CHAPTER THIRTEEN

A dreadful shock

THE FIVE stood panting outside the entrance of the caves, feeling decidedly sheepish at having run away from a noise.

'Whew!' said Julian, mopping his forehead. 'That was decidedly weird. That whistling – it got inside my head. It was like a – like a police whistle gone mad or something. As for the howling . . . well.'

'It was horrible,' said Anne, looking quite pale. 'Like wild animals. I'm not going into those caves again for anything. Let's get back to the camp.'

They walked soberly down the chalk-strewn path that led away from the caves and made their way back to their camp. The rain had stopped now, and the clouds were beginning to break.

The Five sat down inside a tent, and discussed the matter. 'We'll ask Toby if it's usual for noises like that to be heard,' said Dick. 'I wonder anyone ever visits the cave if it *is* infested with horrible whistles and screeches like that.'

'All the same, we were a bit cowardly,' said Julian, now feeling rather ashamed of himself.

'Well, go back and do a bit of howling yourself,'

suggested George. 'It may frighten the howler as much as his howling scared *you*.'

'Nothing doing,' said Julian promptly. 'I'm not going in for any howling matches.' He burrowed down under the rug for his field-glasses and slung them round his neck.

'I'm going to have a squint at the airfield,' he said. 'Just to see if I can spot Cousin Jeff.' He put the glasses to his eyes and focused them on the airfield below them. He gave a sudden exclamation.

'There's quite a lot going on at the airfield this morning!' he said in surprise. 'Dozens of people there! I wonder what's up. There are quite a lot of planes, too – they must all have arrived this morning!'

Each of the others took a turn at looking through the glasses. Yes – Julian was right. There was certainly something going on at the airfield today. Men hurried about, and then came the noise of yet another aeroplane, which zoomed neatly down to the runway.

'Gosh – *another* plane!' said Dick. 'Where did all the others come from? We never heard them.'

'They must have arrived while we were in the caves,' said Julian. 'I wish we could ask Toby's Cousin Jeff what all the excitement is about.'

'We could go down to the farm after our lunch and see if he has heard anything,' suggested Anne, and the others agreed.

'Thank goodness the sun's coming out again,' said George, as a shaft of warm sunlight burst out from behind a cloud, and the sun sailed into a patch of blue sky. 'The heather will soon dry now. Let's have the news on – we may just catch the weather forecast. I don't want to carry my anorak about if it's going to clear up.'

They switched on the little radio set – but they had missed the weather news. 'Blow!' said Dick and raised his hand to switch off – and then he heard two words that stopped him. They were 'Billycock Hill'! He left his hand suspended in the air and listened, full of surprise. The announcer's voice came clearly to the four.

'The aeroplanes stolen from Billycock Hill airfield were two valuable ones, into which had been incorporated new devices,' said the voice from the radio. 'It is possible that they were stolen because of these. We regret that it appears that two of our best pilots flew them away – Flight-Lieutenant Jeffrey Thomas and Flight-Lieutenant Ray Wells. No news has been received of either plane. Both disappeared during a storm over Billycock Hill during the night.'

There was a pause, and then the announcer went on to another item of news. Dick switched off the radio and looked blankly at the others. No one had a word to say at first.

'To think that *Jeff* could do a thing like that – Jeff a traitor – flying off with a plane of ours to sell to an enemy!' said Julian at last, voicing the thought of all the others.

'We heard the planes go!' said Dick. 'Two of them. Gosh – we ought to go to the police and tell what we know. Not that it's much. But, I say – fancy JEFF doing that! I liked him so much.'

'So did I,' said Anne, turning her head away.

'So did Timmy,' said George. 'And he hardly ever makes a mistake in anyone.'

'What will poor Toby do?' said Dick. 'He thought the world of Jeff.'

Timmy suddenly ran off a few yards and began barking – a welcoming bark this time. Julian looked to see who was coming. It was Toby!

He came up to them and sat down beside them. He looked pale and shocked, though he tried to smile at them.

'I've got awful news,' he said in a funny, croaking voice.

'We know,' said Dick. 'We've just heard it on the radio. Oh, Toby – fancy – *Jeff*!'

To everyone's horror Toby's face crumpled up and tears poured down his cheeks. He made no attempt to wipe them away; indeed, he hardly seemed to know that they were there. Nobody knew what to do – except Timmy. Dear old Tim scrambled over Julian and most sympathetically licked Toby's wet face, whining as he did so. Toby put his arm round the dog's neck and began to speak.

'It *wasn't* Jeff! Jeff couldn't have done such a thing. He couldn't! You know he couldn't, don't you?' He turned quite fiercely on the others as he spoke.

'*I* can't believe that he did,' said Julian. 'He seemed to me to be absolutely straight and trustworthy, even though I only met him that once.'

'He was – well – a sort of hero to me,' said Toby, beginning to mop his cheeks with his hanky, and staring in surprise to see it so damp. 'Gosh, I'm a sissy to go on like this! But when the military police came to our farm this morning to ask questions about Jeff – he's my dad's nephew, you know – I couldn't believe my ears. I was so furious with one idiot that I punched him – and Mother sent me out of the room.'

'I suppose both Jeff and the other fellow have definitely *gone*?' asked Julian. 'No other pilots are missing, are they?'

'No, I asked that,' said Toby dismally. 'Everyone answered roll-call at the camp this morning except Jeff and Ray. Ray is Jeff's best friend, you know.'

'It looks bad,' said Dick, after a long pause.

'But it's *not true* that Jeff's a traitor!' cried Toby, up in arms again. 'Are you suggesting that he is?'

'No, I'm not,' said Dick. 'Don't be an ass. I don't . . .' Then he stopped as Timmy ran off and barked fiercely. *Now* who was coming?

A deep voice called to Timmy. 'Down, boy, down! Where are your friends?'

Julian scrambled up and saw two military policemen standing facing the excited Timmy. 'Here, Tim,' called Julian. 'It's all right. Friends!'

Timmy ran to him and the two burly men came up. 'You the children camping on this hill?' asked the first one. 'Well, we want to ask you a few questions about last night. You were here then, weren't you?'

'Yes. We know what you've come about, too,' said Julian. 'We'll tell you all we know – but we're pretty certain that Flight-Lieutenant Thomas hadn't anything to do with it.'

'That's as may be,' said the man. 'Well, sit down, all of you, and we'll have a little talk.'

Soon they were sitting down in the heather, while Julian told all they knew, which wasn't much – just the sound of the two aeroplanes flying off together.

'And you heard nothing suspicious last night – nothing at all?' asked the first man.

'Nothing,' said Julian.

'Nobody about at all, I suppose?' asked the second man,

looking up from his notebook in which he had been writing.

'Oh – well, yes – there were people about,' said Julian, suddenly remembering the butterfly man, Mr Brent, who had said that he and Mr Gringle were out looking at their moth-traps.

The first policeman asked some rapid questions and Julian and the others told them what little they knew – though Julian knew the most, of course.

'You're sure it was Mr Brent you saw?' asked the policeman.

'Well – he *said* he was,' said Julian. 'And he carried a butterfly net on his shoulder – and he wore the same dark glasses I saw him wearing earlier. Of course, it was pretty dark – but I honestly *think* it was Mr Brent. I didn't see or hear Mr Gringle. Mr Brent said he was some way off. They're both mad on moth and butterfly hunting.'

'I see,' said the policeman, and the second one shut his notebook. 'Thanks very much. I think we'll just go and pay a call on these – er – what do you call them – butterfly men? Where do they hang out?'

The children offered to guide them on their way, and the whole company went with the two burly men almost to the butterfly farm.

'Well, thanks a lot,' said the first policeman as they came near the tumbledown cottage. 'We'll go on alone, now. You get back to your camp.'

'Will you send us word as soon as *you* know it wasn't

my Cousin Jeff?' asked Toby, forlornly. 'He'll be getting in touch with you, I know, as soon as he hears what he's suspected of.'

'It's bad luck on you, son – he's your cousin, isn't he?' said the big policeman kindly. 'But you'll have to make up your mind to it – it was Jeff Thomas all right that flew off in one of those aeroplanes last night. There isn't a doubt of it!'

CHAPTER FOURTEEN

Mr Gringle is annoyed

THE MILITARY police went off down the hill to the butterfly farm, and the five children stood disconsolately watching them, with Timmy staring, too, tail well down. He didn't quite know what had happened but he was sure it was something dreadful . . .

'Well – it's no good waiting about here, I suppose,' said Julian. 'I bet the police won't get anything useful out of the butterfly men – *they* wouldn't have noticed anything when they were out last night, except their precious moths!'

They were just turning away when they heard someone screaming in a high voice, and they stopped to listen in surprise. 'It must be old Mrs Janes,' said Dick. 'What's up with her?'

'We'd better see,' said Julian, and he and the others, with Timmy at their heels, went quickly down to the cottage. They heard the voices of the two policemen as they came near.

'Now, now, old lady – don't take on so!' one was saying in a kindly voice. 'We've only come to ask a few questions.'

'Go away, go away!' screamed the old woman, and actually battered at the men with her little bony hands. 'Why are you here? Go away, I tell you!'

'Now listen, Ma – don't take on so,' said the other man patiently. 'We want to talk to Mr Gringle and Mr Brent – are they here?'

'Who? Who did you say? Oh, them! They're out with their nets,' mumbled the old woman. 'I'm all alone here, and I'm scared of strangers. You go away.'

'Listen,' said one policeman. 'Were Mr Gringle and Mr Brent out on the hills last night?'

'I'm in my bed at night,' she answered. 'How would *I* know? You go away and leave me in peace.'

The policemen looked at one another, and shook their heads. It was clearly quite useless to find out anything from this frightened old woman.

'Well, we'll go, Ma,' said one, patting her shoulder gently. 'Sorry we've scared you – there's nothing to be afraid of.'

They turned away and came back up the slope of the hill, seeing the children standing silently there. 'We heard old Mrs Janes screaming,' said Julian. 'So we came to see what was happening.'

'The butterfly men, as you call them, are out with their nets,' said one policeman. 'A funny life, I must say – catching insects and looking after their eggs and caterpillars. Well – I don't suppose they know anything about last night's job. Not that there's anything to know! Two pilots flew off with the planes, we know who they were – and that's that!'

'Well, one was NOT my Cousin Jeff,' said Toby,

fiercely. The men shrugged their shoulders and went off together.

The five children went off up the hill again, very silent. 'I think we'd better have something to eat,' said Julian at last. 'We've had no lunch – and it's long past our usual time. Toby, stay and have some with us.'

'I couldn't eat a thing,' said Toby. 'Not a thing!'

'Let's get out what we've got,' said Julian, and the girls and Timmy went to the little 'larder'. Nobody really felt like eating – but when the food was there, in front of them, they found that they were quite hungry – except poor Toby, who sat forlorn and pale-faced, trying to chew through a sandwich made for him by Anne, but not making a very good job of it!

Timmy began to bark in the middle of the meal, and everyone looked to see who was coming now. Julian thought he saw a movement some way down the hill, and took his field-glasses and put them to his eyes.

'I *think* it's Mr Gringle,' he said. 'I can see his net too. He's out butterflying, I suppose.'

'Let's shout to him,' said Dick. 'We can tell him why the police went to call at his cottage this morning, when he wasn't there. He'll never get any sense out of old Mrs Janes.'

Julian cooeed, and there came an answering call. 'He's coming up,' said Dick. Timmy ran to meet him, and soon the man was just below them, panting as he made his way up the steep slope.

'I hoped I'd see you,' he said. 'I want you to look out for some special moths for me – another day-flying one like the six-spot burnet you saw the other day. It's the cinnabar moth – it's got rich crimson underwings, and – and—'

'Yes – I know that one,' said Julian. 'We'll look out for it. We just wanted to tell you that two military policemen went to your cottage a little while ago to ask you some questions about last night – and as we're sure old Mrs Janes won't be able to explain anything to you, we thought we'd better tell you ourselves.'

Mr Gringle looked absolutely blank and bewildered. 'But – but why on earth should military policemen come to our cottage?' he said at last.

'For nothing much,' said Julian. 'Only to ask you if you saw anything suspicious when you were out looking at your moth-traps last night – you see, two aeroplanes were—'

Mr Gringle interrupted in a most surprised voice. 'But – but, dear boy, I wasn't out at all last night! It wouldn't have been a bit of good looking for moths anywhere, on our moth-traps or anywhere else, on a night like that.'

'Well,' said Julian, also surprised, 'I saw your friend Mr Brent, and he *said* you were both out looking at your moth-traps.'

Mr Gringle stared at Julian as if he were mad, and his mouth fell open in amazement. 'Mr *Brent*!' he said at last. 'But Peter – that's Mr Brent – was at home with *me*! We were busy writing up our notes together.'

There was a silence after this surprising statement. Julian frowned. What was all this? Was Mr Gringle trying to hide the fact that he and his friend had been out on the hills the night before?

'Well – I certainly saw Mr Brent,' said Julian at last. 'It was very dark, I admit – but I'm sure I saw his butterfly net – and his dark glasses.'

'He doesn't *wear* dark glasses,' said Mr Gringle, still more astonished. 'What *is* this tale? Is it a joke of some sort? If you can't talk better sense than this, I'm going.'

'Wait!' said Dick, something else occurring to him. 'You say that Mr Brent doesn't wear dark glasses – then who was the man that took the butterfly from us yesterday evening about six o'clock and gave us fifty pence? He *said* he was Mr Brent, your friend!'

'This is all nonsense!' said Mr Gringle, getting up angrily. 'Wasting my time on a poor joke of this kind! Brent doesn't wear dark glasses, I tell you – and he wasn't at home at six o'clock yesterday – we'd been to buy some tackle in the next town. He was with *me*, not at the cottage. You couldn't possibly have seen him! What do you mean by all this nonsense – dark glasses, fifty pence for a butterfly – and seeing Brent on the hillside last night when he didn't stir out of the house!'

He was now standing up, looking very fierce, his brilliant eyes flashing behind his thick glasses. 'Well,' said Julian, 'all this is extremely puzzling, and . . .'

'Puzzling! You're nothing but a pack of nitwitted, ill-mannered children!' suddenly roared Mr Gringle, quite losing his temper. Timmy gave a warning growl, and stood up – he didn't allow anyone to rave at his friends!

Mr Gringle went off angrily, trampling down the heather as if he were trampling down the children. They heard him muttering to himself as he went off. They looked at one another in really great surprise.

'Well – I simply don't know what to make of all this!' said Julian helplessly. 'Was I dreaming last night? No – I *did* see that fellow – half-see him, anyway – and he *did* say he was Mr Brent, and that Gringle was somewhere near. But – if he wasn't Brent, who was he? And what was he doing on a stormy night, hunting moths?'

Nobody could make even a guess. Toby spoke first.

'Perhaps the man you saw was mixed up in the stealing of those aeroplanes – you never know?'

'Impossible, Toby!' said Julian. 'That's *too* far-fetched. I can't say that I understand it at all – but honestly, he didn't seem like a man who could steal an aeroplane!'

'Who was the man that gave us the fifty pence then, if he wasn't Brent?' said Dick, puzzled.

'Could it have been Mrs Janes's son, pretending he was Brent – just for a silly joke?' said George.

'What was he like?' asked Toby at once. 'I know Will Janes – I told you he's often been to our farm. We don't have him now because he drinks so much and he isn't reliable any more. What was this man Brent like – I'd soon know if he was Will Janes pretending to be someone else!'

'He was small and thin, with dark glasses,' began Dick – and Toby interrupted him at once.

'Then it wasn't Will Janes! He's tall and burly – with a thick neck and, anyway, he doesn't wear dark glasses – or any glasses at all!'

'Then who in the world was it? And *why* did he pretend to be Brent, Gringle's friend?' wondered Dick. Everyone frowned and puzzled over the whole thing – but nobody could think of a sensible reason for anyone wanting to pretend to be Mr Brent!

'Well – for goodness' sake, let's get on with our meal,' said George at last. 'We stopped in the middle of it – and the rest is still waiting for us. Have another ham sandwich, Julian?'

They all munched in silence, thinking hard. Toby sighed. 'I don't really feel that this mix-up with the butterfly men and somebody else, whoever he is, has anything to do with the stealing of the aeroplanes. I wish it had!'

'All the same – it wants looking into,' said Dick seriously. 'And what's more – I vote we keep our eyes and ears open. *Something's* going on at the butterfly farm!'

CHAPTER FIFTEEN

More news – and a night trip

THE FIVE spent most of the afternoon talking about the mystery of the man who had pretended to be Mr Brent. It really was difficult to understand why anyone should do such a foolish thing, especially as it could be so easily found out.

'I can only think there's a madman about who has got it into his head that he is Mr Brent!' said Dick at last. 'No wonder he didn't seem to recognise that butterfly we took him!'

'Do you know what I think would be a good idea?' suddenly said George. 'Why don't we slip down to the butterfly farm tonight, when it's getting dark, and see if the false Mr Brent is there, *and* the real one – whom we've never seen, by the way – *and* Mr Gringle?'

'Hm – yes – quite an idea,' said Julian, seriously. 'But only Dick and I will go – not you or Anne.'

'I'll come, too,' said Toby.

'Right,' said Julian. 'But we'll have to be jolly careful – because if there *is* something funny going on down there, we don't want to be caught. It wouldn't be at all pleasant, I fear!'

'Take Timmy with you,' said George at once.

'No. He might bark or something,' said Dick. 'We'll be all right, George. Gracious – we've had enough adventures by now to teach us how to go about things like this! Ha – I shall look forward to tonight!'

Everyone suddenly felt much more cheerful, even Toby. He managed a very small smile, and stood up to brush the crumbs off his jersey.

'I'm going now,' he said. 'I've a lot of farm jobs to do this afternoon – I'll meet you at the big oak tree behind the butterfly farm – did you notice it?'

'Yes – an enormous one,' said Julian. 'Right. Be there at – say – ten o'clock. No, eleven – it will be dark by then, or almost.'

'So long!' said Toby and plunged down the hill, accompanied for a little way by Timmy.

'Well – I feel much better now we've made a definite plan,' said Dick. 'My goodness, it's half past five already! *Don't* suggest tea, George – we had our lunch so late!'

'I wasn't going to,' said George. 'We'll miss it out and have a really good supper later on. And don't let's forget to listen to the news at six o'clock – there *might* be something about Jeff and his friend Ray – and the aeroplanes.'

So, just before six o'clock, they switched on the little radio set, and listened intently for the news. It came at last – and almost the first piece was about the stolen aeroplanes. The children listened, holding their breath, bending close to the set.

'The two aeroplanes stolen from Billycock airfield last night, flown away by Flight-Lieutenant Jeffrey Thomas and Flight-Lieutenant Ray Wells, have been found. Both planes apparently crashed into the sea, but were seen, and there is a chance of their being salvaged. The pilots were not found, and are presumed to have been drowned. At Edinburgh this afternoon there was a grand rally of . . .'

Julian switched off the news and looked at the others soberly. 'Well – that's that! Crashed, both of them! That was because of the storm, I suppose. Well, at least no enemy will be able to get hold of the new devices that were incorporated in the planes.'

'But – that means Toby's cousin is drowned – or killed,' said Anne, her face very white.

'Yes. But remember, if he flew away in that plane, he was a traitor,' said Dick gravely.

'But Toby's cousin didn't *seem* like a traitor,' said George. 'He seemed so – well, so *very* honest, and I can't say anything finer than that. I feel as if I shall never trust my judgment of anyone again. I liked him so very much.'

'So did I,' said Dick, frowning. 'Well, these things happen – but I just wish it hadn't been Toby's cousin. He was such a hero to him. I don't feel as if Toby will ever be quite the same after this – it's something so absolutely *beastly*!'

Nobody said anything for a little while. They were all profoundly shocked – not only by the idea of Cousin Jeff being a traitor, but also by the news that he had been drowned. It seemed such a horrible end to come to that bright-eyed smiling young airman they had joked with only the other day.

'Do you think we ought to pack up and go home?' said Anne. 'I mean – won't it be awkward for the Thomases to have us hanging round when they must feel shocked and unhappy?'

'No, we don't need to bother them much at the farm,' said Julian. 'And I don't think we can desert old Toby at the moment. It will help him to have friends around, you know.'

'Yes. You're right,' said Dick. 'This is the sort of time to have good friends – poor old Toby. He'll be knocked out by this last piece of news.'

'Will he be waiting for you at the old oak tree tonight, do you think?' asked George.

'Don't know,' said Julian. 'It doesn't matter if he's not there, anyway – Dick and I can do all the snooping round that is necessary. And it will take our minds off this shock a bit – to try and solve the mystery down at the butterfly farm!'

They went for a walk round the hill, with Timmy leaping over the heather in delight. He couldn't understand the lack of laughter and the unusual solemnity shown by his four friends, and he was pleased to be able to forget any troubles and sniff for rabbits.

They had their suppers at eight o'clock and then turned on the radio to listen to a programme. 'We'll hear the news at nine,' said Dick. 'Just in *case* there might be any more.'

But the nine o'clock news only repeated what had been said about the two planes in the six o'clock broadcast, and not a word more. Dick switched off and gazed down at the airfield below.

There were still quite a lot of planes there, though some of them had taken off and flown away during the day. Julian trained his field-glasses on the field.

'Not so many men scurrying about now,' he said. 'Things are quietening down. My word – what a shock it must have been for everyone there last night, to hear the planes revved up, and then flown away! They *must* have been amazed!'

'Maybe they didn't hear them go, in the storm,' said George.

'They must have,' said Julian. '*We* heard them up here. Well, what about you girls turning in? Dick and I don't want to, in case we fall off to sleep – we've got to slip away about half past ten or we shan't be down at the oak tree at eleven.'

'I wish you'd take Timmy with you,' said George uneasily. 'I don't *like* the butterfly farm – or the witch-like old woman there – or the man you met with dark glasses who wasn't Mr Brent, or the son you haven't seen.'

'Don't be an ass, George,' said Julian. 'We shall be back by twelve, I expect – and Timmy is sure to bark in welcome, so you'll know we're safe.'

The girls wouldn't go to their tent to sleep, so they all sat and talked, and watched the sun slip behind the clear horizon. The weather was now perfect again, and there wasn't a cloud in the sky. It was difficult to imagine the sweeping rain and howling wind of last night's storm.

'Well,' said Julian at last, looking at his watch. 'Time we went. Timmy, look after the girls as usual.'

'Woof,' said Timmy, understanding perfectly.

'And you look after *your*selves,' said Anne. 'We'll come down a little way with you – it's such a lovely evening.'

They all set off together, and the girls went halfway to the butterfly farm and then turned back with Timmy. 'Well, Tim – mind you bark at twelve, when they come back,' said Anne. 'Though somehow I think that both George and I will still be awake!'

The two boys went on down the hill and round to the right across towards the butterfly farm. It was almost dark now, though the June night was very clear and bright. 'Better be careful we're not seen,' muttered Julian. 'It's such a clear night.'

They made their way to the big old oak tree that stood at the back of the butterfly farm. Toby was not there – but in about two minutes they heard a slight rustling noise, and saw Toby, panting a little, as if he had been hurrying. Then he was close beside them.

'Sorry I'm a bit late,' he whispered. 'I say – did you hear the six o'clock news?'

'Yes – we were awfully sorry about it,' said Julian.

'Well – as I still don't believe that Cousin Jeff stole the aeroplanes with Ray Wells, but that somebody else did, I wasn't any more upset than before,' said Toby. 'If Jeff didn't steal the plane, he wasn't in it when it crashed, so he's not drowned. See?'

'Yes. I see,' said Julian, glad that Toby had taken the news in that way, but convinced himself that there wasn't really much hope.

'What are your plans?' whispered Toby. 'There are lights in the cottage windows – and I don't think any curtains are pulled. We could go and peep into each one and see exactly who is there!'

'Good idea,' said Julian. 'Come on – and, for goodness'

sake, don't make a noise. Single file, of course. I'll lead the way.'

And silently and slowly they went round the oak tree and down to the tumbledown cottage. What would they see there, when they looked through those lit windows?

CHAPTER SIXTEEN

Looking through windows

The three tiptoed quietly up to the cottage. 'Don't go too near when you look in,' whispered Julian. 'Keep a little distance away. We shall be able to see who is in the rooms, but they mustn't be able to see us outside. I sincerely hope they won't!'

'Look in the downstairs rooms,' said Dick. 'See, that's the kitchen window over there. Old Mrs Janes may be there, if she's still up.'

They crept to the uncurtained window. The room was lit by only a candle, and was full of shadows. The boys gazed in.

Old Mrs Janes *was* there, sitting up in a brown rocking-chair, clad in a dirty dressing-gown. She rocked herself to and fro, and although the boys could not see her face, they sensed that the old woman was frightened and unhappy. Her head was sunk on her chest, and when she put her wispy hair back from her face, her hand shook.

'She's no witch, poor old thing!' whispered Dick, feeling quite sad to see her rocking to and fro all by herself so late at night. 'She's just a poor frightened old woman.'

'Why is she up so late?' wondered Julian. 'She must be waiting for someone.'

'Yes. She might be. We'd better look out then,' said Toby at once, looking behind him as if he expected to see someone creeping up.

'Now let's go round to the front,' said Dick. So they

tiptoed there, and saw another lit window – much more brightly lit than the kitchen window had been. They kept a little way from the pane, afraid of being seen. They looked in and saw two men there, sitting at a table, poring over some papers.

'Mr Gringle!' said Julian, in a low voice. 'No doubt about that – and the other one must be his friend, Mr Brent, I suppose. Certainly he isn't wearing dark glasses, as that man was we gave the butterfly to and who gave us fifty pence. He isn't a *bit* like him!'

They all looked intently at the friend. He was a perfectly ordinary man, with a small moustache, dark hair and a rather big nose. Not in the least like the 'Mr Brent' they had seen the day before.

'What are they doing?' whispered Toby.

'It looks as if they're making lists of something – probably making out bills for their customers,' said Julian. 'Anyway – I must say they look perfectly ordinary sitting there, doing a perfectly ordinary job. I think Mr Gringle was speaking the truth when he said that it wasn't Mr Brent who gave us the fifty pence and it certainly wasn't him either that I saw on the hillside last night with a butterfly net.'

'Then who *was* it?' asked Dick, pulling the others right away from the window, in order to talk more easily. 'And why did he carry the butterfly net and tell that lie about moth-traps? Why was he on the hill, the night the planes were stolen?'

'Yes – why *was* he? I'd like to ask him that!' said Toby in too loud a voice. The others nudged him at once, and he spoke more softly. 'Something funny was going on last night – something people don't know anything about. I'd like to find that phony Mr Brent you met on the hillside, Julian!'

'Well, maybe we shall,' said Julian. 'Now – any other window lit? Yes – one up there, under the roof. Who's there, I wonder?'

'Perhaps it's Mrs Janes's son,' said Dick. 'It would be just like him to take one of the three bedrooms and make her sleep downstairs in the old rocking-chair! I expect the other two little rooms up there are used by the butterfly men.'

'How can we see into the lit room?' wondered Toby. 'Look – if we got up in that tree there, we'd see in.'

'There's an easier way!' said Julian, switching his torch on and off very quickly, giving the others just half a second to see a ladder leaning against a nearby wood-shed.

'Good – yes, that would be much easier,' said Dick. 'But we'll have to be jolly quiet. Whoever is in there would come to the window at once if he so much as heard the top of the ladder grating against the window-ledge!'

'Well, we'll manage it all right,' said Julian. 'The window isn't very high, and the ladder isn't very heavy. Between us we can place it very gently against the wall without disturbing anyone!'

The ladder was certainly quite light. The boys found no

difficulty in carrying it slowly and carefully across to the cottage. They placed it against the wall without a sound.

'I'll go up,' whispered Julian. 'Hold the ladder steady – and for goodness' sake keep a lookout! Give me a signal if you hear anything at all, because I don't want to be trapped at the top of the ladder!'

The others held the sides as he climbed the rather rickety rungs. He came to the lit window and very cautiously and slowly lifted his head until he could see right into the room.

It was lit by a candle, a very small and untidy room, poorly furnished. A man sat on the bed there, a big hulking man, with broad shoulders and a neck like a bull. Julian gazed at him – yes, that must be Mrs Janes's son, who, she said, was so unkind to her. Julian remembered the old mumbling voice saying that her son was cruel. 'He hits me. He twists my arm!' Yes, the man on the bed could be a nasty bully, no doubt about that.

He was reading a newspaper close to the candle.

As Julian looked at him, he pulled out a big watch from his pocket and stared at it, muttering something that Julian couldn't hear. He stood up, and the boy was so afraid that he might come to the window, that he slithered down the ladder as quickly as possible.

'The son's in there,' he whispered to the others. 'I was afraid he was coming to the window to look out; that's why I slid down so quickly. Blow! I've got a splinter in the palm of my hand doing that! Toby – could you creep

up to the top in a minute or two and look in – just to make sure I'm right, and that it *is* Will Janes, the old woman's son?'

Toby went up the ladder as soon as they were certain that Will Janes was not going to look out. He came down almost at once.

'Yes – that's Will – but, my word, he *has* changed!' whispered Toby. 'He looks a brute now – and yet he was a kind decent fellow not so long ago. Mother said he'd fallen in with some bad men, and had taken to drinking – so I suppose he's quite different now.'

'He looked at his watch as if he was expecting someone,' said Julian. 'I wonder – now, I wonder – if the man who paraded about the hillside last night with a net is coming here tonight? I must say I'd like to get a good look at him. He can't be up to any good.'

'Well – let's hide somewhere and wait,' suggested Toby. 'Nobody knows I've slipped out to be with you, so I shan't be missed. Anyway, Mother wouldn't mind if she knew I was on a night trip with you two!'

'We'll hide in that barn over there,' said Julian, and, on tiptoe again, they crossed to an old ruined barn, whose roof was partly off, and whose walls were falling in. It smelt dirty and there seemed no clean place to sit in, but at last Julian pulled out some dusty sacks and laid them in a corner and they sat there waiting in the dark.

'Pooh!' said Dick. 'What a horrible smell in here – old rotting potatoes, or something. I wish we'd chosen somewhere else.'

'Sh!' said Julian suddenly, giving him a nudge that made him jump. 'I can hear something.'

They all sat silent and listened. They could certainly hear something – yes – quiet footsteps, very quiet – made by rubber-soled shoes. The soft sounds passed by the barn, and they could no longer hear them. Then came a soft, low whistle.

Julian stood up and looked through the broken barn window. 'I think there are two men standing below Will Janes's bedroom,' he whispered. 'They must be the men he was waiting for. He'll be coming down. I hope to goodness they don't come into this barn to talk!'

This was a horrible thought, but there was no chance of

going anywhere else, because at that moment the front door opened and Will Janes came out. Julian, still looking through the broken pane, could see him dimly outlined in the light that came from Mr Gringle's front window.

The three men went off very quietly round the cottage. 'Come on,' said Julian. 'Let's shadow them. We might hear something to explain what's up.'

'What's the time?' asked Dick. 'I hope the girls won't start worrying about us. It must be gone twelve by now.'

'Yes. It is,' said Julian, looking at the luminous hands of his watch. 'It can't be helped. They'll guess we're on to something!'

They crept after the three men, who went to a clump of trees on the other side of the glasshouses. There they began to talk, but in such low tones that the three boys could hear nothing but the murmur of the voices.

Then one man raised his voice. It was Will Janes – Toby recognised it at once and told the others. 'It's Will. He's furious about something. He always loses his temper when he thinks people have treated him badly in any way – and it sounds as if he thinks those two men have.'

The two men tried to quiet him, but he would not be pacified. 'I want my money!' the boys heard him say. 'I helped you, didn't I, I hid you here, didn't I, till the job was done. Then give me my money!'

His voice rose almost to a shout, and the two men with him grew frightened. Exactly what happened next the boys never knew, but quite suddenly there was the sound of a

blow and a fall – then another blow and a fall – Will Janes laughed. It was not a nice laugh.

In a few seconds there came an anxious voice from the window of the room where Mr Gringle and his friend were at work. 'Who's there? What's happening?'

CRASH! That was the sound of breaking glass! Will Janes had picked up a big stone and flung it at the nearby glasshouse. It made the three boys almost jump out of their skins.

'It's all right! I came out to see who was prowling about!' shouted Will Janes. 'And whoever it was has broken some of the glass in your butterfly house. I've been out here shouting, trying to catch him.'

He came blundering towards the house – and then, as luck would have it, his torch picked out the three crouching boys. He gave a yell!

'Who's this? Here they are, kids who've been trying to smash the glass! Catch them – that's right – I've got two of them – you catch the third!'

CHAPTER SEVENTEEN

Quite a lot happens

THINGS THEN happened so quickly that, to their utter amazement, the three boys found themselves captives quite unable to escape.

Big Will Janes had hold of both Dick and Toby – and he was so strong, and held them in such a vice-like grip, one in each hand, that it was hopeless to try to get away.

Julian had run straight into Mr Gringle and Mr Brent, and the men had captured him between them. They were very angry.

'What do you mean by coming here and snooping around, smashing our glasshouses!' yelled Mr Gringle, shaking Julian in his rage. 'We shall lose all our butterflies through that broken pane!'

'Let me go. We didn't break your glass,' shouted Julian.

'He did! I saw him!' shouted Will Janes.

'You didn't!' cried Toby. 'Let me go, Will. I'm Toby Thomas, from Billycock Farm. You let me go or my father will have something to say!'

'Oho – so it's Toby Thomas, is it?' said Will in a sneering voice. 'Toby Thomas, whose father won't employ Will Janes now because he turns his nose up at him. You wait till I tell the police tomorrow what I've caught you doing – I'll say you're the kids that have been taking our hens!'

Will dragged the angry boys over to a shed, calling out to the other two men. 'Bring them here. Chuck them in and we'll lock the door and let them cool off till tomorrow morning!'

Julian struggled valiantly against the two men, but short of kicking them viciously there was nothing he could do to escape – and he didn't really want to harm them. It was all a mistake!

And then – oh, joy – there came a sound that made Julian's heart leap – the bark of a dog!

'Timmy! It's Timmy!' yelled Julian to the others. 'Call him! He'll soon make Janes drop you!'

'Tim, Tim!' shouted Dick, and Timmy ran to him at once, and began to growl so ferociously that Will Janes stopped dragging the boys to the shed.

'Set us free or he'll spring at you,' warned Dick. Timmy growled again, and nipped Will's ankle just to let him know he had teeth. Will let both boys go, and they staggered away from him in relief. Then Timmy ran to Julian – but Mr Gringle and Mr Brent had already heard his fierce growls and did not wait for any more! They gave Julian a shove away from them, and retreated into the cottage.

Will Janes also went into the cottage and lumbered up the stairs. The boys saw his figure outlined against the candlelight.

'Well, thank goodness he didn't go and scare his poor old mother,' said Julian, shaking his clothes straight. They had been twisted and pulled in the struggle. 'We'd better go and see if Will knocked those two men out – gracious, what a night! Good old Timmy – you just came in time!'

'I bet the girls sent him after us when twelve o'clock came,' said Dick. 'He'd smell our tracks easily. Dear old Tim. Now, go carefully – it's about here that Will floored those two men, whoever they were.'

But there was no sign of them at all. They must have got up from the ground very quickly and made themselves scarce. 'They went while the going was good!' said Toby grimly. 'What do we do next?'

'Get back to the camp,' said Julian. 'We're really not much wiser now than when we came – except that we know that Gringle and Brent *are* butterfly men, and that Janes is a bad lot and in with those two fellows he knocked out . . .'

'And that he helped them in some way, and hid them here – and hasn't been paid,' finished Dick. 'But how did he help them and why?'

'I've no idea,' said Julian. 'I can't think any more tonight – my mind just won't work. Go back home, Toby. We'll talk it all out tomorrow.'

Toby went off to the farm, puzzled and excited. What an evening! What would Cousin Jeff say when he told him – but no, he couldn't tell him. People said he had gone off in that plane, and that he was now at the bottom of the sea.

'But I won't believe it,' thought the tired boy, stoutly. 'I will – not – believe it!'

The girls were most relieved to hear the boys and Timmy coming back. 'What's happened? Why are you so late?' said George. 'Timmy found you all right, of course?'

'Couldn't have come at a better moment,' said Julian, grinning in the light of George's torch. 'I suppose you sent him after us?'

'We did,' said George. 'He wanted to go, anyway. He kept whining and whining as if you needed help – so we sent him off.'

'And we *did* need help!' said Dick, flinging himself down in the heather. 'Listen to our tale!'

He and Julian told it, and the girls listened, astonished. 'What *has* been going on down there?' said George, puzzled. 'What has Will Janes been up to with those fellows? How can we find out?'

'*He* won't talk,' said Julian. 'Nobody can make him, either. But I think maybe if we went down tomorrow morning and found that he'd gone out, we might persuade old Mrs Janes to tell us a few secrets.'

'Yes – that's a good idea,' said George. 'She *must* know what her son has been up to – especially if he has been hiding people there. She would have to feed them of course. Yes – old Mrs Janes would tell you – if she could!'

'But now,' said Julian, snuggling down in the heather on his rug, 'now, you two gabblers, I want to go to sleep. Goodnight!'

'Well! *Who's* been doing the gabbling!' said George. 'We have hardly been able to get a word in! Come on, Anne – we can go to sleep all right now. I wonder if Toby's home safely, and fast asleep in bed!'

Yes, Toby was home, but he wasn't asleep! He was still brooding over his Cousin Jeff. If only he could *do* something – but he couldn't. Cousin Jeff had disappeared, and he, and he only, could clear himself of the hateful charge of traitor . . . but people said he was drowned.

Next morning the Five awoke late, even Timmy. There wasn't a great deal left in the larder, and Julian hoped that Toby would bring up some more food. If not, they must certainly go down to Billycock Farm and get some. They breakfasted on bread and butter and cheese, with water to wash it down and a humbug from the tin to follow!

'We'll go straight down to the butterfly farm, I think,' said Julian, taking the leadership as he always did when there was any quick decision to be made. 'Dick, you'd better take on the asking of questions – the old lady was so touched when you gave her that money! She's probably got a soft spot for you now.'

'Right,' said Dick. 'Well, are we ready?'

They set off to the butterfly farm, Timmy at their heels. When they came near, they slowed their steps, not wanting to run into Will Janes. But there did not seem to be anybody about at all, not even the butterfly men themselves.

'They've probably gone off butterfly-hunting, I should

think,' said Dick. 'Look – there's poor old Mrs Janes trying to peg up her washing – dropping half of it on the ground.'

Anne ran over to the little woman. 'I'll peg up the things for you,' she said. 'Here, let me have them.' Mrs Janes turned to her and Anne was shocked to see that her right eye was black and bruised.

'However did you get that black eye?' she began. 'Here give me the whole basket. Gracious, what a lot of washing!'

Mrs Janes seemed a little dazed. She let Anne peg up the things without a word – she just stood and watched her. 'Where are Mr Gringle and Mr Brent?' asked Anne as she pegged.

Mrs Janes mumbled something. Anne made out with some difficulty that they had gone butterfly-hunting. 'And where is your son, Will?' she asked, having been prompted to ask this by signs from Julian.

To her dismay Mrs Janes began to sob. The old woman lifted her dirty apron and covered her head with it, and then, half-blinded by it, she stumbled towards the kitchen door, her arms stretched out in front of her.

'Gracious – whatever's the matter with her this morning?' said Anne to the others. Dick ran to the kitchen door and guided the old lady in, sitting her down in her rocking-chair. Her apron slid down from her head and she looked at him.

'You're the one that give me fifty pence,' she mumbled,

and patted his hand. 'Kind, you are. Nobody's kind to me now. My son's cruel. He hits me.'

'Did he give you that black eye?' asked Dick, gently. 'When? Today?'

'Yes. He wanted money – he always wants money,' wept Mrs Janes. 'And I wasn't going to give him that fifty pence. And he hit me. And then the police came and took him away.'

'What! The police took him – this morning do you mean?' asked Dick astonished. The others came a little closer, astonished, too. Why – it was only last night that Will Janes had captured two of them!

'They said he'd been thieving,' sobbed Mrs Janes. 'Robbed old Farmer Darvil of his ducks. But it's those bad men that changed my son. He was a good son once.'

'What men?' asked Dick, patting the skinny old hand. 'You tell us everything. We understand. We'll help you.'

'You're the one that give me fifty pence, aren't you?' she said once more. 'You'll help a poor old woman, won't you? It was those men, I tell you, that changed my son.'

'Where are they now? Did he hide them here?' asked Dick. Mrs Janes clung to his hand and pulled him closer.

'There were four men,' she mumbled, in such a low voice that Dick could hardly hear. 'And my son, he was promised money if he hid them here, on Billycock Hill. They all had a secret, see? And they only talked about it when they were hiding up in my bedroom there – but I listened and I heard.'

'What was the secret?' asked Dick, his heart beating fast. Now perhaps he would hear what all this mystery was about.

'They were watching something,' whispered Mrs Janes. 'Watching something out on the hills. Sometimes daytime, sometimes night-time, always watching. And they hid up there in my little old room, and cook for them I did and got nothing for it. Bad men they were.'

She sobbed again, and the four children felt sad and embarrassed. 'Don't worry her any more,' said Anne.

Then there came the sound of feet outside and Mr

Gringle walked by the window. He looked in and was astounded to see such a crowd in the little kitchen.

'What! You again!' he cried, when he saw Julian and Dick. 'You just look out! I told the police about you when they fetched Will Janes this morning. They'll be after *you* next, and you'll be punished for prowling round here at night and smashing my glasshouse! How *dare* you come here again!'

CHAPTER EIGHTEEN

Nobody knows where to look

'LET'S GO,' said George. 'We can't find out any more from the poor old woman. I'm glad that son of hers has been arrested for thieving. At least he won't be here to knock her about any more!'

Mr Gringle began to talk angrily again, but the Five had had enough. Timmy growled and made him retreat.

'We're going, Mr Gringle,' said Julian coldly. 'We shall be very *glad* to see the police, if you have really sent them after us. Quite a lot has been going on here that you don't know anything about. You've noticed nothing but your butterflies and moths.'

'Anything wrong in that, you uncivil boy?' shouted Mr Gringle.

'Well, it would have been a good thing if you had noticed how that fellow Janes knocked his poor mother about,' said Julian. 'I suppose you haven't even seen the bruised black eye she has this morning? No? I thought not. Well, maybe the police will be asking you a few questions soon – about the four strangers that have been hiding in that little bedroom up there!'

'What? What's that you say? What do you mean?' stammered Mr Gringle, astonished. 'Men? Where from? Who?'

'I've no idea,' said Julian. 'I wish I had.' And then the Five walked off together, leaving a very puzzled and worried Mr Gringle behind them.

'It serves him right,' said Julian. 'To think that he could make that miserable little woman slave for him, and never even notice how frightened and unhappy she was – or even see that she had a black eye from that scoundrel of a son. Let him get back to his butterflies!'

'What did Mrs Janes mean – mumbling about men hidden in that room – *four* of them she said,' wondered Anne. 'And why did they go and watch on the hillside? What *for*? That must have been one of them you saw that night of the storm, Julian – the one you spotted with the butterfly net, who said he was Mr Brent. I suppose he pretended to be him, so that nobody would ask him why he was prowling out there!'

'Yes, you're right,' said Julian. 'Of course, they may have been watching the airfield, you know – yes, of course that's what they *were* doing! Why didn't I think of that before? They were watching it night and day – two by day, I suppose, and two by night – and paid Janes to keep them hidden in that room. What were they up to?'

'Julian – could it – could it *possibly* be anything to do with the stolen aeroplanes?' asked George, with sudden excitement in her voice.

'It might. It certainly might,' said Julian. 'But I don't know how it ties up with Jeff Thomas and Ray Wells flying them away. That doesn't seem to fit somehow. You know – I do really believe we are on to something here! Let's go down to Billycock Farm and see if Mr Thomas, Toby's father, is about. I think we ought to tell him all we know.'

'Yes, that's a fine idea,' said Anne, pleased. 'We do want a bit of help over this now.'

'Well, come on then,' said Julian, and off they went at top speed down the hill, taking the path to Billycock Farm. They soon came to the farmyard and called Toby.

'Toby! Where are you? We've got a bit of news.'

Toby appeared at the barn door, looking rather pale for he had had a bad night. 'Oh, hallo – what news? The only news *I* want to hear is about Jeff. I can't get it out of my mind.'

'Where's your father?' asked Julian. 'We think he ought to hear what we've got to say. He'll know what to do. I'm afraid we don't – it's a puzzle we can't seem to fit together!'

'I'll call Dad,' said Toby at once, and sent a shout over the field where red-and-white cows were grazing. 'Da-ad! Da-ad! You're WANTED!'

His father came hurrying over the field. 'What is it? I'm busy.'

'Dad – Julian and Dick have got something to tell you,' said Toby. 'It won't take very long – but they're a bit worried.'

'Oh – well, what is it, lads?' said Mr Thomas, turning his kindly face to the boys. 'Got into any trouble?'

'Oh no, not exactly,' said Julian. 'I'll tell you as shortly as I can.' And he began to tell him the tale of the butterfly farm – and of the man he had seen at night on the hill – of the old woman at the butterfly farm, and of Will Janes, who treated her so badly. The farmer nodded at that.

'Ay!' he said. 'Will's changed this last year. Got into bad company, of course.'

'We've met some of the "bad company",' said Julian and told of their adventure the night before – and then ended by telling Mr Thomas what the old woman had said to them that morning.

'*Now* what has Will Janes been up to?' said the farmer. 'Bad enough to get into ill company – but worse to ill-treat his poor old mother! He'll have to say who these men are that he's been harbouring up there at the butterfly farm – and why they go out at night – watching the airfield, as you say, I don't doubt. Why, maybe they've even had a hand in the stealing of those planes!'

Toby became very excited at this and his face grew crimson. 'Dad! Maybe it was those men who took the planes! There were *four*, weren't there? They would be strong enough to capture Jeff and Ray and take them off somewhere – and then two of them could fly off the planes, and the other two watch poor Jeff and Ray, wherever they are!'

'You know – you may be right, young Toby,' said his father. 'This is a matter for the police – and at once, too. They must get on to Will, and get everything out of him – make him confess. If Jeff and Ray are held prisoner anywhere, they must be freed.'

Toby was dancing round in excitement. 'I *knew* it wasn't Jeff! I knew he couldn't do a thing like that! I'm sure it was two of those men. Dad, get on to the police at once.'

Mr Thomas hurried indoors to the telephone, and was

soon telling the police all he knew. They listened in astonishment, and at once saw the tremendous importance of the information the children had given.

'We'll question Will Janes at once,' they said. 'He's held on a matter of thieving, so we've got him under our thumb. We'll call you back in about half an hour.'

That half-hour was the very longest the children had ever known. Julian looked at his watch a score of times and nobody could sit still, least of all Toby. Anne was fidgety, and thought she would play with Benny. But neither Benny nor the pigling was there, so she had to wait in patience.

When the telephone bell at last shrilled out everyone jumped violently. Mr Thomas ran to it. 'Yes – yes – that's the police speaking, is it? Yes, I'm listening. What's the news? Oh . . . yes . . . yes . . .'

The farmer held the telephone close to his ear, nodding as he listened intently. The children watched him just as intently, trying to glean something from his few words, and from his face.

'I see. Well – that's very disappointing,' they heard Mr Thomas say, and their hearts sank. 'Thank you. Yes, very worrying indeed. Goodbye!'

He put down the receiver and faced the children. Toby called out to him. 'Was it Jeff who stole the plane, Dad? Was it?'

'No!' said his father, and Toby gave a wild yell of joy, and leapt into the air.

'Then nothing else matters!' he cried. 'Oh I *knew* it wasn't Jeff!'

'Wait a minute, wait a minute,' said Mr Thomas. 'There's something very worrying.'

'What?' said Toby, startled.

'Will Janes has confessed that those four men were sent to steal those two planes,' he said. 'Two of them were first-class pilots. The other two were thugs – bullies – sent to capture Jeff and Ray that night in the storm. They knocked them out and dragged them away from the airfield, and hid them somewhere. Then the pilots got out the two planes, and flew away. When the alarm was raised, it was too late.'

'So – when the planes crashed into the sea, it was the *first-class* pilots who were drowned, not Jeff and Ray?' said Julian.

'Yes. But here's the worrying part. The other two men, the ones who captured Jeff and Ray, have hidden them away, but didn't tell Janes *where*!' said Mr Thomas. 'They refused to pay him any money for his help, because the planes had crashed and their plans had failed – and they also refused to tell him where Jeff and Ray were hidden . . .'

'And now I suppose the two thugs have left the district – made their escape – and left Jeff and Ray to starve in some place where they may never be found!' said Toby, sitting down heavily and looking suddenly subdued.

'Exactly,' said Mr Thomas. 'And unless we find out

where they are pretty quickly, things will go hard with them – they're probably bound hand and foot – and are dependent on the two bullies for food and water. Once the men are gone, there is no one to bring them anything!'

'Oh, I say!' said Toby, horrified. 'Dad, we must find them, we *must*!'

'That's what the police think,' said his father. 'And what I think, too. But nobody knows where to look!'

'Nobody knows where to look!' The words repeated themselves in everyone's mind. Nobody knows where to look!

CHAPTER NINETEEN

A morning of work

THERE WAS a dead silence after Mr Thomas had said those despairing words – 'Nobody knows where to look!' Where *were* Jeff and Ray lying, worried and anxious, knowing their planes to be stolen, picturing them in the hands of an alien country, being dismantled to discover the new and secret devices built into them!

'They must be absolutely furious to think how easily it was all done!' said Dick. 'Taken by surprise like that! Surely there must be someone on the airfield who was in the secret?'

'Bound to be,' said Mr Thomas. 'These things are carefully planned to the very last detail – and, of course, it was a bit of luck for the men to have a storm going on just at the time when they needed something to make their getaway unseen and unheard – unheard, that is, until the planes were actually up in the air, and then it didn't matter!'

'Yes – the rain poured down that night,' said George, remembering. 'Nobody would be out in it – even the guards on the airfield would be under shelter somewhere. It *was* a bit of luck for those fellows!'

'I expect they were delighted to look out of the tiny

little window at the cottage and see a storm blowing up on the very night they wanted one!' said Dick.

'It beats me how Mr Gringle and Mr Brent never heard or suspected anything – with four strange men hanging about the butterfly farm,' said Julian.

'There can't be *anything* in their heads but butterflies or moths,' said Toby. 'I bet the police will have something to say to *them*!'

'The thing is – what's to be done now?' said Julian, frowning. He turned to Mr Thomas, who was deep in thought. 'What do *you* think? Is there anything we can do?'

'I doubt it,' said Mr Thomas. 'The police have had reports of two men driving a closed van at a fast speed – the number was taken by two or three people who complained – and they think that it might have been the one used to transport Jeff and Ray to some distant hiding-place – somewhere in a disused quarry – or in some deserted cellar. Likely places of that sort.'

Everyone groaned. There certainly was absolutely nothing they could do, then – it would be impossible to hunt for miles for old quarries or other hiding-places!

'Well – I must get on with my work,' said Mr Thomas. 'Where's your mother, Toby? You'd better tell her about all this.'

'She's gone shopping,' said Toby, looking at the clock. 'She'll be back just before dinner-time.'

'I suppose Benny has gone with her,' said Mr Thomas,

going to the door. 'Where's Curly, his pigling? Surely he hasn't taken him, too!'

'I expect he has,' said Toby. He looked at the other four children, suddenly remembering something. 'I say – aren't you a bit short of food up at the camp? Shall I get you some to take back with you?'

'Well – if it isn't a bore,' said Julian, apologetically. It seemed rather dreadful to think about food when probably Jeff and Ray were lying tied up somewhere, hungry and thirsty, with no chance of food of any sort.

'I'll get some. You come with me, Anne, and say what you want,' said Toby, and he and Anne went off together to the kitchen, and opened the door of the immense larder. Soon Anne was choosing what she wanted, trying to cheer up poor, downcast Toby at the same time.

'Can we stay and help you this morning, Toby?' asked Julian, when he and Anne came back. He knew that Toby had many jobs to do on the farm, although it was a holiday week – and he thought, too, that it would be good for the boy to have company that worrying morning.

'Yes. I'd like you to!' said Toby, brightening at once. 'I told Dad I'd limewash the hen-houses today – it's just the kind of day for that, nice and dry with a little breeze. You and Dick could help and we'd get them all done by dinner-time.'

'Right. We'll help you all morning, then we'll go back to our camp and have a picnic lunch,' said Julian. 'If you've finished all the jobs you have to do, you could come back with us – and we could go on a hike or something this afternoon.'

'Oh *yes*!' said Toby, cheering up considerably. 'Come on, then – we'll get the lime and find the brushes. Hey Binky, come and help us – and you, too, Timmy.'

'Wait a minute – can't *we* help?' said George. 'I can limewash hen-houses as well as anyone!'

'Oh, no, George – it's a messy job – a job for *boys* not girls,' said Toby, and went off with Dick and Julian, leaving George looking furious.

'Now you've offended George,' said Dick, grinning. Toby was genuinely surprised.

'Have I really?' he said. 'Oh, of course – I forgot she doesn't like to be girlish! Half a minute!' He ran back to the window of the sitting-room and called through it.

'Hi, George! What about doing a job for my mother? She never has time to weed her flower-garden and she is always upset because it's so untidy. I suppose you and Anne couldn't do something about that?'

'Yes, of course!' called Anne, going out of the door. 'Let's find a trowel each, and something to put weeds in. George! Don't look so gloomy! Let's weed the whole bed and make it marvellous for Mrs Thomas. She's so kind and generous, I'd like to do something for her.'

'All right. So would I,' said George, more graciously, and went with her cousin into the garden.

'I wish little Benny was at home,' said Anne, as she and George began their task a few minutes later, complete with trowels and two old tin pails for the weeds. 'I'd like him running round us, asking questions in that dear little high voice of his. And Curly, his pigling, running about like a funny little pig-puppy!'

'Yes. I like Benny, too,' said George, pulling up a handful of weeds. 'My word – there are more weeds than flowers in this bed.'

'Let's take Benny up to the camp with us this afternoon, if Toby comes,' said Anne. 'Then Toby can take him back with him when he goes. I love little Benny – I could look after him while you and the boys go hiking this afternoon.'

'All right,' said George, torn between wanting to stay with Anne and little Benny and his pig and going with the boys. 'Help – I've been stung by a most *vicious* nettle!'

All the children worked hard that morning. The hen-houses had been scrubbed down and well and truly lime-washed. Now they were drying quickly, the doors flung open to sun and wind. The girls had practically cleared the big flower-bed of weeds and were feeling rather pleased with it – and with themselves too!

There came the sound of a car at about a quarter to one. 'That must be Mrs Thomas coming back from her shopping,' said George. 'Quick, let's finish this bed before she sees us – we've only about ten minutes' more work.'

'Benny will soon come running to see what we are doing,' said Anne. 'And little Curly, too. My word – I've just filled my ninth pail of weeds!'

The three boys came by just then, swinging their empty

pails and carrying their big brushes. Timmy came, too, with quite a few white patches on his coat!

'Hallo, girls!' said Dick. 'My word, you've done a fine job on that bed – you can actually see the flowers now!'

The girls sat back pleased. 'Yes, it looks a bit better,' said Anne, pushing back her hair. 'Your mother's home, I think, Toby. We'd better go now, because you'll soon be having your dinner, and we'll be as hungry as hunters by the time we get back to our camp.'

'Right,' said Toby. 'Here, I'll take those pails of weeds for you – and the trowels!'

'Oh – thanks,' said George. 'Dick, Anne and I will go off to the camp now, with Timmy, and take the salad and stuff that wants washing under the spring – you bring the rest of the food, will you?'

'Of course,' said Dick. 'You take one basket, and we'll take the other.'

They went off with Toby. Anne and George went to look for Mrs Thomas, but she had gone into the dairy and was not to be seen.

'Never mind – she'll be busy,' said Anne. 'We'll go off straight away and get our lunch ready.'

They went off to the farm gate and up the path on to the steep slopes of Billycock Hill, the basket between them. Soon they were out of sight.

The boys washed their hands under a pump in the yard. Toby had gone to see his mother and to tell her what the police had said – but his father had already told her. She was very worried indeed.

'Poor Jeff! Poor Ray!' she said. Then she looked round as she heard the footsteps of Dick and Julian. 'Oh,' she said, 'I thought it was Benny. Where is he?'

'Benny – well, he was with you, wasn't he?' said Toby. 'You didn't leave him in the car, did you?'

'What do you mean, Toby?' said Mrs Thomas, looking startled. 'I left Benny here at the farm. I didn't take him with me – I never do when I have a lot of shopping, he gets so bored!'

'But, Mother – I haven't seen him all morning!' said Toby. 'He's not at the farm. I've not seen him for *hours*!'

'Oh, *Toby*!' said his mother, looking frightened. 'Toby, what's happened to him then? I thought you'd look after him, as you usually do!'

'And I thought he'd gone with *you*,' groaned Toby. 'Dick – Julian, have you seen Benny, or Curly?'

'No – we haven't set eyes on him this morning!' said Dick. 'Gosh – where's he got to? He may have gone up Billycock Hill to try and find our camp – I know he wanted to.'

'Toby – the horse-pond!' said Mrs Thomas, looking pale. 'Go there – he may have fallen in. Look in the loft of the barn, too – and go into the machinery shed. Oh, Benny, Benny, where are you?'

She turned to Dick and Julian, standing anxiously beside her. 'Go up to your camp,' she said. 'Hunt and call all the way. He may be lost on the hillside. My little Benny! Perhaps his pigling "runned away" again as he so often tells us – and he followed and got lost! Oh, dear, whatever shall I do?'

CHAPTER TWENTY

A peculiar message

TOBY RACED off to the horse-pond, very frightened. The pond was deep in the middle and Benny couldn't swim. Dick and Julian went off hurriedly through the farm gate and up to Billycock Hill, calling as they went.

'Benny! Benny, where are you? Benny!'

They toiled up the steep, heathery slopes, looking for any sign of the small boy, but there was none. They were both anxious. Benny was such a little wanderer and his pig made such a good excuse for going long distances!

'Benny! BENNY!' they called, and sometimes the echo came back to them, calling the name too.

'Perhaps he will be at the camp,' said Dick. 'I know he wanted to visit it. He *may* be there, the little monkey – with Curly, too.'

'I hope so,' said Julian, soberly. 'But it's a long way for his small legs to go. I don't see how he could possibly find the way without someone to guide him – he has never been there yet!'

'Well, maybe the girls spotted him on their way up,' said Dick. 'My word – this is a day, isn't it? – nobody knows where Jeff and Ray are – and nobody knows where little Benny is either – I don't call this a very good holiday!'

'Exciting – but decidedly worrying,' said Julian. 'Why do we always run into something like this? We *never* seem to have a really peaceful time!'

Dick glanced sideways at Julian and gave a fleeting smile. 'Would you *like* a really peaceful time, Ju?' he said. 'I don't think you would! Come on – let's shout again!'

They came to the camp at last, not having seen a sign of Benny or the pigling. He was not at the camp either, that was quite clear. The girls and Timmy were alone.

They were horrified when they were told about Benny. Anne went pale. 'Let's go and look for him at once,' she said. 'We must!'

'Well, can you make some sandwiches very quickly?' asked Dick. 'We're all hungry, and it won't take a minute. We can munch them as we go. Let's make a plan of campaign while you're cutting them.'

George and Anne set to work with the sandwiches. Anne's fingers were all thumbs, she was so shocked to hear that little Benny was missing. 'Oh, I hope nothing's happened to him!' she said. 'Missing all the morning – for hours! Poor Mrs Thomas!'

'The sandwiches are ready,' said George. 'Now, what's the plan, Julian? We all separate, I suppose, and search the hill, shouting all the time?'

'That's it,' said Julian, beginning on his sandwiches hungrily, and slipping some tomatoes and radishes into his pocket. 'You go round that side, Anne and George, one of you high up on the hill, and one lower down, so that your shouts cover as much distance as possible. And Dick and I will do the same on this side. We'll go down to the butterfly farm too, in case he has wandered there.'

They all set off, and soon the hill echoed to loud shouts. 'BENNY! BE-ENNY! BENNY! Coo-ee Benny! Coo-ee!'

Over the heather scrambled the four, with Timmy excitedly leaping about, too. He knew that Benny was lost, and he was sniffing for some smell of the small boy – but his sharp nose could find nothing.

Julian went to the butterfly farm and searched all about, but there was no sign of the boy there. In fact there was no sign of anyone, not even old Mrs Janes. She had gone off somewhere, and the two men were out butterflying as usual. In fact, George and Anne saw them as they searched their side of the hill and called to them.

'Have you seen anything of a small boy and a little pig?'

The two men were curt and unhelpful. 'No. No sign at all.'

'I suppose they're annoyed because they still think the boys broke the glass of their butterfly house!' said George. 'Well, I wish they would hunt for Benny instead of butterflies.'

It was two hours before Benny was found, and the Five had almost given up looking for him. They had met together as they came round the hill, and were standing in despair, wondering what to do next, when Timmy suddenly pricked up his ears. Then he barked – an excited little bark that said as plainly as possible, 'I've heard something interesting.'

'What is it then, Tim, what is it?' cried George at once. 'Go find, go find!'

Timmy trotted off, his ears well pricked. He stopped every now and again and listened, then went on again. The children listened, too, but they could hear nothing – no call, no groan, no whimper.

'Why – he's going downhill towards the caves,' said Julian at last. '*The caves!* Why didn't we think of those? But how could that tiny little fellow have found the way there – it's a long and complicated way from Billycock Farm?'

'He might have followed Curly, the pig,' said Anne. 'We always thought that he only *pretended* that the pig ran away, so that he could wander where he liked and blame it on the pig. But this time the pig might *really* have "runned away"!'

'Let's hope it's Benny that Timmy can hear,' said Julian. 'I must say I can't hear a single sound and I've got pretty sharp ears!'

And then the next minute they *all* heard something – a small, tired voice calling high and clear – 'Curly! Curly! I want you!'

'BENNY!' yelled everyone and leapt ahead so fast that the heathery ground shook beneath their trampling feet.

Timmy was there first, of course, and when the four children came up, they saw him gently licking the golden-haired little boy, who had put his arms round the dog's neck in delight. Benny was sitting just outside the entrance of the caves, all by himself – his pigling was not there.

'Benny! Oh, Benny darling, we've found you,' cried Anne, and knelt down beside him. He looked up at the others, not seeming at all surprised to see them.

'Curly runned away,' he said. 'He runned *right* away. Curly went in there,' and he pointed into the caves.

'Thank goodness you didn't follow him!' said George. 'You might never have been found! Come along – we must take you home!'

But as soon as she lifted up the child he began to kick and scream. 'No! No! I want Curly! I want Curly!'

'Darling, he'll come along when he's tired of the caves,' said Anne. 'But your mummy wants you now – and your dinner is waiting for you.'

'I'm hungry,' announced Benny. 'I want my dinner – but I want Curly, too. Curly! Curly! Come here!'

'We *must* take Benny back,' said Dick. 'His mother will be so terribly worried. Curly will eventually come out if he's got sense enough to remember the way – if not well – it's just too bad! We daren't go wandering down the unroped paths in case *we* get lost. Come on, bring Benny, George.'

'Curly will come when he's ready,' George said, as she carried the little boy away from the entrance to the caves. 'But now your mummy wants you, and your dinner's waiting.'

With Timmy jumping up delightedly beside her, she carried the small boy down the chalky path, talking to him. They were all so thankful to have found him that they felt quite cheerful, forgetting Jeff and Ray for a time. They teased little Benny, trying to make him forget his lost pet.

Mrs Thomas was overjoyed to see the small boy again. She cried over him as she took him into her arms. 'Oh, Benny, Benny – what a bad pair you are, you and your pigling.'

'He runned away,' said Benny, of course. He was set down at the table to have his dinner and began to eat very fast indeed because he was so hungry. Everyone sat and watched him, so glad to have him safe again that they hardly took their eyes off him while he gobbled his meal.

He finished at last. 'I'm going to look for Curly,' he announced as he got down from his chair.

'Oh, no, you're not,' said his mother. 'You're going to stay with me. I want you to help me to make some cakes. Curly will come home when he's ready.'

And in an hour's time, when Julian, Dick, Anne, George and Toby were busy at the messy job of cleaning out the duck-pond, Curly did come back. He trotted into the farmyard, making his usual funny little squeals, and everyone looked round at once.

'CURLY! You *have* come back! Oh, you bad little pig!' cried George, and Timmy ran up to the pigling and sniffed him and licked him. The pig turned himself round to look for Benny – and Julian laughed.

'Someone's written something on him – in black! Come here, Curly, and let's see.'

Curly trotted over to him, and Julian examined the rather smudged black lettering. 'Can't make it out,' he said. 'Somebody's printed something on his pink little body – silly thing to do – but it will wash off.'

'Wait!' said Dick sharply, as Julian bent to get one of the rags they were using, to wash the pigling's body. 'WAIT, I say! Look – isn't that a J and a T and below those are letters that look like R and V – no, W, because half that letter has been rubbed off by the heather or something.'

Now everyone was staring in excitement. 'J . . . T, and R . . . W!' said Toby in a breathless voice. Then it rose to a shout. 'They stand for JEFF THOMAS AND RAY WELLS. What does it *mean* – who put those letters there?'

'There are some more letters, smaller and rather smudged,' said Julian. 'Hold the pigling still, Dick. We must, we *must* make out what they are! It's some kind of message from Jeff and Ray. The pigling must have been where they are hidden!'

They all looked earnestly at the smudgy letters, which appeared to be five in number. They were almost unreadable – but Dick's sharp brain got hold of them at last.

'The word is CAVES!' he said. 'See – the first letter might be G or O or C – but the third one is certainly V and last is S. I'm sure it's CAVES – and that's where Curly went, we know.'

'Whew! That's where Jeff and Ray are hidden then,' said Julian. 'Quite near, after all – and we thought they had been taken away by car and hidden miles away! Quick – where's your father, Toby?'

Mr Thomas was found and was shown Curly, with the smudgy black letters on his back. He was astounded. 'So Curly went wandering in the caves, did he – what a pig he is! Can't keep his nose out of anything! And somehow he went to where Jeff and Ray were. What a strange way to send a message – they could surely have tied one on to his tail, or round his neck – these letters are almost unreadable!'

'I nearly washed them off, thinking that somebody had played a silly joke on Curly,' said Julian. 'My word – if I had, we'd not have known where Jeff and Ray were. What shall we do now? Go to the caves at once? Telephone the police?'

'Both!' said Mr Thomas. 'The police must know because they are searching everywhere, of course. Now – you start off to the caves – but take a ball of string with you, because Jeff and Ray won't have been hidden in any of the roped tunnels, where sightseers so often go, and without string you might not be able to find your way back down the unroped ones. You may find that you need to unwind the string in order to get back safely. And take Timmy. He'll be useful.'

'He certainly will!' said Julian. 'And we'll take the little pig, too, so that Timmy can smell him, and then smell the tracks Curly made as he wandered through the caves, and follow them! We shan't have to wander all about wondering where Jeff and Ray are then.'

The Five set off at once, with Toby, too, all as excited as they could possibly be.

'Good old Jeff! Good old Ray!' Toby kept saying. 'We're coming! Hang on, we're coming!'

CHAPTER TWENTY-ONE

An exciting finish

UP THE heathery hill panted the five children and Timmy. Julian carried the frightened little pig, who was not at all sure what was happening to him. He kicked and squealed but nobody took any notice of him – he would be of importance when they reached the caves, but not till then!

At last they reached the chalky roadway to the caves and pounded along it, the loose bits of chalk flying between their feet. They came to the entrance where the warning notice stood.

'Timmy!' called George as Julian put down the trembling little pig and held him tightly. 'Timmy – come here! Smell Curly – that's right – smell him all over – now follow, follow, follow! Smell where he went in the caves – and follow, Tim, follow!'

Timmy knew perfectly well what tracking meant and obediently smelt Curly thoroughly, and then put his nose to the ground to follow the scent of the pigling's footsteps. He soon picked it up, and began to run into the first cave.

He stopped and looked back enquiringly. 'Go on, Tim, go on – I know this seems peculiar to you when we've got Curly here – but we want to know where he *went*!' called George, afraid that Timmy might think it was just a silly game and give up. Timmy put his nose to the ground again.

He came to the magnificent cave, full of gleaming 'icicles', the stalactites and stalagmites, some of them looking like shining pillars. Then into the next cave, which, with its glowing rainbow colours, had reminded Anne of a Fairyland cave. Then through the next cave they went – and came to the forking of the ways.

'Here we are – at the three tunnels,' said George. 'I bet Timmy won't go down the usual roped one that all visitors would take . . .'

As she spoke the words Timmy, nose to ground, still following the scent of the pigling's footsteps, took the left-hand, unroped way – and everyone followed, torches shining brightly.

'I thought so!' said George, and her voice began to echo round. 'Thought so, thought so, so, so . . .'

'Do you remember those awful noises we heard the other day – that piercing whistling, and those howls?' said Dick. 'Well, I bet they were made by the bullies who dragged Jeff and Ray here! I expect they heard Timmy barking – *he* must have heard the men, probably, though we didn't – and they were scared in case we were coming. So they made those frightful noises to scare us off, and the echoes magnified them horribly.'

'Well, they certainly scared us away all right,' said Anne, remembering. 'Yes – it must have been those men – there aren't any awful noises today! My word, what a long, winding tunnel this is – and look, it's forking into two!'

'Timmy will know which way to take,' said George – and, of course he did. With his nose to the ground, he chose the left-hand one without any hesitation.

'You didn't really need to bring a ball of string, Julian,' said Toby. 'Timmy will easily be able to take us the right way back, won't he?'

'Yes,' said Julian. 'He's better than any unwinding ball of string! But without Tim we'd *never* find the way back – there are so many caves, and so many tunnels. We must be well into the heart of the hill now.'

Timmy suddenly stopped in his tracking, raised his head, and listened. Could he hear Jeff and Ray? He barked loudly – and from somewhere in the near distance came a shout. 'Hoy! Hoy! This way! This way!'

'It's Jeff!' shouted Toby, dancing in the dark tunnel with excitement. 'JEFF! CAN YOU HEAR ME? JEFF!'

And a voice came back at once. 'Hi, Toby! This way, this way!'

Timmy ran down the passage and stopped. At first the children could not see why – and then they saw that the passage came to an end there – a blank wall faced them just beyond Timmy – and yet Jeff's voice came quite clearly to them!

'Here we are, here!'

'Why – there's a hole in the floor of the tunnel just by

Timmy!' cried Julian, shining his torch on it. 'That's where Jeff and Ray are – down that hole. Hey, Cousin Jeff – are you down there?'

Julian shone his torch right through the hole – and there, lying on the floor of a cave below was Ray – and standing beside him, looking up eagerly, was Jeff!

'Thank God you've found us!' he said. 'Those fellows told us they were leaving us here and not coming back. Ray's got a twisted ankle – he can't stand on it. They pushed us down this hole without any warning, and he fell awkwardly. But with your help we can get him up.'

'Jeff, oh, Jeff – I'm so glad we've found you!' yelled Toby, trying to look down into the hole with Julian. 'What's the best way to get you up? This entrance hole isn't very big.'

'If you can manage to pull *me* up, that's the first thing to do,' said Jeff, considering the matter. 'Then two of you boys can go down to Ray, and help him to stand, and I think I could haul *him* up. This is an awful place – no outlet except through that small hole up there, which was too high for me to jump up to – and Ray couldn't stand, of course, to help me!'

There was soon a great deal of acrobatic work on the part of Jeff, Julian and Dick! The two boys managed to haul up Jeff by lying down on the floor above, and putting their arms and shoulders through the hole to drag him up! Toby and George had to hold on to their legs to prevent them from being pulled into the hole! And Anne had to hold the little pig, which did its best to try and get down the hole, too!

At last Jeff was up through the hole, and then the two boys, Julian and Dick, leapt down to Ray. He seemed

rather dazed and Jeff said that he thought he had hurt his head as well as his leg when the men pushed them down the hole. Julian pulled him gently to his feet and then he and Dick lifted him until he could reach Jeff's swinging hands as he leant down through the hole.

Poor Ray was pulled up at last, and then up went Julian and Dick in the same way. Timmy thought the whole procedure was most extraordinary, and produced volleys of excited barks, scaring the little pig almost out of its skin!

'Phew!' said Jeff, when at last Ray was up, and being helped by the others. 'I never thought we'd get out of there. Let's get away from this nightmare place as quickly as possible. What we want is a little fresh air and food – *and* water! Those brutes haven't been near us for what seems like weeks!'

They made their way back to the cave entrance, Timmy leading the way confidently, not even troubling to smell it. He never forgot a path once he had been along it.

They came out into the bright June sunshine, and it was so very dazzling to the two men who had been so long in pitch-black darkness that they had to shade their eyes.

'Sit down a bit till you get used to it,' said Julian. 'And tell us how you wrote your message on the pig! Did he suddenly appear down the hole?'

Jeff laughed. 'Well,' he said, 'there we were down in that awful hole, Ray and I – with no watch to tell us the time, no means of knowing if it was night or day, or even if it was last Thursday or next Monday! And suddenly we heard a pitter-pattering noise – and the next thing we knew was that something had fallen down through the hole and landed on top of us! It began to squeal like billy-o, so we guessed it was a little pig – though *why* a pig should suddenly descend on us out of the dark tunnel above us we simply couldn't imagine!'

Everyone laughed, even Ray. 'Go on,' said Dick. 'What did you do?'

'Well, we felt the pig all over and knew it was a baby,' said Jeff, 'but it didn't occur to us for some time that we might use it as a messenger! That was Ray's bright idea!'

'We could hardly read your message,' said Dick. 'It was just touch and go that we made it out.'

'I dare say – but when you consider that we had been robbed of everything – even my pencil and pen – to say nothing of my money, my watch and my torch – and Ray's, too – and that it was pitch-dark in the hole, I'm sure you will agree that we didn't make a bad job of printing that message!' said Jeff.

'But what did you print it with if your pockets had been emptied?' asked George, in wonder.

'Well, Ray found a tiny bit of black chalk at the bottom of his trouser pocket,' said Jeff. 'It's chalk we use to mark out our air-routes, on big maps – and that was all we had to use! Ray held the pigling and I printed our initials and the word CAVES on his back. I couldn't see what I was doing in the dark, but I just hoped for the best. Then I stood up and tossed the poor little pig through the hole! It was a jolly good shot, I must say – I heard him scrambling on the edge, and then away he trotted, the finest little pig in the world!'

'What a tale!' said Julian. 'My word, you're lucky, Jeff, that the pigling came home all right! It's a wanderer, that pig, always running away. And to think that I nearly washed your message off his back before we read it.'

'Whew! It gives me the creeps to hear that,' said Jeff. 'Now tell me what happened when it was discovered that we'd disappeared from the airfield – wasn't there an uproar?'

'Rather! You knew your planes were stolen, didn't you?' said Dick.

'I guessed that, when I heard two planes take off, just as some great thugs were hauling us up the hill,' said Jeff. 'I heard a dog barking as we were being kicked and dragged up – was it Timmy? I did hope he would come to our rescue.'

'Oh, *yes* – that must have been the time when he began to bark that night of the storm!' said George, remembering. 'So it was you and those thugs we heard – oh, what a pity we didn't know it!'

'Those two stolen planes crashed into the sea during the storm, Jeff,' said Toby. 'The pilots weren't found.'

'Oh,' said Jeff and was silent for a moment. 'I shall miss my dear old bus – well, let's hope I get another plane – and Ray, too. Ray! How do you feel now? Can you hobble along again or not?'

'Yes – if the boys can help me as they did just now,' said Ray, who was already looking much better since he had been in the open air. 'Let's get along.'

It was very slow going – but fortunately the police met them halfway, on their way to the caves! Mr Thomas had telephoned them and they had come along immediately. They took Ray in hand, and the little party made better progress.

'Put that pig down, Anne, you must be tired of carrying it,' said Dick. 'You look like Alice in Wonderland. She carried a pig, too!'

Anne laughed. 'I think it's gone to sleep, just like Alice's pig!' she said. And so it had!

They were all very thankful when at last they arrived at Billycock Farm. What a welcome they had from Mrs Thomas, her husband and Benny. The little boy dragged his pigling from Anne's arms and hugged it. 'You runned away, you're bad, you runned fast!' he scolded, and set it down. It immediately scampered over to the barn, with Benny in pursuit and Anne went to fetch them back.

'Now we'll all have tea – I've got it ready, hoping that everyone would be back in time from their extraordinary adventures!' said Mrs Thomas. 'I know Jeff and Ray must be starved – you look quite thin in the face, Jeff.'

They all sat round the big table, Toby next to his hero, Cousin Jeff. They gazed with pleasure at the food there – surely never, never had there been such a spread before!

'Mother!' said Toby, his eyes gleaming. 'Mother, this isn't

a meal – it's a BANQUET! Jeff – what will you have?'

'Everything!' said Jeff. 'Some of every single thing. I'll start with two boiled eggs, three slices of ham, two thick pieces of bread and butter, and some of that wonderful salad. My word, it's almost worth being down that hole for ages to end up with a feast like this!'

It was a most hilarious tea, and for once Benny sat at the table throughout the whole meal, and didn't slip from his chair to go and find Curly. Why didn't they have parties like this every day? Why, even his father was there, roaring with laughter! What a pity the two policemen hadn't been able to stop to tea, too – Benny had a lot of questions to ask policemen! Where was Timmy? Yes, he was under the table – Benny could feel him with his foot. And, yes, Binky was there, too, just by Toby.

He slid his hand down with a large piece of cake in it, and immediately it was taken gently from his hand by a hairy mouth – Timmy was having a wonderful time, too!

Everyone was sorry when the grand meal was over. Jeff and Ray now had to report to the airfield, and Mr Thomas offered to take them in his car. The children went to see them off.

'It will seem awfully dull now, up in our camp on the hillside,' said Dick. 'So many things have happened in the last few days – and now nothing will happen at all!'

'Rubbish!' said Jeff. 'I *promise* you something will happen – something grand!'

'What?' asked everyone eagerly.

'I shall see that you're all given a free flight in a plane as soon as possible – perhaps tomorrow,' said Jeff. 'And – *I* shall pilot it! Now then – anyone want to loop the loop with me?'

What shouts and squeals from everyone! Jeff made a face and put his hands to his ears.

'Me too, me too – and Curly!' came Benny's little high voice.

'Where *is* Curly?' said Jeff, looking out of the car. 'I really must shake hooves with him – he's been a wonderful friend to me and Ray! Wherever is he?'

'I don't know,' said Benny, looking all round. 'He must

have . . .'

'Runned away!' chorused everyone, and Timmy barked at the sudden shout. He put his paws up on the car and licked Jeff's hand.

'Thanks, old boy,' said Jeff. 'We couldn't have done without you either! So long, everybody – see you tomorrow – and then whoooops! – up in the clouds we'll go!'

Enid Blyton®

is one of the most popular children's authors of all time. Her books have sold over 500 million copies and have been translated into other languages more often than any other children's author.

Enid Blyton adored writing for children. She wrote over 700 books and about 2,000 short stories. *The Famous Five* books, now 75 years old, are her most popular. She is also the author of other favourites including *The Secret Seven*, *The Magic Faraway Tree*, *Malory Towers* and *Noddy*.

Born in London in 1897, Enid lived much of her life in Buckinghamshire and loved dogs, gardening and the countryside. She was very knowledgeable about trees, flowers, birds and animals. Dorset – where some of the Famous Five's adventures are set – was a favourite place of hers too.

Enid Blyton's stories are read and loved by millions of children (and grown-ups) all over the world. Visit enidblyton.co.uk to discover more.

THE FAMOUS FIVE

FIVE GET INTO A FIX

Have you read all THE FAMOUS FIVE books?

1. Five on a Treasure Island
2. Five Go Adventuring Again
3. Five Run Away Together
4. Five Go to Smuggler's Top
5. Five Go Off in a Caravan
6. Five on Kirrin Island Again
7. Five Go Off to Camp
8. Five Get Into Trouble
9. Five Fall Into Adventure
10. Five on a Hike Together
11. Five Have a Wonderful Time
12. Five Go Down to the Sea
13. Five Go to Mystery Moor
14. Five Have Plenty of Fun
15. Five on a Secret Trail
16. Five Go to Billycock Hill
17. Five Get Into a Fix
18. Five on Finniston Farm
19. Five Go to Demon's Rocks
20. Five Have a Mystery to Solve
21. Five Are Together Again

The Famous Five Colour Short Stories

1. Five and a Half-Term Adventure
2. George's Hair is Too Long
3. Good Old Timmy
4. A Lazy Afternoon
5. Well Done, Famous Five
6. Five Have a Puzzling Time
7. Happy Christmas, Five
8. When Timmy Chased the Cat

Enid Blyton®

THE FAMOUS FIVE

FIVE GET INTO A FIX

Illustrated by Eileen A. Soper

HODDER CHILDREN'S BOOKS

First published in Great Britain in 1958 by Hodder & Stoughton
This edition published in 2016

20

A CIP catalogue record for this book is available from the British Library.

ISBN 978 1 444 93647 6

Printed and bound in Great Britain by Clays Ltd, Elcograf S.p.A.

The paper and board used in this book are made from wood from responsible sources.

Hodder Children's Books
An imprint of
Hachette Children's Group
Part of Hodder & Stoughton
Carmelite House
50 Victoria Embankment
London EC4Y 0DZ

An Hachette UK Company
www.hachette.co.uk
www.hachettechildrens.co.uk

CONTENTS

1	A MISERABLE CHRISTMAS	1
2	OFF TO MAGGA GLEN	9
3	THE END OF THE JOURNEY	19
4	IN THE OLD FARMHOUSE	28
5	THINGS MIGHT BE WORSE!	37
6	A FUNNY LITTLE CREATURE	45
7	BACK AT THE FARM AGAIN	54
8	OFF TO THE LITTLE HUT	63
9	A STRANGE TALE	72
10	IN THE MIDDLE OF THE NIGHT	80
11	STRANGE HAPPENINGS	89
12	OUT ON THE HILLS	98
13	AILY IS SURPRISING	107
14	MORGAN IS SURPRISING TOO	116
15	'WHAT'S UP, TIM?'	124
16	AILY CHANGES HER MIND	134
17	THE 'BIG, BIG HOLE'	143
18	INSIDE OLD TOWERS	152
19	A LOT OF EXCITEMENT	161
20	IN THE HEART OF THE HILL	172
21	AN ASTOUNDING THING	181
22	ALL'S WELL THAT ENDS WELL!	191

CHAPTER ONE

A miserable Christmas

'I DO think these Christmas holidays have been the worst we've ever had,' said Dick.

'Bad luck on George, coming to stay with us for Christmas – and then us all going down with those awful colds and coughs,' said Julian.

'Yes – and being in bed on Christmas Day was *horrible*,' said George. 'The worst of it was I couldn't *eat* anything. Fancy not being hungry on Christmas Day! I never thought that would happen to *me*!'

'Timmy was the only one of us who didn't get ill,' said Anne, patting him. 'You were a pet, Tim, when we were in bed. You divided your time between us nicely.'

'Woof!' said Timmy, rather solemnly. He hadn't been at all happy this Christmas. To have four of the Five in bed, coughing and sneezing, was quite unheard of!

'Well, anyhow, we're all up again,' said Dick. 'Though my legs don't really feel as if they belong to me yet!'

'Oh – do *yours* feel like that too?' asked George. 'I was quite worried about mine!'

'We all feel the same,' said Julian, 'but we shall be quite different in a day or two – now we're up. Anyway – we get back to school next week – so we'd *better* feel all right!'

Everyone groaned – and then coughed. 'That's the worst of this germ we've had, whatever it is,' said George. 'If we laugh – or speak loudly – or groan – we start coughing. I shall go completely mad if I don't get rid of my cough. It keeps me awake for hours at night!'

Anne went to the window. 'It's been snowing again,' she said. 'Not much – but it looks lovely. To think we might have been out in it all last week. I do think it's too bad to have holidays like this.'

George joined her at the window. A car drew up outside and a burly, merry-looking man got out and hurried up the steps to the front door.

'Here's the doctor,' said Anne. 'I bet he'll say we're all quite all right to go back to school next week!'

In a minute or two the door opened and the doctor came into the room, with the mother of Julian, Dick and Anne. She looked tired – and no wonder! Looking after four ill children and a most miserable dog over Christmas had not been an easy job!

'Well, here they are – all up and about now!' said the children's mother. 'They look pretty down in the mouth, don't they?'

'Oh – they'll soon perk up,' said Dr Drew, sitting down and looking at each of the four in turn. 'George looks the worst – not so strong as the others, I suppose.'

George went red with annoyance, and Dick chuckled. 'Poor George is the weakling of the family,' he said. 'She had the highest temperature, the worst cough, and the loudest groans, and she . . .'

But whatever else he was going to say was lost beneath the biggest cushion in the room, which an angry George had flung at him with all her might. Dick flung it back, and everyone began to laugh, George too. That set all the four coughing, of course, and the doctor put his hands to his ears.

'*Will* they be well enough to go to school, Doctor?' asked Mrs Barnard anxiously.

'Well, yes – they would – but they ought to get rid of those coughs first,' said the doctor. He looked out of the window at the snow. 'I wonder now – no – I don't suppose it's possible – but . . .'

'But what?' said Dick, pricking up his ears at once. 'Going to send us to Switzerland for a skiing holiday, Doc? Fine! Absolutely smashing!'

The doctor laughed. 'You're going too fast!' he said. 'No – I wasn't actually thinking of Switzerland – but perhaps somewhere hilly, not far from the sea. Somewhere really bracing, but not too cold – where the snow will lie, so that you can toboggan and ski, but without travelling as far as Switzerland. Switzerland is expensive, you know!'

'Yes. I suppose it is,' said Julian. 'No – we can't expect a holiday in Switzerland just because we've had beastly colds! But I must say a week somewhere would be jolly nice!'

'Oh *yes*!' said George, her eyes shining. 'It would *really* make up for these miserable holidays! Do you mean all by ourselves, Doctor? We'd love that.'

'Well, no – someone ought to be there, surely,' said Dr Drew. 'But that's up to your parents.'

'I think it's a jolly good idea,' said Julian. 'Mother – don't *you* think so? I'm sure you're longing to be rid of us for a while. You look worn out!'

His mother smiled. 'Well – if it's what you need – a short holiday somewhere to get rid of your coughs – you must have it. And I won't say that I shan't enjoy a little rest while you're enjoying yourselves having a good time! I'll talk it over with your father.'

'Woof!' said Timmy, looking inquiringly at the doctor, both ears pricked high.

'He says – *he* needs a rest somewhere too,' explained George. 'He wants to know if he can come with us.'

'Let's have a look at your tongue, Timmy, and give me your paw to feel if it's too hot or not,' said Dr Drew, gravely. He held out his hand, and Timmy obediently put his paw into it.

The four children laughed – and immediately began to cough again. How they coughed! The doctor shook his head at them. 'What a din! I shouldn't have made you laugh. Now I shan't be coming to see you again until just before you go back to school. I expect your mother will let me know when that day comes. Goodbye till then – and have a good time, wherever you go!'

'We will!' said Julian. 'And thanks for bothering about us so much. We'll send you a card when our coughs are gone!'

As soon as Dr Drew had driven off in his car, there was a conference. 'We *can* go off somewhere, can't we, Mother?' said Dick, eagerly. 'The sooner the better! You must be tired to death of our coughs, night and day!'

'Yes. I think you *must* go somewhere for a few days,' said his mother. 'But the question is – *where*? You could go off to George's home, I suppose – Kirrin Cottage . . . but it's not high up . . . and besides, George's father would certainly not welcome four coughs like yours!'

'No. He'd go mad at once,' said George. 'He'd fling open his study door – and stride into our room – and shout "Who's mak—" '

But as George began to shout, she coughed – and that was the end of her little piece of acting! 'That's enough, George,' said her aunt. 'For goodness' sake, go and get a drink of water.'

There was much debating about where they could go for a little while, and all the time they were talking the snow fell steadily. Dick went to the window, pleased. 'If *only* we could find a place high up on a hill, just as the doctor said, a place where we could use our toboggans, and our skis,' he said. 'Gosh, it makes me feel better already to think of it. I do hope this snow goes on and on.'

'I think I'd better ring up a travel agency and see if they can offer us something sensible,' said his mother. 'Maybe a summer camp set up on a hill would do – it would be empty now, and you could have a choice of a hut or a chalet or something.'

But all her telephoning came to nothing! 'No,' said the agencies. 'Sorry – we haven't anything to suggest. Our camps are all closed down now. No – we know of no winter ones in this country at all!'

And then, as so often happens, the problem was suddenly solved by somebody no one had thought of asking . . . Jenkins, the old man who helped in the garden! There was nothing for him to do that day except sweep a path through the snow. He saw the children watching him from the window, grinned and came up to them.

'How are you?' he shouted. 'Would you like some apples? They've ripened nicely now, those late ones. Your mother said you weren't feeling like apples – or pears either. But maybe you're ready for some now.'

'Yes! We are!' shouted Julian, not daring to open the window in case his mother came in and was angry to see him standing with his head out in the cold. 'Bring them in, Jenkins. Come and talk to us!'

So old Jenkins came in, carrying a basket of ripe, yellow apples, and some plump, brown-yellow pears.

'And how are you now?' he said, in his soft Welsh voice, for he came from the Welsh mountains. 'You're pale, and thin too. Ah, it's the mountain air of Wales you want!'

He smiled all over his wrinkled face, handing round his basket. The children helped themselves to the fruit.

'Mountain air – that's what the doctor ordered!' said Julian, biting into a juicy pear. 'I suppose you don't know somewhere like that we could go to, do you, Jenkins?'

'Well, my aunt lets rooms in the summertime!' said Jenkins. 'And she's a good cook, my Aunt Glenys. But I don't know if she'd do it in the wintertime, what with the snow and all. Her farm's on the hillside, and the slope runs right down to the sea. A fine place it is in the summer – but there'll be nothing but snow there now.'

'But – it sounds *exactly* right,' said Anne, delighted. 'Doesn't it, Ju? Let's call Mother! Mother! Mother, where are you?'

Her mother came running in, afraid that one of the children was feeling ill again. She was most astonished to see old Jenkins there – and even more astonished to hear the four children pouring out what he had just told them. Timmy added a few excited barks, and Jenkins stood twirling his old hat, quite overcome.

The excitement made Julian and Dick cough distressingly. 'Now listen to me,' said their mother, firmly. 'Go straight upstairs and take another dose of your cough medicine. *I'll* talk to Jenkins and find out what all this is about. No – don't interrupt, Dick. GO!'

They went at once, and left their mother talking to the bewildered man. 'Blow this cough!' said Dick, pouring out his usual dose. 'Gosh. I hope Mother fixes up something with Jenkins's aunt. If I don't go off somewhere and lose this cough, I shall go mad – stark, staring mad!'

'I bet we'll go to his old aunt,' said Julian. 'That's if she'll take us. It's the kind of sudden idea that clicks – don't you think so?'

Julian was right. The idea did 'click'. His mother had actually met Jenkins's old aunt that spring, when she had come to visit her relations, and Jenkins had brought her proudly up to the house to introduce her. So when Dick and Julian went downstairs again, they were met with good news.

'I'm telephoning Jenkins's aunt, old Mrs Jones,' said their mother. 'And if she'll take you – well, off you can go in a day or two – coughs and all!'

CHAPTER TWO

Off to Magga Glen

EVERYTHING WAS soon settled. Old Mrs Jones, whose voice came remarkably clearly over the long-distance line, seemed delighted to take the four children.

'Yes, I understand. Oh, their coughs won't last a day here, don't you worry. And how's my nephew, Ivor Jenkins?'

'Mother! Tell her we're bringing a dog, too,' said Julian, in his mother's ear. George had been making wild gestures to him, pointing first to Timmy, then to the telephone, where her aunt stood patiently listening to old Mrs Jones's gossipy talk.

'Oh – er – Mrs Jones – there'll be a dog, too!' said her aunt. 'What – you've seven dogs already? Good gracious! Oh, for the sheep, of course . . .'

'*Seven* dogs, Timmy!' said George, in a low voice to Tim, who wagged his tail at once. 'What do you think of that? Seven! You'll have the time of your life!'

'Sh!' said Julian, seeing his mother glance crossly at George. He felt thankful that this unexpected holiday had been so quickly fixed up. Like the others, he was beginning to feel very down and dull. It would be wonderful to go away. He wondered where their skis were . . .

Everyone looked brighter when things had been settled. No school for some time! No lounging about the house wishing something would happen! Timmy would be able to go for long walks at last. They would be on their own again, too, a thing the Five loved.

Jenkins was very helpful in looking out toboggans and skis. He brought them all into the house to be examined and cleaned. Something exciting to do at last! Their exertions made them all cough badly, but they didn't mind so much now.

'Only two days to wait – then we're off!' said Dick. 'Ought we to take our skates, do you think?'

'No. Jenkins says there's no skating round about the farm,' said George. 'I asked him. I say – look at that mound of woollen clothes your mother's just brought in, Ju! We might be going to the North Pole!'

'Whew, Mother! If we wear all those, we'll never be able to ski!' said Julian. 'Gosh, look – *six* scarves! Even if *Timmy* wears one, that's one too many.'

'One or two may get wet,' said his mother. 'It won't matter how many clothes you take – you're going by car, and we can easily get everything in.'

'I'll take my field-glasses, too,' said Dick. 'You never know when they might be useful. George, old thing, I do hope Timmy will be friends with the farm dogs. It would be awful if he quarrelled with them – and he does sometimes get fierce with other dogs, you know – especially if we make a fuss of them!'

'He'll behave *perfectly*,' said George. 'And there's no *need* to make a fuss of other dogs if we've got Timmy.'

'All right, teacher!' said Dick, and George stopped her polishing and threw her duster at him. Yes – certainly things were getting normal again!

When the time came for the children to set out on their journey they were feeling a good deal better – though their coughs were still almost as bad! 'I do hope you'll lose those awful coughs, Julian, before you come back,' said his mother. 'It worries me to hear you all cough, cough, cough, day and night!'

'Poor old Mother – you *have* had a time!' said Julian,

giving her a hug. 'You've been great. What a sigh of relief you'll give when we're all safely away in the car!'

At last the car came, driving up the snowy path to the house. It was a hired car, a very big one, and that was fortunate, as the children's luggage was truly colossal! The driver was a cheerful man, and he and Jenkins soon had the suitcases, toboggans, skis and all the rest either in the boot of the car, or strapped on top.

'There we are!' said the driver at last. 'Everything made fast. We're making a nice early start, and we should be safe in Magga Glen before it's dark.'

'We're all ready to start!' said Julian and the man nodded and smiled, climbing into the driving seat. Dick sat beside him, and the other three sat at the back, with Timmy on their feet. Not that he would stay there long! He liked to look out of the window just as much as the children did!

Everyone heaved a sigh of relief as the car slid down the drive. They were off at last! Jenkins was at the gate, and waved as they went past.

'Remember me to my old aunt now!' he shouted, as he shut the gate.

The driver was very chatty. He soon heard all about their miserable holidays, and how much they were looking forward to their unexpected break before going back to school. In return he told them all about himself and his family – and as he had eleven brothers and sisters, his tale lasted for a good part of the journey!

They stopped for a meal in the car after some time, and found that they were hungry for the first time since they had been ill.

'Good gracious – I can really *taste* these sandwiches!' said George, in a surprised voice. 'Can you, Anne?'

'Yes – they don't taste of cardboard – like all our meals have lately,' said Anne. 'Timmy – you're not going to fare so well, now that we're getting our appetites back!'

'He was a very good dustbin while we were ill, wasn't he?' said Dick. 'He simply *gobbled* up all the bits and pieces we couldn't eat. Ugh – that boiled fish! It tasted like stewed knitting!'

They laughed – and that set them off coughing again. The driver listened and shook his head. 'Nasty coughs you've got!' he said. 'Reminds me of the time when me and my family got whooping cough – twelve of us together. My, when we all whooped, it sounded like a lot of fire-sirens going off!'

That made the children laugh again, and cough. But somehow nobody minded the irritating coughs now – they would surely soon be gone, once they could get out into the country and try their legs at running and racing and skiing once again.

It was a long drive. All the children fell asleep in the car after their meal, and the driver smiled to see them lolling back against one another, looking very peaceful. Only Timmy was awake, and he climbed cautiously up between George and the window, wishing the window was open, so that he could put his big nose out into the wind, as he loved to do.

They stopped for a very early tea at a teashop in a village. 'Better stretch your legs a bit,' said the driver, getting out. 'I know I want to stretch mine. Look – I'm going into that place over there for my tea. There's plenty of my pals there, and I'd enjoy a chat. You go and tuck in at this teashop here, and ask for their buttered crumpets. They're the best in the world! Be back for you in a quarter of an hour – not longer, or we shan't be at the farmhouse before dark. It's still about an hour's run, but there'll be a moon later on.'

They were all glad to stretch their legs. Timmy bounded out as if he were on springs, barking madly. He was disappointed to find that they were only making a short stop – he had hoped they were at the end of their journey. But he was pleased to be given a buttery crumpet all to himself in the teashop. He licked every scrap of butter off first, much to the children's amusement.

'I'd rather like to do that myself, Timmy,' said Anne. 'But it's not really good manners, you know! Oh, *don't* make my shoe buttery – take your crumpet a bit farther away.'

They had time for two crumpets each, and a cup of hot tea. Julian bought some chocolate biscuits, as he felt unexpectedly hungry, even after two crumpets.

'Marvellous to feel even a *bit* hungry, after not being able to look even bread and butter in the face!' he said. 'I knew we must be jolly ill that day we couldn't eat even ice-cream though Mother tried to tempt us with some!'

'My legs are still a bit funny,' said Anne, walking back to the car. 'But they're beginning to feel as if they *belong* to me, thank goodness!'

They set off again. They were in Wales now, and mountains were beginning to loom up in the distance. It was a very clear evening, and although the mountains were white with snow, the countryside they passed was not nearly as snowy as their own home had been when they left.

'I hope to goodness the snow doesn't begin to melt, just as we've arrived,' said Dick. 'It seems all right up on the mountains at present – but down here in the valleys there's hardly any.'

They passed a signpost, and Julian looked to see what it said. He made out a word that looked like 'Cymryhlli', and called to the driver.

'Did you see that signpost? Should we look out for Magga Glen now?'

'Yes. We must be getting on that way,' said the driver. 'I've been looking out for it myself. I wonder I haven't seen it yet.'

'Goodness! I hope we haven't lost our way,' said Anne. 'It will soon be dark.'

The car went on and on. 'Better look out for a village,' said Julian. But they didn't come to one – nor did they see any other signposts. The night was now coming on, but there was already a small moon, which gave a little light.

'Are you sure we're right?' Dick asked the driver. 'The road seems to be getting a bit rough – and we haven't passed even a farmhouse for ages.'

'Well – maybe we are on the wrong road,' admitted the driver, slowing down. 'Though where we took the wrong turning I simply don't know! I reckon we're near the sea now.'

'Look – there's a turning up to the right!' shouted George, as they went slowly on. 'It's got a signpost, too!'

They stopped by the signpost, which was only a small one. 'It doesn't say Magga Glen,' said Dick, disappointed. 'It says Old Towers – just that. Would it be the name of a place, do you think – or a building? Where's a map?'

The driver hadn't one. 'I don't usually need a map,' he said. 'But this countryside isn't signposted as it should be, and I wish I'd brought my map with me. I guess we'd better turn right and go up to see this Old Towers. Maybe they can put us on our road!'

So they swung up to the right, and the car went slowly, crawling up a long, steep, winding road.

'It's quite a mountain,' said Anne, peering out of the window. 'Oh – I can see something – a building on the side of the hill, look – with towers. This must be it.'

They came to stout wooden gates. On them was a large notice, with just two words on it in large black letters:

KEEP OUT

'Well – that's nice and polite!' said the driver, angrily.

'Keep out! Why should we? Wait a bit – there's a little lodge here. I'll go and ask our way.'

But the lodge was no more helpful than the big gate. It was in complete darkness, and when the driver banged on the door, there was no answer at all. Now what could they do?

CHAPTER THREE

The end of the journey

'WELL – WE'D better turn round and go back down the hill,' said Dick, as the driver came back to the car.

'No, wait, I'll just hop out and see if there are any lights anywhere,' said Julian, and jumped out of the car. 'I could go up the drive a little way and see if I can spot the house itself. It can't be *very* far. After all, we spotted it just now as we came up the winding road.'

He went to the gates, and looked at them in the light from the car's headlamps. 'They're padlocked,' he called. 'But I think I can climb over. There's certainly a light somewhere beyond – though how far, I don't know.'

But before he could climb over the gate there came the sound of running footsteps behind it – and then a loud and savage howl came on the night air, and some animal hurled against the other side of the gate.

The driver got back hurriedly into the car and slammed the door. Julian also ran to the car, finding his legs could go quickly if he wanted them to, for all their feebleness!

Timmy began to bark fiercely, and tried to leap through the closed car window. The howling and barking behind the gates went on and on, and the dog there, which must have been a very big one, continually hurled itself against the gates, shaking them from top to bottom.

'Better turn round and go,' said the driver, scared. 'Whew! I'm glad I'm this side of those gates. What a din! That dog of yours is almost as bad, too!'

Timmy was certainly furious. Why wasn't he allowed to get out and tell the other dog what he thought of him? George tried to pacify him, but he wouldn't stop barking. The driver began to turn the car round, cautiously backing a little and then going forward, and backing again. The road was fairly wide, but there was a very steep slope to the right of the car. Old Towers was certainly built on a mountainside!

'The people there must be jolly scared of burglars to have a dog like that,' said Dick. 'Yet it's such a lonely place you wouldn't think many people would come near it. What's up, driver?'

'There's something wrong,' said the driver, who now had the car facing back down the road again. 'The car seems very heavy to drive, all of a sudden. As if I'd got my brakes on.'

'Perhaps you have,' said Julian.

'Well, I haven't,' said the driver, shortly. 'That is, only just a little, to make sure the car doesn't shoot off down the hill – you can see it's pretty steep here, and there's almost a cliff, your side. Don't want to drive down *there* in the dark! What *can* be the matter with the car? It will only crawl.'

'I thought it came *up* the hill terribly slowly, too,' said Dick. 'I know the road was steep and winding – but didn't it seem to *you* as if the car was making heavy work of it?'

'Well, yes, it did,' admitted the driver. 'But I just thought the hill must be steeper than I imagined. What *is* the matter with the car? I've got no brake on at all, and I'm pushing the accelerator down hard – and still she crawls! As if she'd got a ton weight to pull!'

It really was a puzzle. Julian felt worried. He didn't want them to have to spend the night in the car, lost in a cold countryside – especially as now it was beginning to snow lightly! The moon had disappeared behind heavy clouds, and everything looked very dark indeed.

They reached the bottom of the hill at last, and came on to the level road again. The driver heaved a sigh of relief – and then gave a sudden exclamation.

'What's happened? The car's all right again! She's going like a bird! Whew – that's a load off my mind! I thought she was going to pack up, and leave us to spend the night here.'

The car sped along well now, and everyone was most relieved. 'Must have been something wrong with her works somewhere,' said the driver. 'But I'm blessed if I know what it was! Now – look out for a house or a signpost.'

They actually came to a signpost not long after that, and George yelled out at once. 'Stop! Here's a signpost. STOP!'

The car slid to a stop beside it, and everyone looked at it and gave a shout of delight. 'Magga Glen! Hurrah!'

'Up to the left,' said the driver, and swung his car into the lane. It was rather rough, and obviously only a farm road – but there, right up the hill they were now climbing, was a house, with lights shining in the windows. That must be old Mrs Jones's farmhouse.

'Thank goodness!' said Julian. 'This must be it. I'm glad we got here before the snow set in properly. It's quite difficult to see through the windscreen now.'

Yes – it was the farmhouse. Dogs set up a terrific barking as the car drew near, and Timmy at once answered, almost deafening everyone in the car!

The driver drew up at the farmhouse door, and looked out cautiously to make sure that none of the barking dogs was leaping about round the car. The front door opened, and framed in the light stood a little old woman, as upright as any of the children!

'Come in, come in!' she called. 'Out of this cold and snow! Morgan will help with the luggage. Come in, now!'

The four children, suddenly feeling very tired, got out of the car. Anne almost stumbled, because once again her legs felt as if they didn't belong to her, and Julian caught her arm. They went in wearily, only Timmy seeming to have any energy! A tall man hurried out to help the driver with the luggage, saluting them as he passed.

The old lady took them into a big, warm living room and made them sit down. 'What a journey for you!' she said. 'You look worn out and poorly. It's late too, and I had a good tea laid for you. But now it's supper you'll be wanting, poor children!'

Julian caught sight of a loaded table not far from the fire, set to one side. Although he was tired, the sight of the good food there made him suddenly feel hungry. He smiled at the kind old woman. Her hair gleamed like silver, and her fine old face was wrinkled all over – but her eyes were as sharp and bright as a blackbird's.

'I'm sorry we're so late,' he said. 'We lost our way. This is my sister Anne – this is our cousin George – and this is my brother Dick.'

'And this is Timmy,' said George, and Timmy at once offered his paw to the old woman.

'Well, now, it's a wonder to see a dog with such good manners,' she said. 'We've seven – but not one of them would shake hands – no, not if the Queen herself came here, God bless her!'

The barking of the dogs had now died down. Not one of them was to be seen in the house, and the children thought they must be outside in kennels somewhere. Timmy trotted about round the room, sniffing into every corner with much interest. Finally he went to the table, put his paws up and had a good look at the food there. Then he went to George and whined.

'He says he likes the look of the food there,' George said to the old woman. 'I must say I agree with him! It looks good!'

'Go and wash and get yourselves a bit tidy, while I make some hot tea,' said Mrs Jones. 'You look cold and hungry. Go through that door, look – and up the little flight of stairs. The rooms up there are all yours – no one will disturb you.'

The Five went out of the door and found themselves in a little stone passage, lit by a candle. A narrow flight of stone steps led upwards to a small landing on which another candle burned. The steps were very steep, and the children stumbled up them, their legs stiff after their long drive.

Two bedrooms opened off the little landing, opposite to one another. They seemed exactly alike, and were furnished in the same way too. There were washstands with basins, and in each basin was a jug of hot water, wrapped around with a towel. Wood fires burned in the little stone fireplaces, their flames lighting the rooms almost more than the single candles there.

'You'll have this room, girls, and Dick and I will have the other,' said Julian. 'Gosh – wood fires in our bedrooms! What a treat!'

'I shall go to bed early, and lie and watch the flames,' said Anne. 'I'm glad the rooms aren't cold. I know I should cough if they were.'

'We haven't coughed *quite* so much today,' said Dick, and immediately, of course, had a very bad fit of coughing! The old woman downstairs heard him, and called up at once.

'You hurry up, now, and come down into the warm!'

They were soon downstairs, sitting in the warm living room. Nobody was there except old Mrs Jones, pouring out tea.

'Isn't anyone else coming in to tea?' asked George, looking all round. 'Surely all this food isn't just for us?'

'Oh yes it is,' said the old woman, cutting some ham in long thin slices. 'This is your own room – the room I let out to families for themselves. We've got our big kitchen over there for ourselves. You can do what you like here – make as much noise as you like – no one will hear you – our stone walls are so thick!'

After she had served them, she went out of the room, nodding and smiling. The children looked at one another.

'I like her very much,' said Anne. 'How old she must be, if she is Jenkins's aunt! But her eyes are so bright and young!'

'I feel better already,' said Dick, tucking into the ham. 'George, give Timmy something. He keeps poking me with his paw, and I really can't spare him any of my ham.'

'He can have some of mine,' said George. 'I thought I was hungry – but I'm not, after all. I suddenly feel tired.'

Julian looked at her. She did look tired, and her eyes were ringed with black shadows. 'Finish your meal, old thing,' said Julian, 'and go up to bed. You can unpack tomorrow. You're tired out with the long drive! Anne doesn't look nearly so tired as you do!'

Old Mrs Jones came in again, and approved highly of

Julian's idea that they should all go up to bed when they had finished. 'Get up tomorrow when you like,' she said. 'And just come into my kitchen and tell me when you're down. You can do just what you like here!'

But all they wanted to do at that moment was to get into bed and go to sleep by the light of the crackling wood fires! What a relief it was to slip in between the rather rough sheets and shut their eyes! All except Timmy. He kept guard by the door for a long time before he crept on to George's bed. Good old Timmy!

CHAPTER FOUR

In the old farmhouse

THE FOUR children slept like logs all night long. If they coughed they didn't know it! They lay in their beds, hardly moving – and only Timmy opened an eye occasionally, as he always did on the first night in a strange place.

He jumped when a burning log fell to one side in the fireplace. He stared sternly at a big bright flame licking up the chimney, as the log burned fiercely. He cocked up an ear when an owl hooted outside the window.

But at last he too fell asleep, lying as usual on George's feet – though old Mrs Jones would not have approved of that at all!

Julian awoke first in the morning. He heard the sounds of the farm coming through the closed window. Shouts of one man to another – the lowing of cows – the barking of one dog after another, and then all together – and the peaceful sound of hens clucking and ducks quacking. It was nice to lie and hear it all, feeling warm and lazy.

He looked at his watch. Good gracious, it was almost nine o'clock! Whatever *would* Mrs Jones think of them? He leapt out of bed, and awoke Dick with the quick movement.

'It's almost nine!' said Julian, and went to the washstand. This time there was only cold water in the big china jug, but he didn't mind. The bedroom was still warm with the burnt-out wood fires. The sun shone outside, but in the night the snow must have fallen heavily, for everywhere was white.

'Good,' said Julian, looking out. 'We shall be able to use our toboggans soon. Wake the girls, Dick.'

But the girls were already awake, for Timmy had heard the boys stirring, and had gone whining to the door. George stretched herself, feeling quite different from the night before.

'Anne – how do you feel? I feel really fine!' said George, pleased. 'Do you know it's nine o'clock? We've slept for more than twelve hours. No wonder we feel better!'

'Yes. I certainly do too,' said Anne, with an enormous yawn. 'Oh look, I've made Timmy yawn too! Timmy, did *you* sleep well?'

'Woof!' said Timmy, and pawed impatiently at the door.

'He wants his breakfast,' said George. 'I wonder what there is. I feel rather like bacon and egg – goodness, I thought I'd *never* feel like eating that again. Brrrr – this water's cold to wash in.'

They all went downstairs together and found their living room warm with a great wood fire. Breakfast was laid, but only a big crusty loaf, butter and home-made marmalade were there, with an enormous jug of cold, creamy milk.

Mrs Jones came in almost at once, beaming at them. 'Well, good morning to you now,' she said, 'and a nice morning it is too, for all the snow we had in the night.

What would you like for breakfast now? Ham and eggs – or home-made pork sausages – or meat patties – or . . .'

'I'd like ham and eggs,' said Julian, at once, and the others said the same. Mrs Jones went out of the room, and the children rubbed their hands.

'I feared we were only going to have bread and butter and marmalade,' said Dick. 'I say, look at the cream on the top of this milk! Me for a farm life when I grow up!'

'Woof!' said Timmy, approvingly. He kept hearing the other dogs barking, and going to the windows to look out. George laughed at him. 'You'll have to remember you're just a visitor, when you meet those dogs,' she said. 'No throwing your weight about, and barking your head off!'

'They look pretty big dogs,' said Dick, joining Timmy at the window. 'Welsh collies, I should think – they're so good with the sheep. I say, I wonder what that dog was that barked at us so fiercely last night, behind that gate at Old Towers? Do you remember?'

'Yes. I didn't much like it,' said Anne. 'It was rather like a nasty dream – losing our way – going up that steep hill – only to find that horrid notice on the gates – and nobody to ask the way – and then that hidden dog barking ferociously just the other side of the gates! And then the car *crawling* down the hill in that strange way.'

'Yes. It *was* a bit strange,' said Dick. 'Ah – here comes our breakfast. Mrs Jones, you've brought in enough for eight people, not four!'

She was followed by an enormous man, with a mass of black hair, bright blue eyes, and a stern mouth.

'This is my son, Morgan,' she said. The four children looked at the giantlike man in awe.

'Good morning,' said Julian and Dick together, and Morgan nodded his head, after giving them one quick look. The girls gave him polite smiles, and he nodded at them too, but didn't speak a word. He went out at once.

'He's not much of a one for talking,' said the old woman. 'Not my Morgan. But the voice he's got when he's angry! I'm telling the truth when I say you could hear him a mile away! Sends the sheep skittering off for miles when he shouts!'

Julian felt that he could quite believe it. 'Those are his

dogs you can hear barking,' said the old woman. 'Three of them. They go about with my Morgan everywhere. He's all for dogs, he is. Doesn't care much about people! He's got four more dogs on the hills with the sheep – and, believe you me, if Morgan went out in the yard there, and shouted, those four dogs with the sheep on the hills far away would hear him and come tearing down here like a flash of lightning!'

The children felt as if they could well believe this of the giantlike Morgan. They rather wished he *would* call his dogs. His voice would certainly be worth hearing!

They set to work on their breakfast, and although they couldn't eat quite all that Mrs Jones had brought, they managed to do very well indeed! So did Timmy. They especially liked the bread, which was home-made and very good.

'I could really make a meal just of this home-made bread and fresh butter,' said Anne. 'Our bread at home doesn't taste a bit the same. I say – wouldn't Mother be amazed to see the breakfast we've eaten today?'

'She certainly would – considering that we haven't felt like eating even a boiled egg for days,' said Dick 'I say – oughtn't we to telephone home, Julian, and say we're safely here?'

'Gosh, yes,' said Julian. 'I meant to last night. I'll do that now, if Mrs Jones will let me. Hallo, look – isn't that our last night's driver going off? He must have spent the night here.'

The driver was about to get into his car when he heard Julian knocking at the window. He came over to the farmhouse, and walked in at the front door, and soon found the children's living room.

'I'm just off,' he announced. 'The old lady gave me a bed in the barn last night – never been so cosy in my life! And I say – I've found out why the car crawled so slowly up and down that hill to Old Towers last night!'

'Oh, have you? Why was it then?' asked Julian, with interest.

'Well, it wasn't anything to do with the *car*,' said the driver, 'and wasn't I thankful to know that! It was to do with the hill itself.'

'Whatever do you mean?' said Dick, puzzled.

'Well, the shepherd's wife told me they think there must be something magnetic down under that hill,' said the driver. 'Because when the postman goes up on his bicycle, the same thing happens. His bicycle feels like lead, so heavy that he can't even cycle up – and if he *pushes* his bike, it feels just as heavy too. So now he leaves his bike at the bottom and just walks up!'

'I see – so the magnetic whatever-it-is got hold of the car last night, and pulled so much that it made it go slow too,' said Julian. 'Peculiar! There must be some deposit of powerful metal in that hill. Does it affect all cars like that?'

'Oh yes – no one goes up there in a car if they can help it,' said the driver. 'Funny thing, isn't it? Odd hill altogether, if you ask me – that notice on the gate and all!'

'I wonder who lives there?' said Dick.

'Only an old lady,' said the driver. 'She's off her head, so they say – won't let anyone in! Well – *we* know that all right. Sorry I lost my way last night – but you're all right now. You're in clover here!'

He moved to the door, raised his hand in salute, and went out. They saw him through the window getting into his car and driving away, waving a leather-gloved hand out of the window.

'Is the snow thick enough to toboggan on?' wondered George. 'It doesn't look like it. Let's go out and see. Better wrap up well though – I bet the wind's cold out on this hill, and I don't want to start sniffling again. I've had enough of that.'

Soon they were all clad in heavy coats, scarves and woollen hats. Mrs Jones nodded her head when she saw them, and smiled. 'Sensible children you are,' she said. 'It's cold today, with a biting wind, but healthy weather! Be careful of that dog of yours, my boy – don't you let him loose till you're well away from the farm, in case he goes for one of my Morgan's dogs.'

George smiled, pleased to be addressed as a boy. They began to wander round the farm, Timmy cross because he was on the lead. He pulled at it, wanting to run round and explore on his own. But George wouldn't let him. 'Not till you've made friends with all the other dogs,' she said. 'I wonder where they are?'

'Must have gone out with Morgan,' said Dick. 'Come

on – let's go and look at the cows in the sheds. I do love the smell of cows.'

They wandered round the farm, enjoying the pale sun, the keen wind, and the feeling that their legs belonged to them at last, and were not likely to give way at any moment. They hardly coughed at all, and felt quite annoyed when one or other suddenly began.

'I shall let old Timmy off the lead a bit now,' said George. 'I can't see a dog about anywhere.' So she slipped the lead off his collar and he ran off joyfully at once, sniffing here, there and everywhere. He disappeared round a corner, his tongue hanging out happily.

And then the most appalling barking began! The children stopped as if they had been shot. It wasn't one dog, or even two – it sounded like a dozen! The four rushed round the corner of a barn at once – and there was poor Timmy, standing with his back to the barn, growling and barking and snarling at three fierce dogs!

'No, George, no, don't go to Timmy,' shouted Julian, seeing that George was going to rescue Tim, whatever happened. 'Those dogs are savage!'

But what did George care for that? She raced to Timmy, stood in front of him, and yelled at the three surprised dogs snarling there. 'HOW DARE YOU! GET AWAY! GO HOME! I SAID GO HOME!'

CHAPTER FIVE

Things might be worse!

THE THREE snarling dogs took no notice of George. It was Timmy they wanted. Who was this strange dog who dared to come wandering round their home? They tried to get at him, but George stood there, swinging the leather lead, and giving first one dog and then another a sharp flick. Julian rushed to help her – and then Timmy gave a sharp yelp. He had been bitten!

Someone came rushing round the corner. It was Mrs Jones, running as if she were a twelve-year-old!

'Tang! Bob! Dai!' she called, but the three dogs took no notice of her. And then, from somewhere, came a voice. What a voice! It echoed all round the farmyard as if it had come through a megaphone.

'DAI! BOB! TANG!'

And at the sound of that booming voice the three dogs stopped as if shot. Then they turned about and tore off at top speed.

'Thank God! That was Morgan,' panted the old woman, clutching her shawl round her. 'He must have heard the barking. Oh, my little dear – are you hurt?' She took hold of George's arm, and looked at her anxiously.

'I don't know. I don't think so,' said George, looking

rather white. 'It's Timmy that's hurt. Oh, Tim, darling Tim, where did they bite you?'

'Woof!' said Timmy, who, though extremely startled, didn't seem at all frightened. It had all happened so suddenly. George dropped down on her knees in the snow, and gave a little scream. 'He's been bitten on the neck – oh look! Poor, poor Timmy. *Why* did I let you off the lead?'

'It's not much, George,' said Julian, looking at the bleeding place. 'The other dog bit just where his collar is, look – and his teeth went through the collar, not really into Tim's neck. It's really not much more than a graze.'

Anne was leaning against the wall, looking sick, and Dick suddenly felt as if his legs were wobbly again. He couldn't help thinking what would have happened if the three savage dogs had bitten George instead of Timmy. Good old George! She was as brave as a lion!

'What a thing to happen!' said old Mrs Jones, upset. 'Why for did you let him loose, my boy? You should have waited for my Morgan to come along with his dogs, and tell them your Timmy was a friend.'

'I know,' said George, still on her knees beside Timmy. 'It was all my fault. Oh, Timmy, I'm so thankful you've only got that one small bite. Mrs Jones, have you any TCP? I must put some on at once.'

But before Mrs Jones could answer, the giantlike figure of Morgan came round the corner of the barn, his three dogs, extremely subdued now, at his heels.

'Hey?' he said, inquiringly, looking at the four children and his mother.

'The dogs attacked this one,' explained his mother. 'You shouted just in time, Morgan. But he's not much hurt. You should have seen this boy here – the one the dog belongs to – he stood in front of his dog and fought off Tang, Bob and Dai!'

Julian couldn't help smiling to hear George continually called a boy – but, standing there in snow-trousers and coat, a woollen cap on her short hair, she looked very like a sturdy boy.

'Please come and get the TCP,' said George, anxiously, seeing a drop of blood drip from Timmy's neck on to the white snow. Morgan took a step forward and bent down to look at Timmy.

He made a small scornful sound and stood up again. '*He's* all right,' he said, and walked off.

George stared after him angrily. It was *his* dogs that had attacked and hurt Timmy – and he hadn't even been sorry about it! She felt so angry that tears came suddenly into her eyes. She blinked them away, ashamed.

'I don't think I want to stay here,' she said loudly, and clearly. 'Those dogs will be sure to attack Timmy again. They might kill him. I shall go home.'

'Now, now, you're just upset,' said kind old Mrs Jones, taking George's arm. George shook off her hand, scowling. 'I'm *not* upset. I'm just angry to think my dog should have been attacked for nothing – and I'm sure he'll be attacked again. And I want to see to his neck. I'm going indoors.'

She stalked off with Timmy at her heels, her head well up, bitterly ashamed of two more tears that suddenly ran down her cheeks. It wasn't like old George to cry! But she was still not quite herself after being ill. The other three looked at one another.

'Go with her, Anne,' said Julian, and Anne obediently ran after George. Julian turned to the worried old woman.

'You shouldn't stand out here in the cold,' he said, seeing that she was shivering, and pulling her shawl more closely round her. 'George will soon be all right. Don't take any notice of what she says.'

'*She!* What, isn't she a *boy*, then?' said Mrs Jones, in surprise. 'But now, surely she won't go home, will she?'

'No,' said Julian, hoping he was right. You never could tell with George! 'She'll soon get over it. If we could get some TCP it would help, though! She's always terrified of wounds going bad, where Timmy is concerned.'

'Come away in, then,' said Mrs Jones, and hurried back to the farmhouse, refusing Julian's hand over the snow.

George was in the living room with Timmy. She had got some water and was bathing the wound with her handkerchief, having first taken off Tim's collar.

'I'll fetch you the TCP, boy,' said Mrs Jones, forgetting again that George was a girl. She ran to her kitchen, and came back with a big bottle of antiseptic. George took it gratefully, and dabbed some on Timmy, who stood still,

quite enjoying all the fuss. He jumped a little when it stung him, and George patted him and praised him.

'He wouldn't mind having stuff dabbed on him all day long, George, if you would only make a fuss of him,' said Dick, with a laugh.

George looked up. 'He might have been killed,' she said. 'And if those dogs get him again, he certainly will be! I'm going to go back home – not to *your* home, Ju – but to my own, at Kirrin Cottage.'

'Oh, don't be silly, George,' said Dick, exasperated. 'Anyone would think Timmy had been injured for life or something. He's only got a skin wound! Why spoil what may be a jolly good holiday just for that?'

'I don't trust those three dogs,' said George, stubbornly. 'They'll be out to get Tim now – I know they will. I tell you I'm going home. I'm not spoiling *your* holiday – only my own.'

'Well, listen – stay one more day,' said Julian, hoping that if she did, George would see how stupidly she was behaving. 'Just *one* more day. That's not much to ask. It will upset old Mrs Jones dreadfully if you rush off like this – and it will be difficult to make arrangements for you to go back today, now that everywhere is under snow again.'

'All right,' said George, ungraciously. 'I'll stay till tomorrow. It will give Timmy a bit of time to get over his fright. But ONLY till tomorrow.'

'Tim's not frightened,' said Anne. 'George, he would have taken on all three dogs by himself if you hadn't gone to his help. Wouldn't you, Timmy?'

'Woof, woof!' said Timmy, agreeing at once. He wagged his tail vigorously. Dick laughed. 'Good old Tim!' he said. '*You* don't want to go home, do you?'

'Woof!' said Timmy, obligingly, and wagged his tail again. George put on one of her scowls, and Julian nudged the others to warn them to stop teasing her. He didn't want George suddenly to change her mind and rush off home straight away!

'I vote we go for a walk,' said Dick. 'It's a shame to stick indoors like this on this sunny, snowy day. Anne, are you coming?'

'I will if George does,' said Anne. But George shook her head.

'No,' she said. 'I'll stay in with Tim this morning. You go off together.'

Anne wouldn't come, so the boys left the two girls and went out into the keen, invigorating mountain air once more. Already they felt better, and were not coughing at all. What a pity this had happened! It spoilt things for everyone – even for old Mrs Jones, who now appeared at her front door, looking anxious.

'Don't you worry now, Mrs Jones,' said Julian. 'I expect our cousin will be all right soon. She's given up the idea of rushing home today at any rate! My brother and I are going for a walk up the mountain. Which way is best?'

'Well now, take that path,' said the old woman, pointing. 'And go on till you come to our summer chalet. You can rest there before coming back – and if you don't want to come back for dinner, well, you'll find food in the cupboard there. Here is the key to get into the little place!'

'Oh thanks,' said Julian, surprised. 'That sounds good. We'd love to have our lunch up there, Mrs Jones – we'll be back before dark. Tell the girls for us, will you?'

And away they went, whistling. It was fun to have a day all to themselves, just the two of them, together!

They took the snowy path and began to climb up the slope of the mountain. The sun was now melting the snow a little, so they could make out the path fairly easily. Then they discovered that big black stones marked the way here and there – a guide to the farmer and his men, when the snow covered the path and everything!

The view was magnificent. As they climbed higher, they could see the tops of more and more hills, all of which sparkled snowy-white in the pale January sun. 'I *say* – if only we had a bit more snow, what tobogganing we could have down these slopes,' said Dick, longingly. 'I wish I'd brought my skis this morning – the snow is deep enough for them down that hill – we'd whizz along like lightning!'

They were glad when they at last came to the little hut or chalet that old Mrs Jones had spoken about. After two hours' climbing it was nice to think of having something to eat, and a good rest!

'It's quite a place,' said Julian, slipping the key into the lock. 'A little wooden house, with windows and all!'

He opened the door and went inside. Yes – it was a very fine little place indeed, with bunk beds let into the wooden walls, a stove for heating – and cupboards full of crockery – and tins of food! The two boys had the same idea at once, and swung round to one another.

'Couldn't we stay here – on our own? George would love it too,' said Julian, putting into words what Dick was already thinking. Oh – if only they *could*!

CHAPTER SIX

A funny little creature

THE BOYS were tired, but not too tired to examine the little hut thoroughly – though it really was more like a one-roomed house. It faced across the deep valley, and the sun shone straight into it. Julian opened cupboard after cupboard, exclaiming in delight.

'Bedding! Towels! Crockery – and cutlery! And look at these tins of food – and bottles of orangeade and the rest! My word, people who come to stay at Magga Glen in the summer must have a fantastic time!'

'We could light the stove to heat the room,' suggested Dick, pulling the oil-stove into the middle of the room.

'No. We don't need to,' said Julian. 'The sun is pouring in, and it really isn't cold in here. We could wrap ourselves round in rugs from that cupboard if we want to.'

'Do you think we'd be allowed to come up here, instead of living down at the farm?' said Dick, opening a tin of ham with a tin-opener that hung on a nail by the cupboard. 'It's so *much* nicer to be quite on our own and independent! George would simply love it!'

'Well, we can *ask*,' said Julian, taking the cap off a bottle of orangeade. 'Can we find some biscuits to eat with this ham? Oh yes – here are some cream-cracker biscuits. I *say* – I'm really ravenous!'

'So am I,' said Dick, his mouth full. 'Pity George was so silly – she and Anne could have enjoyed this too.'

'Well – perhaps on the whole it's as well they didn't come,' said Julian. 'I think Anne would have been too tired to come all this way on her first day – and George certainly had a worse cold and cough than anyone. A day at the farm will probably do her good. Gosh – she's absolutely fearless, isn't she? I'll never forget her standing up to those three savage dogs! I was jolly scared myself.'

'I'm going to get a rug and wrap it round me and sit out on the doorstep in the sun,' said Dick. 'That view is too marvellous for words!'

He and Julian took a rug each, and then sat out on the wooden doorstep, munching their ham and biscuits. They stared across at the great hill opposite.

'Is that a house on the slope over there – near the top, look?' said Dick, suddenly.

Julian stared across at the opposite hill, but could make out nothing.

'It can't be,' he said. 'The roof would be covered with snow, and we'd never see it. Besides, who would build a house so high up?'

'Plenty of people,' said Dick. 'It's not everyone who likes towns and shops and cinemas and traffic and the rest. I can imagine an artist building a house on one of these mountains, just for the view! He'd be quite happy looking at it and painting it all day long.'

'Well – I like a bit of company, I must say,' said Julian. 'This is all right for a week or two – but you'd need to be an artist or a poet – or a shepherd or something, to stand it all the time!'

He yawned. Both boys had finished their meal, and felt comfortably full and at peace. Dick yawned too, and lay back on his rug. But Julian pulled him upright.

'Oh no! We're not going to take naps up here! We'd sleep like logs again, and wake up in the dark. The sun's going down already, and we've got all that long walk back to the farm – and no torch to light our way if we go wrong!'

'There are those black stones,' said Dick, with another yawn. 'All right, all right – I agree with you! I certainly don't want to stumble down this mountain in the pitch dark!'

Julian suddenly clutched Dick's arm, and pointed upwards, where the path still wound on and on. Dick turned – and stared. Someone was up there, skipping down the path towards them, with a lamb gambolling around, and a small dog scampering after.

'Is it a boy or a girl?' said Julian, in wonder. 'My word – it must be cold, whichever it is!'

It was a small girl coming along, a wild-looking little creature with a mass of untidy black curls, a face as brown as an oak-apple – and very few clothes! She wore a dirty pair of boys' shorts, and a blue shirt. Her legs were bare, and she had old shoes on her feet. She was singing as she came, in a high sweet voice like a bird's.

The dog with her began to bark, and she stopped her song at once. She spoke to the dog, and he barked again, facing towards the hut. The lamb gambolled round without stopping.

The little girl looked towards the hut, and saw Julian and Dick. She turned at once and ran back the way she had come. Julian got up and shouted to her.

'It's all right! We shan't hurt you! Look – here's a bit of meat for your dog!'

The girl stopped and looked round, poised ready to run again at once. Julian waved the bit of ham left over from their meal. The little dog smelt it on the wind, and came running up eagerly. He snapped at it, got it into his mouth and ran back to the girl. He didn't attempt to eat it, but just stood there by her, looking up.

She bent down eagerly, and took it. She tore it in half and gave one piece to the eager dog, who swallowed it at once – and the other piece she ate herself, keeping a sharp eye on the two boys as she did so. The lamb came nosing round her, and she put one thin arm round its neck.

'What a funny little thing,' said Julian to Dick. 'Where *can* she have come from? She must be absolutely frozen!'

Dick called to the child.

'Hallo! Come and talk to us!'

She shot off at once as soon as he shouted. But she didn't go very far. She half hid behind a bush, peeping out now and again.

'Get some of those biscuits,' said Julian to Dick. 'We'll hold some out to her. She's like a wild thing.'

So Dick held out a handful of biscuits, and called:

'Bicuits! For you! And your dog!'

But only the lamb came gambolling up, a toy-like creature, with a tail that frisked and whisked all the time. It tried to get on to Dick's knee, and bumped its little black nose against his face.

'Fany, Fany!' called the small girl, in a high, clear voice. The lamb tried to get away but Dick held on to it. It seemed to be all legs!

'Come and get it!' shouted Dick. 'We shan't hurt you!'

The little girl couldn't bear to leave her lamb. She came out from the bush, and took a few hesitating steps towards the boys. The dog ran right up to them, snuffing at their hands for more ham. Julian gave him a biscuit and he crunched it up at once, giving sidelong glances at his watching mistress as if to apologise for eating it all himself. Julian patted the little thing and it licked him joyfully.

The little girl came nearer. Her legs looked blue with cold, but although she had so little on, she didn't seem to be shivering. Julian held out another biscuit. The dog jumped up and took it neatly in his mouth, running up to the little girl with it. The boys burst into laughter, and the small girl smiled suddenly, her whole face lighting up.

'Come here!' called Julian. 'Come and get your pretty lamb. We've got some more biscuits for you and your dog.'

At last the child came near to them, as watchful as a hare, ready to turn at a moment's notice. The boys sat still and patient, and soon the girl was near enough to snatch a biscuit and retreat again. She sat down on one of the black stones marking the path, and munched her biscuit, staring at them all the time out of her big dark eyes.

'What's your name?' asked Dick, not moving from his place, afraid that the child would leap off like a frightened goat.

The girl didn't seem to understand. Dick repeated his question, speaking slowly.

'What – is – your – name? What – are – you – called?'

The child nodded her head and then pointed to herself.

'Me – Aily,' she said.

She pointed at the dog.

'Dai,' she said, and he leapt up at his name and covered her with licks. Then she pointed to the lamb, which was now gambolling round the boys like a mad thing. 'Fany,' she said.

'Ah – Aily – Dai – Fany,' said Julian, solemnly, and he too pointed at first one then the other. Then he pointed to himself. 'Julian!' he said, and then pointed to Dick. 'Dick!'

The little girl gave a high, clear laugh, and suddenly poured out quite a long speech. The boys couldn't understand a word of it.

'She's speaking in Welsh, I suppose,' said Dick, disappointed. 'What a pity – it sounds lovely, but I can't make head or tail of it.'

The child saw that they had not understood. She frowned, as if thinking hard.

'My da – he up high – sheep!' she said.

'Oh – your father's a shepherd up there!' said Dick. 'But you don't live with him, do you?'

Aily considered this, then shook her head.

'Down!' she said, pointing. 'Aily down!' Then she turned to the dog and the lamb, and cuddled them both. 'Dai mine,' she said, proudly. 'Fany mine!'

'Nice dog. Nice lamb,' said Julian, solemnly, and the little girl nodded in delight. Then, for no reason that the boys could see, she stood up, leapt down the hill, followed by the lamb and the dog, and disappeared.

'What a funny little creature!' said Dick. 'Like a pixie of the hills, or an elf of the woods. I quite expected her to disappear in smoke, or something. I should think she runs completely wild, wouldn't you? We'll ask Mrs Jones about her when we get back!'

'My goodness – come on, the sun's getting quite low,' said Julian, getting up in a hurry. 'We've got to put the things away, and fold up the rugs, and lock up. Buck up – once the sun goes it will be dark almost at once, and we've quite a long way to go.'

It didn't take them long to tidy up and lock the little house carefully. Then down the path they went at top speed. The sun had melted most of the snow farther down, and the going was easy. The boys felt exhilarated by their day on the mountainside and sang as they went, until they were quite out of breath.

'There's the farmhouse,' said Dick, and both boys were glad to see it. Their legs were tired now, and they longed for a good meal and a rest in a warm room.

'I hope George has recovered a bit by now – and is *still* at the farm!' said Julian, with a laugh. 'You never know with old George! I hope she'll like the sound of that hut. We'll ask Mrs Jones about it tonight, when we've talked it over with Anne and George.'

'Here we are,' said Dick, thankfully, as they went up to the house. 'Anne! George! We're back – where are you?'

CHAPTER SEVEN

Back at the farm again

ANNE CAME running to meet Dick and Julian.

'Oh, I'm glad you're back!' she said. 'It's beginning to get dark, and I was afraid you'd lose your way!'

'Hallo, George!' said Julian, seeing her behind Anne, in the darkness of the passage. 'How's Timmy?'

'All right, thank you,' said George, sounding quite cheerful. 'Here he is!'

Timmy barked loudly and jumped at the boys in welcome. He was very glad to see them, for he had been afraid that they had gone back home. They all went into the living room, where there was an enormous wood fire, looking very cheerful indeed. Julian and Dick fell into the two most comfortable chairs and spread their legs out to the fire.

'Ha! This is good!' said Dick. 'I couldn't have walked another step. I don't believe I can even go up the stairs to wash. We've walked MILES!'

They told the girls about their day, and when they described the little summer chalet, the two girls listened eagerly.

'Oh – I wish we'd gone with you,' said Anne, longingly. 'Timmy would have been quite all right, wouldn't he, George? We've decided it's only a skin wound. Actually, you can hardly see it now.'

'But all the same, I'm going back home tomorrow,' said George, determinedly. 'I'm sorry I made such a fuss this morning – but *honestly* I thought Timmy had been badly bitten. Thank goodness he wasn't. Still, I'm not risking such a thing again. If I stay on here with him, he's sure to have those three dogs attacking him sometime or other, and he might be killed. I don't want to upset your holiday – but I can NOT stay on here with Tim.'

'All right, old thing,' said Julian, soothingly. 'Don't get so up-in-the-air about it. There – you've gone and started your cough again! Do you know, Dick and I haven't coughed once today!'

'Nor have I,' said Anne. 'The air is marvellous here. I think I ought to go back with George, though, Ju. She'd be miserable all by herself at home.'

'Listen,' said Julian. 'We've got an idea, Dick and I – one that means old George won't have to go home, and . . .'

'Nothing will make me stop here,' interrupted George at once. 'NOTHING!'

'Give me a chance to tell you what I've got up my sleeve,' protested Julian. 'It's about that mountain hut we've been to – Dick and I thought it would be a marvellous idea if we could all five of us go and spend our time there – instead of here. We'd be ABSOLUTELY on our own then – the way we like to be!'

'Oh *yes*!' said Anne at once, delighted. They all three looked at George. She smiled suddenly.

'Yes – that *would* be fun. I'd like that. I don't suppose those dogs would come near there. And how heavenly to be on our own!'

'Mrs Jones said that her son Morgan told her we're going to have heavy falls of snow!' said Anne. 'We could spend all day long on those slopes with our toboggans and skis. Oh, George – what a pity Timmy can't ski! We'll have to leave him at the hut when we go off skiing!'

'Do you suppose Mrs Jones will mind us going off there?' said Dick.

'I don't think so,' said Anne. 'She was telling us today that parties of children go there alone in the summer, while their parents stay and have a peaceful time down here. I don't see why she shouldn't let us go. We'll ask her when she comes in with our high tea. I said we wouldn't have tea *and* supper – we'd just have one big meal. We didn't know what time you'd be back – and George and I had such an enormous dinner in the middle of the day that we knew we wouldn't want tea.'

'Yes. *I'd* rather have a big meal now, too,' said Julian, yawning widely. 'I'm afraid all I shall want to do afterwards is to go up to bed and fall asleep. I'm *marvellously* tired. In fact, I could go to sleep this very minute! I suppose you girls have been indoors all day long because of Timmy?'

'No. We took it in turns to go for a walk without him,' said Anne. 'George hasn't let him put his nose outside the door. Poor Timmy – he just couldn't understand it, and he whined and whined!'

'Never mind – he'll enjoy himself if we can go up to that hut,' said George, who was very cheerful indeed now. 'I *do* hope we can. It would be glorious fun.'

'Ju – come and wash,' said Dick, seeing that Julian had his eyes closed already. '*Julian!* Come and wash, I tell you – you don't want to miss your meal, do you?' Julian groaned and dragged himself up the stone stairway. But once he had sluiced himself in cold water he felt much better, and very hungry indeed. So did Dick.

'We didn't tell the girls about the funny little creature – what was her name now – Aily! And Dai her dog and

Fany the lamb. We mustn't forget to ask Mrs Jones about them,' said Julian.

They went downstairs, feeling much fresher and were delighted to see that Mrs Jones had been in and laid the table. They went to see what there was for their high tea.

'Pork pie – home-made, of course,' said Dick. 'And what's this – golly, it's a cheese! How enormous! Smell it, Julian – it's enough to make you start eating straight away! And more of that home-made bread! Can't we start?'

'No – there are new-laid boiled eggs to begin with,' said Anne, with a laugh. 'And an apple pie and cream to end with. So I hope you really *are* hungry, you two!'

Mrs Jones came in with a pot of hot tea. She smiled at the boys as she set the big brown teapot down on the table. 'Have you had a nice day away up on the mountain?' she said. 'You look fine, both of you. Did you find the hut all right?'

'Yes, thank you,' said Julian. 'Mrs Jones, it's a marvellous hut. We . . .'

'Yes, yes – it's a good hut,' said Mrs Jones, 'and I was sorry that the two girls didn't go with you, such a fine day as it was, and the dog not really hurt! And to think that the girls want to go back home! I've been feeling sad about it all day.'

She really did seem hurt and grieved, and George looked very guilty. Julian patted Mrs Jones on the arm, and spoke comfortingly.

'Don't you worry about us, Mrs Jones. I've got a fine

idea to tell you. What we'd *really* like is to go and live up at that hut, the five of us – then we'd be out of your way and Timmy would be out of the way of the farm dogs too! Do you think we might do that? Then George wouldn't have to go home, as she had planned to do.'

'Well now! To go to that hut in this weather! What an idea!' said Mrs Jones. 'You'd be most uncomfortable, with no one to look after you, and see to your wants, and cook for you this cold weather. No, no . . .'

'We're used to looking after ourselves,' said Dick. 'We're awfully good at it, Mrs Jones. And, my word, the food you've got up there is enough to feed an army! And there are cups and plates and dishes – and knives and forks – and all kinds of bedding . . .'

'We'd have a *smashing* time,' said George, joining in eagerly. 'I don't really want to go home, Mrs Jones. It's so lovely in these mountains – and if the snow comes down, as your Morgan says, we'd be able to have winter sports all on our own!'

'Oh, do say it's all right,' begged Anne. 'We shall be quite safe and happy there – and we do promise to come down here again if we can't manage, or if anything goes wrong.'

'I'll see that things go all right,' said Julian, speaking in his most grown-up voice.

'Well – well, it's a funny idea,' said Mrs Jones, still taken aback. 'I'll have to talk to my Morgan about it first. Now sit you down and eat your meal. I'll get my Morgan to decide.'

She went out of the room, shaking her head, her mouth pursed up in disapproval. No fire! No hot meals! No one to 'manage' for them. What a dreadful time those children would have up in that hut in this weather!

The five set to work to demolish the good food on the table. George allowed Timmy to sit up on a chair too, and fed him with titbits for a treat. He was perfectly good and very well-mannered indeed.

'I almost expect him to hand me a plate of something!' said Anne, with a giggle. 'Tim, dear – do pass me the salt!'

Timmy put a paw on the table exactly as if he meant to obey Anne, and George hastily made him put it down again! What a meal that was! The pork pie was so good that everyone had two slices, as well as their boiled eggs. Then they started on the cheese, which even Timmy liked. There was very little room indeed for the apple pie that Mrs Jones brought in at the end!

'My goodness – I forgot that an apple pie was coming,' said Anne, in dismay, as the old woman walked in with a tray on which was a big apple pie and a jug of cream.

'Mrs Jones – when we were up at the hut, we saw such a funny little creature,' said Dick. 'She said her name was Aily and she had a lamb and . . .'

'Oh, Aily! That mad little thing!' said Mrs Jones, picking up the dirty plates. 'She's the shepherd's daughter – a little truant she is, runs off from school, and hides away in the hills with her dog and her lamb. She always has a lamb each year – it follows her about everywhere. They say there isn't a rabbit hole or a blackberry bush or a bird's nest that child doesn't know!'

'She was singing when we first saw her,' said Julian. 'Singing like a bird.'

'Ah, yes – she has a lovely voice,' said Mrs Jones. 'She's wild as a bird – there's nothing to be done with her. If she's scolded she goes off for weeks, no one knows where. Don't you let her come round that hut now, when you're there – she might steal from you!'

'Oh, yes – the hut! Have you spoken to Morgan about it?' said Dick, eagerly.

'Yes, I have indeed,' said Mrs Jones. 'And he says yes, to let you go. *He* doesn't want trouble with the dogs either.

He says snow is coming for sure, but you'll be safe up there and you can all take your toboggans for there'll be a chance to use them! He'll help you up with your things.'

'Oh good! Thanks!' said Julian, and the others smiled and looked at one another joyfully. 'Thanks most awfully, Mrs Jones. We'll go tomorrow after breakfast!'

Tomorrow! After breakfast! Up to that lonely hut on the mountainside, just the Five of them together. What could be better than that?

CHAPTER EIGHT

Off to the little hut

JULIAN AND Dick were so sleepy after their long day in the cold air, and their enormous meal, that they could not keep their eyes open for long.

'Go to bed, both of you!' said Anne, seeing them lying tired out in their chairs, when Mrs Jones had cleared away everything.

'Yes. I think we'd better,' said Julian, staggering up. 'Oh, my legs! They're stiff as sticks! Good night, you two girls, and Timmy. See you tomorrow – if we wake up!'

The two boys stumbled up the stone stairs to bed. George and Anne stayed downstairs, talking and reading. Timmy lay on the hearth rug, listening, his ears twitching towards Anne when she spoke, and then towards George as she answered. This little habit of his always made them laugh.

'It's *exactly* as if he was listening, but too lazy to join in our conversation!' said Anne. 'Oh, George – I really am glad you're not going home tomorrow. It would be the first time you'd ever done a thing like that! I'd just have *had* to come with you!'

'Don't let's talk about it,' said George. 'I feel rather ashamed of making such a fuss now. All the same I shall be terrified if I see any of those dogs again when I'm with Timmy. What a bit of luck the boys went up to that hut today, Anne – we'd never have known about it if they hadn't.'

'Yes. It sounds fun,' said Anne. 'Don't let's be too late to bed, George. It will be quite a pull up the mountainside tomorrow, with all our things!'

George went to the window.

'It's snowing hard,' she said. 'Just as Morgan said it would. I don't like him, do you?'

'Oh – I think he's all right,' said Anne. 'And what a voice he's got! He nearly made me jump out of my skin when he called his three dogs. He must have the loudest voice in the world!'

'Timmy – you're yawning!' said George, as Timmy opened his mouth widely and made a yawning noise. 'How's your neck?'

Timmy was getting rather tired of having his neck examined. He lay still while George had another look at it.

'Healing beautifully!' she said. 'You'll be quite all right tomorrow. Will you like going off to that hut all by ourselves, Tim?'

Timmy gave her a loving lick and yawned again. Then he got up and trotted over to the door that led to the stone stairs, looking back inquiringly at George.

'Right. We're coming,' said George, laughing, and she and Anne blew out the lamp on the table, and followed Timmy up the stairs. They peeped in at the boys' room –

and saw Julian and Dick absolutely sound asleep, dead to the world!

'A thunderstorm wouldn't wake them tonight!' said Anne. 'Come on – let's buck up and get into bed ourselves. We've a nice wood fire again, and I shall undress in front of it. Move over, Timmy. I want to stand on the rug.'

In the morning the world was very white indeed! As Morgan had prophesied, the snow had fallen thickly in the night, and everywhere was covered in a thick white blanket, that gleamed and sparkled in the weak January sun.

'This is something like it!' said Dick, as he looked out of his bedroom. 'Get up, Ju – it's a marvellous morning! Remember, we've got to take all our things up to that hut today! Do stir yourself!'

Mrs Jones gave them a fine breakfast – eggs, bacon and sausages.

'It's the last hot meal you'll have, if you're going up to that hut,' she said. 'Though you'll be able to cook eggs in the little saucepan up there, if you set it on top of the oilstove. And mind you don't get playing about round that stove when it's alight, or the whole place might go up in flames!'

'We'll be very careful,' promised Julian. 'I'll send anyone back if they upset the stove – yes, I will, so just look out, Timmy!'

'Woof!' said Tim, amiably. He was pleasantly excited with all the preparations for going, and ran sniffing from one parcel to another.

The children were not taking all their things, of course, but Mrs Jones had made them pack a complete change of clothes each, besides their warmest night-clothes and dressing-gowns. They had torches too, and plenty of rope for hauling things up and down the hills. And also they had six loaves of new-baked bread, a large cheese, about three dozen eggs and a ham. So they were truly well provided for.

'And there's plenty of butter packed in with the loaves,' said Mrs Jones, 'and a large pot of cream. I'll try and send up some milk if the shepherd comes down. He'll pass the hut when he goes up again. There's only a quart in the bottle there – but you'll find plenty of orangeade and lemonade in the hut – and you can boil snow if you want to make cocoa or tea!'

It was quite clear that Mrs Jones had no idea how many times the Five had gone off on their own! They smiled and winked at one another, and took all her advice in good part. She really was so kind, so very concerned about them all. She even packed some bones and dog biscuits for Timmy!

'Here's my Morgan now,' said Mrs Jones, when every single thing had been put in a pile outside the front door, toboggans and skis as well. 'He's brought his snow-slide with him, to take all your goods.'

The snow-slide was like a long flat cart with runners instead of wheels – an elongated sleigh. The children piled on to it all the parcels and two suitcases. They were all going to walk up as the snow was not yet too thick. Timmy danced round in great excitement – though both he and George kept a wary eye out for the other dogs, and Timmy did not venture very far from George.

The giantlike Morgan arrived, his breath puffing before him like a smoke-cloud! He nodded at the children.

'Morning,' he said, and that was all. He took hold of the ropes at the front of the snow-slide and ran them over his shoulders.

'I'll take one,' said Julian. 'It's much too heavy for one person to pull!'

'Ha!' said Morgan, scornfully, and walked off with the two ropes over his shoulder. The snow-slide followed easily.

'Strong as a horse, is my Morgan,' said old Mrs Jones, proudly.

'Strong as *ten* horses!' said Julian, wishing he was as big and as strong as the broad-shouldered farmer.

George said nothing. She hadn't yet forgiven the farmer for being scornful about Timmy's bite the day before. She followed the others, carrying her skis, and waved to kind old Mrs Jones as she stood anxiously watching them leave.

It seemed a long trek up the mountainside, when things had to be pulled or carried! Morgan went first, pulling the big snow-slide easily. Julian went next, pulling a toboggan and carrying his skis. Dick was next with another toboggan and skis, and the girls came last with their skis only.

Timmy ran at the front or the back as he liked, enjoying everything.

Morgan said nothing at all. Julian addressed a few polite remarks to him, and received a grunt in reply, but that was all. He looked curiously at the great, strong fellow, wondering about him and his silence. He *looked* intelligent and even kindly – but he seemed so dour and rough in his manners and behaviour! Oh well – they would soon say goodbye to him and be on their own!

They came at last to the little hut. The girls ran ahead to it, exclaiming in delight. George looked through the windows.

'Oh – it's a proper little house inside! Oh, look at those bunks on the walls! And there's even a carpet on the floor! Quick, Julian, where's the key?'

'Morgan's got it,' said Julian, and they all stood by and waited while Morgan unlocked the door for them.

'Thanks so much for helping to bring up our things,' said Julian, politely. 'It was very kind of you.'

Morgan grunted, but looked pleased.

'Shepherd comes by at times,' he said, in his great deep voice, and the Five felt quite surprised to hear him saying even a short sentence to them! 'He'll take messages for you if you want.'

And with that he set off down the hill back to the farm, with enormous swinging steps, like a giant from an old-time tale.

'He's peculiar,' said Anne, looking after him. 'I don't know if I like him or not.'

'What does it matter?' said Dick. 'Come on, Anne, old girl, give a hand. There's plenty to do. What about you and George seeing what blankets and things are in those cupboards, so we can make up some beds for tonight.'

Anne loved that kind of thing, though George didn't. She would much rather have carried in the things. But she went to the cupboards with Anne, and examined all their contents with much interest.

'Plenty of rugs and blankets and pillows,' said Anne. 'And enough china and cutlery for half a dozen families too! I suppose old Mrs Jones has dozens of people here in the summer! George, I'll put the food away, if you'll see to the beds.'

'Right,' said George, and went to make up four of the bunk beds. There were six of these altogether, in rows of three – three on one wall, three on another, one above the other. George was soon struggling with blankets and pillows, while Anne set out the food they had brought with them, arranging it neatly on the cupboard shelves. Then she went to look at the stove to see if it had oil in it, for it would be very cold that night.

'Yes, it's full,' she said. 'I'll light it tonight, because I expect we'll be out as long as it's daylight, won't we, Dick?'

'You bet!' said Dick, unpacking some of the things out of his suitcase. 'By the way, there's a little wooden bunker outside, with a can of extra oil and an enamel jug. I suppose the jug's for fetching water from some spring or other in the summertime – but we can easily melt snow for water. Will you two girls be long, Anne?'

'No. We're almost finished,' said Anne. 'Do you want something to eat before we go? Or shall we take some bread and ham with us, and have a good meal when we come back?'

'Oh, take some sandwiches,' said Julian. 'I don't want to stop for a meal. Besides, we can't be hungry yet. Let's make sandwiches – and we'll take some of those apples with us too!'

The sandwiches were quickly made, and the boys filled their pockets with apples. Timmy danced round in delight.

'You won't be quite so pleased, Tim, when you find yourself in *deep* snow!' said Dick. 'I wonder if he'll like travelling down the hill on a toboggan, George!'

'Oh, he'll love it!' said George. 'Won't you, Tim? Are we ready? Well, lock the door, Ju, and off we go!'

CHAPTER NINE

A strange tale

THE CHILDREN did not bother about their skis that first day. For one thing the snow was not quite thick or smooth enough for skiing, and for another thing they longed for the swift excitement of tobogganing. Dick took George on his toboggan and Julian took Anne on his. Timmy wouldn't come on either of them.

'Race you to the bottom!' Julian shouted. 'One, two, three, go!' And away they went, swishing over the clean white snow at top speed, shouting with laughter.

Julian won easily, because Dick's toboggan caught on a root or small bush under the snow, which upset it very suddenly. Dick and George were flung headlong into the snow, and sat up, blinking, and spitting out the cold snow from their mouths.

Timmy was terribly excited. He came plunging down the hillside after the toboggans, annoyed at the way his legs went into the snow, barking madly. He was most astonished to see Dick and George fly into the air when their toboggan upset, and pranced round them, licking them and leaping on them in a most aggravating way.

'Oh, *get* away, Timmy!' said Dick, trying to get up, and being knocked down again by the excited dog. 'Go and knock George over, not me! Call him, George!'

Pulling the toboggans back up the hill was a tiring job – but the swift flight down over the snow was worth all the pullings-up! The four children soon had glowing faces and tingling limbs, and wished they could throw off their coats and scarves!

'I can't pull up our toboggan one more time!' said Anne, at last. 'I really can't. You'll have to pull it up yourself, Julian, if you want to toboggan any more.'

'Well, I do want to – but my legs will hardly walk up the hill now,' said Julian, panting. 'Hey, Dick – Anne and I have had enough. We'll go up and eat our sandwiches at the top of the slope, where we can watch you.'

The other two soon joined them, and Timmy was glad to sit down too. His long pink tongue hung out of his mouth, and he puffed his white breath out like rolling mist! At first he had been puzzled by what he thought was 'smoke' coming out of his mouth so continually, but now, seeing that everyone was apparently puffing it out too, he didn't worry!

The Five sat at the top of the slope, eating their sandwiches hungrily, very glad of the rest. Julian grinned round at them all.

'Pity Mother can't see us now!' he said. 'We look marvellous! And nobody's coughed once. I bet we'll be stiff tomorrow though!'

Dick was looking across the slope to the opposite hill, rising steeply up a mile or so away.

'*There's* that building I thought I saw yesterday,' he said. 'Isn't that a chimney sticking up?'

'You've got sharp eyes!' said George. 'Nobody could surely see a building as far away as that, when the snow is on it!'

'Did we bring the field-glasses?' asked Julian. 'Where are they? We could soon find out if there's a house there or not, if we look through those.'

'I put them into a cupboard,' said Anne, getting up. 'Ooooh, I'm stiff! I'll just go and get them.'

She soon came back with the glasses and handed them to Dick. He put them to his eyes and adjusted them, till they were properly focused on the faraway hill opposite.

'Yes,' he said. 'I was right. It *is* a building – and I'm pretty sure it must be Old Towers, too. You know – the place we went to by mistake two nights ago when we lost our way.'

'Let's have a look,' said Anne. 'I think I might recognise it. I caught a glimpse of the towers when we swung round a corner on the way up Old Towers Hill.' She put the glasses to her eyes and gazed through them.

'Yes. I'm sure that's the place,' she said. 'Wasn't it odd – that big rude notice on the gate – and that fiercely barking dog – and nobody about! How lonely the old lady must be living there all by herself!'

As they sat there, nibbling their apples, Timmy suddenly began to bark. He stood up, turning his head towards the path that ran higher up the hill.

'Perhaps it's Aily, that funny child, coming,' said Julian, hopefully. But it wasn't. It was a small, wiry-looking woman, a shawl over her head, neatly dressed, walking swiftly.

She didn't seem very surprised to see the children. She stopped and said 'Good day'.

'You'll be the boys my Aily was telling me of last night,' she said. 'Are you staying in the Jones's hut?'

'Yes,' said Julian. 'We were staying at the farm first – but our dog didn't get on with the others, so we've come up here. It's fine. Marvellous view, too!'

'If you see that Aily of mine, tell her not to stay out tonight,' said the woman, wrapping her shawl more tightly round her. 'Her and her lamb! She's as mad as the old lady in the house over there!' and she pointed in the direction of Old Towers.

'Oh – do you know anything about that old place?' asked Julian, at once. 'We went to it by mistake, and . . .'

'Well, you didn't get into it, I'll be bound,' said Aily's mother. 'Notices on the gate and all! And to think I used to go up there three times a week, and never anything but kindness shown me! And now old Mrs Thomas, she won't see a soul except those friends of her son's. Poor old lady – she's out of her mind, so they say. Must be – or she'd see me, who worked for her for years!'

This was all very interesting.

'Why do they say "Keep out" on the gates?' asked Julian. 'They've a fierce dog there, too.'

'Ah well, young man, you see some of the old lady's friends would like to know what's going on,' said Aily's mother. 'But nobody can do a thing. It's a strange place now – with noises at night – and mists – and shimmerings – and . . .'

Julian began to think that was an old wives' tale, made up because the villagers were angry that they were now kept out of the big old house. He smiled.

'Oh, you may smile, young man,' said the woman, sounding cross. 'But ever since last October, there have been strange goings-on there. And what's more, vans have been there in the dead of night. What for, I'd like to know?

Well, if you ask me, I reckon they've been taking away the poor old thing's belongings – furniture and pictures and such. Poor Mrs Thomas – she was sweet and kind, and now I don't know what's happened to her!'

There were tears in the woman's eyes, and she hastily brushed them away.

'I shouldn't be telling you all this – you'll be scared sleeping here alone at night now.'

'No – no, we shan't,' Julian assured her, amused that she should think that a village tale might frighten them. 'Tell us about Aily. Isn't she frozen, going about with so few clothes on?'

'That child! She's a one, I tell you,' said Aily's mother. 'Runs about the hills like a wild thing – plays truant from school – goes to see her father – he's a shepherd, up there where the sheep are – and doesn't come home at nights. You tell her there's a good scolding waiting for her at home if she doesn't come back tonight. She's like her father, she is – likes to be alone all the time – talks to the lambs and the dogs as if they were human – but never a word to me!'

The children began to feel uncomfortable, and wished they hadn't spoken to the grumbling gossipy woman. Julian got up.

'Well – if we see Aily, we'll certainly tell her to go home – but not about the scolding, because I expect she *wouldn't* go home then,' he said. 'If you pass by the farmhouse will you be kind enough to step in and tell Mrs Jones we are quite all right, and enjoying ourselves very much? Thank you!'

The woman nodded her head, muttered something, and went off down the hill, walking as swiftly as before.

'She said some funny things,' said Dick, staring after her. 'Was that a silly village tale she told us – or do you suppose there's something in it, Ju?'

'Oh – a village tale of course!' said Julian, sensing that Anne hadn't liked it much. 'What a strange family – a shepherd who spends all his time on the hills – a child who wanders about the countryside with a lamb and a dog – and a mother who stops and tells such angry tales to strangers!'

'It's getting dark,' said Dick. 'I vote we go in and light the oil-stove and get the hut warm – and light the table lamp too. It'll be cosy in there. I'm feeling a bit chilled now, sitting out here so long.'

'Well, don't begin to cough,' said Julian, 'or you'll set us all off! Indoors, Tim! Come on!'

Soon they were all in the hut, the oil-stove giving out a lovely warmth and glow, and the table lamp shining brightly.

'We'll play a game, shall we?' said Dick. 'And have a sort of high tea later. Let's have a *silly* game – snap, or something!'

So they sat down to play – and soon Dick's cards had all been 'snapped' by the others. He yawned and went to the window, looking out into the darkness that hid all the snowy hills. Then he stood tense for a moment, staring in surprise. He spoke to the others without turning.

'Quick! Come here, all of you! Tell me what you make of *this*! Did you ever see such an extraordinary thing! QUICK!'

CHAPTER TEN

In the middle of the night

'WHAT IS it, Dick? What can you see?' cried George, putting down her cards as soon as she heard Dick's call. Julian rushed to stand beside him at once, imagining all sorts of things. Anne went too, with Timmy leaping excitedly. They all stared out of the window, Anne half afraid.

'It's gone!' cried Dick, in disappointment.

'But what *was* it?' asked George.

'I don't know. It was over there – on the opposite slope, where Old Towers is,' said Dick. 'I don't know how to describe it – it was like a – like a rainbow – no, not quite like that – how *can* I describe it?'

'Try,' said Julian, excited.

'Well – let me think – you know how, on a very hot day, all the air *shimmers*, don't you?' said Dick. 'Well, that's what I saw on the hill over there – rising high into the sky and then disappearing. A shimmering!'

'What colour?' asked Anne, amazed.

'I don't know – all colours it seemed,' said Dick. 'I don't quite know how to explain – it's something I've never seen before. It just came suddenly – and the shimmering rose all the way up into the sky, and then disappeared. That's all.'

'Well – that's what Aily's mother said – mists – and shimmerings,' said Julian, remembering. 'Gosh – so that *wasn't* just a tale she told us. There was some truth in it. But what in the wide world can this shimmering be?'

'Had we better go back to the farm and tell them there?' asked Anne, hopefully, not at all wanting to spend the night in the hut now.

'No! They've probably heard the tale already,' said Julian. 'Besides – this is exciting. We might be able to find out something more about it. We can easily watch Old Towers from here – it's one of the very few places where anyone can look straight across at it. As the crow flies, it's less than a mile away – though it's many miles by road.'

They all gazed towards the opposite hill again, though they couldn't see it, of course, hoping something would happen. But nothing did happen. The sky was pitch black, for heavy clouds had come up – and the distant hill couldn't be seen.

'Well – I'm tired of looking out in the darkness,' said Anne, turning away. 'Let's get on with our game.'

'Right,' said Julian, and they all sat down again, Dick watching the others play, but occasionally glancing out of the window into the black darkness there.

Anne was out of the game next, and she got up and went to the food cupboard.

'I think I'll start preparing a meal,' she said. 'We'll have boiled eggs, shall we, to begin with – and I'll boil a kettle too and make some cocoa – or would you rather have tea?'

'Cocoa,' said everyone, and Anne got out the tin.

'I'll want some snow, for the kettle,' she said.

'Well, there's some nice clean snow just behind the hut,' said Dick. 'Oh wait, Anne – you won't like going out in the dark now, will you? I'll get it! If you hear me yell, you'll know there's something going on!'

Timmy went out with him, much to Anne's relief. She held the kettle, waiting for the snow – and then suddenly there came a loud yell!

'Hey! Who's that?'

Anne let go the kettle in fright, and it dropped on the floor with a crash, making the other two jump violently. Julian rushed to the door.

'Dick! What's up?'

Dick appeared at the doorway, grinning, with Timmy beside him.

'Nothing much. Sorry if I frightened you. But I was just scraping up some snow in the basin here, when something rushed at me, and butted me!'

'Whatever was it?' said George, startled. 'And why didn't Timmy bark?'

'Because he knew it was harmless, I suppose,' said Dick, grinning aggravatingly. 'Here, Anne – here's the snow for the kettle.'

'*Dick!* Don't be so annoying!' said George. 'Who was out there?'

'Well – I couldn't really see much, because I'd put my torch down to scrape up the snow,' said Dick. 'But I rather *think* it was Fany the lamb! It was gone before I had time to call out. I got quite a shock!'

'Fany the lamb!' said Julian. 'Well – that must mean that little Aily is about. What *can* she be doing out in the darkness at this time of night?'

He went to the door and called:

'Aily! Aily, if you're there, come in here and we'll give you something to eat.'

But there was no answering call. Nobody appeared out of the darkness, no lamb came frisking up.

Timmy stood by Julian, looking out into the darkness, his ears pricked. He had been surprised when the tiny lamb trotted up out of the darkness, and had had half a mind to bark. But who would bark at a lamb? Not Timmy!

Julian shut the door.

'If that kid is out there on this frosty night, with only the few clothes she had on yesterday, I should think she'll catch her death of cold,' he said. 'Cheer up, Anne – and for goodness' sake, don't be scared if you hear a noise outside or see a little face looking in at the window. It will only be that mad little Aily!'

'I don't want to see *any* faces looking in at the window, whether it's Aily or not,' said Anne, putting snow into the kettle. 'Honestly I think she *must* be mad, wandering about these snowy hills alone at night. I don't wonder her mother was cross.'

It wasn't long before they were all sitting round the small table eating a very nice meal. Boiled eggs, laid that morning, cheese and new bread and butter, and a jar of home-made jam they found in the cupboard.

They drank steaming hot cups of cocoa, into each of which Anne had ladled a spoonful of cream.

'No King or Queen in all the world could possibly have enjoyed their meal more than I have,' said Dick. 'Anne, shall I take the milk and cream out into the snow – they'll keep for ages out there.'

'All right. But for goodness' sake don't put them where the lamb can get them – if it *was* a lamb that butted you,' said Anne, giving them to Dick. 'And *don't* yell again if you can help it!'

However, Dick didn't see anything this time, nor did anything come up and butt him. He was quite disappointed!

'I'll wash the plates and cups out in the snow tomorrow,' said Anne. 'How long are you all going to stay up? It's awfully early, I know – but I'm half asleep already! The air up here is so very strong!'

'All right. We'll all pack up,' said Julian. 'You take those two bunks over there, girls, and we'll have these. Shall we have the little oil-stove on, or not?'

'Yes,' said Dick. 'This place will be an ice-box if we don't!'

'I'd like it on too,' said Anne. 'What with shimmerings and buttings and yellings I feel I'd like a little light in the room, even if it only comes from an oil-stove!'

'Well – I know you don't believe my "shimmerings",'

said Dick. 'But I swear they're true! And what's more, I bet we'll all see them before we leave this hut! Well – good night, girls – I'm for bed!'

In a few minutes' time the bunks were creaking as the four children settled into them. They were not as comfortable as beds, but quite good. George's bunk creaked more than anyone's.

'I suppose you've got *Timmy* in your bunk, making it creak like that!' said Anne sleepily. 'Well, I'm glad I'm in the bunk *above* yours, George. I bet Tim falls out in the night!'

One by one they fell asleep. The oil-stove burned steadily. It was turned rather low, and shadows quivered on the ceiling and walls. And then something made Timmy's ears prick up as he lay asleep on George's feet. First one ear pricked up – and then the other – and suddenly Timmy sat up straight and growled in his throat. Nobody awoke – they were all too sound asleep.

Timmy growled again and again – and then he barked sharply. 'WOOF!'

Everyone awoke at once. Timmy barked again, and George put out a hand to him.

'Sh! What's the matter? Is there someone about, Tim?'

'What's up, do you think?' said Julian, from his bunk on the other side of the room. Nobody could hear or see anything out of the ordinary. Why was Timmy barking, then?

The oil-stove was still burning, its light throwing a small

round pattern of yellow on the ceiling. It made a small cosy noise as it burnt, a kind of bubbling. There was nothing else to be heard at all.

'It must be someone prowling outside,' said Dick at last. 'Shall we let Timmy go and see?'

'Well – let's lie down and see if he barks again,' said Julian. 'For all we know a mouse may have run across the floor. Tim would bark at that just as soon as he would bark at an elephant!'

'Yes. You're right,' said George. 'All right – we'll lie down again. Timmy's lying down too. Now, for goodness' sake, Tim, if it is a mouse somewhere, do use your common sense, and let it play if it wants to – and don't wake us up.'

Timmy licked her face. He kept his ears well up for a while. The others all went to sleep except Anne. She lay with her eyes open, wondering what had startled Timmy. She didn't believe it was a mouse!

So it was the wakeful Anne who heard the noise when it came again. She thought at first that it was just a noise in her ears, the kind she often heard when she lay down to sleep, and the room was quiet. But then she felt certain that it *wasn't* in her ears – it was a *real* noise. But what a peculiar one!

'It's a kind of deep, deep, grumbling noise,' thought Anne, sitting up. Timmy gave a little whine as if to say he was hearing something again too. 'A sort of thunder-rumble, but far below me, not above!'

It grew a little louder, and Timmy growled.

'It's all right, Tim,' whispered Anne. 'It *must* be far-off thunder, I think!'

But then the shuddering began! This was so astonishing that Anne didn't know what to make of it. At first she thought it was herself, beginning to shiver with the cold. But no – even her bunk vibrated to her fingers when she touched the wooden side!

Then she really *was* frightened. She called out loudly.

'Julian! Dick! Wake up – something odd is happening. Do wake up!'

And Timmy began to bark again. Woof, woof, woof! WOOF, WOOF!

CHAPTER ELEVEN

Strange happenings

EVERYONE AWOKE at Anne's call. Julian thought he was in bed, and leapt out, forgetting that he was in the top bunk. He landed with a crash on the floor, shaken and alarmed.

'Oh, Ju! You forgot you were in the top bunk!' said George, half scared and half amused. 'Are you hurt? Anne, whatever is the matter? Why did you call out? Did you see something?'

'No. I *heard* something – and *felt* something!' said Anne, glad that the others were awake. 'So did Timmy. But it's all gone now.'

'Yes, but what *was* it?' asked Julian, sitting on the edge of Dick's bunk, and rubbing his knee, which had struck the floor when he fell.

'It was a . . . a . . . well . . . a kind of very, very deep *rumbling*,' said Anne. 'A *deep-down* rumbling – very far away. Not like thunder up in the sky. More like a thunderstorm underground! And then there was a . . . *shuddering*! I felt the edge of my bunk and it seemed to be sort of – well – *quivering*. I can't quite explain it. I was awfully scared.'

'Sounds like a small earthquake,' said Dick, wondering if Anne had dreamt all this. 'Anyway – you can't hear or feel it now, can you? You're sure you didn't dream all this, Anne?'

'*Quite* sure!' said Anne. 'I . . .' And just at that very moment it all began again! First the curious grumbling, muffled, and 'deep-down', as Anne had described it – then the equally strange 'shuddering'. It crept through their bodies till they were all shuddering a little too, and could not stop.

'It's as if we were shivering in every part of us,' said Dick, in wonder. 'Sort of vibrating as if we had tiny dynamo engines working inside us.'

'Yes! You've described it exactly!' said George. 'Goodness – when I put my hand on Timmy I can *feel* him doing the "shudders" – and it's just like putting my hand on something working by electricity! You know the sort of small vibrations you feel then.'

'It's gone!' said Dick, just as George finished speaking. 'I'm not "shuddering" any more. It suddenly stopped. And I can't hear that grumbling, far-off noise now. Can you?'

Everyone agreed that both the noise and the shuddering had stopped. What in the wide world could it be?

'It must be something to do with that curious "shimmering" I saw in the sky over Old Towers Hill tonight,' said Dick, remembering. 'I've a good mind to go and look out of the window that faces the hill opposite, and see if it's there again.'

He leapt out of his bunk and ran to the window. At once he gave a loud cry. 'Come and look! Whew! Just come and look!'

All the others, Timmy as well, rushed to the window at once, Timmy standing on his hind legs to see. Certainly there was something weird to look at!

Over the hill opposite hung a mist – a curious glowing mist, that stood out in the pitch black darkness of the night! It swirled heavily, not lightly as a mist usually does.

'Look at that!' said Anne, in wonder. 'What a strange colour – not red – not yellow – not orange. What colour *is* it?'

'It's not a shade I've ever seen before,' said Julian, rather solemnly. 'I call this jolly strange. What's *happening* here? No wonder Aily's mother told us those stories – there's really something in them! We'd better make a few inquiries tomorrow.'

'It's funny that both the shimmering I saw and that cloud too are over Old Towers Hill,' said Dick. 'You don't think it's something that's happening in Old Towers House, do you?'

'No. Of course not,' said Julian. 'What could happen there that would make us feel the effects here, in this hut – that strange shuddering, for instance? And how in the world could we hear a rumbling from a mile or so away, if it were not thunder? And that certainly wasn't.'

'The mist is going,' said Anne. 'Look – it's changing colour – no, it's just going darker. It's gone!'

They stood looking out for a while longer, and then Julian felt Anne shivering violently beside him.

'You're frozen!' he said. 'Come on, back to bed. You

don't want to get another awful cold and cough. My word – this is all very peculiar. But I expect there's a sensible explanation – probably there are mines around here, and work is being done at night as well as day.'

'We'll find out,' said Dick, and they all climbed thankfully back into their bunks, feeling very cold. Julian turned up the stove a little more to heat the room better.

George cuddled Timmy and was soon as warm as toast, but the others lay awake, trying to get their cold hands and feet warm again. Julian felt very puzzled. So there *was* a lot of truth in that woman's peculiar tale, after all!

They awoke late the next morning, for they had been tired out with their exertions the day before, and with the excitements in the night. Julian leapt out of his bunk when he found that it was actually ten to nine, and dressed quickly, calling to the others. He went out to get some snow to put into the kettle.

Soon breakfast was ready, for Anne was next to get up, and she began quickly to prepare some food. Boiled eggs and ham, bread, butter and jam – and good hot cocoa again. Soon they were all eating and chattering, talking over the happenings of the night, which somehow didn't seem nearly so remarkable now that daylight was everywhere, brilliant with snow, and the sun trying to come from behind the clouds.

As they sat round the table, eating and talking, Timmy ran to the door and began to bark. 'Now what's up?' said Dick. Then a face looked in at the window!

It was a remarkable face, old, lined and wrinkled yet curiously young-looking too. The eyes were as blue as a summer day. It was a man's face, with a long, raggedy beard and a moustache.

'Gracious – he looks like one of the old prophets out of the Bible,' said Anne, really startled. 'Who is he?'

'The shepherd, I expect,' said Julian, going to the door. 'We'll ask him in for a cup of cocoa. Maybe he can answer a few questions for us!'

He opened the door. 'Are you the shepherd?' he said. 'Come in. We're having breakfast and we can give you some too, if you like.'

The shepherd came in, and smiled, making many more wrinkles appear on his weather-beaten face. Julian wondered if he spoke English, or only Welsh. He was a fine-looking fellow, tall and straight, and obviously much younger than he looked.

'You are kind,' he said, standing there with his crook, and Anne suddenly felt that there must have been men just like this all through the history of the world, ever since there had been sheep on the hills, and men to watch them.

The shepherd spoke slowly, as English words were not easy for him. 'You want to send – to send – words – to the farm?' he said, in the lilting Welsh voice so pleasant to hear.

'Oh yes – please take a message to the farm,' said Julian, handing him some bread and butter, and a dish of cheese. 'Just say we're fine, and all is well.'

'All is well, all is well,' repeated the shepherd, and refused the bread and cheese. 'No. I won't eat now. But I would like a drink, please, for the morning is cold.'

'Shepherd,' said Julian, 'did you hear curious noises last night – rumblings and grumblings – and did you feel shudderings and see a coloured mist over the hill there?'

The shepherd listened intently, trying to follow the strange English words. He understood that Julian was asking him something about the opposite hill. He took a sip of his cocoa, and looked over to the hill. 'It has always been a strange hill,' he said slowly, pronouncing some of his words oddly, so that they were hard to understand. 'My grandad told me a big dog lay below, growling for food, and my nan said witches lived there and made their spells, and – and the smock rose up . . .'

'Smock? What does he mean by that?' said George.

'He means "smoke" I should think,' said Julian. 'Don't interrupt. Let him talk. This is very interesting.'

'The smock rose up, and we saw it in the sky,' went on the shepherd, his forehead wrinkled with the effort of using words he was not familiar with. 'And it comes still, young ones, it comes still! The big dog growls, the witches cook in their pots, and the smock rises.'

'We heard the big dog growling last night, and saw the witches' smoke,' said Anne, quite under the spell of the lilting voice of the old shepherd.

The man looked at her and smiled. 'Yes,' he said. 'Yes.

But the dog is worse now and the witches are more evil – more wicked, much more wicked . . .'

'More wicked?' said Julian. 'How?'

The shepherd shook his head. 'I am not clever,' he said. 'I know few things – my sheep, and the wind and the sky – and I know too that the hill is wicked – yes, *more* wicked. You must not go near it, young ones! For there the plough will not plough the fields, the spade will not dig, and neither will the fork.'

This somehow sounded so much like a piece out of the Old Testament that the children felt quite solemn. What a strange and impressive old man!

'He thinks long, long thoughts all the hours he sits watching his sheep,' thought Julian, gazing at him. 'No wonder he says extraordinary things. But what does he mean about the plough not ploughing the fields, I wonder?'

The shepherd put his cup down on the table. 'I go now,' he said, 'and I take your words to Mrs Jones. And thank you for your kindness. Good day!'

He went out with great dignity, and the children saw him striding past the window, his beard being blown backwards by the wind.

'Well!' said Dick. 'What a character! I almost felt that I was in church, listening to a preacher. I liked him, didn't you? But what did he mean about ploughs not ploughing and spades not digging? That's nonsense!'

'Well – it may not be,' said Julian. 'After all, we know

that our car wouldn't go down that hill fast – and you remember that Aily's mother – the shepherd's wife – said that the postman had to leave his bicycle at the bottom of the hill – even that wouldn't work! So it's quite likely that in the old days ploughs went too heavily and too slowly to plough properly, and that spades were the same.'

'But why?' said Anne, puzzled. 'Surely you don't *really* believe these things? I know our own car went crawling down – but that *might* have been because something went wrong in its works for a little while!'

'Anne doesn't *want* to believe in ploughs and spades and forks that won't do their jobs!' said Dick, teasingly. 'Come on – let's forget the weird happenings last night and put on our skis. I feel pretty stiff after yesterday – but a bit of skiing down those slopes will do me good. What about it?'

'Yes! Come on!' said Julian. 'Buck up with the clearing away, and we can get out the skis. Hurry!'

CHAPTER TWELVE

Out on the hills

TIMMY DIDN'T find skiing any fun at all, because, not being fitted with skis, he couldn't keep up with the others, when they tore down the hill at top speed!

At first he plunged after them, but when he jumped into a great soft heap of snow, and buried himself completely, he decided that this kind of winter sport was not for him! He clambered out of the snow-heap, shook the snow off his coat, and stared forlornly after the shouting children.

They had skied before, and were quite good at it. The hill down which they went was very long, and had a fine slope. It ran smoothly into the upward slope of the next hill, on which Old Towers House had been built.

Julian did a marvellous run down, and went swinging on up the opposite hill. He called to the others.

'I say – what about going up to the top of *this* hill, because we're already part of the way up – and skiing down, and partly up our own slope again. It would save time, and give us a jolly good second ski-run.'

All but Anne thought this was a very good idea. She said nothing, and Dick looked at her.

'She's scared of going up Old Towers Hill!' he said. 'Are you afraid of the big, big dog, Anne, who lies under it and growls at night, or of the lank-haired witches that sit on the hill and make their smoky spells?'

'Don't be silly,' said Anne, cross with Dick for reading her thoughts. She didn't believe in either dogs or witches, but somehow she did *not* like that hill! 'I'm coming too, of course!'

So she toiled up the opposite hill with the others, quite ready to enjoy the lovely run down, and to end halfway up their own hill.

'Look – you can see Old Towers quite clearly now,' said George to Julian. She was right. There, not far off, was the great old house, set with towers, built cosily into the side of the steep hill.

They stood still and looked at it. 'We can even see down into a few of the rooms,' said Julian. 'I wonder if the old lady is still there – Mrs Thomas – the one that Aily's mother used to go and work for?'

'Poor old thing – I'm sorry for her if she is,' said George. 'Seeing nobody – keeping out all her friends! I wish we could go and inquire at the house for something – pretend we've lost our way, and snoop round a bit. But there's that fierce dog.'

'Yes – we don't want any more fights,' said Julian. 'Now – we're almost at the top. We'll wait for the others and then have a race. What a wonderful slope!'

'Julian, look – is that someone at one of the tower windows – the one to the right?' said George suddenly, as they stood waiting, looking down at the big old house some way off below them. Julian looked at the tower at once, just in time to see someone disappear.

'Yes. It *was* someone!' he said. 'Someone staring at us, I think. I expect no one ever comes near this hill, and it must have been a surprise to look out and see *us*! Did you make out if it was a man or a woman?'

'A woman, I *think*,' said George. 'Could it have been old Mrs Thomas, do you think? Oh, Ju – you don't suppose she's being kept prisoner in that tower, do you – while her horrid son and his friends gradually steal everything? You know we heard that vans went up to the house in the middle of the night.'

'Hallo, you two!' said Dick, labouring up with Anne. 'What a climb! Still, the run down will be worth it. I simply *must* have a rest first, though!'

'Dick, George and I thought we saw someone at the tower window there – the one on the right,' said Julian. 'When we get back we'll get our field-glasses and train them on to that window. We might *possibly* see some sign of someone there!'

Dick and Anne stared hard at the tower window – and as they looked, someone drew the curtains swiftly across!

'There – we've been seen – and we're not going to be encouraged to look at the old place!' said Julian. 'No wonder there are strange stories about it! Come on, now – let's start our run down!'

They set off together, each taking a different line. Whoooooosh! The wind blew in their faces as they flew down the white slope, gasping in delight at their speed. Julian and Anne slid swiftly all the way down the first slope and halfway up the next – but Dick and George were not so fortunate. They both caught their skis in something, and shot into the air and then down into the soft snow. They lay there breathless, almost dazed with the sudden stoppage.

'Whew!' said Dick, at last. 'What a shock! Is that you, George? Are you all right?'

'I think so,' said George. 'One ankle feels a bit funny – no, I think it's all right! Hallo, here's Tim! He must have seen us fall, and come rushing down to help. It's all right, Tim. We're not hurt. It's all part of the fun!'

As they lay there, getting their breath, halfway down the first slope, a loud voice shouted in the distance.

'Hey there! You keep off this slope!'

Dick sat up straight at once. He saw a tall fellow wading through the snow towards them, coming from the direction of Old Towers, looking angry.

'We're only skiing!' shouted back Dick. 'And we're not doing any harm! Who are you?'

'I'm the caretaker,' shouted the man, nodding his head towards Old Towers. 'This field belongs to the house. So keep off it!'

'We'll come and ask permission of the owners,' yelled Dick, standing up, thinking this might be a good way of having a look at the house.

'You can't. There's no one else here but me!' shouted

back the man. 'I'm the caretaker, I tell you. I'll set my dog on you all, if you don't do what I say!'

'That's funny,' said Dick to George, as the man waded back through the snow. 'He says he's the only one in the house – and yet we saw someone in the right-hand tower only a few minutes ago! The caretaker wouldn't have had time to have got here from the tower – so he *isn't* the only one in the house. There is someone in the tower as well. Odd, isn't it?'

George had held Timmy by the collar all the time the man was speaking. Timmy had growled at the man's angry voice, and George was afraid he might fly at him. Then, if the other dog appeared, there might be a fight! That would be dreadful! Timmy might get bitten again.

She and Dick tried their skis to see if they were still properly fixed after their fall – and then went gliding smoothly off again. The others were waiting for them at the top of the hill.

'Who was that man? What was he shouting about?' demanded Julian. 'Did he actually come from Old Towers?'

'Yes – and a surly fellow he was, too,' said Dick. 'He ordered us to keep off that slope – said it belonged to Old Towers and he was the caretaker – and when we said we'd go and ask permission from the owners, he said he was the only one in the house! But *we* know different.'

'Yes. We do,' said Julian, puzzled. 'Why should it matter to anyone if we ski down that particular slope? Are they afraid we might see something in the house – as we did! And why tell a lie and say there was no one else there? Did he *sound* like a caretaker?'

'Well – he didn't sound *Welsh*!' said George. 'And I should have thought that any owners would have chosen someone trustworthy from the village, someone Welsh, wouldn't you? This is all rather mysterious!'

'And if you add to it all the strange noises and things, it's extremely *curious*,' said Dick. 'In fact, I feel it might be worth inquiring into!'

'No,' said Anne. 'Don't let's spoil our holiday. It's such a short one.'

'Well – I don't see how we *can* inquire into the matter,' said George. 'I'm certainly not going to that house while the dog is there – and there's no other way of making inquiries – even if they would get us anywhere, which I'm pretty sure they wouldn't!'

'I say – do you know that it's almost one o'clock?' said Anne, pleased to change the subject. 'Isn't *any*body hungry?'

'Yes – I'm *ravenous*!' said Julian. 'But as I thought it was only about half past eleven, I didn't like to mention it! Let's go in and have dinner. I vote we finish up that ham!'

They went to the hut, and there, standing in the snow outside it, were two quart bottles of milk, and a large parcel which Timmy at once went to, wagging his tail eagerly. He gave a little bark.

'He says it's meat, so it must be for him,' said George with a laugh.

Julian tore off the paper and laughed too. 'Well, Timmy's

right,' he said. 'It's a big piece of cold roast pork. No ham for me then. I'll have some of this!'

'Pity we haven't any apple sauce,' said Dick. 'I love it with pork.'

'Well, if you like to wait while I make some on the stove, with a few of the apples we brought . . .' began Anne. But the others refused at once. No one was going to wait one minute longer for their meal than they could help, apple sauce or not!

It was a merry meal, and certainly the pork was good. Timmy had a piece and thought that George was very mean not to give him the rest of the joint when they had finished with it.

'Oh no, Tim!' said George, as he put an inquiring paw on her knee. 'Certainly not. *We're* going to finish it up tomorrow! You shall have the bone then.'

'There's more snow coming,' said Julian, looking out of the window. 'I say – who brought the meat and the milk here, do you think?'

'The shepherd, I should imagine, on his way back,' said Dick. 'Jolly nice of him. I wonder where that kid Aily is? I'd be scared of her getting caught in the snow, and having to sleep on the hills in it.'

'I expect she'll look after herself all right *and* her lamb and dog!' said Julian. 'I'd like to see her again – but unless she's hungry, I don't expect we shall!'

'Talk of an angel and hear the rustle of her wings!' said Anne. 'Here she is!' And sure enough, there was Aily, looking in at the window, holding up her lamb for him to take a peep too!

'Let's get her in and feed her – and ask her if *she* knows who lives in Old Towers,' said George. 'She might have seen someone in that right-hand tower too, as we did!'

'Right. I'll call her in,' said Julian, going to the door. 'She *might* know something – always scouring round about the countryside!'

He was right! Aily *did* know something – something that interested everyone very much!

CHAPTER THIRTEEN

Aily is surprising

AILY WAS not shy this time. She did not run away when Julian opened the door. She was still dressed in the same few clothes, but her face glowed, and she certainly didn't *look* cold!

'Hallo, Aily!' said Julian. 'Come along in. We're having dinner – and there is plenty for you!'

Her dog ran right up to the door and into the room, when he smelt the dinner there. Timmy looked most surprised, and gave a very small growl.

'No, Tim, no – he's your guest,' said George. 'Remember your manners, please!'

The small dog wagged his tail vigorously. 'There, Timmy! He's telling you not to be afraid of him; *he* won't hurt you!' said Anne, which made everyone laugh. Timmy wagged his tail vigorously, too, and the pair were friends at once.

Aily came in then, the lamb in her arms, in case Timmy might object to him. But Timmy didn't. He was very interested in the little creature, and when Aily set him down and let him run about the room, Timmy ran sniffing after him, his tail still wagging fast.

Anne offered the untidy little girl some of the meat but

she shook her head and pointed at the cheese. 'Aily like,' she said, and looked on in delight as Anne cut her a generous piece. She sat down on the floor to eat it, and the lamb came along and nibbled at it too. It really was a dear little thing.

'Fany bach!' said the child, and kissed his little nose.

'"Bach" is Welsh for "little", isn't it?' said Anne. She touched Aily on the arm. 'Aily bach!' she said, and the child smiled a sudden sweet smile at her.

'Where did you sleep last night, Aily?' asked George. 'Your mother was looking for you.'

But she had spoken too quickly, and Aily didn't understand. George repeated her words slowly.

Aily nodded. 'In the hay,' she said. 'Down at Magga Farm.'

'Aily, listen – who lives at Old Towers?' said Julian, speaking as slowly and clearly as he could.

'Many people,' said Aily, pointing to the cheese, to show that she wanted another piece. 'Big men, little men. Big dog, too. More big than him!' and she pointed at Timmy.

The others looked at one another in surprise. Many men! Whatever were they doing at Old Towers?

'And yet the caretaker fellow said he was the only one there!' said George.

'Aily, listen – is there – an – old – lady – there?' asked Julian, slowly. 'An – old – lady?'

Aily nodded her head. 'Yes – one old lady – I see her

high up in tower – sometimes she does not see Aily. Aily hide.'

'Where do you hide?' asked Dick, curiously.

'Aily won't tell, will never tell,' said the child, looking through half-closed eyes at Dick, as if she kept her secrets behind them.

'Did you see the old lady when you were in the fields?' asked Julian. Aily considered this, and shook her head.

'Well, where then?' asked Julian. 'Look – you shall have some of this chocolate if you can tell me.' He held the bar of chocolate just out of her reach. She looked at it with bright eyes. Obviously chocolate was a rare treat for

her. She reached out suddenly for it, but Julian was too quick for her.

'No. You tell me what I ask you,' he said. '*Then* you shall have the chocolate.'

Aily suddenly hit out with her hands and gave him a good punch in the chest. He laughed and took both her small hands in his big one.

'No, Aily, no. I am your friend. You do not hit a friend.'

'I know where you were, when you saw the old lady!' said Dick, slyly. 'Aily – you were in the grounds – in the garden!'

'How do you know?' cried Aily. She dragged her hands out of Julian's hand, and leapt to her feet, facing Dick, looking furious and frightened.

'Here – don't get so upset,' said Dick, astonished.

'How do you know?' demanded Aily again. 'You haven't told anyone?'

'Of course I've told no one,' said Dick, who had only just thought of the idea that very moment. 'Aha! So you get into the grounds of Old Towers, do you? How do you get in?'

'Aily won't tell,' said the little girl, and suddenly burst into tears. Anne put her arm round her to comfort her, but the child pushed it roughly away. 'He – Dai went there, not me, not Aily. Poor Dai – big dog bark, wuff-wuff, like that – and . . . and . . .'

'And so you went in to get Dai, didn't you?' said Dick. 'Good little Aily, brave Aily.'

The little girl rubbed her tears away with a grubby hand, and left black streaks down her cheeks. She smiled at Dick, and nodded. 'Good Aily!' she repeated, and took the little dog on her knee and hugged him. 'Poor Dai bach!'

'So she got into the grounds, did she?' said Julian, in a low voice to Dick. 'I wonder how? Through the hedge perhaps. Aily – we want to see this old lady. Can we get through the hedge round the garden?'

'No,' said Aily, shaking her head vigorously. 'There's a fence – a big, high fence that bites.'

Everyone laughed at the idea of a biting fence. But George guessed what she meant. 'An electric fence!' she said. 'So that's what they've put round. My word – the place is like a fort! Locked gates, a fierce dog, an electric fence!'

'How on earth did Aily get in, then?' said Dick. 'Aily – have you seen this old woman many times? Has she seen *you*?'

Aily didn't understand and he had to ask his question again, more simply. The child nodded her head.

'Aily see her many times – up high – and one time she see Aily. She throw out papers – little bits – out of the window.'

'Aily – did you pick them up?' said Julian, sitting up straight at once. 'Was there writing on them?' Everyone waited for Aily's answers. She nodded her head.

'Yes. Writings like they do at school – pen writings.'

'Did you read any of them?' asked Dick.

Aily suddenly wore a hunted expression. She shook her head – then she nodded it. 'Yes, Aily read them,' she said. 'They say "Good morning, Aily. How are you, Aily?"'

'Does the old woman *know* you then?' asked Dick, surprised.

'No, she doesn't know Aily – only Aily's mam,' said the child. 'She wrote on her papers "Aily, you good girl. Aily, you very good!"'

'She's not telling the truth now,' said Dick, noticing that the child would not look at them when she spoke. 'I wonder why?'

'I think *I* know,' said Anne. She took a piece of paper and wrote on it clearly. 'Good morning, Aily.' Then she showed it to the child. 'Read that, Aily,' she said.

But Aily couldn't! She had no idea what was written on the paper.

'She can't even *read*,' said Anne. 'And she was ashamed, so she pretended she could. Never mind, Aily! Listen – have you any of those bits of paper that the old woman dropped?'

Aily felt about in her few clothes, and at last produced a piece of paper that looked as if it had been torn from the top of a page in a book. She gave it to Dick.

All the four bent over it, reading what was written there, in small, rather illegible writing.

'I want help. I am a prisoner here, in my own house, while terrible things go on. They have killed my son. Help me, help me! Bronwen Thomas.'

'Good gracious!' said Julian, very startled. 'I say – this is extraordinary, isn't it! Do you think we ought to show it to the police?'

'Well – there is probably only one policeman shared between three or four of these little places,' said Dick. 'And there's another thing – the old lady *might* be off her head, you know. What she says may not be true.'

'How can we possibly find out if it is or not?' said George.

Dick turned to Aily. 'Aily – we want to see the old lady – we want to take her something nice to eat – she is all by herself, she is sad. Will you show us the way into the grounds?'

'No,' said Aily, shaking her head vigorously. 'Big dog there – dog with teeth like this!' And she bared her own small white teeth and snarled, much to Timmy's astonishment. The children laughed.

'Well – we can't *make* her tell us,' said Julian. 'And anyway, even if we got into the grounds, that dog would be there – and I don't fancy him, somehow.'

'Aily show you way into house,' suddenly said the small girl, much to everyone's astonishment. They all stared at her.

'Into the *house*!' said Dick. 'But – you'd have to show us the way into the *grounds* first if we are to get into the house, Aily!'

'No,' said Aily, shaking her head. 'Aily show you way to house. Aily do that. No big dog there!'

Just then Timmy began to bark, and someone came by the door, looking in as she passed. It was Aily's mother, who had again been to take some things to her shepherd husband. She saw Aily sitting on the floor and gave an angry shout. Then standing at the door she poured out a long string of Welsh words which the children didn't understand. In a great fright Aily ran straight to a cupboard, her dog and lamb with her.

But it was no good. Her mother stormed into the hut and dragged Aily out, shaking her well. Timmy growled, but Aily's little dog was as frightened as she was, and the lamb bleated pitifully in the child's arms.

'I'm taking Aily home!' said her angry mother, glaring at the four children as if she thought they were responsible for the child's keeping away from home. 'I'll scold her well!'

And out she went, holding the protesting child firmly by one arm. The children could do nothing. After all, she was Aily's mother, and the child really was a little monkey, the way she wandered round the countryside.

'You know – I think we'd better go down to the farm and tell *Morgan* what we know,' said Julian, making up his mind. 'I really do. If this thing is serious – and if the old lady is really a prisoner – I don't see how *we* can do a thing – but Morgan might be able to. He'd know the police for one thing. Come on – let's go down now. We can stay at the farm for the night if it gets dark. Buck up – let's go straight away!'

CHAPTER FOURTEEN

Morgan is surprising too

George did not particularly want to go down to the farm, as she was afraid of Timmy meeting the farm dogs again, and being attacked. Julian saw her doubtful face and understood.

'Would you like to stay here by yourself with Timmy, George, till we come back?' he said. 'You should be all right with Tim – he'll look after you. The only thing is, will you be scared if any more tremblings and shudderings and shimmerings come again tonight?'

'I'll stay with George,' said Anne. 'It would really be best if you two boys went alone. I'm a bit tired and I don't think I could go as fast as you'd want to.'

'Right. Then Dick and I will go together, and leave you two girls here with Timmy,' said Julian. 'Come on, Dick. If we hurry, we *might* get back before dark.'

They set off together, and went swiftly down the winding mountain path, still white with snow. They were glad when at last they saw the farmhouse. A light was already in the kitchen, and looked very welcoming!

They went in at the front door, and made their way to the big kitchen, where Mrs Jones was washing up at the sink. She turned in astonishment when they came in, stamping the snow from their shoes.

'Well now – this is a surprise!' she said, drying her hands on a towel. 'Is there something wrong? Where are the girls?'

'They're up at the hut – they're fine,' said Julian.

'You have come for something more to eat?' said Mrs Jones, feeling certain this was the reason for their sudden visit.

'No, thank you – we've got plenty!' said Julian. 'We just wondered if we could talk to your son – Morgan. 'We – well, we've got something to tell him. Something rather urgent.'

'Well now – what could that be?' said Mrs Jones, all curiosity at once. 'Let me see – yes, Morgan will be up at the big barn.' She pointed out of the window, where a big and picturesque old barn stood, outlined against the evening sky. 'It is there you will find my Morgan. Will you be staying the night, now? You'll like supper – a good supper?'

'Well – yes, we should,' said Julian, suddenly realising that they had missed out tea altogether. 'Thanks awfully. We'll just go and find Morgan.'

They made their way out to the big old barn. Morgan's three dogs at once ran out when they heard strange footsteps, and growled. But they recognised the boys immediately and leapt round them, barking.

The giantlike Morgan came out to see what the dogs

were barking about. He was surprised to find the two boys there, fondling the dogs.

'Hey?' he said, questioningly. 'Anything wrong?'

'We think there is,' said Julian. 'May we tell you about it?'

Morgan took them into the almost dark barn. He had been raking it over and he went on with his raking as Julian began his tale.

'It's about Old Towers,' said Julian, and Morgan stopped his raking at once. But he went on again almost immediately, listening without a word.

Julian told him his story. He told him about the rumbling noises, the shimmering in the sky that Dick had seen, the 'shuddering' they had all felt – then about the old woman they had seen in the tower – and how Aily had told of the pieces of paper, and shown them one, which proved that old Mrs Thomas was a prisoner in her own house.

For the first time Morgan spoke. 'And where is this paper?' he asked in his deep bass voice.

Julian produced it and handed it over. Morgan lit a lamp to look at it, for it was now practically dark.

He read it and put it into his pocket. 'I'd rather like it back,' said Julian, surprised. 'Unless you want it to show the police. What do you think about it all? And is there anything we can do? I don't like to think of . . .'

'I will tell you what you are to do,' said Morgan. 'You are to leave it to *me*, Morgan Jones. You are children, you know nothing. This matter is not for children. I can tell

you that. You must go back to the hut, and you must forget all you have heard and all you have seen. And if Aily comes again you must bring her down here to me, and I will talk to her.'

His voice was so hard and determined that the two boys were startled and shocked.

'But, Morgan!' said Julian. 'Aren't you going to do anything about this . . . go to the police, or . . .'

'I have told you this is not a matter for children,' said Morgan. 'I will say no more. You will go back to the hut, and you will say nothing to anyone. If you are not willing to do this, you will go home tomorrow.'

With that the giant of a man put his rake over his shoulder, and left the two boys alone in the barn. 'What do you make of *that*?' said Julian, very angry. 'Come on – we'll go back to the hut. I'm not going to the farm for supper. I don't feel as though I want to meet that rude, dour Morgan again this evening!'

Feeling angry and disappointed the boys made their way out of the barn, towards the path that led up to the hill. It was almost dark now, and Julian felt in his pocket for his torch.

'Blow! I didn't bring it with me!' he said. 'Have you one, Dick?'

Dick hadn't one either, and as neither of them felt like making their way up the mountainside in the darkness Julian decided to go back to the farm, slip up to his bedroom there, and find the extra torch he had put in one of the drawers.

'Come along,' he said to Dick. 'We'll try and get in and out without seeing Morgan or old Mrs Jones.'

They went quietly back to the farmhouse, keeping a lookout for Morgan. Julian slipped up the stone stairway to the bedroom he had been given a few nights before, and rummaged in the drawer for his torch. Good – there it was!

He went downstairs again – and bumped into old Mrs Jones at the bottom. She gave a little scream.

'Oh, it's you, Julian bach! Now what have you been telling my Morgan to put him into such a temper! Enough to turn the milk sour his face is! Wait now, while I get you some supper. Would you like some pork and . . .'

'Well – we've decided to go back to the hut, after all,' said Julian, hoping that the kind old woman wouldn't be upset. 'The girls are alone, you know – and it's dark now.'

'Oh yes, yes – then you shall go back!' said Mrs Jones. 'Wait for one minute – you shall have some of my new bread, and some more pie. Wait now.'

The boys stood in the doorway, waiting, hoping that Morgan would not come by. They suddenly heard him in the distance, yelling at a dog, in his loud, really fierce voice.

'Taking it out on the dogs, I suppose,' said Julian to Dick. 'Gosh – I wouldn't like to come up against him, if I was one of his men! Strong giant that he is, he could take on a dozen men if he wanted to – or a score of dogs!'

Mrs Jones came up with a net bag full of food. 'Here you are,' she said. 'Take care of those girls – and don't go near Morgan now. He's in a fine temper, is my Morgan, and he is not nice to hear!'

The two boys thoroughly agreed. Morgan was *not* nice to hear. They were glad when they were away up the path, out of reach of his enormous voice!

'Well, that's that,' said Julian. 'No help to be got from *this* quarter! And we're forbidden to do anything at all about the matter. As if we were kids!'

'He kept telling us we were only children,' said Dick, sounding disgusted. 'I can't make it out. Ju, WHY was he so annoyed about it all? Didn't he believe us?'

'Oh yes – he believed us all right,' said Julian. 'If you ask me, I think he knows much more than *we* were able to tell him. There's some kind of racket going on at Old Towers – something peculiar and underhand – and Morgan is in it! That's why he shut us up and told us not to interfere, and to forget all about it! He's in whatever's going on, I'm sure of it.'

Dick whistled. 'My word! So that's why he was so angry. He thought we might be putting a spoke in his wheel. And of course the last thing he would want us to do would be to go to the police! Well – whatever do we do next, Ju?'

'I don't know. We'll have to talk it over with the girls,' said Julian, worried. 'This *would* crop up just when we're all set for a jolly holiday!'

'Julian, what do you *think* is going on at Old Towers?' asked Dick, puzzled. 'I mean – it isn't only a question of locking up an old lady in a tower – and selling off her goods and taking the money. It's all the other things too – the rumblings and shudderings and that strange mist.'

'Well – apparently *those* things have been going on for some time,' said Julian. 'They may have nothing whatever to do with what Morgan is mixed up in which is, I'm sure, to do with robbing the old lady. In fact, those old tales may be a very good way of keeping people away from the place. In these country places people are much more afraid of strange happenings than townspeople are.'

'It all sounds very convincing when you put it like that,'

said Dick. 'But somehow I don't *feel* convinced. I just can't help feeling there's something *strange* about it all – something we don't know!'

They fell silent after that, walking one behind the other on the mountain path, seeing the big black stones looming up one after the other in the light of Julian's torch. It seemed a long, long way in the dark, much longer than in the daylight.

But at last they saw the light in the window of the hut. Thank goodness! They were both very hungry now, and were glad that Mrs Jones had presented them with more food. They could really tuck in.

Timmy barked as soon as they came near, and George let him out of the door. She knew by his bark that it was the boys coming back.

'Oh, we *are* glad you came back, instead of staying down at the farm!' cried Anne. 'What happened? Is Morgan going to the police?'

'No,' said Julian. 'He was angry. He told us not to interfere. He took that bit of paper with the message on, and never gave it back to us. *We* think he's mixed up with whatever is going on!'

'Very well then,' said George at once. '*We'll* take up the matter ourselves! *We'll* find out what's going on and *MOST CERTAINLY we'll* get poor old Mrs Thomas out of that tower. I don't know how – but we'll do it! Won't we, Timmy?'

CHAPTER FIFTEEN

'What's up, Tim?'

THE FOUR children sat and talked for a long time, sitting round the little oil-stove, eating a good supper. What would be the best thing to do? It was all very well for George to flare up and say *they* would see to things, *they* would rescue the old lady from the tower – but how could they even *begin* to do anything? For one thing they didn't know how to get into the house! No one was going to risk a battle with that fierce dog!

'If only that kid Aily would help us!' said Julian, at last. 'She's really our only hope. It's no good going to the police – it would take us ages to go down to the village at the bottom of the mountain, and find out where the nearest police station is – and we'd *never* get a village policeman to believe our tale!'

'I wonder the villagers don't do something about Old Towers,' said Dick, puzzled. 'I mean – all those peculiar vibrations we felt last night – and the noises we heard – and the light in the sky when that mist hung over the place . . .'

'Yes – but I suppose all those things are seen and heard up here in the mountains much more clearly than down in the valley below,' said Anne, sensibly. 'I don't expect that weird shuddering would be felt in the valley nor would the rumblings be heard, and even the strange mist over Old Towers might not be seen.'

'That's true,' said Julian. 'I never thought of that. Yes – we up here would see a lot . . . and possibly the shepherd higher up on the hills would, as well. I dare say the farm down below us would see something, too . . . Well, we *know* they did, because of Morgan's behaviour to us tonight! He obviously knew what we were talking about!'

'He's also obviously hand in glove with the men in that place – the big men and little men that Aily spoke of. Gosh – I *wish* she'd show us how to get into that house. How does she get in? I'm blowed if I can think of any way. With that electric fence all round, it sounds impossible.'

'The fence that *bites*!' said George, with a laugh. 'Fancy that child touching the fence and getting a shock. She's an extraordinary creature, isn't she – quite wild!'

'I hope she didn't get told off,' said Anne. 'She *is* a naughty little truant, of course – but you can't help liking her. Does anybody want more cheese? And there are still some apples left – or I could open a tin of pears.'

'I vote for the pears,' said Dick. 'I feel like something really sweet. I say – this stay up here is turning out rather exciting, isn't it?'

'We always seem to run into trouble,' said Anne, going to the cupboard to fetch the tin of pears.

'Give it a better name, Anne, old thing,' said Dick. 'Adventure! *That's* what we're always running into. Some people do, you know – they just can't help it. And we're those sort of people. Jolly good thing too – it makes life exciting!'

Timmy suddenly began to bark, and everyone started up at once. *Now* what was up?

'Let Timmy out,' said Dick. 'With all these funny goings-on I feel as if it would be just as well to let Tim examine anyone coming by here at night!'

'Right,' said George, and went to the door – but as she was about to open it, she heard a dog barking outside, just beyond the hut. She swung round.

'I'm not letting Timmy out! That might be Morgan with his dogs! I seem to recognise that deep bark!'

'Someone's coming by,' said Anne, half scared. 'My word – it *is* Morgan!'

So it was. He passed by the window, and they saw his great shoulders and head bent against the wind as he went on up the hill. He didn't even glance in at them – but the three dogs, who were with him, began to bark furiously as they sensed another dog in the hut. Timmy barked back furiously too.

Then all was quiet. Morgan had gone by and the dogs with him. 'Whew – I'm glad you didn't let Tim out as I suggested,' said Dick. 'He'd have been torn to pieces!'

'Where do you suppose Morgan's going?' she asked Anne. 'It's funny he should be going *up* the hill – not even in the direction of Old Towers!'

'Probably going to talk to the shepherd,' said Julian. 'He's farther up the hill with his sheep. I say – I wonder if *he's* in this too!'

'Oh *no*,' said Anne. 'He's good – I could feel it in my bones. I can't *imagine* him mixed up with a gang of any sort.'

Nobody could, of course. They had all liked the shepherd. But why else would Morgan be going up to him at this time of night?

'He might be going to tell him that we know too much,' suggested Julian. 'He might ask him to keep an eye on us.'

'Or he might be going to complain of Aily, and her doings inside the grounds of Old Towers,' said Dick. 'Goodness – do you suppose that kid will get into trouble because we told Morgan about her – and gave him the bit of paper she found?'

They all stared at one another in dismay. Anne nodded soberly. 'Yes – that's it, of course. Aily will certainly get into trouble over this – oh, *why* did we think of telling Morgan what we knew? Poor little Aily!'

They all felt uncomfortable about Aily. They liked the wild, otherworldly little creature with her pet lamb and little dog. Now what would happen to her thanks to them?

None of them felt like playing cards just then. They sat and talked, wondering if they would hear Morgan coming back. They knew Timmy would bark if he did.

Sure enough he began to bark about half past eight, and made them all jump. 'That will be Morgan coming back,' said Julian, and they watched the window to see if his head and shoulders would pass by again. But they didn't. Neither did any dog bark outside.

Then George saw that Timmy was sitting with his ears pricked up, and his head on one side. Why? And if he could really hear something, why didn't he bark again? She was puzzled.

'Look at Tim,' she said. 'He's heard *something* – and yet he's not barking. And he doesn't look very worried either. What's up, Tim?'

Timmy took no notice. He sat there listening intently, still with his head on one side. What *could* he hear? It was most tantalising to the others, because not one of them could hear anything at all. The countryside seemed to be absolutely quiet at that moment.

Then suddenly Tim jumped up and barked joyfully! He ran to the door and whined, scraping at the bottom of it with his paw. He looked back at George and barked again, as if to say 'Buck up! Open the door!'

'Well!' said Dick, in surprise. 'What's up, Timmy? Has your best friend come to call? Shall we open the door, Julian?'

'I'll go,' said Julian, and went to open the door cautiously. Timmy leapt out at once, barking and whining.

'There's nobody here,' said Julian, astonished. 'Nobody at all! Hey, Tim, what's all the fuss about? Give me that torch, Dick, will you? I'll go out after him and see what the excitement is.'

Out he went, and flashed the torch around to find Timmy. Ah – there he was, scraping at the little wooden bunker that held the oil-cans and the big enamel jug. Julian was astonished.

'Whatever's come over you, Tim?' he said. 'There's nothing here in this bunker – look, I'll lift the lid so that you can peep inside and see, silly dog!'

He lifted up the lid, and shone his torch inside, to show Timmy that it was empty.

But it wasn't! Julian almost let the lid drop down in his surprise! Someone was there – someone small and half-frozen! It was Aily!

'Aily!' said Julian, hardly believing his eyes. 'What on earth – Aily – what *are* you doing here?'

Aily blinked up at him, looking scared to death. She clutched the lamb and the dog, and didn't say a word. Julian saw that she was shivering, and crying bitterly.

'Poor little Aily bach!' he said, using the only Welsh word he knew. 'Come into the hut – we'll get you warm and make you better.'

The child shook her head and clutched her animals closer. But Julian was not going to leave her there in the little oil-bunker on that cold night! He lifted her up, animals and all, and cuddled her. Aily strove to get free but his arms were strong and held her close.

George's voice came impatiently from the hut. 'Ju! Tim! Where are you? Have you found anything?'

'Yes,' called back Julian. 'We have. We're bringing it along – it's quite a surprise!'

He carried the shivering child into the hut, and the others stared in the utmost astonishment. Aily! A cold, forlorn and miserable little Aily, pale and shivering! And the lamb and dog too!

'Bring her near the stove,' said Anne, and stroked the child's thin arm. 'Poor Aily!'

Julian tried to set her down, and the animals as well, but she clung to him. She sensed that he was good and kind and strong, and his arms were very comforting. Julian sat down on a chair, still holding the little creature closely.

The dog and lamb slid off his knee and ran sniffing round the room.

'She was in the oil-bunker out there – she and the lamb and dog,' he said. 'All cuddled up together. Partly hiding, I should think, and partly for shelter. Maybe she's slept there before, with these two. Isn't she a poor little mite? She seems very unhappy. Let's give her something to eat.'

'I'll make some hot cocoa,' said Anne. 'George, get some bread and butter and cheese for her – and hadn't we better get the lamb and dog something too? What do you give lambs?'

'Milk out of a bottle,' said Dick. 'But we haven't got a feeding-bottle! I dare say it will lap milk. Good gracious – the things that happen here!'

Aily felt warm and comforted in Julian's arms. She lay there like a little animal, too cold and tired to be scared. Julian was glad to hold her and comfort her. Poor little thing – what had made her come this long way so late at night?

'She must have gone home with her mother,' he said, watching the little dog hobnobbing with a delighted Timmy. 'And probably got a good telling-off, and was shut up somewhere. And then my guess is that Morgan went down to see if she was there, and to scold her, and tell her mother to be sure and not let her out, and . . .'

'Morgan!' repeated Aily, sitting up in fear, looking all round as if he might be there. 'Morgan! No! No!'

'It's all right, little thing,' said Julian. 'We'll look after you. Morgan shan't get you!'

'See?' he said to the others. 'I bet I'm right! It was he who went and scared her – as soon as he was gone, I expect she escaped from her mother's house and came up here to hide. That horrible fellow! If he shouted at her as he shouted at us, she'd be scared stiff. I bet he was afraid she'd go and give more of the game away unless she was shut up – might even show us the way into the old house over on the opposite hill!'

Timmy suddenly gave a bark – but not a joyful one this time! Anne cried out at once, 'That may be Morgan coming back! Hide Aily, for goodness' sake – or he'll drag her out of here and take her back with him! Quick – where shall we hide her?'

CHAPTER SIXTEEN

Aily changes her mind

AILY LEAPT out of Julian's arms as quickly and surely as a cat, when she heard that it might be Morgan coming. She looked round the room like a hunted thing, and then darted to the bunk beds. With an amazing leap, she was up on one of the top ones in a trice, and pulled a rug over her. She lay absolutely still. The lamb looked up in surprise and bleated.

Then it too leapt up the bunks, as sure-footed as a goat, and cuddled down with its little mistress. Only Dai the dog was left below, whining miserably. 'Gosh!' said Dick amazed at these incredibly sudden happenings. 'Look at that! Did you ever see such leaping! Shut up barking, Tim. We want to hear if Morgan *is* coming. Ju – where shall we hide Aily's dog? He mustn't be seen – or heard either!'

Julian lifted the dog up to the top bunk and put him with the other two there. 'That's about the only place where he'll keep quiet!' he said. 'Aily – lie quite still till we tell you everything is safe.'

There was no reply from the bunk – not a word or a bark or a bleat. Then Timmy began to bark loudly again, and ran to the door.

'I'm going to *lock* the door,' said Julian. 'I'm not having

Morgan and his dogs in here, hunting for Aily! My guess is that he knows she's escaped from her mother's – or maybe she ran off when he scolded her – and thinks she went to her father, the old shepherd! He's got to get hold of her, to stop her from spreading what she knows!'

'Well – for goodness' sake don't let those dogs in here!' said George, desperately. 'I can hear them barking away in the distance.'

'Quick – let's sit round the table with the cards, and pretend to be playing a game!' said Dick, snatching the cards from a shelf. 'Then if Morgan looks in, he'll think everything is normal – and won't guess we've got Aily here. I bet he'll be sly enough to try and peep in without us seeing him – hoping to spot Aily if we've got her!'

They sat round the table, and Dick dealt out the cards. Anne's hands were trembling, and George felt a bit weak at the knees. Anne kept dropping her cards, and Dick laughed at her.

'Butterfingers! Cheer up – Morgan won't eat you! Now – if I suddenly say "What ho!" you'll know I can see Morgan peeping in at the window, and you must laugh and play like anything. See?'

Dick was the one facing the window, and he kept a sharp eye on it as they played snap. There was no sound of dogs barking now, though Tim sat by the door, his ears cocked, as if he could hear *some*thing.

'Snap!' said Julian, and gathered up the cards. They went on playing.

'Snap! I say, don't grab like that – you've almost broken my nail!'

'Snap! I said it first!'

'*What ho!*' said Dick, and that put everyone on their guard at once. They went on playing, but without giving much attention to the game now. What could Dick see?

Dick could see quite a lot. He could see a shadowy face some way from the window, looking in – yes, it was Morgan all right.'

'What ho!' said Dick again, to warn the others that there was still danger. 'WHAT HO!'

Morgan's face had now come quite near to the window. He evidently thought that no one saw him, and that they were all too engrossed in their game to notice anything else. His eyes swept the room from corner to corner. Then his face disappeared.

'He's gone from the window,' said Dick, in a low voice. 'But go on playing. He may come to the door.'

KNOCK! KNOCK!

'Yes – there he is,' said Dick. 'Ju – you take charge now.'

'Who's there?' yelled Julian.

'Morgan. Let me in,' said Morgan's deep, growling voice.

'No – we've got our dog here, and we don't want him set on again,' said Julian, determined not to let Morgan in at any cost.

Morgan turned the handle – but the door was locked. He growled again.

'Sorry! But we can't unlock it!' shouted Julian. 'Our dog might rush out and bite you. He's growling like anything already!'

'Bark, Tim,' said George, in a low voice, and Timmy obligingly barked the place down!

Morgan gave up. 'If you see Aily, send her home,' he said. 'She's gone again, and her mam's worried. I've been looking for her this cold night.'

'Right!' called Julian. 'If she comes we'll give her a bed here.'

'No. You send her home,' shouted Morgan. 'And pay heed to what I told you down at the barn, or it will be the worse for all of us!'

'For *all* of us! I like *that*!' said Dick, in disgust. 'It will certainly be the worse for him and his friends when the secret's out! Awful fellow! Has he gone, Tim?'

Timmy came away from the door and lay down peacefully. He gave a little bark as if to say 'All clear!'

When the dogs began to bark right away in the distance Tim took no notice. 'That means they're going down the hill with Morgan, back to the farm,' said George, thankfully. 'We can get Aily down now, and give her something to eat.'

She went to the bunk. 'Aily!' she called, 'Morgan is gone. Gone right away! Come down and have a meal. We will give the lamb some milk and your dog some meat and biscuits!'

Aily's head peered cautiously over the side of the little bunk bed. With a leap she was down on the floor, as lightly as the lamb itself, which followed at once, landing squarely on its four tiny hooves. The little dog had to be lifted out – he was much too scared to jump!

To everyone's amusement, Aily ran straight to Julian, and held up her arms to be taken into his. She felt safe with this big, kind boy. He sat down with her on his knees and she cuddled up to him like a kitten.

George put some bread and butter and cheese on the table in front of her, and Anne put down a dish of milk for the lamb, which lapped it greedily but most untidily. The dog tried to get the milk too, but soon went to the dish of cut-up meat and biscuits put down by Anne.

'There – the Aily-family is fed,' she said. 'My word – what an excitement all this is! Julian, don't let Aily gobble like that – she'll be sick. I never did see anyone eat so quickly. She can't have had anything since the bit of cheese we gave her this afternoon!'

Aily snuggled back into Julian's arms contentedly, when she had eaten every scrap of her meal. She looked up at him, wanting to please him.

'Aily tell how to get into big, big house,' she said suddenly, taking everyone completely by surprise. Julian looked down at her. He had the dog on his knee now too, though he would not allow the lamb to climb on as well.

'Aily tell me?' he said gravely. 'Good little Aily bach!'

Aily began to try and tell him. 'Big, big hole,' she began. 'Down, down, down . . .'

'Where's this big hole?' asked Julian.

'High up,' said Aily. 'Down it goes down . . .'

'But where *is* it?' asked Julian again.

Aily went off into a long stream of Welsh and the children listened helplessly. How maddening to have Aily willing to tell them her secret – and then not be able to follow what she said.

'Good little Aily,' said Julian, when she came to a stop – at last. 'Where is this big, big hole?'

Aily gazed at him in reproach. 'Aily tell you, tell you, tell you!' she said.

'Yes, I know – but I don't understand Welsh,' said Julian, gently, despairing of trying to make the child understand. 'Where is this big hole – that's all I want to know.'

Aily stared at him. Then she smiled. 'Aily show,' she said, and slipped of his knee. 'Aily show! Come!'

'Good gracious! Not *now*,' said Julian. 'Not in all this snow and darkness. No, Aily – tomorrow – in the morning – not now!'

Aily took a look out of the window into the darkness. She nodded. 'Not now. In the morning, yes? Aily show in the morning.'

'Well, thank goodness that's settled!' said Julian. 'I'd dearly love to see this big, big hole, whatever it is, now, straight away – but we'd only get lost on these hills in the dark. We'll look forward to it tomorrow!'

'Good!' said Dick, yawning. 'I must say that I think that's best too. What a bit of luck that Aily's so grateful to you, Ju! I believe she'd do anything in the world for you now.'

'I believe she would too, funny little creature,' said Julian, looking at Aily as she curled up on the rug near the stove, with her lamb and dog beside her. 'How could Morgan scare such a harmless little thing? He's a brute!'

'Jolly good thing he didn't see her when he looked in,' said George. 'He'd probably have broken the door down! One blow of his fist and it would have cracked from top to bottom!'

Everyone laughed. 'Well – good thing it didn't come to that!' said Julian. 'Now then, let's get to bed. We may have *quite* an exciting day tomorrow!'

'I hope we manage to get to that poor old woman in her tower,' said Anne. 'That's the most important thing to do. Aily, you can sleep in that topmost bunk, where you hid. I'll give you some rugs, and a blanket and a pillow.'

It wasn't long before the hut was quiet and peaceful, with all five children in their bunks, and Timmy with George. The lamb and the little dog were with Aily. Julian looked out from his bunk and smiled. What a collection of people and animals in the hut tonight! Well – he was quite glad there were two dogs!

No one woke in the night except George. She felt Timmy stir and sat up, resting on her elbow. But he didn't bark. He gave her a small lick, and sat with her, listening.

The strange rumbling noise was coming again – and then the 'shuddering', though not so strongly as before. George felt the wooden edge of her bunk – it vibrated as if machinery was in the room below, shaking everything a little.

She leant out of her bunk and looked out of the window. Her eyes widened as she saw what Dick had seen the other night – the 'shimmering' in the sky. She could think of no other name for that strange quivering that rose and rose and finally ended very high up indeed, seeming to lose itself in the stars that were now shining brightly.

George didn't wake the others. As soon as the weird happenings stopped, she lay down again. Perhaps tomorrow they would know what caused such strange things – yes, tomorrow would be *very* exciting!

CHAPTER SEVENTEEN

The 'big, big hole'

NEXT MORNING everyone was awake early. They had slept well, and were full of beans – and excited to think that an adventure lay ahead. To get into that old house, with its many secrets, would be marvellous!

Aily followed Julian about the room like a little dog. She wanted to have her breakfast on his knee, just as she had her supper the night before, and he let her. He was ready to do anything she wanted – if only she would show them the way into Old Towers!

'We'd better set off pretty soon,' said Anne, looking out of the window. 'It's snowing pretty fast again – we don't want to get lost!'

'No. That's true. If Aily is going to take us across country, we shan't have the faintest idea where we're going in this heavy snow!' said Julian, rather anxiously.

'I'll just clear up a bit, then we'll go, shall we?' said Anne. 'Do we take any food with us, Ju?'

'We certainly do – all of us,' said Julian, at once. 'Goodness knows what time we'll get back to this hut. George, you make sandwiches with Anne, will you? And put in some bars of chocolate too, and some apples if there are any left.'

'And for pity's sake, let's remember our torches,' said Dick.

Aily watched while the sandwiches were made, and scraped up the bits that fell on the table to give to Dai, her small dog. The lamb frisked about, quite at home, getting into everyone's way. But nobody minded it – it was such a charming little long-leggitty creature!

At last all the sandwiches were made and put into two bags. The hut was cleared up and tidied, and the children got into their outdoor clothes.

'I think it would be easiest to toboggan down the slope, and halfway up Old Towers' slope,' said Julian, looking out into the snow. 'It would take us ages to walk – and it's no good skiing, because Aily hasn't any skis – and couldn't use them if she had!'

'Oh yes – let's take the toboggans!' said George, pleased. 'What do we do with the lamb? Leave it here? And must we take Dai the dog, too?'

However, that was not for them to settle! Aily absolutely refused to go without her lamb and dog. She gathered them up into her arms, looking mutinous, when Julian suggested they should be left in the warm hut. Neither would she allow herself to be wrapped up warmly – and only consented to wear a scarf and a woollen hat because they happened to be exactly the same as Julian was wearing!

They set off at last. The snow was still falling, and Julian felt seriously doubtful whether they would be able to find their way down the hill and up the other slope without losing their sense of direction.

The toboggans were rather crowded! Julian and Dick were on the first one, with Aily and the lamb between them, and Anne and George were on the second one, with Timmy and Dai between *them*. George was at the front, and Anne had the awkward job of hanging on to both the dogs and keeping her balance too!

'I know we shall all roll off,' she said to George. 'Good gracious – I half wish we had waited a bit! The snow is falling very fast now!'

'Good thing!' called Julian. 'No one will spot us when we are near Old Towers – they won't be able to see a thing through this snow!'

Julian's toboggan shot off down the snowy slope. It gathered speed, and the boys gasped in delight at the pace. Aily clung to Julian's back, half frightened, and the lamb stared with astonished eyes, not daring to move from its place, squashed in between Aily and Julian!

Whoooooooosh! Down the slope to the bottom, and up the opposite slope, gradually slowing down! Julian's toboggan came to a stop, and then, not far behind, came George's, slowing down too. George got out and dragged her toboggan over to Julian.

'Well,' she said, her face glowing, 'what do we do now? Wasn't that a wonderful run?'

'Wonderful!' said Julian. 'I only wish we could have a few more! Did you like that, Aily?'

'No,' said Aily, pulling her woollen cap to exactly the

same angle that Julian wore his. 'No. It makes my nose cold, so cold.'

She cupped her hand over her nose to make it warm. George laughed.

'Fancy complaining about a cold nose when she's hardly wearing anything on her skinny little body – you'd think the *whole* of her would feel cold – not just her nose!'

'Aily – do you know where the big hole is?' asked Julian, looking about in the snow. The snowflakes were quite big now, and nothing that was more than a few yards away could be seen. Aily stood there, her feet sinking into the snow. She looked all round, and Julian felt certain that she was going to say that she didn't know which way to go, in this thick snow. Even he was rather doubtful which was the way back up the hill!

But Aily was like a dog. She had a sure sense of direction, and could go from one place to another on a dark night or in the snow without any difficulty at all!

She nodded.

'Aily know – Dai know, too.'

She walked a few steps, but her feet sank into the snow about her ankles, and her thin shoes were soon soaked through.

'She'll get her feet frost-bitten,' said Dick. 'Better put her on one of the toboggans and pull her, Ju. Pity we didn't have any snow-boots small enough to lend her. I say – this is a bit of a crazy expedition, isn't it! I hope to goodness Aily knows where's she's taking us. I haven't the foggiest idea at the moment which is east or west, north or south!'

'Wait – I've got a compass in one of my pockets,' said Julian, and did a lot of digging in his clothes. At last he pulled out a small compass. He looked at it.

'That's south,' he said, pointing, 'so that's where Old Towers Hill is – south is directly opposite our hut; we know that because the sun shone straight in at our front windows. I reckon we walk this way, then – due south.'

'Let's see which way Aily points,' said Dick. He set her on his toboggan, and wrapped her scarf more closely round her. 'Now – which way, Aily?'

Aily at once pointed due south. Everyone was most impressed.

'That's right,' said Julian. 'Come on, Dick – I'll pull Aily's toboggan, you can pull the girls' for them.'

They all set off up the rest of the slope of Old Towers Hill, Aily on the toboggan with Dai and Fany the lamb, and Timmy sitting in state on George's toboggan, the girls walking behind. Timmy was enjoying himself. He didn't like the way his legs went down into the snow when he tried to run – it was much easier to sit on the toboggan and be pulled along!

'Lazy thing!' said George, and Timmy wagged his tail, not caring a bit what anyone said!

Julian looked at his compass as he went, and walked due south for some time. Then Aily gave a call, and pointed to the right.

'That way, that way,' she said.

'She wants us to go westwards now,' said Julian, stopping. 'I wonder if she's right. By my reckoning we're going dead straight for Old Towers now – but we shall be going up the hill to the right of it, if we go *her* way.'

'That way, that way,' repeated Aily, imperiously, and Dai barked as if to say she was right!

'Better follow her way,' said Dick. 'She seems so jolly certain of it.'

So Julian swerved to the right a little, and the others followed. They went a good way up the steep hill, and Julian began to pant.

'Is it far now?' he asked Aily, who was petting her lamb, and apparently taking no notice of the way they were going. Not that there was anything much to take notice of except snow on the ground and snowflakes in the air!

Aily looked up. Then she pointed again, a little more to the right, and said something in Welsh, nodding her head.

'Well – it looks as if we're getting near this place of hers – this "big, big hole", whatever it is,' said Julian, and on he went.

In about a minute Aily suddenly leapt off the toboggan and stood there, looking round with a frown.

'Here,' she said. 'Big hole here.'

'Well – it may be – but I'd like to see it a bit more *clearly*, Aily,' said Julian. Aily began to scrape down through the snow, and Timmy and Dai obligingly went to help her, imagining that she was after rabbits or a hidden hare.

'I'm afraid the poor kid's led us on a wild-goose chase,' said Dick. 'Why *should* there be a big hole here?'

Timmy and Aily had now got down through the snow to the buried clumps of heather that grew all over the slopes of the mountains in that district. Julian could see the clumps sticking up, stiff and wiry, in the clearing that Aily and the dogs had made.

'Timmy – you take Timmy!' said Aily, suddenly to George. 'He'll fall down, down – he'll fall like Dai one day – down, down!'

'I *say*! I believe she's looking for an old pot-hole!' said Dick, suddenly. 'You know – those strange holes that are sometimes found on moors – sudden holes that drop right down underground. They're called dean-holes I think, in some places. We found one once on Kirrin Island – don't you remember?'

'Oh *yes* – that was in the heather too!' said George, remembering. 'And it led to a cave below, by the seashore! *That's* what Aily meant by a big, big hole! A pot-hole on the moors! Timmy – for goodness' sake come away – you may drop right down it!'

Timmy very nearly *did* go down the hole! George just caught his collar in time! But Dai was wary – he had fallen down once before!

'Hole!' said Aily, pleased. 'Big, big hole! Aily find for you!'

'Well – certainly you've found your hole – but how does it get us into Old Towers?' said Dick. Aily didn't understand. She knelt there, looking down at the hole she had uncovered under the heather and the snow.

'I must say that was a marvellous feat,' said Julian. 'Coming straight to this place and finding the hole when she couldn't see a thing through the falling snow. She really is as good as a dog. Good little Aily bach!'

Aily gave one of her sudden smiles, and slipped her hand in Julian's.

'Go down, yes?' she said. 'Aily show way?'

'Well – we'd better go down if it's possible,' said Julian, not much liking the idea, for he could see nothing but darkness inside the hole, and had no idea of what lay below.

Fany the lamb was tired of waiting about. She gave a little leap to the edge of the big, round hole, and then put her small head in. She kicked up her heels – and was gone!

'She's jumped into the hole!' said George, amazed. 'Here, wait, Aily – you can't jump too – you'll hurt yourself!'

But Aily slithered into the hole, then let herself go.

'Aily here,' came a small voice from below. 'You come quick!'

CHAPTER EIGHTEEN

Inside Old Towers

'WELL! DID you see that – she just let go and dropped!' said George, amazed. 'I wonder she didn't break her legs. Julian, shine your torch down.'

Julian shone it down.

'It's a pretty good drop,' he said. 'I think we'll take the ropes off our toboggans and let ourselves down on those. I don't particularly want to break a leg or sprain an ankle just at present.'

'If we pull our toboggans over the hole, and let their ropes hang down into it, they will hold us safely,' said Dick, and pulled his toboggan right across the hole.

Then Julian pulled the other toboggan across as well, and soon the ropes were dangling down, ready to take each of the four children.

'What about Timmy?' asked George, anxiously. 'Dai has jumped down – though I wonder *he* didn't break a leg!'

'I'll wrap my coat over him and tie one of the ropes round him,' said Julian. 'Then we can let him down easily. Come here, Tim.'

Tim was soon tied up in the coat with the rope. Then Dick slithered down on another rope, and stood on the floor of the hole, ready to take Timmy when Julian let him down. It really wasn't very difficult. Aily looked rather scornful as the four children used the ropes.

Julian laughed, and patted her shoulder.

'We're not all goat-like, you know,' he said. 'We don't gambol about the mountains all day long, like you, Aily. Well – that was your big, big hole. What next?'

He shone his torch round.

'Yes – it's a pot-hole. There's a small underground cave here. Look – is that a tunnel leading out of it?'

'Yes,' said George, as Aily and the lamb skipped off together down into the darkness of the tunnel. 'Look at that – no torch, no lamp – and yet she goes off into the darkness without any fear! I'd be scared stiff!'

'She's got eyes like a cat,' said Anne. 'Well, do we follow her? We'd better or we shall lose her!'

'Come on, Timmy,' said George, and all Five went down the dark, winding little tunnel after Aily. Anne glanced up at the rocky roof and thought with wonder of the thick masses of heather growing on its upper surface, all covered with thick snow.

Aily was nowhere to be seen! Julian grew worried.

'Aily! Come back!'

But there was no answer.

'Never mind,' said Dick. 'There's probably only one way to go, and she knows we must take it! If we come to a fork, we'll shout again.'

But they didn't come to a fork. The tunnel wound on and on, going steadily downhill. Its roof was of rock, and so were the walls, but underfoot was sandy soil alternating with rock ridges that made the going rather rough.

Julian looked at his compass.

'We've been going in a north-easterly direction more or less,' he said. 'And that *should* be in the direction of Old Towers. I think *I* know how Aily gets into the house!'

'Yes – this tunnel must pass right under the fence-that-bites, and under the grounds, and end somewhere near the cellars of the house,' said Dick. 'Or possibly *in* them. Where *is* that child?'

They caught sight of her just then, in the light of Julian's

torch. She was waiting for them in a corner of the passage with Dai and Fany.

She pointed upwards.

'Way to garden!' she said. 'Little hole there – big for Aily! Not for you!'

Julian shone his torch upwards. Sure enough there was a small hole there, which appeared to be overgrown with weeds or heather – he couldn't tell what. He looked at the rocky sides of the upward passage to the hole, and saw how easily Aily could have climbed up to squeeze out of it, and roam the gardens! So that was how it was she had been able to pick up the notes that the poor old woman had thrown out so hopefully! Aily must surely have been the only person who managed to get into the grounds without permission!

'This way,' said Aily, and led them past the garden-hole and downwards again.

'We must be under the house now,' said Julian. 'I wonder if . . .'

But before he could finish his sentence he saw that the passage had led them into some old, half-ruined cellars. It went through a half-fallen cellar wall, and Aily proudly led them into a dark, cluttered-up cellar which, with its many barrels and old bottles, must once have been the wine-cellar.

'What cellars!' exclaimed Dick, in amazement, as they went through one after another. 'Dozens of them. Hey – what's this, Aily?'

He had come to where one high wall had been broken down completely – but the breakage seemed to have been done by human hands, for the breaks looked new, and were not covered with grime and mould as were the other fallen-down walls. A vast opening had been made into what seemed at first glance to be a low-walled cave.

Then a curious sound came to their ears. The sound of water – water gurgling and splashing! Julian took a step forward to peer into the cave beyond the broken walls.

But Aily tugged at his hand in terror.

'No, no! Not go there! Bad men, very bad men. Bad place there!'

'I say, look!' said Julian, amazed, taking no notice of Aily's tugging hand. 'An underground river – not just a stream – a *river*! Flowing down through the mountain, probably fed by springs on the way – and I bet it goes right down to the sea somewhere! We know the sea isn't far away!'

'Bad men down there,' said Aily, in panic, pulling back Dick and George too. 'Bang-bang – big fires – big noise. Come into the house, quick!'

'Gosh – isn't this extraordinary!' said Julian, quite astounded. 'What *is* going on here? We really shall have to find out. What in the world does Aily mean?'

Anne and George were astonished too, but had no desire to go along the river and find out!

'Better leave this for now, and go up into the house,' said George. 'After all, the old lady is the important thing at the moment. No wonder they imprisoned her in one of the towers, so that she wouldn't know what is going on!'

'Well, I'm blowed if *I* know what's going on,' said Dick. 'I'm not quite sure if I'm in some peculiar kind of nightmare or not!'

'Come into the house,' said Aily again, and this time, to her great relief, they followed her, Timmy trotting at the back with George, not quite knowing what to make of it all.

Aily led them unerringly back through the smashed walls, through the musty cellars, and into some that looked as if they had recently been used for store-places. Tins of food stood about, old furniture, old tins and baths and cans, barrels of all sizes and shapes.

'We go soft!' said Aily, meaning that they were now to walk quietly. They followed her up a long flight of stone cellar steps to a great door that stood half open. Aily stood at the top listening – probably for the tall caretaker, Julian thought. He wondered if the fierce dog was anywhere about the house. He whispered to Aily.

'Big dog in house, Aily?'

'No, big dog in garden, big dog there all day and night,' whispered back the little girl, and Julian felt most relieved.

'Aily find man,' said Aily, and shot off by herself, motioning to the others to wait.

'She's gone to find out where the caretaker is,' said Julian. 'My word – did you ever know anyone like her? Gosh, she's back again already!'

So she was, smiling mischievously all over her face.

'Man asleep,' she said. 'Man safe.' She took them through the door from the cellar into a perfectly enormous kitchen, with a colossal range at one end, black and empty now. A larger door nearby was open and Aily darted into it. She brought out a meat pie and offered it to Julian. He shook his head at once.

'No. You mustn't steal!' he said. But Aily either didn't understand, or didn't want to, for she bit into the pie herself, gobbling great pieces down, and then put it on the floor for the animals to finish, which they were very pleased to do!

'Aily – take us to the old woman,' said Dick, not wanting to waste time on things like this. 'Aily – you are *sure* there is no one else in the house?'

'Aily know!' said the little girl. 'One man to watch – he in there!' and she pointed towards the door of a nearby room. 'He watch old woman, and dog watch garden. Other men don't come in here.'

'Oh – well, where do *they* live then, these strange "other men"?' asked Julian, but Aily didn't understand. She led them to a great hall, from which two wide stairways swept up, meeting above at an even wider landing.

The lamb gambolled up, and the little dog Dai barked joyfully.

'Sh!' said all the four children at once, but Aily laughed. She seemed quite at home in the house and Dick wondered how many times she had let herself down into the pot-hole and come wandering in here. No wonder she spent so many nights away from home – she could always come and hide away in some corner of this big house! They followed her up the wide stairs.

But Aily would come no farther than the second floor. She had brought them up two flights of stairs – and now before them stretched a great picture gallery, that led to another stairway at the far end. The child hung back and refused to take Julian's hand.

'What's the matter?' he asked.

'Aily not come here before,' said the child, shrinking back. 'Not come here, not ever. Those people see Aily!' And she pointed at the rows of great pictures, each a portrait of some long-dead owner of the house.

'She's afraid of the portraits!' said Anne. 'Afraid of all their eyes following her as she runs down the long gallery! Funny little thing. All right – you stay here, Aily. We'll go on up to the towers.'

They left Aily curled up behind a curtain, with Dai and Fany. Anne glanced at the rows of grave portraits as the four of them, with Timmy, walked softly down the long gallery. She shivered a little, for their eyes seemed to follow her as she passed, looking grave and disapproving.

Up another flight of stairs, and yet another. And now they were in a long passage that ran from tower-room to tower-room. Which was the tower they wanted?

It was very easy to find out! All of them had their doors wide open but one!

'This must be it!' said Julian, and knocked at the door.

'Who knocks?' said a weak, sorrowful voice. 'Surely not you, Matthew – you have no manners! Unlock the door and do not mock me with your knocking!'

'The key's in the door,' said Dick. 'Unlock it, Julian – quick!'

CHAPTER NINETEEN

A lot of excitement

JULIAN TURNED the key in the lock and opened the door. A stately old woman sat in a chair beside the window, reading a book. She did not turn round.

'And why have you come at this time of the morning, Matthew?' she said, without turning round. 'And how did you find the manners to knock? Are you remembering the time when you knew how to behave to your elders and betters?'

'It isn't Matthew,' said Julian. 'It's us – we've come to set you free.'

The old woman turned at once, gaping in amazement. She got up and went over to the door, and the Five saw that she was trembling.

'Who are you? Let me out of that door before Matthew comes! Let me out, I tell you!'

She pushed by the four children and the dog, and then stood uncertainly in the passage.

'What shall I do? Where shall I go? Are those men here still?'

She went back into her room and sank down in her chair again, covering her face with her hands.

'I feel faint. Get me some water.'

Anne sprang to pour out a glass of water from a jug on a table. The old woman took it and drank it. She looked at Anne.

'Who are you? What is the meaning of this? Where is Matthew? Oh, I must be going mad!'

'Mrs Thomas – you *are* Mrs Thomas, aren't you?' said Julian. 'Little Aily, the shepherd's daughter, brought us here. She knew you were locked up. You remember her mother, don't you? She told us she used to work for you.'

'Aily's mother – Maggy – yes, yes. But what has Aily to do with this? I don't believe it. It's another trick. Where are the men who killed my son?'

Julian looked at Dick. It was clear that the poor old lady was not herself – or else this sudden appearance of the children had upset her.

'Those men that my Llewellyn brought here – they wanted to buy my house,' she said. 'But I wouldn't sell it, no, I wouldn't. Do you know what they said to me? They said that in this hill, far, far below my house, was a rare metal – a powerful metal – worth a fortune. What did they call it now?'

She looked at the children, as if expecting them to know. She shook her head as they didn't answer.

'Why should you know about it – you are only children. But I wouldn't sell it – no, I wouldn't sell my house – nor the metal below. Do you know what they wanted it for? For bombs to kill people with! And I said NO, never will I sell this place so that men can dig the metal and make bombs. It is against the law of God, I said, and I, Bronwen Thomas, will not do such a thing!'

The children listened in awe. The old lady seemed beside herself, and rocked to and fro as she spoke.

'So they asked my son, and he said no, as I had. But they took him away and killed him – and now they are at work below. Yes, yes, I hear them – I hear the noises creeping up, I feel my house shake, I see strange things. But who are you? And where is Matthew? He keeps me here, locked in my room. He told me about Llewellyn, my poor dead son; he is a wicked man, Matthew, he works with those men, those evil men!'

She seemed to forget the four children for a little while. They wondered what to do. Julian saw that the poor woman was not fit to take down the stairs with them, and through the tunnel – and certainly she could not get out of the pot-hole. He began to wish that he hadn't been so hasty in his ideas of rescue. It would really be best to lock the door again and leave her here in safety until he could get the police – for certainly now the police must come.

'We will leave you now,' he said, 'and send someone soon to bring you out of here. We are sorry we disturbed you.'

And, to the astonishment of the others, he pushed them out of the room, turned the key in the lock again, and put it into his pocket!

'Aren't we going to take her with us?' said George, surprised. 'Poor, poor old thing!'

'No. How can we?' said Julian, troubled. 'We must go to the police, no matter what Morgan says. I see it all now, don't you? The mother forbidding the son to sell the old place, in spite of the enormous amount of money offered – the son refusing too – and the men making a plot to get in somehow and down to this metal, whatever it is – and work it . . .'

'And killing the son?' said Dick. 'Well, it may be so – but I should have thought that was a pretty drastic thing to do! Surely the son would have been reported missing very quickly, and the police would have made inquiries. Nobody said the son was missing or dead, did they, except the old lady?'

'Well, let's not talk about it now,' said Julian. 'We've got to *do* something. I'm sorry to leave old Mrs Thomas still locked up in that room, but I honestly think she would be safer there than anywhere else.'

They went down the two flights of stairs to the picture gallery. Aily was there, still cuddling her two pets. She was pleased to see them, and ran up smiling. She didn't seem to notice that they hadn't the old woman with them.

'Man down there very cross!' she said, and laughed. 'He awake now – he shout and bang!'

'Goodness – I hope he won't see us,' said Julian. 'We've got to get out of here, quick, and go to the police. Let's hope he won't come rushing at us, or call in that fierce dog.'

They went downstairs at top speed, looking out for

Matthew. But there was no sign of him in person – though there was a most tremendous row going on somewhere, of shouting and banging.

'Aily lock door,' said Aily, suddenly, pointing in the direction of the sounds. 'Man lock old woman – Aily lock man!'

'*Did* you? Did you *really* lock him in?' said Julian, delighted. 'You really are a monkey – but what a good idea! I wish *I'd* thought of it!'

He went to the door of the room in which the angry Matthew was.

'Matthew!' he called sternly. There was a dead silence, and then Matthew's astonished voice came through the shut door.

'Who's that? Who locked me in? If it's one of you men, you'll be sorry for it! Silly joke to play on me, when you know I've got to go up and see to old Mrs Thomas!'

'Matthew – this isn't one of the men,' said Julian, and how the others admired his cool, determined voice! 'We have come to rescue Mrs Thomas from that tower – and now we are going to the police to report all this, and to report too that her son has been killed by the men who are working far below this house.'

There was an astonished silence. Then Matthew's voice came again.

'What's all this? I don't understand! The *police* can't do anything. Llewellyn, the son, isn't dead – my word, no, he's all alive and kicking – and won't be very pleased with *you*, whoever you are. Clear off at once – but let me out before you go. I'm surprised that Alsatian outside didn't get you, that I am!'

It was the children's turn to be amazed now. So the son *wasn't* dead! Then where was he? And why had Matthew told old Mrs Thomas such a cruel untruth? Julian asked him at once.

'Why did you tell Mrs Thomas her son was dead then?'

'What's it to do with you? Llewellyn told me to tell his mother that. The old lady wouldn't let him sell that stuff deep down under the house – the stuff that gets hold of cars and bicycles, and ploughs, and makes them heavy as lead. Magnetises them, so they say. Well, if *he* wants to sell it, why shouldn't he? But what I say is this – he shouldn't sell it to strangers, no, that he shouldn't! If I'd have known that – well – I wouldn't have taken money from him to act like I did!'

The voice rose and fell as Matthew told his extraordinary tale. Then the man banged frantically on the door again.

'Who are you? You let me out! I've been kind to the old lady – you ask her – though she's difficult, and strange in her ways. I've been loyal to Llewellyn, though he's not easy, no, that he's not. Who are you, I say? Let me out, let me out! If Llewellyn catches me locked in here, he'll kill me! He'll say I've let his secret out. He'll say . . . LET ME OUT, I say!'

'He sounds angry,' said Julian, thankful that the man was locked up. 'He must be a bit daft too, to believe all that the son told him, and do everything he was told to do. Well – we'd better go to the police. Come on – we'll go back the way we came.'

'Let's just have a look down that river to see what the men are up to,' said Dick. 'Just you and I, Julian. It's such a chance – we needn't be seen, and it would only take a few minutes. The girls could wait somewhere with Tim.'

'I don't think we ought to stop now,' said Julian. 'I really don't.'

'No, don't let's,' said Anne. 'I don't like this house. It's got a horrid feel about it. And I can't *imagine* what the "shuddering" would be like, when the men start their work again, deep down below – whatever it is!'

'Well, come along then,' said Julian, and, completely ignoring Matthew's yells and bangs, the children made their way through the kitchen and down the cellar steps, flashing on their torches to light their way.

'I bet Matthew is wild that we've left him locked up,' said Dick, as they went through the vast cellars. 'Serves him right! Taking bribes from the son – and telling lies to that poor old woman. Hallo, we've come to where the men smashed the walls here to get along the river tunnel. I suppose they found that was the easiest way to go down to where the precious metal was – whatever it is!'

They stood looking through the smashed walls at the gurgling river.

'Come, come,' said Aily, dragging at Julian's hand. 'Bad men there!'

She was holding Dai, her little dog, in case he fell into the rushing river, but Fany the lamb was gambolling loose as usual. And, quite suddenly, she skipped off down the river tunnel, her tail whisking behind her madly.

'Fany, Fany!' cried Aily. 'Fany come back!'

But the lamb, thinking that she was going the right way, gambolled on, deafened by the rushing of the water. Aily ran after her, as sure-footed as the lamb, hopping and skipping over the rough, rocky bank of the river.

'Come back!' yelled Julian. But Aily either did not or would not hear, and she disappeared into the blackness of the tunnel almost at once.

'She hasn't got a torch, Ju – she'll fall in and drown!' yelled George in a panic. 'Timmy, go after her. Fetch her back!'

And away went Timmy obediently, running as fast as he could beside the black, churning water, hurrying on its way downwards to the sea.

Julian and the others waited anxiously. Aily didn't come back, nor did any of the animals – and George began to be very panicky about Timmy.

'Oh, Julian – what's happened to Tim – and Aily?' she said. 'With no torch – oh, why did I let Timmy go? We all ought to have gone!'

'They'll come back all right,' said Julian, much more confidently than he felt. 'That child Aily can see in the dark, I really do believe – and she knows her way about like a dog.'

But when, after five minutes, not one of the four had come back, George started forward, flashing her torch on the rocky path beside the river.

'I'm going to find Timmy,' she said. 'And nobody's going to stop me!'

And she was gone before the boys could get hold of her! Julian gave a shout of aggravation.

'George! Don't be stupid! Timmy will find his own way back. Don't go down there – you don't know what you may find!'

'Come on,' said Dick, starting off down the river too. 'George won't come back, we know that – not unless she finds Tim and the others. We'd better go quickly before anything awful happens!'

Anne had to follow the boys, her heart beating fast. What a thing to happen! Just the very worst possible!

CHAPTER TWENTY

In the heart of the hill

IT SEEMED like a bad dream to the four children, making their way over the rocky edge of the underground river. Their torches had good batteries, fortunately, and gave a bright light, so that they could see their way alongside the river. But at times this rocky 'path' they had to walk on grew very narrow indeed!

'Oh dear!' thought Anne, trying to keep up with the boys. 'I know I shall slip! I wish I hadn't these heavy snowboots on. What a noise the river makes, booming along, and how fast it goes!'

Some way in front of the two boys and Anne was George, still calling for Timmy. She was very worried because he didn't come back to her, as he always did when she called him. She didn't realise that Timmy couldn't hear her! The river made such a noise in the enclosed rocky tunnel that Timmy heard nothing at all but the sound of the churning waters!

Quite suddenly the tunnel widened tremendously – the river making a big, broad pool before it tore on down the tunnel again. The walls opened out into an enormous cave, half of which was water and the other half a stretch of rough, rocky floor. George was most astonished.

But she was even more astonished at other things she saw!

Two rafts, sturdy and immensely strong, were moored at the side of the deep pool! And on the floor of the cave were what looked like tin barrels, standing in rough rows – presumably waiting to be packed on to the rafts.

At one side of the cave were stacked great heaps of tins and bottles and cans, none of them opened – and on the other side an equally vast heap of discarded ones – all opened and thrown to one side. Big wooden crates stood about too – though George could not imagine what they were for.

The cave was dimly lit by electricity of some kind – probably from a battery fixed up somewhere. Nobody seemed to be about at all! George gave a call, hoping that Timmy was somewhere there.

'Timmy! Where are you?'

And at once Timmy came from behind one of the big crates, his tail wagging hard! George was so glad that she fell on one knee and hugged him tight.

'You naughty dog,' she said, fondling him. 'Why didn't you come when you were called? Did you find the others? Where is Aily?'

A small face peeped from behind the crate nearby, the one from which Timmy had appeared. It was Aily. She looked terrified, and tears were on her cheeks. She clasped her lamb to her, and Dai was at her heels. She ran straight across to George, crying out something in Welsh, pointing back up the tunnel. George nodded.

'Yes. We'll go back straight away! Look – here come the others!'

Aily had already seen them. She ran to Julian with a cry of delight, and he swung her up in his arms, lamb and all. He was very glad to see George and Timmy too.

They all had a good look round the strange cave.

'*I* see what the idea is,' said Julian. 'Jolly clever too! They are mining that precious metal down here somewhere – and putting it on those rafts there, so that the underground river can take it right down to the sea. I bet they've got barges or something waiting down at some secret creek, to take the stuff away at night!'

'Whew!' said Dick. 'Very ingenious! And they count on the strange noises and shudderings and things to frighten people and keep them away from this hill – nobody dares to come prying round to see what's up!'

'The nearest farm is Magga Glen Farm, where the Joneses live,' said Julian. 'They would really be the only people who could find out anything definite.'

'Which they obviously did!' said Dick. 'I bet Morgan knows all about this, and is in with the son who sold the precious metal to the men who came after it – though it was his mother's.'

'There's no strange noise or anything down here – no noise at all except the sound of the river,' said Julian. 'Do you suppose the works aren't going just now?'

'Well,' began Dick, and then suddenly stopped as Dai and Timmy began to growl, Timmy in a deep voice and

Dai in a smaller one. Julian at once pulled Aily and George behind a big crate, and Dick pushed Anne there. They listened intently. What had the dogs heard? Was there time to rush back to the tunnel and make their way out before they were seen?

Timmy went on growling in a low voice. The children's hearts began to beat fast – and then they heard voices. Where did they come from? Dick peeped cautiously round the crate. It was in a dark corner and he hoped he could not be seen.

The voices seemed to come from the direction of the great pool, and Dick looked over to it. He gave a sudden exclamation.

'Ju! Look over there! Do you see what *I* see?'

Julian looked – and was filled with astonishment. Two men had come *up* the tunnel, from the sea – evidently walking on the rocky edge of the river, just as they themselves had done – and were now wading in the shallows of the pool.

'One is *MORGAN*!' whispered Julian. 'And who's the other man! Gosh! – it's the shepherd – Aily's father! Would you believe it? Well – we always thought *Morgan* was mixed up in this – but I didn't think the shepherd was.'

Aily had seen both Morgan and her father. She made no move to go to the shepherd – she was far too scared of Morgan!

Morgan and the shepherd stood and gazed round a little, as if looking for someone. Then, keeping to the shadows, they made their way across the great cave right to the back of it, where another tunnel, very wide, led downwards into the hill.

As they went, a strange noise began.

'The rumbling!' whispered George, and Timmy growled again. 'But oh – doesn't it sound near. What a terrific noise – it's got right inside my head!'

It was no use whispering now! They had to shout if they wanted to say anything and then the shuddering began! Everything shuddered and vibrated, and when the children touched one another, they could feel the vibration in the other's hands and arms.

'It's as if we're being run by electricity ourselves!' said Dick, astonished. 'I wonder if it's anything to do with that strange metal that is under this hill – that makes steel things heavy, so that ploughs won't plough, and spades won't dig!'

'Let's follow Morgan and the shepherd,' said Julian, so excited now that he felt he must see everything possible. 'We can keep well in the shadows. Nobody would ever guess we were here!'

'Aily – you stay here,' said Julian. 'Big noise, big, big noise frighten Fany and Dai.'

Aily nodded. She settled down behind the crate with her pets.

'Aily wait,' she said. She had no desire at all to go any nearer that strange noise! In her mind she imagined that possibly the thunder itself came from this hill and was made here. Yes, perhaps the lightning too!

Morgan and the shepherd had now disappeared into the tunnel right at the back of the cave, on the opposite side to the great pool. The Five went quickly over to it and looked down. It was very wide and very steep but rough steps had been cut in it, so that it was not difficult to go down.

They trod warily down the steep tunnel, astonished because it was dimly lit – and yet there were no lamps of any sort to be seen.

'I think it's the reflection of some great glare far below,' shouted Julian, above the rumbling. The noise was so loud that it was almost like walking in the middle of thunder.

Down and down they went, and the tunnel curved and wound about, always steep, rocky and dimly lit. Suddenly the noise grew louder, and the tunnel grew lighter. The children saw the end of it, the exit outlined in brilliant light – a light that shimmered and shook in a most curious way.

'We're coming to the works – the mine – where that strange metal is!' shouted Dick, so excited that he felt his hands trembling. 'Be careful we aren't seen. JU! BE CAREFUL WE AREN'T SEEN!'

They went cautiously to the end of the tunnel and peered out. They were looking into a vast pit of light, round which men stood, working some curious-looking machines. The children could not make out what they were – and, indeed, the light was so blinding that it was only possible to look with their eyelids almost closed. All the men were wearing face-guards.

Suddenly the loud rumbling stopped and the light disappeared as if someone had turned off an electric switch! Then, in the darkness, a glow formed, a strange glow that came upwards and outwards, and seemed to go right through the roof itself! Dick clutched at Julian.

'That's the kind of glow we saw the other night!' he said. 'My word – it begins down here, goes right up through the hill in some strange way, and hangs above it! That shimmering must come from here too – some kind of rays that can go through anything – like X-rays or something!'

'It's like a dream,' said Anne, feeling George to make sure it wasn't! 'Just like a dream!'

'Where are Morgan and the shepherd?' said Dick. 'Look – there they are – in that corner, not far off. Look out – they're coming back!'

The four children moved back quickly into the tunnel, afraid of being seen. They suddenly heard shouts, and stumbled up the rocky steps even faster. *Had* they been seen? It sounded like it!

'I can hear someone coming up the tunnel behind us!' panted Dick. 'Quick, quick! I wish that noise would begin again. I know we can be heard!'

Someone was climbing swiftly up behind them. There were shouts and yells from below too. It sounded as if all the men were disturbed and angry. Why, oh why had they followed Morgan and the shepherd? They could so easily have gone back to the cellars!

They came to the top of the steep, rocky tunnel at last, and ran to hide behind the crates, hoping to slip into the river-tunnel without being seen. They had to get Aily before they fled! Where was she?

'Aily, Aily!' shouted Julian. 'Where's she gone? We daren't leave her here. AILY!'

It was difficult to remember exactly where they had left her, in this great cave.

'There's the lamb!' cried Julian, thankfully, as he saw it on the other side of a crate. 'AILY!'

'Look out! There's Morgan!' shouted George, as the big farmer came out of the tunnel and ran across the cave. He saw the children and stopped in the utmost amazement.

'What are you doing here?' he roared. 'Come with us, quickly! You're in danger!'

The shepherd now appeared too, and Aily ran from behind her crate to him. He stared as if he could not believe his eyes, and then picked her up, calling something to Morgan in Welsh.

Morgan swung round on Julian again.

'I told you not to interfere!' he roared. 'I was handling this! Now we shall all be caught! Fool of a boy! Quick – we must hide and hope that the men will think we've gone down the tunnel. If we try to escape now, they will overtake us, and bring us back!'

He swept the astonished children into a dark corner and pulled crates round them.

'Stay there!' he said. 'We will do what we can!'

CHAPTER TWENTY-ONE

An astounding thing

THE FIVE children crouched behind the pile of crates. Morgan pushed another crate up, so that they were completely hidden. Dick clutched Julian.

'Julian! We've made fools of ourselves! Morgan was trying to find out the secret of Old Towers himself – with the help of the shepherd! They were about the only people in the neighbourhood who could guess what was going on. The shepherd could see all the strange things *we* saw, while watching his sheep on the mountainside – and he told Morgan . . .'

Julian groaned.

'Yes. No wonder he was angry when he thought we were meddling in such a serious matter. No wonder he forbade us to do anything more! Gosh – we've been idiots! Where is Morgan now? Can you see him?'

'No. He's hiding somewhere. Listen – here come the men!' said Dick. 'There's a crack between two crates here – I can see the first man. He's got an iron bar or something. He looks pretty grim!'

The men came out cautiously, evidently not sure how many people they were after. They advanced across the cave, seven of them, all with weapons of some kind. Two went to the upper river tunnel, two went to the one that led down to the sea, and the others began to hunt among the crates.

They found the children first! It was Aily's fault, poor child. She gave a sudden scream of fright – and in a trice the man had pulled away the crates. Crash – one by one they fell to the ground – and the amazed men found themselves looking at five children! But not for long! With a terrifying bark Timmy flung himself on the first man!

He yelled and began to fight him off, but Timmy held on like grim death. Morgan appeared from the shadows and surprised another of the men, jumping on him and getting him on the ground, at the same time catching hold of a second man and tossing him away. He had the strength of a giant!

'Run!' he yelled to the children, but they couldn't. Two of the men had penned them into a corner, and although Julian leapt at one of them, he was simply thrown back again. These men were strong miners, and though not a match for the giantlike Morgan, they could certainly take everyone else prisoner – including the gentle shepherd! He too was penned into a corner – only Morgan and Timmy were fighting now.

'Timmy will be hurt,' said George, in a trembling voice, and she tried to push one of the men away to get to him. 'Oh look, Ju – that man is trying to hit him with that bar!'

Timmy dodged the bar and sprang at the man, who

turned and ran for his life. Timmy shot after him and got him on the ground. But there were too many men – and more were now coming up from the tunnel at the back of the cave, pouring in, with weapons of all kinds. All of them were amazed to see the five children!

The men seemed mostly to be from another place, and spoke a language the children couldn't understand. But one man was not – he was obviously the boss, and gave his orders as if he expected them to be obeyed. He hadn't joined in the fight at all.

The shepherd was soon overpowered, and his hands bound behind his back. Morgan fought for some time – but then had to surrender. He was like an angry bull, stamping here, pulling there, roaring with rage as three men tried to tie his hands.

The boss came up and faced him.

'You will be sorry for this, Morgan,' he said. 'All our lives we have been enemies – you down at the farm – and I here at Old Towers.'

Morgan suddenly spat at him.

'Where is your old mother?' he shouted. 'A prisoner in her own house! Who has robbed her? You, Llewellyn Thomas!' Then he went off into a spate of Welsh, his voice rising high as he denounced the man in front of him.

Julian admired the fearless Morgan enormously, as he stood with his hands bound, defying the man who had been a lifelong enemy. How many quarrels had these two had, living in the same countryside, trying their strength against one another? Julian wished intensely that he had obeyed Morgan's command and left everything to him. But he had thought Morgan was on the side of the enemy! How stupid he had been!

'It's all because of us that he's caught,' thought the boy,

remorsefully. 'I've been a fool – and I thought I was doing something clever – and right! And now we're all landed in this mess – the girls too! What will they do with us? I suppose the only *safe* thing for them to do is to keep us prisoner till they've finished this mining job, collected a fortune from the metal, whatever it is, and gone.'

Llewellyn Thomas was now giving some sharp orders, and the men were listening. Timmy was growling, held by the collar in a stranglehold by one of the men. If he tried to squirm away, the man twisted his hand in the collar a little more and poor Timmy was half-choked.

George was wild with despair. Julian had to keep stopping her from trying to make a dash to Timmy. He was afraid that these rough men would strike her. Aily sat in a corner, hugging her lamb and Dai, who had been far too scared even to take a *little* nip at any of the men!

Morgan was held by two hefty miners – but, quite suddenly, he hurled himself sideways at one of them and sent him flying – and then at the other, who staggered away and fell over a tin.

With a great roar Morgan stumbled to the pool, and waded to the entrance of the tunnel that led to the sea, his hands still tightly tied behind his back.

'The fool!' said Llewellyn Thomas. 'If he thinks he can get along that tunnel with his hands tied, he is mad! He will fall into that rushing river – and without his hands to help him, he will drown! No – don't go after him. Let him go – let him drown! We shall be well rid of him!'

The shepherd struggled to his feet to go after his master, knowing quite well that Llewellyn was right – no man could get along that rough edge to the river without his hands to steady him, feeling along the wall at the side – and one slip would put him into the churning, hurrying river, that ran at full-pelt down to the sea far below, at the bottom of the hill.

But Morgan did not mean to escape. He was not going to struggle along beside that treacherous torrent! He had come all the way up beside it, with the shepherd, and knew how easy it was to slip on the wet rocky edge. No – Morgan had another plan!

Julian watched him disappear into the tunnel, and his heart sank. He too knew that no one could walk along there without free hands to help him. But what could anyone do?

The boss turned to the other men, who were still staring after Morgan. He was just about to say something to them, when a roar came to their ears.

Not the roar of the torrent in the underground tunnel. Nor the roar of the strange rumbling mine. No – the roar of a giant voice, that crashed out of the tunnel, and echoed round the cave.

It was Morgan's enormous voice. Morgan, calling the names of his seven great dogs! The children listened in amazement to this unbelievable voice.

'DAI! BOB! TANG! COME TO ME! DOON! JOLL! RAFE! HAL!'

The names echoed round and round the cave, and it seemed as if the place was full of giant voices. Aily, who was used to hearing the dogs called, didn't turn a hair – but the others crouched back in amazement at the sound of such a voice. Surely no one in all the world had ever shouted so loudly before!

'DAI! DAI! RAFE! RAFE!'

The great voice boomed again and again, seeming to be louder each time. At first Llewellyn Thomas, the boss, was taken aback – but then he laughed sneeringly.

'Does he think he can get his dogs up from the beach?' he said. 'All that way down the tunnel. He's mad! Let him be!'

Then again the great voice roared out the names of the seven dogs belonging to Morgan and the shepherd.

'DAI! BOB! TANG! DOON! JOLL! RAFE! HAL!'

At the last name, Morgan's voice seemed to crack. The shepherd raised his head in dismay. Morgan had overstrained that great voice of his, and no wonder. No megaphone could possibly have been louder!

There was silence after that, Morgan called no more. Neither did he appear again. The children felt scared and depressed, and Aily began to whimper.

The curious shuddering vibration began to creep into everything again, and the boss turned sharply, giving some more orders. Two of the men ran to the tunnel at the back of the cave and disappeared. Then things took on a curious shimmer, as if a heat-haze had spread everywhere, and it began to feel very warm in the cave.

Suddenly something happened. At first it sounded far off in the distance, a confused noise that made Timmy tug at his collar again and prick his ears. He barked, and the man who was holding him hit at him.

'What's that noise?' said Llewellyn Thomas, sharply, looking all round. There was no telling where it came from. But it grew louder – and louder – and then suddenly Julian knew what it was!

It was the loud barking of seven angry dogs! The shepherd knew it too, and a glad smile came over his face. He glanced at Llewellyn to see if he recognised it as well.

Yes – the boss had certainly recognised that dreadful sound now. He could hardly believe it! Surely it was not possible that Morgan's voice, enormous as it was, had echoed all the way down the tunnel, and been heard by the sharp, pricked-up ears of the dogs who loved him?

But so it was! Dai, the oldest dog, who loved his master more than any of them, had stood tense and listening ever since Morgan and the shepherd had left them. And, from somewhere far distant, echoing down to the end of the tunnel they were guarding, Dai had heard the faint echoes of his master's beloved voice!

His bark had told the other dogs the news – and, led by Dai, they had all rushed up the rocky tunnel, sure-footed on the slippery, rocky path beside the racing river.

They came to Morgan, sitting beside the river, not far

from the big cave, a little way down the tunnel. It was a moment of joy for Morgan and his dogs!

Dai soon snuffed at his hands and bit the ropes in half. Morgan was free!

'Down now – and hush!' commanded Morgan. He began to walk steadily back to the cave, then motioned the dogs before him.

'Attack!' he cried in Welsh.

And then, to the men's horror, the seven dogs raced out of the tunnel at a great speed, barking, growling, snarling – with a triumphant Morgan behind them, so tall that he had to bend double to leave the tunnel.

The men fled, every one of them. Llewellyn had turned to run even before the dogs appeared, and was gone. Dai leapt at one man and got him down, and Tang leapt at another. The cave was filled with snarls and growls and excited barking.

Timmy delightedly joined in, for his captor had rushed away too. Even little Dai ran to join this wonderful fight, while the children stood amazed and thankful to see their enemy defeated!

'Who would have thought of this?' said Dick, sending the crates crashing down. 'What an *astounding* thing! Hurrah for Morgan and his seven dogs!'

CHAPTER TWENTY-TWO

All's well that ends well!

MORGAN WOULD not let the children stay underground any longer.

'We have things to do,' he said, in his deep voice, which sounded rather hoarse now. 'You will go back to the farm and telephone to the police for me. You will say "Morgan has won" and tell them to send a boat to the little creek I have already told them of. There I will bring these men all the way down the tunnel to the sea. Go now, at once. Obey me this time, boy.'

'Yes,' said Julian. This man was a hero! And he had thought him a villain! He was ready to obey his smallest command now. Then a thought struck him, and he turned back.

'The old woman,' he said. 'Mrs Thomas – that man's mother. What about her? And we've locked the caretaker up in his room!'

'You will not do anything but go to the farm and telephone,' said Morgan, sternly. 'I will do everything there is to be done. Take Aily with you to the farm. She must not be here. Now *go*.'

And Julian went! He and the others took one last look round at the men, all pinioned by the dogs, lying still and panic-stricken. Then, with Aily and her lamb and dog, he led the others up the tunnel again, and at last back into the cellars.

'I don't like leaving that old lady up there, in the tower,' said Dick.

'No. But obviously Morgan has his plans,' said Julian, who was not going to disobey orders in any way this time. 'I expect he has arranged something with the police. We can't interfere now. We messed things up a bit, I'm afraid.'

They climbed soberly up to the place where they had left their toboggans. It took them some time, and they were beginning to feel very hungry. But Julian wouldn't let them stop even to eat some sandwiches.

'No,' he said. 'I've to telephone to the police as soon as ever I can. No stopping now! We'll munch our sandwiches on the way down to the farm.'

It wasn't very difficult to get out of the pot-hole, for they had left the ropes dangling down. Julian and Dick helped the two girls up by pushing them, and they in turn helped to pull up the boys from the top of the hole.

Aily scrambled up easily, swinging delightedly on a rope, and then flinging herself out of the hole. The lamb leapt up in a miraculous manner, and Julian handed Dai to the small girl.

Timmy was hauled up in the same way as he had been let down. He had badly wanted to stay with the other dogs – but nothing would make him leave George!

'Well, that's that,' said Julian, scrambling out last of all. 'Now let's see. We could toboggan down this slope, and halfway up our own slope. That would save a lot of time. Aily, you're to come with us to the farm.'

'No,' said Aily.

'Yes, Aily bach,' said Julian. 'I want you to.' He took her small hand in his and she smiled her sudden little smile, quite content to go along with this big, kind boy, even though she was afraid of going down to the farm for fear she should meet her mother.

'Aily good girl,' said Julian, setting the little thing on his toboggan.

They tobogganed down the slope at a great speed without any mishap, and halfway up the opposite slope. It seemed odd to be out in the dazzling daylight after the dark tunnels underground. Their adventure below began to seem slightly unreal!

'We'll leave the toboggans at the hut,' said Julian, as they dragged them up the rest of the slope. 'Anyone thirsty? I am. I think it must be something to do with that mine – my mouth got as dry as anything as soon as we were down there.'

Everyone said the same.

'I'll run into the hut and pour out some orangeade,' said Anne. 'You stack the toboggans in their place, Ju, and just see if there's enough oil in the can out in the bunker – we'll need to fill the stove tonight. And if there isn't enough we must bring some up with us.'

Julian gave her the key of the hut and she unlocked it and went in with George. They poured orangeade into five cups, and drank thirstily. Their mouths were drier than they had ever been before! Anne felt thankful that she didn't have to wait any longer for a drink.

'I think the roof of my mouth would have stuck to my tongue!' she said, putting down her cup. 'That was lovely!'

'There's plenty of oil,' reported Julian, coming to drink his orangeade. 'My word – I needed this. I'd not like to work down in that mine.'

They locked the hut and set off down to the farm, munching their sandwiches hungrily. They tasted very good indeed, and even Aily asked for one after another. Timmy had his share, and once they missed him, and had to stop and call him.

'Has he lost his bit of meat in the snow?' wondered Anne. But no – he, like the rest of them, was suffering from a very dry mouth and was busy licking the snow, letting it melt in his mouth and trickle down his dry throat!

Mrs Jones was most surprised to see them. When she heard Julian's request to telephone to the police, she looked worried.

'It's all right, Mrs Jones,' said Julian, comfortingly. 'It's a message to them from Morgan. Everything is fine. We'll tell you what's happened as soon as he comes home. He might not like us to say anything till then!'

The police did not seem at all surprised to hear Julian's message – they appeared to be expecting it!

'We will see to the matter,' said the sergeant, in his deep, stolid voice. 'Thank you.' And he rang off at once. Julian wondered what would happen next – what had Morgan arranged?

They were pleased to see Mrs Jones bringing in bowls of hot chicken soup, as they sat talking round the wood fire she had hurriedly lit in the living room.

'Oh! Just what we feel like!' said Anne, gratefully. 'I'm still awfully thirsty – aren't you, George? And look, Timmy – there's a nice meaty bone for you! You *are* kind, Mrs Jones!'

'You know – I feel pretty awful about all this now,' said Julian. 'We shouldn't have interfered after Morgan said we weren't to. I wish we hadn't. He can't think much of us!'

'I vote we all apologise humbly,' said Dick. 'How *could* we have thought he was the villain of the piece? I know he's dour and silent – but he didn't look mean or cruel.'

'We'd better stay down here at the farm till Morgan comes back,' said George. 'Quite apart from wanting to say I'm sorry, I'd like to know what happened!'

'So would I,' said Anne. 'And Aily ought to wait for her father. He'll want to know that she's safe.'

So they asked Mrs Jones if they could stay till Morgan came home. She was delighted.

'Of course, now,' she said. 'We've a roasting turkey today – and you shall come and have supper with us in our room for a change!'

This all sounded rather good. The children gathered round their fire to talk, and Timmy rested his head on George's knee. She looked at his neck.

'That man almost choked him,' she said. 'Oh look, Julian – he's bruised all round his poor neck!'

'Now don't start moaning over Timmy's neck again, for goodness' sake!' said Dick. 'Honestly, George, I'm sure Tim thinks the adventure was worth a bruised neck! *He's* not grumbling. He was jolly brave, I think – and didn't he enjoy himself when the other dogs rushed into the cave, and he joined in the fight!'

'I wonder what they'll do about that poor old woman,' said Anne. 'She will be glad her son is alive, I suppose – but what a shock for her to know he'd lied to her, and sold what is really hers – that strange metal under the hill!'

'Well – I imagine it won't be allowed to be sold now,' said Julian. 'What a plan that was! To get men up that tunnel to mine the stuff – and to send it down by rafts to waiting ships, hidden in that creek. We ought to go down and examine the creek – it would be interesting to see what sort of a place it is down there. It must be well hidden in a fold of the cliff, I should think.'

'Yes – let's do that tomorrow,' said George, thrilled. 'I vote we stay here tonight. I feel tired after such an adventure! Don't you?'

'I do a bit,' said Julian. 'Well – I suppose there won't be quite so much shuddering and shimmering and rumbling now! Funny that that hill should always have been so peculiar, isn't it – "ploughs that will not plough, spades that will not dig!" Must be some kind of iron, I suppose, that magnetises things. Oh well – it's all beyond me!'

Morgan came back with the shepherd when it was dark. Julian went straight up to the burly farmer.

'We want to apologise for being such idiots,' he said. 'We shouldn't have interfered after what you said.'

Morgan gave a broad smile. He seemed to be in a very good humour indeed.

'Forget it, boy,' he said. 'All's well now. The police came up the river tunnel, and all the men are safe in jail. Llewellyn Thomas is a sad man tonight. His mother is free and is staying with friends – poor lady, she doesn't

understand what has happened, and that is as well. And maybe now the right people will get that strange metal – it's worth a hundred times its weight in gold!'

'Come in for your supper, Morgan bach, and shepherd too!' said Mrs Jones, in her lilting voice. 'The children are coming too. We've a roasting turkey – it's your birthday, Morgan boy!'

'Well there now, I didn't know it!' said Morgan and gave his mother such a hug that she squealed. 'Let's go in to the turkey. I've had nothing all day.'

Soon they were all sitting down before the most enormous turkey that the children had ever seen in their lives! Morgan carved it swiftly. Then he said something to his mother in Welsh and she smiled and nodded.

'Yes, you do that,' she said.

Morgan collected some slices of turkey on a big enamel dish, and then went to the door that led from the living room into the farmyard. He roared loudly and the children jumped. What a voice!

'DAI! TANG! BOB! DOON! RAFE! JOLL! HAL!'

'He's calling the dogs,' said Anne. 'Just as he called them up the tunnel. Well – they certainly deserve a good dinner!'

Then down to the door came the seven dogs, jostling each other, barking excitedly. Morgan threw them the slices of turkey, and they gobbled the tasty bits up greedily.

'Woof!' said Timmy politely from behind him, and

Morgan turned. He solemnly cut a big slice and a little slice.

'Here!' he said to Timmy and little Dai. 'You did well too! Catch!'

'There'll not be much left of your birthday turkey!' said his mother, half-cross, half-amused. 'Now fill your glasses again, children, and we will drink to my Morgan – a better son there never was!'

Anne poured home-made lemonade into the empty glasses, while Morgan sat and smiled, listening to his seven dogs still barking together outside.

'Happy birthday, happy birthday!' shouted everyone, raising their glasses, and Julian added his own few words.

'Happy birthday – and may your voice NEVER grow less!'

Join the adventure!

If you can't wait to explore further with **THE FAMOUS FIVE**, read the next book in the series:

Enid Blyton®

is one of the most popular children's authors of all time. Her books have sold over 500 million copies and have been translated into other languages more often than any other children's author.

Enid Blyton adored writing for children. She wrote over 700 books and about 2,000 short stories. *The Famous Five* books, now 75 years old, are her most popular. She is also the author of other favourites including *The Secret Seven*, *The Magic Faraway Tree*, *Malory Towers* and *Noddy*.

Born in London in 1897, Enid lived much of her life in Buckinghamshire and loved dogs, gardening and the countryside. She was very knowledgeable about trees, flowers, birds and animals. Dorset – where some of the Famous Five's adventures are set – was a favourite place of hers too.

Enid Blyton's stories are read and loved by millions of children (and grown-ups) all over the world. Visit enidblyton.co.uk to discover more.

Illustration by Laura Ellen Anderson.

THE FAMOUS FIVE

FIVE ON FINNISTON FARM

Have you read all THE FAMOUS FIVE books?

1. Five on a Treasure Island
2. Five Go Adventuring Again
3. Five Run Away Together
4. Five Go to Smuggler's Top
5. Five Go Off in a Caravan
6. Five on Kirrin Island Again
7. Five Go Off to Camp
8. Five Get Into Trouble
9. Five Fall Into Adventure
10. Five on a Hike Together
11. Five Have a Wonderful Time
12. Five Go Down to the Sea
13. Five Go to Mystery Moor
14. Five Have Plenty of Fun
15. Five on a Secret Trail
16. Five Go to Billycock Hill
17. Five Get Into a Fix
18. Five on Finniston Farm
19. Five Go to Demon's Rocks
20. Five Have a Mystery to Solve
21. Five Are Together Again

The Famous Five Colour Short Stories

1. Five and a Half-Term Adventure
2. George's Hair is Too Long
3. Good Old Timmy
4. A Lazy Afternoon
5. Well Done, Famous Five
6. Five Have a Puzzling Time
7. Happy Christmas, Five
8. When Timmy Chased the Cat

Enid Blyton®

THE FAMOUS FIVE

FIVE ON FINNISTON FARM

Illustrated by Eileen A. Soper

HODDER CHILDREN'S BOOKS

First published in Great Britain in 1960 by Hodder & Stoughton
This edition published in 2016

20

A CIP catalogue record for this book is available from the British Library.

ISBN 978 1 444 93648 3

Printed and bound in Great Britain by Clays Ltd, Elcograf S.p.A.

The paper and board used in this book are made from wood from responsible sources.

Hodder Children's Books
An imprint of
Hachette Children's Group
Part of Hodder & Stoughton
Carmelite House
50 Victoria Embankment
London EC4Y 0DZ

An Hachette UK Company
www.hachette.co.uk
www.hachettechildrens.co.uk

CONTENTS

1 THE FIVE ARE ALL TOGETHER AGAIN 1
2 FINNISTON FARM 10
3 OUT IN THE BARN 19
4 JUNIOR! 28
5 EVENING AT THE FARM 37
6 A LITTLE EXCITEMENT FOR BREAKFAST 47
7 THE TWINS CHANGE THEIR MINDS 57
8 ALL ROUND THE FARM 65
9 A VERY INTERESTING TALE 76
10 QUITE A BIT OF SHOUTING 84
11 A MOST EXCITING TALE 93
12 REALLY VERY THRILLING 103
13 JUNIOR SPRINGS A SURPRISE 113
14 SNIPPET AND NOSEY ARE VERY HELPFUL 123
15 DIGGING FOR THE SECRET TUNNEL 132
16 UP THE TUNNEL AND INTO THE CELLARS 140
17 TRAPPED! 151
18 A GREAT STORY TO TELL! 161
19 'THE MOST EXCITING ADVENTURE WE'VE EVER HAD!' 169

CHAPTER ONE

The Five are all together again

'PHEW!' SAID Julian, mopping his wet forehead. 'What a day! Let's go and live at the equator – it would be cool compared to this!'

He stood leaning on his bicycle, out of breath with a long steep ride up a hill. Dick grinned at him. 'You're out of training, Ju!' he said. 'Let's sit down for a bit and look at the view. We're pretty high up!'

They leant their bicycles against a nearby gate and sat down, their backs against the lower bars. Below them spread the Dorset countryside, shimmering in the heat of the day, the distance almost lost in a blue haze. A small breeze came wandering round, and Julian sighed in relief.

'I'd never have come on this biking trip if I'd guessed it was going to be as hot as this!' he said. 'Good thing Anne didn't come – she'd have given up the first day.'

'George wouldn't have minded,' said Dick. 'She's game enough for anything.'

'Good old Georgina,' said Julian, shutting his eyes. 'I'll be glad to see the girls again. Fun to be on our own of course – but things always seem to happen when the four of us are together.'

'*Five*, you mean,' said Dick, tipping his cap over his

eyes. 'Don't forget old Timmy. What a dog! Never knew one that had such a wet lick as Tim. I say – won't it be fun to meet them all! Don't let's forget the time, Julian. Hey, wake up, stupid! If we go to sleep now we won't be in time to meet the girls' bus.'

Julian was almost asleep. Dick looked at him and laughed. Then he looked at his watch, and did a little calculating. It was half past two.

'Let's see now – Anne and George will be on the bus that stops at Finniston Church at five past three,' he thought. 'Finniston is about a mile away, down this hill. I'll give old Julian fifteen minutes to have a nap – and hope to goodness I don't fall asleep myself!'

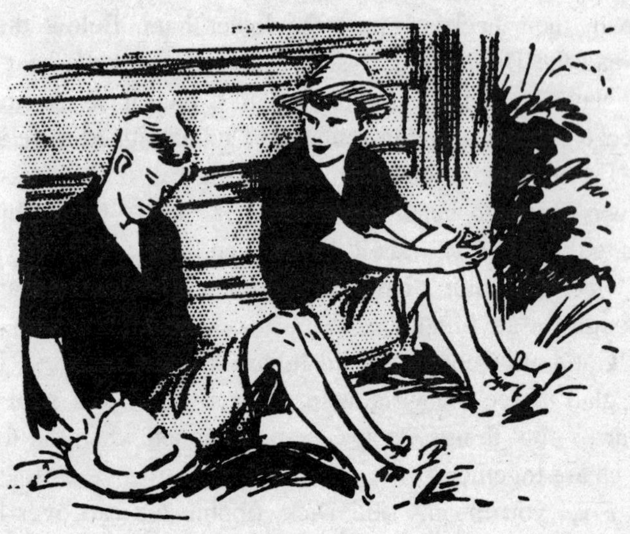

He felt his own eyes closing after a minute, and got up at once to walk about. The two girls and Tim *must* be met, because they would have suitcases with them, which the boys planned to wheel along on their bicycles.

The Five were going to stay at a place called Finniston Farm, set on a hill above the little village of Finniston. None of them had been there before, nor even heard of it. It had all come about because George's mother had heard from an old school friend, who had told her that she was taking paying guests at her farmhouse – and had asked her to recommend visitors to her. George had promptly said she would like to go there with her cousins in the summer holidays.

'Hope it's a good place!' thought Dick, gazing down into the valley, where cornfields waved in the little breeze. 'Anyway, we shall only be there for two weeks – and it *will* be fun to be together again.'

He looked at his watch. 'Time to go!' He gave Julian a push. 'Hey – wake up!'

''Nother ten minutes,' muttered Julian, trying to turn over, as if he were in bed. He rolled against the gate-bars and fell on to the hard dry earth below. He sat up in surprise. 'Gosh – I thought I was in bed!' he said. 'I could have gone on sleeping for hours.'

'Well, it's time to go and meet that bus,' said Dick. 'I've had to walk about all the time you were asleep, I was so afraid I'd go off myself. Come on, Julian – we really must go!'

They rode down the hill, going cautiously round the sharp corners, remembering how many times they had met herds of cows, wide farm carts, tractors and the like, on their way through this great farming county. Ah – there was the village, at the bottom of the hill. It looked old and peaceful and half-asleep.

'Thank goodness it sells ginger-beer and ice-creams!' said Dick, seeing a small shop with a big sign in the window. 'I feel as if I want to hang out my tongue, like Timmy does, I'm so thirsty!'

'Let's find the church and the bus stop,' said Julian. 'I saw a spire as we rode down the hill, but it disappeared when we got near the bottom.'

'There's the bus!' said Dick, as he heard the noise of wheels rumbling along in the distance. 'Look, here it comes. We'll follow it.'

'There's Anne in it – and George, look!' shouted Julian. 'We're here exactly on time! Hey, George!'

The bus came to a stop by the old church, and out jumped Anne and George, each with a suitcase – and out leapt old Timmy too, his tongue hanging down, very glad to be out of the hot, jerky, smelly bus.

'There are the boys!' shouted George, and waved wildly as the bus went off again. 'Julian! Dick! I'm so glad you're here to meet us!'

The two boys rode up, and jumped off their bikes, while Timmy leapt round them, barking madly. They thumped the girls on their backs, and grinned at them. 'Just the same old couple!' said Dick. 'You've got a spot on your chin, George, and why on *earth* have you tied your hair into a ponytail, Anne?'

'You're not very polite, Dick,' said George, bumping him with her suitcase. 'I can't think why Anne and I looked forward so much to seeing you again. Here, take my suitcase – haven't you any manners?'

'Plenty,' said Dick, and grabbed the case. 'I just can't get over Anne's new hair-do. I don't like it, Anne – do you, Ju? Ponytail! A donkey tail would suit you better Anne!'

'It's all right – it's just because the back of my neck was so hot,' said Anne, shaking her hair free in a hurry. She hated her brothers to find fault with her. Julian gave her arm a squeeze.

'Nice to see you both,' he said. 'What about some ginger-beer and ice-cream? There's a shop over there that sells them. And I've a sudden longing for nice juicy plums!'

'You haven't said a word to Timmy yet,' said George, half offended. 'He's been trotting round you and licking your hands – and he's so dreadfully hot and thirsty!'

'Shake paws, Tim,' said Dick, and Timmy politely put up his right paw. He shook hands with Julian too and then promptly went mad, careering about and almost knocking over a small boy on a bicycle.

'Come on, Tim – want an ice-cream?' said Dick, laying his hand on the big dog's head. 'Hark at him panting, George – I bet he wishes he could unzip his hairy coat and take it off! Don't you Tim?'

'Woof!' said Tim, and slapped his tail against Dick's legs.

They all trooped into the ice-cream shop. It was half dairy, half baker's. A small girl of about ten came to serve them.

'Mum's lying down,' she said. 'What can I get you? Ice-creams, I suppose? That's what everyone wants today.'

'You supposed right,' said Julian. 'A large one each, please – five in all – and four bottles of ginger pop as well.'

'*Five* ice-creams – do you want one for that dog, then?' said the girl in surprise, looking at Timmy.

'Woof,' he said at once.

'There you are,' said Dick, 'he said yes!'

Soon the Five were eating their cold ice-creams, Timmy licking his from a saucer. Before he had had many licks, the ice-cream slid from the saucer, and Timmy chased it all the way round the shop, as it slid away from his vigorous licks. The little girl watched him, fascinated.

'I must apologise for his manners,' said Julian, solemnly. 'He hasn't been very well brought up.' He at once had a glare from George, and grinned. He opened his bottle of ginger-beer. 'Nice and cold,' he said. 'Here's a happy fortnight to us all!' He drank half the glass at top speed, and set it down with a great sigh.

'Well, blessings on the person who invented ice-cream, ginger pop and the rest!' he said. 'I'd rather invent things like that any day than rockets and bombs. Ha – I feel

ORANGE
DELIGHT
THE BEST
DRINK FOR
ALL TIMES.

better now. What about you others? Do you feel like going to find the farm?'

'Whose farm?' asked the little girl, coming out from behind the counter to pick up Timmy's saucer. Timmy gave her a large, wet and loving lick as she bent down.

'Ooooh!' she said, pushing him away. 'He licked all down my face!'

'Probably thought you were an ice-cream,' said Dick, giving her his hanky to wipe her cheek. 'The farm we want is called Finniston Farm. Do you know it?'

'Oh *yes*,' said the little girl. 'You go down the village street, right to the end, and turn up the lane there – up to the right. The farmhouse is at the top of the lane. Are you staying with the Philpots?'

'Yes. Do you know them?' asked Julian, getting out some money to pay the bill.

'I know the twins there,' said the girl. 'The two Harries. At least, I don't know them *well* – nobody does. They're just wrapped up in each other, they never make any friends. You look out for their old great-grandad – *he's* a one he is! He once fought a mad bull and knocked it out! And his *voice* – you can hear it for miles! I was real scared of going near the farm when I was little. But Mrs Philpot, she's nice. You'll like her. The twins are very good to her – and to their dad, too – work like farm hands all the holidays. You won't know t'other from which, they're so alike!'

'Why did you call them the two Harries?' asked Anne, curiously.

'Oh, because they've both . . .' began the child, and then broke off as a plump woman came bustling into the shop.

'Janie – you go and see to the baby for me – I'll see to the shop now. Run along!'

Away went the small girl, scuttling through the door.

'Little gasbag she is!' said her mother. 'Anything more you want?'

'No thanks,' said Julian, getting up. 'We must go. We're to stay at Finniston Farm, so we may be seeing you again soon. We liked the ice-creams!'

'Oh – so you're going there, are you?' said the plump woman. 'I wonder how you'll get on with the Harries! And keep out of Grandad's way – he's over eighty, but he can still give a mighty good thumping to anyone who crosses him!'

The Five went out into the hot sun again. Julian grinned round at the others. 'Well – shall we go and find the nice Mrs Philpot – the unfriendly Harries, whoever they might be – and the fearsome great-grandad? Sounds interesting, doesn't it?'

CHAPTER TWO

Finniston Farm

THE FOUR children, with Timmy trotting beside them, walked down the hot, dusty village street until they came to the end, and then saw the lane turning off to the right, just as the little girl had told them.

'Wait a minute,' said Anne, stopping at a curious little shop at the end of the village street. 'Look – here's an interesting shop. It sells antiques. Look at those old horse-brasses – I'd like to get one or two of those. And just see those lovely old prints!'

'Oh *no* – not now, Anne,' said Julian, with a groan. 'This awful craze of yours for second-hand shops has been going on too long! Horse-brasses! You've got stacks of them already! If you think we're going to go into that dark, smelly little shop and . . .'

'Oh, I'm not going in *now*,' said Anne, hurriedly. 'But it does look rather exciting. I'll come by myself sometime and browse round.' She glanced at the name on the shop front. 'William Finniston – how funny to have the same name as the village! I wonder if . . .'

'Oh come *on*,' said George impatiently, and Timmy tugged at her skirt. Anne gave one backward glance at the fascinating little shop window, and hurried after the others, making up her mind to slip down to the shop one day when she was alone.

They all went up the little winding lane, where red poppy-heads jigged about in the breeze, and after a while they came in sight of the farmhouse. It was a big one, three storeys high, with whitewashed walls, and the rather small windows belonging to the age in which it was built. Old-fashioned red and white roses rambled over the porch, and the old wooden door stood wide open.

The Five stood on the scrubbed stone entrance, looking into the dim hall. An old wooden chest stood there, and a carved chair. A rather threadbare rug lay on the stone floor, and a grandfather clock ticked slowly and loudly.

Somewhere a dog barked, and Timmy at once barked back. 'WOOF, WOOF!'

'Be quiet, Timmy,' said George sharply, afraid that a horde of farm dogs might come rushing out. She looked for a bell or a knocker, but couldn't see either. Then Dick spotted a beautiful wrought-iron handle hanging down from the roof of the porch. Could it be a bell?

He pulled it, and at once a bell jangled very loudly somewhere in the depths of the farmhouse, making them all jump. They stood in silence, waiting for someone to come. Then they heard footsteps and two children came up the hallway.

They were *exactly* alike! The most twinny twins I've ever seen, thought Anne, in amazement. Julian smiled his friendliest smile. 'Good afternoon – I – er – I hope you're expecting us.'

The twins stared at him without a smile. They nodded together. 'Come this way,' they both said, and marched back down the hall. The four stared at one another in surprise.

'Why so stiff and haughty?' whispered Dick, putting on a face exactly like the twins'. Anne giggled. They all followed the twins, who were dressed exactly alike in navy shorts and navy shirts. They went right down the long hall, passed a stairway, round a dark corner, and into an enormous kitchen, which was obviously used as a sitting-room as well.

'The Kirrins, Mother!' said the twins, together, and at once disappeared through another door, shoulder to shoulder. The children found themselves facing a pleasant-looking woman standing by a table, her hands white with flour. She smiled, and then gave a little laugh.

'Oh, my dears! I didn't expect you quite so soon! Do forgive my not being able to shake hands with you – but I was just making scones for your tea. I'm so pleased to see you. Did you have a good journey here?'

It was nice to hear her welcoming voice and see her wide smile. The Five warmed to her at once. Julian put down the suitcase he was carrying and looked round the room.

'What a lovely old place!' he said. 'You carry on with your scone-making, Mrs Philpot – we'll look after ourselves. Just tell us where to go. It's nice of you to have us.'

'I'm glad to,' said Mrs Philpot. 'I expect your aunt told you the farm's not doing too well, and she kindly said she'd send you here for two weeks. I've some other boarders too – an American and his son – so I'm pretty busy.'

'Well, you don't need to bother too much about *us*,' said Dick. 'In fact, we'll camp out under a haystack if you like – or in a barn. We're used to roughing it!'

'Well – that *might* be a help,' said Mrs Philpot, going on with her mixing. 'I've a bedroom that would do for the girls all right – but I'm afraid you boys would have to share one with the American boy – and – er – well, you mightn't like him.'

'Oh, I expect we'll get on all right,' said Julian. 'But my brother and I would certainly *prefer* to be by ourselves, Mrs Philpot. What about putting up camp-beds or something in a barn? We'd love that!'

Anne looked at Mrs Philpot's kind, tired face, and felt suddenly sorry for her. How awful to *have* to have your home invaded by strangers, whether you liked them or not! She went over to her.

'You tell Georgina and me anything you'd like us to do to help,' she said. 'You know – making the beds and dusting and things like that. We're used to doing things at home, and . . .'

'I'm going to enjoy having *you*!' said Mrs Philpot, looking round at them all. 'And you won't need to help very much. The twins do a great deal – too much, I think, bless them – because they help on the farm too. Now, you go up the stairs to the very top of the house, and you'll see two bedrooms, one on each side of the landing – the left-hand one is yours, girls – the other is where the American boy is sleeping. And as for you two boys, you can slip out to the barn, and see if you'd like a couple of camp-beds there. I'll get the twins to take you.'

The twins came back at this minute, and stood silently shoulder to shoulder, as alike as peas in a pod. George looked at them.

'What's your name?' she said to one twin.

'Harry!' was the answer. She turned to the other. 'And what's yours?'

'Harry!'

'But surely you don't have the same name?' exclaimed George.

'Well, you see,' explained their mother, 'we called the boy Henry, and he became Harry, of course – and we called the girl Harriet, and *she* calls herself Harry for short – so they're known as the Harries.'

'I thought they were both *boys*!' said Dick in amazement. 'I wouldn't know which is which!'

'Well, they felt they *have* to be alike,' said Mrs Philpot, 'and as Harry can't have long hair like a girl Harriet has to have shorter hair to be like Harry! I very often don't know one from the other myself.'

Dick grinned. 'Funny how some girls want to be boys!' he said, with a sly glance at George, who gave him a furious look.

'Twins, show the Kirrins up to the top bedroom,' said Mrs Philpot, 'and then take the boys out to the big barn. They can have the old camp-beds, if they like the look of the barn.'

'*We* sleep out there,' said the Harries, both together, and scowled just like George.

'Well, you shouldn't,' said their mother. 'I told you to take your mattresses to the little room off the dairy.'

'It's too stuffy,' said the twins.

'Hang on – we don't want to cause trouble,' said Julian, feeling that the twins were too unfriendly for words. 'Can't *we* sleep in the room off the dairy?'

'Certainly not,' said Mrs Philpot, and sent the Harries a warning glance. 'There's room for you all in the big barn. Go on now, twins, do as I tell you, take the four up to the top bedroom, with the cases, and then out to the barn.'

The twins went to pick up the suitcases, still looking mutinous. Dick interposed himself between them and the cases. '*We'll* carry them,' he said stiffly. 'We don't want to be any more trouble to you than we can help.'

And he and Julian picked up a suitcase each, and set off after the Harries, who looked suddenly surprised. George followed with Timmy, more amused than cross. Anne went to pick up a spoon that Mrs Philpot had dropped.

'Thank you, dear,' said Mrs Philpot. 'Look – don't get upset by the twins. They're a funny pair – but good at heart. They just don't like strangers in their home, that's all. Promise you won't mind them? I do want you to be happy here.'

Anne looked at the kindly, tired face of the woman beside her, and smiled. 'We'll promise not to worry about the twins – if you'll promise not to worry about *us*!' she said. 'We can look after ourselves, you know – honestly, we're used to it. And please do tell us when you want anything done!'

She went out of the room and up the stairs. The others were already in one of the two bedrooms at the top of the house. It was a fairly big room, white-washed, with rather a small window and boarded floors. Julian looked at the boards he was standing on. 'I say! Look at the wood this floor's made of – solid old oak, worn white with the years! This farmhouse must be very old. And look at the beams running across the walls and into the roof. Hey, twins, this is a wonderful old house!'

The twins unbent enough to nod in time together. 'Seems as if you two go by clockwork – you speak the same words at the same time, you walk in time, you nod your heads in time!' said Dick. 'But, I say – do you *ever* smile?'

The twins looked at him with dislike. Anne nudged Dick. 'Stop it, Dick! Don't tease them. Perhaps they'd show you the barn now. We'll unpack some clean things we've brought for you in our case, and come down with them when we're ready.'

'Right,' said Dick, and he and Julian went out of the room. Opposite, with its door open, was the other room, where the American boy slept. It was so very untidy that Dick couldn't help exclaiming. 'Gosh – how does he get his room into all that mess?' He and Julian went down the stairs, and Dick turned back to see if the Harries were following. He saw them standing at the top, each shaking a furious fist at the door of the American boy's room. And what a furious look on their faces, too!

'Whew!' thought Dick. 'The Harries have got some sort of grudge against him – let's hope they don't get one for us, too.'

'Well – now for the barn,' he said aloud. 'Don't go so fast, Ju. Wait for the twins – they're just falling over themselves to look after us!'

CHAPTER THREE

Out in the barn

THE TWINS stalked out of the farmhouse and took the two boys round the dairy shed, and up to an enormous barn. One of them pushed open the great door.

'I *say*!' said Julian, gazing into the dark barn. 'I never saw such a great barn in all my life! It's as old as the hills – look at those beams soaring up into the roof – it reminds me of a cathedral, somehow. I wonder why they built the roof so high. What do you store in here, twins?'

'Sacks of meal,' said the Harries together, opening and shutting their mouths as one. The two boys saw a couple of camp-beds in a corner of the barn.

'Look,' said Julian, 'if you really would rather sleep here alone, we'll sleep in the little room off the dairy that your mother spoke of.'

Before the twins could answer, a shrill barking came from the direction of the camp-beds, and the boys saw a tiny black poodle there, standing up, quivering in every hair.

'What a tiny thing!' said Julian. 'Is he yours? What's his name?'

'Snippet,' came the answer from both at once. 'Come here, Snippet!'

At once the tiny black poodle hurled himself off the camp-bed and raced over to them. He fawned on them all, barking in delight, licking everyone in turn. Dick picked him up, but the twins at once clutched Snippet themselves.

'He's OUR dog!' they said so fiercely that Dick backed away.

'All right, all right – you can have him. But be careful Tim doesn't eat him!' he said. A look of fear came over the faces of the Harries, and they turned to one another, anxiously.

'It's all right,' said Julian, hastily. 'Tim's gentle with small things. You needn't be afraid. I say – why do you have to be so *silly*? It really wouldn't hurt you to be a bit friendly. And do let us sleep in your old room – we really don't mind.'

The twins looked at each other again, as if reading one another's thoughts, and then they turned gravely to the boys, not looking quite so unfriendly.

'We will *all* sleep here,' they said. 'We will fetch the other camp-beds.' And off they marched, Snippet running excitedly at their heels.

Julian scratched his head. 'Those twins make me feel peculiar,' he said. 'I don't feel they are quite *real*. The way they act and speak together makes me feel as if they're puppets or something.'

'They're just jolly rude and unfriendly,' said Dick, bluntly. 'Oh well – they won't get in our way much. I vote we explore the farm tomorrow. It looks quite a big one – spreading out over the hill slopes everywhere. I wonder if we could get a ride on a tractor?'

At that moment a bell rang loudly from the direction of the house. 'What's that for?' said Dick. 'Tea, I hope!'

The twins came back at that moment with two more camp-beds, which they proceeded to set up as far from their own as possible. Dick went to give a hand, but they waved him off, and put up the beds most efficiently and quickly by themselves.

'Tea is ready,' they said, standing up when the beds were finished, and blankets and pillows set out on them. 'We will show you where to wash.'

'Thanks,' said Dick and Julian together, and then grinned at one another. 'Better be careful,' said Julian, 'or we'll catch their habit of speaking exactly at the same moment. I say – isn't that poodle funny – look at him stalking that jackdaw!'

A black jackdaw, the nape of his neck showing grey as he ran in front of Snippet, had flown down from somewhere in the roof of the barn. As Snippet danced after him he ran behind sacks, scurried into corners and led the little dog such a dance that the two boys roared. Even the twins smiled.

'Chack!' said the jackdaw, and rose into the air. He settled himself on the middle of the poodle's back, and Snippet promptly went mad, and tore about the barn at top speed.

'Roll over, Snippet!' shouted the Harries, and Snippet at

once flung himself on his back – but the jackdaw, with a triumphant 'chack' rose at once into the air, and alighted on one twin's head.

'I say, is he tame?' said Dick. 'What's his name?'

'Nosey. He's ours. He fell down a chimney and broke his wing,' said the twins. 'So we kept him till it was well and now he won't leave us.'

'Gosh!' said Dick, staring at them. 'Did you *really* say all that – or was it the jackdaw? You *can* talk properly, after all.'

Nosey pecked at the twin's ear nearest to him, and the twin gave a yell. 'Stop it, Nosey!' The jackdaw rose into the air, with a 'chack-chack-chack' that sounded very like a laugh, and disappeared somewhere in the roof.

Just then the two girls came to find the boys in the barn, sent by Mrs Philpot, who was sure they hadn't heard the bell. Timmy was with them, of course, sniffing into every corner, enjoying the farm smells everywhere. They came to the barn and looked in.

'Oh, there you are!' called Anne. 'Mrs Philpot said we . . .'

Timmy began to bark, and she stopped. He had caught sight of Snippet sniffing behind the sacks, still hunting for the cheeky jackdaw. He stood still and stared. What in the wide world was that funny little black creature? He gave another loud bark and shot over towards the poodle, who gave a terrified yelp and leapt into the arms of one of the twins.

'Take your dog away,' said both twins, fiercely, glaring at the four.

'It's all right – he won't hurt Snippet,' said George, advancing on Timmy and taking hold of his collar. 'He really won't.'

'TAKE YOUR DOG AWAY!' shouted the twins, and up in the roof somewhere the jackdaw said, 'CHACK, CHACK, CHACK!' just as fiercely.

'All right, all right,' said George, glaring as angrily as the twins. 'Come on, Tim. That poodle wouldn't be more than a mouthful for you, anyway!'

They all went back to the farmhouse in silence, Snippet having been left behind on the camp-bed belonging to one of the twins. They cheered up when they came into the big, cool kitchen. Tea was now laid on the farmhouse table, a big solid affair of old, old oak. Chairs were set round and it all looked very home-like.

'Hot scones,' said George, lifting the lid of a dish. 'I never thought I'd like hot scones on a summer's day, but these look heavenly. Running with butter! Just how I like them!'

The four looked at the home-made buns and biscuits and the great fruit cake. They stared at the dishes of home-made jam, and the big plate of ripe plums. Then they looked at Mrs Philpot, sitting behind a very big teapot, pouring out cups of tea.

'You mustn't spoil us, Mrs Philpot,' said Julian, thinking that really his hostess was doing too much. 'Please don't let us make too much work for you!'

A loud, commanding voice suddenly made them all jump. Sitting in a big wooden armchair near the window was someone they hadn't seen – a burly old man with a shock of snowy white hair and a luxuriant white beard almost down to his waist. His eyes were startlingly bright as he looked across at them.

'TOO MUCH WORK! What's that you say? TOO MUCH WORK? Ha, people nowadays don't know what work is, they don't! Grumble, grumble, GRUMBLE, asking for this and expecting that! Pah! PAH, I say!'

'Now now, Grandad,' said Mrs Philpot, gently. 'You just sup your tea and rest. You've been out on the farm all day, and it's too much work for you.'

That set the old man off again. 'TOO MUCH WORK! Now let me tell you something. When I was a young lad, I . . . hallo, who's this?'

It was Timmy! He had been startled by the sudden shouting of the old man, and had stood up, his hackles rising, and a low growl down in his throat. And then a very curious thing happened.

Timmy walked slowly over to the fierce old man, stood by him – and laid his head gently on his knee! Everyone stared in astonishment, and George could hardly believe her eyes!

At first the old man took no notice. He just let Timmy stay there, and went on with his shouting. 'No one knows anything these days. They don't know a good sheep or a good bull or a good dog. They . . .'

Timmy moved his head a little, and the old man stopped again. He looked down at Timmy, and patted him on the head. 'Now *here's* a dog – a REAL dog. A dog that could be the best friend any man ever had. Ah, he reminds me of my old True, he does.'

George was staring in amazement at Timmy. 'He's never done a thing like that before,' she said.

'All dogs are like that with old Grandad,' said Mrs Philpot softly. 'Don't mind his shouting. He's like that. See – your Timmy is lying down by Grandad – now they'll both be happy. Grandad will have his tea and be nice and quiet. Don't take any notice of him now.'

Still astonished, the children ate a marvellous tea, and were soon talking eagerly to Mrs Philpot, asking her questions about the farm.

'Yes, of course you can go on the tractor. And we've an old Land Rover too – you can motor round the farm in that, if you like. Wait till my husband comes in – he'll tell you what you can do.'

Nobody saw a little black shadow come in at the door, and sidle softly over to Grandad – Snippet the poodle! He had left the barn and come to the kitchen he loved. It was only when Mrs Philpot turned round to ask the old man to have another cup of tea that she saw a very strange sight indeed. She nudged the twins, and they hurried to look.

They saw Timmy lying peacefully down on Grandad's big feet – and Snippet the poodle lying between Timmy's great front paws! Well – what an astonishing sight to be sure!

'Grandad's happy now,' said Mrs Philpot. 'Two dogs at his feet. And now, look – here's my husband! Come along in, Trevor – we're all here, the dogs as well!'

CHAPTER FOUR

Junior!

A BIG MAN came into the kitchen, very like the twins to look at. He stooped, and seemed tired. He didn't smile, but just nodded.

'Trevor, here are the visitors I told you about,' said Mrs Philpot. 'Look, this is Julian and . . .'

'More visitors?' said Trevor with a groan. 'Good heavens – what a crowd of children! Where's that American boy? I've got a bone to pick with him. He tried to set the tractor going by himself this morning, and . . .'

'Oh, Trevor – never mind about that now. Just wash and come and have your tea,' said Mrs Philpot. 'I've kept some of your favourite scones for you.'

'Don't want any tea,' said her husband. 'Can't stop – except for just one cup, and that I'll take in the dairy. I've got to go and see to the milking. Bob's off today.'

'We'll help, Dad!' said the twins speaking together, as usual, and they got up from the table at once.

'No – you sit down,' said their mother. 'You've been on the go from seven o'clock this morning. Sit down and finish your tea in peace.'

'I could do with your help, twins,' said their father, as he went through the door towards the dairy, 'but now your mother's got so many on her hands, she'll need you more than I do!'

'Mrs Philpot – let the twins go if they want to,' said Julian at once. 'We can help, you know – we're used to helping at home.'

'And what's more, we like it,' said Anne. 'Do let us, Mrs Philpot – we'll feel much more at home then. Can't we clear away and wash up and all that, while the twins go and help with the milking?'

'YOU LET 'EM HELP!' shouted old Great-Grandad suddenly from his corner, making Timmy and Snippet leap to their feet, startled. 'WHAT ARE CHILDREN COMING TO NOWADAYS – WAITED ON HAND AND FOOT? PAH!'

'Now, now, Grandad,' said poor Mrs Philpot. 'Don't you start worrying. We can manage fine.'

The old man made a loud, explosive noise, and banged his hand down on the arm of his chair. 'WHAT I SAY IS THIS . . .'

But he got no further, for the sound of footsteps could be heard in the hall, coming towards the kitchen, and loud, American voices came nearer and nearer.

'See here, Pop – I wanna come with you! This place is dead. You take me up to London with you, aw, Pop, go on, do!'

'That the Americans?' asked Dick, turning to the twins. Their faces had gone as dark as thunder. They nodded. In came a burly man, looking rather odd in smart town

clothes, and a plump pasty-faced boy of about eleven. The father stood at the door and looked round rubbing his hands.

'Hiya, folks! We've been over to that swell old town and picked up some fine souvenirs – my, my, they were cheap as dirt! We late for tea? Hallo, who're all these folks?'

He grinned round at Julian and the others. Julian stood up politely. 'We're four cousins,' he said. 'We've come to stay here.'

'Stay here? Where you gonna sleep, then?' demanded the boy, pulling up a chair to the table. 'This is a one-eyed place, ain't it, Pop.'

'Shut up,' said the twins together, and gave the boy such a glare that Anne stared in astonishment.

'Aw, go on, I can say what I like, can't I?' said the boy. 'Free country, isn't it? Gee, you should just see America! That's something! Mrs Philpot, I'll have a bit of that cake – looks good to me.'

'CAN'T YOU SAY PLEASE?' roared a voice from the corner. That was Great-Grandad of course! But the boy took no notice, and merely held out his plate, while Mrs Philpot cut him an enormous slice of cake.

'I'll have the same as Junior, Mrs Philpot ma'am,' said the American, and sat down at the table. He held out his plate too. 'Say, you should see the things we've bought. We've had a day, haven't we, Junior?'

'Sure, Pop,' said Junior. 'Say, can't I have an iced drink? Look here – who's going to drink hot tea on a day like this!'

'I'll get you some iced lemonade,' said Mrs Philpot, rising.

'LET HIM GET IT HIMSELF! LITTLE BRAT!' That was Great-Grandad again, of course. But the twins were already up and on their way to fetch the lemonade themselves. George caught sight of their faces as they passed her, and had a shock of surprise. Goodness – how those twins hated that boy!

'That old grand-daddy of yours must be a bit of a nuisance to you,' said the American in a low voice to Mrs Philpot. 'Always butting in, isn't he? Rude old fellow, too.'

'NOW DON'T YOU SIT THERE WHISPERING!' shouted Grandad. 'I CAN HEAR EVERY WORD!'

'Now, now, Grandad, don't upset yourself,' said poor Mrs Philpot. 'You just sit there and have a nap.'

'No. I'm going out again,' said Great-Grandad heaving himself up. 'There's some people here that fair make me ill!'

And out he went leaning on his stick, a magnificent figure with his head of snow-white hair and his long beard.

'Like someone out of the Old Testament,' said Anne to Dick. Timmy got up and followed the old man to the door, with Snippet close behind him. Junior saw Timmy at once.

'Hey! Look at that big dog!' he said. 'Who's he? I've not seen him before. Hey, you, come and have a bun.'

Timmy took not the slightest notice. George addressed Junior in an icy voice. 'That's my dog Timmy. I don't allow anyone to feed him except me.'

'Shucks!' said Junior and threw the cake down on the floor, so that it slid to Tim's feet. 'That's for you, dog!'

Timmy looked down at the cake, and stood perfectly still. Then he looked at George. 'Come here, Timmy,' said George, and he walked straight to her. The cake lay on the floor half-broken into crumbs.

'My dog is not going to eat that,' said George. 'Better pick it up, hadn't you? It's made a bit of a mess on the floor.'

'Pick it up yourself,' said Junior, helping himself to another bun. 'Gee – what a glare you've got! Makes me want my sunglasses, brother!' He gave George a sudden sharp dig in the ribs, and she gasped. Timmy was beside her in a moment, growling so deeply that Junior slid out of his seat in alarm.

'Say, Pop – this dog's fierce!' he said. 'He tried to bite me!'

'He did not,' said George. 'But he *might* bite if you don't do what I said, and pick up that bun!'

'Now, now,' said Mrs Philpot, really distressed. 'Leave it – it can be swept up afterwards. Will you have another piece of cake, Mr Henning?'

It really was an embarrassing meal, and Anne longed for it to be over. Junior quietened down considerably when he saw Timmy lying down between his chair and George's, but his father made up for that by talking non-stop about the 'wunnerful' things he had bought that day. Everyone was extremely bored. The twins came back with a jug of orangeade, which they placed on the table, with two glasses, in case Mr Henning wanted some. They then disappeared.

'Where have they gone?' demanded Junior, having poured a glass of orangeade straight down his throat in a most remarkable manner. 'Gee, that was good.'

'The twins have gone to help with the milking, I expect,' said Mrs Philpot, looking suddenly very weary. Julian

looked at her. She must find these meals very tiring, he thought, coping with so many people. Junior piped up at once.

'I'll go and help with the milking,' he said, and slid off his chair.

'I'd rather you didn't, Junior,' said Mrs Philpot. 'You upset the cows a bit last time, you know.'

'Aw gee – that was because I was new to it,' said Junior. Julian looked at Mr Henning, expecting him to forbid Junior to go, but he said nothing. He lit a cigarette and threw the match down on the floor.

George scowled when she saw Junior heading for the door. How dare he go out to the milking against the wishes of his hostess? She murmured a few words to Timmy, and he got up at once and ran to the door, barring it against Junior.

'Get out of my way, you,' said Junior, stopping. Timmy growled. 'Say, call him back, will you?' said Junior, turning round. No one said anything. Mrs Philpot rose and began to gather things together. It seemed to George as if she had tears in her eyes. No wonder, if this kind of thing happened every day!

As Timmy stood like a statue in the doorway, giving small threatening growls every now and again, Junior decided to give up. He dearly longed to give the dog a kick, but didn't dare to. He walked back to his father.

'Say, Pop – coming for a walk?' he said. 'Let's get out of here.'

Without a word father and son walked out of the other

door. Everyone heaved a sigh of relief.

'You go and sit down and have a rest, Mrs Philpot,' said Anne. 'We'll do the washing-up. We'd love to!'

'Well – it's really kind of you,' said Mrs Philpot. 'I've been on the go all day, and twenty minutes' rest will do me good. I'm afraid Junior gets on my nerves. I do *hope* Timmy won't bite him!'

'He'll give him a nip before long,' said George cheerfully, collecting cups and saucers with Anne. 'What are you boys going to do? Go to the milking shed?'

'Yes. We've milked cows plenty of times,' said Dick. 'Nice job! I like the smell of cows. See you later, girls – and if that little pest tries any tricks, just give us a call! I'd love to rub his face into that crumby mess on the floor!'

'I'm just going to sweep it up,' said Anne. 'See you at supper-time!'

The boys went out, whistling. Mrs Philpot had disappeared. Only George, Anne and Timmy were left, for Snippet had gone out with the Harries.

'I rather wish we hadn't come,' said George, carrying out a tray to the scullery. 'It's an *awful* lot for Mrs Philpot to do. Still – if she needs the money . . .'

'Oh well – we can help – and we'll be out most of the day,' said Anne. 'We shan't see much of Junior – little beast!'

You're wrong, Anne. You'll see far too much of him! It's a good thing Timmy's there – he's the only one that can manage people like Junior!

CHAPTER FIVE

Evening at the farm

GEORGE AND Anne went out to find the others in the milking shed. There were plenty of cows there, swishing their tails. The milking was almost finished, and the twins were driving some of the cows back to the field.

'Hallo – how did you get on?' asked Anne.

'Fine – it was fun,' said Dick. 'My cows did better than Julian's, though – I sang to them all the time, and they loved it!'

'Silly!' said George. 'Did you have a talk with the farmer?'

'Yes – he says he's got an old Land Rover and he'll take us all over the farm tomorrow,' said Dick, pleased. '*And* we can ride on that tractor, if Bill – that's one of his farm hands – will let us. He says Bill won't have Junior on the tractor at any price – so maybe there'll be a row if he sees us on it!'

'Well, I'm all ready for a row, and so is Timmy,' said George grimly. 'Sooner or later I'm going to tell Junior a few home-truths.'

'We'd all like to do that,' said Julian. 'But let's hold our horses till a good moment comes – I don't want that nice Mrs Philpot upset – and you know, if we caused her to lose the two Americans she might suffer badly – in her pocket! I bet they pay well.'

'Well – *I* understand all that too, Ju,' said George. 'But Timmy doesn't. He's longing to have a go at Junior!'

'And how I share that feeling!' said Dick, rubbing Timmy's big head. 'What's the time? Shall we go for a walk?'

'No,' said Julian. 'My legs feel stiff with cycling up so many Dorset hills today. I vote we just stroll around a bit, not go for miles.'

The Five set off together, wandering round the farm buildings. They were all very old, some of them falling to pieces. The roofs had great Dorset tiles, made of stone, uneven and roughly shaped. They were a lovely grey, and were brilliant with lichen and moss.

'Aren't they gorgeous?' said George, stopping to look at the tiles on a small outhouse. 'Look at that lichen. Did you ever see such a brilliant orange? But what a pity – half of them have gone from this roof, and someone has replaced them with horrid new tiles!'

'Maybe the Philpots sold them,' said Julian. 'Old tiles like that, brilliant with lichen, can fetch quite a bit of money – especially from Americans. There's many a barn out in America covered with old tiles from this country, moss and all. A bit of old England!'

'If I had a lovely old place like this I wouldn't sell one single tile, or one single bit of moss!' said George, quite fiercely.

'Maybe you wouldn't,' said Dick. 'But some would – if they loved their farm enough and didn't want to see it go to pieces for lack of money. Their fields would be worth more than old tiles to them!'

'I bet old Grandad wouldn't sell them if he could help it!' said Anne. 'I wonder if the American has tried to buy any of these tiles? I guess he has.'

They had an interesting time wandering round. They found one old barn-like shed stacked with ancient castaway junk, and Julian rummaged in it with great interest.

'Look at this giant cart-wheel!' he said, peering into a dark corner. 'It's almost as tall as I am! My word – they must have made all their own wheels here in the old days – in this very shed, perhaps. And maybe their own tools too. Look at *this* old tool – what in the *world* is it?'

They gazed at the curious curved tool, still as strong and as good as it had been two or three centuries before. It was heavy and Julian thought that he wouldn't have liked to use it for more than ten minutes at a time!

'But I bet old Grandad could use it for a whole day and never get tired,' he said. 'When he was a young man, I mean. He must have been as strong as an ox, then.'

'Well, you remember what the girl at the dairy said,' put in Anne. 'She said he had once fought a bull and knocked it out. We must ask him about that. I bet he'd love to tell us.'

'He's a real old character!' said Julian. 'I like him, shouts and temper and all. Come on – it's getting lateish. We didn't ask about the evening meal. I wonder what time we ought to get back for it?'

'Half past seven,' said George. 'I asked. We'd better go back now, because we'll have to get ourselves clean – and Anne and I want to help lay the table.'

'Right. Back we go,' said Julian. 'Come on, Tim. Stop sniffing about that old rubbish. Surely you can't smell anything exciting there!'

They went back to the farmhouse, and the girls went to wash at the kitchen sink, seeing Mrs Philpot already preparing for supper. 'Won't be a minute!' called Anne. 'We'll do those potatoes for you, Mrs Philpot. I say, what a lovely farm this is. We've been exploring those old sheds.'

'Yes – they need clearing out,' said Mrs Philpot, who looked better for the rest she had had. 'But old Great-Grandad, he won't have them touched. Says he promised *his* grandad not to let them go to anyone! But we did sell some of those lovely old grey tiles once – to an American, of course, a friend of Mr Henning's, and Grandad almost went out of his mind. Shouted day and night, poor old chap, and went about with a pitchfork in his hand all the time, daring any stranger even so much as to walk over the fields! We had such a time with him.'

'Good gracious!' said Anne, having a sudden vision of

the grand old man stalking about his fields, shouting, and waving a great pitchfork.

Supper was really a very pleasant meal, for Mr Henning and Junior didn't come in. There was much talk and laughter at the table, though the twins, as usual, said hardly anything. They puzzled Anne. Why should they be *so* unfriendly? She smiled at them once or twice, but each time they turned their eyes away. Snippet lay at their feet, and Timmy lay under the table. Great-Grandad was not there, nor was Mr Philpot.

'They're both making the best of the daylight,' said Mrs Philpot. 'There's a lot to do on the farm just now.'

The children enjoyed the meat-pie that Mrs Philpot had baked, and the stewed plums and rich cream that followed. Anne suddenly yawned a very large yawn.

'Sorry!' she said. 'It just came all of a sudden. I don't know why I feel so sleepy.'

'You've set *me* off now,' said Dick, and put his hand in front of an even larger yawn. 'Well, I don't wonder we feel sleepy. Ju and I set off at dawn this morning – and I know you girls had a jolly long bus ride!'

'Well, you go to bed, all of you, as early as you like,' said Mrs Philpot. 'I expect you'll want to be up bright and early in the morning. The Harries are always up about six o'clock – they just will *not* stay in bed!'

'And what time does Junior get up?' asked George with a grin. 'Six o'clock too?'

'Oh, not before nine o'clock, usually,' said Mrs Philpot. 'Mr Henning comes down about eleven – he likes his breakfast in bed. So does Junior.'

'WHAT? You don't mean to say you take breakfast up to that lazy little pest?' said Dick, astounded. 'Why don't you go and drag him out by the ankles?'

'Well – they are guests and pay well for being here,' said Mrs Philpot.

'*I'll* take Junior his breakfast,' said George, much to everyone's astonishment. 'Timmy and I together. We'd like to. Wouldn't we, Timmy?'

Timmy made a most peculiar noise from under the table. 'That sounded like a *laugh* to me,' said Dick. 'And I'm not surprised! I'd just like to see Junior's face if you and Tim walked in on him with his breakfast!'

'Do you bet me I won't do it?' demanded George, really on the defensive now.

'Yes. I do bet you,' said Dick at once. 'I bet you my new pocket-knife you won't!'

'Taken!' said George. Mrs Philpot looked puzzled. 'No, no, my dears,' she said. 'I can't have one guest waiting on another. Though I must say those stairs are a trial to my legs, when I'm carrying up trays!'

'*I'll* take up Junior's tray *and* Mr Henning's too, if you like,' said George, in a half-kind, half-fierce voice.

'*Not* Mr Henning's,' said Julian, giving George a warning look. 'Don't go too far, old thing. Just Junior's tray will be enough.'

'All right, all right,' said George, rather sulkily. 'Aren't Junior and Mr Henning coming in to supper?'

'Not tonight,' said Mrs Philpot, in a thankful voice. 'They're dining at some hotel in Dorchester, I think. I expect they get a bit tired of our simple farmhouse meals. I only hope they won't be too late back. Great-Grandad likes to lock up early.'

The children were really glad when the evening meal was cleared away and washed up, for they all felt heavy with sleep. The good strong air, the exciting day and the many jobs they had done had really tired them.

'Goodnight, Mrs Philpot,' they said, when everything was done. 'We're off to bed. Are the twins coming too?'

The twins actually condescended to nod. They looked tired out. Julian wondered where Mr Philpot and old Great-Grandad were – still out working, he supposed. He yawned. Well, he was for bed – and even if he had had to sleep on the bare ground that night, he knew he would sleep well! He thought longingly of his camp-bed.

They went their various ways – the twins and Julian and Dick to the big barn – the girls upstairs to the room opposite Junior's. George peeped into it. It was even untidier than before, and obviously Junior must have been eating nuts up there, for the floor was strewn with shells.

They were soon in bed – the girls together in the big, rather hard, old bed, the boys in their separate camp-beds. Timmy was on George's feet, and Snippet slept first on one twin's feet, and then on the other's. He was always perfectly fair in his favours!

A crashing noise awoke the girls about two hours later, and they sat upright in bed, alarmed. Timmy began to bark. George crept to the top of the stairs, hearing Grandad's loud voice below, and then crept back to Anne.

'It's Mr Henning and Junior come back,' she said. 'Apparently old Grandad had locked up, and they crashed and banged on the knocker. My, what a to-do! Here comes

Junior!' And indeed, here Junior did come, stamping up the stairs and singing loudly.

'Little pest!' said George. 'Wait till I take him his breakfast tomorrow!'

CHAPTER SIX

A little excitement for breakfast

It was fun to sleep in the barn. Dick tried to keep awake for a while, and enjoy the barn smell, and the sight of the stars in the sky seen through the open door, where a cool little night breeze came wandering in.

Julian fell asleep at once, and did not even hear the crashing of the knocker at the front door of the farmhouse when the Hennings came in, or the loud voices. He awoke with a start at about one o'clock in the morning, and sat straight up in bed, his heart beating fast. What on earth was that noise he had heard?

He heard it again and laughed. 'What an ass I am! It's only an owl. Or maybe more than one. And gosh, what was that high little scream? A mouse – or a rat? Perhaps the owls are hunting in here?'

He lay still and listened. He suddenly felt a rush of cool air over his face, and stiffened. That must have been an owl's soft-feathered wings! Owls' wings made no noise, he knew. The feathers were so soft that not even a quick-eared mouse could hear an owl swooping silently down!

There came another little high-pitched squeak. The owl's doing his job well, thought Julian. What a fine hunting place for him – a barn where food stuffs are stored

– overrun with mice and rats, of course. I bet this owl is worth his weight in gold to the farmer. Well, owl, do your job – but for goodness' sake don't mistake my nose for a mouse! Ah – there you go again – just over my head. I saw you then – a shadow passing by!

He fell asleep once more and didn't wake until the sun streamed into the barn, lighting up hundreds of tiny motes floating in the air. Julian looked at his watch.

'Half past seven! And I meant to be up at seven. Dick! Wake up!'

Dick was so sound asleep that he didn't wake even when Julian shook him. He merely rolled over and settled down again. Julian glanced across the barn, and saw that the twins' camp-beds were empty. They had stacked their pillows and bedclothes in neat piles, and disappeared silently out of the door. Without waking us! thought Julian, pulling on his socks. I wonder if I can wash at the big kitchen sink. 'Dick – *will* you wake up?' he said loudly. 'It might be TEN O'CLOCK for all you care!'

Dick heard the two shouted words and sat up at once, looking aghast. 'Ten o'clock? Oh *no*! Gosh, I must have slept all round the clock. Oh, I *say* – I didn't mean to be late for breakfast. I . . .'

'Calm down,' grinned Julian, brushing his hair. 'I only said, "It might be ten o'clock for all you care!" Actually, it's just gone half past seven.'

'Thank goodness for that,' said Dick, lying back in bed. 'Oh for ten minutes more!'

'The twins have gone already,' said Julian. 'I wonder if the girls are up. Oh, my goodness, what's that?'

Something had jabbed him sharply in the back, making him jump violently. Julian swung round, expecting it to be Junior or one of the twins playing a silly joke.

'Oh – it's *you* – Nosey the jackdaw!' he said, looking at the cheeky bird, now perched on his pillow. 'You've got a jolly sharp beak!'

'Chack!' said the jackdaw, and flew to his shoulder. Julian felt flattered – until the jackdaw pecked his ear! 'Here – you take the bird,' he said to the unwary Dick, and handed Nosey to him. Nosey promptly pounced on the watch lying beside Dick's pillow and flew off with it. Dick gave an angry yell.

'Bring that back, you crazy bird! Don't you know a watch when you see one? He's taken my watch, Ju – goodness knows where he'll hide it!'

'He's gone into the roof,' said Julian. 'We'd better tell the twins. Perhaps they can deal with him. Now WHY doesn't he take Junior's watch – that would be a trick I should *really* applaud!'

'CHACK, CHACK CHACK,' said Nosey, exactly as if he agreed. He had to open his beak to say 'chack' and the watch promptly fell out. It bounced on to a sack far below, and the bird swooped down to get it. Dick also swooped, and as the watch had now slipped between two sacks, he managed to get it before the jackdaw.

Nosey flew up into the roof, and 'chacked' angrily. 'Don't use such bad language,' said Dick severely, strapping on his watch. 'You ought to be ashamed of yourself!'

They went out of the barn and round to the farmhouse. There were sounds of people about, and the two boys felt quite ashamed of being so late! Breakfast was on the table, but already quite a number of people seemed to have had it!

'The girls haven't had theirs,' said Dick, looking at the places set in front of the chairs where George and Anne had sat the night before. 'But the twins have. It looks as if *everyone* has, except us four, apparently! Ah – here's Mrs Philpot. Sorry we're late. We overslept, I'm afraid.'

'That's all right!' said Mrs Philpot, smiling. 'I don't

expect my visitors to be up early. Anyone can sleep late on a holiday!'

She held a tray in her hands, and set it down on the table. 'That's for Mr Henning – he'll ring when he wants his breakfast. That's Junior's tray over there. I make the coffee when they ring,' she said, and went out again.

There was cold ham for breakfast, boiled eggs and fruit. The two boys tucked in, and looked round reprovingly when the two girls came, with Timmy behind them, still sleepy-eyed. 'Overslept, I suppose?' said Dick, pretending to be shocked. 'Sit down, I'll pour you some coffee.'

'Where's Junior – not down yet, I hope?' said George anxiously. 'I haven't forgotten my bet about taking up his breakfast!'

'I say – do you think it's all right to let George take up Junior's breakfast?' said Julian, after a pause. 'George, don't throw the tray at him or anything, will you?'

'I might,' said George, eating a boiled egg. 'Anything to get your new pocket-knife from you!'

'Well, don't go too far teasing Junior,' said Julian warningly. 'You don't want to make the Henning family walk out and leave Mrs Philpot high and dry!'

'All right, all right,' said George. 'Don't nag. I think I'll have another egg, Dick. Pass one over, please. I don't know why I'm so hungry.'

'Leave a bit of room for this ham,' said Dick, who had cut himself two good slices. 'It's out of this world! Simply too good to be true! I could eat it all day.'

The two girls tucked into their breakfast, and just as they were finishing, a bell rang very loudly in the kitchen, jangling just above their heads. They jumped violently. Mrs Philpot came into the room at once. 'That's Mr Henning's bell,' she said. 'I must make his coffee.'

'I'll take up his tray,' said Anne. 'George is going to take up Junior's.'

'Oh no – I *really* don't like you to do that,' said Mrs Philpot, distressed. Just then another bell rang. It jangled to and fro for a very long time.

'That's Junior's bell,' said Mrs Philpot. 'He always seems to think I'm quite hard of hearing!'

'Bad-mannered little beast!' said Dick, and was pleased to find that Mrs Philpot didn't disagree!

Anne waited till Mr Henning's tray was ready, and then firmly put her hands to the sides. '*I'm* going to take it to Mr Henning,' she said in a most determined voice, and Mrs Philpot smiled gratefully and let her lift it. 'Bedroom on the left of the stairs, first floor!' she said. 'And he likes his curtains pulled, too, when his breakfast is brought.'

'And does Junior like *his* pulled as well?' inquired George, in such a sugary voice that the two boys looked round at her suspiciously. What was she up to now?

'Well – I do pull them for him,' said Mrs Philpot, 'but don't *you* pull them if you don't feel like it! Thank you very much, dear!'

Anne had already gone upstairs with Mr Henning's tray, and now George set off with Junior's. She winked at Dick. 'Get that pocket-knife ready for me!' she said, and disappeared through the door, grinning wickedly. She went carefully upstairs with Timmy close at her heels, wondering whatever George was doing with a tray!

George came to Junior's door. It was shut. She gave it a violent kick and it flew open. She entered, clattering with her feet, and set the tray down on a table with a jolt that upset the coffee. She went whistling to the windows, and pulled the curtains back across the poles so that they made a loud clattering noise.

Junior had apparently fallen asleep again, his head under the clothes. George upset a chair with a crash. That made Junior sit up, half scared. 'What's going on here?' he began. 'Can't you bring my breakfast without . . .' Then he saw that it was George in the room, not the kindly Mrs Philpot.

'Get out!' he said angrily. 'Crashing about like that! Pull the curtains across again. The sun's too strong. And look how you've spilt the coffee! Why didn't Mrs Philpot bring my breakfast? She usually does. Here – put the tray on my knees, like she does!'

George whipped the bed clothes off him, took up the tray and set it down violently on his pyjamaed knees. The hot coffee got a violent jerk and some drops fell on to his bare arm. They were hot, and he yelled loudly. He lashed out at George, and hit her on the shoulder.

That was a very great mistake. Timmy, who was at the door watching, leapt on to the bed at once, growling. He

pulled the terrified boy on to the floor, and kept him lying there, standing over him, deep growls coming from the depths of his great body.

George took absolutely no notice. She went round the room, humming a little tune, putting this and that straight, tidying the dressing-table, not seeming to notice what Timmy was doing. She shut the door so that no one would hear Junior's howls.

'George – take this dog off me!' begged Junior. 'He'll kill me! GEORGE! I'll tell my Pop on you. I'm sorry I hit you. Oh, *do* take this dog off me, PLEASE do!'

He began to weep, and George looked scornfully down at him. 'You nasty spoilt little pest,' she said. 'I've a good mind to leave you here all morning, with Timmy on guard! But this time I'll be generous to you. Come here, Tim. Leave that funny little worm there on the floor!'

Junior was still weeping. He crept into bed and wrapped the blankets round him. 'I don't want any breakfast,' he wept. 'I'll tell Pop about you. He'll get you all right.'

'Yes, you tell him,' said George, tucking him in so tightly that he couldn't move. 'You tell him – and I'll whisper into Timmy's ear that you've told tales on me – and honestly, I simply don't know what *he'll* do!'

'You are the most horrible boy I've ever met,' said Junior, knowing when he was beaten. George grinned. So he thought she was a boy, did he? Good!

'Mrs Philpot isn't going to bring up your breakfast any more,' she said. '*I'm* going to – with Timmy. See? And if you dare to ring that bell more than once each morning, you'll be sorry!'

'I don't *want* my breakfast brought up,' said Junior, in a small voice. 'I'd rather get up and go downstairs for it. I don't *want* you to bring it.'

'Right. I'll tell Mrs Philpot,' said George. 'But if you change your mind, just tell me. I'll bring it up any morning – with Timmy!'

She went out and banged the door, Timmy trotting down the stairs in front of her, puzzled but pleased. He didn't like Junior any more than George did.

George went into the kitchen. Dick and Julian were still there. 'You've lost your bet, Dick,' said George. 'Pocket-knife, please. I not only took up his breakfast, and accidentally spilt hot coffee on him, but Timmy here pulled him out of bed and stood over him, growling. What a sight that was! Poor Junior doesn't want his breakfast in bed any more! He's coming down for it each morning.'

'Good for you, George!' said Dick, and slid his pocket-knife across the table. 'You deserve to win. Now – sit down and finish *your* breakfast and mind – I'm not betting anything else for a long, long time!'

CHAPTER SEVEN

The twins change their minds

THE TWINS, Harry and Harriet, had had their breakfast some while ago. They now came into the big kitchen, Snippet at their heels, and scowled to see the Five *still* having breakfast there. Anne was in fits of laughter over George's account of the way she dealt with Junior.

'You *should* have seen his face when I plonked the breakfast tray on his knees, and the hot coffee splashed him!' said George. 'He let out a yell that startled even old Timmy. And when he hit me, and Timmy leapt on the bed and dragged him out on to the floor, his eyes nearly fell out of his head!'

'No wonder he's decided to come down to breakfast each morning, then,' said Julian. 'He'll be scared stiff of you appearing with a breakfast tray again!'

The twins listened to this in amazement. They looked at one another, and nodded. Then they walked up to the breakfast table, and for once, only one twin spoke. Whether it was Harry or Harriet, nobody knew, for they both looked so much alike.

'What's happened?' said the twin to George. 'Why did *you* take up Junior's breakfast tray?'

'Because we were all so fed up with the way Junior –

and his Pop – impose on your mother,' said George. 'Fancy a *boy* having breakfast in bed!'

'So old George took it into her head to take up his breakfast herself, and said she'd teach him such a lesson he'd be a bit more considerate of your mother in future,' said Dick. 'What's more, I was idiotic enough to bet George she wouldn't do it – and now she's won my best pocket-knife off me – look!'

George proudly displayed the knife. The twins each gave a sudden loud laugh, which surprised the others very much. 'Well!' said Dick. 'Fancy you being able to *laugh*! You always look so fierce and unfriendly. Well, now that you've condescended to talk to us, let me tell you this – we think your mother is absolutely tops, and far from giving her more trouble, we're all going to help as much as we can. Got that?'

Both twins were smiling broadly now. They took it in turns to speak, which was really much more friendly than their usual stiff way of talking in unison.

'We hate Junior!' said one twin. 'He thinks our mother is a kind of servant, to come when he rings for her, or shouts for her.'

'His father's the same,' said the other twin. 'Wanting this and that, and sending our mother all over the place to fetch and carry for him. Why doesn't he go and stay at a hotel?'

'He doesn't because he's so set on snooping out our old things and buying them,' said the other twin. 'I know for

a fact that Mother has sold him some of her own things – but she just *had* to have some money; things are so expensive, and we grow out of our clothes so quickly.'

'It *is* nice to hear you talking properly,' said Julian, clapping the twin on the back. 'And now would you mind letting us know how to tell which of you is which? I know one's a boy and one's a girl, but you both look exactly alike to me – you might be two boys!'

The twins gave sudden, mischievous grins. 'Well – don't you tell Junior, then,' said one. 'You can always tell *me* by this scar on my hand, see? Harriet hasn't any scar. I'm Harry.'

The four looked at the long thin scar on the boy's hand.

'I got that by tearing the back of my hand on barbed wire,' said Harry. 'Now you'll know us from each other! But tell us all about George and the breakfast tray, from beginning to end. Good old George. She looks just as much a boy as Harriet does.'

It was very pleasant to find the twins so friendly, after their stiff, sullen dislike. The four warmed to them – and when Mrs Philpot suddenly appeared in the kitchen to clear away breakfast, she was astounded to see her twins talking and laughing happily with the others. She stood and stared, a delighted smile on her face.

'Mother! Junior's not going to have breakfast in bed any more!' said Harry. 'Listen why!' And the story had to be told all over again. George went red. She was afraid that Mrs Philpot would be displeased. But no, she threw back her head and laughed.

'Oh, that really does me good,' she said. 'But I hope Junior doesn't tell his father, and they don't both go off in a hurry! We do need their money, you know, much as I hate having them here. Now I *must* clear away breakfast!'

'No, you mustn't. That's *our* job,' said Anne. 'Isn't it, twins?'

'YES!' said both twins together. 'We're all friends now, Mother – let them belong to the family.'

'Well, I'll go and see to the chickens, then, if you're going to clear away,' said Mrs Philpot. 'You can wash up, too, bless you!'

'Look – how would you like to go round the farm in our

old Land Rover today?' said Harry to the others. 'It's the best way to see over the farm. I think Bill's got to go round this morning, and check on the fields and the stock. He'll take you, if I ask him.'

'Fine!' said Julian. 'What time?'

'In about half an hour,' said Harry. 'I'll find Bill – and when you hear a horn hooting, come on out. By the way, Bill isn't much of a talker, but if he takes to you, he'll be quite pally.'

'Right,' said Julian. 'Can Dick and I do something while the others are clearing away?'

'Gosh yes, there's *always* something to do on a farm,' said Harry. 'Come on up to the chicken-houses – Harriet and I are patching them up to stop the rain leaking in.'

Julian and Dick, with Timmy behind them, immediately went off with the twins, now as merry and friendly as before they had been dour and sullen! What a change!

'Well, thank goodness I took Junior's breakfast up to him, and put him in his place,' said George, folding up the tablecloth. 'It was apparently just the one thing that would make the twins friendly! Listen, Anne, I believe that's Junior coming.'

She slipped behind the dresser, while Anne set the chairs straight round the table. Junior came creeping in very quietly indeed, and looked round fearfully. He seemed very relieved to find only Anne there. He considered that she was *quite* harmless!

'Where's that dog?' he asked.

‘What dog?’ said Anne innocently. ‘Snippet?’

‘No – that great ugly mongrel – and that awful boy he belongs to,’ said Junior, still fearful.

‘Oh, you mean George, I suppose,’ said Anne, amused that Junior thought George was a boy. ‘Well, look over there!’

Junior saw George advancing on him from behind the dresser, gave one agonised yell and fled, fearing that she had Timmy behind her. George laughed.

‘We shan’t have much trouble with *him* in future,’ she said. ‘I just hope he doesn’t say too much to his Pop!’

After a while they heard the sound of a hooter outside. ‘That’s the Land Rover,’ said George, excited. ‘Well, we’ve just finished the washing-up. Hang up the teacloths to dry, Anne. I’ll pop these dishes into the cupboard . . .’

Soon they were out of the great kitchen door and down the passage that led to the yard. Not far off was a van-like car, the Land Rover. It was an old one, very dirty, and a bit lopsided. Dick and Julian yelled to the girls.

‘Buck up! Didn’t you hear us hooting?’

The girls ran to the Land Rover. Bill, the farm hand, was at the wheel. He grinned at them and nodded. Timmy greeted George as if he hadn’t seen her for a year and almost knocked her down in his playfulness.

‘Tim! Don’t be so silly!’ said George. ‘Planting your great muddy paws all over me! Where are the twins? Aren’t they coming?’

'Naw,' said Bill. 'They be busy.'

They all got in, and were just about to set off when someone else appeared. 'Wait! I'm coming! Wait, I say!'

And up ran Junior, full of himself as usual. 'Jump down, Tim – go to him,' said George, in a low voice. And very willingly indeed Timmy leapt down and ran straight towards the unsuspecting Junior. He gave one loud yell, turned, and fled for his life.

'Well, that's got rid of *him*!' said Dick, with much satisfaction. 'Look at Timmy – he's laughing all over his hairy old face! You love a joke, don't you, Tim?'

It did indeed look as if Tim was laughing, for he had his mouth wide open, showing all his teeth, and his tongue was hanging out happily. He leapt back into the car.

'Sensible dog, that,' said Bill, and then relapsed into his usual silence as he started up the Land Rover with a really shattering noise. It moved off towards the fields.

How it jolted! The four clung to the sides of the van, almost bumped off their seats as the Land Rover jerked its way over field paths, up hill and down hill, jolting in and out of deep ruts, appearing to be on the point of overturning at any minute. Anne wasn't sure that she liked it much, but the others enjoyed every minute.

'Now you'll see the farmland,' said Bill, as they came to the top of the hill. 'Look yonder! Could be the finest farm in the country, if Mr Philpot had the money!'

CHAPTER EIGHT

All round the farm

THE FIVE thoroughly enjoyed their ride over the big farm. It spread out in all directions over undulating hills, and the van swung up and down and continually lurched round corners. It stopped every now and again so that the children might see the magnificent views.

Bill told them the names of the great fields as they passed them. 'That's Oak Tree Field – that's Hangman's Copse over there – that's Tinkers' Wood Field – and that's Faraway Field – the farthest from the farmhouse.'

Name after name came from his lips, and it seemed as if the sight of the fields he knew and loved suddenly set his tongue going. He told them about the stock too. 'They're the new cows over there – give good milk they do – helps a farmer no end to get money every week for milk, you know. And they're the bulls, down in that field. Fine creatures, too – cost a mint of money. But Mr Philpot, he believes in good animals. He'd rather go without a new car than buy poor stock. They're the sheep right away over there – see, dotted about on those slopes. Can't take you to see 'em today, though. You'd like Shepherd. He's been here so long, and is so old, he knows every inch of the farm!'

He relapsed into silence after his unusual spate of talk, and turned down a path that took the children back towards the farmhouse, using a different route, to show them even more fields.

There were glorious fields of corn, golden in the sun, waving in the breeze with a wonderful rustling noise. 'I could sit here for hours and look at that, and listen,' said Anne.

'Then don't you marry a farmer, if you want to do that, for a farmer's wife has no time to sit!' said Bill dryly, and was silent again.

They jolted along, shaken to the bones, but loving every minute. 'Cows, calves, sheep, lambs, bulls, dogs, ducks, chickens,' chanted Anne. 'Corn, kale, beet, cauliflower – ooh, Bill, look out!'

The van had gone at such speed into a deep rut that Anne was nearly flung out. Timmy shot through the back entrance of the van, and landed on the ground, rolling over and over. He got slowly to his feet, looking most amazed.

'Timmy! It's all right! It was only a bigger hole than usual!' shouted George. 'Buck up – jump in!'

As the Land Rover didn't stop, Timmy had to gallop after it, and enter with a flying leap from the back. Bill gave a snort of laughter, which made the wheel wobble dangerously. 'This old car's almost human,' he said. 'Just jigs about for joy on a day like this!'

And he drove headlong over a slanting path and straight

down into a hollow, making poor Anne groan again. 'All very well for Bill!' she said, in Julian's ear. '*He's* got the wheel to hang on to!'

In spite of the jolting and bumping the Five enjoyed their ride round the farm immensely. 'Now we really know what it's like!' said Julian, as the Land Rover came to a very sudden stop near the farmhouse, throwing them all on top of one another. 'My word – no wonder old Great-Grandad and Mr and Mrs Philpot love the place. It's *grand*! Thanks awfully, Bill. We've enjoyed it tremendously! Wish *my* family had a farm like this!'

'Farm like this? Ay. It's taken centuries to grow,' said Bill. 'All the names I told you – they're centuries old too. Nobody knows now who was hanged down in Hangman's Copse – or who came to Tinkers' Wood. But they're not forgot as long as the fields are there!'

Anne stared at Bill in wonder. Why, that was almost poetry, she thought. He turned and saw her gazing at him. He nodded at her.

'You understand all right, don't you?' he said. 'There're some that don't, though. That Mr Henning, he raves about it all – but he don't understand a thing. As for that boy of his!' And to Anne's surprise he turned and spat into the ditch. 'That's what I think of *him*!'

'Oh – it's just the way he's been brought up, I expect,' said Anne. 'I've met heaps of fine American children, and . . .'

'Well, *that* one needs punishing!' said Bill, grimly.

'And if it wasn't that Mrs Philpot begged me not to, he'd be well punished, that boy! I tell you! Trying to ride on the nervy calves and chasing the hens till they're scared off egg-laying – and stoning the ducks, poor critters – and slitting sacks of seed just for the fun of seeing it dribble out and waste! Hoo, wouldn't I like to shake him till his bones rattled!'

The four listened in silence, horrified. Junior was much worse than they had thought, then. George felt very very pleased that she had taught him a lesson that morning.

'Don't you worry any more about Junior,' said Julian grimly. '*We'll* keep him in order while we're here!'

They said goodbye and walked back to the farm-house, stiff and sore from the bumpy, bone-shaking ride, but with their minds full of the lovely sloping hills, the blue distance, the waving corn, and the feel of a farmland in good heart.

'That was good,' said Julian, voicing the feelings of the others. 'Very good. I somehow feel more English for having seen those Dorset fields, surrounded by hedges, basking in the sun.'

'I like Bill,' said Anne. 'He's so – so solid and real. He *belongs* to the land, just as the land belongs to him. They're one!'

'Ah – Anne has discovered what farming really means!' said Dick. 'I say, I'm starving, but I really don't like to go and ask for anything at the farmhouse. Let's go down to the village and get buns and milk at the dairy.'

'Oh *yes*!' said Anne and George, and Timmy gave a few sharp, short barks as if he thoroughly agreed. They set off down the lane that led to the village, and soon came to the little ice-cream shop, half baker's half dairy. Janie, the small talkative girl, was there again. She smiled at them in delight.

'You're here again!' she said, in pleasure. 'Mum's made some macaroons this morning. See – all gooey and fresh!'

'Now how did you guess that we are all very partial to macaroons?' said Dick, sitting down at one of the two little tables there. 'We'll have a plateful, please.'

'What, a *whole* plateful?' exclaimed Janie. 'But there's about twenty on a plate!'

'Just about right,' said Dick. 'And an ice-cream each, please. Large. And don't forget our dog, will you?'

'Oh no, I won't,' said Janie. 'He's a very *nice* dog, isn't he? Have you noticed what lovely smiley eyes he has?'

'Well, yes, we have. We know him quite well, you see,' said Dick, amused. George looked pleased. She did so like Timmy to be praised. Timmy liked it too. He actually went up to Janie and licked her hand!

Soon they had a plateful of delicious macaroons in front of them – and they were indeed nice, and *very* 'gooey' inside, as Janie had so rightly said. George gave Timmy one, but it was really wasted on him, because he gave one crunch, and then swallowed it! He also chased his ice-cream all over the floor again, much to Janie's delight.

'How do you like it at Mrs Philpot's?' she asked. 'Kind, isn't she?'

'Very!' said everyone together.

'We love being at the farm,' said Anne. 'We've been all over it this morning, in the Land Rover.'

'Did Bill take you?' asked Janie. 'He's my uncle. But he don't usually say much to strangers.'

'Well, he said plenty to us,' said Julian. 'He was most interesting. Does he like macaroons?'

'Oooh yes,' said Janie, rather astonished. 'Everyone likes Mum's macaroons.'

'Could he eat six, do you think?' asked Julian.

'Ooooh *yes*,' said Janie, still astonished, her blue eyes opened wide.

'Right. Put six in a bag for me,' said Julian. 'I'll give them to him in return for a great ride.'

'That's right down nice of you,' said Janie, pleased. 'My uncle's been on Finniston Farm all his life. You ought to get him to tell you about Finniston Castle before it was burnt down, and . . .'

'Finniston *Castle*!' exclaimed George, in surprise. 'We went all over the farm this morning, and saw every field – but we didn't see any ruined castle.'

'Oh no, you wouldn't *see* anything!' said Janie. 'I told you – it was burnt down. Right to the ground, ages ago. Finniston Farm belonged to it, you know. There're some pictures of it in a shop down the road. I saw them, and . . .'

'Now, Janie, Janie, how many times have I told you not to chatter to customers?' said Janie's mother, bustling in, frowning. 'That tongue of yours! Can't you learn that people don't want to hear your chatter, chatter, chatter?'

'We like talking to Janie,' said Julian, politely. 'She's most interesting. Please don't send her away.'

But Janie had fled, red-cheeked and scared. Her mother began to arrange the goods on the counter. 'Let's see now – what did you have?' she said. 'Good gracious, where have all those macaroons gone? There were at least two dozen there!'

'Er – well – we had almost twenty – and the dog helped, of course – and Janie put six in a bag for us – let's see now . . .'

'There were twenty-four on that plate,' said Janie's mother, still amazed. 'Twenty-four! I counted them!'

'And five ice-creams,' said Julian. 'How much is that altogether? Most *delicious* macaroons they were!'

Janie's mother couldn't help smiling. She totted up the bill, and Julian paid. 'Come again,' she said, 'and don't you let that little gas-bag of mine bore you!'

They set off down the street, feeling very pleased with life. Timmy kept licking his lips as if he could still taste macaroon and ice-cream! They walked to the end of the street, and came to the little lane that led up to the farm. Anne stopped.

'I'd like to go and look at the horse-brasses in this little antique shop,' she said. 'You go on. I'll come later.'

'I'll come in with you,' said George, and she turned to the little shop window. The boys walked on by themselves. 'We'll probably be helping on the farm somewhere!' shouted back Dick. 'So long!'

Just as Anne and George were going into the shop, two people came out and almost bumped into them. One was Mr Henning, the American, the other was a man they hadn't seen before. 'Good morning,' Mr Henning said to them, and went into the street with his friend. Anne and George walked into the dark little shop.

There was an old man there, drumming on the counter,

looking quite angry. He gave the two girls such a glare that they felt quite frightened!

'That man!' said the old man, and frowned so fiercely that his glasses fell off. Anne helped him to find them among the clutter of quaint old trinkets on his counter. He fixed them on his nose again and looked sternly at the two girls and Timmy.

'If you've come to waste my time, please go,' he said. 'I'm a busy man, children are no good to me. Just want to nose round and touch this and that and never buy anything! That American boy now – he's . . . ah, but you don't know what I'm talking about, do you? I'm upset. I'm *always* upset when people want to buy our beautiful old things and take them away to a country they don't belong to. Now . . .'

'It's all right, Mr Finniston,' said Anne, in her gentle voice. 'You *are* Mr Finniston, aren't you? I just wanted to look at those lovely old horse-brasses please. I won't bother you for long. We're staying at Finniston Farm, and . . .'

'Ah – at Finniston Farm, did you say?' said the old man, his face brightening. 'Then you've met my great friend, dear old Jonathan Philpot. My very great friend!'

'Is that Mr Philpot, the twins' father?' said George.

'No, no, no – it's old Great-Grandad! We were at school together,' said the old man, excited. 'Ah – I could tell you some tales of the Finnistons and the castle they once owned. Yes, yes – I'm a descendant of the owners of that castle, you know – the one that was burnt down. Oh, the tales I could tell you!'

And it was just at that moment that the adventure began – the Finniston Farm adventure that the Five were never to forget!

CHAPTER NINE

A very interesting tale

ANNE AND GEORGE looked at the old man, fascinated, as he talked to them. He stood there behind the counter of his little, dark antique shop, surrounded by things even older than himself, a little, bent old man with only a few hairs on his head. He had a kindly, wrinkled face with eyes so hooded with drooping lids that they seemed to look out through slits.

The two girls were thrilled to hear that old Mr Finniston was actually descended from the long-ago Finnistons, who lived in Finniston Castle.

'Is that why your name's Finniston?' asked Anne. 'Tell us about the castle. We only heard about it for the first time today. But we don't even know exactly whereabouts it stood. I didn't see a single stone when we went round the farm this morning!'

'No, no, you wouldn't,' said Mr Finniston. 'It was burnt right down to the ground, you see – and through the centuries people have taken the old stones for building walls. Ah well – it was a long time ago!'

'How long?' asked George.

'Let's see now – it was burnt down in 1192 – the twelfth century,' said Mr Finniston. 'Norman times, you know.

Ever heard of the Normans? Schooling isn't what it was, I know, so maybe . . .'

'Of *course* we've heard of the Normans!' said George, indignantly. 'Every child knows them! They conquered England, and the first Norman king was William the First, 1066!'

'Hmmm – that's right. You've had *some* schooling then,' said Mr Finniston. 'Well, it was a Norman castle – look, like that one in this picture, see?' And he showed them a copy of an old print. They gazed at the stone castle pictured there.

'Yes. It's a Norman castle,' said George. 'Was Finniston Castle just like that?'

'I've got a copy of an old drawing of it somewhere,' said the old fellow. 'I'll find it and show it to you sometime. A small castle, of course – but a very fine specimen. Well, well, you won't be interested in such details, I know. *How* it was burnt down, I don't know. Can't find out for certain. The story goes that it was attacked at night by the enemy, and there were traitors in the castle itself who set fire to it – and while the castle folk were fighting the fire, the enemy walked in and slew nearly all of them.'

'So the castle was no use for living in after that, I suppose,' said Anne. 'But it's strange there isn't even a stone to be seen anywhere.'

'Oh, but that's where you're wrong!' said Mr Finniston, triumphantly. 'There *are* stones from the castle – all over the farm. But only I and old Great-Grandad know where they are now! There's an old wall with some of the castle stones at the bottom – and there's a well – but no, I mustn't tell you those secrets. You might tell them to the Americans who come here and buy up all our old treasures!'

'We won't! We promise!' said both girls at once, and Timmy thumped his tail on the floor, as if he too agreed.

'Well, maybe Great-Grandad will show you one or two of the old castle stones,' said Mr Finniston. 'But I doubt it – I doubt it! I'll tell you one thing you can see at the farmhouse, though – everybody knows about it, so it's no secret. Have you seen the old kitchen door that leads out into the yard?'

'Yes. That oak door, studded with iron knobs, do you mean?' said Anne at once. 'They're quite fashionable now as front doors in ordinary houses, you know. Surely that farmhouse door isn't a real old one?'

Mr Finniston put his head into his hands and groaned as if he were in pain.

'Fashionable! FASHIONABLE! What will they do next? Surely you can't mix up that fine old door with the trashy copies you've seen in modern houses? What's the world coming to? Couldn't you *feel* that that door was real – was as old as the centuries – and once hung on great hinges in a *castle*? Don't you *know* when things are grand with the weight of years?'

'Well,' said Anne, rather out of her depth, 'I did notice the door – but you see, it's very dark just there, and we really can't see it very clearly.'

'Ah – well – most people go about with their eyes shut half the time!' said Mr Finniston. 'You have a look at that door – feel it – look at the great knocker on it. Think of the old Norman folk who hammered on the door with it, all those ages ago!'

George sighed. This kind of thing didn't interest her as much as it interested Anne. A thought suddenly struck her.

'But, Mr Finniston – if the castle was built of *stone* – how was it burnt to the *ground*?' she said. 'What happened?'

'I can't find out,' said Mr Finniston sadly. 'I've been into every old library in the county, and looked up every old book of that period – and I've delved into the old records in Finniston church. As far as I can make out, the castle was stormed by enemies – and, as I said, traitors inside set fire to it at the same time. The floors fell in, and the castle was left blazing from top to bottom. The great walls fell inwards and covered the base – and the Finniston family fled. Lord Finniston was killed – but his Lady took the children and hid them – it's said she hid them in the old chapel, near the barns of the farm. Maybe she took them down a secret underground passage, leading from the dungeons to the old chapel itself.'

'An old *chapel* – is it still there?' asked Anne. 'Or was it burnt too?'

'No – it wasn't burnt. It's still standing,' said Mr Finniston. 'Old Great-Grandad will show you.' He shook his head sorrowfully. 'It's a storehouse for grain now. Sad, sad. But, mind you – it's still full of prayer!'

The girls stared at him, wondering what he meant. They began to think he must be a little mad. He stood with his head bent, saying nothing for a while. Then he looked up.

'Well, that's the story, my dears – and it's not only a story, it's history! It happened eight hundred years ago. And I'll tell you something else . . .'

'What?' asked the two girls.

'That castle had cellars – and dungeons!' said the old man. 'The fire only burnt down to the ground floor, which was made of earth flattened down, not wood, so it wouldn't burn. The cellars and dungeons can't have been destroyed. Are they still there, undamaged? That's what's been in my mind all these long years. What was down in those cellars – and *is it still there*?'

He spoke in such a hollow voice that that the girls felt quite scared. George recovered herself first. 'But why were the dungeons never uncovered?' she asked. 'I mean, surely someone must have thought of them and wondered about them?'

'Well, when the castle fell and the walls collapsed, any underground entrances must have been completely covered with enormously heavy stones,' said Mr Finniston, peering at them earnestly. 'The peasants and farm hands living around couldn't possibly move them, and maybe they were too scared to, anyhow. They probably lay there for years, till the wind and weather broke them up. Then they were taken to build walls and line wells. But by that time everyone had forgotten about dungeons. Might have been centuries later, you see.'

He stood and brooded for a while, and the girls waited politely for him to go on. 'Yes – everyone forgot . . . and everyone still forgets,' he said. 'Sometimes I wake up in the night and wonder what's underground there. Bones of prisoners? Chests of money? Things stored away by the Lady of the castle? I wake up and wonder!'

Anne felt uncomfortable. Poor old man! He lived absolutely in the past! His mind had woven for him a living fantasy, a story that had no certain foundation, no real truth. She was sorry for him. She wished she could go and see the place where the old castle had once stood! It would be overgrown with grass and weeds, nettles would wave there, and poppies dance in the summer. There would probably be nothing at all to show where once a proud castle had stood, its towers high against the sky, flags flying along the battlements. She could almost hear the cries of the enemy, galloping up on horseback, and the fearful clash of swords! She shook herself and stood up straight.

'I'm as bad as this old man!' she thought. 'Imagining things! But what a *tale*! The others will love to hear it. I wonder if the American knows it.'

'Does that American, Mr Henning, know the old story?' she asked, and the old man straightened up at once.

'Not the whole of it – only what he has heard in the village!' he said. 'He comes here and pesters me. He'd like to bring in men and dig up the whole thing! I know him! He'd buy up all the farm, just for the sake of getting that castle site – if he really *knew* there was something worth having, deep under the ground where it once stood. You won't tell him what I've told you, will you? I've talked too much. I always do when someone's upset me. Ah, to think my ancestors once lived in Finniston Castle – and here I am now, a poor old man in a little antique shop that nobody comes to!'

'Well, *we've* come to it,' said Anne. 'I did want to buy some horse-brasses, but I'll come another time. You're upset now. You go and have a rest!'

They went out of the little shop, almost on tiptoe! 'My

word!' said George, thrilled. 'I just can't *wait* to tell the boys! What a story – and it really sounded true, Anne, didn't it? I vote we find out where that old castle really stood, and then go and have a look round. Who knows what we might find! Come along – let's get back to the farm as quickly as we can!'

CHAPTER TEN

Quite a bit of shouting

ANNE AND GEORGE, with Timmy running in front, went back to the farm to find the boys, but they couldn't see them anywhere and gave up. Then they went indoors and found Mrs Philpot shelling peas. They took over the job at once.

'The boys are still helping to mend the hen-house,' said Mrs Philpot. 'The Harries are pleased to have two more pairs of hands to help them! Something always seems to need repairing! If only we could get a few things we need so badly – a new tractor, for instance. But they cost so much! The barns want mending too and the hen-houses are almost falling down!'

'I hope the harvest will be good for you,' said Anne. 'That will help, won't it?'

'Oh yes – we'll keep our fingers crossed for fine weather from now on!' said Mrs Philpot. 'Thank goodness the cows are such good milkers! What we should do without our milk money, I really don't know! But there – why should I bother you with *my* troubles when you're here for a nice holiday!'

'You don't bother us – and we think it's awfully nice of you to let us help,' said Anne. 'We shouldn't like it if you didn't!'

The girls had no chance of telling the boys what old Mr Finniston had told them, until the afternoon came. They were up at the hen-houses with the two Harries and Snippet, happily hammering and sawing. Snippet was delighted to have so many people whistling cheerily round him, and busily took bits of wood from one boy to another, under the mistaken impression that he was a great help!

Nosey the jackdaw was there too, but he wasn't nearly so popular as Snippet! He pounced on any bright nail or screw he saw, and flew off with it, heedless of the exasperated shouts that followed him.

'Blow that jackdaw!' said Julian, looking up crossly. 'He's just taken the very nail I wanted! Nosey by name and nosey by nature!'

The twins laughed. They seemed entirely different children now that they were friendly – amusing, helpful and most responsible. Julian and Dick admired them – no work was too hard, no hours were too long, if they could help their mother or father.

'We hated you coming here because we knew it would give Mother so much more work,' said Harry. 'We thought if we were beastly to you, you'd go. But you don't make more work! You help an awful lot. It's fun to have you here.'

'I hope the girls are back,' said Dick. 'I know your mother wants help with the peas – such a lot of people to shell for – let me see – counting in your great-grandad,

there will be about a dozen people in to dinner. Whew! I certainly *do* hope the girls are in. Ah – here comes that nosey jackdaw again. Look out, Julian, he's after those screws. Snippet, chase him!'

Away went the tiny poodle after the cheeky jackdaw, barking in his high little voice, thoroughly enjoying having so many children round him. Nosey flew up on to the top of the hen-house, and flapped his wings, chacking rude things in a very loud voice indeed.

Dinner was rather a crowded meal, for everyone was there. Great-Grandad frowned when he saw Mr Henning come in with Junior. Junior strutted to his place at table, giving George his best scowl. However, she was just as good at scowling as Junior, and Mr Henning, who happened to catch sight of her giant-size scowl, had quite a shock.

'Now, now, my boy,' he said to her. 'Why pull such an ugly face?'

Nobody told him that George was a girl. Mrs Philpot was really very much amused. She liked George, and couldn't help thinking she would have made a very good boy indeed!

'Er – Mrs Philpot – would it be all right if I bring a friend to lunch here tomorrow?' asked Mr Henning. 'He's called Durleston – Mr Durleston – and he's a great authority on antiques. He's going to give me some advice. You'll remember that you told me you had a quaint old hole in the wall in one of the bedrooms – where in the old days people used to heat embers for warming-pans, and bricks to put in between the bedsheets. I thought I . . .'

'You thought you could buy 'em, I suppose!' old Great-Grandad suddenly shouted from his place at the head of the table. He thumped on the cloth with the handle of his knife. 'Well, you ask my permission first, see? This place is still mine. I'm an old man, I'm nearly ninety, but I've still got all my wits about me. I don't like this selling of things that have been in our family for donkey's years! That I don't! And . . .'

'Now, now, Grandad, don't excite yourself,' said Mrs Philpot, in her gentle voice. 'Surely it's better to sell old things that we shall never use, in order to buy new tools, or wood to mend the barns?'

'Why can't we sell 'em to our *own* folks, then?' shouted Great-Grandad, banging with his fork as well. 'Taking them out of the country! Part of our history, they are! Selling our birthright, that's what we're doing – for a mess of potage! That's out of the Bible, let me tell you, Mr Henning, in case you don't know.'

'SURE I KNOW,' said Mr Henning, getting up and shouting back at Great-Grandad. 'I'm not as ignorant as you seem to think. You ought to be glad that a poor, run-down, back-dated country like Britain has got anything to sell to a fine upstanding one like America! You . . .'

'That's enough, Mr Henning,' said Mrs Philpot, with such dignity that Mr Henning blushed red and sat down in a great hurry. 'Sorry, ma'am,' he said. 'But that old man, he gets under my skin; he sure does! What's gotten into him? All I want is to buy things you want to sell. You want new tractors – I want old junk and I'm willing to pay for it. That's all there is to it – buying and selling!'

'OLD JUNK!' shouted Great-Grandad again, banging with his glass now. 'Do you call that great old cart-wheel you bought OLD JUNK? Why, that's more than two hundred years old! *My* great-grandad made it – he told me so, when I was a mite of a boy. You won't find another wheel like it in England. HOO – that wheel was made before the first American was born! I tell you . . .'

'Now, now, Grandad, you know you'll feel ill if you go on like this,' said Mrs Philpot, and she got up and went to the old man, who was shaking with fury. 'You belong to old times, and you don't like the new times, and I don't blame you. But things change, you know. Calm yourself, and come with me and have a lie-down.'

Surprisingly, the old fellow allowed Mrs Philpot to lead him out of the room. The seven children had all sat silent while the shouting had been going on. Mr Philpot, looking worried, broke his habitual silence and addressed a few words to the equally worried-looking Mr Henning.

'Storm in a teacup,' he said. 'Soon blow over.'

'Hmmmm,' said Mr Henning. 'Spoilt my dinner! Selfish, ignorant, rude old man.'

'He's not,' said one of the twins, in a voice trembling with anger. 'He's . . .'

'Enough, Harry!' said his father, in such a stern voice that Harry subsided at once, but began to grind his teeth to show that he was still angry, making a most remarkable noise at the now silent table. Junior had sat as still as a mouse all the time, scared of the angry old man. Timmy had given a few small growls, and Snippet had shot straight out of the kitchen as soon as Great-Grandad had begun to shout!

Mrs Philpot came back, and sat down, looking sad and tired. Julian began to talk to her about Janie and the macaroons, and soon succeeded in making her smile. She even laughed out loud when George told her that they had six macaroons to give Bill for taking them out in the Land Rover.

'I know those macaroons,' announced Junior. 'I buy about thirty of them a week. They're just wunnerful!'

'Thirty! No wonder you're so pasty-faced, then,' said George, before she could stop herself.

'Aw shucks! Pasty-face yourself!' retorted Junior, feeling safe with his father near him.

He heard a sudden ominous growl under the table, felt hot breath on his leg, and decided to say no more. He had forgotten all about the watchful Timmy!

Julian thought it was about time to have some bright conversation, and began to tell Mrs Philpot about the hen-houses and what a good job they were making of patching them to make them rain-proof. Mr Philpot listened too, nodded, and actually joined in.

'Yes – you're good with your hands, you boys. I had a look when I came by. Fine work!'

'Harriet's good, too,' said Harry at once. 'She did that corner where the rats get in. Didn't you, Harry?'

'*I* wanted to help, Pop, but they shooed me off, like I was a hen!' said Junior in an aggrieved tone. 'Seems as if they don't want me around. That makes it pretty lonely, Pop. Can't I come out with you this afternoon?'

'No,' said Pop, shortly.

'Aw, *c'mon*, Pop,' said Junior, in a whiny voice. 'Aw shucks, Pop, lemme come!'

'NO!' said Pop, exasperated. Timmy gave a growl again. He didn't like cross voices. He couldn't imagine why there was so much quarrelling here, and sat up, tense and still, until George gave him a gentle push with her toe. Then he lay down again, his head across her feet.

Everyone was glad when the meal was over, delicious though the food had been. The girls and Harriet insisted that Mrs Philpot should go and have a rest while they did all the clearing away and washing-up. 'Now, try not to be unkind to Junior this afternoon,' she said, as she went. 'He'll be all alone when his father's gone. Do let him be with you.'

Nobody answered. They hadn't the least intention of allowing Junior to be with them. 'Spoilt, bad-mannered little idiot!' thought George, clearing away with such vigour that she almost knocked Anne over.

'Julian,' she said in a low voice, catching him at the door as he went out, 'Anne and I have something interesting to tell you. Where will you be this afternoon?'

'Up in the hen-houses, I expect,' said Julian. 'We'll watch out for you and Anne. See you in about half an hour.'

Junior had sharp ears. He heard exactly what George had said, and he was full of curiosity at once. What was this interesting thing George wanted to tell the boys? Was it a secret? All right – he'd be on hand somewhere to hear it!

And so, when the girls had finished their work, and set off to the hen-houses, Junior followed discreetly behind! He kept well out of sight until he saw George and Anne disappear into a hen-house, where the others were working – and then he crept to a corner outside and put his ear to a knot-hole in the wood. 'I'll get my own back now!' he thought. '*I'll* make them smart for leaving me out of things! Just see if I don't!'

CHAPTER ELEVEN

A most exciting tale

THE BOYS were busy hammering and sawing and the girls sat and waited till the noise died down. Snippet was there, leaping about ridiculously with little bits of wood in his mouth, and Nosey the jackdaw had suddenly taken a fancy to the shavings that now covered the floor, and ran about chacking and picking them up.

Outside the hens clucked and squawked, and not far off the ducks quacked loudly. 'Those are the kind of noises I like to hear,' said Anne, settling herself on a sack in a corner. She raised her voice and shouted above the hammering to Dick. 'WANT ANY HELP, DICK?'

'No thanks,' said Dick. 'We'll just finish this job, then sit down and have a rest, and listen to what you have to say. You sit and watch our wonderful carpentering! Honestly, I'd make pounds a week if I took it up!'

'Look out – Nosey has got your nails again!' shouted George. Timmy leapt up as if he was going to chase Nosey, and the jackdaw promptly flew up to a crossbeam, and sat there chacking with laughter. Timmy thought him a very exasperating bird indeed. He lay down again with a thump.

At last the boys had finished the job they were on, and

sat down, rubbing their hands over their wet foreheads. 'Well, now you can tell us your news,' said Dick. 'Good thing we got rid of that little pest of a Junior – I might have hammered a few nails into him by mistake if he'd come worrying us this afternoon.' He imitated Junior's whining drawl. 'Aw shucks, Pop, lemme come with you!'

Outside, his ear to the hole, Junior clenched his fists. He would willingly have stuck a few nails into Dick at that moment!

George and Anne began to tell the four listening children what old Mr Finniston had told them that morning. 'It's about Finniston Castle,' said Anne. 'The old castle that gave the village its name – and the farm as well. The old fellow who told us about it is called Finniston, too – and will you believe it, he's a descendant of the Finnistons who lived in the castle centuries ago!'

'He seems to have spent most of his life trying to discover everything possible about the old castle,' said George. 'He said he'd delved into old libraries – and into the church records here – anywhere that might help him to piece together the castle's history!'

Outside the hen-house, Junior held his breath so as not to miss a single word. Why – his Pop had told him that he couldn't get *anything* out of that old Mr Finniston at the antique shop – not a word about the castle, and its history, or even where the site was. Then why had he told Anne,

and the horrible boy George? Junior felt angry, and listened even more keenly.

'The story goes that the twelfth-century enemies came to attack the castle one night – and there were traitors already inside it who set it on fire, so that the castle folk would be busy trying to put out the fire, and wouldn't be prepared for a fight,' said George. 'The inside of it was burnt down to the ground – and then the great stone walls outside collapsed inwards, and lay in enormous heaps there, covering the place where the castle had stood.'

'Whew!' said Dick, visualising it all. 'What a night that must have been! Everybody killed or burnt, I suppose?'

'No, the Lady of the castle wasn't killed and it is said that she took her children to the little chapel near the farmhouse – we really must go and see that, twins – and they stayed there in safety. Anyway, *some* of the family must have escaped, because it is one of their descendants who keeps that little antique shop – old Mr Finniston!'

'This is tremendously interesting,' said Julian. 'Where's the site of the castle? It should easily be known, because of the great mass of stones that fell there when the walls collapsed.'

'No, they're *not* there now,' said George. 'Mr Finniston said he thought that when the wind and weather had broken them up small enough to be lugged away by the farmers and peasants living nearby, they were taken to build field-walls, or to line wells. He said there were some on this farm. He didn't know himself where the castle once stood because the site would be all grown over, and with no stones left to mark it, it wouldn't be easy to find.'

'But oh, Julian, I *wish* we could find it!' cried Anne, her voice rising in excitement. 'Because, so Mr Finniston says, the cellars and dungeons are probably still there, quite untouched. You see, no one could uncover them for years, because of the heavy stones there – and when the stones were taken away, people had forgotten about the castle and the dungeons!'

'Gosh! So they may *still* be there – with whatever was stored in them hundreds of years ago,' said Dick, thrilled. 'My *word* – there might be priceless things there, as old as the hills! I mean, even an old broken sword would be worth its weight in gold, because it would be so very, very old. I say – don't say a word of all this in front of that American, or he'd dig up the whole farm!'

'We shouldn't *dream* of it,' said George. 'He shan't get to hear a word of this.'

Alas! George little knew that every single word had been overheard by Junior, whose left ear was still pinned to the knot-hole in the wood! His face was red with surprise and delight. WHAT A SECRET! Whatever would his pop say? Dungeons! Perhaps full of gold and jewels and all kinds of things! He rubbed his hands together in delight, thinking that he would soon get even with those annoying children now – as soon as Pop came home, he'd spill everything to him. GEE!

Timmy heard the small sound of Junior rubbing his hands together and sat up, growling, his ears pricked. Snippet growled too, a miniature little sound that nobody took seriously. Timmy then heard Junior creeping away, afraid because he had heard the big dog growling. Timmy growled again and then barked sharply, running to the shut door of the hen-house, scraping at it with his foot.

'Somebody's outside – quick! If it's Junior, I'll throw him on to the muck-heap!' yelled Dick, and flung open the door. They all trooped out and looked round – but there was nobody there! Junior had shot off at top speed, and was now safely behind the nearest hedge.

'What was it, Tim?' said George. She turned to the others. 'He may have heard those hens scratching near the door,' she said. 'There's no one about. Gosh, I was so afraid that it was that little sneak of a Junior! He'd tell his pop every single thing!'

'Twins, listen – Mr Finniston told us that one of the things that *was* saved from the castle – or found afterwards, perhaps – was a great old oak door, iron-studded,' said Anne, suddenly remembering. 'Is that one of your kitchen doors?'

'Yes – that must be the door leading into the dark little passage,' said Harry. 'You wouldn't have noticed it particularly because it's usually kept open, and it's very dark just there. Gosh, I suppose it *could* have come from the castle. It's enormously thick and strong. I wonder if Dad knows.'

'We'll tell him,' said Harriet. 'I say – shall we go and look for the site of the castle sometime? If only we could find it! Do you suppose that if we found the cellars and dungeons, full of chests and things, they'd belong to *us*? The farm belongs to our family, of course, and all the land around.'

'Does it? Well then, perhaps anything found on this land would be yours!' said Julian.

'We might be able to buy a new tractor!' said the twins, both together, in the same excited voice.

'Let's go and look for the castle site *now*,' said George, her voice sounding so excited that Timmy sat up and barked.

'No. We must finish this job,' said Julian. 'We promised we would. There's plenty of time to hunt around, because nobody knows about this except us.'

Julian was wrong, of course. Junior knew – and Junior meant to tell the whole secret to his father as soon as ever he could! He could hardly wait for him to come home.

'Well, we'd better be getting back to the house,' said George. 'We told Mrs Philpot we'd pick some raspberries for supper tonight, so we'd better fetch baskets, and begin. Oh, I do HOPE we find that castle site. I shall dream about it tonight, I know I shall.'

'Well, try and dream where it *is*,' said Julian, with a laugh. 'Then you can lead us straight to it tomorrow morning. I suppose *you* haven't any idea where it might be, have you, twins?'

'No,' they said together, frowning. 'No idea at all!' And Harriet added, 'You see, the farm's so big – and I suppose it might have been built *any*where on our land.'

'Yes – but probably near the top of a hill,' said Julian. 'Castles used to overlook surrounding land, you know, so that approaching enemies could easily be seen. And then again, George said Mr Finniston told them that the Lady of the castle escaped with her children and took them in safety to the chapel, which wouldn't be very far away. I should guess that the castle site must be not further than a quarter of a mile from the chapel, so that narrows the search down a bit. By the way, we really must look at the chapel – it sounds interesting, even though it has been used as a storehouse for years!'

The girls picked raspberries for the rest of the afternoon, and the boys finished their jobs. They went back to the farmhouse for tea, feeling pleasantly tired. The girls were already there, laying the table. They pounced on the twins, and George spoke excitedly.

'Twins! We've been looking at the old studded door. It's MAGNIFICENT! Come and see it, Julian and Dick. If it isn't from the old castle, I'll eat my hat – *and* my shoes as well!'

She took them to the great door that opened from the kitchen into the passage that led to the yard. With much difficulty she swung it shut. They all gazed at it. It had been almost too heavy for George to move! Great iron studs had been driven into it, so deeply and firmly that only by destroying the door itself could they ever be removed. There was a curious iron handle in the middle of the outer side, and George raised it and brought it down smartly. A loud bang resounded through the kitchen, and made the others jump.

'The knocker that visitors used when they came to the castle, I suppose!' said George, laughing at their surprised faces. 'Noise enough to rouse everyone, and alert any guard at once. Do you suppose it was the *front* door of the castle – it's big enough! It must be worth hundreds of pounds!'

'Look out – there's Junior!' said Anne, in a low voice. 'He's grinning all over his face. What do you suppose he's been up to? I wish I knew!'

CHAPTER TWELVE

Really very thrilling

AT TEATIME Julian spoke to Mrs Philpot about the old kitchen door. 'That's a fine old door,' he said. 'Did it come from the castle, do you suppose?'

'Yes – so it's said,' answered Mrs Philpot. 'Great-Grandad here knows more about it than I do, though.'

Great-Grandad was not at the table. He was sitting in his enormous old chair in the window, with Snippet at his feet. He was pulling contentedly at his pipe, a cup of tea on the windowsill beside him.

'What's that?' called the old man. 'Speak up!' Julian repeated what Mrs Philpot had said, and the old fellow nodded.

'Oh ay! That door's from the castle all right. Made of the same oak as the beams in the barns, and the floors of the bedrooms above! Ay, and that American fellow's been at me about it, too! Hoo! Offered me fifty pounds for it. FIFTY POUNDS. I wouldn't take a thousand. What – have that old door hanging in some newfangled house out in that American country, wherever it is? NO. I say NO, and I'll say it till I'm blue in the face!'

'All right, Grandad – don't upset yourself,' said Mrs Philpot. She spoke to Julian in a low voice. 'Change the

subject, quickly, or Grandad will go on and on, poor old fellow!'

Julian racked his brain for a change of subject, and fortunately remembered the hen-houses. He at once began to tell Great-Grandad all they had done that afternoon, and the old fellow calmed down at once, and listened with pleasure. Snippet, who had run in fright to the twins as soon as Great-Grandad had begun to shout, ran back to him, and settled on his feet. Timmy also decided to join them, and soon Great-Grandad was completely happy again, drawing on his old pipe, with one dog at his feet, the other resting a great head on his knee. Timmy certainly did love Great-Grandad!

Mr Henning did not come back that night, much to everyone's relief, but arrived next day just before lunch, bringing with him a dried-up fellow wearing thick glasses, whom he introduced as Mr Richard Durleston.

'The *great* Mr Durleston!' he said proudly. 'Knows more about old houses in England than anyone else in the country. I'd like him to see that old door after lunch, Mrs Philpot – and the strange opening in the wall of the bedroom upstairs, which was used to heat embers and bricks for warming beds years ago.'

Fortunately Great-Grandad was not there to object, and after they had had dinner, Mrs Philpot took Mr Durleston to the old studded door. 'Ah, yes,' he said. 'Quite genuine. Very fine specimen. I should offer two hundred pounds, Mr Henning.'

How Mrs Philpot longed to accept such an offer! What a difference it would make to her housekeeping! She shook her head. 'You'd have to talk to old Great-Grandad,' she said. 'But I'm afraid he'll say no. Now I'll take you to see the strange old opening up in one of the bedrooms.'

She took Mr Henning and Mr Durleston upstairs, and the four followed, with Timmy. It was indeed a strange opening in the wall! It had a wrought-iron door rather like an old oven door. Mrs Philpot opened it. Inside was a big cavity, which had obviously been used as a kind of oven to heat bricks for placing into cold beds; some of the old bricks were actually still there, blackened with long-ago heating! Mrs Philpot took out what looked like a heavy iron tray with an ornamental raised edge. On it were old, old embers!

'This tray was used for heating and holding the embers before they were put into warming-pans,' she said. 'We still have one old warming-pan left – there on the wall, look.'

The four, just as interested as the two men, looked at the copper warming-pan, glowing red-gold on the wall. 'The red-hot embers were emptied into that,' Mrs Philpot told the children, 'and then the pan was carried by its long handle into all the bedrooms, and thrust into each bed for a few minutes to warm it. And that funny little opening in the wall is, as I said, where people years and years ago heated the embers – and the bricks too, which were wrapped in flannel and left in each bed.'

'Hmmmmm. Very interesting. Quite rare to see one in such a well-preserved state,' said Mr Durleston, peering into the opening through thick glasses. 'You could make an offer for this too, Mr Henning. Interesting old place. We'll have a look at the barns too, I think, and the outbuildings. Might be a few things there you could pick up with advantage.'

George thought it was a good thing the twins were not with them to hear all this. They seemed to share with their great-grandad a hatred of parting with any of the treasures belonging to the old farmhouse!

Mrs Philpot took the two men downstairs again, and the four followed.

'I'll just take Mr Durleston to the old chapel, ma'am,' said Mr Henning, and Mrs Philpot nodded. She left them and hurried back into the kitchen, where she had a cake baking. The four looked at one another, and Julian nodded his head towards the two men, now making their way out of doors. 'Shall we go too?' he said. 'We haven't seen this chapel yet, either!'

So they followed the two men, and soon came to a tall, quaint old building with small and beautifully arched windows set high up in the wall. They went in at the door, a few paces behind the two men, and stared in wonder.

'Yes – you can see it was once a chapel!' said Julian, instinctively speaking in a low voice. 'Those lovely old windows – that arch there . . .'

'And the *feel* of it!' said Anne. 'I know now what old Mr Finniston down at that little shop meant, when he said that though it was now a storehouse, it was still full of prayer! You can *feel* that people have been here to pray, can't you? What a lovely little chapel. Oh, I do wish it wasn't used as a storehouse!'

'I was told by an old fellow down in the village antique shop that a Lady Phillippa, who was once the Lady of the castle, brought each of her fifteen children here to learn their prayers,' said Mr Durleston, surprisingly. 'Hmm, hmm – nice old story. Probably true. Chapels were often built near to castles. Wonder which path they took from the castle to the chapel. All gone now, no castle, nothing! Hmm, hmm.'

'I'd like to buy this chapel, knock it down, and take it stone by stone to my place in the States,' said the American enthusiastically. 'Fine specimen, isn't it? It would look wonderful in my place.'

'Can't advise that,' said Mr Durleston, shaking his head. 'Not in good taste. Let's go to those outbuildings over there. Might see something in the old junk there.'

They went off, and the children stayed behind, entranced with the little chapel. Sacks upon sacks of grain and what looked like fertiliser were arranged in rows all over the floor. A cat had three kittens cuddled together on one sack, and a dove cooed somewhere high up in the arched roof. It was a very peaceful sound, somehow just right for the silent little place. The children trooped out quietly, not feeling inclined to follow the brash Mr Henning round any more.

'At least the other man stopped him from his mad idea of removing the chapel stone by stone,' said Anne. 'I couldn't *bear* that beautiful old place to be torn up by its roots and replanted somewhere else.'

'You sound quite angry, Anne – almost as fierce as old Great-Grandad!' said Julian, slipping his arm through his sister's. 'I don't somehow think the old chapel will be sold to Mr Henning – even if he offered a million dollars for it!'

'Well, I like most Americans very much,' said Anne. 'But not Mr Henning. He – he wants to buy history just as if it were chocolate or toffee!'

That made the others laugh. 'I say!' said Julian. 'What

about having a snoop round, now we're out, and just see if we can decide where to hunt for the site of the castle? I presume we all agree that it can't be *very* far away from the chapel?'

'Yes – that's agreed,' said Dick. 'And it's also agreed that the site is probably on a hill. The snag is that there are rather a lot of hills on this undulating farmland!'

'Let's make our way over there – up the nearest slope,' said George. 'Hallo, here are the twins. We'll call them. They might like to come.'

The twins soon joined them, and said yes, they would certainly like to hunt for the castle site. 'But it might take years!' said Harry. 'It might be anywhere on the farm!'

'Well, we plan to examine this slope first,' said Julian. 'Heel, Tim, heel, Snippet. Oh gosh, here's Nosey the jackdaw too. NOT on my shoulder, if you don't mind, Nosey. I rather value my ears!'

'Chack!' said the jackdaw, and flew to the twins.

They made their way up the slope. There was, however, absolutely nothing to be seen except grass, grass, grass! They came to a big mound and stood looking at it.

'A very *large* mole must have made that!' said Dick, which made them all laugh, for the mound was as high as their shoulders. Rabbit holes could be seen at the bottom, though it was probable that very few burrowed there now – the great rabbit disease, myxomatosis, had wiped them practically out of existence on Finniston Farm.

Timmy couldn't see a rabbit hole without scraping at it, and soon he and Snippet were scattering earth over everyone. Snippet was small enough to disappear into one hole, and came out carrying – of all things – an oyster shell! Julian took it out of his mouth in amazement.

'Look here – an *oyster* shell – and we're miles from the sea. How did it get there? Go in again, Snippet. Scrape hard, Timmy. Buck up! An idea is glimmering in my brain!'

Before long, what with Timmy's excited scraping and Snippet's explorations deep into the burrow, quite a collection of oyster shells, and small and large bones lay on the grass!

'Bones!' said Anne. 'Not bones of *people* surely. Don't tell me this is a mound covering an old grave or something. Ju.'

'No. But it *is* something rather exciting!' said Julian. 'I'm pretty sure it's an old kitchen-midden.'

'A *kitchen-midden*? What on earth's that?' said George. 'Oh look – Timmy's got another mouthful of oyster shells!'

'A kitchen-midden is what you might call the rubbish-heap of the old days,' explained Julian, picking up some oyster shells. 'It was often very big, when it comprised the rubbish thrown out from large houses – or castles! Things like bones and shells wouldn't rot away like other rubbish – and I do believe we've found the kitchen-midden of the old castle. My word – what a find! Now we know something very important!'

'What?' asked everyone, in excitement.

'Well – we know now that the site of the castle must be somewhere on this slope!' said Julian. 'The kitchen-midden was probably not far from its walls. We're on the scent, scouts, we're on the scent! Come on – let's go further on. Spread out, examine every inch of the ground!'

CHAPTER THIRTEEN

Junior springs a surprise

THE SIX children felt a sudden surge of excitement, and Timmy felt it too and barked loudly. Snippet joined in, and the jackdaw danced up and down on Harry's shoulder, chacking hoarsely. Junior, who had seen them start out and was tracking them, stared in surprise from behind a bush in a nearby hedge. NOW what was all the excitement about? What had Timmy and Snippet found?

He saw the six children spread out and begin to go slowly up the great slope of the hill. Timmy followed them, rather puzzled. He wished he knew what they were looking for – then he could hunt too! Junior kept safely behind the bush. He knew that if he followed too closely after the children, Timmy would hear him, and bark.

Suddenly the Harries gave a shout. 'Hey!' The others looked up from their search, and saw them beckoning in excitement. 'What about THIS? Come and look!'

Everyone hurried over to the twins, who were standing on a little ridge about two hundred metres below the top of the gently sloping hill. 'Look!' said Harry, sweeping his arm in a circle. 'Would *this* be a likely place for the castle site?'

The four looked at the great shallow depression that the

twins pointed to. In shape it was like a very shallow soup plate, certainly big enough for a castle to have been built there! It was covered with thick, closely growing grass, which was a little darker in colour than the grass around.

Julian clapped Harry on the shoulder. 'Yes! I bet this is where the castle once stood! Why should the ground here suddenly have this great depression in it, as if it had sunk down for some reason? The *only* reason could be that some enormously heavy building once stood here – and it *must* have been the castle!'

'It's not too far from the kitchen-midden, where they threw their rubbish, is it?' asked Anne, anxiously, looking back to see how far away that was.

'No – just about right,' said Julian. 'They would be sure to have it some distance away because it would smell, especially in the hot weather. Yes, twins – I think you really have hit on the castle site – and I bet if we had the machinery to excavate here, we'd come across dungeons, cellars, underground passages – and all they contain!'

The twins went red with excitement, and stared solemnly at the great basin-like circle, green with grass. 'What *will* our mother say?' they said, both together.

'Plenty!' said Dick. 'This might be the saving of your farm! But look – let's not say a word about it yet, in case it gets round to Mr Henning. Let's get Bill and ask him if he'll lend us spades and things. We'll tell him we've found some interesting old shells and bones on the hill and want to do a little digging. We'll soon know if this really *is* the site of the castle.'

'Good idea,' said Julian, excited at the thought of being one of the first to dig down into the old dungeons! 'Let's pace round this old site and see how big it is.'

They walked round and round it and decided it was more than big enough for even a large castle. They thought it was strange that the grass should be a different colour there.

'But it does sometimes happen that grass marks out where old buildings once stood,' said Julian. 'I say – this is just about the most exciting thing that ever happened to us – and I'm so glad it was the twins who first recognised the site! After all, it's on their farm!'

'Isn't that Junior running over there?' said George suddenly, as she saw Timmy prick up his ears, and turn his nose to the wind. 'Yes, it is. He's been spying on us, the little beast! There he goes, look!'

'Well, he can't know *much*,' said Julian, gazing after the running figure. 'I don't expect he even knows that a castle was once built here, at the top of this hill – and he certainly wouldn't know we were looking for the site. He's just snooping, that's all.'

But Junior *did* know all about the old castle, for he had overheard the children talking in the hen-house! And he *did* know what they had been looking for. He had followed them as closely as he dared, listening to their shouts – and now he felt that he must get back to his father and tell him what he knew!

He found his father still with Mr Durleston, examining an old fireplace. 'Now that's worth buying,' Mr Durleston was saying. 'You could rip that out, and use it in your own house – a beautiful thing. Very old! And . . .'

'Pop! I say, Pop! Listen!' cried Junior, bursting in. Mr Durleston looked annoyed. That boy again! But Junior took no notice of the old man's annoyance, and pulled urgently at his father's arm. 'Dad! I know where the place is that the castle once stood on! And there's dungeons and cellars underneath, full of treasure, I know there are. Pop, those kids found the place, but they don't know I saw them!'

'What *is* all this, Junior?' said his father, half-annoyed

too. 'Silly talk! You don't know anything about castle sites and dungeons and the rest!'

'I do, I do! I heard them all talking in the hen-house – I told you I did!' cried Junior, tugging at his father's sleeve again. 'Pop, they've found an old rubbish-heap too, that belonged to the castle – they called it – a – let me see now – a . . .'

'A midden?' asked Mr Durleston, suddenly taking an interest.

'Yes! That's it. A kitchen-midden!' said Junior triumphantly. 'With bones and shells. And then they looked for where the old castle might have been built – they said it couldn't have been far away, and . . .'

'Well, they were right,' said Mr Durleston. 'A kitchen-midden would certainly pinpoint the castle area! Mr Henning, this is extremely interesting. If you could get permission to excavate, it would be a . . .'

'Oh boy!' said Mr Henning, interrupting, his eyes almost staring out of his head. 'Can't you see the papers – "American discovers old castle site – unknown for centuries! Excavates dungeons – finds bones of long-ago prisoners – chests of gold coins . . ."'

'Not so fast, not so fast,' said Mr Durleston, disapprovingly. 'There may be nothing at all there. Let us not count our chickens before they're hatched. And mind – not a word to the newspapers, Henning. We don't want a crowd of people rushing to pry over the farm, sending up its price!'

'I didn't think of that,' said Mr Henning, a little cast down. 'All right – we'll go carefully. What do you advise?'

'I should advise you to approach Mr Philpot – *not* the old great-grandad, but the farmer himself – and offer to put down, say, £250 for the right to excavate up on the hill there,' said Mr Durleston. 'Then if you strike anything interesting, you can offer a further sum for whatever's down there – say another £250. If there *is* anything there, it will be *extremely* valuable – so very, very old. Hmmm. Hmmm. Yes, that is my advice to you.'

'And it sounds pretty good to me,' said Mr Henning, excitement flooding him again. 'You'll stay here and advise me, won't you, Durleston?'

'Certainly, certainly, if you are prepared to pay my fee,' said Durleston. 'I think it would perhaps be advisable if *I* approached Mr Philpot, Mr Henning, not you. You might – er – well – give something away in your excitement. You will come with me, of course – but let me do the talking.'

'Right, old man, you do everything!' said Mr Henning, feeling friendly with the whole world. He clapped the listening Junior on the back. 'Well done, son! You may have let us into something good. Now don't you breathe a word to *anyone*, see?'

'Aw shucks!' said Junior. 'What do you think I am? My mouth's sewn up from now on! Think I'd split, Pop, when there's a chance of getting even with those snooty kids? You go on up that hill when they've gone, and have a look yourself. Mr Durleston will know if it's the real thing or not!'

So, when the six children and dogs were safely out of sight, gone to help with various jobs of work on the farm, Mr Henning and Mr Durleston went with Junior to see the kitchen-midden and the supposed site of the old castle. Mr Henning became very excited indeed, and even the weary-looking Mr Durleston brightened up and nodded his head several times.

'*Looks* the real thing!' he said. 'Yes, we'll get going this evening – after that fierce old fellow – the old great-grandad – has gone to bed. He might put a spoke in our wheels. He's as old as the hills, but as quick as a jackdaw!'

And so, that evening, when Great-Grandad was safely in bed, Mr Henning and Mr Durleston had a private, very private talk with Mr and Mrs Philpot together. The farmer and his wife listened, amazed. When they heard that Mr Henning proposed to hand them a cheque for £250 merely for the right to do a little digging, Mrs Philpot almost cried!

'And I have advised Mr Henning that he should offer you further sums, if he finds anything he would like to take back to the States with him, as – er – as mementos of a very pleasant stay here,' finished Mr Durleston.

'It sounds too good to be true,' said Mrs Philpot. 'We could certainly do with the money, couldn't we, Trevor?'

Mr Henning took out his cheque book and produced his

pen before Mr Philpot could say anything else. He wrote out the sum of £250, and signed the cheque with a flourish. He then presented it to Mr Philpot.

'And I hope there'll be more cheques to come,' he said.

'Thank you, sir. I'll get men along tomorrow to start digging.'

'I'll have a formal agreement drawn up,' put in Mr Durleston, thinking that he saw a rather doubtful look coming over Mr Philpot's face as he took the cheque. 'But you can cash the cheque straight away. Well, we'll leave you to talk it over!'

When the twins and the four heard of this the next morning, they were astounded. Mrs Philpot told the twins first, and Harry and Harriet ran at once to find the others. They listened, amazed and angry.

'How did they know all that? How did they guess where to find the castle site?' said Dick, fiercely. 'I bet it's that snoopy little Junior who put them on to this! I bet he spied on us! I *thought* I saw two people up on that hill after tea yesterday. It must have been Mr Henning and that friend of his – with Junior. Gosh, I could pull that kid's hair out!'

'Well, I suppose there's absolutely nothing we can do now!' said George, angrily. 'The next thing we'll see is lorries rolling up with men inside, and spades and drills and goodness knows what!'

She was quite right! That very morning the hill became quite a busy place! Four men had already been hired by Mr Henning, and they all went up the hill in their lorry,

bumping slowly along, past the kitchen-midden mound, and on up to the shallow basin-like depression near the summit of the hill. Spades, forks and drills rattled in the lorry. Junior was mad with joy, and danced about at a safe distance, yelling defiance at the six children.

'You thought I didn't know anything, didn't you! I heard *everything*! Serves you right! Yah!'

'Timmy – chase him!' ordered George, in a furious voice. 'But don't hurt him, mind. Go on!'

And off went Timmy at a gallop, and if Junior hadn't leapt into the lorry and picked up a spade, Timmy would certainly have rolled him over and over on the ground!

Now what was to be done? The children almost gave up – but not quite! There *might* be something they could do – there might! *Why* was Julian suddenly looking so excited?

CHAPTER FOURTEEN

Snippet and Nosey are very helpful

'LISTEN!' SAID Julian, lowering his voice, and looking all about to make sure that no one was near. 'Do you remember what you told us, George, about a secret passage from the castle to the old chapel?'

'Yes! Yes! I do!' said George, and Anne nodded, her eyes bright. 'You mean the story that old Mr Finniston told us, down at the little antique shop, about the Lady of the castle taking her children in safety from the burning castle, by way of an underground passage to the old chapel? Gosh, I'd forgotten that!'

'Oh, Julian! Yes, George is right!' said Anne. 'Are you thinking that the passage might still be there, hidden underground?'

'What I think is this,' said Julian. 'If the Lady and her children escaped *underground*, they must first have fled down into the cellars of the castle – and so the passage or tunnel must have *started* from there. They couldn't have escaped in any other way because the castle was itself surrounded by enemies. So she must have gone with her children to hide in the cellars – and then, when the castle fell, she took them safely down the secret passage that led to the old chapel. So *that* means . . .'

'That means that if we can find the secret passage, we can get into the cellars ourselves – perhaps before the workmen do!' cried George, almost shouting with excitement.

'Exactly,' said Julian, his eyes shining. 'Now don't let's lose our heads and get too excited. Let's talk about it quietly – and for GOODNESS' sake keep a watch for Junior.'

'Timmy – on guard!' said George, and Timmy at once went some paces away, and stood up straight, looking now in this direction, and now in that. Nobody could come within sight now, without Timmy giving a warning bark!

The children settled down beside a hedge. 'What's the plan?' asked Dick.

'I vote we go to the old chapel, take a line from there to the castle site, and walk slowly up that line,' said Julian. 'We might *possibly* see something that would guide us as to where the secret passage is. I don't know what – maybe the grass might be slightly different in colour – a bit darker than the surrounding grass, just as it was on the castle site. Anyway, it's worth trying. If we *do* see a line of darker grass, or something like that, we'll dig down underground ourselves, hoping the secret passage is underneath!'

'Oh, *Ju*! What a wonderful idea!' said Anne. 'Come on, let's go down to the chapel straight away!'

So off they all went, Timmy, Snippet and Nosey the jackdaw too. He loved being with Snippet, though he teased him unmercifully. They arrived quickly at the chapel door and went in. 'I always feel as if there ought to be an organ playing when I'm inside,' said Anne, looking round the stacked sacks of grain.

'Never mind about organs,' said Julian, standing at the open door, and pointing up the hill. 'Now, see, there's the place where the old castle stood – where the men are already at work – and if we take a fairly straight line to it, we *should* be more or less walking over the old passage. I should think the men who made it would drive as straight a tunnel as they could, to save themselves work. A winding one would take a long time.'

'I can't see that the grass is any different in colour, along the line I'm looking,' said Dick, squinting, and everyone agreed, very disappointed.

'So there's nothing to help us!' said George, mournfully. 'All we can do is to work in a straight line up the hill, and hope to find something that will tell us if we're over a tunnel. Hollow-sounding footsteps, perhaps!'

'That's very doubtful, I'm afraid,' said Julian. 'Still, I can't see that we can do anything else. Come on, then. All right, Tim, you can come back to us. Look at Nosey, on Snippet's back again! That's right, Snippet, roll over and get him off.'

'Chack!' said Nosey, crossly, as he flew up in the air. 'Chack!'

The six children walked up the slope in as straight a line as they could. They came right up to where the men were digging, without having seen or heard anything of any help at all. It was most disappointing. Junior saw them, and yelled loudly.

'Children not allowed here! Keep off! My dad's bought this place!'

'Liar!' shouted back the two Harries at once. 'You've got the right to dig and that's all!'

'Yah!' yelled Junior. 'You wait! Now don't you set that great dog on me again! I'll tell my pop, see?'

Timmy barked loudly, and Junior disappeared in a hurry. George laughed. 'Silly little idiot! Why doesn't somebody box his ears? I bet one of the men will before he's many hours older. Look at him trying to use that drill!'

Junior was certainly not at all popular. He made himself a great nuisance, and in the end his father put him roughly into a lorry and told him to stay there. He howled dismally, but as no one paid any attention, he soon stopped!

The six children went slowly back down the gentle slope of the hill, taking a slightly different line, still hopeful. The jackdaw flew down to Harry's shoulder, chacking loudly, bored with all this walking! He suddenly saw Snippet sitting down to scratch his neck, and at once launched himself at him. He knew that the poodle always shut his eyes when he scratched himself, and that that was a very good time to give him a well-placed peck!

But, unfortunately for Nosey, the poodle opened his eyes too soon, and saw the jackdaw just about to perch on him! He snapped at him – and got him by the wing! 'Chack-chack-CHACK!' cried the jackdaw, urgently calling for help. 'CHACK!'

Harry ran to Snippet, shouting, 'Drop him, Snippet, drop him! You'll break his wing!' Before he could reach the pair, the jackdaw managed to free himself by giving Snippet a sudden peck on his nose, which made him bark in pain. As soon as he opened his mouth to bark, the jackdaw dropped on the ground, and scuttled away, his wing drooping, unable to fly.

The poodle was after him in a second! The twins yelled in vain. He meant to catch that exasperating jackdaw if it was the last thing he did! The squawking bird looked anxiously for a hiding-place – and saw one! A rabbit hole – just the thing to hop down in a trice! In he went with another loud squawk, and disappeared from sight.

'He's gone down that rabbit hole!' said Dick, with a shout of laughter. 'Clever old bird. You're outwitted, Snippet!'

But no – Snippet wasn't! He disappeared down the hole too! He was as small as a rabbit, and could easily run down a burrow. He had never done more than sniff at one before, being rather scared of dark tunnels – but if Nosey had gone down, well, he would too!

The children stared in surprise. First the jackdaw – now Snippet! The twins bent down by the hole and yelled. 'Come back, Snippet, you idiot! The hill's honey combed with old warrens – you'll get lost for ever. Come back! Snippet. Snip-Snip-Snippet, can you hear us! COME HERE!'

There was silence down the rabbit hole. No chack, no bark. 'They must have gone deep down,' said Harry, anxiously. 'There's a perfect maze of burrows in this hill. Dad said there used to be thousands of rabbits here at one time. Hey, Snippet – COME HERE!'

'Well, we'd better sit down till they come back,' said Anne, feeling suddenly tired with excitement and with climbing up hill and down.

'Right,' said Julian. 'Anyone got any sweets?'

'I have,' said George, as usual, and took out a rather grimy packet of peppermints. 'Here you are; have one, twins?'

'Thanks,' they said. 'We really ought to be getting back – we've plenty of work to do!'

They sat sucking their peppermints, wondering what in the world the jackdaw and Snippet were up to. At last Timmy pricked up his ears and gave a small bark, looking at the entrance of the burrow as he did so. 'They're coming,' said George. 'Timmy knows!'

Sure enough, Timmy was right. Out came first Snippet, and then Nosey, apparently quite good friends again. Snippet rushed to the twins and flung himself on them as if he hadn't seen them for days. He put something down at their feet. 'What's this you've found?' said Harry, picking it up. 'Some dirty old bone?'

Julian suddenly took it from him, almost snatching it. 'Bone? No – that's not a bone. It's a small carved dagger with a broken handle – old as the hills! SNIPPET! Where did you find it?'

'The jackdaw's got something too!' cried Anne, pointing to him. 'Look – in his beak!'

Harriet caught the jackdaw easily, for he still could not fly. 'It's a ring!' she said. 'With a red stone in it – look!'

All six children gazed at the two strange articles. An old carved knife, black with age – and an old ring, with a stone still set in it! They could have come from only one place! George said what everyone was thinking.

'Snippet and the jackdaw have been to the cellars of the castle! They must have! That burrow must have led *straight* into the tunnel that goes to the dungeons and the cellars – and they've been there! Oh, Snippet – you clever, clever dog – you've told us *just* what we want to know!'

'George is right!' said Dick, jubilantly. 'We know quite a lot of things now, because of Snippet and Nosey. We know there must be plenty of things still in those castle cellars – and we know that *some*where near the end of this burrow is the secret passage – because that's the only way they could have got into the cellars – by using the passage! The burrow led into the passage! Don't you agree, Julian?'

'You bet!' said Julian, flushed with excitement. 'My word, this *is* a bit of good luck! Hurray for Snippet and Nosey. Look, the jackdaw's trying to fly, his wing isn't badly hurt – just bruised, I expect. Good old Nosey – little did he know what his bit of mischief would lead to!'

'What happens now?' said George, her eyes shining. 'Do *we* dig, too – now that we know where the passage is? It can't be very far; and once we've got down to it, we can easily get into the cellars – before that American does!'

What an excitement! Timmy really thought everyone had gone completely mad!

CHAPTER FIFTEEN

Digging for the secret tunnel

'HOW CAN we get permission to dig?' asked Anne. 'I mean – will we be allowed to?'

'I don't see why not – Mr Henning has only been given permission to dig in one place,' said Julian. 'I bet we'd get permission to dig just here – it's a pretty good way from the castle site, anyway.'

'Why shouldn't we just dig and see if anyone stops us?' said George. 'If Mr Philpot stops us, we could tell him what we're *really* doing. He'd probably let us, then. But whatever happens, we don't want *Mr Henning* to know what we've discovered – or *think* we've discovered!'

'Well, what shall we say then, if he asks why we're digging?' said Anne.

'Say silly things – joke about it!' said Dick. 'Twins, have you work to do this morning? Can you find us spades, do you think?'

'Yes – you can have our spades, and Dad's old ones, too!' said Harry. 'We wish we could help – but we've tons to do, and we're very late already.'

'Oh dear – and I promised that George and I would help in the kitchen!' said Anne. 'And pick peas for dinner and pod them – and get more raspberries! Can you and Dick dig all on your own, Ju?'

'Good heavens, yes!' said Julian. 'It'll be slower with just two of us digging, but we'll soon get deep down, you'll see! Anyway, we could all take turns this afternoon, perhaps, if the twins finish their work.'

'We will! We'll do it at top speed!' said Harry and Harriet together. 'Now we'll get some spades for you.'

They raced off, with Snippet beside them, and the two girls went down the hill more slowly, feeling very thrilled. If only, only they could dig down and find the secret passage from the chapel to the cellars of the old castle! Timmy felt the excitement and wagged his tail happily. He was always happy when George was thrilled about anything.

Harriet soon brought two big spades and two smaller ones to the boys. They were heavy, and she panted as she carried them up the hill.

'Good girl – or is it good boy?' asked Dick, as he took the spades. 'Wait – it's Harriet, isn't it? You've no scar on your hand!'

Harriet grinned and ran off swiftly to join her brother in the farm work that was their task. Julian gazed after her. 'They're good kids,' he said, as he turned to drive his spade into the earth. 'Worth a hundred Juniors! Funny how some children are made of such good stuff, and others aren't worth a penny. Well, Dick – go to it! This earth is pretty hard. I wish we could borrow one of those machines the men are using up there!'

They dug hard, and were soon very hot indeed. They stripped themselves to their shorts, but were still far too hot. They greeted Anne with joy when she laboured up the slope, carrying a jug of cool lemonade and some buns.

'I say! You've made quite a hole already!' she said. 'How far down do you think the tunnel will be?'

'Well, not too far down, really,' said Dick, taking a long drink of the lemonade. 'This is super, Anne. Thanks a lot. We've dug into the burrow, and we're following it at the moment – hoping it will enter the secret tunnel before we're too tired to dig any more!'

'I say – here comes Junior!' said Anne suddenly, looking up the slope. Sure enough, it was the American boy,

feeling quite brave now that neither Timmy nor Snippet was about.

He stopped a little way away and shouted: 'What do you think you're doing, digging in our hill?'

'Go away and lose yourself!' shouted back Dick. 'This isn't your hill! If you can dig, so can we!'

'Copy-cats!' shouted Junior. 'My pop's laughing his head off about you!'

'Well, tell him to pick it up before it rolls down the hill!' yelled Dick. 'Clear off!'

Junior watched them for a little while, puzzled, and then went off up the hill, presumably to report to his father. Anne laughed and went back to the farmhouse.

'As his pop doesn't know a thing about the secret passage, he must think we're off our heads, digging here,' said Julian, with a chuckle. 'Well, let him think so. He'll be off *his* head with rage when he finds out what we're really doing – and he won't know that till we're in the cellars!'

Dick laughed, and wiped his forehead again. 'I wish this burrow would come to an end. And I hope to goodness it *does* lead into the side of the tunnel. I don't want to have to dig up half the hillside. The ground's so hard and dry.'

'Well, thank goodness it's getting sandy here,' said Julian, driving his spade deeper down. He suddenly gave a cry. 'I say! My spade went right down by itself, then! I believe I've come to the secret passage! The burrow must go right through one side of it!'

He was right! The rabbit hole ran sideways and down – and into a passage! The boys dug feverishly now, panting, their hair falling over their foreheads, perspiration dripping off their faces.

Soon they had a deep hole, fairly wide – and at the bottom of it a way into the tunnel beneath! They lay down and peered into it. 'It's just over a metre below the surface,' said Dick. 'We might have had to do much more digging than this! Whew, I'm hot!'

'It must be dinner-time,' said Julian. 'I don't really like to leave our hole, now that we've got down to the tunnel. And yet we simply *must* have something to eat. I'm ravenous!'

'So am I. But if we leave the hole unguarded, that pest of a Junior might come along and climb down and find the passage!' said Dick. 'Look – here comes George – with old Tim. I wonder if she'd leave him here to guard the hole.'

George was delighted to hear their news. She gazed down the hole in great excitement. 'How deeply you've dug!' she said. 'No wonder you're hot. My word – if Mr Henning knew what you've found, he'd be down here in two shakes of a duck's tail!'

'He certainly would,' said Julian, soberly. 'That's what we're afraid of. Or that snoopy Junior might climb down into the hole, if he came along. He's been here already to see what we're doing.'

'We're scared of going in to dinner, in case one of them comes along and investigates the hole while it's unguarded,' said Dick. 'And we wondered if—'

But George interrupted him, almost as if she knew what he was going to say. 'I'll leave Timmy here on guard, while you come down to dinner,' she said. 'He won't let anyone come within metres of it!'

'Thanks, old thing,' said the boys gratefully, and went off down the hill with George, leaving Timmy behind. 'On guard, Timmy,' said George. 'On guard. Don't let *anyone* come near that hole.'

'Woof,' said Timmy, understanding at once, and looking fiercely all round and about him. He lay down with a small growl. Let anyone come near the boys' hole, if they dare!

They did dare – but when they saw Timmy leaping to his feet, the hackles on his neck thick and upright, and heard his deep, continuous growl, Junior and his father thought better of it, and went on down the hill to have dinner at the farmhouse. Poor Mr Durleston trailed behind them, almost knocked out by the heat of the sun.

'Silly kids,' said Mr Henning to Junior. 'Thinking it's clever to dig just because *we're* digging? What do they suppose they'll find down there? Another kitchen-midden?'

Junior sent a stone scudding along towards Timmy – and then fled for his life as the dog came bounding angrily down the slope. Even Mr Henning hurried. He didn't like Timmy either!

That afternoon the twins, Julian, Dick, George, Anne

and Snippet all climbed the hill to the hole, where Tim still lay watching for intruders. They brought him two fine bones, and a jug of water. He was very pleased indeed. Snippet danced round, hoping for a bite at a bone, and the jackdaw, his wing apparently quite recovered now, dared to go and peck at the bigger bone, even though Timmy growled warningly!

The twins were thrilled to see the deep hole. 'Can't we go down now?' they said eagerly, both together.

'Yes – it would be a jolly good time to let ourselves slide into the tunnel,' said Julian. 'All the men working on the castle site have gone off to have dinner at the little village pub, and haven't yet come back – and the Hennings and Mr Durleston are safely at the farmhouse.'

'I'll go first,' said Dick, and lowered himself into the hole. He held on to the grassy edges and poked hard with his feet, to widen the opening into the tunnel. Then he let himself slide down until his legs were out of the rabbit hole, and dangled through the wall of the tunnel.

'Here we go!' he said, and let himself drop. Whoooooosh! He slid right into a dark, musty tunnel, and landed on soft earth. 'Chuck me down a torch,' he shouted. 'It's pitch-dark in here. Did you remember to bring our torches, George?'

Yes, George had four! 'Look out!' she said. 'Here comes one!' And she dropped it down the hole. She had already switched it on, so Dick saw it coming and caught it neatly. He shone it into the dark place around him.

'Yes! It *is* a tunnel!' he shouted. 'The secret passage, no doubt about it! I say – isn't this great? Come on down, all of you, let's share in the find together. Let's walk right up to the castle cellars. Come on, everybody! Come on!'

CHAPTER SIXTEEN

Up the tunnel and into the cellars

DICK HELD up his torch to the hole, so that the others might see their way. One by one they slid into the dark tunnel, too excited for words. Timmy came too, and so did Snippet, but the jackdaw thought better of it, and remained at the enlarged opening of the burrow, chacking loudly.

The children swung their torches to and fro. 'That must be the way down to the old chapel,' said Julian, his torch shining down the dark tunnel. No one could stand upright just there except Timmy, for the roof was low. He sniffed suspiciously here and there, and kept close to George.

'Well – come on!' said Julian, his voice shaking a little with excitement. 'We'll go straight up, and see where the passage ends. My word – I can hardly wait to see what's at the top!'

They made their way slowly up the passage. There had been roof-falls here and there, but not enough to matter. Tree roots, withered and twining, sometimes caught their feet. 'Funny!' said Harry, in astonishment. 'There aren't any trees growing on the hillside here – why the roots, then?'

'They may be the remains of the roots of long-ago trees that did once grow on the hill,' said Julian, shining his torch up the passage, hoping against hope that there would be no serious obstacle to their journey. 'Hallo – what's this at my feet? *Two feathers!* Now how in the world did *they* get here!'

It was a puzzle! The children examined them earnestly by the light of their torches. Feathers – looking quite new too – how *did* they get there? Was there any other way into the passage – and had the birds found it?

Dick gave a shout of laughter that made everyone jump. 'We're idiots! They're two of the *jackdaw's* feathers – they must have dropped out of his bitten wing when he went down the burrow and up this passage with Snippet after him!'

'Of *course*! Why on earth didn't I think of that?' said Julian. They went on upwards once more, and then Julian suddenly stopped again. A curious humming noise had come down the dark, low tunnel, a throbbing that seemed to get right inside their heads.

'What's that?' said Anne, in great alarm. 'I don't like it.'

They all stood there, and felt, like Anne, that the noise was indeed inside their heads. They shook them, put their fingers into their ears – but it was no good. The strange throbbing went on and on.

'This is a bit too mysterious for me,' said Anne, scared. 'I don't think I want to go on.'

The noise stopped, and they all felt better at once – but almost immediately it started again. To everyone's surprise, George began to laugh.

'It's all right! It's only those men at work on the castle site. It's their drills we can hear – throbbing through the hillside, and down this passage right into our ears. They must be back from lunch. Cheer up, everybody!'

They all smiled in relief, though Anne's hands were still shaking a little as she held up her torch to shine through the black darkness. 'There's not an awful lot of air here,' she said. 'I hope we soon get into the cellars!'

'They can't be far,' said Julian. 'This tunnel goes in a pretty straight line, just as we thought it would. Where it curves, it's probable that the men of long ago who made it were forced to burrow round tree roots that blocked their way. Anyway, as we can hear the drills so loudly now, we can't be far from the castle site.'

They were nearer than they thought! Julian's torch suddenly shone on the remains of a great door, lying on the ground before him – the door that once shut off the cellars from the passage! The tunnel ceased just there, and the torches shone on a vast underground place, silent, full of shadows.

'We're there!' said Julian, in a whisper that went scurrying round in the darkness and came back as a strange echo that said: 'There-there-there-there-there.'

'That fallen door must have been one made all those years gone by!' said Anne, in awe. She touched a corner of it with her foot, and the wood crumbled into dust with a strange little sigh.

Snippet pushed in front of them and ran into the cellars. He gave a short bark as if to say, 'Come on – don't be afraid. *I've* been here before.'

'Oh, Snippet, be careful!' said Anne, half-afraid that everything would crumble away at the sound of Snippet's pattering feet!

'Let's go on – but carefully,' said Julian. 'Everything will be ready to crumble into dust – unless it's made of metal! It's a marvel that door was preserved like that – it looks good enough – but I'm sure if any of us sneezed it would be gone.'

'Don't make me laugh, please, Ju,' said Dick, stepping carefully round the fallen door. 'Even a laugh might do damage down here!'

Soon they were all in the blackness of the underground cellars. They flashed their torches around. 'What a vast place!' said Julian. 'Can't see any dungeons, though!'

'Thank goodness!' said Harriet and Anne together. They had both dreaded coming across old bones of long-forgotten prisoners!

'Look – there's an archway,' said George, shining her torch to the right. 'A fine, semicircular arch it is, too, made of stone – and there's another, look. They must lead into a main underground chamber, I should think. There's nothing much to see just here, except heaps of dirt. It all smells so musty, too!'

'Well, follow me carefully,' said Julian, and led the way towards the stone archways, his torch shining brightly. They came to one of the beautiful rounded arches and stood there, all four torches shining brightly into a large underground room.

'No cellars here – but just one great underground storeroom,' said Julian. 'The roof was shored up with great beams – see, some of them have fallen. And those stone arches must have borne much of the weight, too. Not one of those has fallen! They must have stood there for centuries – what wonderful workmanship!'

Dick and the twins were more interested in the great mass of jumble scattered about round the walls. It was covered with dust that rose lightly into the air when Timmy brushed against anything. Snippet ran round happily, sniffing everywhere, and sneezing every now and again as the fine dust went up his nose.

'Any treasures, do you think?' whispered Anne, and the echo came back weirdly, whispering too.

'Whispers seem to echo back more than our ordinary voices!' said Julian. 'Hallo – what's this?'

They shone their torches on to the floor where lay what looked like a heap of blackened metal. Julian bent down and then gave a loud exclamation. 'Do you see what this is? A suit of armour! Almost perfect still. Look, though, it must be ages old – and here's another – and another! Were they old ones, thrown out – or spare ones? Look at this helmet – *grand*!'

He kicked it gently with his foot, and it gave out a metallic sound and rolled away a little. 'Would that be valuable now?' asked Harry, anxiously.

'Valuable! Worth its weight in gold, I should think!' said Julian, such excitement in his voice that everyone felt even more thrilled. Harriet called to him urgently.

'Julian – here's a chest of some sort. Quick!'

They went slowly over to where she stood, for they had already learnt that any quick movement raised clouds of fine, choking dust. She pointed to a great dark chest, its corners bound with iron, and with iron strapping all round it.

It was made of wood, as black with age as the iron itself. 'What's inside, do you think?' whispered Harriet, and at once her whisper echoed from every corner: 'You think, you think, you think . . .'

Timmy went to sniff at the chest – and to his amazement it disintegrated at once! Slowly, softly, the sides and the great lid fell into dust that settled gently on the ground around. Only the iron corners and strapping were left. It was strange to watch something crumble away before their eyes. Like magic! thought Anne.

As the wooden sides of the chest crumbled, something shone out brightly in the light of the torches – something that moved and slid out of the chest, as the sides fell away – fell with a jingling, clinking, sound, curious to hear in that silent darkness.

The children stared in astonishment, hardly believing their eyes. Anne clutched Julian and made him jump. 'Ju! What is it? Is it gold?'

Julian bent to pick up one of the rolling pieces. 'Yes! It's *gold*. No doubt about it. Gold never tarnishes, it keeps bright for ever. These are gold coins of some sort, treasured and hidden away. There couldn't have been time to take them, when the Lady fled with her children – and no one else would be able to get them, for the castle was burnt down and buried by the falling walls! This hoard of gold must have lain here untouched all these long years.'

'Waiting for *us* to come!' said George. 'Twins – your mother and father needn't worry about their farm any more! With the proceeds from the treasures down here they will be able to buy all the tractors and equipment they could possibly need! Julian, there's another chest, look – like this one, but smaller, and beginning to fall to pieces. Let's see what's inside that! More gold, I hope.'

But the second chest did not hold gold pieces – it held a different kind of treasure! One side had burst open, and its contents had dribbled out.

'Rings!' said Anne, picking up two from the dust in which they lay.

'A golden belt!' said George. 'And look – these tarnished chains must be necklaces, because they're set with blue stones. This must be where the jackdaw found that ring!'

'*We've* found something else, too!' called Harry, his excited voice making everyone jump. 'Look – racks of swords and daggers! Some are beautifully carved, too!'

Clamped to the wall were iron racks, held in place by great iron rods driven deep into the hard earth of the wall. Some had loosened and the racks hung crooked, their knives and swords askew, or lay on the floor. Snippet ran to pick one up – just as he had done before when he and Nosey first went into the cellars by themselves!

'What wonderful swords!' said Julian, picking one up. 'My word, this one's heavy! I can hardly hold it! Good gracious – what's that?'

Something had fallen from the roof of the cellar in which they were standing – a great piece of old wood, that had originally been placed there as part of the roofing. At the same time the continual hum of the drilling above rose to a roar that made the children jump.

Julian gave a shout. 'Out of here, quickly!' he yelled. 'Those men will soon be through the roof, and it may suddenly fall and bury us! We'll have to go at once!'

He snatched a dagger from the rack, and still with the sword in his hand, ran back to the entrance of the secret passage, pulling Anne with him. The twins were last of all, for they had run to get a handful of the gold, and two of the necklaces and rings. They *must* show their mother a few of the treasures, they must!

Just as they reached the entrance, more of the roof fell. 'We'll have to stop this excavating,' panted Julian, looking back. 'If the roof falls in, it may destroy many of the old treasures there!'

They hurried into the dark, low tunnel, feeling more excited than they had ever felt in their lives! Timmy led the way, glad to think they were going out into the open air once more!

'What will Mother say?' the twins kept saying to one another. 'What*ever* will she say!'

CHAPTER SEVENTEEN

Trapped!

THE SIX children stumbled down the tunnel, still hearing the far-off sound of the drills, and fearing that at any moment the cellars would be discovered by Mr Henning, who, no doubt, would be anxiously watching from above!

They came to where they thought the burrow must be, that Dick had dug through – but instead, there was nothing but a great mass of earth, some of it seeping into the tunnel! Julian gazed at it by the light of his torch, dismayed.

'The burrow's fallen in!' he said, his voice shaking. 'What are we to do? We've no spades to dig ourselves out!'

'We can use our hands,' said Dick, and began to scrabble at the fallen earth, sweeping it into the tunnel. But as he scrabbled, more and more earth fell into the widened burrow, and Julian stopped Dick at once. 'No more of that, Dick – you might start an earthfall, and we'd all be buried alive. Oh gosh – this is awful! We'll have to go back up the passage and try to make the men hear us shouting. BLOW! That means Mr Henning will know what we're up to.'

'I don't believe the men will be there much longer,' said Dick, looking at his watch. 'They pack up at five, and it's almost that now. My word, we've been ages – Mrs Philpot will wonder where we all are.'

'The drilling has just stopped,' said Anne. 'I haven't got that awful noise inside my ears any longer.'

'In that case, it's certainly no good going back up the tunnel,' said Julian. 'They'd be gone before we got there. I say, you know – this is serious. I ought to have thought of this – any idiot knows that ground entrances to passages should be strengthened, if they're newly dug!'

'Well, we can always go back to the cellars and wait for the men to come tomorrow,' said George, sounding more cheerful than she felt.

'How do we know they'll be there tomorrow?' said Dick. 'Henning may have paid them off today, if he's disappointed in his hopes!'

'Don't be such a dismal Jimmy!' said George, sensing that the twins were getting panicky. They certainly *were* worried – but more because they were certain that their mother would be scared to death if they didn't come home, than for their own safety.

Timmy had been standing patiently beside George, waiting to get out of the hole. At last, tired of waiting, he trotted away – but *down* the tunnel – not up!

'Timmy! Where are you going?' cried George, and shone her torch on him. He turned his head and looked at her, showing quite clearly by his manner that he was tired of standing about, and intended to find out where the tunnel led!

'Ju, look at Timmy! He wants us to go *down* the tunnel!' cried George. 'Why didn't we think of that?'

'I don't know! I'm afraid I thought it would be a sort of blind alley!' said Julian. 'I fear it will, too. Nobody knows where the chapel entrance to the tunnel is, do they, twins?'

'No,' they said, both together. 'It's never been discovered, as far as *we* know.'

'Anyway, it's worth trying,' said George, her voice sounding muffled as she went down the passage after the impatient Timmy. 'I'm getting suffocated in here!'

The others followed, Snippet dancing along behind, thinking the whole thing was a huge joke. The tunnel, as the children had imagined, went downwards in more or less a straight line. It had fallen in slightly here and there, but by bending their heads and crouching low, they managed to get through. Finally they came to a bad fall of earth from the roof, and had to crawl through on hands and knees. Anne didn't like that part at all!

They came at last into a strange little place, where the tunnel ended abruptly. It was like a stone vault – a little chamber about one and a half metres high and two metres square. Julian looked up fearfully at its low roof. Was it of stone? If so, they were trapped. They would never be able to lift a heavy stone slab!

No – not all the roof was made of stone. A piece in the middle about a metre square was made of strong stout wood, which rested on ledges cut in the stone.

'It looks like a trap-door,' said Julian, examining it by the light of his torch. 'I wonder if we are just below the floor of the old chapel? Dick, if you and I and Harry all heave at the same time, we might be able to move this trap-door.'

So they all heaved, George, too – but although the door did lift a little at one corner, it simply could *not* be moved upwards.

'I know why we can't move it,' said Harry, red in the face with heaving. 'There are sacks of grain and fertiliser and all kinds of stuff spread over the floor of the old chapel! They're heavy as lead! We'd never be able to move that trap-door if two or three sacks are on it!'

'Gosh – I didn't think of that,' said Julian, his heart sinking. 'Didn't you know of this entrance into the tunnel, twins?'

'Of course not!' said Harry. 'Nobody did. I can't think why it wasn't known, though. Except, of course, that a storehouse like this has its floor always covered with sacks of something, and with the spillings out of those sacks! It may not have been cleaned out or swept for hundreds of years!'

'Well, what are we to do now?' demanded Dick. 'We can't stay here in this stuffy little place!'

'Listen – I can hear something!' said George suddenly. 'Noises overhead.'

They listened intently, and, through the tightly fitting oak trap-door above them, they heard a loud voice shouting. 'GIVE US A HAND, BILL, WILL YOU?'

'It's Jamie – the men are working overtime this week!' said Harry. 'He's come to get something out of the chapel. Quick, let's all yell and hammer on the trap-door with whatever we've got that'll make a noise!'

At once there was a riot of sound from the little vault – yells, shouts, barks, and the hammering of sword handles and fists on the wooden slab overhead. Then the children ceased their hammering, and fell silent, listening. They heard Jamie's voice, lifted in wonder.

'Bill! What in the name of goodness was that? A rat-fight, do you suppose?'

'They heard us,' said Julian, excited. 'Come on – once again. And bark the place down, Timmy!'

Timmy was only too ready to oblige, for he was very tired of tunnels and dark, echoing places by now! He barked long and fiercely, frightening Snippet so much that the little poodle actually ran back up the tunnel! What with Tim's barking, and everyone's yelling, and the constant hammering, the noise was even louder than before, and Bill and Jamie listened in amazement.

'Comes from over there,' said Bill. 'Something's going on there. Beats me what it is though. If it were night-time,

I'd think it were ghosties having a game! Come on – we'll have a look.'

The place was so full of sacks that the two men had to clamber over the rows, disturbing the cat and her kittens. She had curled herself round them, scared of the unexpected noise.

'This corner, Bill,' said Jamie, standing on top of two layers of sacks. He put his hands to his mouth and bellowed like a bull.

'ANYONE ABOUT?'

The six below answered frantically at the tops of their voices, Timmy barking too.

'There's a dog barking down there,' said Bill, scratching his head, puzzled, looking down at the sacks as if he thought there might be a dog in one of them.

'A dog! There're folks as well,' said Jamie, astounded. 'Where are they? Can't be under these sacks!'

'Maybe they're in that little old store place we found one day, in the floor,' suggested Bill. 'Remember? Under an old trap-door, it were, that were covered by a great slab of stone. You remember, man!'

'Oh ay,' said Jamie, and then the clamour began again, for the children were now getting near despair. 'Come on, Bill,' said Jamie, hearing the note of urgency, though he couldn't make out a word from below. 'Heave over these here sacks. We've got to get to the bottom of this!'

They heaved a dozen sacks away, and then at last the

trap-door was uncovered. The stone slab that had once hidden it had been taken up some years ago by the two men and now stood against the wall. They had not bothered to replace it, not guessing that the 'little old store place' as they had thought it, was really an entrance to a secret, long-forgotten passage. It was fortunate indeed for the children that only the old wooden trap-door was between them and the men, for if the stone slab had been there too, no sound of their shouting would have been heard in the old chapel above!

'Now for this here trap-door,' said Bill. He tapped on it with his great boot. 'Who's down here?' he demanded, wondering what the answer would be.

'US!' shrieked the twins, and the others joined in, with Timmy barking frantically again.

'Bless us all – that's the twins' voices I heard!' said Jamie. 'How did they climb into the storeroom without moving these here sacks?'

With a great heave the two men pulled up the heavy wooden slab, and looked down in the greatest astonishment at the little crowd below! They couldn't believe their eyes! Timmy was the first out. He leapt upwards and landed beside the men, wagging his great tail and licking them lavishly.

'Oh, thanks, Bill, thanks, Jamie,' cried the twins as the two men pulled them up. 'Gosh, I'm thankful you were working overtime – and happened to come in here!'

'Your ma's been hollering for you,' said Bill,

disapprovingly. 'And didn't you say you were going to help me with those poles?'

'How did you get down there?' demanded Jamie, pulling up the others one by one. Julian was the last, and he handed up poor scared little Snippet, who really felt he had had quite enough adventures for one day!

'Oh – it's too long a story to tell you just now,' said Harry. 'But thanks again most awfully, Bill and Jamie. Can you put that slab back? Don't tell anyone we were down there till we tell you how it happened, see? Now we'll have to rush and tell Mother we're all right!'

And away they all went, longing for tea, tired out, full

of thankfulness at their escape from the little stone room under the chapel floor. What *would* everyone say when they displayed the treasures they had brought back with them?

CHAPTER EIGHTEEN

A great story to tell!

THE TWINS tore down to the farmhouse, and saw their mother still looking for them. They flung themselves on her, and she gave them a loving shake.

'Where have you been? You're an hour late for tea, all of you. I've been so worried. Mr Henning told me some story about you digging up on the hillside!'

'Mother! We're ravenous, so let's have tea and we'll tell you some great news,' said the twins, both together. 'Mother, you *will* be astonished. Where's Dad – and Great-Grandad too?'

'They're still at the tea-table – they were late too,' said Mrs Philpot. 'They've been out looking for you all! Great-Grandad isn't very pleased. What in the world have you brought with you? Surely those are not *swords*?'

'Mother, let's have tea first and we'll tell you *everything*!' said the twins. '*Must* we wash? Oh blow – all right, come on, everyone, let's wash. And we'll put our treasures down in the darkest corner, so that Dad and Great-Grandad won't see them till we're ready to show them!'

Soon they were all sitting down at the tea-table, glad to see a wonderful spread! Great slices of thickly buttered bread, home-made jam, home-made cheese, a fat ginger cake, a fruit cake, a dish of ripe plums, and even a home-cooked ham if anyone wanted something more substantial!

Mr Philpot and old Great-Grandad were still at the table, drinking a last cup of tea. Mrs Philpot had told them that the children had to wash, but would tell all that had happened when they came to their tea.

'Hoo!' said Great-Grandad, frowning till his great bushy eyebrows almost covered his nose. 'When I was a boy I daren't come in one minute late for my meals! You twins have worried your mother – that's bad!'

'We're awfully sorry, Great-Grandad,' said the twins, in unison. 'But just wait till you hear our story. Julian – you tell it!'

And so, between great munches of bread and butter, ham sandwiches, and slices of cake, the story was told, all the children joining in now and again.

Great-Grandad already knew that Mr Henning had been given permission to excavate, and that a cheque for £250 had been given to Mr Philpot. He had flown into a terrible temper, and only when Mrs Philpot had sobbed and said that she would give it back, though she could hardly bear to part with it, had Great-Grandad given in. Now ready to fly into another rage, he listened to the children's story. He forgot to drink his cooling tea. He forgot to fill his pipe. He even forgot to ask a single question! Never had he heard such a wonderful, glorious tale in his life!

Julian told the story well, and the others filled in any

bits he left out. Mrs Philpot's eyes almost fell out of her head when she heard how Snippet and Nosey had gone into the rabbit burrow and come out with a broken dagger and a ring!

'But – but where did . . .' she began, and listened again, to hear how Dick and Julian had enlarged the burrow, crawled right through it, and slid down into the long-lost secret tunnel!

'HA!' said Great-Grandad, getting out his great red handkerchief, and dabbing his forehead with it. 'HA! Wish I'd been there. Go on, go on!'

Julian had stopped to drink his tea. He laughed and went on, describing how they had all gone up the tunnel with their torches, the dogs with them.

'It was dark and smelly, and suddenly we heard a terrific noise!' he said.

'It got right inside our heads!' put in Anne.

'What was it, what was it?' said Great-Grandad, his eyes almost as big as the saucer in front of him.

'The noise of the men drilling up on the old castle site,' said Julian, and Great-Grandad exploded in wrath. He pointed his pipe at his grandson, the farmer. 'Didn't I tell you I wouldn't have those men on my farm?' he began, and then calmed down as Mrs Philpot patted his arm, shushing him. 'Go on, Julian,' she said.

And then came the really exciting part, the story of how they came into the actual cellars of the castle – the stone archways – the age-old dust . . .

'And the echoes!' said Anne. 'When we whispered, a hundred other whispers came back!'

When Julian described their finds – the old armour, still good, but black with age – the rack of swords and knives and daggers – the chest of gold . . .

'GOLD! I don't believe you!' shouted Great-Grandad. 'You're making that up, young man. Don't you pile up your tale too much, now. Stick to the truth.'

The twins promptly took some of the gold coins out of their pockets, still brilliant and shining. They laid them on the table in front of the three amazed grown-ups.

'There you are! *They* will tell you if we are making up

all this or not – these gold coins! They will speak more loudly than words!'

In awe Mr Philpot picked them up, and passed them one by one to the old man, and to his wife. Great-Grandad was astounded and speechless. He simply could not say a single word. He could only grunt and puff as he turned the coins over in his great horny hand.

'Are they really gold?' said Mrs Philpot, quite overcome at the sudden appearance of the shining coins. 'Trevor – will they belong to *us*? Does it mean – does it mean that we'll be well enough off to buy a new tractor for you – and . . .'

'Depends how much of this stuff there is, up in those old cellars,' said Mr Philpot, trying to keep calm. 'And depends on how much we're allowed to keep, of course. Might belong to the Crown by now.'

'THE CROWN!' roared Great-Grandad, standing up suddenly. 'The CROWN! No, SIR! It's mine! Ours! Found on my land, put there by our ancestors. Yes – and I'll give old Mr Finniston down in the village a share, so I will. He's been a good friend of mine for years!'

The children thought that was quite a good idea! They then showed the jewellery they had brought, and Mrs Philpot marvelled at it, tarnished though it was.

But the swords and dagger brought the greatest excitement to old Great-Grandad and his grandson, Mr Philpot! As soon as they heard that the children had actually brought back some of the old weapons, the two men got up and went to get them. Great-Grandad picked up the biggest and heaviest of the swords, and swung it dangerously round his head, looking like a reincarnation of some fearsome old warrior, with his great beard and blazing eyes.

'No, no, Grandad!' said Mrs Philpot in fright. 'Oh, you'll knock down the things on the dresser – there, I knew you would! Bang goes my meat dish!'

And down it went, CRASH! Timmy and Snippet almost jumped out of their skins, and began to bark frantically.

'Sit DOWN, all of you!' cried Mrs Philpot to the excited dogs and the men. 'Let Julian finish his story! Great-Grandad, SIT DOWN!'

'Ha,' said Great-Grandad, a broad smile on his face, sitting down in his chair. 'HA! Did me good to swing that sword. Where's that American? I might try it out on him!'

The children roared with delight. It was great to see the old man so delighted. 'Go on with that tale of yours,' he said to Julian. 'You tell it well, boy. Go on! Now, Ma, don't you take my sword away. I'm keeping it here, between my legs, in case I want to use it. HA!'

Julian quickly finished his tale, and told how they had walked back down the passage and found their burrow entrance fallen in – and then gone right down the rest of the tunnel and come at last into the little stone-walled room.

'And we couldn't get out,' said Julian. 'There was a

great wooden trap-door over our heads, and on it lay a dozen or so sacks – heavy as lead! We couldn't lift it. So we yelled!'

'So *that's* where the secret passage led to!' said Mr Philpot. 'How did you get out?'

'We yelled and hammered, and Bill and Jamie heard us, and pulled off the sacks, and lifted up the old trapdoor,' said Julian. 'Gosh, we were glad to see them! We thought we might be lost for ever! Jamie knew about the little stone vault down under the chapel floor – but he thought it was just an old storeroom!'

'I've never heard of it before,' said Mrs Philpot, and old Great-Grandad nodded his head in agreement.

'No more have I,' he said. 'For as long as I can remember the floor of that old chapel has been piled with sacks, and what bits I could see of the floor were covered with thick dust. Yes, even when I was a boy, playing hide and seek in the old place, it was full of sacks – and that's every bit of eighty-five years ago now! Well, well – seems like yesterday I was playing in there with a cat and her kittens!'

'There's a cat and her kittens there now,' said Anne.

'Ay, little lass – and there'll be a cat and her kittens there when you're an old, old woman!' said Great-Grandad. 'There's some things never change, thanks be to the Lord. Well, well – I can sleep easy of a night now – I reckon you and the farm will be all right, Trevor, with the money you'll make out of those old finds – and I'll live to see the twins growing up and handling the finest farm in Dorset, so I shall – with everything newfangled they want, bless their bonny faces! And now I'll just have one more swing with that sword!'

The children fled! Great-Grandad looked years younger already – and goodness knows *what* damage he would do with that great sword! What an afternoon it had been – one they would never forget!

CHAPTER NINETEEN

'The most exciting adventure we've ever had!'

AFTER ALL the excitement of the afternoon the children felt lazy. The twins went off to feed the chickens. 'Better late than never!' they said, together.

'Where are Mr Henning and Mr Durleston and that awful Junior, Mrs Philpot?' asked George, getting up to help with the washing of the tea-things.

'Oh, Mr Henning came in to say he and Mr Durleston were going to a meal at a hotel, and taking Junior too,' said Mrs Philpot. 'He seemed very pleased with himself indeed. He said that they had broken through to the cellars of the old castle, and expected great things – and that maybe a second cheque of £250 would be coming soon!'

'You won't take it, though, will you, Mrs Philpot?' said Julian quickly, overhearing what was being said. 'The things down in that cellar will be worth much more than any money Mr Henning is likely to offer you. He'd only take them to America and sell them for vast sums and make a huge profit. Why should you let him do that?'

'That nice old man, Mr Finniston, down in the little antique shop, would know what everything was worth,' said George. 'And he's a descendant of the long-ago

Finnistons of Finniston Castle, isn't he – he'll be thrilled to bits when he hears what's been happening!'

'We'll send word for him to come up tomorrow,' decided Mrs Philpot. 'After all, Mr Henning has *his* adviser – that surly Mr Durleston. We'll have Mr Finniston for ours. Great-Grandad would be pleased about that – they're great friends, those two.'

There was, however, no need to send for Mr Finniston, for Great-Grandad had himself gone down straight away to tell the great news to his old crony. What a talk they had together!

'Gold coins – jewellery – suits of armour – swords – and goodness knows what else!' said Great-Grandad for

the twentieth time, and old Mr Finniston listened gravely, nodding his head. 'That splendid big sword!' went on Grandad, remembering. 'Just right for me, William! Look, if ever I've lived before, that old sword once belonged to me! I feel it! That's one thing I won't sell, mind! I'll keep it just for the sake of swinging it round my head, when I lose my temper!'

'Yes, yes – but I hope you'll be sure to stand in the middle of an empty room if you do that,' said Mr Finniston, a little alarmed at the fierce look in the old man's eye. 'You won't be allowed to keep all the gold, I'm afraid – there's such a thing as treasure trove, you know – some finds go to the Crown, and I fear that will be one of them. And the jewellery too perhaps. But you'll get the value back; and the suits of armour and the swords – you'll be able to make a mint of money on those!'

'Enough for *two* new tractors?' said Great-Grandad. 'Enough for a new Land Rover? That one my grandson has, it jolts every bone in my body! Look now, William – we've got to get men digging on that site – uncovering all those cellars. What say we keep on the men that fellow Henning's got? We shan't let *him* excavicate, or whatever it's called, any more. HA! That fellow gets under my skin, and sets me itching all over. Now I can scratch him out! And see here, William, you'll shut up this shop of yours and be my adviser, won't you? I won't have that American talking me down – or that fellow Durleston!'

'*You'd* better stop talking for a bit, Grandad, you're

getting too red in the face,' said Mr Finniston. 'You'll go pop if you excite yourself much more! Go home now, and I'll be up tomorrow morning. I'll arrange about the workmen too. And don't you play about with that old sword too much – you might cut off somebody's head by mistake!'

'So I might, so I might,' said Great-Grandad, with a sly look in his eye. 'Now, if that Junior got in the way when I was swinging my sword . . . it's all right, William, it's all right! Just my joke, you know, just my joke!'

And chuckling deep down in his long beard, Great-Grandad strode off, turned up the little lane, and walked back to the farmhouse, feeling very pleased indeed with life!

Mr Henning, Mr Durleston and Junior did not come back that night. Apparently they were all so excited over the excavations they had made in the drilling down through the cellar roof, that they stayed too long at the hotel and decided to spend the night there, much to Mrs Philpot's relief.

'Most farm people like to go to bed about nine o'clock,' said Mr Henning, 'and it's already gone that now. We'll go over tomorrow morning and we'll get them to sign that agreement you've drawn up, Durleston. They're so short of money they'd sign anything. And mind you cry down what we think we've found, so that they won't expect any *more* than £250. We're going to make our fortunes over this!'

So, next morning, the two men, with an excited Junior whom Mr Durleston found most annoying, arrived at the farmhouse at about ten o'clock. They had telephoned to say they would be there then, and would bring the agreement with them, '. . . and the cheque, Mrs Philpot, the cheque!' purred Mr Henning down the phone.

When they arrived there was quite a company there to greet them! There was old Great-Grandad, his grandson Mr Philpot and his wife, the twins, of course, and old Mr Finniston, sniffing a fight, his dull eyes bright this morning for the first time in years! He sat at the back, wondering what was going to happen.

All the Five were there too, Timmy wondering what the excitement was. He kept as close to George as he could, and growled at Snippet every time the excited little poodle came near. Snippet didn't mind! He could always growl back!

A car purred up the drive, and in came Mr Henning, Mr Durleston and Junior, whose face was one big grin.

'Hallo, folks!' said Junior, in his usual jaunty manner. 'How's tricks?'

Nobody answered except Timmy, and he gave a small growl, which made Junior skip out of the way quickly. 'You shut up,' he said to Timmy.

'Did you have your breakfast in bed at the hotel, little boy?' said George suddenly. 'Do you remember the last time you had it in bed here, and Timmy pulled . . .'

'Aw shucks!' said Junior, sulkily. 'Skip it, sister!' He

subsided after that, and sat down by his father. Then began a short, sharp and satisfactory meeting – from Mr Philpot's point of view!

'Er – Mr Philpot – it's my very great pleasure to say that I have been advised by Mr Durleston to offer you a further cheque for £250,' said Mr Henning smoothly. 'While we are rather *disappointed* in what appears to be in the cellars of the castle, we feel it would only be fair to offer you the sum we suggested before. Is that right, Mr Durleston?'

'Absolutely,' said Mr Durleston in a business-like voice, and glared round through his horn-rimmed glasses. 'I've the agreement here. Mr Henning is being very generous. Very. The cellars are *most* disappointing.'

'I'm sorry about that,' said Mr Philpot. 'I hold a different opinion – and my adviser, Mr Finniston, upholds me in this. We are going to excavate the site ourselves, Mr Henning – and then, if any disappointment lies in wait, *we* shall be the ones to suffer, not you.'

'What's all this?' said Mr Henning, glaring round. 'Durleston, what do you say to that? Bit of double-crossing, isn't it?'

'Offer him £500,' said Mr Durleston, looking startled at this unexpected set-back.

'You can offer me five thousand if you like, but I tell you, I prefer to do the excavation myself on my own land,' said Mr Philpot. 'What is more, I will return the cheque you gave me yesterday – and as I intend to keep on the men you engaged, I will pay them myself for their work. So do not trouble to dismiss them. They will now be working for *me*.'

'But this is MONSTROUS!' shouted Mr Henning, losing his temper, and jumping to his feet. He banged on the table, and glared at Mr and Mrs Philpot. 'What do you expect to find in those derelict old cellars? We drilled right through yesterday, and there's practically *nothing* there! I made you a very generous offer. I'll raise it to a thousand pounds!'

'No,' said Mr Philpot, quietly. But Great-Grandad had had enough of Mr Henning's shouting and raging. He stood up too, and bellowed so loudly that everyone jumped, and Timmy began to bark. Snippet at once fled to the kitchen cupboard and hid there.

'HA! NOW YOU LISTEN TO ME!' bellowed Great-Grandad. 'This farm belongs to ME, and my GRANDSON, and it'll go to my GREAT-GRANDSON, sitting yonder. A finer farm there never was, and my family's had it for hundreds of years – and sad it's been for me to see it go downhill for lack of money! But now I see money, much money – down in those cellars! HA! All the money we want for tractors and bailers and combines and the Lord knows what! We don't want *your* money. No, SIR! You keep your dollars, you keep them. Offer me a *five* thousand if you like, and see what I'll say!'

Mr Henning turned swiftly and looked at Mr Durleston, who at once nodded. 'Right!' said the American to Great-Grandad. 'Five thousand! Done?'

'NO!' bawled Great-Grandad, enjoying himself more than he had done for years. 'There's *gold* down in those

cellars – jewels – suits of armour – swords, daggers, knives – all of them centuries old . . . and . . .'

'Don't hand *me* stories like that,' said Mr Henning, sneeringly. 'You old liar!'

Great-Grandad banged his clenched fist down on the table and made everyone almost fall off their chairs. 'TWINS!' he roared. 'Fetch those things you got yesterday – go on, fetch them here. I'll show this American I'm no liar!'

And then, before the astounded eyes of Mr Henning and Mr Durleston, and of Junior, too, the twins laid the gold coins, the jewellery, and the swords and knives on the table. Mr Durleston stared as if he couldn't believe his eyes.

'Well – what do you say to *that*?' demanded Great-Grandad, banging on the table again.

Mr Durleston sat back and said one word. 'Junk!'

Then it was old Mr Finniston's turn to stand up and say a few words! Mr Durleston, who hadn't noticed the quiet old man sitting at the back, was horrified to see him there. He knew he was learned and knowledgeable, for he himself had tried to pick his brains about the old castle site.

'Ladies and gentlemen,' said Mr Finniston, just as if he were addressing a well-conducted meeting, 'I regret to say that, speaking as well-known antiquarian, I do not consider that Mr Durleston knows what he is talking about if he calls these articles junk! The things on the table are worth a small fortune to any genuine collector. I could myself sell them in London tomorrow, for far more than any sum Mr Durleston has advised Mr Henning to offer. Thank you, ladies and gentlemen!'

And he sat down, bowing courteously to the assembled company. Anne felt as if she wanted to clap him!

'Well, I don't think there's any more to say,' said Mr Philpot, getting up. 'If you'll tell me what hotel you'll be staying at, Mr Henning, I'll have your things sent there. You will certainly not wish to stay here any longer!'

'Pop, I don't *wanna* go, I wanna stay here!' howled Junior, most surprisingly. 'I wanna see the cellars exca-exculpated! I wanna dig down! I wanna STAY!'

'Well, we don't *want* you!' said Harry, fiercely. 'You and your peeping and prying and listening and boasting and tale-bearing. Cissy-boy! Breakfast in bed! Can't clean his shoes! Howls when he can't get his own way! Screams when . . .'

'That's enough, Harry,' said his mother sternly, looking quite shocked. 'I don't mind Junior staying on if he'll behave himself. It's not his fault that all this has happened.'

'I wanna *stay*!' wept Junior, and kicked out peevishly under the table. He unfortunately caught Timmy on the nose, and the dog rose in anger, growling and showing his teeth. Junior fled for his life.

'Do you *wanna* stay now?' shouted George, as he went, and the answer came back at once.

'NO!'

'Well, thanks, Timmy, for helping him to make up his mind,' said George, and patted the big dog.

Mr Henning looked as if he were about to burst. 'If that dog bites my boy, I'll have him put to sleep,' he said. 'I'll sue you, I'll . . .'

'Please go,' said Mrs Philpot, suddenly looking tired out. 'I have a lot of baking to do.'

'I shall take my time,' said Mr Henning, pompously. 'I will *not* be turned out suddenly, as if I hadn't paid my bills.'

'Seen this sword, Henning?' said old Great-Grandad, suddenly, and snatched from the table the big sword that he so much liked. 'Beauty, isn't it? The men of old knew how to deal with their enemies, didn't they? They swung at them like this – and like THAT – and . . .'

'Here, stop! You're dangerous! That sword nearly cut me!' cried Mr Henning, in a sudden panic. 'WILL you put it down?'

'No. It's mine. I'm not selling this,' said Great-Grandad, swinging the sword again. It hit the light-bulb above his head, and the glass fell with a clatter. Mr Durleston deserted Mr Henning and fled out of the kitchen at top speed, colliding violently with Bill, who was just coming in.

'Look out – he's mad – that old man's mad!' shouted Mr Durleston. 'Henning, come along before he cuts off your head!'

Mr Henning fled too. Great-Grandad pursued him to the

door, breathing blood and thunder, and the two dogs barked in delight. Everyone began to laugh helplessly.

'Grandad – what's got into you?' said Mr Philpot, as the old fellow swung the sword again, his eyes bright, a broad grin on his wrinkled old face.

'Nothing! I just thought that only this sword would get rid of those fellows. Do you know what *I* call them? JUNK! Ha – wish I'd thought of that when they were here! JUNK! William Finniston, did you hear that?'

'Now you put that sword down before you damage it,' said Mr Finniston, who knew how to manage Great-Grandad, 'and you and I will go down to the old inn and talk over what we're going to do about all this treasure trove. You just put that sword down first – NO, Grandad, I am NOT going to take you into the inn carrying that sword!'

Mrs Philpot heaved a sigh of relief when the two old fellows went off down the lane, leaving the sword safely behind. She sat down, and, to the children's horror, began to cry!

'Now, now – don't take any notice of me!' she said, when the twins ran to her in dismay. 'I'm crying for joy – to have got rid of them – and to know I've not got to pinch and scrape any more – or to take in visitors. To think that your dad can buy the farm machinery he wants – and . . . oh dear, what a baby I am, acting like this!'

'I say, Mrs Philpot – would you like *us* to leave too?' asked Anne, suddenly realising that she and the others were ranked as 'visitors', and must have been an added burden for poor Mrs Philpot.

'Oh no, my dear, no – you're not really visitors, you're *friends*!' said Mrs Philpot, smiling through her tears. 'And what's more I shan't charge your mothers a single penny for having you here – see what good fortune you've brought us!'

'All right – we'll stay. We'd love to,' said Anne. 'We wouldn't miss seeing what else is down in those castle cellars for anything. Would we, George?'

'Gosh, no!' said George. 'We want to be in on everything. This is just about the most exciting adventure we've ever had!'

'We always say that!' said Anne. 'But the nice part about this one is – it isn't finished yet! We'll be able to go and watch the workmen and their drills. We'll be able to help in moving all the exciting old things out of their hiding-places – we'll hear what prices you get for them – and see the new tractor! Honestly, I really do believe the *second* part of this adventure will be better than the first! Don't you think so, Timmy?'

'WOOF!' said Timmy, and wagged his tail so hard that he knocked Snippet right over.

Well, goodbye, Five! Enjoy the rest of your adventures, and have a good time – and *do* make sure that Grandad is careful with that great old sword!

Join the adventure!

If you can't wait to explore further with **THE FAMOUS FIVE**, read the next book in the series:

Do you want to solve a mystery?

Enid Blyton

The Secret Seven

Join Peter, Janet, Jack, Barbara, Pam, Colin, George and Scamper as they solve puzzles and mysteries, foil baddies, and rescue people from danger – all without help from the grown-ups. Enid Blyton wrote fifteen stories about the Secret Seven. These editions contain brilliant illustrations by Tony Ross, plus extra fun facts and stories to read and share.

Enid Blyton®

is one of the most popular children's authors of all time. Her books have sold over 500 million copies and have been translated into other languages more often than any other children's author.

Enid Blyton adored writing for children. She wrote over 700 books and about 2,000 short stories. *The Famous Five* books, now 75 years old, are her most popular. She is also the author of other favourites including *The Secret Seven*, *The Magic Faraway Tree*, *Malory Towers* and *Noddy*.

Born in London in 1897, Enid lived much of her life in Buckinghamshire and loved dogs, gardening and the countryside. She was very knowledgeable about trees, flowers, birds and animals. Dorset – where some of the Famous Five's adventures are set – was a favourite place of hers too.

Illustration by Laura Ellen Anderson.

Enid Blyton's stories are read and loved by millions of children (and grown-ups) all over the world. Visit enidblyton.co.uk to discover more.

THE FAMOUS FIVE

FIVE GO TO DEMON'S ROCKS

Have you read all THE FAMOUS FIVE books?

1. Five on a Treasure Island
2. Five Go Adventuring Again
3. Five Run Away Together
4. Five Go to Smuggler's Top
5. Five Go Off in a Caravan
6. Five on Kirrin Island Again
7. Five Go Off to Camp
8. Five Get Into Trouble
9. Five Fall Into Adventure
10. Five on a Hike Together
11. Five Have a Wonderful Time
12. Five Go Down to the Sea
13. Five Go to Mystery Moor
14. Five Have Plenty of Fun
15. Five on a Secret Trail
16. Five Go to Billycock Hill
17. Five Get Into a Fix
18. Five on Finniston Farm
19. Five Go to Demon's Rocks
20. Five Have a Mystery to Solve
21. Five Are Together Again

The Famous Five Colour Short Stories

1. Five and a Half-Term Adventure
2. George's Hair is Too Long
3. Good Old Timmy
4. A Lazy Afternoon
5. Well Done, Famous Five
6. Five Have a Puzzling Time
7. Happy Christmas, Five
8. When Timmy Chased the Cat

Enid Blyton®

THE FAMOUS FIVE

FIVE GO TO DEMON'S ROCKS

Illustrated by Eileen A. Soper

HODDER CHILDREN'S BOOKS

First published in Great Britain in 1961 by Hodder & Stoughton
This edition published in 2016

20

A CIP catalogue record for this book is available from the British Library.

ISBN 978 1 444 93649 0

Printed and bound in Great Britain by Clays Ltd, Elcograf S.p.A.

The paper and board used in this book are made from wood from responsible sources.

Hodder Children's Books
An imprint of
Hachette Children's Group
Part of Hodder & Stoughton
Carmelite House
50 Victoria Embankment
London EC4Y 0DZ

An Hachette UK Company
www.hachette.co.uk
www.hachettechildrens.co.uk

CONTENTS

1 THREE VISITORS ARRIVE 1
2 A LITTLE EXCITEMENT 8
3 MISCHIEF, TINK – AND TIMMY! 16
4 TINK HAS A WONDERFUL IDEA 24
5 TINK'S LIGHTHOUSE 32
6 MAKING PLANS 39
7 OFF AT LAST! 47
8 THERE'S THE LIGHTHOUSE! 54
9 INSIDE THE LIGHTHOUSE! 62
10 SETTLING IN 70
11 JEREMIAH BOOGLE 78
12 JEREMIAH'S TALE 86
13 A PLEASANT MORNING – AND A SHOCK! 94
14 THE OLD, OLD MAP 103
15 JACOB IS IN TROUBLE 113
16 DOWN IN THE CAVES 121
17 MISCHIEF AGAIN – AND A SURPRISE! 131
18 BACK IN THE LIGHTHOUSE – AND AN EXCITING TALK! 140
19 A NASTY SHOCK! 148

20 DOWN THE SHAFT AND
INTO THE TUNNEL 157
21 A WONDERFUL IDEA 169
22 THE END OF THE ADVENTURE 179

CHAPTER ONE

Three visitors arrive

'FANNY!' SHOUTED Uncle Quentin, running up the stairs with a letter in his hand. 'FANNY! Where are you?'

'Here, dear, here, helping Joanna with the dusting,' said Aunt Fanny, appearing out of a bedroom. 'Don't shout like that. What's the matter?'

'I've a letter here from that old friend of mine, Professor Hayling,' said Uncle Quentin. 'You remember him, don't you?'

'Do you mean the man who came here to stay a few years ago, and kept forgetting to come in for meals?' said Aunt Fanny, flicking some dust off her husband's coat.

'Fanny, don't flick at me like that,' said Uncle Quentin crossly. 'Anyone would think I was covered in dust. Listen – he's coming to stay today. He's going to stay for a week.'

Aunt Fanny stared at her husband in horror. 'But he *can't* do that!' she said. 'George is coming home today – and her three cousins with her, to stay. You know that!'

'Oh – I'd forgotten,' said Uncle Quentin. 'Well, ring up and tell George to stay where she is – we can't have them while Professor Hayling is here. I shall want to be quite undisturbed – he and I have to confer about some new invention of his. Don't look like that, my dear – this may be very, very important.'

'Well, it's important to the Five that *their* plans shouldn't be spoilt,' said Aunt Fanny. 'After all, George only went to stay with Dick, Julian and Anne because you had some urgent papers to write, and you didn't want to be disturbed – and you *knew* today was the day they were due home. Quentin, you must ring up your professor friend and say he can't come.'

'Very well, my dear, very well,' said Uncle Quentin. 'But he won't like it. He won't like it at all!' He went off to his study to use the telephone, and Aunt Fanny hurried up the stairs to get ready the rooms for the four cousins.

'Anne can sleep with George as usual,' she said to Joanna. 'And the two boys can sleep in the guest room.'

'It will be nice to have all the Five back again,' said Joanna, pushing the vacuum cleaner up and down the landing. 'I miss them – and you should see the cakes I made yesterday – two whole tins full!'

'You're too good to those children, Joanna,' said Aunt Fanny. 'No wonder they're so fond of you. Now, we'll – oh dear – there's my husband calling me again. All right, dear, I'm coming, I'm coming!'

She ran downstairs to the hall, and into the study. Uncle Quentin was standing there, holding the telephone receiver. 'What shall I do?' he almost shouted. 'Professor Hayling has left and is already on his way here. I can't stop him coming. And he's bringing his son with him, so there are two of them.'

'His *son*! Well, really!' said Aunt Fanny. 'There isn't room for them here, with the four cousins as well, Quentin. You know that.'

'Well, ring up George and tell *her* not to come back for a week, but to stay with her cousins,' said Uncle Quentin, crossly. 'There's no reason why they should ALL come here.'

'But, Quentin, you *know* perfectly well that George's aunt and uncle are shutting up the house today, and going on a cruise somewhere,' said Aunt Fanny. 'Oh dear, oh dear! Well, I'll ring up George, and try to stop them all coming!'

So once more the telephone was used, and Aunt Fanny tried anxiously to get in touch with George. For a long time nobody answered, and then at last a voice came. 'Hallo – who's there?'

'Mrs Kirrin here – may I speak to George, please?'

'Oh – I'm sorry – they've already left, on their bicycles,' said the voice. 'And the house is empty except for me. I'm a neighbour come in to lock everything up. I'm so sorry I can't get George for you.'

'Oh – thank you. Never mind!' said Aunt Fanny, and put back the receiver. She gave a heavy sigh. NOW what was to be done? Professor Hayling and his son were on their way to Kirrin Cottage – and so were the Five – and none of them could be stopped. What a household it would be!

'Quentin,' she said, going into the study where her

husband was tidying up enormous piles of papers. 'Quentin, listen – George and all the others are on their way here. And *how* I am going to put everyone up, I do not know. It looks as if somebody will have to sleep in Timmy's kennel, and I've a good mind to make a bed up for *you* in the coal-house!'

'I'm busy,' said Uncle Quentin, hardly listening. 'I've all these papers to get in order before Professor Hayling comes. And by the way, my dear, will you *please* tell the children to be quiet while the professor is here – he's rather short-tempered, and . . .'

'Quentin, *I'm* beginning to feel rather short-tempered too,'

said Aunt Fanny. 'And if . . .' She stopped very suddenly and gazed through the study window in horror. Then she pointed her finger at it. 'Look! What's that at the window?'

Her husband turned and stared in amazement. 'It looks like a *monkey*!' he said. 'Where on earth did it come from?'

A voice called down the stairs. It was Joanna. 'There's a car at the door – I think it's your visitors – a man and a boy!'

Aunt Fanny was still staring in astonishment at the monkey, who was now scratching at the window-pane, chattering in a funny little prattle. He pressed his nose to the glass, just like a child.

'Don't tell me that your friend owns a monkey – and has brought *him* to stay too!' groaned poor Aunt Fanny. She jumped as a loud bang came from the front door, and went to open it.

Yes – there stood Professor Hayling, the man who had so often forgotten to come in for meals when he had stayed at Kirrin Cottage years before. And by him was a boy of about nine, with a face a little like that of the monkey now on his shoulder!

The professor strode in, calling to the taxi driver behind. 'Bring the luggage in, please. Hallo, Mrs Kirrin – nice to see you again. Where's your husband? My word, I've some interesting news to tell him. Ah, Quentin, there you are! Got your papers all ready for me?'

'My dear old friend!' said Uncle Quentin, shaking hands warmly. 'Fine to see you! So glad you could come.'

'This is Tink, my son,' said Professor Hayling, clapping

the boy on the back, and almost knocking him over. 'I always forget what his real name is – we call him Tink because he's always tinkering with cars – mad on them, you know! Shake hands, Tink. Where's Mischief?'

Poor Aunt Fanny hadn't been able to get in a word. The professor was now in the hall, still talking. The monkey leapt off the boy's shoulder, and was on the hallstand, swinging on a hat-peg.

'Really, it's like a circus!' thought poor Aunt Fanny. 'And the rooms not prepared yet – and what about lunch? Oh my goodness – and all the cousins coming as well. What *is* that monkey doing now? Making faces at himself in the hall mirror!'

Somehow or other the visitors were pushed into the living room, and they sat down. Uncle Quentin was so anxious to discuss some mighty problems with the professor that he actually fetched a great sheaf of papers and immediately spread them over the table.

'*Not* in here, dear – in your study, please,' said Aunt Fanny, firmly. 'Joanna! Will you help me take the bags up to the guest room? And we can make up a bed there on the couch for the little boy. There won't be room anywhere else.'

'What about the monkey?' asked Joanna, eyeing it warily. 'Is he to have a bed too?'

'He sleeps with me,' said Tink, in an astonishingly loud voice, and suddenly leapt up the stairs, making a most extraordinary purring noise as he went. Mrs Kirrin stared after him in amazement.

'Is he in pain, or something?' she said.

'No, no – he's just being a car,' said his father. 'I told you he was mad about cars. He can't help pretending to be one now and again.'

'I'm a car, a Jaguar car!' yelled Tink, from the top of the stairs. 'Can't you hear my engine! R-R-R-R-R-R-R! Hey, Mischief, come and have a ride!'

The little monkey scampered up the stairs and leapt on to the boy's shoulder, chattering in its funny little voice. The Jaguar car then apparently made a tour of all the bedrooms, occasionally giving a very loud honk.

'Does your boy always behave like that?' asked Uncle Quentin, amazed. 'How do you manage to do any work?'

'Oh, I have a soundproof workroom in my garden,' said the professor. 'I hope your workroom is soundproof, too?'

'No, it isn't,' said poor Uncle Quentin, still hearing the 'car' upstairs. What a boy! How could anyone bear him for more than two minutes? And to think he had come to STAY!

He shut the study door after the professor – but no door could shut out the sound of the small boy honking upstairs!

Poor Aunt Fanny was eyeing all the luggage brought in. Why hadn't the professor gone to a hotel? What was life going to be like, with the Five here, and the professor, and a small boy who apparently thought he was some kind of car all the time. To say nothing of a monkey called Mischief! And *where* were they all going to sleep?

CHAPTER TWO

A little excitement

GEORGE AND her three cousins were already on their way back to Kirrin. They cycled along the lanes with Timmy, George's dog, loping easily beside them.

'Won't it be fun to be at Kirrin Cottage again!' said Anne. 'It's so lovely to look out of a window and see Kirrin Bay, blue as the sky! I vote we go over to the island for a picnic!'

'You'll like to have your own kennel again, won't you, Timmy?' said George, and Timmy gave her ankle a quick lick, and barked.

'It's always so peaceful at Kirrin Cottage,' said Dick. 'And your mother's so kind and jolly, George. I hope we shan't upset Uncle Quentin with our talk and fun.'

'I don't *think* Father has any very important work on hand,' said George. 'Anyway, he'll only have you for a week – it's a pity that professor friend of his is coming in a week's time, or you could have stayed longer.'

'Well, a week is quite a nice long time,' said Julian. 'Hallo – there's our first glimpse of Kirrin Bay, look – as blue as ever!'

They were all glad to see the little blue bay, and to catch sight of Kirrin Island lying there peacefully in the sun.

'You're lucky, George, to have an island all of your own,' said Anne. 'One that is really and truly yours!'

'Yes, I *am* lucky!' said George. 'I was never so pleased in all my life as the day Mother gave it to me. It's belonged to our family for years, of course – and now it's mine! We'll go over there tomorrow!'

At last they came to the end of their journey. 'I can see the chimneys of Kirrin Cottage!' said Julian, standing up on the pedals of his bicycle. 'And the kitchen fire is going – I can see smoke. I hope dinner's cooking!'

'I can smell it!' said Dick, sniffing. 'I think it's sausages.'

'Idiot!' said the other three together, and laughed. They rode up to the back gate, and leapt off their bicycles. They put them into the shed, and George gave a shout!

'Mother! We're *home*! Where are you?'

She had hardly finished yelling when Anne suddenly clutched her arm.

'George – what's that? Look! Peeping out of the window there!'

They all looked – and George shouted in astonishment: 'It's a monkey! A MONKEY! No, Timmy. No – come back! TIMMY!'

But Timmy too had seen the quaint little face peering out of the window, and had shot off to investigate. Was it a small dog? Or a strange sort of cat? Anyway, whatever it was, he was going to chase it away! He barked at the top of his voice as he galloped indoors, and almost knocked over a small boy there. The monkey, terrified, at once leapt

on to the picture-rail than ran round the room.

'You leave my monkey alone, you big bully, you!' cried a furious voice; and through the open door George saw a small boy give Timmy a sharp smack. She raced indoors, and gave the small boy a smack as sharp as the one he had given Timmy! Then she glared at him angrily.

'What are you doing here? How DARE you hit my dog? It's a good thing he didn't eat you up. And what's that creature doing up there?'

The little monkey was terrified. It sat clinging to the picture-rail, trembling, making a piteous chattering noise. Julian came in just as Joanna arrived from upstairs.

'What's all this?' she said. 'You'll have your father racing out of his study in a minute, George. Stop barking at the little monkey, Timmy, for goodness' sake! And stop crying, Tink, and take your monkey away before Timmy eats him.'

'I'm *not* crying,' said Tink fiercely, rubbing his eyes. 'Come here, Mischief. I won't let that dog hurt you! I'll – I'll . . .'

'You take your monkey away,' said Julian gently, thinking that the small boy was very brave to imagine he could fight old Timmy. 'Run along.'

Tink made a clicking sound and the monkey dropped at once on to his shoulder, and nuzzled there. It put its tiny arms round the boy's neck, and made a little choking noise.

'Oh – poor little mite – it's crying!' said Anne. 'I didn't

know monkeys could cry. Timmy, don't frighten it again, please don't. You mustn't bully tiny things.'

'Timmy never bullies anything!' said George at once, frowning at Anne. 'But after all, what do you expect him to do when he comes home and finds a strange boy *and* a monkey here. Who are you, boy?'

'I shan't tell you,' said Tink, and marched out of the room, the monkey still whimpering into his neck.

'Joanna – who on earth is he?' asked Dick. 'And what is he doing here?'

'I thought you wouldn't like it,' said Joanna. 'It's that professor friend of your father's, George – the one who visited a few years ago. He telephoned this morning to say he was coming to stay for a week. He arrived today, and brought his boy as well!'

'Are they *staying* here?' said George, in horror. 'How *can* Mother let them – she *knew* we were all coming today! How *mean* of her, how . . .'

'Be quiet, George,' said Julian. 'Let Joanna go on.'

'Well, they arrived before anything could be done to stop them,' said Joanna. 'And now your father is shut up in his study with Professor Hayling – the boy's father – and your mother and I are at our wits' end to know where to put you all. The boy and his father – and I suppose the monkey too – are sharing the guest room.'

'But that's where Julian and Dick were going to sleep!' said George, losing her temper again. 'I'll go and tell Mother that boy can't stay, I'll . . .'

'Don't be silly, George,' said Julian. 'We'll manage somehow. We can't go back home because our house will be all shut up now.'

'You could sleep up in the loft,' said Joanna, sounding rather doubtful. 'But it's very dusty and terribly draughty. I could put a couple of mattresses up there for you.'

'All right,' said Julian. 'We'll make do up in the loft. Thanks, Joanna. Where's Aunt Fanny? Does she mind all this?'

'Well – she's a bit rushed,' said Joanna. 'But you know what your aunt is – always so kind, never thinks of herself. That Professor Hayling! Just walked into the house as if he owned it, bringing luggage and that most peculiar little boy – and a *monkey*! Though the monkey seems a nice enough little thing. It came and watched me wash up, and bless me if it didn't try to dry the plates for me!'

The kitchen door swung open and George's mother came in. 'Hallo, dears!' she said smiling. 'I thought I heard Timmy barking. Dear Timmy – wait till you see the monkey!'

'He's seen him already,' said George, scowling. 'Mother, how *could* you take people in when you knew we were coming home today?'

'That's enough, George,' said Julian, who saw how worried his aunt looked. 'Aunt Fanny, we won't be ANY trouble! We'll keep out of the house as much as we can, we'll do the shopping for you, we'll go across to Kirrin Island and keep out of your way, we'll . . .'

'You're kind, Julian,' said his aunt, and smiled at him. 'Things *will* be rather difficult – especially as Professor Hayling never can remember to come to meals on time, and you know what your uncle is! He could forget breakfast, dinner and supper for a whole year, and then wonder why he felt hungry!'

That made everyone laugh. Julian slipped his arm round his aunt and gave her a hug. 'We'll sleep in the loft,' he said, 'and enjoy it, too. We will help with the housework and we'll do any odd jobs too. You've no idea how fine I look with an apron round my waist, and a broom in my hand!'

Even George smiled at the idea of Julian wearing an apron. Then Timmy went suddenly to the half-open door and barked. He could smell that monkey again. He heard a high chattering noise, and pushed the door open at once. What! Was that monkey calling him rude names?

He saw the little creature sitting on the top of the rail at the foot of the stairs. It saw Timmy, and danced up and down, sounding as if it were laughing. Timmy raced to the rail and leapt up, barking fiercely.

The study door flew open and out marched not one angry professor, but two!

'WHAT'S ALL THIS NOICE? CAN'T WE HAVE A MOMENT'S PEACE?'

'Oh *dear*!' said Aunt Fanny, foreseeing this kind of thing happening twenty times a day, now that Timmy and the others were here. She shushed the two angry men.

'Now, now – Timmy just isn't used to the monkey yet. Go back, please, and shut the door. I'll see you aren't disturbed again!'

'WOOF-WOOF!' shouted Timmy, using his very loudest bark, and Professor Hayling shot back into the study at top speed!

'Any more rudeness from Timmy and I'll have him sent away!' roared Uncle Quentin, and he too disappeared.

'Well!' said George, her face red with anger. 'What does he mean by *that*, Mother? If Timmy goes, I go too! Oh, *look* at that monkey – he's sitting on top of the grandfather clock now! *He* ought to be sent away, horrid little mischievous thing – not old Timmy!'

CHAPTER THREE

Mischief, Tink – and Timmy!

JULIAN AND Dick set to work to take a couple of old mattresses up to the loft, and some rugs and a couple of cushions for pillows. It *was* rather draughty! But what else was to be done? It was still too cold to sleep outside in a tent.

George was very sulky. 'That scowl will *grow* on your face, George, if you aren't careful,' said Dick. 'Cheer up, for goodness' sake. It's worse for your mother than it is for any of us. She's going to be very busy this week.'

She certainly was! Meals for nine people, five of them very hungry children, were not easy to provide. Joanna did an enormous amount of cooking. The four children helped with the housework and cycled off to Kirrin village in the mornings to do the shopping.

'Why can't that boy Tink help?' demanded George, on the second day they were at home. 'What on earth does he think he's doing now? Look at him out in the garden rushing all round, making a frightful noise. Tink, shut up! You'll disturb your father and mine.'

'You shut up yourself!' called back Tink, rudely. 'Can't you see I'm a Mercedes car, with a very powerful engine? And see how well it stops when I put on the brakes – no jerk at all! And hear the horn – marvellous!'

He gave a remarkably good imitation of a powerful car horn. At once the study window shot up and two very angry men shouted together:

'TINK! What do you think you're doing, making that noise? You've been told to be QUIET!'

Tink began to explain about the Mercedes, but as this didn't seem to satisfy either of the angry men, he offered to be a little Mini. 'You see, it goes like this,' said Tink, beginning to move off, making a low purring noise, 'and it . . .'

But the window was slammed shut, so the little Mini drove itself into the kitchen, and said it was very hungry, could it have a bun?

'I don't feed cars,' said Joanna. 'I have no petrol. Go away.'

The Mini purred out of the kitchen on its two legs, and went to look for passengers. Mischief the monkey scampered up, and ran up Tink's body to his shoulder.

'You're my passenger,' said Tink, and Mischief held on to his hair as he drove all round the garden at top speed, honking every now and again, but very quietly indeed.

'He's a funny child,' said Joanna to Mrs Kirrin, when she came into the kitchen. 'Not bad really – him and his cars! I've never seen a child so mad on them in my life! One of these days he'll turn into one!'

It began to rain next day and Tink couldn't go out. He nearly drove everyone mad, rushing about all over the house hooting, and purring like a car engine.

'Now look,' Joanna said to him, when, for the twentieth time, he drove himself all round her kitchen. 'I don't care if you're a Morris Minor, or an Austin, or a Consul or even a Rolls – you just keep out of my kitchen! It's a funny thing to think that a fine car like a Rolls can steal a bun out of my tin – it ought to be ashamed of itself!'

'Well, if I can't get petrol, I've got to get *something* to run on, haven't I?' demanded Tink. 'Look at Mischief – *he's* helping himself to apples in the larder, but you don't say anything to him!'

'Oh, lands sakes, is that creature in the larder again?' cried poor Joanna, rushing across the kitchen. 'Who left it open, I'd like to know?'

'Timmy did,' said Tink.

'You little liar!' said Joanna as she shooed Mischief out

of the larder. 'Timmy would never do a thing like that. He's as honest as the day, not like that little thief of a monkey of yours!'

'Don't you like him?' said Tink, sorrowfully. 'He likes *you.*'

Joanna glanced across at the tiny monkey. He sat huddled in a corner, his arms over his face, looking very small and sad. One small brown eye peeped out at Joanna.

'You're a humbug, you are!' said Joanna. 'Looking as if you're the unhappiest monkey in the world, when all the time you're thinking what mischief to do next. Here – come and get this biscuit, you rascal – and don't you dare to go near Timmy this morning. He's very very angry with you.'

'What did Mischief do to Timmy?' asked Tink, surprised.

'He went to Timmy's dish and stole one of the bones there,' said Joanna. 'Timmy growled like a roll of thunder! I really thought he would bite off the monkey's tail. My word, you should have seen Mischief skedaddle!'

Mischief had now crept up cautiously to Joanna, eyeing the biscuit she held. He had had one or two taps from her for stealing, and he was rather wary of her quick right hand.

'Here you are – take the biscuit, for goodness' sake,' said Joanna. 'And don't look such a little misery, or I might suddenly find myself giving you another biscuit. Hallo – where's he gone?'

The monkey had snatched the biscuit with one of his tiny paws, and had scampered away to the door. It was shut, so Tink opened it for him. At once Timmy came in. He had been lying outside the door, sniffing the good smell of soup cooking on the stove.

Mischief leapt to the top of a chair back and made a strange little whinnying sound – rather apologetic and sad. Timmy stood still and pricked up his ears. He understood animal language very well!

Mischief still held the biscuit. He leapt down to the seat of the chair – and then, to Joanna's enormous surprise, he held out the biscuit to Timmy! He chattered in a very small voice, and Timmy listened gravely. Then the big dog took the biscuit gently, threw it into the air, chewed it once, and swallowed it!

'Well, did you ever see anything like *that* before!' said Joanna, marvelling. 'For all the world as if Mischief was apologising to Timmy for stealing his bone – and offering him his biscuit to make up! Well, whatever will George say when she hears!'

Timmy licked his lips to see if any biscuit crumbs were left, and then put his big head forward, and gave the monkey a sudden lick on the tip of his funny little nose.

'Timmy's saying thank you!' cried Tink, in delight. 'Now they'll be friends – you see if they won't!'

Joanna was astonished and pleased. Well, well – to think of that monkey being clever enough to present Timmy with a biscuit that he very much wanted to eat himself! He wasn't a bad little thing! She went upstairs to find George and tell her.

But George didn't believe her. 'Timmy would never take a biscuit from that silly little monkey!' she said. 'Never! You made all that up, Joanna, just because you're getting fond of Mischief. You wait till he runs off with your toasting-fork again!'

All the same, George went down with Joanna, curious to see if the two animals *were* becoming friendly – and she saw a very strange sight indeed!

Mischief was on Timmy's back, and Timmy was solemnly trotting round the kitchen, giving him a ride! The monkey was chattering in delight, and Tink was shouting in glee.

'Go faster, Tim, go faster! You're a very fine horse! You'd easily win the Derby! Go on, gallop!'

'I don't want Timmy to give rides to the monkey,' said George. 'Stop it, Timmy! You look silly.'

The monkey suddenly leant forward and hugged Timmy round the neck. Then he slid off and looked at George as if to say, 'All right! I won't make your dog look silly!'

Timmy knew that George was cross and he went to lie down on the rug. At once Mischief came sidling across to him, and settled himself between Timmy's big front paws, cuddling there without fear. Timmy bent his big head and licked him very gently.

Tears came suddenly to Joanna's eyes. That Timmy! He

was just about the nicest dog in the whole world. 'See that!' she said to George. 'Big-hearted and kind that dog of yours is! Don't you scold him now for being great enough to make friends with a little creature who stole his bone!'

'I'm not *going* to scold him!' said George, astonished and proud. 'He's a marvel – the best dog in the world! Aren't you, Timmy darling?'

And she went over to Timmy and stroked his big soft head. He whined lovingly and licked her, looking up as if to say, 'Well, everything's all right now – we're *all* friends!'

Tink had been watching from a corner of the kitchen, saying nothing. He was rather afraid of George and her quick temper. He was delighted when he saw her go over and pat Timmy, without even disturbing the monkey. In his joy he began to honk like a lorry, and startled everyone so much that they yelled at him:

'Stop it, Tink!'

'Be quiet, you little nuisance!'

'Woof!' That was from Timmy.

'You'll have Mr Kirrin in here if you honk like that,' said Joanna. 'Can't you be something quiet for a change – a bicycle, for instance?'

Tink thought that was quite a good idea. He ran round the kitchen and out into the hall, making a hissing noise like the sound of a bicycle's wheels on the road. Then he decided to make a noise like a bicycle bell, and produced a very loud ringing noise indeed! It was so like the ringing of a bell that Aunt Fanny ran out of the living room, thinking there was someone at the front door!

Then the study door flew open and out came Uncle Quentin and Tink's father. Poor Tink was caught, and his father shook him so hard that two pencils shot out of his pocket and rolled over the floor.

Tink began to yell – and *how* he could yell! George came out of the kitchen to see what was happening, and Dick, Julian and Anne raced down the stairs. Joanna rushed out into the hall, too, and almost sent Uncle Quentin flying.

Then George did a very silly thing. She began to laugh – and when George laughed properly, her laugh was wonderful to hear! But neither Uncle Quentin nor Professor Hayling thought it wonderful – they merely thought it rude! George was laughing at *them* – and that wouldn't do at all!

'This is absolutely the last straw!' shouted Uncle Quentin, his face red with rage. 'First this boy ringing bells all over the place – and George encouraging him by laughing! I won't have it! Don't you know that very, very important work is going on here, in Kirrin Cottage – work that may bring great benefits to the world! Fanny, send these children away somewhere. I won't have them in the house, disturbing us when we are doing such important work. Do you hear? SEND THEM AWAY! And that's my LAST word!'

And he and the professor stalked back to the study and banged the door. Well! Now what was to be done?

CHAPTER FOUR

Tink has a wonderful idea

AUNT FANNY had appeared during the row, and sighed when she heard her husband shouting. Oh, dear, dear – these scientists who liked to do wonderful things for the world – and yet often made their own families unhappy! She smiled at George's angry face, and took her arm.

'Come into the living room, dear, and bring the others with you. We'll have to decide what can be done. Your father really *is* doing wonderful work, you know – and I must say that Tink and Mischief and Timmy don't help very much! All right, all right, George – I know it isn't Timmy's fault – but he does have a very loud bark, you know!'

She took the five children and Timmy into the living room. The monkey, scared at the shouting, had gone into hiding and was nowhere to be seen. Aunt Fanny called to Joanna.

'Joanna – come and help us to discuss what's to be done. This kind of thing can't go on.'

They all sat down, looking rather solemn. Timmy flopped down under the table, and put his nose on his paws. Where was that little monkey who had given him his biscuit?

The discussion began. George spoke first, most indignantly.

'Mother, this is our *home*. Why do we have to go away just because Father wants this scientist friend to stay with him? I have to do holiday homework, and I don't make a row every time Father bangs a door when I'm studying. But if I so much as . . .'

'That will do, George,' said her mother. 'You ought to understand your father better than you seem to. You are both exactly the same – impatient, short-tempered, bangers-of-doors, and yet both so kind, too! Now – let's see if we can find a way out.'

'I only wish we could stay at *my* home,' said Julian, feeling awkward. 'But it's all shut up, now that my parents have gone away.'

'Can't we take tents over to Kirrin Island?' said George. 'Yes, Mother, yes – I know what you're going to say – it's only the beginning of April, and it's far too cold and all the rest of it, and . . .'

'The forecast for the weather is very bad,' said her mother. 'Rain, rain, nothing but rain. You can't possibly go and camp in the pouring rain – and row to and fro, getting drenched each day – I'd have you all in bed with bronchitis before three days had gone – and *then* what should we do!'

'All right, Mother – have *you* any good suggestions?' said George, still cross.

'Hey – what's that monkey doing?' said Dick, suddenly. 'Stop him!'

'He's only poking the fire,' said Tink. 'He thinks it's cold in here.'

'Well, what next!' said Joanna and took the poker firmly from the monkey's little paw. 'Do you want to set the house on fire, you – you little . . .'

'Monkey!' finished Dick, with a grin. 'I must say that Mischief is always up to mischief! Can't keep your eye off him for a moment!'

'Well, now – if we can't go to Kirrin Island, or back home, or stay here – where *can* we go?' said Julian, looking serious. 'Hotels are too expensive – and which of our friends would like to have five of us to stay, plus a wicked little monkey and a big dog with an enormous appetite?'

There was a silence. What a problem! Then suddenly Tink spoke up.

'*I* know where we could go – and we'd jolly well have some fun, too!' he said.

'Oh – and where is this wonderful place?' asked George disbelievingly.

'Well – I was thinking of my lighthouse,' said Tink, most surprisingly. And then, as no one said anything, but merely stared at him in astonishment, he nodded at them. 'I said my *lighthouse* – don't you know what a lighthouse is?'

'Don't be silly, please,' said Dick. 'This is no time for jokes.'

'It's *not* a joke,' said Tink, indignantly. 'It's perfectly true. You ask my father.'

'But, Tink dear – you can't possibly *own* a lighthouse,' said Aunt Fanny, smiling.

'Well, I do,' said Tink, quite fiercely. 'You see, my father had some very special work to do, that couldn't be done on land – so he bought an old empty lighthouse, and did his work there. I went to stay with him – my, it was grand there, with the wind and the waves crashing about all the time.'

'But – surely he didn't *give* it to you, did he?' said Julian, disbelievingly.

'Yes, he did. Why shouldn't he, if I wanted it badly?' demanded Tink. '*He* didn't want it any more, and nobody would buy it – and I wanted it terribly, so he gave it to me on my last birthday. And it's mine, I tell you.'

'Well, I'm blessed!' said Julian. 'Here's old George owning an island given to her by her mother – and Tink owning a lighthouse given to him by his father! I wish my parents would present me with a volcano, or something really thrilling!'

George's eyes shone as she looked at the surprising Tink. 'A lighthouse – of your very own! Where is it?'

'About twenty miles along this coast to the west,' said Tink. 'It's not an awfully *big* one, you know – but it's smashing! The old lamp is still there, but it's not used now.'

'Why not?' asked Dick.

'Well, because a big new lighthouse was built farther along the coast, in a better position for warning ships,' explained Tink. 'That's how it was this old one was put up for sale. It was fine for my father to work in. Nobody ever disturbed him there – though he did get very angry with the seagulls sometimes. He said they mewed like great cats all the time, and made him feel he ought to put out milk for them.'

This made everyone burst into loud laughter, and Tink sat beaming round proudly. How clever he must be to make these children laugh like that – yes, and even Joanna and Aunt Fanny too! He broke into their laughter by banging on the table.

'You do believe me now, don't you?' he said. 'It's quite true that the lighthouse is mine. You ask my father. Do let's all go and stay in it till our two fathers have finished their work. We could take Timmy and Mischief too – there's plenty of room.'

This proposal was so astonishing that no one answered for a few moments. Then George gave him a friendly dig in the chest.

'*I'll* come! Fancy living in a *lighthouse*! I bet the girls at school won't believe *that*!'

'Aunt Fanny! May we go?' said Anne, her eyes shining too.

'Well – I don't know,' said her aunt. 'It really is a most extraordinary idea. I shall have to discuss it with your uncle, and with Tink's father too.'

'My father will say yes, I know he will!' said Tink. 'We left some stores there – and some blankets – I *say*, wouldn't it be grand to run a lighthouse ourselves!'

The idea certainly appealed to all the Five – even Timmy thumped his tail on the floor as if he had understood every word. He probably had – he never missed anything that was going on!

'I've a map that shows where my lighthouse is,' said Tink, scrabbling in one of his pockets. 'It's rather crumpled and dirty because I've looked at it so often. Look – here's a map of the coastline – and just there, built on rocks – is my lighthouse. It's marked by a round dot, look!'

Everyone pored over the grubby map. Nobody had the least doubt but that this was the answer to all their problems! Dick stared at the excited Tink. How lucky he was to own a *lighthouse*! Dick had never before met a lighthouse owner – and to think it should be this funny little Tink!

'The rocks that the lighthouse is built on used to wreck many ships,' said Tink. 'Wreckers used to work along that coast, you know – they would shine a light as if to guide ships along the coast, and make them go on the rocks. Crash! They'd be broken to pieces, and everyone drowned – and the wreckers would wait till the ship was washed up on the shore, and then take everything they could from her.'

'The wicked wretches!' said Dick, horrified.

'There's a Wreckers' Cave there, too, where the wreckers stored the things they stole from the wrecked ships,' said Tink. 'I haven't been very far into it – I'm too scared to. They do say there's an old wrecker or two there still.'

'Oh, nonsense!' said Aunt Fanny, laughing. 'That's probably just a tale to keep children away from dangerous caves and rocks. Well, dears – I really don't see any reason why you shouldn't go to Tink's lighthouse, if his father agrees.'

'Mother! THANK YOU!' cried George, and gave her mother a hug that made her gasp. 'I *say* – living in an old *lighthouse* – it's too good to be true! I shall take my binoculars and keep watch for ships!'

'Well, Julian had better take his record-player as well,' said Mrs Kirrin. 'If it's stormy weather, it may be a bit duller than you think, cooped up in a lonely lighthouse!'

'It will be marvellous!' cried Tink, and he suddenly became a racing car, tearing round the room at top speed, making a most extraordinary noise. Timmy barked and Mischief began to chatter loudly.

'Shush!' said Aunt Fanny. 'You'll make your father cross, Tink, and that will be the end of your fine idea. Switch your engine off, please, and sit down quietly! I'll talk to your father as soon as I can!'

CHAPTER FIVE

Tink's lighthouse

MRS KIRRIN thought that she might as well go immediately to the study, and see if her husband and Professor Hayling could talk about the children going away to this lighthouse of Tink's. Could it really be true? She knocked discreetly at the closed door.

She could hear voices inside the room, but nobody called 'come in'. She knocked again.

'What is it *now*?' shouted Uncle Quentin. 'If it's you, George, go away and keep away. And if it's Tink, tell him to go to the garage and park himself there. I suppose it's he who has been making all that row this morning!'

Aunt Fanny smiled to herself. Well, well – if all scientists were like her husband and Professor Hayling, it was a wonder they were ever calm enough to get any work done!

She went away. Perhaps she could bring up the subject of the lighthouse at dinner-time. What a relief it would be to have a peaceful house for a few days!

She went into the kitchen to find Joanna. The monkey was there, helping her! He had slipped away from Tink and gone to see if there were any titbits about. Joanna was talking away to him as she rolled out pastry.

'See, I roll it like this – and like that – and I pick off a tiny bit for you!' And she gave Mischief a snippet for himself. He was very pleased, and leapt on Joanna's shoulder. He lifted a piece of her hair and whispered in her ear. Joanna pretended to understand.

'Yes, Mischief. If you're good I'll give you another titbit in a minute. Now get off my shoulder, and stop whispering. It tickles!'

'Well, Joanna – I never thought to see you rolling pastry with a monkey on your shoulder!' said Aunt Fanny. 'Joanna, what do you think about this lighthouse idea? I haven't been able to get into the study yet! My husband thought I was Tink, and told me to go and park myself in the garage!'

'And a very good idea too,' said Joanna, rolling her pastry vigorously. 'Isn't that Tink out in the hall now – sounds like a car of some sort! Well, I'd say that if the lighthouse is habitable, why shouldn't the Five go there, with Tink and the monkey? They'd enjoy themselves all right, and Timmy would look after them. Sort of thing that they love – rushing off to a lighthouse! Ugh! Nasty lonely place, with waves crashing round and a wind fit to blow your head off!'

'Yes, but do you think they'd be all right all alone there, Joanna?' said Aunt Fanny.

'Well, Julian and Dick are old enough to look after the others – though I must say I wouldn't like the job of being in charge of that Tink,' said Joanna. 'All I hope is that he doesn't imagine he's an aeroplane all of a sudden, and take off from the top of the lighthouse!'

Aunt Fanny laughed. 'Don't say that to *him*!' she said. 'His idea of being a car is bad enough. Well, Joanna, I feel very mean sending George and the others away immediately they come here – but with two excitable scientists in the house, I don't see that there's anything else to do. Look out for that monkey – he's found your bag of raisins!'

'Oh, you little mischief!' said Joanna, and made a grab at the monkey. He shot off to the top of a cupboard with the bag of raisins firmly held in one paw. He made a tiny chattering noise, as if he were scolding Joanna.

'You come down with those raisins!' said Joanna, advancing to the cupboard. 'Else I'll tie you to a chair with that long tail of yours. You little monkey!'

Mischief said something in his funny little voice that sounded rather cheeky. Then he put his paw into the bag and took out a raisin. But he didn't eat it – he threw it straight at Joanna! It hit her on the cheek, and she stared at Mischief in astonishment.

'What! You'd pelt me with my own raisins! Well, that I will *not* have!' She went to the sink and filled a cup with water, while Mischief pelted both her and Aunt Fanny with raisin after raisin! He danced about on the top of the cupboard, screeching loudly in glee!

A bowl on the top of the cupboard fell off as the monkey danced about, and crashed to the ground. The noise scared him, and, with a flying leap, he shot off the cupboard and landed on the top of the half-open door. He pelted the two women from there, making the most extraordinary noises.

The study door was flung open, and out came Uncle Quentin, followed by the professor. 'What was that crash? What's happening here? How *can* we w . . .'

It was most unfortunate that Joanna should have thrown the cup of water at Mischief at that moment. He sat there on the top of the door – and the water fell all over him, splashed over the top of the door – and down on to Uncle Quentin's head as he pushed the door open!

Joanna was horrified. She disappeared into the scullery at once, not knowing whether to laugh or to make her apologies.

Uncle Quentin was astounded to find himself dripping wet. He stared angrily up at Mischief, absolutely certain that it was the monkey who had emptied the water over him.

By this time the Five had come out of the living room, wondering what the noise was. 'It's old Mischief,' said Tink. 'Throwing water, I should think!'

'Well, actually, *I* threw the water,' began Joanna apologetically, peeping out of the scullery, 'because . . .'

'YOU threw it?' said Uncle Quentin, amazed. 'What *is* happening in this house? Things have come to a pretty pass if *you* start flinging water at people, Joanna. You ought to be ashamed of yourself! Are you mad?'

'Listen, Quentin,' said his wife. 'Nobody's mad at present, but pretty soon we all shall be, if this sort of thing goes on! Quentin, are you listening? I've something important to say to you – and to you too, Professor.'

The professor remembered his manners. 'Please go on,' he said politely, and then flinched as a raisin hit him squarely on the head. Mischief had found one on the floor, and had taken a pot shot at the professor. Dick looked at the monkey admiringly – he really was a very good shot!

'What's that little idiot of a monkey throwing!' said Uncle Quentin, fiercely, and knew at once when a raisin hit him smartly on the nose. 'Get rid of him! Put him in the dustbin! Why have I to put up with monkeys that throw things and boys that chug about the house like cars gone mad? I tell you Fanny, I will NOT have it!'

Aunt Fanny looked at him very sternly. 'Listen Quentin, I have something to say. *Listen*! Tink says his father gave him a lighthouse for his own, and he suggests that he and all the others should leave here and go and stay in the lighthouse. Quentin, are you listening?'

'A lighthouse! Are you mad? What, that little monkey of a boy says he owns a *lighthouse*? And you believed him?' said Uncle Quentin amazed.

'Tink's quite right, as it happens,' said Professor Hayling. 'I bought a lighthouse to work in when I wanted to get right away from everywhere and concentrate – and when I'd finished, I couldn't sell it – so as Tink pestered me for it, I gave it to him. But not to *live* in!'

'A *lighthouse* to work in!' said Uncle Quentin, thinking what a truly marvellous idea this was. 'I'll buy it from you! I'll . . .'

'No, Quentin, you won't do anything of the sort,' said his

wife, firmly. 'Will you *please* listen to me, both of you. Professor Hayling, is the lighthouse fit for these five to stay in – and if so, they want to know if they can go there until you two have finished your work here. They're a nuisance to you – and to be quite honest, you're a nuisance to *them*!'

'Fanny!' said her husband, astonished and angry.

'Father, listen. We'll all get out of your way as soon as possible, if you'll say we can go to Tink's lighthouse,' said George, planting herself firmly in front of her father. 'Say one word – "*yes*" – that's all we want.'

'YES!' shouted Uncle Quentin, suddenly tired of all the argument, and longing to get back to his papers with the professor. 'YES! Go to the lighthouse – go to the Tower of London – go and live at the zoo, if you like! The monkeys will welcome that mischievous little creature, sitting grinning up there on the cupboard! But go *somewhere*!'

'Oh, thank you, Father!' said George, joyfully.

'We'll go off to the lighthouse as soon as we can. HURRAY! THREE CH—'

But before she could continue, the study door shut with a bang behind the two exasperated men. George bent down, took Timmy's two front legs, and proceeded to dance all round the living room with him, shouting, 'HURRAY! THREE CHEERS!' over and over again.

Aunt Fanny sat down suddenly in a chair, and began to laugh. Joanna laughed too. 'If we don't laugh, we shall cry!' she said. 'What a hullabaloo! Well, it's a good thing they'll soon be off. That loft is much too draughty for the boys, you know. Look at poor Julian – he's got such a stiff neck he can hardly turn it this morning.'

'Who cares?' said Julian. 'We'll soon be off again together, all the Five – and two more to keep us company. It will be quite an adventure!'

'An adventure?' said Tink, surprised. 'But you can't have adventures in a lighthouse – it's out on the rocks, all by itself, as lonely as can be! There aren't any adventures to be found *there*!'

Ah – you wait and see, Tink! You don't know the Five! If there's any adventure about, they're bound to be right in the middle of it!

CHAPTER SIX

Making plans

IT WAS very exciting making plans to go to the lighthouse. Tink told them all about it, time and time again. 'It's very tall, and there's an iron stairway – a spiral one – going from the bottom up to the top. And at the top is a little room for the lamp that used to flash to warn ships away.'

'It sounds smashing,' said George. 'What about Timmy, though? Can he climb up a spiral stairway?'

'Well, he can live down at the bottom, can't he, if it's too difficult for him to climb up?' said Tink. 'Mischief can climb it easily – he simply *races* up!'

'If Timmy has to live at the bottom, I shall live there with him,' said George.

'Why not wait and see the lighthouse before you arrange the sleeping places?' said Julian, giving her a friendly punch. 'Now first we must find out exactly where it is – and the way to get there. It's a pity Tink can't turn into a *real* car – he could run us there in no time!'

Tink at once imagined himself to be a large van, taking the Five and all their luggage along the road. He raced round the room, making his usual car noise, and hooting so loudly that he made everyone jump. Julian caught him as he raced round the table and sat him down firmly.

'Any more of that and we leave you behind,' he said. 'Now – where's that map of yours – let's have a look at it – and then we'll get Aunt Fanny's big map of the coast, and track down the road to your lighthouse.'

Soon Tink and the Five were studying a large-scale map of the coast, Mischief sitting on Dick's shoulder and tickling his neck.

'See – that's the way to go,' said Julian. 'It really wouldn't be far by sea – look, round the coast here, cut across this bay, round the headland – and just there are the rocks on which the old lighthouse stands. But by road it's a very long way.'

'Better go by car, though,' said Dick. 'We've a good bit of luggage to take – not only our clothes, but crockery and things like that. And food.'

'There are still some stores there,' said Tink, eagerly. 'Dad left some when we went away from the lighthouse.'

'They'll probably have gone bad,' said Julian.

'Well – don't take too much,' said Tink. 'It's a pretty rough way over the rocks to the lighthouse – there isn't a road that runs right up to it, you know. We shall have to carry everything ourselves, once we get to the place. We can always get fresh food if we want it – the village isn't all that far away – but there are some days when you can't even leave the lighthouse! You see the waves splash house-high over the rocks when there's a rough wind. We'd have to get across by boat if the tide's in – the rocks are covered then!'

'This sounds too exciting for words!' said Dick, his eyes shining. 'What do *you* think about it, Anne? You haven't said a word!'

'Well – I do feel just a *bit* scared!' said Anne. 'It sounds so lonely. I do hope no ships will be wrecked on those awful rocks while *we're* there!'

'Tink said there was a fine new lighthouse farther along the coast,' said Julian. 'Its light will keep every ship away from that wicked stretch of rocks. Look, Anne, you *would* like to come, wouldn't you? If not, Aunt Fanny wouldn't mind just *you* staying here – you're a little mouse, you wouldn't bother Uncle Quentin or the professor at all!'

'I shouldn't *dream* of not coming with you,' said Anne, indignantly. 'Julian – you don't think there are still wreckers about do you? I should hate that.'

'They belong to years gone by,' said Julian. 'Cheer up, Anne – this is just a little visit we're going to pay to Tink's seaside house! He is kindly taking in visitors this spring!'

'Well, let's get on with our plans,' said Dick. 'We go there by car – er, *what* was that you just said, Tink?'

'I said I'll drive you, if you like,' said Tink. 'I could dr . . .'

'You haven't a driving licence, so don't talk nonsense,' said George, crossly.

'I know I haven't – but all the same I *can* drive!' said Tink. 'I've driven my father's car round and round our garden, see? And . . .'

'Oh, do shut up,' said Dick. 'You and your pretend cars!

Julian, when shall we go to his lighthouse?'

'Well, why not tomorrow morning?' said Julian. 'I'm sure everyone would be glad if we left as soon as possible! It's hard on Aunt Fanny and Joanna to have so many here. We'll see about a car and someone to drive us, and then we'll pack and make our getaway!'

'Hurray,' said George in delight, and pounded on the table, making Mischief leap up to the top of a bookcase in fright. 'Oh, sorry, Mischief – did I scare you? Timmy tell him I'm sorry, I didn't mean it. He probably understands your doggy language.'

Timmy looked up at Mischief, gave two little whines and a comforting wuff. Mischief listened with his head on one side, and then leapt down, landing neatly on Timmy's back.

'Thanks for giving him my message, Tim,' said George, and everyone laughed. Good old Timmy! He wagged his long tail and put his head on George's knee, looking up at her beseechingly.

'All right, old thing – I understand your language, whether you talk with your voice or your eyes,' said George, patting him. 'You want a walk, don't you?'

'Woof!' said Timmy joyfully, and tore to the door.

'Let's walk down to the garage and see if they have a car or a van to hire out to us,' said Julian. 'We'll have to have a driver too, because someone has to take back the car. Come on, Timmy-dog!'

They all set off to the garage in the village. The rain

held off for a while, and the sun came out, making Kirrin Bay sparkle and shine.

'I wish we could have gone to stay on my island,' said George. 'But it really is too damp to camp out. Anyway, a lighthouse will be nice for a change!'

The man at the garage listened to Julian's tale of wanting a car to go to the lighthouse. 'It's the old lighthouse at Demon's Rocks, not the new one at High Cliffs,' he said. 'We're going to stay there.'

'Stay at a *lighthouse*!' said the man. 'This isn't a joke, is it?'

'No. It happens to belong to one of us,' said Julian. 'We have a few things to take there, of course, and we hoped you'd have a taxi tomorrow for us. We'd let you know somehow when we are ready to come back from the lighthouse, and you can send the same car for us then.'

'Right,' said the man. 'And you're staying at Kirrin Cottage now, you say? Oh – your uncle is Mr Kirrin? Well, I know George here, of course – but I wasn't certain who *you* were. Some funny people order cars, you know!'

George was pleased to be called George. It was nice to be thought a boy. She dug her hands deep down in the pockets of her shorts, and decided to have her hair cut even shorter – if only her mother would allow it!

'We'd better take a few rugs and cushions,' said Julian. 'And some cardigans and sweaters. I can't imagine it's very warm in the lighthouse.'

'There's an oil-heater there,' said Tink. 'I think it was

for the lighthouse lamp when it was in use. We can use that for warmth, if we're cold.'

'What sort of stores did you and your father leave there?' asked Dick. 'We'd better order some foodstuffs at the grocer's – and some ginger-beer or something – and take it all in the car.'

'Well – there's plenty of tinned food, I think,' said Tink, trying to remember. 'We left it there in case my father wanted to come back at any time and work again in peace and quiet.'

'Hm. It's a pity he didn't fix up with Uncle Quentin to have him there with him,' said Julian. 'Then everyone would have been happy!'

They went to the grocer's and Anne tried her best to order what she thought they would need, outside of tinned food. 'Sugar – butter – eggs – oh dear – help me, George. How much shall I order?'

'Don't forget we *can* go shopping in Demon's Rocks village,' said Tink. 'Only it's a bit of a nuisance if there's windy weather – the path over the rocks isn't very safe then. We might have to stay in the lighthouse for a day or two without leaving it. Even a boat might be too risky.'

'It sounds thrilling!' said George, picturing them all marooned by fierce storms, waiting to be rescued from peril and starvation! 'Get some biscuits, Anne. And bars of chocolate. And lots of ginger-beer. And a big bottle of lemonade. And a . . .'

'Wait a minute – do you know who's paying for all

this?' said Julian. '*I* am. So don't ruin me completely!' He took out his wallet. 'Here's five pounds,' he said. 'That's all I can spare at present! Dick can buy the next lot of food we want!'

'Well, I've plenty of money too,' said Tink, taking out a handful from his pocket.

'You would have!' said George. 'I suppose your father just hands out money whenever you ask him. He's so vague he wouldn't know if he paid you three times a day!'

'Well, *yours* seems pretty vague too,' said Tink, smartly. 'He poured the coffee over his porridge this morning, instead of the milk. I saw him. And what's more, he ate it without even *noticing* it was coffee!'

'That's enough,' said Julian. 'We don't tell tales about our parents in public. Tink, don't you want to take anything for Mischief to eat while we're in the lighthouse? George has bought biscuits for Timmy, and we're going to lay in a supply of bones, too.'

'I'll buy Mischief's food myself, thank you,' said Tink, not very pleased at being ticked off by Julian. He gave an order for a packet of raisins, a packet of currants, five pounds of apple rings and some oranges. Mischief eyed all these with very great *pleasure*.

'Paws off!' said George, sharply, as the little monkey slyly slid his paw into the bag of biscuits put ready for Timmy. Mischief jumped on to Tink's shoulder and hid his face in his tiny paws, as if he were ashamed!

'We'll just buy some more fruit,' said Julian, 'and then I

think we'll have enough. We'll take it all round to the garage, and put it in the car ready to take away tomorrow.'

'Tomorrow!' said George, her eyes shining. 'Oh, I hope it comes soon. I can't *wait* for it!'

CHAPTER SEVEN

Off at last!

It was very exciting that evening to talk about the next day – the taxi coming to fetch them – the drive round the coast to Demon's Rocks – exploring the lighthouse – looking out over the endless sea, and watching the great waves coming in to pound on the rocks!

'What *I'm* looking forward to is our first night there,' said George. 'All alone, high up in that old lighthouse! Nothing but wind and waves around! Snuggling down in our rugs, and waking up to hear the wind and waves again.'

'And the gulls,' put in Tink. 'They cry all the time. You can watch them from the lighthouse top. I wish I had wings like a gull – spread out wide – sitting on the wind as they glide!'

'Sitting on the wind – yes, that's exactly what they do!' said Anne. 'I just wish their cry didn't sound so mournful though.'

Aunt Fanny was half-inclined not to let the children go after all! The weather forecast was bad, and she pictured them sitting half-frozen, and perhaps very scared, in the old deserted lighthouse. But no sooner did she begin to wonder out loud if she ought to let them go than the children raised their voices in indignant chorus!

'But we've ordered the TAXI!'

'And heaps of food! And Joanna has packed up a big tin of all kinds of things. She even baked a special cake for us!'

'*Mother!* How *could* you think of saying no when you've already said yes!'

'All right, all right, dears!' said Aunt Fanny. 'I wouldn't really stop you going. But do send me a card or two, will you? That's if there's anywhere to post one!'

'Oh, there's a tiny post office in the village,' said Tink. 'We'll send a card every day. Then you'll know we're all right.'

'Very well – but if a card doesn't come I'll be very worried,' said Aunt Fanny. 'So please do keep your word! You won't forget your mackintoshes will you – and your rubber boots, and . . . ?'

'Mother! I feel as if you're going to mention *umbrellas* next!' said George. 'But honestly, we'd be blown out to sea if we put an umbrella up on Demon's Rocks. Tink says there's always a gale blowing round the coast there.'

'You can think of us playing snap with our packs of cards, and having a fine time in the lighthouse while storms rage round and howl like demons!' said Dick. 'We'll be sitting snug in our rugs, with ginger-beer beside us, and chocolate biscuits all round . . .'

'Woof,' said Timmy, at once, pricking his ears up at words he knew so well.

'Ha – you think you're going to feed on chocolate biscuits, do you, Tim?' said Dick, ruffling the dog's hairy head. 'And please don't interrupt the conversation. It's not good manners.'

'Woof,' said Timmy apologetically, and licked Dick's nose.

'I think you'd all better go to bed early tonight,' said Aunt Fanny. 'You've still some packing to do tomorrow – and you say you've ordered the taxi for half past nine.'

'We'll be down to breakfast at eight o'clock sharp,' said Julian. 'I bet the professor won't be down till about eleven, and forget all about his bacon and eggs! Tink, does your father *ever* have a really hot meal? I mean – it seems to me he either forgets them altogether, or wanders in hours late, and then doesn't know if he's having breakfast, dinner, or supper!'

'Well, I can always eat up everything that's there, if I think he's forgotten to come,' said Tink, sensibly. 'Mischief helps too. You'd be surprised how fond Mischief is of fat bacon.'

'I'm not a *bit* surprised at anything Mischief does,' said Julian. 'I'm just wondering how we are going to put up with his tricks when we're all cooped up in the lighthouse together! We can't send him out into the garden then, to work off some of his high spirits. Aunt Fanny, do you know he took my pencil this morning and scribbled monkey words all over my wallpaper? It's a good thing I can't read monkey language for I'm sure he wasn't scribbling anything polite!'

'You're not to say things like that about Mischief,' said

Tink, offended. 'He's very good-mannered for a monkey. You should see *some* monkeys I know!'

'I'd rather not, thanks,' said Julian.

Tink was cross. He picked up Mischief and went out of the room. Soon there was the noise of a car out in the hall – one that needed repairing by the sound of it!

'R-r-r-RRRRRR-r-r-r, OOOOOOPH, Rrrrrr, PARP!' Aunt Fanny rushed to the door. 'You *know* you've been told not to be a car out in the hall. Come back before your father hears you, Tink. My goodness me, this house will be an entirely different place, once it is rid of all the cars that have driven about in it since you came!'

'I was only being a tractor,' said Tink, surprised. 'I always feel as if I *must* go and be a car when people are horrid to me or Mischief.'

'Oh, be your age!' said George.

'I shall go up to bed,' said Tink, offended again.

'Well, that's not a bad idea, seeing that you have to be punctual tomorrow morning,' said Aunt Fanny. 'Good night, then, Tink dear. Good night, Mischief.'

Tink found himself gently propelled to the door. He went up the stairs, grumbling, Mischief on his shoulder. But he soon stopped frowning as he undressed and thought of the next day. Off to the lighthouse – HIS lighthouse! Ha, that would make George and the others sit up. He snuggled down in bed with Mischief nestling beside him, one little paw down the front of Tink's pyjama jacket.

Next morning George awoke first. She sat up, afraid that the weather forecast might be right, and that it would be pouring with rain. No – it was wrong for once – the sun shone down and she could not hear the sound of the sea – that meant that there was not much wind to blow up big waves that pounded on the shore.

She awoke Anne. 'Lighthouse day!' she said. 'Buck up – it's half past seven.'

They were all down very punctually to breakfast – except Professor Hayling! As usual he did not appear until breakfast was over, and then he sauntered in at the front door!

'Oh – you *are* up then,' said Aunt Fanny, 'I thought you were still asleep in bed.'

'No – Tink woke me up at some very early hour,' complained the professor. 'Or else it was the monkey – I really don't know. They both look alike to me in the early morning.'

Uncle Quentin was already down, but hadn't come into breakfast. He was in his study as usual. 'George – go and fetch your father,' said Aunt Fanny. 'His breakfast will soon be inedible.'

George went to the study door and knocked. 'Father! Don't you want your breakfast?'

'I've had it!' said a surprised voice. 'Very nice – couple of boiled eggs.'

'Father! That was your *yesterday's* breakfast!' said George, impatiently. 'It's bacon and *fried* eggs today.

You've forgotten as usual. Do come. We're leaving for the lighthouse soon.'

'Lighthouse – what lighthouse?' said Uncle Quentin, in tones of great astonishment. But he had no answer. George had gone back to the dining-room, not knowing whether to laugh or frown. Really! Father was so forgetful that he would forget where he lived next!

There was great excitement after breakfast. Rugs – coats – night clothes, the warmest that could be found – tins of cakes and mince-pies packed by Joanna – sandwiches to eat on the way – books – games – as George said, anyone would think they were going away for a month!

'The car's late!' said Dick, impatiently. 'Or else my watch is fast.'

'Here it comes!' said Anne, excited. 'Oh, Aunt Fanny, I wish you were coming too! We're going to have such fun! Where's Mischief – oh, there he is! And Timmy – Timmy, we're going to live in a lighthouse! You don't even know what that is, do you?'

The car came up to the front gate of Kirrin Cottage, and the driver blew his horn, making Uncle Quentin almost jump out of his skin. He turned on poor Tink at once. 'Was that *you* up to your silly tricks of pretending to be a car, and hooting again? Own up, now!'

'No, it wasn't, on my honour it wasn't,' said Tink indignantly, hopping out of the way of what looked as if it might be a very powerful slap. 'See – it's that car!'

'I'll just ask the driver what he means by driving up

here and hooting fit to scare us all!' said Uncle Quentin indignantly. 'What's he come here for, anyway?'

'Father! It's the taxi that's come to take us to the lighthouse!' said George, not knowing whether to laugh or be cross.

'Ah yes,' said Uncle Quentin. 'Why didn't you tell me before? Well, goodbye, goodbye! Have a good time, and don't forget to dry yourselves well after a bathe.'

They piled into the car, and the man put their luggage into the big boot. He stared as Timmy and Mischief leapt in. 'Sure you've all got enough room?' he said. 'What a carful!'

Then to the accompaniment of a loud R-r-r-r-RRR from the car's engine, and an equally loud one from the delighted Tink, the car turned and drove away down the sandy lane.

'We're off,' said George, in a happy voice. 'Off all by ourselves again. It's the thing I like best of all. Do you like it too, Tim?'

'WOOF!' said Timmy, agreeing heartily, and lay down with his head on George's foot. Ah – now for a lovely holiday with George. Timmy didn't mind where he went – even to the end of the world – so long as he was with George!

CHAPTER EIGHT

There's the lighthouse!

ONCE THEY were out on the main road, Tink began to talk to the driver, asking him questions about all kinds of cars. The others listened, amused.

'Well, I don't think much of the new cars,' said Tink. 'All gadgets!'

'Some of the new gadgets are very good,' said the driver, amused with the cocky little boy, and he touched a little lever beside him. At once the window next to Tink went down smoothly, with a curious low moan. Tink was extremely startled.

'Oh, don't open that window,' said Anne, as a rough wind swooped in. 'For goodness' sake shut it, Tink.'

Tink shut it and began to talk about cars again. Once more the driver touched the lever beside him, and once more Tink's window slid mournfully down, and a cold draught came in.

'TINK! Don't mess about with the windows,' ordered Julian.

'I never touched the thing,' said Tink, eyeing the window with suspicion. It suddenly shut itself, sliding upwards very smoothly. Tink began to feel uncomfortable. He watched the window closely, afraid that it might play tricks again. The others, knowing perfectly well that the driver could open and shut any of the windows automatically from his own seat, nudged one another, and giggled. 'That shut up poor old Tink!' murmured Dick.

It had. Not another word about new cars or old came from Tink during the whole drive! It was a very pleasant one, mostly round the coast, and very little inland. The views were magnificent.

'That dog of yours seems to like the views,' said the driver. 'His head has been out of the window all the time.'

'Well – I always thought it was because he liked the fresh air,' said George. 'Timmy, is it because you enjoy the views?'

'Woof,' said Timmy, and withdrew his head to give George a lick. He also gave the little monkey a lick. Poor Mischief didn't much like the motion of the car. He sat very still indeed, afraid that he might be sick. The car purred along, sounding just like Tink's usual imitation!

They stopped for an early lunch, and ate their sandwiches hungrily, sitting on a cliff. The driver had brought his own, and once Mischief had discovered that half the man's sandwiches were made of tomato, he sat on his knee in a very friendly manner, sharing his sandwiches in delight.

'We'll be there in about ten minutes,' said the man. 'Where are you staying at Demon's Rocks? The garage didn't tell me.'

'At the lighthouse,' said Julian. 'Do you know it?'

'Yes – but people don't *stay* there!' said the driver, thinking that Julian was pulling his leg. 'What hotel are you going to – or are you staying with friends?'

'No. We really *are* going to the lighthouse,' said Tink. 'It's mine. My very own.'

'Well – you've certainly got a place with a fine view!' said the driver. 'I was born at Demon's Rocks. My old great-grandad is still in the same cottage where I was born. My word – the stories he used to tell me of that old lighthouse – and how the wreckers got into it one night and grabbed the keeper there, and doused the light, so that a great ship might go on the rocks.'

'How horrible – and *did* it get wrecked?' asked Dick.

'Yes. Smashed to bits,' said the driver. 'Ab-so-lutely – smashed – to bits! And then they waited for the tide to wash up the wreckage. You ought to look up my old great-grandad, and get him to tell you his tales. He might even show you the Wreckers' Cave . . .'

'Oh – we heard about that,' said George. 'Is it really true – *can* we see it? And is there someone in there still?'

'No – no, all the old wreckers are gone long ago,' said the driver. 'As soon as the new lighthouse was built, the wreckers' day was done. It's so powerful, you see. Its beams can be seen even in the fiercest storm. The beam from the lighthouse you're going to wasn't very good – but it saved a good many ships, all the same!'

'What's your great-grandad's name?' asked George,

making up her mind to look him up as soon as she could. 'Where does he live?'

'Ask for Jeremiah Boogle,' said the driver, carefully skirting a herd of cows. 'You'll find him sitting somewhere on the quay, smoking a long pipe, and scowling at anyone that comes near him. But he likes children, so don't you be afraid of his scowl. He'll tell you a few tales, will my old great-grandad! Well, bless us all, if there isn't *another* herd of cows coming round the corner.'

'Hoot at them,' said Tink.

'Ever heard the rhyme about the cow that jumped over the moon, boy?' said the driver. 'Well, someone hooted when it came by, see? And that's what it did – jumped over the moon! No good driver hoots at cows. It scares them silly, and they jump like hares. Look – see that cliff round the curve of the coast there? Well, that's the first bit of Demon's Rocks. We'll soon be there now.'

'Why is it called that?' asked George.

'Well, the rocks there are so wicked that it was reckoned they could only have been put there by some kind of savage demon,' said the driver. 'Some are just below the water so that they catch the keel of a boat and rip it. Others stick up sharp as sharks' teeth – and there's a great ledge of rocks where a boat can be pounded to bits by the waves. Ah, they're Demon's Rocks all right!'

'When shall we see the lighthouse?' asked Tink. 'We ought to see it soon.'

'Wait till another bit of the coast comes in sight as soon

as we get to the top of this hill,' said the driver. 'And just tell that monkey of yours to take his paw out of my coat pocket. I've no more tomatoes there!'

'Behave yourself, Mischief,' said Tink, so sternly that the little creature hid its face in its paws and whimpered.

'Little humbug!' said George. 'There's not a *tear* in his eye! Oh look – is *that* the lighthouse?'

'Yes. That's it,' said the driver. 'You get a good view of it now, from this hill. Fine one, isn't it, for an old one? Ah, they could build well in those days. That one's made of stone. It's wave-swept so it has to be fairly tall, or the shining of the lamp would have been hidden by the spray falling on the windows.'

'Where did the lighthouse keeper live?' asked Dick.

'Oh, there's a cosy enough room just under the lamp room,' said the driver. 'My grandad took me up there once. I never saw such a view of a stormy sea in my life!'

'My father lived there all one summer,' boasted Tink. 'I was with him most of the time. It was grand.'

'Why did your father want to live in a lighthouse?' asked the driver, curiously. 'Was he hiding, or something?'

'Of course not. He's a scientist, and he said he wanted peace and quiet, with no telephones ringing, and no one coming to see him,' said Tink.

'And do you mean to say he had peace and quiet with *you* there?' said the driver teasingly. 'Well, well!'

'It's not so quiet there really,' said Tink. 'The waves

make such a noise, and so does the wind. But my father didn't really notice those. He only notices things like bells ringing, or people talking, or somebody knocking at the door. Things like that drive him mad. He loved the lighthouse.'

'Well – I hope you enjoy yourselves there,' said the driver. 'It's not my cup of tea – hearing nothing but waves and gulls crying. Better you than me!'

They descended the other side of the hill and the lighthouse was no longer to be seen. 'Soon be there now,' said Tink. 'Mischief, will you like to be at the lighthouse again? How quickly you could go up the spiral staircase and down – do you remember?'

The car swept down almost to the edge of the sea. The lighthouse was now plainly to be seen, a good way out from the shore. A small boat bobbed at a stone jetty, and Tink pointed it out with a scream of joy. 'That's the boat we had – the one that took us to and from the lighthouse when the tide was in! It's called *Bob-About*, and it does bob about too.'

'Is it yours?' asked George, rather jealously.

'Well, it was sold with the lighthouse, so I suppose it is,' said Tink. 'Anyway, it's the one we'll use when we can't wade over the rocks.'

'Well, see you don't get storm-bound in the lighthouse,' said the driver, bringing the car to a stop. 'The sea between Demon's Rocks and the jetty will be too rough for that little boat, in stormy weather.'

'I can manage boats all right,' said George. 'I've had one since I was small.'

'Yes. You're pretty good with them, that I do know,' said the driver. 'Well – here we are. Are you going to go straight to the lighthouse – in that boat? Shall I help you carry your things to it?'

'Well, thanks,' said Julian, and between them they carried everything to the little boat. An old man sat nearby, and he touched his cap to them. 'Message came through from Kirrin to say I was to get the old boat out for you,' he said. 'Which of you's Master Hayling?'

'I am,' said Tink. 'And that's *my* boat, and *that's* my lighthouse! Come on, everyone – let's row to the lighthouse – come on! I can hardly wait to get there!'

CHAPTER NINE

Inside the lighthouse!

THE FIVE children jumped down into the boat, which was certainly acting up to its name of *Bob-About*! Timmy leapt in after George, but Mischief the monkey cried in terror when Tink took him into the bobbing boat and sat down, holding him firmly.

'It's all right, Mischief,' said Tink. 'Don't you remember this little boat of mine? You never did like going in a boat, though, did you?'

There were two pairs of oars. Julian took one pair, and George was going to take the other, when Dick quietly took them himself, grinning at George's angry face.

'Sorry – there's a good old swell on the sea, and we've to row through some pretty good waves. I'm just a *bit* stronger than you, George!'

'I row *just* as well as you do,' said George. The boat gave a great roll to one side just then, and she just managed to save one of their suitcases from toppling overboard.

'Well saved!' said Julian. 'And only just in time too! What a swell there is just here!'

'Are you going to row right over the rocks?' asked Anne peering down into the water. 'They are covered by the water

now – we shan't scrape the bottom of the boat at all.'

'These are the rocks that we can walk over when the tide's out,' said Tink. 'Lovely pools there are in them, too! I used to wallow in a nice warm one that was so well-heated by the sun that I wished I had a cold tap to turn on when the water felt too hot!'

Anne chuckled. 'I wish it was warm enough to bathe now,' she said. 'My word – look down and see what horrible rocks there are, just beneath the boat!'

'Yes – I bet they ripped up many a poor ship in the old days,' said Julian. 'No wonder they called them Demon's Rocks! It's a bit of a pull over them, isn't it, Dick?'

'Let *me* have a turn,' said George, grabbing at one of Dick's oars.

'Nothing doing,' said Dick, with a grin. 'You just look after those bags, old thing!'

'Is it a very *old* lighthouse?' asked Anne, as they swung over the hidden rocks, and the lighthouse came nearer and nearer. 'It *looks* old!'

'Yes, it is,' said Tink. 'It's an odd little lighthouse, really – built by a rich man years and years ago. His daughter was drowned in a ship that was wrecked on these rocks – so he built a lighthouse, partly as a memorial to the girl, and partly to prevent other shipwrecks.'

Anne gazed at it. It was sturdily built and seemed very tall to her. Its base was firmly embedded in the rocks below it. Dick thought that the foundations must go very deep down into the rocks, to hold the lighthouse firmly in the great gales that must blow in bad weather. A gallery, rather like a verandah, ran round the top, just below the windows through which the lighthouse lamp once shone. 'What a view there would be from that gallery,' thought Anne.

They came near to the lighthouse, which had stone steps running from the rocks up to a doorway built some way above the crashing waves.

'Will the door be locked?' asked Dick, suddenly. 'I wouldn't want to row all this way and then find we can't get into the place!'

'Of course the door will be locked,' said Tink. 'Anyone got the key?'

'Oh, don't be a donkey!' said Julian, resting his oars, and glaring at Tink. 'Do you mean to say we can't get in, after all this?'

'It's all right!' said Tink, grinning at Julian's dismayed face. 'I just wanted to pull your leg. Here's the key! It's *my* lighthouse, you see, so Dad gave me the key, and I always carry it about with me. It's very precious.'

It was an extremely large key, and George marvelled that Tink could keep it in his pocket. He flourished it at them, grinning again. 'I'm looking forward to unlocking *my* lighthouse with *my* key!' he said. 'I bet *you* wish you had a lighthouse of your own, George.'

'Well, yes, I do,' said George, gazing up at the towering lighthouse, now so near to them.

'You'd better be a bit careful now,' said Tink to the boys. 'Wait till a big waves swells up, then ride over it, and make for that rock over there – the one standing out of the water. There's a calm bit beyond it, for some reason, and you can row up to the steps quite safely. Look out for a stone post there, and chuck the rope round it, George. You're in a better position than I am for that.'

It was all done much more easily than the Five hoped. The boat swung into a stretch of fairly calm water, and the two boys rowed hard for the steps. George neatly threw the loop of rope over the post – and there they were, at the foot of the lighthouse, with only a few rocks to climb over to reach the steps. These rocks were not under water, and one by one the children and Timmy jumped out, and stared up at the lighthouse. It seemed much bigger now that they were just at the bottom!

'I'll unlock the door,' said Tink, proudly, and climbed up the steep stone steps. 'Look at the enormous great stones that my lighthouse is made of. No wonder it has stood so long!'

He thrust the great key into the lock of the stout wooden door, and tried to turn it. He struggled for a minute, and then turned to the others with a scared face. 'I can't open the door!' he said. '*Now* what do we do?'

'I'll have a try,' said Julian. 'It's probably stuck.' He took hold of the key, gave it a strong twist – and opened the door! Everyone was most relieved. Julian pushed the others in out of the wind and the spray, and shut the door firmly.

'Well – here we are!' he said. 'Isn't it dark! Good thing I brought a torch!'

He shone the torch round, but all that was to be seen was a steep iron staircase spiralling up the middle of the lighthouse!

'The staircase goes right up to the top, to the lamp-room,' explained Tink. 'It passes through a few rooms on the way. I'll show you. Hang on to the railing of the staircase, you may feel giddy going up round and round so steeply.'

Tink proudly led the way up the steep little staircase, that went round and round and round! They came to a hole through which the stairway passed into a little dark room. 'One of the storerooms,' said Tink, and flashed his torch

INSIDE THE LIGHTHOUSE!

round. 'See – there are tins of food that I told you my father and I left here. Now we go on up to the oil-room – that's not very big.'

'What's the oil-room?' asked Anne.

'Oh it was just where tins of paraffin oil used to be kept – the oil they used for the light at the top of the lighthouse. The old lamp had to burn oil, you see – there wasn't electricity in those days. Look – here's the oil-room.'

The oil-room had a very low ceiling, no window, and was packed with old tins. It had a nasty smell, and Anne held her nose with her fingers.

'I don't like this room,' she said. 'It has a horrid smell and a horrid *feel* about it! Let's go on up the staircase.'

The next room had one of the few little windows in the lighthouse, and as the sun came through it, it was much lighter and more cheerful.

'This was where my father and I slept,' said Tink. 'Look, we forgot to take that old mattress away with us. What a bit of luck! We can use it!'

Up the spiral staircase they went once more, and this time they came to a room with a higher ceiling than the others, and a good window, though small. The sun came through this one too, and it looked quite homely! It had a table, and three chairs, and a box. It also had an old desk, and a little paraffin stove for boiling water or frying food.

'There's my old frying-pan!' said Tink. 'We'll find that jolly useful. And a kettle – and a saucepan. And we left spoons and forks and knives behind, though not enough for all five of us, I'm afraid. And there's crockery too – though not as much as there ought to be. I broke rather a lot. But there are some tin cups and plates – I used just to wipe them clean with a cloth. Water's precious in a lighthouse you know.'

'Where is the water tank?' asked George. 'We'll have to have some water.'

'My father arranged a catch-tank on the west side of the lighthouse,' said Tink, proudly. 'It catches rainwater, and runs into a pipe that goes through one of the windows and fills a little tank over a sink. I forgot to show you that. There's a tap to turn the water on and off. My father's very clever, you know – and a thing like that is as simple as ABC. He didn't want to have to fetch water every day for washing in! Gosh, we did have fun here!'

'Well, it looks as if you'll have some *more* fun!' said Dick. 'You've plenty of company this time! You must have been jolly lonely before.'

'Oh, well – I had Mischief,' said Tink, and when he heard his name, the little monkey came scampering over to him, and leapt into the boy's arms, cuddling into him lovingly.

'And what's the next room in this marvellous little lighthouse?' asked Julian.

'There's only one more – and that's the lamp-room. I'll show you that – it used to be the most important room in the place – but now it's lonely – never used – quite forgotten! Come and see!' And up the last spiral of the stairway went Tink. How very, very proud he was of his lighthouse!

CHAPTER TEN

Settling in

ONCE MORE they all climbed up the spiral stairway, Timmy rather slowly, for he found the winding stairs difficult. Mischief shot up in front of them, almost as if *he* were the owner of the lighthouse, and was showing off his home!

The lamp-room was a high room with big windows all round it. It was very bright, for the sun shone steadily into it. The view was magnificent!

Anne gave a shout of wonder. The lighthouse was so high that the children could see for miles and miles over the heaving dark blue sea. They went all round the lamp-room, looking in every direction.

'Look! There's a door here!' cried Dick. 'Does it open on to that little balcony, or gallery, or whatever it is that runs all round this room?'

'Yes. The gallery goes completely round the lamp-room,' said Tink. 'You should see it sometimes when the weather's rough, and the gulls go seeking somewhere out of the storm. They perch on that gallery by the dozen! But you can't go out there except in calm weather – you might be blown right off! You've no idea what it's like when there's a storm. Honestly, one night when my father and I were here I thought I felt the lighthouse rocking!'

'This is about the most exciting place I've ever stayed in,' said Anne, her eyes shining. 'Tink, I think you are the luckiest boy in the world!'

'Do you really?' said Tink, pleased. He gave Anne a little pat. 'I hoped you'd like it. Mischief loves it – don't you, Mischief?'

Mischief was up on top of the great lamp. He chattered down to Timmy as if he were telling him all about it. Timmy listened, his ears cocked, his head on one side.

'He looks just as if he understood that monkey-gabble!' said George. 'Tink – this lamp is never lit now, is it?'

'No, never,' said Tink. 'I told you there is a fine new lighthouse a bit farther down the coast. It has a terrific lamp – run by electricity. We shall see its beams sweeping the sea at night.'

'Why don't people build lighthouses and live in them?' wondered George, as she gazed out over the wide blue sea.

'Anyone feeling hungry?' asked Tink, rubbing his tummy. 'I feel jolly empty. Oh gosh – we haven't taken the things out of my boat! Come on – let's carry them all indoors, and have a meal. What's the time? Past four o'clock! No wonder I feel empty. Come on, Mischief – to work! You can carry some of the things in too.'

They ran down the spiral stairway, through room after room, and came to the great door. 'I suppose it had to be built as thickly and strongly as possible, because of the sea dashing against it in storms,' said Julian, pulling it open. The wind rushed in and almost knocked him over! They pushed their way out, and climbed back over the rocks to where they had left the boat. It was bobbing gently up and down in the little stretch of calm water.

'Hallo, *Bob-About*!' said Tink. 'Did you think we were never coming? Got all our goods safely? Good little boat!'

'Idiot!' said Dick, grinning. 'Come on, Ju – I'll take half the heavy things, you take the rest. The girls and Tink can manage the smaller things. Hey, Mischief, what do you think you're doing?'

Mischief had picked up a parcel or two, and was bounding off with them. 'It's all right! He's used to helping!' shouted Tink. 'He often goes shopping with me, and carries bags and things. Let him help, he likes it.'

The monkey certainly was very useful. He scampered to and fro with all kinds of little things, and chattered happily. Timmy stood staring at him, his tail down, wishing he could use his paws as nimbly as Mischief could. George gave him a loving pat.

'It's all right, Timmy, darling. Here – take this basket.'

Timmy took the basket in his mouth by the handle and leapt happily up the steps of the lighthouse. He might not be able to pick up the little things that Mischief so easily managed – but at least he could carry baskets!

'We'll leave the boat bobbing up and down,' said Tink. 'It will be quite all right there, tied to the post, unless the sea gets terribly rough – then we'll have to pull it halfway up the steps.'

'Let's have our meal and unpack before we arrange our things,' said Anne. 'I really do feel very hungry now. What sort of a meal shall we have? I feel as if I want something more than a tea-time meal!'

'That's the worst of living in a lighthouse,' said Tink, quite seriously. 'You're awfully hungry nearly all the time. I used to have five or six meals a day when I stayed here with my father.'

'Sounds all right to *me*,' said Dick, with a grin. 'Let's have a "tea-sup" meal, shall we? A mixture of tea and supper! Tea-sup!'

Some of the things were put into the bedroom and some into the living room. Soon Tink popped a saucepan of water on the stove to boil. Because of the rainy weather, the little rain catch-tank had provided plenty of water for the small inside tank set over the sink, which was most conveniently put in the living room. When Tink turned on the tap, out came clear rainwater!

'Magic!' said Anne, delighted. 'I feel as if I'm in a dream!'

Eggs were put into the saucepan, and were soon boiled. 'Exactly three minutes and a half,' said Anne, ladling out each one with a spoon. '*Two* eggs each! At this rate we shall have to go shopping every day! George, you cut some bread-and-butter. The bread's in that bag – but goodness knows where the butter is. I know we bought some.'

'What about having a few of Joanna's famous mince pies too?' said Dick, taking the lid off a big square tin. 'Whew! Dozens! And cherry buns as well! And homemade macaroons – Joanna's speciality! I *say* what a meal!'

'What shall we have to drink?' said Julian. 'Ginger-beer? Lemonade? Or shall we make some tea?'

Everyone voted for ginger-beer. It was a very pleasant and cheery meal that the Five had in the old lighthouse, with Mischief and Tink. The gulls called outside, the wind gave the lighthouse an occasional buffet, and the sound of the sea was mixed with all the other noises – lovely! Anne hugged her knees as she waited for her ginger-beer. To think they were going to stay here for days and days. All by themselves.

When the meal was over, Anne and George washed up

in the little sink. 'Oh don't wash up – just give the things a quick wipe-over!' said Tink. 'Like this!'

'Oh *no*!' said Anne. 'That's just like a boy! You'd better leave this side of things to me. I *like* doing jobs like this, see?'

'Just like a girl!' said Tink, with a grin.

'No, it isn't,' said George. 'I hate doing them, and *I'm* a girl – though I wish I wasn't!'

'Never mind – you *look* like a boy, and you're often as *rude* as a boy, and you haven't an awful lot of manners,' said Tink, quite thinking that he was comforting George.

'I've more manners than *you*,' said George, and stalked off in a huff to look out of the windows. But nobody could be in a huff for long, with that wonderful view – sea for miles and miles, tipped here and there with white breakers. George gave a sigh of pleasure. She forgot that she was annoyed with Tink, and turned to him with a smile.

'If I could own this view, I'd feel I was the richest person in all the world!' she said. 'You're very lucky, Tink.'

'Am I?' said Tink, thinking it over. 'Well, you can have half the view, if you like. I don't want it all.'

Julian laughed, and clapped the boy on the back. 'We'll all share it, while we're here!' he said. 'Come on – let's unpack and arrange everything. Girls, you had better sleep here in this living room – and we three boys will sleep down in the bedroom. That all right by you, Tink?'

'Fine – so long as you don't mind Mischief sleeping

with us,' said Tink. 'Anyway I expect Timmy will sleep with the girls.'

'Woof,' said Timmy, agreeing. He was certainly not going to sleep anywhere without George!

They all had fun unpacking, and putting the things in the different places. 'Storeroom for that,' Julian said, 'and living room for this and this – and bedroom for these rugs – though these two had better go to the living room, because the girls will sleep there.'

'Cards for the living room,' said Dick, handing them to Anne. 'And books. And papers. Gosh, we mustn't forget to send a card each day to Aunt Fanny. We promised we would.'

'Well, she'll know we arrived safely today because the taxi driver will be sure to send a message to her,' said George. 'But tomorrow we'll go down to the village and buy a stock of postcards – and we'll send one every single day. I know Mother will worry if we don't.'

'All mothers are worriers,' said Dick. 'It's a nuisance – but on the other hand it's one of the nice things about them. Now then – what about a game of cards?'

And there they all are in the lighthouse, playing cards with shouts and laughter, Timmy and Mischief watching. You do have fun together, Five, don't you?

CHAPTER ELEVEN

Jeremiah Boogle

When it began to get dark, Tink left the card table, and fetched an old-fashioned oil-lamp. He shook it.

'It's still got some oil in,' he said. 'Good. I'll light it, then we can see properly.'

'What a pity we can't light the great oil-lamp at the top of the lighthouse,' said George. 'That must have been the lighthouse keeper's great moment – lighting up the lamp to warn ships away. I wonder who first thought of a lighthouse – someone whose folk sailed, and might be wrecked on rocks, I suppose?'

'One of the first great lighthouses was built ages ago on an island called Pharos at the mouth of the Nile, not far from the great port of Alexandria,' said Julian.

'What was it built of – stone, like this one?' asked Tink.

'No. It was built of white marble,' said Julian. 'I thought of it today when we went up the spiral staircase here – because the Pharos lighthouse had one too – much, much bigger than ours.'

'What was their lamp like?' asked Tink.

'I don't know if it had a *lamp*,' said Julian. 'It's said that an enormous fire was built each night on the top of the

lighthouse, whose flames could be seen by ships a hundred miles away!'

'Goodness – it must have been a pretty high lighthouse, then, this Pharos!' said Dick.

'Well, it was supposed to be about 180 metres high!' said Julian.

'Whew! I wonder the wind didn't blow it down!' said Dick. 'Let's go and see it one day – if it's still there.'

'Idiot!' said Julian. 'It's gone long since. After all, it was built over twenty-two hundred years ago! An earthquake came along one day and the magnificent lighthouse was shaken to bits – completely destroyed!'

There was a shocked silence. Everyone looked round at the walls of the lighthouse they were in. An earthquake! What a catastrophe that would be for even a *little* lighthouse!

'Cheer up, Anne!' said Julian, with a laugh. '*We're* not likely to be visited by an earthquake tonight! That old lighthouse on Pharos Island was one of the Seven Wonders of the Ancient World. No – *don't* ask me the others – I'm getting too sleepy to remember!'

'I wish we could light the lamp in *this* lighthouse,' said Anne. 'It can't like being a *blind* lighthouse, after shining brightly for so many years. *Could* the lamp be lit, Tink, or is it broken now?'

'Anne – if you think we're going to scramble round that lamp-room and light the lamp just because you feel sorry about it, you're mistaken,' said Dick, firmly. 'Anyway, it's sure to be out of order after all these years.'

'I don't see why it should be,' objected Tink. 'The lamp's never been interfered with.'

'Look – are we going to go on with our game, or are we not?' said Julian. 'I may as well remind you that I have won practically every game so far! Unless someone else wins a game soon I shall consider that I'm playing with a bunch of nitwits!'

That was quite enough to make everyone pick up their cards, and see if they couldn't possibly beat Julian!

'We'll jolly well play till you're well and truly beaten!' said Dick.

But no – nobody could beat Julian that night. Luck went his way all the time. At the end of the fifth game Anne yawned loudly.

'Oh, sorry!' she said. 'Don't think I'm bored. That yawn came too suddenly for me to stop it!'

'Well, I feel decidedly yawny too,' said Dick. 'What about a snack of something – and then we'll go to bed. We had such an enormous tea-sup that I feel I can't manage another *meal* – but a chocolate biscuit or two would be quite welcome.'

'Woof!' said Timmy at once, agreeing heartily, and Mischief said something in his little chattering voice, and tugged at Tink's sleeve.

'I'll bring you a snack or two,' said Anne, getting up. She soon came back with a tray on which she had put lemonade, large slices of Joanna's new cake, and a chocolate biscuit for everyone, including Timmy and Mischief.

They ate with enjoyment, feeling lazy and comfortable. 'And now to bed!' said Julian. 'Girls, do you want any help with your mattress or rugs or anything?'

'No, thanks,' said Anne. 'Do you boys want to wash, and clean your teeth at the sink here? Because if so, do it now.'

Before a quarter of an hour had gone, everyone was bedded down comfortably. The three boys curled up in rugs in the bedroom below, with Mischief cuddled into

Tink's neck. The two girls and Timmy lay on a mattress, with a blanket over them, Timmy lay beside George, occasionally licking her ear with his big tongue.

'*Dear* Timmy!' said George, sleepily. 'I love you – but do please keep your tongue to yourself!'

And soon they were all asleep, boys, girls, and animals too. Outside, the sea sighed and splashed and swirled, and the wind cried like the daytime gulls. But all was peace and quiet inside the old lighthouse. Not even Mischief the monkey stirred in his sleep.

It was fun to wake up in the morning, and hear the gulls screaming round; fun to have breakfast of eggs and bread and butter, and apples to crunch afterwards – fun to plan what to do that day.

'I vote we do a bit of shopping and buy some more eggs, and fresh bread, and a bottle or two of creamy milk,' said Anne.

'And we might try and find the taxi driver's great-grandad, and ask him a few things about the lighthouse, and the wreckers that came in the old days,' said Dick.

'Yes – and he might show us the Wreckers' Cave!' said Julian. 'I'd like to see that! Let's buck up with whatever jobs there are to do, and we'll go over the rocks to the jetty. The tide should be out, so we ought to be able to walk over.'

'Well, we *must* be back before the tide comes in, then,' said Tink. 'Because if we leave the boat tied up here by

the lighthouse, we shan't be able to get back once the sea sweeps over the rocks and cuts us off!'

'Right,' said Julian. 'Be ready as soon as you can.'

Everyone was ready very quickly, and the little party set off over the rocks that at low tide lay between the lighthouse and the shore. Wicked rocks they were too – with sharp edges and points that would hole a ship at once!

Soon the children were on the little stone jetty. 'What was the name of old Great-Grandad?' said Dick frowning.

'Jeremiah Boogle,' said Anne. 'And he smokes a long pipe, and scowls at people.'

'Well – he *should* be easy to find!' said Julian. 'Come along. He's probably somewhere on the quay.'

'There he is!' said George, spotting an old man with a long pipe in his mouth. 'That's Jeremiah, I'm sure!'

Yes, there he was, sitting with his legs stretched out in front of him, an old, old man, smoking a very long pipe! He had a fine beard, a yachting cap askew on his head, and such enormous shaggy eyebrows that it was difficult to see his eyes beneath them!

The Five went up to him, with Timmy trotting behind, and Mischief on Tink's shoulder. The old man spotted Mischief at once.

'Well, well – a monkey!' he said. 'Many's the little monkey I've brought home from my voyages.' He snapped his fingers and made a curious noise in his throat. Mischief stared at him, listening. Then he leapt from Tink's shoulder on to the old man's, and rubbed his head against the old sailor's hairy ear.

'Mischief!' said Tink, amazed. 'Look at that, George. He never goes to a stranger!'

'Well, maybe I knew his great-grandfather!' said the old sailor, laughing, and scratching Mischief's neck.

'All monkeys like me – and I like them!'

'Er – are you Mr Jeremiah Boogle?' asked Julian.

'Jeremiah Boogle, that's me,' said the old fellow, and touched his cap. 'How do you know my name?'

'Well, Jackson, the taxi driver, told us he was your great-grandson,' said Julian. 'You see we're staying at the old lighthouse – and Jackson said you could tell us a few things about it – its history, you know. And about the wreckers that lived here before the lighthouse was built.'

'Oh, I can tell you tales all right!' said Jeremiah, puffing out a cloud of smoke, and making Mischief cough. 'That's more than that silly young great-grandson of mine can! He don't know nothing, nothing at all – except about cars. Well, who wants cars, nasty, smelly noisy things? Pah! That young George Jackson is a ninny!'

'He's not. He's the cleverest mechanic in the place!' said George, at once. 'There's not a thing he doesn't know about cars!'

'*Cars*! There now, what did I say – nasty, noisy, smelly things!' said Jackson's great-grandad, with a snort.

'Well, look – we don't want to talk about cars,' said Julian. 'You tell us about the old days – the wreckers and all that!'

'Ah – the old days!' said Great-Grandad. 'Well, I knew some wreckers myself, once – there was One-Ear Bill, now . . .' And then old Jeremiah told a story that the Five could hardly believe!

CHAPTER TWELVE

Jeremiah's tale

'NOW WHEN I was a boy,' began the old man, 'a boy not much older than this here youngster,' and he poked Tink with his horny forefinger, 'there wasn't a lighthouse out there – but there were always those wicked rocks! And many's the time in a stormy season when ships have been caught by their teeth, a-glittering there, waiting. You know what they're called, don't you?'

'Yes. Demon's Rocks,' said Tink.

'Well, up on that high cliff there, lived a wicked old man,' said Jeremiah. 'And he had a son as bad as himself, and a nephew too. The Three Wreckers, they was called, and I'll tell you how they came by their name.'

'Did you know them?' asked Dick.

'That I did! And if I was hidden behind a bush when they came marching by, I'd send a stone skedaddling after them!' said the old man. 'Mean and cruel and wicked they were. And everyone was scared of them, right down afraid! There was One-Ear, the old man. They say his left ear was chewed off by a monkey, but do I blame that monkey? No, I do not, not more than I'd blame *your* monkey for chewing off the ear of somebody else I know – but I won't mention no names, he might hear me.'

The old fellow looked over his shoulder as if the man he was thinking of might be about.

'Well – there was One-Ear, the old man – and there was Nosey, the son – and Bart, his nephew – and not a pin to choose between them for meanness. There was only one thing they was after – and that was money! And a mighty wicked way they chose to get it.' The old man stopped and spat in disgust on the pavement.

'Pah! I'll tell you how they got rich, oh yes, I'll tell you. And I'll tell you what happened to them in the end too. Be a lesson to you and to everyone! Well now, you see that high cliff away down the coast there – the one with the flag-post and the flag a-waving in the wind?'

'Yes,' said everyone, looking at the waving flag.

'Now ships mustn't hug the coast beyond that point!' said Great-Grandad. 'If they do, they'll be forced inland by the current, and thrown on those rocks down there – Demon's Rocks. And that's the end of them. No ship has ever been able to escape the sharp teeth of those wicked rocks, once she's caught in that current. Well now, to stop the ships going near to the cliff in those days, they flew a flag in the daytime – and lit a lamp up there at night. And both said as plain as could be, "BEWARE! KEEP OUT! DANGER!"

'Of course, all sailors knew the flag and the lamp too, and many a one blessed them, and took their ships out to sea, away from Demon's Rocks. But that didn't suit old One-Ear Bill. *He* didn't mind a wreck or two! He'd be down on the beach picking up what he could, if a ship came smashing down on the rocks. And would he save a single soul – not he! There were some people who said he was the Demon of Demon's Rocks himself!'

'What a wicked old man!' said Anne horrified.

'Aye, you're right, missie,' said the old fellow. 'Well, the wrecks didn't come often enough for him and Nosey and Bart. So they put their ugly heads together and thought up as wicked a plan as any man could think of!'

'What was it?' said Tink, his eyes almost falling out of his head.

'Well, on a stormy night he put out the lamp shining brightly on the far cliff, and he and Nosey carried it to that bit of cliff over there, see?' And the old man pointed to a jutting-out piece nearby. 'And you know what's just below *that* cliff, don't you – all round the lighthouse!'

'Rocks! Sharp, horrible rocks – the Demon's Rocks!' said George, horrified.

'Do you mean to say that One-Ear Bill and the others deliberately shone the lamp there on stormy nights, to guide ships straight on to the rocks?' said Julian.

'Aye, that's exactly what I mean,' said Jeremiah Boogle. 'And what's more I met old One-Ear Bill myself one dark night when the storms were on – and what was he carrying between himself and Nosey – the lamp! They'd doused the light, of course, but I'd my own little lantern with me, and I saw the lamp plain enough. Aye, that I did! And when they saw me, they set Bart on to me, to push me over the cliff, so I wouldn't tell on them. But I got away, and I DID tell on 'em! Ho, yes, I told all right. And One-Ear Bill went to prison, and serve him right, the wicked man. But he didn't care – and why should he? He was rich! RICH!'

'But how was he rich?' asked Dick.

'Well, young man, the ships that came sailing round this coast in those days, came from far-off countries, and many of them carried treasure,' said Jeremiah. 'And One-Ear Bill stole so much gold and silver and pearls and other things from the wrecks, that he knew he wouldn't need to do another day's work when he came out of prison. A rich man he would be – he wouldn't even need to wreck a ship again!'

'But why weren't the stolen goods taken from him?' said Julian.

'He'd hidden them!' said the old man. 'Ah he'd hidden them well, too. Not even Nosey his son, nor Bart his nephew, knew where he'd put them. They were sure he'd got everything hidden in one of the caves in the cliff – but search as they might, they never found the treasure! They went to prison too, but they came out long before old One-Ear Bill was due out – and how they hunted for the gold and silver, and all that One-Ear had hidden away!'

'Did One-Ear Bill get it when he came out of prison?' asked Dick, thinking this was a much more exciting story than he had ever read in a book – and a true one too!

'No. No, he didn't get it,' said Jeremiah, puffing out a cloud of smoke. 'And glad I am to say that. He died in prison, the wicked old man.'

'Well then – what happened to the treasure from the wrecked ships?' asked George. 'Who found it?'

'No one,' said the old man. 'No one at all! It's still

there, hidden wherever that old rascal put it. His secret went with him. Bart looked for it, and Nosey too – ho, I've seen 'em in those caves day after day, and with a lamp night after night. But they never found even a pearl necklace. Ho – that was a good joke, that was! They're dead and gone now – but there're relatives of theirs still living in Demon's Rocks, who could do with a bit of that treasure – poor as church mice they are, with two children as skinny as ever you'd see!'

'Doesn't anyone even have an *idea* where the loot from the wrecked ships is?' asked Julian. 'What about the cave we've been hearing about – the Wreckers' Cave?'

'Oh aye – we've a Wreckers' Cave, all right,' said the old man, knocking out his pipe. 'And I reckon about five thousand people have been in it, scouting round, looking into holes and corners hoping to find what Bart and Nosey never did find! Or maybe ten thousand, who knows? I don't mind telling you, I've been there meself – but not a smell of a little gold coin did I ever see! I'll take you there myself some day if you like. But mind – don't you hope to find anything. It's my belief that One-Ear Bill never did hide his treasure there – he just said it was there to fool Nosey and Bart!'

'We'd love to go and see the cave,' said Dick, and George nodded her head in delight. 'Not to hunt for treasure, of course – it's pretty obvious it's not there now – maybe somebody *did* find it, and took it away secretly!'

'Maybe,' said Jeremiah. 'All right, young man – you come and tell me when you're ready. I'm sitting here most days. And if you've any nice sweets you don't have any use for, think of me, see?'

'We'll go and buy you some straight away,' said Julian. He couldn't help laughing. 'What kind do you like?'

'Oh, you tell Tom the sweetshop owner it's for old Jeremiah Boogle – he'll give you what I like,' said the old man. 'And mind now – don't you go snooping round them old caves by yourselves – you might get lost. It's a proper laby – laby . . .'

'Labyrinth,' said Julian, smiling. 'Right – we'll be careful.'

The Five went off, Timmy glad to be on the move again. He couldn't understand the old man's story of course, and he wondered why George hadn't taken him for his usual after-breakfast walk. He gave a little whine, and she patted his big head.

'Sorry, Timmy!' she said. 'That old man told such an interesting story that I quite forgot you were longing for a walk. We'll go for one now.'

'Let's call in at the sweetshop first, shall we?' said Julian. 'That old chap deserves an extra something for his tale. Goodness knows how much was true – but he certainly told it well!'

'Of *course* it was true!' said George. 'Why ever should he tell lies?'

'Well – he might have, to get some sweets, you know!'

said Julian, smiling. 'I don't blame him! It's a jolly good story – but please don't think there's any treasure still hidden somewhere, George. It's no use believing that.'

'Well, I do believe it!' said George, defiantly. 'I think he was telling the truth, sweets or no sweets. Don't you, Tink?'

'Oh *yes*,' said Tink. 'You wait till you see the caves round about here! Hoo – there might be any *amount* of treasure there, and no one would ever know! I did hunt round a bit myself – but those caves are scary, and when I coughed once, my cough came echoing back to me a hundred times and I was so scared I ran for my life – and fell splash into a pool!'

Everyone laughed. 'Let's buck up and do our shopping,' said Dick. 'And then what about going for a good long walk?'

'Well, *I* don't want to carry eggs and bread and milk for miles,' said George. 'I say a walk first – and then we'll come back, have ice-creams, do our shopping – and go back to the lighthouse.'

'Right!' said Julian. 'Come on, Timmy. We're off for a walk – a *walk*! Ha, that's the word to set your tail wagging, isn't it? Look at it, Mischief. Don't you wish you could wag *your* tail like that!'

CHAPTER THIRTEEN

A pleasant morning – and a shock!

'WHERE SHALL we go for our walk?' said George, as they wandered through the village. 'Oh look – there's a tiny little shop with Tom's Sweetshop written over the door. Let's get the sweets while we remember.'

So in went Julian, and rapped on the counter. A very small man, like a hobgoblin, appeared out of a dark corner.

'I want some sweets for Jeremiah Boogle, please,' said Julian. 'I think you know the kind he wants.'

'I do that!' said Tom, scrabbling about on a shelf. 'The amount that old Jeremiah has eaten since I've been here would keep an army going for years. There you are, young man!'

'He tells a fine story,' said Julian, putting down the money for the sweets.

Tom laughed. 'He's been going on about Bart and Nosey and all them old folks, I suppose,' he said. 'He's a funny one, is old Jeremiah. Never forgets a thing, even if it happened eighty or more years ago! Never forgives, either. There're two folk in this village that he spits at when he passes by them. Naughty old man, he is.'

'What have they done to earn his spite?' asked Dick, in surprise.

'Well, they're some kin of his old enemy, One-Ear Bill,' said Tom. 'I reckon he told you about him all right, didn't he?'

'Yes, he did,' said Julian. 'But all that business about the wrecking happened years and years ago! Surely Jeremiah doesn't vent his anger on any descendants of the wicked One-Ear Bill!'

'Oh, but he *does*!' said Tom. 'You see, these two fellows he spits at have the job of showing people round the caves here – especially the Wreckers' Cave – and I reckon old Jeremiah still broods about One-Ear's hidden treasure, and is scared in case these two chaps ever find it. Find it! It's nearly seventy years since all that happened. Why, that lighthouse over there was built over sixty years ago – after that wrecking business went on. No one will come across any treasure now!'

'But surely they *might*,' said George. 'It depends where it was hidden. If it was in some dry, watertight place, it should still be all right. After all, gold and silver don't decay, do they? Wherever it was hidden, it must still be there!'

'That's what all you visitors say!' said Tom. 'And that's what Ebenezer and Jacob say – they're the two chaps who show people round the caves. But they only say that to make a bit of a thrill for the visitors, you know. Same as old Jeremiah does. Takes them in properly! Well – you believe what you like, youngsters – but you won't find any treasure! I reckon the sea took that years ago!

Good day to you! I'll give Jeremiah the sweets when he calls in.'

'Well,' said Dick, as soon as they were outside the shop, 'this is all very interesting! I think probably old Tom's right. The reason why the treasure was never found is because it was probably hidden where the sea managed to get at it – in some water-hole, or somewhere like that.'

'I still believe it's somewhere safe,' said George. 'So does Tink.'

'Oh well . . . I should think probably Timmy believes it as well,' said Dick. 'He has a childlike mind too!'

Dick at once received a hard punch on the back from George. He laughed. 'All right! We'll give you a chance to hunt for the treasure, won't we, Ju? We'll visit the Wreckers' Cave as soon as we can. Let's go up on the cliffs for our walk, and see if we can spot where the first old lamp used to be, that warned ships to swing out to sea, and avoid Demon's Rocks.'

It was a lovely walk along the cliffs. The celandines and tiny dog violets were out, and clumps of pale yellow primroses were everywhere. The breeze blew strongly, and Mischief held tightly to Tink's right ear, afraid of being blown off his shoulder. Timmy enjoyed himself thoroughly, bounding along, tail flourishing happily, sniffing at everything.

They came to the flag-post set high on the cliff, its great red flag waving vigorously in the breeze. A notice-board was beside it. George read it.

'This flag warns ships off Demon's Rocks by day. By night the great lighthouse at High Cliffs, farther along the coast, gives warning. In the old days a lamp shone from this spot to give the ships warning, and later a small lighthouse was built out on Demon's Rocks. It is still in existence, but is no longer in use.'

'Ha – they're wrong there!' said Tink, pointing to the last sentence. '*We're* using it! I'll alter the notice!' and Tink actually took a pencil to scratch out the last six words!

Julian took it from him. 'Don't be silly. You can't mess about with public notices. Don't say you're one of the idiots who like to scribble all over the place!'

Tink held out his hand for the pencil. 'All right. It was just that I thought it wanted correcting. I'm *not* the kind of idiot who scribbles on walls or public notices.'

'Right,' said Julian. 'Tink, can we see Demon's Rocks – the rocks themselves, I mean, with our lighthouse – from these cliffs?'

'No,' said Tink. 'The cliff swings away to the left, look, and the Demon's Rocks are away right round the corner, if you see what I mean – so no ship should follow the coastline here, but should keep well out at sea, or it'd be on the rocks. You can see quite well that if the wreckers took the lamp from its warning place here, and put it much farther back, along the way we've come, the ships would swing too far inland, and find themselves wrecked!'

'I think *I* should have hated old One-Ear Bill as much as old Jeremiah does,' said George, imagining the beautiful ships being ground to pieces all those years ago – just because of a greedy man who liked the pickings from wrecks!

'Well, we'd better go back,' said Julian, looking at his watch. 'We've some shopping to do, remember! Better buck up too – it looks like rain all of a sudden!'

He was right. It was pouring by the time they reached the village! They crowded into a little shop that said 'Morning Coffee' and ordered a cup each, and buns. The buns were so nice that they bought some to take back to the lighthouse with them. Then Anne remembered postcards.

'We *must* buy some,' she said, 'and send one off today. Better get some now, and write one and post it while we're here.'

Dick slipped out of the coffee shop and returned with a packet of very gaudily coloured cards. 'Some of them show the lighthouse,' he said. 'We'll send one of those – and you choose a card to send to your father too, Tink.'

'It would be a waste,' said Tink. 'He wouldn't even bother to read it.'

'Well, send one to your mother,' said Anne.

'I haven't one,' said Tink. 'She's dead. She died when I was born. That's why my father and I always go about together.'

'I'm very, very sorry, Tink,' said Anne, shocked. The others were sorry too. No wonder Tink was so wild. No mother to teach him anything! Poor Tink! Anne felt as if she wanted to buy him every bun in the shop!

'Have another bun, Tink,' she said. 'Or an ice-cream. I'll pay. Mischief can have one too.'

'We're *all* going to have another bun each, *and* an ice-cream,' said Julian. 'Timmy and Mischief too. Then we'll do our shopping and go home – home to the lighthouse. That sounds grand, doesn't it!'

They wrote three cards – one to Uncle Quentin and Aunt Fanny – one to Joanna – and one to the professor. 'Now they'll know we are safe and happy!' said Anne, sticking on the stamps.

The rain had stopped, so they went to do their shopping – fresh bread, more butter and eggs, two bottles of milk, some fruit and a few other things. Then off they went down to the little jetty.

'Tide will soon turn,' said Julian, as they jumped down from the jetty to the rocky little beach. 'Come on – we'll just have time to walk over the rocks to the lighthouse. PLEASE don't drop the eggs, Tink!'

They made their way over the rocks, jumping over little pools here and there and avoiding the slimy strands of seaweed that in places covered the rocks. The lighthouse seemed very tall as they came up to it.

'It's *tiny* compared to the great new one away at High Cliffs,' said Tink. 'You ought to go over that! The revolving lamp at the top is magnificent! Its light is so powerful that ships can see it for miles!'

'Well, this little lighthouse looks nice enough to me at the moment,' said Dick, climbing up the stone steps to the strong wooden door. 'Hallo! Look – two bottles of milk on the top step! Don't tell me the milkman's been!'

'He used to call when my father and I were here,' said Tink. 'Only when the tide was out in the morning though, because he hasn't a boat. I suppose he heard *we* were all staying here, and came to see if we wanted milk – and left two bottles when he found we were out. He probably yelled through the letter-box and when we didn't answer he just left the milk, on chance.'

'Sensible fellow!' said Dick. 'Get out your key, Tink, and unlock the door.'

'I don't remember locking it behind us when we went out this morning,' said Tink, frantically feeling in all his pockets. 'I must have left it in the lock on the inside of the door. Let's see now – we locked the door last night, and left the key in the lock. So I *must* have unlocked it this morning for us all to get out.'

'That's right – but after you unlocked it you ran straight down the steps with George, and the rest of us followed,' said Julian. 'Anne was last. Did *you* lock the door after you, Anne?'

'No. I never thought of it!' said Anne. 'I just shut the door with a bang and raced after you all! So the key must still be on the other side of the door!'

'Well, if we push the door, it should open!' said Julian, with a grin. 'And the key will be on the inside, waiting for us! Let's go in!'

He pushed hard, for the door shut very tightly – and sure enough, it swung open. Julian put his hand round to the inside lock to feel for the key.

It wasn't there! Julian looked at the others, frowning.

'*Someone's been here* – and found the door unlocked – taken the key – and probably plenty of other things as well!' he said. 'We'd better go and look. Come on!'

'Wait – there's something on the doormat,' said Dick, picking up a letter. 'The postman has visited the lighthouse too – here's a letter forwarded from Kirrin – so at least *two* people came while we were out! But surely neither of them would take the key – or anything else either!'

'Well – we'll soon see!' said Julian, grimly, and up the first bend of the spiral stairway he went, at top speed!

CHAPTER FOURTEEN

The old, old map

JULIAN AND Dick went into each room of the lighthouse, racing up the spiral stairway from one to the other. Why, oh why, hadn't they watched to see that Tink locked the door and took the key!

Yes – a few things *had* been taken!

'My rug!' said George. 'That's gone!'

'And my purse,' said Anne. 'I left it here on the table. That's been taken, too!'

'So has my little travelling clock,' groaned Julian. 'Why did I bring it? I could have used my watch!'

There were a few other things gone, all small. 'Horrible fellow, whoever he is, to creep into the lighthouse while we were out and take our things!' said Anne, almost crying. 'Who would come here – they would surely be seen from the quay, wouldn't they?'

'Yes – you're right there,' said Julian. 'Though probably the thief slipped in when it was pouring with rain, and the quay was deserted! I think we'll have to tell the police, you know. Let's have our dinner, and then I'll take the boat and slip across to the village. The tide will be in then, and I shan't be able to walk over the rocks. Blow that thief! I was looking forward to a nice quiet read this afternoon!'

After their meal, Julian took the boat and rowed across to the jetty. He went straight to the police station, where a stolid-looking policeman listened to him, and wrote slowly in a book.

'Have you any idea who the thief might be?' asked the policeman. 'Or if anyone came to the lighthouse while you were out?'

'Well, two people seem to have come,' said Julian. 'The milkman, because we were surprised to find milk bottles on the step. And the postman. There was a letter for us on the mat inside the door. I don't know of anyone else.'

'Well, as far as I can tell you, both Willy the Milkman, and Postie are as honest as the day,' said the policeman, scratching his chin with his pencil. 'There may have been a third visitor – one who didn't leave milk or a letter! I'll see if anyone was on the quay this morning, who saw the thief going over the Demon's Rocks. Er – do you suspect anyone?'

'Good gracious, no!' said Julian. 'I don't know anyone here – unless you can count Jeremiah Boogle, or Tom the sweetshop owner!'

'No. No, I think we can rule both of them out,' said the policeman, smiling. 'Well, I'll do what I can, and let you know if I hear of anything. Good afternoon, and by the way, as you can't lock that lighthouse door now, and it's plain there are thieves about, I shouldn't leave the lighthouse empty, see?'

'Yes. Yes, I'd already thought of that,' said Julian. 'I

can jam the door all right with something when we're *in* the lighthouse – but I can't do that when we're out.'

'Well – it looks as if we're in for a wet spell,' said the policeman. 'So maybe it won't be much hardship to keep indoors. I hope you're comfortable in the lighthouse – seems a funny place to stay, really.'

'Oh we're *very* comfortable, Constable,' said Julian, smiling. 'Why not pay us a call sometime, and see us?'

'Thanks,' said the policeman, and took Julian to the door.

The constable was right in forecasting a wet spell. It poured all that afternoon, and the little company in the lighthouse whiled away the time playing cards. Julian and Dick had managed to find a heavy piece of wood in the storeroom to jam the door from the inside. They all felt much safer when they knew that had been done! Now no one could get in without making a terrific noise!

'I'm stiff,' said George, at last. 'I want to stretch my legs. I've a good mind to run up and down the stairway half a dozen times.'

'Well, go on, then,' said Dick. 'Nobody's stopping you!'

'How far down does the lighthouse go, Tink?' asked George. 'We always scoot up the first bit of the spiral stairway and never think about the lighthouse foundations deep down in the rock. *Are* they deep down?'

'Oh, they are,' said Tink, looking up from his book. 'My father told me that when the lighthouse was built, they drilled right down into the rock for a long way – made a kind of shaft. And he said that under these rocks there are all kinds of peculiar holes and tunnels – the drill kept shooting downwards when it came to a sudden space.'

'*Really?*' said Dick interested. 'I hadn't thought of what would have to be done to make a high lighthouse safe from the gales and storms. It would *have* to have deep foundations, of course!'

'My father found an old map somewhere,' said Tink. 'A sort of plan made when the lighthouse was first built.'

'Like architects draw when they plan how to build a house?' said Anne.

'Something like that,' said Tink. 'I can't remember much about it. I know it showed all the rooms in the lighthouse, connected by the spiral stairway – and it showed the big lamp-room at the top – and at the bottom of the map the foundation shaft was drawn.'

'Can you go down the shaft?' asked Dick. 'Is there a ladder, or anything?'

'I don't know,' said Tink. 'I've never been down there. I never thought about it!'

'Do you know where the old map is – the one made by the architect who drew up plans for the lighthouse builder to follow?' said Julian. 'Where did your father put it?'

'Oh, I expect he threw it away,' said Tink. 'Wait a minute though – it may be in the lamp-room! I remember him taking it up there, because it had a drawing of how the lamp worked.'

'Well, I'd rather like to go and see if I can find it,' said

Julian, interested. 'Come up with me, Tink. Thank goodness you don't keep turning into some sort of car now – you must be growing up!'

So the two of them went up the spiral stairway to the lamp-room at the very top of the tower. Again Julian marvelled at the magnificent views all around. The rain had stopped for a time, and the sea, swept by strong winds, was a swirling tumult of angry waters.

Tink scrabbled about in a little dark space under the lamp. He at last brought up a roll of something white and waved it at Julian. 'Here's the map. I thought it would be in the lamp-room.'

Julian took it down to the others, and they spread it out. It showed the plan of the lighthouse, and was very clearly and beautifully drawn.

'How is it that architects draw so marvellously?' said George. 'Are they architects because they can do this kind of thing so well – or do they draw beautifully because they are architects?'

'A bit of both, probably,' said Julian, bending over the finely drawn plan. 'Ah – here are the foundations, look – my goodness, they do go down a long way into the rock!'

'Great tall buildings like this *always* have deep, strong foundations,' said Dick. 'Last term at school we studied how . . .'

'Let's not talk of school,' said Anne. 'It's already looming in the distance! Tink – can anyone get down into this foundation place?'

'I told you – I don't know,' said Tink. 'Anyway I should think it would be a horrible place down there – dark and smelly, and narrow, and . . .'

'Let's go and see,' said George, getting up. 'I'm so bored at the moment that if I don't do something, I'll fall asleep for a hundred years.'

'Idiot,' said Dick. 'Still – quite a good idea of yours. We'd have a bit of peace and quiet while you were sleeping! Oooooch – don't jab me like that, George!'

'Come on,' said George. 'Let's trot down and find out what's down the shaft.'

Anne didn't want to go down the shaft, but the others ran down the stairway, Timmy too, and soon came to the bottom, opposite the entrance door of the lighthouse.

Tink showed them a large, round trap-door in the floor there. 'If we open that, we'll be looking down into the foundation shaft,' he said.

So they pulled up the large, round, wooden trap-door, and gazed downwards. They could see nothing at all except darkness! 'Where's my torch?' said Julian. 'I'll fetch it!'

Soon his torch was lighting up the round shaft, and they saw an iron ladder going down it on one side. Julian climbed down a few steps and examined the walls of the shaft.

'They're cement!' he called. 'And they must be enormously thick, I should think. I'm going on down.'

So down he went, and down, marvelling at the sturdy cement lining of the enormous shaft. He wondered why it had not been filled in. Perhaps a hollow cement-lined shaft was stronger than a filled-in one? He didn't know.

He came almost to the bottom – but he didn't go down the last steps of the iron ladder. A peculiar noise came from below him! A gurgling, choking noise! What in the world could it be?

He shone his torch down to see – and then stared in amazement! There was water at the bottom of the shaft, water that swirled and moved around, making a strange, hollow, gurgling noise. Where did it come from?

As he watched it, it disappeared – then it came back again! He shone his torch here and there to find out how the water made its way into the shaft.

'There must be a tunnel or a passage of some sort down there, that the sea can enter,' he thought. 'It's high tide now – so the water is swirling in. I wonder – now I *wonder* – if it's free of water when the tide is out! And if so where does that tunnel, or whatever it is, lead to? Or is it always under water? I'll go back and tell the others – and have another look at that old map!'

He climbed back, glad to be out of the smelly darkness of the old shaft. The others were at the top, looking down rather anxiously.

'Here he is!' said George. 'See anything interesting, Julian?'

'I did, rather,' said Julian, climbing out of the shaft. 'Got that old map with you? I want to look at something, if so.'

'Come upstairs, then,' said Dick. 'We can see better there. What was down there, Ju?'

‘Wait till we’re up in the living room,’ said Julian. He took the map from Tink as soon as he arrived there, and sat down to look at it. He ran his finger down the shaft to the bottom, and then jabbed at a round mark drawn there.

‘See that? That’s a hole at the bottom of the shaft, through which sea-water comes in. It’s high tide now, so the water is seeping into the shaft – but it’s not very deep. At low tide there wouldn’t be a single drop coming in. Wouldn’t I love to know where that water-tunnel went to – up to the surface of the rocks? Through them to somewhere a good way off? Or what?’

‘An undersea tunnel!’ said George, her eyes bright. ‘Why don’t we explore it sometime when the tide is out?’

'Well – we'd have to be pretty certain we wouldn't suddenly be drowned!' said Julian, rolling up the map. 'Very interesting, isn't it? I suppose the hole was left in case the constant push of water there, when the tide was in, might undermine the foundations. Better to have the shaft half-full of water than eaten away by constant tides!'

'Well,' began Anne, and then suddenly stopped in fright. A very loud voice came up the stairway, and made everyone jump violently.

'ANYONE AT HOME? HEY, ANYONE AT HOME?'

CHAPTER FIFTEEN

Jacob is in trouble

'WHO'S THAT shouting like that?' said Anne, fearfully. 'It can't be the robber, can it?'

'Of course not,' said Julian, and went to the door of the living room. He yelled down the stairway:

'Who is it? What do you want?'

'It's the police!' shouted back the enormous voice.

'Oh. Come on up, then,' said Julian, relieved. Footsteps could be heard coming up the iron stairway, accompanied by loud puffs and pants. Then a policeman's helmet appeared, followed by his shoulders and the rest of him. Soon he was standing in the living room, beaming round at the surprised company, panting with the effort of climbing so many stairs.

'How did you get in?' asked George. 'We jammed the door shut from the inside.'

'Well, I managed to unjam it,' said the policeman, mopping his forehead, and smiling. He was the same policeman that Julian had seen that afternoon. 'Not much protection that, really. You ought to get a new key made.'

'How did you get over here? The tide's in,' said Julian. 'You couldn't have walked over Demon's Rocks.'

'No. I got Jem Hardy's boat,' said the policeman. 'By the way, my name's Sharp – Police Constable Sharp.'

'A very good name for a policeman,' said Julian, with a cheerful grin. 'Well, have you caught the thief who took our key, and the other things?'

'No. But I've a pretty good idea who it is,' said Sharp. 'I couldn't find anyone who'd been sitting on the quay during the time you were away from the lighthouse, but I did by chance find a lady whose windows look down on the jetty, and she happened to see someone standing about there. She said he went over the rocks to the lighthouse.'

'Who was it? The milkman, the postman?' asked Dick.

'Oh no, I told your friend they were good fellows,' said the constable, looking quite shocked. 'It was er – well, a man who's a bit of a bad lot.'

'Who's that?' asked Julian, suddenly afraid it might be old Jeremiah. *Could* he be a bad lot – he had sounded such a good fellow!

'Well, it's no one you know,' said Sharp. 'It's one of a family with rather a bad name – a man called Jacob – Jacob Loomer. He comes of a family that used to do a bit of wrecking, and . . .'

'Wrecking! Old Jeremiah was telling us of long-ago wreckers!' said Dick. 'One was called Nosey – and another was called Bart – relations of a well-known wrecker called One-Ear – er, One-Ear . . .'

'Bill,' said Sharp. 'Ah, yes – One-Ear Bill. He lived a long time ago, when old Jeremiah was a young man. This here Jacob, the one that was seen going into your lighthouse today, would be his great-great-great grandson, I reckon – something like that. Living image of old One-Ear Bill, according to Jeremiah. There's a bad strain in that family – can't seem to get it out!'

'Well – you say it was Jacob who came into the lighthouse? Why can't we have him arrested then?' said Julian. 'And make him give up the key he took – and the other things?'

'Well, if you'll come along with me and identify your things, maybe I can do something about it,' said the constable. 'But he may have hidden them all by now – though he's that free-handed I wouldn't be surprised if he hasn't *given* them all away. A bit of a fool, Jacob is, as well as a rogue. Ah – he'd have liked the job of wrecking ships, he would – right up his street.'

'I'll come with you now,' said Julian. 'The others don't need to, do they?'

'Oh no – you'll do,' said the policeman, and he and Julian went down the spiral stairway to the entrance. The others heard the door bang, and looked at one another.

'Well! To think that a great-great-great grandson of that horrid old One-Ear Bill is still living in the same place that the old wrecker himself did!' said Dick. '*And* he's a rogue too. History repeating itself!'

'We *must* go and see the Wreckers' Cave tomorrow, if we can,' said George. 'Jeremiah Boogle said he would show it to us.'

'So long as there isn't an old, old wrecker hiding there!' said Anne. 'Older than Jeremiah Boogle – with a beard down to his feet – a sort of Old Man of the Sea – with a horrid gurgling voice, and eyes like a fish!'

'*Really*, Anne!' said George astonished. 'I'll be scared to go into caves if you say things like that!'

'I wonder how Julian's getting on,' said Tink. 'Mischief, stop jigging up and down – you make me feel out of breath!'

Julian was at Jacob's house, and there, sure enough, were the things he had stolen – the rug, the clock and Anne's purse – empty now!'

'And what about the key?' demanded the constable. 'Come on now, you took the key out of the door of the lighthouse, we know you did. Give it here, Jacob.'

'I didn't take it,' said Jacob, sullenly.

'I'll have to take you in, you know, Jacob,' said the constable. 'You'll be searched at the police station. Better give up the key now.'

'Search me all you like!' said Jacob. 'You won't find that key on me. I tell you. I didn't take it. What would I want that key for?'

'For the same reason that you usually want keys for,' said the constable. 'For breaking in and stealing. All right, Jacob. If you won't let this young gentleman have his key, I'll have you searched at the police station. Come along with me.'

But alas, no key was found on the surly Jacob, and the constable shrugged his shoulders and raised his eyebrows at Julian.

'If you take my advice, I'd get a different lock put on your door. Jacob's got your key somewhere. He'll be at the lighthouse again as soon as he sees you all go out.'

'Bah!' said Jacob, rudely. 'You and your keys. I tell you I didn't take it. There wasn't a key there . . .'

'Come along with me, Jacob,' said the constable. He turned to Julian. 'Well, that's all. We'll have his house searched. The odds are that he's hidden the key somewhere. He's an artful dodger, this one!'

Julian went back to the lighthouse, rather worried. It

might take a few days, in a little place like this, to have a new lock put in. In the meantime they would either have to keep themselves prisoners in the lighthouse – or leave a front door that anyone could open!

The others listened excitedly to his tale, when he went back. They were glad to have the rug, the clock and the purse again – though Anne was sad that all her money was gone.

'We'll have to get a new lock and key,' said Julian. 'After all, this lighthouse has only been *lent* to us, and it's our responsibility to look after it and all it contains. It's a good thing it was only *our* things that were taken – not Professor Hayling's!'

'It's getting rather late,' said Anne, jumping up. 'We haven't had our tea yet! I'll get it. Anyone feel like buns with butter and jam?'

Everyone did, and soon Anne produced a large plate of delicious-looking buns. They talked as they drank their tea, and ate the buns.

'I vote we go and find Jeremiah Boogle tomorrow, and see if he's heard of the robbery, and if he has anything interesting to say about it,' said George.

'And also we really must get him to show us the Wreckers' Cave,' said Julian. 'By the way, what were the names of the two men who have the job of showing the visitors round the caves? I'm pretty sure one was Jacob!'

'You're right – it was – and the other man was called

Ebenezer!' said Dick. 'Well – let's hope Jacob is locked up, or out of the way somewhere when we go to see the caves. We shall get some dark looks from him, if not!'

'Well, we can give him some back!' said George, putting on a terrific scowl, and making Timmy give a sudden whine. She patted him. 'It's all right, Timmy – that scowl wasn't for you!'

'We'd better go to the caves tomorrow morning when the tide will be more or less out,' said Julian. 'And I'd better see if I can find a locksmith here who can give us a new lock and key quickly!'

'Why not slip out now?' said Dick. 'I'll come with you for a bit of fresh air. Want to come, girls?'

'No, I'd like to finish my book,' said Anne, and George said the same. Tink was playing with Mischief, and he didn't want to come either.

'Well, you and the lighthouse will be safe with Timmy and Mischief to look after you!' said Julian, and down the stairway he went, with Dick close behind him.

The locksmith promised to come and look at the door in the next day or two. 'Can't leave my shop just now,' he said. 'Nobody to see to it! It'll take me a few days to do the job for you, I'm afraid.'

'Oh, blow!' said Julian. 'We've already had a thief in the lighthouse! We don't like to go out and leave it empty now!'

They rowed back to the lighthouse, shut and jammed the door as best they could, and went up to the girls.

Timmy gave them an uproarious welcome, and Mischief took a flying leap from a chair back on to Dick's shoulder.

'No lock or key for a few days,' said Dick, sitting down and tickling the delighted little monkey. 'I did want to go and see the caves tomorrow – especially the famous Wreckers' one – but we can't possibly leave the lighthouse empty.'

'Woof,' said Timmy at once.

'He says, why not leave *him* behind, and let him guard it,' said George, solemnly, and Timmy at once said, 'Woof', again.

They all laughed. Dick patted Timmy, and ruffled the fur behind his ears. 'Dear old Tim – all right, *you* guard the lighthouse – you shall have a Very Special Bone for a reward!'

'That's settled then. We leave Timmy here on guard, and we all go off to the caves,' said Julian. 'Well, one of the brothers who show visitors round will be missing tomorrow, I fear – Jacob will *not* be there!'

'I bet we'll get some scowls from the other brother – what's his name now – Ebenezer?' said Anne. 'We'll have to be careful that we don't get pushed into a deep pool of water!'

'Dear me, yes,' said Julian. 'One never knows! We'll certainly be on our guard!'

CHAPTER SIXTEEN

Down in the caves

Next morning George awoke with a jump. Timmy was pushing her gently with his nose. 'What is it, Tim?' said George. Timmy gave a bark, and ran to where the spiral stairway led downwards.

'Go down and tell the boys what it is you want,' said George, sleepily. So down the stairway went Timmy, and into the room where the boys were sleeping. He trotted in

and nudged Julian with his nose, but Julian was so fast asleep that he didn't stir.

Timmy pawed at him, and Julian awoke with a jump. He sat up. 'Oh, it's you, Tim – what on earth do you want? Is anything wrong with the girls?'

'Woof,' said Timmy, and ran to the spiral stairway. He disappeared down it, barking.

'Blow! He's heard someone!' said Julian, yawning. 'Well, if it's Ebenezer or Jacob – no, it can't be Jacob, of course – I'll tell him what I think of people who steal!'

He unjammed the door of the lighthouse and opened it. On the step stood two milk bottles! 'Well, really, Timmy, fancy waking me because the milkman came!' said Julian, taking in the bottles. 'Good old milkman – I wonder if he had to come by boat – the sea's pretty high this morning – but I suppose he *could* just about have waded over the rocks!'

At breakfast the Five remembered that they meant to see the caves that morning. They had a very fine meal of fried bacon, bought the day before, and eggs, with buttered toast and marmalade to follow. Anne had made some good hot coffee, and they all enjoyed themselves immensely. Mischief made himself a real nuisance by putting a paw deep in the marmalade jar and then, when shooed, running all over the place leaving sticky marmaladey marks everywhere!

'We'd better all take a wet rag with us as we go about the room,' said Anne, in disgust. 'He's run over the table and desk and everything. BAD Mischief! I do so hate feeling sticky.'

Mischief was sad to feel himself in disgrace, and leapt on to Tink's shoulder, putting his sticky paws lovingly round the boy's neck. 'That's right!' said Tink. 'Rub all your stickiness off on *me*, you little monkey!'

'We'll wash up in the sink, and you boys can tidy up the rooms,' said Anne. 'Then we'll all go out. It's a lovely day.'

'Looks a bit stormy to me,' said Dick. 'What do *you* say, Tim?'

Tim agreed. He thumped his tail vigorously on the floor, making Mischief pounce on it in joy. Anne gathered up the crockery and took it to the sink.

In an hour or so they were ready to go out. 'Let's write a card to Aunt Fanny before we leave,' said Anne. 'Then *that* will be done. We won't say a word about the things that were stolen, though. She might feel upset, and tell us to go back! And *then* what would Uncle Quentin and Professor Hayling say?'

'I bet they're having a wonderful time, arguing all day long, working out figures, and studying papers!' said Julian. 'And I'm pretty certain that Aunt Fanny will have to call them to a meal at least twenty times before they arrive at the table!'

Anne wrote the postcard and put on a stamp. 'Now I'm ready,' she said, standing up. Timmy ran to the top of the stairs, glad that everyone seemed to be on the move at last. He did so love a walk.

'Darling Timmy,' said George, 'I'm afraid you'll have to be left behind to guard the lighthouse! You see, we haven't a key – and we can't jam the door from outside. So please, Timmy dear, stay behind – on guard. You know what *that* means, don't you? On guard!'

Timmy's tail went right down. He gave a small whine. He did so hate being left out of anything – especially a walk. He pawed gently at George as if to say, 'Do please change your mind.'

'On guard, Timmy, now,' said George. 'The lighthouse is in your charge. Don't let *anyone in*. You'd better lie on the mat just inside the entrance.'

Timmy ran slowly down behind Julian and the others, looking very mournful indeed. 'Now lie there,' said George, and gave him a pat on the head. 'We'll take you out again soon, and then one of *us* will stay to guard the lighthouse – but this time we *all* want to go out. On guard!'

Timmy lay down on the mat, and put his head on his paws, his brown eyes looking up at George. 'Dear old faithful,' she said ruffling the hair on his head. 'We won't be very long!'

They slammed the door and went down the lighthouse steps. The tide was still out far enough for them to be able to wade over the rocks to the jetty. 'We must be back before it's well in,' said Julian. 'Or we'll have to stay ashore till it's out again. Our boat is tied to the lighthouse post, remember!'

They went for a stroll along the quay and who should be there, sitting on a stone seat, but old Jeremiah Boogle, smoking his long pipe, staring solemnly out to sea.

'Good morning, Jeremiah,' said Dick, politely. 'I hope we bought the right kind of sweets for you from Tom.'

'Oh aye,' said Jeremiah, puffing out very strong-smelling smoke. 'Hallo, little monkey – so you've come to my shoulder again, have you? Well, what's the news from Monkey Lane?'

The others laughed as Mischief at once poured out a stream of monkey chatter into the old man's ear. 'We thought we would go and see the caves today,' said Julian. 'Especially the old Wreckers' Cave.'

'Now don't you let that Ebenezer take you round!' said the old man, at once. 'You won't find Jacob there – oho – I know what's happened to *him*. And serve him right. Never could keep his fingers to himself, that one! Ebenezer's as bad. He could steal the buttons off your coat, and you'd never know! Now look – what about *me* showing you the caves? I know them inside out, and I can show you things that that rat of an Ebenezer doesn't even know of.'

'Well – we'd certainly much rather *you* took us, and not Ebenezer,' said Julian. 'Ebenezer may be feeling rather angry because we told the police about his brother stealing things. We'll give you some more sweets if *you'll* guide us round.'

'Well, let's go now,' said Jeremiah, getting up very spryly. 'This way!'

And off they went, Mischief too. The little monkey did Jeremiah the honour of sitting on his shoulder all the way down the village street. The old man was delighted to see how everyone stared and laughed.

He took them round the foot of some very high cliffs. They came to a rocky beach farther along, and walked over it. 'There's the entrance,' said the old man, pointing to a large hole in the cliff nearby. 'That's the way to the caves. Got a torch?'

'Yes – we brought one each,' said Julian, patting his pocket. 'Do we have to pay to go in?'

'No. People give Ebenezer a tip – a shilling or so – if he shows them round – or Jacob, when he's there,' said Jeremiah. '*I'll* deal with Ebby, though. Don't you waste your money on that scoundrel!'

The hole in the cliff led to the first cave, which was a big one. Lighted lanterns hung here and there, but gave very little light.

'Mind your step, now,' warned Jeremiah. 'It's really slippery in places. This way – through this old arch.'

It was cold and damp in the cave, and the children had to go carefully, and avoid the puddles left by the sea. Then suddenly Jeremiah turned a corner and went in a completely different direction! Down and down and down they went!

'Hey – we're going towards the *sea* now surely?' said Julian, in surprise. 'Do the caves go *under* the sea, then? Not away back into the cliff?'

'That's right,' said Jeremiah. 'This is a real rocky coast

– and the way we're taking leads down a tunnel under the rocks, and then into the caves deep underground. See the rocky roof over our heads – well, if you listen, you can hear the sea now, mumbling and grumbling over it – that roof is the bed of the sea!'

That was a very strange thought indeed, and rather alarming! Anne gazed fearfully up at the rocky roof overhead, and shone her torch on it, half-expecting to see a few cracks leaking salt water from the sea rolling over the rocky roof! But no – there was a little moisture shining on it, and that was all.

'Are we soon coming to the Wreckers' Cave?' asked George. 'Mischief, stop making those noises. There's nothing to be scared of!'

Mischief didn't like this cold, dark, strange walk underground, and had begun to make harsh, frightened noises, and then suddenly gave a loud scared screech.

'Don't! You made me jump!' said Anne. 'Goodness – listen to the monkey's screech echoing all along the tunnel and back! Sounds like a hundred monkeys chattering at once! *Our* voices echo too!'

Mischief was most alarmed to hear the enormous amount of screeches and chattering noises that now filled the tunnel. He began to cry almost like a baby, and clung to Tink as if he would never let him go.

'I expect he thinks this place is absolutely full of screeching monkeys,' said Anne, sorry for the terrified little creature. 'It's only the echo, Mischief.'

'He'll soon get used to it,' said Tink, hugging the monkey close to him.

'You want to hear the echo just round the next bend of the tunnel!' said Jeremiah, stroking the little monkey, and very foolishly gave an enormous yell just as they got there!

The yell came back ten times as loud, and the tunnel seemed suddenly full of shouts tumbling over one another. Everyone jumped violently, and Mischief leapt high in the air in terror. He sprang to the ground, and scampered away at top speed, wailing in his little monkey voice. He tore down the tunnel, tail in air, and disappeared round the corner. Tink was very upset.

'Mischief! Come back!' he yelled. 'You'll get lost!'

And along came the echo at once. 'Get lost, get lost, get lost – lost – lost!'

'Don't you worry about your monkey,' said Jeremiah, comfortingly. 'I've had a score of monkeys in my time – and they always come back!'

'Well, I'll jolly well stay down here till Mischief *does* come back!' said Tink, in rather a shaky voice.

They came out into a cave. This too was lit by lanterns, though very poorly. They had all heard the murmur of voices as they came to it, and wondered who was there.

Three other visitors were in the cave, sightseeing, like the children. A big burly fellow was with them, with jet-black hair, deep-set dark eyes, and a surly mouth – so like Jacob that Julian guessed at once that he was the brother, Ebenezer.

As soon as Ebenezer set eyes on Jeremiah, he roared in fury.

'You get out! This is *my* job – you get out. *I'll* show the caves to those youngsters!'

And with that such a battle of words followed that the children were almost deafened, especially as the echo repeated everything very loudly indeed! The three visitors fled away up the tunnel, fearing a fight. Anne was very frightened, and clung to Julian.

Ebenezer came shouting up to old Jeremiah, his hand raised. 'Haven't I told you more than a hundred times to keep out of these caves? Haven't I told you *I'm* the one to show folks around – and Jacob too?'

'Don't listen to him!' said Jeremiah, turning his back on the angry man. 'He's nothing but a big-mouth, same as his brother Jacob!'

'Look out!' yelled Julian, as the angry Ebenezer rushed at Jeremiah, his fist raised to strike him. 'LOOK OUT!'

CHAPTER SEVENTEEN

Mischief again – and a surprise!

JEREMIAH SAW the angry man coming at him, and very neatly side-stepped. Ebenezer couldn't stop, stepped heavily on a strand of very slippery seaweed – and went sprawling into a corner!

'Ho!' said Jeremiah, delighted. 'Very nice, Ebenezer! Get up, and run at me again!'

'He'd better not,' said Julian, in his most grown-up

voice. 'I shall report him to the police if he does – and that will make a pair of them in two days. Jacob got into trouble yesterday – and now it will be Ebenezer.'

Ebenezer got up, scowling, and glared at Jeremiah, who grinned back in delight. 'Coming at me again, Ebby?' he said. 'It's grand fun to hit an old man, isn't it?'

But Ebenezer was very much afraid that Julian would do what he had threatened, and report him to the police. He rubbed his shoulder where it had struck a piece of rock, and debated what to do.

'Come along,' said Jeremiah, to the five watching children. 'I'll take you down to the Wreckers' Cave. Ebby can come too, if he can behave himself. But maybe he'd like to run away home, and get his shoulder looked to!'

That was enough for Ebby! He was determined to follow the little company and made rude remarks all the time. So he tailed them, and shouted at them from a safe distance. How they wished they had Timmy with them! He would have made short work of the rude Ebenezer!

'Don't take any notice of him,' said Julian. 'Lead on, Jeremiah. My word, isn't it dark in this tunnel! Good thing we all brought good torches!'

The tunnel came to an end at last and opened out into an extraordinary cave. The roof was unexpectedly high, and the irregular sides were ridged with shelves of rocks. On the shelves were dirty old boxes, a crate or two and some sacks.

'What in the world are those?' asked Dick, shining his torch on them.

'Well, young sir, they're just what they look like – ordinary boxes and sacks,' said Jeremiah. 'Put there by Ebenezer and Jacob to fool people! They tells everybody they're what the old wreckers got out of ships they wrecked, years ago! Hoo-hoo-hoo! Anybody that believes those lies *deserves* to be fooled. They're all from Ebby's backyard. Seen them lying there myself! Hoo-hoo-hoo!'

His hoo-hooing laugh echoed round the cave, and Ebenezer made an angry growling noise rather like a dog.

'*I'm* not going to fool these kids,' said Jeremiah. 'You and your sacks and boxes! I know where the old things are, the real old things – oh yes I do!'

'They're no better than the sacks and boxes there, wherever they are!' said Ebby, in a growling voice. 'You're lying, old Jeremiah – you don't know nothing!'

'Take us on farther,' said Dick. 'There must be more caves. I think this is exciting. Is this really where the old wreckers hid the things they salvaged from the wrecks they caused – or just a tale?'

'Oh, this is their cave, that's true enough. Dressed up a bit by Ebby there!' said Jeremiah. 'But *I* know the caves farther on. Ebby doesn't! He's too scared to go farther under the sea. Aren't you, Ebby?'

Ebby said something that sounded rude. Julian turned to Jeremiah eagerly. 'Oh, do take us farther – if it isn't dangerous!'

'Well, *I'm* going farther on, anyway,' said Tink suddenly. 'Mischief hasn't come back – so he must be lost – and *I'm* going to find him!'

Julian saw that Tink was quite determined. 'Right,' he said. 'We'll come with you. Jeremiah, lead the way! But it's not *really* dangerous, is it? I mean – we don't want to find the sea sweeping through these caves, right up to where we are!'

'Tide's not on the turn yet,' said Jeremiah. 'We're all right for a while. When it comes in, it swirls up this passage here – but it stops at the Wreckers' Cave – that's just too high for it, see? The tunnel runs downwards fast now. It goes right under your lighthouse. Have you seen it down at the bottom of the shaft?'

'Good gracious, yes!' said Julian, remembering. 'I went down it – and the sea was swirling in and out at openings in the bottom of the shaft. Do you mean to say that the sea that rises in the shaft at high tide comes racing up into these tunnels too?'

'Aye, that it does,' said Jeremiah. 'You can get from here to the lighthouse under the rocky seabed right to that foundation shaft. But nobody dares! Tide comes in so quickly, you might get caught and drowned!'

Ebby at once shouted something rude again – it sounded as if he was telling Jeremiah to go and get drowned too!

'Do let's go on farther,' said Dick. 'Come on, Jeremiah.'

So Jeremiah led them farther on under the rocky bed of

the sea. It was strange and rather frightening to hear the constant noise of the water racing over the roof of the winding tunnel. Their torches lit up slimy walls, and rocky shelves and hollows.

'You know – this would have been a very good place to hide treasure,' said Julian, glancing up at a dark hollow in the roof of the tunnel. 'Though I don't know how anyone would set about looking for it – there are hundreds of nooks and crannies – and isn't it *cold* in this tunnel!'

'Well, the sun's rays never penetrate down *here*,' said Dick. 'My word, the sea sounds pretty loud now!'

'I wish we could find Mischief,' said Anne to George. 'Look at poor Tink. He's crying. He's pretending not to, but I could see the tears rolling down his cheeks last time I flashed my torch on him.'

They stopped to look at something – a strange jelly-like thing, like an enormous sea anemone. Ebby caught them up, and bumped into Dick. He rounded on Ebby at once.

'Keep off! Follow us if you like, but don't come so near. We don't like you!'

Ebby took no notice but kept as close behind everyone as he possibly could, and Dick realised that he was probably feeling very scared! Then, as they rounded another corner of the tunnel, and saw yet another cave, Tink gave a yell that echoed everywhere.

'MISCHIEF! LOOK! THERE HE IS! MISCHIEF!'

And sure enough, there was the little monkey, crouched under a small shelf of rock, shivering in fright. He wouldn't even go running to Tink. Tink had to pick him up and hug him.

'Mischief! Poor Mischief – were you very frightened?' he said. 'You're trembling all over! You shouldn't have run away! You might have been lost for ever!'

Mischief had something clutched in his tiny paw. He chattered to Tink, and put his furry little arms round his neck. As he did so, he opened one paw – and something fell out and rolled over the rocky floor.

'What have you dropped, Mischief?' said Dick, and shone his torch down on to the floor of the cave. Something was glittering there – something round and yellow! Everyone stared, and a shock of excitement went through Julian, who was nearest. 'A gold coin!' he cried, and picked it up. 'As bright as when it was minted. Mischief, where did you get it from? Look, Dick, look, George – it's gold all right!'

Immediately everyone was full of the greatest excitement, one thought only in their heads.

The treasure! Mischief must have found the treasure! It was an old coin – very old. Where *could* Mischief have found it?

'Oh, let's go farther on and see!' cried Dick. 'Jeremiah, it *must* be the treasure! Mischief will lead us to it!'

But Mischief would do nothing of the sort. He was *not* going to lose himself again. He was going to sit on Tink's shoulders, with an arm safely round the boy's neck! He hadn't liked being lost, all by himself in the dark.

Jeremiah would not go any farther, either. He shook his head. 'No – not today. Tide will soon be sweeping up these tunnels – faster than we can walk. Better turn back now, in case we're caught. Many's the visitor that's had to run for his life, when the tide came up all of a sudden!'

George's sharp ears caught the sound of a 'swooshswoosh'! Somewhere the tide had crept in! 'Come on!' she said. 'We'd better do what Jeremiah says. The sea's coming up the tunnel now as well as over it – and soon it will be sweeping up the beach too, and in at the cliff passages. We'll be caught in the middle, and have to stay here for ages!'

'No need for alarm, missy,' said old Jeremiah. 'There's a bit of time yet. Halloo – where's Ebenezer gone?'

'Blow – he must have heard us talking about Mischief's gold piece,' said George. 'I forgot all about him! Now he knows that Mischief has found a gold coin, he'll feel sure that the treasure *may* be somewhere down here – and he'll look for it as soon as ever he can! WHY didn't we keep quiet about it?'

'I forgot he was standing near us,' groaned Dick. 'Well I suppose the whole of Demon's Rocks village will know by now that a monkey has found the treasure – and hordes of sightseers will swarm down here, hoping to find it. It must have been put in a pretty dry place, surely, for that coin to be so bright and untarnished.'

'Buck up – we'd better go back as quickly as possible,' said Julian. 'Look at old Jeremiah – he's too thrilled for words! He's planning to find the treasure himself at the earliest possible moment!'

'Well, I vote we have a shot at it ourselves tomorrow,' said Dick, excitement welling up in him at the thought. 'Good old Mischief! You're better than any detective!'

Then away up the tunnels they went, making all kinds of plans. *What* an excitement!

CHAPTER EIGHTEEN

Back in the lighthouse – and an exciting talk!

OLD JEREMIAH was as excited as the others, but he said very little. He was angry to think that Ebenezer should have been there to see the find. He didn't trust that Ebby – nor that Jacob either! They'd be ferreting after that treasure as sure as nuts were nuts, and monkeys were monkeys! Ha – wouldn't they like to know where it was! He stumped on, up the old tunnels, thinking hard, and at last they came out into the welcome daylight again!

'Here, Jeremiah – buy yourself some more sweets,' said Julian, putting some money into the old man's hand. 'And don't count too much on that treasure! I expect it's just an odd coin that Mischief found in a dry corner somewhere!'

'Thank you!' said the old man. 'I don't want the treasure myself – I'm just hoping that Ebby and Jacob don't find it. They'll be hunting all the time for it now!'

They were glad to be out in the open again. The sun had gone now, and the wind had whipped up. It was raining hard.

'I say – we'd better buck up, else we shan't be able to walk back to the lighthouse over the rocks!' said Julian, worried. But fortunately the wind was against the tide and they just had time to wade over to the lighthouse steps.

'There's our little boat bobbing about,' said Tink. 'And listen – I can hear old Timmy barking! He's heard us coming!'

So he had. He had been lying on the doormat, his ears glued to the crack under the door, listening. Nobody had come near the lighthouse and not a sound did old Timmy hear but the wind and the sea, and a few gulls gliding by.

'We're back, Timmy!' yelled George, and she pushed at the door. It opened, and Timmy leapt out, almost knocking her over. Mischief sprang on to the dog's back, and chattered at him without stopping.

'He's telling him about the gold coin he found,' said Tink, with a laugh. 'Oh, I *wish* you'd been with us, Timmy. It was grand!'

'It feels as if we've been away for ages,' said George. 'But it isn't very late after all – unless my watch is slow! I'm hungry. Let's have something to eat and talk about everything – and what we're going to do!'

So, over biscuits and sandwiches and coffee, they talked and talked. 'We must get down to the caves again as soon as possible!' said George. 'I'm absolutely certain that Jacob and Ebby will be down there, hunting for coins, as soon as the tide's out again.'

'Well, we can't do anything today, that's certain,' said Dick. 'For one thing the tide's in now – and for another thing it's blowing up for a storm. Just *listen* to the wind!'

Timmy was sitting as close to George as he possibly could. He hadn't liked her going out without him. She sat with her arm round him, eating her biscuits, occasionally giving him half of one. Tink was doing the same with Mischief!

The children talked and talked. Where could Mischief have found that coin? Was it one on its own, that the sea had swept into the tunnel? Or was it part of a whole lot of coins? Had it come from an iron-bound box whose wooden sides had rotted away? They talked endlessly, their eyes bright, the round gold coin on the table in front of them.

'I suppose it would be treasure trove if we found it?' said Dick. 'I mean – it would be so old that it would belong to the Crown, and not to anyone in particular.'

'I expect we'd be allowed to keep a few coins ourselves,' said George. 'If only we could go straight away now and hunt in that tunnel! I feel as if I can't wait!'

'Woof,' said Timmy, agreeing though he really hadn't much idea of what they were talking about!

'I say – Listen to the sea crashing over the rocks between us and the jetty!' said Julian, startled at the sudden booming. 'The wind must be working up to a gale!'

'Well, bad weather's been forecast for some time,' said Dick gloomily. 'Blow! It'll be jolly difficult rowing to and fro in that little *Bob-About* boat. I doubt if we'd be able to walk across the rocks, even at low tide, with a big sea running before the wind.'

'Oh, don't be so gloomy!' said Anne.

'Well, do you want us to be prisoners here in the lighthouse?' demanded Dick.

'It wouldn't matter – there's plenty of food,' said Anne.

'No there isn't! Remember there are five of us – and Timmy and Mischief as well,' said Dick.

'Shut up, Dick,' said Julian. 'You're scaring Anne and Tink. This storm will soon blow over – we'll be able to pop out and do some shopping tomorrow.'

But the storm grew fiercer, and the sky became so dark that Anne lit the lamps. Rain slashed against the lighthouse, and the wind made a loud howling noise that made Timmy growl deep down in his throat.

Anne went to look out of the window. She felt frightened when she saw the great waves that came surging over the rocks below. Some of them broke on the rocks, and the spray flew so high that it spattered the window out of which she was looking! She drew back in alarm.

'Do you know what hit the window then? It was spray from a great wave!'

'Whew!' said Julian, and went to the window himself. What a wonderful sight! The sea was grey now, not blue, and it raced along towards the shore, great waves curling over into white manes, spray flying. Out to sea there were angry waves too, topped with white, which turned into spray as the strong wind caught them. Only a few gulls were out, screaming in excitement, allowing the wind to take them along on their great white wings.

'Well, I certainly wouldn't mind being a gull today,' said Dick. 'It must be a wonderful feeling to ride on a storm – no wonder they are screaming in joy!'

'Ee-oo, Ee-oo, EE-OOO, EE-OOOOO!' cried the gulls, sounding like cats mewing in hunger.

'I'm sorry for the ships out in this,' said Julian. 'Goodness – think of the sailing ships in the olden days, caught on this rocky coast in a wind like this – it's almost a hurricane!'

'And think of that wicked old One-Ear Bill, gloating when he saw a ship sailing nearer and nearer the rocks!' said George. 'And even taking the warning lamp out of its place on the cliff, and bringing it near here to make sure that any ship out that night would make straight for the rocks – CRASH!'

'Don't,' said Anne. 'I hate to think of things like that.'

'Let's have a game,' said Julian. 'Where are the cards? Move that lamp a bit closer to the table, Dick. It's getting so jolly dark. Now no more talk of wrecks! Think of something cheerful – tea-sup, for instance – the treasure – and . . .'

'You know, I think it would be quite easy to find the treasure,' said Dick, bringing the lamp close to the table. 'Mischief is a very clever little thing. I'm sure he would remember where he found that coin, and lead us straight to the place.'

'It might have been just an odd coin, dropped by the man who hid the hoard,' said Anne.

'It might – but wherever it was found I think we can safely say that the main hoard wouldn't be very far away,' said Dick.

'Well, if we do go hunting we'll have to go when the tide is well out,' said Julian. 'I don't really fancy scrabbling about in those caves and tunnels under the rocky seabed, when I know that somehow or other when the tide is coming in the water gets *under* the seabed, as well as on it.'

Dick sat frowning, thinking out something. 'Ju,' he said at last, 'you remember the direction we went in, as soon as we were underground this morning? We went leftish all the way, didn't we?'

'Yes, we did,' said Tink, at once. 'I had my little

compass with me – look – it clips to my wristwatch – and we went sharp west all the time.'

'Towards the lighthouse, that would be,' said Julian, and drew a quick plan. 'See – here's the lighthouse, say – and just here is the entrance into the cliff, where we first went – here's the path we took, curving right back to the sea again, under the rocky beach here it goes – and that's a cave, see, then more tunnel, and caves – the way always curving sharply to the left . . .'

'A bit farther on and we'd have been almost under the lighthouse!' said Dick, in amazement.

'That's right,' said Julian. 'And maybe in the old days, before this lighthouse was built, and ships were sent crashing on the rocks on which it now stands, there was a tunnel down from those lighthouse rocks that joined up with the tunnel we were in this morning – so that the wreckers would find it very easy to stow away anything valuable they found in a wrecked ship, without being seen!'

'Whew! You mean they waited till the ship smashed up, then waded over the rocks, as we do, took what they could find, and disappeared down a tunnel there to hide it!'

'And came out the other end!' said Anne.

George stared at Julian, and her eyes were bright.

'Maybe the tunnel is *still* somewhere in these rocks!' she said. 'Somewhere down at the edge of them, because we know the sea gets into the tunnel. Julian, let's look for it tomorrow. I think you're right. There *may* be a hole in the rocks here somewhere, that drops down into the tunnel we were in.'

Nobody wanted to play a game after that! They felt much too excited. They studied Julian's plan again and again, glad that Tink's little compass had shown him so clearly that morning that the undersea passages had led due west to the lighthouse rocks.

'Do you suppose that everyone has forgotten the old hole?' said Dick. 'Nobody has told us anything about it, not even Jeremiah. Do you think it may have been blocked up?'

Julian frowned, thinking hard.

'Well, yes – it may have been,' he said. 'It *is* odd that Jeremiah didn't say anything about it. Anyway we'll have a good hunt tomorrow.'

'And if we find it, we'll drop down and hunt for the treasure!' said Tink, his eyes shining. '*What* a shock for Ebenezer and Jacob if we find it first!'

CHAPTER NINETEEN

A nasty shock!

THE STORM blew itself out that evening, and next day was much calmer. The sky still looked angry, and rain fell now and again, but it was possible to get out of the lighthouse door in the morning, and go down the steps on to the rocks.

'Shall we go shopping first – or look for the hole?' said Julian.

'Look for the hole,' said Dick, promptly. 'The wind is still pretty strong, and the storm might blow up again – just look at that angry sky! We wouldn't be able to mess about round the edge of the rocks if the sea gets any rougher.'

They spread out and went cautiously over the great rocks on which the lighthouse was built. At low tide the rocks stood well up, out of the sea. The lighthouse was built on the highest part, and seemed to tower over the searchers as they clambered here and there, seeking for any hole that looked as if it might lead down into some tunnel below.

'Here's a hole!' called Anne, suddenly, and they all clambered over to her in excitement, Timmy too. Julian looked down to where Anne was pointing. 'Yes – it does look a likely one,' he said. 'Big enough to take a man, too. I'll climb down and see.'

He slid down the hole, holding on to projecting pieces of rock as he went. The others watched, thrilled. Timmy barked. He didn't like to see Julian disappearing like this!

But before Julian quite disappeared, he shouted again: 'I'm afraid it's no good! It's come to a sudden end! I'm standing on firm rock, and though I've felt all round with my feet, there's no opening anywhere. It's a dead end!'

What a disappointment! 'Blow!' said Dick, lying down on the rocks and putting his arm down the hole to help Julian to climb up again. 'I had high hopes then! Julian – here's my hand. Do you want any help?'

'Thanks – it is a bit difficult!' said Julian. He climbed up with difficulty, and squeezed out of the hole thankfully. 'I wouldn't like to get *wedged* in here!' he said. 'Especially with the tide coming in!'

'It's beginning to pour with rain again!' said Anne. 'Shall we go shopping now – or wait a bit?'

'Oh, let's wait,' said George. 'I'm cold and wet now. Let's go into the lighthouse and make some hot coffee. *What* a disappointment! Never mind – we can always go down the tunnels we were in yesterday and search around – maybe Mischief will show us where he found the gold coin!'

They all went into the lighthouse, and once more Julian jammed the door. 'I wish that locksmith would come,' he said. 'If we go down into the caves, we'll have to leave old Timmy behind on guard – and it is such a shame!'

'Woof,' said Timmy, heartily agreeing. They all went upstairs and Anne began to make the coffee. As they were sitting drinking it, Timmy suddenly sprang to his feet with a most blood-curdling growl. Everyone jumped, and Anne spilt her coffee.

'Timmy! What's up?' said George, in alarm. Timmy was standing with his nose towards the closed door of the room, his hackles rising up on his neck. He looked truly fierce!

'What on *earth* is the matter, Tim?' said Julian, going to the door. 'There can't be anyone on the stairway – the entrance door's jammed!'

Timmy raced out of the door as soon as Julian opened it and tore down the spiral stairway at such a speed that he fell, and rolled to the bottom. George gave a terrified scream. 'Timmy! Have you hurt yourself?'

But Timmy leapt to his feet at once, and ran to the entrance door, growling so ferociously that Anne felt really frightened. Julian ran down and went to the door. It was still well and truly jammed.

'Timmy! Maybe it's just the poor milkman, come with some milk again,' he said, and unjammed the door. He took hold of the handle to open it.

It wouldn't open! Julian pulled and tugged, but it was of no use. The door simply would not open!

By this time everyone was down beside him. 'Let *me* try,' said Dick. 'The door must just have stuck.'

No – he couldn't open it either! Julian looked gravely

round at everyone. 'I'm afraid – very much afraid – that *somebody* has locked us in!' he said.

There was a horrified silence. Then George cried out in anger. 'Locked us in! How dare they! Who's done this?'

'Well – I think we can guess,' said Julian. 'It was whoever came and stole our key the other day!'

'Ebenezer – no, Jacob!' cried Dick. 'One of the two, anyway. How *dare* they? What are we going to do? We can't get out. Why have they done this – this – silly – *wicked* thing?'

'I'm afraid it's because they think we might go looking for the treasure – and find it,' said Julian, his face grave. 'We felt sure that Mischief might remember where he had found the gold coin – and lead us there – and I'm pretty sure they think the same. So this is their way of making sure *they* have time to find the treasure, before we do!'

'They're wicked, they're wicked!' cried George, taking hold of the handle of the door, and pulling it violently. 'We're prisoners!'

'Don't pull the handle off, old thing,' said Julian. 'That wouldn't help at all. Let's go upstairs and talk about it. We'll have to think of some way out of this unexpected difficulty.'

They went soberly upstairs again, and sat down in the living room. Yes – they were certainly prisoners!

'What are we going to do?' said Dick. 'We are in a real fix, Julian.'

'Yes. You're right,' said Julian, looking worried. 'We can't get out of the lighthouse, that's certain. On the other hand – how can we get help? No telephone. Shouting would never be heard. Can't use our boat. No one would ever know we are prisoners – they've seen us going in and out of the lighthouse, and if we suddenly don't appear any more they'll simply think we have gone home, and that the lighthouse is empty again!'

'We shall die of starvation!' said Anne, scared.

'Oh no – I expect we shall think of something,' said Dick, seeing that Anne was really frightened. 'All the same, it's a puzzle. We can't get *out* – and no one can get *in*! Whoever locked that door has certainly taken the key away with him.'

They talked and they talked, and finally they felt hungry, so they had a meal – though they felt that they ought to eat sparingly, in case their food ran short too quickly.

'And I feel so hungry,' complained George. 'I *keep* feeling hungry here.'

'That's what I told you. Living in a lighthouse somehow makes you feel hungry all the time!' said Tink.

'We'll try and catch the milkman tomorrow morning,' said Julian, suddenly. 'Let's see, now – we could write a note, and push it under the door, so that he would see it tomorrow when he comes. We could put HELP – WE ARE LOCKED IN.'

'It would blow away,' said George. 'You know it would.'

'We could pin it down our side – and then it wouldn't,' said Anne. 'Half of it would still stick out under the door.'

'Well, it's worth trying,' said Dick, and immediately wrote out the note on a large sheet of paper. He shot downstairs to pin it to the mat – and shoved half the paper underneath so that it stuck out on the other side of the door.

He ran back upstairs. 'I don't for a moment think that the milkman will come across the rocks in this weather,' he said. 'They'll be almost impassable. Still we'll hope for the best.'

There didn't seem anything else to do. The evening came early, for the sky was dark again, and the wind once more got up, and howled dismally. Even the gulls decided that it was no longer a good idea to glide to and fro.

They played games that evening, and tried to laugh and make jokes. But secretly everyone was worried. Suppose that the stormy weather went on and on, and nobody guessed they were locked in the lighthouse, and the milkman didn't bring any milk, and didn't see the note – and they ate all their food and . . .

'Cheer up, everyone,' said Julian, seeing the dismal looks around the table. 'We've been in worse fixes than this.'

'Well, *I* don't think we have!' said Anne. 'I just can't see *any* way out of this one!'

There was rather a long silence during which Timmy sighed heavily, as if he too was worrying! Only the monkey seemed cheerful, and went head-over-heels at top speed round the room, sitting up for laughs at the end. But nobody laughed. Nobody even seemed to notice him. Mischief felt very sad, and crept over to Timmy for comfort.

'There is one idea that *might* be a good one,' said Julian, at last. 'It's been running round in my head for a while – and I'm not sure whether it's possible or not. Anyway, it's one we might try tomorrow, if help doesn't come.'

'What?' asked everyone at once, and Timmy lifted his head and whined, as if he too quite understood.

'Well, do you remember that I went down that foundation shaft,' said Julian, 'and saw the water swirling at the bottom? Now – do you suppose it's at all possible that that shaft was bored down through a *natural* hole – and the lighthouse builders chose to put the foundation shaft there because there was a ready-made shaft they could use? – a fine hole going right down through the rock! And they made the hole into a cement-lined shaft, strong and everlasting, so that the lighthouse would never be at the mercy of the waves and wind – but would stand firm, whatever happened?'

This was a new idea to everyone, and it took a little while to sink in. Then Dick smacked the table top and made them all jump.

'Julian! You've got it! Yes – that strong cement-lined shaft runs down a *natural* hole – and that hole must be the one we've been looking for! The one that connects up with the tunnels we were in yesterday! No wonder we couldn't

find it when we hunted all over the rocks! The shaft-makers used it!'

There was silence again. Everyone was taking this in, even Tink. Julian looked round the table and smiled. 'Have you all jumped to it?' he said. 'If that *is* the hole we were looking for – what about one of us going down that iron ladder again to the bottom – and finding out if it *does* lead into the tunnel we were in yesterday?'

'And walking through it, and up the passage and coming out through the cliff entrance we used yesterday!' said George. 'Julian! What an absolutely wonderful idea! We could escape that way! What a shock for Ebby and Jacob! We'll do it somehow – we'll *do* it!'

CHAPTER TWENTY

Down the shaft and into the tunnel

IT WAS a most exciting idea to think that the iron ladder in the great cement-lined shaft might possibly lead to the tunnel they had been into yesterday. Julian had seen water swirling at the bottom, when the tide was in – possibly if they went down it when the tide was going out, there would be no danger of being trapped!

The storm was very fitful now – sometimes it came back again, and then the wind blew so hard that it seemed as if the buffeted lighthouse must fall! Rain fell in torrents that night, and during the dark early hours of the morning, when the tide was in, great waves pounded over the rocks, sending spray almost over the top of the lighthouse. Julian awoke and looked out of the bedroom window in awe.

'I hope there's no ship out anywhere near here tonight,' he said, and then gave a sudden exclamation. 'What's that – something swept right across the sky!'

'It's the beam from the new lighthouse at High Cliffs,' said Dick. 'I saw it last night. It must have a very powerful beam, mustn't it, to show even on a night like this?'

They watched for a little while, and then Julian yawned.

'Let's try to go to sleep,' he said. 'We thought we were

going away for a nice little holiday – and BANG – we're in the middle of something again!'

'Well, let's hope that we come out of it all right,' said Dick, settling down in his rugs once more. 'I must say that I feel a bit cut off from civilisation at the moment. 'Night, Julian.'

In the morning the storm was still about, and the wind was terrific. Julian ran down to the entrance door to see if the milkman could possibly have come – and had seen their message for help.

But no – the paper was still half on their side, flapping on the mat. Obviously the milkman hadn't dared to cross the rocks that morning, either on foot or by boat!

Dick had looked out of the window to make sure that their boat was still safely moored to the post – and to his surprise and distress, it was no longer there! Tink was very upset.

'Where's my little boat gone? Has somebody stolen it?'

'Maybe – or possibly the storm broke the mooring rope, and the boat was smashed to pieces on the rocks,' said Julian. 'Anyway, it's gone. Poor old Tink. What a shame!'

Tink was very sad, and Mischief tried to comfort him, doing all sorts of silly tricks to make him laugh. But Tink wouldn't laugh. He really was right down in the dumps.

They had rather a sparse breakfast, and were very silent. Anne cleared away and washed up, and then Julian called them all together.

'Well, now we must decide about this descent down the shaft to what we hope will be the tunnel we were in,' he said. 'I am going down myself.'

'Toss for it!' said Dick, at once. 'There's no reason why *I* shouldn't go, is there? Or what about us both going, in case one gets into trouble, and needs help?'

'Not a bad idea,' said Julian. 'Except that there won't be anyone to look after the girls and Tink.'

'WOOF!' said Timmy, indignantly, standing up at once. Julian laughed and patted him.

'It's all right, Timmy. I just wanted to see if you thought *you* could guard them well. All right – Dick and I will go down the shaft. The sooner the better. We simply must go while the tide is out. What about now, Dick?'

Solemnly they all went down the spiral stairway to the entrance door, where the trap was that opened on to the great shaft. Julian pulled up the lid and gazed down into blackness. He shone his torch down, but he could not see the bottom. 'Well – here goes,' he said, and lowered himself down into the shaft, his feet seeking the rungs of the iron ladder. 'Keep cheerful, girls. We'll get through the tunnels and passages, and to the entrance in the cliff – and fetch help for you in no time at all!'

'Julian, please take care,' said Anne, in a shaky voice. 'Please, please do take care!'

Down went Julian, his torch now held between his teeth. After him went Dick. The girls shone their own torches down the shaft, but soon the boys were so far down that they could not be seen. Only their voices came up now and again, sounding very hollow and peculiar.

'We're at the bottom!' shouted Julian, at last. 'It's rock, and there's no water at present! We've a clear way to follow! I crawled out of the hole at the bottom, and there's some kind of tunnel there all right. We're off now – crawling out, and into the tunnel. Cheer up, all of you! See you soon!' And then the peculiar hollow voice stopped, and the girls and Tink heard nothing more. Timmy began to whine. He couldn't understand these strange goings-on at all!

Julian and Dick were feeling pleased with themselves. It hadn't been very difficult to squeeze out of the arches at the bottom of the shaft. Now they were in a dark narrow tunnel, whose roof sometimes came down so low that they had to bend double. It smelt damp and seaweedy, but there seemed to be plenty of air. In fact at times quite a little breeze seemed to flow round them.

'I shall be glad when we come into a tunnel we recognise!' said Julian, at last. 'We surely must be near where we were yesterday. Hallo, what's this? Dick – look, Dick!'

Dick looked to where Julian's torch was shining and gave a shout. 'A gold coin – another one! We must be near where old Mischief ran off to. Look – there's another – and another. Where on earth did they come from?'

The boys shone their torches all around, and saw at last where the coins had fallen from. Above their heads was a dark hole, running up into the rock. As they shone their torches on it, a gold coin slid out and dropped down to join the others.

'*This* is where Mischief found the coin!' cried Dick. 'Julian there must be a box or something up there which is rotting away, and letting out the money it contains bit by bit.'

'Whoever would have guessed at such a hiding-place!' said Julian, marvelling as he shone his torch above his head. 'There's absolutely nothing to be seen except that dark hole – no box, nothing. It must have been pushed right into a recess at the side of the hole, by someone who knew a good hiding-place was there.'

'Give me a leg-up so that I can put in my hand and feel,' said Dick. 'Buck up – this is too exciting for words!'

Julian gave him a leg-up, and Dick put his head and shoulders into the hole. He felt to one side – nothing – felt to the other side, and his hand came across something hard and cold – an iron band perhaps? He ran his hand over it and touched something soft and crumbly – old, old wood rotting away, maybe – possibly a wooden chest – only held together by the iron bands. He scrabbled about and Julian gave a sudden shout.

'Hey – you've showered me with money! Whew – I never saw so many gold coins in my life!'

'Julian – I think there's more than one box or chest up there,' said Dick, jumping down, and looking at the big heap of shining coins at his feet. 'There may be a fortune there! Talk about treasure trove! Look – let's not disturb anything else up that hole. No one knows about it except ourselves. Better gather up these coins though, just in *case* that awful Ebby takes it into his head to come down this way!'

So they filled their pockets with the coins and then made their way onwards again. To their joy they soon recognised one of the tunnels they had been in before. 'Plain sailing now,' said Dick joyfully. 'We'll soon be out, and then we'll get the locksmith to pick the lock of the lighthouse, so that we can get in.'

'Sh!' said Julian, suddenly. 'I think I can hear something.' They listened, but went on again, thinking that Julian was mistaken.

But he wasn't! As they turned a dark corner that led into a cave, someone leapt at them! Julian went down to the ground at once, and Dick followed. He just had time to see that Ebenezer was there with someone else – Jacob perhaps?

As Dick fell, gold coins spilt out of his pocket. Ebenezer gave a cry and bent down to them at once. Julian tried to take his chance and slip by him – but the other man caught him and sent him spinning backwards. 'Where did you find that money? You tell us or you'll be sorry!' shouted Ebenezer, and the echo came back at once, 'Sorry – sorry – sorry!'

'Run, Dick!' panted Julian. 'It's our only chance!' He gave Ebenezer a terrific shove, which sent him into the other man – yes, it *was* Jacob, who must somehow have

escaped from police custody – and then he and Dick were off at once, running as fast as they could, back along the way they had come. 'You come here!' yelled Ebenezer, and they heard him pounding after them.

'Hurry!' panted Dick. 'If only we can get to the shaft, we're all right.'

But alas, they took the wrong turning, and soon found themselves in a cave they had never seen before. Ebenezer and Jacob blundered past without seeing them. 'Better stay here a while,' said Julian. 'Let them get a good way off.'

So they stayed still and quiet, and then at last ventured out of their hiding-place and tried to find their way back to the right path.

'You know – if we get lost down here, we're done for!' said Julian. 'And once the tide flows in, we shall be in a pretty poor way! Somehow we've got to get out through the cliff way or back to the shaft. Hang on to me, Dick. We mustn't get separated, whatever happens!'

They stumbled on, not really knowing whether they were going in the right direction or not. They seemed to go through endless tunnels and caves – what a labyrinth there was in that great stratum of rocks! Then they heard voices!

'That's Ebby's voice – and Jacob's too,' whispered Julian. 'They're coming this way. Hide here, and keep still!'

So they hid quietly, and listened to Ebby and Jacob.

'Those boys have *got* to come back here,' said Ebby. 'We'll wait. Don't make a sound!'

'We'll have to make a dash for it, and hope for the best!' whispered Julian. 'Come on! We'll be caught by the tide soon if we're not quick!'

They both made a sudden rush, and passed the surprised Ebby and Jacob at a run. Then down the tunnel beyond them they went as fast they could, bumping their arms and legs and heads against the rocky walls, but holding their torches steadily in front of them. On they went and on – and behind them, breathing heavily, came Ebby and Jacob.

'I think this must be a bad dream!' panted Dick. 'JULIAN! JULIAN! Look – there's water coming along this tunnel! The tide's coming in!'

'Come *on*,' said Julian. 'I feel as if the shaft isn't far away now. I seem to know this tunnel – and this cave. Come *on*, Dick, we haven't a minute to spare! We've *got* to get to the ladder!'

'Look! There's the shaft!' yelled Dick at last. 'Come on – we shall just about be able to squeeze under the arch at the bottom! Hurry, Julian – the water's up to our ankles now!'

They reached the shaft and squeezed under the small archway that let the water run through from side to side over the rocky bottom of the shaft. They began to mount the ladder, and then stopped to hear if there were any sounds from Ebby or Jacob.

They heard yells. 'EBBY! COME BACK! Tide's

flowing in!' and then they heard Ebby's angry voice.

'I'm coming! They've gone farther down – and they won't like it! They'll be drowned before they get much farther!'

Dick grinned. 'Come on, Ju, – up we go! I can see the light through the trap-door at the top. The girls have left it open, bless them.'

And soon the two boys were clambering out of the trap-door, with Timmy barking madly and licking their necks, the girls and Tink too excited for words!

'What happened? Didn't you get out of the tunnel to find help for us? Were those men there? What *happened*?'

'Plenty!' said Julian. 'But unfortunately we didn't get past Ebby and Jacob, who were lying in wait for us. So we're *still* stuck in this lighthouse, with nobody to help us. BUT—'

'But what?' asked George, shaking his arm. 'Julian, you look excited. What's happened?'

'We found the treasure!' said Julian. 'Come on – we'll tell you all about it!' And he led the way up the spiral stairway, with Tink and the excited girls close behind.

Soon the boys were telling their story, and George and Anne and Tink listened and exclaimed and danced about, and were altogether marvellous listeners to a marvellous tale.

'It *must* have been the treasure – in an iron-bound chest – oh, Ju, weren't you excited when the coins poured out?'

'Yes. It was certainly a very fine moment,' said Julian.

'Mischief, stop pulling my hair. Wow! It's been an exciting morning! What about a drink of lemonade – and by the way, what's the weather been like? We couldn't see a thing down below!'

'Oh, it's *awful* again, Julian!' said Anne. 'There's another storm coming – look at those scurrying black clouds.'

'It does look bad,' said Julian, his excitement leaving him, as he saw clearly that another big storm was blowing up. 'We certainly shouldn't be able to get out of here today, even if we could get out of the door!'

'Julian, Tink found his father's old pocket radio in a cupboard,' said Anne. 'And it still works. We listened to the weather report, and it gave an important warning to all ships at sea or by the coast. It said they must run to safety as soon as they could.'

'Well, I'm blessed if I know what to do for the best,' said Julian, looking out of the window. 'How in the world are we to let people know we're here, marooned in the lighthouse? We'll simply *have* to think of something!'

But that was easier said than done! How did one get help when there was no way to get help? How did one escape out of a locked lighthouse when there was no key?

CHAPTER TWENTY-ONE

A wonderful idea

'I'M THIRSTY,' said Tink. 'I'll get some lemonade.'

'Well, go slow with it, then,' said Dick. 'You don't know how long we may be locked up here – and we haven't endless food and drink!'

Tink looked alarmed. 'Might we be locked up here for weeks and weeks?' he said.

'If people thought we had left the lighthouse and gone back home because of the bad weather, we might easily be here for some time,' said Julian, soberly. 'Nobody would bother about us – they'd think we were safe at home.'

'But Mother would soon feel worried if she didn't hear from us,' said George. 'We said we'd send her a card each day, you know – and if she doesn't have one for a day or two, she would be sure to get worried, and send someone over here.'

'Hurrah for mothers!' said Dick, relieved. 'All the same – I don't fancy a week or so here with hardly anything to eat. We'll have plenty of one thing though – and that's rainwater!'

'There must be *some* way out of this,' said Julian who had been sitting silent, frowning at his thoughts. 'Can't we get a message out *somehow*? Are there any flags here, Tink, that we could wave out of the window?'

'No,' said Tink. 'I've never seen any. What about a white tablecloth? We've one of those.'

'Yes. That would do,' said Julian. 'Fetch it, Tink.'

Tink pulled it off the table and gave it to Julian. Julian went to the window and looked through the glass, which was misted with spray. 'I don't expect anyone will notice a tablecloth being shaken out of this window,' he said. 'But I'll try it. My word – the window's hard to open. It seems to have stuck.'

He opened it at last, and immediately an enormous gust of wind came in, and everything went flying – papers, books, carpets – chairs fell over, and poor Mischief was blown from one side of the lighthouse room to the other. Timmy barked in fright and tried to catch the flying papers as they went by his nose. The tablecloth disappeared at once!

Julian managed to close the window again after a terrific effort, and once more the room became peaceful. 'Whew!' said Julian. 'I didn't guess there was such a gale outside. I should think that tablecloth is about five miles away by now! The gulls will get a surprise when it comes flapping along in the sky.'

George couldn't help laughing at that, frightened though she was. 'Oh, Julian – it was a jolly good thing you didn't fly off with the tablecloth! My WORD, what a gale! I wonder the lighthouse stands it.'

'Well, we do feel a buffet now and again,' said Dick. 'There – did you feel that? It was either a wave bumping into the rocks or spray forced against us – I distinctly felt the lighthouse shake a little.'

'Rubbish!' said Julian, seeing Anne's scared face. 'Don't make silly jokes like that.'

'You're quite *sure* that the lighthouse can't be blown down?' said Anne, in a small voice.

'Dear Anne, use your common sense,' said Julian. 'Would it have stood for all these years if it hadn't been strong enough to stand against storms far worse than this?'

'Mischief is feeling frightened too,' said Tink. 'He's gone and hidden, look.'

'Well, long may he stay there,' said Julian. 'At least, he's not trying to open the biscuit tin, or delve into the bag of sweets! I should just like to know how many of our sweets he has eaten up to now!'

WHOOOOOOOOOSH!

That was an extra big gale of wind that buffeted the lighthouse, and made Timmy stand up and growl. Rain pattered against the window, sounding as if someone was throwing pebbles.

Julian was very worried. It really did look as if the stormy weather was going on and on. It might quite well continue for a few days, and their food certainly would not last long. There were still some tins left, and they had plenty of water, of course – the rain saw to that – but somehow they were all always so *hungry*!

'Cheer up, Julian,' said George. 'You do look grim.'

'I feel it,' said Julian. 'I cannot for the life of me think of any way to escape from here, or even to get help. We've no way of signalling . . .'

'Pity the lighthouse lamp is no longer going,' said Tink.

'That would have been a fine signal.'

To Tink's enormous surprise Julian suddenly gave a shout, leapt up, came over to Tink, and gave him such a clap on the back that the surprised boy almost fell off his chair!

'W-w-what's the matter?' stammered Tink, rubbing his shoulder.

'Don't you *see* – perhaps we can set the old lamp going, and make it shine out as it used to do – not to warn ships, of course – but to make people realise that we are prisoners in the lighthouse!' said Julian, jubilantly. 'Tink – do you know if it's *possible* to light the lamp?'

'I think so,' said Tink. 'My father showed me how it worked, and I think I remember. Oh – and there's a bell that can be struck, too!'

'Better and better!' said Julian. 'Where is the bell?'

'It was dismantled and put away,' said Tink. 'It used to hang in that sort of verandah place that runs outside, round the lamp-room – there's a big hook for it there.'

'Oh – it hung in that outside gallery, did it?' said Julian. 'Well – that means that one of us would have to go out there in the wind and hang it up – not too good! There must be a ninety-mile-an-hour gale up there. Anyway, let's get the bell and have a look at it.'

The great bell was down in the storeroom, covered up. It was made of brass, and once had had a hammer that struck it at intervals, worked by some simple machinery. But the machinery was in pieces – no good at all!

'We'll take the bell upstairs,' said Julian. 'Gosh, it's heavy as lead. Dick, I'll want your help.'

Between them the two boys carried the heavy bell up to the living room, and Tink brought up the old hammer that used to strike it. Julian and Dick held up the bell by its loop of iron. 'Hit it with the hammer, Tink,' said Julian. 'See if it still sounds loudly.'

Tink struck it hard with the hammer – and at once a great deep clang filled the room from side to side, making Timmy jump almost out of his skin. He and Mischief left the room at top speed and fell down the spiral stairway together. All the others jumped too, and stared at one another in awe. The sound of the bell went booming round and round the room, filling their ears so that they had to shake their heads to try and get rid of the sound. Julian at last clasped the rim of the bell with both his hands and the sound died away.

'What a *wonderful* bell!' he said, in awe. 'Look how old it is, too – see, it says, "Cast in 1896"! If only we could get it hung up in its place on the gallery, the sound of it would go right to the village and beyond! I wonder how many ships heard it in the old days, booming out every now and again as the hammer struck it.'

Tink raised the hammer again, but Dick stopped him. 'No – you saw how scared Timmy and Mischief were. They'll probably jump through a window, glass and all, if we sound the bell again!'

'We'll wait till we think the wind has died down a bit, and then try to hang the bell,' said Julian. 'Now let's look at the lamp. Will it want oil, Tink?'

'It may do – though I think there's some still in it, left when the lighthouse was closed down,' said Tink. 'But there is plenty down in the storeroom.'

'Good,' said Julian, feeling decidedly more cheerful. 'Now – if the gale dies down at all, we'll try to hang the bell. We can strike that as soon as it's hung, and not wait till we light the lamp.'

But the gale seemed to get worse, and Julian really did wonder if the old lighthouse would stand up to it! Should he take everyone down to the storeroom? Just in case? 'I will if the gale gets worse,' he thought. 'Though if the lighthouse should fall, there wouldn't be much chance for us, whatever part of it we're in!'

They went up to the lamp-room in the afternoon and looked at the great old lamp. Tink explained how it worked. 'It used to go round and round mechanically,' he said, 'and there were screens here – and here – that shut out the light in places as it went round – so that the light seemed to go on and off, if any ship was watching it – it seemed to *flash*, you see, instead of to shine steadily. Ships noticed it more quickly then.'

The screens were broken in pieces. There was still some oil in the lamp, but Julian added more. The wick seemed perfectly good. Now, if only they could light the lamp, and keep it going, someone would be sure to see it, and wonder about it!

Julian felt in his pocket for matches. As the lamp-room was enclosed in glass, it was easy to keep the match alight. He touched the oily wick with it – and, hey-presto, the lamp was lit!

It was a very big lamp, and, close to, the light was quite blinding. Dick crowed with delight. 'We've done it! Old lighthouse, you're going to shine once more tonight! You're alive again!'

'Now to hang the bell,' said Julian, and he cautiously opened the door leading on to the gallery outside, having waited until the wind died down for a moment. He and Dick lifted the bell up to the hook there and slipped the iron loop over it. It hung there, swinging, and Julian lifted

the hammer – but at that moment a great gust took him and he staggered, almost falling over the railing!

Dick caught him just in time, and, with George's help, dragged him into the lamp-room. They were all very white-faced! 'That was a narrow escape,' said George, her hands shaking and her body trembling. 'We'll have to be careful if we go out on the gallery again! Perhaps we had better rely only on the lamp.'

'I vote we all go down and have some hot tea,' said Julian, thankful for his escape. His legs felt shaky as he went down the stairs. He was most surprised! Julian was seldom scared, and it was peculiar to have legs that suddenly gave at the knees!

However, everyone soon recovered when they were drinking hot tea and eating ginger biscuits. 'I wish it was dark so that we could see how bright the light is from the lamp when it shines,' said Dick. 'It will be dark very quickly today.'

It was! So dark that the light streaming from the old lamp at the top of the lighthouse was brilliant! It cut a shining path through the night, gleaming yellow.

And through the roar of the sea went a great clanging, as Julian, with Dick holding on to him, struck the old bell hanging in the gallery.

'Listen!' said George, her hand on Timmy's collar. 'Listen! BOOM! BOO-OOO-OOM! BOOOOM! Tim, that bell must feel happy tonight – it's found its voice again!'

BOOOOOOOOOM! Has anyone heard that old bell on this stormy night? Has anyone seen the light from the old, old lamp?

BOOOOOOOOOM!!!

CHAPTER TWENTY-TWO

The end of the adventure

DOWN IN the village of Demon's Rocks that night, people drew their curtains, made up their fires, and sat down in their armchairs. They were thankful not to be out in the wind and the rain.

Old Jeremiah Boogle was lighting his pipe, sitting by his own roaring fire, when he heard a sound that made him drop the flaring match, and listen in amazement.

BOOOOOOM! BOOOOOOM!

'A bell! A bell I've not heard for nearly forty years!' said old Jeremiah, standing up, hardly able to believe his ears. 'No – it *can't* be the lighthouse bell. That's been gone for many a day!'

BOOOOOOM!

Jeremiah went to his window and pulled aside the old curtain. He stared out – and could not believe his eyes! He gave a yell. 'MILLIE! Where's that granddaughter of mine? MILLIE!'

'What is it, Grandad, now?' said a plump little woman, bustling in.

'Look, Millie – am I seeing right – isn't that the lighthouse lamp shining there?' said Jeremiah.

'Well – there's a bright light shining out there high

above Demon's Rocks,' said Millie. 'But I never in *my* life saw the lighthouse lamp shining out before! And what's that booming noise, Grandfather – like a wonderful great bell?'

'That's the old bell in the lighthouse!' said Jeremiah. 'I couldn't mistake that! Many's the time I heard it booming out to warn ships off Demon's Rocks in the old days. Millie, it can't be! It doesn't hang there any more. And the light doesn't shine any more. What's happening?'

'I don't know, Grandad,' said Millie, scared. 'There isn't anyone in the lighthouse, far as *I* know!'

Old Jeremiah smacked his hand down on the windowsill, knocking over a plant pot. 'There *are* folk there – three boys and two girls, and a monkey too – and a dog as well!'

'Well, there now!' said Millie. 'And what would they be there for? Did *they* set the lamp going and sound that bell? BOOOOM – there it goes again – enough to wake all the babies in Demon's Rocks village!'

Millie was right. It did wake all the babies, and the children – and amazed every man and woman in the place, including Ebenezer and Jacob. They had leapt to their feet when they had heard the bell, and were astounded to see the great light shining out steadily in the night.

They heard people hurrying by their cottage, on their way to Demon's Rocks jetty. They heard Jeremiah's big voice booming out too. 'It's those children up there in the lighthouse, banging that bell, and setting that light shining.

Something's wrong! It's help they're needing, folks! Something's wrong!'

Ebenezer and Jacob knew quite well what was wrong! The children were locked in the lighthouse and couldn't get out! They might be ill or hurt – or starving – but they couldn't get out to fetch help. And now the whole village was aroused, and when the morning came, a boat would bob out on the great waves and find out what had happened!

Ebby and Jacob disappeared that night! It wasn't Constable Sharp they feared – it was the people of the village! They slipped away in the dark and the rain, and were gone. But you'll be caught, Ebby, you'll be caught, Jacob! And no one will be sorry for you. No one at all!

When daylight came, there were many people on the jetty, ready to go across to the lighthouse. The wind was so rough that great waves still rolled over the rocks on which the lighthouse stood. Soon a boat was launched, and Jeremiah, Constable Sharp and the village doctor went across, the boat careering from side to side like a mad thing, as the waves caught it.

They went up the steps to the lighthouse and banged at the door – and from the other side came Julian's glad voice: 'You'll have to break down the door. Ebby and Jacob locked us in and took the key. We can't get out, and we're running short of food!'

'Right. Stand back,' shouted Jeremiah. 'Constable and I are going to break in!'

Jeremiah was old but he was still hefty, and Constable Sharp was heftier still. The lock suddenly splintered under their enormous shoves, and the door flew wide open! Jeremiah and the policeman shot inside and bumped into Julian and the rest, sending them flying. Timmy barked in astonishment and Mischief fled up the stairway!

Soon they were all in the living room, and Julian was pouring out his story. Anne made tea and handed round steaming cups. Jeremiah listened open-mouthed, and the policeman busily took notes. The doctor, glad that no one was ill or hurt, sipped his tea and listened, too.

'We didn't know *how* to get out when we were locked in,' said Julian, coming to the end of his long story. 'So in the end we lit the old lamp, and hung up the old bell, and struck it with the hammer. I could hardly stand in the gallery, though, there was such a wind! I struck it for half an hour, and then my brother here went on till he felt too cold. The lamp didn't burn all night – it went out early this morning.'

'But both bell and light did their job well, son,' said Jeremiah, looking twenty years younger, he was so excited. 'Ah, to think that old lamp shone again, and that old bell sounded – I thought I must be dreaming!'

'We'll be after that Ebenezer and Jacob,' said the policeman, shutting his notebook. 'And it seems to me you'd all better go home. This weather's going on for a bit – and there's nothing to keep you here, is there?'

'Well,' said Julian, 'actually there *is* something to keep

us here. You know the old wreckers' lost treasure you told us about, Jeremiah? Well – we've found it!'

Jeremiah was so astounded that he couldn't say a word! He goggled at Julian, and opened and shut his mouth like a fish. Julian took some golden coins out of his pocket and showed them to the policeman and the doctor, and to Jeremiah.

'There you are!' he said. 'We know where there are thousands of these – they are in iron-bound boxes and chests down in one of the tunnels in the rock. What do you think of that? We can't leave here till we've given the treasure into the hands of the police! It belongs to the Crown, doesn't it?'

'Yes, it does,' said Constable Sharp, gazing at the bright gold coins. 'But you'll get a fine reward – all of you will! Where's this treasure? I'd better get it straight away.'

'Well – you have to go down the foundation shaft of the lighthouse,' said Julian, gravely, but with a twinkle in his eye, 'and crawl under the archway at the bottom, and then make your way down the tunnel – but be careful the sea doesn't catch you – and then when you come to . . .'

The policeman stopped scribbling down what Julian was saying, and looked startled. Julian laughed.

'It's all right – Dick and I will fetch it ourselves today, and give it to you, complete with every single gold coin,' he said. 'We don't *need* to go down the shaft – there's another way in – the way *you* took us, Jeremiah. We'll go this morning, for a last excitement. And then – home!

Perhaps you would kindly telephone Kirrin Garage for a car to fetch us at twelve o'clock, Constable?'

'Oh *good*!' said Anne. 'An adventure is always exciting but I've really had enough at the moment! This was such a bad-weather one! Oh, Constable, look out – that monkey has pulled out your whistle!'

So he had – and what is more he blew it – PHEEEEEEEEE! Jeremiah almost jumped out of his skin, and Mischief got a telling-off that almost made *him* jump out of his skin too!

'Goodbye, Jeremiah,' said Julian. 'It's been fine meeting you – and thanks for coming to rescue us. We'll see you again some day. Come along, Constable – we'll go and find the treasure with you now.'

'I don't think I'll come,' said Anne, who really didn't like dark, smelly tunnels and caves. 'I'll do the packing.'

'Timmy and I will help you,' said George, who knew that Anne wouldn't like to be left alone in the lighthouse.

The boys went off with Jeremiah, the doctor and Constable Sharp, rowing over the rocks to the jetty. The doctor and Jeremiah said goodbye at the jetty, and the three boys and Mischief took Constable Sharp to find the treasure. They had to push their way through quite a crowd of people who had collected on the quay, anxious to know why the light had shone out from the lighthouse in the night, and why the bell had sounded.

'Make way, please,' said the policeman, politely. 'Everything is all right. These children were locked in the lighthouse and couldn't get out. Make way, please. There is no need for any excitement!'

'No – that's all over now – isn't it, Ju?' said Dick. 'Whew – it was just a bit *too* exciting at times! I shall be quite glad to be at Kirrin Cottage again, with peace and quiet all around us.'

'You've forgotten that Uncle Quentin and his friend will still be there,' said Julian, with a grin. 'There'll be plenty going on while they're around! I'm afraid they won't be at all pleased to see us back!'

Oh yes, they will, Julian – especially when they hear the exciting story you have to tell! You'll have some fun showing round a gold coin or two. Timmy is to have one hung on his collar, as a reward for guarding you so well – how proud he will be!

Well, goodbye to you all! Goodbye, Julian and Dick, and a good journey home! Goodbye, Anne and George – and Tink too, and Mischief, you funny little monkey!

And goodbye, dear old Timmy, best of friends. How we wish we had a dog like you! See you all again some day!

THE FAMOUS FIVE

FIVE HAVE A MYSTERY TO SOLVE

Have you read all THE FAMOUS FIVE books?

1. Five on a Treasure Island
2. Five Go Adventuring Again
3. Five Run Away Together
4. Five Go to Smuggler's Top
5. Five Go Off in a Caravan
6. Five on Kirrin Island Again
7. Five Go Off to Camp
8. Five Get Into Trouble
9. Five Fall Into Adventure
10. Five on a Hike Together
11. Five Have a Wonderful Time
12. Five Go Down to the Sea
13. Five Go to Mystery Moor
14. Five Have Plenty of Fun
15. Five on a Secret Trail
16. Five Go to Billycock Hill
17. Five Get Into a Fix
18. Five on Finniston Farm
19. Five Go to Demon's Rocks
20. Five Have a Mystery to Solve
21. Five Are Together Again

The Famous Five Colour Short Stories

1. Five and a Half-Term Adventure
2. George's Hair is Too Long
3. Good Old Timmy
4. A Lazy Afternoon
5. Well Done, Famous Five
6. Five Have a Puzzling Time
7. Happy Christmas, Five
8. When Timmy Chased the Cat

Enid Blyton®

THE FAMOUS FIVE

FIVE HAVE A MYSTERY TO SOLVE

Illustrated by Eileen A. Soper

HODDER

HODDER CHILDREN'S BOOKS

First published in Great Britain in 1962 by Hodder & Stoughton
This edition published in 2016

20

A CIP catalogue record for this book is available from the British Library.

ISBN 978 1 444 93650 6

Printed in Great Britain by Clays Ltd, Elcograf S.p.A.

The paper and board used in this book are made from wood from responsible sources.

Hodder Children's Books
An imprint of
Hachette Children's Group
Part of Hodder & Stoughton
Carmelite House
50 Victoria Embankment
London EC4Y 0DZ

An Hachette UK Company
www.hachette.co.uk
www.hachettechildrens.co.uk

CONTENTS

1 EASTER HOLIDAYS 1
2 A VISITOR TO TEA 8
3 THE COTTAGE ON THE HILL – AND WILFRID 18
4 SETTLING IN 28
5 WILFRID IS MOST ANNOYING – AND ANNE IS MOST SURPRISING! 37
6 LUCAS – AND HIS TALE 46
7 UP ON THE GOLF COURSE 56
8 MOSTLY ABOUT WILFRID 64
9 OFF TO WHISPERING ISLAND 73
10 THE FIVE ARE IN A FIX 82
11 A STRANGE DISCOVERY 90
12 A GREAT SURPRISE – AND A SHOCK FOR GEORGE 99
13 A MEAL – A SLEEP – AND A DISAPPEARANCE 108
14 WILFRID HAS AN ADVENTURE ON HIS OWN 116
15 JULIAN HAS AN EXCITING PLAN! 124
16 A JOURNEY UNDERGROUND 134
17 IN THE TREASURE CHAMBER 142

18 A MOST EXCITING TIME! 153
19 ANNE IS A TIGER! 161

Special note from Enid Blyton

My readers will want to know if Whispering Island is real, set in the great blue harbour in the story – and if the little cottage on the hills is there still – and the golf course in the story – and Lucas, who tells the children about the island. Yes, the island is real, and lies in the great harbour, still full of whispering trees. The little cottage on the hills is still there, with its magnificent view and its old well – and Lucas can be found on the golf course, nut-brown and bright-eyed, telling stories of the animals and birds he loves so much. I have taken them all and put them into this book for you – as well as the friends you know so well – The Famous Five.

CHAPTER ONE

Easter holidays

'THE NICEST word in the English language is holidays!' said Dick, helping himself to a large spoonful of marmalade. 'Pass the toast, Anne. Mother, do you feel downhearted to have us all tearing about the place again?'

'Of course not,' said his mother. 'The only thing that *really* worries me when holidays come is Food – Food with a capital F. We never seem to have enough in the house when all three of you are back. And by the way – does anyone know what has happened to the sausages that were in the larder?'

'Sausages – sausages – let me think!' said Julian, frowning. Anne gave a sudden giggle. She knew quite well what had happened.

'Well, Mother – you said we could get our own meal last night, as you were out,' said Julian. 'So we poked about and decided on sausages.'

'Yes, but, Julian – two *whole* packets of sausages!' said his mother. 'I know Georgina came over to spend the evening – but even so . . . !'

'She brought *Timmy*,' said Anne. '*He* rather likes sausages too, Mother.'

'Well, that's the last time I leave the larder door

unlocked, when I go out!' said her mother. 'Fancy cooking those lovely pork sausages for a *dog* – especially Timmy, with his enormous appetite! Really, Anne! I meant to have them for our lunch today.'

'Well – we rather thought we'd go and spend the day at Kirrin, with George and Timmy,' said Dick. 'That's if you don't want us for anything, Mother.'

'I *do* want you,' said his mother. 'Mrs Layman is coming to tea, and she said she wants to see you about something.'

The three groaned, and Dick protested at once. 'Oh, *Mother* – the first day of the holidays – and we have to be in for tea! It's too bad – a glorious spring day like this, too!'

'Oh – we'll be in for tea all right,' said Julian, giving Dick a sharp little kick under the table, as he saw his mother's disappointed face. 'Mrs Layman's a nice old thing – she's been so kind since we moved near to Kirrin.'

'And she gave me a present last birthday,' said Anne. 'Do you think we could ask George over too – with Timmy? George will be awfully disappointed if we aren't with her the first day of the hols.'

'Yes, of course you can,' said her mother. 'Go and ring her up now, and arrange it. And don't forget to put our old Tibby-cat in the shed, with a saucer of milk. She's scared stiff of Timmy – he's so enormous. And please, all of you, TRY to look clean at teatime.'

'*I'll* see to Dick and Anne,' said Julian, with a grin. 'I must remember to find their overalls!'

'I'm going to phone George now, this very minute,' said Anne, getting up from the table. 'Do you mind, Mother? I've finished – and I'd like to catch George before she takes Tim for a walk, or does some shopping for Aunt Fanny.'

'Uncle Quentin will be glad to be rid of George, even for a meal,' said Dick. 'He fell over her lacrosse stick yesterday, and wanted to know why she left her *fishing* net about! George didn't know what he was talking about!'

'Poor old Georgina,' said his mother. 'It's a pity that both she and her father have exactly the same hot tempers. Her mother must find it difficult to keep the peace! Ah – here's Anne back again. Did you get George on the phone, dear?'

'Yes. She's thrilled,' said Anne. 'She says it's just as well we're not going to spend the day with her, because Uncle Quentin has lost some papers he was working on, and he's turning the house upside-down. George said she will probably be mad as a hatter by the time she arrives this afternoon! Uncle Quentin even made Aunt Fanny turn out her knitting bag to see if the papers were there!'

'Dear old Quentin,' said her mother. 'Such a truly brilliant scientist – remembers every book he's ever read – every paper he's ever written – and has the finest brain I know – and yet loses some valuable paper or other almost every week!'

'He loses something else every day of the week too,' said Dick, with a grin. 'His temper! Poor old George – she's always in some sort of trouble!'

'Well, anyway, she's jolly glad to be coming over here!' said Anne. 'She's biking over, with Timmy. She'll be here for lunch. Is that all right, Mother?'

'Of course!' said her mother. 'Now – seeing that you had today's dinner for last night's supper, you'd better do a little shopping for me. What shall we have?'

'SAUSAGES!' said everyone, at once.

'I should have thought you were quite literally *fed up* with sausages, after last night's feast,' said their mother, laughing. 'All right – sausages. But Timmy can have a bone – a nice meaty bone. I am NOT going to buy any more sausages for him, that's quite certain.'

'And shall we get some nice cakes for tea as Mrs Layman is coming?' said Anne. 'Or are you going to make some, Mother?'

'I'll make a few buns,' said her mother. 'And you can choose whatever else you like – so long as you don't buy up the shop!'

The three went off shopping, cycling along the lane to the village. It was truly a lovely spring day. The celandines were golden in the ditches, and daisies were scattered everywhere. Dick burst into song as they went, and the cows in the nearby fields lifted their heads in surprise as Dick's loud voice swept round them.

Anne laughed. It was good to be with her brothers again. She missed them very much when she was at school. And now they would have almost a whole month together with their cousin George too. She was suddenly overwhelmed with joy, and lifted up her voice and joined Dick in his singing. Her brothers looked at her with affection and amusement.

'Good old Anne,' said Dick. 'You're such a quiet little mouse, it's nice to hear you singing so loudly.'

'I am NOT a quiet little mouse!' said Anne, surprised and rather hurt. 'Whatever makes you say that? You just wait – you may get a surprise one day!'

'Yes – we may!' said Julian. 'But I doubt it. A mouse can't suddenly turn into a tiger! Anyway, one tiger's enough. *George* is the tiger of our family – my word, she can put out her claws all right – and roar – and rant and rave!'

Everyone laughed at the picture of George as a tiger. Dick wobbled as he laughed and his front wheel touched Anne's back wheel. She turned round fiercely.

'LOOK OUT, IDIOT! You nearly had me over! Can't you see where you're going? Be sensible, can't you?'

'Hey, Anne – whatever's the matter?' said Julian, amazed to hear his gentle little sister lashing out so suddenly.

Anne laughed. 'It's all right. I was just being a tiger for a moment – putting out my claws! I thought Dick and you might like to see them!'

'Well, well!' said Dick, riding beside her. 'I've never heard you yell like that before. Surprising – but quite pleasing! What about you showing old George your claws sometime when she gets out of hand?'

'Stop teasing,' said Anne. 'Here's the butcher's. For goodness' sake go and get the sausages, and be sensible. I'll go and buy the cakes.'

The baker's shop was full of new-made buns and cakes, and smelt deliciously of home-made bread. Anne enjoyed herself choosing a vast selection. 'After all,' she thought, 'there will be eight of us – counting Timmy – and if we're all hungry, cakes soon disappear.'

The boys were very pleased to see all the paper bags.

'Looks like a good tea today,' said Dick. 'I hope the old lady – what's her name now? – Layman – who's coming to tea today, has a good appetite. I wonder what she's going to tell us about.'

'Did you buy a nice meaty bone for Timmy?' asked Anne. 'He'll like that for his tea.'

'We bought such a beauty that I'm pretty sure Mother will say it's good enough to make soup from,' said Dick, with a grin. 'So I'll keep it in my saddle-bag till he comes. Dear old Tim. He deserves a jolly good bone. Best dog I ever knew!'

'He's been on a lot of adventures with us,' said Anne, bicycling beside the boys, as the road was empty. 'And he seemed to enjoy them all.'

'Yes. So did we!' said Dick. 'Well – who knows? An adventure may be lying in wait for us these hols too! I seem to smell one in the air!'

'You don't!' said Anne. 'You're just making that up. *I'd* like a bit of peace after a hectic term at school. I worked really hard this last term.'

'Well – you were top of your form, and captain of games – so you deserve to have the kind of holiday you like,' said Julian, proud of his young sister. 'And so you shall! Adventures are OUT! Do you hear that, Dick? We keep absolutely clear of them. So that's that!'

'Is it, Ju?' said Anne, laughing. 'Well – we'll see!'

CHAPTER TWO

A visitor to tea

GEORGE AND Timmy were waiting for Julian, Dick and Anne when they arrived home. Timmy was standing in the road, ears pricked, long tail waving. He went quite mad when he saw their bicycles rounding the corner, and galloped towards them at top speed, barking madly, much to the horror of a baker's boy with a large basket.

The boy disappeared into the nearest garden at top speed, yelling, 'Mad dog, mad dog!' Timmy tore past, and forced the three to dismount, for they were afraid of knocking him over.

'*Dear* Timmy!' said Anne, patting the excited dog. 'Do put your tongue in – I'm sure it will fall out some day!'

Timmy ran to each of them in turn, woofing in delight, licking everyone, and altogether behaving as if he hadn't seen them for a year!

'Now, that's enough, old boy,' said Dick, pushing him away, and trying to mount his bicycle once more. 'After all, we did see you yesterday. Where's George?'

George had heard Timmy barking, and had now run out into the road too. The three cycled up to her, and she grinned happily at them.

'Hallo! You've been shopping, I see. Shut up barking,

Timmy, you talk too much. Sorry you couldn't come over to Kirrin Cottage – but I'm jolly glad you asked me to come to *you* – my father still hasn't found the papers he's lost, and honestly, our place is like a madhouse – cupboards being turned out, even the kitchen store-cupboard – and I left poor Mother up in the loft, looking there – though *why* Father should think they might be there, I don't know!'

'Poor old George – I can see your father tearing his hair, and shouting, and all the time he's probably put the papers into the waste-paper basket by mistake!' said Dick, with a chuckle.

'Gracious – we never *thought* of that!' said George. 'I'd better phone Mother at once, and tell her to look. Bright idea of yours, Dick.'

'Well, you go and phone, and we'll put our bikes away,' said Julian. 'Take your nose away from that bag of sausages, Timmy. You're in disgrace over sausages, let me tell you. You're suspected of eating too many last night!'

'He did eat rather a lot,' said George. 'I took my eye off him, and he wolfed quite a few. Hey, who's this Mrs Layman who's coming to tea? Have we *got* to stay in and have tea with her? I hoped we might be going off for a picnic this afternoon.'

''Fraid not,' said Dick. 'Mrs Layman is apparently coming to talk to *us* about something. So we have to be in – with clean hands, nice manners, and everything. So behave yourself, George!'

George gave him a friendly shove. 'That's unfair,' said Dick. 'You know I won't shove you back. My word, you should have seen Anne this morning, George – yelled at me like a tiger howling, and showed her teeth, and . . .'

'Don't be an idiot, Dick,' said Anne. 'He called me a mouse, George – he said we had *one* tiger – you – and that was enough in the family. So I went for him – put out my claws for a moment, and gave him such a surprise. I rather liked it!'

'Good old Anne!' said George, amused. 'But you're not really cut out to be a tiger, and rage and roar, you know.'

'I could be, if I had to,' said Anne, obstinately. 'One of these days I'll surprise you all. You just wait!'

'All right. We will,' said Julian, putting his arm round his sister. 'Come on, now – we'd better get indoors before Timmy gets some of the cakes out of the bags. Stop licking that bag, Tim – you'll make a hole in it.'

'He can smell the cherry buns inside,' said Anne. 'Shall I give him one?'

'NO!' said Julian. 'Cherry buns are wasted on him, you know that. Don't you remember how he chews the bun apart and spits out the cherries?'

'Woof,' said Timmy, exactly as if he agreed. He went to sniff at the bag with his bone inside.

'That's your dinner, Tim,' said Anne. 'Plenty of meat on it, too. Look, there's Mother at the window, beckoning. I expect she wants the sausages. NO, Timmy – the sausages are NOT for you. Get down! Good gracious, I never in my life knew such a hungry dog. Anybody would think you starved him, George.'

'Well, they'd think wrong, then,' said George. 'Timmy, come to heel.'

Timmy came, still looking round longingly at the various bags that the others were now taking from their saddle-bags.

They all went indoors, and deposited the goods on the kitchen table. Doris, the lady who helped their mother in the holidays, opened the bags and looked inside, keeping a sharp eye on Timmy.

'Better take that dog of yours out of my kitchen,' she said. 'Funny how sausages always disappear when he's around. Get down, now – take your paws off my clean table!'

Timmy trotted out of the kitchen. He thought it was a pity that cooks didn't like him. He liked *them* very much indeed – they always smelt so deliciously of cooking, and there were always so many titbits around which he longed for, but was seldom offered. Ah well – he'd trot into the kitchen again when Doris had gone upstairs for something! He might perhaps find a few bits and pieces on the floor then!

'Hallo, Georgina dear!' said her aunt, coming into the kitchen, Timmy following her in delight. 'Timmy, go out of the kitchen. I don't trust you within a mile of sausages. Go on – shoo!'

Timmy 'shooed'. He liked Anne's mother, but knew that when she said 'Shoo!' she meant it. He lay down on a rug in the living room, with a heavy sigh, wondering how long it would be before he had that lovely meaty bone. He put his head on his paws, and kept his ears pricked for George. He thought it most unfair that George shouldn't be shooed out of the kitchen too.

'Now, for goodness' sake keep out of my way while I cook the lunch,' said Doris to the children milling round her kitchen. 'And shut the door, please. I don't want that great hungry dog sniffing round me all the time, making out he's starving, when he's as fat as butter!'

'He's *not*!' said George, indignantly. 'Timmy has never been fat in his life. He's not that kind of dog. He's *never* greedy!'

'Well, he must be the first dog ever born that wasn't greedy,' said Doris. 'Can't trust any of them! There was that pug-dog of Mrs Lane's – crunched up lumps of sugar whenever it could reach a sugar bowl – and that fat poodle next door – came and knocked over the cream that the milkman left outside the back door – *deliberately* knocked it over, mark you – and then licked up every drop. Ha – his mistress tried to make out he didn't like cream – but you should have seen his nose – covered in cream up to his eyes!'

Timmy looked in at the kitchen door, his nose in the air, for all the world as if he were deeply offended at Doris's remarks. Julian laughed. 'You've wounded his pride, Doris!' he said.

'I'll wound him somewhere else, too, if he comes sniffing round me when I'm cooking,' said Doris. That made George give one of her scowls, but the others couldn't help laughing!

The morning went very pleasantly. The Five went down to the beach and walked round the high cliffs, enjoying the stiff breeze that blew in their faces. Timmy raced after every seagull that dared to sit on the smooth sand, annoyed that each one rose up lazily on great wings as soon as he almost reached it.

They were all hungry for their dinner, and not one single

morsel was left when they had finished! Doris had made a tremendous steamed pudding, with lashings of treacle, which was, as usual, a huge success.

'Wish I had a tongue like Timmy's and could lick up the lovely treacle left on the bottom of the dish,' said George. 'Such a waste!'

'You certainly won't be able to eat any tea, I'm sure of that!' said her aunt. But, of course, she was wrong. When teatime came they all felt quite ready for it, and were most impatient when Mrs Layman was late!

The tea looked lovely, laid on a big table covered with a white lace cloth. The children sat and looked at it longingly. When would Mrs Layman arrive?

'I begin to feel I'm not going to like Mrs Layman,' said George, at last. 'I can't *bear* looking at those cream cakes when I'm hungry.'

The front door bell rang. Hurrah! Then in came a cheerful, smiling old lady nodding to everyone, very pleased to see such a nice little party waiting for her.

'Here's Mrs Layman, children,' said Julian's mother. 'Sit down, Mrs Layman. We're delighted to have you.'

'Well, I've come to ask the children something,' said Mrs Layman. 'But we'll have tea first, and then I'll say what I've come to say. My, my – what a wonderful tea! I'm glad I feel hungry!'

Everyone else was hungry too, and soon the bread and butter, the sandwiches, the buns, the cakes and everything else disappeared. Timmy sat quietly by George, who

slipped him a titbit now and again when no one was looking. Mrs Layman chatted away. She was a most interesting person, and the children liked her very much.

'Well now,' she said, when tea was finished, 'I'm sure you must be wanting to know why I asked to come to tea today. I wanted to ask your mother, Julian, if there was any chance of you three . . . and this other boy here, what's his name – George! . . . would you like to help me out of a difficulty?'

Nobody pointed out that George was a girl, not a boy, and that George was short for Georgina. George, as usual, was pleased to be taken for a boy. They all looked at Mrs Layman, listening to her with interest.

'It's like this,' she said. 'I've a dear little house up on the hills, overlooking the harbour – and I've a grandson staying with me there – Wilfrid. Well, I have to go to look after a cousin of mine, who's ill – and Wilfrid can't bear to be left alone. I just wondered if your mother would allow you children to share the little house with Wilfrid, and, well, keep him company. He feels a bit scared being on his own. There's a nice woman there, who comes in to cook and clean – but poor Wilfrid's really scared of being in such a lonely place, high up on the hill.'

'You mean that lovely little house with the wonderful view?' said Julian's mother.

'Yes. It's rather *primitive* in some ways – no water laid on, only just a well to use – and no electricity or gas – just candles, or an oil-lamp. Maybe it sounds too old-fashioned for words – but honestly the view makes up for it! Perhaps the children would like to come over and see it, before they decide?' Mrs Layman looked earnestly round at everyone, and nobody knew quite what to say.

'Well – we'll *certainly* come and see it,' said Julian's mother. 'And if the children feel like it, well, they can stay there. They do like being on their own, of course.'

'Yes,' said Julian. 'We'll come and see it, Mrs Layman. Mother's going to be busy with a bazaar soon – she'll be glad to get us out of the way – and, of course, we *do* like being on our own!'

Mrs Layman looked extremely pleased. 'Tomorrow, then?' she said. 'About ten o'clock. You'll love the view. Wonderful, wonderful! You can see right over the great harbour, and for miles around. Well – I must be going now. I'll tell Wilfrid you children may be keeping him company. He's *such* a nice lad – so helpful. You'll love him.'

Julian had his doubts about the nice, helpful Wilfrid. He even wondered if Mrs Layman wanted to get away from Wilfrid, and leave him to himself! No – that was too silly. Anyway, they'd soon see what the place was like, tomorrow.

'It *would* be fun to be on our own again,' said George, when Mrs Layman had gone. 'I don't expect this Wilfrid would be any bother. He's probably just a silly kid, scared of being left alone – though apparently there *is* a woman there! Well – we'll go tomorrow! Maybe the view will make up for dear Wilfrid!'

CHAPTER THREE

The cottage on the hill – and Wilfrid

NEXT DAY the children prepared to go and see the cottage belonging to Mrs Layman. 'You coming too, Mother?' asked Julian. 'We'd like your advice!'

'Well, no, dear,' said his mother. 'I've rather a lot to do – there's a meeting on at the village hall, and I promised to go to it.'

'You're full of good works, Mother,' said Julian, giving her a hug. 'All right, we'll go by ourselves. I daresay we shall know at once whether we'd like to stay in the cottage – or not. Also, we *must* know what this Wilfrid is like! It's a quarter to ten, and George is already here, with Timmy. I'll call the others and we'll get our bikes.'

Soon the four were on their bicycles, with Timmy, as usual, running alongside, his long tongue out, his eyes bright and happy. This was Timmy's idea of perfect happiness – to be with the four children all day long!

They went along a road that ran on the top of a hill. They swung round a corner – and there, spread far below them, was a great sea vista that included a wonderful harbour, filled with big and little ships. The sea was as blue as the Mediterranean, quite breath-taking. Anne jumped off her bicycle at once.

'I must just feast my eyes on all this before I go any further!' she said. 'What a panorama! What miles of sea and sky!'

She put her bicycle against a gate and then climbed over and stood by herself, gazing down at the view. Dick joined her.

Then suddenly a voice shouted loudly 'FORE! FORE!' A small white thing came whizzing through the air and landed just by Anne's foot. She jumped in surprise.

'It's a golf ball,' said Dick. 'No, don't pick it up. Whoever's playing with it has to come and hit it from exactly where it fell. Good thing you weren't hit, Anne. I didn't realise that this gate led on to a golf course!'

'We ought to have a walk over it,' said Anne. 'Just look at those gorsebushes over there, absolutely flaming with yellow blossom – and all the tiny flowers springing up everywhere – speedwell and coltsfoot and daisies and celandines – beautiful. And what a view!'

'Yes – and if Mrs Layman's cottage has a view anything like this, I'd certainly like to stay there!' said Dick. 'Think of getting out of bed in the morning and seeing this enormous view out of the window – the harbour – the sea beyond – the hills all round – the great spread of sky . . .'

'You ought to be a poet, Dick!' said Anne, in surprise. The golfers came up at that moment, and the children stood aside and watched one of them address the ball, and then strike it easily and strongly. The ball soared through the air, and landed far away on a smooth green fairway.

'Good shot!' said the man's partner, and the two sauntered off together.

'Funny game, really,' said Anne. 'Just hitting a ball all round the course.'

'Wish I had some clubs!' said Dick. 'I'm sure I could hit some smashing shots!'

'Well, if that cottage is anywhere near the golf course perhaps you could pay to have a lesson,' said Anne. 'I bet you could hit a ball as far as that man!'

The others were now yelling for them to come back, so they went to fetch their bicycles. Soon they were all riding along the road again. 'We have to look for a small white gate, with "Hill Cottage" painted on it,' said George. 'On the hillside facing the sea.'

'There it is!' cried Anne. 'We'll pile our bicycles together against the hedge, and go in at the gate.'

They left their bicycles in a heap and went through the gate. Not far to their left stood a funny old cottage, its back to them, its front looking down the steep hill that ran towards the great harbour and the sea beyond.

'It's like a cottage out of an old fairy-tale,' said Anne. 'Funny little chimneys, rather crooked walls, a thatched roof, all uneven – and what tiny windows!'

They walked down a little winding path that led to the cottage. They soon came to a well, and leant over it to see the water deep down. 'So that's the water we'd have to drink!' said Anne, wrinkling up her nose. 'And we'd have to let down the bucket by winding this handle – and down it would go on the rope! Do you suppose the water is pure?'

'Well, seeing that people must have drunk it for years on end – the ones living in that cottage, anyway – I should imagine it's all right!' said Julian. 'Come on – let's find the front door of the cottage – if it has one!'

It had a wooden door, hung rather crooked, with an old brass knocker. It faced down the hill, and was flanked on each side by small windows. Two other small windows were above. Julian looked at them. 'The bedrooms would be very small,' he thought. 'Would there *really* be room for them all?'

He knocked at the door. Nobody came to open it. He

knocked again, and then looked for a bell, but there wasn't one.

'See if the door is unlocked,' said Anne. So Julian turned the handle – and at once the door gave under his hand! It opened straight into a room that looked like a kitchen-living room.

Julian gave a shout. 'Anyone at home?'

There was no answer. 'Well – as this is obviously the cottage we were meant to see, we'd better go in,' said Julian and they all went.

It was old, very old. The carved wooden furniture was old too. Ancient oil-lamps stood on two tables in the room, and in a recess there was an oil-stove with a saucepan on top. A narrow, crooked stairway made of wood curved up to the floor above. Julian went up, and found himself in a long, darkish room, its roof thatched with reed and held up by black beams.

'This place must be hundreds of years old!' he called down to the others. 'I don't think it's big enough for us four and the others too – Wilfrid and the helper.'

Just as he finished calling down the stairs, the front door was flung open and someone came in.

'What are you doing here?' he shouted. 'This is *my* cottage!'

Julian went quickly down the stairs, and there, facing them all, stood a boy of about ten, a scowl on his sunburned face.

'Er – are you Wilfrid, by any chance?' asked Dick, politely.

'Yes, I am. And who are you? And where's my grandmother? She'll soon chuck you out!' said the boy.

'Is your grandmother Mrs Layman?' asked Julian. 'If so, she asked us to come and see her cottage, and decide if we'd like to keep you company. She said she had to go away and look after a sick relative.'

'Well, I don't want you!' said the boy. 'So clear off. I'm all right here alone. My grandmother's a nuisance, always fussing around.'

'I thought there was a lady who looks after you too,' said Julian. 'Where is she?'

'She only comes in the morning, and I sent her off,' said Wilfrid. 'She left me some food. I want to be alone. I don't want *you*. So clear off.'

'Don't be an idiot, Wilfrid,' said Julian. 'You can't live all alone here. You're just a kid.'

'I shan't be living all alone. I've plenty of friends,' said Wilfrid, defiantly.

'You *can't* have plenty of friends here in this lonely place, with only the hills and sky around you,' said Dick.

'Well, I *have*!' said Wilfrid. 'And here's one – so look out!' And, to the horror of the two girls, he put his hand into his pocket, and brought out a snake!

Anne screamed, and tried to hide behind Julian. Wilfrid saw her fright and came towards her, holding the snake by its middle, so that it swayed to and fro, its bright little eyes gleaming.

'Don't be scared, Anne,' said Julian. 'It's only a harmless grass-snake. Put the creature back into your pocket, Wilfrid, and don't play the fool. If that snake is the only friend you have, you'll be pretty lonely here by yourself!'

'I've *plenty* of friends, I tell you!' shouted Wilfrid,

stuffing the snake back into his pocket. 'I'll get you if you don't believe me.'

'Oh no, you won't,' said Dick. 'Just show us your other friends. If they're kids like you, it's just too bad!'

'Kids? I don't make friends with *kids*!' said Wilfrid, scornfully. '*I'll* show you I'm speaking the truth. Come out here on the hillside, and see some of my other friends.'

They all trooped out of the little cottage, on to the hillside, amazed at this fierce, strange boy. When they were in the open, they saw that he had eyes as bright blue as the speedwell in the grass, and hair almost as yellow as the celandines.

'Sit down and keep quiet,' he ordered. 'Over there, by that bush. And don't move a finger. I'll soon make you believe in my friends! How dare you come here, doubting my word!'

They all sat down obediently beside the gorsebush, puzzled and rather amused. The boy sat down too, and drew something out of his pocket. What was it? George tried to see, but it was half-hidden in his right hand.

He put it to his mouth, and began to whistle. It was a soft, weird whistle that grew loud and then died away again. There was no tune, no melody, just a kind of beautiful dirge that pulled at the heart. 'Sad,' thought Anne. 'Such a sad little tune – if you could *call* it a tune!'

Something stirred a little way down the hill – and then to everyone's astonishment, an animal appeared – a hare!

Its great ears stood upright, its big eyes stared straight at the boy with the curious little pipe. Then the hare lolloped right up to Wilfrid – and began to dance! Soon another came, but this one only watched. The first one then seemed to go mad, and leapt about wildly, utterly unafraid.

The tune changed a little – and a rabbit appeared. Then another and another. One came to Wilfrid's feet and sniffed at them, its whiskers quivering. Then it lay down against the boy's foot.

A bird flew down – a beautiful magpie! It stood nearby, watching the hare, fascinated. It took no notice of the children at all. They all held their breath, amazed and delighted.

And then Timmy gave a little growl, deep down in his throat. He didn't really mean to, but he just couldn't help it! At once the hares, the rabbits and the magpie fled, the magpie squawking in fright.

Wilfrid faced round at once, his eyes blazing. He lifted his hand to strike Timmy – but George caught his fist at once.

'Let go!' yelled Wilfrid. 'That dog scared my friends! I'll get a stick and whip him. He's the worst dog in the world, he's . . .'

And then something strange happened. Timmy came gently over to Wilfrid, lay down, and put his head on the angry boy's knee, looking up at him lovingly. The boy, his hand still raised to strike, lowered it, and fondled Timmy's head, making a curious crooning noise.

'Timmy! Come here!' ordered George, amazed and angry. To think that *her* dog, her very *own* dog, should go to a boy who had been about to strike him! Timmy stood up, gave Wilfrid a lick, and went to George.

The boy watched him, and then spoke to them all. 'You *can* come and stay in my cottage,' he said, 'if you'll bring that dog too. There aren't many dogs like him – he's a *wonderful* dog. I'd like him for one of my friends.'

Then, without another word, Wilfrid sprang up and ran away down the hill, leaving four most astonished people – and a dog who whined dismally because the boy had gone. Well, well, Timmy – there must indeed be something about that boy, if you stand looking after him as if you had lost one of your very best friends!

CHAPTER FOUR

Settling in

THE FIVE stared after Wilfrid in silence. Timmy wagged his tail and whined. He wanted the boy to come back.

'Well, thank you, Timmy, old thing,' said Anne, patting the big dog on the head. 'We certainly wouldn't have had this lovely little cottage, with its incredible view, if you hadn't made friends with Wilfrid. What a funny boy he is!'

'Rather peculiar, *I* think!' said George, still amazed at the way that Timmy had gone to Wilfrid, when the boy had been about to strike him. 'I'm not sure that I like him!'

'Don't be silly, George,' said Dick, who had been very much impressed by the boy's handling of the hares, the rabbits and the magpie. 'That boy must have a wonderful love for animals. They would never come to him as they did, if they didn't trust him absolutely. Anyone who loves animals as he does must be all right.'

'I bet I could make them come to *me* if I had that pipe,' said George, making up her mind to borrow it if she could.

Anne went back into the cottage. She was delighted with it. 'It must be very, very old,' she thought. 'It stands dreaming here all day long, full of memories of the people who have lived here and loved it. And how they must all have loved this view – miles and miles of heather, great stretches of sea – and the biggest, highest widest sky I've ever seen. It's a happy place. Even the clouds seem happy – they're scurrying along, so white against the blue!'

She explored the cottage thoroughly. She decided that the room above, under the thatch, should be for the three boys. There were two mattresses – one small, one larger. 'The little one for Wilfrid – the big one for Dick and Julian,' she thought. 'And George and I can sleep down in the living room, with Tim on guard. I wonder if there are any rugs we could sleep on. Ah – wait a bit – this couch is a pull-out bed – just right for us two girls! Good!'

Anne enjoyed herself thoroughly. This was the kind of problem she liked – fixing up this and that for the others! She found a little larder, facing north. It had a few tins in it, and a jug of milk, slightly sour. It also had two loaves of extremely stale bread, and a tin of rather hard cakes.

'Mrs Layman doesn't seem to be a very good housekeeper for herself and Wilfrid,' thought Anne, seriously. 'We'll have to go down to the village and put in a stock of decent food. I might get a small ham – the boys would like that. Goodness – this *is* going to be fun!'

Julian came to the door to see what she was doing. When he saw her happy, serious face, he chuckled. 'Acting "mother" to us, as usual?' he said. 'Deciding who's going to sleep where, and which of us is to do the shopping, and which the washing-up? Dear old Anne – what should we do without you when we go off on our own?'

'I love it,' said Anne, happily. 'Julian, we need another rug or two, and a pillow, and some food. And . . .'

'Well, we'll have to go back home and collect a few clothes and other things,' said Julian. 'We can shop on the way back, and get whatever we want. I wonder if that woman that Mrs Layman spoke about will be coming in to help?'

'Well – Wilfrid said he sent her off,' said Anne. 'And I think perhaps as the cottage is so small, it might be better if we managed it ourselves. I think I could do a bit of cooking on that oil-stove in the corner – and anyway we can pretty well live on cold stuff, you know – ham and salad and cheese and fruit. It would be easy enough for any of us to pop down to the village on our bikes, to fetch anything we needed.'

'Listen!' said Julian, cocking his head to one side. 'Is that somebody calling us?'

Yes – it was. When Julian went outside, he saw Mrs Layman at the gate that led on to the hillside where the cottage stood. He went over to her.

'We *love* the cottage!' he said. 'And if it's all right, we'd like to move in today. We can easily pop home and bring back anything we want. It's a glorious old place, isn't it – and the view must be the finest anywhere!'

'Well, that harbour is the second biggest stretch of water in the whole world,' said Mrs Layman. 'The only stretch that is any bigger is Sydney Harbour – so you have something to feast your eyes on, Julian!'

'You bet!' said Julian. 'It's amazing – and so *very* blue! I only wish I could paint – but I can't. At least, not very well!'

'What about Wilfrid?' said Mrs Layman, anxiously. 'Is he behaving himself? He's – well – he's rather a *difficult* boy at times. And he can be very rude. He hasn't any brothers to rub off his awkward corners, you see.'

'Oh, don't you worry about Wilfrid!' said Julian, cheerfully. 'He'll have to toe the line, and do as he's told. We all do our bit when we're away together. He's a wonder with animals, isn't he?'

'Well – yes, I suppose he *is*!' said Mrs Layman. 'Though I can't say I like pet snakes, or pet beetles, and owls that come and hoot down the chimney at night to find out if Wilfrid will go out and hoot back at them!'

Julian laughed. 'We shan't mind that,' he said. 'And he's managed to get over what might have been our biggest difficulty – he has made friends with our dog, Timmy. In fact, he informed us that if Timmy stayed, we could *all* stay – but *only* if Timmy stayed!'

Mrs Layman laughed. 'That's so like Wilfrid,' she said. 'He's an odd boy. Don't stand any nonsense from him!'

'We shan't,' said Julian, cheerfully. 'I'm surprised he wants to stay on with us, actually. I should have thought he would rather go home than be with a lot of strangers.'

'He can't go home,' said Mrs Layman. 'His sister has measles, and his mother doesn't want Wilfrid to catch it. So you'll have to put up with him, I fear.'

'And he'll have to put up with us!' said Julian. 'Thanks very much for letting us have the cottage, Mrs Layman. We'll take great care of everything.'

'I know you will,' said the old lady. 'Well, goodbye, Julian. Have a good time. I'll get back to my car now. Give Wilfrid my love. I hope he doesn't fill the cottage with animals of all kinds!'

'We shan't mind if he does!' said Julian, and waited politely until Mrs Layman had disappeared and he could hear the noise of a car starting up.

He went back to the cottage and stood outside, looking down at the amazing view. The harbour was full of boats, big and little. A steamer went busily along, making for a great seaside town far away on the other side.

Anne came to join Julian. 'Glorious, isn't it?' she said. 'We're so very high up here that it seems as if we can see half the world at our feet. Is that an island in the middle of the harbour, Ju?'

'Yes – and a well-wooded one too!' said Julian. 'I wonder what it's called – and who lives there. I can't see a single house there, can you?'

Dick called to Anne. 'Anne! George and I are going to fetch our bikes and ride down to the village. Give us your shopping list, will you? Julian, is there anything special you want us to pack for you at home, and bring back, besides your night things and a change of clothes?'

'Yes – don't go off yet!' called Julian, hurrying into the cottage. 'I've made a list somewhere. I think I'd better go with you. There will be food and other things to bring back – unless Mother would bring everything up by car this afternoon.'

'Yes – that's a good idea,' said Dick. 'We'll go to Kirrin Cottage first and get George's things – and then home to get ours. I'll leave all the shopping with Mother, and all our luggage, so that she can pop up here in the car with it. She'll love the view!'

'I'll stay behind and tidy up the cottage, and find out how the stove works,' said Anne, happily. 'I'll have everything neat and tidy by the time Mother comes this afternoon, Dick. Oh, here's Julian with the list. Why don't you go off on your bike with George and Dick, Julian? I'll be quite happy here messing about.'

'Yes, I'm going to,' said Julian, putting his list into his pocket. 'Look after yourself, Anne! We'll take Timmy with us, to give him a run.'

Off went the three, Timmy loping behind, very glad of the run. Anne waited till they were out of sight, then went happily back to the cottage. She was almost there when she heard someone calling her. She turned and saw a fresh-faced woman waving.

'I'm Sally!' she called. 'Do you want any help with the cooking and cleaning? Wilfrid told me not to come any more, but if you want me, I will.'

'Oh, I think we can manage, Sally,' said Anne. 'There's so many of us now, we can all do the jobs. Did you sleep here?'

'Oh no!' said Sally, coming up. 'I just came in to help, and then went back home. You tell me if you want me any time, and I'll gladly come. Where's that monkey of a Wilfrid? He spoke to me very rudely this morning, the little devil! I'll tell his grandmother of him – not that that's much good! He just laughs at her! Don't you stand any nonsense from him!'

'I won't,' said Anne, smiling. 'Where do you live, in case we *do* want you?'

'Just the other side of the road, in the small wood there,' said Sally. 'You'll see my tiny cottage when you go by the wood on your bikes.'

She disappeared up the hill and across the road there. Anne went back happily to her household tasks. She cleaned out the little larder, and then found a pail and went to the well. She hung the pail on the hook at the end of the rope, and then worked the old handle that let the pail down to the water, swinging on the rope. Splash! It was soon full, and Anne wound it up again. The water looked crystal clear, and was as cold as ice – but all the same Anne wondered if she ought to boil it.

Someone came quietly behind her – and jumped at her with a loud howl! Anne dropped the pail of water, and gave a scream. Then she saw it was Wilfrid, dancing round her, grinning.

'Idiot!' she said. 'Now you just go and get me some more water.'

'Where's that big dog?' demanded Wilfrid, looking all round. 'I can't see him. You can't any of you stay here unless you have that dog. I like him. He's a wonderful dog.'

'He's gone down to the village with the others,' said Anne. 'Now will you please pick up that pail and get more water?'

'No, I won't,' said Wilfrid. 'I'm not your servant! Get it yourself!'

'Very well, I will. But I'll tell George, who owns Timmy, how rude you are – and you may be *quite* sure that Timmy won't be friends with you,' said Anne, picking up the pail.

'I'll get the water, I'll get the water!' shouted Wilfrid, and snatched the pail. 'Don't you dare to tell George or Timmy tales of me. Don't you dare!'

And off he went to the well and filled the pail. Well! What a time they were all going to have with such a very peculiar boy! Anne didn't like him at all!

CHAPTER FIVE

Wilfrid is most annoying – and Anne is most surprising!

WILFRID BROUGHT back the pail to Anne, and dumped it down. 'Like to see my pet beetles?' he said.

'No thank you,' said Anne. 'I don't like beetles very much.'

'Well, you ought to!' said Wilfrid. 'I've two very beautiful ones. You can hold them if you like. The tiny feet feel very funny when they walk all over your hand.'

'I don't *mind* beetles, but I don't want them walking over my hand,' said poor Anne, who really was a bit afraid of what she called 'creepy-crawly' things. 'Do get out of my way, Wilfrid. If you had any manners, you'd carry that pail indoors for me.'

'I *haven't* any manners,' said Wilfrid. 'Everybody tells me that. Anyway, I don't want to carry your pail if you don't want to see my beetles.'

'Oh, go away!' said Anne, exasperated, picking up the pail herself. Wilfrid went to a little thick bush and sat down by it. He put his face almost on the grass, and looked under the bush. Anne felt uncomfortable. Was he going to call his beetles out? She couldn't help putting down her pail, and standing still to watch.

No beetles came out from under the bush – but something else did. A very large, awkward-looking toad came crawling out, and sat there, looking up at Wilfrid with the greatest friendliness. Anne was amazed. How did Wilfrid know the toad was there? And why in the world should it come out to see *him*? She stood and stared – and shivered, because she really did *not* like toads. 'I know they have beautiful eyes, and are intelligent, and eat all kinds of harmful insects, but I just can't go near one!' she thought. 'Oh goodness – Wilfrid's tickling its back – and it's scratching where he's tickled – just like *we* would!'

'Come and say how-do-you-do to my pet toad,' called Wilfrid. 'I'll carry your pail for you then.'

Anne picked up her pail in a hurry, afraid that Wilfrid might whistle up a few snakes next. What a boy! How she wished the others would come back! Why, Wilfrid might own a boa constrictor – or have a small crocodile somewhere – or . . . but no, she was being silly! If *only* the others would come back!

To her horror the toad crawled right on to Wilfrid's hands, and looked up at him out of its really beautiful eyes. That was too much for Anne. She fled into the cottage, spilling half the water as she went.

'I wish I was like George,' she thought. 'She wouldn't really mind that toad. I'm silly. I ought to try and like *all* creatures. Oh my goodness, look at that enormous spider in the corner of the sink! It's sitting there, looking at me out of its eight eyes!'

'Wilfrid, Wilfrid – *please* come and get this spider out of the sink for me!'

Wilfrid sauntered in, fortunately without the toad. He held his hand out to the spider and made a curious clicking, ticking noise. The spider perked up at once, waved two curious little antennae about, and crawled across the sink to Wilfrid's hand. Anne shuddered. She simply couldn't help it! She shut her eyes and when she opened them, the spider had gone and so had Wilfrid.

'I suppose he's now teaching it to dance, or something,' she thought, trying to make herself smile. 'I can't *think* how insects and animals and birds like him. I simply can't *bear* him. If *I* were a rabbit or a bird or beetle, I'd run miles away from him. What's this curious attraction he has for creatures of all kinds?'

Wilfrid had completely disappeared, and Anne thankfully went on with her little jobs. 'I'll tidy up the loft where the boys will sleep,' she thought. 'I'll wash this living room floor. I'll make a list of the things in the larder. I'll clean that dirty window over there. I'll . . . good gracious, what's that noise?'

It was the sound of magpies chattering noisily – a harsh but pleasant noise. Anne peered out of the little cottage window. Well, what a sight! There stood Wilfrid in front of the window, a magpie on each outstretched hand – and one on the top of his head! It stood there, chattering loudly, and then turned round and round, getting its feet mixed up in the boy's thick hair.

'Come out here and I'll tell one of my magpies to sit on your head too!' shouted Wilfrid. 'It's such a nice feeling. Or would you like a young rabbit to cuddle? I can call one for you with my little pipe!'

'I don't *want* a magpie on my head,' said Anne, desperately. 'For goodness' sake get a nice little baby rabbit. I'd like that.'

Wilfrid jerked the magpies off his hands and shook his head violently so that the third one flew up, squawking cheerfully. He then sat down and pulled out his funny little whistle-pipe, as Anne called it. She watched, fascinated, as the strange little dirge-like tune came to her ears. She found her feet walking to the door. Good gracious – could there be some peculiar kind of magic in that pipe that made *her* go to Wilfrid, just as the other creatures did?

She stopped at the door, just as a baby rabbit came lolloping round a tall clump of grass. It was the funniest, roundest, dearest little thing, with a tiny bobtail and big ears.

It went straight to Wilfrid and nestled against him. The boy stroked it and murmured to it. Then he called to Anne softly.

'Well – here's the baby rabbit you asked for. Like to come and stroke it?'

Anne went softly over the grass, expecting the rabbit to bolt at once. Wilfrid continued to fondle it, and the little thing looked at him with big, unwinking eyes. Anne bent down to stroke it – but immediately it leapt in fright and fled into the grass.

'Oh *dear* – why did it do that?' said Anne, disappointed. 'It was quite all right with *you*! Wilfrid, how do you get all these creatures to come to you?'

'Shan't tell you,' said Wilfrid, getting up. 'Is there anything to eat in the cottage? I'm hungry.'

He pushed Anne aside and went into the cottage. He opened the larder door, and took down a tin. There was a cake inside and he cut off a huge piece. He didn't offer Anne any.

'Couldn't you have cut *me* a piece too?' said Anne. 'You really are a rude boy!'

'I *like* being rude,' said Wilfrid, munching his cake. 'Especially to people who come to my cottage when I don't want them.'

'Oh, don't be so *silly*!' said Anne, exasperated. 'It *isn't* your cottage – it belongs to your grandmother. She told us so. Anyway, you said we could stay if Timmy stayed too.'

'I'll soon make Timmy *my* dog,' said Wilfrid, taking another bite. 'You'll see! Soon he won't want that girl George any more – and he'll follow at my heels all day and night. *You'll* see!'

Anne laughed scornfully. Timmy following at this boy's heels? That could never happen! Timmy loved George with all his doggy heart. He would never desert her for Wilfrid, no matter how much he whistled on pipes, or put on his special croony voice. Anne was absolutely certain of that!

'If you laugh at me, I'll call up my grass-snake *and* my adder!' said Wilfrid, fiercely. 'Then you'll run for miles!'

'Oh no I won't!' said Anne, hurrying into the cottage. 'Just watch *yourself* run!' She picked up the pail of water, went out with it, and threw it all over the astonished Wilfrid! Somebody else was *most* astonished too – and that was Julian, who had arrived back before the others, anxious not to leave Anne alone in the cottage for too long.

He came just in time to see Anne drenching Wilfrid, and stared in the utmost amazement. *Anne* behaving like that? Anne looking really *fierce* – quiet, peaceful Anne! What in the world had happened?

'Anne!' he called. 'What's the matter? What's Wilfrid been doing?'

'Oh – *Julian*!' said Anne, glad to see him, but horrified that he had come just then. Wilfrid was drenched from head to foot. He stood there, gasping, taken aback, bewildered. Why, Anne had seemed such a *quiet*, frightened little thing – scared even of a spider!

'That girl!' said Wilfrid, half-choking, shaking the water off himself. 'That bad, wicked girl! She's like a tiger! She sprang at me, and threw the water all over me! I won't let her stay in my cottage!'

The boy was so angry, so wet, so taken aback, that Julian had to laugh! He roared in delight, and clapped Anne on the back. 'The mouse has turned into a tiger! Well, you said you might one day, Anne – and you haven't lost much time! Let me see if you've grown claws!'

He took Anne's hands and pretended to examine her nails. Anne was half-laughing, half-crying now, and pulled her hand away. 'Oh, Julian, I shouldn't have soaked Wilfrid – but he was so *irritating* I lost my temper, and . . .'

'All right, all right – it's quite a good thing to do sometimes,' said Julian. 'And I bet young Wilfrid deserved all he got. I only hope the water was icy cold! Have you a change of clothes here, Wilfrid? Go and get into them, then.'

The boy stood there, dripping wet, and made no effort to obey. Julian spoke again. 'You heard what I said, Wilfrid. Jump to it! Go and change!'

The boy looked so wet and miserable that Anne felt suddenly sorry for what she had done. She ran to him and felt his wet shoulders. 'Oh, I'm *sorry*!' she said. 'Truly I am. I don't know *why* I turned into a tiger so suddenly!'

Wilfrid gave a little half-laugh, half-sob. 'I'm sorry too,' he mumbled. 'You're nice – and your nose is like that baby rabbit's – it's – it's a bit woffly!'

He ran into the cottage and slammed the door. 'Let him be for a while,' said Julian, seeing that Anne made a move to go after him. 'This will do him good. Nothing like having a pail of cold water flung over you to make you see things as they really are! He was really touched when you said you were sorry. *He's* probably never apologised to anyone in his life!'

'*Is* my nose like a rabbit's?' said Anne, worried.

'Well, yes – just a bit,' said Julian, giving his sister an affectionate pat. 'But a rabbit's nose is very nice, you know – very nice indeed. I don't think you'll have much trouble with Wilfrid after this little episode. He didn't know that you had the heart of a tiger, as well as a nose like a rabbit's!'

Wilfrid came out of the cottage in about ten minutes, dressed in dry clothes, carrying his wet ones in a bundle.

'I'll hang those out on the bushes for you, to dry in the sun,' said Anne, and took them from him, smiling. He suddenly smiled back.

'Thanks,' he said. 'I don't know how they got so wet! Must have been *pouring* with rain!'

Julian chuckled and smacked him gently on the back. 'Rain can do an awful lot of good at times!' he said. 'Well, Anne, we've brought you back a whole lot of goods for your larder. Here come the others. We'll carry everything in for you – with Wilfrid's help too!'

CHAPTER SIX

Lucas – and his tale

IT WAS fun storing all the shopping away. Anne enjoyed it more than anyone, for she really was a most domesticated little person.

'A real home-maker!' said Dick, appreciatively, when he saw how neat and comfortable she had made the loft, where the three boys were to sleep. 'Just about room for the three of us, plus all the baggage in the corner! And how good the larder looks!'

Anne looked at her well-stocked larder, and smiled. Now she could give her little 'family' really nice meals. All those tins! She read the names on them. Fruit salad. Tinned pears. Tinned peaches. Sardines. Ham. Tuna. A new cake in that round tin, big enough to last for at least three days. Biscuits. Chocolate wafers – good old Julian – he knew how much she loved those – and George did, too!

Anne felt very happy as she arranged all her goods. She no longer felt guilty at drenching poor Wilfrid. Indeed she couldn't help feeling a little thrill when she remembered how she had suddenly turned into a tiger for a minute or two! It was fun to be a tiger for once. 'I might even be one again, if the chance arose,' thought Anne. 'How surprised

Wilfrid was – and Julian too! Oh dear – poor Wilfrid. Still, he's much nicer now.'

And indeed he was! He was most polite to both the girls, and, as Dick said, he didn't 'throw his weight about' nearly so much. They all settled down very well together in the little cottage.

They had most of their meals out of doors, sitting on the warm grass. It was rather a squeeze indoors, for the cottage really was very small. Anne enjoyed herself preparing the meals, with sometimes a little help from George – and the boys carried everything out. Wilfrid did his share, and was pleased when he had a clap on the back from Julian.

It was glorious sitting out in the sun, high up on their hill. They could look down on the harbour, watch the yachts and the busy little boats, and enjoy the wonderful views all around.

George was very curious about the island that lay in the middle of the harbour. 'What's it called?' she asked Wilfrid. But he didn't know. He did know, however, that there was a strange story about it. 'It belonged to a lonely old man,' he said. 'He lived in a big house in the very middle of the wood. The island was given to his family by a king – James the Second, I think. This old man was the very, very last one of his family. People kept wanting to buy his island, and he had some kind of watchmen to keep people from landing on it. These watchmen were pretty fierce – they had guns.'

'Gosh – did they shoot people who tried to land, then?' asked Dick.

'Well – they just shot to frighten them off, not to hurt them, I suppose,' said Wilfrid. 'Anyway, a lot of sightseers had an awful fright when they tried to land. BANG-BANG! Shooting all round them! My granny told me that someone she knew, who had a lot of money, wanted to buy part of the island – and *he* had his hat shot right off when his boat tried to land!'

'Is there anyone there now?' asked Julian. 'I suppose the old fellow is dead? Has he a son or anyone to follow him?'

'I don't think so,' said Wilfrid. 'But I don't know an awful lot about it. I tell you who does, though – one of the groundsmen on the golf course, called Lucas. He was once one of the watchmen who kept visitors away from the island.'

'It might be rather interesting to talk to him,' said Dick. 'I'd rather like to walk over the golf course, too. My father plays a good game of golf, and I know something about it.'

'Well, let's go now,' said George. 'Timmy is longing for a good long walk, even though he ran all the way down to the village and back yesterday! Walk, Timmy? Walk?'

'Woof-woof,' said Timmy, and leapt up at once. Walk? Of *course* he was ready for a walk! He leapt all round George, pretending to pounce at her feet. Wilfrid tried to catch hold of him, but couldn't. 'I wish you were *my* dog,' he told Timmy. 'I'd never let you out of my sight.'

Timmy ran up to him then, and gave him a loving lick.

It was astonishing how he seemed to like Wilfrid. Nobody could understand it. As George said, 'Timmy is usually so particular about making friends! Still, Wilfrid *is* nicer than he was!'

The Five, with Wilfrid too, went up the hill, crossed over the road that ran along the top, and climbed over a stile. They found themselves on one of the fairways of the golf course not far from a green, in which stood a pole with a bright red flag waving at the top.

Wilfrid knew very little about the game of golf, but the others had watched their parents play many a time. 'Look out – someone's going to pitch his ball on this green,' said Julian, and they stood by the hedge to watch the man play his ball. He struck it beautifully with his club, and the ball rose, and fell right on to the green. It rolled very close to the hole in which the flag-pole stood.

Timmy ran forward a few steps, as he always did when a ball rolled near him. Then he remembered that this was golf, and he must never, never touch a ball on the fairway or on the green.

The players passed, and went on with their game. Then they disappeared, to play off another tee.

'Well, let's see if we can find Lucas now,' said Wilfrid, crossing the fairway to where he could get a good look over the course. 'You'll like him. There's not much he doesn't know about the animals and birds here. *I* think he's a wonderful man!'

Wilfrid stood on the slope of a hill and looked all round.

'There he is!' he said, pointing to where a man was trimming up a ditch. 'See? Down there. He's using his billhook to make things tidy.'

They went down the hill towards the ditch at the bottom. 'I bet there's an awful lot of balls in that ditch,' said Wilfrid. 'Hey, Lucas! How are you?'

'Morning, young man,' said the groundsman, turning towards them. His face was as tanned as a well-ripened nut, and his arms and shoulders were sunburned. He wore no shirt or vest, and his dark, deep-set eyes twinkled as they took in the five children and the dog.

He held out a tanned hand to Timmy, who licked it gravely, wagging his tail. Then Timmy smelt Lucas all over and finally lay down with his head on the man's feet.

'Ha!' said Lucas to Timmy, and gave a loud, hearty laugh. 'Think I'm going to stand here all morning, do you? Well, I'm not. I've got work to do, old dog, so get up! You're a right good-un, you are, lying on my foot so I can't move a step! Want me to stop and have a rest, don't you?'

'Lucas, we came to ask you something,' said Wilfrid. 'About the island in the harbour. What's its name – and does anyone live there now?'

'We can see it from that little cottage almost at the top of the hill on the other side of the road,' said Dick. 'It looks awfully quiet and lonely.'

'And so it is,' said Lucas, sitting down on the bank of the ditch. Timmy at once sat up beside him, sniffing him with pleasure. He put his arm round the dog, and began to talk, his bright eyes going from one to another of the children. He was so friendly, and so completely natural, that the children felt he was an old, old friend. They sat down too, sniffing the smell of the gorsebushes nearby. ‘They smell like coconut,’ thought Anne. ‘Yes – just like coconut!’

'Well, now,' said Lucas, 'that island's always been a mystery place. It's called Wailing Island by some folks because the wind makes a right strange wailing noise round some of its high cliffs. And others call it Whispering Island because it's full of trees that whisper in the strong winds that always blow across it. But most of us call it Keep-Away Island – and that's the best name of all, for there's never been any welcome there, what with the dark cliffs, the cruel rocks, and the dense woods.'

Lucas paused, and looked at the listening faces around him. He was a born storyteller, and knew it. How often Wilfrid had listened to his tales of the birds and animals he met during his work on the course! Lucas was one of the few people that the boy admired and loved.

'Do go on, Lucas!' said Wilfrid, touching the man's bare, warm arm. 'Tell us about the rich old man who hated everyone, and bought the island years ago.'

'I'm telling the story my own way,' said Lucas, with great dignity. 'Be patient now, or I'll start my ditching again. Sit like this dog, see – he doesn't even twitch a muscle, good dog that he is. Well now, about this rich old man. He was so afraid of being robbed that he bought that lonely island. He built himself a great castle right in the middle of the thick woods. Cut down about a hundred trees to make room for it, so the story goes, and brought every single stick and stone from the mainland. Did you see the old quarry on this here golf course, as you came along to me?'

'Yes, we did,' said Julian, remembering. 'I felt sorry for anyone who sent a golf ball there!'

'Well, out of that quarry came the great stones that the old man used for his castle,' said Lucas. ''Tis said that big, flat-bottomed boats had to be made to ferry the stones across to the island – and to this day the road through this golf course is the one made by horses dragging the great stones down to the water's edge.'

'Were you alive then?' said Wilfrid.

'Bless you, boy, no, of course not,' said Lucas, with a great chuckle of a laugh. 'Long before my time, that was. Well, the stone house – or castle, whatever you like to call it – was built. And the old man brought to it all kinds of treasures – beautiful statues, some of gold, it was said, but I don't believe that. There are many strange tales I've heard of what that rich old man took over to Whispering Island – a great bed made of pure gold, and set with precious stones – a necklace of rubies as big as pigeons' eggs – a wonderful sword with a jewelled handle, worth a king's fortune – and other things I can't remember.'

He paused and looked round. Julian asked him a quick question. 'What happened to all these things?'

'Well now, he fell foul of the king of the land, and one morning, what did he see landing on the shores of his island but ships of all kinds,' said Lucas, enjoying the rapt attention of his audience. 'A lot of them were sunk by the wicked rocks but enough men were left to storm the strange stone castle in the wood, and they killed the old man and all his servants.'

'Did they find the treasures the old fellow had collected?' asked Dick.

'Not one thing!' said Lucas. 'Not one thing. Some say it was all a tale – the old man never did bring any wonders there, and some say they're still there, on Whispering Island. I think it's all a yarn – but a good yarn at that!'

'Who owns the island now?' asked Dick.

'Well, an old fellow and his wife went to live there. Maybe they paid rent to the Crown for it, maybe they bought it – but they didn't care for anything except for the birds and the animals there,' said Lucas, picking up his curved billhook again, and hacking lightly at some briars. 'They wouldn't allow anybody there, and it was they who kept the gamekeepers with guns to frighten away sightseers. They wanted peace and quiet for themselves, and for all the wildlife on the island – and a fine idea too. Many a time when I was there with the other keepers – three of us there were – many a time I've had rabbits gambolling over my feet, and snakes gliding by me – and the birds as tame as canaries.'

'I'd *love* to go there,' said Wilfrid, his eyes shining. 'I'd have a good time with all the wild creatures! Can anyone go there now?'

'No,' said Lucas, getting up. 'Not a soul has lived in the old stone castle since the old man and his wife fell ill and died. The place is empty. The island belongs to a great-nephew of the old couple now, but he never goes there. Just keeps a couple of men on the island to frighten off visitors – pretty fierce they are, so I've been told. Well, there you are, that's the story of Whispering Island – not very pleasant – a bit grim and ugly. It belongs to the birds and the beasts now, and good luck to them!'

'Thank you for telling us the story,' said Anne, and the old countryman smiled down at her, his eyes wrinkling, and his hand patting her cheek.

'I'll be off to my hedging and ditching again,' he said, 'and I'll feel the sun warm on my bare back, and hear the birds singing to me from the bushes. That's happiness enough for anyone – and it's a pity that more folks don't know it!'

CHAPTER SEVEN

Up on the golf course

THE CHILDREN walked round the golf course together, after talking to old Lucas. 'We must keep out of the way of anyone playing,' said Dick, 'or we might get hit on the head with a ball! Hey, Timmy, what are you doing in the bracken?'

Timmy came out with something in his mouth. He dropped it at George's feet. It was a golf ball, fairly new. George picked it up. 'What do we do with this?' she said. 'There's no golfer near us. It must be a lost ball.'

'Well, all balls lost on golf courses should be taken in to the pro,' said Julian. 'By right they belong to him if found on the course.'

'What's a pro?' asked Anne.

'A professional golfer – a man who's very, very good at the game, and is in charge of a golf course,' explained Julian. 'Hey, look! Here comes old Tim again with *another* ball. Timmy, we ought to hire you out to golfers who keep losing their balls – you'd save them no end of trouble!'

Timmy was pleased to be patted and praised. He set off into the rough again at once, sniffing here and there.

'Anyone would think that golf balls smelt like rabbits or something, the way Timmy sniffs them out!' said Anne, as

Timmy ran up with yet another ball. 'Golfers must be jolly careless, losing so many balls!'

They went on round the course, which was set with great stretches of gorse, full of brilliant blossom. A baby rabbit fled from the bracken as Timmy nosed there for balls. Timmy chased it, and the frightened little creature dodged this way and that, trying to escape. 'Let it go, Tim, let it go!' yelled George, but Timmy was much too excited to pay any attention.

Wilfrid suddenly bent down as the rabbit raced near him, and gave a curious low whistle. The rabbit swerved, came straight towards him, and leapt into his arms, lying there trembling. Timmy jumped up to it at once, but George dragged him away.

'NO, Timmy. Sorry, but NO, you can't have the little thing. Down! DOWN, I say!'

Timmy gave George a disgusted look, and pattered off into the bracken, nosing for balls again. He was very cross with George. Rabbits were meant to be chased, weren't they? Why did George have to spoil his fun?

George stared at Wilfrid. The rabbit was still nestling in his arms, and he was making a curious noise to it. The tiny thing was trembling from head to tail. Everyone watched it, glad that it was safe. They were all silent, astonished at the way that Wilfrid had rescued the little creature. How had the rabbit known that Wilfrid's arms were ready to save it?

He took it to the bracken, dropped it gently, and watched it race like lightning to the nearest burrow. Then he turned and patted Timmy, who stood silently by, watching.

'Sorry, Tim,' he said. 'It's so little, and you're so big!'

'Woof,' said Tim, exactly as if he understood, and he gave Wilfrid's hand a quick lick. Then he pranced round the boy, barking, as if he wanted a game, and Wilfrid raced off with him at top speed.

The others followed, impressed once again by Wilfrid's uncanny way with animals. He was such a horrid little boy in some ways – so rude, so mannerless, so selfish – then how was it that animals liked him so much? George frowned. She thought it was all wrong that animals should love Wilfrid and go to him – why, even Timmy was all over him! If she wasn't careful he would spend more time with Wilfrid than with her! That would never do!

Timmy found five more balls, and soon Julian's pockets were heavy with them. They made their way to the small clubhouse in the distance, meaning to give in the balls. It was set in a little dip, and looked friendly and welcoming. They all went in at the door, and Julian walked over to the pro, who was checking some scorecards. He emptied his pockets of balls and grinned. 'A present from our dog!' he said.

'My word – did he find all those?' said the pro, pleased. 'Not bad ones, either. I'll stand you all some lemonade or orangeade – which will you have?'

They all had orangeade, and the pro sent a packet of biscuits to Timmy, who was waiting patiently outside. He was delighted!

'We're staying in that little cottage up on the hillside,' said Dick. 'Do you know it?'

''Course I do!' said the pro. 'My grandmother lived there once upon a time. You've a wonderful view there, haven't you? One of the finest in the world, I reckon! You can see Whispering Island from there, too. Ought to be called Mystery Island! It's said that folks have gone there and never come back!'

'What happened to them?' asked Anne.

'Oh well – maybe it's all a tale!' said the pro. 'There's supposed to be priceless things there, packed away somewhere – and collectors from all over the world have come here, and tried to get over to that island – not to steal, you understand, but just to see if they could find anything worthwhile and buy it for museums – or maybe for their own collections. It's said there are statues in the wood, white as snow – but that I never did believe!'

'And didn't the collectors ever come back?' asked Julian.

'It's said that a lot of them didn't,' said the pro, 'but that may all be silly tales. But I do know that two men came down here from some museum in London, and hired a boat to go across. They took a white flag with them so that the two keepers wouldn't shoot them – and after that nobody heard a word about them. They just disappeared!'

'Well – what could have happened to them?' asked Julian.

'Nobody knows,' said the pro. 'Their boat was found miles out to sea, drifting – and empty. So the police reckoned a mist came down, they lost direction, and ended by drifting way out to sea.'

'But did they jump out of their boat, and try to swim back – and get drowned?' asked Dick. 'Or did a passing steamer or yacht save them?'

'They weren't picked up, that's certain,' said the pro. 'Else they'd have arrived safely back at their homes, sometime or other. But they didn't. No – I reckon the poor fellows were drowned. Of course, maybe they were shot by the keepers, when they tried to land, and their boat was set adrift!'

'Didn't the police do anything?' asked Julian, puzzled.

'Oh, yes – they went across to the island in the coast-guard patrol boat,' said the pro. 'But the keepers swore they'd seen nobody arriving, and that they were the only people on the place. The police landed and searched everywhere, and they found nothing except the great white castle-like house in the woods and hundreds of wild animals, so tame that they'd sit and watch you as you walked by.'

'All very mysterious,' said Julian, getting up. 'Well, thanks for the welcome orangeade, and for your information! We'd already heard a bit from a groundsman of yours – Lucas – a real old countryman, and a born storyteller!'

'Ah, Lucas – yes, he knows that island well,' said the pro. 'He was once one of the keepers, I believe! Well – come and see me again some time – thanks for the balls. It isn't everyone who's honest enough to come and give them in when they find them!'

They all said goodbye and went out. Timmy pranced along in joy. Sitting down outside the club-house didn't suit him at all!

'Did you enjoy your biscuits, Tim?' asked George, and he ran up and gave her hand a quick lick. What a question! He *always* enjoyed biscuits! He ran off into the bracken and began to nose about there again, hunting for balls.

The others went to walk up the hill, talking about the island. 'I wonder what really *did* happen to those two collector men who were never heard of again,' said Anne. 'Funny that their boat was found adrift and empty.'

'They must have been drowned, of course,' said Dick. 'I wonder if anything *is* left of the old treasures that were once taken there. No – there wouldn't be – the police would have made a very thorough search!'

'I wish *we* could go to the island!' said George. 'I don't expect the keepers would shoot at *us*, would they? They might even let us on, to make change for them – they must be so bored with only themselves to talk to.'

'That's *very* wishful thinking, George,' said Julian. 'We are CERTAINLY not going near the island, so put that right out of your head.'

'Well – I knew it was impossible, really,' said George. 'But wouldn't it be a *grand* adventure if we managed to get on the mysterious Whispering Island and explore it without the keepers knowing!'

'Not such a grand adventure if we were all peppered with shot from the keepers' guns!' said Dick. 'Anyway, we wouldn't find anything of interest – the treasures must have been removed long ago. The only possible things of interest would be the very tame wild creatures there! Wilfrid would go mad with joy – wouldn't you, Wilfrid?'

'I'd like it very much,' said the boy, his eyes shining. 'What's more, I might hire a boat myself and row round the island to see if I could spot any animals there.'

'You'll do nothing of the sort!' said Julian, at once. 'So don't try any silly tricks, see?'

'I shan't promise! said Wilfrid, irritatingly. 'You just never know!'

'Oh yes, I do know! You're just trying to sound big!' said Julian. 'Come along quickly, everyone – it's past our dinner-time, and I'm ravenous! What's for lunch, Anne?'

'We'll open a tin of tuna,' said Anne, 'and there's plenty of bread left, and lettuce, which I left in water. And tomatoes. And heaps of fruit.'

'Sounds good!' said George. 'Dinner, Timmy, dinner!'

And, hearing that welcome word, Timmy shot up the steep hill at top speed, his tail waving joyously.

'Wish I was a dog and could tear up a hill like that!' said Anne, panting. 'Give me a push, Julian! I'll *never* get to the top!'

CHAPTER EIGHT

Mostly about Wilfrid

TIMMY WAS waiting for the children at the top of the hill, his tail waving, his mouth open as he panted. He picked something up, as the children came, threw it into the air, and caught it.

'Another golf ball, Timmy?' said Dick, as Timmy threw the ball into the air again with a toss of his big head.

'No – it's too big for that,' said George. 'Drop it, Timmy. What have you found?'

Timmy dropped the ball at George's feet. It was bigger than a golf ball, and had a hole right through it. 'Oh, it's one of those balls that children throw up and try to catch on a stick,' said George. 'Somebody must have dropped it. All right, Tim, you can have it.'

'He won't swallow it, will he?' said Wilfrid, anxiously. 'It's not *awfully* big – and I once saw a dog swallow something by mistake, that he threw into the air to catch.'

'Timmy's *much* too sensible to swallow *any* ball,' said George. 'You needn't worry about *him*. Anyway, *I* can do any worrying necessary. He's *my* dog.'

'All right, all right, all right!' said Wilfrid. 'Miss High-and-Mighty can look after her own dog. Fine!'

George looked round at him furiously and he made a

face at her. Then he whistled to Timmy – yes, he actually dared to whistle to him!

'Nobody whistles for my dog except me,' said George. 'And anyway, he won't come to *you*.'

But, to her surprise and horror, Timmy *did* go to Wilfrid, and pranced all round him, expecting a game. George called him sternly, and he looked at her in surprise. He began to trot over to her when Wilfrid whistled again, and obediently Timmy turned as if to go to him.

George caught hold of the dog's collar, and aimed a punch at the whistling boy. It missed him, and he danced round, laughing.

'Stop it now, you two,' said Julian, seeing George's look of fury. 'I said STOP IT! Wilfrid, go on ahead, and *keep* going. George, don't be an ass. He's only teasing you to make you lose your temper. Don't please him by losing it!'

George said nothing more, but her eyes blazed. 'Oh dear!' thought Anne. 'Now we shan't have any peace! She won't forgive Wilfrid for making Timmy go to him! Blow Wilfrid – he really is a little pest at times.'

They were all very hungry for their lunch and very pleased with everything that Anne provided. Dick went into the little cottage to help her, because George insisted on keeping her hand on Timmy's collar all the time, in case Wilfrid should entice him to his side.

'He's making some of his peculiar noises now,' said Dick to Anne. 'Noises that animals can't seem to resist! I don't wonder that George has got Timmy tightly by the

collar! I'm not a dog, but I find those little whiny noises Wilfrid is making very curious indeed, and I'd love to go nearer!'

'Well, I hope we're not going to have dark looks from George from now on,' said Anne. 'Wilfrid's an awful little idiot at times, and MOST irritating – but he's not bad underneath, if you know what I mean.'

'Well, I don't really,' said Dick, cutting some tomatoes in half. 'I think he's a badly brought-up little pest – and if I were a dog, I'd bite him, not fawn on him! Have I cut up enough tomatoes, Anne?'

'Good gracious, yes!' said Anne. 'How ever many do you think we're going to eat – forty or fifty? Look, you open this tin for me, Dick. I hate opening tins. I nearly always cut myself.'

'Don't you ever open one again, then,' said Dick. 'I'm the official tin-opener from now on! Dear old Anne, whatever should we do without you? You take everything on your shoulders, and we just *let* you! We all ought to help you more.'

'No, don't,' said Anne, in alarm. 'I *like* doing things on my own. You lot would only break things or upset them. You're all so ham-handed when it comes to washing-up or setting out crockery, though I know you *mean* well.'

'So we are all ham-handed, are we?' said Dick, pretending to be offended. 'When have *I* ever broken anything, I'd like to know? I'm just as careful as you when I handle crockery!'

Alas for Dick! The glass he was holding suddenly slipped from his hand, fell to the floor, and broke! Anne looked at him and gave a sudden delighted giggle. 'Old ham-hand!' she said. 'Can't pick up a glass without dropping it! Look, take out this tray for me, and for goodness' sake don't drop *that*!'

They all had a delicious lunch, and ate practically everything. Wilfrid sat a little away from everyone, scattering crumbs around as he ate. Birds of all kinds were soon round him, even hopping on to his hands. A magpie flew down to his left shoulder. Wilfrid greeted it like an old friend. 'Hallo, Maggie Pie! How's the family? I hope Polly Pie has recovered from her cold. And is Peter Pie's bad leg better? And what about old Grandpa Pie – does he still chase you young ones?'

The magpie put its glossy head on one side and chattered back to him in bird language, which Wilfrid appeared to understand. He stroked the bird's gleaming breast, and fondled it lovingly. George deliberately didn't watch. She turned her back on Wilfrid and the magpie, and talked to Timmy. The others couldn't help being amused.

The magpie put an end to Wilfrid's conversation very suddenly. The boy was about to put half a tomato into his mouth when the bird bent down its head and snatched away the tomato with its powerful beak. Then it rose quickly into the air on its big wings, making a noise exactly as if it were laughing!

Everyone roared with laughter except the surprised Wilfrid. 'He's gone to take your tomato to Polly Pie, I should think,' said Anne, and that made everyone laugh again.

'I'll have another tomato now, please,' said Wilfrid.

'Sorry. You're unlucky. They're all gone,' said Dick.

It was lovely sitting up on the hillside, watching the

boats in the harbour, and seeing the beautiful white-sailed yachts bending to and fro in the strong wind that blew there. They could all see Whispering Island quite clearly, and noticed that no boats went anywhere near it. Clearly everyone knew that men might be there, watching for intruders.

'There might be badgers there,' said Wilfrid, suddenly. 'I've never been really *close* to a badger.'

'I shouldn't think anyone but you would *want* to be!' said George. 'Smelly things! There's one thing – you can't call one with your whistle-pipe – there aren't any here!'

'Wilfrid – get out your pipe and make the little rabbits

come again,' said Anne, suddenly. 'While we're all sitting here quietly. Would they come?'

'Yes, I think so,' said Wilfrid, and felt in his pocket. He felt in another pocket, and looked worried. Then he stood up and patted himself all over, looking really distressed. He stared round at the others, anguish on his face.

'It's gone,' he said. 'I must have lost it! It's gone. I'll never have another one like it, never.'

'Oh, it *must* be in one of your pockets,' said Dick, touched by the look on the boy's face. 'Here, let *me* feel.'

But no – the pipe wasn't there. Wilfrid looked as if he were about to burst into tears. He began to hunt all round, and everyone helped him. No – not quite everyone. George didn't. Dick glanced at her, and frowned. George was *pleased* that the precious pipe was lost. How she must dislike poor Wilfrid! Well, he *was* dislikeable at times, no doubt about it – but he was so distressed now that surely nobody could help feeling sorry for him!

George got up and began to clear away the remains of the meal. She carried plates and glasses to the cottage, and after a while Anne followed her.

'I'm sorry for poor old Wilfrid, aren't you?' she said.

'No, I'm not,' said George, shortly. 'Serves him right! I hope he never finds his silly pipe. That will teach him not to try and get Timmy away from me!'

'Oh, don't be silly! He only does it for fun!' said Anne, shocked. 'Why do you take things so seriously, George? You know Timmy loves you better than anyone in the world and always will. He's your dog and nobody, nobody else's! Wilfrid's only teasing you when he tries to get Timmy to go to him.'

'Timmy goes, though,' said George, desperately. 'And he shouldn't. He *shouldn't*.'

'He can't help it, I think,' said Anne. 'Wilfrid has some peculiar attraction for animals – and that little whistle-pipe of his is like a magic call to them.'

'I'm *glad* it's gone!' said George. 'Glad, glad, glad!'

'Then I think you're silly and unkind,' said Anne, and walked off, knowing that she could do nothing with George in this mood. She worried a little as she went. Did George *know* where the pipe was? Had *she* found it – and hidden it – or destroyed it? No – no! George could be difficult and unkind at times, but she wasn't *mean*. And *what* a mean thing it would be, to destroy the beautiful little pipe with its magic trills!

Anne went back to the others, meaning to try and comfort Wilfrid – but he wasn't there. 'Where's he gone?' asked Anne.

'To look for his precious whistle-pipe,' said Dick. 'He's really heartbroken about it, I think. He says he's going to walk back the way we came from the golf course, and then he's going to walk everywhere there that we walked this morning, and hunt and hunt. He's even going down to the clubhouse to see if he dropped it there. He'll never find it!'

'Poor old Wilfrid!' said Anne, tender-hearted as ever. 'I wish he'd waited for me. I'd have gone with him. He's awfully upset, isn't he? Won't he be able to call the wild animals to him any more?'

'I've no idea,' said Dick. 'Er – I suppose old George doesn't know anything about it? Perhaps that's a mean thing to say – but George might have found it and kept it just for a joke.'

'No. No, I don't think she'd do that,' said Anne. 'It would be a *very* poor joke. Well – we'll just have to hope Wilfrid finds it. What are you going to do this afternoon? Sleep, by the look of you!'

'Yes – sleep out in the warm sun here, till three o'clock,' said Julian. 'Then I'm going for a walk – down to the harbour. I might even have a bathe.'

'We'll all go,' said Dick, sleepily. 'Oh how lovely it is to feel lazy – and warm – and well-fed – and sleeeeeeepy! So long, everyone! I'm asleep!'

CHAPTER NINE

Off to Whispering Island

THE TWO boys, and Anne and George, slept soundly in the sun until just past three o'clock. Then a large fly buzzed around Anne's head and awoke her. She sat up and looked at her watch.

'Gracious! It's ten past three!' she said, in surprise. 'Wake up, Julian! Dick, stir yourself! Don't you want to go and bathe?'

Yawning loudly the two boys sat up, and looked all round. George was still asleep. Wilfrid hadn't yet come back.

'Still hunting for his precious pipe, I suppose,' said Anne. 'Get up, you two boys. Dick, you're *not* to lie down, you'll only go to sleep again. Where are your bathing things? I'll get them. And does anyone know where our bathing towels are? We'll probably have to dress and undress with them round us!'

'They're up in our room, chucked into a corner,' said Dick, sleepily. 'Gosh, I *was* sound asleep. I really thought I was in my bed when I awoke!'

Anne went to fetch the bathing towels and the bathing things. She called back to the boys. 'I've got everything. Buck up, Julian, *don't* go to sleep again!'

'Right!' said Julian, sitting up and stretching himself. 'Oh, this sun – it's GLORIOUS!'

He poked Dick with his toe. 'Get up! We'll leave you behind if you snore again. George, goodbye – we're going!'

George sat up, yawning, and Timmy stood over her and licked her cheek. She patted him. 'All right, Timmy, I'm ready. It's so warm that I'm *longing* for a dip – and you'll love it too, Tim!'

Carrying their bathing things they made their way down the hill, and across a stretch of moorland to the edge of the sea, Timmy running joyously behind them. Beyond lay Whispering Island, a great tree-clad mass, and all around and about little boats plied, and yachts sailed in the wind, enjoying themselves in the great harbour which stretched far beyond the island to a big seaside town on the opposite coast.

The four went behind some rocks, and stripped off their clothes, emerging three minutes later in their scanty bathing things. Anne raced to the edge of the water, and let it lap over her toes. 'Lovely!' she said. 'It's not a bit cold! I *shall* enjoy my swim!'

'Woof!' said Timmy and plunged into the water. He loved the sea too, and was a fine swimmer! He waited for George to come in and then swam to her. She put her arms round his neck and let him drag her along with him. 'Dear Timmy! How strong he was,' thought George.

They had a wonderful time in the water. Further out the waves were big and curled over like miniature waterfalls, sweeping the children along with them. They yelled in joy, and choked when the water splashed into their mouths. It was an ideal day for bathing.

When they came out, they lay on the sand in the sun, Timmy beside George, keeping guard as usual. It was really warm. George sat up and looked longingly out to sea, where the wind was whipping up the waves tremendously.

'Wish we had a boat!' she said. 'If we were back home, I could get out my own boat, and we could go out in the cool breeze and get dry.'

Julian pointed lazily to a big notice not far off. It said 'BOATS FOR HIRE. ENQUIRE AT HUT.'

'Oh good!' said George. 'I'll go and enquire. I'd *love* a good row!'

She slipped on her sandals, and went to the hut to which the sign pointed. A boy of about fifteen sat there, staring out to sea. He looked round as George came along.

'Want a boat?' he said.

'Yes, please. How much?' asked George. 'For four of us – and a dog.'

'Three pounds an hour,' said the boy. 'Or six pounds a day. Or fifteen pounds a week. Better to take it by the week if you're staying here. It works out very cheap then.'

George went back to the boys and Anne. 'Shall we take the boat by the week?' she said. 'It'll cost fifteen pounds. We could do lots of rowing about, and it would be fun.'

'Right,' said Dick. 'Anyone got any money?'

'There's some in my pocket, but not enough, I'm afraid,' said Julian. 'I'll go and fix up the boat for us to have tomorrow – we'll take it for a whole week. I can easily bring the money with me in the morning.'

The boat boy was very obliging. 'You can have the boat today and onwards, if you like, you needn't wait till tomorrow,' he said. '*I* know you'll bring me the money all right! So, if you'd like to have it this afternoon, it's up to you. Choose which boat you like. They're all the same. If you want to take it out at night too and do some fishing, you can – but tie it up safe, won't you?'

'Of course,' said Julian, going to look at the boats. He beckoned to the others, and they all came over.

'Any boat we like, day *or* night!' said Julian. 'Which do you fancy? *Starfish – Splasho – Adventure – Seagull – Rock-a-bye*? They all look good, sound little boats to me!'

'I'd like *Adventure*, I think,' said George, thinking that that particular little boat looked sturdy, clean and sound. 'Nice name – and nice little boat!'

So *Adventure* it was! 'And a jolly good name for any boat of ours!' said Dick, pushing it down to the sea with Julian. 'Whoooooosh! There she goes! Steady, my beauty – we want to get in! Chuck in all clothes, George! We can dress when we feel cold.'

Soon they were all in the boat, bobbing about on the waves. Julian took the oars and pulled out to sea. Now they were in the full breeze – and a strong one it was too! 'I'm certainly not hot any more!' said George, pulling her bathing towel round her shoulders.

The tide was running out, and pulled the boat strongly out to sea. Whispering Island suddenly seemed very much nearer! 'Better look out!' said George, suddenly. 'We don't know if a keeper's on guard somewhere on the shore of the island. We're getting pretty near.'

But the outgoing tide swept the boat on and on towards the island, so that very soon they could see a sandy shore. Dick then took one oar, and Julian the other, and they tried to row against the tide and take the boat back into calm water.

It was no good. The tide was far too strong. Very soon the boat was quite near the shore of the island, and then an enormous wave flung them right up the sand and left the boat grounded as it went back again. It slid over to one side, and they all promptly fell out!

'Whew!' said Julian. 'What a tide! I'd no idea it ran so strongly, or I'd never have brought the boat out so far.'

'What shall we do!' said Anne, rather scared. She kept looking all round for a keeper with a gun. Suppose they got into real trouble through coming right on to the island?

'I think we'll have to stay on the island till the tide turns, and we can row back on it,' said Julian. 'I can't think why that boat boy didn't warn us about the tide. I suppose he thought we knew.'

They pulled the boat a little further up on the firm sand, took out their bundles of clothes and hid them under a bush. They walked up the beach towards a wood, thick with great trees. As they neared them, they heard a strange, mysterious sound.

'Whispering!' said George, stopping. 'The trees are *really* whispering. Listen! It's just as if they were talking to one another under their breath! No wonder it's called Whispering Island!'

'I don't like it much,' said Anne. 'It almost sounds as if they're saying nasty things about us!'

'Shooey, shooey, shooey, shooey!' said the trees, nodding towards one another as the wind shook them. 'Shooey, shooey!'

'*Just* the noise of whispering!' said George. 'Well – what do we do now? We'll have to wait an hour or two till the tide turns again!'

'Shall we explore?' said Dick. 'After all, we've got Timmy with us. No one is likely to attack us if they see *him*!'

'They can shoot him, can't they, if they have guns?' said George. 'If he growled one of his terrifying growls, and ran at them showing his teeth, they'd be scared to bits and fire at him.'

'I think you're right,' said Julian, angry with himself for landing them all into what might be serious trouble. 'Keep your hand on Timmy's collar, George.'

'You know what I think?' said Dick suddenly. 'I think we ought to try and find the guards, and tell them the tide swept us on to the island quite by accident – we couldn't stop the boat surging on! We're not grown-ups, come to snoop around, so they're sure to believe us – and we'd be safe from any chasing or shooting then.'

They all looked at Julian. He nodded. 'Yes – good idea. Give ourselves up, and ask for help! After all, we hadn't any real intention of actually *landing* – the tide simply *threw* the boat into that sandy cove!'

So they walked up to the back of the cove and into the wood, whose whispering was very loud indeed once they were actually among the trees. No one was to be seen. The wood was so thick that it was in parts quite difficult to clamber through. After about ten minutes' very hard walking and clambering, Julian came to a stop. He had seen something through the trees.

The others pressed behind him. Julian pointed in front, and the others saw what looked liked a great grey wall, made of stone.

'The old castle, I imagine!' Julian whispered, and at once the trees themselves seemed to whisper even more loudly! They all made their way to the wall, and walked alongside it. It was a very high wall indeed, and they could hardly *see* the top! They came to a corner and peeped round. A great courtyard lay there – quite empty.

'Better shout, I think,' said Dick, beginning to feel rather creepy, but before they could do that two enormous men suddenly came down a flight of great stone steps. They looked so fierce that Timmy couldn't help giving a blood-curdling growl. They stopped short at once and looked all round, startled.

'The noise came from over there,' said one of the men, pointing to his left – and, to the children's great relief, both swung off in the wrong direction!

'We'd better get back to the cove,' whispered Julian. 'I don't like the look of those men at all – they look like proper thugs. Quiet as you can, now. George, don't let Timmy bark.'

They made their way back beside the stone wall, through the whispering trees, and there they were at the cove.

'We'd better row back as quickly as we can,' said Julian. 'I think there's something wrong here. Those men certainly weren't gamekeepers. I wish we hadn't come.'

'Ju – where's our boat?' said Dick in a shocked voice.

'It's gone. This can't be the right cove!'

The others stared round. Certainly there was no boat! They *must* have come to the wrong cove.

'It looks the same cove to *me*,' said George. 'Except that the sea has come in a bit more. Do you think it took our boat away – gosh, look at that big wave sweeping right in – and sucking back!'

'My word, yes! Our boat could easily have been dragged out on a wave like that!' said Julian, very worried. 'Look out – here comes another!'

'It *is* the same cove!' said Anne, looking under a bush at the back. 'Here are our clothes, look! We hid them here!'

'Take them out quickly!' called Julian, as another big wave swept right in. 'What an idiot I am! We should have pulled our boat as far up as we could.'

'I'm cold now,' said Anne. 'I'm going to dress. It will be easier to carry a bathing-suit than a heap of clothes!'

'Good idea!' said Dick, and they all promptly dressed, feeling warmer at once.

'We might as well leave our bathing things under the bush where we left our clothes,' said George. 'At least we'll know it's the same cove if we find them there!'

'The thing is – what are we going to do *now*?' said Julian, worried. 'No boat to get back in – and why on earth did we choose one called *Adventure*! We might have *known* something would happen!'

CHAPTER TEN

The Five are in a fix

JULIAN WENT to the mouth of the cove and looked out over the waves, hoping that he might see their boat bobbing somewhere. 'I could swim out to it if so,' he thought, 'and bring it in. No – there's not a sign of a boat! I could kick myself for being so careless!'

Dick came up, looking worried. 'I suppose it's too far to swim back to the mainland, isn't it?' he said. 'I could have a shot – and get another boat and come back for everyone.'

'No. Too far,' said Julian. 'The tide's too strong for any swimmer at the moment. We're certainly in a fix!'

'We can't signal, I suppose?' said Dick.

'What with?' asked Julian. 'You could wave a shirt for an hour and it wouldn't be seen from the mainland!'

'Well – we must think of *something*!' said Dick, exasperated. 'What about trying to find a boat *here*? Surely those men must have one to get to and fro.'

'Of course!' said Julian, clapping Dick on the back. 'Where are my brains? They seem to be going soft or something! We could snoop round and about tonight, to see if there's a boat anywhere. They may have two or three. They'd have to get food from the mainland at times.'

The two girls and Timmy came up then, and Timmy whined. 'He doesn't seem to like this island,' said George. 'I think he smells danger!'

'I bet he does!' said Dick, putting his hand on Timmy's firm head. 'I'm jolly glad he's with us. Can you girls think of any good ideas? We can't!'

'We could signal,' said George.

'No good. A signal from here couldn't be seen,' said Dick. 'We've already thought of that.'

'Well – if we lit a fire here on the beach tonight, when the tide's out, surely *that* would be seen?' said Anne.

Dick and Julian looked at one another. 'Yes!' said Julian. 'If we lit it on a hilly bit it would be better still – on that cliff up there, for instance.'

'Wouldn't the guards see it?' asked Dick.

'We'd have to chance that,' said Julian. 'Yes – we could do that. Good idea, Anne. But we're going to get jolly hungry, aren't we? Anyone got anything to eat?'

'I've two bars of chocolate – a bit soft now though,' said George, digging into the pocket of her shorts.

'And I've some peppermints,' said Anne. 'What about you boys? You always take barley-sugars about with you, Dick – don't say you haven't any just when we could all do with them!'

'I've a new packet!' said Dick. 'Let's all have one now!' He pulled the packet from his pocket and handed it round. Soon they were all sucking barley-sugars. Timmy was given one too, but his was gone in a flash!

'Wasted on you, Tim, absolutely *wasted*!' said Anne. 'Crick, crack, swallow – that's all a barley-sugar means to you! Why can't dogs suck a sweet as we do! They never seem to suck *anything*. No, Timmy, don't go sniffing into Dick's pocket for another!'

Timmy was disappointed. He went snuffling round the cove, and then, scenting a rabbit smell, he followed it with his nose to the ground. The children didn't notice that he had disappeared but went on talking, trying to solve their very real difficulty.

No boat. No food. No way of getting help except by signalling in some way. '*Not* very funny,' thought Dick.

And then, very suddenly, a loud sound broke the silence – CRACK!

Everyone jumped up at once. 'That was a gunshot,' said Dick. 'The keepers! But what are they shooting at?'

'Where's Timmy?' cried George, looking all round. 'Tim, Tim, where are you TIM!'

Everyone's heart went cold. Timmy! No, the shot couldn't have been meant for old Timmy! Surely the keepers wouldn't shoot a *dog*!

George was nearly mad with dread. She clutched at Dick, tears streaming down her cheeks. 'Dick! It couldn't be Timmy, could it? Oh, Timmy, where are you? TIMMY! Come to me!'

'Listen! Listen a minute, George!' said Dick, as shouts came from the distance. 'I thought I heard Tim whine then. Isn't that him coming through the bushes?'

There was the noise of rustling as some creature pressed through the last year's bracken fronds – and then Timmy's head appeared, his bright eyes looking for them.

'Oh, Timmy, darling Timmy, I thought you'd been shot!' cried George, hugging the big dog. '*Did* they shoot at you? Are you hurt anywhere?'

'I bet I know why he was shot at,' said Dick. 'Look what he's got in his mouth – half a ham! Drop it, you robber, you!'

Timmy stood there, the ham in his mouth, wagging his tail joyously. He had felt hungry, and was sure the others did too – so he had gone hunting!

'Where did you get that, you bad dog?' said Julian. Timmy wished he could tell him. He would have said, 'Well, I went sniffing after a rabbit – and I came to a shed stored with tins of food – and one was open with this piece of ham inside, waiting for me. And here it is!'

He dropped the ham at George's feet. It smelt extremely good. 'Well, thanks, old fellow,' said Julian. 'We could do with some of that – though we'll have to pay for it when we meet the owner, whoever he is!'

'Julian – he *has* been shot at!' said George, in a trembling voice. 'Look – his tail's bleeding, and some fur is gone.'

'Oh, yes!' said Julian, examining Timmy's tail. 'Good gracious – those fellows mean business. I really think I'd better find them and tell them we're here, in case they take a pot-shot at us too!'

'Well, let's go *now* – all of us,' said Dick. 'They

probably thought Timmy was a wolf or a fox or something, slinking through the trees. Poor old fellow!'

Timmy was not at all disturbed. He was so proud of finding and bringing back the ham that he even wagged his wounded tail!

'It's quite certain that no animals or birds will be tame and friendly on this island now,' said Anne. 'They'll have been scared stiff by the gamekeepers potting at this and that.'

'You're right,' said Julian. 'It rather makes me think that the fellows on the island are no longer merely gamekeepers, put in to preserve the wildlife, and to frighten sightseers away – but real, fierce guards of some kind. Like those two horrible men we saw in the courtyard!'

'Well, what *are* they guarding then?' said George.

'That's what I'd very much like to find out,' said Julian. 'And I think perhaps I'll snoop round a bit and see what I can discover. When it's getting dark, though, not now.'

'I wish we hadn't come,' said Anne. 'I wish we were safe in our cottage with Wilfrid. I wonder if he's found his whistle-pipe. Goodness, it seems *ages* since we hired that boat!'

'Can't we go quietly through the woods and explore a bit?' asked George. 'Or walk round the shore to see if there's a boat anywhere? I'm getting bored, sitting here, talking.'

'Well – I suppose old Tim would give us warning at once if he heard anyone near,' said Julian, who was also longing to stretch his legs. 'We'll go in single file and make as little noise as we can. Timmy can go ahead. He'll give us instant warning if we come near any of the keepers.'

They all stood up, and Timmy looked at them, wagging his nicked tail. 'I'll look after you,' said his two bright eyes. 'Don't be afraid!'

They made their way carefully and quietly through the whispering trees. 'Sh, sh, sh, shoo, shooey,' said the leaves above their heads, as if warning everyone to go as quietly as possible. And then suddenly Timmy stopped and gave a low, warning growl. They all stood still at once, listening.

They could hear nothing. They were in a dense part of the wood, and it was dark and sunless. What was Timmy growling at? He took a step forward, and growled softly again.

Julian went forward too, as silently as he could. He stopped suddenly and stared. What in the world was that strange figure, gleaming out of the shadows? His heart began to beat loudly. The figure stood there, silently, an arm outstretched as if pointing at something!

He thought it moved and he took a step backwards in fear. Was it a ghost or something? It was so very, very white and shone so strangely. The others, coming up behind, suddenly saw it too and stopped in fright. Timmy growled again, and all the hackles on his neck rose up. What was *this*?

Everyone stood absolutely still, and Anne gave a gulp. She took hold of Dick's arm, and he held it tightly against him. And then George gave a very small laugh. To everyone's horror she went forward, and touched the hand of the gleaming figure.

'How do you do?' she said. 'It is so nice to meet a well-mannered statue!'

Well! A statue! Only a *statue*! It had looked so real standing there, and yet so ghostly. Everyone heaved a sigh of relief, and Timmy ran forward and sniffed at the statue's flowing robes.

'Look around you,' said Julian. 'The wood's full of statues just here – and aren't they *beautiful*! I hope they don't suddenly come alive – they really look as if they might!'

CHAPTER ELEVEN

A strange discovery

THE CHILDREN were astonished to see so many gleaming statues standing in the darkness of the wood. They wandered round them, and then came to a large shed. They peeped inside.

'Look here!' said Dick, excited. 'Long, deep boxes, strong as iron! And see what's in these two!'

They all came to look. In the first, packed in what looked like sawdust, was a beautifully carved statue of a boy. The next box seemed to be entirely full of sawdust, and Anne had to scrape quite a lot away to see if anything was packed there too.

'It's a little stone angel!' she said, scraping sawdust from a quaint little face, a small crown and the tips of small wings. 'Lovely! Why are these statues being packed away like this?'

'Use your brain!' said Dick. 'It's obvious that they're works of art – and are probably very old. They're being packed to send away in some boat or ship – to be transported somewhere where they'll fetch a lot of money – America, probably!'

'Did they come from the old castle, do you think?' asked George. 'It's quite near. I expect this shed belongs

to it. But how was it that the police didn't find them in the castle when they searched? They must have gone there, and looked into every corner! And what about the statues in the wood outside – why haven't *they* been packed away?'

'Too big, probably,' said Julian. 'And too heavy. A small boat wouldn't be strong enough to take great things like that. But those little statues are quite perfect for transporting – they don't weigh as much as the big ones – and they aren't marked by the weather, through standing in rain, sun and snow! Not a mark on them!'

'You're right,' said Anne. 'I noticed that those big ones outside were green here and there, and some had bits knocked off them. I wish we could get inside the castle and see the things there!'

'The man at the golf club, the one we took those lost balls to – *he* said something about statues as white as snow, standing in this wood – do you remember?' said Dick.

'Yes. They must have stood there for some time,' said Julian. 'I don't feel they can be very valuable, else they would be put carefully indoors, under cover. But these little beauties – I guess they're worth a lot of money!'

'Who do you suppose packed them in here?' said Anne.

'Maybe those big men we saw,' said Julian. 'Even small statues like these need someone very strong indeed to carry them here to this shed, and pack them like this. Then, of course, they would have to be carried to some boat – or ship – probably to a boat first and then rowed out to a waiting ship. But I don't think those guards are the men behind all this – someone with a great knowledge of old things must be the ringleader. He probably heard the old legend of the island, came to have a look round, and made quite a lot of interesting discoveries!'

'*Where?*' asked George. 'In the castle?'

'Probably – though carefully hidden away!' said Julian. 'For all we know there may be scores of really valuable old treasures hidden there still. That sword with a jewelled handle, for instance! And the bed made of gold, and . . .'

'To think they might all be quite near us, somewhere on Whispering Island!' said Anne. 'Wouldn't I love to be able to say I'd slept on a bed of pure gold!'

'Well, I think you'd find it jolly hard,' said Dick.

Timmy suddenly gave a small whine, and licked George's hand. 'What is it?' she said. 'What do you want, Timmy?'

'Perhaps he's hungry,' said Anne.

'Thirsty, more likely!' said Julian. 'Look at his tongue hanging out!'

'Oh, *poor* Tim – you haven't had a drink for hours!' said George. 'Well – where on earth can we get you one? We'll have to look for a puddle, I'm afraid. Come on!'

They left the shed where the beautiful little statues were lying in their sawdust, and went out into the sunshine. Everywhere was dry. Julian felt worried.

'We shall *all* be thirsty soon!' he said. 'I wonder where we can get some water?'

'Would it be too dangerous to go near the castle and see if there's a tap anywhere?' asked George, ready to face almost anything to get her dog a drink!

'Yes, it would,' said Julian, in a very decided voice. 'We're not going near any of those men with guns. They might have been told to shoot on sight, and that wouldn't be very pleasant. We'd be peppered all over with shot!'

'Look – what's that round thing over there – like a little circular wall?' said Dick, pointing to something behind the shed where the statues lay in their boxes.

They all went over to it – and Anne guessed what it was at once! 'A well! An old well!' she said. 'Look, it has an old wooden beam over the top, with a pulley to wind and unwind a bucket. *Is* there a bucket – let's hope so! We can let it down to the water and fill it for Timmy then.'

Timmy put his paws on the rim of the wall and sniffed. Water! That was what he wanted more than anything. He began to whine.

'All right, Timmy – we'll send the bucket down,' said George. 'It's still on the hook! Julian, this handle's awfully stiff – can you turn it to let down the bucket?'

Julian tried with all his strength – and quite suddenly the rope loosened, and the bucket gave a sudden jerk and jump. Alas – it jumped right off the hook, and with a weird echoing, jangling sound, fell from the top to the bottom of the well – landing in the water with a terrific splash!

'Blow, blow, blow!' said Julian, and Timmy gave an anguished howl. He peered down at the lost bucket, now on its side in the water at the bottom of the well, gradually filling itself.

'It'll probably sink below the water now,' said Julian with a groan. 'Is there a ladder down the well? If so I could shin down and get the bucket.'

But there wasn't, though it looked as if there had been at some time, for here and there were staples in the brick side of the well wall.

'What can we do?' asked Anne. 'Can we possibly pull up the bucket?'

'No – I'm afraid we can't,' said Dick. 'But wait a minute – I could shin down the rope, couldn't I, and pick the bucket out of the water? And easily get up again, because

George and Julian could turn the well handle, and pull me up that way!'

'Righto. Down you go then,' said Julian. 'The rope's good and strong, not frayed or rotten. We'll wind you and the bucket up all right!'

The boy sat on the side of the well wall, and reached out for the rope. He swung himself on to it, and swayed there a moment or two, looking down the long, dark hole below him, with the water at the bottom. Then down he went, hand-over-hand, just as he often did at school in the gym.

He came to the bottom, reached down, took hold of the bucket handle, and filled the bucket full. The water felt as cold as ice to his hand. 'All right. Pull me up!' he shouted, his voice sounding very hollow and strange as it rose up through the well walls.

Dick was heavy to pull up. Julian and George turned the handle valiantly, but it was slow work. Gradually Dick came up nearer and and nearer to the top. When he was halfway they heard him give an exclamation, and call out something; but they couldn't make out what it was and went on winding the groaning rope, slowly but surely.

They reached down and took the bucket from Dick as soon as his head appeared at the top. Timmy fell on it with excited barks, and began to lap vigorously.

'Didn't you hear me yelling to you to stop when I was halfway up?' demanded Dick, still swinging on the rope. 'Don't let go that handle. Hang on to it for a minute.'

'What's the excitement?' asked Julian, in surprise. '*Why* did you yell to us? We couldn't make out what you said.'

Dick swung himself to one side, caught hold of the well top and hauled himself up, so that he could sit on the well wall. 'I shouted because I suddenly saw something quite peculiar as I came up the well,' he said. 'And I wanted to stop and see what it was!'

'Well – what *was* it?' asked Julian.

'I don't quite know. It looked awfully like a little door! An iron door,' said Dick. 'Hey, don't let Timmy drink all that water – he'll be ill. We'll let the pail down again in a minute and get some more for ourselves.'

'Go on about what you saw,' said George. 'How *could* there be a door in the side of a well going deep down into the earth?'

'Well, I tell you, there *was* one,' said Dick. 'Look, Timmy's gone and upset the pail now! Let's send it down on the pulley to be filled again, and I'll go down on the rope again too. But when I come up and you hear me shout "Stop" just stop winding, see?'

'Here's the bucket for the hook,' said Julian. 'I'll be careful not to jerk it off this time. Ready?'

Down went Dick and the bucket again. Splash went the bucket and filled with water once more. Then up came Dick again, wound up by Julian and George as before. As soon as they heard him shout 'Stop', they stopped their winding and peered down.

They saw Dick peering hard at the side of the well wall, and pulling at it with his fingers. Then he shouted again. 'All right. Up we go!'

They hauled him up to the top, and he clambered off the rope, swung himself on to the well wall and sat there.

'Yes. It *is* some kind of opening in the well wall – it *is* a door – and it has a bolt this side to undo, but it was too stiff for my fingers. I'd have to go down and jiggle it about with my knife before I could loosen it.'

'A door in a well! But where on earth would it lead to?' said Julian, astonished.

'That's what we're going to find out!' grinned Dick, rather pleased with himself. 'Who would ever think of putting a door in the side of a well? *Some*body did – but why? Very cunning – and mysterious – and unguessable. I rather think I'll go straight down again and see if I can't open that door – and discover what it leads to!'

'Oh *do*, Dick, do!' said George. 'If you don't, *I* will!'

'Hang on to the rope. Down I go again!' said Dick. And down he went, much to Timmy's surprise. The others looked down anxiously. Could Dick open the well door? What would he find behind it? Quick, Dick, quick – everybody's waiting for you!

CHAPTER TWELVE

A great surprise – and a shock for George

As soon as Dick shouted 'Stop', Julian and George hung on to the rope to stop it going down any further. Dick was swinging just opposite the strange door. He began to feel round it, and to jiggle it. It had no lock, apparently, but there was a bolt on his side. He tried to push back the bolt – and suddenly it came away from the door, and dropped down into the well. It had rusted so much that it could not even hold to the door, once it was handled!

The door felt loose, now the bolt was gone. Dick ran his hands round it, trying to loosen it further and banged it with his fist. Rust fell off it, and Dick's hands were soon brown with the old, old rust.

He saw a little knob at the top of the door and gave it a tug. Ah – the door felt looser now. He ran his knife all round the edges, scraping away all the rust he could find. Then he managed to get his strongest knife-blade in between the door edge and the well wall, and used it as a lever to force the door open.

It opened slowly and painfully, with creaks and groans. It was about fifty centimetres high and not quite so much wide. Dick pulled it back with difficulty and then peered through the hole.

He could see nothing at all but black darkness – how very disappointing! He fumbled in his pocket to see if he had a torch. Yes – good! He shone it through the little door, his hand trembling with excitement. What would he see?

His torch was small and not very powerful. The light fell first of all on a face with gleaming eyes, and Dick had such a shock that he almost fell down the well. The eyes seemed to glare up at him in a very threatening manner! He switched his torch to the right – and yet another face gleamed up to him. 'An odd face,' thought Dick. 'Yellow as can be! YELLOW! YELLOW! I believe that face is made of gold!'

His hand was trembling even more. He shone his torch here and there through the opening, catching first one yellow face in its light, and then another. The faces had yellow bodies too, and their eyes glinted very strangely.

'I believe – yes, I really do believe – that I've found the hiding-place of the golden statues,' thought Dick. 'And those gleaming eyes must be precious jewels. I did have a shock when I saw them all looking at me! Whatever is this place they're in?'

'DICK! What can you see? Do tell us!' yelled Julian, and poor Dick almost fell off the rope when the shouts echoed round him. 'Pull me up!' he shouted. 'It's too extraordinary for words. Pull me up and I'll tell you!'

And before a minute had passed he was standing by the others, his eyes gleaming almost as brightly as the eyes of the golden statues, his words tumbling over one another.

'That door leads into the place where all the treasures are hidden. The first thing I saw was a golden statue staring at me – brilliant eyes in a yellow face – a golden face, real gold! There are dozens of them. I don't think they liked me very much – they glared so! Thank goodness they didn't say a word – though I half expected them to. What a hiding-place – right down under the earth!'

'There must be another entrance to it,' said Julian, thrilled to hear such extraordinary news. 'The well door must be a secret one. Statues couldn't be pushed through it. My word, what a find, Dick.'

'Let's all go down in turn and look through the door!'

said George. 'I can't believe it. I think I must be dreaming it. Quick, let me go down!'

One by one they all went down on the rope and looked through the door. Anne came back rather scared. She had felt very strange when she had seen the silent statues looking at her. 'I know they're not *really* looking, it's only that their eyes gleam,' she said. 'But I kept expecting one or other to take a step forward and speak to me!'

'Well – the next thing to do is to climb through the door, and see exactly where the statues are underground,' said Julian. 'And find out the opening *they* were brought in by. There must be a door the other end of their room, through which they were brought. What a hiding-place, though! No wonder the police could find nothing in the way of statues or other treasures.'

'We might find the golden sword there, with the jewelled handle!' said Anne. 'And the golden bed.'

She had hardly finished speaking when there came a loud noise from behind them. Timmy was barking his head off! Whatever was the matter?

'Sh!' said George, fiercely. 'You'll bring the guards here, you idiot! Stop it!'

Timmy stopped barking and whined instead. Then he ran off towards the wood, his tail waving happily. 'Who in the world is he going to meet?' said George, amazed. 'Someone he knows, by the look of his tail!'

The others all followed Timmy, who raced along

towards the cove where they had landed – and lost their boat. And there, in the cove, was another boat! A small one, to be sure, but still a boat – and by it, fondling Timmy, was Wilfrid! Wilfrid! What an amazing thing!

'WILFRID! How did you get here – did you hire that boat? Did you come all by yourself? Did you . . .'

Wilfrid grinned round in delight, thrilled at the surprise he was giving everyone. Timmy licked him without stopping, and George didn't even seem to notice!

'Well,' he said, 'you didn't come back, so I guessed something was wrong – and when the boat boy told me you'd taken one of his boats and it had been reported tossing about, empty, on the water near the island, I guessed what had happened – I said, "Aha! they didn't make the boat fast when they got to the island – and now they're marooned there!" You were pretty mean to go without me – but I guessed you'd be pleased to see me if I borrowed a boat and came over!'

Anne was so pleased that she gave the boy a hug. 'Now we can go back whenever we want to,' she said.

'But we *don't* want to, at the moment,' said Dick. 'We've made some startling discoveries, Wilfrid – and I'm jolly pleased you'll be able to share in them! Er – what have you got in your pocket? Something keeps poking its head out at me.'

'Oh, that's only a baby hedgehog,' said Wilfrid, taking it out gently. 'It got trodden on – by a horse, I think – so I'm just caring for it for a day or two.' He put it back into his pocket. 'But go on – tell me what you've found. Not the lost treasures, surely?'

'Yes!' said Anne. 'We saw them when we went down a well near the castle.'

'Gracious – did somebody throw them into the water there?' said Wilfrid, amazed.

'No,' said Dick, and told him about the curious door in the side of the well wall. Wilfrid's eyes nearly fell out of his head.

'I *am* glad I came!' he said. 'I nearly didn't. I thought you wouldn't really want me – and I knew George wouldn't be pleased, because of Timmy. I can't help him coming round me – and anyway he'd feel hurt if I pushed him off.'

Timmy came nosing round him at that moment, with his ball. He wanted Wilfrid to throw it for him. But Wilfrid didn't notice the ball. He just patted the soft head, and went on talking.

'The boat boy wasn't very pleased when he heard that the boat you hired was loose on the sea. He said you'd hired it for a week, and there it was, back the same day, wet and empty! His cousin brought it in. No damage done.'

'I'll make it up to him when I see him,' said Julian. 'I haven't paid him for the hire of it either, but he knows I will, when I get back. I had no idea that the sea would throw up waves here whose backwash would drag out an unmoored boat.'

'You ought to have taken me with you,' said Wilfrid, grinning. Timmy, tired of trying to make him throw his ball, went off to George, who was only too pleased to. She threw it into the air, and Timmy leapt up and caught it.

Then, very suddenly, he made a horrible noise and rolled over, kicking as if he were in great pain. 'What's the matter, Timmy?' cried George, and rushed to him. Wilfrid ran too. The dog was choking, and his eyes were almost starting out of his head.

'That ball's stuck in his throat!' cried Wilfrid. 'I knew it was dangerous! I told you it was! Cough it up, Timmy, cough it up. Oh, you poor, choking thing! Oh, Timmy, Timmy!'

The boy was beside himself with fear that the dog would choke, as he had once seen another dog do, and as for George, she was wild with terror. Poor Timmy's eyes looked terrible as he choked and choked, trying to get the ball out of his throat.

'He'll choke to death,' cried Wilfrid. 'Julian, force his mouth open, and hold it. I must try to get out the ball. Quick!'

Timmy was growing weaker, and it was not too difficult to force his mouth wide open. Wilfrid could see the ball down the dog's throat – the ball with the hole in the middle. He put his small hand into the dog's big mouth, and forced his forefinger into the hole in the ball. His finger joint stuck there – Wilfrid gently drew back his hand – and the ball came too, on his finger! There it was, with his finger still stuck in the hole! Timmy began to breathe again, great panting breaths, while George stroked his head and cried for joy that he was all right.

'I shouldn't have given you that ball, I shouldn't!' she said. 'It was too small for a big dog like you – and you *will* throw them up in the air and catch them. Oh, Timmy, Timmy, I'm very very sorry. Timmy, are you all right?'

Wilfrid had gone off, but now came back with some water in the pail. He dipped his hand in it and let drops of water drip into the dog's mouth. Timmy swallowed it gratefully. His throat was sore, but the water was cool and soothing. George let Wilfrid do this without a word. She looked rather white and shaken. Why – Timmy might be dead by now if Wilfrid hadn't put his finger into that hole in the ball and drawn it out!

'Thank you, Wilfrid,' she said, in a low voice. 'You were very clever.'

'Thank goodness the ball had a hole through it,' said Wilfrid, and he put his arms round Timmy's neck. The dog licked him gratefully. Then he turned and licked George too.

'He says he belongs to both of us now,' said George. 'I'll share him with you. You saved his life.'

'Thanks,' said Wilfrid. 'I'd love to have just a *bit* of him – he's the nicest dog I know!'

CHAPTER THIRTEEN

A meal – a sleep – and a disappearance

'I FEEL hungry again,' said George, who always had a very good appetite indeed. 'We've finished all that ham, haven't we? I *had* to give old Timmy some. What about a barley-sugar, Dick?'

'Two more left for each of us – just ten,' said Dick, counting. 'Sorry, Timmy, old thing – none for you this time. Have one, everybody. We'll have five left then!'

'Oh, I quite forget to tell you,' said Wilfrid, taking a barley-sugar. 'I brought some food in my boat! I didn't think you'd taken any, and I guessed you'd soon be jolly hungry!'

'You're a marvel, Wilfrid!' said Julian, wondering why he had ever disliked the boy. 'What have you brought?'

'Come and see,' said Wilfrid, and they all went over to the boat, Timmy walking as close to the boy as he could. Higgledy-piggledy in the boat was a pile of tins, a large loaf of bread, and some butter, looking rather soft.

'Oh good!' said Anne, in delight. 'But how in the world did you carry all this from the cottage to your boat? Look, everyone, Wilfrid has even brought some plates and spoons!'

'I put everything into a sack, and carried it over my shoulder,' said Wilfrid, enjoying everyone's delighted surprise. 'I fell over going down the hill to the shore and all the tins rolled out, and *shot* down the slope!'

Everyone laughed at the thought of tins rolling at top speed down the hill. Anne slipped her arm through Wilfrid's and gave it a squeeze.

'You did really well,' she said and Wilfrid beamed at her, astonished and pleased at everyone's warm friendliness. Timmy went up to the boat and began sniffing at the bread. Then he turned and barked as if to say, 'Is there anything here for *me*?'

Wilfrid understood at once. 'Oh *yes*, Timmy!' he said. 'I brought a special tin of dog-meat for you – here you are – a large tin of Waggomeat!'

Timmy recognised the tin at once, and barked joyfully. He pawed Wilfrid as if to say, 'Come on, then – open it! I'm hungry!'

'Anyone got a tin-opener?' said George. 'It would be too dreadful if we couldn't open the tins!'

'Gosh – I never even *thought* about that!' said Wilfrid. 'What an idiot I am!'

'It's all right. I've got a thing on my pocket-knife that's *supposed* to open tins,' said Dick, taking out a very large closed knife. 'I've never bothered to use it – so let's hope it *will* do the trick. Chuck me a tin, Wilfrid.'

Wilfrid threw him the tin of Waggomeat. With everyone watching very anxiously indeed, Dick opened a peculiar-looking tool in his knife, and jabbed the point into the top of the tin. It worked!

'First time I've ever used it,' said Dick, running the gadget round the tin top. 'Three cheers for the man who thought of including it in a knife!'

'Will Timmy be able to swallow yet?' asked George, anxiously. 'His throat must still be hurting him where that wooden ball choked him.'

'Oh, Timmy will be able to judge that for himself,' said Julian. 'If I know anything about him not even a sore throat will stop him from wolfing half that tin!'

Julian was right. As soon as Dick scraped out a third of the meat with his knife on to a flat stone nearby, Timmy was wolfing it in great gulps!

'Nothing much the matter with your throat now, Tim!' said Anne, patting him. 'Dear old Tim. Don't ever choke again. I simply couldn't bear it!'

'Let's have a meal ourselves now,' said George. 'We'll open more of those tins. We don't need to be stingy about them because we can leave in Wilfrid's boat at any time, and get back to the mainland.'

Soon they had opened a tin of tuna, two tins of fruit and a large tin of baked beans. They cut the big loaf into six pieces (one for Timmy, of course) and then sat down at the back of the cove to feast.

'Best meal I ever had in my life!' said Dick, enjoying himself. 'Tasty food – fresh air – sea nearby – sun on our heads – and friends sitting all round me!'

'Woof!' said Timmy, at once, and gave Dick a very wet lick.

'He says he couldn't agree more,' said Anne with a laugh.

'The sun's going down,' said George. 'What are we going to do? Go back to the mainland in Wilfrid's boat – or stay here for the night?'

'Stay here,' said Julian. 'Nobody knows we're here, and I want to snoop round a bit tonight, when those men can't see me. There's a lot of things that puzzle me. For instance, how on earth do they send away the things from here – such as those packed statues we saw? It must mean that a fairly big vessel comes along to collect them, I suppose. And I'd like to know how many men there are on the island – presumably the guards we saw, with guns – and the men who have found that underground cave, where everything was hidden. Then we'll go back, tell the police, and leave things to them!'

'Couldn't Wilfrid take the two girls back to the mainland then come back with the boat?' said Dick. 'I don't think we ought to let them run any risk.'

Before Julian could reply, George spoke quickly – and crossly. 'We're staying here – though Anne can go back if she wants to. But Timmy and I are staying with you boys, so that's that.'

'All right, all right, no need to shout!' said Dick, pretending to cover his ears. 'What about you, though, Anne? You're the youngest, and . . .'

'I'm staying,' said Anne. 'I'd be worried stiff all night if I left you on the island. And I certainly don't want to miss any excitement!'

'Right,' said Julian. 'We all stay then. Wilfrid, did you know that Timmy has his nose in the pocket where you keep your hedgehog?'

'Yes. They're just making friends,' said Wilfrid. 'Anyway, the hedgehog's only a baby – his quills won't prick Timmy's nose, they're still too soft. He's a dear little thing. I thought I'd call him Spiky.'

'Wuff,' said Timmy, quite agreeing. He was sitting between George and Wilfrid, very happy indeed, for both fondled him and patted him at the same time.

'I think I'll take a walk round the island,' Wilfrid announced suddenly. 'Timmy, like to come with me?'

Timmy got up at once, but George pulled him down. 'Don't be an idiot, Wilfrid,' she said. 'Timmy's been shot at once by the men here – and I'm not going to risk it again – besides, we don't want them to know we're here.'

'I'd be very careful,' persisted Wilfrid. 'I wouldn't let them spot me. They didn't spot me coming over in the boat.'

Julian sat up very suddenly. 'How do we know they didn't?' he said. 'I never thought of that! They might have a telescope – they might keep watch all the time – they might even have seen *us* in *our* boat! After all, they can't risk being spied on!'

'I don't *think* they could have seen us,' said Dick. 'They would have made a search.'

'I'm jolly sure they didn't see *me*,' boasted Wilfrid. 'They'd have been waiting for me on the shore, if they had.' He got up and looked all round. 'I think I'll go for my walk now,' he said.

'No! You are *definitely* not to go for a walk, Wilfrid,' said Julian, and lay back in the sun again. It was sinking now, but still very bright. Dick began to think of the night, and how he and Julian would snoop round and find the way into that strange place underground where those golden statues stood silently in the darkness.

Then he fell asleep, and only awoke when Anne gave

him a friendly punch. He sat up and began a long and leisurely conversation with his sister – and then Anne suddenly looked all round.

'Where's Wilfrid?' she said. They *all* sat up then, and looked startled. Wilfrid was nowhere to be seen!

'He must have slipped away without a sound! said Dick, angrily. 'The little idiot. He's been gone quite a long time! He'll get caught, as sure as can be. Good thing Timmy didn't go with him – he might have been caught too – and shot!'

George put her arms round Timmy in fear. 'Timmy would never go with Wilfrid if I wasn't there too,' she said. 'What a little fool he is! Those men will guess there's someone else on the island with Wilfrid, won't they? They might even *make* him tell all he knew – and where the boat is, and everything!'

'What shall we do?' said Anne. 'We'd better go after him.

'Timmy will track him for us,' said George, getting up. 'Come on, Tim. Find Wilfrid. Find that silly disobedient boy Wilfrid!'

Timmy understood at once. He put his nose to the ground, found Wilfrid's scent, and began to walk away. 'Not too fast, Timmy,' said George, and he at once slowed down. George looked round at the little place among the bushes where they had been sitting. 'Had we better take a tin or two with us?' she said.

'Yes. Good idea,' said Julian. 'You just never know!'

He and Dick took a couple of tins each, stuffed uncomfortably into their pockets. Stupid Wilfrid!

'He must have gone in this direction,' said Dick. 'I never spotted him slinking away, the little nuisance! I'm surprised Timmy didn't make a sound! Track him, Tim, track him!'

'Listen!' said Anne, suddenly, and she stopped. 'Listen!' They all listened – and didn't at all like what they heard. It was Wilfrid's voice, yelling in fright.

'Let me go! Let me go!'

And then a stern, loud and threatening voice came. 'Who are you with? Where are they? You're not alone, we're certain of that!'

'Quick – we must hide!' said Julian, angry and worried. 'Dick, look about for a good place and I will too.'

'No good,' said Dick. 'They'll beat everywhere for us. Better climb trees.'

'Good idea!' said Julian. 'Anne, come with me. I'll give you a shove up. Hurry, everybody! Hurry!'

CHAPTER FOURTEEN

Wilfrid has an adventure on his own

'WHAT ABOUT Timmy? He can't climb,' said George, fearfully. 'He might be shot.'

'Put him under a bush and tell him to sit, sit, sit!' said Julian, urgently. 'He knows perfectly well what that means. Go on, George, quick.'

George took Timmy by the collar and led him to a very thick bush. She pushed him under it. He turned himself round, poked his nose out of the leaves, and looked at her in surprise.

'Sit, Timmy! Sit, and keep quiet!' said George. 'Sit, sit, sit – and keep *quiet*. Understand?'

'Woof,' said Timmy, very quietly, and withdrew his nose so that nothing of him could be seen at all. He knew perfectly well what George meant. Clever old Timmy!

Dick was giving Anne a shove up a tree with drooping branches thick with leaves. 'Get as high as you can,' he said, in a low voice. 'And then stay put till you hear me call you. Don't be afraid. Old Timmy's down here to protect you!'

Anne gave him rather a small smile. She was not like George, fearless and always ready to rush into trouble. Anne was all for a peaceful life – but how could she have that if she was one of the Five!

The boys and George were now high up in trees, listening to the shouting going on. Apparently Wilfrid was not going to give away his friends – one up to him!

'How did you get here?' a man was shouting.

'In a boat,' said Wilfrid.

'Who was with you?' shouted another man.

'Nobody. I came alone,' said Wilfrid, perfectly truthfully. 'I wanted to visit the island. I'm an animal lover and I heard that all the wild creatures here were tame.'

'A likely story that!' sneered a man's voice. 'Huh! Animal lover!'

'All right then – look what I've got here in my pocket,' said Wilfrid, and apparently showed the man his baby hedgehog. 'He was trodden on by a horse – and I've been looking after him.'

'Very well – you can go back to your boat, and row away,' said the man. '*At once*, mind. And don't look so scared. We shan't hurt you. We've business of our own here, and we don't want strangers round – not even silly little kids with hedgehogs in their pockets!'

Wilfrid took to his heels and fled. He felt lost now. He would never find the others – or the cove where his boat was. *Why* had he disobeyed Julian? Had the others heard the men shouting at him? Which way should he go?

He had entirely lost his sense of direction and had no idea whether to go to the left or the right. He began to panic. Where could the others be? He *must* find them, he must! He ran through the trees, wishing that Timmy was

with him. Then he stopped. Surely this was quite the wrong way? He turned and went in a different direction. No, this couldn't be right either, he didn't recognise a thing!

He thought he heard voices in the distance. He stood and listened. Could it be the others? If only George would tell Timmy to find him! But she wouldn't, in case he was shot at. *Was* that noise voices – or was it just the wind? Perhaps it was the others looking for him. Wilfrid rushed off towards the distant sound. But alas, it died down. It was only the wind!

The trees thinned out into bushes – and then Wilfrid suddenly saw the sea in the distance! Good! If he could get to it, he could walk round the shore till he came to his cove. He would know where he was then. He began to run towards the blue sea.

Through the bushes he went, and came out at last on to what seemed to be a very high cliff. Yes – there was the sea, below and beyond. If only he could scramble down the cliff he could bear to the right and at last come to his cove. He came to the edge of the cliff and looked down – and then he started back in fear. What was that noise – that awful, dreadful noise? It was like a giant wailing and wailing at the top of his voice, the wailing going up and down in the wind. Wilfrid found his knees were shaking. He simply didn't dare to go on. He sat down and tried to get his breath, putting his hands over his ears to keep out the horrible wailing.

And then he suddenly remembered something and heaved a sigh of heartfelt relief. 'Of course – these must be the Wailing Cliffs we were told about,' he thought thankfully. 'We heard about the Whispering Wood – and it *does* whisper – and the Wailing Cliffs – and they *do* wail! At least, it's really the wind, of course. But goodness, what a strange sound!'

He sat for a while longer, then, feeling much bolder, he went to the edge of the great cliff, and looked over. He stared down in surprise.

'There's somebody down there – three or four people! Mustn't let them see me – they must belong to the men on the island! What are they doing down there?'

He lay down and peered over. Four men were there – but, as Wilfrid watched, they disappeared. Where had they gone? He craned over the cliff to see. 'There must be caves in the cliff, I suppose,' he said to himself. 'That's where they've gone! Gosh, I wish this wailing would stop. I shall start wailing myself in a minute!'

After some time voices came faintly up to him, as he lay watching, and he saw two men coming out on to the rocks below again. What are they carrying? A long, deep box – why, it looked like one of the boxes in which the others had seen those beautiful little statues, packed in sawdust!

'So *that*'s how they get them away from here – take them down through some passage in the cliffs to a waiting boat. Where's the boat, though? I can't see one. Not arrived yet, perhaps.'

He watched with intense interest as the men carried out box after box and piled them on a great flat rock that abutted a stretch of fairly calm water.

'Big boxes – little ones – those men have been busy lately!' thought Wilfrid, wishing and wishing and wishing that the others were with him. 'I wonder what's in them.

Not the bed of gold, that's certain. I bet it would be far too big to put into a boat. Have to be pulled to pieces first! Hallo – here comes another box – a small one this time. Wow, they'll soon need a steamer to take all these!'

Almost as he thought it, he saw a small steamer in the far distance! 'Well! There's the steamer, just as I said! I bet the boat will appear soon, and be loaded – and then chug off to the waiting steamer!'

But the steamer came no nearer, and no boats appeared. 'Waiting for the tide, I expect,' thought Wilfrid. 'What *will* the others say when I tell them all this! They won't believe me! And I bet they won't scold me for going off by myself!'

He decided to go back and find the others and tell them what he had seen. He set off, trying to remember the way. Surely he must be near the place where he had left them? And then quite suddenly, someone leapt out from behind a tree and caught hold of him!

'Let me go, let me go!' shouted Wilfrid, in a panic. And then he gave a cry of relief as he suddenly saw Timmy running towards him.

'Timmy! Save me!'

But Timmy didn't come running to save him. He stood there, looking up at him, rather puzzled, while poor Wilfrid went on struggling, really frightened!

Then Wilfrid heard a giggle. A GIGGLE? Who in the world could be giggling just then? He forced himself to look round – and saw Dick and Anne, doing their best not

to laugh, and George holding her sides. His captor let go of him and began to laugh too. It was Julian!

'This is too bad! You gave me an awful fright,' said Wilfrid. 'I've already been captured once this afternoon. Whatever do you think you're doing?'

'Where have you been, Wilfrid?' said Julian, rather sternly. 'I forbade you to go for a walk – and you went.'

'I know. I went off by myself – and a man caught me and scared me. Then I ran away and lost myself. I couldn't find any of you,' said poor Wilfrid. 'But I saw something very very interesting on that walk of mine!'

'What?' asked Julian, at once.

'Let's sit down, and I'll tell you,' said Wilfrid. 'I feel quite shaky. You really were beasts to jump on me like that.'

'Never mind, Wilfrid,' said Anne, feeling sorry for the boy, who really did look rather shaken. 'Now go on, tell us everything that happened.'

Wilfrid sat down. He was still trembling a little. Everything seemed to have happened at once. He began to tell the others about the Wailing Cliffs, and all he had seen.

They all listened with intense interest. 'So *that's* the other way to the underground treasure chamber – through a passage in the cliffs!' said Julian. 'I never thought of that! That is something to know! I vote we go and explore the cliffs ourselves, when there's nobody about.'

'Well, it had better be in the evening,' said Wilfrid. 'Just in case we were spotted climbing down the cliffs to find the passage – if there *is* one, and I think there must be! Those men might be on the watch, now they know there's someone on the island. I bet they guess I'm not the only one – even though I told them I came alone.'

'I vote we have something to eat,' said George. 'We can talk over everything then. It's ages since we had a meal. Let's go and open some more tins, and plan what we're going to do tonight. This is getting too exciting for words. Isn't it, Timmy?'

'Woof,' agreed Timmy. '*Too* exciting,' he thought. 'Yes – and dangerous, too.' He'd keep close to George that evening, as close as ever he could! If she went into danger, Timmy would be close by her side!

CHAPTER FIFTEEN

Julian has an exciting plan!

THE FIVE children talked and talked, as they opened more tins and had a most peculiar meal of ham spread with fruit salad and beans. They finished up with another barley-sugar each. George gave hers to Timmy who disposed of it with a crick-crack, swallow!

'Have we all got torches?' asked Julian. 'I know it will be bright moonlight tonight, but as we shall presumably be getting down – or up – dark caves, we shall want torches.'

Yes – they each had a torch. Wilfrid, for some reason, had two, rather small but quite efficient.

'What's the plan going to be, Ju?' asked George, and Timmy gave a little whine, as if to say, 'Yes, tell us.' He sat by George, listening earnestly, with Wilfrid on the other side of him. At times he sniffed at the baby hedgehog still in the boy's pocket, and apparently quite happy there. Wilfrid had been busy catching insects for it, much to Timmy's interest.

'I propose that we go to the cliffs – the Wailing Cliffs – as soon as it's twilight, and make our way down,' said Julian. 'There is probably some kind of pathway down, I should think – even if only a rabbit path. I'll lead the way down, of course. Anne and Wilfrid are to come between me and Dick, with George and Timmy behind.'

'Right!' said everyone.

'We are, of course, to make as little noise as possible,' said Julian. 'And do try not to send stones hurtling down the path or cliff, just in *case* anyone's about! When we get down to the rocks, we'll let Wilfrid go ahead, because he saw where the men went in and out earlier on.'

Wilfrid felt suddenly important – it was like planning an exploration! He suddenly remembered something – the wailing noise.

'I hope the girls won't be scared when they hear the awful wailing noise,' he said. 'It's only the wind screaming in and out of the holes and corners of the great cliffs.'

George made a scornful noise. 'Who's scared of the wind!' she said.

'Timmy might be,' said Julian, smiling. 'We *know* what makes the wailing. He doesn't! You may have to hold him when it begins, George. He'll be a bit uneasy.'

'He won't!' said George. 'Timmy's not afraid of anything in the world!'

'Oh yes, he is,' said Dick, at once. 'I know something that scares him dreadfully – makes him put his tail down and flop his ears.'

'You do not!' said George, angrily.

'Well, haven't you seen him when you speak sharply to him?' said Dick, with a chuckle. 'He goes all shaky in the legs!'

Everyone laughed except George. 'He does not,' she said. 'Nothing scares Timmy, not even me. So shut up, Dick.'

'It may be that it would be best for only one or two of us to go right into the depths of the caves,' went on Julian. 'If so, the rest must wait in hiding. Just keep on the lookout for any signal from me. I don't expect we shall see a soul down there tonight, but you never know. If there is a way through the cliffs to that underground chamber where we saw the golden statues, we shall be in real luck. We shall then be absolutely certain how things can be taken in and out.'

'Taken *in*? But I thought they had been there for ages,' said Dick, 'and were probably only taken out to sell. *Smuggled* out.'

'Well, I think it may be more than that,' said Julian. 'It might even be a central clearing-ground for a great gang of high-class thieves, who would hide valuable stolen goods there till it was safe to sell them. However, that's only guessing!'

'*I* think somebody's discovered the underground chamber, full of that rich old man's treasures, and is taking them out bit by bit,' said Dick. 'Anyway, whatever it is, it's awfully exciting. To think we know so much!'

'All because we went down the well to get some water!' said Anne.

'I wish we'd put sweaters on,' said Julian. 'It will be freezing cold in the wind that rages round those cliffs!'

'I'm longing to start!' said George. 'It's an adventure, this – do you hear that, Timmy? An adventure!'

'Anything more, Julian?' asked Anne. Julian always sounded so very grown-up when he gave them a plan of campaign. She felt very proud of him.

'That's the lot,' said Julian, 'except that we'll have some sort of a meal before we go this evening. Wilfrid will have to lead the way for us, as he's the only one who knows it – but when we come to the cliff, *I'll* lead you down. Can't have anyone missing a footstep and rolling headlong, frightening any robber or smuggler!'

'Do you hear that, Timmy?' said George, and Timmy whined, and put a paw on George's knee as if to say: 'It's a pity you haven't sure feet like mine, with rubber pads beneath, so that *your* footing is always sure!'

George patted his paw. 'Yes – you've fine sure feet, Tim. I wish I could buy some like them!'

The time seemed to go very, very slowly after that. Everyone was eager to start, and kept looking at their watches! The sun left a bright glow in the sky, so they would probably start more or less in daylight, which would, however, soon fade into twilight.

They had another meal, but strangely enough, nobody felt very hungry! 'We're too excited!' said Julian, giving Timmy a biscuit. Timmy was the only one who didn't seem at all excited. As for George, she fidgeted and fidgeted until everyone was quite tired of her!

At last they started off. Wilfrid led them at first, as he

knew the way. Actually he found that he didn't really know it – it was the loud wind that guided him, just as it had done before. 'Awfully like far-off voices shouting to one another,' he said, and everyone at once agreed.

When they came near to the cliff, the sound gradually changed into the mournful wailing noise that gave the cliffs their name. 'EEE-ee-OOOOO-oo-EEEEEEEEAH-OOO!'

'Not very nice,' said Anne, shivering a little. 'It sounds as if someone is crying and sobbing and howling!'

'Good name for this place – Wailing Cliffs,' said Dick. 'Wow – what a wind up here! I'm glad my hair's my own! It would certainly be blown off if it weren't! Hang on to old Timmy, George – he's more blowable than we are – not so heavy!'

George put her hand on Timmy's collar at once. How DREADFUL if Timmy were to be blown over the cliff! He gave a grateful lick. He didn't like the wind here very much – it had a truly miserable voice!

They came to the edge of the cliff and looked down cautiously, in case anyone should be on the rocks below. But, except for some big gulls preening their feathers there, there was no sign of life.

'No boats about – no steamer – nothing,' said Dick. 'All clear, Julian!'

Julian had been looking for a good path down the cliff. There didn't seem to be a continuous one. 'We'll have to go so far – then climb down a bit – then walk along that ledgy bit, see – then climb down that slanting rock – the great big one – and get down on to the more level rocks. OK everyone?'

'I'll let Timmy go first,' said George. 'He is so sure-footed and will know the best way. Go on, Timmy – lead us down!'

Timmy understood at once and went in front of Julian. He took the first little path down the cliff, slid down the next bit, walked along the ledge that Julian had pointed out, and then stood and waited for everyone. He gave a little bark as if to say, 'Come along. It's easy! Follow me!'

They all followed, some more carefully than others. George and Wilfrid were least careful, and poor Wilfrid lost his footing and slid quite a long way on his behind. He didn't like it at all, and looked quite scared!

'Watch your feet, now, Wilfrid,' said Julian. 'It's getting a bit dark, so don't try any funny tricks. You tried to *jump* over that big stone instead of stepping over carefully. I really don't want to send Timmy down to the bottom of the cliff to pick up your pieces!'

At last they were all down the cliff and on the rocks below. The tide was out, so that waves did not splash up and soak them. Anne suddenly slipped into a pool and made her shoes wet, but that didn't matter. They were only plastic ones.

'Now – exactly where did you see those men, Wilfrid?' asked Julian, stopping on a big flat rock. Wilfrid jumped beside him, and pointed.

'See the cliff over there? See that funny rock shaped rather like a bear? Well, that's where I saw the men. They went by that rock, and disappeared.'

'Right,' said Julian. 'Now, no more talking, please – though this wailing sound would drown almost anything. Follow me!'

He went over the rocks towards the big bear-like one that Wilfrid had pointed to. The others followed, a little tide of excitement welling up inside them. Anne caught hold of Wilfrid's hand, and squeezed it. 'Exciting, isn't it?' she said, and Wilfrid nodded eagerly. He knew he would have been scared stiff by himself – but with the others it was an adventure – a really exciting adventure!

They came to the bear-like rock. Near it was a dark place in the cliff – a way in? 'That's where the men came out, Julian,' said Wilfrid, keeping his voice low. 'Do we go in there?'

'We do,' said Julian. 'I'm going in first and I'm going to stand quite still and listen, as soon as I get the sound of the wind and sea out of my ears. If I hear nothing I'll whistle, see? Then you can all come in too.'

'Right!' said everyone, thrilled. They watched as Julian went to the dark slit-like opening. He paused and looked inside. It was so dark that he knew they would all need their torches! He switched on his powerful one and shone it into the passage. He saw a channel that ran slanting upwards for some way, and on either side a rocky ledge, not too rough. Water ran down the rocky channel and bubbled out beside him, to join the sea over the rocks.

'I'm just going into the cliff tunnel a little way, to see if I can hear anything or anyone,' he said. 'Wait here.' He disappeared inside the dark opening and everyone waited in impatient excitement.

A gull suddenly swooped down close to their heads. 'Ee-ooo, ee-ooo, EEE-OOO!' it screeched, and made them all jump violently. Wilfrid almost fell off his rock, and clutched at George. Timmy growled, and looked up angrily at the seagull. Silly bird, frightening everyone like that!

There came a low whistle, and Julian appeared again, his torch switched on. 'All clear,' he said. 'I can't hear a sound inside the opening, and I've been some way along. It's not hard going. There's a funny little stream flowing down, and a ledge either side we can walk on. Very

convenient! Now, no talking, please – and be careful even of your whispers – every sound seems to be magnified in here. Keep hold of Timmy, George, in the steepest places.'

Timmy gave a little whine of surprise when George took him inside the cliff. At once his whine was magnified all round them, and everyone jumped. Timmy didn't like it at all.

George took firm hold of Timmy's collar. 'You're to keep close by me,' she whispered, 'and you're not to make a sound. This is an adventure, Timmy – a big adventure – and you're in it as much as any of us. Come along!'

And there they go, all of them, climbing up the dark passage into the cliff! What will they find – what will they see? No wonder their hearts beat fast and loudly, no wonder Timmy keeps close to George. An adventure? He must be on guard then – *anything* might happen in an adventure!

CHAPTER SIXTEEN

A journey underground

It was very dark inside the cliff. The children's torches made bright streaks everywhere, and were very useful indeed for seeing the safest places to tread. As Julian had told the others, there was a curious little stream flowing down the middle of the steep passage, with uneven ledges on each side of it. It had worn this little channel for itself during the many, many years it had flowed down inside the cliff.

'It's probably water draining from the surface of the cliffs,' said Julian in a low voice, picking his way carefully. 'Be careful here – the ledges are *very* slippery!'

'Oooh!' said Wilfrid, treading on a slippery bit, and finding one of his feet in ice-cold water.

The echo took up the noise at once, 'OOOOH-OOOOOOH-OOOOOH!' Poor Wilfrid's little 'Oooh' echoed up and down and all round them! It was very weird indeed and nobody liked it. Anne pressed close to Julian, and he squeezed her arm comfortingly.

'Sorry about my "Oooh",' said Wilfrid, in a low voice. 'My oooh, oooh, oooh!' said the echo at once, and George simply couldn't *help* giving a giggle, which at once repeated itself a score of times!

'You really will have to be quiet now,' came Julian's voice, almost in a whisper. 'I have a feeling we're coming to some big opening. There's suddenly a great draught blowing down this steep passage – I can feel it round my head.'

The others felt it too, as they climbed higher up the steep passage, trying to avoid the tiny stream that splashed down its worn channel. It made a nice little noise – 'very cheerful,' Anne thought – and gleamed brightly in the light of their torches.

Julian wondered how in the world anyone could take crates or boxes down such a steep dark passage! 'It's *wide* enough, I suppose,' he thought. But only just – and the bends in it must be very awkward for boxes to get round! I do hope we don't meet anyone round a bend, carrying a crate or two! Wow, the draught is quite a wind now! There *must* be an opening somewhere.

'Ju – we've not only gone upwards, we've gone a good way forward too,' whispered Anne. 'Wasn't the old castle somewhere in this direction?'

'Yes – I suppose it would be,' answered Julian, stopping to think. 'Gosh – I wonder if this passage comes up in one of its cellars! An old castle like that would have huge cellars – and probably a dungeon or two for prisoners! Let me think – we must have left the cliff behind now – and yes – I think we *may* be heading for the castle. Why didn't I think of that before!'

'Well, then – the well wall must run down beside the

castle foundations!' said Dick, in much too loud a voice. The echo made everyone jump violently, and Julian stopped climbing and hissed at Dick. 'Whisper, can't you, idiot! You nearly made me jump out of my skin!'

'Skin, skin, skin!' said the echo, in a peculiar whisper that made George want to laugh.

'Sorry!' whispered back Dick.

'I think you may be right about the well wall running down beside the foundations of the castle,' Julian said, whispering again. 'I never thought of that. The castle wasn't very far from the well. It would probably have enormous cellars spreading underground.'

'The wall in the well, that that funny little door was in, was terrifically thick,' said Dick. 'I bet I was looking into one of the castle cellars, when I peeped through it!'

This was all very interesting. Julian thought about it as they went on and on through the endless passage. It ran more or less level now, and was easy to walk through, for it was much wider.

'I think this part of the passage was man-made,' said Julian, stopping and facing the others, his face bright in the light of their torches. He went on in a loud whisper, 'Up through the cliff the passage was a natural one, awfully difficult to climb – but here it's quite different – look at these old bricks here – probably put there to strengthen the tunnel.'

'Yes – a secret way from the castle to the sea!' said

Dick, almost forgetting to keep his voice down, in his excitement. 'Isn't it thrilling!'

Everyone began to feel even more excited – all except Timmy, who didn't much like dark, secret passages, and couldn't imagine why Julian was taking them for such a gloomy and peculiar walk. He had splashed solemnly through the stream the whole time, finding the stone ledges much too slippery for his paws.

The draught grew stronger and was very cold indeed. 'We're coming near to the opening where the draught comes from,' whispered Julian. 'All quiet, now, please!'

They were as quiet as possible, and Anne began to feel almost sick with excitement. Where were they coming to? Then suddenly Julian gave a low exclamation.

'Here we are! An iron gate!'

They all tried to crowd round Julian to see. The gate was a big strong one, with criss-cross bars of iron. They could easily see between the bars, and they shivered in the draught that swept through the great gate.

Julian shone his torch through the bars, his hand shaking in excitement. The bright ray of light ran all round what looked like a stone room – quite small – with a stout, nail-studded door at the far end. This door was wide open, and it was through this that the steady draught blew.

'This is a cellar – or a dungeon, more likely!' said Julian. 'I wonder if the gate is locked.'

He shook it – and it swung open quite easily, as if it had been well-oiled! Julian stepped into the dungeon, flashing his torch all round the dark and dismal little place.

He shivered. 'It's cold as ice, even on this warm day!' he said. 'I wonder how many poor, miserable prisoners have been kept down here in the cold!'

'Look – here's a staple in the wall,' said Dick, standing beside him, examining the half-hoop of iron deeply embedded in the stone wall. 'I suppose the unhappy prisoner was tied up to this, to make his punishment even worse.'

Anne shivered. 'How could people be so cruel?' she said, her vivid imagination seeing wretched men here, with perhaps only crusts of bread to eat, water to drink, no warmth, no bed, only the stone floor!

'Perhaps some of them escaped out of the gate and went down the cliff passage,' she said, hopefully.

'No – it's much more likely that the passage was used to get *rid* of the prisoners,' said Dick. 'They could be dragged down to the sea and drowned – and nobody would ever know.'

'Don't tell me things like that,' said Anne. 'It makes me feel I shall hear groans and cries. I don't like this place. Let's go.'

'I hate it too,' said George. 'And Timmy's tail is right down. I feel as if this horrid dungeon is full of miserable memories. Julian, *do* let's go.'

Julian walked over to the nail-studded door and went through the doorway. He looked out on to a stone-paved passage, with stone walls and ceiling. He could see other doors, iron-barred, along a dismal stone passage. He came back to the others.

'Yes – these *are* the castle dungeons,' he said. 'I expect the castle cellars are somewhere near too – where they stored wine and food and other things. Come on – let's explore. I can't hear a sound. I think this place is absolutely empty.'

They all followed Julian down the stone passage, looking in at each miserable dungeon as they passed. Horrible! Dirty, damp, cold, bare – poor, poor prisoners of long ago!

At the end of the passage was another iron-barred door, but that too was wide open. They went through it and came out into an enormous cellar. Old boxes were there, old worm-eaten chests, broken chairs, loose papers that rustled as their feet touched them – the kind of junk that can be found in a thousand cellars! It all smelt rather musty – though, as Julian said, the draught that blew everywhere took away some of the smell.

They came to some stone steps and went up them. At the top was another great door, with an enormous bolt on it. 'Fortunately the bolt is *our* side,' said Julian, and slid it out of its socket. He was surprised that it went so smoothly – he had expected it to be rusted and stiff. 'It's been oiled recently,' he said, shining his torch on it. 'Well, well – other people have been here not long ago, and used this door. We'd better go quietly in case they are *still* here!'

Anne's heart began to beat loudly again. She hoped there was no one waiting round a corner to jump out at them! 'Be careful, Julian,' she said. 'Somebody may have heard us! They may be waiting to ambush us. They . . .'

'All right, Anne – don't worry!' said Julian. 'Old Timmy would give us a warning growl if he heard a single footstep!'

And good gracious – at that very moment Timmy *did* give a growl – an angry, startled growl that made everyone jump, and then stand still, holding their breath.

Dick looked round at Timmy, who was growling again. His head was down and he was looking at something on the floor. What was it? Dick swung down his torch to see. Then he gave a small laugh. 'It's all right. We don't need to be scared yet. Look what Timmy's growling at!'

They all looked down – and saw a great fat toad, its brilliant eyes staring steadily up at them. As they exclaimed at it, it turned aside, and crawled slowly and clumsily to a little damp spot in the corner of the wall.

'I've never seen such a big toad in my life!' said Anne. 'It must be a hundred years old! Goodness, Timmy, you made me jump when you suddenly growled like that!'

The toad squatted down in its corner, facing them. It seemed to glare at poor Timmy. 'Come away, Tim,' said Dick. 'Toads can ooze out a very nasty-smelling, nasty-tasting stuff. Never bite a toad!'

Julian had now gone through the door at the top of the steps. He gave a loud exclamation – so loud that the others rushed to him in alarm, wondering what was exciting him.

'Look!' said Julian, shining his torch into the dark space beyond. 'See where we've come to! Did you ever see such a storehouse of wonders!'

CHAPTER SEVENTEEN

In the treasure chamber

JULIAN'S TORCH shone steadily into the vast room, which seemed to have no end! The others shone their torches too, and Timmy pressed between their legs to see what the excitement was.

What a sight! They were actually in the enormous chamber that the boys had seen through the opening in the well wall! 'What a place it was – absolutely *vast*,' thought Anne, awed at the size, the height and the great silence.

'There are the golden statues!' said Dick, going over to a group of them. 'Wonderful! Strange faces they have, though – not like ours. And look how their slanting eyes gleam when we shine our torches on them. Makes them look as if they're almost alive, and looking at us.'

Anne suddenly gave a cry and rushed over to something. 'The golden bed!' she said. 'I *wished* I could lie on one – and now I shall!' And with that she climbed on to a vast four-poster bed with a great canopy, now rotting to pieces.

The bed gave a mournful creak, and the part that Anne was lying on suddenly subsided. The canopy collapsed and Anne disappeared in a cloud of dust. The bed had, quite literally, fallen to pieces! Poor Anne.

The others helped her up and Timmy looked at the clouds of dust in surprise. What was Anne doing, making such a dust! He sneezed loudly, and then sneezed again.

Anne sneezed too. She scrambled quickly out of the collapsed bed and dusted herself down.

'It has a carved gold headpiece, and gold legs and endpiece,' said Dick, shining his torch on it. 'What a monster of a bed, though – I should think *six* people could sleep in it at once! What a pity it has been lost here so long – all the hangings fell to pieces as soon as Anne climbed on the bed part! *What* a dust!'

There was no doubt about it, there were priceless treasures in this vast underground cellar. The children could not find the sword with the jewelled handle, nor the necklace of rubies, which Julian thought were probably locked away in one of the chests. But they found many other wonderful things.

'Look in this chest – this beautiful carved chest!' called Anne. 'Gold cups and plates and dishes. Still bright and clean!'

'And look what's in here!' shouted George. 'Wrapped up in stuff that falls to pieces when I touch it!'

They crowded round a great enamelled box. In it was a set of animals carved out of some lovely green stone. They were absolutely perfect, and, when Anne tried to stand them up, each of them stood as proudly as once they did many years ago when little princes and princesses played with them.

'They're made of green jade,' said Julian. 'Beautiful! Goodness knows how much they're worth! They should be in some museum, not mouldering away in this cellar.'

'Why didn't those collectors take these – and the golden statues – and all the other things?' wondered Anne.

'Well, that's obvious,' said Julian. 'For one thing this is a secret cellar, I should think, and nobody would be able to get into it unless they knew the secret way to it. There's probably a sliding panel or hidden door that leads to it, somewhere in the castle above. It's very old, and ruined in many parts – and some of the walls have fallen in – so I suppose it was pretty impossible to get to the cellars even if the secret way was known!'

'Yes – but what about the way *we* came up,' said Dick. 'From the sea – up the cliff passage!'

'Well – I don't know exactly why that hasn't been used before,' said Julian, 'though I could make a guess! Did you notice that great heap of fallen rocks near the entrance to the cliff passage? I should think that that part of the cliff fell at one time, and hid the passage completely – blocked it up. Then maybe a storm came, and the sea shifted some of the rocks – and lo and behold, there was the secret passage – open again!'

'And somebody found it – somebody, perhaps, who had heard the old legends about the castle of Whispering Island!' said Anne.

'A collector of old things, do you think?' asked George. 'What about those two men on the island – the ones we saw in the courtyard – do you suppose *they* know of this entrance?'

'Yes, probably,' said Julian. 'And it's likely they were

put on guard in case anyone else found it and came to rob the secret chamber. The things here are priceless! Those men are not there to guard the animals on the island, as they were in the old couple's day. They had *genuine* keepers, like that nice old man Lucas who told us about this island this morning.'

'You think these men are in somebody's pay then – somebody who knows about this great chamber under the castle, and wants to get the centuries-old treasures?' said Dick.

'Yes,' said Julian. 'And what's more I don't believe that the real owner of the island – the great-nephew of the old couple who owned it – even *knows* they're here, or that anyone is taking things from the island. For all we know he may live in America or Australia, and not care tuppence about his island!'

'How extraordinary!' said Anne. 'If *I* owned an island like this, I'd live here and never leave it. And all the animals and birds would be protected as they once were, and . . .'

'Dear Anne – what a pity it *isn't* yours!' said Julian, ruffling her hair. 'But now, the thing is – what are we going to *do* about this? We'll talk about it when we're back at the cottage. Hey, it's getting late! It will be pitch dark outside, unless the moon is up and the sky is clear of clouds!'

'Well, come on then, let's go,' said Dick, making for the great nail-studded door. Then, as Timmy suddenly gave a blood-curdling growl, he stopped in fright. They had *shut*

the door – but now it was opening. Somebody was coming into the great underground chamber! Who *could* it be?

'Quick – hide!' said Julian, and he pushed the two girls behind a great chest. The others were near the golden bed and they crouched behind it at once, Dick's hand on Timmy's collar. He had managed to stop the dog from growling, but was afraid that Timmy would begin again at any moment!

A man came into the room – one of the two big fellows that the children had seen in the courtyard. He didn't seem to have heard Timmy growling, for he sauntered in, whistling lightly. He shone his torch all round, and then called loudly.

'Emilio! Emilio!'

There was no answer at all. The man yelled again, and then an answer came from beyond the door, and hurrying footsteps could be heard. Then in came the other big rough fellow, and looked round, shining his torch. He lighted an oil-lamp on a box, and switched off his torch.

'You're always sleeping, Emilio!' growled the first man. 'You are always late! You know the boat comes tonight to take the next batch of goods – have you got the list? We must wrap them up quickly and take them to the shore. That little statue has to go, I know!'

He went over to the statue of a boy whose eyes gleamed with emeralds. 'Well, boy,' said the man, 'you're going out into the world! How'll you like that after being in the dark so long? Don't glare at me like that, or I'll box your ears!'

Apparently the golden boy went on glaring, for the man gave his head a tap. The other fellow came over and shifted a long, deep box over from the wall to the little golden statue. Then he began to wrap it up carefully, rolling material round and round it from head to foot while the golden boy stood patiently.

'What time is Lanyon coming for it?' asked Emilio. 'Have I time to wrap another?'

'Yes – that one over there,' said the first fellow, pointing. Emilio went whistling over to it, passing the chest behind which the girls were hiding. They crouched right to the floor, afraid of being seen. But Emilio was sharp-eyed, and thought he saw something move as he passed by the chest. He stopped. What was that poking out by the side of the chest – a foot! A *foot*!

Emilio rushed round the chest, his torch switched on again. He gave a loud shout. 'Carlo! There's someone here! Come quickly!'

Carlo, the second man, dropped what he was holding and raced round to Emilio, who had now pulled the girls roughly to their feet.

'What are you doing here? How did you get in?' shouted Emilio.

Julian shot out from his hiding-place at once, followed by Dick and Wilfrid. George was doing all she could to hold back Timmy, who was now deafening everyone with his angry barks. He did his best to get away from George, but she was afraid he might fly at Emilio's throat. The two men were full of amazement to see the five children and Timmy!

'Keep that dog back or I'll shoot him,' said Carlo, producing a gun. 'Who are you? What do you mean by coming into this place?'

'We came by boat – but the boat got washed out to sea,' said Julian. 'We've been camping on the island. We just – er – wandered into this place by mistake.'

'By mistake! Well, I can tell you that you've certainly made the biggest mistake in your life!' said Carlo. 'You'll have to stay here for quite a long time – till our job's done, at any rate!'

'What's your job?' asked Julian, bluntly.

'Wouldn't you like to know!' said Carlo. 'Well – one part of it is to guard the island, and keep off strangers! Now, we've jobs to do tonight and tomorrow, and I'm afraid you're going to have a miserable time! You'll stay down here in this old cellar till we come back again – and what will happen to you after that, I don't know, because I'll have to tell my employer you've been spying down here. I wouldn't be surprised if he doesn't hand you over to the police – or lock you up down here for a month, on bread and water!'

Timmy growled very fiercely indeed, and tugged hard to get away from George and fly at this hateful man. She hung on to him for all she was worth, though how she longed to let him leap at the man and get him on the ground!

'Better go, Carlo, or we'll miss that boat out there,' said Emilio, grumpily. 'We'll deal with these kids when we get back!' He shouldered the box into which he had put the wrapped statue, and started for the door. Carlo followed him, backing all the time to make sure that George did not set Timmy on to him. He shut the great door with a loud bang, and shot the bolt.

'Don't say anything for a minute in case they are listening outside the door,' said Julian. So they all stood in silence, Anne's knees trembling a little. Oh dear – how unlucky to be caught like this!

'Relax!' said Julian at last. 'You all look so stiff and tense!'

'Well, I should *think* so!' said Dick. 'I don't particularly want to stay shut up here till those men deign to come back and do a bit more stealing. Suppose they *never* come back! We'd be here for keeps!'

'No, Dick!' said Anne, and to everyone's surprise, she began to laugh. 'We can *easily* escape!'

'What – through that locked and bolted door?' said Dick. 'Not a hope!'

'But we *can* easily escape!' said Anne, and George suddenly brightened up and nodded her head, smiling. 'Oh yes – of course! Don't look so solemn, Dick! Look up there!'

Dick looked up to where Anne was pointing. 'What am I supposed to look at?' he said. 'The old stone wall?'

'No – just there – over the top of that tall chest,' said Anne.

Dick looked – and then a large smile came over his face. '*What* an idiot I am! That's the old iron door in the side of the old well wall, isn't it – the opening I looked through! It looks just like an ordinary ventilation hole from down here – and I don't really believe anyone would ever notice it except us, who know what it is. I see what you're getting at, Anne!'

'Good old Anne!' said George, realising what Anne had in mind. 'Of course – we've only got to climb up to that hole in the wall, open the door there, and then go up the well – and we're safe!'

'Yes. But it's easier said than done,' said Julian, soberly. 'We've got to get hold of the rope, and climb right up it to the top – *not* very easy!'

'Suppose the rope's at the top, with the bucket hanging on the hook,' said Anne. 'We'd never reach it then!'

'We'll think of something!' said Julian. 'Anyway, it's our only hope of escape. Now – we'll push that huge, high chest or wardrobe or whatever it is, right over against the wall, under that opening into the well – there's a sturdy little one over there. Come on! We'll be through that opening in no time, and up the well. What a shock for dear Emilio and Carlo, when they come back and find that the birds have flown!'

CHAPTER EIGHTEEN

A most exciting time!

IT WAS quite a job pushing the heavy chest over towards the stone wall of the castle. It took all of them shoving with all their might, to do it.

'We seem to be making an awful noise with the chest scraping over the floor,' panted Dick. 'I hope we're not heard!'

Timmy wished he could help. He kept jumping up and pressing his paws on the side of the chest, but Dick stopped him. 'You're getting in the way,' he said. 'You go and sit near the door and warn us if you hear those men coming.'

So Timmy ran to the door and sat there, his head cocked to one side listening, while the others went on shoving the heavy chest along. At last it was in position. Then came the job of hoisting a stout little wooden table on top. Julian climbed up to the top of the chest to take the table from Dick, but just couldn't manage it, it was so heavy and solid. So Wilfrid climbed up beside him, and between the two of them they pulled up the little oblong table, and set it firmly on top of the chest. Julian stood on it – and found he could easily reach the little iron door that led into the old well.

'Good,' he said, and he gave the door a hard shove. It shook a little but didn't budge. He gave it another hard push. 'What's up?' said Dick, climbing up beside Julian. 'It *must* open – the bolt's not there any more – it fell off into the well. I expect it's rusted a little again. We'll both shove it together.'

The girls watched the boys anxiously, dreading every moment to hear the two men returning. Together the boys pushed at the iron door – and it groaned and then gave way, swinging open inside the well wall! To the boys' delight, there was the rope, hanging near them!

'We've done it!' Dick called down softly to the girls. 'We'll come down and help you up to the table here – then we'll try our luck up the well.'

The girls were soon on the chest top. There wasn't room for everyone on the table, and the boys were debating what to do next.

'*You* go up the rope, Julian,' said Dick. 'You can climb up to the top and get out and look around and make sure there's no one about. Then Wilfrid can climb up – do you think you can, Wilfrid?'

'Of course,' said the boy. 'Then I can help Julian to wind up the girls!'

'Right!' said Dick. I'll stay here with the girls, and help each of them on to the rope, first Anne – and you two can wind the rope up, with her on it. Then George can go – and I'll follow last of all and shut the well door.'

'And when the men come they won't know how in the world we got out of the treasure chamber!' said Anne, grinning. 'What a shock for them!'

'When you've all gone up safely, I'll climb in myself and shut the door,' said Dick. 'Ready, Ju? I'll shine my torch for you!'

Julian nodded. He squeezed through the old iron door, reached out for the rope, and swung on it for a moment. Then up he went, hand-over-hand, till he reached the top, a little out of breath, but delighted to be out in the open air and the bright moonlight. It seemed almost as light as day!

He called down the well. 'I'm at the top, Dick, and all's well. Moon's out, and all is quiet.'

'You next, Wilfrid,' said Dick. 'Can you get hold of the rope all right, do you think? For *pity's* sake don't fall into the water. My torch will give you plenty of light.'

'Don't worry about *me*! It's just like being on the ropes at gym in school,' said Wilfrid, scornfully. He swung his legs into the opening, leapt at the rope, hung on, and began to climb up just like a monkey.

Julian's voice came down the well again, echoing hollowly, sounding rather odd. 'Wilfrid's safely up. Now send Anne – we'll wind up the rope for her so that she doesn't need to climb, only to hang on.'

Through the opening went Anne, and sat on its ledge. 'Can you swing the rope a bit, Julian?' she called. 'It's rather far for me to jump.'

'Watch out! For goodness' sake be careful!' called Julian, in alarm. 'Tell Dick to help you.'

But the well wall opening was so small that Dick couldn't even look through it while Anne was sitting there.

'Don't jump till you've got firm hold of the rope, Anne,' he told his sister, anxiously. 'Is Ju swinging it to and fro? Can you see it clearly? It's so dark in the well, and my torch isn't too good now!'

'Yes. I can see it,' said Anne. 'It bumped against my legs then, and I just missed getting it. Here it comes again – I've got it! I'm going to hold on to it tightly and drop off the ledge. Here I go!'

She sounded very much braver than she felt. She let herself drop off the ledge, and there she swung on the thick rope, with the black water far below! 'Wind me up, Ju!' she called, and held on as the two boys at the top exerted all their strength. Dick saw her disappear up the well, and heaved a sigh of relief. Now for George.

He climbed down from the table and chest and looked for George and Timmy, shining his torch everywhere. To his utmost surprise he couldn't see them! He called softly, 'Timmy!'

A small stifled whine came from somewhere. Dick frowned. 'George – where are you? For goodness' sake buck up and come out from where you're hiding. Those men might come back at any time! Don't play the fool.'

A dark curly head poked out from behind a large box near the door, and George spoke in a very fierce voice. 'You *know* Timmy can't hang on to a rope! He'd fall and be drowned. I think you are all horrid to forget that he can't climb. I'm staying here with him. You go on up the well.'

'Certainly *not*!' said Dick at once. 'I shall stay here with you. I suppose it's no use asking you to let *me* stay with Tim, while you climb up?'

'Not the slightest use. He's *my* dog, and I'm jolly well sticking by him,' said George. 'He'd never desert *me*, I'm sure of that.'

Dick knew George only too well when she was in one of her determined moods. Nothing, absolutely nothing, would make her change her mind!

'All right, George – I expect I'd feel the same if Timmy was mine,' said Dick. 'I'm staying here with you, though!'

'No,' said George. 'We'll be all right, Tim and I.'

Dick ran to the chest and table that he had used to get up to the opening in the well wall, and climbed quickly to the top. He swung himself through, sat on the edge of the opening and called up the well.

'Julian? Are you there? Listen – George won't leave Timmy because he can't climb up the rope. So I'm staying with her!'

No sooner had he said these words than he heard someone unlocking the door of the room they were in! Timmy growled so fiercely that Dick's heart jumped in fear. Suppose Tim leapt at those men – and one of them had a gun!

George heard the noise and the key turning in the door, and quick as lightning she went behind a pile of boxes with Timmy. 'Go for them, Timmy, just as soon as you can!' she said. 'Get them down before they can hurt you.'

'Woof,' said Timmy, understanding every word. He stood beside George, ears cocked, showing his teeth in a snarl. The door opened, and a man came in, carrying a lantern. 'I've brought you a light,' he began – and then Timmy leapt at him!

Crash! Down went the lantern and the light went out. Down went the man too, shouting in fear as the big dog leapt on his chest, his hairy face so close that the man could feel the dog's hot breath. The man's head struck against the edge of a chest, and he was suddenly still and silent.

'Knocked out, I do believe!' said Dick to himself, and very cautiously shone his torch round. Yes – there was the man on the floor, eyes closed, unmoving!

George was at the open door, looking out, Timmy by her side. 'Dick! I'm taking Timmy down the secret way through the cliffs. I'll be perfectly safe with him.'

'I must tell Julian,' said Dick. 'He's still at the top of the well, expecting you and Timmy. You go as quickly as you can – and be careful. Timmy will look after you.'

George disappeared at top speed, her shoes making no sound. She looked anxious but not afraid. 'She's so brave!' thought Dick, for the hundredth time. 'Doesn't turn a hair! Now I'd better get back to that opening in the well, and tell Julian that George and Timmy have gone down the secret way. That man is still knocked out, thank goodness!'

He was soon on top of the chest and table, and peering through the hole. He could see the light from Julian's torch far away at the top, the light flashing on and off as if signalling. Dick called up, 'Julian!'

'Oh, so you're still there,' said Julian, sounding very relieved. 'Anything happened?'

'Yes,' said Dick. 'I'll tell you in a minute. Swing the rope a bit, Ju.'

The rope swung near Dick, and he caught it, and was just about to swing himself into the well when he heard a

noise. He looked back into the vast room, which was now in darkness, for he had switched off his torch.

Someone came in hurriedly. 'What's happened? Why didn't you . . .' Then he stopped as the light from the lantern he carried picked out the figure of the man on the floor. He gave an exclamation and knelt down by him. Dick grinned to himself – what about a nice little shock for this fellow? He reached down to the sturdy little table, gave it a shove that sent it hurtling down to the floor, and then swung himself into the well on the rope. He was just in time to see the table fall with a crash by the man with the lantern, and to hear him shout in fear – and then Julian and Wilfrid hauled him up the well, still grinning to himself. 'Bit of a shock for those men!' he thought. 'George and Timmy disappeared – and the rest of us gone most mysteriously! Pull, Julian, pull! I've a nice little story to tell you!'

And soon he was up on the well wall, telling the others what had happened. They laughed in delight.

'Good old George! Good old Timmy!'

'George knows the way down the cliff passage all right – and if she didn't Timmy would take her safely,' said Julian. 'We'll go down on the rocks and meet her, I think. She should be all right because the moon's out now, and everything is as light as day!'

And off they all went through the wood, laughing when they thought how puzzled and mystified those men would be!

CHAPTER NINETEEN

Anne is a tiger!

IN THE meantime, George was hurrying down the secret way through the cliffs. Timmy ran first in front and then behind, his ears pricked for any possible pursuer or danger. He could hear no one. Good! Both he and George were glad to hear the babbling of the funny little underground stream as it ran swiftly down towards the sea. 'It's a nice friendly sound, Tim,' said George. 'I like it.'

Once or twice they slipped from the wet ledges into the water, and George felt a bit afraid of falling and breaking her torch. 'It wouldn't be much fun if we had to go down this passage in the pitch dark!' she told Timmy, and he gave a little woof of agreement.

'What's that bright light?' said George, suddenly, stopping in the passage. 'Look, Tim – *aw*fully bright. Is it someone coming with a lantern?'

Timmy gave a loud bark and rushed in front. *He* knew that lantern all right! It was the one that somebody sometimes hung in the sky, and that George called the moon. Didn't she know?

George soon did know, of course, and cried out in delight. 'Oh, it's the *moon*, of course, dear old moon. I'd forgotten it was a moonlit night tonight. I wonder where

the others are, Timmy. You'll have to smell them out!'

Timmy already knew where they were! He had caught their scent on the wind. They weren't very far away! He barked joyously. Soon they would all be together again!

He and George came out of the tunnel in the cliff and found themselves on the rocks. The sea was splashing over them, and the waves gleamed brightly in the bright moonlight.

George saw something moving in the distance. She put her hand on Timmy's collar. 'Careful, Tim,' she said. 'Is that someone coming over there? Stay by me.'

But Timmy disobeyed for once! He leapt away and splashed through the pools, over seaweed, over slippery rocks, barking madly. 'Timmy!' called George, not recognising who was coming. 'TIMMY! COME BACK!'

And then she saw who were coming over the rocks in the bright moonlight, picking their way through the slippery seaweed. She waved and shouted joyfully.

'Here I am! I've escaped all right!'

What a joyful meeting that was! They all sat down on a convenient rock and talked nineteen to the dozen, telling each other what had happened. And then a big wave suddenly came up and splashed all over them!

'Blow!' said Julian. 'Tide's coming in, I suppose. Come on – let's get back to Whispering Wood.'

Anne gave a most enormous yawn. 'I don't know what the time is,' she said. 'And it's so bright everywhere that I'm not sure if it's day or night. All I know is that I'm suddenly most awfully *sleepy*.'

Julian glanced at his watch. 'It's very late,' he said. 'Long past our bedtime. What shall we do – risk sleeping here on the island – or find Wilfrid's boat and row across to the mainland – and have a nice, long, peaceful snooze in that dear little cottage?'

'Oh, don't let's stay on the island!' said Anne. 'I'd never go to sleep! I'd be afraid those men would find us.'

'Don't be silly, Anne,' said George, trying not to yawn. 'They wouldn't have the remotest idea where to look for us! I honestly don't fancy looking for Wilfrid's boat, rowing all the way to the mainland, and then climbing up that steep hill to the cottage!'

'Well – all right,' said Anne. 'But oughtn't somebody to be on guard – oughtn't we each to take a turn?'

'Why so fussy, Anne?' asked George. 'Timmy would hear anyone!'

'I suppose he would,' said Anne, giving way. 'We'll stay here then.'

They were all very tired. The boys pulled up armfuls of old dry bracken and spread it on a sheltered patch of grass, where bushes surrounded them and sheltered them from the wind. It was not far from the cove where Wilfrid's boat lay. They snuggled into the bracken.

'Nice and cosy!' said George, yawning. 'Ohhh! I've never felt so sleepy in my life!' And in three seconds she was sound asleep! Wilfrid dropped off at once too, and Dick and Julian were soon giving little gentle snores.

Anne was still awake. She felt nervous. 'I'd dearly like to know if those men are safely underground,' she thought. 'I can't imagine that they are very pleased at us getting away – they'll know we'll go to the mainland as soon as we can and tell everyone what we have found! I should have thought they would try to stop us leaving. They must *know* we have a boat!'

She lay and worried, keeping her ears open for any strange sound. Timmy heard her tossing and turning and crept over to her very quietly, so as not to wake George. He lay down beside Anne, giving her a loving lick, as if to say, 'Now, you go to sleep, and I'll keep watch!'

But still Anne didn't fall asleep. Still she kept her ears wide open for any unusual sound – and then, quite suddenly, she heard something. So did Timmy. He sat up, and gave a very small growl.

Anne strained her ears. Yes – it was certainly voices she could hear – low voices, that didn't want to be heard. It was the men coming to find Wilfrid's boat! Once they had that, the children couldn't get away from Whispering Island!

Timmy ran a little way from the bushes, and looked round at Anne as if to say, 'Coming with me?'

Anne got up quietly and went to Timmy. He ran on in front, and she followed. She really *must* see what was happening, then if it was anything important, she could run back and rouse everyone. Timmy was taking her to the cove where Wilfrid had left his boat, hauled high up on the sand for fear of big waves.

They were both as quiet as they could be. Timmy growled a little when he heard the voices again, much nearer this time.

The men had come quietly round the island in their own boat, to set Wilfrid's boat adrift. Anne saw them pushing Wilfrid's boat down the sand towards the sea. Once it was adrift, she and the others would be prisoners on the island! She yelled at the top of her voice.

'You stop that! It's OUR boat!' And Timmy began to bark his head off, prancing round the men, and showing

his big white teeth. The barking awoke all the others and they leapt up at once. 'That's Timmy!' shouted Julian. 'That's Timmy barking! Come on, quickly – but be careful!'

They ran at top speed to the cove. Timmy was still barking madly – and someone was yelling. It sounded like Anne. '*Anne* – no, no, it couldn't be quiet little Anne!' thought Julian.

But it was! For when the four arrived at the cove, there was Anne yelling to Timmy to bite the men, and dancing about in a rare old temper!

'How DARE you come and take our boat! I'll tell Timmy to bite you! And he will too! Get them, Tim, get them! How DARE you take our boat! *Bite* them, Timmy!'

Timmy had already bitten both the men, who were now rowing away in their own boat at top speed. Anne picked up a stone and sent it whizzing after them. It struck their boat and made them jump.

Anne jumped too when she turned and saw Julian, George, Wilfrid and Dick. 'I'm so glad you've come!' she said. 'I *think* Timmy and I have frightened them off. The beasts!'

'Frightened them off! You've scared them stiff!' said Julian, hugging his sister. 'You even scared *me*! Good gracious – the mouse has certainly turned into a fearsome tiger! I can almost see smoke coming out of your nostrils.'

'A tiger? Did I *really* sound like a tiger?' said Anne. 'I'm glad! I hated you all thinking I was a mouse. You'd better be careful now, I *might* turn into a tiger again!'

The men were now out of sight, and Timmy sent a volley of barks after their vanished boat. What chance had any men against a dog and a tiger? WOOF!

'Julian – why can't we row back to the mainland *now*?' demanded Anne. 'I'm so hungry and there's nothing to eat here now. And I wasn't really very comfortable in the brackeny bed. I'm longing to sleep in a *proper* bed. I've a good mind to take that boat of Wilfrid's and row myself back, if you don't want to come.'

Julian couldn't help laughing at this new fierce Anne. He put his arm round her.

'I believe it's dangerous to say no to a tiger,' he said. 'So you shall have your way, Anne. *I'm* awfully hungry too – and I bet the others are.'

And, in five minutes' time, the six of them were out on the sea, Julian taking one oar, and Dick the other. 'Swish-swash – swish-swash,' went the oars, and the boat rocked as it sped along.

'I bet if those men spot us out on the sea in a boat, going across to the mainland, they will feel pretty uncomfortable!' said Julian. 'They'll know we'll be going to the police first thing tomorrow. This has been quite an adventure, hasn't it? I shall be glad of a little peace now!'

Well – you'll soon have it, Julian! That little cottage is waiting for you all, with its glorious view over the harbour and Whispering Island. You'll have quite a bit of excitement tomorrow, of course, when the police take you back to the island in their boat, and you show them the old well, the vast treasure chamber, the secret passage, and all the rest. You'll be there when all the men are rounded up, you'll watch them chugging off, prisoners, in the police boat, amazed that the Famous Five should have defeated them. What an adventure! And what a relief when all the excitement is over, and you lie peacefully on the hillside, with the little cottage just behind you.

'Now for a real lazy time!' said Anne, when the Five had seen the last of the police. 'Let's all go out on the hill in the sunshine, and have orangeade and biscuits and fruit salad – and Wilfrid shall play his magic pipe and bring his furred and feathered friends to see us.'

'Has he found his pipe then?' said Dick, pleased.

'Yes. He took the well bucket to get some water to drink – and lo and behold, the pipe was in the bottom of the bucket!' said Anne. 'He thinks it must have fallen there the last time he went to fetch water from the well – and nobody noticed it!'

'Oh *good*!' said George, thankfully. 'Wilfrid, what about playing a tune on your little pipe? I'm so glad it's found. I'd like to hear it again.'

Wilfrid was pleased. 'All right,' he said. 'I'll see if my friends here still remember me!'

He sat down on the hillside a little away from the others and began to blow down the pipe – and out came the strange little tune! At once the birds in the trees around turned their heads. In the bushes, the lizards raised themselves, put their quaint heads on one side and listened. Rabbits stopped their play. The big hare bounded up the hill, its great ears taking in every note. A magpie flew down to the boy's foot and sat there.

Wilfrid didn't stir. He just went on playing as the creatures came to listen. Timmy listened too, and went to the boy, pressing against him, licking his ear. Then he went back to George.

We'll leave them all there in the sunshine, quiet and peaceful, watching the little creatures that Wilfrid can always bring around him.

Julian is lying back, looking at the April sky, glad that their adventure ended so well. Dick is looking down at Whispering Island, set in the brilliant blue harbour. Anne is half asleep – quiet little Anne who *can* turn into a tiger if she has to!

And George, of course, is close to Timmy, her arm round his neck, very happy indeed. Goodbye, Five – it *was* fun sharing in your grand adventure!

THE FAMOUS FIVE

FIVE ARE TOGETHER AGAIN

Have you read all THE FAMOUS FIVE books?

1. Five on a Treasure Island
2. Five Go Adventuring Again
3. Five Run Away Together
4. Five Go to Smuggler's Top
5. Five Go Off in a Caravan
6. Five on Kirrin Island Again
7. Five Go Off to Camp
8. Five Get Into Trouble
9. Five Fall Into Adventure
10. Five on a Hike Together
11. Five Have a Wonderful Time
12. Five Go Down to the Sea
13. Five Go to Mystery Moor
14. Five Have Plenty of Fun
15. Five on a Secret Trail
16. Five Go to Billycock Hill
17. Five Get Into a Fix
18. Five on Finniston Farm
19. Five Go to Demon's Rocks
20. Five Have a Mystery to Solve
21. Five Are Together Again

The Famous Five Colour Short Stories

1. Five and a Half-Term Adventure
2. George's Hair is Too Long
3. Good Old Timmy
4. A Lazy Afternoon
5. Well Done, Famous Five
6. Five Have a Puzzling Time
7. Happy Christmas, Five
8. When Timmy Chased the Cat

Enid Blyton®

THE FAMOUS FIVE

FIVE ARE TOGETHER AGAIN

Illustrated by Eileen A. Soper

HODDER CHILDREN'S BOOKS

First published in Great Britain in 1963 by Hodder & Stoughton
This edition published in 2016

20

A CIP catalogue record for this book is available from the British Library.

ISBN 978 1 444 93651 3

Printed and bound in Great Britain by Clays Ltd, Elcograf S.p.A.

The paper and board used in this book are made from wood from responsible sources.

Hodder Children's Books
An imprint of
Hachette Children's Group
Part of Hodder & Stoughton
Carmelite House
50 Victoria Embankment
London EC4Y 0DZ

An Hachette UK Company
www.hachette.co.uk
www.hachettechildrens.co.uk

CONTENTS

1 BACK FOR THE HOLIDAYS 1
2 PLANS FOR THE FIVE 11
3 BIG HOLLOW – AND TINK AND MISCHIEF AGAIN! 20
4 JENNY HAS A VERY GOOD IDEA 29
5 THE TRAVELLING CIRCUS 40
6 GETTING READY FOR CAMPING OUT 50
7 IN THE CIRCUS FIELD 60
8 CHARLIE THE CHIMP IS A HELP! 69
9 A WONDERFUL EVENING 78
10 ROUND THE CAMP-FIRE 88
11 IN THE DARK OF THE NIGHT 100
12 A SHOCK FOR TINK 110
13 QUITE A LOT OF PLANS! 121
14 LADDERS – AND A LOT OF FUN! 133
15 A HAPPY DAY – AND A SHOCK FOR JULIAN 143
16 NIGHT ON KIRRIN ISLAND 154
17 AND AT LAST THE MYSTERY IS SOLVED! 167

CHAPTER ONE

Back for the holidays

'GEORGE, CAN'T you sit still for even a minute!' said Julian. 'It's bad enough to have the train rocking about all over the place, without you falling over my feet all the time, going to look out of first one window and then the other.'

'Well, we're nearly at Kirrin – almost home!' said George. 'I can't *help* feeling excited. I've missed old Timmy so *much* this term, and I just can't *wait* to see him! I love to look out of the window and see how much nearer we are to Kirrin. Do you think Timmy will be on the station to meet us, barking madly?'

'Don't be an idiot,' said Dick. 'He's a clever dog, but not clever enough to read railway timetables.'

'He doesn't need to,' said George. 'He *always* knows when I'm coming home.'

'I really believe he does,' said Anne, seriously. 'Your mother always says how excited he is on the day you are arriving home from school – can't keep still – keeps going to the front gate and looking down the road.'

'Dear, dear Timmy!' said George, falling over Julian's feet again, as she scrambled once more to the window. 'We're nearly there. Look, there's the signal-box, and the signal is down. Hurrah!'

Her three cousins looked at her in amusement. George was always like this on the way home from school. Her thoughts were full of very little else but her beloved Timmy all the way home. Julian thought how much she looked like a restless boy just then, with her short, curly hair, and her determined expression. George had always longed to be a boy, but as she wasn't, she made up for it by trying to speak and act like one, and would never answer to her full name of Georgina.

'We're coming into Kirrin station!' yelled George, almost falling out of the window. 'I can see Peter, the guard. Hey, we're back again. WE'RE BACK AGAIN!'

The train slid into Kirrin station, and Peter waved and grinned. He had known George since she was a baby. George opened the door and leapt out of the carriage.

'Home again! Back at Kirrin! Oh, I do hope Timmy will be at the station!' she said.

But there was no Timmy there. 'He must have forgotten you were coming,' said Dick, with a grin, and at once got a scowl from George. Peter came up, smiling all over his face, and gave them his usual welcome. Everyone in Kirrin village knew the Five – which, of course, included Timmy the dog.

Peter helped the children with their luggage, and wheeled it down the platform on his trolley. 'Had a good term?' he asked.

'Fantastic!' said Dick. 'But it seemed very long, as Easter is so late this year. Gosh – look at the primroses on the railway banks.'

But George had no eyes for anything just then. She was still looking out for Timmy. Where was he? *Why* hadn't he come to the station to meet them? He came last time and the time before! She turned a troubled face to Dick.

'Do you think he's ill?' she asked. 'Or has he forgotten me? Or . . . ?'

'Oh, don't be silly, George,' said Dick. 'He is probably in the house somewhere and can't get out. Look out – the trolley nearly ran you over then.'

George skipped out of the way, glaring. *Where* was Timmy? She was sure he was ill – or had had an accident – or was tied up and couldn't get away. Perhaps Joanna, who helped her mother in the house, had forgotten to let him loose.

'I'm going to take a taxi home, if I've enough money,' she said, taking out her purse. 'You others can walk. I must see if anything's happened to Timmy – he's *never* missed meeting our train before.'

'But, George, it's such a lovely walk to Kirrin Cottage!' said Anne. 'You know how you love to see your island – dear old Kirrin Island – as we walk to your mother's house – and the bay – and hear the waves crashing on the rocks.'

'I'm taking the station taxi,' said George, obstinately, counting the money in her purse. 'If you'd like to come with me, you can. It's Timmy I want to see, not islands and waves and things! I'm *sure* he's ill or has had an accident or something!'

'All right, George, do as you please,' said Julian. 'Hope

you find dear old Timmy is perfectly well – and has only forgotten the time of the train. See you later.'

The two brothers and their sister Anne set off together, looking forward to the walk to Kirrin Cottage. How lovely to see Kirrin Bay again, and George's island!

'Isn't she lucky to have a real island of her very own!' said Anne. 'Fancy it belonging to her family for years and years – and then one day her mother suddenly gives it to George! I bet she worried and worried dear Aunt Fanny until she gave in to old George. I do so hope Timmy is all right; we shan't enjoy our holidays with George's mother if there's anything wrong with Timmy.'

'Oh, George will probably go and live in Timmy's kennel with him,' said Dick, with a chuckle. 'Ha – look! The sea – and Kirrin Bay – *and* the little old island as lovely as ever!'

'With its gulls circling round, and mewing like cats,' said Julian. 'And the old ruined castle there, just exactly the same as usual. Not a single stone fallen out of it, as far as I can see.'

'You can't *possibly* see that at this distance,' said Anne, screwing up her eyes. 'Oh, isn't the first day of the hols heavenly? We seem to have all the time in the world in front of us!'

'Yes. But, after a few days, the holidays *rush* by,' said Julian. 'I wonder if George is home by now.'

'Well, her taxi passed us going at a tremendous pace!'

said Dick. 'I bet old George was shouting at the driver to go as fast as possible!'

'Look – there's Kirrin Cottage – I can just see the chimneys in the distance,' said Dick. 'Smoke is coming from one of them.'

'Funny – why only one?' said Julian. 'They usually have the kitchen fire going, and a fire in Uncle Quentin's study. He's such a cold mortal when he's working out all his wonderful figures for his inventions.'

'Perhaps he's away,' said Anne, hopefully. She was rather afraid of George's hasty-tempered father. 'I should think Uncle Quentin could do with a holiday at times – he's always buried in rows and rows of figures.'

'Well, let's hope we don't disturb him too much,' said Julian. 'It's hard on Aunt Fanny if he keeps yelling at everyone. We'll try and be out of doors most of the time.'

They were nearly at Kirrin Cottage now. As they came near to the front gate, they saw George come running down the garden path. To Julian's horror, she was crying bitterly.

'I say – it does look as if something has happened to old Timmy,' he said. 'It's not like George to cry – she *never* cries! What *can* have happened?'

In great alarm they began to run, and Anne shouted as she ran, 'George! George, what's the matter? Is something wrong with Timmy? What's happened?'

'We can't stay at home,' wept George. 'We've got to go away somewhere. Something awful's happened!'

'What is it? Tell us, you idiot!' said Dick, in alarm. 'For goodness' sake, what's happened? Is Timmy run over, or something?'

'No – it isn't Timmy,' said George, wiping her eyes with her hand, because, as usual, she had no handkerchief. 'It's Joanna – Joanna, our dear, darling Joanna!'

'What's the matter with her?' asked Julian, thinking of all kinds of dreadful things. 'George, will you please *tell us*!'

'Joanna's got scarlet fever,' said George, sniffing dolefully. 'So we can't be at Kirrin Cottage.'

'Why not?' demanded Dick. 'Joanna will have to go to hospital – and we can all stay at Kirrin Cottage and help your mother. Poor old Joanna! But cheer up, George, scarlet fever isn't much of a thing to have nowadays. Come on – let's go in and see if we can comfort your mother. Poor old Aunt Fanny, she *will* be in a stew – with all of us four cousins at Kirrin Cottage too! Never mind, we can . . .'

'Stop jabbering, Dick,' said George, exasperated. 'We *can't* stay at Kirrin Cottage. Mother wouldn't even let me go in at the front door! She shooed me away, and said I was to wait in the garden, the doctor was coming in a minute or two.'

Someone called to them from a window of Kirrin Cottage. 'Are you all there, children? Julian, come here, will you?'

They all went into the garden, and saw their Aunt Fanny, George's mother, leaning out of a bedroom window.

'Listen, dears,' she said. 'Joanna has scarlet fever, and is waiting for an ambulance to take her to the hospital, and . . .'

'Aunt Fanny – don't worry. We'll all turn to and help,' called back Julian, cheerfully.

'Dear Julian – you still don't understand,' said his aunt. 'You see, neither your uncle nor I have had scarlet fever – so we are in quarantine, and mustn't have anyone near us, in case we get it, and give it to them – and that might mean we'd give it to all you four.'

'Would Timmy get it?' asked George, still sniffing dolefully.

'No, of course not. Don't be silly, George,' said her

mother. 'Did you ever hear of dogs getting measles or whooping-cough or any of *our* illnesses? Timmy isn't in quarantine. You can get him out of his kennel as soon as you like.'

George's face lit up immediately, and she shot round the back of the house, yelling Timmy's name. At once there came a volley of barks!

'Aunt Fanny – what do you want us to do?' asked Julian. 'We can't go to my home, because Mummy and Daddy are still in Germany. Should we go to a hotel?'

'No, dear, I'll think of somewhere you can all go,' said his aunt. 'Good gracious, what a row Timmy is making! Poor Joanna – she has such a splitting headache.'

'Here's the ambulance,' cried Anne, as a big hospital van drew up outside the gate. Aunt Fanny disappeared from the window at once to tell Joanna. The ambulance man went up to the front door, his mate behind him carrying a stretcher. The four children watched in surprise. 'He's gone to fetch dear old Joanna,' said Julian. And sure enough the stretcher was soon carried out with Joanna lying on it, wrapped round in blankets. She waved to the children as the men carried her out.

'Soon be back!' she said, in rather a croaky voice. 'Help Mrs Kirrin if you can. So sorry about this!'

'Poor Joanna,' said Anne, with tears in her eyes. 'Get better quickly, Joanna. We shall miss you so!'

The ambulance door closed and the van went off very smoothly and quietly.

'Whatever shall we do?' said Dick, turning to Julian. 'Can't go home – can't stay here! Oh, here's Timmy! How are you, Tim, old thing? Thank goodness *you* can't get scarlet fever. Don't knock me over, old boy. Down! Gosh, what a licky dog you are!'

Timmy was the only one in high spirits. The others felt really down in the dumps. Oh dear – what was to be done? Where could they go? What a horrid beginning to a holiday! Down, Timmy, DOWN! What a dog! Anyone would think he had never even *heard* of scarlet fever! WILL you get down, Timmy!

CHAPTER TWO

Plans for the Five

George was still looking upset. What with her fears that Timmy might be ill or hurt, and now her distress at Joanna being carried off in the ambulance, she wasn't much help to anyone.

'Do stop sniffing, George,' said Anne. 'We've just got to be sensible and think of some way out of this.'

'I'm going to find Mother,' said George. 'I don't care if she's in quarantine or not.'

'Oh no you're not,' said Julian, taking her firmly by the arm. 'You jolly well know what quarantine means. When you had whooping-cough *you* weren't allowed to come near any of us, in case we caught it too. You were infectious, and that meant that you didn't have close contact with anybody for at least a few weeks. I think it's only two weeks for scarlet fever, so it won't be too bad.'

George went on sniffing, trying to pull away from Julian's hand. Julian winked at Dick, and said something that made George pull herself together at once.

'Well, *really*, George!' he said. 'You're acting *just* like a weepy girl. Poor Georgina! Poor little old Georgina!'

George stopped sniffing immediately and glared at Julian in fury. If there was one thing she really hated it was to be told she was acting like a silly *girl*! And how *awful* to be called by her real name, Georgina! She gave Julian a hefty punch, and he grinned at her, warding her off.

'That's better,' he said. 'Cheer up! Just look at Timmy staring at you in amazement. He's hardly ever heard you crying before.'

'I'm *not* crying!' said George. 'I'm – well, I'm upset about Joanna. And it's awful to have nowhere to go.'

'I can hear Aunt Fanny telephoning,' said Anne, who had very sharp ears. She fondled Timmy's head, and he licked her hand. He had already given everyone a wonderful welcome, whining with pleasure, and licking lavishly. He had been mad with joy to see George again, and was surprised and sad to find her looking so miserable now. Dear Timmy – he certainly belonged to the Five!

'Let's sit down and wait for Aunt Fanny,' said Julian, settling himself on the grass. 'We look a bit silly standing staring at Kirrin Cottage like this. Aunt Fanny will come to the window in a minute. She is sure to have thought of a good idea for us. TIMMY! I shan't stay sitting down for long if you keep licking my neck like that. I shall send you for a towel in a minute, so that I can wipe it dry!'

The little joke made everyone feel better. They were all sitting on the grass now, and Timmy went lovingly from one to the other. All his family back again – it was too good to be true! He settled down at last, his head on George's knee, George's hand caressing his ears.

'Aunt Fanny's put down the telephone,' said Anne. 'Now she'll come to the window.'

'You've got ears like a dog – just as good as Timmy's,' said Dick. '*I* couldn't hear a thing!'

'Here's Mother!' said George, and leapt to her feet as Aunt Fanny came to the window and leant out.

'It's all right, dears,' she called. 'I've been able to arrange something for you. I have been telephoning the scientist that your father has been working with, George – Professor Hayling. He was coming here for a day or two, and when I told him he couldn't, because we're in quarantine, he at once said that *you* must all go *there* – and that Tink, his son – you remember him, don't you – would be delighted to have your company!'

'Tink! Goodness, yes, I shall never forget him – or his monkey either!' said Julian. 'He's the boy who owns that old lighthouse at Demon's Rocks, isn't he? We went to stay there with him, and had a marvellous time.'

'Well – you're not staying at the lighthouse, I'm afraid,' said his aunt, from the window. 'Apparently a storm blew up one night and damaged it, and it's not safe to live in any more.'

Groans from all the Five, of course, Timmy joining in as usual! 'Where are we to go then? To Tink's *home*?' said Dick.

'Yes. You can get a bus from here, at Little Hollow, that will take you almost to Big Hollow, where Professor Hayling lives,' said Aunt Fanny. 'You're to go today. I'm so very sorry about this, dears, but it's just one of those things we have to put up with. I'm sure you'll have a good time with Tink, and that monkey of his. What was it called now?'

'Mischief,' said everyone together, and Anne smiled in delight to think of being with the naughty little creature, and watching its wicked ways.

'The bus will pass in ten minutes,' said her aunt. 'And have a good time, dears, and send me a card or two. I'll let you know how we get on – but I really don't think that either your uncle or I will catch scarlet fever, so don't worry. And I'll send you some money to spend. You'd better run for the bus now.'

'Right, Aunt Fanny, and thank you!' called Julian. 'I'll look after everyone and keep them in order – especially old George. Don't worry at all – and I do hope you or Uncle don't go down with the fever. Goodbye.'

They all went to the front gate where the luggage still stood. 'Anne, go out into the road and stop the bus when it comes,' ordered Julian. 'Then Dick and I will heave our bags aboard. Gosh, I wonder what it will be like with old Tink at Big Hollow. I've a feeling it might be rather exciting!'

'*I* don't think so,' said George, mournfully. 'I like Tink all right – he's funny – and that little monkey is a darling – such a *naughty* little thing too. But oh dear, don't you remember what it was like when Tink's *father* came to stay with us? It was *awful*! He never remembered to come to meals, and was always losing his coat or his hanky or his money, and losing his temper too. I got very tired of him.'

'Well, he'll probably get very tired of *us*!' said Julian. 'He won't find it very funny to have four kids parked on him, especially if he's in the middle of difficult work – to say nothing of a rather large, licky dog leaping round the house as well.'

'Timmy isn't likely to lick *him*,' said George, at once, and put on one of her scowls. '*I* didn't like Tink's father at all.'

'Well, don't look like a thunderstorm,' said Julian. 'I don't expect he'll like any of *us* either. But it's kind of him to let us come and stay at Big Hollow, and we're jolly well going to behave ourselves, see? There's to be no back-chat from *you*, George – even if he dares to disapprove of Timmy!'

'He'd better *not*,' said George. 'In fact, I've a good mind not to go. I think I'll live in the summer-house with Timmy, at the bottom of the garden!'

'You will NOT!' said Julian, taking firm hold of her arm. 'You'll play fair, come with us, and behave properly! Listen, there's the bus. Come on, we'll all wave, and hope there are a few empty seats.'

Anne had already stopped the bus, and run round to ask the driver if he would help with the bags. He knew the children very well, and leapt down at once.

'You're going back to school pretty quick!' he said. 'I

thought the schools had only just broken up.'

'They have,' said Julian, 'but we're off to stay at Big Hollow. The bus goes there, doesn't it?'

'Yes, we go right through the village of Big Hollow,' said the driver, carrying three bags at once, much to Julian's envy. 'Whereabouts are you staying there?'

'At Professor Hayling's house,' said Julian. 'I think that's called Big Hollow too, like the village.'

'Ah, we pass it,' said the driver. 'I'll stop the bus just outside and give you a hand with your things again. My word – you'll have to mind your ps and qs there – old Professor Hayling's a bit peculiar, you know. Goes off the handle properly if things don't go his way! Once a horse got into his garden and believe it or not he chased that horse for two miles, shouting at it all the way. And bless me, when he got back home, tired out, there was that horse, chewing up his garden again. The horse was cute – he'd taken a short cut back. Yes – you be careful how you behave at Big Hollow. The old man might get cross and pop you into one of his strange machines and grind you up into little pieces!'

The four children laughed. 'Oh, the old Professor is all right,' said Julian. 'A bit forgetful, like most people who work with their brains all the time. My brain goes fairly slowly – but my Uncle Quentin's goes about a hundred miles an hour, and I bet the Professor's does too! *We'll* be all right!'

Away went the bus, bumping over the road from Kirrin

and Little Hollow, and on to Big Hollow. The four children gazed out of the windows as they passed alongside the shore, where the sea shone as blue as cornflowers, and once more saw Kirrin Island out in the big bay.

'Wish we were going *there*!' sighed George. 'We'll have to take a picnic meal there sometimes, and enjoy ourselves. I'd like old Tink to visit my island. He may have a lighthouse of his own, but having an island is *much* better!'

'I think I agree with you,' said Julian. 'Tink's lighthouse is certainly lovely and all on its own, and the view from it is amazing – but there's something about Kirrin Island that I *love*. Islands are quite different from anything else!'

'Yes. They are,' said Anne. '*I'd* like one too. A very little one, so that I could see all round it at one glance. And I'd like one little cave to sleep in – just big enough for *me*.'

'You'd soon be lonely, Anne,' said Dick, giving his sister a friendly pat. 'You love to have people round you, you like to be friendly!'

'So does Timmy!' said Julian, as Timmy left his place by George's knee and went to sniff at a string bag held by an old man, who at once fondled the big dog, and fumbled for a biscuit out of a paper bag. 'Timmy doesn't mind how many people there are around, so long as one or two of them have a biscuit or a bone to hand out!'

'Come to heel, Timmy,' said George. 'You're not to go

round begging, telling people you are half-starved! I should think you eat more than any other dog in Kirrin. Who eats the cat's dinner whenever he can, I should like to know?'

Timmy gave George a loving lick and settled down beside her, his head on her toes. He got up politely every time someone entered or left the bus. The driver was most impressed.

'I wish all dogs were as good on my bus as yours,' he told George. 'You'd better get ready to jump out. Our next stop is supposed to be a little way beyond Big Hollow, but I'll stop for a moment, and you can get out.'

'Thanks a lot,' said Julian, gratefully, and when the bus stopped with a jerk a minute later, all the Five were ready to jump out.

The bus went on, and left them standing outside a large wooden gate. The drive from it led steeply downwards, and a large house could just be seen hidden in a hollow by great trees.

'Big Hollow!' said Julian. 'Well – here we are. What a strange place – sort of mysterious and brooding. Now to find old Tink! I bet he'll be pleased to see us all, especially Timmy! Help me with the bags, Dick!'

CHAPTER THREE

Big Hollow – and Tink and Mischief again!

THE FOUR children and Timmy went through the big heavy gate, which groaned loudly. Timmy was very startled to hear the mournful creak, and barked sharply.

'Sh!' said George. 'You'll get into trouble with the Professor, Timmy, if you raise your voice like that. I expect we'll have to talk in whispers, so as not to disturb the Professor – so just see if you can whisper too.'

Timmy gave a small whine. He knew he couldn't whisper! He trotted at George's heel as they all went down the steep drive to the house. It was a curious house, built sideways to the drive, and had astonishingly few windows.

'I expect Professor Hayling is afraid of people peering in at his work,' said Anne. 'It's very, very secret, isn't it?'

'I know he uses miles and miles of figures,' said Dick. 'Tink told me one day that his monkey Mischief once chewed up a page of figures when he was very small – and Professor Hayling chased him for a whole hour, hoping to catch him and find even a *few* bits of paper still in his mouth, so that he could rescue at least part of his figures. But Mischief fled down a rabbit hole and didn't come up for two days, so it wasn't any good.'

Everyone smiled at the thought of poor Mischief hiding down a rabbit hole. '*You* couldn't do that, Timmy old thing!' said Julian. 'So just be careful of any paper *you* eat.'

'He wouldn't be so silly,' said George, at once. 'He knows perfectly well what's eatable and what's not.'

'Ha! *Does* he?' said Anne. 'Well, I'd just like to know what kind of food he thought my blue slipper was that he chewed up last hols!'

'Don't tell tales on him,' said George. 'He only chewed it because someone shut him in your bedroom and he hadn't anything else to do.'

'Woof,' said Timmy, quite agreeing. He gave Anne's hand a little lick, as if to say, 'Very sorry, Anne – but I was so *bored*!'

'*Dear* Timmy! I wouldn't mind if you chewed up *all* my slippers!' said Anne. 'But it would be nice if you chose the very *oldest* ones!'

Timmy suddenly stopped and looked into the bushes. He gave a low growl! George put her hand on his collar at once. She was always afraid of snakes in the springtime.

'It might be an adder!' she said. 'The dog next door trod on one last year, so I heard, and his leg swelled up terribly, and he was in great pain. Come away now, Timmy – it's an adder, with poison in its fangs!'

But Timmy went on growling. Then he suddenly stood still and sniffed hard. He gave an excited whimper and pulled away from George, jumping into the bushes – and out came, not a snake, but Mischief, Tink's bright-eyed little monkey!

He at once leapt on to the dog's broad back, put his little monkey fingers under Timmy's collar, and chattered in delight. Timmy nearly dislocated his neck to twist his head round to lick him!

'Mischief!' cried everyone at once, in real delight. 'You've come to welcome us!'

And the little monkey, jabbering away excitedly in monkey language, leapt first on to George's shoulder, and then on to Julian's. He pulled Julian's hair, twisted his right ear round, and then leapt from him to Dick, and on to Anne's shoulder. He cuddled into her neck, his eyes bright and brown, looking very happy.

'Oh! *Isn't* he pleased to see us again!' said Anne, delighted. 'Mischief, where's Tink?'

Mischief jumped off Anne's shoulder and scampered down the drive as if he quite understood all that Anne had said. The children raced after him – and then a loud voice suddenly roared at them from one side of the drive.

'What are you doing here? Clear out! This is private ground. I'll fetch the police. Clear OUT!'

The Five stopped still in fright – and then Julian saw who it was – Professor Hayling! He stepped forward at once. 'Good afternoon,' he said. 'I hope we didn't disturb you, but you did tell my aunt we could come here.'

'Your aunt? Who's your aunt? I don't know any aunt!' roared the Professor. 'You're sightseers, that's what you are! Come to pry into my work, just because there was a piece about it in some silly paper! You're the third lot today.

Clear out, I tell you – and take that dog too. How DARE you!'

'But – don't you *really* know us?' said Julian very startled. 'You came to stay at our house, you know, and . . .'

'Stuff and nonsense! I haven't been away for years!' shouted the Professor. Mischief, the monkey, was so frightened that he leapt away into the bushes, making a funny little crying noise.

'I hope he fetches Tink,' said Julian, in a low voice to Dick. 'The Professor has forgotten who we are, and why we've come. Let's retreat a bit.'

But as they went cautiously back up the steep path, followed by the angry Professor, a loud voice hailed them, and Tink came racing up with Mischief on his shoulder, clinging to his hair. So the little monkey had gone to fetch him. 'Good for *him*!' thought Julian, pleased.

'Dad! Don't yell at our friends like that!' cried Tink, dancing about in front of his angry father. 'You asked them here yourself, you know you did!'

'I DID NOT!' said the Professor. 'Who are they?'

'Well, George, that girl, is the daughter of Mr Kirrin, and the others are his niece and nephews. And that's their dog, Timmy. And you asked them all here because Mr and Mrs Kirrin are in quarantine for scarlet fever,' shouted Tink, still dancing about in front of his father.

'Stop jigging about like that,' said the Professor, crossly. '*I* don't remember asking them. I would have told Jenny the housekeeper if I had.'

'You did tell her!' shouted Tink, still jigging about, with Mischief the monkey jigging too in delight. 'She's angry because you left your breakfast and now it's almost dinner-time. She's cleared it away.'

'Bless us – so *that*'s why I feel so hungry and cross!' said Professor Hayling, and he began to laugh. He had a tremendous laugh, and the children couldn't help laughing too. What an odd fellow – so brainy, such a fine scientist – with the most enormous amount of knowledge in his head – and yet no memory for such ordinary things as breakfast and visitors and telephone calls.

'It was just a misunderstanding,' said Julian, politely. 'It was very, very kind of you to invite us here when we can't be at home because of the scarlet fever. We'll try not to be a nuisance, and if there's anything we can do to help you, please ask us. We'll make as little noise as possible, and keep out of your way, of course.'

'You hear that, Tink?' said Professor Hayling, suddenly swinging round on the startled Tink. 'Why can't you do the same – make very little noise, and keep out of my way? You know I'm very busy now – on a *most important* project.' He turned to Julian. 'You'll be very welcome if you keep Tink out of my way. And *nobody* – absolutely nobody – is to go up into that tower. Understand?'

They all looked up to where he was pointing, and saw a tall, slender tower rising up amid the trees. It had curious tentacle-like rods sticking out at the top, and these shook slightly in the breeze.

'And don't ask me questions about it,' went on the Professor, looking fiercely at George. 'Your father's the only other man who knows what it's for, and *he* knows how to keep his mouth shut.'

'None of us would *dream* of prying,' said Julian. 'It's very, very kind of you to offer to have us here, and do believe me when I say we shan't be any trouble to you at all – but a help if you'll allow us.'

'Ah well, you sound a sensible fellow, I must say,' said the Professor, who had now calmed down, and looked quite peaceable. 'Well, I'll say goodbye for now and go and have my breakfast. I hope it's fried eggs and bacon. I'm very hungry.'

'Dad – Jenny's cleared your breakfast *away*! I told you that before!' said Tink in despair. 'It's almost dinner-time, now.'

'Ah good – good!' said the Professor. 'I'll come at once.'

And he led the way indoors, followed by the five children, with Timmy and Mischief, all looking rather worried. Really, nobody *ever* knew what the Professor was going to do or say next!

Jenny certainly had a good dinner for them all. There was a large and delicious stew with carrots, onions and peas swimming in the gravy, and plenty of potatoes. Everyone tucked in well, and Mischief, who loved the peas, took quite a few from Tink's plate, his little paw creeping up, and neatly snatching a pea from the gravy.

The girls went out to help bring in the next course, which was a big steamed pudding with plenty of raisins in it. Mischief at once jigged up and down in delight, for he loved raisins. He leapt on to the table, and received a sharp tap from the Professor, who unfortunately smacked the pudding dish at the same time, making the pudding jump in the air.

'Good gracious, Dad – we nearly lost the pudding!' cried Tink. 'And it's my favourite. Oh, don't give us such *small* pieces! Mischief, get off the table. You are NOT to put your paw into the sauce!'

So Mischief disappeared under the table, where he received quite a lot of raisins from various kindly hands, unseen by the Professor. Timmy felt rather left out. He was under the table too, having been rather scared by the Professor's angry voice, but as he didn't very much like raisins, he wasn't as lucky as Mischief.

'Ha – I enjoyed that!' said the Professor, having cleaned his plate thoroughly. 'Nothing like a good breakfast!'

'It was midday dinner, Dad!' said Tink. 'You don't have pudding at breakfast.'

'Dear me, of course not – that was pudding!' said his father, and laughed his great laugh. 'Now you can all do exactly what you like, so long as you do *not* go into my study, or my workroom, or that tower. AND DON'T MEDDLE WITH ANYTHING! Mischief, get off the water jug, you'll upset it. Can't you teach that monkey some table manners, Tink?'

And with that he marched out of the room, and disappeared into some mysterious passage that apparently led to his study or workroom. Everyone heaved a sigh of relief.

'We'll clear away and then I'll show you your rooms,' said Tink. 'I do hope you won't find it too dull here.'

Dull, Tink! You needn't worry! There is far too much excitement waiting for the Five – and you too! Just wait a bit, and see!

CHAPTER FOUR

Jenny has a very good idea

TINK RACED out to the kitchen to fetch a tray or two. He made a most peculiar noise as he went, and for a moment Timmy looked extremely startled.

'Goodness – don't say that Tink *still* has that awful habit of pretending to be some kind of car!' groaned Julian. 'How on earth does his father put up with it? What's he think he is now? A motorbike by the sound of it.'

There was a sudden crash and a loud yell. The Five raced down the kitchen passage to find out what had happened, Timmy at the front.

'Accident!' bellowed Tink, scrambling up from the floor. 'I took the bend too quickly, and my front wheel skidded, and I went bang into a wall! I've bent my mudguard.'

'Tink – do you mean to say you're *still* being silly enough to pretend to be cars and motorbikes and tractors and lorries?' demanded Julian. 'You nearly drove us all mad, driving about all over the house, when you stayed with us. Have you *got* to be a machine of some sort?'

'Yes,' said Tink, rubbing one of his arms. 'It sort of

comes over me, and away I go. You should have heard me yesterday, being a lorry absolutely *loaded* with new cars for delivery. Dad *really* thought it was a great lorry and he rushed out into the drive to send it away. But it was only me. I hooted too – like this!'

And the sound of a loud and a deep hooter immediately filled the passage! Julian shoved Tink into the kitchen and shut the door.

'I should have thought that your father would have been driven completely mad by now!' he said. 'Now, you just shut up. Can't you grow up a bit?'

'No,' said Tink, sullenly. 'I don't want to grow up. I might be like my father and forget to eat my meals, and go out with one sock on and one off. And I'd hate to forget my meals. Just think how *awful* it would be! I'd always be hungry.'

Julian couldn't help laughing. 'Pick up your tray, and help to clear away!' he said. 'And if you simply can't *help* being a car sometimes, for goodness' sake go outside! It sounds terrible in the house. You're much too good at awful noises.'

'Oh, am I *really* good?' said Tink, pleased. 'I suppose you wouldn't like to hear me being one of those new planes that go over here sometimes, making a funny droning noise?'

'No, I would not!' said Julian, firmly. 'Now will you *please* get that tray, Tink. And tell Mischief to get off my right foot. He seems to think it's a chair.'

But Mischief clung to Julian's ankle and refused to move. 'All right, all right,' said Julian. 'I shall just have to walk about all day with you riding on my foot.'

'If you *stamp* as you walk, he soon gets off,' remarked Tink.

'Why didn't you tell me that just now?' asked Julian, and stamped a few steps round the room. Mischief leapt off his foot at once and sat on a table, making an angry noise.

'He sits on Dad's foot for ages, even when he walks about,' said Tink. 'But Dad doesn't even notice him there! He even sat on Dad's head once, and Dad thought he was wearing his hat indoors and tried to take it off. But it was only Mischief there!'

That made everyone laugh. 'Now come on,' said Julian, briskly. 'We really must clear away the dinner things. We three boys will carry out the loaded trays and you girls can wash up. And *don't* let Mischief think he can carry teapots or milk jugs.'

Jenny was very pleased with their help. She was short and plump, and waddled rather than walked, but managed to get here and there remarkably quickly.

'I'll show your visitors their bedrooms after we've cleared,' she said. 'But, you know, Tink, those mattresses we sent to be remade haven't come back yet. I've told your father a dozen times to telephone about them, but I'm sure he hasn't remembered.'

'Oh, Jenny!' said Tink, in dismay. 'That means that the two beds for visitors can't be slept in! What ever are we to do?'

'Well, your dad will have to ring up for new mattresses to be sent today,' said Jenny. 'Maybe they would send them out by van.'

Tink immediately became a furniture van and rushed down the passage, into the dining-room and back again, Mischief following him in delight. He made a noise exactly like a slow-moving van, and the children couldn't help laughing.

The Professor shot out of his study, his hands to his ears. 'TINK! COME HERE!'

'No thanks,' said Tink, warily. 'Sorry, Father. I was a van bringing the mattresses you forgot to order for the beds for visitors.'

But the Professor didn't seem to hear. He advanced on Tink, who fled upstairs with Mischief leaping after him. Professor Hayling turned on Jenny.

'Can't you keep the children quiet? What do I pay you for?'

'Cleaning, cooking and washing,' she said, briskly. 'But I'm not a nurse for children. That Tink of yours could do with half a dozen nurses, and he'd still be a nuisance to you while he was in the house. Why don't you let him take his tent and camp out in the field with his friends? It's hot weather and those new mattresses haven't come, and they'd all love it. I can cook for the children and take them out meals – or they could come and fetch them.'

The Professor looked as if he could give Jenny a big hug. The children waited eagerly to see what he would say. Camping out – that would be fun in this weather – and honestly, living in the same house as the Professor wasn't going to be much fun. Timmy gave a little whine as if to say, 'Fine idea! Let's go at once!'

'Good idea, Jenny, *very* good idea!' said Professor Hayling. 'But that monkey's to camp out too. Then perhaps he won't jump in at my workroom window and fiddle about with my models!'

He marched back into his study and slammed the door so hard that the whole house shook. Timmy was startled and gave a yelp. Mischief the monkey leapt up the stairs again, howling in fright. Tink began to dance round in joy, and very firmly Jenny took hold of him and propelled him into her big, clean kitchen.

'Wait, Jenny, I've remembered something. We've only one tent, and that's mine, a small one. I'll have to ask Dad if I can get two big ones!' And before anyone could stop him he was banging at the Professor's door, then flung it open, and shouted out his request.

'WE WANT TWO MORE TENTS, DAD. CAN I BUY THEM?'

'For goodness' sake, Tink, clear out and leave me alone!' shouted his father. 'Buy SIX tents if you want them, but GET OUT!'

'Ooh, thanks, Dad!' said Tink, and was just slipping out of the door when his father yelled again.

'BUT WHAT ON EARTH DO YOU WANT *TENTS* FOR?'

Tink slammed the door and grinned at the others. 'I'd better buy Dad a new memory. He's only *just* told us we can camp out, and he knows there's only my very small tent – almost a toy one.'

'I'm glad we shan't be in the house,' said Anne. 'I know what a nuisance it is to *George's* father to have us around, playing about. We'll be better out of the way.'

'Camping out again!' said George, very pleased. 'Let's catch the bus back home and get our own tents. I've got them all stored away in the garden shed. We can just ask Jim the carrier to take them in his van, when we've found them.'

'He's calling here today – I'll give him the message for you, if you like,' said Jenny. 'The sooner you get the tents, the better. It was a kind thought of the Professor's to ask you all here, but I just knew it wouldn't work! You'll be all right out in the field at the back of the house – he won't hear a thing, not even if you all yell together! So you get your tents and put them up, and I'll see what I can find in the way of ground-sheets and rugs.'

'Don't bother, Jenny,' said Julian. 'We've got all those things – we've often camped out before.'

'I only hope there aren't any cows in the field,' said Anne. 'Last time we camped, a cow put its head into my tent opening, and mooed. I woke up with such a jump, and I was too scared to move.'

'I don't think there are any cows,' said Jenny, laughing. 'Now I *must* get on with the washing-up, so will you bring out the dinner things please – but don't let that monkey carry anything breakable, for goodness' sake! He tried to balance the teapot on his head last week – and that was the end of the teapot!'

Soon everyone was hard at work, clearing away, and helping Jenny with the washing-up.

'I shall like camping out,' Anne told her. 'I'd be scared of staying here in the house. Professor Hayling is a bit like my Uncle Quentin, you know – forgetful, and quick-tempered and a bit shouty.'

'Oh, you don't want to be scared of him,' said Jenny, handing Anne a dish to dry. 'He's kind, for all his crossness when he's upset. Why, when my mother was ill, he paid for her to go into a really good nursing-home – and believe it or not, he gave me money to buy her fruit and flowers!'

'Oh goodness – that reminds me – we MUST send Joanna some flowers,' said George. 'She has scarlet fever, you know. That's why we're here.'

'Well, you go and telephone the florist,' said Jenny. 'I'll finish this job.'

But George was rather afraid that Professor Hayling might rush out to see who was using the telephone!

'I'm sure we can buy flowers in Kirrin village, and have

them sent,' she said. 'We've got to go and get our things ready for Jim, and I can order the flowers then. We might as well come back on our bicycles – they'd be useful here.'

'Well, you'd better go now,' said Jenny, 'or you won't be back in time for tea, and *then* there'd be trouble.'

'*I'll* bring back Anne's bicycle,' said Julian. 'I can easily manage it beside mine as I ride back.'

'Look, George,' said Dick, 'you needn't come. I'll order the flowers and I can bring your bike back too. So you stay with Anne.' Reluctantly George agreed.

Off went Julian and Dick, leaving Tink and the girls to help Jenny. But Jenny soon sent Tink off, afraid that he would drop things and break them.

'You go and be a nice, quiet, purring Rolls-Royce at the bottom of the garden,' she said. 'And when you think you've done thirty miles or so, come back for petrol.'

'Lemonade, you mean!' said Tink, with a grin. 'All right. I haven't been a Rolls-Royce for a long time. Dad won't hear me right at the bottom of the garden!'

Off he went, and Jenny and the girls finished the washing-up. Mischief was a nuisance and went off with the teaspoons. He leapt to the top of a high cupboard, and dropped them there.

Tink suddenly put his head in at the window. 'Come on out to the field where we're going to put up our tents,'

he called to Anne and George. 'We'll choose a nice sheltered spot. Buck up! You must have finished washing-up by now. I'm tired of being a Rolls-Royce!'

'You go with him, Anne,' said George. 'I don't feel like it just now.'

So down the garden went the two children and out through a gate at the bottom into a big field.

'Good gracious!' said Tink, staring. 'Look at all those caravans coming in at the gate the other end of the field. I'll soon send them off. It's *our* field!' And away he marched to the gate in the distance.

'Come BACK, Tink,' shouted Anne. 'You'll get into trouble if you interfere. COME BACK!'

But Tink marched on, his head held high. Ha – he'd soon tell the caravan folk it was *his* field!

CHAPTER FIVE

The travelling circus

ANNE WATCHED anxiously as Tink went on and on over the field. There were now four caravans trundling in the far gate, and behind them, in the lane, were vans – enormous vans – all with enormously large words painted on them.

TAPPER'S TRAVELLING CIRCUS

'Hoo! I'll tell Mr Tapper what I think of him, coming into *my* field!' said Tink to himself. Mischief the monkey was on his shoulder, jogging up and down as Tink marched along, muttering furiously.

Four or five children from the caravans looked at him curiously as he marched along. One small boy rushed up to him, shouting in delight to see the monkey.

'A monkey, look, a monkey!' he cried. 'Much smaller than our chimp. What's he called, boy?'

'Mind your own business,' said Tink. 'Where's Mr Tapper?'

'Mr Tapper? Oh, you mean our grandad!' said the boy. 'He's over there, look, beside that big van. Better not talk to him now. He's busy!'

Tink walked over to the van and addressed the man there. He was rather fierce-looking and had a long, bushy beard, enormous eyebrows that hung down over his eyes, a rather small nose, and only one ear. He looked inquiringly down at Tink, and put out his hand to Mischief.

'My monkey might bite you,' said Tink, at once. 'He doesn't like strangers.'

'I'm no stranger to *any* monkey,' said the man, in a deep-down voice. 'There's isn't a monkey in the world, nor a chimp either, that wouldn't come to me if I called it. Nor a gorilla, see?'

'Well, *my* monkey won't come to you,' said Tink, angrily. 'But what I've come to say is . . .'

Before he could finish his sentence, the man made a curious noise in his throat – rather like Mischief did when he was pleased about anything. Mischief looked at the man in surprised delight – and then leapt straight from Tink's shoulder to his, nuzzling against his neck, making little crooning noises. Tink was so amazed that he stared without saying a word.

'See?' said the man. 'He's my little friend already. Don't gawp so, little fellow. I've trained the monkey family all my life. You lend me this little chap and I'll teach him to ride a small tricycle in two days.'

'Come here, Mischief!' said Tink, amazed and angry at the monkey's behaviour. But Mischief cuddled down still farther into the big man's neck. The man hauled him out and handed him to Tink.

'There you are,' he said. 'Nice little fellow he is. What is it you wanted to say to me?'

'I've come to say that this field belongs to my father, Professor Hayling,' said Tink. 'And you've no right to bring your caravans here. So please take them all out. My friends and I are planning to camp out here.'

'Well, I've no objection to that,' said the big man, good-temperedly. 'You choose your own corner, young man. If you don't interfere with us, we shan't interfere with you!'

A boy of about Tink's age came sidling up, and looked at Tink and Mischief with interest. 'Is he selling you that monkey, Grandad?' he asked.

'No I'm *not*!' almost shouted Tink. 'I came to tell you and your caravans to clear out. This field belongs to my family.'

'Ah, but we've an old licence to come here every ten years, and show our circus,' said the bearded man. 'And believe it or not, there's been a Tapper's circus in this field every ten years since the year 1648. So you just run home and make no silly fuss, young man.'

'You're a fibber!' cried Tink, losing his temper. 'I'll tell the police! I'll tell my father! I'll . . .'

'Don't you talk to my grandad like that!' shouted the boy, standing beside the old man. 'I'll hit you if you do!'

'I'll say what I like!' shouted Tink, his temper now quite lost. 'And just you shut up!'

The very next moment Tink found himself flat on his

back on the grass. The boy had shot out his fist and hit Tink in the chest! He struggled to his feet, red in the face, quite furious.

The old man fended him away. 'Don't you be silly now, boy,' he said. 'This youngster is a Tapper, like me, and he'll never give in. You go home and be sensible. We're not going to take notice of a hot-headed little kid like you. Our circus is coming in this here field, just like it has for years and years!'

He turned and walked to the nearest caravan. It was drawn by horses, and he clicked to them. They strained forward and the caravan followed. Others behind began to move too. The circus boy put his tongue out at Tink. 'Sucks to you!' he said. 'Nobody gets the better of my grandad – or of me either! Still – it was plucky of you to go for him. I enjoyed it.'

'Shut up!' said Tink, alarmed to find himself very near to tears. 'You just wait till my dad tells the police! You'll all go out much quicker than you came in – and one of these days I'll knock *you* down!'

He turned and ran back to the gate. He wondered what to do. He had so often heard his father say that the field behind their house belonged to him, and that he had let this or that farmer have the grazing rights for his horses and cattle. How *dare* the travelling circus come into his father's field?

'I'll tell Dad,' he said to Anne, who was waiting at the gate. '*He* ought to turn them out! It's *our* field and I love it, especially just now when it's so green and beautiful, and the hedges are just going to be covered in white may. I'll tell Dad the boy knocked me down – shot out his fist just like *that* – and down I went. I'd like to do the same to *him*!'

He went into the house, followed by a puzzled Anne. He looked into the sitting-room and saw George there.

'Tink! That boy knocked you down!' said Anne, in a horrified voice. 'Why did he do that?'

'Oh – just because I told his grandad to take his caravans away,' said Tink, feeling rather grand. 'He didn't hurt me at all – just punched me on the chest. Still – I said what I had gone to say.'

'But *will* they take the caravans away out of the field?' asked Anne.

'I told them I'd tell the police,' said Tink. 'So I bet they'll skedaddle. They haven't any right to be there. It's *our* field!'

'*Are* you going to the police?' asked George, disbelievingly. 'I really don't see why you have to make such a fuss about it all, Tink. They might make it difficult for *us* to go camping there.'

'But I tell you it's *my* field – Dad's always said so!' said Tink. 'He said it wasn't any use to him, so I could consider it my own. And I do. And we're going to camp in it, whatever anyone says! It's a travelling circus that's coming there, so the old man said.'

'Oh, Tink! How marvellous to have a circus at the bottom of the garden!' said George, her eyes shining, and Anne nodded too. Tink glared at them.

'Just like girls to say a thing like that!' he said. 'Would *you* want people trespassing all over a field that belonged to you, with horses neighing and tigers and lions roaring, and bears grunting, and chimpanzees stealing things – and nasty circus boys being rude all the time, ready to knock you down?'

'Oh, Tink! You *do* make it sound so exciting!' said George. 'Will there really be lions and tigers? Suppose one escaped – what a thrill!'

'Well – *I* shouldn't like that,' said Anne, at once. 'I don't particularly want a lion peering in at my window, or a bear clomping round my bedroom!'

'Neither do I,' said Tink, in a most decided voice. 'That's why I'm going to tell Dad about it. He's got the old document that sets out our rights to that field. He showed me it one day. I'll ask him about it, and if he'll let me see it, I'll take it straight to the police and let them turn out that rude old man and his horrible circus.'

'How do you *know* it's horrible?' asked George. 'It might be really good. I'm sure they'd let us camp in the corner nearest the garden, and we'd get a great view of what's going on all the time. Look – there's your father strolling down the path, smoking a pipe. He never does that if he's busy. It would be a good time to go and ask him about the document. He might even show it to us.'

'All right,' said Tink, rather sulkily. 'But you'll see I'm right. Come on.'

However, Tink proved to be quite, quite wrong! His father went to fetch the old, yellowed piece of parchment at once. 'Ha! Here it is!' he said. 'It's pretty valuable too, because it's so old. It dates back quite a few centuries.'

He undid the rather dirty piece of ribbon round it and unrolled it. Neither the girls nor Tink could read the old-fashioned lettering.

'What does it all say?' asked Anne, with great interest.

'It says that the field known as "Cromwell's Corner" is to be held by the Hayling Family for always,' said Professor Hayling. 'It was given to them by Cromwell because our family allowed them to camp in that field when they sorely needed a rest after battle. It's been ours ever since.'

'So *nobody* else is allowed to camp in it, or use it for grazing or anything, unless we say so!' said Tink, triumphantly.

'Quite right,' said his father. 'But wait a minute – I seem to remember an odd clause that said something about a travelling show – a show that had rights to camp in the field since about 1066. Not even Cromwell could alter that – it was in the original deeds, long before Cromwell battled in that district. Now let's see – that piece would come about the end, I expect.'

The two girls and Tink waited while the Professor pored over the old and beautiful lettering. He jabbed his finger on to three lines towards the end.

'Yes. There it is. I'll quote it. Listen! "And let it be known that Ye Travelling Show so-named 'Tapper's Travelling Show', which has always had camping rights, shall still have the right to claim these once every ten years so long as the show travels the country ways – Given under my hand . . ." and so on and so on. Well – I don't expect that Tapper's Travelling Show is going now, all these years and years after the document was drawn up and signed in the year 1648. See – here's the date – if you can read the old figures!'

The children stared at the date, and then glanced up at Tink. He looked angry and very red in the face. 'You might have told me all that before, Dad,' he said.

'Why?' asked his father, astonished. 'What possible interest can it have for you children?'

'Only that there's a circus called Tapper's Travelling Circus in that field this very minute,' said Anne. 'And the old man with it is called Tapper – and he said it was his right to be there, and . . .'

'He was rude to me and I want you to turn out this circus this very day!' said Tink. '*We* want to camp there.'

'I'm sure Mr Tapper would have no objection to you camping there,' said his father. 'Aren't you being rather silly, Tink? *You* weren't rude to any of the circus folk, were you?'

Tink went very red, turned his back and stalked out of the room, Mischief clinging to his neck. He rubbed his chest where the circus boy had punched him. 'Just you wait!' he said in a whisper. 'I'll punch *you* one day!'

'Anne, if you and the others want to camp in the field, I'll go and speak to Mr Tapper,' said the Professor, puzzled by Tink's behaviour.

'Oh no – it's all right,' said Anne, hastily. 'He has already said that it didn't matter if we camped there. Oh – there are the boys back again. I'll just go and see if they have brought back all our bicycles safely. Thank you for showing us that marvellous old document, Professor!'

And away she went looking rather hot and bothered!

CHAPTER SIX

Getting ready for camping out

DICK AND Julian were most interested to hear about Tink and the travelling circus – and the old, old document.

'You made a bit of a fool of yourself,' said Julian, looking at Tink. 'Still, there's no harm done, apparently. I vote we go and see where we can put up our tents. Personally, I shall be thrilled to see a bit of circus life so close to me! I wonder how they'll manage to put on a show. I suppose they've everything with them, and can put up a circus ring and a tent and anything else necessary.'

'There are a lot of big vans,' said Anne. 'I went down to have a look about half an hour ago. The field is almost full now, except for one corner near our hedge that I suppose they have left for our tents.'

'I saw the posters about the circus as we cycled back,' said Dick. 'Dead-Shot Dick – Chimpanzee that plays Cricket – the Boneless Man – Madelon and her Beautiful Horses – Monty and Winks, the Clowns – the Dancing Donkey – Mr Wooh, the Wonder Wizard – gosh, it sounded *quite* a circus. I'm glad we can camp in the same field – we shall really see behind the scenes, then.'

'Don't forget there was Charlie the Chimp, and the Bonzo Band,' said Julian. 'What fun if the chimp got loose and peeped in at the kitchen window!'

'It wouldn't be at *all* funny,' said Anne. 'Jenny would run for miles! So would Tink's monkey!'

'What about putting up our own tents after tea?' said Dick. 'Jim said he'd have them here by tea-time. It's hotter than ever today. I don't feel I can do much at the moment. I just want to laze.'

'Woof,' said Timmy, who was lying down with his head on his paws, panting.

'You feel the same, old chap, don't you?' said Julian, poking him with his toe. 'You're tired out with your long run back from Kirrin, aren't you?'

'The roads were so *dusty*!' said Dick. 'He kept sneezing whenever a car passed us, because the dust got up his nose. Poor old Tim. You really are tired out with that long, long run!'

'Woof!' said Tim, suddenly sitting up straight and pawing vigorously at George. Everyone laughed.

'He says he's not at *all* tired, he wants a walk,' chuckled Dick.

'Well, if he's not tired, I *am*,' said Julian. 'It really was a job sorting out all our things at Kirrin – and cycling all the way back. NO, Timmy – I am NOT going to take you for a walk!'

Timmy whined, and at once Mischief the monkey leapt down from Tink's shoulder and went to cuddle against the big dog, making small comforting noises. He even put his thin little arms round Timmy's neck!

'You're being just a *little* soppy, Mischief,' said Tink, but Mischief didn't care. His big friend was sad about something, or he wouldn't have whined. Timmy put out a big red tongue and licked the little creature delicately on his nose. Then he suddenly pricked up his ears, and sat straight up. He had heard a noise from somewhere. So had all the others.

'It's music of some kind,' said Anne. 'Oh – I believe I know what it is!'

'What?' said the others.

'It must be Tapper's Travelling Circus Band practising for opening night,' said Anne.

'Well, that's tomorrow,' yawned George. 'Yes – it does sound like a band. Maybe we shall see the bandsmen after tea, when we put up our tents. I'd like to see the Boneless Man, wouldn't you?'

'No!' said Anne. 'He'd be all limp and wriggly and horrid – like a worm or a jellyfish! I shan't go and see him. But I'd love to see the horses and the Dancing Donkey. Does he dance to the band, do you think?'

'We'll find out when we go,' said Dick, 'as it opens tomorrow. If Mr Tapper isn't annoyed about Tink trying to turn them out, he might let us wander round.'

'I don't think I want to come,' said Tink. 'Mr Tapper was rude – and that boy knocked me flat.'

'Well, I expect I'd do the same if I thought you were

being rude to *my* grandad,' said Julian, lazily. 'Now – it's settled, is it, that we go down with our things to the field after tea, and see if we can put up our tents in some sheltered corner?'

'Yes,' said everyone. Dick idly tickled Mischief's nose with a thin blade of grass. The monkey sneezed at once, and then again. He rubbed his little paw across his nose and stared disapprovingly at Dick. Then he sneezed once more.

'Borrow a hanky, old thing,' said Julian. And, to everyone's intense amusement, Mischief leapt across to Dick and neatly pulled his handkerchief out of his pocket! Then he pretended to blow his nose.

Everyone roared with laughter, and Mischief was delighted. 'You'll be stolen to act in a circus one day, if you behave like that!' said Dick, snatching back his hanky. 'The Pickpocket Monkey!'

'He'd be very good in a circus,' said Julian.

'I'd *never* let him join a circus!' said Tink at once. 'He might have a dreadful life.'

'No. I don't think he would,' said Julian. 'Circus folk love their animals and are proud of them. And after all, if they treated them unkindly, the animals wouldn't be happy or healthy, and couldn't enjoy their acts. *Most* circus people treat their animals like one of the family.'

'What! Even a chimpanzee!' said Anne, in horror.

'They're nice creatures – and very clever,' said Julian. 'Mischief, do *not* remove my handkerchief, please. It was funny the first time, but *not* a second time. Look at him now, trying to undo Timmy's collar.'

'Come and sit quietly by me, Mischief,' ordered Tink, and the little creature obediently went to him and cuddled on to his knee, making a soft, crooning noise.

'You're a humbug,' said Tink, fondling him. 'You be careful I don't give you away to the circus, and get an elephant in exchange!'

'Idiot!' said Dick, and everyone laughed at the thought of Tink and an elephant. What in the world would he do with it?

A voice called from the house. 'Tink! Jim's here with all the camping things. He's put them in the hall, *just* where your father will fall over them. You'd better come and see to them now.'

'In a few minutes, Jenny!' called back Tink. 'We're busy.'

'You're a real fibber, Tink,' said Dick. 'We are *not* busy. You could easily go to find out where the things are, and see if they're all there. There are quite a lot.'

'We'll go in twenty minutes or so,' said Anne, yawning. 'I bet Tink's father is asleep this hot afternoon. He won't stir out of his study.'

But she was wrong. Professor Hayling was wide awake, and when he had finished his work, he wanted a drink of very cold water. He threw open his study door, strode out towards the kitchen – and fell over a pile of all kinds of camping gear, bringing them down with a tremendous noise.

Jenny rushed out of the kitchen with loud screams of fright, and the Professor bellowed in anger as he took a ground-sheet off his head, and a tent-pole off his back. 'What ARE these things? I will NOT have them in the hall! Jenny! JENNY! Take them down to the bonfire and burn the lot!'

'Our camping things!' cried George, listening in horror. 'Quick! We must get them! Oh, I do hope Tink's father hasn't hurt himself. Bother, bother, bother!'

While Julian and Dick deftly removed everything that had fallen on to the angry Professor and took it all down the garden, Anne and George comforted him, and made such a fuss of him that he began to feel decidedly less angry. He sat down in a chair and wiped his forehead. 'I hope you've taken all those things down to the bottom of the garden,' he said after a while.

'Yes,' said Tink, truthfully. 'Er – they're all by the bonfire, but it's not lit yet.'

'I light it myself tomorrow,' said his father, and Tink heaved a sigh of relief. His father would forget, of course – and anyhow, everything was going to be taken into the camping field after tea.

'Have a cup of nice hot tea,' said Jenny, appearing with a tray of tea-things. 'Sit down and drink this. It's newly made. Best thing to have after a fall and a shock.'

She turned and whispered crossly to Tink, 'Didn't I call to you and tell you the Professor would trip over those things, the poor man? Now you just get your own tea, while I take him into the dining-room and comfort him with a nice hot scone, and a cup of tea!'

'I'll get *our* tea,' said Anne. 'Then we'll set up the tents down in the field, and enjoy ourselves. And Tink, don't you get into any more trouble with the circus folk.'

'I'll see he doesn't,' said George, firmly. 'Come on – let's go down to the field while Anne gets the tea. I could do with a bun or two!'

Between them, Dick and Julian had lugged all the things down the garden – two tents, ground-sheets, blankets, tent-pegs and all the rest. Timmy ran with them in excitement, wondering what all the fuss was about. Mischief, of course, leapt to the top of whatever was being carried, and chattered excitedly all the way down the garden.

He got into trouble when he ran off with a tent-peg, but Timmy managed to catch him and make him drop it. Then, very solemnly, Timmy carried the tent-peg to Julian.

'Good dog!' said Julian. 'Just keep an eye on that wicked little monkey, Tim, will you? There are all sorts of things he might run off with!'

So Timmy kept an eye on Mischief, nosing him away whenever he thought the monkey was going to pick up something he shouldn't. Finally Mischief became tired of Timmy's nose and leapt on his back, where, clinging to the dog's collar, he rode just as if he were on horseback. 'Only it's dogback, not horseback,' said George, with a laugh.

'They would make quite a good pair for the circus,' said Dick. 'I bet Mischief could hold on to reins, if Timmy had any!'

'Well, he's not *going* to have any,' said George. 'The next thing would be a whip! Whew! What a lot of things we've got – is that the lot?'

It was, thank goodness. A bell rang out from the house at that moment, and everyone heaved a sigh of relief.

'Tea at last!' said Dick. 'I could drink a whole potful. Come on – we've finished piling up all the things. We'll get busy after tea with them. I can't do a thing more. Don't you agree, Timmy?'

'WOOF!' said Timmy, heartily, and galloped up the

garden path at top speed, with Mischief scampering after him.

'Talk about a circus!' said Dick. 'We've a ready-made one here! All right, Anne – we're coming! We're coming!'

CHAPTER SEVEN

In the circus field

Nobody wanted to spend a long time over tea. They all longed to go down to the field and set up their little camp.

'We shall have a wonderful look-in at what goes on in a circus camp,' said Dick. 'We shall be living so near the circus folk! I do hope Mischief won't get too friendly with the people there. They might take him away with them when they leave.'

'*Indeed* they won't!' said Tink, fiercely. 'What a thing to say! As if Mischief would go with them, anyhow! I don't expect he'll mix with the circus crowd at all.'

'You wait and see!' grinned Dick. 'Now buck up with your tea – I'm longing to go and set our camp in the field, and see what's going on there.'

It wasn't long before they were ready. They were soon down by the fence, and gazed over it in amazement. Great vans were in the field, all with Mr Tapper's name on and all painted in bright colours. There were caravans too, much smaller than the great vans, and these had windows, each with neat lace curtains. The circus folk lived in the caravans, of course, and George found herself wishing that she herself could go about in one, instead of living in a house that couldn't move anywhere!

'Look at the horses!' cried Dick, as a bunch of them appeared with tossing heads and beautiful long thick tails. The boy who had knocked Tink down was with them, whistling. They were all coming from a big horse-van, and were delighted to be in a field with lush green grass.

'Is that gate properly shut?' yelled an enormous voice, and the boy yelled back, 'Yes, Grandad. I shut it. There's nowhere the horses can get out. Don't they like this grass!'

Then he saw Julian and the others all looking over the fence, and waved to them. 'See our horses? Aren't they a great lot?'

And, just to show off a little, he leapt on to the back of the nearest one, and went all round the edge of the field with it. George watched him enviously. If only *she* could have a horse like that!

'Well, let's take our camp things into the field,' said Tink. 'The nearer we are to the circus the better. We ought to have some fun.'

He climbed over the fence and Dick followed. 'I'll hand everything over,' said Julian. 'George can help me – she's a strong old thing!'

George grinned. She loved to hear anyone say that! It was quite a job getting some of the things over the fence. The tents, neatly wrapped though they were, were heavy, awkward things to handle, but at last everything was safely over, lying on the grass.

Then Julian, Anne and George climbed over the fence too, and stood in the field, looking round for a good corner to set up their things.

'What about near those bushes over there?' said Julian. 'There's that big tree behind as well to protect us from the wind – and we aren't *too* near the circus folk – they might not like us right on top of them – and yet we're near enough to see what's going on.'

'Oh, it's going to be *fun*!' said Anne, her eyes shining.

'I think I'd better go and find the old grandad – Mr Tapper,' said Julian. 'Just to tell him we're here, in case he thinks we're intruders and have no right to be here.'

'You haven't got to ask his permission for us to be in *my* field!' said Tink, at once.

'Now don't keep flying off the handle like that, Tink,' said Julian. 'This is merely a question of good manners – something you don't seem to know much about! How do we know that the circus folk won't resent us camping so near them? Much better to show ourselves friendly from the start.'

'All right, all right,' said Tink, sulkily. 'But it is *my* field, after all! You'll be telling me to be friends with that nasty circus boy next!'

'Well, you'd better be – else he might knock you flat again!' said George. 'Anyway, be sensible, Tink – it's not often people have a circus just at the bottom of their garden, and can pop over the fence and mix with the circus folk.'

Julian walked over to the nearest caravan. It was empty – no one answered his knock.

'What you want, mister?' called a high little voice, and a small girl with tangled, untidy hair came running up.

'Where's Mr Tapper?' asked Julian, smiling at the bright-eyed little thing.

'He's with one of the horses,' said the small girl. 'Who are you?'

'We're your neighbours,' said Julian. 'Will you take us to Mr Tapper?'

'Old Grandad's this way,' said the child, and slipped a dirty little hand into Julian's. 'I'll show you. I like you.'

She led the children to the middle of the camp. A mournful howl came from somewhere behind them and George stopped suddenly. 'That's Timmy! He must have found out that we've got out of the garden. I'll go back for him.'

'Better not,' said Julian. 'There might be ructions if he met the chimpanzee. A big chimp would make mincemeat of him!'

'It *wouldn't*!' said George, but all the same she didn't go back to fetch Timmy. Julian hoped that the dog wouldn't jump over the fence and come to find them.

'There's old Grandad Tapper on those steps,' said the

little girl, smiling up at Julian, whose hand she still held. 'I like you, mister.' Then she shouted loudly to the old fellow sitting on the steps of a nearby caravan. 'Grandad! Here's folks to see you!'

Grandad was looking at a beautiful chestnut-brown horse, tethered close to him. He had one of the horse's hooves in his hand. The children stood and gazed at him – black beard, frowning eyebrows – and, 'Oh dear!' thought Anne. 'Only one ear, poor man. What *could* have happened to the missing one?'

'GRANDAD!' called the girl again. 'SOME FOLKS TO SEE YOU!'

Mr Tapper looked round, his eyes very bright under his black eyebrows. He set the horse's hoof down, and gave the lovely creature a pat. 'You don't need to limp any more, my beauty,' he said. 'I've taken out the stone that was in your hoof. You can dance again!'

The horse lifted up its magnificent head and neighed as if it were saying thank you. Tink almost jumped out of his skin, and Mischief slipped from his shoulder and cuddled under his arm in terror.

'Now, now, little monkey, don't you know a horse's voice when you hear one?' said Grandad, and Mischief poked his head out from under Tink's arm to listen.

'Does that horse *really* dance?' said Anne, longing to stroke its long, smooth nose.

'Dance! It's one of the finest dancing horses in the

world!' said Grandad, and began to whistle a lively little tune. The horse pricked up its ears, gazed at Grandad, and then began to dance! The children watched in astonishment.

There it went, round and round, nodding its head to the tune, its feet tapping the grass in perfect time to Grandad's whistling.

'Oh, the lovely thing!' said George. 'Do *all* your horses dance as well as this one?'

'Yes. Some a good deal better,' said Grandad. 'This one has a fair ear for music, but not as good an ear as some. You wait till you see them dressed up, with feathery plumes nodding on their heads. Horses – there's nothing in the world as beautiful as a good horse.'

'Mr Tapper – we come from the house over the fence there,' said Julian, feeling that it was time to explain their visit. 'As you probably know, Tink's father owns this field, and . . .'

'Yes, yes – but we have an old right to come every so often,' said the old man, raising his voice. 'Now don't you start arg . . .'

'I haven't come to argue with you,' said Julian, politely. 'I've only just come to say that we – that is my friends here and I – would like to come and camp in this field, but we shouldn't annoy you in any way, and . . .'

'Oh well – if that's what you want, you're more than welcome!' said the old man. 'More than welcome! I thought maybe you'd think you could turn us out – like that youngster there would like to do!' And he nodded at Tink.

Tink went red and said nothing. The old man laughed. 'Ha! My grandson didn't think much of that idea, did he, youngster? He hit out, and down you went on your back. He's got a temper, he has, young Jeremy. But another time maybe he'll find himself on *his* back, eh?'

'Yes. He will,' said Tink, at once.

'Right. Well, you'll be even with one another then, and you can shake hands like gentlemen,' said the old man, his eyes twinkling. 'Now – what about you bringing your gear right into the field, and setting up your tents? I'll get old Charlie the Chimp to help you. He's as strong as ten men!'

'The *chimpanzee*! Is he tame enough to help us to put up our *tents*?' said Anne, disbelievingly.

'Old Charlie is cleverer than all of you put together, and as tame as you are!' said Grandad. 'And he could beat you three boys at cricket any day! You bring your bat along one morning and watch him. I'll call him to help you. CHARLIE! CHARLIE! Where are you? Snoozing I suppose!'

But no Charlie came. 'You go and fetch him,' said the old man, pointing to a corner of the field where stood a big, strong cage, with a tarpaulin roof to keep out the rain. 'He'll do anything you want him to do, so long as you give him a word of praise now and again!'

'Let's get him, Ju,' said Dick, eagerly. 'Fancy having a chimpanzee to help us!'

And off they all went to the great cage. CHARLIE! CHARLIE! Wake up, you're wanted! CHARLIE!

CHAPTER EIGHT

Charlie the Chimp is a help!

TINK CAME to the big cage first. He peered inside. Charlie the Chimp was there all right, sitting at the back of his cage, his brown eyes looking at the children with curiosity. He got up and went over to where Tink was peering in and pressed his nose against the strong wire, almost against Tink's. Then he blew hard and Tink backed away, surprised and cross.

'He *blew* at me!' he said to the others, who were laughing at Tink's disgust. The chimp made a funny noise that Mischief the monkey immediately tried to imitate. The chimpanzee stared at Mischief, then he grew very excited. He rattled his cage, jumped up and down, and made some very odd noises indeed.

A boy came running up at once. It was the boy who had knocked Tink down. 'Hey – what are you doing to the chimp?' he called. 'Oh – aren't you the boy who shouted at my grandad – the one I knocked down?'

'Yes. And don't you dare try that on again, or you'll be sorry!' said Tink in a fierce voice.

'Shut up, Tink,' said Julian. He turned to the boy. 'Your name's Jeremy, isn't it?' he said. 'Well, we've just been talking to your grandad over there, and he said we could get the chimpanzee to help us with our camping gear. It's all right for him to come out of his cage, isn't it?'

'Oh yes – I take him out two or three times a day,' said Jeremy. 'He gets bored in his cage. He'd love to help put up your tents – he's always helping us with things like that. He's as strong as a lion.'

'Is he – er – is he safe?' asked Dick, eyeing the big animal doubtfully.

'Safe? What do you mean – safe?' asked Jeremy, surprised. 'He's as safe as I am! Charlie, come on out! Go on, you can undo your cage perfectly well, you know you can!'

The chimpanzee made a funny little chuckling noise, put his hand through the wire, reached the bolt, pulled it, took his hand back – and pushed open the cage door.

'See! Easy, isn't it?' said Jeremy, grinning. 'Charlie boy, come along. Your help's wanted!'

Charlie lumbered out of his cage, and went with the children to where they had left their tents and ground-sheets and the rest. He walked with his fists on the ground in a most inelegant manner, making a funny little groaning noise all the time. Mischief was rather afraid of him, and kept well to the back – but the chimpanzee suddenly turned round, caught hold of Mischief, and sat him up on his shoulder! Mischief held on, not knowing whether to be scared or jubilant!

'I wish I had my camera here,' said Anne to George. 'Just look at them – Mischief is as pleased as can be!'

They arrived at the pile of camping gear. 'Carry this, Charlie, and follow us,' ordered Jeremy. The chimp grabbed at this, that and the other, and, with his great arms full, followed the children to where they thought they could camp, with the great tree to shelter them from the wind.

'Drop those things, Charlie,' said Jeremy, 'and go back for the rest. Buck up. Don't stand there staring! You've got work to do!'

But Charlie still crouched there, staring straight at Mischief. 'Oh! He wants Mischief the monkey to go with him!' cried George. 'Go on, Mischief, have a ride again!'

Mischief leapt up on to the chimpanzee's shoulders. Charlie put up a great paw to steady him and then lumbered off to fetch the rest of the things. One of the ground-sheets came undone and slithered over his head like a tent, so that he couldn't see where he was going. In a rage he leapt on it and began to jump up and down, up and down, growling most terrifyingly. The children felt rather scared.

'Charlie, don't be silly!' said Jeremy, and pulled it away from him, rolling it up swiftly. The chimpanzee could manage it then, and his good temper immediately came back again.

Everything was soon piled up in one place, and Julian and Dick began to put up the tents. Charlie watched them with the greatest interest, and helped most intelligently when he saw that he could.

'He's a good sort, isn't he?' said Jeremy, proud that his friend the chimpanzee could show off like this. 'Did you see him put that tent-pole in exactly the right place? And you ought to see him fetch the pails of water for the horses each day. He carries a full pail in each hand!'

'He ought to get wages,' said Tink.

'He does!' said Jeremy. 'He gets eight bananas a day and as many oranges as he likes. And he loves sweets!'

'Oh! I think I've got some!' said Tink and delved into one of his pockets. He brought up a peculiar mixture of things, among which was a screwed-up sweet bag. Inside was a mass of half-melted boiled sweets.

'You can't give him *those*!' said Anne. 'They're old and sticky and messy!'

But Charlie thought differently. He took the paper bag straight out of Tink's hand, sniffed it – and then put the whole thing into his mouth at once!

'He'll choke!' said Julian.

'Not Charlie!' said Jeremy. 'Let him be. He'll go straight back to his cage, get in, shoot the bolt and sit there sucking sweets till they're gone. He'll be as happy as can be.'

'Well – he certainly deserved a reward,' said George. 'He did all the heavy work! Come on, let's finish putting everything straight. Hey – won't it be fun sleeping out in tents tonight! We'd better have supper first.'

'You can come and join *us*, if you like,' said Jeremy. 'We don't have posh food like you, of course – but it's good food, all the same. Old Grandma cooks it in her pot. She's two hundred years old.'

The children laughed in disbelief. 'Two hundred! Nobody lives as long as that!' said George.

'Well, that's what she tells everyone,' said Jeremy. 'And

she looks it, too! But her eyes are as sharp as needles still! Shall I tell her you'll be here to supper?'

'Well – would there be enough for so many extra?' said Julian. 'We meant to bring our own meal. Should we bring that and share everything with you? We've more than enough. Jenny said she would have it all ready for us to bring down tonight – a meat pie, cold sausages, and apples and bananas.'

'Sh! Don't say bananas in front of Charlie,' said Jeremy. 'He'll worry you for them all the time. All right – you bring your food and we'll share with you round our camp-fire. I'll tell old Grandma. We're having a sing-song tonight, and Fred the Fiddler's playing his fiddle. Ah, that fiddle! Its tunes get into your feet and away you go!'

This all sounded very exciting. Julian thought they ought to go back home before anyone began to be worried about their complete disappearance, and pack up the food for supper that night.

'We'll be back as soon as we can,' said he. 'And thanks a lot for all your help. Come on, Mischief. Say goodbye to Charlie for the moment, and don't look so gloomy. We're coming back here tonight!'

They all went back over the fence, feeling a little tired now, but full of their plans for the evening. 'It's almost like *belonging* to the circus, going back to sit round a camp-fire and eat supper from that old black stewpot on the fire,' said Tink. 'I bet the supper will taste delicious. I hope Dad won't mind us popping off to the circus camp.'

'I don't expect he'll even notice that we've gone,' said George. 'My father never notices things like that. Sometimes he doesn't even notice when people are there, in front of his nose!'

'Well, that must be useful at times if they're people he doesn't like,' said Tink. 'Now – let's see what Jenny's got that we can take back with us.'

Jenny listened wide-eyed to all they had to say. 'Well, well, well!' she said. 'Camping out with the circus folk! Whatever next? I'd like to know what your parents would think of *that*!'

'We'll ask them, next time we see them,' said Julian, with a grin. 'What do you have for our supper? We're taking it down to our camp.'

'I thought maybe you'd do that,' said Jenny. 'It's all cold. A meat pie, cold sausages, a cucumber and lettuce hearts and tomatoes, rolls, and apples and bananas. Will that be enough?'

'Gosh, yes,' said Tink, thrilled. 'What about something to drink?'

'You can take lemonade or orangeade with you, whichever you like,' said Jenny. 'But listen now – don't go bursting into your father's workroom. He's worked hard all day, and he's tired.'

'And cross, I expect,' said Tink. 'People are always cross when they're tired. Except you, dear, dear Jenny.'

'Ha! You want something else out of my cupboard, calling me your dear, dear Jenny,' she said with a twinkle.

'Could we have some sugar lumps?' asked Tink. 'Oh, Jenny, there are the loveliest horses you ever saw down in the circus field. I want to give them a sugar lump each.'

'And yourself a few as well!' said Jenny. 'All right. I'll pack up everything for you, and give you a few enamel plates and mugs and knives. What about Timmy? Doesn't he want a meal too?'

'Wuff!' said Timmy, glad that someone had remembered him. Jenny patted his big head. 'It's all ready in the larder for you,' she said. 'George, you go and get it. He must be hungry.'

George fetched a plate of meat and biscuits from the larder and Timmy fell on it with happy little barks. Yes – he was very, *very* hungry!

At last all the food was ready, packed to take down the garden to the field. What a lot there seemed! Well, they would certainly have plenty to spare for their circus friends. They said good night to Jenny, and set off down the garden again. They thought they had better not disturb Professor Hayling.

'He might be cross and forbid us to go and eat with the circus folk,' said Tink. 'Mischief, come off that basket, and don't pretend you weren't fishing in it for a banana. And please put on your best table manners tonight, or Charlie the Chimp will be ashamed of you!'

It was fun going back down the garden and over the fence into the field again. The sun was sinking fast and soon the shadows would fall. How lovely to sit round a fire and eat supper with the kindly circus folk – and perhaps to sing old songs with them – and hear Fred the Fiddler fiddle his old, old tunes! What fun to creep into a tent, and sleep with the cries of owls around, and stars shining in at the tent opening!

There they go, over the fence, handing the food one to another. Take your paw out of that basket, Mischief! That's right, Timmy, nibble his ear if he's as mischievous as his name! You're all going to have some fun tonight!

CHAPTER NINE

A wonderful evening

AS SOON as Jeremy saw the visitors climbing over the fence, he ran to help them. He was very excited at the thought of having guests. He took them over to old Grandad first, to be welcomed.

'Now I expect your friends will like to see round a bit,' said Grandad. 'Charlie the Chimp can go with you. We've a rehearsal on tonight, so the ring has been set up. You can watch some of the show.'

This was great news. The children saw that curved pieces of painted wood had been set together to make a great ring in the field, and as they went across the grass, the Musical Horses began to troop into the ring, the leading one ridden by Madelon, a lovely girl dressed in shimmering gold.

'How beautiful they are!' thought Anne, as she watched. 'Look at their great feathery plumes, nodding on their magnificent heads.'

The Bonzo Band struck up just then, and the horses at once trotted in perfect time to the music. The band looked a little peculiar as the bandsmen had not put on their smart uniforms. They were saving those for the opening night!

The horses trotted prettily out of the ring after two or three rounds, the beautiful Madelon on the leading horse. Then in came Fred the Fiddler and played his violin for a few minutes. First the music was slow and solemn, then Fred began to play quickly, and the children found themselves jigging about, up and down and round about. 'I can't keep still!' panted Anne. 'The tune's got into my feet.'

Charlie the Chimp came up just then, walking on hind legs, and looking unexpectedly tall. He usually walked on all fours. He began to jig about too, looking very funny. He ran right into the ring and put his arms round Fred the Fiddler's legs. 'He loves Fred,' said Jeremy. 'Now he's going to rehearse his cricket act. I must go and bowl to him.'

And off went Jeremy into the ring. The chimpanzee rushed over to him and hugged him. A bat was thrown into the ring, and Charlie picked it up and made a few swipes into the air with it, making delighted noises all the time.

Then a cricket ball was thrown to Jeremy, who caught it deftly. A small girl appeared from somewhere and set up three stumps for a wicket. 'Can't find the bails, Jeremy!' she called. 'Have you got them in your pocket?'

'No,' said Jeremy. 'Never mind, I'll knock the stumps right over!'

But that wasn't so easy with Charlie the Chimp at the wicket! He took a terrific swipe at the ball and it went right over Jeremy's head, too high to catch. The chimp lost his balance and sat down on the wicket, knocking the stumps out of the ground.

'OUT!' yelled Jeremy, but the chimp wasn't having that. He carefully put up the stumps again, and then set himself in front once more, waggling the bat.

It was the funniest cricket that the children had ever seen! The chimpanzee was very, very clever with the bat, and sent poor Jeremy running all over the place. Then he chased the boy all round the ring with the bat, making curious chortling noises. The children didn't know if he was amused or angry! Finally he threw the bat at Jeremy and walked off, scratching himself under one arm.

The children roared with laughter at him. 'He's as good as any clown!' said Dick. 'Jeremy, does he do this cricket act every night when the circus is open?'

'Oh yes – and sometimes he hits the ball into the audience,' said Jeremy. 'There's great excitement then. Sometimes, for a treat, we let one of the boys in the audience come down and bowl to Charlie. One bowled him right out once, and Charlie was so cross that he chased him all round the ring three times – just as he chased *me* just now. The boy didn't like it much!'

Charlie came up to Jeremy and put his great arms round him, trying to swing him off the ground. 'Stop that, Charlie,' said Jeremy, wriggling free. 'Look out – here comes the Dancing Donkey! Better get out of the ring – goodness knows what antics *he'll* be up to!'

In came the Dancing Donkey. He was dark grey, and tossed his head as he came galloping in. He stood and looked round at everyone. Then he sat down, lifted up a leg and scratched his nose. The children stared in astonishment. They had never in their lives seen a donkey do *that* before! Then, when the band suddenly began to play, the donkey stood up and listened, flapping his ears first one way and then another, and nodding his head in time to the music.

The band changed its tune to a march. The donkey listened again, and then began to march round the ring in perfect time – clip-clop-clip-clop-clip-clop. Then it apparently felt tired, and sat down heavily on its back legs.

The children couldn't help laughing. The donkey got up, and somehow its back legs became entangled with its front ones and it fell down, looking most ridiculous.

'Has it hurt itself?' asked Anne, anxiously. 'Oh dear – it will break one of its legs if it goes on like this. Look, it can't untangle them, Jeremy.'

The donkey gave a mournful bray, tried to get up, and flopped down again. The band changed its tune, and the donkey leapt up at once, and began to do a kind of tap dance – clickety-click, clickety-click, clickety-click – it was marvellous!

'I shouldn't have thought that a donkey could possibly have been taught to tap dance,' said George.

Soon the donkey seemed to feel tired again. It stopped dancing, but the band still went on playing. The donkey ran towards it and stamped a foot.

A weird voice suddenly came from it. 'Too fast! TOO FAST!' But the band took no notice and went on playing. The donkey bent down, wriggled hard – and its head fell off on to the grass in the ring! Anne gave a shriek of fright.

'Don't be an idiot, Anne,' said Dick. 'You didn't think the donkey was a *real* one, did you?'

'*Isn't* it?' said Anne, relieved. 'It looks *just* like that donkey that used to give rides to children on Kirrin beach.'

The donkey now split in half and a small man climbed out of each half, both taking their legs carefully out of the donkey's legs. The donkey-skin fell to the ground and lay there, flat and collapsed.

'Wish *I* had a donkey-skin like that,' said Tink. 'I've got a friend at school who could be the back legs and I'd be the front legs. The things we'd do!'

'Well, I must say you'd make a first-class donkey, the way you behave sometimes,' said George. 'Look, this must be Dead-Shot Dick coming on.'

But before Dead-Shot Dick could do any of his shooting tricks, the two donkey-men had run to the band and begun a loud argument with them.

'Why play so fast? You *know* we can't do our tricks at top speed. Are you trying to mess up our turn?'

The bandleader shouted something back. It must have been rude, because one of the donkey-men shook his fist and began to run towards the band.

A loud voice crashed in on the argument and made everyone jump. It was Mr Tapper, old Grandad, giving his orders in an enormous voice.

'ENOUGH! You, Pat, and you, Jim, get out of the ring. I give the orders, not you. ENOUGH, I SAY!'

The two donkey-men glared at him, but did not dare to say a word more. They stalked out of the ring, taking the donkey-skin with them.

Dead-Shot Dick looked very ordinary, dressed in a rather untidy flannel suit. 'He's not going to go all through his act,' said Jeremy. 'You'll see him another night, when the show's on for the public – he shoots at all kinds of things – even a sixpenny bit dangling on a long string from the roof – and never misses! He's got a smashing rig-out too – sequins sewn all over his trousers and jersey – and his little horse is a wonder – goes round and round the ring and never turns a hair when Dead-Shot Dick fires his gun! Look – there he is, peeping in to see if Dick's coming back to him.'

A small white horse was looking anxiously at the ring, its eyes fixed on Dead-Shot Dick. It pawed the ground as if to say, 'Buck up! I'm waiting for you! Am I to come on or not?'

'All right, Dick – you can go off now,' shouted Grandad. 'I hear your horse has hurt a foot – give him a good rest tonight. We'll want him on tomorrow.'

'Right, sir!' said Dead-Shot Dick. He saluted smartly, and ran off to his little horse.

'What's next, Jeremy?' asked George, who was enjoying everything very much.

'Don't know. Let's see – there's the acrobats – but the trapeze-swings aren't put up yet, so they won't come on tonight. And there's the Boneless Man – look, there he is. Good old Boney! I like him. He's free with his money, he is, not like some of the other folk!'

The Boneless Man looked very peculiar. He was remarkably thin, and remarkably tall. He walked in, looking quite extraordinary. 'He can't be boneless!' said Dick. 'He couldn't walk if he was!'

But the Boneless Man soon began to seem absolutely

boneless. His legs gave way at the knees, and his ankles turned over so that he sank down to the ground, unable to walk. He could bend his arms all kinds of different ways, and turned his head almost completely round on his neck. He did a few peculiar things with his apparently boneless body, and finally wriggled along the ground exactly like a snake!

'He'll be dressed in a sort of snake-skin when he does his act properly,' said Jeremy. 'Funny, isn't he?'

'How on earth does he do it?' wondered Julian amazed. 'He bends his arms and legs all the wrong ways! Mine would break if I did that!'

'Oh, it's easy for *him*!' said Jeremy. 'It's just that he's completely double-jointed – he can bend his arms both ways, and his legs both ways, and make them seem so loose that it looks as if he really *is* boneless. He's a nice chap. You'd like him.'

Anne felt a bit doubtful. What strange people made up a circus! It was a world of its own. She jumped suddenly as there came the sound of a trumpet blowing loudly.

'That's for supper,' said Jeremy, gleefully. 'Come on – let's go to old Grandma and her pot! Buck up, all of you!'

CHAPTER TEN

Round the camp-fire

JEREMY LED the way out of the circus ring. It had been well-lit, and the night seemed very dark outside the ring. They went over the field to where a large fire was burning, cleverly set about with stones. An enormous cooking pot was hung over it, and a very, very nice smell came to their noses as they went near.

Old Grandma was there, of course, and she began stirring the pot when she saw them. 'You've been a long time in the ring,' she grumbled to Grandad. 'Anything gone wrong?'

'No,' said Grandad, and sniffed the air. 'I'm hungry. That smells good. Jeremy, help your grandma.'

'Yes, Grandad,' said Jeremy, and took a pile of plates to the old lady, who at once began ladling out pieces of meat and potatoes and vegetables from the steaming pot. Old Grandad turned to Julian.

'Well – did you like our little rehearsal?' he asked.

'Oh *yes*!' said Julian. 'I'm only sorry you didn't rehearse *all* the turns. I badly wanted to see the acrobats and the clowns. Are they here? I can't see them.'

'Oh yes – there's one clown over there – look – with Madelon, who had the horses,' said Grandad.

The children looked – and were very disappointed. 'Is he a *clown*?' said Dick, disbelievingly. 'He doesn't look a bit funny. He looks miserable.'

'That's Monty all right,' said Grandad. 'He always looks like that out of the ring. He'll make you double up with laughter when the circus is on – he's a born clown. But a lot of clowns are like Monty when they're not performing – not much to say for themselves, and looking miserable. Winks is a bit livelier – that's him, pulling Madelon's hair. He'll get a smacked face in a minute – he's a real tease. There – I knew he'd get a clip on the ear!'

Winks went howling over to the children, boohooing most realistically. 'She smacked me!' he said. 'And she's got such p-p-p-pretty hair!'

The children couldn't help laughing. Mischief ran to the clown, jumped up on his shoulder and chattered comforting monkey words into his ear. Charlie the Chimp let himself out of his cage, and came to put his great paw into Winks' hand. They both thought that Winks really was hurt.

'That's enough, Winks,' said Grandad. 'You'll have the horses comforting you next! You do that in the ring tomorrow when we open, and you'll bring the house down. Sit down and have your supper.'

'Mr Tapper,' said Julian. 'There's another member of your circus we didn't see at the rehearsal – and that's Mr Wooh, the Wonder Magician. Why wasn't he there?'

'Oh, he never rehearses,' said Mr Tapper. 'He keeps himself to himself, does Mr Wooh. He may come and join us for supper, and he may not. As we're opening the circus tomorrow night, maybe he'll turn up tonight. He's Charlie's owner, you know? I'm a bit scared of him, to tell you the truth.'

'But he's not a *real* wizard, is he?' asked Tink.

'Well, when I talk to Mr Wooh I feel as if he is,' said Mr Tapper. 'There isn't a thing he doesn't know about figures, there isn't a thing he can't do with them. Ask him to multiply any number by any other number, running into dozens of figures, and he'll tell you in a second. He shouldn't be in a circus. He should be an inventor of some sort – an inventor whose invention needs pages and pages of figures. He'd be happy then.'

'He sounds a bit like my father,' said Tink. '*He's* an inventor, you know, and sometimes when I creep into his study I see papers *full* of millions of tiny figures and plans and diagrams with tiny figures all over them too.'

'Very interesting,' said Grandad. 'Your father and Mr Wooh ought to meet. They would probably talk figures all day long! My word – what's that you're handing round, young lady?'

'Some of the food *we* brought,' said Anne. 'Have a sausage or two, Mr Tapper – and a roll – and a tomato.'

'Well, thanks,' said Mr Tapper, pleased. 'Very kind of you. Nice to have met you all. You might be able to teach Jeremy a few manners!'

'Grandad – here's Mr Wooh!' said Jeremy, suddenly, and got up. Everyone turned round. *So this* was Mr Wooh, the Wonder Magician. Well, he certainly looked the part.

He stood there, with a half-smile on his face, tall, commanding and handsome. His hair was thick and black as soot, his eyes gleamed in the firelight, half hidden by great eyebrows, and he wore a thin, pointed beard. He had a curiously deep voice, and spoke with an accent.

'So we have visitors this night?' he said, and showed a row of gleaming white teeth in a quick smile. 'May I join you?'

'Oh do, Mr Wooh,' said Anne, delighted to have the

chance of talking to a Wonder Magician. 'We've brought plenty of food. Do you like cold sausage – and tomato – and a roll?'

'Most deelicious!' said the magician, and sat down cross-legged to join the group.

'We were disappointed not to see you at the rehearsal,' said Dick. 'I'd have liked to hear you doing all kinds of wizard sums in your head, as quick as lightning!'

'My father can do that too,' said Tink proudly. 'He's a wizard at figures as well. He's an inventor.'

'Ha! An inventor? And what does he invent?' asked Mr Wooh, eating his roll.

That was enough to set Tink describing at once how wonderful his father was. 'He can invent *any*thing he's asked for,' said the boy, proudly. 'He invented a wonderful thing for keeping aeroplanes dead straight in the right direction – better than any idea before. He invented the sko-wheel, if you know what that is – and the electric trosymon, if you've ever heard of that. I don't suppose you have, though. They're too . . .'

'Wait, boy!' said Mr Wooh, sounding most interested. 'These things I have heard of, yes. I do not know them, but I have certainly heard of them. Your father must be a very, very clever man, with a most unusual brain.'

Tink swelled with pride. 'Something got into the papers about his inventions a little while ago,' he said, 'and reporters came down to see Dad, and his name was in the papers – but Dad was awfully cross about it. You see, he's

in the middle of the biggest idea he's ever thought of and it messed up his work to have people coming to interview him – some of them even peered through the window, and went to see his wonderful tower, with its . . .'

'Tower? He has a tower?' said Mr Wooh, full of surprise. Before Tink could answer, he received a hard poke from Julian's finger. He turned crossly, to see Julian frowning fiercely at him. So was George. He went suddenly red in the face. Of course – he had been told never to talk about his father's work. It was secret work, very secret.

He pretended to choke over a piece of meat, hoping that Julian would take the chance of changing the subject – and Julian did, of course!

'Mr Wooh, could you do a bit of magic reckoning with figures?' he asked. 'I've heard that you can give the answers to any sum as quick as lightning.'

'That is true,' said Mr Wooh. 'There is nothing that I cannot do with figures. Ask me anything you like, and I will give you the answer at once!'

'Well, Mr Wooh, answer this then,' cried Tink. 'Multiply sixty-three thousand, three hundred and forty-two by eighty thousand, nine hundred and fifty-three! Ha – you can't do that in a hurry!'

'The answer is, in figures, 5127724926,' said Mr Wooh at once, with a slight bow. 'That is an easy question, my boy.'

'Crumbs!' said Tink, astounded. He turned to Julian. 'Is that right, Ju?'

Julian worked out the sum on paper. 'Yes. Absolutely correct. Whew!' he said. 'You said that as quick as lightning!'

'Let *me* give him a sum to do!' cried George. 'What do you get if you multiply 602491 by 352, Mr Magician?'

'I get the figures 2–1–2–0–7–6–8–3–2,' said Mr Wooh, immediately. And once more Julian worked out the sum on paper. He raised his head and grinned. 'Yes – correct. How do you do it so quickly?'

'Magic – just a little elementary magic!' answered Mr Wooh. 'Try it sometime yourself. I am sure that this boy's father would be as quick as I am!' He looked at Tink. 'I should much like to meet your clever father, my boy,' he said in his deep voice. 'We would have much, so much to talk about. I have heard about his wonderful tower. A monument to his genius! Ah, you see, even we know of your father's great work. Surely he is afraid of having his secrets stolen?'

'Oh, I don't think so,' said Tink. 'The tower is a pretty good hiding-place, and . . .' He stopped suddenly, and went red again as he received an even harder kick from Julian. How *could* he be so stupid as to give away the fact that his father's secret plans and models were hidden in the tower!

Julian thought it was time to take Tink firmly away from Mr Wooh and give him a good lecture on keeping his mouth shut. He looked at his watch, and pretended to be horrified at the time. 'Look. Do you know what the time is? Jenny will be ringing up the police if we don't get back straight away. Come on, Tink, and you others, we *must* go. Thanks a lot, Grandad, for letting us share your supper.'

'But we haven't yet finished!' said Grandad. 'You haven't had enough to eat.'

'We really couldn't eat any more,' said Dick, following

Julian's determined lead. 'See you tomorrow, Grandad. Good night, Grandma. Thanks very much indeed.'

'We've still got bananas and apples to eat,' said Tink, feeling obstinate.

'Oh, we brought those for Charlie the Chimp,' said Dick, not quite truthfully. He could have boxed Tink's ears! Silly little idiot, couldn't he realise that Julian wanted to get him away from this cunning Mr Wooh? Wait till he got Tink by himself!

Tink found himself hustled on all sides, and felt a bit scared. Julian sounded rather fierce, he thought. Old Grandad was most astonished at the sudden departure of his guests – but Charlie the Chimp didn't mind! The guests had left behind a generous supply of fruit!

Over the fence they all went, with Julian hustling Tink in front of him. Once over the fence and out of Mr Wooh's hearing, Julian and George rounded on the boy angrily.

'Are you mad, Tink?' demanded Julian. 'Didn't you guess that that man was trying to pump you about your father's hush-hush job?'

'He wasn't,' said Tink, almost in tears. 'You're just exaggerating!'

'Well, I hope *I* never try to give away *my* father's secret work!' said George, in a tone of such disgust that Tink could have howled.

'I don't like him and I don't trust him,' said Julian, sounding suddenly very grown up. 'But there you sat lapping up everything he said, ready to pour out all he wanted to know. I'm ashamed of you. You'd be in so much trouble if your father had heard you. I only hope you haven't already said too much. You know how angry your father was when a report of his latest ideas got into the papers, and swarms of people came prying round the house . . .'

Tink could stand it no longer. He gave a forlorn howl that made Mischief jump, and fled up the garden to the house, the little monkey running swiftly behind him. He wanted to comfort Tink. What was the matter? Poor little Mischief felt bewildered, and tried his best to catch up with the sobbing Tink. He caught him up at last, leapt to the boy's shoulder and put his little furry arms round Tink's neck, making a funny comforting noise.

'Oh Mischief,' said Tink. 'I'm glad *you're* still my friend. The others won't be now, I know. Aren't I an *idiot*, Mischief? But I was only being proud of my father, I was, really!'

Mischief clung to Tink, puzzled and upset. Tink stopped outside the tall tower. There was a light at the top. His father must still be working there. A faint humming noise came to his ears. He wondered if it was those strange, spindly tentacles right at the very top of the tower that made the noise.

Suddenly the light at the top of the tower went out.

'Dad must have finished his work for tonight,' thought Tink. 'He'll be coming to the house. I'd better go. He

might wonder why I'm all upset. Gosh, I never heard Julian be so angry before. He sounded as if he absolutely *despised* me!'

He crept up the path that led to the house, and in at the garden door. Better not go and see Jenny. She might worm everything out of him, and be as disgusted with him as Julian was. She would wonder why he wasn't camping out with them! He'd go upstairs and sleep in his own bed tonight!

'Come on, Mischief,' he said, in a mournful voice. 'We'll go to bed, and you can cuddle down with me. You'd never be mean to me, would you? You'd always be my friend.'

Mischief jabbered away, and the funny little monkey voice comforted Tink all the time he undressed. He flung himself into bed, and Mischief lay at the bottom, on his feet. 'I shall never be able to get to sleep tonight,' said Tink, still miserable. 'Never!'

But he fell asleep at once – which was a great pity, really. He might have shared in quite a bit of excitement, if he hadn't slept so soundly! Poor Tink!

CHAPTER ELEVEN

In the dark of the night

JULIAN AND the others made no attempt to follow Tink. 'Let him go, the little idiot!' said Julian. 'Come into one of the tents and have a low pow-wow before we get undressed and go to sleep.'

'I'm sorry poor old Tink isn't going to camp out with us, our first night in the field,' said Anne. 'I don't think he *meant* to give anything away.'

'That's no excuse, Anne,' said George. 'He can be really stupid at times, and he's got to learn not to be. Let's go to our tent. I feel quite tired. Come along, Timmy!'

She yawned and Dick yawned too. Then Julian found himself yawning. 'Awfully catching, this yawning business!' he said. 'Well, it's turned out to be a lovely night as regards weather – warm and dry – and there's a nice little half-moon to look at. Good night, girls, sleep tight! And don't scream if a spider wakes you, because I warn you, I am NOT going to get up to deal with a harmless spider!'

'You wait till one runs all over *your* face!' said Anne, 'and starts making a web from your nose to your chin and catches flies in it!'

'Don't, Anne,' said George. 'I'm not a bit scared of

spiders, but that's a horrible idea of yours! Timmy, please watch out for spiders, and give me warning of them!'

Everyone laughed. 'Well, good night, girls,' said Dick. 'Pity about young Tink. Still, he's got to learn a few things, and keeping his mouth shut is one of them.'

They were all quite tired, and it wasn't long before everyone's torch was out, and peace and quiet descended on the little camp. Much farther up the field the circus was also peaceful and quiet, though there were still lights here and there in the tents. Someone belonging to the circus band was strumming a banjo, but not loudly, and the sound was pleasant to hear – strum-a-strum – strum-a-strum – strummmm . . .

A few clouds blew up and slid across the moon. One by one the lights went out in the circus tents. The wind blew softly through the trees, and an owl hooted.

Anne was still awake. She lay listening to the wind, and to the owl's 'Too-whoo-too-whit', and then she, too, fell asleep. Nobody heard someone stirring in the circus camp. Nobody saw a shadowy figure creep out when the moon was safely behind a cloud. It was late, very late, and the two camps were lost in dreams.

Timmy was fast asleep too – but in his sleep he heard a faint sound, and at once he was awake. He didn't move, except for his ears which switched themselves to listen. He gave a little growl, but not enough to wake George. So long as the person who was moving about in the circus camp did not come near to George's tent, or the boys' tent,

Timmy did not mean to bark. He heard a tiny grunt and recognised it at once. Charlie the Chimp! Well, that was all right! Timmy fell asleep again.

Tink, too, was fast asleep in his bed up at the house, Mischief at his feet. He had thought he would be too miserable to sleep, but found himself half-dreaming in no time. He didn't hear a small noise outside, a very small noise indeed – a little scrape, as if someone's foot had caught against a stone. Then there came other very small noises – and a whisper of a voice – and more noises again.

Nobody heard anything at all until Jenny woke up thirsty, and stretched out her hand to get a glass of water from her bed table. She didn't switch her light on, and was about to lie down again when her quick ears caught a little sound.

She sat up. 'That can't be the children,' she thought. 'They're camping down in the field. Oh my goodness me, I hope it's not a burglar – or someone trying to steal the Professor's secrets. He's got papers all over the place. Thank goodness he keeps most of them in that tower of his!'

She listened, and then lay down again. But soon she heard another little noise, and sat up, scared. 'It sounds as if it comes from the tower,' she thought, and got out of bed. No – there was no light in the tower – no light anywhere, that she could see. The moon was behind a cloud. She'd just wait till it slid out and lit up the courtyard

below, and the tower. There! That was another little noise. Could it be the wind? No, it couldn't. And now, what was *that*? It sounded just like someone whispering down there in the courtyard. Jenny felt really frightened, and began to shake. She must go and wake the Professor! Suppose it was someone after his precious papers? Or his wonderful new invention!

The moon swung out from behind the cloud and Jenny peered cautiously out of the window again. She gave a loud scream, and staggered back into her room, still screaming. 'There's a man! Help! Help! He's climbing up the wall of the tower! Professor! PROFESSOR HAYLING! Come quickly! Thieves, robbers, help, help! Get the police!'

There came a long slithering sound, and before Jenny dared to look out again, the moon had gone behind another cloud, and she could not see a thing in the sudden darkness. There was a deep silence after the slithering noise, and Jenny couldn't bear it. She rushed out of her bedroom, yelling at the top of her voice. 'THIEVES! ROBBERS! COME QUICKLY!'

The Professor woke with a jump, threw off his bedclothes and rushed out into the passage, almost colliding with Jenny. He clutched at her, thinking she was the thief, and she screamed again, sure that one of the intruders had got hold of her. They struggled together, and then the Professor realised that he wasn't holding a thief, he was holding poor, plump Jenny!

'JENNY! What on earth are you doing, waking up the whole household!' said the Professor, switching on the passage light. 'Have you had a bad dream – a nightmare?'

'No, no,' panted Jenny, out of breath with her struggle. 'There's robbers about. I saw one climbing up the tower wall – and there must have been others below. I heard them whispering. Oh, I'm scared! What shall we do? Can you telephone for the police?'

'Well,' said the Professor, doubtfully. 'Are you quite sure, Jenny, that you didn't have a nightmare? I mean – if there really *are* robbers, I'll certainly telephone – but it's rather a long way for the police to come out here, and . . .'

'Oh – then won't you just take a torch and look round the place?' begged Jenny. 'You know there's your precious papers in that tower. And isn't there that new invention of yours? Oh yes, I know I'm not supposed to know anything about it, but I do dust your rooms thoroughly, you know, and I see quite a lot, though I keep my mouth shut, and . . .'

'Yes, yes, Jenny, I know,' said poor Professor Hayling, trying to stop Jenny's stream of talk. 'But honestly, everything seems quiet now. I've looked out into the courtyard. There's no one there. And you know as well as I do that nobody can get into my tower. It has three different keys – one to unlock the bottom door – one for the middle door, halfway up – and one for the top door. Jenny, be sensible. Nobody could have used my three keys. Look, there they are on my dressing-table.'

Jenny began to calm down, but she still wasn't satisfied. 'I *did* hear whispering, and I *did* see someone halfway up the wall of the tower. Please do come down with me, and let's look around. I daren't go on my own. But I shan't sleep again tonight till I know nobody's forced the tower door, or taken a ladder to go up the tower.'

'All right, Jenny,' said the Professor, with a sigh. 'Put on your dressing-gown, and I'll put mine on too – we'll try the doors, and we'll look for a ladder – though, mind you, it would have to be an absolutely colossal one to reach the top of that tower. Nobody could possibly bring one that size and length into our small courtyard! All right, all right – we'll go.'

And so, a few minutes later, Jenny and the Professor were down in the courtyard. There was no sign of any ladder at all – no sign of anyone climbing up the wall – and the downstairs tower door was safely locked! 'You unlock the door, and go up to the top room and see if that door's locked too,' begged Jenny.

'I think you're being rather silly now, Jenny,' said the Professor impatiently. 'Here, take the keys yourself. This one's locked, of course – and if the middle door is still locked, you'll know nobody could have got into my top room. Hurry, Jenny.'

So Jenny, still trembling, slid a key into the bottom lock, opened the door, and began to climb the spiral stair that led upwards. Halfway was another door, also safely locked.

She unlocked this too. She began to feel rather silly. Nobody could have gone through locked doors. And there now – the top one was well and truly locked also! She gave a sigh of relief and ran down the spiral stairway, locking the middle door, and then the bottom one. She gave the keys to the Professor, who by now was feeling rather chilly!

'All locked,' said Jenny. 'But I'm still sure someone was about. I could have sworn I saw someone up that tower wall, and heard somebody else whispering below.'

'I expect you were so scared that you imagined things, Jenny,' said the Professor, yawning. 'I think you'll agree with me that the wall is far too steep for anyone to climb – and I'm pretty certain I'd have heard it if a ladder had been dragged about the courtyard!'

'Well, I'm sure I'm very sorry,' said poor Jenny. 'It's a good thing we didn't wake Tink – though I'm surprised Mischief didn't hear something and come running down the stairs.'

'But Mischief is surely with Tink, camping out in the field!' said the Professor in surprise.

'No – Tink and Mischief are back. I found them asleep in bed – but not the others!' said Jenny. 'Maybe Tink had quarrelled with them. Funny that Mischief didn't come running out to see what was up – he must have heard us!'

'Mischief is clever – but not clever enough to open Tink's bedroom door,' said the Professor, yawning again.

'Good night, Jenny. Don't worry. You'll feel all right in the morning, and that will be that!'

The Professor went sleepily to his room. He looked out of the window down into the courtyard and then across at the tower, and smiled. Dear Jenny! She did rather let her imagination run away with her! As if anyone in the world could get up into that tower room without a ladder! And HOW could a long, long ladder be brought into that small courtyard without either being seen or heard? The Professor yawned once more and climbed into bed.

But someone *had* been in the tower room! Someone very clever, someone very light-fingered! What a shock for poor Professor Hayling next morning when he crossed the courtyard, unlocked the bottom door of the tower – walked up the spiral stairway – unlocked the middle door, and went on up the stairway again – and finally unlocked the top door and opened it wide.

He stood and stared in horror. The place was upside down! All his papers were scattered everywhere. He crouched down at once to see if any were missing. Yes – quite a lot! But they seemed to have been taken quite haphazardly – a few pages from this notebook – a few pages from that – some letters he had written and left on his desk to post – and good gracious, the ink was spilt all over the place – and the little clock was gone from the mantelpiece. So Jenny was right – a thief *had* been about last night. A thief that could apparently get through three locked doors – or else could climb up a long, long ladder that he had put outside without being seen – and taken away again!

'I'll have to ring the police,' he thought. 'But I must say it's a mystery! I wonder if Tink heard anything in the night? No, he couldn't have, or he would have run to fetch me. It's a mystery – a real puzzle of a mystery!'

CHAPTER TWELVE

A shock for Tink

Tink was horrified when Jenny told him the next morning what had happened. 'Your father's in a rare old state,' she said. 'He came down early this morning because he wanted to finish some work up in the tower – and as soon as he unlocked the top door into the tower room, he saw the whole room upside down and some of his precious papers gone, and . . .'

'JENNY! How awful!' said Tink. 'Dad kept his most precious papers there – with all the figures for that new electric thing of his. It's a wonderful thing, too marvellous for words, Jenny, it's for . . .'

'Now don't you give away any of your father's plans, not even to *me*,' said Jenny. 'You've been told that before. Maybe you've been talking too much already, and somebody's ears took it all in!'

Tink suddenly felt sick. *Was* it because of something he had been silly enough to say in public? In the bus, perhaps? Or in the circus field? What would the others say – especially Julian – when they heard that someone had come in the night and stolen precious papers containing figures and diagrams for some of his father's inventions? Julian would be sure to say that it was *his* fault for not

keeping his mouth shut! Oh dear – would *this* be in the papers – and would hordes of people come visiting the place again, staring and whispering and exclaiming in awe at his father's curious tower with its waving tentacles?

He dressed quickly and ran downstairs. Jenny had told him that she was sure she had heard whispering down in the courtyard the night before, and had seen someone climbing up the tower. 'Your father says nobody could have brought a long ladder into that courtyard,' she said. 'Not without us seeing it, anyway, or hearing some kind of noise when it was dragged in. But it might have been a sliding ladder, mightn't it? That would be a smallish thing, with ropes to pull out the sliding part.'

'Yes. Like the window cleaner uses,' said Tink. 'It couldn't have been the window cleaner, could it?'

'No. He's a really decent fellow,' said Jenny. 'I've known him for twenty years. So put *that* out of your head. But the ladder could certainly have been the sort that window cleaners use. We'll go out into the courtyard as soon as I've finished washing-up, and see if we can find the marks where the ladder was dragged over the courtyard. Though I must say I didn't hear any *dragging* noises. I heard whispering – and a kind of slithery noise – but that's all.'

'The slithery noise *might* have been made by the ladder when it was dragged along!' said Tink. 'Hey – look at old Mischief. He's listening as if he understood every word. Mischief, why didn't you wake me up last night when all this was going on? You usually wake if anything unusual happens, or you hear a strange noise.'

Mischief leapt into Tink's arms and cuddled there. He didn't like it when Tink was upset about anything; he knew by the boy's voice that he was worried. He made small comforting noises, and rubbed his monkey nose against the boy's chin.

'You'd better go to your father,' said Jenny. 'You might be able to comfort him a little. He's very upset indeed. He's up in the tower room, trying to sort out his papers. My word, they were left in a state – scattered all over the room!'

Tink stood up to go, and was astonished to find that he

was shaky at the knees. Would his father ask him if he had been talking about the work he was doing? Oh dear – he had even boasted about it just the day before, and talked about his father's sko-wheel, and the wonderful new machine, the electric trosymon! Tink's knees became shakier than ever.

But, fortunately, his father was far too upset about his muddled room and missing papers to worry about anything Tink had said or done. He was up in the tower room, trying to discover which of his papers were missing.

'Ah, Tink,' he said, when the boy came into the tower room. 'Just give me a hand, will you? The thief who came last night must have knocked the whole bunch of papers off the table, down on the floor – and fortunately he seems not to have seen some that went under the table. So I doubt very much if the papers he *did* take away with him will be of any use. He'd need to be quite a scientist to understand them, without having the ones he left behind.'

'Will he come back for the others, then?' asked Tink.

'Probably,' said his father. 'But I shall hide them somewhere. Can you think of a good hiding-place, Tink?'

'Dad – don't *you* hide them,' begged Tink. 'Not unless you tell *me* where they are! You know how you forget things! You might forget where you'd put this bunch of papers, and then you wouldn't be able to go on with your inventions. Have you copies of the stolen sheets of figures and diagrams?'

'No. But they're all in my head as well as on paper,' said his father. 'It will take me a bit of time to work them all out again, but it can be done. It's a nuisance – especially as I'm working to a date. Now run along, Tink, please. I've work to do.'

Tink went down the spiral staircase of the tower. He'd have to make sure that his father *did* hide away those papers very carefully indeed – in some really good place. 'Oh dear – I hope he won't do what he did with the last lot of papers he wanted to hide,' he thought. 'He stuffed them up the chimney – and they nearly went up in flames because Jenny thought she'd light the fire the next night, it was unexpectedly so cold. Good thing they fell down when she laid the fire and she rescued them before they got burnt! Why are brainy people like Dad so silly about ordinary things! I *bet* he'll either forget where he puts them – or go and hide them in some easy place where anyone could find them!'

He went to talk to Jenny. 'Jenny – Dad says that the thief only took *some* of his papers – and that he can't make much use of the ones he took, unless he has the whole lot. And Dad says he thinks that when the thief finds this out, he'll try to steal the rest of the papers.'

'Well, let him try!' said Jenny. '*I* could hide them in a place where no thief would find them – if your Dad would let *me* have them. I shan't tell you where!'

'*I'm* afraid he might hide them up a chimney again, or some silly place like that,' said Tink, looking so worried that Jenny felt really worried too! 'They've got to be hidden somewhere *nobody* would think of looking. And if Dad finds a place like that he'll promptly forget all about it, and never be able to find them again! But a thief might find them – he'd know *all* the places to look in.'

'Let's go up to the tower room and clear up the mess that the spilt ink made, and see if your father has taken his precious papers and hidden them somewhere there,' said Jenny. 'It would be just like him to hide them in the very room that the thief went to last night! Up the ladder, in at the window – left wide open, I've no doubt – snatched up every paper he could see, the rogue, and then raced down the ladder again!'

'Come on up to the tower, then,' said Tink. 'I only hope Dad isn't there!'

'He's just crossing the courtyard, look,' said Jenny, leaning out of the window. 'See, there he is – carrying something under his arm.'

'His morning newspapers,' said Tink. 'It looks as if he's going to have a jolly good read, doesn't it? Oh dear, I do hope all this won't be printed in the newspapers – it would bring hordes of people down here again. Do you remember how awful it was last time, Jenny – people even walked over the flower-beds!'

'Hoo – some people like to poke their nose into everything!' said Jenny. 'I don't mind telling you that I emptied my dirty washing water out of the window on to a few of them – quite by mistake, of course. How was *I* to know they were out there, staring up and down?'

Tink gave a shout of laughter. 'I wish I'd seen that!' he said. 'Oh, Jenny – if people come poking their noses into Dad's business again, *do* let's empty water on their silly heads! Come on, Jenny – let's go up to the tower room now Dad's out of the way. Quick!'

They were soon out in the courtyard and, as they crossed it, Jenny stopped and looked hard at the ground.

'What are you looking for?' asked Tink.

'Just to see if there are any marks that might have been made by someone dragging a ladder across,' said Jenny. 'I heard a funny slithering sound, you know but it didn't *sound* like a ladder being dragged across.'

The two of them looked all over the courtyard, but could see no marks there that could possibly have been made by a ladder.

'Funny,' said Jenny. 'It worries me, that slithery sound.' She looked up at the tall, steep wall of the tower. It was made of flint-stones of all shapes and sizes, the kind found in the countryside round about Kirrin and Big Hollow.

'Well, I suppose a *cat* might climb up,' said Jenny, doubtfully. 'But not a *man*. He'd slip sooner or later. It would be far too dangerous. I doubt if even a cat would get far.'

'And yet you say you thought you saw someone up the tower wall!' said Tink. 'Go on, Jenny – it must have been the shadow of a passing cloud that you saw! Look up this wall – now can you imagine *anyone* climbing up it at night, when it was dark?'

Jenny stared up. 'No – you're right. Only a madman would even try. Well, my eyes must have played me up, then, when I looked out last night – but I really *did* think I saw a dark shadow climbing up the tower wall. Still, it's easy to be mistaken at night. And I don't believe there was a ladder, either! There *would* be marks on the paving-stones of the courtyard if there had been a ladder. Oh well – let's hurry on up to the tower room before your dad decides to go back to it again!'

They went up the spiral stairway. All the doors were unlocked, as it was plain that the Professor was going to come back again after he had read his papers.

'All the same – he shouldn't leave the doors unlocked, even for a minute!' said Jenny. 'Well, here we are – just look at the ink splashes everywhere – and that dear little clock that kept such good time is gone. Now what would the thief want with a clock, I'd like to know?'

'It would be small and neat enough to pop into his pocket,' said Tink. 'If he was dishonest enough to steal Dad's papers, he would certainly not say no to a nice little clock like that! He's probably taken other things too!'

They went right into the room, and Jenny at once gave a loud exclamation. 'LOOK! Aren't those some of the papers your father was working on – on the table there? All covered with tiny figures?'

Tink looked closely at them. 'Yes – they're his very

latest papers. He showed me them the other day. I remember this diagram. Jenny – how *could* he leave them on the table with the door unlocked this morning – when only last night the thief was here! How could he? He *said* he was going to hide them away so carefully, because, if the thief found them, he could use them with the other papers that were stolen – but as long as the thief only had half of them, they wouldn't be much use – and now he's forgotten all about hiding them, after all!'

'Look now, Tink – let's hide them away ourselves,' said Jenny, 'and not tell him where they are. These thieves will have another try for them, no doubt about that. Let's think of some place where they'd be absolutely safe.'

'*I* know!' said Tink. 'We could hide them on Kirrin Island! Somewhere in the old ruined castle! *Nobody* would guess they were there.'

'Now that's a *fine* idea!' said Jenny. 'I'd be glad to think they were out of the house.' She gathered up the papers quickly. 'Here you are. You'd better tell Julian and the others, and go across to the island with them as soon as you can. My, what a relief to think they'll be well away from here. I'll be able to sleep soundly in my bed at nights then!'

Tink stuffed the precious papers under his jersey, and he and Jenny ran at top speed down the spiral stairway. They saw the Professor not far off, and he turned and hailed them. 'Tink! Jenny! I know what you're going to ask me! You want to know where I've hidden those papers of mine. Come here and I'll whisper!'

Not knowing quite what to say, the two went rather guiltily over to Tink's father. He whispered loudly, 'I've wrapped them up, and put them under the coal at the back of the coal-cellar – right at the *very* back!'

'And a fine mess you've made of your trousers,' said Jenny, disgusted. 'And good gracious – you must have sat down in the coal yourself! You look a right mess. Come along and let me brush you down. Not indoors, though, or the place will be thick with coal-dust!'

'Don't you think it was a good hiding-place, Jenny?' asked the Professor. 'Ha – you thought I'd forget to hide them, didn't you?'

He went off, looking very pleased with himself. Jenny chuckled in delight. 'Dear old Professor! He's hidden all his *newspapers* there, but not a single one of his own precious papers. And now whatever shall we tell him when he wants the morning papers? Tink, you cycle out to the paper shop and get another lot. My goodness – what it is to have a brainy man in the house! Whatever will he do next?'

CHAPTER THIRTEEN

Quite a lot of plans!

AFTER TINK had fetched a new supply of morning papers, he decided to go down to the camp in the field and tell the others all that had happened that morning. He still felt angry about being ticked off by Julian the night before – but he simply couldn't wait to tell the others about the robbery – and about the grand idea he, Tink, had of hiding the rest of his father's papers on Kirrin Island.

So off he went, with Mischief happily on his shoulder, holding tightly to his hair. The others were all there in the field. They had just come back from a shopping expedition, and Tink's eyes gleamed when he saw the various tinned meats and tinned fruits, fresh rolls, tomatoes and apples and bananas that had been brought back from the shops at Big Hollow.

Julian was glad to see that Tink looked bright and cheerful. He was afraid that the boy might have sulked, and that would have spoilt things for the others.

'Hi!' said Tink. 'I've got news!' And he proceeded to tell the others all about the happenings of the night before, ending up with his father solemnly going off to hide his morning newspapers under the coal at the back of the

coal-cellar, under the impression that he was hiding the rest of his precious papers.

'But why on earth didn't you tell him he had left his valuable papers behind and hidden his newspapers?' asked George.

'Because, if he knew that, he'd go and hide the *precious* papers somewhere, and forget where he'd put them – and they might be lost for ever!' said Tink.

'Well, what are *you* going to do with them?' asked Dick.

'I've had rather a brainwave,' said Tink, as modestly as he could. 'Er – I thought that *we'd* hide them away ourselves, where nobody could *possibly* find them.'

'And where is this wonderful hiding-place?' asked Dick.

'On Kirrin Island!' said Tink, triumphantly. 'Who'd think of looking *there*? And as we shall *all* know the hiding-place, we can't possibly forget it. The papers will be absolutely safe. Dad can get on with the rest of his ideas without worrying about anything!'

'Have you told him all this?' asked Julian.

'Well, no,' said Tink. 'Jenny thought we'd better just keep it to ourselves. She's pretty certain the thieves will try their hand at breaking in to get the rest of the papers, though.'

'Ha! Well, I vote we scribble some papers ourselves,' said Dick. 'Complete with wonderful diagrams, and all kinds of peculiar figurings and numberings. I feel I could do that very well! And we'd leave them up in the tower room for the thieves to take – they'd think they were the ones they'd missed!'

Everyone chuckled. 'Idiot!' said Julian. 'Still – it's not a bad idea to leave something behind for the thieves that isn't worth a moment's look – and hide the genuine figures where they'd never dream of finding them – on Kirrin Island!'

'When shall we go?' asked George. 'It's ages since I've visited my island – and will you believe it, last time I rowed over *day-trippers* had been there and left their beastly mess everywhere! Paper bags, broken glass, lettuce leaves, orange peel, ugh!'

'Why *do* people do that?' asked Anne. 'They'd hate to have to sit in the midst of *other* people's mess – so why in the world can't they clear up their own?'

'Oh, they're probably just like that in their own homes,' said Dick. 'All mess and litter – and yet it takes so little time to clear up a picnic mess, and leave the place decent for the next comers.'

'What did you do with all the mess left on Kirrin Island?' asked Julian.

'I buried it deep in the sand at the back of one of the beaches,' said George. 'Where the tide can't turn it all up again. And with every dig of my spade I said, "Blow you, you awful day-trippers without manners, blow you – and next time you go anywhere, may you find someone else's litter to make you feel sick. Blow you!"'

George looked and sounded so very fierce that everyone burst out laughing. Timmy sat there with his tongue lolling out, looking as if he were laughing too, and Mischief made a funny little noise rather like a giggle.

'Good old George. She always says straight out what she thinks!' said Julian.

They sat and talked over their plans for some time. 'Dick and Julian had better make the fake plans and figures,' said George. 'They'd be better at that kind of thing than anyone else. And Tink can plant them somewhere in his father's tower room for the thief to take if he goes there again – and I bet he will. He found it easy enough last night!'

'And George could take Tink's father's papers with the *correct* figures and plans over to Kirrin Island,' said Anne.

'Not till night-time, though,' said Dick. 'If anyone were on the watch, and saw George rowing over there, they might guess she was taking something important to hide. They might be watching her father too. By the way – where *are* these papers? You did not leave them behind at home, did you, Tink?'

'I didn't dare to,' said Tink. 'I felt as if there might be eyes peeping at me, watching and hoping I'd go out and leave the papers behind. I've got them under my jersey, just here!' And he patted the top of his stomach.

'Oh – so *that*'s why you look as if you've had too much breakfast!' said George. 'Well – what shall our plans be?'

'We'd better make out the false papers straight away, with figures and diagrams,' said Julian. 'Just in case thieves come sooner than we think. Tink, we'd better go into *your* house to do those. If we go to George's her father might spot us and wonder what on earth we were doing. We'd probably be sent off, anyway, because of the scarlet fever business.'

'Well, what about *my* father?' said Tink. '*He* might spot us too. Anyway, he's not keen on my having anyone there this week, because he's so busy with his new invention. It's awfully good, and . . .'

'*Tink* – don't start spilling beans again!' said Julian, warningly. 'I say it would be best to go to your house.'

'What about *me* going indoors and bringing out Dad's big drawing-board, and some of his paper, and his mapping pens and ink, and doing the diagrams and things out here in the tent?' said Tink. 'Honestly, I never know when Dad is going to come into my room. He'd wonder what on *earth* we were doing if he found us all there! We can have a good look at the papers I've got under my jersey, and do a whole lot in the same style – not the *same* figures, naturally – and we could do some diagrams too.'

'All right,' said Julian, giving way, as he saw that Tink was genuinely afraid that his father might see them making the false papers. 'Go and get the drawing-board and come back with it, and anything else we'll need. You go with him, George.'

'Right,' said George, and she and Tink went up Tink's garden to the house. Tink scouted round to see if his father was anywhere about, but couldn't see him. He found a large drawing-board, some big sheets of paper used by his father for working out his figures, and a book of odd but easy-to-copy diagrams. He also brought mapping pens, Indian ink and blotting-paper, and even remembered drawing-pins to pin the sheets of paper to the board. George carried half the things, and kept a sharp lookout for Tink's father.

'It's all right. He's asleep somewhere – can't you hear that noise?' asked Tink; and sure enough George could – a gentle snoring from some room not far off!

They went back down the garden and over the fence, handing everything to the others before they climbed over. 'Good!' said Julian. 'Now we can produce some beautiful charts of figures that mean absolutely nothing at all – and diagrams that will look perfect and not mean a thing either!'

'Better come into the tent,' said George. 'If anyone wanders down from the circus camp, they might ask us what we're doing.'

So they all went into the boys' tent, which was the bigger one, Timmy too, and Mischief, who was delighted to be with the big dog. Julian soon set to work, though he found the space rather cramped. They were all watching him in admiration as he set out rows of beautiful, meaningless, figures when Timmy suddenly gave a deep growl, and all his hackles rose up on his neck.

Julian turned the drawing-board over at once, and sat on it. The canvas doorway of the tent was pulled aside and in poked the grinning face of Charlie the Chimp!

'Oh, it's *you*, Charlie!' said Julian. 'Well, well, well, and how are you today?'

The chimpanzee grinned even more widely, and held out his hand. Julian shook it solemnly, and the chimpanzee went carefully all round the tent, shaking hands with everyone.

'Sit down, Charlie,' said Dick. 'I suppose you've let yourself out of your cage as usual, and come to see what we've got for our dinner. Well, you'll be glad to hear we've got enough for you as well as ourselves.'

Charlie squashed himself between Timmy and Tink, and with much interest watched Julian at work with his pen and ink. 'I bet that chimp could draw, if you gave him a piece of paper and a pencil,' said Anne.

So, to keep him quiet, he was given a pencil, and a notebook. He at once began to scribble in it very earnestly.

'Goodness – he's doing a whole lot of funny figures!' said Anne. 'He's trying to copy *you*, Ju!'

'If he's not careful, I'll hand the whole job over to him!' said Julian, with a chuckle. 'George, let's talk about your plans for tonight. I think, if you are going over to Kirrin Island to hide those papers, you must take Timmy with you.'

'Oh, I will!' said George. 'Not that there will be a single soul on the island, but I'd like old Tim just for company. I'll take the papers straight to the island, land, and hide them.'

'Where?' asked Julian.

'Oh, I'll decide that when I'm there,' said George. 'Somewhere cunning! I know my own little island from top to bottom. And there those papers will stay until all danger is past. We'll let Professor Hayling think he has hidden them somewhere himself, and forgotten where! It will be fun to row across to my island at night, with Timmy.'

'The thieves can make do with *my* figures and diagrams if they come to the tower room again,' said Julian. 'Don't they look professional?'

They certainly did! Everyone looked at the neat figures and carefully drawn diagrams with admiration.

Timmy suddenly sat up and gave a deep growl again. Charlie the Chimp patted him as if to say, 'What's wrong, old boy?' but Timmy took no notice and went on growling. He suddenly shot out of the tent, and there was a shout from someone outside. 'Get off! Get down! GET DOWN!'

George swung back the tent opening. Mr Wooh was there, looking extremely frightened as Timmy growled menacingly round his ankles. Charlie the Chimp ran up to him on all fours and, angry because Timmy was snarling at his friend, showed his teeth suddenly at the big dog. George was terrified. 'Don't let them fight!' she cried, afraid that Timmy would get decidedly the worst of it. Charlie was jumping up and down in a most alarming way.

'Charleee!' said Mr Wooh in his deep voice. 'Charleee!'

And Charlie stopped jumping up and down and making horrible noises, and leapt straight on to Mr Wooh's back, putting his arms round his neck.

Mr Wooh bowed courteously to them all. 'I trust I have not disturbed you, my friends,' he said. 'I'll now take a little walk with my friend Charleee. You come again to see our show, I hope. Yes? No?'

'Probably,' said Dick, noticing that the magician had taken a quick and interested look at Julian's figures and diagrams. Julian covered them up immediately, as if he didn't want the magician to see them. He had seen something in the man's eyes that puzzled him. Could Mr Wooh

possibly have had anything to do with the theft of the papers the night before? After all, he was a wizard at figures himself – he might be able to read the Professor's figures and diagrams and understand them perfectly. Well – he wouldn't gather much from the ones Julian was now doing – they were more or less nonsense made up by Julian himself to deceive anyone interested in the real ones.

'I interrupt you? Pardon me!' said Mr Wooh, and bowed himself politely away from the group in the tent. Charlie the Chimp followed him, hoping that Mischief would too, so that they could have a game. But Mischief didn't want to. He didn't like Mr Wooh.

'Well, I didn't realise that anyone from the circus would walk down the field so quietly, and be able to hear what we were saying inside the tent,' said Julian, worried. 'I didn't like the look in his eyes. Dick – you don't suppose he heard anything we were saying, do you?'

'Would it matter?' said Dick.

'It might,' said Julian. 'Do you think he heard what George said about going over to Kirrin Island with the other papers – the valuable ones that the thieves didn't see in the tower room last night? I wouldn't let George go if I thought he had heard. In fact, I think she'd better *not* go. She might run into danger.'

'Don't be silly, Ju,' said George. 'I *am* going. And Timmy will be with me.'

'You heard what I said, George. You are *not* to go!' said Julian. '*I'll* take the papers and hide them on the island.

I'll get them when it's dark, fairly late. I'll cycle over to Kirrin and untie the boat you keep there, and row over to the island.'

'All right, Julian,' said George, astonishingly meekly. 'Shall we have a meal now? We've only to open the tins, and empty the tomatoes and lettuces out of the basket there. And the drinks are in that cool corner over there.'

'Right,' said Julian, glad that George had given way to him so easily. *He* would go across in George's boat and find a good hiding-place. If danger was about, he reckoned he could deal with it better than George could.

Yes, Julian, you may be right. But don't be too sure about tonight!

CHAPTER FOURTEEN

Ladders – and a lot of fun!

THE CHILDREN stared after Mr Wooh and the chimpanzee. They saw Charlie pick up two empty buckets, one in each strong paw, and race off to the right with them.

'Where's he going?' said Anne, astonished at the rate he was running along.

'I bet he's going to get some water from the stream in those pails, and take them to whoever washes down the

horses,' said George. She was right! Charlie soon came back again, walking this time, holding a heavy pail of water in each hand!

'Well, I must say that chimpanzee is jolly useful!' said Dick. 'Look – there's Madelon who trains those beautiful horses that paraded round the ring last night. She's wearing old trousers this morning – she looks quite different. There – Charlie has set the pails of water down beside her. I bet that as soon as she wants any more water, he'll be off again to the stream!'

'I rather like old Charlie,' said Anne. 'I didn't at first – but now I do. I wish he didn't belong to Mr Wooh.'

Julian stood up, looking down at the paper on which he had so carefully written lines of small figures and drawn many peculiar diagrams. 'I somehow feel this isn't much good now,' he said. 'I think Mr Wooh must have guessed it was all a make-up as soon as he saw it. He gave himself away a bit, though – I saw him looking at the paper in a rather startled way, as if he'd seen something very like it very recently indeed!'

'So he had, the wretch, if he'd sent someone up to get my dad's papers out of the tower room!' said Tink. 'Hey! What about having a look round the circus to see if we can spot a ladder anywhere – one tall enough to reach the tower room!'

'Good idea!' said Dick. 'Come on – we'll go now. Chuck that drawing-board and diagram paper over our fence, Ju. I hardly think it's worth your while to finish it.'

The Five, with Tink and Mischief, wandered down the field to where the circus was encamped. Dick spotted a ladder lying in the grass, and nudged Julian.

'Julian! See that? Would it reach the tower?' Julian walked over to it. It certainly was very, very long – but *would* it be long enough? No – he didn't think it would. Still – he might as well find out who owned it. At that moment up came the Boneless Man, walking perfectly. He grinned at the children – and then suddenly put all his double-joints to work, bent his knees into peculiar positions, twisted his head round so that he was looking over his own back, and then bent his double-jointed arms the wrong way, so that he looked very odd indeed!

'Don't! I don't like it!' said Anne. 'You look so peculiar and strange! Why are you called the *Boneless* Man? You aren't boneless – you just make yourself *look* as if you were, with all those funny double-joints of yours!'

The Boneless Man seemed suddenly to lose all his bones, and crumpled up on the grass in a funny heap. The children couldn't help laughing. He didn't look as if he had any bones at all then!

'Er – can you climb ladders if you're double-jointed?' asked Julian, suddenly.

'Of course!' said the Boneless Man. 'Run up them backwards, forwards, sideways – any way you like.'

'Is that *your* ladder, then?' asked Dick, nodding his head towards the ladder in the grass.

'Well – I use it, but so does everyone else!' said the

Boneless Man, turning his head the wrong way round, so that it seemed as if it was put on back to front. It was odd to speak to someone whose head did that – one minute they were talking to his face, the next to the back of his head!

'I *wish* you wouldn't do that,' said Anne. 'It makes me feel giddy.'

'Do you use that ladder to put the flag on the top of the circus tent?' asked Dick. 'It doesn't look long enough for that.'

'It isn't,' said the Boneless Man, turning his head the right way round, much to Anne's relief. 'There's a much longer one over there – it takes three men to carry it, it's so heavy – but the centre circus pole is very tall, as you see. One man couldn't *possibly* carry the long ladder.'

The children looked at one another. That ruled out the very long ladder too, then. If it needed three men to carry it, Jenny would certainly have heard a lot more noise last night!

'Are there any more ladders in the circus camp?'

'No – just the two. Why? Thinking of buying one?' said the Boneless Man. 'I must go. The Boss is beckoning to me.' Off he went, walking in a most peculiar fashion, using his double-joints for all he was worth!

'What about the acrobats?' said Julian. '*They* must be used to climbing and clambering everywhere. I wonder if any of *them* could have climbed the wall?'

'I don't think so,' said Tink. 'I had a good look at it this morning – and although there *is* a kind of creeper climbing up the wall, it stops halfway – and above that there's just the stone wall. Even an acrobat would have to have some help up the tower wall!'

'Could the *clowns* have found a way?' said George. 'No – I suppose they're not as good even as the acrobats at climbing. I don't believe the thief *could* have been anyone from the circus after all. Look – what's that on the ground over there – outside that tent?'

They all went over to see. It looked like a pile of dark-grey fur. George touched it with her toe. 'Oh – *I* know what it is – the donkey-skin!'

'Golly – so it is!' cried Tink in delight, and picked it up – or tried to. It was much too heavy for him to hold up all of it.

In a trice Dick and George were inside that donkey-skin! Dick had the head, and found that he *could* see quite well where he was going, for the donkey neck had neat eye-holes in it – the head itself was stuffed with paper. George was the back legs, and kicked up her feet and made the donkey look extremely lively. The others roared with laughter.

Someone shouted loudly. 'Hey – you leave that donkey-skin alone!'

It was Jeremy. He came running up, looking furious. He had a stick in his hand, and hit out at the donkey's hind parts, giving poor George a good old whack, and making her yell.

LING CIRCUS

'Hey! Stop that, it hurt!'

Tink looked furiously at Jeremy. 'How dare you do that?' he shouted. 'Dick and George are in the donkey-skin. Put down that stick!'

But Jeremy gave the donkey's hind legs another whack and George yelled again. Tink gave a shout too, and flung himself on Jeremy, trying to get the stick out of his hand. The boy struggled, holding on to the stick, but Tink gave him a straight blow on the chest, and down he went!

'Ha! I *said* I'd knock you down sometime, and I have!' yelled Tink. 'Get up and fight. *I'll* teach you not to hit animals!'

'Now stop it, Tink,' said Julian. 'Come out of the skin, you two idiots, before old Grandad comes up. He looks as if he's on his way now!'

Jeremy was up now, and danced round Tink with doubled fists. Before either boy could exchange a blow, Grandad's great voice came to them.

'NOW THEN! STOP IT!'

Jeremy swung his fist at Tink, who dodged, and then in his turn hit out at Jeremy, who ran back – straight into old Grandad, who at once clutched him.

By this time George and Dick were out of the donkey-skin, looking rather ashamed of themselves. Old Grandad grinned at them, still holding on to the furious Jeremy. 'Fight's off,' said Grandad to Tink and Jeremy. 'If you want to go on, either of you, you can fight *me*, not each other.'

However, neither of the boys wanted to take on old Grandad. He might be old, but he could still give some mighty slaps, as Jeremy very well knew. They stood staring at one another, looking rather sheepish.

'Go on – shake hands and be friends,' said Grandad. 'Quick, now, or I'll do a little fighting myself!'

Tink held out his hand just as Jeremy held out his. They shook, grinning at one another. 'That's right!' said old Grandad. 'No harm done. No bones broken. You're quits now, so no more knocking each other about.'

'Right, Grandad,' said Jeremy, giving him a friendly punch. The old man turned to Dick and George. 'And if *you* want to borrow that donkey-skin, you're welcome,' said old Grandad. 'But it's manners to ask the owner's permission first.'

'Yes. Sorry,' said Dick, grinning. He wondered what Professor Hayling and Jenny would say if he and George did borrow it, and galloped into Hollow House at top speed. But no – he decided reluctantly that Jenny might be scared stiff and give notice, and that would never do. She wouldn't at all like being chased by an apparently mad donkey, nor would Professor Hayling.

Grandad went off, and Julian spoke to Jeremy, who wasn't quite sure whether to go or to stay. 'We saw old Charlie carrying pails of water for the horses,' he said. 'Isn't he strong!'

Jeremy grinned, glad to be friends again, and to be able to stay with the Five and Tink. They wandered all round the field together, looking at the magnificent horses and at Dead-Shot Dick doing a little practising at shooting, and then watched one small acrobat practising amazing jumps and somersaults.

Mischief the monkey came with them. He was absolutely at home with everyone in the circus now, man, woman or animal. He leapt on to the horses' backs, and they didn't mind! He pretended to help Charlie the Chimp to carry one of the pails of water – he ran off with Dead-Shot Dick's cap. He went into the chimp's cage and cuddled up in the straw with him, scrabbling about as if the cage belonged to him. He even went into Grandad's tent and came out with a small bottle of lemonade! He couldn't get the top off, and took it to Charlie, who was watching nearby! Charlie promptly forced it off with his strong front paws – and then, to Mischief's disgust, tipped up the bottle and drank the lot!

Mischief was very angry indeed. He ran to Charlie's cage, which was open, and sent the straw flying everywhere. Charlie sat outside his cage and enjoyed the fun, grinning happily.

'Come out, Mischief!' called Tink. 'You're making a nuisance of yourself!'

'Let him be,' said one of the acrobats, who was standing nearby. 'Old Charlie enjoys a bit of temper – when it's someone else's! Look at him sitting grinning there.'

They watched for a few seconds more, to make sure that Mischief wasn't annoying the big chimpanzee, and then turned to watch Monty and Winks, the clowns, having an argument, which ended in Monty throwing water over Winks, and Winks emptying a basket of rubbish over Monty. What a pair!

When they turned to see if Mischief was still annoying Charlie, they saw that the little monkey had left the cage, and was tearing down the field to the fence. He leapt up, and over, and disappeared.

'He must think it's dinner-time,' said Tink, looking at his watch. 'And gosh, so it is. Come on everyone, Jenny will be in a fine old fury if we're really late – it's hot dinner today.'

Away they all went in a hurry. Hot dinner! Over the fence, then, and up the garden at top speed. They mustn't keep a hot dinner waiting – or Jenny either!

CHAPTER FIFTEEN

A happy day – and a shock for Julian

TINK AND the Five were two minutes late for their dinner. Jenny was just taking it in, looking a little grim, as she had not been able to find the children anywhere. 'Ah – here you are at last!' she said. 'I looked down the garden but you were nowhere to be seen. It's a good thing you came in when you did – five minutes more and I'd have taken the dinner back again.'

'*Dear* Jenny, you know you wouldn't,' said Tink, giving her a sudden squeeze that made her squeal. 'Oh, how good it smells! Mmmmm-mmmmm!'

'You and your mmmmms!' said Jenny, pushing Tink away. 'And I've told you before, that I don't mind a gentle hug, but those *squeezes* of yours take all my breath away. *No*, Tink, keep away from me – another squeeze like that and I'll feel like a lemon!'

Everyone laughed at that. Jenny did say the most amusing things. Anne felt sorry that she hadn't offered to stay and help her with the dinner. Oh dear – the time went so quickly, once they were all out together.

The talk at dinner-time was very lively. So was Mischief the monkey! He took bits from everyone's plate and handed some of them down to Timmy, who was lying under the table as usual. Timmy appreciated these titbits very much!

'Well! *I* didn't see a single ladder in the circus camp that was tall enough to reach up to the tower room,' said George.

'No. If there was one, it was jolly well hidden,' said Dick. 'Pass the mustard, someone!'

'In front of you, idiot,' said Julian. 'You know I'm beginning to wonder if Mr Wooh had anything to do with the stealing of your father's papers, Tink. I can't somehow see him climbing high ladders – he's so – so . . .'

'Polite and proper,' said Anne. 'Actually, I can't think of *any*one in the circus who would either *want* the papers, or is nasty enough to steal them. They're all so nice.'

'I still think Mr Wooh is the most *likely* one,' said Julian. 'He's interested in complicated figures and clever inventions. But all the same, I'm beginning to think I'm wrong. He could NOT have got up to the tower room as there is no ladder long enough – and I really doubt if he'd *dare* to take a ladder into the courtyard and risk putting it up to the tower. He might so easily be caught.'

'Right. We'll rule him out,' said Tink. 'But if nobody went up the spiral stairway, because all doors were locked, and nobody used a ladder, I don't see *how* those papers disappeared.'

'Wind took them out of the window, perhaps?' suggested Anne. 'Would that be possible?'

'No. For two reasons,' said Julian. 'One is that the

window wasn't wide enough open for the wind to blow in with enough strength to blow papers *out*. And secondly, we'd have been sure to have found some of them down in the courtyard if they'd been blown out. But we didn't find a single one there.'

'Well – if nobody got through the three locked doors, and nobody got through the window, *how* did those papers get stolen?' demanded George. 'It would have been a miracle for those papers to have hopped away by themselves – and I don't believe in that kind of miracle!'

There was a long silence. What a mystery it was! 'I suppose Tink's father couldn't *possibly* have gone walking in his sleep, and taken them, could he?' asked Anne.

'Well – I don't know if a sleep-walker can unlock doors with the right keys, and steal his own papers, leaving some on the floor, and then walk carefully down the spiral stairway still fast asleep, locking all the doors behind him, and then go to his own bedroom, get into bed, and then wake up in the morning without remembering a single moment of the whole thing!' said Julian.

'No. It can't be possible,' said Dick. 'Have you ever known your father to walk in his sleep, Tink?'

Tink considered. 'No, I can't say I have,' he said. 'He's a very light sleeper, usually. No. I don't believe Dad did all that in his sleep. It was somebody else.'

'It must have been some sort of miracle man, then,' said George. 'No *ordinary* person could do it. And whoever planned it wanted those papers very, very badly, or he would never have risked getting them against so many odds.'

'And if he wanted them so *very* badly, he'll certainly make an effort to get the ones he left behind under the table,' said Julian. 'Good thing we've got those! He will probably try to get up into the tower the same way as he did before – but goodness knows what it was!'

'Well – those papers will be safely out of his way, tonight!' said George. 'On my island!'

'Yes,' said Julian. 'I'll find a most unlikely hiding-place – somewhere about the ruined castle, I think. By the way – I hope you haven't *still* got them under your jersey, Tink. No – you don't look large any more. What have you done with them?'

'George said I'd better give them to her to keep, in case they slipped out of my jersey,' said Tink. 'You took them, didn't you, George?'

'Yes,' said George. 'Don't let's talk about it any more.'

'Why not? The thief's not here. He can't be listening to us!' said Tink. 'I believe you're cross, George, because Julian won't let you take the papers yourself!'

'Oh, do shut up, Tink,' said George. 'I shall be jolly cross with *you* in a minute, if you let Mischief upset your glass of lemonade again, all over my bread. Take him off the table! His manners are getting worse!'

'They aren't – but your temper is!' said Tink and promptly received a kick under the table from Julian. He was about to kick back but thought better of it. Julian could kick very much harder than he could! He decided to take Mischief off the table in case George smacked him. He put the little monkey under the table where Timmy was sitting quietly. Mischief immediately cuddled up to him, putting his little furry arms round the big dog's neck. Timmy sniffed him all over, and then gave him two or three licks. He was very fond of the naughty little monkey.

'What shall we do this afternoon?' asked Dick, when they had all helped Jenny to clear away and wash up. 'What about a bathe in the sea? Is it warm enough?'

'Not really. But that doesn't matter. We always feel warm when we come out of the water and run about and then rub ourselves down,' said Anne. 'Jenny – do *you* feel like a bathe?'

'Good gracious, no!' said Jenny, shivering at the thought. 'I'm a cold mortal, I am. The thought of going into that cold sea makes me shudder. If you want your towels, they are all in the airing cupboard. And don't you be late for tea, if you want any, because I've a lot of ironing to do afterwards.'

'Right, Jenny,' said Tink, about to give her one of his 'squeezes' but thinking better of it when he saw her warning look. 'Julian, may I come with you to Kirrin Island tonight? I'd like a bit of fun.'

'You may not,' said Julian. 'Anyway, there won't be any fun.'

'There might be if Mr Wooh did hear George say she was taking those papers over,' said Tink. 'He'd be waiting on the island – and you might be glad to have me with you!'

'I should *not* be glad to have you with me,' said Julian. 'You'd just be in the way. It would be much easier to look after myself than to see what *you* were up to all the time. I am going by myself. Please don't scowl at me like that, George.'

He got up from the table and went to look out of the window. 'Wind's died down a bit,' he said. 'I think I'll have a bathe in an hour's time. If any of you others want to come, we'll go down together.'

They all went down to the beach after a while and bathed, except Mischief, who put one small paw into the water, gave a howl and scampered back up the beach as fast as ever he could, afraid that Tink might catch him and make him go in! Timmy went in, of course. He swam marvellously, and even gave Tink a ride on his back, diving down when the boy felt heavy, so that Tink suddenly found himself sprawling in the water! 'You wretch, Timmy!' yelled the boy. 'The water's gone up my nose. Wait till I catch you! I'll put *you* under!'

But he couldn't possibly catch old Timmy, who really enjoyed the joke. The big dog gave a joyful bark, and swam after George. How he loved being with them all!

The rest of the day went quickly. Jenny had a fine tea for them, with slices of ham, and salad, and fruit to end with, and said afterwards that she had time to play a game

of Scrabble with them if they liked. Mischief sat on the table to watch.

'I don't mind you *watching*,' said Anne. 'But you are NOT to scrabble, Mischief. You sent all my little ivory tiles on the floor last time we played, and I lost the game.'

Timmy watched gravely, sitting on a chair beside George. He simply could *not* understand what made the children play games like this when they could go for a nice long walk with him. They took pity on him when the game was over and went out for a two-mile walk along by the sea. How Timmy loved that!

'I shall cycle to Kirrin Village as soon as it's dark,' announced Julian. 'I suppose your boat is tied up in the usual place, George? I'm sorry I can't take you with me, but there *might* be a bit of danger, as we said. However I won't run into any if I can help it. I shan't feel comfortable until those secret papers are safely out of the way! You can give them to me just before I go, George.'

Anne suddenly yawned. 'Don't start too late or I shall fall asleep!' she said. 'It's getting dark already. All that swimming has made me feel tired!'

Dick yawned too. 'I'm jolly sleepy as well,' he said. 'I shall bed down in our tent as soon as you've gone, Ju. I'll see you off safely first, papers and all! You'd better go to your tent, too, girls – you look tired.'

'Right!' said Anne. 'You coming, George?'

'We'll all go,' said George. 'Come on, Tink. Bet you I get over the fence and down to our tents first! Good night, Jenny. We're off!'

She and Anne and Tink, with Timmy running behind, went off down the darkening garden. Dick and Julian helped Jenny to tidy up, and to draw all the curtains. 'Well, good night, Jenny,' said Dick. 'All you have to do is to lock the door behind us and go safely up to bed. We'll go down to our tents now. Sleep well!'

'Oh, I always do,' said Jenny. 'Look after yourselves now and don't get into any mischief! Hide those papers well, where nobody can find them!'

Julian and Dick went off down the garden, having heard Jenny carefully locking the door behind them.

Tink and the girls were already over the fence, Mischief on Tink's shoulder. Anne spoke anxiously to

George. 'I do hope Julian will be all right going over to Kirrin Island,' she said. 'I wish he'd take Dick with him.'

'If he took anyone it should be *me*!' burst out George. 'It's *my* island!'

'Oh, don't be silly, George. The papers would be much safer with Julian,' said Anne. 'It would be an awful business for you, cycling by yourself to Kirrin, getting your boat into the water, and rowing over in the dark!'

'It would not!' said George. 'If Julian can do it, then so could I. You go into our tent, Anne, and get ready for bed. I'll come in a minute, after I've taken Timmy for a run.'

She waited till Anne had disappeared through the tent opening. Then she went quietly off by herself in the dark, Timmy trotting beside her, rather surprised.

Soon there came the sound of voices, as Julian and Dick reached the fence and leapt over it. They went to their tent and found Tink there, yawning and getting ready for bed.

Soon the three boys were all rolled up in their rugs, Mischief cuddled up to Tink. After some time Julian sat up and looked at his watch, and then peeped out of the tent opening. 'Quite dark!' he said. 'But the moon's coming up, I see. I think I'll get the papers from George now, and set off on my bicycle to Kirrin. I can easily get it out of the shed.'

'You know where George keeps her boat,' said Dick. 'You won't have any difficulty in finding it. Got your torch, Ju?'

'Yes – and a new battery,' said Julian. 'Look!'

He switched on his torch. It gave a good, powerful beam. 'Shan't miss the island if I put *this* on!' he said. 'Now – I'll get those papers. Hey, George – I'm coming to your tent for the papers!'

He went over to the girls' tent. Anne was there, only half-awake. She blinked as Julian's torch shone into her eyes.

'George!' said Julian. 'Give me those papers now, please – hallo – *Hey*, Anne – where is George?'

Anne started looking all round the tent. George's rugs were there, piled in an untidy heap; but there was no George – and no Timmy either!

'Oh, Ju! Do you know what George has done – she's slipped out with the precious papers – and taken Timmy too! She must have gone to fetch her bike, and ridden off to Kirrin to get her boat – and row over to Kirrin Island! Julian, whatever will happen if she rows over and finds somebody waiting to grab those papers from her?' Poor Anne was very near to tears.

'I could *shake* her!' said Julian, very angry indeed. 'Going off alone like that in the dark – cycling to Kirrin – rowing over to the island – and back! She must be mad! Suppose Mr Wooh and his friends are waiting there for her! The – silly – little – idiot!'

'Oh, Julian, quick! You and Dick get your cycles and try to catch her,' begged Anne. 'Oh please do! Anything might happen to her! Dear, silly old George! Thank goodness Timmy's gone with her.'

'Well, that's a blessing, anyway,' said Julian, still angry. 'He'll look after her as much as he can. Oh, I could shake George till her teeth rattled! I *thought* she was rather quiet tonight. Thinking out this plan, I suppose!'

He went up to the house with Dick and Tink to tell Jenny about George, and then he and Dick at once went to get their bicycles. This was serious. George had no right to be out alone at night like this – and go rowing over to Kirrin Island – *especially* if there was any chance of someone lying in wait for her!

Jenny was very worried indeed. She watched the two boys cycling off in the dark. Tink begged her to let him go too, but she wouldn't. 'You and Mischief would just be nuisances,' she said. 'Oh, won't I shake that rascal of a George when she gets back. What a girl! Well, well – thank goodness Timmy's with her. That dog's as good as half a dozen policemen!'

CHAPTER SIXTEEN

Night on Kirrin Island

It was certainly very dark when the half-moon went behind the clouds. George was glad that her bicycle lamp shone so brightly. The shadows in the hedges were deep and mysterious – 'as if they hid people ready to jump out at us,' she said to Timmy. 'But you'd go for them at once, wouldn't you, Timmy!'

Timmy was too much out of breath to bark an answer. George was going pretty fast, and he didn't mean to let her get out of sight. He was sure she shouldn't be out by herself on a dark night like this. He couldn't *imagine* why she had suddenly taken it into her head to go for a long night ride! He raced along, panting.

They met cars with dazzling headlamps, and George had to keep pulling to the side. She was terribly afraid that Timmy might be hit by one of the cars. 'Oh dear – I'd never, never forgive myself if anything happened to Timmy,' she thought. 'I half wish I hadn't set out now. But I'm NOT going to let Julian hide anything on *my* island. That's my job, not his.'

'Timmy darling, PLEASE keep on my left side. You'll be safe then.'

So Timmy kept on her left, still mystified by this sudden

journey out into the night. They came at last to Kirrin village, where windows were still lit here and there. Through the village and on to Kirrin Bay – ah, there was the bay! The half-moon slid out from behind a cloud and George saw the dark sea, shining here and there as the moonlight caught the crests of the waves.

'There's my island, look, Timmy,' said George, feeling a swelling of pride as she looked over the dark heaving sea to a darker stretch, which she knew was Kirrin Island. 'My very *own* island. Waiting for me tonight!'

'Woof,' said Timmy, rather quietly, because he really hadn't any breath to waste. *Now* what was George going to do? Why had she come out on this lonely ride without the others? Timmy was puzzled.

They came to the stretch of beach where boats were kept. George rode down a ramp to the beach, jumped off her bicycle, and put it by a bathing-hut in the deep shadows. No one would see it there. Then she went to stare over the sea at her island.

She had only looked for a moment or two when she clutched Timmy's collar, and gave an exclamation.

'TIMMY! There's a *light* on my island! Look, to the right there. Can you see it? Timmy, there's somebody camping there. How *dare* they? It's *my* island and I don't allow *any*one on it unless they have my permission.'

Timmy looked – and yes, he could see the light too. Was it made by a camp-fire – or a lantern? He couldn't tell. All he knew was that he didn't want George to go over there

now. He pawed at her, trying to make her understand that he wanted her to go back home with him.

'No, Timmy. I'm *not* going back till I've found out who's there!' she said. 'It would be cowardly to turn back now. And if it's somebody waiting for me to turn up with the papers, they can think again. Look – I'm hiding them here under the tarpaulin in this boat. It would be idiotic to try and hide them on the island if there's someone there who *might* rob me of anything I've got – it might be one of the thieves who climbed into the tower room, and left some of the papers behind. If *he*'s waiting for me, he won't get any papers!'

George stuffed the parcel of papers under the tarpaulin as she spoke. 'It's Fisherman Connell's boat, called *Stormrider*,' she said, reading the name on the boat by the light of her torch. '*He* won't mind me hiding something in it!'

She covered up the papers with the tarpaulin, and then looked over to the island again. Yes – that light was still there. Anger welled up in George again, and she went to look for her own boat, which should be somewhere near where they were.

'Here it is,' she said to Timmy, who leapt in at once. She ordered him out for she had to pull the boat down to the water. Fortunately it was a small, light boat and as the tide was almost fully in, she didn't have very far to drag it. Timmy took hold of the rope with his teeth and helped too. At last it was on the water, bobbing gently about in the dim light of the half-moon. Timmy leapt in, and soon George was in too, though with very wet feet!

She took the oars and began to pull away from the shore. 'Tide's almost on the turn,' she told Timmy. 'It won't be too hard a row. Now we can find those campers and tell them what we think of them. You're to bark your very loudest and scare them, Timmy – in fact, you can chase them to their boat, if you like.'

Timmy answered with a small bark. He knew quite well that George didn't want him to make much noise. He thought it was odd that she was going over to her island tonight, all by herself. Why hadn't she taken the others? He was sure that Julian would be very cross!

'Now don't bark or whine, Timmy,' she said, in a

whisper. 'We're almost at my landing place – but I'm going under those trees there, not landing here. I want to hide my boat.'

She guided the boat towards some trees whose branches overhung a tiny creek that ran a little way inland. She leapt out, and flung the mooring rope round the trunk of the nearest tree, and made it fast.

'There, little boat,' she said. 'You'll be safe there. No one will see you. Come on, Tim – we'll tackle those campers now.'

She turned to go, and then stopped. 'I wonder where *their* boat is,' she said. 'Let's have a look round, Timmy. It must be here somewhere.'

She soon found the boat lying on the sands, its rope thrown round a nearby rock. The tide was almost up to it. She grinned to herself. 'Timmy!' she whispered. 'I'm going to untie this boat and set it loose on the tide. It will soon be far away. Ha – what will those awful campers say?'

And, to Timmy's amazement, she undid the rope from the rock, rolled it up, and threw the coil inside the boat. Then she gave the boat a push – but it was still embedded in the wet sand.

'Never mind,' she said. 'Another ten minutes and the tide will be right under it – and then it will turn and take the boat with it!'

She began to make her way up the beach, Timmy close to her side. 'Now let's go after those campers, whoever they are,' she said. 'Where's their light gone? I can't see it now.'

But in a minute or two she saw it again. 'It's not from a camp-fire – it's from a lantern of some sort,' she whispered to Timmy. 'We'll have to be careful now. Let's see if we can creep up behind them.'

The two of them made their way silently towards the middle of the little island. Here there was an old ruined castle – and there, in the courtyard of the castle, sitting in the midst of thick, overgrown weeds, were two men. George had her hand on Timmy's collar, and tugged it gently. He knew that meant, 'No barking, no growling, Tim,' and he stood perfectly still, the hackles on his neck rising fast.

The two men were playing cards by the light of a fairly powerful lantern, which they had set on a ruined stone wall. Timmy couldn't help giving a surprised growl when he saw one of them, but George hushed him at once.

Mr Wooh, the magician from the circus, was there, dealing out the cards! The other man she didn't know. He was well-dressed, and seemed bored. He flung down his cards as Timmy and George watched from a dark corner of the old castle, and spoke to his companion in an irritated voice.

'Well, whoever it is you said was bringing the rest of those papers here to the island doesn't seem to be turning up. The papers you've given me are good – very good – but of no use without the others. This scientist fellow you've stolen them from is a genius. If we get the complete

set of papers, they will be worth a tremendous sum of money, which I can get for you – but without the other papers, there will be no money for you – the first set would be useless!'

'I tell you, someone will be here with them. I heard them say so,' said Mr Wooh in his stately voice.

'Who stole them – you?' asked the other man, shuffling the cards quickly.

'No. I did not steal them,' said Mr Wooh. 'Me, I keep my hands clean – I do not steal.'

The second man laughed. 'No. You let other people do your dirty work for you, don't you! Mr Wooh, the World's Most Wonderful Magician, does not soil his hands! He merely uses the hands of others – and charges enormous prices for the goods they steal. You're a cunning one, Mr Wooh. I wouldn't like you for an enemy! How did you manage to get the papers?'

'By using my eyes and my ears and my cunning,' answered Mr Wooh. 'They are better than most people's. So many people are stupid, my good friend.'

'I'm not your good friend,' said the other man. 'I've *got* to do business with you, Mr Wooh, but I wouldn't like to have you for a friend. I'd rather have that chimpanzee of yours! I don't even like playing cards with you! *WHY* doesn't this fellow come?'

George put her mouth to one of Timmy's ears. 'Timmy, I'm going to tell them to clear off my island,' she whispered furiously to the listening dog. 'Fancy fellows like *that* daring to set foot here – rascals and rogues! Don't come with me – wait till I call you, then if you have to rescue me, come at once!'

Leaving a most unwilling Timmy standing beside part of the old castle wall, she suddenly appeared before the two astonished men by the light of their lantern.

They leapt to their feet at once. 'It's the girl who's come – I shouldn't have thought that the boys would have let her,' said Mr Wooh, astonished. 'I am . . .'

'WHAT ARE YOU DOING ON MY ISLAND?' demanded George, angrily. 'It belongs to *me*. I saw your light and came over with my dog. Be careful of him – he's big and strong and fierce. Clear off at once, or I'll report you to the police!'

'Easy, easy, now!' said Mr Wooh, standing very straight and looking immensely tall. 'So the boys sent *you* to hide the papers instead of daring to come themselves. How cowardly of them! Where are the papers? Give them to me.'

'I've hidden them,' said George. 'They're not very far away. You didn't think I'd be silly enough to come along to you with them in my hands when I saw your light and knew that people were here, did you? No – I've hidden them somewhere on the shore – where *you* won't find them. Now you just clear off, both of you!'

'A very brave and determined young lady!' said Mr Wooh, bowing solemnly to George.

'Do you mean to tell me that's a *girl*!' said the other man, amazed. 'Well! She's a plucky kid, I must say! Look here, kid, if you've got those papers, hand them over, and I'll give you a whole lot of money which you can give to Professor Hayling with my best wishes.'

'Come and get them,' said George, turning as if to go. The two men looked at one another, eyebrows raised. Mr Wooh nodded, and then winked. If George had seen his face she would have known what that wink meant. It meant let's humour this silly kid, follow her – see the hiding-place, snatch the papers and clear off in our boat without paying a penny! But LOOK OUT for the dog!

George led the way, Timmy walking between her and the two men. He was growling all the time, deep down in his throat, as if to say 'Just you lay a finger on George and

I'll bite it off!' The men took care not to go too near him! They shone the lantern on him all the time, making sure that he was not going to leap at them.

George led them to the shore, to the place where they had left their boat. Mr Wooh gave a cry. 'Where's our boat? It was tied to that rock!'

'Is this it over this ridge?' called George climbing up a steep bank that overhung the water, which was now quite deep with the surging tide.

The men went to look – and then George gave them the surprise of their lives! She ran at Mr Wooh and gave him such a push that he fell right over the high bank into the sea below, landing with a yell and a terrific splash. George shouted a command to Timmy, who was now very excited, and the big dog did the same to the other man, leaping at him and pushing him over. He, too, shot over the ridge and fell into the sea with a splash. Timmy stood on the little cliff and barked madly, as excited as George.

'You'll have to swim to the shore of the mainland if you want to escape!' yelled George. 'The tide has taken away your boat – I set it loose! You'd better not get back on my island yet – Timmy's on the watch for you – and he'll fly at either of you if you try to set a foot on it again!'

Both men could swim, though not very well, and both were exceedingly angry and very frightened. They were sure they could never swim to the mainland – but how to get on the island to safety, they didn't know. That great, fierce dog was there, barking as if he wanted to bite them

into small bits. Their boat had been set loose, there was no way to escape. They swam round in circles, not knowing what to do!

'I'm going back to the mainland now!' yelled George, climbing into her boat. 'I'll send the police to rescue you in the morning. You can get on my island now – but you're in for a *very* cold night! Goodbye!'

And off went George in her boat, with Timmy standing at the back, watching to make sure those men didn't swim after them. He gave George an admiring lick. She wasn't afraid of *anything*! He'd rather belong to *her* than to anyone else in the world. WOOF, WOOF, W-O-O-F!

CHAPTER SEVENTEEN

And at last the mystery is solved!

GEORGE COULDN'T help singing loudly as she rowed back to the shore in her boat. Timmy joined in with a bark now and again. He was glad that George was so happy. He stood in the prow of the boat, wishing it was not night-time, so that he could see clearly where he was going. The moon clouded over, and the sea looked endless in the dark. Very few lights showed on the mainland at that time of night – just one or two from houses where people were still up.

Wait, though – what was that bright light suddenly shining out from the mainland? Was it someone trying to pick out their boat? Timmy barked at the light, and George, who, of course, was rowing with her back to the shore, shipped her oars for a moment and looked round.

'It's someone on the quay,' she said. 'Maybe a late fisherman. Good! He'll be able to help me drag my boat up out of the way of the tide!'

But it wasn't a fisherman. It was Julian and Dick. They had arrived about five minutes ago, and had looked at once for George's boat and hadn't found it. 'Bother! We're too late to stop her, then. She's gone over to the island!' said

Julian and began to examine all the other tied-up boats to see if he could find one that he could borrow, belonging to a friend. *Somehow* they must get over to Kirrin Island, and rescue George. He felt sure she would be in danger of some kind.

Then suddenly the two boys heard the sounds of oars splashing not far out to sea. Well, if that was a fisherman coming home, maybe Julian could ask *him* to lend him his boat to go to Kirrin Island in. He could tell him that he was afraid his cousin might be in need of help.

Timmy, in George's boat, suddenly recognised the two boys when the moon swam out from a cloud, and gave a delighted volley of barks. George, wondering if it *was* Julian and Dick, rowed as quickly as she could. She came into shore, jumped out and began to drag in her boat. The boys were beside her at once, and the boat was soon in its usual place, carefully made safe in case the tide was a high one.

'George!' said Julian, so overjoyed to see his cousin safe and sound that he couldn't help giving her a bear hug. 'You wicked girl! You went to the island – just what I said you *weren't* to do. You might have found the thieves on the island, and *then* you would have been in trouble!'

'I *did* find them – but it's *they* who are in trouble, not me!' said George. 'I saw a light over there, took my boat and went over to the island – and there they were – Mr Wooh the Magician and another man – ON MY ISLAND! Did you ever hear such cheek? They asked me for the papers at once!'

'Oh, George – did you give them to the men?' asked Dick.

'Of *course* not! I'd already hidden them where those men couldn't possibly find them. I wasn't idiotic enough to take them over to hide on the *island* when I saw somebody was there – probably waiting for me – *and* for the papers!' said George.

'But, George – if you knew somebody was there, why on *earth* did you risk going over to Kirrin Island then?' asked Julian, puzzled. 'It was a very dangerous thing to do.'

'I wanted to turn off whoever it was, of course,' said George. 'As if I'd allow just *anyone* on my island! It's mine, my very own, and I only allow people on it that I like. You know that.'

'I just *never* know what you'll do next, George,' said Julian, patting Timmy on the head. 'How did you *dare* to go and tackle those men? Oh, I know Timmy was with you, but even so . . . why in the world didn't the men row after you, and ram your boat?'

'Well, you see, they couldn't,' said George. 'I found their boat, untied it, and set it adrift on the tide. It's probably half a mile away by now!'

The boys were so astonished that they couldn't even laugh at first. But then, when they thought of the two men marooned on Kirrin Island, their boat gone goodness knows where, they laughed till tears came into their eyes!

'George, I don't know how you can *think* of doing such things!' said Julian. 'Weren't the men furious?'

'I don't know,' said George. 'I didn't tell them about their boat. I pretended that I'd take them to where I'd hidden the papers – and then when we got on to a nice high ridge overlooking the sea, they looked over it to see if their boat was all right, and I gave Mr Wooh a jolly good push, and Timmy leapt at the man with him – and in they went – SPLASH! SPLASH!'

Julian really *had* to sit down and have another bout of laughing till the stitch in his side grew so bad that he was forced to get up and walk about. George suddenly saw the funny side of it all too, and she began to laugh as heartily as Julian. Dick joined in as well, and Timmy barked madly, enjoying the fun.

'Oh dear!' said Julian, feeling weak with laughter, 'and then I suppose you said a polite farewell and left them to their fate?'

'Well, actually I yelled out to tell them I'd send the police to rescue them in the morning,' said George. 'I'm afraid they'll both spend a very uncomfortable night – they were soaking wet, you see!'

'George – I'm beginning to think it was a good thing *you* went with the papers to the island, and not me, after all,' said Julian. 'I should *never* have thought of doing all the things you did – pushing the men into the sea – really, how *could* you and Timmy dare to do such things? And setting their boat loose! What on earth will the police say when we tell them?'

'I don't think we'd better tell them, had we?' said

George. 'I mean – they might think I'd gone too far. Anyway, why not let the two men kick their heels on the island all night, and we'll decide what to do about the police in the morning. It's funny – I suddenly feel awfully tired.'

'I bet you do!' said Dick. 'Come on, let's get our bikes. Oh, and those precious papers – where are they?'

'Under the tarpaulin in Fisherman Connell's boat,' said George, and suddenly gave the most enormous yawn. 'I hid them there.'

'I'll get them,' said Julian. 'Then off we go back to Big Hollow House. The others will be getting awfully worried by now!'

He found the papers in the fishing boat and then the three of them rode off quickly along the road from Kirrin to Big Hollow, Timmy running behind them. Julian kept laughing to himself. George was amazing! Fancy tackling those two fellows like that – pushing them into the water, and setting their boat adrift. Julian was sure he would never have thought of doing such daring things himself.

At last they were back at the tents, and the others crowded round them to hear what had happened. Anne looked very white. Jenny was with her, comforting her – she had *just* made up her mind to telephone the police, and was *most* relieved to see George again.

'We'll tell you all the details in the morning,' said Julian. 'But all I'll say now is that the papers are safe all right, here in my pocket – the thieves were probably Mr

Wooh and another man. They were on the island tonight, waiting for George. They *had* overheard what she said in the tent! However, George and Timmy pushed them both into the water and set their boat adrift, so things are settling down nicely! They will have to spend the night on the island, cold and wet through!'

'*George* did all that!' said Jenny, amazed. 'Well! I never knew she was so *dangerous*! Good gracious! I feel right-down scared of her! Settle down to sleep in your tent, dear – you look tired out!'

George was glad to flop down on her rugs. Now that the excitement was all over she felt too sleepy for words! She fell asleep at once – but Julian and Dick didn't. They lay awake for some time, chuckling over George's deeds of daring. What a cousin to have!

When they were up at the house at breakfast next morning, Jeremy came up the garden and put his head in at the dining-room window. 'Hey!' he said. 'Mr Wooh's not in his tent this morning! He's disappeared! And poor old Charlie the Chimp is too miserable for words.'

'Ah – we can tell you *exactly* where Mr Wooh is,' said Julian. 'But – wait a bit, Tink, where are you going? You haven't finished your . . .'

But Tink had gone off with Jeremy at top speed! He was very fond of Charlie. Oh dear, would the chimpanzee weep for his master and refuse to take his food? Tink called Mischief and they both ran down to the fence with Jeremy and climbed over it. Tink went straight to

Charlie's cage. The chimpanzee sat with his head in his hands, rocking himself to and fro, making sad, crying noises.

'Let's get into the cage with him,' said Tink. 'He'll like to be comforted. He must be missing Mr Wooh very, very much.'

They crawled into the cage and sat down in the straw, each putting an arm round the sad chimpanzee. Old Grandad was very surprised to see them both there.

'Don't know what's happened to Mr Wooh,' he said. 'Didn't come home last night! Here, Jeremy, you come on out. I can't spare you to cry over Charlie all morning. He'll soon perk up. *You* can stay with him, Tink, if you like.'

Jeremy crawled out of the cage and went off crossly. Tink sat with his arm round Charlie, wishing he didn't look so terribly sad. As he sat there, he heard a funny little noise going on all the time. Tick-tick-tick-ticka-ticka-tick-tick-tick-tick-ticka-ticka-tick. 'Sounds like a watch or something,' said Tink, and scrabbled about in the straw. Perhaps Mr Wooh's big gold watch had fallen into Charlie's cage?

His hand felt something small and round and smooth at the bottom of the cage. He riffled away the thick straw, and drew out the object underneath it. He stared and stared at it in the utmost surprise. Charlie saw him looking at it, snatched it away and hid it in the straw again. He made a few growly noises as if he were angry.

'Charlie, *where* did you get that little clock?' said Tink. 'Oh, Charlie! Well, as you're so sad this morning, I'll give it to you for your very own. Just to cheer you up. But oh, Charlie, I *am* surprised at you!'

He slid out of the cage and went back over the fence and into his own garden. Up the path he ran and burst into the dining-room, where the others were still finishing their breakfast.

'What's up?' said Dick.

'Listen! I know who the thief was who climbed in at the tower window . . . I KNOW WHO HE WAS!' cried Tink, almost shouting in his excitement.

'Who?' said everyone, in amazement.

'It was *Charlie the Chimp*!' said Tink. 'Why didn't we think of him before? He can climb anything! It would be quite easy for *him* to swing himself up that rough-stoned wall, hanging on to the bits of creeper here and there – and to the uneven stones – and climb through the window into the tower room, collect all the papers he could hold – and climb down again – *slither* down again, probably . . .'

'*That* must have been the slithering sound I heard!' said Jenny. 'I *told* you I heard a strange slithering noise!'

'And the whispering you heard must have been Mr Wooh trying to make him go up the tower wall and into the window!' said Julian. 'Gosh – I bet poor old Charlie's been taught to get into all sorts of windows and take whatever he sees. Mr Wooh must have known Tink's father worked out all his ideas up in the tower.'

'Wooh could easily teach him to take papers,' said Julian. 'But there were, of course, too many for old Charlie in the tower room. He wouldn't be able to carry them *all* in his front paws, for he needed *all* his paws to climb down that steep wall – so he must have crammed as many as he could into his mouth – and dropped the rest under the table! Charlie the Chimp – well! Who would have thought *he* could be the thief!'

'Wait a bit – how on earth do you know it was Charlie?' said Dick. 'Nobody saw him. It was at night.'

'Well, I *do* know it was Charlie,' said Tink. 'You remember that a dear little clock was stolen from the tower room mantelpiece, on the night when those papers were stolen? Well *I* found it hidden in the straw in Charlie's cage this morning! He snatched it away from me, and almost cried – so I let him keep it! It was ticking loudly just like it always did. It was the loud ticking that told me it was there in the cage!'

'Who wound it up at nights, to keep it going?' said Julian, at once, most astonished.

'Charlie, I suppose,' said Tink. 'He's very clever with his paws! The clock was quite safe, hidden in his cage. Nobody would be likely to get into the chimp's cage and sit there with him – but *I* did this morning, and that's how I found it. I heard it ticking, you see. I bet old Charlie was clever enough to pop his precious clock into his mouth when he saw any of the men coming to clean out his cage!'

'Well, I'm blessed!' said Jenny. 'How was it that Mr Wooh never saw him bringing it along with the papers that night, when he stole them?'

'Well, as Tink told you – my guess is that old Charlie must have put the little clock in his mouth then, along with the papers,' said Dick. 'He needed all his four paws, climbing – or rather *slithering* down that wall – and he's got a jolly big mouth! You should see what a lot of food he can stuff into it!'

'Yes. And Mr Wooh would take the papers, of course – Charlie would just take them from his mouth and hand them to him – but he'd be crafty enough to keep his precious new toy hidden in his mouth! Poor old Charlie! Can't you see him listening to the clock, and cuddling it – like a child with a new toy!' said George.

'He sounded exactly as if he were crying this morning,' said Tink. 'I couldn't bear it. Poor old Charlie! He couldn't understand *why* Mr Wooh didn't go and see him today. He was *so* miserable!'

'I think we'll *have* to get the police along now,' said Julian. 'Not only to catch Mr Wooh and his friend, left so conveniently marooned by George on her island – but also because Mr Wooh should be charged with stealing your father's irreplaceable charts and diagrams, Tink. Goodness knows what else he has taught poor old Charlie to steal. I bet he's sent the chimp into a lot of houses, and up many walls, and into many windows.'

'Yes. There's probably been a trail of robberies wherever

the circus went,' said Jenny. 'And many innocent people must have been suspected.'

'What a shame!' said Anne. 'But, oh dear – if Mr Wooh goes to prison, whatever will become of poor old Charlie the Chimp?'

'I bet Jeremy will take him,' said Tink. 'He loves him, and old Charlie adores Jeremy! He'll be all right with Jeremy and old Grandad!'

'Well, Tink, I think you'd better go and tell your father all this,' said Jenny. 'I know he's busy – he always is – but this is a thing *he* ought to deal with and nobody else. If you'd like to fetch him, George could tell him the whole story – and then I rather guess *he'll* ring up the police – and Mr Wooh will find himself in a whole lot of trouble.'

So there goes Tink, with Mischief on his shoulder, to find his father, down the hall – up the stairs – along the landing – into his father's bedroom . . . R-r-r-r-r-r-r-r-r-r-r! Tink, you sound like a motor-scooter going up a steep hill! PARP-PARP! *Don't* hoot like that, you'll make your father so angry that he won't listen to a word you say!

But the Professor *did* listen – and soon Jenny heard him telephoning the police. They're coming straight away, and that means that Mr Wooh the Magician is in for a most unpleasant time, and his magic won't help him at all! He'll have to give back the papers that he made Charlie steal – and plenty of other things, too! There he is, marooned on the island, quite unable to escape, waiting fearfully with his companion, for the police!

'Another adventure over!' said George, with a regretful sigh. 'And a jolly exciting one too! I'm glad you solved the mystery, Tink – it was clever of you to find the little tower room clock. I bet Mr Wooh wouldn't have let Charlie keep it, if he'd known he'd taken it from the tower room! Poor old Charlie the Chimp!'

'I'm just wondering if Dad would let me keep Charlie here, while Mr Wooh is in prison,' began Tink, and stopped as Jenny gave a horrified shriek.

'*Tink!* If you so much as *mention* that idea to your father, I'll walk straight out of this house and NEVER COME BACK!' said Jenny. 'That chimp would be in my kitchen all day long – oh yes, he would – and things would be disappearing out of my larder, and my cupboards, and my drawers, and he'd dance up and down and scream at me if I so much as said a word, and . . .'

'All right, dear, dear Jenny, I won't ask for Charlie, honest I won't,' said Tink. 'I do love you a *bit* more than I'd love a chimp – but think what a companion he would be for Mischief!'

'I'm not thinking anything of the sort!' said Jenny. 'And what about you taking a bit of notice of that monkey of yours – bless us all if he hasn't helped himself to half that jar of jam – just *look* at his sticky face! Oh, what a week this has been, what with chimps and monkeys and children and robberies, and George disappearing, and all!'

'Dear old Jenny,' said George, laughing as she went off into the kitchen. 'What an exciting time we've had! I really did enjoy every minute of it!'

So did we, George. Hurry up and fall into another adventure. We are longing to hear what you and the others will be up to next. How we wish we could join you! Goodbye for now – and take care of yourselves, Five. Good luck!

Join the adventure!

Have you read the first adventure in
THE FAMOUS FIVE series?

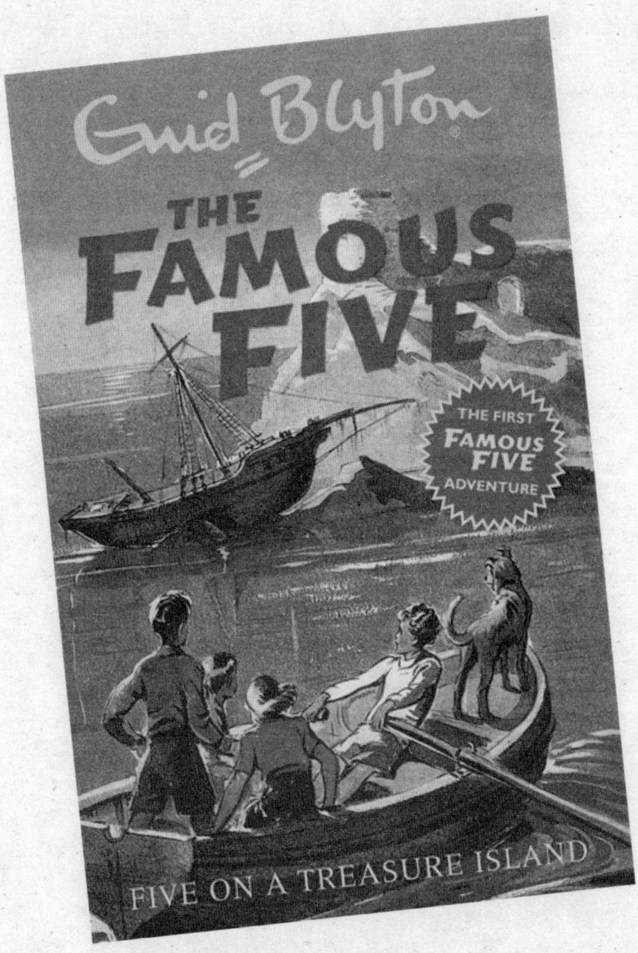

Do you want to solve a mystery?

Enid Blyton

The Secret Seven

Join Peter, Janet, Jack, Barbara, Pam, Colin, George and Scamper as they solve puzzles and mysteries, foil baddies, and rescue people from danger – all without help from the grown-ups. Enid Blyton wrote fifteen stories about the Secret Seven. These editions contain brilliant illustrations by Tony Ross, plus extra fun facts and stories to read and share.

More classic stories from the world of

Enid Blyton

The Naughtiest Girl

Elizabeth Allen is spoilt and selfish. When she's sent away to boarding school she makes up her mind to be the naughtiest pupil there's ever been! But Elizabeth soon finds out that being bad isn't as simple as it seems. There are ten brilliant books about the Naughtiest Girl to enjoy.

Enid Blyton®

is one of the most popular children's authors of all time. Her books have sold over 500 million copies and have been translated into other languages more often than any other children's author.

Enid Blyton adored writing for children. She wrote over 700 books and about 2,000 short stories. *The Famous Five* books, now 75 years old, are her most popular. She is also the author of other favourites including *The Secret Seven*, *The Magic Faraway Tree*, *Malory Towers* and *Noddy*.

Born in London in 1897, Enid lived much of her life in Buckinghamshire and loved dogs, gardening and the countryside. She was very knowledgeable about trees, flowers, birds and animals. Dorset – where some of the Famous Five's adventures are set – was a favourite place of hers too.

Enid Blyton's stories are read and loved by millions of children (and grown-ups) all over the world. Visit enidblyton.co.uk to discover more.